WHISPERS

As quickly as it had come, his anger went. He picked her up and held her.

'I'm sorry. Oh, I'm sorry. I didn't mean to. But I was terrified, Lynn. You could have been kidnapped – yes, in broad daylight – dragged down an alley, whisked into a car, raped, God knows what. This country is full of thugs.' He kissed her tears. 'I was beside myself. Don't you understand?'

He kept kissing her cheeks, her forehead, her hands, and when at last she turned to him, her lips.

'If anything were to happen to you, I wouldn't want to live. I was so frightened. I love you so.'

She put her arms around his neck. 'All right. All right, darling. Robert, forget it, it's over. We misunderstood each other. It's nothing. Nothing.'

And it was as it had been, as glorious as ever except for the ugly dark blue blotches on her arms.

*Also by Belva Plain
and available from Coronet Books*

Evergreen
Random Winds
Blessings
Harvest
Treasures
Daybreak

About the author

Belva Plain is one of the world's best-loved writers. Her first novel, *Evergreen*, was published in 1978, and she has since entranced an international audience with nine further best-sellers, including, most recently, *Blessings*, *Harvest*, *Treasures* and *Daybreak*.

Whispers

Belva Plain

CORONET BOOKS
Hodder and Stoughton

First published in Great Britain in 1993
by New English Library Hardbacks
A division of Hodder Headline PLC

Coronet edition 1994
This editiion 1995

10 9 8 7 6 5 4

British Library C.I.P.

A CIP catalogue record for this title is available from
the British Library

ISBN 0 340 59985 5

Printed and bound in Great Britain by
Cox & Wyman Ltd, Reading, Berkshire

Hodder and Stoughton
A division of Hodder Headline PLC
338 Euston Road
London NW1 3BH

Part One

Spring 1985

1

In dodging Robert's hand, the furious hand aimed at her face, she fell and struck the edge of the closet's open door instead. Now on the floor, stunned by a rush of pain, she leaned against the wall, touched her cheek, and, in a kind of astonishment, stared at the blood on her hand.

Robert's eyes and his mouth had become three dark, round holes in his face.

'Oh, good God!' He knelt beside her. 'Let me look. No, let me, Lynn! Thank goodness it's nothing. Just a break in the skin. An accident ... I'll get a washcloth and ice cubes. Here, let me pull you up.'

'Don't touch me, damn you!' Thrusting his hand away, she pulled herself up and sat down on the bed between the suitcases. Her face burned, while her cold fingers felt for the rising lump on her cheekbone. Another lump, thick with outrage and tears, rose in her throat.

Robert bustled between the bedroom and the bathroom. 'Damn, where's the ice bucket? In a first-class hotel like this you'd think they'd put – oh, here it is. Now just lie back. I'll fix the pillows. Hold this to your face. Does it hurt much?'

His expressions of anxiety were sickening. She closed her eyes. If she could have closed her ears, she would have done so. His voice, so rich, so beautifully modulated, was trying to soothe her.

'You tripped. I know I raised my hand but you tripped.

3

I'm sorry, but you were so angry, you were almost hysterical, Lynn, and I had to stop you somehow.'

She opened her eyes. 'I? *I* was so angry? *I* was almost hysterical? Think again and tell the truth if you can.'

'Well, I did lose my temper a little. I'll admit that. But can you blame me? Can you? When I depended on you to do the packing and you know how important this convention is, you know this could be my chance for promotion to the New York headquarters, the main chance of a lifetime maybe, and here I am without a dinner jacket.'

'I didn't do it on purpose. Now I'll tell you for the third time that Kitty Lombard told me the men won't be wearing tuxedos. I specifically asked about it.'

'Kitty Lombard! She steered you wrong on purpose and you're too stupid to know it. How often have I told you that people like nothing better than to see somebody else look like a fool? Especially in the business world. They all want to sabotage you. When will you learn to stop trusting every Tom, Dick, and Harry you come across? Never, I suppose.' Striding across the room, in his powerful indignation, Robert looked about ten feet tall. 'And by the way, may I remind you again that it's not called a "tuxedo"? It's a "dinner jacket."'

'All right, all right. I'm a hick, a small-town hick, remember? My dad ran a hardware store. I never saw a dinner jacket except in pictures until I met you. But I never saw a man raise his hand to a woman either.'

'Oh, let's stop this, Lynn! There's no sense going over it all night. It's almost six, and the dinner's at seven. Your ice is melting. Let me have a look again.'

'I'll take care of myself, thanks. Let me alone.'

In the bathroom she closed the door. The full-length mirror reflected a small, freckled woman, still girlish at thirty-six, with bangs and a curving cap of smooth sandy

4

hair worn as she had in high school. The face, pleasing yet unremarkable except for a pair of rather lovely light eyes, was disfigured now by the bruise, much larger than she had imagined and already more hideously, brightly blue and green than one would have thought possible. She was horrified.

Robert opened the door. 'Jesus! How can you possibly go downstairs looking like that! Unless –' He frowned over his thoughts.

'Unless what, if you please?'

'Well – I don't know. I could say the airline lost the bag with my clothes, and that you have a stomach virus, one of those twenty-four-hour things. Make yourself comfortable, take a hot bath, keep the ice on your face, get in bed, and read. Call room service and have a good dinner. Relax. It'll do you good. A nice quiet dinner without kids.'

Lynn stared at him. 'Mr Efficiency. You have it figured out, as always.'

Everything was ruined, this happily anticipated weekend away, the new dress, spring-green silk with crystal buttons, the new bottle of perfume, the manicure, all the joy gone. Sordid ruination. And he could stand there, confident, handsome, and secure, ready to cope, to go forward again.

'I hate you,' she said.

'Oh, Lynn, cut it out. I am not, I repeat, not going to go over this business ad infinitum. Just pull yourself together. I have to pull myself together for both our sakes, make an appearance and make the best of this opportunity. All the top brass will be here, and I can't afford to be rattled. I have to think clearly. Now I'm going to get dressed. Thank God my other suit is pressed.'

'I know. I pressed it.'

'Well, you got one thing straight, at least.'

'I keep *your* whole life straight every day of *my* life.'

'Will you lower your voice? People can hear you in the hall. Do you want to disgrace us both?'

Suddenly, as water is sucked down a drain, her strength rushed out. Her arms, her legs, even her voice refused to work and she dropped facedown onto the wide bed between the open suitcases. Her lips moved silently.

'Peace, peace,' they said.

Robert moved about, jingling keys as he dressed. When he was ready to go he came to the bed.

'Well, Lynn? Are you going to stay there like that all rumpled up in your street clothes?'

Her lips moved, but silently, again. 'Go away. Just go away,' they said.

The door clicked shut. And at that moment the tension broke. All the outrage at injustice, the humiliation of helpless defeat, flowed out in torrential tears, tears that she could never have shed while anyone was watching.

You were always a proud, spunky little thing, Dad used to say. Oh, such a proud, spunky little thing! she thought as she collapsed into long, heaving, retching sobs.

Much later, as abruptly as the torrent had started, it ceased. She was emptied, calmed, relieved. Cold and stiff from having lain so long uncovered, she got up and, for lack of any other purpose, went to the window. Forty floors below lights moved through the streets; lights dotted the silhouettes of Chicago's towers; light from the silver evening sky sprayed across Lake Michigan. Small, dark, fragmented clouds ran through the silver light and dissolved themselves within it. The whole scene was in motion, while the invisible wind rattled at the window glass.

Behind her the room was too still. Hotel rooms, when you were alone, were as desolate as a house emptied out after death. And Lynn, shuddering, ran to her carry-on bag, took out the photo of her children, and put it on

6

the dresser, saying aloud, 'There!' They had created an instant's presence.

And she stood looking, wanting most terribly these two girls whom she had left home in St Louis only that morning and whom, like any other mother, she had been glad to leave behind for a while. Now, if she possibly could, she would repack her bag and fly back to them. Her beautiful Emily, the replica of Robert, would be at the sophomore dance tonight. Annie would just about now be going back to Aunt Helen's house from a third-grade birthday party. Smart Annie, funny, secretive, sensitive, difficult Annie. Yes, she would fly home to them right now if she could. But Robert had the tickets and the money. She never did have any cash beyond the weekly allowance for the household. And anyway, she thought, remembering, how could I just walk in with this face and without their father?

The silence began to buzz in Lynn's ears. A sensation of fear as of some desperate, unexplainable menace came flooding. The walls closed in.

'I have to get out of here,' she said aloud.

Putting on her travel coat, she drew the collar up and wrapped a scarf around her head, drawing it like a peasant's babushka over her cheeks as far as it would go, which was not far enough. Luckily there were only two other people in the elevator during its long descent, a very young couple dressed for some gala event, and so tenderly engrossed with each other that they truly did not give a glance to Lynn's face. In the marble lobby people were either hurrying from cocktails to dinner or else lingering at the vitrines with their displays of glittering splendors, their jewels, leathers, satins, and furs.

Outdoors, cold spring air stung the burning bruise. At a drugstore she stopped to get something for it, a gauze bandage or some ointment, anything.

'I bumped into a door. Isn't that stupid?' she said. Then,

7

shocked at the sight of her swollen eye in the mirror behind the man's head, she added clumsily, 'And on top of that, I have this miserable allergy. My eyes –'

The man's own eyes, when he handed her a little package of allergy pills and a soothing ointment, reflected his disbelief and his pity. Overcome with shame at her own naïveté, she rushed away into the anonymity of the street.

Then, walking in the direction of the lake, she remembered vaguely from a previous visit to the city that there would be a green space there with walks and benches. It was really too cold to sit still, but nevertheless she sat down, tightened the coat around her, and gazed out to where the water met the sky. Couples strolled, walking their dogs and talking peaceably. It hurt so much to watch them that she could have wept, if she had not already been wept out.

The day had begun so well. The flight from home was a short one, so there had been time enough for a walk on Michigan Avenue before going back to the room to dress. Robert was a window-shopper. He loved dark, burnished wood in fine libraries, eighteenth-century English paintings of fields and farms, classic sculpture, and antique rugs, all quiet, dignified, expensive things. Often he stopped to admire a beautiful dress, too, like the one they had seen this afternoon, a peach silk ballgown scattered with seed-pearl buds.

'That would be perfect on you,' he had observed.

'Shall I wear it to the movies on Saturday night?' she had teased back.

'When I am a chief executive officer, there will be occasions for a dress like that,' he had replied, and added then, 'It suits you. Airy and delicate and soft, like you.'

It had begun so well . . . Their life together had begun so well . . .

*   *   *

'Why do they call you "Midge"?' he had asked her. He had never noticed her before that day. But then, he was the head of the department, while she only sat at a typist's desk. 'Why? On the list it says your name is Lynn Riemer.'

'I was always called that. Even at home. It's short for "midget." I guess it was because my sister's tall.'

'You're nowhere near being a midget.' He looked her up and down quite seriously. 'Five foot two, I'd estimate.'

It was his eyes that held her, the brilliant blue, darkening or lightening according to mood, that held every woman in the office, for that matter, and possibly, in a different way, the men too. The men had to have serious respect for authority; authority could praise and promote; authority could also discharge a man to creep home in defeat to his family. But the women's fear of Robert Ferguson was diluted with a tremulous, daring, sexual fervor. This fervor had to be secret. Each would have been embarrassed to admit to another, for fear of seeming ridiculous: Robert Ferguson was totally beyond their reach, and they all knew it, worlds apart from the men with whom they had grown up and whom they dated.

It was not only that with those vivacious eyes and his long, patrician bones he was extraordinarily handsome. It was an aura about him. He was absolutely confident. His diction was perfect, his clothes were perfect, and he demanded perfection of everyone around him. Lateness was not tolerated. Papers put on his desk for his signature had to be flawless. His initials had to be accurate: V. W. Robert Victor William Ferguson. His car must be kept in a quickly accessible place in a parking lot. Yet, for all of this, he was considerate and kind. When he was pleased, he was generous with a compliment. He remembered birthdays, making happy occasions in the office. When anyone was sick, he became earnestly involved. It was known that he volunteered at the men's ward at the hospital.

'He's an enigma,' Lynn had once remarked when

Robert was being discussed, and he often was discussed.

'I'm going to call you "Lynn" from now on,' he said that day, 'and tell everyone here to do the same.'

She had no idea why he should have paid enough attention to her to remark upon her name. It was silly. Yet she was sufficiently flustered by the happening to tell her sister Helen that she would not answer to 'Midge' anymore.

'Why? What's wrong with it?'

'I have a perfectly good name, and I'm not a midget. Even my boss says it's ridiculous.'

Helen had given her a look of amusement that she remembered clearly long afterward. Ever since her marriage and the birth of two babies, Helen had assumed a superior air of motherly protectiveness.

'Your boss? It seems to me you talk about him a good deal.'

'I do not.'

'Oh, yes, you do. You may not realize it, but you do. 'My boss has a stereo in his office. My boss treated us all to pizza for lunch. My boss got a big raise from the main office –'

It was true that he was more and more in Lynn's thoughts, that she watched without seeming to do so for his every arrival and departure. She had begun to have passionate fantasies. So Helen was probably right . . .

Then one day Robert asked her to go to dinner with him.

'You look as if you were floating on air,' Helen said.

'Well, I am. I thought, I still am thinking, Why me?'

'Why not you? You have more life and more energy than any six people put together. Why do you think boys all –'

'You don't understand. This man is different. He's distinguished. His face looks like the ones you see on statues or on those old coins in Dad's collection.'

'By the way, how old is he?'

'Twenty-seven.'

'And you're twenty. Twenty, going on fourteen. Filled with dreams.'

Lynn still kept the dress she had worn that night. Sentimental almost to a fault, she held on to everything, from her wedding dress and her children's christening gowns to the pressed flowers from the bouquet that Robert had sent after that first dinner, a splendid sheaf of white roses tied with pink ribbon.

'Tell me about yourself,' he had begun when they sat down with the candlelight between them.

She had responded lightly, 'There isn't much to tell.'

'There always is, in every life. Start from the beginning. Were you born here in the city?'

'No, in Iowa. In a farming town south of Des Moines. My mother died, and my father still lives there. My sister moved here when she was married, and I guess that's why, after graduation from high school, I came here too. There were no jobs at home anyway. This is my first one, and I hope I'm doing well.'

'I'm sure you are.'

'I wanted to see the city, to see things, and it's been fun. Having the apartment, going to the concerts –'

He nodded. 'A world-class orchestra. As fine as anything in New York.'

'I've never been there.'

'When I was at the Wharton School, I went often to the theater. It's only a short train ride from Philadelphia.'

Her tongue was loosening. The wine might be helping. 'I'd like to see the east. I'd like to see Europe, England, France, Rome.'

His eyes were shining and smiling at her. 'The places that you read about in *Portrait of a Lady* last week?'

She was astonished. 'How did you know?'

11

'Simple. I saw the book on your desk. Don't they call me "Hawkeye" in the office?'

She laughed and blushed. 'How on earth can you know that? Nobody ever says –'

'I've also got sharp ears.'

She struck out boldly. 'Is that why you invited me tonight? Is that what gave you the idea, that I read Henry James?'

'That had a little to do with it. I was curious. You must admit that the rest of them on the staff don't go much beyond movie magazines, do they?'

'They're my friends. I don't pay attention to things like that,' she said loyally. 'They're not important.'

'Don't think I'm a snob. I don't judge people by their knowledge of what's in books either. But you have to admit that it's pleasant to be with people who like the same things you like. Besides, you're beautiful. That must have had something to do with it, don't you think?'

'Thank you.'

'You don't believe you are beautiful, do you? Your eyes say that you're doubtful. I'll tell you. You're a porcelain doll. Your skin is white as milk.'

She parried, 'Is it good to look like a porcelain doll?'

'I think so. I meant it as a compliment.'

This dialogue was certainly different from any she had ever had before, with Bill or anyone else. And she was not sure what she ought to say next.

'Well, go on with your story about yourself. You've only just begun.'

'There isn't much more. Dad couldn't afford college, so I went to a very good secretarial school that had courses in English lit. I'd always loved to read, and it's there that I learned what to read. So I read and I cook. That's my second hobby. Maybe it's boasting, but the fact is, I'm a very good cook. And that's all, I guess. Now it's your turn.'

'Okay. Born and grew up in Pittsburgh. No brothers or sisters, which made for a bit of lonesomeness. I had a good home, though. My parents were especially loving. They spoiled me a little, I think. In their way they were unusual people. My mother played the piano and taught me to play. I'm not all that good, but I play because it makes me think of her. My father was a learned man and very quiet and kindly, with an old-fashioned sort of dignity. His business took him around the world. Every summer they went to Salzburg for the music festival.' He paused. 'They were killed in an auto accident the summer I was graduated from college.'

She felt a stab of horror. 'How awful for you! It's bad enough when someone has a heart attack, as my mother did. But a car accident's so – so unnecessary, so wrong!'

'Yes. Well, life goes on.' His face sank into sadness, the mouth and eyes gone still.

At the back of the room, just then the pianist was singing, 'A tale told by a stranger, by a new love, on a dark blue evening in a rose-white May.'

The poignant words of the forties, so long ago, coming at this moment of Robert's revelations, filled her chest with a longing almost painful, a confusion of sadness and thrilling joy. Tears came to her eyes.

When he saw them, he touched her hand. 'Gentle girl . . . But enough of this. Come, we'll be late for the movie.'

She went home and lay awake half the night. I want to live with him for the rest of my life, she thought. He is the one. But I'm an idiot. We had an evening together, that's all. He won't seriously want me. How can he? I'm not nearly good enough for him. He won't want me.

He had wanted her, though, wanted her badly. In the office they hid their intense emotion; passing each other, their eyes turned away. Joyously, she kept their secret. She alone came to know the other side of this man whom others found imperious, the part of him that was so very tender. She alone knew about the high tragedy of his parents' deaths, and about his lesser sorrows too.

He confided. 'I've been married.'

She felt a rush of disappointment, a pang of jealousy.

'We met at college and were married in commencement week. Looking back, I wonder how it ever happened. She was very beautiful and very rich, but spoiled and irresponsible, too, so we were completely unsuited to each other. Querida – her mother was Spanish – was 'artistic'. She did watercolors. I don't mean to disparage her, but she was just a dabbler. She took a job in a small gallery and on her day off was a volunteer docent at the museum. Anything to get out of the house. She hated the house. The place was a mess, no meals, the laundry not even sent out half the time, nothing done. I could never bring anybody home from the office, never solidify the contacts one needs to make it in the business world.' He shrugged. 'What can I say except that hers was an entirely different way of life from what I was used to? We grated on each other's nerves, and so of course we argued almost daily. She disliked my friends, and I wasn't fond of hers, I can tell you that.' He smiled ruefully. 'We would have parted even sooner if it hadn't been for the child. Jeremy. He's six now.'

'What happened to him?'

'I haven't seen him since he was a year old. But I support him, although he wouldn't be in want if I didn't. Querida went back to live with her parents, so he's growing up in a mansion. She didn't want joint custody, said it was too confusing for a child, and I didn't want to fight her decision.'

'Still, how awful for you not to see him! Or for him not to know you.'

Robert sighed. 'Yes. Yes, it is. But he can't remember me, so for him at his age I suppose it's as if I had died. I hope so much, though, that he'll want to see me when

14

he's old enough to understand.' And he sighed again.

'I'm sure he will,' Lynn said, in her pity.

'Well, he'll know how to find me. His money goes into the bank every month. So that's the end of my little story.'

'It's a sad story.'

'Yes, but it could be worse, Lynn. It seems like something that happened a lifetime ago,' he said earnestly. 'I've never talked about it to anyone before this. It's too private. And I'm a very private person, as you know by now.'

Inevitably, the affair of Robert and Lynn had to come to notice. In the second month she took him to Helen's house. Helen's husband, Darwin, was a good-natured man, round featured with an extra chin. Beside him Robert sparkled with his white collar glistening above his dark blue blazer. Darwin looked rumpled, as if he had been napping in his clothes. In a nice way – or perhaps not such a nice way? – Lynn was proud to let Helen see the contrast between the two, proud and a little ashamed of being proud.

The next day Helen said, 'Of course you want to know what I thought of your new man. I'm going to tell you right out flat: I didn't like him much.'

Lynn screamed into the telephone. 'What?'

'I'm always honest with you, Lynn. I know I can be too blunt – but he's not your type. He can be sarcastic, I notice, and I have a hunch he's a snob. He thinks he's better than other people.'

Lynn was furious. 'Have you anything else nice to say about a man you don't even know? Any more hunches?'

'He has a critical, sharp tongue.'

'I've never noticed it.'

'I thought it was in poor taste, even cruel of him, to talk about that girl in the office and her long nails. "Filthy long nails. Can you imagine the bacteria snuggled under

15

them?" It was belittling to name her, and Darwin thought so too.'

'Oh, dear! I am so sorry you and Darwin don't approve. Really sorry.'

'Don't be angry at me, Lynn. Who wishes you more joy in life than I do? Dad and I. I just don't want you to make a mistake. I see that you're infatuated. It's written all over you.'

'I'm not infatuated.'

'I feel in my bones that he's not right for you.'

'Does it possibly occur to your bones that I might not be right for him? Robert's brilliant. He's head of computer marketing for the whole region. I hear the salesmen talking –' Indignation made Lynn almost breathless. 'An international company –'

'Is it that that impresses you? Listen, Lynn. You never know about big corporations. You're on top today and out tomorrow. It's better to be your own boss, even in a small way, instead of at other people's mercy.'

Helen's husband had a little plumbing business with five employees.

'Are you accusing me of being ambitious? Me? You think that's what I see in Robert?'

'No, no, I didn't mean that at all. You're one of the least materialistic people. I didn't express myself well. I meant that perhaps you felt – a kind of admiration, hero worship, just because he is so successful and – I only meant, don't get too serious so fast.'

'Do you know what I think? I think you're an idiot,' Lynn said before she hung up.

But it was not in her nature to hold a grudge very long. Helen was transparent. She was undoubtedly not even aware of it, and would deny it, but her motive was envy, even though she lived happily with Darwin. Pure and simple envy. And Lynn forgave her.

Almost three months passed before they went to bed

together; Lynn had to wait for her roommates to go out of town.

On the weekend this finally happened, the two women had scarcely reached the airport before she had a lavish dinner prepared, and he arrived with flowers, record albums, and champagne. In the first moment they stood staring at each other as if this sudden marvelous freedom had transfixed them; in the next moment everything happened, everything moved. The flowers in their green tissue paper were flung onto the table, Robert's overcoat was flung over a kitchen chair, and Lynn was lifted into his arms.

Quickly, deftly, in the dim light of the wintry day, he removed her clothes, the sweater and the white blouse with the lace collar, the plaid skirt and the underthings. Her heart was speeding. She could hear its beat.

'I never – this is the first time, Robert.'

'I'll be very gentle,' he murmured.

And he was. Persistent, warm, and gentle, he spoke soft, endearing words while he held her.

'So sweet ... So beautiful ... I love you so.'

Whatever little fear there had been now dissolved, and she gave herself into total passionate trust.

Much later when they released each other, Lynn began to laugh. 'I was just thinking, it's a good thing I hadn't yet turned the oven on when you arrived. We'd be having cinders for dinner.'

Over her expert ratatouille and *tarte normande* they talked about themselves.

'Twenty-year-old virgins are becoming very rare these days,' said Robert.

'I'm glad I waited.' She was still too shy to say: It makes me belong all the more to you. Because, would this last? She trusted, and yet there were no guarantees. Nothing had been said. But I shall die if he leaves me, she thought.

They went back to bed. This time there was no need

17

to be as gentle. She worshiped his strength. For a man so slender he was exceedingly strong. And, surprisingly, she found herself responding with a strength and a desire equal to his. They slept, until long before dawn she felt him return to her and, with willing arms, received him. Sleeping again past dawn, they awoke to see that a heavy snowfall was darkening the world.

'Let's stay indoors the whole day,' he whispered. 'Indoors, in bed.'

All through Saturday and Sunday they knew no surfeit.

'I'm obsessed with you,' Robert said. 'You are the most erotic woman – I've never known anything like you. And you look so innocent in your sweaters and skirts. A man would never guess.'

On Sunday evening Lynn looked at the clock. 'Robert, their plane gets in at ten. I'm afraid you have to leave in a hurry.'

He groaned. 'When can we do this again?'

'I don't know,' she said mournfully.

'This is no way to live!' he almost shouted. 'I hate a hole-and-corner business, skulking in highway motels. And I don't want "living together" either. We need to be permanent. Lynn, you're going to marry me.'

They set the wedding for June, taking advantage of Robert's vacation to have a honeymoon in Mexico.

'Of course, you'll have to quit your job,' he told her. 'We can't be in the same office.'

'I'll find another one easily.'

'Not yet. You'll need time to furnish an apartment. It should be done carefully. Buy things of quality that will last.'

Helen generously offered their house for the reception. 'You can't very well have it at Dad's, since he's only got three rooms now,' she said. 'With luck, if the weather's right, we can have the whole thing in our yard. Darwin has plans for a perennial border, and you know his green thumb. It should be beautiful.'

To give her fullest credit Helen did not speak one disparaging word from the moment the engagement was announced. She kissed Lynn, admired the ring, which was a handsome one, and wished the couple every happiness.

'Every happiness,' she said now as a chill blew in over Lake Michigan, loudly enough, apparently, for the couple with the poodles, who had circled back, to turn and stare. An eccentric woman, huddled there talking to herself, that's what she was. An object to be stared at. Ah, well, there was no stopping memory once it got started back and back . . .

Robert endeared himself to everyone during that expectant enchanted spring before the wedding. Helen's little boys adored him; he bought small bats, taught them to pitch, took them to ball games, and showed them how to wrestle. While the ice held, they all went skating, and when the days warmed, had picnics in the country.

In Helen's kitchen Lynn cooked superb little dinners, quiches, cassoulets, and soufflés out of Julia Child's new book.

'You put me to shame,' Helen said.

After dinner Robert would sit at the old upright piano and play whatever was called out to him: jazz, show tunes, or a Chopin waltz.

At his suggestion the two couples went to hear the St Louis symphony. Darwin had never gone before and was surprised to find that he liked it.

'Once you acquire the taste, you'll never be without music,' Robert told him. 'For me it's another kind of food. We've got to get season tickets next year, Lynn.'

Naively, kindly, Darwin praised Robert. 'It beats me, Lynn, how he *knows* so much. I can just about make it through the daily paper. And he sure knows how to get fun out of life, too, and knows how to fit in with people.'

Her father approved. 'I like him,' he said after Lynn and Robert's weekend visit. 'It'll be good to have a new son. And good for him to have a family. Hard on a young fellow to lose his parents like that. What kind of people were they? Do you know anything about them?'

'What is there to find out? They're dead,' Lynn answered, feeling impatient.

'That's all he has, the old aunt back in Pittsburgh?'

'And an uncle in Vancouver.'

'Practically alone in the world,' Dad said with sympathy.

In the hardware store, being introduced as customers came in, most of them from the farms, Robert knew how to meet their jovial simplicity in kind. She saw that they approved of him, as did her father.

'I like him, Midge,' Dad kept saying. 'You've got yourself a man, not like the kids who used to hang around you. No offense meant. They were all good boys, but wet behind the ears. This one's a man. What I like is, he hasn't let the education or the job go to his head. I'll be glad to dance at your wedding.'

A woman remembers every detail of her wedding day. She remembered the long ride, the organ singing, and the faces turned to watch her marching toward the altar.

Her hand had trembled on her father's arm. *Easy now*, he said, feeling the trembling hand. *There's Robert waiting for you. There's nothing to fear.* And then it was Robert who took her hand, while they stood together listening to the gentle, serious admonitions: *Be patient and loving with each other.*

The rest of that day was jollity, music, dancing, kissing, teasing, and ribald, friendly jokes. The office crowd came, of course, and friends from the hometown came. Darwin's and Helen's friends were all there and Robert had invited the friends he had made in St Louis; he had been away from Pittsburgh too long to expect people he scarcely knew anymore to come to his wedding.

One relative came, Aunt Jean from Pittsburgh, the uncle in Vancouver not being well enough to travel. It was curious, Lynn reflected now, that such a pleasant, rather self-effacing little woman, with graying curls and a conventional print dress, should have been the cause of one out of the two false notes in the wedding.

It was not her fault. It was Robert's. They were at the family table after the ceremony when Aunt Jean remarked, 'Someday I'll have to get at my pile of photographs, label them, and bring them when I come to visit you. There are some of Robert that you just must have, Lynn. You'd never believe it, but his hair –'

'For once, Aunt Jean,' Robert interrupted, 'will you spare us a description of the blond curls I had when I was a year old? Really, nobody cares.'

Chastised, she said nothing more, so that Lynn, with a gentle look of reproach in Robert's direction, said gaily, 'I care, Aunt Jean. I want to hear anything you can tell me about Robert and all the family, father, mother, grandparents, cousins –'

'It's a small family,' Jean said. 'We don't have any cousins at all, on either side.'

Then Dad, who had heard only this last remark, cried out, 'No cousins? Heck, we'll be glad to lend you some. I've got a dozen on my side alone, in Iowa, Missouri, even two in California.' And in his friendly way he inquired whether Jean was related to Robert's mother or his father.

'His mother was my sister.'

'He got his music from her, didn't he?' Lynn said. 'And his father must have been remarkable, from what Robert tells me.'

'Indeed.'

21

'It was such a tragedy, the way they died.'

'Yes. Yes, it was.'

Dad remarked, 'It must have been lonesome when Robert was a kid. Christmas with just his parents and you.'

'Well, we did our best,' said Jean, 'and he grew up, and here he is.' She gave Robert a fond smile.

'Yes, here we all are, and let's look forward. Reminiscences are for the old,' Robert responded, after which he patted his aunt's hand.

He was making amends for having been sharp toward her. But the mild old woman annoyed him. And there seemed to be no reason why she should.

On a day like this, at a moment of lonely desperation, Lynn thought now, you remember these false notes.

There had been dancing on the deck that Darwin had built with his own hands. In the yard his perennial border was rich with pinks and reds; peonies and phlox, tiger lilies and oriental poppies, fired the blue dusk. Robert was at the railing, looking down at them.

'Isn't it just lovely what Darwin's done with this house?' Lynn asked.

He smiled – she remembered the smile – and said, 'It's all right, I guess, but it's really a dump. I'll give you so much better. You'll see.'

He meant it well, but just as it had hurt to hear him reprimand his aunt, it hurt to hear him scoff at Darwin's garden, at Helen's little house. Small things to have remembered for so long...

Each night as they traveled through Mexico, when the door closed on their room, Robert said again, 'Isn't it wonderful? Not having to scrounge around for a place to go? Here we are, forever and ever.'

Yes, it was wonderful, all of it. The sunny days when, in sneakers and broad straw hats, they climbed Mayan ruins in the Yucatán, when they drank tequilas on the

22

beach, or drove through stony mountain villages, or dined most elegantly in Mexico City.

And there were fourteen nights of passion and love. 'Happy?' Robert would inquire in the morning.

'Oh, darling! How can you even ask?'

'You know,' he told her one day, 'your father's a fine old soul. Guess what he said to me when we were leaving for the airport? "Be good to my girl," he said.'

She laughed. 'That's a sweet, old-fashioned thing to say.'

'It's all right. I knew what he meant. And I will be good to you.'

'We'll be good to each other. We're on top of the world, you and I.'

On the very last day they went shopping in Acapulco. Robert saw something in the window of a men's shop, while at the same time Lynn saw something in the window of another shop just down the street.

'You do your errand while I do mine, and I'll meet you down there,' he said.

So they separated. Since she was quickly finished, she walked back up the street to meet him. When some minutes had passed and he had not appeared, she went into the men's shop and learned that he had left a while ago. Puzzled, she walked back. By now a rush of tourists just discharged from a cruise ship filled the sidewalks and spilled out into the traffic on the street. It was impossible to see through the jostling mass. She began to feel the start of alarm. But that was absurd, and fighting it down, she reasoned: He has to be here. Perhaps on the other side of the street. Or down that alley, out of the crowd. Right now he's looking for me. Or maybe, not finding what he wanted, he had gone to the next block.

Alarm returned. When an hour had passed, she decided that her search was making no sense. What made sense, she reasoned, was to go back to the hotel where

23

he had probably also gone and where he would be waiting for her.

When her taxi drew up to the entrance, he was indeed
waiting. And she laughed with relief.

'Isn't this the silliest thing? I looked all over for you.'

'Silly?' he replied very coldly. 'I would hardly call it
that. Come upstairs. I want to talk to you.'

His unexpected anger dismayed her. And wanting to
soothe, she replied lightly, 'We must have been walking
in circles, looking for each other. A couple of idiots, we
are.'

'Speak for yourself.' He slammed the door of their
room. 'I was about to go to the front desk and have them
call the police when you arrived.'

'Police! Whatever for? I'm glad you didn't.'

'I told you to wait for me in front of that store, and
you didn't do it.'

Now, resenting his tone, she countered, 'I walked up
to meet you. What's wrong with that?'

'I should think the result would tell you what's wrong
with it. Disorderly habits, and this is the result. Saying
one thing and doing something else.'

She said angrily, 'Don't lecture me, Robert. Don't make
such a big deal out of this.'

He was staring at her. And at that moment she realized
he was furious. Not angry, but furious.

'I don't believe it!' she cried when he seized her. His
hands dug into the flesh of her upper arms and ground
it against the bones. In his fury he shook her.

'Let go!' she screamed. 'You're hurting me! Let go of
my arms!'

His hands pressed deeper; the pain was shocking. Then
he flung her onto the bed, where she lay sobbing.

'You hurt me ... You hurt me.'

As quickly as it had come, his anger went. He picked
her up and held her.

'I'm sorry. Oh, I'm sorry. I didn't mean to. But I was terrified, Lynn. You could have been kidnapped – yes, in broad daylight – dragged down an alley, whisked into a car, raped, God knows what. This country is full of thugs.' He kissed her tears. 'I was beside myself. Don't you understand?'

He kept kissing her cheeks, her forehead, her hands, and when at last she turned to him, her lips.

'If anything were to happen to you, I wouldn't want to live. I was so frightened. I love you so.'

She put her arms around his neck. 'All right. All right, darling. Robert, forget it, it's over. We misunderstood each other. It's nothing. Nothing.'

And all was as it had been, as glorious as ever except for the ugly dark blue blotches on her arms.

Two days later they were home, visiting her father. It was hot, and forgetting her raw bruises, she put on a sundress.

'What the dickens are those marks?' Dad asked at once. They were alone in the house.

'Oh, those? I don't know. I don't remember how I got them.'

Dad removed his glasses and came closer. 'Identical, symmetrical bruises on both arms. Somebody did that to you with strong, angry hands. Who was it, Lynn?'

She did not answer.

'Was it Robert? Tell me, Lynn, or I'll ask him myself.'

'No. No. Oh, please! It's nothing. He didn't mean it, it's just that he was so scared.' The story spilled out. 'It was my fault, really it was. He was terrified that something had happened to me. He had told me to wait on the street, and I wandered around the corner and lost my way. My sense of direction –'

'Has nothing to do with these marks. Don't you think I was ever upset with your mother from time to time? You can't be married without getting mad at each other.

But I never laid a hand on her. It isn't civilized. No, damn it, it's not. I want to have a little talk with Robert – nothing nasty, just a sensible little talk.'

'No, Dad. You can't. Don't do this to me. Robert is my husband, and I love him. We love each other. Don't make a big thing out of this.'

'It is a big thing to me.'

'It's not, and you can't come between us. You mustn't.'

Her father sighed. 'It was easier when people married somebody from the same town. You could have a pretty fair idea of what you were getting.'

'Dad, we can't go back to George Washington.'

He sighed again. 'I feel,' he said, 'I don't feel – the same about things.'

'Meaning that you don't feel the same about Robert.'

Now it was he who did not answer. And that exasperated her. The thing was being carried much too far. She saw a crisis looming, one that might change, might color, all their future. So she made herself speak patiently and quietly.

'Dad, this is foolish. Don't worry about me. You're making a big deal out of something that happened once. All right, it shouldn't have, but it did. I want you to put it completely out of your mind, because I have. Okay?' She put her hand on his shoulder. 'Okay? Promise?'

He turned, giving her his familiar, reassuring smile. 'Well, well, since you want me to, I'll promise. We'll just leave it at that. Since you want me to, Midge.'

It was never mentioned again. But neither Helen nor Dad ever had reason to raise any questions about the marriage of Robert and Lynn. They were to any beholder a successful, beautiful pair.

Emily was born eleven months after the wedding. They had scarcely equipped an apartment before Robert bought a house, a ranch house not far from Helen's but twice the size.

26

'We'll have more children, so we might as well do it now as later,' he said.

They went together to furnish the house. Whatever he liked, he bought, and Lynn had only to admire a chair or a lamp, and before she had even glanced at the price, he bought it. In the beginning she worried that money was flowing out too fast. But she saw Robert was earning bonuses as business expanded. And besides, he kept telling her not to worry. Finances were his concern. She never had cash. She charged things and he paid the bills without complaint.

'I wouldn't like that,' Helen said once.

'Why should I mind?' Lynn responded, glancing around the pretty nursery where the pretty baby was waking up from a nap. 'I have everything. This most of all.' And she picked up her daughter, the daughter who already had Robert's bones and black silk hair and dark blue eyes.

Because Robert had been so aware of names, she had chosen the child's name with subtle care. 'Names have colors,' she told him. ' "Emily" is blue. When I say it with my eyes closed, I see a very high October sky without a cloud.'

Caroline was eighteen months later. 'Caroline' was a gold so light that it was almost silver.

And memory, a reel of pictures in reverse, sped on . . .

'What a fabulous house!' Lynn exclaimed.

The house belonged to her neighbor's parents, who were giving the birthday party for their granddaughter, aged five. The terrace was bordered by a lawn, the lawn extended to a distant meadow, and the meadow attached to a pond, which was barely visible at the foot of the slope.

'What a wonderful day for a party!' she exclaimed again.

And it was a wonderful summer day, a cool one, with everything in bloom and a breeze rustling through the

27

oaks. Under these oaks the tables were set for lunch, the children's table dressed in crepe paper with a balloon tied to every chair. It looked, she thought, like a scene in one of those British films where women, wearing silk or white linen, moved against a background of ivy-covered walls. She, whose daily garb was either shorts or jeans, wore yellow silk, and her girls wore pink sister dresses and white Mary Janes.

'They look almost like twins,' one of the women remarked. 'Caroline's tall for her age, isn't she?'

'We sometimes think she's three going on ten. She's strong and fast and into everything,' Lynn said comfortably.

There was probably nothing more satisfying to a parent than knowing that her children were admired. No book, no symphony, no work of art, she was certain, could rival the joy, the pride, and, she reminded herself, the gratitude that came from these creations, these two bright, sweet, healthy little girls.

Gratitude grew when she thought of two friends who were unable to have a child. And all through the lunch and the pleasant gossip she was aware, deep inside, of thankfulness. Life was good.

After lunch a clown arrived to entertain the children, who sat in a circle on the grass. For a little while the mothers watched him, but since the children were absorbed and fascinated, they went back to their tables in the shade.

'Talk about attention span,' someone said. 'He's kept them amused for more than half an hour.'

It was just about time for the party to break up. Emily came trotting to Lynn with a bag full of favors and a balloon.

'Where's Caroline?' asked Lynn.

'I don't know,' said Emily.

'But you were sitting together.'

'I know,' said Emily.

'Well, where can she be?' asked Lynn, feeling a faint rise of alarm and in the same instant driving it down, because of course there could be no reason for alarm here in this place.

'She must have gone to the bathroom.'

So they looked in the downstairs bathroom and all through the house; they searched the bushes where possibly she might be hiding, to tease them. Alarm turned to panic. Kidnappers? But how could anybody have come among all these people without being seen? They searched the fields, treading through the long grass. Then they thought, although no one wanted to voice the thought, that perhaps, being an adventurous little girl, Caroline had gone as far as the pond.

And there she lay facedown, in her ruffled pink dress. Quite near the shore she lay in water so shallow that she could have stood up and waded back.

One of the women there was a Red Cross lifesaver. Laying Caroline on the grass, she went to work while Lynn knelt, staring at her child, not believing ... no, no it was not possible!

People drew the children away from the sight. Someone had called for an ambulance; someone else had called the doctor in the next house. There was a bustle and hurry and yet it was silent; you could almost hear the hush and a following long, collective sigh.

Men came, two young ones wearing white coats. Lynn staggered to her feet, grasped a white sleeve, and begged, 'Tell me! Tell me!'

For answer he put a gentle arm around her shoulders. And so she knew. Hearing the women cry, she knew. And yet, 'It isn't possible,' she said. 'No. I don't believe it. No.'

She looked around at all the faces, all of them shocked and pitying. And she screamed, screamed at the fair sky, the waving grass, the summer world. Screamed and screamed. Then people took her home.

She was wild with despair and denial. She *knew*, and yet she would not let herself know. They had to hold her down and sedate her.

When she woke up, she was in her living room. The house was crowded. It seemed as if a thousand voices were speaking; doors were opening and closing; the telephone kept ringing and being answered, only to ring again.

Helen said, 'Leave her alone, Robert. She's not even awake.'

Robert said, 'How can she have been so stupid, so careless? She will never forgive herself for this.'

She could not decide whether or not to wake up. In one way the dream was unbearable, so perhaps it would be better to open her eyes and be rid of it; but on the other hand perhaps it was not a dream, in which case it would be better to sink into a sleep so deep that she would know nothing.

Still she heard Robert's sobs, repeating, 'She will never forgive herself.'

There came another voice, belonging to someone who was holding her wrist: 'Quiet, please. I'm taking her pulse,' it said sharply, and she recognized Bill White, their family doctor.

'You'd better stop this talk about forgiveness,' said Bill White. 'First of all it's hogwash. This could have happened just as easily if you had been there, Robert. Secondly, you'd better stop it if you don't want to have a very sick woman here for the rest of her life. Don't you think she will torture herself enough as it is?'

And so she had, and so she did still, here on this bench beside Lake Michigan. The images were imprinted on her brain. Caroline laughing at the clown, Caroline – how many minutes later – dead in the water. Emily's little face puckered in tears and terror. She herself surrounded by kind arms and soft words at the heartbreaking funeral.

'I don't know why my aunt had to come,' Robert complained. 'Who sent for her, anyway?'

'Helen got her number out of my book. She's your family, she's all you have, and she belongs here.'

It was strange that he never wanted Jean. She annoyed him, he said. Well, perhaps. Perhaps her very kindness irritated him. Men were like that sometimes. But Jean had been so helpful during those first awful days, comforting Emily in her warm arms and clearing Caroline's room, which neither Lynn nor Robert could have borne to enter.

Somehow they had endured.

'If a marriage can survive this,' people declared, 'it can survive anything. Imagine the guilt!'

Yes, imagine it if you can, Lynn thought. But Robert had taken Bill White's words to heart. Through many cruel nights he had held her close. And for a long time they had moved softly about the house, speaking in whispers; she had walked on tiptoes until he had gently called her attention to what she was doing. It was he who had saved her sanity. She must remind herself of that whenever things went wrong . . .

Yet how could a man as forgiving as he had been, so caring of his family, give way to such dreadful rages? Like this one tonight, like all the other sporadic outbursts through the years? To live with Robert was to dwell in sunlight for months and months; then suddenly a flashing storm would turn everything into darkness. And as quickly as it had come the storm would pass, leaving a memory growing fainter in the distance, along with the hope that this time had been the last.

The children never knew, nor must they ever know. For how could she explain to them the thing that she did not herself understand?

Annie especially, Annie so young and vulnerable, must

31

never know! She had been different and difficult from the start. A red baby, dark, raging, squalling red, she was to some extent like that still, a child of moods who could be childishly sweet or curiously adult; one felt at such times that she was seeing right through one's slightest evasion or excuse. Yet she did rather poorly at school. She was overweight and clumsy at sports, although Robert, who did everything so well, tried hard to teach her. She was a secret disappointment to him, Lynn knew. A child of his, although not yet nine, to show not the smallest indication of doing anything well at all!

The full wealth of his love went to Emily, so like himself, tenacious, confident, competent in everything from mathematics to tennis. Beside all that, at fifteen she was already charming the boys. Life would be easy for Emily.

My children ... Oh, God, if it weren't for them, Lynn cried to herself, I wouldn't go home at all. I'd get on a plane and fly and fly – anywhere, to Australia and beyond. But that was stupid. Stupid to dwell on the impossible. And if she had packed the suit none of this would have happened. It was her own fault ...

It was growing colder. A sharper wind blew in suddenly from the lake. Rushing through the trees, it brought the piercing scent of northern spring. Thrusting her hands more deeply into her pockets, Lynn drew the coat tighter against the chill. Her cheek throbbed.

She was a fool to sit here shivering, waiting to be mugged. But she was too sunken in spirit to move or to care. If only there were another woman to hear her woe tonight! Helen, or Josie, wise, kind Josie, the best friend either Helen or she had ever had. They called themselves the three musketeers.

'We've transferred a new man to be my assistant for marketing,' Robert had announced one day more than seven years ago. 'Bruce Lehman from Milwaukee. Jewish and very pleasant, but I'm not wildly enthusiastic. He

32

strikes me as kind of a lightweight. No force. It's hard to describe, but I recognize it when I see it in a man. You'd like him, though. He's well read and collects antiques. His wife's a social worker. No children. You'll have to call and ask them over to the house. It's only right.'

That was the start of their friendship. If I could only talk to her now, thought Lynn. Yet when the moment came, I probably wouldn't tell the truth. Josie would analyze, and I would shrivel under her clinical analysis.

As for confiding this to Helen, that's impossible. She warned me against Robert once long, long ago, and I will not go whimpering to her or anyone. I will handle this myself, although God knows how.

She stiffened. Her heart pounded. Out of the violet shadows beyond the lamplight a slatternly woman, drunken or drugged, came shuffling toward her and stopped.

'Sitting alone in the dark? And you've got a black eye,' she said, peering closer. When she touched Lynn's arm, Lynn, shrinking, looked into an old, sad, brutal face.

'I suppose you ran into a door. A door with fists.' The woman laughed and sat down on the bench. 'You'll have to think of a better one than that, my dear.'

Lynn got up and ran to the avenue, where traffic still streamed. The woman had given her such a fright that, in spite of the cold, she was sweating. There was no choice but to go back to the hotel. When the elevator stopped at her floor, she felt an impulse to turn about and go down again. Yet she could not very well sleep on the street. And maybe Robert was so angry that he would not even be in the room. She put the key in the lock and opened the door.

Fully dressed, he was sitting on the bed with his face in his hands. When he saw her he jumped up, and she saw that he was frantic.

'I looked for you everywhere. It's midnight,' he cried.

'Long past midnight. In God's name, where were you? I looked for you all through the hotel, up and down the streets, everywhere. I thought – I don't know what I thought.' His face was haggard, and his hoarse voice shook.

'What's the difference where I was?'

'I didn't know what you might have done. I was terrified.'

'There's no need to be. I'm all right.' In one piece, anyway, she thought.

When she took the scarf off and moved into the full glare of lamplight, Robert looked away. He got up and stood at the window, staring out into the darkness. She watched his stooped shoulders and felt shame for him, for herself, and for the entity known as Mr and Mrs Robert Ferguson, respectable and respected parents and citizens.

Presently, still with his back turned to her, he spoke. 'I have a quick temper. Sometimes I overreact. But I've never really hurt you, have I? Other than a slap now and then? And how often have I done that?'

Often enough. Yet not all that often. But the sting of humiliation far outlasted the momentary physical sting. The bruise of humiliation far outlasted the bruise on the upper arms where fingers had gripped and shaken. And a deep sigh came out of her very heart.

'When did it happen last?' he asked, as if he were pleading. 'I don't think you can even remember, it was so long ago.'

'Yes, yes I can. It was last Thanksgiving week, when Emily didn't get home till two A.M. and you were in a rage. And I thought, after we talked it over and you were so sorry, that it was to be really the last time, that we were finished with all that.'

'I meant it to be. I did,' he replied, still in the pleading tone. 'But we don't live in a perfect world. Things happen that shouldn't happen.'

34

'But why, Robert? Why?'

'I don't know. I hate myself afterward, every time.'

'Won't you go and talk to someone? Get some help. Find out why.'

'I don't need it. I'll pull myself up by my own boot-straps.' When she was silent before this familiar reply, he continued, 'Tell the truth, Lynn. You know I'm a loving, good husband to you all the rest of the time, and a good father too. You know I am.' He turned to her then, pleading, 'Don't you?'

She was silent.

'I did wrong tonight, even though some of it was an accident. But I told you how awfully important it was. I could only think of what it could mean to us. New York with a fifty-percent raise, maybe. And after that, who knows?' His hands were clenched around the wooden rail of the chair's back as though he would break it. The pleading continued. 'It's hard, Lynn, a struggle every day. I don't always tell you, I don't want to burden you, but it's a dog-eat-dog world. That's why that woman steered you wrong about the suit. People do things like that. You can't imagine it because you're so honest, so decent, but believe me, it's true. You have to be alert every minute of your life. There's never a minute that I'm not thinking of us, you and me and the girls. We're one, a tight little unit in an indifferent world. In the last analysis we're the only ones who really care about each other.'

At his urging she was slipping inch by inch back into reality, and she knew it. Children, family, house. And the man standing here to whom all these ties connected her. Impulsive thoughts of airplanes flying to the ends of the earth, of floating free and new, were not reality . . . Home, children, friends, job, school, home, children –

A sudden thought interrupted this litany. 'What did you tell Bruce?'

'What I told everybody, that the bag with my dinner jacket was lost.'

She heard him making an easy joke of it. *My suit may be on a plane to the Fiji Islands, or more likely, it's still in St Louis.* He was laughing, making everyone else laugh with him.

'That's not what I meant. What did you say about me?'

'Just said you weren't feeling well. I was vague about it.'

'Yes, I daresay you would have to be,' she said bitterly.

'Lynn, Lynn, can't we wipe the slate clean? I promise, promise, that I will guard my temper and never, never, so help me, God –' His voice broke.

Exhausted, she sat down on the bed. Let the night be over fast, she prayed. Let morning come, let's get out of this hateful room.

He sat down next to her. 'I stopped at a drugstore and got some stuff,' he said with a bottle of medicine in hand.

'I don't want it.'

'Please let me.'

She was too tired to struggle. He had taken a first-aid course and knew how to touch her cheek with care. Softly, softly, his fingers bathed her temples with coolness.

'Doesn't that feel better?'

Unwilling to give him satisfaction, she conceded only, 'It's all right.'

Relaxed against the pillows, she saw through half-closed eyes that he had unpacked her overnight bag and, meticulous as always, had hung up her robe and night-gown in the closet.

'Your poor, darling, lovely face. I wish you would hit me. Make a fist and let me have it.'

'What good would that do?'

'Maybe you'd feel better.'

'I don't need to get even. That's not me, Robert.'

36

'I know. I know it isn't.' He closed the bottle. 'There, that's enough. There won't be any mark, I can tell. That damn door had a mighty sharp edge, though. The management ought to be told. It's so easy to trip there.'

It was true. She had tripped. But would she have if his hand had not threatened? It was hard to be accurate in describing an accident. The event flashes past in seconds and the recollection is confused.

She sighed and mourned, 'I'm so tired. I don't think I've ever been so tired.'

'Turn over and let me undo your dress. I'll rub your back.'

Anger still boiled in her chest, a sorrowful, humiliated anger. Yet at the same time, a subtle, physical relief was beginning to wear it down. Robert's persisting hands, slowly, ever so slowly and firmly, were easing the tension in her neck and between her shoulder blades. Her eyes closed. As if hypnotized, she floated.

How intimately he knew her body! It was as if he knew it as well as she knew it, as if he knew it as well as he knew his own, as if they were one body. One . . .

Minutes passed, whether a few or many or even half an hour, she could not have said. But as finally he turned her over, she felt no resistance. Half waking, half dreaming, her willing arms accepted.

When she awoke, he was already dressed.

'I've been up for an hour. It's a bright, beautiful day. I've been watching boats far out on the lake. Would you like to take a walk down there? We can always get a later flight home.'

She saw that he was testing her mood.

'Whatever you want. I don't mind either way.'

It was not important. She was testing her own mood, which was important. Last night the darkness had been a horror down there near the lake. But those were morbid, useless thoughts now. And something she had read only a short time ago now crossed her mind: A majority of Americans, even in these days, still see nothing so terrible about a husband's occasional blow. Surely this was a curious thing to be remembering now. Perhaps it was a lesson for her. What do you want of life, Lynn? She might as well ask. Perfection? And she admonished herself: Grow up. Be realistic. Look forward, not back.

Besides, you love him . . .

He sat down on the bed. He smoothed her hair. 'I know you must be thinking you look awful, but you don't, take my word for it.'

Gingerly, she felt her cheekbone. It did seem as though the swelling had diminished.

'Go put on some makeup. I'll order room service for breakfast. You must be starved.'

'I had a sandwich yesterday at lunch.'

'A big breakfast, then. Bacon, eggs, the works.'

When she came out of the bathroom, he was moving the table on which the breakfast had been laid. 'These waiters never do it just right. You'd think they'd know enough to put the table where one can enjoy the view. There, that's better. As soon as we're finished, I want you to go out with me. We've an errand on the avenue.'

'What is it?'

'A surprise. You'll see.'

In the elevator they met Bruce Lehman.

'I thought you'd have gone home by now,' Robert said.

'No, I've got to pick up something first. Remember? How are you feeling, Lynn? We missed you last night.' He was carefully not looking straight at her.

Robert answered. 'She fell and was too embarrassed to go to the dinner with a lump on her face.'

'A bruise can't spoil you, as pretty as you are,' Bruce said, now turning his full gaze to her.

Josie liked to say that she had married him because his eyes had a friendly twinkle, and he liked cats. This twinkle was visible even behind his glasses. He reminded Lynn of a photograph in some advertisement of country life, a sturdy type in a windbreaker, tramping a field, accompanied by a pair of little boys or big dogs.

'Mind if we go with you?' asked Robert. 'You gave me a very good idea last night.'

'Of course not. Come along. I bought a bracelet yesterday for Josie,' Bruce explained to Lynn. 'I wanted them to engrave her initials on it and it will be ready this morning.'

'I was going to surprise Lynn,' Robert chided lightly. 'Well, no matter. We'll be there in a minute, anyway.'

She was disturbed. There was a right time for gifts, a right mood for receiving them. And she remonstrated, 'Robert, I don't need anything. Really.'

'No one ever *needs* jewelry. But if Bruce can have the pleasure, why can't I have it?'

In the shop, which was itself a small jewel of burnished wood, velvet carpet, and crystal lights, Bruce displayed the narrow gold bangle he had ordered.

'Like it, Lynn? Do you think Josie will?'

'It's lovely. She'll be so happy with it.'

'Well, it won't make up for the mastectomy, God knows, but I thought – a little something, I thought –' His voice quavered and he stopped.

Robert had gone to the other side of the shop and now summoned Lynn.

'Come here, I want you to look at this.'

Set in a web of woven gold threads was a row of cabochon stones – rubies, sapphires, and emeralds in succession.

'This,' Robert said, 'is what I call a bracelet.'

'Byzantine,' the salesman explained. 'Handwoven. The originals are in museums.'

'Try it on, Lynn.'

The price tag was too small to be legible, but she knew enough without asking, and so replied, 'It's much too expensive.'

'Let me be the judge of that,' Robert objected. 'If I'm going to buy, I'm not going to buy junk. Either the best or nothing. Try it on.'

Obeying, she went to the mirror. Unaccustomed to such magnificence, she felt an awkwardness; she had the air of a young girl.

When Bruce came over, Robert commanded her, 'Show Bruce what you're getting.'

'It's Robert's idea. I really don't –' she began.

Bruce laid his hand on her arm and quite oddly, she thought, corrected her. 'It's beautiful. Take it. You deserve it,' and to Robert added, 'We have good wives. They deserve our best.'

So the purchase was concluded.

'Keep the bracelet in your pocketbook,' Robert said. 'It's not insured yet, and the suitcase might get lost.'

'Like yours,' Bruce said.

'You didn't want the bracelet,' Robert said when they were flying home, 'because you think I was trying to make up for what I did yesterday. But you're wrong. And it's nothing compared with what I'll be giving you someday.' He chuckled. 'On the other hand, compared with what that cipher bought for Josie –'

'Why do you call Bruce a cipher? He's one of the most intelligent people we know.'

'You're right, and I used the wrong word. What I meant was that he'll never set the world on fire. That much I can tell you.'

'Maybe he doesn't want to,' she retorted with mild indignation.

'He does his work at the office all right and makes a good impression, but in my opinion he lacks brilliance, the kind that keeps a man staying late and coming back on Saturday when everyone else is taking it easy.'

'He's had to be home a lot with Josie when she was so awfully sick, you know that. Now that she's so much better, it'll be different.'

'Well, they're an odd couple, anyway. She effervesces like a bottle of fizz, while he has the personality of a clam.'

'That's not true. He's just not talkative. He listens.' And she said quietly, 'You've never liked Bruce and Josie, have you?'

'Now, that's not true either.' Robert clasped her hand, which lay on the armrest. 'Oh, the dickens with everybody except us, anyway. Lynn, I've got a good hunch that there's a big change in the air for us. Things were said last night both to me and about me that make it fairly sure I'll be tapped for the New York post. What have you got to say about that?'

'That I'm not surprised. If anyone deserves it, you do.'

'I'll be in charge of marketing the whole works from the Mississippi to the Atlantic.'

She was having a private thought, vaguely lonesome: I shall miss Helen and Josie.

'They may be sending one or two others from here, under me, of course. There's a general switching going on all over the map.'

'I hope Bruce goes.'

'Because of Josie, naturally. You depend too much on her, Lynn.'

'I don't depend on her at all. I don't know how you can say that.'

'I can say it because I see it.' After a minute he mused. 'New York. Then, who knows? The international division. Overseas. London. Paris. Up and up to the very top. Company president when I'm fifty. It's possible, Lynn. Just have faith in me.'

He was an exceptional man, not to be held back. Everyone knew it, and she, his wife, knew it most of all. Again he clasped her hand, turning upon her his infectious, brilliant smile.

'Love me? With all my faults?'

Love him. Joined to him, no matter what. From the very first day. No matter what. Explain it? As soon explain the force of the rising tide.

'Love me?' he persisted.

'Yes,' she said. 'Oh, yes.'

Part Two

Spring 1988

2

The house lay comfortably on a circle of lawn and spread its wings against the dark rise of hills behind it. The architect, who had built it for himself, had brought beams from old New England barns and pine paneling from old houses to recreate the eighteenth century within commuting distance of Manhattan. The windows had twelve lights; and the fanlight at the front door was authentic.

Robert had found the property on his initial visit to New York and had come home filled with nervous enthusiasm. Connecticut was the place! It had charm. It had atmosphere. The schools were good. The neighborhoods were safe. There were wonderful open spaces. Imagine three wooded acres on a narrow, rural road with no one in sight except for the house directly opposite, and that, too, a treasure out of *Architectural Digest*.

Of course, it was expensive. But with his salary and his prospects a mortgage would be no problem. She had only to read the items about his promotion in *The Wall Street Journal* and in *Forbes* magazine to know where he was headed. Besides, a house like this one was an investment, a setting for entertaining – to say nothing of its being an investment in happy living for themselves. Once Lynn had seen the place, and if she liked it, then she must get busy right away and furnish it well. There must be no piecemeal compromises; a first-class decorator must do it all.

She would fall in love with it, he was certain; already

he could see her working in the flower beds with her garden gloves and her big straw sun-hat on.

So they got out a bottle of champagne and, sitting at the kitchen table, toasted each other and their children and General American Appliance and the future.

Now in late spring, the evening air blew its fragrance through the open windows in the dining room. And lilacs, the source of this fragrance, reared their mauve heads and their healthy leafage above the sills.

'Listen, a mockingbird! I can't imagine when he ever sleeps,' Lynn said. 'I hear him the last thing when I fall asleep, and in the morning when I wake, he's still singing.'

Josie's black eyes, too prominent in her thin, birdlike face, smiled at Lynn.

'You do love this place, don't you?'

'Oh, I do. I know I felt in the beginning that the house was too big, but Robert was right, we really do spread out so comfortably here. And as for its being too expensive, I still have a few doubts, but I leave all that to him.'

'My wife is frugal,' said Robert.

'A lot of men would like to have that complaint,' Josie remarked. She spoke quickly, as was her habit. And again it seemed to Lynn that her remarks to Robert, however neutral, so often had a subtle edge.

Then again it seemed to her that whenever Bruce followed Josie in his so different, deliberate way, it was with an intention to smooth that edge.

'You've done a wonder with the house.' His gaze went over Robert's head toward the wide hall in which rivers, trees, and mountains repeated themselves on the scenic wallpaper, and then beyond to the living room where on chairs and rugs and at the windows a mélange of cream, moss-green, and dusty pink evoked the gardens of Monet.

Lynn followed his gaze. The house had indeed been done to a refined perfection. Sometimes, though, when

46

she was left alone in it to contemplate these rooms, she had a feeling that they were frozen in their perfection as if preserved in amber.

'As for us,' Bruce was saying, 'will you believe that after two years we still have unopened cartons of books in the basement? We left St Louis in such a hurry, we just threw things together, we never expected to be transferred, it was all so unexpected –' He laughed. 'The truth is that we aren't known for our neatness, anyway, neither Josie nor I.'

Josie corrected him. 'When you have work to do for the company, you're one of the most efficient people I've ever seen.'

Robert shook his head. 'We were completely settled in a week. I personally can't function with disorder around me. I'm internally compelled toward order. I know that about myself. If a sign says KEEP OFF THE GRASS, I have to obey, while there are other people who have to challenge the sign by walking on the grass.' He sighed. 'People are crazy.'

'I can attest to that,' said Josie. 'The things I see and hear in my daily work –' She did not finish.

'I wish you'd tell me some of them, Aunt Josie. I keep asking you.'

Everyone turned to Emily. There was a fraction of a second's silence, no longer than a collective indrawn breath, as if the four adults had simultaneously been struck by an awareness of the girl's beauty in her yellow dress, with her black silk hair flowing out under a cherry-colored bandeau and the shaft of evening sunshine on her eager face.

'I will, whenever you want. But so much is tragedy, sordid tragedy.' And with gentle curiosity Josie asked, 'What makes you so interested?'

'You know I'm going to be a doctor, and doctors need to understand people.'

There was a fullness in Lynn's throat, a silent cry: How lovely she is! How dear they both were, her girls! And she was thankful for their flourishing; they had taken the move so well and found their places in the new community.

'Emily did incredibly on her PSATs,' Robert said. 'Oh, I know you don't like me to boast about you, darling, but sometimes I can't help it. So forgive me. I am just so proud of you.'

Annie's round face under its halo of pale, kinky hair turned to her father. And Lynn said, 'Our girls both work hard. Annie comes home from school, goes right to the piano to practice, and then to her homework. I never have to remind you, do I, Annie?'

The child turned now to her mother. 'May I have the rest of the soufflé before it collapses? Look, all the air's going out of it.'

Indeed the remaining section of the chocolate fluff was slowly settling into a moist slab at the bottom of the bowl.

'No, you may not,' Robert answered as Annie shoved her plate under Lynn's nose. 'You're fat enough. You shouldn't have had any in the first place.'

Annie's mouth twisted into the square shape of tragedy, an outraged sob came forth, she sprang up, tumbling her chair onto its back, and fled.

'Come back at once and pick up your chair,' commanded Robert.

In reply the back door slammed. Everyone took care not to look at anyone else until Emily spoke, reproaching gently, 'You embarrassed her, Dad.'

'What do you mean? We're not strangers here. Aunt Josie and Uncle Bruce knew her before she was born.'

'But you know how she hates being told she's fat.'

'She has to face reality. She is fat.'

'Poor little kid,' Lynn murmured. A little kid who didn't like herself, not her fat, nor the kinky hair that she had inherited from some unknown ancestor. Who could know her secret pain? 'Do go after her, Robert. She's probably in the usual place behind the toolshed.'

Robert stood up, laid his napkin on the table, and nodded toward the Lehmans. 'If you'll excuse me. She's impossible . . .' he said as he went out, leaving a dull silence behind him.

At the sideboard Lynn poured coffee. Robert had bought the heavy silver coffee service at Tiffany as a 'house gift to ourselves'. At this moment its formality in the presence of Bruce and Josie made her feel awkward; it would have been natural to bring the percolator in from the kitchen as they had always done. But Robert wanted her to use all these fine new things, 'Or else, why have them?' he always said, which, she had to admit, did make some sense. Her hand shook the cup, spilling a few drops. It was an uneasy moment, anyway, in this humming silence.

It was Emily who broke through it. At seventeen she already had social poise. 'So you're all going to the Chinese auction for the hospital tonight?'

'I've been racking my brains,' Josie reported, 'and the best thing I can come up with is to offer three nights of baby-sitting.'

'Well, if you need references,' Emily said gaily, 'tell them to call me. You and Uncle Bruce sat for us often enough, goodness knows.'

Lynn had recovered. 'I'll give a "dinner party for eight at your house."'

'Dad's offering three tennis lessons. He's better than the coach we had last year at school.'

'What's this about me?' asked Robert. He came in with his arm around Annie's shoulder and, without waiting for an answer, announced cheerfully, 'We've settled the problem, Annie and I. Here it is. One luscious, enormous dessert, as enormous as she wants, once a week, and no sweets, none at all, in between. As a matter of fact, that's a good rule for all of us, no matter what we weigh. Good idea, Lynn?'

'Very good,' she said gratefully. As quickly as Robert could blunder into a situation, so quickly could he find the way out.

He continued. 'Annie, honey, if you finish your math homework tonight, I'll review it tomorrow and then we'll go ahead to the next assignment so you'll have a leg up on the rest of the class. You will surprise the teacher. How's that?' The child gave a nod. 'Ah, come, Annie, smile a little.' A small smile crossed the still mottled cheeks. 'That's better. You staying with Annie tonight, Emily?'

'Going to the movies, Dad, it's Friday.'

'Not with that boy Harris again?'

'Yes, with that boy Harris again.'

Robert did not answer. Emily must be the only person in the world who can cause him to falter, Lynn thought.

'Eudora's going to sit tonight,' she said. 'Emily dear, I think I hear Harris's car.'

'You can hear it a mile away. It needs a new muffler,' Robert said.

An instant later Emily admitted Harris. He was a tall, limber youth with a neat haircut, well-pressed shirt, and a friendly, white-toothed greeting. It seemed to Lynn that health and cheer came with him. Now he was holding by the collar a large, lumbering dog whose long, ropy hair was the shape and color of wood shavings.

'Hello, Mr Ferguson, Mrs Ferguson, Mr and Mrs Lehman. I think your Juliet's got something in her ear. She was wriggling around outside trying to rub it on the grass. If somebody'll hold her, I'll try to take a look.'

'Not in the living room on the light carpet, please,' Robert said.

'No, sir. Is it all right here in the hall?'

'Yes, lay her down.'

It was not easy to wrestle with Juliet. Emily held her legs and Robert pressed on her shoulders. Harris probed through the hairy tangle of her ear.

'Be careful. She may snap,' Lynn warned.

Harris shook his head. 'Not Juliet. She knows I'm trying to help.' His fingers searched. 'If it's inside the ear – no, I don't see anything, unless it's something internal, but I don't think so – if it is, she'll have to see the vet – sorry, poor girl – am I hurting you? Oops, I think I felt – yes, I did – hey, I've got it, it's a tiny burr stuck in the hair – ouch, that hurts – wait, old lady – I'll need a scissors, Mrs Ferguson. I'll need to cut some hair.'

'She won't miss it,' Lynn told him, handing the scissors. 'I've never seen such a hairy dog.'

'You'd make a fine vet,' Bruce said, 'or MD, either one.'

Harris, still on his knees, looked up and smiled. 'That's what I plan. Emily and I are both in Future Doctors of America.'

'Well, you've certainly got a way with animals. Juliet even seems to be thanking you,' Bruce said kindly.

'We've always had animals in our house, so I'm used to them,' Harris explained, stroking the dog's head. 'Just last week we lost one old dog. He was sixteen, almost as old as I am, and I do miss him.'

Bruce nodded. 'I know what you mean. What kind was he?'

'Just Heinz 57, the all-American dog.'

'Juliet is a Bergamasco,' Robert said. 'I had a hard time finding one, I can tell you.'

'I'd never even heard the name until Emily told me what she was.'

'Not many people have. It's a very rare breed in this country. Italian.'

Lynn laughed. 'I don't think she gives a darn about being rare, do you, Juliet?'

51

The dog yawned, settling back under the boy's stroking hand. Harris spoke to her.

'You feel a lot better now that you're rid of that thing, don't you?'

'Oh, Juliet, we do love you, you funny-looking, messy girl!' Emily exclaimed. 'Although I always did want an Irish setter.'

'Everybody has an Irish setter,' Robert said. He looked at his watch. 'Well, shall we go? Leave your car here, Bruce. You can pick it up on your way home. And, Emily, don't be too late.'

'That's a nice boy,' Bruce remarked as always, when they were in the car.

Lynn agreed. 'Yes, he's responsible and thoughtful. I never worry about Emily when he drives. Some of the others –'

'What others?' Robert interrupted. 'It seems to me that she's always with him. And I don't like it. I don't like it at all.'

'You read too much into it,' Lynn said gently. 'They're just high school kids.'

'Emily is not "just" anything. She's an exceptional, gifted girl, and I don't want to see her wasting her time. Yes, the boy's nice enough, and his family's probably respectable. The father's a policeman –'

'Is that what you object to?' Josie said bluntly. 'That his father's a policeman?'

Lynn cringed. Intimate as she was with her old friend, the secret of Robert's and Josie's dislike for each other remained unacknowledged between them. Neither woman wanted to open this particular Pandora's box.

Bruce gave his wife a mild rebuke. 'Of course he doesn't mean that.'

It seemed to Lynn that Bruce and she were too often called upon to smooth rough passages. And she said impatiently, 'What a waste of words! A pair of seventeen-year-olds.'

'Well, I don't know,' Bruce said somewhat surprisingly. 'Josie and I fell in love when we were in high school.'

'That was different,' Robert grumbled. 'Emily's different. She has a future in the world, and she can't afford to play with it.'

'I thought you were still one of those men who think women are better off in the house,' Josie told him.

Again Lynn had to cringe. It was a relief that before Robert could reply, the car arrived at the entrance to the country club.

The membership had gotten behind the hospital's gigantic fund drive. Actually, it had been Robert who had brought about the liaison between the club and the hospital's trustees. It was remarkable that after only two years in this community, he had become well enough known for at least ten people to stop and greet him before he had even passed through the lobby.

The auction, in the long room that faced the golf course, was about to begin. Flanking the podium, two tables held sundry donations: glass candlesticks, dollhouse furniture, and an amateurish painting of ducks floating on a pond. On one side there hung a new mink jacket, a contribution from one of the area's best shops.

Robert paused to consider it. 'How about this?' he whispered.

Lynn shook her head. 'Of course not. You know how I feel about fur.'

'Okay, I won't force it on you. On second thought, if you should ever change your mind, I wouldn't buy this one. It looks cheap.' He moved on. 'How about the dollhouse furniture for Annie?'

'She hasn't got a dollhouse.'

'Well, buy her one for her birthday. Let her fix it up

herself. Annie needs things to occupy her mind. What's this? Do I recognize a menorah?'

'You do,' said Bruce from behind him. 'I inherited three from various relatives, and since we hardly need three, I thought I'd contribute one. It's a Czech piece, about a hundred years old, and should bring a very good price.'

'I doubt it. There are no Jews in this club.'

'But there are some in the neighborhood, and they always give generously,' Bruce said, sounding unusually firm.

'That's well known,' Lynn offered, worrying that Robert's remark might have sounded too brusque.

Robert moved on again. 'Hey, look here. Two Dickenses from 1890. *Bleak House* and *Great Expectations*. These are finds, Lynn.' He lowered his voice. 'We have to buy something. It wouldn't look right if we didn't. Anyway, I want these.'

With the appearance of the auctioneer the audience ceased its rustle and bustle. One by one, with approval and jokes, various offers were made and accepted: Josie to baby-sit, Robert to give tennis lessons, Lynn to give a dinner, and a few dozen more. All went for generous prices. A delighted lady with blue-rinsed hair got the mink jacket, the doll furniture went to the Fergusons, as did the two volumes of Dickens. And Bruce's menorah brought three thousand dollars from an antiques dealer.

Robert said only, 'I could use a cup of coffee,' as the crowd dispersed into the dining room, where dessert was to be served.

Robert and Lynn saved places for the Lehmans.

'It gets a little sticky,' he whispered as they sat down. 'We should be mingling with people here, and yet I should be with Bruce too.'

'He seems to be doing all right,' Lynn observed, for

Bruce and Josie were standing in an animated little group. 'They make friends easily,' she went on.

'Yes, when he makes the effort. He should make it more often for his own good. Well, I'm not going to waste time sitting here waiting for them. There are a dozen people I ought to see, and I want to get the tally besides. We must have made over twenty thousand, at least. I want to get hold of a local editor, too, and make sure that my name is in the write-up and that General American Appliance gets credit.'

Robert's fingers drummed on the table. 'No. Tomorrow morning will be better for that. A few private words over the telephone away from this crowd will accomplish more.'

Josie, Bruce, and another man had detached themselves from their group and now came over to the table. Bruce made introductions.

'This is Tom Lawrence, who bought your dinner offer, Lynn, so I thought you two ought to meet.'

Robert said cordially, 'Please join us, Mr Lawrence, you and Mrs Lawrence.'

'Thanks, I will. But there is no Mrs Lawrence. Not anymore.' The man's smile had a touch of mischief, as if he were amused at himself. 'You assumed I had a wife, or else why would I be bidding on a dinner party? I can't blame you, but the fact is that although I keep a bachelor's house, I like to entertain.' He turned to Lynn. 'Bruce told me that you're a fabulous cook and I ought to bid on your dinner. So I did.'

'You bid more than it's worth,' Lynn said. 'I hope you won't be disappointed.'

'I'm sure I won't be.' Now Lawrence turned to Robert. 'And you're the man, I noticed, who got my Dickens. A fair exchange.'

'Not really. They're handsome books. I wonder that you parted with them.'

'For the same reason that Bruce here parted with his candle holder – menorah, I mean. Both my grand-fathers were book collectors, and since I'm not a collector of anything, it seemed to me that I didn't need duplicates. Also,' he said somewhat carelessly, 'one of my grandfathers helped found this club and the hospital, too, so the cause has extra-special meaning for me.'

'Ah, yes. Lawrence Lawrence. The plaque in St Wilfred's lobby.'

Lynn, watching, knew that Robert was taking the man's measure. He would recognize assurance and alacrity. Now Robert was asking how Bruce and he had become acquainted.

'We met while jogging on the high school track,' Law-rence responded. 'We seem to keep pretty much the same schedule.'

'You must live near the school, then.'

'I do now. I gave up a bigger house after my divorce. I used to live out on Halsey Road,' he said in the same careless way.

'That's where we are!' Lynn exclaimed. 'We bought the Albright house.'

'Did you? Beautiful place. I've been at many a great party there.'

'You should see it now. We've done so much with it that you might not recognize it,' Robert said. 'It needed a lot of work.'

'Really,' said Lawrence. 'I never noticed.'

He doesn't like Robert, Lynn thought. No, that's absurd. Why shouldn't he? I'm always imagining things.

Suddenly Josie laughed. 'Do you know something funny? Look at Lynn and look at Tom. Does anybody see what I see?'

'No, what?' asked Robert.

'Why, look again. They could be brother and sister.

The same smooth sandy hair, the short nose, the cleft chin – it's uncanny.'

'If so, I'm honored.' And Lawrence made a little bow toward Lynn.

'I don't see it at all,' Robert said.

The instant's silence contained embarrassment, as if a social blunder had been made. Yet Josie's remark had been quite harmless.

And Lynn said pleasantly, 'You must tell me when you want your dinner for eight, Mr Lawrence.'

'Tom's the name. I'll get my list together and call you. Will the week after next be all right?'

'Don't forget we are taking Emily to visit Yale,' Robert cautioned.

'I won't forget. The week after next will be fine.'

Presently, the room began to empty itself. People looked at their watches and made the usual excuses to depart. The evening had played itself out.

'Who is this fellow Lawrence, anyway?' Robert inquired on the way home.

Bruce explained. 'He's a bright guy, and partner in a big New York law firm.'

'That doesn't tell me much. There are a lot of bright guys in big New York firms.'

'I don't know much more than that, except that he's been divorced a couple of times, he's close to fifty, and looks a lot younger. And I know he comes from what you'd call an important family,' Bruce added with what Lynn took to be a touch of humor.

'I'm not happy about having Lynn go over to a strange man's house.'

'Oh,' Lynn said, 'don't be silly. Does he look like a rapist?'

'I don't know. What does a rapist look like?' Robert gave a loud, purposeful sigh. 'My wife is still an innocent.'

'It's a dinner party for eight. And I'm planning to take

57

Eudora to help. So that should make you feel better. Really, Robert.'

'All right, all right, I'll feel better if you want me to.'

'People were saying some nice things about you tonight, Robert,' Bruce said. 'About the hospital, of course, and also the big pledge you got GAA to make to the Juvenile Blindness campaign.'

'Yes, yes. You see, you people used to think all that had nothing to do with marketing electronic appliances, but I hope you see now that it does. Anything that connects the name of GAA to a good cause counts. And the contacts one makes in the country club all connect to these causes and their boards. You really ought to join a club, Bruce.'

'You know I can't join this one.'

'That's disgusting,' Lynn said. 'It makes me want to stand up and fight.'

'You may want to but you'd better not. I keep reminding you,' Robert told her, 'that reality has to be faced. Bruce is smart enough to accept it. Join a Jewish club, Bruce. There are a couple just over the Westchester line. And the company'll pay. They'll be glad to.'

Lynn, looking back from the front seat, could see Bruce's shrug.

'Josie and I never did go for club life, Jewish or not.'

'It's time you began, then.' Robert spoke vigorously. 'You need to get on some of these boards, go to the dinners and have your wife go to the luncheons. You owe it to the firm and to yourself.'

'I do what I can,' Bruce answered.

'Well, think about what I'm telling you. And you, too, Josie.'

Lynn interjected, 'Josie works. And anyway, I can't imagine her exchanging gossip with company wives. You have to be careful of what you say. They judge everything, your opinions, your clothes, everything. Some of those afternoons can wear one out.'

'It's the price you pay for being who you are and where you are. You'll think it a small enough price, too, if it leads to a big job in Europe,' Robert declared.

A small chilly dread sank in Lynn's chest. She knew the pattern of promotion: two or three years in each of several European countries, then possibly the home office in New York again. Or else a spell in the Far East with another return. And no permanence, no roots, no place to plant a maple sapling and see it grow. There were myriads of people who would forgo a thousand maples for such opportunities, and that was fine for them, but she was not one of those people.

Yet Robert was. And he would well deserve his rewards when they came. Never, never, she thought as always, must she by the slightest deed or word hold him back.

As if he were reading her mind, at that very moment Bruce remarked, 'When there's another big job in Europe, and with all that's happening abroad, there's bound to be one soon, you're the man to get it, Robert. Everybody knows that.'

Later when they were reading in bed, Robert asked, 'What are you doing tomorrow?'

'I'm taking Josie and a few friends to lunch, remember? It's her birthday.'

'Missing the women's tennis tournament?'

'I have to. Josie works all week, so Saturday is the only day we can make it.'

After a moment Robert, laying his book aside, said decidedly, 'Josie's too opinionated. I've always said so. It's a wonder to me why he isn't sick of her, except that he's too much of a weakling, a yes-man, to do anything about it.'

'Sick of her! Good Lord, he's no yes-man, he adores

her! And as to being opinionated, she's not. She's merely honest, that's all. She's outspoken.'

'Well, well, if you say so. I guess I'm just a male chauvinist who's uncomfortable with outspoken women.'

Lynn laughed. 'Our Emily's a pretty outspoken woman, I'd say.'

'Ah, that's different.' And Robert laughed too. 'She's my daughter. She can do anything she wants.'

'Except choose her own boyfriends?'

'Lynn, I only want what's best for her. Wouldn't I give my life for her? For all of you?'

'Dear Robert, I know that.'

He picked up his book and she went back to hers. Presently Robert laid his down again.

'By the way, did you have the fender fixed where you scraped it?'

'Yes, this morning.'

'Did they do a good job?'

'You'd never know there'd been a mark.'

'Good. There's no sense riding around in a marked-up car.' Then he thought of something else; it was as if he kept a memo book in his head, Lynn often told him.

'Did you send a birthday present to my aunt?'

'Of course I did. A beautiful summer bag.'

'That's right, considering all those sweaters she knits for the girls.'

There was a hurtful, grudging quality in this comment that Lynn was unable to ignore.

'Robert, I think you treat her very badly.'

'Nonsense. I was perfectly nice to her last year at Christmas.'

'You were polite, that's all, and it wasn't last year, it was the year before. The reason she didn't come last year was that she felt you didn't want her. You, not I. I actually like her. She's a kind, gentle lady.'

'She may be kind and gentle, but she's a garrulous old fool and she gets on my nerves.'

'Garrulous! She hardly opens her mouth when you're around.'

He did not answer. And Lynn persisted.

'Emily's very fond of her. She had a lovely afternoon tea when Jean was visiting in New York last month.'

'All right. Leave me alone about Aunt Jean, will you? It's unimportant.'

He turned and, in pulling the blanket with him, dropped the book with a loud thump onto the floor.

'Sorry. Damn! I'm restless.'

She put her hand on his arm. 'Tell me what's really bothering you.'

'Well, you may think it's foolish of me, you probably will think so. But I told you, I don't like the idea of your going to cook dinner in another man's house where there's no wife. I wish to hell you had thought of something else to contribute to the auction.'

'But cooking is what I do best. It'll be fun. Didn't you watch the bidding? He paid a thousand dollars for my services, I want you to know.'

'Bruce shoved him onto you. That's what happened.'

'You're surely not going to be annoyed with Bruce. Robert, how silly can you be?'

'I don't like the man's looks. Divorced, and divorced again, and –'

Trying to tease him out of his mood, she said, 'Apparently he looks like me, so you should –'

'So yes, he is something like you, and you –'

He turned again, this time toward Lynn, to meet her eyes, so that she could see close up his darkening blue irises, black lashes, white lids, and her own reflection in his pupils. 'You grow more lovely with each year. Some women do.'

She was pleased. 'I do believe you're jealous.'

'Of course I am. Isn't it only natural? Especially when I have never once in all our life together – I swear it – I have never been unfaithful to you.'

The white lids, like shell halves, closed over the blue. And with a violent motion he buried his head in her shoulder.

'Ah, Lynn, you don't know. You don't know.'

That he could want her still with such fierce, sudden spasms of desire, and that she could respond as she had first done when they began together, was a marvel that flashed upon her each and every time, as now . . .

The wind fluttered the curtains, the bedside clock ticked, and a car door cracked lightly, quickly shut. Robert roused from his doze.

'Emily?'

'She's home. I kept awake to be sure.'

'She stays out too late.'

'Hush. Go to sleep. Everything's all right.'

With all safe, Emily and Annie in their beds, now she could sleep too. Her thoughts trembled on the verge of consciousness, her body was warmed by the body beside which she had been sleeping for thousands of nights. Thousands.

There went the mockingbird again. Trilling, trilling its heart out without a care in the world, she thought, and then abruptly thought no more.

Tom Lawrence asked, 'Are you sure I'm not in your way?'

Perched on a barstool in his glossy black-and-white kitchen, he was watching Lynn's preparations.

'No, not at all.'

'This is a new experience for me. Usually when I have guests, I have a barbecue outdoors. Steaks, and ice cream for dessert. Fast and easy.'

Since this was quite a new experience for Lynn, too, she had to grope for something to say, however banal, to avoid a stiff silence. 'It's a pity not to use all these beautiful things more often,' she remarked as she filled the cups of a silver epergne with green grapes.

'That's a great idea, putting fruit in that thing. I forgot I had it. You know, when we split up and I moved, my former wife and I agreed to divide all the stuff we owned, stuff from her family and mine, plus things we'd bought together. I didn't pay any attention, just let her do it all. The whole business was a mess. The move. The whole business.' Abruptly, he slid from the stool. 'Here, let me carry that. Where does it go?'

'It's the centerpiece. Careful, the arms detach.'

The dining table stood at the side of a great room with a fireplace at each end. One saw that there was no more to the house than the splendid kitchen and what must be two bedrooms leading off this great room. A quick glance encompassed paintings, bookshelves, a long glass wall with a terrace, and thick foliage, dense as a forest, beyond it.

'What an elegant little house!' she exclaimed.

'Do you think so? Yes, after almost three years I can say I finally feel at home here. When I first moved in, my furniture looked alien. I hardly recognized it.'

'I know what you mean. When the van comes and sets your things down in a strange place, they look forlorn, don't they? As if they knew and missed their own home. Then when the empty van drives away – oh, there's something final about it that leaves one just a trifle sad, I think.' And for an instant she was back in the little house in St Louis – 'little', contrasted with the present one – with the friendly neighbors on the familiar, homelike street. Then she said briskly, 'But of course one gets over it.'

His reply was wholly unexpected. 'I imagine that you make yourself 'get over' things pretty quickly, though. You make yourself do what's right.'

Astonished, she looked up to meet a scrutiny.

Returning it, she saw that except for some superficial features, this man did not resemble her at all; he was keen and worldly wise, which she definitely was not; he would see right through a person if he chose to.

'What makes you say that?' she asked curiously.

He smiled and shrugged. 'I don't know. Sometimes I get a sudden insight, that's all. Unimportant. And possibly wrong.'

'Maybe you sense that I'm a little nervous about this evening. I'm hoping I haven't bitten off more than I can chew.'

He followed her back into the kitchen. 'Please don't be nervous. These are all real people tonight, a few old friends driving out from New York and not a phony among them. They'll be stunned when they see this table. I'm sure they're expecting Tom Lawrence's usual paper plates.'

Arrayed on the counters were bowls and platters of food that Lynn had already prepared at home: a dark red ham in a champagne sauce, stuffed mushroom caps, plump black olives and silver-pale artichokes tossed into a bed of greens, golden marinated carrots, rosy peaches spiced with cinnamon and cloves. Back and forth from the pantry to the refrigerator she moved. Then to the oven, into which she slid a pan of crisp potato balls, and to the mixer for the topping of whipped cream on a great flat almond tart.

When all was finished and she was satisfied, full confidence returned. 'This kitchen's absolutely perfect,' she told Tom, who was still there quietly observing her work. 'The restaurant-sized oven, the freezer – all of it. I'm really envious.'

'Well, you deserve a perfect kitchen, you're that expert. Have you ever thought of going professional?'

'I've thought about it sometimes, I'll admit. I've even thought of a name, "Delicious Dinners." But what with a lot of volunteering and the PTA and our big house taking time out of every day, I don't know how – ' She paused and finished, 'Robert is very fastidious about the house.' She paused again to add, 'Anyway, I'm not in a hurry,' and was immediately conscious of having sounded defensive. 'I need a last look at the table,' she said abruptly.

'Excuse me.' Tom was apologetic. 'But the silver – I mean, aren't the forks and spoons upside down, inside out?'

Lynn laughed. 'When the silver's embossed on the back, you're supposed to let it show.'

'Oh? Now I've learned something,' he said. His eyes smiled at her.

They're like Bruce's eyes, she thought. There isn't another thing about him that's like Bruce, but that. Her hands moved, smoothing the fine cloth, rearranging the candlesticks. There aren't that many people whose eyes can smile like that.

'You've suddenly grown thoughtful, Lynn. May I call you that?'

'Of course. Oh, thoughtful? I was remembering,' she said lightly, 'when Robert bought the etiquette book so I'd learn how to give proper dinners when we moved here. I thought it was silly of him, but I find it's come in handy, after all.'

The doorbell rang. 'Oh, that's Eudora. She cleans and baby-sits for us. I've asked her to help. I'll let her in.'

When Lynn returned, Tom said, 'I wish you'd set another place at table, one for yourself, now that you've got help in the kitchen.'

'I'm here to work. I'm not a guest,' she reminded him. 'Thank you, anyway.'

'Why shouldn't you be a guest? There'll be all couples tonight except for me. And I really should have a female to escort me, shouldn't I?'

'That wasn't the arrangement.'

His smile subsided as again he gave her his quick scrutiny. 'I understand. You mean, if you were to be a guest, then your husband would be here too.'

She nodded. 'Anyway, I couldn't depend upon Eudora in the kitchen. She'll be fine to bring in the plates after I fix them and to clean up with me afterward.'

She hurried away into the kitchen. Why was she flustered? Actually, the man had said nothing so startling. And she turned to Eudora, who was waiting for instructions.

'They'll be here in a minute. Turn the oven on low to warm up the hors d'oeuvres. Half an hour for drinks. I'll toss the salad. It goes on the blue plates – no, not those, take the other ones.'

'They're having a good time,' Eudora said much later. The swinging door opened and closed on genial laughter as she went in and out. 'I never did see people clean plates like this.'

'Good. Now carry the cake in so they can see it first. Then you can bring it back, and I'll slice it.'

'You sure are some cook, Mrs Ferguson. I'm old enough to be your mother, and I never even heard of the things you fix.'

'Well, I'd never seen some of your good Jamaican dishes, either, until I knew you.'

Although she had been standing on her feet all day, Lynn suddenly received a charge of energy. What had begun as a lark, an adventure, had become a test, and she had passed it. She had been paid for her skill, and she felt happy. So, when the door opened and Tom said his guests were demanding to see the cook, she was quite ready to go with him.

'Just do let me fix my face first. I'm all flushed from the stove.'

'Yes, it's awful to be flushed like a rose,' he retorted, pulling her with him.

In a moment she appraised the group: they were sophisticated, successful, bright New Yorkers, the kind who
wear their diamonds with their blue jeans when they
want to. They marry and divorce with equal ease when
they want to. Good natured and accepting, it takes a lot
to shock them. Robert would despise their type. All this
went through her head.

They were most kind, heaping praise on Lynn. 'What
a talent ... You could work for Le Cirque or La Grenou-
ille ... I ruined my diet tonight ... Absolutely marvelous.'

The evening rose to a peak. Warmed by the food and
wine, the group left the table in a high, restless mood.
Tom turned on the record player, the men pushed back
the scatter rugs, and dancing began.

He held his hands out to Lynn. 'Come, join the party.'

'It's rock and roll. I'm awful at it,' she protested.

'Then it's time you learned,' he answered, and pulled
her out onto the floor.

At first she felt foolish. If Emily, who danced like a
dervish, could see her mother, she'd die laughing. The
best Lynn could do was to watch the others' dizzy twists
and gyrations and try to imitate them.

Then after a while, the drumming, primitive, blood-
pounding beat began to speak to her. Quite unexpectedly, she caught the beat.

'Why, you've got it!' Tom cried. 'You've got it!'

This whirling, which should have been exhausting, was
instead exhilarating. When Lynn became aware that
Eudora was standing at the door to signal her departure,
it surprised her to find that it was already almost eleven
o'clock. She would have guessed the time to be no later
than nine. Pressing some bills into Eudora's hand, she
whispered, 'You remembered to leave the crystal?'

'Oh, I hate to leave you with it, Mrs Ferguson, but I'd
hate to be responsible for it too.'

'That's all right, Eudora. I'll wash it fast and start right home.'

Back in the kitchen with the apron on again, Lynn was rinsing the goblets when Tom, with eyes alight and in a merry mood, came looking for her.

'Hey! What are you doing in here?'

'Eudora was afraid to touch your Baccarat. She knows what it costs.'

'Oh, leave it. We're all going to dance outdoors. It's a perfect night.'

'I can't. Really. I can't.'

'Yes, you can. I insist. For ten minutes. Come on.'

The outdoor lanterns gave the effect of moonglow, barely glimmering toward the edge of darkness, where the hemlock grove fenced the little clearing on which the terrace lay. It had rained during the day, and the smell of damp grass was tart.

One of the men complained, 'Age is creeping up, Tom, because I'm beat. How about some slow golden oldies for a change?'

'No problem. I've got all the tunes your parents danced to. Now, this is really nice,' he said as his arm brought Lynn close. 'When you come down to it, the old way is better.'

Unlike Robert, he was not much taller than she, so that their faces almost touched. Their feet moved in skillful unison to the swing of the sentimental music.

'You have a sweet mouth,' Tom said suddenly, 'and sweet eyes.'

An uneasy feeling stiffened Lynn, and he felt it at once.

'You didn't like me to say that, did you?'

'I didn't expect it.'

'Why not? If a compliment is sincere, it should be spoken and accepted.'

'Well, then, thank you.'

'You still look uncomfortable. You're thinking I'm just

a smooth talker. But you are really someone special, I have to tell you. Refreshing. Different.'

She could feel his breath on her neck. The hand on the small of her back pressed her so close to him that she could feel his heartbeat. And the dreamy charm of the night changed into nervous misgiving.

'It's after eleven,' she cried. 'I have to go right away. Please – '

'So there you are!'

The harsh voice rang as Robert came from around the corner of the house into the light. Just then the music stopped, leaving the dancers stopped, too, arrested in motion, all turned toward the voice.

'I telephoned, I got no answer, I came over and rang the doorbell and still got no answer.'

'This is my husband,' Lynn said. 'Tom Lawrence – but how stupid of me! Of course you know each other. I'm not thinking.' And she moistened her lips, to which there had suddenly come a curious, salty taste, like that of blood, as if blood had drained upward from her heart.

'I'm so sorry. We've been out here, and the music's drowned out all the bells. Come in and join us,' Tom said cordially. 'Your wife made a marvelous dinner. You've got to sample some of the dessert. I hope there's some left, Lynn?'

'Thank you, but cake is hardly what I need. It's going on twelve, and I'm not usually out at this hour rounding up my wife at a dance.'

Crazy thoughts went through Lynn's head: He looked sinister and black, a figure in mask and cape from an old melodrama, angry-dark, why can't he smile, I'll die of shame before these people. And in a shrill, gay tone not her own, she cried out, 'What an idiot I am, I forgot to wear my watch, all these nice people made me come out of the kitchen and dance with them, I'll just get my bowls and things – '

'Yes, you do that,' Robert said. 'You do just that. I'll wait in front.' He turned about and walked away through the shrubbery.

Tom and the whole company, men and women both, went into the kitchen with Lynn. Rattling and prattling, she let them help gather her possessions, and load her car, while Robert sat stiffly at the wheel of his car, and the hot, awful shame went prickling along her spine.

'You follow me home,' he said.

Past quiet houses already at rest in the shadows of new-leaved trees, his car sped like a bullet aimed at the heart of the friendly countryside. She knew that he sped so because he was furious, and knowing it, her own anger grew. What right had he? Who did he think he was?

'Damn!' she cried. That an evening, having begun so nicely, could end in such miserable confusion, with Tom Lawrence's unwelcome attention and Robert's nastiness!

He had already driven his car into the garage and was waiting for her in the driveway when she arrived home. I want the first word, she thought, and I'm going to have it. Nevertheless, she spoke with quiet control.

'You were unbelievably rude, Robert. I almost didn't recognize you.'

'Rude, you say? Rude? I went there as any other husband would, looking for his wife.'

'You embarrassed me terribly. You know you did.'

'I was concerned. Close to midnight, and no word from you.'

'If you were so concerned, you could have telephoned.'

'I did telephone, I told you. Where's your head? Didn't you listen to me? And then I went over to find you, not in the kitchen doing this ridiculous dinner, and where were you? Dancing, if you please. Dancing.'

'I had been dancing for a couple of minutes, and I was just leaving that very second when you came.'

'You had been dancing much longer than a couple of

minutes. And don't try to deny it because I was there.'

Caught in her lie, no, not a lie, a fib, an innocent fib, such an innocent business altogether in which to be embroiled, she lashed out.

'You were standing there behind the trees snooping? It's degrading. I should think you'd be ashamed, Robert. The way you just burst out of the dark, enough to scare the life out of people. Don't you think they all knew you must have been spying? You were horrible. You wouldn't have put on an act like that if any of them could be of use to you in your business. Otherwise, you don't care what you say to people.'

'That's not true. But it is true that I don't give a damn about a lot of pseudosophisticated phonies. I recognize the type at a glance. I wouldn't trust one of them any farther than I can throw a grand piano, and that includes Lawrence.'

'You're so critical. You're always carping. You don't approve of anybody.'

The headlights of her car, which she had forgotten to turn off, blazed up on Robert. And he seemed, as he stood there, as strong as the dark firs behind him.

'Turn those lights off,' he snapped, 'or you'll have a dead battery.' And turning his back, he climbed the steps to the deck at the back of the house.

She turned the lights off. She was too tired to put one foot ahead of the other, too tired to fight this war of words that she knew was far from over. But with a long sigh she followed him to the deck.

'Pseudosophisticated phonies,' he repeated.

'What is it, Robert?' she asked. 'Tell me what it is that makes you despise people you don't even know. What makes you so angry? Don't you like yourself?' And saying so, she felt the faint sting of her own tears.

'Please,' he said, 'spare me your pop psychology, Mrs Freud.'

He took out his keys and unlocked the house door. Juliet came bounding, barking fiercely, but, seeing who was there, jumped up on Robert and wagged her tail instead. He thrust her away.

'Not in the mood, Juliet. Down.' And abruptly returning to Lynn, he demanded, 'I want an apology. There'll be no sleep for either of us tonight until I get one.'

How a handsome face can turn so ugly! she thought. In the half-dark his cheeks were faintly blue, and his eyes were sunk in their sockets.

'An apology, Lynn.'

'For what? For overstaying my time by an hour? For having a little fun? You could have come in and joined the party. Tom asked you to.'

'Oh, of course, if Tom asks.'

'What does that sarcastic tone mean, I'd like to know?'

'It means that I don't like the way he was looking at you, that's what.'

'The way he looked at me,' she scoffed. 'I don't know how he did because I wasn't studying his expressions, I assure you. But if,' she cried indignantly, 'if he or anyone should take it into his head to admire me a little, you'd have no right to object. Not you. You love it when women fawn on you. Don't tell me you don't, because I've seen it a thousand times.'

'Now, you listen to me and don't change the subject. But no, on the other hand now that you've brought up the subject, I'll tell you this: I have never encouraged any woman. Never. Nor done anything in any way that I couldn't do right in front of you. I'll swear on the Bible.'

'The Bible! All of a sudden the Bible. When were you last in church?'

'Never mind. I believe. I have my moral standards. One mistake, one misstep down a slippery slope, and you can't –'

'What is this? Who's made any missteps? What in

72

heaven's name are you talking about? I can't figure you out.'

'Damn it, if you'll stop interrupting me, I'll figure it out for you.'

From the roof peak the mockingbird began a passionate crescendo, then a trill and a plaintive diminuendo. The sweetness of it went to Lynn's heart and pierced it.

'Let's stop this,' she said, trembling. 'I've had enough. There's no sense in it. I'm going inside.'

He clutched her sleeve. 'No, you're not. You'll hear me first.'

She pulled, and hearing the sleeve rip, the fine sleeve of a cherished dress, she was enraged.

'Let go of me this minute, Robert.'

'No.'

As she wrenched it away, the sleeve tore off at the shoulder.

A muffled cry came from his throat. And he raised a menacing hand. His arm shot out, grasping her shoulder, and she spun, fled, and fell headfirst off the deck into the hawthorn hedge. She heard her own terrible scream, heard the dog going wild, heard Robert's outcry, thought, *my face!* and knew not to break the fall with her hands but to protect her eyes instead.

'Oh, God,' Robert said.

When he lifted her, she screamed. She was flayed, stripped, skinned on the backs of her hands, her legs, her cheeks ... She screamed.

'I have to get you up,' he said, sounding as if he were speaking through clenched teeth. 'If you can't bear it, I'll have to call an ambulance.'

'No. No. We'll try ... Try loosening one at a time. I'll bear it.'

Annie was out on a sleep-over at a friend's house. And Emily must not be home yet, or she would have heard by now and come running. And she gave thanks that they were not seeing this, a happening that must seem both hideous and absurd, with the dog now leaping, now howling, as if it, too, were in pain, shattering the quiet of the night.

Weeping and whimpering she lay and, while Robert brought a flashlight from the car and set to work on her torn arms and legs, tried not to scream. One by one the thorns were parted from her flesh. Only once or twice did she cry out loud.

When finally he raised her and she stood wavering on the grass, they were both sweating and stained with bloody droplets. Wordless, they simply stared at one another. Then she stumbled up the shallow steps, moaning softly.

'I've turned my ankle. I can hardly walk.'

'I'll carry you.'

He picked her up and bore her as lightly as he would have borne a child. He laid her on the bed and took her clothes off.

'Soap and water first,' he said. 'Don't be afraid, I'll be very careful. Then antibiotic cream. That'll do until you see a doctor in the morning.'

'I'm not going to see any doctor. You don't need a doctor for a sprained ankle or a thorn.'

'You had eighteen thorns. I counted.'

'All the same, I'm not going,' she insisted feebly, and was perfectly aware that this was masochism, that it was her intent to make him feel his guilt, guilt for the wounded hands clasped on her naked, wounded breast, for the ruined yellow dress that lay on the floor like dirty laundry, guilt for the whole horror of this night.

'Well, suit yourself,' he said. 'If you change your mind and don't want to drive, call a taxi. I can't take you. My desk in the office is piled with work, and work won't wait just because it's Saturday.'

When she crept under the blanket, he was still standing looking down at her.

'What do you want?' she whispered. 'Anything you want to say?'

He lowered his eyes and took a long breath. 'Yes. I was angry. But I didn't throw you into the hedge.'

'You pushed me. You were going to hit me, you were inches from my face.'

'I was not.'

'You were, Robert.'

'Are you a crystal gazer or something, who can foretell what a person's going to do?'

'You grabbed my shoulder and shoved me. And I saw your face. It was ugly with rage.'

'In the first place, it was too dark for you to see whether my face was ugly or not. This is garbage, Lynn.'

All she wanted was to lie in the darkness and rest. 'Why don't you let me alone?' she cried. 'Haven't you any mercy? At least let me try to sleep if I can.'

'I won't bother you, Lynn.' He walked to the door. 'I hope you can sleep. I doubt that I can. A miserable night. These miserable misunderstandings! Go downstairs, Juliet. Stop pestering.'

'Leave the dog here. I want her.'

Now darkness filled the room. The little sounds of the night were soft, a rustle in the oak near the window and the tinkle of Juliet's tags. The dog came to the bed, reached up, and licked Lynn's sore hand, as if comfort were intended; as always, then, comfort brought the most grateful tears. And Lynn lay still, letting them flow, feeling them cool and slippery on her cheeks. After a while the dog thumped down on the floor near the bed, the tears stopped, and she closed her eyes.

Still no sleep came. Emily was not home yet. It must be very late, she thought. But it was too painful to turn over in the bed and look at the clock. From downstairs there drifted the pungent smell of pipe tobacco, and she knew that Robert was sitting in the corner of the sofa watching television or reading, or perhaps just sitting. No matter. She didn't want to think of him at all. Not yet.

After a time she heard the small thud of a car door being closed, followed by Emily's feet creeping down the hall to her room. Where had the girl been so late? But she was home and safe.

At last it seemed that blessed sleep might come. It had not yet come when Robert entered the room and got into bed, but she pretended that it had.

In the morning, still feigning sleep, she waited until he had dressed and gone downstairs. Then she got up and limped painfully to the mirror, which confirmed what she had expected to see: a swollen face with small, reddened eyes sunk into bloated cheeks. The whole unsightly face was puffed, and there were dark droplets of dried blood on the long scratch. Merely to look like this was another undeserved punishment.

She was standing there applying useless makeup and trying to decide whether the wearing of dark glasses would help or whether it would be better simply to brave things out, when Robert came in.

'I hope you feel better,' he said anxiously.

'I'm fine. I'm just fine. Can't you see?'

'I see only that you're hurt. And that hurts me, even though right now you may not think it does. But I am just so sorry, Lynn. So sorry it happened. I can't tell you.'

'It didn't just happen: I'm not going to accept that stuff anymore. Somebody made it happen, and I'm not the somebody.'

'I understand how you feel.' Robert was patient now, and contrite. 'I realize how it must appear to you. I was angry – we can talk about that some other time – I scared you with my anger, which was wrong of me, and so you ran and then –'

She interrupted. 'And then I don't want to hear any more.'

'All right. Come down and eat your breakfast. Let's keep things normal in front of the girls. Annie's just been brought home. I've told them about your accident, so they're prepared.'

'My accident. Ah, yes,' Lynn mocked, wiping off the eye makeup, which made her look like a sick owl. She would just honestly let the girls see she had been crying. They'd see the injuries anyway.

Emily had set the table in the breakfast room. Coffee bubbled in the percolator and bread was in the toaster. Evidently, she had gone outside and picked a spray of lilacs for the green bowl. Emily was a take-charge person.

'You're up early for someone who went to bed late,' Lynn said pleasantly.

'A bunch of us are driving to the lake,' said Emily, carefully not looking at Lynn's face, 'where Amy's folks keep the boat. What's wrong with your foot? You've hurt that too?'

'It's nothing much. I just can't get a shoe on, so I'll stay home today.'

Annie was staring at Lynn. 'You look awful,' she said. 'You've been crying too.'

Emily admonished her, 'Mind your business, silly.'

Robert spoke. 'Your mother hurt herself. Don't you cry when you're hurt?'

No one answered. The silence was unhappy, restless with the awareness that it would have to end, and the fear that it would end badly.

'It was twenty minutes after twelve when you walked in last night,' Robert said, addressing Emily. 'Did you know that?' he asked, addressing Lynn, who nodded.

'I forgot to look at the time. A bunch of us were studying at Sally's,' Emily explained.

'That won't do,' Robert said. 'You're damaging your

77

reputation, if nothing more, coming home at that hour.'

'We'll talk about it this morning, Emily,' Lynn said.

'No.' Robert looked at his watch. 'I have to run. Emily, you are not to leave the house tonight. *I* want to talk to you. You and I are going to have a very serious talk, straight from the shoulder, one that you won't forget in a hurry. When I'm through, you'll know what's expected of you.'

The emphasis on the 'I' was directed at Lynn; she understood that clearly, having been told often enough that she wasn't firm, didn't consider appearances, and the girls would never learn from her.

'Oh, what an awful mood,' Emily said when Robert had left.

Annie got up. 'I promised Dad I'd practice this morning, and since he's in a bad mood, I guess I'd better do it,' she said in a tone of resignation.

'That's not why you should,' Lynn said gently. 'You should do it because – well, because you should do it,' she finished with a smile.

When Annie was in the living room drumming out a minuet, Lynn said to Emily, 'Sit down while I have my second cup. You shouldn't stay out so late. You know that without my telling you. Were you really at Sally's all that time?'

'I was. Believe it or not, we were studying for finals, Mom.'

Robert's blue eyes looked candidly back at her from Emily's face.

'I believe you.' And thoughtfully, as if she had weighed whether or not to ask the question, she ventured it. 'Was Harris there?'

'Yes. He brought me home.'

'After twelve, your father said.'

'He was sitting in the dark when I came in. Then he

78

came to the hall and stood there just glaring at me. He didn't say a word, and neither did I.'

'That was wrong of you.'

'I'm sorry, Mom. But he needn't have looked so ferocious. I know I should have phoned, but I forgot to look at the time. That's not a crime.'

'I suppose Sally's mother wasn't there, as usual?'

'Well, she's divorced, she goes on dates.' Again the clear eyes met Lynn's. 'So, no, she wasn't there.'

'Wrong. All wrong,' Lynn said. 'And Harris – he's a fine boy, I see that, and it's not that we don't trust you, but –'

'But what, Mom?'

'Your father is very, very angry. You must try to do the right thing, you understand, or you'll be grounded. You really will, Emily, and there'll be nothing I can do about it.'

There was a silence except for the balanced cadence of Annie's minuet.

Emily reached across the table and touched Lynn's hand. 'Mom?' And now the clear, the honest, the lustrous eyes were troubled. 'Mom? What's wrong with Dad? I wish he were like other people's fathers. He gets so mad. It's weird.'

On guard now, Lynn answered as if she were making light of the complaint.

'Why? Because he's going to give you a scolding that you deserve?'

'No. It has nothing at all to do with that.'

'What, then?'

'Oh, things. Just things. He gets so mad sometimes.'

'Everybody gets cranky now and then. He works very hard. Sometimes he's terribly tired and as you say, it's only sometimes.'

Emily shook her head. 'That's not what I mean.'

Lynn feared, although she did not want to think

specifically of what it was that she feared. So she spoke with a touch of impatience.

'You'll have to give me an example, since I have no idea what you're talking about.'

Still Emily hesitated, with a wary, doubtful glance at Lynn. Finally she said, 'Remember when I met Aunt Jean in the city and she took me to tea? Something happened that I didn't tell you about.'

'Yes?'

'Don't be scared, it's nothing awful. What happened is, we were talking and you know how she likes to tell about old times, when the neighbor's house burned down and what a cute little boy Dad was, and then suddenly she let something slip about Dad's first marriage – Mom, how is it we never knew he was married before?'

So that's all it was. Nothing, or comparatively nothing . . .

Carefully, Lynn explained, 'I don't really understand why it had to be such a secret, but it's your father's life and he wants it that way. That must have been a terribly hard time for him and he simply doesn't want to be reminded of it. People often do that; they just bury their bad memories.'

'The second Aunt Jean said it she looked horrified, she was so scared that I felt sorry for her. She kept saying how sorry *she* was, and begged me to promise not to tell, to forget that I'd heard it. And of course I promised.' Emily turned away for a moment and then, turning back to Lynn, admitted with shame that she had broken the promise. 'I held back as long as I could, but last week I told Dad.'

'Oh, that was wrong, Emily.'

'I know, and I feel bad about it. You asked about Dad being so angry at me, though, and –'

'And?' Lynn prodded.

'He was absolutely furious. I've never seen him like

that. Mad, Mom! I couldn't believe it. He glared at me. "That's no business of yours," he told me, "and I don't want the subject to be mentioned ever again. Is that clear?" It stunned me.'

'I hope he won't take it out on poor Aunt Jean.'

'I made him promise not to let her know I had told on her. So I guess it will be all right. I hope so.'

Now Lynn wondered whether Jean had said anything more, anything about Robert's boy, for instance. There must be more pain in that loss than he had ever admitted; it was natural, then, that he would want to forget the boy's existence. And, worrying, she asked, 'Is that all Jean said?'

'Two or three words, and clapped her hand over her mouth. I told you.' Emily frowned in thought, and shook her head in doubt.

'Don't you ever feel strange about it? If I were you – I mean, you might be passing each other on the street, and not know.'

'Hardly likely. This is a big country. Besides, why should we know each other, in the circumstances? It's far better that we don't. Most times a divorce is a closed chapter – understandably.'

'But aren't you even the least bit curious? I know I would be.'

'You don't know. One doesn't know how to act in a situation, or how to feel, until it happens.'

No, I never would have wanted to connect in any way with Robert's glamor girl, Lynn thought, as always with a slight bitterness, but this morning with an extra bitterness. She remembered when she had first known Robert, raw little girl that she had been, an innocent so unsure of herself, how she had flinched at the thought of Robert making love to her predecessor, so rich, so beautiful and careless, that she could afford to toss such a man away.

81

It was strange to be having these thoughts at the kitchen table this morning, on this particular morning.

Nervously, Emily played with a spoon. 'All the same,' she said, 'Dad can be very odd.'

'He's not, Emily. I don't want you to say that or think it.'

And suddenly the girl began to cry. 'Oh, Mom, why am I afraid to say what I really want to say?'

Again fear, hot as fire, struck Lynn's heart.

'Emily darling, what is it?'

'Something happened to you last night.'

'Yes, yes, of course it did. I fell in the dark, fell into the hedge.' She laughed. 'It was a mess, falling into the hedge. Clumsy.'

'No,' Emily said. The word seemed to choke in her throat. 'No. Dad did it. I know it.'

'What? What?' Lynn's hands clenched together in her lap so that her rings dug into the flesh. 'That's ridiculous. However did you get such an idea? Emily, that's ridiculous,' she repeated in a high, unnatural tone.

'One time before we moved here, once when you came home from Chicago, I remember, I heard Aunt Helen say something to Uncle Darwin about how awful you looked. She said she thought maybe –'

'Emily, I'm surprised. Really, I am. I'm sure you didn't hear right. But even if you did, I can't help what Aunt Helen may have dreamed up.'

'You wouldn't have cried so last night if it were only the pain. It's got to be more than that.'

'Only the pain! All those thorns? Well, maybe I'm a coward and a crybaby. Maybe I am, that's all.'

Emily must not lose faith in her father. It's damaging forever. A woman remembers her father all her life. My own dearest memories are of my dad. He taught me how to stand up for my rights and how to forgive; when he had to scold he was gentle . . .

82

Lynn quieted her hands, resting them on the tabletop, and made a firm appeal.

'Trust me, Emily. Have I ever lied to you?'

But disbelief remained in the girl's quivering lips. Two lines formed on her smooth forehead.

'He was so ferocious this morning.'

'Darling, you keep using that nasty word. He was in a hurry to get to the office, I told you. He was distressed.' She spoke rapidly. 'Your father's such a good man! Need I tell you that, for heaven's sake? And you're so like him, a hard worker, determined to succeed, and you always do succeed. That's why you've been so close, you two. You've had such a special relationship. It hurts me to think you might lose it.'

'Don't you think it hurts me too? But you have to admit Dad can be very strange.'

'Strange? After all the caring, the loving attention he's given you all your life?'

'You don't convince me, Mom.'

'I wish I could.'

'I feel something. It's stuck inside my head. But I can understand why you're talking to me this way.'

The kettle whistled, and Emily got up to turn it off. She moved with elegance, even in jeans and sneakers; her slender waist, rounding into the swell of her hips, was womanly, while her skin was as unflawed as a baby's. Suddenly it seemed to Lynn that she was being condescended to, as if the young girl, out of a superior wisdom, were consoling or patronizing the older woman. Her very stance as she turned her back to stack the dishwasher, the very flip of her ponytail, gave rise in her mother to resentment. And she said somewhat sharply, 'I trust you'll keep these unbecoming thoughts to yourself. And keep them especially away from Annie. That's an order, Emily.'

Emily spun around. 'Do you really think I would hurt

83

Annie any more than she's already hurt? Annie's a wreck. I don't think you realize it.'

This stubborn persistence was too much like Robert's. Lynn was under attack. Arrows were flying. It was too much. Yet she replied with formal dignity. 'You exaggerate. I'm well aware that Annie is going through a difficult stage. But Annie will be just fine.'

'Not if Dad keeps picking on her about being fat,' Emily said, and added a moment later, 'I wish things seemed as simple as they used to seem.'

Her forced smile was sad, and it affected Lynn, changing the earlier flash of resentment into pity.

'You're growing up,' she said wistfully.

'I'm already grown, Mom.'

Across the hall Annie was still pounding at the minuet. Suddenly, as if two hands had come down in full angry force, the melody broke off into a cacophony of shrill chords, as if the piano were making violent protest.

The two women frowned, and Emily said, 'She hates the piano. She only does it because he makes her.'

'It's for her own good. She'll be glad someday.'

They gave each other a searching look that lasted until Emily broke the tension.

'I'm sorry I said anything this morning. Maybe this is only a mood that will wear away.' From outside came the light tap of a horn. 'That's Harris. I'm off.' The girl leaned down and kissed her mother's cheek. 'Don't worry about me. I won't make any trouble. Forget what I said. Maybe I don't know what I'm talking about. But take care of yourself, Mom. Just take care of yourself.'

The kitchen was very still after Emily went out. Then the screen door slammed on the porch. The dog rose, shook itself, and followed Annie outside. In the silence a plaintive repetition sounded in Lynn's ears. *Dad can be very strange. Take care of yourself, Mom.* And as if in a trance she sat with her fingers clasped around the coffee cup, which had long grown cold.

She tried to concentrate on errands to be done, the house to be tidied and clothes to take to the cleaners, all the small ways in which living continues even when the worst things have happened, for if the pipes break on the day of the funeral, one still has to call the plumber. And yet she did not rise to do any of these things.

The doorbell brought her out of her lethargy. Expecting the delivery of some packages, she put her sunglasses back on; they were light and concealed very little, but the United Parcel man would probably not even look at her, and if he did look, wouldn't care. Barefooted, in her housecoat, she opened the door into the glare of revealing sunlight and faced Tom Lawrence.

'You forgot this,' he said, holding out her purse, 'so I thought I'd –' His eyes flickered over her and away.

'Oh, how stupid of me. How nice of you.' Absurd words came out of her mouth. 'I look a mess, I fell, sprained my ankle, and can't get a shoe on.'

He was looking at the tubbed geraniums on the top step. That was decent of him. He had seen, and was embarrassed for her.

'Oh. A sorry end to a wonderful evening. Ankles turn so easily. It takes a few days to get back to normal. I hope you'll feel better.'

She closed the door. Mortified, she thought, I wish I could dig a hole and crawl into it. What can he be thinking! I never want to see him again. Never.

After a while, with main effort, she recovered. Alone in the house, she could admonish herself out loud.

'What are you doing, not dressed at eleven o'clock? Get moving, Lynn.'

So, slowly and painfully, she limped through the house doing small, unimportant chores, raised or lowered shades according to need, wrote a check at the desk, and threw out faded flowers, allowing these ordinary acts to soothe her spirit as best they could.

Presently she went into the kitchen. For her it had always been the heart of the house, her special place. Here she could concentrate a troubled mind on a difficult new recipe, here feel the good weight of copper-bottom pots in her hands, and here feel quietness.

A lamb stew simmered, filling the room with the smell of rosemary, and an apple pie had cooled on the counter when, late in the afternoon, she heard Robert's car enter the driveway.

Robert's mouth was as expressive as his eyes; she could always tell by it what was to come next. Now she saw with relief that his lips were upturned into a half smile.

'Everybody home?'

'The girls will be home in a minute. Emily went to the lake, and Annie's at a friend's house.'

'And how are you? You're still limping. Wouldn't it feel better with a tight bandage?'

'It's all right as it is.'

'Well, if you're sure.' He hesitated. 'If that's Emily' – for there came the sound of wheels on gravel – 'I want to talk to her. To both of them. In the den.'

'Can't it wait until after dinner? I have everything ready.'

'I'd rather not wait,' he answered, walking away.

She thought, He will take out his guilt over me in anger at them.

'Your father wants to see you both in the den,' she told the girls when they came in. As they both grimaced, she admonished them. 'Don't make faces. Listen to what he has to say.'

Never let them sense any differences between their parents about discipline. That's a cardinal rule for their own good. Rule number one.

Now again her heart was beating so rapidly that she

felt only a need to flee, yet she followed them to the den, where Robert stood behind his desk.

He began at once. 'We need more order in this house. It's too slipshod. People come and go as they please without having even the decency to say where they're going or when they're coming back. They have no sense of time. Coming home at all hours as they please. You'd think this was a boardinghouse.'

The poor children. What had they done that was so bad? This was absurd. And she thought again: It is his conscience. He has to turn the tables to put himself in the right.

'I want to know whenever and wherever you go to another house, Annie. I want to know with whom you are associating.'

The child stared. 'The other fathers aren't like you. You think this is the army, and you're the general.'

It was an oddly sophisticated observation to come from the mouth of an eleven-year-old.

'I won't have your impudence, Annie.'

Robert never raised his voice when he was angry. Yet there was more authority in his controlled anger than in another man's shouts; memory carried Lynn suddenly back to the office in St Louis and the dreaded summons from Ferguson to be 'reamed out'; she had never received that summons herself, but plenty of others had and never forgot it afterward.

'You'd better get hold of yourself, Annie. You're no baby anymore, and you're too fresh. Your schoolwork isn't good enough, and you're too fat. I've told you a hundred times, you ought to be ashamed of the way you look.'

Gooseflesh rose on Lynn's cold arms, and she stood there hugging them. It was unbearable to be here, weakened as she was today, but still she stayed as if her presence, silent as she was, was some protection for her children, although she was certainly not protecting them against these words, and there was no need to guard them from anything else. Never, never had Robert, nor would he ever, raise a hand to his girls.

Her mind, straying, came back to the present. He had been saying something about Harris, calling him a 'character.' That nice boy. She could not hear Emily's murmured answer, but she plainly heard Robert's response.

'And I don't want to see him every time I walk into my home. I'm sick of looking at him. If I wanted a boy, I'd adopt one.'

Annie, whose face had turned a wounded red, ran bawling to the door and flung it open so violently that it crashed against the wall.

'I hate everybody! I hate you, Dad!' she screamed. 'I wish you would die.'

With her head high, tears on her cheeks and looking straight ahead, Emily walked out.

In Robert's face Lynn saw the reflection of her own horror. But he was the first to lower his eyes.

'They needed what they got,' he said. 'They're not suffering.'

'You think not?'

'They'll get over it. Call them back down to eat a proper dinner in the dining room.'

'No, Robert. I'm going to bring their supper upstairs and leave them in peace. But yours is ready for you.'

'You eat if you can. I have no appetite.'

She went upstairs with plates for Emily and Annie, which they both refused. Sick at heart, she went back to the kitchen and put the good dinner away. Even the clink of the dishes was loud enough to make her wince. When it grew dark, she went outside and sat down on the steps with Juliet, who was the sole untroubled creature in that house. Long after the sky grew dark, she sat there, close to the gentle animal, as if to absorb some comfort from its gentleness. I am lost, she said to herself. An image came to her of someone fallen off a ship, alone on a raft in an empty sea.

And that was the end of Saturday.

On Sunday the house was still in mourning. In their rooms the girls were doing homework, or so they said when she knocked. Perhaps, poor children, they were just sitting in gloom, not doing much of anything. In the den Robert was bent over papers at the desk, with his open briefcase on the floor beside him. No one spoke. The separation was complete. And Lynn had a desolate need to talk, to be consoled. She thought of the people who loved her, and had loved her: her parents, both gone now, who would have forfeited their lives for her just as she would do for Emily and Annie; of Helen, who – and here she had to smile a bit ruefully – would give a little scolding along with comfort; and then of Josie. But to none of these would she or could she speak. Her father would have raged at Robert. And Helen would think, even if she might not say, 'You remember, I never liked him, Lynn.' And Josie would analyze. Her eyes would search and probe.

No. None of these. And she thought as always: Marriage is a magic circle that no outsider must enter, or the circle will never close again. Whatever is wrong must be solved within the circle.

She walked through the house and the yard doing useless makework, as she had done the day before. In the living room she studied Robert's photo, but today the rather austere face told her nothing except that it was handsome and intelligent. In the yard the two new garden benches that he had ordered from a catalog stood near the fence. He was always finding ways to brighten the house, to make living more pleasant. He had hung thatched-roof birdhouses in secluded places, and one was already occupied by a family of wrens. He had bought a book of North American birds and was studying it with Annie, or trying to anyway, for the child's attention span was short. But he tried. So why, why was he – how, how could he –

The telephone rang in the kitchen, and she ran inside to answer it.

'Bruce went fishing yesterday,' Josie reported, 'and brought home enough for a regiment. He wants to do them on the outdoor grill. How about all of you coming over for lunch?'

Lynn lied quickly. 'The girls are studying for exams, and Robert is working at his desk. I don't dare disturb him.'

'Well, but they do need to eat,' Josie said sensibly. 'Let them come, eat, and run.'

She was always sensible, Josie was. And at that moment this reasonableness of hers had its effect on Lynn, so that she said almost without thinking, 'But I'll come by myself, if that's all right with you.'

'Of course,' said Josie.

Driving down Halsey Road through the estate section, and then through the town past the sportswear boutiques, the red-brick colonial movie, and the saddlery shop, all at Sunday-morning rest, she began to regret her hasty offer. Since she had no intention of confiding in Josie, she would have to make small talk, or at least Josie's version of small talk, which would involve the front page of *The New York Times*. Yet she did not go back, but drove through the little town and out to where the great estates had long ago been broken up, where new tract houses stood across from the pseudo-Elizabethan tract houses that had been put there in the twenties.

It was one of these that the Lehmans had bought, a little

house with mock-oak beams and leaded glass windows. It was a rather cramped little house.

'He can afford better,' Robert had remarked with some disdain.

And Lynn had answered innocently, 'Josie told me they couldn't afford anything better because of her medical expenses.'

Robert had exclaimed, 'What? Well, that's undignified, to say the least, going all over the neighborhood telling people about one's business.'

'She's not going all over the neighborhood. We're friends.'

'Friends or not, the woman talks too much. I hope you don't learn bad habits from her.' And then he had said, 'Bruce is cheap. He thinks small. I saw that from the beginning.'

But Bruce wasn't 'cheap.' Josie's sickness had cost a small fortune, and as Josie herself had said, who knew what was yet to come? It was she who hadn't let him spend more. He would have given the stars to her if he could.

He was in the backyard when she drove up, sanding a chest of drawers, concentrating with his glasses shoved up into his curly brown hair.

He summoned Lynn. 'Come, look at my find. What a job! I picked it up at an antiques barn way past Litchfield last week. Must have twenty coats of paint on it. I have a hunch there's curly maple at the bottom. Well, we'll see.'

His enthusiasm was appealing to her. His full lips were always slightly upturned, even in repose; she had the impression that he could sometimes hardly contain a secret inner happiness. A cleft in his chin gave sweetness to a face that, with its high cheekbones and jutting nose, might best be described as 'rugged.' A 'man's man,' you could say; but then she thought, a 'man's man' is all the more a woman's man too.

'You've really been having a great time with your antiques since you moved east,' she said.

When she moved from the shade into the glare he saw her face. For an instant his eyes widened before he bent back over his work and replied, as though he had seen nothing.

'Well, of course, New England's the place. You can't compare it with Missouri for early Americana. You'd think that the old villages had been combed through so long now that there'd be nothing left, but you'd be surprised. I even found a comb-back Windsor. It needs a lot of work, but I've got weekends, and with daylight saving I can squeeze in another hour when I get back from the city. Where's Robert? Still working, I think Josie said?'

'Yes, as usual, he's at his desk with a pile of papers,' she replied, sounding casual.

'I admire his energy. To say nothing of his headful of ideas. There's no stopping him.' Smiling, Bruce turned back to the sander. 'As for me, I'm driving my wife crazy with this stuff. She doesn't care about antiques.'

'She cares about you, and that's what matters,' Lynn told him, and went inside conscious of having blurted out something too serious for the time and place.

Josie was on the sun porch with the paper and a cup of tea. She looks thin, Lynn thought, thinner since I last saw her a week ago. Still, her bright expression of welcome and her strong voice were the same as always. The body had betrayed the spirit. And this thought, coming upon her own agitation, almost brought tears to Lynn.

'Why, whatever's happened to you?' Josie cried, letting the paper slide to the floor. 'Your face! Your legs!'

'Nothing much. I slipped and fell. Clumsy.'

'Is that why you've been crying?'

'That, and a silly mood. Forget it.'

'It would be sillier to forget it. You came for a reason.'

Lynn tucked her long cotton skirt over her spotted legs. 'I fell into the hawthorn hedge in the dark.'

'So it hurts. But what about the mood?'

'Oh, it's just been a bad day. The house is in turmoil, perhaps because they got upset over me. And we just don't seem to know sometimes how to handle the girls. Although it will straighten out, I'm sure. When you called, I suppose at that moment I needed a shoulder to cry on, but now that I'm here, I know I shouldn't have come.'

Josie regarded her from head to foot. 'Yes, you should have come. Let me get you a cup of tea, and then you can tell me what's on your mind. Or not tell me, as you please.' She went quickly to the door and turning, added, 'I hope you will tell me.'

'We don't seem to know how to handle the girls,' Lynn repeated. 'But you know our problems already. I needn't tell you that Robert doesn't approve of Emily's boyfriend. And Annie won't try to lose weight, she stuffs herself, and Robert can't stand that.'

She stopped, thinking again, I shouldn't have come here to dump all this on her. She looks so tired, I'm tired myself, and nothing will come of all these prattling half-truths, anyway.

'I do know all that,' Josie said. 'But I don't think you're telling me the whole story,' she added, somewhat sternly.

Like my sister, Lynn thought, she can be stern and soft at the same time, which is curious. I never could be.

'They're good girls –'

'I know that too.'

'Maybe I'm making a mountain out of a molehill. These are hard times in which to rear children. I'm sure lots of families have problems worse than ours. Yes, I am making too much of it,' Lynn finished, apologizing.

'I don't think you are.'

There was a silence in which Lynn struggled first with

words that were reluctant to be said, and finally with words that struggled equally hard to be released.

'Yesterday Robert was furious because Emily came home too late.'

'Do you think she did?'

'Yes, only I wouldn't have been so angry about it. And Annie, you know she wants to have her hair straightened and Robert says that's ridiculous, and there is always something going on between Robert and Annie, although he does try hard. Yesterday she screamed at him. She was hysterical, almost. She hates everybody. She hates him.' And Lynn, ceasing, gave Josie an imploring look.

'Tell me, is it only Robert who is having this trouble with the girls? Just Robert?'

'Well, yes. It's hard for a man to come home from a trying day and have to cope with children, when what he needs most is rest. Especially a man with Robert's responsibilities.'

'We all have our responsibilities,' Josie said dryly.

For a moment neither woman said more. It was as if they had reached an impasse. Lynn shifted uncomfortably in the chair. When Josie spoke again, she was careful to look away from Lynn and down at her own fingernails, saying with unusual softness, 'Isn't there anything more?'

Lynn drew back in alarm. 'Why, no. What should there be?'

'I only asked,' said Josie.

And suddenly Lynn began to cry. Muffled broken phrases came through her tears.

'It wasn't just the children this time. It was because of me – at Tom Lawrence's house – it was too late, and Robert came – and I was dancing – Robert was angry, really so awfully – of course I knew I shouldn't have been dancing, but –'

'Now, wait. Let me get this straight. You were dancing with Tom, and Robert –'

'He was furious,' sobbed Lynn, wiping her eyes.

'What the hell was wrong with dancing? You weren't in bed with the man. What do you mean, you shouldn't have been? I've never heard anything so ridiculous,' Josie said hotly. She paused, frowned as if considering the situation, and then spoke more quietly. 'And so you went home and had an argument near the thorn hedge and –'

Lynn put up her hand as if to stop traffic. 'No, no, it wasn't–' she began. For a red warning had flashed in her head. Robert is Bruce's superior in the firm. It won't do, no matter how much I care about Bruce and Josie, for me to undermine Robert at his work. I've said too much already. Stupid. Stupid.

It was just then that Bruce came into the room.

'I'm taking time out. You don't mind, Boss?' he began, and stopped abruptly. 'Am I interrupting anything? You two look so sober.'

Lynn blinked away the moisture that had gathered again in her eyes. 'I was spilling out some minor troubles, that's all.'

Josie corrected her. 'They are not minor, Lynn.'

'I'll leave you both,' Bruce said promptly.

But Lynn wanted him. It would have been inappropriate and subject to misinterpretation for her to tell him: Your presence helps me. You are so genuine. So she said only, 'Please stay.'

'You've told me, and since I would tell Bruce anyway after you left, he might as well hear it from me now.' And as Lynn sat like a patient, listening miserably while a pair of doctors discussed her case, Josie repeated the brief, disjointed story.

Bruce had sat down in an easy chair. His legs rested on an ottoman, while his arms were folded comfortably behind his head. This informal posture, and his deliberate, considering manner of speech, were reassuring.

'So you had a row over the girls. Does it happen often?'

'Oh, no, not at all. Annie and Robert –'

Bruce put his hand up. 'I don't think you should be talking to me about Robert,' he said gently.

Lynn felt the rebuke. She ought to have remembered Bruce's sense of ethics. And she stood up, saying quickly, 'I've really got to run home and see about lunch. We can talk another time.'

'Wait,' said Bruce. 'Josie, do you agree with me that Lynn needs advice? You're much too close to her to give it, but don't you think somebody should?'

'Definitely.'

'What's the name of that fellow you knew who went into counseling, Josie? You had such a high opinion of him, and he settled in Connecticut, I think.'

'Ira Miller,' Josie said promptly. 'You'd like him, Lynn. I can get you the address from my alumni bulletin. I'll just run upstairs.'

'I'm not sure I want to do this,' Lynn told Bruce when they were alone.

'You have lovely girls,' he said quietly. 'Your little Annie is my special person. You know that. And if they're a problem or making trouble, you need to find out why, don't you?'

He was trying not to look at her face or her dreadful legs when he repeated the question. 'Don't you?'

'I suppose so.'

'You know so, Lynn.'

'Yes.' They were right. She had to talk to somebody. There was a volcano in her head, ready to erupt in outrage and grief. Relief must come. It must. And it was true that to a stranger she would be able to say what she could not say to these old friends: My husband did this to me.

'I called him for you,' Josie reported. 'I took the liberty of making an appointment for you tomorrow afternoon. He couldn't have been nicer. Here's the address.'

As they walked Lynn to her car, Bruce said, 'I hear your dinner was a big success.'

'Goodness, how did you hear that?'

'Tom Lawrence. I met him yesterday morning jogging.'

'Oh, dear, I suppose he told you how awful I looked when he came to the house to return my purse? I was still in my housecoat, and –'

'The only thing he told me was that you should do something with your talent, and I agree.'

'It'll be about half an hour's drive tomorrow,' Josie said. She smiled encouragement. 'And that's even allowing time for getting lost.'

'Good luck,' Bruce called as Lynn drove away.

Robert, finding the reminder on Lynn's writing desk, demanded, 'Dr Miller, three o'clock. What kind of doctor is this?'

These were the first words he had spoken to her that Sunday, and she gave him a short answer. 'What are you doing at my desk?'

'I was looking in your address book for a periodontist that somebody asked about.'

'I don't look at things on your desk.'

'I never said you shouldn't. I have no secrets.' He strode to the large flattop on the other side of the room. 'Come on. Look. Open any drawer you want.'

'I don't want to open any drawer, Robert. All right, I'll tell you. Dr Miller is a therapist. That's what we've come to.'

'That's not necessary, Lynn.' He spoke quietly. 'You don't need it.'

'But I do. And you need to go too. Will you?'

'Definitely not. We had a disagreement. What's so extraordinary? People have disagreements all the time and get over them. No doubt this is some bright idea of Josie's.'

'It is not,' she answered truthfully.

'Bruce's, then.'

Hating to lie, she did not answer.

'I'm not spending money on this stuff, Lynn. I work too hard for it. Paying some stranger to listen to your troubles.' His voice rose now, not in anger but in plaint. 'I've never prevented you from buying anything you wanted, have I? Just look around at this house.' His arm swept out over the leather chairs, the tawny rug, and the golden light on the lawn beyond the windows.

'Furniture isn't everything, or rings either,' she responded, twisting the diamond on her finger.

'I should think you'd be ashamed to go and spill out your personal affairs. You're overreacting, you're over emotional. A man and wife have a nasty argument, and you behave as if the end of the world had come. No, I don't want you to go. Listen to me, Lynn –'

But she had already left the room.

In midafternoon the turnpike was an almost vacant path through a pastel landscape, pink cherry bloom, white apple bloom, and damp green leafage. The station wagon rolled along so easily that Lynn, turning off at the exit, found herself an hour too early for her appointment.

She drew up before a square house on a quiet street of developer's houses, all alike, except that this one possessed a wing with a separate entrance. A dirt bike propped against the wall of the garage and a glimpse of a jungle gym in the backyard were encouraging; the man would be experienced, and his words would not all come out of books.

Thinking it absurd to sit in the car for an hour, she rang the bell. A nondescript woman in a purple printed dress, who might have been either the doctor's wife or his mother, opened the door. No, the doctor was not in yet, but Lynn might come inside and wait.

The wait felt very, very long. Now that she had taken this great step, now that she was actually here, an anxious haste overcame her. Let me get this over with, it pleaded. As the minutes went by so slowly, so slowly, a faint fear began to crawl up from the pit of her stomach, to quicken her heart and lump itself in her throat. And she tried to stamp the fear out with reassurance: It is like waiting for your turn at the dentist's, that's all it is.

But this office was too small. There was no willing stranger to talk with or even to observe.

Her heart was racing now. She crossed the little room, took a couple of magazines, and was unable to read. Nothing made sense, neither the summer fashions nor the economic development of Eastern Europe. Nothing. She got up to examine the pictures on the wall, skillful portraits and pictures of places where the subjects of the portraits had been. Here they were posed on beaches, in ski clothes, and smiling under the iron arches of the Eiffel Tower. When she had seen all these, she sat down again with her heart still racing.

What was she to say to this unknown man? How to start? Perhaps he might ask why she had come to him. How, then, would she explain? Opening sentences formed and reformed silently on her lips. Well, on Saturday night there was a terrible scene. Cruel, bitter words were spoken, words that I had not dreamed could be said in our home, where we loved – love each other. But on the other hand, don't all children sometimes say that they hate their parents? So that it means nothing, really? Really? But Emily said that Robert ... that Robert ...

A husky middle-aged man appeared at the inner door. They matched, he and the woman in the purple print, so she must be his wife, Lynn thought absurdly, and was at the same instant aware that she was not thinking straight.

'Will you come in, please, Mrs Ferguson?'

When she stood up, the walls whirled, and she had to grasp the back of the chair.

'I'm suddenly not feeling well, Doctor.' The words

came brokenly. 'Maybe it's the flu or something. I don't know. I'm dizzy. It just came over me. If you'll excuse me, I'll come again. I'll pay for this visit. I'm sorry,' she stammered.

The man's eyes, magnified by thick glasses, regarded her gravely. And she was suddenly reminded of her bruises, the unsightly marks on which scabs had not yet formed.

'I had – you can see – I had a little accident. I fell. We have a thorn hedge, so pretty, but those thorns, like needles –'

'Oh? An accident?' He paused. 'Well, you mustn't drive while you're dizzy, you know. Please come in and rest in a comfortable chair until you feel better.'

Feeling forced to obey, she took her seat in a large leather chair, laid her head back, and closed her eyes. She could hear papers rustling on the desk, the opening and closing of a drawer, and the pounding of her blood in her ears.

After a while a pleasant voice caused her to open her eyes.

'You don't have to talk if you don't want to.'

'It does seem foolish to sit here and say nothing. Really, really, I think I should go,' she repeated, as if she were begging permission.

'If you like, of course. But I don't think you're coming down with the flu.'

'The dizziness is gone at least, so perhaps not.'

'I am curious to know why you came here at all. Can you tell me that much?'

'It's strange. I imagined you would ask me that.'

'And did you imagine what your answer would be?'

'Josie – Josie Lehman said I should ask advice.' She wiped her sweating palms on a handkerchief. 'We don't, I mean, sometimes my husband and I don't seem to handle the children, I mean we don't always agree. We

100

have a teenage daughter and a girl of eleven, she's very sensitive, too fat, and my husband wants her to lose weight, and of course he's right, and you see – well, this weekend there were, there were misunderstandings, a quarrel, you see, and Annie, she's the younger one, told Robert she hated him, and I didn't quite know what to do.'

And Emily said: Dad did it to you.

I can't, I can't say that.

Lynn's eyes filmed. Fiercely she wiped the damned humiliating tears away. She had vowed not to cry.

'I'm sorry,' she murmured.

'That's all right. Why not cry if you need to?'

'So. So that's what it is, you see. Maybe I'm exaggerating. Now that I hear myself, I think I probably am. It's one of my faults. I get too emotional.'

There were a few moments of silence until the pleasant voice addressed her again.

'You haven't told me anything about your husband.'

'Oh, Robert, Robert is an unusual man. You don't often meet anyone like him, a Renaissance man, you might say. People do say. He has so many talents, everyone admires him, his scholarship and energy, he does so much good in the community and takes so much time with the children, their education, so much time –'

I hate you.

Dad did it to you.

'Yes?' said the voice, encouraging.

'I don't know what else to say. I –'

'You've told me what your husband does for the children and for the community, but not what he does for you.'

'Well, he's very generous, very thoughtful and –' She stopped. It was impossible; she was not able to say it; she should not have come here.

'Is that all? Tell me, for instance, whether you are often angry at each other.'

101

'Well, sometimes Robert gets angry, of course. I mean, people do, don't they? And often it's my fault – '

Nausea rose into her throat, and she was cold. On a blazing summer afternoon she felt gooseflesh on her arms. And she stood abruptly in a kind of panic, wanting only to flee.

'No, I can't say any more today. No, no, I'm not dizzy now, truly I'm not. I can drive. It's just a headache, a touch of fever. I am coming down with something after all. I *know* I am. But I'll come back,' she said. 'I surely will. I know I should.'

Asking no more, the doctor stood and opened the door.

'I'll give you an appointment, Mrs Ferguson. I'm going away for three weeks. When I come back, if you want to keep the appointment, I will be glad to talk to you. And in the meantime it would be a good idea to keep a daily record of everything you all do together. Write it down, the happy hours as well as the other kind. Then we'll talk. If you wish,' he repeated. 'Will you do that?'

'Yes, yes, I will. And thank you, thank you so much,' she said.

Safely alone in the car, safely away from the measuring eyes behind the thick glasses, she felt at first a deep relief. But very gradually, as the distance between herself and those eyes increased, and the distance between herself and home diminished, she began to feel instead the heat of a cowardly shame, as if she had been caught in some dishonorable act, a harmful lie, a demeaning theft, or as if she had been found wandering demented through the streets in her underwear. Why, why, had she not told the whole truth? The man had known there was something else. He had seen right through her.

The after-work traffic was heavy, so it was past the dinner hour when she reached home to find Robert's car already in the garage. Ready for a confrontation, she steadied herself and walked into the house. Well, I did it, she would say, and I'll face right up to him. Yes, I'll say, I'm going again, and there's nothing you can do about it.

They were all still at table. Robert got up and pulled out Lynn's chair, Annie smiled, and Emily said, 'I put your chicken casserole into the microwave and made a salad, Mom. I hope you weren't saving the casserole for anything. I didn't know.'

'Saving it for all of you, dear. And thank you, Emily. You're as helpful as my right hand.'

'Annie set the table,' Emily said pointedly.

'If I had two right hands, then you'd be the other one, Annie.'

The atmosphere was tranquil. One could always sense something as palpable as wind or temperature in a room where any strong emotions, healthy or otherwise, had stirred the air. Here, now, a breeze rippled the white silk curtains, Juliet dozed under the table, and three calm faces turned to Lynn. Can they all have forgotten? she asked herself incredulously. It was true that Robert's black moods could quickly, with the flip of a coin, turn golden. Also it was true that, when in his own golden mood, he knew how to charm a person whom he had just hurt and angered. Besides, the girls had the wonderful, forgetful resilience of youth. For that at least, she should be thankful. Still, it was astonishing to see them all sitting there like that.

Annie inquired, 'Where were you so late, Mommy?'

'Oh, I had the usual errands and didn't look at my watch.'

Unconsciously, Lynn glanced toward Robert, whose glance, above the rim of his cup, met hers. He put the cup down, and she looked away.

'Aren't you going to tell Mom now?' asked Emily, addressing Robert.

At once alarmed, Lynn gave a little cry. 'Tell Mom what? Has something happened?'

'Something very nice, I think,' Emily said.

Robert, reaching into his jacket pocket, drew out a long envelope and, with a satisfied air, handed it to Lynn.

'Plane tickets,' he told her.

'Kennedy to San Juan and transfer to St –' she read. 'Robert! What on earth?'

'Ten days in the Caribbean. We leave Saturday morning. That gives you a few days to get ready and to feel better. He wore a proud smile. 'Now, what do you say to that?'

What I want to say, she thought, is: How dare you! What do you think I am? Instead, and only because the girls were present, she replied, 'The girls can't miss school, Robert. I don't know what can be in your mind.'

'They aren't going to miss school. This vacation is for you and me.'

It was a cheap – no, an expensive – bribe. She could feel the heat in her cheeks. And still for the girls' sake, she said evenly, 'It makes no sense. Who'll be in charge here? I'm not walking away and leaving a household to fend for itself.'

'Of course not. That's all been taken care of. I've spent the whole day making arrangements. Eudora will sleep in while we're gone. The girls use the school bus, and if there's need to go anyplace, Eudora'll take them in her car or Bruce and Josie will, on the weekends. I talked to Bruce,' Robert explained. 'They'll be glad to take the girls to the town pool, and Bruce will drive Annie to her tennis lesson. I don't want her to miss it, and he doesn't mind.'

Annie, who returned Bruce's love tenfold, now interjected a plea. 'You know I like going with Uncle Bruce, Mommy. Please say yes, Mommy.'

'So you see, it's all arranged. No problems. Nothing to do but pack a few clothes,' Robert said positively.

Feeling trapped, Lynn pushed away from the table, saying only, 'We'll talk about it later. I don't like having things sprung on me like this. Now, you have homework, girls. Leave the kitchen; I'll clean up by myself.'

When she went upstairs, Robert followed. Once in their room, she turned on him.

'You think you can bribe me, don't you? It's unspeakable.'

'Please. There's no bribe intended, only a cure. A cure for what ails us.'

'It'll take more than ten days in the island paradise,' she said sarcastically. 'A whole lot more, to do that.'

At the window she stood with her back to him. The view of trees and hill, always so restful to her soul, was melancholy now as the hill hid the lowering sun and shadowed the garden.

'The girls want us to go. You heard them.'

Of course they do, she thought. It will be an adventure for them to lord it over the house with their parents away. Why not? And she thought, too, now with a twinge of unease, Emily will stay out too late with Harris.

Robert persisted. 'I'm not worried about them, you know. Bruce and Josie are as dependable as you and I are.'

Yes, she thought, when they can be useful, you will use the Lehmans, even though you don't like them. Still she said nothing, only, for some unconscious reason, turned up her palms, on which tiny dark-red scabs like polka dots had begun to form.

'I don't want to go,' she said abruptly.

'You saw that man today,' he said.

'I did,' she retorted, 'and what of it?'

'I didn't believe you would. I'm completely shocked. I didn't think you really meant to.'

'I meant to, Robert.'

'And what did he –'

'Oh, no!' she cried. 'You don't ask a question like that. Don't you know any better? Unless you will consent to go with me.'

'If it will satisfy you,' he said, seizing her words. 'I don't believe we need anything except to get away together. But if it will satisfy you, I will do anything,' he finished humbly.

And she stood there still staring at her hands.

'We're tired, both of us.' He, whose speech was always so deliberate, now rushed and stumbled. 'This last year or two has been hectic, there's been no rest, you and I have scarcely had an hour alone together. The new house for you, new office and work for me. New faces for me, new schools, friends, all these hard adjustments –'

In the face of his distress she felt triumphant, and yet something in her had to pity that distress.

'Listen. I know my temper's hot, but I don't lose it often, you have to admit. And I'm always sorry as hell afterward. Not that that does much good, I know. But I'm not a bad sort, Lynn, and I love you.'

From below came the sound of Annie's plodding minuet. Emily came bounding upstairs to answer her ringing phone. As if he had read Lynn's mind – as he almost always could – Robert said softly, 'They need us, Lynn. Our children need us both. We can't punish them. Let's put this crazy business behind us. Please.'

'Oh,' she said with a heavy sigh.

He paced the room while again his words rushed.

'I was jealous, I was furious that night. The sight of you dancing with that man when I had been worried about you made me frantic. You looked so intimate together. I realize now how stupid it was of me. You're an innocent woman, you could never –' And he stopped while his eyes went bright with the start of tears. 'Then you said there was something wrong with me.'

'I was very, very angry, Robert, and I still am.'

106

'All right. Angry or not, will you go? For the family's sake, will you go?' He laid the thick envelope on the dresser. 'I was lucky to get these tickets. They're all booked up for honeymooners this time of year, but there was a cancellation. So you see, it was meant to be. Oh, Lynn, forgive me.'

He was still standing there, with the tears still brilliant on his lashes, when without replying, she turned away.

Down the long road beside the marshes the plane sped, raised itself mightily into the bright air, and circled southward.

'Well, here we are,' said Robert.

Lynn said nothing. Nothing was required. Resentment was still sore in her, burning like ill-digested food. Because of her wish to be finished with a hideous anger, to conceal from her children whatever could be concealed, she had been led and inveigled, tricked, into sitting where she now sat.

'You'll be glad you've gone,' he said soothingly.

She turned the full force of her scorn upon him. 'Glad? That'll be the day.'

Robert, with a look of appeal, pursed his lips to caution: Shh. They were sitting three abreast. An old man, so hugely fat that his bulk hung over his seat into Robert's space, sat by the window. The aisle seat was Lynn's.

'Miserably cramped,' Robert murmured. 'First class was taken up, dammit.'

Ignoring him, she took a book out of her carry-on and settled back. It had always been her way to 'make the best' of things, and whether she liked to admit it to herself or not, there was, even in these circumstances, a certain anticipation of pleasure in the sight of palms and blue water. Having spent most of her life in the Midwest, she still found these a marvelous novelty; she had visited the lovely, lazy Caribbean islands only twice before. There's

107

no point, she argued now, in wearing a hair shirt. I shall swim, I've brought three great books, and luckily for me, I'm thin enough so that I can afford to eat; I hope the food will be good. And I don't have to talk to Robert.

He mumbled again, 'I'm going to try for first class going home. I can't tolerate this. It's worse than the subway.'

When she did not comment, he made no further effort, and little more was said between them all the rest of the way.

From the balcony on the first morning, she looked out upon water and sky. There was no one in sight except for the beachboys, who were setting up a row of yellow umbrellas, and far out a little bobbing boat with a Roman-striped sail. I suppose, she thought idly, if one were to head straight east from here, one would land someplace in northern Africa.

'Why, you're up early,' Robert said brightly. 'You beat me this morning. Wonderful, isn't it?'

'Yes. I'm going for a walk on the beach.'

'If you'll wait a minute, I'll go with you.'

'Thank you, but I want to walk by myself.'

'All right,' he said agreeably.

The sun had not been up long, and the air was still cool. She walked easily on the firm sand at the water's edge, left the hotel's property behind, and continued along what seemed to be an unending stretch of beach edged by pine grove, beach grape, and clustered green-ery nameless to her. Occasionally, she passed what must be the winter homes of American or British millionaires, low, gracious houses steeped in the shade of banyan and flamboyant trees.

Rounding an abrupt curve, she faced a grassy hill that blocked her path, steep as a ladder, with water on three sides. It would be a struggle to the top, but not daunted, she began the climb. Once there and breathless, she sat down to look about and gaze and was struck with the kind of wonder that fills the soul in some ancient, high cathedral.

No, not so. For here was a far greater splendor. Such blue! Almost green at the shore where the green hill was reflected, this water shaded into purest turquoise; then three quarters of the way to the horizon lay a broad band of cobalt so even as to have been drawn with a ruler. On the farthest outer edge the horizon was a thin, penciled line, above which there spread another blue, the calm, eternal blue of a sky without cloud.

The wind rushed and the tide in soporific rhythm splashed on the rocks below. Before her lay an immense dazzle, the mysterious power of brilliant light; so it had been for untold eons and would be for untold eons more, she thought, until the sun should burn itself out and the earth freeze. The thought was hardly original, but that made it no less awesome.

Lying back on the rough sweet grass, she looked up at the shimmering sky. All the transient things, the injustice, the hurt, the unfairness, what were they in the end that we should waste our lives on them? My God, how short life was!

Now came a flock of seabirds, racing from nowhere, turning and turning in their descent to skim the water and soar again upward. They were so joyous – could birds be joyous? – and she laughed at herself for thinking so and at her own pleasure in watching them. And her first thoughts returned with a thrill of sorrow, repeating: How short life is. And we walk with blinders on.

For half an hour or maybe longer, she lay while the hilltop breeze cooled the sun's burning. Stretching, she felt how young and healthy her body was. Even her foot was beginning to ease, and the heat seemed to soothe her wounds. She felt a surge of strength, as if she had absorbed the power of the light, as if she possessed the power to do anything, to bear anything, to solve anything.

Then she lectured aloud. After all, Lynn, he didn't want, he didn't try, to hurt you. He's beside himself now with regret and guilt. This can go on forever, this rage of yours, if you allow it to. But it will corrode you if you do. Listen, he could have been eaten up with rage at you because of our tragedy, our Caroline . . .

And she reflected, I shouldn't have stayed late at that damn-fool dinner. That's what began it all. I should not have let myself be lured into staying. What if I had been waiting at home for Robert and then found him having a careless good time with a pretty woman?

She remembered Tom Lawrence's cheek so close to her own, almost touching, his mischievous, clever eyes, bright like his hair and his fresh skin, and the cheerful effects of this brightness. *You have such sweet eyes, a sweet mouth, Lynn.* Flattery, all flattery, possibly with the hope that it might lead to something, and possibly not that at all. How was she to know? I know so little, she thought. Married at twenty and sheltered ever since, when and where could I have learned about the world?

No, she said then to herself, and sat up. Naïveté like that is inexcusable. I should have known better. I should at least have been smart enough to foresee consequences. My husband has a temper, that shouldn't be news to me . . .

Our children need us, he'd said. It's true, she thought now, he is never too tired or busy to do something for them. Waiting in Washington between planes, he hails a taxi to the National Gallery of Art. *We can show them a good many pictures in ninety minutes*, he says, imbuing us all with his energy. He gets out of the hammock where he has been resting and runs into the house to fetch the encyclopedia because he wants to make sure he has given his daughter the best answer to her question. He sits up all night with Annie when she has her tonsils out.

110

He could also be harsh with them, and too demanding. Yes, yes, I know. But they were quite fine the last two days before we came here. Regardless of everything, they do love him. People say things they don't really mean.

Our children need us. They need us both.

There's nothing that can't be worked out by applying some simple common sense.

Back in the room, a note lay on a table next to a book. The note said, *Gone to breakfast. I'll be in the dining room or else on the beach.* The book was opened to a poem, a poem that Lynn did not need to read because she almost knew it by heart. Nevertheless, she read it again.

> '*O fierce and shy, Your glance so piercing-true*
> *Shot fire to the struck heart that was as tinder—*
> *The fire of your still loveliness, the tender*
> *High fortitude of the spirit shining through.*
> *And the world was young. O—*'

She laid the book down and shivered. He had given these poems to her when they were first married, and they had often read them together; sometimes he had read aloud in his grave, expressive voice; they had been so madly in love.

> '*The high fortitude of the spirit shining through.*
> *And the world was young—*'

'Oh, Robert,' she said.

She found him reading on the beach. At her approach he looked up, questioning.

'I've come to bury the hatchet,' she told him shyly.

Two poor tears sprang into the corners of his eyes, and he took her hand into his and held it. It seemed to her that a stream of common blood was running through their joined hands. She felt the pride and relief of calm forgiveness.

'You read the poem?' When she nodded, he cried anxiously, 'Lynn, Lynn, you're everything in the world to me. Without you I'm nothing. You do know that, don't you? Are we all right again? Are we?'

'Let's not talk about it anymore. It's over.'

'We can have our bad times, but at least they don't last. Right, darling?' He jumped up. 'Well, as you say, enough. What shall we do first, now? Jog or swim?'

'Let's walk. There's something I want to show you, where I've been.'

So they retraced her path between the incoming tide and the silver twisted branches of the sea grape, past the fine houses in their gardens, Robert speculating on the price of each.

'Hey! How far is this thing you want to show me? Aren't you tired yet? This is your second trip.'

'No, I'm a walker, and it's worth ten trips. You'll see.'

'You're as young as you ever were.'

It was true. Her body in the scarlet swimsuit was as taut and limber as it had been when she was twenty. And rejoicing in this health, in the breezy morning and the decent peace she had made, she strode, ignoring her slight limp, up the hill.

They stood quite still at the top.

'I see what you mean,' Robert whispered.

This time, though, there was a sign of life in view: a white yacht moving sedately on a line with the horizon.

'Look at that grand thing,' he said. 'Wouldn't you love to own it? We could go off to the South Seas, all around the world.'

'No,' she responded seriously, 'even if we could afford it, which we likely never will, I wouldn't want it.'

He shook his head as if she were beyond under-standing.

'What do you want? Don't you ever want anything?'

Still very seriously, she told him, 'Only peace and love, that's all. Peace and love.'

'You have them. You shall have them.' He dropped down on the grass. 'Sit here. Let's stay a minute.' When she complied, he turned serious too. 'I know I'm not always easy to live with. I'm not home enough. I'm a workaholic. And you're very patient, I know that too. At the office and on the commuter train I hear stories that can make one's hair stand on end, about women having nervous breakdowns, drinking alone during the day, or else having an affair with a hairdresser.' He laughed. 'Imagine you having an affair! I think you'd flee in terror if a man were to lay a hand on you. And when I hear all this, don't think I fail to appreciate what you are, the time and effort you put in with the children, your solid health, your good cheer, everything. I should do more. I should take more upon myself.'

'You do plenty. More than many fathers do. Much more,' she said sincerely.

'No, I should do better. You don't play piano, so you can't help Annie with it. I was thinking she should switch to popular music. It will help her socially when she's a few years older.' He sighed. 'And I worry about Emily and that boy. I know you don't like to hear it, but –'

'Not now, Robert. It's too beautiful here to think of worries, even though I don't agree that Harris is a worry. Shall we go back?'

Half walking, half sliding, they descended the hill and trudged along the shoreline, their feet slapping through the wet sand.

For a time neither spoke, until Robert said, 'Oh, I just want to say one thing more and then – you're right that this is no place or time for problems – but is Emily just being an average teenager, growing away as she's supposed to grow, or is there something else? Lately when we're together I've had the feeling that she's annoyed with me.' And when Lynn did not reply at once, he said, sounding wistful, 'I wish you'd be truthful if there's anything you know.'

She hesitated. 'She feels that you weren't always open with her and shut her out.'

'Shut her out? From what?'

'Oh, things. Little things. For instance, she said – when she mentioned Querida a while ago you were furious. You shouted at her. You wouldn't tell her anything.'

He protested. 'Of course I wouldn't. Why does she need to know? That brilliant aunt of mine! It's a wonder she didn't let slip about the boy too. There'd be a hundred questions about that, wouldn't there? Well, my conscience is clear. I've done right by him, but he's no part of my life. The bank informs me that he lives in Europe. I don't even know in what country. I don't support him anymore. He's an adult. It's a complete separation. There's nothing unusual about that these days, with families dispersed over the globe.' Stopping his agitated walk, he stood still, looking out over the water. 'Why are we talking about this foolishness, anyway?'

'You asked about Emily.'

'Yes. Yes, I did. Well,' he said, looking down at her with a troubled expression, 'is there anything else?'

I've gone partway, and I might as well go all the way, she told herself. And fixing her eyes upon Robert, she said quietly, 'She thinks you did that to me the other night.'

He took a deep breath, and she saw how her words had struck him.

'And what did you say? Did you – explain? Did you –'

She answered steadily, still with her eyes fixed on his.

114

'I told her that was arrant nonsense. That I was astonished she could ever have such a thought.'

Robert bowed his head. They were two people in pain. How odd, Lynn thought, to stand here in this streaming sunlight, with all this animated life around us, children on floats, people splashing into the waves, calling and laughing, while we have a dialogue so tragic, so profound. No one seeing them here could possibly guess. She pitied the man who stood there with bowed head, and she touched his arm.

'Enough, Robert. I've had no breakfast, and I'm starved. Is there a place on the terrace where I might get a cup of coffee and a roll?'

His response was a grateful, a humble, smile. 'Of course. I've explored the whole place and all its hidden corners. There's a hidden corner with umbrella tables in the shade near the pool. Let's go. And after that, a swim. And after that,' he said, recovering, 'there's a fishing trip scheduled for this afternoon, a short one to an out island in a catamaran. Or we might sign up tomorrow for an all-day trip with snorkeling and a picnic lunch on one of the farther islands. Or would you like a water-ski lesson? I looked over the schedule this morning.'

She had to smile. It was so like Robert to organize, to account for every minute.

'Swim first, then take the others as they come. Remember, you said we needed to relax.'

'Right. Right you are.'

Later in the afternoon they came back laughing at themselves after their first lesson on water skis, and took seats in the shade near the pool. Little groups of young couples were chatting at surrounding tables.

'Honeymooners, most of them,' Robert observed. 'You could be a bride yourself. You don't look any different from them.'

'Brides are older these days.'

'You're turning just faintly brown,' he remarked.

'In spite of sunblock and a shady hat? I'll go home looking like a lobster. Ah, well, since that's the case, I might as well be fat too. I'll have ice cream.'

She was aware as she ate that he was watching her, as if he were enjoying her enjoyment. She finished the ice cream with a feeling of satisfaction, thinking, How physical we are! The taste buds are satisfied, the stomach is filled, the air is fresh, not too hot and not too cool, and somehow all our troubles vanish – for a while, anyway.

A lizard, green as a gem, slid along a wall. Blackbirds stalked among the tables picking up fallen crumbs. A tiny yellow bird alighted on the table, paused on the edge, and then, on its frail, twiggy legs, hopped to the ice cream dish where lay a small, melted puddle. Totally still, Lynn sat watching the little beak thrust and thrust again; with the other part of her vision she was still aware of Robert watching her with the same affectionate concentration that she was giving to the bird.

'It's adorable,' she said. 'That little brain can't be any bigger than half a pea.'

'It's you who are adorable,' he told her.

An elderly couple sitting at the next table overheard him, for the man, catching Robert's eye, smiled and nodded.

'We were watching you two on water skis,' he said with a heavy German accent.

'Oh, we were both awful,' Robert answered. 'It was our first time.'

'So you were very brave, then. My wife and I' – he raised gray eyebrows in an expression of mock sorrow – 'we are too old to learn new things.'

And so a conversation began. Introductions were made, and brief biographical sketches drawn. The Hummels were from Stuttgart; he was a banker, semiretired, but only semi; they did a good deal of traveling, mostly in Eastern Europe of late, where so many astonishing changes were occurring. This trip, their first to the Caribbean, was purely for pleasure, to celebrate their fiftieth wedding anniversary. Later, at home, there would be a party with family and friends, but first they wanted this time alone.

'And is today the day?' asked Robert.

'Today is the day,' Herr Hummel acknowledged, and his wife, a portly woman with beautiful upswept white hair and no devices behind which to hide her age, nodded and smiled.

'It's so lovely here,' she said. 'Usually we go to the Riviera for sun, but it is nothing like this. All these strange, wonderful flowers –' And she waved toward a clump of shrubbery that bore in clusters what looked like red beads, each the size of a pinhead. 'What do you call those?'

'Ixora,' Robert answered.

'Ah, you study flowers,' said Mrs Hummel.

'Not really.' Robert laughed. 'I just happened to pass some on my way to breakfast this morning and saw a marker with the name.'

'He remembers everything,' said Lynn.

'So you have,' Mr Hummel remarked, 'a memory like – what is the word? Like a camera, you know.'

'A photographic memory,' Lynn said. 'Yes, he has.'

'Perhaps,' said Mr Hummel, 'you will tell me if I go too far, intrude on your time, but perhaps you will have a drink of champagne with us tonight? It is tomorrow we leave. Perhaps you will have dinner with us, a table for four?'

'Why, that would be very nice,' Robert answered cordially.

When they were alone, Lynn was curious. 'Why did you say yes to dinner with them?'

117

'Well, he's a banker with connections in the new republics. It never hurts to pick up information and connections wherever you can. Besides, they're nice people, and you can see they're feeling a little bit lonesome.'

She was amused. Even away on vacation his mind was with General American Appliance.

'It's dress up tonight,' he said. 'I read it on the bulletin in the lobby. Dancing and entertainment.'

'Limbo and calypso, I'm sure. Funny, I keep loving calypso no matter how often I hear it.'

'That dress is perfect, well worth the money.'

White silk was even whiter and pearls more luminous against sun-tinged skin. She was pleased with herself.

'Where's the bracelet?' Robert asked.

'Which one?' she replied, knowing which one he meant because he always asked about it.

'The cabochons. The good one.'

'It's much too valuable to take traveling,' she told him.

It was indeed a special piece, always remarked upon whenever she wore it, and yet she wore it only when he reminded her to. It made her remember the sinking despair of that bleak windy night on the bench overlooking Lake Michigan. It wasn't healthy to relive a night like that one.

The Hummels had reserved a table near the dining-room balcony overlooking the sea. Champagne was already in a cooler. They were beaming, he in a summer dinner jacket and she in light blue chiffon, rather too fancy. A pair of solid burghers, Lynn thought, and felt kindly disposed to them. Fifty years married!

'It is so nice to be with young people for our little celebration,' said Mrs Hummel. 'You must tell us more about yourselves. You have babies at home?'

'Not babies,' Lynn answered. 'Not babies. A daughter of seventeen and an eleven-year-old.'

'My goodness, we have grandchildren older. A boy

twenty-seven. He works in Franz's bank,' she added proudly.

The conversation now divided, Mrs Hummel describing to Lynn every member of her large family, while the men, led by Robert, pursued a different direction. With half an ear Lynn, who was hardly interested in the Hummel grandchildren, was able to hear some of the men's talk.

'I'm starting a course in Hungarian,' Robert said. 'I don't know where I'll get the time, but I'll have to make the time.'

'A man of your type makes the time. I know your type.'

'Thank you, but it's a difficult language. An Ugric language, related to Finnish, I'm told. I decided to start with it because, by comparison, Hungary is already somewhat prosperous. My firm deals in home appliances, as you know, and as the country gets richer, the demand will grow.'

'Have you been in Hungary yet?'

'No, I want to prepare a team for Russia, Poland, and the whole area before I talk to the top brass – the president, that is. I've got to get a better handle on the languages, though. It makes an impression if you can show your contacts that you're at least making the effort to learn their language.'

'You're right. It's true that not everybody speaks English. People seem to think that everybody does.'

' – often think boys are easier to bring up,' Mrs Hummel was saying. 'I suppose your husband would love to have a boy.'

'I guess he would, but two are enough, and he adores our girls.'

'Actually, I'm in marketing, but one needs to broaden one's scope. I have to know what they're doing in product development if I'm to do a competent job in marketing, don't I?'

'Ya, ya. Technology changes by the hour. You give me your card, I'll give you mine, and if I can be of any help, who knows, we may work some good things out together. No?'

'I'd be delighted. Now I think we're neglecting your great occasion. I'm going to order another bottle, and we're going to drink to the next fifty years.'

'Your husband is a very ambitious, very intelligent young man, Mrs Ferguson,' Mr Hummel told Lynn.

'It's heartwarming,' Mrs Hummel said, 'to see a couple still young and beautiful together. All these discontented couples, I never understand, so many of them. Franz and I are seventy-three. I'm seven months older, but we never tell anybody.' All four laughed, and Lynn said politely, 'Neither one of you looks his age.'

'Really?' Mrs Hummel was gratified. 'If it's so, it's because we have been so happy with each other. My mother always told me – there is a *sprichwort* – a saying, about not going to sleep angry.'

'Never let the sun go down on your anger,' Lynn said. 'My mother told me that too.'

'Ah, yes. And it works, it really does.'

'Interesting types,' Robert said when they got up to dance.

'Rather out of fashion these days in this world.'

'Well, if they are, it's too bad about this world.'

They were in the open courtyard. When the music paused, one heard the swish of the waves, hushed now at low tide. Into the perfumed night the music blended. 'Smoke Gets in Your Eyes' and 'Always and Always' they played.

It might be corny, Lynn said to herself, and yet the music is as lovely as the day it was written before I was born. And it still appeals to a longing that doesn't die, no matter what the style or the generation and whether people admit it or not.

'Do I dance as well as Tom Lawrence does?' Robert whispered.

She drew back and reproached him. 'For someone who can be so tactful when he wants to be, I'm surprised at you.'

'I'm sorry. It was meant to be funny, and it wasn't at all. I'm sorry.' He kissed her ear and held her more closely. 'Forgive me.'

Passing the Hummels, who were dancing stiffly apart, the two couples smiled at each other.

'Never let the sun go down on your anger,' Robert murmured. 'We're going to remember that.'

Yes. Yes. A whole fresh start. The champagne is going to my head. Such a lovely feeling. And above Robert's shoulder the sky was suddenly filled with blinking stars.

'Are there more stars here? Is that possible, Robert? Or am I drunk?'

'You may be drunk, but it does seem as if there are more because there's no pollution, and the sky is clear. Anyway, the constellations are different here. We're close to the equator.'

'You know so much,' she whispered.

And she looked around at the men moving to the music in slow circles. Not one could compare with Robert, so distinguished, so admired, so full of knowledge, with such marvelous eyes, now gazing into hers with that long, long look.

'*I can't help falling in love with you.*' Their bodies moved to the nostalgia and the yearning, were led by it, slowly, closer and closer; as one body, they were barely moving, swaying together in one spot.

'I can't help falling in love with you,' he sang into her ear. And she thought: I was so angry that I wished he would die. Oh, God, oh, God, and overcome with tears, she reached up to his mouth, and there on the dance floor, kissed him over and over.

'Oh, my dear, my dearest.'

'Let's get out of here,' he whispered. 'Say good-night to those people and get out of here. Quick, I can't wait.'

In the room he slammed and fastened the door, crying, 'Hurry, hurry!'

'I am. Don't tear my dress.'

'I'll buy you another one.'

He seized her and carried her to the wide, cool bed. Palms rattled at the window and the sea wind blew all through the first time and the second, and then all night, long after they had fallen asleep.

They swam and went deep-sea fishing, then played tennis, took long runs on the beach, and lay resting in the shade. Others went to the free-port shops and returned with the usual bags of liquor and perfume, but Lynn and Robert went no farther than a sailboat could carry them. After the Hummels departed, they were always, by tacit agreement only, together.

In the mornings when the first tree frogs began to peep, they made love again.

'No work, no errands, no telephone, no clock, no kids,' he whispered.

It was delicious, unhurried luxury. It was like being remade, like being married all over again. Robert had been right. This was what they had needed.

Part Three

Summer 1988 – Spring 1989

3

No one was home when they arrived except Juliet, who gave them a tongue-licking welcome and then turned over to have her belly scratched.

'Where is everybody?' Lynn wondered.

'Maybe there's a note on the bulletin board in the kitchen.'

She opened the kitchen door, stood a second in total bewilderment, and gasped.

'Oh, my God! What have you done?'

Robert came in grinning. 'Like it? Like it?'

'How on earth did you ever do this?'

'It was easy. Just paid an arm and a leg for their guarantee to finish it in ten days, that's all.'

A glistening new kitchen had been installed with a restaurant-sized stove, a double-sized refrigerator-freezer, a trash compactor, and a center island above which hung the best new European cookware. Closets and glass-fronted cabinets had been expertly reorganized and consolidated; a library of cookbooks stood in vivid jackets on the shelves, and African violets in lavender bloom flourished on the broad new windowsills.

'I think I'm going to faint,' Lynn said.

'Well, don't do that. You're supposed to produce good meals here, not faint.'

'It's perfect. It's gorgeous, you're a magician, you're Santa Claus, you're an angel.'

'A talented worker deserves a good workroom. I've

125

done some thinking, and I truly realize what this means to you, so if you want to do some sort of baking or catering on a small scale, if it will make you happy, why, now you've got the place to do it in. And if not, well, you've got a handsome kitchen, that's all.'

'You couldn't, you absolutely couldn't, have given me anything more wonderful.'

She was hugging him when the front door opened to a chorus, 'Welcome home!' and the girls, with Josie and Bruce and Harris, came in with arms full.

'Chinese takeout,' Emily said. 'We didn't expect you to make dinner in this palace the minute you got home.'

'I came over every day to watch the miracle take shape,' Josie said.

'Girls, I hope you didn't make any trouble for Uncle Bruce and Aunt Josie,' Robert said.

'We had a fine time,' Bruce assured him. 'We ate out, we ate at our house, and last Sunday Harris took us to the woods and made a meal from scratch. He started a fire without matches.'

'Without matches,' Lynn repeated, turning to Harris, who was actually blushing.

'Well, I was an Eagle Scout. You have to know how to survive in the wilderness.'

'The Connecticut wilderness?' asked Robert.

Josie corrected him. 'It's the same thing whether you're here or in the wilderness of Timbuktu.'

Bruce laughed. 'Timbuktu is not a wilderness, Josie.'

'Harris,' said Emily, 'tell them about you-know-what at school.'

'No, they're your parents, you tell them,' Harris answered quietly.

'We both got an A in the advanced chemistry finals. The only ones in the class.'

Harris corrected her. 'You got an A, and I got an A-minus.'

126

Robert put his arm about his daughter's shoulder. 'I'm so proud of you, Emily.'

Bruce spoke to Harris, who was standing a little apart. 'You must be coming close to a college decision. Have you any special place in mind?'

'Wherever I can get the best scholarship,' the boy replied seriously. 'They're kind of scarce these days.'

'Well, summer vacation's almost upon you, so just relax awhile and leave those worries for September,' Lynn said cheerfully. 'And you know what we're going to do? Next Sunday I'm going to inaugurate this kitchen. I'm going to make a big supper. All of you come. Annie, bring a friend or two, and, Bruce, if your cousin should be in town by then, bring him along. We'll eat on the deck.'

'It's been raining all week,' Annie said, pouting.

'Well, all the better. That means we're due for a long spell of sunshine,' Lynn told her.

A long spell, a lasting spell of sunshine in many ways, she assured herself.

It was as she had predicted, the proverbial day in June, cool and blue. All the previous afternoon and all morning she had been working and humming to herself in the new kitchen, and the result was a summer banquet, 'fit for the gods,' as Robert put it.

On the big round table in the kitchen's bay window stood a lobster ragout fragrant with herbs, crisp green peppers stuffed with tomatoes and goat cheese, warm French bread, a salad of raw vegetables in an icy bed of lettuce, a pear tart glazed with apricot jam, and a chocolate torte garnished with fresh raspberries and *crème anglaise*. In a pair of antique crystal carafes, bought by Robert, were red wine and white, while for Annie and her friend Lynn had set out a bowl of ginger-ale punch in which there floated a few balls of vanilla ice cream.

'If you'd like me to grill a couple of hamburgers outside for the little girls, I'd be glad to, Mrs Ferguson,' Harris offered.

She looked at him and laughed. 'You're just too polite to tell me that those kids won't like the lobster ragout, and you're right. I should have thought of that myself.'

Harris laughed back. What a nice boy, she thought, handing him a plate of raw hamburgers.

Bruce had brought his cousin, who was visiting from the Midwest. He was a quiet man, much like Bruce himself, who taught physics at a high school in Kansas City. Harris and Emily immediately got talking to him about physics and premeds. Annie and her friend were full of giggles over some private joke. It gladdened Lynn to see Annie having an intimate friend.

Bruce's cousin admired the view. 'You have a beautiful place here,' he told Robert, who sat across from him.

'It needs a lot of work yet. I'm thinking of putting a split-rail fence along the boundaries. And of course, we should have a pool. I want a naturalistic pool, not one of those ordinary rectangular affairs, but something free form with woodsy landscaping. It'll be a big job.'

'I'm perfectly content with the pool at the club,' Lynn reminded Robert.

'My wife is easily satisfied,' Robert said.

'You always say that,' Josie remarked.

And Robert remarked, 'Well, it's true.'

'There's nothing wrong with the pool at the club,' Lynn insisted, out of a certain consideration for the feelings of the school-teacher, whose income, one could be sure, did not provide either for a private pool or a country club membership, adding, 'especially when the company pays for the club. Otherwise, I wouldn't even want that.'

'Let's all help carry things back to the kitchen,' Bruce suggested. 'Having stuffed ourselves like this, we need the exercise.'

Robert sprang up. 'After that, how about badminton, or croquet? I've just set up a game on the side lawn, so take your choice.'

When the table had been cleared, Lynn sat down to rest.

'Do you know the best thing about vacations, Josie? That they stay with you. Here I am, happy to be home, and yet a part of me is still down on the island. I can still feel that soft, damp air.'

'I'm glad,' said Josie.

'I can't thank you and Bruce enough for taking care of the girls.'

'Don't be silly. We love them, and they were wonderful.'

Juliet, having been unlawfully fed with hamburger scraps, came sniffing to Josie now in hopes of more.

'Yes, yes, you're a good dog,' she said almost absently, while her hand played in the thick ruff of hair around the dog's neck. 'A good dog,' she repeated, and then suddenly she raised her hand to confront Lynn with what Lynn knew she had been meaning to say all the time. 'So. You have an appointment with my friend, I think.'

'I'm not going to keep it. I must call him.'

'I think you should keep it,' Josie said.

'Things change, Josie. Being away together, you get a different perspective. Robert's right. When we moved, we all had too many adjustments to make. It's been especially hard for the girls, unsettling, bad for the nerves, even though on the surface they handled it well. It's foolish to take every blow-up too seriously, as if the end had come. In this last week alone since we've been home, why – I can't tell you how good it's been. Robert's even been so nice to Harris. I convinced him that he shouldn't worry, that they're just kids having their first crush, and he finally agreed that I'm right, that Harris is a very fine person. And Robert's gotten the girls interested in the hospital fund drive, so they're selling tickets to everybody they know. They'll be calling you next, I'm sure.'

'It's nice to hear all that, but I still think you ought to go, Lynn.'

'I wouldn't know what to say to the man. I'd feel like a fool,' Lynn said firmly. 'No. I'm canceling the appointment. To tell the truth, I forgot about it or I would have done it already.'

So she closed the subject. She regretted the day she had run to Josie and complained. She was a big girl, for heaven's sake, and would solve her own problems. She already had solved them.

June was a crowded month, a month of rituals. Annie had a birthday party complete with pink crepe-paper, pink icing, and a new pink dress. Friends had weddings and proud commencements. It was a time of graceful ceremonies, set about with flowers. And through these festive days Lynn moved with a fresh sense of well-being.

On a hot Saturday, the last in the month, Robert went to the city for a morning's work. Lynn, knowing that he would never alter his habits, agreed to meet him later in the afternoon at the club's pool. Arriving early, she found a chair in the shade and, glad of the privacy afforded by Annie's and Emily's occupation elsewhere, settled down to read until Robert should arrive. She was somewhat irritated, therefore, when she saw a man approach carrying a folding chair, and more than irritated when he turned out to be Tom Lawrence.

Lawrence was dressed for golf, wearing a light straw hat, which he now tipped to her, replaced, and removed again, this confusion giving her the impression that he was as discomfited as she was.

'In this heat you've got to be crazy to go out on the fairway,' he complained. 'I need to cool off in the shade. Do you mind?'

'Not at all.'

He sat down, and she returned to her book with a finality intended to discourage any further conversation. For a few moments he waited, saying nothing, and then spoke.

'Actually, I was on my way out, when I caught a glimpse of you. I wanted to talk to you. I wanted to apologize.'

She raised her eyes from the book and looked at him. The happy thought came to her that this time, unlike the last, she could face him confidently; she was wearing the scarlet swimsuit that had been so successful on the Caribbean beach; her body was unblemished and her face unmarked by having wept.

'What for?' she asked.

'I was to blame for making you late that night and making your husband furious.'

'He wasn't furious,' she said, resenting the man's intrusion.

'Oh, come.' The tone was gentle. 'He was furious. Everyone saw it.'

'I can't help what everyone saw,' she said coldly. 'And it was none of their business, anyway.' To her shame angry tears began to form, as they always did whenever her emotions, grieving or joyous, were stirred. Damn tears. She blinked them back, but not before he had seen.

He shook his head. 'It's a pity for you to be unhappy.'

She turned upon him then. 'How can you talk to me this way? What do you know about me? I'm not unhappy. Not.'

'You were miserable when I saw you the next morning. And I do know something about you. I know that your husband lays a heavy hand on you, and I don't mean just psychologically either.'

She was appalled. She was totally shocked. She had a positively Victorian impulse to say something like 'How dare you?' and then flounce off in seething indignation. But of course, that would be ridiculous. There were

131

people sitting all around the pool who would notice. All this rushed through her head, and she said only, 'I have never heard anyone talk so outrageously in all my life. You're making a fool of yourself too. You don't know what you're saying.'

'But I do know. I used to do divorce work, and I've seen the signs too often to be mistaken.'

Her heart was pounding. She pulled herself up into a haughty posture and said, making each word sharply distinct, 'My husband happens to be a useful, respected citizen with a good name. He's a senior officer with one of the world's largest corporations, General American Appliance. Perhaps,' she added sarcastically, 'you have possibly heard of it?'

'Yes, I've been a stockholder for years. As a matter of fact, the president, Pete Monacco, is a friend of mine. He married my cousin. A sort of third cousin, I believe.'

'Well, good for you. With connections like that you should know better than to cast aspersions on a man who does what Robert does, in this community alone. The hospital, AIDS, the new town library –' She was almost sputtering. 'You ought to be ashamed of yourself!'

Lawrence was undaunted. 'The one has nothing to do with the other. A man can be a distinguished citizen and still be violent toward his wife.'

His voice and face were kind. He sat there, easily, cradling the straw hat on his knee. He might have been talking about something as trivial as the heat. But his words were blunt and hard as a hammer.

'You don't know how good Robert is, how totally devoted to his family. You don't understand.'

For answer Tom simply shook his head. And this stubborn refusal to retract his words made her anger boil afresh.

'What's the matter with me? What kind of a fool am I? Why am I even *talking* like this to a stranger? Allowing

132

you to say such things to me. It's degrading to us both. And I'll tell you something: If you're still around, we'll invite you to our fiftieth anniversary and dare you to come. Dare you.'

He stood up. 'I admire you for your defense, Lynn. I know your kind of woman. You have a vision of romance. "Till death do us part," no matter what. It's the "no matter what" that's wrong. Otherwise I'm all in favor of fiftieth anniversaries, I assure you.'

She got up and walked toward the pool. Only a dive into the water would silence this man.

'Romantic visions of everlasting love. That's what you're living by.'

'Yes,' she said over her shoulder, 'yes, I believe in that. I live by it.'

'Take care you don't die by it, Lynn.'

Those were the last words she heard before the water splashed over her.

'You seem disturbed about something,' Robert said, when, not long afterward, he joined her.

'This sickening heat is enough to disturb anybody.'

Later he remarked, 'I thought I saw Tom Lawrence leaving the club when I drove in.'

'Yes, he was here.'

'Did you talk to him?'

'A few words. Not much more than hello and good-bye.'

Still later, at dinner, he said, 'The company president is flying in on Monday to give a talk. He's some impressive guy. Powerful. It's easy to see how he got where he is. Funny how things change, though,' he mused. 'A generation ago nobody with an Italian name would have headed a company like ours.'

'What's wrong with an Italian name?'

'It just didn't use to happen, that's all. Now it happens every day.'

What made her say what she next said, Lynn could not have explained. 'Tom Lawrence is related to him.'

'How do you know that?'

'He told me so today.'

'You must have had quite a talk with him, then,' Robert said after a moment.

'Not at all. I told you that we said a few words. And he happened to mention Mr Monacco.'

Robert looked amused. 'I don't mind that you talked to him, Lynn, since that's what you're thinking of. So he told you he's related to Monacco? That's odd. I had the impression that Lawrence was old American stock.'

'It's his second cousin who's married to Monacco.'

'Oh.' Robert looked reflective. 'I wish I had a connection like that, distant or not. Business is contacts, it's channels. I've got a head full of ideas, but how to get to the right ears with them? One department overlaps another –' With a small, self-deprecating frown he paused. 'Too bad. I would have done differently if I had known about Lawrence. But I'll make up for it. We're certain to run into him again at the club.'

Lynn was aghast. 'You surely aren't going to ask for an introduction to Mr Monacco, are you?'

'No, no, no. That's not the way things are done. You get acquainted with somebody, invite him to dinner, get talking, and after a while – after a while, who knows what can happen?'

What can happen, she repeated to herself, is too awful to think about.

Still she could not help but think about it. The unmitigated gall of that man! Who was he to play detective-psychologist, and to pry into the innermost heart of a stranger's life? She could only dread the next time she would have to see Tom Lawrence.

*　　*　　*

134

Indeed, she was so agitated for a week or more that she kept waking up in the middle of the night to relive the scene at the pool's edge. She felt actually ill. Her stomach churned. And suddenly, one morning as the kitchen warmed with the pungent smells of coffee and bacon, she had to run from the room.

'I can't stand the smell of food,' she complained when she came back. 'Even the sight of it makes me sick.'

'That certainly doesn't sound like you.' Robert looked at her thoughtfully. 'I don't suppose you could possibly be –'

She stared at him. 'Oh, no. What are you saying?'

'We had some pretty good times down on the island.'

She was barely able to absorb the possibility. Why, Emily was already seventeen!

'Would it be awful if I were? Would you mind awfully?'

'Do I look as if I would mind?' He chuckled.

'Maybe I am a little late,' she admitted. 'But since I often am, it hasn't occurred to me that it could be anything.'

'Don't look so terrified. We always wanted three, and would have had them if we hadn't lost Caroline.' Robert kissed her cheek. 'It may be nothing, but see a doctor tomorrow, anyway. Or this afternoon, if you can.'

She went to the doctor, received an affirmative answer, and came home in a state of shock despite what Robert had said. Her head was full of troublesome possibilities. How would Annie take the news? And she'd heard that at Emily's stage of life, a mother's pregnancy could be a painful embarrassment.

But Robert held her close. 'Darling, darling. I'm delighted.' Back and forth, he strutted, across the bedroom. He laughed. 'Maybe it will be a boy. Not that it wouldn't be wonderful either way, but it would be fun to have a boy for a change. This is absolutely the best news, Lynn. You'll have to postpone your business venture for a while, but I guess there couldn't be a better reason. And don't you worry about the girls. Annie will have a live toy, and Emily's a real woman. She'll be a help, you'll see. Let's go downstairs and tell them.'

'Oh, let it wait, Robert, this is much too soon.'

'Why wait? Come on,' he insisted.

His delight overflowed and was contagious.

'Well, Annie, you've been wanting us to let Juliet have puppies, so will this do instead?' He swung the heavy child off the floor and hugged her. 'Room for one more, hey, girls? Always room for one more and plenty of love left over.'

'Wait till I tell people in school,' said Annie. 'I'll bet I'm the only one of my friends who'll be having a new baby.'

'Not yet, dear,' Lynn warned. 'It's not till the end of February. I'll let you know when you can talk about it. And, Emily, are you sure you don't feel "funny"?'

She was moved when, unknowingly, Emily repeated Robert's words about Caroline, the little sister whom she could barely remember. 'There would have been three of us if Caroline hadn't died.'

The little white coffin, the overwhelming scent of white roses, enough to make you faint, hushed words meant to comfort, and arms supporting her.

Now again it was as if all of them, husband and children, were rallying to support her. She felt a sudden strong sense of unity among them, and a surge of excitement, a physical vibration, went through her body. On all their faces she seemed to see a look of curiosity, of respect and tenderness. And it came to her that, in this roundabout way, she might possibly be making up to Robert, in part, for the child who through her fault had been lost.

'Let's drive over to tell Josie and Bruce,' she said suddenly.

'No, no. This is private talk between women. You run

to see Josie, since I see you're bursting to tell. Just don't stay too long.'

Bruce was in the backyard putting the finishing touches on the chest of drawers.

'That's beautiful,' Lynn said.

'I was right. It's curly maple.' He shoved his glasses up into his hair and looked at her quizzically. 'Josie didn't expect you, did she? She's got a late meeting at the office.'

'No. I was passing nearby and remembered something. Not important. That's a beautiful piece,' she repeated. 'What are you going to do with it?'

'Darned if I know. Maybe keep it and give it to Emily someday when she gets married. She likes old things. Feel the wood.' He guided her hand over the top of the chest. 'I've been working two months on this. Feels like satin, doesn't it?'

She smiled. 'Like satin.'

He was so steady, so relaxed, working there near the shed in the cool of the late afternoon. She wondered what it would be like to live with a man who moved and spoke without haste. He never seemed to be *going* anywhere, but rather to be already *there*, and content to be there. She imagined that he must be a considerate lover.

'You look preoccupied,' he said while his hand moved up and down with the waxing cloth.

'I am, somewhat.'

'Nothing bad, I hope.'

'Not at all.' A smile, quite involuntary, spread across her face and quickly receded as she told herself: It is utterly selfish of me to bring this news with such pleasure when they have – at least I know Bruce has – always wanted children so badly.

He had seen the quick flash of her smile. 'What is it? Tell me.'

'I'm going to have – I'm pregnant.'

137

His wide mouth opened and shut. He laid the cloth down. And because his face went blank, with no readable expression, she was puzzled and vaguely hurt.

'Aren't you going to say anything? Is it so startling that you can't?'

'Well, it is a bit of a surprise.'

Naturally, he would be remembering the day when she had come here with tear-swollen eyes and a pathetic story of trouble at home. But that was past. This baby was testimony to the start of a new understanding, a whole new era. And she said lightly, almost frivolously, 'Why? I'm not that old.'

'That's not what I meant.'

'Oh, that! That's old business. It's over, Bruce, completely healed.'

'Josie and I only want you to be happy, Lynn.'

'I am happy.'

'Then let me congratulate you.' He gave her a quick hug. 'I'll tell Josie the minute she comes in.'

When she got back into the car, he was still watching her with that first blank look on his face. And as the car moved away, she heard him call after her, 'God bless you, Lynn.'

Now came a time of bloom. Nausea went as abruptly as it came. She felt strong and able, animated by good health. Because it had been so unexpected and because she was older, this new life seemed more marvelous than any of the others had. When, after amniocentesis, the doctor asked her whether she wanted to know the sex of the baby, she declined. She wanted to have all the delights, the suspense, and the surprise.

Once Robert told her she looked 'exalted.' He had come upon her in a quiet moment listening to music, and she had laughed, making light of her own profound feeling.

'It's only hormones,' she had answered.

In the garden, working through a drowsy noon, and in the beautiful new kitchen, she often sang. From time to time she had a recall of that almost mystical experience when, on the top of the cliff, she had stood looking out upon the silence of sea and sky.

For Josie and Bruce's anniversary Robert proposed taking them to the dinner dance at the country club. This suggestion surprised Lynn because it was always she who arranged their social times with the Lehmans, and she remarked upon it.

'Well,' he replied, 'they were so nice to the girls while we were away, so it's only right to do something for them in return. I don't like being indebted. Wear that white dress again,' he said. 'Maybe it was the dress that got me started on Robert junior one of those nights.'

'You really do want it to be Robert junior, don't you?'

'Or Roberta, or Susie, or Mary, will be just as wonderful. Wear the bracelet, too, will you?'

'Of course.' For the first time she clasped it on without any ugly memory. After all, it was stupid, it was almost superstitious, to let such memories persist. Chicago was long past. Her heart – or whatever it is that makes a person different from every other person on earth – was glad. And Robert owned it.

But she never entered the club without feeling a small dread of encountering Tom Lawrence. The very thought made her face burn. And for some inexplicable reason she had a premonition that tonight was to be the night.

So it was. They had just sat down when she saw him in the dining-room doorway. Unaccompanied, he hesitated as if he were looking for somebody. She could only hope that Robert would not catch sight of him, but of course, Robert was too alert to miss anything.

'I was standing there hoping I'd see somebody I know,'

Tom said when Robert hailed him. 'My date had to leave town in a hurry, a family illness, and at the last minute I thought I'd come alone anyway. How are you all?'

His light, skeptical eyes roved around the table, skimmed past Lynn, who was doing her best to look indifferent, and came to rest on Bruce, who replied. 'I can answer for Josie and myself. It's our anniversary and we are feeling absolutely great, thank you.'

'Congratulations. How long?'

'Twenty years.'

'That's marvelous. Nice to hear that in these days.'

I wonder, Lynn thought, whether he is remembering my invitation to our fiftieth?

'Do you care to join us?' Robert asked. 'Since you and Bruce are old friends, or I should say old jogging companions, at least.'

'Yes, pull up a chair,' Bruce said.

The evening was ruined at the outset. Unless she could contrive to keep her eyes down on her plate, she would be looking straight at Tom, who now sat across from her. And she was furious with him for foisting himself upon them; surely he knew what he must be doing to her.

When the three men took over the conversation, the two women subsided into listening. First came the usual generalities about the state of the economy; then almost imperceptibly, talk veered to the personal as Robert skillfully led it where he wanted it to go.

'I understand you're related to our boss, Bruce's and mine.'

'Yes, we're good friends,' acknowledged Lawrence. 'I don't see him that often unless I happen to be in San Francisco or I'm invited to their Maine camp in the fall, which I generally am. They like to go for the foliage season. There isn't much of a foliage season in California, as we all know,' he finished agreeably.

'I have to admire a man like Monacco,' Robert said,

'working his way up from the bottom to where he is today. These modern heroes amaze me, these men who create jobs, make the country strong, and let people live better. Heroes,' he repeated.

No one contradicted him, and Robert continued, 'I heard him speak in New York not long ago and was vastly impressed. He talked about what we're all concerned with, the future of the European community, especially the new eastern republics. I've been exploring a lot of ideas myself. The rapidity of change is astounding. Who could ever have predicted it?'

Lawrence said that no one could have, not to this extent, anyway.

'Establishing a company, a brand name, isn't going to be as easy as some think. We're talking about a huge, backward area with poor transportation, and it's all so fragmented. Czechoslovakia is different from Hungary, and they're both worlds removed from Romania. Worlds apart.' And Robert made a wide gesture. 'But I find it all fascinating, a history book in reverse, the future unfolding before your eyes. Fascinating.'

Lawrence agreed that it was.

Lynn could only wonder about the thoughts that Tom must be having as he listened, with head politely inclined toward Robert. And Robert, all unaware of the other man's opinion of him, continued smoothly.

'I'm having fun with some ideas of my own. One thing I'm doing is studying Hungarian, and that's not the easiest language in the world.'

'Where do you get the time?' asked Lawrence.

'It's not easy. I have to squeeze it in somehow, mostly on Saturday mornings.'

'That's when I go jogging with your colleague here.' Lawrence motioned toward Bruce. 'We're out conditioning our flab, while you're in town conditioning your brain.' He laughed.

Bruce defended Robert. 'He watches his flab, too, as you can see. He watches everything. He's known for it in the firm.'

Tom said, 'You've got a fine name there yourself, Bruce. Monacco's aware of it. I told him you were my jogging partner, and he recognized your name, your good name.'

'Thanks,' Bruce said. 'I like my work, but I also like to forget business over the weekend, stay home or go out into the country, picking up old furniture. Then I spend Sunday afternoon puttering around restoring it. I'm teaching myself to weave cane. Maybe I should have been a cabinetmaker. Who knows, I might end up being one when I retire.'

'You can't be serious,' Robert said.

For the first time Josie spoke. 'He could be. I guess you still don't know Bruce that well.'

Here we go again, Lynn thought. What is it about those two? Impatiently, she twisted in the uncomfortable chair while trying to avoid Tom Lawrence's eyes.

'Well, maybe I don't know Bruce.' And Robert demanded of him, 'Do you mean to say you'd leave one of the biggest firms in the world to become a cabinetmaker?'

'Probably not,' Bruce replied mildly. 'Just a thought. But there is something rewarding about working with your hands. I love the feel of old wood. It almost comes alive under your fingers.' And he looked around the table with his wide, slow smile.

And Lynn thought, as always, So cheerful, never in a hurry, and still he gets things done.

'I have never been especially ambitious,' Bruce said as if he were thinking aloud. 'I just keep going step by step.'

'For someone who's not especially ambitious, I should say you've come mighty far,' Josie remarked, with the combination of affection and gentle rebuke that was so typical of her.

For answer Bruce took her hand, and they sat united,

142

content with each other. He is thankful that she's here, Lynn knew. She's had four good years. If you can get through five, you're home free, they say.

When the dance band struck up, Bruce rose. 'Excuse us. It's not the anniversary waltz, but it will do just the same.'

Tom's eyes followed them. 'I like them,' he said simply.

Robert acknowledged the remark. 'Yes. Salt of the earth.'

'You two go and dance. Don't mind me.' For the first time Tom addressed Lynn. 'I always do seem to lack a partner, don't I?'

Compelled to make some reply, she gave him a faint smile. Then Robert said hastily, 'Why don't you dance with Lynn? I want to make some inquiry about the cake I ordered for the Lehmans and check on the champagne.'

'You're sure you don't mind?' asked Tom.

Asking Robert whether he minds, as though I were an object that can be borrowed or lent! She was hotly indignant.

'No, no. Go ahead,' Robert said. And a second later she was on the dance floor with Tom Lawrence's arm around her waist.

'Why are you doing this?' The final word emerged with a hiss. 'It's not even decent, what you're doing tonight.'

'Why? I want to apologize, that's all.'

'What? Not again?'

'Yes. I've been making too many bad mistakes involving you. When I left you at the pool that day, it didn't take me long – as a matter of fact, I was only halfway home – to realize that I had said some horrendous things. I've been hoping to meet you so that I could tell you I'm sorry. I hurt you. I interjected where I had no business to be.'

'No, you didn't have any business.'

'I am dreadfully, dreadfully sorry.'

He drew far enough away so that he could look into her face, and she saw in his an expression of genuine contrition and concern. She thought wryly, I've had so many apologies these past months, Robert's and now this. And she wondered, too, whether it could be the body contact while dancing that made it easier for people to make these intimate revelations. Who would think now that these two people, strangers to each other, were saying such serious things to the tune of a society dance-band?

'In my work I seem to have acquired a kind of intuition. It works like a flash, and as a rule I find I can depend on it. But that's no excuse for using it. I must learn to keep my mouth shut even when I'm sure I'm right.'

'But you were wrong that time. Your intuition failed you. Look at me,' she commanded with a proud lift of her head. 'How do I look to you?'

'Very, very lovely, Lynn.'

'Robert treats me very, very well, Tom.'

'Does he?'

'I'm going to have a baby.'

The skeptical eyes looked straight into hers while two pairs of feet moved expertly, not missing a step. Then the music stopped and Tom released her.

'God bless you, Lynn,' he said.

The blessing jolted her. It was what Bruce had given her when she had brought him the news, and it had seemed fitting on his lips. But on Tom Lawrence's it seemed ironic.

Nevertheless, the evening turned out not badly after all.

Bruce and Josie received their cake and their champagne toast. At Robert's request the band played 'The Anniversary Waltz,' Bruce kissed Josie, everyone applauded, and then they all went home.

'Very smooth, that Lawrence,' Robert remarked on the way back.

'Does that mean you don't like him?'

'I can't make up my mind.'

'That's unusual for you. You generally know right away what you think about people.'

'Maybe that's a failing. Maybe I shouldn't be so sure of my judgment. Oh, he's sharp as a tack. Congenial, a thorough gentleman, but somehow I can't make up my mind what he thinks about me. I almost think he dislikes me. But that's absurd. Why should he? Oh, but that Bruce! He makes such an idiot of himself with his remarks about furniture when, if he were more attuned to what's going on, he should have seen that I was leading the conversation somewhere. I looked up Lawrence's law firm. They have offices in Brussels, London, and Geneva. You never know what might come of that. Besides, the connection with Pete Monacco is no bad thing. Good Lord, a man has to keep his eyes wide open! That's Bruce's failing. I saw it the first day he came to the St Louis office. Remember when I came home and told you? A lightweight, I said. A nice guy who'll never get very far. Oh, he's done all right, but he's stuck where he is. Stuck.'

'That's not what Tom Lawrence said. Remember? He said Bruce has a very good name in your firm.'

'Fine. But I'm there on the spot and I think I should be a better judge than Lawrence is.'

Jealous. Jealous of Tom because I was foolish that night, and of Bruce because he is a handsome man. He wants to be the only handsome man, I suppose. Lord, men can be such babies!

'All the same,' Lynn said amusedly, 'if I had a brother, I'd want him to be like Bruce.'

'As long as you wouldn't want your husband to be like Bruce. Or like anyone else, including Tom Lawrence. Right, Mrs Ferguson?'

'Right,' she said.

Josie telephoned with thanks for the anniversary celebration.

'It was lovely, perfect. They even played our songs, our specials.'

'That was Robert's doing. You know he never forgets anything.'

They gossiped briefly, and then Josie said, 'Tom Lawrence really admires you.'

'How can you know that?'

'He told Bruce.'

'Oh, he admires my cooking.'

'No, you.'

'Well, that's generous of him.'

'He's a generous person.'

'I didn't realize you knew him that well.'

'I don't know him *that* well. He stops in for a cold drink or a hot drink after he's met Bruce on the track. I find him interesting. Hard to pin down, like quicksilver. But very decent, very honorable.'

'How can you know if you say you don't know him well?' Lynn asked, wanting for some reason to argue the point.

'I just know. It's not important either way. I only wanted to pass on a compliment.'

When the conversation ended and she hung up the phone, she sat for a moment or two staring into the mirror on the opposite wall. An odd little smile flickered over her lips.

A few weeks later Robert telephoned from the office at midday. He never called from the office, and she was startled.

'Is anything wrong?'

'Wrong? I should say not.' There was glee in his voice. 'In a million years you'd never guess. I got a call

146

from California from the big boss. I almost fell off the chair.'

'Not Monacco? He called you?'

'Himself. I can't imagine what Tom told him about me. He seems to have described me as some kind of genius, some sort of phenomenon. So, Monacco says he'd like to meet me and have a talk. We've been invited for the weekend to his place in Maine. His wife will call you.'

Robert was chuckling; she knew that he was wearing an enormous smile and that his eyes would be brilliant with excitement.

'I haven't mentioned it to anyone here. It's a bad policy to seem boastful. Being casual about it is much the better way.'

'Does that mean not to tell Josie?'

'Oh, they'll know. We'll have to ask them to keep an eye on the girls again, anyway, won't we? But, uh, keep it light, as if it's nothing much. It'd be nasty to rub this under Bruce's nose, since he wasn't invited. Now I'm beginning to get nervous. I do have some good ideas, it's true, but I hope the man won't be expecting so much from me that I'll fall flat on my face. Well, at least you'll be there to help charm him. I think you must have charmed Lawrence.'

'Don't be silly.'

Robert laughed. He was absolutely euphoric. 'In a nice way, I meant.'

'I didn't charm him, any way, nice or not. I danced with him once, at your behest, if you remember, and we hardly spoke.'

'Okay, okay. Don't keep the phone tied up too long in case Mrs Monacco should call.'

When she hung up, her feelings were mixed. Of course this was a mavelous thing for Robert, an unprecedented summons to the man's home. Small wonder that he was

147

ecstatic. She could only be glad for him, and she was glad. Yet at the same time she was slightly vexed and vaguely troubled.

She made excuses to avoid the country club, although she knew Robert liked to go there for dinner. But apparently Tom Lawrence also liked to go there...

Robert urged her. 'As new in the community as we are, it's important to keep being seen. Otherwise, people forget you're alive.'

'Your name's all over this community, on practically every committee. They couldn't forget you if they wanted to,' she told him.

'Speaking of remembering people, we really should show some appreciation to Tom Lawrence. Let's have him over for dinner one night. I mean, when have you heard of anyone's doing such an extraordinary favor for a man he scarcely knows? Of course I called him at once to thank him, and I mentioned that we'd like to have him come over soon.'

'I will, but first I want to get a few things out of the way. That root canal's been bothering me, which means a few visits to the man in the city. And I want to get the baby's room finished, too, before I get so big that I won't want to go into the city. But I will,' she promised.

It disturbed her to think of seeing Tom again; it was disturbing in itself that she should feel that way. She was a literal person, one who needed a clear explanation for everything, even for the workings of her own mind. So it was with some dismay that one afternoon not long afterward she encountered him on a New York street. Having done her errands, she was on the way to Grand Central Terminal and home. She had stopped in front of a small picture gallery, attracted by a painting of sheep on a hillside, as well as by the name above the entrance: Querida. An unusual name. The name of Robert's first wife. It gave her a small, unpleasant flutter. And then, turning away from the window, she had seen Tom Lawrence.

'What are you doing in the city?' he inquired, as though they were old friends who reported their doings to each other.

She replied casually, 'I go to a dentist in the neighborhood. And today I bought nursery furniture.'

'That must be a happy thing, although I wouldn't know, would I?'

Again, she had a sense of being brightly, although not disagreeably, scrutinized.

'You're looking wonderful. They tell me there are women who actually thrive on being pregnant. Are you buying pictures?'

'No, just admiring.' And wanting to divert that scrutiny, she remarked, 'These sheep are lovely.'

'She does have nice things. I've priced some, and the prices are very fair, but she's a cranky kind of oddball. Are you on your way home? Yes? So am I. We'll go together. Are you walking or cabbing?'

'I always walk as much as I can when I'm in the city.'

'Yes, it's wonderful this time of year. Everything seems to be waking up. And the shops! I can see why women go crazy in the shops.'

Tweeds and silks, silver, mahogany, and burnished leather made a passing show of the windows as they walked down Madison Avenue. The most brilliant blue, as deep as cobalt, overhung the towers, and where distance disguised grime, the towers shone white.

'Am I going too fast for you?' Tom asked.

'No, I'm fine.'

They were keeping an even pace. Always with Robert she had to hurry to keep up with his long strides, but then, she thought idly, Robert was half a head taller than this man.

'I never take the train home this early,' Tom explained, 'but I made myself take time off to do some shopping today.' He went on making small talk. 'My days are pretty long. I take the seven-thirty every morning, so I guess I'm entitled to treat myself now and then.'

'Robert takes the six-thirty.'

'He's a hard worker.'

And suddenly she cut through the small talk, saying, 'I must thank you for that incredible invitation to Maine. I know Robert's told you how much it means to him.'

'Oh, that. It was all Pete's idea. He says there's never much time during his flying visits to New York, what with all the meetings and stuff, so Maine's a much better place to talk.'

'I didn't mean Maine, specifically. I meant the whole business.' She raised her eyes to Tom, inquiring directly, 'Why did you do anything at all for Robert? Did he,' she asked, not flinching, 'did he by any chance ask you to?'

'Lord, no. Don't you know he wouldn't do that? But I knew he wanted something all the same.'

Troubled, she went further. 'Was he so obvious?'

'I suppose not really. I guess maybe it was my famous intuition that I told you about,' Tom said rather mischievously.

'No, really. I'm serious. Because you don't like Robert.'

'Robert's very smart, very competent, very diligent. I knew I wouldn't go wrong by recommending him.'

'But Bruce wasn't invited.'

'I didn't mention Bruce.'

'Why not? You like him very much. You said so; I heard you.'

'Ah, don't ask so many questions, lady!'

Embarrassed, she murmured only, 'It was awfully good of you.'

In the train Tom read the newspaper, and Lynn read her book, until the train had passed the dark brown tene-

150

ments in the uptown reaches of the city, then the cheerful towns with their malls and parks, and crossed the Connecticut line. At that point he laid the paper aside and spoke.

'Lynn ... I have another apology to make.'

'Oh, no, not another! For what this time?'

'For that first night at my house. If your husband could have read my thoughts, which fortunately he couldn't, he'd have had a right to be furious.' Tom paused. 'The truth is, I was hoping that you and I'd get together. Oh, not that night,' he amended quickly, 'of course not. But I thought perhaps the next time.'

She turned her face away toward the window to hide her exasperating blush. Naturally, it was flattering to be propositioned after all these years, to know that she could tempt someone else beside Robert. She supposed, though, that she ought to feel angry; whatever had made this man dare to think that she would be open to his proposition? And she felt guilty because she was not angry.

Rather mildly, she said, 'But you knew I had Robert.'

'I made a mistake. I misread you, which I don't usually do. Maybe it was the wine or the spring night or something. Anyway, a sexual attraction doesn't have to disrupt a man's or a woman's other life. Do I shock you?' For she had turned to him and saw now his rueful smile. 'Yes, of course I do. You'd eat yourself alive with guilt if you ever – you'd say "cheated." Well, I respect that. Maybe someday you'll feel different about it.'

'Never.' She shook her head decisively. 'Robert and I are permanent.' She looked down at her little swollen belly and repeated, 'Permanent.'

Tom followed her glance. 'I understand. And I've made my apology for my thoughts and intentions that night. I wanted to clear my own mind. So –' She remembered that he had that funny way of saying 'so' when he changed

151

the subject. 'So. You'll have a good time in Maine. Pete and Lizzie are easygoing, not formal at all. Paper-plate people like me. And it's beautiful this time of year. Over near the New Hampshire line the mountains turn red and gold. I'll be sorry to miss it.'

She was surprised. 'You're not going?'

'No. I've too much on the fire at the office.'

She was not sure whether she was sorry or glad that he would not be there.

Robert laid careful plans for the weekend. 'We'll need a house gift, you know.'

'Wine?' she suggested. 'Or I'll find something suitable for the country, a rustic bowl for flowers or fruit or something like that.'

'No, definitely not. That's banal. Besides, they already have their own wine and no doubt a couple of dozen bowls or whatnots too.'

'Well, what then?'

'I'll tell you what. An enormous box of your best cookies. Those almond things, you know the ones, and the lemon squares, and some chocolate brownies. Everybody loves them. That will be just the right gesture, friendly, simple, and elegant. As for clothes: sweaters, naturally, and heavy shoes. They'll probably take us tramping through the woods. And raincoats, and don't forget an umbrella. Something silk for the two nights in case they dress for dinner.'

'They won't dress for dinner up in the woods, and besides, I haven't a thing that fits anymore. I never did show this early, but I do show now.'

He regarded her thoughtfully. 'You look like a woman who needs to lose a little weight around the middle, that's all.'

'That's just it. My things don't fit around the middle, and it's too early for maternity clothes.'

152

'Well, buy something. For myself, tweed jackets, not new. A relaxed, used look.' Robert unfolded his plans systematically. 'We'll start the afternoon before and stay overnight on the road. Then we'll arrive rested and fresh before noon. And we'll take the station wagon. The Jaguar might look – I'm not sure, but it might look overdone. If the boss drives one, it certainly will. Yes, the station wagon.'

In midmorning they arrived exactly as planned. A long log house set about with cleared fields lay on a rise above a small lake. At the side were two tennis courts. On a wide veranda looking down on a bathhouse and a dock was a row of Adirondack chairs. The driveway was a rutted dirt road with a worn, grassy circle for parking; half a dozen cars were already there, station wagons, plain American sedans, and not an import in sight.

Lynn looked at Robert and had to laugh. 'Are you ever wrong?' she inquired.

'Ah, welcome, welcome,' cried Pete Monacco, descending the steps. 'How was the trip?' His voice boomed, his handshake was painful, and his smile showed square teeth that looked as granite hard as the rest of his large body. 'Beautiful scenery here in the East. I wouldn't miss this for the world. California is home and we love it, but for color you've got to see New England. Just look out there! My wife, she's Lizzie and I'm Pete, we're all first-name folks when we're up here, has taken everybody sailing, but they'll be back for lunch. Here, let me give you a hand with the bags.'

In their room Robert beamed. 'I don't know what the hell that fellow Tom can have said about me. Call him 'Pete'! You wouldn't guess he's the same man as the one who flies in with an entourage like the President's, gives a talk that's part pep and part scolding, leaves his commands, shakes your hand in the reception line, and then flies back across the Mississippi. Well, here we are. Can you believe it?'

He looked around the sparsely furnished room. A rag rug covered the floor, the walls were pine, the bed had Indian blankets and a huge comforter folded at the foot. The only ornament was the view that was framed by the single window.

'There's a sailboat coming in,' Lynn said.

Robert peered over her shoulder. 'Pretty sight, isn't it? Yes, all you need is money. Well, and taste too,' he conceded. 'Knowing how to use it.'

'We ought to go down and meet everybody,' she said as Robert began to unpack.

'No. Tidy up first. It'll take five minutes, if that. Let's get a move on.'

Hot coffee and doughnuts were being served on the veranda when they came downstairs. Lizzie Monacco, in jeans and a heavy sweater, shook hands.

'Excuse my freezing hands. There's a real wind out there. But it's great fun. Would you people like a ride around the lake this afternoon?' Like her husband she was voluble, with curly gray windblown hair and a candid expression. 'My goodness, how young you are! Lynn, isn't it? You are the youngest female here, and we shall all feel like old hags next to you.'

'No, no.' Lynn smiled. 'I have a daughter who'll be going to college next year.'

'For goodness' sake, and you're pregnant too. I hope it's not a secret, but Tom told me, anyway. I hope you're feeling well, but if you're not, don't feel you have to keep up with our crazy pace. Just take a book and relax.'

Robert answered for her. 'Lynn's in good shape. She plays a great game of tennis too.'

'You do? Good. We're all tennis freaks here. So maybe after lunch and a hike – there's a lookout place just down the lake where you can climb and see for miles, really

154

'splendid – maybe when we come back, we can play.'

'This is what you love. Busy, busy, busy,' Lynn murmured later to Robert.

'I know. It makes me feel like a kid. And the air, the pine smell. I feel great.'

These men came from the company's top echelon, chiefly from Texas and points west of Texas. If there were any women in the top echelon, they weren't at this party; these women were all wives. They didn't, Lynn noted, wear the same anxious look that she had so often seen on the women at the country club, whose husbands were still on the way up and always fearful of falling back down. These people seldom fell back or fell very hard if they did; there was always a golden parachute. She listened as the older women talked of volunteering, of the Red Cross and the United Way. Those slightly younger had gone to work in real estate or travel agencies and were pleased with themselves, since they did not have to work and yet did so.

'Tom told me that you're a fabulous cook,' said Lizzie Monacco, drawing Lynn into the conversation. 'I took a look at that gorgeous box of cookies. We're going to serve them at dinner tonight. It was darling of you.'

Lynn was thinking: Tom has surely done a lot of talking. He had put effort into this weekend. Pete Monacco was not a man who was readily open to suggestion, that was obvious. So Tom must have been very, very persuasive.

After the hike, tennis, and cocktails, they dressed for dinner. Lizzie had been most tactful.

'We do change for dinner. But nothing fancy, just anything you'd wear to your club on a weekday night. Anything at all.' And she had given Lynn her candid smile.

'You were right again,' Lynn said as she took a dark red silk dress off the hanger. She laid a string of pearls and the bracelet on the dresser.

'Don't wear that,' Robert cautioned.

155

'Not? But you always want me to.'

'Not here. It looks too rich. The pearls are enough. Modest. Sweet. I'm sorry you wore your ring, come to think of it. Ah, well, too late.'

'You beat him at tennis. Should you have?' she asked.

'That's different. People respect a winner. They respect sports. It may seem silly, and I suppose it is when you really think about it, but the idea of excelling in a sport sort of stamps a man. He won't forget me.' With his head tilted back he stood knotting his tie and exuding confidence. 'That's what I keep telling the girls. That's what I shall tell him.' He pointed at her abdomen, laughed, and corrected himself. 'Sorry, I don't want to be sexist. But I don't know why I'm sure it's a him. Come on, you look lovely as always. Let's go down. I'm starved.'

In the long dining room on a pine sawbuck table, pewter plates were set on rough linen mats. The utensils were plain stainless steel. But the candles were lit, and the dinner was served by two maids in uniform. A pair of handsome golden retrievers lay patiently in a corner.

'The great thing about the airplane,' Lizzie said contentedly, 'is that you can bring your household across country, dogs and all.'

The airplane? No, the private company jet, thought Lynn, and was amused. A variety of conversations crossed the table, and she tried to catch some of them. There was talk of travel, not to London or Paris, but to the Fiji Islands and Madagascar. One couple had been on an expedition to the South Pole. It was like peering through a crack in the door, to a new world. Robert wanted to push the door open and walk into that world. It seemed to her as she overheard him at the other end of the table that he had already gotten one foot through the crack.

His rich voice and his eager expression were very attractive. At any rate, three or four of the men were paying attention, leaning to catch his remarks, which were addressed, of course, to Monacco.

'– we should, I've been thinking a lot about it, and we should train our own people in languages before we send them over. We should do our own public relations. Our outside PR in one office alone costs twenty-five thousand a month, minimum, and it won't be any less over there. I've been getting some figures together. Seems to me we know our own product best and should be able to do our own PR.'

Then Monacco asked something that Lynn, caught in the crossfire of conversations, could not hear. But he had asked a question; that meant he was listening carefully.

'– met a German banker recently from Stuttgart. He's just the man to give us the answer to that. He travels all through the new republics. Yes, he's a good friend of mine. I can get in touch with him as soon as I get back to the office.'

'Oh, that house where the light's on?' Lizzie was saying. 'Across the lake, you mean. That's the caretaker's light.' Through the autumn dusk there sparked one point of fire; it danced in the black water. 'They left, and the place is for sale. We had a real scandal around here,' she explained to Lynn. 'This perfectly wonderful couple – we've known them for years and their place is really beautiful – well, she left him. It seems he knocked her around once too often. All those years it had been going on and none of us ever had the faintest suspicion. Isn't that amazing?'

Lynn's neighbor, with eager eyes and voice, supplemented the story. 'They were a stunning couple. How could we have guessed? He had the best sense of humor too. He absolutely *made* a party. You'd never think to talk to him that he could do things like that.'

'Well, it goes to show, doesn't it? You never know what goes on behind closed doors.'

'No,' said Lynn.

Her heart had leapt as though a gun had sounded. Now, just calm down, she said to herself. Just stop it. That business is all past. It ended months ago on the island. It's finished, remember? Finished.

Robert's voice sounded again over the chatter. 'Of course, advertising's cheapest during the first quarter of the year, we know that. Television and radio are hungry then. I think we should find out how that works abroad before we make any definite commitments.'

Almost unconsciously, Lynn glanced toward him, and at that very instant he glanced toward her, so that she caught his familiar, endearing smile. Things are going well, it declared.

'Oh, here come your marvelous cookies,' cried Lizzie.

'You didn't make these yourself?' asked Lynn's neighbor.

'Yes, she did. I know all about her. She's professional.' Lynn corrected her. 'No, no, I'd only like to be.'

'Well, why don't you? I have a friend whose daughter – she must be about your age – makes the most exquisite desserts for people, bombes and –'

'Lynn's pregnant,' Lizzie interrupted. 'She'll have other things to do.'

'Really? Congratulations! You have a daughter ready for college and you're having another. That's marvelous.'

All eyes were on her. An earnest woman said, 'You set an example, starting again just at the age when practically everybody's breaking up. Your baby's lucky.'

'I hope so.'

'One thing's sure, between you and that handsome husband of yours, it'll be good looking.'

Presently, everyone got up and went into the living room for drinks. A vigorous fire flared under the great stone mantel, drawing Lynn to stand and gaze at it.

'You're looking thoughtful,' said Pete Monacco.

'No, just hypnotized. Fountains and fires do that, don't they? And this has been such a lovely day.'

He raised his glass to her as if making a toast. 'We're glad you came. Robert's got interesting ideas. I'm glad he was brought to my attention. Unfortunately, some very bright guys get lost in the crowd – not often, but it can happen. He'll be making his mark in the firm. Hell, he has made it.'

'I think I've left an impression,' Robert said later. They were in bed under the quilt. 'He asked me to put some of my ideas in writing and send them to him. What was he saying to you?'

'Nice things. That you were going to make your mark on the firm.'

The window was low. When she raised her head, she had a clear view far down to the lake, where the diamond point of light still glistened from the vacant house that belonged to 'the perfectly wonderful couple.'

Robert stroked her stomach. 'It won't be long before this fellow will be kicking you.'

'Who is he? What will he be?' she wondered. She had also begun to think of the baby as 'he.' 'It's all so mysterious. When I look back upon where we've been and then look ahead, even only as far as a year from now . . . Yes, it's all so mysterious.'

It had grown very cold outside, and the wind had risen, sounding a melancholy wail through the trees. Even under the quilt it was cold, and Robert drew her close.

'Listen to that wind,' he whispered. 'It's a great night for sleeping, all snug in here. And it's been a great day. Things are really looking up for us, Mrs Ferguson.' He sighed with pleasure. 'I love you, Mrs Ferguson. I take it you're aware of that?' He chuckled, drawing her even closer.

'I am,' she answered, thought following swiftly: It is

absurd to let a piece of gossip affect me. What have Robert and I to do with those people? I know nothing about them, anyway. I am I and Robert is Robert.

He yawned. 'Can't keep my eyes open. Let's sleep. Tomorrow'll take care of itself.'

That was certain. They unfold, those unknown tomorrows, with their secrets curled like the tree that lies curled within the small, dry seed.

They started home right after dawn on Sunday. That way, Robert said, they'd be back before dinner with some time left over to be with the girls.

The house was deserted when they arrived. There wasn't even a light on.

'Ah, poor Juliet! They left her in the dark,' said Lynn as the dog came forward into the dark hall. 'They're probably over with Bruce and Josie. I guess they didn't expect us back this early.'

'I never asked you what Josie said about our going up to Monacco's place.'

'She didn't say much.'

'I wonder what they really thought. You can't tell me there isn't some sort of envy, in a nice way at least.'

'I don't think so. You know Josie is the last person to disguise her feelings, especially to me. So I'd know if there were.'

'Did you know we've been invited to Monacco's in Maine?' Lynn had asked her, wanting no cat-and-mouse game between them, no dishonesty posing as tact.

And Josie had replied that yes, Robert had told Bruce, and she had said, 'Don't feel uncomfortable on account of Bruce. I know you.' She had smiled. 'Bruce wasn't made to shine or sparkle. He knows himself.'

That was true. You could see that Bruce knew who he was and didn't need to measure his worth by other people's accomplishments.

'Robert's exceptional,' Josie had said. 'He works like a demon and deserves whatever he may get.'

Robert said now, 'I did feel a little sorry, a little uncomfortable, when I told him.'

'Well, you needn't have. Josie told me you deserve whatever you get.'

Robert laughed. 'One can take that in two ways.'

'They mean it in one way only.'

'Of course. Just a joke.' He started upstairs with the two suitcases. 'Come on, let's unpack before they all come home.'

'I'll do it in the morning.'

'You always say that. Who wants to wake up and find suitcases staring you in the face? Never put off till tomorrow what you can do today. That's my motto.'

She followed him. The first room at the top of the stairs was the new nursery, and she couldn't pass it without peering in. The furniture had arrived, the crib and dresser in light yellow; the walls matched; there were large Mother Goose pictures in maple frames and spring-green gingham curtains, a refreshing change from pink and blue. A large, soft polar bear sat in one corner of the crib. At the window there was a rocking chair, where she would sit to nurse the baby. The thought of doing this again brought a renewal of youth, an affirmation of womanhood. None of the theories that one read, with all their political or psychological verbiage, could come within miles of describing the real sweetness of the fuzzy head and the minuscule splayed fingers against the breast.

In the bedroom, where Robert had already begun to unpack, the telephone rang. He was standing by the bed holding the phone when she came in.

'What? What?' he said. A dreadful look passed over his face. 'What are you saying, is she –'

And Lynn, seeing him, turned ice cold.

161

'We'll be there. In the parking lot. Yes. Yes.' He put the phone down. He was shaking. 'That was Bruce. Emily's had a hemorrhage. From menstruation, he thought. She's in the hospital. Hurry. He'll meet us there.'

The car squealed around the corner at the foot of the drive.

'Take it easy, Robert. Not so fast. Listen, listen, it was just her period, that's all it was ... But why a hemorrhage?' She babbled. 'But it can't be anything too bad. She's in perfect health ...'

'They don't admit people to the hospital for nothing at all,' he said grimly.

She wrung her hands in her lap and was quiet, while, in a frenzy, they rode through the town and into the hospital parking lot, where Bruce was waiting. Robert slammed the car door and began to run toward the entrance.

'Stop, I have to talk to you first,' Bruce cried. 'No, no, she's not – you're thinking she died, and I'm breaking it to you easily – but no, no, she's upstairs and she'll be fine, only she's terrified.' The kind, earnest eyes matched the kind, earnest voice. 'The fact is – well, I have to tell you, Emily had a miscarriage.'

There was a total silence, as when the sounds of the world are drowned by a heavy snowfall. Traffic on the avenue and bustle in the parking lot all receded, leaving the three in that pool of silence, looking from one to the other.

'She's terrified,' Bruce repeated, and then begged Robert, 'don't be hard on her.'

'How –' Lynn began.

Bruce resumed steadily. 'She telephoned us around noon. She was more worried about Annie than about herself. She didn't want Annie to know. So Josie took Annie to our house, and I brought Emily here. The doctor says' – Bruce laid his hand on Lynn's arm – 'he said she was in the third month. Are you all right, Lynn?'

Robert groaned, and at the piteous sound she turned to him. So he had been justified, more than justified, in his fears. And she cried inwardly: Oh, Emily, I trusted you! And she cried: Was this my fault? Robert will say it's my fault.

'Shall we go?' asked Bruce.

On the long walk from the parking lot she rallied. I'm the one who is good in emergencies, remember? Say the mantra: Good in emergencies ... Her legs were weak, yet they moved. Then it seemed as if the elevator would never come. When it did, they shared space with a patient on a stretcher; so Mom had been carried that day with the white sheet drawn up to a drained white face. No one spoke as they ascended, then stepped out into a foreboding wave of hospital smells, of disinfectant and cleaning fluids. Ether too? No, it couldn't be, not in a corridor. But it sickened her, whatever it was, and she swallowed hard.

'I asked for a private room,' Bruce said when they stopped at the end of the corridor. His voice rose half an octave, cheerfully. 'Emily, your dad and mom are here.'

A hot sunset light lay over the bed where Emily lay. Her body made only a slight ridge under the blanket, and the one arm that was exposed was frail; nothing of Emily had ever before seemed frail.

Lynn took a cold, sweating hand in hers and whispered, 'We're here. Darling? We're here.'

She wanted to say, It's going to be all right, it's not the end of the world, nor the end of you, God forbid. There's nothing that can't be solved, can't be gotten over, nothing, do you hear me? Nothing. She wanted to say all these, but no sounds came from her dry lips.

Emily's beautiful eyes wandered toward the ceiling. Tears rolled on her cheeks. And Robert, who had been

163

standing on the other side of the bed, said faintly, 'I have to sit down.'

He's going to be sick, Lynn thought, while Bruce and the nurse, who had been at the window, must have had the same thought, because the nurse shoved a chair across the room, and Bruce took Robert's arm.

'Put your head down. Sit,' he murmured.

Robert laid his head on Emily's coverlet, and the others walked toward the door out of his hearing.

'Poor man.' The nurse clucked her tongue. 'It's funny how often men take things harder than we do. She's going to be fine, Mrs Ferguson. Mr Lehman called Dr Reeve. He's the chief of gynecology here, you couldn't get better.'

Lynn's voice quivered. 'I'm so scared. Tell me the truth. She looks so awful. Please tell me the truth.'

'She's very weak, and she's in quite some pain. This is like giving birth, you know, the same pains. But there's nothing to be afraid of, you understand? Here, rest till the doctor comes back.'

Rapid steps came purposefully down the hall. Dr Reeve looked like a doctor, clean shaven, compact, and authoritative. He could play the part in a soap opera, Lynn thought hysterically; a foolish laugh rose to her throat and was silenced there. Were they really in a hospital room talking to this man about Emily?

Robert stood up. 'Bruce, you talk, you do it,' he said, and then sat down again.

Bruce conferred briefly with the doctor, who then turned back to the parents.

'She's losing a lot of blood,' he said, wasting no words. 'We'll need to do a D and C. She says she hasn't eaten since breakfast. Can I rely on that? Because if she's had food within the last few hours, we'll have to wait.'

Lynn replied faintly, 'I don't know. We've been away. We just got home.'

'You can rely on it,' Bruce said.

'Fine. Then we'll take her up right away.' Dr Reeve looked keenly at Robert and Lynn. 'Why don't you two go out with your brother and –'

Bruce prompted. 'I'm just a friend.'

'Well, take them out and get something to eat.' He looked again at Robert, who was wiping his eyes with the back of his hand. 'Have a drink too. You can come back later in the evening.'

'A good idea,' said Bruce, assenting. 'We'll do just that.'

'No,' Robert said. 'I'm not leaving here. No, we'll stay.'

'All right,' Bruce said quickly. 'There's a sun parlor at the end of the hall. We'll sit there. And if you need us for anything, Doctor, that's where we'll be.'

'Fine. I suggest you go there now, then.' The professional smile was sympathetic, but firm.

He means, Lynn knew, that we are not to stand here watching them wheel Emily into the operating room. It's plain to see that Robert can barely cope with this. Poor Robert. And she took his hand, twining her fingers through his as they went down the hall with Bruce.

In restless, forlorn silence they waited. Bruce and Lynn thumbed through magazines, not reading, while Robert stared through the window wall at the treetops. It was long past visiting hours, and steps were few in the hall, when a familiar, distinctive clicking sound approached: Josie's high heels, worn because Bruce was so much taller than she.

'I got permission to come in,' she whispered. 'I tracked Eudora down, and she went straight to your house, so I could bring Annie back there. Eudora's a princess. Annie was having her bath and getting ready for bed when I left.'

Josie was wise. She gave no comforting words, no

165

warm hug that would have brought on tears. She simply did whatever was needed.

Robert, with head in hands, was huddled in the sofa. All six feet four of him looked small. Lynn got up and caressed his bent head.

'Our beautiful girl, our beautiful girl,' he moaned, and clearly she recalled his cry when Caroline's tiny body lay before them. Our baby. Our beautiful baby.

'She's going to be fine. I know. Oh, darling, she will.'

'I'd like to get my hands on that rotten little bastard. I'd like to kill him.'

'I know. I know.'

Time barely moved. Eventually it grew dark. Bruce stood up and turned on the lights, then returned to sit with Josie. They spoke in whispers, while Lynn and Robert sat hand in hand. No one looked at his watch, so no one knew what time it was when Dr Reeve appeared in the doorway. He looked different in his crumpled green cotton pants, with a pinched face and circled eyes. Authority had come from the suit and the tie and the brisk walk. Now he looked like a tired workman. Such scattered thoughts went through Lynn's head as he came toward them.

'Your girl is all right,' he said. 'She's in the recovery room, but she'll be back in her own room shortly. Mr Lehman asked for a nurse through tonight and as long as needed. Good idea if you can afford it. Now, I suggest that you go home and come back again in the morning. Emily won't know you for hours, and it's already close to midnight.' He glanced at Robert. 'If – it's highly unlikely – if it should be necessary to call anyone, shall –' He glanced toward Bruce.

Robert got up. It was as if the news had brought him back to life. 'No, we're the parents. We're over the first shock, and we can handle whatever comes next. You can imagine what a shock it was, being away and finding this when we got home.'

'Of course. But it must be good to have friends like these to handle an emergency for you.'

'We appreciate them. Bruce and Josie are the best.'

'Well,' Bruce said brightly now, 'all's well that ends well. What I suggest is that we get something to eat. I personally could eat shoe leather at this point.'

Josie went considerately on tiptoe through the corridor. 'Darn heels sound like hammers,' she whispered. 'Listen. We're all too tired to go home and forage for food. What about the all-night diner on the highway? We can get a quick hamburger or something.'

When they were settled in a booth, she explained, 'I told Annie that Emily had a sick stomach, a little problem. She was scared at first, but then she accepted my story and seems fine.'

'She mustn't ever know, of course,' Lynn said.

'I knew you would feel that way about it, and that's why I told her what I did.'

The emphasis on *you* prompted Lynn to ask, 'Why? Wouldn't you feel that way?'

'I'm not sure. Kids know much more about what's going on around them than you may think.'

'I'm sure Emily didn't tell her about – about what was going on between herself and Harris, for God's sake!'

'I'm sure Emily didn't, but as I said, kids are smart, and Annie is especially so. Smart and secretive,' Josie added. 'Annie could say a lot of things if she wanted to or dared to.'

Robert, who had said nothing since he sat down, now burst out. 'Never mind what Annie knows or doesn't know! It's Emily who's tearing me to shreds. The thought of her –' He turned upon Lynn. 'I want you to know, I blame you as much as Emily. I told you when she was

167

only fifteen years old that you were too lax with her. You have no backbone. You let people walk all over you. And you're not alert. You don't look around and watch what's going on. You never did.'

Caroline, Lynn thought, and her will ebbed hopelessly.

'Now here we are,' Robert said. 'Yes, here we are.'

'That's hardly fair, Robert,' Josie protested angrily, 'and not true. I don't know of a wiser, more caring mother than Lynn. You mustn't do this to her.'

'I don't care. This was all avoidable. Is this what I work for, to see my daughter ruined, thrown away on a penniless bastard? Ruined – ruined.'

The fluorescent bulbs above them glared on Robert, turning his exhausted face dark green.

Bruce said quietly, 'You mustn't think of Emily as being ruined, Robert. This is a terrible thing, I know it is, but still, at seventeen she has a wonderful long life ahead. You mustn't,' he said more sternly, 'allow her to think otherwise.'

Robert flexed his fingers. 'I want to get my hands on the bastard. I just want to get my hands on him.'

Despair sank like a stone in Lynn's chest. A few hours before they had been feeling – or she had been feeling on Robert's behalf – the glow of his success. They had been driving home through the bright fall afternoon with music on the radio, the new baby on the way, and –

'I could kill him,' Robert said again. 'Home now, sleeping like a log, not giving a damn, while Emily is –' He broke off. 'Does the bastard even know, I wonder?'

'Of course he does,' Bruce said. 'He's quite frantic. He wanted to go to the hospital, but I told him he couldn't. I told him to call me for information. As a matter of fact, I will telephone him when we get home. He's waiting up.'

Lynn was inwardly saying her mantra again: Good in emergencies. Now she made inquiry. 'The third month.

168

What was she – what were they – intending to do? Did she say? I don't understand,' she whispered.

Bruce answered her. 'On the way to the hospital Emily told me that she hadn't known really what to do. She had intended to get up courage to talk to you both this week, but she didn't want to spoil her father's important trip to Maine, to get him upset before the big meeting.'

Robert made correction. 'It wasn't a big meeting. I don't know where she got that idea. It wasn't that important.'

'Well, anyway, that's the story. They were, I gather, quite beside themselves this last month, the two of them. They didn't know where to turn.'

Lynn burst into tears and covered her face. 'Poor baby. The poor baby.'

Bruce and Josie got up. 'Let's go. Get whatever rest you can,' Josie commanded. 'I have to go to work in the morning, although I suppose I could phone in.'

Lynn recovered. 'No. Go to work. You've done enough. You've been wonderful.'

'Rubbish,' said Bruce. 'If you need either of us, you know where we are. You two will come through this all right, though, and so will Emily. Only one thing: Be kind to each other tonight. No recriminations. This is not your fault. Not yours, Robert, and not Lynn's. Have I got your word?' he asked, leaning into the car where Robert had already started the engine. 'Robert? Have I got your word?' he repeated sternly.

'Yes, yes,' Robert muttered, and grumbled as he drove away. 'I don't know what he thinks I'm going to do to you.'

That you are going to go on blaming me, she said to herself. That's what he thought. But now you won't, thank God. I don't think I can bear a harsh word tonight. And yet, was any of it my fault? Perhaps . . .

Home again, she walked restlessly through the house. Setting the table for breakfast, she thought: Disaster strikes and yet people eat, or try to. She let the dog out and, while Juliet rummaged in the bushes, watched the stars. The sky was sprinkled with them; far off at a distance beyond calculation, could there be some living, thinking creature like herself, and in such pain?

She went upstairs to Emily's room, wanting to feel her presence, wanting to find some clue to her child's life. The closet and the desk were neat, for Emily was orderly, like Robert. There hung the shirts, not much larger than a hand towel. There stood the shoes, sneakers next to a pair of three-inch heels. On the bedside table lay a copy of *Elle* and a book: *Studies of Marital Abuse*.

Lynn opened the book to the first chapter: 'The Battered Woman in the Upper Middle Class.' She closed the book.

Are we now marked by this forever? Is it engraved on Emily's mind forever?

'Come,' Robert said from the doorway. 'This won't do you any good.' He spoke not unkindly. 'What's that she's reading?' And he took hold of the book before Lynn could hide it. 'What the devil is this trash? The battered woman! She'd have done better to read about the pregnant high school girl.'

'The one has nothing to do with the other.'

Yet perhaps it had. Things are entwined, braided into each other . . .

'Somebody comes out with a "study,"' Robert scoffed. 'Then somebody else has to write another. It's all a money-making, publicity-seeking lot of trash. Exaggerations. Lies, half of it. Throw the damn book out.'

'No. It belongs to Emily. Don't you touch it, Robert.'

'All right,' he grumbled. 'All right. We've got enough trouble tonight. Come to bed.'

Neither of them slept. It began to rain. Drops loud as an onslaught of stones beat the windows, making the night cruel. Turning and turning in the bed, Lynn saw

170

the hall light reflected upward on the ceiling. Robert would be sitting downstairs in his usual corner, his 'mournful' corner, alone. If anything were to happen to Emily, it would kill him. But she had poor Annie – why did she always think 'poor Annie,' as if the child were some neglected misfit, disabled and deserted, when she was none of these? And then there was this baby, the boy Robert wanted. But nothing would happen to Emily, the doctor had said. He'd said it. Her thoughts ran, circled, and returned all night.

The doctor was just leaving Emily's room after early rounds when Robert and Lynn came down the hall. He spoke to them quickly in his succinct, flat manner. For after all, Emily could mean no more to him than another problem to be solved as skillfully as he could.

'She's still in some pain, but it's lessening. She has anemia from the blood loss, and we've just given her a transfusion, so don't be shocked when you see her. It's all to be expected.' He swung away, took a few steps, and turned back. 'I have a daughter her age, so I know.' He stopped. 'She'll have her life,' he said then with an abrupt smile, and this time walked away.

A lump in Lynn's throat was almost too painful to admit speech, but she called after him.

'Thank you for everything. Thank you.'

The nurse, who had been sitting by the bed, stood up when, with questioning faces, they entered the room.

'Come in. She's not sleeping, just resting. She'll be glad to see you.'

Lynn stood over the bed. Glad, she thought bitterly. Glad, I doubt. Bruce said she was terrified.

The girl's face was dead white, frozen, carved in ice.

Robert said softly, 'Emily, it's Dad. Dad and Mom.'

'I know. I'm very tired,' Emily whispered with her eyes shut.

'Of course you are. Emily, we love you,' Robert said.

171

'We love you so.' His voice was so low that he repeated the words. He wanted to make certain that she had heard him. Kneeling on the floor, he brought his face level with hers. 'Emily, we love you.' Then he put his face down again on the coverlet.

Everything spun too fast. The way life moved and sped was extraordinary. It was fearful. One was, after all, quite helpless. First there was Emily trying for Yale with all the honors. And then there was this scene. A sudden vertigo overcame Lynn and she grasped the back of the bed to steady herself.

The nurse whispered, 'She'll sleep now. The night nurse said she was up most of the night in spite of the medication.'

So they waited all day in the room. Late in the afternoon Emily awoke and stirred in the bed.

'I'm better,' she said clearly.

And indeed, some faint color flowed under her skin, and her eyes were bright, their pupils large and dark as after recovery from fever.

Next she said, 'You're very angry.'

They spoke in unison. 'No, no.'

She sighed. 'You need to be told.'

'Not now,' Robert said. 'You don't need to talk now.'

But Emily insisted. 'I want to.' In a tone of bewilderment, as if she were telling a stranger's story, one that she did not really understand, she began. 'At first I didn't know. I didn't think, it was only about the middle of the second month. I didn't know. And after that, I was so scared. I couldn't believe it.'

Her thin hands clung together on the coverlet. On her little finger she wore the initialed gold ring that had been too large even for her middle finger when it was new. She had been eight, seven or eight, Lynn thought; my sister gave it to her for her birthday; we had a clown at the party, I remember.

172

'I – we didn't know what to do. We kept talking about what to do. I was going to tell you, honestly. I just couldn't seem to get my courage up.'

And Lynn thought of the day she had learned about the baby who, it now seemed, was at this minute making its first movements within her, of how she had brought the news home and the house had turned into a holiday house.

'I didn't want an abortion, I couldn't do that.'

'What then would you have done?' Robert asked softly.

'We thought – I'll be eighteen this month, we'll be in college next year. They have married couples in college, lots of people marry that young. We'd want to be married, we'd want the baby to have proper parents.' Emily's eyes turned toward the ceiling for a moment, reflecting. 'You see, we're not that modern. Maybe I am, but Harris isn't. He comes from a very religious family. They go to church every Sunday. He does, too, and they'd want things done right. They're very good people, really. Harris wouldn't be what he is if they weren't.'

Robert raised his head, looked across the bed toward Lynn. His lips formed a sneer; she understood the sneer. But he said nothing. And she herself was as yet incapable of making any judgment at all.

'You won't believe this,' Emily said, 'but it was only one time. I swear it.' When neither parent answered, she continued, 'I loved him. I love him now. So it happened. It was one day when we were going to the lake, and –'

'No.' Robert spoke roughly. 'No. We don't have to hear about that.'

He did not want to imagine his daughter with a man, to think of Emily and sex at the same time. Well, that was understandable, Lynn supposed.

Now Emily reached for her hand. 'You know, Mom,' she said. 'You understand about loving, even when there are times one shouldn't.' And she gave her mother a serious, meaningful look, holding her so long with that look that Lynn, struck by painful memory, was the first to turn away. It was as if Emily wanted to remind her of something, as if there were some complicity between her daughter and herself.

Then the nurse came back. It was five o'clock, dinnertime, and visiting hours were over until the evening, she said, apologizing.

'Anyway, now that Emily's doing fine, you must feel better yourselves.'

'You must be awfully tired, Mom.' Emily smiled. 'You're starting the fifth month, aren't you? Go home and rest.'

When they were halfway home, it occurred to Lynn that Emily had not spoken one direct word to Robert.

A car was parked in front of their house when they entered the driveway. Two men got out and walked toward them. One was Harris in his neat chinos, and the other, of equal height, with the same thick brown hair, but older and broader, was undoubtedly his father, wearing a policeman's uniform.

'Oh, no,' Lynn said aloud.

Robert heard her and gave an order. 'Be quiet. I'll handle this.'

They met beside Robert's car. The boy, like Lynn, was afraid, but his father came forward frankly.

'I'm Lieutenant Weber. My son has come to talk to you. Speak up, Harris.'

Robert gave a stop signal with his raised hand. 'There is nothing you can tell me that I want to hear. Nothing.'

The boy flushed. The blood, surging from neck to scalp, looked as though it must burn him.

'I'd like to beat you to a pulp,' Robert said, making a fist with the raised hand.

'Mr Ferguson,' the father said, 'perhaps if we go inside and talk together –'

'No. My little girl is in there, and anyway, I don't want

174

you – him – in my house. I don't want to talk to him.'

'Let him speak here, then. Please, Mr Ferguson. It'll only take a few minutes.'

'I just want you to know,' Harris said, 'it's hard to find the words, but – I am so terribly sorry, I'll never forget this as long as I live.' His whole body was shaking, but he raised his head and threw his shoulders back. 'I'm ashamed. I am so terribly ashamed, and so sad for Emily because I love her. I don't know what else to say, Mr Ferguson, Mrs Ferguson.' He gave a little sob, and his Adam's apple bobbed. 'You've always been so nice to me, and –'

His father continued for him. 'I have always told him, always since he was grown, that he had two little sisters and that he must treat girls as he'd want somebody to treat them.'

Robert interrupted. 'Look, Lieutenant, this is all very sweet talk, but there's no point in it. Talk can't undo the facts or make us feel any better. The facts are that Emily came close to dying –'

'No, Robert,' Lynn said softly. 'No, don't make it worse than it is.'

'My wife's a sentimental woman. She doesn't want to hear the truth spoken. It's all right for you to talk sweetly, young fellow. You're not the one lying in pain.'

Harris's eyes glistened, and with her eyes Lynn tried to communicate with him. Certain thoughts were taking shape in her mind. He hadn't raped Emily, after all. And it did take two.

Lieutenant Weber said it for her. 'It does, after all, take two,' he reminded them gently. He gazed out toward the hill where darkness already lay on the trees. 'And it's not the first time this has happened, God knows.'

A dialogue spun itself out between the two men while Lynn and Harris stood by.

'That doesn't concern me. I'm only concerned about this time.'

175

'Of course. As the father of girls I surely understand. The question is, what is to happen now to these young folks?'

The man was sorrowful and yet not humble, Lynn saw. Somehow the onus is always put on the boy, so it must be hard to be standing in his shoes. Yet he does it honorably. And Robert was making it harder, offering no way for minds to meet.

'He's heard plenty from me and his mother, too, about this, you can bet, enough so he'll never forget it,' Lieutenant Weber persisted.

'He didn't hear enough. If he were my son, I'd break his neck.'

The father laid his hand on his son's arm. 'What good would that do?'

'Let him suffer a little, that's what.'

'Don't you think he is suffering? He's a good kid, same as Emily. She's been at our house, and we know her well. She's a fine girl, the finest. They made a mistake, a bad one, but not the worst. Now it's up to us to help them.'

'I'm going inside,' Robert said coldly. 'We've been through hell, my wife and I, and we're wasting our strength listening to drivel. If you'll excuse us.' The gravel crunched under his heel as he moved.

'I'm sorry you think it's drivel, Mr Ferguson. Harris came here like a man to face you. In our family he's been taught to have respect. Never mind this modern stuff. He goes to church, he's not the kind who goes banging – pardon the expression' – this with a bow toward Lynn – 'every girl he –'

Robert's anger blazed. 'No,' he said, 'not every girl. Only a girl from a family like this one, a home like this one.' He waved his arm toward the house. 'Not such a dumb idea to come snooping and sneaking around a place like this so he can raise himself up from the bottom.'

176

Lynn cried in horror. 'Robert! Robert!'

'You stay out of this, Lynn. People like him there think they'll better themselves by creeping in where they don't belong.'

'Now, wait a minute, Mr Ferguson. Don't you take that superior tone with me. I won't stand for it.'

'Dad! For God's sake, don't! Please don't argue,' Harris pleaded.

'Don't you worry, son. You go sit in the car. Go now. I won't be long.'

When the boy was out of hearing, he resumed. 'I came here like a gentleman with my son. I planned to go into your house so your neighbors across the road wouldn't recognize me in my uniform. I wanted to spare you again, the way I spared you before. I wasn't going to tell you this, for Emily's and Harris's sakes I wasn't, but you've asked for it. On the bottom, are we? You're hardly one to talk.'

'Explain yourself,' Robert said. 'And lower your voice while you're at it.'

'Yes, that would be a good idea,' replied the other man, and lowered it. 'It would have been better for you if you had lowered yours that night a while back when you were battering your wife.'

'Oh, Lieutenant, oh, please,' Lynn begged.

'Mrs Ferguson, I'm sorry, but I have to. I'm a man too. Maybe it's just as well that Mr Ferguson hears the truth.'

Lynn's heart raced. It crossed her mind that even at her age, one could have a heart attack. How fast could a heart beat before it gave up?

'Let me tell you,' Weber said, 'I was called here, I was on duty, when a call came a while back in the summer. The people across the road were out taking an evening walk when they passed your house and heard something going on. So they phoned the station, and up I came. I stood in the dark, and I heard enough to know what it was, all right. I could have taken you in right then and there. But I wasn't about to make trouble for Emily. I figured she already had enough because it can't be the greatest thing for a girl to grow up here, grand as it is.'

Robert was breathing heavily, and Weber continued.

'We're very fond of Emily. We know what she is. True blue. I wouldn't hurt her for the world. So I told the people across the road that it was a mistake, and back at the station I buried the record. Buried it. So don't you talk to me about fine family, Mr Ferguson, or coming up from the bottom.' He turned to Lynn, who was crying. 'I know you're expecting, Mrs Ferguson, and this isn't good for you. I'm awfully sorry about it. About everything. If there's anything I can ever do for you, you know where I am, where we are, Harris and –'

'Yes, you can do something,' Robert said. He was shaking. 'You're a lying bastard, cop or no. You saw nothing when you were here, and you know you didn't. You're trying to intimidate me. Well, it won't work. Now get out of here, you and your precious son. And never come back, either one of you. That's what you can do, and that's all I have to say.'

'That's just what I intended to do all along, Mr Ferguson. Good night, Missus.'

For a minute the two were speechless. Lynn was as shocked and immobile as in that first second when Bruce had told them about Emily. The sound of Weber's chugging old engine died away down the road before Robert spoke.

'Stop crying. Cry about Emily, not about that garbage.' He bent down in the dusk to stare at her. 'Don't tell me you're feeling sorry for that wretched kid. Yes, I wouldn't be surprised. I suppose you are.'

'Yes, Robert, I am.'

'It figures. That's you.'

'Maybe it is.'

178

Pity, like a wave, flooded over her, pity for everything, for a child lost in the crowd and crying for its mother, for a shivering dog abandoned on the roadside, for Emily, so afraid, so ashamed, and for that young fellow, too, with his scared eyes, paying such a price for his few moments of a natural passion. And now, unmistakably this time, the baby moved within her, flexing its tiny arm or leg, stretching and readying itself for a hard world.

'We've seen the last of them, at any rate,' Robert said as they went toward the house. 'If he ever comes here, you're to throw him out. But he won't dare.' They went inside, where Robert poured a drink. His hand was shaking. 'My heart's pounding like a trip-hammer. This sort of thing doesn't do you any good, that's for sure.'

'No,' she said, wiping her wet cheeks.

There was a terrible shame in the room, as if two strangers, a man and a woman, had blundered into a place where one of them was naked. It was not quite clear to her who the naked one was here, Robert, so painfully proud, or she herself, who had for the first time seen another human being stand up to Robert and win. For Weber had won; there could be no doubt of that.

He swallowed the drink and went to the foot of the stairs, calling Annie.

'We're home, honey. What are you doing?'

'Homework,' came the answer.

'What homework?'

'Geography.'

'Have you got the atlas up there with you?'

'Yes.'

'Good. Good girl. Well, stay up there and finish it.'

Returning, Robert said, 'We need to talk before she comes down.'

'About what?'

'About what we're going to do, naturally. I'd like to take her out of that school. Put her in private school, where she won't have to see him. I don't want her to see him even passing in the halls.'

'You can't do that to her, you can't break up a term in senior year, Robert!'

He considered, then conceded, 'I suppose you're right. But I'm going to have a talk with Emily – oh, don't worry, I see the worry on your face. It's going to be very peaceable, with no recriminations, because she's been through enough. But I'm going to make things quite clear, all the same. I want her to rest at home for a week or so, and when she goes back to school, she'll say she had the flu.' He walked back and forth across the room with steps so firm that the crystals on the wall sconces made a musical tinkle as he passed. 'I want you to keep a strict watch over her free time, Lynn. I want to know where she's going, with whom, and when she'll be home, and no nonsense about it. You get the idea.' He increased his pace so that the crystals complained. 'Damn! Damn! And life was looking so good. The fates just can't let you enjoy what they give without taking something away at the same time, or so it seems. However, there's no use lamenting about the fates.'

Lynn agreed that there was not, and he continued, 'I want to keep up with what I started in Maine, keep up the momentum. If it weren't for all that, I'd like to take the lot of us away over Thanksgiving and again at Christmas, and again in February, spend every damn school vacation away from here. But as it is . . . well, we'll have to find other things to do, a ski weekend, theater tickets, Saturdays in the city, anything to keep that girl out of harm's way.'

So he walked the length of the room like a general organizing his campaign. That which had been darkly, safely buried, that which Weber had dug up and brought into a cruel glare, had been dismissed from Robert's mind: It was an outrageous lie, it had never happened.

180

At least, Lynn thought wryly, at least Weber's done one thing; he's had a sobering effect; Robert hasn't said anything more about my being to blame for Emily's trouble.

The words repeated themselves in pitying silence: Emily's trouble.

'I am so terribly tired,' she said involuntarily.

Robert gave her a glance. 'Yes, you do look done in. Go to bed. I'll see how Annie's doing.'

She moved heavily. It was an effort to raise her arms and slip the dress over her head, to pull the spread back and get into the bed. Yet it was not long before she fell into a thick, dark sleep. Toward morning when the windows turned gray, she dreamed. She tumbled, hurling from some great height while grabbing in terror at the empty air, while below, sharp, pointed things – knives, sticks, thorns? – were aimed at her open eyes, and there was no way, no way she could –

She screamed, screamed, and was jolted awake. Robert was holding her, saying softly, 'What is it?'

'Nothing, nothing,' she whispered.

He comforted her shaking body, stroking the back of her neck.

'Nerves. Nerves. And why not? You've been through too much. Take it easy. I'm here. I'm here.'

'Then I have your promise, Emily?' Robert asked.

'I have already given it to you,' she answered, lying back on the pillowed sofa.

'It is for your own good, Emily. You've had a very narrow escape. As terribly hard as it was, the miscarriage' – here he seemed to gulp over the word – 'was easier than the other way would have been. Your whole life, your ambition, everything, would have turned inside out.' He made a gesture of hopeless dismissal. 'So now the rest is up to you,' he said, standing up and producing a

181

smile meant to encourage. 'I have to run for the late train. My desk must be loaded.' At the door he turned back again. 'Oh, yes, I meant to tell you, I've bought tickets to the opera, Saturday matinees. But you'll be able to squeeze in your homework all day Sunday. And Annie will too.'

'He's so well oiled,' said Emily when Robert had gone. 'Everything planned. You press a button and the answers to all your problems just pop out. Quick and easy.'

'That's nasty, Emily. Your father means so well. You never thought he'd be so understanding, now, did you?'

'Does he think I don't see through him? Do your home-work all day Sunday, meaning, Don't leave this house. I'm keeping an eye on you.'

'That's not true. You heard him say you should go out with other boys.'

'I don't want to go out with other boys. I want to be with Harris. I want to be trusted.'

Lynn raised an eyebrow. 'Trusted? Well, really, Emily.'

'It happened once, Mom. We're hardly ever alone together in the first place. All summer we were at the lake with a crowd, you know that. You believe me, don't you?'

Her blue eyes, moist as petals, are so beautiful, that it's a wonder he could resist her at all, Lynn thought.

'You believe me?' the girl repeated.

'Yes. But you see what happened from just that once.'

'We want to get married.'

'Oh, my God, Emily, you're much too young.'

'Eighteen! You were only twenty.'

'That was different. Your father was older.'

'My father? Yes, and look what you got.'

Lynn, choosing to ignore the sarcasm, said only, 'Harris, or you, or both of you, may change your minds, you know.'

'Not any more than we'll change our minds about

182

medical school. And it was horrible, what Dad said about Harris wanting to better himself because our family has more money,' Emily said bitterly. 'It was a cheap and cruel and stupid thing to say. Harris phoned me at the hospital just before you got there to take me home, and he told me.'

'Your father was beside himself with worry over you. I've never seen him so desperate. People say things when they're desperate.'

Lynn felt as if she were being driven toward a trap. But Harris had not been present, he had been sent to wait in the car when his father had talked about that night last spring. Her mind moved swiftly in recollection. Obviously, then, Weber hadn't wanted Harris to hear that part. He was a decent human being who had done his best to conceal what had happened. 'I buried it,' he had said. 'Buried it.' No, he would not have told Harris. And Lynn's fear subsided.

'Harris said his parents have told him he mustn't see me, that he must even avoid me in school.'

'They're right, Emily. It's wiser that way.'

'It's all Dad's fault. It goes back to him.'

Lynn protested, 'There's no logic in that remark. I don't understand it at all.'

'Don't you? I could tell you, but you wouldn't want to hear it. There's no use talking when you won't be open with me, Mom.'

Lynn, folding her hands on her lap, looked down on the backs that had been covered with puncture wounds. What Emily wanted was a confirmation, an admission about those wounds, now long healed. But she was not going to get it. A mother hides her private pain from her children. For their own good she does this.

For my own good, too, she thought. Abruptly a tinge of anger colored her feeling for Lieutenant Weber. He should not have said those things! He should have known how they would hurt. But then, there were the things that Robert had said ... Her head throbbed.

'I'll tell you, Emily,' she said somewhat crisply, 'I can't play verbal games with you. You say you're a woman, so I'll talk to you as one woman talks to another. I'll tell you frankly that I'm not feeling my best right now, and I don't want to argue about anything. I only want to help you, and I want you to help me too.'

Emily got up and took her mother into her arms. 'All right, Mom, we won't talk about this anymore. Just have a wonderful, healthy baby and be well.' She smiled at Lynn. 'Don't worry about me. I'll work hard the rest of the year and graduate with honors too. You'll see. And I won't make any trouble for anybody. I've made enough already.'

4

'What's the matter with Emily?' Annie asked again. 'Why won't anybody tell me?'

'There's nothing to tell. She's just working terribly hard these days. She has to keep her grades up if she wants to get into Yale,' Lynn answered cheerfully.

'She cries a lot. Her eyes were red last night.' Annie's own small, worried eyes were suspicious. 'Didn't you see?'

'She has a little cold, that's all.'

The weight of Emily's sadness lay heavily on Lynn. Of course she cried, why wouldn't she, poor child? The double shocks, to the body and to the spirit, had aged and changed her. Hardened her too? she wondered.

She hesitated at the door of Emily's room. Conscious of her own pregnancy's pronounced visibility, she could not help but think of its effect on the wounded girl.

But she opened the door, and in the cheerful, artificial tone that had by now become a habit, inquired, 'Busy? Or may I come in?'

Emily put the book down. 'I'm busy, but come in.'

'I don't want to disturb you. I thought – you've been isolated lately with all this studying. Of course, it's necessary, I know.' Floundering so, she came suddenly to the point. 'Tell me. Do you need to talk about your feelings, about Harris? Because if you want to, I'm here. I'm always here for you.'

'Thanks, but there's nothing to talk about.'

Emily's shoulders appeared to straighten, and her chin rose a proud inch or two. This small display of pride seemed to shut Lynn out, and she repeated gently.

'Nothing?'

'No. We stay completely away from each other, so if that's why you're worried, don't.'

'I'm not worried about that. I know you'll keep your word.'

'He sent me a birthday card with a lace handkerchief in it. And we do talk on the phone.' Emily paused as if, Lynn thought, she expects me to protest about that. When no protest came, Emily said proudly, 'He works every day. He even has a Sunday job. I suppose it's part of his punishment.'

'Oh! I shouldn't think punishment was necessary. I mean ... Our feeling is that you should have fun, you know that.' And when Emily was once more silent, Lynn continued, 'I know boys call you.'

'Because they know Harris and I are through.'

'But you never accept.'

Emily gave her a twist of a smile. 'If I wanted to, and I don't, there wouldn't be time, would there? My days are filled up. Aren't they?'

Indeed. True to his word, Robert had provided an activity for every available hour; they had gone to the opera, to country fairs, and the local dog show; they had skated on the season's first ice at Rockefeller Center and seen the exhibit at the Metropolitan Museum. Vigorously, tenaciously, he fulfilled his plan, and with equal tenacity and her new cool courtesy, Emily had complied.

But how she must ache!

So the autumn passed, a long, slow season this year, the ground covered with black leaves rotting under steady rain, a season sliding downhill toward a frozen winter, as if the chilly gloom wanted to reflect the cold that underlay the sham politeness in the house.

186

By tacit agreement the trouble was covered over. At meals Robert led the talk to current events, the day's headlines. Alone with Lynn the talk was chiefly about the firm. It was as if, for him, nothing else of any import had happened or was happening.

'They're thinking of sending me abroad,' he told her one night. 'There's a group from the West Coast going, from Monacco's office, and they want me to go with them for a meeting in Berlin. After that I go alone to meet the people whom we've contacted in Budapest.' Excited, stimulated, he paced the bedroom floor and came to rest behind Lynn, who was brushing her hair at the mirror. 'It'll take two weeks probably, if I go. I'm pretty sure I will, though. It'll be some time in December. I hate to leave you.' He studied her face. 'You look tired.'

'I'm fine. We'll be fine.'

'You're pretty heavy this time, that's what it is. By March you'll be yourself again.'

She agreed. 'I'm sure.'

Yet she felt a weakness that she had never felt before. It was hard to get out of bed in the morning, and so hard to keep running between activities, the train to New York, the car to the country fair, going, going all the time. With Robert away there would at least be some rest.

Josie said, 'It's not the pregnancy. You're emotionally wrung out. Emily's trouble was enough to do it, God knows.'

But you don't know the half of it, thought Lynn. Involuntarily, she sighed.

Josie remarked the sigh. 'You never went back to my friend – Dr Miller, I mean.' The tone was accusatory.

'No.' Go back to tell him about Lieutenant Weber and – and all the rest? Wake that up yet again? And for what? What could he do, that man, except make her feel like two cents, sitting there? And biting the thread with which she was mending Annie's skirt, she remarked only,

187

'That child tears everything. She's always bumping into things.'

'How do she and Robert get along these days?'

'All right. No problems.'

Not on the surface, anyway. He kept them all too busy, she thought. But perhaps that was healthy? Healthy and wholesome. You want to think so ... but is it?

'Robert's leaving for Europe on Tuesday, you know,' she said, feeling slightly awkward because Bruce was not leaving. Yet to ignore the fact before Josie would be more awkward.

'Yes, I know.'

No more was said about that. Then Josie asked about Emily.

'She never mentions Harris, and I don't ask anymore. "It's over," she told me. So maybe Robert was right when he said it would pass and the scars would fade. I guess so. I don't know.' She reflected. 'Anyway, she's working long hours, half the night, for the science fair. It's all voluntary. I think she's doing too much, but Robert says I should leave her alone. Well, of course, he's so proud of her achievement. And I am, too, but mostly I want her to be happy. I feel' – Here Lynn put the sewing down and clasped her hands – 'I feel so terribly sorry for her, Josie, and for the boy too.'

'Bruce has seen him a few times when he passes the soccer field on the way to the jogging track. He asks about Emily.'

'Yes, I'm sorry for him,' Lynn repeated, and, with a little laugh, added, 'You can imagine that Robert isn't. His anger over this has gone too deep. There's no forgiveness in it.'

'Robert's an angry man to begin with,' Josie said. 'Listen, Lynn, I don't want to come after you with a sledgehammer, but I wish you would listen to me. You *need* to talk to somebody. Keeping your secrets – and I know you do

188

– will only harm you in the end. God only knows what may happen.' And she repeated, 'Robert is an angry man.'

Her comments only offended Lynn; Josie's comments always had. They were exaggerated, and anyway it was unseemly to disparage a woman's husband to her face, no matter what you thought.

Yet this was the only flaw in the long friendship. She had always to consider that. And she had also to consider the nasty things Robert said about Josie. So she made her defense a calm one.

'Robert has always worked under very high pressure. Right now he's got his heart set on building a future for this baby, for the son he's convinced it is.'

'Oh, naturally he'd want a son.'

'Well, we already do have two girls, Josie. Anyway, Robert's a workaholic. I worry sometimes that he'll work himself to death.'

'If he does, it'll be by his own choice.'

'Oh, no, he plans to live and rear this boy. He's got such plans, it's really amazing to hear him; you'd think having a baby was the grandest thing that can happen. Well, I guess it is, after all.' Stricken with embarrassment before this barren woman, she stopped.

Josie's response was quick. 'Don't be sorry about me. I've long accepted that other women have babies and I don't. You have to face the realities, one right after the other, all through life.'

Lynn was immediately sober. 'Well, you surely face them,' she amended. 'I remember how you were when you had your operation. You were amazing.' She smiled. 'Thank goodness, you're fine now.'

'Is that a statement or a question?'

'Well, both, I guess.' Lynn was startled. 'You are fine now, aren't you?'

'You can't know that positively,' Josie answered quietly. 'Can you ever know anything positively?'

189

'I suppose not. But are you telling me something – something bad about yourself?'

'No. I'm only telling you that facing reality isn't the easiest thing for most of us to learn.'

There was a silence until Josie rose to depart. She left a vague discomfort in the room, a hollow space, a chilled draft, an enigmatic message. Lynn felt as if she had been scolded.

On Monday, the night before he was to leave, Robert came home early. He had bought new luggage and laid it on the bed ready to pack. His passport and traveler's checks were on the dresser, the new raincoat hung on the closet door, and his list was at hand.

They had dinner. He was euphoric, filled with a sense of novelty and adventure.

'This is much more than a question of profits, you understand. The world's peace, its future, hang on whether we can make the European Community work. We need to take all these eastern republics into some sort of attachment to NATO. That's why it's so important to lay an economic foundation.' He talked and talked. His eyes were brilliant.

Upstairs again after dinner, he went on talking while folding and packing; he would not allow Lynn to do it for him, preferring his own method. As he called out, she checked off the list.

'Notebook, camera, film, dictionary. There, that's it.' He turned to her. 'God, I'll miss you.'

'You'll be too busy to miss anyone.'

'Only you,' he said gravely. 'Hey, I guess the girls have gone to bed. I'll kiss them good-bye in the morning unless they're still asleep.'

'They'll be up.'

'I'm leaving at the crack of dawn. Where's Juliet?'

'Right there on the other side of the bed. I'll go put her out.'

'No, no, I will. Come on, girl, let's go,' he said as the dog, stretching and yawning, lumbered behind him.

It was not half a minute later when Lynn heard the voices exploding in the kitchen, and she raced downstairs. Robert was standing over Annie, trembling in her nightgown, with a face all puckered in tears. In front of her on the kitchen table was a soup bowl piled high with ice cream, whipped cream, fudge sauce and salted almonds; the base of the tower was encircled by a ring of sliced bananas, and the peak was adorned with a maraschino cherry.

'Look! Will you look at this!' Robert cried. 'No wonder she can't lose weight. You're a pig, Annie. You're worse than a pig because you're supposed to have some intelligence. You're disgusting, if you want to know.'

Annie sobbed. 'You – you've no right to say things like that. I haven't murdered anybody. If I want to be fat, I'll be fat, and it's my business.'

Lynn mourned, stroking the child's head. 'Oh, Annie. You had a good dinner. You were supposed to be in bed.'

Robert interrupted. 'Stop the coaxing and caressing. That's been the whole trouble here anyway. No discipline. No guts. Anything they want to do, they do.'

He snatched the soup bowl, Annie snatched, too, and the contents slopped over onto the table.

Annie screamed. 'Don't touch it! I want it!'

'Oh, this is awful,' Lynn lamented. 'I can't stand this! Robert, for heaven's sake, let her have a spoonful, a taste. Then she'll let you throw it away, I know she will.'

'Let' me? What do you mean? Nobody 'lets' me do anything in this house. I'm the father. Here,' he shouted with the bowl now firmly in his grasp, 'this is going where it belongs, into the garbage pail.'

The lid clanged shut, and Annie howled. 'That was mean! You're the worst father. Mean!'

'I may be mean, but you're a mess. A total, absolute mess. A disappointment. You'd better get hold of yourself.'

Lynn protested, 'Robert, that's cruel. It's true that Annie needs to watch her weight, but she is not a mess. She's a lovely girl, and –'

'Lynn, cut out the soft soap. It's sickening. I gag on it.'

'Don't you yell at Mommy! Leave Mommy alone!'

The two confronted each other, the trim, tall man opposed to the square little girl whose stomach bulged under her nightdress and whose homely, pallid face was mottled red with rage. Lynn summoned every ounce of control.

'Come upstairs with me. Come to bed,' she repeated quietly. 'There's no sense in this.'

When she had pacified Annie and seen her into bed, she went to her own bedroom, where Robert was reading.

'Well,' she said, 'a nice good-bye on your last night. Very nice to remember.'

A stack of Christmas cards waiting to be addressed lay on a table beside his chair. He held up a photograph of the Ferguson family, standing in front of the holly garlands on the living room mantel; they were all smiling; even Juliet, with lolling tongue, looked happy. Then he snapped the card back onto the pile and mocked:

'The perfect American family. There they are. Perfect.'

'Losing your temper like that over a dish of ice cream,' she protested.

'You know very well it was more than that. It was the principle of the thing, the disobedience, her defiance.'

'You called her a 'mess.' That was unforgivable. Brutal.'

'It's the truth. I work with her, you see how much time I spend trying to lift her out of her slovenly habits, I try

192

my darnedest, and still she comes home with C's on her report card. I don't know what to say anymore.'

Robert stood up, walked to the dresser, where he arranged his combs and brushes in parallels, then walked to the window, where he brought the shade even with the sill.

The baby made a strong turn or kick inside Lynn. Its weight pulled her so hard, she had to sit down.

'I can't stand this,' she said.

'Well, what do you want me to do? Go around pussy-footing, pretending not to see what I see? Maybe if you kept better order here –'

'Order? What's disorderly? Do you mind giving me an example other than the ice cream tonight?'

'Okay. That business last week when she went to school with a ten-cent-store ring on each finger. She looked ridiculous, and I said so, but you let her do it anyway.'

'Oh, for heaven's sake, it's the style in her grade. So it looks ridiculous – what difference? So I let her do it, and now I'm a failure as a mother.'

'Don't put words in my mouth. I didn't call you a failure.'

But you've thought it. I know. Ever since I let the baby drown.

'You implied it,' she said.

'What's all this quibbling? What are we doing here?' Exasperated, he punched his fist into his palm.

She should really not argue with him. Just don't talk back, she told herself. He's tense, he has to leave early in the morning, he needs his rest. Annie will forget about this, I'll forget, and it will all pass if I just keep quiet.

Yet a quick answer leapt from her mouth. 'I don't know what you're doing, but I know what I'm doing. I'm trying to cope.'

He stared as if in astonishment. 'You? You are? Coping? While I'm working my head off on the brink of the biggest opportunity of my life – of our lives – calmly keeping myself together and doing an expert job in spite of the disaster here at home, the disaster that you allowed to happen –'

She sprang up. 'Back again to Emily, are you? This is too much. It's insane.'

'Insane? You don't want to hear it, I know. And if you notice, I haven't talked about it. Purely out of consideration for your condition, Lynn. Purely.'

'Louder! Speak louder so she'll be sure to hear this.'

He strode to the door, closed it, and said in a lower voice, 'I warned you and warned you about her and that bastard, but in your laissez-faire way you did nothing. You didn't watch her, you ruined a beautiful girl, you ruined her life.'

Lynn's anger mounted. 'Listen here, you with your phony accusations. I could have done some accusing, too, in my time if I'd wanted to, and my accusations wouldn't have been phony either. You know darn well what –'

Robert sprang up, grabbed her arms, and shook her. 'If you weren't pregnant, I know what I'd –'

'Take your hands off me, Robert. You're hurting me. Now, you let me alone, you hear?'

'Goddamn crazy house,' he muttered, walking away. 'I'll be glad to get out of it in the morning.'

She lay down, hoping for sleep. Anger was disaster. Some people throve on it, but it sapped her; some bodies just were not programmed for anger. She lay awake while Robert undressed and did his small last-minute chores. She heard his shoelace break as he sat on the side of the bed removing his shoes; she heard him fumble in the weak lamplight, searching for another lace.

When at last he got into bed, she did not turn to him, as was their custom, nor did he turn to her.

In the morning when she woke, he was gone.

It was a brilliant morning. It turned the view from

194

the kitchen window into a Japanese print: Brittle black branches on the hill's crest cut patterns against the sky. Lynn stared at it, unseeing; on this day it could give her no pleasure. Nothing could. A faint nausea rose to her throat, and she pushed her cup away. Too much coffee. Too many heavy thoughts.

The house was quiet, and the hum of its silence was unbearably mournful. She got up, moving her clumsy body to the appointment book on the desk. There was nothing much for today except the monthly visit to the obstetrician, who would scold her for not having gained weight; years ago they used to scold you for gaining it. Other than that, there were just a few little errands and marketing. Lunch with Josie had been crossed out because Josie had a cold, and that was just as well, for she was in no mood for sociability.

Dr Rupert having been called away, Lynn was to see an associate, a young man, younger than she, his curly hair hanging almost to shoulder length over his white coat. The look had gone out in the eighties, but now, in the nineties, it was apparently coming back. Wrapped in white sheeting, she sat on the examining table observing him while he read her record.

'Nausea last month, I see. How is it now?' he asked her.

'I still have it now and then.'

'It's not usual in the sixth month.'

'I know. I didn't have it the other times.'

'It says here that you feel unusually tired too.'

'Sometimes.' She didn't feel like talking. If he would just get on with it and let her go! 'I'm much larger than I was with my other babies, so I guess there's just more to carry.'

He looked doubtful. 'Could be. But your blood pressure's up this morning. Not terribly, but definitely up. Is there any reason that you can think of?'

Alarmed, she responded quickly. 'Well, no. Is it bad?'

'No. I said not terribly. Still, one has to wonder why it's up at all. Has anything upset you?'

His smile wanted to persuade her, but she would neither be persuaded nor tricked into any admission. Yet, some answer had to be given.

'Perhaps it's because my husband has just left for Europe, and that worries me a little. I can't think of anything else.'

He was looking straight into her eyes. His own were shrewd, narrowed under eyebrows drawn together as they might be if he were doing a mathematical computation or working a puzzle.

'I was wondering,' he said slowly. 'Those marks on your upper arms –'

'Marks?' she repeated, and glancing down, saw above her elbows the blue-green spots where Robert's thumbs had pressed last night.

'Oh, those.' She shrugged. 'I can't imagine. I bruise easily. I'm always finding bruises and can't remember how I got them.'

'Symmetrical bruises. Somebody made them,' he said, flashing the same easy smile.

As if she didn't see through him! His deliberately casual manner, coaxing, as if he were speaking to a child!

The father said to the new bride, 'Somebody made those marks. Lynn, I want to know.'

'Is there something you want to tell me?' the doctor asked her now.

Thinking she heard a note of curiosity in his voice, she felt the hot sting of indignation. It was the new style these days; you got it on television and in print, people saying whatever came into their heads without manners or tact, prying and snooping with no respect for privacy; *just let it all hang out*.

'What can you mean?' she retorted. 'What should I possibly want to tell you?'

The young man, catching her expression, which must have been fierce, retreated at once.

'I'm sorry. I only asked in case you had something else on your mind. So, that's all for today. Next month Dr Rupert will see you as usual.' And he turned back to the chart.

Her heart was still pounding when she left the office. Meddler. Officious busybody. She wondered whether he would write, *Two bruises, upper arms*, on the chart.

Even as she pushed the cart through the supermarket a little while later, she was still aware of her heartbeat. Then, in the parking lot as she was unloading the cart, she caught sight of Harris Weber and his mother in the next row of cars. And her heart began its race again. They hadn't seen her yet, and she bent lower over the bags so that they might leave without noticing her. This avoidance was not because of any ill feeling toward them, for she had almost none toward Harris and certainly none at all toward his mother; it was because the unknown woman knew things about her, about her and Robert ... And she wanted to hide, not to look the woman in the face and have to see there – what would she see there? Curiosity? Pity? Contempt?

But they were taking so long that by now the boy must have recognized her car and would know she was leaning ostrichlike over the groceries in order to avoid them. Something told her to look up, not to hurt the boy.

'Hello,' she said, and raised her arm in a slight wave.

He gave her his bright, familiar look, that candid look with the masculine sweetness in it, whose appeal she had felt from the very first.

'Hello, Mrs Ferguson.'

'How are you?' she called across the car's hood.

'Fine, thanks. And you?'

197

She nodded and smiled; the mother nodded and gave in return a smile that said nothing; it was merely polite and perhaps a trifle shy. That was all. And they drove away, the old car sputtering out of the parking lot.

There, Lynn told herself, that wasn't so bad. It had to be done. Yet the little encounter had given her another kind of sadness – not for herself, but for Emily. She went home, put the groceries away, sat down to read the mail, mostly bills and Christmas cards, and with the sadness still in her, listened to the drowsy hum of the silence.

The telephone rang. She must have been dozing, for it startled her, and she jumped.

'Hello,' said Robert.

'Where are you?' she cried.

'In London. I told you, we took the day flight so we're staying the night here, and we leave for Berlin in the morning. It was a fine flight.'

'That's nice,' she said stiffly.

'Lynn, it's night here, but I couldn't go to sleep without talking to you. I waited till you'd be back from the doctor's. How are you?'

'How is my health, do you mean, or my state of mind?'

'Both.'

'My health is all right. The other is what you might expect.'

'Lynn, I'm sorry. I'm so awfully sorry. I said it was a good flight, but it wasn't, because I kept thinking about us all the way. About us and Annie. I didn't want to hurt her feelings, God knows. I never do.'

'You hurt her because she isn't Emily. She isn't beautiful, and –'

'No, no, that's not true. I do everything for her, everything I can. But I'm not as patient as you are, I'll admit that. I always do admit when I'm wrong, don't I?'

She wanted to ask: Shall I count the times you do, the

198

times you don't, and give you the ratio? But that kind of hairsplitting led nowhere. It was like jumping up and down on the same spot.

She sighed. 'I suppose so.'

'I get frustrated. I want so much for her, and she doesn't understand. Annie's not easy.'

There she had to agree. Yet she fenced with her reply, saying sternly, 'Nobody is, Robert.'

'That's not so. You are. You are the kindest, the gentlest, the most reasonable, sensible, wonderful woman, and I don't deserve you.'

Was this the frowning, hostile man who had shouted last night in the kitchen, hurt her arms, and turned his back on her in the bedroom? Yes, of course he was. And somewhat scornfully she admonished herself: Don't tell me again that you're surprised.

'Lynn, are you there?'

'I'm here, I'm here.'

'Tell Annie I'm sorry, will you?'

'Yes, I'll tell her.'

'The whole thing was stupid, the way we turned away from each other without saying good-night as we always do, or without saying good-bye this morning. What if one of us should have an accident like the Remys and we were never to see each other again?'

The Remys, who had lived across the street. Linda and Kevin. The words pierced her. She could still hear Linda's terrible cry when they called to tell her of the accident; the sound had rung down the block so that people had come running, and Linda had gone mad.

'He left for work an hour ago!' she screamed, and had kept screaming. 'He left for work an hour ago!'

'That angry night would have been our last one. Think about it,' Robert said.

A heart attack. A plane crash, or a car crash on a foreign road in fog and rain. His mangled body. They would return it to America. He would never sit in that chair again.

'Lynn, are you all right? What is it?'

'I'm all right.'

But he had pierced her. It felt like internal bleeding. She was seeing herself in the house alone – because what are one's children, more than an extension of oneself? These vulnerable girls, this unborn infant to care for, and he not coming back. No man's voice, no man's dependable step coming up the stairs at the end of the day. No man's strong arms.

'I guess my nerves wore thin,' she said. 'I should have brought you and Annie together before night. But I was just plain mad. And then, I'm not twenty years old anymore,' she finished ruefully.

'Yes, you are, as you were when I met you. You'll always be twenty. Tell me you love me a little. Just tell me that, and it'll hold until I come back. Tell me you're not angry anymore.'

Her very flesh could feel the vibrations in his voice, the quiver of his pain.

'I love you all so much, but you first of all. I'm nothing without you, Lynn. Forgive me for the times I've hurt you. Forgive me, please.'

'Yes. Yes.'

The marks on the arms, the hot-tempered words so dearly repented of – what are they in the end compared with all the goodness? Nothing. Nothing.

Thousands of miles apart, we are, and still this tie renews itself as if he were in this room or I in that strange room in London, and we were touching one another. Astonishing!

So her anger dissolved. It lifted the chill that had clung like a wet pall all that day, and comfort began to warm her.

'And you love me, Lynn?'

200

'Yes, yes I do.'

In spite of everything, I do.

'Take care, then, darling. Give my love to the girls. I'll call again in a couple of days.'

Relief was still flooding, and she was still sitting there cradling the plastic instrument in her hands as if it could still hold some essence of that relief, when it rang again.

'Hello, this is Tom Lawrence. How are you?'

'I'm fine, thank you.' And she actually heard the lilt in her own voice.

'I'll tell you why I'm calling. I wonder whether you can do me a favor. My sister's in town with her daughter. They live in Honolulu, and she thought it was time for Sybil to see what lies beyond Hawaii. Sybil's twelve. Don't you have a girl about twelve?'

'Yes, Annie. She's eleven.'

'That's great. May we borrow her? Do you think she'd like to go into the city? We'd see a show, maybe a museum or maybe the Statue of Liberty. How does that sound?'

'It sounds lovely.'

'Well, then, we'll pick Annie up tomorrow morning, if that's all right, and we'll take the train in.'

'Annie'll be thrilled. She loves New York.'

'It'll be a new experience for me, with two ladies that young. My sister wants the morning off by herself to do the shops, so I'll be on my own with the girls for a while.'

'You'll do very well, I'm sure.'

'She'll like Sybil. A nice kid, even if she is my niece.'

A faint worry passed through Lynn. For some reason she imagined the sister to be like the excessively smart young women whom she had seen at that party in Tom's house. She would be incredibly thin, and her daughter would be, too, dressed in French clothes, and looking sixteen years old. There were plenty of girls like that, but Annie was not one of them.

So it was with some relief that she greeted the party

201

at the door the next morning. Tom's sister, who might have been his twin, was pretty and proper and friendly. Sybil, like her, was neither thin nor fat, although not as pretty as her mother. Annie would have a good day.

Lynn's prediction turned out to be right. Annie had a wonderful Saturday. At dinnertime she repeated triumphantly, 'I had chocolate cake with raspberries and cream. I told them my father says I'm too fat, and Tom said when I'm older I'll want to diet and not to worry too much in the meantime.'

' "Tom"? You called Mr Lawrence "Tom"?'

'He told me to. Because Sybil calls him "Uncle Tom." '

Light snow, mixed with rain, had begun to freeze. In the moment of quiet it could be heard tinkling on the windowpanes.

'It's nice eating here in the kitchen,' Emily said. 'Cozy.'

It was true. In the dining room with only four at the table, it always seemed that ten or twelve more were missing, for the table, an original Sheraton, was long enough to seat eighteen. The room always seemed to echo. Robert said, though, that a dining room was meant to be dined in.

Annie was still full of her day. 'I told him I hate my hair, it's so kinky. And he said I can have it straightened if I want to. I said my father won't let me, and he said I could do it when I was grown up because I could do whatever I wanted then. He said he knew a lady who had it done, and she loved it afterward.' Annie giggled. 'I'll bet he meant one of his wives.'

Lynn and Emily glanced at each other. And Emily scoffed, 'You don't know anything about his wives.'

'Yes, I do. Sybil told me. He's had two. Or maybe three, she thinks.' Annie, looking thoughtful, stopped the fork midway to her mouth. 'You know what? If you ever divorce Dad, I think you should marry Tom.'

'Why, Annie! As if I would ever divorce Daddy.'

'I should think you would pick Uncle Bruce,' Emily remarked. 'You love him so much.'

She had a twitch at the corner of her mouth as she spoke, that might have been humorous, or cynical, or both. Lynn looked away.

And Annie said seriously, 'Yes, of course I love him, silly, but he has Aunt Josie.'

Lynn rebuked them. 'This is all silly. And don't you dare say anything as idiotic as that in front of Daddy either. He's coming home the week after next on Wednesday.'

'Eleven more days. Only eleven more days,' Annie said. 'I thought he was going to stay longer.'

'Well, he'll be finished with his work by then,' Lynn explained, 'so it will be time to come home.'

Annie grumbled. 'He just left. What's the use of going away when he just turns around and comes right back? He can't be doing very much. I hope they give him a bigger job next time.'

'Go let Juliet out. She needs to go,' Lynn said.

On the Monday, when school reopened, Emily came home without Annie, grumbling, 'That kid! She missed the bus again. Now I suppose I'll have to get in the car and go back for her. And she'll be soaked, too, standing outside in this mess.'

Lynn looked out of the window where sleet was slanting as if it, too, like the trees, were leaning against the wind. A high, dangerous glaze lay on the white slope.

'No, I'll go, Emily. The roads are slippery, and you haven't been driving long enough to manage.'

Emily looked at her mother's enormous belly. 'And if the car gets stuck and you have to get out and you fall? No, I'll go, Mom. I'll be careful.'

When you come down to it, she is still the most responsible girl, Lynn thought as she watched the car move cautiously down the drive, slide into the road, and move almost inch by inch out of sight. Nevertheless, she remained at her anxious post by the window, mentally timing the trip to the school and return.

When the telephone rang – always at the most inconvenient moments, it seems, the telephone has to ring – she picked it up. An unfamiliar voice came over the wire.

'Lynn Ferguson? This is Fay Heller, your sister Helen's neighbor in St Louis. Do you remember me?'

Lynn's insides quivered. 'Yes, yes. Has anything – Where's Helen?'

'Helen's fine. The whole family's away on a ski trip. I'm calling because they're away, and your little girl Annie's here at my house.'

Lynn sank down onto a chair. 'Annie? There with you? I don't understand.'

A very calm, soothing voice explained. 'Don't be frightened. She's quite all right, unharmed. She arrived in a taxi around three o'clock. I saw her ringing Helen's bell, and naturally getting no answer, so I went over and brought her here. She doesn't want to explain herself, and so I haven't pressed, but –'

Oh, my God, she's run away. What else is going to happen? To run away makes no sense . . .

'I can't imagine whatever got into her head!' Lynn cried, the trite words coming automatically, while her thoughts ran opposite. You don't have to imagine, you know. Robert is coming home . . .

The ice cream episode had been horrible, and yet . . . To run away . . . Annie, Annie . . .

Her head pounded. Her sweaty, cold hand shook, holding the receiver.

'Kids do surprise us sometimes, don't they?' The woman was trying to make light of the affair, trying to console. 'I guess we did the same to our parents in our time.'

Lynn's thoughts were racing. However had Annie bought a ticket and gotten onto the plane? An unaccompanied child, going all that distance? They would never sell her a ticket.

'May I talk to her, please?'

'I did suggest that she call you right away, but she was a bit upset, naturally, so I thought it better not to insist.'

'She's not afraid to talk to me? Tell her I won't scold her. I only want to know how she is. Tell her, please, please.'

'Well, the fact is, I wouldn't say she's afraid, but she was really awfully tired, and I sent her upstairs to lie down. After she ate, I mean. She was hungry.'

Now the woman is being tactful. The truth is, Annie doesn't want to talk to me.

'She wants to go home. Do you want me to see whether there's a plane we can get her on this evening?'

So she does want to come back! Oh, thank God for that.

'No, in the circumstances, I don't want her to fly alone. I'll find out how I can fly from here instead.'

'Actually, the weather's very bad on this end. Why don't you let me keep her overnight? It's late in the day now, anyway.'

Tears were gathering; Lynn's throat was tightening. And the other woman, apparently sensing this, said gently, 'You're thinking she's a trouble to us, but she isn't. And she's quite fine here. You remember my three, don't you? They're grown and gone, but I still know what to do with a young girl. So don't worry.'

A little sob broke now. 'I'm terrified thinking what might have happened if it hadn't been you who discovered her. God knows who else might have come along.'

'Well, no one else did. Wait a minute, my husband's

saying something. Oh, I'm right. Nothing's flying out of here tonight. You'll have to wait till tomorrow.'

'All right, then, I'll take the first plane in the morning. And, oh, I want to thank you. How can I even begin?'

'Don't bother. You would do the same for someone. Just get a good night's sleep if you can.'

She must wipe her eyes and compose her face before Emily came back. The mother is strong in emergencies, not shaken. A mother hides her fears and hurts. But she hadn't been able to hide them from the doctor that morning . . .

In the back entry Emily stamped snow from her boots and called, 'Mom? Mom? She wasn't there. I looked all over. The darn kid must have gone home with one of her friends. You'd think she could at least call up. Why, what's the matter?'

'What on earth do you think that foolish child has gone and done?' Lynn wanted to express, instead of her total dismay, a kind of mock exasperation as if to say, with hands thrown up, What will she do next?

But Emily did not respond in kind. 'She's very frightened. Her dark thoughts frighten her,' she said gravely.

The two women looked at each other. It occurred to Lynn that they, too, were exchanging such rather enigmatic looks quite often lately. It occurred to her, too, that it was always she herself who first dropped her eyes or turned away.

'Annie was never an easy child, not like you,' she said, since a comment of some kind was needed.

That, of course, was just what Robert had said when he called from London. And Emily's reply was the very one that she, Lynn, had given to Robert.

'Nobody's easy.'

She was not up to a philosophical argument, not now. 'I'll fly out tomorrow on the first flight I can get.' Since Emily still stood there looking uncertain, she added, 'I remember the Hellers. They're good friends of Aunt Helen's. So let's try not to worry too much.'

Emily said only, 'Well, I've a ton of work. I'd better get to it.'

Sometimes, not often, it can seem that there's no comfort in Emily, Lynn thought. In fact, she even has a way of making me feel uncomfortable, almost as if, right now, I'm the one who made Annie run away.

The dog whined to go out. She stood at the kitchen door while Juliet ran to the shrubbery, where each twig was now glassy with ice. The dog squatted, ran back, and shook the wet from her fur, sprinkling the kitchen floor. On sudden impulse, oblivious of the wetness, Lynn knelt and hugged her. She needed living warmth.

'Oh, God,' she said, letting the dog lick her hand.

But she needed words, too, warm words, and these the animal could not give. So she went to the telephone. She had to tell Josie.

'Are you all right?' asked Josie when she had finished her short account.

'Yes, yes, I only needed to talk. I'm sorry to be dumping on you when you're sick.'

'It's only this nasty cold that I still can't shake, and you are not dumping. Hold on a minute. Bruce is here and he wants to know what this is all about.'

First Lynn heard them conferring in the background. Then Bruce came to the telephone.

'Lynn, take it easy,' he said. 'I'll go bring her back. The weather's bad, and you can't risk a fall. I'll go in the morning.'

She protested, was overruled with utmost firmness, and, suddenly exhausted, went upstairs to lie down on the bed.

In a rowboat, alone and terror stricken, struggling and straining somewhere on turbulent high seas with no land in sight, she suddenly saw the flare of light and heard someone speak. Emily was standing beside the bed.

'Mom dear, wake up. You've been asleep for more than an hour. You've got to eat something. I've made dinner.'

In midmorning Tom Lawrence called with an invitation to Annie for a good-bye dinner with Sybil, who was going back home. The normalcy of this request, made in Tom's jocular way, but arriving in these abnormal circumstances, made Lynn's answer choke in her throat.

'Annie's not here.' Her voice slipped into a high falsetto. 'Annie's run away.'

There was a pause. What should, what could, anyone reply to news like that?

He asked her quietly whether she could tell him anything more.

'Yes. She went back to St Louis to my sister. Only, my sister wasn't there –' Her voice broke, and he had to wait for her to resume. 'Bruce has gone to bring her home.'

'Robert's not back, then?'

'No. The day after tomorrow.'

'Who's with you, Lynn?'

'Nobody. I made Emily go to school, and Josie has a terrible cold, flu or something. And I don't want anyone else to know.'

'Of course not. You shouldn't be there by yourself, though. I'm coming over.'

'Oh, no! You needn't. I'm all right, really.'

She must look frightful, a pregnant elephant with dark circles under the eyes ... Strange that she should care at all, at a time like this, how she would appear before this man. 'Your work, your office –'

'I'm coming over.'

The pile of logs in the fireplace was ready to be ignited. For a moment she regarded it uncertainly, feeling a little foolish for even having the thought, as though she were being a hostess preparing for guests. Then, deciding, she lit the fire, went to the kitchen to prepare coffee, took a cup of violets from the windowsill and put it on the tray with the cups and the coffeepot. By the time Tom arrived, the fire was lovely, the coffee was fragrant, and a little plate of warm muffins lay on the table before the fire.

In jeans and a flannel shirt he looked like a college boy, belying his years. Robert never wore jeans. Her thoughts were disconnected.

'Do you want to talk about it?' he asked. 'Or shall we talk instead about the day's headlines? Or shall we not talk at all?'

She put out her hands, palms up, expressing confusion, and began to string together the adjectives that seemed to come automatically with every description of Annie. 'I don't know how to say it . . . She's a difficult, secretive, moody child.' She had to stop.

Tom nodded. 'She's a great little kid, all the same. My sister couldn't get over how much she knows compared with Sybil.'

And Robert complains that she's stupid.

'She's a sweet little girl, your Annie.'

There was a very gentle compassion in Tom's face. His eyes were leaf shaped; funny, she had not noticed that before.

'You gave her a wonderful time. She loved it.'

He took a muffin. 'Banana. It's different. What's in it?'

'Orange peel. I thought I'd try it. Is it any good?'

'Wonderful. I told you, you ought to be in business. But of course, this is hardly the time.'

The fire crackled, drawing them with its ancient lure to watch its tipsy dance. Presently, Tom spoke again.

'May I talk frankly? Annie's worried about herself, isn't she? About her weight and her hair?'

'Yes, you were very kind to reassure her.'

And as she remembered Annie saying, 'You should

marry Tom,' a tiny smile, in spite of herself, quickly came and went.

He opened his mouth and closed it.

'You were going to say something, Tom.'

'No, I changed my mind.'

'Why? Please say it.'

He shook his head. 'I got in a lot of trouble with you once, remember?'

'Yes, because you said things that weren't true.'

She had to tell him that. Had to. Framed in silver on the table beside the sofa, Robert was regarding her gravely. On his hand the wedding band showed prominently. It had been his idea to wear joint rings.

Tom had followed her gaze. And, as if he had made a resolve, continued. 'I was only going to say that Annie repeated several times that her father was upset about her weight. That's all I was going to say. I thought it might be a useful clue to what's happened.'

Upset. That dreadful scene. *You're a mess.* The child's blotchy, tear-smeared face. And then: *I would never hurt her feelings. I love you all.*

'I don't know what to think,' she murmured, as if Tom weren't there.

He took a swallow of coffee, put the cup down, took it up again, replaced it once more, and then said, 'I'm your friend, Lynn. We haven't known each other very long or closely, but I hope you feel that I'm your friend.'

Clearly, he was trying to pull from her some admission, some confession of need, and some appeal for his help. Even in the midst of this day's turmoil she was alert enough to be aware of that. Yet she felt no resentment toward him for trying, which was strange, and because it was necessary to respond to his generosity, she murmured, 'I know you would help if you could. The fact that you're sitting here is enough to tell me that.'

'And you're sure I can't help?'

She shook her head. 'It is something we shall have to work on with patience. Robert always used to talk Annie out of her – her moods – but lately, they've been having their troubles. Well, she's growing up, and growing up is harder for some children than it is for others.'

'Oh, yes. Well, I wouldn't know, not having had any children, only wives.'

She leapt toward the change of subject. 'How many, may I ask?'

'Two and a half.'

'A half!'

'Yes, I lived with one for a year. You might call that having half a wife.' He laughed. 'Oh, it was all very friendly. We made a mutual decision to call it quits.'

Lynn thought: If I had him, I don't think I would, or could, easily let him go. And she remembered how when she first had seen him, she had felt a kind of lightness about him, a bright illumination, shedding happiness.

He gave her now a quizzical look, saying, 'You don't approve?'

'I? I don't judge. But Robert wouldn't –' And she stopped.

That was wrong. Her mention of Robert's trouble with Annie was wrong. One kept one's problems to oneself, within the family. And she looked again at Robert's photograph, which, although it was of ordinary size, dominated the room. This time, Tom followed her glance.

'I talked to Pete Monacco the other day. He wanted me to know how much they're all impressed with Robert. Of course, he thinks Robert and I are very close friends.'

At the 'close friends,' Lynn flushed. She said quickly, 'Well, Robert's impressive. I don't know where he gets all his energy. In addition to everything else he does, he's taken on a new project, fund-raising for AIDS research.'

'Incredible energy.'

There was a pause, as if they had both been brought

211

up short at a line that neither one must cross. Then a telephone call came, easing the moment.

'Yes, Bruce? Oh, thank God. Yes, hurry. Don't miss it.' She hung up. 'That was Bruce, phoning from the airport. They're on the way home. Annie's cheerful, and I'm not to worry.' She wiped her eyes. 'Not to worry. Imagine.'

'But you do feel a lot better.'

'Yes. I'll talk to Annie very, very seriously. As you say, she's a bright girl. We'll talk heart to heart. I can reach her.' As she spoke, it seemed to her that this was a reasonable attitude. You talk things out, you reached understanding. True, Annie had run off on a crazy impulse, but she had come back; it was not the end of the world.

'Yes, I do feel better,' she repeated.

He stood up, saying, 'That being the case, I'll leave you. It's my sister's last day.'

'Of course. You were wonderful to come at all.'

'You're a lovely woman, Lynn. But you're all out of style. Oh, I don't mean your clothes. When you're a normal shape you look like Fifth Avenue. I mean, you still have a sort of old-fashioned, small-town trustfulness. I'm not making myself clear, am I?'

Answering his smile, she said, 'Not really.'

'What I mean is, trust is out of fashion now.'

He took her hand and raised it to his lips.

'Something I learned last year in Vienna. They still do it there. "I kiss your hand, honored lady."'

At the front door, puzzled and slightly embarrassed, she could think of only one thing to say, and repeated, 'It was wonderful of you to come. Thank you so much.'

'I'm here for you anytime you need me. Remember that,' he said, and went down the path.

She was left with the same puzzlement. Was this just unusual kindness on his part, or was there anything more to it? She was, after all, so inexperienced. She had hardly

212

spoken to another man or been alone in a room with any man but Robert since she was twenty years old. But she let herself feel flattered anyway. For a pregnant woman with a burdened mind it was a pleasant feeling.

'Well, here we are,' cried Bruce when Emily opened the front door.

Lynn held out her arms, and Annie rushed into them, hiding her face against her mother's shoulder. Bruce looked on, his smile combining triumph with relief, while a gleam of moisture fogged his glasses.

'Why did you do it, darling?' Lynn cried. 'You scared us all so terribly. Why? You should have talked to me first!'

'Don't be angry at me. I was scared too.' Annie's plea was muffled in Lynn's sweater. 'I was scared when I was on the plane. I wished I hadn't done it, but I couldn't get off the plane, could I?'

'No, no, darling, not without a parachute.' And Lynn pressed the child closer. Then she cried, 'How ever did you get a ticket at your age?'

'There were some big girls going to college and they let me say I was their sister. Then when I got there I wanted to go back again, only I didn't have enough money. I used up everything in my piggy bank for one way. So I had to go to Aunt Helen's house. And I rang the bell, and nobody was there, and' – the recital ended in a wail – 'I wanted to go home!'

'Of course you did. And now you are home.'

But the courage of the child! To make this plan, to carry it out by herself, took brains and courage.

Annie drew away, wiped her running nose with the back of her hand, and shook her head. Tears had streaked her face. Her rumpled collar was twisted inside the neck of her coat. If the girl were beautiful, Lynn told herself in that instant, one would not feel quite so much anguish,

213

such protective pity. And she repeated softly, 'Why didn't you tell me, Annie, whatever it was?'

Annie burst out. 'You wouldn't answer. Anyway, it's awful here. It's so full of secrets in this house. You're sick –'

At that Lynn had to interrupt, protesting, 'Darling, I'm not sick. Sometimes when a woman is pregnant, her stomach acts funny, that's all. That's not being sick. You know. I've explained it to you.'

'But that's not the kind of sick I mean. And besides, there's something wrong with Emily too. She's different. She's always in her room. She hardly talks to me anymore.'

Now it was Emily who interrupted. 'That's not so, Annie. I have to study in my room. And anyway, I do talk to you.'

'You won't let me come in, and I know why. You're crying, and you don't want me to see it. Nobody ever tells me the truth. When you went to the hospital, you said it was something you ate, infectional flu or something.'

'Intestinal flu,' said Lynn.

'And that's all it was,' said Emily.

'I don't believe you! Do you want to know what I think? It was something Dad did.'

'Oh, what a dreadful idea!' Lynn cried.

Perhaps they ought to have listened to Josie and told the truth to Annie. These days kids knew everything. They knew about abortions and miscarriages, homosexuality, AIDS, everything. But Emily would not have wanted it. And it was Emily's life, after all.

'How can you think such a thing?' Lynn cried out again.

'Because he's mean, that's why. You never want anybody to say things about him, but I don't want him to come home. I don't. I don't.'

And this was what his tumultuous angers had produced. What mattered all his steady, persistent efforts to

214

teach tennis or piano? Lynn wanted to cry again, but knew she must not.

Like strangers on an unfamiliar street, uncertain which way to turn, the little group stood hesitantly in the hall.

Bruce broke into the uncertain silence. 'Let's get our coats off at least and sit down.'

'You must be hungry,' Emily said promptly. 'I can fix something in a couple of minutes.'

'No,' Bruce answered. 'We had dinner on the plane. I think we should talk instead.'

They followed him into the den, where Lynn had kept the fire burning all day. He walked toward it and stood with head down and an intent expression, as if he were seeing something hidden in the fire's ripple and flare. Then he turned about and, still with the same grave face, began rapidly to speak.

'We had a few words about all this on the flight home. But then I realized it wasn't the place for the things I wanted to say. So let's have an open talk now. What I want to explain to Annie is something she has already found out, that people, every one of us, are a mixture of all the people who came before us. This one's eyes and hair, that one's talent for the piano, another one's sense of humor or short temper or patience or impatience.'

Except for the jingle of Juliet's collar as she scratched herself, the room had gone very still. Not used to seeing him so solemn, they were all drawn to Bruce.

'And when you get people together in a family, in the same house, you come up against these differences every day. In my house Josie thinks I'm messy, and I am. I get sawdust on my clothes and in my pockets. Then I come in and sit down on the sofa and leave sawdust between the pillows. Josie can't stand that. I think she makes too much of a fuss because I don't think the sofa is that important, but she does, and she thinks I ought to see

215

that it's important. So we're just different, that's the way we are.'

He paused with his eyebrows drawn together and looked them over keenly. 'And every one of you here does things that the others can't stand.' He raised his hand as if to halt anyone who was about to speak. 'No, I'm not looking for confessions. I just wanted to make my point. Annie, have you any idea what my point is? I mean, why Josie and I don't pull each other's hair out over the sawdust? Or one of us doesn't run away?'

Annie gave a small smile.

'Makes you want to laugh, doesn't it? Tell me. Why do you think we don't?'

'I guess,' she said weakly, 'because you love each other.'

'You guessed right, Annie. That's the whole answer. You say your father's "mean." Maybe he seems so, but I'm not here, and I don't know. But if he does say mean things, the truth is he also says very good things, too, doesn't he? And does good things for you too?'

Receiving no answer, Bruce pressed again. 'Come now. Doesn't he?'

'I guess so.'

'Ah, Annie, you know so. I've been here often enough. I've seen you two play piano duets together, and that's wonderful. I've watched him teach you to play tennis, too, and I've met you both at the library on Saturday mornings, getting books. Do you think he does all those things because he's mean?'

Lynn had seldom heard Bruce speak at such length and with such intensity; he was known for his brevity. When they were together, it was Josie who, earnest and positive, did most of the talking.

'So maybe, I'm not saying he has, but you say he has a terrible way of scolding. But, Annie, what can you do about it? He isn't likely to change. People rarely do, Annie. Most of us stay pretty much the way we're made. So running away won't help. This is your home, here's your mother, here's your sister. You'll have to make a go of it right here.'

Emily was looking straight ahead. Her face held sadness; the parted lips were tired. And what were the thoughts that had drawn a line across her forehead? Lynn's own head was heavy with scattered recollections. Did Bruce really mean what he was saying?

'It comes back to love, as you just said about Josie and me. You have to remember that people can scold and yell and still love. Your father loves you, Annie. He would do anything for you. Always think of that, even if it's sometimes hard to do. Try not to let words hurt you, even if they seem unfair and perhaps really are unfair. If it's his way to speak harshly sometimes, well then, that's his particular fault, that's all, and you'll have to live with it.'

All this time Bruce had been standing, and now he sat down, wiping his forehead as if he had been making a great effort. Again Lynn saw the gleam of moisture behind his glasses. Today is a day, she thought, that I'd like to forget. This desolate day. And yet, he has managed to put some heart into it.

'I was wondering,' he said now slowly, his remark directed at Lynn as much as to Annie, 'whether it might not be a good thing for Annie to have someone to talk to when she feels troubled? There's a Dr Miller, a friend of Josie's –'

'It would be a wonderful help to you, Annie,' Lynn said. 'I agree with Uncle Bruce.'

Immediately, Annie objected. 'No! I know what you mean. A psychologist. I know all about that, and I'm not going, not, not, not!'

Lynn waited for Bruce to respond. It seemed quite natural to trust the decision to him.

He said gently, 'You don't have to decide this minute.

217

Think about it carefully, and when you change your mind let your mother know.'

'I won't change my mind,' Annie said.

This defiance sounded exactly like Robert. Curious thought. If Annie should agree, though, there would be another tussle, strong objections from Robert, almost impossible to override. And yet, Lynn thought fiercely, if need be, I will override them.

'Okay, okay,' Bruce said. 'Nobody's going to force you to do anything. We're just glad you're home. Your family can't get along without you, Annie, even Aunt Josie and I can't. We depend on you for those Sunday mornings when you help with the furniture.'

Bruce had a project, repairing old furniture that had been donated for the needy, a quiet project that brought no acclaim. And Lynn recalled again, as she so often did, her father's old expression: He is the salt of the earth.

The fire had died into a pile of white ash, yet its friendly heat seemed to linger. Bruce was standing before it with hands outstretched toward the warmth. And a bizarre thought flashed into Lynn's head: What if I were to get up and put my arms around him? Bizarre! Have I lost my mind? The man is Josie's husband, for God's sake. And I am Robert's wife. And it is Robert whom I love.

She said cheerfully, 'You're hungry, no matter what you say. Stay a minute. I made vegetable soup this afternoon while I was waiting for you.'

'That sounds good after all,' Bruce admitted. 'Airline food leaves you hollow.'

So they came to a little spread in the kitchen, soup and biscuits, a dish of warm fruit and a plate of chocolate chip cookies. To Lynn's surprise Annie refused the cookies. Could it be that when sweets were freely offered, Annie found that she didn't want them as badly as when they were refused? One had to ponder that.

At the front door she took Bruce's hand between both of hers.

'This is the second time you've been a lifesaver. Do you realize that?'

'It's what friends are for, Lynn.'

'I am so very rich in friends.' And for no known reason she told him that Tom Lawrence had come that morning too. 'I was so surprised.'

'Why? He thinks the world of you,' Bruce said. 'But then, we all do.'

When he had gone and Annie was upstairs, Lynn asked Emily, 'What was Bruce saying while I was in the kitchen?'

'Nothing much.'

'You all suddenly stopped talking when I came in. Don't hide anything from me, Emily.'

'Okay. He only said that you need us at this time. That it's not right for you to be under stress, not good for you or for the baby.'

Lynn frowned. 'I hate to seem like an invalid, for heaven's sake. As if you shouldn't feel free to express yourselves naturally. I don't want that.'

'Is it true about the baby?'

'I don't really know. They say it may be.'

'I've never seen him so stern,' Emily said. 'He seemed almost angry at us.'

'Why, what do you mean?'

'He said we are to keep this house peaceful no matter what anyone – what anyone says or does. Ever. We are to keep things smooth and happy.' Emily reflected. 'It's true, I have never seen him so stern. He actually commanded us. It didn't seem like Uncle Bruce talking.' She laid her cheek against Lynn's. She was taller than Lynn, who had not been aware until this instant how much taller. 'We – both of us – took him very seriously. Annie won't do anything wild again. He helped her a lot. Don't worry, Mom.'

'If you say so, I won't.'

'Promise?'

'I promise.'

But it is all too simply said, Lynn told herself. How many of Bruce's own words he really believed, she thought again, or what he truly thought, she could not know.

Nevertheless, when Robert came home, it was as if the two previous days had been wiped out of memory.

Having been delayed at customs to pay for all the gifts he had bought, he was late in arriving. It took two men, the driver and Robert, to maneuver a tall carton up the walk and set it down in the hall.

'Why, what on earth have you brought?' Lynn cried.

'You'll see.'

His eyes sparkled; the long trip, the exertions, had only lifted his high spirits. He had hugs and kisses for them all. For an instant, as Annie was pulled to him, Lynn, watching and inwardly imploring, thought she saw refusal in her eyes, but it vanished, and perhaps she had only imagined it. Laughing, he held Lynn's hands and stepped back at arm's length to examine her.

'Oh, my, you've grown! Look at your mother, girls. I swear it looks as if she had twins in there, or triplets. If so, we'll have to build an addition onto this house, or move. But how are you, darling?' And not waiting for an answer, 'How is she, girls? Has she been feeling well? Because she'd never tell me if she hadn't been.'

'She's been fine,' Emily assured him.

'Then you've been taking good care of her.' He rubbed his hands together. 'It's freezing outside, but nowhere near what it is in Central Europe. Oh, I've got a million things to tell you. It's hard to know where to begin.'

'How about beginning with dinner?'

'Ah, dinner! Ah, good to be home.'

Lynn had prepared a feast of rich, hot food for a winter's night: mushroom soup, brown slivers floating in the golden broth, duckling with dark cherries, spinach soufflé with herbs and onions, and apple pudding in wine sauce. Champagne stood in a nest of ice, and everyone drank except Annie, who tasted and made a face. Even Lynn, in spite of her pregnancy, took a sip. The table was set with the best china and the Baccarat crystal that Robert had bought. In the center Lynn had arranged a low cluster of white roses. All this excellence did not go unappreciated.

'Your mother!' Robert exclaimed. 'Your mother. Just look at all this.' He was exultant.

'What a fantastic experience! Of course, it was hard work, late hours, talking and translating, meeting all sorts of people, some cooperative and eager, some stubborn – but that's life, isn't it? All in all, though, I should say it was a great success. Budapest, as you walk through the old quarter, is somewhat dark and dingy to our eyes, but wonderfully quaint, all the same. And then suddenly you come up against a modern glass tower. The company's office is as modern as anything we have in New York. You walk away, and there's a Chinese restaurant, next a pizza place, and there you see what's ahead, you see the future.'

Robert paused to cut off a piece of duckling, swallowed it, and could barely wait to continue his tale.

'Hungary is a full democracy now. Knowing some history of its past, you can only feel the marvel of what's happening. Eventually, they'll be in NATO, or in some sort of association with it. No doubt of that. What the country needs now, what all these countries need, is management training, and that's where the West, where we, come in. Oh, say, I almost forgot. I brought a real Hungarian strudel. I bought it yesterday morning. It's in my carry-on. Well, we can eat it tomorrow. It'd be too much with this dessert too. You should see the little coffee-houses, Lynn. All the pastries! You would get recipes galore. I sat in one of them and looked out onto a square with palaces and a huge Gothic church. Marvelous. You're going to love it, girls.'

'What about college?' Emily asked anxiously.

'Don't worry, just you get into Yale. Nothing's going to interfere with that.' Robert smiled. 'You'll just fly over whenever there's a vacation. I'll be earning enough to afford it, don't worry.'

'And what about me?' inquired Annie.

'Don't you worry. We'll have a fine school for you, with diplomats' children and all sorts of interesting people and – '

He had brought home his full vigor and his old magic. It was contagious. And in her daughters' faces, Lynn saw that they were feeling the contagion too.

'And of course we won't be limited to Hungary. It's so quick and easy to get around Europe, and you'll have a chance to see it all. You'll see Greece and the Parthenon, and you'll know why I wanted you to study the Greek gods, Annie. Rome, Paris, of course, and' – he made a wide sweep of his hand – 'the world! Why not?'

After dinner they opened the packages. Standing in the center of a circle of chairs, Robert unwrapped and displayed his finds. He had bought with care. For Annie there was a cuckoo clock. 'I remember you said once that you wanted one, and this one's a beauty.' For Emily there was a watercolor of a castle on a hill. For Lynn there were Herend figurines, all in green and white and large size: a kangaroo, an elephant, and a unicorn.

'I thought awhile about whether I should get them in the red or the green. What do you think, did I do right, Lynn?' he asked.

And without waiting for her reply he set them on the mantel-piece, then stepped back, regarding them with a slight frown. 'No, not that way.' He moved them. 'They should be clustered at the side. Symmetry is boring.'

Lynn remarked, 'I don't know where you got the time for shopping.'

'I don't know myself. When you want to do something, you make the time. That's about it.'

The evening went on long past Annie's bedtime and usurped Emily's homework hours.

'. . . and we should have at least a few days' skiing in Chamonix. From what I've read the French Alps have a special charm. Oh, I'll manage to get days off.' Robert laughed. 'The boss of the office can always wangle a few days, especially when he's overworked all the rest of the time. Say, look at the clock. All of a sudden jet lag has got to me. Shall we go up?'

In their bedroom as he undressed, Robert said, 'Things are looking so good, Lynn, so good. You know what they say about getting sand in your shoes, so you'll want to return? Well, there may not be any sand over there, but I can't wait to go back.'

As he emptied the suitcase and sorted the contents, he moved fast and spoke fast, leaping from one subject to the next.

'I faxed a report to Monacco and got a very pleased reply . . . I noticed something different about Emily tonight. That sort of remote look she's been having is quite gone. She seemed warmer toward me. Yes, as I predicted, she's gotten over that fellow. Thank God . . . And Annie, too, was really sweet, I thought . . .'

He hung his ties up on the rack and, turning, suddenly exclaimed, 'Oh, but I missed you all so much, hectic as it was. Did you miss me as much, Lynn?'

She was telling herself: He's bound to find out, so I might as well get it over with now. So as briefly as possible she began to relate the story of Annie, making sure not to disclose any of Annie's remarks about him.

Robert was startled, vexed, and dismayed, all together.

'Good God,' he said, 'the minute my back is turned some disaster befalls my children.'

Lynn's heart sank.

'I didn't want to spoil your homecoming, and I hope this hasn't, because, as you see, we're all right now.' And she improvised, for to tell the tragic story with complete accuracy would only provoke an argument. 'It seems she had been worried about me. Well, I suppose it's only natural for her to have mixed feelings about this pregnancy. And then she was upset about Emily last summer. She thought Emily was terribly sick and we were hiding the truth. It all seems to have been preying on her mind, and so she just –'

And why am I hiding the truth myself? she asked now as she fell suddenly silent. Am I still so torn about Caroline that I fear to take any more blame for anything? He has already said that Emily's trouble was my fault . . .

Robert had sat down heavily. 'And Bruce brought her home,' he said.

'Yes, it was wonderful of him, wasn't it?'

He slumped in the chair. In the weak light of the lamp on the bedside table, his face went sallow, as if the vigor had just drained out.

Anxiously, Lynn explained, repeating herself, 'He was wonderful. He talked to Annie, to both of them, so beautifully.'

'What did he talk about?'

'Oh, life in general, meeting challenges, optimism, understanding one another. He did them a lot of good.'

'That may be, but I'm not happy about it.'

'No, there's nothing to be *happy* about. I really do believe, Robert, that Annie should have some help, some counseling. And so should we.'

'That's nonsense. I've told you my opinion of that stuff. Anyway, Annie's not the first kid who got a notion in her

224

head and ran off. It happens all the time. I'm sure she was sorry before she was halfway there.'

Well, that much was true . . .

'But I'm thinking about Bruce. He's my subordinate in the office, and he knows my family's most private affairs, Emily's mess last summer, and now this. Dammit all.'

'He was very kind,' Lynn said, and then, wanting to clear the record entirely, she added, 'Tom Lawrence was very kind too. He came over that morning.'

'Oh, for God's sake, he too? How did that happen?'

'He didn't want me to be alone when he heard. You shouldn't mind, Robert. These are good friends.'

'Good friends, but they know too much.'

'They're fine men. They would never talk about our children. You know that.'

'The fact that they themselves know is enough,' he grumbled.

As she leaned to take off her shoes, she could barely reach her feet. Seeing her struggle, he got up to help her. The baby was active; its movement under her sheer slip was visible to him, and she saw that he pitied her; he would not argue.

'Poor girl,' he said. 'What a time you've had with me away! Poor girl. Now I'm home, you relax and let me take care of things.'

The baby turned and turned. Through these last frantic days she had scarcely been able to give thought to it, but now awareness of its imminent arrival shocked her. Only another eight or nine weeks from now, it would be separated from her, separated and yet in another way closer, because of its demands, which would and should come before any others. She must, she must, keep calm and hopeful for its sake.

Calm and hopeful. All right, then. Relax and let Robert take care of things. He wants to, anyway.

*　　*　　*

Robert V. W. Ferguson, Jr., was born early on a windy morning in between winter and spring. Rough and tough as he had been in the womb, his exit from it was remarkably easy. He weighed nine pounds, came with a full head of hair, and was the first of the Ferguson babies not to be bald. His hair was sandy like Lynn's; his face gave promise of length and would probably be aquiline like Robert's.

'All in all a nice compromise,' said Robert. He stood against a background of spring bouquets arrayed on the windowsill. 'Have you counted the flowers? That basket of green orchids on the end is from Monacco. He wired it from California.' He watched his son feeding at Lynn's breast. 'What a bruiser!' he cried. 'What a bruiser. Just look at that boy.'

Scarcely containing his jubilation, he made Lynn feel like a queen.

Back at home she lay in bed like a queen.

'You're going to take it easy, you're going to rest and be waited on at least till the end of the week,' Robert insisted.

The bassinet, skirted in white net, stood beside the bed, and Lynn thanked Josie for its blue bows.

'The minute we heard from Robert that it was a boy,' Bruce said, 'she came over here. And I want you to know that I'm the one responsible for the bows being blue.'

'So sexist,' Josie said.

'You surely weren't going to put pink ones on, were you?' asked Lynn.

'Why not?' was Josie's cheerful reply. 'Still, I did what my husband ordered.'

Their funny mock bickering amused Lynn. The short hour that she had been home had already filled her with a fresh sense of well-being. New books in their bright jackets were stacked on the bedside table, next to the box of chocolates – now no longer on the forbidden list

– and a cluster of lilies of the valley in a tiny cup. Husband, friends, and daughters, all of them fascinated by the baby in his soft wool nest, were gathered around her. Annie and Emily spoke in whispers.

'You don't have to whisper, darling,' Lynn told them. 'Talking won't disturb him a bit.'

Annie asked anxiously, 'When can we hold him?'

'When he wakes up, I'll let you hold him.'

And shyly, Annie said, 'Isn't it funny? I don't know him at all, but I love him already.'

Lynn's eyes filled. 'Oh, Annie, that's lovely.'

'Why? Did you think I wouldn't love him? I'm much too old to have sibling rivalry with the baby.'

Everyone laughed. Bruce patted Annie on the back, and Emily said, 'Annie, where are the boxes that came this morning?'

'Right here, behind the door. Open them, Mom. They're probably more sweaters. He's got seven already. And there's a big box downstairs that came yesterday. I haven't opened it.'

Robert went down and a few minutes later returned with a childsize wing chair upholstered in needlepoint.

'Queen Anne! Isn't that adorable? A formal chair for our living room,' cried Lynn. 'Whoever thought of that?'

'Tom Lawrence's card, with best wishes.' Robert frowned. 'Why such a lavish present? We hardly know him. He's not an intimate.'

Lynn, feeling the rise of heat, hoped it wouldn't flow out on her cheeks. Tom had outdone himself; the gift was original, in perfect taste – and expensive.

As if Bruce had read her mind, he came to the rescue.

'It's not so lavish for a man in Tom's position. Expense is relative. And obviously he likes you both.'

'Well, it's only that I don't like feeling beholden,' Robert explained.

A puzzled look crossed his face. Lynn knew that he

was thinking back to the weekend in Maine, and to all the things Lawrence had done for him, the good words he had put in for him.

'You'll have to write to him tomorrow at the latest, Lynn.'

'I don't feel up to it. I'm more tired than I thought I was,' she said untruthfully.

A letter to Tom, if indeed he had any ideas – and the more she thought, the more certain it appeared that he might have some, even though she had certainly made her own position quite clear – might be unwise. The situation was a little bit exciting, but it was also disturbing. No, not a letter.

'You write,' she told Robert, 'and I'll sign it along with you.' And she turned to Emily as if she had abruptly remembered something. 'Hasn't Aunt Helen even phoned?'

Annie, Emily, and Robert all looked around at each other.

'No? How strange. I don't understand it.'

'Oh,' Robert said, 'it was supposed to be a surprise, but we might as well tell you. They're on the way, both of them. They should be here in an hour or two. They're renting a car at the airport.'

'Darwin too?' Lynn was touched. 'How good of him to take the time!'

'His time.' Robert laughed. 'Bathtubs and toilets. Important business.'

'I shouldn't care to be without either one,' Bruce remarked, laughing.

Josie said firmly, 'I like Darwin. I always did. He's kind.'

'Oh, kind, yes,' Robert agreed. 'A diamond in the rough.'

If only Robert would not always, always, say things like that!

And Robert said, 'I might as well break the news. Aunt Jean has taken it into her head to come too.'

'Don't look so glum! I think it's darling of her to want to see the baby. I'm glad she's coming, and I'm going to show her I'm glad.' But then immediately Lynn worried. 'Where's everybody going to sleep? And what's everyone going to eat? They'll be here for a couple of days, I'm sure, and –'

'Not to worry.' Emily assured her. 'I've fixed a nice bed in the little third-floor room for Aunt Jean, Uncle Darwin and Aunt Helen will have the guest room, and we've a ton of food. Uncle Bruce went marketing with us this morning before you got home, to help carry all the stuff. Enough for an army.'

'And the dinner table's set already,' Annie said. 'We even made a centerpiece out of the flowers you brought home.'

So they all came and went, up and down the stairs all day, in and out of the room where the queen lay back on embroidered pillows, the best set, kept for sickness in bed and so, fortunately, never used before.

Annie brought Juliet up to let her sniff at the bassinet. 'To get used to the baby's smell,' she explained. Robert brought a supper tray. 'Don't I make a good butler?' he asked, wanting praise. And then came Helen and Darwin, he as pudgy and beaming as ever, she as welcome as ever.

'I feel as if I haven't seen you for a century,' Lynn cried as they hugged each other.

'Well, it's been almost two years. No matter what they say about planes getting people back and forth in a couple of hours, it's a big trip. It's traveling.'

'This family's going to get used to traveling,' announced Robert, who in his pride was standing with a hand on the bassinet. 'This little boy is going to see the world.' And when Helen looked blank, he asked, 'Do you mean to say Lynn hasn't told you? Yes, we're going to be living abroad for a while. Two years, three, five – who knows?' And he gave an enthusiastic account of his project.

'How is it that you never told me about all this?' asked Helen when the two were alone. Then, before Lynn could reply, and in her quick, penetrating way that so much resembled Josie's way, said, 'You had too much else on your mind, that's why.'

'Well, it wasn't the easiest pregnancy, I'll admit. But isn't he darling? His head is so beautifully shaped, don't you think so?'

Helen smiled. 'He's lovely. Mine looked like little monkeys for the first month or so. But I wasn't thinking of the pregnancy. I meant – you must know that I meant Annie.'

Lynn had no wish to reveal the doubts and worries that, even though Annie did seem to be much steadied, still flickered in her consciousness. She especially did not want to admit them to Helen. So she spoke lightly, in dismissal.

'Annie's over all that.'

'Yes, until the next time.'

Helen was always reaching for clues, for signals and alarms; of course it was because she had never liked, and still didn't like, Robert. But she was too decent to say so.

There was a note of petulance in Lynn's voice when she replied. She heard it herself and even knew the reason for it: I've said things are different now, but I've said it often enough before too; I don't want to be reminded of that today; I just want a little time to be purely happy with my baby.

'Annie's fine, Helen. Delighted about Bobby. Can't you see?'

Helen's silence told Lynn that she did not believe her.

'You can ask Bruce if you don't trust me,' Lynn added stubbornly. 'He knows Annie well.'

230

'I want to trust you,' Helen said, her lips making the tight pucker that always gave a shrewd look to her pretty face. 'I want to. But I know that if things were bad, you would never admit it.'

Probing, probing, Lynn thought resentfully.

'You've always been so secretive. One has to worry about you.'

Lynn's impatience mounted. 'Look at me. What do you see? Look around at the house. What do you see?'

'I see that you look the same as ever and your house has everything of the best.'

From downstairs there came the sounds of a piano accompanying lively song.

'That's Robert playing, and the girls are singing. They made up a funny song to welcome me at the door when we came home from the hospital. Doesn't that tell you anything?' demanded Lynn.

'Well ... It tells me that we all love you.' And Helen, apparently accepting defeat, changed the subject. 'Do you know what? I'm starved. I'm going down to see what there is to eat.'

'May I come in, or will I tire you?' Jean hesitated, as was her way. At least it was her way when she was in Robert's house.

'Of course come in. I'm not the least bit tired and it's ridiculous for me to be lying on this bed, but the doctor said, "Two days rest, positively."'

When Jean had admired the baby for the second time, she sat down in the rocking chair by the bed. For a few moments she said nothing, merely smiling at Lynn with the expression that Robert called 'meek'; instead Lynn had always seen, and saw now, not meekness but a stifled sorrow.

Jean folded her old, brown-spotted hands together; lying in her flowered lap – did she never wear anything but flowers? – they were patient and strong.

'It's nice to have a time alone with you, Lynn,' she said. 'And this is likely to be the last time. I'm moving to Vancouver.'

'But so far away! Why?'

'I'm going to live with my brother. We're both pretty old and all we have is each other.'

'You have us. You could move here, near us.'

'No, dear. Let's be truthful. Robert doesn't like to have me around.'

There was nothing meek about the statement. It had been delivered with a rather stern lift of the curly gray head and an expression that, although grave, was yet without rancor.

The statement demanded an honest reply. Or a more-or-less honest reply.

'Robert can be irritable sometimes with anyone, Aunt Jean, when he's in the mood. But you must know, his bark is worse than his bite.'

'I know. He was a darling little boy, and so smart. We used to play games together, checkers and dominoes. He loved to beat me, but, oh, his temper was terrible when he lost! We had fun together ... but things change. It's a pity, isn't it? After my sister was gone, and he moved away ... You would have liked Frances,' Jean said abruptly. 'She was a gentle person. And she would have loved having you for a daughter. You've always reminded me of her. You're soft and you're kind, like her.'

Very much touched, Lynn said simply, 'Thank you.'

The rocking chair swayed; there was a quaintness in its regular creak, an old-fashioned peacefulness as in the presence of the old woman herself.

'I'm sorry you and I haven't seen more of each other, Lynn. But I'm glad to see how well things are going for you. They are going well, aren't they?'

'Why, yes,' replied Lynn, wondering.

'And Robert is still a good husband to you.'

232

Was that a question or a statement?

'Why, yes,' Lynn said again.

Jean nodded. 'I'll think of you here in this lovely house and it will be a pleasure to me. I've put that photo of Emily and Annie into a flowered frame. I like to have flowers everywhere. I guess you've learned that about me, haven't you? I do hope you'll send me a nice photo of Bobby sometime.'

'As soon as he grows some more hair. I promise.'

'And that you'll still call me every week – even in Vancouver.'

'Of course we will. You know that.'

'I like your sister,' Jean said, 'and your friends Josie and Bruce. There's something special about him, although I don't know yet what it is.'

Lynn smiled. 'You like everybody, I think.'

'No, not everybody. But I do try to find the good in people if I can. Frances was like that – too much so for her own good – oh, well, tell me, does the baby need an afghan for his carriage?'

So the conversation veered away from people into the neutral area of things, things knitted, woven, cooked, and planted. The comfortable ease that Jean had brought into the room was ever so vaguely troubled when she left.

I wish people wouldn't be so – so enigmatic, Lynn said to herself.

Now Emily came and sat on the edge of the bed.

'Mom, you're so especially beautiful when you're happy,' she said.

She had a charming way of widening her eyes to express emotion. Today her hair was twisted and piled on top of her head; she wore the heart-shaped gold earrings that Robert had given her on her last birthday. Just to look at her brought an undiluted joy that Lynn needed just then.

'I'm happy when you all are.' The baby grunted in his

233

sleep. 'Turn him onto the other side of his face for a change,' she said.

'Oh, Lord, I don't know how. I'm scared to touch him.'

Lynn laughed. 'I know. When you were born, I was afraid to pick you up, afraid you'd break. Just raise his head gently,' she directed, 'and turn it. He's not that fragile.'

'He sighed,' Emily said. 'Did you hear him? It sounded just like a sigh when I turned him.'

'He's probably worrying about the international situation,' Lynn said cheerfully.

But Emily was grave. 'Mom,' she said, 'I never realized what a serious thing it is.'

'Serious?'

'To care for a baby, I mean. A person should think about it very, very long before doing it.'

She spoke very low, not looking at her mother, but away toward the window where a dark blue evening was coming on. And Lynn understood her meaning: that what had happened last summer must not happen again.

Still speaking toward the darkness, Emily continued, 'All the plans you must have for him, his health and his school, the cozy room that he was brought to, and the quiet home. You have to plan, don't you? And keep to the plan.'

Lynn was putting herself into her daughter's place, trying to imagine her remorse, to feel the fright that must still be hers when she considered some of the turns her life could have taken. And hesitating, she said softly, 'There will be a right time for you, Emily. You know that now, don't you?'

Emily turned back to her. 'I know. And I'm fine, Mom. I really am. Believe me.'

She was an achiever, competent and strong. A young woman with purpose, Lynn thought as always, certainly not your usual high-school senior.

'Yes,' she said. 'Yes, I do believe you.' And then to relieve the poignancy of the moment, 'But have you had your dinner?'

'Half of it. I thought you might not like being alone.'

'I don't mind at all. Go down and finish. Just hand Bobby to me first. He's going to be hungry in a minute, I can tell.'

And sure enough, the boy woke just then with a piteous wail.

'Turn on the lamps before you go. Thanks, darling.'

When Emily walked out she left no suspicions and no enigmas behind to fog the air. Lynn took a deep, pure breath. From belowstairs came the pleasant buzz of talk. She could imagine them sitting at the table; Robert at its head was carving and serving the meat in the old-fashioned style to which he kept. The back door banged; somebody was letting Juliet out. Someone was walking through the halls; heels struck the bare floor between the rugs. These were the sounds of the family, the rhythms of the house, the home.

Let Helen peer and delve; she means well, but never mind it. And never mind poor, dear old Jean's *And Robert is still a good husband to you?* It is the natural curiosity of a lonesome woman, that's all it is.

These last few days, these last few months, had been so rich! Before then it had been a cruel year, God knew, but was pain not a part of life too? Miraculously now, a new spirit seemed to have come over them all, over Robert and the girls, and because of them, over herself.

And she lay with the hungry baby at her breast. Little man! Such a little creature to have, by his simple presence, brought so much joy into this house! Lynn was feeling a cleansing gratitude, a most remarkable peace.

Part Four

Spring 1989 – Fall 1990

5

The enormous room was packed. Every table had been taken, and, reflected in the mirrored wall of this somewhat typically gaudy hotel ballroom, the audience was impressive in its size.

'This man,' said the mayor, 'this man on whom we gratefully bestow the Man of the Year Award, has accomplished more for our community in the few years he has been among us than many, including myself, who were born here, have done for it.'

Affectionate and friendly laughter approved of the mayor's modesty. Nevertheless, thought Lynn at the pinnacle of pride, it is true.

'The list of his activities fills a long page of single-spaced type. There's his work on behalf of the hospital, the cancer drive, the new library, so sorely needed, for AIDS, education, for the whole recycling program that has set an example to the towns around us. I could go on and on, but I know you are waiting to hear from Robert Ferguson himself.'

Robert had grace. Beside him on the podium the town's dignitaries, three men and a pleasant-faced woman with blue-white curls, looked nondescript. It was always so. Wherever he went, he was superior.

'Mayor Williams spoke of a list,' he said. 'My lists are much longer. They contain the names of the ones who are really responsible for the success of whatever good causes I have been helping. It would take hours to tell

239

you who they are, and I might miss some, and I mustn't do that. So I'll simply tell you that we owe a debt of hearty thanks to all those people who manned telephones, gathering the funds we needed, who stuffed envelopes, gave benefit dinners, wrote reports, and stayed up nights to get things done.'

His voice was richly resonant, his diction clear and pure, but unaffected. There wasn't a cough or whisper or creaking chair among the audience.

'And above all, I must give full credit to the company of which I am fortunate to be a part, to General American Appliance, of whose magnanimous gifts, not only here in our community but all over the country, you are certainly aware. The extraordinary generosity of such great American corporations is the wonder of the world. And GAA has always been outstanding for its public service. *We care*. And here in this relatively little corner of the United States, you have been seeing the fruits of our caring.

'And so I thank my superiors at GAA for encouraging my little undertakings here and covering for me whenever necessary, so making it possible for me to find the time I need.

'Last – my family. My wonderful wife, Lynn –'

All eyes turned to Lynn in her daisy-flowered summer dress; Robert had been right to insist on a smashing new dress. Across from her at the round table sat Bruce and Josie, flanked by town officials. Bruce smiled as he caught her eye; Josie, who seemed to be regarding the chandeliers, had no expression. And a thought fled through Lynn's mind: Robert has not mentioned Bruce.

'. . . and my lovely daughters, Emily and Annie, who never complain when I have to take some of the hours I owe them to go to a meeting. Emily will be graduating from high school on Tuesday, and entering Yale in the fall.'

Emily, serene in white, inclined her head to acknowledge the applause with the simple dignity of a royal personage. Her father's dignity.

'. . . and our Bobby, four months old today, has been very cooperative too. He tolerates me –'

Laughter followed, then more applause, a concluding speech, a shuffling of chairs, and the emptying of the room. In the lobby people crowded around Robert; he had charmed them.

'How about a drink? Come back to our house. It's early yet.'

'Thanks, but my wife's a real mother, a nursing mother, and Bobby's waiting,' Robert said.

He was glowing. It was as if there were a flame in him, heating his very flesh. She felt it when she stood beside him at the crib, watching the baby settle back to sleep after feeding. And surely she felt it when afterward in bed he turned to her.

'All those months we've missed because of the baby,' he whispered. 'We have to make up for them.'

In the close darkness of the bed, without seeing, she yet knew that his eyes were thrilled, that their blue had gone black with excitement. She put her hand out to feel his racing heart, the heat and the flame.

The graduates, in alphabetical order, came marching down the football field through the lemon-yellow light of afternoon.

'Good thing that kid's name begins with W,' Robert whispered.

He may be at the end of the line, Lynn thought, but he's still the valedictorian.

It was the finality of all this ceremony that was so moving. Childhood was indisputably over. These boys and girls would all disperse; these young ones, a little proud, a little embarrassed in their gowns and mortarboards, would be gone. The bedroom would be vacant, the customary chair at the table unoccupied, and the family diminished by one. Nothing would ever be the same. Two weak tears gathered in Lynn's eyes. Reaching for her purse to find a tissue, she was touched on the arm.

'Here, take mine,' said Josie. 'I need one too.'

Josie knew. Bruce knew, too, for he had taken Josie's other hand and clasped it on his knee. Last year at this time things had looked rather different for Emily, alone and desperate with her secret. Now they were calling her name, handing the rolled white document: 'Emily Ferguson, with highest honors.'

But Robert was chuckling, bursting. His girl. His girl. He was the first to scramble down from the benches to take her picture and rejoice.

Everywhere were cameras, kissing and laughing and calling. The PTA had set up tables on the grass for punch and cookies. People crowded in knots and got separated, parents making much of teachers, younger brothers and sisters finding their own friends.

Lynn, as she stood at a table to replenish her cup of punch, heard Bruce's voice a few feet away.

'Yes, of course it's a science and an art. You're lucky at your age to be so sure of what you want to do.'

'Well, it's useful,' she heard Harris say. 'That and teaching are the only truly essential things' – and then, so apologetically that she imagined his fair skin flushing – 'I don't mean that business isn't useful, Mr Lehman. I don't express myself very well sometimes.'

'Don't apologize. I quite agree with you. If I'd had the ability, I would have wanted to be a doctor or perhaps a teacher of some sort.'

They caught sight of Lynn, who had filled her cup. Sure enough, Harris was brick-red.

'Congratulations, Harris,' she said.

'Thanks. Thanks very much. I seem to have lost my folks. I'd better run.'

They watched him dart back into the crowd.

'It touches you to see a boy like him. You just hope life will be good to him,' Bruce said.

'I know. I feel the same.'

'Robert would slaughter us if he heard us.'

'I know.'

She oughtn't to have agreed; it was complicity with Bruce against Robert. And as they stood there drinking out of their paper cups, she avoided his eyes. It occurred to her suddenly that they had never had a dialogue; they were always in a foursome or more.

Presently, Lynn said, 'Emily's having a little party tonight. Want to come and supervise the fun? They're all over eighteen, and Robert's allowing one glass of champagne apiece. One small glass.'

'Thanks, but I think not. We'll call it a day.'

That was strange. She was wondering about the refusal, when she met up with Robert.

'Did you see Bruce talking to young Weber?' he demanded.

'Only for a second.'

'Well, I watched. Bruce deliberately sought him out. Your fine friend. I consider that disloyalty. Unforgivable.'

Not liking the sarcasm of 'your fine friend,' she answered, 'But you'll have to forgive it, won't you, since there's nothing you can do about it.'

'More's the pity.'

'It's all over, anyhow. Emily's started a new chapter. Let's go home for her party.'

The next day in the middle of the afternoon, Bruce telephoned, alarming Lynn, who thought at once of Robert.

He understood. 'Don't be frightened. It's nothing to do with Robert, and I'm not at the office. I didn't go in today.'

His voice was clearly strained, as if there were something wrong with his larynx. 'Josie was operated on this morning. I'm at the hospital in her room. She's still in recovery.'

'Why? What is it?' Lynn stammered. 'It's not—'

'Yes,' he said, still in that strangled voice. 'Yes. The lymph. The liver. It's all through her.'

A wave of cold passed through Lynn. *Footsteps on my grave*, my grandmother had used to say. No, Josie's grave. And she is thirty-nine.

She burst into tears. 'I can't believe it. You wake up suddenly one morning, and there's death looking into your face? Just like that? Yesterday at the graduation she was so happy for Emily. She never said ... There's no sense in what you're telling me. I can't make any sense of it.'

'Wait. Hold on, Lynn. We have to be calm for her. Listen to me. It wasn't sudden. It's been going on for months. All those colds she said she had, that time I went to St Louis last winter to fetch Annie, all those were excuses. She was home, too sick to move; she almost didn't get to the graduation yesterday. She wouldn't have chemo—'

'But why? She had it before and came through it so well!'

'This is different. We went to New York, we went to Boston, and they were all honest with us. Try chemo, but without much hope. That's what it came down to, underneath the tactful verbiage. So Josie said no to it, and I can understand why, God knows.'

Lynn asked desperately, 'Then why the operation now?'

'Oh, another man saw her and had an idea, something new. She wanted to refuse that, too, but you grasp at straws and I made her try it. I was wrong.' And now Bruce's voice died.

'All these months. Why did she hide it? What are friends for? You should have told us, Bruce, even if she wouldn't.'

'She absolutely wouldn't let me. She made me promise

not to worry you. She said you had enough with the new baby and . . .' He did not finish.

'But Josie's the one who always says you should face reality.'

'Your own reality. She's facing hers, and very bravely. She just didn't want to inflict *her* reality on other people as long as she could face it alone. Don't you see?'

'"Other people"! Even her best friend? I would have helped her . . .' And afraid of the answer, Lynn murmured the question, 'What's to happen?'

'It won't be very long, they told me.'

She wiped her eyes, yet a tear slipped through and dropped on the desk, where it lay glistening on the dark leather top.

'When can I see her?' she asked, still murmuring.

'I don't know. I'll ask. Maybe tomorrow.'

'Does Robert know?'

'I called him this morning at the office. They needed to cancel my appointments. I have to go now, Lynn.'

'Bruce, we all love you so, Emily and Annie . . . I don't know how to tell Annie.'

'I'll talk to her. Annie and I, you know we have a special thing.'

'I know.'

'I have to go now, Lynn.'

She put the receiver back and laid her hand on the desk, saying aloud, 'I am heartsick.' And the words made literal sense, for her chest was heavy, and the cold tremble would not stop. Josie, my friend. Josie, the sturdy, the wise, fast moving, fast talking, always there. Josie, aged thirty-nine.

She might have sat in a fog of sorrow all that afternoon if Bobby's cry had not rung through the fog. When she had taken him up from his nap and fed him, she carried him outdoors to the playpen on the terrace. With a full stomach and content in his comfortable, fresh diaper, he lay waving a rattle. Dots of light flickering through the emerald shade seemed to please him, for every now and then his babble broke into something that sounded like a laugh. At four months! She stood looking down at his innocence, knowing that there was no way on earth he could ever be shielded from heartbreak.

After a while she rolled the playpen over to the perennial border, where he could watch as she knelt to weed. A different reaction had begun in her, a need to move, to assure herself of her own vitality.

From a tough central root, purslane shot its multiple rubbery arms and legs like an octopus, crawling like cancer among the phlox and iris, peonies and asters, all the glad and glorious healthy life. With fierce hatred she dug out the roots and threw them away.

The sun had gone behind the hill, and the grass had turned from jade to olive when tires crunched the gravel. Robert, on his way from the station, had called for the girls at the pool, and the three were coming toward her as she rose from her knees. By their faces she saw that he had given the news to the girls.

'Is she going to die?' asked Annie, never mincing words.

The truth was as yet unspeakable. She could think it and know it, but not say it. So Lynn answered, 'We don't know anything except that she's very sick.'

'Perhaps,' said Emily, 'the operation will have cut it all away. My math teacher in junior year had cancer when he was thirty-five, and he's old now.'

'Perhaps,' said Robert. 'We shall hope.'

Alone with Lynn he gave a long, deep sigh. 'Poor guy. Poor Bruce. Oh, if it were you . . .'

'Are we maybe rushing to a conclusion?' She clasped her hands as if imploring him. 'Is it really hopeless?'

'Yes. He told me the only hope left is that it may go fast.'

* * *

Measured by the calendar it went fast, covering as it did only the short span of summer. And yet it seemed as if each day contained twice the normal count of hours, so slowly did they move.

Once on a weekend they tried bringing Josie home. She was so light that Bruce, carrying her, was able to run up the steps into the house. At the window, where she could look out into the trees, he set her down and brought an ottoman for her feet. The day was warm, but she was shivering, and he put a shawl around her frail shoulders.

The cat bounded onto her lap and she smiled.

'He hasn't forgotten me. I thought maybe he would have.'

'Forgotten you? Of course not,' Bruce said heartily.

We are all acting, thought Lynn. We know we dare not show tears, so we talk loud and briskly, we fear a moment's silence, we bustle around and think we're being normal.

A fine rain had begun to fall, so that the summer greenery was dimmed behind a silvery gray gauze. Josie asked to have the window opened.

'Listen,' she said. 'You can hear it falling on the leaves.' And she smiled again. 'It's the most beautiful kind of day in the most beautiful time of the year.'

This time next year, Lynn thought, and had to look away. She had brought a dinner, light, simple food, white meat of chicken in herbs. Josie took a few mouthfuls and laid the fork down.

'No appetite,' she said, apologizing, and added quickly, 'but as always, your food is marvelous. Someday you'll do something really big with your talent. You should be trying it now.'

Robert corrected her. 'She has her hands full at home. Right, Lynn?'

'I don't know,' said Lynn, thinking that Josie's skin,

her lovely skin, was like old yellowed newspaper.

'But I know,' said Josie, wanting her way.

In the evening she asked to go back to the hospital, and Bruce took her.

Her flesh fell off, leaving her eyes sunken into their round bony sockets and her teeth enormous in the cup of her jaws. Yet in a brief spurt of energy a lovely smile could bring harmony to this poor face. More often, it seemed as though the medication was loosening her tongue. Indeed, when she was lucid, she admitted as much.

'Yesterday I said something I perhaps should not have said,' she told Lynn one afternoon. 'I remember it now quite clearly, isn't that odd?'

'I don't remember anything,' Lynn assured her, although she did remember and quite clearly too.

'It was when I showed you the roses that Tom Lawrence brought. I was so surprised. I didn't expect a visit from him. We don't know him all that well.'

'He likes Bruce, that's no mystery.'

'That's what you answered me yesterday. I said, "No, he likes you, Lynn." We are his contact with you, since he can't very well see you when Robert's not there, and he doesn't want to see you when he is there. That's what I said, and it upset you.'

'Not at all. Why should it upset me, since it's so silly?'

'It's you who know the answer to that. But you would never tell me what you think about Tom. You would never tell me anything that really touches you in the deepest part of your heart. You're too secretive, Lynn.'

'Secrets, Josie?' Lynn queried gently. 'What about you? You've been sick for six months and never said a word.'

'There was nothing you could do!' And as Lynn began to protest, she cried, 'Now, don't scold me again about that!'

The plaintive tone, so unlike Josie's clear, brisk way of speaking, was hopeless and, like the wasted hands on the coverlet, helpless.

And Lynn burst out, 'Was I so wrapped up in myself, my new baby, my own life, that I didn't see what was happening to you? How can I have been so blind to your need?'

'Lynn dear, no. I had good days and bad ones. I just didn't let you or anyone see the bad ones. And you are the last person to be accused of self-absorption. It would be better for you if you did think more about yourself.'

'But I do,' Lynn protested.

'No, you don't. You've built a wall around yourself. Even your sister knows that. No one can really get through to you. But a person can't do what you're doing forever.' Josie turned in the bed, seemed to find a more bearable position, and resumed, 'That's why I wish – I wish you had a man like Tom. I could die knowing that you were being treated well. That you were safe . . .'

'Josie, Josie, I'm fine. I'm safe, dear. And don't talk about dying!' And don't talk about Robert . . .

'Yes, now I must. There's a right time to speak out. Six months ago it wasn't necessary. Now it is.'

Lynn looked at the walls, the depressing hospital-green walls that, if they could talk, would tell of a thousand griefs and partings. Now here was another. It was too hard to imagine a day on which she would pick up the telephone to call Josie and have to tell herself that Josie was no longer here.

'You've been my support,' she said, ready to weep. 'Whenever I'm worried about Annie, and I worry so about her, you're my support. You've borne all my troubles.'

Josie's wan smile was faintly bitter. 'No, not all. You skirt around the truth about Robert.'

'About Robert?' Lynn admonished gently. 'But we are very happy, Josie . . . Everything's fine now.'

'No, no.' Josie's head rolled back on the pillow. 'I'm a social worker, you forget. I see things you could never imagine. I see things as they really are.' Suddenly her fingers clawed at the sheet, and her body writhed. 'Oh, why can't you be honest with me when I'm in such pain, when I have to die and leave Bruce? Oh, God, this pain!'

Lynn's heart was bursting. 'I'll get the nurse,' she said, and ran, and ran.

Even now, half raving, Josie probes, she thought on the way home.

Josie and Helen.

It was all too much to contend with. Her deep thoughts ran like an underground river.

The summer plodded on, creating its own routine. At Robert's insistence Bruce came almost every evening for dinner before going to the hospital.

'He must have lost fifteen pounds,' Robert had observed. 'We can't let him go on like that. It's a question of decent responsibility. He's part of the firm of GAA, after all.'

Annie left for scout camp, and Lynn said, 'I'm glad she's gone. It would be too hard for her when –' and glancing at Bruce, she stopped.

He finished for her. 'When the end comes? Annie and I have had some very truthful talks about that, and I don't think you need to worry about her. She's quite prepared,' he said firmly, 'as I must be.' He smiled. 'And am not.'

No one at the table spoke until Emily said gravely, 'This makes everything else in the world seem small, doesn't it?'

A heat wave, striking the countryside, struck the human body with intent to draw its breath out. Petunias went limp in the border, and birds were still. Even the dog, after a minute or two outside, panted to get back into the house. And in the air-conditioned house the air was stale. It was as if the very weather had conjoined with events to stifle them all.

'It takes too long to die,' said Emily.

And then one morning at breakfast Emily had something else to say, something very serious.

'You'll be shocked. I'm scared to tell you,' she began.

Two startled faces looked up from their plates.

'I don't know how to begin.'

'At the beginning,' Robert said impatiently.

The girl's hands clung to the table's edge as if she needed support. Her eyes were darkly circled, as if she had not slept. She gulped and spoke.

'I'm not going to go to Yale.'

Robert stood up, his chair screeching on the floor, and threw his balled napkin onto his plate.

'What? What? Not going to Yale?'

'I wrote to them. I want to go to Tulane.'

My God, Robert's going to have a stroke, Lynn thought, while into her own neck, the blood came rushing. She could see the beat of the pulses at his temples and put her hand on his arm to warn him.

'Tulane? Why,' he said, 'of course, it's the southern climate, isn't it? You like that better. Oh, of course, that must be it.' And he made an elaborate sweep of his arm in mocking courtesy.

Emily said quietly, 'No, Dad. It's because Harris got a scholarship there.' And she looked without flinching at her father.

Robert stared back. Two pairs of steady eyes confronted one another, and Lynn glanced toward the girl, so frightened yet firm, and back to the furious man and back to the girl. How could she be doing this to them? She had given her word. How could she be doing this

251

to herself? After all that had been said, all the reasoned explanations, the kind, sensible advice; had it all passed into deaf ears and out again?

As if she were reading Lynn's thoughts, Emily said, 'I have not lied to you, since that's what you must be thinking. I have not seen him even once since – since what happened. We do talk on the phone. You know that, Mom.'

'What?' cried Robert. 'You knew they had telephone communication and you allowed it!'

His anger, like a diverted stream, now rushed torrentially toward Lynn. She braced herself. 'Why, yes. I saw no harm in it.' His eyes were hot and were cold; the cold burned like dry ice. 'I thought, I mean –'

'You didn't think and you don't know what you meant. It's just another example of your ineptitude. This whole affair was mismanaged from the start. I should have done what I wanted to do, sent her away to a private school.'

'A school without telephones?'

'That could have been managed,' Robert said grimly. He picked up the ball of napkin and hurled it back onto the plate. If it had been hard, it would have shattered the plate. 'Dammit, I don't know how I manage to keep my head. A thousand things on my mind, and now this! If I should have a stroke, you'll have a lot of questions to ask yourselves, both of you. That's all –'

'No. Don't blame Mom,' Emily said, interrupting. 'That's not fair. The fault is mine. The decision is mine. Dad, I'm nineteen. Please let me have some say in my own life. I'm not trying to defy you, I only want to be happy. We don't want to be away from each other for four years. No, please listen to me,' she said hurriedly. 'There won't be a repeat of what happened last year. I understand that's what you're afraid of. We'll be very careful, we'll be so busy keeping our grades up, that we'll keep all that to an absolute minimum, anyway –'

Robert roared. 'I don't want to hear about your sex life.'

'We haven't had any for a year. I only meant –'

'I'm not interested, I said!'

'This is disgusting!' Lynn cried.

She closed her eyes. How ugly, the three of them on a summer morning filling the blue light with their dark red rage! Her eyelids pressed against her eyeballs, wanting to shut the rage out.

The dining-room clock struck the half hour.

'Good Christ,' Robert said. 'I've got fifteen minutes to get to the station. With luck maybe a truck will hit me on the way, and you'll all be free to take the road to hell without my interference.' He picked up his attaché case and, at the door, turned around. 'You did say you wrote to Yale, didn't you?'

'Yes. I gave up my place.'

'Well. Well, I'll tell you what. I'm not going to pay your bill anywhere but at Yale. Is that clear, young lady? You just write to them again and phone or go there and straighten the mess out with them, or you won't go anywhere. I'm not paying my good money so that you can go and shack up with that boy again.'

'We won't ... I told you ... I promise. I've kept my promise, haven't I? If only you would listen . . .' Emily whimpered.

'And I told you: no tuition. I hope that's clear. Is it clear?'

Wordlessly, Emily nodded.

'Fine. So don't waste your energy or mine asking me again. No tuition. Not a penny. That's it. And it's your own doing. Now let me get out of here.'

They stood, each behind her chair, as if frozen there, while the front door sounded its solid thud, and the car's engine raced, its tires spurted gravel on the drive and squealed around the curve.

Lynn sat down again, and Emily followed. A conference, it seemed, was called for, although Lynn was too distraught, too confused, to begin one. Emily, with her head down, fiddled with the silverware at her place. Its tiny clash and clink were unbearable, and Lynn scolded.

'Do stop that.' Then more quietly, she said, 'Well, you've managed to set the house on fire once again, haven't you?'

It was rotten of Emily. Rotten.

'It's Dad. He's unforgiving,' Emily replied.

'No. He's crushed, that's what it is. And don't dodge the issue. Giving up Yale! After all your effort and our hopes. Why weren't you at least open about it? We could have talked it over. This is really – it's really unspeakable. I trusted you. Now you've put me in the position of a fool. No, what am I saying? I don't mean to talk about myself, about your father and me. Never mind us. What about you? What are you doing with your life, you foolish, foolish, capricious, thoughtless girl?'

'I don't think I'm foolish or thoughtless, Mom.' The tone was earnest and reasoned, belying the tears that, unwiped, rolled over reddening eyelids. 'We want to be married. Oh, not yet. We know it's much too soon. But we mean it, Mom. Why didn't I talk about this before I canceled Yale? Because you know as well as I do that Dad would have talked me out of doing what I want to do. He's so powerful, he gets his way. Oh, I wish our family was like Harris's family!'

How that hurt! What else had Lynn ever wanted but to build a life for her children that they would happily remember? And now this girl, across whose face and therefore in whose mind there passed the most delicate and subtle feelings, could wish that they were 'like Harris's family.'

'Yes? What are they like?' she asked in a dull monotone.

'Well, we told them how we feel. They aren't exactly

thrilled about our being at college together, but they think we're old enough to make our own mistakes. His mother said we made one mistake, so probably that would be a warning not to make another. And she's right. Oh, you think –'

'You don't know what I think,' Lynn said with bitterness. And it was a bitter thing to stand between this enmity, daughter against father.

'Well, Dad thinks –'

'Yes, try to imagine what he thinks. He works so hard for us all.'

'He works for his own pleasure, Mom. The way you put it, anytime a person opposes Dad, you lay guilt on the person because Dad 'works hard.' Harris's father works hard too. Do you think a policeman's life is easy?' Emily's words came tumbling. 'And you needn't think they're eager to have Harris marry me. They think too much of their son to have him marry into a family that doesn't want him. They're pleased that we're going to wait. But they do understand that we don't want to be separated. Is that so bad? Is it?'

Yes, it was pretty bad, a pretty bad trick this canny girl had played.

'This is all academic,' Lynn said, 'since without money you can't get to Tulane or any other place.' At that her voice caught in a little sob. 'So there go college and medical school. Both. Just like that.'

'Won't you give it to me, Mom?'

'Money? I haven't got any.'

'He would really do that,' Emily said, asking a question and declaring a fact at the same time.

'You know he would.'

'Then will you give me the money, Mom? Even though you don't approve?'

'I just told you, I have none. I haven't a cent of my own.'

'Not a cent? None!' Emily repeated in astonishment.

'I never have had. Your father gives me everything I need or want.'

The girl considered that. And Lynn, who knew so well the nuances of her daughter's expression, saw unmistakable distaste and was humiliated by it.

'Aunt Helen, maybe? For the first semester, at least!'

'Don't be silly. Aunt Helen can't afford it.'

That was not true. Darwin had been doing well of late, well enough for them to buy a bigger house in a prettier suburb. But she wasn't going to exhibit her dirty linen to Helen.

'If I have enough for the first semester, I'm sure I could get a student loan. And I'd find work. I'd take any kind I could get.'

'It's not so easy to get a loan. When they find out your father's position and income, you'll never get one.'

'Oh, Mom, what am I going to do?'

'If I were you, I'd go back to Yale and be thankful.'

'But you see – I can't! It's too late. They've already filled my place from the wait list.'

Stupid, stupid girl ... This crushing disappointment, this disaster, made Lynn hard.

'Then you've burned your bridges, so I guess that's the end of it.'

Emily stood up. 'Then there's nothing you can tell me.'

'What can I tell you? Except,' she added, knowing it was cruel to her, 'that I'm on my way to visit a dying woman. You may come if you want to.'

'No. I'm going upstairs.'

Lynn sat with her face in her hands. She was furious with Emily, and yet felt her daughter's pain as if it were scarring her own flesh. I suppose, she thought, eventually I will have to go crawling to Helen. I will have to endure her sardonic questions: *What are you telling me? That Robert refuses?* But it was also likely that Helen would

256

refuse. They had their own children to educate; one son was going to graduate school. The new house was certainly mortgaged; Darwin couldn't be doing *all* that well ... Her thoughts unraveled. Maybe as long as it wasn't where that boy was going, Robert would pay for some other place. But no, he wouldn't; he had had his heart set on Yale for this brilliant daughter. Robert never changed his mind.

She got up from the table and went to the window. Outside in the yard Eudora was singing while she hung clothes on the line. Eudora believed that white goods should dry in sunlight. Bobby was sitting up in the playpen. Falling backward, he would struggle up again, as if proud of his newfound ability to look at the world from a different angle. Eudora bent to talk to him. The scene was cheerful. It was wholesome. Wholesome. A good word.

The house inside was unwholesome. From the bottom of the stairs she could see the closed door to Emily's room and could well imagine that behind the door, Emily was lying facedown on her bed in despair. A part of her wanted to go up and give comfort, to stroke the poor, trembling shoulders. Meager comfort that would be! cried the part of Lynn in which anger was still stone hard.

She grabbed her car keys and started for the hospital. In the rearview mirror she practiced a noncommittal face, the only decent face to present to a sufferer, surely not tears, not even gravity.

And yet her resolution failed her. Josie, this day and for a brief hour, was wide awake. Bruce was telling her something about the new cat when Lynn came in.

'I'm so furious at myself,' she began. 'It's beastly hot, and I made a sherbet for you with fresh raspberries. It even looks cool, and I thought you'd love it, but then I went and forgot it. My mind –' And she clapped her hand to her forehead.

Josie looked quizzical. 'So? What's your trouble? You never forget things, especially things for me. What is it?'

'Oh, nothing much, really.'

But she was bursting; the trouble could scarcely be confined.

'Tell us,' said Josie.

So Lynn did. When she had finished her account, Bruce and Josie were somber.

'She's tenacious, all right,' Josie said. 'You have to admire that much, anyway.'

Lynn sighed. 'Yes, like Robert.'

'No.' Josie corrected her. 'Like herself.'

It was clear that she didn't want Emily to resemble Robert. Now in some way, Lynn had to defend him.

'Emily tricked us into thinking she was finished with Harris. She lied to us.'

'I don't remember,' Bruce remarked calmly, 'that she ever said she was "finished." She said she wouldn't see him all year, and she hasn't done so.'

'A lie by omission, then, wasn't it?'

'When you were a year older than Emily is now, and someone had told you to stay away from Robert for another four years, and probably lose him in doing so, would you have obeyed?' asked Bruce.

Her glance fell under his chastisement. 'No,' she said, and then, recovering, protested, 'but that was different. Robert was older. He was a man.'

'Nonsense,' said Josie. The voice was tired, but the word was crisp. 'Nonsense.' She raised herself on the pillow. 'If I've ever seen a real man, I've seen one in young Harris.'

'But Yale,' Lynn lamented. 'To give that up! It has crushed Robert.' She appealed, 'Don't you understand that?'

'But Emily,' said Josie. 'It is a question of priorities.'

Bruce's eyebrows drew together in his familiar expression of concern as he spoke.

'Yes, I can understand Robert. She should have told you, she should have been candid, but she wasn't. She was afraid to be candid, and that has to be understood too.'

'You are leaving her alone with her mistake,' Josie remonstrated. 'Leaving her alone to pick up the pieces by herself.'

In their quiet way they were scolding Lynn.

'She's an extraordinary girl,' Josie said, making a little show of vigor. 'Of all people Robert knows that. I must have heard him say so a thousand times at least. Does he want to take everything away, her chance at medical school, all that, so he can have the miserable satisfaction of saying later: "I told you so. You transgressed, so you've paid for it, paid for it with the rest of your life"?'

How she hated Robert! Hatred had given her strength enough to speak out, and now having spoken, she lay back, exhausted.

And something happened to Lynn that had never happened before in her life: Thoughts that should not have been revealed took shape in speech, and she heard herself saying without any rancor at all, 'You have always despised Robert.'

'Yes,' Josie said simply. 'I have,' and closed her eyes.

Lynn was feeling faint. It was the overpowering scent of gardenias, a little pot of them on the window ledge. Josie would not have said that if it were not for the medication and the pain. Bruce, shaking his head and with silent lips, spelled out the same: It is the medicine.

'Let her go,' said Josie, faintly now.

They had to lean toward her, not sure they had heard correctly. Lynn stroked the hot forehead and pushed back the tousled hair.

'What did you say, darling?' Bruce asked.

'Let her go. She had highest honors . . .' Josie's breathing was hard. 'A good girl . . . woman . . . Let her get away . . . She needs . . . Take my money for her.'

Lynn struggled against tears. 'No, darling. We can't do that. You are an angel, but we can't do that.'

'Yes, I said!' Josie's hands went frantic as pain struck again. 'Bruce, listen to me.'

'Dearest, I'm listening. We'll do what you say. I promise I'll give whatever Emily needs. She'll take it from me.'

'No,' Josie gasped. 'Mine . . . Power of attorney . . . Not your name . . . Not you involved . . . at office. Not you.'

Bruce turned helplessly to Lynn. 'She means that my interference would complicate things between Robert and me. Yes, I see. And it would be terribly hard for you too. Lynn, will you let me take it for Emily out of Josie's account? Will you?'

Past reasoning about what was right, and yet feeling somehow that it probably was right, confused and troubled and in anguish for Josie, she bowed her head in assent.

As she went out and met the nurse who came hurrying in, she heard Josie's anguished cry repeated. 'Let Emily go!'

Robert was beaten. Emily, swollen eyed and half sick, had taken a bowl of cereal to her room, so that Lynn sat alone with him at the dinner table. Unspeaking, they sat over the barely eaten food.

Only once he groaned, 'Ruined her life. Ruined it.'

'Would you consider another place, someplace where Harris wasn't?' Lynn asked.

'No. Maybe in a year or two. I'll see. She must learn a lesson. Parents cannot be defied. No.'

Lynn's father had been full of old-time sayings: *The rigid tree breaks in the storm, but the soft one bends and bounces back.*

She would have liked to tell that to Robert out of compassion, to console and warn, but it would have been useless this night, so she said nothing and waited instead until he had fallen asleep before going in to Emily.

The girl wept when Lynn told her what Josie was going to do. She wept and was glad and grateful. Also, she was hesitant.

'Does Dad know?'

'I hadn't the heart to tell him tonight.'

'The heart?'

'The strength, I should have said. He will be very, very angry.'

The two looked at each other. And Lynn said honestly, 'I was angry, too, you know that. It was Josie and Bruce who said, mostly Josie –' She could not go on.

'I know, Mom. I understand.'

'Do you, Emily?'

'More than you have ever realized.'

The morning began with dread. In the kitchen Lynn made the coffee and orange juice, moving on tiptoe, moving the utensils without a sound, to let Robert sleep another minute and to postpone the moment when he would appear and she would have to speak.

Perhaps with the same motive Emily came in on tiptoe, whispering.

'Uncle Bruce called on my phone. I have to rush over now with the college bill to get the check before he leaves for the hospital. They are so good to me, Mom! I don't understand why they want to do this for me.'

'They love you, that's why.' And she said also, 'They trust you.'

'And you? Do you trust me too?'

'You're old enough to be trusted, so I will have to.'

'You won't be sorry, Mom. I promise. And I'm going to pay back every cent. I can't tell how long it will take me, but I'll do it.'

261

So young and so sure of herself! Well, the world wouldn't survive for very long if people weren't sure of themselves at nineteen. And her heart ached over Emily's youth and courage.

'If I had money of my own I would do anything and everything for you. You know that, Emily. Oh, I wish I had money of my own! But –' She stopped before completing the sentence in her head. Your father never let me, he said it wasn't necessary because he gave me whatever I wanted, which was true, but it was being treated like a child, an imbecile, damn it –

She took a deep breath and spoke aloud.

'You'd better leave if Bruce is waiting.'

'Was that Emily going out?' asked Robert as he entered the kitchen. 'I heard her phone ring a while ago. That young bastard, I suppose.'

'No, it was Bruce. Josie is going to pay for Emily at Tulane.' And she waited for the explosion.

He sat down. 'You can't really have said what I think you said. Maybe you should say it again.'

She drew a deep breath. 'When I was at the hospital, I told them about Emily. Josie can't bear' – she must be careful not to bring Bruce into this affair – 'Josie can't bear to have Emily waste a year, and so she offered, she insisted on paying.'

Robert's right hand made a fist. 'That damnable woman! That damnable, interfering witch of a woman! I had her number the first time I saw her, and you know I did.' The fist came down hard on the table, rattling the empty cups. 'I'd like to smash this fist into her. I hope she rots. I'd like her to tell me to my face how I should deal with my own family.'

'She's dying. She can hardly talk.'

'Hardly talk? Then who masterminded this scheme? It must have been Bruce.'

'No, it was Josie. She asked him, since he has power

262

of attorney, to write a check, and he simply agreed. It was her idea, not his. She meant so well,' Lynn pleaded.

'The hell it was only her idea! It was his too. And yours too. You could have put a stop to it. You're only the girl's mother, aren't you? You could have said, if you had any respect for your husband's judgment, for his wishes, you could have said no. Positively no. Well, say something. Why don't you?'

'Because I've been thinking, probably we were too harsh. It's Emily's life, after all,' she said disconsolately. 'Her life.'

'God, I'm cursed! My wife, my daughter, the whole lot of you. The only one who hasn't disappointed me is the boy, and who knows how he'll turn against me when his time comes?' Robert sprang up so abruptly that he upset the coffeepot, which, as it smashed, sent a brown river meandering across the floor. And Juliet, who had been lying under the table, ran with her tail between her legs. 'The humiliation! Think of it: that weakling, that excuse for a man, comes into my home and takes over. The next thing, he'll be sleeping with my wife.'

'You're revolting, Robert. Let me tell you, I have no desire to sleep with Bruce. But if you had a few of his qualities, it might be better for us all.'

'His qualities! You have the gall to say it would be better for the family if I were like him?'

'Yes, and better for you too.'

Robert's eyes burned right through Lynn. He took a deep breath, a long step, and slapped her. Pressed as she was against the wall, she had no room to evade him, but could only twist helplessly. His open palm struck swiftly, stinging one cheek, then the other, and then the first, in succession; his ring, his marriage band, grazed her cheek as her head slammed against the wall, and she cried out. The dog came flying and yelping back into the kitchen. The backyard gate swung shut with a clang.

Eudora's key turned in the lock at the kitchen door, and her face appeared in the upper half. Robert fled. Lynn fled . . .

Panting and groping in the closet for his attaché case, he mumbled, 'Fine condition for the commuter train. Smile the good-morning greeting, read the newspaper, act like all the other men, after a scene like this. Yes, fine condition,' he repeated as the front door closed upon him.

On the sofa in the back den she sobbed. The attack had pained, but that was not the whole reason for her sobs. Not at all. A sudden light had flared in her head. It was so hot that it hurt.

For this attack was different from all the others. It had brought an end to the excuses and dodges, the conceal-ment that had made the reality tolerable. There was no doubt that Eudora had seen, and now she knew. And it was this knowing that would take away Lynn's dignity. It had stripped her at last. It had damaged her very soul, or whatever you wanted to name the thing that, apart from blood or bone, was your self.

So she lay, and cried, and tried to think.

There came a knock at the door and a call. 'Mrs Fer-guson? Are you all right? Is anything the matter?'

'Yes, thank you, I'm all right.'

The door opened, and Lynn was revealed in her rumpled wet-eyed state. Now she had to sit up and make the best of it.

'I'm upset,' she said. 'I've been crying because of Mrs – of my friend, Josie.'

'Oh, sure, it's awful hard.' Eudora's face was kind – she was a kind woman – but her eyes spoke, too, and they were saying plainly, 'I know the truth, but I will pretend for your sake that I don't.'

Kind as she was, she would talk at her other jobs. It was only human nature. The story was too juicy to be withheld. It would be all over the country club. It would be whispered behind Lynn's back. Whispered.

Up and down she walked now, past Robert's austere face framed in sterling silver, and past her own soft, childish face, her dreaming eyes beneath blond bangs and a bridal veil held by clustered lilies of the valley.

'I will leave him,' she said aloud. And the sound of her voice, the sound of those daring, impossible words, those unthinkable words, stopped her in her walk, and the shock chilled her bones.

Eudora was singing as she carried Bobby down the stairs.

'Big fat boy. Beautiful, big fat boy, Eudora's boy. You beautiful—'

They went into the kitchen. And Lynn stood listening, asking herself, How much should I bear? How much can I bear? I shall have to keep my head. Am I to tear the roof down over his head?

'Beautiful big fat boy—'

Josie is dying. Emily is leaving. Let me take one day at a time. That's it. One day at a time.

She went into the kitchen, into the light near the window, and inquired anxiously, 'Do I look all right, Eudora? I don't want Josie to see that I've been crying because of her.'

Eudora considered. 'You look all right. Put a little powder on, maybe. Up on your left cheek,' she explained with tact.

In the hospital's corridors there are the smells of antiseptics and anxiety. So many large things are compressed in a narrow space, in a short time, as one walks: the night they came in their terror, rushing to see Emily, the gusty morning when Bobby came squalling into the world, and now, as the door opens off the corridor, there is Josie on the high bed with her wasted hands, on which the plain wedding band has been tied with a string.

265

Bruce got up from his chair in the corner.

'She went into a coma last night,' he said, answering Lynn's unspoken question.

The sorrow in him was tangible. It made her chest ache to look at him. All the clichés were true; the heart does weigh heavily in the chest, heavy and sorely bruised.

'Why? Why?' she asked.

He shook his head, and they sat down together on either side of Josie's bed, where she lay as in peaceful sleep. As if a loving hand had passed across her face, the agony and torment were wiped away.

After a long time the noontime sun came glaring into the room. Someone pulled the shade, making a watered-green gloom on the walls. When later the room became too dark, the shades were raised again to let in a tawny summer afternoon.

A doctor came, murmuring something to Bruce, and then more audibly, he addressed them both.

'This can go on for days, or it may not. We can't tell. In any case, there's no point in staying here around the clock. I think you should go home, Bruce. You were here until three o'clock this morning, they tell me. Go home.'

At the hospital's front steps they met the other world where cars passed, glittering in the light, and small girls played hopscotch and a couple strolled, thoughtfully eating double ice cream cones.

'Can you give me a lift?' Bruce asked. 'My car's in the shop. I was lucky to get a taxi last night.'

'Of course.'

There was little to talk about until Lynn was compelled to say something about Emily.

'How can anyone say thank you? Thank you for saving a person when he was drowning, thank you for curing a person's blindness? How does one say such things?'

'How do I say thank you for being my support? We don't need words, Lynn.'

266

Numbed by her dual sorrow, she drove without thinking, as if the car, like an obedient, well-trained horse, knew the route by itself.

'We go back a long time,' Bruce said suddenly. 'Eighteen years. Emily was a baby.' He placed his hand over Lynn's. 'Don't worry too much about her. I have a feeling that she will do very, very well.'

'Perhaps. But do you know,' she said sadly, 'that I am glad she's leaving? I never thought I could say that, but I can.' And a little sob escaped from her throat.

The car had stopped in front of his house, and he gave her a quick look, saying, 'You don't want to go home like this. Come in and we'll talk.'

'No, I'm not going to burden you with my troubles. You have enough and far more.'

'Let's say I don't want to be alone.'

'In that case, I will.'

The house, though tidy, had the abandoned air that comes when there is no woman in it. The curtains that were usually drawn at night were still drawn, and the philodendron on the mantel were turning yellow. Lynn shuddered in the gloom and pulled the curtains back.

In the bay stood Josie's prize gardenias that she had nourished and brought all the way here when they moved.

'Gardenias need water,' Lynn said. 'It would be a pity to lose these.'

That was a foolish remark. What could it matter to this man if the plant should die? But she was restless, and it soothed her at this moment to fuss with it.

'Bruce, I see a couple of mealybugs. I need cotton swabs and some alcohol. Where does Josie keep all that stuff?'

'I'll get it.'

A nervous exchange of trivia came next.

'You can't ever seem to get rid of them,' said Lynn as she rubbed each dark leaf.

'Josie told me.'

'It's her pet plant. A miracle that it survived the move at all.'

'So she says.'

'I've never had any luck with gardenias. Josie has a green thumb.'

'That's true.'

In the bay, when Lynn had cleaned each leaf, topside and under, they stood looking out at the yard, where a flock of pigeons had taken possession of the bird feeder.

'See that one?' Bruce pointed. 'The white one? It's her favorite. She claims it knows her.'

He can barely see the bird, Lynn thought, with those blurred eyes.

'I want a brandy,' he said, he who scarcely drank even wine. 'What about you?'

She smiled wanly. 'It wouldn't hurt.'

They sat on either side of the fireplace, she on the sofa, he in his easy chair. He removed his glasses; she did not remember having ever seen him without them, and it seemed to her now that perhaps she had never really seen him before. The glasses had in some way given him a benevolent look; the simplicity of the man she had pictured in her head, striding on a hill alongside a bevy of large dogs, or else the one whom she had actually known, as he sanded old wood and looked up with that benevolent smile, was gone. This man was bitter.

He caught her studying him.

'What is it?' he asked.

She could say only, 'I'm so sorry for you. My heart hurts.'

'No, feel sorry for her. She gave so much to everybody. Everyone who really knew her . . . And now they're taking her short life away. Feel sorry for her.'

'Oh, God, I do! But you, she worries about you, Bruce. She told me. About leaving you alone.'

'She worries about you too.'

'There's no need to,' Lynn said, wanting to seem, and wanting to be, courageous.

He did not answer. Perhaps it was the positioning of the furniture and the fireplace and the same tension of immediate grief that restored abruptly the day when Bruce had brought Annie home. And she told him so, saying, 'You have always been there when I needed you. I know that you talked to the girls when I was out of the room that day.'

'I only tried to mend, to find a way for you all to survive together.'

He swirled the brandy, tilting and tipping and studying the little amber puddle.

Then abruptly he inquired, 'Has it worked?'

Lynn's courage left. She felt herself broken. She saw herself backed against the kitchen wall this morning, so small and weak, so insignificant in the face of Robert's anger. No one must ever know of that insignificance.

Bruce's eyes were studying her with a gravity almost severe. He asked again, 'Has it?'

Faltering, she replied, 'Yes, but now because of Emily, he –'

The cat came in, Josie's exquisite white cat; curling itself around Bruce's ankle, it made a diversion for which Lynn was grateful.

He smoothed the cat's fur and looked over again at her.

'What did he do?'

'He was quite – quite furious. He –' And now she was truly broken, unable to go on.

'He struck you, didn't he? This morning, before you came to the hospital.'

She stared at him.

'Dear Lynn, dear Lynn, do you really think we don't know? And haven't known for I can't remember how long? That day in Chicago I knew, and even before that we both did. Oh, when first we suspected, we told ourselves we must be wrong. It's hard to think of Robert's using force; he's always so coldly polite when it's plain that he has a rage inside. One doesn't imagine him being common enough to be violent.'

Bruce's laugh was sardonic. And Lynn could only keep staring at him.

'I remember when we first met. We were invited to your house. You had made a wonderful dinner, coq au vin. And we had never had it before, although it was a fashionable dish then. How trustful you were! It was what we both thought of you. The way you looked at Robert. How can I put it? I'm floundering. It's hard to make clear what I mean. Josie and I, we are – how shall I say it – more equal in our marriage. But you seemed so tender to him, and there's so much love in you, even for that plant over there.'

'But there's love in him too,' she said, choking. 'You don't know. I've loved him so. You don't know – or maybe you do have some little idea how good he was when I let Caroline die. He never blamed me, although anybody else would –'

'Now, stop right there. Anybody else would say it was an accident. Accidents happen. A child pulls away from you and runs into the street. An adult stumbles and falls down the stairs in front of your eyes. Are we supposed to be infallible? And as for not blaming you – ah, Lynn, admit it, in a hundred subtle ways he lets you know it was your fault, but he – he the magnanimous – forgives you! Crap, Lynn. Crap. Stop the guilt. You did not kill Caroline!'

Bruce was on a talking jag. It was as if all the pent-up fear and grief and anger at the fates that were taking Josie away were storming within him, lashing to be released.

'Maybe I'll be sorry to have talked to you like this, but right now I'm sorry I didn't do it a long time ago. Only, if I had you wouldn't have listened and then you'd have ended up by hating me.'

'No,' she said truthfully, 'no, I could never hate you. Not you.'

For there was something about him that had always touched her heart: the candor, the simplicity, the vigorous bloom of a man who was healthy in body and in mind.

'That day you came over,' he continued, 'that morning when you told us you had fallen into the thorn hedge, don't you think we knew what had really happened? Tom Lawrence told us about the dinner at his house, and how he found you when he brought back your purse the next day. Oh, don't worry!' He flung up his hand. 'Tom never talks. He's too decent for that. He was only concerned that you were in trouble.'

Lynn put her face into her hands. And he went on relentlessly.

'The day when you came to tell us you were pregnant, we could hardly believe that you would tie yourself up again. Josie was sick over it.'

'Why are you doing this to me, Bruce?' she burst out.

'I don't know. I suppose I hope you will start to think.'

'Oh, my God, oh, my God!' she cried.

He jumped to his feet and, sitting down on the sofa, took both her hands in his.

'Oh, Lynn, I've hurt you. Forgive me, I'm clumsy, but I mean well. Don't you think I'm glad you had Bobby? That's not what I meant at all.'

Her baby. Her little boy. She wanted to hide. And in her despair she turned and put her head on Bruce's shoulder.

'Yes, he struck me this morning. We had some words about Emily, and he was furious.'

271

'I'm sorry, I'm sorry. Poor little Lynn.'

'It wasn't – it wasn't so much that my face was hurt, it was that I felt, I feel, like nothing. Can you understand? Like nothing.'

His big hands smoothed the back of her head softly, over and over.

'Yes,' he murmured, 'yes.'

'Maybe you can't. It's so different with you and Josie.'

'It is. It is.'

His voice was bleak. Like an echo, it came from far off, detached from the warm, living shoulder to which she clung, detached from the warm hand that cradled her head.

'This morning I hated him,' she whispered. 'His filthy temper. And still there is love. Am I crazy? Why am I so confused? Why is living just so awfully hard?'

'Lynn, I don't know. I don't know why dying is so hard either. On this day, all of a sudden I don't know anything at all.'

She raised her head and looked into his expressive face, on which, over the short season of this summer, deep lines had been written. And it seemed to her that they two, on this hollow, emptying day, must be among the most miserable people in the world.

He pushed her bangs aside and stroked her forehead, saying with a small rueful smile, 'How good you are, how sweet. You mustn't give up, you mustn't despair.'

'Please don't be kind to me. I can't bear it.'

Yet, how clearly she needed the kindness of encircling arms, of human warmth! And so, impulsively, she raised her arms around his neck; he pulled her to him, and she lay against his heart. It was consolation . . .

So they held to each other, each sunk in grief, not speaking. In unison they felt the rise and fall of breath, and in unison heard the beat of the other's heart.

The room was still. From the yard came pigeons'

throaty gurgles, a peaceful sound of untroubled life. A clock somewhere else in the house struck the half hour with a musical ping, leaving a sweet, glittering chime in the air. Neither moved. In this quiet, one could simply float, assuaging against each other's limp and weary body the need for comfort.

Then, little by little, there began a response. Up and down her spine, perhaps unconsciously, his hand moved. It was so soft, this fluttering touch, this delicate caress, and yet from it a subtle pleasure began to travel through her nerves. After a time – how long a time she could not have said and never afterward remembered – there came from the deepest core of sensation a familiar fire. And she knew that he was feeling it as well.

It was as if, outside of the self that was Lynn Ferguson, she was observing ever so curiously a film in slow motion.

The film gathered speed. The actors moved inexorably, his lips on her neck, his fingers unfastening her blouse, her skirt falling into a yellow heap on the floor. Neither of them spoke. She lost all thought. He lost all thought. Desperate and famished, they hastened; it was a kind of collapse into each other, a total fusion . . .

When she awoke, he was gently shaking her. Startled, disoriented in time and place, it was a moment before she understood where she was. In that moment, as she later recalled it, she was free of care; the knot of tension at the nape of her neck had disappeared; she was *normal*.

That moment ended, and she knew what had happened, knew that after it had happened, she had dozed, resting in this man's arms as if she belonged there. Appalled, she met his eyes and saw in them a duplication of her own horror.

He had dressed himself, but she was naked, covered only by the plaid knit throw that he had put over her.

Through long evenings and on rainy afternoons she had watched Josie knit that throw. Knit, cable, purl, rose and cream and green.

'I have to get to the hospital,' he said dully.

'You have no car,' she said.

'They've brought mine back.'

This dialogue was absurd. It was surreal.

The afternoon had faded. From the window where Josie's beautiful white cat slept on the sill came an almost imperceptible movement of air and a creeping shade. The room became a place where, helplessly, one waited for some onrushing, unstoppable disaster.

'Oh, God,' she groaned.

He turned away, saying only, 'I'll let you get dressed,' and left the room.

Shaking, with nausea rising to her throat, she put on her clothes. On the opposite wall there hung a mirror, one of Bruce's antiques, with a surface of wavy glass that distorted her face as she passed it. This ugly distortion seemed fitting to her, and she stopped in front of it. Ugly. Ugly. That's what I am. I, Lynn, have done this while she lies dying. I, Lynn.

And Robert said, 'On the health and lives of our children, I swear that I have never been unfaithful to you.' He would not have sworn it so if it were not true. Whatever else he was, he was not a liar.

She had expected Bruce to be in a hurry, but when he returned, he sat down on the chair across from the sofa. So she sat down, too, neat, proper Lynn Ferguson with the shaking stomach, the knot as tight as ever it had been at the nape of her neck, and her feet neatly placed on the floor. She waited for him to speak.

Several times he began, and as his voice broke, had to stop. Finally he said, 'I think we must forget what happened, put it out of our minds forever. It was human . . . We are both under terrible strain.'

'Yes,' she said, looking down at her feet, the suburban lady's nice brown-and-white summer pumps.

His voice broke again. 'That this could happen – I don't know – my Josie – I love her so.'

'I am so ashamed,' she whispered, looking not at Bruce but at the white cat.

'We will have to forget it,' he repeated. 'To try to forget it. But before that, I must apologize.'

She gave a little shrug and a painful frown as if to say, There is no need, the burden is just as much mine.

'And something else: I should never have told you what I did about Robert and forced your answer.'

'It doesn't matter. What you said was true.'

'All the same, you will be sorry you admitted it. I know you, Lynn. I know you very well.'

'I have admitted it to no one but you, and I trust you.'

He put on his glasses, restoring the old Bruce, the one she had known, the brotherly friend with whom such a thing as had just passed between them would have been an impossibility. And he said, 'Perhaps that's your mistake.'

'What? Trusting you?'

'Oh, God, no, Lynn. I meant your mistake in not admitting it to anyone else.'

'Such as who?'

'Well, once I would have said – I did say – a counselor. But now I would say "Tom Lawrence."'

To ask for advice, for help, from Tom? And she remembered the scene at the club pool, remembered the humiliation and her own defiant invitation to the golden wedding.

'A lawyer? No.'

'He's not only a lawyer, Lynn. He would care. He admires you. Believe me, I know.'

He is also the man who thinks I belong in the nineteenth century, an anachronism, part charming, part absurd. That, no doubt, is what he finds interesting, only because it's different from what he sees around him, those blunt, independent women at his party that night. If he knew what I have done just now in this room, he would have to laugh through his amazement. 'The joke's on me,' he would say. She could hear him say it and see the crinkles forming around his light, bright eyes.

Her mind leapt: What if Robert knew! And terror seized her as if she were alone in a stalled car at midnight, or as if, alone in a house, she heard footsteps on the stairs at midnight.

She stood up, fighting it off. 'I've been gone all day. The baby . . . And Emily, I must talk to Emily.'

He saw her to the door and took her hand. 'Go home. Drive carefully.' The lines in his forehead deepened with anxiety. 'Are you all right? Really?'

'I am. I really am.'

Naked with a man who wasn't Robert. With Josie's husband . . .

'We've done no harm, Lynn. Remember that. It was just something that happened. We're both good people. Remember that too.'

'Yes,' she said, knowing that he hoped she would forget because, not believing it himself, he needed to have someone else believe it. But he himself would remember this betrayal of his darling Josie.

'I have to get to the hospital,' he said.

'Yes, go.'

'I'll call you if anything –'

'Yes, do.'

So she left Josie's house.

It was Bobby who relieved the silence at the table, which Eudora had thoughtfully set before leaving, although it was not her job to do so. From the freezer she had taken one of Lynn's pot pies and heated it. Lynn thought, It is because she pities me.

Emily had eaten earlier by herself and gone to her room.

'Emily said to tell you she has a headache. But you're not to worry, it's nothing,' Eudora said, while her eyes told Lynn, I pity you.

Eyes told everything. Eyes averted told of guilt or shame or fear. Robert's glance fell on Lynn's cheek, where the split skin showed a thin red thread. Lynn looked down at her plate. Robert fed soft pieces of potato to the baby.

The baby bounced in the infant seat. When he dropped his toy, Robert retrieved it; when he threw his toy, Robert had to get up and fetch it from under the table.

'Toughie,' Robert said. 'Little toughie.'

Lynn said nothing. The boy was beautiful; the hair with which he had been born and that he had lost soon after birth was now growing back, silky and silver white.

She imagined herself saying to this child: Your father, whom I loved – love still, and God alone can explain that – I wish He would because I am incapable of understanding it myself – your father has struck me once too often.

Is it Josie who has made this time different from the other times? Or Eudora who has made it seem like the last straw? Or simply that it is, it truly is, the last straw for me, and me alone.

The telephone rang. 'Shall I take it or will you?' asked Robert.

'You, please.'

Any hour the phone could bring the news of Josie's death. Her legs were too weak to carry her to the telephone; her hand would not be able to hold it.

But it was only from the PTA. 'A Mrs Hargrove,' Robert reported as he sat down again. 'You're asked to be class mother for Annie. I said you'd call back.'

He spoke without inflection or tone. Then he stretched his arm to reach the basket of bread, as if he could not bring himself to ask for the bread, he who was contemptuous of anyone who had poor table manners, of what he would call 'the boardinghouse reach.' So she handed the basket to him, their hands grazing, their eyes meeting blankly.

The evening light lay delicately on mahogany and turned the glittering pendants on the chandelier to ice. The baby, out of some secret bliss of his own, spread his adorable arms and crowed. And Emily was hiding in her room. And Annie, fragile Annie, would soon be coming home.

It was unbearable.

Emily looked up from the open suitcase on the bed when Lynn came in. The doorknobs were hung with clothes and the chairs were strewn with more; sweaters, shoes, skirts, and slacks were heaped together. On the floor along with Emily's Walkman were piles of books, and her tennis racket leaned against the wall.

'So soon?' asked Lynn.

'Mom, I wanted you to know beforehand, not shock you by having you walk in like this. The thing is, I delayed telling about Tulane, I delayed because I dreaded it, and now I'm at the last minute. Freshman indoctrination starts the day after tomorrow, and I'll have to leave tomorrow morning. Oh, Mom!'

'It's all right,' Lynn said, swallowing the inevitable pain.

'I tried to call you at the hospital this afternoon, but you weren't there. I didn't know where else to try.'

'It's all right.'

'The nurse in Josie's room said you and Uncle Bruce had left.'

'We didn't leave, we only went to the cafeteria for coffee and a doughnut.' And Lynn, suddenly aware of

278

exhaustion, shoved a shoe aside and sat down on the edge of a chair.

'I was hoping you'd get home early so we could talk.'

'I went back to Josie's room and stayed late.'

Emily's eyes filled. 'Poor Josie! She was always so good to me, now more than ever. It's not fair for her to die.'

Youth, youth, still astonished that life can be unfair.

'I wish I could see her again to tell her how much I love her and how much I thank her for what she's doing. But I did thank Uncle Bruce. I thanked him a thousand times.'

'Josie wouldn't hear you if you did go. She's in a coma.'

'Like a deep sleep.'

'Like death.'

On the pillow lay the face, the head so small now that the hair had fallen; under the blanket lay the body, so slight that it barely made a displacement. And while she lay there, where had her husband been, where her dearest friend?

With enormous effort Lynn pulled her mind back from the edge of the cliff. 'Have you talked to your father at all?'

'I tried to, but he wouldn't answer me, wouldn't even look at me. I don't like to leave home this way, Mom,' Emily said, now crying hard.

Lynn stood up to put her arms around her daughter. 'Darling, this isn't the way I planned it either. Things will work out. They always do. Just have patience. Believe me.'

How often, not knowing what else to say, you had to rely on platitudes!

'Patience isn't going to help you, Mom.'

'I don't understand,' Lynn said.

'I know he hit you this morning. Eudora told me.'

'Oh, my God!'

A shiver passed along Lynn's spine and ran like cold

fingers through her nerves. Her arms dropped; like bewildered rabbits or deer caught on the road at night by the sudden glare of headlights, unsure whether to stand or run, the two women paused.

'She said I mustn't let you know she told me.'

'So why did she do it?' Lynn wailed.

'Well, somebody ought to know, and I'm your oldest child.'

'How could she have done this? She had no right.'

'Don't be angry at her, Mom. She feels so bad for you. She told me you're the nicest, kindest person she ever worked for.'

Lynn was not mollified. What a terrible thing for Emily to be leaving home for the first time with this fresh information in her poor young head! This unnecessary information! It was mine to give when I was ready to give it, and not before, she thought.

'Promise you won't be angry at Eudora?'

Emily knelt at the chair onto which Lynn now fell and laid her head on her mother's knee, her wet cheeks dampening the thin silk skirt. Over and over, Lynn smoothed her daughter's hair, from the beating temples to the nape where the ribbon held the ponytail. A scent of perfume came from the hair, and she had to smile through her tears; Emily had been at her bottle of Joy again.

She stroked and stroked, thinking that this was to be another home broken in America. A statistic. This girl was a statistic, as were Annie and the baby in the crib across the hall. And her mind, as it went back to the beginning, asked almost reproachfully: Who would have believed it could end like this?

Her mind turned pages in an album, the pages rustling as they flashed disjointed pictures. Their first dinner, his wonderful face in candlelight, and she herself bewitched. People praising him, and she in a kind of awe that he belonged to her. The wedding music, the double ring, and the blaze of sunshine on the church steps when they came out together. The hotel room in Mexico and his dark rage. The death of Caroline and his arms around her. Slaps and shoves, falls and tears. The snowman on the lawn, hot chocolate afterward, and Robert at the piano with the girls. The bench in Chicago and the half-crazed beggar woman laughing at her. The rapture of the night when Bobby was conceived. This morning. Now.

Again Emily asked, 'You won't be angry at Eudora?'

'No, I won't be.'

What difference did it make, after all? When the end came, Emily would find out a whole lot more. And a great sigh came out of Lynn's heavy chest.

The unthinkable was happening, or was about to. Leaving Robert! Just yesterday she would have said, would have said in spite of everything, that there is always a way; there is so much good here too; there is always hope that the last time really was the last. But today was different. A great, unheralded, unexpected change had taken place within her. She was a good woman, deserving of a better life, and she was going to have it from now on.

Ah, yes! But how to do it? Ways and means. She calculated: In a short while, a few months, Robert would be sent abroad. It would be quite logical then for him to go ahead to prepare for their housing while she stayed behind to settle last-minute business here at home. Then, from a safe distance, she would let him know they were not going to follow him, and that she was through. Finished.

But where to go, with a baby still in arms and without a penny of her own? How to prepare? Bruce had said: Talk to Tom Lawrence. Well, perhaps she would. But she could see his bright, ironic face. He would be remembering, although surely he would never say, I told you so. Bruce had said: He admires you. Tom had said that brutal morning when Annie ran away: When you need help, I will be here for you. In a queer and subtle way, and in spite of the anguish of this day, she felt now a faint touch of self-esteem.

Emily got up, wiped her face, and began to fold sweaters.

'Let me help you,' Lynn said. This movement, the physical action of emptying drawers and packing a suitcase, was a physical pain. It was too final for them both.

'Oh, Mom, I can't bear to leave you like this. Why do you put up with it? Why?' Emily cried, her tone high and piercing.

The tension had to be eased, the girl must get a night's sleep and leave in relative calmness to take the plane. So Lynn said softly, 'Honey, don't worry about what Eudora told you. I'm sure she exaggerated.'

'It isn't only what happened this morning. Before Bobby was born, something happened. I know the truth about that too.'

Startled, Lynn stopped folding. 'What do you mean?'

'The night you got into the thorn hedge and the people across the road, the Stevenses, called the police.'

'Who told you that? Did Lieutenant Weber?' And a terrible anger rose in Lynn. Was the whole world conspiring to spread the news?

'No, no, he wouldn't do that, ever. Harris heard his father telling his mother. They didn't know he was sitting on the porch and could hear them in their living room. And when they found out that he'd overheard, his father asked him not to let me know. He said I mustn't be embarrassed or hurt in any way. But Harris did tell me. I suppose he shouldn't have, but he was worried, and he thought I ought to know. Not that I didn't already have my own ideas about it.'

'I see,' Lynn said.

282

She glanced at the wall where Emily's camp photo hung. Eight girls sat on a cabin's steps with Emily in the middle of the row, eight girls who perhaps knew more dreadful things than their naive expressions revealed. My girl, my Emily.

'I was sick. I was so ashamed before him when he told me. I was so ashamed for all of us, for the family that's supposed to be so respectable, with people all impressed by Dad's awards and his charities and this house and everything. I was so ashamed, I was sick. How could my father do that to you? But I'd been right the morning after when I didn't believe your explanation. Why didn't I believe it? Why ever did I suspect that there was something more? When I love Dad so? Then you denied it so strongly and I thought I mustn't think about my parents this way, it doesn't make sense. And when you came back from your trip and seemed so happy together, I thought surely that I'd been all wrong. I was even ashamed of myself because of the thoughts I'd had.

'You were already pregnant with Bobby when Harris told me. We were walking in the woods up at the lake. I guess I fell apart, and he took me in his arms to comfort me. He was so strong and kind! That's when it happened, when we made love. We'd planned not to do it until we were older, honestly we had. A lot of the kids start sex even in junior high, everybody knows that. But you never see things in the papers or on TV about all the kids who don't, even in high school.' And Emily, giving a little sob, continued, 'It's funny, Mom, when I go over it in my mind, how making love just seemed to grow out of the comfort and the kindness. It just seemed to be all one thing, do you know? And it happened just like that. I guess I'm not explaining it very well. I guess maybe you can't understand how it was.'

Lynn was still looking at the photograph; that was the year Emily got braces on her teeth; there were elastic

283

bands on the wires, and she'd gone around to show them off to her friends. She could not look at Emily when she answered.

'I understand,' she said.

'It took so long for your hands and your arms to heal last summer, and every time I saw the scabs, I wanted to tell you that I knew. But I'd made so much trouble for you already, that I felt I had no right to make more. And that time Annie ran away, you remember that Uncle Bruce told us both to keep things peaceful for the baby's sake, for all our sakes?'

'You told me.'

'And then,' Emily said, 'when Bobby came, he was so darling. You looked so beautiful holding him. And Dad was so nice, too, really himself. I thought, well, just forget what happened and keep your secret. It's the best you can do. Keep the peace, as Uncle Bruce said you should.'

'And how well you have done it.'

'I tried. But now that I'm going away, there's something I want to tell you. You were looking at that camp picture a minute ago. Now I have a picture I want to show you.'

From a folder in her desk drawer she drew a photograph, evidently an enlarged snapshot, of a little boy not more than a year old. He was sitting on the floor; holding a striped ball three times the size of the tiny face under its full head of straight black hair.

'He looks like an Indian,' Lynn said. 'He's cute.'

Emily turned the picture over.

'Read the name.'

'Jeremy Ferguson, with love from Querida,' Lynn read, and paused. It was a long pause. Then, 'Where did you get this?' she asked.

'When Bobby was born and Aunt Jean came to visit, she brought me a box of pictures. There was Dad from birth to college, there were my grandparents and their grandparents, taken in the eighteen eighties, really interesting, and then I found this, which looks modern. When I asked who the boy was, she said very quickly, "Oh, some distant cousin in your father's family, I'm not sure who. I cannot think how it ever came to me," and changed the subject. But she was flustered and of course there has to be more to it. Who is he, Mom?'

Lynn was unnerved. There was too much happening all at once, too much to endure without adding a long, fruitless explanation and questions that she was in no mood to answer.

'I have no idea,' she said.

'Mom dear, look me in the eye and tell me that's the truth.'

Lynn closed her eyes, shook her head, and pleaded, 'What difference does it make? Do we need any more trouble? Don't complicate things. You have no need to know.'

Emily persisted. 'Well, you're telling me in spite of yourself. You're telling me Dad has another child.'

Lynn sighed and gave up. 'Yes, all right. There was a boy born to his first marriage. I'm surprised Jean kept the picture. She must have been very fond of him.'

'And Querida? Is she his mother?'

'Yes. Listen, Emily, if your father finds out that Jean gave this to you, he'll be wild.'

'She didn't give it to me. I distracted her, and later when she looked for it, she couldn't find it.'

'Emily! Why on earth do you do these things?' Lynn lamented.

'Because I want to understand. I have a half brother and I never even knew it. This secrecy makes no sense, unless there's a whole lot behind it, in which case it may make sense.'

'You're looking for trouble. Your father's angry enough without your making things worse. Besides, he has a right

285

to privacy, regardless of anything else. So do put that thing away. Please.'

'All right, Mom, since it upsets you.' With a swift tear Emily destroyed the photo. 'There, that's over. But I have one more thing to tell you. Querida is in New York.'

'How on earth do you know that?'

'I don't know it for a fact, but I'm making connections, Sherlock Holmes stuff. That time in New York before Bobby was born, when I met Aunt Jean there, we were in a taxi on my way to Grand Central to go home, and she got out first a few blocks before. We stopped at the corner for a red light, so I was able to see where she went. It was a store with the name "Querida." Mom, it's got to be the same person.'

Lynn had a sudden picture of herself standing on the street with Tom on the day they had ridden home together on the train. In the window of the shop there had been a painting of sheep, and the name on the sign was QUERIDA. And she remembered the twinge of recognition, the stab of jealousy and curiosity, the wanting to know, the wanting not to know. But all that meant nothing, after this morning.

She said so now. 'It means nothing, Emily. I don't care where she is or who she is. So please forget Sherlock Holmes, will you?'

'Okay.'

Emily was packing a small stuffed polar bear among the sweaters. Her profile was grave, and her face when she turned back to Lynn was suddenly older than her years, so she questioned.

'May I ask you something, Mom?'

This child with the stuffed animal, this little woman . . .

'Anything, my darling. Ask.'

'Why didn't you ever call the police?'

As if by an automatic reflex Lynn had to attempt a defense.

'Your father's not some drunkard who comes home and beats his wife every Saturday night,' she said quietly, realizing in the instant that these had been Robert's very own words.

'But that night? That one night? The neighbors heard, and they called, so it must have been pretty bad.'

'I couldn't, Emily. Don't ask for an answer I can't give. Please don't.'

In a flood came the terrible sensation of the night when Weber had confronted Robert. Her one thought then had been that her children must be spared this hideous shame. Beyond her understanding were the women who could let their children watch their father being taken away by the police, unless of course they had been beaten most awfully ... This was not Lynn's case, and Emily knew it was not.

'I feel sorry for all of us,' said Emily. 'And in a queer way, for Dad too.'

In a queer way, yes.

'Tell me, Mom, may I ask what you are going to do?'

'I am going to leave him,' replied Lynn, and burst into tears.

The polar bear's black eyes looked astonished. The very stillness was astonished.

'When did you decide?'

'This morning. It came to me this morning. Why today and not the other times? I don't know. I don't know anything.'

'It had to be sometime,' said Emily with pity.

Lynn covered her face again, whispering as if to herself alone, 'He was – he is – was – the love of my life.'

The sentimental, melodramatic words were the purest truth.

'Sometimes I think I'm dreaming what's happened to us all,' Emily said.

Lynn raised her head, pleading, 'Don't commit yourself and your free will to any man. Don't.'

'To no one? Ever? You can't mean that, Mom.'

'I suppose not. Certainly don't do it yet. Don't let Harris disappoint you. Don't let him hurt you.'

'He never will. Harris is steady. He's level. There are no extremes in him.'

Yes, one could see that. There was no sparkle in him, either, thought Lynn, recalling the young Robert, who had lighted up her sky.

'If I tell you something, you won't laugh?' And before Lynn could promise not to laugh, Emily continued, 'We made a list, each of us did, of all the qualities we'd need in the person we marry and whether the other one had those qualities. Then we read the list aloud to see how they matched. And they did, almost exactly. Now wasn't that very sensible of us? Harris said his parents did that, too, when they were young, so that's how he got the idea. They're really such good people, the Webers. You can feel the goodness in their house. I think a person's family is so important, don't you?'

'It's not everything.'

'It helps, though,' said Emily, as wisely as if she had had a lifetime's experience with humanity's woes.

The confident assertion was a childish one, and yet, perhaps ... I knew really nothing about Robert, Lynn told herself. He came as a stranger. And comparing the wild, thoughtless passion she had felt for him with her daughter's 'sensible' list, she felt only bafflement.

'I think Bobby's crying,' said Emily, tilting her head listening.

'He's probably wet.'

'I'll go, Mom. You're too upset.'

'No, I'll go. You finish packing.'

'I want to hold him. He might be asleep when I leave in the morning.'

288

The night-light sent a pink glow into the corner where the crib stood. While Lynn watched, Emily soothed the baby, changed him, and cradled him in her arms.

'Look at his hair! I should have been the blonde,' she complained with a make-believe pout.

'You'll do as you are.'

So these were her children, this young woman in all her grace, and this treasure of a baby boy, the son of Robert, from whom she was about to part.

Emily whispered, swaying lightly while Bobby fell back to sleep on her shoulder, 'When are you going to do what you said?'

'I have to think. I have to think of Annie and you and him.'

'We'll be fine. We'll still be a family, Mom.'

'Oh, my God!' Lynn exclaimed.

'It must be awful for you, but you have to do it. Eudora said it was terrible –'

Lynn raised her hand for silence. A sudden vision of the scene with Bruce that afternoon, a recurring shock, had produced the exclamation. If Emily knew *that*! If Robert knew it! And yet in a curious way, she wished he could be told and be wounded in the very heart of his pride, wounded and bloodied.

She steadied herself. 'I'll drive you to Kennedy in the morning. Have you called Annie at camp to say good-bye?'

'No, I'll phone her when I get there. And I'll write often. I'll be so worried about you all, Mom.'

'You mustn't be. I want you to concentrate on what you have to do. I want you to see yourself as Dr Ferguson in your white coat with a stethoscope around your neck.' And Lynn forced a smile. Then she thought of something else. 'Will you talk to your father too? I'm sure his anger will fade if you give him a little time. And he is still your father, who loves you, no matter what else.'

When they closed Bobby's door, the hall light shone on Emily's wet eyes.

'Just give me a little time first too,' she said, 'and then I will.'

A familiar smoky scent drifted up the stairs. Robert must be smoking his pipe. Without looking Lynn knew that he was sitting in the corner chair by the window, brooding in the meager light of one lamp, in a room filled with shadows, and with a mind filled with shadows too. At the top of the stairs she hesitated; a part of her wanted to go down and tell him, in what is called a 'civilized' fashion – as if anything as brutal as the termination of a marriage begun in passion and total trust could, no matter how many fine words were summoned, be anything but a devastation – that she was unable to continue this way. But another part of her knew that the attempt would lead to a horrified protest, to apologies and promises, then to tears – her own – and perhaps even more frantic blows. Who could be sure anymore? So she turned about and went to bed.

Every muscle, every nerve, was stretched. There was no sleep in her. Her ears picked up every sound, the swish of a passing car, the far high drone of a plane, and Emily's slippered steps from the bathroom back to her room. Clearly, she constructed tomorrow's departure, the final embrace, the giving of the boarding pass to the attendant, the ponytail and the red nylon carry-on disappearing down the jetway.

'I shall not cry,' she said aloud. 'I shall send her off with cheer.'

And she reminded herself that Emily knew twice as much about the world as she had known at Emily's age . . .

The screen door clicked shut as Robert brought Juliet inside. A moment later they came upstairs, the dog with tinkling collar tags and Robert with a heavy, dreary tread.

Always, his footsteps had revealed his mood, and she knew what was to follow: He would sit down in the darkness and talk.

He began, 'I'm sorry about this morning, Lynn. It was nasty, and I know it.'

'That it was. Very nasty, and that hardly describes it.'

He was probably waiting for her to say more, probably bracing himself for an attack of rage such as she had made in the past; he could not know that she was beyond such agonized rage, far beyond it, that she had reached a tragic conclusion.

Breathing hard, he began again. 'It was Emily. I don't think my spirit has ever sunk so low in all my life. It crushed me, Lynn. And so I lashed out. I was beside myself. That's my only excuse.'

Yes, she thought, it's your only and your usual excuse. When haven't you had a reason for being 'beside yourself'? It's never been your fault, but always somebody else's, usually mine.

'Aren't you going to say something? Yell at me if you want to. But try to understand me too. Please, Lynn. Please.'

'I don't feel like yelling. I've had a terrible day.'

'I'm sorry.' Sighing, he said, 'I suppose we just have to tell ourselves that Emily will survive her mistake. What else can we do? What do you think?'

'I'm too tired to think.'

Yes, but tomorrow she would weep storms. Weep for Emily, for the turmoil that had thrown her into the arms of Bruce, and for the collapse of this marriage that had been the focus of, the reason for, the central meaning of, her life.

'Maybe I can give you a piece of good news to make up for the rest,' Robert said now, speaking almost humbly. 'Monacco flew in today. He told me they'll be sending me back across the pond right around the start of the year.'

And he waited again, this time no doubt for some enthusiasm or congratulations, but when she gave neither, he resumed, letting his own enthusiasms mount.

'I've been thinking that I should go a month or so ahead of you and get things ready. They have some very comfortable houses with gardens in back, very pleasant. We'd need a furnished place, naturally. I'll have it all cleaned up and ready by the time you arrive with Annie and Bobby. And maybe by that time Emily might –' He broke off.

'I'm tired,' Lynn said again. 'I really want to sleep.'

'Okay.'

He turned on the night-light and quietly began to undress. But he was too charged to be still for very long; he was a quivering high-tension wire.

'I've been thinking, too, that we could rent this house. We're not going to spend the rest of our lives in Europe, and we may want to come back right here. We can put everything in storage. What do you think?'

'Fine.'

Emily's departure had 'crushed him,' and yet here he was, hale and strong enough to make his rosy plans. That's called 'putting things into perspective,' I suppose, thought Lynn. I am so bitter. I am so bitter.

'Did you know that our government sponsors a training program for bankers in Hungary so they can learn investment methods? They have no personnel. No accountants, for instance, a handful in the entire country. It's shocking to us how ignorant they are. Well, a whole generation lived under communism, after all, so all the more of a challenge, I say.'

The bed creaked as Robert got in. He moved so near to Lynn that she could smell his shaving lotion. If he touches me, she thought, shuddering, if he touches my breasts, if he kisses me, I'll hit him. I will not be tricked

292

into anything anymore. I will remember my head being slammed against the wall. I will remember Bruce this afternoon. No ... no, I don't want to remember that.

'Sleeping?' murmured Robert.

'I would if you didn't keep waking me up.'

'I'm sorry,' he apologized, and turned over.

Yes, tomorrow she would weep storms, tomorrow she would weep for the waste, for the loss of the central meaning of her life. She would set free all the grief that was imploding within the little bony cage where her heart lay, and let it explode instead, to shatter the very walls of this house.

Then, somehow, she would pick herself up and keep going. If Josie could face death with quiet courage, surely she, Lynn, could face life.

On the third day Josie died. On the fourth day they saw her home to her grave. It was Josie's own kind of day; the air was soft after recent rain, pearl-gray clouds hung low, and the smell of wet grass rose among the tombstones. Lynn, almost blindly, read names that were meaningless to her and inscriptions that could only be ineffectual: BELOVED WIFE, DEAR FATHER. For how can a mere adjective describe wretched pain and endless loss?

And always, always, came the pictures: rain pelting the hearse when they followed her mother through the town and uphill to the burial ground; white flowers on Caroline's tiny coffin ...

'Astonishing,' Robert whispered as the crowd gathered. 'The whole office staff is here. Half the country club, too, it seems, and they didn't even belong.'

'Josie had friends,' Lynn said. 'Everybody liked her and Bruce.'

Bruce's name caught on her tongue. She winced and feared to look at him. He looked like a man of seventy, like a man stricken and condemned.

'My heart, my right hand,' she overheard him say to someone offering condolences.

'I know what this means to you,' Robert whispered.

'How can you know? You never liked her. You were furious with her.'

'Well, she loved you, and I can appreciate that, at least.'

Up the small rise people streamed from the parking lot, all kinds and colors and ages of them, the fashionable, the workers and, too, the poor, who must have come to Josie in their need and been comforted, so that they remembered her.

The many voices were muted. All was muted: the spray of cream-colored roses on the coffin, and even the simple language of the prayers, giving thanks for the blessing of Josie's life and the memories she had left to those who loved her.

The brief service came, then, to an end. Too shaken to cry, Lynn looked up into the trees where a flock of crows were making a great stir. And turning her head, she met Tom Lawrence's somber gaze.

'If you need help,' Bruce had advised, 'ask Tom Lawrence.'

'I know women inside out,' Tom had told her once. 'You'd eat yourself alive with guilt if you ever –'

And Robert took her arm, saying, 'Come. It's over.' They got into the car and he said, looking almost curious, 'You really loved her, didn't you? Funny, I should still be mad at her because of Emily, but what's done is done, and why waste energy? Besides, you'd have to be heartless to look at Bruce's face just now and not feel something. Who knows what goes through a person's head at a time like this? I suppose people recall the times they fought and the things they said that now they wish they hadn't said. But that's only natural. Nobody's perfect. Anyway, he looks like a cadaver. He looks as if he'd been starving himself. He hasn't come to dinner these last few days, and maybe we should keep asking him over for a while until he can straighten himself out.'

'That's kind of you,' she said, somewhat surprised. And then, induced perhaps by this compassion that he now showed for a man whom he had never liked, she had a sudden insight into herself: If Eudora hadn't been a witness, if Bruce hadn't revealed that he and Josie had always known, might she not have gone on as before, burying the memory, denying it, as indeed she had been doing for years? Maybe she would even have gone on making love to Robert, as he had wanted her to the other night before Emily left, when she had by her silence and immobility rebuffed him. It was an odd, uncertain insight.

They drove on, while Robert ruminated: 'I wonder what he'll do now. He's the kind who may never marry again. God forbid, if anything were to happen to you, I never would.'

She had to say something. 'You can't know that,' she said.

'Yes, I can. I know myself. If I had to stand there in that awful cemetery the way he just did and watch you – I can't even say it.'

She was thinking: He will suffer when I leave.

'I suppose he'll just go back to the office in a couple of days, back to his old plodding routine.'

She thought then: But Robert will have his work. He will get the news, be stunned and furious, and suffer most awfully. She saw him now as clearly as if it had already happened; standing in some strange room on a strange street with a view, perhaps, of cobblestones and medieval towers, he would open her long, sad, careful letter; in expectation of loving words, he would start to read and, not believing his own senses, would read again ... And someday he would become the head of the company and have all the glory he so dearly wanted.

Her hands, faintly brown, lay on her lap. When she turned them over, the scars, smooth, white pinhead spots, were unmistakable. And on her cheek this morning, the thin red cut was just closing.

She turned her head to look at Robert, at the lean, fine face. He had scarcely changed. He was as fascinating as he had been when she first had seen him. For her there was something aphrodisiac about the white collar and the dark suit as, so many women admit, there is about a military uniform.

What you have done to me, to us! she thought. You had so much, we had so much, and could have kept it, but you have thrown it away. What you have done with your filthy rage!

The house was bleak. Almost it seemed a dangerous place with hazards and avoidances, as if one were walking through a minefield.

First there was Annie, who, fresh from scout camp, where unfortunately she had not lost a pound, had to be faced with two stupendous changes, the departure of Emily and the death of Josie. The matter of Emily was eased by some telephone calls, but the matter of Josie could only be eased, it seemed, by Bruce.

Lynn drove her to his house, where she spent the day and came out looking relatively cheerful in spite of her swollen eyelids.

'Uncle Bruce said it's all right to cry. He said after I've cried, I'll feel better, and I do. He said Aunt Josie wouldn't want me to be too sad. She'd want me to remember nice things about her, but she'd mainly want me to do good work in school and have friends and be happy. Why didn't you come inside, Mom?'

'I had a lot of errands, and Bobby's cutting a tooth. He's cranky.'

'I think you should tell Uncle Bruce to come to dinner. There's nothing in his refrigerator.'

'No? What did you have for lunch?'

'He opened a can of beans.'

'He hasn't got his appetite back. It's much too soon.'

'Aren't you going to tell him to have dinner with us?'

'He'll come when he's ready.'

If Lynn knew anything at all about Bruce, she knew he would never be ready. The prospect of sitting down to dinner, the two of them facing Robert, would be as dismaying to him as it was to her.

'Do you suppose he'll get married now that Aunt Josie's dead?' asked Annie.

'How on earth should I know that?' And then, because she had shown such irritation at the question, Lynn made amends. 'How about taking Bobby up the road in the stroller? He'd like that. He adores you.'

The adoration was mutual, for Annie's reply was prompt. 'Okay! You know I'm still the only person in my class who's got a new baby at home?'

'Oh? That makes you sort of special, doesn't it?'

That night Robert said, 'I've been making inquiries about schools for Annie. We should really prepare her now and get her used to the idea. We don't want a too sudden disruption at midterm.'

Lynn replied quickly, 'Not now. She hasn't been back at school a week yet. Leave her alone for a while.'

'I suppose you've heard from our other daughter?'

The tone had a knife edge, a serrated knife edge, she thought, saying calmly, 'Yes. She likes the place. She's taking biology, of course, sociology, psychology –'

Robert stopped her, raising the newspaper like a fence in front of his face.

'I don't want the details of her curriculum, Lynn.'

'Are you never going to relent?' she asked.

The newspaper crackled angrily as he shifted it. 'Don't pin me down. "Never" is a long time.'

A bleak house indeed.

*   *   *

297

As she drove back from a PTA meeting, Lynn's mind was filled not with its agenda, the school fair and back-to-school night, but with her own uncertainties. Would she be staying in this house? Almost certainly not, for Robert would hardly support a place like this one after she had left him. So there would be a new home to prepare; should it be here where the family's roots had gradually been taking hold, or would it be better to turn to the older, deeper roots in the Midwest?

And then there loomed the larger, ominous problem: the severance itself. She had no experience at all with the law. How exactly did one go about this severance? Here on the road, dancing ahead of the car, she seemed to see a swirling cloud of doubt and menace, rising like some dark genie released from its jar.

The road curved. She was not often in this part of town, but she recognized a turreted Victorian house.

'It has two hideous stone lions at the foot of the driveway,' Tom Lawrence had said. 'Take the next left after you pass it. I'm a quarter of a mile from the turn.'

The genie threatened to tower over the car, to descend and crush it ... Lynn broke into a chill and a sweat; she drove left beyond the lions and drew up in breathless fear before Tom's house.

It had not occurred to her, unthinking as she was just then, that he might not be home. But his car was there, and he answered her ring. She was taken aback at the sight of him. It had been crazy to come here, yet it would have been crazier to turn now and run.

'I was just passing,' she said.

That was absurd, and she knew it as she was saying it.

'Well, then, come in. Or rather, come in and out again. It's too beautiful to be indoors. Shall we sit in the sun or the shade?'

'It doesn't matter.' The chill wanted sun, while the sweat wanted shade.

He was wearing tennis whites, and a racket lay on a table alongside an open book. A bed of perennials, of delphinium, phlox, and cosmos, pink and blue and mauve, bordered the terrace; from a little pool lying in a grotto came the cool trickle of a tiny fountain. Upon this peace she had intruded, and she was too embarrassed to explain herself.

'An unexpected visit. An unexpected pleasure,' Tom said, smiling.

'Now that I'm here, I feel a fool. I'm sorry. I don't really know why I came.'

'I do. You're in trouble, and you need a friend. Isn't that so?'

Her eyes filled, and she blinked. Considerately, Tom gazed out toward the garden.

When she was able, she said in a low, tremulous voice, 'I am going to leave Robert.'

Tom turned quickly. 'A mutual agreement, or are you adversaries?'

A lawyer's questions, Lynn thought, and said aloud, 'He doesn't know yet. And he will not agree, you may be sure.'

'Then you'll need a very good lawyer.'

'You told me once that if I ever needed help, I should call you.'

'I meant it. I don't take matrimonial cases anymore, but I'll get you somebody who does.'

'You don't seem surprised. No, of course you aren't. You're thinking of my invitation to our golden wedding.'

Mechanically, she twisted the straps of her handbag and, in the same low voice, continued, 'He struck me. But this time something different happened. I knew I couldn't – I know I can't – I can't take it again.'

He nodded.

'I know you think I'm stupid to have put up with what I did. One reads all those articles about battered

299

women and thinks, "You idiots! What are you waiting for?"'

'They're not idiots. There are a hundred different reasons why they stay as long as they do. Surely,' Tom said gently, 'you can think of some very cogent reasons yourself. In your own case –'

She interrupted. 'In my own case I never thought of myself as a battered woman.'

'You didn't want to. You thought of yourself as a romantic woman.'

'Oh, yes! I loved him . . .'

'From a woman's point of view I daresay he's a very attractive man. A powerful man. Admired.'

'I wish I could understand it. He can be so loving and, sometimes, so hard. Poor Emily –' And briefly she related, without mention of the pregnancy, what had occurred.

Tom commented, 'That sounds just like Bruce's generosity. You've seen him since the funeral, of course.'

'No.'

'Now I am surprised, close as you've been.'

Close, she thought, wincing.

'I don't think he wants to see me,' she said, and at once corrected this slip of the tongue. 'To see anyone yet, I meant.'

Tom inquired curiously whether Bruce knew of her plans.

'I haven't really made them yet,' she evaded. 'I've only been thinking about them. Robert will be sent abroad in a couple of months. He will go ahead of the rest of us, and I thought I would send him a letter with my decision.'

'That gets complicated. Wouldn't it be better to have it all out now and have the wheels turning before he leaves?'

'No. He'll be crushed as it is – but if I do it now, he'll

never leave, and his chance will be lost. This chance is all he talks about. I can't be that cruel. I can't destroy him utterly.'

She was still twisting the strap of her purse. Tom reached over and put the purse on the table.

'Let me get you a drink. Liquor or no liquor? Personally, I think you could use a stiff drink.'

'Nothing. Nothing, thank you.'

They had sat on either side of the fireplace. The white cat had wound itself around his ankle. He had stirred his brandy. And after the brandy . . .

'So in spite of everything you don't want to hurt him. You still feel something,' Tom said.

'Feel! Oh, yes. How can I not, after twenty years?' She had not expected to weep, to make a scene. Nevertheless, tears came now in a flood. 'I can't believe this is happening. These last days have been a nightmare.'

Tom got up and went into the house. When he returned, he held a damp washcloth, with which, most tenderly, he wiped Lynn's face. Like a child or a patient she submitted, talking all the while.

'I should be ashamed of myself to come here and bother you. I should solve my own problem. God knows I'm old enough. It's ridiculous, it's stupid to be talking like this . . . But I'm miserable. Though why shouldn't I be? Millions of other people are miserable. Am I any different? Nobody ever said life is supposed to be all wine and roses.'

She started to get up. 'I'm all right, Tom. See, I've stopped crying. I'm not going to cry anymore. I'm going home. I apologize.'

'No, you're too agitated.' Tom pressed her shoulders back against the chair. 'Stay here until you wind down. You don't have to talk unless you want to.'

A cloud passed over the sun, dimming the garden's colors, quieting the nerves. And she said more calmly,

'The truth is, I'm afraid, Tom. How is it that I'm determined to do this, and at the same time I'm so scared? I don't want to face life alone. I'm too young to live without love. And there may never be anyone else who will love me.'

'What makes you think that?'

'I'm almost forty, and I have responsibilities, a baby, a teenager who can be troublesome, and Emily. And it's not as if I had a career or were free with an independent fortune and were a ravishing beauty besides.'

Tom smiled. 'I know one man who thinks you are. Bruce thinks so.'

A flush tingled up Lynn's neck into her face. If Tom had told her this two weeks ago, she would have shrugged. 'Oh,' she would have said, 'Bruce is as prejudiced in my favor as if I were his sister.' But such a reply would have stuck in her throat if she were to try it now.

'I just realized,' Tom said, 'that I've made a tactless remark. I've said "one man" – although,' he added with his usual mischievous twinkling around the eyes, 'I myself wouldn't really call you "ravishing" either. It sounds too rouged and curly, too flirtatious, to suit a lovely woman like you.'

'I'm not lovely,' she protested, feeling stubborn. 'My daughter Emily is. You saw her. She looks like Robert.'

'Oh, yes, oh, yes. Robert's your standard, I see that.' The rebuke was rough. 'Get your mirror out.'

She was puzzled. 'Why?'

'Get it out. Here's your purse. Now look at yourself,' he commanded, 'and tell me what you see.'

'A woman's who's distraught and dreary. That's what I see.'

'That will pass. When it does, you will be – well, almost beautiful. It's true that your face is a shade too wide at the cheekbones, at least for some tastes. And maybe your nose is too short.' Tilting his head to study her from

302

another angle, he frowned slightly, as if he were criticizing a work of art. 'It's interesting, though, that you have dark lashes when your hair's so light.'

'Don't tease me, Tom. I'm too unhappy.'

'All right, I was teasing. I thought I could tease you out of your mood, but I was wrong. What I really want is to rejoice with you, Lynn. You're finally going to end this phase of your life, get strong, and go on to something better.'

'I'm going to end this phase, that's true. But as to the rest, I just don't know.' She looked at her watch. 'I have to go. I like to be home when Annie gets out of school.'

'How's Annie doing?'

'Well, I worry. I always feel uneasy. But at least there haven't been any more episodes. No running away, thank God. She seems calm enough. And Robert has been doing all right with her. As a matter of fact, he's so tired and busy, so preoccupied these last few weeks with his big promotion, that he doesn't have much time for her or anything else.'

Not even for sex, she thought wryly, and I don't know what I shall do when he does make an attempt.

Sunk as she was in the deep lounge chair, she had to struggle upward. Tom pulled her and, not relinquishing her hands, admonished her.

'I want you to be everything you can be. Listen to me. You're too good a human being to be so unhappy.' Then he took her face between his hands and kissed her gently on the forehead. 'You're a lovely woman, very, very attractive. Robert knows it too. That's why he was so furious when he came here and saw you dancing that night.'

'I can barely think. My head's whirling,' she whispered.

'Of course it is. Go home, Lynn, and call me when you need me. But the sooner you leave him, the better, in my opinion. Don't wait too long.'

In a state of increasing confusion she started for home.

What did she feel for Tom? What did he feel for her? Twice now her need for comfort and support had led to a complication – in Bruce's case rather more than a 'complication'!

But then, as she drove on through the leafy afternoon, she began to have some other thoughts, among them a memory that loosened her lips and even produced a wan little smile.

'I wish you would marry Tom,' Annie had said once when she was at odds with Robert. 'Of course, you could marry Uncle Bruce if he didn't already have Aunt Josie.'

It was the babble of a child, and yet there was, for a woman in limbo, a certain sense of security in knowing that at least two men were out there in the great unknown world of strangers who found her attractive, and she would not be going totally unarmed into that world.

And she asked herself whether anyone, at the start of this short summer, could have imagined where they would all be at its waning. On graduation day Emily had been on a straight course to Yale, or so it had seemed; Josie had been smiling her congratulations, and now she was dead; Robert and Lynn, husband and wife, had sat together holding hands.

Robert, home early, explained, 'I decided to call it a day at the office and shop for luggage. We haven't nearly enough. I was thinking, maybe we should buy a couple of trunks to send the bulk of our stuff on ahead. What do you think?'

It was strange that he could look at her and talk of normal things without seeing the change in her. 'We have plenty of time,' she said.

'Well, but there's no sense leaving things to the last minute either.'

A while later Emily telephoned. 'Mom, I just got back from my sociology lecture, and what do you think the

304

subject was? Abused women.' Her voice was urgent and agitated. 'Oh, Mom! What are you waiting for? The lesson is: They never change. This is *your life*, the only one you'll ever have, for heaven's sake. And if you've been staying on because of us, as I believe you have, you're wrong. I have nightmares now, I see your scarred hands and the bruise on your face. Do you want Annie to find out too?'

'I told you what I'm going to do,' Lynn said. 'And if you have any feeling that you're responsible for my staying, you're mistaken. I've stayed this long because I loved him, Emily.'

Neither spoke until Emily, her voice barely breaking, said, so that Lynn knew she was in tears, 'My father, my father . . .'

There was another silence until Lynn responded, 'Darling, if it's the last thing I do, I'll take care of you all. I will.'

'Not me. Don't worry about me, just Annie and Bobby.'

'All right, darling, I won't worry about you.'

Nineteen, and she really believes she doesn't need anybody anymore.

'Have you seen Uncle Bruce? How is he?'

She dreaded a face-to-face meeting with Bruce. It would be stiff and strange . . . It would be guilty . . . 'Not for the last few days. He's doing as well as one might expect,' she answered.

'Be sure to give him my love.'

When she had hung up the phone, Lynn sat for a little while watching darkness creep across the floor. From upstairs in Bobby's room came the sound of Annie, singing. Bobby, delighted with this attention, would be holding on to the crib's railing while he bounced. Annie's high voice was still childish, so that its song at that moment was especially poignant.

A juggler must feel as I do now, Lynn told herself, when

he steps out onto the stage to start his act. One ball missed, and they would all come tumbling...

'But I shall not miss,' she said aloud.

Eudora was waiting for her in the garage when Lynn came home with the groceries.

'Mrs Ferguson! Mrs Ferguson,' she called even before the engine had been shut off. 'They want you at the school, somebody telephoned about Annie – no, no, she's not sick, they said don't be scared, they need to talk to you, that's all.'

Everything in the body from the head down sinks to the feet; so went Lynn's thought. Yet she was able to speak with uncommon quietness.

'They said she's all right?'

'Oh, yes. They wouldn't lie, Mrs Ferguson.'

Perhaps, though, they would. They might well want to break bad news gently...

But Annie was sitting in the principal's office when Lynn rushed in. The first thing she saw was a tear-smeared face and a blouse ripped open down the front.

Mr Siropolous began, 'We've had some trouble here today, Mrs Ferguson, a fight in the schoolyard at recess, and I had to call you. For one thing, Annie refuses to ride home on the school bus.'

Lynn, with her first fears relieved, sat down beside her child.

'Yes, you look as if you've been in a fight. Can you tell me about it?'

Annie shook her head, and Lynn sighed. 'You don't want to ride home in the bus with the girl, is that it? I'm assuming it's a girl.'

Annie folded her lips shut.

'Don't be stubborn,' Lynn said, speaking still mildly. 'Mr Siropolous and I only want to help you. Tell us what happened.'

306

The folded lips only tightened, while Annie stared at the floor. The principal, who looked tired, urged with slight impatience, 'Do answer your mother.'

Lynn stood up and grasped Annie firmly by the shoulders. 'This is ridiculous, Annie. You're too old to be stubborn.'

'It seems,' Mr Siropolous said now, 'that some of the girls were taunting Annie about something. She punched one of them in the face, and there was a scuffle until Mr Dawes managed to separate them.'

In dismay Lynn repeated, 'She punched a girl in the face!'

'Yes. The girl is all right, but of course we can't allow such behavior. Besides, it's not like Annie. Not like you at all, Annie,' he said, kindly now.

Lynn was ashamed, and the shame made her stern.

'This is horrible, Annie,' she chided. 'To lose your temper like that, no matter what anyone said, is horrible.'

At that the child, clenching her pathetic little fists, burst forth. 'You don't know what they said! They were laughing at me. They were all laughing at me.'

'About what, about what?' asked the two bewildered adults.

'They said – "Your father hits your mother all the time, and everybody knows it. Your father hits your mother." ' Annie wailed. 'And they were laughing at me!'

Mr Siropolous looked for an instant at Lynn and looked away.

'Of course it's not true,' Lynn said firmly.

'I told them it was a lie, Mom, I told them, but they wouldn't listen. Susan said she heard her mother tell her father. They wouldn't let me talk, so I hit Susan because she was the worst, and I hate her anyway.'

Lynn took a handkerchief from her purse, with a hand that shook wiped Annie's face, and said, still firmly, 'Children – people – do sometimes say things that hurt most terribly and aren't true, Annie. And I can understand why you were angry. But still you shouldn't have hit Susan. What is to be done, do you think, Mr Siropolous?'

For a moment he deliberated. 'Perhaps tomorrow you and Susan, maybe some others, too, will meet in my office and apologize to each other, they for things they said, and you for punching. We'll talk together about peace, as they do at the United Nations. In this school we do not speak or act unkindly. How does that sound to you, Mrs Ferguson?'

'A very good idea. Very fair.' The main thing was to get out of there as quickly as possible. 'And now we'd better get home. Come, Annie. Thank you, Mr Siropolous. I'm awfully sorry this happened. But I suppose you must be used to these little – little upsets.'

'Yes, yes, it's all part of growing up, I'm afraid,' said the principal, who, also pleased to end the affair as quickly as possible, was politely holding the door open.

'She's such a good child,' he murmured to Lynn as they went out. 'Don't worry. This will pass over.'

'Susan,' Lynn reflected aloud when they were in the car. 'Susan who? Perhaps I know her mother from PTA?'

'She's awful. She thinks she's beautiful, but she isn't. She's growing pimples. Her aunt lives across the road.'

'Across our road?'

'Mrs Stevens,' Annie said impatiently. 'Mrs Stevens across the road.'

Lynn, making the swift connection, frowned. But Lieutenant Weber had told the Stevenses that night that there was nothing wrong.

'She's afraid of dogs, the stupid thing. I'm going to send Juliet over to scare her the next time she visits.'

Needing some natural, light response, Lynn laughed. 'I don't really think anybody would be afraid of our clumsy, flop-eared Juliet.'

'You're wrong. She was scared to death the day Juliet

followed Eudora to the Stevenses. She screamed, and Eudora had to hold Juliet by the collar.'

'Oh? Eudora visits the Stevenses?'

'Not them. The lady who comes to clean their house is Eudora's best friend.'

Was that then the connection, or had it been only Weber, or was it both? It surprised her that no hot resentment was rising now toward whomever it was who had spread the news. People would always spread news; it was quite natural; she had done it often enough herself.

Then came a sudden startling query. 'But, Mom – did Dad ever?'

'Ever what?'

'Do what Susan said,' Annie mumbled.

'Of course not. How can you ask?'

'Because he gets so angry sometimes.'

'That has nothing to do with what Susan said. Nothing.'

'Are you sure, Mom?'

'Quite sure, Annie.'

An audible sigh came from the child. And Lynn had to ask herself how she would set about explaining the separation when it came, how she might explain it without telling the whole devastating truth; some of it, yes, but spare the very worst.

Well, when the time came, and it was approaching fast, some instinct would certainly show her the way, she assured herself now. But for the present she could feel only a deep and tired resignation.

6

The baby was being dried after his evening bath when
Robert, hours late, came home. Lynn, stooping beside the
tub, was aware of his presence in the doorway behind
her, but did not turn to greet him; the time for loving
welcomes was past, and she waited for him to speak first,
after which she would give her civil response.

'I'm home,' he said.

Then some quality in his voice made her glance up,
and she saw that he looked like death. He had opened
his collar and loosened his tie; he, Robert Ferguson, to
be disheveled like that in the commuter train!

'What's the matter?' she cried.

'You will not believe it,' he said.

'I will believe it if you tell me.'

'Ask Annie to put Bobby to bed. She won't mind. And
come downstairs. I need a drink.'

He's ill, she thought, that's what it is. They've told him
he has cancer or is going blind. Pity, shuddering and
chill, ran through her.

'Glenfiddich. Toss it down,' he said, as if he were talking to himself. 'And toss another.'

The bottle made a little clink on the silver tray. He sat
down.

'Well, Lynn, I've news. General American Appliance and
I are finished. Parted. Through.'

'Through?' she repeated, echoing the word that had,
in the instant, no meaning.

'I didn't get the promotion, so I quit. That's why I'm late. I was cleaning out my desk.'

'I don't understand,' she said.

He stood up and walked to the long bow window that faced the road and the lighted lantern at the foot of the Stevenses' long drive. Like a sentry on duty he spun around, walked the length of the room to the opposite window, and stood there looking out into the dark lawn and the darker bulk of the hill beyond. When he turned again to face Lynn, she saw that his eyes were bright with tears. Then he sat down and began to talk in rapid, staccato bursts.

'Yes, cleaning out my desk. Twenty-three years of my life. And do you know how I got the news? In the elevator coming back to the office late in the afternoon. I hadn't been there all day. I'd gone straight from the train to an appointment. And a couple of kids were talking, clerks or mailroom kids; they didn't even recognize me. They were talking about Budapest, and Bruce Lehman going there to head the office. It sounded crazy. I didn't pay any attention to it, except to be amused. And then Warren called me in. He showed me a fax from Monacco, and I saw it was true. And still I couldn't believe it.'

Robert put his hands over his face. His elbows rested on his knees, and his head sank. She was staring at a beaten man, as out of place in this rich room as any beggar sprawled upon marble stairs.

'I told him there had to be some ridiculous mistake, that everybody knew it had been promised to me. Why Lehman? It made no sense. I said I wanted to speak to Monacco then and there. So Warren phoned California, but we didn't reach Monacco. I demanded that Warren tell me what he knew. I wasn't going to spend a sleepless night trying to figure out what had gone wrong. Damn! It'll be a sleepless night anyway.'

And again, Robert got up to pace the length of the

311

room. At the mantel he paused to adjust the Herend figurines, which Eudora had moved when she dusted.

'I remember the day I bought these,' he said. 'I thought I had the world at my feet. I did have it too. Excuse me. These damn tears. I'm ashamed that you should see them.'

'There's nothing to be ashamed of, Robert. A man has a right to show his grief too.'

She spoke softly, not out of compassion alone, but also out of her own bewilderment in the face of this stunning complication.

'And Warren? Did he tell you why?'

'Oh, yes. Oh, yes. He was delicate about it, you know, very much the gentleman. But how he was enjoying it! He's home now, I'll bet on it, regaling his wife or maybe the crowd at the club, with the story. God, as hard as I've worked, brought marketing farther along than anyone else had ever done; and what has Lehman ever accomplished compared with me? A drudge, without imagination –'

'You haven't told me the reason,' Lynn said patiently.

'The reason? Oh, yes. I said he was delicate about it. Very tactful. It seems that people – that someone has been saying things, personal things, exaggerations – God! Everybody, every marriage, has problems of one sort or another, problems that people overcome, put behind them. I told him the stuff bore no resemblance to reality, none at all. What right anyway do strangers have to draw conclusions about what goes on between a man and his wife? You'd think a man like Monacco would have more sense than to listen to idle gossip.'

'Idle,' Lynn murmured, so faintly that he did not hear her.

All the whispering had united into one tearing shout, loud enough to reach to California. It was a confirmation of sorts, but useless to her, for to what end would it lead?

And her path that had seemed so clear, though painful, had brought her into a blind alley.

'Would you believe a man like Monacco could stoop so low? What have I done that's so terrible, after all?' When she was silent, a note of faint suspicion came into his voice. 'I wonder who could have spread this dirty stuff. You couldn't – you didn't ever run to the Lehmans with anything, did you?'

She interrupted. 'Don't dare say such a thing to me!'

'Ah, well, I believe you. But then, how and who?'

The question hung between them, and he was expecting an answer, but she was numb and could give none. In all this horror there was the kind of fascination that draws a person unwillingly to look at an accident, to stare at bloody wreckage.

Robert resumed, 'Warren said – and he was speaking for Monacco "according to instructions," he said, that of course I was free to stay on in my present position. "Of course,"' Robert mocked.

'And you're not going to,' she said, recognizing the mockery.

'Good God, Lynn! I wrote out my resignation then and there. What do you take me for? After a slap in the face like that, do you think I could stay on? While Bruce Lehman enjoys the reward that belongs to me?'

'Bruce never wanted it,' she said.

'He's damn well accepted it now.'

The world is spinning around me, and I make no sense of it, Lynn thought. Then, for want of something to say, she inquired, 'Are you sure you're doing the right thing by leaving?'

'No doubt of it. Anyhow, they want me to go, don't you see that? They'd find a way to ease me out. They'd make it so miserable that I'd want to leave.' Robert's face contorted itself into the mask of tragedy, with cheeks puffed, brows upward drawn, and mouth gaping. 'I'm ruined,

Lynn! Destroyed. Disgraced. Thrown out like trash, a piece of trash.'

It was all true. He had done it to himself, but it was still true. What could she, what should she, say? She could think of nothing but some trivial creature comfort.

'Shall I fix you something? You've had no dinner.'

'I can't eat.' He looked at the clock. 'It's half past eight. Not too late to see Bruce. Come on.'

'See Bruce? But why?'

'To offer congratulations, naturally.'

Dismayed, she sought a sensible objection. 'He won't want us to visit. We'll be intruding, Robert.'

'Nonsense. He'll appreciate congratulations. We'll bring a bottle of champagne.'

'No, no. He's in mourning. It's not fitting,' she protested.

'This has nothing to do with Bruce's mourning. It's a question of Robert Ferguson's honor and good taste, of his sportsmanship. I want him to see that I can take this like a man.'

'Why torture yourself to make a point, Robert? A phone call will do as well.'

'No. Get the champagne. He can chill it in his freezer for half an hour.'

Silently she asked: Whom are you fooling with this show of bravado? By your own admission you're dying inside.

'If it's a celebration you want,' she said, not unkindly, 'button your collar and change your tie. It's stained.'

Bruce wouldn't care, but Robert would see himself in a mirror and be appalled.

She had not been in Bruce's house since that day. He had been reading when they arrived; the book was in his hand when he opened the door. The evening was cold and windy, a harbinger of winter, and apparently he had been using Josie's knitted afghan on the very sofa where they had lain together, where he had covered her nakedness with that afghan.

And she wondered whether the same thought was in his mind, too, and could not look at him or at the sofa, but made instead a show of greeting the white cat.

Bruce asked whether they would mind if he saved the wine for another time together, explaining, 'I am not quite up to it. It's been a rather bad day for me, Robert.'

'Now, why should that be?'

'It's very simple. The post was yours. You earned it, and it should have gone to you.'

Robert shrugged. 'That's generous of you, Bruce, but it wasn't in the cards, that's all.'

The remark was almost flippant; it could have aroused compassion for its attempt at bravery, or, given the fact that the others present knew why 'it wasn't in the cards,' it could arouse anger.

Bruce, though, was compassionate. 'I have to tell you that I'm overwhelmed. It won't be easy to follow in your footsteps, Robert. I only hope I can do the job.'

'I'll be available for advice if you need it anytime. It might be a good idea for you to come over one night soon and let me give you some background on what's already been done over there.'

'Well, thanks, but not just yet. This has come down on me like a ton of bricks, while I'm still buried under a mountain of bricks. I'm not thinking very clearly.'

'I understand,' Robert said sympathetically.

'At least, though, this will force me to get away. I'd been wishing there was someplace where I could get away from myself, Outer Mongolia, maybe, or the South Pole. So now it's to be Hungary. Not that it makes any difference where. I'll still be taking myself with myself, and myself's pretty broken down.'

Bruce had not given Lynn a glance, but now he turned fully toward her and made a request.

'I'm worried about Barney.' The cat, lying curled in front of the fireplace, looked like a heap of snow. At hearing his name he raised his head. 'I can't take him with me, and Josie would haunt me for the rest of my days if I didn't get a good home for him. So do you suppose you could take him, Lynn? I don't want to give you any more work or any problem, but I'm stumped.'

'You don't know Lynn if you can say that,' Robert declared. 'She'd take in any four-legged creature you can name.'

'Of course I will,' Lynn said quickly.

'No, you don't know Lynn,' repeated Robert.

But he does know Lynn, and very well too. The words, on the tip of her tongue, came so close to slipping out that she was shocked.

'What's your schedule?' Robert asked.

'Sometime in December, I think.' And Bruce said again, 'It's all so sudden ... I'll keep Barney till I go ... It's good of you ... I'm grateful ... Josie would be grateful.'

'He's in a fog. He'll never measure up. Doesn't know what he's in for,' Robert said when they left.

At home he resumed his agitated pacing, saying, 'He'll never measure up.'

Annie came quietly into the room, so quietly that they were startled by her voice.

'What's wrong? Has something awful happened? Is Emily sick again?'

Robert made a choking sound. 'Oh, Annie. Oh, my little girl, no, Emily's well, thank God. Thank God, we're all well.' And pulling Annie to him, he kissed the top of her head and held her, saying tenderly, 'I'll find a way to take care of you. They think they've ruined me, but they can't crush my spirit, no –' He began to weep.

'You're terrifying her!' Lynn cried. 'Daddy's upset, Annie, because of some trouble at work. He's leaving the firm. He's upset.'

316

The child wriggled free of Robert and stared at him as if she had never seen him before. A variety of expressions moved across her face, ranging through curiosity and distaste to fear.

'I need to talk to Emily,' Robert said. 'Get me her number, Lynn.'

'You'll scare her to death too. Wait till you calm down.'

'I'm calm,' he said through his tears. 'I'm calm. I need to talk to her, to tell her I'm sorry. We're a family, we make mistakes, we have to stand together now. What's the number, Annie?'

If I hadn't seen how little he drank of it, I would have said it's the Scotch, Lynn thought.

'Emily, Emily,' Robert was saying into the telephone. 'No, don't be frightened, we're all right here, it's just that I quit GAA. It's a long story, too long to explain over the phone, but – excuse me, I'm very emotional at the moment, I feel that the stars have fallen – But I'm going to pull myself together and I – well, I want to apologize, to straighten things out between you and me. I've been heartsick over the situation. I want to apologize for not understanding you, not trying to understand. I just want to say, don't worry about the tuition, I'll pay it, I'm not broke yet. You just stay there and do your work and God bless you, darling. I love you, Emily. I'm so proud of you. Tell me, how's Harris?'

Later, in their bedroom, he became subdued, sighing and questioning, 'Tell me, do I – do we – deserve this? I wanted everything for you, and now – now what?'

In bed he turned and, pulling her gently from where she had been lying with her back toward him, drew her close. And she knew it was assurance that he wanted, a bodily relief from tension, some sweet recompense for loss. He wanted proof that he was still a man, her man. Had he asked this of her even a few hours ago, before disaster had befallen him, she would, she knew, have

317

scratched and fought him. Now, though, she hadn't the heart to inflict another hurt; what did it matter, after all? A woman could lie like a stone and feel nothing. In a few minutes it would be over, anyway.

So often during these past weeks she had imagined the humbling of Robert Ferguson, and yet now that he had been humbled beyond imagining, the sight was almost too dreadful to be borne. And she felt his pain as if she were herself inside his skin.

In the tight little world of the company, many of whose officers lived in the town, news spread. On Saturday in the supermarket a group of women had obviously been talking about the Fergusons, because when they saw Lynn, they stopped and abruptly gave an unusually cordial greeting.

Not that it makes any difference, she thought, and it's probably absurd of me to ask, yet I have to know how this happened. And going to a pay phone, she telephoned Tom. Perhaps he would know; if he did not, he would find out.

'It's about Robert. Have you heard that he's left the firm? They found out that . . .' Her voice quavered.

'Yes, I know. Come over, Lynn. I'm home all morning.'

In the large room where the table had glittered on that night from which the present trouble had stemmed, she felt suddenly very small. She felt like a petitioner.

'How did you hear?' she asked.

'Monacco phoned me. He's always had the impression, for some unfathomable reason, that Robert and I are close friends.'

'But why did he phone you? To ask or to tell?'

'Both. He told me that a letter had come to him, and he asked me whether the accusations in it were true, whether I knew anything about them.'

'A letter,' Lynn echoed.

318

'I don't know who sent it. It was a woman's letter, anonymous. But it sounded authentic, Monacco said, as if the wife of one of the firm's officers had written it. It had a good deal of corroborating evidence, one thing being a report from some neighbors.'

Tom lowered his eyes to study his shoes before saying anything further. Then, looking directly at Lynn, as if he had had to consider the decision to say more, he continued, 'It was about what happened the night you came here to make dinner.'

'An anonymous letter. How dirty!'

She was thinking rapidly: Who, except the Stevenses, could have known what happened that night? And they were related to that child Susan's family. And Eudora, who had seen too much, was a friend of the woman who worked for the Stevenses.

'And since the letter said there'd been a call to the police, Monacco had a check made.'

Weber. He hadn't 'buried' it, after all. Weber had wanted to get back at Robert for the things Robert had said.

'So they made the check and found that there had indeed been a complaint, and that somebody in the police department had tried to hide it, had actually hidden it, as a matter of fact.'

Then she had misjudged Weber. At once guilty and pitying, she asked Tom, 'Did he get into trouble, the man who had hidden it?'

'No. The police chief is a friend of mine, and we had a talk.'

'Then you know about Emily and his son,' she said softly.

'Nothing except that they've been going together.' Tom smiled. 'Do they still say "going steady"? My teenage vocabulary is definitely out of date.'

'I don't really know. It's all a tangle,' lamented Lynn.

Tom nodded. '*Tangled* is the word. Even the cop at the club knew all about it. He used to be my gardener before he joined the police force, and he tells me things. You'd be surprised how many people know about Robert, things true and untrue. That's what happens in these towns; you find your way into the stream of gossip, and soon everybody knows what kind of breakfast cereal you eat.'

'The meanness of it!'

It seemed to her as if, in exposing Robert, the slack-tongued mob, inquisitive and gloating, had exposed them all, herself and the girls and even the baby boy. Anger exploded, and she protested, 'You would think people might find better things to do than to probe into other people's trouble!'

'You would think, but that's not the way it is.' And Tom added, 'Monacco won't tolerate scandal, you see, not even the slightest.'

'It isn't fair! The thing's all blown out of proportion. It's between Robert and me, anyway, isn't it? Not GAA, or the town. Why should any wrong done to me affect his job? Why?' she ended, demanding.

Tom's expression, as he raised his eyebrows and shook his head, seemed to be saying, I give up!

'Oh, you think I'm naive?'

'Yes, very. Corporations have an image, Lynn. There's morale to maintain. How can you get respect from a subordinate when your own behavior is – shall we say "shady"?'

'All right, it was a silly question. All right.'

Then, following Tom's glance, she became aware that she had been twisting her rings, working her nervous fingers on her lap. And she planted her hands firmly on the arms of the chair. But she ought to go home; having heard what she had, there was nothing more to wait for.

'Monacco was really distressed,' Tom said gently. 'This

isn't anything a man likes to do to someone he admires. And of course he said what you might expect, that this was the last thing he would have believed of Robert, as brilliant as he is, with such a future ahead.'

'Like seeing a murderer's picture in the paper, I suppose. "Oh, my, he's got such a nice face!" Is that it?' And Lynn's fingers went back to the rings, twirling and twisting.

Tom reached over and held one of her hands quietly. 'It's the devil for you, I know.'

'One has to ache for Robert, regardless of everything. He can't sleep, just walks around the house all night, upstairs and down. He barely eats. He looks older by ten years. The rejection ... The humiliation...'

'Especially because Bruce is the one who got his place?'

'Well, naturally. He certainly never thought that Bruce, of all people, could be his competition.'

'Why do you say "of all people"?'

'I didn't say it, Robert did. He always said Bruce was not competitive.'

'He was dead wrong. When the Hungarian project was first conceived, Bruce was right up among the top prospects.'

'How do you know all this? Even if you're connected with Monacco, you still don't work for GAA. So how do you know?'

'I never did know or care about GAA. But this one time I made it my business to. I wanted Robert to get a promotion. I did it for you.'

At that Lynn slipped her hand out of his so quickly that he, too, spoke quickly.

'I knew, it didn't take much to see, in spite of your protests, Lynn, that the marriage wouldn't last. And then you'd be needing a decent settlement. Courts aren't giving much to wives these days.'

The room was absolutely quiet. A phone rang somewhere in the house and stopped when Tom did not answer it. A man passing on the walk outside gave a rumbling laugh, and a woman laughed in return. Then the sound faded. So people were still finding humor in the world! The thought came to her that she might never again have anything to laugh about. And another thought came, a questioning: If I were free now, unencumbered by events, would I accept this humorous, quirky, kindly man who's sitting here carefully looking at his shoes again and not at me? Surely his last words meant something: *I did it for you*.

'How good you are!' she exclaimed, and would have said more, but was fearful of tears.

'Well,' he said. 'Well, I like to set things straight. Lawyers, you know. They're orderly. So tell me, where do we go from here? Or I should say first, where do you go?'

'Where can I go, Tom? The man is ill. He begs forgiveness – oh, not only for the bad things, but for his failure. There's been very little money put aside. I was surprised how little. He needs a position, he'll need one soon, but first he'll have to get back some pride and courage. He wants to move away from here, to start fresh. I don't know. I don't know anything. I'm sick at heart myself, Tom. It's a whole strange, sad new page. He's so humble, so changed.'

'No, Lynn. He's not changed.'

'You can't say that. You haven't seen him. On the telephone, talking to Emily, he sobbed.'

'I don't need to see him. You're too good,' Tom said. 'That's the trouble.'

'Does one step on a person when he's already fallen down?'

Tom did not answer, and she hid her face in her hands, thinking that Tom, after all, couldn't know what was churning inside her. Twenty years together, with so much

322

good! Oh, yes, bad too, bad too. And yet grown together, one flesh even when he hurt her, so that now she could feel his suffering as no outsider, no matter how sensitive or how subtle, could ever feel.

She raised her face, appealing for understanding. 'I can't leave a sinking ship, Tom. I can't leave.'

He nodded. 'But you will eventually,' he said.

It was a time of waiting, an uneasy suspension of customary life. The days went slowly, and although it was autumn, they were long. From this house, surrounded by heavy foliage, Lynn looked out into a haze of faded colors, of greens gentled into gray and reds turned rusty, mournful yet lovely in their melancholy. It seemed to her that the earth was reflecting the mood of the house, for the fall should be bright and blazing. But it is all in the mind, she told herself; one sees what one needs to see.

On the far lawn under a maple Annie was doing her English assignment, reading *Huckleberry Finn*. Robert, kneeling on the grass, extended his arms toward Bobby, who, now going on ten months old, had already taken a few independent steps. Robert was proud; the boy would be athletic; the boy would be a strong tennis player, a swimmer, a track star.

If that gives him comfort, Lynn thought, let him have comfort. It was strange to see him here at home in the middle of the afternoon. Eudora, as she passed now between the garage and the grape arbor, must think so too.

Poor woman, only a week ago she had come, hesitant and shy, to make a confession.

'There's something I have to tell you, Mrs Ferguson. All Mr Ferguson's trouble, I heard about it from my friend, she shouldn't have talked, but I shouldn't have talked, either, I know I shouldn't. It was just that we were all having lunch at church, and you know when people work in other people's houses, they hear things, and they talk. I didn't mean to hurt you all, honestly I didn't. Even Mr Ferguson, he's a gentleman, and I really liked him until he —'

Lynn had stopped her. 'Dear Eudora, I understand. And it wasn't just you or your friend at the Stevenses'. Even the policeman at the country club knew, it seems that a great many people did. Oh, don't cry, please. Don't make it harder for me.'

There had been no stopping the contrition. 'I wouldn't hurt you for the world, you've been so good to me, all those clothes, and not just your old ones, but the new things for my birthday and last Christmas. You've been my *friend*. I couldn't stand it that morning when I came in and saw what he was doing to you, such a little thing you are, can't be more than a hundred pounds. Such a little thing.'

The mild, anxious eyes had been asking a question that Eudora dared not ask aloud: 'Are you staying, Mrs Ferguson? Are you really?'

Lynn, raising her chin ever so slightly to show determination, had replied to the unspoken question. 'We always need to look ahead in life, not back. What's past is past, isn't it?'

And in the saying she was conscious of maturity and strength.

'It's between Robert and me, our affair alone,' she had told Tom Lawrence.

But of course, it was not. It was the proverbial stone thrown into a pond, with the widening ripples. It was Emily and Annie . . .

Annie had been the surprise. The resilience of this so-often-troubled child was always a surprise. Unless she was holding it all in . . .

'Uncle Bruce told me not to believe what the kids said. He told me not even to answer them. "They want you to cry and get angry," he told me. "But if you don't do either, you'll spoil their fun, and they'll stop." We talk on the phone a lot.' And she had finished with assurance, 'Uncle Bruce gives me good advice.' Then abruptly switching, she had demanded, 'Why doesn't he come here anymore?'

'He's been busy getting ready to go away,' Lynn had explained.

It was a question whether Bruce was more concerned to avoid Robert or to avoid her.

She wished Bruce would talk to Emily, but then was almost positive that his remarks to her would be quite different from his advice to Annie. Anyway, Emily was determined not to be moved.

Speaking to her sometime after the day of Robert's first frantic telephoned appeal, Lynn had come up against a wall of resistance.

'Mom, you're making a dreadful mistake,' she had said in a sorry tone of disapproval. 'Dreadful. I've done a lot of reading about marriages like yours.'

'I know. I saw a book in your room. Those statistics don't fit every case. Emily. *People* aren't statistics.'

'But there's a pattern, no matter how different each case may seem. We're still discussing wife abuse in my sociology course and I tell you, I've felt cold chills. You've got to take care of yourself, Mom. You can't depend on Dad anymore. You need to leave, and soon, Mom.'

'No. If you could see your father, you'd know what I'm seeing. He's a different man. This has done something drastic to him, something terrible.'

'You may be looking at him, but you're not seeing him.'

'Have you no mercy or forgiveness, Emily? No pity?'

'Yes. Pity for you.' And at the end Emily had said, 'Well, Mom, you have to do what you think best.'

Offended and defeated, Lynn had replied rather coolly,

'Of course I must. Don't we all?' Then, softening, she had tried again. 'In spite of his worries Dad's looking forward to Christmas, to the family being together. Would you like to bring Harris to dinner too? I'll make a feast, a *bûche de Noël* and everything.'

'Harris has his own family dinner,' Emily had replied, in the dry tone she seemed lately to have acquired.

'Well, one other day during vacation, then.'

'We'll see,' said Emily.

Stubborn! When Robert was really trying so hard to make amends!

'Don't tell Emily I'm worried about what I'm going to do,' he kept saying. 'I don't want her work to be affected. She needs a clear mind.'

'But what are you really going to do?' Lynn had asked again only last night.

'I don't know yet. I need more time to think. In the meantime we can manage with my severance pay.' The tone was dispirited, and the words were certainly vague. 'Something, I'll find something.'

On her birthday he had laid a long-stemmed rose at her plate.

'It's the best I can afford right now. I won't buy jewelry unless it's flawless, you know that. So, a flawless rose instead.' Straightening his shoulders, and with a smile intended to be brave, he had said, 'But next year at this time there'll be a shiny box tied with ribbon.'

Something within Lynn had been displeased with this image; she had picked up the rose, so alive in its perfect simplicity, and held it against her cheek, saying only, 'This is perfect, Robert. Thank you.'

She could have said, 'I don't measure things by shine and ribbon, don't you know that?'

But it would have come out prissy and righteous-sounding, which was not her intent at all, so she had just

326

let him go to the piano, where, while she ate her breakfast, he played a birthday song.

Yesterday when it rained, she thought now, watching the baby stagger across the grass and fall into Robert's arms, he had spent the whole afternoon at the piano playing dreamy nocturnes. How long could the man go on this way? He went nowhere, not even on simple errands to the shopping center, where he feared to meet anybody he knew.

'You have to go out and hold your head up,' she kept saying. 'After all, you're not a murderer out on bail, are you? This is a seven-day wonder, anyhow. There's something new every week for people to chew over. Already, I'll take a bet on it, your departure from GAA is old stuff, forgotten.'

But that was not true. At the supermarket there were no more curious glances and conversations broken off at her approach, but the telephone at home, an instrument that had once rung steadily, was now silent. And she recalled the conversation at Monacco's dinner table, the caretaker's light in the vacant house across the lake where had lived that couple about whom 'you'd never guess it was possible.'

Now Robert, seeing her at the window, waved, and she opened the casement.

'Bruce phoned while you were out,' he called. 'He's cleaning the house out and has some stuff he wants to give us, though I can't imagine what. Will you go over in the station wagon? He'd bring it himself, but his car's too small. Can you go now?'

'Can't you do it?'

'I'd rather not get into conversation with him in the circumstances,' Robert pleaded.

Dismay was her instant reaction. Clothed though she was, she knew that she would feel naked in that room with Bruce, with no third person there to draw attention away from her. And yet, as she closed the casement, another thought came: I have neglected him, and he was, he is, or he and Josie were, our dearest friends. Shameful to have been so engrossed in her own trouble when his loss was so much greater! Yes, on one hand, came the argument: You have to remember that afternoon; how can you face each other, Lynn, tell me how? But on the other hand ... So she stood, fearing to go, not wanting to, then in a queer, shamefaced fashion, wanting to.

Some time ago, before Josie's death, she had meant to give her a collection of pictures that they had taken together over the years. In the hall chest lay this folder, this record of the radiant hours that people want to save, the picnic on the Fourth of July, the birthdays, the company outing, and the silly hats on New Year's Eve. Surely Bruce would want this treasure. He would want every scrap and crumb of memory. Yes.

He was standing in a house half stripped when Lynn arrived. The first thing she noticed was that the living-room sofa was gone. A pair of early American matching chests were all that remained in the room.

'The new owners bought the best stuff,' Bruce said. 'The tall clock under the stairs, the stretcher table – stuff. The rest I gave away to the homeless project. Come, I'll show you what I thought might look nice in your garden. The new people don't want it.'

Through the garden door, which stood open, he pointed to the birdbath that had been bought during his and Josie's only trip abroad. It was a large marble basin, on the rim of which there stood a pair of marble doves, drinking. Bruce laughed about it.

'Damn thing cost more to ship home from Italy than I paid for it! But Josie fell in love with the doves. And it is rather nice, I have to admit.'

Now he added, 'Would you like to have it? If you do,

I can ask my neighbor's boy to help me load it into your car.'

'It's beautiful, Bruce. But are you sure –?' she began.

'That I won't ever use it? Yes, Lynn. Quite sure. I've had my time for a home, and my time's passed.'

What a pity, she thought, to feel so old at his age. He was beginning to look himself, though; the haggard desperation that had marked his face during these hard months had lessened; the body tries to heal even when the spirit cannot. Rest healed, and so did the sun that was now glinting on his curly, summer-bleached hair. Funny, she thought, I never noticed his lashes are golden.

They were standing in the doorway. A white butterfly fluttered and poised itself on a clump of dead, still-yellow marigolds.

'Butterflies,' murmured Lynn, 'and it's almost Thanksgiving.'

He, apparently not inclined to speak anymore, stood there with his hands in the pockets of his jeans, his glasses thrust up into his curly hair, and eyes that seemed to be seeing, not the quiet surrounding afternoon, but something different, something far away.

And she, feeling superfluous, made a move to leave, asking hesitantly, 'Did you say your neighbor will help carry?'

'Yes, his son. They're across the street. I'll go out the front door and get him.'

The kitchen cabinets had been almost all cleaned out, Lynn saw as she followed him. The floor was littered, a broom stood in a corner with a new trunk next to it, and a pile of books stood waiting to be packed into stout crates.

'I'm taking my books and Josie's, the only things I want to save.'

'Oh,' Lynn said, 'I almost forgot, I've got a collection of pictures that you'll want. I left them in my car. They go all the way back to when you first came to St Louis. Oh, my head's a sieve.'

'You've had a few other things to fill your head with,' Bruce said. 'How is Robert these days?'

'Subdued. You wouldn't know him. Subdued and worried, but nothing like what he was in the first days, thank God. I'll never forget how he cried on the telephone to Emily. I'd never seen a man show grief that way, although there's no reason why men shouldn't. But still, my father, even after my mother's funeral –' Abruptly, shocked at her own tactlessness in mentioning funerals, she stopped.

'I take it that you're staying, Lynn.' And when she nodded, he said quite gently, 'I thought you probably would.'

'He's changed,' she told him, aware as she spoke it that she had used the same word, *changed*, both to Emily and to Tom.

Unlike either of those two he made no protest but looked at her with an expression of utmost sweetness. Leaning against a kitchen counter, he faced her as she leaned against the counter opposite, the two of them standing among the disarray of an abandoned home. Neither one would venture to speak of what surely must have been in each of their minds; she was thinking, as she regarded him, that it had always been a total impossibility for her to have sex with any man but Robert, and yet it had happened with this man.

'It is your loyalty,' Bruce said suddenly, as if he were thinking aloud. 'You feel his pain as if it were your own.'

'Yes,' she said, surprised that he had expressed her feelings so exactly. 'I suppose it makes no sense to you. You can't understand it. And Josie would be furious with me if she could know.'

'You're mistaken. Josie would try to talk you out of it,

but she would understand. There are very few things that Josie failed to understand or forgive.'

He meant what had happened between the two of them, on that day when she lay in such pain that even morphine could not assuage it. That's what he meant.

'Oh, she was no saint,' Bruce said. 'I don't want to draw false pictures. She deserves to be remembered as she really was.'

Indeed, not saintly, with that sharp scrutiny of hers and that peppery tongue! Only good, purely good, to the very last day.

Bruce made a little gesture with both hands, a movement implying emptiness.

'They say an amputated limb still aches. So I suppose it doesn't really do any good to go away, since the ache will only go along with me. Still, I'm relieved to be given this chance, although not at Robert's expense, it's true.'

'When are you going?'

'Next week. Tuesday.'

'And how long will you be gone?'

'Years, I hope. They tell me I'm climbing up the ladder. I don't know. If I do well in Budapest, there'll be more places, they say. Moscow, maybe. I don't care, Lynn. But the communists have left a lot of ecological cleaning up to be done, and I care about that.' He smiled. 'For the Emilies and the Annies and the Bobbies of the world, I care.'

The cat roused itself from where it had been sleeping in an empty box, crossed the room, and rubbed against Lynn's ankle. Extremely moved by the words and the memories that had just passed, she stooped to stroke its back, and the cat, to acknowledge the soft stroke, raised its small face, its pink mouth, and its astounding periwinkle eyes.

'You did ask us to take him, didn't you, Bruce?'

'If you still want to.'

'He can come with me now,' she said, wanting a reason not to have to see Bruce again, only to leave quietly now, to say the last good-bye and have it over with. 'I'll take good care of him. Don't worry.'

'Do you remember how she used to say she married me because I liked cats?'

'I remember.' And she thought, but did not say, It was because your eyes smiled too. She said instead, 'Are there – do you have instructions about Barney's food and things?'

'I'll write them out. Where's a pencil?' He went rummaging and, in an obvious attempt at cheer, kept talking. 'Let's see: litter box, carrier, collar and leash, almost never used but good to have, some canned food, his favorite kind. Of course, he likes scraps whenever you have fish for dinner.'

'Dover sole?' she asked, forcing a laugh, needing to seem light-hearted.

He responded in kind. 'Oh, naturally. Only the best. And you might let him have a couple of spoons of ice cream now and then, any flavor but coffee. He doesn't like coffee.'

Standing on the walk, she watched while Bruce and the neighbor's son put the birdbath and the unprotesting cat with his belongings into the station wagon. Then the moment of departure came, and suddenly there was nothing to say. Uncomfortable with this vacuum, she remarked that the neighbor's son seemed to be a fine boy, rather mature for fifteen.

'That's what you have to look forward to with Bobby,' he replied.

'I hope so. I'll do my best.'

'I know you will.'

'So, I guess it's good-bye,' she said, and, absurdly, held out her hand.

'A handshake, Lynn?' Holding her face, he softly

332

touched her lips with his own. Then he put his arms around her, held her close, and kissed her again.

'Take care of yourself, Lynn. Take good care.'

'And you. You do the same.'

'I worry so about you. I have for a long time.'

'There's no need. I'm fine. I'm strong.'

'Well, but if you ever need anything, call Tom Lawrence, will you?'

'I won't need anything. Honestly. Believe me.'

'Tom cares about you, Lynn.'

Tom, she thought, says the same about you. It would be comical if things weren't all so mixed up. And, turning from him so that he might not see her wet, blinking eyes, she climbed into the driver's seat.

'Be sure to write to us now and then, especially to Annie.'

'My special Annie. I'll always be there for her.'

'You are the best, the kindest,' she said, and, able to say no more, started the engine.

The last she saw of Bruce as the car moved off was the sunlight striking his glasses and his arm upraised in farewell. The last she saw of the little house was the kitchen window, where Josie's red gingham curtains still hung. Her eyes were so wet that she could barely see to drive.

Robert is probably right about him, she thought. He's the kind who really may never marry again. He's lost. And the word echoed: lost. It was a tolling bell, grave and sorrowful and final. She would probably never see him again. He would drift and she would drift, and they would not meet.

At home there was hustle and bustle. Annie at once took over the care of the cat.

'Barney knows me best,' she insisted. 'He should be my cat. I'll be responsible for his food and his vet appointments and everything.'

333

'And will you clean the litter box too?' Lynn asked.

'Absolutely. Now I have to introduce him to Juliet. I really don't think there'll be any trouble, do you?'

'I don't think so. If there is, we'll learn how to handle it.'

Robert was still in the yard with Bobby. At the moment the little boy was stretched on the grass with Juliet, and both were watching Robert hammer a playhouse into shape. He does everything well, Lynn thought, observing the swift competence and the masculine grace.

Seeing her, he called, 'Like it? He'll be able to use it before you know it.'

'It's time for his bath.' She walked out and picked up the baby. 'Oh, my, wet through. You do need a bath.'

The boy laughed and caught hold of her hair. Robert gave them a look of such intensity that she had to ask curiously, 'What is it?'

'You. Both of you together. Your lovely, tranquil spirit. I don't deserve you.'

She did not want her heart to be touched or moved. She wanted just peace, calm and practical and friendly.

'Dinner will be heating while I bathe Bobby. Then I have Annie's scout meeting tonight. It's for mothers and daughters, so will you put him to bed?'

'Of course I will.'

'Come see when you're finished there,' she called back from the kitchen door. 'I've brought Bruce's cat.'

Then she closed the door and carried Bobby upstairs. *I worry about you,' Bruce had said, with the implication that she was somehow in peril. But it was not so, for she was going to be in control. I can run this house and this family like clockwork, she told herself, holding her child. I can keep a happy order here, and I can cope with anything.*

She was strong, and she was proud.

* * *

A few days later she went to New York for the pre-Christmas sales. Now that their financial future was uncertain, she had to shop with a particular care, to which for a long time she had been unaccustomed. Hurrying homeward past Salvation Army Santa Clauses and shop windows festooned with glass balls and tinsel arabesques, she worried whether the coat and skirts would fit Annie properly.

But there was something else on her mind, something that, because of her preoccupation with Josie's death and Robert's depression, she had locked away in the dark. However, it did not accept the darkness, but struggled out again and again, as if to force her to examine it.

There was something odd about Aunt Jean's connection to Querida. Or there would be, provided that Emily's report was correct. Or provided that the name over the shop's door belonged to *the* Querida – which it might well not, she thought now, summoning common sense and probabilities.

She was passing through the neighborhood, and it gave her immediate recall, such as follows a chord, a flavor, or a scent; it brought back the day when events had crashed upon each other like cars on a foggy highway; there had been Robert's attack in the kitchen, her flight into Bruce's arms, and Emily's sorrowful leavetaking. And it seemed to her that all these were somehow linked in ways that she could not fathom, that these things had their origin in one place, one time.

I have to know, she thought, as she came to the street, to the shop, and, with a thumping of the heart like a pounding on a door, stood there looking in the window.

A row of dog paintings was on display. They were all the fashion these days; the English-country-house look was the right look, casual elegance among rural acres for the homes of people who had never owned either an acre or a dog and possibly would never want to, she thought, surveying the haughty pugs, Queen Victoria's favorites, and the sporting setters, flaunting their proud tails. But there among them hung an unfamiliar creature, a strange beast, looking so much like Juliet that it could have been Juliet.

Abruptly her feet made the decision to enter and she found herself inside.

A small, dark woman limped across the room and took Juliet out of the window.

'It's not old,' she said in reply to Lynn's query. 'I've put it with the old ones because it has a nineteenth-century look. Actually, it's the work of a man who simply likes to paint dogs, any kind.'

'It's charming.'

The dog, sitting on a doorstep, had the same alert, faintly concerned expression that Juliet wore whenever the family drove away without her.

'Yes, I see by your face how much you like it,' the woman said.

'It's the image of our dog.'

Lynn's heart was pounding, and while she was seeing the painting, she was also seeing the woman. Had Robert not spoken about 'a job in a gallery,' and 'a dabbler'? Still, his 'beauty' could certainly not be this person, whose angular face with its flat black eyes was topped by a dome of coarse black hair. Relief and disappointment met and mingled. In one way she 'had to know', she wanted to behold the woman who had first occupied her place; but in another way there was dread.

She returned to the picture. It would be a fine surprise for Robert, something to enliven him. They might hang it in his den at home or better still in his office. For an instant she forgot that at present he did not have an office.

'It's not expensive. The price is on the tag.'

The price was most fair. Since the painting was small

336

enough, she could carry it home right now. And she handed over her credit card.

The woman looked hard at the card and slowly turned her eyes up toward Lynn.

'Robert V. W. Ferguson. So now you've come too,' she said. 'I was wondering whether you would.'

Lynn's knees went so weak that she had to perch on the stool that stood beside the counter, and she stammered. 'I don't understand.'

'Your daughter Emily was here a while back, the day after Thanksgiving.'

Emily in New York? But Emily was in New Orleans! We talked on the phone on Thanksgiving day. She must have flown in to see this woman, and gone back to college without telling us . . .

The woman was staring at Lynn in open curiosity.

'She had a lot of questions, but I didn't answer them. She's too young, sweet and young. Besides, it's up to you to tell her whatever you want her to know.'

Lynn's voice came in a whisper. 'I know nothing.'

'Nothing?'

'Not much. Only that you didn't get along.'

'Didn't get along! There's a bit more to it than that, you can be sure.'

The black eyes bored into Lynn. 'You're a pretty woman. He liked blondes, I remember.'

Lynn was in panic. She had come here wanting to find out – what? To find out something about Robert that other people – Aunt Jean – knew and had kept hidden. And now that she was here she was in panic.

'He must have told you something about me.'

'That there was a child, a boy,' Lynn whispered again.

'Yes. He's a man now, living in England. He's had a good life: I saw to that. And you? Do you have other children?'

'Another girl, and a boy ten months old.'

337

'A nice family.'

The air in the confined and cluttered space held bad vibrations; there was an impending intimacy from which Lynn now shrank. What she must do was to stand up and leave the place, picture and all. But she was unable to move.

Querida's eyes roved over her, coming to rest on the fur coat and the fine leather bag. 'I see that he has accomplished what he wanted to.'

And Lynn, mesmerized, submitted to inspection. The brusque remark, that could have been offensive, was somehow not. It was merely odd. Whatever could Robert have seen in this woman? Two more ill-matched people one could hardly imagine.

As if she had read Lynn's mind, Querida said, 'I don't know how we ever got mixed up. It was just one of those things, I guess. He was brilliant, won all the scholarships, and God knows he was good looking. I was Phi Beta Kappa, and I suppose he was impressed by that. I was no beauty, although somewhat better looking than I am now, that's for sure. We were together only three or four times and I got pregnant. I didn't want an abortion, and I'll say this much for him, he did the right thing for those days, anyway. He married me.'

Had she no inhibitions? Why was she telling these things to a person who had not asked to hear them?

'We were dirt poor, both of us. Hadn't anything, never had had anything.'

Poor? The trips to Europe and Querida's prominent family? What of them?

'Why do you look surprised? Are you surprised?'

'Yes,' Lynn murmured.

'I suppose he told you I was beautiful. He always liked to tell me about his former lovers, how exceptional they were. And I suppose he drew you a picture of his distinguished patrician background. Poor Robert. He did it so often that he really believed it. Anyway, by your time they were dead, so what difference? But I knew. I knew the mother with the doilies and the tea wagon. The genteel poor. Pretense, all pretense. She was pathetic, a decent little woman, half the size of her husband, and helpless under his fists.'

'I don't want to hear this!' cried Lynn, shuddering.

'But maybe you should.'

You could feel the anger burning in this queer woman, as if her very skin would be hot to the touch. She was eccentric, neurotic, or even perhaps a trifle mad . . . And still you had to listen.

'Jean worries about you. Oh, yes, she's kept in touch with me over the years. She's a good soul, like her sister, and she's never been sure about you and Robert.'

This was too much, this infringement of the decent privacy that Lynn had guarded all her life.

'People have no right –' she blurted, but the other, ignoring her indignation, continued.

'Do you know how Robert's mother died? They were in their car on the turnpike, the two of them. A man at a tollbooth notified the police when he saw what was wrong, but by the time the police caught up with them it was too late. She had been trying to jump out of the moving car, away from him. The people in the car behind had seen it. The car swerved and hit a tree. They were both killed. Good for him, and none too soon. And those,' Querida said, 'are the distinguished Fergusons.'

Oh, the horror! And the woman would not stop the gush of words. Perhaps she could not.

'Do you see this leg? My hip was broken. Yes, the story repeats itself, although not all the way, because I knew enough to get free. Yes, Robert did this to me.'

Now Lynn recognized that she herself was in a state of physical shock; her mouth went dry, her palms wet, and her heart was audibly drumming in her ears. She sat quite still, not having moved from the support of the counter at her back, sat and stared as the nervous voice resumed.

'It wasn't the first time, although it was the worst. We were ice skating. He asked me what there was for dinner, and I said we'd pick up some fast food on the way home. I wasn't a good housekeeper. I'm still not, and that infuriated him. But he infuriated me with his compulsive ways, so neat, so prompt, so goddamn perfect. So he went absolutely mad about the dinner. A thing like that could trigger him.'

Lynn's dry lips formed a statement: *I told you I don't want to hear any more*. Yet no sound came out.

'It was almost dark, and we were the last ones on the lake. So he slapped my face, and his gloves had buckles on the wrists. He shoved me, and I fell on the ice. He kicked me, and I couldn't get up. Then he was scared, and he ran to a public phone to call an ambulance. When they came, I was almost fainting with the pain. I heard him say, "She fell."'

If she would just stop and let me get out of here, Lynn thought, and then rebuked herself: You know you have to stay to the end, to hear it all.

'A neighbor woman cared for the baby while I was in the hospital. When he came and started talking about the 'accident,' I told him I never wanted to see him again. So I took my child and left. I had a friend in Florida who gave me a job, and I let him get the divorce on the grounds of desertion. I didn't care, I wanted no part of him. I said if he ever came near me or the child, I would expose him and ruin him forever.' Again there came that forced, grim laugh. 'I must say he has supported the boy generously – not me, because I wouldn't take a penny of his anyway. Now my son is twenty-four and independent.

'My hip wasn't set right. They tell me it should be broken again and reset. But I don't want to go through

340

all that. I keep it this way as a remembrance of Robert.'

Why was she revealing this terrible story after all these years? It was to take revenge for her suffering. It was to destroy Robert's marriage, especially if it should be a good one.

'And do you think it does any good to go to the police? Do you? Well, I'll tell you. It doesn't. I went once. They didn't even take me seriously. I came in a nice car. We both had jobs then, and we had pooled our money for it. We had a neat apartment in a decent neighborhood. 'What are you complaining about?' they asked me. 'The guy can't be all bad. You should see the things we see. Straighten it out. Don't make him angry. Of course, if you want to swear out a complaint, we can arrest him and make a big stink. Then maybe he'll lose his job, and where'll you be? Nah, think it over. You women don't know when you're well off.' That's what they told me. I see I've upset you.'

'What did you expect?' Lynn's pity and horror collided. Her head reeled, and her voice filled with tears. 'You had no right to dump all this stuff on me. I came in to buy a picture, and –'

The other woman's tight face softened. 'I suppose I shouldn't have talked,' she said. 'I shouldn't be involved in this at all. But when your daughter came I suspected – never mind. Do you still want the picture? I'll let you have it for nothing. My way of apologizing.'

Lynn slid off the stool. 'Yes, I want it. And I want to pay for it.'

'As you wish. I'll wrap it.'

Although her heart was still pounding, she was beginning to recover and take command of herself. With a show of casual dignity she walked around the walls as if to examine the paintings hung there, yet, in her agitation, scarcely seeing them at all.

After a moment the voice pursued her. 'You don't believe me.'

Lynn turned and went back to the counter. 'Whether I do or not,' she said quietly, 'doesn't matter. Just give me the picture, please, so I can go.'

In the silence, now throbbing with the words that had been spoken there, she waited while the package was being wrapped. Querida's fingers delicately handled paper, cardboard, and twine; she had oval nails and a strong profile as she bent over the work. An intelligent face, thought Lynn.

The silence broke abruptly. 'He made her life a hell. I'm talking about Robert's father and mother. Her people hated him. They begged her to leave him, but she wouldn't. A little bit proud, a little too ashamed. I know. I've seen them, the soft ones who listen to the sweet apology and believe it won't happen again. You, too, I'm thinking.'

Now words came, choking in Lynn's throat. 'You don't know anything about me!'

'But I do. I know that lovely girl of yours wouldn't have sought me out unless she had a great trouble on her mind. She knows plenty, but she wants to know more. I saw. Pull yourself together, my dear; take care of yourself and your children. I know you think I'm queer and maybe I am, but I mean well.'

The door slammed and cold air struck Lynn's face. A blast of wind from Canada rounded the stone corner and almost knocked her over as she ran toward Grand Central. Her legs barely held her.

The soft ones – the sweet apology . . .

A strange woman, with those wild eyes. How they must have hated each other! Not like Robert and me because we – in spite of all, we –

But he lied to me. All those lies. And yet she – is everything she said true?

342

Faintly dizzy, she struggled through the wind and the crowds. Within the vast cavern of the terminal 'Good King Wenceslaus' reverberated heartily. People returning to their suburban homes were normal; there was reassurance in the cheerful sound of greetings; a fat man clapped another on the back and two matrons squealed with delight at seeing one another. These were common, everyday noises. These were ordinary, everyday people.

The train clicked over the tracks. It's true, it's not, it's true, it's not, said the wheels. This had been the worst day ... Lynn laid her head back against the seat. And the woman next to her, young and fashionable with no troubles on her face, asked anxiously, 'Are you not feeling well?'

'It's only a headache, thank you. I'm all right.' Embarrassed, Lynn smiled.

The car was parked at the station. When she got in and drove through the town, which looked the same as it had that morning, it seemed astonishing that everything should be the same. Station wagons were parked in the supermarket lot, the yellow school buses were returning to the garage, and the windows were prepared here, too, for the holiday as if nothing of any importance had happened since the morning.

It seemed too early to go home. Actually, it was early, for she had wanted to make another stop in the city on the way to the train. But after what had happened, she had needed only to rush away. So she stopped the car at a dingy luncheonette on the fringe of the center and sat down to order a pot of tea with a bun. Tea was soothing.

He kicked me while I lay on the ice with my hip broken. Now, that, that's hard to believe. Yes, he had bursts of rotten temper – how well I know! But sadism like that, never. No, that's hard to accept. Out of a kernel of truth, a large kernel, she has developed this sickly growth, this enormous exaggeration.

She's odd, filled with rage and, in some way that I can't diagnose, disturbed. But if she were more, let's say for want of more accurate words, more reasonable, temperate, sweeter, *acceptable*, then would I be more apt to believe her?

Yet even if only some of it is true, how terrible and sad it is that he has needed to conceal it all these years! Why, when I would have tried to help him? Didn't he know that I would have tried?

But weigh the sin of his concealment against all our years together, all the good, all the good ...

The warm cup, held between Lynn's hands, brought remembrance of her parents, sitting at the kitchen table on other winter afternoons. They had used to hold their cups just so, and the cups had had daisies around the rims. It had been a simple time ... Her eyes flooded, and she thrust the tea away.

Someone put money in a jukebox left over, probably, from the fifties, and canned voices, moaning over love lost or remembered or found, swelled out into the gray, depressing room. Lynn got up and paid her bill. It was time to pull herself together and go home. It was time, Josie would say, to face reality. Go home and, making no fuss, ask him what you want to know, and tell him what you have found out.

Robert had put a candle bulb in each window, so that the house appeared to float through the early darkness like a ship with lighted portholes. Through the bow window, where the curtains were still open, she could see him sitting in his big leather chair with Bobby on one knee; they were looking at a book spread on the other knee.

The little boy adored the man: His dark blue eyes were rounder than Emily's and Robert's; they were round like his dear head and his little fat hands. She felt a twinge of pain, like a tender wound, a soft something that was both merciful and sorrowful. For a moment she was almost within their skins, that of the vulnerable baby, and that of the man who perhaps had once known such grievous hurt that he was unable to admit its existence.

Opening the door, she heard Annie practicing her piano lesson at the other end of the hall, and she paused a moment to listen. Annie was really doing better, doing better at everything. It might be that the new quietness in Robert, the slowing of the house's rhythm, had affected the child too. It was a strange irony that the father's most cruel defeat should have brought about a subtle kind of peace that had not been there before, whose absence she had not even been aware of until it occurred.

The dog jumped to announce her presence and Robert looked up in surprise.

'Hello! We didn't hear you come in.'

'I've been watching you. You're so cozy, you two.'

'We're halfway through Mother Goose, up to Little Jack Horner.' He got up, set the baby in the playpen, and kissed Lynn. 'You've been shopping, I see. Did you buy anything nice?'

'I hope you'll think so. It's your Christmas present.'

'Didn't we promise each other just books this year? And now you've gone and broken your promise,' he said with a rueful smile.

'This wasn't horribly expensive, honestly. It's a picture. Open it.'

'Why not wait till Christmas?'

'Because I don't want to wait.'

Bobby, attracted by the crackle of paper as Robert cut the string, stretched out his arms as if he could reach the bright redness and the crackle. And something caught again in Lynn's chest, in her heart and throat, at the sight of the merry child and the father's dark head bent over the package.

Surely this family's path would straighten and all the past evil be forgotten! This was only a sharp turning in the path, a crooked obstacle to be got over, and she would get over it. There was so much else to be thankful for; no one had cancer, no one was blind...

'Wherever did you find this?' Robert cried. 'It's Juliet to the life. Fantastic!'

'I thought you would love it.'

'It's wonderful. Dog portraits are always the same, spaniels or hounds or faithful collies. Thanks a million, Lynn.'

'You'll never believe where I found it. Quite by accident, I saw it in a window on the way to the train, in a tiny gallery called "Querida."'

Robert's face changed. As if a hand had passed over it, the eyes' lively shine, the smile crinkles at their corners, the smile pouches of the cheeks, and the happy lift of the lips were wiped away. And she saw that he was waiting for the words that would come next, saw that, quite understandably, she had stunned him.

'The odd thing is that it really was she. I couldn't believe it. It was when I showed the American Express card and she recognized the name.'

Say nothing about Emily having been there. Be careful. Nothing.

'Very interesting.' He clipped the words like a stage Englishman. 'Interesting, too, that you didn't turn right around and walk out.'

'But I wanted the painting,' she protested, and was aware, even as she spoke them, that the words were too innocent. Then she added, 'Besides, it would have been awkward just to turn on my heel and leave.'

'Oh, awkward, of course. Much easier to stay and have a cozy chat with the lady.'

Robert's eyes narrowed, and he straightened his posture. As always, it seemed that he grew taller when he was angry. And in dismay she knew that he was very, very angry.

This was not what she had expected; perhaps she'd been foolish to think he would defend himself. Instead he was on the attack.

'There was no chat. I was only there for the time it took to pay and have this wrapped. It was only a minute. A couple of minutes,' she said, stumbling over the defense.

'So you didn't open your mouths, either of you.' He nodded. 'After that astonishing revelation there was total silence, I'm sure.'

'Well, not exactly.'

'I suppose you got quite an earful about me.'

It was he who was to have been on the defensive, he who was to have been scared. How had the tables been turned like this? And she murmured, almost coaxing now, 'Why no, Robert, not at all.'

'I don't believe it. Your curiosity would have kept you listening, with your ears open and your mouth hanging open, while your husband was smeared with filth. Don't tell me not, Lynn, because I know better.' He was trembling. 'Talk about loyalty! If you had any, you wouldn't have entered there in the first place.'

'How would I know? How could I have known?'

'You knew damn well that that – creature – played around with art and worked in a gallery. You didn't forget that, Lynn. And the name – you didn't forget that either. You could have thought, when you saw that name – it wasn't Susan, it wasn't Mary; do you see it on every street corner? You could have thought, Well, maybe it's possible, I won't take a chance. But your curiosity got the better of you, didn't it?'

The iota of accuracy in what he said brought a flush of heat that ran up her neck and scorched her cheeks.

'Well, didn't it?'

His voice rose and filled the room so that Bobby, hearing the unfamiliar tone, turned a puzzled face to his father.

Now Lynn had to go over to the attack. 'You're impossible! How can you have so little understanding, when my only thought was to bring you something that might make you a little bit happy in these hard days? And I did cut her short. I didn't want to hear anything, so I walked out when she –'

'You cut her short? But you just told me nothing was said. You'd better get your story straight.'

'You get me all mixed up. You tie my tongue. When you're like this, I can't even think straight. I get so muddled, I don't know what I'm saying.'

'You're muddled, all right. Now, listen to me – I want to know exactly what was said, and you had better tell me exactly.'

Like a whip he sprang and grasped her arms at the place where he had always grasped before, in the soft flesh above the elbow. His hard fingers pressed his thumbs against the very bone.

In the playpen the baby now pulled himself up and stood swaying against the railing. His wide eyes stared at them.

'Let go,' Lynn said, keeping her voice low for Bobby's sake.

'I want an answer, I said.'

The pain was horrible, but she still spoke evenly. 'Keep your voice down, Robert. The baby's terrified. And do you want Annie to hear this too?'

'I want to know what that crazy woman said, that's what I want. Answer me!'

He shook her. There was a fierceness in his expression that she had never seen there before, something desperate and grim, something fanatical. And, more frightened than she had ever been, she began to cry.

'Ah, the tear machine. Don't answer a simple question. Just turn on the tear machine.'

He shook her so violently that her neck jerked.

'Robert, let go! I'll have to scream, and everybody will know. This is insane. Look at the baby!'

Bobby's wet pink mouth hung open and his round cheeks were puckering toward tears. 'Look what you're doing to the baby!'

'Then talk.'

'All you do is find fault with me! I can't stand it!'

In a nasal whine he mocked her. 'All I do is find fault with you. You can't stand it.'

The baby rattled the playpen, fell on his back, and wailed. And Lynn, frantic now with fright and pain and concern over Bobby, screamed out, 'Let go of me, Robert! Damn you –'

'Talk, and I will.'

There was a tumult within her, the desperation of a captive who has been wrongly accused, a victim of terror. And this desperation exploded.

'All right, I'll talk! Enough of lies! Let the truth blare! Why have you hidden yourself from me all these years? I had thought to talk to you in a civil way and ask you why you never trusted me enough to be open with me. Why did you hide what your father did to your mother? Oh, I see now why Aunt Jean was never welcome! It's you! You didn't want her around for fear she would say too much. And why? Did you think so little of me as to believe I wouldn't understand about your family? Did you think so little of yourself that you had to invent a family? Why do you feel that you have to be without flaw, descended from saints or something?'

She saw the pulses throbbing in his temples, where suddenly on each a crooked blue vein had swelled. And now that she had begun, now that the pressure of Robert's

349

hands was unbearable, she, too, screamed, not caring or able to care who heard.

'Why did you tell me Querida was beautiful and rich? To make me jealous? Why didn't you tell me about her broken hip? Why have you lived with all these lies, so that I've had to live with them too? Now I see, I see it all. My life, my whole life . . . What's the matter with you? What have you done?'

Her words tumbled and raced and would not cease.

'A sham, a cover-up, all the excuses I made because I wanted not to admit anything. I needed to keep the dream. She told me everything you did to her, Robert, everything. She said –'

He let her go. He picked up the painting, raised it high, and brought it down hard, splintering the frame and ripping the canvas from top to bottom over the back of a chair. The baby screamed; in a distant room the piano sounded a smashing discord and stopped. The vandalism was atrocious. He was panting like an animal.

'You disgust me!' she cried. 'People should know this, should see what you can do! Yes, you disgust me.'

He struck her. A violent blow landed on her neck, and she fell back, crashing into the playpen. When she picked herself up, he struck her again, grazing her eye as she turned, gasped, and tried to flee. With his left hand he seized her collar; his right fist smashed her nose so hard that the crack was audible, as bone met bone. Blood gushed; she reached for support, but there was only empty air. The room slowly circled and tilted around her as she fell, and was still.

She had fallen or been laid upon the sofa. Vomit and blood had smeared her white silk shirt, and for some reason that later she was to find incredible, this damage to the shirt was the first thing she saw. It was a terrible humiliation. She heard herself wail, 'Oh, look!' She sobbed. In a confusion of sound and sight she seemed to see Eudora clutching Robert's coat and screaming at him, 'What the hell have you done?' At the same time she seemed to see Eudora holding Bobby on one arm while Annie, somewhere at her side, was crying.

Next came the pain in a wave of fire, so that, as if to cool it, she pressed her hands to her face, then drew them away in revulsion over her own sticky blood.

The room was filled with a swelling crowd of many people, many voices making a vast, low roar. But after a while she knew that the roar was only in her head. When she opened her eyes again, she began to distinguish among the faces. Eudora was still holding Bobby. Annie was at the foot of the sofa. Somebody was wiping her face with a cold towel; the hands were gentle and very careful. She focused her eyes. The room had stopped circling, and things had righted themselves so that she began to see quite clearly. It was Bruce who stood over her holding the towel.

'What are you doing here?' she whispered.

'Annie called me.' He took his glasses off and wiped them. His eyes were moist, as though they might have held tears; yet at the same time they were fierce. His mouth, his full-lipped, easy mouth, was a hard line. 'You fainted,' he said.

Annie knelt and laid her face on Lynn's shoulder, whimpering, 'Mommy. Oh, Mommy.'

'Careful, dear. Her face is sore,' said Bruce.

Now came Robert's voice. 'I've got the ice bag. Move away a little, Annie.'

'Don't you touch her,' Bruce commanded. 'The ice bag can wait a minute.'

'I have a first-aid certificate,' protested Robert.

'You know what you can do with your goddamn certificate! She'll see a doctor after she's pulled herself together. You keep away from her, hear?'

Now Robert moved into view, his eyes and his voice making joint appeal.

'Oh, God, Lynn, I don't know how to say what I feel. I never intended ... But things just got out of hand ... We were both angry...'

Bruce shouted, 'Oh, why don't you shut up!'

'Yes, why don't you?' Annie repeated. Her head was buried in her mother's shoulder while her mother's arm held her.

'Annie dear,' Bruce said, 'your mother will be happier, I think, if you go upstairs. I know this is awfully hard for you, but if you'll just try to be a little patient, we'll talk about it in the morning, I promise.'

Robert coaxed. 'Don't worry about Mom. It looks worse than it is. I'll see that she's taken care of. Do go up, darling.'

When he moved toward her, as if to take her away from the sofa, Annie scrambled up out of his reach and, with her hands on her chubby hips and her eyes streaming tears, defied him.

'I'm not your darling. You're an awful father, and Susan was right. You do hit Mom. I saw you just now, I saw you. And, and – I never told anybody, but sometimes I have a dream about you, and I hate it because it wakes me up and I feel so bad, and I tell myself it's only a dream, but now, now,' she sputtered, 'look what you did! It's as horrible as the dream!'

'What dream, Annie? Can you remember it?' asked Bruce.

'Oh, yes. I see Mom in a long white dress, wearing a crown on her head and he – he is hitting her.'

This blow, this other kind of blow, struck Lynn again between the eyes. And it had struck Robert hard, too, for, dazed as she was, she was able to see how clearly he was recalling that night of the New Year's Eve costume party, so long ago. Annie had been no more than three...

And she gave Robert a terrible look. She wanted to say, So, this explains a good deal about Annie, doesn't it?

But instead she whispered, summoning the top of her strength, 'You're *my* darling. So will you do something for me and go up with Eudora? Tomorrow I'll tell you about the dream, about everything.'

'Come, Annie,' said Eudora, 'come up and help give Bobby his bottle. I'm going to sleep on a cot in your room with you. I'm staying here tonight.'

Annie raised her head, and Lynn, too miserable to speak, gave the child a look of appeal.

'Juliet has to sleep in my room too.'

'Of course she will,' said Eudora.

And the little group shuffled out, the woman holding the baby and the girl, for comfort, holding on to the dog.

And we were sure, thought Lynn, silent in bitter grief, that we had kept the children from knowing.

The doorbell rang just as Eudora started up the stairs.

'That's Tom Lawrence,' Bruce said. 'I called him.'

'What? He has no business here. Don't open the door, Eudora,' commanded Robert.

Bruce countermanded the order. 'Yes, please open it, Eudora. I'd do it myself, only I don't want to step away from Mrs Ferguson.'

'What in blazes –' said Tom. Stunned, he stood in the doorway and stared at the scene. 'What in blazes –'

He walked over and looked down at Lynn, grimaced, shut his eyes for an instant from the sight, and turned to Robert.

'So, you bastard, it's finally happened. It took a while coming, but I knew it would. You ought to be strung up.'

'You don't know what you're talking about! We had some upset here, an argument, and I only meant –'

The words diminished and faded. As shocked and foggy as Lynn's brain was then, still there came a lucid thought: He is considering that Tom is a lawyer, and he's scared.

'You 'only' nothing, Ferguson.' Tom walked toward Robert, who drew back. It was strange to see him drawing back from a man whose head barely reached past his shoulder. 'I'm calling the police.'

Lynn struggled up against the pillows. Her eye throbbed. When her tongue touched her front teeth, one moved. She tried again. Definitely, it had been loosened. And she spoke through swollen lips.

'No. No police. Please, Tom.' She wanted him to understand that Annie had already seen horror enough. 'All I want is for – him,' she said, motioning toward Robert, 'for him to get out.' She lay back again. 'I'm so dizzy.'

'Ah, you see? Even Lynn doesn't want the police,' said Robert.

'I'd like to overrule you, Lynn,' Tom said gravely. 'This is a public matter now. A man can't be allowed to get away with this kind of thing.'

'Stay out of it, Lawrence,' Robert said. 'Nobody invited you here.'

Bruce jumped to the attack. 'I invited him. Lynn needs friends, and she needs legal advice, which I can't give.'

'My advice again is to call the police,' Tom urged. 'They need only to take one look at her, and it'll be worth a thousand words for future use.'

Robert pounced. 'Future use?'

'It would be in the newspapers,' Lynn murmured. 'My children have been hurt badly enough without that too.'

'You're not thinking,' Bruce said quietly. 'Everyone knows about it, anyway. In the office now –'

At that Robert shouted out. 'In the office? Yes, yes, do you think I don't know about the lies you've spread? You wanted to tear me down, you wanted to take my place.'

Bruce pointed to Lynn. 'Lies? Look at your wife's face. If I had talked, and I never did, which you know quite well, there would have been no lies. No. Robert, if I had ever wanted to talk, I could have done it long ago, that morning in Chicago, or maybe even before that, and you would never have gotten as far as New York. Let alone Europe,' he shouted. His rage and contempt had set him on fire. 'You aren't fit to live, after what you've done here tonight. You ought to be taken out and shot.'

I'm not here, Lynn was saying to herself. All this has nothing to do with me. It's not happening to me.

Tom took her hand, which was cold, as one chill after another began to shake her.

'What do you want us to do, Lynn? Tell us. There's no point in arguing who said or did not say what. You're too exhausted.'

She answered him softly, as if she feared Robert's wrath if he should overhear. 'Just make him go. I don't want to see him ever, ever, ever.'

But Robert had heard. 'You don't mean that, Lynn,' he cried. 'You know you don't.'

Tom gave an order. He was a small, active terrier badgering a Great Dane. 'You heard what she said. Go! Get your coat and get out.'

Robert, clasping his hands, beseeched her. 'Lynn, hear me. These people, these strangers, are egging you on. I'll spend the rest of my days making up to you for this, I swear I will. And telling me to go is no solution. These people – it's no business of theirs.'

'Tom and Bruce, whom you call "these people," are my friends,' she answered, finding voice. 'I wanted them here. I need them. And I want you to go. It's I who want it. I.'

He beat his clenched hands on his breast. 'You and I have lived a life together. Can any third person know what we have had, you and I? The things that have been between us? I'll change. I'll go anywhere you want, talk to anyone you want, take any counsel. I promise, I swear.'

'Too late,' she cried. 'Too late.'

'I beg you, Lynn.'

His shame and his agony were contagious; absurd as it was, as her intelligence told her it was, he could still elicit pity. It was odd that when he was angry, he could seem so tall; now between the other two men, pleading, he shrank.

Bruce held out his hand, commanding, 'Give me your house keys, Robert. Does he have duplicates?' he asked Lynn.

Still overcome with the shame of this, she told him, 'In the drawer of the table behind you.'

'I'll take them.' Bruce put them in his pocket. 'I'll throw them out when I get home. You'll change your locks tomorrow. Now get out of here, Robert. Now. This minute.'

'You may come back tomorrow morning at nine o'clock for your clothes,' Tom said. 'But you heard Bruce, so go, and hurry up about it. Lynn needs rest and attention.'

'I want to hear that from Lynn,' Robert answered.

His face had gone gray. She thought: He knows I pity him, even now. But I am not wavering. If I had any tendency to do it, and I do not, the thought of Annie alone would stop me.

And drawing herself upright, she said sternly, 'I will tell you, Robert. Leave now, or weak as I am, I shall take Annie and Bobby and sit at the airport until the first plane leaves for my sister's in St Louis, and you'll have the damned house to yourself.'

Tom cried, 'Oh, no! This house is yours as much as his. You'll stay in it until your lawyer says you may leave it. I'm getting a fine Connecticut lawyer for you tomorrow. And you had better get going, Ferguson,' he threatened. 'Otherwise, no matter what Lynn says, I'll have the police here in ten minutes.'

The two men stood side by side in front of Robert. He looked them up and down, then looked at Lynn for so long that she had to shut her eyes. His face was like that of a man who has come upon a ghastly slaughter and is helpless. She supposed that her expression might be the same. Then he turned on his heel and went rapidly from the house.

The door closed. There was the sound of wheels on the gravel drive, and then nothing.

The two men took charge. First came a doctor, a friend of Tom's who, in a situation like this one, was willing to make a house call.

Bruce explained. 'Mrs Ferguson doesn't want to press charges, and if she goes to the hospital –'

The doctor understood. 'There would be questions. As long as there's no damage to the retina, I think we'll be able to manage here at home.' Plainly shocked, he bent over Lynn and flashed a light into her eye. 'No, there's not. You're lucky. It almost –' And he shook his head.

When he had gone, Tom and Bruce made decisions for the morning. New door locks must be installed. Appointments with a dentist and an attorney must immediately be made. Bruce would talk to Annie and assess the damage to her.

'I'm staying all night,' he said. 'I can stretch out on the sofa in the den.'

He would certainly not stretch out on this one. Lynn's blood had ruined the moss-green damask, ruined it forever. And Robert had always worried about their guests' palms on the armrests.

'Your flight's tomorrow night. You need some sleep,' she protested.

'It doesn't matter. There's no sleep in me now, anyhow. I'll make up for it on the plane.'

357

Until long past midnight they talked. Bruce wanted to know what had led to such horror, and she told him everything, starting with the painting, which still, in its innocence, lay wrecked on the floor.

His comment, when she had finished, was thoughtful and sorrowful. 'He was afraid that, after what you had heard, you would leave him. He was terrified. Don't you see?'

'I see that he went into an insane rage. It was unimaginable,' she said, shivering again. 'He could have killed me.'

Bruce said grimly, 'He might well have if Eudora hadn't been here.'

'Such rage! I can't comprehend such rage.'

Bruce shook his head. 'You have to look deeper. Robert has always been filled with fear. He's one of the most fearful people I've ever known.'

'Robert?'

'Oh, yes. He doesn't think much of himself. That's why he has always had to be the dominant one.'

She thought. Doesn't think much of himself? But it was I who looked to him! I who always felt, so secretly that I could hardly acknowledge it even to myself except in a pensive moment now and then, that I was never quite good enough, neither accomplished nor beautiful enough for him.

'Have you just thought of this now, Bruce? Tell me.'

'No, it was clear a long time ago, almost at the beginning.'

She raised her swollen, tired eyes to Bruce and asked him quietly, 'So that's what you saw in Robert. What did you see in me?'

'That you were always too terribly anxious to please. That you deferred to him. It was plain to see, if one looked only a little beneath the surface.'

'And you looked.'

'No, strictly speaking it was Josie who looked and saw.

I learned from her. I learned a great many things from Josie.'

'Did she think it would ever come to what happened here tonight?'

'We both feared it very much, Lynn.'

'And yet you must have seen so many of our happy times, our good times.'

Lamplight struck her ring when she moved her hand, so that the diamond came to life; absently, nervously, she twirled it around and around her finger, playing, as was her habit, with needles and sparks of light. Good times and undercurrents ... Annie playing duets with Robert and Annie having nightmares, concealing her nightmares ...

'What is to become of Annie?' she asked, lifting her eyes from the ring. 'I am so afraid, so worried about her.'

'I think now you really must take her for counseling. I have always thought so, anyway. You know that.'

'Yes, but will you talk to her too?'

'In the morning, I told you.'

'We shall all miss you so, Bruce.'

'I'll miss you too.' And in a familiar gesture he pushed his glasses up into his hair. 'But I'm ready to go, Lynn. I couldn't even wait to get the furniture out of the house. The chairs she sat in, the address book in her handwriting, everything – I can't look at the things.'

It would be years before he got over Josie, if ever. But I, too, Lynn thought, in my very different way I, too, face loss. I am opening a door and stepping into darkness, to a flight of stairs and a fall into darkness.

'I have lost my courage,' she said suddenly. 'This morning I still had it, and now it's gone.'

'And no wonder. But you haven't really lost it. You've been under attack. Your good mind will recover and pull you through. I know it will.' He stood up. 'Go on to bed, Lynn. It's late. Do you need help up the stairs?'

'Thanks, I'll manage.' Stretching her sore cheeks, she tried to smile. 'I must look awful. I'm afraid to look in the mirror.'

'Well, you certainly don't look your best. But you'll mend. By the way, you should sleep in some other room, in Emily's. He'll be coming for his clothes, and they're probably in your room, aren't they? I want to keep him out of your way. And, oh, yes, you should take a sleeping pill. Are there any in the house?'

'Robert kept them for the times when he felt keyed up. But I've never taken one.'

'Well, take one tonight.'

Painfully, she pulled herself upstairs and got into bed. It crossed her mind, as some hours later she fell into the mercy of sleep, that she had quite forgotten to be ashamed before Bruce.

A stream of sunlight had already crossed the room at a noontime angle when Lynn awoke. Groggy and unwashed, she had fallen into bed, and now, still groggy and unwashed, she got up to go to the mirror.

The sight stunned her. She could hardly bear to look, and yet she had to keep on looking. That a human being could do this to another human face! One's identity, one's face that is like no other among all the billions on the earth! This violation of the most intimate property – it's rape in a dark alley, it's a sleeping household entered through a broken window, it's a freight car filled with half-crazed refugees, a prisoner led to a torture cell, it's every hideous thing that men do to one another.

She sobbed: Oh, my life ... I wanted to make everything so beautiful for all of us. I did. I tried. I did ...

And then, a terrible fury took over. If he had been in the room and she had had a knife, she would have plunged it into his heart. Thank God, then, that he wasn't there, for

360

she must preserve herself, get well, and be strong. She had brought three dependent lives into the world. *She* had. Not *he*. She, alone now. He had forfeited those lives, whether he knew it or not, had given them up forever. And Lynn gritted her teeth on that.

Then she ran the shower. Gingerly she cleansed her swollen, livid face of the blood that had dried black around her lips and nostrils. Carefully she pried open the eye that was half shut and bathed it. Then she powdered herself all over, put on scent, and fastidiously cleaned her nails. Let the body, at least, be presentable, even if the face was not. This was a question of self-respect.

When she came out into the bedroom, Eudora was straightening the bed. Most tactfully, she did not focus upon Lynn, but reported instead the events of the household.

'Mr Lehman said to tell you good-bye. He had a long talk with Annie before he left, I didn't hear it, but Annie was willing to go to school, I didn't think she would be, but she was, and he drove her himself. Mr Lawrence phoned, the doctor's coming again this afternoon, unless you need him sooner, then Mr Lawrence will send a cab to take you to the office. Bobby's fine, he's already had his lunch, and I put him down for his nap. And Emily's on the way, she phoned from the airport, Annie called her last night, I couldn't stop her. So I guess that's about all.'

'Oh, dear. She's in the middle of exams.'

'Well, they'll wait. You're her mother,' Eudora said firmly.

The house trembled when Emily arrived. The front door banged, and feet clattered up the stairs; she plunged into the room and, halfway toward Lynn, stopped.

'Oh, my God,' she whispered, and began to cry.

'Oh, don't,' said Lynn.

Poor child. She shouldn't have come, shouldn't see this.

'Emily darling, don't cry so. It looks worse than it is. Honestly.'

'You would say that! I don't believe you. What are you doing, protecting him again?'

'No, no. That's over.'

'Oh, my God, this is a nightmare! But it was only to be expected. It was only a question of time.'

'Was it? I suppose so.'

'Oh, Mom, what are you going to do?'

Emily sat down on the edge of the bed. There was such anguish in her question that for an instant Lynn had to turn away without answering.

'Do? Many things. My head's swimming with all I have to do.'

'How did it happen? What led to it this time?' Emily asked, emphasizing *this time*.

'I'll tell you the whole thing, but first tell me how you came to that place. I was there too. I bought a picture, and she told me about you. You were in New York without letting me know. What happened? Why?'

So many secrets. So much going on behind each other's back.

'You knew what my thoughts have been, Mom. Suddenly I wasn't able to rest any longer while they were whirling in my head. So I took a plane to New York, spent a couple of hours, and flew right back.'

'Whatever was in your mind when you went there? What did you expect to learn?'

'Maybe I felt there was some dark secret, I don't know. I was curious about Jeremy, though, and there wasn't any other way to find out about him.'

'Well, did you find out anything?'

'He lives in England, and in a nice enough way, terse but still nice, she made it clear that he should be let alone. Obviously she doesn't want Dad to learn where he is. But who knows? Maybe someday – or maybe never – he'll want to know Annie and Bobby and me.'

The winter afternoon was closing in and Lynn pulled the lamp cord to lighten the gloom.

'You're wondering what brought me there,' she said, conscious that each of them had avoided saying the name 'Querida.' 'When I considered what you had learned through Aunt Jean – it took me a while – I knew I had to reach back into the past. I had deliberately closed my mind. I realize that. And so I had to open it. Perhaps,' Lynn said ruefully, 'perhaps in a way I hoped, when I went in, that the woman would turn out not to be – to be Querida, and then I would not have to face facts. If there were any facts. And of course there were.'

Now, having made herself say the name, Lynn made herself continue to the end of the horrifying story.

There was a long silence when she'd finished. Emily wiped her eyes, got up, walked to the window, and stood there looking out into the oncoming night. Lynn's heart ached at sight of the girl's bowed head; revelations like these are not what you want your nineteen-year-old daughter to hear.

'Poor Aunt Jean,' Emily said. 'She must have struggled all these years with herself: to tell or not to tell?'

'She couldn't possibly have told. There are some things too awful to let loose. It would be like opening a cage and letting a lion out.'

'The lion got out anyway last night.'

And again there was a silence; it was as if there were no words for the enormity of events.

Lamplight made a pale circle on the dark rug, laying soft, contrasting shadows in the far corners of the flowery room, with its well-waxed chests, its photographs and books.

And almost absently, Emily remarked, 'You love this house.'

'I don't know. I love the garden.' The roof had caved in. Everything was shattered. 'It will be sold.'

'What's going to happen to Dad, do you think?'

'It's a big world. He'll find a place, I'm sure,' Lynn said bitterly.

'I meant – will he go to jail for this?'

'No. He could, but I don't want that.'

'I'm glad. It's true that he deserves it. Still, I should hate to see it.'

'I know. I guess we're just that kind of people.'

There was a tiredness in the room. They were both infected with it. They were people who had come, breathless after a steep climb, to the top of a hill, only to find another hill ahead.

'I had to come and see you.' Emily spoke abruptly. 'I thought I would lose my mind when I heard last night.'

'But you have exams this week.'

'I'll take a makeup on the one I missed today. Once I've seen the doctor, if he says you're all right, I'll go back. Harris came with me,' she added.

Lynn was surprised. 'Harris?'

'He insisted. He wouldn't let me go alone.'

Lynn considered that. 'I always liked him, you know.'

'I do know, and he knows it too.'

'So then, how are things with you both?'

'The same. But we're not rushing.'

'That's good. Where is he?'

'Downstairs. He didn't think he ought to come into the house, but I made him.'

'What, freezing as it is? Of course he should have come in. I'll put on some decent clothes and go down.'

'Downstairs?' Emily repeated.

'It's just my face that's awful, not my legs.'

'I meant – I thought, knowing how you are about yourself, that you wouldn't want anyone to see you like this.'

Go down, put out your hand, and don't cringe. Don't hide. That time's over, and all the burden of pride is over too.

'No,' Lynn said. 'I don't mind. It's out in the open now.'

She had spent so many hours in this chair across from this man Kane, whose ruddy cheeks, gray-dappled hair, and powerful shoulders were framed by a wall of texts and law reviews, that she was able to feel almost, if not entirely, comfortable.

'It's funny,' she said, 'although I know perfectly well that it's not true, I still, after all these months, have the feeling that something like this only happens among the miserable, helpless poor. How can it have happened to me? I ask myself. Ridiculous of me, isn't it?'

Kane shrugged. 'I guess it is, although most people like you would be surprised to learn that twenty percent of the American people, when polled, believe it's quite all right to strike one's spouse on occasion. Do you know that every fifteen seconds another woman is being battered by her husband or her boyfriend in this country? There's nothing new about it either. Have you ever heard of the "rule of thumb"? It's from the English common law, and it says that a man may beat his wife as long as the stick is no thicker than his thumb.'

'What a fool I was! A weakling and a fool,' she said softly, as if to herself.

'I keep telling you, stop the blame. It's easy enough for the world to see you as having been weak, for staying on so long. You saw yourself, though, as strong, keeping the home intact for your children. You wanted a house with two parents in it. In that sense you really were strong, Lynn.'

Her mind was racing backward into a blur of years, as in an express train, seated in reverse direction, one sees in one swift glimpse after the other where one has just been. At the same time her passive gaze out of the window at her side fell upon a street where a cold, late April rain was sliding across a stationer's window, still filled with paper eggs and chicks, although Easter was long past. Holiday decorations were inexpressibly depressing when the holiday was over ... Robert had used to dye the eggs and hide them in the garden.

'And besides, in your case,' Kane was saying, 'one could say you had plausible reason for hope. One could, that is, if one hadn't the benefit of knowledge and experience with these cases.'

His fingers formed a steeple; the pose was pontifical. Men in authority liked to make it, she thought, observing him.

'He is an extraordinarily intelligent man, according to Tom Lawrence and to his own counsel. And of course, there was his status. I don't mean that status was anything you sought, but he was admirable in the public's eyes, and that had to have had its effect on you.'

'I guess so. But how unhappy he must have been in his youth!'

'Yes, but that's no excuse for making other people – a wife – pay for it. *If* that's the explanation at all.'

'When he lost that promotion, he lost everything. I had an idea that he might even kill himself.'

'More likely to kill you, it seems.'

Kane shrugged again. It was an annoying habit, and yet she liked the man. He was sensible and plain spoken.

'I understand he has the offer of a job with some firm that's opening an office in Mexico. He's probably glad enough to go, even with a deal less money. But he's lucky, and his counsel knows it. You've let him off easily. No criminal charges and no publicity.'

'I did it for my children. They have a terrible memory of this as it is. Annie's still having bad dreams, even with therapy.'

'Well, he's out of their lives, even without Mexico. His attorney says he's satisfied about custody – he damn well better be! Your children are all yours. He said he thinks it will be better for them and for himself not to see them.'

'My daughters don't want to see him. But it's a terrible thing for a man to lose his children, so if they should ever want to see him, I would not stand in the way. Right now, though, they refuse.'

'He knows that. I believe he meant the little boy.'

The little boy, now surefooted, could run all over the house. The first week or so after Robert's disappearance he had called 'Daddy,' but now whenever Tom came, he seemed to be just as comfortable playing on the floor with him as he had been with Robert.

'Bobby will not remember,' she said, thinking. This is the second time that Robert has lost a son.

'So there being no contest, this will move along easily. You'll be free before you know it, Lynn.' He regarded her with a kindly, almost fatherly smile. 'How's the baking going? That cake you sent for my twins' birthday was fabulous. They're still talking about it.'

'I've been doing some. One friend tells another and I get orders. But my mind's been too disturbed to do much of anything.'

'And no wonder. Is there anything else you want to ask today?'

'Yes, I have something.' And from the floor beside her chair she picked up a cardboard box and, handing it over to Kane, said only, 'Will you please give this to Robert's lawyer for me? It belongs to Robert.'

'What is it? I need to know.'

'Just jewelry, some things I no longer want.'

'All your jewelry?'

'All.'

'Come, Lynn. That's foolish. Let me look at it.'

'Open it if you want.'

Each in its original velvet container lay the diamond wedding band, the solitaire, pearls, bracelets, and earrings, twenty years' worth of shimmering accumulation.

'Heavy. The best,' he said as he spread the array on the desk.

'Robert never bought anything cheap,' she said dryly.

Kane shook his head. 'I don't understand you. What are you doing? These things are yours.'

'They were mine, but I don't want them anymore.'

'Don't be foolish. You'll have a pittance when this is over, you know that. There must be over one hundred thousand dollars' worth of stuff here.'

'I couldn't wear any of it. Every time I'd touch them, I'd think' – and she put her finger on the bracelet, on the smooth, deep-toned cabochons in a row, emerald, ruby, sapphire, emerald, ruby – 'I'd remember too much.'

She would remember the diamond band on the white wedding day: flowers, taffeta, and racing clouds. She would remember the earrings bought that week when Bobby was conceived, when the night wind rustled the palms. She would remember the bench by the lake in Chicago, the cold windy night, the despair, and the crazy woman laughing. And she withdrew her finger as if the jewels were poisonous.

'Then sell the lot and keep the cash. You won't have anything to remind you of anything.' Kane laughed. 'Cash is neutral.'

'No. I want to make a clear, clean break. Just get all you can for my children from the man who fathered them. For myself, I will take nothing except the house,

369

or what's left of the sale after the mortgage is paid off.'

Kane shook his head again. 'Do you know you're incredible? I can't decide what to think about you.'

He looked at Lynn so long and hard that she wondered whether he was seeing her with admiration or writing her off as some sort of pitiable eccentric.

'I've never had a client like you. But then, Tom Lawrence told me you were unique.'

She smiled. 'Tom exaggerates.'

'He's always concerned about you.'

'He has been a true friend in all this trouble. To me and to my children. Annie adores him.'

Annie asks: 'Will you every marry Tom, Mom? I hope you do.'

And Emily, even Eudora, too, put on such curious expressions whenever his name is mentioned, just as Kane is doing now.

Well, it's wonderful to be wanted, she thought, and I daresay I can have him when I'm free, but right at the moment I am not ready.

'By the way, his lawyer mentioned something about Robert's books. He'll want to come for them. I'll let you know when. Perhaps you can have them packed so he can remove them quickly. And you should certainly have someone in the house when he comes.'

'I'll do that.'

'The house should sell fast. Even in this market the best places are snapped up. It's a pity that the mortgage company is going to get most of it.'

'A pity and a surprise to me.'

She stood up and gave him her hand. When he took it, he held it a moment, saying kindly, 'You've had more surprises in your young life than you bargained for, I'm afraid.'

'Yes. And the mystery is the most surprising.'

'The mystery?'

'That when all is said and done, all the explanations asked for and given, I still don't really know why.'

'Why what, Lynn?'

'Why I loved him so with all my heart.'

'You need to get married again,' said Eudora some months later. 'You're the marrying kind.'

'Do you think so?'

Eudora had gradually become a mother hen, free with advice and worries. She had taken to sleeping several nights a week at the house, ostensibly because she 'missed Bobby,' but more probably because she feared that somehow, regardless of new locks and burglar alarms, Robert might find his way in.

It was natural, then, that a pair of women in a house without a man should develop the kind of intimacy that enabled Eudora to say what she had just said.

'I was thinking maybe you shouldn't sign any papers to sell the house just yet.' She spoke with her back turned, while polishing Lynn's best copper-bottomed pots. 'You might want to stay here, you never know,' she said, and discreetly said no more.

Of course they all knew what she meant. Tom Lawrence was in all their minds, as in Lynn's own. The two girls, Annie and Emily, home for Thanksgiving, were having lunch at the kitchen table and giving each other a sparkling, mischievous look.

'I shall never stay in this house,' Lynn said firmly. She was breaking eggs for a sponge cake. 'Eight, nine – no, eight. You've made me lose count. I have only stayed here this long because I've been instructed to until everything becomes final.'

Divorce was a cold, ugly word, and she avoided it. *Everything* said it all just as well.

'And when will that be?' asked Emily.

'Soon.'

'Soon,' shouted Bobby, who was pushing a wooden automobile under people's feet.

'He repeats everything. And he knows dozens of words. Do you suppose he always understands what he says?' asked Annie.

Eudora's reply came promptly. 'He certainly does. That's one smart little boy. One smart little boy, aren't you, sweetheart?'

'He's crazy about Tom,' Annie informed Emily. 'You haven't seen them together as much as I have. Tom spends half an hour on the floor with him every time he comes to take Mom out.'

They were pressing her for information, and Lynn knew it. What they wanted was some certainty: along with the relief of knowing that the shock, the plural shocks, they had undergone were never to be repeated, they were feeling a certain looseness. There was neither anchor nor destination; the family was merely floating. So they were really asking her what was to come next, and she was not prepared to answer the question.

'I'm trying out a new recipe with the leftover turkey,' she told them instead. 'It's a sauce with black Mission figs. Sounds good, doesn't it?'

'Why, what's the celebration?' Emily wanted to know. 'Who's coming?'

'Nobody but us. It's celebration enough to have you home. Do you want to invite Harris for leftover turkey?'

'Oh, thanks, Mom, I'll call him.'

'Is Tom coming?'

'No, but he's coming tomorrow afternoon. It's the day your father will be here for his books.'

In spite of herself Lynn felt a tremor of fear. She had not seen Robert since that horrendous night. And dread mounted now even as she stood stirring the yellow dough. Still, Tom would be there . . .

'Eudora's going to put Bobby in his room while he's

372

here, and I'd like you two to be out of the house. Go visit friends, or maybe there's a decent movie someplace.'

Emily said cheerfully, 'Okay.' She got up and laid her cheek against Lynn's. 'I know you worry about us. But we're both, Annie and I, pretty solid by now. As solid as we'll ever be, I guess, and that seems to be good enough.'

'Thank you, darling, thank you.'

As solid as they'd ever be. No, one never 'got over' what they had seen. It would be with them for the rest of their lives, and they would just have to work around it. That was what they were doing; now in her second year, Emily had a 3.6 average, and Annie – well, Annie was trudging along in her fashion.

Alone in the kitchen a short while later, Lynn's thoughts found a center: Tom. No man could be more attentive. All through this troubled time he had been there, solid as a rock, for her to lean on. And as the trouble began, ever so gradually, to recede into the past, during these last few months especially, she had begun to feel again the stirrings of pure fun. They had danced and laughed and drunk champagne to commemorate the day when her last scar faded away. He had brought her again the brightness that had surrounded him on the fateful night of the dinner in his house.

He never made love to her, and that puzzled her, for how many times since they met had he not told her that she was lovely? It was not that she wanted him to attempt it; indeed, she would have stopped him, for something had died in her. Perhaps it was that that he sensed, and he was simply being patient. But it troubled her to think that she might never again be the passionate woman she once had been.

And Robert had always said, 'Funny, but to look at you, no man would guess.'

Yet she felt sure that ultimately Tom would ask her what the girls were hoping he would ask. Sometimes it

seemed that when that moment came, she would
have to say no to him, for what was lacking, she supposed, was the painful, wonderful yearning that says:
You and no other for the rest of our lives. Yet, why not he,
with his intelligence, his humor, charm, and kindness?
A woman ought to have a man, a good man. It was a
terrible thing to be alone, to face long years going downhill alone.

She would have to make up her mind, and soon. For
only this morning on the telephone, he had answered
her invitation to stay for lunch after Robert's coming: 'Yes,
I'll stay. I've been wanting to have a talk with you.'

The day was bright. She had carefully considered what
she was to wear, dark red if it should be raining, or else,
in the sun, the softest blue that she owned. When she
was finished dressing, she examined herself from the
pale tips of her matching blue flats to the pale cap of her
shining hair, and was more pleased with herself than she
had been in a long time. Simplicity could be alluring
without any jewels at all.

Eudora appraised her when she came downstairs.

'You look beautiful, Mrs Ferguson.' And she nodded
as if there was complicity between the two women.

Eudora thought the dress was for Tom's benefit, which
it was, but in a queer way, it was also to be for Robert's;
let him see, especially with Tom in the house, that Lynn
was still desired and desirable.

The books had been packed, and the cartons put in the
front hall. Tom was already there when the car stopped in
the driveway.

'He's got a driver with him to help him carry,' he
reported to Lynn, who stood half hidden in the living
room. 'Are you afraid? Why don't you go back into the
den?'

'No.' She could not have explained why she wanted

to look at Robert, other than to say it was just morbid curiosity.

He wore a dark blue business suit out of the proverbial bandbox. She did not know whether it was surprising or not that he should be as perfect in his handsome dignity as he had ever been.

No greeting passed between him and Tom. It took several trips from the house to the car before the books were removed, and they were all accomplished in silence. She had thought and feared that perhaps he might try to talk to her and to plead, but he did not even seem to notice where she was standing.

On the last trip Eudora came out of the kitchen to give him a vindictive smile as she passed.

Ah, don't, Eudora! It is so sad. So very sad. You don't understand. How can you, how can anyone, except Robert and me?

At the doorstep Juliet came from the back of the house, wagging her tail at the sight of the man who had been her favorite in the family. When Lynn saw him stoop to caress the dog, she ran to the door. Something compelled her, and Tom's wavering touch did not restrain her.

'Robert,' she said, 'I'm sorry, so sorry that our life ended like this.'

He looked up. The blue eyes, his greatest beauty, had turned to ice; without replying he gave her a look of such chilling fury, of such ominous, unforgiving power, that involuntarily, she stepped back out of his reach.

Tom closed the door. She went to the window to watch Robert walk down the path; it was as if she wanted to make sure that he had really gone away.

When Tom put a comforting hand on her shoulder, she was whispering, 'To think he was my entire world. I can't believe it.'

With his other hand on her other shoulder he turned her about to face him.

'Listen to me. It's over,' he said quietly. 'Let it be over. And now, I believe you promised me some lunch.'

On a little table in front of the long window, she had set two places with a bowl of pink miniature chrysanthemums between them.

'If I can't eat outdoors when cold weather comes, I can at least look at the outdoors,' she said, to start conversation.

And she followed his gaze across the grass, which was still dark emerald, although the birches, spreading their black fretwork against the sky, were quite bare.

They talked, and Lynn knew it was prattle, that, comfortable as they appeared to be, there was an underlying nervousness in each of them. The moment was approaching. At some time before they were to leave this room, she was certain, a momentous question would have been put. It was incredible that even now, she could be still uncertain of her answer, although it seemed more and more as the minutes passed that her answer ought to be yes.

Thoughtfully, Tom peeled a pear, took a bite, pushed it aside, and began.

'We've had a rather special understanding, a feel for each other, haven't we?' And he paused as if waiting for confirmation, which she gave.

'That's true.'

'There are things I want to say, things I've thought about for quite a time. What's brought it all to a head is that you've reached a turning point. Kane told me the other day that you're about to be free.' He picked up the pear and then put it back on the plate. 'I'm being really awkward . . .'

Lynn said lightly, 'That's not usual for you.'

'No, it's not. I'm usually pretty sure of myself. Blunt, like a sledgehammer.'

'Oh, yes,' she said, still lightly, 'I found that out one day at the club pool.'

He laughed, and she thought, He's acting like a boy, a kid scared to be turned down.

'Well,' Tom resumed, 'perhaps I should organize my thoughts, begin from the beginning. You remember, I think I've told you about that night at my house when we were dancing and I confessed I'd had the intention of dancing you right into bed – you were so blithe, so sweet, so fresh-from-the-farm, and I had always been rather successful with women. That's an awful thing to say in 1990, so forgive me for saying it, will you? I hope you're not going to take it too badly.'

'No, go on.'

'Well, aside from that, I was mistaken in being so sure of you that night. I knew that later and was ashamed of myself, too, especially when on the very next morning I saw what trouble you were in. I surely wasn't going to add any other complications to your life. I suppose you're wondering what the point of all this rambling talk can possibly be.'

'That you want to be honest about your feelings. Isn't that the point?'

'Precisely. Honest and open, which brings me to the present.'

He stopped to take a drink of water that she knew he must not really want; it was only a means of delay. His forehead had creased itself into three deep, painful lines.

'So what I want to say is – oh, hell, it's difficult – I think we've come to the time we should stop seeing each other.'

'Stop?' she echoed.

'Oh, Lynn, if you could know how I have anguished over this! I've thought and thought. Probably I should have ended this months ago but I couldn't bring myself to do it because I didn't *want* to end it, and I still don't *want* to now. But I know I must. It wouldn't be fair to you – or to myself – to go on misleading us both.'

Tom took another drink of water and, to cover his agitation, adjusted his watch strap. Lynn was tingling and hot with shame; the blood beat in her neck.

'You haven't misled me, not at all,' she cried. 'I can't imagine how you ever got such an idea!'

Suddenly he reached and grasped both her hands. She tried to wrench them away, but he held them fast.

'You wouldn't want an affair, Lynn, while I would. But I don't want to get married again. I'm not the man to start another life rearing an adolescent girl and a toddler. Playing with Bobby for an hour is something very different. It wouldn't be right for any of us.'

The irony of this, she was thinking. How foolish of me to have been so sure, to have misread –

He was tightening his hold on her hands; his voice was urgent and sad.

'Lynn, if I were starting life again now without all these experiences I've had, I would look for a wife like you. There's no one with whom I'd rather have spent my life. If I had met you in the beginning, I would have learned things about myself ... I've had two divorces, as you know, and other involvements besides. I live a certain way now, without obligations. It's a long story. No, don't pull your hands away, please don't. I know you haven't asked me to psychoanalyze myself, but I have to tell you ... I wouldn't do for you, Lynn, not in the long run. In the kind of life I lead, with the people I know, we are wary with each other. We don't expect things to last.'

'I don't expect anything either. Not anymore. And you don't have to tell me all this.'

'I wanted to. I did have to, because someday, I hope you'll find someone steady and permanent, not like me. I could have been that, I know that much about myself.

But now – well, now I'm not the faithful type, and I know that too.'

'Robert was faithful,' she said for no reason at all, and her lips twisted.

'Yes. Confusing, isn't it?'

She pulled her hands away, and this time he released them.

'I've hurt you. I've hurt your pride, and that's not at all what I intended to do.'

'Pride!' she said derisively.

'Yes, why not? You have every reason for it. Oh, I knew I'd be too damned clumsy to make this clear! But I couldn't simply stop calling or seeing you, could I? Without any explanation? It would have been far worse to leave you wondering what was wrong.'

She said nothing, because that much was true.

'I only want you to move on now, Lynn, and you can't very well do that with me or any one man hanging around.'

Still she said nothing, thinking, I have been rejected, and the thought stung hard. *A woman scorned*.

Yet he had not scorned her.

'Lynn? Listen to me. I only wanted not to mislead you, even though you say you expected nothing.'

'That's so,' she said with her head high.

'Then I'm glad. You've had betrayals enough.'

When he stood up from the table, she rose, too, asking with dignity whether he was leaving now.

'No. Let's sit down somewhere else if you will let me. I have more things to say.'

He took a chair near the unlit fire and sighed. She had never seen him so troubled.

'I told you once, didn't I, that I used to do matrimonial work? I quit because it wore me down. Too many tears, too much rage and suffering. The price was too high. But one thing it did was to teach me to see people,

379

and that includes myself, far more clearly than I ever had.'

'So you've told me I must find a man to marry me who will be faithful and permanent, ready to cope with my children. But that's not what I want. Right now I don't ever want to depend on a man again.'

'Right!' The syllable exploded into the room. 'Right! What I was going to tell you is that you shouldn't look for any man at all. Not now. You should look to yourself only. Put yourself in order. You don't *need* anyone. That's been your trouble, Lynn.'

'What are you doing, scolding me?' The day was awful, first seeing Robert and now undergoing this humiliation, for say what one would, it was humiliation. 'If you are scolding, it's inhuman of you.'

'I'm sorry. I don't mean it that way. It's only that I know what you are and what you can be. I want you to be your best, Lynn.' He finished quietly. 'Robert didn't. He wanted you to be dependent on him.'

Her right hand, reaching for her left, tried to twirl the rings that were no longer there. Remembering, she put her hands on the arms of the chair. And, meeting Tom's look of concern, admitted, 'Until he left, I had never balanced a bank statement. I had hardly ever written a check.'

'But now you do both.'

'Of course. I've had to.'

'Tell me, whatever happened to Delicious Dinners?'

'You know what happened. I had Bobby instead.'

'Why can't you have both?' he asked gently.

Lynn shook her head. 'The very thought is staggering. Money and child care, a place and time – I don't know how to begin.'

'This very minute you don't, but you can learn. There are people who can tell you how to start a business, where to get the right child care, everything you'd need

380

to know. Step out into the world, Lynn. It's not as unfriendly as it often seems.'

For an instant the crinkles smiled around his eyes, until the look of concern replaced them again, and he asked, almost as if he were asking a favor, 'Don't you think you can try? Look squarely at the reality of things?'

She smiled faintly. 'Yes, that's what Josie used to say.'

'And she was right.'

The cat plodded in from the kitchen, switched its tail, and lay down comfortably at Tom's feet.

'He's made himself at home here, hasn't he? What do you hear from Bruce?'

The change of subject relieved Lynn. 'Postcards with picturesque scenery. He writes to Annie and me, he tells about his work, which seems to be going well, but doesn't really say much, if you know what I mean.'

'I had a card from him, too, just a few lines, rather melancholy, I thought.'

'He'll never get over Josie.'

'I don't think I ever felt anything that intense,' Tom said soberly. 'I suppose I've missed something.'

'No. I'd say you're fortunate.'

'You don't really mean that.'

'Well, maybe I don't.'

'Will you think seriously about what I've just said? Will you, Lynn?'

It was his look, affectionate and troubled, that finally touched her and lessened her chagrin. Aware that he was making ready to leave, she got up then and went over to take his hand.

'You are, when all is said and done, one of the best friends a person could ever want. And yes, I will think seriously about what you said.'

So it ended, and for the second time that day she stood at the window to watch a man walk out of her life.

381

He had told her some rough truths. *Put yourself in order. Be your best.*

In a certain way these admonitions were frightening. Indeed, she could, she wanted, and would need to be an earner again. She had already been thinking about refreshing her secretarial skills, renting an apartment, and squirreling away for the inevitable emergencies whatever might remain to her after the mortgage company got its share.

It would be a meager livelihood for a woman with a family, yet it would be manageable; the hours would be regular, which meant that good day care for Bobby would not be too hard to find. But this was not at all what Tom had meant by 'be your best.'

She walked into the kitchen and stood there looking around. Everything sparkled, everything was polished, from the pots to the flowered tile, from the wet leaves of the African violets to the slick covers of the cookbooks on their shelves. Peaches displayed their creamy cheeks in a glass bowl on the countertop, and fresh, red-tipped lettuce drained from a colander into the sink. It came to her that this place was the one room in the house that had been completely her own; here she had worked hour upon hour, contented and singing.

For no particular reason she took a cookbook from a shelf; it fell open to the almond tart that she had made for that fateful dinner at Tom Lawrence's. And she kept standing there with the book in hand, thinking, thinking . . .

Le Cirque, they'd said, applauding. The finest restaurants in Paris . . . Well, that's a bit of an exaggeration, a bit absurd, isn't it?

She walked back into the hall and through the rooms and back to where Tom had sat. 'Put yourself in order,' he said. So possibilities were there. You started simply, took courses, studied, learned. People did it, didn't they?

You took what you might call a cautious chance . . .

And after a while she knew what she must do. The thing was to move quickly. Hesitation would only produce too many reasons not to move. She went to the telephone and dialed her sister Helen's number.

'I have a surprise for you,' she said.

Helen's voice had the upward lilt of eager curiosity. 'I'll bet I know what it is.'

'I'm sure you don't.'

'It's about a man named Tom. Emily and Annie have both told me things. Isn't he the one who sent the needle-point chair for Bobby?'

'You have a memory like an elephant. No, it's not about him or any other man. It's about me and what I'm to do with my life. I'm going into business for myself.'

And a kind of excitement bubbled up into Lynn's throat. It was astonishing how an idea, taking shape in spoken words, could become all at once so plausible, so inevitable, so alive.

She could almost feel Helen's reaction, as though the wire were able to transmit an intake of breath, an open mouth, and wide eyes, as Helen shrieked.

'Business! What kind, for goodness' sake?'

'Catering, naturally. Cooking's what I do best, after all. I've been baking cakes to order, but we can't live on that.'

'When did you decide on this?'

'Just an hour or two ago.'

'What next? Out of the blue, just like that?'

'Well, not exactly. You know it's been in and out of my mind for ages. I've toyed with it. And now things have come together, that's all. Opportunity and necessity.'

'And courage,' Helen said, rather soberly. 'It takes money to open a business. Is your lawyer getting any more out of Robert or something?'

'Nothing more than you already know.'

'It's not much, Lynn.'

'I wouldn't want more from him even if he had it.'

'Well, I would. You are the limit, you are. Where's this business going to be, anyway?'

'Somewhere in Connecticut. Not this town, though. I want to get away.'

There was a silence.

'Helen? Are you there?'

'I'm here. I'm thinking. Since you want to get away from where you are, why not make a big move while you're at it?'

'Such as?'

'Such as coming back here. You've been away only four years, and everybody knows you. People will give you a start here. Doesn't that make sense?'

Lynn considered it for a long minute. It did seem to make practical sense. She had perhaps not thought of going 'home' because it might seem like going back for the refuge of family and a familiar place. But then, what was wrong with that?

'Doesn't it make sense?' Helen repeated.

'Yes. Yes, I believe it does.'

'It will be wonderful to have you here again! Darwin,' Lynn heard her call. 'Come hear the news. Lynn's coming home.'

The house, with its furnishings, was sold overnight. A formal couple, impressed by Robert's formal rooms, walked through it once and made an acceptable offer the next day.

Except for the kitchen's contents and the family's books, there was little to take with them. There were Emily's desk and Annie's ten-speed bicycle; to Lynn's surprise she also asked to keep the piano, although she had not touched it since the night when that final dissonant chord had crashed. Carefully, in a carton lined with tissue paper, Lynn packed pictures and photographs, treasured remembrances of her parents on their wedding day, of her grandparents, and her children from birth to graduation. When these were done, she stood uncertainly, holding the portrait of Robert in its ornate silver frame. As if they were alive, his eyes looked back at her. She had an impulse on the one hand to throw it, silver and all, into the trash, while on the other hand she reflected that posterity, perhaps at the end of the twenty-first century, might be curious to behold a great-grandfather. By that time probably no one alive would know what Robert Ferguson had really been, and his descendants would be free to praise and be pleased by his distinguished face. So she would let the thing lie wrapped up in an attic until then.

Two unexpected events occurred just before moving day. The first was a Sunday-afternoon visit from Lieutenant Weber and his wife.

'We weren't sure you would welcome us,' said the lieutenant when Lynn opened the door. 'But Harris said you would. He wanted us to come over and say goodbye.'

'I'm glad you did,' Lynn answered, meaning the words, meaning that it was good to depart from a place without leaving any vague resentments behind.

When they sat down, Mrs Weber explained, 'Harris thought, well, since you are moving away, he thought we ought to be, well, not strangers,' she concluded, emphasizing *strangers* almost desperately. And then she resumed, 'I guess he meant in case he and Emily –' and stopped again.

Lynn rescued her. 'In case they get married, he wants us to be friends. Of course we will. Why wouldn't we? We've never done each other any harm.'

'I'm thankful you feel that way,' Weber said. 'I know I tried to do my best, but I'm sorry it didn't work.'

'All of that is beginning to seem long ago and far away.'

Lynn smiled. 'Can you believe they're already halfway through their sophomore year?'

'And doing so well with their A's,' said Weber. 'They seem to kind of run a race with each other, don't they? On the last exam Emily beat, but Harris doesn't seem to mind. It's different these days. When I was a kid, I'd've been sore if my girlfriend ever came out ahead of me.'

'Oh, it's different, all right,' Lynn agreed.

Talking to this man and this woman was easy, once the woman had recovered from her first unease. Soon Lynn found herself telling them about her plans, about the store she had rented and the house that Darwin had found for them.

'My brother-in-law's aunt and uncle have moved to Florida, but they don't want to sell their house in St Louis because the market is so bad. So they'll let me stay there for almost nothing, just to take care of it. We'll be house-sitters.'

Almost unconsciously, Mrs Weber glanced around the living room, which was as elegant as it had ever been except for the slipcover on the blood-stained sofa. The glance spoke to Lynn, and she answered it.

'I shan't miss this at all, not even the kitchen.'

'Yes, Emily told us about your kitchen.'

'I'll show it to you before you leave. Yes, it's gorgeous. I'm taking my last money, my only money, to fix one like it in the shop. It's a gamble, and I'm taking the gamble.'

So the conversation went; they talked a little more about Emily and Harris, talked with some pride and some natural parental worry. They admired the kitchen and left.

'No false airs there,' Lynn said to herself after the couple had gone. 'If anything should come of it, Emily will be in honest company. Good stock.'

The second unexpected event concerned Eudora. She wept.

'I never thought you'd go away from here. I was sure that you and Mr Lawrence – '

'Well, you were wrong. You all were.'

'I'll miss my little man. And Annie too. And you, Mrs Ferguson. I'll think of you every time I make the crepes you taught me to make. You taught me so much. I'll miss you.'

'We'll miss you, too, don't you know we will? But I can't afford you. And the house isn't at all like this one. It's a little place that any woman can keep with one hand tied behind her back.'

For a moment Eudora considered that. Then her face seemed to brighten with an idea.

'You'll need somebody in the shop, won't you? How can you do all the cooking and baking and serving by yourself?'

'I can't, of course. I'll need to find a helper, or even two, if I should be lucky enough to see the business grow that much.'

'They wouldn't have to be an expert like you, would they? I mean, they would be people to do easy things and people you could teach.'

There was a silence. And suddenly Lynn's face brightened too. Why not? Eudora learned fast, and she was so eager, waiting there with hope and a plea in her eyes.

'Eudora, are you telling me that you would – '

'I'm telling you that I wish you would take me with you.'

The day arrived when the van that was to take the piano and the sundries rumbled up the drive. It was a colorless day under a motionless sky. The little group, almost as forlorn as the gray air, stood at the front door watching their few possessions being loaded into the van.

'Wait!' Lynn cried to the driver. 'There's something in the yard in back of the house. It's a birdbath, a great big thing. Do you think you can make room?'

387

The man gave a comical grin. 'A birdbath, lady?'

'Yes, it's very valuable, it's marble, with doves on it, and it mustn't be cracked or chipped.'

'Okay. We'll fit it in.'

'Mom, what do you want with it?' asked Annie.

'I don't know. I just want it, that's all.'

'Because Uncle Bruce gave it to you?'

That canny child was trying to read her mind.

'Maybe. Now bring out Barney in the carrier and put on Juliet's leash. Don't forget their food and a bowl for water. We've a long way to travel.'

So the final moment came. The van rumbled away, leaving the station wagon alone in the drive. For a moment they all took a last look at the house. Aloof as ever, it stood between the long lawns and the rising hill, waiting for new occupants as once it had waited for those who were now leaving it.

'The house doesn't care about us,' Lynn said, 'and we won't care about it. Get in, everybody.'

The station wagon was full. Annie sat in the front, Eudora and Bobby had the second row, and in the third, alongside Barney in his carrier, sat Juliet, so proud in her height that her head almost touched the roof.

'We're off!' cried Lynn. And not able, really, to comprehend the tumult of regret and hope and courage that whirled through her veins, she could only repeat the cry, sending it bravely through the quiet air: 'We're off!'

The car rolled down the drive, turned at the end, and headed west.

Part Five

Winter 1992–1993

8

Emily, who was home for spring break, propped her chin in her hands and leaned on the kitchen table as she watched Lynn put another pink icing rosebud on a long sheet cake.

'It seems so strange to have it still cold in March,' she remarked. 'Right now in New Orleans the tourists are sitting in the French Market having a late breakfast, beignets and strong, dark coffee. Do you know how to make beignets, Mom?'

'I've never made any, but I can easily find out how.'

'That cake's absolutely gorgeous. Where and when did you ever learn to be so professional?'

'At that three-week pastry course I took last year.'

'I'm so in awe of what you've done in just two years.'

'Two years and five months. But talk about awe! Harvard Medical School! I'm so proud of you, Emily, that I want to walk around with a sign on my back.'

'Wait till next September when I'll actually be there.'

Cautiously, Lynn inquired, 'How is Harris taking it?'

'What? My going to Harvard? He wasn't admitted there, so I'll go to Harvard and he'll be at P & S, which is mighty good too. I don't feel happy about it, but I certainly wasn't going to turn down an opportunity like this one.'

You turned Yale down, Lynn thought, but said instead, 'I wouldn't expect you to. And if you still keep on loving each other, the separation won't alter things.'

'Exactly,' agreed Emily.

She had come a long way. Yet she still looked like a high school girl with her jeans and sneakers and the red ribbon holding her hair back from her radiant face. From her father she had received some intellectual gifts and the handsome bone structure, but thank God, nothing more. She would do well with or without Harris or anyone else.

Never tell a daughter, Lynn thought now, that she'll find a wonderful man who will love and take perfect care of her forever. That's what my mother told me, but then it was in another time, another age.

With the last rose firmly affixed she stepped back to appraise her work.

'Well, that's finished. I like to do jobs like this one here in my own kitchen. There's too much going on at the shop for me to concentrate on fancy work.'

The kitchen smelled of warm sugar and morning peace. It was quiet time while Annie was in school and Bobby in nursery school, time for a second cup of coffee. And she sat down to enjoy one.

In their big basket five puppies squealed and tumbled, digging at their mother in their fight for milk.

'They're so darling,' Emily said. 'Are you going to keep them all?'

'Heavens, no. Annie wants to, of course, but we'll have to find homes for four of them. I've consented to keep one. Then we'll have Juliet spayed.'

Emily was amused. 'How on earth did such a thing happen to our pure-bred Bergamasco lady?'

'She got out somewhere, maybe before I had this yard fenced in. Or maybe somebody got in. I have my suspicions about a standard poodle who lives near here, because a couple of pups have long poodle noses. They're going to be enormous.'

One of them fell out of the basket just then and made

a small puddle on the floor. Lynn jumped, replaced the pup, and cleaned the puddle, while Emily laughed.

'Mom, I was thinking, wouldn't Dad be furious that Juliet had mongrel puppies?'

'He wouldn't approve, that's sure. He wouldn't approve of this whole house, anyway.'

She looked out into the hall, where Bobby's three-wheeler was parked and a row of raincoats hung on an old-fashioned clothes tree. How relaxing it was not to be picture perfect all the time, neat to the last speck of dust, prompt to the last split second . . .

Emily remarked, 'I rather like old Victorians with the wooden gingerbread on the front porch and all the nooks. Of course, this furniture's pretty awful.'

'If I buy the house, I'll certainly not buy the furniture. And I might buy it. They've decided to sell, and since they're Uncle Darwin's relatives, they've offered easy terms. Maybe I shouldn't do it, but the neighborhood's nice, the yard's wonderful for Bobby, and I am finally meeting expenses with a little bit left over. So maybe I should.' Lynn smiled. 'Live dangerously! Have I told you that I've given Eudora a ten percent interest in the business, plus a salary? She's my partner now, and she's thrilled. She learns fast when I teach her. And, of course, she has her own Jamaican dishes that people love, her rice-and-peas, her banana pies, all good stuff. She can oversee the shop while I'm home baking or, if I'm busy at the shop, she'll come back here to let Annie and Bobby in after school. So it's been working out well for all of us.'

Emily, absorbed in this account, marveled at the way the business had just 'leapt off the ground' and 'taken flight.'

'There's a big demand,' responded Lynn. 'With so many women working now, it's not just a question of dinners and parties, it's also all the food we freeze and cook daily to sell over the counter. Besides, it was a good idea to come back here where dozens of people remembered me.'

Emily asked, 'Does Uncle Bruce write often?'

'Well, I wouldn't say often, but he certainly writes.'

His friendly chatty letters. His work, his travels. And nothing more.

'The latest news is that they want him to open a new office in Moscow. He's been taking lessons in Russian.'

Emily opened her mouth, made a sound, and closed her mouth.

'What is it? What is it you want to say?'

'I wanted to ask – to ask whether you ever heard from Dad.'

'The only contact I have or will ever want to have is with the bank, when they forward his remittances for all of you. Apparently he has a very good job.' Lynn hesitated over whether to say anything more, and then, deciding to, went ahead. 'Have you heard from Dad?'

'A birthday present, a check, and a book of modern poetry. He didn't say anything much about himself, just hoped I was happy.'

His girls, his Emily, Lynn thought, and, in a moment of painful empathy, felt Robert's loss. But it was done, there was no undoing it ...

She stood up and removed her apron, saying briskly, 'I have to go to the shop now. Oh, Aunt Helen's going to come by to pick up the cake.'

'Twenty-five years married!'

'Yes, and happily.'

'Dad always thought Uncle Darwin was an idiot, didn't he?'

'He thought a lot of people were, and he was wrong.'

It was uncomfortable to be reminded of Robert's scorn, the twist of his mouth, the sardonic wit at other people's expense, the subtle digs about the Lehmans' being Jewish

394

or even about Monacco's being Italian. And it was obvious that Emily, too, had been uncomfortable asking.

On sudden impulse Lynn bent to stroke her daughter's forehead. 'What are you going to do while I'm gone, honey?'

'Nothing. Just be lazy. It's vacation.'

'Good. You need to be lazy. Enjoy it.'

Let life be sweet, let it be tranquil, Lynn thought as she drove through the quiet suburban streets. As best we can, we must plaster over the taint and the stain. Bobby would not remember that night, and Annie always would; but her intelligence, which Robert had so disparaged, would help her. It had already helped her. And therapy had helped, but chiefly she had improved because Robert was gone. It was as simple as that. She had lost twenty pounds, so that her face, no longer pillowed in fat, had developed a kind of piquant appeal. Her hair had been straightened, and now, for the first time, she was pleased with herself. She had even gone back, entirely unbidden, to the piano!

They had come far since the day the station wagon had crossed the Mississippi and they had spent their first night in the strange house. It had been after midnight, raining and very cold. Darwin had started the furnace, and Helen had made up the beds into which they had all collapsed.

The rain had beaten at the window of the strange room where Lynn lay. From time to time she had raised her head to the bedside alarm clock. Three o'clock ... Her heart had jumped in a surge of pure panic. Here she was, responsible for all these people, for her children and even for Eudora, so hopeful, so faithful, and so far from home. Panic spoke: You can't go it alone. It's too much and too hard. You don't know anything. All right, you can cook, but you're no five-star genius. What makes you think you can do this? How dare you think you can? Fool, fool, you can't. And the rain kept beating. Even the rain, as it told of the relentless world outside, was hostile.

Then dawn came, a dirty gray dawn, to spill its dreary light upon the ugly furniture in the strange room.

What are you thinking of? You can't do it alone.

But she had done so. She had admonished herself: Head over heart. You won't accomplish anything lying here in bed and shivering with fear. So she had gotten up, and in that same dreary dawn, had taken pen and paper to make a list.

First there was school registration and continued counseling for Annie. Then a visit to the store that was, she had thought wryly, to make her fortune, to see there what needed to be done. Next, a visit to one of those volunteer businessmen's groups where someone would show her how to go about starting a business; she had read that these groups could be very helpful.

'The world is not as unfriendly as it often seems to be,' Tom had assured her. Maybe, she had thought in that gray dawn, maybe it's true. I shall find out soon enough.

And now Lynn had to smile, remembering how very friendly it could be. For the man who had helped her the most, a fairly young man, retired in his mid-forties, had been sufficiently admiring of what he called her 'enterprise,' to become very serious, serious enough to propose marriage.

'I like you,' she had told him, 'and I thank you. I like you very much, but I am not interested in getting married.'

It was one thing and very natural to desire the joy of having a man in the bed; it was one thing to welcome the trust and commitment of a man as friend; but to be *possessed* in marriage, to be *devoured* in marriage as she had been, even discounting Robert's violence, was another thing. He had *devoured* her. It was this that she feared. The day might come when equality in marriage might seem a possibility and she would have lost her fear, but not yet. Not yet. At least not with any of the men she had been seeing.

There had been men to whom Helen and their old friends had introduced her, men decent, intelligent, and acceptable. Some of them had been fun in many ways. Yet that was all. She was not ready.

She liked to say, laughing a little at the excuse, although it was obviously a true one, that she simply hadn't the time! When people, usually women, inquired and urged, 'Why don't you? George or Fred or Whoever is really so nice, so right for you,' she would protest that she had Annie and an active little boy, she had the business, she hadn't an hour; couldn't everyone see that?

Sometimes – often – she thought of Bruce. She relived the day, the only day, they had made love. Time had faded the guilt and left her with the memory of a singular joy. She thought about it long and deeply now, wanting to relive it and to understand it. And, ultimately, she came to understand the subtle difference between sex that was giving and sex that was all taking, sex that was ownership. Robert had *owned* her, while Bruce had not. And she knew in her heart that Bruce would never want to own a woman; he would want her to be free and equal.

But it was useless to be thinking at all about him. Except for those brief letters and postcards with pictured castles from Denmark or Greece, he had disappeared into another life, vanished from the stage on which Lynn's life was being played.

Once, a month ago, she had been surprised by the appearance of Tom Lawrence. He had been in St Louis to take a deposition and had telephoned the shop.

'I took a chance on "Delicious Dinners" and looked it up in the phone book,' he said. 'Will you have dinner with me?'

And she had gone, feeling both gratitude and pride in being able to show him how well she had carried out his advice. Gratitude and pride, but nothing more.

She had been completely honest with him.

'I would have married you if you had asked me that day. I was prepared to,' she said. 'Now I thank you for telling me it would have been a mistake.'

He answered seriously, 'As I told you then, it would have been different if I had met you when I was twenty years younger and maybe wiser.'

She laughed. 'You would have spared me a ton of trouble if you had.'

'Why? Would you have taken me then instead of Robert?'

Considering that with equal seriousness, she shook her head.

'No. At that time the Prince of Wales probably couldn't have gotten me away from him.'

'Lynn, it's so good to see you! And you're looking so lovely, younger; all the tension seems to have been wiped away.'

She said playfully, 'You don't think running a business is tension?'

'Yes, but it's a very different kind.' He smiled at her with the old brightness, not mischievous now, but affectionate. 'I like your suit. I like your pearls. I thought you had given back all the jewelry.'

'I did. I bought these myself.'

'They're handsome. Pure white, European taste. Americans prefer creamy ones. You see how much I know?'

She had been passing a jeweler's on the day that her bank loan, obtained through Darwin's willingness to cosign the note, had been paid off. She was then in the black. And she had stood for a minute staring at the marvelous blue-white pearls, struggling with herself. She didn't need them. But she loved them. She wanted them. So she went in and walked out with the pearls in hand, *her* pearls, for which there was no reason to thank anyone but herself.

'What do you hear from Bruce?' Tom had inquired.

It had seemed that everyone in town who had ever known Bruce was always asking that, and now she replied as always, 'Not very much. He seems to be frightfully busy.'

'He is. I happened to mention him the last time I saw Monacco and he told me. Actually he said Bruce is a "brilliant guy. Quiet, with no brag about him".'

'I'm glad for him. At that rate I don't suppose we'll ever see him again.'

Tom had looked at her keenly. 'What makes you say that?'

'The paths life takes. You meet, you stay for a while, and you part.'

'He was very fond of you.'

'And I of him.'

'I understand you went back a long time together.'

'That's true.'

A long time. Back and back into the dimmest corners of the mind and memory. Young days in the sun, easy and familiar as brother and sister. Snatches of memory popping like switchboard lights. The morning Robert bought the bracelet and Bruce said, 'Take it, you deserve it.' She had not known then what he meant. The day he phoned from the hospital where he had taken Emily. The day he fetched Annie after she had run away. The day they had made love in Josie's house; wrong as it had been, it had been comforting, it had been voluptuous, it had been happy. It had been right. And then had come the night when, awakening from unconsciousness, she felt him washing her damaged face.

Memory, going back and back.

But she had not wanted to speak of these things to Tom, had herself been troubled because she was not sure what they really meant, and because, after all, they were useless.

The car came to a stop on a pleasant street bordered

with prosperous shops and trees that would in a few months give summer shade. Between a florist's and a bookstore hung a bright blue sign on which in fine old-fashioned script was written DELICIOUS DINNERS. Beneath the sign, in a bow window, stood a table, beautifully set with a spring-yellow cloth, black-and-white china, and a low bowl of the first daffodils. Customers were going in and customers were coming out at the bright blue door.

Two young girls in starched white were busy at the counter when Lynn went in. At the rear, behind swinging doors, the work was being done; a woman was cleaning vegetables, and Eudora was arranging a fish platter for a ladies' luncheon.

'Well, I finished the cake,' Lynn said. She looked at her watch. 'Plenty of time for me to do the salad bowl and the cornbread sticks. I told her that a French bread would be better, but she wanted the sticks. Is that my apron on the knob?'

An hour later she was taking the corn sticks out of the oven when one of the salesgirls opened the swinging door.

'There's a man here who insists on seeing you. I told him you were busy, but he –'

'Hello,' Bruce said.

'Oh, my God!' Lynn cried, and dropped the pan on the table.

'Yes, it's who you think it is.' And he opened his arms.

She was laughing, she was crying, as he hugged her and the astonished onlookers gaped.

'I thought you were in Russia! What are you doing here?'

'I was supposed to go to Russia, had my things ready, had my tickets, but then I changed my mind, changed the airline, and arrived at Kennedy this morning instead. Then I made this connection. I didn't have time to shave. Sorry.'

400

'Who cares? I can't believe it. No warning, nothing.' She babbled. 'Emily's here on spring break. Guess what! She got into Harvard Med. She'll be so glad to see you. She'll be bowled over. And Annie keeps wondering whether you'll ever come to see how well she's taking care of Barney. Oh,' she repeated, 'I can't believe it.' And pulling away from the hug, she cried, 'And look who's here! Eudora!'

'Eudora? What are you doing here in the Midwest?'

'She's my partner,' Lynn answered before Eudora could get the words out. 'She has an interest in this place.'

Bruce looked around. 'You never told me when you wrote that it was anything like this. I had no idea.'

He saw the shelves, the enormous, gleaming stove and freezer, the trays of cookies, the people at the counter waiting to be served.

'Why, it's stupendous, Lynn. I expected you would be doing, oh, I don't know. I expected –'

'That I'd be making dinners single-handedly? Well, I started that way. There were only Eudora and I the first few months, but business grew. It just grew.'

In his excitement Bruce had pushed his glasses back into his hair, and she had to laugh.

'You never keep them on your eyes.'

'What? These? Oh, I don't know why I do it. Tell me, can we have lunch? Can I drag you away from here?'

Lynn appealed to Eudora. 'Can you manage without me? I don't want to run out on you, but –'

'No, no, it's fine. I only need to toss the salad and make some pea soup. You go.' Eudora was enjoying the surprise. 'Better take off your apron before you do, though.'

'I'll use my car,' Bruce said. 'I rented one at the airport. I've already taken my stuff to the hotel. I got a suite. I had too much stuff to fit into one room. Let's go back there for lunch, I'm starved. I only had coffee this morning.'

'You brought all your things out to St Louis? I don't understand.'

'It's a long story. Well, not so long. I'll tell you when we sit down.'

He was all charged up; it was entirely unlike him to talk so fast.

'Well,' he began when they were seated in the dining room, quiet and hushed by carpets and curtains. 'Well, here I am. It feels like a century since I was last in this place. Remember our farewell party here before we all left for New York? You look different,' he said quizzically. 'I don't know exactly what it is, but I like it. You look taller.'

She was suddenly self-conscious. 'How can I possibly look taller?'

'It's something subtle, perhaps the way you stand, the way you walked in here just now. Something spirited and confident. Not that I didn't like the way you looked and walked before. You know that, Lynn.'

She did not answer. Tom, too, had given many a compliment, and she no longer took much stock in compliments.

'You look peaceful,' Bruce said, studying her face. 'Yes, I see that too.'

'Well, I've made peace with a lot of things. I think you'll be glad about one of them. A while back I went with some of the women to a tea at that house where Caroline fell into the pond. I made myself go to look at the pond, and for the first time I was able to remember what happened without blaming myself. I accepted, and felt free.' She finished quietly, 'That was your doing, Bruce, that afternoon in your house.' She smiled. 'Now tell me about yourself, what's been happening.'

He began. 'I took the position, as you know, because

I wanted to get away. And I threw myself into the work. It was a godsend. We worked like beavers, all of us did, and I do think we've made great strides. The company was pleased. I even got a letter from Monacco, offering me the post in Moscow. Well, I almost took it. But then I decided to go home.'

'What made you do that? You were on the way to bigger things, like wearing Monacco's shoes one day,' she said, thinking of how Robert had coveted those shoes.

'That's the last thing I'd want, heading an international corporation, with all its politics. It's good that some people want it, just the way some people want to be President of the United States, but I don't want either. I told them I'd like to go back to my old place here in St Louis, only this time I'd be the boss. That much authority, I'd like.'

'Why not New York, at least?'

'I never liked New York. Again, it's a fine place for some people, for the millions who live there and love it and for the millions more who would like to be there. But millions more, including me, wouldn't,' he ended firmly.

Curiosity drove Lynn further. 'So why did you go there in the first place? You didn't have to.'

This time he replied less firmly, almost sheepishly, 'I guess I wanted to show I was as good as Robert. It was pride, but I think I wanted to prove that I could do whatever he could, and do it just as well. I knew he never liked me and had a low opinion of me.'

Astonished, she pursued him. 'But why should you have cared about Robert's opinion?'

'I told you. Pride. Human beings are foolish creatures. So now that I've proved what I can do, I don't care anymore.'

This strange confession touched her heart in an unexpected way. She felt hurt on his behalf, hurt for him.

403

He looked down at his plate and then, raising his eyes, said somewhat shyly, 'I had a letter from Tom Lawrence after he came here to see you a couple of months ago.'

'Yes, he was here.'

And still shyly, Bruce said, not asking a question but making a statement, 'Then you and Tom have something serious going.'

'I don't know what makes you think that. He didn't come to see me. He had business in the city and looked me up, that's all. He's a fine man, and he has his charm.' She smiled. 'But he's not for me, and I'm not for him either.'

'Really?' The brown eyes widened and glowed. 'I thought he had come on purpose to see you. Not that he said anything definite, but anyway, I'd been expecting something of the sort.' Bruce stumbled. 'I always thought you and he –'

She said stoutly, 'For a while I had some fleeting thoughts, too, but it was very halfhearted, a sort of desperation, I guess, still thinking that a woman can't survive without a man. I've got over that. God knows it took me long enough.'

'You can't mean that you're writing men off because of what you've been through?'

'I didn't say that.'

They were sparring. If they had been fencing, they would have just tipped their weapons and retreated, tipped again and retreated. She became aware that her heartbeat was very fast.

'I'm glad it's not Tom,' Bruce said suddenly.

'Are you?'

'Is it – is there anybody else?'

'No. There could be, there could've been more than one, but I didn't, I don't, want any of them.'

She looked away at the tables where people were talking in low voices about the Lord knew what, the movie they had seen last night or maybe what they were going to do with their whole lives. And as she sat with her forlorn hands resting on the table, she wished that Bruce had not returned to live here where she would be bound to encounter him, bound to treat him like a cousin or a good old friend. Until this moment, in spite of her intermittent longings, she had not realized how deep those longings were; they had always been stifled. Here she sat and there, only inches away, were his warm lips and warm arms. They would have their lunch and smile and part until the next time, and that would be all.

She wanted to get up and run out. But people don't do things like that. They conceal and suffer politely.

'A few weeks ago I went over that batch of pictures you gave me,' he said. 'I spread them out so I could travel through the years. I had – I guess I had – an epiphany.'

Startled by the word, Lynn raised her eyes, which met a long, grave gaze.

'I saw everything, saw you and saw myself quite clearly. I shocked myself with my sudden knowledge of what I had to do.' Leaning over the table, he placed his hand on hers. 'You've always been very dear to me, I don't know whether you felt it or not. But don't misunderstand; I don't need to tell you how I loved Josie. So how could I admit that there was still room for you? How could I?'

Her eyes filled with tears and she did not answer.

'Tell me, am I too late? Or perhaps too early? Tell me.'

Very low, she replied, 'Neither. Neither too early nor too late.'

A smile spread from his mouth to his eyes; they radiated an amber light. The smile was contagious; Lynn began to laugh while her tears dropped.

'How I love you, Lynn! I must have loved you for years without knowing it.'

'And I – I remember the day you left. I turned the corner and you were waving –'

'Don't. Don't cry. It's all right now.' He shoved the coffee cup aside. 'Let's go upstairs. It's time.'

And to think that only this morning on the way to work she had been thinking of him, with such desire and so wistful a sense of 'never again'!

'Love in the afternoon,' she whispered. This time there was no sorrow, no search for comfort, no guilt, only the most honest, trusting, naked joy. Tightly together, they lay back on the pillows.

'I'm so contented.' Bruce sighed. 'Let's not go back to your house this minute. We need to talk.'

'All right. What shall we talk about?'

'I'm just letting my mind wander. Maybe someday when we're tired of doing what we're doing we could open a country inn. What do you think?'

'Darling, all the options are open.'

'We could furnish it with antiques. I got some old things in Europe, Biedermeier, it's being shipped. You'd be surprised how well it looks with other things, I never liked it before, but –'

Suddenly he laughed his loud, infectious laugh.

'What's funny?'

'I was thinking of the times I must have been gypped. Those old pieces that I so lovingly restored . . . A fellow told me of a place in Germany where they manufacture them and send them over here, all battered and marred with five coats of peeling paint. I used to spend hours removing it to get down to the original. Remember how Annie used to help me? Oh, Lord!' He shook with laughter. 'Lynn, I'm so happy. I don't know what to do with myself.'

'I'll tell you what. Let's get dressed after all and go back to the house. I want you to see everybody, and I want them to see you.'

'Okay.' He kept talking. 'You know, I think another

reason why I took that post in Budapest was that I had always envied Robert for having you without deserving you. I was pleased to see him punished when he saw me take his place. Very small minded, I know.'

'Very human too.'

And she pondered, while combing her hair before the mirror, 'I wonder, do you believe Robert became what he did because of his father?' The name 'Robert' sounded strange when spoken in her own voice. She had no occasion anymore to use it. 'Of course he could easily have done just the opposite to prove himself different, couldn't he?'

'He could have, but he didn't, and that's all that matters.'

Bruce came behind her, and the two faces looked back out of the mirror.

'Bruce and Lynn. It's funny how there's really never any one person for any of us. In my case, if it hadn't been Josie, it could have been you.'

She thought, Tom Lawrence said something like that, not quite the same, but almost.

'But Josie and I are so different,' she replied.

'That's what I mean. Tell me, if it hadn't been Robert, could it have been me?'

She answered truthfully, 'I don't know what I would have done then. Someone else once asked me that question, and I answered that not even the Prince of Wales could have gotten me away from him. I was bewitched – then. I wasn't the person I am now.'

'But if you had been the person you are now? Or is that an impossible, a foolish, question?'

'Foolish, yes. Because, can't you see, don't you know, that if I had had my present head on my shoulders –' She turned about and took his face between her hands. 'Oh, my dear, oh, my very dear, you know it would have been yes. A thousand times yes.'

* * *

407

In the living room Annie was practicing scales. Downstairs in the makeshift playroom that would have to be made over, Bobby and two four-year-old friends were playing some raucous game.

'I hope,' Lynn said, 'you think you can get used to a very noisy household.'

'I lived in a very quiet one for a long, long time. I will get used to it with gratitude.'

They were standing in the little sun parlor overlooking the yard. She had shown him around the house, he had been welcomed by the family, who, perhaps guessing what was afoot, had left them in this room by themselves.

'Look out there,' Lynn said. 'What do you see?'

'Don't tell me you moved the birdbath with you.'

'At the last minute I couldn't leave it.'

A mound of grainy, half-melted snow lay at the marble base, while the rest of the lawn was bare, ready for spring.

'I have it heated in the winter. Birds need water in the winter too.'

'It's like you to think of that. Nine out of ten people wouldn't.'

'Look, look at that lovely thing! It's the first robin, first of the season. Watch it drink. It must be tired and thirsty after its long flight from the south.'

The bird fluttered into the water, shook itself, and flew away into the trees.

'I wonder what it thinks. That there's a whole bright summer ahead, maybe.'

'I can't imagine, but I know what I'm thinking.'

She looked up into the dear face. The glasses were pushed back again into the curly brown hair, and the eyes sparkled.

'I'm thinking of our own bright summer, and all the years ahead.'

BELVA PLAIN

BLESSINGS

Life was at last going well for Jennie. Her recent engagement to Jay promised happiness beyond dreams. Her legal work in the poorest parts of the city was profoundly satisfying. And now she had the extra challenge of protecting a thousand acres of wilderness from the developers.

Just that one phone call changed everything.

Long forgotten memories awaken a hurt so deep, they threaten the loss of the man she loves. In danger both at home and at work, Jennie finds she must face the hard decisions she evaded so many years before.

'The suspense is real enough. And so are the emotions'
New York Daily News

HODDER AND STOUGHTON PAPERBACKS

MORE BELVA PLAIN TITLES AVAILABLE
FROM CORONET BOOKS

All these books are available at your local bookshop or newsagent, or can be ordered direct from the publisher. Just tick the titles you want and fill in the form below.

Prices and availability subject to change without notice.

HODDER AND STOUGHTON PAPERBACKS, P.O. Box 11, Falmouth, Cornwall.

Please send cheque or postal order for the value of the book, and add the following for postage and packing:

U.K. including B.F.P.O. – £1.00 for one book, plus 50p for the second book, and 30p for each additional book ordered up to a £3.00 maximum.

OVERSEAS INCLUDING EIRE – £2.00 for the first book, plus £1.00 for the second book, and 50p for each additional book ordered.

OR Please debit this amount from my Access/Visa Card (delete as appropriate).

Card Number ☐☐☐☐☐☐☐☐☐☐☐☐☐☐☐☐☐☐

Amount £ ....

Expiry Date...

Signed ....

Name ....

Address ....

....

D1435712

VOX

SPANISH
and
ENGLISH
School Dictionary

Second Edition

VOX

SPANISH
and
ENGLISH
School Dictionary

Second Edition

New York   Chicago   San Francisco   Athens   London   Madrid
Mexico City   Milan   New Delhi   Singapore   Sydney   Toronto

2 3 4 5 6 7 8 9 10 11 12 13   QLM/QLM   1 0 9 8 7 6 5 4

ISBN   978-0-07-181665-6   (hardcover)
MHID   0-07-181665-8

ISBN   978-0-07-181664-9   (paperback)
MHID   0-07-181664-X

Library of Congress Cataloging-in-Publication Data

Vox Spanish and English school dictionary / Larousse Editorial. — Second Edition.
        pages cm. — (VOX Dictionaries)
    ISBN 0-07-181665-8 (hard cover) — ISBN 0-07-181664-X (pbk.)
1. Spanish language—Dictionaries—English.   2. English language—
Dictionaries—Spanish.   I. Larousse (Firm)   II. Title: Spanish and English
school dictionary.
    PC4640.V6966   2014
    463'.21—dc23
                                                          2013033383

Dirección editorial: Jordi Induráin Pons
Coordinación editorial: Ma José Simón Aragón, Jordi Tebé Soriano
Asesoría pedagógica: Lluís Figueras Havidich, Ma Rosa Raméntol Estela
Realización: dos més dos edicions, s.l.
Ilustraciones: Juanjo Barco (Alins ilustración), Estudi Farrés
Cartografía: Santi Maicas
Diseño de cubierta: Francesc Sala

Table of Contents

INTRODUCTION

Maybe you are already in the habit of using a dictionary, or maybe this is the first time you've looked at one. Whatever the case, it will be useful for you to read these pages to discover all that you can learn from it. First some figures: you'll find 30,000 words or entries (17,000 of them English) and 70,000 translations. Of course, there are bigger dictionaries, but, unlike this one, they are not specially designed for your grade or language level. Let time take its course and the day will come when you'll be ready for them; for the moment, you're better off with the words our experts and panel of teachers have selected to meet your specific needs. That way, you'll learn gradually and solidly, improving your knowledge day by day.

Almost without realizing it, you learn new vocabulary every day: in class, watching a film, listening to a song, or surfing the Internet. Sometimes you can deduce the meaning of a new word because it belongs to the same family as another one you have already studied, but sometimes it isn't so easy. This is when you should reach for your dictionary: you'll find the meaning of the new word, examples of how to use it, and other information that, with your teacher's help, will allow you to improve your Spanish.

Maybe you've wondered what it would be like to speak only Spanish to your teachers and classmates. In these pages, you'll find a selection of phrases organized by subject that you can practice. No doubt you'll enjoy learning expressions that you'd like to be able to use in Spanish, but which you can't find in your books! Your teachers will help you to get the most out of these words and phrases.

And now that you know your dictionary better, get as much out of it as you can. *¿Estás preparado?*

How to Use This Dictionary

Perhaps you think that a dictionary does nothing
more than show you the translation of a word.
Well, we're going to show you all that you can do with it,
because some of it's bound to be new to you:

▶ Have you seen a word that was spelled differently from the way
you thought? Every day we use lots of words, but sometimes
we don't know how to spell them or we feel lazy about looking
them up. Remember every word that you look up, it will help you
to build up a solid vocabulary base.

appearance [ə'pɪərəns] *n* **1** *(becoming visible)* aparición *f.* **2** *(before a court, etc)* comparecencia. **3** *(look)* apariencia.

aparcamiento *nm* **1** *(acción)* parking. **2** *(en la calle)* place to park, parking place…

arithmetic [*(n)* ə'rɪθmətɪk; *(adj)* ærɪθ-metɪk] *n* aritmética.
▶ *adj* aritmético,-a.

aproximación *nf* **1** *(gen)* approximation. **2** *(acercamiento)* bringing together; *(de países)* rapprochement.

▶ Do you see the square brackets [ ] immediately after the English
headword? Here you will find the exact pronunciation of the
English headword. Maybe there are some symbols that you don't
understand, but we'll explain what they mean in another section.

achievement [ə'tʃiːvmənt] *n* **1** *(completion)* realización *f.* **2** *(attainment)* logro. **3** *(feat)* hazaña, proeza.

▸ Have you seen the abbreviation that comes right after the Spanish headword? This tells you the part of speech of the headword: if it's a feminine or masculine noun, a transitive or intransitive verb, and so on. Your language teachers will have taught you what these words mean. Here you can put into practice what they have explained to you: sometimes a word can be a noun and an adjective and have different meanings. You should pay attention to a word's part of speech so that you don't make mistakes when you are translating.

behind [bɪˈhaɪnd] *prep* detrás de.
▸ *adv* **1** detrás, atrás. **2** *(late)* atrasado,-a.
▸ *n fam (buttocks)* trasero.

alemán,-ana *adj* German.
▸ *nm & nf (persona)* German.
▸ *nm* **alemán** *(idioma)* German.

▸ Have you noticed that in some entries there are numbers? These show you the different meanings of the word. The number **1** indicates the commonest meaning, but the others are important too; all of them can help you to find the translation you're looking for.

capital [ˈkæpɪtəl] *n* **1** *(of country, etc)* capital *f*. **2** FIN capital *m*: *starting capital* capital inicial. **3** *(letter)* mayúscula: *write it in capitals* escríbelo con mayúsculas.

ampliar *vt* **1** to enlarge, extend. **2** ARQUIT to build an extension onto. **3** *(fotografía)* to enlarge. **4** *(capital)* to increase. **5** *(estudios)* to further. **6** *(tema, idea)* to develop, expand on.

▸ There are some words that are used only in a certain expression, or which require a certain preposition. Others have some peculiarity, such as an irregular plural. Because of this, you must be sure to read everything in the entry. You're bound to learn something new that will help you to understand what the word means and how it's used.

capability [keɪpəˈbɪlɪtɪ] *n* capacidad *f* (to, para/de).
① *pl* capabilities.

absorto,-a *adj* **1** *(pasmado)* amazed, bewildered. **2** *(ensimismado)* absorbed (en, in).

▶ Have you seen a box with the letters COMP? This means that the word is often used with another word and that together they have a different meaning. Have you see the letters LOC too? Now you can learn phrases and expressions with this word and see what verbs normally go with it.

elementary [elɪ'mentərɪ] *adj* **1** *(basic)* elemental, básico,-a. **2** *(easy)* fácil, sencillo,-a. COMP **elementary education** enseñanza primaria.
faithfully ['feɪθfʊlɪ] *adv* fielmente. LOC **yours faithfully** *(in letter)* atentamente.

accidente *nm* **1** accident: *sufrir un accidente* to have an accident. **2** *(terreno)* unevenness. LOC **por accidente** by chance. COMP **accidente de trabajo** industrial accident. ▌**accidente de tráfico** road accident. ▌**accidentes geográficos** geographical features.

▶ Have you seen some letters (for example, GB) after one of the numbers that indicate the different meanings? They tell you whether the word is used only in British English, in the United States, Canada, or Australia. If there are other letters after these, these tell you the field the word is used in, for example cookery or medicine.

dresser ['dresəʳ] *n* **1** GB *(in kitchen)* aparador *m*. **2** US *(chest of drawers)* tocador *m*.
fail [feɪl] *n* EDUC suspenso.
▶ *vt* **1** *(let down)* fallar, decepcionar; *(desert)* fallar, faltar. **2** EDUC suspender.

ADN *abrev* MED (ácido desoxirribonucleico) desoxyribonucleic acid; *(abreviatura)* DNA.
adobar *vt* **1** CULIN to marinate, marinade. **2** *(pieles)* to tan.

▶ If you see a box with this symbol ☒, read it carefully; this information is very interesting. Some Spanish words look very similar to English words, but they do not always mean the same thing and you can make a mistake.

fabric ['fæbrɪk] *n* **1** *(material)* tela, tejido. **2** *(structure)* fábrica, estructura.
☒ **Fabric** no significa 'fábrica', que se traduce por **factory**.

▸ Sometimes a dictionary is like a mini-encyclopedia. If you see a text with a shaded background and a globe symbol, here you will find information about customs and culture.

> **GCSE** ['dʒiː'siː'esˈiː] *abbr* GB (General Certificate of Secondary Education) ≈ Enseñanza Secundaria Obligatoria; *(abbreviation)* ESO *f*.
>
> 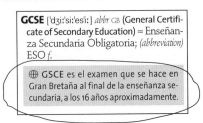 GSCE es el examen que se hace en Gran Bretaña al final de la enseñanza secundaria, a los 16 años aproximadamente.

▸ Have you looked up a word you didn't know and found an arrow and another word you didn't know? Well, you're in luck! You're going to learn two new words. The arrow means that to find the meaning of the word, you have to go to another more important word which it comes from or is related to. You will find what you're looking for at the second word.

> **got** [gɒt] *pt & pp* → **get**.

> **adecuado,-a** *pp* → **adecuar**.
> ▸ *adj* adequate, suitable.

▸ You will also find a lot of other information about words: their plural, if they are irregular or not, or explanations about how to use them. So that you can find this information quickly, it is marked with an ① or a ✎.

> **enseguida** *adv* at once, straight away, immediately.
> 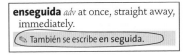 ✎ También se escribe en seguida.

We hope that this explanation has been helpful to you and that you will use it. Now you are ready and can start to use your dictionary.

ABBREVIATIONS USED IN THIS DICTIONARY

abr	abreviatura, abbreviation	*fam*	familiar use, uso familiar
adj	adjective, adjetivo	*fig*	figurative use, uso figurado
abbr	abbreviation, abreviatura	FIN	finance, finanzas
adv	adverb, adverbio	FÍS	física, physics
AER	aeronautics, aeronáutica	*fml*	formal use, uso formal
AGR	agriculture, agricultura	*fut*	future, futuro
AM	American Spanish, español americano	GB	British English, inglés británico
ANAT	anatomy, anatomía	*gen*	in general, en general
ARCH	architecture, arquitectura	GEOG	geography, geografía
arg	argot, slang	GEOL	geology, geología
ARQ	arquitectura, architecture	*ger*	gerund, gerundio
ART	art, arte	GRAM	grammar, gramática
art	article, artículo	HIST	history, historia
art def	artículo definido, definite article	*imperat*	imperative, imperativo
art indef	artículo indefinido, indefinite article	*imperf*	imperfect, imperfecto
AUTO	automobiles, automóvil	*indef art*	indefinite article, artículo indefinido
AV	aviation, aviación	*indic*	indicative, indicativo
BIOL	biology, biología	*inf*	infinitive, infinitivo
BOT	botany, botánica	INFORM	informática, computing
CHEM	chemistry, química	*interj*	interjection, interjección
CINEM	cinema, cinematografía	*iron*	ironic, irónico
COM	comercio, commerce	*irón*	irónico, ironic
COMM	commerce, comercio	JUR	law, derecho
comp	comparative, comparativo	LING	linguistics, lingüística
COMPUT	computing, informática	LIT	literature, literatura
conj	conjunction, conjunción	*loc*	locución, phrase
contr	contraction, contracción	MAR	maritime, marítimo
COST	costura, sewing	MAT	matemáticas, mathematics
CULIN	cookery, cocina	MATH	mathematics, matemáticas
def art	definite article, artículo definido	MED	medicine, medicina
DEP	deporte, sport	METEOR	meteorology, meteorología
EDUC	education, educación	MIL	military, militar
ELEC	electricity, electricidad	MUS	music, música
etc	etcetera, etcétera	MÚS	música, music
euf	uso eufemístico, euphemistic use	*n*	noun, nombre
euph	euphemistic use, uso eufemístico	*neut*	neuter, neutro
		nf	feminine noun, nombre femenino

nf pl	plural feminine noun, nombre femenino plural	*v aux*	auxiliary verb, verbo auxiliar
nm	masculine noun, nombre masculino	*vi*	intransitive verb, verbo intransitivo
nm o nf	masculine or feminine noun, nombre de género ambiguo	*vpr*	pronominal verb, verbo pronominal
nm & nf	masculine and feminine noun, nombre de género común	*vt*	transitive verb, verbo transitivo
nm pl	masculine plural noun, nombre masculino plural	*vt insep*	inseparable transitive phrasal verb, verbo preposicional transitivo inseparable
npl	plural noun, nombre plural	*vt sep*	separable transitive phrasal verb, verbo preposicional transitivo separable
pej	pejorative, peyorativo		
pers	person, persona		
pey	peyorativo, pejorative		
phr	phrase, locución	ZOOL	zoology, zoología
PHYS	physics, física	≈	approximately equivalent to, aproximadamente equivalente a
POL	politics, política		
pp	past participle, participio pasado	→	see, véase
pref	prefix, prefijo	►	different part of speech, cambio de categoría gramatical
prep	preposition, preposición		
pres	present, presente		
pron	pronoun, pronombre	◆	phrasal verb
pt	past, pasado	LOC	block of idioms and phrases, bloque de frases y locuciones
QUÍM	química, chemistry		
RAD	radio		
REL	religion, religión	COMP	block of compound nouns, bloque de compuestos
SEW	sewing, costura		
sím	símbolo, symbol		
sing	singular	①	note about some type of irregularity, nota sobre algún tipo de irregularidad morfológica
sl	slang, argot		
SP	sport, deporte		
subj	subjunctive, subjuntivo		
superl	superlative, superlativo	✎	note about a peculiarity of the headword, nota sobre alguna particularidad de la palabra
symb	symbol, símbolo		
TEAT	teatro, theatre		
TÉC	técnica, technical		
TECH	technical, técnica	✖	note about a false friend, nota sobre un «falso amigo»
THEAT	theatre, teatro		
TV	television, televisión		
US	American English, inglés norteamericano	⊕	cultural note, nota de tipo cultural

ENGLISH
SPANISH

A

A, a [eɪ] *n* **1** *(the letter)* A, a. **2** MUS la.
COMP **A road** carretera principal.

a [eɪ, *unstressed* ə] *indef art* **1** un, una: *a man and a woman* un hombre y una mujer. **2** *(not translated)*: *I'm a history teacher* soy profesor de historia; *two and a half litres* dos litros y medio. **3** *(per)* por: *three times a week* tres veces por semana; *£3 a kilo* tres libras el kilo. **4** *(a certain)* un tal, una tal: *a Mr Fletcher would like to see you* un tal Sr. Fletcher quiere verle.

✎ Se usa delante de las palabras que empiezan con sonido no vocálico. Consulta también **an**.

aback [əˈbæk] *adv* hacia atrás. LOC **to be taken aback** asombrarse.

abacus [ˈæbəkəs] *n* ábaco.

abandon [əˈbændən] *vt* abandonar.

abate [əˈbeɪt] *vi (gen)* reducirse; *(storm, anger)* amainar; *(wind)* cesar.
▶ *vt (reduce)* reducir; *(stop)* acabar con.

abattoir [ˈæbətwɑːʳ] *n* matadero.

abbey [ˈæbɪ] *n* abadía.

abbot [ˈæbət] *n* abad *m*.

abbreviate [əˈbriːvɪeɪt] *vt* abreviar.

abbreviation [əbriːvɪˈeɪʃən] *n* **1** *(shortening)* abreviación *f.* **2** *(shortened form)* abreviatura.

abdicate [ˈæbdɪkeɪt] *vi* abdicar.

abdomen [ˈæbdəmən] *n* abdomen *m*.

abdominal [æbˈdɒmɪnəl] *adj* abdominal. COMP **abdominal muscles** músculos abdominales.

abduct [æbˈdʌkt] *vt* raptar, secuestrar.

abhor [əbˈhɔːʳ] *vt* aborrecer, detestar.
ⓘ *pt & pp* **abhorred**, *ger* **abhorring**.

abide [əˈbaɪd] *vt (bear, stand)* soportar, aguantar: *I can't abide that woman* no aguanto a esa mujer.
◆ **to abide by** *vt insep (promise)* cumplir con; *(rules, decision)* acatar.

ability [əˈbɪlɪtɪ] *n* **1** *(capability)* capacidad *f,* aptitud *f.* **2** *(talent)* talento.
ⓘ *pl* **abilities**.

ablation [əˈbleɪʃən] *n* ablación *f.*

ablaze [əˈbleɪz] *adj* ardiendo, en llamas.

able [ˈeɪbəl] *adj* **1** que puede: *those able to escape did so* aquéllos que podían se escaparon. **2** *(capable)* hábil, capaz, competente: *he's a very able administrator* es un gestor muy competente. LOC **to be able to** poder.

✎ En pasado, **to be able to** se emplea en vez de **could** para expresar una capacidad relacionada con un acontecimiento concreto: *we weren't able to go* no pudimos ir.

abnormal [æbˈnɔːməl] *adj* **1** *(not normal)* anormal. **2** *(unusual)* inusual.

aboard [əˈbɔːd] *adv (ship, plane)* a bordo; *(train)* en el tren; *(bus)* en el autobús.
▶ *prep (ship, plane)* a bordo de; *(train, bus)* en. LOC **to go aboard 1** *(ship, plane)* embarcar, subir a bordo. **2** *(train, bus)* subir.

abode [əˈbəʊd] *n* LOC **of no fixed abode** sin domicilio fijo.

abolish [əˈbɒlɪʃ] *vt* **1** abolir, suprimir. **2** JUR derogar.

abominable [əˈbɒmɪnəbəl] *adj* abominable; *(terrible)* terrible, horrible. COMP **the Abominable Snowman** el Yeti.

aborigine [æbəˈrɪdʒɪnɪ] *n* aborigen *mf.*

abort [əˈbɔːt] *vi* abortar.
▶ *vt* **1** *(foetus)* abortar. **2** *(mission, program, etc)* abortar.

abortion [əˈbɔː(ʃ)ən] n 1 (of foetus) aborto. 2 (of mission, etc) interrupción f.

abound [əˈbaʊnd] vi abundar.

about [əˈbaʊt] prep 1 (concerning) sobre, acerca de: to speak about... hablar de...; what is the book about? ¿de qué trata el libro? 2 (showing where) por, en; (around) alrededor de: he's somewhere about the house está por algún rincón de la casa.
▶ adv 1 (approximately) alrededor de: at about three o'clock a eso de las tres; it cost about £500 costó unas quinientas libras. 2 fam (almost) casi: she's about finished está a punto de acabar. 3 (near) por aquí, por ahí: there was nobody about no había nadie... LOC to be about to ... estar a punto de... ‖ how/what about + noun ¿qué te parece + sustantivo?: how about a pizza? ¿qué te parece si tomamos una pizza? ‖ how/what about + -ing ¿y si + subj?: how about going to Paris? ¿y si fuéramos a París?

above [əˈbʌv] prep 1 (higher than) por encima de: above our heads por encima de nuestras cabezas. 2 (more than) más de, más que: above 5,000 people más de 5.000 personas.
▶ adv 1 arriba, en lo alto: the palace, seen from above el palacio, visto desde arriba. 2 (in writing) arriba: see above véase arriba. LOC above all sobre todo.

above-board [əbʌvˈbɔːd] adj legítimo,-a, legal.

abreast [əˈbrest] adv LOC to walk abreast caminar uno al lado de otro; to keep abreast of things estar al tanto de las cosas.

abridge [əˈbrɪdʒ] vt resumir, abreviar.

abroad [əˈbrɔːd] adv (position) en el extranjero; (movement) al extranjero.

abrupt [əˈbrʌpt] adj 1 (sudden) repentino,-a. 2 (rude) brusco,-a, arisco,-a. 3 (slope) empinado,-a.

ABS [ˈeɪbiːˈes] abbr (anti-lock braking system) sistema m de antibloqueo; (abbreviation) ABS.

abscess [ˈæbses] n (gen) absceso; (on gum) flemón m.

abscond [əbˈskɒnd] vi fugarse.

abseil [ˈæbseɪl] vi hacer rappel.

absence [ˈæbsəns] n 1 (of person) ausencia. 2 (of thing) falta, carencia.

absent [(adj) ˈæbsənt; (vb) æbˈsent] adj 1 ausente. 2 (expression) distraído,-a.

absentee [æbsənˈtiː] n ausente mf.

absenteeism [æbsənˈtiːɪzəm] n absentismo.

absent-minded [æbsəntˈmaɪndɪd] adj distraído,-a, despistado,-a.

absolute [ˈæbsəluːt] adj 1 (gen) absoluto,-a. 2 (total) total: there was absolute silence hubo silencio total. COMP absolute zero cero absoluto.

absolutely [æbsəˈluːtlɪ] adv completamente, totalmente.
▶ interj (agreement) ¡por supuesto!, ¡desde luego!: I think we should sell. What about you John? – Oh, absolutely! creo que deberíamos vender. ¿Y tú John? –Oh, ¡por supuesto!

absolution [æbsəˈluːʃən] n absolución f.

absolutism [ˈæbsəluːtɪzəm] n absolutismo.

absolve [əbˈzɒlv] vt absolver (of/from, de).

absorb [əbˈzɔːb] vt 1 (liquids, etc) absorber; (shock) amortiguar. 2 (time) ocupar.

absorption [əbˈzɔːpʃən] n absorción f.

abstain [əbˈsteɪn] vi abstenerse (from, de).

abstemious [æbˈstiːmɪəs] adj abstemio,-a, sobrio,-a.

abstention [æbˈstenʃən] n abstención f.

abstinence [ˈæbstɪnəns] n abstinencia.

abstract [(adj-n) ˈæbstrækt; (vb) æbˈstrækt] adj (not concrete) abstracto,-a.
▶ n (summary) resumen m.

absurd [əbˈsɜːd] adj absurdo,-a.

abundance [əˈbʌndəns] n abundancia.

abundant [əˈbʌndənt] adj abundante.

abuse [(n) əˈbjuːs; (vb) əˈbjuːz] n 1 (verbal) insultos mpl; (physical) malos tratos mpl. 2 (misuse) abuso.
▶ vt 1 (verbally) insultar; (physically) maltratar. 2 (misuse) abusar de.

abyss [əˈbɪs] n abismo.

abysmal [əˈbɪzməl] adj pésimo,-a.

AC [ˈeɪˈsiː] abbr ELEC (alternating current) corriente f alterna; (abbreviation) CA f.

academic [ækəˈdemɪk] adj 1 (gen) académico,-a. 2 (theoretical) teórico: it's a *purely academic question* es una cuestión puramente teórica.

▶ *n (scholar)* académico,-a; *(lecturer)* profesor,-ra universitario,-a. COMP **academic year** año académico.

academy [əˈkædəmɪ] *n* **1** academia. **2** *(in Scotland)* instituto de enseñanza media.

ⓘ *pl* **academies**.

accelerate [ækˈseləreɪt] *vt* acelerar.

▶ *vi* acelerarse.

acceleration [æksɛləˈreɪʃˀn] *n* aceleración *f*.

accelerator [əkˈseləreɪtəʳ] *n* acelerador *m*.

accent [*(n)* ˈæksənt; *(vb)* ækˈsent] *n* acento.

▶ *vt* acentuar.

accentuate [ækˈsentʃueɪt] *vt* acentuar.

accentuation [æksentʃuˈeɪʃˀn] *n* acentuación *f*.

accept [əkˈsept] *vt* aceptar, admitir.

acceptable [əkˈseptəbˀl] *adj* aceptable, admisible.

acceptance [əkˈseptəns] *n* **1** *(act of accepting)* aceptación *f*. **2** *(approval)* acogida.

access [ˈækses] *n* acceso.

▶ *vt* COMPUT acceder a, entrar en. COMP **access code** código de acceso. ❙ **access road** carretera de acceso.

accessibility [æksesɪˈbɪlɪtɪ] *n* accesibilidad *f*.

accessible [ækˈsesɪbˀl] *adj* **1** accesible. **2** *(person)* asequible, tratable.

accessory [ækˈsesərɪ] *n* **1** *(gadget)* accesorio. **2** JUR *(accomplice)* cómplice *mf*.

▶ *n pl* **accessories** *(bag, gloves, etc)* complementos *mpl*.

ⓘ *pl* **accessories**.

accident [ˈæksɪdənt] *n* accidente *m*. LOC **by accident** por casualidad.

accidental [æksɪˈdentˀl] *adj* fortuito,-a.

acclaim [əˈkleɪm] *n* **1** *(welcome)* aclamación *f*. **2** *(praise)* elogios *mpl*, alabanza.

▶ *vt* **1** *(welcome)* aclamar. **2** *(praise)* elogiar, alabar.

acclimatize [əˈklaɪmətaɪz] *vt* aclimatar.

▶ *vi* aclimatarse.

accommodate [əˈkɒmədeɪt] *vt* alojar.

accommodation [əkɒməˈdeɪʃˀn] *n* alojamiento.

accomplice [əˈkɒmplɪs] *n* cómplice *mf*.

accomplish [əˈkɒmplɪʃ] *vt* lograr.

accomplishment [əˈkɒmplɪʃmənt] *n* **1** *(act of achieving)* realización *f*. **2** *(achievement)* logro.

▶ *n pl* **accomplishments** *(skills)* aptitudes *fpl*, dotes *fpl*, habilidades *fpl*.

accord [əˈkɔːd] *n* *(agreement)* acuerdo: *the Oslo accords* los acuerdos de Oslo. LOC **of one's own accord** espontáneamente, por propia voluntad.

▶ *vt (award)* conceder, otorgar.

❌ To accord no significa 'acordar', que se traduce por to agree.

accordance [əˈkɔːdˀns] LOC **in accordance with** de acuerdo con.

according [əˈkɔːdɪŋ] *prep* **according to 1** según: *according to Philip/the paper/my watch* según Philip/el periódico/mi reloj. **2** *(consistent with)* de acuerdo con: *it went according to plan* salió tal como se había previsto.

accordion [əˈkɔːdɪən] *n* acordeón *m*.

account [əˈkaunt] *n* **1** *(in bank)* cuenta. **2** *(report)* relación *f*, relato, informe *m*: *he gave us an account of his experiences* nos contó sus experiencias. LOC **on account of** por, a causa de: *don't leave on my account* no te vayas por mí. ❙ **on no account** bajo ningún concepto. ❙ **to keep the accounts** llevar las cuentas. ❙ **to take into account** tener en cuenta. COMP **accounts department** sección *f* de contabilidad.

◆ **to account for** *vi* explicar.

accountable [əˈkauntəbˀl] *adj* LOC **to be accountable to sb for sth** ser responsable ante ALGN de ALGO.

accountant [əˈkauntənt] *n* contable *mf*.

accumulate [əˈkjuːmjuleɪt] *vt* acumular.

▶ *vi* acumularse.

accumulation [əkjuːmjuˈleɪʃˀn] *n* acumulación *f*.

accumulator [əˈkjuːmjuleɪtəʳ] *n* acumulador *m*.

accuracy [ˈækjurəsɪ] *n* **1** *(of numbers, instrument, information)* exactitud *f*, precisión *f*. **2** *(of shot)* certeza.

accurate ['ækjʊrət] *adj* **1** *(numbers, etc)* exacto,-a, preciso,-a. **2** *(instrument)* de precisión. **3** *(shot)* certero,-a.

accusation [ækjuːˈzeɪʃᵊn] *n* acusación *f*.

accuse [əˈkjuːz] *vt* acusar (of, de).

accused [əˈkjuːzd] *n* **the accused** *(man)* el acusado; *(woman)* la acusada.

accustom [əˈkʌstəm] *vt* acostumbrar (to, a).

accustomed [əˈkʌstəmᵊd] *adj* [LOC] **to be accustomed to** esar acostumbrado a.

ace [eɪs] *n* **1** *(gen)* as *m*. **2** *(tennis)* ace *m*.

acetic [əˈsiːtɪk] *adj* acético,-a. [COMP] **acetic acid** ácido acético.

acetone ['æsɪtəʊn] *n* acetona.

acetylene [əˈsetɪliːn] *n* acetileno.

ache [eɪk] *n* dolor *m*.
▶ *vi* doler: *my head aches* me duele la cabeza, tengo dolor de cabeza.

📎 Ache se usa para formar palabras compuestas como **headache** *(dolor de cabeza)*, **toothache** *(dolor de muelas)*, **earache** *(dolor de oídos)* o **stomach-ache** *(dolor de estómago)*.

achieve [əˈtʃiːv] *vt* **1** *(finish)* realizar, llevar a cabo. **2** *(attain)* lograr, conseguir.

achievement [əˈtʃiːvmənt] *n* **1** *(completion)* realización *f*. **2** *(attainment)* logro. **3** *(feat)* hazaña, proeza.

Achilles [əˈkɪliːz] *n* Aquiles. [COMP] **Achilles' heel** *fig* talón *m* de Aquiles. ▮ **Achilles' tendon** ANAT tendón *m* de Aquiles.

acid ['æsɪd] *adj* **1** CHEM ácido,-a. **2** *(taste)* agrio,-a. [COMP] **acid rain** lluvia ácida.
▶ *n* CHEM ácido,-a.

acknowledge [əkˈnɒlɪdʒ] *vt* **1** *(admit)* admitir, reconocer. **2** *(be thankful)* agradecer, expresar agradecimiento por. [LOC] **to acknowledge receipt of** acusar recibo de.

acknowledgement [əkˈnɒlɪdʒmənt] *n* **1** *(recognition)* reconocimiento. **2** *(thanks)* muestra de agradecimiento. [COMP] **acknowledgement of receipt** acuse *m* de recibo.

acknowledgment [ækˈnɒlɪdʒmənt] *n* → acknowledgement.

acne ['ækni] *n* acné *f*.

acorn ['eɪkɔːn] *n* bellota.

acoustic [əˈkuːstɪk] *adj* acústico,-a.

acoustics [əˈkuːstɪks] *n* *(science)* acústica.
▶ *n pl* *(sound conditions)* acústica *f sing*.

acquaint [əˈkweɪnt] *vt* informar (with, de). [LOC] **to acquaint os with** STH familiarizarse con ALGO. ▮ **to be acquainted with** SB conocer a ALGN, tener trato con ALGN.

acquaintance [əˈkweɪntəns] *n* *(person)* conocido,-a: *an acquaintance of mine* un conocido mío. [LOC] **to make SB's acquaintance** conocer a ALGN.

acquiesce [ækwɪˈes] *vi* consentir (in, en), conformarse (in, con).

acquire [əˈkwaɪəʳ] *vt* adquirir.

acquisition [ækwɪˈzɪʃᵊn] *n* adquisición *f*.

acquit [əˈkwɪt] *vt* absolver, declarar inocente.
ⓘ *pt & pp* acquitted, *ger* acquitting.

acquittal [əˈkwɪtᵊl] *n* absolución *f*.

acre ['eɪkəʳ] *n* acre *m*.

📎 Un acre equivale a 40,47 hectáreas.

acrobat ['ækrəbæt] *n* acróbata *mf*.

acrobatic [ækrəˈbætɪk] *adj* acrobático,-a.

acronym ['ækrənɪm] *n* sigla.

acropolis [əˈkrɒpəlɪs] *n* acrópolis *f*.

across [əˈkrɒs] *prep* **1** *(movement)* a través de, de un lado a otro de: *to swim across a river* cruzar un río nadando/a nado. **2** *(position)* al otro lado de: *they live across the road* viven enfrente.
▶ *adv* de un lado a otro: *it's 4 metres across* mide 4 metros de lado a lado.

📎 Con verbos como **walk, run, swim**, etc, se suele traducir por 'cruzar' o 'atravesar'.

acrylic [əˈkrɪlɪk] *adj* acrílico,-a.

act [ækt] *n* **1** acto, acción *f*. **2** THEAT acto. **3** *(of parliament)* ley *f*. [COMP] **act of God** fuerza mayor.
▶ *vi* **1** *(do something)* actuar. **2** *(behave)* portarse, comportarse: *she acts like a little girl* se comporta como una niña. **3** *(in theatre)* actuar, hacer teatro; *(in cinema)* actuar, hacer cine.

▸ *vt* hacer el papel de: *she's acting (the part of) Portia* ella hace el papel de Portia.
◆ **to act as** *vt insep* hacer de: *I had to act as interpreter* tuve que hacer de intérprete.

acting ['æktɪŋ] *adj* en funciones.
▸ *n* **1** THEAT *(profession)* teatro. **2** *(performance)* interpretación *f*, actuación *f*.

actinium [æk'tɪnɪəm] *n* actinio.

action ['ækʃən] *n* **1** *(gen)* acción *f*. **2** JUR demanda. COMP **action replay** repetición *f* de la jugada. ▮ **action stations** zafarrancho de combate.

❌ Action no significa 'acción' (de una empresa), que se traduce por share.

activate ['æktɪveɪt] *vt (mechanism, bomb)* activar.

activation [æktɪ'veɪʃən] *n (of mechanism, bomb)* activación *f*.

active ['æktɪv] *adj* activo,-a. COMP **the active voice** la voz activa.

activism ['æktɪvɪzəm] *n* activismo.

activist ['æktɪvɪst] *n* activista *mf*.

activity [æk'tɪvɪtɪ] *n* actividad *f*.
ⓘ *pl* activities.

actor ['æktər] *n* actor *m*.

actress ['æktrəs] *n* actriz *f*.

actual ['æktʃʊəl] *adj* real, verdadero,-a.

❌ Actual no significa 'actual', que se traduce por present, current o up-to-date.

actually ['æktʃʊəlɪ] *adv* **1** en realidad, realmente, de hecho: *I haven't actually decided what to do yet* en realidad, todavía no he decidido qué hacer. **2** *(indicating surprise)* incluso, hasta: *she actually accused me of stealing her bag* hasta me acusó de robarle el bolso.

❌ Actually no significa 'actualmente', que se traduce por nowadays, at present.

acupuncture ['ækjʊpʌŋktʃə] *n* acupuntura.

acupuncturist ['ækjʊpʌŋktʃərɪst] *n* acupunturista *mf*.

acute [ə'kjuːt] *adj* **1** *(gen)* agudo,-a. **2** *(angle)* agudo,-a. **3** *(hearing, etc)* muy

fino,-a, muy desarrollado,-a. COMP **acute accent** acento agudo. ▮ **acute triangle** triángulo acutángulo.

AD ['eɪ'diː] *abbr* **(Anno Domini)** después de Cristo; *(abbreviation)* d.J.C.

ad [æd] *n fam* anuncio.

Adam ['ædəm] *n* Adán *m*. COMP **Adam's apple** nuez *f* (de la garganta).

adamant ['ædəmənt] *adj* firme, inflexible. LOC **to be adamant about** STH mantenerse firme en ALGO.

adapt [ə'dæpt] *vt* adaptar.
▸ *vi* adaptarse.

adaptable [ə'dæptəbəl] *adj (person)* capaz de adaptarse.

adaptation [ædəp'teɪʃən] *n* adaptación *f*.

adapter [ə'dæptər] *n* ELEC → **adaptor**.

adaptor [ə'dæptər] *n* ELEC ladrón *m*.

add [æd] *vt* **1** *(gen)* añadir, agregar. **2** *(numbers)* sumar.
◆ **to add to** *vt insep* aumentar.
◆ **to add up** *vt sep (numbers)* sumar.
▸ *vi fig* cuadrar: *there's something funny going on; it doesn't add up* pasa algo raro; es que no cuadra.

addend ['ædənd] *n* MAT sumando.

adder ['ædər] *n* ZOOL víbora.

addict ['ædɪkt] *n* **1** adicto,-a. **2** *fam (fanatic)* fanático,-a.

addicted [ə'dɪktɪd] *adj* adicto,-a.

addiction [ə'dɪkʃən] *n* adicción *f*.

addictive [ə'dɪktɪv] *adj* que crea adicción: *nicotine is addictive* la nicotina crea adicción.

addition [ə'dɪʃən] *n* **1** adición *f*, añadidura. **2** MATH adición *f*, suma. LOC **in addition to** además de.

additional [ə'dɪʃənəl] *adj* adicional.

additive ['ædɪtɪv] *n* aditivo.

additive-free ['ædɪtɪv'friː] *adj* sin aditivos.

address [ə'dres] *n* **1** *(on letter)* dirección *f*, señas *fpl*. **2** *(speech)* discurso, alocución *f*.
▸ *vt* **1** *(problem)* abordar. **2** *(person)* dirigirse a. COMP **address book** libro de direcciones. ▮ **form of address** tratamiento.

adductor [əˈdʌktəʳ] *n* ANAT aductor,-ra.

adenoids [ˈædənɔɪdz] *n pl* adenoides *mpl*, vegetaciones *fpl*.

adept [əˈdept] *adj* experto,-a, diestro,-a.

❌ Adept no significa 'adepto, seguidor', que se traducen por **follower, supporter**.

adequate [ˈædɪkwət] *adj* **1** *(enough)* suficiente. **2** *(satisfactory)* satisfactorio,-a.

adhere [ədˈhɪəʳ] *vi* *(stick)* adherirse, pegarse.

adherent [ədˈhɪərənt] *adj* adherente.

adhesive [ədˈhiːsɪv] *adj* adhesivo,-a.
▶ *n* adhesivo.

adipose [ˈædɪpəʊz] *adj* adiposo,-a.

adjacent [əˈdʒeɪsənt] *adj* adyacente.
COMP **adjacent angles** ángulos adyacentes.

adjective [ˈædʒɪktɪv] *n* adjetivo.

adjoin [əˈdʒɔɪn] *vt* lindar con.
▶ *vi* colindar.

adjoining [əˈdʒɔɪnɪŋ] *adj* **1** *(building)* contiguo,-a. **2** *(land)* colindante.

adjourn [əˈdʒɜːn] *vt* aplazar, suspender.
▶ *vi* suspenderse.

adjournment [əˈdʒɜːnmənt] *n* aplazamiento, suspensión *f*.

adjust [əˈdʒʌst] *vt* ajustar, arreglar.
▶ *vi* *(person)* adaptarse.

adjustable [əˈdʒʌstəbəl] *adj* regulable.
COMP **adjustable spanner** llave *f* inglesa.

adjustment [əˈdʒʌstmənt] *n* **1** ajuste *m*, arreglo. **2** *(person)* adaptación *f*. **3** *(change)* cambio.

administer [ədˈmɪnɪstəʳ] *vt* **1** *(control)* administrar. **2** *(give)* administrar, dar; *(laws, punishment)* aplicar.

administration [ədmɪnɪsˈtreɪʃ°n] *n* **1** administración *f*. **2** *(of law, etc)* aplicación *f*.

administrator [ədˈmɪnɪstreɪtəʳ] *n* administrador,-ra.

admirable [ˈædmɪrəbəl] *adj* admirable.

admiral [ˈædmərəl] *n* almirante *m*.

admiration [ædmɪˈreɪʃ°n] *n* admiración *f*.

admire [ədˈmaɪəʳ] *vt* admirar.

admirer [ədˈmaɪərəʳ] *n* *(gen)* admirador,-ra; *(suitor)* pretendiente *mf*.

admissible [ədˈmɪsɪbəl] *adj* admisible.

admission [ədˈmɪʃ°n] *n* **1** *(gen)* admisión *f*; *(to hospital)* ingreso. **2** *(price)* entrada. **3** *(acknowledgement)* reconocimiento.

admit [ədˈmɪt] *vt* **1** *(allow in)* admitir; *(to hospital)* ingresar. **2** *(acknowledge)* reconocer.
① *pt & pp* admitted, *ger* admitting.

admittance [ədˈmɪt°ns] *n* entrada. LOC «No admittance» «Prohibida la entrada».

admittedly [ədˈmɪtɪdlɪ] *adv* es verdad que, lo cierto es que.

admonish [ədˈmɒnɪʃ] *vt* amonestar.

ado [əˈduː] *n* LOC **without further ado** sin más preámbulos.

adobe [əˈdəʊbɪ] *n* adobe *m*.

adolescence [ædəˈles°ns] *n* adolescencia.

adolescent [ædəˈles°nt] *adj* adolescente.
▶ *n* adolescente *mf*.

adopt [əˈdɒpt] *vt* adoptar.

adoption [əˈdɒpʃ°n] *n* adopción *f*.

adoptive [əˈdɒptɪv] *adj* adoptivo,-a.

adore [əˈdɔːʳ] *vt* adorar.

adorn [əˈdɔːn] *vt* adornar.

adrenalin [əˈdrenəlɪn] *n* adrenalina.

Adriatic [eɪdrɪˈætɪk] *adj* adriático,-a. COMP **the Adriatic (Sea)** el (mar) Adriático.

adrift [əˈdrɪft] *adj* a la deriva.

adulate [ˈædjʊleɪt] *vt* adular.

adult [ˈædʌlt] *adj* **1** *(gen)* adulto,-a. **2** *(film, etc)* para adultos.
▶ *n* adulto,-a.

adulterate [əˈdʌltəreɪt] *vt* adulterar.

adultery [əˈdʌltərɪ] *n* adulterio.

advance [ədˈvɑːns] *n* **1** *(gen)* avance *m*. **2** *(payment)* anticipo. LOC **in advance 1** *(gen)* antes. **2** *(rent, etc)* por adelantado.
▶ *vt* **1** *(gen)* avanzar. **2** *(money, date)* adelantar.

advantage [ədˈvɑːntɪdʒ] *n* **1** ventaja. **2** *(benefit)* provecho. LOC **to take advantage of 1** *(thing)* aprovechar. **2** *(person)* aprovecharse de.

advantageous [ædvən'teɪdʒəs] *adj* ventajoso,-a, provechoso,-a.

adventure [əd'ventʃər] *n* aventura. COMP **adventure playground** parque *m* infantil.

adverb ['ædvɜ:b] *n* adverbio.

adversary ['ædvəsərɪ] *n* adversario,-a.
① *pl* adversaries.

adversative [æd'vɜ:sətɪv] *adj* adversativo,-a.

adverse ['ædvɜ:s] *adj* desfavorable.

adversity [əd'vɜ:sɪtɪ] *n* adversidad *f*.
① *pl* adversities.

advert ['ædvɜ:t] *n fam* anuncio.

advertise ['ædvətaɪz] *vt* anunciar.
▶ *vi* hacer publicidad.

advertisement [əd'vɜ:tɪsmənt] *n* anuncio.
▶ *n pl* **advertisements** *(on television)* publicidad *f*, anuncios *mpl*.

X Advertisement no significa 'advertencia', que se traduce por **warning**.
---

advertiser ['ædvətaɪzər] *n* anunciante *mf*.

advertising ['ædvətaɪzɪŋ] *n* publicidad *f*. COMP **advertising agency** agencia de publicidad. ▌ **advertising campaign** campaña publicitaria.

advice [əd'vaɪs] *n* consejos *mpl*. COMP **a piece of advice** un consejo.

advise [əd'vaɪz] *vt* aconsejar.

X To advise no significa 'avisar', que se traduce por **to warn**.
---

adviser [əd'vaɪzər] *n* consejero,-a.

advocate [*(n)* 'ædvəkət; *(vb)* 'ædvəkeɪt] *n* **1** *(supporter)* partidario,-a. **2** *(lawyer)* abogado,-a defensor,-ra.
▶ *vt* abogar por, propugnar.

Aegean [ɪ'dʒiːən] *adj* egeo,-a. COMP **the Aegean (Sea)** el (mar) Egeo.

aerial ['eərɪəl] *adj* aéreo,-a.
▶ *n* antena.

aerobe ['eərəub] *n* aerobio.

aerobics [eə'rəubɪks] *n* aerobic *m*, aeróbic *m*.

aerodrome ['eərədrəum] *n* aeródromo.

aerodynamics [eərəudaɪ'næmɪks] *n* aerodinámica.

aeronautics [eərə'nɔ:tɪks] *n* aeronáutica.

aeroplane ['eərəpleɪn] *n* aeroplano, avión *m*.

aerosol ['eərəsɒl] *n* aerosol *m*.

aerostatic [eərə'stætɪk] *adj* aerostático,-a.

aesthetic [i:s'θetɪk] *adj* estético,-a.

aesthetics [i:s'θetɪks] *n* estética.

affair [ə'feər] *n* **1** *(matter)* asunto: *that's your affair* eso es asunto tuyo. **2** *(case)* caso: *the Watergate affair* el caso Watergate. COMP **current affairs** actualidad *f sing*.

affect [ə'fekt] *vt* **1** *(gen)* afectar. **2** *(feign)* fingir, afectar: *he affected indifference* fingió indiferencia.

affection [ə'fekʃən] *n* afecto, cariño.

affectionate [ə'fekʃənət] *adj* afectuoso,-a, cariñoso,-a.

affiliate [ə'fɪlɪət] *n* afiliado,-a.
▶ *vt* afiliar.
▶ *vi* afiliar.

affinity [ə'fɪnɪtɪ] *n* afinidad *f*.
① *pl* affinities.

affirm [ə'fɜ:m] *vt* afirmar, asegurar.

affirmation [æfə'meɪʃən] *n* afirmación *f*.

affirmative [ə'fɜ:mətɪv] *adj* afirmativo,-a.

affix [ə'fɪks] *vt* *(stamp)* poner; *(poster)* fijar.

afflict [ə'flɪkt] *vt* afligir.

affluence ['æfluəns] *n* riqueza, prosperidad *f*.

affluent ['æfluənt] *adj* rico,-a.

afford [ə'fɔ:d] *vt* permitirse, costear: *I can't afford to pay £750 for a coat* no puedo (permitirme) pagar 750 libras por un abrigo.

afforestation [əfɒrɪ'steɪʃən] *n* repoblación *f* forestal.

affricate ['æfrɪkət] *n* africada.

Afghan ['æfgæn] *adj* afgano,-a.
▶ *n* **1** *(person)* afgano,-a. **2** *(language)* afgano.

Afghanistan [æfgænɪ'stæn] *n* Afganistán *m*.

afield [ə'fiːld] *adv* LOC **far afield** lejos: *they went as far afield as Canada* llegaron hasta Canadá.

afloat [ə'fləʊt] *adj* a flote.

afoot [ə'fʊt] *adv* en marcha, en proceso.

afraid [ə'freɪd] *adj* temeroso,-a. LOC **to be afraid 1** *(frightened)* tener miedo. **2** *(sorry)* temer, sentir, lamentar: *I'm afraid so/not* me temo que sí/no. ❙ **to be afraid of** STH/SB tener miedo de ALGO/ALGN.

afresh [ə'freʃ] *adv* de nuevo: *he had to start afresh* tuvo que volver a empezar.

África ['æfrɪkə] *n* África. COMP **South Africa** Sudáfrica.

African ['æfrɪkən] *adj* africano,-a.
▶ *n* africano,-a. COMP **South African** sudafricano,-a.

Afro ['æfrəʊ] *adj & n (hairstyle)* afro.

Afro-American [æfrəʊə'merɪkᵊn] *adj* afroamericano,-a.
▶ *n* afroamericano,-a.

⊕ Afro-American es el término más adecuado para referirse a los estadounidenses cuyos antepasados eran originarios del África subsahariana y que, en su mayoría, fueron llevados como esclavos a América entre los siglos XVI y XIX.

after ['ɑːftəʳ] *prep* **1** *(time)* después de: *after class* después de la clase. **2** *(following)* detrás de: *the police are after us* la policía nos está persiguiendo. **3** US *(past)* y: *it's a quarter after four* son las cuatro y cuarto.
▶ *adv* después: *the day after* el día después.
▶ *conj* después que, después de que: *after he left, I went to bed* después de que se marchara, me acosté.
▶ *n pl* **afters** GB *fam* postre *m*.

afterbirth ['ɑːftəbɜːθ] *n* placenta.

after-effect ['ɑːftərɪfekt] *n* efecto secundario, secuela.

afterlife ['ɑːftəlaɪf] *n* más allá *m*.

afternoon [ɑːftə'nuːn] *n* tarde *f*: *in the afternoon* por la tarde.

after-sales service [ɑːftə'seɪlzsɜːvɪs] *n* servicio posventa.

aftershave ['ɑːftəʃeɪv] *n* loción *f* para después del afeitado.

aftertaste ['ɑːftəteɪst] *n* regusto.

afterwards ['ɑːftəwədz] *adv* después, luego.

again [ə'gen, ə'geɪn] *adv* **1** *(once more)* otra vez, de nuevo: *play me that song again* tócame esa canción otra vez. **2** *(in questions)*: *where do you live again?* ¿dónde has dicho que vives? LOC **again and again** repetidamente. ❙ **now and again** de vez en cuando.

against [ə'genst, ə'geɪnst] *prep* **1** *(gen)* contra: *against the wall* contra la pared; *Leeds played against Liverpool* Leeds jugó contra Liverpool. **2** *(opposed to)* en contra de: *I voted against the proposal* voté en contra de la propuesta.

age [eɪdʒ] *n* edad *f*. LOC **of age** mayor de edad. ❙ **under age** menor de edad.
▶ *vt & vi* envejecer.

aged [eɪdʒd] *adj* de (tantos años de) edad: *a boy aged ten* un muchacho de diez años. COMP **the aged** los ancianos *mpl*.

agency ['eɪdʒᵊnsɪ] *n* **1** *(commercial)* agencia: *a travel/advertising/employment agency* una agencia de viajes/publicidad/empleo. **2** *(governmental, etc)* organismo.
① *pl* **agencies**.

agenda [ə'dʒendə] *n* orden *m* del día.

❌ Agenda no significa 'agenda', que se traduce por **diary**.

agent ['eɪdʒᵊnt] *n* agente *mf*.

aggravate ['ægrəveɪt] *vt* **1** *(make worse)* agravar. **2** *fam (annoy)* irritar, molestar.

aggression [ə'greʃᵊn] *n* **1** *(act)* agresión *f*. **2** *(feeling)* agresividad *f*.

aggressive [ə'gresɪv] *adj* **1** *(gen)* agresivo,-a. **2** *(dynamic)* emprendedor,-ra.

aggressor [ə'gresəʳ] *n* agresor,-ra.

aghast [ə'gɑːst] *adj* horrorizado,-a.

agile ['ædʒaɪl] *adj* ágil.

agility [ə'dʒɪlɪtɪ] *n* agilidad *f*.

agitate ['ædʒɪteɪt] *vt* agitar.

agnostic [æg'nɒstɪk] *adj* agnóstico,-a.
▶ *n* agnóstico,-a.

ago [ə'gəʊ] *adv* hace: *ten days ago* hace diez días; *it happened a long time ago* ocurrió hace mucho tiempo.

✎ Ago se usa siempre con el verbo en pasado. Consulta también **for, since**.

agonise ['ægənaɪz] *vi* → **agonize**.

agonize ['ægənaɪz] *vi* agonizar.

agony ['ægənɪ] *n* **1** *(pain)* dolor *m* muy agudo. **2** *(anguish)* angustia.
ⓘ *pl* agonies.

X Agony no significa 'agonía (antes de morir)', que se traduce por dying breath.

agora ['ægərə] *n* ágora.
ⓘ *pl* agoras o agorae ['ægəraɪ, 'ægəri:].

agree [ə'gri:] *vi* **1** *(be in agreement)* estar de acuerdo (with, con): *do you agree with me?* ¿estás de acuerdo conmigo? **2** *(reach an agreement)* ponerse de acuerdo (on, en): *they can't agree on a name for the baby* no se ponen de acuerdo en el nombre del bebé. **4** *(food, climate, etc)* sentar bien (with, -): *the prawns didn't agree with me* las gambas no me sentaron bien.
► *vt (grammatically)* concordar (with, con).

agreeable [ə'gri:əbəl] *adj* **1** *(pleasant)* agradable. **2** *(in agreement)* conforme.

agreement [ə'gri:mənt] *n* **1** acuerdo: *the two men reached an agreement* los dos hombres llegaron a un acuerdo. **2** *(grammatical)* concordancia.

agricultural [ægrɪ'kʌltʃərəl] *adj* agrícola.

agriculture ['ægrɪkʌltʃəʳ] *n* agricultura.

agronomy [ə'grɒnəmɪ] *n* agronomía.

aground [ə'graund] *adj* encallado,-a.
LOC **to run aground** encallar.

ahead [ə'hed] *adv (in front)* delante: *there's a police checkpoint ahead* hay un control de policía aquí delante; *we finished ahead of schedule* acabamos antes de lo previsto. LOC **go ahead!** ¡adelante!

aid [eɪd] *n (help)* ayuda; *(rescue)* auxilio. COMP **humanitarian aid** ayuda humanitaria.
► *vt* ayudar, auxiliar.

AIDS [eɪdz] *n* (Acquired Immune Deficiency Syndrome) sida *m*.

aileron ['eɪlərɒn] *n* alerón *m*.

ailing ['eɪlɪŋ] *adj* enfermo,-a.

ailment ['eɪlmənt] *n* dolencia, achaque *m*.

aim [eɪm] *n* **1** *(marksmanship)* puntería: *his aim is good* tiene buena puntería. **2** *(objective)* meta, objetivo: *what's your aim in life?* ¿qué objetivo tienes en la vida?

► *vt* **1** *(gun)* apuntar (at, a). **2** *(attack)* dirigir (at, a).

ain't [eɪnt] *contr fam* → am not, is not, are not, has not, have not.

air [eəʳ] *n* aire *m*. LOC **by air 1** *(send letter)* por avión. **2** *(travel)* en avión. COMP **air hostess** azafata. ‖ **air lane** ruta aérea. ‖ **air pressure** presión *f* atmosférica. ‖ **air rifle** escopeta de aire comprimido. ‖ **air terminal** terminal *f* aérea. ‖ **air traffic controller** controlador,-ra aéreo,-a.
► *vt* **1** *(gen)* airear. **2** *(room)* ventilar.

airbag ['eəbæg] *n* airbag *m*.

airbase ['eəbeɪs] *n* base *f* aérea.

air-bed ['eəbed] *n* GB colchón *m* de aire.

air-conditioned [eəkən'dɪʃ°nd] *adj* con aire acondicionado, refrigerado,-a.

air-conditioning [eəkən'dɪʃ°nɪŋ] *n* aire *m* acondicionado.

aircraft ['eəkrɑ:ft] *n (gen)* aeronave *f*; *(plane)* avión *m*.
ⓘ *pl* aircraft.

aircraft-carrier ['eəkrɑːftkærɪəʳ] *n* portaaviones *m inv*.

airfield ['eəfiːld] *n* campo de aviación.

airforce ['eəfɔːs] *n* fuerza aérea, fuerzas *fpl* aéreas.

airline ['eəlaɪn] *n* línea aérea.

airliner ['eəlaɪnəʳ] *n* avión *m* de pasajeros *(grande)*.

airmail ['eəmeɪl] *n* correo aéreo.

airplane ['eəpleɪn] *n* US aeroplano, avión *m*.

airport ['eəpɔːt] *n* aeropuerto.

airship ['eəʃɪp] *n* dirigible *m*.

airsick ['eəsɪk] *adj* mareado,-a. LOC **to be airsick** marearse.

airspace ['eəspeɪs] *n* espacio aéreo.

airstrip ['eəstrɪp] *n* pista de aterrizaje.

airtight ['eətaɪt] *adj* hermético,-a.

airway ['eəweɪ] *n* **1** *(route)* ruta aérea, vía aérea. **2** *(airline)* línea aérea.

airy ['eərɪ] *adj* **1** *(ventilated)* bien ventilado,-a. **2** *(light)* ligero,-a.
ⓘ *comp* airier, *superl* airiest.

aisle [aɪl] *n* **1** *(between seats, shelves, etc)* pasillo. **2** *(section of church)* nave *f* lateral.

aitch [eɪtʃ] *n* hache *f*.

ajar [ə'dʒɑːʳ] *adj* entreabierto,-a.

akimbo [ə'kɪmbəʊ] *adv* en jarras.

akin [ə'kɪn] *adj* parecido,-a (to, a).

alabaster ['æləbɑːstəʳ] *n* alabastro.

alarm [ə'lɑːm] *n* **1** *(device)* alarma. **2** *(fear)* temor *m*, alarma. COMP **alarm clock** despertador *m*.
▶ *vt* alarmar, asustar.

alarmism [ə'lɑːmɪzᵊm] *n* alarmismo.

Albanian [æl'beɪnɪən] *adj* albanés,-esa.
▶ *n* **1** *(person)* albanés,-esa. **2** *(language)* albanés *m*.

albatross ['ælbətrɒs] *n* albatros *m*.

albino [æl'biːnəʊ] *adj* albino,-a.
▶ *n* albino,-a.
ⓘ *pl* albinos.

album ['ælbəm] *n* álbum *m*.

albumen ['ælbjʊmɪn, US æl'bjuːmən] *n* **1** *(white of egg)* clara de huevo. **2** *(in plants)* albumen *m*.

albumin ['ælbjʊmɪn, US æl'bjuːmən] *n* albúmina.

alcohol ['ælkəhɒl] *n* alcohol *m*.

alcohol-free ['ælkəhɒlfriː] *adj* sin alcohol.

alcoholism ['ælkəhɒlɪzᵊm] *n* alcoholismo.

aldehyde ['ældɪhaɪd] *n* aldehído.

ale [eɪl] *n* cerveza.

alert [ə'lɜːt] *adj* **1** *(quick to act)* alerta, vigilante. **2** *(lively)* vivo,-a.
▶ *n* alarma.
▶ *vt* alertar, avisar.

A-level ['eɪlevᵊl] *abbr* GB (Advanced level) ≈ segundo curso de bachillerato.

alfalfa [æl'fælfə] *n* alfalfa.

algae ['ældʒiː] *n pl* algas *fpl*.
ⓘ *sing* alga ['ælgə].

algebra ['ældʒɪbrə] *n* álgebra.

algebraic [ældʒɪ'breɪɪk] *adj* algebraico,-a.

Algeria [æl'dʒɪərɪə] *n* Argelia.

Algerian [æl'dʒɪərɪən] *adj* argelino,-a.
▶ *n* argelino,-a.

algorithm ['ælgərɪðᵊm] *n* algoritmo.

alias ['eɪlɪəs] *adv* alias.
▶ *n* alias *m*.

alibi ['ælɪbaɪ] *n* coartada.

alien ['eɪlɪən] *adj* **1** *(foreign)* extranjero,-a. **2** *(extraterrestrial)* extraterrestre. **3** *(strange)* extraño,-a, ajeno,-a: *his ideas are alien to me* sus ideas me son ajenas.
▶ *n* **1** *(foreigner)* extranjero,-a. **2** *(extraterrestrial)* extraterrestre *mf*.

alight [ə'laɪt] *adj* encendido,-a, ardiendo.

align [ə'laɪn] *vt* alinear (with, con).

alike [ə'laɪk] *adj (the same)* iguales; *(similar)* parecidos,-as: *they are alike in all respects* son iguales en todo.
▶ *adv* igual: *they dress alike* visten igual.

alimentary [ælɪ'mentᵊrɪ] *adj* alimenticio,-a. COMP **alimentary canal** tubo digestivo.

alimony ['ælɪmənɪ] *n* pensión *f* alimenticia.

alive [ə'laɪv] *adj* vivo,-a.

alkaline ['ælkəlaɪn] *adj* alcalino,-a.

all [ɔːl] *adj (singular)* todo,-a; *(plural)* todos,-as: *all the chairs* todas las sillas; *all day/month/year* todo el día/mes/año.
▶ *pron* **1** *(everything)* todo, la totalidad *f*: *all was lost in the fire* se perdió todo en el incendio. **2** *(everybody)* todos *mpl*, todo el mundo: *all of them helped/they all helped* ayudaron todos.
▶ *adv* completamente, totalmente: *she was dressed all in leather* iba vestida toda de cuero. LOC **after all 1** *(despite everything)* después de todo. **2** *(it must be remembered)* no hay que olvidarlo. ▎ **all over** en todas partes. ▎ **all over** acabar: *in ten minutes it was all over* en diez minutos todo había acabado. ▎ **all right 1** *(acceptable)* bien, bueno,-a: *the film's all right, but I've seen better ones* la película no está mal, pero las he visto mejores. **2** *(well, safe)* bien: *are you all right?* ¿estás bien? **3** *(accepting suggestion)* vale, bueno: *are you coming? –all right* ¿te vienes? –vale. ▎ **all that** tan: *he's not all that fast* no es tan rápido. ▎ **all the + comp** tanto + adj/adv, aún + adj/adv: *all the better* tanto mejor. ▎ **all the time** todo el rato, siempre. ▎ **at all** en absoluto. ▎ **in all** en total. ▎ **not at all** no hay de qué.

Allah ['ælə] *n* Alá *m*.

alleged [ə'ledʒd] *adj* presunto,-a.

allegory ['ælɪgərɪ] *n* alegoría.
ⓘ *pl* allegories.

allergic [ə'lɜːdʒɪk] *adj* alérgico,-a (to, a).

allergy ['ælədʒɪ] *n* alergia.
ⓘ *pl* allergies.

alleviate [ə'liːvɪeɪt] *vt* aliviar, mitigar.

alley ['ælɪ] *n* callejuela, callejón *m*.

alliance [ə'laɪəns] *n* alianza.

allied ['ælaɪd] *adj* **1** POL aliado,-a. **2** *(related)* relacionado,-a, afín.

alligator ['ælɪgeɪtə'] *n* caimán *m*.

alliteration [əlɪtə'reɪʃ°n] *n* aliteración *f*.

allocate ['æləkeɪt] *vt (money)* destinar; *(time, space, job, etc)* asignar.

allocation [ælə'keɪʃ°n] *n* **1** *(distribution)* asignación *f*; *(of money)* distribución *f*. **2** *(money given)* cuota.

allot [ə'lɒt] *vt* asignar.
ⓘ *pt & pp* allotted, *ger* allotting.

all-out [ɔːl'aʊt] *adj* total.

allow [ə'laʊ] *vt* **1** *(permit)* permitir, dejar. **2** *(set aside)* conceder, dar, dejar. **3** *(admit)* admitir, reconocer.
◆ **to allow for** *vt insep* tener en cuenta.

allowance [ə'laʊəns] *n* **1** *(from government)* subsidio, prestación *f*. **2** *(from employer)* dietas *fpl*, asignación *f*. **3** US *(pocket money)* paga semanal. LOC **to make allowances for 1** *(take into account)* tener en cuenta. **2** *(be permissive)* tener paciencia con.

alloy ['ælɔɪ] *n* aleación *f*.

all-purpose [ɔːl'pɜːpəs] *adj* multiuso.

all-star ['ɔːlstɑː'] *adj* estelar: *an all-star cast* un reparto estelar.

all-terrain [ɔːltə'reɪn] *adj* todo terreno.

allude [ə'luːd] *vi* aludir (to, a).

allure [ə'ljʊə'] *n* atractivo, encanto.
▶ *vt* atraer, seducir.

alluring [ə'ljʊərɪŋ] *adj* seductor,-ra.

allusion [ə'luːʒ°n] *n* alusión *f*.

alluvial [ə'luːvɪəl] *adj* aluvial.

ally ['ælaɪ] *n* aliado,-a.
ⓘ *pl* allies.
▶ *vt* aliar (with, con).
▶ *vi* aliarse (with, con).
ⓘ *pt & pp* allied, *ger* allying.

almighty [ɔːl'maɪtɪ] *adj* todopoderoso,-a.
▶ *n* the Almighty el Todopoderoso.

almond ['ɑːmənd] *n* almendra. COMP **almond tree** almendro.

almost ['ɔːlməʊst] *adv* casi.

alone [ə'ləʊn] *adj (unaccompanied)* solo,-a.
▶ *adv (only)* solo, solamente. LOC **to leave** STH **alone** no tocar ALGO. ▌**to leave** SB **alone** dejar a ALGN en paz.

along [ə'lɒŋ] *prep* **1** por, a lo largo de: *we walked along the riverbank* caminamos por la orilla del río. **2** *(in)* en: *his office is along this corridor* su despacho está en este pasillo.
▶ *adv* adelante, hacia adelante: *move along, please* circulen, por favor. LOC **along with** junto con. ▌**come along 1** *(sing)* ven. **2** *(plural)* venid.

alongside [əlɒŋ'saɪd] *prep* al lado de.
▶ *adv* al costado, al lado.

aloof [ə'luːf] *adj* distante.
▶ *adv* a distancia.

alopecia [ælə'piːʃə] *n* alopecia.

aloud [ə'laʊd] *adv* en voz alta.

alpha ['ælfə] *n* alfa. COMP **alpha ray** rayo alfa.

alphabet ['ælfəbet] *n* alfabeto, abecedario.

alphabetical [ælfə'betɪk°l] *adj* alfabético,-a. LOC **in alphabetical order** por orden alfabético.

alphanumeric [ælfənjuː'merɪk] *adj* alfanumérico,-a.

alpine ['ælpaɪn] *adj* alpino,-a.

Alps [ælps] *n pl* the Alps los Alpes *mpl*.

already [ɔːl'redɪ] *adv* ya: *they've already left* ya se han ido.

also ['ɔːlsəʊ] *adv* también.

altar ['ɔːltə'] *n* altar *m*.

altarpiece ['ɔːltəpiːs] *n* retablo.

alter ['ɔːltə'] *vt (gen)* cambiar; *(clothes)* arreglar.
▶ *vi* cambiar, cambiarse.

alteration [ɔːltə'reɪʃ°n] *n* modificación *f*.
▶ *n pl* **alterations** reformas *fpl*.

alternate [*(adj)* ɔːl'tɜːnət; *(vb)* 'ɔːltɜːneɪt] *adj* alterno,-a.
▶ *vt* alternar.
▶ *vi* alternarse.

alternating ['ɔːltɜːneɪtɪŋ] COMP alternating current corriente f alterna.

alternative [ɔːl'tɜːnətɪv] adj alternativo,-a.
▸ n (option) opción f, alternativa.

alternator ['ɔːltəneɪtər] n alternador m.

although [ɔːl'ðəʊ] conj aunque.

altimeter ['æltɪmiːtər] n altímetro.

altitude ['æltɪtjuːd] n altitud f, altura.

altogether [ɔːltə'geðər] adv 1 (completely) del todo. 2 (on the whole) en conjunto. 3 (in total) en total.

altruism ['æltruɪzəm] n altruismo.

aluminium [æljʊ'mɪnɪəm] n aluminio. COMP **aluminium foil** papel m de aluminio, papel m de plata.

aluminum [ə'luːmɪnəm] n US aluminio.

alveolar [ælvɪ'əʊlər] adj alveolar. COMP **alveolar sacs** ANAT sacos alveolares.

alveolus [æl'vɪələs] n alveolo, alvéolo.
① pl **alveoli** [æl'vɪəlaɪ].

always ['ɔːlweɪz] adv siempre.

am [æm] pres → be.

a.m. ['eɪ'em] abbr (ante meridiem) de la mañana.

amass [ə'mæs] vt acumular.

amateur ['æmətər] adj aficionado,-a.
▸ n aficionado,-a.

amateurism ['æmətʃərɪzəm] n amateurismo.

amaze [ə'meɪz] vt asombrar, pasmar.

amazement [ə'meɪzmənt] n asombro, pasmo.

amazing [ə'meɪzɪŋ] adj asombroso,-a, pasmoso,-a.

Amazon ['æməzən] n **the Amazon 1** (river) el Amazonas m. **2** (basin) Amazonia.

ambassador [æm'bæsədər] n embajador,-ra.

amber ['æmbər] n ámbar m.
▸ adj ámbar.

ambience ['æmbɪəns] n ambiente m.

ambiguity [æmbɪ'gjuːɪtɪ] n ambigüedad f.
① pl **ambiguities**.

ambiguous [æm'bɪgjʊəs] adj ambiguo,-a.

ambition [æm'bɪʃən] n ambición f.

ambitious [æm'bɪʃəs] adj ambicioso,-a.

ambulance ['æmbjʊləns] n ambulancia.

ambush ['æmbʊʃ] n emboscada.
▸ vt poner una emboscada a.

ameba [ə'miːbə] n US → amoeba.

ameliorate [ə'miːlɪəreɪt] vt mejorarse.
▸ vi mejorar.

amelioration [əmiːlɪə'reɪʃən] n mejora.

amen [ɑː'men] interj amén.

amenable [ə'miːnəbəl] adj tratable, bien dispuesto,-a.

amend [ə'mend] vt (law) enmendar; (error) corregir.

amendment [ə'mendmənt] n enmienda.

amenities [ə'miːnɪtɪz] n pl servicios mpl, prestaciones fpl.

America [ə'merɪkə] n América. COMP **Central America** América Central, Centroamérica. ‖ **Latin America** América Latina, Latinoamérica. ‖ **North America** América del Norte, Norteamérica. ‖ **South America** América del Sur, Sudamérica.

✎ Los estadounidenses suelen referirse a su propio país (Estados Unidos), como America y a ellos, como Americans.

American [ə'merɪkən] adj 1 (gen) americano,-a. 2 (from USA) estadounidense. COMP **American football** fútbol m americano.
▸ n 1 (gen) americano,-a. 2 (from USA) estadounidense mf.

⊕ En Estados Unidos, llaman football al fútbol americano (más parecido al rugby que al fútbol europeo) y denominan soccer a lo que nosotros llamamos «fútbol».

americium [æmə'rɪsɪəm] n americio.

amethyst ['æməθɪst] n amatista.

amiable ['eɪmɪəbəl] adj afable, amable.

amicable ['æmɪkəbəl] adj amistoso,-a, amigable.

amid [ə'mɪd] prep en medio de, entre.

amidst [ə'mɪdst] prep → amid.

amine [ə'miːn] n amina.

amino acid [æmi:nəʊˈæsɪd] *n* aminoácido.

amiss [əˈmɪs] *adv* mal. LOC **to take amiss** tomar a mal.

ammonia [əˈməʊnɪ] *n* amoníaco.

ammunition [æmjʊˈnɪʃən] *n* municiones *fpl*.

amnesia [æmˈni:zɪə] *n* amnesia.

amnesty [ˈæmnəstɪ] *n* amnistía.
① *pl* amnesties.

amniotic [æmnɪˈɒtɪk] *adj* amniótico,-a.

amoeba [əˈmi:bə] *n* ameba.
① *pl* amoebae [əˈmi:bi:].

amok [əˈmɒk] LOC **to run amok** volverse loco,-a y causar destrozos.

among [əˈmʌŋ] *prep* entre.

amongst [əˈmʌŋst] *prep* → among.

amorphous [əˈmɔ:fəs] *adj* amorfo,-a.

amount [əˈmaʊnt] *n* cantidad *f*.
◆ **to amount to** *vt insep* **1** ascender a. **2** *fig* equivaler a.

amp [æmp] *n* (*abbr of* ampere) amperio, ampere *m*.

ampere [ˈæmpeə'] *n* amperio.

amphetamine [æmˈfetəmi:n] *n* anfetamina.

amphibian [æmˈfɪbɪən] *n* anfibio.

amphibious [æmˈfɪbɪəs] *adj* anfibio,-a.

amphitheater [ˈæmfɪθɪətə'] *n* US anfiteatro.

amphitheatre [ˈæmfɪθɪətə'] *n* anfiteatro.

amphora [ˈæmfərə] *n* ánfora.
① *pl* amphoras o amphorae [ˈæmfəri:].

ample [ˈæmpəl] *adj* **1** (*enough*) bastante. **2** (*plenty*) más que suficiente. **3** (*large, generous*) amplio,-a.

amplification [æmplɪfɪˈkeɪʃən] *n* amplificación *f*.

amplifier [ˈæmplɪfaɪə'] *n* amplificador *m*.

amplify [ˈæmplɪfaɪ] *vt* **1** (*sound*) amplificar. **2** (*statement*) ampliar.
① *pt & pp* amplified, *ger* amplifying.

amplitude [ˈæmplɪtju:d] *n* amplitud *f*.

amputate [ˈæmpjuteɪt] *vt* amputar.

amputation [æmpjuˈteɪʃən] *n* amputación *f*.

amuck [əˈmʌk] *adv* → amok.

amulet [ˈæmjʊlət] *n* amuleto.

amuse [əˈmju:z] *vt* entretener, divertir.

amusement [əˈmju:zmənt] *n* **1** (*enjoyment*) diversión *f*, entretenimiento. **2** (*pastime*) pasatiempo. COMP **amusement arcade** salón *m* de juegos. ▌ **amusement park** parque *m* de atracciones.

amusing [əˈmju:zɪŋ] *adj* entretenido,-a, divertido,-a.

an [ən, æn] *indef art* **1** un, una. **2** (*per*) por.

> ✎ Se usa delante de las palabras que empiezan con sonido vocálico. Consulta también a.

anabolism [əˈnæbəlɪzəm] *n* anabolismo.

anachronistic [ənæˈkrɒnɪk] *adj* anacrónico,-a.

anaconda [ænəˈkɒndə] *n* anaconda.

anaemia [əˈni:mɪə] *n* anemia.

anaemic [əˈni:mɪk] *adj* anémico,-a.

anaerobic [æneəˈrəʊbɪk] *adj* anaerobio,-a.

anaesthesia [ænəsˈθi:zɪə] *n* anestesia.

anaesthetic [ænəsˈθetɪk] *adj* anestésico,-a.
▶ *n* anestésico.

anaesthetise [əˈni:sθətaɪz] *vt* → anaesthetize.

anaesthetize [əˈni:sθətaɪz] *vt* anestesiar.

anagram [ˈænəgræm] *n* anagrama *m*.

anal [ˈeɪnəl] *adj* anal.

analgesic [ænəlˈdʒi:zɪk] *adj* analgésico,-a.
▶ *n* analgésico.

analog [ˈænəlɒg] *adj-n* US → analogue.

analogue [ˈænəlɒg] *adj* analógico,-a.
▶ *n* análogo.

analogy [əˈnælədʒɪ] *n* analogía, semejanza.
① *pl* analogies.

analyse [ˈænəlaɪz] *vt* analizar.

analysis [əˈnælɪsɪs] *n* análisis *m*.
① *pl* analyses [əˈnælɪsi:z].

analyst [ˈænəlɪst] *n* analista *mf*.

anarchism [ˈænəkɪzəm] *n* anarquismo.

anarchist [ˈænəkɪst] *n* anarquista *mf*.

anarchy [ˈænəkɪ] *n* anarquía.
① *pl* anarchies.

anatomy [ə'nætəmɪ] *n* anatomía.
ⓘ *pl* anatomies.

ancestor ['ænsəstər] *n* antepasado.

anchor ['æŋkər] *n* ancla.
▶ *vt* **1** *(ship)* anclar. **2** *(make secure)* sujetar.

anchovy ['æntʃəvɪ] *n (salted)* anchoa; *(fresh)* boquerón *m*.
ⓘ *pl* anchovies.

ancient ['eɪnʃ°nt] *adj* **1** antiguo,-a; *(monument)* histórico,-a. **2** *fam* viejísimo,-a. COMP ancient history historia antigua.

> ✎ Ancient no se emplea en el sentido de 'anterior' con el que a menudo se usa «antiguo» en español (*mi antiguo jefe*). La palabra inglesa para este sentido de «antiguo» es *former* (*my former boss*).

and [ænd, *unstressed* ənd] *conj* **1** y; *(before i- and* hi-) e: *black and white* blanco y negro; *opinions and ideas* opiniones e ideas. **2** *(with infinitives)*: *go and look for it* ve a buscarlo; *wait and see what happens* espera a ver lo que pasa. **3** *(expressing repetition, increase)*: *it rained and rained* no paró de llover. **4** *(with numbers)*: *a hundred and twenty* ciento veinte; *two thousand and eighty four* dos mil ochenta y cuatro. **5** *(in sums)* más: *four and six are ten* cuatro más seis son diez.

Andes ['ændi:z] *n pl* the Andes los Andes *mpl*.

Andorra [æn'dɔːrə] *n* Andorra.

Andorran [æn'dɔːrən] *adj* andorrano,-a.
▶ *n* andorrano,-a.

android ['ændrɔɪd] *n* androide *m*.

anecdote ['ænɪkdəʊt] *n* anécdota.

anemia [ə'niːmɪə] *n* US → anaemia.

anemic [ə'niːmɪk] *adj* US → anaemic.

anemometer [ænɪ'mɒmɪtər] *n* anemómetro.

anemone [ə'nemənɪ] *n* BOT anémona.

anesthesia [ænəs'θiːzɪə] *n* → anaesthesia.

anesthetic [ænəs'θetɪk] *adj-n* → anaesthetic.

anesthetize [ə'niːsθətaɪz] *vt* → anaesthetize.

angel ['eɪndʒ°l] *n* ángel *m*.

anger ['æŋgər] *n* cólera, ira, furia.
▶ *vt* encolerizar, enojar, enfurecer.

angina [æn'dʒaɪnə] [also angina pectoris] *n* angina de pecho.

> ✖ Angina no significa 'anginas', que se traduce por sore throat.

angiosperm ['ændʒɪəspɜːm] *n* angiosperma.

angle¹ ['æŋg°l] *n* ángulo.

angle² ['æŋg°l] *vi* pescar con caña.

anglepoise lamp ['æŋg°lpɔɪzlæmp] *n* flexo.

angler [ændlər] *n* pescador,-a.

Anglican ['æŋglɪkən] *adj* anglicano,-a.
▶ *n* anglicano,-a.

angling ['æŋglɪŋ] *n* pesca con caña.

Anglo-Saxon [æŋgləʊ'sæks°n] *adj* anglosajón,-ona.
▶ *n* **1** *(person)* anglosajón,-ona. **2** *(language)* anglosajón *m*.

Angola [æn'gəʊlə] *n* Angola.

Angolan [æn'gəʊlən] *adj* angoleño,-a.
▶ *n* angoleño,-a.

angry ['æŋgrɪ] *adj* enojado,-a, enfadado,-a.
ⓘ *comp* angrier, *superl* angriest.

angstrom ['æŋgstrəm] *n* ángstrom *m*.

anguish ['æŋgwɪʃ] *n* angustia.

angular ['æŋgjʊlər] *adj* angular.

anhydride [æn'haɪdraɪd] *n* anhídrido.

animal ['ænɪm°l] *adj* animal.
▶ *n* animal *m*.

animate [*(adj)* 'ænɪmət; *(vb)* 'ænɪmeɪt] *adj* animado,-a, vivo,-a.
▶ *vt* **1** animar. **2** *fig* estimular.

animation [ænɪ'meɪʃ°n] *n* **1** animación *f*. **2** *(life)* vida, marcha.

animator ['ænɪmeɪtər] *n* animador,-ra.

animism ['ænɪmɪz°m] *n* animismo.

anion ['ænaɪən] *n* anión *m*.

anise ['ænɪs] *n (plant)* anís *m*.

ankle ['æŋk°l] *n* tobillo.

annelid ['ænəlɪd] *n* anélido.

annexe ['æneks] *n* anexo, anejo.

annihilate [ə'naɪəleɪt] *vt* aniquilar.

anniversary [ænɪ'vɜːsərɪ] *n* aniversario.
ⓘ *pl* anniversaries.

announce [ə'naʊns] *vt* anunciar.

announcement [ə'naʊnsmənt] *n* anuncio.

announcer [ə'naʊnsə'] *n (on TV, radio)* presentador,-ra, locutor,-ra.

annoy [ə'nɔɪ] *vt* molestar, fastidiar.

annoying [ə'nɔɪɪŋ] *adj* molesto,-a.

annual ['ænjʊəl] *adj* anual.

annul [ə'nʌl] *vt* anular.
ⓘ *pt & pp* annulled, *ger* annulling.

annular ['ænjʊlə'] *adj* anular.

anode ['ænəʊd] *n* ánodo.

anomaly [ə'nɒməlɪ] *n* anomalía.
ⓘ *pl* anomalies.

anonymous [ə'nɒnɪməs] *adj* anónimo,-a.

anopheles [ə'nɒfəliːz] *n* anofeles *m*.

anorak ['ænəræk] *n* anorak *m*.

anorexia [ænə'reksɪə] *n* anorexia.

another [ə'nʌðə'] *adj* otro,-a.
▶ *pron* otro,-a.

answer ['ɑːnsə'] *n* respuesta, contestación *f*.
▶ *vt & vi* responder, contestar.
◆ **to answer back** *vt sep & vi* replicar.
◆ **to answer for** *vt insep* **1** *(guarantee)* responder por, garantizar. **2** *(accept responsibility)* responder de.

answering machine ['ɑːnsərɪŋməʃiːn] *n* contestador *m* automático.

answerphone ['ɑːnsəfəʊn] *n* contestador *m* automático.

ant [ænt] *n* hormiga. COMP **ant hill** hormiguero.

Antarctic [ænt'ɑːktɪk] *adj* antártico,-a.
▶ *n* **the Antarctic** la Antártida. COMP **Antarctic Circle** Círculo polar antártico.

Antarctica [ænt'ɑːktɪkə] *n* Antártida.

anteater ['ænti:tə'] *n* oso hormiguero.

antecedent [æntɪ'si:d°nt] *n* antecedente *m*.

antediluvian [æntɪdɪ'lu:vɪən] *adj* antediluviano,-a.

antenatal [æntɪ'neɪt°l] *adj* prenatal.

antenna [æn'tenə] *n* **1** [*pl* antennae [æn'teni:]] *(of insect)* antena. **2** [*pl* antennas] *(aerial)* antena.

anterior [æn'tɪərɪə'] *adj* anterior.

anthem ['ænθəm] *n* motete *m*.

anther ['ænθə'] *n* antera.

anthology [æn'θɒlədʒɪ] *n* antología.
ⓘ *pl* anthologies.

anthracite ['ænθrəsaɪt] *n* antracita.

anthropology [ænθrə'pɒlədʒɪ] *n* antropología.

antibiotic [æntɪbaɪ'ɒtɪk] *adj* antibiótico,-a.
▶ *n* antibiótico.

antibody ['æntɪbɒdɪ] *n* anticuerpo.
ⓘ *pl* antibodies.

anticipate [æn'tɪsɪpeɪt] *vt* **1** *(expect)* esperar. **2** *(get ahead of)* adelantarse a. **3** *(foresee)* anticiparse a, prever.

anticipation [æntɪsɪ'peɪʃ°n] *n* **1** *(expectation)* expectación *f*. **2** *(foresight)* previsión *f*.

anticline ['æntɪklaɪn] *n* anticlinal *m*.

anticlockwise [æntɪ'klɒkwaɪz] *adj* en el sentido contrario a las agujas del reloj.

anticyclone [æntɪ'saɪkləʊn] *n* anticiclón *m*.

antidote ['æntɪdəʊt] *n* antídoto.

antifreeze ['æntɪfri:z] *n* anticongelante *m*.

antigen ['æntɪdʒen] *n* antígeno.

Antilles [æn'tɪliːz] *n pl* Antillas *fpl*.

antimony ['æntɪmənɪ] *n* antimonio.

antipodes [æn'tɪpədiːz] *n pl* antípodas *fpl*.

antipyretic [æntɪpaɪ'retɪk] *n* antipirético.

antique [æn'ti:k] *adj* antiguo,-a. COMP **antique shop** tienda de antigüedades.
▶ *n* antigüedad *f*.

antiquity [æn'tɪkwɪtɪ] *n* antigüedad *f*.
ⓘ *pl* antiquities.

antiseptic [æntɪ'septɪk] *adj* antiséptico,-a.
▶ *n* antiséptico.

antiviral [æntɪ'vaɪr°l] *adj* MED antivirus.

antivirus [æntɪ'vaɪrəs] *adj* INFORM antivirus.

antlers ['æntlə'] *n pl* cornamenta *f sing*.

antonym ['æntənɪm] *n* antónimo.

anus ['eɪnəs] *n* ano.

anvil ['ænvɪl] *n* yunque *m*.

anxiety [æŋ'zaɪətɪ] *n* ansiedad *f*.
ⓘ *pl* anxieties.

anxious ['æŋkʃəs] *adj* **1** *(worried)* preocupado,-a (about, por). **2** *(desirous)*
ansioso,-a.

any ['enɪ] *adj* **1** *(in questions)* algún,-una:
are there any biscuits left? ¿queda alguna
galleta? **2** *(negative)* ningún,-una: *he
hasn't bought any milk/biscuits* no ha comprado leche/galletas; *without any difficulty* sin ninguna dificultad. **3** *(no matter
which)* cualquier,-ra: *any old rag will do*
cualquier trapo sirve.
▶ *pron* **1** *(in questions)* alguno,-a: *there are
foxes round here, have you seen any?* hay
zorros por aquí, ¿has visto alguno? **2**
(negative) ninguno,-a: *they're very cheap,
but I haven't sold any* son muy baratos,
pero no he vendido ninguno. **3** *(no matter which)* cualquiera: *any of these books
will do* cualquiera de estos libros sirve.
▶ *adv no suele traducirse: I don't work there
any more* ya no trabajo allí; *do you want
any more?* ¿quieres más?.

🖎 En preguntas y frases negativas, con los
sustantivos contables en singular no se
usa any sino a o an.

anybody ['enɪbɒdɪ] *pron* **1** *(in questions)*
alguien: *has anybody seen my car?* ¿ha
visto alguien mi coche? **2** *(negative)* nadie: *there isn't anybody in the room* no hay
nadie en la sala. **3** *(no matter who)* cualquiera: *anybody would tell you the same*
cualquiera te diría lo mismo.

anyhow ['enɪhaʊ] *adv* **1** → **anyway**. **2**
(carelessly) de cualquier forma, de
cualquier manera.

anyone ['enɪwʌn] *pron* → **anybody**.

anyplace ['enɪpleɪs] *adv* US → **anywhere**.

anything ['enɪθɪŋ] *pron* **1** *(in questions)*
algo, alguna cosa: *is there anything left?*
¿queda algo? **2** *(negative)* nada: *there
isn't anything left* no queda nada. **3** *(no
matter what)* cualquier cosa: *anything
will do* cualquier cosa sirve; *they can cost
anything from £5 to £5,000* el precio va
desde cinco libras a cinco mil.

anyway ['enɪweɪ] *adv* **1** *(in any case)* de
todas formas, de todos modos. **2** *(in
conversation)* bueno, bueno pues, to-

tal, en cualquier caso: *anyway, as I was
saying, ...* bueno pues, como te decía, ...

anywhere ['enɪweə'] *adv* **1** *(in questions
- situation)* en algún sitio, en alguna
parte; *(- direction)* a algún sitio, a alguna parte: *have you seen my keys anywhere?*
¿has visto mis llaves en alguna parte?;
are you going anywhere this weekend? ¿vas
a algún sitio el fin de semana? **2** *(negative
- situation)* en ningún sitio, en ninguna parte; *(- direction)* a ningún sitio, a
ninguna parte: *I can't find him anywhere*
no lo encuentro en ninguna parte; *we're
not going anywhere* no vamos a ningún
sitio. **3** *(no matter where - situation)* donde
sea, en cualquier sitio; *(- direction)* a
donde sea, a cualquier sitio: *I'd live
anywhere as long as it's with you* viviría en
cualquier sitio mientras sea contigo;
she'd travel anywhere to see Bruce viajaría a
cualquier sitio para ver a Bruce.

aorta [eɪ'ɔ:tə] *n* aorta.

apart [ə'pɑ:t] *adv* **1** *(not together)*
separado,-a; *(distant)* alejado,-a. **2** *(in
pieces)* en piezas. ⌐LOC⌐ **apart from** aparte de. ▌**to fall apart** deshacerse. ▌**to
tell apart** distinguir.

apartheid [ə'pɑ:taɪt] *n* apartheid *m*.

apartment [ə'pɑ:tmənt] *n* piso, apartamento. ⌐COMP⌐ **apartment block / apartment building** bloque *m* de pisos.

apathetic [æpə'θetɪk] *adj* apático,-a.

apathy ['æpəθɪ] *n* apatía.

ape [eɪp] *n* simio.
▶ *vt* imitar.

Apennines ['æpənaɪnz] *n* **the Apennines** los (montes) Apeninos *mpl*.

aperitif [əperɪ'ti:f] *n* aperitivo.

aperture ['æpətjə'] *n* abertura.

❌ Aperture no significa 'apertura (de
una tienda)', que se traduce por opening.

apex ['eɪpeks] *n* ápice *m*; *(of triangle)* vértice *m*.
ⓘ *pl* apexes o apices.

apiculture ['eɪpɪkʌltə'] *n* apicultura.

apiece [ə'pi:s] *adv* cada uno,-a: *she gave
us three apiece* nos dio tres a cada uno.

apocalypse [ə'pɒkəlɪps] *n* apocalipsis *m*.

apogee ['æpədʒi:] *n* apogeo.

apologise [əˈpɒlədʒaɪz] vi → **apologize**.

apologize [əˈpɒlədʒaɪz] vi disculparse, pedir perdón.

apology [əˈpɒlədʒɪ] n **1** (for mistake) disculpa. **2** fml (of beliefs) apología.
ⓘ pl **apologies**.

apoplexy [ˈæpəpleksɪ] n apoplejía.
ⓘ pl **apoplexies**.

apophthegm [ˈæpəθem] n apotema.

apostle [əˈpɒsl] n apóstol m.

apostrophe [əˈpɒstrəfɪ] n apóstrofo.

apothegm [ˈæpəθem] vt → **apophthegm**.

appal [əˈpɔːl] vt horrorizar.
ⓘ pt & pp **appalled**, ger **appalling**.

Appalachians [æpəˈleɪʃəns] n the Appalachians los (montes) Apalaches mpl.

appall [əˈpɔːl] vt US → **appal**.

appalling [əˈpɔːlɪŋ] adj **1** (horrific) horroroso,-a. **2** (bad) malísimo,-a.

apparatus [æpəˈreɪtəs] n **1** (equipment) aparatos mpl; (piece of equipment) aparato. **2** (structure) aparato.

apparent [əˈpærənt] adj **1** (obvious) evidente. **2** (seeming) aparente.

apparently [əˈpærəntlɪ] adv **1** (obviously) evidentemente. **2** (seemingly) aparentemente.

appeal [əˈpiːl] n **1** (request) ruego, llamamiento; (plea) súplica. **2** (attraction) atractivo. **3** JUR apelación f.
▶ vi **1** (request) pedir, solicitar; (plead) suplicar. **2** (attract) atraer: it doesn't appeal to me no me atrae. **3** JUR apelar (against, -), recurrir (against, -).

appealing [əˈpiːlɪŋ] adj **1** (moving) suplicante. **2** (attractive) atractivo,-a.

appear [əˈpɪər] vi **1** (become visible) aparecer. **2** (before a court, etc) comparecer (before, ante). **3** (seem) parecer.

appearance [əˈpɪərəns] n **1** (becoming visible) aparición f. **2** (before a court, etc) comparecencia. **3** (look) apariencia.

appendices [əˈpendɪsiːz] n pl → **appendix**.

appendicitis [əpendɪˈsaɪtɪs] n apendicitis f.

appendix [əˈpendɪks] n **1** [pl appendices] (in book) apéndice m. **2** [pl appendixes] MED apéndice m.

appetite [ˈæpɪtaɪt] n apetito.

appetizer [ˈæpɪtaɪzər] n aperitivo.

appetizing [ˈæpɪtaɪzɪŋ] adj apetitoso,-a.

applaud [əˈplɔːd] vi (clap) aplaudir.
▶ vt **1** (clap) aplaudir. **2** (praise) alabar.

applause [əˈplɔːz] n aplauso.

apple [ˈæpəl] n manzana. COMP apple pie tarta de manzana. ‖ apple tree manzano. ‖ the Big Apple Nueva York.

applet [ˈæplət] n COMPUT applet m.

appliance [əˈplaɪəns] n **1** (device) aparato. **2** (fire engine) coche m de bomberos.

applicable [ˈæplɪkəbəl] adj aplicable.

applicant [ˈæplɪkənt] n (for job) candidato,-a, solicitante mf.

application [æplɪˈkeɪʃən] n **1** (for job) solicitud f. **2** (of ointment, theory, etc) aplicación f. **3** (effort) diligencia.

apply [əˈplaɪ] vt aplicar.
▶ vi **1** (be true) aplicarse, ser aplicable. **2** (for job) solicitar.
ⓘ pt & pp **applied**, ger **applying**.

appoint [əˈpɔɪnt] vt **1** (person for job) nombrar. **2** (day, date, etc) fijar, señalar.

appointment [əˈpɔɪntmənt] n **1** (meeting - with lawyer, etc) cita; (- with hairdresser, dentist, doctor) hora. **2** (person for job) nombramiento.

apposition [æpəˈzɪʃən] n aposición f.

appraisal [əˈpreɪzəl] n valoración f, evaluación f.

appraise [əˈpreɪz] vt valorar, evaluar.

appreciate [əˈpriːʃɪeɪt] vt **1** (be thankful for) agradecer. **2** (understand) entender, comprender. **3** (value) valorar, apreciar.
▶ vi revalorizarse, valorizarse.

appreciation [əpriːʃɪˈeɪʃən] n **1** (thanks) agradecimiento, gratitud f. **2** (understanding) comprensión f. **3** (appraisal) evaluación f. **4** (increase in value) apreciación f, aumento en valor.

apprehend [æprɪˈhend] vt **1** (arrest) detener, capturar. **2** (understand) comprender.

apprehension [æprɪˈhenʃən] n **1** (arrest) detención f, captura. **2** (fear) aprensión f, temor m, recelo.

apprehensive [æprɪˈhensɪv] adj (fearful) aprensivo,-a.

apprentice [əˈprentɪs] n aprendiz,-za.

approach [əˈprəʊtʃ] n **1** (coming near) aproximación f, acercamiento; (arrival) llegada. **2** (way in) acceso, entrada. **3** (to problem) enfoque m.
► vi (come near) acercarse, aproximarse.
► vt **1** (come near) acercarse a, aproximarse a. **2** (tackle - problem) enfocar, abordar; (- person) dirigirse a. COMP approach road vía de acceso.

appropriate [əˈprəʊprɪət] adj apropiado,-a, adecuado,-a, indicado,-a.

approval [əˈpruːvəl] n aprobación f.
LOC on approval a prueba.

approve [əˈpruːv] vt aprobar.

⊠ To approve no significa 'aprobar (un examen)', que se traduce por to pass.

approximate [(adj) əˈprɒksɪmət; (vb) əˈprɒksɪmeɪt] adj aproximado,-a.
► vi aproximarse (to, a).

apricot [ˈeɪprɪkɒt] n (fruit) albaricoque m. COMP apricot tree albaricoquero.

April [ˈeɪprɪl] n abril m. COMP April Fool's Day el día 1 de abril (≈ día de los Santos Inocentes).

📎 Para ejemplos de uso, consulta May.

apron [ˈeɪprən] n **1** (garment - domestic) delantal m; (- workman's) mandil m. **2** (at airport) pista de estacionamiento.

apse [æps] n ábside m.

apt [æpt] adj **1** (suitable) apropiado,-a; (remark) acertado,-a. **2** (liable to) propenso,-a.

APT [ˈeɪpiːˈtiː] abbr GB (Advanced Passenger Train) ≈ AVE m.

aptitude [ˈæptɪtjuːd] n aptitud f.

aquarium [əˈkweərɪəm] n acuario.
ⓘ pl aquaria o aquariums.

Aquarius [əˈkweərɪəs] n Acuario.

aquatic [əˈkwætɪk] adj acuático,-a.

aqueduct [ˈækwɪdʌkt] n acueducto.

aquifer [ˈækwɪfər] n acuífero.

Arab [ˈærəb] adj árabe.
► n (person) árabe mf.

Arabia [əˈreɪbɪə] n Arabia.

Arabian [əˈreɪbɪən] adj árabe, arábigo,-a.

► n árabe mf. COMP Arabian Peninsula Península Arábiga. ‖ Arabian Sea Mar m Arábigo.

Arabic [ˈærəbɪk] adj Árabe.
► n (language) Árabe m. COMP arabic numerals números mpl arábigos.

arachnid [əˈræknɪd] n arácnido.

aragonite [əˈrægənaɪt] n aragonito.

arbitrary [ˈɑːbɪtrərɪ] adj arbitrario,-a.

arbitrate [ˈɑːbɪtreɪt] vt & vi arbitrar.

arc [ɑːk] n arco.

arcade [ɑːˈkeɪd] n pasaje m. COMP shopping arcade galerías fpl comerciales.

arch [ɑːtʃ] n **1** (gen) arco; (vault) bóveda. **2** (of foot) empeine m.
► vt **1** (back, eyebrows) arquear, enarcar **2** (vault) abovedar.

archaeological [ɑːkɪəˈlɒdʒɪkəl] adj arqueológico,-a.

archaeologist [ɑːkɪˈɒlədʒɪst] n arqueólogo,-a.

archaeology [ɑːkɪˈɒlədʒɪ] n arqueología

archaic [ɑːˈkeɪɪk] adj arcaico,-a.

archaism [ˈɑːkeɪɪzəm] n arcaísmo.

archangel [ˈɑːkeɪndʒəl] n arcángel m.

archbishop [ɑːtʃˈbɪʃəp] n arzobispo.

archeological [ɑːkɪəˈlɒdʒɪkəl] adj US → archaeological.

archeologist [ɑːkɪˈɒlədʒɪst] n US → archaeologist.

archeology [ɑːkɪˈɒlədʒɪ] n US → archaeology.

archer [ˈɑːtʃər] n arquero.

archery [ˈɑːtʃərɪ] n tiro con arco.

archipelago [ɑːkɪˈpeligəʊ] n archipiélago.
ⓘ pl archipelagos o archipelagoes.

architect [ˈɑːkɪtekt] n arquitecto,-a.

architecture [ˈɑːkɪtektʃər] n arquitectura.

archives [ˈɑːkaɪvz] n pl archivo m sing.

archivist [ˈɑːkaɪvɪst] n archivero,-a.

Arctic [ˈɑːktɪk] adj ártico,-a.
► n the Arctic el Ártico. COMP the Arctic Circle el Círculo Polar Ártico. ‖ the Arctic Ocean el océano Ártico.

ardor [ˈɑːdər] n US → ardour.

ardour [ˈɑːdər] n ardor m.

arduous [ˈɑːdjʊəs] *adj* arduo,-a.

are [ɑːʳ, əʳ] *pres* → be.

area [ˈeərɪə] *n* **1** *(extent)* área, superficie *f*. **2** *(region)* región *f*; *(of town)* zona. **3** *(field)* campo.

arena [əˈriːnə] *n* **1** *(stadium)* estadio. **2** *(in amphitheatre)* arena. **3** *fig* ámbito.

☒ Arena no significa 'arena', que se traduce por sand.

aren't [ɑːnt] *contr* → are not.

Argentina [ɑːdʒənˈtiːnə] *n* Argentina.

Argentine [ˈɑːdʒəntaɪn] *adj* argentino,-a.
▶ *n* the Argentine Argentina.

Argentinian [ɑːdʒənˈtɪnɪən] *adj* argentino,-a.
▶ *n* argentino,-a.

argon [ˈɑːgɒn] *n* argón *m*.

argot [ˈɑːgəʊ] *n* jerga.

argue [ˈɑːgjuː] *vi* **1** *(quarrel)* discutir (with, con). **2** *(reason)* argüir, argumentar, sostener.

argument [ˈɑːgjʊmənt] *n* **1** *(quarrel)* discusión *f*, disputa. **2** *(reasoning)* argumento. LOC **to have an argument with sB** discutir con ALGN.

arid [ˈærɪd] *adj* árido,-a.

aridity [əˈrɪdɪtɪ] *n* aridez *f*.

Aries [ˈeəriːz] *n* Aries.

arise [əˈraɪz] *vi* surgir (from, de).
ⓘ *pt* arose [əˈrəʊz], *pp* arisen [əˈrɪzən].

aristocracy [ærɪsˈtɒkrəsɪ] *n* aristocracia.
ⓘ *pl* aristocracies.

aristocrat [ˈærɪstəkræt, US əˈrɪstəkræt] *n* aristócrata *mf*.

arithmetic [(n) əˈrɪθmətɪk; (adj) ærɪθˈmetɪk] *n* aritmética.
▶ *adj* aritmético,-a.

arithmetical [ærɪθˈmetɪkəl] *adj* aritmético,-a. COMP **arithmetical progression** progresión *f* aritmética.

ark [ɑːk] *n* arca.

arm [ɑːm] *n* **1** ANAT brazo. **2** *(of coat, etc)* manga. **3** *(of chair)* brazo.
▶ *vt* armar.
▶ *n pl* arms *(weapons)* armas *fpl*.

armadillo [ɑːməˈdɪləʊ] *n* armadillo.
ⓘ *pl* armadillos.

armchair [ɑːmˈtʃeəʳ] *n* sillón *m*.

Armenia [ɑːˈmiːnɪə] *n* Armenia.

Armenian [ɑːˈmiːnɪən] *adj* armenio,-a.
▶ *n* **1** *(person)* armenio,-a. **2** *(language)* armenio.

armistice [ˈɑːmɪstɪs] *n* armisticio.

armor [ˈɑːməʳ] *n* US → armour.

armour [ˈɑːməʳ] *n* **1** armadura. **2** *(on vehicle)* blindaje *m*.

armpit [ˈɑːmpɪt] *n* sobaco, axila.

armrest [ˈɑːmrest] *n* brazo.

army [ˈɑːmɪ] *n* ejército.
ⓘ *pl* armies.

aroma [əˈrəʊmə] *n* aroma *m*.

aromatic [ærəˈmætɪk] *adj* aromático,-a.

arose [əˈrəʊz] *pt* → arise.

around [əˈraʊnd] *adv* **1** *(near, in the area)* alrededor: *is there anybody around?* ¿hay alguien cerca? **2** *(from place to place)*: *they cycle around together* van juntos en bicicleta. **3** *(approximately)* alrededor de: *it costs around £5,000* cuesta unas cinco mil libras.
▶ *prep* **1** *(near)*: *there aren't many shops around here* hay pocas tiendas por aquí. **2** *(all over)*: *there were clothes around the room* había ropa por toda la habitación. **3** *(in a circle or curve)* alrededor de: *he put his arms around her* la rodeó con los brazos. **4** *(at)* sobre, cerca de: *they came around seven* vinieron sobre las siete.

arouse [əˈraʊz] *vt* **1** *(awake)* despertar. **2** *(sexually)* excitar.

arrange [əˈreɪndʒ] *vt* **1** *(gen)* arreglar; *(furniture, etc)* colocar, ordenar. **2** *(plan)* planear, organizar. **3** *(marriage)* concertar.

arrangement [əˈreɪndʒmənt] *n* **1** *(agreement)* acuerdo, arreglo. **2** MUS arreglo.
▶ *n pl* arrangements *(plans)* planes *mpl*; *(preparations)* preparativos *mpl*.

array [əˈreɪ] *n* **1** *(selection)* surtido. **2** *(series)* serie *f*. **3** COMPUT matriz *f*.

arrears [əˈrɪəz] *n pl* atrasos *mpl*.

arrest [əˈrest] *n* arresto, detención *f*.

arrival [əˈraɪvəl] *n* llegada.

arrive [əˈraɪv] *vi* llegar.

arrogant [ˈærəgənt] *adj* arrogante.

arrow [ˈærəʊ] *n* flecha.

arsenal [ˈɑːsənəl] *n* arsenal *m*.

arsenic ['ɑːsˤnɪk] *n* arsénico.

arson ['ɑːsˤn] *n* incendio provocado.

arsonist ['ɑːsənɪst] *n* pirómano,-a.

art [ɑːt] *n (painting, etc)* arte *m*.
  ▶ *n pl* **arts** *(branch of knowledge)* letras *fpl*. COMP **art deco** art deco *m*. **l art gallery 1** *(museum)* pinacoteca. **2** *(commercial)* galería de arte. **l art nouveau** art nouveau *m*, modernismo.

artefact ['ɑːtɪfækt] *n* artefacto.

arterial [ɑːˈtɪərɪəl] *adj* **1** ANAT arterial. **2** *(road)* principal, importante.

artery ['ɑːterɪ] *n* ANAT arteria.
  ① *pl* arteries.

artesian well [ɑːtiːzɪənˈwel] *n* pozo artesiano.

arthritis [ɑːˈθraɪtəs] *n* artritis *f*.

arthropod [ɑːˈθrəpɒd] *n* artrópodo.

artichoke ['ɑːtɪtʃəʊk] *n* alcachofa.

article ['ɑːtɪkˤl] *n* artículo. COMP **article of clothing** prenda de vestir. **l definite article** artículo determinado. **l indefinite article** artículo indeterminado. **l leading article** editorial *m*.

articulate [*(adj)* ɑːˈtɪkjʊlət; *(vb)* ɑːˈtɪkjʊleɪt] *adj (person)* que se expresa con facilidad; *(speech)* claro,-a.
  ▶ *vt* **1** articular. **2** *(pronounce)* pronunciar.

articulated [ɑːˈtɪkjʊleɪtɪd] *adj* articulado,-a. COMP **articulated lorry** camión *m* articulado.

articulation [ɑːtɪkjʊˈleɪʃˤn] *n* articulación *f*.

artifact ['ɑːtɪfækt] *n* US → **artefact**.

artificial [ɑːtɪˈfɪʃˤl] *adj* artificial.

artillery [ɑːˈtɪlərɪ] *n* artillería.

artisan ['ɑːtɪzæn] *n* artesano,-a.

artist ['ɑːtɪst] *n* **1** artista *mf*. **2** *(painter)* pintor,-ra.

artistic [ɑːˈtɪstɪk] *adj* artístico,-a.

artwork ['ɑːtwɜːk] *n* ilustraciones *fpl*.

as [æz, *unstressed* əz] *prep* como: *he works as a clerk* trabaja de oficinista.
  ▶ *adv (in comparatives)*: *eat as much as you like* come tanto como quieras.
  ▶ *conj* **1** *(while)* mientras; *(when)* cuando: *as he painted, he whistled* mientras pintaba, silbaba; *as he grew older he became more tolerant* a medida que iba envejeciendo se

volvía más tolerante. **2** *(because)* ya que, como: *as there were no seats we had to stand* como no había asientos tuvimos que estar de pie. **3** *(although)* aunque: *tall as he was, he still couldn't reach the shelf* aunque era alto no podía alcanzar el estante. LOC **as far as** hasta. **l as far as I know** que yo sepa. **l as for** en cuanto a. **l as if** como si. **l as long as** mientras. **l as of** desde. **l as soon as** tan pronto como. **l as though** como si. **l as well as** además de. **l as yet** hasta ahora, de momento.

asbestos [æsˈbestəs] *n* amianto.

ascend [əˈsend] *vt* ascender, subir a.
  ▶ *vi* ascender, subir.

ascendancy [əˈsendənsɪ] *n* predominio, supremacía.
  ① *pl* ascendancies.

ascension [əˈsenʃˤn] *n* ascensión *f*.

ascent [əˈsent] *n* **1** *(slope)* subida. **2** *(climb)* ascensión *f*.

ascribe [əsˈkraɪb] *vt* atribuir (**to**, a).

aseptic [əˈseptɪk] *adj* aséptico,-a.

asexual [eɪˈsekʃʊəl] *adj* asexual.

ash¹ [æʃ] *n* ceniza. COMP **Ash Wednesday** miércoles *m* de ceniza.
  ① *pl* ashes.

ash² [æʃ] *n (tree)* fresno.
  ① *pl* ashes.

ashamed [əˈʃeɪmd] *adj* avergonzado,-a.

ashbin ['æʃbɪn] *n* US cubo de la basura.

ashtray ['æʃtreɪ] *n* cenicero.

Asia ['eɪʃə, 'eɪʒə] *n* Asia.

Asian ['eɪʃˤn, 'eɪʒˤn] *adj* asiático,-a.
  ▶ *n* asiático,-a.

Asiatic [eɪʃɪˈætɪk, eɪʒɪˈætɪk] *adj* asiático,-a.

aside [əˈsaɪd] *adv* al lado, a un lado. LOC **aside from** aparte de.

ask [ɑːsk] *vt* **1** *(inquire)* preguntar. **2** *(request)* pedir: *we have to ask permission* debemos pedir permiso. **3** *(invite)* invitar, convidar: *he asked her to go out with him* la invitó a salir con él.
  ◆ **to ask after** *vt insep* preguntar por.
  ◆ **to ask for** *vt insep (thing)* pedir; *(person)* preguntar por.
  ◆ **to ask out** *vt sep* invitar a salir.

asleep [ə'sliːp] *adj (person)* dormido,-a. LOC **to fall asleep** dormirse.

asparagus [æs'pærəgəs] *n (plant)* espárrago; *(shoots)* espárragos *mpl*. COMP **an asparagus tip** una punta de espárrago.

aspect ['æspekt] *n* **1** *(gen)* aspecto. **2** *(of building)* orientación *f*.

asphalt ['æsfælt] *n* asfalto.

asphyxia [əs'fɪksɪə] *n* asfixia.

asphyxiate [əs'fɪksɪeɪt] *vt* asfixiar.

aspic ['æspɪk] *n* CULIN gelatina.

aspire [əs'paɪəʳ] *vi* aspirar **(to**, a).

aspirin® ['æspɪrɪn] *n* aspirina®.

ass [æs] *n (animal)* burro,-a, asno,-a; *(person)* burro,-a, imbécil *mf*.

assail [ə'seɪl] *vt* **1** *(physically)* atacar. **2** *(doubts, problems, etc)* asaltar.

assailant [ə'seɪlənt] *n* atacante *mf*.

assassin [ə'sæsɪn] *n* asesino,-a.

assassinate [ə'sæsɪneɪt] *vt* asesinar.

assassination [əsæsɪ'neɪ[ə]n] *n* asesinato.

✎ Assassin, assassinate y assassination sólo se emplean cuando se trata del asesinato de un personaje importante. En los demás casos, se usan las palabras murderer, murder.

assault [ə'sɔːlt] *n* **1** MIL asalto, ataque *m*. **2** JUR agresión *f*.
▶ *vt* JUR *(gen)* agredir; *(sexually)* abusar de.

assemble [ə'semb[ə]l] *vt* **1** *(bring together)* reunir. **2** *(put together)* montar. **3** COMPUT ensamblar.
▶ *vi* reunirse.

assembly [ə'semblɪ] *n* **1** *(meeting)* reunión *f*. **2** *(group, body)* asamblea. **3** TECH *(putting together)* montaje *m*; *(unit)* unidad *f*. COMP **assembly hall** sala de actos. ‖ **assembly line** cadena de montaje.
ⓘ *pl* assemblies.

assent [ə'sent] *n* asentimiento.
▶ *vi* asentir **(to**, a).

assert [ə'sɜːt] *vt* aseverar, afirmar.

assertion [ə'sɜː[ə]n] *n* afirmación *f*.

assess [ə'ses] *vt* **1** *(value)* tasar, valorar. **2** *(calculate)* calcular. **3** *fig* evaluar.

assessment [ə'sesmənt] *n* **1** *(valuation)* tasación *f*, valoración *f*. **2** *(calculation)* cálculo. **3** *fig* evaluación *f*.

asset ['æset] *n* calidad *f* positiva, ventaja.
▶ *n pl* assets COMM activo *m sing*.

assign [ə'saɪn] *vt* asignar, atribuir.

assignment [ə'saɪnmənt] *n* **1** *(mission)* misión *f*. **2** *(task)* tarea.

assimilate [ə'sɪmɪleɪt] *vt* asimilar.
▶ *vi* asimilarse.

assist [ə'sɪst] *vt & vi* ayudar.

❌ To assist no significa 'asistir, ir', que se traducen por to attend, to go.

assistance [ə'sɪstəns] *n* ayuda.

assistant [ə'sɪstənt] *n* **1** *(helper)* ayudante *mf*. **2** *(in shop)* dependiente *mf*.

associate [*(adj-n)* ə'səʊʃɪət; *(vb)* ə'səʊʃɪeɪt] *adj* **1** *(company)* asociado,-a. **2** *(member)* correspondiente.
▶ *n (partner)* socio,-a.
▶ *vt* asociar.
▶ *vi* relacionarse **(with**, con).

association [əsəʊsɪ'eɪ[ə]n] *n* asociación *f*.

associative [ə'səʊʃɪətɪv] *adj* asociativo,-a.

associativity [əsəʊʃɪə'tɪvɪtɪ] *n* propiedad *f* asociativa.

assonance ['æsənəns] *n* asonancia.

assorted [ə'sɔːtɪd] *adj* surtido,-a, variado,-a.

assortment [ə'sɔːtmənt] *n* surtido, variedad *f*.

assume [ə'sjuːm] *vt* **1** *(suppose)* suponer. **2** *(power, responsibility)* tomar, asumir. **3** *(attitude, expression)* adoptar.

assurance [ə'ʃʊərəns] *n* **1** *(guarantee)* garantía. **2** *(confidence)* seguridad *f*, confianza. **3** *(insurance)* seguro. COMP **life assurance** seguro de vida.

assure [ə'ʃʊəʳ] *vt* asegurar.

asterisk ['æstərɪsk] *n* asterisco.

asteroid ['æstərɔɪd] *n* asteroide *m*.

asthma ['æsmə] *n* asma.

astonish [əs'tɒnɪʃ] *vt* asombrar, sorprender.

astonishing [əsˈtɒnɪʃɪŋ] *adj* asombroso,-a, sorprendente.

astonishment [əsˈtɒnɪʃmənt] *n* asombro.

astound [əsˈtaʊnd] *vt* asombrar.

astral [ˈæstrəl] *adj* astral.

astray [əˈstreɪ] *adv* extraviado,-a. LOC **to go astray 1** *(err)* descarriarse. **2** *(be lost)* extraviarse.

astrolabe [ˈæstrəleɪb] *n* astrolabio.

astrologer [əsˈtrɒlədʒəʳ] *n* astrólogo,-a.

astrology [əsˈtrɒlədʒɪ] *n* astrología.

astronaut [ˈæstrənɔːt] *n* astronauta *mf*.

astronomer [əsˈtrɒnəməʳ] *n* astrónomo,-a.

astronomical [æstrəˈnɒmɪkəl] *n* astronómico,-a.

astronomy [əsˈtrɒnəmɪ] *n* astronomía.

astute [əsˈtjuːt] *adj* astuto,-a, sagaz.

asylum [əˈsaɪləm] *n* **1** *(political)* asilo, refugio. **2** *(for mentally ill)* manicomio.

asymmetric [æsɪˈmetrɪk] *adj* asimétrico,-a. COMP **asymmetric bars** barras *fpl* asimétricas.

at¹ [æt, *unstressed* ət] *prep* **1** *(position)* en, a: *at home/school/work/church* en casa/el colegio/el trabajo/la iglesia; *she's at the dentist's* ha ido al dentista. **2** *(time)* a: *at two o'clock* a las dos; *at night* por la noche. **3** *(direction, violence)* a, contra: *she's always shouting at them* no para de gritarles. **4** *(with numbers)* a: *at 50 miles an hour* a 50 millas la hora,. **5** *(state)*: *he's at breakfast/lunch/dinner* está desayunando/comiendo/cenando; *men at work* hombres trabajando. **6** *(ability)*: *he's good at French* va bien en francés. LOC **at first** al principio. **at last!** ¡por fin! **at least** por lo menos. **at most** como máximo. **at the moment** ahora.

at² [æt] *n* *(Internet)* arroba

ate [et, eɪt] *pt* → **eat**.

atheism [ˈeɪθɪɪzəm] *n* ateísmo.

atheist [ˈeɪθɪɪst] *n* ateo,-a.

Athens [ˈæθənz] *n* Atenas.

athlete [ˈæθliːt] *n* atleta *mf*.

athletic [æθˈletɪk] *adj* **1** atlético,-a. **2** *(sporty)* deportista.

athletics [æθˈletɪks] *n* atletismo.

Atlantic [ətˈlæntɪk] *adj* atlántico,-a. COMP **the Atlantic (Ocean)** el (océano) Atlántico.

atlas [ˈætləs] *n* atlas *m inv*.

atmosphere [ˈætməsfɪəʳ] *n* **1** atmósfera. **2** *(ambience)* ambiente *m*, atmósfera.

atmospheric [ætməsˈferɪk] *adj* atmosférico,-a. COMP **atmospheric pressure** presión *f* atmosférica.

atoll [ˈætɒl] *n* atolón *m*.

atom [ˈætəm] *n* átomo. COMP **atom bomb** bomba atómica.

atomic [əˈtɒmɪk] *adj* atómico,-a.

atrium [ˈeɪtriːəm] *n* atrio.
ⓘ *pl* **atriums** o **atria** [ˈeɪtrɪə].

atrocity [əˈtrɒsɪtɪ] *n* atrocidad *f*.
ⓘ *pl* **atrocities**.

attach [əˈtætʃ] *vt* **1** *(fasten)* sujetar. **2** *(tie)* atar. **3** *(stick)* pegar. **4** *(document)* adjuntar.

attachment [əˈtætʃmənt] *n* **1** TECH accesorio. **2** *(to an e-mail)* anexo. **3** *(fondness)* cariño, apego.

attack [əˈtæk] *n* *(gen)* ataque *m*; *(terrorist)* atentado.
▶ *vt* **1** atacar.

attain [əˈteɪn] *vt* **1** *(goal)* lograr. **2** *(rank, age)* llegar a.

attempt [əˈtempt] *n* *(try)* intento, tentativa.
▶ *vt* intentar.

attend [əˈtend] *vt* **1** *(be present at)* asistir a: *all her friends attended the funeral* todos sus amigos asistieron al funeral. **2** *(care for)* atender, cuidar.
▶ *vi* asistir.
◆ **to attend to** *vt insep* **1** ocuparse de. **2** *(in shop)* despachar.

attendance [əˈtendəns] *n* **1** *(being present)* asistencia. **2** *(people present)* asistentes *mpl*.

attendant [əˈtendənt] *n* *(in car park, museum)* vigilante *mf*; *(in cinema)* acomodador,-ra.

attention [əˈtenʃən] *n* atención *f*.
▶ *interj* **attention!** MIL ¡firmes! LOC **to pay attention** prestar atención.

attentive [əˈtentɪv] *adj* **1** *(paying attention)* atento,-a. **2** *(helpful)* solícito,-a.

attic ['ætɪk] n desván m.

attire [ə'taɪəʳ] n atuendo, atavío.

attitude ['ætɪtjuːd] n **1** (way of thinking) actitud f. **2** (pose) postura, pose f.

attorney [ə'tɜːnɪ] n US abogado,-a. COMP **Attorney General** GB ≈ Ministro,-a de Justicia.

attract [ə'trækt] vt atraer.

attraction [ə'trækʃ°n] n atracción f.

attractive [ə'træktɪv] adj **1** (person) atractivo,-a. **2** (offer) interesante, tentador,-ra.

attribute [(n) æ'trɪbjuːtɪ (vb) ə'trɪbjuːt] n atributo.
▶ vt atribuir.

attribution [ætrɪ'bjuːʃ°n] n atribución f.

attributive [ə'trɪbjutɪv] adj atributivo,-a.

atypical [eɪ'tɪpɪk°l] adj atípico,-a.

aubergine ['əʊbəʒiːn] n berenjena.

auction ['ɔːkʃ°n] n subasta.
▶ vt subastar.

audacious [ɔː'deɪʃəs] adj **1** (daring) audaz, intrépido,-a. **2** (rude) descarado,-a, osado,-a.

audible ['ɔːdɪb°l] adj audible.

audience ['ɔːdɪəns] n (spectators) público; (radio) audiencia; (television) telespectadores mpl.

audio-visual ['ɔːdɪəʊ'vɪzjuəl] adj audiovisual.

audit ['ɔːdɪt] n auditoría.
▶ vt auditar.

audition [ɔː'dɪʃ°n] n prueba.

auditor ['ɔːdɪtəʳ] n auditor,-ra.

auditorium [ɔːdɪ'tɔːrɪəm] n auditorio.
ⓘ pl auditoriums o auditoria [ɔːdɪ'tɔːrɪə].

augment [ɔːg'ment] vt fml aumentar.
▶ vi fml aumentarse.

augmentative [ɔːg'mentətɪv] adj aumentativo,-a.

August ['ɔːgəst] n agosto.

✎ Para ejemplos de uso, consulta May.

aunt [ɑːnt] n tía.

auntie ['ɑːntɪ] n fam tía, tita.

au pair [əʊ'peəʳ] n au pair f. COMP **au pair girl** au pair f.

aura ['ɔːrə] n aura.

auricle ['ɒrɪk°l] n **1** (of heart) aurícula. **2** (of ear) aurícula, pabellón m de la oreja.

aurora [ɔː'rɔːrə] n aurora. COMP **aurora australis** aurora austral. ∎ **aurora borealis** aurora boreal.

auscultate ['ɔːskʌlteɪt] vt auscultar.

auscultation [ɔːskʌl'teɪʃ°n] n auscultación f.

austere [ɒs'tɪəʳ] adj austero,-a.

austerity [ɒs'terɪtɪ] n austeridad f.

Australia [ɒ'streɪlɪə] n Australia.

Australian [ɒ'streɪlɪən] adj australiano,-a.
▶ n australiano,-a.

Austria ['ɒstrɪə] n Austria.

Austrian ['ɒstrɪən] adj austríaco,-a, austriaco,-a.
▶ n austríaco,-a, austriaco,-a.

authentic [ɔː'θentɪk] adj auténtico,-a.

author ['ɔːθəʳ] n autor,-ra, escritor,-ra.

authoritarian [ɔːθɒrɪ'teərɪən] adj autoritario,-a.

authority [ɔː'θɒrɪtɪ] n **1** (gen) autoridad f. **2** (permission) autorización f, permiso.
ⓘ pl authorities.

authorisation [ɔːθəraɪ'zeɪʃ°n] n → authorization.

authorise ['ɔːθəraɪz] vt → authorize.

authorization [ɔːθəraɪ'zeɪʃ°n] n autorización f.

authorize ['ɔːθəraɪz] vt autorizar.

autism ['ɔːtɪz°m] n autismo.

autistic [ɔː'tɪstɪk] adj autista.

auto ['ɔːtəʊ] n US fam coche m.
ⓘ pl autos.

autobiography [ɔːtəbaɪ'ɒgrəfɪ] n autobiografía.
ⓘ pl autobiographies.

autograph ['ɔːtəgrɑːf] n autógrafo.
▶ vt autografiar.

automatic [ɔːtə'mætɪk] adj automático,-a. COMP **automatic pilot** piloto automático.

automation [ɔːtə'meɪʃ°n] n automatización f.

automobile [ɔːˈtəməbiːl] *n* automóvil *m*, coche *m*.

autonomous [ɔːˈtɒnəməs] *adj* autónomo,-a.

autonomy [ɔːˈtɒnəmɪ] *n* autonomía.
① *pl* autonomies.

autopsy [ˈɔːtɒpsɪ] *n* autopsia.
① *pl* autopsies.

autumn [ˈɔːtəm] *n* otoño.

auxiliary [ɔːgˈzɪljərɪ] *adj* auxiliar. COMP auxiliary verb verbo auxiliar.

available [əˈveɪləbəl] *adj* disponible.

avalanche [ˈævəlɑːnʃ] *n* **1** alud *m*. **2** *fig* avalancha.

avarice [ˈævərɪs] *n* avaricia.

avenge [əˈvendʒ] *vt* vengar.

avenue [ˈævənjuː] *n* **1** *(street)* avenida. **2** *(means)* vía.

average [ˈævərɪdʒ] *n* promedio, media. LOC above average por encima de la media. ▌below average por debajo de la media. ▌on average por término medio.
▸ *adj* **1** medio,-a. **2** *(not special)* corriente, regular.
▸ *vt* hacer un promedio de: *I average 10 kilometres an hour* hago un promedio de 10 kilómetros por hora.

aversion [əˈvɜːʒən] *n* aversión *f*.

avert [əˈvɜːt] *vt* *(avoid)* evitar. LOC to avert one's eyes apartar la vista.

aviary [ˈeɪvjərɪ] *n* pajarera.
① *pl* aviaries.

aviation [eɪvɪˈeɪʃən] *n* aviación *f*.

aviator [ˈeɪvɪeɪtər] *n* aviador,-ra.

avid [ˈævɪd] *adj* ávido,-a.

avocado [ævəˈkɑːdəʊ] [also avocado pear] *n* aguacate *m*.
① *pl* avocados.

avoid [əˈvɔɪd] *vt* **1** evitar. **2** *(question)* eludir. **3** *(person)* esquivar.

awake [əˈweɪk] *adj* despierto,-a.
▸ *vi* **1** despertar. **2** despertarse.
① *pt* awoke [əˈwəʊk], *pp* awoken [əˈwəʊkən].

awaken [əˈweɪkən] *vt-vi* → awake.
① *pt & pp* awakened.

award [əˈwɔːd] *n* **1** *(prize)* premio; *(medal)* condecoración *f*; *(trophy)* tro-

feo. **2** *(grant)* beca. **3** *(damages)* indemnización *f*.
▸ *vt* **1** *(prize, grant)* otorgar, conceder. **2** *(damages)* adjudicar.

aware [əˈweər] *adj* **1** consciente. **2** *(informed)* informado,-a, enterado,-a. LOC to be aware of ser consciente de. ▌to become aware of darse cuenta de.

away [əˈweɪ] *adv* **1** lejos, fuera, alejándose: *he lives 4 km away* vive a 4 km (de aquí); *the wedding is 6 weeks away* faltan 6 semanas para la boda. **2** *(indicating continuity)*: *they worked away all day* trabajaron todo el día. LOC to go away irse, marcharse. ▌to put away guardar. ▌to run away irse corriendo.

awe [ɔː] *n* sobrecogimiento.

awful [ˈɔːfʊl] *adj* **1** *(shocking)* atroz, horrible. **2** *fam (very bad)* fatal, horrible, espantoso,-a.

awfully [ˈɔːfʊlɪ] *adv fam* terriblemente.

awhile [əˈwaɪl] *adv* un rato.

awkward [ˈɔːkwəd] *adj* **1** *(clumsy - person)* torpe; *(- expression)* poco elegante. **2** *(difficult)* difícil; *(uncooperative)* poco cooperativo,-a: *it's an awkward place to get to* es difícil llegar hasta allí. **3** *(embarrassing)* embarazoso,-a, delicado,-a. **5** *(uncomfortable)* incómodo,-a.

awning [ˈɔːnɪŋ] *n* toldo.

awoke [əˈwəʊk] *pt* → awake.

awoken [əˈwəʊkən] *pp* → awake.

ax [æks] *n* US → axe.

axe [æks] *n* hacha.

axiom [ˈæksɪəm] *n* axioma *m*.

axis [ˈæksɪs] *n* eje *m*.

axle [ˈæksəl] *n* eje *m*.

axon [ˈæksəm] *n* axón *m*.

Azerbaijan [æzəbaɪˈdʒɑːn] *n* Azerbaiyán *m*.

Azerbaijani [æzəbaɪˈdʒɑːnɪ] *adj* azerbaiyano,-a, azerí.
▸ *n* **1** *(person)* azerbaiyano,-a, azerí *mf*. **2** *(language)* azerí *m*, azerbaiyano.

azimuth [ˈæzɪməθ] *n* acimut *m*.

Aztec [ˈæztek] *adj* azteca.
▸ *n* **1** *(person)* azteca *mf*. **2** *(language)* azteca *m*.

B

B, b [biː] *n* **1** *(the letter)* B, b *f*. **2** *(musical note)* si *m*. COMP **B road** carretera secundaria.

babble ['bæbəl] *vi* balbucear.
► *vt* farfullar.
► *n* murmullo, rumor *m*.

baboon [bə'buːn] *n* mandril *m*, babuino.

baby ['beɪbɪ] *n* **1** bebé *m*. **2** *(of animal)* cría. LOC **to have a baby** dar a luz, tener un niño. COMP **baby carriage** US cochecito de niño. ‖ **baby tooth** diente *m* de leche.
ⓘ *pl* babies.

baby-sit ['beɪbɪsɪt] *vi* hacer de canguro, cuidar niños.
ⓘ *pt & pp* baby-sat ['beɪbɪsæt], *ger* babysitting.

baby-sitter ['beɪbɪsɪtəʳ] *n* canguro *mf*.

baby-walker ['beɪbɪwɔːkəʳ] *n* andador *m*, tacataca *m*, tacatá *m*.

bachelor ['bætʃələʳ] *n* soltero. COMP **bachelor flat** piso de soltero.

⊠ Bachelor no significa 'bachiller', que no tiene una traducción directa en inglés.

bacillus [bə'sɪləs] *n* bacilo.
ⓘ *pl* bacilli [bə'sɪlaɪ].

back [bæk] *n* **1** *(of person)* espalda. **2** *(of animal, book)* lomo. **3** *(of chair)* respaldo. **4** *(of hand)* dorso. **5** *(sport - player)* defensa *mf*; *(- position)* defensa.
► *adj* trasero,-a, de atrás.
► *adv* *(at the rear)* atrás; *(towards the rear)* hacia atrás. LOC **back to front** al revés.
► *vt* **1** *(support)* apoyar, respaldar. **2** *(finance)* financiar.
◆ **to back away** *vi* retirarse.
◆ **to back off** *vi* apartarse.
◆ **to back out** *vi* volverse atrás.
◆ **to back up** *vt sep* *(support)* apoyar; *(vehicle)* dar marcha atrás a.

backache ['bækeɪk] *n* dolor *m* de espalda.

backbone ['bækbəʊn] *n* columna vertebral.

backbreaking ['bækbreɪkɪŋ] *adj* *(work)* agotador,-ra.

backcloth ['bækklɒθ] *n* telón *m* de fondo.

backdated [bæk'deɪtɪd] *adj* con efecto retroactivo.

backer ['bækəʳ] *n* **1** FIN promotor,-ra. **2** *(guarantor)* fiador,-ra. **3** *(supporter)* partidario,-a.

backfire [bæk'faɪəʳ] *vi* fallar: *our plan backfired* nos salió el tiro por la culata.

background ['bækgraʊnd] *n* **1** fondo. **2** *fig* *(origins)* orígenes *mpl*, antecedentes *mpl*. COMP **background knowledge** conocimientos *mpl* previos. ‖ **background music** música de fondo.

backhand ['bækhænd] *n* revés *m*. COMP **backhand shot** revés *m*.

backhanded [bæk'hændɪd] *adj* *(compliment)* equívoco,-a.

backhander [bæk'hændəʳ] *n* fam soborno.

backing ['bækɪŋ] *n* **1** *(support)* apoyo, respaldo. **2** MUS acompañamiento.

backlash ['bæklæʃ] *n* reacción *f* violenta y repentina.
ⓘ *pl* backlashes.

backlog ['bæklɒg] n acumulación f de trabajo, trabajos mpl pendientes.

backpack ['bækpæk] n US mochila.
▶ vi viajar por un país o continente: my sister's backpacking around Europe mi hermana está de viaje por Europa.

back-seat ['bæksi:t] n asiento trasero.

backside [bæk'saɪd] n fam trasero.

backslash ['bækslæʃ] n barra inversa.

backslide ['bækslaɪd] vi reincidir.
ⓘ pt & pp backslid ['bækslɪd].

backstage [bæk'steɪdʒ] n 1 (area) bastidores mpl. 2 (dressing-rooms) camerinos mpl.

backstroke ['bækstrəʊk] n (swimming) espalda.

backtrack ['bæktræk] vi 1 (retrace one's steps) desandar lo andado, volverse atrás. 2 (reverse opinion) desdecirse.

backup ['bækʌp] n 1 (moral support) apoyo. 2 COMPUT copia de seguridad. COMP backup file archivo de seguridad.

backward ['bækwəd] adj 1 hacia atrás. 2 (child) atrasado,-a. 3 (shy) tímido,-a.
▶ adv → backwards.

backwards ['bækwədz] adv 1 hacia atrás. 2 (the wrong way) al revés: he always does things backwards siempre hace las cosas al revés.

backyard [bæk'jɑːd] n patio de atrás.

bacon ['beɪkən] n tocino, bacón m.

bacteria [bæk'tɪərɪə] n pl bacterias fpl.
ⓘ sing bacterium.

bacterium [bæk'tɪərɪəm] n bacteria.
ⓘ pl bacteria.

bad [bæd] adj 1 malo,-a; (before masc noun) mal: he made a bad decision tomó una mala decisión. 2 (rotten) podrido,-a. 3 (serious) grave: they had a bad accident tuvieron un accidente grave. 4 (naughty) malo,-a, travieso,-a. 5 (aches, illnesses) fuerte, intenso,-a: he's got a bad headache tiene un fuerte dolor de cabeza. LOC to be bad at (skill, subject) ser malo,-a en: he's bad at English es malo en inglés. ∎ to come to a bad end acabar mal. ∎ to have a bad leg tener la pierna lisiada. COMP bad cheque cheque m sin fondos.
ⓘ comp worse, superl worst.

▶ adv mal. LOC to feel bad encontrarse mal. ∎ to look bad 1 (person) tener mala cara. 2 (situation) pintar mal.
▶ n lo malo. LOC too bad! ¡mala pata!, ¡qué lástima!

baddy ['bædɪ] n fam malo,-a de la película.
ⓘ pl baddies.

bade [beɪd] pt → bid.

badge [bædʒ] n 1 insignia, distintivo. 2 (metallic) chapa. COMP lapel badge pin m.

badger ['bædʒə'] n tejón m.

badly ['bædlɪ] adv 1 mal: he behaved badly at the party se portó mal en la fiesta. 2 (seriously) gravemente: he was badly hurt in the bombing fue gravemente herido en el atentado. 3 (very much) mucho,-a: he badly needs your help tiene mucha necesidad de tu ayuda.

bad-mannered [bæd'mænəd] adj maleducado,-a.

bad-tempered [bæd'tempəd] adj (permanently) de mal genio; (temporarily) malhumorado,-a, de mal humor.

baffle ['bæfəl] vt 1 (perplex) dejar perplejo,-a, desconcertar. 2 (frustrate) frustrar.

bag [bæg] n 1 (paper, plastic) bolsa; (large) saco. 2 (handbag) bolso. 3 (for school) cartera.
▶ n pl bags (under eyes) ojeras fpl. LOC bags of montones de.

baggage ['bægɪdʒ] n equipaje m.

baggy ['bægɪ] adj holgado,-a, ancho,-a.
ⓘ comp baggier, superl baggiest.

bagpipes ['bægpaɪps] n pl gaita f sing.

bail¹ [beɪl] n fianza. LOC to be on bail estar en libertad bajo fianza.
◆ to bail out vt sep 1 pagar la fianza a. 2 fig sacar de un apuro.

bail² [beɪl] vt (water) achicar.

bailiff ['beɪlɪf] n (court officer) alguacil m.

bait [beɪt] n cebo.
▶ vt 1 cebar. 2 (torment) atosigar. LOC to take the bait picar.

bake [beɪk] vt cocer (en el horno).
▶ vi cocerse.

baked [beɪkt] *adj* cocido al horno. COMP **baked apple** manzana al horno. | **baked beans** alubias *fpl* guisadas en salsa de tomate. | **baked potato** patata asada.

baker ['beɪkə'] *n* (*of bread*) panadero,-a; (*of cakes*) pastelero,-a.

bakery ['beɪkərɪ] *n* (*for bread*) panadería; (*for cakes*) pastelería.
ⓘ *pl* bakeries.

baking ['beɪkɪŋ] *n* cocción *f*. COMP **baking powder** levadura en polvo. | **baking soda** bicarbonato sódico.

balaclava [bælə'klɑːvə] *n* pasamontañas *m*.

balance ['bæləns] *n* **1** equilibrio. **2** (*scales*) balanza. **3** (*of account, etc*) saldo. **4** (*remainder*) resto.
▶ *vi* **1** mantenerse en equilibrio. **2** FIN cuadrar.

balanced ['bælənst] *adj* equilibrado,-a.

balcony ['bælkənɪ] *n* **1** balcón *m*. **2** (*in theatre*) anfiteatro; (*gallery*) gallinero.
ⓘ *pl* balconies.

bald [bɔːld] *adj* **1** calvo,-a. **2** (*tyre*) desgastado,-a. **3** (*style*) escueto,-a. **4** (*statement*) directo,-a, franco,-a.

Balearic [bælɪ'ærɪk] *adj* balear, baleárico,-a. COMP **the Balearic Islands** las (islas) Baleares.

ball [bɔːl] *n* **1** (*gen*) pelota; (*football, etc*) balón *m*; (*golf, billiards*) bola. **2** (*of paper*) bola; (*of wool*) ovillo. **3** (*of eye*) globo ocular. **4** (*dance*) baile *m*, fiesta. LOC **to play ball 1** US (*sport*) jugar a la pelota. **2** (*cooperate*) cooperar, colaborar. COMP **gala ball** baile *m* de etiqueta.

ballad ['bæləd] *n* balada.

ball-and-socket ['bɔːlən'sɒkɪt] COMP **ball-and-socket joint** articulación *f* de rótula.

ballast ['bæləst] *n* (*boat, balloon*) lastre *m*.

ballerina [bælə'riːnə] *n* bailarina.

ballet ['bæleɪ] *n* ballet *m*.

ballistics [bə'lɪstɪks] *n* balística.

balloon [bə'luːn] *n* **1** globo. **2** (*in cartoon*) bocadillo. **3** (*glass*) copa grande.

☒ Balloon no significa 'balón', que se traduce por **ball**.

ballot ['bælət] *n* **1** (*vote*) votación *f*. **2** (*votes recorded*) número de votos escrutados. LOC **to take a ballot on** STH someter algo a votación. COMP **ballot box** urna. | **ballot paper** papeleta.

ballpoint ['bɔːlpɔɪnt] [también **ballpoint pen**] *n* bolígrafo.

ballroom ['bɔːlruːm] *n* sala de baile. COMP **ballroom dancing** baile *m* de salón.

balm [bɑːm] *n* bálsamo.

balmy ['bɑːmɪ] *adj* **1** (*weather*) suave. **2** (*soothing*) balsámico,-a.
ⓘ *comp* balmier, *superl* balmiest.

balsam ['bɔːlsəm] *n* → **balm**.

balsamic [bɔːl'sæmɪk] *adj* balsámico,-a.

Baltic ['bɔːltɪk] *adj* báltico,-a. COMP **the Baltic (Sea)** el (mar) Báltico.

bamboo [bæm'buː] *n* bambú *m*.

ban [bæn] *n* prohibición *f*.
▶ *vt* prohibir.
ⓘ *pt & pp* banned, *ger* banning.

banal [bə'nɑːl] *adj* banal, trivial.

banality [bə'nælɪtɪ] *n* banalidad *f*.
ⓘ *pl* banalities.

banana [bə'nɑːnə] *n* **1** (*fruit*) plátano, banana. **2** (*tree*) bananero, AM banano.

band [bænd] *n* **1** (*gen*) banda; (*pop*) conjunto; (*jazz*) orquesta. **2** (*strip*) tira. **3** (*around arm*) brazalete *m*. **4** (*wrapper*) faja. **5** PHYS banda, frecuencia. **7** TECH correa.

bandage ['bændɪdʒ] *n* venda, vendaje *m*.
▶ *vt* vendar.
◆ **to bandage up** *vt sep* vendar.

Band-Aid® ['bændeɪd] *n* tirita®.

B and B ['biːən'biː] *abbr* (**bed and breakfast**) casa de huéspedes que ofrece habitación con desayuno incluido.

⊕ Los **B and B** son una alternativa por lo general más asequible a los hoteles. Tradicionalmente, estos establecimientos solían estar situados en casas grandes cuyos dueños obtenían así una fuente adicional de ingresos. Hoy en día, el concepto se ha ampliado y hay **B and B** para todos los gustos y bolsillos.

bandit ['bændɪt] *n* bandido,-a.

bandstand [ˈbændstænd] *n* quiosco de música.

bandwidth [ˈbændwɪdθ] *n* ancho de banda.

bandy [ˈbændɪ] *vt* SP *(ball)* pasarse. LOC **to bandy sɐ's name about** difamar ALGN, hablar mal de ALGN.
ⓘ *pt & pp* bandied, *ger* bandying.

bandy-legged [ˈbændɪləgˀd] *adj* patizambo,-a.

bang [bæŋ] *n* **1** *(blow)* golpe *m*. **2** *(noise)* ruido; *(of gun)* estampido; *(explosion)* estallido; *(of door)* portazo.
▸ *vt* golpear, dar golpes en.
▸ *adv fam* justo: *bang in the middle* justo en medio. LOC **to bang the door** dar un portazo.
▸ *n pl* **bangs** US flequillo.

banger [ˈbæŋəʳ] *n* **1** *(firework)* petardo. **2** GB *fam (sausage)* salchicha. **3** *fam (car)* tartana, trasto.

bangle [ˈbæŋgəl] *n* brazalete *m*.

banish [ˈbænɪʃ] *vt (expel)* desterrar.

banishment [ˈbænɪʃmənt] *n* destierro, exilio.

banister [ˈbænɪstəʳ] *n* barandilla.

bank¹ [bæŋk] *n* banco. COMP **bank holiday** GB festivo, día festivo.
▸ *vt (deposit money)* ingresar, depositar.

bank² [bæŋk] *n* **1** *(of river)* ribera; *(edge)* orilla: *on the banks of the Manzanares* a orillas del Manzanares. **2** *(mound)* loma; *(embankment)* terraplén *m*.
▸ *vt* **1** *(soil, earth)* amontonar. **2** *(river)* encauzar.

bankbook [ˈbæŋkbʊk] *n* libreta de ahorro, cartilla de ahorro.

banker [ˈbæŋkəʳ] *n* banquero,-a.

banking [ˈbæŋkɪŋ] *n* banca.

banknote [ˈbæŋknəʊt] *n* billete *m* de banco.

bankruptcy [ˈbæŋkrʌptsɪ] *n* quiebra, bancarrota.
ⓘ *pl* bankruptcies.

banner [ˈbænəʳ] *n* **1** *(flag)* bandera. **2** *(placard)* pancarta. **3** *(on web page)* banner *m*, anuncio.
▸ *adj* US excelente, de primera. COMP **banner headlines** grandes titulares *mpl*.

banns [bænz] *n pl* amonestaciones *fpl*.

banquet [ˈbæŋkwɪt] *n* banquete *m*.

banter [ˈbæntəʳ] *n* bromas *fpl*, guasa.
▸ *vi* bromear, estar de guasa.

baptise [bæpˈtaɪz] *vt* → baptize.

baptism [ˈbæptɪzəm] *n* bautismo.

baptize [bæpˈtaɪz] *vt* bautizar.

bar [bɑːʳ] *n* **1** *(iron, gold)* barra. **2** *(in prison)* barrote *m*. **3** *(soap)* pastilla. **4** *(obstacle)* obstáculo. **5** *(counter)* barra, mostrador *m*. **6** *(room)* bar *m*. **7** *(in court)* tribunal *m*: *the prisoner at the bar* el acusado, la acusada. COMP **bar chart** gráfica de barras.
▸ *vt* **1** *(door)* atrancar; *(road, access)* cortar. **2** *(ban)* prohibir, vedar; *(from a place)* prohibir la entrada. **3** *(prevent)* impedir.
ⓘ *pt & pp* barred, *ger* barring.
▸ *prep* excepto, salvo: *they all came, bar his parents* acudieron todos, excepto sus padres.
▸ *n* **the Bar** JUR el colegio de abogados.

barbarian [bɑːˈbeərɪən] *adj* bárbaro,-a.
▸ *n* bárbaro,-a.

barbecue [ˈbɑːbəkjuː] *n* barbacoa.
▸ *vt* asar a la parrilla.
ⓘ *ger* barbecuing.

barbed [bɑːbd] *adj* **1** con púas, punzante. **2** *fig* mordaz, incisivo,-a.

barber [ˈbɑːbəʳ] *n* barbero. COMP **barber's shop** barbería.

barbiturate [bɑːˈbɪtʃərət] *n* barbitúrico.

bare [beəʳ] *adj* **1** *(naked)* desnudo,-a; *(head)* descubierto,-a. **2** *(land)* raso,-a; *(tree, plant)* sin hojas. **3** *(empty)* vacío,-a; *(unfurnished)* sin muebles. **4** *(scanty)* escaso,-a. **5** *(worn)* gastado,-a, raído,-a.
▸ *vt* desnudar; *(uncover)* descubrir.

barefaced [ˈbeəfeɪst] *adj* descarado,-a.

barefoot [ˈbeəfʊt] *adj* descalzo,-a.
▸ *adv* descalzo,-a.

barely [ˈbeəlɪ] *adv* apenas.

bargain [ˈbɑːgən] *n* **1** *(agreement)* trato, acuerdo. **2** *(good buy)* ganga.
▸ *vi* **1** *(negotiate)* negociar. **2** *(haggle)* regatear. COMP **bargain offer** oferta especial. ‖ **bargain price** precio de oferta, precio de saldo.

barge [bɑːdʒ] *n* gabarra, barcaza.

baritone ['bærɪtəʊn] *n* barítono.

barium ['beərɪʌm] *n* bario.

bark¹ [bɑːk] *n* **1** (of dog) ladrido. **2** (cough) tos *f* fuerte.
 ▶ *vi* ladrar.

bark² [bɑːk] *n* (of tree) corteza.

barley ['bɑːlɪ] *n* cebada.

barmaid ['bɑːmeɪd] *n* camarera.

barman ['bɑːmən] *n* camarero, barman *m*.
 ⓘ *pl* barmen ['bɑːmen].

barn [bɑːn] *n* (for grain) granero.

barnacle ['bɑːnəkəl] *n* percebe *m*.

barnyard ['bɑːnjɑːd] *n* corral *m*.

barometer [bə'rɒmɪtər] *n* barómetro.

baron ['bærən] *n* barón *m*.

baroness ['bærənəs] *n* baronesa.

baroque [bə'rɒk] *adj* barroco,-a.
 ▶ *n* barroco.

barrack ['bærək] *vt* (jeer) abuchear.

barracks ['bærəks] *n pl* cuartel *m*.

✎ Puede considerarse singular o plural: *where is/are the barracks* ¿dónde está el cuartel.

barrage ['bærɑːʒ] *n* presa, embalse *m*.

barrel ['bærəl] *n* **1** (of beer) barril *m*; (of wine) tonel *m*, cuba. **2** (of gun) cañón *m*. **3** (of pen) depósito. **4** TECH tambor *m*.

barren ['bærən] *adj* **1** (land, woman) estéril. **2** (meagre) escaso,-a.

barricade [bærɪ'keɪd] *n* barricada.
 ▶ *vt* poner barricadas en.

barrier ['bærɪər] *n* barrera. COMP **barrier reef** banco de coral, arrecife *m*.

barrister ['bærɪstər] *n* abogado,-a *(capacitado,-a para actuar en tribunales superiores)*.

barrow ['bærəʊ] *n* (wheelbarrow) carretilla; (for carrying goods) carro.

barstool ['bɑːstuːl] *n* taburete *m* de bar.

bartender ['bɑːtendər] *n* US camarero, barman *m*.

barter ['bɑːtər] *n* trueque *m*.
 ▶ *vt* trocar.

basalt ['bæsɔːlt] *n* basalto.

base¹ [beɪs] *n* **1** (gen) base *f*. **2** ARCH (of column) basa, base *f*. **3** (of word) raíz *f*.
 ▶ *vt* basar.

base² [beɪs] *adj* **1** bajo,-a, vil. **2** (metal) común, de baja ley.

baseball ['beɪsbɔːl] *n* béisbol *m*.

baseline ['beɪslaɪn] *n* **1** SP (tennis) línea de saque. **2** (diagram) línea cero. **3** ART punto de fuga.

basement ['beɪsmənt] *n* sótano.

bash [bæʃ] *vt fam* golpear, aporrear.
 ▶ *n* **1** *fam* (blow) golpe *m*. **2** *fam* (try) intento.

bashful ['bæʃfʊl] *adj* vergonzoso,-a, tímido,-a, modesto,-a.

basic ['beɪsɪk] *adj* **1** básico,-a. **2** (elementary) elemental, para principiantes.

basil ['bæzəl] *n* BOT albahaca.

basilica [bə'zɪlɪkə] *n* basílica.

basin ['beɪsən] *n* **1** (bowl) cuenco; (washbowl) palangana. **2** (washbasin) lavabo. **3** GEOG cuenca.

basis ['beɪsɪs] *n* base *f*, fundamento. LOC **on the basis of ... 1** (according to) según. **2** (in accordance with) de acuerdo con. **3** (starting from) a partir de. **2** (because of) por, a causa de.
 ⓘ *pl* bases ['beɪsiːz].

✎ En ocasiones, basis puede traducirse al español mediante un adverbio: *on a temporary/regular/weekly basis* temporalmente/regularmente/semanalmente.

bask [bɑːsk] *vi* tumbarse al sol.

basket ['bɑːskɪt] *n* **1** cesta, cesto. **2** (basketball) canasta, cesta. **3** (of balloon) barquilla.

basketball ['bɑːskɪtbɔːl] *n* baloncesto.

Basque [bɑːsk] *adj* vasco,-a.
 ▶ *n* **1** (person) vasco,-a. **2** (language) vasco, euskera *m*.

bas-relief [bæsrɪ'liːf] *n* bajorrelieve *m*.

bass¹ [beɪs] *n* **1** MUS (singer) bajo. **2** MUS (notes) graves *mpl*. **3** MUS (guitar) bajo.
 ▶ *adj* MUS bajo,-a.

bass² [bæs] *n* (fish) róbalo, lubina; (freshwater) perca.

bassoon [bə'suːn] *n* fagot *m*.

bastard ['bɑːstəd] *adj & n* bastardo,-a.

baste [beɪst] *vt* CULIN rociar, bañar.

bastion ['bæstɪən] *n* baluarte *m*.

bat¹ [bæt] *n* ZOOL murciélago.

bat² [bæt] n SP bate m; *(table tennis)* pala.
▶ vi batear.
ⓘ pt & pp batted, ger batting.

batch [bætʃ] n *(gen)* lote m, remesa; *(of bread, etc)* hornada.

bath [bɑːθ] n **1** baño. **2** *(tub)* bañera.
▶ vi bañarse.
▶ n pl **baths** piscina f sing municipal.
[LOC] **to have a bath / take a bath** bañarse. **ǁ to run a bath** preparar un baño.

bathe [beɪð] vt **1** MED *(cut, wound)* lavar. **2** *(eyes)* bañarse. **3** fig *(with light)* bañar.
▶ vi *(in sea)* bañarse.

⊕ La diferencia entre los verbos bath y bathe es que este último se emplea para referirse a un baño en el mar, un río o un lago, es decir, sin un objetivo higiénico.

bather ['beɪðər] n bañista mf.

bathing ['beɪðɪŋ] n baño. [LOC] **"No bathing"** «Prohibido bañarse». [COMP] **bathing costume** traje m de baño. **ǁ bathing suit** traje m de baño.

bathrobe ['bɑːθrəʊb] n albornoz m.

bathroom ['bɑːθruːm] n cuarto de baño.

bathtub ['bɑːθtʌb] n US bañera.

bathyscaph ['bæθɪskæf] n batiscafo.

baton ['bætən, 'bætɒn] n **1** *(truncheon)* porra. **2** MUS batuta. **3** SP testigo.

batrachian [bəˈtreɪkjən] adj batracio,-a.
▶ n batracio.

battalion [bəˈtæljən] n batallón m.

batter¹ ['bætər] n CULIN rebozado.

batter² ['bætər] vt *(person)* golpear, apalear; *(bruise)* magullar; *(object)* maltratar, estropear.

batter³ ['bætər] n SP *(baseball, cricket)* bateador,-ra.

battery ['bætərɪ] n **1** ELEC *(wet)* batería; *(dry)* pila. **2** MIL *(of artillery)* batería. **3** *(series)* batería.
ⓘ pl batteries.

battle ['bætəl] n batalla.
▶ vi pelearse, batirse.

battlefield ['bætəlfiːld] n campo de batalla.

battleship ['bætəlʃɪp] n acorazado.

bauble ['bɔːbəl] n **1** *(trinket)* baratija. **2** *(Christmas decoration)* bola de Navidad.

bawl [bɔːl] vi chillar, gritar.

bay¹ [beɪ] n GEOG bahía; *(large)* golfo.
[COMP] **Bay of Biscay** golfo de Vizcaya.

bay² [beɪ] n *(tree)* laurel m.

bay³ [beɪ] vi *(howl)* aullar.

bay⁴ [beɪ] n **1** ARCH *(recess)* hueco, nicho. **2** *(in factory)* nave f.

bayonet ['beɪənət] n MIL bayoneta.

bazaar [bəˈzɑːr] n bazar m.

BBC ['biːˈbiːˈsiː] abbr (British Broadcasting Corporation) compañía británica de radiodifusión; *(abbreviation)* BBC f.

BC ['biːˈsiː] abbr (before Christ) antes de Cristo.

be [biː] vi **1** *(permanent or essential characteristic)* ser: *she's clever* es inteligente. **2** *(nationality, origin)* ser: *John's English* John es inglés. **3** *(occupation)* ser: *we are both teachers* los dos somos profesores. **4** *(ownership, authorship)* ser: *it's my pencil* es mi lápiz. **5** *(composition)* ser: *this cupboard is oak* este armario es de roble. **6** *(use)* ser: *this product is for tiles* este producto es para baldosas. **7** *(location)* estar: *Whitby is on the coast* Whitby está en la costa. **8** *(temporary state)* estar: *your supper's cold* tu cena está fría; *how are you?* ¿cómo estás? **9** *(age)* tener: *Philip is 22* Philip tiene 22 años. **10** *(price)* costar, valer: *a single ticket is £9.50* un billete de ida cuesta 9,50 libras. **11** tener: *he's hot/cold* tiene calor/frío; *he's right* tiene razón. [LOC] **to be about to + inf** estar para + inf, estar a punto de + inf: *the train is about to arrive* el tren está a punto de llegar.
▶ aux **1** be + pres part *(action in progress or near future)* estar: *it is raining* está lloviendo; *the train is coming* viene el tren; *I am going on Thursday* iré el jueves. **2** to be + pp *(passive)* ser: *she was arrested at the border* fue detenida en la frontera, la detuvieron en la frontera. **3** be + to + inf *(future)*: *the King is to visit Egypt* el Rey visitará Egipto. [LOC] **there is / there are** hay.
◆ **to be after** vi querer, estar buscando: *what are you after?* ¿que estás buscando?
◆ **to be off** vi *(leave)* salir, marcharse; *(be stale, bad)* estar pasado,-a.
◆ **to be in** vi **1** *(at home)* estar en casa. **2** *(in fashion)* estar de moda.

◆ **to be out** *vi (away)* no estar, estar fuera: *John's out at the moment* John no está en estos momentos.

◆ **to be away** *vi* estar fuera.

◆ **to be back** *vi* estar de vuelta, haber vuelto.

◆ **to be over** *vi* haber acabado.
ⓘ *pres 1ª pers* **am**, *2ª pers sing y todas las del pl* **are**, *3ª pers sing* **is**; *pt 1ª y 3ª pers sing* **was**, *2ª pers sing y todas del pl* **were**; *pp* **been**.

beach [biːtʃ] *n* playa.
ⓘ *pl* **beaches**.

beacon [ˈbiːkən] *n* **1** *(fire)* almenara. **2** *(light)* baliza. **3** *(lighthouse)* faro.

bead [biːd] *n* **1** *(on rosary, necklace)* cuenta; *(glass)* abalorio. **2** *(of liquid)* gota.

beak [biːk] *n* pico.

beaker [ˈbiːkəʳ] *n* **1** taza alta. **2** *(for measuring, playing dice)* cubilete *m*. **3** CHEM vaso de precipitación.

beam [biːm] *n* **1** *(wooden)* viga. **2** *(of light)* rayo. **3** *(width of ship)* manga. **4** *(smile)* sonrisa radiante. **5** PHYS haz *m*.
▸ *vi* **1** *(shine)* brillar. **2** *(smile)* sonreír.
▸ *vt* irradiar, emitir. COMP **electron beam** haz *m* de electrones.

bean [biːn] *n* **1** *(vegetable)* alubia, judía, haba. **2** *(of coffee)* grano.

beansprout [ˈbiːnspraʊt] *n* brote *m* de soja.

bear¹ [beəʳ] *n* ZOOL oso. COMP **bear cub** ZOOL osezno. **‖ grizzly bear** oso pardo. **‖ the Great Bear** la Osa Mayor. **‖ the Little Bear** la Osa Menor.

bear² [beəʳ] *vt* **1** *(gen)* llevar. **2** *(show signs of)* mostrar, revelar. **3** *(weight)* soportar, aguantar; *(responsibility, cost)* asumir. **4** *(fruit)* producir. **5** FIN *(interest)* devengar.
ⓘ *pt* **bore** [bɔːʳ], *pp* **borne** [bɔːⁿ].

bearable [ˈbeərəbəl] *adj* soportable, llevadero,-a.

beard [bɪəd] *n* **1** *(on face)* barba. **2** *(of corn)* arista, raspa.

bearded [ˈbɪədɪd] *adj* barbudo,-a.

bearing [ˈbeərɪŋ] *n* **1** *(posture)* porte *m*. **2** *(relevance)* relación *f*. **3** *(importance)* trascendencia. **4** TECH cojinete *m*. **5** ARCH soporte *m*, columna. **6** MAR rumbo, orientación *f*.

bearskin [ˈbeəskɪn] *n (hat)* birretina.

beast [biːst] *n* bestia, animal *m*.

beastly [ˈbiːstlɪ] *adj* **1** bestial. **2** *(unpleasant)* antipático,-a. **3** *sl (damn)* dichoso,-a, maldito,-a.
ⓘ *comp* **beastlier**, *superl* **beastliest**.

beat [biːt] *n* **1** *(of heart)* latido. **2** *(noise)* golpe *m*, ruido; *(of rain)* tamborileo; *(of wings)* aleteo. **3** MUS ritmo. **4** *(of policeman)* ronda.
▸ *adj fam* agotado,-a, rendido,-a.
▸ *vt* **1** *(hit)* golpear; *(metals)* martillear; *(person)* azotar; *(drum)* tocar. **2** CULIN batir. **3** *(defeat)* vencer, derrotar; *(in competition)* ganar.
▸ *vi* **1** *(heart)* latir. **2** *(wings)* batir.

◆ **to beat down** *vt sep* **1** *(door)* derribar, echar abajo. **2** *(price)* conseguir un precio más bajo.

◆ **to beat up** *vt sep* dar una paliza a.
ⓘ *pt* **beat**, *pp* **beaten** [ˈbiːtən].

beater [ˈbiːtəʳ] *n* **1** CULIN batidora. **2** *(in hunting)* ojeador,-ra.

beating [ˈbiːtɪŋ] *n* **1** *(thrashing)* paliza. **2** *(defeat)* derrota. **3** *(of heart)* latidos *mpl*.

beautician [bjuːˈtɪʃən] *n* esteticista *mf*.

beautiful [ˈbjuːtɪful] *adj* **1** *(person, object, place)* hermoso,-a, bonito,-a, precioso,-a; *(person)* guapo,-a. **2** *(wonderful)* maravilloso,-a, magnífico,-a. **3** *(delicious)* delicioso,-a.

beauty [ˈbjuːtɪ] *n* belleza. COMP **beauty spot 1** *(on face)* lunar *m*. **2** *(place)* lugar *m* pintoresco.
ⓘ *pl* **beauties**.

beaver [ˈbiːvəʳ] *n* castor *m*.

became [bɪˈkeɪm] *pt* → **become**.

because [bɪˈkɒz] *conj* porque.
▸ *prep* **because of** a causa de: *they were late because of the snow* llegaron tarde a causa de la nieve.

become [bɪˈkʌm] *vi* **1** *(with noun)* convertirse en, hacerse, llegar a ser: *to become a doctor/teacher* hacerse médico,-a/maestro,-a; *to become friends* hacerse amigos. **2** *(change into)* convertirse en, transformarse en: *chrysalises become butterflies* las crisálidas se transforman en mariposas. **3** *(irrevocable state)* volverse; *(temporary state)* ponerse; *(involuntary state)* quedarse: *to become mad* volverse loco,-a, *to become fat* engordar; *to become sad* ponerse triste.

ⓘ *pt* became [bɪ'keɪm], *pp* become.

becoming [bɪ'kʌmɪŋ] *adj* **1** *(dress, etc)* que sienta bien, favorecedor,-ra. **2** *(behaviour, language)* apropiado,-a.

bed [bed] *n* **1** cama. **2** *(for animals)* lecho. **3** *(of flowers)* arriate *m*, macizo. **4** *(of river)* lecho, cauce *m*; *(of sea)* fondo. **5** GEOL capa, yacimiento. LOC **to go to bed** acostarse. ■ **to put sb to bed** acostar a ALGN. ■ **to make the bed** hacer la cama. COMP **bunk bed** litera. ■ **double bed** cama de matrimonio. ■ **single bed** cama individual. ■ **twin beds** camas *fpl* separadas. ■ **bed and board** pensión *f* completa. ■ **bed and breakfast** alojamiento con desayuno incluido.

✎ Consulta B and B.

bedbug ['bedbʌg] *n* chinche *f*.

bedclothes ['bedkləʊðz] *n pl* ropa de cama.

bedding ['bedɪŋ] *n* **1** ropa de cama. **2** *(for animals)* lecho.

bedpan ['bedpæn] *n* cuña, orinal *m* de cama.

bedridden ['bedrɪdən] *adj* postrado,-a en cama.

bedroom ['bedru:m] *n* dormitorio, habitación *f*.

bedside ['bedsaɪd] *n* cabecera.

bedsit [bed'sɪt] *n* estudio.

⊕ El bedsit es un tipo de alojamiento de alquiler asequible típico del Reino Unido. Consiste en una sola habitación que hace de dormitorio, sala de estar y comedor. Se suele compartir el baño con otras personas y a veces se tiene derecho a una cocina.

bedsore ['bedsɔ:] *n* MED llaga, úlcera.

bedspread ['bedspred] *n* cubrecama.

bedtime ['bedtaɪm] *n* la hora de acostarse.

bee [bi:] *n* abeja.

beech [bi:tʃ] *n* *(wood)* haya. COMP **beech grove** hayal *m*, hayedo. ■ **beech tree** haya.

bee-eater ['bi:i:tə'] *n* abejaruco.

beef [bi:f] *n* **1** *(meat)* carne *f* de buey, carne *f* de vaca. **2** *(animal)* buey *m*, vaca; *(cattle)* ganado vacuno. COMP **corned beef** carne *f* de vaca en conserva.

beefburger ['bi:fbɜ:gə'] *n* hamburguesa.

beefeater ['bi:fi:tə'] *n* alabardero de la Torre de Londres.

beefsteak ['bi:fsteɪk] *n* bistec *m*.

beehive ['bi:haɪv] *n* colmena.

beekeeper ['bi:ki:pə'] *n* apicultor,-ra.

beekeeping ['bi:ki:pɪŋ] *n* apicultura.

beeline ['bi:laɪn] *n* línea recta. LOC **to make a beeline for...** irse directamente a...

been [bi:n, bɪn] *pp* → be.

beep [bi:p] *n* pitido.
► *vi* pitar, tocar el pito. LOC **to beep the horn** tocar el claxon.

beer [bɪə'] *n* cerveza.

beeswax ['bi:zwæks] *n* cera de abejas.

beet [bi:t] *n* remolacha.

beetle ['bi:təl] *n* escarabajo.

beetroot ['bi:tru:t] *n* **1** *[pl* beet] remolacha azucarera. **2** US *[pl* beets] remolacha.

before [bɪ'fɔ:'] *prep* **1** *(earlier)* antes de. **2** *(in front of)* delante de; *(in the presence of)* ante; *(for the attention of)* ante: *he's before me in the queue* va delante de mi en la cola; *he appeared before the judge* compareció ante el juez. **3** *(rather than)* antes que. **4** *(ahead)* por delante. **5** *(first)* primero: *ladies before gentlemen* las señoras primero.
► *conj* **1** *(earlier than)* antes de + *inf*, antes de + *subj*: *don't forget to say goodbye before you go* no te olvides de despedirte antes de irte. **2** *(rather than)* antes de + *inf*: *he would starve before he asked them for money* preferiría morir de hambre antes de pedirles dinero.
► *adv* **1** *(earlier)* antes. **2** *(previous)* anterior. **3** *(already)* ya: *we've seen it before* ya lo hemos visto.

beforehand [bɪ'fɔ:hænd] *adv* **1** *(earlier)* antes. **2** *(in advance)* de antemano, con antelación: *payment must be made a month beforehand* los pagos deben efectuarse con un mes de antelación. **3** *(before)* antes: *they arrived two hours beforehand* llegaron dos horas antes.

befriend [brˈfrend] *vt* ofrecer su amistad a.

beg [beg] *vt* **1** mendigar. **2** *(ask for)* pedir. **3** *lit (beseech)* suplicar, rogar. ⃞LOC **I beg your pardon** ¿cómo ha dicho?
▸ *vi* **1** mendigar. **2** *(dog)* sentarse *(con las patas delanteras levantadas).*
ⓘ *pt & pp* **begged**, *ger* **begging**.

began [brˈgæn] *pt* → **begin**.

beggar [ˈbegəʳ] *n* **1** mendigo,-a, pordiosero,-a. **2** *fam* tipo, individuo,-a: *he's a funny beggar* es un tipo raro.

begin [brˈgɪn] *vt* empezar, comenzar.
ⓘ *pt* **began** [brˈgæn], *pp* **begun** [brˈgʌn], *ger* **beginning**.

beginner [brˈgɪnəʳ] *n* principiante *mf*.

beginning [brˈgɪnɪŋ] *n* **1** principio, comienzo. **2** *(cause)* origen *m*, causa.

begrudge [brˈgrʌdʒ] *vt* **1** *(envy)* envidiar. **2** *(disapprove)* desaprobar.

beguile [brˈgaɪl] *vt* **1** *(seduce)* seducir, atraer; *(bewitch)* embrujar. **2** *(cheat)* engañar.

begun [brˈgʌn] *pp* → **begin**.

behalf [brˈhɑːf] *phr* **on behalf of** *(acting for)* en nombre de, de parte de; *(in favour of)* por, en favor de; *(for the benefit of)* por, en beneficio de.

behave [brˈheɪv] *vi* **1** *(people)* comportarse, portarse. **2** *(equipment, machinery)* funcionar bien: *this computer won't behave* este ordenador no funciona bien.

behavior [brˈheɪvjəʳ] *n* US → **behaviour**.

behaviour [brˈheɪvjəʳ] *n* **1** *(of person)* conducta, comportamiento. **2** *(of equipment, machine)* funcionamiento. **3** *(treatment)* trato.

behead [brˈhed] *vt* decapitar.

behind [brˈhaɪnd] *prep* detrás de.
▸ *adv* **1** detrás, atrás. **2** *(late)* atrasado,-a. **3** *(with payment)* retrasado,-a: *he's behind with the payments* está retrasado en los pagos.
▸ *n fam (buttocks)* trasero.

behindhand [brˈhaɪndhænd] *adv* en retraso, retrasado,-a.

beige [beɪʒ] *n* beige *m*.

▸ *adj* (de color) beige.

being [ˈbiːɪŋ] *n* **1** *(living thing)* ser *m*. **2** *(existence)* existencia. ⃞LOC **being as** ya que, puesto que: *being as they arrived late …* puesto que llegaron tarde … ‖ **for the time being** por ahora, de momento. ⃞COMP **human being** ser *m* humano.

Belarus [ˈbelərʌs] *n* Bielorrusia.

belated [brˈleɪtɪd] *adj fam* tardío,-a.

belay [brˈleɪ] *vt (boat)* amarrar; *(rope in mountaineering)* asegurar, fijar.

belch [beltʃ] *n* eructo.
▸ *vi* eructar. ⃞LOC **to belch (out)** vomitar, arrojar: *the burning building belched out smoke* el edificio en llamas arrojaba humo.

beleaguer [brˈliːgəʳ] *vt* **1** *(beseige)* sitiar, cercar. **2** *(harass)* perseguir, hostigar.

belfry [ˈbelfrɪ] *n* campanario.
ⓘ *pl* **belfries**.

Belgian [ˈbeldʒən] *adj* belga.
▸ *n* belga *mf*.

Belgium [ˈbeldʒəm] *n* Bélgica.

belie [brˈlaɪ] *vt* **1** *(contradict)* mostrar como falso. **2** *(misrepresent)* no reflejar, ocultar. **3** *(fail to justify)* defraudar.

belief [brˈliːf] *n* **1** *(gen)* creencia. **2** *(opinion)* opinión *f*. **3** *(confidence)* confianza: *he has no belief in the legal system* no tiene confianza en el sistema jurídico. ⃞LOC **to the best of my belief** que yo sepa. ‖ **it is beyond belief** parece mentira.

believable [brˈliːvəbəl] *adj* creíble, verosímil.

believe [brˈliːv] *vt* **1** *(accept as true, think)* creer. **2** *(suppose)* suponer.
▸ *vi* **1** creer (in, en). **2** *(trust)* confiar (in, en). **3** *(support, be in favour of)* ser partidario,-a (in, de). **4** REL tener fe. ⃞LOC **it is believed that** se cree que.

believer [brˈliːvəʳ] *n* **1** creyente *mf*. **2** *(supporter)* partidario,-a.

belittle [brˈlɪtəl] *vt* menospreciar.

bell [bel] *n* **1** *(church, etc)* campana. **2** *(handbell)* campanilla. **3** *(on bicycle, door, etc)* timbre *m*. **4** *(on toy, hat)* cascabel *m*. **5** *(cowbell)* cencerro *m*. **6** *(flower)* campanilla. ⃞LOC **to ring the bell** tocar el timbre.

B

bell-bottoms [bel'bɒtəmz] *n pl* pantalones *mpl* acampanados.

bellboy ['belbɔɪ] *n* botones *m*.

bellhop ['belhɒp] *n* US botones *m*.

belligerent [bɪ'lɪdʒərənt] *adj* beligerante.

bellow ['beləʊ] *n* bramido.
▶ *vi* bramar.
▶ *n pl* **bellows** fuelle *m sing*.

belly ['belɪ] *n* **1** (*person*) vientre *m*, barriga. **2** (*animal*) panza. COMP **belly button** ombligo. ‖ **belly laugh** carcajada.
ⓘ *pl* bellies.

bellyache ['belɪeɪk] *n fam* dolor *m* de barriga.
▶ *vi fam* quejarse.

bellybutton ['belɪbʌtən] *n fam* ombligo.

belong [bɪ'lɒŋ] *vi* **1** pertenecer (to, a), ser (to, de). **2** (*be a member of a club*) ser socio,-a (to, de); (*be a member of a political party*) ser miembro (to, de). **3** (*have suitable qualities*) ser apto,-a (in, para).

belongings [bɪ'lɒŋɪŋz] *n pl* pertenencias *fpl*, bártulos *mpl*.

beloved [(*adj*) bɪ'lʌvd; (*n*) bɪ'lʌvɪd] *adj* querido,-a, amado,-a.
▶ *n* amado,-a.

below [bɪ'ləʊ] *prep* **1** debajo de, bajo. **2** por debajo (de). **3** (*lower than*) bajo. LOC **below sea level** por debajo del nivel del mar.
▶ *adv* **1** abajo. **2** de abajo. LOC **see below** véase abajo.

belt [belt] *n* **1** cinturón *m*. **2** TECH correa. **3** (*area*) zona.
▶ *vt fam* (*hit*) arrear un tortazo.
◆ **to belt along** *vi fam* ir a todo gas.
◆ **to belt up** *vi fam* cerrar el pico.

bemused [bɪ'mjuːzd] *adj* perplejo,-a.

bench [bentʃ] *n* **1** banco. **2** JUR tribunal *m*. **3** SP banquillo. LOC **to be on the bench** ser juez,-za.
ⓘ *pl* benches.

bend [bend] *n* **1** (*in road, etc*) curva. **2** (*in pipe*) ángulo.
▶ *vt* **1** doblar, curvar. **2** (*head*) inclinar; (*back*) doblar, encorvar; (*knee*) doblar, flexionar.
▶ *vi* **1** doblarse, combarse: *the legs of the chair bent when he sat down* las patas de la silla se combaron cuando se sentó. **2** (*head*) inclinarse; (*back*) encorvarse. **3** (*road*) torcer.
◆ **to bend down** *vi* agacharse.
◆ **to bend over** *vi* inclinarse.
ⓘ *pt & pp* bent [bent].

beneath [bɪ'niːθ] *prep* **1** bajo, debajo de. **2** por debajo de: *the underground line runs beneath our house* la línea de metro va por debajo de nuestra casa. **3** *fig* indigno,-a de, no digno,-a de: *it's beneath you to behave like this* es indigno de ti comportarte de esta manera.
▶ *adv* de abajo: *she lives in the flat beneath* vive en el piso de abajo.

benefactor ['benɪfæktə'] *n* benefactor *m*.

beneficial [benɪ'fɪʃəl] *adj* beneficioso,-a, provechoso,-a.

beneficiary [benɪ'fɪʃərɪ] *n* beneficiario,-a.
ⓘ *pl* beneficiaries.

benefit ['benɪfɪt] *n* **1** (*advantage*) beneficio, provecho. **2** (*good*) bien *m*. **3** (*allowance*) subsidio. **4** (*charity performance*) función *f* benéfica; (*charity game*) partido benéfico.
▶ *vt* beneficiar.
▶ *vi* beneficiarse (from, de).
ⓘ *pt & pp* benefited (US benefitted), *ger* benefiting (US benefitting).

benevolence [bɪ'nevələns] *n* benevolencia.

benevolent [bɪ'nevələnt] *adj* benévolo,-a. COMP **benevolent society** sociedad *f* benéfica.

beneficence [bɪ'nefɪsəns] *n* beneficencia.

benign [bɪ'naɪn] *adj* benigno,-a.

bent [bent] *pt & pp* → **bend**.
▶ *adj* **1** torcido,-a, doblado,-a. **2** *sl* (*corrupt*) corrupto,-a.
▶ *n* (*innate ability*) facilidad *f*, don *m*: *she's got a bent for maths* tiene facilidad para las matemáticas.

benzene ['benziːn] *n* CHEM benceno.

benzine ['benziːn] *n* CHEM bencina.

bequest [bɪ'kwest] *n* legado.

bereaved [bɪ'riːvd] *adj* desconsolado,-a, afligido,-a: *his bereaved wife* su desconsolada esposa.

bereavement [bɪˈriːvmənt] *n* **1** *(loss)* pérdida. **2** *(mourning)* duelo.

beret [ˈbereɪ] *n* boina.

berry [ˈberɪ] *n* baya.
① *pl* berries.

✎ Hay muchas frutas cuyo nombre se forma con **berry**, ya que se trata de bayas. Por ejemplo: **blackberry** *(mora)*, **gooseberry** *(grosella espinosa)*, **raspberry** *(frambuesa)* o **strawberry** *(fresón)*.

---

berserk [bəˈzɜːk] *adj* enloquecido,-a.

berth [bɜːθ] *n* **1** *(in harbour)* amarradero. **2** *(on ship)* camarote *m*, litera.
▶ *vi* atracar.

beryl [ˈberəl] *n* GEOL berilo.

beryllium [bəˈrɪlɪəm] *n* CHEM berilio.

beseech [bɪˈsiːtʃ] *vt lit* implorar, suplicar.
① *pt & pp* besought [bɪˈsɔːt] o beseeched.

beset [bɪˈset] *vt* **1** *(attack, harass)* acosar, asaltar. **2** *(hem in, surround)* acorralar, cercar.
① *pt & pp* beset, *ger* besetting.

beside [bɪˈsaɪd] *prep* **1** al lado de. **2** *(compared to)* frente a, comparado,-a con. LOC **to be beside os** estar fuera de sí. ▌ **that's beside the point** esto no viene al caso.

besides [bɪˈsaɪdz] *prep (as well as)* además de, aparte de.
▶ *adv* además.

besiege [bɪˈsiːdʒ] *vt* **1** MIL sitiar. **2** *fig* asediar, inundar.

besought [bɪˈsɔːt] *pt & pp* → beseech.

best [best] *adj (superl of* good) mejor. LOC **the best part of** casi: *it cost me the best part of £5,000* me costó casi 5.000 libras. COMP **best man** padrino de boda. **the best one** el mejor, la mejor.
▶ *adv* **1** *(superl of* well) mejor. **2** *(to a greater extent)* más: *of all the girls she is the one he likes best* de todas las chicas ella es la que le gusta más. LOC **best before ...** consumir preferentemente antes de …
▶ *n* **1** lo mejor: *the best is yet to come* lo mejor aún está por venir. **2** *(person)* el mejor, la mejor: *she's the best in the class at maths* es la mejor de la clase en mates. **3** *(in*

sport) plusmarca. LOC **all the best! 1** ¡que te vaya bien! **2** *(in letter)* un saludo. ▌ **it's for the best** más vale que sea así.

bestial [ˈbestɪəl] *adj* bestial, brutal.

bestow [bɪˈstəʊ] *vt (honour, award)* otorgar (on, a); *(favour)* hacer (on, a); *(title)* conferir (on, a).

best-seller [bestˈselə'] *n* best seller *m*, superventas *m*.

bet [bet] *n* apuesta. LOC **to make a bet** hacer una apuesta.
▶ *vt & vi* apostar.
① *pt & pp* bet o betted, *ger* betting.

beta [ˈbiːtə] *n* beta. COMP **beta rays** rayos *mpl* beta.

betray [bɪˈtreɪ] *vt* **1** traicionar. **2** *(secret)* revelar. **3** *(show signs of)* dejar ver, acusar. **4** *(deceive)* engañar.

betrayal [bɪˈtreɪəl] *n* **1** traición *f*. **2** *(deceit)* engaño.

better¹ [ˈbetə'] *adj* **1** *(comp of* good) mejor: *his new novel is better than his last one* su última novela es mejor que la anterior. **2** *(more healthy)* mejor: *he's feeling better today* hoy se encuentra mejor. LOC **to get better** recuperarse, mejorarse. ▌ **better and better** cada vez mejor.
▶ *adv* **1** *(comp of* well) mejor. **2** *(to a greater extent)* más: *I like this one better* me gusta más éste. LOC **had better + *inf*** más vale que + *subj*: *we'd better be going* más vale que nos vayamos. ▌ **to like STH/SB better** preferir ALGO/a ALGN.
▶ *vt* **1** *(improve)* mejorar: *he has bettered their working conditions* ha mejorado sus condiciones de trabajo. **2** *(surpass)* superar: *he bettered his own record* superó su propio récord.
▶ *n pl* **betters** superiores *mpl*: *you must listen to your betters* debes escuchar a tus superiores.

betting [ˈbetɪŋ] *n* apuestas *fpl*. LOC **what's the betting that he "(she, it, etc)...?"** ¿qué te apuestas a que …?: *what's the betting that he arrives late?* ¿qué te apuestas a que llega tarde? COMP **betting shop** GB administración *f* de apuestas hípicas.

between [bɪˈtwiːn] *prep* entre: *choose a number between one and ten* escoge un número entre uno y diez.

▶ *adv* [también **in between**] de en medio: *we could see the sea if it wasn't for the houses (in) between* podríamos ver el mar si no fuera por las casas de en medio.

bevel ['bevəl] *n* bebida.

beverage ['bevərɪdʒ] *n* bebida.

bevy ['bevɪ] *n (of birds)* bandada.
ⓘ *pl* **bevies**.

beware [bɪ'weə'] *vi* tener cuidado (of, con): *beware of the dog!* ¡cuidado con el perro!

bewilder [bɪ'wɪldə'] *vt* desconcertar, dejar perplejo,-a.

bewitch [bɪ'wɪtʃ] *vt* **1** hechizar, embrujar. **2** *fig* hechizar, fascinar.

beyond [bɪ'jɒnd] *prep* **1** más allá de: *they live beyond the mountains* viven más allá de las montañas. **2** *(outside)* fuera de: *it's beyond my jurisdiction* está fuera de mi jurisdicción. LOC **it's beyond doubt** es indudable, es seguro, no cabe duda.
▶ *adv* más allá, más lejos.
▶ *n* **the beyond** el más allá.

bias ['baɪəs] *n* **1** *(prejudice)* parcialidad *f*, prejuicio. **2** *(inclination)* tendencia, predisposición *f*. **3** *(in statistics)* margen *f* de error.
▶ *vt* predisponer, influenciar.
ⓘ *pt & pp* **biased** o **biassed**, *ger* **biasing** o **biassing**.

biased ['baɪəst] *adj* parcial.

bib [bɪb] *n* **1** *(for baby)* babero. **2** *(top of apron, overall)* peto.

Bible ['baɪbəl] *n* Biblia.

bibliography [bɪblɪ'ɒɡrəfɪ] *n* bibliografía.
ⓘ *pl* **bibliographies**.

bicarbonate [baɪ'kɑ:bənət] *n* CHEM bicarbonato.

biceps ['baɪseps] *n* bíceps *m*.

bicker ['bɪkə'] *vi* discutir, porfiar.

bicycle ['baɪsɪkəl] *n* bicicleta. LOC **to ride a bicycle** montar en bicicleta. COMP **bicycle pump** bomba de bicicleta.

bid [bɪd] *n* **1** *(at auction)* puja. **2** *(attempt)* intento. **3** *(offer)* oferta.
▶ *vi (at auction)* pujar (for, por).
ⓘ *pt & pp* **bid**, *ger* **bidding**.

bidder ['bɪdə'] *n* postor,-ra, pujador,-ra, licitador,-ra.

bidding ['bɪdɪŋ] *n* **1** *(at auction)* puja, oferta. **2** *(order)* orden *f*.

bide [baɪd] *vt* **to bide one's time** esperar el momento oportuno.
ⓘ *pt* **bided** o **bode** [bəʊd], *pp* **bided**, *ger* **biding**.

bidet ['bi:deɪ] *n* bidé *m*.

bifocal [baɪ'fəʊkəl] *adj* bifocal.
▶ *n pl* **bifocals** lentes *fpl* bifocales.

bifurcate ['baɪfəkeɪt] *vi* bifurcarse.

big [bɪɡ] *adj* **1** *(size, importance)* grande; *(before sing noun)* gran. **2** *(older)* mayor.
ⓘ *comp* **bigger**, *superl* **biggest**.

bigamy ['bɪɡəmɪ] *n* bigamia.

big-head ['bɪɡhed] *n* sabihondo,-a, creído,-a.

big-hearted [bɪɡ'hɑ:tɪd] *adj* de buen corazón, generoso,-a.

bigmouth ['bɪɡmaʊθ] *n* bocazas *mf*.

bigot ['bɪɡət] *n* fanático,-a.

☒ **Bigot** no significa 'bigote', que se traduce por **moustache**.

bigotry ['bɪɡətrɪ] *n* fanatismo.

bigwig ['bɪɡwɪɡ] *n fam* pez *m* gordo.

bike [baɪk] *n* **1** *fam (bicycle)* bici *f*. **2** *(motorcycle)* moto *f*.

bikeway ['baɪkweɪ] *n* carril-bici *m*.

bikini® [bɪ'ki:nɪ] *n* biquini® *m*, bikini® *m*.

bilateral [baɪ'lætərəl] *adj* bilateral.

bile [baɪl] *n* bilis *f*, hiel *f*. COMP **bile duct** conducto biliar.

biliary ['bɪlɪərɪ] *adj* biliar.

bilingual [baɪ'lɪŋɡwəl] *adj* bilingüe.

bilirubin [bɪlɪ'ru:bɪn] *n* bilirrubina.

bill¹ [bɪl] *n* **1** factura; *(in restaurant)* cuenta. **2** *(law)* proyecto de ley. **3** US *(banknote)* billete *m*. **4** *(poster)* cartel *m*. COMP **bill of exchange** letra de cambio. ‖ **Bill of Rights** declaración *f* de derechos.
▶ *vt* **1** facturar, pasar la factura. **2** THEAT programar.

bill² [bɪl] *n* **1** *(of bird)* pico. **2** *(headland)* cabo, promontorio.

billboard ['bɪlbɔ:d] *n* US valla publicitaria.

billfold ['bɪlfəʊld] *n* US billetero, cartera.

billing [ˈbɪlɪŋ] *n* **1** *(invoicing)* facturación *f*. **2** THEAT *orden de aparición en cartel*.

billion [ˈbɪlɪən] *n* **1** mil millones *mpl*. **2** GB *(formerly)* billón *m*.

✎ En el uso actual, tanto en EE UU como en Gran Bretaña, un **billion** equivale a mil millones. Antiguamente, el **billion** británico tenía el mismo significado que en español, es decir, 'un millón de millones'

billionaire [bɪlɪəˈneəʳ] *n* multimillonario,-a.

billow [ˈbɪləʊ] *n* **1** *(of water)* ola. **2** *(of smoke)* nube *f*.
▸ *vt* **1** *(sea)* ondear. **2** *(sail)* hincharse.

billy goat [ˈbɪlɪɡəʊt] *n* macho cabrío.

bin [bɪn] *n* **1** *(for rubbish)* cubo de la basura; *(for paper)* papelera. **2** *(large container)* recipiente *m*.

binary [ˈbaɪnərɪ] *adj* binario,-a. COMP **binary fission** bipartición *f*, fisión *f* binaria.

bind [baɪnd] *n fam* fastidio, molestia.
▸ *vt* **1** *(tie up)* atar; *(cereals, corn)* agavillar. **2** CULIN *(sauce)* ligar. **3** *(book, etc)* encuadernar. **4** *(bandage)* vendar. **5** *(require)* obligar.
ⓘ *pt & pp* **bound** [baʊnd].

binder [ˈbaɪndəʳ] *n* **1** *(file)* carpeta. **2** *(of books)* encuadernador,-ra.

binding [ˈbaɪndɪŋ] *n* **1** *(of book)* encuadernación *f*. **2** SEW ribete *m*. **3** *(of skis)* fijación *f*.
▸ *adj* obligatorio,-a (on, para).

binge [bɪndʒ] *n* *(drinking)* borrachera; *(eating)* atracón *m*.
▸ *vi* atiborrarse, hartarse de comida.

bingo [ˈbɪŋɡəʊ] *n* bingo.
ⓘ *pl* **bingos**.

binnacle [ˈbɪnəkəl] *n* bitácora.

binoculars [bɪˈnɒkjʊləz] *n pl* prismáticos *mpl*, gemelos *mpl*.

biochemistry [baɪəʊˈkemɪstrɪ] *n* bioquímica.

biodegradable [baɪəʊdɪˈɡreɪdəbəl] *adj* biodegradable.

biography [baɪˈɒɡrəfɪ] *n* biografía.
ⓘ *pl* **biographies**.

biological [baɪəˈlɒdʒɪkəl] *adj* biológico,-a.

biologist [baɪˈɒlədʒɪst] *n* biólogo,-a.

biology [baɪˈɒlədʒɪ] *n* biología.

biomass [ˈbaɪəʊmæs] *n* biomasa.

biomechanics [baɪəʊmɪˈkænɪks] *n* biomecánica.

biometry [baɪˈɒmətrɪ] *n* biometría.

bionic [baɪˈɒnɪk] *adj* biónico,-a.

biophysics [baɪəʊˈfɪzɪks] *n* biofísica.

biopsy [ˈbaɪɒpsɪ] *n* biopsia.
ⓘ *pl* **biopsies**.

biorhythm [ˈbaɪərɪðəm] *n* biorritmo.

biosphere [ˈbaɪəsfɪəʳ] *n* biosfera.

biotope [ˈbaɪətəp] *n* biotopo.

biped [ˈbaɪped] *adj* bípedo,-a.
▸ *n* bípedo.

biplane [ˈbaɪpleɪn] *n* biplano.

bipolar [baɪˈpəʊləʳ] *adj* bipolar.

birch [bɜːtʃ] *n* **1** *(tree)* abedul *m*. **2** *(rod)* vara de abedul.
▸ *vt* azotar.

bird [bɜːd] *n* **1** *(large)* ave *f*; *(small)* pájaro. **2** GB *sl (girl)* chica. **3** *sl (person)* tipo. COMP **bird of prey** ave *f* de rapiña, ave *f* de presa.

birdcage [ˈbɜːdkeɪdʒ] *n* jaula de pájaro.

birdie [ˈbɜːdɪ] *n* **1** *(little bird)* pajarito. **2** *(in golf)* birdie *m*.

birdseed [ˈbɜːdsiːd] *n* BOT alpiste *m*.

bird's-eye view [bɜːdzaɪˈvjuː] *n* vista panorámica.

bird-watcher [ˈbɜːdwɒtʃəʳ] *n* ornitólogo,-a *(cuya afición es observar las aves)*.

Biro® [ˈbaɪrəʊ] [also written **biro**] *n fam* boli *m*.
ⓘ *pl* **Biros**.

birth [bɜːθ] *n* **1** nacimiento. **2** MED parto. **3** *(descent)* linaje *m*. LOC **to give birth to 1** *(child)* dar a luz a. **2** *fig* dar lugar a. COMP **birth certificate** partida de nacimiento.
▌ **birth control** control *m* de la natalidad.
▌ **birth rate** tasa de natalidad.

birthday [ˈbɜːθdeɪ] *n* cumpleaños *m*.

birthmark [ˈbɜːθmɑːk] *n* mancha de nacimiento, antojo.

birthplace [ˈbɜːθpleɪs] *n* lugar *m* de nacimiento.

biscuit [ˈbɪskɪt] *n* galleta.

bisection [baɪˈsekʃən] *n* bisección *f*.

bisectrix [baɪˈsektrɪks] *n* bisectriz *f*.
ⓘ *pl* **bisectrices** [baɪˈsektrɪsiːz].

B

bisexual [baɪˈseksjʊəl] *adj* bisexual.
▸ *n* bisexual *mf*.

bishop [ˈbɪʃəp] *n* **1** obispo. **2** *(chess)* alfil *m*.

bison [ˈbaɪsən] *n* bisonte *m*.

bissextile [baɪˈsekstaɪl] *adj* bisiesto,-a.

bit[1] [bɪt] *n* **1** *(small piece)* trozo, pedacito. **2** *(small amount)* poco. **3** *fam (time)* un poco, un ratito. LOC **a bit** *fam (rather)* algo, un poco. I **a bit of** algo de. I **quite a bit / a good bit** *fam* bastante. **to come to bits** hacerse pedazos, romperse.

bit[2] [bɪt] *n* **1** *(of bridle)* bocado. **2** *(of drill)* broca.

bit[3] [bɪt] *n* COMPUT bit *m*.

bit[4] [bɪt] *pt* → bite.

bite [baɪt] *n* **1** *(act)* mordisco. **2** *(of insect)* picadura. **3** *(of dog, etc)* mordedura. **4** *(of food)* bocado.
▸ *vt* **1** morder.**2** *(insect, snake)* picar. **3** *(grip)* agarrar.
▸ *vi* **1** morder. **2** *(insect, snake)* picar. **3** *(fish)* picar.
① *pt* bit, *pp* bitten [ˈbɪtən].

biting [ˈbaɪtɪŋ] *adj* **1** *(wind)* cortante, penetrante. **2** *(comment)* mordaz.

bitten [ˈbɪtən] *pp* → bite.

bitter [ˈbɪtəʳ] *adj* **1** *(gen)* amargo,-a; *(fruit)* ácido,-a, agrio,-a. **2** *(weather)* glacial. **3** *(person)* amargado,-a. **4** *(fight)* enconado,-a.
▸ *n* cerveza amarga.

bitterly [ˈbɪtəlɪ] *adv* **1** con amargura, amargamente: *she complained bitterly* se quejó amargamente. **2** *(very)* muy: *it's bitterly cold* hace un frío glacial.

bitterness [ˈbɪtənəs] *n* **1** *(gen)* amargura; *(of fruit)* acidez *f*. **2** *(of weather)* crudeza. **3** *(resentment)* rencor *m*, resentimiento.

bittersweet [ˈbɪtəswiːt] *adj* agridulce.

bitumen [ˈbɪtjʊmɪn] *n* betún *m*.

bivalent [baɪˈveɪlənt] *adj* bivalente.

bivalve [ˈbaɪvælv] *adj* bivalvo,-a.
▸ *n* bivalvo.

bizarre [bɪˈzɑːʳ] *adj* **1** raro,-a, extraño,-a.

blab [blæb] *vi* **1** *fam (gossip)* cotillear, chismear. **2** *fam (talk constantly)* rajar, parlotear.
① *pt & pp* blabbed, *ger* blabbing.

black [blæk] *adj* **1** negro,-a. **2** *(dirty)* sucio,-a. **3** *(threatening)* amenazador,-ra. LOC **black and white** blanco y negro. COMP **black economy** economía sumergida.
▸ *n* **1** *(colour)* negro. **2** *(person)* negro,-a.
▸ *vt* **1** *(make black)* ennegrecer. **2** *(boycott)* boicotear.
◆ **to black out** *vt sep* **1** *(windows of house)* tapar; *(electrical supply)* apagar el alumbrado. **2** *(cause power cut)* dejar sin luz, causar un apagón.
▸ *vi* *(faint)* desmayarse.

blackberry [ˈblækbərɪ] *n* zarzamora, mora. COMP **blackberry bush** zarza.
① *pl* blackberries.

blackbird [ˈblækbɜːd] *n* mirlo.

blackboard [ˈblækbɔːd] *n* pizarra.

blackcurrant [blækˈkʌrənt] *n* grosella negra.

blacken [ˈblækən] *vt* **1** ennegrecer. **2** *fig (defame)* manchar.

blackhead [ˈblækhed] *n* espinilla.

blackjack [ˈblækdʒæk] *n* *(card game)* veintiuna.

blackleg [ˈblækleg] *n* esquirol *m*.

blacklist [ˈblæklɪst] *n* lista negra.

blackmail [ˈblækmeɪl] *n* chantaje *m*.
▸ *vt* hacer chantaje a, chantajear.

blackmailer [ˈblækmeɪləʳ] *n* chantajista *mf*.

blackout [ˈblækaʊt] *n* **1** *(through electrical fault)* apagón *m*; *(in wartime)* oscurecimiento general de una ciudad. **2** *(fainting)* pérdida de conocimiento, desmayo.

blacksmith [ˈblæksmɪθ] *n* herrero. COMP **blacksmith's forge** herrería.

blackthorn [ˈblækθɔːn] *n* BOT endrino.

bladder [ˈblædəʳ] *n* **1** vejiga. **2** *(in tyre, football)* cámara de aire.

blade [bleɪd] *n* **1** *(of sword, knife, etc)* hoja. **2** *(of ice skate)* cuchilla. **3** *(of propeller, fan, oar, hoe)* pala. **4** *(of grass)* brizna.

blame [bleɪm] *n* culpa.
▸ *vt* culpar, echar la culpa a.

blanch [blɑ:ntʃ] vt CULIN escaldar.
▶ vi palidecer.

bland [blænd] adj soso,-a.

> ❌ Bland no significa 'blando', que se traduce por **soft**.

blank [blæŋk] adj **1** (page, etc) en blanco. **2** (look, etc) vacío,-a. **3** (cassette, tape) virgen. COMP **blank cheque** cheque m en blanco.
▶ n **1** (on paper) espacio en blanco. **2** (bullet) bala de fogueo.

blanket ['blæŋkɪt] n **1** manta, AM frazada. **2** (layer) capa, manto: a blanket of snow una capa de nieve.

blare [bleəʳ] n **1** (loud noise) estruendo, fragor m. **2** (of trumpet) trompetazo.
▶ vi resonar, sonar.
◆ **to blare out** vi sonar muy fuerte.

blaspheme [blæs'fi:m] vi blasfemar (against, contra).

blasphemy ['blæsfəmɪ] n blasfemia.
ⓘ pl blasphemies.

blast [blɑ:st] n **1** (of wind) ráfaga. **2** (of water, air, etc) chorro. **3** (of horn) toque m. **4** (of trumpet) trompetazo. **5** (explosion) explosión f, voladura. **6** (shock wave) onda expansiva. **7** (reprimand) bronca.
▶ vt **1** (explode) volar, hacer volar. **2** (criticize) criticar. **3** (reprimand) echar una bronca. **4** (ruin, spoil) echar a perder, dar al traste con. **5** (shoot) pegar un tiro a. **6** (shrivel, wither) marchitar.

blasted ['blɑ:stɪd] adj maldito,-a, dichoso,-a.

blast-off ['blɑ:stɒf] n (of rocket, missile) despegue m.

blatant ['bleɪtənt] adj descarado,-a.

blaze [bleɪz] n **1** (fire) incendio. **2** (flame) llamarada. **3** (of light) resplandor m. **4** (outburst) arranque m, acceso.
▶ vi **1** (fire) arder. **2** (sun) brillar con fuerza. **3** (light) resplandecer.

blazer ['bleɪzəʳ] n americana de sport, blazer m.

bleach [bli:tʃ] n lejía.
▶ vt blanquear.

bleachers ['bli:tʃəz] n pl US gradas fpl.

bleak [bli:k] adj **1** (countryside) desolado,-a. **2** (weather) desapacible. **3** (fu-ture) poco prometedor,-ra. **4** (welcome, reception) frío,-a.

bleary ['blɪərɪ] adj **1** (from tears) nubloso,-a. **2** (from tiredness) legañoso,-a.
ⓘ comp blearier, superl bleariest.

bleat [bli:t] n balido.
▶ vi balar.

bled [bled] pt & pp → bleed.

bleed [bli:d] vi MED sangrar.
ⓘ pt & pp bled [bled].

bleep [bli:p] n pitido.
▶ vi pitar.
▶ vt localizar con un busca.

bleeper ['bli:pəʳ] n busca m, buscapersonas m.

blemish ['blemɪʃ] n **1** desperfecto, imperfección f.
▶ vt **1** (spoil) estropear, desmejorar. **2** fig (reputation) manchar, tiznar. LOC **without a blemish** fig intachable.

blench [blenʃ] vi **1** (recoil) retroceder. **2** (flinch) pestañear, inmutarse.

blend [blend] n mezcla, combinación f.
▶ vt **1** (mix) mezclar, combinar. **2** (match) matizar, armonizar.

blender ['blendəʳ] n CULIN batidora, minipímer® m.

bless [bles] vt bendecir. LOC **bless you!** (on sneezing) ¡Jesús!

blessed ['blesɪd] adj **1** (holy) bendito,-a, santo,-a. **2** (content, happy) bienaventurado,-a.

blessing ['blesɪŋ] n bendición f.

blew [blu:] pt → blow.

blight [blaɪt] n **1** (mildew) tizón m. **2** (calamity) plaga.

blind [blaɪnd] adj ciego,-a.
▶ n (on window) persiana.
▶ vt **1** cegar, dejar ciego,-a. **2** (dazzle) deslumbrar.

blindfold ['blaɪndfəʊld] n venda.
▶ vt vendar los ojos a.
▶ adv con los ojos vendados.

blink [blɪŋk] n **1** parpadeo. **2** (gleam, glimmer) destello. LOC **on the blink** fam averiado,-a.

blinkers ['blɪŋkəz] n pl anteojeras fpl.

bliss [blɪs] n felicidad f, dicha.

B

blister ['blɪstə'] n 1 (on skin) ampolla. 2 (on paint, surface) burbuja.

blizzard ['blɪzəd] n tempestad f de nieve, ventisca.

bloated ['bləʊtɪd] adj hinchado,-a.

blob [blɒb] n 1 (drop) gota. 2 (smudge) borrón m. 3 (of colour) mancha.

bloc [blɒk] n POL bloque m.

block [blɒk] n 1 bloque m. 2 (of wood, stone) taco. 3 (group of buildings) manzana. 6 (obstruction) obstrucción f. COMP block letters mayúsculas fpl. ‖ block of flats bloque m de pisos. ‖ note block taco, bloc m de notas.
▶ vt 1 (pipe, etc) obstruir, atascar. 2 (streets, etc) bloquear.

blockade [blɒ'keɪd] n MIL bloqueo m.
▶ vt bloquear.

blockage ['blɒkɪdʒ] n obstrucción f, atasco.

blockbuster ['blɒkbʌstə'] n 1 fig (novel) best seller m, éxito de ventas. 2 fig (film) película de acción.

bloke [bləʊk] n GB fam tipo, tío.

blond [blɒnd] (suele escribirse blonde cuando se refiere a una mujer) adj rubio,-a.
▶ n rubio,-a.

blonde [blɒnd] adj-n → blond.

blood [blʌd] n sangre f. 2 (ancestry) parentesco, alcurnia. COMP blood pressure tensión f arterial. ‖ blood vessel vaso sanguíneo.

bloodhound ['blʌdhaʊnd] n sabueso.

bloodshed ['blʌdʃed] n derramamiento de sangre.

bloodstream ['blʌdstriːm] n corriente f sanguínea.

bloodthirsty ['blʌdθɜːstɪ] adj sanguinario,-a, ávido,-a de sangre.
① comp bloodthirstier, superl bloodthirstiest.

bloody ['blʌdɪ] adj 1 (battle) sangriento,-a. 2 sl (damned) puñetero,-a, mierda de.
① comp bloodier, superl bloodiest.

bloody-minded [blʌdɪ'maɪndɪd] adj 1 (stubborn) tozudo,-a, terco,-a. 2 (bad-tempered) de malas pulgas.

bloom [bluːm] n 1 (flower) flor f. 2 (on fruit) pelusa.
▶ vi florecer.

bloomer ['bluːmə'] n GB fam metedura de pata, pifia.

blossom ['blɒsəm] n flor f.
▶ vi florecer.
◆ to blossom out vi alcanzar su plenitud.

✎ Blossom se refiere a las flores de los árboles; para el resto de flores, se emplea la palabra flower.

blot [blɒt] n (of ink) borrón m; (on reputation) mancha.
▶ vt 1 (stain) manchar. 2 (dry) secar.
◆ to blot out vt sep 1 (hide) ocultar. 2 (memory) borrar.
① pt & pp blotted, ger blotting.

blotch [blɒtʃ] n mancha.
▶ vi 1 (become stained) mancharse. 2 (skin) salir manchas.

blotting-paper ['blɒtɪŋpeɪpə'] n papel m secante.

blouse [blaʊz] n blusa.

blow¹ [bləʊ] n golpe m.

blow² [bləʊ] vi 1 (wind) soplar. 2 (instrument) tocar, sonar; (whistle) pitar. 3 (fuse) fundirse. 4 (tyre) reventarse.
▶ vt fam (money) despilfarrar, malgastar.
◆ to blow away vt sep 1 arrastrar. 2 fam fig mandar al otro barrio.
◆ to blow in vt sep derribar.
◆ to blow off vi (lid, hat) salir volando.
◆ to blow out vt sep 1 (flame) apagar, (candle) soplar. 2 (cheeks) hinchar.
◆ to blow over vt sep derribar.
▶ vi 1 derrumbarse. 2 (storm) amainar.
◆ to blow up vt sep 1 (explode) (hacer) volar: they blew up the building hicieron volar el edificio. 2 (inflate) hinchar. (photograph) ampliar.
▶ vi 1 (explode) explotar. 2 (lose one's temper) salirse de sus casillas.
① pt blew [bluː], pp blown [bləʊn].

blowhole ['bləʊhəʊl] n 1 (of whale) orificio nasal. 2 (hole, air vent) respiradero.

blowlamp ['bləʊlæmp] n soplete m.

blown [bləʊn] pp → blow.

B

blowout [ˈbləʊaʊt] *n* **1** AUTO reventón *m*, pinchazo. **2** *sl* comilona, atracón *m*.

blowtorch [ˈbləʊtɔːtʃ] *n* soplete *m*.

blow-up [ˈbləʊʌp] *n* (photograph) ampliación *f*.

blue [bluː] *adj* **1** azul. **2** (sad) triste. **3** (depressed) deprimido,-a. **4** (obscene) verde: *a blue joke* un chiste verde.
▶ *n* azul *m*.
▶ *n pl* **blues** MUS blues *m*.
▶ *n pl* **the blues** la depresión *f*.

bluebell [ˈbluːbel] *n* BOT campanilla.

blueberry [ˈbluːbəri] *n* BOT arándano.
ⓘ *pl* blueberries.

blue-collar [ˈbluːkɒləʳ] *adj* obrero,-a.

blueprint [ˈbluːprɪnt] *n fig* anteproyecto.

blues [bluːz] *n pl* → blue.

blunder [ˈblʌndəʳ] *n* metedura de pata.
▶ *vi* meter la pata.

blunt [blʌnt] *adj* **1** (knife) desafilado,-a; (pencil) despuntado,-a. **2** *fig* (person) que no tiene pelos en la lengua.
▶ *vt* desafilar, embotar; (pencil) despuntar. COMP **blunt angle** MATH ángulo obtuso.

blur [blɜːʳ] *n* borrón *m*, mancha.

blurb [blɜːb] *n fam pej* información *f* publicitaria.

blurred [blɜːd] *adj* **1** borroso,-a. **2** *fig* (memories) vago,-a, confuso,-a.

blurt [blɜːt] LOC **to blurt** STH **out** soltar ALGO bruscamente, espetar algo.

blush [blʌʃ] *n* rubor *m*, sonrojo.
▶ *vi* ruborizarse, sonrojarse.

blusher [ˈblʌʃəʳ] *n* colorete *m*.

blustery [ˈblʌstəri] *adj* (windy) ventoso,-a.

boa [ˈbəʊə] *n* ZOOL boa.

boar [bɔːʳ] *n* ZOOL verraco.

board [bɔːd] *n* **1** (piece of wood) tabla, tablero. **2** (food) comida, pensión *f*. **3** (committee) junta, consejo. **4** (company) compañía: *the gas board* la compañía del gas. LOC **on board** MAR a bordo. **I to take on board 1** (responsibility) asumir. **2** (concept, idea) abarcar. COMP **board and lodging** pensión completa. **I board of directors** junta directiva. **I board of trade** US cámara de comercio.

▶ *vt* (ship, etc) subirse a, embarcar en.
▶ *vi* (lodge) alojarse; (at school) ser interno,-a.

boarder [ˈbɔːdəʳ] *n* **1** (gen) huésped *mf*. **2** (at school) interno,-a.

boarding [ˈbɔːdɪŋ] *n* **1** (ship, plane, etc) embarque *m*. **2** (lodging) pensión *f*, alojamiento. COMP **boarding card** tarjeta de embarque. **I boarding house** casa de huéspedes. **I boarding school** internado.

boast [bəʊst] *n* jactancia.
▶ *vi* jactarse (about, de), presumir (about, de).
▶ *vt fig* presumir de.

boat [bəʊt] *n* barco, nave *f*; (small) bote *m*, barca; (large) buque *m*, navío; (launch) lancha.

boatswain [ˈbəʊsən] *n* contramaestre *m*.

boatyard [ˈbəʊtjɑːd] *n* astillero.

bob¹ [bɒb] *n* **1** (jerking movement) sacudida; (bouncing movement) rebote *m*. **2** (curtsy) reverencia.
▶ *vi* **1** (jerk) moverse a sacudidas; (bounce) rebotar. **2** (curtsy) hacer una reverencia.

bobbin [ˈbɒbɪn] *n* (for textiles, wire, etc) carrete *m*, bobina; (for lace) bolillo, palillo.

bobby [ˈbɒbi] *n* GB *fam* poli *m*.
ⓘ *pl* bobbies.

⊕ Este término, aunque hoy poco utilizado, se usa para referirse a los agentes de policía del Reino Unido. El nombre proviene del fundador del cuerpo, sir Robert Peel, ya que Bobby es el diminutivo de Robert.

bobsleigh [ˈbɒbslei] *n* bobsleigh *m*.

bode [bəʊd] *pt* → bide.
▶ *vt* (foretell) presagiar, augurar. LOC **to bode ill/well** ser de buen/mal agüero.

bodice [ˈbɒdɪs] *n* corpiño.

body [ˈbɒdi] *n* **1** cuerpo. **2** (corpse) cadáver *m*. **3** (organization) organismo, entidad *f*, ente *m*; (association) agrupación *f*. **4** (of wine) cuerpo. **5** (of people) grupo, conjunto. **6** AUTO (of car) carrocería. **7** AV fuselaje *m*.
ⓘ *pl* bodies.

body-blow [ˈbɒdɪbləʊ] *n* revés *m*.

body-building ['bɒdɪbɪldɪŋ] *n* SP culturismo.

bodyguard ['bɒdɪgɑːd] *n* guardaespaldas *m*.

bodywork ['bɒdɪwɜːk] *n* carrocería.

bog [bɒg] *n* **1** pantano, cenagal *m*. **2** *sl (toilet)* meódromo.

◆ **to bog down** *vt sep* atascar.

bogey ['bəʊgɪ] *n (golf)* bogey *m*.

bogus ['bəʊgəs] *adj* **1** *(fake)* falso,-a, apócrifo,-a. **2** *(fictitious)* ficticio,-a. **3** *(sham)* simulado,-a, fingido,-a.

boil¹ [bɔɪl] *n* MED furúnculo, forúnculo.

boil² [bɔɪl] *vt (liquid)* hervir; *(food)* hervir, cocer; *(egg)* pasar por agua, cocer.
▶ *vi* **1** *(liquid)* hervir; *(food)* hervir, cocerse. **2** *fig (undulate, seethe)* bullir.

◆ **to boil down to** *vt insep fig* reducirse a.

boiler ['bɔɪləʳ] *n* **1** caldera. **2** *(fowl)* gallina *(que solo sirve para el caldo)*.

boiling ['bɔɪlɪŋ] *adj* hirviendo, hirviente. COMP **boiling point** punto de ebullición.

boisterous ['bɔɪstərəs] *adj* **1** *(noisy, rowdy)* bullicioso,-a, alborotador,-ra. **2** *(weather)* borrascoso,-a; *(sea)* agitado,-a.

bold [bəʊld] *adj* **1** *(brave)* valiente. **2** *(daring)* audaz, atrevido,-a. **3** *(cheeky)* descarado,-a, fresco,-a. **4** *(vivid)* vivo,-a. **5** *(print)* en negrita.

Bolivia [bə'lɪvɪə] *n* Bolivia.

Bolivian [bə'lɪvɪən] *adj* boliviano,-a.
▶ *n* boliviano,-a.

bolster ['bəʊlstəʳ] *n* **1** *(pillow)* cabezal *m*, travesaño. **2** TECH soporte *m*.
▶ *vt* reforzar.

bolt [bəʊlt] *n* **1** *(on door, etc)* cerrojo; *(small)* pestillo. **2** *(screw)* perno, tornillo. **3** *(lightning)* rayo.
▶ *vt* **1** *(lock)* cerrar con cerrojo, cerrar con pestillo. **2** *(screw)* sujetar con pernos, sujetar con tornillos. **3** *fam (food)* engullir.
▶ *vi (person)* escaparse; *(horse)* desbocarse.

bolus ['bəʊləs] *n* bolo alimenticio.

bomb [bɒm] *n* **1** bomba. **2** US *(failure)* fracaso.
▶ *vt* MIL bombardear; *(terrorist)* colocar una bomba en.
▶ *vi* US *fam (fail)* fracasar.

bombard [bɒm'bɑːd] *vt* bombardear.

bombardment [bɒm'bɑːdmənt] *n* bombardeo.

bombastic [bɒm'bæstɪk] *adj* rimbombante, ampuloso,-a.

bomber ['bɒməʳ] *n* **1** MIL bombardero. **2** *(terrorist)* terrorista *mf* que coloca bombas.

✕ Bomber no significa 'bombero', que se traduce por **fireman**.

bombing ['bɒmɪŋ] *n* **1** MIL bombardeo. **2** *(terrorist act)* atentado con bomba.

bombshell ['bɒmʃel] *n* **1** *fig* bomba. **2** MIL *(artillery bomb)* obús *m*. **3** *fam (attractive woman)* mujer *f* explosiva.

bona fide [bəʊnə'faɪdɪ] *adj* genuino,-a, auténtico,-a.

bond [bɒnd] *n* **1** *(link)* lazo, vínculo: *bonds of friendship* vínculos de amistad. **2** FIN bono, obligación *f*. **3** JUR fianza. **4** *(agreement)* pacto, compromiso.
▶ *vt* **1** *(stick, join)* pegar, unir. **2** *(deposit in customs)* depositar.
▶ *vi (stick, join)* pegarse, unirse.

bondage ['bɒndɪdʒ] *n* esclavitud *f*, servidumbre *f*.

bone [bəʊn] *n* **1** hueso. **2** *(of fish)* espina, raspa; *(of whale)* barba. **3** *(of corset)* ballena.
▶ *vt (meat)* deshuesar; *(fish)* quitar la espina.
▶ *n pl* **bones** *(remains)* huesos *mpl*, restos *mpl* mortales. COMP **bone marrow** médula ósea.

◆ **to bone up on** *vt insep* empollar.

bonfire ['bɒnfaɪəʳ] *n* hoguera. COMP **Bonfire night** GB *la noche del cinco de noviembre; se celebra con hogueras y fuegos artificiales.*

⊕ Es la noche del 5 de noviembre que se celebra en Inglaterra con hogueras y fuegos artificiales. Conmemora el intento fallido en el año 1605, de Guy Fawkes y otros conspiradores, de volar el edificio del parlamento. También se llama **Guy Fawkes Night**.

bonkers ['bɒŋkəz] *adj* GB *sl* chalado,-a.

bonnet ['bɒnɪt] n **1** (child's, woman's) gorro, gorra. **2** (maid's) cofia. **3** AUTO capó m.

bonus ['bəʊnəs] n **1** (gratuity) plus m, sobresueldo, prima. **2** (benefit) beneficio.
ⓘ pl bonuses.

bony ['bəʊnɪ] adj **1** (thin) esquelético,-a. **2** (with a lot of bone) huesudo,-a. **3** (like bone) óseo,-a. **4** (meat) lleno,-a de huesos; (fish) lleno,-a de espinas.
ⓘ comp bonier, superl boniest.

bonze [bɒnz] n bonzo.

boo [buː] n abucheo.
▶ vi abuchear.

booby ['buːbɪ] n alcatraz m.
ⓘ pl boobies.

booby-trap ['buːbɪtræp] n trampa explosiva.

book [bʊk] n **1** libro. **2** (of tickets) taco; (of matches) cajetilla.
▶ vt **1** (table, room, holiday) reservar; (entertainer, speaker) contratar. **2** (police) multar; (football) advertir, amonestar.
▶ n pl **books** COMM libros mpl, cuentas fpl. LOC **to be booked up 1** (hotel, restaurant) estar completo. COMP **savings book** libreta de ahorro.
◆ **to book in** vt sep (in hotel) hacer la reserva.
▶ vi registrarse.

bookcase ['bʊkkeɪs] n librería, estantería.

booking ['bʊkɪŋ] n (table, room, holiday) reserva; (entertainer, speaker) contratación f. COMP **booking office** taquilla.

bookkeeping ['bʊkkiːpɪŋ] n contabilidad f, teneduría de libros.

bookmaker ['bʊkmeɪkəʳ] n GB corredor,-ra de apuestas.

bookmark ['bʊkmɑːk] n (for book) punto de libro; (electronic) marcador.
▶ vt (electronically) agregar un marcador.

bookseller ['bʊkseləʳ] n librero,-a.

bookshelf ['bʊkʃelf] n estante m.
▶ n pl **bookshelves** estantería.
ⓘ pl bookshelves.

bookshop ['bʊkʃɒp] n librería.

bookstand ['bʊkstænd] n **1** (stall) quiosco de periódicos. **2** (bookrest) atril m.

bookstore ['bʊkstɔːʳ] n US librería.

bookworm ['bʊkwɜːm] n fig ratón m de biblioteca.

boom¹ [buːm] n (noise) estampido.
▶ vi tronar, retumbar.
▶ interj ¡bum!

boom² [buːm] n **1** MAR botalón m. **2** (of microphone) jirafa. **3** (of crane) brazo. **4** (barrier) barrera.

boom³ [buːm] n fig (prosperity, increase) boom m, auge m.

boomerang ['buːməræŋ] n **1** bumerán m. **2** fig resultado contraproducente.

boost [buːst] n **1** (incentive) incentivo, estímulo. **2** (promotion) promoción f, fomento. **3** (increase) aumento.
▶ vt **1** (create an incentive) incentivar, estimular. **2** (promote) promocionar, fomentar. **3** (increase) aumentar.

booster ['buːstəʳ] n **1** ELEC elevador m de voltaje. **2** RAD repetidor m. **3** TECH motor m auxiliar de propulsión. COMP **booster injection** MED revacunación f.

boot [buːt] n **1** (footwear) bota. **2** GB (of car) maletero, portaequipajes m. **3** (kick) patada.
▶ vt **1** (kick) dar una patada a. **2** COMPUT cargar el sistema operativo.
◆ **to boot out** vt sep echar, echar a patadas.

bootblack ['buːtblæk] n US limpiabotas m, AM lustrabotas m.

booth [buːð] n **1** cabina. **2** (at fair) puesto. COMP **telephone booth** locutorio.

bootleg ['buːtleg] n (illegal recording) grabación f pirata.

bootlegger ['buːtlegəʳ] n contrabandista mf de licores.

booty ['buːtɪ] n botín m.
ⓘ pl booties.

booze [buːz] n fam trinque m, alcohol m.
▶ vi fam mamar.

bop [bɒp] n **1** fam (dance) baile m. **2** fam (thump) cachete m.
▶ vi fam (dance) bailar.
ⓘ pt & pp bopped, ger bopping.

border ['bɔːdəʳ] n **1** (of country) frontera. **2** (edge) borde m. **3** (in sewing) ribete m, orla. **4** (of flowers, plants) arriate m.
◆ **to border on** vt insep **1** lindar con. **2** fig rayar en.

bore¹ [bɔːʳ] pt → **bear**.

bore² [bɔːʳ] n **1** (of gun) ánima, alma; (calibre) calibre m. **2** (hole) taladro.
▸ vt & vi perforar, taladrar.

bore³ [bɔːʳ] n (person) pelmazo,-a, pesado,-a; (thing) lata, rollo, tostón m.
▸ vt aburrir, fastidiar.

bored [bɔːd] adj aburrido,-a. LOC **to get bored** aburrirse.

boredom ['bɔːdəm] n aburrimiento.

borer ['bɔːrəʳ] n **1** (tool) taladro, barrena. **2** (machine) taladradora.

boric ['bɔːrɪk] adj CHEM bórico,-a. COMP **boric acid** ácido bórico.

boring ['bɔːrɪŋ] adj aburrido,-a.

born [bɔːn] adj nato,-a: she's a born leader es una líder nata. LOC **to be born** nacer.

borne [bɔːn] pp → **bear²**.

borough ['bʌrə] n **1** (district) barrio, distrito. **2** (town, city) ciudad f.

borrow ['bɒrəʊ] vt pedir prestado,-a, tomar prestado,-a: can I borrow your pen? ¿me dejas tu boli?; you can borrow it if you like te lo presto si quieres.

Bosnia ['bɒznɪə] n Bosnia.

Bosnian ['bɒznɪən] adj bosnio,-a.
▸ n bosnio,-a.

bosom ['buzəm] n **1** pecho. **2** (centre) seno: in the bosom of the family en el seno de la familia. COMP **bosom friend** amigo,-a del alma.

boss [bɒs] n jefe,-a.
◆ **to boss around** vt sep mangonear.

bosun ['bəʊsən] n MAR contramaestre m.

botanic [bəˈtænɪk] adj botánico,-a.

botanical [bəˈtænɪkəl] adj botánico,-a. COMP **botanical gardens** jardín m botánico.

botany ['bɒtənɪ] n botánica.

botch [bɒtʃ] n chapuza.
▸ vt [also **to botch up**.] (bungle) pifiarla, fastidiarla.

both [bəʊθ] adj ambos,-as, los dos, las dos.
▸ pron ambos,-as, los dos, las dos: both of us nosotros,-as dos; both of you vosotros,-as dos; both of them los dos, las dos, ambos,-as. LOC **both ... and** tanto ... como: both she and her sister are teachers tanto ella como su hermana son profesoras.
▸ adv a la vez: it's both cheap and good es bueno y barato a la vez.

bother ['bɒðəʳ] n **1** (nuisance) molestia, fastidio. **2** (problems) problemas mpl.
▸ vt **1** (be a nuisance) molestar, fastidiar. **2** (worry) preocupar.
▸ vi **1** (take trouble) molestarse, tomar la molestia. **2** (worry) preocuparse.

Botswana [bɒtˈswɑːnə] n Botsuana.

Botswanan [bɒtˈswɑːnən] adj botsuanés,-esa, botsuano,-a.
▸ n botsuanés,-esa, bostuano,-a.

bottle ['bɒtəl] n **1** botella; (small) frasco; (for baby) biberón m; (for gas) bombona. **2** sl (nerve) agallas fpl.
▸ vt (wine, etc) embotellar; (fruit) envasar.

bottle-bank ['bɒtəlbæŋk] n contenedor m de vidrio.

bottled ['bɒtəld] adj (wine, etc) embotellado,-a; (fruit) envasado,-a. COMP **bottled gas** gas m butano.

bottom ['bɒtəm] n **1** (gen) fondo; (of bottle) culo; (of hill, steps, page) pie m; (of ship) quilla. **2** (of dress) bajo; (of trousers) bajos mpl. **3** (buttocks) trasero, culo. **4** (last) último,-a. **5** (underneath) parte f inferior, parte f de abajo.
▸ adj **1** (position) de abajo. **2** (number, result) más bajo,-a.

bottomless ['bɒtəmləs] adj sin fondo, insondable.

boudoir ['buːdwɑːʳ] n tocador m.

bough [baʊ] n rama.

bought [bɔːt] pt & pp → **buy**.

bouillon ['buːjɒn] n CULIN caldo.

boulder ['bəʊldəʳ] n canto rodado.

boulevard ['buːləvɑːd] n bulevar m.

bounce [baʊns] n bote m.
▸ vi (ball) rebotar, botar.
▸ vt **1** (cheque) ser rechazado por el banco. **2** (ball) hacer botar.

bouncer ['baʊnsəʳ] n sl gorila m.

bound¹ [baʊnd] *pt & pp* → **bind**.
► *adj* **1** *(tied)* atado,-a. **2** *(forced)* obligado,-a. **3** *(book)* encuadernado,-a. ⊡ᴏᴄ **to be bound to** ser seguro que.

bound² [baʊnd] *adj (destined)* destinado,-a: *he knew he was bound to succeed* sabía que estaba destinado a tener éxito. ⊡ᴏᴄ **to be bound for** ir con destino, navegar con rumbo a. ❙ **-bound** con rumbo a: *Paris-bound* con rumbo a París.

bound³ [baʊnd] *n (jump)* salto, brinco.
► *vi* saltar.

boundary [ˈbaʊndərɪ] *n* límite *m*, frontera. ᴄᴏᴍᴘ **boundary stone** hito, mojón *m*. ① *pl* **boundaries**.

boundless [ˈbaʊndləs] *adj* sin límites.

bounds [baʊndz] *n pl (border)* frontera; *(boundary)* límites *mpl*.

bouquet [buːˈkeɪ] *n* **1** *(flowers)* ramo. **2** *(wine)* aroma *m*, buqué *m*.

bourgeois [ˈbʊəʒwɑːˈ] *adj* burgués,-esa.
► *n* burgués,-esa.

bourgeoisie [bʊəʒwɑːˈziː] *n* burguesía.

bout [baʊt] *n* **1** *(period)* rato. **2** ᴍᴇᴅ *(of flu, measles, etc)* ataque *m*. **3** *(boxing)* combate.

boutique [buːˈtiːk] *n* boutique *f*, tienda.

bovine [ˈbəʊvaɪn] *adj* bovino,-a.
► *n* bovino.

bow¹ [bəʊ] *n* **1** *(for arrows)* arco. **2** *(of violin)* arco. **3** *(knot)* lazo. ᴄᴏᴍᴘ **bow saw** sierra de arco.

bow² [baʊ] *n* ᴍᴀʀ proa.

bow³ [baʊ] *n (with body)* reverencia.
► *vt* inclinar: *he bowed his head* inclinó la cabeza.

bowel [ˈbaʊəl] *n* intestino.
► *n pl* **bowels** *(entrails)* entrañas *fpl*.

bowl [bəʊl] *n* **1** *(for food, etc)* cuenco, fuente *f*, bol *m*; *(large drinking bowl)* tazón *m*. **2** *(for washing)* palangana, barreño. **3** *(of toilet)* taza.

bow-legged [bəʊˈlegd, bəʊˈlegɪd] *adj* patizambo,-a.

bowler¹ [ˈbəʊləˈ] *n (hat)* bombín *m*.

bowler² [ˈbəʊləˈ] *n (cricket)* lanzador,-ra.

bowling [ˈbəʊlɪŋ] *n* bolos *mpl*. ᴄᴏᴍᴘ **bowling alley** bolera.

bow-tie [bəʊˈtaɪ] *n* pajarita.

box¹ [bɒks] *n* **1** caja; *(large)* cajón *m*. **2** *(of matches)* cajetilla. **3** ᴛʜᴇᴀᴛ palco. **4** *(for sentry)* garita. **5** *(of coach)* pescante *m*. **6** ɢʙ *fam (telly)* tele *f*. ᴄᴏᴍᴘ **box number** número de apartado de correos. ❙ **box office** taquilla. ❙ **post-office box** apartado de correos.

box² [bɒks] *vi* boxear.

boxcar [ˈbɒkskɑːˈ] *n* ᴜs furgón *m*.

boxer [ˈbɒksəˈ] *n* **1** boxeador,-ra. **2** *(dog)* bóxer *m*.

boxing [ˈbɒksɪŋ] *n* boxeo. ᴄᴏᴍᴘ **Boxing Day** ɢʙ *el día 26 de diciembre*.

⊕ El 26 de diciembre es festivo en Gran Bretaña. Las tiendas inician las rebajas, se disputan partidos de fútbol y se celebran carreras de caballos.

boy [bɔɪ] *n (baby)* niño; *(child)* chico, muchacho; *(youth)* joven *m*.

boycott [ˈbɔɪkɒt] *n* boicoteo, boicot *m*.
► *vt* boicotear.

boyfriend [ˈbɔɪfrend] *n* **1** *(fiancé)* novio. **2** *(male friend)* amigo.

boyhood [ˈbɔɪhʊd] *n* infancia, niñez *f*.
► *adj* de la infancia.

bra [brɑː] *n* sostén *m*, sujetador *m*.

brace [breɪs] *n* **1** *(clamp)* abrazadera. **2** ᴀʀᴄʜ *(support)* riostra. **3** *(drill)* berbiquí *m*. **4** *(on teeth)* aparato.
► *n pl* **braces** tirantes *mpl*.

bracelet [ˈbreɪslət] *n* pulsera, brazalete *m*.

bracken [ˈbrækən] *n* ʙᴏᴛ helechos *mpl*.

bracket [ˈbrækɪt] *n* **1** *(round)* paréntesis *m*. **2** *(for shelf)* escuadra, soporte *m*. **3** *(group, category)* grupo, categoría *m*. ᴄᴏᴍᴘ **square bracket** corchete *m*.

brag [bræg] *n* jactancia, fanfarria.
► *vi* jactarse (**about**, de).
① *pt & pp* **bragged**, *ger* **bragging**.

braggart [ˈbrægət] *n* fanfarrón,-ona.

braid [breɪd] *n* **1** *(on clothing)* galón *m*. **2** *(plait)* trenza.

Braille [breɪl] *n* braille *m*.

brain [breɪn] *n (organ)* cerebro, seso.

▶ *n pl* **brains 1** *(intellect)* cerebro, seso, inteligencia. **2** *(as food)* sesos *mpl.* [LOC] **to have brains** ser un cerebro, ser inteligente. [LOC] **brain death** muerte *f* cerebral. ∎ **brain drain** fuga de cerebros. ∎ **brain scan** electroencefalograma *m.*

brain-dead ['breɪndɛd] *adj* clínicamente muerto,-a.

brainstorming ['breɪnstɔːmɪŋ] *n* reunión *f* creativa, lluvia de ideas.

brainy ['breɪnɪ] *adj fam* inteligente, sesudo,-a.

ⓘ *comp* brainier, *superl* brainiest.

braise [breɪz] *vt* CULIN freír y luego cocer a fuego lento.

brake [breɪk] *n* freno. [COMP] **brake arm** palanca del freno. ∎ **brake block** pastilla de freno. ∎ **brake fluid** líquido de freno.

▶ *vt* frenar, hacer frenar.

bramble ['bræmbəl] *n* BOT zarzamora, mora. [COMP] **bramble bush** zarza.

bran [bræn] *n* salvado.

branch [brɑːntʃ] *n* **1** *(tree)* rama. **2** *(of family)* ramo. **3** *(road, railway)* ramal *m;* *(stream, river)* brazo. **4** *(of shop)* sucursal *f;* *(of bank)* oficina, sucursal *f.* **5** *(field of science, etc)* ramo. **6** *(of candelabra)* brazo.

▶ *vi* *(road)* bifurcarse.

brand [brænd] *n* **1** marca. **2** *(type)* clase *f,* tipo.

brand-new [bræn'njuː] *adj* flamante, de estreno.

brandy ['brændɪ] *n* brandy *m.*

ⓘ *pl* brandies.

brass [brɑːs] *n* **1** latón *m.* **2** *sl (money)* pasta. **3** MUS metales *mpl.*

▶ *adj* de cobre.

brassiere ['bræzɪəʳ] *n* sujetador *m,* sostén *m.*

brat [bræt] *n fam pej* mocoso,-a.

brave [breɪv] *adj* valiente.

▶ *n* guerrero indio.

▶ *vt* **1** *(defy)* desafiar. **2** *(confront)* afrontar, hacer frente a.

bravo [brɑː'vəʊ] *interj* ¡bravo!

brawl [brɔːl] *n* reyerta, pelea.

▶ *vi* pelearse.

bray [breɪ] *vi* **1** *(donkey, ass)* rebuznar. **2** *(laugh)* carcajearse.

Brazil [brə'zɪl] *n* Brasil.

Brazilian [brə'zɪlɪən] *adj* brasileño,-a.

▶ *n* brasileño,-a.

breach [briːtʃ] *n* **1** *(opening)* brecha, abertura. **2** *(in promise, undertaking)* incumplimiento; *(in law)* violación *f,* infracción *f.* **3** *(in relationship)* ruptura.

bread [brɛd] *n* pan *m.* [COMP] **wholemeal bread** pan *m* integral.

bread-and-butter ['brɛdənbʌtəʳ] *adj (commonplace)* rutinario,-a, corriente y moliente.

breadth [brɛdθ] *n* **1** *(broadness)* ancho, anchura. **2** *(space)* extensión *f,* amplitud *f.*

break [breɪk] *n* **1** *(in leg, etc)* rotura. **2** *(in relationship)* ruptura. **3** *(in meeting)* descanso, pausa; *(at school)* recreo. [LOC] **to take a break** tomarse un descanso. ∎ **without a break** sin descanso, sin parar. ∎ **at break of day** al amanecer.

▶ *vt* **1** romper. **2** *(record)* batir.

▶ *vi* **1** romperse. **2** *(storm)* estallar.

◆ **to break away** *vi* *(escape)* escaparse, darse a la fuga; *(leave family, job)* irse.

◆ **to break down** *vt sep* **1** *(door)* derribar, echar abajo. **2** *(resistance)* vencer.

▶ *vi* **1** *(car)* averiarse; *(driver)* tener una avería. **2** *(burst into tears)* romper a llorar. **3** *(talks, negotiations)* fracasar.

◆ **to break in** *vi (force entry)* entrar por la fuerza.

◆ **to break off** *vt sep* **1** *(relationship)* romper. **2** *(discussions, negotiations)* interrumpir.

◆ **to break out** *vi* **1** *(prisoners)* escaparse. **2** *(war, fire, etc)* estallar.

◆ **to break up** *vt sep* *(chair, table, etc)* romper; *(ship, boat)* desguazar.

▶ *vi* **1** *(couple)* separarse. **2** *(gathering, meeting)* disolverse. **3** *(school)* empezar las vacaciones.

ⓘ *pt* broke [brəʊk], *pp* broken ['brəʊkən]

breakable ['breɪkəbəl] *adj* frágil, rompible.

breakage ['breɪkɪdʒ] *n* rotura.

breakdown ['breɪkdaʊn] *n* **1** *(of car, machine)* avería. **2** MED crisis *f* nerviosa. **3** *(in negotiations)* ruptura. **4** *(chemical analysis)* análisis *m.* [COMP] **breakdown service** (ser vicio de) asistencia en carretera. ∎ **breakdown van / breakdown truck** grúa.

breakfast ['brekfəst] *n* desayuno. [LOC] **to have breakfast** desayunar.
▶ *vi* desayunar.

break-in ['breɪkɪn] *n* entrada forzada.

breaking ['breɪkɪŋ] *n* **1** (*of leg, object*) rotura. **2** (*of relationship*) ruptura.

break-out ['breɪkaʊt] *n* (*from prison*) fuga.

breakthrough ['breɪkθruː] *n* avance *m* importante.

break-up ['breɪkʌp] *n* (*of relationship, negotiations*) ruptura; (*of couple*) separación *f*.

breakwater ['breɪkwɔːtəʳ] *n* rompeolas *m*.

bream [briːm] *n* (*river fish*) brema. [COMP] **gilt-head bream** dorada. ∎ **red bream** besugo.

breast [brest] *n* **1** (*chest*) pecho; (*of woman*) pecho, seno. **2** (*of chicken, etc*) pechuga.

breastbone ['brestbəʊn] *n* ANAT esternón *m*.

breast-feed ['brestfiːd] *vt* amamantar, dar el pecho a.
ⓘ *pt & pp* breast-fed ['brestfed].

breaststroke ['breststrəʊk] *n* (*swimming*) braza.

breath [breθ] *n* **1** (*of person*) aliento. **2** (*of air*) soplo. **3** (*breathing*) resuello, respiración *f*. [LOC] **out of breath** sin aliento. [COMP] **breath test** GB prueba del alcohol.

Breathalyser® ['breθəlaɪzəʳ] *n* alcoholímetro.

breathe [briːð] *vt* (*air, etc*) respirar.
▶ *vi* **1** (*air, etc*) respirar. **2** (*be alive*) respirar, vivir: *is he still breathing?* ¿respira aún? [LOC] **to breathe in** aspirar. ∎ **to breathe out** espirar.

breathing ['briːðɪŋ] *n* respiración *f*.

bred [bred] *pt & pp* → **breed**.

breeches ['brɪtʃɪz] *n pl* **1** (*knee-length trousers*) calzones *mpl*. **2** *fam* (*trousers*) pantalones *mpl*.

breed [briːd] *n* (*of animal*) raza; (*of plant*) variedad *f*.
▶ *vt* (*animals*) criar.
▶ *vi* (*animals*) reproducirse.
ⓘ *pt & pp* bred [bred].

breeze [briːz] *n* METEOR brisa.

brew [bruː] *n* **1** (*tea, etc*) infusión *f*. **2** (*potion*) brebaje *m*.
▶ *vt* **1** (*beer*) elaborar. **2** (*tea, etc*) preparar.
▶ *vi* **1** (*tea, etc*) reposar. **2** (*storm*) prepararse, acercarse.

brewer ['bruːəʳ] *n* fabricante *mf* de cerveza, cervecero,-a. [COMP] **brewer's yeast** levadura de cerveza.

brewery ['bruːərɪ] *n* fábrica de cerveza, cervecería.
ⓘ *pl* breweries.

briar ['braɪəʳ] *n* BOT (*heather*) brezo.

bribe [braɪb] *n* soborno.
▶ *vt* sobornar.

bribery ['braɪbərɪ] *n* soborno.

bric-a-brac ['brɪkəbræk] *n* baratijas *fpl*.

brick [brɪk] *n* **1** ladrillo. **2** (*toy*) cubo (de madera).

bricklayer ['brɪkleɪəʳ] *n* albañil *m*.

bridal ['braɪdəl] *adj* nupcial. [COMP] **bridal gown** vestido de novia.

bride [braɪd] *n* novia, desposada. [COMP] **the bride and groom** los novios.

bridegroom ['braɪdgruːm] *n* novio.

✎ Bridegroom o groom sólo se emplean para referirse al novio durante el día de la boda.

bridesmaid ['braɪdzmeɪd] *n* dama de honor.

bridge [brɪdʒ] *n* **1** puente *m*. **2** (*of nose*) caballete *m*.

bridle ['braɪdəl] *n* brida.
▶ *vt* (*horse*) embridar.
▶ *vi* mostrar desagrado (at, por).

brief [briːf] *adj* (*short*) breve; (*concise*) conciso,-a; (*scanty*) diminuto,-a.
▶ *n* **1** (*report*) informe *m*. **2** JUR expediente *m*. **3** MIL instrucciones *fpl*.
▶ *vt* **1** (*inform*) informar (about, sobre). **2** (*instruct*) dar instrucciones a.

briefcase ['briːfkeɪs] *n* maletín *m*, cartera.

briefing ['briːfɪŋ] *n* reunión *f* informativa, briefing *m*.

brigade [brɪ'geɪd] *n* MIL brigada.
▶ *vt* MIL formar una brigada con.

bright [braɪt] *adj* **1** (*gen*) brillante. **2** METEOR (*sky, day*) claro,-a, despejado,-a;

(sunny) soleado,-a, de sol. **3** *(colour)* vivo,-a. **4** *(cheerful)* alegre, animado,-a.

◆ **to brighten up** *vt sep* 1 METEOR despejar. **2** *(room, house)* dar un aspecto más alegre a. **3** *(enliven)* alegrar, animar.

brightness ['braɪtnəs] *n* **1** *(light)* luminosidad *f*. **2** *(of sun)* resplandor *m*. **3** *(of day)* claridad *f*. **4** *(of colour)* viveza. **5** *(cleverness)* inteligencia.

brilliant ['brɪljənt] *adj* **1** *(gen)* brillante. **2** *(colour)* vivo,-a. **3** *fam* estupendo,-a, fantástico,-a.

brim [brɪm] *n* **1** *(of cup, glass, etc)* borde *m*. **2** *(of hat)* ala.

▶ *vi* rebosar (**with**, de): *he was brimming with pride* rebosaba de orgullo.

brine [braɪn] *n* salmuera.

bring [brɪŋ] *vt* **1** traer. **2** *(lead)* llevar, conducir.

◆ **to bring about** *vt sep* *(accident, change, etc)* provocar, causar.

◆ **to bring back** *vt sep* **1** *(book, record, etc)* devolver. **2** *(past experience, childhood, etc)* recordar, hacer recordar.

◆ **to bring down** *vt sep* **1** *(chair, book, etc)* bajar. **2** *(door, house, government)* derribar. **3** *(prices, temperature)* hacer bajar.

◆ **to bring forward** *vt sep* **1** *(meeting, appointment)* adelantar. **2** *(theme, question)* presentar, plantear.

◆ **to bring in** *vt sep* **1** *(person)* hacer pasar. **2** *(coal, food, etc into house)* traer. **3** JUR *(verdict)* emitir, pronunciar.

◆ **to bring off** *vt sep* *(victory, result)* conseguir, lograr.

◆ **to bring on** *vt sep* *(illness)* provocar.

◆ **to bring out** *vt sep* *(record)* sacar al mercado, sacar; *(book)* publicar.

◆ **to bring to** *vt sep* hacer volver en sí.

◆ **to bring up** *vt sep* **1** *(chair, book, etc)* subir. **2** *(child)* criar, educar. **3** *(subject, topic)* plantear. **4** *(vomit)* devolver.

ⓘ *pt & pp* **brought** [brɔːt].

brink [brɪŋk] *n* borde *m*.

brisk [brɪsk] *adj* enérgico,-a.

bristle ['brɪsəl] *n* cerda.

▶ *vi* **1** *(hair)* erizarse, ponerse de punta. **2** *(show annoyance)* mosquearse.

Britain ['brɪtən] *n* Gran Bretaña. COMP **Great Britain** Gran Bretaña.

British ['brɪtɪʃ] *adj* británico,-a.

▶ *n pl* **the British** los británicos *mpl*.

Briton ['brɪtən] *n* británico,-a.

brittle ['brɪtəl] *adj* quebradizo,-a, frágil.

broach [brəʊtʃ] *n* **1** *(drill bit)* broca. **2** *(roasting-spit)* espetón *m*.

broad [brɔːd] *adj* **1** *(street, avenue)* ancho,-a; *(surface, water, plateau)* extenso,-a. **2** *fig (field of study, debate)* amplio,-a. **3** *(measurement)* de ancho. **4** *(general)* general. **5** *(main)* principal. **6** *(accent)* marcado,-a, cerrado,-a. **7** *(vowel)* abierto,-a.

broadcast ['brɔːdkɑːst] *n* *(by TV, radio)* emisión *f*.

▶ *vt* **1** *(by TV, radio)* emitir, transmitir. **2** *(make known)* difundir.

ⓘ *pt & pp* **broadcast**.

broadcasting ['brɔːdkɑːstɪŋ] *n* **1** RAD radiodifusión *f*. **2** TV transmisión *f*.

broaden ['brɔːdən] *vt* ensanchar.

broadly ['brɔːdlɪ] *adv* en términos generales.

broad-minded [brɔːd'maɪndɪd] *adj* liberal, tolerante.

broccoli ['brɒkəlɪ] *n* brécol *m*, brócoli *m*.

brochette [brə'ʃet] *n* brocheta.

brochure ['brəʊʃər] *n* folleto.

broil [brɔɪl] *vt* US asar a la parrilla.

broiler ['brɔɪlər] *n* **1** CULIN pollo. **2** *(gridiron)* parrilla.

broke [brəʊk] *pt* → **break**.

▶ *adj* *fam* sin un duro, sin blanca.

broken ['brəʊkən] *pp* → **break**.

▶ *adj* **1** *(plate, window, etc)* roto,-a. **2** *(machine)* estropeado,-a. **3** *(bone)* fracturado,-a. **4** *(person)* destrozado,-a. **6** *(language)* chapurreado,-a: *he speaks broken Spanish* chapurrea el español.

broker ['brəʊkər] *n* COMM corredor,-ra agente *mf* de Bolsa.

brolly ['brɒlɪ] *n* GB *fam* paraguas *m*.

ⓘ *pl* **brollies**.

bromine ['brəʊmaɪn] *n* CHEM bromo.

bronchial ['brɒŋkɪəl] *adj* ANAT bronquial. COMP **bronchial tubes** ANAT bronquios *mpl*.

bronchitis [brɒŋ'kaɪtəs] *n* MED bronquitis *f*.

bronchus ['brɒŋkəs] n bronquio.
ⓘ pl **bronchi** ['brɒŋkaɪ].

brontosaurus [brɒntə'sɔːrəs] n brontosaurio.

bronze [brɒnz] n bronce m. COMP the **Bronze Age** HIST la Edad del Bronce.
▶ vi (get a suntan) broncearse.

brooch [brəʊtʃ] n broche m.

brood [bruːd] n 1 (birds) nidada. 2 fam fig (children) prole f.
▶ vi 1 (hen) empollar. 2 fig (worry) apurarse, preocuparse.

brook [brʊk] n arroyo, riachuelo.

broom [bruːm] n 1 (for sweeping) escoba. 2 BOT hiniesta.

broomstick ['bruːmstɪk] n 1 (handle) palo de escoba. 2 (of witch) escoba.

Bros [brɒs] abbr (Brothers) Hermanos mpl; (abbreviation) Hnos: Jones Bros Hnos Jones.

broth [brɒθ] n CULIN caldo.

brothel ['brɒθəl] n burdel m.

brother ['brʌðəʳ] n 1 (gen) hermano. 2 US fam (friend) colega m, tío: what's happening brother? ¿qué pasa tío?

brotherhood ['brʌðəhʊd] n hermandad f, cofradía.

brother-in-law ['brʌðərɪnlɔː] n cuñado.
ⓘ pl **brothers-in-law** ['brʌðərɪnlɔː].

brought [brɔːt] pt & pp → bring.

brow [braʊ] n 1 (eyebrow) ceja. 2 (forehead) frente f. 3 (of hill) cresta.

browbeat ['braʊbiːt] vt intimidar.
ⓘ pt **browbeat**, pp **browbeaten** ['braʊbiːtən].

brown [braʊn] adj 1 marrón. 2 (hair, etc) castaño,-a. 3 (skin) moreno,-a.
▶ vi CULIN dorarse.

brownie ['braʊnɪ] n US pastelito de chocolate y nueces.

browse [braʊz] vi 1 (grass) pacer. 2 (person in shop) mirar.
◆ to **browse through** vt insep (book, magazine) hojear.

browser ['braʊzəʳ] n (Internet) navegador m, explorador m.

bruise [bruːz] n morado, magulladura, contusión f.
▶ vt magullar, contusionar.
▶ vi magullarse.

brunch [brʌnʃ] n brunch m.

✎ El brunch es una especie de copioso desayuno que se toma a última hora de la mañana y hace asimismo las veces de almuerzo.

brunette [bruː'net] n morena.
▶ adj moreno,-a.

brush [brʌʃ] n 1 (for teeth, clothes, etc) cepillo. 2 (artist's) pincel m; (house painter's) brocha. 3 (unpleasant encounter) roce m: he had a brush with the police tuvo un roce con la policía.
▶ vt 1 (gen) cepillar. 2 (touch lightly) rozar.
◆ to **brush away** vt sep (dirt, dust) quitar, limpiar.
◆ to **brush up** vt sep (knowledge) refrescar, repasar.

brush-off ['brʌʃɒf] n (rebuff, snub) desaire m.

brushwood ['brʌʃwʊd] n 1 (twigs) broza. 2 (undergrowth) maleza.

brusque [brʌsk] adj brusco,-a.

Brussels ['brʌsəlz] n Bruselas. COMP **Brussels sprouts** coles fpl de Bruselas.

brutal ['bruːtəl] adj brutal, cruel.

brute [bruːt] n bruto,-a, bestia mf.
▶ adj brutal, bruto,-a.

✗ Brute no se utiliza en el sentido de '(importe) bruto', que se traduce por gross.

bubble ['bʌbəl] n (in liquid) burbuja; (of soap) pompa.

bubonic [bjuː'bɒnɪk] adj MED bubónico,-a. COMP **bubonic plague** peste f bubónica.

buck¹ [bʌk] n (rabbit, hare) macho; (deer) ciervo; (goat) macho cabrío.
▶ adj (animal) macho.

buck² [bʌk] n US fam dólar m.

bucket ['bʌkɪt] n cubo.

buckle ['bʌkəl] n (on shoe, belt) hebilla.
▶ vt (belt) abrochar.
▶ vi 1 (metal, object) torcerse, combarse. 2 (knees) doblarse.

bucolic [bjuː'kɒlɪk] adj bucólico,-a.

bud¹ [bʌd] n (on tree, plant) brote m, yema; (of flower) botón m, capullo.

bud² [bʌd] n US fam colega mf.
Buddhism ['budɪzəm] n REL budismo.
budding ['bʌdɪŋ] adj en ciernes.
buddy ['bʌdɪ] n US fam amigote m, colega mf.
ⓘ pl buddies.
budge [bʌdʒ] vt **1** (move) mover. **2** (make change opinion) hacer cambiar de opinión.
budgerigar ['bʌdʒərɪgɑːʳ] n ZOOL periquito.
budget ['bʌdʒɪt] n presupuesto.
► adj (good-value) bien de precio.
► vt **to budget for** presupuestar.
budgie ['bʌdʒɪ] n ZOOL fam periquito.
buff [bʌf] n **1** (leather) piel f de ante. **2** (colour) color m de ante. **3** (enthusiast) aficionado,-a.
buffalo ['bʌfələu] n ZOOL búfalo.
ⓘ pl buffalo o buffaloes.
buffer ['bʌfəʳ] n **1** (for train) tope m. **2** COMPUT memoria intermedia. **3** CHEM regulador m.
buffet ['bʌfeɪ] n **1** (bar) bar m; (at station) bar m, cantina. **2** (meal) bufé m libre, bufé m. **3** (sideboard) aparador m.
bug [bʌg] n **1** (insect) bicho. **2** fam (microbe) microbio. **3** (microphone) micrófono oculto. **4** fam (interest) afición f. **5** (in computer program) error m.
► vt **1** fam ocultar micrófonos en. **2** US (annoy) molestar, fastidiar: what's bugging her? ¿qué mosca le ha picado?
ⓘ pt & pp bugged, ger bugging.
bugle ['bjuːgəl] n MUS corneta.
build [bɪld] n (physique) constitución f, complexión f: a strong build una complexión fuerte.
► vt construir.
ⓘ pt & pp built [bɪlt].
builder ['bɪldəʳ] n **1** (owner of company) constructor,-ra. **2** (bricklayer) albañil m.
building ['bɪldɪŋ] n **1** edificio. **2** (action) construcción f, edificación f. COMP **building society** sociedad f hipotecaria. **‖ the building industry / the building trade** la construcción.
build-up ['bɪldʌp] n **1** (increase) aumento: a build-up in pollution un aumento de la contaminación. **2** (of gas) acumulación f.

built [bɪlt] pt & pp → build.
built-in [bɪlt'ɪn] adj **1** (as component) incorporado,-a. **2** (recessed) empotrado,-a.
built-up [bɪlt'ʌp] adj urbanizado,-a.
bulb [bʌlb] n **1** BOT bulbo. **2** ELEC bombilla.
Bulgaria [bʌl'geərɪə] n Bulgaria.
Bulgarian [bʌl'geərɪən] adj búlgaro,-a.
► n búlgaro.
bulge [bʌldʒ] n bulto.
bulimia [bjuː'liːmɪə] n bulimia.
bulk [bʌlk] n **1** (mass) masa, bulto, (amount, quantity) volumen m, cantidad f. **2** (greater part) mayor parte f.
bulk-buying ['bʌlkbaɪɪŋ] n compra en grandes cantidades.
bull¹ [bul] n **1** toro. **2** (elephant, whale, etc) macho. **3** FIN alcista mf.
► adj **1** (elephant, whale, etc) macho. **2** FIN alcista, en alza.
bull² [bul] n REL (papal) bula.
bulldog ['buldɒg] n bulldog m.
bulldozer ['buldəuzəʳ] n bulldozer m.
bullet ['bulɪt] n bala.
bulletin ['bulɪtɪn] n **1** (publication) boletín m. **2** (medical, etc) parte m.
bulletproof ['bulɪtpruːf] adj antibalas. COMP **bulletproof vest** chaleco antibalas.
bullfight ['bulfaɪt] n corrida de toros.
bullfighter ['bulfaɪtəʳ] n torero,-a.
bullfighting ['bulfaɪtɪŋ] n los toros mp. (art) tauromaquia.
bullion ['buljən] n (gold) oro en lingotes; (silver) plata en lingotes.
bullock ['bulək] n buey m.
bullring ['bulrɪŋ] n plaza de toros.
bull's-eye ['bulzaɪ] n **1** (target) diana. **2** (score) acierto. **3** MAR (porthole) portilla. LOC **to score a bull's-eye** dar en el blanco.
bullshit ['bulʃɪt] n taboo (nonsense) chorradas fpl.
bully ['bulɪ] n matón,-ona.
ⓘ pl bullies.
bum¹ [bʌm] n GB fam (bottom) culo.
bum² [bʌm] n **1** US fam (tramp) vagabundo,-a. **2** US fam (idler) vago,-a, holgazán,-ana.

▶ vt fam (scrounge) gorrear, sablear.

bumblebee ['bʌmbəlbiː] n ZOOL abejorro.

bummer ['bʌmər] n fam lata, latazo.

bump [bʌmp] n **1** (blow) golpe m, batacazo. **2** (on head) chichón m; (swelling) hinchazón m; (lump) bulto. **4** (dent) abolladura. **5** (on road) bache m.
▶ vt **1** darse un golpe en: he bumped his head se dio un golpe en la cabeza. **2** dar un golpe a.
▶ vi **1** chocar (into, con), topar (into, contra). **2** (collide) chocar, colisionar.
◆ **to bump into** vt insep fam encontrar por casualidad, tropezar con.
◆ **to bump off** vt sep sl liquidar.

bumper ['bʌmpər] n parachoques m.
▶ adj abundante.

bumpy ['bʌmpɪ] adj **1** (surface) desigual, accidentado,-a. **2** (road) lleno,-a de baches.
ⓘ comp bumpier, superl bumpiest.

bun [bʌn] n **1** (bread) panecillo; (sweet) bollo. **2** (cake) ma(g)dalena. **3** (hair) moño.

bunch [bʌntʃ] n **1** manojo. **2** (flowers) ramo. **3** (fruit) racimo. **4** fam (group of people) grupo; (gang) pandilla.

bundle ['bʌndəl] n **1** (clothes) fardo, bulto. **2** (wood) haz m. **3** (papers, banknotes) fajo. **4** (keys) manojo.

bung [bʌŋ] n (stopper) tapón m.

bungalow ['bʌŋgələʊ] n bungalow m.

bungle ['bʌŋgəl] vt chapucear.

bungler ['bʌŋglər] n chapucero,-a.

bunion ['bʌnjən] n MED juanete m.

bunk [bʌŋk] n (bed) litera.

bunk-bed ['bʌŋkbed] n litera.
ⓘ pl bunk-beds.

bunker ['bʌŋkər] n **1** MIL búnker m. **2** (golf) búnker m.

bunny ['bʌnɪ] n fam conejito.
ⓘ pl bunnies.

buoy [bɔɪ] n boya, baliza.

buoyant ['bɔɪənt] adj **1** flotante. **2** (cheerful) animado,-a. **3** (optimistic) optimista.

burden ['bɜːdən] n carga.
▶ vt cargar.

bureau ['bjʊərəʊ] n **1** (desk) escritorio. **2** US (office) oficina. **3** US (agency) agencia. **4** US (chest of drawers) cómoda. **5** US departamento del estado.
ⓘ pl bureaus o bureaux ['bjʊərəʊ].

bureaucracy [bjʊəˈrɒkrəsɪ] n burocracia.
ⓘ pl bureaucracies.

burger ['bɜːgər] n hamburguesa.

burglar ['bɜːglər] n ladrón,-ona.

burglary ['bɜːglərɪ] n (gen) robo.
ⓘ pl burglaries.

burgle ['bɜːgəl] vt robar.

burial ['berɪəl] n entierro. COMP **burial ground** cementerio.

burn¹ [bɜːn] n quemadura.
▶ vt quemar.
▶ vi **1** arder.
◆ **to burn down** vt sep incendiar.
◆ **to burn out** vi **1** (fire) extinguirse. **2** (fuse, bulb) fundirse.
ⓘ pt & pp burnt [bɜːnt] o burned.

burn² [bɜːn] n (stream) arroyo.

burner ['bɜːnər] n quemador m.

burning ['bɜːnɪŋ] adj **1** (on fire) en llamas, ardiendo. **2** (sun) abrasador,-ra, de justicia; (heat) achicharrante. **3** (desire, need) ardiente. COMP **burning issue / burning question** cuestión f candente.

burnt [bɜːnt] pt & pp → **burn**.

burnt-out ['bɜːntaʊt] adj **1** (building, car) carbonizado,-a. **2** fig (person) quemado,-a, caduco,-a.

burp [bɜːp] n fam eructo.
▶ vi fam eructar.

burrow ['bʌrəʊ] n madriguera.

bursary ['bɜːsərɪ] n (scholarship) beca.
ⓘ pl bursaries.

burst [bɜːst] n **1** (of balloon, pipe) reventón m; (of tyre) pinchazo, reventón m. **2** (explosion) estallido, explosión f. **3** (of applause) salva. **4** (of gunfire) ráfaga.
▶ vi (balloon, pipe) reventarse; (tyre) pincharse, reventarse.
ⓘ pt & pp burst.

bury ['berɪ] vt enterrar.
ⓘ pt & pp buried, ger burying.

bus [bʌs] n **1** autobús m, bus m. **2** COMPUT bus m. COMP **bus conductor** cobrador. ▌ **bus conductress** cobradora. ▌ **bus lane** carril m de autobuses. ▌ **bus route** línea de autobús. ▌ **bus shelter**

parada de autobús cubierta. **I bus station** estación *f* de autobuses. **I bus stop** parada de autobús.

ⓘ *pl* buses (US busses).

bush [buʃ] *n* **1** *(plant)* arbusto. **2** *(land)* breña.

▶ *n pl* **bushes** matorral *m*, maleza.

Bushman ['buʃmən] *n & adj* bosquimano,-a.

ⓘ *pl* Bushmen ['buʃmen].

bushy ['buʃɪ] *adj* espeso,-a, tupido,-a.

ⓘ *comp* bushier, *superl* bushiest.

business ['bɪznəs] *n* **1** *(commerce)* negocios *mpl*: *the business world* el mundo de los negocios. **2** *(firm)* negocio, empresa: *he's got a small business on the coast* tiene un pequeño negocio en la costa. **3** *(affair)* asunto, tema *m*: *I've got business to discuss with the manager* tengo asuntos que tratar con el director. LOC **it's my "(your, etc)" business to ...** me *(te, etc)* incumbe .... **I to go out of business** quebrar. **I to run a business** llevar un negocio. **I to set up a business** montar un negocio. **I mind your own business!** ¡no te metas donde no te llaman! LOC **business card** tarjeta de presentación, tarjeta comercial. **I business trip** viaje *m* de negocios.

businesslike ['bɪznəslaɪk] *adj* formal, serio,-a.

businessman ['bɪznəsmən] *n* hombre *m* de negocios, empresario.

ⓘ *pl* businessmen ['bɪznəsmen].

businesswoman ['bɪznəswumən] *n* mujer *m* de negocios, empresaria.

ⓘ *pl* businesswomen ['bɪznəswɪmɪn].

busker ['bʌskəʳ] *n* GB músico callejero,-a.

bust¹ [bʌst] *n* busto.

bust² [bʌst] *adj fam* roto,-a. LOC **to go bust** *fam* quebrar.

▶ *vt fam* romper.

▶ *vi* romperse.

ⓘ *pt & pp* bust [bʌst] o busted.

bustard ['bʌstəd] *n* avutarda.

bustle ['bʌsəl] *n* bullicio, ajetreo.

busy ['bɪzɪ] *adj* **1** *(person)* ocupado,-a, atareado,-a. **2** *(street, place)* concurrido,-a. **3** *(day)* ajetreado,-a. **4** US *(telephone)* comunicando: *the line was busy*

estaba comunicando. LOC **to get busy 1** *fam (work)* ponerse a trabajar. **2** *(hurry)* darse prisa.

ⓘ *comp* busier, *superl* busiest.

busybody ['bɪzɪbɒdɪ] *n* entremetido,-a, fisgón,-ona.

ⓘ *pl* busybodies.

but [bʌt] *conj* **1** pero: *it's cold, but dry* hace frío, pero no llueve; *I'd like to, but I can't* me gustaría, pero no puedo. **2** *(after negative)* sino: *not two, but three* no dos, sino tres. **3** *(after negative with verb)* sino que: *she told him not to wait, but to go home* le dijo que no se esperara, sino que se fuera para casa. LOC **but for** de no ser por, si no fuera por: *but for him, we would have failed* de no ser por él, habríamos fracasado.

▶ *adv* (nada) más que, no ... sino, solamente, solo,: *he spoke nothing but the truth* no dijo nada más que la verdad.

▶ *prep* excepto, salvo, menos: *everyone but me* todos menos yo; *I can meet you any day but Friday* te puedo ver cualquier día excepto el viernes.

▶ *n* pero: *there are no buts about it* no hay pero que valga.

butane ['bju:teɪn] *n* CHEM butano. COMP **butane bottle** bombona (de butano). **I butane gas** gas *m* butano.

butcher ['butʃəʳ] *n* carnicero,-a.

butcher's ['butʃəz] *n* carnicería.

butchery ['butʃərɪ] *n* carnicería.

butt¹ [bʌt] *n (with head)* cabezazo.

butt² [bʌt] *n* **1** *(of rifle)* culata. **2** *(of cigarette)* colilla. **3** US *fam (bottom)* culo.

butt³ [bʌt] *n (target)* blanco.

butt⁴ [bʌt] *n* **1** *(barrel)* tonel *m*. **2** *(for water)* aljibe *m*.

butter ['bʌtəʳ] *n* mantequilla.

▶ *vt* untar con mantequilla. COMP **butter dish** mantequera. **I**

◆ **to butter up** *vt sep fam* dar coba a.

buttercup ['bʌtəkʌp] *n* BOT botón *m* de oro, ranúnculo.

butterfingers ['bʌtəfɪŋgəz] *n* manazas *mf*, torpe *mf*.

butterfly ['bʌtəflaɪ] *n* **1** mariposa. **2** SP *(swimming)* mariposa.

ⓘ *pl* butterflies.

buttock ['bʌtək] n 1 (of person) nalga. 2 (of animal) anca.
► n pl **buttocks** (bottom) trasero, nalgas fpl.

button ['bʌtən] n 1 (on clothing, machine) botón m; (on doorbell) pulsador m, botón m: press the button pulse el botón. 2 BOT (bud) botón m, yema.
► vi abrocharse.
► vt **to button (up)** abrochar, abrocharse: button (up) your coat abróchate el abrigo.

buttonhole ['bʌtənhəʊl] n ojal m.

buttress ['bʌtrəs] n ARCH contrafuerte m.

butty ['bʌtɪ] n fam bocata m.
ⓘ pl **butties**.

buy [baɪ] n compra.
► vt 1 comprar: they've just bought a new flat acaban de comprar un piso nuevo. 2 (bribe) sobornar. 3 fam (accept, believe) tragárselo: he's so gullible he bought it es tan ingenuo que se lo tragó.
ⓘ pt & pp **bought** [bɔːt].

buyer ['baɪəʳ] n comprador,-ra.

buying power ['baɪɪŋpaʊəʳ] n poder m adquisitivo.

buzz [bʌz] n 1 zumbido. 2 (of voices) murmullo. 3 fam telefonazo, toque m: give me a buzz dame un toque.
► vi zumbar.

buzzard ['bʌzəd] n ratonero.

buzzer ['bʌzəʳ] n timbre m.

buzzing ['bʌzɪŋ] n zumbido.

buzz-saw ['bʌzsɔː] n sierra circular.

buzz-word ['bʌzwɜːd] n palabra pegadiza, palabra que está de moda.

by [baɪ] prep 1 (agent) por: painted by Constable pintado por Constable. 2 (means) por: by air/sea por avión/mar; by car/train en coche/tren; by hand a mano; by heart de memoria. 3 (showing difference) por: I won by 3 points gané por tres puntos; better by far muchísimo mejor. 4 (not later than) para: I need it by ten lo necesito para las diez. 5 (during) de: by day/night de día/noche. 6 (near) junto a, al lado de: sit by me siéntate a mi lado. 7 (according to) según: by the rules según las reglas. 8 (measurements) por: 6 metres by 4 6 metros por 4. 9 (rate) por: paid by the hour

pagado por horas. 10 MATH por: 12 divided by 3 12 dividido por 3. 11 (progression) a: day by day día a día; little by little poco a poco. 12 (in sets) en: two by two de dos en dos. 13 (introducing gerund) : you can find out by reading the papers te enterarás leyendo los periódicos. LOC **to go by** pasar delante. ‖ **by** os solo,-a.
► adv al lado, delante. LOC **to go by** pasar delante.

bye [baɪ] interj fam ¡adiós!, ¡hasta luego!

bye-bye ['baɪbaɪ] interj fam ¡adiós!, ¡hasta luego! LOC **to say bye-bye** fam decir adiós. ‖ **to go to bye-byes** ir a dormir, ir a la cama.

Byelorussia [bjeləʊˈrʌʃə] n → Belarus.

bygone ['baɪgɒn] adj pasado,-a: a bygone age tiempos pasados.
► n (object) antigualla. LOC **in bygone times** antiguamente. ‖ **let bygones be bygones** lo pasado, pasado está.

bylaw ['baɪlɔː] n ley f municipal.

bypass ['baɪpɑːs] n 1 AUTO variante f. 2 TECH tubo de desviación. 3 MED bypass m.
► vt 1 (traffic, road) desviar. 2 (avoid) esquivar, evitar.

by-product ['baɪprɒdʌkt] n 1 subproducto, derivado. 2 fig consecuencia.

byre ['baɪəʳ] n establo.

by-road ['baɪrəʊd] n carretera secundaria.

bystander ['baɪstændəʳ] n espectador,-ra, curioso,-a.

byte [baɪt] n COMPUT byte m.

by-way ['baɪweɪ] n 1 (road) carretera secundaria. 2 (remote path) camino poco frecuentado.

byword ['baɪwɜːd] n 1 arquetipo, mayor mf exponente. 2 (proverb) refrán m, proverbio. LOC **to be a byword in** ser sinónimo de: their products are a byword in luxury sus productos son sinónimo de lujo.

Byzantine [bɪˈzæntaɪn] n bizantino,-a.
► adj bizantino,-a.

Byzantium [bɪˈzæntɪəm] n Bizancio.

C

C, c [siː] *n* **1** *(the letter)* C, c *f.* **2** MUS do.

c. [ˈsentʃərɪ] *abbr* **(circa)** hacia; *(abbreviation)* h.: *Ramses III c. (800 BC)* Ramsés III (h. 800 a. d. C.).

cab [kæb] *n* **1** *(taxi)* taxi *m.* **2** *(in vehicle)* cabina. COMP **cab driver** taxista *mf.* ▌ **cab rank** parada de taxis.

cabaret [ˈkæbəreɪ] *n* cabaret *m.*

cabbage [ˈkæbɪdʒ] *n* col *f*, repollo, berza.

cabin [ˈkæbɪn] *n* **1** *(wooden house)* cabaña. **2** *(on ship)* camarote *m.* **3** *(on plane)* cabina. COMP **cabin crew** personal *m* de cabina.

> ☒ Cabin no significa 'cabina (telefónica)', que se traduce por phone box.

cabinet [ˈkæbɪnət] *n* **1** *(furniture - gen)* armario; *(glass fronted)* vitrina. **2** POL gabinete *m* (ministerial), consejo de ministros. COMP **cabinet meeting** consejo de ministros.

cable [ˈkeɪbəl] *n* **1** *(rope, wire)* cable *m.* **2** *(telegram)* cable *m*, telegrama *m.* COMP **cable television** televisión por cable.

cacao [kəˈkɑːəʊ] *n* BOT cacao.

cache [kæʃ] *n* **1** *(store)* alijo. **2** *(computer memory)* caché *m.* COMP **cache memory** memoria caché.

cackle [ˈkækəl] *n* **1** *(of hen)* cacareo. **2** *(of person)* risotada, carcajada.
▸ *vi* **1** *(of hen)* cacarear. **2** *(of person)* reírse a carcajadas.

cacophony [kəˈkɒfənɪ] *n* cacofonía.

cactus [ˈkæktəs] *n* cactus *m.*
ⓘ *pl* cacti [ˈkæktaɪ] o cactuses.

caddie [ˈkædɪ] *n* *(in golf)* cadi *m.* COMP **caddie car / caddie cart** carrito de golf.

cadence [ˈkeɪdəns] *n* cadencia.

cadet [kəˈdet] *n* cadete *m.*

cadge [kædʒ] *vt fam* gorronear.
▸ *vi fam* gorronear **(from/off,** a).

cadger [ˈkædʒəʳ] *n fam* gorrón,-ona.

cadmium [ˈkædmɪəm] *n* cadmio.

caecum [ˈsiːkəm] *n* ANAT intestino ciego.
ⓘ *pl* caeca [ˈsiːkə].

Caesarean [sɪˈzeərɪən] [also Caesarean section] *n* cesárea.

caesium [ˈsiːzɪəm] *n* cesio.

café [ˈkæfeɪ] *n* cafetería, café *m.*

cafeteria [kæfəˈtɪərɪə] *n* *(in factory, college, etc)* cafetería, cantina; *(restaurant)* autoservicio, self-service *m.*

caffeine [ˈkæfiːn] *n* cafeína.

cage [keɪdʒ] *n* *(gen)* jaula.
▸ *vt* enjaular.

cagey [ˈkeɪdʒɪ] *adj fam* reservado,-a, cauteloso,-a, precavido,-a.
ⓘ *comp* cagier, *superl* cagiest.

cagoule [kəˈɡuːl] *n* chubasquero.

cajole [kəˈdʒəʊl] *vt* engatusar.

cake [keɪk] *n* **1** CULIN pastel *m*, tarta, torta. **2** *(of soap)* pastilla.

calamity [kəˈlæmɪtɪ] *n* calamidad *f.*
ⓘ *pl* calamities.

calcite [ˈkælsaɪt] *n* calcita.

calcium [ˈkælsɪəm] *n* calcio.

calculate [ˈkælkjəleɪt] *vt & vi* calcular.

calculation [kælkjəˈleɪʃən] *n* cálculo.

calculator [ˈkælkjəleɪtəʳ] *n* calculadora.

calculus [ˈkælkjələs] *n* **1** MATH cálculo matemático. **2** [*pl* calculi [ˈkælkjəlaɪ]] MED cálculo.

calendar [ˈkælɪndəʳ] *n* calendario.

calf¹ [kɑːf] *n* ZOOL *(of cattle)* ternero,-a, becerro,-a; *(of whale)* ballenato; *(of other animals)* cría.
ⓘ *pl* calves.

calf² [kɑ:f] *n* ANAT pantorrilla.
ⓘ *pl* calves.

caliber ['kælɪbər] *n* US → **come**.

calibre ['kælɪbər] *n* calibre *m*.

caliph ['keɪlɪf, 'kælɪf] *n* califa *f*.

call [kɔ:l] *n* **1** (shout, cry) grito, llamada. **2** (by telephone) llamada (telefónica). **3** (demand) demanda; (need) motivo. LOC **to be on call** estar de guardia. ‖ **to give SB a call** llamar a ALGN. COMP **call box** GB cabina telefónica.
▶ *vt* **1** (shout) llamar. **2** (by telephone) llamar. **3** (summon - meeting, strike, election) convocar; (announce - flight) anunciar.
▶ *vi* **1** (shout) llamar. **2** (by phone) llamar. **3** (visit) pasar, hacer una visita: *I called round at Martin's this afternoon* he pasado por casa de Martin esta tarde. **4** (train) parar (at, en). LOC **to call for STH/SB** pasar a recoger ALGO/a ALGN.
◆ **to call back** *vi* (by phone) volver a llamar; (visit) volver a pasar.
◆ **to call on** *vt insep* visitar, ir a ver a.
◆ **to call out** *vt sep* (summon - fire brigade) llamar; (doctor) hacer venir; (workers) llamar a la huelga.

caller ['kɔ:lər] *n* **1** (visitor) visita, visitante *mf*. **2** (by telephone) persona que llama.

calligraphy [kə'lɪɡrəfɪ] *n* caligrafía.

calling ['kɔ:lɪŋ] *n* (vocation) vocación *f*, llamada; (profession) profesión *f*. COMP **calling card** US tarjeta de visita.

callous ['kæləs] *adj* duro,-a, insensible.
☒ Callous no significa 'callos', que se traduce por tripe.

callus ['kæləs] *n* callo.
ⓘ *pl* calluses.

calm [kɑ:m] *adj* **1** (sea, weather) en calma, tranquilo,-a. **2** (person) tranquilo, -a, calmado,a: *keep calm!* ¡tranquilo!
▶ *n* **1** (of sea, weather) calma. **2** (peace and quiet) tranquilidad *f*.
▶ *vt* calmar, tranquilizar, sosegar.
◆ **to calm down** *vt* tranquilizar, calmar.
▶ *vi* tranquilizarse, calmarse.

Calor Gas® ['kæləɡæs] *n* (gas *m*) butano.

caloric [kə'lɒrɪk] *adj* calórico,-a.

calorie ['kælərɪ] *n* caloría.

calvary ['kælvərɪ] *n* calvario.

calves [kɑ:vz] *npl* → **calf**.

calyx ['keɪlɪks, 'kælɪks] *n* cáliz *m*.
ⓘ *pl* calices o calixes.

Cambodia [kæm'bəʊdɪə] *n* Camboya.

Cambodian [kæm'bəʊdɪən] *adj* camboyano,-a.
▶ *n* **1** (person) camboyano,-a. **2** (language) camboyano.

camcorder ['kæmkɔ:dər] *n* videocámara.

came [keɪm] *pt* → **come**.

camel ['kæməl] *n* ZOOL camello,-a.

camellia [kə'mi:lɪə] *n* BOT camelia.

camera ['kæmərə] *n* cámara.

cameraman ['kæmərəmən] *n* cámara *mf*.

Cameroon [kæmə'ru:n] *n* Camerún *m*.

Cameroonian [kæmə'ru:nɪən] *adj & n* camerunés,-esa.

camomile ['kæməmaɪl] *n* BOT manzanilla, camomila.

camouflage ['kæməflɑ:ʒ] *n* camuflaje *m*.

camp [kæmp] *n* **1** (gen) campamento. **2** (group, faction) bando.
▶ *vi* acampar.

campaign [kæm'peɪn] *n* campaña.
▶ *vi* hacer una campaña (for, en favor de).

camper ['kæmpər] *n* **1** (person) campista *mf*. **2** (vehicle) caravana.

campfire ['kæmpfaɪər] *n* fogata, hoguera.

camping ['kæmpɪŋ] *n* camping *m*. LOC **«No camping»** «Prohibido acampar». ‖ **to go camping** ir de camping. COMP **camping site** camping *m*, campamento.

campus ['kæmpəs] *n* campus *m*.
ⓘ *pl* campuses.

can¹ [kæn] *n* **1** (tin - for food, drinks) lata, bote *m*. **2** (container - for oil, petrol, etc) bidón *m*.

can² [kæn] *aux* **1** (gen) poder: *can you come tomorrow?* ¿puedes venir mañana?. **2** (know how to) saber: *he can speak Chinese* sabe hablar chino; *can you swim?* ¿sabes nadar?. **3** (be allowed to) poder, estar permitido,-a: *you can't smoke here* no se puede fumar aquí; *you can go now* ya te puedes ir. **4** (with verbs of perception or mental activity): *she couldn't see anything* no veía nada; *I can smell burning* huele a quemado.
ⓘ *pt & cond* could [kʊd].

C

Canada ['kænədə] n Canadá.

Canadian [kə'neɪdɪən] adj canadiense.
► n (person) canadiense mf.

canal [kə'næl] n canal m.

canapé ['kænəpeɪ] n canapé m.

canary [kə'neərɪ] n canario.
ⓘ pl canaries.

cancel ['kænsəl] vt 1 (gen) cancelar. 2 (stamp) matasellar. 3 (delete) tachar. 6 MATH eliminar.
ⓘ pt & pp cancelled (US canceled), ger cancelling (US canceling).

cancellation [kænsə'leɪʃən] n 1 (gen) cancelación f. 2 (of stamp) matasellos m.

cancer ['kænsə'] n MED cáncer m.
► n Cancer (constellation, sign) Cáncer m.

cancerous ['kænsərəs] adj canceroso,-a.

candid ['kændɪd] adj franco,-a, sincero,-a. COMP **candid camera** cámara indiscreta.

☒ Candid no significa 'cándido', que se traduce por ingenuous.

candidacy ['kændɪdəsɪ] n candidatura.
ⓘ pl candidacies.

candidate ['kændɪdət] n candidato,-a.

candidature ['kændɪdətʃə'] n candidatura.

candle ['kændəl] n (gen) vela; (in church) cirio.

candlestick ['kændəlstɪk] n (gen) candelero, palmatoria.

candy ['kændɪ] n US (sweets) caramelos mpl, golosinas fpl; (a sweet) caramelo.
ⓘ pl candies.

candyfloss ['kændɪflɒs] n GB algodón m de azúcar.

cane [keɪn] n 1 BOT caña. 2 (stick) bastón m. 3 (furniture) mimbre m.

canine ['keɪnaɪn] adj ZOOL canino,-a. COMP **canine tooth** (diente m) canino, colmillo.

canister ['kænɪstə'] n (for tea, coffee, etc) bote m, lata.

canned [kænd] adj enlatado,-a. COMP **canned food** conservas fpl.

cannelloni [kænə'ləʊnɪ] n pl canelones mpl, canalones mpl.

cannibal ['kænɪbəl] n caníbal mf.

canning ['kænɪŋ] n enlatado. COMP **canning factory** fábrica de conservas. I **canning industry** industria conservera.

cannon ['kænən] n 1 MIL cañón m. 2 (in billiards) carambola.
ⓘ pl cannon o cannons.

cannonball ['kænənbɔːl] n bala de cañón.

cannot ['kænɒt] aux = can not.

canoe [kə'nuː] n canoa, piragua.

canonization [kænənaɪ'zeɪʃən] n canonización.

can-opener ['kænəʊpənə'] n abrelatas m.

can't [kɑːnt] aux = can not.

canteen [kæn'tiːn] n 1 (restaurant) cantina, comedor m. 2 (set of cutlery) juego de cubiertos. 3 (flask) cantimplora.

cantilever ['kæntɪliːvə'] n ARCH voladizo. COMP **cantilever bridge** puente m voladizo.

canton ['kæntɒn] n cantón m.

canvas ['kænvəs] n 1 (cloth) lona. 2 ART lienzo.

canvass ['kænvəs] vi POL hacer propaganda electoral (for, a favor de), hacer campaña (for, a favor de).

canyon ['kænjən] n GEOG cañón m.

canyoning ['kænjənɪŋ] n barranquismo.

cap [kæp] n 1 (type of hat) gorra. 2 (cover - of pen) capuchón m; (- of bottle) tapón m, chapa. 3 GEOG casquete m.

capability [keɪpə'bɪlɪtɪ] n capacidad f (to, para/de).
ⓘ pl capabilities.

capable ['keɪpəbəl] adj 1 (able) capaz (of, de): he's capable of breaking the world record es capaz de batir el récord mundial. 2 (competent) competente, capaz: a very capable person una persona muy competente.

capacity [kə'pæsɪtɪ] n capacidad f.
ⓘ pl capacities.

cape¹ [keɪp] n (garment) capa.

cape² [keɪp] n cabo. COMP **Cape Verde** Cabo Verde.

caper¹ ['keɪpə'] n alcaparra.

caper² ['keɪpə'] n 1 (jump) brinco. 2 fam (prank) travesura, broma.

capillary [kə'pɪlərɪ] n capilar m.
ⓘ pl capillaries.

capital [ˈkæpɪtəl] n **1** (of country, etc) capital f. **2** FIN capital m: starting capital capital inicial. **3** (letter) mayúscula: write it in capitals escríbelo con mayúsculas.
▶ adj **1** (gen) capital. **2** (letter) mayúscula: capital A A mayúscula. COMP **capital goods** bienes mpl de equipo.

capitalism [ˈkæpɪtəlɪzəm] n capitalismo.

capitol [ˈkæpɪtəl] n capitolio.

capitulation [kəpɪtjəˈleɪʃən] n capitulación f.

Capricorn [ˈkæprɪkɔːn] n (constellation, sign) Capricornio.

capsicum [ˈkæpsɪkəm] n pimiento.

capsize [kæpˈsaɪz] vi zozobrar.
▶ vt hacer zozobrar.

capsule [ˈkæpsjuːl] n cápsula.

captain [ˈkæptɪn] n capitán,-ana.

caption [ˈkæpʃən] n **1** (under picture) leyenda, pie m de foto. **2** CINEM subtítulo.

captivate [ˈkæptɪveɪt] vt cautivar, fascinar.

captivating [ˈkæptɪveɪtɪŋ] adj encantador,-ra, cautivador,-ra.

captive [ˈkæptɪv] adj & n cautivo,-a.

captivity [kæpˈtɪvɪtɪ] n cautiverio, cautividad f.

capture [ˈkæptʃər] n (seizure - of person) captura, apresamiento; (of town) toma, conquista.
▶ vt **1** (seize - person) capturar, apresar; (- town) tomar. **2** fig (attract) captar.

car [kɑːr] n **1** AUTO coche m, automóvil m. **2** US (railway carriage) vagón m, coche m. LOC **to go by car** ir en coche.

caramel [ˈkærəmel] n **1** CULIN (burnt sugar) azúcar m quemado. **2** (toffee) caramelo.

carapace [ˈkærəpeɪs] n caparazón m.

carat [ˈkærət] n quilate m.

caravan [kærəˈvæn] n caravana.

caravel [ˈkærəvel] n carabela.

carbohydrate [kɑːbəʊˈhaɪdreɪt] n hidrato de carbono, carbohidrato.

carbon [ˈkɑːbən] n CHEM carbono. COMP **carbon dioxide** dióxido de carbono. ‖ **carbon monoxide** monóxido de carbono. ‖ **carbon paper** papel m carbón.

☒ Carbon no significa 'carbón', que se traduce por coal.

carbonated [ˈkɑːbəneɪtɪd] adj (fizzy) gaseoso,-a, con gas.

Carboniferous [kɑːbəˈnɪfərəs] adj GEOL carbonífero,-a. COMP **the Carboniferous period** el carbonífero.

carburettor [kɑːbəretər] n carburador m.

carcass [ˈkɑːkəs] n res f muerta.

carcinogenic [kɑːsɪnəˈdʒenɪk] adj MED cancerígeno,-a, carcinógeno,-a.

card [kɑːd] n **1** (gen) tarjeta. **2** (greetings card) tarjeta de felicitación, felicitación f. **3** (of membership, identity) carnet m, carné m. **4** (stiff paper) cartulina. **5** carta, naipe m.

cardboard [ˈkɑːdbɔːd] n cartón m.

cardiac [ˈkɑːdɪæk] adj cardíaco,-a. COMP **cardiac arrest** paro cardíaco. ‖ **cardiac sphincter** cardias.

cardigan [ˈkɑːdɪgən] n rebeca.

cardinal [ˈkɑːdɪnəl] adj (most important) capital, fundamental, principal.
▶ n REL cardenal m. COMP **cardinal number** número cardinal. ‖ **cardinal point** punto cardinal. ‖ **cardinal sin** pecado capital.

cardiologist [kɑːdɪˈɒlədʒɪst] n cardiólogo,-a.

cardiology [kɑːdɪˈɒlədʒɪ] n cardiología.

care [keər] n **1** (gen) cuidado: take care when driving at night (ten) cuidado al conducir de noche; I left the baby in the care of my mother dejé al bebé al cuidado de mi madre. **2** (worry, grief) preocupación f.
▶ vi (be worried, be concerned) preocuparse (about, por), importar: I don't care no me importa, me da igual.
▶ vt (feel concern, mind) importar: no-one cares if you're late a nadie le importa si llegas tarde. LOC «Handle with care» «Frágil». ‖ **take care! 1** (be careful) ¡ten cuidado! **2** (look after yourself) ¡cuídate! COMP **medical care** asistencia médica.
◆ **to care for** vt insep **1** (look after) cuidar, atender. **2** (like) gustar; (feel affection for) querer, sentir cariño por.

career [kəˈrɪər] n **1** (profession) carrera. **2** (working life) vida profesional.

carefree [ˈkeəfriː] adj despreocupado,-a, libre de preocupaciones.

careful [ˈkeəful] *adj* **1** *(cautious)* prudente, cuidadoso,-a: *a careful driver* un conductor prudente. **2** *(painstaking)* cuidadoso,-a. LOC **to be careful** tener cuidado.

carefully [ˈkeəfulɪ] *adv* **1** *(cautiously)* con cuidado, con precaución: *drive carefully* conduce con cuidado. **2** *(with great attention)* cuidadosamente.

careless [ˈkeələs] *adj (inattentive, thoughtless - person)* descuidado; *(driving)* negligente.

caress [kəˈres] *n* caricia.
▶ *vt* acariciar.

caretaker [ˈkeəteɪkəʳ] *n* conserje *m*, portero,-a.

cargo [ˈkɑːgəʊ] *n (goods)* carga; *(load)* cargamento.
ⓘ *pl* cargoes o cargos.

ⓧ Cargo no significa 'cargo (empleo)', que se traduce por **position**.

Caribbean [kærɪˈbɪən, US kəˈrɪbɪən] *adj* caribeño,-a. COMP **the Caribbean (Sea)** el (mar) Caribe.

caribou [ˈkærɪbuː] *n* caribú *m*.

caricature [ˈkærɪkətjʊəʳ] *n* caricatura.

caries [ˈkeərɪz] *n* caries *f*.

carnage [ˈkɑːnɪdʒ] *n* carnicería.

carnal [ˈkɑːnəl] *adj* carnal.

carnation [kɑːˈneɪʃən] *n* clavel *m*.

carnival [ˈkɑːnɪvəl] *n* carnaval *m*.

carnivore [ˈkɑːnɪvɔːʳ] *n* carnívoro,-a.

carnivorous [kɑːˈnɪvərəs] *adj* carnívoro,-a.

carol [ˈkærəl] *n* villancico.

carotene [ˈkærətiːn] *n* caroteno.

carousel [kærəˈsel] *n* **1** US *(roundabout)* tiovivo, caballitos *mpl*, carrusel *m*. **2** *(for baggage)* cinta transportadora. **3** *(for slides)* carrete *m* de diapositivas.

carp¹ [kɑːp] *n (fish)* carpa.

carp² [kɑːp] *vi (complain)* quejarse (about/at, de).

carpenter [ˈkɑːpɪntəʳ] *n* carpintero,-a.

carpentry [ˈkɑːpɪntrɪ] *n* carpintería.

carpet [ˈkɑːpɪt] *n* **1** *(gen)* alfombra; *(fitted)* moqueta. **2** *fig* alfombra.

ⓧ Carpet no significa 'carpeta', que se traduce por **folder**.

carriage [ˈkærɪdʒ] *n* **1** HIST *(horse-drawn)* carruaje *m*. **2** GB *(railway vehicle)* vagón *m*, coche *m*. **3** *(of typewriter)* carro. **4** *(cost of transport)* porte *m*, transporte *m*.

carriageway [ˈkærɪdʒweɪ] *n* GB calzada.

carrier [ˈkærɪəʳ] *n* **1** *(company, person)* transportista *mf*. **2** AV compañía aérea, línea aérea. **3** MED *(of disease)* portador,-ra. COMP **aircraft carrier** MAR portaaviones *m*. ‖ **carrier pigeon** paloma mensajera.

carrion [ˈkærɪən] *n* carroña.

carrot [ˈkærət] *n* zanahoria.

carrousel [kærəˈsel] *n* **1** *(roundabout)* tiovivo, carrusel. **2** *(for baggage reclaim)* cinta.

carry [ˈkærɪ] *vt* **1** *(gen)* llevar. **2** *(goods, load, passengers)* transportar. **3** *(disease)* ser portador,-ra de. **4** *(blame, responsibility)* cargar con. **5** *(entail, involve)* conllevar **8** MATH llevar(se).

◆ **to carry forward / carry over** *vt sep* llevar a la columna siguiente, llevar a la página siguiente: *carry this figure forward to the next page* lleva esta cifra a la página siguiente.

◆ **to carry off** *vt sep* **1** *(part, action, duty)* realizar con éxito, salir airoso,-a de: *she carried the speech off well* salió airosa del discurso. **2** *(prize)* llevarse, hacerse con.

◆ **to carry on** *vt insep* continuar con, seguir con.

◆ **to carry through** *vt sep (plan, etc)* llevar a cabo.
ⓘ *pt & pp* carried, *ger* carrying.

carry-out [ˈkærɪaʊt] *n* **1** US *(food)* comida para llevar. **2** *(drink)* bebida para llevar.

carsick [ˈkɑːsɪk] *adj* mareado,-a (al ir en coche). LOC **to get carsick** marearse en coche.

cart [kɑːt] *n* **1** *(horse-drawn)* carro, carreta; *(handcart)* carretilla. **2** US *(for shopping)* carrito, carro.

cartel [kɑːˈtel] *n* cártel *m*.

Cartesian [kɑːˈtiːʒən] *adj* cartesiano,-a.

Carthaginian [kɑːθəˈdʒɪnɪən] *adj* cartaginense.
▶ *n* cartaginense *mf*.

cartilage [ˈkɑːtɪlɪdʒ] *n* cartílago.

cartography [kɑːˈtɒgrəfɪ] *n* cartografía.

carton ['kɑːtˀn] *n (of cream, yoghurt)* bote *m; (of milk, juice, cigarettes)* cartón *m; (of cereals, etc)* caja.

☒ Carton no significa 'cartón', que se traduce por cardboard.

cartoon [kɑːˈtuːn] *n* **1** *(drawing)* viñeta, chiste *m; (strip)* tira cómica, historieta. **2** *(animated)* dibujos *mpl* animados.

cartridge ['kɑːtrɪdʒ] *n* **1** MIL cartucho. **2** *(for pen)* recambio.

carve [kɑːv] *vt* **1** *(wood, stone)* tallar; *(statue, etc)* esculpir; *(initials)* grabar. **2** *(meat)* cortar, trinchar.

cascade [kæsˈkeɪd] *n* cascada.

case¹ [keɪs] *n* **1** *(gen)* caso. **2** JUR *(lawsuit)* causa, litigio, pleito. LOC **in case ...** por si..., en caso de que... ∥ **in no case** bajo ninguna circunstancia.

case² [keɪs] *n* **1** *(suitcase)* maleta. **2** *(box)* caja, cajón *m; (small, hard container)* estuche *m; (soft container)* funda.

cash [kæʃ] *n* dinero (en) efectivo, metálico.
▶ *vt (cheque)* cobrar, hacer efectivo.

cashier [kæˈʃɪəʳ] *n* cajero,-a.

cashmere [kæʃˈmɪəʳ] *n* cachemira.

casino [kəˈsiːnəu] *n* casino.
ⓘ *pl* casinos.

cask [kɑːsk] *n* tonel *m*, barril *m*.

☒ Cask no significa 'casco (para la cabeza)', que se traduce por helmet.

casket ['kɑːskɪt] *n* **1** *(box)* cofre *m*. **2** *(coffin)* ataúd *m*.

casserole ['kæsərəul] *n* **1** *(dish)* cazuela. **2** *(food)* guiso, guisado.

cassette [kəˈset] *n* casete *f*.

cast [kɑːst] *n* **1** THEAT reparto. **2** TECH *(mould)* molde *m; (product)* pieza.
▶ *vt* **1** *(gen)* lanzar. **2** *(shadow, light)* proyectar. **3** *(vote)* emitir. **4** THEAT *(part, role)* asignar el papel a. LOC **to be cast away** naufragar. ∥ **to cast a spell on TH/SB** hechizar ALGO/a ALGN.
▶ **to cast about for / cast around for** *vt insep* buscar, andar buscando.
▶ **to cast out** *vt sep fml* expulsar.
ⓘ *pt & pp* cast.

castaway ['kɑːstəweɪ] *n* náufrago,-a.

caste [kɑːst] *n* casta.

caster ['kɑːstəʳ] *n (wheel)* ruedecilla.

Castilian [kæˈstɪlɪən] *adj* castellano,-a.
▶ *n* **1** *(person)* castellano,-a. **2** *(language)* castellano.

casting ['kɑːstɪŋ] *n* **1** TECH *(process)* fundición *f; (object)* pieza fundida. **2** THEAT *(selection)* selección *f*, casting *m*.

cast-iron ['kɑːstaɪən] *adj* de hierro fundido, de hierro colado.

castle ['kɑːsˀl] *n* **1** *(gen)* castillo. **2** *(chess)* torre *f*.
▶ *vi (chess)* enrocar.

castor¹ ['kɑːstəʳ] *n* → **caster**.

castor² ['kɑːstəʳ] *n* COMP **castor oil** aceite *m* de ricino.

castrate [kæˈstreɪt] *vt* castrar, capar.

casual ['kæʒjuəl] *adj* **1** *(chance - visit, visitor)* ocasional; *(- meeting)* fortuito,-a, casual. **2** *(superficial)* superficial; *(reader)* ocasional. **3** *(informal)* informal.

casually ['kæʒjuəlɪ] *adv* **1** *(dress)* de manera informal. **2** *(unconcernedly)* despreocupadamente.

☒ Casually no significa 'casualmente', que se traduce por by chance.

casualty ['kæʒjuəltɪ] *n (of accident)* herido,-a; MIL baja
ⓘ *pl* casualties.

☒ Casualty no significa 'casualidad', que se traduce por chance.

cat [kæt] *n (domestic)* gato,-a; *(lion, tiger)* felino,-a

Catalan ['kætəlæn] *adj* catalán,-ana.
▶ *n* **1** *(person)* catalán,-ana. **2** *(language)* catalán *m*.

catalogue ['kætəlɒg] *n* catálogo.
▶ *vt* catalogar.

catalyst ['kætəlɪst] *n* catalizador *m*.

catapult ['kætəpʌlt] *n* **1** *(gen)* catapulta. **2** *(toy)* tirachinas *m*.

cataract ['kætərækt] *n* **1** *(waterfall)* catarata. **2** MED catarata.

catarrh [kəˈtɑːʳ] *n* catarro.

catastrophe [kəˈtæstrəfɪ] *n* catástrofe *f*.

catch [kætʃ] *n* **1** *(of ball)* parada. **2** *(of fish)* presa. **4** *(fastener on door)* pestillo.

▶ vt **1** *(gen)* coger, agarrar; *(fish)* pescar. **2** *(train, plane - take)* coger, tomar: *I just caught the last train* cogí el último tren con el tiempo justo. LOC **to catch a cold** resfriarse, coger un resfriado.

◆ **to catch on** vi **1** *(understand)* entender, darse cuenta (to, de). **2** *(become popular)* ponerse de moda, imponerse.

◆ **to catch out** vt sep *(doing something wrong)* pillar, sorprender; *(trick)* hacer que uno caiga.

◆ **to catch up** vt sep *(person)* alcanzar.
ⓘ pt & pp **caught** [kɔːt].

catching ['kætʃɪŋ] adj contagioso,-a.
catchword ['kætʃwɜːd] n eslogan m.
catechism ['kætəkɪzəm] n catecismo.
categoric [kætə'gɒrɪk] adj categórico,-a.
category ['kætəgərɪ] n categoría.
ⓘ pl categories.
cater ['keɪtər] vi *(food)* proveer comida *(for, para)*.

◆ **to cater for** vt insep *(needs, interests, tastes)* atender a, satisfacer.
caterer ['keɪtərər] n proveedor,-ra.
catering ['keɪtərɪŋ] n *(business, course)* hostelería; *(service)* catering m.
caterpillar ['kætəpɪlər] n oruga.
cathedral [kə'θiːdrəl] n catedral f.
catheter ['kæθətər] n catéter m.
cathode ['kæθəʊd] n cátodo. COMP **cathode ray** rayo catódico.
Catholic ['kæθəlɪk] adj & n REL católico,-a.
Catholicism [kə'θɒlɪsɪzəm] n REL catolicismo.
cattle ['kætəl] n pl ganado (vacuno).
caught [kɔːt] pt & pp → **catch**.
cauldron ['kɔːldrən] n caldero.
cauliflower ['kɒlɪflaʊər] n coliflor f.
cause [kɔːz] n **1** *(gen)* causa **2** *(reason, grounds)* razón f, motivo.
▶ vt causar.
caustic ['kɔːstɪk] adj cáustico,-a. COMP **caustic soda** sosa cáustica.
cauterize ['kɔːtəraɪz] vt cauterizar.
caution ['kɔːʃən] n **1** *(care, prudence)* cautela, precaución f, prudencia. **2** *(warning)* aviso, advertencia.
▶ vt **1** *(warn)* advertir. **2** GB *(judge, etc)* amonestar.

cautious ['kɔːʃəs] adj cauteloso,-a prudente, cauto,-a.
cavalry ['kævəlrɪ] n caballería.
ⓘ pl cavalries.
cave [keɪv] n cueva. COMP **cave painting** pintura rupestre.

◆ **to cave in** vi *(roof, etc)* hundirse, derrumbarse; *(opposition, etc)* ceder.
caveman ['keɪvmæn] n cavernícola m hombre m de las cavernas.
cavern ['kævən] n caverna.
caviar ['kævɪɑːr] n caviar m.
caving ['keɪvɪŋ] n espeleología.
cavity ['kævɪtɪ] n **1** *(hole)* cavidad f. **2** *(tooth)* caries f.
ⓘ pl cavities.
caw [kɔː] n graznido.
▶ vi graznar.
cayman ['keɪmən] n caimán m.
CD ['siː'diː] abbr (compact disc) disc compacto; *(abbreviation)* CD m.
CD-ROM ['siː'diː'rɒm] abbr (compac disc read-only memory) CD-ROM m.
cease [siːs] vt suspender. LOC **to ceas fire** MIL cesar el fuego.
▶ vi cesar.
cease-fire [siːs'faɪər] n alto el fuego.
ceaseless ['siːsləs] adj incesante.
cecum ['siːkəm] n US → caecum.
cedar ['siːdər] n BOT cedro.
ceiling ['siːlɪŋ] n **1** *(of room)* techo. **2** *(up per limit)* tope m, límite m.
celebrate ['selɪbreɪt] vt & vi celebrar.
celebrated ['selɪbreɪtɪd] adj célebr famoso,-a.
celebration [selɪ'breɪʃən] n *(event)* fies ta, festejo; *(activity)* celebración f.
▶ n pl **celebrations** festividades fp festejos mpl.
celebrity [sə'lebrɪtɪ] n celebridad personaje m famoso.
ⓘ pl celebrities.
celery ['selərɪ] n apio.
celestial [sɪ'lestɪəl] adj **1** *(heavenly)* c lestial. **2** *(of the skies)* celeste.
cell [sel] n **1** *(in prison, monastery)* celda. *(of honeycomb)* celdilla. **3** *(of organism* célula. **4** ELEC *(in battery)* pila.

cellar ['selə'] *n* **1** *(basement)* sótano. **2** *(for wine)* bodega.

cellist ['tʃelɪst] *n* violoncelista *mf.*

cello ['tʃeləʊ] *n* violoncelo.
ⓘ *pl* cellos.

Cellophane® ['seləfeɪn] *n* celofán® *m.*

cellphone ['selfəʊn] *n* US teléfono móvil.

cellular ['seljələ'] *adj* celular. COMP **cellular telephone** teléfono móvil.

cellulite ['seljʊlaɪt] *n* *(fat)* celulitis *f.*

celluloid® ['seljəlɔɪd] *n* celuloide® *m.*

cellulose ['seljələʊs] *n* celulosa.

Celsius ['selsɪəs] *adj* Celsius: *30 degrees Celsius* 30 grados Celsius.

Celt [kelt] *n* celta *mf.*

cement [sɪ'ment] *n* **1** *(in building)* cemento. **2** *(glue)* adhesivo; *(for filling teeth)* empaste *m.* COMP **cement mixer** hormigonera.

cemetery ['semətrɪ] *n* cementerio.
ⓘ *pl* cemeteries.

censor ['sensə'] *n* censor,-ra.
▶ *vt* censurar.

censorship ['sensəʃɪp] *n* censura.

censure ['senʃə'] *n fml* censura.
▶ *vt fml* censurar.

census ['sensəs] *n* censo, padrón *m.*

cent [sent] *n* centavo, céntimo.

centenary [sen'ti:nərɪ] *n* centenario.
ⓘ *pl* centenaries.

centennial [sen'tenɪəl] *n* US centenario.

center ['sentə'] *n & vb* US → **centre.**

centigrade ['sentɪgreɪd] *adj* centígrado,-a.

centigram ['sentɪgræm] *n* centigramo.

centilitre ['sentɪli:tə'] *n* centilitro.

centimetre ['sentɪmi:tə'] *n* centímetro.

centipede ['sentɪpi:d] *n* ciempiés *m.*

central ['sentrəl] *adj* **1** *(government, bank, committee)* central. **2** *(of, at or near centre)* céntrico,-a. COMP **central nervous system** sistema *m* nervioso central.

centre ['sentə'] *n* centro.
▶ *vt (put in centre)* centrar.
▶ *vi (focus on)* centrarse (on/upon, en).

centrifugal [sentrɪ'fju:gəl] *adj* centrífugo,-a.

centripetal [sen'trɪpɪtəl] *adj* centrípeto,-a.

century ['sentʃərɪ] *n* siglo: *the twentieth century* el siglo veinte.
ⓘ *pl* centuries.

ceramic [sə'ræmɪk] *adj* de cerámica.
▶ *n* cerámica.

ceramics [sə'ræmɪks] *n (art)* cerámica; *(objects)* objetos *mpl* de cerámica.

cereal ['sɪərɪəl] *n (plant, grain)* cereal *m;* *(breakfast food)* cereales *mpl.*

cerebellum [serɪ'beləm] *n* cerebelo.

cerebral ['serɪbrəl] *adj* cerebral. COMP **cerebral palsy** parálisis *f* cerebral.

cerebrum ['serəbrəm] *n* cerebro.

ceremony ['serɪmənɪ] *n* ceremonia.
ⓘ *pl* ceremonies.

certain ['sɜːtən] *adj* **1** *(gen)* seguro,-a: *she's certain to pass* seguro que aprobará. **2** *(specific, particular)* cierto,-a. **4** *(named)* tal: *a certain Pedro Díaz* un tal Pedro Díaz.

certainly ['sɜːtənlɪ] *adv* **1** *(definitely, surely)* seguro. **2** *(when answering questions)* desde luego, por supuesto.

certainty ['sɜːtəntɪ] *n* certeza, seguridad *f.*
ⓘ *pl* certainties.

certificate [sə'tɪfɪkət] *n (gen)* certificado: *birth certificate* partida de nacimiento.

certify ['sɜːtɪfaɪ] *vt* certificar.
ⓘ *pt & pp* certified, *ger* certifying.

cervical ['sɜːvɪkəl] *adj* **1** *(of neck)* cervical. **2** *(of uterus)* del (cuello del) útero. COMP **cervical cancer** cáncer *m* de útero. ‖ **cervical vertebrae** vértebras cervicales.

cervix ['sɜːvɪks] *n* **1** *fml (neck)* cerviz *f,* cuello. **2** *(uterus)* cuello del útero.
ⓘ *pl* cervixes o cervices.

cesium ['si:zɪəm] *n* US → **caesium.**

cesspit ['sespɪt] *n* pozo negro.

cetacean [sɪ'teɪʃ³n] *adj* cetáceo,-a.
▶ *n* cetáceo.

chafe [tʃeɪf] *vt* **1** *(make sore)* rozar, excoriar. **2** *(make warm)* frotar, friccionar.
▶ *vi* irritarse.

chain [tʃeɪn] *n* **1** *(metal rings)* cadena. **2** *(of shops, hotels, etc)* cadena; *(of events)* cadena, serie *f.* COMP **chain reaction** reacción en cadena. ‖ **mountain chain** cordillera, cadena montañosa.
▶ *vt* encadenar, atar.

chair [tʃeəʳ] *n (gen)* silla; *(with arms)* sillón *m*, butaca. LOC **to address the chair** dirigirse al presidente, dirigirse a la presidencia. COMP **chair lift** telesilla.
▸ *vt (meeting)* presidir.

chairman [ˈtʃeəmən] *n* presidente *m*.
ⓘ *pl* chairmen [ˈtʃeəmen].

chairmanship [ˈtʃeəmənʃɪp] *n* presidencia.

chairperson [ˈtʃeəpɜːsᵊn] *n* presidente,-a.

chairwoman [ˈtʃeəwʊmən] *n* presidenta.
ⓘ *pl* chairwomen [ˈtʃeəwɪmɪn].

chaise longue [ʃeɪzˈlɒŋ] *n* diván *m*.

chalet [ˈʃæleɪ] *n* chalet *m*, chalé *m*.

chalice [ˈtʃælɪs] *n* cáliz *m*.

chalk [tʃɔːk] *n* **1** *(mineral)* creta, roca caliza. **2** *(for writing)* tiza.
◆ **to chalk up** *vt insep fam (victory, success)* apuntarse.

challenge [ˈtʃælɪndʒ] *n* reto, desafío.
▸ *vt* **1** *(invite to compete)* retar, desafiar. **2** *(statement)* poner en duda, cuestionar.

challenger [ˈtʃælɪndʒəʳ] *n (for title, leadership)* aspirante *mf*; *(opponent, rival)* contrincante *mf*, rival *mf*.

challenging [ˈtʃælɪndʒɪŋ] *adj (task, job, problem)* que supone un reto; *(idea)* estimulante; *(look, tone)* desafiante.

chamber [ˈtʃeɪmbəʳ] *n* **1** *(gen)* cámara. **2** *(of gun)* recámara.

chambermaid [ˈtʃeɪmbəmeɪd] *n* camarera (de hotel).

chameleon [kəˈmiːlɪən] *n* camaleón *m*.

champagne [ʃæmˈpeɪn] *n (French)* champán *m*, champaña; *(Catalan)* cava *m*.

champion [ˈtʃæmpɪən] *n* **1** campeón, -ona. **2** *fig (defender)* defensor,-ra, paladín,-ina.
▸ *adj* premiado,-a.
▸ *vt fig* defender, abogar por.

championship [ˈtʃæmpɪənʃɪp] *n* SP campeonato.

chance [tʃɑːns] *n* **1** *(fate, fortune)* azar *m*, casualidad *f*. **2** *(opportunity)* oportunidad *f*, ocasión *f*: *you won't get another chance like this* no se te presentará otra oportunidad como ésta. **3** *(possibility, likelihood)* posibilidad *f*. LOC **by chance** por casualidad.
▸ *adj (meeting, discovery, occurrence)* fortuito,-a, casual.
▸ *vt (risk)* arriesgar.

chancellor [ˈtʃɑːnsᵊləʳ] *n* **1** POL canciller *m*. **2** GB *(of university)* rector,-ra. COMP **Chancellor of the Exchequer** GB ministro,-a de Hacienda.

chancy [ˈtʃɑːnsɪ] *adj fam* arriesgado,-a.
ⓘ *comp* chancier, *superl* chanciest.

chandelier [ʃændəˈlɪəʳ] *n* araña.

change [tʃeɪndʒ] *n* **1** *(gen)* cambio. **2** *(of clothes)* muda. **3** *(coins)* cambio, monedas *fpl*; *(money returned)* cambio, vuelta.
▸ *vi* cambiar, cambiarse.

changeable [ˈtʃeɪndʒəbᵊl] *adj* variable.

changeless [ˈtʃeɪndʒləs] *adj* inmutable.

changing [ˈtʃeɪndʒɪŋ] *adj* cambiante.
COMP **changing room** vestuario.
▸ *n* MIL cambio, relevo.

channel [ˈtʃænᵊl] *n* **1** *(gen)* canal *m*. **2** *(on television)* canal *m*, cadena.

chant [tʃɑːnt] *n* **1** REL canto litúrgico, cántico. **2** *(of crowd)* eslogan *m*, consigna.

chaos [ˈkeɪɒs] *n* caos *m*.

chaotic [keɪˈɒtɪk] *adj* caótico,-a.

chap [tʃæp] *n fam* tío, tipo.

chapel [ˈtʃæpᵊl] *n* capilla.

chaplain [ˈtʃæplɪn] *n* capellán *m*.

chapter [ˈtʃæptəʳ] *n* capítulo.

char [tʃɑːʳ] *vt* chamuscar, carbonizar.
ⓘ *pt & pp* charred, *ger* charring.

character [ˈkærəktəʳ] *n* **1** *(gen)* carácter *m*. **2** *(in film, book, play)* personaje *m*.

characteristic [kærəktəˈrɪstɪk] *adj* característico,-a.
▸ *n* característica.

characterize [ˈkærəktəraɪz] *vt (gen)* caracterizar; *(describe character of)* calificar (as, de).

chard [tʃɑːd] *n* acelgas *fpl*.

charge [tʃɑːdʒ] *n* **1** *(price)* precio; *(fee(s))* honorarios *mpl*. **2** *(responsibility)* cargo. **3** JUR cargo, acusación *f*. **4** MIL *(attack)* carga. **5** *(explosive)* carga explosiva. **6** ELEC carga.
▸ *vt* **1** *(ask as a price - customer, amount)* cobrar; *(record as debit)* cargar. **2** JUR

acusar (with, de). **3** ELEC cargar. **4** MIL cargar contra, atacar.

charger ['tʃɑːdʒəʳ] *n* **1** ELEC cargador *m*. **2** *(horse)* corcel *m*.

chariot ['tʃærɪət] *n* cuadriga, carro.

charisma [kə'rɪzmə] *n* carisma *m*.

charitable ['tʃærɪtəbəl] *adj* **1** *(person)* caritativo,-a. **2** *(organization)* benéfico,-a.

charity ['tʃærɪtɪ] *n* **1** *(gen)* caridad *f*. **2** *(organization)* institución *f* benéfica.
ⓘ *pl* charities.

charlatan ['ʃɑːlətᵊn] *n* embaucador,-a.

> ✗ Charlatan no significa 'charlatán (que habla mucho)', que se traduce por chatterbox.

charm [tʃɑːm] *n* **1** *(quality)* encanto. **2** *(object)* amuleto. **3** *(spell)* hechizo.
▶ *vt* encantar.

charmer ['tʃɑːməʳ] *n* **1** *(charming person)* persona encantadora. **2** *(of snakes)* encantador,-ra.

charming ['tʃɑːmɪŋ] *adj (delightful)* encantador,-ra.

chart [tʃɑːt] *n* **1** *(table)* tabla; *(graph)* gráfico *m*. *(map)* carta, mapa *m*. **2** *(navigational)* carta de navegación.
▶ *vt (make a map of)* trazar un mapa de; *(plan, plot on map)* trazar.
▶ *n pl* **the charts** MUS la lista de éxitos, el hit parade *m*.

charter ['tʃɑːtəʳ] *n* **1** *(gen)* estatutos *mpl*; *(of town)* fuero. **2** *(constitution)* carta. **3** *(hiring of plane, etc)* fletamiento.
▶ *vt* **1** *(grant rights, privileges to)* aprobar los estatutos de. **2** *(hire plane, boat, etc)* fletar, alquilar.

chartered ['tʃɑːtəd] *adj (qualified)* colegiado,-a. COMP **chartered accountant** contable *mf* diplomado,-a.

chase [tʃeɪs] *n* *(gen)* persecución *f*; *(hunt)* caza.
▶ *vt (gen)* perseguir; *(hunt)* cazar.

chasm ['kæzᵊm] *n* **1** GEOG sima. **2** *fig* abismo.

chassis ['ʃæsɪ] *n* chasis *m*.
ⓘ *pl* chassis.

chaste [tʃeɪst] *adj* **1** *(pure)* casto,-a, puro, -a. **2** *(not ornate)* sobrio,-a, sencillo,-a.

chastise [tʃæs'taɪz] *vt fml* castigar.

chastity ['tʃæstɪtɪ] *n* castidad *f*.

chat [tʃæt] *n* **1** *(in general)* charla. **2** *(on Internet)* charla, chat *m*.

chatter ['tʃætəʳ] *n* **1** *(rapid talk)* cháchara, parloteo. **2** *(of teeth)* castañeteo.
▶ *vi* **1** *(talk rapidly)* chacharear, parlotear, cotorrear. **2** *(teeth)* castañetear.

chatterbox ['tʃætəbɒks] *n fam* parlanchín,-ina, charlatán,-ana.

chatty ['tʃætɪ] *adj (person)* hablador,-ra, parlanchín,-ina.
ⓘ *comp* chattier, *superl* chattiest.

chauffeur ['ʃəʊfəʳ] *n* chófer *mf*, chofer *mf*.

chauvinism ['ʃəʊvɪnɪzᵊm] *n* chovinismo.

cheap [tʃiːp] *adj* **1** *(gen)* barato,-a. **2** *(of poor quality, shoddy)* ordinario,-a. **3** *(contemptible - trick, gibe, crook)* vil, bajo,-a; *(vulgar - joke, remark)* de mal gusto.
▶ *adv* barato.

cheapen ['tʃiːpᵊn] *vt* **1** *(in price)* abaratar. **2** *(degrade)* degradar, rebajar.

cheat [tʃiːt] *n* **1** *(gen)* tramposo,-a; *(swindler)* estafador,-ra. **2** *(trick)* trampa; *(swindle)* estafa, timo.
▶ *vt (trick, deceive)* engañar; *(swindle)* estafar, timar.
▶ *vi (gen)* hacer trampa(s); *(in exam)* copiar.

check [tʃek] *n* **1** *(gen)* revisión *f*, control *m*; *(of machine)* verificación *f*, inspección *f*; *(of results, facts, information)* comprobación *f*, verificación *f*. **2** *(stop, restraint)* control *m*, freno. **3** US → **cheque**. **4** US *(bill)* cuenta, nota. **5** *(chess)* jaque *m*.
▶ *vi (make sure)* comprobar, verificar.
◆ **to check in** *vi (at airport)* facturar el equipaje; *(at hotel)* registrarse.
▶ *vt sep* facturar.
◆ **to check out** *vi* pagar la cuenta e irse, dejar el hotel.
▶ *vt sep (facts, information)* verificar, comprobar; *(place)* ir a ver; *(person)* hacer averiguaciones sobre.

checked [tʃekt] *adj* a cuadros.

checkers ['tʃekəz] *n pl* US damas *fpl*.

checkmate ['tʃekmeɪt] *n* (jaque *m*) mate *m*.
▶ *vt* dar (jaque) mate a.

checkout ['tʃekaʊt] *n* *(in supermarket)* caja.

checkpoint ['tʃekpɔɪnt] *n* control *m*.

checkroom ['tʃekruːm] *n* US guardarropa.

check-up ['tʃekʌp] *n (by doctor)* chequeo, reconocimiento médico.

cheek [tʃiːk] *n* **1** ANAT mejilla. **2** *fam (nerve, impudence)* descaro, cara.

cheekbone ['tʃiːkbəʊn] *n* pómulo.

cheeky ['tʃiːkɪ] *adj (person)* descarado, -a, fresco,-a; *(remark)* impertinente.
① *comp* cheekier, *superl* cheekiest.

cheer [tʃɪəʳ] *n* **1** *(shout of joy)* viva *m*, vítor *m*, hurra *m*. **2** *(happiness)* alegría.
▶ *vt* **1** *(applaud with shouts)* vitorear, aclamar. **2** *(gladden)* animar, alegrar.
◆ **to cheer up** *vt sep* animar, alegrar.
▶ *vi* animarse, alegrarse: *cheer up!* ¡ánimo!

cheerful ['tʃɪəfʊl] *adj* alegre.

cheerio ['tʃɪərɪˈəʊ] *interj* GB *fam* ¡adiós!, ¡hasta luego!

cheerleader ['tʃɪəliːdəʳ] *n* animador, -ra (de un equipo deportivo).

cheers [tʃɪəz] *interj* **1** *fam (as toast)* ¡salud! **2** *fam (thanks)* ¡gracias! **3** *fam (goodbye)* ¡adiós!, ¡hasta luego!

cheese [tʃiːz] *n* queso.

cheetah ['tʃiːtə] *n* guepardo.

chef [ʃef] *n* chef *m*, jefe,-a de cocina.

chemical ['kemɪkəl] *adj* químico,-a.
▶ *n* sustancia química.

chemist ['kemɪst] *n* **1** CHEM químico, -a. **2** GB *(pharmacist)* farmacéutico,-a.
COMP **chemist's (shop)** GB farmacia.

chemistry ['kemɪstrɪ] *n* química.

chemotherapy [kiːməʊˈθerəpɪ] *n* quimioterapia.

cheque [tʃek] *n* cheque *m*, talón *m*.

chequebook ['tʃekbʊk] *n* talonario de cheques.

chequered ['tʃekəd] *adj* **1** *(cloth, pattern)* a cuadros. **2** *fig (past, history, career)* con altibajos, accidentado,-a.

chequers ['tʃekəz] *n pl* damas *fpl*.

cherish ['tʃerɪʃ] *vt* **1** *(person)* apreciar, querer. **2** *(hope, memory, illusion)* abrigar.

cherry ['tʃerɪ] *n (fruit)* cereza, guinda; *(wood)* cerezo. COMP **cherry tree** cerezo.
① *pl* cherries.

chess [tʃes] *n* ajedrez *m*: *a game of chess* una partida de ajedrez.

chessboard ['tʃesbɔːd] *n* tablero de ajedrez.

chessmen ['tʃesmən] *n pl* piezas *fpl* de ajedrez.

chest [tʃest] *n* **1** *(large)* arca, arcón *m*; *(small)* cofre *m*. **2** ANAT pecho.

chestnut ['tʃesnʌt] *n* **1** BOT *(tree, wood)* castaño; *(nut)* castaña. **2** *(colour)* castaño. **3** *(horse)* alazán,-ana.
▶ *adj (colour)* castaño,-a; *(horse)* alazán,-ana.

chew [tʃuː] *vt (food)* mascar, masticar; *(nails, pencil)* morder.

chewing gum ['tʃuːɪŋɡʌm] *n* chicle *m*.

chic [ʃiːk] *adj* chic, elegante.
▶ *n* elegancia.

chick [tʃɪk] *n* polluelo.

chicken ['tʃɪkɪn] *n* **1** *(hen)* gallina; *(food)* pollo. **2** *fam (coward)* gallina *mf*.
▶ *adj fam* gallina.

chickenpox ['tʃɪkɪnpɒks] *n* varicela.

chickpea ['tʃɪkpiː] *n* garbanzo.

chicory ['tʃɪkərɪ] *n* achicoria, chicoria.

chief [tʃiːf] *n (gen)* jefe,-a; *(of party)* líder *mf*; *(of tribe)* cacique *m*.
▶ *adj* principal.

chiefly ['tʃiːflɪ] *adv (mainly)* principalmente; *(especially)* sobre todo.

chieftain ['tʃiːftən] *n* cacique *m*, jefe,-a.

chiffon ['ʃɪfɒn] *n* gasa.

chilblain ['tʃɪlbleɪn] *n* sabañón *m*.

child [tʃaɪld] *n* **1** *(boy)* niño; *(girl)* niña. **2** *(son)* hijo; *(daughter)* hija.
① *pl* children.

childbirth ['tʃaɪldbɜːθ] *n* parto.

childhood ['tʃaɪldhʊd] *n* infancia.

childish ['tʃaɪldɪʃ] *adj (of a child)* infantil; *(immature)* pueril, infantil.

childlike ['tʃaɪldlaɪk] *adj* infantil.

children ['tʃɪldrən] *n pl* → **child**.

chili ['tʃɪlɪ] *n* US → **chilli**.

chill [tʃɪl] *n* MED *(cold)* resfriado; *(shiver)* escalofrío.
▶ *adj (wind, etc)* frío,-a.
▶ *vt* enfriar.

chilli ['tʃɪlɪ] *n* chile *m*.

chilling ['tʃɪlɪŋ] *adj* **1** glacial. **2** *fig* espeluznante, escalofriante.

chilly ['tʃɪlɪ] *adj (gen)* frío,-a.
① *comp* chillier, *superl* chilliest.

chime [tʃaɪm] *n (bells)* carillón *m*; *(sound of bells)* repique *m*; *(of clock)* campanada; *(of doorbell)* campanilla.
▶ *vi (bells)* sonar, repicar; *(clock)* dar la hora, sonar.

chimney ['tʃɪmnɪ] *n* chimenea.

✎ Chimney sólo se refiere al conducto por donde sale el humo. El hogar se traduce por fireplace.

chimpanzee [tʃɪmpænˈziː] *n* chimpancé *m*.

chin [tʃɪn] *n* barbilla, mentón *m*.

china ['tʃaɪnə] *n* **1** *(white clay)* loza; *(fine)* porcelana. **2** *(crockery)* vajilla, objetos *mpl* de porcelana, loza.

China ['tʃaɪnə] *n* China.

Chinese [tʃaɪˈniːz] *adj* chino,-a.
▶ *n* **1** *(person)* chino,-a. **2** *(language)* chino.

chink¹ [tʃɪŋk] *n* grieta, abertura.

chink² [tʃɪŋk] *n (noise)* tintineo.
▶ *vt* hacer tintinear, hacer sonar.

chip [tʃɪp] *n* **1** GB *(fried potato)* patata frita. **2** US patata frita (de bolsa). **3** COMPUT chip *m*. **4** *(of wood)* astilla; *(of stone)* lasca. **5** *(flaw - in plate, glass)* desportilladura. **6** *(in gambling)* ficha.
▶ *vt* **1** GB *(potatoes)* cortar. **2** *(china, glass)* desportillar; *(paint)* desconchar.
① *pt & pp* chipped, *ger* chipping.

chipboard ['tʃɪpbɔːd] *n* aglomerado, madera aglomerada.

chiropodist [kɪˈrɒpədɪst] *n* podólogo, -a, pedicuro,-a, callista *mf*.

chirp [tʃɜːp] *vi (insect)* chirriar; *(bird)* gorjear.

chisel ['tʃɪzəl] *n (for stone)* cincel *m*.
▶ *vt (stone)* cincelar; *(wood, metal)* labrar, tallar.
① *pt & pp* chiselled *(US* chiseled*)*, *ger* chiselling *(US* chiseling*)*.

chit [tʃɪt] *n fam (note)* nota.

chitchat ['tʃɪttʃæt] *n fam* palique *m*, cháchara.

chives [tʃaɪvz] *n pl* BOT cebollino, cebolleta.

chloride ['klɔːraɪd] *n* cloruro.

chlorine ['klɔːriːn] *n* cloro.

chloroform ['klɒrəfɔːm] *n* cloroformo.

chlorophyll ['klɒrəfɪl] *n* clorofila.

chock [tʃɒk] *n* calzo, cuña.

chock-a-block [tʃɒkəˈblɒk] *adj fam* hasta los topes, de bote en bote.

chock-full [tʃɒkˈful] *adj fam* hasta los topes.

chocolate ['tʃɒkələt] *n* **1** *(substance)* chocolate *m*: *a bar of chocolate* una chocolatina, una tableta de chocolate. **2** *(individual sweet)* bombón *m*.

choice [tʃɔɪs] *n* **1** *(act)* elección *f*, opción *f*. **2** *(person, thing chosen)* elección *f*. **3** *(variety, range)* surtido, selección *f*.
▶ *adj* **1** *(top quality)* selecto,-a, de primera calidad.

choir ['kwaɪəʳ] *n* coro.

choke [tʃəuk] *vt* **1** *(person)* ahogar, asfixiar, estrangular. **2** *(block - pipe, drain, etc)* atascar, obstruir.
▶ *n* estárter *m*.

☒ Choke no significa 'choque', que se traduce por collision.

cholera ['kɒlərə] *n* cólera *m*.

cholesterol [kəˈlestərɒl] *n* colesterol *m*.

choose [tʃuːz] *vt* **1** *(select)* escoger, elegir; *(elect)* elegir. **2** *(decide)* decidir, optar por.
① *pt* chose [tʃəuz], *pp* chosen ['tʃəuzən], *ger* choosing.

choosy ['tʃuːzɪ] *adj fam* exigente.
① *comp* choosier, *superl* choosiest.

chop [tʃɒp] *n* **1** *(blow)* tajo, golpe *m*; *(with axe)* hachazo. **2** CULIN chuleta.
▶ *vt* cortar (up, -).
◆ **to chop down** *vt sep (tree, etc)* talar.
◆ **to chop off** *vt sep* cortar.
① *pt & pp* chopped, *ger* chopping.

choppy ['tʃɒpɪ] *adj (sea)* picado,-a.
① *comp* choppier, *superl* choppiest.

chopsticks ['tʃɒpstɪks] *n pl* palillos *mpl*.

choral ['kɔːrəl] *adj* coral. COMP **choral society** coral *f*, orfeón *m*.

chorale [kəˈrɑːl] *n* coral *f*.

chord[1] [kɔːd] n **1** MATH cuerda. **2** ANAT → cord.

chord[2] [kɔːd] n MUS acorde m.

chore [tʃɔːʳ] n (job) quehacer m, tarea; (boring job) lata.

choreography [kɒrɪˈɒgrəfɪ] n coreografía.

chorister [ˈkɒrɪstəʳ] n corista mf.

chorus [ˈkɔːrəs] n **1** (choir) coro. **2** (of song) estribillo.

chose [tʃəʊz] pt → choose.

chosen [ˈtʃəʊzən] pp → choose.
▸ adj elegido,-a, escogido,-a.

Christ [kraɪst] n Cristo, Jesucristo.

christening [ˈkrɪsənɪŋ] n (ritual) bautismo; (celebration) bautizo.

Christian [ˈkrɪstɪən] adj & n cristiano,-a.

Christmas [ˈkrɪsməs] n Navidad f, Navidades fpl. COMP **Christmas Eve** Nochebuena. ❙ **Christmas Day** día m de Navidad.

chrome [krəʊm] n cromo.

chromosome [ˈkrəʊməsəʊm] n cromosoma m.

chronic [ˈkrɒnɪk] adj **1** (disease, person, problem) crónico,-a. **2** GB fam (terrible) malísimo,-a, terrible.

chronicle [ˈkrɒnɪkəl] n crónica.

chronological [krɒnəˈlɒdʒɪkəl] adj cronológico,-a.

chronology [krəˈnɒlədʒɪ] n cronología.

chronometer [krəˈnɒmɪtəʳ] n cronómetro.

chrysalis [ˈkrɪsəlɪs] n crisálida.
ⓘ pl chrysalises.

chrysanthemum [krɪˈsænθəməm] n crisantemo.

chubby [ˈtʃʌbɪ] adj (person) regordete,-a, gordinflón,-ona.
ⓘ comp chubbier, superl chubbiest.

chuck [tʃʌk] vt **1** fam (throw) tirar. **2** fam (give up) dejar, plantar.
◆ to **chuck away** vt sep (rubbish) tirar; (money) derrochar.

chuckle [ˈtʃʌkəl] vi reírse (entre dientes).
▸ n risita.

chum [tʃʌm] n fam compinche mf.

church [tʃɜːtʃ] n iglesia. COMP **Church of England** Iglesia Anglicana.

churchyard [ˈtʃɜːtʃjɑːd] n cementerio, camposanto.

churn [tʃɜːn] n **1** GB (for milk) lechera. **2** (for butter) mantequera.
▸ vt **1** (butter) hacer; (milk, cream) batir. **2** (water, earth) agitar (up, -), revolver (up, -).
◆ to **churn out** vt sep producir en serie, hacer como churros.

chute [ʃuːt] n (slide) tobogán m.

cicada [sɪˈkɑːdə] n cigarra.

cider [ˈsaɪdəʳ] n sidra.

cigar [sɪˈgɑːʳ] n puro, cigarro.

cigarette [sɪgəˈret] n cigarrillo.

cinder [ˈsɪndəʳ] n ceniza, pavesa.

Cinderella [sɪndəˈrelə] n (la) Cenicienta.

cinema [ˈsɪnəmə] n cine m.

cinnamon [ˈsɪnəmən] n canela.

cipher [ˈsaɪfəʳ] n **1** (code) código, clave f. **2** (zero) cero; (numeral) cifra.

circle [ˈsɜːkəl] n círculo.
▸ vt (encircle) rodear, cercar; (move in a circle) dar vueltas alrededor de.

circuit [ˈsɜːkɪt] n **1** (route, journey round) recorrido; (of running track) vuelta. **2** ELEC circuito. **3** SP (series of tournaments) circuito.

circular [ˈsɜːkjələʳ] adj circular.

circulate [ˈsɜːkjəleɪt] vi circular.
▸ vt hacer circular.

circulation [sɜːkjəˈleɪʃən] n **1** (gen) circulación f. **2** (of newspaper, magazine) tirada.

circulatory [sɜːkjəˈleɪtərɪ] adj circulatorio,-a.

circumcision [sɜːkəmˈsɪʒən] n circuncisión f.

circumference [səˈkʌmfərəns] n circunferencia.

circumflex [ˈsɜːkəmfleks] n circunflejo.

circumstance [ˈsɜːkəmstəns] n (condition, fact) circunstancia.
▸ n pl **circumstances** (financial position) situación f económica.

circus [ˈsɜːkəs] n **1** (entertainment) circo. **2** GB (in town) glorieta, plaza redonda.

cistern [ˈsɪstən] n cisterna.

cite [saɪt] vt citar.

citizen [ˈsɪtɪzən] n ciudadano,-a.

citizenship [ˈsɪtɪzənʃɪp] n ciudadanía.

citric [ˈsɪtrɪk] adj cítrico,-a.

city ['sɪtɪ] n ciudad f. ⸤COMP⸥ **city council** GB ayuntamiento, municipio. ∥ **the City** GB el centro financiero de Londres. ① pl **cities**.

⊕ La City de Londres es el barrio original a partir del cual creció la actual metrópoli. Hoy en día, concentra las sedes de las grandes empresas y es unos de los centros económicos más importantes del mundo.

civic ['sɪvɪk] adj (duty, pride) cívico,-a; (leader, event) municipal.

civics ['sɪvɪks] n educación f cívica.

civil ['sɪvɪl] adj 1 (of citizens) civil. 2 (polite) cortés,-esa, educado,-a. ⸤COMP⸥ **civil servant** funcionario,-a. ∥ **the Civil Service** la administración pública.

civilian [sɪ'vɪljən] adj civil. ⸤LOC⸥ **in civilian dress** de paisano.
  ► n civil mf.
  ► n pl **civilians** población f sing civil.

civility [sɪ'vɪlɪtɪ] n cortesía.

civilization [sɪvɪlaɪ'zeɪʃ°n] n civilización f.

civilize ['sɪvɪlaɪz] vt civilizar.

clad [klæd] pt & pp → **clothe**.
  ► adj vestido,-a.

claim [kleɪm] n 1 (demand - for insurance) reclamación f; (for benefit, allowance) solicitud f. 2 (assertion) afirmación f.
  ► vt 1 (gen) reclamar. 2 (apply for) solicitar. 3 (of disaster, accident, etc) cobrar. 4 (assert) afirmar, sostener, decir.
  ► vi presentar un reclamación.

claimant ['kleɪmənt] n 1 (of benefit, allowance) solicitante mf; (of insurance) reclamante mf. 2 (to throne) pretendiente mf. 3 JUR demandante mf.

clam [klæm] n almeja.

clamber ['klæmbər] vi trepar gateando (over, a).

clammy ['klæmɪ] adj (weather) bochornoso,-a; (hands) pegajoso,-a. ① comp **clammier**, superl **clammiest**.

clamor ['klæmər] n US → **clothe**.

clamour ['klæmər] n clamor m.
  ► vi clamar.

clamp [klæmp] n abrazadera.
  ► vt sujetar con abrazaderas.

◆**to clamp down on** vt insep poner freno a, tomar medidas drásticas contra.

clan [klæn] n clan m.

clandestine [klæn'destɪn] adj clandestino,-a.

clang [klæŋ] n sonido metálico (fuerte).
  ► vi sonar.

clap [klæp] n 1 (noise) ruido seco. 2 (applause) aplauso. 3 (slap) palmada.
  ► vt 1 (applaud) aplaudir. 2 (slap) dar una palmada a.

◆**to clap on** vt sep (add) agregar.

clapperboard ['klæpəbɔːd] n claqueta.

clapping ['klæpɪŋ] n aplausos mpl.

claret ['klærət] n (wine) clarete m.

clarify ['klærɪfaɪ] vt aclarar.
  ① pt & pp **clarified**, ger **clarifying**.

clarinet [klærɪ'net] n clarinete m.

clarity ['klærɪtɪ] n claridad f.

clash [klæʃ] n 1 (fight) enfrentamiento, choque m; (disagreement, argument) desacuerdo. 2 (conflict - of interests) conflicto; (- of personalities, cultures, opinions) choque m. 3 (loud noise) sonido.
  ► vi 1 (opposing forces - fight) chocar; (- disagree) discutir, enfrentarse (with, a). 2 (interests) estar en conflicto. 3 (dates, events) coincidir. 4 (colours) desentonar (with, con). 5 (cymbals) sonar.

clasp [klɑːsp] n (on necklace) broche m; (on belt) cierre m, hebilla.
  ► vt agarrar, sujetar.

class [klɑːs] n clase f.
  ► vt clasificar, catalogar.

classic ['klæsɪk] adj clásico,-a.
  ► n (novel, film, play) clásico.
  ► n pl **classics** (literature) clásicos mpl; (languages) clásicas fpl.

classical ['klæsɪk°l] adj (gen) clásico,-a.

classification [klæsɪfɪ'keɪʃ°n] n clasificación f.

classified ['klæsɪfaɪd] adj 1 (categorized) clasificado,-a. 2 (secret) secreto,-a, confidencial.

classify ['klæsɪfaɪ] vt clasificar.
  ① pt & pp **classified**, ger **classifying**.

classmate ['klɑːsmeɪt] n compañero,-a de clase.

classroom ['klɑːsrʊːm] n aula, clase f.

classy [ˈklɑːsɪ] *adj sl* con clase.
  ① *comp* **classier**, *superl* **classiest**.

clatter [ˈklætəʳ] *n* ruido.
  ▶ *vi* hacer ruido.

clause [klɔːz] *n* **1** *(in document)* cláusula. **2** LING oración *f*.

claustrophobia [klɔːstrəˈfəʊbɪə] *n* claustrofobia.

claustrophobic [klɔːstrəˈfəʊbɪk] *adj* claustrofóbico,-a.

clavichord [ˈklævɪkɔːd] *n* clavicordio.

clavicle [ˈklævɪkəl] *n* clavícula.

claw [klɔː] *n* **1** *(of lion, tiger, etc)* garra, zarpa; *(of cat)* uña; *(of bird)* garra; *(of crab, lobster)* pinza.
  ▶ *vi (scratch)* arañar (at, -).

clay [kleɪ] *n* arcilla.

clean [kliːn] *adj* limpio,-a.
  ▶ *vt (gen)* limpiar.
  ▶ *vi* limpiarse.
  ◆ **to clean out** *vt sep* **1** *(room, etc)* limpiar a fondo. **2** *fam (take all money)* dejar limpio,-a, dejar sin blanca.
  ◆ **to clean up** *vt sep* **1** *(room, mess, etc)* limpiar. **2** *fam (money, fortune)* hacer, sacar.
  ▶ *vi* **1** *(room, etc)* limpiar. **2** *fam (make money)* forrarse, barrer con todo.

clean-cut [kliːnˈkʌt] *adj (outline, feature)* bien definido,-a, nítido,-a; *(person, appearance)* limpio,-a, muy cuidado,-a.

cleaner [ˈkliːnəʳ] *n* **1** *(person)* encargado, -a de la limpieza. **2** *(product)* limpiador *m*.
  ▶ *n* **cleaner's** *(place, shop)* tintorería.

cleanse [klenz] *vt* limpiar (of, de).

cleanser [ˈklenzəʳ] *n (detergent)* producto de limpieza; *(lotion for skin)* leche *f* limpiadora, crema limpiadora.

cleansing [ˈklenzɪŋ] *n* limpieza.

clear [klɪəʳ] *adj* **1** *(glass, plastic, liquid)* transparente; *(sky, day, etc)* despejado,-a. **2** *(not blocked - road, desk)* despejado,-a; *(free - time)* libre. **3** *(picture, outline)* nítido, -a. **4** *(voice, sound, explanation)* claro,-a.
  ▶ *adv* **1** *(clearly - speak)* claramente; *(hear)* bien. **2** *(not touching)* a distancia.
  ▶ *vt* **1** *(table)* quitar; *(floor, road)* despejar; *(pipe, drain)* desatascar; *(building, room - of people)* desalojar, desocupar;

(house, room - of furniture) vaciar. **2** *(accused person)* absolver, exculpar; *(one's name)* limpiar. **3** *(debt)* liquidar, saldar. **4** *(obstacle)* salvar. **5** SP *(ball)* despejar.
  ◆ **to clear away** *vt sep (dishes, etc)* recoger, quitar.1

  ◆ **to clear off** *vi fam* largarse.
  ▶ *vt sep (debt)* liquidar.

  ◆ **to clear out** *vi fam* largarse.
  ▶ *vt sep (cupboard, drawers, room)* vaciar; *(old things)* tirar.

  ◆ **to clear up** *vt sep* **1** *(mystery, crime)* resolver, esclarecer; *(issue, misunderstanding)* aclarar; *(loose ends)* atar. **2** *(tidy)* recoger.
  ▶ *vi* **1** *(tidy)* ordenar. **2** *(weather)* despejar, mejorar.

clearance [ˈklɪərəns] *n* **1** SP despeje *m*. **2** *(permission)* autorización *f*. COMP **clearance sale** liquidación *f*.

clear-cut [klɪəˈkʌt] *adj* claro,-a, bien definido,-a.

clear-headed [klɪəˈhedɪd] *adj* lúcido,-a, despejado,-a.

clearing [ˈklɪərɪŋ] *n (in wood)* claro.

clearness [ˈklɪənəs] *n* claridad *f*.

clear-sighted [klɪəˈsaɪtɪd] *adj* perspicaz, lúcido,-a.

clef [klef] *n* MUS clave *f*: *bass/treble clef* clave de fa/de sol.

cleft [kleft] *adj (chin, lip)* partido,-a.
  ▶ *n* hendidura, grieta.

clementine [ˈklem.əntaɪn] *n* clementina.

clench [klentʃ] *vt* **1** *(teeth, fist)* apretar. **2** *(grip)* apretar, agarrar.

clergy [ˈklɜːdʒɪ] *n* clero.

clergyman [ˈklɜːdʒɪmən] *n* clérigo.
  ① *pl* **clergymen** [ˈklɜːdʒɪmən].

clerical [ˈklerɪkəl] *adj* **1** REL clerical, eclesiástico,-a. **2** *(of a clerk)* de oficina, administrativo,-a.

clerk [klɑːk, US klɜːrk] *n* **1** *(office worker)* oficinista *mf*, administrativo,-a. **2** US *(in a shop)* dependiente,-a *mf*.

clever [ˈklevəʳ] *adj* **1** *(person - intelligent)* listo,-a, inteligente; *(skilful)* hábil. **2** *(idea, plan, gadget)* ingenioso,-a; *(move)* hábil.

cliché [ˈkliːʃeɪ] *n* cliché *m*, tópico.

click [klɪk] n *(sound - gen)* clic m; *(of tongue, fingers)* chasquido.
　▸ vt *(tongue, fingers)* chasquear.
　▸ vi **1** *(make noise)* hacer clic. **2** *(understand, realize)* caer en la cuenta, darse cuenta de.

client ['klaɪənt] n cliente,-a.

cliff [klɪf] n acantilado, precipicio.

cliffhanger ['klɪfhæŋəʳ] n situación f de suspense.

climate ['klaɪmət] n **1** GEOG clima m. **2** *fig* clima m, situación f.

climatic [klaɪˈmætɪk] adj climático,-a.

climatological [klaɪmətəˈlɒdʒɪkəl] adj climatológico,-a.

climatology [klaɪməˈtɒlədʒɪ] n climatología.

climax ['klaɪmæks] n clímax m.

climb [klaɪm] n **1** *(gen)* subida. **2** SP escalada.
　▸ vt subir (a).
　▸ vi trepar.
　◆ **to climb down** vi **1** *(descend)* bajar. **2** *fig (admit mistake, withdraw)* ceder, volverse atrás.

climber ['klaɪməʳ] n **1** SP alpinista mf, escalador,-ra. **2** BOT enredadera.

climbing ['klaɪmɪŋ] n SP alpinismo, montañismo.

clinch [klɪntʃ] n **1** *fam (embrace)* abrazo apasionado. **2** SP *(in boxing)* cuerpo a cuerpo.
　▸ vt *fam (deal)* cerrar; *(argument)* resolver; *(title)* hacerse con.
　▸ vi SP *(in boxing)* abrazarse.

cling [klɪŋ] vi **1** *(hold tightly)* agarrarse (to, a). **2** *(stick - clothes)* pegarse, ceñirse; *(- smell)* pegarse.
　① pt & pp **clung** [klʌŋ].

clingfilm ['klɪŋfɪlm] n film m transparente.

clinic ['klɪnɪk] n **1** *(private, specialized)* clínica. **2** *(in state hospital)* ambulatorio, dispensario.

clink [klɪŋk] n *(noise)* tintineo.
　▸ vt hacer tintinear.
　▸ vi tintinear.

clip¹ [klɪp] n **1** *(with scissors)* tijeretada. **2** *(of film)* fragmento. **3** *fam (blow)* cachete m.

　▸ vt **1** *(cut - gen)* cortar; *(ticket)* picar; *(animals)* esquilar. **2** *(cut out)* recortar. **3** *fam (hit)* dar un cachete a.
　① pt & pp **clipped**, ger **clipping**.

clip² [klɪp] n **1** *(for papers, etc)* clip m; *(for hair)* pasador m, clip m. **2** *(brooch)* broche m, alfiler m de pecho.

clipboard ['klɪpbɔːd] n INFORM portapapeles m.

clippers ['klɪpəz] n pl *(for nails)* cortaúñas m sing; *(for hair)* maquinilla f sing.

clipping ['klɪpɪŋ] n *(cutting)* recorte m de periódico, recorte m de prensa.

clique [kliːk] n *pej* camarilla f.

clitoris ['klɪtərɪs] n clítoris m.

cloak [kləʊk] n **1** *(garment)* capa. **2** *fig (cover)* capa, manto.

cloakroom ['kləʊkruːm] n **1** *(gen)* guardarropa. **2** GB *euph (toilet)* lavabo, servicios mpl.

clock [klɒk] n reloj m (de pared).
　▸ vt **1** *(time - athlete, race)* cronometrar. **2** *(register - speed, time)* registrar, hacer.
　◆ **to clock in/on** vi fichar (al llegar al trabajo).
　◆ **to clock out/off** vi fichar (al salir del trabajo).
　◆ **to clock up** vt insep *(miles, hours)* hacer.

clockwise ['klɒkwaɪz] adv en el sentido de las agujas del reloj.

clog [klɒg] n *(shoe)* zueco.
　▸ vt [also **clog up**] obstruir, atascar.
　▸ vi [also **clog up**] obstruirse, atascarse.
　① pt & pp **clogged**, ger **clogging**.

cloister ['klɔɪstəʳ] n claustro.

clone [kləʊn] n clon m.
　▸ vt clonar.

close¹ [kləʊz] n **1** *(end)* fin m, final m. **2** *(precincts)* recinto.
　▸ vt cerrar.
　▸ vi **1** *(gen)* cerrar, cerrarse. **2** *(end)* concluir, terminar.
　◆ **to close up** vi **1** *(of wound)* cicatrizar, cerrarse. **2** *(shop, etc)* cerrar.

close² [kləʊs] adj **1** *(near)* cercano,-a (to, a), próximo,-a (to, a). **2** *(friend)* íntimo,-a; *(relation, family)* cercano,-a.
　▸ adv **1** *(in position)* cerca. **2** *(in time)* cerca.

closed [kləʊzd] adj cerrado,-a.

close-knit [kləʊsˈnɪt] *adj* unido,-a.

closely [ˈkləʊslɪ] *adv* **1** *(connect)* estrechamente, muy. **2** *(resemble)* mucho. **3** *(carefully - watch, listen)* atentamente; *(follow)* de cerca; *(question)* a fondo.

closet [ˈklɒzɪt] *n* US armario.

close-up [ˈkləʊsʌp] *n* primer plano.

closing [ˈkləʊzɪŋ] *n* cierre *m*.

closure [ˈkləʊʒəʳ] *n (gen)* cierre *m*; *(debate)* clausura.

clot [klɒt] *n* **1** *(of blood)* coágulo. **2** GB *fam* tonto,-a, bobo,-a.
► *vt* coagular.
► *vi (blood)* coagularse; *(cream)* cuajar.
ⓘ *pt & pp* clotted, *ger* clotting.

cloth [klɒθ] *n* **1** *(fabric)* tela; *(thick)* paño. **2** *(rag)* trapo.

✎ Consulta también clothes.

clothe [kləʊð] *vt* **1** *(dress, provide clothes for)* vestir (in/with, de). **2** *(cover)* revestir (in, de), cubrir (in, de).
ⓘ *pt & pp* clothed o clad [klæd], *ger* clothing.

clothes [kləʊðz] *n pl* ropa *f sing*.

clothing [ˈkləʊðɪŋ] *n* ropa.

cloud [klaʊd] *n* nube *f*.
◆ **to cloud over** *vi (sky)* nublarse; *(face, eyes)* empañarse.

cloudy [ˈklaʊdɪ] *adj* **1** *(sky, weather, day)* nublado,-a. **2** *(liquid)* turbio,-a.
ⓘ *comp* cloudier, *superl* cloudiest.

clout [klaʊt] *n* **1** *fam* tortazo. **2** *fam (influence)* influencia, peso.

clove¹ [kləʊv] *n (spice)* clavo.

clove² [kləʊv] *n (of garlic)* diente *f*.

clover [ˈkləʊvəʳ] *n* trébol *m*.

cloverleaf [ˈkləʊvəliːf] *n* BOT hoja de trébol.

clown [klaʊn] *n* payaso, clown *m*.

club [klʌb] *n* **1** *(gen)* club *m*. **2** *(stick)* porra. **3** SP *(in golf)* palo. **5** *(in cards - English pack)* trébol *m*; *(- Spanish pack)* basto.

cluck [klʌk] *n* cloqueo.
► *vi* cloquear.

clue [kluː] *n* pista.

clump [klʌmp] *n* **1** *(of trees)* grupo; *(of plants)* mata, macizo. **2** *(of earth)* terrón *m*.

clumsy [ˈklʌmzɪ] *adj* **1** *(gen)* torpe. **2** *(tool, shape)* pesado,-a y difícil de manejar; *(furniture)* mal diseñado,-a.
ⓘ *comp* clumsier, *superl* clumsiest.

clung [klʌŋ] *pt & pp* → cling.

cluster [ˈklʌstəʳ] *n (of trees, stars, buildings, people)* grupo; *(of berries, grapes)* racimo; *(of plants)* macizo.
► *vi* agruparse, apiñarse (round, alrededor de/en torno a).

clutch [klʌtʃ] *n* **1** AUTO embrague *m*. **2** *(grasp, grip)* agarrón *m*.
► *vt (seize)* agarrar; *(hold tightly)* estrechar, apretar.

clutter [ˈklʌtəʳ] *n (things)* cosas *fpl*, trastos *mpl*; *(untidy state)* desorden *m*.
► *vt [also* **to clutter up**] llenar, atestar, abarrotar.

cm [ˈsiːˈem] *symb* (centimetre) centímetro; *(symbol)* cm.

coach [kəʊtʃ] *n* **1** GB *(bus)* autocar *m*. **2** *(carriage)* carruaje *m*, coche *m* de caballos. **3** *(on train)* coche *m*, vagón *m*. **4** EDUC *(tutor)* profesor,-ra particular. **5** SP *(trainer)* entrenador,-ra.
► *vt* **1** EDUC dar clases particulares a, preparar. **2** SP entrenar.

coagulate [kəʊˈægjəleɪt] *vt* coagular.
► *vi* coagularse.

coagulation [kəʊægjəˈleɪʃən] *n* coagulación *f*.

coal [kəʊl] *n* carbón *m*, hulla.

coalition [kəʊəˈlɪʃən] *n* coalición *f*.

coarse [kɔːs] *adj* **1** *(fabric)* basto,-a; *(skin)* áspero,-a; *(sand, salt)* grueso,-a. **2** *(language, joke)* grosero,-a, vulgar.

coast [kəʊst] *n* costa, litoral *m*.
► *vi (in car)* ir en punto muerto; *(on bicycle)* ir sin pedalear.

coastal [ˈkəʊstəl] *adj* costero,-a.

coastguard [ˈkəʊstgɑːd] *n* guardacostas *mf*.

coat [kəʊt] *n* **1** *(overcoat)* abrigo; *(short)* chaquetón *m*. **2** *(of paint)* capa, mano *f*; *(of dust)* capa. **3** *(of animal)* pelo, pelaje *m*.
► *vt* **1** cubrir (in/with, de).

coating [ˈkəʊtɪŋ] *n* **1** CULIN capa, baño. **2** *(of paint, dust, wax)* capa; *(of metal)* revestimiento.

coax [kəuks] *vt (person)* engatusar.

coaxial [kəu'æks[ə]l] *adj* coaxial.

cob [kɒb] *n (of corn)* mazorca (de maíz).

cobble [kɒb°l] *n* adoquín *m*.
▶ *vt (street)* adoquinar.

cobblestone [kɒb°lstəun] *n* adoquín *m*.

cobweb [kɒbweb] *n* telaraña.

cocaine [kə'keɪn] *n* cocaína.

coccyx [kɒksɪks] *n* coxis *m*, cóccix *m*.
ⓘ *pl* coccyxes o coccyges.

cochineal [kɒtʃɪ'ni:l] *n* cochinilla.

cochlea [kɒklɪə] *n* caracol *m* del oído.

cock [kɒk] *n* **1** *(rooster)* gallo; *(any male bird)* macho. **2** *(on firearm)* percutor *m*.

cockle [kɒk°l] *n* berberecho.

Cockney [kɒknɪ] *adj del barrio obrero del este de Londres.*
▶ *n* **1** *(person) persona del barrio obrero del este de Londres.* **2** *(dialect) dialecto que se habla en el barrio obrero del este de Londres.*

cockpit [kɒkpɪt] *n (in plane)* cabina del piloto, carlinga; *(in racing car)* cabina.

cockroach [kɒkrəutʃ] *n* cucaracha.

cocktail [kɒkteɪl] *n* cóctel *m*.

cocoa [kəukəu] *n (powder)* cacao; *(drink)* chocolate *m*.

coconut [kəukənʌt] *n* coco.

cocoon [kə'ku:n] *n* capullo.
▶ *vt fig* envolver, arropar.

cod [kɒd] *n* bacalao.
ⓘ *pl* cod.

code [kəud] *n* **1** *(gen)* código. **2** *(telephone)* prefijo; *(postal)* código (postal).
▶ *vt* poner en clave, cifrar.

codification [kəudɪfɪ'keɪʃ°n] *n* codificación *f*.

codify [kəudɪfaɪ] *vt* codificar.
ⓘ *pt & pp* codified, *ger* codifying.

coeducation [kəuedjə'keɪʃ°n] *n* enseñanza mixta.

coefficient [kəuɪ'fɪʃ°nt] *n* coeficiente *m*.

coexist [kəuɪg'zɪst] *vi* coexistir.

coffee [kɒfɪ] *n* café *m*.

coffeepot [kɒfɪpɒt] *n* cafetera.

coffer [kɒfə'] *n* arca, cofre *m*.

coffin [kɒfɪn] *n* ataúd *m*, féretro.

cog [kɒg] *n* **1** *(on wheel)* diente *m*. **2** *fig* pieza.

cogent [kəudʒənt] *adj* convincente, contundente.

cognac [kɒnjæk] *n* coñac *m*.

cognitive [kɒgnɪtɪv] *adj* cognitivo,-a.

coherent [kəu'hɪərənt] *adj* coherente.

coil [kɔɪl] *n* **1** *(of rope, wire)* rollo; *(of cable)* carrete *m*; *(of hair)* rizo, moño; *(of smoke)* espiral *m*, voluta. **2** *(single loop)* vuelta, lazada. **3** TECH bobina.
▶ *vt* [also **to coil up**] enrollar.

coin [kɔɪn] *n* moneda.
▶ *vt* acuñar.

coincide [kəuɪn'saɪd] *vi* coincidir (with, con).

coincidence [kəu'ɪnsɪdəns] *n* coincidencia, casualidad *f*.

Coke® [kəuk] *n* Coca Cola®.

coke [kəuk] *n (coal)* coque *m*.

colander [kʌləndə'] *n* colador *m*.

cold [kəuld] *adj* frío,-a.
▶ *n* **1** *(weather)* frío. **2** MED resfriado, catarro, constipado. COMP **cold cuts** US embutidos *mpl*, fiambres *mpl*.

cold-blooded [kəuld'blʌdɪd] *adj* **1** ZOOL de sangre fría. **2** *fig (person)* frío,-a, insensible; *(crime)* a sangre fría.

coleslaw [kəulslɔ:] *n* ensaladilla de col y zanahoria.

colic [kɒlɪk] *n* cólico.

coliseum [kɒlɪ'si:əm] *n* coliseo.

collaborate [kə'læbəreɪt] *vi* colaborar (with, con).

collaborator [kə'læbəreɪtə'] *n* **1** colaborador,-ra. **2** *(with enemy)* colaboracionista *mf*.

collage [kɒlɑ:dʒ] *n* ART collage *m*.

collapse [kə'læps] *n* **1** *(falling down)* derrumbamiento; *(falling in)* hundimiento. **2** *(failure, breakdown)* fracaso. **3** *(prices, currency)* caída en picado; *(business, company)* quiebra. **4** MED colapso.
▶ *vi* **1** *(building, bridge, etc)* derrumbarse, desplomarse; *(roof)* hundirse, venirse abajo. **2** MED *(person)* sufrir un colapso.
▶ *vt (table)* plegar.

collapsible [kə'læpsəb°l] *adj* plegable.

collar ['kɒlə^r] n **1** (of shirt, etc) cuello. **2** (for dog) collar m. **3** TECH collar m, abrazadera.
▸ vt fam pescar, pillar.

☒ Collar no significa 'collar (de persona)', que se traduce por necklace.

collarbone ['kɒləbəʊn] n clavícula.
collateral [kə'læt^ərəl] adj colateral. LOC collateral damage daños mpl colaterales.
colleague ['kɒliːg] n colega mf, compañero,-a.
collect [kə'lekt] vt **1** (glasses, plates, belongings, etc) recoger; (information, data) reunir, recopilar. **2** (stamps, records, etc) coleccionar. **3** (taxes) recaudar; (rent) cobrar. **4** (pick up, fetch) ir a buscar, recoger.
▸ vi **1** (dust, water) acumularse; (people) reunirse, congregarse. **2** (for charity) recaudar dinero, hacer una colecta.
collection [kə'lek^ən] n **1** (of stamps, paintings, etc) colección f; (of poems, short stories) recopilación f; (of people) grupo. **2** (range of new clothes) colección f. **3** (for charity) colecta. **4** (of mail, of refuse) recogida. **5** (of taxes) recaudación f; (of rent) cobro.
collective [kə'lektɪv] adj colectivo,-a.
▸ n (enterprise) cooperativa.
collector [kə'lektə^r] n **1** (of stamps, etc) coleccionista mf. **2** (of rent, debts, tickets) cobrador,-ra.
college ['kɒlɪdʒ] n **1** (for higher education) escuela, instituto mf. **2** US (university) universidad f, facultad f. **3** GB (within university) colegio universitario.

☒ College no significa 'colegio (de niños)', que se traduce por school.

collide [kə'laɪd] vi chocar.
colliery ['kɒljərɪ] n mina de carbón.
ⓘ pl collieries.
collision [kə'lɪʒ^ən] n (between cars, trains, etc) colisión f, choque m; (between ships) abordaje m.
colloquial [kə'ləʊkwɪəl] adj coloquial.
cologne [kə'ləʊn] n colonia.
Colombia [kə'lʌmbɪə] n Colombia.
Colombian [kə'lʌmbɪən] adj & n colombiano,-a.

colon¹ ['kəʊlən] n ANAT colon m.
colon² ['kəʊlən] n LING dos puntos mpl.
colonel ['kɜːn^əl] n coronel m.
colonial [kə'ləʊnɪəl] adj colonial.
▸ n colono,-a.
colonialism [kə'ləʊnɪəlɪz^əm] n colonialismo.
colonist ['kɒlənɪst] n (inhabitant) colono; (colonizer) colono,-a, colonizador,-ra.
colonize ['kɒlənaɪz] vt colonizar.
colony ['kɒlənɪ] n (gen) colonia.
ⓘ pl colonies.
color ['kʌlə^r] n US → colour.
colossal [kə'lɒs^əl] adj colosal.
colossus [kə'lɒsəs] n coloso.
colour ['kʌlə^r] n color m.
▸ adj (television, film, etc) en color.
▸ vt **1** (with pen, paint, crayon) pintar, colorear; (dye) teñir. **2** fig (affect negatively, influence) influir en.
▸ vi **1** (blush) ruborizarse, sonrojarse, ponerse rojo,-a. **2** (of leaves) ponerse amarillo,-a; (fruit) coger color.
▸ n pl colours GB (worn by team, school) colores mpl; MIL (flag) bandera, enseña.
◆ to colour in vt sep pintar, colorear.
colour-blind ['kʌləblaɪnd] adj daltónico,-a.
coloured ['kʌləd] adj de color, de colores.
colourful ['kʌləfʊl] adj **1** (full of colour, bright) lleno,-a de color, vistoso,-a; (brightly coloured) de colores vivos. **2** (person) pintoresco,-a.
colouring ['kʌlərɪŋ] n **1** (substance, dye) colorante m. **2** (person's skin, hair and eye colour) color m. **3** (of animal's skin, fur, plumage) color m.
colourless ['kʌlələs] adj **1** (without colour) incoloro,-a, sin color; (pale) pálido,-a. **2** fig (dull, uninteresting) soso,-a, anodino,-a, gris.
colt [kəʊlt] n potro.
column ['kɒləm] n (gen) columna.
columnist ['kɒləmnɪst] n columnista mf.
coma ['kəʊmə] n MED coma m. LOC to go into a coma caer en coma, entrar en coma.

comb [kəum] *n* **1** *(for hair)* peine *m*. **2** *(for wool, cotton)* carda. **3** *(of bird)* cresta. **4** *(of honeycomb)* panal *m*.
▶ *vt* **1** *(hair)* peinar. **2** *(wool, cotton)* cardar, peinar. **3** *(search - area)* rastrear, peinar.

combat ['kɒmbæt] *n* combate *m*.
▶ *vt* combatir, luchar contra.

combination [kɒmbɪ'neɪʃ°n] *n* combinación *f*.

combine [*(vb)* kəm'baɪn; *(n)* 'kɒmbaɪn] *vt* combinar.
▶ *vi* (gen) combinarse; *(teams, forces)* unirse; *(companies)* fusionarse.
▶ *n* COMM grupo industrial, asociación *f*.

combined [kəm'baɪnd] *adj* combinado,-a, conjunto,-a.

combustible [kəm'bʌstɪb°l] *adj* combustible, inflamable.

combustion [kəm'bʌstʃ°n] *n* combustión *f*.

come [kʌm] *vi* **1** (gen) venir. **2** *(arrive, reach)* llegar. **3** *(happen)* suceder.
▶ *vt* *(behave, play the part)* hacerse: *don't come the innocent with me* no te hagas el inocente conmigo.
◆ **to come about** *vi* *(happen)* ocurrir, suceder.
◆ **to come across** *vt insep* *(thing)* encontrar, tropezar con.
▶ *vi* **1** *(be understood)* ser comprendido, -a. **2** *(make an impression)* causar una impresión.
◆ **to come after** *vt insep* seguir.
◆ **to come along** *vi* **1** *(progress)* ir, marchar. **2** *(hurry up)* darse prisa. **3** *(arrive)* venir, llegar; *(appear)* aparecer.
◆ **to come back** *vi* **1** *(return)* volver *(from, de)*. **2** *(remember)* volver a la memoria. **3** *(return to topic, question, idea)* volver *(to, a)*; *(reply, retort)* replicar, contestar.
◆ **to come before** *vt insep* **1** JUR comparecer ante. **2** *(be more important than)* ser más importante que.
◆ **to come down** *vi* **1** (gen) bajar; *(collapse)* caerse, hundirse, venirse abajo; *(fall - rain, snow)* caer. **2** *(plane - land)* aterrizar; *(- fall)* caer.
◆ **to come down with** *vt insep* *(illness)* caer enfermo,-a de, contraer, coger.

◆ **to come in** *vi* *(enter)* entrar.
◆ **to come on** *vi* **1** *(make progress)* avanzar. **2** *(hurry up)* darse prisa.
◆ **to come out** *vi* **1** *(leave)* salir *(of, de)*; *(tooth, hair)* caerse; *(stain)* salir, quitarse; *(colour, dye)* desteñirse. **2** *(sun, moon, stars)* salir. **3** *(new book, record, magazine, figures)* salir, publicarse; *(film)* estrenarse.
◆ **to come through** *vt insep* *(operation, accident)* sobrevivir, salir con vida de; *(illness)* recuperarse de; *(difficult period)* pasar por, atravesar.
◆ **to come up to** *vt insep* **1** *(equal)* alcanzar, llegar a, estar a la altura de. **2** *(approach - in space)* acercarse a; *(- in time)* ser casi.
◆ **to come up with** *vt insep* *(idea)* tener, ocurrirse; *(solution)* encontrar; *(plan)* idear; *(proposal)* presentar, plantear.
◆ **to come upon** *vt insep* encontrarse con, encontrar.
ⓘ *pt* **came** [keɪm], *pp* **come**[kʌm], *ger* **coming**.

comeback ['kʌmbæk] *n* **1** *fam* *(of person)* reaparición *f*, vuelta, retorno. **2** *(way of obtaining compensation)* reclamación *f*. **3** *(reply)* réplica, respuesta.

comedian [kə'mi:dɪən] *n* cómico, humorista *m*.

comedienne [kəmi:dɪ'en] *n* cómica, humorista.

comedy ['kɒmədɪ] *n* comedia.
ⓘ *pl* **comedies**.

comet ['kɒmɪt] *n* cometa *m*.

comfort ['kʌmfət] *n* **1** *(well-being)* comodidad *f*, confort *m*, bienestar *m*. **2** *(thing, luxury)* comodidad *f*. **3** *(consolation)* consuelo.
▶ *vt* consolar.

comfortable ['kʌmf°təb°l] *adj* **1** *(furniture, clothes, etc)* cómodo,-a. **2** *(life)* desahogado,-a, acomodado,-a.

comforting ['kʌmfətɪŋ] *adj* reconfortante.

comic ['kɒmɪk] *adj* cómico,-a.
▶ *n* **1** *(comedian)* cómico,-a, humorista *mf*. **2** *(magazine)* tebeo, cómic *m*.

coming ['kʌmɪŋ] *adj* (gen) próximo,-a; *(generation)* venidero,-a, futuro,-a.
▶ *n* llegada.

comma ['kɒmə] *n* coma. LOC **inverted comma** comilla.

command [kə'mɑ:nd] *n* **1** *(order)* orden *f*. **2** *(control, authority)* mando. **3** *(knowledge, mastery)* dominio. **4** INFORM comando, instrucción *f*.
▶ *vt* **1** *(order)* mandar, ordenar. **2** MIL *(have authority over)* estar al mando de, comandar.

commander [kə'mɑ:ndər] *n* **1** MIL comandante *m*. **2** MAR capitán *m* de fragata.

commanding [kə'mɑ:ndɪŋ] *adj* **1** *(voice, manner, appearance)* autoritario,-a. **2** *(position)* dominante, de superioridad.

commandment [kə'mɑ:ndmənt] *n* REL mandamiento.

commando [kə'mɑ:ndəʊ] *n* comando.
ⓘ *pl* commandos o commandoes.

commemorate [kə'memərett] *vt* conmemorar.

commend [kə'mend] *vt* *(praise)* alabar (for, por), elogiar (for, por); *(recommend)* recomendar.

comment ['kɒment] *n* comentario, observación *f*. LOC **no comment** sin comentarios.
▶ *vt* comentar, observar.

commentary ['kɒmənt°rɪ] *n* **1** *(spoken description)* comentario, comentarios *mpl*. **2** *(set of written remarks)* comentario, crítica.
ⓘ *pl* commentaries.

commentator ['kɒmənteɪtər] *n* comentarista *mf*.

commerce ['kɒmɜ:s] *n* comercio.

commercial [kə'mɜ:ʃl] *adj* comercial.
▶ *n* *(advertisement)* anuncio, spot *m* publicitario.

commercialization [kə'mɜ:ʃəlaɪzeɪʃ°n] *n* comercialización *f*.

commercialize [kə'mɜ:ʃəlaɪz] *vt* comercializar.

commission [kə'mɪʃ°n] *n* **1** COMM comisión *f*. **2** *(piece of work)* encargo.
▶ *vt* *(order)* encargar.

commissioner [kə'mɪʃənər] *n* **1** *(public official)* comisario. **2** *(member of a commission)* comisionado,-a.

commit [kə'mɪt] *vt* **1** *(crime, error, sin)* cometer. **2** *(send to prison, etc)* internar. **3** *(bind)* comprometer, obligar; *(pledge)* asignar, consignar, destinar.
ⓘ *pt & pp* committed, *ger* committing.

commitment [kə'mɪtmənt] *n* **1** *(undertaking, obligation)* compromiso, obligación *f*; *(responsibility)* responsabilidad *f*. **2** *(dedication)* dedicación *f*, entrega.

committed [kə'mɪtɪd] *adj* *(to a cause)* comprometido,-a; *(dedicated)* dedicado,-a, entregado,-a.

committee [kə'mɪtɪ] *n* comité *m*

commode [kə'məʊd] *n* cómoda.

commodity [kə'mɒdɪtɪ] *n* **1** COMM producto, artículo, mercancía. **2** FIN materia prima.
ⓘ *pl* commodities.

❌ Commodity no significa 'comodidad', que se traduce por comfort.

common ['kɒmən] *adj* **1** *(ordinary, average)* corriente. **2** *(usual, not scarce)* común, corriente. **3** *(shared, joint)* común. **4** *pej (vulgar)* ordinario,-a.
▶ *n* *(land)* tierras *fpl* comunales.

commoner ['kɒmənər] *n* plebeyo,-a.

commonplace ['kɒmənpleɪs] *adj* común, corriente.
▶ *n* *(platitude)* lugar *m* común, tópico.

Commons ['kɒmənz] *n pl* **the Commons** GB los Comunes. COMP **the House of Commons** la Cámara de los Comunes.

⊕ La Cámara de los Comunes británica es el equivalente al Congreso español y es el órgano legislativo más importante del Reino Unido.

Commonwealth ['kɒmənwelθ] *n* GB Commonwealth *f*.

⊕ La Commonwealth es una organización compuesta por 53 naciones con fuertes vínculos con el Reino Unido por haber pertenecido en algún momento de su historia al Imperio británico.

commotion [kə'məʊʃ°n] *n* *(scandal)* escándalo; *(noise, excitement)* alboroto, jaleo; *(confusion)* confusión *f*.

communal [ˈkɒmjənəl] *adj (shared)* comunal; *(of a community)* comunitario,-a.

commune [ˈkɒmjuːn] *n* comuna.

communicate [kəˈmjuːnɪkeɪt] *vt* **1** *(make known, convey)* comunicar. **2** MED transmitir, contagiar.
▶ *vi* comunicarse (**with**, con).

communication [kəmjuːnɪˈkeɪʃən] *n* **1** *(gen)* comunicación *f*. **2** *(message)* comunicado.
▶ *n pl* **communications** comunicaciones *fpl*.

communicative [kəˈmjuːnɪkətɪv] *adj* comunicativo,-a.

communion [kəˈmjuːnjən] *n fml* comunión *f*.
▶ *n* **Communion** REL Comunión *f*.

communiqué [kəˈmjuːnɪkeɪ] *n* comunicado.

communism [ˈkɒmjənɪzəm] *n* comunismo.

communist [ˈkɒmjənɪst] *adj* comunista.
▶ *n* comunista *mf*.

community [kəˈmjuːnɪtɪ] *n* comunidad *f*.
ⓘ *pl* **communities**.

commute [kəˈmjuːt] *vi* desplazarse diariamente al lugar de trabajo.
▶ *vt* conmutar.

commuter [kəˈmjuːtər] *n* persona que se desplaza diariamente a su lugar de trabajo. COMP **the commuter belt** los barrios *mpl* periféricos.

compact [*(adj-vb)* kəmˈpækt; *(n)* ˈkɒmpækt] *adj (gen)* compacto,-a; *(style)* conciso,-a.
▶ *n* **1** *(for powder)* polvera de bolsillo. **2** US coche *m* utilitario.
▶ *vt* compactar, comprimir.

companion [kəmˈpænjən] *n* **1** *(partner, friend)* compañero,-a. **2** *(person employed)* persona de compañía. **3** *(either of pair or set)* compañero,-a, pareja.

companionship [kəmˈpænjənʃɪp] *n* compañerismo, camaradería.

company [ˈkʌmpənɪ] *n* **1** *(companionship)* compañía. **2** *(visitors)* visita. **3** *(business)* empresa, compañía, sociedad *f*. **4** THEAT compañía. **5** MIL compañía.
ⓘ *pl* **companies**.

comparable [ˈkɒmpərəbəl] *adj* comparable (**to**, a) (**with**, con).

comparative [kəmˈpærətɪv] *adj* **1** *(relative)* relativo,-a. **2** *(making a comparison)* comparado,-a. **3** LING comparativo,-a.
▶ *n* LING comparativo.

compare [kəmˈpeər] *vt* comparar (**to/with**, con).

comparison [kəmˈpærɪsən] *n* comparación *f*.

compartment [kəmˈpɑːtmənt] *n (in wallet, fridge, desk)* compartimento; *(in train)* departamento, compartimiento.

compass [ˈkʌmpəs] *n* **1** *(magnetic)* brújula, compás *m*: *the points of the compass* los puntos cardinales. **2** [se usa como *sing* or *pl*] *(for drawing)* compás *m*: *a pair of compasses, a compass* un compás. COMP **compass rose** rosa de los vientos.

compassion [kəmˈpæʃən] *n* compasión *f*.

compassionate [kəmˈpæʃənət] *adj* compasivo,-a.

compatibility [kəmpætəˈbɪlɪtɪ] *n* compatibilidad *f*.

compatible [kəmˈpætɪbəl] *adj* compatible (**with**, con).

compatriot [kəmˈpætrɪət] *n* compatriota *mf*.

compel [kəmˈpel] *vt* **1** *(force)* obligar. **2** *fig (inspire)* infundir, inspirar.
ⓘ *pt & pp* **compelled**, *ger* **compelling**.

compensate [ˈkɒmpənseɪt] *vt* **1** *(recompense, indemnify)* indemnizar (**for**, por), compensar (**for**, por). **2** *(counterbalance)* compensar.
▶ *vi* compensar (**for**, -).

compensation [kɒmpənˈseɪʃən] *n* **1** *(money, damages)* indemnización *f* (**for**, por). **2** *(way of compensating)* compensación *f* (**for**, por).

compere [ˈkɒmpeər] *n* GB presentador, -ra.
▶ *vt* GB presentar.

compete [kəmˈpiːt] *vi (try to win)* disputarse; *(take part in)* competir, participar.

competence [ˈkɒmpɪtəns] *n* **1** *(ability)* competencia, capacidad *f*, aptitud *f*: *a fair level of competence in German* un buen nivel de alemán. **2** JUR *(legal author-ity)* competencia.

❌ Competence no significa 'compe-tencia (en el mercado)', que se traduce por competition.

competent ['kɒmpɪtənt] *adj* **1** *(person)* competente; *(work, novel, etc)* acepta-ble, bastante bien. **2** JUR competente.

competition [kɒmpə'tɪʃ°n] *n* **1** *(gen)* concurso; *(race, sporting event)* compe-tición *f*. **2** *(rivalry)* competencia.

competitive [kəm'petɪtɪv] *adj* competitivo,-a.

competitor [kəm'petɪtə'] *n* **1** COMM *(ri-val)* competidor,-ra, rival *mf*. **2** SP *(in race, etc)* participante *mf*; *(opponent)* contrincante *mf*. **3** *(in quiz, etc)* concur-sante *mf*, participante *mf*; *(in competitive examination)* opositor,-ra.

compilation [kɒmpɪ'leɪʃ°n] *n* **1** *(gen)* compilación *f*. **2** *(record, etc)* recopila-ción *f*.

compile [kəm'paɪl] *vt* **1** *(produce book, list, etc)* compilar; *(collect information)* reco-pilar. **2** COMPUT compilar.

complain [kəm'pleɪn] *vi* quejarse (about/of, de).

complaint [kəm'pleɪnt] *n* **1** *(gen)* queja (about, de); *(formal)* reclamación *f*. **2** MED enfermedad *f* (leve), achaque *m*.

complement ['kɒmplɪmənt] *n (gen)* complemento (to, de).
► *vt* complementar.

complementary [kɒmplɪ'ment°rɪ] *adj (gen)* complementario,-a.

complete [kəm'pliːt] *adj* **1** *(entire)* completo,-a. **2** *(finished)* acabado,-a, terminado,-a.
► *vt* **1** *(make whole)* completar. **2** *(finish)* acabar, terminar. **3** *(fill in - form)* rellenar.

completion [kəm'pliːʃ°n] *n (act, state)* fi-nalización *f*, terminación *f*.

complex ['kɒmpleks] *adj* complejo,-a.
► *n* complejo.

complexion [kəm'plekʃ°n] *n (quality of skin)* cutis *m*; *(colour or tone of skin)* tez *f*.

❌ Complexion no significa 'complexión (física)', que se traduce por constitution.

complexity [kəm'pleksɪtɪ] *n* compleji-dad *f*.
ⓘ *pl* complexities.

complicate ['kɒmplɪkeɪt] *vt* complicar.

complicated ['kɒmplɪkeɪtɪd] *adj* complicado,-a.

complication [kɒmplɪ'keɪʃ°n] *n* com-plicación *f*.
► *n pl* **complications** MED complicacio-nes *fpl*.

complicity [kəm'plɪsɪtɪ] *n* complici-dad *f* (in, en).

compliment ['kɒmplɪmənt] *vt* felicitar (on, por).
► *n (praise)* cumplido, halago.
► *n pl* **compliments** saludos *mpl*, felici-taciones *fpl*.

comply [kəm'plaɪ] *vi (order)* obedecer (with, -), cumplir (with, con); *(request)* acceder (with, a); *(law)* acatar (with, -); *(standards)* cumplir (with, con).
ⓘ *pt & pp* **complied**, *ger* **complying**.

component [kəm'pəʊnənt] *adj* com-ponente.
► *n* **1** *(gen)* componente *m*. **2** AUTO pieza.

compose [kəm'pəʊz] *vt* **1** *(music, poem)* componer; *(letter)* redactar. **2** *(consti-tute)* componer. **3** *(one's thoughts)* poner en orden.
► *vi* MUS componer.

composed [kəm'pəʊzd] *adj (calm)* sereno,-a, sosegado,-a, tranqui-lo,-a.

composer [kəm'pəʊzə'] *n* composi-tor,-ra.

composite ['kɒmpəzɪt] *adj* compuesto,-a.
► *n* combinación *f*, conjunto.

composition [kɒmpə'zɪʃ°n] *n* **1** *(gen)* composición *f*. **2** *(essay)* redacción *f*. **3** *(substance)* mezcla.

compost ['kɒmpɒst] *n* abono orgáni-co, abono vegetal, compost *m*.

composure [kəm'pəʊʒə'] *n* calma, se-renidad *f*, compostura *f*.

compound¹ [*(adj-n)* 'kɒmpaʊnd; *(vb,* kəm'paʊnd] *adj* compuesto,-a.
► *n* **1** CHEM compuesto. **2** *(substance,* mezcla. **3** LING palabra compuesta.

▶ vt **1** *(mix)* componer, combinar, mezclar. **2** *(worsen, exacerbate - problem)* agravar; *(- difficulty)* aumentar.

compound² ['kɒmpaʊnd] *n (enclosed area)* recinto.

comprehend [kɒmprɪ'hend] *vt* **1** *(understand)* comprender. **2** *fml (include)* comprender, abarcar.

comprehensible [kɒmprɪ'hensəbºl] *adj* comprensible.

comprehension [kɒmprɪ'henʃºn] *n* comprensión *f*.

comprehensive [kɒmprɪ'hensɪv] *adj (thorough)* detallado,-a, global, completo,-a; *(broad)* amplio,-a, extenso,-a.

☒ Comprehensive no significa 'comprensivo (tolerante)', que se traduce por understanding.

compress [(n) 'kɒmpres; (vb) kəm'pres] *n* compresa.

▶ vt **1** *(air, straw)* comprimir. **2** *(text, argument, speech)* condensar.

compressibility [kəmprəsɪ'bɪlɪtɪ] *n* compresibilidad *f*.

compression [kəm'preʃºn] *n* compresión *f*.

compressor [kəm'presəʳ] *n* compresor *m*.

comprise [kəm'praɪz] *vt (consist of, be made up of)* comprender, constar de; *(constitute, form)* componer, constituir.

compromise ['kɒmprəmaɪz] *n* acuerdo mutuo, solución *f* de compromiso.

▶ vi llegar a un acuerdo, transigir.

▶ vt *(endanger, weaken)* comprometer.

☒ Compromise no significa 'compromiso (obligación o promesa de matrimonio)', que se traducen por commitment y engagement.

compulsion [kəm'pʌlʃºn] *n* **1** *(force)* obligación *f*, coacción *f*. **2** *(urge)* compulsión *f*.

compulsive [kəm'pʌlsɪv] *adj* **1** *(compelling, fascinating)* fascinante, irresistible, absorbente. **2** *(obsessive)* obsesivo,-a.

compulsory [kəm'pʌlsərɪ] *adj (subject, military service)* obligatorio,-a; *(retirement, redundancy)* forzoso,-a.

computation [kɒmpjʊ'teɪʃºn] *n* cálculo, cómputo.

compute [kəm'pju:t] *vt* computar, calcular.

computer [kəm'pju:təʳ] *n* ordenador *m*, computadora.

computerization [kəmpju:tərəɪ'zeɪʃºn] *n (of data)* computerización *f*; *(of system, business)* informatización *f*.

computerize [kəm'pju:təraɪz] *vt (data)* computarizar, computerizar; *(system, business)* informatizar.

computing [kəm'pju:tɪŋ] *n* informática.

comrade ['kɒmreɪd] *n* POL camarada *mf*, compañero,-a.

con¹ [kɒn] *n fam* estafa, timo.

▶ vt *fam (money)* estafar, timar; *(person)* embaucar, engañar.

① *pt & pp* conned, *ger* conning.

con² [kɒn] *n (disadvantage)* contra *m*.

✎ Consulta también pro.

concave ['kɒnkeɪv] *adj* cóncavo,-a.

concavity [kɒn'kævɪtɪ] *n* concavidad *f*.

conceal [kən'si:l] *vt (gen)* ocultar; *(facts)* encubrir; *(feelings)* disimular.

concede [kən'si:d] *vt* **1** *(admit)* reconocer, admitir. **2** *(allow, give away)* conceder.

▶ vi ceder, rendirse.

conceit [kən'si:t] *n (pride)* vanidad *f*.

conceivable [kən'si:vəbºl] *adj* concebible, imaginable.

conceive [kən'si:v] *vt* **1** *(gen)* concebir. **2** *(understand)* entender.

concentrate ['kɒnsºntreɪt]

▶ vt *(gen)* concentrar (on, en).

▶ vi **1** *(person)* concentrarse (on, en).

concentration [kɒnsºn'treɪʃºn] *n* concentración *f* (on, en).

concentric [kən'sentrɪk] *adj* concéntrico,-a.

concept ['kɒnsept] *n* concepto.

conception [kən'sepʃºn] *n* **1** *(of child, idea, plan)* concepción *f*. **2** *(idea)* concepto, idea, noción *f*.

concern [kən'sɜːn] *n* **1** *(worry)* preocupación *f*, inquietud *f*. **2** *(interest)* interés *m*; *(affair)* asunto. **3** COMM *(company, business)* negocio.

▶ vt **1** *(affect, involve)* afectar, concernir. *(interest)* interesar. **2** *(worry)* preocupar. **3** *(book, film, article, etc)* tratar de.

concerned [kən'sɜːnd] *adj (worried)* preocupado,-a (about/for, por).

concerning [kən'sɜːnɪŋ] *prep* referente a, con respecto a, en cuanto a.

concert ['kɒnsət] *n* concierto.

concerted [kən'sɜːtɪd] *adj* concertado,-a, coordinado,-a.

concerto [kən'tʃeətəʊ] *n* concierto.
① *pl* concertos o concerti [kən'tʃeətɪ].

✎ Concerto se refiere específicamente a conciertos de música clásica para uno o varios instrumentos solistas y una orquesta.

concession [kən'seʃ³n] *n* concesión *f* (to, a).

concessionaire [kənseʃə'neəʳ] *n* concesionario,-a.

conciliate [kən'sɪlɪeɪt] *vt & vi* conciliar.

concise [kən'saɪs] *adj* conciso,-a.

concision [kən'sɪʒ³n] *n* concisión *f*.

conclude [kən'kluːd] *vt* **1** *(end)* concluir, finalizar. **2** *(settle - deal)* cerrar; *(- agreement)* llegar a; *(- treaty)* firmar. **3** *(deduce)* concluir, llegar a la conclusión de.
▶ *vi* concluir, terminar.

conclusion [kən'kluːʒ³n] *n* conclusión *f*.

conclusive [kən'kluːsɪv] *adj* concluyente.

concoct [kən'kɒkt] *vt* **1** *(dish, sauce, drink)* confeccionar, preparar. **2** *(story, excuse, explanation)* inventar, inventarse.

concord ['kɒŋkɔːd] *n* **1** *fml (harmony)* concordia. **2** LING concordancia.

concourse ['kɒŋkɔːs] *n (hall)* vestíbulo; *(in station)* explanada.

❌ Concourse no significa 'concurso (competición)', que se traduce por competition.

concrete ['kɒŋkriːt] *adj* **1** *(definite, not abstract)* concreto,-a. **2** *(made of concrete)* de hormigón.
▶ *n* hormigón *m*.

concur [kən'kɜːʳ] *vi (agree)* estar de acuerdo, coincidir.
① *pt & pp* concurred, *ger* concurring.

concurrence [kən'kʌrəns] *n* acuerdo, coincidencia.

concussion [kən'kʌʃ³n] *n* MED conmoción *f* cerebral.

condemn [kən'dem] *vt* condenar.

condemnation [kɒndem'neɪʃ³n] *n* condena.

condensation [kɒnden'seɪʃ³n] *n* CHEM *(process)* condensación *f*; *(on glass)* vaho.

condense [kən'dens] *vt* condensar.

condenser [kən'densəʳ] *n* condensador *m*.

condescend [kɒndɪ'send] *vi* **1** *(deign,* condescender, dignarse. **2** *(patronize,* tratar con condescendencia.

condescending [kɒndɪ'sendɪŋ] *adj (attitude, answer)* condescendiente.

condiment ['kɒndɪmənt] *n* condimento.

condition [kən'dɪʃ³n] *n* **1** *(state)* condición *f*, estado. **2** *(requirement, provision* condición *f*. **3** MED afección *f*, enfermedad *f*.
▶ *vt* **1** *(determine, accustom)* condicionar **2** *(treat - hair)* acondicionar, suavizar.

conditional [kən'dɪʃ³n'l] *adj* condicional.
▶ *n* the conditional LING el condicional *m*.

conditioner [kən'dɪʃ³nəʳ] *n (for hair* acondicionador *m*, suavizante *m*.

condolences [kən'dəʊlənsɪs] *n pl* pésame *m sing*.

condom ['kɒndəm] *n* condón *m*, preservativo.

condominium [kɒndə'mɪnɪəm] *n* **1** PC condominio. **2** US *(apartment block* bloque *m* de pisos; *(apartment)* apartamento, piso.

condone [kən'dəʊn] *vt (person)* aprobar consentir.

condor ['kɒndɔːʳ] *n* cóndor *m*.

conducive [kən'djuːsɪv] *adj* propicio,-(to, para).

conduct [*(n)* 'kɒndʌkt; *(vb)* kɒn'dʌkt] *n (behaviour)* conducta, comportamiento. **2** *(management)* dirección *f*, gestió *f*, administración *f*.
▶ *vt* **1** *(direct - survey, campaign)* llevar cabo, realizar; *(- business)* administra

2 *(lead, guide)* conducir, guiar. **3** *(transmit - heat, etc)* conducir. **4** MUS dirigir.
▶ *vi* MUS dirigir.

conduction [kənˈdʌkʃən] *n* PHYS conducción *f*.

🗵 Conduction no significa 'conducción (de un vehículo)', que se traduce por **driving**.

conductivity [kənˈdʌktɪvɪtɪ] *n* conductividad *f*.

conductor [kənˈdʌktər] *n* **1** *(of heat, electricity)* conductor *m*. **2** *(of orchestra)* director,-ra de orquesta. **3** *(on bus)* cobrador,-ra. **4** US *(on train)* jefe,-a de tren.

🗵 Conductor no significa 'conductor (de un vehículo)', que se traduce por **driver**.

conductress [kənˈdʌktrəs] *n* *(on bus)* cobradora *f*.

conduit [ˈkɒndjuɪt] *n* conducto.

cone [kəʊn] *n* **1** *(shape, for traffic)* cono. **2** *(for ice cream)* cucurucho. **3** BOT *(fruit of pine tree)* piña.

confectioner [kənˈfekʃənər] *n* confitero,-a, pastelero,-a.

confectionery [kənˈfekʃənrɪ] *n* dulces *mpl*.

confederacy [kənˈfedərəsɪ] *n* confederación *f*.
① *pl* confederacies.

confederation [kənfedəˈreɪʃən] *n* confederación *f*.

confer [kənˈfɜːr] *vt* *(award, grant, bestow)* conferir, conceder.
▶ *vi* *(consult, discuss)* consultar (with, con) (about/on, sobre).
① *pt & pp* conferred, *ger* conferring.

conference [ˈkɒnfərəns] *n* **1** *(large event, convention)* congreso. **2** *(meeting)* reunión *f*, junta.

🗵 Conference no significa 'conferencia (discurso)', que se traduce por **lecture**.

confess [kənˈfes] *vt & vi* confesar.

confessed [kənˈfest] *adj* declarado,-a.

confession [kənˈfeʃən] *n* confesión *f*.

confessional [kənˈfeʃənəl] *n* confesionario.

confessor [kənˈfesər] *n* REL confesor *m*.

confetti [kənˈfetɪ] *n* confeti *m*.

confidant [ˈkɒnfɪdænt] *n* confidente *m*.

confidante [ˈkɒnfɪdænt] *n* confidenta.

confide [kənˈfaɪd] *vt* confiar.
◆ **to confide in** *vi* confiar en.

confidence [ˈkɒnfɪdəns] *n* **1** *(trust, faith)* confianza (in, en), fe *f* (in, en). **2** *(self-confidence)* confianza, seguridad *f*. **3** *(secrecy)* confianza. **4** *(secret)* confidencia.

confident [ˈkɒnfɪdənt] *adj* **1** *(certain)* seguro,-a. **2** *(self-confident)* seguro,-a de sí mismo,-a.

confidential [kɒnfɪˈdenʃəl] *adj* confidencial.

confine [kənˈfaɪn] *vt* **1** *(person)* confinar, recluir; *(animal)* encerrar. **2** *(limit, restrict)* limitar.

confinement [kənˈfaɪnmənt] *n* **1** *(imprisonment)* reclusión *f*. **2** MED *(in childbirth)* parto.

confines [ˈkɒnfaɪnz] *n pl* límites *mpl*, confines *mpl*.

confirm [kənˈfɜːm] *vt* confirmar.

confirmation [kɒnfəˈmeɪʃən] *n* confirmación *f*.

confirmed [kənˈfɜːmd] *adj* *(inveterate)* empedernido,-a.

confiscate [ˈkɒnfɪskeɪt] *vt* confiscar.

conflict [*(n)* ˈkɒnflɪkt; *(vb)* kənˈflɪkt] *n* conflicto.
▶ *vi* chocar (with, con), estar en conflicto (with, con).

conflicting [kənˈflɪktɪŋ] *adj* *(evidence, accounts)* contradictorio,-a; *(opinions, interests)* contrario,-a, opuesto,-a.

confluence [ˈkɒnfluəns] *n* confluencia.

conform [kənˈfɔːm] *vi* **1** *(comply with rules, standards, regulations)* ajustarse (to/with, a), cumplir (to/with, con). **2** *(agree, be consistent with)* conformarse (to/with, con), concordar (with, con). **3** *(fit in, behave like other people)* ser conformista.

conformist [kənˈfɔːmɪst] *adj* conformista.
▶ *n* conformista *mf*.

conformity [kənˈfɔːmɪtɪ] *n* conformidad *f*.

confront [kənˈfrʌnt] *vt* hacer frente a, enfrentarse a.

confuse [kənˈfjuːz] *vt* confundir.

confused [kən'fjuːzd] *adj* **1** *(person)* confundido,-a. **2** *(mind, ideas, account)* confuso,-a.

confusing [kən'fjuːzɪŋ] *adj* confuso,-a.

confusion [kən'fjuːʒən] *n* confusión *f*.

congeal [kən'dʒiːl] *vi (blood)* coagularse; *(fat)* solidificarse.

congenial [kən'dʒiːnɪəl] *adj* agradable.

congenital [kən'dʒenɪtəl] *adj* MED congénito,-a.

congested [kən'dʒestɪd] *adj* congestionado,-a.

congestion [kən'dʒestʃn] *n* congestión *f*.

conglomerate [*(n)* kən'glɒmərət; *(vb)* kən'glɒməreɪt] *n* **1** COMM conglomerado (de empresas). **2** GEOL conglomerado.

congratulate [kən'grætjəleɪt] *vt* felicitar (on, por).

congratulation [kən'grætjəleɪʃənz] *n* felicitación *f*.
▸ *interj* **congratulations!** ¡felicidades! *fpl*, ¡enhorabuena!

congregate ['kɒŋgrɪgeɪt] *vi* congregarse.

congregation [kɒŋgrɪ'geɪʃn] *n* REL *(people gathered)* fieles *mpl*; *(parishioners)* feligreses *mpl*.

congress ['kɒŋgres] *n* congreso.
▸ *n* **Congress** US el Congreso.

congruent ['kɒŋgruənt] *adj* MATH congruente.

conic ['kɒnɪk] *adj* cónico,-a.

conifer ['kɒnɪfər] *n* conífera.

conjecture [kən'dʒektʃər] *n* conjetura, suposición *f*.
▸ *vi* hacer conjeturas.

conjugal ['kɒndʒəgəl] *adj* conyugal.

conjugate ['kɒndʒəgeɪt] *vt* conjugar.
▸ *vi* conjugarse.

conjugation [kɒndʒə'geɪʃn] *n* conjugación *f*.

conjunction [kən'dʒʌŋkʃn] *n* conjunción *f*. [LOC] **in conjunction with** conjuntamente con.

conjure ['kʌndʒər] *vi* hacer magia, hacer juegos de manos.

◆ **to conjure up** *vt sep (evoke - memories)* evocar, traer a la memoria; *(summon - spirits)* invocar.

☒ Conjure no significa 'conjura (conspiración)', que se traduce por plot.

conjurer ['kʌndʒərər] *n* mago,-a, prestidigitador,-ra.

connect [kə'nekt] *vt* **1** *(gen)* conectar. **2** *(associate)* relacionar, asociar. **3** *(on telephone)* poner (with, con).

connection [kə'nekʃn] *n* **1** *(gen)* conexión *f*. **2** *(train, plane)* conexión *f*, enlace *m*.
▸ *n pl* **connections** *(professional)* contactos *mpl*; *(relatives)* familia, parientes *mpl*.

connector [kə'nektər] *n* conector *m*.

connoisseur [kɒnə'sɜːr] *n* entendido,-a, conocedor,-ra.

connotation [kɒnə'teɪʃn] *n* connotación *f*.

conquer ['kɒŋkər] *vt (country, mountain, heart)* conquistar; *(enemy, fear)* vencer.

conqueror ['kɒŋkərər] *n* conquistador,-ra, vencedor,-ra.

conquest ['kɒŋkwest] *n* conquista.

consanguinity [kɒnsæŋ'gwɪnɪtɪ] *n* consanguinidad *f*.

conscience ['kɒnʃəns] *n* conciencia.

conscientious [kɒnʃɪ'enʃəs] *adj (work)* concienzudo,-a; *(person)* aplicado,-a, serio,-a.

conscientiousness [kɒnʃɪ'enʃəsnəs] *n* escrupulosidad *f*.

conscious ['kɒnʃəs] *adj* **1** MED consciente. **2** *(aware)* consciente. **3** *(intentional, deliberate)* deliberado,-a.

conscript [*(n)* 'kɒnskrɪpt; *(vb)* kən'skrɪpt] *n* recluta.
▸ *vt* reclutar.

conscription [kən'skrɪpʃn] *n* servicio militar obligatorio.

consecrate ['kɒnsɪkreɪt] *vt* consagrar.

consecutive [kən'sekjətɪv] *adj* consecutivo,-a.

consensus [kən'sensəs] *n* consenso.

consent [kən'sent] *n* consentimiento
▸ *vi* consentir (to, en), acceder (to, en)

consequence ['kɒnsɪkwəns] *n* **1** *(result)* consecuencia. **2** *(importance)* importancia, trascendencia.

consequent ['kɒnsɪkwənt] *adj* consiguiente.

conservation [kɒnsə'veɪʃᵊn] *n* conservación *f*.

conservationist [kɒnsə'veɪʃᵊnɪst] *n* ecologista *mf*.

conservatism [kən'sɜ:vətɪzᵊm] *n* POL conservadurismo.

conservative [kən'sɜ:vətɪv] *adj* **1** *(traditional)* conservador,-ra. **2** *(cautious)* cauteloso,-a, prudente.
▶ *n (traditionalist)* conservador,-ra.
▶ *adj* **Conservative** POL conservador,-ra.
▶ *n* **Conservative** POL conservador,-ra.

conservatoire [kən'sɜ:vətwɑ:ʳ] *n* conservatorio.

conservatory [kən'sɜ:vətrɪ] *n* **1** MUS conservatorio. **2** *(greenhouse)* invernadero.
ⓘ *pl* conservatories.

conserve [kən'sɜ:v] *vt (nature, wildlife, etc)* conservar, proteger; *(save)* conservar, ahorrar.
▶ *n* CULIN *(jam)* confitura.

consider [kən'sɪdəʳ] *vt* considerar.

considerable [kən'sɪdᵊrəbᵊl] *adj* considerable.

considerate [kən'sɪdᵊrət] *adj* considerado,-a, atento,-a.

consideration [kənsɪdə'reɪʃᵊn] *n* **1** *(gen)* consideración *f*. **2** *(factor to consider)* factor *m* a tener en cuenta.

considering [kən'sɪdərɪŋ] *prep* teniendo en cuenta.
▶ *conj* teniendo en cuenta que.
▶ *adv* después de todo.

consign [kən'saɪn] *vt* **1** COMM *(send - goods)* consignar. **2** *fml (entrust)* confiar.

consignment [kən'saɪnmənt] *n* COMM remesa, envío.

consist [kən'sɪst] *vi* **1** *fml (have as chief element)* consistir (in, en). **2** *(comprise, be composed of)* constar (of, de), estar compuesto,-a (of, de).

consistency [kən'sɪstənsɪ] *n (of actions, behaviour, policy)* coherencia, lógica. **2** *(of mixture)* consistencia.

consistent [kən'sɪstənt] *adj (of person, behaviour, beliefs)* coherente (with, con), consecuente (with, con); *(denial, improvement)* constante.

consolation [kɒnsə'leɪʃᵊn] *n* consuelo.

console¹ ['kɒnsəʊl] *n (electrical)* consola; *(video games)* consola.

console² [kən'səʊl] *vt* consolar.

consolidate [kən'sɒlɪdeɪt] *vt* **1** *(gen)* consolidar. **2** COMM *(merge)* fusionar.

consolidation [kənsɒlɪ'deɪʃᵊn] *n* **1** *(gen)* consolidación *f*. **2** COMM fusión *f*.

consommé ['kɒnsɒmeɪ] *n* consomé *m*.

consonant ['kɒnsᵊnənt] *n* consonante *f*.

conspicuous [kəns'pɪkjʊəs] *adj (clothes)* llamativo,-a; *(mistake, difference, lack)* evidente, obvio,-a.

conspiracy [kəns'pɪrəsɪ] *n* conspiración *f*: *a conspiracy to murder* una conspiración de asesinato.
ⓘ *pl* conspiracies.

conspirator [kəns'pɪrətəʳ] *n* conspirador,-ra.

conspire [kəns'paɪəʳ] *vi* conspirar.

constable ['kʌnstəbᵊl] *n* policía *mf*, guardia *mf*, agente *mf* (de policía).

constabulary [kən'stæbjələrɪ] *n* GB policía.
ⓘ *pl* constabularies.

constant ['kɒnstənt] *adj* **1** *(gen)* constante. **2** *(unchanging)* constante.
▶ *n* constante *f*.

constellation [kɒnstə'leɪʃᵊn] *n* constelación *f*.

consternation [kɒnstə'neɪʃᵊn] *n* consternación *f*.

constipated ['kɒnstɪpeɪtɪd] *adj* estreñido,-a.

> ☒ To be constipated no significa ' estar constipado (acatarrado)', que se traduce por to have a cold.

constipation [kɒnstɪ'peɪʃᵊn] *n* estreñimiento.

> ☒ Constipation no significa 'constipado (catarro)', que se traduce por cold.

constituency [kən'stɪtjʊənsɪ] *n* circunscripción *f*, distrito electoral.
ⓘ *pl* constituencies.

constituent [kənˈstɪtjuənt] *adj* constituyente.
▶ *n (component)* componente *m*.

constitute [ˈkɒnstɪtjuːt] *vt* constituir.

constitution [kɒnstɪˈtjuːʃən] *n* **1** *(gen)*
constitución *f*. **2** *(of person)* constitución *f*, complexión *f*.

constitutional [kɒnstɪˈtjuːʃənəl] *adj*
constitucional.

constrain [kənsˈtreɪn] *vt* **1** *(oblige, force)*
constreñir, obligar, forzar. **2** *(restrict,
hold back)* contener.

constraint [kənˈstreɪnt] *n* **1** *(compulsion,
coercion)* coacción *f*, obligación *f*. **2** *(restriction)* restricción *f*, limitación *f*.

constrict [kənˈstrɪkt] *vt* **1** *(blood vessels)*
estrangular; *(breathing, movement)* dificultar; *(neck)* apretar, oprimir. **2** *fig
(action, behaviour)* limitar, coartar.

construct [kənsˈtrʌkt] *vt* construir.

construction [kənˈstrʌkʃən] *n* **1** *(gen)*
construcción *f*. **2** *fig (meaning)* interpretación *f*.

constructive [kənˈstrʌktɪv] *adj* constructivo,-a.

constructor [kənˈstrʌktər] *n* constructor,-ra.

construe [kənˈstruː] *vt* interpretar.

consul [ˈkɒnsəl] *n* cónsul *mf*.

consulate [ˈkɒnsjələt] *n* consulado *m*.

consult [kənˈsʌlt] *vt* consultar.
▶ *vi* consultar.

consultant [kənˈsʌltənt] *n* **1** *(expert, advisor)* asesor,-ra, consultor,-ra. **2** GB
(doctor) especialista *mf*.

consultation [kɒnsəlˈteɪʃən] *n* consulta.

consulting [kənˈsʌltɪŋ] *adj (architect, engineer)* asesor,-ra, consultor,-ra. COMP
consulting room MED consulta.

consume [kənˈsjuːm] *vt* consumir.

consumer [kənˈsjuːmər] *n* consumidor,-ra.

consummate [*(adj)* ˈkɒnsəmət; *(vb)*
ˈkɒnsəmeɪt] *adj fml* consumado,-a.
▶ *vt fml* consumar.

consumption [kənˈsʌmpʃən] *n* consumo.

contact [ˈkɒntækt] *n* contacto. COMP
contact lenses lentes *fpl* de contacto.
▶ *vt* ponerse en contacto con.

contagion [kənˈteɪdʒən] *n* contagio.

contagious [kənˈteɪdʒəs] *adj* contagioso,-a.

contain [kənˈteɪn] *vt* contener.

container [kənˈteɪnər] *n* **1** *(receptacle)* recipiente *m*; *(packaging)* envase *m*. **2** *(fo
transporting goods)* contenedor *m*, contáiner *m*.

containment [kənˈteɪnmənt] *n* con
tención *f*.

contaminate [kənˈtæmɪneɪt] *vt* conta
minar.

contamination [kəntæmɪˈneɪʃən]
contaminación *f*.

contemplate [ˈkɒntempleɪt] *vt* con
templar.

contemporaneous [kɒntempəˈreɪ
nɪəs] *adj fml* contemporáneo,-a.

contemporary [kənˈtempərərɪ] *ad*
contemporáneo,-a.
▶ *n* contemporáneo,-a.
ⓘ *pl* contemporaries.

contempt [kənˈtempt] *n* desprecio
desdén *m*, menosprecio.

contemptible [kənˈtemptəbəl] *adj* des
preciable.

contend [kənˈtend] *vi* **1** *(compete)* con
tender, competir. **2** *(deal with, strugg
against)* enfrentarse a, lidiar con.
▶ *vt (claim, state)* sostener, afirmar.

contender [kənˈtendər] *n* contendien
te *mf* (for, por).

content¹ [ˈkɒntent] *n* contenido.
▶ *n pl* **contents** contenido *m sing*.

content² [kənˈtent] *adj* contento,-a
satisfecho,-a: *he's content to watch th
match at home* se conforma con ver el pa
tido en casa.
▶ *n* contento.
▶ *vt* contentar, satisfacer.

contented [kənˈtentɪd] *adj* contento,-a
satisfecho,-a.

contention [kənˈtenʃən] *n* **1** *(opinion, a
sertion)* opinión *f*. **2** *(dispute, disagreemen
discusión *f*, controversia.

contentious [kənˈtenʃəs] *adj* polé
mico,-a.

contest [*(n)* ˈkɒntest; *(vb)* kənˈtest] *n
(competition - gen)* concurso; *(- sports)* con

petición f; (- boxing) combate m. **2** (struggle, attempt) contienda, lucha.

▶ vt **1** (championship, seat) competir por, luchar por, disputarse; (election) presentarse como candidato,-a. **2** (dispute) refutar, rebatir. **3** JUR (appeal against) impugnar.

❌ To contest no significa 'contestar', que se traduce por to answer.

contestant [kən'testənt] n (in competition, quiz, game) concursante mf; (for post, position) candidato,-a, aspirante mf.

context ['kɒntekst] n contexto.

contiguous [kən'tɪgjuəs] adj contiguo,-a.

continent ['kɒntɪnənt] n continente m.

continental [kɒntɪ'nentəl] adj continental.

▶ adj Continental GB europeo,-a.

contingency [kən'tɪndʒənsɪ] n contingencia. COMP contingency plan plan m de emergencia.

contingent [kən'tɪndʒənt] adj contingente.

▶ n contingente m.

continual [kən'tɪnjuəl] adj continuo,-a, constante.

continuation [kəntɪnju'eɪʃən] n continuación f.

continue [kən'tɪnjuː] vt & vi continuar, seguir.

continuous [kən'tɪnjuəs] adj continuo,-a.

contort [kən'tɔːt] vt (face) contraer.

▶ vi contraerse.

contortion [kən'tɔːʃən] n contorsión f.

contour ['kɒntuər] n contorno.

contraband ['kɒntrəbænd] n contrabando.

contraception [kɒntrə'sepʃən] n anticoncepción f.

contraceptive [kɒntrə'septɪv] adj anticonceptivo,-a.

▶ n anticonceptivo.

contract [(n) 'kɒntrækt; (vb) kən'trækt] n (gen) contrato; (for public work, services) contrata.

▶ vt **1** (place under contract) contratar. **2** (make smaller) contraer. **3** fml (debt, habit, illness) contraer.

contraction [kən'trækʃən] n contracción f.

contractor [kən'træktər] n contratista mf.

contradict [kɒntrə'dɪkt] vt & vi contradecir.

contradiction [kɒntrə'dɪkʃən] n contradicción f.

contradictory [kɒntrə'dɪktərɪ] adj contradictorio,-a.

contraption [kən'træpʃən] n fam cacharro, artefacto, artilugio.

contrary [(adj) 'kɒntrərɪ; (n) kɒn'treərɪ] adj **1** (opposite) contrario,-a. **2** (stubborn) terco,-a, obstinado,-a, tozudo,-a.

▶ n the contrary lo contrario.

contrast [(n) 'kɒntrɑːst; (vb) kən'trɑːst] n contraste m.

▶ vt & vi contrastar.

contribute [kən'trɪbjuːt] vt **1** (money) contribuir (to, a; towards, para); (ideas, information) aportar. **2** (article, poem, etc) escribir.

▶ vi **1** (gen) contribuir (to, a; towards, para); (in discussion) participar (to, en). **2** (to newspaper, magazine, etc) colaborar (to, en), escribir (to, para).

contributor [kən'trɪbjətər] n **1** (to charity, appeal, etc) donante mf. **2** (to newspaper, magazine, etc) colaborador,-ra.

contrive [kən'traɪv] vt **1** (way, device) idear, inventar; (meeting) arreglar; (meal, dress, etc) improvisar. **2** (manage) conseguir.

contrived [kən'traɪvd] adj artificial.

control [kən'trəul] vt controlar.

▶ n **1** (power, command) poder m, dominio, mando; (authority) autoridad f. **2** (restriction, means of regulating) control m. **3** (place, people in control) control m. **4** (switch, button) botón m, mando. COMP control tower torre f de emergencia.

▶ n pl controls (of vehicle) mandos mpl.

controller [kən'trəulər] n **1** (financial) interventor,-ra. **2** (in broadcasting) director,-ra de programación.

controversy [kən'trɒvəsɪ] n controversia, polémica.

ⓘ pl controversies.

contusion [kən'tjuː'ʒ°n] n contusión f.
convalesce [kɒnvə'les] vi convalecer.
convalescence [kɒnvə'les°ns] n convalecencia.
convalescent [kɒnvə'les°nt] adj convaleciente.
convenience [kən'viːnɪəns] n conveniencia, comodidad f. COMP **convenience food** plato precocinado.
convenient [kən'viːnɪənt] adj (time, arrangement) conveniente, oportuno,-a; (thing) práctico,-a, cómodo,-a.
convent ['kɒnvənt] n convento.
convention [kən'venʃ°n] n convención f, congreso.
converge [kən'vɜːdʒ] vi (lines, roads) convergir (on, en), converger (on, en); (people) reunirse.
conversant [kən'vɜːs°nt] adj familiarizado,-a (with, con), versado,-a (with, en).
conversation [kɒnvə'seɪʃ°n] n conversación f.
converse ['kɒnvɜːs] adj opuesto,-a, contrario,-a.
conversion [kən'vɜːʃ°n] n conversión f (to, a; into, en).
convert [(vb) kən'vɜːt; (n) 'kɒnvɜːt] vt (gen) convertir (into, en; to, a).
  ▶ n REL converso,-a.
convertible [kən'vɜːtəb°l] adj (gen) convertible; (car) descapotable.
  ▶ n AUTO descapotable m.
convex ['kɒnveks] adj convexo,-a.
convey [kən'veɪ] vt 1 (goods, people, electricity) transportar, conducir; (sound) transmitir, llevar. 2 (opinion, feeling, idea) comunicar, transmitir.
conveyance [kən'veɪəns] n 1 (transport) transporte m. 2 fml (vehicle) vehículo. 3 JUR traspaso, transferencia.
conveyor belt [kən'veɪə'belt] n cinta transportadora.
convict [(n) 'kɒnvɪkt; (vb) kən'vɪkt] n presidiario,-a, recluso,-a.
  ▶ vt JUR declarar culpable, condenar.
conviction [kən'vɪkʃ°n] n 1 (belief) convicción f, creencia. 2 JUR condena (for, por).
convince [kən'vɪns] vt convencer.

convincing [kən'vɪnsɪŋ] adj convincente.
convoy ['kɒnvɔɪ] n convoy m.
cook [kuk] n cocinero,-a.
  ▶ vt (food) guisar, cocinar; (meals) preparar, hacer.
cooker ['kukə'] n (stove) cocina.
cookery ['kukərɪ] n cocina: Spanish cookery cocina española. COMP **cookery book** libro de cocina.
cookie ['kukɪ] n 1 US (biscuit) galleta. 2 (in computing) cookie m & f, galleta.
cooking ['kukɪŋ] n cocina: home cooking cocina casera.
cool [kuːl] adj 1 (gen) fresco,-a. 2 (unfriendly, reserved) frío,-a. 3 (calm) tranquilo,-a, sereno,-a. 4 fam (great) guay.
coop [kuːp] n gallinero.
cooperate [kəʊ'bpəreɪt] [also written co-operate] vi cooperar, colaborar.
coordinate [(vb) kəʊ'ɔːdɪneɪt; (n) kəʊ'ɔːdɪnət] [also written co-ordinate] vt coordinar.
  ▶ n MATH coordenada.
coordination [kəʊɔːdɪ'neɪʃ°n] [also written co-ordination] n coordinación f.
cop [kɒp] n sl (policeman) poli mf.
cope [kəʊp] vi arreglárselas, poder.
copious ['kəʊpɪəs] adj copioso,-a, abundante.
copper ['kɒpə'] n 1 (metal) cobre m. 2 GB fam (coin) penique m, pela, perra. 3 sl (policeman) poli mf.
copse [kɒps] n arboleda, bosquecillo.
copulate ['kɒpjəleɪt] vi copular.
copy ['kɒpɪ] n 1 (reproduction) copia. 2 (of book, magazine, etc) ejemplar m.
  ① pl copies.
  ▶ vi copiar.
copycat ['kɒpɪkæt] n fam copión,-ona.
  ▶ adj (crime) inspirado,-a en otro.
copyright ['kɒpɪraɪt] n copyright m, derechos mpl de autor.
coral ['kɒr°l] n coral m.
cord [kɔːd] n 1 (string, rope) cuerda. 2 ELEC cable m. 3 (corduroy) pana.
cordon ['kɔːd°n] n cordón m.
corduroy ['kɔːdərɔɪ] n pana.

core [kɔːʳ] n **1** (gen) núcleo. **2** (of apple, pear, etc) corazón m.

coriander [kɒrɪˈændəʳ] n cilantro.

cork [kɔːk] n (material) corcho.

corkscrew [ˈkɔːkskruː] n sacacorchos m.

corm [kɔːm] n bulbo.

corn¹ [kɔːn] n (gen) cereales mpl; (wheat) trigo; (oats) avena; (maize) maíz m.

corn² [kɔːn] n MED callo.

corncob [ˈkɔːnkɒb] n mazorca de maíz.

cornea [ˈkɔːnɪə] n córnea.

corned beef [kɔːndˈbiːf] n carne f en conserva.

corner [ˈkɔːnəʳ] n **1** (of street) esquina; (bend in road) curva; (of table, etc) esquina, punta. **2** (of room, cupboard, etc) rincón m; (of mouth) comisura; (of eye) rabillo; (of page, envelope) ángulo. **3** SP (kick - in football) córner m, saque m de esquina.
▶ vt arrinconar, acorralar; (person) arrinconar.

cornet [ˈkɔːnɪt] n **1** MUS corneta. **2** GB (for ice-cream) cucurucho.

cornflakes [ˈkɔːnfleɪks] npl copos de maíz.

cornice [ˈkɔːnɪs] n cornisa.

corolla [kəˈrɒlə] n corola.

coronation [kɒrəˈheɪʃən] n coronación f.

coroner [ˈkɒrənəʳ] n juez mf de instrucción.

corporal [ˈkɔːpərəl] n MIL cabo.

corporate [ˈkɔːpərət] adj **1** (collective) colectivo,-a. **2** (of a corporation) de la empresa, de la compañía.

corporation [kɔːpəˈreɪʃən] n corporación f.

corps [kɔːʳ] n cuerpo.
ⓘ pl corps [kɔːz].

corpse [kɔːps] n cadáver m.

corpus [ˈkɔːpəs] adj **1** (of texts) corpus m. **2** ANAT cuerpo. COMP ANAT **corpus callosum** cuerpo calloso.

corpuscle [ˈkɔːpəsəl] n corpúsculo, glóbulo.

correct [kəˈrekt] adj correcto,-a.
▶ vt corregir.

correspond [kɒrɪsˈpɒnd] vi **1** (gen) corresponderse (with, con). **2** (write) escribirse (with, con).

correspondence [kɒrɪsˈpɒndəns] n correspondencia.

correspondent [kɒrɪsˈpɒndənt] n corresponsal mf.

corridor [ˈkɒrɪdɔːʳ] n pasillo.

corrode [kəˈrəʊd] vt corroer.
▶ vi corroerse.

corrosion [kəˈrəʊʒən] n **1** (process) corrosión f. **2** (substance) herrumbre f, orín m.

corrupt [kəˈrʌpt] adj corrompido,-a, corrupto,-a.
▶ vt corromper; (bribe) sobornar.

corruption [kəˈrʌpʃən] n corrupción f.

corset [ˈkɔːsɪt] n corsé m.

cortex [ˈkɔːteks] n corteza.

cos [ˈkəʊsaɪn] abbr (cosine) coseno; (abbreviation) cos.

cosine [ˈkəʊsaɪn] n MATH coseno.

cosmetic [kɒzˈmetɪk] adj cosmético,-a.
COMP **cosmetic surgery** cirugía estética.

cosmic [ˈkɒzmɪk] adj cósmico,-a.

cosmonaut [ˈkɒzmənɔːt] n cosmonauta mf.

cosmopolitan [kɒzməˈpɒlɪtən] adj cosmopolita.

cosmos [ˈkɒzmɒs] n cosmos m.

cost [kɒst] vt costar, valer.
ⓘ pt & pp cost [kɒst].
▶ n (price) coste m, precio. COMP **cost of living** coste de la vida.

costal [ˈkɒstəl] adj costal.

co-star [ˈkəʊstɑːʳ] n coprotagonista mf.

Costa Rica [kɒstəˈriːkə] n Costa Rica.

Costa Rican [kɒstəˈriːkən] adj costarricense.
▶ n (person) costarricense mf.

cost-effective [kɒstɪˈfektɪv] adj rentable.

costly [ˈkɒstlɪ] adj costoso,-a.
ⓘ comp costlier, superl costliest.

costume [ˈkɒstjuːm] n traje m.
▶ n pl **costumes** THEAT vestuario.

cosy [ˈkəʊzɪ] adj **1** (room, house, atmosphere) acogedor,-ra. **2** (chat) íntimo,-a y agradable.
ⓘ comp cosier, superl cosiest.

cot [kɒt] n **1** (for baby) cuna. **2** US (camp bed) cama de campaña.

cotton [ˈkɒtˀn] *n* **1** *(cloth, plant)* algodón *m*. **2** *(thread)* hilo (de coser).
▶ *adj (shirt, etc)* de algodón. COMP **cotton bud** bastoncillo de algodón. ∥ **cotton wool** algodón *m* hidrófilo.

couch [kaʊtʃ] *n (sofa)* canapé *m*, sofá *m*.

couchette [kuːˈʃet] *n* litera.

✎ Couchette se refiere específicamente a las literas de los trenes. Las literas que puede haber en una casa se llaman **bunk beds**.

cougar [ˈkuːgəʳ] *n* puma *m*.

cough [kɒf] *n* tos *f*.
▶ *vi* toser.

could [kʊd] *pt* → **can**.

council [ˈkaʊnsˀl] *n* **1** *(elected group)* consejo. **2** GB *(of town, city)* ayuntamiento. **3** REL concilio.

councillor [ˈkaʊnsˀləʳ] *n* concejal,-la.

counsel [ˈkaʊnsˀl] *n* **1** *(advice)* consejo. **2** JUR abogado,-a.

counsellor [ˈkaʊnsˀləʳ] *n* **1** *(adviser)* consejero,-a, asesor,-ra. **2** US *(lawyer)* abogado,-a.

count¹ [kaʊnt] *n (act of counting)* recuento; *(of votes)* escrutinio; *(total)* total *m*, suma.
▶ *vt* **1** *(gen)* contar. **2** *(consider)* considerar.

✗ To count no significa 'contar (relatar)', que se traduce por to tell.

count² [kaʊnt] *n (nobleman)* conde *m*.

countable [ˈkaʊntəbˀl] *adj* contable.

countdown [ˈkaʊntdaʊn] *n* cuenta atrás.

counter [ˈkaʊntəʳ] *n* **1** *(in shop)* mostrador *m*; *(individual)* ventanilla. **2** *(in board games)* ficha.

counteract [kaʊntəˈrækt] *vt* contrarrestar.

counterattack [ˈkaʊntˀrətæk] *n* contraataque *m*.
▶ *vt* contraatacar.

counterclockwise [kaʊntəˈklɒkwaɪz] *adj* US en sentido contrario a las agujas del reloj.

counterfeit [ˈkaʊntəfɪt] *adj* falso,-a, falsificado,-a.
▶ *n* falsificación *f*.
▶ *vt* falsificar.

counterfoil [ˈkaʊntəfɔɪl] *n* matriz *f*.

counterpart [ˈkaʊntəpɑːt] *n* homólogo,-a.

counterproductive [kaʊntəprəˈdʌktɪv] *adj* contraproducente.

countess [ˈkaʊntəs] *n* condesa.

countless [ˈkaʊntləs] *adj* incontable, innumerable.

country [ˈkʌntrɪ] *n* **1** *(state, nation)* país *m*; *(people)* pueblo. **2** [no se usa en *pl*] *(rural area)* campo. **3** [no se usa en *pl*] *(region, area of land)* región *f*, zona, territorio. **1** [también **country music**] MUS música country, country *m*.
ⓘ *pl* countries.
▶ *adj (rural - life, lane)* rural; *(- house)* de campo.

countryman [ˈkʌntrɪmən] *n* **1** *(man from country)* campesino. **2** *(compatriot)* compatriota *m*.
ⓘ *pl* countrymen [ˈkʌntrɪmən].

countryside [ˈkʌntrɪsaɪd] *n* *(area)* campo, campiña; *(scenery)* paisaje *m*.

countrywoman [ˈkʌntrɪwʊmən] *n* **1** *(woman from the country)* campesina. **2** *(compatriot)* compatriota.
ⓘ *pl* countrywomen [ˈkʌntrɪwɪmɪn].

county [ˈkaʊntɪ] *n* condado.
ⓘ *pl* counties.

coup [kuː] *n* golpe *m*. COMP **coup d'état** golpe *m* de estado.

couple [ˈkʌpˀl] *n* **1** *(two things)* par *m*; *(a few)* unos,-as. **2** *(two people)* pareja.
▶ *vt* conectar, acoplar.

coupon [ˈkuːpɒn] *n* **1** COMM *(for discount, free gift, etc)* cupón *m*, vale *m*. **2** GB *(for competition, football pools)* boleto.

courage [ˈkʌrɪdʒ] *n* coraje *m*, valor *m*, valentía.

courageous [kəˈreɪdʒəs] *adj* valiente.

courgette [kʊəˈʒet] *n* calabacín *m*.

courier [ˈkʊərɪəʳ] *n* **1** *(messenger)* mensajero,-a. **2** *(guide)* guía *mf* turístico,-a.

course [kɔːs] *n* **1** *(gen)* curso; *(of ship)* rumbo. **2** EDUC *(year - long)* curso; *(- short)* cursillo; *(at university)* carrera; *(individual subject)* asignatura. **3** *(of meal)* plato. **4** SP *(for golf)* campo. LOC **of course** desde luego, por supuesto. COMP **main course** segundo plato.

court [kɔːt] n **1** JUR (place, people) tribunal m; (building) juzgado. **2** (royal) corte f. **3** SP (tennis, squash, etc) pista, cancha. **4** (courtyard) patio.

courteous [ˈkɜːtɪəs] adj cortés.

courtesy [ˈkɜːtəsɪ] n **1** (good manners) cortesía, educación f. **2** (polite act or remark) favor m, atención f.
ⓘ pl courtesies.

courthouse [ˈkɔːthaʊs] n juzgado.

courtroom [ˈkɔːtruːm] n sala de justicia, tribunal m.

courtyard [ˈkɔːtjɑːd] n patio.

cousin [ˈkʌzən] n primo,-a.

cove [kəʊv] n cala, ensenada.

covenant [ˈkʌvənənt] n JUR (formal agreement) convenio, pacto; (clause) cláusula, provisión f.

cover [ˈkʌvəʳ] n **1** (lid) tapa, cubierta. **2** (thing that covers - gen) funda. **3** (outside pages - of book) cubierta, tapa; (- of magazine) portada. **4** (insurance) cobertura. **5** (shelter, protection) abrigo, protección f.
▸ vt **1** (place over - gen) cubrir (with, de); (- floor, wall) revestir (with, de); (- sofa) tapizar; (- book) forrar. **2** (with lid, hands) tapar. **3** (hide) tapar.

coverage [ˈkʌvərɪdʒ] n cobertura.

coveralls [ˈkʌvərɔːlz] n pl US → overalls.

covering [ˈkʌvərɪŋ] n (protective) cubierta, envoltura; (layer) capa.

covert [ˈkʌvət] adj secreto,-a.

cover-up [ˈkʌvərʌp] n encubrimiento.

covet [ˈkʌvət] vt codiciar.

cow [kaʊ] n vaca.

coward [ˈkaʊəd] n cobarde mf.

cowardly [ˈkaʊədlɪ] adj cobarde.

cowboy [ˈkaʊbɔɪ] n vaquero.

cox [kɒks] n timonel mf.

coy [kɔɪ] adj tímido,-a, recatado,-a.

coyote [kaɪˈəʊtɪ] n coyote m.

cozy [ˈkəʊzɪ] adj US → cosy.
ⓘ comp cozier, superl coziest.

crab [kræb] n (shellfish) cangrejo.

crack [kræk] vt **1** (break - cup, glass, etc) rajar; (- bone) fracturar, romper. **2** (break open - safe) forzar; (- egg, nut) cascar; (- bottle) abrir, descorchar. **3** (hit) pegar, golpear.
▸ vi **1** (break - cup, glass) rajarse, resquebrarse; (- rock, plaster, paint, skin) agrietarse. **2** (relationship, system) venirse abajo; (person) sufrir una crisis nerviosa.
▸ n **1** (in cup, glass) raja; (in ice, wall, ground, pavement, etc) grieta. **2** (slit, narrow opening) rendija. **3** (of whip) restallido, chasquido.
▸ adj (troops, regiment, shot) de primera.

cracked [krækt] adj fam (mad, crazy) chiflado,-a, chalado,-a.

cracker [ˈkrækəʳ] n **1** (biscuit) galleta seca. **2** (firework) petardo m.

cracking [ˈkrækɪŋ] adj fam (shot, goal) de primera; (pace) muy rápido,-a.

crackle [ˈkrækəl] n (of twigs, etc) crujido, chasquido.
▸ vi (twigs, etc) chasquear; (fire) chisporrotear, crepitar; (radio, telephone) hacer ruido.

cradle [ˈkreɪdəl] n cuna f.
▸ vt (baby) acunar (en los brazos), mecer.

craft [krɑːft] n **1** (occupation) oficio. **2** (art) arte m; (skill) habilidad f, destreza. **3** (boat) embarcación f.
▸ vt trabajar.

craftsman [ˈkrɑːftsmən] n artesano.
ⓘ pl craftsmen [ˈkrɑːftsmən].

craftswoman [ˈkrɑːftswʊmən] n artesana.
ⓘ pl craftswomen [ˈkrɑːftswɪmɪn].

crafty [ˈkrɑːftɪ] adj (person) astuto,-a; (child) pillo,-a; (method, idea, etc) hábil.
ⓘ comp craftier, superl craftiest.

crag [kræg] n peña, risco, peñasco.

cram [kræm] vt (stuff, fill) atestar (with, de), atiborrar (with, de).
▸ vi fam (learn for exam) empollar.
ⓘ pt & pp crammed, ger cramming.

cramp¹ [kræmp] n MED calambre m.
▸ n pl cramps (gen) retortijones mpl

cramp² [kræmp] vt obstaculizar.

cranberry [ˈkrænbərɪ] n arándano.
ⓘ pl cranberries.

crane [kreɪn] n **1** ZOOL grulla común. **2** (machine) grúa.

cranium [ˈkreɪnɪəm] n cráneo.
ⓘ pl craniums o crania [ˈkreɪnɪə].

crank [kræŋk] n **1** (crankshaft) cigüeñal m. **2** (starting handle) manivela.

crash [kræʃ] n **1** (noise) estrépito; (of thunder) trueno, estallido. **2** (collision) choque m, accidente m. **3** COMM (collapse) quiebra.

crate [kreɪt] n caja, cajón m.
▶ vt embalar.

crater [ˈkreɪtəʳ] n cráter m.

crave [kreɪv] vt ansiar, tener ansias de.

craving [ˈkreɪvɪŋ] n (gen) ansia (for, de), ansias fpl (for, de); (in pregnancy) antojo (for, de).

crawfish [ˈkrɔːfɪʃ] n → crayfish.

crawl [krɔːl] vi **1** (move slowly - person, snake) arrastrarse; (- baby) gatear. **2** (car, traffic) ir a paso de tortuga.
▶ n SP (in swimming) crol m.

crayfish [ˈkreɪfɪʃ] n cangrejo de río.
ⓘ pl crayfish.

crayon [ˈkreɪɒn] n lápiz m de cera.

craze [kreɪz] n (fashion) moda; (game, sport, hobby, etc) manía.

crazy [ˈkreɪzɪ] adj fam loco,-a.
ⓘ comp crazier, superl craziest.

creak [kriːk] vi (floorboard, stairs, joints) crujir, hacer un crujido; (door, hinge) chirriar.

cream [kriːm] n **1** (of milk) nata, crema (de leche). **2** (cosmetic) crema; (medical) pomada, crema.

crease [kriːs] n **1** (wrinkle) arruga; (fold) pliegue m; (ironed) raya. **2** SP (in cricket) línea.

create [kriːˈeɪt] vt **1** (gen) crear. **2** (cause) producir, causar.

creation [kriːˈeɪʃən] n creación f.

creature [ˈkriːtʃəʳ] n **1** (animal) criatura. **2** (human being) ser m.

credentials [krɪˈdenʃəlz] n pl **1** (qualifications) credenciales fpl. **2** (documents) cartas fpl credenciales.

credible [ˈkredɪbəl] adj creíble.

credit [ˈkredɪt] n **1** (praise, approval) mérito, reconocimiento. **2** (belief, trust, confidence) crédito. **3** FIN (gen) crédito; (in accountancy) haber m; (on statement) saldo acreedor. **5** EDUC crédito.
▶ n pl credits (of film, programme) ficha técnica.

creditor [ˈkredɪtəʳ] n acreedor,-ra.

creed [kriːd] n credo.

creek [kriːk] n **1** GB cala. **2** US riachuelo, arroyo.

creep [kriːp] vi **1** (move quietly) moverse sigilosamente, deslizarse. **2** (move with the body close to the ground) arrastrarse, reptar.
ⓘ pt & pp crept [krept].

creeper [ˈkriːpəʳ] n (planta) trepadora.

cremate [krɪˈmeɪt] vt incinerar.

crematorium [kreməˈtɔːrɪəm] n (horno) crematorio.
ⓘ pl crematoriums o crematoria [kreməˈtɔːrɪə].

crepe [kreɪp] n crepe m.

crept [krept] pt & pp → creep.

crescent [ˈkresnt] n (shape) medialuna.
▶ adj creciente. COMP crescent moon luna creciente.

cress [kres] n berro.

crest [krest] n **1** (of cock) cresta. **2** (of hill) cima, cumbre f; (of wave) cresta.

crestfallen [ˈkrestfɔːlən] adj abatido,-a.

crevice [ˈkrevɪs] n grieta, raja.

crew¹ [kruː] n **1** (of ship, etc) tripulación f. **2** (working team) equipo.

crew² [kruː] pt → crow.

crib [krɪb] n **1** (manger) pesebre m; (Nativity scene) belén m, pesebre m. **2** (for baby) cuna. **3** (for cheating) chuleta.
▶ vt plagiar, copiar.
ⓘ pt & pp cribbed, ger cribbing.

crick [krɪk] n (in neck) tortícolis f.

cricket¹ [ˈkrɪkɪt] n (insect) grillo.

cricket² [ˈkrɪkɪt] n SP cricket m.

cried [kraɪd] pp → cry.

crime [kraɪm] n crimen m.

criminal [ˈkrɪmɪnəl] adj criminal.
▶ n delincuente mf, criminal mf.

cringe [krɪndʒ] vi encogerse, agacharse.

crinkle [ˈkrɪŋkəl] n arruga.
▶ vt arrugar.

cripple [ˈkrɪpəl] n lisiado,-a, tullido,-a.
▶ vt **1** (person) dejar cojo,-a, lisiar. **2** fig (industry, country) paralizar.

crisis [ˈkraɪsɪs] n crisis f.
ⓘ pl crises [ˈkraɪsiːs].

crisp [krɪsp] *adj* **1** *(pastry, biscuits, etc)* crujiente; *(lettuce)* fresco,-a. **2** *(weather, air)* frío,-a y seco,-a.
▶ *n* GB patata frita *(de bolsa o churrería)*.

✎ Son las patatas de bolsa o de churrería que se comen frías, pues las que se comen calientes se llaman **chips** en inglés británico y **french fries** en inglés americano.

crisscross [ˈkrɪskrɒs] *vt* entrecruzar.
critic [ˈkrɪtɪk] *n (reviewer)* crítico,-a.
critical [ˈkrɪtɪkəl] *adj* crítico,-a.
criticism [ˈkrɪtɪsɪzəm] *n* crítica.
criticize [ˈkrɪtɪsaɪz] *vt* criticar.
croak [krəʊk] *n* **1** *(of raven)* graznido; *(of frog)* canto. **2** *(of person)* voz *f* ronca.
Croatia [krəʊˈeɪʃə] *n* Croacia.
Croatian [krəʊˈeɪʃən] *adj* croata.
▶ *adj (person)* croata *mf; (language)* croata *m.*
crochet [ˈkrəʊʃeɪ] *n* ganchillo.
crockery [ˈkrɒkəri] *n* loza, vajilla.
crocodile [ˈkrɒkədaɪl] *n* cocodrilo.
crocus [ˈkrəʊkəs] *n* azafrán *m.*
crony [ˈkrəʊnɪ] *n fam* compinche *mf.*
ⓘ *pl* cronies.
crook [krʊk] *n* **1** cayado, gancho. **2** *fam (criminal)* sinvergüenza *mf,* delincuente *mf.*
▶ *vt (finger, arm)* doblar.
crop [krɒp] *n* **1** *(plant)* cultivo; *(harvest)* cosecha. **2** *(group, batch)* tanda. **3** *(hairstyle)* corte *m* al rape.
cross [krɒs] *n* **1** *(gen)* cruz *f.* **2** BIOL *(hybrid)* cruce *m.*
▶ *vt (street, river, bridge,)* cruzar, atravesar; *(arms, legs)* cruzar.
▶ *vi (walk across)* cruzar (over, -); *(intersect, pass each other)* cruzarse.
crossbar [ˈkrɒsbɑːʳ] *n (of goal)* travesaño, larguero; *(of bicycle)* barra.
crossing [ˈkrɒsɪŋ] *n* **1** MAR travesía. **2** *(intersection, crossroads)* cruce *m.* COMP **border crossing** paso fronterizo.
cross-reference [krɒsˈrefərəns] *n* remisión *f.*
▶ *vt* remitir.
crossroads [ˈkrɒsrəʊdz] *n* encrucijada, cruce *m.*

crossword [ˈkrɒswɜːd] [también crossword puzzle] *n* crucigrama *m.*
crotch [krɒtʃ] *n* entrepierna.
crotchet [ˈkrɒtʃɪt] *n* MUS negra.
crouch [kraʊtʃ] [también crouch down] *vi (person)* agacharse, ponerse en cuclillas; *(cat)* agazaparse.
crow¹ [krəʊ] *n (bird)* cuervo.
crow² [krəʊ] *vi (cock)* cantar, cacarear.
ⓘ *pt* crowed o crew [kruː], *pp* crowed.
crowbar [ˈkrəʊbɑːʳ] *n* palanca.
crowd [kraʊd] *n* **1** *(large number of people)* multitud *f,* muchedumbre *f,* gentío; *(at match, concert, etc)* público. **2** *(particular group)* gente *f; (clique)* pandilla.
crowded [ˈkraʊdɪd] *adj* abarrotado,-a de gente, concurrido,-a.
crown [kraʊn] *n* **1** *(of king, queen)* corona. **2** ANAT *(of head)* coronilla; *(of tooth)* corona. **3** *(top - of hat, tree)* copa.
crucial [ˈkruːʃəl] *adj* crucial.
crucifix [ˈkruːsɪfɪks] *n* crucifijo.
crucify [ˈkruːsɪfaɪ] *vt* crucificar.
ⓘ *pt & pp* crucified, *ger* crucifying.
crude [kruːd] *n* **1** *(manners, style)* tosco,-a, grosero,-a; *(joke)* grosero,-a, ordinario,-a. **2** *(oil)* crudo,-a.

❌ Crude no significa 'crudo (sin hacer)', que se traduce por raw.

cruel [ˈkruːəl] *adj* cruel.
ⓘ *comp* crueller, *superl* cruellest.
cruelty [ˈkruːəltɪ] *n* crueldad *f* (to, hacia).
ⓘ *pl* cruelties.
cruise [kruːz] *vi* MAR hacer un crucero.
▶ *n* crucero.
cruiser [ˈkruːzəʳ] *n* **1** *(warship)* crucero. **2** *(pleasure boat)* yate *m.*
crumb [krʌm] *n* miga, migaja.
crumble [ˈkrʌmbəl] *vt (gen)* desmenuzar, deshacer; *(bread)* desmigajar.
crumple [ˈkrʌmpəl] *vt (clothes)* arrugar; *(paper)* estrujar.
crunch [krʌntʃ] *vt* **1** *(food)* mascar. **2** *(with feet, tyres)* hacer crujir.
crusade [kruːˈseɪd] *n* cruzada.
crush [krʌʃ] *vt* **1** *(squash - gen)* aplastar; *(squeeze)* estrujar. **2** *(smash, pound - gen)* triturar; *(- ice)* picar.

► *n* **1** *(of people)* aglomeración *f*. **2** GB *(soft drink)* refresco.

crust [krʌst] *n* corteza.

crustacean [krʌˈsteɪʃᵉn] *n* crustáceo.

crutch [krʌtʃ] *n* **1** *(for walking)* muleta.

crux [krʌks] *n* quid *m*, meollo.

cry [kraɪ] *vt* **1** *(shout, call)* gritar. **2** *(weep)* llorar.
ⓘ *pt & pp* cried, *ger* crying.

crying [ˈkraɪɪŋ] *n* *(weeping)* llanto.

crypt [krɪpt] *n* cripta.

crystal [ˈkrɪstᵉl] *n* cristal *m*.

crystallize [ˈkrɪstəlaɪz] *vt* cristalizar.

cub [kʌb] *n* ZOOL cachorro,-a

cube [kjuːb] *n* **1** *(shape)* cubo; *(of sugar)* terrón *m*; *(of ice)* cubito; *(of cheese, meat, etc)* dado. **2** MATH cubo. COMP cube root raíz *f* cúbica.
► *vt* MATH elevar al cubo.

cubic [ˈkjuːbɪk] *adj* cúbico,-a.

cubism [ˈkjuːbɪzᵉm] *n* cubismo.

cuckoo [ˈkuku:] *n* cuco.
ⓘ *pl* cuckoos.

cucumber [ˈkjuːkʌmbəʳ] *n* pepino.

cuddle [ˈkʌdᵉl] *vt* abrazar, acariciar.

cue¹ [kjuː] *n* **1** *(for actor)* pie *m*; *(for musician)* entrada. **2** *(signal)* señal *f*. **3** *(example)* ejemplo.

cue² [kjuː] *n* *(in billiards, etc)* taco. COMP cue ball bola blanca.

cuff¹ [kʌf] *n* **1** *(of sleeve)* puño. **2** US *(of trousers)* dobladillo.
► *n pl* cuffs *sl* esposas *fpl*.

cuff² [kʌf] *vt* dar un bofetada a.
► *n* bofetada, cachete *m*, bofetón *m*.

cufflinks [ˈkʌflɪŋks] *n pl* gemelos *mpl*.

cuisine [kwɪˈziːn] *n* cocina.

cul-de-sac [ˈkʌldəsæk] *n* calle *f* sin salida.

culminate [ˈkʌlmɪneɪt] *vi* culminar.

culottes [kjuːˈlɒts] *n pl* falda pantalón *f sing*.

culprit [ˈkʌlprɪt] *n* culpable *mf*.

cult [kʌlt] *n* *(gen)* culto; *(sect)* secta.

cultivate [ˈkʌltɪveɪt] *vt* cultivar.
ⓘ *pt & pp* cupped, *ger* cupping.

culture [ˈkʌltʃəʳ] *n* **1** *(gen)* cultura. **2** *(growth)* cultivo.

cumbersome [ˈkʌmbəsəm] *adj* **1** *(thing)* incómodo,-a, voluminoso,-a, pesado,-a. **2** *(procedure)* torpe, engorroso,-a.

cumin [ˈkʌmɪn] *n* comino.

cunning [ˈkʌnɪŋ] *adj* astuto,-a
► *n* astucia.

cup [kʌp] *n* **1** *(for drinking)* taza. **2** SP *(trophy)* copa.

cupboard [ˈkʌbəd] *n* armario.

curator [kjuˈreɪtəʳ] *n* *(of museum)* conservador,-ra.

curb [kɜːb] *n* **1** *(for horse)* barbada. **2** *(control)* freno. **3** US bordillo.

curd [kɜːd] *n* *(from milk)* cuajada. COMP curd cheese requesón *m*.

curdle [ˈkɜːdᵉl] *vi* *(form curds)* cuajarse; *(go bad)* cortarse.

cure [kjuəʳ] *vt* curar.
► *n* cura.

cure-all [ˈkjuərɑːl] *n* panacea.

curfew [ˈkɜːfjuː] *n* toque *m* de queda.

curiosity [kjuərˈɒsətɪ] *n* curiosidad *f*.
ⓘ *pl* curiosities.

curious [ˈkjuərɪəs] *adj* **1** *(inquisitive)* curioso,-a. **2** *(strange, odd)* curioso,-a, extraño,-a; *(interesting)* interesante.

curl [kɜːl] *vt* rizar.
► *vi* rizarse.
► *n* *(of hair)* rizo; *(ringlet)* bucle *m*, tirabuzón *m*; *(of smoke)* espiral *f*, voluta.

curly [ˈkɜːlɪ] *adj* rizado,-a.
ⓘ *comp* curlier, *superl* curliest.

currant [ˈkʌrənt] *n* **1** *(dried grape)* pasa (de Corinto). **2** *(fruit)* grosella.

currency [ˈkʌrənsɪ] *n* FIN moneda. COMP foreign currency divisa.
ⓘ *pl* currencies.

current [ˈkʌrənt] *adj* **1** *(present, existing - gen)* actual; *(- month, year)* en curso; *(most recent - issue)* último,-a. **2** *(generally accepted)* corriente, común, habitual, general. COMP current account cuenta corriente.
► *n* *(gen)* corriente *f*.

currently [ˈkʌrəntlɪ] *adv* **1** *(at present)* actualmente, en la actualidad. **2** *(commonly)* comúnmente.

curriculum [kəˈrɪkjələm] *n* EDUC plan *m* de estudios. COMP curriculum vitae currículum *m*, historial *m*.

curry [ˈkʌrɪ] n CULIN curry m.
ⓘ pl curries.

curse [kɜːs] n 1 (evil spell) maldición f. 2 (oath) palabrota.

cursor [ˈkɜːsəʳ] n cursor m.

curt [kɜːt] adj seco,-a, brusco,-a.

curtain [ˈkɜːtən] n 1 (gen) cortina. 2 THEAT telón m.

curvature [ˈkɜːvətʃəʳ] n 1 (of surface) curvatura. 2 MED encorvamiento.

curve [kɜːv] n (gen) curva.
▶ vi (of road, river, ball) describir una curva, torcer.

cushion [ˈkʊʃən] n (gen) cojín m; (large) almohadón m.
▶ vt fig suavizar, amortiguar.

custard [ˈkʌstəd] n (cold, set) natillas fpl; (hot, liquid) crema. COMP **custard apple** chirimoya.

custom [ˈkʌstəm] n costumbre f: it's a typical Spanish custom es una típica costumbre española.

customary [ˈkʌstəmərɪ] adj (habitual) acostumbrado,-a, habitual.

customer [ˈkʌstəməʳ] n cliente mf.

customize [ˈkʌstəmaɪz] vt hacer por encargo, hacer a la medida.

custom-made [kʌstəmˈmeɪd] adj (clothes, etc) hecho,-a a medida.

customs [ˈkʌstəmz] n aduana.

✎ Puede ser tanto singular como plural.

cut [kʌt] n 1 (ge) corte m; (knife wound) cuchillada. 3 (share) parte f, tajada. 4 (reduction - in budget, services, wages) recorte m; (- in level, number, price) reducción f. 6 ELEC corte m, apagón m.
▶ vt 1 (gen) cortar 2 (reduce - level, number) reducir; (- budget, spending) recortar; (- price) rebajar, reducir.
◆ **to cut down** vt sep (tree) talar, cortar; (kill) matar.
◆ **to cut off** vt sep 2 (disconnect, discontinue) cortar: our phone's been cut off nos han cortado el teléfono. 3 (isolate, separate) aislar: she felt cut off se sentía aislada.
◆ **to cut out** vt sep 1 (from newspaper) recortar; (in sewing) cortar. 2 (exclude) suprimir, eliminar.
ⓘ pt & pp cut, ger cutting.

cutaneous [kjuːˈteɪnɪəs] adj cutáneo,-a.

cute [kjuːt] adj 1 (sweet) mono,-a, rico, -a; (good-looking) guapo,-a, lindo,-a. 2 US (clever) listo,-a.

cutlery [ˈkʌtlərɪ] n cubiertos mpl, cubertería.

cutlet [ˈkʌtlət] n CULIN chuleta.

cutout [ˈkʌtaʊt] n 1 (shape) recortable m. 2 (device, switch) cortacircuitos m.

cutter [ˈkʌtəʳ] n (tool) cúter m.

cutting [ˈkʌtɪŋ] n 1 (from newspaper) recorte m. 2 BOT esqueje m.

cuttlefish [ˈkʌtəlfɪʃ] n jibia, sepia.

cyanide [ˈsaɪənaɪd] n cianuro.

cybernetics [saɪbəˈnetɪks] n cibernética.

cycle [ˈsaɪkəl] n 1 (series of events, of songs, etc) ciclo; (of washing machine) programa m. 2 (bicycle) bicicleta; (motorcycle) moto f. COMP **cycle lane/path/way** carril m bici. ❙ **cycle track** velódromo.
▶ vi ir en bicicleta.

cyclic [ˈsɪklɪk, ˈsaɪklɪk] adj cíclico,-a.

cyclical [ˈsɪklɪkəl, ˈsaɪklɪkəl] adj cíclico,-a.

cycling [ˈsaɪklɪŋ] n ciclismo.

cyclist [ˈsaɪklɪst] n ciclista mf.

cyclone [ˈsaɪkləʊn] n ciclón m.

cygnet [ˈsɪgnət] n pollo de cisne.

cylinder [ˈsɪlɪndəʳ] n 1 (gen) cilindro. 2 (for gas) bombona.

cylindrical [sɪˈlɪndrɪkəl] adj cilíndrico,-a.

cymbal [ˈsɪmbəl] n címbalo, platillo.

cynic [ˈsɪnɪk] n cínico,-a.

cynical [ˈsɪnɪkəl] adj cínico,-a.

cynicism [ˈsɪnɪsɪzəm] n cinismo.

cypress [ˈsaɪprəs] n ciprés m.

Cypriot [ˈsɪprɪət] adj chipriota,-a.
▶ n 1 (person) chipriota mf. 2 (language) chipriota m.

Cyprus [ˈsaɪprəs] n Chipre m.

cyst [sɪst] n quiste m.

cystitis [sɪˈstaɪtɪs] n cistitis f.

czar [zɑːʳ] n zar m.

Czech [tʃek] adj checo,-a.
▶ n 1 (person) checo,-a. 2 (language) checo. COMP **Czech Republic** República Checa.

Czechia [ˈtʃekɪə] n Chequia.

D

D, d [diː] *n* **1** *(the letter)* D, d *f.* **2** MUS re *m.*

'd [əd] *aux* **1** → **would.** *I'd go* iría. **2** → **had:** *he'd seen* había visto. **3** *fam* → **did.** *what'd you do?* ¿qué hiciste?

dab [dæb] *n (of paint)* toque *m; (of perfume)* gota; *(of butter)* poquito.
▶ *vi* dar ligeros toques (at, en).
▶ *n pl* **dabs** GB *sl* huellas *fpl* dactilares.

dabble ['dæbəl] *vi (in activity)* aficionarse (in, a), tener escarceos (in, con).
▶ *vt (in water)* chapotear.

dad [dæd] *n fam* papá *m.*

daddy ['dædɪ] *n fam* papá *m,* papi *m.*
ⓘ *pl* **daddies.**

daffodil ['dæfədɪl] *n* narciso.

dagger ['dægəʳ] *n* **1** *(weapon)* daga, puñal *m.* **2** *(obelisk)* cruz *f.*

daguerreotype [də'gerəʊtaɪp] *n* daguerrotipo.

dahlia ['deɪljə] *n* dalia.

daily ['deɪlɪ] *adj (newspaper, prayers)* diario,-a; *(routine)* diario,-a, cotidiano,-a.
▶ *adv* diariamente, a diario.
▶ *n (newspaper)* diario.
ⓘ *pl* **dailies.**

dainty ['deɪntɪ] *adj* **1** *(delicate - thing)* delicado,-a, fino,-a; *(- person)* precioso,-a, delicado,-a, refinado,-a.
ⓘ *comp* **daintier,** *superl* **daintiest.**
▶ *n pl* **dainties** *(small cakes)* pastelitos *mpl.*

dairy ['deərɪ] *n* **1** *(on farm)* vaquería. **2** *(shop)* lechería; *(company)* central *f* lechera. COMP **dairy products** productos lácteos. ‖ **dairy products** productos lácteos.
ⓘ *pl* **dairies.**

✎ No hay que confundir las palabras **dairy** con **diary,** que significa 'diario, agenda'.

dairymaid ['deərɪmeɪd] *n* lechera.

dairyman ['deərɪmən] *n* lechero.
ⓘ *pl* **dairymen** ['deərɪmən].

dais [deɪz] *n* tarima.
ⓘ *pl* **daises.**

daisy ['deɪzɪ] *n* margarita.
ⓘ *pl* **daisies.**

daltonism ['dɔːltənɪzəm] *n* daltonismo.

dam¹ [dæm] *n* **1** *(barrier)* dique *m.* **2** *(reservoir)* embalse *m,* presa.
◆ **to dam up** *vt sep* **1** *(river)* represar, embalsar. **2** *(emotions)* reprimir, contener.
ⓘ *pt & pp* **dammed,** *ger* **damming.**

dam² [dæm] *n* ZOOL madre *f.*

damage ['dæmɪdʒ] *n (gen)* daño; *(to reputation, cause, health)* perjuicio, daños *mpl; (destruction)* destrozos *mpl,* daños *mpl.*

dame [deɪm] *n* **1** US *fam* mujer *f,* tía. **2** *(in pantomime)* vieja *(representada por un hombre).*
▶ *n* **Dame** GB *(title)* título honorífico concedido a una mujer.

damn [dæm] *interj fam* ¡mecachis!, ¡caray!
▶ *adj fam* maldito,-a, condenado,-a.
▶ *adv fam* muy, sumamente: *you were damn lucky* tuviste mucha suerte.
▶ *vt* **1** REL condenar. **2** *(curse)* maldecir: *damn it!* ¡maldita sea!

damned [dæmd] *adj* **1** *fam* maldito,-a, condenado,-a. **2** REL condenado,-a.

damp [dæmp] *adj (gen)* húmedo,-a; *(wet)* mojado,-a. COMP **damp course** aislante *m* hidrófugo.
▶ *n* humedad *f.*

dampen ['dæmpən] *vt* **1** *(make damp)* humedecer. **2** *fig (enthusiasm, ardour, etc)* hacer perder, apagar, enfriar; *(person's spirits)* desanimar.

damsel ['dæmzəl] *n* doncella.

dance [dɑːns] *n (gen)* baile *m; (classical, tribal)* danza.
▸ *vi* bailar.

dancer ['dɑːnsəʳ] *n* bailarín,-ina; *(flamenco)* bailaor,-ra.

dandelion ['dændɪlaɪən] *n* diente *m* de león.

dandruff ['dændrəf] *n* caspa.

dandy ['dændɪ] *n* dandy *m*, petimetre *m*.
ⓘ *pl* dandies.
▸ *adj* US *fam* estupendo,-a.

danger ['deɪndʒəʳ] *n (peril, hazard)* peligro; *(risk)* riesgo.

dangerous ['deɪndʒərəs] *adj (gen)* peligroso,-a; *(risky)* arriesgado,-a; *(illness)* grave.

dangle ['dæŋgəl] *vt (hang)* colgar; *(swing)* balancear.
▸ *vi* colgar, pender.

Danish ['deɪnɪʃ] *adj* danés,-esa.
▸ *n (language)* danés *m*.
▸ *n pl* **the Danish** los daneses *mpl*.

dank [dæŋk] *adj* húmedo,-a y frío,-a.

dare [deəʳ] *vi* atreverse (**to**, a), osar (**to**, -).
▸ *vt (challenge)* desafiar.
▸ *n* desafío, reto.

daredevil ['deədevəl] *n* atrevido,-a, temerario,-a.

daring ['deərɪŋ] *adj (bold, brave)* audaz, osado,-a, atrevido,-a.
▸ *n* osadía, atrevimiento, audacia.

dark [dɑːk] *adj* **1** *(without light)* oscuro,-a. **2** *(hair, skin)* moreno,-a; *(eyes)* negro,-a. **3** *(gloomy)* triste, sombrío,-a. **4** *(sinister)* siniestro,-a, tenebroso,-a. **5** *(secret)* misterioso,-a.
▸ *n* **1** *(darkness)* oscuridad *f*. **2** *(nightfall)* anochecer *m*.

darken ['dɑːkən] *vt* **1** oscurecer, hacer más oscuro,-a. **2** *fig* entristecer, ensombrecer.

darkness ['dɑːknəs] *n* oscuridad *f*.

darling ['dɑːlɪŋ] *n (lover)* querido,-a, amor *m*, cariño; *(popular person)* niño,-a mimado,-a.
▸ *adj* **1** *(loved)* querido,-a. **2** *fam (charming)* precioso,-a, encantador,-ra, mono,-a.

darn [dɑːn] *n* zurcido.
▸ *vt (sock, etc)* zurcir.

darnel ['dɑːnəl] *n* cizaña.

dart [dɑːt] *n* **1** *(object)* dardo, flechilla. **2** *(rush)* movimiento rápido. **3** SEW *(fold)* pinza.
▸ *vt (look, glance)* lanzar; *(tongue)* disparar.
▸ *vi (move quickly - person)* lanzarse, precipitarse; *(- butterfly, etc)* revolotear.

dartboard ['dɑːtbɔːd] *n* diana, blanco de tiro.

dash [dæʃ] *n* **1** *(sudden run)* carrera. **2** *(small amount)* poco; *(of salt, spice)* pizca; *(of liquid)* chorrito, gota. **3** *(horizontal mark)* raya; *(hyphen)* guion *m; (in Morse code)* raya. **4** *(style, panache)* elegancia; *(energy, vitality)* brío, dinamismo. **5** US *(dashboard)* salpicadero.
▸ *vt* **1** *(hit)* lanzar, arrojar; *(smash)* romper, estrellar. **2** *(hopes)* truncar.

dashboard ['dæʃbɔːd] *n* salpicadero.

data ['deɪtə] *n pl* datos *mpl*, información *f*.
ⓘ *sing* datum.

database ['deɪtəbeɪs] *n* COMPUT base *f* de datos.

date¹ [deɪt] *n* **1** *(in time)* fecha. **2** *(appointment)* cita, compromiso: *I've got a date with David tonight* tengo una cita con David esta noche. **3** US *(person)* ligue *m*, amigo,-a, pareja. **4** *(performance, booking)* actuación *f*.
▸ *vt* **1** *(write a date on)* fechar. **2** *(determine the date of)* datar. **3** *(show the age of)* demostrar la edad de. **4** US *fam (go out with)* salir con.
▸ *vi* **1** *(have existed since)* datar (**from**, de), remontarse (**back to**, a). **2** *(go out of fashion)* pasar de moda. **3** US *(go out together)* salir juntos, ser novios.

date² [deɪt] *n (fruit)* dátil *m*.

dated ['deɪtɪd] *adj* anticuado,-a.

dative ['deɪtɪv] *n* LING dativo.

datum ['deɪtəm] *n* dato.
ⓘ *pl* data.

daub [dɔːb] *n* **1** *(small bit, smear)* mancha. **2** *(bad painting)* pintarrajo.
▸ *vt* embadurnar.

daughter ['dɔːtəʳ] *n* hija.

daughter-in-law ['dɔːtərɪnlɔː] *n* nuera.

daunt [dɔ:nt] *vt (frighten)* intimidar; *(dishearten)* desanimar, desalentar.

dauphin [ˈdɔ:fɪn] *n* delfín *m*.

dawn [dɔ:n] *n* alba, aurora, amanecer *m*.
▶ *vi* amanecer, alborear, clarear.

day [deɪ] *n* día *m*. LOC **the day after tomorrow** pasado mañana. ‖ **the day before tomorrow** anteayer. COMP **day off** día libre.
▶ *n pl* **days** *(period)* época, tiempos *mpl*.

daybreak [ˈdeɪbreɪk] *n* amanecer *m*, alba.

daydream [ˈdeɪdri:m] *n* ensueño, ensoñación *f*.
▶ *vi* soñar despierto,-a, fantasear.

daytime [ˈdeɪtaɪm] *n* día *m*.
▶ *adj (flight)* diurno,-a.

daze [deɪz] *n* aturdimiento.
▶ *vt* aturdir.

D-day [ˈdi:deɪ] *n* **1** *(in war)* día *m* D. **2** *(important date)* el día *m* señalado.

deacon [ˈdi:kən] *n* diácono.

deactivate [di:ˈæktɪveɪt] *vt* desactivar.

dead [ded] *adj* **1** *(not alive)* muerto,-a. **2** *(obsolete - language)* muerto,-a; *(- custom)* desusado,-a, en desuso; *(finished with - topic, issue, debate)* agotado,-a, pasado,-a; *(- glass, bottle)* terminado,-a, acabado,-a. **3** *(numb)* entumecido,-a, dormido,-a. **4** *(not functioning - telephone)* desconectado,-a, cortado,-a; *(- machine)* averiado,-a; *(- battery)* descargado,-a, gastado,-a; *(- match)* gastado,-a. **5** *fam (very tired)* muerto,-a. **6** *(dull, quiet, not busy)* muerto,-a. **7** *(sounds)* sordo,-a; *(colours)* apagado,-a. **8** SP *(ball)* muerto,-a. **9** *(total)* total, completo,-a, absoluto,-a.
▶ *adv* **1** *(completely, absolutely)* completamente, sumamente; *(as intensifier)* muy: *I'm dead sure* estoy segurísimo. **2** *(exactly)* justo: *we arrived dead on time* llegamos puntualísimos.
▶ *n* **the dead** los,-las muertos,-as.

deaden [ˈdedən] *vt (pain)* calmar, aliviar; *(noise, blow)* amortiguar.

deadline [ˈdedlaɪn] *n (date)* fecha límite, fecha tope, plazo de entrega; *(time)* hora límite, hora tope.

deadlock [ˈdedlɒk] *n* punto muerto, impasse *m*.

deaf [def] *adj* sordo,-a.
▶ *n* **the deaf** los sordos *mpl*.

deaf-aid [ˈdefeɪd] *n* audífono.

deafen [ˈdefən] *vt* ensordecer.

deaf-mute [ˈdefmju:t] *n* sordomudo,-a.

deafness [ˈdefnəs] *n* sordera.

deal [di:l] *n* **1** *(agreement)* trato, acuerdo, pacto; *(financial)* acuerdo. **2** *(treatment)* trato. **3** *(amount)* cantidad *f*. **4** *(in card games)* reparto.
▶ *vt* **1** *(cards)* repartir, dar. **2** *(drugs)* traficar.
◆ **to deal with** *vt insep* **1** COMM *(trade with)* tratar con, tener relaciones comerciales con. **2** *(tackle - problem, etc)* abordar, ocuparse de; *(- task)* encargarse de; *(- person)* tratar (con), lidiar con.
ⓘ *pt & pp* **dealt** [delt].

dealer [ˈdi:lər] *n* **1** COMM comerciante *mf*, negociante *mf*. **2** *(illegal - in drugs)* traficante *mf*; *(- in stolen goods)* perista *mf*. **3** FIN corredor,-ra de bolsa, corredor,-ra de valores.

dealt [delt] *pt & pp* → **deal**.

dean [di:n] *n* **1** REL deán *m*. **2** EDUC decano,-a.

deanery [ˈdi:nərɪ] *n* decanato.

dear [dɪər] *adj* **1** *(loved - person)* querido,-a; *(- thing)* preciado,-a. **2** *(as form of address)* querido,-a. **3** *fam (in letter)* querido,-a; *(more formally)* apreciado,-a, estimado,-a. **4** *(expensive)* caro,-a.
▶ *interj* ¡Dios mío!
▶ *adv* caro.

dearly [ˈdɪəlɪ] *adv* **1** *(very much)* mucho. **2** *(at a cost)* caro.

death [deθ] *n* **1** *(gen)* muerte *f*; *(decease, demise)* fallecimiento, defunción *f*. **2** *(end - of custom, institution)* fin *m*. COMP **death penalty** pena de muerte.

deathtrap [ˈdeθtræp] *n fam* lugar peligroso.

debacle [deɪˈbɑ:kəl] *n* debacle *m*.

debate [dɪˈbeɪt] *n* debate *m*.
▶ *vt* **1** *(discuss)* debatir, discutir. **2** *(consider, think over)* considerar, dar vueltas a.

debit ['debɪt] *n* FIN débito.
▶ *vt* cargar en cuenta.

debrief [di:'bri:f] *vt* interrogar.

debris ['deɪbri:] *n (ruins)* escombros *mpl*; *(wreckage)* restos *mpl*.

debt [det] *n (something owed)* deuda; *(indebtedness)* endeudamiento.

debtor ['detər] *n* deudor,-ra.

debug [di:'bʌg] *vt* **1** *(computer programme, system)* depurar. **2** *(room, building, etc)* quitar los micrófonos ocultos de.
① *pt & pp* debugged, *ger* debugging.

debunk [di:'bʌŋk] *vt fam (person)* desmitificar, desenmascarar; *(idea, belief)* desacreditar, desprestigiar.

debut ['deɪbju:] *n* debut *m*.

decade ['dekeɪd] *n* década, decenio.

decadence ['dekədəns] *n* decadencia.

decaffeinated [di:'kæfɪneɪtɪd] *adj* descafeinado,-a.

decagon ['dekəgɒn] *n* decágono.

decagonal [dɪ'kægənəl] *adj* decagonal.

decahedron [dekə'hi:drən] *n* decaedro.

decalitre ['dekəli:tər] *n* decalitro.

decanter [dɪ'kæntər] *n* decantador *m*.

decapitation [dɪkæpɪ'teɪʃən] *n* decapitación *f*.

decapod ['dekəpɒd] *n* decápodo.

decasyllable [dekə'sɪləbəl] *n* decasílabo.

decathlete [dɪ'kæθli:t] *n* decatleta *f*.

decathlon [dɪ'kæθlɒn] *n* decatlón *m*.

decay [dɪ'keɪ] *n* **1** *(of organic matter)* descomposición *f*; *(of teeth)* caries *f*. **2** *(of building)* deterioro, desmoronamiento. **3** *fig (of culture, values)* decadencia.

decease [dɪ'si:s] *n* fallecimiento, defunción *f*.

deceit [dɪ'si:t] *n (trick)* engaño; *(deceiving)* falsedad *f*.

deceive [dɪ'si:v] *vt* engañar.

decelerate [di:'seləreɪt] *vi* reducir la velocidad, desacelerar.

December [dɪ'sembər] *n* diciembre *m*.

✎ Para ejemplos de uso, consulta **May**.

decency ['di:sənsɪ] *n* **1** *(seemliness)* decencia, decoro. **2** *(politeness)* buena educación *f*, cortesía, consideración *f*.
① *pl* decencies.

decennial [dɪ'senɪəl] *n* decenal.

decent ['di:sənt] *adj* decente.

decentralize [di:'sentrəlaɪz] *vt* descentralizar.

deception [dɪ'sepʃən] *n (trick)* engaño; *(deceiving)* falsedad *f*.

⌧ Deception no significa 'decepción', que se traduce por disappointment.

deceptive [dɪ'septɪv] *adj* engañoso,-a: *appearances can be deceptive* las apariencias engañan.

decibel ['desɪbel] *n* decibelio.

decide [dɪ'saɪd] *vt* decidir.

deciduous [dɪ'sɪdjʊəs] *adj* de hoja caduca.

decigram ['desɪgræm] *n* decigramo.

decilitre ['desɪli:tər] *n* decilitro.

decimal ['desɪməl] *n* decimal *m*. COMP decimal point coma decimal.

decimate ['desɪmeɪt] *vt* diezmar.

decimation [desɪ'meɪʃən] *n* reducción *f* catastrófica, acción de diezmar.

decimetre ['desɪmi:tər] *n* decímetro.

decipher [dɪ'saɪfər] *vt* descifrar.

decision [dɪ'sɪʒən] *n* **1** *(choice, verdict)* decisión *f*. **2** *(resolution)* resolución *f*, decisión *f*, determinación *f*.

decisive [dɪ'saɪsɪv] *adj* **1** *(conclusive - gen)* decisivo,-a; *(- victory)* contundente. **2** *(firm, resolute - person)* decidido,-a, resuelto,-a; *(- reply, action)* firme.

deck [dek] *n* **1** *(of ship)* cubierta. **2** *(of bus, coach)* piso. **3** US *(of cards)* baraja. **4** *(of record player)* plato. **5** US *(raised roofless area)* terraza.

deckchair ['dektʃeər] *n* tumbona.

declaim [dɪ'kleɪm] *vt* declamar.
▶ *vi* declamar.

declamation [deklə'meɪʃən] *n* declamación *f*.

declarant [dɪ'kleərənt] *n* declarante *mf*.

declaration [deklə'reɪʃən] *n* declaración *f*.

declare [dɪ'kleər] *vt* **1** *(gen)* declarar; *(opinion)* manifestar. **2** *(at customs)* declarar.

declassify [dɪ'klæsɪfaɪ] *vt* desclasificar.
① *pt & pp* declassified, *ger* declassifying.

declination [deklɪ'neɪʃ°n] *n* declinación *f*, variación *f*. COMP **magnetic declination** variación *f* magnética.

decline [dɪ'klaɪn] *n* **1** *(decrease)* disminución *f*, descenso. **2** *(deterioration - gen)* deterioro, declive *m*, decadencia; *(in health)* deterioro, empeoramiento.

decode [di:'kəʊd] *vt* decodificar, descodificar.

decompose [di:kəm'pəʊz] *vt* descomponer.
▸ *vi* **1** descomponerse, pudrirse. **2** CHEM descomponerse.

decomposer [di:kəm'pəʊzə'] *n* saprótrofo.

decompress [dɪkəm'pres] *vt* someter a descompresión.

decompression [dɪkəm'preʃ°n] *n* descompresión *f*.

decongestion [di:kən'dʒetʃ°n] *n* descongestión *f*.

decontaminate [di:kən'tæmɪneɪt] *vt* descontaminar.

decor ['deɪkɔ:'] *n* **1** *(furnishings)* decoración *f*. **2** THEAT decorado.

decorate ['dekəreɪt] *vt* **1** *(adorn, make beautiful)* decorar (with, con), adornar (with, con). **2** *(paint)* pintar; *(wallpaper)* empapelar. **3** *(honour)* condecorar (for, por).

decoration [dekə'reɪʃ°n] *n* **1** *(act, art)* decoración *f*. **2** *(ornament)* adorno. **3** *(medal)* condecoración *f*.

decorator ['dekəreɪtə'] *n* *(designer)* decorador,-ra, interiorista *mf*; *(painter)* pintor,-ra; *(wallpaperer)* empapelador,-ra.

decoy ['di:kɔɪ] *n* **1** *(bird)* cimbel *m*; *(in hunting)* señuelo, reclamo. **2** *fig (lure)* señuelo, carnada, gancho.

decrease [dɪ'kri:s] *n* disminución *f*, descenso.
▸ *vt* disminuir, reducir.

decreasing [dɪ'kri:sɪŋ] *adj* decreciente.

decree [dɪ'kri:] *n* **1** *(command)* decreto. **2** US *(judgement)* sentencia.
▸ *vt* decretar.

decriminalize [di:'krɪmɪn°laɪz] *vt* despenalizar.

dedicate ['dedɪkeɪt] *vt* dedicar.

dedicatory ['dedɪkət°rɪ] *adj* dedicatorio,-a.

deduce [dɪ'dju:s] *vt* deducir (from, de).

deduct [dɪ'dʌkt] *vt* *(gen)* descontar, deducir; *(from taxes)* desgravar.

deduction [dɪ'dʌkʃ°n] *n* **1** *(subtraction)* deducción *f*, descuento; *(from taxes)* desgravación *f*. **2** *(reasoning)* deducción *f*.

deed [di:d] *n* **1** *lit (act)* acto, acción *f*, obra; *(feat)* hazaña, proeza. **2** JUR escritura.

deejay ['di:dʒeɪ] *n* pinchadiscos *mf*, discjockey *mf*.

deep [di:p] *adj* **1** *(river, hole, well, etc)* hondo,-a, profundo,-a. **2** *(shelf, wardrobe)* de fondo; *(hem, border)* ancho,-a. **3** *(sound, voice)* grave, bajo,-a; *(note)* grave; *(breath)* hondo,-a.
▸ *adv* **1** *(to a great depth)* profundamente. **2** *(far from the outside)* lejos. **3** *(far in time, late)* tarde.

deepen ['di:p°n] *vt* **1** *(well, channel, river)* profundizar, hacer más profundo,-a. **2** *(knowledge)* profundizar, ahondar; *(sympathy)* aumentar; *(colour, emotion)* intensificar; *(sound, voice)* hacer más grave.

deep-freeze ['di:p'fri:z] *n* congelador *m*.
▸ *vt* *(at home)* congelar; *(commercially)* ultracongelar.
① *pt* **deep-froze** [di:p'frəʊz], *pp* **deep-frozen** [di:p'frəʊz°n].

deep-sea ['di:psi:] *n* *(fishing, diving)* de altura.

deer [dɪə'] *n* ciervo, venado.
① *pl* **deer**.

default [dɪ'fɔ:lt] *n* **1** *(failure to act)* omisión *f*, negligencia. **2** *(failure to pay)* incumplimiento de pago, mora, demora.
▸ *vi* **1** *(fail to act)* faltar a sus compromisos, incumplir un acuerdo. **2** *(fail to pay)* no pagar (on, -), demorarse (on, en).

defeat [dɪ'fi:t] *n* **1** *(of army, team)* derrota; *(of motion, bill)* rechazo. **2** *fig (of hopes, plans)* fracaso.
▸ *vt* **1** *(gen)* derrotar, vencer. **2** *fig (hopes, plans)* frustrar.

defect [*(n)* 'di:fekt; *(vb)* dɪ'fekt] *n* *(gen)* defecto; *(flaw)* desperfecto, tara.

▶ *vi (party, team)* desertar, pasarse al bando contrario; *(country)* huir.

defective [dɪˈfektɪv] *adj* **1** *(faulty)* defectuoso,-a; *(flawed)* con desperfectos; *(incomplete, lacking)* deficiente. **2** LING defectivo,-a.

defence [dɪˈfens] *n* defensa.

defend [dɪˈfend] *vt* defender.
▶ *vi* SP jugar de defensa.

defendant [dɪˈfendənt] *n* JUR *(in civil case)* demandado,-a; *(in criminal case)* acusado,-a.

defender [dɪˈfendəʳ] *n* **1** *(gen)* defensor,-ra. **2** SP defensa *mf*.

defense [dɪˈfens] *n* US → **defence**.

defensive [dɪˈfensɪv] *adj* defensivo,-a.

defer¹ [dɪˈfɜːʳ] *vt (postpone)* aplazar, posponer, retrasar.
ⓘ *pt & pp* **deferred**, *ger* **deferring**.

defer² [dɪˈfɜːʳ] *vi (submit to)* deferir (to, a).
ⓘ *pt & pp* **deferred**, *ger* **deferring**.

defiance [dɪˈfaɪəns] *n* desafío.

defiant [dɪˈfaɪənt] *adj* desafiante.

deficiency [dɪˈfɪʃənsɪ] *n* **1** *(lack)* deficiencia; *(shortage)* escasez *f*, falta, déficit *m*. **2** *(fault, shortcoming)* defecto, deficiencia.
ⓘ *pl* **deficiencies**.

deficient [dɪˈfɪʃənt] *adj* deficiente.

deficit [ˈdefɪsɪt] *n* déficit *m*.

define [dɪˈfaɪn] *vt* definir.

definite [ˈdefɪnət] *adj* **1** *(final, fixed - gen)* definitivo,-a; *(- opinions)* fijo,-a. **2** *(clear, distinct)* claro,-a.

definitely [ˈdefɪnətlɪ] *adv* **1** *(without doubt)* sin duda, seguramente. **2** *(definitively)* definitivamente.
▶ *interj* ¡desde luego!, ¡claro que sí!

definition [defɪˈnɪʃən] *n* definición *f*.

definitive [dɪˈfɪnɪtɪv] *adj* **1** *(final, conclusive)* definitivo,-a. **2** *(ultimate - study, etc)* de mayor autoridad.

deflate [dɪˈfleɪt] *vt (balloon, tyre)* desinflar, deshinchar.

deflation [dɪˈfleɪʃən] *n* **1** *(of balloon, tyre)* desinflamiento. **2** *(economic)* deflación *f*.

deflect [dɪˈflekt] *vt* desviar.
▶ *vi* desviarse.

deforest [diːˈfɒrɪst] *vt* deforestar.

deform [dɪˈfɔːm] *vt* deformar.

deformation [diːfɔːˈmeɪʃən] *n* deformación *f*.

deformed [dɪˈfɔːmd] *adj* deforme.

defraud [dɪˈfrɔːd] *vt* estafar.

> ☒ To defraud no significa 'defraudar (decepcionar), que se traduce por to disappoint.

defrost [diːˈfrɒst] *vt* **1** *(freezer, food)* descongelar. **2** US *(windscreen)* desempañar.

deft [deft] *adj* diestro,-a, hábil.

defunct [dɪˈfʌŋkt] *adj* difunto,-a.

defy [dɪˈfaɪ] *vt* **1** *(gen)* desafiar; *(disobey - law, order, authority)* desobedecer, desacatar. **2** *(make impossible)* ser imposible.
ⓘ *pt & pp* **defied**, *ger* **defying**.

degenerate [*(adj-n)* dɪˈdʒenərət; *(vb)* dɪˈdʒenəreɪt] *adj* degenerado,-a.
▶ *n* degenerado,-a.
▶ *vi* degenerar (into, en).

degenerative [dɪˈdʒenərətɪv] *adj* degenerativo,-a.

degradation [degrəˈdeɪʃən] *n* degradación *f*.

degrade [dɪˈgreɪd] *vt* degradar.

degree [dɪˈgriː] *n* **1** *(unit of measurement)* grado. **2** *(extent, level, point)* nivel *m*, punto; *(amount)* algo. **3** EDUC título.

dehumanize [diːˈhjuːmənaɪz] *vt* deshumanizar.

dehydrate [diːhaɪˈdreɪt] *vt* deshidratar.
▶ *vi* deshidratarse.

de-icing [diːˈaɪsɪŋ] *n* deshielo.

deification [diːɪfɪˈkeɪʃən] *n* deificación *f*.

deign [deɪn] *vi* dignarse (to, a).

deity [ˈdeɪɪtɪ] *n* deidad *f*.
ⓘ *pl* **deities**.

dejection [dɪˈdʒekʃən] *n* abatimiento, desaliento, desánimo.

delay [dɪˈleɪ] *n* retraso.
▶ *vt* **1** *(gen)* aplazar, retrasar. **2** *(make late - flight, train)* retrasar, demorar; *(person)* entretener.

delayed [dɪˈleɪd] *adj* con retraso.

delegate [*(adj-n)* ˈdelɪgət; *(vb)* ˈdelɪgeɪt] *n* delegado,-a.
▶ *vt (duties, responsibility, etc)* delegar (to, en).

delegation [delɪˈgeɪʃən] *n* delegación *f*.

delete [dɪ'li:t] *vt (remove)* eliminar, suprimir; *(cross out)* tachar.

deliberate [*(adj)* dɪ'lɪbªrət; *(vb)* dɪ'lɪbəreɪt] *adj* **1** *(intentional)* deliberado,-a, intencionado,-a; *(studied)* premeditado,-a. **2** *(slow, unhurried)* pausado,-a, lento,-a; *(careful)* reflexivo,-a.
▸ *vi* deliberar (on, sobre).

delicacy ['delɪkəsɪ] *n* **1** *(softness, tenderness)* delicadeza. **2** *(fragility)* fragilidad *f*. **3** *(food)* exquisitez *f*.
ⓘ *pl* delicacies.

delicate ['delɪkət] *adj* **1** *(fine - gen)* delicado,-a; *(- embroidery, handiwork)* fino,-a, esmerado,-a. **2** *(easily damaged)* frágil. **3** *(sensitive - instrument)* sensible; *(- sense of smell, taste)* fino,-a.

delicatessen [delɪkə'tesªn] *n* charcutería.

delicious [dɪ'lɪʃəs] *adj* delicioso,-a.

delight [dɪ'laɪt] *n* **1** *(great pleasure, joy)* placer *m*, gusto, alegría, deleite *m*. **2** *(source of pleasure)* encanto, delicia, placer *m*.
▸ *vi* deleitarse (in, en/con).

delighted [dɪ'laɪtɪd] *adj (person)* encantado,-a, contentísimo,-a; *(smile, shout, look)* de alegría.

delinquency [dɪ'lɪŋkwənsɪ] *n* **1** *(behaviour)* delincuencia. **2** *(act)* delito.

delinquent [dɪ'lɪŋkwənt] *adj* **1** *(youth)* delincuente; *(activity)* delictivo,-a. **2** FIN *(person)* moroso,-a.
▸ *n* delincuente *mf*.

delirious [dɪ'lɪrɪəs] *adj* **1** MED delirante. **2** *fig (happy)* loco,-a de alegría.

deliver [dɪ'lɪvəʳ] *vt* **1** *(gen)* entregar; *(distribute)* repartir (a domicilio). **2** *(hit, kick, push)* dar; *(shot, fast ball)* lanzar. **3** *(say)* pronunciar. **4** *(produce, provide, fulfil)* cumplir. **5** MED *(baby)* asistir en el parto de, atender en el parto de.

delivery [dɪ'lɪvʳrɪ] *n* **1** *(act - gen)* entrega, reparto; *(- of mail)* reparto. **2** *(consignment)* partida, remesa. **3** *(manner of speaking)* modo de hablar. **4** *(of baby)* parto. **5** *(throwing, launching - of ball, missile)* lanzamiento. COMP **delivery note** albarán de entrega.
ⓘ *pl* deliveries.

delta ['deltə] *n* **1** GEOG delta *m*. **2** *(Greek letter)* delta.

deltoid ['deltoɪd] *adj* deltoides.
▸ *n* deltoides *m*.

delude [dɪ'lu:d] *vt* engañar.

deluge ['delju:dʒ] *n* **1** *(rain)* diluvio; *(flood)* inundación *f*. **2** *fig* avalancha, alud *m*.

delusion [dɪ'lu:ʒªn] *n* **1** *(false belief)* falsa ilusión *f*; *(mistaken idea)* error *m*. **2** *(act, state)* engaño.

de luxe [də'lʌks] *adj* de lujo.

demagogue ['deməgɒg] *n* demagogo,-a.

demagogy ['deməgɒgɪ] *n* demagogia.

demand [dɪ'mɑ:nd] *n* **1** *(request)* solicitud *f*, petición *f*; *(claim)* exigencia; *(for pay rise, rights, etc)* reclamación *f*. **2** COMM demanda. **3** *(note, warning)* aviso.
▸ *vt (call for, insist on)* exigir; *(rights, conditions, etc)* reclamar.

demanding [dɪ'mɑ:ndɪŋ] *adj* **1** *(person - gen)* exigente; *(awkward)* difícil. **2** *(tiring - job, etc)* agotador,-ra.

dementia [dɪ'menʃɪə] *n* demencia.

demise [dɪ'maɪz] *n* **1** *(death)* fallecimiento, defunción *f*. **2** *fig (end)* desaparición *f*; *(failure)* fracaso.

demist [di:'mɪst] *vt* desempañar.

demo ['deməʊ] *n* **1** *(recording, tape)* maqueta. **2** *fam (demonstration)* manifa *f*, manifestación *f*. **3** INFORM demo.
ⓘ *pl* demos.

demobilize [di:'məʊbɪlaɪz] *vt* desmovilizar.

democracy [dɪ'mɒkrəsɪ] *n* democracia.
ⓘ *pl* democracies.

democrat ['deməkræt] *n* demócrata *mf*.

demography [dɪ'mɒgrəfɪ] *n* demografía.

demolish [dɪ'mɒlɪʃ] *vt* derribar, demoler, echar abajo.

demolition [demə'lɪʃªn] *n* demolición *f*, derribo.

demon ['di:mən] *n* demonio, diablo.

demonstrate ['demənstreɪt] *vt* demostrar.
▸ *vi (protest)* manifestarse.

demonstration [demən'streɪʃ°n] *n* **1** *(act of showing)* demostración *f*, muestra. **3** *(march)* manifestación *f*.

demonstrative [dɪ'mɒnstrətɪv] *adj* **1** *(person - showing feelings)* abierto,-a, expresivo,-a. **3** LING demostrativo,-a.

demonstrator ['demənstreɪtəʳ] *n* POL manifestante *mf*.

demoralize [dɪ'mɒrºlaɪz] *vt* desmoralizar.

den [den] *n* **1** *(of animals)* guarida. **2** *(secret meeting-place)* antro. **3** *fam (room)* cuarto; *(for study)* estudio.

denarius [dɪ'neərɪəs] *n* denario.
ⓘ *pl* **denarii** [dɪ'neərɪɪ].

denaturize [di:'neɪtʃəraɪz] *vt* desnaturalizar.

dendrite ['dendraɪt] *n* dendrita.

denial [dɪ'naɪəl] *n* **1** *(of accusation)* mentís *m*, desmentido **2** *(of principle)* negación *f*. **3** *(of rights, justice)* denegación *f*. **4** *(of request)* negativa, rechazo.

denim ['denɪm] *n* tela vaquera.
▶ *n pl* **denims** vaqueros *mpl*, tejanos *mpl*.

Denmark ['denmɑːk] *n* Dinamarca.

denominate [dɪ'nɒmɪneɪt] *vt* denominar.

denomination [dɪnɒmɪ'neɪʃ°n] *n* **1** REL confesión *f*. **2** *(standard of value)* valor *m*. **3** *(classification)* denominación *f*.

denominator [dɪ'nɒmɪneɪtəʳ] *n* MATH denominador *m*.

denounce [dɪ'naʊns] *vt* denunciar.

dense [dens] *adj* denso,-a.

density ['densɪtɪ] *n (gen)* densidad *f*.
ⓘ *pl* **densities**.

dent [dent] *n (in car, metal)* abolladura.
▶ *vt (car, metal)* abollar.

dentist ['dentɪst] *n* dentista *mf*.

dentistry ['dentɪstrɪ] *n* odontología.

denture ['dentʃəʳ] *n (plate)* prótesis *f* dental.
▶ *n pl* **dentures** dentadura *f sing* postiza.

deny [dɪ'naɪ] *vt* **1** *(repudiate - accusation, fact)* negar; *(rumour, report)* desmentir; *(charge)* negar. **2** *(refuse - request)* denegar; *(- rights, equality)* privar de; *(- access)* negar.
ⓘ *pt & pp* **denied**, *ger* **denying**.

deodorant [di:'əʊdərənt] *n* desodorante *m*.

deoxyribonucleic [di:ɒksɪraɪbəʊnjuː'kleɪɪk] *n* desoxirribonucleico,-a.

depart [dɪ'pɑːt] *vi fml* partir, salir.

department [dɪ'pɑːtmənt] *n* **1** *(in shop)* sección *f*; *(in company, organization)* departamento, sección *f*; *(in government)* ministerio. **2** *fam (responsibility)* campo, esfera, terreno.

departure [dɪ'pɑːtʃəʳ] *n* **1** *(of person)* partida, marcha; *(of plane, train, etc)* salida. **2** *fig (divergence)* desviación *f*; *(venture, type of activity)* innovación *f*.

depend [dɪ'pend] *vi* depender.
◆ **to depend on** *vt* confiar en.

depict [dɪ'pɪkt] *vt* **1** *(portray visually, in music)* pintar, representar, retratar. **2** *(describe in writing)* describir, retratar.

deplore [dɪ'plɔːʳ] *vt* deplorar.

deploy [dɪ'plɔɪ] *vt* **1** MIL desplegar. **2** *(use effectively)* utilizar, hacer uso de.

deport [dɪ'pɔːt] *vt* deportar.

deportee [di:pɔː'tiː] *n* deportado,-a.

depose [dɪ'pəʊz] *vt* **1** *(remove from power - leader, president)* deponer, destituir; *(- king)* destronar. **2** JUR declarar, deponer.

deposit [dɪ'pɒzɪt] *n* **1** *(sediment)* sedimento, depósito; *(layer)* capa. **2** *(mining - of gold,etc)* yacimiento. **3** FIN *(payment into account)* depósito, ingreso.

> ☒ Deposit no significa 'depósito (recipiente)', que se traduce por tank.

depot ['depəʊ] *n (storehouse)* almacén *m*.

depreciate [dɪ'priːʃɪeɪt] *vi* FIN depreciarse.
▶ *vt* FIN depreciar, amortizar.

depress [dɪ'pres] *vt* **1** *(make sad)* deprimir. **2** *(reduce - prices, sales, wages)* reducir, disminuir. **3** *fml (press down)* pulsar, apretar.

depression [dɪ'preʃ°n] *n* depresión *f*.

depressive [dɪ'presɪv] *adj* depresivo,-a.

deprive [dɪ'praɪv] *vt* privar (of, de).

depth [depθ] *n (of hole, swimming pool, mine, etc)* profundidad *f*; *(of cupboard, shelf)* fondo; *(of hem, border)* ancho.

deputation [depjʊˈteɪʃ³n] *n* delegación *f*.

deputy [ˈdepjətɪ] *n* **1** *(substitute)* sustituto,-a, suplente *mf*. **2** POL diputado,-a. **3** US ayudante *mf* del shérif. COMP **deputy head** EDUC subdirector,-ra. ① *pl* deputies.

derby [ˈdɑːbɪ] *n* **1** SP *(between two local teams)* derby *m*. **2** US *(horse race)* carrera (de caballos). **3** US *(bowler hat)* bombín *m*, sombrero (de) hongo. ① *pl* derbies.

derelict [ˈderɪlɪkt] *adj (building)* abandonado,-a, en ruinas.

deride [dɪˈraɪd] *vt* burlarse de, ridiculizar, reírse de.

derive [dɪˈraɪv] *vt (get, obtain)* sacar, recibir.
▶ *vi* **1** LING *(word)* derivar, derivarse (from, de). **2** *(stem from - problem, attitude)* provenir (from, de).

dermatitis [dɜːməˈtaɪtɪs] *n* dermatitis *f*.

dermis [ˈdɜːmɪs] *n* dermis *f*.

derogatory [dɪˈrɒgət³rɪ] *adj (remark, attitude, article)* despectivo,-a; *(meaning, sense)* peyorativo,-a.

derrick [ˈderɪk] *n* **1** *(crane)* grúa. **2** *(tower over oil well)* torre *f* de perforación.

descend [dɪˈsend] *vt* descender, bajar.

descent [dɪˈsent] *n (by plane, climbers, etc)* descenso, bajada; *(slope)* pendiente *f*, declive *m*.

describe [dɪˈskraɪb] *vt* **1** *(depict in words)* describir. **2** *(call, characterize)* calificar, definir. **3** *(move in shape)* describir; *(draw)* trazar.

desert¹ [ˈdezət] *n* desierto.

desert² [dɪˈzɜːt] *vt (family, person, place)* abandonar; *(political party, idea)* desertar (from, de).

deserve [dɪˈzɜːv] *vt* merecer, merecerse.

desiccation [desɪˈkeɪʃ³n] *n* desecación *f*.

design [dɪˈzaɪn] *n* **1** ART *(gen)* diseño, dibujo. **2** *(plan, drawing)* plano, proyecto; *(sketch)* boceto; *(of dress)* patrón *m*; *(of product, model)* modelo. **3** *fig (purpose, intention)* plan *m*, intención, proyecto.
▶ *vt* **1** *(gen)* diseñar, proyectar; *(fashion, set, product)* diseñar; *(course, programme)* planear, estructurar. **2** *(develop for a purpose)* concebir, idear; *(intend, mean)* pensar, destinar.

designate [*(vb)* ˈdezɪgneɪt; *(adj)* ˈdezɪgnət] *vt* **1** *fml (indicate, mark, show)* indicar, señalar. **2** *(appoint)* designar, nombrar.

desire [dɪˈzaɪə³] *n* deseo.
▶ *vt fml* desear.

desist [dɪˈzɪst] *vi fml* desistir (from, de).

desk [desk] *n* **1** *(in school)* pupitre *m*; *(in office)* escritorio. **2** *(service area)* mostrador *m*. **3** *(newspaper office)* sección *f*.

desktop [desktɒp] *n* escritorio. COMP **desktop computer** ordenador de sobremesa. ❙ **desktop publishing** autoedición.

desolate [ˈdesələt] *adj* **1** *(place)* deshabitado,-a, desierto,-a. **2** *(person - sad)* triste, desconsolado,-a; *(lonely)* solitario,-a.
▶ *vt* desolar.

despair [dɪsˈpeə³] *n* desesperación *f*.
▶ *vi* desesperar (of, de), desesperarse (of, por).

desperado [despəˈrɑːdəʊ] *n* forajido,-a.

desperate [ˈdesp³rət] *adj (reckless, risky)* desesperado,-a.

despicable [dɪˈspɪkəb³l] *adj (person, act)* despreciable, vil; *(behaviour)* indigno,-a.

despise [dɪˈspaɪz] *vt* despreciar, menospreciar.

despite [dɪˈspaɪt] *prep* a pesar de: *she went to work despite having a bad cold* se fue a trabajar a pesar de estar muy resfriada.

despondent [dɪˈspɒndənt] *adj* desalentado,-a, desanimado,-a, abatido,-a.

despot [ˈdespɒt] *n* déspota *mf*.

dessert [dɪˈzɜːt] *n* postre *m*.

destabilize [diːˈsteɪbəlaɪz] *vt* desestabilizar.

destination [destɪˈneɪʃ³n] *n* destino.

destined [ˈdestɪnd] *adj* **1** *(intended, meant)* destinado,-a. **2** *(fated)* condenado,-a, destinado,-a. **3** *(bound)* con destino (for, a).

destiny ['destɪnɪ] *n* destino, sino.
① *pl* destinies.

❌ Destiny no significa 'destino (punto de llegada)', que se traduce por **destination**.

destitute ['destɪtjuːt] *adj* indigente, mísero,-a.

❌ To destitute no significa 'destituir', que se traduce por **to dismiss**.

destroy [dɪ'strɔɪ] *vt* destruir.
destruction [dɪ'strʌkʃ°n] *n* destrucción *f*.
detach [dɪ'tætʃ] *vt* **1** *(separate, remove)* separar, quitar; *(unstick)* despegar: *you can detach the collar from the coat* se puede quitar el cuello del abrigo. **2** MIL destacar.

detached [dɪ'tætʃt] *adj* **1** *(separated - gen)* separado,-a, suelto,-a. **2** *(person, manner - impartial)* objetivo,-a, imparcial; *(- aloof)* distante, indiferente. COMP **detached house** vivienda unifamiliar.

detail ['diːteɪl] *n* detalle *m*, pormenor *m*.
▶ *vt* **1** *(describe)* detallar. **2** MIL destacar.
▶ *n pl* **details** *(information)* información *f*; *(particulars)* datos *mpl*.

detain [dɪ'teɪn] *vt* **1** *(hold - in custody)* detener. **2** *(delay)* entretener, demorar.
detainee [diːteɪ'niː] *n* detenido,-a.
detect [dɪ'tekt] *vt* **1** *(gen)* detectar. **2** *(discover - crime, criminal, fraud)* descubrir.
detective [dɪ'tektɪv] *n* *(private)* detective *mf*; *(in police force)* agente *mf*, oficial *mf*.
detector [dɪ'tektə'] *n* detector *m*.
detente ['deɪtɒnt] *n* distensión *f*.
detention [dɪ'tenʃ°n] *n* **1** JUR *(of suspect)* detención *f*, arresto. **2** EDUC *(of pupil)* castigo.

deter [dɪ'tɜː'] *vt* **1** *(person - dissuade)* disuadir (from, de). **2** *(prevent, stop)* impedir.
① *pt & pp* deterred, *ger* deterring.
detergent [dɪ'tɜːdʒ°nt] *n* detergente *m*.
deteriorate [dɪ'tɪərɪəreɪt] *vi* *(economy, health, situation, relations, material)* deteriorarse; *(weather, work)* empeorar.
deterioration [dɪtɪərɪə'reɪʃ°n] *n* *(gen)* empeoramiento; *(of material)* deterioro.

determination [dɪtɜːmɪ'neɪʃ°n] *n* determinación *f*.
determine [dɪ'tɜːmɪn] *vt* determinar.
determined [dɪ'tɜːmɪnd] *adj* *(person)* decidido,-a, resuelto,-a; *(attempt, effort)* enérgico,-a, persistente.

❌ Determined no significa 'determinado (cierto)', que se traduce por **particular**.

determiner [dɪ'tɜːmɪnə'] *n* LING determinante *m*.
deterrent [dɪ'terənt] *adj* disuasivo,-a, disuasorio,-a.
▶ *n* fuerza disuasoria, fuerza disuasiva.
detest [dɪ'test] *vt* detestar, odiar, aborrecer: *I detest cooking* odio cocinar.
detonate ['detəneɪt] *vi* estallar, detonar, explotar.
▶ *vt* hacer estallar, hacer explotar.
detonation [detə'neɪʃ°n] *n* detonación *f*.
detour ['diːtʊə'] *n* *(in traffic)* desvío.
detract [dɪ'trækt] *vt* **to detract from** *(achievement)* quitar mérito(s) a, restar valor a; *(beauty)* deslucir.
detractor [dɪ'træktə'] *n* detractor,-ra.
detritus [dɪ'traɪtəs] *n* **1** GEOL detrito, detritus *m*. **2** *(debris)* deshechos *mpl*.
deuce [djuːs] *n* *(in tennis)* cuarenta *mpl* iguales.
devaluation [diːvæljuː'eɪʃ°n] *n* FIN devaluación *f*, desvaloración *f*.
devalue [diː'væljuː] *vt* **1** FIN *(currency)* devaluar, desvalorizar. **2** *(person, achievement)* subvalorar.
devastate ['devəsteɪt] *vt* **1** *(city, area, country)* devastar. **2** *fam fig (person)* anonadar, apabullar.
devastation [devə'steɪʃ°n] *n* devastación *f*
develop [dɪ'veləp] *vt* **1** *(gen)* desarrollar; *(foster - trade, arts)* fomentar, promover. **2** *(acquire - habit, quality, feature)* contraer, adquirir; *(- talent, interest)* mostrar; *(get - illness, disease)* contraer. **3** *(exploit - resources)* explotar; *(- site, land)* urbanizar. **4** *(film, photograph)* revelar.
▶ *vi* **1** *(gen)* desarrollarse; *(- system)* perfeccionarse. **2** *(evolve - emotion)* conver-

D

tirse (into, en), transformarse (into, en); *(plot, novel)* desarrollarse. **3** *(appear - problem, complication, symptom)* aparecer, surgir; *(situation, crisis)* producirse. **4** *(of film, photograph)* salir.

developer [dɪ'veləpəʳ] *n* **1** *(of land, property - company)* promotora inmobiliaria, empresa constructora; *(- person)* constructor,-ra. **2** *(for photographs)* revelador *m*.

developing [dɪ'veləpɪŋ] *adj (country)* en vías de desarrollo.

development [dɪ'veləpmənt] *n* **1** *(gen)* desarrollo; *(- of skill, system)* perfección *f*; *(fostering)* fomento, promoción *f*; *(evolution)* evolución *f*. **2** *(invention - of product)* creación *f*. **4** *(event, incident)* acontecimiento, suceso; *(advance)* avance *m*, conquista. **5** *(of resources)* explotación *f*; *(of site, land, etc)* urbanización *f*.

deviance ['di:vɪəns] *n* desviación *f*.

deviant ['di:vɪənt] *adj* anormal.
▶ *n* pervertido,-a.

deviate ['di:vɪeɪt] *vi* desviarse (from, de).

device [dɪ'vaɪs] *n* **1** *(object, equipment)* aparato, artefacto; *(mechanism)* mecanismo, dispositivo. **2** *(scheme, trick)* ardid *m*, estratagema.

devil ['devəl] *n* diablo, demonio.

devious ['di:vɪəs] *adj* tortuoso,-a, sinuoso,-a.

devise [dɪ'vaɪz] *vt (plan, scheme)* idear, concebir, crear; *(object, tool)* inventar.

devoid [dɪ'vɔɪd] *adj* carente (of, de), desprovisto,-a (of, de).

devote [dɪ'vəut] *vt (time, effort)* dedicar, consagrar.

devoted [dɪ'vəutɪd] *adj (loyal - friend)* fiel (to, a), leal (to, a); *(- couple)* unido,-a; *(- follower, supporter)* ferviente; *(selfless)* abnegado,-a: *your devoted daughter* tu hija que te quiere.

devotion [dɪ'vəuʃən] *n* **1** *(loyalty)* lealtad *f*, fidelidad *f*; *(love)* cariño, afecto, amor *m*. **2** *(to work, research, cause)* dedicación *f*, entrega. **3** REL *(devoutness)* devoción *f*.

devour [dɪ'vauəʳ] *vt* devorar.

dew [dju:] *n* rocío.

dexterity [dek'sterɪtɪ] *n (manual)* destreza, maña; *(intellectual)* habilidad *f*.

diabetes [daɪə'bi:ti:z] *n* diabetes *f*.
ⓘ *pl* diabetes.

diabolical [daɪə'bɒlɪkəl] *adj* **1** *(evil)* diabólico,-a. **2** GB *fam (extremely bad)* espantoso,-a, atroz.

diabolo [dɪ'æbələu] *n* diábolo.

diacritic [daɪə'krɪtɪk] *adj* diacrítico,-a.
▶ *n* signo diacrítico.

diadem ['daɪədem] *n* diadema.

diaeresis [daɪ'erəsɪs] *n* diéresis *fpl*.
ⓘ *pl* diaereses [daɪ'erəsiːz].

diagnose ['daɪəgnəuz] *vt* MED diagnosticar.

diagnosis [daɪəg'nəusɪs] *n* MED diagnóstico.
ⓘ *pl* diagnoses [daɪəg'nəusi:s].

diagonal [daɪ'ægənəl] *adj (line)* diagonal; *(path)* en diagonal.
▶ *n* diagonal *f*.

diagram ['daɪəgræm] *n (gen)* diagrama *m*; *(graph)* gráfico, gráfica; *(of process, system)* esquema *m*.

dialect ['daɪəlekt] *n* dialecto.

dial ['daɪəl] *n* **1** *(of clock)* esfera. **2** *(of radio)* dial *m*.
▶ *vt* marcar. [COMP] **dialling code** prefijo (telefónico). ‖ **dialling tone** señal *f* de llamada.

dialogue ['daɪəlɒg] *n* diálogo.

diameter [daɪ'æmɪtəʳ] *n* diámetro.

diamond ['daɪəmənd] *n* **1** *(stone)* diamante *m*, brillante *m*. **2** *(shape)* rombo. **3** *(in cards)* diamante *m*.

diaper ['daɪəpəʳ] *n* US pañal *m*.

diaphragm ['daɪəfræm] *n* diafragma *m*.

diarrhoea [daɪə'rɪə] *n* diarrea.

diary ['daɪərɪ] *n* **1** *(of thoughts, events, etc)* diario. **2** *(for appointments)* agenda.
ⓘ *pl* diaries.

❌ Diary no significa 'diario (periódico)', que se traduce por **newspaper**.

diastole [daɪəs'təlɪ] *n* diástole *f*.

dice [daɪs] *n* dado.
ⓘ *pl* dice.

dichotomy [daɪ'kɒtəmɪ] *n* dicotomía.
ⓘ *pl* dichotomies.

dictate [*(vb)* dɪk'teɪt; *(n)* 'dɪkteɪt] *vt* **1** *(letter, etc)* dictar. **2** *(state, lay down - law, demands, trends)* ordenar; *(terms, conditions)* imponer.
▸ *vi (read out)* dictar.
▸ *n* mandato.

dictation [dɪk'teɪʃᵊn] *n* dictado.

dictator [dɪk'teɪtər] *n* dictador,-ra.

dictatorship [dɪk'teɪtəʃɪp] *n* dictadura.

dictionary ['dɪkʃənᵊrɪ] *n* diccionario.
ⓘ *pl* dictionaries.

did [dɪd] *pt* → **do**.

didn't ['dɪdənt] *pt* → **do**.

didactic [dɪ'dæktɪk] *adj* didáctico,-a.

die [daɪ] *vi* morir, morirse.
◆ **to die away** *vi (noise)* desvanecerse, irse apagando; *(breeze)* amainar.

die-hard ['daɪhɑːd] *n* intransigente *mf*.

dieresis [daɪ'erəsɪs] *n* US → **diaeresis**.

diesel ['diːzᵊl] *n* **1** *(fuel)* gasóleo, gasoil *m*. **2** *(car)* coche *m* diesel.

diet ['daɪət] *n (food)* dieta (alimenticia), alimentación *f*. **2** *(restricted food)* régimen *m*, dieta. [loc] **to be on a diet** estar a régimen. I **to go on a diet** ponerse a régimen.
▸ *adj (food)* de régimen, bajo,-a en calorías.
▸ *vi* estar a régimen, estar a dieta, hacer régimen, hacer dieta.

differ ['dɪfər] *vi* **1** *(be unlike)* ser distinto,-a (from, de), ser diferente (from, de), diferir (from, de). **2** *(disagree)* discrepar (about/on, en).

difference ['dɪfᵊrəns] *n* diferencia.

different ['dɪfᵊrənt] *adj* diferente (from, de), distinto,-a (from, de).

differential [dɪfə'renʃᵊl] *adj* diferencial.
▸ *n* **1** FIN diferencial *m*. **2** [también differential gear] AUTO diferencial *m*.

differentiate [dɪfə'renʃɪeɪt] *vt* diferenciar (from, de), distinguir (from, de).
▸ *vi* distinguir (between, entre).

difficult ['dɪfɪkᵊlt] *adj* difícil.

difficulty ['dɪfɪkᵊltɪ] *n* dificultad *f*.
ⓘ *pl* difficulties.

diffuse [*(adj)* dɪ'fjuːs; *(vb)* dɪ'fjuːz] *adj (light, gas)* difuso,-a.
▸ *vt (light, heat, news)* difundir.

diffusion [dɪ'fjuːʒᵊn] *n* difusión *f*.

dig [dɪg] *n* **1** *(poke, prod)* codazo. **2** *fam (gibe)* pulla; *(hint)* indirecta. **3** *(by archaeologists)* excavación *f*.
▸ *vt (ground, garden)* cavar (en); *(by machine - tunnel, trench)* excavar; *(by hand - hole)* hacer, cavar; *(site)* excavar.
◆ **to dig into** *vt insep* **1** *(investigate, examine)* investigar. **2** *(resources, savings, reserves)* echar mano de.
◆ **to dig out** *vt sep (trapped person, car)* sacar, desenterrar.
ⓘ *pt & pp* dug, *ger* digging.

digest [*(n)* 'daɪdʒest; *(vb)* dɪ'dʒest] *n (summary)* resumen *m*, compendio.
▸ *vt* digerir.

digestion [dɪ'dʒestʃᵊn] *n* digestión *f*.

digestive [daɪ'dʒestɪv] *adj* digestivo,-a.

digger ['dɪgər] *n* excavadora.

digit ['dɪdʒɪt] *n* **1** MATH dígito. **2** ANAT *(finger)* dedo; *(thumb)* pulgar *m*.

digital ['dɪdʒɪtᵊl] *adj* **1** *(watch, display, recording)* digital. **2** ANAT dactilar, digital.

dignify ['dɪgnɪfaɪ] *vt* dignificar.
ⓘ *pt & pp* dignified, *ger* dignifying.

dignitary ['dɪgnɪtᵊrɪ] *n* dignatario,-a.
ⓘ *pl* dignitaries.

dignity ['dɪgnɪtɪ] *n* dignidad *f*.

dilapidated [dɪ'læpɪdeɪtɪd] *adj (furniture)* desvencijado,-a, en mal estado; *(building)* ruinoso,-a; *(car)* desvencijado,-a, destartalado,-a.

> ✖ Dilapidated no significa 'dilapidado (malgastado)', que se traduce por **wasted**.

dilate [daɪ'leɪt] *vt* dilatar.

dilation [daɪ'leɪʃᵊn] *n* dilatación *f*.

dilemma [dɪ'lemə] *n* dilema *m*.

diligence ['dɪlɪdʒəns] *n* diligencia.

dill [dɪl] *n* eneldo.

dilute [daɪ'luːt] *vt* **1** *(liquid, concentrate)* diluir. **2** *fig (criticism, effect, influence)* atenuar, suavizar.
▸ *adj* diluido,-a.

dilution [daɪ'luːʃᵊn] *n* dilución *f*.

dim [dɪm] *adj* **1** *(light)* débil, tenue; *(room, corridor, corner)* oscuro,-a. **2** *fam (person)* tonto,-a, corto,-a (de luces).
ⓘ *comp* dimmer, *superl* dimmest.

▸ *vt (light)* atenuar, bajar; *(eyes)* nublar, empañar; *(memory)* borrar, difuminar.
ⓘ *pt & pp* **dimmed**, *ger* **dimming**.

dime [daɪm] *n* US moneda de diez centavos.

dimension [dɪ'menʃən] *n* dimensión *f*.
▸ *n pl* **dimensions** dimensiones *fpl*.

diminish [dɪ'mɪnɪʃ] *vt* disminuir, reducir.

diminution [dɪmɪ'njuːʃən] *n* disminución *f*, reducción *f*.

diminutive [dɪ'mɪnjətɪv] *adj* **1** diminuto,-a. **2** LING diminutivo,-a.
▸ *n* LING diminutivo.

dimmer ['dɪmə'] [también **dimmer switch**] *n* regulador *m* de intensidad (de la luz).

dimple ['dɪmpəl] *n* hoyuelo.

din [dɪn] *n (of voices)* barullo, alboroto; *(of traffic)* estruendo, ruido.

dine [daɪn] *vi fml (gen)* comer (on, -); *(in evening)* cenar (on, -).
◆ **to dine out** *vi* cenar fuera.

diner ['daɪnə'] *n* **1** *(person)* comensal *mf*. **2** US restaurante *m* barato.

dinghy ['dɪŋgɪ] *n* bote *m*.
ⓘ *pl* **dinghies**.

dingy ['dɪndʒɪ] *adj (dark, depressing - room, house, street)* lúgubre, deprimente, sórdido,-a; *(drab - colour, wall, curtains)* deslucido,-a; *(dirty)* sucio,-a.
ⓘ *comp* **dingier**, *superl* **dingiest**.

dining car ['daɪnɪŋkɑː'] *n* vagón *m* restaurante.

dining room ['daɪnɪŋruːm] *n* comedor *m*.

dinner ['dɪnə'] *n (at midday)* comida; *(in evening)* cena. LOC **to have dinner** cenar. COMP **dinner jacket** esmoquin *m*, smoking *m*.

⊕ En los países anglosajones la cena se sirve mucho más temprano que en España (entre las 17 h 30 y las 19 h) y es la comida más importante del día.

dinosaur ['daɪnəsɔː'] *n* dinosaurio.

diocese ['daɪəsɪs] *n* diócesis *f*.

dioxide [daɪ'ɒksaɪd] *n* dióxido.

dip [dɪp] *n* **1** *(downward slope)* declive *m*, pendiente *f*; *(drop - in prices, temperature, sales, production, profits)* caída, descen-

so. **2** *fam (quick swim)* chapuzón *m*. **3** CULIN *(sauce)* salsa.
▸ *vt* **1** *(put into liquid - pen, brush, bread)* mojar; *(- hand, spoon)* meter. **2** *(lower - head)* agachar, bajar.
▸ *vi* bajar.
ⓘ *pt & pp* **dipped**, *ger* **dipping**.

diphthong ['dɪfθɒn] *n* LING diptongo.

diploma [dɪ'pləʊmə] *n* diploma *m*.

diplomacy [dɪ'pləʊməsɪ] *n* diplomacia.

diplomat ['dɪpləmæt] *n* **1** *(ambassador, etc)* diplomático,-a. **2** *(tactful person)* persona diplomática.

diplomatic [dɪplə'mætɪk] *adj* diplomático,-a.

dire ['daɪə'] *adj* **1** *(desperate, extreme)* extremo,-a, urgente. **2** *(serious, ominous)* serio,-a, grave. **3** *(terrible, dreadful)* terrible, atroz.

direct [dɪ'rekt, daɪ'rekt] *adj* **1** *(gen)* directo,-a. **2** *(exact, complete)* exacto,-a. **3** *(straightforward - person)* franco,-a, sincero,-a; *(- question)* directo,-a; *(- answer)* claro,-a.
▸ *adv (go, write, phone)* directamente; *(broadcast)* en directo.
▸ *vt* **1** *(gen)* dirigir. **2** *(show the way)* indicar el camino a.

direction [dɪ'rekʃən, daɪ'rekʃən] *n* dirección *f*.
▸ *n pl* **directions** instrucciones *f pl* de uso. LOC **to ask for directions** preguntar cómo se va.

directive [dɪ'rektɪv] *n* directiva, directriz *f*.

director [dɪ'rektə', daɪ'rektə'] *n* director,-ra.

directory [dɪ'rektərɪ, daɪ'rektərɪ] *n* **1** *(telephone)* guía telefónica, listín *m* (de teléfonos); *(book, lost, index)* directorio, guía. **2** [también **street directory**] callejero.
ⓘ *pl* **directories**.

dirt [dɜːt] *n* **1** *(dirtiness)* suciedad *f*. **2** *(earth)* tierra. **3** *fam (scandal, gossip)* chismes *mpl*, trapos *mpl* sucios.

dirty ['dɜːtɪ] *adj* **1** *(gen)* sucio,-a; *(stained)* manchado,-a. COMP **dirty word** palabrota.
ⓘ *comp* **dirtier**, *superl* **dirtiest**.
▸ *vt* ensuciar.

disability [dɪsəˈbɪlɪtɪ] *n (state)* invalidez *f*, discapacidad *f*, minusvalía; *(handicap)* desventaja, handicap *m*.
ⓘ *pl* disabilities.

disabled [dɪsˈeɪbəld] *adj* minusválido,-a. COMP **disabled access** acceso para minusválidos.
▶ *n pl* **the disabled** los minusválidos.

disadvantage [dɪsədˈvɑːntɪdʒ] *n (drawback)* desventaja; *(obstacle)* inconveniente *m*.

disadvantaged [dɪsədˈvɑːntɪdʒd] *adj* desfavorecido,-a.
▶ *n pl* **the disadvantaged** los desfavorecidos *mpl*.

disagree [dɪsəˈɡriː] *vi* **1** *(not agree)* no estar de acuerdo (on, en), (with, con), disentir (with, de), discrepar (with, de), (on, en). **3** *(food)* sentar mal (with, a); *(weather)* no convenir (with, a).

disagreeable [dɪsəˈɡriəbəl] *adj* desagradable.

disagreement [dɪsəˈɡriːmənt] *n* **1** *(difference of opinion)* desacuerdo; *(argument)* discusión *f*, riña, altercado. **2** *(lack of similarity)* discrepancia.

disappear [dɪsəˈpɪər] *vi* desaparecer.

disappearance [dɪsəˈpɪərəns] *n* desaparición *f*.

disappoint [dɪsəˈpɔɪnt] *vt* decepcionar, defraudar, desilusionar.

disappointed [dɪsəˈpɔɪntɪd] *adj* decepcionado,-a.

disappointment [dɪsəˈpɔɪntmənt] *n* desilusión *f*, decepción *f*.

disapprove [dɪsəˈpruːv] *vt* desaprobar (of, -).

disarm [dɪsˈɑːm] *vt* **1** *(gen)* desarmar; *(bomb)* desactivar.

disarmament [dɪsˈɑːməmənt] *n* desarme *m*.

disaster [dɪˈzɑːstər] *n* desastre *m*.

disbelief [dɪsbɪˈliːf] *n* incredulidad *f*.

disc [dɪsk] *n* disco. COMP **disc jockey** pinchadiscos *m sing*.

discard [dɪsˈkɑːd] *vt* desechar, deshacerse de.

discern [dɪˈsɜːn] *vt* percibir, distinguir.

discernment [dɪˈsɜːnmənt] *n* (buen) criterio, discernimiento.

discharge [*(n)* ˈdɪstʃɑːdʒ; *(vb)* dɪsˈtʃɑːdʒ] *n* **1** descarga. **2** *(of prisoner)* liberación *f*, puesta en libertad; *(of patient)* alta. **3** *(of worker)* despido.
▶ *vt* **1** *(give, send out - sewage, waste, oil)* verter; *(smoke, fumes)* despedir; *(- electric current)* descargar. **2** *(prisoner)* liberar, poner en libertad; *(patient)* dar de alta. **3** *(dismiss)* despedir.

disciple [dɪˈsaɪpəl] *n* discípulo,-a.

disciplinary [ˈdɪsɪplɪnərɪ] *adj* disciplinario,-a.

discipline [ˈdɪsɪplɪn] *n* **1** *(behaviour)* disciplina. **2** *(punishment)* castigo.

disclose [dɪsˈkləʊz] *vt* **1** *(make known)* revelar, dar a conocer. **2** *(show)* mostrar, dejar ver.

disco [ˈdɪskəʊ] *n fam* disco *f*, discoteca.
ⓘ *pl* discos.

discomfort [dɪsˈkʌmfət] *n* **1** incomodidad *f*. **2** inquietud *f*, desasosiego.

disconnect [dɪskəˈnekt] *vt (from mains)* desconectar; *(gas, electricity, etc)* cortar.

disconsolate [dɪsˈkɒnsələt] *adj* desconsolado,-a.

discontent [dɪskənˈtent] *n* descontento.

discontinue [dɪskənˈtɪnjuː] *vt (service)* suspender, interrumpir; *(model)* dejar de fabricar.

discotheque [ˈdɪskətek] *n fml* discoteca.

discount [*(n)* ˈdɪskaʊnt; *(vb)* dɪsˈkaʊnt] *n* descuento.
▶ *vt (goods)* rebajar; *(price)* reducir; *(amount, bill of exchange)* descontar.

discourage [dɪsˈkʌrɪdʒ] *vt* **1** *(dishearten)* desanimar, desalentar. **2** *(dissuade)* disuadir (from, de).

discouragement [dɪsˈkʌrɪdʒmənt] *n* desaliento, desánimo.

discover [dɪsˈkʌvər] *vt (find - gen)* descubrir; *(mistake, loss, fact)* descubrir, darse cuenta de.

discoverer [dɪsˈkʌvərər] *n* descubridor,-ra.

discovery [dɪsˈkʌvərɪ] *n* descubrimiento.
ⓘ *pl* discoveries.

discredit [dɪs'kredɪt] *n (dishonour, disgrace)* descrédito.

discreet [dɪ'skriːt] *adj (gen)* discreto,-a; *(distance)* prudencial.

discrepancy [dɪ'skrepənsɪ] *n* discrepancia.
ⓘ *pl* discrepancies.

discrete [dɪs'kriːt] *adj* diferenciado,-a, distinto,-a.

❌ Discrete no significa 'discreto', que se traduce por discreet.

discretion [dɪ'skreʃən] *n* **1** *(quality of being discreet)* discreción *f*; *(prudence)* prudencia. **2** *(judgement)* criterio, juicio.

discriminate [dɪ'skrɪmɪneɪt] *vi (treat differently)* discriminar (against, a; between, entre).
▶ *vt (see a difference)* distinguir (from, de), discriminar.

discrimination [dɪskrɪmɪ'neɪʃən] *n* **1** *(bias)* discriminación *f*. **2** *(distinction)* diferenciación *f*, distinción *f*. **3** *(judgement)* discernimiento, criterio.

discus ['dɪskəs] *n (object)* disco.
▶ *n* the discus *(event, sport)* el lanzamiento de disco.
ⓘ *pl* discuses o disci ['dɪskaɪ].

discuss [dɪ'skʌs] *vt (talk about - person)* hablar de; *(- subject, topic)* hablar de, tratar de; *(- plan, problem)* discutir.

❌ To discuss no significa 'discutir (pelearse)', que se traduce por to argue.

discussion [dɪ'skʌʃən] *n* discusión *f*, debate *m*.

❌ Discussion no significa 'discusión (pelea)', que se traduce por argument.

disdain [dɪs'deɪn] *n* desdén *m*, desprecio.
▶ *vt* desdeñar, despreciar.

disease [dɪ'ziːz] *n* enfermedad *f*.

disembark [dɪsɪm'bɑːk] *vt* desembarcar.

disembarkation [dɪsɪmbɑː'keɪʃən] *n (of people)* desembarco; *(of goods)* desembarque *m*.

disenchanted [dɪsɪn'tʃɑːntɪd] *adj* desencantado,-a, desilusionado,-a.

disenchantment [dɪsɪn'tʃɑːntmənt] *n* desencanto, desilusión *f*.

disengage [dɪsɪn'geɪdʒ] *vt* **1** *(free - gen)* soltar (from, de); *(gears, mechanism)* desconectar. **2** MIL *(troops)* retirar (from, de).

disentangle [dɪsɪn'tæŋgəl] *vt (unravel)* desenredar, desenmarañar.

disfavour [dɪs'feɪvəʳ] *n* desaprobación *f*.

disfigure [dɪs'fɪgəʳ] *vt (face, person)* desfigurar; *(building, town, landscape)* afear, estropear.

disgrace [dɪs'greɪs] *n* **1** *(loss of favour)* desgracia; *(loss of honour)* deshonra, deshonor *m*. **2** *(shame)* escándalo, vergüenza.
▶ *vt* **1** *(bring shame on)* deshonrar. **2** *(discredit)* desacreditar.

disgraceful [dɪs'greɪsful] *adj* vergonzoso,-a: *it's disgraceful* es vergonzoso, es una vergüenza.

disguise [dɪs'gaɪz] *n* disfraz *m*. LOC in disguise disfrazado,-a.
▶ *vt (person)* disfrazar (as, de); *(voice, handwriting)* disimular.

disgust [dɪs'gʌst] *n (revulsion)* asco, repugnancia; *(strong disapproval)* indignación *f*.
▶ *vt (revolt)* repugnar, dar asco a; *(disapprove)* indignar.

❌ To disgust no significa 'disgusto', que se traduce por displeasure o sorrow.

disgusting [dɪs'gʌstɪŋ] *adj* asqueroso,-a, repugnante.

dish [dɪʃ] *n* **1** *(plate)* plato; *(for serving)* fuente *f*. **2** CULIN *(food)* plato. **3** TV antena parabólica.
▶ *n pl* dishes *(crockery)* platos *mpl*, vajilla *f sing*. LOC to do the dishes lavar los platos.

dishcloth ['dɪʃklɒθ] *n* trapo, bayeta.

dishearten [dɪs'hɑːtən] *vt* descorazonar, desanimar, desalentar.

dishevel [dɪ'ʃevəl] *vt* despeinar.
ⓘ *pt & pp* dishevelled *(US* disheveled*)*, *ger* dishevelling *(US* disheveling*)*.

dishonest [dɪs'ɒnɪst] *adj (person, answer)* deshonesto,-a, poco honrado,-a; *(means, etc)* fraudulento,-a.

dishonour [dɪsˈɒnəʳ] *n* deshonra, deshonor *m*.
▶ *vt* deshonrar.

dishonourable [dɪsˈɒnərəbəl] *adj* deshonroso,-a.

dishwasher [ˈdɪʃwɒʃəʳ] *n (machine)* lavaplatos *m*, lavavajillas *m*; *(person)* lavaplatos *mf*.

disillusion [dɪsɪˈluːʒən] *vt* desilusionar.

disinfect [dɪsɪnˈfekt] *vt* desinfectar.

disinfection [dɪsɪnˈfekʃən] *n* desinfección *f*.

disinherit [dɪsɪnˈherɪt] *vt* desheredar.

disintegration [dɪsɪntɪˈgreɪʃən] *n* desintegración *f*.

disinter [dɪsɪnˈtɜːʳ] *vt fml* desenterrar.
ⓘ *pt & pp* disinterred, *ger* disinterring.

disk [dɪsk] *n (gen)* disco. COMP **disk drive** COMPUT disquetera.

diskette [dɪsˈket] *n* COMPUT disquete *m*.

dislike [dɪsˈlaɪk] *n* aversión *f*, antipatía.

dislocation [dɪsləˈkeɪʃən] *n* MED dislocación *f*.

dislodge [dɪsˈlɒdʒ] *vt* **1** *(object)* sacar. **2** *(person)* desalojar (from , de).

disloyal [dɪsˈlɔɪəl] *adj* desleal (to, a/ con).

dismal [ˈdɪzməl] *adj* sombrío,-a, deprimente, lúgubre.

dismantle [dɪsˈmæntəl] *vt (take apart - machinery)* desmontar; *(- furniture)* desarmar.

dismay [dɪsˈmeɪ] *n* consternación *f*.
▶ *vt* consternar.

☒ To dismay no significa 'desmayo', que se traduce por faint.

dismiss [dɪsˈmɪs] *vt* **1** descartar, desechar. **2** *(sack)* despedir.

dismissal [dɪsˈmɪsəl] *n* **1** descarte *m*, abandono. **2** *(sacking - of employee)* despido; *(- of official, minister)* destitución *f*.

dismissive [dɪsˈmɪsɪv] *adj* desdeñoso,-a.

dismount [dɪsˈmaʊnt] *vi* desmontarse (from, de), apearse (from, de).

disobedience [dɪsəˈbiːdɪəns] *n* desobediencia.

disobedient [dɪsəˈbiːdɪənt] *adj* desobediente.

disobey [dɪsəˈbeɪ] *vt* desobedecer.

disorder [dɪsˈɔːdəʳ] *n* desorden *m*.

disordered [dɪsˈɔːdəd] *adj* desordenado,-a.

disorganisation [dɪsɔːgənaɪˈzeɪʃən] *n* → disorganization.

disorganization [dɪsɔːgənaɪˈzeɪʃən] *n* desorganización *f*.

disorganize [dɪsˈɔːgənaɪz] *vt* desorganizar.

disorganized [dɪsˈɔːgənaɪzd] *adj* desorganizado,-a.

disorientate [dɪsˈɔːrɪənteɪt] *vt* desorientar.

disorientation [dɪsɔːrɪənˈteɪʃən] *n* desorientación *f*.

disown [dɪsˈəʊn] *vt* renegar de, repudiar.

disparity [dɪˈspærɪtɪ] *n fml (inequality)* disparidad *f*; *(difference)* discrepancia.
ⓘ *pl* disparities.

dispatch [dɪˈspætʃ] *n* **1** mensaje, despacho. **2** *(journalist's report)* noticia, reportaje *m*.
▶ *vt* **1** *(send)* enviar, expedir. **2** *(finish quickly)* despachar.

☒ To dispatch no significa 'despachar (despedir)', que se traduce por to dismiss.

dispel [dɪˈspel] *vt* disipar.
ⓘ *pt & pp* dispelled, *ger* dispelling.

dispensary [dɪˈspensərɪ] *n (in hospital)* dispensario; *(in school)* enfermería.
ⓘ *pl* dispensaries.

dispense [dɪˈspens] *vt* **1** *(distribute)* distribuir, repartir. **2** JUR *(justice)* administrar. **3** *fml (public service)* suministrar, administrar.
◆ **to dispense with** *vt insep* prescindir de, pasar sin.

dispenser [dɪˈspensəʳ] *n* máquina expendedora.

disperse [dɪˈspɜːs] *vt* dispersar.

dispersed [dɪsˈpɜːst] *adj* disperso,-a.

displace [dɪs'pleɪs] *vt* **1** *(gen)* desplazar; *(bone)* dislocar. **2** *(replace)* sustituir, reemplazar.

display [dɪ'spleɪ] *n* **1** exposición *f*, muestra. **2** COMPUT visualización *f*.
▸ *vt* **1** exhibir, exponer. **5** COMPUT visualizar.

displease [dɪs'pli:z] *vt fml* disgustar.

displeasure [dɪs'pleʒə'] *n* disgusto.

disposable [dɪ'spəʊzəb'l] *adj* desechable, de usar y tirar.

disposal [dɪ'spəʊz'l] *n* **1** eliminación *f*. **2** disponibilidad *f*.

dispose [dɪ'spəʊz] *vt* **1** disponer, colocar. **2** *fml* predisponer (**to/towards**, hacia).
◆ **to dispose of** *vt insep* **1** tirar, deshacerse de.

☒ To dispose no significa 'disponer de (tener)', que se traduce por to have.

disposition [dɪspə'zɪʃ'n] *n* **1** *fml* carácter *m*. **2** disposición *f*.

dispossess [dɪspə'zes] *vt* desposeer, despojar.

disproportionate [dɪsprə'pɔ:ʃ'nət] *adj* desproporcionado,-a (**to**, a).

disprove [dɪs'pru:v] *vt (theory)* refutar, rebatir.

disputable [dɪ'spju:təbəl] *adj* discutible.

dispute [*(n)* 'dɪspju:t; *(vb)* dɪ'spju:t] *n* discusión *f*.
▸ *vi* discutir.

disqualification [dɪskwɒlɪfɪ'keɪʃ'n] *n* descalificación *f*.

disqualify [dɪs'kwɒlɪfaɪ] *vt* descalificar.
① *pt & pp* disqualified, *ger* disqualifying.

disregard [dɪsrɪ'gɑ:d] *n* indiferencia (**for**, hacia); despreocupación *f*.
▸ *vt (danger, difficulty)* ignorar, despreciar.

disrespect [dɪsrɪ'spekt] *n* falta de respeto.

disrespectful [dɪsrɪ'spektful] *adj* irrespetuoso,-a; irreverente.

disrupt [dɪs'rʌpt] *vt* interrumpir.

disruption [dɪs'rʌpʃ'n] *n (of meeting)* interrupción *f*; *(of traffic)* problemas *mpl*.

disruptive [dɪs'rʌptɪv] *adj* perjudicial, nocivo,-a; perturbador,-ra.

dissatisfaction [dɪssætɪs'fækʃ'n] *n* insatisfacción *f*, descontento.

dissatisfied [dɪs'sætɪsfaɪd] *adj* insatisfecho,-a, descontento,-a.

dissect [dɪ'sekt, daɪ'sekt] *vt* diseccionar.

disseminate [dɪ'semɪneɪt] *vt fml* divulgar, difundir, diseminar.

dissemination [dɪsemɪ'neɪʃ'n] *n fml* diseminación *f*, difusión *f*.

dissent [dɪ'sent] *n* desacuerdo, disconformidad *f*.
▸ *vi* disentir, discrepar.

dissenting [dɪ'sentɪŋ] *adj* discrepante.

dissertation [dɪsə'teɪʃ'n] *n* **1** *(formal discourse)* disertación *f*. **2** EDUC *(for lower degree, master's)* tesina; *(for PhD)* tesis *f* (doctoral).

dissidence ['dɪsɪd'ns] *n* disidencia.

dissident ['dɪsɪdənt] *adj* disidente.
▸ *n* disidente *mf*.

dissimilar [dɪ'sɪmɪlə'] *adj* diferente (**to**, de), distinto,-a (**to**, de/a).

dissimilarity [dɪsɪmɪ'lærɪtɪ] *n* diferencia.

dissimulate [dɪ'sɪmjəleɪt] *vt fml* disimular; ocultar, encubrir.
▸ *vi fml* disimular.

dissipate ['dɪsɪpeɪt] *vt* dispersar; difundir.
▸ *vi* disiparse, desvanecerse.

dissipated ['dɪsɪpeɪtɪd] *adj* disoluto,-a, disipado,-a.

dissociate [dɪ'səʊʃɪeɪt] *vt (separate)* disociar (**from**, de), separar (**from**, de).

dissolve [dɪ'zɒlv] *vt* disolver.

dissuade [dɪ'sweɪd] *vt* disuadir (**from**, de).

dissuasion [dɪ'sweɪʒ'n] *n* disuasión *f*.

dissuasive [dɪ'sweɪsɪv] *adj* disuasorio,-a.

distance ['dɪstəns] *n (gen)* distancia. LOC **from a distance** desde lejos. **in the distance** a lo lejos.
▸ *vt* distanciar.

distant ['dɪstənt] *adj* lejano,-a, distante.

distaste [dɪsˈteɪst] n aversión f, desagrado.

distasteful [dɪsˈteɪstful] adj (idea, task) desagradable; (joke, remark) de mal gusto.

distend [dɪˈstend] vt dilatar, hinchar.
▶ vi dilatarse, hincharse.

distil [dɪsˈtɪl] vt destilar.
ⓘ pt & pp distilled, ger distilling.

distill [dɪsˈtɪl] vt US → distil.

distillation [dɪstɪˈleɪʃən] n destilación f.

distiller [dɪsˈtɪlər] n destilador,-ra.

distillery [dɪsˈtɪlərɪ] n destilería.
ⓘ pl distilleries.

distinct [dɪˈstɪŋkt] adj distinto,-a (from, a), diferente (from, de).

distinction [dɪˈstɪŋkʃən] n 1 diferencia, distinción f. 3 GB ≈ matrícula de honor.

distinctive [dɪˈstɪŋktɪv] adj distintivo,-a, característico,-a; personal, inconfundible.

distinctly [dɪˈstɪŋktlɪ] adv con claridad.

☒ Distinctly no significa 'de forma distinta', que se traduce por differently.

distinguish [dɪˈstɪŋgwɪʃ] vt distinguir.
▶ vi distinguir (between, entre).

distinguished [dɪˈstɪŋgwɪʃt] adj distinguido,-a.

distort [dɪˈstɔːt] vt deformar.

distortion [dɪˈstɔːʃən] n deformación f.

distract [dɪˈstrækt] vt distraer (from, de).

distracting [dɪˈstræktɪŋ] adj (noise) molesto,-a; (presence) que distrae.

distraction [dɪˈstrækʃən] n distracción f. 2 desconsuelo, aflicción f.

distraught [dɪˈstrɔːt] adj afligido,-a.

distress [dɪˈstres] n (mental) aflicción f, angustia; (physical) dolor m; (exhaustion) agotamiento, COMP distress call señal de socorro.
▶ vt (upset) afligir; (grieve) consternar.

distressing [dɪˈstresɪŋ] adj penoso,-a, angustioso,-a.

distribute [dɪˈstrɪbjuːt] vt distribuir.

distribution [dɪstrɪˈbjuːʃən] n distribución f.

distributor [dɪˈstrɪbjətər] n distribuidor,-ra.

district [ˈdɪstrɪkt] n (of town, city) distrito, barrio; (of country) región f, zona.

distrust [dɪsˈtrʌst] n desconfianza, recelo.
▶ vt desconfiar de, no fiarse de.

disturb [dɪˈstɜːb] vt molestar.

disturbed [dɪˈstɜːbd] adj perturbado,-a.

disturbing [dɪˈstɜːbɪŋ] adj inquietante.

disuse [dɪsˈjuːs] n desuso.

ditch [dɪtʃ] n (gen) zanja; (at roadside) cuneta; (for irrigation) acequia.
▶ vt fam deshacerse de.
▶ vi AV hacer un aterrizaje forzoso.

dither [ˈdɪðər] vi vacilar, titubear.

ditto [ˈdɪtəʊ] n (in list) ídem m.

diuretic [daɪjəˈretɪk] adj diurético,-a.

diurnal [daɪˈɜːnəl] adj diurno,-a.

divan [dɪˈvæn] n (couch) diván m, canapé m.

dive [daɪv] n 1 (into water) zambullida; (in competition) salto (de trampolín); (underwater) buceo; (whale) inmersión f. 2 (of plane, bird) picado.
▶ vi [US pt dove [dəʊv]] 1 (into water) zambullirse, tirarse (de cabeza); (in competition) saltar; (underwater) bucear; (whale) sumergirse. 2 (birds, planes) bajar en picado. 3 (move suddenly) precipitarse hacia.
◆ to dive in vi zambullirse, tirarse de cabeza.

diver [ˈdaɪvər] n buzo, submarinista mf.

diverge [daɪˈvɜːdʒ] vi (gen) divergir; (roads) bifurcarse.

divergence [daɪˈvɜːdʒəns] n divergencia.

divergent [daɪˈvɜːdʒənt] adj divergente.

diverse [daɪˈvɜːs] adj diverso,-a, variado,-a.

diversification [daɪvɜːsɪfɪˈkeɪʃən] n 1 (variety) variedad f. 2 COMM diversificación f.

diversify [daɪˈvɜːsɪfaɪ] vt diversificar.
ⓘ pt & pp diversified, ger diversifying.

diversion [daɪˈvɜːʃ(ə)n] *n* desvío, desviación *f*.

diversity [daɪˈvɜːsɪtɪ] *n* diversidad *f*.

divert [daɪˈvɜːt] *vt* **1** desviar. **2** divertir.

divest [daɪˈvest] *vt* despojar, privar (of, de).

divide [dɪˈvaɪd] *vt* dividir, separar.
 ▸ *vi* dividirse, bifurcarse.
 ▸ *n fml* división *f*, diferencia.

divided [dɪˈvaɪdɪd] *adj (opinion)* dividido,-a.

dividend [ˈdɪvɪdend] *n* dividendo.

divider [dɪˈvaɪdəʳ] *n (in file)* separador *m*; *(in room)* mampara.

dividers [dɪˈvaɪdəz] *n pl* compás *m* de punta (fija).

divine [dɪˈvaɪn] *adj* divino,-a.

diviner [dɪˈvaɪnəʳ] *n* zahorí *m*.

diving [ˈdaɪvɪŋ] *n* **1** buceo, submarinismo. **2** *(in competition)* saltos *mpl* (de trampolín). COMP **diving board** trampolín *m*. ‖ **diving mask** gafas *f pl* de bucear.

divinity [dɪˈvɪnɪtɪ] *n* **1** *(quality, state)* divinidad *f*. **2** *(subject)* teología.
 ① *pl* **divinities**.

divisible [dɪˈvɪzəbəl] *adj* divisible.

division [dɪˈvɪʒ°n] *n* división *f*, reparto.

divisor [dɪˈvaɪzəʳ] *n* divisor *m*.

divorce [dɪˈvɔːs] *n* divorcio.
 ▸ *vi* divorciarse.

divorced [dɪˈvɔːst] *adj* divorciado,-a.

divulge [daɪˈvʌldʒ] *vt* divulgar, revelar.

DIY [ˈdiːaɪˈwaɪ] *abbr* GB (do-it-yourself) bricolaje *m*.

dizziness [ˈdɪzɪnəs] *n* mareo, vértigo.

dizzy [ˈdɪzɪ] *adj* **1** *(person)* mareado,-a. **2** *(speed, pace)* vertiginoso,-a; *(height)* de vértigo.
 ① *comp* **dizzier**, *superl* **dizziest**.

DJ¹ [ˈdiːˈdʒeɪ] *abbr* GB *fam* (dinner jacket) esmoquin *m*, smoking *m*.

DJ² [ˈdiːˈdʒeɪ] *abbr* (disc jockey) pinchadiscos *m*, disc-jockey *m*.

DNA [ˈdiːˈenˈeɪ] *abbr* (deoxyribonucleic acid) ácido desoxirribonucleico; *(abbreviation)* ADN *m*.

do [duː] *vt* **1** *(gen)* hacer. **2** *(as job)* dedicarse. **3** *(be sufficient for)* ser suficiente; *(be satisfactory for, acceptable to)* ir bien a. **4** *fam (cheat, swindle)* estafar, timar. LOC **how do you do?** *(greeting)* buenos días, buenas tardes; *(answer)* mucho gusto.

✎ Do es el verbo auxiliar que se emplea en inglés con la mayoría de los verbos para formar las preguntas (do you like dancing? ¿te gusta bailar?; does she live in Spain? ¿vive en España?) y formar las frases negativas (I don't want to go no quiero ir; he doesn't play tennis no juega a tenis). También sirve para sustituir al verbo principal en las respuestas (did you see the film? – no I didn't ¿viste la película – no, no la vi) y para otros usos, como en las question tags o como manera de enfatizar una afirmación.

◆ **to do away with** *vt insep* abolir, suprimir.

◆ **to do for** *vt insep (manage)* arreglárselas para conseguir.

◆ **to do in** *vt sep fam* matar, agotar.

◆ **to do up** *vt sep* **1** *fam (fasten, belt)* abrochar(se). **2** *(wrap)* envolver. **3** *(dress up)* arreglar.

◆ **to do with** *vt insep (need)* venir bien a.

◆ **to do without** *vt* arreglárselas sin.
 ① *pt* **did** [dɪd], *pp* **done** [dʌn], *ger* **doing**.

doc [dɒk] *n fam* doctor,-ra.

docile [ˈdəʊsaɪl] *adj* dócil.

dock¹ [dɒk] *n* **1** MAR *(gen)* muelle *m*; *(for cargo)* dársena. **2** JUR banquillo (de los acusados).
 ▸ *vt (ship)* atracar (at, a); *(spaceship)* acoplar.
 ▸ *n pl* **docks** puerto.

dock² [dɒk] *vt* **1** *(animal's tail)* cortar. **2** *(wages)* descontar dinero de.

docker [ˈdɒkəʳ] *n* estibador,-ra, cargador,-ra.

dockland [ˈdɒklænd] *n* zona del puerto, zona portuaria.

⊕ En Londres Docklands es la antigua zona portuaria cerca del río Támesis donde se han establecido muchas grandes empresas, sobre todo del sector financiero.

dockside ['dɒksaɪd] *n* dársena.

dockyard ['dɒkjɑːd] *n* astillero.

doctor ['dɒktə'] *n* médico,-a, doctor,-ra.
▶ *vt pej* falsificar, amañar.

doctorate ['dɒktˀrət] *n* doctorado.

doctrine ['dɒktrɪn] *n* doctrina.

document ['dɒkjəmənt] *n* documento.
▶ *vt* documentar.

documentary [dɒkjə'mentˀrɪ] *adj* documental.
▶ *n* documental *m*.
ⓘ *pl* documentaries.

documentation [dɒkjəmən'teɪ[ˀn] *n* documentación *f*.

dodder ['dɒdə'] *vi fam* andar tambaleándose.

doddery ['dɒdərɪ] *adj fam* chocho,-a.

doddle ['dɒdˀl] COMP it's a doddle *fam* es pan comido, está chupado.

dodecagon [dəʊ'dekəgɒn] *n* dodecágono.

dodecahedron [dəʊdekə'hiːdrən] *n* dodecaedro.

dodecasyllable [dəʊdekə'sɪləbˀl] *n* dodecasílabo.

dodge [dɒdʒ] *n* **1** *(quick movement)* regate *m*. **2** *fam (trick)* truco, treta, artimaña.
▶ *vt* esquivar.

dodgems ['dɒdʒəmz] *n pl* coches *mpl* de choque, autos *mpl* de choque.

dodgy ['dɒdʒɪ] *adj* **1** *fam (risky)* arriesgado,-a. **2** *fam (person)* que no es de fiar.
ⓘ *comp* dodgier, *superl* dodgiest.

doe [dəʊ] *n (of deer)* gama; *(of rabbit)* coneja.

does [dʌz] *pres* → do.

doesn't [dʌz'ˀnt] *contr (does + not)* → do.

dog [dɒg] *n* perro,-a.
▶ *vt (pursue)* perseguir.
ⓘ *pt & pp* dogged, *ger* dogging.

dogged ['dɒgɪd] *adj* terco,-a, obstinado,-a.

doggie ['dɒgɪ] *n* → doggy.

doggy ['dɒgɪ] *n* perrito,-a.
ⓘ *pl* doggies.

doghouse ['dɒghaʊs] *n* US caseta del perro.

dogma ['dɒgmə] *n* dogma *m*.

dogmatic [dɒg'mætɪk] *adj* dogmático,-a.

dogmatism ['dɒgmətɪzˀm] *n* dogmatismo.

dog-tired ['dɒgtaɪəd] *adj* rendido,-a, hecho,-a polvo.

doh [dəʊ] *n* MUS do.

do-it-yourself [duːɪtjɔː'self] *n* bricolaje *m*.

dole [dəʊl] *n* **the dole** GB *fam* el subsidio de desempleo, el paro.
◆ **to dole out** *vt sep* repartir, dar.

doll [dɒl] *n* muñeca.
◆ **to doll up** *vt sep fam* poner guapo,-a.

dollar ['dɒlə'] *n* dólar *m*.

dolly ['dɒlɪ] *n (doll)* muñeca.
ⓘ *pl* dollies.

dolmen ['dɒlmən] *n* dolmen *m*.

dolphin ['dɒlfɪn] *n* delfín *m*.

domain [də'meɪn] *n* **1** *(lands)* dominios *mpl*. **2** *(in computing)* dominio. **3** *(sphere of knowledge)* campo, esfera; *(area of activity)* ámbito.

dome [dəʊm] *n* ARCH *(roof)* cúpula; *(ceiling)* bóveda.

domestic [də'mestɪk] *adj* **1** doméstico,-a: *domestic animal* animal doméstico. **2** hogareño,-a, casero,-a. **3** *(news, flight)* nacional; *(trade, policy)* interior; *(affairs, policy, market)* interno,-a.

domesticate [də'mestɪkeɪt] *vt* domesticar.

domicile ['dɒmɪsaɪl] *n* JUR domicilio.

dominance ['dɒmɪnəns] *n* dominio.

dominant ['dɒmɪnənt] *adj* dominante.

dominate ['dɒmɪneɪt] *vt* dominar.
▶ *vi (predominate)* predominar.

domination [dɒmɪ'neɪ[ˀn] *n* dominación *f*.

domineer [dɒmɪ'nɪə'] *vi* avasallar.

domineering [dɒmɪ'nɪərɪŋ] *adj* dominante.

Dominica [dɒmɪ'niːkə] *n* Dominica.

Dominican [də'mɪnɪkən] *adj* dominicano,-a.
▶ *n* dominicano,-a. COMP **Dominican Republic** República Dominicana.

D

dominion [dəˈmɪnjən] n dominio.

domino [ˈdɒmɪnəʊ] n ficha de dominó.
▸ n pl **dominoes** (game) dominó m.
ⓘ pl **dominoes**.

donate [dəʊˈneɪt] vt donar.

donation [dəʊˈneɪʃ°n] n 1 (act) donación f. 2 (gift) donativo.

done [dʌn] pp → **do**.
▸ adj 1 (finished) terminado,-a, hecho,-a. 2 bien visto,-a.

donkey [ˈdɒŋkɪ] n burro,-a, asno.

donor [ˈdəʊnəʳ] n donante m.

don't [dəʊnt] aux (do + not) → **do**.

donut [ˈdəʊnʌt] n → **doughnut**.

doodle [ˈduːd°l] vi garabatear.
▸ n garabato.

doom [duːm] n (fate) destino; (ruin) fatalidad f; (death) muerte f.
▸ vt (destine) destinar; (condemn) condenar.

door [dɔːʳ] n 1 (gen) puerta. 2 (entrance) puerta, entrada.

doorbell [ˈdɔːbel] n timbre m.

doorknob [ˈdɔːnɒb] n pomo.

doorman [ˈdɔːmən] n portero.

doormat [ˈdɔːmæt] phr felpudo.

doorstep [ˈdɔːstep] n 1 peldaño, umbral m. 2 GB fam (thick slice of bread) rebanada gruesa de pan.

doorstop [ˈdɔːstɒp] n cuña, tope.

door-to-door [dɔːtəˈdɔː] adj de puerta en puerta, a domicilio.

doorway [ˈdɔːweɪ] n entrada, portal m.

dope [dəʊp] vt 1 fam (food, drink) adulterar con drogas, poner droga en. 2 SP (athlete, horse) dopar, drogar.

doping [ˈdəʊpɪŋ] n dopaje m, doping m.

dormant [ˈdɔːmənt] adj 1 (volcano) inactivo,-a; (animal, plant) aletargado,-a. 2 fig (idea, emotion, rivalry) latente.

dormer [ˈdɔːməʳ] [también dormer window] n buhardilla.

dormitory [ˈdɔːmɪt°rɪ] n 1 (in boarding school, hostel) dormitorio. 2 US residencia de estudiantes, colegio mayor.
ⓘ pl **dormitories**.

✖ Dormitory no significa 'dormitorio (de una casa)', que se traduce por **bedroom**.

dormouse [ˈdɔːmaʊs] n lirón m.
ⓘ pl **dormice** [ˈdɔːmaɪs].

dorsal [ˈdɔːs°l] adj dorsal.

dosage [ˈdəʊsɪdʒ] n (amount) dosis f; (on medicine bottle) posología.

dose [dəʊs] n dosis f.
▸ vt medicar.

doss [dɒs] n fam (short sleep) cabezada.
◆ **to doss down** vi GB fam echarse a dormir.

dossier [ˈdɒsɪeɪ] n expediente m, dossier m.

dot [dɒt] n (spot) punto.
▸ vt 1 (letter) poner el punto a. 2 (scatter) esparcir, salpicar.
ⓘ pt & pp **dotted**, ger **dotting**.

dote [dəʊt] vi **to dote on** adorar.

dotted [ˈdɒtɪd] adj (line) de puntos.

dotty [ˈdɒtɪ] adj GB fam chiflado,-a.
ⓘ comp **dottier**, superl **dottiest**.

double [ˈdʌb°l] adj doble. COMP **double bass** contrabajo. ❙ **double bed** cama de matrimonio. ❙ **double room** habitación doble.
▸ n doble.
▸ vt 1 (increase twofold) doblar, duplicar. 2 (fold in half) doblar por la mitad.
▸ n pl **doubles** (tennis) partido de dobles.
◆ **to double back** vi volver sobre sus pasos.
◆ **to double up** vt sep doblar.
▸ vi 1 (with pain, laughter) doblarse; (with laughter) partirse, mondarse. 2 (share) compartir la habitación.

double-click [dʌb°lˈklɪk] vi hacer doble clic.

double-cross [dʌb°lˈkrɒs] vt fam engañar, traicionar.

double-dealing [dʌb°lˈdiːlɪŋ] n doble juego.

double-decker [dʌb°lˈdekəʳ] n [también **double-decker bus**] GB autobús m de dos pisos.

🌐 Double-decker es cualquier vehículo de dos pisos. Sin embargo el **double-decker** por antonomasia es el clásico autobús londinense que se retiró del servicio en 2005.

double-edged [dʌbəl'edʒd] *adj* de doble filo.

double-park [dʌbəl'pɑːk] *vt* aparcar en doble fila.

doubt [daʊt] *n (gen)* duda; incertidumbre *f*.
► *vi* dudar.

doubtful ['daʊtfʊl] *adj* dudoso,-a, incierto,-a.

doubtless ['daʊtləs] *adv* sin duda, indudablemente.

dough [dəʊ] *n* 1 CULIN masa. 2 *sl (money)* pasta.

doughnut ['dəʊnʌt] *n* rosquilla, donut® *m*.

Douro ['dʊərəʊ] *n* el Duero.

douse [daʊs] *vt* 1 *(extinguish - light, candle)* apagar. 2 *(soak)* mojar, empapar.

dove¹ [dʌv] *n (bird)* paloma (blanca).

dove² [dəʊv] *pt* US → **dive**.

dovecote ['dʌvkəʊt] *n* palomar *m*.

dowdy ['daʊdɪ] *adj pej* sin gracia, sin estilo
ⓘ *comp* dowdier, *superl* dowdiest.

down¹ [daʊn] *prep* 1 *(to a lower level)* (hacia) abajo. 2 *(at a lower level)* abajo. 3 *(along)* por: *cut it down the middle* córtalo por la mitad.
► *adv* 1 *(to lower level)* (hacia) abajo. 2 *(on paper, in writing)*: *she wrote his phone number down* apuntó su teléfono.
► *vt* 1 *(knock over, force to ground)* derribar, tumbar. 2 *fam (drink)* beberse rápidamente: *he downed the glass in one* se bebió el vaso de un trago.

down² [daʊn] *n (on bird)* plumón *m*; *(on peach)* pelusa; *(on body)* vello.

downcast ['daʊnkɑːst] *adj* abatido,-a.

downer ['daʊnəʳ] *n* 1 *fam (drug)* calmante *m*, sedante *m*. 2 *(blow, depressing experience)* palo.

downfall ['daʊnfɔːl] *n* 1 *fig (of person)* perdición *f*, ruina. 2 *(of regime, dictator, etc)* caída.

downgrade [daʊn'greɪd] *vt* 1 *(demote)* bajar de categoría. 2 *(make seem unimportant)* restar importancia a.

downhearted [daʊn'hɑːtɪd] *adj* desanimado,-a, desmoralizado,-a.

downhill [daʊn'hɪl] *adv* cuesta abajo.
► *n (in skiing)* descenso.

download ['daʊnləʊd] *vt* bajar; *(internet)* descargar.

downpour ['daʊnpɔːʳ] *n* chaparrón *m*, aguacero.

downright ['daʊnraɪt] *adj fam* descarado,-a.
► *adv fam* muy, absolutamente.

downs [daʊnz] *n pl* GB colinas *fpl*.

Down's syndrome ['daʊnz sɪndrəʊm] *n* MED síndrome *m* de Down.

downstairs [daʊn'steəz] *adv (down the stairs)* abajo.
► *adj (room)* (del piso) de abajo.
► *n* planta baja.

downstream [daʊn'striːm] *adv* río abajo.

downtown [daʊn'taʊn] *adj* US céntrico,-a.
► *n* US centro de la ciudad.

downward ['daʊnwəd] *adj (movement)* descendente; *(direction, pressure)* hacia abajo.

downwards ['daʊnwədz] *adv* hacia abajo.

downy ['daʊnɪ] *adj* aterciopelado,-a.
ⓘ *comp* downier, *superl* downiest.

dowry ['daʊərɪ] *n* dote *f*.
ⓘ *pl* dowries.

doze [dəʊz] *n* cabezada.
► *vi* dormitar, echar una cabezada.
◆ **to doze off** *vi* quedarse dormido,-a.

dozen ['dʌzᵊn] *n* docena.

dozy ['dəʊzɪ] *adj* 1 *(sleepy)* adormilado,-a. 2 GB *fam (stupid)* tonto,-a.
ⓘ *comp* dozier, *superl* dozier.

Dr ['dɒktəʳ] *abbr* (**Doctor**) Doctor,-ra; *(abbreviation)* Dr., Dra.

drab [dræb] *adj* 1 *(colour)* apagado,-a; *(appearance)* soso,-a, sin gracia. 2 *(dreary - life)* monótono,-a, gris.

draft [drɑːft] *n* 1 *(rough copy - of letter, speech, etc)* borrador *m*; *(of plot)* esbozo; *(of plan, project)* anteproyecto. 2 FIN *(bill of exchange)* letra de cambio, giro. 3 US *(conscription)* (reclutamiento para el)

D

servicio militar obligatorio. **4** US →
draught.
▶ *adj (version, copy)* preliminar.

draftsman [ˈdrɑːftsmən] *n* US → **draughts-**
man.

drag [dræg] *n (hindrance)* estorbo (on,
para), carga (on, para).
▶ *vt (pull, cause to trail)* arrastrar, llevar a
rastras.
◆ **to drag on** *vi* alargarse, prolongarse, hacerse interminable.
◆ **to drag out** *vt sep* alargar, prolongar.
◆ **to drag up** *vt sep (revive, recall)* sacar a
relucir.
ⓘ *pt & pp* **dragged**, *ger* **dragging**.

dragon [ˈdrægən] *n* **1** *(mythology)* dragón *m*. **2** *fam (woman)* bruja.

dragonfly [ˈdrægənflaɪ] *n* libélula.
ⓘ *pl* **dragonflies**.

drain [dreɪn] *n* desagüe *m*, alcantarilla.
▶ *vt* **1** *(empty)* vaciar; *(- wound, blood)*
drenar. **2** *(rice, pasta, vegetables, etc)* escurrir.
▶ *vi* **1** *(discharge - pipes, rivers)* desaguar. **2**
(dry out) escurrir (off, -), escurrirse (off, -).
3 *fig (strength, energy, etc)* irse agotando.
▶ *n pl* **the drains** *(of town)* el alcantarillado *m sing*; *(of building)* las tuberías *fpl*
del desagüe.
◆ **to drain away** *vi (liquid - empty)* va-
ciarse.

drainage [ˈdreɪnɪdʒ] *n* **1** drenaje, desagüe *m*. **2** *(drains - of town)* alcantarillado; *(of building)* desagüe *m*. ⬚ⓒⓞⓜⓟ drain-
age basin cuenca hidrográfica.

drainpipe [ˈdreɪnpaɪp] *n (pipe)* tubo de
desagüe.

drake [dreɪk] *n* pato (macho).

drama [ˈdrɑːmə] *n* **1** THEAT *(play)* obra
de teatro; *(plays, literature)* teatro, drama *m*. **2** *(as school subject)* expresión *f*
corporal; *(at drama school)* arte *m* dramático.

dramatic [drəˈmætɪk] *adj* dramático,-a,
teatral, emocionante.

dramatist [ˈdræmətɪst] *n* dramatur-
go,-a.

drank [dræŋk] *pt* → **drink**.

drape [dreɪp] *vt* **1** *(decorate)* drapear;
(cover) cubrir (in/with, con). **2** *(part of*
body) descansar, acomodar.
▶ *n pl* **drapes** US *(curtains)* cortinas *fpl*.

drastic [ˈdræstɪk] *adj* drástico,-a.

draught [drɑːft] *n* **1** *(of cold air)* corriente *f* (de aire). **2** *(swallow of beer, etc)* trago. **3** *(medicine)* pócima. **4** *(piece in game,*
dama, pieza.
▶ *n pl* **draughts** GB damas *fpl*.

draughtboard [ˈdrɑːftbɔːd] *n* tablero
de damas.

draughtsman [ˈdrɑːftsmən] *n* **1** *(artist)*
delineante *mf*. **2** GB *(in game)* ficha de
damas.
ⓘ *pl* **draughtsmen** [ˈdrɑːftsmən].

draughtswoman [ˈdrɑːftswʊmən] *n*
ARCH delineante.
ⓘ *pl* **draughtswomen** [ˈdrɑːftswɪmɪn].

draw [drɔː] *n* **1** *(raffle, lottery)* sorteo. **2**
SP *(tie - gen)* empate *m*. **3** *(attraction,*
atracción *f*.
▶ *vt* **1** *(sketch - picture)* dibujar; *(- plans*
trazar. **2** *(move)* llevar. **3** *(pull out, tak*
out - gen) sacar, extraer; *(bow)* tensar. **4**
SP *(tie)* empatar. **5** *(attract)* atraer. **6** *(pro*
duce, elicit) provocar, obtener; *(- praise*
conseguir.
◆ **to draw back** *vi* **1** *(move away)* retirar
se, retroceder. **2** *(pull out)* echarse
atrás, volverse atrás.
◆ **to draw in** *vi* **1** *(of days)* acortarse. **2**
(train) llegar.
◆ **to draw off** *vt sep (liquid)* sacar, extraer
◆ **to draw on** *vt insep (make use of - exper*
ence, etc) recurrir a, hacer uso de; *(- mon*
ey, savings) utilizar, recurrir a.
▶ *vi (approach - winter, night, etc)* acercarse
◆ **to draw up** *vt sep (draft - contract, treaty*
etc) preparar, redactar; *(- list)* hacer; *(*
plan) esbozar.
▶ *vi (of vehicle)* detenerse, pararse.
ⓘ *pt* **drew** [druː], *pp* **drawn** [drɔːn].

drawback [ˈdrɔːbæk] *n* inconveniente
m, desventaja.

drawbridge [ˈdrɔːbrɪdʒ] *n* puente *m*
levadizo.

drawer [ˈdrɔːəʳ] *n* **1** *(in furniture)* cajón *m*
2 *(draughtsperson)* dibujante *mf*.

drawing ['drɔ:ɪŋ] *n* dibujo: *she's good at drawing* dibuja muy bien. LOC **to go back to the drawing board** volver a empezar, empezar de nuevo. COMP **drawing board** tablero de dibujo. **drawing pin** GB chincheta. **drawing room** sala de estar, salón *m*.

drawn [drɔ:n] *pp* → draw.
▶ *adj* **1** *(face - tired, haggard)* ojeroso,-a, cansado,-a; *(- worried)* preocupado,-a. **2** SP *(match, etc)* empatado,-a.

dread [dred] *n* terror *m*, pavor *m*.
▶ *vt* temer, tener terror a: *he's dreading the exam*, el examen le da terror.

dreadful ['dredful] *adj* **1** *(shocking)* terrible, espantoso,-a, atroz. **2** *fam (awful)* fatal, horrible, malísimo,-a: *how dreadful!* ¡qué horror!

dream [dri:m] *n* **1** *(while asleep)* sueño: *I had a bad dream* tuve una pesadilla; *sweet dreams!* ¡felices sueños! **2** *(daydream)* ensueño, sueño: *he lives in a dream* vive en las nubes. **3** *(hope, fantasy)* sueño (dorado), deseo, ilusión *f*: *the house of your dreams* la casa de tus sueños.
▶ *adj (imaginary)* imaginario,-a; *(ideal)* ideal, de ensueño: *your dream holiday* las vacaciones de tus sueños.
▶ *vt* **1** *(while asleep)* soñar: *I dreamt that I was flying* soñé que volaba. **2** *(imagine)* imaginarse: *I never dreamt you'd actually do it* nunca me imaginé que lo harías de verdad.
▶ *vi* **1** *(while asleep)* soñar (about/of, con); *(daydream)* soñar (despierto,-a): *I dreamt about you last night* soñé contigo anoche; *dream on* sigue soñando. **2** *(imagine)* soñar (of, con); *(contemplate)* soñar despierto: *I dream of having my own business* sueño con tener mi propia empresa.
◆ **to dream up** *vt sep fam pej (excuse)* inventarse; *(plan)* idear.
① *pt & pp* dreamed o dreamt [dremt].

dreamer ['dri:mə'] *n* soñador,-ra.

dreamt [dremt] *pt & pp* → dream.

dreary ['drɪərɪ] *adj* **1** *(gen)* triste, deprimente. **2** *fam (dull, uninteresting)* pesado,-a, aburrido,-a.
① *comp* drearier, *superl* dreariest.

dredge¹ [dredʒ] *vt & vi (river, lake, etc)* dragar, rastrear.

dredge² [dredʒ] *vt* CULIN *(with sugar)* espolvorear; *(with flour)* enharinar, rebozar.

drench [drentʃ] *vt* empapar. LOC **to be/get drenched** empaparse. **to be drenched to the skin** estar calado,-a hasta los huesos.

dress [dres] *n* **1** *(for women)* vestido. **2** *(clothing)* ropa, vestimenta.
▶ *adj (shirt, suit)* de etiqueta. COMP **dress rehearsal** THEAT ensayo general.
▶ *vt* **1** *(person)* vestir. **2** MED *(wound)* vendar. **3** CULIN *(poultry, crab)* aderezar, preparar; *(salad)* aliñar. **4** *(shop window)* arreglar, decorar; *(Christmas tree)* decorar, adornar; *(hair)* arreglar.
▶ *vi (gen)* vestirse; *(formally)* vestirse de etiqueta. LOC **to get dressed** vestirse.
◆ **to dress down** *vt sep (scold)* regañar; *(rebuke)* echar una bronca.
▶ *vi (dress informally)* vestirse informalmente.
◆ **to dress up** *vi (in fancy dress)* disfrazarse (as, de); *(dress formally)* ponerse de tiros largos.
▶ *vt sep fig (truth, facts, etc)* disfrazar.

dresser ['dresə'] *n* **1** GB *(in kitchen)* aparador *m*. **2** US *(chest of drawers)* tocador *m*.

dressing ['dresɪŋ] *n* **1** *(gen)* apósito; *(bandage)* vendaje *m*. **2** *(act of getting dressed)* el vestir(se) *m*. **3** CULIN *(for salad)* aliño. **4** US *(stuffing)* relleno. COMP **dressing gown** bata. **dressing room** THEAT camerino. **dressing table** tocador *m*.

dressmaker ['dresmeɪkə'] *n (woman)* modista *f*, modisto; *(man)* modista *m*, modisto.

dressmaking ['dresmeɪkɪŋ] *n* costura.

drew [dru:] *pt* → draw.

dribble ['drɪbəl] *n* **1** *(saliva)* saliva, baba. **2** *(of water, blood)* gotas *fpl*, hilo, chorrito. **3** SP dribling *m*.
▶ *vi* **1** *(baby)* babear. **2** *(liquid)* gotear.
▶ *vt* driblar, regatear.

dried [draɪd] *pp* → dry.
▶ *adj (fruit)* seco,-a; *(milk)* en polvo.

drier ['draɪə'] *n* → dryer.

drift [drɪft] *n* **1** *(of snow)* ventisquero; *(of sand)* montón *m*. **2** MAR *(flow of water)* deriva. **3** *(movement)* movimiento; *(tendency)* tendencia. **4** *(meaning, gist)* significado, sentido, idea: *do you get my drift?* ¿entiendes lo que quiero decir?
▶ *vi* **1** *(float on water)* ir a la deriva. **2** *(pile up - of snow, sand, leaves, etc)* amontonarse.

drill¹ [drɪl] *n* **1** *(handtool)* taladro; *(large machine)* barreno, perforadora; *(dentist's)* fresa; *(drill head, bit)* broca. **2** MIL instrucción *f*. **3** EDUC *(exercise)* ejercicio. **4** *(rehearsal, practice)* simulacro; *(procedures to be followed)* procedimiento: *fire drill* simulacro de incendio; *safety drill* instrucciones de seguridad.
▶ *vt* **1** *(wood, metal, etc)* taladrar, perforar; *(hole)* hacer, perforar. **2** MIL instruir.
▶ *vi* **1** *(for oil, coal)* perforar. **2** MIL entrenarse. LOC **to drill STH into SB** inculcarle ALGO a ALGN.

drill² [drɪl] *n* *(material)* dril *m*.

drink [drɪŋk] *n* *(gen)* bebida; *(alcoholic drink)* copa, trago; *(soft drink)* refresco: *let's go for a drink!* ¡vamos a tomar algo!, ¡vamos a tomar una copa!
▶ *vt* *(gen)* beber, tomar: *you haven't drunk your tea* no te has bebido el té; *what do you want to drink?* ¿qué quieres beber? LOC **to drink a toast to SB** brindar por ALGN. ‖ **to drink to STH/SB** brindar por ALGO/ALGN. ‖ **to have STH to drink** tomar(se) ALGO.
▶ *vi* beber: *she doesn't drink (alcohol)* no bebe (alcohol); *don't drink and drive* si bebes, no conduzcas.
◆ **to drink in** *vt sep* *(scene, sights, sounds, etc)* apreciar, empaparse de; *(success)* saborear.
ⓘ *pt* **drank** [dræŋk], *pp* **drunk** [drʌŋk].

drinkable ['drɪŋkəbəl] *adj* *(water)* potable; *(wine, beer, etc)* aceptable.

drinker ['drɪŋkəʳ] *n* bebedor,-ra.

drinking ['drɪŋkɪŋ] *n* *(alcohol)* bebida; *(action)* beber *m*. COMP **drinking fountain** fuente *f* de agua potable. ‖ **drinking water** agua potable.

drip [drɪp] *n* **1** *(drop of liquid)* goteo; *(sound)* gotear *m*. **2** MED gota a gota *m*: they put him on a drip le pusieron el gota a gota. **3** *fam* *(person)* soso,-a.
▶ *vi* *(fall in drops)* gotear, caer; *(fall heavily)* chorrear: *the tap drips* el grifo gotea.
▶ *vt* dejar caer gota a gota.
ⓘ *pt & pp* **dripped**, *ger* **dripping**.

drive [draɪv] *n* **1** *(trip)* paseo en coche; *(journey)* viaje *m*: *we went for a drive* dimos una vuelta en coche; *it's a two-hour drive* es un viaje de dos horas. **2** *(road)* calle *f*. **3** SP *(golf, tennis)* drive *m*. **4** *(campaign)* campaña: *sales drive* promoción; *membership drive* campaña para atraer socios; *a no-smoking drive* una campaña antitabaco. **5** *(energy, initiative)* energía. **6** *(propulsion system)* transmisión *f*, propulsión *f*; *(of wheeled vehicle)* tracción *f*: *front-wheel drive* tracción delantera; *four-wheel drive* tracción en las cuatro ruedas.
▶ *vt* **1** *(operate - vehicle)* conducir: *he drives a bus* es conductor de autobús. **2** *(take - person)* llevar (en coche). **3** *(cause to move - person)* llevar, obligar a; *(- animal)* arrear. **4** *(provide power for, keep going)* hacer funcionar, mover: *the river drives the waterwheel* el río mueve el molino. **5** *(force, compel to act)* forzar, obligar; *(cause to be in state)* llevar: *you're driving me crazy* me estás volviendo loco.
▶ *vi* *(vehicle)* conducir: *can you drive?* ¿sabes conducir?; *he's learning to drive* está aprendiendo a conducir; *I drove here* vine en coche.
◆ **to drive at** *vt insep* insinuar.
◆ **to drive away** *vt sep* *(fend off - attacker, animal)* ahuyentar; *(throw out)* alejar.
◆ **to drive off** *vt sep* ahuyentar.
▶ *vi* *(car, driver)* irse.
◆ **to drive out** *vt sep* expulsar.
ⓘ *pt* **drove** [drəʊv], *pp* **driven** ['drɪvˀn].

drivel ['drɪvˀl] *n* tonterías *fpl*, bobadas *fpl*, memeces *fpl*.

driven ['drɪvˀn] *pp* → **drive**.

driver ['draɪvəʳ] *n* **1** *(of bus, car)* conductor,-ra; *(of taxi)* taxista *mf*; *(of lorry)* camionero,-a; *(of racing car)* piloto *mf*; *(of train)* maquinista *mf*: *he's a very good driver* conduce muy bien. **2** SP *(golf club)* madera número 1. COMP **driver's licence** US carnet *m* de conducir, permiso de conducir.

driving ['draɪvɪŋ] n AUTO conducción f: *we shared the driving* nos turnamos para conducir.
▶ adj COMP driving licence carnet m de conducir, permiso de conducir. **I** **driving school** autoescuela. **I** **driving test** examen m de conducir.

drizzle ['drɪzəl] n llovizna.
▶ vi lloviznar.

droll [drəʊl] adj (amusing) gracioso,-a, chistoso,-a; (odd, quaint) curioso,-a.

dromedary ['drɒmədərɪ] n dromedario.
① pl dromedaries.

drone¹ [drəʊn] n (bee) zángano.

drone² [drəʊn] n **1** (noise) zumbido. **2** (monotonous talk) cantinela, sonsonete m.
▶ vi (bee, plane, engine) zumbar.

drool [druːl] n **1** (of baby) baba, babas fpl. **2** (drivel) tonterías fpl, bobadas fpl.
▶ vi (of baby, dog) babear.

droop [druːp] n (of shoulders) caída, inclinación f,.
▶ vi **1** (head) inclinarse, caerse; (shoulders) encorvarse; (eyelids) cerrar. **2** (flower) marchitarse; (branches) inclinarse.

drop [drɒp] n **1** (of liquid) gota: *she carried the cup without spilling a drop* llevó la taza sin derramar ni una gota; *we could do with a drop of rain* nos iría bien un poco de lluvia. **2** (sweet) pastilla, caramelo. **3** (descent, distance down) desnivel m, caída. **4** (fall - gen) caída; (in temperature) descenso.
▶ vt **1** (let fall - accidentally) caérsele a uno: *he dropped the glass* se le cayó el vaso; *don't drop it!* ¡que no se te caiga!. **2** (let fall - deliberately) dejar caer, tirar; (let go of) soltar; (launch - bomb, supplies) lanzar: *she dropped her handkerchief by his chair* dejó caer su pañuelo al lado de su silla; *drop it!* ¡suéltalo! **3** (lower - gen) bajar; (- speed) reducir. **4** fam (set down - passenger) dejar (off, -); (- delivery) dejar, pasar a dejar (off, -): *where shall I drop you?* ¿dónde quieres que te deje? **5** (give up, abandon) dejar, abandonar. **6** (omit, leave out - in speaking) no pronunciar, comerse; (in writing) omitir: *don't drop your "h"s* no te comas las «haches». **7** SP (player from team) echar, sacar, no seleccionar; (lose) perder. LOC to drop

dead caerse muerto,-a. **I** **to drop sb a line / drop sb a note** escribir cuatro/unas líneas a ALGN.
▶ vi **1** (fall - object) caer, caerse; (- person) dejarse caer, tirarse. **2** (prices, temperature, voice) bajar; (wind) amainar; (speed) reducirse, disminuir. **3** (lapse) dejar: *let it drop!* ¡déjalo ya!, ¡basta ya!
◆ **to drop away** vi **1** (support, interest) disminuir. **2** (ground) caer.
◆ **to drop by** vi pasar.
▶ vt insep pasar por.
◆ **to drop in** vi (visit) pasar.
◆ **to drop off** vi **1** fam (fall asleep) dormirse. **2** (sales, interest, etc) disminuir.
◆ **to drop out** vi (of school, etc) dejar los estudios; (of group) dejar el grupo; (of race, competition) abandonar; (of society) marginarse.
① pt & pp dropped, ger dropping.

droplet ['drɒplət] n gotita.

drought [draʊt] n sequía.

drove [drəʊv] pt → drive.
▶ n **1** (of cattle) manada. **2** (of people) multitud f.

drown [draʊn] vt **1** (gen) ahogar. **2** (submerge - place) inundar, anegar.
▶ vi ahogarse.

drowse [draʊz] vi dormitar.

drowsy ['draʊzɪ] adj (person, look) somnoliento,-a: *these tablets make me drowsy* estas pastillas me dan sueño. LOC to feel drowsy tener sueño.
① comp drowsier, superl drowsiest.

drug [drʌg] n **1** (medicine) medicamento. **2** (narcotic) droga: *hard/soft drugs* drogas duras/blandas. LOC to be on/do/take drugs drogarse. COMP drug addict drogadicto,-a, toxicómano,-a. **I** **drug dealer** traficante mf de drogas. **I** **drug pusher** camello mf.
▶ vt **1** (person, animal) drogar. **2** (food, drink) adulterar con drogas.
① pt & pp drugged, ger drugging.

druggist ['drʌgɪst] n US farmacéutico,-a.

drugstore ['drʌgstɔːr] n US *establecimiento donde se puede comprar medicamentos, cosméticos, periódicos y otras cosas.*

drum [drʌm] n **1** (instrument) tambor m.
2 (container) bidón m. **3** TECH tambor.
▶ vi **1** tocar el tambor.
ⓘ pt & pp **drummed**, ger **drumming**.
▶ n pl **drums** (set) batería.

drummer ['drʌmə'] n (in marching band)
tambor mf; (in pop group, jazz band) batería mf.

drumstick ['drʌmstɪk] n **1** MUS baque-
ta, palillo (de tambor). **2** CULIN muslo
(de ave).

drunk [drʌŋk] pp → **drink**.
▶ adj borracho,-a. LOC **to get drunk**
emborracharse.

drunkard ['drʌŋkəd] n borracho,-a.

drunken ['drʌŋkən] adj borracho,-a.

dry [draɪ] adj **1** seco,-a. COMP **dry dock**
dique m seco. ‖ **dry goods 1** GB comestibles mpl no perecederos. **2** US
artículos mpl de mercería. ‖ **dry land**
tierra firme.
ⓘ comp **drier**, superl **driest**.
▶ vt secar.
▶ vi secarse (off, -).
ⓘ pt & pp **dried**, ger **drying**.

dry-clean [draɪ'kliːn] vt limpiar en seco.

dry-cleaner's [draɪ'kliːnəz] n tintorería, tinte m.

dryer ['draɪə'] n (for clothes) secadora;
(for hair) secador m.

dryness ['draɪnəs] n sequedad f.

dual ['djuːəl] adj (gen) doble. COMP **dual
carriageway** GB carretera de doble
calzada.

dub¹ [dʌb] vt (soundtrack) doblar (into, a).
ⓘ pt & pp **dubbed**, ger **dubbing**.

dub² [dʌb] vt (give nickname) apodar.
ⓘ pt & pp **dubbed**, ger **dubbing**.

dub³ [dʌb] n MUS dub m.

dubbing ['dʌbɪŋ] n (of soundtrack) doblaje m.

duchess ['dʌtʃəs] n duquesa.

duck¹ [dʌk] n pato,-a.

duck² [dʌk] vi (bend down) agacharse;
(hide) esconderse: she ducked behind the
sofa se escondió detrás del sofá.

duckling ['dʌklɪŋ] n patito.

duct [dʌkt] n conducto.

ductile ['dʌktaɪl] adj dúctil.

ductility [dʌk'tɪlətɪ] n ductilidad f.

dud [dʌd] n **1** fam (object) trasto inútil,
engañifa; (person) desastre m, inútil
mf. **2** (grenade, bomb, firework, etc) granada, bomba, fuego artificial, etc. que
no estalla.
▶ adj (defective) defectuoso,-a; (worthless, useless) inútil,; (valueless - note, coin)
falso,-a; (grenade, bomb, firework) que
no estalla. COMP **dud cheque** cheque m
sin fondos.

due [djuː] adj (expected) esperado,-a:
her new book is due out in December su
nuevo libro saldrá en diciembre; the train
is due (in) at five o'clock el tren debe llegar
a las cinco. LOC **due to** debido a. COMP
due date (fecha de) vencimiento.
▶ n merecido.
▶ adv derecho hacia: due north derecho hacia el norte.
▶ n pl **dues** cuota.

duel ['djuːəl] n duelo.
▶ vi batirse en duelo (with, con).
ⓘ pt & pp **duelled** (US **dueled**), ger **duel-
ling** (US **dueling**).

duet [djuː'et] n dúo.

dug [dʌg] pt & pp → **dig**.

duke [djuːk] n duque m.

dull [dʌl] adj **1** (boring - job) monótono,-a,
pesado,-a; (- person, life, film) pesado,-a,
aburrido,-a, soso,-a; (- place, town)
aburrido,-a. **2** (not bright - colours)
apagado,-a; (weather, day) gris, triste,
feo,-a. **3** (sound, pain) sordo,-a. **4** (slow-
witted) torpe, lerdo,-a.
▶ vt (pain) aliviar, calmar; (sound)
amortiguar; (hearing) embotar.

duly ['djuːlɪ] adv **1** fml (properly) debidamente. **2** (as expected) como era de
esperar.

dumb [dʌm] adj **1** (unable to speak)
mudo,-a. **3** US fam (stupid) tonto,-a.

dummy ['dʌmɪ] n **1** (in shop window,
dressmaker's) maniquí m. **2** (fake) imitación f. **3** GB (for baby) chupete m. **4** fam
imbécil mf.
ⓘ pl **dummies**.

dump [dʌmp] n vertedero, basurero.
▶ vt (drop, unload - rubbish) verter, descargar; (leave) dejar, poner: he dumped

his dirty washing on the floor dejó su ropa sucia en el suelo.

dumping ['dʌmpɪŋ] *n* vertido. LOC «No dumping» «Prohibido arrojar basuras».

dune [djuːn] [también **sand dune**] *n* duna.

dung [dʌŋ] *n* estiércol *m*.

dungarees [dʌŋɡəˈriːz] *n (garment)* peto; *(overalls)* mono.

dungeon ['dʌndʒən] *n* mazmorra.

duo ['djuːəʊ] *n* dúo.
ⓘ *pl* duos.

duodena [djuːəˈdiːnə] *n pl* → **duodenum**.

duodenum [djuːəˈdiːnəm] *n* duodeno.
ⓘ *pl* duodenums o duodena [djuːəˈdiːnə].

dupe [djuːp] *n* ingenuo,-a.
▶ *vt* engañar, embaucar.

duplex ['djuːpleks] *n* US *(house)* casa adosada; *(flat, apartment)* dúplex *m*.

duplicate [*(adj)*'djuːplɪkət; *(n)*'djuːplɪkeɪt] *adj* duplicado,-a.
▶ *n* copia, duplicado. LOC **in duplicate** por duplicado.
▶ *vt* duplicar, hacer copias de.

durable ['djʊərəbˀl] *adj* duradero,-a.

duration [djʊəˈreɪʃˀn] *n* duración *f*.

during ['djʊərɪŋ] *prep* durante: *I lived in France during the war* viví en Francia durante la guerra; *she's out at work during the day* trabaja fuera de casa durante el día.

dusk [dʌsk] *n* anochecer *m*. LOC **at dusk** al anochecer.

dust [dʌst] *n* polvo.
▶ *vt* quitar el polvo a.

dustbin ['dʌstbɪn] *n* GB cubo de la basura. COMP **dustbin man** basurero.

dustcart ['dʌstkɑːt] *n* camión *m* de la basura.

duster ['dʌstəʳ] *n (for dusting)* paño, trapo (del polvo); *(for blackboard)* borrador *m*.

dustman ['dʌstmən] *n* GB basurero.

dustpan ['dʌstpæn] *n* recogedor *m*.

Dutch [dʌtʃ] *adj* holandés,-esa, neerlandés,-esa. LOC **to go Dutch (with sb)** pagar a escote.
▶ *n (language)* holandés *m*.

Dutchman ['dʌtʃmən] *n* holandés *m*, neerlandés *m*.
ⓘ *pl* Dutchmen ['dʌtʃmən].

Dutchwoman ['dʌtʃwʊmən] *n* holandesa.
ⓘ *pl* Dutchwomen ['dʌtʃwɪmɪn].

duty ['djuːtɪ] *n* 1 *(obligation)* deber *m*, obligación *f*: *I feel it's my duty to go* creo que es mi obligación ir. 2 *(task)* función *f*, cometido: *her duties include dealing with the public* sus funciones incluyen atender al público. 3 *(service)* guardia, servicio. 4 *(tax)* impuesto. LOC **to be off duty 1** *(doctor, nurse, etc)* no estar de guardia. 2 *(police, firefighter, etc)* no estar de servicio. ▌**to be on duty 1** *(doctor, nurse, etc)* estar de guardia. 2 *(police, firefighter)* estar de servicio. COMP **customs duties** derechos *mpl* de aduana, aranceles *mpl*.
ⓘ *pl* duties.

duty-free ['djuːtɪfriː] *adj & adv* libre de impuestos. COMP **duty-free shop** duty-free *m*, tienda libre de impuestos.

duvet ['duːveɪ] *n* GB edredón *m*. COMP **duvet cover** funda de edredón.

DVD ['diːviːˈdiː] *n* (Digital Video Disc) DVD *m*. COMP **DVD player** lector *m* de DVD.

dwarf [dwɔːf] *n* enano,-a.
ⓘ *pl* dwarfs o dwarves [dwɔːz].
▶ *adj* enano,-a.

dwell [dwel] *vi fml* habitar, vivir.
ⓘ *pt & pp* dwelt [dwelt].

dweller ['dweləʳ] *n* habitante *mf*.

dwelling ['dwelɪŋ] *n fml* morada.

dwelt [dwelt] *pt & pp* → **dwell**.

dye [daɪ] *n* tinte *m*, tintura, colorante *m*.
▶ *vt* teñir.

dying ['daɪɪŋ] *adj* moribundo,-a.

dyke [daɪk] *n (bank)* dique *m*, barrera; *(causeway)* terraplén *m*.

dynamic [daɪˈnæmɪk] *adj* dinámico,-a.

dynamics [daɪˈnæmɪks] *n* dinámica.

dynamite ['daɪnəmaɪt] *n* dinamita.

dynamo ['daɪnəməʊ] *n* dinamo *f*.
ⓘ *pl* dynamos.

dynasty ['dɪnəstɪ] *n* dinastía.
ⓘ *pl* dynasties.

dyne [daɪn] *n* dina.

dysentery ['dɪsˀntrɪ] *n* disentería.

dyslexia [dɪsˈleksɪə] *n* dislexia.

dyslexic [dɪsˈleksɪk] *adj* disléxico,-a.

dystrophy ['dɪstrəfɪ] *n* distrofia.

E

E, e [iː] *n* **1** *(the letter)* E, e *f.* **2** MUS mi *m.*

each [iːtʃ] *adj* cada: *each day* cada día, todos los días.

▶ *pron* cada uno,-a: *they each have their own car* cada uno tiene su coche.

▶ *adv* cada uno,-a: *apples cost 15p each* las manzanas cuestan 15 peniques la pieza.

✎ Each y every tienen significados muy similares. Each se emplea cuando se considera cada cosa por separado. Every, cuando se considera cada cosa en función del todo del que forma parte.

eager [ˈiːgəʳ] *adj (anxious)* ávido,-a (to, de), ansioso,-a (to, de); *(desirous)* deseoso,-a (to, de).

eagle [ˈiːgəl] *n* **1** *(bird)* águila. **2** *(in golf)* eagle *m.*

eaglet [ˈiːglət] *n* aguilucho.

ear¹ [ɪəʳ] *n* **1** ANAT oreja. **2** *(sense)* oído. ∎ ear canal conducto auditivo. ∎ **ear flap** orejera. ∎ **ear lobe** lóbulo. ∎ **ear, nose and throat specialist** otorrinolaringólogo,-a.

ear² [ɪəʳ] *n (of cereal)* espiga.

earache [ˈɪəreɪk] *n* dolor *m* de oídos.

eardrum [ˈɪədrʌm] *n* tímpano.

earflap [ˈɪəflæp] *n* orejera.

earl [ɜːl] *n* conde *m.*

early [ˈɜːlɪ] *adj* **1** *(before expected)* temprano,-a, pronto,-a: *we were early* llegamos temprano. **2** *(initial)* primero,-a: *take the early train* coge el primer tren de la mañana. **3** *(near beginning)*: *in the early 1960's* a principios de los sesenta.

① *comp* **earlier**, *superl* **earliest**.

▶ *adv* **1** *(before expected)* temprano, pronto; *(soon)* pronto: *she got up early* se levantó temprano. **2** *(in good time)* con tiempo, con anticipación: *we got there early to get a good seat* llegamos con tiempo para coger buen sitio.

earn [ɜːn] *vt* ganar, ganarse: *how much do you earn a month?* ¿cuánto ganas al mes?

✎ Cuando se habla de dinero, la diferencia entre earn y win (ambos, 'ganar') es que earn se refiere al dinero que se gana trabajando y win al que se obtiene por azar, como en la lotería.

earner [ˈɜːnəʳ] *n* **1** *(person)* persona que gana dinero: *I'm the only earner in the family* soy el único de la familia que gana un sueldo. **2** *(thing)* cosa rentable.

earnest [ˈɜːnɪst] *adj* serio,-a, formal.

earnings [ˈɜːnɪŋz] *n pl* **1** *(personal)* ingresos *mpl.* **2** *(of company)* ganancias *fpl.*

earphones [ˈɪəfəʊnz] *n pl* auriculares *mpl.*

earplug [ˈɪəplʌg] *n* tapón *m* para los oídos.

earring [ˈɪərɪŋ] *n* pendiente *m.*

earth [ɜːθ] *n* **1** *(gen)* tierra. **2** GB toma de tierra, tierra. **3** GB *(of fox, badger)* madriguera.

✎ Cuando se refiere al planeta Tierra se suele escribir con mayúscula: Earth.

earthen [ˈɜːðən] *adj* **1** *(of earth)* de tierra. **2** *(of baked clay)* de barro, de arcilla.

earthquake [ˈɜːθkweɪk] *n* terremoto.

earthworm [ˈɜːθwɜːm] *n* lombriz *f.*

earwax [ˈɪəwæks] *n* cerumen *m*, cera.

earwig [ˈɪəwɪg] *n* tijereta.

ease [iːz] *n* **1** *(lack of difficulty)* facilidad *f.* **2** *(natural manner)* soltura, naturalidad *f.* **3** *(freedom from pain)* alivio. **4** *(leisure, affluence)* comodidad *f*, desahogo.

▸ *vt* **1** *(relieve, alleviate)* aliviar (of, de), calmar. **2** *(improve)* mejorar, facilitar; *(make easier)* facilitar.

▸ *vi* **1** *(pain)* aliviarse, calmarse; *(tension, etc)* disminuir. **2** *(become easier)* mejorar.

◆ **to ease off / ease up** *vi* **1** *(pain)* aliviarse, calmarse; *(tension, etc)* disminuir; *(rain)* amainar. **2** *(slow down)* ir más despacio.

◆ **to ease up on** *vt insep fam (go easy, be more moderate)* aflojar, no pasarse con.

easel [ˈiːzəl] *n* caballete *m*.

easily [ˈiːzɪlɪ] *adv* **1** *(without difficulty)* fácilmente, con facilidad. **2** *(by far)* con mucho; *(without doubt)* sin duda.

east [iːst] *adj (gen)* este, oriental; *(wind)* del este.

▸ *adv* hacia el este.

▸ *n* este *m*.

▸ *n* **the East** *(Asia)* Oriente *m*; *(Eastern Europe)* el Este *m*.

Easter [ˈiːstəʳ] *n* **1** REL Pascua (de Resurrección). **2** *(holiday)* Semana Santa.

easterly [ˈiːstəlɪ] *adj* **1** *(to the east)* al este, hacia el este. **2** *(from the east)* del este.

▸ *n* viento del este.

ⓘ *pl* easterlies.

eastern [ˈiːstən] *adj* oriental, del este.

eastward [ˈiːstwəd] *adj* hacia el este.

eastwards [ˈiːstwədz] *adv* hacia el este.

easy [ˈiːzɪ] *adj* **1** *(not difficult)* fácil, sencillo. **2** *(comfortable)* cómodo,-a, holgado,-a. **3** *(unworried, relaxed)* tranquilo,-a.

ⓘ *comp* easier, *superl* easiest.

▸ *adv* con cuidado, con calma.

easy-going [iːzɪˈgəʊɪŋ] *adj (relaxed)* tranquilo,-a; *(easy to please)* fácil de complacer, poco exigente.

eat [iːt] *vt* comer.

▸ *vi* comer.

◆ **to eat away** *vt sep (mice)* roer; *(termites)* carcomer; *(acid)* corroer.

◆ **to eat out** *vi (lunch)* comer fuera; *(dinner)* cenar fuera.

◆ **to eat up** *vt sep* **1** *(finish food)* comerse: *eat it all up!* ¡cómetelo todo!. **2** *(consume)* consumir, tragar, devorar.

ⓘ *pt* ate [et, eɪt], *pp* eaten [ˈiːtən].

eaten [ˈiːtən] *pp* → eat.

eavesdrop [ˈiːvzdrɒp] *vi* escuchar a escondidas (on, -).

ⓘ *pt & pp* eavesdropped, *ger* eavesdropping.

ebb [eb] *n* reflujo.

▸ *vi* **1** *(water)* bajar. **2** *fig* disminuir.

ebonite [ˈebənaɪt] *n* ebonita.

ebony [ˈebənɪ] *n* ébano.

eccentric [ɪkˈsentrɪk] *adj* excéntrico,-a.

▸ *n (person)* excéntrico,-a.

echinoderm [ɪˈkaɪnəʊdɜːm] *n* equinodermo.

echo [ˈekəʊ] *n* eco.

ⓘ *pl* echoes.

▸ *vt* **1** repetir (back, -). **2** *fig (words)* repetir, imitar; *(opinions)* hacerse eco de.

eclectic [ɪˈklektɪk] *adj fml* ecléctico,-a.

▸ *n* ecléctico,-a.

eclipse [ɪˈklɪps] *n* eclipse *m*.

▸ *vt* eclipsar.

ecofriendly [ekəʊˈfrendlɪ] *adj* que no perjudica el medio ambiente.

ecological [iːkəˈlɒdʒɪkəl] *adj* ecológico,-a. COMP **ecological footprint** huella ecológica.

ecologist [ɪˈkɒlədʒɪst] *n* ecologista *mf*.

ecology [ɪˈkɒlədʒɪ] *n* ecología.

economic [ekəˈnɒmɪk, iːkəˈnɒmɪk] *adj* **1** *(gen)* económico,-a. **2** *(profitable)* rentable.

economically [ekəˈnɒmɪklɪ, iːkəˈnɒmɪklɪ] *adv* económicamente: *economically speaking* en términos económicos.

economics [ekəˈnɒmɪks, iːkəˈnɒmɪks] *n* **1** *(science)* economía. **2** EDUC económicas *fpl*, ciencias *fpl* económicas.

economist [ɪˈkɒnəmɪst] *n* economista *mf*.

economize [ɪˈkɒnəmaɪz] *vi* economizar (on, en), ahorrar (on, en).

economy [ɪˈkɒnəmɪ] *n* **1** *(saving)* economía, ahorro. **2** *(science)* economía.

ⓘ *pl* economies.

ecosystem [ˈiːkəʊsɪstəm] *n* ecosistema *m*.

Ecuador [ˈekwədɔːʳ] *n* Ecuador *m*.

Ecuadorian [ekwəˈdɔːrɪən] *adj* ecuatoriano,-a.

▸ *n* ecuatoriano,-a.

eczema [ˈeksɪmə] *n* eccema *m*.

edema [ɪˈdiːmə] *n* US → oedema.

Eden [ˈiːdən] *n* el Edén *m*.

edge [edʒ] *n* **1** *(of cliff, wood, etc)* borde *m*. **2** *(of coin, step, etc)* canto. **3** *(of knife)* filo. **4** *(of water)* orilla. **5** *(of town)* afueras *fpl*. **6** *(of paper)* margen *m*.
▸ *vt* **1** *(supply with border)* bordear. **2** SEW ribetear.
◆ **to edge away** *vi* alejarse poco a poco.
◆ **to edge forward** *vi* avanzar lentamente, avanzar poco a poco.

edible [ˈedɪbəl] *adj* comestible.

edict [ˈiːdɪkt] *n* **1** edicto. **2** JUR decreto.

edit [ˈedɪt] *vt* **1** *(prepare for printing)* preparar para la imprenta. **2** *(correct)* corregir; *(put together)* editar. **3** *(run newspaper, etc)* dirigir. **4** *(film, programme)* montar, editar.
◆ **to edit out** *vt sep* cortar.

edition [ɪˈdɪʃən] *n* edición *f*.

editor [ˈedɪtəʳ] *n* **1** *(of book)* editor,-ra; *(writer)* redactor,-ra; *(proofreader)* corrector,-ra. **2** *(of newspaper, etc)* director,-ra. **3** *(of film, programme)* montador,-ra.

editorial [edɪˈtɔːrɪəl] *adj* editorial.
▸ *n* editorial *m*. COMP **editorial staff** redacción *f*.

educate [ˈedjʊkeɪt] *vt* educar.

educated [ˈedjʊkeɪtɪd] *adj* culto,-a, cultivado,-a.

ⓧ Educated no significa 'educado (de buenos modales)', que se traduce por polite.

education [edjʊˈkeɪʃən] *n* **1** *(system of teaching)* educación *f*, enseñanza. **2** *(training)* formación *f*, preparación *f*. **3** *(acquisition of knowledge)* estudios *mpl*, formación *f* académica. **4** *(theory of teaching)* pedagogía. **5** *(knowledge, culture)* cultura.

ⓧ Education no significa 'educación (buenos modales)', que se traduce por manners.

educational [edjʊˈkeɪʃənəl] *adj* educativo,-a.

eel [iːl] *n* anguila.

eerie [ˈɪərɪ] *adj* misterioso,-a.

effect [ɪˈfekt] *n* efecto.
▸ *vt fml* efectuar, provocar.
▸ *n pl* **effects** *(property)* efectos *mpl*.

effective [ɪˈfektɪv] *adj* **1** *(successful)* eficaz. **2** *(real, actual)* efectivo,-a. **3** *(operative)* vigente. **4** *(impressive)* impresionante; *(striking)* llamativo,-a.

effervescent [efəˈvesənt] *adj* efervescente.

efficiency [ɪˈfɪʃənsɪ] *n* **1** *(of person)* eficiencia, competencia. **2** *(of system, product)* eficacia. **3** *(of machine)* rendimiento.

efficient [ɪˈfɪʃənt] *adj* **1** *(person)* eficiente, competente. **2** *(system, product)* eficaz. **3** *(machine)* de buen rendimiento.

effigy [ˈefɪdʒɪ] *n* efigie *f*.
ⓘ *pl* effigies.

effort [ˈefət] *n* **1** *(exertion)* esfuerzo. **2** *(attempt, struggle)* intento, tentativa. **3** *(achievement)* obra.

egg¹ [eg] *n* **1** *(laid by birds, etc)* huevo. **2** BIOL *(ovum)* óvulo. COMP **boiled egg** huevo pasado por agua.

egg² [eg] *vt* **to egg on** animar, incitar.

eggplant [ˈegplɑːnt] *n* US berenjena.

eggshell [ˈegʃel] *n* cáscara de huevo.

ego [ˈiːgəʊ] *n* ego.
ⓘ *pl* egos.

egocentric [iːgəʊˈsentrɪk] *adj* egocéntrico,-a.

egoism [ˈiːgəʊɪzəm] *n* egoísmo.

egoist [ˈiːgəʊɪst] *n* egoísta *mf*.

Egypt [ˈiːdʒɪpt] *n* Egipto.

Egyptian [ɪˈdʒɪpʃən] *adj* egipcio,-a.
▸ *n* **1** *(person)* egipcio,-a. **2** *(language)* egipcio.

eider [ˈaɪdəʳ] *n* [also eider duck] *n* eider *m*.

eiderdown [ˈaɪdədaʊn] *n* edredón *m*.

eight [eɪt] *adj* ocho.
▸ *n* ocho.
✎ Consulta también six.

eighteen [eɪˈtiːn] *adj* dieciocho.
▸ *n* dieciocho.
✎ Consulta también six.

eighteenth [eɪˈtiːnθ] *adj* decimoctavo,-a.
▸ *adv* en decimoctavo lugar.

▶ *n* **1** *(in series)* decimoctavo,-a. **2** *(fraction)* decimoctavo; *(one part)* decimoctava parte *f*.

✎ Consulta también sixth.

eighth [eɪtθ] *adj* octavo,-a.
▶ *adv* en octavo lugar.
▶ *n* **1** *(in series)* octavo,-a. **2** *(fraction)* octavo; *(one part)* octava parte *f*.

✎ Consulta también sixth.

eightieth ['eɪtɪɪθ] *adj* octogésimo,-a.
▶ *adv* en octogésimo lugar.
▶ *n* **1** *(in series)* octogésimo,-a. **2** *(fraction)* octogésimo; *(one part)* octogésima parte *f*.

✎ Consulta también sixtieth.

eighty ['eɪtɪ] *adj* ochenta.
▶ *n* ochenta.

✎ Consulta también sixty.

either ['aɪðər, 'iːðər] *pron* **1** *(affirmative)* cualquiera: *either of them* cualquiera de los dos. **2** *(negative)* ni el uno ni el otro, ni la una ni la otra, ninguno de los dos, ninguna de las dos: *I can't stand either* no aguanto ni el uno ni el otro.
▶ *adj* **1** cualquier. **2** *(both)* cada, los dos, las dos, ambos,-as. **3** *(neither)* ninguno de los dos, ninguna de las dos.
▶ *conj* **1** *(affirmative)* o: *he'll arrive either today or tomorrow* llegará u hoy o mañana. **2** *(negative)* ni: *I didn't go to either the wedding or the party* no fui ni a la boda ni a la fiesta.
▶ *adv* *(after negative)* tampoco: *Ann didn't come either* tampoco vino Ann.

ejaculation [ɪdʒækuˈleɪʃən] *n* **1** *(ejection)* eyaculación *f*. **2** *(exclamation)* exclamación *f*.

eject [ɪˈdʒekt] *vt* expulsar, echar.
▶ *vi* AV eyectar(se).

ejection [ɪˈdʒekʃən] *n* **1** *(gen)* expulsión *f*. **2** *(from plane)* eyección *f*.

elaborate [*(adj)* ɪˈlæbərət; *(vb)* ɪˈlæbəreɪt] *adj* **1** *(detailed, extensive)* detallado,-a. **2** *(ornate, intricate)* muy trabajado,-a, esmerado,-a. **3** *(complex, intricate)* complicado,-a.
▶ *vt* *(work out in detail, refine)* elaborar.

▶ *vi* *(discuss in detail)* explicar detalladamente; *(expand)* ampliar, dar más detalles.

elaboration [ɪlæbəˈreɪʃən] *n* **1** *(working out in detail)* elaboración *f*. **2** *(additional detail)* complicación *f*, detalle *m*.

elastic [ɪˈlæstɪk] *adj* elástico,-a. COMP **elastic band** goma elástica.

elasticity [ɪlæˈstɪsətɪ] *n* elasticidad *f*.

Elastoplast® [ɪˈlæstəplɑːst] *n* tirita®.

elbow ['elbəʊ] *n* **1** ANAT codo. **2** *(bend)* recodo.

elder ['eldər] *adj* mayor.
▶ *n* **1** mayor *m*. **2** REL anciano,-a.

elderly ['eldəlɪ] *adj* mayor, anciano,-a.
▶ *n* **the elderly** los ancianos *mpl*.

eldest ['eldɪst] *adj* mayor.
▶ *n* el mayor, la mayor.

elect [ɪˈlekt] *adj* electo,-a.
▶ *vt* **1** *(vote for)* elegir. **2** *(choose, decide)* decidir.

election [ɪˈlekʃən] *n* elección *f*.
▶ *adj* electoral.

elector [ɪˈlektər] *n* elector,-ra.

electoral [ɪˈlektərəl] *adj* electoral. COMP **electoral college** colegio electoral. **electoral roll** / **electoral register** censo electoral.

electorate [ɪˈlektərət] *n* electorado.

electric [ɪˈlektrɪk] *adj* eléctrico,-a.

electrical [ɪˈlektrɪkəl] *adj* eléctrico,-a.

electrician [ɪlekˈtrɪʃən] *n* electricista *mf*.

electricity [ɪlekˈtrɪsɪtɪ] *n* electricidad *f*.

electrocute [ɪˈlektrəkjuːt] *vt* electrocutar.

electrode [ɪˈlektrəʊd] *n* electrodo.

electrolysis [ɪlekˈtrɒləsɪs] *n* electrólisis *f*.

electrolyte [ɪˈlektrəlaɪt] *n* electrolito, electrólito.

electromagnet [ɪlektrəʊˈmægnɪt] *n* electroimán *m*.

electromagnetism [ɪlektrəʊˈmægnɪtɪzəm] *n* electromagnetismo.

electromagnetic [ɪlektrəʊmægˈnetɪk] *adj* electromagnético,-a.

electron [ɪˈlektrɒn] *n* electrón *m*. COMP **electron microscope** microscopio electrónico.

electronic [ɪlek'trɒnɪk] *adj* electrónico,-a.

electronics [ɪlek'trɒnɪks] *n (science, technology)* electrónica.
▸ *n pl (circuits and devices)* componentes *mpl* electrónicos.

elegance ['elɪgəns] *n* elegancia.

elegant ['elɪgənt] *adj* elegante.

element ['elɪmənt] *n* **1** CHEM elemento. **2** *(necessary part of a whole)* parte *f*, componente *m*. **5** ELEC resistencia. **4** *(group, section)* fracción *f*.
▸ *n pl* **elements 1***(weather)* los elementos *mpl*. **2***(basics)* rudimentos *mpl*.

elementary [elɪ'mentərɪ] *adj* **1** *(basic)* elemental, básico,-a. **2** *(easy)* fácil, sencillo,-a. COMP **elementary education** enseñanza primaria.

elephant ['elɪfənt] *n* elefante *m*. COMP **elephant seal** elefante *m* marino.

elevate ['elɪveɪt] *vt fml (raise)* elevar; *(promote)* ascender, promover.

elevated ['elɪveɪtɪd] *adj fml (fine, noble)* elevado,-a, noble.

elevation [elɪ'veɪʃən] *n* **1** *fml (gen)* elevación *f*. **2** *fml (in rank)* ascenso. **3** *(height)* altitud *f*, altura. **4** ARCH alzado.

elevator ['elɪveɪtər] *n* **1** US ascensor *m*. **2** *(machine)* montacargas *m*.

eleven [ɪ'levən] *adj* once.
▸ *n* once *m*.

✎ Consulta también six.

eleventh [ɪ'levənθ] *adj* undécimo,-a.
▸ *adv* en undécimo lugar.
▸ *n* **1** *(in series)* undécimo,-a, onceno,-a. **2** *(fraction)* onceavo, undécimo; *(one part)* onceava parte *f*, undécima parte *f*.

✎ Consulta también sixth.

elicit [ɪ'lɪsɪt] *vt* **1** *fml (facts, information)* sonsacar, obtener. **2** *(reaction, response)* provocar.

elide [ɪ'laɪd] *vt* elidir.
▸ *vi* elidirse.

eligible ['elɪdʒəbəl] *adj* **1** *(qualified, suitable)* idóneo,-a, apto,-a. **2** *(desirable)* deseable.

eliminate [ɪ'lɪmɪneɪt] *vt* eliminar.

elision [ɪ'lɪʒən] *n* elisión *f*.

elite [eɪ'liːt] *n* elite *f*.
▸ *adj* exclusivo,-a, selecto,-a.

elk [elk] *n* alce *m*.

ellipse [ɪ'lɪps] *n* elipse *f*.

ellipsis [ɪ'lɪpsɪs] *n* elipsis *f*.
① *pl* **ellipses** [ɪ'lɪpsiːz].

elliptic [ɪ'lɪptɪk] *adj* elíptico,-a.

elm [elm] *n* olmo.

elongated ['iːlɒŋgeɪtɪd] *adj* alargado,-a.

eloquence ['eləkwəns] *n* elocuencia.

eloquent ['eləkwənt] *adj* elocuente.

else [els] *adv* más, otro,-a: *anything else?* ¿algo más?; *where else have you been?* ¿en qué otro(s) sitio(s) has estado?

elsewhere [els'weər] *adv* en otro sitio, en otra parte.

elude [ɪ'luːd] *vt* **1** *(escape from)* escaparse de. **2** *(avoid)* eludir. **3** *(not remember)* no recordar, no acordarse; *(not understand)* no entenderse.

elusive [ɪ'luːsɪv] *adj* **1** *(difficult to capture)* huidizo,-a, esquivo,-a. **2** *(difficult to remember)* difícil de recordar; *(difficult to understand)* difícil de entender.

e-mail ['iːmeɪl] *n* correo electrónico.

emancipate [ɪ'mænsɪpeɪt] *vt* emancipar.

emancipation [ɪmænsɪ'peɪʃən] *n* emancipación *f*.

embankment [ɪm'bæŋkmənt] *n* **1** *(wall, earth, etc)* terraplén *m*. **2** *(river bank)* dique *m*.

embargo [em'baːgəʊ] *n* embargo.
① *pl* **embargoes**.
▸ *vt* **1** *(prohibit)* prohibir. **2** *(seize)* embargar.
① *pt & pp* **embargoed**, *ger* **embargoing**.

embark [ɪm'baːk] *vt* embarcar.
◆ **to embark on** *vt insep* emprender.

embarrass [ɪm'bærəs] *vt (make ashamed)* avergonzar, hacer pasar vergüenza a; *(make awkward)* desconcertar.

embarrassed [ɪm'bærəst] *adj (behaviour, action)* embarazoso,-a; *(person)* avergonzado,-a, molesto,-a.

⊠ Embarrassed no significa 'embarazada', que se traduce por **pregnant**.

embarrassing [ɪmˈbærəsɪŋ] *adj* embarazoso,-a, violento,-a, desconcertante.

embarrassment [ɪmˈbærəsmənt] *n* **1** *(state)* vergüenza, desconcierto. **2** *(person, object)* vergüenza, estorbo. **3** *(event, situation)* disgusto, vergüenza.

embassy [ˈembəsɪ] *n* embajada.
ⓘ *pl* embassies.

embed [ɪmˈbed] *vt* *(jewels, stones)* incrustar; *(weapon, nails)* clavar (in, en).
ⓘ *pt & pp* embedded, *ger* embedding.

embellish [ɪmˈbelɪʃ] *vt* adornar, embellecer.

ember [ˈembər] *n* brasa, ascua.

emblem [ˈembləm] *n* emblema *m*.

emblematic [embləˈmætɪk] *adj* emblemático,-a.

emboss [ɪmˈbɒs] *vt* *(leather, metal)* repujar; *(initials)* grabar en relieve.

embrace [ɪmˈbreɪs] *n* abrazo.
▶ *vt* **1** *(hug)* abrazar, dar un abrazo a. **2** *(include)* abarcar, incluir. **3** *fml (accept - opportunity, etc)* aprovechar; *(- offer)* aceptar. **4** *fml (adopt - religion, etc)* convertirse a; *(- new idea)* abrazar.

embroidery [ɪmˈbrɔɪdəɪ] *n* SEW bordado.

embryo [ˈembrɪəʊ] *n* embrión *m*.
ⓘ *pl* embryos.
▶ *adj* embrionario,-a.

emerald [ˈemərəld] *n* esmeralda *f*.
▶ *adj* (de color) esmeralda.

emerge [ɪˈmɜːdʒ] *vi* **1** *(come out)* emerger, aparecer, salir. **2** *(become known)* resultar.

emergence [ɪˈmɜːdʒəns] *n* aparición *f*.

emergency [ɪˈmɜːdʒənsɪ] *n* **1** emergencia. **2** MED urgencia.
ⓘ *pl* emergencies.
▶ *adj* de emergencia, de urgencia.

emergent [ɪˈmɜːdʒənt] *adj* **1** *(emerging)* emergente. **2** *(of countries, nations)* en vías de desarrollo.

emery [ˈeməɪ] *n* esmeril *m*.

emigrant [ˈemɪɡrənt] *n* emigrante *mf*.

emigrate [ˈemɪɡreɪt] *vi* emigrar.

emigration [emɪˈɡreɪʃən] *n* emigración *f*.

eminence [ˈemɪnəns] *n* eminencia.

eminent [ˈemɪnənt] *adj* **1** *(of person)* eminente. **2** *(of qualities)* destacado,-a.

emir [eˈmɪər] *n* emir *m*.

emirate [ˈemɪrət] *n* emirato. COMP **United Arab Emirates** Emiratos *mpl* Árabes Unidos.

emissary [ˈemɪsərɪ] *n* emisario,-a.
ⓘ *pl* emissaries.

emission [ɪˈmɪʃən] *n* emisión *f*.

❌ Emission no significa 'emisión (de televisión)', que se traduce por programme.

emit [ɪˈmɪt] *vt* *(signal, heat, light, smoke)* emitir, producir; *(sound, noise)* producir; *(smell)* despedir; *(cry)* dar.
ⓘ *pt & pp* emitted, *ger* emitting.

emoticon [ɪˈmɒtɪkɒn] *n* COMPUT emoticón *m*, emoticono.

emotion [ɪˈməʊʃən] *n* **1** *(feeling)* sentimiento. **2** *(strong feeling)* emoción *f*.

emotional [ɪˈməʊʃənəl] *adj* **1** *(connected with feelings)* emocional, afectivo,-a. **2** *(moving)* conmovedor,-ra, emotivo,-a. **3** *(sensitive)* emotivo,-a, sentimental.

emotive [ɪˈməʊtɪv] *adj* emotivo,-a.

emperor [ˈempərər] *n* emperador *m*.

emphasis [ˈemfəsɪs] *n* énfasis *m*.
ⓘ *pl* emphases [ˈemfəsiːs].

emphasize [ˈemfəsaɪz] *vt* enfatizar.

emphatic [emˈfætɪk] *adj* **1** *(forceful - tone, gesture)* enfático,-a, enérgico,-a. **2** *(insistent - refusal, rejection, assertion)* categórico,-a, rotundo,-a.

empire [ˈempaɪər] *n* imperio: *the British Empire* el Imperio Británico.

empirical [emˈpɪrɪkəl] *adj* empírico,-a.

employ [ɪmˈplɔɪ] *n fml* empleo.
▶ *vt* **1** *(give work to)* emplear; *(appoint)* contratar. **2** *fml (make use of, use)* emplear, usar. **3** *(occupy)* ocupar.

employed [emˈplɔɪd] *adj* **1** *(in work)* empleado,-a. **2** *(busy)* ocupado,-a.

employee [emˈplɔɪiː, emplɔɪˈiː] *n* empleado,-a.

employer [emˈplɔɪər] *n* **1** *(manager, boss)* empresario,-a; *(of domestic worker)* patrón,-ona. **2** *(company, organization)* empresa, organismo.

employment [em'plɔɪmənt] *n* **1** *(work)* trabajo; *(availability of work)* empleo. **2** *(use)* empleo, uso.

empress ['emprəs] *n* emperatriz *f*.

empty ['emptɪ] *adj* **1** *(gen)* vacío,-a; *(place)* desierto,-a; *(house)* desocupado,-a, deshabitado,-a; *(seat, table, place)* libre. **2** *fam (hungry)* hambriento,-a.
ⓘ *comp* emptier, *superl* emptiest.
▶ *vt* vaciar.
▶ *n pl* empties envases *mpl*, cascos *mpl*.

emulsifier [ɪ'mʌlsɪfaɪəʳ] *n* emulsionante *m*.

emulsify [ɪ'mʌlsɪfaɪ] *vt* emulsionar.
ⓘ *pt & pp* emulsified, *ger* emulsifying.

emulsion [ɪ'mʌlʃən] *n* emulsión *f*.

enable [ɪ'neɪbəl] *vt* permitir.

enact [ɪ'nækt] *vt* **1** *(law)* promulgar. **2** *(play)* representar.

enamel [ɪ'næməl] *n* esmalte *m*.
▶ *vt* esmaltar.
ⓘ *pt & pp* enamelled (US enameled), *ger* enamelling (US enameling).

encephalic [ensɪ'fælɪk] *adj* encefálico,-a.

enchant [ɪn'tʃɑːnt] *vt* **1** *(delight)* encantar, cautivar. **2** *(cast spell on)* hechizar.

enchanted [ɪn'tʃɑːntɪd] *adj* encantado,-a.

enchanting [ɪn'tʃɑːntɪŋ] *adj* encantador,-ra.

enchantment [ɪn'tʃɑːntmənt] *n* **1** *(delight)* encanto. **2** *(spell)* hechizo.

encircle [ɪn'sɜːkəl] *vt* rodear, cercar.

enclitic [en'klɪtɪk] *adj* enclítico,-a.

enclose [ɪn'kləʊz] *vt* **1** *(surround)* encerrar; *(with wall or fence)* cercar, rodear. **2** *(include in letter)* adjuntar.

enclosure [ɪn'kləʊʒəʳ] *n* **1** *(land)* cercado; *(area)* recinto. **2** *(with letter)* anexo, documento adjunto.

encode [ɪŋ'kəʊd] *vt* codificar.

encore ['ɒŋkɔːʳ] *interj* ¡otra!.
▶ *n* repetición *f*, bis *m*.

encounter [ɪn'kaʊntəʳ] *n* encuentro.
▶ *vt (meet)* encontrar, encontrarse con; *(be faced with)* tropezar con.

encourage [ɪn'kʌrɪdʒ] *vt* **1** *(cheer, inspire)* animar, alentar. **2** *(develop, stimulate)* fomentar, favorecer, estimular.

encouragement [ɪn'kʌrɪdʒmənt] *n* **1** *(act)* aliento, ánimo. **2** *(development)* fomento, estímulo.

encrypt [en'krɪpt] *vt* cifrar.

encyclopaedia [ensaɪklə'piːdɪə] *n* enciclopedia.

encyclopedia [ensaɪklə'piːdɪə] *n* enciclopedia.

end [end] *n* **1** *(extremity - of rope)* cabo; *(- of street)* final *m*; *(- of table, sofa)* extremo; *(- of stick, tail)* punta; *(- of box)* lado. **2** *(final part, finish)* fin *m*, final *m*. **3** *(aim)* objeto, objetivo, fin *m*. **4** *(of cigarette)* colilla.
▶ *adj* final, último,-a.
▶ *vt* **1** *(conclude)* acabar, terminar. **2** *(stop)* terminar, poner fin a, acabar con.
◆ **to end in** *vi* acabar en.
◆ **to end off** *vt sep* acabar.
◆ **to end up** *vi* acabar, terminar.

endanger [ɪn'deɪndʒəʳ] *vt* poner en peligro.

endangered [ɪn'deɪndʒəd] *adj* en peligro. COMP endangered species especie *f* en peligro (de extinción).

endeavor [ɪn'devəʳ] *n* US → endeavour.

endeavour [ɪn'devəʳ] *n fml* esfuerzo, empeño.
▶ *vi* esforzarse, intentar, procurar.

endemic [en'demɪk] *adj* endémico,-a.

ending ['endɪŋ] *n* **1** final *m*, conclusión *f*, desenlace *m*. **2** LING terminación *f*.

endive ['endaɪv] *n* **1** GB escarola. **2** US endibia.

endless ['endləs] *adj* interminable.

endocarp ['endəʊkɑːp] *n* endocarpio.

endocrine ['endəʊkrɪn] *adj* endocrino,-a. COMP endocrine gland glándula endocrina.

endorse [ɪn'dɔːs] *vt* **1** *(of cheque, etc)* endosar. **2** *(approve)* aprobar, apoyar.

endow [ɪn'daʊ] *vt* **1** *(bless)* dotar. **2** *(give money)* dotar (de fondos).

endurance [ɪn'djʊərəns] *n* resistencia, aguante *m*.
▶ *adj* de resistencia.

endure [ɪn'djʊəʳ] *vt* soportar, aguantar.

▶ vi *(continue to exist, survive)* durar.

enemy ['enəmɪ] n enemigo,-a.
ⓘ pl enemies.
▶ adj enemigo,-a.

energetic [enəˈdʒetɪk] adj enérgico,-a.

energy ['enədʒɪ] n energía.
▶ n pl **energies** *(efforts)* energías fpl, fuerzas fpl.
ⓘ pl energies.

enforce [ɪnˈfɔːs] vt 1 *(force to obey)* hacer cumplir. 2 *(impose)* imponer.

engage [ɪnˈgeɪdʒ] vt 1 *(hire)* contratar. 2 *(take up, occupy)* ocupar, entretener. 3 *(attract)* llamar, atraer, captar. 5 AUTO *(gear)* engranar, meter; *(clutch)* apretar. 6 TECH engranar con.

engaged [ɪnˈgeɪdʒd] adj 1 *(to be married)* prometido,-a. 2 *(busy)* ocupado,-a.

engagement [ɪnˈgeɪdʒmənt] n 1 *(to be married)* petición f de mano; *(period)* noviazgo. 2 *(appointment)* compromiso, cita. 3 MIL combate m. 4 *(employment)* contrato, empleo.

engaging [ɪnˈgeɪdʒɪŋ] adj atractivo,-a.

engine ['endʒɪn] n 1 motor m. 2 *(of train)* máquina, locomotora. COMP **engine driver** maquinista mf.

engineer [endʒɪˈnɪəʳ] n 1 *(graduate)* ingeniero,-a; *(technician)* técnico,-a. 2 US maquinista mf.
▶ vt *(contrive)* maquinar, tramar, urdir.

engineering [endʒɪˈnɪərɪŋ] n ingeniería.

England ['ɪŋglənd] n Inglaterra.

English ['ɪŋglɪʃ] adj inglés,-esa.
▶ n *(language)* inglés m.

Englishman ['ɪŋglɪʃmən] n inglés m.
ⓘ pl Englishmen.

English-speaking ['ɪŋglɪʃspiːkɪŋ] adj de habla inglesa.

Englishwoman ['ɪŋglɪʃwumən] n inglesa.
ⓘ pl Englishwomen ['ɪŋglɪʃwɪmɪn].

engrave [ɪnˈgreɪv] vt grabar.

engrossed [ɪnˈgrəust] adj absorto,-a *(in, en)*.

engulf [ɪnˈgʌlf] vt envolver.

enhance [ɪnˈhɑːns] vt 1 *(beauty, taste)* realzar; *(quality, chances)* mejorar; *(power, value)* aumentar. 2 COMPUT procesar.

enigma [ɪˈnɪgmə] n enigma m.

enigmatic [enɪgˈmætɪk] adj enigmático,-a.

enjoy [ɪnˈdʒɔɪ] vt 1 *(get pleasure from)* disfrutar de; *(like)* gustarle a uno. 2 *(benefit from)* gozar de.

enjoyment [ɪnˈdʒɔɪmənt] n placer m.

enlarge [ɪnˈlɑːdʒ] vt *(gen)* extender, aumentar; *(photograph)* ampliar.

enlargement [ɪnˈlɑːdʒmənt] n 1 *(photograph)* ampliación f. 2 extensión f.

enlighten [ɪnˈlaɪtən] vt 1 *(free from ignorance)* iluminar, ilustrar. 2 *(inform)* informar, instruir.

enlightenment [ɪnˈlaɪtənmənt] n 1 fml *(act)* aclaración f, explicación f. 2 *(liberalism)* tolerancia.
▶ n the Enlightenment la Ilustración f.

enliven [ɪnˈlaɪvən] vt avivar, animar.

enormous [ɪˈnɔːməs] adj enorme.

enough [ɪˈnʌf] adj bastante, suficiente.
▶ adv bastante, suficientemente.

enquire [ɪŋˈkwaɪəʳ] vt preguntar.
▶ vi 1 preguntar, informarse. 2 JUR investigar *(into, -)*.

enquiry [ɪŋˈkwaɪərɪ] n 1 pregunta. 2 JUR investigación f.
ⓘ pl enquiries.

enrage [ɪnˈreɪdʒ] vt enfurecer.

enrich [ɪnˈrɪtʃ] vt enriquecer.

enrol [ɪnˈrəul] vt matricular, inscribir.
▶ vi matricularse, inscribirse.
ⓘ pt & pp enrolled, ger enrolling.

enroll [ɪnˈrəul] n US → enrol.

enrollment [ɪnˈrəulmənt] n US → enrolment.

enrolment [ɪnˈrəulmənt] n matrícula, inscripción f.

ensemble [ɒnˈsɒmbəl] n conjunto.

ensue [ɪnˈsjuː] vi 1 *(follow)* seguir. 2 *(result)* resultar *(from, de)*.

ensure [ɪnˈʃuəʳ] vt 1 *(make sure)* asegurarse. 2 *(assure)* asegurar.

entail [ɪnˈteɪl] vt *(involve, mean)* suponer, implicar; *(make necessary)* ocasionar.

entangle [ɪnˈtæŋgəl] vt enredar.

enter ['entəʳ] vt 1 *(gen)* entrar en. 3 *(participate)* participar en; *(register)* inscribirse en. 4 *(write down, record)* anotar, apuntar.

enterprise ['entəpraɪz] *n* **1** *(venture)* empresa, proyecto. **2** *(initiative)* iniciativa. **3** *(firm)* empresa.

entertain [entə'teɪn] *vt* **1** *(amuse)* entretener, divertir. **2** *fml (suggestion, etc)* considerar, tener en cuenta; *(doubts, etc)* abrigar. **3** *(invite)* recibir, invitar.
► *vi (act as host)* tener invitados.

☒ To entertain no significa 'entretener (distraer)', que se traduce por to occupy.

entertaining [entə'teɪnɪŋ] *adj* divertido,-a, entretenido,-a.
entertainment [entə'teɪnmənt] *n* **1** *(amusement)* entretenimiento, diversión *f*. **2** THEAT espectáculo, función *f*.
enthral [ɪn'θrɔːl] *vt* cautivar.
  ① *pt & pp* enthralled, *ger* enthralling.
enthrall [ɪn'θrɔːl] *vt* US → enrol.
enthrone [ɪn'θrəʊn] *vt* entronizar.
enthusiasm [ɪn'θjuːzɪæzəm] *n* entusiasmo (about/for, por).
enthusiast [ɪn'θjuːzɪæst] *n* entusiasta *mf*.
enthusiastic [ɪnθjuːzɪ'æstɪk] *adj* **1** *(reaction)* entusiástico,-a, caluroso,-a. **2** *(person)* entusiasta.
entice [ɪn'taɪs] *vt* persuadir, tentar.
entire [ɪn'taɪə'] *adj* entero,-a.
entitle [ɪn'taɪtəl] *vt* **1** *(give right to)* dar derecho (to, a). **2** *(book, etc)* titular.
entity ['entɪtɪ] *n* entidad *f*.
  ① *pl* entities.
entourage [ɒntʊ'rɑːʒ] *n* séquito.
entrails ['entreɪlz] *n pl* entrañas *fpl*, tripas *fpl*, vísceras *fpl*.
entrance ['entrəns] *n* **1** *(gen)* entrada; *(door, gate)* puerta; *(hall)* vestíbulo, hall *m*. **2** *(admission)* entrada, admisión *f*; *(to school, university)* ingreso.
entrant ['entrənt] *n* *(competitor)* participante *mf*; *(applicant)* aspirante *mf*.
entrepreneur [ɒntrəprə'nɜː'] *n* *(business person)* empresario,-a.
entrust [ɪn'trʌst] *vt* confiar.
entry ['entrɪ] *n* **1** *(entrance)* entrada; *(joining)* ingreso. **2** *(right to enter)* admisión *f*. **3** US *(door, gate)* puerta. **4** *(item in accounts)* asiento; *(in diary)* anotación *f*; *(in diction-*

ary) entrada. **5** *(in competition - participant)* participante *mf*.
  ① *pl* entries.
entryphone ['entrɪfəʊn] *n* portero automático.
enumerate [ɪ'njuːməreɪt] *vt* enumerar.
enunciate [ɪ'nʌnsɪeɪt] *vt* **1** *(pronounce)* pronunciar, articular. **2** *(express)* expresar, enunciar.
envelop [ɪn'veləp] *vt* envolver.
envelope ['envələʊp] *n* *(of letter)* sobre *m*; *(covering)* envoltura.
enviable ['envɪəbəl] *adj* envidiable.
envious ['envɪəs] *adj* *(person)* envidioso,-a; *(look, etc)* de envidia.
environment [ɪn'vaɪrənmənt] *n* **1** *(ecology)* medio ambiente *m*: we need to protect the environment hemos de proteger el medio ambiente. **2** *(surroundings)* ambiente *m*, entorno; *(habitat)* hábitat *m*.
environmental [ɪnvaɪrən'mentəl] *adj* **1** *(ecological)* del medio ambiente, ambiental: environmental pollution contaminación del medio ambiente. **2** *(of surroundings)* ambiental.
environs [ɪn'vaɪrənz] *n pl* alrededores *mpl*.
envisage [ɪn'vɪzɪdʒ] *vt* **1** *(foresee)* prever. **2** *(imagine)* imaginarse.
envoy ['envɔɪ] *n* enviado,-a.
envy ['envɪ] *n* envidia (at/of, de).
  ① *pl* envies.
  ► *vt* envidiar, tener envidia de.
  ① *pt & pp* envied, *ger* envying.
enzyme ['enzaɪm] *n* enzima *m & f*.
ephemeral [ɪ'femərəl] *adj* efímero,-a.
epic ['epɪk] *adj* épico,-a.
epicentre ['epɪsentə'] *n* epicentro.
epidemic [epɪ'demɪk] *n* epidemia.
  ► *adj* epidémico,-a.
epidermis [epɪ'dɜːmɪs] *n* epidermis *f*.
epiglottis [epɪ'glɒtɪs] *n* epiglotis *f*.
epigraph ['epɪgrɑːf] *n* epígrafe *m*.
epilepsy ['epɪlepsɪ] *n* epilepsia.
epileptic [epɪ'leptɪk] *adj* epiléptico,-a.
  ► *n* epiléptico,-a.
epilogue ['epɪlɒg] *n* epílogo.
episode ['epɪsəʊd] *n* **1** episodio. **2** *(of series)* capítulo.

epitaph ['epɪtɑːf] *n* epitafio.

epithelial ['epɪθeliəl] *adj* epitelial.

epithet ['epɪθet] *n* epíteto.

epoch ['iːpɒk] *n* época.

equal ['iːkwəl] *adj* **1** *(identical)* igual; *(same)* mismo,-a. **2** *(capable)* capaz.
  ▶ *n* igual *mf*.
  ▶ *vt* **1** MATH ser igual a, equivaler a. **2** *(match)* igualar.

equality [ɪ'kwɒlɪtɪ] *n* igualdad *f*.
  ⓘ *pl* equalities.

equalize ['iːkwəlaɪz] *vi* SP empatar.
  ▶ *vt* igualar.

equanimity [ekwə'nɪmɪtɪ] *n* ecuanimidad *f*.

equate [ɪ'kweɪt] *vt* equiparar (with, con), comparar (with, con).

equation [ɪ'kweɪʒən] *n* **1** MATH ecuación *f*. **2** *fml (relationship)* relación *f*.
  COMP **simple equation** ecuación *f* de primer grado.

equator [ɪ'kweɪtər] *n* ecuador *m*.

equestrian [ɪ'kwestrɪən] *adj* ecuestre.
  ▶ *n (man)* jinete *m*; *(woman)* amazona.

equidistant [iːkwɪ'dɪstənt] *adj* equidistante.

equilateral [iːkwɪ'lætərəl] *adj* equilátero,-a. COMP **equilateral triangle** triángulo equilátero.

equilibrium [iːkwɪ'lɪbrɪəm] *n* equilibrio.

equine ['ekwaɪn] *adj* equino,-a.

equinox ['iːkwɪnɒks] *n* equinoccio.

equip [ɪ'kwɪp] *vt* **1** *(fit out, supply)* equipar (with, con), proveer (with, de). **2** *(prepare)* preparar (for/to, para).
  ⓘ *pt & pp* equipped, *ger* equipping.

equipment [ɪ'kwɪpmənt] *n* **1** *(materials)* equipo, material *m*. **2** *(act of equipping)* equipamiento.

equitable ['ekwɪtəbəl] *adj fml* equitativo,-a.

equivalence [ɪ'kwɪvələns] *n* equivalencia.

equivalent [ɪ'kwɪvələnt] *adj* equivalente.
  ▶ *n* equivalente *m*.

era ['ɪərə] *n* era, época.

eradicate [ɪ'rædɪkeɪt] *vt* erradicar.

eradication [ɪrædɪ'keɪʃən] *n* erradicación *f*.

erase [ɪ'reɪz] *vt* borrar.

eraser [ɪ'reɪzər] *n* goma de borrar.

erect [ɪ'rekt] *adj* **1** *(upright)* derecho,-a, erguido,-a. **2** ANAT erecto,-a.
  ▶ *vt (build)* erigir, levantar; *(put up - tent)* armar; *(- flagstaff)* izar.

erection [ɪ'rekʃən] *n* erección *f*.

ergonomic [ɜːgə'nɒmɪk] *adj* ergonómico,-a.

erode [ɪ'rəud] *vt* **1** *(rock, soil)* erosionar. **2** *(metal)* corroer, desgastar.

erosion [ɪ'rəuʒən] *n* **1** *(of rock, soil)* erosión *f*. **2** *(of metal)* corrosión *f*.

erotic [ɪ'rɒtɪk] *adj* erótico,-a.

errand ['erənd] *n* encargo, recado.

error ['erər] *n* error *m*, equivocación *f*.

erupt [ɪ'rʌpt] *vi* **1** *(volcano)* entrar en erupción. **2** *fig (war, violence, fire)* estallar. **3** MED *(rash, spots, etc)* brotar, salir; *(tooth)* salir.

eruption [ɪ'rʌpʃən] *n* **1** *(volcano)* erupción *f*. **2** *fig (war, anger)* estallido. **3** *(disease)* brote *m*, epidemia; *(rash, spots, etc)* erupción *f*.

escalator ['eskəleɪtər] *n* escalera mecánica.

escalope ['eskəlɒp] *n* escalope.

escapade ['eskəpeɪd, eskə'peɪd] *n* aventura.

escape [ɪ'skeɪp] *n* **1** *(flight)* fuga, huida (from, de). **2** *(of gas)* fuga, escape *m*.
  ▶ *vi* **1** *(get free, get away)* escaparse, fugarse, huir. **2** *(gas, etc)* escapar.
  ▶ *vt* **1** *(avoid)* escapar a, librarse de. **2** *(be forgotten or unnoticed)* no recordar.

escort [*(n)* e'skɔːt; *(vb)* ɪ'skɔːt] *n* **1** acompañante *mf*. **2** MIL escolta.
  ▶ *vt* **1** acompañar: *I'll escort you home* te acompañaré a casa. **2** MIL escoltar.

Eskimo ['eskɪməu] *n* **1** *(person)* esquimal *mf*. **2** *(language)* esquimal *m*.
  ⓘ *pl* Eskimos o Eskimo.
  ▶ *adj* esquimal.

esophagus [ɪ'sɒfəgəs] *n* US → **oesophagus**.

esoteric [esəu'terɪk] *adj* esotérico,-a.

espadrille [espə'drɪl] *n* alpargata.

especial [ɪ'speʃəl] *adj* especial.

especially [ɪˈspeʃəlɪ] *adv* especialmente, sobre todo.

espresso [esˈpresəʊ] *n* café *m* exprés.
ⓘ *pl* espressos.

essay [ˈeseɪ] *n* **1** *(school)* redacción *f*; *(university)* trabajo. **2** *(literary)* ensayo. **3** *fml (attempt)* intento.
▸ *vt fml* intentar.

essence [ˈesəns] *n* esencia.

essential [ɪˈsenʃəl] *adj* esencial.
▸ *n (necessary thing)* necesidad *f* básica.
▸ *n pl* **essentials** lo esencial *m sing*, lo fundamental *m sing*.

establish [ɪˈstæblɪʃ] *vt* **1** *(gen)* establecer. **2** *(find out, determine)* determinar, averiguar.

established [ɪˈstæblɪʃt] *adj* **1** *(practice, custom)* consolidado,-a. **2** *(person - set up)* establecido,-a; *(- well known)* reconocido,-a. **3** *(fact)* comprobado,-a.

establishment [ɪˈstæblɪʃmənt] *n* **1** *(setting up)* establecimiento, fundación *f*. **2** *(premises)* establecimiento; *(business)* negocio. **3** *(staff)* plantilla, personal *m*.
▸ *n* the Establishment GB el sistema.

estate [ɪˈsteɪt] *n* **1** *(land)* finca. **2** GB *(with houses)* urbanización *f*. **3** *(money and property)* propiedad *f*, bienes *mpl*; *(inheritance)* herencia.

⊠ Estate no significa 'estado', que se traduce por state o condition.

esteem [ɪˈstiːm] *vt* estimar.
▸ *n* aprecio, estima.

esthetic [iːsˈθetɪk] *adj* US → aesthetic.

estimate [*(n)* ˈestɪmət; *(vb)* ˈestɪmeɪt] *n* **1** *(calculation - of amount, size)* cálculo, estimación *f*; *(- of value, cost)* valoración *f*, estimación *f*; *(- for work)* presupuesto. **2** *(judgement)* evaluación *f*, juicio, opinión *f*.
▸ *vt* **1** *(calculate)* calcular. **2** *(judge, form opinion about)* pensar, creer, estimar.
▸ *vi (for work)* hacer un presupuesto (for, de).

⊠ To estimate no significa 'estimar (querer)', que se traduce por to respect.

estimation [estɪˈmeɪʃən] *n* **1** opinión *f*, juicio. **2** *(esteem)* estima, aprecio.

Estonia [eˈstəʊnɪə] *n* Estonia.

Estonian [eˈstəʊnɪən] *adj* estonio,-a.
▸ *n* **1** *(person)* estonio,-a. **2** *(language)* estonio.

estrogen [ˈiːstrədʒən] *n* US → **oestrogen**.

estuary [ˈestjʊərɪ] *n* estuario.
ⓘ *pl* estuaries.

etching [ˈetʃɪŋ] *n* aguafuerte *m & f*.

eternal [ɪˈtɜːnəl] *adj* **1** *(everlasting)* eterno,-a. **2** *fam (unceasing)* incesante. **3** *(immutable)* inmutable.

eternity [ɪˈtɜːnətɪ] *n* eternidad *f*.

ether [ˈiːθər] *n* éter *m*.

ethic [ˈeθɪk] *n* ética.

ethical [ˈeθɪkəl] *adj* ético,-a, moral.

ethics [ˈeθɪks] *n (science)* ética.
▸ *n pl (moral correctness)* moralidad *f*.

Ethiopia [iːθɪˈəʊpɪə] *n* Etiopía.

Ethiopian [iːθɪˈəʊpɪən] *adj* etíope.
▸ *n* **1** *(person)* etíope *mf*, etiope *mf*. **2** *(language)* etíope *m*.

ethnic [ˈeθɪk] *adj* étnico,-a. COMP ethnic minority minoría étnica.

ethnography [eθˈnɒɡrəfɪ] *n* etnografía.

ethnology [eθˈnɒlədʒɪ] *n* etnología.

ethyl [ˈiːθaɪl, ˈeθɪl] *n* CHEM etilo. COMP ethyl alcohol alcohol *m* etílico.

etiquette [ˈetɪket] *n* protocolo, etiqueta.

⊠ Etiquette no significa 'etiqueta (rótulo)', que se traduce por label.

etymological [etɪməˈlɒdʒɪkəl] *adj* etimológico,-a.

etymology [etɪˈmɒlədʒɪ] *n* etimología.
ⓘ *pl* etymologies.

eucalyptus [juːkəˈlɪptəs] *n* eucalipto. COMP eucalyptus tree eucalipto.

EU [ˈiːˈjuː] *abbr* (European Union) Unión *f* Europea; *(abbreviation)* UE *f*.

euphemism [ˈjuːfəmɪzəm] *n* eufemismo.

euro [ˈjʊərəʊ] *n* euro.

Europe [ˈjʊərəp] *n* Europa.

European [jʊərəˈpɪən] *adj* europeo,-a.
▸ *n (person)* europeo,-a. COMP European Economic Community Comunidad *f* Económica Europea. ‖ European Parliament Parlamento Europeo. ‖ European Union Unión *f* Europea.

euthanasia [juːθəˈneɪzɪə] n eutanasia.
evacuate [ɪˈvækjʊeɪt] vt **1** (people) evacuar. **2** (place) desalojar; (mil) desocupar.
evacuation [ɪvækjuˈeɪʃən] n **1** (of people) evacuación f. **2** (of place) desalojo.
evade [ɪˈveɪd] vt **1** evadir, eludir.
evaluate [ɪˈvæljʊeɪt] vt (assess) evaluar, juzgar; (estimate value) valorar, calcular (el valor de), tasar.
evaluation [ɪvæljuˈeɪʃən] n evaluación f.
evaporate [ɪˈvæpəreɪt] vt evaporar.
▶ vi evaporarse.
evaporation [ɪvæpəˈreɪʃən] n evaporación f.
evasion [ɪˈveɪʒən] n **1** (gen) evasión f. **2** (excuse, etc) evasiva.
evasive [ɪˈveɪsɪv] adj evasivo,-a.
eve [iːv] n víspera, vigilia. LOC on the eve of STH en vísperas de ALGO.
even [ˈiːvən] adj **1** (level, flat) llano,-a, plano,-a; (smooth) liso,-a: this surface isn't even esta superficie no es plana. **2** (regular, steady) uniforme, regular, constante. **3** (evenly balanced) igual, igualado,-a. **4** (number) par. **5** (placid-character) apacible. **7** (on the same level as) a nivel (with, de).
▶ adv **1** hasta, incluso, aun: it's always sunny, even in winter siempre hace sol, incluso en invierno. **2** (with negative) siquiera, ni siquiera: she never even said hello ni siquiera me saludó. **3** (before comparative) aun, todavía: she's even more beautiful than I remembered es aun más guapa de lo que recordaba. LOC even if aun si, aunque. ‖ even so aun así. ‖ even though aunque, aun cuando.
▶ vt **1** (level) nivelar, allanar. **2** (score) igualar; (situation) equilibrar.
◆ to even out vt sep (make level) nivelar; (make equal) igualar; (spread equally) repartir equitativamente.
evening [ˈiːvənɪŋ] n (early) tarde f; (late) noche f. LOC good evening! ¡buenas tardes!, ¡buenas noches!

✎ Evening comprende la parte final de la tarde y el principio de la noche, antes de que anochezca del todo.

evenly [ˈiːvənlɪ] adv **1** (uniformly) uniformemente. **2** (fairly, equally) equitativamente, igualmente. **3** (of voice) en el mismo tono,.
event [ɪˈvent] n **1** (happening) suceso, acontecimiento. **2** SP prueba.
eventual [ɪˈventʃʊəl] adj **1** (final, ultimate) final. **2** (resulting) consiguiente. **3** (possible) posible.

☒ Eventual no significa 'provisional', que se traduce por temporary.

eventually [ɪˈventʃʊəlɪ] adv finalmente, con el tiempo.
ever [ˈevəʳ] adv **1** (in negative sentences) nunca, jamás. **2** (in questions) alguna vez. **3** (always) siempre. **4** (after comparative and superlative) nunca. **5** (emphatic use): how ever did you lose your coat? ¿cómo has podido perder el abrigo? LOC for ever para siempre.
evergreen [ˈevəɡriːn] adj BOT de hoja perenne.
▶ n árbol m de hoja perenne.
everlasting [evəˈlɑːstɪŋ] adj **1** (eternal, lasting for ever) eterno,-a. **2** (lasting for a long time) duradero,-a.
every [ˈevrɪ] adj **1** (each) cada; (all) todos,-as: every day cada día, todos los días. **3** (all possible): we encourage people to help in every way animamos a la gente a que ayude de cualquier manera. LOC every other day un día sí un día no, cada dos días.

✎ Consulta también each.

everybody [ˈevrɪbɒdɪ] pron todos,-as, todo el mundo.
everyday [ˈevrɪdeɪ] adj (day-to-day) diario,-a; (ordinary) corriente, cotidiano,-a: for everyday use para uso diario.
everyone [ˈevrɪwʌn] pron → everybody.
everyplace [ˈevrɪpleɪs] adv → US everywhere.
everything [ˈevrɪθɪŋ] pron todo.
everywhere [ˈevrɪweəʳ] adv **1** (place) en todas partes, por todas partes: he's been everywhere ha estado en todas partes. **2** (movement) a todas partes.

evidence ['evɪdəns] n 1 (proof) prueba, pruebas fpl. 2 (sign, indication) indicio, indicios mpl, señal f. 3 JUR (testimony) testimonio, declaración f.
▶ vt 1 (prove) demostrar, probar. 2 (give proof of) justificar.

evident ['evɪdənt] adj evidente.

evil ['iːvəl] adj 1 (gen) malo,-a. 2 (foul - smell) fétido,-a, repugnante; (- temper, weather) terrible, de perros. 4 (unlucky) aciago,-a, de mal agüero.
▶ n (wickedness) mal m, maldad f.

evoke [ɪ'vəʊk] vt 1 (bring to mind) evocar. 2 fml (produce, cause) provocar.

evolution [iːvə'luːʃən] n evolución f.

evolve [ɪ'vɒlv] vt 1 (develop) desarrollar. 2 (give off) desprender.
▶ vi evolucionar.

ewe [juː] n oveja.

exact [ɪg'zækt] adj 1 (precise) exacto,-a. 2 (meticulous) meticuloso,-a. 3 (accurate) preciso,-a. 4 (specific, particular) justo.
▶ vt (demand, insist on) exigir (from, a).

exacting [ɪg'zæktɪŋ] adj exigente.

exaggerate [ɪg'zædʒəreɪt] vt exagerar.

exalt [ɪg'zɔːlt] vt 1 fml (elevate) exaltar, elevar. 2 (praise, extol) ensalzar.

exam [ɪg'zæm] n fam examen m.

examination [ɪgzæmɪ'neɪʃən] n 1 EDUC examen m. 2 (inspection) inspección f, examen m; (of house, room) registro. 3 MED reconocimiento. 4 JUR interrogatorio.

examine [ɪg'zæmɪn] vt 1 (inspect) inspeccionar, examinar; (check) comprobar; (consider) examinar, estudiar. 2 (customs) registrar. 3 EDUC examinar (in/on, de). 4 MED hacer un reconocimiento a. 5 JUR interrogar.

examiner [ɪg'zæmɪnər] n examinador,-ra.

example [ɪg'zɑːmpəl] n (gen) ejemplo.

exasperate [ɪg'zɑːspəreɪt] vt exasperar, irritar. [LOC] for example por ejemplo.

excavate ['ekskəveɪt] vt excavar.

excavation [ekskə'veɪʃən] n excavación f.

excavator ['ekskəveɪtər] n (machine) excavadora.

exceed [ɪk'siːd] vt exceder.

excel [ɪk'sel] vt (surpass) superar.
▶ vi (be very good at) destacar (at/in, en), sobresalir (at/in, en).
ⓘ pt & pp excelled, ger excelling.

excellence ['eksələns] n excelencia.

excellent ['eksələnt] adj excelente.
▶ interj fam ¡estupendo!, ¡fantástico!.

except [ɪk'sept] prep excepto, salvo.
▶ vt fml excluir, exceptuar.

exception [ɪk'sepʃən] n excepción f.

exceptional [ɪk'sepʃənəl] adj excepcional.

excerpt ['eksɜːpt] n extracto.

excess [ɪk'ses] n 1 exceso. 2 COMM excedente m.
▶ adj excedente, sobrante.

excessive [ɪk'sesɪv] adj excesivo,-a.

exchange [ɪks'tʃeɪndʒ] n 1 (gen) cambio. 2 (of ideas, information, etc) intercambio. 3 (of prisoners) canje m. 4 FIN cambio. 5 EDUC (reciprocal visit) intercambio.
▶ vt 1 (gen) cambiar. 2 (ideas, information, etc) intercambiar. 3 (prisoners) canjear.

exchequer [ɪks'tʃekər] n (treasury) tesoro público.
▶ n the Exchequer Hacienda.

excite [ɪk'saɪt] vt 1 (enthuse, thrill) emocionar, apasionar. 2 fml (bring about) provocar. 3 (stimulate) excitar.

excited [ɪk'saɪtɪd] adj 1 emocionado,-a, ilusionado,-a. 2 (sexually) excitado,-a.

excitement [ɪk'saɪtmənt] n 1 (strong feeling) emoción f, entusiasmo, ilusión f. 2 (commotion) agitación f, conmoción f, revuelo.

exciting [ɪk'saɪtɪŋ] adj emocionante.

exclaim [ɪk'skleɪm] vt exclamar, gritar.
▶ vi exclamar.

exclamation [eksklə'meɪʃən] n exclamación f. [COMP] exclamation mark signo de admiración. ‖ exclamation point US signo de admiración.

exclude [ɪk'skluːd] vt 1 (leave out, not include) excluir, no incluir. 2 (debar, prevent from entering) no admitir.

excluding [ɪkˈsklu:dɪŋ] *prep (excepting)* excepto, con excepción de.

exclusive [ɪkˈsklu:sɪv] *adj* **1** *(gen)* exclusivo,-a. **2** *(press)* en exclusiva.
▸ *n (press)* exclusiva.

excrement [ˈekskrɪmənt] *n* excremento.

excrete [ɪkˈskri:t] *vt* excretar.

excretory [ɪkˈskrəi:təəɪ] *adj* excretor,-ra. COMP **excretory system** sistema excretor.

excruciating [ɪkˈskru:ʃɪeɪtɪŋ] *adj* **1** insoportable. **2** *euph* fatal, horrible.

excursion [ɪkˈskɜ:ʒən] *n (outing)* excursión *f*, viaje *m*.

excuse [*(n)* ɪkˈskju:s; *(vb)* ɪkˈskju:z] *n* **1** *(apology)* disculpa. **2** *(pretext)* excusa.
▸ *vt* **1** perdonar, disculpar. **2** *(justify)* justificar. **3** *(exempt)* eximir.

execute [ˈeksɪkju:t] *vt* **1** *(put to death)* ejecutar. **2** *(carry out)* ejecutar; *(orders)* cumplir; *(tasks)* realizar. **3** *(music, etc)* interpretar.

execution [eksɪˈkju:ʃən] *n* **1** *(carrying out)* ejecución *f*; *(of order)* cumplimiento; *(of task)* realización *f*. **2** *(putting to death)* ejecución *f*. **4** *(of music, etc)* interpretación *f*.

executioner [eksɪˈkju:ʃənəʳ] *n* verdugo.

executive [ɪgˈzekjətɪv] *adj* ejecutivo,-a.
▸ *n (person)* ejecutivo,-a; *(committee)* ejecutiva.
▸ *n* **the executive** el (poder) ejecutivo.

exemplify [ɪgˈzemplɪfaɪ] *vt* ejemplificar.
ⓘ *pt & pp* **exemplified**, *ger* **exemplifying**.

exempt [ɪgˈzempt] *adj* exento,-a, libre (from, de).
▸ *vt* eximir, dispensar (from, de).

exemption [ɪgˈzempʃən] *n* exención *f* (from, de).

exercise [ˈeksəsaɪz] *n* ejercicio. COMP **exercise book** cuaderno.
▸ *vt* **1** *(employ, make use of)* ejercer, emplear. **2** *(give exercise to - dog)* sacar de paseo; *(- horse)* entrenar.
▸ *vi* hacer ejercicio, entrenarse.

exert [ɪgˈzɜ:t] *vt* ejercer.

exhalation [ekshəlˈeɪʃⁿn] *vt* exhalación *f*.

exhale [eksˈheɪl] *vt (breathe out)* exhalar.
▸ *vi (give off)* despedir.

exhaust [ɪgˈzɔ:st] *n* **1** *(pipe)* (tubo de) escape *m*. **2** *(fumes)* gases *mpl* de combustión.
▸ *vt* **1** *(gen)* agotar. **2** *(empty)* vaciar.

exhausted [ɪgˈzɔ:stɪd] *adj* agotado,-a.

exhausting [ɪgˈzɔ:stɪŋ] *adj* agotador,-ra.

exhaustive [ɪgˈzɔ:stɪv] *adj* exhaustivo,-a.

exhibit [ɪgˈzɪbɪt] *n* ART objeto expuesto.
▸ *vt* **1** *(display, show)* exponer, presentar. **2** *fml (manifest)* manifestar, mostrar.
▸ *vi (of artist)* exponer.

exhibition [eksɪˈbɪʃən] *n* **1** *(art, etc)* exposición *f*. **2** *(display)* demostración *f*, muestra.

exhibitionist [eksɪˈbɪʃənɪst] *n* exhibicionista *mf*.

exhilarating [ɪgˈzɪləreɪtɪŋ] *adj (invigorating)* estimulante; *(exciting)* emocionante.

exhume [eksˈhju:m] *vt* exhumar.

exile [ˈeksaɪl] *n* **1** *(action)* destierro, exilio. **2** *(person)* desterrado,-a, exiliado,-a.
▸ *vt* desterrar, exiliar.

exist [ɪgˈzɪst] *vi* **1** *(gen)* existir. **2** *(subsist)* subsistir (on, a base de).

existence [ɪgˈzɪstəns] *n* existencia.

existent [ɪgˈzɪstənt] *adj* existente.

exit [ˈeksɪt] *n* **1** *(gen)* salida. **2** THEAT mutis *m*.
▸ *vi* THEAT hacer mutis.

Ⓧ **Exit** no significa 'éxito', que se traduce por **success**.

exodus [ˈeksədəs] *n* éxodo.

exorbitant [ɪgˈzɔ:bɪtənt] *adj* exorbitante.

exorcism [ˈeksɔ:sɪzəm] *n* exorcismo.

exotic [egˈzɒtɪk] *adj* exótico,-a.

expand [ɪkˈspænd] *vt* **1** *(enlarge - business)* ampliar; *(- number)* aumentar, incrementar. **2** *(gas, metal)* dilatar, expandir.
▸ *vi* **1** *(grow larger)* crecer, aumentar. **2** *(metal)* dilatarse; *(gas)* expandirse. **3** *(spread out)* extenderse.

◆ **to expand on** *vt insep* ampliar, desarrollar.

expanse [ɪk'spæns] *n* extensión *f*.

expansion [ɪk'spænʃən] *n* **1** crecimiento, aumento. **2** *(gas, metal)* dilatación *f*, expansión *f*. **3** *(trade)* desarrollo.

expansive [ɪk'spænsɪv] *adj* **1** *(friendly, talkative)* hablador,-ra, comunicativo,-a. **2** *(able to expand)* expansivo,-a.

expect [ɪk'spekt] *vt* **1** *(anticipate)* esperar: *I never expected to win* no esperaba ganar. **2** *(demand)* esperar, contar con. **3** GB *fam (suppose)* suponer, imaginar.

expectancy [ɪk'spektənsɪ] *n* *(anticipation)* expectación *f*, expectativa; *(hope)* ilusión *f*.

expectation [ekspek'teɪʃən] *n* *(hope, firm belief)* esperanza.
▶ *n pl* **expectations** *(confident feelings)* expectativas *fpl*.

☒ Expectation no significa 'expectativa', que se traduce por excitement.

expedient [ɪk'spiːdɪənt] *adj* conveniente, oportuno,-a.
▶ *n* expediente *m*, recurso.

expedition [ekspɪ'dɪʃən] *n* **1** *(gen)* expedición *f*. **2** *fml (speed)* aceleración *f*, prontitud *f*.

expel [ɪk'spel] *vt* expulsar.
① *pt & pp* **expelled**, *ger* **expelling**.

expend [ɪk'spend] *vt* **1** *fml (spend, use)* gastar, emplear. **2** *fml (use up, exhaust)* agotar.

expendable [ɪk'spendəbəl] *adj fml* prescindible.

expenditure [ɪk'spendɪtʃər] *n* gasto, desembolso.

expense [ɪk'spens] *n* gasto, desembolso.
▶ *n pl* **expenses** gastos *mpl*.

expensive [ɪk'spensɪv] *adj* caro,-a.

experience [ɪk'spɪərɪəns] *n* experiencia.
▶ *vt (sensation, situation, etc)* experimentar; *(difficulty)* tener; *(loss)* sufrir.

experienced [ɪk'spɪərɪənst] *adj* experimentado,-a, con experiencia.

experiment [ɪk'sperɪmənt] *n* experimento.

▶ *vi* experimentar, hacer experimentos.

experimental [ɪksperɪ'mentəl] *adj* experimental.

expert ['ekspɜːt] *n* experto,-a (at/in/on, en).
▶ *adj* experto,-a.

expertise [ekspɜː'tiːz] *n* *(skill)* pericia, habilidad *f*; *(knowledge)* conocimiento (práctico).

expire [ɪk'spaɪər] *vi* **1** *(come to end)* terminar, acabarse; *(die)* expirar, morir. **2** *(run out - contract)* vencer; *(- passport, ticket)* caducar. **3** MED *(breathe out)* espirar.

expiry [ɪk'spaɪərɪ] *n* **1** *(ending)* expiración *f*, terminación *f*. **2** *(of contract, bill of exchange)* vencimiento; *(of passport, driving licence, etc)* caducidad *f*.

explanation [eksplə'neɪʃən] *n* explicación *f*.

explicit [ɪk'splɪsɪt] *adj* explícito,-a.

explode [ɪk'spləʊd] *vt* **1** *(blow up - bomb, etc)* hacer estallar, hacer explotar. **2** *(refute - theory)* refutar; *(- rumour)* desmentir.
▶ *vi* **1** *(blow up)* estallar, explotar. **2** *(react violently)* reventar, explotar, estallar.

exploit [*(n)* 'eksplɔɪt; *(vb)* ɪk'splɔɪt] *n* hazaña, proeza.
▶ *vt* **1** *(work, develop fully)* explotar. **2** *(use unfairly)* aprovecharse de, explotar.

exploitation [eksplɔɪ'teɪʃən] *n* explotación *f*.

exploration [eksplə'reɪʃən] *n* exploración *f*.

explore [ɪk'splɔːr] *vt* **1** *(gen)* explorar. **2** *(examine)* examinar.
▶ *vi* explorar.

explorer [ɪk'splɔːrər] *n* explorador,-ra.

explosion [ɪk'spləʊʒən] *n* **1** *(gen)* explosión *f*, estallido. **2** *(violent outburst)* ataque *m*, arrebato.

explosive [ɪk'spləʊsɪv] *adj* explosivo,-a.

exponent [ɪk'spəʊnənt] *n* **1** *(gen)* exponente *m*; *(supporter)* defensor,-ra (of, de), partidario,-a (of, de). **2** *(performer)* intérprete *mf*; *(expert)* experto,-a. **3** MATH exponente *m*.

exponential [ekspə'nenʃəl] *adj* MATH exponencial.

export [(n) 'ekspɔːt; (vb) ɪk'spɔːt] *n* **1** *(trade)* exportación *f*. **2** *(article)* artículo de exportación.
▶ *vt* exportar.

exporter [ek'spɔːtəʳ] *n* exportador,-ra.

expose [ɪk'spəʊz] *vt* **1** *(uncover, make visible)* exponer. **2** *(make known - secret, etc)* revelar, descubrir; *(- person)* desenmascarar. **3** *fig (lay open)* exponerse. **4** *(photo)* exponer.

exposure [ɪk'spəʊʒəʳ] *n* **1** *(being exposed)* exposición *f*. **2** *(revelation, disclosure)* revelación *f*, descubrimiento. **3** *(in photography - picture)* fotografía; *(- time)* exposición *f*. **4** *(position of house, etc)* situación *f*, orientación *f*. **5** *(publicity)* publicidad *f*; *(coverage)* cobertura.

express [ɪk'spres] *adj* **1** *(explicit)* expreso,-a, claro,-a. **2** *(fast - mail)* urgente; *(- train, coach)* expreso.
▶ *adv* urgente.
▶ *n (rail)* (tren *m*) expreso.
▶ *vt* **1** expresar. **2** *fml (juice)* exprimir.

expression [ɪk'spreʃən] *n* **1** *(gen)* expresión *f*; *(manifestation)* manifestación *f*. **2** MATH expresión *f*.

expressive [ɪk'spresɪv] *adj* expresivo,-a.

expressway [ɪk'spresweɪ] *n* US autopista.

expulsion [ɪk'spʌlʃən] *n* expulsión *f*.

exquisite [ek'skwɪzɪt, 'ekskwɪzɪt] *adj* **1** *(delicate, etc)* exquisito,-a, perfecto,-a. **2** *fml (of emotion)* intenso,-a; *(of power to feel)* delicado,-a.

extend [ɪk'stend] *vt* **1** *(enlarge)* ampliar; *(lengthen - line, road)* prolongar, alargar. **2** *(over time)* prolongar, alargar; *(deadline)* prorrogar. **3** *(stretch out - arm, hand)* alargar, tender; *(- leg)* estirar; *(- wing)* desplegar, extender.
▶ *vi* **1** *(in space)* continuar, extenderse, llegar hasta. **2** *(in time)* prolongarse, alargarse, durar. **3** *(become extended - ladder, etc)* extenderse. **4** *(include, affect)* incluir, abarcar, extenderse a.

extension [ɪk'stenʃən] *n* **1** *(widening)* ampliación *f*, extensión *f*. **2** *(of line, road, etc)* prolongación *f*. **5** *(telephone line)* extensión *f*; *(telephone)* supletorio.

extensive [ɪk'stensɪv] *adj* **1** *(area)* extenso,-a, amplio,-a. **2** *(wide-ranging)* vasto,-a, amplio,-a, extenso,-a; *(thorough)* exhaustivo, minucioso,-a. **3** *(very great in effect, widespread)* importante, múltiple.

extensor [ɪk'stensəʳ] *n* extensor.

extent [ɪk'stent] *n* **1** *(expanse)* extensión *f*. **2** *(range, scale, scope)* amplitud *f*, alcance *m*. **3** *(point)* punto.

extenuate [ɪk'stenjʊeɪt] *vt fml* atenuar.

exterior [ɪk'stɪəɪəʳ] *adj* exterior, externo,-a-: *exterior walls* paredes exteriores.
▶ *n* **1** exterior *m*. **2** *(of person)* aspecto externo, apariencia.

exterminate [ɪk'stɜːmɪneɪt] *vt* exterminar.

extermination [ɪkstɜːmɪ'neɪʃən] *n* exterminación *f*, exterminio.

external [ek'stɜːnəl] *adj* externo,-a, exterior. COMP **external ear** oído externo.

extinct [ɪk'stɪŋkt] *adj* **1** *(of animal)* extinguido,-a. **2** *(of volcano)* extinguido,-a, apagado,-a.

extinction [ɪk'stɪŋkʃən] *n* extinción *f*.

extinguish [ɪk'stɪŋgwɪʃ] *vt* extinguir.

extinguisher [ɪk'stɪŋgwɪʃəʳ] *n* extintor *m*.

extort [ɪk'stɔːt] *vt (money)* sacar, conseguir a la fuerza; *(promise, confession)* arrancar, obtener.

extortion [ɪk'stɔːʃən] *n* extorsión *f*.

extra ['ekstəə] *adj (additional)* extra, más, otro,-a; *(spare)* de sobra; *(on top)* aparte.
▶ *adv (more than usually)* extra, muy; *(additional)* aparte.
▶ *n* **1** *(additional thing)* extra *m*, complemento; *(additional charge)* suplemento; *(luxury)* lujo. **2** CINEM extra *mf*. **3** *(press)* edición *f* especial.

extract [(n) 'ekstrækt; (vb) ɪk'strækt] *n* extracto.

▶ *vt* **1** *(pull out)* extraer, sacar. **2** *(obtain - confession, promise, etc)* arrancar, obtener; *(- information, passage, quotation)* extraer, sacar. **3** *(produce)* extraer, sacar.

extraction [ɪkˈstrækʃən] *n* **1** *(gen)* extracción *f*. **2** *(of tooth)* extracción *f*. **3** *(descent)* origen *m*.

extractor [ɪkˈstræktəʳ] *n* extractor *m*. COMP **extractor fan** extractor *m* de humos.

extradite [ˈekstrədaɪt] *vt* extraditar, extradir.

extradition [ekstrəˈdɪʃən] *n* extradición *f*.

extramarital [ekstrəˈmæəɪtəl] *adj* extramatrimonial.

extraordinary [ɪkˈstrɔːdənəɪ] *adj* extraordinario,-a.

extrasensory [ekstrəˈsensəəɪ] *adj* extrasensorial.

extraterrestrial [ekstrətəˈrestrɪəl] *adj* extraterrestre.
▶ *n* extraterrestre *mf*.

extravagance [ɪkˈstrævəgəns] *n* *(spending)* derroche *m*, despilfarro, lujo; *(behaviour)* extravagancia.

extravagant [ɪkˈstrævəgənt] *adj* **1** *(wasteful - person)* derrochador,-ra, despilfarrador,-ra; *(- thing)* ineficaz, ineficiente. **2** *(extreme)* extravagante. **3** *(luxurious)* lujoso,-a.

extreme [ɪkˈstriːm] *adj* **1** *(gen)* extremo,-a. **2** *(severe, unusual)* excepcional.
▶ *n* extremo.

extremism [ɪkˈstriːmɪzəm] *n* extremismo.

extremist [ɪkˈstriːmɪst] *n* extremista *mf*.

extremity [ɪkˈstremɪtɪ] *n* **1** *fml (furthest point)* extremo. **2** *fml (extreme degree, situation)* situación *f* extrema.
▶ *n pl* **extremities** ANAT extremidades *fpl*.
ⓘ *pl* **extremities**.

extricate [ˈekstrɪkeɪt] *vt* *fml* librar, sacar. LOC **to extricate os** lograr salir (from, de).

extrinsic [ɪkˈstrɪnzɪk] *adj* extrínseco,-a.

extrovert [ˈekstrəvɜːt] *adj* extrovertido,-a.
▶ *n* extrovertido,-a.

exuberance [ɪgˈzjuːbəəəns] *n* *(vigour)* exuberancia; *(high spirits)* euforia.

exuberant [ɪgˈzjuːbəəənt] *adj* **1** *(of person)* eufórico,-a. **2** *(of plants)* exuberante.

exude [ɪgˈzjuːd] *vt* **1** *fml (of sweat, etc)* exudar, rezumar. **2** *fig (of feeling)* rebosar: *she exudes confidence* rebosa de confianza.
▶ *vi (of sweat, etc)* exudar, rezumar.

exultant [ɪgˈzʌltənt] *adj* exultante.

eye [aɪ] *n* **1** ANAT ojo. **2** *(sense)* vista. **3** *(of needle, potato, storm)* ojo.
▶ *vt (observe)* mirar, observar; *(look at longingly)* echar el ojo a.

eyeball [ˈaɪbɔːl] *n* globo ocular.

eyebolt [ˈaɪbəʊlt] *n* armella, hembrilla.

eyebrow [ˈaɪbəaʊ] *n* ceja.

eye-catching [ˈaɪkætʃɪŋ] *adj* llamativo,-a.

eyelash [ˈaɪlæʃ] *n* pestaña.

eyelid [ˈaɪlɪd] *n* párpado.

eyeliner [ˈaɪlaɪnəʳ] *n* lápiz *m* de ojos.

eyesight [ˈaɪsaɪt] *n* vista.

eyesore [ˈaɪsɔːʳ] *n* monstruosidad *f*.

eyestrain [ˈaɪstreɪn] *n* vista cansada.

eyetooth [aɪˈtuːθ] *n* colmillo.

eyewash [ˈaɪwɒʃ] *n* **1** MED colirio. **2** *fam (nonsense)* tonterías *fpl*: *it's all eyewash!* ¡eso son disparates!.

eyewitness [ˈaɪwɪtnəs] *n* testigo presencial, testigo ocular.

F

F, f [ef] n **1** (the letter) F, f f. **2** MUS fa m.

F [ˈfærənhaɪt] abbr (Fahrenheit) Fahrenheit; (abbreviation) F.

fable [ˈfeɪbəl] n fábula.

fabric [ˈfæbrɪk] n **1** (material) tela, tejido. **2** (structure) fábrica, estructura.

☒ Fabric no significa 'fábrica', que se traduce por **factory**.

fabulous [ˈfæbjələs] adj fabuloso,-a.

façade [fəˈsɑːd] n fachada.

face [feɪs] n **1** (gen) cara. **2** (surface) superficie f. **3** (of dial) cuadrante m. **4** (of watch) esfera. LOC **face down** boca abajo. ▌**face up** boca arriba.
  ▶ vt **1** (look towards) mirar hacia. **2** (look onto) estar orientado,-a hacia, dar a. **3** (be opposite to) estar enfrente de. **4** (confront) presentarse, plantearse; (deal with) enfrentarse a. **5** (tolerate) soportar.
  ◆ **to face up to** vt insep afrontar, enfrentar, enfrentarse a.

faceless [ˈfeɪsləs] adj anónimo,-a.

facelift [ˈfeɪslɪft] n **1** lifting m. **2** fig (building) lavado de cara.

facet [ˈfæsɪt] n faceta.

facial [ˈfeɪʃəl] adj facial.

facilitate [fəˈsɪlɪteɪt] vt facilitar.

facility [fəˈsɪlɪti] n facilidad f.
  ▶ n pl **facilities 1** (equipment) instalaciones fpl, servicios mpl. **2** (means) facilidades fpl.
  ① pl **facilities**.

fact [fækt] n **1** (event, happening) hecho. **2** (the truth) realidad f. LOC **as a matter of fact** en realidad. ▌**in fact** de hecho.

faction [ˈfækʃən] n facción f.

factor [ˈfæktəʳ] n factor m.

factorize [ˈfæktəraɪz] vt descomponer en factores.

factory [ˈfæktərɪ] n fábrica.
  ① pl **factories**.

faculty [ˈfækəltɪ] n **1** (power, ability) facultad f. **2** (at university) facultad f. **3** US (at university) profesorado.
  ① pl **faculties**.

fad [fæd] n **1** (fashion) moda pasajera. **2** (personal) manía.

fade [feɪd] vt (colour) descolorar, descolorir, desteñir.
  ◆ **to fade away** vi **1** (become less intense, strong, etc) desvanecerse, esfumarse. **2** (die) morirse.

faecal [ˈfiːkəl] adj fecal.

faeces [ˈfiːsiːz] n pl heces fpl.

fag [fæg] n **1** GB fam (cigarette) pitillo. **2** sl (drag) lata, rollo.

Fahrenheit [ˈfærənhaɪt] adj Fahrenheit.

fail [feɪl] n EDUC suspenso.
  ▶ vt **1** (let down) fallar, decepcionar; (desert) fallar, faltar. **2** EDUC suspender.
  ▶ vi **1** (neglect) dejar de. **2** (not succeed) fracasar, no hacer algo. **3** (crops) fallar, echarse a perder. **4** (stop working) fallar. **5** (light) acabarse, irse apagando. **6** (become weak) debilitarse, fallar. **7** COMM (become bankrupt) quebrar, fracasar.

failing [ˈfeɪlɪŋ] n (fault) defecto, fallo; (weakness) punto débil.
  ▶ prep a falta de.

fail-safe [ˈfeɪlseɪf] adj (device, mechanism) de seguridad; (plan) infalible.

failure [ˈfeɪljəʳ] n **1** (lack of success) fracaso. **2** COMM quiebra. **3** EDUC suspenso. **4** (person) fracasado,-a. **5** (breakdown) fallo, avería. **6** (of crops) pérdida.

faint [feɪnt] *adj* **1** *(sound, voice)* débil, tenue. **2** *(colour)* pálido,-a. **3** *(slight - memory, etc)* vago,-a.
  ▶ *n* mareo.
  ▶ *vi* desmayarse (from, de).

fair¹ [feəʳ] *adj* **1** *(just)* justo,-a; *(impartial)* imparcial; *(reasonable)* razonable. **2** *(considerable)* considerable. **3** *(idea, guess, etc)* bastante bueno,-a. **4** *(weather)* bueno,-a. **5** *(hair)* rubio,-a; *(skin)* blanco,-a.

fair² [feəʳ] *n* **1** *(market)* mercado, feria. **2** *(show)* feria; *(funfair)* parque *m* de atracciones.

fairground ['feəgraund] *n* *(site)* recinto ferial; *(show)* feria; *(funfair)* parque *m* de atracciones.

fairly ['feəlɪ] *adv* **1** *(justly)* justamente. **2** *(moderately)* bastante. **3** *(completely)* completamente.

fairway ['feəweɪ] *n* **1** *(golf)* calle *f*. **2** *(sea)* canal *m* navegable.

fairy ['feərɪ] *n* hada. [COMP] **fairy story/ tale** cuento de hadas.
  ⓘ *pl* fairies.

faith [feɪθ] *n* **1** fe *f*. **2** *(trust, confidence)* confianza (in, en), fe *f* (in, en). **3** REL fe *f*.

faithful ['feɪθful] *adj* **1** *(loyal)* fiel (to, a), leal (to, a/con). **2** *(accurate)* exacto,-a.

faithfully ['feɪθfulɪ] *adv* fielmente. [LOC] **yours faithfully** *(in letter)* atentamente.

fake [feɪk] *n* **1** falsificación *f*. **2** *(person)* impostor,-ra, farsante *mf*.
  ▶ *adj* falso,-a, falsificado,-a.
  ▶ *vt* **1** *(falsify)* falsificar. **2** *(pretend)* fingir: *she faked illness* fingió estar enferma.

falcon ['fɔːlkən] *n* halcón *m*.

fall [fɔːl] *n* **1** *(act of falling)* caída. **2** *(of rock)* desprendimiento; *(of snow)* nevada. **3** *(decrease)* baja, descenso, disminución *f*. **4** *(defeat)* caída. **5** US *(autumn)* otoño.
  ▶ *vi* **1** *(gen)* caer, caerse. **2** *(decrease)* bajar, descender. **3** *(be defeated)* caer; *(be killed)* perecer. [LOC] **to fall asleep** quedarse dormido. **‖ to fall in love** enamorarse.
  ▶ *n pl* **falls** *(waterfall)* cascada *f sing*, cataratas *fpl*.
  ◆ **to fall apart** *vi* romperse, deshacerse, caerse a pedazos.
  ◆ **to fall back** *vi* *(retreat)* retroceder, retirarse.

  ◆ **to fall back on** *vt insep* *(resort to)* recurrir a.
  ◆ **to fall behind** *vi* *(be overtaken)* retrasarse, rezagarse.
  ◆ **to fall down** *vi* **1** *(gen)* caer, caerse. **2** *(fail)* fallar.
  ◆ **to fall for** *vt insep* **1** *(be tricked)* dejarse engañar por, picar. **2** *fam* *(fall in love)* enamorarse de.
  ◆ **to fall off** *vi* **1** *(decrease in quantity)* bajar, disminuir; *(in quality)* empeorar. **2** *(become detached)* desprenderse, caerse.
  ◆ **to fall out** *vi* *(quarrel)* reñir (with, con), pelearse (with, con).
  ▶ *vi* *(drop)* caerse.
  ◆ **to fall over** *vt insep* caer, tropezar con.
  ⓘ *pt* fell [fel], *pp* fallen ['fɔːlən].

fallen ['fɔːlən] *pp* → **fall**.
  ▶ *adj* *(not virtuous)* perdido,-a.

Fallopian tube [fələupɪən'tjuːb] *n* trompa de Falopio.

fallout ['fɔːlaut] *n* lluvia radiactiva.

fallow ['fæləu] *adj* en barbecho.

false [fɔːls] *adj* **1** *(untrue)* falso,-a. **2** *(artificial)* postizo,-a. [COMP] **false alarm** falsa alarma. **‖ false start** salida nula. **‖ false teeth** dentadura postiza.

falsify ['fɔːlsɪfaɪ] *vt* **1** *(alter falsely)* falsificar. **2** *(misrepresent)* falsear.
  ⓘ *pt & pp* falsified, *ger* falsifying.

falter ['fɔːltəʳ] *vi* *(person)* vacilar, titubear; *(voice)* fallar.

fame [feɪm] *n* fama.

familiar [fəˈmɪlɪəʳ] *adj* **1** *(well-known)* conocido,-a (to, a). **2** *(aware)* familiarizado,-a (with, con). **3** *(intimate)* íntimo,-a.

  ☒ Familiar no significa 'familiar (de la familia)', que se traduce por family.

familiarity [fəmɪlɪˈærɪtɪ] *n* familiaridad *f*.

familiarize [fəˈmɪlɪəraɪz] *vt* *(become acquainted)* familiarizarse (with, con).

family ['fæmɪlɪ] *n* familia.
  ⓘ *pl* families.
  ▶ *adj* familiar. [COMP] **family name** apellido.

famine ['fæmɪn] *n* hambruna, hambre *f*.

famous ['feɪməs] *adj* famoso,-a (for, por).

famously ['feɪməslɪ] *adv* *fam* estupendamente.

fan [fæn] n **1** (object) abanico. **2** ELEC ventilador m. **3** (follower) aficionado,-a; (of pop star, etc) admirador,-ra, fan mf. **4** (of football) hincha mf.
► vt (face) abanicar; (elec) ventilar.
ⓘ pt & pp fanned, ger fanning.

fanatic [fəˈnætɪk] n fanático,-a.
► adj fanático,-a (about, de).

fancier [ˈfænsɪəʳ] n aficionado,-a.

fanciful [ˈfænsɪful] adj **1** (idea) imaginario,-a, fantástico,-a. **2** (extravagant) caprichoso,-a, estrafalario,-a.

fancy [ˈfænsɪ] n **1** (imagination) fantasía, imaginación f. **2** (whim) capricho, antojo.
ⓘ pl fancies.
► adj **1** (jewels, goods, etc) de fantasía. **2** (high-class, posh) elegante, de lujo.
► vt **1** (want) apetecer, querer. **2** (find attractive) encontrar atractivo,-a. **3** (think) creer, suponer.
ⓘ pt & pp fancied, ger fancying.

fanfare [ˈfænfeəʳ] n fanfarria.

fang [fæŋ] n colmillo.

fantastic [fænˈtæstɪk] adj fantástico,-a.

fantasy [ˈfæntəsɪ] n fantasía.
ⓘ pl fantasies.

FAQ [ˈefeɪˈkjuː] n (frequently asked questions) preguntas frecuentes.

far [faːʳ] adj **1** (distant) lejano,-a, remoto,-a. **2** (more distant) opuesto,-a, extremo,-a.
ⓘ comp farther o further, superl farthest o furthest.
► adv **1** (a long way) lejos. **2** (a long time) lejos. **3** (much) mucho. LOC as far as hasta: as far as I am concerned por lo que a mí se refiere. ❙ far away lejos. ❙ so far hasta ahora.

faraway [ˈfaːrəweɪ] adj lejano,-a, remoto,-a; (look) distraído,-a.

farce [faːs] n farsa.

fare [feəʳ] n (price) tarifa, precio del billete; (boat) pasaje m.
► vi (progress, get on) desenvolverse.

✎ Fare se refiere sólo a los billetes de transporte público.

farewell [feəˈwel] interj ¡adiós!
► n despedida.

farm [faːm] n granja.
► adj agrícola, de granja.
► vt **1** (use land) cultivar, labrar. **2** (breed animals) criar.
► vi (grow crops) cultivar la tierra.

farmer [ˈfaːməʳ] n granjero,-a, agricultor,-ra.

farmhouse [ˈfaːmhaus] n granja.

farming [ˈfaːmɪŋ] n agricultura. LOC farming industry industria agropecuaria.

farmland [ˈfaːmlænd] n tierra de cultivo.

farmyard [ˈfaːmjaːd] n corral m.

far-reaching [faːˈriːtʃɪŋ] adj de gran alcance.

farrier [ˈfærɪəʳ] n herrero.

far-sighted [faːˈsaɪtɪd] adj previsor,-ra.

fart [faːt] n **1** fam pedo. **2** (fool) carcamal m, carroza m.
► vi tirarse un pedo.

farther [ˈfaːðəʳ] adj comp → far: Santander is farther than Murcia Santander está más lejos que Murcia.

farthest [ˈfaːðɪst] adj → far: Pluto is the farthest planet from the Sun Plutón es el planeta más alejado del Sol.
► adv → far: who lives farthest from the school? ¿quién vive más lejos de la escuela?

fascinate [ˈfæsɪneɪt] vt fascinar.

fascinating [ˈfæsɪneɪtɪŋ] adj fascinante.

fascination [fæsɪˈneɪʃən] n fascinación f.

fascism [ˈfæʃɪzəm] n fascismo.

fascist [ˈfæʃɪst] n fascista mf.
► adj fascista.

fashion [ˈfæʃən] n **1** (style) moda. **2** (way) modo. LOC in fashion de moda. ❙ out of fashion pasado de moda.
► vt (clay) formar; (metal) labrar.

fashionable [ˈfæʃənəbəl] adj de moda.

fast¹ [faːst] adj **1** (gen) rápido,-a. **2** (tight, secure) firme, seguro,-a. **3** (clock) adelantado,-a.
► adv **1** rápidamente, deprisa. **2** (securely) firmemente; (thoroughly) profundamente.

fast² [faːst] n ayuno.
► vi ayunar.

fasten [ˈfaːsən] vt **1** (attach) fijar, sujetar. **2** (tie) atar. **3** (box, door, window) cerrar; (belt, dress) abrochar.
► vi (box, door, etc) cerrarse; (dress, etc) abrocharse.

fastener ['fɑːsənər] n cierre m.
fastidious [fæ'stɪdɪəs] adj quisquilloso,-a, melindroso,-a.

❌ Fastidious no significa 'fastidioso
(molesto)', que se traduce por annoying.

fat [fæt] adj gordo,-a.
ⓘ comp fatter, superl fattest.
▶ n 1 (of meat) grasa; (of person) carnes
fpl. 2 (for cooking) manteca; (lard) lardo.
fatal ['feɪtəl] adj 1 (causing disaster) fatal,
funesto,-a; (serious) grave. 2 (causing
death) mortal. 3 (fateful) fatídico,-a.

❌ Fatal no significa 'fatal (muy malo)',
que se traduce por awful.

fatality [fə'tælɪtɪ] n víctima mortal.
ⓘ pl fatalities.
fate [feɪt] n 1 (destiny) destino. 2 (person's
lot) suerte f.
fated ['feɪtɪd] adj predestinado,-a.
fateful ['feɪtful] adj fatídico,-a.
father ['fɑːðər] n 1 (male parent) padre m.
2 (priest) padre m.
▶ vt engendrar.
father-in-law ['fɑːðərɪnlɔː] n suegro.
fatherland ['fɑːðəlænd] n patria.
fatherly ['fɑːðəlɪ] adj paternal.
fatigue [fə'tiːg] n 1 fatiga, cansancio. 2
TECH fatiga.
▶ vt fml fatigar, cansar.
fat-soluble [fæt'sɒljəbəl] adj liposoluble.
fatten ['fætən] vt 1 (animal) cebar (up, -).
2 (person) engordar (up,-).
fattening ['fætənɪŋ] adj que engorda:
biscuits are fattening las galletas engordan.
fatty ['fætɪ] adj (greasy) graso,-a.
ⓘ comp fattier, superl fattiest.
▶ n fam pej gordinflón,-ona.
ⓘ pl fatties.
faucet ['fɔːsɪt] n US grifo.
fault [fɔːlt] n 1 (gen) defecto. 2 (blame)
culpa. 4 (mistake) error m, falta. 5 (in
earth) falla. 6 (in tennis, etc) falta.
▶ vt criticar, encontrar defectos a.

❌ Fault no significa 'falta (carencia)',
que se traduce por lack.

faultless ['fɔːltləs] adj perfecto,-a, intachable, impecable.

faulty ['fɔːltɪ] adj defectuoso,-a.
ⓘ comp faultier, superl faultiest.
fauna ['fɔːnə] n fauna.
faux pas [fəʊ'pɑː] n metedura de pata.
ⓘ pl faux pas.
favor ['feɪvər] n-vt US → favour.
favorite ['feɪvərɪt] n US → favorite.
favour ['feɪvər] n 1 (kindness) favor m. 2
(approval) aprobación f, favor m. 3 (favouritism) parcialidad f, favoritismo.
▶ vt 1 (prefer) preferir, inclinarse por.
2 (benefit, aid) favorecer.
favourable ['feɪvərəbəl] adj favorable
(to/towards, a).
favourite ['feɪvərɪt] n favorito,-a.
▶ adj favorito,-a.
favouritism ['feɪvərɪtɪzəm] n favoritismo.
fawn [fɔːn] n 1 ZOOL cervato. 2 (colour)
beige m.
▶ adj beige.
◆ to fawn on vt insep adular, lisonjear.
fax [fæks] n fax m.
▶ vt enviar por fax. COMP fax machine
fax m.
fear [fɪər] n miedo, temor m.
▶ vt temer, tener miedo a.
▶ vi temer, tener miedo.
◆ to fear for vt insep temer por: I fear for
the children's safety temo por la seguridad
de los niños.
fearful ['fɪəful] adj 1 (frightened) temeroso,-a (of, de). 2 (terrible) terrible, espantoso,-a.
fearless ['fɪələs] adj audaz.
fearsome ['fɪəsəm] adj temible.
feasibility ['fiːzəbɪlɪtɪ] n viabilidad f.
feasible ['fiːzəbəl] adj 1 (viable) factible,
viable. 2 (plausible) verosímil.
feast [fiːst] n 1 festín m, banquete m. 2
fam comilona. 3 REL fiesta de guardar,
día m de fiesta.
▶ vi banquetear, festejar.
feat [fiːt] n proeza, hazaña.
feather ['feðər] n pluma.
feature ['fiːtʃər] n 1 (of face) rasgo, facción
f. 2 (characteristic) rasgo, característica. 3
(press) artículo especial, especial m
COMP feature (film) largometraje m.

▶ *vt (have)* tener; *(film)* tener como protagonista: *this car features the latest safety devices* este coche incorpora los últimos dispositivos de seguridad.

▶ *vi (appear)* figurar (in, en): *his name featured in the police report* su nombre figuró en el informe policial.

February ['februərɪ] *n* febrero.

✎ Para ejemplo de uso, consulta **May**.

fecal ['fiːkəl] *adj* US → **faecal**.

feces ['fiːsiːz] *n* US → **faeces**.

fed [fed] *pt & pp* → **feed**. LOC **to be fed up with** *fam* estar harto,-a de.

federal ['fedərəl] *adj* federal.

federation [fedə'reɪʃən] *n* federación *f*.

fee [fiː] *n* **1** *(doctor's, etc)* honorarios *mpl*; *(for tuition)* derechos *mpl* (de matrícula). **2** *(membership)* cuota, cuota de socio. COMP **registration fee** matrícula.

feeble ['fiːbəl] *adj* **1** *(person)* débil. **2** *(light, sound)* tenue, débil. **3** *(argument, excuse)* de poco peso.

feed [fiːd] *n* **1** comida. **2** *fam* comilona. **3** *(for cattle)* pienso. **4** TECH alimentación *f*.

▶ *vt* **1** alimentar: *could you feed our cat while we're away?* ¿podrías dar de comer a nuestro gato mientras estamos fuera? **2** *(breastfeed)* dar de mamar a; *(bottle-feed)* dar el biberón a. **3** TECH alimentar, suministrar. **4** *(insert)* introducir; *(coins)* meter.

▶ *vi (people)* comer, alimentarse (on, de); *(animals)* pacer.

◆ **to feed up** *vt sep (animal)* cebar; *(person)* engordar.

ⓘ *pt & pp* fed [fed].

feedback ['fiːdbæk] *n* **1** TECH retroalimentación *f*, retroacción *f*. **2** *fig* reacción *f*, respuesta.

feeder ['fiːdər] *n* **1** TECH alimentador *m*. **2** *(road)* ramal *m*, carretera.

feel [fiːl] *n* **1** *(sense, texture)* tacto. **2** *(atmosphere)* aire *m*, ambiente *m*.

▶ *vt* **1** *(touch)* tocar, palpar. **2** *(search with fingers)* buscar. **3** *(sense, experience)* sentir, experimentar. **4** *(believe)* creer.

▶ *vi* **1** *(be)* sentir(se), encontrarse. **2** *(seem)* parecer: *it feels like leather* parece piel. **3** *(perceive, sense)* sentir: *she could feel*

all eyes upon her sentía que todos la miraban. **4** *(opinion)* opinar, pensar: *how do you feel about exams?* ¿qué opinas de los exámenes?

◆ **to feel for** *vt insep (have sympathy for)* compadecer a, compadecerse de.

ⓘ *pt & pp* felt [felt].

feeler ['fiːlər] *n* antena.

feeling ['fiːlɪŋ] *n* **1** *(emotion)* sentimiento, emoción *f*. **2** *(sensation)* sensación *f*. **3** *(sense)* sensibilidad *f*. **4** *(impression)* impresión *f*: *I have the feeling that …* tengo la impresión de que …

▶ *adj* sensible, compasivo,-a.

▶ *n pl* **feelings** sentimientos *mpl*.

feet [fiːt] *n pl* → **foot**.

feign [feɪn] *vt* fingir, aparentar: *she feigned illness to get off school* fingió estar enferma para no ir a la escuela.

feint [feɪnt] *n fml (fencing)* finta; *(boxing)* treta, estratagema.

▶ *adj (paper)* rayado,-a.

feldspar ['feldspɑːr] *n* feldespato.

feline ['fiːlaɪn] *adj* felino,-a.

▶ *n* felino,-a.

fell¹ [fel] *vt* **1** *(tree)* talar. **2** *(enemy)* derribar.

fell² [fel] *pt* → **fall**.

fellow ['feləʊ] *n* **1** *fam (chap)* tipo, tío: *old fellow* viejo amigo; *poor fellow!* ¡pobrecito! **2** *(companion, comrade)* compañero,-a, camarada *mf*. **3** *(member)* socio,-a.

fellowship ['feləʊʃɪp] *n* **1** *(group)* asociación *f*, sociedad *f*. **2** *(companionship)* compañerismo, camaradería. **3** EDUC *(scholarship)* beca.

felspar ['felspɑːr] *n* feldespato.

felt¹ [felt] *pt & pp* → **feel**.

felt² [felt] *n* fieltro.

▶ *adj* de fieltro.

felt-tip ['felttɪp] [also **felt-tip pen**] *n* rotulador *m*.

female ['fiːmeɪl] *n* **1** hembra. **2** *(woman)* mujer *f*; *(girl)* chica.

▶ *adj* **1** femenino,-a. **2** ZOOL hembra.

feminine ['femɪnɪn] *adj* femenino,-a.

▶ *n* femenino,-a.

feminism ['femɪnɪzəm] *n* feminismo.

feminist ['femɪnɪst] *n* feminista *mf*.

femoral ['fiːmərəl] *adj* femoral.

femur ['fiːməʳ] *n* fémur *m*.

fence [fens] *n* valla, cerca. LOC **to sit on the fence** ver los toros desde la barrera.
▶ *vi* **1** SP practicar la esgrima. **2** *(land)* cercar.

fencing ['fensɪŋ] *n* **1** SP esgrima. **2** *(structure)* cercado.

fend [fend] *vi* **to fend for os** valerse por uno mismo,-a.
◆ **to fend off** *vt sep (blow)* parar, desviar; *(question)* esquivar; *(attack)* rechazar, defenderse de.

fender ['fendəʳ] *n* **1** *(for fire)* pantalla. **2** US *(on automobile)* parachoques *m*.

fennel ['fenəl] *n* hinojo.

ferment [*(n)* 'fɜːment; *(vb)* fəˈment] *n* **1** *(substance)* fermento. **2** *(unrest)* agitación *f*.
▶ *vt & vi* fermentar.

fermentation [fɜːmenˈteɪʃən] *n* fermentación *f*.

fern [fɜːn] *n* helecho.

ferocious [fəˈrəʊʃəs] *adj* feroz.

ferocity [fəˈrɒsɪtɪ] *n* ferocidad *f*.

ferret ['ferɪt] *n* hurón *m*.
◆ **to ferret out** *vt sep* descubrir.

ferrous ['ferəs] *adj* ferroso,-a.

ferry ['ferɪ] *n (small)* barca de pasaje; *(large)* transbordador *m*, ferry *m*.
ⓘ *pl* **ferries**.
▶ *vt* transportar.
ⓘ *pt & pp* **ferried**, *ger* **ferrying**.

ferryboat ['ferɪbəʊt] *n* → **ferry**.

fertile ['fɜːtaɪl] *adj* fértil.

fertility [fəˈtɪlɪtɪ] *n* fertilidad *f*.

fertilization [fɜːtəlaɪˈzeɪʃən] *n* **1** *(soil)* fertilización *f*. **2** *(egg)* fecundación *f*.

fertilize ['fɜːtɪlaɪz] *vt* **1** *(soil)* fertilizar, abonar. **2** *(egg)* fecundar.

fertilizer ['fɜːtɪlaɪzəʳ] *n* fertilizante *m*, abono.

ferule¹ ['feruːl] *n* férula.

fervent ['fɜːvənt] *adj* fervoroso,-a.

fervor ['fɜːvəʳ] *n* US → **fervour**.

fervour ['fɜːvəʳ] *n* fervor *m*.

fester ['festəʳ] *vi* **1** MED supurar, enconarse. **2** *fig* amargarse.

festival ['festɪvəl] *n* **1** *(event)* festival *m*. **2** *(celebration)* fiesta.

fetal ['fiːtəs] *n* US → **foetal**.

fetch [fetʃ] *vt* **1** *(go and get)* ir por, ir a buscar, buscar; *(bring)* traer. **2** *fam (sell for)* venderse por, alcanzar.
◆ **to fetch up** *vi* ir a parar.

fête [feɪt] *n (party)* fiesta; *(fair)* feria.
▶ *vt* festejar.

fetid ['fetɪd] *adj* fétido,-a.

fetish ['fetɪʃ] *n* fetiche *m*.

fetter ['fetəʳ] *vt* **1** encadenar. **2** *fig* estorbar, poner trabas a.
▶ *n pl* **fetters** grilletes *mpl*, cadenas *fpl*.

fetus ['fiːtəs] *n* US → **foetus**.

feud [fjuːd] *n* enemistad *f* (duradera): *there's been a feud between the two families for years* hace años que existe una enemistad entre ambas familias.
▶ *vi* disentir, reñir, pelear.

☒ Feud no significa 'feudo (dominio)', que se traduce por **fief**.

feudal ['fjuːdəl] *adj* feudal.

feudalism ['fjuːdəlɪzəm] *n* feudalismo *m*.

fever ['fiːvəʳ] *n* fiebre *f*.

feverish ['fiːvərɪʃ] *adj* febril.

few [fjuː] *adj* **1** *(not many)* poco,-a, pocos,-as: *very few cars* muy pocos coches. **2** *(some)* uno,-as cuantos,-as, algunos,-as: *in the next few days* en los próximos días.
▶ *pron* **1** *(not many)* pocos,-as: *many try but few succeed* muchos lo intentan pero pocos lo consiguen. **2** *(some)* unos,-as cuantos,-as, algunos,-as: *there are a few left* quedan unos cuantos.

fiancé [fɪˈænseɪ] *n* prometido, novio.

fiancée [fɪˈænseɪ] *n* prometida, novia.

fiasco [fɪˈæskəʊ] *n* fiasco, fracaso.
ⓘ *pl* **fiascos**.

fib [fɪb] *n fam* bola, trola.
▶ *vi fam* contar bolas, contar trolas.
ⓘ *pt & pp* **fibbed**, *ger* **fibbing**.

fibre ['faɪbəʳ] *n* fibra. COMP **fibre optics** fibra óptica. ▌**man-made fibre** fibra artificial.

fibreglass ['faɪbəglɑːs] *n* fibra de vidrio.

fibrosis [faɪˈbrəʊsɪs] *n* fibrosis *f*.

fibrous ['faɪbrəs] *adj* fibroso,-a.

fibula ['fɪbjələ] *n* peroné *m*.

fickle ['fɪkəl] *adj* inconstante, voluble.

fiction [ˈfɪkʃən] n **1** (novels) novela, narrativa. **2** (invention) ficción f.

fictitious [fɪkˈtɪʃəs] adj ficticio,-a.

fiddle [ˈfɪdəl] n **1** fam violín m. **2** fam (fraud) estafa, trampa.
▶ vi **1** tocar el violín. **2** fam (play) juguetear (with, con).
▶ vt fam (cheat) amañar, falsificar.
◆ **to fiddle about / fiddle around** vi fam perder el tiempo.

fiddler [ˈfɪdləʳ] n **1** fam (violinist) violinista mf. **2** fam (cheat) tramposo,-a.

fidelity [fɪˈdelɪtɪ] n fidelidad f.

fidget [ˈfɪdʒɪt] n persona inquieta.
▶ vi (move about) moverse, no poder estar(se) quieto,-a; (play about) jugar (with, con).

fief [fiːf] n feudo.

field [fiːld] n **1** (gen) campo. **2** (for mining) yacimiento. **3** (subject, area) campo, terreno. **4** SP (competitors) competidores mpl; (horses) participantes mpl.

fierce [fɪəs] adj **1** (gen) feroz. **2** fig (heat, competition, etc) fuerte, intenso,-a; (argument) acalorado,-a.

fiery [ˈfaɪərɪ] adj **1** (colour) encendido,-a, rojo,-a. **2** (burning) ardiente. **3** (food) muy picante; (drink) muy fuerte.
① comp **fierier**, superl **fieriest**.

fifteen [fɪfˈtiːn] adj quince.
▶ n quince m.
✎ Consulta también **six**.

fifteenth [fɪfˈtiːnθ] adj decimoquinto,-a.
▶ adv en decimoquinto lugar.
▶ n **1** (in series) decimoquinto,-a. **2** (fraction) decimoquinto; (one part) decimoquinta parte f.
✎ Consulta también **sixth**.

fifth [fɪfθ] adj quinto,-a.
▶ adv quinto, en quinto lugar.
▶ n **1** (in series) quinto,-a. **2** (fraction) quinto; (one part) quinta parte f.
✎ Consulta también **sixth**.

fiftieth [ˈfɪftɪəθ] adj quincuagésimo,-a.
▶ adv en quincuagésimo lugar.

▶ n **1** (in series) quincuagésimo,-a. **2** (fraction) quincuagésimo; (one part) quincuagésima parte f.
✎ Consulta también **sixtieth**.

fifty [ˈfɪftɪ] adj cincuenta.
▶ n cincuenta m.
✎ Consulta también **sixty**.

fifty-fifty [ˈfɪftɪˈfɪftɪ] adv fam mitad y mitad, a medias.

fig [fɪg] n higo. COMP **fig tree** higuera.

fight [faɪt] n **1** (struggle) lucha. **2** (physical violence) pelea; (quarrel) riña; (argument) disputa. **3** (boxing) combate m.
▶ vi **1** (quarrel) pelear(se) (about/over, por), discutir (about/over, por). **2** (in boxing) pelear (against, contra). **3** (with physical violence) pelearse (with, con) (against, contra), luchar (with, con) (against, contra).
▶ vt **1** (bull) lidiar. **2** (engage in - battle) librar; (- war) hacer; (- election) presentarse a. **3** (with physical violence) pelearse, luchar.
◆ **to fight back** vi defenderse, resistir.
▶ vt sep (tears) contener.
◆ **to fight off** vt sep vencer, rechazar.
① pt & pp **fought** [fɔːt].

fighter [ˈfaɪtəʳ] n **1** (war) combatiente mf. **2** (boxing) boxeador,-ra. **3** fig luchador,-ra.

fig-leaf [ˈfɪgliːf] n hoja de parra.

figurative [ˈfɪgərətɪv] adj figurado,-a.

figure [ˈfɪgəʳ] n **1** (number, sign) cifra, número. **2** (money, price) cantidad f, precio. **3** (in art, shape, human form) figura. **4** (personality) figura, personaje m.
▶ vi (appear) figurar, constar.
▶ vt US (think) suponer, imaginarse.
◆ **to figure out** vt sep fam (gen) comprender, enterarse; (problem) resolver, calcular.

filament [ˈfɪləmənt] n filamento.

file [faɪl] n **1** (tool) lima. **2** (folder) carpeta. **3** (archive) archivo, expediente m. **4** COMPUT archivo. **5** (line) fila.
▶ vt **1** (smooth) limar. **2** (put away) archivar; (in card index) fichar. **3** JUR presentar.
▶ vi (walk in line) desfilar.

filigree [ˈfɪlɪgriː] n filigrana.

fill [fɪl] *vt* **1** *(make full)* llenar (with, de). **2** *(time)* ocupar. **3** *(cover)* cubrir. **4** CULIN rellenar. **5** *(tooth)* empastar. **6** *(hold a position)* ocupar; *(appoint)* cubrir. **7** *(fulfil)* satisfacer.
▶ *vi* llenarse (with, de).
◆ **to fill in** *vt sep* **1** *(space, form)* rellenar. **2** *(inform)* poner al corriente (on, de).
◆ **to fill in for** *vt insep* sustituir a.
◆ **to fill up** *vt sep* llenar.
▶ *vi* llenarse.

fillet ['fɪlɪt] *n* filete *m*.

filling ['fɪlɪŋ] *n* **1** *(in tooth)* empaste *m*. **2** CULIN relleno. COMP **filling station** gasolinera.

film [fɪlm] *n* **1** CINEM película, filme *m*, film *m*. **2** *(coating of dust, etc)* capa, película. **3** *(of photos)* carrete *m*, rollo.
▶ *vt* **1** CINEM rodar, filmar; *(tv programme)* grabar. **2** *(event)* filmar.
▶ *vi* CINEM rodar.

filter ['fɪltər] *n* filtro.
▶ *vt* filtrar.

filth [fɪlθ] *n* **1** *(dirt)* suciedad *f*, porquería. **2** *fig (obscenity)* obscenidades *fpl*, porquerías *fpl*.

filthy ['fɪlθɪ] *adj* **1** *(dirty)* sucio,-a, asqueroso,-a. **2** *(obscene)* obsceno,-a, grosero,-a, asqueroso,-a.
① *comp* filthier, *superl* filthiest.

fin [fɪn] *n* aleta.

final ['faɪnəl] *adj* final.
▶ *n* SP final *f*.
▶ *n pl* **finals** *(at university)* exámenes *mpl* finales.

finale [fɪ'nɑːlɪ] *n* final *m*.

finalist ['faɪnəlɪst] *n* finalista *mf*.

finality [faɪ'nælətɪ] *n* carácter *m* definitivo.

> ✗ Finality no significa 'finalidad (objetivo)', que se traduce por purpose, aim.

finalize ['faɪnəlaɪz] *vt (plans, arrangements)* ultimar; *(date)* fijar.

finally ['faɪnəlɪ] *adv* **1** *(at last)* por fin, al final. **2** *(lastly)* por último, finalmente.

finance ['faɪnæns] *n (management of money)* finanzas *fpl*.
▶ *vt* financiar.
▶ *n pl* **finances** *(money available)* fondos *mpl*.

financial [faɪ'nænsɪəl] *n* financiero,-a, económico,-a.

find [faɪnd] *n (act, thing found)* hallazgo.
▶ *vt* **1** *(gen)* encontrar. **2** *(declare)* declarar.
◆ **to find out** *vt sep* **1** *(enquire)* preguntar, averiguar; *(discover)* descubrir, enterarse de.
▶ *vi* **1** *(enquire)* informarse (about, sobre), averiguar. **2** *(discover)* enterarse (about, de), (llegar a) saber.
① *pt & pp* found [faʊnd].

finding ['faɪndɪŋ] *n* **1** *(of inquiry)* conclusión *f*, resultado. **2** JUR fallo, veredicto.

> ✎ Se usa en plural con el mismo significado.

fine¹ [faɪn] *adj* **1** *(gen)* fino,-a. **2** *(high-quality)* excelente. **3** *(weather)* bueno,-a. **4** *(healthy)* bien. **5** *fam (all right)* bien.
▶ *adv* **1** *(in small bits)* fino, finamente. **2** *fam (very well)* muy bien.

fine² [faɪn] *n (punishment)* multa.
▶ *vt* multar.

finger ['fɪŋgər] *n* dedo.
▶ *vt* tocar.

fingernail ['fɪŋgəneɪl] *n* uña.

fingerprint ['fɪŋgəprɪnt] *n* huella digital, huella dactilar.

fingertip ['fɪŋgətɪp] *n* punta del dedo, yema del dedo.

finish ['fɪnɪʃ] *n* **1** fin *m*, final *m*. **2** SP llegada, meta. **3** *(for surface)* acabado.
▶ *vt* acabar, terminar.
◆ **to finish up** *vi (end up)* ir a parar a/en.

finite ['faɪnaɪt] *adj* finito,-a.

Finland ['fɪnlənd] *n* Finlandia.

Finn [fɪn] *n (person)* finlandés,-esa.

Finnish ['fɪnɪʃ] *adj* finlandés,-esa.
▶ *n (language)* finlandés *m*.

fiord [fɪ'ɔːd] *n* fiordo.

fir [fɜːr] *n* abeto.

fire ['faɪər] *n* **1** *(gen)* fuego. **2** *(blaze)* incendio, fuego. **3** *(heater)* estufa. **4** MIL fuego. LOC **to be on fire** estar ardiendo. I **to catch fire** prenderse. COMP **fire brigade** los bomberos. I **fire engine** coche *m* de bomberos. I **fire escape** escalera de incendios. I **fire extinguisher** extintor *m*. I **fire hydrant** boca de incendios. I **fire station** parque *m* de bomberos.

► *vt (weapon)* disparar; *(rocket)* lanzar. **2** *fam (dismiss)* despedir.
► *vi* **1** *(shoot)* disparar **(at, sobre)**, hacer fuego. **2** AUTO encenderse.
► *interj* ¡fuego!

firearm ['faɪɑːm] *n* arma de fuego.

firebreak ['faɪəbreɪk] *n* cortafuego.

firecracker ['faɪəkrækəʳ] *n* petardo.

firefighter ['faɪəfaɪtəʳ] *n* bombero *mf*.

firefly ['faɪəflaɪ] *n* luciérnaga.
① *pl* fireflies.

fireman ['faɪəmən] *n* bombero.
① *pl* firemen ['faɪəmən].

fireplace ['faɪəpleɪs] *n* **1** *(structure)* chimenea. **2** *(hearth)* hogar *m*.

fireproof ['faɪəpruːf] *adj* a prueba de fuego.

firewall ['faɪəwɔːl] *n* cortafuego.

firewood ['faɪəwʊd] *n* leña.

fireworks ['faɪəwɜːks] *n pl* fuegos *mpl* artificiales, fuegos *mpl* de artificio.

firing ['faɪərɪŋ] *n* tiroteo.

firm¹ [fɜːm] *n (business)* empresa.

✗ Firm no significa 'firma (escrita)', que se traduce por signature.

firm² [fɜːm] *adj* **1** *(strong, solid, steady)* firme, sólido,-a. **2** *(strict, strong)* duro,-a. **3** FIN *(steady)* firme, estable.

first [fɜːst] *adj* primero,-a.
► *adv* **1** *(before anything else)* primero. **2** *(for the first time)* por primera vez. **3** *(in preference to)* antes. LOC **at first** al principio. I **first of all** primero.
► *n* **1** la primera vez. **2** *(gear)* primera: *I can't put it into first* no puedo meter primera.

first-aid [fɜːst'eɪd] *adj* de primeros auxilios. COMP **first-aid kit** botiquín *m*.

first-born ['fɜːstbɔːn] *adj* primogénito,-a.
► *n* primogénito,-a.

first-class ['fɜːstklɑːs] *adj* **1** de primera clase. **2** *fig* de primera, excelente.
► *adv* en primera.

first-hand [fɜːst'hænd] *adj* de primera mano.

firstly ['fɜːstlɪ] *adv* en primer lugar.

first-rate ['fɜːstreɪt] *adj* de primera.
► *adv* de primera.

fiscal ['fɪskəl] *adj* fiscal.

fish [fɪʃ] *n* **1** pez *m*. **2** CULIN pescado. COMP **fish farm** piscifactoría. I **fish finger** palito de pescado rebozado. I **fish shop** pescadería.
① *pl* fish o fishes.
► *vi* pescar **(for, -)**.

✎ Cuando significa 'pez', fish es un nombre contable y su plural es fish, aunque también se puede emplear la forma menos frecuente fishes. Cuando significa 'pescado', es incontable y, por lo tanto, no tiene plural.

fishbowl ['fɪʃbəʊl] *n* pecera.

fisherman ['fɪʃəmən] *n* pescador *m*.
① *pl* fishermen ['fɪʃəmən].

fish-hook ['fɪʃhʊk] *n* anzuelo.

fishing ['fɪʃɪŋ] *n* pesca. LOC **to go fishing** ir de pesca. COMP **fishing line** sedal *m*. I **fishing net** red *f* de pesca. I **fishing rod** caña de pescar.

fishmonger ['fɪʃmʌŋgəʳ] *n* GB pescadero,-a. COMP **fishmonger's** pescadería.

fission ['fɪʃən] *n* fisión *f*.

fissure ['fɪʃəʳ] *n* fisura, grieta.

fist [fɪst] *n* puño.

fistful ['fɪstfʊl] *n* puñado.

fit¹ [fɪt] *n* **1** MED ataque *m*, acceso. **2** *(of laughter, rage)* ataque *m*.

fit² [fɪt] *adj* **1** *(suitable, appropriate)* adecuado,-a, apropiado,-a; *(qualified for)* capacitado,-a, capaz. **2** *(in good health)* sano,-a, bien de salud; *(physically)* en forma. **3** *fam (ready)* a punto de.
① *comp* fitter, *superl* fittest.
► *n* **1** *(of clothes)* : *it's a perfect fit* me va perfectamente. **2** *(in space)*: *it'll be a tight fit* vamos a estar muy apretados.
► *vt* **1** *(be right size for)* sentar bien, quedar bien. **2** *(try (clothing) on sb)* probar. **3** *(key)* abrir. **4** *(install)* instalar, poner. **5** *(adapt)* ajustar, adaptar, adecuar.
◆ **to fit in** *vi* **1** *(get on)* llevarse bien, integrarse. **2** *(suit)* encajar; *(harmonize)* pegar, quedar bien; *(tally)* cuadrar.

▸ *vt sep* **1** *(physically)* hacer sitio para. **2** *(in timetable)* hacer un hueco para. **3** *(harmonize)* encajar, cuadrar.
ⓘ *pt & pp* fitted, *ger* fitting.

fitness ['fɪtnəs] *n* **1** *(health)* buena forma física, buen estado físico. **2** *(suitability)* capacidad *f* (for, para).

fitted ['fɪtɪd] *adj* *(cupboard)* empotrado,-a; *(room)* amueblado,-a. COMP fitted carpet moqueta.

fitting ['fɪtɪŋ] *adj (appropriate, proper)* apropiado,-a, adecuado,-a.
▸ *n* SEW prueba.
▸ *n pl* fittings **1** *(accessories)* accesorios *mpl*. **2** *(furnishings)* muebles, cortinas y alfombras.

five [faɪv] *n* cinco.
▸ *adj* cinco.

✎ Consulta también six.

fix [fɪks] *n* **1** *fam (difficult situation)* apuro, aprieto. **2** *(position of ship, aircraft)* posición *f*. **3** *(dishonest arrangement)* tongo.
▸ *vt* **1** *(gen)* fijar. **2** *(decide)* decidir; *(date, meeting, etc)* fijar. **3** *(organize)* arreglar, organizar. **4** *(dishonestly)* amañar. **5** *(repair)* arreglar.
◆ to fix on *vt insep (decide, select - person)* decidir, optar por, escoger; *(- date)* fijar.
◆ to fix up *vt sep* **1** *(accommodate, provide with)* proveer (with, de), conseguir. **2** *(organize)* arreglar, organizar. **3** *(repair, redecorate)* arreglar; *(install)* poner.

fixation [fɪk'seɪʃən] *n* obsesión *f*.

fixture ['fɪkstʃəʳ] *n* SP encuentro.
▸ *n pl* fixtures *(furniture)* muebles *mpl* empotrados.

fizz [fɪz] *n* burbujeo, efervesencia.
▸ *vi* burbujear.

fizzle ['fɪzəl] *vi* burbujear.
◆ to fizzle out *vi* esfumarse, perder fuerza, quedar en nada.

fizzy ['fɪzɪ] *adj (gen)* gaseoso,-a, con gas; *(wine)* espumoso,-a.
ⓘ *comp* fizzier, *superl* fizziest.

fjord [fɪ'ɔːd] *n* fiordo.

flabbergasted ['flæbəgɑːstɪd] *adj* pasmado,-a, atónito,-a.

flabby ['flæbɪ] *adj (part of body)* fofo,-a.
ⓘ *comp* flabbier, *superl* flabbiest.

flaccid ['flæksɪd] *adj* fláccido,-a.

flag¹ [flæg] *n (paving slab)* → flagstone.

flag² [flæg] *n* **1** *(gen)* bandera. **2** MAR pabellón *m*. **3** *(for charity)* banderita.
◆ to flag down *vt sep* hacer señales para que un coche se detenga.

flagellum [flə'dʒɛləm] *n* flagelo.
ⓘ *pl* flagellums o flagella [flə'dʒɛlə].

flagpole ['flægpəʊl] *n* asta de bandera.

flagship ['flægʃɪp] *n* buque *m* insignia.

flagstone ['flægstəʊn] *n (large)* losa; *(small)* loseta.

flair [fleəʳ] *n* talento, don *m*, facilidad *f*.

flake [fleɪk] *n* **1** *(of snow, oats)* copo. **2** *(of skin, soap)* escama. **3** *(of paint)* desconchón *m*, trozo desprendido.
▸ *vi* to flake away/off *(gen)* descamarse; *(paint)* desconcharse.

flamboyant [flæm'bɔɪənt] *adj* llamativo,-a, extravagante.

flame [fleɪm] *n* llama.
▸ *vi* **1** *(burn)* arder. **2** *(glow, shine)* brillar. **3** *(become angry)* montar en cólera.

flame-thrower ['fleɪmθrəʊəʳ] *n* lanzallamas *m*.

flamingo [flə'mɪŋgəʊ] *n* flamenco.
ⓘ *pl* flamingos o flamingoes.

flammable ['flæməbəl] *adj* inflamable

flan [flæn] *n* CULIN tarta rellena.

❌ Flan no significa 'flan', que se traduce por crème caramel.

flange [flændʒ] *n (on wheel)* pestaña; *(of pipe)* reborde *m*.

flank [flæŋk] *n* **1** *(of animal)* ijada, ijar *m*. **2** MIL flanco. **3** *(of building, mountain, etc)* lado, falda.

flannel ['flænəl] *n (material)* franela.

flap [flæp] *n* **1** *(of envelope, pocket)* solapa. **2** *(of tent)* faldón *m*. **3** *(of plane)* alerón *m*.
▸ *vt (wings)* batir; *(arms)* agitar.
▸ *vi* **1** *(wings)* aletear. **2** *(flag, sails)* ondear. **3** *fam* inquietarse.
ⓘ *pt & pp* flapped, *ger* flapping.

flare [fleəʳ] *n* **1** *(flame)* llamarada. **2** *(signal)* bengala.
▸ *vi* **1** llamear. **2** *fig* estallar, encenderse.
◆ to flare up *vi (blow up, erupt)* estallar, encenderse; *(get angry)* enfadarse, montar en cólera.

flared ['fleəd] adj acampanado,-a.

flash [flæʃ] n 1 (of light) destello, centelleo; (of lightning) relámpago. 2 (from firearm) fogonazo. 3 fig destello, rayo. 4 (photography) flash m.
▶ vi brillar, destellar.
▶ vt (shine - light) dirigir, lanzar; (- torch) encender, dirigir.

flashback ['flæʃbæk] n flashback m.

flashlight ['flæʃlaɪt] n 1 (torch) linterna. 2 (photo) flash m.

flashy ['flæʃɪ] adj llamativo,-a.
ⓘ comp flashier, superl flashiest.

flask [flɑːsk] n 1 frasco. 2 CHEM matraz m.

flat¹ [flæt] n (apartment) piso.

flat² [flæt] adj 1 (level, even) llano,-a, plano,-a; (smooth) liso,-a. 2 (shoes) sin tacón. 3 (tyre, ball, etc) desinflado,-a. 4 (battery) descargado,-a. 5 (drink) sin gas. 6 MUS (key) bemol; (voice, instrument) desafinado,-a.
ⓘ comp flatter, superl flattest.
▶ n 1 (plain) llano, llanura. 2 (of hand) palma. 3 MUS bemol m. 4 US (tyre) pinchazo.

flatly ['flætlɪ] adv 1 (categorically) categóricamente, rotundamente. 2 (voice) con voz monótona.

flatten ['flætən] vt 1 (make flat) allanar, aplanar (out, -); (smooth) alisar. 2 (crush) aplastar; (knock down) derribar, tumbar; (knock over) atropellar.

flatter ['flætəʳ] vt 1 (praise) halagar, adular. 2 (suit) favorecer.

flattering ['flætərɪŋ] adj 1 (words) lisonjero,-a, halagüeño,-a. 2 (clothes, etc) favorecedor,-ra.

flattery ['flætərɪ] n adulación f, halagos mpl.

flaunt [flɔːnt] vt hacer alarde de, hacer ostentación de.

flautist ['flɔːtɪst] n flautista mf.

flavor ['fleɪvəʳ] n US → flavour.

flavour ['fleɪvəʳ] n sabor m, gusto.
▶ vt sazonar, condimentar (with, con).

flavouring ['fleɪvərɪŋ] n condimento.

flaw [flɔː] n 1 (fault - in material, product, etc) defecto, tara. 2 (failing - in character) defecto; (- in argument) error m.

flawless ['flɔːləs] adj sin defecto, impecable, perfecto,-a.

flax [flæks] n lino.

fleck [flek] n mota, punto.

fled [fled] pt → flee.)

flee [fliː] vt (run away) huir de.
▶ vi 1 (run away, escape) huir. 2 (vanish) desaparecer.
ⓘ pt & pp fled [fled].

fleece [fliːs] n 1 (sheep's coat, fabric) lana. 2 (sheared) vellón m.

fleet [fliːt] n 1 (of ships) flota. 2 (of vehicles) flota, parque m móvil.

fleeting ['fliːtɪŋ] adj fugaz, efímero,-a.

flesh [fleʃ] n 1 (of animals, humans) carne f. 2 (of fruit) carne f, pulpa.

flew [fluː] pt → fly¹.

flex [fleks] n GB cable m.
▶ vt (body, joints) doblar; (muscles) flexionar.

flexibility [fleksɪ'bɪlɪtɪ] n flexibilidad f.

flexible ['fleksəbəl] adj flexible.

flexor ['fleksəʳ] n flexor.

flexitime ['fleksɪtaɪm] n horario flexible.

flick [flɪk] n 1 (jerk) movimiento rápido, movimiento brusco. 2 (of fingers) capirotazo; (of whip) latigazo, chasquido; (of tail) coletazo. 3 (of pages) hojeada.
◆ **to flick away** vt sep quitar, sacudirse.
◆ **to flick through** vt insep hojear.

flicker ['flɪkəʳ] n 1 (of flame, eyelids) parpadeo; (of light) titileo, parpadeo. 2 fig (slight sign) señal f, muestra; (faint emotion) chispa, pizca.
▶ vi 1 (gen) parpadear; (shadow) bailar. 2 (eyelids) parpadear. 3 (smile) esbozarse.

flies [flaɪs] pt → fly³.

flight [flaɪt] n 1 (journey by air) vuelo: our flight has been delayed nuestro vuelo se ha retrasado. 2 (path) trayectoria. 3 (flock of birds) bandada. 4 (of stairs) tramo. 5 (escape) huida, fuga. COMP **flight attendant** auxiliar mf de vuelo.

flimsy ['flɪmzɪ] adj 1 (thin) fino,-a, ligero,-a. 2 (structure) poco sólido,-a. 3 fig (unconvincing) flojo,-a, pobre, poco convincente.
ⓘ comp flimsier, superl flimsiest.

flinch [flɪntʃ] vi 1 (wince) estremecerse. 2 (shun) retroceder (from, ante).

fling [flɪŋ] *n* **1** *(throw)* lanzamiento. **2** *(wild time)* juerga. **3** *(affair)* aventura (amorosa), romance *m*.
▶ *vt* **1** *(throw)* arrojar, tirar, lanzar. **2** *(move)* echar, lanzar. **3** *(say)* lanzar.
ⓘ *pt & pp* flung [flʌŋ].

flint [flɪnt] *n* **1** *(stone)* sílex *m*; *(piece)* pedernal *m*. **2** *(of lighter)* piedra.

flip [flɪp] *n* **1** *(light blow)* golpecito. **2** *(somersault)* voltereta (en el aire).
▶ *interj fam* ¡ostras!
▶ *vt* **1** *(toss - gen)* echar, tirar al aire; *(coin)* echar a cara o cruz. **2** *(turn over)* dar la vuelta a.
▶ *vi fam (get angry)* perder los estribos; *(go mad)* volverse loco,-a.
ⓘ *pt & pp* flipped, *ger* flipping.

flip-flop [ˈflɪpflɒp] *n* chancla.

flipper [ˈflɪpəʳ] *n* aleta.

flirt [flɜːt] *n* coqueto,-a, ligón,-ona.
▶ *vi (coquette)* flirtear (with, con), coquetear (with, con).

float [fləʊt] *n* **1** *(for fishing)* boya, flotador *m*. **2** *(for swimming)* flotador *m*. **3** *(vehicle - in procession)* carroza; *(- for delivery)* furgoneta.
▶ *vi (gen)* flotar.

flock [flɒk] *n* **1** *(of sheep, goats)* rebaño; *(of birds)* bandada. **2** *fam (crowd)* multitud *f*, tropel *m*.

flood [flʌd] *n* **1** *(overflow of water)* inundación *f*. **2** *(of river)* riada.
▶ *vt* **1** *(gen)* inundar, anegar; *(engine)* ahogar. **2** *fig (with calls, applications, etc)* llover, inundar (with, de).
▶ *vi* **1** *(river)* desbordarse. **2** *fig (cover, fill)* invadir, inundar.

floodgate [ˈflʌdgeɪt] *n* compuerta.

flooding [ˈflʌdɪŋ] *n* inundación *f*.

floodlight [ˈflʌdlaɪt] *n* foco.

floor [flɔːʳ] *n* **1** *(surface)* suelo. **2** GEOG fondo. **3** *(storey)* piso, planta. **4** *(dance)* pista.

❌ Floor no significa 'flor', que se traduce por **flower**.

flop [flɒp] *n fam* fracaso.
▶ *vi* **1** *(fall clumsily)* abalanzarse, arrojarse (into, en); *(sit or lie clumsily)* tumbarse, dejarse caer. **2** *fam (fail)* fracasar.
ⓘ *pt & pp* flopped, *ger* flopping.

floppy [ˈflɒpɪ] *adj* blando,-a, flexible.
COMP **floppy disk** COMPUT disco flexible, disquete *m*.
ⓘ *comp* floppier, *superl* floppiest.

flora [ˈflɔːrə] *n* flora.

florist [ˈflɒrɪst] *n* florista *mf*. COMP **florist's (shop)** floristería.

flounce [flaʊns] *n* SEW volante *m*.

flounder [ˈflaʊndəʳ] *n* *(fish)* platija.
▶ *vi* **1** *(struggle, move with difficulty)* forcejear. **2** *fig (hesitate, dither)* vacilar.

flour [flaʊəʳ] *n* harina.
▶ *vt* enharinar.

flourish [ˈflʌrɪʃ] *n* **1** *(gesture)* ademán *m*, gesto exagerado. **2** *(signature)* rúbrica.
▶ *vt (wave about)* agitar, blandir.
▶ *vi* **1** *(be successful)* florecer, prosperar. **2** *(plant)* crecer bien.

flow [fləʊ] *n* **1** *(gen)* flujo. **2** *(of river)* corriente *f*. **3** *(of traffic)* circulación *f*.
▶ *vi* **1** *(gen)* fluir. **2** *(pour out - blood)* manar; *(- tears)* correr. **3** *(tide)* subir. **4** *(traffic)* circular.
◆ **to flow into** *vi (river)* desembocar en: *the Ebro flows into the sea at Amposta* el Ebro desemboca en el mar en Amposta.

flower [flaʊəʳ] *n* flor *f*.
▶ *vi* florecer.

flowerbed [ˈflaʊəbed] *n* parterre *m*, macizo.

flowerpot [ˈflaʊəpɒt] *n* maceta, tiesto.

flown [fləʊn] *pp* → **fly**.

flu [fluː] *n* gripe *f*: *he's got (the) flu* tiene la gripe.

fluctuate [ˈflʌktjʊeɪt] *vi* fluctuar.

fluency [ˈfluːənsɪ] *n* **1** fluidez *f*. **2** *(of language)* dominio (in, de).

fluent [ˈfluːənt] *adj* **1** *(gen)* fluido,-a. **2** *(language)* fluido,-a: *he speaks fluent English* habla inglés con soltura.

fluff [flʌf] *n* **1** *(down, material)* pelusa, lanilla. **2** *fam (mistake, blunder)* pifia, fallo.
▶ *vt fam (do badly, fail)* hacer mal.

fluffy [ˈflʌfɪ] *adj* **1** *(feathery)* mullido,-a. **2** *(toys)* de peluche.
ⓘ *comp* fluffier, *superl* fluffiest.

fluid [ˈfluːɪd] *adj* **1** *(not solid)* fluido,-a, líquido,-a. **2** *(smooth, graceful)* natural, con soltura. **3** *(not fixed)* flexible.
▶ *n* fluido, líquido.

fluke [flu:k] *n fam* chiripa.

flung [flʌŋ] *pt & pp* → fling.

fluorescent [fluə'resənt] *adj* fluorescente. COMP **fluorescent light/lamp** fluorescente *m*.

flurry ['flʌrɪ] *n* **1** (of wind) ráfaga; (of snow) nevisca. **2** fig (burst) nerviosismo.
ⓘ *pl* flurries.

flush¹ [flʌʃ] *n* (in cards) color *m*.

flush² [flʌʃ] *n* **1** (blush) rubor *m*. **2** (of emotion) acceso, arrebato. **3** (of toilet) cisterna.
▶ *vt* **1** (cause to blush) ruborizar, sonrojar. **2** (clean) limpiar con agua. **3** (toilet) tirar (de) la cadena.
▶ *vi* **1** (blush) ruborizarse. **2** (toilet) funcionar.

fluster ['flʌstər] *vt* poner nervioso,-a.
▶ *n* confusión *f*, agitación *f*.

flute [flu:t] *n* flauta.

flutter ['flʌtər] *n* **1** (excitement) agitación *f*, emoción *f*. **2** (of wings) aleteo. **3** (of eyelashes) pestañeo. **4** fam (bet) apuesta.
▶ *vt* **1** (eyelashes) parpadear. **2** (wings) aletear.
▶ *vi* **1** (flag) ondear. **2** (wings) aletear. **3** (flit) revolotear. **4** (heart) palpitar.

fluvial ['flu:vɪəl] *adj* fluvial.

fly¹ [flaɪ] *vi* **1** volar. **2** (go by plane) ir en avión. **3** (flag, hair) ondear. **4** fam (flee) largarse.
▶ *vt* **1** (plane) pilotar. **2** (send by plane) transportar. **3** (kite) hacer volar. **4** (flag) enarbolar.
ⓘ *pt* flew [flu:], *pp* flown [fləʊn], *ger* flying.
▶ *n pl* flies (on trousers) bragueta *f sing*.
◆ **to fly away / off** *vi* irse volando.

fly² [flaɪ] *adj* GB fam (smart) astuto,-a.
ⓘ *comp* flier, *superl* fliest.

fly³ [flaɪ] *n* mosca.
ⓘ *pl* flies.

flying ['flaɪɪŋ] *n* **1** AV aviación *f*. **2** (action) vuelo.
▶ *adj* **1** (soaring) volante; (animal, machine) volador,-ra, que vuela. **2** (quick) rápido,-a.

flyover ['flaɪəʊvər] *n* GB paso elevado.

foal [fəʊl] *n* potro,-a.
▶ *vi* parir.

foam [fəʊm] *n* espuma.

foamy ['fəʊmɪ] *adj* espumoso,-a.
ⓘ *comp* foamier, *superl* foamiest.

fob [fɒb] *vt* engañar, engatusar.
ⓘ *pt & pp* fobbed, *ger* fobbing.

focal ['fəʊkəl] *adj* focal.

focus ['fəʊkəs] *n* **1** foco. **2** (centre) centro.
ⓘ *pl* focuses o foci ['fəʊsaɪ].
▶ *vt* **1** (camera, etc) enfocar (on, -). **2** fig (concentrate) fijar (on, en), centrar (on, en).
ⓘ *pt & pp* focused o focussed, *ger* focusing o focussing.

fodder ['fɒdər] *n* pienso, forraje *m*.

foetal ['fi:təl] *adj* fetal.

foetus ['fi:təs] *n* feto.

fog [fɒg] *n* niebla.
▶ *vt* **1** (mirror, etc) empañar. **2** (photo) velar. **3** fig complicar.
▶ *vi* empañarse (up/over, -).
ⓘ *pt & pp* fogged, *ger* fogging.

foggy ['fɒgɪ] *adj* **1** de niebla: *it's foggy* hay niebla. **2** (confused) confuso,-a.
ⓘ *comp* foggier, *superl* foggiest.

foglamp ['fɒglæmp] *n* faro antiniebla.

foil¹ [fɔɪl] *vt* (prevent, frustrate) frustrar.

foil² [fɔɪl] *n* **1** (metal paper) papel *m* de plata. **2** (contrast) contraste *m*.

fold¹ [fəʊld] *n* (for sheep) redil *m*, aprisco.

fold² [fəʊld] *n* **1** (crease) pliegue *m*, doblez *m*. **2** GEOG pliegue *m*.
▶ *vt* **1** doblar, plegar (up, -). **2** (wrap) envolver.
▶ *vi* **1** doblarse, plegarse. **2** (go bankrupt) quebrar.

folder ['fəʊldər] *n* carpeta.

folding ['fəʊldɪŋ] *adj* plegable.

folk [fəʊk] *n pl* gente *f sing*.
▶ *adj* popular.
▶ *n pl* **folks** fam (family) familia *f sing*; (friends) amigos *mpl*.

folklore ['fəʊklɔ:r] *n* folklor(e) *m*.

follicle ['fɒlɪkəl] *n* folículo.

follow ['fɒləʊ] *vt* **1** (gen) seguir. **2** (pursue) perseguir. **3** (take interest in) seguir, estar al corriente de.
▶ *vi* **1** (gen) seguir. **2** (understand) entender. **3** (be logical) resultar, derivarse.
◆ **to follow up** *vt sep* **1** (develop) profundizar en. **2** (investigate) investigar.

following ['fɒləʊɪŋ] *adj* siguiente
▸ *prep* después de.
▸ *n (supporters)* seguidores *mpl*.

folly ['fɒlɪ] *n fml* locura, desatino.
ⓘ *pl* follies.

fond [fɒnd] *adj* **1** *(loving)* cariñoso,-a. **2** *(indulgent)* indulgente. **3** *(hope, belief)* vano,-a.

fondle ['fɒndəl] *vt* acariciar.

fondness ['fɒndnəs] *n* **1** cariño (for, a). **2** *(liking)* afición *f* (for, a/por).

font [fɒnt] *n* pila (bautismal).

food [fuːd] *n* comida, alimento.

foodstuffs ['fuːdstʌfs] *n pl* alimentos *mpl*, productos *mpl* alimenticios.

fool [fuːl] *n* **1** tonto,-a, loco,-a. **2** *(jester)* bufón,-ona. [LOC] **to make a fool of** poner en ridículo a. ‖ **to play the fool** hacer el tonto.
▸ *vt* engañar.
▸ *vi* bromear.
◆ **to fool about / fool around** *vi* **1** *(be stupid)* hacer el tonto, hacer el payaso. **2** *(waste time)* perder el tiempo neciamente.

foolish ['fuːlɪʃ] *adj* **1** *(silly)* tonto,-a. **2** *(stupid)* estúpido,-a; *(unwise)* imprudente. **3** *(ridiculous)* ridículo,-a.

foolproof ['fuːlpruːf] *adj* **1** *(plan, method, idea)* infalible. **2** *(machine)* seguro,-a.

foot [fʊt] *n* **1** ANAT pie *m*. **2** *(measurement)* pie *m*. **3** *(bottom)* pie *m*. **4** *(of animal)* pata. [LOC] **on foot** a pie.
ⓘ *pl* feet.

football ['fʊtbɔːl] *n* **1** *(game)* fútbol *m*. **2** *(ball)* balón *m*. [COMP] **football player** futbolista *mf*. ‖ **football pools** quinielas.

🌐 En inglés americano football a secas se refiere al 'fútbol americano'; el 'fútbol' tal como se conoce en Europa se suele llamar soccer.

football ['fʊtbɔːlər] *n* futbolista *mf*.

footlights ['fʊtlaɪts] *n pl* candilejas *fpl*.

footloose ['fʊtluːs] *adj* libre.

footnote ['fʊtnəʊt] *n* nota a pie de página.

footpath ['fʊtpɑːθ] *n* sendero, camino.

footprint ['fʊtprɪnt] *n* huella, pisada.

footstep ['fʊtstep] *n* paso, pisada.

footwear ['fʊtweər] *n* calzado.

for [fɔːr] *prep* **1** *(intended)* para. **2** *(purpose)* para: *what's this for?* ¿para qué sirve esto? **3** *(destination)* para. **4** *(in order to help, on behalf of)* por: *do it for me* hazlo por mí. **5** *(because of, on account of)* por, a causa de. **6** *(past time)* durante; *(future time)* por; *(specific point in time)* para: *I walked for five miles* caminé cinco millas. **8** *(in exchange, as replacement for)* por. **9** *(in favour of, in support of)* por, a favor de. **10** *(despite)* a pesar de, para; *(considering, contrast)* para: *she's very tall for her age* es muy alta para su edad. **11** *(as)* de, como, por. **12** *(in order to obtain)* para: *for further details ...* para más información…
▸ *conj* **6** *fml lit* ya que, puesto que.

forage ['fɒrɪdʒ] *n (food)* forraje *m*.

forbade [fɔːˈbeɪd] *pt* → **forbid**.

forbid [fəˈbɪd] *vt* **1** *(prohibit)* prohibir. **2** *(make impossible)* impedir.
ⓘ *pt* forbade [fɔːˈbeɪd], *pp* forbidden [fɔːˈbɪdən], *ger* forbidding.

forbidden [fɔːˈbɪdən] *pp* → **forbid**.

forbidding [fəˈbɪdɪŋ] *adj (stern)* severo,-a; *(unfriendly)* formidable.

force [fɔːs] *n* **1** *(strength, power, violence)* fuerza. **2** PHYS fuerza. **3** MIL cuerpo.
▸ *vt (oblige)* forzar, obligar.

forceful ['fɔːsfʊl] *adj (person, manner)* enérgico,-a; *(speech)* contundente; *(argument)* convincente.

forceps ['fɔːseps] *n pl* fórceps *m inv*.

ford [fɔːd] *n* vado.
▸ *vt* vadear.

forearm ['fɔːrɑːm] *n* antebrazo.

foreboding [fɔːˈbəʊdɪŋ] *n* presentimiento.

forecast ['fɔːkɑːst] *n* pronóstico, previsión *f*.
▸ *vt* pronosticar.
ⓘ *pt & pp* forecast o forecasted.

forefinger ['fɔːfɪŋgər] *n* (dedo) índice *m*.

forefront ['fɔːfrʌnt] *n* vanguardia.

forego¹ [fɔːˈgəʊ] *vt (precede)* preceder.
ⓘ *pt* forewent [fɔːˈwent], *pp* foregone ['fɔːgɒn], *ger* foregoing.

forego² [fɔːˈgəʊ] *vt* → **forgo**.
ⓘ *pt* forewent [fɔːˈwent], *pp* foregone ['fɔːgɒn], *ger* foregoing.

foregoing [fɔːˈɡəʊɪŋ] *adj* precedente.
foregone [ˈfɔːɡɒn] *pp* → **forego**.
▸ *adj* inevitable.
foreground [ˈfɔːɡraʊnd] *n* primer plano, primer término.
forehead [ˈfɒrɪd, ˈfɔːhed] *n* frente *f*.
foreign [ˈfɒrɪn] *adj* **1** *(from abroad)* extranjero,-a. **2** *(dealing with other countries)* exterior. **3** *(strange)* ajeno,-a, extraño,-a.
foreigner [ˈfɒrɪnəʳ] *n* extranjero,-a.
foreman [ˈfɔːmən] *n* **1** *(of workers)* capataz *m*. **2** *(of jury)* presidente *m* del jurado.
ⓘ *pl* **foremen** [ˈfɔːmən].
foremost [ˈfɔːməʊst] *adj* principal.
forename [ˈfɔːneɪm] *n* nombre *m* (de pila).
forensic [fəˈrensɪk] *adj* forense.
forerunner [ˈfɔːrʌnəʳ] *n* precursor,-ra.
foresaw [fɔːˈsɔː] *pt* → **foresee**.
foresee [fɔːˈsiː] *vt* prever.
ⓘ *pt* **foresaw** [fɔːˈsɔː], *pp* **foreseen** [fɔːˈsiːn], *ger* **foreseeing**.
foreseen [fɔːˈsiːn] *pp* → **foresee**.
foresight [ˈfɔːsaɪt] *n* previsión *f*.
foreskin [ˈfɔːskɪn] *n* prepucio.
forest [ˈfɒrɪst] *n* **1** *(gen)* bosque *m*. **2** *(jungle)* selva.
▸ *adj* forestal.
forestall [fɔːˈstɔːl] *vt* **1** *(preempt)* anticiparse a. **2** *(prevent)* prevenir.
forestry [ˈfɒrɪstrɪ] *n* silvicultura.
foretell [fɔːˈtel] *vt* predecir, pronosticar.
ⓘ *pt & pp* **foretold** [fɔːˈtəʊld].
forethought [ˈfɔːθɔːt] *n* **1** previsión *f*. **2** JUR premeditación *f*.
foretold [fɔːˈtəʊld] *pt & pp* → **foretell**.
forever [fəˈrevəʳ] *adv* **1** *(all the time)* siempre. **2** *(for good)* para siempre.
forewarn [fɔːˈwɔːn] *vt* prevenir.
forewent [fɔːˈwent] *pp* → **forego**.
foreword [ˈfɔːwɜːd] *n* prólogo.
forfeit [ˈfɔːfɪt] *n* **1** *(penalty)* pena, multa. **2** *(in games)* prenda.
▸ *vt* perder, perder (el derecho de).
forgave [fəˈɡeɪv] *pt* → **forgive**.
forge [fɔːdʒ] *n* **1** *(apparatus)* fragua. **2** *(smithy)* forja.

▸ *vt* **1** *(counterfeit)* falsificar. **2** *(metal)* forjar, fraguar.
forgery [ˈfɔːdʒərɪ] *n* falsificación *f*.
ⓘ *pl* **forgeries**.
forget [fəˈɡet] *vt* **1** *(gen)* olvidar, olvidarse de. **2** *(leave behind)* dejar.
ⓘ *pt* **forgot** [fəˈɡɒt], *pp* **forgotten** [fəˈɡɒtən], *ger* **forgetting**.
▸ *vi* olvidarse de, no recordar.
forgive [fəˈɡɪv] *vt* **1** *(pardon)* perdonar. **2** *(let off debt)* perdonar.
ⓘ *pt* **forgave** [fəˈɡeɪv], *pp* **forgiven** [fəˈɡɪvən].
forgiven [fəˈɡɪvən] *pp* → **forgive**.
forgiveness [fəˈɡɪvnəs] *n* perdón *m*.
forgo [fɔːˈɡəʊ] *vt* renunciar a, sacrificar.
ⓘ *pt* **forwent** [fɔːˈwent], *pp* **forgone** [ˈfɔːɡɒn], *ger* **forgoing**.
forgone [fɔːˈɡɒn] *pp* → **forgo**.
forgot [fəˈɡɒt] *pt* → **forget**.
forgotten [fəˈɡɒtən] *pp* → **forget**.
fork [fɔːk] *n* **1** *(for eating)* tenedor *m*. **2** AGR horca, horquilla. **3** *(in road, river, etc)* bifurcación *f*.
▸ *vi* **1** *(road, river, etc)* bifurcarse. **2** *(person, car)* torcer, girar.
▸ *n* **forks** *(on bike)* horquilla.
forlorn [fəˈlɔːn] *adj* **1** *(forsaken)* abandonado,-a. **2** *(desolate)* triste. **3** *(hopeless)* desesperado,-a.
form [fɔːm] *n* **1** *(shape, mode, etc)* forma. **2** *(kind)* clase *f*, tipo. **3** *(formality)* formas *fpl*; *(behaviour)* educación *f*. **4** *(physical condition)* forma. **5** *(mood, spirit)* humor *m*. **6** *(document)* formulario, impreso, hoja. **7** EDUC *(age group)* curso; *(class)* clase *f*.
▸ *vt* **1** *(mould)* moldear; *(make)* hacer, formar. **2** *(be, constitute)* formar, constituir. **3** *fig (idea)* hacerse, formarse.
formal [ˈfɔːməl] *adj* **1** *(gen)* formal. **2** *(dress, dinner)* de etiqueta.

✗ Formal no significa 'formal (serio)', que se traduce por **serious**.

formality [fɔːˈmælɪtɪ] *n* *(correctness)* formalidad *f*; *(convention)* ceremonia.
ⓘ *pl* **formalities**.
format [ˈfɔːmæt] *n* formato.
▸ *vt* COMPUT formatear.
ⓘ *pt & pp* **formatted**, *ger* **formatting**.

formation [fɔːˈmeɪʃən] *n* **1** *(gen)* formación *f*. **2** *(establishment)* creación *f*.

former [ˈfɔːməʳ] *adj* **1** *(earlier)* antiguo,-a; *(person)* ex. **2** *(of two)* primero,-a.
▶ *pron* **the former** aquél, aquélla.

formerly [ˈfɔːməlɪ] *adv* *(previously)* antiguamente, antes.

formidable [ˈfɔːmɪdəbəl] *adj* **1** *(impressive)* formidable. **2** *(daunting)* temible, imponente.

❌ Formidable no significa 'formidable (magnífico)', que se traduce por wonderful.

formula [ˈfɔːmjələ] *n* fórmula.
ⓘ *pl* formulas o formulae [ˈfɔːmjuliː].

formulate [ˈfɔːmjəleɪt] *vt* formular.

formulation [fɔːmjəˈleɪʃən] *n* formulación *f*.

fort [fɔːt] *n* fuerte *m*.

forth [fɔːθ] *adv* *(onwards)* en adelante.

forthcoming [fɔːθˈkʌmɪŋ] *adj* **1** *fml (happening in near future)* próximo,-a. **2** *(available)* disponible. **3** *(communicative)* comunicativo,-a, dispuesto,-a a hablar.

fortieth [ˈfɔːtɪəθ] *adj* cuadragésimo,-a.
▶ *adv* en cuadragésimo lugar.
▶ *n (fraction)* cuadragésimo; *(one part)* cuadragésima parte *f*.

✎ Consulta también sixtieth.

fortification [fɔːtɪfɪˈkeɪʃən] *n* fortificación *f*.

fortify [ˈfɔːtɪfaɪ] *vt* **1** MIL fortificar. **2** *(strengthen)* fortalecer.
ⓘ *pt & pp* fortified, *ger* fortifying.

fortnight [ˈfɔːtnaɪt] *n* GB quincena, quince días *mpl*.

fortress [ˈfɔːtrəs] *n* fortaleza.

fortunate [ˈfɔːtʃənət] *adj* afortunado,-a.

fortunately [ˈfɔːtʃənətlɪ] *adv* afortunadamente, por suerte.

fortune [ˈfɔːtʃən] *n* **1** *(fate)* fortuna; *(luck)* suerte *f*. **2** *(money)* fortuna.

fortune-teller [ˈfɔːtʃənteləʳ] *n* adivino,-a.

forty [ˈfɔːtɪ] *adj* cuarenta.
▶ *n* cuarenta *m*.

✎ Consulta también sixty.

forum [ˈfɔːrəm] *n* foro.

forward [ˈfɔːwəd] *adv* [como adverbio, también forwards] **1** *(gen)* hacia adelante. **2** *(time)* en adelante.
▶ *adj* **1** *(position)* delantero,-a, frontal; *(movement)* hacia delante. **2** *(future)* a largo plazo. **3** *(advanced)* adelantado,-a, precoz. **4** *(too bold, too eager)* atrevido,-a, descarado,-a, fresco,-a.
▶ *vt* **1** *(send on to new address)* remitir; *(send goods)* enviar, expedir. **2** *fml (further, advance)* adelantar, fomentar.

forwent [fɔːˈwent] *pt* → forgo.

fossil [ˈfɒsəl] *n* fósil *m*.
▶ *adj* fósil.

foster [ˈfɒstəʳ] *vt* **1** *(child)* acoger temporalmente. **2** *(encourage)* fomentar, promover.
▶ *adj* adoptivo,-a.

fought [fɔːt] *pt & pp* → fight.

foul [faʊl] *adj* **1** *(dirty, disgusting)* asqueroso,-a; *(smell)* fétido,-a. **2** *(language)* grosero,-a, obsceno,-a.
▶ *n* SP falta (on, contra).
▶ *vt* **1** *(dirty)* ensuciar; *(pollute)* contaminar. **2** *(snag)* enredar. **3** SP cometer una falta contra.

found¹ [faʊnd] *vt (metals)* fundir.

found² [faʊnd] *vt* **1** *(establish)* fundar. **2** *(base)* basar (on, en).

found³ [faʊnd] *pt & pp* → find.

foundation [faʊnˈdeɪʃən] *n* **1** *(act, organization)* fundación *f*. **2** *(basis)* fundamento, base *f*. **3** *(make-up)* base *f*.
▶ *n pl* **foundations** cimientos *mpl*.

founder¹ [ˈfaʊndəʳ] *vi* **1** *(plan, etc)* fracasar, malograrse. **2** *(ship)* hundirse. **3** *(horse)* dar un traspié.

founder² [ˈfaʊndəʳ] *n* fundador,-ra.

foundry [ˈfaʊndrɪ] *n* fundición *f*.
ⓘ *pl* foundries.

fountain [ˈfaʊntən] *n* **1** fuente *f*. **2** *(jet)* surtidor *m*, chorro.

four [fɔːʳ] *adj* cuatro.
▶ *n* cuatro.

✎ Consulta también six.

fourteen [fɔːˈtiːn] *adj* catorce.
▶ *n* catorce *m*.

✎ Consulta también six.

fourteenth [fɔːˈtiːnθ] *adj* decimocuarto,-a.
► *adv* en decimocuarto lugar.
► *n* **1** *(in series)* decimocuarto,-a. **2** *(fraction)* decimocuarto; *(one part)* decimocuarta parte *f*.

✎ Consulta también sixth.

fourth [fɔːθ] *adj* cuarto,-a.
► *adv* cuarto, en cuarto lugar.
► *n* **1** *(in series)* cuarto,-a. **2** *(fraction)* cuarto; *(one part)* cuarta parte *f*.

✎ Consulta también sixth.

fowl [faʊl] *n* ave *f* de corral.
ⓘ *pl* fowl.

fox [fɒks] *n* zorro,-a.
► *vt* **1** *fam (trick)* engañar. **2** *(confuse)* dejar perplejo,-a, confundir, despistar.

foxy [ˈfɒksɪ] *adj fam* astuto,-a.
ⓘ *comp* foxier, *superl* foxiest.

foyer [ˈfɔɪeɪ, ˈfɔɪəʳ] *n* vestíbulo.

fraction [ˈfrækʃən] *n* **1** *(division)* fracción *f*. **2** *(small part, bit)* poquito.

fractional [ˈfrækʃənəl] *adj* **1** *(in fractions)* fraccionario,-a. **2** *(very small)* muy pequeño,-a, ínfimo,-a.

fracture [ˈfræktʃəʳ] *n* fractura.
► *vt* fracturar.
► *vi* fracturarse.

fragile [ˈfrædʒaɪl] *adj* **1** frágil. **2** *fig (health)* delicado,-a.

fragility [frəˈdʒɪlɪtɪ] *n* fragilidad *f*.

fragment [*(n)* ˈfrægmənt; *(vb)* frægˈment] *n* fragmento.
► *vi* fragmentarse.

fragmentation [frægmənˈteɪʃən] *n* fragmentación *f*.

fragrance [ˈfreɪgrəns] *n* fragancia.

fragrant [ˈfreɪgrənt] *adj* fragante.

frail [freɪl] *adj* **1** frágil, delicado,-a. **2** *(morally weak)* débil.

frame [freɪm] *n* **1** *(of building, machine, tent)* armazón *f*. **2** *(of bed)* armadura. **3** *(of bicycle)* cuadro. **4** *(of spectacles)* montura. **5** *(of window, door, picture, etc)* marco. **6** CINEM fotograma *m*. **7** *(of comic)* viñeta.
► *vt* **1** *(picture)* enmarcar. **2** *(door)* encuadrar.

framework [ˈfreɪmwɜːk] *n* **1** armazón *f*. **2** *fig* estructura, sistema *m*, marco.

franc [fræŋk] *n* franco.

France [frɑːns] *n* Francia.

franchise [ˈfræntʃaɪz] *n* **1** COMM concesión *f*, franquicia. **2** *(vote)* derecho de voto.

frank [fræŋk] *adj* franco,-a.
► *vt* franquear.

frantic [ˈfræntɪk] *adj* **1** *(hectic)* frenético,-a. **2** *(anxious)* desesperado,-a.

fraternal [frəˈtɜːnəl] *adj* fraternal.

fraternity [frəˈtɜːnɪtɪ] *n* **1** *(brotherhood)* fraternidad *f*. **2** *(society)* asociación *f*. **3** REL hermandad *f*, cofradía. **4** US *(university)* club *m* de estudiantes.
ⓘ *pl* fraternities.

fraud [frɔːd] *n* **1** *(act)* fraude *m*. **2** *(person)* impostor,-ra, farsante *mf*.

fraught [frɔːt] *adj* **1** *(filled, charged)* lleno,-a (with, de), cargado,-a (with, de). **2** *fam (worried)* nervioso,-a, alterado,-a, tenso,-a.

fray¹ [freɪ] *vi* **1** *(cloth)* deshilacharse, raerse. **2** *(tempers, nerves, etc)* crisparse.

fray² [freɪ] *n* contienda, lucha.

freak [friːk] *n* *(monster)* monstruo; *(strange person)* bicho raro. **2** *fam (fan)* fanático,-a. **3** *(eccentric)* estrafalario,-a.
► *adj (unusual)* insólito,-a; *(unexpected)* inesperado,-a.
◆ **to freak out** *vt sep* flipar, alucinar.

freckle [ˈfrekəl] *n* peca.

free [friː] *adj* **1** *(gen)* libre. **2** *(without cost)* gratuito,-a, gratis; *(exempt)* libre (from, de).
► *adv* **1** *(gratis)* gratis. **2** *(loose)* suelto,-a.
► *vt* **1** *(liberate, release - person)* poner en libertad, liberar; *(- animal)* soltar. **2** *(rid)* deshacerse (of/from, de), librarse (of/from, de). **3** *(loosen, untie)* soltar, desatar.

freedom [ˈfriːdəm] *n* libertad *f*.

freehand [ˈfriːhænd] *adj* a mano alzada.

freelance [ˈfriːlɑːns] *adj* independiente, autónomo,-a.
► *n* persona que trabaja por cuenta propia.
► *vi* trabajar por cuenta propia.

freestyle ['fri:staɪl] *n (swimming)* estilo libre.

freeway ['fri:weɪ] *n* US autopista.

freewheel [fri:'wi:l] *vi (cycle)* ir a rueda libre; *(car)* ir en punto muerto.

freeze [fri:z] *n* **1** METEOR helada. **2** COMM congelación *f*.
▶ *vt (gen)* congelar.
▶ *vi* **1** *(liquid)* helarse; *(food)* congelarse. **2** METEOR helar.
ⓘ *pt* froze [frəʊz], *pp* frozen [frəʊzən], *ger* freezing.

freezer ['fri:zəʳ] *n* congelador *m*.

freeze-up ['fri:zʌp] *n* helada.

freight [freɪt] *n* **1** *(transport)* transporte *m*. **2** *(goods)* carga, flete *m*. **3** *(price)* flete *m*.
▶ *vt* transportar.

freighter ['freɪtəʳ] *n (ship)* buque *m* de carga; *(aircraft)* avión *m* de carga.

French [frentʃ] *adj* francés,-esa.
▶ *n (language)* francés *m*.
▶ *n pl* the French los franceses *mpl*.

Frenchman ['frentʃmən] *n* francés *m*.
ⓘ *pl* Frenchmen ['frentʃmən].

Frenchwoman ['frentʃwʊmən] *n* francesa.
ⓘ *pl* Frenchwomen ['frentʃwɪmɪn].

frenzy ['frenzɪ] *n* frenesí *m*.
ⓘ *pl* frenzies.

frequency ['fri:kwənsɪ] *n* frecuencia.
ⓘ *pl* frequencies.

frequent [*(adj)* 'fri:kwənt; *(vb)* frɪ'kwent] *adj* frecuente.
▶ *vt* frecuentar.

fresco ['freskəʊ] *n* fresco.
ⓘ *pl* frescos o frescoes.

fresh [freʃ] *adj* **1** *(gen)* fresco,-a. **2** *(water)* dulce. **3** *(air)* puro,-a.

freshen ['freʃən] *vt* refrescar.
▶ *vi* refrescarse.

freshly ['freʃlɪ] *adv* recién: *freshly baked bread* pan recién hecho.

freshness ['freʃnəs] *n* **1** *(brightness)* frescura. **2** *(cool)* frescor *m*. **3** *(newness)* novedad *f*. **4** *fam (cheek)* descaro.

freshwater ['freʃwæɔ:təʳ] *adj* de agua dulce: *freshwater fish* pez de agua dulce.

fret¹ [fret] *vi* preocuparse (about/at/over, por).

▶ *vt (wear away)* raer, desgastar.
ⓘ *pt & pp* fretted, *ger* fretting.
▶ *n (worry)* preocupación *f*.

fret² [fret] *n (on guitar)* traste *m*.

friar [fraɪəʳ] *n* fraile *m*.

fricative ['frɪkətɪv] *adj* fricativo,-a.
▶ *n* fricativa.

friction ['frɪkʃən] *n* **1** *(conflict)* fricción *f*, roces *mpl*. **2** *(rubbing)* rozamiento, roce *m*.

Friday ['fraɪdɪ] *n* viernes *m*.

> ✎ Para ejemplos de uso, consulta Saturday.

fridge [frɪdʒ] *n* nevera, frigorífico.

fried [fraɪd] *pt & pp* → fry.
▶ *adj* frito,-a.

friend [frend] *n* **1** amigo,-a, compañero,-a. **2** *(helper, supporter)* amigo,-a (of/to, de).

friendly ['frendlɪ] *adj* **1** *(person)* simpático,-a, amable. **2** *(atmosphere)* acogedor,-ra. **3** *(smile, manner, etc)* amable.
ⓘ *comp* friendlier, *superl* friendliest.

friendship ['frendʃɪp] *n* amistad *f*.

frieze [fri:z] *n* **1** *(painted)* friso. **2** *(wallpaper)* cenefa.

frigate ['frɪgət] *n* fragata.

fright [fraɪt] *n* **1** *(shock)* susto. **2** *(fear)* miedo.

frighten ['fraɪtən] *vt* asustar, espantar.

frightfully ['fraɪtfʊlɪ] *adv fam* muchísimo.

frigid ['frɪdʒɪd] *adj* **1** *(sexually)* frígido,-a. **2** *(icy)* glacial, muy frío,-a.

frill [frɪl] *n (on dress)* volante *m*.
▶ *n pl* frills *(decorations)* adornos *mpl*.

fringe [frɪndʒ] *n* **1** *(decorative)* fleco. **2** *(of hair)* flequillo. **3** *(edge)* borde *m*.

frisk [frɪsk] *vt (search)* registrar, cachear.
▶ *vi (frolic)* brincar, retozar.

frisky ['frɪskɪ] *adj (child, animal)* juguetón,-ona; *(adult)* vivo,-a, vital.
ⓘ *comp* friskier, *superl* friskiest.

fritter ['frɪtəʳ] *n* CULIN buñuelo.

frivolity [frɪ'vɒlətɪ] *n* frivolidad *f*.
ⓘ *pl* frivolities.

frizzy ['frɪzɪ] *adj* crespo,-a, rizado,-a.
ⓘ *comp* frizzier, *superl* frizziest.

frock [frɒk] *n* vestido.

frog [frɒg] *n* rana.

frolic ['frɒlɪk] *vi* juguetear, retozar.
▶ *n* aventura.

from [frɒm] *prep* **1** *(starting at)* de; *(train, plane)* procedente de: *the train from Madrid* el tren procedente de Madrid. **2** *(origin, source)* de, desde. **9** *(because of)* por, a causa de. **10** *(considering, according to)* según, por. **11** *(indicating difference)* de; *(when distinguishing)* entre. **12** *(indicating position)* desde. LOC **from now on** de ahora en adelante, a partir de ahora.

front [frʌnt] *n* **1** *(forward part)* parte *f* delantera, frente *m*. **2** METEOR frente *m*. **3** *(facade)* fachada. **4** MIL frente *m*. **5** *(promenade)* paseo marítimo.
▶ *adj* delantero,-a, de delante.
▶ *vi (face)* dar (on/onto, a).
▶ *vt* **1** *(lead, head)* encabezar. **2** *(present)* presentar.

frontalis [frən'talɪs] *n* músculo frontal.

frontier [frʌn'tɪər] *n* frontera.
▶ *adj* fronterizo,-a.

front-page [frʌnt'peɪdʒ] *adj* de portada, de primera plana.

frost [frɒst] *n* **1** *(covering)* escarcha. **2** *(freezing)* helada.
▶ *vt* helar, cubrir de escarcha.

frostbite ['frɒstbaɪt] *n* congelación *f*.

frosted ['frɒstɪd] *adj* **1** *(glass)* esmerilado,-a. **2** CULIN recubierto,-a de azúcar glas, escarchado,-a.

frosty ['frɒstɪ] *adj* **1** METEOR *(cold with frost)* de helada; *(very cold)* helado,-a, muy frío,-a. **2** METEOR *(covered with frost)* escarchado,-a, cubierto,-a de escarcha. **3** *fig (unfriendly)* glacial.
ⓘ *comp* **frostier**, *superl* **frostiest**.

froth [frɒθ] *n (gen)* espuma.

frown [fraun] *n* ceño.
▶ *vi* fruncir el ceño.

froze [frəuz] *pt* → **freeze**.

frozen ['frəuzən] *pp* → **freeze**.
▶ *adj* **1** *(water, ground)* helado,-a. **2** *(food)* congelado,-a.

fructose ['frʌktəuz] *n* fructosa.

frugal ['fru:gəl] *adj* frugal.

fruit [fru:t] *n* **1** *(food)* fruta. **2** BOT fruto. **3** *(result, reward)* fruto.
▶ *adj* de fruta. COMP **fruit juice** zumo de fruta. ‖ **fruit salad** macedonia.
▶ *vi* dar fruto.

fruitful ['fru:tful] *adj* fructífero,-a.

frustrate [frʌ'streɪt] *vt* **1** *(thwart)* frustrar. **2** *(upset)* frustrar.

frustration [frʌ'streɪʃən] *n* frustración *f*.

fry¹ [fraɪ] *vt* freír.
▶ *vi* **1** freírse. **2** *fig (in sun)* asarse, achicharrarse.
ⓘ *pt & pp* **fried**, *ger* **frying**.

fry² [fraɪ] *n pl (fish)* alevines *mpl*.

fryer ['fraɪər] *n (frying pan)* sartén *f*.

frying pan ['fraɪɪŋpæn] *n* sartén *f*.

ft ['fut, 'fi:t] *abbr* **(foot, feet)** pie *m*, pies *mpl*.

fuel [fjuəl] *n* **1** *(gen)* combustible *m*. **2** *(for motors)* carburante *m*.
▶ *vt* **1** *(plane)* abastecer de combustible; *(car)* echar gasolina. **2** *fig (make worse)* empeorar; *(encourage)* alimentar.

fugitive ['fju:dʒɪtɪv] *n (from danger, war, etc)* fugitivo,-a; *(from justice)* prófugo,-a.
▶ *adj* fugitivo,-a.

fulcrum ['fulkrəm] *n* fulcro.

fulfil [ful'fɪl] *vt* **1** *(promise, duty)* cumplir. **2** *(task, plan, ambition)* realizar. **3** *(role, function, order)* efectuar, desempeñar. **4** *(need, desire, wish)* satisfacer.
ⓘ *pt & pp* **fulfilled**, *ger* **fulfilling**.

fulfill [ful'fɪl] *vt* US → **fulfil**.

fulfilled [ful'fɪld] *pt & pp* → **fulfill**.
▶ *adj* realizado,-a, satisfecho,-a.

full [ful] *adj* **1** *(gen)* lleno,-a. **2** *(week, day)* cargado,-a, movido,-a. **3** *(entire, complete)* completo,-a. **4** *(highest or greatest possible)* máximo,-a. LOC **full time** a jornada completa. COMP **full board** pensión *f* completa. ‖ **full stop** punto.
▶ *adv (directly)* justo, de lleno.

full-length [ful'leŋθ] *adj* **1** *(mirror, portrait)* de cuerpo entero. **2** *(garment)* largo,-a. **3** *(film)* de largo metraje.

full-scale [ful'skeɪl] *adj* **1** *(actual size)* de tamaño natural. **2** *(complete, total)* completo,-a, total.

full-time [ful'taɪm] *adj* a tiempo completo, de jornada completa.
▶ *adv* a tiempo completo.

fumble ['fʌmbəl] *vt* dejar caer.
▶ *vi* **to fumble for** buscar a tientas.
▶ *vi* **to fumble with** hacer torpemente.

fume [fjuːm] *vi* **1** *(produce smoke, etc)* echar humo. **2** *fig (show anger)* echar humo, subirse por las paredes.
▸ *n pl* **fumes** humos *mpl*.

❌ To fume no significa 'fumar', que se traduce por to smoke.

fumigate ['fjuːmɪɡeɪt] *vt* fumigar.

fun [fʌn] *n* **1** *(enjoyment, pleasure)* diversión *f*: *it'll be good fun when we go camping* lo pasaremos muy bien cuando nos vayamos de camping. **2** *(amusement)* gracia: *it's no fun staying in alone on Saturday night* no tiene gracia quedarse solo en casa el sábado por la noche.
▸ *adj (humorous, amusing)* divertido,-a.

function ['fʌŋkʃən] *n* **1** *(purpose, use, duty)* función *f*. **2** *(ceremony)* acto, ceremonia; *(reception)* recepción *f*. **3** MATH función *f*.
▸ *vi* funcionar. LOC **to fulfil a function** desempeñar una función. COMP **function key** tecla de función.

functional ['fʌŋkʃənəl] *adj* **1** *(operational)* funcional. **2** *(practical, useful)* práctico,-a.

fund [fʌnd] *n* **1** *(sum of money)* fondo. **2** *(supply)* fuente *f*.
▸ *vt* **1** *(finance)* patrocinar. **2** *(debt)* consolidar.
▸ *n pl* **funds** *(financial resources)* fondos *mpl*.

fundamental [fʌndə'mentəl] *adj* fundamental.
▸ *n pl* **fundamentals** *(essential part, basic rule)* fundamentos *mpl*, reglas *fpl* básicas.

fundamentalist [fʌndə'mentəlɪst] *adj* REL fundamentalista, integrista.
▸ *n* REL fundamentalista *mf*, integrista *mf*.

funeral ['fjuːnərəl] *n* entierro, funeral *m*.
▸ *adj* fúnebre.

funfair ['fʌnfeər] *n* GB feria, parque *m* de atracciones.

fungus ['fʌŋɡəs] *n* hongo.
ⓘ *pl* **funguses** o **fungi** ['fʌndʒaɪ].

funicular [fjuː'nɪkjələr] *n* funicular *m*.

funk [fʌŋk] *n* MUS funky *m*.

funky ['fʌŋkɪ] *adj* **1** MUS funky. **2** *fam (fashionable)* guay, chulo,-a.
ⓘ *comp* **funkier**, *superl* **funkiest**.

funnel ['fʌnəl] *n* **1** *(for liquid)* embudo. **2** *(chimney)* chimenea.

▸ *vi* verterse.
▸ *vt fig (channel)* encauzar.

funny ['fʌnɪ] *adj* **1** *(amusing)* gracioso,-a, divertido,-a: *I don't find your remarks at all funny* tus comentarios no son nada graciosos. **2** *(strange)* raro,-a, extraño,-a, curioso,-a: *the funny thing is that …* lo curioso es que … **3** *fam (slightly ill)* rarillo,-a, malito,-a; *(slightly mad)* chiflado,-a: *I feel funny* no me encuentro bien.
ⓘ *comp* **funnier**, *superl* **funniest**.

fur [fɜːr] *n* **1** *(of living animal)* pelo, pelaje *m*. **2** *(of dead animal)* piel *f*. **3** *(garment)* abrigo de piel. **4** *(on tongue)* sarro.
▸ *adj* de piel. COMP **fur coat** abrigo de pieles.

furious ['fjʊərɪəs] *adj (very angry)* furioso,-a: *she'll be furious if we break anything* se pondrá furiosa si rompemos algo; *he's got a furious temper* tiene muy mal genio.

furnace ['fɜːnəs] *n* horno.

furnish ['fɜːnɪʃ] *vt* **1** *(house, etc)* amueblar (with, de): *I'd like to rent a furnished flat* quisiera alquilar un piso amueblado. **2** *fml (supply - material)* suministrar, proveer; *(- information, etc)* facilitar, proporcionar.

furnishings ['fɜːnɪʃɪŋz] *n pl* muebles, cortinas y alfombras.

furniture ['fɜːnɪtʃər] *n* mobiliario, muebles *mpl*: *I need some new furniture* necesito unos muebles nuevos.

furrow ['fʌrəʊ] *n* **1** AGR surco. **2** *(wrinkle)* arruga.
▸ *vt* **1** AGR surcar. **2** *(forehead)* arrugar.

furry ['fɜːrɪ] *adj* **1** *(hairy)* peludo,-a. **2** *(scaly)* sarroso,-a.
ⓘ *comp* **furrier**, *superl* **furriest**.

further ['fɜːðər] *adj* **1** *(farther)* más lejos: *she lives further down the road* vive más abajo de la calle. **2** *(more, additional)* más, adicional; *(new)* nuevo,-a: *I have just one further question* tengo una pregunta más; *this office will remain closed until further notice* esta oficina permanecerá cerrada hasta nuevo aviso; *for further information, please contact …* para más información, póngase en contacto con …
▸ *adv* **1** *(farther)* más lejos: *is it much further?* ¿queda mucho más?; *don't go any further* no vayas más lejos. **2** *(more, to a*

greater degree) más: *the police want to take the matter further* la policía quiere investigar más el asunto; *I'd like to go further into this subject* me gustaría estudiar el tema más a fondo. **3** *fml (besides)* además: *further, I'd like to complain about the lack of parking spaces* además, quisiera quejarme de la falta de aparcamientos.

▶ *vt (advance, promote)* fomentar, promover: *he would have gone to any lengths to further his career* hubiera hecho cualquier cosa para promover su propia carrera. LOC **this must not go any further** esto tiene que quedar entre nosotros, esto no tiene que salir de aquí. **further to** con referencia a, referente a: *further to your letter of the 6th inst* con referencia a su carta del día 6 del corriente. COMP **further education** estudios *mpl* superiores.

✎ Consulta también far.

furthermore [fɜː'ðə'mɔː'] *adv fml* además.

furthest ['fɜː'ðɪst] *adj* → **far, farthest, further.**
▶ *adv* → **far, further.**

furtive ['fɜː'tɪv] *adj* furtivo,-a.

fury ['fjʊəri] *n* furia. LOC **to be in a fury** estar furioso,-a. **to fly into a fury** ponerse hecho,-a una furia.
ⓘ *pl* **furies.**

fuse [fjuːz] *n* **1** ELEC fusible *m*, plomo: *the fuses blew* saltaron los fusibles, se fundieron los plomos. **2** *(wick)* mecha; *(detonator)* espoleta. LOC **to blow a fuse 1** *(appliance)* saltar el fusible de, fundirse el plomo de. **2** *(person)* estallar, explotar. COMP **fuse box** caja de fusibles.
▶ *vt* **1** *(cause to stop working, melt)* fundir- **2** *fig (merge)* fusionar.
▶ *vi* **1** *(stop working, melt)* fundirse: *the lights have fused* se han fundido los plomos. **2** *fig (merge)* fusionarse: *the two companies fused* las dos empresas se fusionaron.

fuselage ['fjuːzəlɑːʒ] *n* fuselaje *m*.

fusillade [fjuːzə'leɪd] *n* tiroteo,.

fusion ['fjuːʒən] *n* fusión *f*.

fuss [fʌs] *n* **1** *(commotion, nervous excitement)* alboroto, jaleo. **2** *(angry scene, dispute)* escándalo, problemas *mpl*; *(complaints)* quejas *fpl*.
▶ *vt (pester, annoy, bother)* molestar: *stop fussing me* no me molestes.
▶ *vi* **1** *(worry, fret)* preocuparse, inquietarse: *don't fuss, we'll get there on time* no te preocupes, llegaremos a tiempo. **2** *(pay excessive attention to)* preocuparse excesivamente (over, de). LOC **to make a fuss / kick up a fuss** *(complain strongly)* armar un escándalo, montar una escena. **to make a fuss of** SB deshacerse por ALGN.

fussy ['fʌsi] *adj* **1** *(concerned with details)* quisquilloso,-a, exigente. **2** *(nervous about small things)* nervioso,-a. **3** *(too elaborate)* recargado,-a.
ⓘ *comp* **fussier**, *superl* **fussiest**.

fusty ['fʌsti] *adj* **1** *(musty)* mohoso,-a, rancio,-a; *(stale)* que huele a cerrado. **2** *(old-fashioned)* chapado,-a a la antigua.
ⓘ *comp* **fustier**, *superl* **fustiest**.

futile ['fjuːtaɪl] *adj* vano,-a, inútil: *a futile attempt to save him* un intento inútil de salvarlo.

future ['fjuːtʃər] *adj* futuro,-a: *my future husband* mi futuro marido; *we arranged to meet at some future time* quedamos para vernos en un futuro. COMP **future tense** futuro.
▶ *n* **1** futuro, porvenir *m*: *the future is promising* el futuro es prometedor. **2** *(verb tense)* futuro. LOC **in future** en el futuro, de aquí en adelante. **in the future** en el futuro. **in the distant future** en un futuro lejano. **in the near future** en un futuro próximo. **in the not too distant future** en un futuro no muy lejano.

fuzz [fʌz] *n (fluff)* pelusa; *(fine hair)* vello.

fuzzy ['fʌzi] *adj* **1** *(frizzy)* rizado,-a, crespo,-a; *(fluffy)* con pelusilla. **2** *(blurred)* borroso,-a, movido,-a.
ⓘ *comp* **fuzzier**, *superl* **fuzziest**.

F

G

G, g [giː] *n* **1** *(the letter)* G, g *f*. **2** MUS sol *m*.

g [græm] *symb* **(gram, gramme)** gramo; *(abbreviation)* g.

gab [gæb] *n* labia, palique *m*. LOC **to have the gift of the gab** tener el pico de oro.
▶ *vi* charlar, parlotear.
ⓘ *pt & pp* **gabbed**, *ger* **gabbing**.

gabardine ['gæbədiːn] *n* gabardina.

gabble ['gæbəl] *n* chapurreo.
▶ *vt* farfullar, charlotear.

gadfly ['gædflaɪ] *n* ZOOL tábano.
ⓘ *pl* **gadflies**.

gadget ['gædʒɪt] *n fam* aparato, artilugio, chisme *m*.

Gaelic ['geɪlɪk] *adj* gaélico,-a.
▶ *n (language)* gaélico.

gaffe [gæf] *n* metedura de pata.

gag [gæg] *n* **1** *(cover for the mouth)* mordaza. **2** *(joke)* chiste *m*, gag *m*, broma.
▶ *vt* amordazar.
▶ *vi* tener náuseas.
ⓘ *pt & pp* **gagged**, *ger* **gagging**.

gaily ['geɪlɪ] *adv* alegremente.

gain [geɪn] *n* **1** *(achievement)* logro. **2** *(profit)* ganancia. **3** *(increase)* aumento.
▶ *vt* **1** *(achieve)* lograr, conseguir. **2** *(obtain)* ganar. **3** *(increase)* aumentar. **4** *(clock)* adelantar.
▶ *vi* **1** *(clock)* adelantar. **2** *(shares)* subir.

gait [geɪt] *n* andares *mpl*.

gaiter ['geɪtəʳ] *n* polaina.

galactic [gə'læktɪk] *adj* galáctico,-a.

galaxy ['gæləksɪ] *n* galaxia.
ⓘ *pl* **galaxies**.

gale [geɪl] *n (wind)* vendaval *m*; *(storm)* tempestad *f*.

gall¹ [gɔːl] *n fig* descaro, caradura. COMP **gall bladder** vesícula biliar.

gall² [gɔːl] *vt* irritar, molestar.

gallant ['gælənt] *adj* **1** *(brave)* valiente. **2** *(chivalrous)* galante.

galleon ['gælɪən] *n* galeón *m*.

gallery ['gælərɪ] *n* **1** *(gen)* galería. **2** *(in theatre)* gallinero.
ⓘ *pl* **galleries**.

galley ['gælɪ] *n* **1** *(ship)* galera. **2** *(kitchen on ships)* cocina.

gallon ['gælən] *n* galón *m*.

✎ Equivale en GB a 4,55 litros y en US 3,78 litros.

gallop ['gæləp] *n* galope *m*.
▶ *vi* galopar.

gallows ['gæləuz] *n pl* horca *sing*, patíbulo *sing*.

galore [gə'lɔːʳ] *adj* en abundancia.

galvanize ['gælvənaɪz] *vt* galvanizar.

gamble ['gæmbəl] *n* **1** *(risky undertaking)* empresa arriesgada. **2** *(risk)* riesgo. **3** *(bet)* jugada, apuesta.
▶ *vt* jugar(se).
▶ *vi* **1** *(bet)* apostar. **2** *(take a risk)* arriesgarse, confiar.

gambler ['gæmbləʳ] *n* jugador,-ra.

gambling ['gæmblɪŋ] *n* juego.

game [geɪm] *n* **1** juego. **2** *(match)* partido. **3** *(of cards, chess, etc)* partida. **4** *(hunting)* caza. COMP **game reserve** coto de caza.
▶ *adj* dispuesto,-a, listo,-a.
▶ *n pl* **games** GB educación *f sing* física.

gamekeeper ['geɪmkiːpəʳ] *n* guardabosque *mf*.

gammon ['gæmən] *n* GB jamón *m (ahumado o curado a la sal)*.

gamut ['gæmət] *n* gama, serie *f*.

gander ['gændəʳ] *n* ganso.

gang [gæŋ] *n* **1** *(criminals)* banda. **2** *(youths)* pandilla.

gangplank ['gæŋplæŋk] n plancha.

gangrene ['gæŋgri:n] n gangrena.

gangster ['gæŋstə'] n gángster m.

gangway ['gæŋweɪ] n 1 GB (aisle, passage) pasillo. 2 (on ship) pasarela.

gaol [dʒeɪl] n GB cárcel f.

✎ Consulta también jail.

gap [gæp] n 1 (hole) abertura, hueco. 2 (crack) brecha. 3 (empty space) espacio. 4 (blank) blanco. 5 (time) intervalo.

gape [geɪp] vi 1 abrirse. 2 (stare) mirar boquiabierto,-a.

garage ['gæra:ʒ, 'gærɪdʒ] n 1 garaje m. 2 (for repairs) taller m mecánico. 3 (for petrol, etc) gasolinera.

garbage ['ga:bɪdʒ] n 1 US basura. 2 GB desperdicios mpl. 3 fig tonterías fpl, majaderías fpl, sandeces fpl.

garbled ['ga:bʰld] adj confuso,-a.

garden ['ga:dʰn] n jardín m.
▶ vi cuidar el jardín.

gardener ['ga:dʰnə'] n (gen) jardinero,-a; (of vegetables) hortelano,-a.

gargle ['ga:gʰl] vi hacer gárgaras.

gargoyle ['ga:gɔɪl] n gárgola.

garish ['geərɪʃ] adj (colour) chillón,-ona, llamativo,-a; (light) cegador,-ra, deslumbrante.

garland ['ga:lənd] n guirnalda.

garlic ['ga:lɪk] n ajo.

garment ['ga:mənt] n (clothes) prenda.

garnet ['ga:nɪt] n granate m.

garnish ['ga:nɪʃ] n guarnición f.
▶ vt guarnecer.

garrison ['gærɪsʰn] n guarnición f.

garter ['ga:tə'] n liga.

gas [gæs] n 1 (substance) gas m. 2 US gasolina. 3 (anaesthetic) anestesia. 4 US fig algo divertido. COMP gas chamber cámara de gas. ▌ gas mask máscara antigás. ▌ US gas station gasolinera.
ⓘ pl gases o gasses.
▶ vt asfixiar con gas.
▶ vi fam charlotear.

gaseous ['gæsɪəs] adj gaseoso,-a.

gash [gæʃ] n cuchillada.

gasket ['gæskɪt] n junta.

gasoline ['gæsəli:n] n US gasolina.

gasp [ga:sp] vi 1 (in astonishment) quedar boquiabierto,-a. 2 (to pant) jadear.

gassy ['gæsɪ] adj gaseoso,-a.
ⓘ comp gassier, superl gassiest.

gastric ['gæstrɪk] adj gástrico,-a.

gastronomy [gæs'trɒnəmɪ] n gastronomía.

gate [geɪt] n 1 (door) puerta, verja. 2 (at airport) puerta; (at stadium) entrada. 3 GB (attendance) asistencia.

gateau ['gætəʊ] n pastel m, tarta.
ⓘ pl gateaux ['gætəʊz].

gatecrash ['geɪtkræʃ] vt fam colarse en.
▶ vi fam colarse.

gateway ['geɪtweɪ] n entrada, puerta.

gather ['gæðə'] vt 1 (collect) juntar. 2 (call together) reunir. 3 (pick up) recoger. 4 (taxes) recaudar. 5 (gain) ganar, cobrar.
▶ vi 1 (come together) reunirse, juntarse. 2 (build up) acumularse. 3 (form) formarse.

gathering ['gæðərɪŋ] n reunión f.

gauche [gəʊʃ] adj (awkward) torpe, desmañado,-a; (tactless) sin tacto.

gaudy ['gɔ:dɪ] adj chillón,-ona.
ⓘ comp gaudier, superl gaudiest.

gauge [geɪdʒ] n 1 (device) indicador m, calibrador m. 2 (measure) medida estándar. 3 (railways) ancho de vía.
▶ vt 1 (measure) medir, calibrar. 2 fig apreciar, calcular.

gaunt [gɔ:nt] adj 1 (lean) demacrado,-a. 2 fig (desolate) lúgubre; (grim) siniestro,-a.

gauze [gɔ:z] n gasa.

gave [geɪv] pt → give.

gay [geɪ] adj 1 fam (homosexual) gay. 2 (happy, lively) alegre. 3 (bright) vistoso,-a.

gaze [geɪz] n mirada fija.
▶ vi mirar fijamente.

gazelle [gə'zel] n gacela.

gazette [gə'zet] n GB boletín oficial.

GCSE ['dʒi:'si:'es'i:] abbr GB (General Certificate of Secondary Education) ≈ Enseñanza Secundaria Obligatoria; (abbreviation) ESO f.

⊕ GCSE es el examen que se hace en Gran Bretaña al final de la enseñanza secundaria, a los 16 años aproximadamente.

GDP [ˈdʒiːˈdiːˈpiː] *abbr* (gross domestic product) producto interior bruto; *(abbreviation)* PIB *m*.

gear [gɪəʳ] *n* **1** TECH engranaje *m*. **2** AUTO marcha, velocidad *f*. **3** *(equipment)* equipo. **4** *fam (belongings)* efectos *mpl* personales, pertenencias *fpl*; *(clothes)* ropa. [COMP] gear lever palanca de cambios.

gearbox [ˈgɪəbɒks] *n* caja de cambios.

gearshift [ˈgɪəʃɪft] *n* AUTO US palanca de cambio.

gearstick [ˈgɪəstɪk] *n* AUTO palanca de cambio.

geese [giːs] *n pl* → goose.

gel [dʒel] *n* **1** gel *m*. **2** *(for hair)* gomina, fijador *m*.

gelatine [ˈdʒelətiːn] *n* gelatina.

gem [dʒem] *n* **1** *(jewel)* gema. **2** *fig (person, thing)* joya, alhaja.

Gemini [ˈdʒemɪnaɪ] *n* Géminis *m*.

gender [ˈdʒendəʳ] *n* género.

gene [dʒiːn] *n* gene *m*, gen *m*. [COMP] gene pool banco genético.

genera [ˈdʒenərə] *n pl* → genus.

general [ˈdʒenʳrəl] *adj* general. [COMP] general election elecciones *fpl* generales. ‖ general knowledge cultura general.
► *n* MIL general *m*.

generalize [ˈdʒenʳrəlaɪz] *vt & vi* generalizar.

generate [ˈdʒenəreɪt] *vt (gen)* generar.

generation [dʒenəˈreɪʃʳn] *n* generación *f*.

generator [ˈdʒenəreɪtəʳ] *n* generador *m*.

generic [dʒəˈnerɪk] *adj* genérico,-a.

generosity [dʒenəˈrɒsətɪ] *n* generosidad *f*.

generous [ˈdʒenʳrəs] *adj* generoso,-a.

genetic [dʒəˈnetɪk] *adj* genético,-a. [COMP] genetic code código genético.

genetically [dʒəˈnetɪklɪ] *adv* genéticamente. [LOC] genetically modified transgénico,-a.

genetics [dʒəˈnetɪks] *n* genética.

genial [ˈdʒiːnɪəl] *adj* afable, amable.

☒ Genial no significa 'genial (brillante)', que se traduce por brilliant.

genital [ˈdʒenɪtʳl] *adj* genital.
► *n pl* genitals (órganos *mpl*) genitales *mpl*.

genitive [ˈdʒenɪtɪv] *adj* genitivo,-a.
► *n* genitivo.

genius [ˈdʒiːnɪəs] *n* **1** *(person)* genio. **2** *(gift)* don *m*. ① *pl* geniuses.

☒ Genius no significa 'genio (carácter)', que se traduce por temper.

genocide [ˈdʒenəsaɪd] *n* genocidio.

genome [ˈdʒiːnəʊm] *n* genoma *m*.

genotype [ˈdʒenətaɪp] *n* genotipo.

genre [ˈʒɑːnrə] *n* género.

gent [dʒent] *n fam* caballero, señor *m*.

gentle [ˈdʒentʳl] *adj* **1** *(person)* bondadoso,-a, dulce, tierno,-a. **2** *(breeze, movement, touch, etc)* suave. **3** *(hint)* discreto,-a. **4** *(noble)* noble.
① *comp* gentler, *superl* gentlest.
► *n pl* gents servicio de caballeros.

gentleman [ˈdʒentʳlmən] *n* caballero, señor *m*.
① *pl* gentlemen [ˈdʒentʳlmən].

gently [ˈdʒentlɪ] *adv* **1** *(smoothly)* suavemente. **2** *(slowly)* despacio, poco a poco. **3** *(kindly)* amablemente.

genuine [ˈdʒenjʊɪn] *adj* **1** *(authentic, true)* genuino,-a, auténtico,-a, verdadero,-a. **2** *(sincere)* sincero,-a.

genus [ˈdʒiːnəs] *n* género.
① *pl* genera [ˈdʒenərə].

geographic [dʒɪəˈgræfɪk] *adj* geográfico,-a.

geography [dʒɪˈɒgrəfɪ] *n* geografía.

geological [dʒɪəˈlɒdʒɪkal] *adj* geológico,-a.

geology [dʒɪˈɒlədʒɪ] *n* geología.

geometric [dʒɪəˈmetrɪk] *adj* geométrico,-a.

geometry [dʒɪˈɒmətrɪ] *n* geometría.

geranium [dʒəˈreɪnɪəm] *n* geranio.

geriatric [dʒerɪˈætrɪk] *adj* geriátrico,-a.

germ [dʒɜːm] *n* germen *m*.

German [ˈdʒɜːmən] *adj* alemán,-ana.
► *n* **1** *(person)* alemán,-ana. **2** *(language)* alemán *m*.

Germany [ˈdʒɜːmənɪ] *n* Alemania.

germinate [ˈdʒɜːmɪneɪt] *vi* germinar.
► *vt* hacer germinar.

germination [dʒɜ:mɪˈneɪʃᵊn] *n* germinación *f.*

gerund [ˈdʒerənd] *n* gerundio.

gestation [dʒesˈteɪʃᵊn] *n* BIOL gestación *f.*

gesticulate [dʒesˈtɪkjəleɪt] *vi* gesticular.

gesture [ˈdʒestʃəʳ] *n* **1** ademán *m*, gesto. **2** *fig (token)* detalle *m*, gesto, muestra.
► *vi* hacer gestos, hacer ademanes.

❌ Gesture no significa 'gesto (de la cara)', que se traduce por **grimace**.

get [get] *vt* **1** *(obtain)* obtener, conseguir: *I want to get a job* quiero conseguir un trabajo; *he got a bank loan* le concedieron un crédito bancario; *what did you get in maths?* ¿qué sacaste en mates?. **2** *(receive)* recibir: *I got your letter yesterday* recibí tu carta ayer. **3** *(buy)* comprar: *where did you get your jeans?* ¿dónde compraste tus vaqueros? **4** *(fetch)* traer: *get the car* traiga el coche. **5** *(catch illnesses, means of transport)* coger: *she got the flu* cogió la gripe. **6** *(receive signal)* captar, recibir. **7** *(ask)* pedir, decir; *(persuade)* persuadir, convencer: *get your brother to help you* pídele a tu hermano que te ayude. **8** *(have sth done)* hacer algo a uno: *she loves getting her hair done* le encanta que le arreglen el pelo.
► *vi* **1** *(become)* ponerse, volverse: *she gets very angry if we're late* se pone furiosa si llegamos tarde. **2** *(go)* ir: *how do you get there?* ¿cómo se va hasta allí? **3** *(arrive)* llegar: *how did you get home?* ¿cómo llegaste a casa? **4** *(come to)* llegar a. **5** *(start)* empezar. [LOC] **to get dressed** vestirse. ‖ **to get lost** perderse. ‖ **to get married** casarse. ‖ **to get old** envejecer, hacerse viejo. ‖ **to get ready** prepararse. ‖ **to get wet** mojarse.
◆ **to get across** *vt insep (cross - street, road)* cruzar; *(- bridge)* atravesar.
► *vi* hacerse entender.
◆ **to get ahead** *vi* adelantar, progresar.
◆ **to get along** *vi* **1** *(manage)* arreglárselas, apañárselas. **2** *(leave)* marcharse, irse.
◆ **to get along with** *vt insep* **1** *(person)* llevarse (bien) con. **2** *(progress)* marchar.
◆ **to get around** *vi* **1** *(person)* moverse; *(travel)* viajar. **2** *(news)* difundirse.
► *vt insep (avoid)* evitar, sortear.
◆ **to get around to** *vi* encontrar tiempo para.

◆ **to get away** *vi* escaparse, irse.
► *vt sep* alejar, quitar, sacar.
◆ **to get away with** *vt insep* salir impune de.
◆ **to get back** *vi* **1** *(return)* volver, regresar. **2** *(move backwards)* moverse hacia atrás, retroceder.
► *vt sep (recover)* recuperar: *did you get your money back?* ¿te devolvieron el dinero?
◆ **to get behind** *vi* atrasarse.
◆ **to get by** *vi* **1** *(manage)* arreglárselas. **2** *(pass)* pasar.
◆ **to get down** *vt sep* **1** *(depress)* deprimir, desanimar. **2** *(gen)* bajar. **3** *(write down)* apuntar, anotar. **4** *(swallow)* tragar.
► *vi (descend)* bajarse.
◆ **to get down to** *vi* ponerse a.
◆ **to get in** *vi* **1** *(arrive)* llegar. **2** *(enter)* entrar; *(car)* subir; *(be elected)* ser elegido,-a.
► *vt sep* **1** *(insert)* meter. **2** *(harvest)* cosechar; *(washing)* recoger; *(supplies)* comprar. **3** *(summon)* llamar.
◆ **to get into** *vi insep* **1** *(arrive)* llegar. **2** *(enter)* entrar en; *(car)* subir a.
◆ **to get off** *vt sep (remove)* quitarse.
► *vt insep (vehicle, horse, etc)* bajarse de.
► *vi* **1** bajarse. **2** *(leave)* salir. **3** *(begin)* comenzar. **4** *(escape)* escaparse.
◆ **to get off with** *vt insep fam* ligar con.
◆ **to get on** *vt insep (vehicle)* subir a, subirse a; *(bicycle, horse, etc)* montar a.
► *vi* **1** *(make progress)* progresar, avanzar, ir. **2** *(succeed)* tener éxito. **3** *(be friendly)* llevarse bien, avenirse, entenderse. **4** *(continue)* seguir, continuar. **5** *(grow old)* hacerse mayor, envejecerse.
◆ **to get out** *vt sep (thing)* sacar; *(stain)* quitar.
► *vi* **1** *(leave)* salir. **2** *(of car, etc)* bajar de, bajarse de. **3** *(escape)* escapar(se). **4** *(news, rumours, etc)* llegar a saberse, hacerse público,-a.
◆ **to get out of** *vt insep (avoid)* librarse de.
► *vi (stop)* dejar, perder la costumbre.
◆ **to get over** *vt insep* **1** *(illness)* recuperarse de. **2** *(recover from)* sobreponerse a; *(forget)* olvidar. **3** *(obstacle)* salvar; *(difficulty)* vencer.
► *vt sep (idea, etc)* comunicar, hacer comprender.
◆ **to get over with** *vt sep* acabar con.

G

◆ **to get round** *vt insep* **1** *(obstacle)* salvar. **2** *(law, regulation)* evitar, soslayar. **3** *(person)* convencer, persuadir.

▶ *vi (news)* difundirse, hacerse público,-a, llegar a saber.

◆ **to get through** *vi* **1** *(gen)* llegar. **2** *(on phone)* conseguir hablar (to, con). **3** *(communicate)* hacerse comprender (to, a).

▶ *vt insep* **1** *(finish)* acabar, terminar. **2** *(consume)* consumir; *(money)* gastar; *(drink)* beber. **3** *(exam)* aprobar.

◆ **to get together** *vi (people)* reunirse, juntarse.

▶ *vt sep* **1** *(people)* juntar, reunir. **2** *(assemble)* montar; *(money)* recoger, reunir.

◆ **to get up** *vi* **1** *(rise)* levantarse; *(climb up)* subir. **2** *(become stronger - wind, storm)* levantarse.

◆ **to get up to** *vt insep* **1** hacer: *what have you been getting up to?* ¿qué has estado haciendo? **2** *(reach)* llegar a.

ⓘ *pt* got [gɒt], *pp* got [gɒt] (US gotten [ˈgɒtⁿn]), *ger* getting.

getaway [ˈgetəweɪ] *n fam* fuga, huida.

get-together [ˈgettəgeðəʳ] *n fam (meeting)* reunión *f*; *(party)* fiesta.

getup [ˈgetʌp] *n fam* atavío, atuendo.

geyser [ˈgiːzəʳ, US ˈgaɪzəʳ] *n* **1** *(natural spring)* géiser *m*. **2** *(water heater)* calentador *m* de agua.

ghastly [ˈgɑːstlɪ] *adj* **1** espantoso,-a, horrible, horroroso,-a. **2** *(pale)* pálido,-a, mortecino,-a.

ⓘ *comp* ghastlier, *superl* ghastliest.

gherkin [ˈgɜːkɪn] *n* pepinillo.

ghetto [ˈgetəʊ] *n* gueto.

ⓘ *pl* ghettos o ghettoes.

ghost [gəʊst] *n* fantasma *m*, espectro.

COMP **ghost train** tren *m* de la bruja.

ghostwrite [ˈgəʊstraɪt] *vt (literature)* hacer de negro, escribir para otro.

giant [ˈdʒaɪənt] *n* gigante,-a.

▶ *adj* gigante, gigantesco,-a.

gibberish [ˈdʒɪbərɪʃ] *n* galimatías *m*.

Gibraltar [dʒɪˈbrɔːltəʳ] *n* Gibraltar *m*.

Gibraltarian [dʒɪbrɔːlˈteərɪən] *adj* gibraltareño,-a.

giddy [ˈgɪdɪ] *adj (dizzy)* mareado,-a.

ⓘ *comp* giddier, *superl* giddiest.

gift [gɪft] *n* **1** *(present)* regalo, obsequio. **2** *(talent)* don *m*. **3** REL ofrenda. **4** JUR donación *f*. COMP **gift shop** tienda de regalos.

gifted [ˈgɪftɪd] *adj* dotado,-a.

gigabyte [ˈgɪgəbaɪt] *n* (giga)byte *m*.

gigantic [dʒaɪˈgæntɪk] *adj* gigantesco,-a.

giggle [ˈgɪgəl] *n* **1** risita, risa tonta. **2** GB *fam* broma, diversión *f*.

gild [gɪld] *vt* dorar.

gill [gɪl] *n (of fish)* agalla, branquia.

gilt [gɪlt] *adj* dorado,-a.

▶ *n* dorado.

gin [dʒɪn] *n* ginebra.

ginger [ˈdʒɪndʒəʳ] *n (spice)* jengibre *m*.

▶ *adj (hair)* rojo,-a; *(person)* pelirrojo,-a.

◆ **to ginger up** *vt sep* animar, estimular.

gingerbread [ˈdʒɪndʒəbred] *n* pan *m* de jengibre.

gipsy [ˈdʒɪpsɪ] *n* gitano,-a.

ⓘ *pl* gipsies.

giraffe [dʒɪˈrɑːf] *n* jirafa.

girdle [ˈgɜːdəl] *n* **1** *(clothes)* faja. **2** *fig* cinturón *m*.

▶ *vt fig* rodear.

girl [gɜːl] *n* **1** chica, muchacha, joven *f*; *(small)* niña. **2** *(daughter)* hija.

girlfriend [ˈgɜːlfrend] *n* **1** *(partner)* novia. **2** *(friend)* amiga, compañera.

girlish [ˈgɜːlɪʃ] *adj (of girl)* de niña; *(effeminate)* afeminado,-a.

giro [ˈdʒaɪrəʊ] *n* GB giro.

ⓘ *pl* giros.

gist [dʒɪst] *n (general idea)* idea general, sentido general; *(fundamental idea)* lo esencial.

give [gɪv] *n (flexibility)* elasticidad *f*, flexibilidad *f*.

▶ *vt* **1** *(gen)* dar, entregar. **2** *(as a gift)* dar, regalar: *he gave her a dress* le regaló un vestido. **3** *(perform a concert, etc)* dar; *(speech)* pronunciar. **4** *(dedicate)* dedicar, consagrar. LOC **to give way** ceder el paso.

▶ *vi (yield)* ceder; *(cloth, elastic)* dar de sí.

◆ **to give away** *vt sep* **1** *(gen)* distribuir, repartir; *(present)* regalar; *(prize)* entregar. **2** *(betray)* delatar, traicionar; *(disclose)* revelar, descubrir.

◆ **to give back** *vt sep (return)* devolver.

◆ **to give in** *vi (admit defeat)* darse por vencido,-a, rendirse; *(yield)* ceder.

▶ *vt sep (hand in)* entregar.

◆ **to give off** *vt sep (smell, heat, etc)* despedir, desprender, emitir.

◆ **to give onto** *vi* dar a.

◆ **to give over** *vt sep (hand over)* entregar; *(allocate)* dedicar, asignar.

▶ *vi fam (stop)* dejar de.

◆ **to give up** *vt sep* **1** *(renounce)* dejar; *(idea)* abandonar, renunciar a. **2** *(devote)* dedicar. **3** *(surrender)* entregarse.

▶ *vi (admit defeat)* darse por vencido,-a, rendirse.

◆ **to give up on** *vt insep* abandonar, desistir.

① *pt* **gave** [geɪv], *pp* **given** ['gɪvªn], *ger* **giving**.

given ['gɪvªn] *pp* → give.

▶ *adj* **1** *(fixed)* dado,-a, determinado,-a. **2** *(prone)* dado,-a, propenso,-a.

▶ *prep* **1** *(considering)* dado,-a, teniendo en cuenta. **2** *(if)* si.

glacial ['gleɪʃªl] *adj* **1** GEOL glacial. **2** *(icy)* glacial.

glacier ['glæsɪər, 'gleɪʃər] *n* GEOL glaciar *m*.

glad [glæd] *adj (pleased)* contento,-a, alegre; *(happy)* feliz.

① *comp* **gladder**, *superl* **gladdest**.

gladden ['glædªn] *vt* alegrar.

gladiator ['glædɪeɪtər] *n* HIST gladiador *m*.

gladly ['glædlɪ] *adv* de buena gana, con mucho gusto.

glamorous ['glæmərəs] *adj* **1** atractivo, -a. **2** *(charming)* encantador,-ra.

glamour ['glæmər] *n* **1** atractivo. **2** *(charm)* encanto.

glance [glɑːns] *n* vistazo, ojeada.

▶ *vi* echar un vistazo **(at, a)**.

gland [glænd] *n* ANAT glándula.

glare [gleər] *n* **1** *(light)* luz *f* deslumbrante. **2** AUTO deslumbramiento. **3** *(look)* mirada furiosa, mirada hostil.

▶ *vi* **1** *(dazzle)* deslumbrar. **2** *(look)* lanzar una mirada furiosa.

glass [glɑːs] *n* **1** *(material)* vidrio, cristal *m*. **2** *(for drinking)* vaso; *(with stem)* copa. **3** GB barómetro.

① *pl* **glasses**.

▶ *n pl* **glasses** gafas *fpl*.

glassware ['glɑːsweər] *n* cristalería.

glaze [gleɪz] *n (for pottery)* vidriado; *(lustre)* brillo, lustre *m*; *(varnish)* barniz *m*, esmalte *m*.

▶ *vt* **1** *(pottery)* vidriar, esmaltar. **2** *(windows)* poner cristales a. **3** CULIN glasear.

gleam [gliːm] *n* **1** destello, rayo. **2** *fig* rayo, resquicio, vislumbre *m*.

▶ *vi* brillar, destellar, relucir.

glean [gliːn] *vt* **1** AGR espigar. **2** *fig* recoger, cosechar.

glide [glaɪd] *n* **1** deslizamiento. **2** AV planeo, vuelo sin motor. **3** LING semivocal *f*.

▶ *vi* **1** deslizarse. **2** AV planear.

glider ['glaɪdər] *n* AV planeador *m*.

glimmer ['glɪmər] *n (light)* luz *f* tenue.

▶ *vi* brillar con luz tenue.

glimpse [glɪmps] *n* visión *f* fugaz.

▶ *vt* vislumbrar, entrever.

glisten ['glɪsªn] *vi* brillar, relucir.

glitter ['glɪtər] *n* brillo.

▶ *vi* brillar, relucir.

global ['gləʊbªl] *adj* **1** mundial. **2** *(total)* global. COMP **global warming** calentamiento global.

globalization [gləʊbªlaɪ'zeɪʃªn] *n* globalización *f*.

globe [gləʊb] *n* globo

☒ Globe no significa 'globo (de niño)', que se traduce por **balloon**.

globe-trotter ['gləʊbtrɒtər] *n fam* trotamundos *mf*.

globule ['glɒbjuːl] *n* glóbulo.

gloom [gluːm] *n* **1** *(darkness)* penumbra *f*. **2** *(sadness)* tristeza, melancolía. **3** *(hopelessness)* desolación *f*, pesimismo.

gloomy ['gluːmɪ] *adj* **1** *(dark)* lóbrego,-a, oscuro,-a, tenebroso,-a. **2** *(sad)* melancólico,-a, triste; *(depressing)* deprimente. **3** *(pessimistic)* pesimista. **4** *(weather)* gris, encapotado,-a.

① *comp* **gloomier**, *superl* **gloomiest**.

glorious ['glɔːrɪəs] *adj* **1** glorioso,-a. **2** *(wonderful)* espléndido,-a, magnífico,-a.

glory ['glɔːrɪ] *n* **1** *(gen)* gloria. **2** *fig* esplendor *m*.

① *pl* **glories**.

gloss [glɒs] n 1 lustre m, brillo. 2 *(explanation)* glosa. 3 *fig* oropel m.
▶ vt *(text)* glosar, comentar.
◆ **to gloss over** vt insep *(play down)* paliar, suavizar; *(hide)* encubrir; *(ignore)* pasar por alto.

glossary ['glɒsərɪ] n glosario.
① pl glossaries.

glove [glʌv] n guante m. COMP **glove compartment** guantera.

glow [gləʊ] n 1 *(of lamp)* luz f; *(of jewel)* brillo. 2 *(of fire)* calor m vivo; *(of sky)* arrebol m; *(of fire, metal, etc)* incandescencia. 3 *(of face)* rubor m. 4 *fig* sensación f de bienestar, satisfacción f.
▶ vi 1 *(jewel, sun, etc)* brillar; *(of metal)* estar al rojo vivo; *(fire)* arder. 2 *fig* rebosar de.

glucose ['glu:kəʊz] n glucosa.

glue [glu:] n cola, pegamento.
▶ vt encolar, pegar.

gluten ['glu:tən] n gluten m.

gluteal ['glu:təl] adj glúteo,-a.

gluteus ['glu:trəs] n glúteo.

glutton ['glʌtən] n glotón,-ona.

glycerine [glɪsəˈrɪn] n glicerina.

GMT ['dʒiːˈemˈdiː] abbr (Greenwich Mean Time) hora media de Greenwich; *(abbreviation)* GMT.

gnat [næt] n ZOOL mosquito.

gnaw [nɔː] vt 1 *(bite)* roer. 2 *fig (worry)* corroer.

gnome [nəʊm] n gnomo.

GNP ['dʒiːˈenˈpiː] abbr (gross national product) producto nacional bruto; *(abbreviation)* PNB m.

gnu [nuː] n ñu m.

go [gəʊ] n 1 *(energy)* energía, empuje m. 2 *(turn)* turno: *it's my go* me toca a mí. 3 *(try)* intento: *I'd like to have a go at hang gliding* me gustaría intentar vuelo con ala delta. 4 *(start)* principio.
▶ vi 1 *(gen)* ir: *to go on holiday* irse de vacaciones. 2 *(leave)* marcharse, irse; *(bus, train, etc)* salir: *let's go!* ¡vámonos! 3 *(vanish)* desaparecer. 4 *(function)* funcionar, marchar: *his business is going very well* su negocio marcha muy bien. 5 *(become)* volverse, ponerse, quedarse: *to go deaf* quedarse

sordo,-a. 6 *(fit)* entrar, caber: *the bed won't go into the room* la cama no cabrá en la habitación. 7 *(break)* romperse, estropearse; *(yield)* ceder; *(blow)* fundirse. 8 *(progress)* ir, marchar, andar: *things aren't going too well for him* no le van muy bien las cosas. 9 *(be available)* quedar, haber: *is there any more meat going?* ¿queda algo de carne?. 10 *(make a noise, gesture, etc)* hacer: *go like this with your head* haz así con la cabeza. 11 *(time - pass)* pasar; *(- be remaining)* faltar: *the years went by slowly* los años pasaron lentamente; *only two weeks to go* solo faltan dos semanas. 16 *(say)* decir: *as the saying goes* según el dicho.
▶ vt 1 *(make a noise)* hacer: *it goes tick-tock* hace tic-tac. 2 *(travel)* hacer, recorrer.
▶ interj go! *(starting races)* ¡ya!: *ready, steady, go!* ¡preparados, listos, ya!.
◆ **to go after** vt insep *(pursue)* perseguir, andar tras.
◆ **to go ahead** vi *(proceed)* proceder: *go ahead!* ¡adelante!.
◆ **to go along with** vt insep estar de acuerdo con.
◆ **to go around** vi → **to go round**.
◆ **to go away** vi marcharse.
◆ **to go back** vi *(return)* volver, regresar; *(date from)* datar de, remontarse a.
◆ **to go back on** vt insep *(break)* romper, no cumplir.
◆ **to go by** vi *(time)* pasar.
▶ vt insep *(rules)* atenerse a, seguir; *(instinct)* dejarse llevar por; *(appearances)* juzgar por.
◆ **to go down** vi 1 *(gen)* bajar; *(tyre)* deshincharse; *(sun)* ponerse; *(ship)* hundirse. 2 *(be received)* ser acogido,-a.
◆ **to go for** vt insep 1 *(attack)* atacar. 2 *(fetch)* ir a buscar. 3 *fam (like)* gustar. 4 *fam (be valid)* valer para.
◆ **to go in** vi entrar.
◆ **to go in for** vt insep *(enter - race, competition)* participar en; *(- exam)* presentarse a; *(- career)* dedicarse a; *(like, agree with)* ser partidario,-a de.
◆ **to go into** vt insep 1 *(gen)* entrar en. 2 *(investigate)* investigar. 3 *(crash)* chocar contra.
◆ **to go off** vi 1 *(leave)* marcharse. 2 *(bomb)* estallar; *(alarm)* sonar; *(gun)* dis-

pararse. **3** *(food)* estropearse, pasarse; *(milk)* cortarse. **4** *(stop operating)* apagarse.

▶ *vt insep (stop liking)* perder el gusto por, perder el interés por.

◆ **to go on** *vi* **1** *(continue)* seguir, continuar. **2** *(happen)* pasar, ocurrir: *what's going on?* ¿qué pasa?. **3** *(complain)* quejarse (about, de); *(talk at length)* hablar sin parar. **4** *(light, etc)* encenderse. **5** *(age)* estar a punto de cumplir: *she's ten going on eleven* está a punto de cumplir los once años.

◆ **to go out** *vi* **1** *(leave)* salir: *he goes out a lot* sale mucho. **2** *(fire, light)* apagarse.

◆ **to go over** *vt insep (check, revise)* revisar, repasar.

◆ **to go over to** *vt insep* **1** *(betray)* pasarse a. **2** *(change to)* cambiar a, pasar a.

◆ **to go round** *vi* **1** *(gyrate)* dar vueltas, girar. **2** *(visit)* pasar por casa de, visitar.

◆ **to go through** *vt insep* **1** *(undergo)* pasar por, sufrir, padecer. **2** *(examine)* examinar; *(search)* registrar; *(spend)* gastar; *(explain)* explicar.

▶ *vi (act, law)* ser aprobado,-a.

◆ **to go through with** *vt insep* llevar a cabo.

◆ **to go under** *vi* **1** *(ship)* hundirse. **2** *fig* fracasar.

◆ **to go up** *vi* **1** *(gen)* subir; *(approach)* acercarse. **2** *(curtain in theatre)* levantarse. **3** *(explode)* estallar; *(burst into flames)* prenderse fuego.

ⓘ *pt* **went** [went], *pp* **gone** [gɒn], *ger* **going**.

goal [gəʊl] *n* **1** SP *(area)* meta, portería. **2** SP *(point)* gol *m*, tanto. **3** *(aim)* fin *m*, objetivo, meta.

goalkeeper ['gəʊlkiːpəʳ] *n* portero,-a, guardameta *mf*.

goat [gəʊt] *n (female)* cabra; *(male)* macho cabrío.

goatee [gəʊ'tiː] *n (beard)* perilla.

gobble ['gɒbəl] *vt* engullir, zamparse.

god [gɒd] *n (deity, idol)* dios *m*.

▶ *n* **God** Dios *m*.

godchild ['gɒdtʃaɪld] *n* ahijado,-a.

ⓘ *pl* **godchildren** ['gɒdtʃɪldrən].

goddaughter ['gɒddɔːtəʳ] *n* ahijada.

goddess ['gɒdəs] *n* diosa.

godfather ['gɒdfɑːðəʳ] *n* padrino.

godmother ['gɒdmʌðəʳ] *n* madrina.

godparents ['gɒdpeərənts] *n pl* padrinos *mpl*.

godsend ['gɒdsend] *n* regalo llovido del cielo.

godson ['gɒdsʌn] *n* ahijado.

goggle ['gɒgəl] *vi* quedarse atónito,-a.

goggles ['gɒgəlz] *n pl* gafas *fpl* protectoras.

going ['gəʊɪŋ] *n* **1** *(departure)* ida, salida. **2** *(pace)* paso, ritmo. **3** *(path, road)* estado del camino.

▶ *adj* **1** *(price, rate)* actual, corriente. **2** *(business)* que marcha bien.

gold [gəʊld] *n (metal)* oro.

▶ *adj* **1** *(colour)* dorado,-a. **2** *(made of gold)* de oro.

golden ['gəʊldən] *adj* **1** de oro. **2** *(colour)* dorado,-a. **3** *(hair)* rubio,-a.

goldfinch ['gəʊldfɪntʃ] *n* jilguero.

goldfish ['gəʊldfɪʃ] *n* pez *m* de colores.

ⓘ *pl* **goldfish** ['gəʊldfɪʃ].

goldsmith ['gəʊldsmɪθ] *n* orfebre *mf*.

golf [gɒlf] *n* golf *m*.

▶ *vi* jugar al golf. COMP **golf course** campo de golf.

golfer ['gɒlfəʳ] *n* jugador,-ra de golf.

gone [gɒn] *pp* → **go**.

▶ *adj* **1** *(time)* pasado,-a. **2** *(dead)* muerto,-a.

gong [gɒŋ] *n* **1** gong *m*. **2** *fam fig (award, prize)* galardón *m*.

good [gʊd] *adj* **1** bueno,-a; *(before m sing noun)* buen. **2** *(healthy)* sano,-a. **3** *(kind)* amable. **4** *(useful)* servible. LOC **for good** para siempre. COMP **Good Friday** Viernes *m* Santo.

ⓘ *comp* **better**, *superl* **best**.

▶ *n* bien *m*: *its for your own good* es por tu propio bien.

▶ *n pl* **goods** *(property)* bienes *mpl*; COMM *(in shop)* género *m sing*, artículos *mpl*; COMM *(merchandise)* mercancías *fpl*.

goodbye [gʊd'baɪ] [also written good-bye] *n* adiós *m*.

▶ *interj* ¡adiós!

G

good-for-nothing ['gʊdfənʌθɪŋ] *n* golfo.

good-hearted [gʊd'hɑːtɪd] *adj* de buen corazón.

good-humoured [gʊd'hjuːməd] *adj* de buen humor, campechano,-a.

good-looking [gʊd'lʊkɪŋ] *adj* guapo,-a, bien parecido,-a.

good-natured [gʊd'neɪtʃəd] *adj* bondadoso,-a.

goodness ['gʊdnəs] *n* **1** *(virtue)* bondad *f.* **2** *(in food)* lo nutritivo.

goodwill [gʊd'wɪl] *n* buena voluntad *f.*

goose [guːs] *n* ganso, oca.
ⓘ *pl* geese.

gooseberry ['gʊzbrɪ, 'guːsbᵊrɪ] *n* **1** BOT grosella espinosa. **2** GB *fam fig (person)* carabina.
ⓘ *pl* gooseberries.

gooseflesh ['guːsfleʃ] *n* piel *f* de gallina.

gore¹ [gɔːʳ] *n* sangre *f* derramada.

gore² [gɔːʳ] *vt* dar una cornada a.

gorge [gɔːdʒ] *n (mountain pass)* desfiladero; *(ravine)* barranco.

gorgeous ['gɔːdʒəs] *adj* **1** magnífico,-a, espléndido,-a. **2** *(person)* guapísimo,-a.
▸ *n fam* guapo,-a.

gorilla [gəˈrɪlə] *n* ZOOL gorila *m.*

go-slow [gəʊ'sləʊ] *n* huelga de celo.

gospel ['gɒspᵊl] *n* **1** REL evangelio. **2** MUS música gospel.

gossip ['gɒsɪp] *n* **1** *(talk)* cotilleo, chismorreo. **2** *(person)* cotilla *mf,* chismoso,-a. COMP **gossip column** crónica de sociedad.
▸ *vi* cotillear, chismorrear.

got [gɒt] *pt & pp* → get.

Gothic ['gɒθɪk] *adj* **1** godo,-a. **2** *(language, architecture, type)* gótico,-a.

gotten ['gɒtᵊn] *pp* US → get.

gourmet ['gʊəmeɪ] *n* gastrónomo,-a, gurmet *m.*

govern ['gʌvᵊn] *vt* **1** gobernar, dirigir. **2** LING regir. **3** *(determine)* dictar.
▸ *vi* **1** gobernar. **2** *(predominate)* predominar, prevalecer.

government ['gʌvᵊnmənt] *n* gobierno.

▸ *adj* **1** *(of government)* del gobierno, gubernamental. **2** *(of a governor)* del gobernador.

governmental [gʌvᵊn'mentᵊl] *adj* gubernamental.

governor ['gʌvᵊnəʳ] *n* **1** *(town, state, bank)* gobernador,-ra. **2** *(prison)* director,-ra. **3** *(school)* administrador,-ra. **4** GB *fam (employer)* jefe *m.*

gown [gaʊn] *n* **1** vestido largo. **2** *(judge's, academic's)* toga. **3** *(surgeon's)* bata.

GP ['dʒiː'piː] *abbr* (general practitioner) médico,-a de cabecera.
ⓘ *pl* GPs.

grab [græb] *vt* **1** *(seize, snatch)* coger, agarrar, asir. **2** *(capture, arrest)* pillar, coger. **3** *fam* entusiasmar.
ⓘ *pt & pp* grabbed, *ger* grabbing.

grace [greɪs] *n* **1** gracia, elegancia. **2** *(deportment)* garbo. **3** *(courtesy)* delicadeza, cortesía. **4** *(blessing)* bendición *f.* **5** REL gracia. **6** *(delay)* plazo.
▸ *vt* **1** *(adorn)* adornar. **2** *(honour)* honrar.

☒ Grace no significa 'gracia (chiste)', que se traduce por joke.

gracious ['greɪʃəs] *adj* **1** gracioso,-a. **2** *(polite)* cortés. **3** *(kind)* amable. **4** *(benevolent)* benévolo,-a.
▸ *interj* ¡Dios mío!.

☒ Gracious no significa 'gracioso (divertido)', que se traduce por funny.

grade [greɪd] *n* **1** *(degree, level)* grado. **2** *(quality)* calidad *f.* **3** *(class, category)* clase *f,* categoría. **4** *(rank)* rango, grado. **5** *(mark)* nota. **6** US *(gradient)* pendiente *f.* **7** US *(form)* clase *f.*
▸ *vt* **1** *(sort, classify)* clasificar. **2** *(road)* nivelar. **3** *(student)* calificar, poner una nota. **4** *(colours)* degradar.
◆ **to grade up** *vt sep* subir de categoría.
◆ **to grade down** *vt sep* bajar de categoría.

gradual ['grædjʊəl] *adj* gradual.

graduate [*(n)* 'grædjʊət; *(vb)* 'grædjʊeɪt] *n* EDUC *(after 3-year course)* diplomado,-a; *(after 5-year course)* licenciado,-a.
▸ *vt (grade, classify)* graduar.

▶ *vi (after 3-year course)* diplomarse (in, en); *(after 5-year course)* licenciarse (in, en).

graduation [grædju'eɪʃˀn] *n* 1 EDUC graduación *f*. 2 TECH graduación *f*.

graft [grɑːft] *n (of plant, tissue)* injerto.
▶ *vt* injertar (onto, en).

grain [greɪn] *n* 1 *(gen)* grano. 2 *(cereals)* cereales *mpl*. 3 *(in wood)* veta, fibra; *(in stone)* filón *m*, veta; *(of leather)* flor *f*.
▶ *vt (give granular texture)* granular.

grammar ['græmər] *n* gramática. LOC **grammar school** instituto de enseñanza media.

gramme [græm] *n* gramo.

granary ['grænəri] *n* granero.
ⓘ *pl* granaries.

grand [grænd] *adj* 1 *(splendid)* grandioso,-a, espléndido,-a, magnífico,-a. 2 *(impressive)* impresionante. 3 *(important - person)* distinguido,-a, importante. 4 *fam (great)* fenomenal. COMP **grand piano** piano de cola.

grandchild ['græntʃaɪld] *n* nieto,-a.
ⓘ *pl* grandchildren [grən'tʃɪldrən].

granddad ['grændæd] *n fam* abuelo.

granddaughter ['grændɔːtər] *n* nieta.

grandfather ['grændfɑːðər] *n* abuelo.

grandma ['grænmɑː] *n fam* abuela.

grandmother ['grænmʌðər] *n* abuela.

grandpa ['grænpɑː] *n fam* abuelo.

grandparents ['grændpeərənts] *n pl* abuelos *mpl*.

grandson ['grændsʌn] *n* nieto.

granite ['grænɪt] *n* granito.
▶ *adj* de granito.

granny ['græni] *n fam* abuela.
ⓘ *pl* grannies.

grant [grɑːnt] *n* 1 EDUC beca. 2 *(subsidy)* subvención *f*. 3 JUR *(rights, property)* cesión *f*.
▶ *vt* 1 conceder, otorgar. 2 JUR ceder, transferir. LOC **to take** STH **for granted** dar ALGO por sentado.

granule ['grænjuːl] *n* gránulo.

grape [greɪp] *n* uva.

grapefruit ['greɪpfruːt] *n* pomelo.
ⓘ *pl* grapefruits o grapefruit.

grapevine ['greɪpvaɪn] *n (gen)* parra; *(vine)* vid *f*.

graph [grɑːf] *n* gráfica, gráfico. COMP **graph paper** papel cuadriculado.

graphic ['græfɪk] *adj* 1 *(gen)* gráfico,-a. 2 *(vivid)* muy gráfico,-a, vívido,-a.

graphite ['græfaɪt] *n* grafito.

grasp [grɑːsp] *vt* 1 *(seize - with hands)* agarrar, asir; *(opportunity, offer)* aprovechar. 2 *(understand)* comprender, captar.

grass [grɑːs] *n (plant)* hierba, yerba; *(lawn)* césped *m*; *(pasture)* pasto; *(dried)* paja.

grasshopper ['grɑːshɒpər] *n* saltamontes *m*.

grassy ['grɑːsi] *adj* cubierto,-a de hierba.
ⓘ *comp* grassier, *superl* grassiest.

grate¹ [greɪt] *vt* 1 CULIN rallar. 2 *(scrape - gen)* rascar; *(- teeth)* hacer rechinar.

grate² [greɪt] *n (metal frame)* rejilla; *(fireplace)* chimenea.

grateful ['greɪtful] *adj (person)* agradecido,-a; *(letter, smile)* de agradecimiento.

grater ['greɪtər] *n* rallador *m*.

gratification [grætɪfɪ'keɪʃˀn] *n* gratificación *f*, satisfacción *f*, placer *m*.

gratify ['grætɪfaɪ] *vt* 1 *(satisfy - desire, etc)* satisfacer. 2 *(give pleasure to)* complacer, gratificar.
ⓘ *pt & pp* gratified, *ger* gratifying.

gratitude ['grætɪtjuːd] *n* gratitud *f*, agradecimiento.

gratuitous [grə'tjuːɪtəs] *adj* gratuito,-a.
☒ Gratuitous no significa 'gratuito (gratis)', que se traduce por free.

grave¹ [greɪv] *n* tumba, sepultura.

grave² [greɪv] *adj* 1 *(gen)* grave. 2 [grɑːv] *(accent)* grave.

gravel ['grævˀl] *n* grava, gravilla, guijo.

gravestone ['greɪvstəʊn] *n* lápida.

graveyard ['greɪvjɑːd] *n* cementerio.

gravity ['grævɪti] *n* 1 PHYS gravedad *f*. 2 *(seriousness)* gravedad *f*; *(of person, manner)* gravedad *f*, circunspección *f*.

gray [greɪ] *adj* US → grey.

graze¹ [greɪz] *n* rasguño, roce *m*.

graze² [greɪz] *vt (sheep, cattle)* pastar, pastorear, apacentar.

grease [griːs] *n (gen)* grasa.
▶ *vt (part of car, machine, device)* engrasar.

G

greasy ['gri:sɪ] *adj* **1** *(oily - hands)* grasiento,-a. **3** *fam pej (smarmy)* pelota.
ⓘ *comp* greasier, *superl* greasiest.

great [greɪt] *adj* **1** *(gen)* grande; *(before sing noun)* gran. **2** *fam (excellent, wonderful)* estupendo,-a, fantástico,-a, sensacional, fabuloso,-a.
▶ *adv fam* muy bien, estupendamente, fenomenal.

great-grandchild [greɪt'græntʃaɪld] *n* bisnieto,-a, biznieto,-a.
ⓘ *pl* great-grandchildren [greɪtgrən'tʃɪldrən].

great-grandfather [greɪt'grændfɑ:ðəʳ] *n* bisabuelo.

great-grandmother [greɪt'grænmʌðəʳ] *n* bisabuela.

Greece [gri:s] *n* Grecia.

greed [gri:d] *n* **1** *(for money, power)* codicia, avaricia. **2** *(for food)* gula, glotonería.

greedy ['gri:dɪ] *adj* **1** *(for money, power)* codicioso,-a. **2** *(for food)* glotón,-ona.
ⓘ *comp* greedier, *superl* greediest.

Greek [gri:k] *adj* griego,-a.
▶ *n* **1** *(person)* griego,-a. **2** *(language)* griego.

green [gri:n] *adj* **1** *(colour)* verde. **2** *(environment friendly)* ecológico,-a. **4** *(pale)* pálido,-a. **5** *(inexperienced)* novato,-a, verde; *(gullible)* ingenuo,-a, crédulo,-a. **6** *(jealous)* envidioso,-a.
▶ *n* **1** *(colour)* verde *m*. **2** *(stretch of grass)* césped *m*; *(in golf)* green *m*; *(in village)* césped público.
▶ *n pl* **greens** *(vegetables)* verduras *fpl*.
▶ *n pl* **the Greens** POL los verdes *mpl*.

greenfly ['gri:nflaɪ] *n* pulgón *m*.
ⓘ *pl* greenflies.

greengrocer ['gri:ngrəʊsəʳ] *n* verdulero, -a. LOC greengrocer's (shop) verdulería.

greenhouse ['gri:nhaʊs] *n* invernadero. COMP greenhouse effect efecto invernadero.

Greenland ['gri:nlənd] *n* Groenlandia.

Greenlander ['gri:nləndəʳ] *n* groenlandés,-esa.

greet [gri:t] *vt* **1** *(wave at, say hello to)* saludar; *(welcome)* dar la bienvenida a; *(receive)* recibir. **2** *(react)* acoger, recibir. **3** *fig (meet)* llegar, presentarse.

greeting ['gri:tɪŋ] *n* saludo.
▶ *n pl* **greetings** saludos *mpl*, recuerdos *mpl*.

gregarious [gre'geərɪəs] *adj* gregario,-a, sociable.

gremlin ['gremlɪn] *n* duende *m*.

Grenada [grə'neɪdə] *n* Granada.

grenade [grə'neɪd] *n* granada.

grew [gru:] *pt* → grow.

grey [greɪ] *adj* **1** *(colour)* gris; *(hair)* cano,-a; *(sky)* nublado,-a, gris. **2** *(gloomy)* triste, gris.
▶ *n* **1** *(colour)* gris *m*. **2** *(horse)* caballo tordo. LOC to go grey encanecer.

greyhound ['greɪhaʊnd] *n* galgo.

grid [grɪd] *n* **1** *(grating)* reja, parrilla, rejilla. **2** ELEC *(network)* red *f* nacional de tendido eléctrico. **3** *(on map)* cuadrícula.

griddle ['grɪdəl] *n* CULIN plancha.

grief [gri:f] *n* dolor *m*, pena.

grieve [gri:v] *vt* afligir, apenar, dar pena a, entristecer.
▶ *vi* apenarse, afligirse.

grill [grɪl] *n* CULIN *(over cooker)* gratinador *m*, grill *m*; *(on charcoal)* parrilla. **4** → grille.

grille [grɪl] *n* reja.

grim [grɪm] *adj* **1** *(serious)* austero,-a, severo,-a; *(look)* ceñudo,-a. **2** *(unpleasant)* horroroso,-a, pesimista; *(- prospect, outlook)* nefasto,-a, desalentador,-ra; *(- reality)* crudo,-a, duro,-a. **3** *(gloomy - landscape, place)* lúgubre, sombrío,-a.
ⓘ *comp* grimmer, *superl* grimmest.

grimace ['grɪməs] *n* mueca.

grin [grɪn] *n* *(genuine)* sonrisa (abierta); *(mocking)* sonrisa burlona.
▶ *vi* sonreír (abiertamente).
ⓘ *pt & pp* grinned, *ger* grinning.

grind [graɪnd] *vt* **1** *(mill)* moler; *(crush)* machacar, triturar; *(lens, mirror)* pulir; *(knife, blade)* afilar. **2** *(mince - beef)* picar. **3** *(teeth)* rechinar. **4** *(press down hard on)* incrustar, aplastar; *(press in)* meter.
▶ *vi* **1** *(crush)* triturarse. **2** *(make harsh noise)* rechinar. **3** US *(swot)* empollar.
ⓘ *pt & pp* ground [graʊnd].
▶ *n* **1** *fam (work)* trabajo pesado; *(effort)* paliza. **2** US *fam (swot)* empollón,-ona.
◆ **to grind down** *vt sep* oprimir.
◆ **to grind out** *vt sep (music)* tocar.

grinder ['graɪndəʳ] n *(machine - for coffee)* molinillo; *(person - for knives, etc)* afilador,-ra.

grindstone ['graɪnstəʊn] n muela, piedra de afilar.

gringo ['grɪŋgəʊ] n *pej* gringo,-a.
ⓘ *pl* gringos.

grip [grɪp] n **1** *(tight hold)* asimiento. **2** *(of tyre)* adherencia, agarre m. **3** *fig (control, force)* control m, dominio. **4** SP *(way of holding)* la forma en que uno coge la raqueta, etc; *(part of handle)* asidero, empuñadura. **5** *(hairgrip)* horquilla.
▶ vt **1** *(hold tightly - gen)* agarrar, asir, sujetar. **2** *(adhere to)* tener agarre, agarrarse, adherirse. **3** *fig (film, story, play)* captar el interés de, captar la atención de.
▶ vi adherirse.
ⓘ *pt & pp* gripped, *ger* gripping.

grit [grɪt] n **1** *(fine)* arena; *(coarse)* gravilla; *(dirt)* polvo. **2** *fam (determination)* valor m, agallas *fpl*.

grizzly ['grɪzlɪ] [also grizzly bear] n oso pardo.

groan [grəʊn] n **1** gemido, quejido. **2** *(creak)* crujido.
▶ vi **1** *(in pain)* gemir, quejarse; *(with disapproval)* gruñir. **2** *(creak)* crujir.

grocer ['grəʊsəʳ] n tendero,-a. COMP **grocer's (shop)** tienda de comestibles.

groceries ['grəʊsərɪz] n pl comestibles *mpl*.

grocery ['grəʊsərɪ] n US tienda de ultramarinos, tienda de comestibles.
ⓘ *pl* groceries.

groggy ['grɒgɪ] adj fam grogui.
ⓘ *comp* groggier, *superl* groggiest.

groin [grɔɪn] n ANAT ingle f.

groom [gruːm] n **1** *(bridegroom)* novio. **2** *(for horses)* mozo de cuadra.

✎ Se usa para referirse al novio sólo durante el día de la boda. Es la forma abreviada de **bridegroom**.

groove [gruːv] n **1** *(gen)* ranura; *(for door)* guía; *(in column)* acanaladura. **2** *(on record)* surco.

groovy ['gruːvɪ] adj fam guay, genial.
ⓘ *comp* groovier, *superl* grooviest.

grope [grəʊp] vi andar a tientas.

gross [grəʊs] adj **1** *(flagrant - injustice)* flagrante; *(- ignorance)* craso,-a; *(- error)* grave. **2** *(fat)* muy gordo,-a, obeso,-a. **3** *(behaviour, manners)* grosero,-a, tosco,-a; *(- language)* soez; *(disgusting)* asqueroso,-a. **4** FIN *(total)* bruto,-a.
▶ vt *(person)* obtener unos ingresos brutos de; *(film, etc)* recaudar.

grotesque [grəʊ'tesk] adj grotesco,-a.

grotto ['grɒtəʊ] n gruta.
ⓘ *pl* grottoes o grottos.

ground¹ [graʊnd] n **1** *(surface of earth)* suelo; *(soil, earth)* tierra; *(terrain, land)* campo, terreno. **2** US *(electrical)* tierra. **3** ART *(background)* fondo. **4** *(matter, subject)* aspecto, punto. COMP **ground floor** planta baja.
▶ n pl **grounds** *(reason, justification)* razón f, motivo; *(of coffee)* poso, posos *mpl*; *(gardens)* jardines *mpl*; *(area of land)* terreno.

ground² [graʊnd] pt & pp → **grind**.
▶ adj **1** *(coffee)* molido,-a. **2** US *(beef)* picado,-a.

grounding ['graʊndɪŋ] n base f, conocimientos *mpl*.

groundwork ['graʊndwɜːk] n trabajo preliminar, trabajo preparatorio.

group [gruːp] n grupo.
▶ vt agrupar.

grouper ['gruːpəʳ] n mero.

groupie ['gruːpɪ] n fam grupi *mf*.

grow [grəʊ] vi **1** *(gen)* crecer. **2** *(increase)* aumentar. **3** *(become)* hacerse, volverse. **4** *(begin gradually)* llegar a. LOC **to grow old** envejecer.
▶ vt **1** *(crop, plant, flower)* cultivar. **2** *(beard, etc)* dejarse (crecer); *(hair, nails)* dejarse crecer.
◆ **to grow into** vt insep *(become)* convertirse en, hacerse.
◆ **to grow on** vt insep llegar a gustar.
◆ **to grow up** vi **1** *(become adult)* hacerse mayor; *(spend childhood)* criarse, crecer. **2** *(spring up)* surgir, nacer, desarrollarse.
ⓘ *pt* grew ['gruː], *pp* grown [grəʊn].

grower ['grəʊəʳ] n *(farmer)* cultivador,-ra.

growl [graʊl] n gruñido.
▶ vi gruñir.

grown [grəʊn] pp → **grow**.
▶ adj adulto,-a.

grown-up [ˈgrəʊnʌp] *adj* mayor, adulto,-a.
► *n* persona mayor.

growth [grəʊθ] *n* **1** *(gen)* crecimiento; *(increase)* aumento; *(development)* desarrollo. **2** MED *(tumour)* bulto, tumor *m*. **3** *(of beard)* barba.

grub [grʌb] *n* *(larva)* larva, gusano.
► *vi* **1** *(by digging)* escarbar, hurgar. **2** *fig* rebuscar.
① *pt & pp* grubbed, *ger* grubbing.

grudge [grʌdʒ] *n* rencor *m*.
► *vt* **1** *(begrudge, resent)* dar a regañadientes, dar de mala gana. **2** *(envy)* envidiar.

grumble [ˈgrʌmbəl] *n* **1** *(complaint)* queja. **2** *(of thunder)* estruendo.
► *vi* **1** *(moan, complain)* refunfuñar, quejarse (about, de). **2** *(rumble - thunder)* retumbar; *(- stomach)* hacer ruido.

grumpy [ˈgrʌmpɪ] *adj* gruñón,-ona, malhumorado,-a, de mal humor.
① *comp* grumpier, *superl* grumpiest.

grunge [grʌndʒ] *n* MUS grunge *m*.

grunt [grʌnt] *n* gruñido.
► *vi* gruñir.

guarantee [gærənˈtiː] *n* **1** *(gen)* garantía; *(certificate)* certificado de garantía.
► *vt* **1** *(gen)* garantizar; *(assure, promise)* asegurar. **2** *(debt)* avalar, garantizar.

guard [gɑːd] *n* **1** *(sentry, soldier)* guardia *mf*; *(security guard)* guarda *mf*, guarda jurado,-a, guarda de seguridad; *(prison officer)* carcelero,-a. **2** *(duty)* guardia. **3** GB *(on train)* jefe,-a de tren. **4** *(on machine)* dispositivo de seguridad; *(on gun)* seguro. LOC to be on guard estar de guardia. ‖ to stand guard montar guardia.
► *vt* **1** *(watch over)* vigilar; *(protect - person, reputation)* proteger; *(keep - secret)* guardar. **2** *(control - tongue)* cuidar, controlar.

❌ To guard no significa 'guardar (en un sitio)', que se traduce por to put away.

guardian [ˈgɑːdɪən] *n* **1** *(defender)* guardián,-ana, defensor,-ra. **2** JUR *(of child)* tutor,-ra.

guava [ˈgwɑːvə] *n* *(fruit)* guayaba.

guess [ges] *n* *(conjecture)* conjetura; *(estimate)* cálculo. LOC to have a guess adivinar.
► *vt* **1** *(gen)* adivinar. **2** US *fam (suppose)* suponer, pensar, creer.
► *vi* adivinar.

guesswork [ˈgeswɜːk] *n* conjeturas *fpl*, suposiciones *fpl*.

guest [gest] *n* **1** *(at home, restaurant, etc)* invitado,-a; *(in hotel)* cliente,-a, huésped,-da. **2** *(on TV programme)* invitado,-a.

guesthouse [ˈgesthaʊs] *n* casa de huéspedes, pensión *f*.

guestroom [ˈgestruːm] *n* cuarto de (los) invitados.

Guiana [gaɪˈænə, gɪˈɑːnə] *n* Guayana.

guidance [ˈgaɪdəns] *n* *(help, advice)* orientación *f*, consejos *mpl*.

guide [gaɪd] *n* **1** *(person)* guía *mf*. **2** *(book)* guía. **3** *(indicator)* guía, modelo. COMP guide dog perro lazarillo.
► *vt* **1** *(show the way)* guiar; *(lead)* conducir. **2** *(advise, influence)* orientar, aconsejar.

guidebook [ˈgaɪdbʊk] *n* guía.

guideline [ˈgaɪdlaɪn] *n* pauta, directriz *f*.

guiding [ˈgaɪdɪŋ] *adj* que guía, que sirve de guía.

guild [gɪld] *n* *(of workers)* gremio; *(association)* asociación *f*, agrupación *f*.

guillotine [ˈgɪlətiːn] *n* guillotina.
► *vt* *(person, paper)* guillotinar.

guilt [gɪlt] *n* **1** JUR culpabilidad *f*. **2** *(blame)* culpa; *(remorse)* remordimiento.

guilty [ˈgɪltɪ] *adj* culpable (of, de). LOC to find SB guilty declarar culpable a ALGN.
① *comp* guiltier, *superl* guiltiest.

Guinea [ˈgɪnɪ] *n* Guinea. COMP Equatorial Guinea Guinea Ecuatorial. ‖ New Guinea Nueva Guinea.

guinea [ˈgɪnɪ] *n* *(coin)* guinea. COMP guinea fowl gallina de Guinea, pintada. ‖ guinea pig conejillo de Indias, cobaya.

Guinea-Bissau [gɪnɪbɪˈsaʊ] *n* Guinea Bissau.

Guinean [ˈgɪnɪən] *adj* guineano,-a.
► *n* guineano,-a.

guitar [gɪˈtɑːʳ] *n* guitarra.

guitarist [gɪˈtɑːrɪst] *n* guitarrista *mf*.

gulf [gʌlf] *n* **1** GEOG golfo. **2** *fig* abismo. COMP Gulf of Mexico golfo de Méjico. ‖ Persian Gulf golfo Pérsico. ‖ Gulf Stream corriente *f* del Golfo.

gull [gʌl] *n* gaviota.

gulley ['gʌlɪ] *n* → **gully**.

gullible ['gʌlɪbªl] *adj* crédulo,-a.

gully ['gʌlɪ] *n* **1** GEOG *(small valley, ravine)* barranco, torrentera. **2** *(deep ditch, waterway, channel)* surco, cauce *m*.
ⓘ *pl* gullies.

gulp [gʌlp] *n (of drink)* trago; *(of air)* bocanada: *he drank his glass in one gulp* se bebió todo el vaso de un trago.
▶ *vt (drink)* beberse de un trago (down, -); *(food)* engullir (down, -).
▶ *vi (swallow air)* tragar aire; *(with fear)* tragar saliva.
◆ **to gulp back** *vt insep* tragarse.

gum¹ [gʌm] *n* ANAT encía.

gum² [gʌm] *n* **1** *(natural substance)* goma, resina. **2** *(chewing gum)* chicle *m*. **3** *(glue)* goma (de pegar), pegamento.
▶ *vt* pegar (con goma).
ⓘ *pt & pp* gummed, *ger* gumming.

gumboil ['gʌmbɔɪl] *n* flemón *m*.

gumboot ['gʌmbuːt] *n* bota de agua.

gumtree ['gʌmtriː] *n* gomero, árbol *m* del caucho.

gun [gʌn] *n* **1** *(gen)* arma de fuego; *(handgun)* pistola, revólver *m*; *(rifle)* rifle *m*, fusil *m*; *(shotgun)* escopeta; *(cannon)* cañón *m*. **2** SP pistola.

gunboat ['gʌnbəʊt] *n* (lancha) cañonera.

gunfire ['gʌnfaɪəʳ] *n (gen)* fuego, disparos *mpl*; *(shooting)* tiroteo; *(shellfire)* cañoneo, cañonazos *mpl*.

gunman ['gʌnmən] *n* pistolero.
ⓘ *pl* gunmen ['gʌnmən].

gunner ['gʌnəʳ] *n* artillero.

gunpoint ['gʌnpɔɪnt] LOC **at gunpoint** a punta de pistola.

gunpowder ['gʌnpaʊdəʳ] *n* pólvora.

gunshot ['gʌnʃɒt] *n* disparo, tiro.

guru ['guːruː] *n* gurú *m*.

gush [gʌʃ] *n* chorro, borbotón *m*.
▶ *vi* **1** *(liquid)* salir a borbotones. **2** *(person)* ser efusivo,-a: *everyone was gushing over her new baby* todos se deshacían en elogios con su nuevo bebé.
▶ *vt* chorrear, derramar.

gust [gʌst] *n* **1** *(of wind)* ráfaga, racha; *(of rain)* chaparrón *m*. **2** *fig (of anger)* arrebato: *gust of laughter* carcajada.
▶ *vi* soplar.

gut [gʌt] *n* **1** ANAT intestino. **2** *fam (belly)* barriga, tripa.
▶ *n pl* **guts** *(entrails)* entrañas *fpl*, tripas *fpl*; *fam (courage)* agallas *fpl*: *it takes guts to do what you did* hay que tener agallas para hacer lo que hiciste.

gutter ['gʌtəʳ] *n (in street)* arroyo, cuneta; *(on roof)* canal *m*, canalón *m*. COMP **gutter press** prensa amarilla.

guy [gaɪ] *n* **1** *fam (man)* tipo, tío: *he's a great guy* es un tío estupendo; *a tough guy* un tipo duro. **2** US *fam (person)* tío,-a: *come on you guys* venga tíos. COMP **Guy Fawkes Night** → **Bonfire night**.

Guyana [gaɪˈænə] *n* Guyana, Guayana.

Guyanan [gaɪˈænən] *adj-n* → **Guyanese**.

guzzle ['gʌzªl] *vt fam (eat)* zamparse, engullirse; *(drink)* chupar, tragar.
▶ *vi fam (eat)* engullir; *(drink)* chupar, tragar.

gym [dʒɪm] *n* **1** *fam (gymnasium)* gimnasio. **2** *(gymnastics)* gimnasia.

gymkhana [dʒɪmˈkɑːnə] *n* gymkhana.

gymnasium [dʒɪmˈneɪzɪəm] *n* gimnasio.
ⓘ *pl* gymnasiums o gymnasia [dʒɪmˈneɪzɪə].

gymnast ['dʒɪmnæst] *n* gimnasta *mf*.

gymnastics [dʒɪmˈnæstɪks] *n* gimnasia.

gymnosperm ['dʒɪmnəʊspɜːm] *n* gimnospermo.

gynaecological [gaɪnəkəˈlɒdʒɪkªl] *adj* ginecológico,-a.

gynaecologist [gaɪnɪˈkɒlədʒɪst] *n* ginecólogo,-a.

gynaecology [gaɪnɪˈkɒlədʒɪ] *n* ginecología.

gypsum ['dʒɪpsəm] *n* yeso.

gypsy ['dʒɪpsɪ] *n* gitano,-a.
ⓘ *pl* gypsies.
▶ *adj* gitano,-a.

gyroscope ['dʒaɪrəskəʊp] *n* giroscopio, giróscopo.

H, h [eɪtʃ] *n (the letter)* H, h *f.*

habit [ˈhæbɪt] *n* **1** *(custom)* hábito, costumbre *f.* **2** REL *(garment)* hábito.

habitable [ˈhæbɪtəbəl] *adj* habitable.

habitat [ˈhæbɪtæt] *n* hábitat *m.*

habitual [həˈbɪtʃuəl] *adj* **1** *(usual)* habitual. **2** *(liar, etc)* empedernido,-a.

hack [hæk] *vt* **1** *(cut)* cortar. **2** COMPUT *(cut)* cortar.

hacker [ˈhækəʳ] *n fam (in computers)* pirata *mf.*

had [hæd] *pt & pp* → **have.**

haddock [ˈhædək] *n (fish)* eglefino.

hadn't [hæd] *pt* → **have.**

haematoma [hiːməˈtəʊmə] *n* hematoma *mf.*

haemorrhage [ˈhemərɪdʒ] *n* hemorragia.

haggis [ˈhægɪs] *n* CULIN *plato típico escocés hecho con las asaduras del cordero.*

haggle [ˈhægəl] *vi* regatear (**over,** -).

hail¹ [heɪl] *n (greeting)* saludo; *(shout)* grito.
▶ *vi* **1** *(call a taxi)* llamar. **2** *(acclaim)* aclamar.

hail² [heɪl] *n* **1** METEOR granizo. **2** *fig* lluvia.
▶ *vi* METEOR granizar.

hailstone [ˈheɪlstəʊn] *n* granizo.

hailstorm [ˈheɪlstɔːm] *n* granizada.

hair [heəʳ] *n* **1** *(on head)* cabello, pelo. **2** *(on body)* vello. **3** *(horse's mane)* crin *f.*

hairbrush [ˈheəbrʌʃ] *n* cepillo para el pelo.

haircut [ˈheəkʌt] *n* corte *m* de pelo.
[LOC] **to have a haircut** cortarse el pelo.

hairdresser [ˈheədresəʳ] *n* peluquero,-a. [COMP] **hairdresser's** peluquería.

hairdryer [ˈheədraɪəʳ] *n* secador *m* (de pelo).

hairspray [ˈheəspreɪ] *n* laca para el pelo.

hairstyle [ˈheəstaɪl] *n* peinado.

hairy [ˈheərɪ] *adj* **1** peludo,-a. **2** *fig (scary)* espeluznante, espantoso,-a.
ⓘ *comp* **hairier,** *superl* **hairiest.**

Haiti [ˈheɪtɪ] *n* Haití *m.*

Haitian [ˈheɪʃən] *adj* haitiano,-a.
▶ *n* haitiano,-a.

hake [heɪk] *n (fish)* merluza; *(young)* pescadilla.

half [hɑːf] *n* **1** mitad *f: a kilo and a half* un kilo y medio. **2** SP *(period)* parte *f,* mitad *f,* tiempo. **3** *(beer)* media pinta.
ⓘ *pl* **halves.**
▶ *adj* medio,-a: *he's been gone for half an hour* lleva fuera media hora. [COMP] **half board** media pensión *f.* ▌ **half term** *vacaciones que se hacen a mitad de trimestre.*
▶ *adv* medio, a medias: *she's half Spanish* es medio española. [LOC] **half past** y media: *it's half past two* son las dos y media.

⊕ **Half term** es una semana de vacaciones que los colegios británicos tienen a mediados de cada trimestre.

half-day [hɑːfdeɪ] *n* media jornada.

half-mast [hɑːfmɑːst] *phr* **at half-mast** a media asta.

half-note [hɑːfnəʊt] *n* US blanca.

half-time [hɑːftaɪm] *n* SP descanso, media parte *f.*

halfway [hɑːfweɪ] *adj* medio,-a, intermedio,-a.
▶ *adv* a medio camino.

hall [hɔːl] *n* **1** *(entrance)* vestíbulo, entrada. **2** *(for concerts, etc)* sala. **3** *(mansion)* casa solariega, mansión *f.* **4** US *(corridor)* pasillo, corredor *m.*

hallo [həˈləʊ] *interj* → **hello.**

Halloween [hæləʊ'iːn] *n* víspera de Todos los Santos.

⊕ Halloween es la fiesta de la víspera de Todos los Santos. Los niños se disfrazan y van de casa en casa. Cuando les abren la puerta dicen «trick or treat!» (truco o trato) y la gente les da golosinas.

hallucinate [hə'luːsɪneɪt] *vi* alucinar.

hallway ['hɔːlweɪ] *n* US vestíbulo.

halo ['heɪləʊ] *n* **1** *(round moon, etc)* halo. **2** REL aureola.
ⓘ *pl* haloes o halos.

halogen ['hælədʒen] *n* halógeno.

halt [hɔːlt] *n* **1** alto, parada. **2** *(railway)* apeadero.
▶ *vt* parar, detener, interrumpir.

halve [hɑːv] *vt* **1** *(cut in two)* partir en dos. **2** *(reduce)* reducir a la mitad. **3** *(share)* compartir. **4** *(golf)* empatar.

halves [hɑːvz] *n pl* → half.

ham [hæm] *n* *(food)* jamón *m*.

hamburger ['hæmbɜːgəʳ] *n* *(food)* hamburguesa.

✎ Lo más habitual es llamar burger a la hamburguesa.

hamlet ['hæmlət] *n* aldea.

hammer ['hæməʳ] *n* **1** *(tool, bone)* martillo. **2** *(gun)* percutor *m*.
▶ *vt* **1** *(gen)* martillar, martillear; *(nail)* clavar. **2** *fam (beat)* dar una paliza, machacar.

hammock ['hæmək] *n* **1** hamaca. **2** MAR coy *m*.

hamster ['hæmstəʳ] *n* ZOOL hámster *m*.

hand [hænd] *n* **1** mano *f*. **2** *(worker)* trabajador,-ra, operario,-a; *(sailor)* tripulante *mf*, marinero,-a. **3** *(of clock)* manecilla, aguja. **4** *(handwriting)* letra. **5** *(of cards)* mano *f*, cartas *fpl*. **6** *(applause)* aplauso. ⌐LOC⌐ **at hand** a mano. **║ hands up!** ¡manos arriba! **║ on the one hand** por un lado **║ by hand** a mano **║ on the other hand** por otro lado **║ to lend a hand** echar una mano.
◆ **to hand back** *vt sep* devolver.
◆ **to hand in** *vt sep (work, etc)* entregar; *(resignation, etc)* presentar, notificar.

◆ **to hand on** *vt sep (traditions, etc)* transmitir, heredar; *(give)* pasar, dar.
◆ **to hand out** *vt sep (distribute)* repartir, distribuir; *(give - gen)* dar; *(- punishment)* aplicar.
◆ **to hand over** *vt sep (give)* entregar; *(one's possessions, etc)* ceder.

handbag ['hændbæg] *n* bolso.

handball ['hændbɔːl] *n* SP balonmano.

handbook ['hændbʊk] *n* *(guidebook)* guía; *(reference book)* manual *m*.

handbrake ['hændbreɪk] *n* freno de mano.

handcuff ['hændkʌf] *vt* esposar.
▶ *n pl* **handcuffs** esposas *fpl*.

handful ['hændfʊl] *n* puñado.

handicap ['hændɪkæp] *n* **1** *(physical)* discapacidad *f*; *(mental)* deficiencia, disminución *f* psíquica. **2** *(in sport)* handicap *m*. **3** *fig* obstáculo.
▶ *vt* obstaculizar, impedir.
ⓘ *pt & pp* handicapped, *ger* handicapping.

handicapped ['hændɪkæpt] *adj* **1** *(physically)* minusválido,-a, discapacitado,-a, disminuido,-a físico,-a; *(mentally)* disminuido,-a psíquico,-a. **2** *fig* desfavorecido,-a.

handicraft ['hændɪkrɑːft] *n* **1** *(job, art)* artesanía; *(objects)* objetos *mpl* de artesanía. **2** *(manual skill)* habilidad *f* manual.

handkerchief ['hæŋkətʃiːf] *n* pañuelo.
ⓘ *pl* handkerchiefs o handkerchieves.

handle ['hændəl] *n* **1** *(of door)* pomo, manilla. **2** *(of drawer)* tirador *m*. **3** *(of cup)* asa. **4** *(of knife)* mango. **5** *(lever)* palanca. **6** *(crank)* manivela.
▶ *vt* **1** *(gen)* manejar, manipular. **2** *(people)* tratar. **3** *(tolerate)* aguantar. **4** *(control)* controlar, dominar. **5** *(manage)* poder con, tener la capacidad para.

handlebar ['hændəlbɑːʳ] *n* manillar *m*.

handmade [hænd'meɪd] *adj* hecho,-a a mano.

handout ['hændaʊt] *n* **1** *(leaflet)* folleto, prospecto; *(political)* octavilla. **2** EDUC material *m*. **3** *(press)* nota de prensa.

H

handshake ['hændʃeɪk] n apretón m de manos.

handsome ['hænsəm] adj 1 (man) apuesto, guapo; (woman) bella, guapa. 2 (elegant) elegante. 3 (generous) considerable, generoso,-a.

hands-on ['hændzɒn] adj (for computers) práctico,-a.

handstand ['hændstænd] n LOC **to do a handstand** hacer el pino.

handwriting ['hændraɪtɪŋ] n letra, escritura.

handy ['hændɪ] adj 1 (person) hábil. 2 (close at hand) a mano, cercano,-a. 3 (useful) práctico,-a, cómodo,-a, útil.
ⓘ comp **handier**, superl **handiest**.

handyman ['hændɪmæn] n manitas mf.
ⓘ pl **handymen** ['hændɪmən].

hang [hæŋ] vt 1 [pt & pp hung [hʌŋ]] (gen) colgar. 2 [pt & pp hung [hʌŋ]] (wallpaper) colocar. 3 [pt & pp hanged.] JUR ahorcar.
▶ n (of dress, etc) caída.
◆ **to hang about / hang around** vi 1 esperar. 2 (waste time) perder el tiempo.
▶ vt insep frecuentar.
◆ **to hang back** vi 1 quedarse atrás. 2 fig vacilar.
◆ **to hang down** vi colgar, caer.
◆ **to hang on** vi 1 (hold tight) agarrarse. 2 (wait) esperar.
◆ **to hang out** vt sep (washing) tender.
▶ vi fam soler estar.
◆ **to hang up** vt sep colgar.

hangar ['hæŋəʳ] n hangar m.

hanger ['hæŋəʳ] n percha.

hang-glider ['hæŋɡlaɪdəʳ] n ala delta.

hang-gliding ['hæŋɡlaɪdɪŋ] n ala m delta.

hangover ['hæŋəʊvəʳ] n 1 (after too much drinking) resaca. 2 (remains) resto, vestigio.

happen ['hæpən] vi 1 (occur) ocurrir, pasar, suceder. 2 (by chance) dar la casualidad de.

happening ['hæpənɪŋ] n acontecimiento.

happily ['hæpɪlɪ] adv 1 (in a happy way) felizmente, con alegría. 2 (luckily) afortunadamente.

happiness ['hæpɪnəs] n felicidad f, alegría.

happy ['hæpɪ] adj 1 (cheerful) feliz, alegre, dichoso,-a, afortunado,-a. 2 (glad) contento,-a, satisfecho,-a. LOC **happy birthday!** !feliz cumpleaños!
ⓘ comp **happier**, superl **happiest**.

harass ['hærəs] vt 1 acosar, hostigar. 2 (military) hostilizar, hostigar. 3 (worries, problems) atormentar, agobiar.

harassment ['hærəsmənt] n acoso, hostigamiento.

harbor ['hɑːbəʳ] n US → harbour.

harbour ['hɑːbəʳ] n puerto.
▶ vt 1 (criminal) encubrir. 2 (doubts) abrigar. 3 (suspicions) tener; (contain, hide) contener, esconder.

hard [hɑːd] adj 1 (gen) duro,-a; (solid) sólido,-a. 2 (difficult) difícil. 3 (harsh) severo,-a. 4 (work) arduo,-a, agotador,-ra. 5 (final decision) definitivo,-a, irrevocable; (person) severo,-a, inflexible. 6 LING fuerte. LOC **hard of hearing** duro,-a de oído. **to work hard** trabajar mucho. COMP **hard court** pista dura. **hard disk** disco duro. **hard labour** trabajos forzados.
▶ adv (forcibly) fuerte; (diligently) mucho, concienzudamente, con ahínco.

harden ['hɑːdən] vt 1 endurecer. 2 fig insensibilizar.

hardly ['hɑːdlɪ] adv (scarcely) apenas, casi; (not easily) difícilmente.

hardness ['hɑːdnəs] n dureza.

hardware ['hɑːdweəʳ] n 1 (goods) artículos mpl de ferretería. 2 COMPUT hardware m, soporte m físico. COMP **hardware store** ferretería.

hard-working ['hɑːdˈwɜːkɪŋ] adj trabajador,-ra.

hare [heəʳ] n ZOOL liebre f.
▶ vi correr muy deprisa.

haricot bean [hærɪkəʊˈbiːn] n alubia, judía.

harm [hɑːm] n mal m, daño.
▶ vt dañar, perjudicar. LOC **to do sb harm** hacerle daño a ALGN. **there's no harm in...** no se pierda nada...

harmful ['hɑːmfʊl] adj dañino,-a, nocivo,-a, perjudicial.

harmless ['hɑ:mləs] *adj* inocuo,-a, inofensivo,-a.

harmonic [hɑ:'mɒnɪk] *adj* armónico,-a.

harmony ['hɑ:mənɪ] *n* armonía.
ⓘ *pl* harmonies.

harp [hɑ:p] *n* MUS arpa.

harpist ['hɑ:pɪst] *n* MUS arpista *mf*.

harpoon [hɑ:'puːn] *n* arpón *m*.
▶ *vt* arponear.

harsh [hɑ:ʃ] *adj* **1** *(cruel)* cruel, duro,-a, severo,-a. **2** *(sound)* discordante. **3** *(rough)* áspero,-a.

harvest ['hɑ:vɪst] *n* **1** *(gen)* cosecha, siega. **2** *(grapes)* vendimia.
▶ *vt* **1** cosechar, recoger. **2** *(grapes)* vendimiar.

harvester ['hɑ:vɪstə'] *n* **1** *(person)* segador,-ra. **2** *(machine)* segadora, cosechadora.

has [hæz] *pres* → have.

haste [heɪst] *n* prisa, precipitación *f*.

hasten ['heɪsən] *vi* darse prisa.

hastily ['heɪstɪlɪ] *adv (quickly)* de prisa.

hat [hæt] *n* sombrero.

hatch [hætʃ] *n* **1** *(on ship)* escotilla. **2** *(of chickens, brood)* pollada.
▶ *vt* **1** *(eggs)* empollar, incubar. **2** *fig (plot, plan)* idear, tramar.
▶ *vi* salir del cascarón, salir del huevo.

hate [heɪt] *n* odio.
▶ *vt* **1** *fam (detest)* odiar, detestar, aborrecer. **2** *fam (regret)* lamentar, sentir.

hatred ['heɪtrəd] *n* odio.

haul [hɔ:l] *n* **1** *(distance)* recorrido, camino. **3** *(fish)* redada. **4** *(loot)* botín *m*.
▶ *vt* **1** *(drag)* tirar de, arrastrar. **2** *(boat)* halar; *(car, caravan, etc)* remolcar.

haunt [hɔ:nt] *n (of people)* sitio preferido; *(of criminals, animals)* guarida.
▶ *vt* **1** *(frequent - gen)* frecuentar; *(- ghost)* aparecer en, rondar por. **2** *(memory, thought)* obsesionar, perseguir.

haunted ['hɔ:ntɪd] *adj* encantado,-a.

have [hæv] *vt* **1** *(gen)* tener, poseer. **2** *(food)* comer, tomar; *(drink)* beber, tomar. **3** *(treatment)* recibir: *she's having physiotherapy* acude a fisioterapia. **4** *(invite)* recibir, invitar. **5** *(borrow)* pedir prestado, dejar. **6** *(party, meeting)* cele-

brar, tener, dar. **7** *(cause to happen)* hacer, mandar: *he had the house painted* hizo pintar la casa. **8** *fam (cheat)* timar.
ⓁⓄⒸ **have got** tener: *he's got two sisters* tiene dos hermanas; *we haven't got any sugar* no tenemos azúcar. ∣ **to have breakfast** desayunar. ∣ **to have dinner** cenar. ∣ **to have just** acabar de: *I have just seen him* acabo de verlo. ∣ **to have lunch** comer, almorzar. ∣ **to have a bath** bañarse. ∣ **to have a shower** ducharse. ∣ **to have a swim** darse un baño.
▶ *aux* haber: *I have seen her* la he visto.
◆ **to have on** *vt sep* **1** *(wear)* llevar puesto,-a. **2** *(tease)* tomar el pelo a.
◆ **to have out** *vt sep (tooth)* sacarse; *(appendix)* operarse de.
ⓘ *3rd pers pres sing* has [hæz], *pt & pp* had [hæd], *ger* having.

✎ Have es el verbo auxiliar que se emplea en inglés para conjugar los tiempos perfectos.

haven ['heɪvən] *n* **1** *fig* refugio, asilo. **2** *(harbour)* puerto.

havoc ['hævək] *n* estragos *mpl*.

hawk¹ [hɔ:k] *n* halcón *m*.

hawk² [hɔ:k] *vt* **1** *(in the street)* vender en la calle; *(door to door)* vender de puerta en puerta. **2** *(gossip, news)* divulgar, pregonar, difundir.
▶ *vi* carraspear.

hay [heɪ] *n* BOT heno. ⓒⓄⓂⓅ **hay fever** fiebre *f* del heno.

hazard ['hæzəd] *n* **1** *(risk)* riesgo, peligro. **2** *(in sports in general)* obstáculo.
▶ *vt* **1** *fml* arriesgar, poner en peligro. **2** *fml (guess, remark)* aventurar, atreverse a hacer.

hazardous ['hæzədəs] *adj* arriesgado,-a, peligroso,-a, aventurado,-a.

haze [heɪz] *n* **1** neblina. **2** *fig* confusión *f*, vaguedad *f*.
▶ *vt* US hacer una novatada a.

hazel ['heɪzəl] *n* BOT avellano.
▶ *adj* (de color de) avellana.

hazelnut ['heɪzəlnʌt] *n* BOT avellana.

hazy ['heɪzɪ] *adj* con neblina.

he [hiː] *pron* **1** él: *he's my brother* (él) es mi hermano. **2** *(gen)* el que, quien.
▶ *n* **1** *(male animals)* macho. **2** *(man)* hombre *m*, varón *m*.

head [hed] *n* **1** *(gen)* cabeza; *(mind)* mente *f*. **2** *(on tape recorder, video)* cabezal *m*. **3** *(of bed, table)* cabecera. **4** *(of page)* principio. **5** *(on beer)* espuma. **6** *(cape)* cabo, punta. **7** *(of school, company)* director,-ra.
▶ *adj* principal, jefe.
▶ *vt* **1** *(company, list, etc)* encabezar. **2** *(ball)* rematar de cabeza, dar un cabezazo a, cabecear.
◆ **to head for** *vt insep* dirigirse hacia.
◆ **to head off** *vi* marcharse, irse.
▶ *vt sep (divert)* interceptar; *(avoid)* evitar.

headache [ˈhedeɪk] *n* dolor *m* de cabeza.

head-first [hedˈfɜːst] *adv* de cabeza.

head-hunter [hedˈhʌntəʳ] *n* **1** cazador,-ra de cabezas, jíbaro,-a. **2** *fam fig* cazatalentos *mf*.

heading [ˈhedɪŋ] *n* **1** *(of chapter)* encabezamiento, título. **2** *(letterhead)* membrete *m*.

headlamp [ˈhedlæmp] *n* AUTO faro.

headlight [ˈhedlaɪt] *n* AUTO faro.

headline [ˈhedlaɪn] *n* titular *m*.

headmaster [hedˈmɑːstəʳ] *n* director *m*.

headmistress [hedˈmɪstrəs] *n* directora.

headphones [ˈhedfəʊnz] *n pl* auriculares *mpl*, cascos *mpl*.

headquarters [ˈhedkwɔːtəz] *n* **1** *(of an organization)* sede *f*; *(main office)* oficina central. **2** *(of a firm)* domicilio social. **3** MIL cuartel *m* general.

✎ Headquarters puede considerarse tanto singular como plural: *our headquarters is/are in New York* nuestra sede está en Nueva York.

headteacher [hedˈtiːʳ] *adj* director,-a.

headword [ˈhedwɜːd] *n* entrada.

heal [hiːl] *vt* **1** *(disease, patient)* curar; *(wound)* cicatrizar, curar. **2** *fig* curar, remediar.

▶ *vi* **1** *(wounds)* cicatrizar, cicatrizarse; *(people)* curarse,. **2** *fig* remediarse.
◆ **to heal up** *vi* curarse, cicatrizarse.

health [helθ] *n* **1** salud *f*. **2** *(service)* sanidad *f*. **3** *fig* prosperidad *f*. COMP **health care** sanidad *f*. ▌ **health centre** centro de salud. ▌ **health food** alimentos *mpl* naturales.

healthy [ˈhelθɪ] *adj* **1** *(gen)* sano,-a. **2** *(good for health)* saludable. **3** *(appetite)* bueno,-a. **4** *(prosperous)* próspero,-a; *(disposition)* sensato,-a.
ⓘ *comp* healthier, *superl* healthiest.

heap [hiːp] *n* montón *m*.

hear [hɪəʳ] *vt* **1** *(gen)* oír. **3** *(lecture)* asistir a; *(a news item)* saber. **3** JUR *(case)* ver; *(witness, defendant)* oír.
ⓘ *pt & pp* heard [hɜːd].

heard [hɜːd] *pt & pp* → **hear**.

hearer [ˈhɪərəʳ] *n* oyente *mf*.

hearing [ˈhɪərɪŋ] *n* **1** *(sense)* oído. **2** *(act of hearing)* audición *f*. **3** JUR audiencia, vista.

heart [hɑːt] *n* **1** ANAT corazón *m*. **2** *(centre of feeling)* corazón *m*. **3** *(courage)* valor *m*, corazón *m*. **4** *(of lettuce, etc)* cogollo; *(of place)* corazón *m*, centro; *(of question)* fondo, quid *m*, meollo. LOC **to learn by heart** aprender de memoria. ▌ **to take heart** animarse. ▌ **to learn by heart** aprender de memoria. COMP **heart attack** ataque *m* de corazón.
▶ *n pl* **hearts** *(cards)* corazones *mpl*; *(Spanish cards)* copas *fpl*.

heartbeat [ˈhɑːtbiːt] *n* latido del corazón.

heartburn [ˈhɑːtbɜːn] *n* ardor *m* de estómago.

hearten [ˈhɑːtən] *vt* animar, alentar.

heartless [ˈhɑːtləs] *adj* cruel, insensible.

heat [hiːt] *n* **1** *(gen)* calor *m*. **2** *(heating)* calefacción *f*. **3** SP eliminatoria, serie *f*. **4** ZOOL celo.
▶ *vt* **1** calentar. **2** *fig* acalorar.
◆ **to heat up** *vi (warm up)* calentarse; *(to raise excitement, etc)* acalorarse.

heater [ˈhiːtəʳ] *n* calentador *m*.

heather [ˈheðəʳ] *n* BOT brezo.

heating [ˈhiːtɪŋ] *n* calefacción *f*.

heatstroke ['hi:tstrəuk] n MED insolación f.

heatwave ['hi:tweɪv] n ola de calor.

heave [hi:v] n (pull) tirón m; (push) empujón m.
▶ vt 1 (pull) tirar; (lift) levantar. 2 (push) empujar. 3 fam (throw) lanzar, arrojar.

heaven ['hevªn] n 1 cielo. 2 fam gloria, paraíso.
▶ n pl **heavens** cielo.

heavily ['hevɪlɪ] adv 1 (fall, move, step, etc) pesadamente; (rain) fuertemente, mucho. 2 (sleep, etc) profundamente; (drink) con exceso, mucho; (breathe) con dificultad f.

heavy ['hevɪ] adj 1 (gen) pesado,-a. 2 (rain, blow) fuerte, pesado,-a. 3 (traffic) denso,-a. 4 (sleep) profundo,-a. 5 (crop) abundante. 6 (atmosphere) cargado,-a. 7 (loss, expenditure) grande, considerable. [COMP] **heavy metal** rock m duro, heavy metal m.
ⓘ comp **heavier**, superl **heaviest**.

heavy-duty ['hevɪ'dju:tɪ] adj (clothes, shoes, etc) de faena, resistente; (equipment, machinery, etc) reforzado,-a, robusto,-a, para grandes cargas.

heavyweight ['heviweit] n 1 SP peso pesado. 2 fig peso pesado.

Hebrew ['hi:bru:] adj hebreo,-a.
▶ n 1 (person) hebreo,-a. 2 (language) hebreo.

hectare ['hektɑ:ʳ] n hectárea.

hectic ['hektɪk] adj agitado,-a, ajetreado,-a, movido,-a.

he'd [hi:z] contr 1 he had. 2 he would.

hedge [hedʒ] n 1 seto vivo. 2 fig protección f, barrera.
▶ vi contestar con evasivas.
▶ vt 1 cercar, separar con un seto. 2 fig (protect) proteger, guardar; (protect OS against) protegerse.

hedgehog ['hedʒhɒg] n ZOOL erizo.

heel [hi:l] n 1 ANAT talón m. 2 (on shoe) tacón m; (of sock) talón m.
▶ vt 1 poner tacón a. 2 (in rugby) talonear. 3 MAR inclinar.
▶ vi MAR escorar.

height [haɪt] n 1 (gen) altura. 2 (altitude) altitud f. 3 (of person) estatura. 4 GEOG cumbre f, cima.

heir [eəʳ] n heredero.

heiress ['eəres] n heredera.

held [held] pt & pp → **hold**.

helicopter ['helɪkɒptəʳ] n helicóptero.

heliport ['helɪpɔ:t] n helipuerto.

helium ['hi:lɪəm] n CHEM helio.

helix ['hi:lɪks] n hélice f.

hell [hel] n infierno.

he'll [hi:l] contr 1 he will. 2 he shall.

hello [he'ləʊ] interj 1 ¡hola! 2 (on telephone - answering) ¡diga!; (- calling) ¡oiga! 3 (to get sb's attention) ¡oiga!, ¡oye!

helm [helm] n MAR timón m.

helmet ['helmɪt] n casco.

help [help] n 1 (gen) ayuda. 2 (servant) asistenta, criada.
▶ interj ¡socorro!
▶ vt 1 (gen) ayudar. 2 (be of use) ayudar, servir. 3 (to relieve) aliviar. 4 (avoid) evitar.
◆ to **help out** vt sep ayudar.

helper ['helpəʳ] n 1 ayudante,-a mf, auxiliar mf. 2 (collaborator) colaborador,-ra.

helpful ['helpful] adj 1 (thing) útil, práctico,-a,. 2 (person) amable.

helping ['helpɪŋ] n ración f, porción f.
▶ adj ayuda.

helpless ['helpləs] adj 1 (unprotected) desamparado,-a, indefenso,-a, desvalido,-a. 2 (powerless) impotente, incapaz, inútil.

hem [hem] n SEW dobladillo.
▶ vt hacer un dobladillo en.
ⓘ pt & pp **hemmed**, ger **hemming**.

hematoma [hi:mə'təʊmə] n US → **haematoma**.

hemisphere ['hemɪsfɪəʳ] n hemisferio.

hemorrhage ['hemərɪdʒ] n US → **haemorrhage**.

hen [hen] n (chicken) gallina; (female bird) hembra.

hence [hens] adv 1 fml (so) por eso, por lo tanto, de ahí. 2 (from now) de aquí a, dentro de.

henceforth [hens'fɔ:θ] adv fml de ahora en adelante.

henhouse ['henhaʊs] n gallinero.

H

henna ['henə] *n* BOT alheña.

heptagon ['heptəgən] *n* heptágono.

heptagonal [hep'tægənªl] *adj* heptagonal.

her [hɜ:ʳ] *pron* **1** *(direct object)* la: *I love her* la quiero. **2** *(indirect object)* le; *(with other third person pronouns)* se: *give it to her* dáselo. **3** *(after preposition)* ella: *go with her* vete con ella. **4** *fam (as subject)* ella: *listen, that's her!* ¡escucha, es ella!
▸ *adj* su, sus; *(emphatic)* de ella.

heraldic [he'rældɪk] *adj* heráldico,-a.

herb [hɜ:b] *n* hierba.

herbaceous [hɜ:'beɪʃəs] *adj* herbáceo,-a.

herbal ['hɜ:bªl] *adj* de hierbas.

herbicide ['hɜ:bɪsaɪd] *n* herbicida *m*.

herbivore ['hɜ:bɪvɔ:ʳ] *n* ZOOL herbívoro,-a.

herd [hɜ:d] *n* **1** *(cattle)* manada; *(goats)* rebaño; *(pigs)* piara. **2** *fam (people)* montón *m*, multitud *f*.

here [hɪəʳ] *adv* aquí. LOC *here you are* aquí tienes.

hereby [hɪə'baɪ] *adv fml* por la presente.

hereditary [hɪ'redɪtªrɪ] *adj* hereditario,-a.

heredity [hɪ'redɪtɪ] *n* herencia.

heresy ['herəsɪ] *n* herejía.
ⓘ *pl* heresies.

heritage ['herɪtɪdʒ] *n* herencia, patrimonio.

hermaphrodite [hɜ:'mæfrədaɪt] *adj* hermafrodita.

hernia ['hɜ:nɪə] *n* hernia.

hero ['hɪərəʊ] *n* **1** *(gen)* héroe *m*. **2** *(in novel)* protagonista *m*.
ⓘ *pl* heroes.

heroic [hɪ'rəʊɪk] *adj* heroico,-a.

heroin ['herəʊɪn] *n (drug)* heroína.

heroine ['herəʊɪn] *n* **1** heroína. **2** *(in novel)* protagonista.

herpes ['hɜ:pi:z] *n* herpe *m*, herpes *m*.

herring ['herɪŋ] *n* arenque *m*.
ⓘ *pl* herring o herrings.

hers [hɜ:z] *pron (sing)* (el) suyo, (la) suya; *(pl)* (los) suyos, (las) suyas; *(emphatic)* de ella: *this pencil is hers* este lápiz es suyo.

herself [hɜ:'self] *pron* **1** *(reflexive use)* se: *she washed herself* se lavó. **2** *(emphatic)* ella misma: *she made it all herself* lo hizo todo ella misma. LOC *by herself* sola.

hertz [hɜ:ts] *n* hertz *m*, hercio.

he's [hi:z] *contr* **1** he is. **2** he has.

hesitate ['hezɪteɪt] *vi* vacilar, dudar.

hesitation [hezɪ'teɪʃªn] *n* duda, indecisión.

heterogeneous [hetərəʊ'dʒi:nɪəs] *adj* heterogéneo,-a.

heterosexual [hetərəʊ'seksjʊəl] *adj* heterosexual.

heterotrophic [hetərəʊ'trɒfɪk] *adj* heterotrófico,-a.

hexagon ['heksəgən] *n* hexágono.

hexagonal [hek'sægənªl] *adj* hexagonal.

hi [haɪ] *interj fam* ¡hola!

hibernate ['haɪbəneɪt] *vi* hibernar.

hiccough ['hɪkʌp] *n-vi* → hiccup.

hiccup ['hɪkʌp] *n* hipo: *to have hiccups* tener hipo.

hid [hɪd] *pt & pp* → hide.

hidden ['hɪdªn] *pp* → hide.
▸ *adj* **1** escondido,-a. **2** *fig* oculto,-a.

hide¹ [haɪd] *n (concealed place)* escondite *m*.
▸ *vt (conceal)* esconder; *(obscure)* ocultar, tapar.
ⓘ *pt* hid [hɪd], *pp* hid [hɪd] o hidden ['hɪdªn].

hide² [haɪd] *n* **1** piel *f*, cuero. **2** *fig (of a person)* pellejo.

hide-and-seek [haɪdªn'si:k] *n* escondite *m*.

hideous ['hɪdɪəs] *adj* **1** *(terrible)* horroroso,-a, atroz. **2** *(ugly)* horrendo,-a, espantoso.

hide-out ['haɪdaʊt] *n* escondrijo, escondite *m*, guarida.

hierarchic [haɪə'rɑ:kɪk] *adj* jerárquico,-a.

hierarchy ['haɪərɑ:kɪ] *n* jerarquía.
ⓘ *pl* hierarchies.

hieroglyphics [haɪərə'glɪfɪks] *n pl* jeroglíficos *mpl*.

hi-fi ['haɪfaɪ] *n* hifi *m*, alta fidelidad *f*.

high [haɪ] *adj* **1** alto,-a, elevado. **2** *(important)* alto,-a, importante; *(strong)* fuerte. **3** *(very good)* bueno,-a. **4** *(going rotten - food)* pasado,-a; *(- game)* mani do,-a. **5** *(of time)* pleno,-a. `COMP` **high jump** salto de altura. ▌ **high school** instituto (de bachillerato). ▌ **high street** calle mayor. ▌ **high tide** marea alta.

⊕ El **high school** es el equivalente a los institutos de bachillerato, sobre todo en Estados Unidos.

high-class [haɪ'klɑːs] *adj (classy)* de categoría; *(superior)* de calidad f.

higher ['haɪəʳ] *adj* **1** → high. **2** superior. **3** *(bigger)* más alto,-a; *(number, velocity, etc)* mayor. `COMP` **higher education** enseñanza superior.

high-heeled ['haɪ'hiːld] *adj* de tacón alto.

highlight ['haɪlaɪt] *vt* **1** destacar, hacer resaltar. **2** *(with pen)* marcar *(con un rotulador fosforescente)*.
▶ *n* **1** ART toque *m* de luz. **2** *(hairdressing)* reflejo. **3** *fig (especially in show business)* atracción f principal; *(most outstanding)* punto culminante; *(aspect or feature)* característica notable.

highly ['haɪlɪ] *adv (very)* muy; *(favourably)* muy bien.

Highness ['haɪnəs] *n* Alteza *mf*.

high-pitched ['haɪ'pɪtʃt] *adj (sound, voice)* agudo,-a; *(roof)* empinado,-a.

high-tech [haɪ'tek] *adj* de alta tecnología.

highway ['haɪweɪ] *n* **1** US autovía. **2** JUR vía pública.

hijack ['haɪdʒæk] *n* secuestro.
▶ *vt* secuestrar.

hijacker ['haɪdʒækəʳ] *n* secuestrador,-a.

hijacking ['haɪdʒækɪŋ] *n* secuestro.

hike [haɪk] *n* **1** *(walk)* excursión f a pie. **2** *fam* aumento de precio.
▶ *vi* ir de excursión, hacer una excursión.
▶ *vt fam* aumentar los precios.

hiker ['haɪkəʳ] *n* excursionista.

hiking ['haɪkɪŋ] *n* excursionismo a pie.

hilarious [hɪ'leərɪəs] *adj* graciosísimo,-a, hilarante, divertidísimo,-a.

hill [hɪl] *n* **1** colina, cerro. **2** *(slope)* cuesta.

hillside ['hɪlsaɪd] *n* ladera.

hilltop ['hɪltɒp] *n* cumbre f, cima.

him [hɪm] *pron* **1** *(direct object)* lo: *I love him* lo quiero. **2** *(indirect object)* le; *(with other pronouns)* se: *give him the money* dale el dinero; *give it to him* dáselo. **3** *(after preposition)* él: *we went with him* fuimos con él. **4** *fam (as subject)* él: *it's him!* ¡es él!

himself [hɪm'self] *pron* **1** *(reflexive)* se; *(alone)* solo, por sí mismo: *he cut himself* se cortó; *he did it by himself* lo hizo solo. **2** *(emphatic)* él mismo, sí mismo, en persona.

hinder ['hɪndəʳ] *vt* dificultar, entorpecer, estorbar, impedir.

Hindu [hɪn'duː, 'hɪnduː] *n* hindú *mf*.
▶ *adj* hindú.

Hinduism ['hɪnduɪzəm] *n* hinduismo.

hinge [hɪndʒ] *n* **1** TECH gozne *m*, bisagra. **2** *(for stamps)* fijasello. **3** *fig* eje *m*.
▶ *vi* girar sobre goznes.

hint [hɪnt] *n* **1** insinuación f, indirecta. **2** *(advice)* consejo, sugerencia. **3** *(clue)* pista. **4** *(trace)* pizca. **5** *(sign)* sombra.
▶ *vt (imply)* insinuar, aludir a.

hip¹ [hɪp] *n* ANAT cadera.

hip² [hɪp] `LOC` **hip hip hooray!** ¡hurra!

hippie ['hɪpɪ] *n fam* hippie *mf*.

hippo ['hɪpə] *n fam* hipopótamo.

hippopotamus [hɪpə'pɒtəməs] *n* ZOOL hipopótamo.

hippy ['hɪpɪ] *n fam* hippie *mf*.
ⓘ *pl* hippies.

hire ['haɪəʳ] *n* alquiler *m*.
▶ *vt* **1** *(rent)* alquilar. **2** *(employ)* contratar.
◆ **to hire out** *vt sep (equipment, vehicles, etc)* alquilar; *(people)* contratar.

his [hɪz] *adj* **1** su, sus: *his dog* su perro. **2** *(emphatic)* de él.
▶ *pron* (el) suyo, (la) suya, (los) suyos, (las) suyas.

Hispanic [hɪs'pænɪk] *adj* hispánico,-a.
▶ *n* US hispano,-a, latino,-a.

hiss [hɪs] *n* **1** *(gen)* siseo. **2** *(air, snake, steam, etc)* silbido. **3** *(protest)* silbido.
▶ *vt* **1** sisear, silbar. **2** *(in protest)* pitar, abuchear.

historic [hɪ'stɒrɪk] *adj* histórico,-a.

historical [hɪ'stɒrɪkəl] *adj* histórico,-a.

history ['hɪstᵊrɪ] n **1** (in general) historia. **2** COMPUT historial m.
ⓘ pl histories.

❌ History no significa 'historia (relato)', que se traduce por story.

hit [hɪt] n **1** (blow) golpe m. **2** (success) éxito, acierto. **3** (shot) impacto. **4** (visit to web page) acceso. **5** fig (damaging remark) pulla.
▸ vt **1** (strike) golpear, pegar. **2** (crash into) chocar contra. **3** (affect) afectar, perjudicar. **4** (reach) alcanzar.
◆ **to hit back** vi (strike in return) devolver golpe por golpe; (reply to criticism) defenderse.
ⓘ pt & pp hit, ger hitting.

hitch [hɪtʃ] n obstáculo, dificultad f.
▸ vt (tie) enganchar, atar.
▸ vi fam hacer autoestop, ir a dedo, hacer dedo.

hitchhike ['hɪtʃhaɪk] vi hacer autoestop.

hitchhiking ['hɪtʃhaɪkɪŋ] vi autoestop m, dedo.

HIV ['eɪtʃaɪ'viː] abbr (human immunodeficiency virus) virus m de inmunodeficiencia humana; (abbreviation) VIH m.

hive [haɪv] n **1** colmena. **2** fig lugar m muy activo.

hoard [hɔːd] n **1** (provisions) reserva. **2** (money) tesoro escondido.
▸ vt **1** (objects) acumular. **2** (money) atesorar.

hoarse [hɔːs] adj ronco,-a, áspero,-a.

hoax [həʊks] n (trick) trampa, engaño; (joke) broma pesada.
▸ vt engañar a, gastar una broma a.

hob [hɒb] n (of cooker) encimera; (next to fireplace) repisa.

hobble ['hɒbᵊl] vi (limp) cojear, andar con dificultad f.
▸ vt **1** (tie) trabar, manear. **2** fig poner trabas a, obstaculizar.

hobby ['hɒbɪ] n afición f, hobby m, pasatiempo favorito.
ⓘ pl hobbies.

hockey ['hɒkɪ] n SP hockey m.

hoe [həʊ] n azada, azadón m.

▸ vt (earth) azadonar, cavar; (weeds) sachar.

hog [hɒg] n **1** cerdo, puerco, marrano. **2** fam pej (not a nice person) indeseable mf.
▸ vt acaparar.
ⓘ pt & pp hogged, ger hogging.

hoist [hɔɪst] n **1** (crane) grúa. **2** (lift) montacargas m.
▸ vt **1** levantar, subir. **2** (flag) izar.

hold [həʊld] n **1** (place to grip) asidero. **2** (in ship, plane) bodega. LOC **to get hold of 1** (grab) agarrar, coger. **2** (obtain) hacerse con, encontrar.
▸ vt **1** (keep in one's hand) aguantar, sostener: hold my bag aguántame el bolso. **2** (opinion) sostener. **3** (contain) dar cabida a, tener capacidad para: the stadium holds a lot of people el estadio tiene capacidad para mucha gente. **4** (meeting) celebrar; (conversation) mantener: political parties often hold meetings in parks los partidos políticos celebran a menudo sus mítines en los parques. LOC **to hold SB** abrazar a ALGN.
◆ **to hold back** vt sep **1** (suspect) retener. **2** (information) ocultar; (restrain) contener; (feelings) reprimir; (keep) guardar.
▸ vi (hesitate) vacilar, no atreverse; (abstain) abstenerse.
◆ **to hold down** vt sep (control) dominar; (job) desempeñar.
◆ **to hold forth** vi hablar largo y tendido.
◆ **to hold off** vt sep mantener alejado,-a.
▸ vi (refrain) refrenarse.
◆ **to hold on** vi **1** (grip tightly) agarrarse fuerte, agarrarse bien. **2** (wait) esperar; (on phone) no colgar.
◆ **to hold over** vt sep aplazar.
◆ **to hold up** vt sep **1** (rob) atracar, asaltar. **2** (delay) retrasar. **3** (raise) levantar. **4** (support) aguantar, sostener.
▸ vi aguantar, resistir.
◆ **to hold with** vt insep estar de acuerdo con.
ⓘ pt & pp held [held].

holder ['həʊldᵊr] n **1** (owner) poseedor, -ra; (of passport) titular mf. **2** (container) recipiente m, receptáculo. **3** (bearer - person) portador,-ra; (- of bonds) tenedor,-ra.

4 *(handle)* asidero. **5** *(tenant - on land)* arrendatario,-a; *(- of a flat)* inquilino,-a.

hold-up ['həʊldʌp] *n* **1** *(robbery)* atraco; *(of train, etc)* asalto. **2** *(delay)* retraso. **3** AUTO atasco.

hole [həʊl] *n* **1** *(gen)* agujero; *(in ground, golf)* hoyo. **2** *(in road)* bache *m*. **3** *(of rabbits)* madriguera; *(cavity)* cavidad *f*. **4** *fam (town)* pueblucho de mala muerte. **5** *fam (place to live)* cuchitril *m*; *(unsavoury place)* antro. **6** *(a tight spot)* aprieto, apuro.
  ▶ *vt* **1** *(make holes - small)* agujerear; *(large)* hacer un boquete en. **2** *(at golf)* meter en el hoyo.

holiday ['hɒlɪdeɪ] *n* **1** *(one day)* fiesta, día *m* de fiesta, día *m* festivo. **2** *(period)* vacaciones *fpl*. LOC **to be on holiday** estar de vacaciones. ‖ **to go on holiday** irse de vacaciones.
  ▶ *vi* GB *(gen)* pasar las vacaciones; *(in summer)* veranear.

Holland ['hɒlənd] *n* Holanda.

hollow ['hɒləʊ] *adj* **1** *(sound, thing)* hueco,-a. **2** *(cheeks, etc)* hundido,-a. **3** *fig (laugh)* falso,-a; *(promise)* vacío,-a.
  ① *comp* **hollower**, *superl* **hollowest**.
  ▶ *n* **1** hueco. **2** GEOG hondonada.

holly ['hɒlɪ] *n* acebo.
  ① *pl* **hollies**.

holocaust ['hɒləkɔːst] *n* holocausto.

holy ['həʊlɪ] *adj* **1** REL *(sacred)* santo,-a, sagrado,-a. **2** *(blessed)* bendito,-a.
  ① *comp* **holier**, *superl* **holiest**.

home [həʊm] *n* **1** *(house)* hogar *m*, casa. **2** *fml* domicilio. **3** *(institution)* asilo. **4** *(country, village, etc)* patria, tierra. **5** ZOOL hábitat *m*. LOC **at home** en casa.
  ▶ *adj* **1** casero,-a. **2** POL *(del)* interior. **3** *(native)* natal.

homeland ['həʊmlænd] *n* *(gen)* patria; *(birthplace)* tierra natal.

homeless ['həʊmləs] *adj* sin hogar, sin techo.

home-made ['həʊmmeɪd] *adj* casero,-a, de fabricación casera, hecho,-a en casa.

homemaker ['həʊmmeɪkər] *n* ama de casa.

homesick ['həʊmsɪk] *adj* nostálgico,-a.

homesickness ['həʊmsɪknəs] *n* añoranza, morriña, nostalgia.

homework ['həʊmwɜːk] *n* deberes *mpl*.

homogeneous [hɒmə'dʒiːnɪəs] *adj* homogéneo,-a.

homograph ['hɒməgræf] *n* homógrafo.

homonym ['hɒmənɪm] *n* homónimo.

homosexual [həʊməʊ'seksjʊəl] *adj & n* homosexual.

honest ['ɒnɪst] *adj* **1** *(trustworthy)* honrado,-a, honesto,-a. **2** *(frank)* sincero,-a, franco,-a. **3** *(fair)* justo,-a.
  ▶ *adv* *fam* de verdad.

honestly ['ɒnɪstlɪ] *adv* **1** *(fairly)* honradamente. **2** *(frankly)* sinceramente, francamente. **3** *(truthfully)* de verdad, a decir verdad.
  ▶ *interj* *(question)* ¿de verdad?; *(exclamation)* ¡hay que ver!

honesty ['ɒnɪstɪ] *n* honradez *f*.

honey ['hʌnɪ] *n* **1** miel *f*. **2** US *fam (dear)* cariño, cielo.

honeycomb ['hʌnɪkəʊm] *n* panal *m*.

honeymoon ['hʌnɪmuːn] *n* luna de miel, viaje *m* de novios.

honor ['ɒnər] *n* US → **honour**.

honour ['ɒnər] *n* **1** *(virtue)* honor *m*, honra. **2** *(title)* Su Señoría.
  ▶ *vt* **1** *(respect)* honrar. **2** *(cheque)* pagar, aceptar; *(promise, word, agreement)* cumplir.

hood [hʊd] *n* **1** *(of clothes)* capucha. **2** *(on pram, etc)* capota. **3** US *(car bonnet)* capó *m*. **4** *(of hawk)* capirote *m*.

hoof [huːf] *n* *(of sheep, cow, etc)* pezuña; *(of horse)* casco.
  ① *pl* **hoofs** o **hooves**.

hook [hʊk] *n* **1** *(gen)* gancho. **2** *(for fishing)* anzuelo.
  ▶ *vt* **1** *(catch)* enganchar. **2** *(fishing)* pescar, coger. **3** *(in boxing)* pegar un gancho.
  ◆ **to hook up** *vt sep (connect)* conectar.

hooligan ['huːlɪgən] *n* gamberro,-a.

hoop [huːp] *n* **1** *(gen)* aro; *(of barrel)* fleje *m*; *(of wheel)* llanta.

hoot [huːt] *n* **1** *(of owl)* ululato, grito. **2** *(of car)* bocinazo. **3** *fam (funny thing)* cosa divertida; *(funny person)* persona divertida.

H

hooter ['huːtəʳ] n 1 (siren) sirena. 2 (on car) bocina, claxon m. 3 GB (nose) narizota, napias fpl.

Hoover® ['huːvəʳ] n GB aspiradora.

hooves ['huːvz] pl → hoof.

hop¹ [hɒp] n 1 salto, brinco. 2 fam (dance) baile m. 3 AV fam vuelo corto.
▶ vi saltar, dar brincos, dar saltos.
▶ vt 1 US fam (train, etc) coger. 2 AV cruzar.
ⓘ pt & pp hopped, ger hopping.

hop² [hɒp] n (plant) lúpulo.

hope [həup] n (gen) esperanza; (false) ilusión f.
▶ vt esperar.

hopeful ['həupful] adj 1 (promising) esperanzador,-ra, prometedor,-ra, alentador,-ra. 2 (confident) optimista.

hopefully ['həupfulɪ] adv 1 (confidently) con esperanza, con ilusión, con optimismo. 2 fam (all being well) ojalá.

hopeless ['həupləs] adj 1 desesperado,-a. 2 fam (useless) inútil.

hopelessly ['həupləslɪ] adv sin esperanza, con desesperación, desesperadamente.

horizon [həˈraɪzən] n horizonte m.

horizontal [hɒrɪˈzɒntəl] adj horizontal.

hormonal [hɔːˈməunəl] adj hormonal.

hormone ['hɔːməun] n hormona.

horn [hɔːn] n 1 ZOOL asta, cuerno. 2 AUTO bocina, claxon m. 3 MUS cuerno, trompa.

horoscope ['hɒrəskəup] n horóscopo.

horrible ['hɒrɪbəl] adj (gen) horrible, horroroso,-a; (person) antipático,-a.

horrid ['hɒrɪd] adj (horrible) horroroso,-a, horrible; (unkind) antipático,-a, odioso,-a; (child) inaguantable, insoportable.

horrific [həˈrɪfɪk] adj horrendo,-a, horroroso,-a.

horrify ['hɒrɪfaɪ] vt horrorizar, espantar.
ⓘ pt & pp horrified, ger horrifying.

horrifying ['hɒrɪfaɪɪŋ] adj escalofriante.

horror ['hɒrəʳ] n horror m, terror m.
COMP horror film película de terror.

hors d'oeuvre [ɔːˈdɜːvʳ] n CULIN entremés m.
ⓘ pl hors d'oeuvre o hors d'oeuvres.

horse [hɔːs] n 1 ZOOL caballo. 2 (in gym) potro. 3 TECH caballete m. 4 sl (heroin) caballo. COMP horse riding equitación f.

horseback ['hɔːsbæk] adj & adv a caballo. LOC on horseback a caballo.

horsepower ['hɔːspauəʳ] n 1 AUTO caballo de vapor, caballo. 2 potencia.

horseshoe ['hɔːsʃuː] n herradura.

hose¹ [həuz] n (pipe) manguera.
ⓘ pl hose.
▶ vt regar, lavar.

hose² [həuz] n pl (socks) calcetines mpl; (stockings) medias fpl.

hosepipe ['həuzpaɪp] n manguera.

hospitable [hɒˈspɪtəbəl] adj hospitalario,-a, acogedor,-ra.

hospital ['hɒspɪtəl] n hospital m.

hospitality [hɒspɪˈtælɪtɪ] n hospitalidad f.

host¹ [həust] n 1 (person) anfitrión,-ona; (place) sede f. 2 (TV presenter) presentador,-ra. 3 (animal, plant) huésped m.
▶ vt 1 TV presentar. 2 celebrar,.

host² [həust] n (large number) multitud f.

Host [həust] n REL hostia.

hostage ['hɒstɪdʒ] n rehén mf.

hostel ['hɒstəl] n residencia, hostal m.

hostess ['həustəs] n 1 (at home) anfitriona. 2 (on plane, etc) azafata. 3 (in club) camarera. 4 TV presentadora.

hostile ['hɒstaɪl] adj hostil, enemigo,-a.

hostility [hɒˈstɪlɪtɪ] n hostilidad f.
ⓘ pl hostilities.

hot [hɒt] adj 1 (gen) caliente. 2 METEOR caluroso,-a, cálido,-a. 3 (food - spicy) picante.
ⓘ comp hotter, superl hottest.

hotel [həuˈtel] n hotel m.

hotline ['hɒtlaɪn] n línea directa.

hound [haund] n perro de caza.
▶ vt (harass) acosar, perseguir.

hour [auəʳ] n hora.

hourly ['auəlɪ] adj cada hora.
▶ adv a cada hora, por horas.

house [(n) haus; (vb) hauz] n 1 (gen) casa; (official use) domicilio. 2 POL cámara. 3 THEAT sala. 4 (company) empresa, casa.
COMP House of Commons Cámara de los Comunes. ▌ House of Lords Cáma-

ra de los Lores. ∎ **House of Representatives** Cámara de Representantes. ∎ **Houses of Parliament** Parlamento.

▶ *vt* **1** *(gen)* alojar, albergar; *(supply housing)* proveer de vivienda. **2** *(store)* guardar, almacenar; *(fit)* dar cabida a.

⊕ Tanto el Reino Unido como Estados Unidos disponen, al igual que nosotros, de un sistema legislativo bicameral, con unas cámaras bajas (equivalentes al Congreso de los diputados), que se llaman **House of Commons** en el Reino Unido y **House of Representatives** en Estados Unidos, y unas cámaras altas (similares a nuestro Senado), que se llaman **House of Lords** en el Reino Unido y **Senate** en Estados Unidos.

housemaster ['haʊsmɑːstər] *n* EDUC tutor *m*.

housemistress ['haʊsmɪstrəs] *n* EDUC tutora.

housewife ['haʊswaɪf] *n* ama de casa.
ⓘ *pl* housewives ['haʊswaɪvz].

housework ['haʊswɜːk] *n* quehaceres *mpl* domésticos.

housing ['haʊzɪŋ] *n* **1** vivienda. **2** TECH bastidor *m*, caja.

hover ['hɒvər] *vi* **1** *(aircraft)* permanecer inmóvil *(en el aire)*. **2** *(bird)* cernerse, revolotear. **3** *(move around)* rondar. **4** *(hesitate)* dudar, vacilar.

hovercraft ['hɒvəkrɑːft] *n* aerodeslizador *m*.
ⓘ *pl* hovercraft.

how [haʊ] *adv* **1** *(in questions - direct)* ¿cómo?; *(- indirect)* cómo: *tell me how to do it* dime cómo se hace. **2** *(in exclamations)* qué: *how odd!* ¡qué extraño!, ¡qué raro! LOC how about...? ¿qué te parece si...? ∎ **how are you?** ¿cómo estás? ∎ **I how many** cuántos,-as ∎ **how much** cuánto

✎ La expresión How do you do? se emplea en inglés formal cuando se encuentran dos personas por primera vez. La respuesta es la misma How do you do? El equivalente en español sería 'encantado'.

however [haʊ'evər] *adv* **1** *(nevertheless)* sin embargo, no obstante. **2** *(with adj)*

por: *however hard it may be* por difícil que sea; *however much* por más que, por mucho que.

howl [haʊl] *n* *(cry)* aullido.
▶ *vi* aullar.
◆ **to howl down** *vt sep* abuchear.

HP ['eɪtʃ'piː] *abbr* **(horsepower)** caballos *mpl* de vapor; *(abbreviation)* cv *mpl*.

HQ ['eɪtʃ'kjuː] *abbr* **1 (headquarters)** cuartel *m* general. **2** *fig* centro de operaciones.

HTML ['eɪtʃ'tiː'em'el] *abbr* **(hypertext markup language)** HTML.

hub [hʌb] *n* **1** AUTO cubo. **2** *fig* centro, eje *m*.

hubcap ['hʌbkæp] *n* AUTO tapacubos *m*.

huddle ['hʌdəl] *n* grupo.
▶ *vi* **1** *(crouch)* acurrucarse, apiñarse, amontonarse. **2** *(cluster)* apiñarse.

hug [hʌg] *n* abrazo.
▶ *vt* **1** abrazar. **2** *fig (kerb, coast)* pegarse a, ceñirse a.
ⓘ *pt & pp* hugged, *ger* hugging.

huge [hjuːdʒ] *adj* enorme, inmenso,-a.

hull [hʌl] *n* **1** *(of ship)* casco. **2** BOT *(shell)* cáscara; *(pod)* vaina.
▶ *vt* *(peas, beans, etc)* desvainar.

hullo [hʌ'ləʊ] *interj* → **hello**.

hum [hʌm] *n* *(of bees, engine)* zumbido.
▶ *vi* **1** *(bees, engine, etc)* zumbar. **2** *(sing)* tararear, canturrear. **3** *(bustling with activity)* hervir.
▶ *vt* *(tune)* tararear, canturrear.
ⓘ *pt & pp* hummed, *ger* humming.

human ['hjuːmən] *adj* humano,-a. COMP **human being** ser *m* humano.
▶ *n* ser *m* humano, humano.

humanitarian [hjuːmænɪ'teərɪən] *adj* humanitario,-a, filantrópico,-a.
▶ *n* filántropo,-a.

humanity [hjuː'mænɪti] *n* **1** *(virtue)* humanidad *f*. **2** *(mankind)* género humano, raza humana.
ⓘ *pl* humanities.

humanize ['hjuːmənaɪz] *vt* humanizar.

humble ['hʌmbəl] *adj* humilde.
▶ *vt* humillar.
ⓘ *comp* humbler, *superl* humbliest.

H

humerus ['hju:mərəs] *n* ANAT *(bone)* húmero.
ⓘ *pl* **humeri** ['hju:mərai].

humid ['hju:mɪd] *adj* húmedo,-a.

☒ Humid no significa 'húmedo (impregnado de agua)', que se traduce por damp, wet.

humidity [hju:'mɪdɪtɪ] *n* humedad *f*.
humiliate [hju:'mɪlɪeɪt] *vt* humillar.
humiliation [hju:mɪlɪ'eɪ[ᵉ]n] *n* humillación *f*.
hummingbird ['hʌmɪŋbɜ:d] *n* colibrí *m*.
humor ['hju:mə'] *n* US → **humour**.
humorous ['hju:mərəs] *adj* **1** *(funny)* gracioso,-a, divertido,-a. **2** *(writer)* humorístico,-a, humorista.
humour ['hju:mə'] *n* **1** humor *m*. **2** *(of a joke)* gracia. **3** *(whim)* capricho.
▶ *vt* complacer, seguir el humor a.

☒ Humour no significa 'humor (estado de ánimo)', que se traduce por mood.

hump [hʌmp] *n* **1** *(on back)* giba, joroba. **2** *(hillock)* montículo.
▶ *vt* **1** GB *fam (carry)* cargar.
humus ['hju:məs] *n* AGR mantillo, humus *m*.
hunchback ['hʌntʃbæk] *n* *(person)* jorobado,-a.
hundred ['hʌndrəd] *n* cien.
▶ *n pl* **hundreds** *(many)* centenares *mpl*, cientos *mpl*.
hundredth ['hʌndrədθ] *adj* centésimo,-a.
▶ *adv* en centésimo lugar.
hung [hʌŋ] *pt & pp* → **hang**.
Hungarian [hʌŋ'geəriən] *adj* húngaro,-a.
▶ *n* **1** *(person)* húngaro,-a. **2** *(language)* húngaro.
Hungary ['hʌŋgərɪ] *n* Hungría.
hunger ['hʌŋgə'] *n* **1** hambre *f*. **2** *fig* sed *f*. COMP **hunger strike** huelga de hambre.
◆ **to hunger after / hunger for** *vt insep* ansiar, anhelar, tener hambre de.
hungry ['hʌŋgrɪ] *adj* **1** hambriento,-a. **2** *fig* ávido,-a, sediento,-a. LOC **to be hungry** tener hambre.
ⓘ *comp* **hungrier**, *superl* **hungriest**.

hunt [hʌnt] *n* **1** *(gen)* caza, cacería. **2** *(search)* búsqueda.
▶ *vt* cazar.
◆ **to hunt down** *vt sep (corner)* acorralar, perseguir; *(to find)* dar con, encontrar.
◆ **to hunt out / hunt up** *vt sep (to find)* encontrar; *(to look for)* buscar.
hunter ['hʌntə'] *n* **1** cazador,-ra *mf*. **2** ZOOL caballo de caza. **3** *(watch)* saboneta.
hunting ['hʌntɪŋ] *n* *(gen)* caza; *(expedition)* cacería, montería.
hurdle ['hɜ:dᵊl] *n* **1** SP valla. **2** *fig* obstáculo.
▶ *vt* SP *(barrier)* saltar.
hurdling ['hɜ:dlɪŋ] *n* SP carrera de vallas.
hurl [hɜ:l] *vt* **1** lanzar, arrojar, tirar. **2** *(insults)* soltar.
hurrah [hʊ'rɑ:] *interj* ¡hurra!: *hurrah for Peter!* ¡viva Peter!
▶ *vt* vitorear, aclamar.
hurray [hʊ'reɪ] *interj* ¡hurra!
hurricane ['hʌrɪkən, 'hʌrɪkeɪn] *n* huracán *m*.
hurry ['hʌrɪ] *n* prisa: *are you in a hurry for the report?* ¿le corre prisa el informe? LOC **to be in a hurry** tener prisa.
▶ *vi* apresurarse, darse prisa.
◆ **to hurry up** *vi* darse prisa.
ⓘ *pt & pp* **hurried**, *ger* **hurrying**.
hurt [hɜ:t] *n* **1** *(harm)* daño, dolor *m*, mal *m*. **2** *(wound)* herida. **3** *fig* daño, perjuicio.
▶ *adj* **1** *(physically)* herido,-a. **2** *(offended)* dolido,-a.
▶ *vt* **1** *(cause injury)* lastimar, hacer daño; *(to wound)* herir: *he has hurt his arm* se ha hecho daño en el brazo. **2** SP lesionar. **3** *(offend)* herir, ofender: *you hurt her feelings* la has ofendido, le has herido los sentimientos.
▶ *vi* **1** doler: *my eyes hurt* me duelen los ojos. **2** *fam* venir mal, ir mal.
ⓘ *pt & pp* **hurt**.
husband ['hʌzbənd] *n* marido, esposo.
hush [hʌʃ] *n* quietud *f*, silencio.
▶ *vt* callar, silenciar.

▸ *interj* ¡silencio! ¡cállate! ¡cállese! ¡chito! COMP **hush money** *fam* soborno *(que se paga para que alguien no hable)*.
◆ **to hush up** *vt sep (affair)* echar tierra a; *(person)* hacer callar.

hustle ['hʌsəl] *n* bullicio. COMP **hustle and bustle** ajetreo.

hut [hʌt] *n* **1** cabaña. **2** *(in garden)* cobertizo. **3** MIL barraca.

hyacinth ['haɪəsɪnθ] *n* BOT jacinto.

hyaena [haɪˈiːnə] *n* hiena.

hybrid ['haɪbrɪd] *adj* híbrido,-a.
▸ *n* híbrido.

hydrant ['haɪdrənt] *n* boca de riego.

hydrate [haɪˈdreɪt] *vt* hidratar.

hydraulic [haɪˈdrɔːlɪk] *adj* hidráulico,-a. COMP **hydraulic brake** freno hidráulico.

hydrocarbon [haɪdrəʊˈkɑːbən] *n* CHEM hidrocarburo.

hydrochloric [haɪdrəˈklɒrɪk] *adj* clorhídrico,-a. COMP **hydrochloric acid** ácido clorhídrico.

hydroelectric [haɪdrəʊˈlektrɪk] *adj* hidroeléctrico,-a. COMP **hydroelectric power station** central *f* hidroeléctrica.

hydrogen ['haɪdrədʒən] *n* CHEM hidrógeno. COMP **hydrogen bomb** bomba de hidrógeno.

hydrography [haɪˈdrɒgrəfɪ] *n* hidrografía.

hydrology [haɪˈdrɒlədʒɪ] *n* hidrología.

hydroplane ['haɪdrəpleɪn] *n* hidroavión *m*, hidroplano.

hydrosphere ['haɪdrəsfəʳ] *n* hidrosfera.

hydroxide [haɪˈdrɒksaɪd] *n* hidróxido.

hyena [haɪˈiːnə] *n* ZOOL hiena.

hygiene ['haɪdʒiːn] *n* higiene *f*.

hygienic [haɪˈdʒiːnɪk] *adj* higiénico,-a.

hymn [hɪm] *n* himno. COMP **hymn book** cantoral *m*.

hyperbola [haɪˈpɜːbələ] *n* hipérbola.
ⓘ *pl* **hyperbole** [haɪˈpɜːbəlɪ] o **hyperbolas**.

hyperbole [haɪˈpɜːbəlɪ] *n* hipérbole *f*.

hyperlink ['haɪpəlɪŋk] *n* hiperenlace.

hypermarket ['haɪpəmɑːkɪt] *n* GB hipermercado.

hypertension [haɪpəˈtenʃən] *n* MED hipertensión *f*.

hypertext ['haɪpətekst] *n* hipertexto.

hyphen ['haɪfən] *n* guion *m*.

hypnosis [hɪpˈnəʊsɪs] *n* MED hipnosis *f*.

hypnotise ['hɪpnətaɪz] *vt* → **hypnotize**.

hypnotize ['hɪpnətaɪz] *vt* hipnotizar.

hypochondriac [haɪpəˈkɒndrɪæk] *n* hipocondríaco,-a.
▸ *adj* hipocondríaco,-a.

hypocrisy [hɪˈpɒkrɪsɪ] *n* hipocresía.

hypocrite ['hɪpəkrɪt] *n* hipócrita *mf*.

hypotension [haɪpəʊˈtenʃən] *n* MED hipotensión *f*.

hypotenuse [haɪˈpɒtənjuːz] *n (geometry)* hipotenusa.

hypothesis [haɪˈpɒθəsɪs] *n* hipótesis *f*.
ⓘ *pl* **hypotheses** [haɪˈpɒθəsiːz].

hypothetic [haɪpəˈθetɪk] *adj* hipotético,-a.

hysteria [hɪˈstɪərɪə] *n* histeria.

hysterical [hɪˈsterɪkəl] *adj* histérico,-a.

H

I, i [aɪ] *n (the letter)* I, i *f.*

I [aɪ] *pron* yo.

Iberian [aɪ'bɪərɪən] *adj (modern)* ibérico,-a; *(historically)* ibero,-a, íbero,-a.
▸ *n* **1** *(person - now)* ibérico,-a; *(- historically)* ibero,-a, íbero,-a. **2** *(language)* ibero, íbero. [COMP] **Iberian Peninsula** Península Ibérica.

ice [aɪs] *n* **1** *(frozen water)* hielo. **2** *(ice-cream)* helado. [COMP] **ice cube** cubito de hielo. **‖ ice hockey** hockey *m* sobre hielo. **‖ ice lolly** polo. **‖ ice ring** pista de hielo.

iceberg ['aɪsbɜːg] *n* **1** iceberg *m*. **2** *fig* persona fría.

icebreaker ['aɪsbreɪkəʳ] *n* rompehielos *m inv.*

ice-cream ['aɪskriːm] *n* helado.

Iceland ['aɪslənd] *n* Islandia.

Icelander ['aɪsləndəʳ] *n (person)* islandés,-esa.

Icelandic [aɪs'lændɪk] *adj* islandés,-esa.
▸ *n (language)* islandés *m.*

ice-skate ['aɪsskeɪt] *vi* patinar sobre hielo.

ice-skating ['aɪskeɪtɪŋ] *n* patinaje *m* sobre hielo.

icicle ['aɪsɪkəl] *n* carámbano.

icing ['aɪsɪŋ] *n* cobertura.

icon ['aɪkɒn] *n* icono.

iconography [aɪkə'nɒgrəfɪ] *n* iconografía.

icy ['aɪsɪ] *adj* **1** *(very cold - hand, etc)* helado,-a; *(- wind)* glacial. **2** *(covered with ice)* cubierto,-a de hielo. **3** *fig* glacial.
ⓘ *comp* icier, *superl* iciest.

ID [aɪ'diː] *abbr* (identification) identificación *f.* [COMP] **ID card** documento nacional de identidad, DNI *m.*

I'd [aɪd] *contr* **1** I would. **2** I had.

idea [aɪ'dɪə] *n* **1** *(gen)* idea; *(opinion)* opinión *f.* **2** *(intuition)* impresión *f*, sensación *f.* **3** *(concept)* concepto.
▸ *n* **the idea** *(aim, purpose)* idea, intención *f*, objetivo.

ideal [aɪ'diːl] *adj* ideal, perfecto,-a.
▸ *n* **1** *(perfect example)* ideal *m*. **2** *(principle)* principio, ideal *m.*

idealize [aɪ'dɪəlaɪz] *vt* idealizar: *we tend to idealize the past* tendemos a idealizar el pasado.

identical [aɪ'dentɪkəl] *adj* **1** *(exactly alike)* idéntico,-a (**to/with**, a). **2** *(the same)* mismísimo,-a.

identification [aɪdentɪfɪ'keɪʃn] *n* **1** *(gen)* identificación *f.* **2** *(papers)* documentación *f.*

identify [aɪ'dentɪfaɪ] *vt* **1** *(gen)* identificar. **2** *(associate)* asociar (**with**, con), relacionar (**with**, con).
ⓘ *pt & pp* identified, *ger* identifying.

Identikit® [aɪ'dentɪkɪt] [COMP] **Identikit picture** retrato robot.

identity [aɪ'dentɪtɪ] *n* identidad *f.* [COMP] **identity card** carnet *m* de identidad.
ⓘ *pl* identities.

ideogram ['ɪdɪəʊgræm] *n* ideograma *m.*

ideological [aɪdɪə'lɒdʒɪkəl] *adj* ideológico,-a.

ideology [aɪdɪ'ɒlədʒɪ] *n* ideología.
ⓘ *pl* ideologies.

idiom ['ɪdɪəm] *n* **1** *(phrase)* locución *f*, modismo, frase *f* hecha. **2** *(language,* lenguaje *m*, idioma *m*; *(style)* estilo.

> ☒ Idiom no significa 'idioma', que se traduce por **language**.

idiomatic [ɪdɪə'mætɪk] *adj* idiomático,-a.

idiot ['ɪdɪət] *n* **1** *fam* idiota *mf*, tonto,-a. **2** MED idiota *mf*.

idle ['aɪdəl] *adj* **1** *(lazy)* perezoso,-a, vago,-a. **2** *(not working - person)* parado,-a, desempleado,-a; *(- machinery)* parado,-a; *(- money)* improductivo,-a.
ⓘ *comp* **idler**, *superl* **idlest**.
▶ *vi (waste time)* gandulear, holgazanear, perder el tiempo.

idol ['aɪdəl] *n* ídolo.

idolatry [aɪˈdɒlətrɪ] *n* idolatría.
ⓘ *pl* **idolatries**.

i.e. ['aɪˈiː] *abbr* (id est) esto es, a saber; *(abbreviation)* i.e.

if [ɪf] *conj* **1** *(supposing)* si: *if it rains, we'll stay at home* si llueve, nos quedaremos en casa; *you can come if you want* puedes venir si quieres. **2** *(whether)* si: *do you know if she got the job?* ¿sabes si consiguió el trabajo? **3** *(used after verbs expressing feelings)* que: *do you mind if I open the window?* ¿te importa que abra la ventana? **4** *(but)* aunque, pero: *it's good, if a little slow at times* es bueno pero algo lento a veces. **5** *(in exclamations)*: *well, if it isn't Jimmy Jazz!* vaya, ¡pero si es Jimmy Jazz! |LOC| **if I were you** yo que tú, yo en tu lugar. ‖ **if only** *(present or future time)* ¡ojalá!, ¡si al menos...!

igloo ['ɪgluː] *n* iglú *m*.
ⓘ *pl* **igloos**.

igneous ['ɪgnɪəs] *adj* ígneo,-a.

ignition [ɪgˈnɪʃən] *n* **1** ignición *f*. **2** AUTO encendido, arranque *m*.

ignorance ['ɪgnərəns] *n* ignorancia.

ignorant ['ɪgnərənt] *adj* **1** *(unaware)* ignorante (of, de). **2** *fam (rude)* descortés, maleducado,-a.

ignore [ɪgˈnɔːr] *vt* **1** *(order, warning)* no hacer caso de, hacer caso omiso de; *(behaviour, fact)* pasar por alto. **2** *(person)* hacer como si no existiese.
☒ **To ignore** no significa 'ignorar (no saber)', que se traduce por **not to know**.

iguana [ɪˈgwɑːnə] *n* iguana.

ilium ['ɪlɪəm] *n* ilion *m*, íleon *m*.

ill [ɪl] *adj* **1** *(sick)* enfermo,-a. **2** *(harmful, unpropitious)* malo,-a.
▶ *n fml (harm, evil)* mal *m*.

▶ *adv* **1** *(badly)* mal. **2** *(unfavourably)* mal. **3** *(with difficulty)* mal, a duras penas.
▶ *n pl* **ills** *(problems, misfortunes)* desgracias *fpl*.

I'll [aɪl] *contr* **1** I will. **2** I shall.

illegal [ɪˈliːgəl] *adj* ilegal.

illegality [ɪlɪˈgælɪtɪ] *n* ilegalidad *f*.
ⓘ *pl* **illegalities**.

illegible [ɪˈledʒɪbəl] *adj* ilegible.

illegitimate [ɪlɪˈdʒɪtɪmət] *adj* ilegítimo,-a.

illicit [ɪˈlɪsɪt] *adj* ilícito,-a.

illiterate [ɪˈlɪtərət] *adj* **1** *(unlettered)* analfabeto,-a. **2** *(uneducated)* ignorante, inculto,-a. **3** *(poor style)* inculto,-a, pobre.
▶ *n (unlettered person)* analfabeto,-a.

ill-mannered [ɪlˈmænəd] *adj* maleducado,-a, descortés.

illness ['ɪlnəs] *n* enfermedad *f*.
ⓘ *pl* **illnesses**.

illogical [ɪˈlɒdʒɪkəl] *adj* ilógico,-a.

illuminate [ɪˈluːmɪneɪt] *vt* iluminar.

illuminated [ɪˈluːmɪneɪtəd] *adj (manuscript)* iluminado,-a.

illumination [ɪluːmɪˈneɪʃən] *n* **1** *(light)* iluminación *f*. **2** *(clarification)* aclaración.

illusion [ɪˈluːʒən] *n* ilusión *f*, falsa impresión *f*.
☒ **Illusion** no significa 'ilusión (esperanza)', que se traduce por **hope**.

illusionist [ɪˈluːʒənɪst] *n* ilusionista *mf*.

illustrate ['ɪləstreɪt] *vt* ilustrar.

illustrated ['ɪləstreɪtɪd] *adj* ilustrado,-a.
☒ **Illustrated** no significa 'ilustrado (culto)', que se traduce por **learned**.

illustration [ɪləsˈtreɪʃən] *n* **1** *(gen)* ilustración *f*. **2** *(example)* ejemplo.

illustrative ['ɪləstrətɪv] *adj* **1** *(gen)* ilustrativo,-a, ilustrador,-ra. **2** *(example)* aclaratorio,-a.

I'm [aɪm] *contr* I am.

image ['ɪmɪdʒ] *n* **1** *(gen)* imagen *f*. **2** *(reputation)* imagen *f*, fama, reputación *f*.

imaginary [ɪˈmædʒɪnərɪ] *adj* imaginario,-a, inventado,-a.

imagination [ɪmædʒɪ'neɪʃ°n] *n (gen)* imaginación *f; (inventiveness)* inventiva.

imaginative [ɪ'mædʒɪnətɪv] *adj (person)* imaginativo,-a, de gran inventiva; *(creation)* lleno,-a de imaginación, lleno,-a de fantasía.

imagine [ɪ'mædʒɪn] *vt* **1** *(visualize)* imaginar. **2** *(suppose)* suponer, imaginar(se), figurarse.

imam [ɪ'mɑːm] *n* imán *m*.

imbalance [ɪm'bæləns] *n* desequilibrio.

IMF ['aɪ'em'ef] *abbr* (International Monetary Fund) Fondo Monetario Internacional; *(abbreviation)* FMI *m*.

imitate ['ɪmɪteɪt] *vt (gen)* imitar, copiar; *(for fun)* imitar.

imitation [ɪmɪ'teɪʃ°n] *n* **1** *(gen)* imitación *f*, copia; *(for fun)* imitación *f*. **2** *(reproduction)* reproducción *f*.
▶ *adj* de imitación.

immaterial [ɪmə'tɪərɪəl] *adj* **1** *(unimportant)* irrelevante. **2** *(incorporeal)* inmaterial, incorpóreo,-a.

immature [ɪmə'tjʊəʳ] *adj* **1** *(gen)* inmaduro,-a; *(- plant)* joven. **2** *(childish)* inmaduro,-a, pueril.

immediate [ɪ'miːdɪət] *adj* **1** *(instant)* inmediato,-a; *(urgent)* urgente. **2** *(nearest)* inmediato,-a, más próximo,-a. **3** *(direct)* primero,-a, principal.

immediately [ɪ'miːdɪətlɪ] *adv (instantly, at once)* inmediatamente, de inmediato, en seguida, en el acto.

immense [ɪ'mens] *adj* inmenso,-a, enorme.

immensely [ɪ'menslɪ] *adv* enormemente, sumamente.

immersion [ɪ'mɜːʃ°n] *n* **1** inmersión *f*, sumersión *f*. **2** *fig* absorción *f*.

immigrant ['ɪmɪɡrənt] *adj* inmigrante.
▶ *n* inmigrante *mf*.

immigrate ['ɪmɪɡreɪt] *vi* inmigrar.

immigration [ɪmɪ'ɡreɪʃ°n] *n* inmigración *f*.

imminent ['ɪmɪnənt] *adj* inminente.

immoral [ɪ'mɒr°l] *adj* inmoral.

immortal [ɪ'mɔːt°l] *adj* **1** *(god, soul, etc)* inmortal. **2** *fig (fame, memory, etc)* imperecedero,-a, perdurable.
▶ *n* inmortal *mf*.

immortality [ɪmɔː'tælɪtɪ] *n* inmortalidad *f*.

immune [ɪ'mjuːn] *adj* **1** *(gen)* inmune (to, a). **2** *(exempt)* exento,-a.

immunity [ɪ'mjuːnɪtɪ] *n* **1** *(gen)* inmunidad *f*. **2** *(exemption)* exención *f*.

immunize ['ɪmjənaɪz] *vt* inmunizar (against, contra).

immunodeficient [ɪmjʊnəʊdɪ'fɪʃ°nt] *adj* inmunodeficiente.

immunodeficiency [ɪmjʊnəʊdɪ'fɪʃ°nsɪ] *n* inmunodeficiencia.

immunology [ɪmjʊ'nɒlədʒɪ] *n* inmunología.

impact [*(n)* 'ɪmpækt; *(vb)* ɪm'pækt] *n* **1** *(gen)* impacto; *(crash)* choque *m*. **2** *(impression, effect)* efecto, impresión *f*, impacto.
▶ *vt* US *(have impact on)* impresionar.

impartial [ɪm'pɑːʃ°l] *adj* imparcial.

impatience [ɪm'peɪʃ°ns] *n* **1** *(eagerness)* impaciencia, ansiedad *f*. **2** *(irritation)* impaciencia, irritación *f*.

impatient [ɪm'peɪʃ°nt] *adj* **1** *(eager)* impaciente, ansioso,-a. **2** *(irritable)* irritable. **3** *fml (intolerant)* intolerante.

impeachment [ɪm'piːtʃmənt] *n* JUR *(accusation)* acusación *f*, denuncia; *(trial)* proceso.

impeccable [ɪm'pekəb°l] *adj (gen)* impecable, perfecto,-a.

impending [ɪm'pendɪŋ] *adj* inminente.

imperative [ɪm'perətɪv] *adj* **1** *(indispensable)* imprescindible. **2** *(authoritative)* imperativo,-a, imperioso,-a. **3** LING imperativo,-a.

imperfect [ɪm'pɜːfekt] *adj* **1** *(gen)* imperfecto,-a; *(goods, sight)* defectuoso,-a. **2** LING imperfecto,-a.
▶ *n* the imperfect LING el imperfecto.

imperfection [ɪmpə'fekʃ°n] *n (gen)* imperfección *f*; *(defect)* defecto, tara, tacha; *(blemish)* mancha.

imperial [ɪmˈpɪərɪəl] *adj* **1** *(gen)* imperial. **2** *(weight, measure)* del sistema métrico británico.

imperialism [ɪmˈpɪərɪəlɪzᵊm] *n* imperialismo.

imperialist [ɪmˈpɪərɪəlɪst] *n* imperialista *mf*.

impersonal [ɪmˈpɜːsᵊnəl] *adj* impersonal.

impersonate [ɪmˈpɜːsᵊneɪt] *vt* **1** *(imitate to deceive)* hacerse pasar por. **2** *(imitate to entertain)* imitar.

impertinent [ɪmˈpɜːtɪnənt] *adj* impertinente, descarado,-a.

implant [*(vb)* ɪmˈplɑːnt; *(n)* ˈɪmplɑːnt] *vt* **1** MED implantar, injertar. **2** *(ideas, etc)* inculcar (in, en).
▶ *n* MED implantación *f*, injerto.

implement [*(n)* ˈɪmpləmənt; *(vb)* ˈɪmplɪment] *n* *(instrument)* instrumento, utensilio; *(tool)* herramienta.
▶ *vt* *(plan, suggestion, etc)* llevar a cabo, poner en práctica; *(law, policy)* aplicar.

implementation [ɪmpləmenˈteɪʃᵊn] *n* *(of plan, etc)* puesta en práctica, desarrollo; *(of law, etc)* aplicación *f*.

implicate [ˈɪmplɪkeɪt] *vt* implicar, (in, en).

implication [ɪmplɪˈkeɪʃᵊn] *n* implicación *f*.

implicit [ɪmˈplɪsɪt] *adj* **1** *(implied)* implícito,-a, tácito,-a. **2** *(absolute)* absoluto,-a, incondicional.

implied [ɪmˈplaɪd] *adj* implícito,-a, tácito,-a.

imply [ɪmˈplaɪ] *vt* **1** *(involve, entail)* implicar, suponer, presuponer. **2** *(mean)* significar, querer decir; *(hint)* insinuar, dar a entender.
① *pt & pp* implied.

impolite [ɪmpəˈlaɪt] *adj* maleducado,-a, descortés.

import [ˈɪmpɔːt] *n* **1** *(article)* artículo de importación. **2** *(activity)* importación *f*.
▶ *vt* importar.

☒ To import no significa 'importar (tener importancia)', que se traduce por to matter.

importance [ɪmˈpɔːtᵊns] *n* importancia.

important [ɪmˈpɔːtᵊnt] *adj* **1** *(gen)* importante. **2** *(influential)* de categoría.

importation [ɪmpɔːˈteɪʃᵊn] *n* importación *f*.

importer [ɪmˈpɔːtəʳ] *n* importador,-ra.

impose [ɪmˈpəʊz] *vt* *(gen)* imponer (on, a).
◆ **to impose on** *vt insep (take advantage of)* abusar de, aprovecharse de.

impossible [ɪmˈpɒsɪbᵊl] *adj* *(gen)* imposible.

impotence [ˈɪmpətᵊns] *n* impotencia.

impoverishment [ɪmˈpɒvᵊrɪʃmənt] *n* empobrecimiento.

imprecise [ɪmprəˈsaɪs] *adj* impreciso,-a, inexacto,-a.

imprecision [ɪmprəˈsɪʒᵊn] *n* imprecisión *f*, falta de precisión.

impress [ɪmˈpres] *vt* **1** *(cause respect)* impresionar. **2** *(emphasize, stress)* subrayar, convencer, recalcar. **3** *fig* grabar.

impression [ɪmˈpreʃᵊn] *n* **1** *(gen)* impresión *f*. **2** *(imitation)* imitación *f*. **3** *(imprint, mark)* marca, señal *f*, impresión *f*; *(in wax, plaster)* molde *m*; *(of foot, etc)* huella. **4** *(reprint)* impresión *f*, edición *f*.

impressionism [ɪmˈpreʃᵊnɪzᵊm] *n* ART impresionismo.

impressionist [ɪmˈpreʃᵊnɪst] *adj* ART impresionista.
▶ *n* **1** ART impresionista. **2** *(mimic)* imitador,-ra.

impressive [ɪmˈpresɪv] *adj* impresionante.

imprison [ɪmˈprɪzᵊn] *vt* encarcelar, meter en la cárcel.

imprisonment [ɪmˈprɪzᵊnmənt] *n* encarcelamiento.

improbable [ɪmˈprɒbəbᵊl] *adj* **1** *(event)* improbable. **2** *(story, explanation)* inverosímil.

improper [ɪmˈprɒpəʳ] *adj* **1** *(behaviour)* impropio,-a; *(method, conditions)* inadecuado,-a. **3** *(language)* indecente. **2** *(proposal)* deshonesto,-a.

improve [ɪmˈpruːv] *vt* **1** *(quality, etc)* mejorar. **2** *(skill, knowledge)* perfeccionar. **3** *(mind)* cultivar. **4** *(property)* hacer mejoras en. **5** *(increase)* aumentar.
▶ *vi (get better)* mejorar, mejorarse.

◆ **to improve on** *vt insep (better)* superar.

improvement [ɪmˈpruːvmənt] *n* **1** *(gen)* mejora, mejoramiento; *(in health)* mejoría. **2** *(in knowledge)* perfeccionamiento. **3** *(increase)* aumento.

improvise [ˈɪmprəvaɪz] *vt* improvisar.

imprudent [ɪmˈpruːdənt] *adj fml (unwise)* imprudente; *(rash)* precipitado,-a.

impudent [ˈɪmpjʊdənt] *adj* insolente, fresco,-a, descarado,-a.

impulse [ˈɪmpʌls] *n* **1** *(sudden urge)* impulso, capricho; *(stimulus, drive)* impulso, estímulo, ímpetu *m*. **2** TECH impulso.

impulsive [ɪmˈpʌlsɪv] *adj* impulsivo,-a, irreflexivo,-a.

impunity [ɪmˈpjuːnɪtɪ] *n* impunidad *f*.

impure [ɪmˈpjʊəʳ] *adj* **1** *(contaminated)* contaminado,-a; *(adulterated)* adulterado,-a. **2** *(morally - act)* impuro,-a; *(- thought)* impúdico,-a, deshonesto,-a.

in¹ [ɪn] *prep* **1** *(place)* en, dentro de: *it's in the box* está en la caja. **2** *(motion)* en, a: *we arrived in Bonn* llegamos a Bonn. **3** *(time - during)* en, durante: *in 1980* en 1980. **4** *(time - within)* en, dentro de. **5** *(wearing)* en, vestido,-a de: *the woman in black* la mujer vestida de negro. **6** *(state, condition)* en. **7** *(ratio, measurement, number)* varias traducciones: *in twos* de dos en dos; *she's in her thirties* tiene treinta y tantos años. **8** *(profession)* en: *she's in television* trabaja en la televisión. **9** *(weather, light)* varias traducciones: *walking in the rain* caminando bajo la lluvia. **10** *(after superlative)* de: *the tallest in the class* el más alto de la clase. LOC **in all** en total.

▶ *adv* **1** *(motion)* dentro. **2** *(tide)* alto,-a. **3** *(fashionable)* de moda: *hats are in* los sombreros están de moda. **4** *(on sale, obtainable)* disponible.

▶ *n pl* **ins and outs** *(details)* detalles *mpl*, pormenores *mpl*.

▶ *phr* **to be in** *(at home)* estar en casa; *(at work)* estar.

inability [ɪnəˈbɪlɪtɪ] *n* incapacidad *f*.

inaccessible [ɪnækˈsesəbəl] *adj* inaccesible.

inaccuracy [ɪnˈækjərəsɪ] *n* **1** *(gen)* inexactitud *f*. **2** *(error)* error *m*, incorrección *f*.
ⓘ *pl* inaccuracies.

inaccurate [ɪnˈækjərət] *adj (gen)* inexacto,-a; *(incorrect)* incorrecto,-a, erróneo,-a.

inactive [ɪnˈæktɪv] *adj* inactivo,-a.

inactivity [ɪnækˈtɪvətɪ] *n* inactividad *f*.

inadequate [ɪnˈædɪkwət] *adj* **1** *(not sufficient)* insuficiente; *(not appropriate)* inadecuado,-a. **2** *(person)* incapaz, incompetente. **3** *(defective)* defectuoso,-a, imperfecto,-a.

inanimate [ɪnˈænɪmət] *adj* inanimado,-a.

inappropriate [ɪnəˈprəʊprɪət] *adj (unsuitable - clothes, behaviour)* poco apropiado,-a, no apropiado,-a; *(- time, remark)* inoportuno,-a, inconveniente.

inarticulate [ɪnɑːˈtɪkjʊlət] *adj* **1** *(person)* incapaz de expresarse. **2** *(speech, words, writing)* mal expresado,-a, incoherente. **3** *(cry, sound)* inarticulado,-a. **4** *(joints)* inarticulado,-a.

inattentive [ɪnəˈtentɪv] *adj (not paying attention)* poco atento,-a, distraído,-a; *(not attentive)* poco atento,-a.

inaudible [ɪnˈɔːdəbəl] *adj* inaudible, imperceptible.

inaugural [ɪˈnɔːgjʊrəl] *adj* inaugural, de inauguración, de apertura.

inaugurate [ɪˈnɔːgjʊreɪt] *vt* **1** *(building, exhibition, etc)* inaugurar. **2** *(president, etc)* investir.

inauguration [ɪnɔːgjʊˈreɪʃən] *n* **1** *(of building, etc)* inauguración *f*. **2** *(of president, etc)* investidura, toma de posesión.

inborn [ˈɪnbɔːn] *adj* innato,-a.

inbox [ˈɪnbɒks] *n* bandeja de entrada.

inbred [ˈɪnbred] *adj* **1** *(innate)* innato,-a. **2** *(produced by inbreeding)* endogámico,-a.

Inc [ɪnˈkɔːpəreɪtɪd] *abbr* US *(Incorporated)* ≈ sociedad *f* anónima; *(abbreviation)* S.A.

incantation [ɪnkænˈteɪʃən] *n* conjuro, ensalmo.

incapable [ɪnˈkeɪpəbəl] *adj* **1** *(unable)* incapaz. **2** *(incompetent)* incompetente.

3 *(helpless)* impotente, imposibilitado,-a.

incapacity [ɪnkəˈpæsɪtɪ] *n* incapacidad *f*.

incense¹ [ˈɪnsens] *n* incienso.

incense² [ɪnˈsens] *vt (make angry)* enfurecer, poner furioso,-a.

incentive [ɪnˈsentɪv] *n* incentivo, estímulo, aliciente *m*.

incest [ˈɪnsest] *n* incesto.

inch [ɪntʃ] *n* **1** *(measurement)* pulgada. **2** *(small amount)* poco, pelo, ápice *m*.
ⓘ *pl* inches.

⚜ Equivale a 2,54 cm.

incidence [ˈɪnsɪdəns] *n* **1** *(occurrence)* frecuencia, extensión *f*. **2** PHYS incidencia.

incident [ˈɪnsɪdnt] *n (event)* incidente *m*; *(violent episode)* altercado.

incidentally [ɪnsɪˈdentlɪ] *adv* **1** *(by the way)* a propósito, por cierto, dicho sea de paso. **2** *(by chance)* por casualidad.

incinerate [ɪnˈsɪnəreɪt] *vt* incinerar, quemar.

incineration [ɪnsɪnəˈreɪʃən] *n* incineración *f*, quema.

incision [ɪnˈsɪʒən] *n* incisión *f*.

incisive [ɪnˈsaɪsɪv] *adj* **1** *(comment, wit)* incisivo,-a, mordaz. **2** *(mind)* penetrante.

incisor [ɪnˈsaɪzər] *n* (diente *m*) incisivo.

inclination [ɪnklɪˈneɪʃən] *n* **1** *(tendency)* inclinación *f*, tendencia; *(disposition)* disposición *f*, propensión *f*. **2** *(slope)* inclinación *f*, pendiente *f*. **3** *(bow)* inclinación *f*.

incline [*(n)* ˈɪnklaɪn; *(vb)* ɪnˈklaɪn] *n* pendiente *f*, inclinación *f*, cuesta.
▶ *vt* **1** *(bend forward)* inclinar. **2** *fml (persuade, influence)* inclinar, predisponer.
▶ *vi* **1** *(slope)* inclinarse, estar inclinado,-a. **2** *(tend)* tender a, tener tendencia a.

inclined [ɪnˈklaɪnd] *adj* **1** *(disposed, encouraged)* dispuesto,-a (to, a). **2** *(tending to)* propenso,-a. **3** *(having natural ability)* dotado,-a. **4** *(sloping)* inclinado,-a.

include [ɪnˈkluːd] *vt* incluir.

including [ɪnˈkluːdɪŋ] *prep* incluso, incluyendo.

inclusion [ɪnˈkluːʒən] *n* inclusión *f*.

inclusive [ɪnˈkluːsɪv] *adj* inclusive.

incognito [ɪnkɒgˈniːtəʊ] *adv* de incógnito.

incoherence [ɪnkəʊˈhɪərəns] *n* incoherencia.

incoherent [ɪnkəʊˈhɪərənt] *adj* incoherente.

income [ˈɪnkʌm] *n (from work)* ingresos *mpl*, renta; *(from investment)* réditos *mpl*.
COMP income tax impuesto sobre la renta.

incompatibility [ɪnkəmpætəˈbɪlɪtɪ] *n* incompatibilidad *f*.
ⓘ *pl* incompatibilities.

incompatible [ɪnkəmˈpætəbəl] *adj* incompatible (with, con).

incompetence [ɪnˈkɒmpətəns] *n* incompetencia, ineptitud *f*, incapacidad *f*.

incompetent [ɪnˈkɒmpətnt] *adj* incompetente, inepto,-a, incapaz.
▶ *n* incompetente *mf*, inepto,-a.

incomplete [ɪnkəmˈpliːt] *adj* **1** *(not whole)* incompleto,-a; *(not finished)* inacabado,-a, sin terminar. **2** *(partial)* parcial.

incomprehensible [ɪnkɒmprɪˈhensəbəl] *adj* incomprensible.

inconceivable [ɪnkənˈsiːvəbəl] *adj* **1** inconcebible. **2** *fam* imposible, increíble.

inconclusive [ɪnkənˈkluːsɪv] *adj* **1** *(debate, vote, etc)* no decisivo,-a. **2** *(evidence, result, etc)* no concluyente.

inconsequent [ɪnˈkɒnsɪkwənt] *adj* **1** *(not following logically)* inconsecuente. **2** *(inconsequential)* de poca importancia, sin trascendencia.

inconsiderate [ɪnkənˈsɪdərət] *adj* desconsiderado,-a, inconsiderado,-a, poco atento,-a.

inconsistent [ɪnkənˈsɪstənt] *adj* **1** *(not agreeing with, at variance with)* inconsecuente; *(contradictory)* contradictorio,-a. **2** *(changeable - weather)* variable; *(- person)* inconstante, voluble, irregular; *(- behaviour)* imprevisible, irregular.

inconstant [ɪn'kɒnstᵊnt] *adj* **1** *(person)* inconstante, veleidoso,-a, mudable. **2** *(not fixed)* variable.

incontinence [ɪn'kɒntɪnᵊns] *n* incontinencia.

inconvenience [ɪnkən'vi:nɪəns] *n* *(gen)* inconveniente *m*; *(trouble, difficulty)* molestia, dificultad *f*; *(hindrance)* estorbo, obstáculo; *(discomfort)* incomodidad *f*: *I'm sorry to cause you so much inconvenience* siento causarle tanta molestia.
▸ *vt (annoy)* causar molestia a, molestar; *(cause difficulty)* incomodar.

inconvenient [ɪnkən'vi:nɪənt] *adj* **1** *(gen)* inconveniente, molesto,-a, incómodo,-a; *(place)* mal situado,-a; *(time)* mal, inoportuno,-a; *(arrangement)* poco práctico,-a. **2** *(fact)* incómodo,-a.

incorporate [ɪn'kɔːpəreɪt] *vt* **1** *(make part of, include in)* incorporar (**in/into**, a), incluir (**in/into**, en); *(include, contain)* incluir, contener. **2** US *(company)* constituir, constituir en sociedad.
▸ *adj* US *(company)* constituido,-a, constituido,-a en sociedad.

⊠ To incorporate no significa 'incorporarse (levantarse)', que se traduce por to sit up.

incorrect [ɪnkə'rekt] *adj* **1** *(wrong, untrue)* incorrecto,-a, erróneo,-a, equivocado,-a. **2** *(- dress)* impropio,-a, inadecuado,-a.

increase [*(n)* 'ɪnkriːs; *(vb)* ɪn'kriːs] *n (gen)* aumento, incremento; *(in price, temperature)* subida, alza.
▸ *vt (gen)* aumentar, incrementar; *(temperature)* subir.

increasing [ɪn'kriːsɪŋ] *adj* creciente.

increasingly [ɪn'kriːsɪŋlɪ] *adv* cada vez más.

incredible [ɪn'kredɪbᵊl] *adj (unbelievable)* increíble, inverosímil; *(amazing)* fantástico,-a.

incredulous [ɪn'kredjələs] *adj* incrédulo,-a.

increment ['ɪnkrɪmənt] *n* aumento, incremento.

incriminate [ɪn'krɪmɪneɪt] *vt* incriminar.

incubate ['ɪnkjʊbeɪt] *vt* incubar.
▸ *vi (of eggs)* incubar; *(of bird)* empollar.

incubation [ɪnkjʊ'beɪʃᵊn] *n* incubación *f*.

incubator ['ɪnkjʊbeɪtᵊr] *n* incubadora.

incurable [ɪn'kjʊərəbᵊl] *adj* **1** *(disease)* incurable. **2** *fig (loss)* irremediable; *(habit, optimist)* incorregible.
▸ *n* enfermo,-a incurable.

indebted [ɪn'detɪd] *adj* **1** *(in debt)* endeudado,-a. **2** *fig (grateful)* agradecido,-a.

indecent [ɪn'diːsᵊnt] *adj* **1** *(obscene)* indecente, indecoroso,-a, obsceno,-a. **2** *(improper)* impropio,-a, indebido,-a, injustificado,-a; *(undue)* excesivo,-a.

indecisive [ɪndɪ'saɪsɪv] *adj* **1** *(hesitant)* indeciso,-a, irresoluto,-a. **2** *(inconclusive)* poco concluyente, no concluyente, no decisivo,-a.

indeed [ɪn'diːd] *adv* **1** *(yes, certainly)* efectivamente, en efecto: *are you Mr Fox? yes, indeed* ¿es el Sr Fox? sí, efectivamente. **2** *(intensifier)* realmente, de veras, de verdad: *thank you very much indeed* muchísimas gracias. **3** *fml (in fact)* realmente, en realidad, de hecho; *(what is more)* es más.

indefinite [ɪn'defɪnət] *adj* **1** *(vague, not precise)* indefinido,-a, vago,-a, impreciso,-a. **2** *(not fixed - period of time, amount, number)* indefinido,-a, indeterminado,-a.

indefinitely [ɪn'defɪnətlɪ] *adv* indefinidamente.

indemnity [ɪn'demnɪtɪ] *n* **1** *(insurance, guarantee)* indemnidad *f* (**against**, contra). **2** *(compensation)* indemnización *f* (**for**, por), reparación *f*, compensación *f*.
ⓘ *pl* indemnities.

indent [*(vb)* ɪn'dent; *(n)* 'ɪndent] *vt (text)* sangrar.
▸ *vi* GB *(order)* hacer un pedido (**for**, de), encargar (**for**, -).
▸ *n* GB *(order)* pedido.

indentation [ɪnden'teɪʃᵊn] *n* **1** *(in text)* sangría. **2** *(notch in edge, mark)* mella, muesca.

independence [ɪndɪ'pendəns] *n* independencia (**from**, de).

independent [ɪndɪˈpendᵊnt] *adj (gen)* independiente.
▸ *n* POL (candidato,-a) independiente *mf*.

in-depth [ɪnˈdepθ] *adj* minucioso,-a, exhaustivo,-a, a fondo.

indeterminate [ɪndɪˈtɜːmɪnət] *adj* indeterminado,-a.

India [ˈɪndɪə] *n* (la) India. COMP **India rubber** caucho.

index [ˈɪndeks] *n* índice. COMP **index finger** dedo índice.
ⓘ *pl* **indixes** o **indices** [ˈɪndɪsiːz].

Indian [ˈɪndɪən] *adj* indio,-a, hindú *mf*.
▸ *n* indio,-a, hindú. COMP **the Indian Ocean** el océano Indico.

indicate [ˈɪndɪkeɪt] *vt* indicar, señalar, marcar.
▸ *vi* AUTO poner el intermitente.

indication [ɪndɪˈkeɪʃᵊn] *n (gen)* indicio, señal *f*, indicación *f*.

indicative [ɪnˈdɪkətɪv] *adj* **1** *fml* indicativo,-a (of, de). **2** LING indicativo,-a.
▸ *n* LING indicativo.

indicator [ˈɪndɪkeɪtəʳ] *n* **1** *(gen)* indicador *m*. **2** AUTO intermitente *m*.

indices [ˈɪndɪsiːz] *n pl* → **index**.

indictment [ɪnˈdaɪtmənt] *n* **1** JUR acusación *f*, sumario. **2** *fig (criticism)* crítica.

indifference [ɪnˈdɪfᵊrəns] *n* indiferencia (to, ante).

indifferent [ɪnˈdɪfᵊrənt] *adj* **1** *(gen)* indiferente (to, a). **2** *(mediocre, average)* mediocre, regular, pobre.

☒ **Indifferent** no significa 'indiferente (irrelevante)', que se traduce por **immaterial**.

indigestion [ɪndɪˈdʒestʃᵊn] *n* indigestión *f*, empacho.

indignation [ɪndɪgˈneɪʃᵊn] *n* indignación *f* (about/over, por) (at, ante/por).

indigo [ˈɪndɪgəʊ] *n* añil *m*.

indirect [ɪndɪˈrekt] *adj* indirecto,-a.

indirectly [ɪndɪˈrektlɪ] *adv* indirectamente.

indissoluble [ɪndɪˈsɒljəbᵊl] *adj fml (cannot be dissolved)* indisoluble; *(cannot be broken)* inseparable.

individual [ɪndɪˈvɪdjʊəl] *adj* **1** *(single, separate)* por separado. **2** *(for one person)* individual. **3** *(particular, personal)* personal, propio,-a. **4** *(different, unique)* personal, original.
▸ *n* **1** *(person)* individuo, persona. **2** *fam* individuo, tipo, tío,-a.

individualism [ɪndɪˈvɪdʒʊəlɪzᵊm] *n* individualismo.

individualist [ɪndɪˈvɪdʒʊəlɪst] *n* individualista *mf*.

individually [ɪndɪˈvɪdʒʊəlɪ] *adv (separately)* individualmente, por separado; *(one by one)* uno por uno.

indivisible [ɪndɪˈvɪzəbᵊl] *adj* indivisible.

indoor [ˈɪndɔːʳ] *adj* **1** *(aerial, plant, photography, etc)* interior; *(clothes, etc)* de estar por casa. **2** SP *(swimming pool, running track)* cubierto,-a.

indoors [ɪnˈdɔːz] *adv (inside house)* dentro (de casa); *(at home)* en casa; *(inside building)* a cubierto, dentro.

induction [ɪnˈdʌkʃᵊn] *n* **1** *(initiation - gen)* admisión *f*, ingreso; *(- of priest)* instalación *f*. **2** US *(recruitment)* reclutamiento. **3** *(logic)* inducción *f*.

inductive [ɪnˈdʌktɪv] *adj* inductivo,-a.

indulgence [ɪnˈdʌldʒᵊns] *n* **1** *(luxury)* (pequeño) lujo; *(bad habit)* vicio. **2** *(of desire, whim)* satisfacción *f*, complacencia; *(partaking - of food, drink)* abuso; *(of person)* consentimiento; *(of child)* mimo. **3** REL indulgencia.

industrial [ɪnˈdʌstrɪəl] *adj* industrial.

industrialize [ɪnˈdʌstrɪəlaɪz] *vt* industrializar.
▸ *vi* industrializarse.

industrious [ɪnˈdʌstrɪəs] *adj (hard-working)* trabajador,-ra, laborioso,-a; *(diligent)* diligente, aplicado,-a.

industry [ˈɪndəstrɪ] *n* **1** *(gen)* industria. **2** *fml (hard work)* diligencia.
ⓘ *pl* **industries**.

inefficiency [ɪnɪˈfɪʃᵊnsɪ] *n* **1** *(gen)* ineficacia. **2** *(of person)* incompetencia, ineficiencia, ineptitud *f*.

inefficient [ɪnɪˈfɪʃᵊnt] *adj* **1** *(gen)* ineficaz. **2** *(person)* incompetente, ineficiente, poco eficiente.

inept [ɪˈnept] *adj (person)* inepto,-a, incapaz; *(remark)* torpe.

inequality [ɪnɪˈkwɒlətɪ] *n* desigualdad *f.*
ⓘ *pl* inequalities.

inequity [ɪnˈekwətɪ] *n* injusticia.
ⓘ *pl* inequities.

inertia [ɪˈnɜːʃə] *n* 1 PHYS inercia. 2 *(lethargy)* inercia, letargo, apatía.

inevitable [ɪnˈevɪtəbəl] *adj* 1 *(unavoidable)* inevitable. 2 *fam (usual)* sempiterno,-a, consabido,-a, de siempre.

inexact [ɪnɪgˈzækt] *adj* inexacto,-a.

inexpensive [ɪnɪkˈspensɪv] *adj* barato,-a, económico,-a.

inexperience [ɪnɪkˈspɪərɪəns] *n* inexperiencia, falta de experiencia.

inexpert [ɪnˈekspɜːt] *adj (person)* inexperto,-a (at, en).

inexplicable [ɪnɪkˈsplɪkəbəl] *adj* inexplicable.

inexpressive [ɪnɪkˈspresɪv] *adj* inexpresivo,-a.

infant [ˈɪnfənt] *n* 1 *(baby)* bebé *m,* niño,-a; *(at infant school)* niño,-a, párvulo,-a. 2 GB menor *mf* de edad.
COMP **infant school** escuela primaria.

infanticide [ɪnˈfæntɪsaɪd] *n* 1 *(crime)* infanticidio. 2 *(person)* infanticida *mf.*

infantry [ˈɪnfəntrɪ] *n* infantería.

infect [ɪnˈfekt] *vt* 1 *(wound, cut, etc)* infectar; *(food, water, etc)* contaminar; *(person)* contagiar. 2 *fig (emotions)* contagiar. 3 *(poison)* envenenar.

infection [ɪnˈfekʃən] *n* 1 *(of wound, cut, etc)* infección *f; (of food, water, etc)* contaminación *f; (with illness)* infección *f,* contagio. 2 *(disease)* infección *f.*

infectious [ɪnˈfekʃəs] *adj* infeccioso,-a, contagioso,-a.

inferior [ɪnˈfɪərɪəʳ] *adj* inferior (to, a).
▶ *n* inferior *mf.*

inferiority [ɪnfɪərɪˈɒrətɪ] *n* inferioridad *f.*

infertility [ɪnfəˈtɪlətɪ] *n* esterilidad *f.*

infidel [ˈɪnfɪdəl] *n* infiel *mf.*

🗙 Infidel no significa 'infiel (con la pareja, un amigo)', que se traduce por **unfaithful**.

infidelity [ɪnfɪˈdelətɪ] *n* infidelidad *f.*
ⓘ *pl* infidelities.

infiltration [ɪnfɪlˈtreɪʃən] *n* infiltración *f.*

infinite [ˈɪnfɪnət] *adj (endless)* infinito,-a; *(very great)* sin límites.
▶ the Infinite Dios *m.*

infinitesimal [ɪnfɪnɪˈtesɪməl] *adj* infinitesimal, infinitésimo,-a.

infinitive [ɪnˈfɪnɪtɪv] *n* LING infinitivo.

infinity [ɪnˈfɪnɪtɪ] *n* 1 *(gen)* infinidad *f.* 2 MATH infinito.

infirmary [ɪnˈfɜːmərɪ] *n* 1 *(hospital)* hospital *m.* 2 *(in school, etc)* enfermería.
ⓘ *pl* infirmaries.

inflammable [ɪnˈflæməbəl] *adj* 1 inflamable. 2 *fam fig* explosivo,-a.

inflammation [ɪnfləˈmeɪʃən] *n* inflamación *f.*

inflate [ɪnˈfleɪt] *vt* 1 inflar, hinchar. 2 *fig* inflar, hinchar, exagerar. 3 *(economy)* inflar.

inflation [ɪnˈfleɪʃən] *n* inflación *f.*

inflexible [ɪnˈfleksɪbəl] *adj* inflexible.

inflict [ɪnˈflɪkt] *vt* 1 *(grief, suffering, pain)* causar (on, a); *(blow)* dar a, asestar a, propinar a; *(defeat, punishment)* infligir (on, a), imponer (on, a); *(grief, suffering, pain)* causar (on, a). 2 *fig (view, etc)* imponer (on, a).

influence [ˈɪnfluəns] *n (gen)* influencia.
▶ *vt (decision, etc)* influir en/sobre; *(person)* influenciar.

influential [ɪnfluˈenʃəl] *adj* influyente.

influenza [ɪnfluˈenzə] *n* gripe *f.*

info [ˈɪnfəʊ] *n fam* información *f.*

inform [ɪnˈfɔːm] *vt* informar, notificar.

informal [ɪnˈfɔːməl] *adj (speech)* informal, familiar; *(discussion)* informal.

🗙 Informal no significa 'informal (poco serio)', que se traduce por **unreliable**.

information [ɪnfəˈmeɪʃən] *n (gen)* información *f; (facts)* datos *mpl.*

informative [ɪnˈfɔːmətɪv] *adj* informativo,-a.

infrared [ɪnfrəˈred] *adj* infrarrojo,-a.

infrastructure [ˈɪnfrəstrʌktʃəʳ] *n* infraestructura.

infringe [ɪnˈfrɪndʒ] *vt (law, rule, etc)* infringir, transgredir, violar; *(copyright,* *agreement, etc)* no respetar; *(liberty, rights)* violar, usurpar.

infuriate [ɪnˈfjʊərɪeɪt] *vt* enfurecer, poner furioso,-a, sacar de quicio.

ingenious [ɪnˈdʒiːnɪəs] *adj (person, thing)* ingenioso,-a; *(idea)* genial.

ingenuity [ɪndʒɪˈnjuːɪtɪ] *n* ingenio, ingeniosidad *f*, inventiva.

ingredient [ɪnˈɡriːdɪənt] *n* **1** CULIN ingrediente *m*. **2** *fig* componente *m*, elemento.

inhabit [ɪnˈhæbɪt] *vt* habitar, vivir en, ocupar, poblar.

inhabitable [ɪnˈhæbɪtəbəl] *adj* habitable.

☒ Inhabitable no significa 'inhabitable', que se traduce por uninhabitable.

inhabitant [ɪnˈhæbɪtənt] *n* habitante *mf*.

inhalation [ɪnhəˈleɪʃən] *n* inhalación *f*.

inhale [ɪnˈheɪl] *vt (air)* aspirar, respirar; *(gas, vapour)* inhalar.

inherit [ɪnˈherɪt] *vt* heredar (from, de).

inheritance [ɪnˈherɪtəns] *n (money, property, etc)* herencia (from, de); *(succession)* sucesión *f*.

inheritor [ɪnˈherɪtər] *n* heredero,-a.

inhibit [ɪnˈhɪbɪt] *vt* **1** *(person)* inhibir, cohibir. **2** *(hold back - attempt)* inhibir. **3** *(prevent)* impedir, restringir.

inhuman [ɪnˈhjuːmən] *adj* inhumano,-a.

initial [ɪˈnɪʃəl] *adj* inicial, primero,-a.
▶ *n* inicial *f*, letra inicial.
▶ *n pl* **initials** *(of name)* iniciales *fpl*; *(of abbreviation)* siglas *fpl*.

initially [ɪˈnɪʃəlɪ] *adv* al principio.

initiate [*(vb)* ɪˈnɪʃɪeɪt; *(n)* ɪˈnɪʃɪət] *vt* **1** *(gen)* iniciar; *(reform, plan, etc)* promover. **2** JUR entablar. **3** *(admit, introduce)* admitir (into, en).
▶ *n* iniciado,-a.

initiative [ɪˈnɪʃɪətɪv] *n* iniciativa.

inject [ɪnˈdʒekt] *vt* **1** *(drug, etc)* inyectar; *(person)* poner una inyección a, pinchar. **2** *fig (new ideas, enthusiasm, etc)* infundir; *(money, resources, etc)* invertir.

injection [ɪnˈdʒekʃən] *n* **1** inyección *f*.

injure [ˈɪndʒər] *vt* **1** herir, lesionar, lastimar. **2** *fig (feelings)* herir; *(health, reputation, etc)* perjudicar.

injured [ˈɪndʒəd] *adj* **1** *(hurt)* herido,-a, lesionado,-a, lastimado,-a. **2** *fig (offended - feeling)* herido,-a; *(- look, tone, etc)* ofendido,-a.
▶ *n pl* **the injured** los heridos.

injury [ˈɪndʒərɪ] *n* **1** herida, lesión *f*. **2** *fig (to feelings, etc)* daño; *(to reputation)* agravio.
ⓘ *pl* **injuries**.

☒ Injury no significa 'injuria', que se traduce por insult.

injustice [ɪnˈdʒʌstɪs] *n* injusticia.

ink [ɪŋk] *n* tinta.
▶ *vt* entintar.

inkblot [ˈɪŋkblɒt] *n* borrón *m*.

inkjet printer [ˈɪŋkdʒet ˈprɪntər] *n* impresora de chorro de tinta.

inkpad [ˈɪŋkpæd] *n* tampón *m* de entintar, almohadilla.

inland [*(adj)* ˈɪnlənd; *(adv)* ɪnˈlænd] *adj* (del) interior.
▶ *adv (travel)* tierra adentro, hacia el interior; *(live)* en el interior. COMP **Inland Revenue** GB Hacienda.

inn [ɪn] *n (with lodgings)* posada, fonda, mesón *m*; *(in country)* venta; *(pub)* taberna.

innate [ɪˈneɪt] *adj* innato,-a.

inner [ˈɪnər] *adj* **1** *(room, region, etc)* interior; *(organization)* interno,-a. **2** *(feelings, etc)* interior, íntimo,-a.

innocence [ˈɪnəsəns] *n* inocencia.

innocent [ˈɪnəsnt] *adj (gen)* inocente; *(harmless)* inocuo,-a, inofensivo,-a; *(naive)* ingenuo,-a.

innovate [ˈɪnəveɪt] *vi* innovar.

innumerable [ɪˈnjuːmərəbəl] *adj* innumerable.

inopportune [ɪnˈɒpətjuːn] *adj* inoportuno,-a.

inorganic [ɪnɔːˈɡænɪk] *adj* inorgánico,-a.

input [ˈɪnpʊt] *n (of power)* entrada; *(of money, resources)* inversión *f*; *(of data)* input *m*.
▶ *vt* COMPUT entrar, introducir.
ⓘ *pt & pp* **input** o **inputted**.

inquire [ɪnˈkwaɪəʳ] *vi fml* preguntar, informarse.

 ◆ **to inquire into** *vt insep* investigar.

inquiry [ɪnˈkwaɪəʳrɪ] *n* **1** *fml (question)* pregunta. **2** *(investigation)* investigación *f*.

 ⓘ *pl* inquiries.

inquisition [ɪnkwɪˈzɪʃ(ə)n] *n* investigación *f*, inquisición *f*. COMP **the Inquisition** HIST la Inquisición *f*.

inquisitive ɪnkwɪˈzɪtɪv] *adj (person)* curioso,-a.

inroads [ˈɪnrəʊds] *n pl (raid)* incursión *f* *sing*.

 ► *n fig (encroachment)* intrusión *f*.

insalubrious [ɪnsəˈlʊːbrɪəs] *adj fml* insalubre.

insane [ɪnˈseɪn] *adj* **1** *(person)* loco,-a, demente; *(act)* insensato,-a. **2** *fam (idea, etc)* loco,-a. LOC **to go insane** volverse loco,-a.

 ⊠ Insane no significa 'insano', que se traduce por unhealthy.

inscription [ɪnˈskrɪpʃ(ə)n] *n (gen)* inscripción *f*; *(in book)* dedicatoria.

insect [ˈɪnsekt] *n* insecto.

insecticide [ɪnˈsektɪsaɪd] *n* insecticida *m*.

insecure [ɪnsɪˈkjʊəʳ] *adj* inseguro,-a.

insecurity [ɪnsɪˈkjʊərɪtɪ] *n* inseguridad *f*.

inseminate [ɪnˈsemɪneɪt] *vt* inseminar.

insensitive [ɪnˈsensətɪv] *adj* insensible.

insert [*(vb)* ɪnˈsɜːt; *(n)* ˈɪnsɜːt] *vt (gen)* introducir en, meter en; *(comment, clause, paragraph, etc)* incluir (in, en), insertar (in, en); *(advertisement)* poner (in, en).

 ► *n (in book, newspaper)* encarte *m*; *(in clothing)* añadido.

inside [ɪnˈsaɪd] *n* **1** interior *m*, parte *f* interior. **2** *(driving on left)* la izquierda; *(driving on right)* la derecha.

 ► *adv (position)* dentro; *(movement)* adentro. LOC **inside out** del revés.

 ► *prep* dentro de.

 ► *n pl* **insides** *fam* entrañas *fpl*, tripas *fpl*.

insight [ˈɪnsaɪt] *n* **1** *(deep understanding, perception)* perspicacia, penetración *f*. **2** *(sudden understanding)* idea.

insignificant [ɪnsɪgˈnɪfɪkənt] *adj* insignificante.

insincere [ɪnsɪnˈsɪəʳ] *adj* poco sincero,-a, insincero,-a, falso,-a.

insinuate [ɪnˈsɪnjʊeɪt] *vt* **1** *(hint, suggest)* insinuar, dar a entender. **2** *(worm, install)* insinuarse (into, en).

insist [ɪnˈsɪst] *vt* **1** *(declare firmly)* insistir en. **2** *(demand forcefully)* exigir.

insolence [ˈɪnsələns] *n* insolencia.

insolent [ˈɪnsələnt] *adj* insolente.

insoluble [ɪnˈsɒljəb(ə)l] *adj* **1** *(of substances)* insoluble, indisoluble. **2** *fig* sin solución, insoluble.

insomnia [ɪnˈsɒmnɪə] *n* insomnio.

inspect [ɪnˈspekt] *vt (gen)* inspeccionar, examinar, revisar.

inspection [ɪnˈspekʃ(ə)n] *n* **1** *(gen)* inspección *f*, examen, revisión *f* **2** *(of luggage)* registro.

inspector [ɪnˈspektəʳ] *n (gen)* inspector,-ra; *(on train)* revisor,-ra; *(in police)* inspector,-ra de policía.

inspiration [ɪnspɪˈreɪʃ(ə)n] *n* **1** *(gen)* inspiración *f*. **2** *fam (good idea)* genialidad *f*.

inspire [ɪnˈspaɪəʳ] *vt* **1** *(gen)* inspirar. **2** *(encourage)* estimular, animar, mover. **3** *(fill with - fear)* infundir; *(- confidence, respect)* inspirar.

 ⊠ To inspire no significa 'inspirar (aire)', que se traduce por to breathe, to inhale.

install [ɪnˈstɔːl] *[also instal] vt* **1** *(equipment, etc)* instalar. **2** *(person)* instalar, colocar.

installation [ɪnstəˈleɪʃ(ə)n] *n* instalación *f*.

installment [ɪnˈstɔːlmənt] *n* US→ **instalment**

instalment [ɪnˈstɔːlmənt] *n* **1** *(of payment)* plazo. **2** *(of book, story, etc)* entrega; *(of collection)* fascículo.

instance [ˈɪnstəns] *n* ejemplo, caso. LOC **for instance** por ejemplo.

 ► *vt* poner por caso, citar como ejemplo.

 ⊠ Instance no significa 'instancia (formulario)', que se traduce por form.

instant [ˈɪnstənt] *n* instante *m*, momento.

▶ *adj* **1** *(at once)* inmediato,-a. **2** *(coffee, etc)* instantáneo,-a. **3** *fml (urgent)* urgente. **4** COMM *(of the present month)* del corriente.

instantly ['ɪnstəntlɪ] *adv* al instante, inmediatamente.

instead [ɪn'sted] *adv* en cambio, en su lugar: *Mrs Jones couldn't do the class so I did it instead* la Señora Jones no pudo dar la clase así que yo la di en su lugar.

▶ *prep* **instead of** en vez de, en lugar de: *we should eat more fish instead of meat* deberíamos comer más pescado en lugar de carne.

instinct ['ɪnstɪŋkt] *n* instinto.

instinctive [ɪn'stɪŋktɪv] *adj* instintivo,-a.

institute ['ɪnstɪtjuːt] *n* **1** *(gen)* instituto, centro. **2** *(professional body)* colegio, asociación *f*; *(educational)* escuela.

▶ *vt fml (organize, establish)* instituir, establecer, fundar; *(initiate - enquiry)* iniciar, empezar; *(- proceedings)* entablar.

institution [ɪnstɪ'tjuːʃən] *n* **1** *(gen)* institución *f* **3** *(home)* asilo; *(asylum)* hospital *m* psiquiátrico, manicomio; *(orphanage)* orfanato.

instruct [ɪn'strʌkt] *vt* **1** *(teach)* instruir, enseñar; *(inform)* informar. **2** *(order)* ordenar, mandar, dar instrucciones. **3** JUR *(solicitor, barrister)* dar instrucciones a; *(jury)* instruir.

instruction [ɪn'strʌkʃən] *n* **1** *(teaching)* instrucción *f*, enseñanza. **2** *(order)* orden *f*, mandato.

instructor [ɪn'strʌktər] *n* *(gen)* instructor,-ra; *(of driving)* profesor,-ra; *(of sport)* monitor,-ra.

instrument ['ɪnstrəmənt] *n* instrumento.

insufficient [ɪnsə'fɪʃənt] *adj* insuficiente.

insulate ['ɪnsjəleɪt] *vt* **1** TECH aislar (against/from, de). **2** *fig (protect)* proteger (against, contra), (from, de).

insulation [ɪnsjə'leɪʃən] *n* TECH aislamiento.

insulator ['ɪnsjəleɪtər] *n* TECH aislante *m*, aislador *m*.

insulin ['ɪnsjəlɪn] *n* insulina.

insult [*(n)* 'ɪnsʌlt; *(vb)* ɪn'sʌlt] *n* insulto.

▶ *vt* insultar, ofender, injuriar.

insurance [ɪn'ʃuərəns] *n* **1** seguro. **2** *fig (safeguard)* salvaguarda, protección *f*, garantía.

insure [ɪn'ʃuər] *vt* **1** asegurar (against, contra). **2** US *(ensure)* asegurar.

insurgent [ɪn'sɜːdʒənt] *adj* insurgente, insurrecto,-a.

insurrection [ɪnsə'rekʃən] *n* insurrección *f*.

intact [ɪn'tækt] *adj* intacto,-a.

intake ['ɪnteɪk] *n* **1** *(of food, etc)* consumo; *(of breath)* inhalación *f*. **2** TECH *(of air, water)* entrada; *(of electricity, gas, water)* toma. **3** *(number of people)* número de personas inscritas.

integer ['ɪntɪdʒər] *n* MATH entero, número entero.

integral ['ɪntɪɡrəl] *adj* **1** *(intrinsic, essential)* integral, esencial, fundamental. **2** *(built-in)* incorporado,-a. **3** MATH integral.

integrity [ɪn'teɡrətɪ] *n* **1** *(honesty)* integridad *f*, honradez *f*. **2** *(completeness)* totalidad *f*.

intellect ['ɪntəlekt] *n* **1** *(intelligence)* intelecto, inteligencia. **2** *(person)* intelectual *mf*.

intellectual [ɪntə'lektjuəl] *adj* intelectual.

▶ *n* intelectual *mf*.

intelligence [ɪn'telɪdʒəns] *n* **1** *(gen)* inteligencia. **2** *(information)* información *f*, espionaje *m*.

intelligent [ɪn'telɪdʒənt] *adj* inteligente.

intend [ɪn'tend] *vt* **1** *(plan, mean, have in mind)* tener la intención de, tener el propósito de, proponerse, pensar, querer. **2** *(destine for)* ir dirigido,-a a.

intense [ɪn'tens] *adj* **1** *(gen)* intenso,-a, fuerte; *(stare)* penetrante. **2** *(emotions)* profundo,-a, grande, vivo,-a. **3** *(person)* muy serio,-a.

intensify [ɪn'tensɪfaɪ] *vt* *(search, campaign)* intensificar; *(effort)* redoblar; *(production, pollution, pain)* aumentar.
ⓘ *pt & pp* intensified, *ger* intensifying.

intensity [ɪn'tensɪtɪ] *n* **1** intensidad *f*. **2** *(of person)* seriedad *f*.
ⓘ *pl* intensities.

intensive [ɪnˈtensɪv] *adj* **1** *(course, training, etc)* intensivo,-a. **2** *(search)* minucioso,-a; *(study)* profundo,-a. `COMP` **intensive care** cuidados *mpl* intensivos.

intention [ɪnˈtenʃən] *n (purpose, aim, plan, determination)* intención *f*, propósito.

interact [ɪntərˈækt] *vi* **1** *(people)* relacionarse, interaccionar. **2** CHEM reaccionar.

interaction [ɪntərˈækʃən] *n* interacción *f*.

interactive [ɪntərˈæktɪv] *adj* interactivo,-a.

inter-city [ɪntəˈsɪti] *adj* interurbano,-a, de largo recorrido.

intercom [ˈɪntəkɒm] *n* interfono.

interconnection [ɪntəkəˈnekʃən] *n* interconexión *f*.

intercontinental [ɪntəkɒntɪˈnentəl] *adj* intercontinental.

intercostal [ɪntəˈkɒstəl] *adj* intercostal.

intercourse [ˈɪntəkɔːs] *n* **1** *(dealings)* trato. **2** *(sexual)* coito, relaciones *fpl* sexuales.

interest [ˈɪntrəst] *n* **1** *(gen)* interés *m*. **2** *(hobby)* afición *f*, interés *m*. **3** *(advantage, benefit)* provecho, beneficio. **4** COMM *(share, stake)* participación *f*, interés *m*. **5** FIN *(money)* interés *m*, rédito. ▶ *vt* interesar.

interested [ˈɪntrəstɪd] *adj* interesado,-a (in, en).

interesting [ˈɪntrəstɪn] *adj* interesante.

interface [ˈɪntəfeɪs] *n* **1** COMPUT interface *f*, interfaz *f*. **2** *fig* terreno común.

interfere [ɪntəˈfɪəʳ] *vi (meddle)* entrometerse (in, en), inmiscuirse (in, en).

interference [ɪntəˈfɪərəns] *n* **1** *(meddling)* intromisión *f*, entrometimiento, injerencia. **2** *(with broadcast)* interferencia.

interior [ɪnˈtɪərɪəʳ] *adj* interior. ▶ *n* interior *m*, parte *f* interior.

interjection [ɪntəˈdʒekʃən] *n* **1** *(part of speech)* interjección *f*. **2** *(comment)* interposición *f*.

intermediate [ɪntəˈmiːdɪət] *adj* intermedio,-a.

internal [ɪnˈtɜːnəl] *adj* interno,-a.

international [ɪntəˈnæʃənəl] *adj* internacional.

internationalize [ɪntəˈnæʃnəlaɪz] *vt* internacionalizar.

Internet [ˈɪntənet] *n* Internet *f*.

interpret [ɪnˈtɜːprət] *vt (gen)* interpretar; *(understand)* interpretar, entender.

interpretation [ɪntɜːprəˈteɪʃən] *n* interpretación *f*.

interpreter [ɪnˈtɜːprətəʳ] *n* intérprete *mf*.

interrogate [ɪnˈterəgeɪt] *vt* interrogar.

interrogation [ɪnterəˈgeɪʃən] *n* interrogatorio.

interrogative [ɪntəˈrɒgəætɪv] *adj fml* interrogativo,-a. ▶ *n* LING *(word)* palabra interrogativa; *(phrase)* oración *f* interrogativa.

interrupt [ɪntəˈrʌpt] *vt* interrumpir. ▶ *vi* interrumpir.

interruption [ɪntəˈrʌpʃən] *n* interrupción *f*.

interstate [ˈɪntəsteɪt] *adj (esp us)* interestatal, entre estados.

interval [ˈɪntəvəl] *n* **1** *(in time, space)* intervalo (between, entre). **2** *(in play, film, etc)* intermedio, descanso; *(in play)* entreacto. **3** *(pause, break)* pausa; *(silence)* silencio; *(rest)* descanso. **4** MUS intervalo.

intervene [ɪntəˈviːn] *vi* **1** *(person)* intervenir (in, en). **2** *(event, etc)* sobrevenir, ocurrir. **3** *fml (time)* transcurrir, mediar.

🗷 To intervene no significa 'intervenir (operar)', que se traduce por to operate on.

interview [ˈɪntəvjuː] *n (gen)* entrevista; *(press)* entrevista. ▶ *vt* entrevistar, hacer una entrevista a, entrevistarse con.

interviewee [ɪntəvjuːˈiː] *n* entrevistado,-a.

interviewer [ˈɪntəvjuːəʳ] *n* entrevistador,-ra.

intervocalic [ɪntəvəˈkælɪk] *adj* intervocálico,-a.

intestinal [ɪnˈtestɪnəl] *adj* intestinal.

intestine [ɪnˈtestɪn] *n* intestino. COMP **large intestine** intestino grueso. ∎ **small intestine** intestino delgado.

intimate¹ [ˈɪntɪmət] *adj* **1** *(gen)* íntimo,-a; *(link, etc)* estrecho,-a. **2** *(knowledge)* profundo,-a.
▶ *n (friend)* amigo,-a íntimo,-a.

intimate² [ˈɪntɪmeɪt] *vi fml* insinuar, dar a entender.

⊠ To intimate no significa 'intimar (conocerse mejor)', que se traduce por to become close.

intimidate [ɪnˈtɪmɪdeɪt] *vt* intimidar.

into [ˈɪntʊ] *prep* **1** *(indicating movement)* en, dentro de, a; *(in direction of)* a, hacia; *(against)* contra, con. **2** *(time, age)* hasta. **3** *(indicating change)* en, a: *he turned water into wine* transformó el agua en vino. **4** MATH entre: *what's four into twenty?* ¿cuánto son veinte entre cuatro?

intolerant [ɪnˈtɒlərənt] *adj* intolerante, intransigente.

intonation [ɪntəˈneɪʃən] *n* entonación *f*.

intoxicate [ɪnˈtɒksɪkeɪt] *vt* **1** *fml* embriagar, emborrachar. **2** *fig* embriagar.

⊠ To intoxicate no significa 'intoxicar', que se traduce por to poison.

intoxication [ɪntɒksɪˈkeɪʃən] *n* embriaguez *f*.

⊠ Intoxicate no significa 'intoxicación', que se traduce por poisoning.

intranet [ˈɪntrənet] *n* red *f* local.

intransitive [ɪnˈtrænsɪtɪv] *adj* LING intransitivo,-a.

intrauterine [ɪntrəˈjuːtəraɪn] *adj* MED intrauterino,-a.

introduce [ɪntrəˈdjuːs] *vt* **1** *(person, programme)* presentar. **2** *(bring in - gen)* introducir; *(- new product, etc)* presentar, lanzar; *(law, procedure, etc)* instituir. **3** *(to hobby, habit)* iniciar (to, en). **4** *(bring up)* proponer, sugerir, plantear. **5** *fml (insert)* introducir, meter, insertar.

introduction [ɪntrəˈdʌkʃən] *n* **1** *(of person, programme)* presentación *f*. **2** *(to book, speech, etc)* introducción *f*. **3** *(- of new product, etc)* presentación *f*, lanzamien-

to; *(- of law, procedure, etc)* introducción *f*, institución *f*. **4** *(first experience)* iniciación *f*. **5** MUS introducción *f*.

introvert [ˈɪntrəvɜːt] *n* introvertido,-a.

intruder [ɪnˈtruːdər] *n* intruso,-a.

intuition [ɪntjuːˈɪʃən] *n* intuición *f*.

intuitive [ɪnˈtjuːɪtɪv] *adj* intuitivo,-a.

invade [ɪnˈveɪd] *vt (gen)* invadir.

invader [ɪnˈveɪdər] *n* invasor,-ra.

invalid¹ [ˈɪnvəlɪd] *n (disabled person)* inválido,-a, minusválido,-a; *(sick person)* enfermo,-a.

invalid² [ɪnˈvælɪd] *adj (gen)* inválido,-a, no válido,-a, nulo,-a; *(out of date)* caducado,-a.

invalidate [ɪnˈvælɪdeɪt] *vt (result, rule, etc)* invalidar, anular; *(argument)* refutar, demostrar el error de.

invasion [ɪnˈveɪʒən] *n (gen)* invasión *f*.

invent [ɪnˈvent] *vt* inventar, inventarse.

invention [ɪnˈvenʃən] *n* **1** *(gen)* invento, invención *f*; *(lying)* invención *f*, mentira. **2** *(capacity for inventing)* inventiva.

inventive [ɪnˈventɪv] *adj* inventivo,-a.

inventor [ɪnˈventər] *n* inventor,-ra.

inventory [ˈɪnvəntrɪ] *n* inventario.
ⓘ *pl* inventories.

inversion [ɪnˈvɜːʒən] *n* inversión *f*.

⊠ Inversion no significa 'inversión (de dinero)', que se traduce por investment.

invert [ɪnˈvɜːt] *vt* invertir. COMP **inverted commas** comillas.

⊠ To invert no significa 'invertir (dinero)', que se traduce por to invest.

invertebrate [ɪnˈvɜːtɪbrət] *adj* invertebrado,-a.

invest [ɪnˈvest] *vt* **1** *(money)* invertir (in, en). **2** *(time, effort, etc)* emplear (in, en), invertir (in, en). **3** *fml (right, rank, power, etc)* investir (with, con), conferir (with, -), otorgar (with, -). **4** *fml (quality, characteristic, etc)* revestir (with, con), envolver (with, de). **5** MIL *dated* sitiar, cercar.

investigate [ɪnˈvestɪgeɪt] *vt (crime)* investigar; *(cause, possibility)* examinar, estudiar.
▶ *vi fam (check)* mirar.

investigation [ɪnvestɪˈgeɪʃən] *n (of crime)* investigación *f* (into, sobre); *(of cause, possibility)* examen *m* (into, de), estudio (into, de).

investigator [ɪnˈvestɪgeɪtəʳ] *n* investigador,-ra.

investment [ɪnˈvestmənt] *n* **1** *(of money)* inversión *f*. **2** *(investiture)* investidura.

investor [ɪnˈvestəʳ] *n* inversor,-ra, inversionista *mf*.

invidious [ɪnˈvɪdɪəs] *adj* **1** *(task, job, etc)* odioso,-a, ingrato,-a. **2** *(comparison, choice, etc)* injusto,-a.

✖ Invidious no significa 'envidioso', que se traduce por envious.

invisible [ɪnˈvɪzəbəl] *adj* invisible.

invitation [ɪnvɪˈteɪʃən] *n* invitación *f*.

invite [*(vb)* ɪnˈvaɪt; *(n)* ˈɪnvaɪt] *vt* **1** *(guest, etc)* invitar, convidar; *(candidate, participant)* pedir, invitar. **2** *(comment, suggestion, etc)* solicitar. **3** *(criticism, disaster, etc)* provocar, incitar.

invoice [ˈɪnvɔɪs] *n* COMM factura.

invoke [ɪnˈvəʊk] *vt* invocar.

involuntary [ˈɪnˈvɒləntərɪ] *adj* involuntario,-a.

involve [ɪnˈvɒlv] *vt* **1** *(entail)* suponer, implicar, conllevar; *(give rise to)* acarrear, ocasionar. **2** *(include, affect, concern)* tener que ver con, afectar a. **3** *(implicate)* implicar, involucrar, meter.

inward [ˈɪnwəd] *adj* interior.
► *adv* hacia dentro.

inwards [ˈɪnwədz] *adv* hacia dentro.

iodine [ˈaɪədiːn] *n* yodo.

ion [aɪən] *n* ion *m*.

ionize [ˈaɪənaɪz] *vt* ionizar.

ionosphere [aɪˈɒnəsfɪəʳ] *n* ionosfera.

IQ [ˈaɪˈkjuː] *abbr* (intelligence quotient) coeficiente *m* de inteligencia; *(abbreviation)* CI *m*.

Iran [ɪˈrɑːn] *n* Irán.

Iraq [ɪˈrɑːk] *n* Irak.

Ireland [ˈaɪələnd] *n* Irlanda. COMP Northern Ireland Irlanda del norte.

iris [ˈaɪˈrɪs] *n* **1** *(of eye)* iris *m inv*. **2** BOT lirio.

Irish [ˈaɪrɪʃ] *adj* irlandés,-esa.

Irishman [ˈaɪrɪʃmən] *n* irlandés *m*.
ⓘ *pl* Irishmen [ˈaɪrɪʃmən].

Irishwoman [ˈaɪrɪʃwʊmən] *n* irlandesa.
ⓘ *pl* Irishwomen [ˈaɪrɪʃwɪmɪn].

iron [ˈaɪən] *n* **1** *(metal)* hierro. **2** *(appliance)* plancha. **3** *(for golf)* hierro, palo de hierro.
► *adj* de hierro.
► *vt (clothes)* planchar.
► *n pl* irons *(fetters)* grilletes *mpl*.
◆ to iron out *vt sep* **1** *(clothes)* planchar. **2** *fig (problem, difficulty, etc)* resolver, solucionar.

ironing [ˈaɪrɒnɪŋ] *n* planchado. LOC to do the ironing planchar. COMP ironing board tabla de planchar.

ironic [aɪˈrɒnɪk] *adj* irónico,-a.

ironmonger [ˈaɪənmʌŋgəʳ] *n* GB ferretero,-a. COMP ironmonger's (shop) ferretería.

ironmongery [ˈaɪənmʌŋgərɪ] *n* GB ferretería.

irony [ˈaɪrənɪ] *n* ironía.
ⓘ *pl* ironies.

irregular [ɪˈregjələʳ] *adj* **1** *(gen)* irregular; *(uneven)* desigual. **2** *(unusual, abnormal)* raro,-a, anormal; *(against the rules)* inadmisible. **3** *(troops)* irregular.

irrelevant [ɪˈrelɪvənt] *adj* **1** *(unimportant - fact, detail, etc)* irrelevante. **2** *(out of place)* que no viene al caso: *that's irrelevant* eso no tiene nada que ver, eso no viene al caso.

irresistible [ɪrɪˈzɪstəbəl] *adj* **1** *(temptation, impulse, etc)* irresistible: *an irresistible urge* un impulso irrefrenable. **2** *(person, thing)* irresistible.

irresponsibility [ɪrɪspɒnsəˈbɪlətɪ] *n* irresponsabilidad *f*, falta de seriedad.

irresponsible [ɪrɪˈspɒnsəbəl] *adj* irresponsable, poco serio,-a.

irrigable [ˈɪrɪgəbəl] *adj* irrigable, regadío,-a.

irrigate [ˈɪrɪgeɪt] *vt* **1** AGR regar, irrigar. **2** MED irrigar.

irrigated [ˈɪrɪgeɪtɪd] *vt* **1** AGR irrigado,-a. **2** MED irrigar.

irrigation [ɪrɪˈgeɪʃən] *n* AGR riego, irrigación *f*. COMP irrigation channel acequia, canal *m* de riego. ▮ **irrigation farming** cultivo de regadío. ▮ **irrigation system** sistema *m* de regadío.

irritate ['ɪrɪteɪt] *vt* **1** *(annoy)* irritar, molestar, fastidiar. **2** MED *(cause discomfort)* irritar; *(make inflamed)* inflamar.

irritating ['ɪrɪteɪtɪŋ] *adj* **1** *(annoying)* irritante, molesto,-a, fastidioso,-a, pesado,-a. **2** MED irritante.

irritation [ɪrɪ'teɪʃ*ə*n] *n* **1** MED irritación *f*. **2** *(cause of annoyance)* molestia, fastidio. **3** *(anger)* mal humor *m*, enfado, irritación *f*.

is [ɪz] *pres* → **be**.

Islam ['ɪzlɑːm] *n* islam *m*.

Islamic [ɪz'læmɪk] *adj* islámico,-a.

island ['aɪlənd] *n* isla.
▸ *adj* isleño,-a. COMP **safety island** US isla de peatones, isleta, refugio. ▮ **traffic island** isla de peatones, isleta, refugio.

isle [aɪl] *n* isla.

islet ['aɪlət] *n* islote *m*.

isobar ['aɪsəbɑː'] *n* isobara.

isolate ['aɪsəleɪt] *vt* aislar (from, de): *scientists have isolated the germ* los científicos han aislado el microbio.

isolated ['aɪsəleɪtɪd] *adj* **1** *(solitary)* aislado,-a, apartado,-a: *an isolated house* una casa aislada; *I live a very isolated life* llevo una vida muy solitaria. **2** *(single)* aislado,-a, único,-a, excepcional: *an isolated case* un caso aislado.

isosceles [aɪ'sɒsəliːz] *adj* isósceles. COMP **isosceles triangle** triángulo isósceles.

isotherm ['aɪsəθɜːm] *n* isotermo.

isotope ['aɪsətəʊp] *n* isótopo.

Israel ['ɪzrɪəl] *n* Israel.

Israeli [ɪz'reɪli] *adj* israelí.
▸ *n* israelí *mf*.

Israelite ['ɪzrɪəlaɪt] *adj* israelita.
▸ *n* israelita *mf*.

issue ['ɪʃuː] *n* **1** *(subject, topic)* tema *m*, cuestión *f*, asunto. **2** *(of newspaper, magazine, etc)* número. **3** *(of stamps, shares, back notes, etc)* emisión *f*; *(of book)* publicación *f*. **4** *(of passport, licence)* expedición *f*. **5** *(of equipment, supplies, etc)* distribución *f*, reparto, suministro.

6 *fml (emergence - of water, blood)* flujo. **7** *fml (children)* descendencia. **8** *fml (result, outcome)* resultado, consecuencia, desenlace *m*.
▸ *vt* **1** *(book, article)* publicar. **2** *(stamps, shares, banknotes, etc)* emitir. **3** *(passport, visa)* expedir. **4** *(equipment, supplies, etc)* distribuir, repartir, suministrar, proporcionar. **5** *(order, instruction)* dar; *(statement, warning)* dar, hacer público; *(writ, summons)* dictar, expedir; *(decree)* promulgar; *(warrant)* expedir.
▸ *vi* **1** *fml (liquid, blood)* fluir, manar; *(smell, etc)* salir. **2** *fml (result)* resultar (from, de), provenir (from, de), derivar(se) (from, de).

isthmus ['ɪsməs] *n* istmo.

it [ɪt] *pron* **1** *(subject)* él, ella, ello: *where's my supper? it's in the oven!* ¿dónde está mi cena? ¡está en el horno!; *whose is this coat? it's mine!* ¿de quién es este abrigo? ¡es mío!; *is it a boy or a girl?* ¿es niño o niña?; *who's that? who is it? it's me!* ¿quién eres? ¿quién es? ¡soy yo! **2** *(object - direct)* lo, la; *(- indirect)* le: *I doubt it* lo dudo; *I've just got this letter. Can you read it for me?* acabo de recibir esta carta. ¿Me la puedes leer?; *do you like skiing? yes, I love it* ¿te gusta esquiar? sí, me encanta; *she went up to the horse and patted it* se acercó al caballo y lo acarició; *can you manage that bag? Give it to me* ¿puedes con esa bolsa? Dámela. **3** *(after prep)* él, ella, ello: *a vase with flowers in it* un florero con flores dentro; *the train was still there so I ran for it* el tren aún estaba allí así que corrí para cogerlo; *you're not frightened of it, are you?* no le tienes miedo, ¿verdad?; *tell me about it* explícamelo, cuéntamelo. **4** *(abstract)* ello: *let's get on with it* vamos a por ello. **5** *(impersonal)* no se traduce: *it's cold* hace frío; *it's too early* es demasiado temprano; *it's six o'clock* son las seis; *it's Wednesday* es miércoles; *it's cloudy* está nublado; *it's not far* no está lejos; *it's impossible* es imposible; *it's important* es importante; *it's worth it* vale la pena; *it doesn't matter* no importa; *what's it like?* ¿cómo es?; *it cost a fiver* costó cinco libras; *it's true* es verdad; *it seems (that) she failed* parece que suspendió.

Italian [ɪˈtælɪən] *adj* italiano,-a.

▶ *n* **1** *(person)* italiano,-a. **2** *(language)* italiano.

italic [ɪˈtælɪks] *adj* (letra) cursiva.

itch [ɪtʃ] *n* **1** MED picazón *f*, picor *m*. **2** *fam fig (strong desire)* deseo, anhelo, ansia: *an itch to travel* un deseo de viajar.

▶ *vi* picar: *my feet itch* me pican los pies; *I'm itching all over* me pica todo; *this blanket itches* esta manta pica.

it'd [ˈɪtəd] *contr* **1** it had. **2** it would.

item [ˈaɪtəm] *n* **1** *(on list)* artículo, cosa; *(in collection)* pieza. **2** *(on agenda)* asunto, punto. **3** *(on bill)* partida, asiento. **4** *(in show)* número. COMP **item of clothing** prenda de vestir.

▶ *adv* también.

itinerary [aɪˈtɪnᵊrərɪ] *n* itinerario, ruta.
ⓘ *pl* itineraries.

it'll [ˈɪtᵊl] *contr* it will.

its [ɪts] *adj* (one thing) su; (more than one thing) sus: *the cat cleaned its paws* el gato se limpió las patas; *the baby's in its pram* el bebé está en su cochecito; *the film has its good points* la película tiene sus puntos buenos.

it's [ɪts] *contr* **1** → it is. **2** → it has.

itself [ɪtˈsɛlf] *pron* **1** *(reflexive)* se: *the bird preened itself* el pájaro se arregló las plumas; *Barcelona has opened itself up to the sea* Barcelona se ha abierto al mar. **2** *(emphatic)* en sí: *the house itself is quite old* la casa en sí es bastante vieja; *the job itself isn't that difficult* el trabajo en sí no es muy difícil; *she is politeness itself* es la cortesía personificada. **3** *(after prep)* sí: *the committee wants to keep all the profits for itself* el comité quiere guardar todos los beneficios para sí; *each dog has a kennel to itself* cada perro tiene su propia casita; *the idea in itself isn't bad* la idea en sí no está mal; *the first course was a meal in itself* el primer plato ya era una comida de por sí. LOC **by itself** solo,-a: *it switches off by itself* se apaga solo, se apaga automáticamente; *the baby did it all by itself* el niño lo hizo él solo.

I've [aɪv] *contr* I have.

ivory [ˈaɪvərɪ] *n (substance)* marfil *m*; *(colour)* color *m* marfil.

▶ *adj* de marfil.

▶ *n pl* **ivories** *(objects)* objetos *mpl* de marfil; *(piano keys)* teclas *fpl*. LOC **an ivory tower** una torre de marfil. COMP **Ivory Coast** Costa de Marfil.

ivy [ˈaɪvɪ] *n* hiedra, yedra. COMP **Ivy League** *ocho prestigiosas universidades privadas del nordeste de los Estados Unidos.*

⊕ La **Ivy League** reúne a las ocho universidades más prestigiosas de Estados Unidos que, además, son de las más antiguas. Un título de cualquiera de estos centros suele ser sinónimo de una excelente formación académica.

J

J, J [dʒeɪ] *n (the letter)* J, j *f.*

jab [dʒæb] *n* **1** pinchazo; *(with elbow)* codazo. **2** *fam (of pain)* pinchazo: *a flu jab* una inyección contra la gripe. **3** *(in boxing)* gancho.

▶ *vt* pinchar; *(with elbow)* dar un codazo a.

ⓘ *pt & pp* jabbed, *ger* jabbing.

jack [dʒæk] *n* **1** AUTO gato. **2** *(in cards)* jota; *(Spanish pack)* sota. **3** *(in bowls)* boliche *m.* **4** ELEC enchufe *m.* [COMP] **jack plug** ELEC jack *m*, clavija.

jackal ['dʒækɔːl] *n* chacal *m.*

jacket ['dʒækɪt] *n* **1** *(in general)* chaqueta; *(of suit)* americana; *(leather, etc)* cazadora. **2** *(of book)* sobrecubierta. **3** US *(of record)* funda. [COMP] **jacket potato** patata asada *(con su piel).*

jackknife ['dʒæknaɪf] *n* navaja.

jackpot ['dʒækpɒt] *n* (premio) gordo. [LOC] **to hit the jackpot** tocarle a ALGN el gordo.

Jacuzzi® [dʒə'kuːzɪ] *n* jacuzzi® *m.*

jade [dʒeɪd] *n* jade *m.*

jagged ['dʒægɪd] *adj* irregular, dentado,-a.

jaguar ['dʒægjuəʳ] *n* jaguar *m.*

jail [dʒeɪl] *n* cárcel *f*, prisión *f.*

▶ *vt* encarcelar: *he was jailed for life* lo condenaron a cadena perpetua.

jailer ['dʒeɪləʳ] *n* carcelero,-a.

jailhouse ['dʒeɪlhaʊs] *n* US cárcel *f.*

jam¹ [dʒæm] *n* mermelada, confitura. [COMP] **jam jar** bote *m* de mermelada.

jam² [dʒæm] *n (tight spot)* aprieto, apuro. [LOC] **to get into a jam** meterse en un apuro. [COMP] **jam session** sesión improvisada de jazz o rock.

▶ *vt* **1** *(fill)* abarrotar, atestar: *thousands of people jammed the streets* miles de personas abarrotaban las calles. **2** *(cram)* embutir, meter a la fuerza: *she jammed all her things into the bag* embutió todas sus cosas en la bolsa. **3** *(block)* bloquear: *the switchboard was jammed with calls of complaint* las llamadas de protesta bloquearon la centralita.

ⓘ *pt & pp* jammed, *ger* jarring.

Jamaica [dʒə'meɪkə] *n* Jamaica.

Jamaican [dʒə'meɪkⁿn] *adj* jamaicano,-a.

▶ *n* jamaicano,-a.

jangle ['dʒæŋgⁿl] *vi* sonar de un modo discordante.

▶ *vt* hacer sonar de un modo discordante.

▶ *n* sonido discordante.

January ['dʒænjʊərɪ] *n* enero.

📝 Para ejemplos de usos, consulta May.

Japan [dʒə'pæn] *n* (el) Japón *m.*

Japanese [dʒæpə'niːz] *adj* japonés,-esa.

▶ *n* **1** *(person)* japonés,-esa. **2** *(language)* japonés *m.*

jar [dʒɑːʳ] *n* **1** *(glass)* tarro, bote *m*: *a jar of strawberry jam* un tarro de mermelada de fresa. **2** *(earthenware)* vasija, tinaja. **3** *(shake, shock)* sacudida: *it gave me a bit of a jar* me chocó bastante. **4** *fam (drink)* copa: *let's go and have a few jars!* ¡vamos a tomar unas copas!

jargon ['dʒɑːgⁿn] *n* jerga, jerigonza.

jasmine ['dʒæzmɪn] *n* jazmín *m.*

jaundice ['dʒɔːndɪs] *n* ictericia.

jaunty ['dʒɔːntɪ] *adj* garboso,-a.

ⓘ *comp* jauntier, *superl* jauntiest.

javelin ['dʒævⁿlɪn] *n* jabalina. [LOC] **to throw the javelin** lanzar la jabalina.

COMP **javelin competition** lanzamiento de jabalina.

jaw [dʒɔ:] n **1** ANAT mandíbula. COMP **upper jaw** maxilar m superior. **lower jaw** maxilar m inferior. **2** ZOOL mandíbula, quijada, carrillera.
  ▶ vi fam (talk) charlar.

jazz [dʒæz] n jazz m. LOC **and all that jazz** y demás, y toda la pesca, y todo el rollo.
  ▶ adj de jazz, jazzístico,-a. COMP **jazz band** conjunto de jazz.
  ◆ **to jazz up** vt sep (in general) hacer más alegre, dar vida a; (party) animar.

jealous ['dʒeləs] adj **1** celoso,-a. **2** (envious) envidioso,-a. LOC **to be jealous of** SB tener celos de ALGN, estar celoso,-a de ALGN. **to make** SB **jealous** poner celoso,-a a ALGN.

jealousy ['dʒeləsɪ] n **1** celos mpl. **2** (envy) envidia.
  ① pl **jealousies**.

jeans [dʒi:nz] n pl vaqueros mpl, tejanos mpl.

jeep® [dʒi:p] n jeep® m, todoterreno.

jeer [dʒɪəʳ] vi (mock) burlarse (at, de), mofarse (at, de).
  ▶ vt (boo) abuchear.
  ▶ vi (boo) abuchear.
  ▶ n pl **jeers** (booing) abucheos mpl; (mocking) burlas fpl, mofas fpl, befas fpl.

jelly ['dʒelɪ] n **1** (in general) jalea. **2** (fruit) gelatina.
  ① pl **jellies**.

jellyfish ['dʒelɪfɪʃ] n medusa.
  ① pl **jellyfishes**.

jeopardy ['dʒepədɪ] n peligro. LOC **to be in jeopardy** estar en peligro, peligrar. **to put in jeopardy** poner en peligro, hacer peligrar.

jerk [dʒɜ:k] n **1** (pull) tirón m; (jolt) sacudida. **2** fam imbécil mf, subnormal mf. LOC **with a jerk** bruscamente.
  ▶ vt dar una sacudida a, tirar de.
  ▶ vi dar una sacudida.

jerrycan ['dʒerɪkæn] n bidón m.

jersey ['dʒɜ:zɪ] n jersey m, suéter m.

jest [dʒest] n broma. LOC **in jest** en broma.
  ▶ vi bromear.

jester ['dʒestəʳ] n HIST bufón m.

Jesus ['dʒi:zəs] n Jesús m, Jesucristo. COMP **Jesus Christ** Jesucristo.

jet [dʒet] n **1** (aircraft) reactor m. **2** (stream) chorro. **3** (outlet) boquilla, mechero. COMP **jet engine** reactor m, propulsor m a chorro. **jet foil** deslizador m. **jet lag** jet lag m, desarreglo horario. **jet set** la jet set f, la jet f. **jet propulsion** propulsión f a chorro.

jetty ['dʒetɪ] n (stone) malecón m; (wooden) embarcadero.
  ① pl **jetties**.

Jew [dʒu:] n REL judío,-a.

jewel ['dʒu:əl] n **1** joya, alhaja. **2** (stone) piedra preciosa. **3** (in watch) rubí m.

jewelled ['dʒu:əld] adj adornado,-a con piedras preciosas.

jeweller ['dʒu:ələʳ] n joyero,-a.

jewellery ['dʒu:əlrɪ] n joyas fpl.

Jewish ['dʒu:ɪʃ] adj judío,-a.

jigsaw ['dʒɪgsɔ:] n **1** (saw) sierra de vaivén. **2** (puzzle) rompecabezas m, puzzle m.

jingle ['dʒɪŋgəl] n **1** tintineo. **2** TV tonadilla publicitaria.
  ▶ vi tintinear.
  ▶ vt hacer sonar.

jinx [dʒɪŋks] n **1** (person) gafe mf. **2** (bad luck) mala suerte f: there's a jinx on this computer este ordenador está gafado.
  ▶ vt gafar.

job [dʒɒb] n **1** (employment) empleo, (puesto de) trabajo: what's your job? ¿en qué trabajas? **2** (piece of work) trabajo; (task) tarea: he did a good job (of work) hizo un buen trabajo. LOC **it's a good job that ...** menos mal que... **on the job** trabajando. **out of a job** parado,-a. **to make the best of a bad job** poner a mal tiempo buena cara. COMP **job centre** oficina de empleo. **job hunting** búsqueda de trabajo.

jobless ['dʒɒbləs] adj parado,-a.

jockey ['dʒɒkɪ] n jockey m.

jog [dʒɒg] n **1** (push) empujoncito, sacudida. **2** (pace) trote m.
  ▶ vt empujar, sacudir.

▶ vi hacer footing. LOC **at a jog trot** a trote corto. **I to go for a jog** (ir a) hacer footing.

◆ **to jog along** vi **1** andar a trote corto. **2** fig ir tirando.

ⓘ pt & pp **jogged**, ger **jogging**.

jogging ['dʒɒgɪŋ] n footing m. LOC **to go jogging** hacer footing.

join [dʒɔɪn] vt **1** (bring together) juntar, unir. **2** (connect) unir, conectar: the two cities are joined by a bridge las dos ciudades están unidas por un puente. **3** (company, etc) incorporarse a: Mr Osuna joined the company last year el Sr Osuna se incorporó a la empresa el año pasado. **4** (armed forces) alistarse en; (police) ingresar en. **5** (club) hacerse socio,-a de. **6** (party) afiliarse a, ingresar en. **7** (be with sb) reunirse con, unirse a: would you like to join us for the evening? ¿les gustaría pasar la tarde con nosotros? LOC **join the club!** ¡ya somos dos etc! **I to join forces** aunar esfuerzos. **I to join hands** cogerse de las manos.

▶ vi **1** juntarse, unirse. **2** (rivers) confluir; (roads) juntarse, empalmar.

◆ **to join in** vi participar.

▶ vt insep (debate) intervenir en.

◆ **to join up** vi alistarse.

joiner ['dʒɔɪnər] n carpintero que se dedica a puertas, ventanas, etc.

joint [dʒɔɪnt] n **1** junta, unión f. **2** ANAT articulación f. **3** sl (drugs) porro. LOC **to put out of joint** (elbow, shoulder, etc) dislocar: she put her shoulder out of joint se dislocó el hombro.

▶ adj colectivo,-a, mutuo,-a. COMP **joint account** cuenta conjunta, cuenta indistinta. **I joint owner** copropietario,-a.

▶ vt CULIN descuartizar.

jointed ['dʒɔɪntɪd] adj **1** articulado,-a. **2** (chicken, etc) cortado,-a a piezas.

jointly ['dʒɔɪntlɪ] adv conjuntamente.

joke [dʒəʊk] n **1** chiste m: shall I tell you a joke? ¿te cuento un chiste? **2** (practical) broma: John can't take a joke John no aguanta una broma. **3** (person) payaso. LOC **to make a joke of** STH reírse de ALGO. **I to play a joke on** SB gastar una

broma a ALGN. **I to tell a joke** contar un chiste.

▶ vi bromear. LOC **you must be joking!** ¡venga ya!

joker ['dʒəʊkər] n **1** bromista mf: some joker put salt in the sugar algún gracioso ha puesto sal en el azúcar. **2** (card) comodín m. **3** fam idiota mf. COMP **the joker in the pack** un elemento desconocido.

jolly ['dʒɒlɪ] adj (cheerful) alegre, animado,-a: she was a very jolly person era una persona muy animada.

ⓘ comp **jollier**, superl **jolliest**.

▶ adv GB fam muy: it's jolly difficult es la mar de difícil; they played jolly well jugaron fenomenal.

◆ **to jolly along** vt sep dar ánimos a, animar.

ⓘ pt & pp **jollied**, ger **jollying**.

jolt [dʒəʊlt] n **1** sacudida. **2** (fright) susto.

▶ vt sacudir.

▶ vi dar tumbos.

Jordan ['dʒɔːdən] n **1** (country) Jordania.

Jordanian [dʒɔːˈdeɪnɪən] adj jordano,-a.

▶ n jordano,-a.

jot [dʒɒt] n pizca: there isn't a jot of truth in it no hay pizca de verdad en esto; I don't care a jot me importa un bledo.

▶ vt apuntar, anotar.

◆ **to jot down** vt sep apuntar.

ⓘ pt & pp **jotted**, ger **jotting**.

joule [dʒuːl] n julio.

journal ['dʒɜːnəl] n **1** (magazine) revista. **2** (diary) diario.

journalism ['dʒɜːnəlɪzəm] n periodismo.

journalist ['dʒɜːnəlɪst] n periodista mf.

journey ['dʒɜːnɪ] n viaje m: it's a 100 mile journey es un viaje de 100 millas.

▶ vi viajar.

joy [dʒɔɪ] n **1** alegría, júbilo: her face was a picture of joy estaba radiante de alegría; he's a joy to work with da gusto trabajar con él. **2** fam (satisfaction) satisfacción f; (luck) suerte f; (success) éxito: you can complain all you like, but you'll get no joy quéjate todo lo que quieras, pero no te servirá de nada.

joyful ['dʒɔɪful] adj jubiloso,-a, alegre.

J

joystick ['dʒɔɪstɪk] *n* **1** AV palanca de mando. **2** COMPUT joystick *m*.

jubilation [dʒuː·bɪ'leɪ[ə]n] *n* júbilo.

☒ Jubilation no significa 'jubilación', que se traduce por **retirement**.

jubilee ['dʒuː·bɪliː] *n* **1** festejos *mpl*. **2** *(anniversary)* aniversario.

Judaism ['dʒuː·deɪɪzəm] *n* judaísmo.
▸ *n* vibración *f (violenta)*.

judge [dʒʌdʒ] *n* **1** *(man)* juez *m*; *(woman)* juez *f*, jueza. **2** *(in competition)* jurado, miembro del jurado.
▸ *vt* **1** *(court case)* juzgar. **2** *(calculate)* calcular: *it's hard to judge how much we need* es difícil calcular cuánto necesitamos.

judgement ['dʒʌdʒmənt] [también se escribe **judgment**.] *n* **1** *(ability)* (buen) juicio, (buen) criterio. **2** *(opinion)* juicio, opinión *f*: *my personal judgement is that...* mi opinión es que ...; *in my judgement...* a mi juicio... **3** *(decision)* fallo. **4** *(criticism)* crítica.

judicial [dʒuː'dɪʃ[ə]l] *adj* judicial. COMP **judicial inquiry** investigación *f* judicial.

judo ['dʒuː·dəʊ] *n* yudo, judo.

jug [dʒʌg] *n* **1** jarra, jarro. **2** *sl (prison)* chirona.

juggle ['dʒʌg[ə]l] *vi* **1** hacer juegos malabares (with, con). **2** *fig (figures, etc)* jugar (with, con).

juggler ['dʒʌg[ə]lə'] *n* malabarista *mf*.

jugular ['dʒʌgjələ'] *adj* yugular. COMP **jugular vein** vena yugular.
▸ *n* yugular *f*. LOC **to go for the jugular** saltarle a ALGN a la yugular.

juice [dʒuːs] *n* **1** *(gen)* jugo. **2** *(of fruit)* zumo, AM jugo. **3** *fam (petrol)* gasolina; *(electricity)* fuerza, luz *f*. COMP **juice extractor** licuadora.

juicy ['dʒuː·sɪ] *adj* **1** jugoso,-a. **2** *fam (gossip, etc)* picante, escabroso,-a.
ⓘ *comp* **juicier**, *superl* **juiciest**.

jukebox ['dʒuː·kbɒks] *n* máquina de discos.

July [dʒuː'laɪ] *n* julio.

✎ Para ejemplos de usos, consulta **May**.

jumble ['dʒʌmb[ə]l] *n* revoltijo, mezcolanza. COMP **jumble sale** rastrillo benéfico.
▸ *vt* desordenar.

jumbo ['dʒʌmbəʊ] *adj* gigante.
▸ *n* [Also **jumbo jet.**] *(plane)* jumbo.

jump [dʒʌmp] *n* **1** salto: *a parachute jump* un salto en paracaídas. **2** *(in prices, etc)* salto, aumento importante, disparo: *there's been a tremendous jump in profits* ha habido un aumento importante de los beneficios. **3** *(fence)* valla, obstáculo: *the horse refused at the first jump* el caballo se plantó en el primer obstáculo. COMP **jump seat** asiento plegable. ▮ **jump suit** mono.
▸ *vi* **1** saltar. **2** *(rise sharply)* dar un salto: *inflation jumped 2% last month* la inflación dio un salto de un 2% el mes pasado. LOC **to jump to conclusions** llegar a conclusiones precipitadas.
▸ *vt* saltar: *he tried to jump the wall, but it was too high* intentó saltar el muro, pero era demasiado alto. LOC **to jump rope** US saltar a la comba. ▮ **to jump the gun** precipitarse, adelantarse. ▮ **to jump the lights** saltarse el semáforo en rojo. ▮ **to jump the queue** colarse.
◆ **to jump at** *vt insep* aceptar sin pensarlo: *when they offered him the job, he jumped at it* cuando le ofrecieron el trabajo lo aceptó sin pensar.

jumper¹ ['dʒʌmpə'] *n* **1** GB jersey *m*. **2** US *(dress)* pichi *m*.

jumper² ['dʒʌmpə'] *n* SP saltador,-ra.

junction ['dʒʌŋk[ə]n] *n* **1** *(railways)* empalme *m*. **2** *(roads)* cruce *m*. **3** *(motorway - entry)* acceso; *(- exit)* salida.

June [dʒuːn] *n* junio.

✎ Para ejemplos de usos, consulta **May**.

jungle ['dʒʌŋg[ə]l] *n* selva, jungla.

junior ['dʒuː·nɪə'] *adj* **1** *(in rank)* subalterno,-a. **2** *(in age)* menor, más joven. **3** US *(after name)* hijo.
▸ *n* **1** *(in rank)* subalterno,-a. **2** *(in age)* menor *mf*: *she is three years my junior* tiene tres años menos que yo. **3** GB alumno,-a de EGB. **4** US hijo: *where's your mom, Junior?* ¿dónde está tu mamá

hijo? COMP **junior college** US *colegio universitario para los dos primeros cursos*. ‖ **junior high school** US instituto de enseñanza secundaria. ‖ **junior school** GB escuela primaria.

junk [dʒʌŋk] *n* trastos *mpl*. COMP **junk food** comida basura. ‖ **junk mail** correo basura. ‖ **junk shop** chamarilería.

Jupiter ['dʒuːpɪtə'] *n* Júpiter *m*.

Jurassic [dʒuˈræsɪk] *adj* jurásico,-a.

jury ['dʒuərɪ] *n* jurado.
ⓘ *pl* juries.

just¹ [dʒʌst] *adj* **1** *(fair)* justo,-a. **2** *(justifiable)* fundado,-a, justificado,-a. **3** *(deserved)* merecido,-a. LOC **to get one's just desserts** llevar su merecido.

just² [dʒʌst] *adv* **1** *(exactly)* exactamente, precisamente, justo: *this is just what I needed* esto es justo lo que necesitaba. **2** *(only)* solamente, solo: *no sugar for me, please, just milk* no quiero azúcar, gracias, solo leche. **3** *(barely)* apenas, por poco: *I ran all the way and (only) just caught the bus* fui corriendo y cogí el autobús por poco. **4** *(right now)* en este momento: *I'm just finishing it* lo acabo ahora mismo. **5** *(simply)* sencillamente:

we could just stay here and wait for her pues, sencillamente podríamos quedarnos aquí y esperarla. **6** *(for emphasis)*: *he's just as clever as you are* él es tan inteligente como tú. **7** *(used to interrupt)*: *just shut up, will you?* ¡cállese, por favor! **8** *fam (really)* realmente, verdaderamente: *the weather's just marvellous* hace un tiempo realmente maravilloso. LOC **just about** prácticamente. ‖ **just in case** por si acaso. ‖ **just like that!** ¡sin más! ‖ **just so 1** *(tidy)* ordenado,-a, arreglado,-a. **2** *(as a reply)* sí, exactamente. ‖ **just then** en ese momento. ‖ **just the same 1** *(not different)* exactamente igual. **2** *(nevertheless)* sin embargo, no obstante.
▸ *phr* **to have just + *pres part*** acabar de + *infin*: *he has just telephoned* acaba de telefonear.

justice ['dʒʌstɪs] *n* **1** justicia. **2** *(judge - man)* juez *m*; *(- woman)* juez *f*, jueza. LOC **to bring to justice** llevar ante los tribunales. ‖ **to do justice to** SB hacer justicia a ALGN.

justify ['dʒʌstɪfaɪ] *vt* justificar.
ⓘ *pt & pp* justified, *ger* justifying.

J

K

K, k [keɪ] *n (the letter)* K, k *f.*

kaleidoscope [kəˈlaɪdəskəʊp] *n* calidoscopio.

kangaroo [kæŋgəˈruː] *n* canguro.
ⓘ *pl* **kangaroos**.

karaoke [kærɪˈəʊkɪ] *n* karaoke *m.*

karate [kəˈrɑːtɪ] *n* kárate *m.*

karstic [ˈkɑːstɪk] *adj* kárstico,-a.

Kazakh [kæˈzæk] *adj* kazajio,-a.
▶ *n* **1** *(person)* kazajio,-a. **2** *(language)* kazajio.

Kazakhstan [kæzækˈstæn] *n* Kazajstán.

keen [kiːn] *adj* **1** *(eager)* entusiasta, aficionado,-a: *he's a very keen pupil* es un alumno muy entusiasta. **2** *(sharp - mind, senses, etc)* agudo,-a, vivo,-a; *(- look)* penetrante; *(- wind)* cortante; *(- edge, point)* afilado,-a. **3** *(feeling)* profundo, -a, intenso,-a. **4** *(competition)* fuerte, reñido,-a. **5** *(price)* competitivo,-a.
LOC **to be keen on** STH ser aficionado,-a a ALGO, gustarle ALGO a ALGN. **I to be keen on** SB gustarle ALGN a ALGN. **I to take a keen interest in** mostrar un gran interés por.

keep [kiːp] *n* **1** *(board)* sustento, mantenimiento: *to earn one's keep* ganarse el pan. **2** *(of castle)* torreón *m*, torre *f* del homenaje.
▶ *vt* **1** *(not throw away)* guardar. **2** *(not give back)* quedarse con: *keep the change* quédese con el cambio. **3** *(have)* tener; *(carry)* llevar. **4** *(look after, save)* guardar: *can you keep me a loaf of bread for Friday?* ¿me guarda una barra de pan para el viernes? **5** *(put away, store)* guardar: *where do you keep the glasses?* ¿dónde guardas los vasos? **6** *(secret)* guardar: *can you keep a secret?* ¿sabes guardar un secreto? **7** *(with adj, verb, etc)* mantener:

these doors must be kept locked estas puertas deben mantenerse cerradas.
▶ *vi* **1** *(do repeatedly)* no dejar de; *(do continuously)* seguir, continuar: *she was exhausted but kept swimming* estaba agotada pero siguió nadando. **2** *(stay fresh)* conservarse. **3** *(continue in direction)* continuar, seguir: *keep left/right* circula por la izquierda/derecha. **4** *(with adj, verb, etc)* quedarse, permanecer: *we must keep calm* debemos mantener la calma. LOC **to keep swimming** seguir (adelante). **I to keep going** seguir (adelante). **I to keep one's head** no perder la cabeza. **I to keep quiet** callarse, no hacer ruido. **I to keep SB from doing** STH impedir que ALGN haga ALGO. **I to keep** STH **from** SB ocultar ALGO a ALGN.
◆ **to keep off** *vi (stay away)* mantenerse a distancia; *(of rain)* no llover: *if the rain keeps off, we'll be able to play tennis* si no llueve, podremos jugar a tenis.
▶ *vt sep (make stay away)* no dejar entrar, no dejar acercarse; *(avoid)* no tocar, no hablar de: *"Keep off the grass"* «No pisar la hierba».
◆ **to keep out** *vt sep* no dejar entrar, no dejar pasar.
▶ *vi* no entrar.
◆ **to keep up** *vt sep* **1** *(gen)* mantener, seguir. **2** *(from sleeping)* mantener despierto,-a, tener en vela.
▶ *vi* **1** *(not fall behind)* aguantar el ritmo. **2** *(stay in touch)* mantenerse al día.
ⓘ *pt & pp* **kept** [kept].

keeper [ˈkiːpəʳ] *n* **1** *(in zoo)* guardián -ana. **2** *(in park)* guarda *mf.* **3** *(in museum)* conservador,-ra; *(in archives)* archivador,-ra.

kennel [ˈkenəl] *n* caseta del perros.
▶ *n pl* **kennels** *(boarding)* residencia *sing* canina.

Kenya [ˈkenjə] n Kenia.

Kenyan [ˈkenjən] adj keniano,-a.
▶ n keniano,-a.

kerb [kɜ:b] n bordillo.

kept [kept] pt & pp → keep.

kernel [ˈkɜ:nəl] n 1 (of nut, fruit) semilla.
2 fig núcleo, grano.

kerosene [ˈkerəsi:n] n US queroseno.

ketchup [ˈketʃəp] n ketchup m, catsup m.

kettle [ˈketəl] n tetera (para hervir agua):
will you put the kettle on to make some tea?
¿quieres poner el agua a hervir para hacer té? LOC **that's a different kettle of fish** eso es harina de otro costal.

key [ki:] n 1 (of door, car, etc) llave f. 2 (of clock, mechanical) llave f. 3 fig (to problem, map, code) clave f; (to exercises) respuestas fpl. 4 (on computer, piano, etc) tecla. 5 MUS (on wind instrument) llave f, pistón m; (set of notes) clave f; (tone, style) tono.
▶ adj clave, principal: tourism is the country's key industry el turismo es la industria principal del país. COMP **key ring** llavero.
◆ **to key in** vt sep introducir, teclear:
she keyed in the data introdujo los datos.

keyboard [ˈki:bɔ:d] n teclado. COMP **keyboard player** teclista mf.
▶ n pl **keyboards** teclados mpl.

keyhole [ˈki:həʊl] n ojo de la cerradura.

khaki [ˈkɑ:kɪ] n caqui m.
▶ adj caqui.

kick [kɪk] n 1 (by person) puntapié m, patada. 2 SP golpe m, tiro. 3 (by animal) coz f. 4 fam (pleasure) diversión f, emoción f: he gets a kick out of playing basketball se divierte jugando al baloncesto.
▶ vt 1 (hit ball) dar un puntapié a, golpear con el pie; (score) marcar. 2 (hit person) dar una patada a; (move legs) patalear. 3 (by animal) dar coces a, cocear.
◆ **to kick off** vi SP sacar, hacer el saque inicial; (begin) empezar, comenzar.
▶ vt sep 1 (begin) empezar, comenzar, iniciar. 2 (remove - shoes) quitarse.
◆ **to kick out** vt sep echar.

kick-off [ˈkɪkɒf] n SP saque m inicial.

kid¹ [kɪd] n 1 fam crío,-a, niño,-a, chico,-a, chaval,-la. 2 (animal) cabrito. 3 (leather) cabritilla. LOC **to treat SB with**

kid gloves tratar a ALGN con guantes de seda.
▶ adj (brother, sister) menor.

kid² [kɪd] vt 1 (deceive, tease) tomar el pelo a, engañar. 2 (fool os) engañarse a sí mismo, hacerse ilusiones.
▶ vi estar de broma: you're kidding! ¡estás de broma!, ¡no me digas!; no kidding! ¡en serio!

kidnap [ˈkɪdnæp] vt secuestrar, raptar.
① pt & pp kidnapped, ger kidnapping.

kidnapper [ˈkɪdnæpəʳ] n secuestrador,-ra.

kidnapping [ˈkɪdnæpɪŋ] n secuestro.

kidney [ˈkɪdnɪ] n riñón m. COMP **kidney machine** riñón m artificial.

kill [kɪl] n (act) matanza; (animal) pieza.
▶ vt 1 matar, asesinar. 2 fig (hope, conversation, etc) destruir, acabar con; (pain) aliviar. 3 (hurt) doler mucho: my back's killing me me duele mucho la espalda. LOC **to kill os** matarse, suicidarse. **I to kill os laughing** morirse de risa. **I to kill time** pasar el rato, matar el tiempo. **I to kill two birds with one stone** matar dos pájaros de un tiro. **I**
◆ **to kill off** vt sep exterminar, rematar.

killer [ˈkɪləʳ] n (person) asesino,-a; (thing) mortal, que mata. COMP **killer whale** orca.

killing [ˈkɪlɪŋ] n matanza; (of person) asesinato. LOC **to make a killing** ganar una fortuna, hacer el negocio del siglo.
▶ adj fig agotador,-ra, duro,-a.

kiln [kɪln] n horno.

kilo [ˈki:ləʊ] n kilo.
① pl kilos.

kilobyte [ˈkɪləbaɪt] n kilobyte.

kilocalorie [ˈkɪləkælərɪ] n kilocaloría.

kilogram [ˈkɪləgræm] n kilogramo.

kilogramme [ˈkɪləgræm] n US → kilogram.

kilometer [kɪˈlɒmɪtəʳ] n US → kilometer.

kilometre [kɪˈlɒmɪtəʳ] n kilómetro.

kilt [kɪlt] n falda escocesa.

kimono [kɪˈməʊnəʊ] n quimono.
① pl kimonos.

K

kin [kɪn] *n* parientes *mpl*, familia. COMP **next of kin** pariente *m* más próximo.

kind [kaɪnd] *adj (person)* amable: *she is the sweetest, kindest person I know* es la persona más dulce y amable que conozco; *that's very kind of you* eres muy amable.
► *n (sort)* tipo, género, clase *f*: *what kind of ...?* ¿qué clase de …? LOC **to be two of a kind** ser tal para cual. ‖ **to pay in kind 1** pagar en especie. **2** *(treatment)* pagar con la misma moneda.
► *adv fam* **kind of** bastante, algo, un poco: *it's kind of difficult* es un poco difícil; *have you finished? – Kind of …* ¿has acabado? –Más o menos; *... and that kind of thing ...* y cosas por el estilo.

kindergarten [ˈkɪndəgɑːtən] *n* parvulario, guardería.

kind-hearted [kaɪndˈhɑːtɪd] *adj* bondadoso,-a.

kindly [ˈkaɪndlɪ] *adj* amable.
ⓘ *comp* kindlier, *superl* kindliest.
► *adv* **1** con amabilidad: *she very kindly lent me £5* tuvo la amabilidad de prestarme cinco libras. **2** *(please)* por favor: *kindly shut up!* ¡haz el favor de callarte!

kindness [ˈkaɪndnəs] *n* **1** bondad *f*, amabilidad *f*. **2** *(favour)* favor *m*.

kinetics [kɪˈnetɪks] *n* cinética.

king [kɪŋ] *n* rey *m*. COMP **the king and queen** los reyes *mpl*. ‖ **the Three Kings** los Reyes *mpl* Magos.

kingdom [ˈkɪŋdəm] *n* reino.

kingfisher [ˈkɪŋfɪʃəʳ] *n* martín pescador *m*.

king-size [ˈkɪŋsaɪz] *adj* extragrande, extralargo,-a.

kiosk [ˈkiːɒsk] *n* **1** quiosco. **2** *(telephone)* cabina telefónica.

kipper [ˈkɪpəʳ] *n* arenque *m*.

Kiribati [kɪrɪˈbætɪ] *n* Kiribati.

kiss [kɪs] *n* beso.
ⓘ *pl* kisses.
► *vt* besar, dar un beso a: *he kissed her on the cheek* le dio un beso en la mejilla.
► *vi* besarse, darse un beso.

kit [kɪt] *n* **1** *(equipment, gear)* equipo, equipaje *m*. **2** *(clothes)* ropa. **3** *(model)* maqueta, kit *m*.
◆ **to kit out** *vt sep* equipar.

kitchen [ˈkɪtʃɪn] *n* cocina. COMP **kitchen garden** huerto.

kite [kaɪt] *n* **1** *(bird)* milano. **2** *(toy)* cometa: *to fly a kite* hacer volar una cometa.

kitten [ˈkɪtən] *n* gatito,-a. LOC **to have kittens** tener un ataque: *I nearly had kittens!* ¡por poco me da un ataque!

kitty [ˈkɪtɪ] *n* **1** *fam (cat)* minino,-a. **2** *(in card games)* bote *m*; *(for bills, drinks)* fondo común.
ⓘ *pl* kitties.

kiwi [ˈkiːwiː] *n* **1** *(bird)* kiwi *m*. **2** *(fruit)* kiwi *m*.

klaxon [ˈklæksən] *n* claxon *m*.

knack [næk] *n* maña, truco. LOC **to get the knack of doing** STH cogerle el tranquillo a ALGO.

knapsack [ˈnæpsæk] *n* mochila.

knead [niːd] *vt* amasar.

knee [niː] *n* **1** ANAT rodilla: *on one's knees* de rodillas. **2** *(of trousers)* rodillera.
► *vt* dar un rodillazo a.

kneecap [ˈniːkæp] *n* rótula.

kneel [niːl] *vi* arrodillarse.
ⓘ *pt & pp* knelt [nelt].

kneepad [ˈniːpæd] *n* rodillera.

knelt [nelt] *pt & pp* → **kneel**.

knew [njuː] *pt* → **know**.

knickers [ˈnɪkəz] *n pl* bragas *fpl*: *she bought three pairs of knickers* compró tres bragas

knife [naɪf] *n (gen)* cuchillo; *(folding)* navaja.
ⓘ *pl* knives.
► *vt* apuñalar, acuchillar.

knight [naɪt] *n* **1** *arch* caballero. **2** *(chess)* caballo. **3** caballero, *(hombre que lleva el título de* Sir*)*. COMP **knight in shining armour** príncipe *m* azul.

knit [nɪt] *vt* tejer.
► *vi* **1** hacer punto, hacer media. **2** MED soldarse. **3** *fig* unirse. LOC **to knit one's brow** fruncir.
ⓘ *pt & pp* knit o knitted, *ger* knitting.

knitting [ˈnɪtɪŋ] *n (material)* punto; *(activity)* labor *f* de punto. COMP **knitting machine** tricotosa. ‖ **knitting needle** aguja de tejer.

knives [naɪvz] *pl* → **knife**.

knitwear [ˈnɪtweəʳ] *n* género de punto

knob [nɒb] *n* **1** *(on door - large)* pomo; *(- small)* tirador *m*. **2** *(on stick)* puño. **3** *(natural)* bulto, protuberancia. **4** *(on radio, etc)* botón *m*.

knock [nɒk] *n* **1** *(blow)* golpe *m*. **2** *(on door)* llamada: *was that a knock at the door?* ¿han llamado a la puerta? **3** *fig (bad luck)* revés *m*.

▶ *vt* **1** *(to hit)* golpear, darse un golpe en. **2** *fam (criticize)* criticar, hablar mal de: *the newspapers are forever knocking the England manager* los periódicos siempre critican al entrenador de la selección inglesa.

▶ *vi* **1** *(at door)* llamar: *please knock before entering* por favor, llamen antes de entrar. **2** *(of car engine)* golpear, martillear.

◆ **to knock down** *vt sep* **1** *(building)* derribar. **2** *(person - with a car)* atropellar; *(- with a blow)* derribar. **3** *(price)* rebajar.

◆ **to knock out** *vt sep* **1** *(make unconscious)* dejar sin conocimiento; *(put to sleep)* dejar dormido,-a; *(boxing)* dejar K.O. **2** *(from competition)* eliminar.

◆ **to knock over** *vt sep* **1** *(overturn)* volcar, tirar. **2** *(run over)* atropellar.

knockdown ['nɒkdaʊn] *adj* rebajado. COMP **knockdown price** precio de saldo.

knocker ['nɒkəʳ] *n* **1** aldaba. **2** *(critic)* detractor,-ra.

knockout ['nɒkaʊt] *n* **1** SP knock-out *m*, fuera de combate *m*. **2** *fam* maravilla: *it's a knockout!* ¡es alucinante!

knot [nɒt] *n* **1** *(gen)* nudo. **2** *(people)* corrillo, grupo.

▶ *vt* anudar.

ⓘ *pt & pp* **knotted**, *ger* **knotting**.

know [nəʊ] *vt* **1** *(be acquainted with)* conocer: *do you know Colin?* conoces a Colin? **2** *(recognize)* reconocer: *I'd know him if I saw him again* lo reconocería si lo volviera a ver. **3** *(have knowledge of)* saber: *I don't know the answer* no sé la respuesta. LOC **as far as I know** que yo sepa. I **don't I know it!** ¿y me lo dices a mí?, ¡ni que lo digas! I **how should I know?** ¿yo qué sé? I **if only I'd known!** ¡haberlo sabido! I **not that I know of** que yo sepa, no. I **you never know** nunca se sabe. I **I know what!** ¡ya lo tengo! I **to be in the know** estar enterado,-a.

I **you know best** tú sabes mejor que yo, sabes lo que más te conviene. I **to know better** tener más juicio. I **to know by sight** conocer de vista. I **to know of** *vt insep* **1** saber de, entender de.

◆ **to know about** *vt insep* **1** saber de, entender de.

◆ **to know of** *vt insep* saber de, haber oído hablar de.

ⓘ *pt* **knew** [nju:], *pp* **known** [nəʊn].

know-all ['nəʊɔːl] *n* sabelotodo *mf*.

know-how ['nəʊhaʊ] *n* saber hacer *m*, conocimiento práctico.

knowledge ['nɒlɪdʒ] *n* **1** *(learning, information)* conocimientos *mpl*: *his knowledge of football is amazing* sus conocimientos de fútbol son increíbles. **2** *(awareness)* conocimiento: *at that time I had no knowledge of what was happening* entonces no tenía conocimiento de lo que estaba pasando. LOC **to my knowledge** que yo sepa. I **to be common knowledge that ...** ser notorio que ..., todo el mundo sabe que ... I **it has come to my knowledge that ...** he llegado a saber que ... I **to have a good knowledge of sth** conocer algo bien.

knowledgeable ['nɒlɪdʒəbl] *adj* entendido,-a: *he's very knowledgeable about music* es muy entendido en música.

known [nəʊn] *pp* → **know**.

knuckle ['nʌkl] *n* nudillo.

◆ **to knuckle down** *vi fam* ponerse a trabajar en serio.

◆ **to knuckle under** *vi* pasar por el aro.

koala [kəʊˈɑːlə] *n* koala *m*.

Koran [kɔːˈrɑːn] *n* Alcorán *m*, Corán *m*.

Korea [kəˈrɪə] *n* Corea. COMP **North Korea** Corea del Norte. I **South Korea** Corea del Sur.

Korean [kəˈrɪən] *adj* coreano,-a.

▶ *n* **1** *(person)* coreano,-a. **2** *(language)* coreano. COMP **North Korean** norcoreano,-a. I **South Korean** surcoreano,-a.

kudos ['kjuːdɒs] *n* prestigio.

Kurd [kɜːd] *adj* kurdo,-a.

▶ *n (person)* kurdo,-a.

Kurdish ['kɜːdɪʃ] *adj* kurdo,-a.

▶ *n (language)* kurdo.

Kuwait [kuˈweɪt] *n* Kuwait.

Kuwaiti [kuˈweɪtɪ] *adj* kuwaití.

▶ *n* kuwaití *mf*.

K

L

L, l [el] n (the letter) L, l f.

l ['liːtəʳ] symb (litre, US liter) litro; (symbol) l.

lab [læb] n fam (abbr of laboratory) laboratorio.

label ['leɪbəl] n **1** etiqueta. **2** (record company) casa discográfica.
▸ vt **1** etiquetar, poner etiqueta a. **2** fig calificar (as, de).
ⓘ pt & pp labelled (US labeled), ger labelling (US labeling).

laboratory [ləˈbɒrətəri, US ˈlæbrətɒrɪ] n laboratorio.
ⓘ pl laboratories.

labor ['leɪbəʳ] n US → labour.

⊕ El Labor Day es el día del trabajo en Estados Unidos. Se celebra del primer lunes de septiembre y marca el final del verano y el inicio del curso escolar.

labour ['leɪbəʳ] n **1** (work) trabajo. **2** (task) labor f, tarea, faena. **3** (workforce) mano f de obra. **4** (childbirth) parto. COMP **labour camp** campo de trabajos forzados. ‖ **Labour Day** día del trabajo. ‖ **labour force** mano f de obra.
▸ vi **1** (work hard) trabajar duro. **2** (move slowly) avanzar penosamente; (engine) funcionar con dificultad.
▸ n **Labour** GB los laboristas mpl, el Partido Laborista.

laborer ['leɪbərəʳ] n US → labourer.

labourer ['leɪbərəʳ] n peón m, jornalero,-a, bracero. COMP **farm labourer** peón m agrícola.

labyrinth ['læbərɪnθ] n laberinto.

lace [leɪs] n **1** (material) encaje m. **2** (shoestring) cordón m.
▸ vt (pull string through) poner los cordones a.

lachrymal ['lækrɪməl] adj lagrimal, lacrimal.

lack [læk] n falta, carencia, escasez f: she has no lack of self-confidence no le falta confianza en sí misma. LOC **for lack of** por falta de.
▸ vt carecer de.

lacquer ['lækəʳ] n laca.
▸ vt (metal, wood) lacar; (hair) poner laca a.

lacrimal ['lækrɪməl] adj → lachrymal.

lactic ['læktɪk] adj láctico,-a.

lactose ['læktəʊs] n lactosa.

lad [læd] n **1** GB fam muchacho, chaval m, chico. **2** GB fam diablillo, pillo: John's a bit of a lad. John es un poco pillo. **3** (stable boy) mozo de cuadra.

ladder ['lædəʳ] n **1** escalera (de mano). **2** GB (in stocking) carrera. **3** fig escala. COMP **rope ladder** escalera de cuerda.
▸ vi GB hacerse una carrera.
▸ vt GB hacerse una carrera en.

laden ['leɪdən] adj cargado,-a (with, de). LOC **to be fully laden** estar lleno,-a hasta el tope.

ladies ['leɪdɪz] n GB (toilet) lavabo (de señoras). COMP **ladies room** US lavabo (de señoras).

ladle ['leɪdəl] n cucharón m.
▸ vt servir con cucharón.
◆ **to ladle out** vt sep repartir.

lady ['leɪdɪ] n señora; (of high social position) dama.
ⓘ pl ladies.

ladybird ['leɪdɪbɜːd] n mariquita.

ladybug ['leɪdɪbʌg] n US mariquita.

lag [læg] n **1** retraso. **2** GB sl preso. COMP **time lag** retraso.

lager ['lɑːgəʳ] n cerveza rubia.

laid [leɪd] pt & pp → lay².

lain [leɪn] *pp* → lie².

lake [leɪk] *n* lago.

lama ['lɑːmə] *n* lama *m*.

lamb [læm] *n* **1** *(animal)* cordero,-a. **2** *(meat)* carne *f* de cordero. **3** *fam (person)* cordero,-a: *poor lamb!* ¡pobrecito,-a!

lame [leɪm] *adj* **1** cojo,-a: *lame in one leg* cojo,-a de una pierna. **2** *fig* débil; *(excuse)* poco convincente; *(business)* fallido,-a. COMP **lame duck** inútil *mf*.

lamp [læmp] *n* **1** lámpara. **2** *(on car, train)* faro.

lamppost ['læmppəʊst] *n* (poste *m* de) farol *m*.

lampshade ['læmpʃeɪd] *n* pantalla (de lámpara).

land [lænd] *n* **1** *(gen)* tierra: *by land and sea* por tierra y por mar. **2** *(soil)* suelo, tierra. **3** *(country, region)* tierra: *in foreign lands* en tierras extranjeras. **4** *(property)* terreno, tierras *fpl*. LOC **land ahoy!** ¡tierra a la vista! COMP **farm land** tierras *fpl* de cultivo. **land-agent** GB encargado,-a de una granja.
▶ *vi* **1** *(plane, etc)* aterrizar, tomar tierra; *(bird)* posarse. **2** *(disembark)* desembarcar. **3** *(fall)* caer.
◆ **to land in** *vt sep* causar, traer: *he's bound to land you in trouble* seguro que te traerá problemas.
◆ **to land up** *vi* acabar.

landing ['lændɪŋ] *n* **1** *(plane)* aterrizaje *m*. **2** *(on stairs)* descansillo, rellano. **3** *(of people)* desembarco. COMP **crash landing** aterrizaje *m* de emergencia. ❙ **landing field** pista de aterrizaje. ❙ **landing gear** tren *m* de aterrizaje.

landlady ['lændleɪdɪ] *n* *(of flat)* propietaria, dueña; *(of house)* casera.
ⓘ *pl* landladies.

landlord ['lændlɔːd] *n* **1** *(of flat)* propietario, dueño; *(of house)* casero.

landowner ['lændəʊnəʳ] *n* propietario,-a, terrateniente *mf*, hacendado,-a.

landscape ['lændskeɪp] *n* paisaje *m*. COMP **landscape gardener** jardinista *mf*, arquitecto,-a paisajista. ❙ **landscape painter** paisajista *mf*.
▶ *vt* ajardinar.

lane [leɪn] *n* **1** *(in country)* camino, sendero; *(in town)* callejuela, callejón *m*. **2**

(on road) carril *m*. **3** *(in athletics, swimming)* calle *f*.

language ['læŋgwɪdʒ] *n* **1** *(faculty, way of speaking)* lenguaje *m*. **2** *(tongue)* idioma *m*, lengua. **3** *(school subject)* lengua. LOC **to use bad language** ser mal hablado,-a. COMP **language laboratory** laboratorio de idiomas. ❙ **language school** escuela de idiomas.

lantern ['læntən] *n* linterna, farol *m*.

Laos [laʊz, laʊs] *n* Laos.

Laotian ['laʊʃɪən] *adj* laosiano,-a.
▶ *n* laosiano,-a.

lap¹ [læp] *n* regazo; *(knees)* rodillas *fpl*; *(skirt)* falda.

lap² [læp] *n* **1** SP vuelta. **2** *fig (stage)* etapa.
▶ *vt* SP *(overtake)* doblar.
▶ *vi* *(go round)* dar la vuelta.
ⓘ *pt & pp* lapped, *ger* lapping.

lap³ [læp] *vt* **1** *(animal)* beber a lengüetadas. **2** *(waves)* lamer, besar.
ⓘ *pt & pp* lapped, *ger* lapping.

lapel [ləˈpel] *n* solapa.

Lapland ['læplænd] *n* Laponia.

lapse [læps] *n* **1** *(in time)* intervalo, lapso. **2** *(slip)* desliz *m*. **3** *(when speaking)* lapsus *m*; *(of memory)* fallo.

laptop ['læptɒp] [also **laptop computer**] *n* ordenador *m* portátil.

lard [lɑːd] *n* manteca de cerdo.

larder ['lɑːdəʳ] *n* despensa.

large [lɑːdʒ] *adj* **1** grande; *(before sing noun)* gran; *(sum, amount)* importante; *(meal)* abundante. **2** *(family)* numeroso,-a. **3** *(extensive)* amplio,-a, extenso,-a. LOC **at large** *(as a whole)* en general. ❙ **by and large** por lo general.

large-scale ['lɑːdʒskeɪl] *adj* **1** de gran escala. **2** *(map)* a gran escala.

lark¹ [lɑːk] *n* *(bird)* alondra.

lark² [lɑːk] *n* *fam (bit of fun)* broma.
◆ **to lark about / lark around** *vi fam* hacer el indio.

larva ['lɑːvə] *n* larva.
ⓘ *pl* larvae ['lɑːviː].

laryngitis [lærɪnˈdʒaɪtəs] *n* laringitis *f*.

larynx ['lærɪŋks] *n* laringe *f*.
ⓘ *pl* larynxes o larynges ['lærɪdʒiːz].

lasagna [lə'zɑːnjə] *n* lasaña.

laser ['leɪzə'] *n* láser *m*.

lash [læʃ] *n* **1** *(blow with whip)* latigazo, azote *m*; *(with tail)* coletazo. **2** *(whip)* látigo; *(thong)* tralla. **3** *(eyelash)* pestaña. ⓘ *pl* lashes.
▸ *vt* **1** *(in general)* azotar. **2** *(fasten)* sujetar.
◆ **to lash out** *vi* **1** arremeter (against/at, contra). **2** *(splurge)* gastarse un montón (de dinero) (on, en).

lass [læs] *n fam* chica, chavala. ⓘ *pl* lasses.

lasso [læ'suː] *n* lazo. ⓘ *pl* lassos o lassoes.

last [lɑːst] *adj* **1** *(final)* último,-a. **2** *(most recent)* último,-a: *the last time* la última vez. **3** *(past)* pasado,-a; *(previous)* anterior: *last Monday* el lunes pasado; *the night before last* anteanoche.
▸ *adv* **1** por última vez: *when he last came to see me* cuando vino a verme por última vez. **2** *(at the end)* en último lugar; *(in race)* en última posición. ᴸᴼᶜ **at last** al fin, por fin. **‖ at long last** por fin.
▸ *n* *(person)* el/la último,-a; *(thing)* lo último: *are you the last?* ¿eres tú el último? ᴸᴼᶜ **last but one** penúltimo,-a.
▸ *vi* *(continue)* durar; *(hold out)* aguantar, resistir.
▸ *vt* durar.
◆ **to last out** *vi* resistir, aguantar.

lasting ['lɑːstɪŋ] *adj* duradero,-a.

lastly ['lɑːstlɪ] *adv* por último, finalmente.

latch [lætʃ] *n* pestillo: *come in, the door's on the latch* entra, el pestillo no está echado.

late [leɪt] *adj* **1** *(not on time)* tardío,-a: *you're ten minutes late* llegas diez minutos tarde. **2** *(far on in time)* tarde: *in late May* a finales de mayo. **3** *euph (dead)* difunto,-a, fallecido,-a. **4** *(former)* anterior. **5** *(last-minute)* de última hora. ᴸᴼᶜ **to get late** hacerse tarde.
▸ *adv* **1** tarde: *I stayed up late last night* anoche me acosté muy tarde. **2** *(recently)* recientemente: *as late as yesterday* ayer mismo. ᴸᴼᶜ **of late** últimamente.

lately ['leɪtlɪ] *adv* últimamente, recientemente.

later ['leɪtə'] *adj* **1** más tardío,-a: *we'll discuss that at a later date* hablaremos de eso más adelante. **2** *(more recent)* más reciente.
▸ *adv* **1** más tarde: *five minutes later* cinco minutos más tarde; *see you later!* ¡hasta luego! **2** *(afterwards)* después, luego. ᴸᴼᶜ **later on** más adelante, más tarde.

lateral ['lætərəl] *adj* lateral.

latest ['leɪtɪst] *adj* último,-a, más reciente.
▸ *n* lo último. ᴸᴼᶜ **at the latest** como máximo.

latex ['leɪteks] *n* látex *m*.

lather ['lɑːðə'] *n* **1** *(of soap)* espuma. **2** *(sweat)* sudor *m*.
▸ *vt* enjabonar.

Latin ['lætɪn] *adj* latino,-a.
▸ *n* **1** *(person)* latino,-a. **2** *(language)* latín *m*. ᶜᴼᴹᴾ **Latin American** latinoamericano,-a.

latitude ['lætɪtjuːd] *n* latitud *f*.

latter ['lætə'] *adj* **1** *(last)* último,-a: *the latter days of his life were very happy* los últimos días de su vida fueron muy felices. **2** *(second)* segundo,-a.
▸ *pron* **the latter** éste,-a, este,-a último,-a.

lattice ['lætɪs] *n* celosía, enrejado.

Latvia ['lætvɪə] *n* Letonia.

Latvian ['lætvɪən] *adj* letón,-ona.
▸ *n* **1** *(person)* letón,-ona. **2** *(language)* letón *m*.

laugh [lɑːf] *vi* reír, reírse: *it makes me laugh* me da risa. ᴸᴼᶜ **he who laughs last laughs longest** quien ríe último ríe mejor. **‖ to laugh one's head off** *fam* partirse de risa, troncharse de risa, desternillarse de risa.
▸ *n* risa: *we had a really good laugh* nos reímos muchísimo.
◆ **to laugh at** *vt insep* reírse de.
◆ **to laugh off** *vt sep* tomar a risa.

laughter ['lɑːftə'] *n* risas *fpl*: *a fit of laughter* un ataque de risa.

launch [lɔːntʃ] *vt* **1** lanzar: *it will be launched on the market next year* se lanzará al mercado el año que viene. **2** *(ship)*

botar; *(lifeboat)* echar al mar. **3** *(film, etc)* estrenar; *(book)* presentar. **4** *(company)* fundar. **5** *(scheme, attack)* iniciar. COMP **launch pad** plataforma de lanzamiento.
▶ *n (boat)* lancha.
ⓘ *pl* launches.

launching ['lɔ:ntʃɪŋ] *n* **1** lanzamiento. **2** *(of ship)* botadura. **3** *(of film)* estreno; *(of book)* presentación f. COMP **launching pad** plataforma de lanzamiento.

launder ['lɔ:ndəʳ] *vt* **1** *(clothes)* lavar (y planchar). **2** *fig (money)* blanquear.

launderette [lɔ:n'dˀret] *n* lavandería automática.

laundry ['lɔ:ndrɪ] *n* **1** *(place)* lavandería. **2** *(dirty)* ropa sucia, colada; *(clean)* ropa limpia, ropa lavada. LOC **to do the laundry** lavar la ropa.
ⓘ *pl* laundries.

lava ['lɑ:və] *n* lava.

lavatory ['lævətˀrɪ] *n* **1** váter m. **2** *(room)* lavabo, baño.
ⓘ *pl* lavatories.

lavender ['lævɪndəʳ] *n* espliego, lavanda.
▶ *adj (colour)* de color lavanda.

law [lɔ:] *n* **1** ley f. **2** EDUC derecho. LOC **against the law** contra la ley. ‖ **by law** por ley. ‖ **to keep within the law** obrar según la ley. COMP **law and order** orden m público. ‖ **law court** tribunal m de justicia.

lawful ['lɔ:ful] *adj* legal.

lawn [lɔ:n] *n* césped m.

lawnmower ['lɔ:nməuəʳ] *n* cortacésped m & f.

lawsuit ['lɔ:sju:t] *n* pleito, juicio.

lawyer ['lɔ:jəʳ] *n* abogado,-a.

laxative ['læksətɪv] *adj* laxante.
▶ *n* laxante m.

lay¹ [leɪ] *adj* **1** REL laico,-a, seglar. **2** *(non-professional)* lego,-a, no profesional.

lay² [leɪ] *vt* **1** *(gen)* poner, colocar; *(spread out)* extender. **2** *(bricks, carpet)* poner; *(cable, pipe)* tender; *(foundations, basis)* echar; *(bomb)* colocar. **3** *(prepare)* preparar; *(curse)* lanzar. **4** *(eggs)* poner.

5 *(bet)* apostar. **6** *(charge)* formular. LOC **to lay the table** poner la mesa.
▶ *vi (hen)* poner huevos.
◆ **to lay by** *vt sep* guardar; *(money)* ahorrar.
◆ **to lay down** *vt sep* **1** *(let go)* dejar, soltar. **2** *(give up)* entregar. **3** *(establish)* imponer, fijar.
◆ **to lay off** *vt sep (worker)* despedir.
▶ *vt insep fam (stop)* dejar en paz.
▶ *vi fam* parar: *lay off!* ¡ya está bien!, ¡para ya!
◆ **to lay on** *vt sep (provide)* suministrar.
▶ *vt insep (burden)* cargar.
◆ **to lay out** *vt sep* **1** *(spread out)* tender, extender. **2** *(arrange)* disponer, colocar. **3** *(present)* presentar, exponer. **4** *(town, etc)* hacer el trazado de; *(garden)* diseñar.
◆ **to lay over** *vi* US *(gen)* hacer una parada (at/in, en); *(plane)* hacer escala (at/in, en).
ⓘ *pt & pp* laid [leɪd].

lay³ [leɪ] *pp* → **lie²**.

lay-by ['leɪbaɪ] *n* área de descanso.
ⓘ *pl* lay-bys.

layer ['leɪəʳ] *n* **1** capa. **2** *(of rock)* estrato. **3** *(hen)* gallina ponedora.

layout ['leɪaut] *n* **1** *(arrangement)* disposición f; *(presentation)* presentación f. **2** *(printing)* composición f, formato. **3** *(plan)* trazado.

laze [leɪz] *vi* gandulear, holgazanear.
◆ **to laze about / laze around** *vi* hacer el vago.

laziness ['leɪzɪnəs] *n* pereza.

lazy ['leɪzɪ] *adj* **1** gandul,-la, vago,-a, perezoso,-a. **2** *(river)* perezoso,-a.
ⓘ *comp* lazier; *superl* laziest.

lazybones ['leɪzɪbəunz] *n* perezoso,-a, gandul,-la.
ⓘ *pl* lazybones.

lb [paund] *abbr* (pound) libra.
ⓘ *pl* lb o lbs.

lead¹ [led] *n* **1** *(metal)* plomo. **2** *(in pencil)* mina. LOC **to swing the lead** *fam* hacer el vago.

lead² [li:d] *vt* **1** *(guide)* llevar, conducir: *our tour guide led the way to the cathedral* la guía nos llevó a la catedral. **2** *(be leader*

of) liderar, dirigir. **3** *(be first in)* ocupar el primer puesto en. **4** *(influence)* llevar: *he is easily led* se deja llevar fácilmente.
► *vi* **1** *(road)* conducir, llevar (to, a). **2** *(command)* tener el mando. **3** *(go first)* ir primero,-a.
ⓘ *pt & pp* led [led].
► *n* **1** *(front position)* delantera. **2** SP liderato; *(difference)* ventaja. **3** THEAT primer papel *m*.

leader ['liːdəʳ] *n* **1** POL líder *mf*, dirigente *mf*. **2** *(in race)* líder *mf* (of/in, de).

leadership ['liːdəʃɪp] *n* **1** *(position)* liderato, liderazgo. **2** *(qualities)* dotes *mpl* de mando. **3** *(leaders)* dirección *f*.

lead-free ['ledfriː] *adj* sin plomo.

leading ['liːdɪŋ] *adj* destacado,-a, principal.

leaf [liːf] *n* **1** *(of plant)* hoja. **2** *(of book)* hoja, página.
ⓘ *pl* leaves [liːvz].

leaflet ['liːflət] *n* *(folded)* folleto; *(single sheet)* octavilla, hoja suelta.
► *vi* GB repartir folletos, repartir octavillas.

league [liːg] *n* liga. LOC **to be in league with** SB estar conchabado,-a con ALGN.

leak [liːk] *vi* **1** *(container)* tener un agujero; *(pipe)* tener un escape. **2** *(roof)* gotear. **3** *(gas, fluid)* escaparse.
► *n* **1** *(hole)* agujero. **2** *(in roof)* gotera. **3** *(of gas)* fuga, escape *m*; *(of liquid)* escape *m*. **4** *fig (of information, etc)* filtración *f*.
◆ **to leak out** *vi* **1** *(gas, fluid)* escaparse. **2** *fig* filtrarse.

leakage ['liːkɪdʒ] *n* fuga, escape *m*.

leaky ['liːkɪ] *adj* **1** *(container)* agujereado,-a; *(pipe)* con un escape. **2** *(roof)* que tiene goteras. **3** *(pipe)* que tiene escapes.
ⓘ *comp* leakier, *superl* leakiest.

lean¹ [liːn] *adj* **1** *(person)* delgado,-a, flaco,-a. **2** *(meat)* magro,-a. **3** *(harvest)* malo,-a, escaso,-a; *(year)* malo,-a, pobre: *it was a lean year for car sales* fue un mal año para la venta de coches.
► *n (meat)* carne *f* magra.

lean² [liːn] *vi* **1** inclinarse. **2** *(for support)* apoyarse (on, en) (against, contra).
► *vt* apoyar.
◆ **to lean on** *vt insep* **1** *(depend on)* depender de. **2** *(pressure)* presionar a.
◆ **to lean towards** *vt insep* estar a favor de, tirar hacia.
ⓘ *pt & pp* leaned o leant [lent].

leaning ['liːnɪŋ] *adj* inclinado,-a.
► *n* inclinación *f*, tendencia.

leant [lent] *pt & pp* → **lean²**.

leap [liːp] *vi* saltar, brincar.
ⓘ *pt & pp* leaped o leapt [lept].
► *n* **1** salto, brinco. COMP **leap year** año bisiesto.

leapfrog ['liːpfrɒg] *n* pídola.
► *vt fig (skip)* saltarse.
ⓘ *pt & pp* leapfrogged, *ger* leapfrogging.

leapt [lept] *pt & pp* → **leap**.

learn [lɜːn] *vt* **1** aprender: *I'd love to learn (how) to ice-skate* me encantaría aprender a patinar sobre hielo. **2** *(find out about)* enterarse de, saber.
► *vi* **1** aprender. **2** *(find out)* enterarse (about/of, de).
ⓘ *pt & pp* learned o learnt [lɜːnt].

learned ['lɜːnəd] *adj* erudito,-a.

learner ['lɜːnəʳ] *n* estudiante *mf*. COMP **learner driver** conductor,-a en prácticas.

learnt [lɜːnt] *pt & pp* → **learn**.

leash [liːʃ] *n* correa.

leasing ['liːsɪŋ] *n* **1** arrendamiento, arriendo. **2** FIN leasing *m*.

least [liːst] *adj* menor, menos: *he makes the least money* es el que gana menos dinero.
► *adv* menos: *when you least expect it* cuando menos lo esperas.
► *n* lo menos: *it's the least I can do* es lo menos que puedo hacer. LOC **at (the) least** por lo menos.

leather ['leðəʳ] *n* piel *f*, cuero.
► *adj* de piel, de cuero.

leave¹ [liːv] *vt* **1** *(go away from)* dejar, abandonar; *(go out of)* salir de: *she left home when she was 16* se marchó de casa a los 16 años. **2** *(stop being with)* irse de, marcharse de. **3** *(forget)* dejarse, olvi-

dar, olvidarse. **4** *(allow to remain)* dejar: *please leave the door open* por favor, deja la puerta abierta. **5** *(cause to remain)* dejar: *the glass left a ring on the table* el vaso dejó un cerco en la mesa. **6** *(bequeath)* dejar, legar. **7** MATH dar: *two from six leaves four* seis menos dos dan cuatro.
▸ *vi* marcharse, irse, partir: *he left for Rome this morning* esta mañana salió hacia Roma.
◆ **to leave off** *vt insep* dejar de: *there was so much noise that I had to leave off studying* había tanto ruido que tuve que dejar de estudiar.
▸ *vi* acabar, terminar.
◆ **to leave out** *vt sep* omitir, excluir.
ⓘ *pt & pp* **left**, *ger* **leaving**.

leave² [li:v] *n* **1** *(time off)* permiso. **2** *(permission)* permiso. LOC **to be on leave** MIL estar de permiso.

leaven ['levªn] *n* levadura.

leaves [li:vz] *pl* → **leaf**.

Lebanese [lebə'ni:z] *adj* libanés,-esa.
▸ *n* libanés,-esa.
▸ *n pl* **the Lebanese** los libaneses *mpl*.

Lebanon ['lebənən] *n* Líbano.

lectern ['lektən] *n* atril *m*; *(in church)* facistol *m*.

lecture ['lektʃəʳ] *n* **1** conferencia. **2** *(in university)* clase *f*. **3** *(telling-off)* reprimenda, sermón *m*.
▸ *vi* **1** dar una conferencia (on, sobre). **2** *(in university)* dar clase.
▸ *vt* *(scold)* sermonear, echar una reprimenda a.

☒ Lecture no significa 'lectura', que se traduce por **reading**.

lecturer ['lektʃərəʳ] *n* **1** conferenciante *mf*. **2** *(in university)* profesor,-ra.

☒ Lecturer no significa 'lector', que se traduce por **reader**.

led [li:vz] *pp & pt* → **lead²**.

ledge [ledʒ] *n* **1** *(shelf)* repisa; *(of window)* antepecho, alféizar *m*. **2** *(of rock)* saliente *m*.

lee [li:] *n* **1** MAR sotavento, socaire *m*. **2** *(shelter)* abrigo. LOC **in the lee of** al abrigo de.

leech [li:tʃ] *n* sanguijuela.

leek [li:k] *n* puerro.

left¹ [left] *adj* **1** izquierdo,-a. **2** POL de izquierdas: *the left wing of the party* el ala izquierda del partido.
▸ *adv* a la izquierda, hacia la izquierda.
▸ *n* **1** izquierda: *keep to the left* manténgase a la izquierda. **2** *(punch)* golpe *m* de la izquierda. LOC **on the left** a mano izquierda.

left² [left] *pt & pp* → **leave¹**. LOC **to be left** quedar: *is there any milk left?* ¿queda leche? ‖ **to be left over** sobrar, quedar. COMP **left luggage office** consigna.

left-hand ['lefthænd] *adj* izquierdo,-a: *the shop is on the left-hand side* la tienda está a mano izquierda.

leftover ['leftəʊvəʳ] *adj* sobrante, restante.
▸ *n pl* **leftovers** sobras *fpl*, restos *mpl*.

leg [leg] *n* **1** ANAT pierna; *(of animal)* pata. **2** CULIN *(lamb, etc)* pierna; *(chicken, etc)* muslo. **3** *(of furniture)* pata, pie *m*. **4** *(of trousers)* pernera. **5** *(stage)* etapa. LOC **to pull sb's leg** *fam* tomarle el pelo a ALGN.

legal ['li:gªl] *adj* **1** legal, lícito,-a. **2** *(relating to the law)* jurídico,-a, legal: *the legal profession* la abogacía. LOC **to take legal action** entablar un pleito (against, contra).

legalize ['li:gªlaɪz] *vt* legalizar.

legend ['ledʒªnd] *n* leyenda.

legendary ['ledʒªndªrɪ] *adj* legendario,-a.

leggings ['legɪŋz] *n pl* *(whole leg)* mallas *fpl*; *(below knee)* polainas *fpl*.

legible ['ledʒəbªl] *adj* legible.

legion ['li:dʒªn] *n* legión *f*.

legionary ['li:dʒªnərɪ] *n* legionario.
ⓘ *pl* **legionaries**.

legionnaire ['li:dʒə'neəʳ] *n* legionario. COMP **legionnaire's disease** enfermedad *f* del legionario.

legislation [ledʒɪs'leɪʃªn] *n* legislación *f*.

legislative ['ledʒɪslətɪv] *adj* legislativo,-a.

legitimate [lɪ'dʒɪtɪmət] *adj* legítimo,-a.

legume ['legjuːm] n legumbre f.

leisure ['leʒəʳ, US 'liːʒəʳ] n ocio, tiempo libre. LOC **at leisure 1** (with free time) en su tiempo libre. **2** (calmly) tranquilamente. COMP **leisure centre** centro recreativo.

lemon ['lemən] n limón m.
▸ adj (colour) de color limón. COMP **lemon squeezer** exprimidor m. ‖ **lemon tree** limonero.

lemonade [leməˈneɪd] n **1** (fizzy - plain) gaseosa; (- lemony-flavoured) limonada. **2** (still) limonada.

lend [lend] vt **1** dejar, prestar: could you lend me some money? ¿me dejas un poco de dinero? **2** fig (add) dotar de, prestar. LOC **to lend os to sth** prestarse a ALGO, prestarse para ALGO. ‖ **to lend (sb) a hand** echar una mano (a ALGN).
① pt & pp lent [lent].

length [leŋθ] n **1** longitud f. **2** (of time) duración f. **3** (piece) trozo; (of cloth) largo. **4** (of road) tramo; (of swimming pool) largo.

lengthen ['leŋθən] vt **1** (skirt, etc) alargar. **2** (lifetime) prolongar.
▸ vi **1** (skirt, etc) alargarse. **2** (lifetime) prolongarse; (days) crecer.

lengthy ['leŋθɪ] adj (in general) largo,-a.
① comp lengthier, superl lengthiest.

lens [lenz] n **1** (of glasses) lente m & f. **2** (of camera) objetivo. **3** ANAT cristalino.
① pl lenses.

lent [lent] pt & pp → lend.

lentil ['lentɪl] n lenteja.

Leo ['liːəʊ] n Leo.

leopard ['lepəd] n leopardo.

leotard ['liːətɑːd] n malla.

Lesotho [lɪˈsuːtuː] n Lesotho.

less [les] adj menos.
▸ pron menos: the less you buy, the less you'll spend cuánto menos compres, menos gastarás. LOC **no less** nada menos.
▸ adv menos: less and less cada vez menos; he was being less than sincere no fue nada sincero. LOC **much less** menos aún.
▸ prep menos.

lessen ['lesən] vt disminuir, reducir.
▸ vi disminuir, reducirse.

lesser ['lesəʳ] adj menor.

lesson ['lesən] n **1** (class) clase f. **2** (warning) lección f.

let [let] vt (allow) dejar: he lets the children watch cartoon videos a los niños les deja mirar vídeos de dibujos animados. LOC **to let sb alone** dejar a ALGN en paz, no molestar a ALGN. ‖ **to let sb know** hacer saber a ALGN, avisar a ALGN.
▸ aux que + subjuntivo: let him come que venga; let's go! ¡vamos!, ¡vámonos!
▸ vt GB (rent) alquilar: «House to let» «Se alquila casa».
▸ n GB (renting) alquiler m.
◆ **to let down** vt sep **1** (lower) bajar. **2** (lengthen) alargar. **3** (deflate) desinflar. **4** (disappoint) fallar, defraudar.
◆ **to let in** vt sep dejar entrar: her father let me in me abrió su padre.
◆ **to let into** vt sep **1** dejar entrar a: this key will let you into the garage con esta llave podrás entrar en el garaje. **2** (reveal) revelar.
◆ **to let off** vt sep **1** (leave off) dejar. **2** (bomb) hacer explotar; (fireworks) hacer estallar. **3** (person - forgive) perdonar; (- let leave) dejar marcharse; (- free) dejar en libertad.
◆ **to let on** vi fam (tell) decir, descubrir.
▸ vt insep fam (pretend) hacer ver.
◆ **to let out** vt sep **1** (in general) dejar salir; (release) soltar (from, de). **2** (utter) soltar.
◆ **to let through** vt sep dejar pasar.
◆ **to let up** vi parar.
◆ **to let up on** vt insep fam dejar en paz.
① pt & pp let, ger letting.

let's [lets] v aux → let.

letter ['letəʳ] n **1** (of alphabet) letra. **2** (message) carta. LOC **to the letter** al pie de la letra. COMP **capital letter** mayúscula. ‖ **letter box** buzón m. ‖ **small letter** minúscula.

lettuce ['letɪs] n lechuga.

leukaemia [luːˈkiːmɪə] n leucemia.

leukemia [luːˈkiːmɪə] n US → leukaemia.

leukocyte ['luːkəsaɪt] n leucocito.

level ['levəl] *adj* **1** *(horizontal)* llano,-a, plano,-a. **2** *(even)* a nivel, nivelado,-a; *(spoonful, etc)* raso,-a: *the table's not level* la mesa no está nivelada. **3** *(equal)* igual, igualado,-a. **4** *(steady)* estable; *(voice)* llano,-a. COMP **level crossing** paso a nivel.
▶ *n* **1** nivel *m*: *above sea level* sobre el nivel del mar. **2** *(flat ground)* llano, llanura. LOC **to be on a level with** estar al mismo nivel que.
▶ *vt* **1** *(make level, survey)* nivelar. **2** *(raze)* arrasar, rasar. **3** *(aim)* apuntar.
▶ *adv* a ras (with, de).
ⓘ *pt & pp* levelled (US leveled), *ger* levelling (US leveling).

lever ['li:vər] *n* **1** palanca. **2** *(in lock)* guarda.

levy ['levɪ] *vt* recaudar; *(fine)* imponer.
ⓘ *pt & pp* levied, *ger* levying.
▶ *n* recaudación *f*; *(of fine)* imposición *f*.
ⓘ *pl* levies.

lexical ['leksɪkəl] *adj* léxico,-a.

liable ['laɪəbəl] *adj* **1** *(likely, susceptible)* propenso,-a (to, a): *the car is liable to stall* el coche tiende a calarse. **2** *(susceptible)* susceptible (to, a).

liar ['laɪər] *n* mentiroso,-a, embustero,-a: *he's such a liar!* ¡menudo embustero está hecho!

liberal ['lɪbərəl] *adj* **1** *(in general)* liberal. **2** *(abundant)* abundante.

Liberal ['lɪbərəl] *adj* POL liberal.
▶ *n* POL liberal *mf*.

liberalize ['lɪbərəlaɪz] *vt* liberalizar.

liberation [lɪbəˈreɪʃən] *n* liberación *f*.

Liberia [laɪˈbɪərɪə] *n* Liberia.

Liberian [laɪˈbɪərɪən] *adj* liberiano,-a.
▶ *n* liberiano,-a.

liberty ['lɪbətɪ] *n* libertad *f*.
ⓘ *pl* liberties. LOC **at liberty** en libertad, libre (to, de). ‖ **to take liberties with sb/sth** tomarse libertades con ALGN/ALGO.

Libra ['li:brə] *n* Libra *m*.

librarian [laɪˈbreərɪən] *n* bibliotecario,-a.

library ['laɪbrərɪ] *n* **1** biblioteca. **2** *(collection)* colección *f*. COMP **newspaper library** hemeroteca.
ⓘ *pl* libraries.

⚠ Library no significa 'librería (tienda)', que se traduce por bookshop, ni 'librería (mueble)', que se traduce por bookcase.

libretto [lɪˈbretəʊ] *n* libreto.
ⓘ *pl* librettos o libretti [lɪˈbreti:].

Libya ['lɪbɪə] *n* Libia.

Libyan ['lɪbɪən] *adj* libio,-a.
▶ *n* libio,-a.

lice [laɪs] *pl* → **louse**.

licence ['laɪsəns] *n* **1** *(permit)* licencia, permiso. **2** *(freedom)* libertad *f*; *(excessive freedom)* licencia. COMP **licence number** matrícula.

license ['laɪsəns] *n* US → **licence**.
▶ *vt* autorizar, dar licencia a.

licensed ['laɪsənst] *adj* autorizado,-a.

lichen ['laɪkən, 'lɪtʃən] *n* liquen *m*.

lick [lɪk] *vt* **1** lamer. **2** *fam (defeat - team)* vencer a, derrotar; *(- problem)* superar, solucionar. LOC **to lick one's lips** relamerse.
▶ *n* **1** lamedura, lengüetada. **2** *fam (of paint)* mano *f*.

licorice ['lɪkərɪs, 'lɪkərɪʃ] *n* regaliz *m*.

lid [lɪd] *n* **1** *(cover)* tapa. **2** *(of eye)* párpado. LOC **to take the lid off sth** *fig* destapar ALGO.

lie¹ [laɪ] *vi* mentir.
ⓘ *pt & pp* lied, *ger* lying.
▶ *n* mentira. LOC **to tell lies** mentir.

lie² [laɪ] *vi* **1** *(adopt a flat position)* acostarse, tumbarse. **2** *(be situated)* estar (situado,-a), encontrarse. **3** *(be buried)* yacer. **4** *(remain)* quedarse, permanecer.
◆ **to lie back** *vi* recostarse.
◆ **to lie down** *vi* acostarse, tumbarse, echarse.
◆ **to lie up** *vi* guardar cama.
ⓘ *pt* lay [leɪ], *pp* lain [leɪn], *ger* lying.

Liechtenstein ['lɪktənstaɪn] *n* Liechtenstein.

lie-down ['laɪdaʊn] *n* siesta.

lieutenant [lefˈtenənt, US lu:ˈtenənt] *n* **1** MIL teniente *m*. **2** *(non-military)* lugarteniente *m*.

life [laɪf] *n* **1** vida. **2** *(of battery)* duración *f*. LOC **it's a matter of life and death** es cuestión de vida o muerte. ∎ **not on your life!** *fam* ¡ni hablar! ∎ **to come to life** cobrar vida. ∎ **to lose one's life** perder la vida. ∎ **to take one's own life** suicidarse, quitarse la vida. ∎ **to take sb's life** matar a ALGN. COMP **life belt / life buoy** salvavidas *m*. ∎ **life jacket** chaleco salvavidas. ∎ **life style** estilo de vida. ① *pl* **lives** [laɪvz].

lifeboat ['laɪfbəʊt] *n* **1** *(on shore)* lancha de socorro. **2** *(on ship)* bote *m* salvavidas.

lifeguard ['laɪfɡɑːd] *n* socorrista *mf*.

lifelong ['laɪflɒŋ] *adj* de toda la vida.

life-saver ['laɪfseɪvə^r] *n* socorrista *mf*.

lifestyle ['laɪfstaɪl] *n* estilo de vida.

lifetime ['laɪftaɪm] *n* **1** vida: *in her lifetime* en su vida. **2** *fam* eternidad *f*.

lift [lɪft] *vt* **1** *(in general)* levantar, coger. **2** *(by plane)* transportar.
▶ *vi (of movable parts)* levantarse:.
▶ *n* GB ascensor *m*. LOC **to give sb a lift 1** *(in car)* llevar a ALGN en coche. **2** *(cheer up)* animar.

liftoff ['lɪftɒf] *n* despegue *m*.

ligament ['lɪɡəmənt] *n* ligamento.

light¹ [laɪt] *n* **1** *(gen)* luz *f*. **2** *(lamp)* luz *f*, lámpara; *(traffic light)* semáforo. **3** *(for cigarette, fire)* fuego. LOC **in (the) light of** GB en vista de, teniendo en cuenta. ∎ **to come to light** salir a luz. ∎ **to throw light on** STH aclarar ALGO. COMP **light bulb** bombilla. ∎ **light switch** interruptor *m* de la luz. ∎ **light year** año luz.
▶ *vt* **1** *(ignite)* encender. **2** *(illuminate)* iluminar, alumbrar.
① *pt & pp* **lighted** o **lit** [lɪt].
▶ *adj* **1** *(colour)* claro,-a; *(complexion)* blanco,-a. **2** *(bright)* con mucha claridad.

light² [laɪt] *adj* **1** *(not heavy)* ligero,-a; *(rain)* fino,-a; *(breeze)* suave. **2** *(sentence, wound)* leve. COMP **light aircraft** avioneta.

lighten¹ ['laɪt°n] *vt* **1** *(colour)* aclarar. **2** *(room)* iluminar.
▶ *vi (colour)* aclararse.

lighten² ['laɪt°n] *vt (make less heavy)* aligerar.
▶ *vi (mood, etc)* alegrarse.

lighter ['laɪtə^r] [also **cigarette lighter**] *n* encendedor *m*, mechero.

lighthouse ['laɪthaʊs] *n* faro.

lighting ['laɪtɪŋ] *n* **1** *(in general)* iluminación *f*. **2** *(system)* alumbrado.

lightly ['laɪtlɪ] *adv* **1** *(not heavily)* ligeramente. **2** *(not seriously)* a la ligera.

lightning ['laɪt°nɪŋ] *n* rayo; *(flash only)* relámpago.

lights-out ['laɪtsaʊt] *n* la hora de apagar las luces.

lightweight ['laɪtweɪt] *n (boxing)* peso ligero.

lignite ['lɪɡnaɪt] *n* lignita.

like¹ [laɪk] *prep* **1** *(the same as)* como: *the flat looks like new* el piso está como nuevo. **2** *(typical of)* propio,-a de: *it isn't like her to make a scene* no es propio de ella armar un escándalo. LOC **to look like** SB parecerse a ALGN. ∎ **something like that** ALGO así, ALGO por el estilo.
▶ *adj* **1** *(such as)* como. **2** *fml* parecido,-a.
▶ *conj fam* como.
▶ *n* ALGO parecido: *I've never seen the like of it* nunca he visto cosa igual.

like² [laɪk] *vt* **1** *(enjoy)* gustar. **2** *(want)* querer, gustar: *I'd like a cup of coffee* me gustaría tomar un café. LOC **to like** STH **better** preferir ALGO.
▶ *vi* querer: *if you like* si quieres.
▶ *n pl* **likes** gustos *mpl*.

likeable ['laɪkəb°l] *adj* simpático,-a.

likelihood ['laɪklɪhʊd] *n* probabilidad *f*.

likely ['laɪklɪ] *adj* probable: *he's likely to leave late* es probable que salga tarde.
▶ *adv* probablemente. LOC **as likely as not** *fam* lo más seguro.
① *comp* **likelier**, *superl* **likeliest**.

likeness ['laɪknəs] *n* **1** *(similarity)* semejanza, parecido. **2** *(portrait)* retrato.

likewise ['laɪkwaɪz] *adv* **1** *(the same)* lo mismo, igualmente: *to do likewise* hacer lo mismo.

liking ['laɪkɪŋ] *n (for thing)* gusto, afición *f*; *(for person)* simpatía; *(for friend)* cariño.

lilac ['laɪlək] *n* **1** BOT lila. **2** *(colour)* lila *m*.
▶ *adj* (de color) lila.

lily ['lɪlɪ] *n* lirio, azucena.
① *pl* **lilies**.

limb [lɪmb] *n* **1** ANAT miembro. **2** *(branch)* rama.
◆ **to limber up** *vi* SP entrar en calor.
▶ *vt sep* calentar.

lime [laɪm] *n* **1** *(citrus fruit)* lima. **2** *(citrus tree)* limero. **3** *(linden)* tilo.

limestone [ˈlaɪmstəʊn] *n* piedra caliza.

limit [ˈlɪmɪt] *n* límite *m*. LOC **that's the limit!** *fam* ¡eso es el colmo! ▌ **to be off limits** estar en zona prohibida (to, para). ▌ **within limits** dentro de ciertos límites.
▶ *vt* limitar, restringir (to, a)

limitation [lɪmɪˈteɪʃ°n] *n* limitación *f*.

limousine [ˈlɪməˈziːn] *n* limusina.

limp¹ [lɪmp] *vi* cojear.
▶ *n* cojera.

limp² [lɪmp] *adj* **1** *(floppy)* flojo,-a, fláccido,-a; *(lettuce)* mustio,-a. **2** *(weak)* débil.

limpet [ˈlɪmpɪt] *n* lapa.

linden [ˈlɪnd°n] *n* tilo.

line [laɪn] *n* **1** *(in general)* línea: *in a straight line* en línea recta. **2** *(drawn on paper)* raya. **3** *(of text)* línea, renglón *m*; *(of poetry)* verso: *new line* punto y aparte. **4** *(row)* fila, hilera. **5** US *(queue)* cola. **6** *(cord)* cuerda, cordel *m*; *(fishing)* sedal *m*; *(wire)* cable *m*. **7** *(route)* vía, LOC **all along the line 1** *(from the beginning)* desde el principio. **2** *(in detail)* con todo detalle. ▌ **in line with** *fig* conforme a. ▌ **to stand in line** US hacer cola. COMP **dotted line** línea de puntos. ▌ **line drawing** dibujo lineal.
▶ *vt* **1** *(draw lines on)* dibujar rayas en. **2** *(mark with wrinkles)* arrugar. **3** *(form rows along)* bordear.
◆ **to line up** *vi* ponerse en fila; *(in queue)* hacer cola.

linen [ˈlɪnɪn] *n* **1** *(material)* lino, hilo. **2** *(sheets, etc)* ropa blanca, lencería. COMP **bed linen** ropa de cama. ▌ **table linen** mantelería.

liner [ˈlaɪnəʳ] *n* *(mar)* transatlántico.

linesman [ˈlaɪnzmən] *n* juez *mf* de línea, linier *m*.
ⓘ *pl* **linesmen** [ˈlaɪnzmən].

line-up [ˈlaɪnʌp] *n* *(of people)* alineación *f*, formación *f*.

lingerie [ˈlɑːnʒəriː] *n fml* lencería.

linguist [ˈlɪŋgwɪst] *n* **1** lingüista *mf*. **2** *(fam)* políglota *mf*.

linguistic [lɪŋˈgwɪstɪk] *adj* lingüístico,-a.

linguistics [lɪŋˈgwɪstɪks] *n* lingüística *f*.

lining [ˈlaɪnɪŋ] *n* forro.

link [lɪŋk] *n* **1** *(in chain)* eslabón *m*. **2** *(connection)* enlace *m*. **3** *fig* vínculo, lazo.
▶ *vt* **1** unir, conectar. **2** *fig* vincular, relacionar.

linkage [ˈlɪŋkɪdʒ] *n* conexión *f*.

lintel [ˈlɪnt°l] *n* dintel *m*.

lion [ˈlaɪən] *n* león *m*.

lioness [ˈlaɪənəs] *n* leona.
ⓘ *pl* **lionesses**.

lip [lɪp] *n* **1** labio. **2** *(of cup, etc)* borde *m*.

lipid [ˈlɪpɪd] *n* lípido.

lip-read [ˈlɪpriːd] *vt* leer en los labios.
▶ *vi* leer en los labios.
ⓘ *pt & pp* **lip-read** [ˈlɪpred].

lipstick [ˈlɪpstɪk] *n* *(stick)* barra de labios, lápiz *m* de labios; *(substance)* pintura de labios.

liquefaction [lɪkwɪˈfækʃ°n] *n* licuefacción *f*, licuación *f*.

liquefy [ˈlɪkwɪfaɪ] *vt* licuar.
▶ *vi* licuarse.
ⓘ *pt & pp* **liquefied**, *ger* **liquefying**.

liqueur [lɪˈkjʊəʳ, US lɪˈkɜːʳ] *n* licor *m*.

liquid [ˈlɪkwɪd] *n* **1** líquido.
▶ *adj* **1** líquido,-a.

liquidate [ˈlɪkwɪdeɪt] *vt* liquidar.

liquor [ˈlɪkəʳ] *n* US licor *m*.

liquorice [ˈlɪkərɪs, ˈlɪkərɪʃ] *n* regaliz *m*.

lira [ˈlɪərə] *n* lira.
ⓘ *pl* **liras** o **lire** [ˈlɪərə].

list [lɪst] *n* lista.
▶ *vt* hacer una lista de: *he listed the contents of the house* hizo una lista de las cosas que había en la casa.

listen [ˈlɪs°n] *vi* escuchar (to, -): *listen to me!* ¡escúchame!
◆ **to listen in** *vi (radio)* escuchar (to, -).
◆ **to listen out** *vi fam* estar a la escucha, estar en escucha (for, de).

listener [ˈlɪs°nəʳ] *n* **1** *(in general)* oyente *mf*. **2** RAD radioyente *mf*.

| **listing** | 222 |

listing ['lɪstɪŋ] *n* listado.

lit [lɪt] *pt & pp* → light.

liter ['li:tə^r] *n* US → litre.

literacy ['lɪt^ərəsɪ] *n* **1** *(ability to read)* alfabetización *f*. **2** *(knowledge)* conocimientos *mpl*, nociones *fpl*.

literal ['lɪt^ərəl] *adj* literal.

literary ['lɪt^ərərɪ] *adj* literario,-a.

literature ['lɪt^ərətʃə^r] *n* **1** literatura. **2** *(bibliography)* bibliografía.

lithium ['lɪθɪəm] *n* litio.

lithograph ['lɪθəgrɑ:f] *n* litografía.

lithosphere ['lɪθəsfɪə^r] *n* litosfera.

Lithuania [lɪθjʊ'eɪnɪə] *n* Lituania.

Lithuanian [lɪθjʊ'eɪnɪən] *adj* lituano,-a.
▶ *n* **1** *(person)* lituano,-a. **2** *(language)* lituano.

litre ['li:tə^r] *n* litro.

litter ['lɪtə^r] *n* **1** *(rubbish)* basura, desperdicios *mpl*; *(paper)* papeles *mpl*. **2** *(of kittens, etc)* camada. [COMP] **litter bin** GB papelera.

little ['lɪt^əl] *adj* **1** *(small)* pequeño,-a: *a little cup* una tacita. **2** *(not much)* poco,-a: *a little milk* un poco de leche. [COMP] **little finger** dedo meñique.
ⓘ *comp* **less**, *superl* **least**.
▶ *pron* poco: *more tea? -just a little, please* ¿quieres más té? -un poco, por favor.
▶ *adv* poco: *I'm a little (bit) tired* estoy un poco cansada. [LOC] **little by little** poco a poco.

liturgy ['lɪtədʒɪ] *n* liturgia.
ⓘ *pl* **liturgies**.

live¹ [lɪv] *vi* vivir: *he lives in the country* vive en el campo.
▶ *vt* vivir: *the old woman had lived a life of luxury* la vieja había llevado una vida llena de lujos. [LOC] **to live it up** *fam* pasárselo bomba.
◆ **to live down** *vt sep* lograr que se olvide.
◆ **to live in** *vi* *(student)* estar internado,-a; *(servant)* vivir con la familia.
◆ **to live off** *vt insep* vivir de.
◆ **to live on** *vi* sobrevivir; *(memory)* seguir vivo,-a.
◆ **to live through** *vt insep* sobrevivir.

live² [laɪv] *adj* **1** *(not dead)* vivo,-a: *it's a real live snake* es una serpiente de verdad. **2** *(still burning)* vivo,-a, candente; *(issue)* candente. **3** *(broadcast)* en directo: *a live concert* un concierto en directo.
▶ *adv* en directo, en vivo.

livelihood ['laɪvlɪhʊd] *n* sustento.

lively ['laɪvlɪ] *adj* **1** vivo,-a, animado,-a; *(interest)* entusiasmado,-a. **2** *(colour)* vivo,-a.
ⓘ *comp* **livelier**, *superl* **liveliest**.

liven ['laɪv^ən] *vt* **to liven up** animar.
▶ *vi* **liven up** animarse.

liver ['lɪvə^r] *n* ANAT hígado.

lives [laɪvz] *pl* → life.

livestock ['laɪvstɒk] *n* ganado. [LOC] **livestock farming** ganadería.

living ['lɪvɪŋ] *adj* vivo,-a: *every living creature* todo bicho viviente.
▶ *n* vida: *what do you do for a living?* ¿cómo te ganas la vida? [COMP] **living room** salón *m*, sala de estar. ‖ **living thing** ser *m* vivo.

lizard ['lɪzəd] *n* lagarto; *(small)* lagartija.

'll [l] *v aux* → will, shall.

llama ['lɑ:mə] *n* ZOOL llama.

load [ləʊd] *n* **1** *(in general)* carga: *a lorry shed its load on the motorway yesterday* ayer un camión perdió su carga en la autopista. **2** *(weight)* peso. [LOC] **a load of ...** / **loads of ...** *fam* montones de..., un montón de...
▶ *vt* cargar (with, de): *they loaded up the van with furniture* cargaron la furgoneta de muebles.
▶ *vi* cargar.
◆ **to load down** *vt sep* cargar (with, de); *(with worries, etc)* agobiar (with, de/por).

loaf [ləʊf] *n* pan *m*; *(French)* barra; *(sliced)* pan *m* de molde.
ⓘ *pl* **loaves** [ləʊvz].

loan [ləʊn] *n* *(of money)* préstamo, crédito. [LOC] **on loan** prestado,-a.

loathe [ləʊð] *vt* odiar, aborrecer.

loaves [ləʊvz] *pl* → loaf.

lobby ['lɒbɪ] *n* **1** *(hall)* vestíbulo. **2** POL grupo de presión.
ⓘ *pl* **lobbies**.

▶ *vi* presionar (**for**, para) (**against**, en contra de).

▶ *vt* POL presionar, ejercer presión sobre.

lobe [ləʊb] *n* lóbulo.

lobster [ˈlɒbstəʳ] *n* bogavante *m*.

local [ˈləʊkəl] *adj* **1** *(in general)* local. **2** *(person)* del barrio, de la zona.

▶ *n* **1** *fam (person)* vecino,-a. **2** GB *fam* bar *m*, pub *m* *(del barrio)*. **3** US *(train)* tren *m* de cercanías; *(bus)* autobús *m*.

☒ Local no significa 'local (establecimiento)', que se traduce por premises.

locality [ləʊˈkælɪtɪ] *n fml* localidad *f*.
　① *pl* localities.

locate [ləʊˈkeɪt] *vt* **1** *fml (find)* localizar. **2** *fml (situate)* situar, ubicar.

location [ləʊˈkeɪʃən] *n* **1** lugar, ubicación *m*. **2** CINEM exteriores *mpl*.

loch [lɒk] *n (in Scotland)* lago.

lock¹ [lɒk] *n* **1** *(gen)* cerradura; *(padlock)* candado. **2** *(in canal)* esclusa. **3** *(in wrestling)* llave *f*.

▶ *vt (with key)* cerrar con llave; *(with padlock)* cerrar con candado.

▶ *vi* **1** *(door, etc)* cerrarse (con llave).

lock² [lɒk] *n (of hair)* mecha, mechón *m*.

locker [ˈlɒkəʳ] *n* armario, taquilla.

locksmith [ˈlɒksmɪθ] *n* cerrajero.

locomotion [ləʊkəˈməʊʃən] *n* locomoción *f*.

locomotive [ləʊkəˈməʊtɪv] *n* locomotora.

▶ *adj* locomotor,-ra.

locomotor [ləʊkəˈmətəʳ] *adj* locomotor,-a.

locust [ˈləʊkəst] *n* langosta.

✎ La palabra locust se refiere al insecto; el marisco se llama lobster.

lodge [lɒdʒ] *n* **1** *(in general)* casita; *(hunter's)* refugio. **2** *(porter's)* portería. **3** *(masonic)* logia.

▶ *vi* **1** *(as guest)* alojarse, hospedarse. **2** *(become fixed)* quedarse atrapado,-a.

▶ *vt (complaint)* presentar.

lodger [ˈlɒdʒəʳ] *n* huésped,-da.

lodging [ˈlɒdʒɪŋ] *n* alojamiento. COMP lodging house casa de huéspedes.

loft [lɒft] *n* desván *m*, buhardilla.

▶ *vt* SP lanzar al aire.

log [lɒg] *n* **1** tronco; *(for fire)* leño. **2** *(on ship)* cuaderno de bitácora; *(on plane)* diario de vuelo. **3** MATH *fam (abbr of* logarithm*)* logaritmo.

▶ *vt* **1** registrar, anotar. **2** *(cover)* recorrer.

◆ **to log in** *vi* COMPUT entrar (en el sistema).

◆ **to log out** *vi* COMPUT salir (del sistema).

　① *pt & pp* logged, *ger* logging.

logarithm [ˈlɒgərɪðəm] *n* logaritmo.

logic [ˈlɒdʒɪk] *n* lógica.

logical [ˈlɒdʒɪkəl] *adj* lógico,-a: *the logical thing would be to say yes* lo lógico sería decir que sí.

logistics [ləˈdʒɪstɪks] *n* logística.

logo [ˈləʊgəʊ] *n* logotipo.
　① *pl* logos.

loin [lɔɪn] *n* CULIN *(of pork)* lomo; *(of beef)* solomillo.

lollipop [ˈlɒlɪpɒp] *n* **1** pirulí *m*, piruleta. **2** GB *(iced)* polo.

lolly [ˈlɒlɪ] *n* **1** GB *fam* pirulí *m*, piruleta. **2** GB *fam (iced)* polo.
　① *pl* lollies.

loneliness [ˈləʊnlɪnəs] *n* soledad *f*.

lonely [ˈləʊnlɪ] *adj* **1** *(person)* solo,-a. **2** *(place)* solitario,-a, aislado,-a.
　① *comp* lonelier, *superl* loneliest.

lonesome [ˈləʊnsəm] *adj* US→ lonely.

long¹ [lɒŋ] *adj* largo,-a: *a long journey* un largo viaje. COMP long jump salto de longitud.

▶ *adv* mucho tiempo: *it takes a long time to climb the mountain* se tarda mucho en escalar la montaña. LOC as long as *(while)* mientras. I long ago hace mucho tiempo.

long² [lɒŋ] *phr* to long to do STH tener muchos deseos de hacer ALGO.

◆ **to long for** *vt insep (yearn)* anhelar; *(nostalgically)* añorar.

long-distance [lɒŋˈdɪstəns] *adj* de larga distancia.

L

longing ['lɒŋɪŋ] n (yearning) ansia, anhelo; (nostalgia) nostalgia.

longitude ['lɒndʒɪtjuːd] n longitud f.

long-life ['lɒŋlaɪf] adj (battery) de larga duración; (milk) UHT, uperizado,-a.

long-range ['lɒŋreɪndʒ] adj **1** (distance) de largo alcance. **2** (plans, forecast) a largo plazo.

long-term ['lɒŋtɜːm] adj a largo plazo, de largo plazo.

long-wearing ['lɒŋweərɪŋ] adj US duradero,-a, resistente.

loo [luː] n GB fam váter m.
ⓘ pl loos.

look [lʊk] vi **1** mirar (at, -). **2** (seem) parecer: he looks tired parece cansado. LOC **look out!** ¡cuidado!
▸ vt **1** mirar: I can't look him in the face no puedo mirarle a la cara. **2** (seem) parecer: he doesn't look his age no aparenta la edad que tiene.
▸ n **1** (glance) mirada: have a look at this mira esto. **2** (appearance) aspecto, apariencia. **4** (fashion) moda: I'm not into the punk look no me va la moda punk.
▸ interj ¡mira!
◆ **to look after** vt insep (deal with) ocuparse de, atender a; (take care of) cuidar (de).
◆ **to look at** vt insep **1** (consider) mirar, considerar. **2** (examine) mirar.
◆ **to look back** vi mirar atrás.
◆ **to look for** vt insep buscar: what are you looking for? ¿qué buscas?
◆ **to look forward to** vt insep esperar (con ansia).
◆ **to look on** vt insep considerar.
◆ **to look like** vt insep parecerse a: he looks like his father se parece a su padre.
◆ **to look out** vi (be careful) ir con cuidado.
◆ **to look through** vt insep (check) revisar (bien); (quickly) ojear.
◆ **to look up** vi fam (improve) mejorar.
▸ vt sep **1** (in dictionary, etc) consultar, buscar.

lookalike ['lʊkəlaɪk] n fam doble mf, sosia m.

loom¹ [luːm] n telar m.

loom² [luːm] vi vislumbrarse; (causing fear) amenazar.
◆ **to loom up** vi surgir.

loony ['luːnɪ] adj fam chiflado,-a, chalado,-a.
ⓘ comp loonier, superl looniest.

loop [luːp] n (in string, etc) lazo.
▸ vi formar un lazo. LOC **to loop the loop** rizar el rizo.

loose [luːs] adj **1** (in general) suelto,-a. **2** (not tight) flojo,-a; (clothes) holgado,-a.
▸ vt lit soltar.

loose-fitting [luːsˈfɪtɪŋ] adj holgado,-a, amplio,-a.

loosen ['luːsən] vt (gen) soltar, aflojar; (belt) desabrochar.
▸ vi **1** soltarse, aflojarse.
◆ **to loosen up** vi (relax) relajarse.

loot [luːt] n botín m.

lord [lɔːd] n **1** señor m. **2** GB (title) lord m. **3** (judge) señoría mf. LOC **good Lord!** ¡ay Dios!, ¡Dios mío! COMP **the Lord** REL el Señor.

lorry ['lɒrɪ] n GB camión m.
ⓘ pl lorries.

lose [luːz] vt **1** (in general) perder: don't lose it no lo pierdas. **2** (clock) atrasar.
▸ vi **1** (in general) perder: Liverpool lost to United el Liverpool perdió ante el United. **2** (clock) atrasarse. LOC **to lose one's way** perderse. ‖ **to lose sight of** STH perder ALGO de vista.
ⓘ pt & pp lost [lɒst], ger losing.

loser ['luːzəʳ] n perdedor,-ra.

loss [lɒs] n **1** (in general) pérdida. **2** MIL (death) baja.
ⓘ pl losses.

lost [lɒst] pt → lose.
▸ adj perdido,-a. LOC **to get lost** perderse. COMP **lost property** objetos perdidos.

lost-and-found [lɒstənˈfaʊnd] [also lost-and-found department] n US oficina de objetos perdidos.

lot [lɒt] n **1** (large number) cantidad f: he talks a lot habla mucho. **2** (group) grupo: the next lot of passengers el próximo grupo de pasajeros. **3** (fate) suerte f. LOC **thanks a lot!** ¡muchísimas gracias!
▸ n **the lot** todo,-a, todos,-as.

▶ *phr* **lots of** mucho,-a, muchos,-as, cantidad de: *there were lots of people* había mucha gente.

lotion ['ləʊʃ°n] *n* loción *f*.

lottery ['lɒt°rɪ] *n* lotería.
ⓘ *pl* lotteries.

loud [laʊd] *adj* **1** *(sound)* fuerte. **2** *(voice)* alto,-a. **3** *(colour)* chillón,-ona.
▶ *adv* fuerte, alto. LOC **out loud** en voz alta.

loudly ['laʊdlɪ] *adv (speak)* alto; *(shout)* fuerte; *(complain)* a voz en grito.

loudness ['laʊdnəs] *n (of sound)* fuerza, intensidad *f*; *(noisiness)* bullicio.

loudspeaker [laʊd'spi:kəʳ] *n* altavoz *m*.

lounge [laʊndʒ] *n* salón *m*. COMP **lounge suit** *fam* traje *m*.
▶ *vi* **1** *(on sofa, etc)* repantigarse. **2** *(idle)* holgazanear.

lounger ['laʊndʒəʳ] *n (chair)* tumbona.

louse [laʊs] *n* **1** piojo. **2** *fam* canalla *mf*.
ⓘ *pl* lice.

lousy ['laʊzɪ] *adj* **1** *fam* fatal, malísimo,-a: *he felt lousy* se encontraba fatal.
ⓘ *comp* lousier; *superl* lousiest.

lovable ['lʌvəb°l] *adj* adorable.

love [lʌv] *n* **1** *(in general)* amor *m*; *(affection)* cariño; *(liking)* afición *f* (**for**, a). **2** GB *fam (person)* guapo,-a, chato,-a. **3** *(regards)* recuerdos *mpl*: *(give my) love to your parents* muchos recuerdos a tus padres. LOC **to be in love with** estar enamorado,-a de. ‖ **to fall in love** enamorarse. ‖ **to make love** hacer el amor (**to**, a). COMP **love affair** aventura amorosa, lío.
▶ *vt* **1** amar, querer: *do you love him?* ¿lo quieres? **2** *(like a lot)* encantarle a uno, gustarle a uno mucho: *I love playing tennis* me encanta jugar a tenis.

lovely ['lʌvlɪ] *adj* **1** *(wonderful)* estupendo,-a, maravilloso,-a. **2** *(beautiful)* hermoso,-a, precioso,-a; *(charming)* encantador,-ra.
ⓘ *comp* lovelier; *superl* loveliest.

lover ['lʌvəʳ] *n* amante *mf*.:

loving ['lʌvɪŋ] *adj* cariñoso,-a: *your loving son, Paul* tu hijo que te quiere, Paul.

low [ləʊ] *adj* **1** *(in general)* bajo,-a; *(neckline)* escotado,-a: *low clouds* nubes bajas. **2** *(battery)* gastado,-a. **3** *(depressed)* deprimido,-a, abatido,-a. **4** MUS grave. LOC **to keep a low profile** ser discreto,-a. COMP **low tide** marea baja. ‖ **the Low Countries** los Países Bajos.
▶ *adv* bajo: *we're running low on petrol* se nos acaba la gasolina.
▶ *n (low level)* punto bajo.

low-calorie [ləʊ'kælərɪ] *adj* bajo,-a en calorías, hipocalórico,-a.

lower ['ləʊəʳ] *adj* inferior. COMP **lower case** caja baja, minúscula.
▶ *vt* **1** *(in general)* bajar; *(price)* rebajar. **2** *(flag)* arriar.

lower-class [ləʊə'klɑːs] *adj* de clase baja.

lowest ['ləʊɪst] *adj* más bajo,-a; *(price, speed)* mínimo,-a.
▶ *n* mínimo: *at the lowest* como mínimo.

low-fat [ləʊ'fæt] *adj* de bajo contenido graso.

loyal ['lɔɪəl] *adj* leal, fiel.

loyalty ['lɔɪəltɪ] *n* lealtad *f*, fidelidad *f*.
ⓘ *pl* loyalties.

lozenge ['lɒzɪndʒ] *n* **1** pastilla. **2** *(geometry)* rombo.

LP ['el'piː] *abbr* (long player) elepé *m*; *(abbreviation)* LP.

lubricant ['luːbrɪkənt] *n* lubricante *m*.

lucerne [luː'sɜːn] *n* GB alfalfa.

luck [lʌk] *n* suerte *f*. LOC **bad luck! / hard luck! / tough luck!** ¡mala suerte! ‖ **good luck! / best of luck!** ¡suerte! ‖ **to be in luck** estar de suerte. ‖ **to try one's luck** probar fortuna.

luckily ['lʌkɪlɪ] *adv* afortunadamente.

lucky ['lʌkɪ] *adj (in general)* afortunado,-a; *(timely)* oportuno,-a: *how lucky you were!* ¡qué suerte tuviste! COMP **lucky charm** amuleto.
ⓘ *comp* luckier; *superl* luckiest.

lucrative ['luːkrətɪv] *adj* lucrativo,-a.

ludo ['luːdəʊ] *n* GB parchís *m*.

luggage ['lʌgɪdʒ] *n* GB equipaje *m*. COMP **luggage rack** portaequipajes *m*. ‖ **luggage van** furgón *m* de equipaje.

L

lukewarm [ˈluːkwɔːm] *adj* tibio,-a, templado,-a.

lullaby [ˈlʌləbaɪ] *n* canción *f* de cuna, nana.
ⓘ *pl* lullabies.

lumbar [ˈlʌmbəʳ] *adj* lumbar.

luminous [ˈluːmɪnəs] *adj* luminoso,-a.

lump [lʌmp] *n* **1** *(chunk)* pedazo, trozo; *(in sauce)* grumo. **2** *(swelling)* bulto, protuberancia; *(in throat)* nudo. **3** *(of sugar)* terrón *m*. **4** *fam (idiot)* burro,-a.

lumpy [ˈlʌmpɪ] *adj* lleno,-a de bultos; *(sauce)* grumoso,-a.
ⓘ *comp* lumpier, *superl* lumpiest.

lunar [ˈluːnəʳ] *adj* lunar. COMP lunar landing alunizaje *m*. ▌ lunar month mes *m* lunar.

lunatic [ˈluːnətɪk] *adj* loco,-a.
▶ *n* loco,-a, lunático,-a. COMP lunatic asylum manicomio. ▌ the lunatic fringe los fanáticos *mpl*.

lunch [lʌntʃ] *n* comida, almuerzo: *we'll have lunch at one* comeremos a la una. COMP business lunch almuerzo de trabajo. ▌ lunch break hora de comer. ▌ lunch hour hora de comer.
▶ *vi fml* comer, almorzar.

lunchtime [ˈlʌntʃtaɪm] *n* hora de comer, hora de almorzar.

lung [lʌŋ] *n* pulmón *m*: *her little girl has a good pair of lungs!* ¡su hijita tiene buenos pulmones! COMP lung cancer cáncer *m* de pulmón.

lurk [lɜːk] *vi* **1** *(wait)* estar al acecho. **2** *(hide)* esconderse.

lust [lʌst] *n* **1** *(sexual)* lujuria. **2** *(greed)* codicia; *(strong desire)* ansia.

lute [luːt] *n* laúd *m*.

Luxembourg [ˈlʌksəmbɜːg] *n* Luxemburgo.

Luxembourger [ˈlʌksəmbɜːgəʳ] *n* luxemburgués,-esa.

luxuriant [lʌgˈzjʊərɪənt] *adj* **1** *(vegetation)* exuberante; *(hair)* abundante.

luxurious [lʌgˈzjʊərɪəs] *adj* lujoso,-a.

luxury [ˈlʌkʃərɪ] *n* lujo.
ⓘ *pl* luxuries.

lychee [ˈlaɪtʃiː] *n* lichi *m*.

lying [ˈlaɪɪŋ] *adj (deceitful)* mentiroso,-a.
▶ *n (lies)* mentiras *fpl*.

lymph [lɪmf] *n* linfa.

lymphatic [lɪmˈfætɪk] *adj* linfático,-a.

lynch [lɪntʃ] *vt* linchar.

lynx [lɪŋks] *n* lince *m*.

lyre [laɪəʳ] *n* lira.

lyric [ˈlɪrɪk] *adj* lírico,-a.
▶ *n* poema *m* lírico.
▶ *n pl* lyrics *(of song)* letra *f sing*.

M, m [em] *n (the letter)* M, m *f.*

mac [mæk] *n* GB *fam (mackintosh)* impermeable *m.*

macaroni [mækəˈrəʊnɪ] *n* macarrones *mpl.*

macaw [məˈkɔː] *n* guacamayo, ara *m.*

mace [meɪs] *n (club, staff)* maza.

macerate [ˈmæsəreɪt] *vt* macerar.
▶ *vi* macerarse.

machine [məˈʃiːn] *n* **1** *(gen)* máquina. **2** *(organization, system)* organización *f*, aparato. COMP **machine gun** ametralladora.
▶ *n pl* **machines** *(machinery)* maquinaria *f sing.*

machinery [məˈʃiːnərɪ] *n* **1** *(machines)* maquinaria. **2** *(workings)* mecanismo.

mackerel [ˈmækərəl] *n* caballa.

mackintosh [ˈmækɪntɒʃ] *n* impermeable *m.*

macro [ˈmækrəʊ] *n* COMPUT macro *f.*

macroeconomics [mækrəʊiːkəˈnɒmɪks] *n* macroeconomía.

macroscopic [mækrəˈskɒpɪk] *adj* macroscópico,-a.

mad [mæd] *adj* **1** *(insane)* loco,-a: *she's quite mad* está completamente loca. **2** *fam (person)* loco,-a; *(crazy - idea, plan)* disparatado,-a, descabellado,-a. **3** *fam (enthusiastic)* loco,-a *(about, por)*, chiflado,-a: *he's mad about her* está loco por ella. **4** *fam (angry)* enfadado,-a, furioso,-a *(at/with, con).* LOC **to drive SB mad / send SB mad** volver a ALGN loco,-a, traer loco,-a a ALGN. ‖ **to get mad** enfadarse. ‖ **to go mad** volverse loco,-a, enloquecer.
ⓘ *comp* **madder**, *superl* **maddest.**

Madagascan [mædəˈgæskən] *adj* malgache.
▶ *n (person)* malgache *mf.*

Madagascar [mædəˈgæskəˈ] *n* Madagascar.

madam [ˈmædəm] *n fml* señora.

made [meɪd] *pt & pp* → **make.**
▶ *adj (produced)* hecho,-a, fabricado,-a: *made in England* hecho,-a en Inglaterra. LOC **to be made from** STH estar hecho, -a de ALGO. ‖ **to be made of** STH ser de ALGO, estar hecho,-a de ALGO, estar compuesto,-a de ALGO.

madly [ˈmædlɪ] *adv* como un loco.

madness [ˈmædnəs] *n* **1** *(insanity)* locura, demencia. **2** *(foolishness)* locura: *it is madness to drive in this weather* es una locura conducir con el tiempo que hace.

magazine [mæɡəˈziːn] *n* **1** *(periodical)* revista. **2** *(on TV, radio)* magacín *m*, magazine *m.* COMP **magazine rack** revistero.

maggot [ˈmæɡət] *n* larva, gusano.

magic [ˈmædʒɪk] *n* magia.
▶ *adj* mágico,-a. COMP **magic wand** varita mágica.

magical [ˈmædʒɪkəl] *adj* mágico,-a.

magician [məˈdʒɪʃən] *n* **1** *(conjurer)* prestidigitador,-ra, ilusionista *mf.* **2** *(wizard)* mago,-a.

magistrate [ˈmædʒɪstreɪt] *n* JUR magistrado,-a, juez *mf.*

magma [ˈmæɡmə] *n* magma.

magnesite [ˈmæɡnesɪt] *n* magnesita.

magnesium [mæɡˈniːzɪəm] *n* magnesio.

magnet [ˈmæɡnət] *n* imán *m.*

magnetic [mæɡˈnetɪk] *adj* **1** *(force, etc)* magnético,-a. **2** *fig (personality, charm)* carismático,-a.

magnetism [ˈmæɡnɪtɪzəm] *n* magnetismo.

magnetized ['mægnɪtaɪzd] *adj* magnetizado,-a. **2** *fig (person)* magnetizar, cautivar.

magnification [mægnɪfɪ'keɪʃ⁰n] *n* **1** *(increase)* aumento, ampliación *f*. **2** *(power of lens, etc)* aumento.

magnificent [mæg'nɪfɪs⁰nt] *adj (splendid)* magnífico,-a, espléndido,-a.

magnify ['mægnɪfaɪ] *vt* **1** *(enlarge)* aumentar, ampliar. **2** *fig (exaggerate)* exagerar, agrandar.
ⓘ *pt & pp* magnified, *ger* magnifying.

magnifying glass ['mægnɪfaɪɪŋglɑːs] *n* lupa.
ⓘ *pl* magnifying glasses.

magnitude ['mægnɪtjuːd] *n (size)* magnitud *f*; *(importance)* magnitud *f*, envergadura.

magnolia [mæg'nəʊlɪə] *n* **1** *(tree)* magnolio, magnolia. **2** *(flower)* magnolia.

magpie ['mægpaɪ] *n* urraca.

mahogany [mə'hɒgənɪ] *n (wood, tree)* caoba; *(colour)* color *m* caoba.

maid [meɪd] *n (servant)* criada, sirvienta; *(in hotel)* camarera.

maiden ['meɪd⁰n] *n (unmarried woman, girl)* doncella.
▶ *adj (first of its kind - speech, voyage)* inaugural.

mail [meɪl] *n* **1** *(system)* correo: *send it by mail* envíalo por correo. **2** *(letters, etc)* correo, cartas *mpl*, correspondencia.
▶ *vt (send)* mandar por correo.

mailbox ['meɪlbɒks] *n* buzón *m*.

mailman ['meɪlmæn] *n* US cartero.
ⓘ *pl* mailmen ['meɪlmæn].

maim [meɪm] *vt* mutilar, lisiar.

main [meɪn] *adj (most important)* principal: *be careful when you cross the main road* ten cuidado al cruzar la carretera principal. [COMP] **main course** plato principal, segundo plato. ‖ **main road** carretera principal.

mainframe ['meɪnfreɪm] [also mainframe computer] *n* unidad *f* central, ordenador *m* central.

mainland ['meɪnlənd] *n continente o isla grande en contraposición a una isla cercana más pequeña.*

mainly ['meɪnlɪ] *adv (chiefly)* principalmente, sobre todo; *(mostly)* en su mayoría.

maintain [meɪn'teɪn] *vt* **1** *(preserve, keep up - gen)* mantener; *(- silence, appearances)* guardar. **2** *(support financially)* mantener, sostener.

maintenance ['meɪntənəns] *n* **1** *(gen)* mantenimiento. **2** *(upkeep of family)* manutención *f*.

maize [meɪz] *n* maíz *m*.

majesty ['mædʒəstɪ] *n* majestad *f*.
ⓘ *pl* majesties.

major ['meɪdʒə'] *adj* **1** *(more important, greater)* mayor, principal: *tourism is the major industry* el turismo es la industria principal. **2** *(important - gen)* importante; *(- issue)* de gran envergadura; *(- illness)* grave. **3** MUS *(key, scale)* mayor.
▶ **1** MIL comandante *m*.

majorette [meɪdʒər'et] *n* majorette *f*.

majority [mə'dʒɒrɪtɪ] *n* mayoría: *the great majority of students* la gran mayoría de los estudiantes. [LOC] **to be in a/the majority** ser mayoría.
ⓘ *pl* majorities.
▶ *adj* mayoritario,-a.

make [meɪk] *n (brand)* marca: *what make is your watch?* ¿de qué marca es tu reloj?
▶ *vt* **1** *(produce - gen)* hacer; *(construct)* construir; *(manufacture)* fabricar; *(create)* crear; *(prepare)* preparar: *she made some sandwiches* hizo unos bocadillos, preparó unos bocadillos; *stop making all that noise* ¡dejad de hacer tanto ruido! **2** *(carry out, perform)* hacer: *I must make a phone call* tengo que hacer una llamada. **3** *(cause to be)* hacer, poner, volver: *the gift made him happy* el regalo lo hizo feliz. **4** *(force, compel)* hacer, obligar; *(cause to do)* hacer: *they make me go to bed early* me obligan a acostarme temprano. **5** *(be, become)* ser, hacer; *(cause to be)* hacer, convertir en: *she'll make a good singer* será buena cantante, tiene madera de cantante.
▶ *vi (to be about to)* hacer como, simular: *he made as if to kiss her* hizo como si la besara. [LOC] **to make sense** tener sentido. ‖ **to make sure (of** STH**)** asegurarse (de ALGO).

◆ **to make for** vt insep **1** (move towards) dirigirse hacia. **2** (result in, make possible) contribuir a, crear, conducir a.

◆ **to make out** vt sep **1** (write - list, receipt) hacer; (- cheque) extender, hacer; (- report) redactar. **2** (see) distinguir, divisar; (writing) descifrar. **3** (understand) entender, comprender.

▶ vt insep fam (pretend, claim) pretender, hacerse pasar por.

◆ **to make up** vt sep **1** (invent) inventar. **2** (put together) hacer; (assemble) montar; (bed, prescription) preparar; (page) componer; (clothes, curtains) confeccionar, hacer. **3** (complete) completar. **4** (constitute) componer, formar, integrar; (represent) representar. **5** (cosmetics) maquillar.

▶ vi **1** maquillarse, pintarse. **2** (become friends again) hacer las paces, reconciliarse.

ⓘ pt & pp made, ger making.

maker ['meɪkə'] n (of product) fabricante mf; (of film, etc) creador,-ra.

make-up ['meɪkʌp] n **1** (cosmetics) maquillaje m: she never wears make-up nunca se maquilla, nunca se pone maquillaje. **2** (composition, combination) composición f. **3** (of person) carácter m.

malaria [mə'leərɪə] n malaria, paludismo.

Malawi [mə'lɑ:wɪ] n Malawi.

Malawian [mə'lɑ:wɪən] adj malawiano,-a.

▶ n malawiano,-a.

Malaysia [mə'leɪzɪə] n Malaysia, Malasia.

Malaysian [mə'leɪzɪən] adj malasio,-a.

▶ n malasio,-a.

Maldives ['mɔ:ldaɪvz] n Maldivas.

Maldivian [mɔ:l'dɪvɪən] adj maldivo,-a.

▶ n maldivo,-a.

male [meɪl] adj **1** (animal, plant) macho; (person, child) varón; (sex, hormone, character, organ) masculino,-a. **2** (manly) varonil, viril.

▶ n **1** (man, boy) varón m; (animal, plant) macho.

Mali ['mɑ:lɪ] n Malí.

Malian ['mɑ:lɪən] adj maliense.

▶ n maliense mf.

mall [mæl, mɔ:l] n US (covered) centro comercial; (street) zona comercial.

malleability ['mælɪəbɪlɪtɪ] n **1** (metal) maleabilidad f. **2** fig (person) docilidad f.

malleable ['mælɪəbºl] adj **1** (metal) maleable. **2** fig (person) dócil.

mallet ['mælət] n mazo.

malnutrition [mælnju:'trɪʃºn] n desnutrición f.

malt [mɔ:lt] n (grain) malta.

Malta ['mɔ:ltə] n Malta.

Maltese [mɔ:l'ti:z] adj maltés,-esa.

▶ n **1** (person) maltés,-esa. **2** (language) maltés m.

▶ n pl the Maltese los malteses mpl.

maltreatment [mæl'trɪtmənt] n malos tratos mpl.

mammal ['mæmºl] n mamífero.

mammary ['mæmərɪ] adj mamario,-a.

[COMP] mammary gland mama.

mammography [mæ'mɒɡrəfɪ] n mamografía.

ⓘ pl mammographies.

mammoth ['mæməθ] n ZOOL mamut m.

mammy ['mæmɪ] n fam mamá.

ⓘ pl mammies.

man [mæn] n **1** (adult male) hombre m, señor m: an old man un hombre mayor, un señor mayor, un viejo. **2** (human being, person) ser m humano, el hombre m: all men are born equal todos los hombres nacen iguales. **3** (husband) marido, hombre m; (boyfriend) novio; (partner) pareja: man and wife marido y mujer.

ⓘ pl men.

manage ['mænɪdʒ] vt **1** (run - business, company) dirigir; (- property) administrar: she manages a shop es la encargada de una tienda, lleva una tienda. **2** (handle, cope with - child, person) llevar, manejar; (- animal) domar; (- work, luggage, etc) poder con. **3** (succeed) conseguir, lograr: we managed it! ¡lo conseguimos! **4** (have room for, have time for) poder.

▶ vi **1** poder: can you manage? ¿puedes? **2** (financially) arreglárselas, apañarse.

manager ['mænɪdʒə'] n **1** (of company, bank) director,-ra, gerente mf. **2** (of shop, restaurant) encargado,-a; (of depart-

M

ment) jefe,-a. **3** *(of actor, group, etc)* representante *mf*, manager *mf*. **4** SP *(of football team)* entrenador *m*, míster *m*.

mandarin ['mændərɪn] *n* **1** mandarina. **2** GB *pej (government official)* mandarín *m*.
► *n* Mandarin *(language)* mandarín *m*.

mandatory ['mændətˀrɪ] *adj (compulsory)* obligatorio,-a.

mandible ['mændɪbˀl] *n* mandíbula.

mane [meɪn] *n (of horse)* crin *f*; *(of lion)* melena.

maneuver [məˈnuːvəʳ] *n & v* US → manoeuvre.

manganese ['mæŋɡəniːz] *n* manganeso.

manger ['meɪndʒəʳ] *n* pesebre *m*.

mangle ['mæŋɡˀl] *vt* **1** *(cut to pieces)* destrozar, despedazar; *(crush)* aplastar.

mango ['mæŋɡəʊ] *n* mango.
ⓘ *pl* mangoes o mangos.

mangrove ['mæŋɡrəʊv] *n* manglar *m*.

maniac ['meɪnɪæk] *n* **1** *fam (wild person)* loco,-a. **2** *fam (fan)* entusiasta *mf*, fanático,-a.

manifestation [mænɪfeˈsteɪˀn] *n fml* manifestación *f*.

⊠ Manifestation no significa 'manifestación (de protesta)', que se traduce por demonstration.

manifesto [mænɪˈfestəʊ] *n* manifiesto.
ⓘ *pl* manifestos o manifestoes.

manioc ['mænɪɒk] *n* mandioca, yuca.

manipulate [məˈnɪpjəleɪt] *vt* **1** *(work - machine)* manejar; *(- knob, lever)* accionar. **2** *(control, influence)* manipular.

mankind [mænˈkaɪnd] *n* la humanidad *f*, el género humano, los hombres *mpl*.

man-made [mænˈmeɪd] *adj* **1** *(lake, etc)* artificial. **2** *(fabric, etc)* sintético,-a.

mannequin ['mænɪkɪn] *n* **1** *(dummy)* maniquí *m*. **2** *dated (model)* modelo *f*.

manner ['mænəʳ] *n* **1** *(way, method)* manera, modo: *in this manner* de esta manera. **2** *(way of behaving)* forma de ser, comportamiento, aire *m*: *she has a pleasant manner* tiene una forma de ser agradable. [LOC] **in a manner of speaking** por decirlo así, hasta cierto punto.

► *n pl* **manners** *(social behaviour)* maneras *fpl*, modales *mpl*; *(customs)* costumbres *fpl*. [COMP] **bad manners** falta de educación. **good manners** buenos modales *mpl*.

manoeuvre [məˈnuːvəʳ] *n* maniobra.
► *vt* **1** *(gen)* maniobrar. **2** *(person)* manipular, manejar.
► *vi* maniobrar.

manometer [məˈnɒmɪtəʳ] *n* manómetro.

manor ['mænəʳ] *n* señorío. [COMP] **manor house** casa solariega.

manpower ['mænpaʊəʳ] *n* mano *f* de obra.

mansion ['mænˀn] *n (gen)* casa grande; *(country)* casa solariega.

mantelpiece ['mæntˀlpiːs] *n* repisa de chimenea.

mantis ['mæntɪs] *n* mantis *f*.
ⓘ *pl* mantis.

manual ['mænjʊəl] *adj* manual.
► *n* manual *m*.

manufacture [mænjəˈfæktʃəʳ] *n (gen)* fabricación *f*; *(of clothing)* confección *f*; *(of foodstuffs)* elaboración *f*.
► *vt* **1** *(gen)* fabricar; *(clothing)* confeccionar; *(foodstuffs)* elaborar. **2** *fig (excuse, etc)* inventar.

manufactured [mænjəˈfæktʃərəd] *adj* manufacturado,-da.

manufacturer [mænjəˈfæktʃərəʳ] *adj* fabricante *mf*.

manure [məˈnjʊəʳ] *n* abono, estiércol *m*.

manuscript ['mænjəskrɪpt] *n* **1** *(historic handwritten book)* manuscrito. **2** *(original copy of text)* original *m*, texto original.

many ['menɪ] *adj* mucho,-a, muchos,-as: *many people never go abroad* mucha gente nunca va al extranjero.
ⓘ *comp* more, *superl* most. [LOC] **as many ... as** tantos,-as… como. **how many?** ¿cuántos,-as? **not many** pocos,-as, no muchos,-as. **too many** demasiados,-as.
► *pron* muchos,-as: *I don't want many* no quiero muchos.

✎ Many se usa sobre todo en las frases negativas y en las preguntas; en las frases afirmativas se usa más a lot of.

map [mæp] n (of country, region) mapa m; (of town, bus, tube) plano. COMP **map of the world** mapamundi m.
► vt (area) trazar un mapa de.
ⓘ pt & pp **mapped**, ger **mapping**.

maple ['meɪpəl] n (tree, wood) arce m.

marathon ['mærəθən] n maratón m.
► adj fig maratoniano,-a, larguísimo,-a.

marble ['mɑ:bəl] n **1** (stone, statue) mármol m. **2** (glass ball) canica.
► n pl **marbles** (game) canicas fpl. ART mármoles mpl.

March [mɑ:tʃ] n marzo.

✎ Para ejemplos de uso, consulta May.

march [mɑ:tʃ] n **1** MIL marcha. **2** (walk) caminata. **3** (demonstration) manifestación f. **4** MUS marcha.
► vi **1** MIL marchar, hacer una marcha.
2 (walk) caminar, marchar.
► vt hacer marchar.

mare [meəʳ] n yegua.

margarine [mɑ:dʒəˈri:n] n margarina.

marge [mɑ:dʒ] n GB fam margarina.

margin ['mɑ:dʒɪn] n **1** (gen) margen m. **2** (difference, leeway) margen m: there is no margin for error no hay margen de error.

marginal ['mɑ:dʒɪnəl] adj **1** (small, minor) menor, pequeño,-a, mínimo,-a. **2** (artist) marginal.

marihuana [mærɪˈhwɑ:nə] n marihuana.

marina [məˈri:nə] n puerto deportivo.

marinate ['mærɪneɪt] vt adobar.

marine [məˈri:n] n (life, flora, etc) marino,-a, marítimo,-a.
► adj (law, stores, etc) marítimo,-a.
► n soldado de infantería de marina.
► n pl **the Marines** GB la infantería de marina.

marionette [mærɪəˈnet] n marioneta, títere m.

marital ['mærɪtəl] adj (relations, problems) matrimonial, marital; (bliss) conyugal. COMP **marital status** estado civil.

maritime ['mærɪtaɪm] adj marítimo,-a.

mark [mɑ:k] n **1** (imprint, trace) huella; (from blow) señal f; (stain) mancha: there's a mark on this blouse esta blusa tie-

ne una mancha. **2** (sign, symbol) marca, señal f: I've put a mark by the things I'm interested in he señalado las cosas que me interesan. **3** EDUC nota, calificación f: he got a good mark in maths sacó una buena nota en mates. LOC **on your marks, get set, go!** ¡preparados, listos, ya!
► vt **1** (gen) marcar. **2** EDUC (correct) corregir; (grade - student) poner nota a; (- exam, essay, etc) puntuar, calificar.
► vi (stain) mancharse.
◆ **to mark down** vt sep **1** (reduce price of) rebajar el precio de. **2** (reduce marks of) bajar la nota de. **3** (note in writing) apuntar.
◆ **to mark out** vt sep **1** (area) marcar, delimitar; (boundary) marcar, trazar. **2** (choose) señalar, seleccionar.

market ['mɑ:kɪt] n **1** (selling fruit, vegetables, etc) mercado; (selling clothes, etc) mercadillo; (marketplace) plaza: I always go to the market on Saturdays siempre voy a la plaza los sábados. **2** (trade) mercado: the property market el mercado inmobiliario. LOC **to be on the market** estar en venta. COMP **market day** día m de mercado. ‖ **market garden** GB huerta. ‖ **market price** precio de mercado.

marketing ['mɑ:kɪtɪŋ] n marketing m, mercadotecnia.

marketplace ['mɑ:kɪtpleɪs] n mercado; (square) plaza.

marksman ['mɑ:ksmən] n tirador m.
ⓘ pl **marksmen** ['mɑ:ksmən].

marmalade ['mɑ:məleɪd] n mermelada (de cítricos).

✎ La palabra **marmalade** sólo se refiere a las mermeladas de cítricos y en especial a la de naranja. Las demás mermeladas se llaman **jam**.

maroon [məˈru:n] adj granate.
► n (color m) granate m.

marquee [mɑ:ˈki:] n (large tent) carpa.

marriage ['mærɪdʒ] n **1** (state, institution) matrimonio. **2** (act, wedding) boda, casamiento, enlace m matrimonial. LOC **to take SB in marriage** casarse con ALGN. COMP **marriage bureau** agencia matrimonial. ‖ **marriage certificate** certificado de matrimonio.

M

married ['mærɪd] *adj* **1** *(person, status)* casado,-a (to, con): *a married couple* un matrimonio. **2** *(life, bliss)* matrimonial, conyugal.

marrow ['mærəʊ] *n* **1** [also bone marrow] ANAT *(of bone)* tuétano, médula. *fig (inner meaning)* meollo. **2** [also vegetable marrow] GB calabacín *m* grande.

marry ['mærɪ] *vt* **1** *(take in marriage)* casarse con. **2** *(unite in marriage)* casar.
▶ *vi* **1** casarse. **2** *fig* unirse. LOC **to get married** casarse (to, con).
ⓘ *pt & pp* **married**, *ger* **marrying**.

Mars [mɑːz] *n* Marte *m*.

marsh [mɑːʃ] *n* **1** *(bog)* pantano. **2** *(area)* zona con pantanos, pantanal *m*.

marshal ['mɑːʃəl] *n* **1** MIL mariscal *m*. **2** *(at sports event, demonstration)* oficial *mf*, organizador,-ra.

martial ['mɑːʃəl] *adj* marcial.

Martian ['mɑːʃən] *n* marciano,-a.
▶ *adj* marciano,-a.

martyr ['mɑːtəʳ] *n* **1** mártir *mf*. **2** *fam* víctima (to, de).

martyrdom ['mɑːtədəm] *n* martirio.

marvel ['mɑːvəl] *n* **1** *(wonder)* maravilla: *it's a marvel no-one was hurt* es un milagro que no hubiera heridos. **2** *(person)* maravilla. LOC **to do marvels / work marvels** hacer maravillas.
▶ *vi* **1** *fml* maravillarse (at, con), asombrarse (at, de).
ⓘ *pt & pp* **marvelled** (US **marveled**), *ger* **marvelling** (US **marveling**).

marvellous ['mɑːvələs] *adj* maravilloso,-a, magnífico,-a, estupendo,-a.

marzipan ['mɑːzɪpæn] *n* mazapán *m*.

mascara [mæˈskɑːrə] *n* rímel *m*.

☒ Mascara no significa 'máscara', que se traduce por **mask**.

mascot ['mæskɒt] *n* mascota.

masculine ['mæskjəlɪn] *adj* masculino,-a.
▶ *n* LING masculino.

mash [mæʃ] *n* CULIN *fam* puré *m* de patatas.
▶ *vt* **1** *(beat, crush)* triturar (up, -), machacar (up, -). **2** CULIN *(potatoes)* hacer un puré de. COMP **mashed potatoes** puré *m* de patatas.

mask [mɑːsk] *n* *(gen)* máscara; *(disguise)* careta, carátula; *(around eyes)* antifaz *m*. COMP **diving mask** gafas *fpl* de bucear.
▶ *vt* *(gen)* enmascarar.

masked [mɑːskt] *adj* enmascarado,-a. COMP **masked ball** baile *m* de disfraces, baile *m* de máscaras.

masking tape ['mɑːskɪŋteɪp] *n* cinta adhesiva.

masochism ['mæsəkɪzəm] *n* masoquismo.

masochist ['mæsəkɪst] *n* masoquista.
▶ *adj* masoquista.

mason ['meɪsən] *n* *(builder)* albañil *m*.

mass [mæs] *n* **1** *(large quantity)* montón *m*, masa; *(of people)* masa, multitud *f*, muchedumbre *f*: *a mass of books* un montón de libros. **2** *(majority)* mayoría.
▶ *vi* *(crowd)* congregarse, reunirse en gran número.
▶ *vt* reunir.
▶ *adj* masivo,-a, multitudinario,-a, de masas: *there was a mass meeting* se celebró un mitin multitudinario. COMP **mass media** medios *mpl* de comunicación (de masas).
▶ *n pl* **masses** *fam* *(lots)* cantidad *f*, montones *mpl*, mogollón *m*.

Mass [mæs] *n* REL misa.

massage ['mæsɑːʒ] *n* masaje *m*.
▶ *vt* **1** *(person, body)* dar un masaje a; *(part of body)* dar un masaje en.

masseter ['mæsətəʳ] *n* masetero.

masseur [mæˈsɜːʳ] *n* masajista *m*.

masseuse [mæˈsɜːz] *n* masajista.

massif [mæˈsiːf] *n* macizo.

massive ['mæsɪv] *adj* **1** *(huge)* enorme, gigantesco. **2** *(solid, weighty)* sólido,-a, macizo,-a.

mast [mɑːst] *n* **1** MAR mástil *m*, palo. **2** *(transmitter)* torre *f*, poste *m*.

master ['mɑːstəʳ] *n* **1** *(of slave, servant, dog)* amo; *(of household)* señor *m*; *(owner)* dueño. **2** MAR *(of ship)* capitán *m*; *(of fishing boat)* patrón *m*. **3** GB *(teacher - infant school)* maestro, profesor *m*; *(- secondary)* profesor *m*. COMP **master bedroom** dormitorio principal. ‖ **master copy** original *m*.
▶ *n* **Master's (degree)** EDUC máster *m*.

▶ *adj (expert, skilled)* maestro,-a, experto,-a.

▶ *vt (learn - subject, skill)* llegar a dominar; *(- craft)* llegar a ser experto,-a en.

mastermind ['mɑːstəmaɪnd] *n (person)* cerebro, genio.

masterpiece ['mɑːstəpiːs] *n* obra maestra.

mastodon ['mæstədɒn] *n* mastodonte *m*.

masturbation [mæstə'beɪʃ°n] *n* masturbación *f*.

mat [mæt] *n* **1** *(rug)* alfombrilla; *(doormat)* felpudo. **2** *(rush mat)* estera; *(beach mat)* esterilla. **3** SP colchoneta.

match¹ [mætʃ] *n (light)* cerilla, fósforo.

match² [mætʃ] *n* **1** SP *(football, hockey, etc)* partido, encuentro. **2** *(equal)* igual *mf*: *when it comes to chess, she's no match for you* ella no puede competir contigo al ajedrez. **3** *(marriage)* casamiento, matrimonio. **4** *(clothes, colour, etc)* juego, combinación *f*.
ⓘ *pl* matches.

▶ *vt* **1** *(equal)* igualar: *nobody can match him* nadie lo iguala. **2** *(go well with)* hacer juego (con), combinar (con): *her shoes match her dress* los zapatos hacen juego con el vestido. **3** *(be like, correspond to)* corresponder a, ajustarse a.

▶ *vi* **1** *(go together)* hacer juego, combinar. **2** *(tally)* coincidir, concordar. **3** *(people)* llevarse bien, avenirse.

matchbox ['mætʃbɒks] *n* caja de cerillas.
ⓘ *pl* matchboxes.

matching ['mætʃɪŋ] *adj* que hace juego, a juego.

mate [meɪt] *n* **1** *(school friend, fellow worker, etc)* compañero,-a, colega *mf*; *(friend)* amigo,-a, colega *mf*, compinche *mf*. **2** *(assistant)* ayudante *mf*, aprendiz,-za. **3** ZOOL pareja; *(male)* macho; *(female)* hembra.

🖉 Mate entra también en la formación de palabras como classmate (compañero de clase), flatmate (persona con la que se comparte un piso), roommate (persona con la que se comparte una habitación) o teammate (compañero de equipo).

material [mə'tɪərɪəl] *n* **1** *(physical substance)* materia, material *m*: *raw material* materia prima; *building materials* materiales de construcción. **2** *(cloth)* tela, tejido.

▶ *adj* **1** *(physical)* material. **2** *(important)* importante.

materialism [mə'tɪərɪəlɪz°m] *n* materialismo.

maternity [mə'tɜːnɪtɪ] *n* maternidad *f*.

math [mæθ] *n fam* US mates *fpl*.

mathematical [mæθə'mætɪk°l] *adj* matemático,-a.

mathematician [mæθ°mə'tɪʃ°n] *n* matemático,-a.

mathematics [mæθ°'mætɪks] *n* matemáticas *fpl*.

maths [mæθs] *n fam* mates *fpl*.

mating ['meɪtɪŋ] *n* ZOOL acoplamiento, apareamiento. COMP **mating call** reclamo. | **mating season** época de celo.

matrix ['meɪtrɪks] *n* matriz *f*.
ⓘ *pl* matrixes o matrices ['meɪtrɪsiːz].

matter ['mætə'] *n* **1** *(affair, subject)* asunto, cuestión *f*: *it's a personal matter* es un asunto personal. **2** *(trouble, problem)* problema *m*: *what's the matter?* ¿qué pasa? **3** PHYS *(physical substance)* materia, sustancia. **4** *(type of substance, things of a particular kind)* materia. LOC **as a matter of fact** en realidad, de hecho. | **to be another matter** ser otra cosa.

▶ *vi (be important)* importar (to, a): *it doesn't matter* no importa, es igual, da igual. LOC **no matter** no importa: *no matter what* pase lo que pase; *no matter what I say* diga lo que diga.

matting ['mætɪŋ] *n* estera.

mattress ['mætrəs] *n* colchón *m*.
ⓘ *pl* mattresses.

mature [mə'tʃʊə'] *adj (gen)* maduro,-a.

▶ *vt* madurar.

▶ *vi & vt* madurar.

maturity [mə'tʃʊərətɪ] *n* madurez *f*.

Mauritania [mɒrɪ'teɪnɪə] *n* Mauritania.

Mauritanian [mɒrɪ'teɪnɪən] *adj* mauritano,-a.

▶ *n* mauritano,-a.

mausoleum [mɔːsə'lɪəm] *n* mausoleo.

mauve [məʊv] *adj* malva.

▶ *n* malva *m*.

M

maverick ['mævᵊrɪk] *n* inconformista *mf*, independiente *mf*.
▶ *adj* inconformista, independiente.

maxilla 'mæksɪlə] *n* maxilar *m*.
ⓘ *pl* maxillae.

maximum ['mæksɪməm] *adj* máximo,-a.
▶ *n* máximo, máximum *m*. LOC **to the maximum** al máximo.

May [meɪ] *n* mayo: *his birthday is on the twentieth of May* su cumpleaños es el veinte de mayo; *at the beginning/end of May* a principios/finales de mayo; *in the middle of May* a mediados de mayo; *last May* en mayo del año pasado; *next May* en mayo del año que viene.

may [meɪ] *aux* **1** *(possibility, probability)* poder, ser posible: *he may come* es posible que venga, puede que venga; *you may laugh, but I think it's serious* tú bien puedes reír, pero yo creo que es grave. **2** *(permission)* poder: *may I help you?* ¿en qué puedo servirle?; *may I go?* ¿puedo irme? **3** *(wish)* ojalá: *may it be so* ojalá sea así.

✎ Cuando **may** expresa una posibilidad se puede traducir por 'quizá', 'quizás', 'a lo mejor', 'tal vez' o 'puede que'; cuando se usa para pedir o conceder permiso se traduce sencillamente por 'poder'. Consulta también **might**.

maybe ['meɪbi:] *adv* quizá, quizás, tal vez: *maybe it'll rain* tal vez llueva; *maybe you're right* quizás tengas razón, a lo mejor tienes razón.

mayday ['meɪdeɪ] *n* señal *f* de socorro, S.O.S. *m*.

mayonnaise [meɪə'neɪz] *n* mayonesa, mahonesa.

mayor [meᵊr] *n* (*man*) alcalde *m*; (*woman*) alcaldesa.

mayoress ['meᵊres] *n* alcaldesa.

maze [meɪz] *n* laberinto.

me¹ [mi:] *n* MUS mi *m*.

me² [mi:] *pron* **1** *(as object of verb)* me: *follow me* sígueme; *give it to me* dámelo; *he looked at me* me miró. **2** *(after prep)* mí: *it's for me* es para mí; *are you talking to me?* ¿me lo dices a mí? **3** *(emphatic)* yo: *it's me!* ¡soy yo!; *it's me, David* soy David.

meadow ['medəʊ] *n* prado, pradera.

meal¹ [mi:l] *n* (*flour*) harina.

meal² [mi:l] *n* (*gen*) comida: *three meals a day* tres comidas al día. LOC **to have a meal 1** *(lunch)* comer. **2** *(supper)* cenar.

✎ **Meal** se refiere a cualquiera de las tres comidas principales que se toman a lo largo del día.

mealtime ['mi:ltaɪm] *n* hora de comer.

mean¹ [mi:n] *adj* **1** *(miserly, selfish - person)* mezquino,-a, tacaño,-a, agarrado, -a. **2** *(unkind)* malo,-a, antipático,-a; *(petty)* mezquino,-a; *(ashamed)* avergonzado,-a. **3** *fam (skilful, great)* excelente, de primera, genial. LOC **to be no mean** ser todo,-a un,-a: *she's no mean singer* es una cantante excelente.

mean² [mi:n] *vt* **1** *(signify, represent)* significar, querer decir; *(to be a sign of, indicate)* ser señal de, significar: *what does «mug» mean?* ¿qué significa «mug»?, ¿qué quiere decir «mug»? **2** *(have in mind)* pensar, tener la intención de: *she didn't mean to do it* lo hizo sin querer. **3** *(involve, entail)* suponer, implicar; *(have as result)* significar: *that means we can't go on holiday* eso significa que no podemos irnos de vacaciones. LOC **to be meant for 1** *(be intended for)* ser para. **2** *(be destined for)* estar dirigido,-a a, ir dirigido,-a a: *these shoes are meant for light walking* estos zapatos son para pasear.
ⓘ *pt & pp* **meant** [ment].

mean³ [mi:n] *adj (average)* medio,-a: *mean temperature* temperatura media.
▶ *n* **1** *(average)* promedio. **2** MATH media. **3** *(middle term)* término medio.

meander [mɪ'ændeᵊr] *vi* **1** *(river, etc)* serpentear. **2** *(person)* vagar, deambular, andar sin rumbo fijo. **3** *fig (conversation)* divagar.
▶ *n* (*of river, etc*) meandro.

meaning ['mi:nɪŋ] *n* **1** *(sense)* sentido, significado. *what's the meaning of «draft»?* ¿qué significa «draft»?, ¿qué quiere decir «draft»? **2** *(significance, importance)* sentido; *(purpose, intention)* intención *f*: *a glance full of meaning* una mirada llena de intención.

meaningless [ˈmiːnɪŋləs] *adj* **1** *(word, phrase, etc)* sin sentido. **2** *(futile)* sin sentido, inútil, vano,-a.

means [miːnz] *n (way, method)* medio, manera: *there's no means of escape* no hay escapatoria, no hay manera de escapar; *a means of transport* un medio de transporte.
▶ *n pl (resources)* medios *mpl* de vida, recursos *mpl*. LOC **a means to an end** un medio de conseguir un objetivo, un medio para lograr un fin. **by all means** naturalmente, por supuesto. **by means of** por medio de, mediante. **by no means / not by any means** de ninguna manera, de ningún modo. **to live beyond one's means** vivir por encima de sus posibilidades.
ⓘ *pl* means.

meant [mærɪˈhwɑːnə] *pp & pt* → **mean**.

meantime [ˈmiːntaɪm] *adv* mientras tanto, entretanto. LOC **in the meantime** mientras tanto.

meanwhile [ˈmiːnwaɪl] *adv* mientras tanto, entretanto.

measles [ˈmiːzᵊlz] *n* MED sarampión *m*.

measurable [ˈmeʒᵊrəbᵊl] *adj* mensurable.

measure [ˈmeʒəʳ] *n* **1** *(system)* medida: *liquid measure* medida para líquidos. **2** *(indicator)* indicador *m*: *it's a measure of her popularity* es un indicador de su popularidad. **3** *(ruler)* regla. **4** *(measured amount, unit)* medida. **5** *(amount, degree, extent)* grado, cantidad *f*: *some measure of happiness* cierta felicidad. **6** *(method, step, remedy)* medida, disposición *f*: *safety measures* medidas de seguridad. LOC **in large measure** en gran parte, en gran medida. **in some measure** hasta cierto punto, en cierta medida. **to take measures** tomar medidas, adoptar medidas.
▶ *vt* **1** *(area, object, etc)* medir. **2** *(person)* tomar las medidas de. **3** *fig (assess)* evaluar; *(consider carefully)* sopesar, pensar bien.
▶ *vi (be)* medir: *it measures 3 feet by 6 feet* mide 1 metro por 2 metros.

✖ Measure no significa 'mesura', que se traduce por moderation.

🌐 Tanto los británicos como los americanos utilizan un sistema de medidas diferente del sistema métrico decimal, que es el que empleamos nosotros. En la páginas centrales de este diccionario encontrarás las equivalencias entre estos dos sistemas de medición.

measurement [ˈmeʒəmənt] *n* **1** *(act)* medición *f*. **2** *(length, etc)* medida.

measuring [ˈmeʒᵊrɪŋ] *n (act)* medición *f*. COMP **measuring tape** cinta métrica, metro.

meat [miːt] *n* carne *f*: *I prefer meat to fish* me gusta más la carne que el pescado. COMP **cold meat / cooked meat** fiambre *m*.

meatball [ˈmiːtbɔːl] *n* albóndiga.

mechanic [məˈkænɪk] *n (person)* mecánico,-a.

mechanical [məˈkænɪkᵊl] *adj* mecánico,-a.

mechanics [məˈkænɪks] *n (science)* mecánica. COMP **the mechanics** *(working parts)* el mecanismo. *(processes)* el funcionamiento.

mechanism [ˈmekənɪzᵊm] *n* mecanismo.

medal [ˈmedᵊl] *n* medalla.

medallist [ˈmedəlɪst] *n* medalla *mf*, campeón,-ona.

media [ˈmiːdɪə] *n pl* **the media** los medios *mpl* de comunicación.

✎ Consulta también media.

mediaeval [medriˈiːvᵊl] *adj* medieval.

median [ˈmiːdɪən] *adj* MATH mediano,-a.
▶ *n* MATH *(line)* mediana; *(quantity)* valor *m* mediano.

mediator [ˈmiːdɪeɪtəʳ] *n* mediador,-ra.

medical [ˈmedɪkᵊl] *adj (treatment, care, examination)* médico,-a; *(book, student)* de medicina.
▶ *n fam (check-up)* chequeo, reconocimiento médico, revisión *f* médica.

medicinal [məˈdɪsɪnᵊl] *adj* medicinal.

medicine [ˈmedɪsᵊn] *n* **1** *(science)* medicina. **2** *(drugs, etc)* medicina, medicamento.

medieval [medriˈiːvᵊl] *adj* medieval.

mediocrity [miːdɪˈɒkrətɪ] *n* mediocridad *f*.

M

meditation [medɪˈteɪʃ(ə)n] *n* meditación *f*.

Mediterranean [medɪtəˈreɪnɪən] *adj* mediterráneo,-a.
▸ *n* the Mediterranean el Mediterráneo.

medium [ˈmiːdɪəm] *adj (average)* mediano,-a, regular, normal. ⎡COMP⎤ **medium wave** onda media.
▸ *n* **1** [*pl* media] *(means)* medio. **2** [*pl* media.] *(environment)* medio (ambiente). **3** [*pl* media] *(middle position)* punto medio, término medio. **4** [*pl* mediums] *(spiritualist)* médium *mf*.

medium-sized [ˈmiːdɪəmˈsaɪzd] *adj (thing)* de tamaño mediano.

meet [miːt] *vt* **1** *(by chance)* encontrar, encontrarse con: *she met an old friend* se encontró con un viejo amigo. **2** *(by arrangement)* reunirse con, quedar con; *(informally)* ver: *I'm meeting Rob tomorrow* he quedado con Rob para mañana. **3** *(meet for first time)* conocer: *I met him at a party* lo conocí en una fiesta. **4** *(collect)* ir a buscar, pasar a buscar; *(await arrival of)* esperar; *(receive)* ir a recibir: *he'll meet me at the station* me vendrá a buscar a la estación.
▸ *vi* **1** *(by chance)* encontrarse: *we'll meet again* nos volveremos a encontrar. **2** *(by arrangement)* reunirse, verse, quedar,; *(formally)* entrevistarse: *we arranged to meet on Saturday* quedamos para el sábado., **3** *(get acquainted)* conocerse: *I think we've already met* creo que ya nos conocemos.
① *pt & pp* met [met].
▸ *n* **1** SP encuentro.

meeting [ˈmiːtɪŋ] *n* **1** *(gen - prearranged)* reunión *f*; *(- formal)* entrevista; *(- date)* cita. **2** *(chance encounter)* encuentro. **3** *(of club, committee, etc)* reunión *f*; *(of assembly)* sesión *f*; *(of shareholders, creditors)* junta. **4** POL *(rally)* mitin *m*. ⎡COMP⎤ **meeting place** lugar *m* de encuentro, lugar *m* de reunión.

megabyte [ˈmegəbaɪt] *n* COMPUT megabyte *m*, megaocteto.

megalith [ˈmegəlɪθ] *n* megalito.

megaphone [ˈmegəfəʊn] *n* megáfono, altavoz *m*.

megawatt [ˈmegəwɒt] *n* megavatio.

melamine [ˈmeləmiːn] *n* melamina.

melodramatic [melədrəˈmætɪk] *adj* melodramático,-a.

melody [ˈmelədɪ] *n* melodía.
① *pl* melodies.

melon [ˈmelən] *n (honeydew, etc)* melón *m*; *(watermelon)* sandía.

melt [melt] *vt* **1** *(ice, snow, butter, etc)* derretir. **2** *(metal)* fundir (**down**, -). **3** *(sugar, chemical)* disolver. **4** *fig* ablandar.
▸ *vi* **1** *(ice, snow)* derretirse (**away**, -). **2** *(metal)* fundirse. **3** *(sugar, chemical)* disolverse.
◆ **to melt away** *vi* **1** *(money, crowd, person)* desaparecer. **2** *fig (confidence, etc)* desvanecerse, esfumarse; *(anger)* disiparse, desaparecer.

melting [ˈmeltɪŋ] *n (of metal)* fundición *f*; *(of snow)* derretimiento. ⎡COMP⎤ **melting point** punto de fusión. **‖ melting pot** crisol *m*.

member [ˈmembər] *n* **1** *(gen)* miembro *mf*; *(of club)* socio,-a; *(of union, party)* afiliado,-a: *the youngest member of the family* el miembro más joven de la familia. **2** POL *(of Parliament)* diputado,-a; *(of European Parliament)* eurodiputado,-a. **3** ANAT miembro.
▸ *adj (country, state)* miembro,-a.

membership [ˈmembəʃɪp] *n* **1** *(of club - state)* calidad *f* de socio,-a, pertenencia; *(- entry)* ingreso. **2** *(of political party, union - state)* afiliación *f*; *(- entry)* ingreso. **3** *(members - of club)* miembros *mpl*, socios *mpl*; *(- of political party)* afiliados *mpl*.

membrane [ˈmembreɪn] *n* membrana

memo [ˈmeməʊ] *n* **1** *(official)* memorándum *m*. **2** *(personal note)* nota, apunte *m*. ⎡COMP⎤ **memo pad** bloc *m* de notas.
① *pl* memos.

memorandum [meməˈrændəm] *n* **1** *(official note)* memorándum *m*, memorando. **2** *(personal note)* nota, apunte *m*.
① *pl* memorandums o memoranda [meməˈrændə].

memorial [məˈmɔːrɪəl] *adj (plaque, etc)* conmemorativo,-a.
▸ *n (monument)* monumento conmemorativo; *(ceremony)* homenaje *m*.

🌐 El **Memorial Day** es una fiesta que se celebra en Estados Unidos el último lunes de mayo en honor de todos los soldados muertos en las distintas guerras en las que ha participado el país americano.

memorize ['meməraɪz] vt memorizar, aprender de memoria.

memory ['meməri] n **1** *(ability, computers)* memoria: *she's got a good memory for names* tiene buena memoria para los nombres. **2** *(recollection)* recuerdo. [LOC] **to lose one's memory** perder la memoria. ▌ **within living memory** que se recuerde.
ⓘ *pl* **memories**.

men [men] *pl* → **man**.

menace ['menəs] n **1** *(threat)* amenaza (**to**, para); *(danger)* peligro (**to**, para). **2** *fam (nuisance - person)* pesado,-a; *(- thing)* lata, molestia.
▸ vt amenazar (**with**, de).

mend [mend] vt **1** *(repair - gen)* reparar, arreglar; *(sew)* coser; *(patch)* remendar; *(darn)* zurcir: *can you mend my watch?* ¿me puedes arreglar el reloj? **2** *(improve)* mejorar. [LOC] **to be on the mend** ir mejorando.
▸ n *(patch)* remiendo; *(darn)* zurcido.

meninges [me'nɪdʒəs] n pl MED meninges *fpl*.

meningitis [menɪn'dʒaɪtəs] n MED meningitis f.

meniscus [mɪ'nɪskəs] n menisco.
ⓘ *pl* **meniscuses** o **menisci** [mɪ'nɪskaɪ].

menopause ['menəupɔːz] n menopausia.

menstrual ['menstruəl] adj menstrual. [COMP] **menstrual cycle** ciclo menstrual. ▌ **menstrual period** regla, período.

menstruation [menstru'eɪʃ°n] n menstruación f, regla.

menswear ['menzweər] n ropa de caballero, ropa de hombres.

mental ['ment°l] adj mental: *mental effort* esfuerzo mental; *mental health* salud mental; *mental arithmetic* cálculo mental. [COMP] **mental age** edad f mental. ▌ **mental handicap** disminución f psíquica. ▌

mental home / mental hospital *(hospital m)* psiquiátrico.

mentality [men'tæləti] n mentalidad f.
ⓘ *pl* **mentalities**.

mention ['menʃ°n] n mención f: *she made no mention of your visit* no mencionó tu visita.
▸ vt mencionar, hacer mención de, aludir a: *he never mentioned the money* no mencionó el dinero. [LOC] **don't mention it!** ¡de nada!, ¡no hay de qué!

menu ['menjuː] n **1** carta, menú m. **2** COMPUT menú m. [COMP] **menu bar** barra de menús.
ⓘ *pl* **menus**.

meow [mɪ'au] n maullido, miau m.
▸ vi maullar.

mercenary ['mɜːs°nərɪ] adj mercenario,-a.
▸ n mercenario,-a.
ⓘ *pl* **mercenaries**.

merchandise ['mɜːtʃ°ndaɪz] n mercancías *fpl*, géneros *mpl*.
▸ vt *(sell)* vender, poner en venta; *(promote)* promocionar.

merchant ['mɜːtʃ°nt] n *(trader)* comerciante *mf*; *(dealer, businessperson)* negociante *mf*. [COMP] **merchant bank** banco comercial. ▌ **merchant navy** marina mercante.

Mercury¹ ['mɜːkjərɪ] n *(planet)* Mercurio.

mercury² ['mɜːkjərɪ] n *(metal)* mercurio.

mercy ['mɜːsɪ] n **1** *(compassion)* misericordia, clemencia, piedad f: *have mercy upon me!* ¡tenga piedad de mí! **2** *fam (good fortune)* suerte f, milagro; *(blessing)* bendición f.
[LOC] **to be at the mercy of** SB/STH estar a la merced de ALGN/ALGO.
ⓘ *pl* **mercies**.
▸ adj de ayuda, de socorro. [COMP] **mercy killing** eutanasia.

mere [mɪər] adj mero,-a, simple, puro,-a.
▸ adj **merest** *(slightest)* el/la más mínimo,-a.

merge [mɜːdʒ] vt *(combine - gen)* unir (**with**, a), combinar (**with**, con); *(- road)* empalmar (**into**, con); *(- river)* desem-

M

bocar (into, en); (- firms, businesses) fusionar.

meridional [məˈrɪdɪənᵊl] adj meridional.

meringue [məˈræŋ] n merengue m.

merit [ˈmerɪt] n mérito.
▶ vt (deserve) merecer.

mermaid [ˈmɜːmeɪd] n sirena.

merry [ˈmerɪ] adj 1 (cheerful) alegre; (amusing) divertido,-a, gracioso,-a. 2 fam (slightly drunk) alegre, achispado, -a. LOC **merry Christmas!** ¡felices Navidades!
ⓘ comp merrier, superl merriest.

merry-go-round [ˈmerɪɡəʊraʊnd] n tiovivo, caballitos mpl.

mess [mes] n 1 (untidy state) desorden m, revoltijo: your room is a complete mess! ¡tu habitación está toda desordenada! 2 (confusion, mix-up) confusión f, lío, follón m; (person, thing) desastre m: what a mess! ¡vaya lío!
▶ vt (untidy) desordenar; (dirty) ensuciar.
◆ **to mess about / mess around** vi 1 (idle) gandulear; (kill time) pasar el tiempo; (potter about) entretenerse. 2 (act the fool) hacer el primo, tontear.
◆ **to mess up** vt sep 1 fam (untidy) desordenar; (dirty) ensuciar. 2 (spoil) estropear, echar a perder.

message [ˈmesɪdʒ] n 1 (communication) recado, mensaje m: could you give her a message? ¿podrías darle un recado? 2 (of story, film, etc) mensaje m. LOC **to get the message** (understand) entender, darse cuenta.

messenger [ˈmesɪndʒəʳ] n mensajero,-a. COMP **messenger boy** recadero.

Messiah [məˈsaɪə] n REL Mesías m.

messy [ˈmesɪ] adj 1 (untidy) desordenado,-a, en desorden; (- dirty) sucio,-a. 2 (confused) complicado,-a, enredado,-a; (awkward) difícil; (unpleasant) desagradable.
ⓘ comp messier, superl messiest.

met [met] pp & pt → **meet**.

metabolism [məˈtæbəlɪzᵊm] n metabolismo.

metal [ˈmetᵊl] n metal m.
▶ adj metálico,-a, de metal.

metallic [məˈtælɪk] adj metálico,-a. COMP **metallic paint** pintura metalizada.

metallurgy [məˈtælədʒɪ] n metalurgia.

metamorphic [metəˈmɔːfɪk] adj metamórfico,-a

metamorphosis [metəˈmɔːfəsɪs] n metamorfosis f.
ⓘ pl **metamorphoses** [metəˈmɔːfəsiːz].

metaphor [ˈmetəfɔːʳ] n metáfora.

metaphysics [metəˈfɪzɪks] n metafísica.

metatarsus [metəˈtɑːsəs] n metatarso.
ⓘ pl **metatarsi** [metəˈtɑːsaɪ].

meteorite [ˈmiːtɪəraɪt] n meteorito.

meteorological [miːtɪərəˈlɒdʒɪkᵊl] adj meteorológico,-a.

meteorologist [miːtɪəˈrɒlədʒɪst] n meteorólogo,-a.

meteorology [miːtɪəˈrɒlədʒɪ] n meteorología.

meter [ˈmiːtəʳ] n 1 US → **metre**. 2 contador m.
▶ vt medir.

methacrylate [meθˈækrɪleɪt] n metacrilato.

methane [ˈmiːθeɪn] n metano.

method [ˈmeθəd] n 1 (manner, way) método, forma. 2 (system, order) sistema m, orden m, lógica.

metonymy [meˈtɒnɪmɪ] n metonimia

metre [ˈmiːtəʳ] n 1 (measure) metro. 2 (in poetry) metro. COMP **cubic metre** metro cúbico.

metric [ˈmetrɪk] adj métrico,-a. COMP **metric system** sistema métrico. I **metric ton** tonelada métrica.

metropolis [məˈtrɒpəlɪs] n metrópoli f, metrópolis f.
ⓘ pl **metropolises**.

metropolitan [metrəˈpɒlɪtᵊn] adj metropolitano,-a.

mew [mjuː] vi maullar.
▶ n maullido.

Mexican [ˈmeksɪkᵊn] adj mejicano,-a.
▶ n mejicano,-a.

Mexico [ˈmeksɪləʊ] n Méjico.

mi [miː] n MUS mi m.

miaow [miːˈaʊ] n maullido.
▶ vi maullar.

mica [ˈmaɪkə] *n* mica.

mice [maɪs] *pl* → **mouse**.

micro [ˈmaɪkrəʊ] *n fam* microordenador *m*.
ⓘ *pl* micros.

microbe [ˈmaɪkrəʊb] *n* microbio.

microbiology [maɪkrəʊbaɪˈɒlədʒɪ] *n* microbiología.

microchip [ˈmaɪkəʊtʃɪp] *n* microchip *m*.

microclimate [ˈmaɪkrəʊklaɪmət] *n* microclima *mf*.

microfilm [ˈmaɪkrəʊfɪlm] *n* microfilme *m*.

micron [ˈmaɪkrɒn] *n* micra.

microphone [ˈmaɪkrəfəʊn] *n* micrófono.

microprocessor [maɪkrəʊˈprəʊsesəʳ] *n* microprocesador *m*.

microscope [ˈmaɪkrəskəʊp] *n* microscopio.

microscopic [maɪkrəˈskɒpɪk] *adj* microscópico,-a.

microwave [ˈmaɪkrəweɪv] *n* microonda. COMP microwave oven horno de microondas, microondas *m inv*.
▶ *vt* cocinar en el microondas.

midday [mɪdˈdeɪ] *n* mediodía *m*.
▶ *adj* de mediodía. LOC at midday al mediodía.

middle [ˈmɪdəl] *adj (central)* de en medio, central; *(medium)* mediano,-a, medio,-a: *he's the middle son* él es el hijo mediano. LOC in the middle of nowhere en el quinto pino. COMP middle age mediana edad *f*. I middle class clase *f* media. I middle finger dedo corazón. I the Middle Ages la Edad Media.
▶ *n* 1 *(centre)* medio, centro: *there's a pond in the middle of the garden* hay un estanque en medio del jardín. 2 *(halfway point of period, activity)* mitad *f*: *in the middle of a storm* en medio de una tormenta. 3 *fam (waist)* cintura.

✎ El apellido se traduce por **surname** o **family name** y el nombre de pila, por **Christian name** o **first name**. Casi todo el mundo tiene dos **Christian names**, aunque se utilice sólo uno. Ese segundo nombre de pila es el **middle name**, que se suele escribir sólo con la inicial.

middle-aged [mɪdəlˈeɪdʒd] *adj* de mediana edad.

middle-class [mɪdəlˈklɑːs] *adj* de la clase media.

middleman [ˈmɪdəlmən] *n* intermediario.
ⓘ *pl* middlemen [ˈmɪdəlmen].

middleweight [ˈmɪdəlweɪt] *n (boxing)* peso medio.

midnight [ˈmɪdnaɪt] *n* medianoche *f*: *we got home at midnight* llegamos a casa a medianoche.

midwife [ˈmɪdwaɪf] *n* comadrona, partera, matrona.
ⓘ *pl* midwives [ˈmɪdwaɪvz].

might [maɪt] *aux* 1 *(possibility)* poder: *it might rain* podría llover. 2 *(in suggestions or requests)* poder: *you might try the hardware shop* podrías probar en la ferretería. 3 *(permission)* poder: *he asked if he might come in* pidió permiso para entrar. LOC I might have known! ¡debí imaginármelo!, ¡típico! I might (just) as well más vale que.

✎ Como expresa una posibilidad también se puede traducir por 'quizá', 'quizás', 'a lo mejor', 'tal vez' o 'puede que'. Consulta también **may**.

mighty [ˈmaɪtɪ] *adj* 1 *(very strong)* muy fuerte; *(powerful)* potente. 2 *(great, imposing)* enorme.
ⓘ *comp* mightier, *superl* mightiest.
▶ *adv* US *fam (very)* muy.

migraine [ˈmaɪgreɪn] *n* jaqueca, migraña.

migrant [ˈmaɪgrənt] *adj* migratorio,-a.
▶ *n (person)* emigrante *mf*; *(bird)* ave *f* migratoria.

migrate [maɪˈgreɪt] *vi* migrar.

migration [maɪˈgreɪʃən] *n* migración *f*.

migratory [ˈmaɪgrətərɪ] *adj* migratorio,-a.

mike [maɪk] *n fam* micro.

mild [maɪld] *adj* 1 *(person, character)* apacible, afable, dulce. 2 *(climate, weather)* benigno,-a, templado,-a, suave, blando,-a; *(soap, detergent)* suave. 3 *(protest, attempt)* ligero,-a; *(punishment, fever)* leve;

M

(illness, attack) ligero,-a, leve; *(criticism, rebuke)* suave, leve.

mile [maɪl] *n* milla (1,6 kms).
▸ *n pl* miles *(much)* mucho, muchísimo: *I'm miles better* estoy mucho mejor; *it's miles away* está muy lejos.

mileage ['maɪlɪdʒ] *n* **1** AUTO *(miles travelled by a car)* ≈ kilómetros *mpl*, kilometraje *m*. **2** *fam fig (benefit, advantage, use)* jugo, partido.

mileometer [maɪ'lɒmɪtəʳ] *n* AUTO cuentakilómetros *m*.

milestone ['maɪlstəʊn] *n* **1** hito, mojón *m*. **2** *fig* hito.

militant ['mɪlɪtənt] *adj* POL militante.
▸ *n* POL militante *mf*.

military ['mɪlɪtʰrɪ] *adj* militar.
▸ *n* **the military** los militares, las fuerzas armadas.

milk [mɪlk] *n (gen)* leche *f*. COMP **milk shake** batido. ‖ **milk tooth** diente *m* de leche.
▸ *adj (bottle, production)* de leche; *(product)* lácteo,-a.

milkman ['mɪlkmən] *n* lechero, repartidor *m* de la leche.
① *pl* **milkmen** ['mɪlkmen].

milky ['mɪlkɪ] *adj* **1** *(liquid, jewel)* turbio,-a. **2** *(coffee, tea)* con mucha leche; *(substance)* lechoso,-a. **3** *(colour)* pálido,-a. COMP **Milky Way** Vía Láctea.
① *comp* **milkier**, *superl* **milkiest**.

mill [mɪl] *n* **1** *(machinery)* molino. **2** *(for coffee, pepper, etc)* molinillo. **3** *(factory)* fábrica.
▸ *vt (crush, grind)* moler.

millennium [mɪ'lenɪəm] *n* milenio, milenario.
① *pl* **millenniums** o **millennia** [mɪ'lenɪə].

millet ['mɪlɪt] *n* mijo.

millimetre ['mɪlɪmiːtəʳ] *n* milímetro.

million ['mɪljən] *n* millón *m*: *one million dollars* un millón de dólares.
▸ *n pl* **millions** *fam (lots)* millones *mpl*.

millionaire [mɪljə'neəʳ] *n* millonario,-a.

millionth ['mɪljənθ] *adj* millonésimo,-a.
▸ *n* millonésima parte, millonésimo.

millipede ['mɪlɪpiːd] *n* milpiés *m inv*.

millstone ['mɪlstəʊn] *n* muela, rueda de molino.

mime [maɪm] *n* **1** *(art)* mimo. **2** *(performance)* pantomima, representación de mimo.
▸ *vt (express by mime)* expresar haciendo mímica.

mimic ['mɪmɪk] *n* imitador,-ra.
▸ *vt (copy)* imitar, remedar.
① *pt & pp* **mimicked**, *ger* **mimicking**.

mince [mɪns] *n* GB *(meat)* carne *f* picada.
COMP **mince pie** pastelito.
▸ *vt (chop, cut)* picar.

mind [maɪnd] *n* **1** *(intellect)* mente *f*. *(mentality)* mentalidad *f*. **3** *(brain, thoughts)* cabeza, cerebro: *her mind was very confused* estaba confusa.
▸ *vt* **1** *(heed, pay attention to)* hacer caso de; *(care about)* importar, preocuparse: *mind what people say* me importa lo que dice la gente. **2** *(be careful with)* tener cuidado con: *mind the step!* ¡cuidado con el escalón! **3** *(look after - child)* cuidar, cuidar de; *(- house)* vigilar; *(- shop)* atender; *(- seat, place)* guardar. **4** *(object to, be troubled by)* tener inconveniente en, importar: *I don't mind staying* no tengo inconveniente en quedarme. **5** *(fancy, quite like)* venir bien: *I wouldn't mind a coffee* me vendría bien un café.
▸ *vi* **1** *(be careful)* tener cuidado: *mind (out)!* ¡cuidado!, ¡ojo! **2** *(object to)* importar, molestar: *do you mind if I open the window?* ¿le importa que abra la ventana?
LOC **never mind 1** *(it doesn't matter)* no importa, da igual. **2** *(don't worry)* no te preocupes. **3** *(let alone)* ni hablar de. ‖ **to be out of one's mind** estar loco,-a. ‖ **to change one's mind** cambiar de opinión, cambiar de parecer. ‖ **to make up one's mind** decidirse. ‖ **to set mind** en la opinión de ALGN.

mine¹ [maɪn] *n (gen)* mina.
▸ *vt* **1** *(coal, gold, etc)* extraer; *(area)* explotar. **2** MIL sembrar minas en, minar.
▸ *vi* explotar una mina.

mine² [maɪn] *pron* (el) mío, (la) mía, (los) míos, (las) mías, lo mío: *he that's mine!* ¡ey! ¡eso es mío!; *a friend of mine* un/una amigo,-a mío,-a.

miner ['maɪnər] *n* minero,-a.

mineral ['mɪnⁿrəl] *adj* mineral.
▶ *n* mineral *m*. COMP **mineral water** agua mineral. ‖ **mineral oil** GB petróleo.

miniature ['mɪnɪtʃər] *n* miniatura.
▶ *adj* (en) miniatura.

minibus ['mɪnɪbʌs] *n* microbús *m*.
ⓘ *pl* minibuses.

minicab ['mɪnɪkæb] *n* GB taxi *m*.

minicomputer [mɪnɪkəm'pjuːtər] *n* microordenador *m*.

minimal ['mɪnɪmⁿl] *adj* mínimo,-a.

minimum ['mɪnɪməm] *adj* mínimo,-a.
▶ *n* mínimo: *a minimum of 20 people* un mínimo de 20 personas.

mining ['maɪnɪŋ] *n* minería, explotación *f* de minas: *coal mining* extracción de carbón.
▶ *adj* (area, town, industry) minero,-a.
COMP **mining engineer** ingeniero,-a de minas.

miniseries [mɪnɪ'sɪəriːz] *n* TV miniserie *f*.

miniskirt ['mɪnɪskɜːt] *n* minifalda.

minister ['mɪnɪstər] *n* **1** (gen) ministro, -a (for, de). **2** GB (priest) pastor,-ra.
▶ *vi* atender (to, a), cuidar (to, a).

ministry ['mɪnɪstri] *n* (gen) ministerio.
▶ *n* **the ministry**
ⓘ *pl* ministries. GB (priesthood) el clero.

minor ['maɪnər] *adj* **1** (unimportant) menor; (secondary) secundario,-a. **2** MUS menor.
▶ *n* JUR menor *mf*.

minority [maɪ'nɒrɪti] *n* **1** minoría. **2** JUR minoría de edad.
ⓘ *pl* minorities.
▶ *adj* minoritario,-a.

mint¹ [mɪnt] *adj* FIN (place) casa de la moneda.
▶ *vt* (coins, words) acuñar.

mint² [mɪnt] *n* **1** BOT menta. **2** (sweet) caramelo de menta.

minus ['maɪnəs] *prep* **1** MATH menos: *four minus three equals one* cuatro menos tres es igual a uno. **2** METEOR bajo cero: *minus five degrees* cinco grados bajo cero.
▶ *adj* negativo,-a. COMP **minus sign** signo de menos *m*.

▶ *n* **1** MATH menos *m*. **2** (disadvantage) desventaja *m*.

minuscule ['mɪnəskjuːl] *adj* minúsculo.

minute¹ [maɪ'njuːt] *adj* (tiny) diminuto,-a, minúsculo,-a.

minute² ['mɪnɪt] *n* **1** (of time) minuto: *it's a five minute walk* es un paseo de cinco minutos. **2** fam (moment) momento; (instant) instante *m*: *I'll be back in a minute* ahora vuelvo, vuelvo en un momento.
▶ *n pl* **minutes** (notes) acta *f sing*, actas *fpl*. LOC **(at) any minute now** en cualquier momento. ‖ **at the last minute** en el último momento, a última hora.

miracle ['mɪrəkⁿl] *n* (gen) milagro.

mirage [mɪ'rɑːʒ] *n* espejismo.

mirror ['mɪrər] *n* (gen) espejo: *stop looking at yourself in the mirror* deja de mirarte en el espejo. COMP **driving mirror** espejo (retrovisor).
▶ *vt* reflejar.

misbehave [mɪsbɪ'heɪv] *vi* portarse mal, comportarse mal.

miscarriage [mɪs'kærɪdʒ] *n* MED aborto (espontáneo).

miscarry [mɪs'kæri] *vi* **1** MED abortar (espontáneamente), tener un aborto. **2** (plans, etc) fracasar, frustrarse, malograrse.
ⓘ *pt & pp* miscarried, ger miscarrying.

miscellaneous [mɪsɪ'leɪnɪəs] *adj* (mixed, varied) variado,-a, vario,-a, diverso,-a, misceláneo,-a.

mischief ['mɪstʃɪf] *n* **1** (naughtiness) travesura, diablura: *I know you're up to some mischief* sé que estás haciendo alguna travesura. **2** fml daño, mal *m*.

miserable ['mɪzⁿrəbⁿl] *adj* **1** (person - unhappy) abatido,-a, triste, deprimido, -a; (- bad-tempered) antipático,-a. **2** (place, etc) deprimente, triste; (weather) horrible. **3** (paltry) miserable, mezquino,-a; (pathetic) lamentable.

misery ['mɪzəri] *n* **1** (wretchedness, unhappiness) desgracia, desdicha, tristeza. **2** (suffering) sufrimiento, dolor *m*, suplicio. **3** (poverty) pobreza, miseria.
ⓘ *pl* miseries.

M

misfortune [mɪsˈfɔːtʃ⁽ə⁾n] *n* infortunio, desgracia, mala fortuna.

miss¹ [mɪs] *n* señorita.

✎ Miss se emplea delante del apellido de una mujer soltera.

miss² [mɪs] *n (catch, hit, etc)* fallo; *(shot)* tiro errado.
► *vt* **1** *(not to hit, score, etc)* fallar: *he missed a penalty* falló un penalti. **2** *(not catch)* perder: *I missed the bus* perdí el autobús. **3** *(not experience)* perderse: *don't miss this concert!* ¡no te pierdas este concierto! **4** *(not see)* perderse: *she doesn't miss anything* no se le escapa nada. **5** *(not attend - meeting, etc)* no asistir a; *(- class, work)* faltar a. **7** *(long for - person)* echar de menos; *(- place)* añorar: *she misses her family* echa de menos a su familia.
► *vi* **1** *(catch, kick, etc)* fallar; *(shot)* errar el tiro. **2** *(engine)* fallar. **3** *(fail)* fallar.
◆ **to miss out** *vt sep (omit, fail to include)* saltarse, omitir; *(overlook, disregard)* pasar por alto, dejarse.
► *vi (lose opportunity)* dejar pasar, perderse.

missile [ˈmɪsaɪl] *n* **1** *(explosive weapon)* misil *m*. **2** *(object thrown)* proyectil *m*.

missing [ˈmɪsɪŋ] *adj* **1** *(object - lost)* perdido,-a, extraviado,-a. **2** *(person - disappeared)* desaparecido,-a; *(- absent)* ausente: *she's been missing for a week* hace una semana que desapareció. ⃞ to be missing faltar. ⃞ missing person desaparecido,-a.

mission [ˈmɪʃ⁽ə⁾n] *n* misión *f*.

missionary [ˈmɪʃ⁽ə⁾nərɪ] *n* misionero,-a.
ⓘ *pl* missionaries.

misspell [mɪsˈspel] *vt* escribir mal.
ⓘ *pt & pp* misspelled o misspelt [mɪsˈspelt], *ger* misspelling.

misspend [mɪsˈspend] *vt* malgastar.
ⓘ *pt & pp* misspent [mɪsˈspent].

mist [mɪst] *n* **1** *(gen)* neblina; *(sea)* bruma; *(haze)* calima. **2** *(on window, mirror, etc)* vaho.

mistake [mɪsˈteɪk] *n (error)* equivocación *f*, error *m*; *(in test)* falta; *(oversight)* descuido: *there must be some mistake* debe haber algún error. ⃞ by mistake 1

(in error) por error. **2** *(unintentionally)* sin querer. ▌ to make a mistake equivocarse, cometer un error.
► *vt* **1** *(misunderstand)* entender mal. **2** *(confuse)* confundir (for, con).
ⓘ *pt* mistook [mɪsˈtʊk], *pp* mistaken [mɪsˈteɪk⁽ə⁾n].

mistaken [mɪsˈteɪk⁽ə⁾n] *pp* → mistake.
► *adj (wrong, incorrect)* equivocado,-a, erróneo,-a. ⃞ to be mistaken equivocarse.

mister [ˈmɪstə⁽ʳ⁾] *n* señor *m*.

mistletoe [ˈmɪs⁽ə⁾ltəʊ] *n* muérdago.

mistook [mɪsˈtʊk] *pt* → mistake.

mistreat [mɪsˈtriːt] *vt* maltratar, tratar mal.

mistress [ˈmɪstrəs] *n* **1** *(owner - gen)* dueña, ama, señora; *(of dog)* ama, dueña. **2** *(lover)* amante *f*. **3** GB maestra, profesora.

mistrust [mɪsˈtrʌst] *n* desconfianza, recelo.
► *vt* desconfiar de.

misty [ˈmɪstɪ] *adj* **1** METEOR neblinoso,-a: *it's misty* hay neblina. **2** *(window, glasses, etc)* empañado,-a.
ⓘ *comp* mistier, *superl* mistiest.

misunderstand [mɪsʌndəˈstænd] *vt (gen)* entender mal; *(misinterpret)* malinterpretar.
ⓘ *pt & pp* misunderstood [mɪsʌndəˈstʊd].

misunderstanding [mɪsʌndəˈstændɪŋ] *n* malentendido (about, sobre).

mite [maɪt] *n (insect)* ácaro, acárido.

miter [ˈmaɪtə⁽ʳ⁾] *n* US → mitre.

mitigating [ˈmɪtɪɡeɪtɪŋ] *adj* mitigador,-ra. ⃞ mitigating circumstance JUR circunstancias *fpl* atenuantes.

mitre [ˈmaɪtə⁽ʳ⁾] *n* **1** REL mitra. **2** TECH inglete *m*.

mitten [ˈmɪt⁽ə⁾n] *n (fingers covered)* manopla; *(fingers exposed)* mitón *m*.

mix [mɪks] *n* **1** *(mixture - gen)* mezcla. CULIN preparado.
► *vt* **1** *(combine)* mezclar, combinar: *mix the sugar with the butter* mezclar el azúcar con la mantequilla. **2** *(make, prepare - plaster, cement)* amasar; *(- cocktail, salad, medicine)* preparar.

▶ vi **1** (substances) mezclarse. **2** (clothes, colours, food) combinar bien, ir bien juntos,-as. **3** (people - come together) mezclarse con la gente; (- get on) llevarse bien (with, con).

◆ **to mix up** vt sep **1** (ingredients) mezclar bien. **2** (confuse) confundir. **3** (mess up, put in disorder) desordenar, revolver.

mixed [mɪkst] adj **1** (of different kinds) variado,-a: mixed biscuits galletas surtidas. **2** (ambivalent) desigual. **3** (for both sexes) mixto,-a.

mixer ['mɪksər] n (for food) batidora.

mixture ['mɪkstʃər] n (gen) mezcla.

mix-up ['mɪksʌp] n fam (confusion) lío, confusión f; (misunderstanding) malentendido.

mm ['mɪlɪmiːtər] symb (millimetre) milímetro; (abbreviation) mm.

moan [məʊn] n **1** (groan) gemido, quejido. **2** (complaint) queja, protesta.
▶ vi **1** (groan) gemir. **2** (complain) quejarse (about, de), protestar (about, por).

moaner ['məʊnər] n quejica m & f.

moat [məʊt] n foso.

mobile ['məʊbaɪl] adj (object, troops, etc) móvil, movible. COMP **mobile home** caravana, remolque m. ▮ **mobile phone** teléfono móvil.
▶ n (hanging ornament) móvil m.

mock [mɒk] adj **1** (object) de imitación. **2** (feeling) fingido,-a, simulado,-a; (modesty) falso,-a.
▶ vt (laugh at, make fun of) burlarse de, mofarse de.
▶ vi burlarse (at, de).

mockery ['mɒkərɪ] n **1** (ridicule) burla, mofa. **2** (farce) farsa; (travesty) parodia. LOC **to make a mockery of** STH poner ALGO en ridículo.

modal ['məʊdl] adj modal. COMP **modal auxiliary** auxiliar m modal. ▮ **modal verb** verbo modal.

model ['mɒdəl] n modelo.
▶ adj **1** (miniature) en miniatura, a escala; (toy) de juguete. **2** (exemplary) ejemplar; (ideal) modelo.
▶ vt (clay, etc) modelar.
ⓘ pt & pp modelled (US modeled), ger modelling (US modeling).

modem ['məʊdem] n COMPUT modem m.

moderate ['mɒdərət] adj **1** (average) mediano,-a, regular: moderate size tamaño mediano. **2** (not extreme) moderado,-a; (reasonable) razonable. **3** (talent, ability, performance) mediocre, regular.
▶ vt moderar.
▶ vi moderarse.

moderation [mɒdəˈreɪʃən] n moderación f.

modern ['mɒdən] adj **1** (up-to-date) moderno,-a. **2** (history, literature, etc) contemporáneo,-a. COMP **modern language** lengua moderna.

modernize ['mɒdənaɪz] vt modernizar.
▶ vi modernizarse.

modest ['mɒdɪst] adj **1** (gen) modesto,-a, humilde. **2** (improvement, increase) modesto,-a; (- price) módico,-a.

modesty ['mɒdɪstɪ] n **1** (humility) modestia, humildad f. **2** (chastity) pudor m, recato.

modify ['mɒdɪfaɪ] vt (change) modificar.
ⓘ pt & pp modified, ger modifying.

module ['mɒdjuːl] n módulo.

moist [mɔɪst] adj (damp) húmedo,-a; (slightly wet) ligeramente mojado,-a: a moist sponge cake un bizcocho tierno.

moisture ['mɔɪstʃər] n humedad f.

mold [məʊld] n → mould.

mole¹ [məʊl] n (on skin) lunar m.

mole² [məʊl] n **1** ZOOL topo. **2** fam (spy) topo mf, espía mf.

molecular [məˈlekjələr] adj molecular.

molecule ['mɒlɪkjuːl] n molécula.

molest [məˈlest] vt **1** (attack - person) atacar, asaltar; (- dog) perseguir, atacar. **2** (sexually) abusar sexualmente.

✖ To molest no significa 'molestar', que se traduce por to bother.

mollusc ['mɒləsk] n molusco.

molt [məʊlt] n US → moult.

mom [mɒm] n US fam mamá f.

moment ['məʊmənt] n (instant) momento, instante m: just a moment un momentito; I didn't believe that story for a moment no me creí ese cuento ni por un momento. LOC **at any moment** de un

M

momento a otro, en cualquier momento. ▌ **at the moment** en este momento. ▌ **at the last moment** a última hora. ▌ **for the moment** de momento, por el momento. ▌ **in a moment** dentro de un momento.

mommy ['mɒmɪ] *n* US *fam* mamá.
ⓘ *pl* mommies.

Monaco ['mɒnəkəu] *n* Mónaco.

monarch ['mɒnək] *n* monarca *m*.

monarchy ['mɒnəkɪ] *n* monarquía.
ⓘ *pl* monarchies.

monastery ['mɒnəstᵊrɪ] *n* monasterio.
ⓘ *pl* monasteries.

Monday ['mʌndɪ] *n* lunes *m inv*.

✎ Para ejemplos de uso, consulta Saturday.

Monegasque ['mɒnəgæsk] *n* monegasco,-a.

monetary ['mʌnɪtᵊrɪ] *adj* monetario,-a.

money ['mʌnɪ] *n* **1** *(gen)* dinero: *how much money have you got?* ¿cuánto dinero tienes? **2** *(currency)* moneda. LOC **to make money 1** *(person)* ganar dinero, hacer dinero. **2** *(business)* dar dinero. ▌ **to put money on** STH apostar por ALGO.

moneybox ['mʌnɪbɒks] *n* hucha.
ⓘ *pl* moneyboxes.

Mongol ['mɒŋgɒl] *n* mongol,-la, mogol,-la.

Mongolia [mɒŋ'gəulɪə] *n* Mongolia.

Mongolian [mɒŋ'gəulɪən] *adj* mongol, -la, mogol,-la.
▶ *n* **1** *(person)* mongol,-la, mogol,-la. **2** *(language)* mongol *m*, mogol *m*.

monitor ['mɒnɪtə'] *n* **1** *(screen)* monitor *m*. **2** *(school pupil)* responsable *mf*, encargado,-a.
▶ *vt (check)* controlar; *(follow)* seguir de cerca; *(watch)* observar.

monk [mʌŋk] *n* monje *m*.

monkey ['mʌŋkɪ] *n (gen)* mono,-a; *(long-tailed)* mico,-a. COMP **monkey nut** cacahuete *m*. ▌ **monkey wrench** llave *f* inglesa.

monogamy [mə'nɒgəmɪ] *n* monogamia.

monographic [mɒnə'græfɪk] *adj* monográfico,-a.

monolith ['mɒnəlɪθ] *n* monolito.

monologue ['mɒnəlɒg] *n* monólogo.

monopoly [mə'nɒpəlɪ] *n* monopolio.
ⓘ *pl* monopolies.

monorail ['mɒnəureɪl] *n* monorraíl *m*, monocarril *m*.

monotheism ['mɒnəuθɪɪzᵊm] *n* monoteísmo.

monotonous [mə'nɒtənəs] *adj* monótono,-a.

monotony [mə'nɒtənɪ] *n* monotonía.

monoxide [mə'nɒksaɪd] *n* monóxido.

monsoon [mɒn'su:n] *n* **1** *(wind)* monzón *m*. **2** *(rainy season)* estación *f* lluviosa. COMP **monsoon rains** lluvias *fpl* monzónicas.

monster ['mɒnstə'] *n (gen)* monstruo.
▶ *adj fam (huge)* enorme, gigantesco,-a.

Montenegrin [mɒntɪ'ni:grɪn] *adj* montenegrino,-a.
▶ *n* montenegrino,-a.

Montenegro [mɒntɪ'ni:grəu] *n* Montenegro.

month [mʌnθ] *n* mes *m*: *I'm going on holiday at the end of the month* me voy de vacaciones a final de mes.

monthly ['mʌnθlɪ] *adj* mensual.
▶ *adv* mensualmente, cada mes.
▶ *n (magazine)* revista mensual.

monument ['mɒnjəmənt] *n* monumento (to, a).

monumental [mɒnjə'mentᵊl] *adj* **1** *(gen)* monumental. **2** *fam (lie, blunder, etc)* garrafal, monumental.

moo [mu:] *n (of cow)* mugido.
▶ *vi* mugir.
◆ **to mooch about / mooch around** *vi* dar vueltas, deambular.
ⓘ *pt & pp* mooed, *ger* mooing.

mood¹ [mu:d] *n* LING modo.

mood² [mu:d] *n* **1** *(humour)* humor *m*: *her moods change very quickly* cambia de humor de repente. LOC **to be in a good/ bad mood** estar de buen/mal humor.

moon [mu:n] *n* luna: *full moon* luna llena. LOC **to be over the moon** estar en el séptimo cielo.

moonlight ['mu:nlaɪt] *n* claro de luna, luz *f* de luna.

Moor [muər] *n* moro,-a.

moor[1] [muər] *n (heath)* brezal *m*.

moor[2] [muər] *vt (with rope)* amarrar; *(with anchor)* anclar.
▸ *vi (with anchor)* anclar; *(with rope)* echar amarras.

mooring ['muərɪŋ] *n (place)* amarradero.
▸ *n pl* **moorings** *(ropes, etc)* amarras *fpl*.

Moorish ['muərɪʃ] *adj* moro,-a.

moorland ['muərlənd] *n* páramo.

moose [muːs] *n* alce *m*.

mop [mɒp] *n* **1** *(for floor)* fregona. **2** *fam (of hair)* mata de pelo.
▸ *vt* **1** *(floor)* fregar, limpiar. **2** *(brow, tears)* enjugarse (with, con), secarse.
◆ **to mope about / mope around** *vi* andar abatido,-a, andar deprimido,-a.
ⓘ *pt & pp* **mopped**, *ger* **mopping**.

moped ['məupəd] *n* ciclomotor *m*.

moral ['mɒrəl] *adj* moral.
▸ *n (of story)* moraleja.
▸ *n pl* **morals** moral *f sing*, moralidad *f sing*.

❌ Moral no significa 'moral (estado de ánimo)', que se traduce por **morale**.

morale [məˈrɑːl] *n* moral *f*, estado de ánimo.

morality [məˈrælɪtɪ] *n* moralidad *f*, moral *f*.

morally ['mɒrəlɪ] *adv* moralmente.

more [mɔːr] *adj* más: *more than half an hour* más de media hora.
▸ *pron* más: *we need some more* necesitamos más. ⌐LOC⌐ **the more ..., the more ...** cuanto más ..., más ... ❙ **what is more** además, lo que es más.
▸ *adv* más: *it's more expensive* es más caro. ⌐LOC⌐ **more and more** cada vez más. ❙ **more or less 1** *(approximately)* más o menos. **2** *(almost)* casi.

✎ Consulta también **many** y **much**.

moreover [mɔːˈrəuvər] *adv fml* además, por otra parte.

morgue [mɔːg] *n* depósito de cadáveres.

morning ['mɔːnɪŋ] *n (gen)* mañana; *(early)* madrugada: *at eight o'clock in the morning* a las ocho de la mañana; *the following morning* a la mañana siguiente.

⌐LOC⌐ **good morning!** ¡buenos días! ❙ **in the morning** *(tomorrow before noon)* mañana por la mañana.
▸ *adv* **mornings** por la mañana, por las mañanas.

Moroccan [məˈrɒkən] *adj* marroquí, -ina.
▸ *n* marroquí,-ina.

Morocco [məˈrɒkəu] *n* Marruecos.

morose [məˈrəus] *adj* malhumorado, -a, hosco,-a, taciturno,-a.

❌ Morose no significa 'moroso', que se traduce por **defaulting**.

morpheme ['mɔːfiːm] *n* LING morfema *m*.

morphine ['mɔːfiːn] *n* morfina.

morphological [mɔːfəˈlɒdʒɪkəl] *adj* morfológico,-a.

morphology [mɔːˈfɒlədʒɪ] *n (gen)* morfología.

Morse [mɔːs] *n* Morse *m*. ⌐COMP⌐ **Morse code** alfabeto Morse.

mortal ['mɔːtəl] *adj (gen)* mortal.
▸ *n* mortal *mf*.

mortality [mɔːˈtælɪtɪ] *n* mortalidad *f*.

mortgage ['mɔːgɪdʒ] *n* hipoteca.
▸ *adj* hipotecario,-a.
▸ *vt* hipotecar.

mosaic [məˈzeɪɪk] *adj* mosaico.

Moslem ['mɒzləm] *adj* musulmán, -ana.
▸ *n* musulmán,-ana.

mosque [mɒsk] *n* mezquita.

mosquito [məsˈkiːtəu] *n* mosquito.
⌐COMP⌐ **mosquito bite** picadura de mosquito. ❙ **mosquito net** mosquitero, mosquitera.
ⓘ *pl* **mosquitoes** o **mosquitos**.

moss [mɒs] *n* BOT musgo.

most [məust] *adj* **1** *(greatest in quantity)* más: *Simon's got the most points* Simon tiene más puntos. **2** *(majority)* la mayoría de, la mayor parte de: *most people live in flats* la mayoría de la gente vive en pisos.
▸ *adv* más: *the most difficult question* la pregunta más difícil.
▸ *pron* **1** *(greatest part)* la mayor parte: *it rained most of the time* llovió durante la mayor parte del tiempo. **2** *(greatest number*

M

or amount) lo máximo. **3** *(the majority of people)* la mayoría.
► *adv* **1** *(superlative)* más: *the most beautiful girl* la chica más guapa. **3** *(very)* muy, de lo más: *it was most kind of you* ha sido muy amable de su parte; *a most delightful evening* una tarde muy agradable. **3** US *(almost)* casi. LOC **for the most part** por lo general. I **most of all** sobre todo.

✎ Consulta también many y much.

mostly ['məʊstlɪ] *adv* **1** *(mainly)* principalmente, en su mayor parte. **2** *(generally)* generalmente; *(usually)* normalmente.

moth [mɒθ] *n* mariposa nocturna. COMP **clothes moth** polilla.

mother ['mʌðəʳ] *n* madre *f*: *a single mother* una madre soltera.
► *vt* **1** *(care for)* cuidar como una madre; *(rear)* criar. **2** *(spoil)* mimar. COMP **Mother Nature** la Madre *f* Naturaleza. I **mother ship** buque *m* nodriza. I **mother tongue** lengua materna.

mother-in-law ['mʌðərɪnlɔ:] *n* suegra. ⓘ *pl* mothers-in-law.

mother-of-pearl [mʌðərəv'pɜːl] *n* madreperla, nácar *m*.

motif [məʊ'tiːf] *n* **1** *(pattern, design)* motivo. **2** *(in music, literature - theme)* tema *m*.

motion ['məʊʃən] *n* **1** *(movement)* movimiento. **2** *(gesture)* gesto, ademán *m*. **3** POL *(proposal)* moción *f*. LOC **in motion** en movimiento. I **in slow motion** CINEM a cámara lenta. COMP **motion picture** película. I **motion pictures** el cine *m*.

motivate ['məʊtɪveɪt] *vt* motivar.

motive ['məʊtɪv] *n* **1** *(reason)* motivo. **2** JUR móvil *m*.
► *adj* motor,-ra, motriz. COMP **motive force / motive power** fuerza motriz.

motocross ['məʊtəkrɒs] *n* SP motocross *m*.

motor ['məʊtəʳ] *n* **1** *(engine)* motor *m*. **2** GB *fam (car)* coche *m*, automóvil *m*. COMP **motor racing** carreras *fpl* de coches. I **motor vehicle** vehículo a motor.
► *adj* **1** TECH motor,-ra. **2** BIOL motor,-ra, motriz.

motorbike ['məʊtəbaɪk] *n fam* motocicleta, moto *f*.

motorboat ['məʊtəbəʊt] *n* lancha motora, motora.

motorcycle ['məʊtəsaɪkəl] *n* motocicleta, moto *f*.

motorcycling ['məʊtəsaɪkəlɪŋ] *n* motociclismo.

motorcyclist ['məʊtəsaɪkəlɪst] *n* motociclista *mf*, motorista *mf*.

motorist ['məʊtərɪst] *n* automovilista *mf*, conductor,-ra (de coche).

motorway ['məʊtəweɪ] *n* GB autopista.

motto ['mɒtəʊ] *n* lema *m*. ⓘ *pl* mottos o mottoes.

mould¹ [məʊld] *n* *(growth)* moho.

mould² [məʊld] *n* **1** *(cast)* molde *m*. **2** *fig (type)* carácter *m*, temple *m*.
► *vt* **1** *(figure)* moldear; *(clay)* modelar.

moult [məʊlt] *vi* ZOOL mudar.
► *n* ZOOL muda.

mound [maʊnd] *n* **1** *(small hill)* montículo. **2** *(pile, heap)* montón *m*.

mount¹ [maʊnt] *n* *(mountain)* monte *m*.

mount² [maʊnt] *n* **1** *(horse, etc)* montura. **2** *(for machine, gun, trophy)* soporte *m*, base *f*; *(for photo, picture)* fondo; *(for jewel)* engaste *m*, engarce *m*; *(for slide)* marquito.
► *vt* **1** montar. *(stairs)* subir.
► *vi* **1** *(go up)* subir, ascender.
◆ **to mount up** *vi* *(accumulate)* amontonarse, acumularse.

mountain ['maʊntən] *n* **1** GEOG montaña. **2** *fig (large amount)* montaña, montón *m*. COMP **mountain bike** bicicleta de montaña. I **mountain range** cordillera, sierra.
► *adj* de montaña.

mountaineer [maʊntə'nɪəʳ] *n* montañero,-a, alpinista *mf*, AM andinista *mf*.

mountaineering [maʊntə'nɪərɪŋ] *n* montañismo, alpinismo, AM andinismo.

mountainous ['maʊntənəs] *adj* **1** *(region)* montañoso,-a. **2** *(huge)* enorme, gigantesco,-a.

mourn [mɔːn] *vt* *(person)* llorar la muerte de; *(thing)* llorar, añorar.

mourning ['mɔːnɪŋ] n luto, duelo. LOC
to be in mourning for SB estar de luto
por ALGN.

mouse [maʊs] n (gen) ratón m.
ⓘ pl mice.

mousse [muːs] n CULIN mousse f.

moustache [məs'tɑːʃ] n bigote m.

mouth [(n) maʊθ; (vb) maʊð] n 1 ANAT
boca. 2 (of river) desembocadura; (of
bottle) boca; (of tunnel, cave) boca, entrada. 3 (person to feed) boca. LOC **to keep
one's mouth shut** mantener la boca
cerrada, no decir nada. COMP **mouth
organ** armónica.

mouthful ['maʊθfʊl] n 1 (of food) bocado; (of drink) trago; (of air) bocanada. 2
fam (long word, phrase) trabalenguas m.

mouth-to-mouth [maʊθtə'maʊθ] [also
mouth-to-mouth resuscitation] n boca
a boca m.

movable ['muːvəbªl] adj movible, móvil.

move [muːv] n 1 (act of moving, movement)
movimiento: he watched my every move
observó todos mis movimientos. 2 (to
new home) mudanza; (to new job) traslado. 3 (in game) jugada; (turn) turno:
whose move is it? ¿a quién le toca jugar? 4
(action, step) paso, acción f, medida;
(decision) decisión f; (attempt) intento.
▶ vt 1 (gen) mover; (furniture, etc) cambiar de sitio, trasladar; (transfer) trasladar; (out of the way) apartar: you've
moved the furniture! ¡habéis cambiado los
muebles de sitio! 2 (affect emotionally)
conmover. 3 (in games) mover, jugar.
▶ vi 1 (gen) moverse; (change - position)
trasladarse, desplazarse; (- house) mudarse; (- post, department) trasladarse:
she was so scared she couldn't move tenía
tanto miedo que no podía moverse.
◆ **to move away** vi 1 (move aside, etc)
alejarse, apartarse. 2 (change house)
mudarse de casa.
◆ **to move in** vi 1 (into new home) instalarse. 2 (prepare to take control, attack, etc)
acercarse.
◆ **to move over** vt sep (step aside) apartarse.
▶ vi (make room) correrse, moverse.

movement ['muːvmənt] n 1 (act, motion)
movimiento; (gesture) gesto, ademán
m. 2 (of goods) traslado; (of troops) desplazamiento; (of population) movimiento. 3 (political, literary) movimiento. 4 (trend) tendencia, corriente f.
▶ n pl **movements** (activities) movimientos mpl, actividades fpl.

movie ['muːvɪ] n US película.
▶ n pl **the movies** el cine m sing. LOC **to
go to the movies** ir al cine.

moving ['muːvɪŋ] adj 1 (that moves) móvil; (in motion) en movimiento, en
marcha. 2 (causing motion) motor,-ra,
motriz. 3 (causing action, motivating) ins-
tigador,-ra, promotor,-ra. 4 (emotional)
conmovedor,-ra.

mow [məʊ] vt (lawn) cortar, segar; (corn,
wheat) segar.
ⓘ pt mowed, pp mowed o mown [məʊn].

mower ['məʊəʳ] n (for lawn) cortacésped m & f; (for fields) segadora.

mown [məʊn] pp → mow.

Mozambique [məʊzæm'biːk] n Mozambique.

Mozambiquean [məʊzæm'biːkªn] adj
mozambiqueño,-a.
▶ n mozambiqueño,-a.

MP ['em'piː] abbr (member of Parliament)
diputado,-a.

mph ['em'piː'eɪt] abbr (miles per hour)
millas por hora.

Mr abbr (Mister) señor; (abbreviation) sr.

Mrs abbr señora; (abbreviation) sra.

Ms abbr (Miss) señorita; (abbreviation)
srta.

much [mʌtʃ] adj mucho,-a: we haven't got
much bread no tenemos mucho pan; he
didn't have much time no tenía mucho
tiempo; we've made too much jam hemos
hecho demasiada mermelada; why is there
so much traffic? ¿por qué hay tanto tráfico?;
take as much time as you need tómate tanto
tiempo como necesites; how much money
have you got? ¿cuánto dinero tienes?
ⓘ comp more, superl most.
▶ pron mucho: there's not much to do
round here no hay mucho que hacer por
aquí; how much is it? ¿cuánto vale? LOC **a
bit much** un poco demasiado, un po-

co excesivo,-a. **▌ as much 1** *(equal)* equivalente a. **2** *(the same)* lo mismo.
▸ *adv* mucho: *he felt much better* se encontraba mucho mejor.

✎ Much se emplea sobre todo en las frases negativas e interrogativas, en las frases afirmativas se emplea a lot.

mucus ['mju:kəs] *n* mucosidad *f*.

mud [mʌd] *n* *(gen)* barro, lodo; *(thick)* fango.

muddle ['mʌdəl] *n* **1** *(mess)* desorden *m*: *everything's in a muddle* todo está en desorden. **2** *(confusion, mix-up)* confusión *f*, embrollo, lío.
▸ *vt* [also **to muddle up**] *(untidy)* revolver, desordenar; *(confuse mentally)* liar, confundir, embarullar; *(confuse, mix up)* confundir.
◆ **to muddle through** *vi* arreglárselas.

muddy ['mʌdɪ] *adj* **1** *(gen)* fangoso,-a, barroso,-a, lodoso,-a. **2** *(colour)* sucio,-a. **3** *(thinking, idea, etc)* confuso,-a, turbio,-a.
ⓘ *comp* muddier, *superl* muddiest.

mudguard ['mʌdɡɑ:d] *n* guardabarros *m inv*.

muesli ['mju:zlɪ] *n* muesli *m*.

muffin ['mʌfɪn] *n* **1** GB *panecillo redondo que se come tostado y con mantequilla.* **2** US *tipo de magdalena.*

mug [mʌɡ] *n* *(large cup)* taza alta, tazón *m*.

mugger ['mʌɡəʳ] *n* atracador,-ra, asaltante *mf*.

mugging ['mʌɡɪŋ] *n* atraco, asalto.

mule [mju:l] *n* ZOOL mulo,-a.

mullet ['mʌlɪθ] COMP **grey mullet** mújol *m*. ▌ **red mullet** salmonete *m*.

multicultural [mʌltɪ'kʌltʃərəl] *adj* multicultural.

multilateral [mʌltɪ'lætərəl] *adj* multilateral.

multinational [mʌltɪ'næʃənəl] *adj* multinacional.
▸ *n* multinacional *f*.

multiple ['mʌltɪpəl] *adj* múltiple.
▸ *n* MATH múltiplo.

multiple-choice [mʌltɪpəl'tʃɔɪs] *adj* tipo test.

multiplex ['mʌltɪpleks] *adj* **1** *(cinema)* multicines *mpl*. **2** TECH múltiple.

multiplication [mʌltɪplɪ'keɪʃən] *n* multiplicación *f*. COMP **multiplication sign** signo de multiplicar. ▌ **multiplication table** tabla de multiplicar.

multiply ['mʌltɪplaɪ] *vt* MATH multiplicar (**by**, por).
ⓘ *pt & pp* multiplied, *ger* multiplying.
▸ *vi* multiplicarse.

multipurpose [mʌltɪ'pɜ:pəs] *adj* multiuso *inv*.

mum [mʌm] *n* GB *fam* mamá *f*.

mumble ['mʌmbəl] *vt* *(gen)* decir entre dientes, mascullar; *(prayer)* musitar.
▸ *vi* hablar entre dientes, farfullar.

mummify ['mʌmɪfaɪ] *vt* momificar.
ⓘ *pt & pp* mummified, *ger* mummifying.

mummy¹ ['mʌmɪ] *n* *(dead body)* momia.
ⓘ *pl* mummies.

mummy² ['mʌmɪ] *n* GB *fam* *(mother)* mamá *f*.
ⓘ *pl* mummies.

mumps [mʌmps] *n* MED paperas *fpl*.

mundane [mʌn'deɪn] *adj* **1** *(worldly)* mundano,-a. **2** *pej* *(banal)* rutinario,-a, banal.

municipal [mju:'nɪsɪpəl] *adj* municipal.

municipality [mju:nɪsɪ'pælɪtɪ] *n* municipio.
ⓘ *pl* municipalities.

mural ['mjʊərəl] *n* pintura mural, mural *m*.

murder ['mɜ:dəʳ] *n* **1** asesinato, homicidio. **2** *fam fig* *(difficult experience)* pesadilla. COMP **murder story** novela negra, novela policíaca.
▸ *vt* **1** *(kill)* asesinar, matar. **2** *fam fig* *(be angry with)* matar.

murderer ['mɜ:dərəʳ] *n* asesino, homicida *mf*.

murmur ['mɜ:məʳ] *n* **1** *(of voice)* murmullo, susurro. **2** *(of traffic)* rumor *m*; *(of insects)* zumbido; *(of wind)* murmullo; *(of water)* susurro. **3** MED soplo.
▸ *vt* murmurar: *they murmured their approval* hubo un murmullo de aprobación.

▶ *vi* **1** murmurar, susurrar. **2** *(complain)* quejarse (**against/at**, de).

❌ To murmur no significa 'murmurar (hablar mal)', que se traduce por **to gossip**.

muscle [ˈmʌsəl] *n* **1** ANAT músculo. **2** *(muscle power)* fuerza. **3** *fig (strength, power)* poder *m*, fuerza. LOC **to not move a muscle** no inmutarse.

◆ **to muscle in** *vi (situation)* entrometerse (**on**, en); *(place)* introducirse por la fuerza.

muscular [ˈmʌskjələr] *adj* **1** *(pain, tissue)* muscular. **2** *(person)* musculoso,-a.

musculature [ˈmʌskjələtʃər] *n* **1** musculatura. **2** *(person)* musculoso,-a.

muse¹ [mjuːz] *vi* meditar (**on/over**, -), reflexionar (**on/over**, sobre).

muse² [mjuːz] *n* musa.
▶ *n pl* **the Muses** las Musas *fpl*.

museum [mjuːˈzɪəm] *n* museo.

mushroom [ˈmʌʃruːm] *n* **1** BOT seta, hongo. **2** CULIN *(button mushroom)* champiñón *m*; *(wild)* seta. COMP **mushroom cloud** hongo nuclear.

✎ La palabra mushroom se usa para designar cualquier seta u hongo comestible; las setas no comestibles se llaman toadstools.

music [ˈmjuːzɪk] *n* música. COMP **music box** caja de música. ‖ **music centre** equipo de música. ‖ **music hall** teatro de variedades. ‖ **music score** partitura. ‖ **music stand** atril *m*.

musical [ˈmjuːzɪkəl] *adj* **1** *(gen)* musical. **2** *(person - gifted)* dotado,-a para la música; *(- fond of music)* aficionado,-a a la música, melómano,-a. COMP **musical box** caja de música. ‖ **musical instrument** instrumento musical.
▶ *n* musical *m*.

musician [mjuːˈzɪʃən] *n* músico,-a.

musk [mʌsk] *n (substance)* almizcle *m*.

musket [ˈmʌskɪt] *n* mosquete *m*.

musketeer [mʌskəˈtɪər] *n* mosquetero.

Muslim [ˈmʌzlɪm] *adj* musulmán,-ana.
▶ *n* musulmán,-ana.

muslin [ˈmʌzlɪn] *n* muselina.

mussel [ˈmʌsəl] *n* mejillón *m*.

must¹ [mʌst] *aux* **1** *(necessity, obligation)* deber, tener que: *I must leave now* tengo que marcharme ahora; *must you play your music so loud?* ¿es necesario poner la música tan fuerte? **2** *(probability)* deber de: *she must be tired* debe de estar cansada; *but someone must have seen her* pero alguien debe de haberla visto. LOC **if I must** si no hay más remedio. ‖ **if you must know, ...** si te empeñas en saberlo, ...
▶ *n (need)* necesidad *f*: *it's an absolute must for all film buffs* es imprescindible para todos los cinéfilos.

mustache [məsˈtaːʃ] *n* US → **moustache**.

mustard [ˈmʌstəd] *n (gen)* mostaza. COMP **mustard gas** gas *m* mostaza.

mutant [ˈmjuːtənt] *n* mutante *mf*.
▶ *adj* mutante.

mutation [mjuːˈteɪʃən] *n* mutación *f*.

mute [mjuːt] *adj (dumb, silent)* mudo,-a. COMP **deaf mute** sordomudo,-a.
▶ *n* **1** LING mudo,-a. **2** *(dumb person)* mudo,-a. **3** MUS sordina.

mutilate [ˈmjuːtɪleɪt] *vt* mutilar.

mutilation [mjuːtɪˈleɪʃən] *n* mutilación *f*.

mutiny [ˈmjuːtɪnɪ] *n* motín *m*, amotinamiento, sublevación *f*, rebelión *f*.
① *pl* **mutinies**.
▶ *vi* amotinarse.
① *pt & pp* **mutinied**, *ger* **mutinying**.

mutter [ˈmʌtər] *n* murmullo, refunfuño.
▶ *vt (mumble)* murmurar, mascullar, decir entre dientes, refunfuñar.
▶ *vi* **1** *(mumble)* murmurar, hablar entre dientes. **2** *(complain)* refunfuñar, rezongar, quejarse.

mutton [ˈmʌtən] *n* carne *f* de oveja.

mutual [ˈmjuːtʃuəl] *adj* **1** *(help, love, etc)* mutuo,-a, recíproco,-a. **2** *(friend, interest, etc)* común.

mutually [ˈmjuːtʃuəlɪ] *adv* mutuamente.

muzzle [ˈmʌzəl] *n* **1** *(snout)* hocico. **2** *(guard)* bozal *m*. **3** *(of gun)* boca.

M

▶ vt **1** *(dog)* poner un bozal a. **2** *fig (person, press, etc)* amordazar.

muzzy ['mʌzɪ] *adj* **1** *(blurred)* borroso,-a. **2** *(groggy)* atontado,-a, espeso,-a.
ⓘ *comp* muzzier, *superl* muzziest.

my [maɪ] *adj* mi, mis: *my book* mi libro; *my records* mis discos; *one of my friends* un amigo mío.
▶ *interj* ¡caramba!, ¡caray!

myopia [maɪ'əʊpɪə] *n* miopía.

myopic [maɪ'ɒpɪk] *adj* miope.

myrtle ['mɜːtəl] *n* BOT arrayán *m*, mirto.

myself [maɪ'self] *pron* **1** *(reflexive)* me: *I cut myself* me corté; *I helped myself* me serví. **2** *(after preposition)* mí (mismo,-a): *I kept it for myself* lo guardé para mí; *I said to myself* me dije a mí mismo. **3** *(emphatic)* yo mismo,-a: *I did it by myself* lo hice yo mismo,-a. LOC **all by myself 1** *(alone)* solo,-a. **2** *(without help)* yo solo,-a. **I to myself** *(private)* para mí solo,-a.

mysterious [mɪ'stɪərɪəs] *adj* misterioso,-a.

mysteriously [mɪ'stɪərɪəslɪ] *adv* misteriosamente.

mystery ['mɪstərɪ] *n* misterio.
ⓘ *pl* mysteries.

mystic ['mɪstɪk] *adj* místico,-a.
▶ *n* místico,-a.

mystical ['mɪstɪkəl] *adj* místico,-a.

myth [mɪθ] *n* **1** *(ancient story)* mito. **2** *(fallacy)* falacia.

mythical ['mɪθɪkəl] *adj* **1** *(of a myth)* mítico,-a. **2** *(not real, imagined)* imaginario,-a, fantástico,-a.

mythological [mɪθə'lɒdʒɪkəl] *adj* mitológico,-a.

mythology [mɪ'θɒlədʒɪ] *n* mitología.

N

N, n [en] *n (the letter)* N, n *f.*

N [nɔːθ] *abbr* (**north**) norte *m; (abbreviation)* N.

naff [næf] *adj fam* hortera.

nag [næg] *vt* **1** *(annoy)* molestar, fastidiar. **2** *(complain)* dar la tabarra a.
▶ *vi* quejarse.
ⓘ *pt & pp* nagged, *ger* nagging.

nail [neɪl] *n* **1** *(on finger, toe)* uña: *to bite/cut/trim one's nails* morderse/cortarse/arreglarse las uñas. **2** *(metal)* clavo.
▶ *vt* **1** clavar, fijar con clavos. **2** *fam* pillar, coger. **▌**COMP **nail clippers** cortaúñas *m.* **▌nail polish** esmalte *m* para las uñas. **▌nail varnish** esmalte *m* para las uñas. **▌nail varnish remover** quitaesmaltes *m.*
◆ **to nail down** *vt sep* **1** *(thing)* clavar, sujetar con clavos. **2** *fig (person)* conseguir que ALGN se comprometa: *I couldn't nail him down to a price* no pude conseguir que me concretara un precio.

naive [naɪˈiːv] *adj* ingenuo,-a.

naked [ˈneɪkɪd] *adj* desnudo,-a.

name [neɪm] *n* **1** *(first name)* nombre *m; (surname)* apellido: *his name's Richard* se llama Richard; *what's your name?* ¿cómo te llamas? **2** *(fame)* fama, reputación *f: she made her name in the theatre* se hizo famosa en el teatro.
▶ *vt* **1** llamar: *they named the child Dominic after his uncle* al niño le pusieron Dominic por su tío. **2** *(appoint)* nombrar: *he was named Minister of Transport* lo nombraron Ministro de Transportes.
LOC **in the name of...** en nombre de...
COMP **big name** pez *m* gordo. **▌name day** santo.

namely [ˈneɪmlɪ] *adv* a saber.

Namibia [nəˈmɪbɪə] *n* Namibia.

Namibian [nəˈmɪbɪən] *adj* namibio,-a.
▶ *n* namibio,-a.

nanny [ˈnænɪ] *n* **1** *(carer)* niñera. **2** GB *fam (grandmother)* yaya, abuela.
ⓘ *pl* nannies.

nap [næp] *n* siesta.
▶ *vi* dormir la siesta. LOC **to have a nap / take a nap** echar la siesta.
ⓘ *pt & pp* napped, *ger* napping.

nape [neɪp] *n* nuca, cogote *m.*

napkin [ˈnæpkɪn] *n* servilleta. COMP **napkin ring** servilletero.

nappy [ˈnæpɪ] *n* GB pañal *m.*
ⓘ *pl* nappies.

narcissus [nɑːˈsɪsəs] *n* narciso.
ⓘ *pl* narcissi o narcissuses.

narcotic [nɑːˈkɒtɪk] *adj* narcótico,-a.
▶ *n* narcótico.

narrate [nəˈreɪt] *vt* narrar.

narrative [ˈnærətɪv] *adj* narrativo,-a.
▶ *n* **1** narración *f.* **2** *(genre)* narrativa.

narrator [nəˈreɪtəʳ] *n* narrador,-ra.

narrow [ˈnærəʊ] *adj* **1** estrecho,-a: *a narrow road* una carretera estrecha. **2** *(restricted)* reducido,-a, restringido,-a: *a narrow circle of friends* un círculo reducido de amigos. **3** *(by very little)* escaso,-a: *by a narrow majority* por una escasa mayoría.
ⓘ *comp* narrower, *superl* narrowest.
▶ *vt* **1** *(make narrower)* estrechar. **2** *(reduce)* reducir, acortar: *Leeds narrowed Hull's lead to only 1 point* el Leeds redujo la ventaja del Hull a 1 solo punto.

nasal [ˈneɪzəl] *adj* **1** nasal. **2** *(way of speaking)* gangoso,-a.

nasty [ˈnɑːstɪ] *adj* **1** *(unpleasant)* desagradable, repugnante, horrible: *what a nasty smell!* ¡qué olor más desagradable! **2** *(malicious)* malintencionado,-a; *(unkind)*

antipático,-a: *she was really nasty to everyone* se mostró muy antipática con todos. **3** *(dangerous)* peligroso,-a: *this bend is really nasty* esta curva es muy peligrosa. **4** *(tricky)* peliagudo,-a: *it's quite a nasty little problem* es un problemita bastante peliagudo. **5** *(serious)* grave: *a nasty cold* un resfriado de cuidado.
ⓘ *comp* **nastier**, *superl* **nastiest.**

nation ['neɪʃən] *n* **1** *(country)* nación *f*, país *m*. **2** *(ethnic group)* pueblo, nación *f*.

national ['næʃ°nəl] *adj* nacional. ᴄᴏᴍᴾ **national anthem** himno nacional.
▶ *n* súbdito,-a, ciudadano,-a.

nationalism ['næʃ°nəlɪz°m] *n* nacionalismo.

nationalist ['næʃ°nəlɪst] *adj* nacionalista.
▶ *n* nacionalista *mf*.

nationality [næʃ°nælɪtɪ] *n* nacionalidad *f*.
ⓘ *pl* **nationalities.**

native ['neɪtɪv] *adj* **1** *(place)* natal; *(language)* materno,-a: *her native country* su país natal; *his native tongue is Danish* su lengua materna es el danés; *we need a native speaker of English* necesitamos un hablante de inglés que sea nativo. **2** *(plant, animal)* originario,-a: *it's native to Australia* es originario de Australia; *native varieties of grape* variedades autóctonas de vid.
▶ *n* **1** natural *mf*, nativo,-a: *she's a native of Orense* es natural de Orense. **2** *(original inhabitant)* indígena *mf*. ᴄᴏᴍᴾ **Native American** indio,-a americano,-a.

⊕ Se llama **Native American** a los descendientes de las tribus aborígenes que habitaban Estados Unidos antes de la llegada de los europeos. Se trata de una multitud de pueblos con lenguas y tradiciones diferentes que fueron diezmados durante la colonización y, posteriormente, recluidos en reservas.

nativity [nə'tɪvɪtɪ] *n* natividad *f*.
ⓘ *pl* **nationalities.**

NATO ['neɪtəʊ] [also written Nato] *abbr* (North Atlantic Treaty Organization) Organización *f* del Tratado del Atlántico Norte; *(abbreviation)* OTAN *f*.

natural ['nætʃ°rəl] *adj* natural. **3** *(usual)* natural, normal: *it's only natural to feel afraid* es normal tener miedo. ᴄᴏᴍᴾ **natural childbirth** parto natural. ▌**natural gas** gas *m* natural. ▌**natural history** historia natural. ▌**natural resources** recursos *mpl* naturales. ▌**natural science** ciencias *fpl* naturales. ▌**natural selection** selección *f* natural.

naturally ['nætʃ°rəlɪ] *adv* **1** *(by nature)* por naturaleza. **2** *(unaffectedly)* con naturalidad. **3** *(not artificially)* de manera natural. **4** *(of course)* naturalmente, por supuesto.

nature ['neɪtʃəʳ] *n* **1** *(gen)* naturaleza. **2** *(character)* carácter *m*, forma de ser: *it's in her nature to be like that* es así por naturaleza. ʟᴏᴄ **by nature** por naturaleza. ᴄᴏᴍᴾ **nature conservation** conservación *f* de la naturaleza. ▌**nature reserve** reserva natural. ▌**nature study** ciencias *fpl* naturales.

naughty ['nɔːtɪ] *adj* **1** travieso,-a, malo,-a. **2** *(risqué)* atrevido,-a.
ⓘ *comp* **naughtier**, *superl* **naughtiest.**

Nauru ['naʊruː, 'nɑːuːruː] *n* Nauru.

Nauruan [naʊ'ruːən] *adj* nauruano,-a.
▶ *n* nauruano,-a.

nausea ['nɔːzɪə] *n* **1** *(physical)* náusea. **2** *(disgust)* asco, repugnancia.

nauseating ['nɔːzɪeɪtɪŋ] *adj* **1** *(physically)* nauseabundo,-a. **2** *(disgusting)* asqueroso,-a, repugnante.

nautical ['nɔːtɪk°l] *adj* náutico,-a. ᴄᴏᴍᴾ **nautical mile** milla náutica.

Navajo ['nævəhəʊ] *adj-n* → **Navaho.**

naval ['neɪv°l] *adj* naval. ᴄᴏᴍᴾ **naval battle** batalla naval. ▌**naval base** base *f* naval.

navel ['neɪv°l] *n* ombligo.

navigate ['nævɪgeɪt] *vt* **1** *(river, sea)* navegar por. **2** *(steer - ship)* gobernar; *(- plane)* pilotar.
▶ *vi (when sailing, flying)* dirigir; *(when driving)* guiar: *you drive, I'll navigate* tú conduce, yo te guiaré.

navigation [nævɪ'geɪʃ°n] *n* navegación *f*.

navigator ['nævɪgeɪtəʳ] *n* MAR navegante *mf*.

navy ['neɪvɪ] *n* marina de guerra, armada. COMP **navy blue** azul marino. ① *pl* navies.

Nazi ['nɑːtsɪ] *adj* nazi.
▶ *n* nazi *mf*.

Nazism ['nɑːtsɪzªm] *n* nazismo.

Neanderthal [nɪ'ændətɑːl] *adj* de Neanderthal. COMP **Neanderthal man** hombre *m* de Neanderthal.

near [nɪəʳ] *adj* **1** cercano,-a: *where is the nearest bank?* ¿dónde está el banco más cercano?; *a near relative* un pariente cercano. **2** *(time)* próximo,-a: *in the near future* en un futuro próximo.
① *comp* nearer, *comp* nearest.
▶ *adv* cerca: *I live quite near (by)* vivo bastante cerca.
▶ *prep* **1** cerca de: *it's near the market* está cerca del mercado. **2** [also near to.] a punto de: *she was near to crying* estuvo a punto de llorar.
▶ *vt* acercarse a: *we are nearing the day when...* nos acercamos al día en que…

nearby [(*adj*) 'nɪəbaɪ; (*adv*) nɪə'baɪ] *adj* cercano,-a: *a nearby hotel* un hotel cercano.
▶ *adv* cerca: *is there one nearby?* ¿hay alguno cerca?

nearly ['nɪəlɪ] *adv* casi. LOC **not nearly** ni mucho menos, ni con mucho: *there's not nearly enough time to finish* el tiempo para acabar es del todo insuficiente.

neat [niːt] *adj* **1** *(room)* ordenado,-a; *(garden)* bien arreglado,-a. **2** *(person)* pulcro,-a; *(in habits)* ordenado,-a. **3** *(writing)* claro,-a. **4** *(clever)* ingenioso,-a, apañado,-a. **5** *(drinks)* solo,-a. **6** US fantástico,-a, estupendo,-a, chulo,-a, guay.

neatness ['niːtnəs] *n* esmero.

necessarily [nesə'serɪlɪ] *adv* **1** necesariamente. **2** *(inevitably)* inevitablemente, forzosamente.

necessary ['nesɪsªrɪ] *adj* **1** necesario,-a. **2** *(inevitable)* inevitable, forzoso,-a. LOC **to do the necessary** hacer lo necesario.
▶ *n pl* **necessaries** lo necesario, cosas *fpl* necesarias.

necessity [nɪ'sesɪtɪ] *n* **1** necesidad *f*: *it's a necessity* es indispensable. **2** *(item)* requisito indispensable.
① *pl* necessities.

neck [nek] *n* cuello. LOC **to be in** STH **up to one's neck** estar metido,-a en ALGO hasta el cuello. ‖ **to break one's neck** desnucarse. ‖ **to risk one's neck** jugarse el tipo.

necklace ['nekləs] *n* collar *m*.

neckline ['neklaɪn] *n* escote *m*. LOC **with a low neckline** muy escotado,-a.

nectarine ['nektərɪn] *n* nectarina.

née [neɪ] *adj* de soltera: *Mrs Hastings, née Lawley* la Sra. Hastings, de soltera Lawley.

need [niːd] *n* **1** necesidad *f*: *there's no need for all of you to come with me* no hace falta que me acompañéis todos; *I have enough to satisfy my needs* tengo suficiente para satisfacer mis necesidades. **2** *(poverty)* necesidad *f*, infortunio: *to help* SB *in time of need* ayudar a ALGN en tiempos de necesidad. LOC **if need be** si hace falta. ‖ **to be in need of** necesitar. ‖ **to have need of** necesitar, tener necesidad de.
▶ *vt* necesitar: *you'll need a pencil* necesitarás un lápiz; *I need to see you* tengo que verte.
▶ *aux* hacer falta: *need we all go?* ¿hace falta que vayamos todos?; *need you drive so fast?* ¿tienes que conducir tan deprisa?; *you needn't come in tomorrow* no hace falta que vengas mañana; *you needn't have bought me a present* no hacía falta que me compraras ningún regalo.

needle ['niːdªl] *n* **1** *(gen)* aguja. **2** GB *fam (friction)* pique *m*. **3** US *fam (injection)* inyección *f*. **4** *(leaf)* hoja: *pine needles* hojas de pino. LOC **it's like looking for a needle in a haystack** es como buscar una aguja en un pajar.
▶ *vt fam* pinchar.

needless ['niːdləs] *adj* innecesario,-a.

needn't ['niːdənt] *v* → need.

negative ['negətɪv] *adj* negativo,-a.
▶ *n* **1** LING negación *f*. **2** *(answer)* negativa. **3** *(photograph)* negativo.

neglect [nɪ'glekt] *n* **1** *(of thing)* descuido, desatención *f*: *the house was in a state of neglect* la casa estaba totalmente descuidada, la casa se encontraba en un estado de abandono. **2** *(of duty)* incumplimiento.

N

▸ vt **1** (not take care of) tener abandonado,-a, desatender: I've been neglecting my friends recently tengo abandonados a mis amigos. **2** (fail to attend to) descuidar: with so much sport you've been neglecting your academic work con tanto deporte tienes los estudios muy descuidados. **3** (forget to do) olvidar: she neglected to lock the safe olvidó cerrar la caja con llave.

neglected [nɪˈglektɪd] adj descuidado,-a.

negligence [ˈneglɪdʒəns] n negligencia.

negotiate [nɪˈgəʊʃɪeɪt] vt negociar.

negotiation [nɪgəʊʃɪˈeɪʃ°n] n negociación f: the agreement is under negotiation el acuerdo se está negociando.

negotiator [nɪˈgəʊʃɪeɪtəʳ] n negociador,-a.

neigh [neɪ] n relincho.
▸ vi relinchar.

neighbor [ˈneɪbəʳ] n US → neighbour.

neighbour [ˈneɪbəʳ] n **1** vecino,-a. **2** (fellow man) prójimo,-a.

neighbourhood [ˈneɪbəhʊd] n **1** vecindad f, barrio. **2** (people) vecindario. COMP **neighbourhood watch** grupo de vigilancia vecinal.

neither [ˈnaɪðəʳ, ˈniːðəʳ] adj ninguno de los dos, ninguna de las dos: neither boy knew the answer ninguno de los dos chicos sabía la respuesta.
▸ pron ninguno de los dos, ninguna de las dos: neither is here ninguno de los dos está aquí.
▸ adv **1** ni: he's neither fat nor thin no es ni gordo ni delgado. **2** tampoco: I don't like it and neither does my wife no me gusta a mí, y a mi mujer tampoco. LOC neither... nor... ni... ni...: she neither smokes nor drinks ni fuma ni bebe.

neolithic [nəʊˈlɪθɪk] adj neolítico,-a.

neon [ˈniːɒn] n neón m. COMP **neon light** luz f de neón. ∎ **neon sign** rótulo con tubos de neón.

Nepal [nəˈpɔːl] n Nepal.

Nepalese [nepəˈliːz] adj nepalés,-esa, nepalí.
▸ n **1** (person) nepalés,-esa, nepalí mf. **2** (language) nepalés m, nepalí m.

Nepali [nəˈpɔːlɪ] adj → Nepalese.

nephew [ˈnevjuː] n sobrino.

Neptune [ˈneptjuːn] n Neptuno.

nerve [nɜːv] n **1** nervio. **2** (daring) valor m. **3** (cheek) descaro, cara: what a nerve! ¡qué cara! LOC **to be a bundle of nerves** estar hecho,-a un manojo de nervios. ∎ **to get on ss's nerves** crispar los nervios a ALGN. ∎ **to lose one's nerve** rajarse. COMP **nerve cell** neurona. ∎ **nerve centre** centro neurálgico. ∎ **nerve gas** gas m nervioso.

nervous [ˈnɜːvəs] adj **1** nervioso,-a. **2** (afraid) miedoso,-a; (timid) tímido,-a. **3** (apprehensive) aprensivo,-a. COMP **nervous breakdown** crisis f nerviosa. ∎ **nervous system** sistema m nervioso. ∎ **nervous wreck** manojo de nervios.

nest [nest] n **1** nido; (hen's) nidal m. **2** (wasp's) avispero; (animal's) madriguera. **3** fig nido, refugio.
▸ vi anidar, nidificar.
▸ vt COMPUT anidar.

net¹ [net] n red f.
▸ vt coger con red.
ⓘ pt & pp netted, ger netting.

net² [net] adj FIN neto,-a: they made a net profit of £1.5M tuvieron beneficios netos de un millón y medio de libras. COMP **net result** resultado final. ∎ **net weight** peso neto.

nether [ˈneðəʳ] adj lit inferior, de abajo.

Netherlander [ˈneðəlændəʳ] n neerlandés,-esa.

Netherlands [ˈneðələndʒ] n the Netherlands los Países mpl Bajos.

netsurfer [ˈnetsɜːfəʳ] n internauta mf.

nettle [ˈnet°l] n ortiga. LOC **to grasp the nettle** coger el toro por los cuernos. COMP **nettle rash** urticaria.

network [ˈnetwɜːk] n red f.
▸ vt COMPUT conectar en red.

neuron [ˈnjʊərɒn] n neurona.

neuter [ˈnjuːtəʳ] adj neutro,-a.
▸ n LING neutro.

neutral [ˈnjuːtrəl] adj **1** (in general) neutro,-a: a neutral colour/shampoo un color/champú neutro. **2** POL neutral: a neutral country un país neutral. **3** (impartial) neutral, imparcial: *a neutral judgment* un juicio imparcial.

► *n* AUTO punto muerto: *leave the car in neutral* deja el coche en punto muerto.

neutron ['njuərɒn] *n* neutrón *m*.

never ['nevər] *adv* nunca, jamás: *I have never been there* jamás he estado allí; *we never go there any more* ya no vamos allí nunca; *never have I heard such rubbish* en mi vida he oído tales tonterías; *he never so much as thanked me* ni siquiera me dio las gracias. LOC **never again** nunca más. ▎**never mind!** ¡no importa!

never-ending [nevə'rendɪŋ] *adj* interminable.

nevertheless [nevəðə'les] *adv* sin embargo.

new [njuː] *adj* **1** *(following - in order)* nuevo,-a: *a new car* un coche nuevo; *new bread* pan recién hecho. **2** *(baby)* recién nacido,-a: *she's got a new baby* acaba de tener un hijo. LOC **what's new?** ¿qué hay de nuevo? COMP **new moon** luna nueva. ▎**New Testament** Nuevo Testamento. ▎**new wave** nueva ola. ▎**New World** Nuevo Mundo. ▎**New Year** Año Nuevo. ▎**New Year's Day** día *m* de Año Nuevo. ▎**New Year's Eve** Nochevieja. ▎**New York** Nueva York. ▎**New Zealand** Nueva Zelanda. ▎**New Zealander** neozelandés,-esa.

newborn ['njuːbɔːn] *adj* recién nacido,-a.

newcomer ['njuːkʌmər] *n* recién llegado,-a.

Newfoundland ['njuːfəndlənd] *n* Terranova.

news [njuːz] *n* noticias *fpl*. LOC **bad news travels fast** las malas noticias corren deprisa. ▎**it's news to me** *fam* ahora me entero. ▎**no news is good news** la falta de noticias son buenas noticias. ▎**to break the news to sb** dar la noticia a ALGN. COMP **a piece of news** una noticia. ▎**news agency** agencia de noticias. ▎**news bulletin** boletín *m* de noticias. ▎**news conference** conferencia de prensa. ▎**news item** noticia.

newsagent ['njuːzeɪdʒənt] *n* vendedor,-ra de periódicos. COMP

newsagent's (shop) quiosco, puesto de periódicos.

newsdealer ['njuːzdiːlər] *n* US vendedor,-ra de periódicos.

newsflash ['njuːzflæʃ] *n* noticia de última hora.

newsgroup ['njuːzgruːp] *n* grupo de discusión.

newsletter ['njuːzletər] *n* hoja informativa, boletín *m*.

newspaper ['njuːspeɪpər] *n* diario, periódico.

newsstand ['njuːzstænd] *n* quiosco, puesto de periódicos.

newt [njuːt] *n* tritón *m*.

newton ['njuːtən] *n* newton *m*.

next [nekst] *adj* **1** *(following - in order)* próximo,-a, siguiente; *(- in time)* próximo,-a, que viene: *the next street on the left* la próxima calle a la izquierda; *it's on the next page* está en la página siguiente; *not this stop, the next* esta parada no, la siguiente; *next Thursday «(Friday, etc)»* el próximo jueves *(viernes, etc)*, el jueves *(viernes, etc)* que viene; *next week/month/year* la semana/el mes/el año que viene. **2** *(room, house, etc)* de al lado: *they live in the next house* viven en la casa de al lado.

► *adv* luego, después, a continuación: *what did you say next?* ¿qué dijiste luego?; *what do you want to do next?* ¿qué quieres hacer ahora?

► *prep* **next to** al lado de: *it's next to the cinema* está al lado del cine. LOC **next to nothing** casi nada. ▎**next door** al lado, la casa de al lado: *they live next door* viven (en la casa de) al lado.

next-door ['nekstdɔːr] *adj* de al lado, de la casa de al lado: *my next-door neighbours* los vecinos de al lado.

NGO ['en'dʒiː'əʊ] *abbr* (Non-Governmental Organization) Organización *f* no gubernamental; *(abbreviation)* ONG *f*.

nibble ['nɪbəl] *n* **1** *(action)* mordisco. **2** *(piece)* bocadito.

► *vi* picar.

Nicaragua [nɪkə'rægjuə] *n* Nicaragua.

Nicaraguan [nɪkə'rægjuən] *adj* nicaragüense.

► *n* nicaragüense.

nice [naɪs] *adj* **1** *(person)* amable, simpático: *he's such a nice boy!* ¡es un chico tan simpático! **2** *(thing)* bueno,-a, agradable: *nice day today, isn't it?* hace buen día, ¿verdad? **3** *(food)* delicioso,-a, bueno,-a. **4** *(pretty)* bonito,-a, mono,-a, guapo,-a.

nicely ['naɪslɪ] *adv* **1** *(well)* bien: *she was very nicely dressed* iba muy bien vestida. **2** *(properly)* bien: *behave nicely, dear* compórtate bien, cariño. **3** *fam (very well)* perfecto, estupendo: *Friday would suit me nicely* el viernes me iría perfecto.

nickel ['nɪkəl] *n* **1** níquel *m*. **2** US moneda de cinco centavos.

nickname ['nɪkneɪm] *n* apodo.
▶ *vt* apodar: *he was nicknamed "Lanky"* lo apodaron «Lanky».

niece [ni:s] *n* sobrina.

Niger [ni:'ʒeə'] *n* Níger.

Nigeria [naɪ'dʒɪərɪə] *n* Nigeria.

Nigerian [naɪ'dʒɪərɪən] *adj* nigeriano,-a.
▶ *n* nigeriano,-a.

night [naɪt] *n* noche *f*. [LOC] **all night long** toda la noche. ▌**at night** de noche. ▌**by night** de noche. ▌**last night** anoche. ▌**late at night** a altas horas de la noche. ▌**night and day** noche y día. ▌**to have a bad night** pasar una mala noche. ▌**to have a good night 1** *(sleep well)* dormir bien. **2** *(have fun)* pasárselo bien. ▌**to have a late night** acostarse tarde. ▌**to have a night out** salir por la noche. ▌[COMP] **night shift** turno de noche. ▌**night watchman** vigilante *m* nocturno.

nightdress ['naɪtdres] *n* camisón *m*.
ⓘ *pl* nightdresses.

nightfall ['naɪtfɔ:l] *n* anochecer *m*.

nightie ['naɪtɪ] *n* camisón *m*.

nightgown ['naɪtgaʊn] *n* camisón *m*.

nightingale ['naɪtɪŋgeɪl] *n* ruiseñor *m*.

nightmare ['naɪtmeə'] *n* pesadilla.

nighttime ['naɪttaɪm] *n* noche *f*.

nil [nɪl] *n* **1** cero, nada: *costs have been reduced to practically nil* los costes se han reducido prácticamente a cero. **2** SP cero: *Lincoln beat Grantham two goals to nil* Lincoln ganó a Grantham por dos goles a cero.

nine [naɪn] *adj* nueve.
▶ *n* nueve *m*.

✎ Consulta también six.

nineteen [naɪn'ti:n] *adj* diecinueve.
▶ *n* diecinueve *m*.

✎ Consulta también six.

nineteenth [naɪn'ti:nθ] *adj* decimonono,-a.
▶ *adv* en decimonono lugar.
▶ *n* **1** *(in series)* decimonono,-a. **2** *(fraction)* decimonono; *(one part)* decimonona parte *f*.

✎ Consulta también sixth.

ninetieth ['naɪntɪəθ] *adj* nonagésimo,-a.
▶ *adv* en nonagésimo lugar.
▶ *n* **1** *(in series)* nonagésimo,-a. **2** *(fraction)* nonagésimo; *(one part)* nonagésima parte *f*.

✎ Consulta también sixtieth.

ninety ['naɪntɪ] *adj* noventa.
▶ *n* noventa *m*.

✎ Consulta también sixty.

ninth [naɪnθ] *adj* nono,-a, noveno,-a.
▶ *adv* en nono lugar, en noveno lugar.
▶ *n* **1** *(in series)* nono,-a, noveno,-a. **2** *(fraction)* noveno; *(one part)* novena parte *f*.

✎ Consulta también sixth.

nip [nɪp] *n* **1** *(pinch)* pellizco: *she gave him a nip* le pegó un pellizco. **2** *(bite)* mordisco, mordedura: *the dog gave me a nip on the ankle* el perro me pegó un mordisco en el tobillo. **3** *(drink)* trago: *a nip of whisky* un trago de whisky.
▶ *vt* **1** *(pinch)* pellizcar: *a crab nipped my finger* un cangrejo me pellizcó el dedo. **2** *(bite)* morder (con poca fuerza): *the dog nipped me* el perro me mordió.
ⓘ *pt & pp* nipped, *ger* nipping.

nipple ['nɪpəl] *n* **1** *(female)* pezón *m*. **2** *(male)* tetilla. **3** *(teat)* tetilla. **4** TECH pezón *m*.

nit [nɪt] *n* **1** liendre *f*. **2** GB *fam* imbécil *mf*.

niter ['naɪtə'] *n* US→ nitre.

nitre ['naɪtə'] *n* salitre *m*.

nitrogen ['naɪtrədʒən] *n* nitrógeno.

no [nəʊ] *adv* no: *have you seen it? –no!* ¿lo has visto? –¡no!; *he's no better than a thief* no es más que un ladrón. ⎡LOC⎤ **no way!** ¡ni hablar!

▸ *adj* ninguno,-a; *(before masc sing)* ningún: *I have no time* no tengo tiempo; «*No smoking*» «Prohibido fumar»; «*No motorcycles*» «Motos no».

▸ *n* no: *there were two noes, nine yeses and one abstention* hubo dos noes, nueve síes y una abstención.

nobility [nəʊˈbɪlɪtɪ] *n* nobleza.

noble [ˈnəʊbəl] *adj* noble.
ⓘ *comp* **nobler**, *superl* **noblest**.
▸ *n* noble *mf*.

nobleman [ˈnəʊbəlmən] *n* noble *m*.
ⓘ *pl* **noblemen** [ˈnəʊbəlmən].

noblewoman [ˈnəʊbəlwʊmən] *n* noble *f*.
ⓘ *pl* **noblewomen** [ˈnəʊbəlwɪmɪn].

nobody [ˈnəʊbədɪ] *pron* nadie: *nobody went to the party* no fue nadie a la fiesta.
▸ *n* don nadie *m*.

nod [nɒd] *n* **1** saludo *con la cabeza*. **2** *(in agreement)* señal *f* de asentimiento.
▸ *vi* **1** saludar *con la cabeza*. **2** *(agree)* asentir *(con la cabeza)*.
ⓘ *pt & pp* **nodded**, *ger* **nodding**.

noise [nɔɪz] *n* ruido, sonido.
▸ *n pl* **noises** comentarios *mpl*. ⎡LOC⎤ **to make a noise** hacer ruido. ⎡COMP⎤ **big noise** *fam* pez *m* gordo.

noisy [ˈnɔɪzɪ] *adj* ruidoso,-a.
ⓘ *comp* **noisier**, *superl* **noisiest**.

nomad [ˈnəʊmæd] *n* nómada *mf*.

no-man's-land [ˈnəʊmænzlænd] *n* tierra de nadie.

nominal [ˈnɒmɪnəl] *adj* **1** nominal. **2** *(price)* simbólico,-a.

nominate [ˈnɒmɪneɪt] *vt* **1** nombrar: *he was nominated team captain* lo nombraron capitán del equipo. **2** *(propose)* proponer: *I nominate Neil as captain* yo propongo a Neil como capitán.

nonconformist [nɒnkənˈfɔːmɪst] *adj* disidente.

none [nʌn] *pron* ninguno,-a: *none of the keys opens the door* ninguna de las llaves abre la puerta; *none of them could do it* nadie supo hacerlo; *I wanted nutmeg, but they had none* quería nuez moscada, pero no tenían.
▸ *adv* de ningún modo: *he's none the worse for his ordeal* no le ha afectado esa

mala experiencia. ⎡LOC⎤ **none but** únicamente, solamente, solo: *none but the strongest survived* sobrevivieron solo los más fuertes..

nonsense [ˈnɒnsəns] *n* tonterías *fpl*: *don't talk nonsense!* ¡no digas tonterías!

nonstick [ˈnɒnstɪk] *adj* antiadherente.

nonstop [ˈnɒnstɒp] *adj* **1** *(continuous)* continuo,-a. **2** *(flight, etc)* directo,-a, sin escalas.
▸ *adv* sin parar.

noodle [ˈnuːdəl] *n* fideo.

noon [nuːn] *n* mediodía *m*.

no-one [ˈnəʊwʌn] [also written **no one**] *pron* nadie: *no-one went to the party* no fue nadie a la fiesta.

no-place [ˈnəʊpleɪs] *adv* US→ **nowhere**.

nor [nɔːr] *conj* **1** ni: *neither you nor I* ni tú ni yo; *I neither know nor care* ni lo sé ni me importa. **2** tampoco: *nor do I* yo tampoco.

Nordic [ˈnɔːdɪk] *adj* nórdico,-a.

normal [ˈnɔːməl] *adj* normal.

normally [ˈnɔːməlɪ] *adv* normalmente.

normality [nɔːˈmælɪtɪ] *n* normalidad *f*.

north [nɔːθ] *n* norte *m*: *to the north of London* al norte de Londres; *in the north of Scotland* en el norte de Escocia.
▸ *adj* del norte: *I live in north London* vivo en el norte de Londres.
▸ *adv* norte, hacia el norte: *we're travelling north* viajamos hacia el norte; *they've moved north* se han trasladado al norte; *it's north of Cambridge* está al norte de Cambridge. ⎡COMP⎤ **North Pole** Polo Norte.

northeast [nɔːθˈiːst] *n* nordeste *m*, noreste *m*.
▸ *adj* del nordeste.
▸ *adv* al nordeste, hacia el nordeste.

northern [ˈnɔːθən] *adj* norte, del norte.

northwest [nɔːθˈwest] *n* noroeste *m*.
▸ *adj* del noroeste.
▸ *adv* al noroeste, hacia el noroeste.

Norway [ˈnɔːweɪ] *n* Noruega.

Norwegian [nɔːˈwiːdʒən] *adj* noruego,-a.
▸ *n* **1** *(person)* noruego,-a. **2** *(language)* noruego.

nose [nəʊz] *n* **1** nariz *f*. **2** *(of animal)* hocico. **3** *(sense)* olfato. **4** *(of car, etc)* morro.

N

LOC **to blow one's nose** sonarse. ▌ **to get up SB's nose** GB *fam* fastidiar a ALGN. ▌ **under SB's very nose / right under SB's nose** ante las propias narices de ALGN.

nosebleed ['nəʊzbliːd] *n* hemorragia nasal.

nostril ['nɒstrəl] *n* fosa nasal.

nosy ['nəʊzɪ] *adj fam* curioso,-a, entrometido,-a.
ⓘ *comp* nosier, *superl* nosiest.

not [nɒt] [la forma contracta es n't: isn't, aren't, doesn't.] *adv* no: *I did not steal it* no lo robé; *she told me not to tell anyone* me dijo que no lo dijera a nadie; *I hope/suppose not* espero/supongo que no; *are you coming or not?* ¿vienes o no? LOC **not likely!** ¡ni hablar! ▌ **not that...** no es que...: *where is he?, not that I mind, of course* ¿dónde está?, no es que me importe, claro está. ▌ **not to say...** por no decir...

✎ Not acompaña al auxiliar del verbo en las oraciones negativas. En el inglés hablado y en los textos escritos informales se suele contraer a -n't: *she isn't English; he doesn't like it.* También se usa para la forma negativa de los verbos subordinados.

notary ['nəʊtərɪ] *n* notario,-a.
ⓘ *pl* notaries.

note [nəʊt] *n* **1** MUS nota; *(key)* tecla. **2** *(message)* nota. **3** *(money)* billete *m*.
▶ *vt* **1** *(notice)* notar, advertir: *I noted a certain reluctance on John's part* noté cierta reticencia por parte de John. **2** *(pay special attention)* fijarse en: *note that the plural of «child» is «children»* fijaos en que el plural de «child» es «children». **3** *(write down)* apuntar, anotar.
▶ *n pl* **notes** apuntes *mpl*.
◆ **to note down** *vt sep* apuntar.

✖ Note no significa 'nota (calificación)', que se traduce por **mark**.

notebook ['nəʊtbʊk] *n* **1** *(book)* libreta, cuaderno. **2** *(computer)* ordenador *m* portátil.

notepad ['nəʊtpæd] *n* bloc *m* de notas.

nothing ['nʌθɪŋ] *n* nada: *there's nothing left* no queda nada; *it's nothing special* no es nada del otro jueves. LOC **for nothing** *fam* gratis. ▌ **nothing but...** únicamente..., solo...
▶ *adv* de ningún modo, de ninguna manera: *it's nothing like a pheasant* no se parece en nada a un faisán.

notice ['nəʊtɪs] *n* **1** *(sign)* letrero: *there's a notice which says «No parking»* hay un letrero que pone «Prohibido aparcar». **2** *(announcement)* anuncio: *there's a notice in the paper about a lost dog* hay un anuncio en el diario acerca de un perro extraviado. **3** *(warning)* aviso: *they gave him a month's notice to quit the flat* le dieron un plazo de un mes para abandonar el piso. LOC **to take no notice of** no hacer caso de. ▌ **until further notice** hasta nuevo aviso. ▌ **without notice** sin previo aviso.
▶ *vt* notar, fijarse en, darse cuenta de.
▶ *vi fam (show)* verse: *don't worry, the stain doesn't notice* no te preocupes, la mancha no se ve.

✖ Notice no significa 'noticia', que se traduce por **news**.

noticeable ['nəʊtɪsəbəl] *adj* que se nota, evidente.

noticeboard ['nəʊtɪsbɔːd] *n* tablón *m* de anuncios.

notify ['nəʊtɪfaɪ] *vt* notificar, avisar.
ⓘ *pt & pp* notified, *ger* notifying.

notion ['nəʊʃən] *n* noción *f*, idea, concepto.
▶ *n pl* **notions** US mercería *f sing*.

notorious [nəʊˈtɔːrɪəs] *adj pej* célebre: *a notorious criminal* un conocido criminal.

✖ Notorious no significa 'notorio (conocido)', que se traduce por **well-known**.

nougat ['nuːgɑː] *n* turrón *m* blando.

nought [nɔːt] *n* cero: *nought point sixty-six* cero coma sesenta y seis. COMP **noughts and crosses** tres en raya *m*.

noun [naʊn] *n* nombre *m*, sustantivo. COMP **noun phrase** sintagma *m* nominal.

nourish ['nʌrɪʃ] *vt* nutrir, alimentar.

nourishing ['nʌrɪʃɪŋ] *adj* nutritivo,-a.

novel¹ ['nɒvəl] *adj* original, novedoso,-a: *what a novel idea!* ¡qué idea más original!

novel² ['nɒvəl] *n* novela.

novelist ['nɒvəlɪst] *n* novelista *mf*.

novelty [ˈnɒvəltɪ] n 1 novedad f: the novelty soon wore off pronto dejó de ser novedad. 2 (trinket) chuchería.
ⓘ pl novelties.

November [nəʊˈvembəʳ] n noviembre m.

✎ Para ejemplos de uso, consulta May.

novice [ˈnɒvɪs] n 1 novato,-a. 2 REL novicio,-a.

now [naʊ] adv 1 (at the present) ahora; (used contrastively) ya: where do you work now? ¿dónde trabajas ahora?; I'm ready now ya estoy listo. 2 (immediately) ya, ahora mismo: do it now! ¡hazlo ya! 3 (in past) ya, entonces. 4 (introductory) bueno, vamos a ver, veamos: now, let's begin bueno, empecemos. **by now** ya: she'll be in Mexico by now ya debe de estar en Méjico. **for now** por el momento. **from now on** de ahora en adelante. **just now 1** (at this moment) en estos momentos, ahora mismo. **2** (a short while ago) hace un momento, ahora mismo: I can't help you just now ahora mismo no puedo ayudarte. **now and then** de vez en cuando. **right now** ahora mismo.
▶ conj [also now that] ahora que, ya que: now (that) we're all here, we can begin ya que estamos todos, podemos empezar.

nowadays [ˈnaʊədeɪz] adv hoy día, hoy en día, actualmente.

nowhere [ˈnəʊweəʳ] adv (position) en ninguna parte, en ningún sitio, en ningún lugar; (direction) a ninguna parte, a ningún sitio: where are you going? – nowhere special ¿dónde vas? –a ningún sitio en especial; there's nowhere to hide no hay donde esconderse. LOC **in the middle of nowhere** en el quinto pino. **nowhere near** muy lejos de.

nozzle [ˈnɒzəl] n (of hose) boquilla; (of oilcan) pitorro; (large calibre) tobera.

nuclear [ˈnjuːklɪəʳ] adj nuclear. COMP nuclear bomb bomba nuclear. **nuclear energy** energía nuclear. **nuclear fission** fisión f nuclear. **nuclear fusion** fusión f nuclear. **nuclear power** energía nuclear. **nuclear power station** central f nuclear. **nuclear reactor** reactor m nuclear. **nuclear waste** residuos nucleares. **nuclear weapon** arma nuclear.

nucleus [ˈnjuːklɪəs] n núcleo.
ⓘ pl nuclei [ˈnjuːklɪaɪ].

nude [njuːd] adj desnudo,-a.
▶ n desnudo.

nudge [nʌdʒ] n 1 (with elbow) codazo. 2 empujón m suave.
▶ vt dar un codazo a.

nuisance [ˈnjuːsəns] n 1 molestia, fastidio, lata. 2 (person) pesado,-a. LOC **to make a nuisance of os** dar la lata.

numb [nʌm] adj entumecido,-a, insensible. LOC **to be numb with cold** estar helado,-a de frío.

number [ˈnʌmbəʳ] n número. LOC **a number of...** varios,-as... **any number of...** muchísimos,-as... **without number** un sinfín de... COMP **number plate** placa de matrícula..
◆ **to number off** vi numerarse.

numeral [ˈnjuːmərəl] n número, cifra.

numerous [ˈnjuːmərəs] adj numeroso,-a.

nun [nʌn] n monja, religiosa.

nurse [nɜːs] n 1 enfermero,-a. 2 (children's) niñera.
▶ vt 1 (look after) cuidar. 2 (suckle) amamantar. 3 (hold) acunar. 4 (feeling) guardar.

nursery [ˈnɜːsərɪ] n 1 (in house) cuarto de los niños. 2 (kindergarten) guardería. 3 (for plants) vivero. COMP **nursery rhyme** canción f infantil, poema m infantil. **nursery school** parvulario.
ⓘ pl nurseries.

nut [nʌt] n 1 BOT fruto seco. 2 TECH tuerca. 3 fam (head) coco. 4 fam (nutcase) chalado,-a, chiflado,-a.

nutcrackers [ˈnʌtkrækəz] n pl cascanueces m inv.

nutmeg [ˈnʌtmeg] n nuez f moscada.

nutrient [ˈnjuːtrɪənt] n nutriente m.

nutrition [njuːˈtrɪʃən] n nutrición f.

nutritious [njuːˈtrɪʃəs] adj nutritivo,-a.

nutshell [ˈnʌtʃel] n cáscara. LOC **in a nutshell** en pocas palabras.

nylon® [ˈnaɪlɒn] n nailon m.
▶ n pl nylons medias fpl de nailon.

nymph [nɪmf] n ninfa.

N

O

O, o [əʊ] *n (the letter)* O, o *f*.

O [əʊ] *n (as number)* cero.

oak [əʊk] *n* **1** BOT roble *m*. **2** *(wood)* roble *m*.
▶ *adj* de roble.

oar [ɔːʳ] *n* remo.

oarsman ['ɔːzmən] *n* remero.
ⓘ *pl* oarsmen ['ɔːzmən].

oasis [əʊ'eɪsɪs] *n* oasis *m*.
ⓘ *pl* oases [əʊ'eɪsiːz].

oats [əʊts] *n pl* avena.

oath [əʊθ] *n* **1** JUR juramento. **2** *(swearword)* palabrota, juramento. LOC **on my oath** lo juro. ▌ **to be on oath / be under oath** estar bajo juramento.

obedience [ə'biːdɪəns] *n* obediencia.

obedient [ə'biːdɪənt] *adj* obediente.

obelisk ['ɒbəlɪsk] *n* obelisco.

obese [əʊ'biːs] *adj* obeso,-a.

obesity [əʊ'biːsɪtɪ] *n* obesidad *f*.

obey [ə'beɪ] *vt* **1** *(gen)* obedecer; *(orders)* acatar. **2** *(law)* cumplir.
▶ *vi (gen)* obedecer.

object [*(n)* 'ɒbdʒekt; *(vb)* əb'dʒekt] *n* **1** *(thing)* objeto, cosa. **2** *(aim, purpose)* objetivo, fin *m*. **3** *(focus of feelings)* objeto: *he was an object of ridicule* fue objeto de burlas. **4** LING complemento: *direct/indirect object* complemento directo/indirecto. COMP **object glass / object lens** objetivo.
▶ *vt* objetar.
▶ *vi* **1** *(oppose)* oponerse (**to**, a), poner reparos (**to**, a).

objection [əb'dʒekʃ°n] *n* objeción *f*, reparo, inconveniente.

objective [əb'dʒektɪv] *adj* objetivo,-a.
▶ *n* **1** *(purpose)* objetivo, fin *m*. **2** *(lens)* objetivo.

objectivity [əbdʒek'tɪvɪtɪ] *n* objetividad *f*.

obligation [ɒblɪ'geɪʃ°n] *n* obligación *f*.

oblige [ə'blaɪdʒ] *vt* **1** *(compel)* obligar: *I felt obliged to attend* me veía obligado a asistir. **2** *(do a favour)* hacer un favor a, ayudar a. LOC **much obliged!** ¡muy agradecido,-a!
▶ *vi (do a favour)* hacer un favor, ayudar.

oblong ['ɒblɒŋ] *adj* oblongo,-a, alargado,-a.
▶ *n* rectángulo.

oboe ['əʊbəʊ] *n* oboe *m*.

obscene [ɒb'siːn] *adj* obsceno,-a, indecente.

obscenity [əb'senɪtɪ] *n* obscenidad *f*.
ⓘ *pl* obscenities.

obscure [əbs'kjʊəʳ] *adj* **1** *(unclear)* oscuro,-a, poco claro,-a. **2** *(vague, indistinct)* vago,-a, confuso,-a; *(hidden)* recóndito,-a.

> ❌ Obscure no significa 'oscuro (un color)', que se traduce por dark.

obsequious [əb'siːkwɪəs] *adj* servil.

> ❌ Obsequious no significa 'obsequioso', que se traduce por obliging.

observant [əb'zɜːv°nt] *adj* observador,-ra.

observation [ɒbzə'veɪʃ°n] *n* **1** *(watching, study)* observación *f*; *(surveillance)* vigilancia. **2** *(remark)* observación *f*, comentario.

observatory [əb'zɜːvət°rɪ] *n* observatorio.
ⓘ *pl* observatories.

observe [əb'zɜːv] *vt* **1** *(see, watch)* observar, ver; *(in surveillance)* vigilar. **2** *(law)* cumplir, respetar. **3** *fml (say)* señalar.
▶ *vi* observar.

obsess [əb'ses] *vt* obsesionar.

obsession [əb'seʃən] *n* obsesión *f* (with/about, con).

obsessive [əb'sesɪv] *adj* obsesivo,-a.
  ▶ *n* obsesivo,-a.

obstacle ['ɒbstəkəl] *n* **1** obstáculo. **2** *fig* obstáculo, impedimento. COMP **obstacle race** carrera de obstáculos.

obstetrics [ɒb'stetrɪks] *n* obstetricia, tocología.

obstinate ['ɒbstɪnət] *adj* obstinado,-a.

obstruct [əb'strʌkt] *vt* **1** (block - gen) obstruir; (- pipe, etc) atascar, bloquear; (- view) tapar. **2** (make difficult) dificultar.

obstruction [əb'strʌkʃən] *n* **1** (gen) obstrucción *f*. **2** (hindrance) estorbo, obstáculo.

obtain [əb'teɪn] *vt* obtener, conseguir.

obtuse [əb'tjuːs] *adj fml* (stupid) obtuso,-a. COMP **obtuse angle** ángulo obtuso.

obvious ['ɒbvɪəs] *adj* (clear) obvio,-a: *for obvious reasons* por razones obvias.

obviously ['ɒbvɪəslɪ] *adv* obviamente, evidentemente.

occasion [ə'keɪʒən] *n* **1** (time) ocasión *f*; (event) acontecimiento. **2** (opportunity) ocasión *f*, oportunidad *f*: *if the occasion arises* si se presenta la ocasión. LOC **on occasion** de vez en cuando. ▌ **on the occasion of** con motivo de. ▌ **to rise to the occasion** estar a la altura de las circunstancias, dar la talla.

occasional [ə'keɪʒənəl] *adj* (not frequent) esporádico,-a, eventual.

occasionally [ə'keɪʒənəlɪ] *adv* de vez en cuando, ocasionalmente.

occipital [ɒk'spɪtəl] *adj* occipital.

occult ['ɒkʌlt] *adj* oculto,-a.

⊠ Occult no significa 'oculto (escondido)', que se traduce por **hidden**.

occupant ['ɒkjəpənt] *n* (gen) ocupante *mf*; (tenant) inquilino,-a.

occupation [ɒkjə'peɪʃən] *n* **1** (job) ocupación *f*, profesión *f*. **2** (pastime) pasatiempo. **3** (act, state of occupying) ocupación *f*.

occupied ['ɒkjəpaɪd] *adj* ocupado,-a.

occupy ['ɒkjəpaɪ] *vt* ocupar.
  ① *pt & pp* occupied, *ger* occupying.

occur [ə'kɜːr] *vi* **1** (happen - event, incident) ocurrir, suceder; (- change) producirse. **2** *fml* (be found, exist) existir, darse. **3** (come to mind) ocurrir, ocurrirse: *it never occurred to me to ask* no se me ocurrió preguntar.
  ① *pt & pp* occurred, *ger* occurring.

occurrence [ə'kʌrəns] *n* **1** (event, incident) suceso. **2** *fml* (frequency) incidencia, frecuencia; (existing amount) cantidad *f*.

⊠ Occurrence no significa 'ocurrencia', que se traduce por **idea**.

ocean ['əʊʃən] *n* océano.
  ▶ *adj* oceánico,-a: *ocean currents* corrientes oceánicas.

oceanic [əʊʃɪ'ænɪk] *adj fml* oceánico,-a.

oceanography [əʊʃən'ɒgrəfɪ] *n* oceanografía.

ocher ['əʊkər] *adj* US → ochre.

ochre ['əʊkər] *adj* (de color) ocre.
  ▶ *n* ochre *m*.

o'clock [ə'klɒk] *adv* : *it's one o'clock* es la una; *at three o'clock* a las tres.

octagon ['ɒktəgən] *n* octágono, octógono.

octagonal [ɒk'tægənəl] *adj* octagonal, octogonal.

octahedron [ɒktə'hiːdrən] *n* octaedro.

October [ɒk'təʊbər] *n* octubre *m*.

Para ejemplos de uso, consulta May.

octopus ['ɒktəpəs] *n* pulpo.
  ① *pl* octopuses.

odd [ɒd] *adj* **1** (strange) extraño,-a, raro,-a: *the odd thing is that...* lo raro es que... **2** (number) impar. **3** (approximately) y pico: *thirty odd people* unas treinta y pico personas. **4** (shoe, glove, etc) suelto,-a, desparejado,-a. LOC **to be the odd man out 1** (be over) estar de más. **2** (be different) ser la excepción. COMP **odd jobs** trabajillos *mpl*.
  ▶ *n pl* **odds 1** (probability, chances) probabilidades *fpl*: *the odds are that...* lo más probable es que... **2** (in betting) apuestas *fpl*. LOC **against (all) the odds** contra todo pronóstico.

odontology [ɒdɒn'tɒlədʒɪ] *n* odontología.

odor ['əʊdər] *adj* US → odour.

odorless ['əʊdələs] *adj* US → odourless.

O

odour ['əʊdə^r] n (smell) olor m; (fragrance) perfume m, fragancia.

odourless ['əʊdələs] adj inodoro,-a.

odyssey ['ɒdɪsɪ] n odisea.

oesophagus [iː'sɒfəgəs] n esófago.
ⓘ pl oesophagi [iː'sɒfəgaɪ].

oestrogen ['iːstrədʒ^ən] n estrógeno.

of [ɒv, unstressed əv] prep **1** (belonging to) de: a friend of mine un amigo mío. **2** (made from) de: Spanish-leather shoes zapatos de piel española. **3** (containing) de: a bag of crisps una bolsa de patatas. **4** (showing a part, a quantity) de: a kilo of apples un kilo de manzanas. **5** (partitive use) de: the two of us nosotros dos. **6** (dates, distance) de: the 7th of August el 7 de agosto. **7** (apposition) de: the city of London la ciudad de Londres. **8** (by) de: the works of Shakespeare las obras de Shakespeare. **9** (with, having) de: a child of five un niño de cinco años. **10** (after superlative) de: best of all was the food lo mejor de todo fue la comida.

off [ɒf] prep **1** (movement) de: he got off the bus bajó del autobús. **2** (indicating removal) de: he cut a branch off the tree cortó una rama del árbol. **3** (distance, situation) diferentes traducciones: a narrow street off the main road una callejuela que sale de la carretera; the ship sank off Malpica el barco se hundió a la altura de Malpica. **4** (away from) diferentes traducciones: the ship went off course el barco se desvió de su rumbo; we're a long way off finding a cure estamos lejos de encontrar una cura. **5** (not wanting) : I'm off coffee ya no tomo café. **6** (not at work) : she comes off duty at 10.00pm acaba el turno a las 10.00. **7** fam (from) a: I bought it off Eva se lo compré a Eva.
  ▶ adv **1** (departure): he ran off se fue corriendo; I'm off me voy. **2** (showing distance) a: the village is three miles off el pueblo está a tres millas. **3** (reduced in price) menos: 70% off! ¡70% menos! **4** (disconnected, not working) diferentes traducciones: turn the light off apaga la luz; she turned the tap off cerró el grifo. **7** (free, on holiday) libre: can I have the afternoon off? ¿puedo tomarme la tarde libre? LOC **off and on / on and off** de vez en cuando, a ratos. ▌ **right off / straight off** acto seguido.

  ▶ adj **1** (event) cancelado,-a, suspendido,-a: the wedding's off la boda se ha suspendido. **2** (not turned on - gas, water) cerrado,-a; (- electricity) apagado,-a. COMP **off season** temporada baja.

offence [ə'fens] n **1** JUR delito, infracción f: a traffic offence una infracción de tráfico. **2** (insult) ofensa. LOC **to take offence at sth** ofenderse por algo, sentirse ofendido,-a por algo.

offend [ə'fend] vt **1** (insult, hurt) ofender: she'll be offended if we don't go se ofenderá si no vamos.
  ▶ vi **1** fml (do wrong to) atentar (against, a). **2** JUR fml (commit crime) cometer un delito.

offender [ə'fendə^r] n **1** JUR (gen) infractor,-ra; (criminal) delincuente mf. **2** (culprit) culpable mf.

offensive [ə'fensɪv] adj **1** (insulting) ofensivo,-a, insultante. **2** (disgusting - gen) repugnante; (- smell) desagradable. **3** (attacking) ofensivo,-a.
  ▶ n MIL ofensiva.

offer ['ɒfə^r] vt **1** (gen) ofrecer: she offered us a coffee nos ofreció un café. **2** (show willingness) ofrecerse (to, para): he offered me a lift to the airport se ofreció para llevarme al aeropuerto. **3** (propose) proponer, sugerir.
  ▶ n **1** (gen) oferta, ofrecimiento; (proposal) propuesta. **2** COMM oferta. LOC **to be on offer 1** (at reduced price) estar de oferta. **2** (available) disponible.

office ['ɒfɪs] n **1** (room) despacho, oficina; (building) oficina; (staff) oficina. **2** GB ministerio: the Foreign Office el Ministerio de Asuntos Exteriores. **3** (post, position) cargo. LOC **to hold office** ocupar un cargo. COMP **office block** edificio de oficinas. ▌ **office boy** recadero. ▌ **office junior** auxiliar mf de oficina. ▌ **office worker** oficinista mf.

officer ['ɒfɪsə^r] n **1** MIL oficial mf. **2** (police officer) agente mf. **3** (in government) funcionario,-a. **4** (of club, society) directivo,-a.

official [ə'fɪʃ^əl] adj (gen) oficial.
  ▶ n funcionario,-a, oficial mf.

⊠ Official no significa 'oficial (militar)', que se traduce por **officer**.

officially [əˈfɪʃ^əlɪ] *adv* oficialmente.

officious [əˈfɪʃəs] *adj (too eager)* oficioso,-a; *(interfering)* entrometido,-a.

☒ Officious no significa 'oficioso (no oficial', que se traduce por **unofficial**.

off-licence [ˈɒflaɪs^əns] *n* GB tienda de bebidas alcohólicas.

offshoot [ˈɒfʃuːt] *n* BOT retoño, vástago.

offshore [ɒfˈʃɔːʳ] *adj* **1** *(at sea)* a poca distancia de la costa. **2** *(breeze)* terral, de tierra. **3** *(overseas)* en el extranjero.
▶ *adv* mar adentro.

offside [ɒfˈsaɪd] *adj* **1** SP fuera de juego. **2** GB *(part of vehicle)* del lado del conductor.
▶ *adv* SP en fuera de juego.
▶ *n* GB *(of vehicle)* lado del conductor.

offspring [ˈɒːfsprɪŋ] *n* **1** *fml (child)* descendiente *mf*; *(children)* descendencia, prole *f*. **2** *(animal - one)* cría; *(- several)* crías *fpl*.
ⓘ *pl* offspring.

off-the-record [ɒfðəˈrekɔːd] *adj* extraoficial, confidencial.

often [ˈɒf^ən, ˈɒft^ən] *adv (frequently)* a menudo, con frecuencia: *we often go to the theatre* vamos al teatro a menudo.

oh [əʊ] *interj* ¡oh!, ¡ay!, ¡vaya!: *oh, really?* ¿de veras?; *oh, look!* ¡eh, mira!

ohm [əʊm] *n* ohmio, ohm *m*.

oil [ɔɪl] *n* **1** *(gen)* aceite *m*: *sunflower oil* aceite de girasol. **2** *(petroleum)* petróleo: *crude oil* crudo. **3** ART *(painting)* óleo, pintura al óleo.
▶ *vt* engrasar, lubricar, lubrificar.
▶ *n pl* **oils** *(paints)* óleo: *she paints in oils* pinta al óleo. COMP **oil painting** cuadro al óleo, óleo. ▌**oil rig** plataforma petrolífera. ▌**oil slick** marea negra. ▌**oil tanker** petrolero. ▌**oil well** pozo petrolífero.

oilcan [ˈɔɪlkæn] *n* aceitera.

oilcloth [ˈɔɪlklɒθ] *n* hule *m*.

oilfield [ˈɔɪlfiːld] *n* yacimiento petrolífero.

oily [ˈɔɪlɪ] *adj* **1** *(food)* aceitoso,-a, grasiento,-a; *(skin, hair)* graso,-a. **2** *pej (manner)* empalagoso,-a.
ⓘ *comp* oilier, *superl* oiliest.

ointment [ˈɔɪntmənt] *n* ungüento, pomada.

okay [əʊˈkeɪ] *interj* ¡vale!, ¡de acuerdo!
▶ *adj* correcto,-a, bien: *are you okay?* ¿estás bien?
▶ *adv* bien, bastante bien: *he's doing okay at school* va bien en el colegio.
▶ *n* visto bueno, aprobación *f*.

old [əʊld] *adj* **1** *(gen)* viejo,-a: *an old man* un anciano, un hombre mayor; *the old part of the city* el casco antiguo de la ciudad; *he's an old friend* es un viejo amigo. **2** *(former)* antiguo,-a: *in my old job* en mi antiguo trabajo. LOC **how old are you?** ¿cuántos años tienes?, ¿qué edad tienes? ▌**to be... years old** tener... años. COMP **old age** vejez *f*. ▌**the Old World** el viejo mundo.
▶ *n* **the old** las personas *fpl* mayores, los ancianos *mpl*.

older [ˈəʊldəʳ] *adj* **1** *(comparative)* → old. **2** *(elder)* mayor.

old-fashioned [əʊldˈfæʃ^ənd] *adj (outdated - gen)* anticuado,-a, pasado,-a de moda; *(- person)* chapado,-a a la antigua.

olfactory [ɒlˈfækt^ərɪ] *adj* olfativo,-a, olfatorio,-a. COMP **olfactory epithelium** epitelio olfativo. ▌**olfactory nerve** nervio olfativo.

oligarchy [ˈɒlɪgɑːkɪ] *n* oligarquía.
ⓘ *pl* oligarchies.

olive [ˈɒlɪv] *n* **1** *(tree, wood)* olivo. **2** *(fruit)* aceituna, oliva. **3** *(colour)* verde *m* oliva. COMP **olive grove** olivo. ▌**olive oil** aceite *m* de oliva. ▌**olive tree** olivo.
▶ *adj (paint)* color aceituna; *(skin)* aceitunado,-a.

Olympiad [əˈlɪmpɪæd] *n* Olimpíada, Olimpiada.

Olympic [əˈlɪmpɪk] *adj* olímpico,-a.
▶ *n pl* **the Olympics** los Juegos Olímpicos, la Olimpíada *f sing*. COMP **Olympic Games** Juegos *mpl* Olímpicos.

omega [ˈəʊmɪgə] *n* omega.

omelette [ˈɒmlət] *n* tortilla. COMP **plain omelette** tortilla francesa.

omit [əʊˈmɪt] *vt* **1** *(not include, leave out)* omitir, suprimir; *(forget to include)* olvi-

O

dar incluir. **2** *(fail to do)* omitir, dejar de; *(forget)* olvidarse.

ⓘ *pt & pp* **omitted,** *ger* **omitting.**

omnivore ['ɒmnɪvɔːʳ] *n* omnívoro.

omnivorous [ɒmˈnɪvərəs] *adj* ZOOL *fml* omnívoro,-a.

on [ɒn] *prep* **1** *(covering or touching)* sobre, encima de, en: *it's on the table* está encima de la mesa. **2** *(supported by, hanging from)* en: *she put the picture on the wall* colgó el cuadro en la pared. **3** *(to, towards)* a, hacia: *on the right/left* a la derecha/izquierda. **4** *(at the edge of)* en: *a village on the coast* un pueblo de la costa. **5** *(days, dates, times)* no se traduce: *on Saturday* el sábado. **6** *(at the time of, just after)* al: *on arriving* al llegar. **7** *(as means of transport)* a, en: *on foot* a pie; *on the train* en el tren. **8** *(regarding, about)* sobre, de: *a book on art* un libro de arte. **9** *(in possession of)* con: *have you got any money on you?* ¡llevas dinero?

▸ *adv* **1** *(not stopping)* sin parar: *she kept on talking* siguió hablando. **2** *(movement forward)* diferentes traducciones: *walk on until you get to the church* sigue hasta que llegues a la iglesia; *it's time we were moving on* es hora de que nos vayamos. **3** *(clothes - being worn)* puesto,-a: *she had a cap on* llevaba puesta una gorra. **4** *(working)* diferentes traducciones: *who left the TV on?* ¡quién dejó la TV encendida?; *don't leave the tap on!* ¡no dejes el grifo abierto! **5** *(happening)* diferentes traducciones: *what time is the film on?* ¿a qué hora ponen la película?; *have we got anything on this weekend?* ¿tenemos plan para este fin de semana? LOC **and so on** y así sucesivamente. ▯ **from that day on** a partir de aquel día.

▸ *adj* **1** *(in use)* diferentes traducciones: *is the heating on?* ¿está puesta la calefacción?; *all the lights were on* todas las luces estaban encendidas. **2** *(happening)* diferentes traducciones: *the strike's on* la huelga sigue convocada; *is the party still on?* ¿se hace la fiesta?; *the match is on after all* después de todo, el partido se celebra. **3** *(performing)* diferentes traducciones: *you're on next!* ¡sales tú el próximo!; *they're bringing the sub on* hacen salir a jugar al suplente. LOC **it's not on** no hay derecho, eso no vale. ▯ **you're on!** ¡trato hecho!

once [wʌns] *adv* **1** *(one time)* una vez: *once a week* una vez por semana. **2** *(formerly)* antes, en otro tiempo: *I was a cook once* antes era cocinero. LOC **at once 1** *(at the same time)* a la vez. **2** *(immediately)* en seguida, inmediatamente, ahora mismo. ▯ **once again** otra vez. ▯ **once and for all** de una vez para siempre, de una vez por todas. ▯ **once in a while** de vez en cuando. ▯ **once more** una vez más. ▯ **once upon a time** érase una vez.

▸ *conj* una vez que, en cuanto: *once everyone gets here, we can start* una vez que lleguen todos, podemos empezar.

▸ *n* vez *f*: *just this once* solo esta vez.

oncoming ['ɒnkʌmɪŋ] *adj* **1** *(traffic)* que viene en dirección contraria. **2** *(event, season)* venidero,-a, futuro,-a.

one [wʌn] *adj* **1** *(stating number)* un, una: *I've got one brother* tengo un hermano. **2** *(unspecified, a certain)* un, una, algún, -una: *one day in January* un día de enero. **3** *(only, single)* único,-a: *it's my one chance* es mi única oportunidad. **4** *(same)* mismo, -a: *in one direction* en la misma dirección.

▸ *pron* **1** *(thing)* uno,-a: *a red one* uno,-a rojo,-a; *this one* éste,-a. **2** *(person)* él, la: *he's the one who I was telling you about* es él de quien te estaba hablando. **3** *(any person, you)* uno, una: *one can't think of everything* uno no puede pensar en todo. LOC **one after another** uno,-a detrás de otro,-a. ▯ **one another** el uno al otro. ▯ **one at a time** de uno en uno. ▯ **one by one** de uno,-a en uno,-a.

▸ *n* *(number)* uno: *my son is one today* mi hijo cumple un año hoy.

oneself [wʌnˈself] *pron* **1** *(reflexive)* se; *(emphatic)* uno,-a mismo,-a; *(after prep)* sí mismo,-a: *to wash oneself* lavarse. **2** *(alone)* solo,-a: *one can't do everything oneself* uno no puede hacerlo todo solo. LOC **(all) by oneself** solo,-a. ▯ **to oneself** para sí, para sí solo,-a.

one-way ['wʌnweɪ] *adj* **1** *(street)* de sentido único, de dirección única. **2** *(ticket)* de ida.

onion ['ʌnɪən] *n* cebolla.

online ['ɒnlaɪn] *adj* COMPUT en línea.

▸ *adv* COMPUT en línea.

onlooker [ˈɒnlʊkəʳ] n espectador,-ra, curioso,-a.

only [ˈəʊnlɪ] adj (sole) único,-a: the only problem is that... el único problema es que... COMP **only child** hijo,-a único,-a.
► adv **1** (just, merely) solo, solamente: he's only a child solo es un niño. **2** (exclusively) solo, solamente, únicamente: only my mother knows mi madre es la única que lo sabe. LOC **not only...** sino también... ‖ **only just 1** (a moment before) acabar de. **2** (almost not, scarcely) por poco. ‖ **only too...** muy...
► conj pero: it's like yoghurt, only better es como el yogur, pero mejor.

onshore [ɒnˈʃɔːʳ] adj (on land) en tierra.
► adv (towards land) tierra adentro.

onto [ˈɒntu] prep **1** (movement) a, en: it fell onto the floor cayó al suelo. **2** (new subject) a: let's move onto a different subject cambiemos de tema.

onwards [ˈɒnwədz] adv GB adelante, hacia adelante: from now onwards de ahora en adelante.

ooze¹ [uːz] vi rezumar.
► vt **1** rezumar. **2** fig rebosar.

ooze² [uːz] n cieno, lodo.

opacity [əʊˈpæsɪtɪ] n **1** (non-transparency) opacidad f. **2** (obscurity) oscuridad f.

opal [ˈəʊpəl] n ópalo.

opaque [əʊˈpeɪk] adj **1** (not transparent) opaco,-a. **2** (difficult to understand, obscure) obscuro,-a, oscuro,-a, poco claro,-a.

open [ˈəʊpən] adj **1** (gen) abierto,-a; I can't keep my eyes open no puedo mantener los ojos abiertos. **2** (not covered) descubierto,-a: an open car un coche descapotable. COMP **open day** jornada de puertas abiertas. ‖ **open letter** carta abierta. ‖ **open season** temporada de caza.
► n SP (competition) open m.
► vt abrir: open your mouth abre la boca. LOC **to open fire** abrir fuego (on/at, contra).
► vi **1** (gen) abrir, abrirse: the door opened la puerta se abrió. **2** (spread out, unfold) abrirse: the roses are opening las rosas se están abriendo. **3** (start - conference, play, book) comenzar, empezar;

(film) estrenarse. **4** (begin business) abrir.
► adj **open to** (susceptible) susceptible a, expuesto,-a a; (receptive) abierto,-a a.
► n **the open** (the outdoors, open air) campo, aire m libre.
◆ **to open into / open onto** vt insep dar a: the back door opens onto the patio la puerta trasera da al patio.

open-air [ˈəʊpˈneəʳ] adj al aire libre.

opener [ˈəʊpənəʳ] n abridor m.

opening [ˈəʊpənɪŋ] n **1** (ceremony - gen) inauguración f, comienzo. **2** (first night) estreno. **3** (process of opening, unfolding) apertura. **4** (hole) abertura; (space) hueco; (gap) brecha; (clearing) claro. **5** (chance) oportunidad f (for, para). **6** (vacancy) vacante f (for, para). COMP **opening hours** horario de apertura. ‖ **opening night** noche f de estreno.
► adj (initial) inicial.

openly [ˈəʊpənlɪ] adv (not secretly) abiertamente; (publicly) públicamente, en público.

open-minded [ˈəʊpənˈmaɪndɪd] adj abierto,-a, de actitud abierta.

openness [ˈəʊpənnəs] n (frankness) franqueza; (receptiveness) actitud f abierta.

opera [ˈɒpərə] n ópera.

operate [ˈɒpəreɪt] vt **1** (machine, etc) hacer funcionar, manejar,. **2** (manage, run - business) dirigir, llevar.
► vi **1** (function - machine, etc) funcionar. **2** (carry on trade) operar; (work) trabajar. **3** MED operar (on, a), intervenir (on, a).

operating [ˈɒpəreɪtɪŋ] adj COMM (losses, costs) de explotación. COMP **operating room** US quirófano. ‖ **operating system** COMPUT sistema m operativo. ‖ **operating theatre** GB quirófano.

operation [ɒpəˈreɪʃən] n **1** MED operación f, intervención f. **2** (of machine - gen) funcionamiento; (- by person) manejo; (of system) uso. **3** (activity) operación f; (planned campaign) campaña. **4** MIL operación f. **5** MATH operación f.

operator [ˈɒpəreɪtəʳ] n **1** (of equipment, machine) operario,-a. **2** (of switchboard) operador,-ra, telefonista mf.

O

ophthalmologist [ɒfθæl'mɒlədʒɪst] *n* oftalmólogo,-a, oculista *mf*.

opinion [ə'pɪnɪən] *n* **1** *(belief)* opinión *f*, parecer *m*. **2** *(evaluation, estimation)* opinión *f*, concepto. LOC **in my opinion** en mi opinión, a mi juicio. COMP **opinion poll** encuesta.

opium ['əʊpɪəm] *n* opio.

opponent [ə'pəʊnənt] *n* adversario,-a, oponente *mf*.

opportunity [ɒpə'tjuːnɪtɪ] *n* **1** *(gen)* oportunidad *f*, ocasión *f*. **2** *(prospect)* perspectiva.
ⓘ *pl* opportunities.

oppose [ə'pəʊz] *vt* oponerse a.

opposite ['ɒpəzɪt] *adj* **1** *(facing)* de enfrente: *she lives on the opposite side of the road* vive al otro lado de la calle. **2** *(contrary, different)* opuesto,-a, contrario,-a.
▸ *prep* enfrente de, frente a: *the building opposite the cinema* el edificio enfrente del cine.
▸ *adv* enfrente: *the family who live opposite* la familia que vive enfrente.
▸ *n* lo contrario, lo opuesto: *the opposite of big is small* lo contrario a grande es pequeño.

opposition [ɒpə'zɪʃ°n] *n* **1** *(resistance)* oposición *f*, resistencia. **2** *(rivals - in sport)* adversarios *mpl*; *(- in business)* competencia.
▸ *n* the Opposition POL la oposición *f*.

oppress [ə'pres] *vt* oprimir.

oppression [ə'preʃ°n] *n* opresión *f*.

oppressor [ə'presər] *n* opresor,-ra.

opt [ɒpt] *vi* optar (for, por).
◆ to opt out *vi (person)* abandonar, dejar de participar.

optic ['ɒptɪk] *adj* óptico,-a.

optical ['ɒptɪk°l] *adj* óptico,-a.

optician [ɒp'tɪʃ°n] *n* óptico,-a, oculista *mf*. COMP **optician's (shop)** óptico.

optics ['ɒptɪks] *n* óptica.

optimism ['ɒptɪmɪz°m] *n* optimismo.

optimist ['ɒptɪmɪst] *n* optimista *mf*.

optimistic [ɒptɪ'mɪstɪk] *adj* optimista.

option ['ɒpʃ°n] *n* **1** *(choice)* opción *f*, posibilidad *f*. **2** EDUC *(optional subject)* asignatura optativa.

optional ['ɒpʃ°nəl] *adj* opcional.

or [ɔːr] *conj* **1** *(alternative - gen)* o; *(- before word beginning with o or ho)* u: *tea or coffee* té o café. **2** *(with negative)* ni: *she can't sing or dance* no sabe cantar ni bailar. **3** *(otherwise)* o: *come on, or we'll be late!* ¡date prisa o llegaremos tarde! LOC **or so** más o menos.

oral ['ɔːrəl] *adj* **1** *(spoken - gen)* oral; *(tradition)* transmitido,-a oralmente. **2** MED *(contraceptive)* oral; *(hygiene)* bucal.
▸ *n (exam)* examen *m* oral.

orange ['ɒrɪndʒ] *n* **1** *(fruit)* naranja. **2** *(colour)* naranja *m*. COMP **orange blossom** azahar *m*. ǁ **orange juice** zumo de naranja. ǁ **orange tree** naranjo.
▸ *adj* naranja, de color naranja.

orang-utan [ɔː'ræŋuː'tæn] *n* orangután *m*.

orbicularis [ɔː'bɪkə'lærɪs] *adj* **1** ANAT orbicular. **2** *fml lit (sphere)* esfera; *(sun)* el sol *m*; *(moon)* la luna.

orbit ['ɔːbɪt] *n* **1** *(of satellite)* órbita. **2** *(area of influence)* órbita, esfera de influencia, ámbito. LOC **to go into orbit** entrar en órbita.
▸ *vt* girar alrededor de, orbitar alrededor de.

orbital ['ɔːbɪt°l] *adj* orbital, orbitario,-a. COMP **orbital road** carretera de circunvalación.

orchard ['ɔːtʃəd] *n* huerto.

orchestra ['ɔːkɪstrə] *n* orquesta.

orchid ['ɔːkɪd] *n* BOT orquídea.

order ['ɔːdər] *n* **1** *(gen)* orden *m*: *in alphabetical/chronological order* por orden alfabético/cronológico. *she put her affairs in order* puso sus asuntos en orden. **2** *(fitness for use)* condiciones *fpl*, estado: *the car's in good working order* el coche funciona bien. **3** *(obedience, authority, discipline)* orden *m*, disciplina. **4** *(rules, procedures, etc)* orden *m*, procedimiento. **5** *(command)* orden *f*. **6** COMM *(request, goods)* pedido: *the waiter took our order* el camarero tomó nota de lo que queríamos. **7** *(group, society)* orden *f*; *(badge, sign worn)* condecoración *f*, orden *f*: *the monastic orders* las órdenes monásticas. LOC **in order that** para que, a fin de que. ǁ **in order to** para, a fin de. ǁ **out of order** *(not working)* que

no funciona. COMP **order book** libro de pedidos. ▌ **order form** hoja de pedido.
▶ vt **1** *(command)* ordenar, mandar. **2** *(ask for)* pedir, encargar: *I've ordered a cake for his birthday* he encargado un pastel para su cumpleaños. **3** *(arrange, put in order, organize)* ordenar, poner en orden.
▶ vi *(request to bring, ask for)* pedir.

ordinal [ˈɔːdɪnəl] *adj* ordinal.
▶ n ordinal *m*.

ordinarily [ˈɔːdənərɪlɪ] *adv* generalmente.

ordinary [ˈɔːdɪnərɪ] *adj (usual, normal)* normal, usual, habitual; *(average)* normal, común. COMP **ordinary seaman** marinero.

☒ Ordinary no significa 'ordinario (vulgar)', que se traduce por vulgar.

ordinate [ˈɔːdɪnət] *n* MATH ordenada.

ore [ɔːˀ] *n* mineral *m*, mena.

☒ Ore no significa 'oro', que se traduce por gold.

oregano [ɒrɪˈɡɑːnəʊ] *n* orégano.

organ [ˈɔːɡən] *n* órgano.

organic [ɔːˈɡænɪk] *adj* **1** *(living)* orgánico,-a. **2** *(without chemicals)* biológico,-a, ecológico,-a.

organism [ˈɔːɡənɪzˀm] *n* organismo.

organization [ɔːɡənaɪˈzeɪʃˀn] *n* organización *f*.

organize [ˈɔːɡənaɪz] *vt* organizar, ordenar.
▶ vi organizar.

organized [ˈɔːɡənaɪzd] *adj (gen)* organizado,-a.

organizer [ˈɔːɡənaɪzəˀ] *n* organizador, -ra.

orgy [ˈɔːdʒɪ] *n (wild party)* orgía.
① *pl* orgies.

Orient [ˈɔːrɪənt] *n* **the Orient** el oriente *m*.

oriental [ɔːrɪˈentˀl] *adj* oriental.
▶ n oriental *mf*.

orientate [ˈɔːrɪənteɪt] *vt* orientar.

orientation [ɔːrɪenˈteɪʃˀn] *n* orientación *f*.

origin [ˈɒrɪdʒɪn] *n* origen *m*.
▶ n pl **origins** origen *m sing*.

original [əˈrɪdʒɪnˀl] *adj* original, originario,-a, primero,-a.
▶ n original *m*.

originally [əˈrɪdʒɪnəlɪ] *adv* **1** *(in the beginning)* originariamente, en un principio. **2** *(in a new way)* con originalidad.

originate [əˈrɪdʒɪneɪt] *vt (create)* originar, crear, dar lugar a.
▶ vi *(arise)* tener su origen (in, en), originarse (in, en), provenir (in, de).

ornament [ˈɔːnəmənt] *n (decoration)* ornamento, adorno; *(object)* adorno.

ornithology [ɔːnɪˈθɒlədʒɪ] *n* ornitología.

orography [ɒˈrɒɡrəfɪ] *n* orografía.

orphan [ˈɔːfˀn] *n* huérfano,-a.
▶ vt dejar huérfano,-a. LOC **to be orphaned** quedar huérfano,-a.

orphanage [ˈɔːfˀnɪdʒ] *n* orfanato.

orthodox [ˈɔːθədɒks] *adj* ortodoxo,-a.

orthography [ɔːˈθɒɡrəfɪ] *n* ortografía.

orthopaedic [ɔːθəˈpiːdɪk] *adj* MED ortopédico,-a.

osmosis [ɒzˈməʊsɪs] *n* ósmosis *f*, osmosis *f*.

osseous [ˈɒzɪəs] *adj* óseo,-a.

ostensible [ɒˈstensɪbˀl] *adj (apparent)* aparente; *(alleged)* pretendido,-a, fingido,-a.

☒ Ostensible no significa 'ostensible', que se traduce por obvious.

ostrich [ˈɒstrɪtʃ] *n* avestruz *m*.

other [ˈʌðəˀ] *adj* **1** *(additional)* otro,-a: *I have one other idea* tengo otra idea. **2** *(different)* otro,-a: *people from other countries* gente de otros países. **3** *(second, remaining)* otro,-a: *it's on the other side of the street* está al otro lado de la calle. LOC **every other day** un día sí, otro no. ▌ **the other day** el otro día.
▶ pron otro,-a. LOC **one after the other** uno tras otro.
▶ prep **other than** *(except)* aparte de, salvo: *there was nobody other than the teacher* aparte del profesor, no había nadie.

otherwise [ˈʌðəwaɪz] *adv* **1** *(differently)* de otra manera, de manera distinta: *she couldn't do otherwise* no podía obrar

O

de otra manera. **2** *(apart from that, in other respects)* aparte de eso, por lo demás.
▶ *conj (if not)* si no, de no ser así, de lo contrario.
▶ *adj* distinto,-a.

otitis [əʊˈtaɪtɪs] *n* otitis *f.*

otter [ˈɒtəʳ] *n* nutria.

ouch [aʊtʃ] *interj* ¡ay!

ought [ɔːt] *aux* ought to **1** *(moral obligation)* deber: *you ought to have helped them* debiste ayudarles. **2** *(recommendation)* deber, tener que. **3** *(expectation)* deber de: *they ought to be home by now* seguramente ya estarán en casa.

ounce [aʊns] *n* **1** *(weight)* onza. **2** *fam (small quantity)* pizca.

✎ La onza equivale a 28,35 gramos.

our [aʊəʳ] *adj* nuestro,-a: *our house* nuestra casa; *our children* nuestros hijos.

ours [aʊəz] *pron* (el) nuestro, (la) nuestra: *a friend of ours* un amigo nuestro.

ourselves [aʊəˈselvz] *pron* **1** *(reflexive)* nos: *we made ourselves comfortable* nos pusimos cómodos. **2** *(emphatic)* nosotros,-as mismos,-as: *we did it ourselves* lo hicimos nosotros mismos.

out [aʊt] *adv* **1** *(gen)* fuera, afuera: *could you wait out there?* ¿podrías esperar allí fuera?; *she ran out* salió corriendo. **2** *(expressing distance)* en: *they live out in the country* viven en el campo. **3** *(expressing removal)* diferentes traducciones: *I've had a tooth out* me han sacado una muela; *she got out a handkerchief* sacó un pañuelo. **4** *(available, existing)* diferentes traducciones: *the film comes out next month* la película se estrenará el mes que viene; *it's the best sandwich out* es el mejor bocadillo que hay. **5** *(protruding)* que sale: *a nail sticking out* un clavo que sobresale. **6** *(clearly, loudly)* en voz alta: *he called out to me* me llamó en voz alta.
▶ *prep* out of **1** *(gen)* fuera de: *out of danger* fuera de peligro; *they are out of the cup* han quedado fuera de la copa. **2** *(from among)* de: *she got five out of ten in French* sacó (un) cinco sobre diez en francés. **3** *(without)* sin: *out of money* sin dinero. **6** *(using, made from)* de: *made out of wood* hecho,-a de madera.

outboard motor [aʊtbɔːˈdməʊtəʳ] *n* MAR motor *m* fueraborda, fuerabordo *m.*

outbreak [ˈaʊtbreɪk] *n* **1** *(of violence, fighting)* brote *m.* **2** *(of disease)* brote *m*, epidemia; *(of spots)* erupción *f.*

outburst [ˈaʊtbɜːst] *n* **1** *(of emotion)* explosión *f*, arrebato *m.* **2** *(of activity)* explosión *f.*

outcast [ˈaʊtkɑːst] *n* marginado,-a.

outclass [ˈaʊtklɑːs] *vt* superar.

outcome [ˈaʊtkʌm] *n* resultado.

outdated [aʊtˈdeɪtɪd] *adj* anticuado,-a.

outdoor [aʊtˈdɔːʳ] *adj (gen)* exterior.

outdoors [aʊtˈdɔːz] *adv* fuera, al aire libre.

outer [ˈaʊtəʳ] *adj* exterior, externo,-a.
[COMP] **outer space** espacio exterior. **‖ outer suburbs** afueras *fpl.*

outgrow [aʊtˈɡrəʊ] *vt (clothes, etc)* hacerse demasiado grande para: *he's outgrown his shoes* se le han quedado pequeños los zapatos.
① *pt* outgrew [aʊtˈɡruː], *pp* outgrown [aʊtˈɡrəʊn].

outing [ˈaʊtɪŋ] *n (trip)* salida, excursión *f.*

outlaw [ˈaʊtlɔː] *n* forajido,-a, proscrito,-a.
▶ *vt* prohibir, declarar ilegal.

outlet [ˈaʊtlet] *n* **1** *(opening - gen)* salida; *(for water)* desagüe *m.* **2** *fig (for emotions)* válvula de escape. **3** COMM *(shop)* punto de venta.

outline [ˈaʊtlaɪn] *n* **1** *(outer edge)* contorno; *(shape)* perfil *m.* **2** *(draft)* bosquejo, esquema *m*; *(summary)* resumen *m.*
▶ *vt* **1** *(draw lines of)* perfilar; *(sketch)* bosquejar. **2** *(summarize)* resumir.

outnumber [aʊtˈnʌmbəʳ] *vt* superar en número, ser más que.

out-of-date [aʊtəvˈdeɪt] *adj (fashion)* pasado,-a de moda; *(technology)* desfasado,-a, obsoleto,-a; *(food, ticket)* caducado,-a.

output [ˈaʊtpʊt] *n* **1** *(gen)* producción *f*; *(of machine)* rendimiento. **2** COMPUT salida.

outrageous [aʊtˈreɪdʒəs] *adj* **1** *(shocking - gen)* escandaloso,-a; *(crime)* atroz; *(language)* injurioso,-a. **2** *(unconventional)* extravagante.

outside [(n) aʊt'saɪd; (prep) 'aʊtsaɪd] n **1** (exterior part) exterior m, parte f exterior: from the outside desde fuera. **2** GB (when driving) derecha.
▶ prep **1** (gen) fuera de. **2** (beyond) más allá de, fuera de: outside working hours fuera del horario laboral. **3** (other than) aparte de, fuera de.
▶ adv (gen) fuera, afuera.
▶ adj **1** (exterior) exterior. **2** (external) externo,-a. **3** (remote) remoto,-a. LOC at the outside como máximo, como mucho.

outsider [aʊt'saɪdə'] n **1** (person- stranger) extraño,-a, forastero,-a, desconocido,-a. **2** (unlikely winner - athlete, etc) competidor,-ra con pocas probabilidades de ganar.

outskirts ['aʊtskɜːts] n pl afueras fpl, alrededores mpl, extrarradio m sing.

outstanding [aʊt'stændɪŋ] adj **1** (excellent) destacado,-a, notable, sobresaliente; (exceptional) excepcional, extraordinario,-a, singular. **2** (gen) sin pagar, pendiente.

outstretched [aʊt'stretʃt] adj extendido,-a.

outward ['aʊtwəd] adj **1** (appearance) exterior; (sign) externo,-a, show. **2** (journey, flight) de ida.

outwards ['aʊtwədz] adv (gen) hacia fuera, hacia afuera; (attention, etc) hacia el exterior.

oval ['əʊvəl] adj oval, ovalado,-a.
▶ n óvalo.

ovary ['əʊvərɪ] n ovario.
① pl ovaries.

ovation [əʊ'veɪʃən] n ovación f.

oven ['ʌvən] n horno.

over ['əʊvə'] adv **1** (down) diferentes traducciones: the boy fell over el niño se cayó; I knocked the glass over tiré la copa (de un golpe). **2** (from one side to another) diferentes traducciones: turn over the page dar la vuelta a la página; he bent over se inclinó. **3** (across) diferentes traducciones: let's cross over crucemos al otro lado; over here/there aquí/allí. **5** (too much) de más: it's 50 grams over pesa 50 gramos de más. LOC over here aquí. ❙ over there allí.

▶ prep **1** (gen) encima de: a sign over the door un letrero encima de la puerta; he wore a jacket over his sweater llevaba una americana encima del jersey. **2** (across); (on the other side of) al otro lado de: he lives over the border vive al otro lado de la frontera. **3** (during) durante: over the past 25 years durante los últimos 25 años. **4** (throughout) por: we travelled all over Italy viajamos por toda Italia. **5** (more than) más de: she's over thirty tiene más de treinta años. **6** (about) por: an argument over money una discusión por dinero. LOC all over en todas partes. ❙ over and above además de.
▶ adj (ended) acabado,-a, terminado, -a: the game is over la partida ha acabado.

overact [əʊvər'ækt] vi exagerar, sobreactuar.

overall [(adj) 'əʊvərɔːl; (adv) əʊvər'ɔːl] adj (general) global, total.
▶ adv (generally, on the whole) en conjunto, por lo general.
▶ n GB (work coat) guardapolvo, bata.
▶ n pl overalls mono m sing.

overambitious [əʊvəræm'bɪʃəs] adj demasiado ambicioso,-a.

overboard ['əʊvəbɔːd] adv por la borda. LOC to fall overboard caer al agua. ❙ to go overboard pasarse.

overbooking [əʊvə'bʊkɪŋ] n sobrecontratación f.

overcame [əʊvə'keɪm] pt → overcome.

overcoat ['əʊvəkəʊt] n abrigo.

overcome [əʊvə'kʌm] vt **1** (defeat) vencer. **2** (overwhelm) agobiar, abrumar, invadir, apoderarse de, vencer: he was overcome by sleep el sueño se apoderó de él.
① pt overcame [əʊvə'keɪm], pp overcome [əʊvə'kʌm].

overdose ['əʊvədəʊs] n sobredosis f.

overflow [(n) 'əʊvəfləʊ; (vb) əʊvə'fləʊ] n **1** (of river, etc) desbordamiento. **2** (pipe) tubo de desagüe; (hole) rebosadero.
▶ vi **1** (river) desbordarse; (bath, etc) rebosar. **2** (people) rebosar. **3** (be full of) rebosar (with, de). LOC to be full to overflowing estar lleno,-a hasta el borde.
▶ vt (liquid) salirse de.

O

overhead [(*adj*) 'əʊvəhed; (*adv*) əʊvə'hed] *adj (cable)* aéreo,-a; *(railway)* elevado,-a.
▶ *adv* arriba, por encima de la cabeza.

overhear [əʊvə'hɪəʳ] *vt* oír por casualidad.
ⓘ *pt & pp* overheard [əʊvə'hɜːd].

overheard [əʊvə'hɜːd] *pt & pp* → **overhear**.

overland [(*adj*) 'əʊvəlænd; (*adv*) əʊvə'lænd] *adj* por tierra.
▶ *adv* por tierra.

overlap [əʊvə'læp] *vi* superponerse, solaparse.
ⓘ *pt & pp* overlapped, *ger* overlapping.
▶ *n* superposición *f*, coincidencia.

overlook [əʊvə'lʊk] *vt* **1** *(not notice)* pasar por alto;. **2** *(excuse)* disculpar. **3** *(have a view of)* tener vistas a.

overnight [əʊvə'naɪt] *adv* **1** *(during the night)* durante la noche; *(at night)* por la noche: *it rained overnight* llovió durante la noche. **2** *fam (suddenly)* de la noche a la mañana.
▶ *adj* **1** *(during the night)* de la noche; *(for the night)* de una noche. **2** *fam (sudden)* repentino,-a.

oversaw [əʊvə'sɔː] *pt* → **oversee**.

overseas [əʊvə'siːz] *adj (person)* extranjero,-a; *(trade)* exterior.
▶ *adv* en ultramar.

oversee [əʊvə'siː] *vt* supervisar.
ⓘ *pt* oversaw [əʊvə'sɔː], *pp* overseen [əʊvə'siːn].

overseen [əʊvə'siːn] *pp* → **oversee**.

oversized [əʊvə'saɪzd] *adj* demasiado grande.

oversleep [əʊvə'sliːp] *vi* quedarse dormido,-a, no despertarse a tiempo.
ⓘ *pt & pp* overslept [əʊvə'slept].

overslept [əʊvə'slept] *pt & pp* → **oversleep**.

overtake [əʊvə'teɪk] *vt* **1** GB *(a vehicle)* adelantar, pasar, AM rebasar: *we overtook a sports car* adelantamos un coche deportivo. **2** *(surpass)* superar. **3** *(happen suddenly to)* adelantarse a; *(surprise)* sorprender.
ⓘ *pt* overtook [əʊvə'teɪkən], *pp* overtaken [əʊvə'tʊk].

overtaken [əʊvə'teɪkən] *pp* → **overtake**.

overtime ['əʊvətaɪm] *n (extra work, extra hours)* horas *fpl* extras.

overtook [əʊvə'tʊk] *pt* → **overtake**.

overturn [əʊvə'tɜːn] *vt* **1** *(vehicle)* volcar; *(boat)* hacer zozobrar; *(furniture)* dar la vuelta a. **2** *(government)* derrocar. **3** *fig (ruling)* anular.
▶ *vi (vehicle)* volcar; *(boat)* zozobrar.

overview ['əʊvəvjuː] *n* perspectiva general.

overweight [əʊvə'weɪt] *adj (thing)* demasiado pesado,-a; *(person)* demasiado gordo,-a.

overwhelm [əʊvə'welm] *vt* **1** *(physically - defeat)* arrollar, aplastar. **2** *fig (emotionally)* abrumar.

overwhelming [əʊvə'welmɪŋ] *adj (defeat, victory)* aplastante, arrollador,-ra; *(generosity)* abrumador,-ra.

ovine [əʊ'vɪn] *adj* ovino,-a.

oviparous [əʊ'vɪpərəs] *adj* ovíparo,-a.

ovulate ['ɒvjəleɪt] *vi* ovular.

ovulation [ɒvjə'leɪʃ°n] *n* ovulación *f*.

ovule ['ɒvjuːl] *n* óvulo.

owe [əʊ] *vt (gen)* deber: *you owe me 10 pounds* me debes 10 libras.

owing ['əʊɪŋ] *adj (due)* debido,-a.
▶ *prep* **owing to** debido a, a causa de.

owl [aʊl] *n* búho, lechuza.

own [əʊn] *adj* propio,-a: *they grow their own vegetables* cultivan sus propios verduras.
▶ *pron* propio,-a: *would you like to borrow mine or do you have your own?* ¿quieres que te deje el mío o ya tienes uno propio? LOC **on one's own 1** *(alone)* solo,-a **2** *(without help)* uno,-a mismo,-a.
▶ *vt (possess)* poseer, ser dueño,-a de.
◆ **to own up** *vi* confesarlo.

owner ['əʊnəʳ] *n* dueño,-a, propietario,-a.

ox [ɒks] *n* buey *m*.
ⓘ *pl* oxen [ɒks°n].

oxen ['ɒksən] *npl* → **ox**.

oxidation [ɒksɪ'deɪʃ°n] *n* oxidación *f*.

oxide ['ɒksaɪd] *n* óxido.

oxygen ['ɒksɪdʒ°n] *n* oxígeno.

oyster ['ɔɪstəʳ] *n (shellfish)* ostra.

ozone ['əʊzəʊn] *n* ozono. COMP **ozone layer** capa de ozono.

ozone-friendly ['əʊzəʊnfrendlɪ] *adj* que no daña la capa de ozono.

P

P, p [pi:] *n (the letter)* P, p *f*.

pace [peɪs] *n* **1** *(rate, speed)* marcha, ritmo, velocidad *f*. **2** *(step)* paso.
▶ *vt* **1** *(room, floor)* ir de un lado a otro de. **2** *(set speed for)* marcar el ritmo a.

pacemaker ['peɪsmeɪkəʳ] *n* **1** SP liebre *f*. **2** MED marcapasos *m*.

pachyderm ['pækɪdɜ:m] *n* paquidermo.

pacifism ['pæsɪfɪzəm] *n* pacifismo.

pacifist ['pæsɪfɪst] *n* pacifista *mf*.

pacify ['pæsɪfaɪ] *vt* **1** *(person)* calmar, tranquilizar. **2** *(country)* pacificar.
ⓘ *pt & pp* pacified, *ger* pacifying.

pack [pæk] *n* **1** *(parcel)* paquete *m*; *(bundle)* fardo, bulto; *(rucksack)* mochila. **2** US *(packet - gen)* paquete *m*; *(of cigarettes)* paquete *m*, cajetilla. **3** GB *(of cards)* baraja. **4** *pej (of thieves)* banda, partida. **5** *(of lies)* sarta. **6** *(of wolves, dogs)* manada; *(of hounds)* jauría.
▶ *vt* **1** *(goods)* empaquetar, envasar. **2** *(suitcase)* hacer; *(clothes, etc)* poner, meter. **3** *(fill)* atestar, abarrotar, llenar: *the disco was packed with young people* la discoteca estaba abarrotada de jóvenes. **4** *(press down)* apretar.
▶ *vi* **1** *(suitcase, etc)* hacer las maletas, hacer el equipaje: *he hasn't packed yet* aún no ha hecho las maletas. **2** *(people)* apiñarse, apretarse, meterse.
◆ **to pack up** *vi* **1** *(stop, give up)* dejarlo. **2** *(machine)* estropearse; *(car)* averiarse.
▶ *vt sep (belongings - in case)* meter en la maleta; *(gather together)* recoger.

package ['pækɪdʒ] *n* **1** *(parcel)* paquete *m*. **2** *(proposals)* paquete *m*; *(agreement)* acuerdo. COMP **package holiday** viaje *m* organizado.
▶ *vt (goods)* empaquetar, envasar.

packaging ['pækɪdʒɪŋ] *n* embalaje *m*.

packed [pækt] *adj (with people)* lleno,-a, abarrotado,-a, repleto,-a; *(with facts, information, etc)* lleno,-a.

packet ['pækɪt] *n* **1** *(small box - gen)* paquete *m*, cajita; *(of cigarettes)* paquete *m*, cajetilla; *(envelope)* sobre *m*. **2** *fam (large amount of money)* dineral *m*.

packing ['pækɪŋ] *n (material)* embalaje *m*.

pact [pækt] *n* pacto.

pad [pæd] *n* **1** *(cushioning)* almohadilla, cojinete *m*. **2** *(inkpad)* tampón *m*. **3** *(of paper)* taco, bloc *m*. **4** *(of animal)* almohadilla. **5** *(platform)* plataforma. COMP **knee pad** rodillera. ▮ **sanitary pad** compresa.
▶ *vt (chair, etc)* acolchar, rellenar, guatear; *(garment)* poner hombreras a.
ⓘ *pt & pp* padded, *ger* padding.

paddle¹ ['pædəl] *n (oar)* pala, remo.
▶ *vt (boat, canoe)* remar con pala.
▶ *vi* remar con pala.

paddle² ['pædəl] *vi (walk or play in water)* mojarse los pies, chapotear.
▶ *n* chapoteo.

paddling pool ['pædlɪŋpu:l] *n* piscina para niños, piscina infantil.

padlock ['pædlɒk] *n* candado.
▶ *vt* cerrar con candado.

padre [pa:dreɪ] *n (priest)* padre *m*.

paediatrician [pi:dɪætrɪʃən] *n* pediatra *mf*.

paedophile ['pi:dəfaɪl] *n* pedófilo,-a.

pagan ['peɪɡən] *adj* pagano,-a.
▶ *n* pagano,-a.

page¹ [peɪdʒ] *n (of book)* página; *(of newspaper)* plana, página. LOC **on the front page** en primera plana.

page² [peɪdʒ] *n* **1** *(boy servant, at wedding)* paje *m*; *(in hotel, club)* botones *m*. **2** HIST escudero.

pagoda [pəˈgəʊdə] *n* pagoda.

paid [peɪd] *pp & pt* → **pay.**
▶ *adj (purchase, holiday)* pagado,-a; *(work)* remunerado,-a.

pail [peɪl] *n* cubo.

pain [peɪn] *n* **1** *(physical)* dolor *m*: *I've got a pain in my stomach* me duele el estómago. **2** *(mental suffering)* sufrimiento, dolor *m*. **3** *(annoying thing)* lata, fastidio; *(person)* pesado,-a, pelmazo. LOC **to be a pain in the neck** ser un,-a pesado,-a.
▶ *vt* doler, dar pena a, apenar.
▶ *n pl* **pains** *(effort)* esfuerzos *mpl*.

⊠ Pain no significa 'pena (tristeza)', que se traduce por **grief, sorrow.**

painful [ˈpeɪnful] *adj (physically)* doloroso,-a; *(mentally)* angustioso,-a.

painkiller [ˈpeɪnkɪləʳ] *n* calmante *m*.

painless [ˈpeɪnləs] *adj* **1** *(without pain)* indoloro,-a, sin dolor. **2** *(without distress)* sencillo,-a, sin complicaciones.

paint [peɪnt] *n* pintura: *a tin of paint* una lata de pintura. LOC **"Wet paint"** «Recién pintado».
▶ *vt (gen)* pintar: *we're going to paint the walls yellow* vamos a pintar las paredes de amarillo.
▶ *vi* pintar: *she paints in oils* pinta al óleo.

paintbrush [ˈpeɪntbrʌʃ] *n* **1** *(for walls, etc)* brocha. **2** *(artist's)* pincel *m*.

painter [ˈpeɪntəʳ] *n* **1** ART pintor,-ra. **2** *(decorator)* pintor,-ra de brocha gorda.

painting [ˈpeɪntɪŋ] *n* **1** ART *(picture)* pintura, cuadro. **2** *(activity)* pintura.

pair [peəʳ] *n* **1** *(of shoes, socks, gloves, etc)* par *m*; *(of cards)* pareja: *a pair of brown eyes* dos ojos castaños. **2** *(of people, animals)* pareja. LOC **in pairs** de dos en dos. COMP **a pair of scissors** unas tijeras. ‖ **a pair of trousers** unos pantalones.
▶ *vt (people)* emparejar; *(animals)* aparear.
▶ *vi (animals)* aparearse.

pajamas [pəˈdʒæməz] *n pl* US → **pyjamas.**

Pakistan [pɑːkɪˈstɑːn] *n* Pakistán *m*.

Pakistani [pɑːkɪˈstɑːnɪ] *adj* pakistaní.
▶ *n* pakistaní *mf*.

pal [pæl] *n fam* amigo,-a, colega *mf*.

palace [ˈpæləs] *n* palacio.

Palaeolithic [pælɪəʊˈlɪθɪk] *adj* paleolítico,-a.

palate [ˈpælət] *n (gen)* paladar *m*.

pale [peɪl] *adj (complexion, skin)* pálido,-a; *(colour)* claro,-a, pálido,-a; *(light)* débil. LOC **to turn pale** ponerse pálido,-a.
▶ *vi* palidecer.

Paleolithic [pælɪəʊˈlɪθɪk] *adj* US → **Palaelothic.**

Palestine [ˈpælɪstaɪn] *n* Palestina.

Palestinian [pælɪˈstɪnɪən] *adj* palestino,-a.
▶ *n* palestino,-a.

palette [ˈpælət] *n* paleta.

palfrey [ˈpɔːlfrɪ] *n* palafrén *m*.

palm¹ [pɑːm] *n* BOT *(tree)* palmera; *(leaf)* palma. COMP **palm tree** palmera.

palm² [pɑːm] *n* ANAT palma.

pamphlet [ˈpæmflət] *n* folleto.

pan [pæn] *n (saucepan)* cacerola, cazuela, cazo; *(cooking pot)* olla.

Panama [ˈpænəmə] *n* Panamá.

Panamanian [pænəˈmeɪnɪən] *adj* panameño,-a.
▶ *n* panameño,-a.

pancake [ˈpænkeɪk] *n* tortita, crepe *f*.

pancreas [ˈpæŋkrɪəs] *n* páncreas *m*.

panda [ˈpændə] *n* (oso) panda *m*.

pane [peɪn] *n* cristal *m*, vidrio.

panel [ˈpænəl] *n* **1** *(of door, wall, car body etc)* panel *m*; *(on ceiling)* artesón *m*. **2** *(of controls, instruments)* tablero. **3** *(group of people)* panel *m*; *(team)* equipo.

panic [ˈpænɪk] *n* pánico: *panic spread throughout the crowd* el pánico cundió entre la gente. LOC **to get into a panic** desjarse llevar por el pánico.
▶ *vt* infundir pánico a.
▶ *vi* entrarle el pánico a, aterrarse.
① *pt & pp* **panicked,** *ger* **panicking.**

panic-stricken [ˈpænɪkstrɪkⁿ] *adj* preso,-a de pánico, aterrorizado,-a.

panorama [pænəˈrɑːmə] *n (view)* panorama *m*.

panoramic [pænəˈræmɪk] *adj* panorámico,-a.

pant [pænt] *vi* jadear, resoplar.

pantheon [ˈpænθɪən] *n* ARCH panteón *m*.

panther [ˈpænθəʳ] *n* pantera.

pantomime ['pæntəmaɪm] *n* **1** *(mime)* pantomima. **2** GB *(play)* representación musical navideña basada en cuentos de hadas.

⊕ Es una representación teatral cómica y musical que se hace por Navidades y que suele contar historias tradicionales como, por ejemplo, Aladdin (*Aladino y la lámpara maravillosa*), Puss in Boots (*El gato con botas*) o Cinderella (*La Cenicienta*).

pantry ['pæntrɪ] *n* despensa.
ⓘ *pl* pantries.

pants [pænts] *n pl* **1** GB *(underpants - men's)* calzoncillos *mpl*; *(- women's)* bragas *fpl*. **2** US *(trousers)* pantalón *m*, pantalones *mpl*.

papaya [pə'paɪə] *n* papaya.

paper ['peɪpəʳ] *n* **1** *(material)* papel *m*: *take a sheet of paper* coge una hoja de papel. **2** *(newspaper)* periódico, diario. **3** *(examination)* examen *m*. **4** *(essay, written work)* trabajo (escrito); *(for conference)* ponencia. LOC **on paper** por escrito. COMP **paper mill** fábrica de papel. ‖ **paper money** papel *m* moneda. ‖ **paper shop** quiosco.
▶ *vt* empapelar.
▶ *n pl* papers *(documents)* documentos *mpl*.

✕ Paper no significa 'papel (en el teatro o el cine)', que se traduce por role, part.

paperclip ['peɪpəklɪp] *n* clip *m*.

paprika ['pæprɪkə] *n* pimentón *m* dulce.

papua ['pæpjuə] *n* Papúa. COMP **Papua New Guinea** Papúa Nueva Guinea.

papuan ['pæpjuən] *adj* papú,-úa.
▶ *n* papú,-úa.

parabola [pə'ræbələ] *n* MATH parábola.

parachute ['pærəʃuːt] *n* paracaídas *m*.
▶ *vi* saltar en paracaídas.

parade [pə'reɪd] *n* **1** *(procession)* desfile *m*: *fashion parade* desfile de modelos. **2** MIL desfile *m*.
▶ *vt* **1** MIL hacer desfilar. **2** *(flaunt - knowledge, wealth)* alardear, hacer alarde de.
▶ *vi* **1** *(gen)* desfilar. **2** MIL pasar revista.

✕ Parade no significa 'parada (detención)', que se traduce por stop.

paradise ['pærədaɪs] *n* paraíso.

paradox ['pærədɒks] *n* paradoja.

paraffin ['pærəfɪn] *n* GB queroseno. COMP **paraffin wax** parafina.

paragraph ['pærəgrɑːf] *n* párrafo. COMP **full stop, new paragraph** punto y aparte.

Paraguay [pærə'gwaɪ] *n* Paraguay.

Paraguayan [pærə'gwaɪən] *adj* paraguayo,-a.
▶ *n* paraguayo,-a.

parallel ['pærəlel] *adj* **1** paralelo,-a (to/ with, a). **2** *fig (similar)* paralelo,-a (to/with, a), análogo,-a (to/with, a).
▶ *n* **1** MATH paralela. **2** GEOG paralelo. **3** *(similarity)* paralelo, paralelismo.

paralyse ['pærəlaɪz] *vt (gen)* paralizar.

paralysis [pə'ræləsɪs] *n* **1** MED parálisis *f*. **2** *fig* paralización *f*.

paralytic [pærə'lɪtɪk] *adj* MED paralítico,-a.
▶ *n* MED paralítico,-a.

parameter [pə'ræmɪtəʳ] *n* parámetro.

paranoia [pærə'nɔɪə] *n* paranoia.

paraplegia [pærə'pliːdʒə] *n* MED paraplejía.

parasite ['pærəsaɪt] *n* parásito,-a.

parasol [pærə'sɒl] *n* sombrilla.

paratrooper ['pærətruːpəʳ] *n* MIL paracaidista *mf*.

parcel ['pɑːsəl] *n* **1** *(package)* paquete *m*. **2** *(piece of land)* parcela. LOC **parcel post** servicio de paquetes postales.

parchment ['pɑːtʃmənt] *n* pergamino.

pardon ['pɑːdən] *n* **1** *(forgiveness)* perdón *m*. **2** JUR indulto. LOC **I beg your pardon!** *fml* ¡perdone! ‖ **I beg your pardon?** *fml* ¿cómo dice?
▶ *vt* **1** *(forgive)* perdonar: *pardon me for interrupting* perdone que le interrumpa. **2** JUR indultar. COMP **pardon?** *(for repetition)* ¿cómo dice?, ¿cómo? ‖ **pardon me!** *(sorry)* ¡perdón!, ¡perdone!, ¡Vd. perdone!

parent ['peərənt] *n (father)* padre *m*; *(mother)* madre *f*.
▶ *n pl* parents padres *mpl*.

✕ Parent no significa 'pariente', que se traduce por relative.

parietal [pə'raɪətəl] *adj* parietal.

parish ['pærɪʃ] n **1** REL parroquia. **2** GB (civil) municipio.

parishioner [pə'rɪʃ[ə]nəʳ] n feligrés,-esa.

park [pɑːk] n parque m, jardín m público.
▸ vt (car) aparcar, estacionar: I'm parked opposite he aparcado enfrente.
▸ vi aparcar, estacionar.

parking ['pɑːkɪŋ] n (act) estacionamiento. LOC "No parking" «Prohibido aparcar». COMP parking meter parquímetro.

parliament ['pɑːləmənt] n (assembly) parlamento.
▸ n Parliament GB (body) Parlamento; (period) legislatura.

parlor ['pɑːləʳ] adj US → parlour.

parlour ['pɑːləʳ] n **1** US (shop) salón m, tienda. **2** dated (room in house) salón m. COMP parlour game juego de salón.

parody ['pærədɪ] n parodia.
① pl parodies.
▸ vt parodiar.
① pt & pp parodied, ger parodying.

parole [pə'rəʊl] n libertad f condicional.
▸ vt poner en libertad condicional.

parquet ['pɑːkeɪ] n parqué m.

parrot ['pærət] n loro, papagayo.

parsimonious [pɑːsɪ'məʊɪəs] adj fml mezquino,-a, tacaño,-a.

☒ Parsimonious no significa 'parsimonioso (lento)', que se traduce por slow.

parsley ['pɑːslɪ] n perejil m.

parsnip ['pɑːsnɪp] n chirivía.

part [pɑːt] n **1** (gen) parte f: we spent part of the day on the beach pasamos parte del día en la playa. **2** (component) pieza. **3** (of serial, programme) capítulo. **4** (measure) parte f. **5** (in play, film) papel m: she plays the part of Scarlett hace el papel de Scarlett. **6** (role, share, involvement) papel m, parte f: I want no part in your dodgy deals no quiero saber nada de tus negocios sucios. LOC for my part por mi parte, en cuanto a mí. ‖ in part en parte. ‖ the best part of / the better part of la mayor parte de, casi todo,-a. ‖ to play a part in desempeñar un papel en.
▸ adv en parte.
▸ adj parcial.
▸ vt (separate) separar (from, de).

▸ vi **1** (separate) separarse; (say goodbye, despedirse: they parted as friends se separaron amistosamente. **2** (open - lips curtains) abrirse.
▸ n pl parts (area) zona, parajes mpl.
◆ to part with vt insep desprenderse de, separarse de.

partial ['pɑːʃ[ə]l] adj **1** (not complete) parcial. **2** (biased) parcial. LOC to be partial to sr ser aficionado,-a a ALGO.

participant [pɑː'tɪsɪpənt] n (gen) partici pante mf; (in competition) concursante m

participate [pɑː'tɪsɪpeɪt] vi participa (in, en).

participation [pɑːtɪsɪ'peɪʃ[ə]n] n partici pación f.

participle ['pɑːtɪsɪp[ə]l] n participio.

particle ['pɑːtɪk[ə]l] n partícula.

particular [pə'tɪkjuləʳ] adj **1** (special) parti cular, especial: for no particular reason pc nada en especial. **2** (specific) concreto particular. **3** (fussy) exigente, especial.
▸ n pl particulars (of event, thing) detalle mpl; (of person) datos mpl personales.

☒ Particular no significa 'particular (privado)', que se traduce por private.

particularly [pə'tɪkjuləlɪ] adv especia mente, particularmente.

partly ['pɑːtlɪ] adv en parte.

partner ['pɑːtnəʳ] n **1** (in an activity compañero,-a; (in dancing, tennis, card etc) pareja. **2** COMM socio,-a, asocia do,-a. **3** (spouse) cónyuge mf; (husban marido; (wife) mujer f; (in relationshi pareja, compañero,-a.

partnership ['pɑːtnəʃɪp] n **1** COMM (com pany) sociedad f. **2** (working relationshi asociación f.

partridge ['pɑːtrɪdʒ] n perdiz f.
① pl partridges o partridge.

part-time [pɑːt'taɪm] adj (work, job) d media jornada, a tiempo parcial.
▸ adv media jornada, a tiempo parcia

part-timer [pɑːt'taɪməʳ] n trabajadc -ra a tiempo parcial.

party ['pɑːtɪ] n **1** (celebration) fiesta: birt day party fiesta de cumpleaños. **2** Pc partido. **3** (group) grupo.
① pl parties.

▶ *adj* **1** *(dress)* de fiesta; *(mood, atmosphere)* festivo,-a. **2** POL *(member, leader)* del partido.

▶ *vi* *(go to parties)* ir a fiestas; *(have fun)* divertirse.

ⓘ *pt & pp* **partied**, *ger* **partying**.

pass [pɑːs] *n* **1** GEOG *(in mountains - gen)* puerto, paso (de montaña); *(narrow)* desfiladero. **2** *(official permit)* pase *m*, permiso. **3** *(in exam)* aprobado. **4** SP pase *m*. COMP **bus pass** abono de autobús.

▶ *vt* **1** *(go past - gen)* pasar; *(person)* cruzarse con: *I passed her in the street* me crucé con ella en la calle. **2** *(overtake)* adelantar. **3** *(cross - border, frontier)* pasar, cruzar. **4** *(give, hand)* pasar: *pass me that screwdriver* pásame ese destornillador. **5** SP *(ball)* pasar. **6** *(exam, test, examinee)* aprobar; *(bill, law, proposal, motion)* aprobar; *(censor)* pasar. **7** *(time)* pasar.

▶ *vi* **1** *(go past - gen)* pasar; *(procession)* desfilar; *(people)* cruzarse: *I was just passing* pasaba por aquí. **2** *(overtake)* adelantar. **3** *(move, go)* pasar: *we passed through Zaragoza* pasamos por Zaragoza. **4** SP hacer un pase. **5** *(exam, test)* aprobar; *(bill, motion)* ser aprobado,-a. **6** *(happen)* ocurrir, acontecer, suceder: *it came to pass that ...* sucedió que…

◆ **to pass away** *vi* *(die)* pasar a mejor vida.

◆ **to pass by** *vi* pasar: *she watched the people passing by* miraba pasar a la gente.

▶ *vt sep* pasar de largo.

◆ **to pass out** *vi* **1** *(faint)* desmayarse. **2** MIL graduarse.

▶ *vt sep* *(distribute)* repartir.

passage ['pæsɪdʒ] *n* **1** *(in street)* pasaje *m*; *(alleyway)* callejón *m*; *(narrow)* pasadizo. **2** *(in building - corridor)* pasillo. **3** *(way, movement - gen)* paso; *(of vehicle)* tránsito, paso. **4** *(of time)* paso, transcurso. **5** MAR *(journey)* travesía, viaje *m*; *(fare)* pasaje *m*. **6** *(writing, music)* pasaje *m*.

passenger ['pæsɪndʒəʳ] *n* pasajero,-a.

passer-by [pɑːsə'baɪ] *n* transeúnte *mf*.

ⓘ *pl* **passers-by**.

passion ['pæʃən] *n* pasión *f*. COMP **passion fruit** granadilla, maracuyá *m*.

passionate ['pæʃənət] *adj* apasionado,-a.

passionately ['pæʃənətlɪ] *adv* apasionadamente, fervientemente.

passive ['pæsɪv] *adj* *(gen)* pasivo,-a.

▶ *n* LING voz *f* pasiva.

passivity [pæ'sɪvətɪ] *n* pasividad *f*.

passport ['pɑːspɔːt] *n* pasaporte *m*.

password ['pɑːswɜːd] *n* contraseña.

past [pɑːst] *adj* **1** *(gone by in time)* pasado,-a; *(former)* anterior. **2** *(gone by recently)* último,-a: *the past few days* los últimos días. **3** *(finished, over)* acabado,-a, terminado,-a: *summer is past* el verano ha pasado. **4** LING pasado,-a. COMP **past participle** participio pasado. **| past tense** pasado.

▶ *n* **1** *(former times)* pasado: *in the past* en el pasado, antes, antiguamente. **2** *(of person)* pasado; *(of place)* historia.

▶ *prep* **1** *(farther than, beyond)* más allá de; *(by the side of)* por (delante de): *it's just past the cinema* está un poco más allá del cine. **2** *(in time)* y: *it's five past six* son las seis y cinco. **3** *(older than)* más de: *he's past forty* pasa de los cuarenta (años). **4** *(beyond the limits of)*: *it's past my comprehension* me resulta incomprensible.

▶ *adv*: *a few joggers ran past* pasaron unos haciendo footing.

pasta ['pæstə] *n* pasta, pastas *fpl*.

paste [peɪst] *n* **1** *(mixture)* pasta; *(glue)* engrudo. **2** CULIN pasta, paté *m*.

▶ *vt* *(stick)* pegar; *(put paste on)* encolar.

pasteboard ['peɪstbɔːd] *n* cartón *m*.

pastel ['pæstəl] *n* **1** *(chalk)* pastel *m*; *(drawing)* dibujo al pastel. **2** *(colour)* color *m* pastel.

▶ *adj* *(drawing)* al pastel; *(colour, tone, shade, etc)* pastel.

🗙 Pastel no significa 'pastel (tarta)', que se traduce por **cake**, **pie**.

pastime ['pɑːstaɪm] *n* pasatiempo.

pastry ['peɪstrɪ] *n* **1** *(dough)* masa. **2** *(cake)* pasta, bollo.

ⓘ *pl* **pastries**.

pasture ['pɑːstʃəʳ] *n* pasto.

pasty¹ ['pæstɪ] *n* CULIN empanadilla.

ⓘ *pl* **pasties**.

pasty² ['peɪstɪ] *adj* **1** *(pale)* pálido,-a. **2** *(like paste)* pastoso,-a.

ⓘ *comp* **pastier**, *superl* **pastiest**.

P

pat [pæt] n **1** (tap) golpecito, palmadita; (touch) toque m; (caress) caricia. **2** (of butter) porción f.
▶ vt (tap) dar palmaditas a; (touch) tocar; (caress) acariciar.
ⓘ pt & pp **patted**, ger **patting**.

patch [pætʃ] n **1** (to mend clothes) remiendo, parche m. **2** (over eye) parche m. **3** (area on surface - gen) trozo, lugar m, zona; (- of colour, damp, etc) mancha. **4** (plot of land) parcela.
▶ vt (mend) remendar; (put patch on) poner un parche a.

patchwork ['pætʃwɜːk] n **1** labor f de retales. **2** fig (of fields) mosaico.
▶ adj de retales.

pâté ['pæteɪ] n paté m.

patella [pə'telə] n rótula.

patent ['peɪtᵊnt] n COMM patente f.
▶ adj (obvious) patente, evidente. COMP **patent leather** charol m.
▶ vt COMM patentar.

paternity [pə'tɜːnɪtɪ] n paternidad f.

path [pɑːθ] n **1** (track) camino, sendero: keep to the path seguir el camino. **2** (course of bullet, missile) trayectoria; (of flight) rumbo. LOC **to be on the right path** ir bien encaminado,-a.

pathetic [pə'θetɪk] adj patético,-a.

pathology [pə'θɒlədʒɪ] n patología.

pathway ['pɑːθweɪ] n camino, sendero.

patience ['peɪʃᵊns] n **1** (quality) paciencia: I lost my patience perdí la paciencia. **2** (card game) solitario.

patient ['peɪʃᵊnt] adj (person - gen) paciente; (long-suffering) sufrido,-a: be patient with him ten paciencia con él.
▶ n paciente mf, enfermo,-a.

patiently ['peɪʃᵊntlɪ] adv pacientemente.

patio ['pætɪəʊ] n patio.
ⓘ pl patios.

patriarch ['peɪtrɪɑːk] n patriarca m.

patrician [pə'trɪʃᵊn] adj patricio,-a.
▶ n patricio.

patrimony ['pætrɪmənɪ] n patrimonio.

patriot ['peɪtrɪət] n patriota mf.

patriotic [pætrɪ'ɒtɪk] adj patriótico,-a.

patrol [pə'trəʊl] n patrulla. LOC **to be on patrol** patrullar, estar de patrulla.

▶ vt (area) patrullar por, estar de patrulla en.
ⓘ pt & pp **patrolled** (US patroled), ger **patrolling** (US patroling).

patron ['peɪtrən] adj **1** (customer) cliente, -a habitual, parroquiano,-a. **2** (sponsor) patrocinador,-ra, mecenas m. COMP **patron saint** patrón m.

Ⓧ Patron no significa 'patrón (jefe)', que se traduce por boss.

pattern ['pætᵊn] n **1** (decorative design) diseño, dibujo; (on fabric) diseño, estampado. **2** (way something develops) orden m, estructura: behaviour pattern patrón de conducta. **3** (example, model) ejemplo, modelo. **4** (for sewing, knitting) patrón m; (sample) muestra.

pause [pɔːz] n **1** (gen) pausa; (silence) silencio; (rest) descanso. **2** MUS pausa.
▶ vi (gen) hacer una pausa; (stop moving) detenerse.

pavement ['peɪvmənt] n GB acera. **2** US calzada, pavimento.

paving ['peɪvɪŋ] n pavimento. COMP **paving stone** baldosa, losa.

paw [pɔː] n **1** ZOOL (foot) pata; (claw - of big cats) zarpa, garra. **2** fam (person's hand) manaza.

pawn [pɔːn] n **1** (in chess) peón m. **2** (unimportant person) juguete m, marioneta, títere m.

pawnshop ['pɔːnʃɒp] n casa de empeños.

pawpaw ['pɔːpɔː] n papaya.

pay [peɪ] n (wages) paga, sueldo, salario. COMP **pay phone** teléfono público.
▶ vt **1** (gen) pagar; (bill, debt) pagar, saldar: I paid him 10 pounds to mend my bike le pagué 10 libras para que me arreglara la bici. **2** (make, give - attention) prestar; (homage, tribute) rendir; (respects) presentar, ofrecer; (compliment, visit, call) hacer. **3** FIN (make, give - interest, dividends) dar. **4** (be worthwhile) compensar, convenir: it'll pay you to keep your mouth shut te conviene no decir ni pío. LOC **to pay attention** prestar atención.
▶ vi **1** (gen) pagar: you don't have to pay to go in no hay que pagar para entrar. **2** fig

(suffer) pagar (for, -): *he'll pay for this!* ¡me las pagará! **3** *(be profitable - business, etc)* ser rentable, ser factible. **4** *(be worthwhile)* compensar, convenir. LOC **to get paid** cobrar. | **to pay in advance** pagar por adelantado. | **to pay cash / pay in cash** pagar al contado, pagar en efectivo.

◆ **to pay back** *vt sep* **1** *(money)* devolver, reembolsar; *(loan, mortgage)* pagar. **2** *fig (take revenge on)* hacer pagar a: *I'll pay you back for this!* ¡te haré pagar por esto!

◆ **to pay off** *vt sep* **1** *(debt)* saldar, liquidar, cancelar; *(loan)* pagar; *(mortgage)* acabar de pagar. **2** *(worker)* dar el finiquito a.

▸ *vi (be successful)* dar resultado; *(prove worthwhile)* valer la pena.

ⓘ *pt & pp* **paid** [peɪd].

payment ['peɪmənt] *n* **1** *(paying)* pago. **2** *(instalment)* plazo.

payroll ['peɪrəʊl] *n* nómina.

pea [pi:] *n* guisante *m*.

peace [pi:s] *n* **1** *(not war)* paz *f*. **2** *(tranquillity)* paz *f*, tranquilidad *f*: *I just want a bit of peace and quiet* solo quiero un poco de paz y de tranquilidad. LOC **at peace / in peace** en paz. | **to make one's peace with SB** hacer las paces con ALGN.

peaceful ['pi:sful] *adj* **1** *(non-violent)* pacífico,-a. **2** *(calm)* tranquilo,-a.

peacefully ['pi:sfʊlɪ] *adv (quietly)* tranquilamente; *(non violently)* pacíficamente.

peacetime ['pi:staɪm] *n* tiempos *mpl* de paz.

peach [pi:tʃ] *n* **1** *(fruit)* melocotón *m*. **2** *(colour)* (color *m*) melocotón *m*.

▸ *adj* de color melocotón. COMP **peach tree** melocotonero.

peacock ['pi:kɒk] *n* pavo real.

peak [pi:k] *n* **1** GEOG *(of mountain)* pico; *(summit)* cima, cumbre *f*. **2** *fig (highest point)* cumbre *f*, punto álgido; *(climax)* apogeo. **3** *(of cap)* visera. LOC **peak hours** horas *fpl* punta.

▸ *adj (maximum)* máximo,-a.

▸ *vi* alcanzar el punto máximo.

peaked [pi:kt] *adj (cap)* con visera.

peanut ['pi:nʌt] *n* cacahuete *m*.

▸ *n pl* **peanuts** *(small amount)* una miseria.

pear [peəʳ] *n (fruit)* pera. COMP **pear tree** peral *m*.

pearl [pɜ:l] *n* perla.

peasant ['pezᵊnt] *adj* campesino,-a, rural.

▸ *n* **1** *(gen)* campesino,-a. **2** *pej (uncultured person)* inculto,-a, palurdo,-a.

pebble ['pebᵊl] *n* guija, guijarro, china.

peck [pek] *n (of bird)* picotazo; *(kiss)* besito.

▸ *vt (bird)* picotear; *(kiss)* dar un besito a.

▸ *vi (bird)* picotear (at, -).

pectin ['pektɪn] *n* pectina.

pectoral ['pektᵊrəl] *adj* pectoral.

peculiar [prˈkju:lɪəʳ] *adj* **1** *(strange)* extraño,-a, raro,-a; *(unwell)* indispuesto,-a. **2** *(particular)* característico,-a (to, de), propio,-a (to, de).

pedagogy ['pedəgɒdʒɪ] *n* pedagogía.

pedal ['pedᵊl] *n (gen)* pedal *m*. COMP **pedal bin** cubo de la basura con pedal.

▸ *vi* pedalear.

ⓘ *pt & pp* **pedalled** *(US* pedaled*), ger* pedalling *(US* pedaling*).

pedalo ['pedᵊləʊ] *n* patín *m*.

ⓘ *pl* **pedalos** o **pedaloes**.

peddle ['pedᵊl] *vt* COMM vender de puerta en puerta.

pederast ['pedəræst] *n* pederasta *m*.

pedestal ['pedɪstᵊl] *n* pedestal *m*.

pedestrian [pəˈdestrɪən] *n* peatón, -ona. COMP **pedestrian crossing** paso de peatones. | **pedestrian precinct** zona peatonal.

▸ *adj (dull)* pedestre.

pediatrician [pi:dɪˈætrɪʃᵊn] *n* US → **paediatrician**.

pedigree ['pedɪgri:] *n (of animals)* pedigrí *m*; *(of people)* linaje *m*.

▸ *adj* de raza.

pedophile ['pi:dəfaɪl] *n* US → **paedophile**.

pee [pi:] *n fam* pis *m*, pipí *m*.

▸ *vi fam* hacer pis, hacer pipí.

peel [pi:l] *n (skin - gen)* piel *f*; *(- of orange, lemon, etc)* corteza, cáscara, monda, mondadura.

▸ *vt* pelar, quitar la piel de.

P

► *vi (skin)* pelarse; *(paint)* desconcharse; *(wallpaper)* despegarse.

peeler ['piːləʳ] [also potato peeler] *n* pelapatatas *m*.

peep¹ [piːp] *n (look)* ojeada, vistazo.
► *vi* espiar, mirar a hurtadillas.

peep² [piːp] *n (noise)* pío: *I don't want to hear another peep out of you!* ¡que no te oiga decir ni pío!

peephole ['piːphəʊl] *n* mirilla.

peer [pɪəʳ] *vi (look closely)* mirar detenidamente (at, -).

peg [peg] *n* **1** *(for hanging clothes on)* percha, colgador *m*. **2** TECH clavija.
► *vt* **1** *(clothes)* tender (out, -); *(tent)* fijar con estacas (down, -). **2** *(prices)* fijar, estabilizar.
ⓘ *pt & pp* pegged, *ger* pegging.

pejorative [pəˈdʒɒrətɪv] *adj* peyorativo,-a, despectivo,-a.

pelican ['pelɪkən] *n* pelícano.

pelvis ['pelvɪs] *n* pelvis *f*.

pen¹ [pen] *n (gen)* pluma; *(ballpoint)* bolígrafo *m*.
► *vt (write - gen)* escribir.
ⓘ *pt & pp* penned, *ger* penning.

✎ Pen es el nombre general que se da a cualquier instrumento que escriba con tinta, por ejemplo, la estilográfica (fountain pen), el bolígrafo (ballpoint pen) o el rotulador (felt tip pen).

pen² [pen] *n* corral *m*.

penal ['piːnəl] *adj* penal.

penalty ['penəltɪ] *n* **1** *(gen)* pena, castigo; *(fine)* multa. **2** SP *(gen)* castigo (máximo); *(football)* penalti *m*. **3** *(disadvantage)* desventaja, inconveniente *m*.
ⓘ *pl* penalties.

pence [pens] *n* → penny

pencil ['pensəl] *n* lápiz *m*: *write in pencil* escribir con lápiz. COMP **pencil case** plumero, estuche *m* de lápices. ‖ **pencil sharpener** sacapuntas *m*.

pending ['pendɪŋ] *adj (waiting to be decided or settled)* pendiente; *(imminent)* próximo,-a, inminente.
► *prep (while awaiting)* en espera de.

penetrate ['penɪtreɪt] *vt* **1** *(gen)* penetrar en; *(clothing)* atravesar, traspasar; *(organization)* infiltrarse en. **2** *(understand)* penetrar, entender.
► *vi (sink in)* causar impresión.

penfriend ['penfrend] *n* amigo,-a por correspondencia.

penguin ['peŋgwɪn] *n* pingüino.

penicillin [penɪˈsɪlɪn] *n* penicilina.

peninsula [pəˈnɪnsjʊlə] *n* península.

penis ['piːnɪs] *n* ANAT pene *m*.
ⓘ *pl* penises o penes ['piːniːs].

penknife ['pennaɪf] *n* cortaplumas *m*, navaja.
ⓘ *pl* penknives ['pennaɪvz].

pennant ['penənt] *n* banderín *m*.

penny ['penɪ] *n* **1** GB penique *m*: *a fifty pence piece* una moneda de cincuenta peniques. **2** US centavo.
ⓘ *pl* penises o pence [pens].

pennyroyal [penɪˈrɔɪəl] *n* poleo.

pension ['penʃən] *n* pensión *f*.

pensioner ['penʃənəʳ] *n* jubilado,-a, pensionista *mf*.

pentagon ['pentəgən] *n* pentágono.

⊕ El Pentagon (Pentágono) es la sede de la secretaría de Defensa de los Estados Unidos y es sinónimo del poderío militar del país. Fue uno de los objetivos de los famosos atentados perpetrados con aviones de pasajeros el 11 de septiembre de 2001.

pentathlon [penˈtæθlən] *n* pentatlón *m*.

penthouse ['penthaʊs] *n* ático.

penultimate [pɪˈnʌltɪmət] *adj* penúltimo,-a.

people ['piːpəl] *n pl* **1** *(gen)* gente *f*, personas *fpl*: *a lot of people* mucha gente; *over a hundred people* más de cien personas; *people say that...* dicen que…, se dice que… **2** *(citizens)* ciudadanos *mpl*; *(inhabitants)* habitantes *mpl*. COMP **old people** los viejos *mpl*, los ancianos *mpl*, la gente *f* mayor. ‖ **the common people** la gente *f* corriente. ‖ **young people** los jóvenes *mpl*, la juventud *f*, la gente *f* joven.
► *n (nation, race)* pueblo, nación *f*.
► *vt* poblar.

✎ Consulta también person.

pepper ['pepər] n 1 (spice) pimienta. 2 (vegetable) pimiento.
▶ vt CULIN echar pimienta a.

peppermint ['pepəmɪnt] n 1 BOT menta. 2 (sweet) caramelo de menta.

per [pɜːr] prep por: 100 miles per hour 100 millas por hora. |LOC| **as per** de acuerdo con, según. ‖ **per annum** por año, al año. ‖ **per cent** por ciento.

perceive [pə'siːv] vt (see) percibir, ver; (notice) notar; (realize) darse cuenta de.

☒ To perceive no significa 'percibir (dinero)', que se traduce por receive.

percentage [pə'sentɪdʒ] n porcentaje m.

perception [pə'sepʃən] n 1 (sense) percepción f. 2 (insight) perspicacia, agudeza. 3 (way of understanding) idea.

perch[1] [pɜːtʃ] n (fish) perca.
① pl perch o perches.

perch[2] [pɜːtʃ] n 1 (for bird) percha. 2 (high position) posición f elevada, posición f privilegiada; (pedestal) pedestal m.
▶ vi (bird) posarse (on, en); (person) sentarse (on, en).

percolator ['pɜːkəleɪtər] n cafetera eléctrica.

percussion [pɜː'kʌʃən] n percusión f.

percussionist [pe'kʌʃənɪst] n percusionista nf.

perennial [pə'renɪəl] adj perenne.

perfect [(adj) 'pɜːfɪkt; (vb) pə'fekt] adj 1 (gen) perfecto,-a. 2 (absolute, utter - fool) perdido,-a, redomado,-a; (- gentleman) consumado; (- waste of time) auténtico,-a: he's a perfect stranger to me me es totalmente desconocido. 3 LING perfecto,-a.
▶ n LING perfecto.
▶ vt perfeccionar.

perfection [pə'fekʃən] n 1 (state, quality) perfección f. 2 (act) perfeccionamiento. |LOC| **to do** STH **to perfection** hacer ALGO a la perfección.

perfectionist [pə'fekʃənɪst] n perfeccionista nf.

perfectly ['pɜːfektlɪ] adv 1 (exactly, faultlessly) perfectamente. 2 (absolutely) totalmente.

perform [pə'fɔːm] vt 1 (task) ejecutar, llevar a cabo; (function) desempeñar, hacer, cumplir. 2 (piece of music) interpretar, tocar; (song) cantar; (play) representar, dar; (role) interpretar.
▶ vi 1 (actor) actuar; (singer) cantar; (musician) tocar, interpretar; (dancer) bailar. 2 (machine) funcionar, marchar; (person) trabajar.

performance [pə'fɔːməns] n 1 (of task) ejecución f, realización f; (of function, duty) ejercicio f. 2 (session - at theatre) representación f, función f; (- of circus, show, etc) número, espectáculo. 3 (action - of song, of musician) interpretación f; (- of play) representación f; (- of actor) interpretación f, actuación f. 4 (of machine) funcionamiento.

performer [pə'fɔːmər] n (gen) artista mf, actor m, actriz f; (musician) intérprete mf.

perfume ['pɜːfjuːm] n perfume m.
▶ vt perfumar.

perhaps [pə'hæps] adv quizá, tal vez: perhaps they've got lost quizá se hayan perdido.

perimeter [pə'rɪmɪtər] n perímetro.

period ['pɪərɪəd] n 1 (length of time) período, periodo. 2 (epoch) época. 3 GEOL período. 4 EDUC (lesson) clase f. 5 (menstruation) regla, período. 6 US (full stop) punto.
▶ adj (dress, furniture) de época.

periodic [pɪərɪ'rɒdɪk] adj periódico,-a. |COMP| **periodic table** CHEM tabla periódica.

periodical [pɪərɪ'rɒdɪkəl] adj periódico,-a.
▶ n publicación f periódica.

peripheral [pə'rɪfərəl] adj 1 (zone, etc) periférico,-a. 2 (secondary) secundario,-a.

periphery [pə'rɪfəri] n 1 (of city) periferia. 2 (of society) margen m.

periscope ['perɪskəup] n periscopio.

perish ['perɪʃ] vi 1 (die) perecer, fallecer. 2 (decay) estropearse.
▶ vt (rubber) deteriorar.

perishable ['perɪʃəbəl] adj perecedero,-a.

peritonitis [perɪtə'naɪtəs] n MED peritonitis f.

perm [pɜːm] n fam (in hair) permanente f.

permanent ['pɜːmənənt] adj 1 (lasting - gen) permanente; (dye, ink) indeleble; (damage) irreparable. 2 (job, address) fijo,-a.

permission [pə'mɪʃ⁹n] *n (gen)* permiso; *(authorization)* autorización *f*. LOC **to ask for permission to do** STH pedir permiso para hacer ALGO.

permit [*(n)* 'pɜːmɪt; *(vb)* pɜː'mɪt] *n* permiso.
► *vt (gen)* permitir; *(authorize)* autorizar: *he was not permitted access to the meeting* no se le permitió la entrada a la reunión.
► *vi* permitir: *weather permitting* si el tiempo lo permite.
ⓘ *pt & pp* **permitted**, *ger* **permitting**.

permutation [pɜːmjuˈteɪʃⁿ] *n* **1** MATH permutación *f*. **2** GB *fam (in football pools)* combinación *f*.

perpendicular [pɜːpənˈdɪkjʊləʳ] *adj* **1** MATH perpendicular (**to**, a). **2** *(upright)* vertical.
► *n* perpendicular *f*.

perpetuity [pɜːpɪˈtjuːtɪ] *n* perpetuidad *f*.

perplexity [pəˈpleksɪtɪ] *n* perplejidad *f*.

persecution [pɜːsɪˈkjuːʃⁿ] *n* persecución *f*.

perseverance [pɜːsɪˈvɪərəns] *n* perseverancia.

persistent [pəˈsɪstənt] *adj* **1** *(person)* insistente. **2** *(cough, pain, fog)* persistente; *(rain)* continuo,-a, persistente; *(denials, rumours, warnings)* continuo,-a, constante, repetido,-a.

person ['pɜːsⁿn] *n* **1** *(gen)* persona: *he's a really nice person* es una persona muy simpática. **2** LING persona. LOC **in person** personalmente.

✎ El plural más usual es **people**, pero **persons** se emplea en el lenguaje jurídico.

personal ['pɜːsⁿnəl] *adj* **1** *(private)* personal, privado,-a: *for personal reasons* por motivos personales. **2** *(own)* particular, personal. **3** *(individual)* personal. **4** *(physical - appearance)* personal; *(hygiene)* íntimo,-a, personal. **5** *(in person)* en persona. LOC **to get personal** hacer alusiones personales. COMP **personal computer** ordenador personal.

personality [pɜːsⁿˈnælɪtɪ] *n* **1** *(nature)* personalidad *f*. **2** *(famous person)* personaje *m*.
ⓘ *pl* **personalities**.

personally ['pɜːsⁿnəlɪ] *adv* **1** *(in person)* personalmente, en persona. **2** *(for my part)* personalmente. **3** *(as a person)* como persona. LOC **to take** STH **personally** ofenderse.

personify [pɜːˈsɒnɪfaɪ] *vt* personificar.
ⓘ *pt & pp* **personified**, *ger* **personifying**.

perspective [pəˈspektɪv] *n* **1** ART perspectiva. **2** *fig (view, angle)* perspectiva.

persuade [pəˈsweɪd] *vt* persuadir, convencer: *she's easily persuaded* se deja convencer fácilmente.

persuasion [pəˈsweɪʒⁿn] *n* **1** *(act)* persuasión *f*. **2** *(ability)* persuasiva.

perturb [pəˈtɜːb] *vt* perturbar.

Peru [pəˈruː] *n* Perú.

Peruvian [pəˈruːvɪən] *adj* peruano,-a.
► *n (person)* peruano,-a.

perversion [pəˈvɜːʃⁿn] *n* **1** *(sexual)* perversión *f*. **2** *(distortion)* tergiversación *f*, distorsión *f*.

perversity [pəˈvɜːsɪtɪ] *n (wickedness)* perversidad *f*; *(stubbornness)* terquedad *f*.
ⓘ *pl* **perversities**.

pessimist ['pesɪmɪst] *n* pesimista *mf*.

pessimistic [pesɪˈmɪstɪk] *adj* pesimista.

pest [pest] *n* **1** plaga: *greenfly and other pests* pulgones y otras plagas. **2** *fam (person)* pelma *mf*, pesado,-a; *(thing)* lata, rollo.

⊠ Pest no significa 'peste (mal olor)', que se traduce por stink.

pester ['pestəʳ] *vt* molestar.

pesticide ['pestɪsaɪd] *n* pesticida.

pet [pet] *n (tame animal)* animal *m* de compañía, mascota. COMP **teacher's pet** enchufado,-a.
► *adj* **1** *(kind person)* sol, cielo; *(term of affection)* cariño, cielo. **2** *(tame)* domesticado,-a. **3** *(favourite - theory, subject, etc)* favorito,-a. COMP **pet name** nombre *m* cariñoso.
❙ **pet shop** tienda de animales.
► *vt (animal)* acariciar.
► *vi fam* tocarse y besuquearse.
ⓘ *pt & pp* **petted**, *ger* **petting**.

petal ['petⁿl] *n* pétalo.

petiole ['petɪəʊl] *n* pecíolo.

petition [pəˈtɪʃⁿn] *n* **1** petición *f*, solicitud *f*. **2** JUR demanda.

▶ *vt* presentar una solicitud a.

▶ *vi* solicitar (for, -).

petrochemical [petrəʊˈkemɪkəl] *adj* petroquímico,-a.

petrol [ˈpetrəl] *n* gasolina. COMP **petrol pump** surtidor *m* de gasolina. ▌ **petrol station** gasolinera.

☒ Petrol no significa 'petróleo', que se traduce por oil.

petroleum [pəˈtrəʊlɪəm] *n* petróleo. COMP **petroleum jelly** vaselina.

petticoat [ˈpetɪkəʊt] *n (underskirt)* enaguas *fpl; (slip)* enagua, combinación *f*.

petty [ˈpetɪ] *adj* **1** *(trivial)* insignificante, sin importancia. **2** *(mean)* mezquino, -a. COMP **petty cash** dinero para gastos *mpl* menores.

ⓘ *comp* pettier, *superl* pettiest.

petulant [ˈpetjʊlənt] *adj* malhumorado,-a.

☒ Petulant no significa 'petulante', que se traduce por vain.

pew [pjuː] *n* banco de iglesia.

phalange [ˈfælændʒ] *n* falange *f*.

phallus [ˈfæləs] *n* falo.

phantom [ˈfæntəm] *n (ghost)* fantasma *m*.

▶ *adj (imaginary)* ilusorio,-a.

Pharaoh [ˈfeərəʊ] *n* faraón *m*.

pharmaceutical [fɑːməˈsjuːtɪkəl] *adj* farmacéutico,-a.

pharmacist [ˈfɑːməsɪst] *n* farmacéutico,-a.

pharmacy [ˈfɑːməsɪ] *n* farmacia.

ⓘ *pl* pharmacies.

✎ Cuando se trata del establecimiento donde se expenden medicamentos, la palabra más usual es chemist's.

pharyngitis [færɪnˈdʒaɪtɪs] *n* faringitis *f*.

pharynx [ˈfærɪŋks] *n* faringe *f*.

phase [feɪz] *n (gen)* fase *f; (stage)* etapa.

▶ *vt* escalonar, realizar por etapas.

pheasant [ˈfezᵊnt] *n* faisán *m*.

phenomenon [fɪˈnɒmɪnən] *n* fenómeno.

ⓘ *pl* phenomenons o phenomena [fɪˈnɒmɪnə].

philately [fɪˈlætəlɪ] *n* filatelia.

philharmonic [fɪlɑːˈmɒnɪk] *adj* filarmónico,-a.

Philippine [ˈfɪlɪpiːn] *adj* filipino,-a.

Philippines [ˈfɪlɪpiːnz] *n* Filipinas.

philology [fɪˈlɒlədʒɪ] *n* filología.

philosopher [fɪˈlɒsəfəʳ] *n* filósofo,-a.

philosophical [fɪləˈsɒfɪkəl] *adj* filosófico,-a.

philosophy [fɪˈlɒsəfɪ] *n* filosofía.

phobia [ˈfəʊbɪə] *n* fobia.

Phoenician [fəˈniːʃən] *adj* fenicio,-a.

▶ *n* **1** *(person)* fenicio,-a. **2** *(language)* fenicio.

▶ *n* fenicio,-a.

phone [fəʊn] *n fam* teléfono. COMP **phone book** listín *m*, guía telefónica. ▌ **phone box** cabina telefónica. ▌ **phone call** llamada telefónica. ▌ **phone number** número de teléfono.

▶ *vt* llamar (por teléfono), telefonear.

▶ *vi* llamar (por teléfono), telefonear.

phonecard [ˈfəʊnkɑːd] *n* tarjeta telefónica.

phonetic [fəˈnetɪk] *adj* fonético,-a.

phonetics [fəˈnetɪks] *n* fonética.

phosphorus [ˈfɒsfərəs] *n* fósforo.

photo [ˈfəʊtəʊ] *n fam* foto *f*.

photocopier [ˈfəʊtəʊkɒpɪəʳ] *n* fotocopiadora.

photocopy [ˈfəʊtəʊkɒpɪ] *n* fotocopia.

ⓘ *pl* photocopies.

▶ *vt* fotocopiar.

ⓘ *pt & pp* photocopied, *ger* photocopying.

photoelectric [fəʊtəʊɪˈlektrɪk] *adj* fotoeléctrico,-a. COMP **photoelectric cell** célula fotoeléctrica, fotocélula.

photograph [ˈfəʊtəgrɑːf] *n* fotografía, foto *f: colour photograph* fotografía en color. LOC **to take a photograph of** STH/SB fotografiar ALGO/a ALGN, hacer/sacar/tomar una fotografía de ALGO/ALGN.

▶ *vt* fotografiar.

photographer [fəˈtɒɡrəfəʳ] *n* fotógrafo,-a.

photographic [fəʊtəˈɡræfɪk] *adj* fotográfico,-a.

photography [fəˈtɒɡrəfɪ] *n* fotografía.

photosynthesis [fəʊtəʊˈsɪnθəsɪs] *n* fotosíntesis *f*.

P

phrasal verb [freɪzˈəlˈvɜːb] *n* verbo compuesto.

📎 Los phrasal verbs son verbos seguidos de una partícula (adverbio, preposición) cuyo significado es muy distinto del significado del verbo por si solo. Existen multitud de phrasal verbs y su traducción suele plantear bastantes problemas a los estudiantes de inglés. En algunos casos, el verbo es separable, es decir, se pueden colocar complementos entre el verbo y la partícula, y en otros no.

phrase [freɪz] *n* 1 LING frase *f*, locución *f*. 2 *(expression)* frase *f*, expresión *f*.
▶ *vt (express)* expresar.

physical [ˈfɪzɪkəl] *adj* 1 *(gen)* físico,-a, material. 2 *(of physics)* físico,-a. 3 *fam euph (rough)* duro,-a: *it was a very physical game* fue un partido muy duro. LOC **physical education** educación *f* física. ∥ **physical geography** geografía física.
▶ *n (medical examination)* reconocimiento médico.

physician [fɪˈzɪʃən] *n* médico,-a.

physicist [ˈfɪzɪsɪst] *n* físico,-a.

physics [ˈfɪzɪks] *n* física.

physiology [fɪzɪˈɒlədʒɪ] *n* fisiología.

physiotherapist [fɪzɪəʊˈθerəpɪst] *n* fisioterapeuta *mf*.

physiotherapy [fɪzɪəʊˈθerəpɪ] *n* fisioterapia.

pianist [ˈpɪənɪst] *n* pianista *mf*.

piano [pɪˈænəʊ] *n (instrument)* piano.
ⓘ *pl* pianos.

piccolo [ˈpɪkələʊ] *n* flautín *m*.
ⓘ *pl* piccolos.

pick¹ [pɪk] *n (tool)* pico, piqueta.

pick² [pɪk] *n (choice)* elección *f*, selección *f*: *take your pick* elige el que quieras, escoge el que quieras. COMP **the pick of the bunch** el/la mejor de todos,-as.
▶ *vt* 1 *(choose - gen)* elegir, escoger; *(team)* seleccionar. 2 *(flowers, fruit, cotton, etc)* coger, recoger. 3 *(remove pieces from - gen)* escarbar, hurgar; *(spots)* tocarse. 4 *(remove from - hair, etc)* quitar. 5 *(open - lock)* forzar, abrir con una ganzúa. 6 *(of birds)* picotear.

◆ **to pick on** *vt insep (victimize)* meterse con; *(choose for task)* elegir, escoger.

◆ **to pick up** *vt sep* 1 *(lift)* levantar; *(from floor)* recoger; *(take)* coger; *(stitch)* coger; *(telephone)* descolgar: *don't forget to pick up all your litter* no os olvidéis de recoger toda la basura. 2 *(learn - language)* aprender; *(- habit)* adquirir, coger; *(- news, gossip)* descubrir, enterarse de. 3 *(illness, cold)* pescar, pillar. 4 *(acquire, get)* conseguir, encontrar. 5 *(collect - person)* recoger, pasar a buscar. *(- hitchhiker)* coger; *(- thing)* recoger: *I'll pick you up at 9.00 pm* te vendré a buscar a las nueve.

pickaxe [ˈpɪkæks] *n* GB pico, piqueta.

picket [ˈpɪkɪt] *n* 1 *(industry)* piquete *m*. 2 *(stick)* estaca.

pickle [ˈpɪkəl] *vt* encurtir, conservar en vinagre.
▶ *n pl* **pickles** *(vegetables)* encurtidos *mpl*.

pickpocket [ˈpɪkpɒkɪt] *n* carterista *mf*.

pick-up [ˈpɪkʌp] *n (on record player)* brazo (del tocadiscos). COMP **pick-up truck** furgoneta, camioneta.

picnic [ˈpɪknɪk] *n* picnic *m*.
▶ *vi (go on a picnic)* ir de picnic; *(eat)* hacer un picnic.
ⓘ *pt & pp* picnicked, *ger* picnicking.

picnicker [ˈpɪknɪkəʳ] *n* excursionista *mf*.

picture [ˈpɪktʃəʳ] *n* 1 *(painting)* pintura, cuadro; *(portrait)* retrato; *(drawing)* dibujo, grabado; *(illustration)* ilustración *f*, lámina; *(photograph)* fotografía, foto *f*: *he painted her picture* la retrató; *I took a picture of them* les saqué una foto. 2 *(account, description)* descripción *f*; *(mental picture)* imagen *f*, idea, impresión *f*. 3 TV *(quality of image)* imagen *f*. 4 GB *(film)* película. LOC **to take a picture** hacer una foto. COMP **picture book** libro ilustrado. ∥ **picture window** ventanal *m*.
▶ *vt* 1 *(imagine)* imaginarse, verse: *I can't picture them married* no me los imagino casados. 2 *(paint)* pintar; *(draw)* dibujar.
▶ *n pl* **the pictures** GB el cine: *we went to the pictures* fuimos al cine.

pie [paɪ] *n* CULIN *(sweet)* pastel *m*, tarta; *(savoury)* pastel *m*, empanada.

piece [piːs] *n* 1 *(bit - large)* trozo, pedazo; *(small)* cacho; *(of broken glass)* fragmento

2 *(part, component)* pieza, parte f: *a thirty-piece dinner service* una vajilla de treinta piezas. **3** *(coin)* moneda. **4** *(in board games)* ficha. **5** *(in newspaper)* artículo. **6** *(item, example of)* pieza: *a piece of advice* un consejo; *a piece of chalk* una tiza; *a piece of furniture* un mueble; *a piece of news* una noticia; *a piece of paper* un papel; *a piece of work* un trabajo. ⎣LOC⎦ **in one piece** *(unharmed)* sano,-a y salvo,-a. ∥ **to be in pieces 1** *(broken)* estar hecho,-a pedazos. **2** *(dismantled)* estar desmontado,-a. ∥ **to break STH in pieces** hacer ALGO pedazos.

pier [pɪəʳ] n **1** *(landing place)* muelle m, embarcadero. **2** ARCH *(pillar)* pilar m, estribo.

pierce [pɪəs] vt **1** *(make hole in)* perforar, agujerear; *(go through)* atravesar, traspasar. **2** *(of light, sound)* penetrar, traspasar.

piercing [ˈpɪəsɪŋ] adj *(sound)* agudo,-a; *(scream)* desgarrador,-ra; *(look)* penetrante; *(wind)* cortante.

piety [ˈpaɪətɪ] n piedad f.

pig [pɪg] n **1** ZOOL cerdo, puerco, marrano. **2** pej *(ill-mannered person)* cerdo, puerco, cochino; *(glutton)* glotón,-ona, tragón,-ona, comilón,-ona.

pigeon [ˈpɪdʒɪn] n *(bird)* paloma; *(for eating)* pichón m.

pigeonhole [ˈpɪdʒɪnhəʊl] n casilla.
▶ vt encasillar.

piggy [ˈpɪgɪ] n cerdito. ⎣COMP⎦ **piggy bank** hucha (en forma de cerdito).
ⓘ pl piggies.

piglet [ˈpɪglət] n cerdito, cochinillo.

pigment [ˈpɪgmənt] n pigmento.

pigsty [ˈpɪgstaɪ] n pocilga.
ⓘ pl pigsties.

pigtail [ˈpɪgteɪl] n coleta.

pilchard [ˈpɪltʃəd] n sardina.

pile¹ [paɪl] n **1** *(heap)* montón m, pila. **2** fam *(a lot of)* montón m, pila: *I've got a pile of essays to mark* tengo que corregir un montón de redacciones.
▶ vt **1** *(form a pile)* amontonar, apilar. **2** *(fill)* llenar, colmar: *the sink was piled high with dishes* el fregadero estaba lleno de platos.
▶ n pl **piles of** montones mpl de.

pile² [paɪl] n ARCH pilote m, pilar m.

pilgrim [ˈpɪlgrɪm] n peregrino,-a.

pilgrimage [ˈpɪlgrɪmɪdʒ] n peregrinación f.

pill [pɪl] n *(gen)* píldora, pastilla.

pillow [ˈpɪləʊ] n almohada.

pillowcase [ˈpɪləʊkeɪs] n funda de almohada.

pilot [ˈpaɪlət] n **1** AV piloto mf. **2** MAR práctico mf. **3** *(TV or radio programme)* programa m piloto. ⎣COMP⎦ **pilot light** piloto.
▶ adj piloto, experimental.
▶ vt **1** *(ship, etc)* pilotar. **2** *(guide)* dirigir. **3** *(test)* poner a prueba.

pimento [pɪˈmentəʊ] n pimiento morrón.
ⓘ pl pimentos.

pimp [pɪmp] n chulo, proxeneta mf.

pimple [ˈpɪmpəl] n *(spot)* grano.

pin [pɪn] n **1** *(gen)* alfiler m. **2** *(badge, brooch)* insignia, pin m, alfiler m. **3** TECH *(peg, dowel)* clavija, espiga. **4** ELEC polo: *a two-pin plug* una clavija de dos patillas. ⎣COMP⎦ **pins and needles** hormigueo.
▶ vt **1** *(garment, hem, seam)* prender (con alfileres); *(papers, etc together)* sujetar (con un alfiler); *(notice on board, etc)* clavar (up, -); *(hair)* recoger (up, -). **2** *(person)* inmovilizar; *(arms)* sujetar.
▶ n pl **pins** fam *(legs)* patas fpl.
◆ **to pin up** vt sep clavar (con chinchetas), sujetar (con alfileres).
ⓘ pt & pp pinned, ger pinning.

pinafore [ˈpɪnəfɔːʳ] n *(apron)* delantal m. ⎣COMP⎦ **pinafore dress** pichi m.

pinball [ˈpɪnbɔːl] n flipper m.

pincer [ˈpɪnsəʳ] n *(of crab, etc)* pinza.
▶ n pl **pincers** *(tool)* tenaza, tenazas fpl.

pinch [pɪntʃ] n **1** *(nip)* pellizco. **2** *(small amount)* pizca.
▶ vt **1** *(nip)* pellizcar; *(shoes)* apretar. **2** fam *(steal)* birlar, afanar, robar.

❎ To pinch no significa 'pinchar', que se traduce por **to prick**.

pine¹ [paɪn] n BOT *(tree, wood)* pino.
▶ adj de pino. ⎣COMP⎦ **pine cone** piña. ∥ **pine nut** piñón m.
◆ **to pine away** vi consumirse, morirse de pena.

pineapple [ˈpaɪnæpəl] n piña.

ping-pong ['pɪŋpɒŋ] n tenis m de mesa, ping-pong m.

pinion ['pɪnɪən] n TECH piñón m.

pink [pɪŋk] adj (de color) rosa, rosado,-a. LOC **to go pink / turn pink** ponerse colorado,-a.
  ► n 1 (colour) (color m) rosa m. 2 BOT clavel m, clavellina.

pint [paɪnt] n (measurement) pinta.
  ► n a pint fam (of beer) una cerveza, una jarra. LOC **to go for a pint** ir a tomar una cerveza.

✎ En Gran Bretaña equivale a 0,57 litros; en Estados Unidos equivale a 0,47 litros.

pioneer [paɪə'nɪər] n pionero,-a.
  ► vt (policy, industry) promover; (technique) iniciar.

pious ['paɪəs] adj piadoso,-a.

pip¹ [pɪp] n (seed) pepita.

pip² [pɪp] n (sound) señal f (corta).

pipe [paɪp] n 1 (for water, gas, etc) tubería, cañería, conducto. 2 (for smoking) pipa: he smokes a pipe fuma en pipa.
  ► n pl pipes gaita f sing.

pipeline ['paɪplaɪn] n (for water) tubería, cañería; (for gas) gasoducto; (for oil) oleoducto.

piper ['paɪpər] n gaitero,-a.

piping ['paɪpɪŋ] n tubería, cañería.

piracy ['paɪˀrəsɪ] n piratería.

piranha [pɪ'rɑːnə] n (fish) piraña.

pirate ['paɪˀrət] n pirata m.
  ► adj pirata.
  ► vt piratear.

pirouette [pɪruˈet] n pirueta.

Pisces ['paɪsiːz] n piscis m.
  ► vi hacer piruetas, piruetear.

pistachio [pɪsˈtɑːʃɪəʊ] n pistacho. COMP **pistachio tree** pistachero.
  ① pl pistachios.

pistil ['pɪstɪl] n pistilo.

pistol ['pɪstˀl] n pistola.

piston ['pɪstˀn] n TECH pistón m, émbolo.

pit¹ [pɪt] n 1 (hole) hoyo, foso; (grave) fosa. 2 (mine) mina, pozo. 3 (mark - on metal, glass) señal f, marca; (- on skin) pi-

cadura, cicatriz f. 4 THEAT (for orchestra) foso de la orquesta.
  ► n pl the pits (in motor racing) los boxes mpl.

pit² [pɪt] n US (seed) pepita; (stone) hueso.

pitch¹ [pɪtʃ] n 1 MUS (of sound) tono; (of instrument) diapasón m. 2 SP (field) campo, terreno; (throw) lanzamiento. 3 (degree, level) grado, punto, extremo. 4 (position, site) lugar m, sitio; (in market) puesto. 5 MAR (movement) cabezada. 6 (slope of roof) pendiente f.
  ► vt 1 MUS (note, sound) entonar. 2 fig (aim, address) dirigir (at, a); (set) dar un tono a. 3 (throw) tirar, arrojar; (in baseball) lanzar. 4 (tent) plantar, montar; (camp) montar.
  ► vi 1 (fall) caerse. 2 (ship, plane) cabecear. 3 SP (in baseball) lanzar.

pitch² [pɪtʃ] n (tar) brea, pez f.

pitched [pɪtʃt] adj (roof) en pendiente, inclinado,-a. COMP **pitched battle** batalla campal.

pitcher¹ ['pɪtʃər] n (of clay) cántaro.

pitcher² ['pɪtʃər] n SP pítcher mf, lanzador,-ra.

pitchfork ['pɪtʃfɔːk] n AGR horca.

pith [pɪθ] n 1 (of bone, plant) médula; (of orange) piel f blanca. 2 fig meollo.

pitiful ['pɪtɪfʊl] adj 1 (arousing pity - sight) lastimoso,-a; (cry) lastimero,-a. 2 (arousing contempt) lamentable.

pituitary [pɪ'tjuːɪtˀrɪ] adj pituitario,-a. LOC **pituitary gland** glándula pituitaria.

pity ['pɪtɪ] n 1 (compassion) piedad f, compasión f: she gave him some money out of pity le dio dinero por compasión. 2 (regret) lástima, pena. LOC **for pity's sake!** ¡por amor de Dios! ▌ **what a pity!** ¡qué lástima!, ¡qué pena!
  ① pl pities.
  ► vt (feel pity for) compadecerse de, tener lástima de, dar lástima.
  ① pt & pp pitied, ger pitying.

pivot ['pɪvət] n 1 pivote m. 2 fig eje m.

pixel ['pɪksəl] n píxel m.

pizza ['piːtsə] n pizza.

pizzeria [piːtsə'rɪə] n pizzería.

placard ['plækɑːd] n pancarta.

place [pleɪs] *n* **1** *(particular position, part)* lugar *m*, sitio: *we visited lots of different places* fuimos a muchos sitios diferentes. **2** *(proper position)* lugar *m*, sitio; *(suitable place)* lugar *m* adecuado, sitio adecuado: *put the book back in its place* devuelve el libro a su sitio. **3** *(building)* lugar *m*, sitio; *(home)* casa, piso: *let's go to my place* vamos a mi casa. **4** *(in book)* página. **5** *(seat)* asiento, sitio; *(at table)* cubierto. **6** *(position, role, rank)* lugar *m*; *(duty)* obligación *f*: *if I were in your place* yo en tu lugar. **7** *(in race, contest)* puesto, lugar *m*, posición *f*; *(in queue)* turno. **8** *(job)* puesto; *(at university, on course)* plaza; *(on team)* puesto. ⌊LOC⌋ **all over the place** por todas partes, por todos lados. ▌**in place** en su sitio. ▌**in place of** SB **/** in SB's **place** en el lugar de ALGN. ▌**out of place** fuera de lugar. ▌**to take place** tener lugar.
▶ *vt* **1** *(put - gen)* poner; *(- carefully)* colocar: *she placed the vase on the shelf* puso el florero en el estante. **2** *(find home, job for)* colocar. **3** *(rank, class)* poner, situar. **4** *(remember - face, person)* recordar; *(- tune, accent)* identificar. ⌊LOC⌋ **to place an order** hacer un pedido.

placenta [pləˈsentə] *n* placenta.
ⓘ *pl* **placentas** o **placentae** [pləˈsentiː].

plague [pleɪg] *n* **1** *(of insects, etc)* plaga. **2** MED peste *f*.
▶ *vt* **1** *(pester)* acosar, asediar. **2** *(afflict)* afligir, asolar, plagar, atormentar.

plain [pleɪn] *adj* **1** *(clear)* claro,-a, evidente: *he made it quite plain* lo dejó muy claro. **2** *(straightforward)* franco,-a, directo,-a: *tell me in plain language* dímelo en lenguaje corriente. **3** *(simple, ordinary)* sencillo,-a; *(without pattern)* liso,-a. **4** *(unattractive)* poco agraciado,-a, feúcho,-a. **5** *(chocolate)* sin leche. ⌊LOC⌋ **in plain clothes** vestido,-a de paisano.
▶ *adv* **1** *(absolutely)* totalmente. **2** *(clearly)* claramente, francamente.
▶ *n* GEOG llanura.

plait [plæt] *n* trenza.
▶ *vt* trenzar.

plan [plæn] *n* **1** *(scheme, arrangement)* plan *m*, proyecto: *a change of plan* un cambio

de planes. **2** *(map, drawing, diagram)* plano; *(design)* proyecto; *(for essay)* esquema *m*.
▶ *vt* **1** *(make plans)* planear, proyectar, planificar; *(intend)* pensar, tener pensado: *they plan to get married next year* tienen planeado casarse el año que viene. **2** *(make a plan of - house, garden, etc)* hacer los planos de, diseñar; *(- economy, strategy)* planificar.
ⓘ *pt & pp* **planned**, *ger* **planning**.

plane¹ [pleɪn] *n* **1** MATH *(surface)* plano. **2** *fig (level, standard)* nivel *m*. **3** *fam (aircraft)* avión *m*: *they went by plane* fueron en avión.
▶ *adj* plano,-a.

plane² [pleɪn] *n* *(tool)* cepillo.
▶ *vt* cepillar.

plane³ [pleɪn] *n* *(tree)* plátano.

planet [ˈplænət] *n* planeta *m*.

planetarium [plænɪˈteərɪəm] *n* planetario.
ⓘ *pl* **planetariums** o **planetaria** [plænɪˈteərɪə].

plank [plæŋk] *n* *(of wood)* tablón *m*, tabla.

plankton [ˈplæŋktən] *n* plancton *m*.

planning [ˈplænɪŋ] *n* planificación *f*.

plant¹ [plɑːnt] *n* BOT planta.
▶ *vt* **1** *(flowers, trees)* plantar; *(seeds, vegetables)* sembrar; *(bed, garden, etc)* plantar (with, de). **2** *(bomb)* colocar; *(blow)* plantar; *(kiss)* dar, plantar. **3** *(ideas, doubt)* inculcar, meter.

plant² [plɑːnt] *n* *(factory)* planta, fábrica; *(machinery)* equipo, maquinaria.

plantation [plænˈteɪʃən] *n* *(for crops)* plantación *f*.

plasma [ˈplæzmə] *n* plasma *m*.

plaster [ˈplɑːstər] *n* **1** *(powder, mixture - gen)* yeso; *(for walls)* revoque *m*, enlucido. **2** MED escayola: *he's got his arm in plaster* tiene el brazo escayolado.
▶ *vt* **1** *(wall, ceiling)* enyesar, enlucir. **2** *(cover, spread)* cubrir (with, de).

plastic [ˈplæstɪk] *adj* **1** *(bag, cup, spoon, etc)* de plástico,-a. **2** *(malleable)* moldeable. ⌊COMP⌋ **plastic surgery** cirugía plástica. ▌ **the plastic arts** las artes *fpl* plásticas.
▶ *n* **1** plástico. **2** *fam (credit cards)* tarjetas de crédito.

Plasticine® [ˈplæstɪsiːn] *n* GB plastilina.

P

| plate 286 |

plate [pleɪt] n 1 (dish, plateful) plato. 2 (sheet of metal, glass) placa; (thin layer) lámina. 3 (illustration) grabado, lámina. [COMP] number plate matrícula. ‖ plate rack escurreplatos.

plateau ['plætəʊ] n 1 GEOG meseta. 2 (state) estancamiento.
ⓘ pl plateaus o plateaux ['plætəʊz].

platform ['plætfɔ:m] n 1 (gen) plataforma; (for speaker) tribuna, estrado; (for band) estrado. 2 (railway) andén m, vía.

platinum ['plætɪnəm] n platino.

platonic [plə'tɒnɪk] adj platónico,-a.

platoon [plə'tu:n] n MIL pelotón m.

platypus ['plætɪpəs] n ornitorrinco.

play [pleɪ] n 1 (recreation) juego: children at play niños jugando. 2 SP (action) juego; (match) partido; (move) jugada. 3 THEAT obra (de teatro), pieza (teatral).
▶ vt 1 (game, sport) jugar a. 2 SP (compete against) jugar contra; (in position) jugar de; (ball) pasar; (card) jugar; (piece) mover. 3 MUS tocar. 4 (joke, trick) gastar, hacer. 5 THEAT (part) hacer el papel de, hacer de; (play) representar, dar: she plays the part of Juliet hace de Julieta. [LOC] to play it cool hacer como si nada. ‖ to play the game jugar limpio.
▶ vi 1 (amuse oneself) jugar (at, a), (with, con). 2 SP (at game) jugar. 3 THEAT (cast) actuar, trabajar; (show) ser representado,-a. 4 MUS tocar.
◆ to play about vi juguetear.
◆ to play around vi (gen) juguetear; (have affairs) tener líos.

player ['pleɪə'] n 1 SP jugador,-ra. 2 THEAT (actor) actor m; (actress) actriz f.

playful ['pleɪfʊl] adj juguetón,-ona, travieso,-a.

playground ['pleɪgraʊnd] n patio de recreo.

playhouse ['pleɪhaʊs] n 1 (theatre) teatro. 2 (for children) casita.

playing card ['pleɪɪŋkɑ:d] n carta, naipe m.

playing field ['pleɪɪŋfi:ld] n campo deportivo.

playmate ['pleɪmeɪt] n compañero,-a de juego, amiguito,-a.

play-off ['pleɪɒf] n SP partido de desempate.

playpen ['pleɪpen] n parque m (para niños).

playtime ['pleɪtaɪm] n recreo.

plead [pli:d] vi suplicar (with, -).
▶ vt (give as excuse) alegar.

pleading ['pli:dɪŋ] adj (tone, voice, look) suplicante.
▶ n súplica, ruego.

pleasant ['plezənt] adj 1 (gen) agradable; (surprise) grato,-a. 2 (person) simpático, -a, amable.
ⓘ comp pleasanter, superl pleasantest.

please [pli:z] vt (make happy, be agreeable to) agradar, gustar, complacer; (satisfy) contentar, complacer: you can't please everyone no se puede complacer a todos.
▶ vi 1 (satisfy) contentar, complacer, satisfacer. 2 (choose, want, like) querer: you can do as you please puedes hacer lo que quieras.
▶ interj por favor: quiet, please silencio, por favor.

pleased [pli:zd] adj (happy) contento,-a; (satisfied) satisfecho,-a. [LOC] pleased to meet you! ¡encantado,-a!, ¡mucho gusto!

pleasing ['pli:zɪŋ] adj agradable, grato,-a.

pleasure ['pleʒə'] n placer m: it's a pleasure to be here es un placer estar aquí. [LOC] my pleasure ha sido un placer. ‖ to have the pleasure of... tener el placer de..., tener gusto de... ‖ with pleasure con mucho gusto.

plebeian [plɪ'bi:ən] adj 1 HIST plebeyo, -a. 2 pej ordinario,-a.

plentiful ['plentɪfʊl] adj abundante.

plenty ['plentɪ] n abundancia.
▶ pron mucho,-a, muchos,-as: we've got plenty of time tenemos tiempo de sobra.

pliers ['plaɪəz] n pl alicates mpl, tenazas fpl.

plinth [plɪnθ] n 1 (of column, pillar) plinto; (of statue) peana.

plod [plɒd] vi 1 (walk slowly) andar con paso lento. 2 (work steadily) hacer laboriosamente.
ⓘ pt & pp plodded, ger plodding.

plot¹ [plɒt] *n* **1** *(conspiracy)* conspiración *f*, complot *m*. **2** *(of book, film, etc)* trama, argumento.
▶ *vt* **1** *(plan secretly)* tramar, urdir. **2** *(course, position)* trazar.
▶ *vi* conspirar, tramar, maquinar.
ⓘ *pt & pp* plotted, *ger* plotting.

plot² [plɒt]

plough [plaʊ] *n* AGR arado.
▶ *vt (land, etc)* arar.

plow [plaʊ] *adj* US → **plough**.

plug [plʌg] *n* **1** *(for bath, sink, etc)* tapón *m*. **2** ELEC *(on lead)* enchufe *m*, clavija; *(socket)* enchufe *m*, toma de corriente. **3** *(publicity)* publicidad *f*.
▶ *vt* **1** *(hole, etc)* tapar (up, -). **2** *(publicize)* dar publicidad a, promocionar.
◆ **to plug away** *vt insep* perseverar (at, en).
◆ **to plug in** *vt sep* enchufar.
▶ *vi* enchufarse.
◆ **to plug into** *vt sep* enchufar a.
ⓘ *pt & pp* plugged, *ger* plugging.

plug-in [plʌgɪn] *n* plug-in *m*, conector *m*.

plum [plʌm] *n* **1** *(fruit)* ciruela. **2** *(colour)* color *m* ciruela. COMP **plum tree** ciruelo.
▶ *adj fam* fantástico,-a.
◆ **to plumb in** *vt sep* instalar, conectar.

plumber [plʌmə] *n* fontanero,-a.

plumbing [plʌmɪŋ] *n* **1** *(occupation)* fontanería. **2** *(system)* tubería, cañería.

plump [plʌmp] *adj* regordete, rollizo,-a.

plunder [plʌndə] *n* **1** *(action)* pillaje *m*, saqueo. **2** *(loot)* botín *m*.
▶ *vt* saquear, pillar.

plunge [plʌndʒ] *n* **1** *(dive)* zambullida, chapuzón *m*. **2** *(fall)* caída, descenso.
▶ *vi* **1** *(dive)* lanzarse, zambullirse; *(fall)* caer, hundirse. **2** *(drop - prices, etc)* caer en picado.
▶ *vt (immerse)* sumergir, hundir; *(thrust)* clavar, meter; *(in despair, poverty, etc)* sumir.

plural [plʊərəl] *adj* plural.
▶ *n* plural *m*.

plus [plʌs] *prep* más: *four plus five is nine* cuatro más cinco son nueve.
▶ *adj* **1** *(ion, number)* positivo,-a. **2** *(and more)* más de, ALGO más de. **3** *(advantageous)* positivo,-a.
▶ *n* **1** MATH *(sign)* signo más. **2** *(advantage)* ventaja, factor *m* positivo, pro.

Pluto [pluːtəʊ] *n* Plutón *m*.

plutonium [pluːtəʊnɪəm] *n* plutonio.
◆ **to ply with** *vt sep (drink, food)* no parar de ofrecer; *(questions)* asediar a, acosar a.

ply [plaɪ] *n (of wood)* chapa; *(of paper)* capa.
ⓘ *pl* plies.

plywood [plaɪwʊd] *n* contrachapado.

pm [piːem] *abbr* (post meridiem) de la tarde. *it is 5.10 p.m.* son las cinco y diez de la tarde.

pneumatic [njuːmætɪk] *adj* neumático,-a.

pneumonia [njuːməʊnɪə] *n* pulmonía.

poach [pəʊtʃ] *vt* CULIN *(fish)* hervir; *(eggs)* escalfar.

poacher [pəʊtʃə] *n (of game)* cazador,-ra furtivo,-a; *(of fish)* pescador,-ra furtivo,-a.

pocket [pɒkɪt] *n* **1** *(gen)* bolsillo. **2** *(small area - of air)* bolsa; *(- of resistance)* foco.
▶ *adj (dictionary, camera, etc)* de bolsillo.
LOC **pocket money** *(for children)* paga, semanada.

pocketknife [pɒkɪtnaɪf] *n* navaja.
ⓘ *pl* pocketknives.

pod [pɒd] *n* BOT vaina.

podium [pəʊdɪəm] *n* podio.
ⓘ *pl* podiums o podia [pəʊdɪə].

poem [pəʊəm] *n* poema *m*, poesía.

poet [pəʊət] *n* poeta *mf*.

poetic [pəʊetɪk] *adj* poético,-a.

poetry [pəʊətrɪ] *n* poesía.

point [pɔɪnt] *n* **1** *(sharp end - of knife, nail, pencil)* punta. **2** *(place)* punto, lugar *m*: *meeting point* punto de encuentro. **3** *(moment)* momento, instante *m*: *at this point* en este momento. **4** *(state, degree)* punto, extremo. **5** *(on scale, graph, compass)* punto; *(on thermometer)* grado. **6** SP *(score, mark)* punto, tanto. **8** *(item, matter, detail)* punto. **9** *(central idea, meaning)* idea, significado: *you've missed the point* no has captado la idea. **10** *(purpose, use)* sentido, propósito: *what's the point?* ¿para qué? **11** *(quality, ability)* cualidad *f*. **12** GEOG punta, cabo. **13** MATH *(in geometry)* punto (de intersección). **14** *(in decimals)* coma: *five point six* cinco coma seis. LOC **to come to the point** ir al grano. COMP **point of view** punto de vista.

P

▶ vi **1** *(show)* señalar: *the girl pointed at the clown* la niña señaló al payaso con el dedo. **2** fig *(indicate)* indicar.

▶ vt **1** *(with weapon)* apuntar. **2** *(direct)* señalar, indicar.

◆ **to point out** vt sep **1** *(show)* señalar. **2** *(mention)* señalar, hacer notar; *(warn)* advertir.

✎ En el sistema inglés, los millares se separan con una coma y los decimales con un punto, así que *tres mil ochocientos treinta y cinco* se escribiría 3,835 y *treinta y ocho coma veinticinco* se escribiría 38.25.

pointed ['pɔɪntɪd] *adj* puntiagudo,-a, en punta.

pointless ['pɔɪntləs] *adj (meaningless)* sin sentido; *(useless)* inútil.

poison ['pɔɪzən] *n* veneno.

▶ vt *(harm, kill - person, animal)* envenenar; *(make ill)* intoxicar; *(river)* contaminar.

poisoning ['pɔɪzənɪŋ] *n* envenenamiento.

poisonous ['pɔɪzənəs] *adj* **1** *(plant, berry, snake)* venenoso,-a; *(drugs, gas)* tóxico, -a. **2** fig pernicioso,-a.

poke [pəʊk] *n (jab)* empujón *m*, golpe *m*; *(with elbow)* codazo; *(with sharp object)* pinchazo.

poker ['pəʊkər] *n (card game)* póquer *m*.

Poland ['pəʊlənd] *n* Polonia.

polar ['pəʊlər] *adj* polar. COMP **polar bear** oso polar.

polarity [pəʊ'lærɪtɪ] *n* polaridad *f*.
ⓘ *pl* polarities.

Pole [pəʊl] *n* polaco,-a.

pole¹ [pəʊl] *n (stick, post)* poste *m*, pértiga. COMP **pole vault** salto con pértiga.

pole² [pəʊl] *n (electrical, geographical)* polo. LOC **to be poles apart** ser polos opuestos.

police [pə'liːs] *n pl (body)* policía *f sing*; *(officers)* policías *mpl*. COMP **police station** comisaría.

✎ Recuerda que el verbo que acompaña a police va en plural.

policeman [pə'liːsmən] *n* policía *m*, agente *m* de policía, guardia *m*.
ⓘ *pl* policemen [pə'liːsmən].

policewoman [pə'liːswʊmən] *n* policía, agente *f* de policía, guardia.
ⓘ *pl* policewomen [pə'liːswɪmɪn].

policy ['pɒlɪsɪ] *n* **1** POL política. **2** *(course of action, plan)* política, estrategia. **3** *(insurance)* póliza (de seguros).
ⓘ *pl* policies.

polish ['pɒlɪʃ] *n* **1** *(for furniture)* cera (para muebles); *(for shoes)* betún *m*; *(for floors)* cera, abrillantador *m* (de suelos); *(for nails)* esmalte *m*. **2** *(shine)* lustre *m*, brillo. **3** fig *(refinement)* refinamiento, brillo.

▶ vt *(floor, furniture)* sacar brillo a, encerar; *(shoes)* limpiar; *(silver, cutlery)* sacar brillo a; *(nails)* pintar con esmalte; *(stone)* pulir.

Polish ['pəʊlɪʃ] *adj* polaco,-a.

▶ *n* **1** *(person)* polaco,-a. **2** *(language)* polaco.

▶ *n pl* **the Polish** los polacos *mpl*.

polite [pə'laɪt] *adj* cortés, educado,-a, cumplido,-a, correcto,-a: *he was very polite to me* me trató con cortesía.
ⓘ *comp* politer, *superl* politest.

politely [pə'laɪtlɪ] *adv* cortésmente, educadamente, correctamente.

politeness [pə'laɪtnəs] *n* cortesía, educación *f*.

political [pə'lɪtɪkəl] *adj (gen)* político,-a.

politician [pɒlɪ'tɪʃən] *n* político,-a.

politics ['pɒlɪtɪks] *n* **1** *(gen)* política: *he's active in politics* es militante (político). **2** *(science)* ciencias *fpl* políticas.

▶ *n pl (view, opinions)* ideas *fpl* políticas.

polka ['pɒlkə] *n (dance)* polca. COMP **polka dot** lunar *m*.

poll [pəʊl] *n* **1** *(voting)* votación *f*. **2** *(survey)* encuesta, sondeo.

▶ vt **1** *(votes - obtain)* obtener. **2** *(ask opinion)* sondear, encuestar.

▶ *n pl* **the polls** las elecciones *fpl*, los comicios *mpl*. LOC **to go to the polls** acudir a las urnas.

pollen ['pɒlən] *n* polen *m*.

pollination [pɒlɪ'neɪʃən] *n* polinización *f*.

polling ['pəʊlɪŋ] *n* votación *f*. COMP **polling station** colegio electoral.

pollute [pə'luːt] vt contaminar.

pollution [pəˈluːʃᵊn] n contaminación f.

polo [ˈpəʊləʊ] n SP polo.

polo-neck [ˈpəʊləʊnek] adj (sweater) de cuello alto, de cuello cisne.

polyester [pɒlɪˈestər] n poliéster m.

polygamy [pɒˈlɪɡəmɪ] n poligamia.

polygon [ˈpɒlɪɡɒn] n polígono.

polytechnic [pɒlɪˈteknɪk] n escuela politécnica, politécnico.

pond [pɒnd] n estanque m.

pony [ˈpəʊnɪ] n póney m, poni m.
ⓘ pl ponies.

ponytail [ˈpəʊnɪteɪl] n cola de caballo.

pool¹ [puːl] n 1 (of water, oil, blood, etc) charco; (of light) foco. 2 (pond) estanque m; (in river) pozo.

pool² [puːl] n 1 (common fund of money) fondo común; (in gambling) bote m. 2 (common supply of services) servicios mpl comunes. 3 US (snooker) billar m americano.
▶ vt (funds, money) reunir, juntar; (ideas, resources) poner en común.
▶ n pl **the pools** las quinielas fpl.

poor [pʊər] adj 1 (person, family, country) pobre. 2 (inadequate) pobre, escaso,-a; (bad quality) malo,-a; (inferior) inferior: you've got a poor memory tienes mala memoria. 3 (unfortunate) pobre: poor Edward el pobre Edward.
▶ n pl **the poor** los pobres mpl.

poorly [ˈpʊəlɪ] adj (ill) indispuesto,-a.
▶ adv (badly) mal: poorly dressed mal vestido,-a.

pop¹ [pɒp] n 1 (of cork) taponazo. 2 fam (drink) gaseosa.
▶ vt 1 (burst) hacer reventar; (cork) hacer saltar. 2 (put) poner, meter.
▶ vi 1 (burst) estallar, reventar; (cork) saltar. 2 (go quickly) ir rápidamente.
ⓘ pt & pp popped, ger popping.

pop² [pɒp] n fam (music) música pop.
COMP **pop art** pop-art m. ‖ **pop star** estrella del pop.

popcorn [ˈpɒpkɔːn] n palomitas fpl de maíz.

pope [pəʊp] n papa m.

poplar [ˈpɒplər] n BOT álamo.

poppy [ˈpɒpɪ] n amapola.
ⓘ pl poppies.

popular [ˈpɒpjʊlər] adj 1 (well-liked - gen) popular; (- person) estimado,-a; (- resort, restaurant) muy frecuentado,-a; (fashionable) de moda: she's popular with her workmates les cae muy bien a sus compañeras de trabajo. 2 (of or for general public) popular; (prices) popular, económico,-a.

popularity [pɒpjʊˈlærɪtɪ] n popularidad f.

population [pɒpjʊˈleɪʃᵊn] n población f.

porcelain [ˈpɔːsᵊlɪn] n porcelana.
▶ adj de porcelana.

porch [pɔːtʃ] n 1 (of church) pórtico; (of house) porche m, entrada. 2 US (veranda) terraza.

porcine [ˈpɔːsaɪn] adj porcino,-a.

porcupine [ˈpɔːkjʊpaɪn] n puerco espín.

pore [pɔːr] n ANAT poro.

pork [pɔːk] n carne f de cerdo. COMP **pork butcher** charcutero,-a.

pornography [pɔːˈnɒɡrəfɪ] n pornografía.

porridge [ˈpɒrɪdʒ] n gachas fpl de avena.

port¹ [pɔːt] n (harbour, town) puerto.
▶ adj portuario,-a.

port² [pɔːt] n (left side) babor m.

portable [ˈpɔːtəbᵊl] adj portátil.

porter [ˈpɔːtər] n 1 (in hotel, block of flats) portero,-a; (in public building, school) conserje m; (in hospital) camillero. 2 (at station, airport) mozo, maletero.

portion [ˈpɔːʃᵊn] n (gen) porción f, parte f; (of food) ración f.
◆ **to portion out**

portrait [ˈpɔːtreɪt] n retrato.

portray [pɔːˈtreɪ] vt 1 (painting) representar, retratar. 2 (describe) describir, retratar. 3 (act) interpretar.

portrayal [pɔːˈtreɪəl] n 1 (painting) representación f. 2 (description) descripción f. 3 (acting) interpretación f.

Portugal [ˈpɔːtjʊɡᵊl] n Portugal.

P

Portuguese [pɔːtjʊˈgiːz] *adj* portugués, -esa.

▶ *n* **1** *(person)* portugués,-esa. **2** *(language)* portugués *m*.

▶ *n pl* **the Portuguese** los portugueses *mpl*.

pose [pəʊz] *n* **1** *(position, stance)* postura, actitud *f*. **2** *pej (affectation)* pose *f*, afectación *f*.

▶ *vt (problem, question, etc)* plantear; *(threat)* representar.

▶ *vi* **1** *(for painting, photograph)* posar. **2** *pej (behave affectedly)* presumir, hacer pose.

[LOC] **to pose as** hacerse pasar por.

posh [pɒʃ] *adj* **1** GB *fam (place, area)* elegante, de lujo; *(accent)* refinado,-a. **2** GB *fam (upper-class)* pijo,-a.

position [pəˈzɪʃən] *n* **1** *(place)* posición *f*. **2** *(right place)* sitio, lugar *m*: **they manoeuvred the piano into position** colocaron el piano en su lugar. **3** *(posture)* postura, posición *f*. **4** *(on scale, in competition)* posición *f*, lugar *m*, puesto; *(social standing)* categoría social, posición *f*. **5** *(job)* puesto. **6** *(situation, circumstances)* situación *f*, lugar *m*. **7** *(opinion, point of view)* postura, posición *f*. **8** SP posición *f*.

▶ *vt (put in place)* colocar, poner.

positive [ˈpɒzɪtɪv] *adj* **1** *(gen)* positivo,-a. **2** *(definite - proof, evidence)* concluyente, definitivo,-a; *(- refusal, decision)* categórico,-a; *(- instruction, order)* preciso,-a. **3** *(effective - criticism, advice)* constructivo,-a; *(- attitude, experience)* positivo,-a. **4** *(quite certain)* seguro,-a (**about**, de): **I'm absolutely positive** estoy segurísimo.

▶ *n* positivo.

possess [pəˈzes] *vt* **1** *(own)* poseer, tener. **2** *(take over - anger, fear)* apoderarse de.

possession [pəˈzeʃən] *n* **1** *(ownership)* posesión *f*, poder *m*. **2** *(thing owned)* bien *m*, posesión *f*.

possessive [pəˈzesɪv] *adj* **1** *(person)* posesivo,-a; *(selfish)* egoísta. **2** LING posesivo,-a.

▶ *n* LING posesivo.

possessor [pəˈzesəʳ] *n* poseedor,-ra.

possibility [pɒsɪˈbɪlɪtɪ] *n* **1** *(likelihood)* posibilidad *f*. **2** *(something possible)* posibilidad *f*.

ⓘ *pl* possibilities.

possible [ˈpɒsɪbəl] *adj* posible. [LOC] **as much as possible** todo lo posible. **as soon as possible** cuanto antes, lo antes posible.

▶ *n* posible candidato,-a.

possibly [ˈpɒsɪblɪ] *adv* **1** *(reasonably, conceivably)* posiblemente: **you can't possibly have finished already!** ¡no es posible que ya hayas acabado! **2** *(in requests)*: **could you possibly give me a lift to the station?** ¿me podría llevar a la estación? **3** *(perhaps)* posiblemente, quizás.

post¹ [pəʊst] *n (of wood)* estaca, poste *m*.

post² [pəʊst] *n* **1** *(job)* puesto, empleo; *(important position)* cargo. **2** MIL puesto.

▶ *vt* **1** MIL destinar, apostar. **2** *(employee)* destinar, mandar.

post³ [pəʊst] *n* GB *(mail)* correo; *(collection)* recogida; *(delivery)* reparto: **it's in the post** ya está enviado.

▶ *vt* **1** GB *(send - letter, parcel)* mandar por correo, echar al correo; *(put in postbox)* echar al buzón. [COMP] **post office** Correos, oficina de correos.

postage [ˈpəʊstɪdʒ] *n* franqueo, porte *m*.

postal [ˈpəʊstəl] *adj* postal.

postbag [ˈpəʊstbæg] *n* **1** *(sack)* saca (de correos). **2** GB *(letters)* correspondencia.

postbox [ˈpəʊstbɒks] *n* GB buzón *m*.

postcard [ˈpəʊstkɑːd] *n* tarjeta postal *f*.

postcode [ˈpəʊstkəʊd] *n* GB código postal.

poster [ˈpəʊstəʳ] *n* póster *m*, cartel *m*.

postgraduate [pəʊstˈgrædjʊət] *n* postgraduado,-a.

▶ *adj* de postgrado.

postman [ˈpəʊstmən] *n* cartero.

ⓘ *pl* postmen [ˈpəʊstmən].

postmark [ˈpəʊstmɑːk] *n* matasellos *m*.

▶ *vt* timbrar, matasellar.

postpone [pəsˈpəʊn] *vt* posponer.

posture [ˈpɒstʃəʳ] *n* **1** *(position of body)* postura, pose *f*. **2** *(attitude)* postura.

▶ *vi* hacer poses, adoptar poses.

postwar [ˈpəʊstwɔːʳ] *adj* de la posguerra.

postwoman [ˈpəʊstwʊmən] *n* cartera.

ⓘ *pl* postwomen [ˈpəʊstwɪmɪn].

pot [pɒt] *n* **1** CULIN *(container)* pote *m*, tarro; *(for cooking)* olla, puchero; *(earthen-*

ware) vasija; *(teapot)* tetera; *(coffee pot)* cafetera. **2** *(of paint)* bote *m*. **3** *(flowerpot)* maceta, tiesto.
► *vt (plant)* plantar en una maceta.
► *n* **the pot** *(in card games)* el bote.

potassium [pə'tæsɪəm] *n* potasio.

potato [pə'teɪtəʊ] *n* patata.
ⓘ *pl* potatoes.

potential [pə'tenʃəl] *adj* potencial.
► *n* potencial *m*.

potholer ['pɒθəʊlər] *n* GB espeleólogo,-a.

potholing ['pɒθəʊlɪŋ] *n* GB espeleología.

potter ['pɒtər] *n* alfarero,-a.

pottery ['pɒtərɪ] *n* alfarería.

potty ['pɒtɪ] *n* orinal *m*.
ⓘ *pl* potties.

pouch [paʊtʃ] *n* **1** *(gen)* bolsa (pequeña); *(for tobacco)* petaca. **2** ZOOL bolsa abdominal.

poultry ['pəʊltrɪ] *n* aves *fpl* de corral.

pounce [paʊns] *n* salto.
► *vi* saltar (on, sobre), abalanzarse (on, sobre).

pound¹ [paʊnd] *vt* **1** *(crush)* machacar. **2** *(strike, beat)* aporrear, golpear.
► *vi* **1** *(strike, beat)* aporrear (at/on, -), golpear (at/on, -); *(of waves)* batir (against, contra). **2** *(heart)* palpitar, latir con fuerza.

pound² [paʊnd] *n* **1** FIN libra: *a five-pound note* un billete de cinco libras. **2** *(weight)* libra: *half a pound of tomatoes* media libra de tomates.

✎ Como medida de peso equivale a 454 gr.

pound³ [paʊnd] *n* *(enclosure - for dogs)* perrera; *(- for cars)* depósito.

pour [pɔːr] *vt* *(liquid)* verter, echar; *(substance)* echar; *(drink)* servir: *she poured the orange juice into a jug* vertió el zumo de naranja en una jarra.
► *vi* **1** *(blood)* manar, salir; *(water, sweat)* chorrear. **2** *fig* moverse en tropel. COMP **to pour (down/with rain)** llover a cántaros: *it's pouring* está lloviendo a cántaros.

pouring ['pɔːrɪŋ] *adj (rain)* torrencial.

poverty ['pɒvətɪ] *n (gen)* pobreza.

powder ['paʊdər] *n (dust)* polvo; *(cosmetic, medicine)* polvos *mpl*.
► *vt* **1** *(put powder on)* poner polvos, empolvar. **2** *(pulverize)* pulverizar, reducir a polvo.

power ['paʊər] *n* **1** *(strength, force)* fuerza; *(of sun, wind)* potencia, fuerza; *(of argument)* fuerza. **2** *(ability, capacity)* poder *m*, capacidad *f*: *it's beyond his power* no está en sus manos. **3** *(faculty)* facultad *f*. **4** *(control, influence, authority)* poder *m*; *(of country)* poderío, poder *m*: *the power of the media* el poder de los medios de comunicación. **5** *(nation)* potencia; *(person, group)* fuerza. **6** PHYS *(capacity, performance)* potencia; *(energy)* energía. **7** ELEC electricidad *f*, corriente *f*. **8** MATH potencia: *six to the power of four* seis elevado a la cuarta potencia.
► *vt* propulsar, impulsar: *it's powered by electricity* funciona con electricidad.

powerful ['paʊəful] *adj* **1** *(strong - athlete, body, current)* fuerte; *(- blow, engine, machine)* potente. **2** *(influential - enemy, nation, ruler)* poderoso,-a. **3** *(effective)* impactante.

powerless ['paʊələs] *adj* impotente.

practical ['præktɪkəl] *adj* **1** *(gen)* práctico,-a. **2** *(good with hands)* hábil.
► *n* *(lesson)* clase *f* práctica. COMP **practical joke** broma.

practically ['præktɪkəlɪ] *adv* **1** *(almost)* casi, prácticamente. **2** *(in a practical way)* de manera práctica.

practice ['præktɪs] *n* **1** *(repeated exercise)* práctica; *(training)* entrenamiento: *I'm out of practice* me falta práctica. **2** *(action, reality)* práctica: *in practice* en la práctica. **3** *(custom, habit)* costumbre *f*. LOC **to be out of practice** haber perdido práctica.
► *vt & vi* US → **practise**.

practise ['præktɪs] *vt* **1** GB *(do repeatedly - language, serve, scales)* practicar; *(song, act)* ensayar. **2** GB *(religion, belief, economy)* practicar. **3** GB *(profession)* ejercer.
► *vi* **1** GB *(gen)* practicar. **2** *(sports team)* entrenar; *(actors)* ensayar. **3** GB *(professionally)* ejercer (as, de/como).

pragmatic [præg'mætɪk] *adj* pragmático,-a.

prairie ['preərɪ] *n* pradera, llanura.

P

praise [preɪz] *n* **1** alabanza, elogio, loa. **2** REL alabanza.
▶ *vt* **1** elogiar. **2** REL alabar.

pram [præm] *n* GB cochecito de niño.

prank [præŋk] *n (trick)* broma; *(of child)* travesura. LOC **to play a prank on** SB gastar una broma a ALGN.

prawn [prɔːn] *n (large)* langostino; *(medium)* gamba; *(small)* camarón *m*.

pray [preɪ] *vi* REL orar, rezar.

prayer [preər] *n* REL *(request)* oración *f*, rezo, plegaria; *(action)* oración *f*, rezo.

preach [priːtʃ] *vt* **1** REL *(gospel)* predicar; *(sermon)* dar, hacer. **2** *(advocate)* aconsejar.
▶ *vi* REL predicar.

preacher [priːtʃər] *n* predicador,-ra.

precaution [prɪˈkɔːʃən] *n* precaución *f*.

precedent [presɪdənt] *n* precedente *m*.

preceding [prɪˈsiːdɪŋ] *adj* anterior.

precinct [priːsɪŋkt] *n* **1** *(of cathedral, hospital, etc)* recinto. **2** GB *(part of town)* zona.
▶ *n pl* **precincts** recinto *m sing*.

⊠ Precinct no significa 'precinto', que se traduce por seal.

precious [preʃəs] *adj* **1** *(jewel, stone, metal)* precioso,-a. **2** *(moment, memory, possession)* preciado,-a, querido,-a. COMP **precious little** poquísimo,-a.

⊠ Precious no significa 'precioso (bonito)', que se traduce por beautiful.

precipice [presɪpɪs] *n* precipicio.

precipitation [prɪsɪpɪˈteɪʃən] *n* **1** *fml (haste)* precipitación *f*. **2** METEOR precipitación.

precise [prɪˈsaɪs] *adj* preciso,-a.

precisely [prɪˈsaɪslɪ] *adv (exactly)* precisamente; *(accurately)* con precisión. LOC **precisely!** ¡exacto!, ¡eso es!

precision [prɪˈsɪʒən] *n* precisión *f*.

precocious [prɪˈkəʊʃəs] *adj* precoz.

precooked [priːˈkʊkt] *adj* precocinado,-a.

predator [predətər] *n* ZOOL depredador *m*.

predecessor [priːdɪsesər] *n* predecesor,-ra, antecesor,-ra.

predict [prɪˈdɪkt] *vt* predecir.

prediction [prɪˈdɪkʃən] *n* predicción *f*.

predominate [prɪˈdɒmɪneɪt] *vi* predominar.

prefect [priːfekt] *n* **1** *(official)* prefecto. **2** GB *(in school)* monitor,-ra.

prefer [prɪˈfɜːr] *vt* preferir: *she prefers coffee to tea* prefiere el café al té.
ⓘ *pt & pp* **preferred**, *ger* **preferring**.

preferable [prefərəbl] *adj* preferible (to, a).

preference [prefərəns] *n* preferencia (for, por).

prefix [priːfɪks] *n* LING prefijo.

pregnancy [pregnənsɪ] *n* embarazo.
ⓘ *pl* **pregnancies**.

pregnant [pregnənt] *n (woman)* embarazada; *(animal)* preñada: *she's six months pregnant* está embarazada de seis meses.

preheat [priːˈhiːt] *vt* precalentar.

prehistoric [priːhɪˈstɒrɪk] *adj* prehistórico,-a.

prehistory [priːˈhɪstərɪ] *n* prehistoria.

prejudice [predʒədɪs] *n* **1** *(unfavourable bias)* prejuicio; *(favourable)* predisposición *f*.
▶ *vt* **1** *(influence, bias)* predisponer (against, contra), (in favour of, a favor de). **2** *(harm)* perjudicar.

prejudiced [predʒʊdɪst] *adj* parcial.

premature [preməˈtjʊər] *adj (gen)* prematuro,-a.

premiere [premɪeər] *n* estreno.

premises [premɪsɪz] *n pl* local *m*. LOC **on the premises** dentro del local.

preoccupy [priːˈɒkjʊpaɪ] *vt (worry)* preocupar; *(think about too much)* pensar demasiado en.
ⓘ *pt & pp* **preoccupied**, *ger* **preoccupying**.

preparation [prepəˈreɪʃən] *n* **1** *(action)* preparación *f*. **2** *(substance)* preparado.
▶ *n pl* **preparations** preparativos *mpl* (for, para).

preparatory [prɪˈpærətərɪ] *adj* preparatorio,-a, preliminar.

prepare [prɪˈpeər] *vt (gen)* preparar; *(report)* redactar.
▶ *vi* prepararse (for, para).

prepared [prɪˈpeəd] *adj* **1** *(gen)* preparado,-a. **2** *(willing)* dispuesto,-a (to, a).

preposition [prepəˈzɪʃən] *n* preposición *f*.

prescribe [prɪsˈkraɪb] *vt* **1** *(medicine, drugs, etc)* recetar; *(holiday, rest)* recomendar. **2** *fml (order)* prescribir.

prescription [prɪsˈkrɪpʃ°n] *n* receta (médica).

presence [ˈprez°ns] *n* **1** *(gen)* presencia; *(attendance)* asistencia. **2** *(spirit)* espíritu *m*.

present¹ [ˈprez°nt] *adj* **1** *(in attendance)* presente. **2** *(current)* actual. **3** LING presente.
▶ *n (now)* presente *m*, actualidad *f*. [LOC] **at present** actualmente, en este momento.
▶ *n* **the present** LING presente *m*. [COMP] **present continuous** presente continuo. **present perfect** presente perfecto. **present tense** presente.

present² [*(vb)* prɪˈzent; *(n)* ˈprez°nt] *vt* **1** *(make presentation)* entregar, hacer entrega de; *(give - as gift)* regalar. **2** *(offer - report, petition, bill, cheque)* presentar; *(- argument, ideas, case)* presentar, exponer. **3** *fml (offer - apologies, respects)* presentar; *(- compliments, greetings)* dar. **4** *(give - difficulty, problem)* plantear; *(constitute)* suponer, constituir, ser. **5** *(introduce)* presentar. **6** *(play)* representar; *(programme)* presentar.
▶ *n (gift)* regalo; *(formal)* obsequio: *he gave me a present* me hizo un regalo.

presentation [prez°nˈteɪʃ°n] *n* **1** *(of awards, prizes, gifts)* entrega. **2** *(way of presenting)* presentación *f*. **3** *(of play)* representación *f*.

presenter [prɪˈzentər] *n (on radio)* presentador,-ra, locutor,-ra; *(on TV)* presentador,-ra.

presently [ˈprez°ntlɪ] *adv* **1** GB *(soon)* pronto, enseguida. **2** US *(at present)* actualmente.

preservation [prezəˈveɪʃ°n] *n (of wildlife)* conservación *f*, preservación *f*; *(of food, works of art, buildings)* conservación *f*.

preservative [prɪˈzɜːvətɪv] *n* CULIN conservante *m*.

preserve [prɪˈzɜːv] *n* CULIN *(fruit)* conserva; *(jam)* confitura, mermelada.
▶ *vt* conservar, proteger.

preset [priːˈset] *vt* programar.
ⓘ *pt & pp* preset, *ger* presetting.

presidency [ˈprezɪdənsɪ] *n* presidencia.
ⓘ *pl* presidencies.

president [ˈprezɪd°nt] *n* presidente,-a.

press [pres] *n* **1** *(newspapers)* prensa. **2** *(machine)* prensa, imprenta. **3** *(act of pressing)* presión *f*; *(of hand)* apretón *m*; *(act of ironing)* planchado. [COMP] **press agency** agencia de prensa. **press conference** conferencia de prensa, rueda de prensa.
▶ *vt* **1** *(push down - button, switch)* pulsar, apretar, presionar; *(- accelerator)* pisar; *(- key on keyboard)* pulsar; *(- trigger)* apretar. **2** *(squeeze - hand)* apretar. **3** *(crush - fruit)* exprimir, estrujar; *(- grapes, olives, flowers)* prensar. **4** *(clothes)* planchar, planchar a vapor. **5** *(record)* imprimir. **6** *(urge, put pressure on)* presionar, instar; *(insist on)* insistir en, exigir.
▶ *vi* **1** *(push)* apretar, presionar. **2** *(crowd)* apretujarse, apiñarse. **3** *(urge, pressurize)* presionar, insistir; *(time)* apremiar.

pressing [ˈpresɪŋ] *adj* urgente, apremiante.

pressure [ˈpreʃər] *n* **1** *(gen)* presión *f*. **5** *(stress)* tensión *f*: *he's under a lot of pressure* está sometido a una gran presión. [COMP] **pressure cooker** olla a presión, olla exprés.

prestige [presˈtiːʒ] *n* prestigio.

prestigious [presˈtɪdʒəs] *adj* prestigioso,-a.

presume [prɪˈzjuːm] *vt* suponer, imaginarse, presumir: *I presume so* supongo que sí.
▶ *vi* **1** suponer. **2** *(venture to)* atreverse a.

[✕] To presume no significa 'presumir (vanagloriarse)', que se traduce por to boast.

pretend [prɪˈtend] *vt (feign)* fingir, aparentar: *the children pretended to be asleep* los niños fingían estar dormidos.
▶ *vi (feign)* fingir.
▶ *adj (make-believe)* de mentirijillas.

[✕] To pretend no significa 'pretender', que se traduce por to want to, to try to.

pretension [prɪˈtenʃ°n] *n* pretensión *f*.

pretentious [prɪˈtenʃəs] *adj* pretencioso,-a.

preterite [ˈpret°rɪt] *n* LING pretérito.

pretty [ˈprɪtɪ] *adj (girl, baby)* bonito,-a, guapo,-a, mono,-a; *(thing)* bonito,-a

P

mono,-a: *what a pretty little girl!* ¡qué niña más bonita!
ⓘ *comp* **prettier,** *superl* **prettiest.**
► *adv* bastante: *I'm pretty sure* estoy bastante seguro,-a. [LOC] **pretty much** más o menos. ▌ **pretty well** casi.

prevailing [prɪˈveɪlɪŋ] *adj* predominante.

prevent [prɪˈvent] *vt (gen)* impedir; *(avoid - accident)* evitar; *(- illness)* prevenir. [LOC] **to prevent** SB **from doing** STH impedir a ALGN hacer ALGO.

prevention [prɪˈvenʃ°n] *n* prevención *f.*

preview [ˈpriːvjuː] *n* preestreno.

previous [ˈpriːvɪəs] *adj* previo,-a, anterior: *the previous day* el día anterior.

prey [preɪ] *n* **1** *(animal)* presa. **2** *fig* presa, víctima.

price [praɪs] *n* **1** *(gen)* precio; *(amount)* importe *m; (value)* valor *m: what's the price of this jacket?* ¿qué precio tiene esta chaqueta? **2** *fig (cost, sacrifice)* precio. [LOC] **at any price** a toda costa, cueste lo que cueste.
► *vt (fix price of)* tener un precio; *(value)* valorar, tasar; *(mark price on)* poner el precio a.

priceless [ˈpraɪsləs] *adj* que no tiene precio, inestimable.

pricey [ˈpraɪsɪ] *adj fam* caro,-a.
ⓘ *comp* **pricier,** *superl* **priciest.**

prick [prɪk] *n (pain)* pinchazo; *(hole)* agujero.
► *vt (with needle, pin, fork)* pinchar.
► *vi (pin, thorn)* pinchar; *(itch, sting)* escocer, picar.

prickly [ˈprɪkl°ɪ] *adj* **1** *(plant)* espinoso,-a; *(animal)* con púas; *(wool, sweater)* que pica. **2** *(irritable, touchy)* enojadizo,-a, irritable, difícil.
ⓘ *comp* **pricklier,** *superl* **prickliest.**

pride [praɪd] *n* **1** *(gen)* orgullo; *(self-respect)* amor *m* propio. **2** *(arrogance)* soberbia, orgullo.

priest [priːst] *n* sacerdote *m,* cura *m.*

priestess [ˈpriːstes] *n* sacerdotisa.

priesthood [ˈpriːsθ°ʊd] *n (clergy)* clero; *(office)* sacerdocio.

primary [ˈpraɪmərɪ] *adj* **1** *(main)* principal, fundamental. **2** *(first, basic)* prima-

rio,-a. [COMP] **primary school** escuela primaria.

primate [ˈpraɪmeɪt] *n* ZOOL primate *m.*

prime [praɪm] *adj* **1** *(main, chief)* principal, primero,-a. **2** *(first-rate - meat)* de primera (calidad); *(example, location)* excelente.
► *n (best time of life)* flor *f* de la vida. [COMP] **Prime Minister** primer,-a ministro,-a.
► *vt* **1** *(engine, pump, bomb)* cebar; *(surface, wood)* imprimar, preparar. **2** *fig (person)* preparar, enseñar.

primitive [ˈprɪmɪtɪv] *adj (man, tribe, culture)* primitivo,-a; *(tool, method, shelter)* rudimentario,-a, primitivo,-a.

prince [prɪns] *n* príncipe *m.*

princess [ˈprɪnses] *n* princesa.
ⓘ *pl* **princesses.**

principal [ˈprɪnsɪp°l] *adj* principal.
► *n* **1** EDUC director,-ra. **2** THEAT protagonista *mf,* primera figura.

principle [ˈprɪnsɪp°l] *n* **1** *(basic idea, rule, law)* principio; *(basis)* base *f.* **2** *(moral rule)* principio: *it's a matter of principle* es cuestión de principios.

print [prɪnt] *n* **1** *(lettering)* letra: *in large print* en letra grande. **2** *(photo)* copia. **3** *(printed fabric)* estampado. **4** *(mark - of finger, foot)* huella.
► *vt* **1** *(book, page, poster, etc)* imprimir; *(publish)* publicar, editar. **2** *(photo - negative)* imprimir; *(- copy)* sacar una copia de. **3** *(write clearly)* escribir con letra de imprenta. **4** *(fabric)* estampar. **5** *(make impression)* marcar.
◆ **to print out** *vt sep* imprimir.

printer [ˈprɪntər] *n (person)* impresor,-ra; *(machine)* impresora.

printing [ˈprɪntɪŋ] *n (act, process)* impresión *f; (industry)* imprenta. [COMP] **printing press** prensa.

print-out [ˈprɪntaʊt] *n* COMPUT impresión *f.*

prior [ˈpraɪər] *adj* anterior, previo,-a. [LOC] **prior to** antes de.

priority [praɪˈɒrɪtɪ] *n* prioridad *f.*
ⓘ *pl* **priorities.**
► *adj* prioritario,-a.

prism [ˈprɪz°m] *n* prisma.

prison ['prɪzⁿn] n prisión f, cárcel f: *he's in prison* está en la cárcel.

prisoner ['prɪzⁿnəʳ] n *(in jail)* preso,-a, recluso,-a; *(captive)* prisionero,-a.

privacy ['prɪvəsɪ] n privacidad f.

private ['praɪvət] adj **1** *(own, for own use - property, house, class)* particular; *(- letter, income)* personal. **2** *(confidential)* privado, -a, confidencial. **3** *(not state-controlled)* privado,-a. **4** *(not official)* privado,-a, personal. **5** *(person)* reservado,-a. COMP
private eye detective mf privado,-a.
▶ n MIL soldado raso.

privatize ['praɪvətaɪz] vt privatizar.

privilege ['prɪvɪlɪdʒ] n privilegio.

prize [praɪz] n *(gen)* premio.
▶ adj *(having won a prize)* premiado,-a; *(excellent)* de primera, selecto,-a.

probability [prɒbə'bɪlɪtɪ] n probabilidad f.
ⓘ pl probabilities.

probable ['prɒbəbⁿl] adj probable.

probably ['prɒbəblɪ] adv probablemente: *it'll probably rain* es probable que llueva.

probation [prə'beɪʃⁿn] n **1** JUR libertad f condicional. **2** *(in employment)* período de prueba.

probe [prəub] n **1** MED sonda. **2** *(investigation)* investigación f.
▶ vt **1** MED sondar. **2** *(investigate - gen)* investigar; *(public opinion)* sondear.

☒ To probe no significa 'probar (demostrar o catar)', que se traducen por **to prove** o **to taste**.

problem ['prɒbləm] n problema m: *no problem!* ¡no hay problema!, ¡ningún problema!

procedure [prə'siːdʒəʳ] n *(set of actions)* procedimiento; *(step)* trámite m, gestión f.

proceed [prə'siːd] vi **1** *(continue)* seguir, continuar. **2** *(progress)* marchar. **3** fml *(go along)* avanzar, circular; *(go towards)* dirigirse a.

☒ To proceed no significa 'proceder (venir de)', que se traduce por **to come from**.

proceedings [prə'siːdɪŋz] n pl **1** *(events at meeting, ceremony, etc)* actos mpl. **2** JUR *(lawsuit)* proceso sing.

process ['prəuses] n **1** *(set of actions, changes)* proceso: *the process of growing old* el envejecimiento. **2** *(method)* procedimiento, proceso.
▶ vt **1** *(raw material, food)* procesar, tratar; *(film)* revelar. **2** *(deal with)* ocuparse de, tramitar. **3** COMPUT procesar, tratar.

processing ['prəusesɪŋ] n **1** *(treatment)* procesamiento, tratamiento; *(of film)* revelado. **2** *(in business, law)* tramitación f. **3** COMPUT procesamiento.

procession [prə'seʃⁿn] n **1** *(gen)* desfile m. **2** REL procesión f.

processor ['prəusesəʳ] n **1** *(for food)* robot m de cocina. **2** COMPUT procesador m.

proclaim [prə'kleɪm] vt proclamar, declarar.

procure [prə'kjuəʳ] vt *(obtain)* conseguir, obtener.

☒ To procure no significa 'procurar (intentar)', que se traduce por **to try**.

prodigy ['prɒdɪdʒɪ] n prodigio.
ⓘ pl prodigies.

produce [*(vb)* prə'djuːs; *(n)* 'prɒdjuːs] vt **1** *(gen)* producir, fabricar. **2** *(give birth to)* tener. **3** *(show)* enseñar, presentar. **4** *(cause)* producir, causar. **5** *(play)* poner en escena, dirigir.
▶ n productos mpl: *produce of Spain* productos de España.

producer [prə'djuːsəʳ] n **1** *(gen)* productor,-ra, fabricante. **2** *(play)* director,-ra de escena.

product ['prɒdʌkt] n producto.

production [prə'dʌkʃⁿn] n **1** *(gen)* producción f, fabricación f. **2** *(of film)* producción f; *(of play)* producción f, puesta en escena. COMP **production line** cadena de montaje.

productive [prə'dʌktɪv] adj productivo,-a.

productivity [prɒdʌk'tɪvɪtɪ] n productividad f.

profession [prə'feʃⁿn] n *(occupation)* profesión f: *he's a baker by profession* es panadero de profesión.

professional [prə'feʃⁿnəl] adj *(gen)* profesional.
▶ n profesional mf.

P

professor [prə'fesər] *n* **1** GB catedrático, -a. **2** US profesor,-ra universitario,-a.

proficiency [prə'fɪʃənsɪ] *n* competencia.

profile ['prəufaɪl] *n* **1** *(side view)* perfil *m*. **2** *(description)* perfil *m*; *(written)* reseña.

profit ['prɒfɪt] *n* **1** COMM ganancia, beneficio. **2** *fml (advantage)* provecho. LOC **to make a profit** sacar beneficios, tener ganancias.

profitable ['prɒfɪtəbəl] *adj* **1** COMM rentable. **2** *(beneficial)* provechoso,-a.

profit-making ['prɒfɪtmeɪkɪŋ] *adj (business)* rentable; *(charity)* con fines lucrativos.

profound [prə'faʊnd] *adj* profundo,-a.

program ['prəugræm] *n* COMPUT programa *m*.
▸ *vt* COMPUT programar.
ⓘ *pt & pp* **programmed**, *ger* **programming**.

programme ['prəugræm] *n (gen)* programa *m*; *(plan)* plan *m*.
▸ *vt (gen)* programar; *(activities)* planear.

programmer ['prəugræmər] *n* programador,-ra.

programming ['prəugræmɪŋ] *n* programación *f*.

progress [*(n)* 'prəugres; *(vb)* prəu'gres] *n (advance)* progreso, avance *m*; *(development)* desarrollo.
▸ *vi* **1** *(advance)* progresar, avanzar, adelantar; *(develop)* desarrollar. **2** *(improve)* mejorar, hacer progresos. LOC **to be in progress** *(work)* estar en curso, estar en marcha.

progression [prə'greʃən] *n* **1** *(development)* evolución *f*, avance *m*. **2** *(series)* serie *f*.

prohibit [prə'hɪbɪt] *vt* prohibir.

prohibition [prəuɪ'bɪʃən] *n* prohibición *f*.

project [*(n)* 'prɒdʒekt; *(vb)* prə'dʒekt] *n* **1** *(gen)* proyecto. **2** EDUC trabajo, estudio.
▸ *vt* **1** *(gen)* proyectar. **2** *(extrapolate)* extrapolar.
▸ *vi* sobresalir, resaltar.

projectile [prə'dʒektaɪl] *n* proyectil *m*.

projection [prə'dʒekʃən] *n* **1** *(gen)* proyección *f*. **2** *(protuberance)* saliente *m*, resalto.

proletariat [prəulə'teərɪət] *n* proletariado.

prologue ['prəulɒg] *n* prólogo.

prolong [prə'lɒŋ] *vt* prolongar, alargar.

promenade [prɒmə'nɑːd] *n* **1** GB *(at seaside)* paseo marítimo. **2** *fml (walk)* paseo.

prominent ['prɒmɪnənt] *adj (important)* importante; *(projecting)* prominente, saliente.

promise ['prɒmɪs] *n* **1** *(pledge)* promesa. **2** *(expectation, hope)* esperanza, esperanzas *fpl*. LOC **to break a promise** romper una promesa. **∎ to keep a promise** mantener una promesa.
▸ *vt* **1** prometer: *you promised to help me* prometiste ayudarme. **2** *(seem likely)* prometer.
▸ *vi (gen)* prometer; *(swear)* jurar: *I promise* te lo prometo.

promote [prə'məut] *vt* **1** *(in rank)* promover, ascender. **2** *(encourage)* promover, fomentar.

promotion [prə'məuʃən] *n* promoción *f*.

prompt [prɒmpt] *adj (quick)* pronto,-a, rápido,-a; *(punctual)* puntual.
▸ *adv* en punto.
▸ *vt* **1** *(cause, incite)* instar, incitar, mover. **2** THEAT apuntar.
▸ *n* THEAT *(line)* apunte *m*.

promptly ['prɒmptlɪ] *adv* rápidamente.

prone [prəun] *adj (face down)* boca abajo. LOC **to be prone to** STH ser propenso,-a a ALGO.

pronoun ['prəunaun] *n* LING pronombre *m*.

pronounce [prə'nauns] *vt* **1** LING pronunciar. **2** *(declare)* declarar.
▸ *vi* pronunciarse (on, sobre).

pronunciation [prənʌnsɪ'eɪʃən] *n* pronunciación *f*.

proof [pruːf] *n* **1** *(evidence)* prueba. **2** *(trial copy, print)* prueba.

propaganda [prɒpə'gændə] *n* propaganda.

⊠ *Propaganda* no significa 'propaganda *(publicidad)'*, que se traduce por **advertising**.

propagation [prɒpə'geɪʃən] *n* propagación *f*.

propane ['prəupeɪn] *n* propano.

propel [prə'pel] vt propulsar, impulsar.
ⓘ pt & pp propelled, ger propelling.

propeller [prə'pelə'] n hélice f.

propelling pencil [prəpelɪŋ'pensəl] n portaminas m.

proper ['prɒpə'] adj 1 (suitable) adecuado,-a, apropiado,-a; (correct) correcto,-a. 2 fam (real, genuine) verdadero,-a, de verdad. 3 fam (thorough) auténtico,-a. 4 (respectable) correcto,-a, decente. COMP **proper name / proper noun** nombre propio.

☒ Proper no significa 'propio (de uno)', que se traduce por own.

properly ['prɒpəlɪ] adv 1 (properly) bien, adecuadamente. 2 (correctly) bien; (as one should) como es debido.

property ['prɒpətɪ] n 1 (possessions, ownership) propiedad f. 2 (buildings, land) propiedad f, bienes mpl; (estate) finca f. 3 fml (building) inmueble m.
ⓘ pl properties.

prophecy ['prɒfəsɪ] n profecía.
ⓘ pl prophecies.

prophet ['prɒfɪt] n profeta m.

prophetic [prə'fetɪk] adj profético,-a.

proportion [prə'pɔ:ʃən] n 1 (ratio) proporción f. 2 (part) parte f; (percentage) porcentaje m. 3 (correct relation) proporción f.
► n pl **proportions** dimensiones fpl, proporciones fpl.

proportional [prə'pɔ:ʃənəl] adj proporcional (to, a).

proposal [prə'pəuzəl] n propuesta.

propose [prə'pəuz] vt 1 (suggest) proponer. 2 (intend) pensar.
► vi declararse, proponer matrimonio a.

prose [prəuz] n LIT prosa.

prosecute ['prɒsɪkju:t] vt JUR procesar.
► vi JUR (bring a charge) entablar una acción judicial; (be prosecutor) llevar la acusación.

prosecution [prɒsɪ'kju:ʃən] n JUR (action) procesamiento, acción f judicial.
► n **the prosecution** JUR (person) la acusación.

prosecutor ['prɒsɪkju:tə'] n JUR fiscal mf, acusador,-ra.

prospect [(n) 'prɒspekt; (vb) prə'spekt] n 1 (picture in mind) perspectiva. 2 (possibility, hope) posibilidad f, probabilidad f. 3 fml (wide view) panorama m, vista, perspectiva.
► vt prospectar, explorar.
► vi buscar (for, -).
► n pl **prospects** perspectivas fpl.

☒ Prospect no significa 'prospecto', que se traduce por leaflet.

prosper ['prɒspə'] vi prosperar.

prosperity [prɒ'sperɪtɪ] n prosperidad f.

prosperous ['prɒspərəs] adj próspero,-a.

prostate ['prɒsteɪt] n próstata.

prosthesis ['prɒsθəsɪs] n prótesis f.

prostitute ['prɒstɪtju:t] n prostituta.

protect [prə'tekt] vt (gen) proteger; (interests) proteger, salvaguardar.

protection [prə'tekʃən] n (gen) protección f; (shelter) protección f, amparo.

protective [prə'tektɪv] adj protector,-ra.

protector [prə'tektə'] n protector,-ra.

protein ['prəuti:n] n proteína.

protest [(n) 'prəutest; (vb) prə'test] n (gen) protesta; (complaint) queja; (demonstration) manifestación f de protesta.
► vt protestar de.
► vi protestar (about, de), (against, contra), (at, por): they protested about the working conditions protestaron de las condiciones de trabajo.

Protestant ['prɒtɪstənt] adj protestante.
► n protestante mf.

proton ['prəutɒn] n protón m.

proud [praud] adj orgulloso,-a: I'm proud of you estoy orgulloso de ti.

proudly ['praudlɪ] adv (with satisfaction) orgullosamente, con orgullo; (arrogantly) arrogantemente, con arrogancia.

prove [pru:v] vt 1 (show to be true) probar, demostrar. 2 (turn out to be) demostrar.
ⓘ pt proved, pp proved o proven [pru:vən], ger proving.

☒ To prove no significa 'probar (comida)', que se traduce por taste.

proven ['pru:vən] pp → prove.
► adj probado,-a, comprobado,-a.

P

proverb ['prɒvɜːb] *n* proverbio, refrán *m*.

provide [prə'vaɪd] *vt* **1** *(supply)* proveer, suministrar, proporcionar: *he provided us with all the information* nos facilitó toda la información. **2** *fig (answer, example)* ofrecer, dar.

provided [prə'vaɪdɪd] [also provided that] *conj* siempre que, con tal que.

province ['prɒvɪns] *n* **1** *(region)* provincia. **2** *fig* terreno, campo, competencia.

provincial [prə'vɪnʃ³l] *adj* **1** *(government)* provincial; *(town)* de provincia(s). **2** *pej* provinciano,-a, pueblerino,-a.

provision [prə'vɪʒ³n] *n* **1** *(supply)* suministro, abastecimiento. **2** *(preparation)* previsiones *fpl*.
  ▶ *n pl* **provisions** *(food)* provisiones *fpl*, víveres *mpl*.

provisional [prə'vɪʒ³nəl] *adj* provisional.

provoke [prə'vəʊk] *vt* **1** *(make angry)* provocar, irritar: *he's not easily provoked* no se irrita fácilmente. **2** *(cause)* provocar.

prowl [praʊl] *vi* merodear, rondar.
  ▶ *vt* merodear por, rondar por.
  ▶ *n* merodeo.

proximity [prɒk'sɪmɪtɪ] *n fml* proximidad *f*.

prune [pruːn] *n* ciruela pasa.

psalm [sɑːm] *n* salmo.

pseudonym ['sjuːd³nɪm] *n* seudónimo.

psychedelic [saɪkɪ'delɪk] *adj* psicodélico,-a.

psychiatric [saɪkɪ'ætrɪk] *adj* psiquiátrico,-a.

psychiatrist [saɪ'kaɪətrɪst] *n* psiquiatra *mf*.

psychiatry [saɪ'kaɪətrɪ] *n* psiquiatría.

psychic ['saɪkɪk] *adj (mental)* psíquico,-a.

psychoanalyst [saɪkəʊ'ænəlɪst] *n* psicoanalista *mf*.

psychological [saɪkə'lɒdʒɪk³l] *adj* psicológico,-a.

psychologist [saɪ'kɒlədʒɪst] *n* psicólogo,-a.

psychology [saɪ'kɒlədʒɪ] *n* psicología.

psychosis [saɪ'kəʊsɪs] *n* psicosis *f*.
  ① *pl* **psychoses** [saɪ'kəʊsiːz].

pub [pʌb] *n* bar *m*, pub *m*, taberna.

puberty ['pjuːbətɪ] *n* pubertad *f*.

pubis ['pjuːbɪs] *n* pubis *m*.

public ['pʌblɪk] *adj* público,-a. COMP **public convenience** servicios *mpl*, aseos *mpl*. ∥ **public holiday** fiesta nacional. ∥ **public house** bar *m*, pub *m*. ∥ **public school 1** GB colegio privado. **2** US colegio público.
  ▶ *n* **the public** el público.

⊕ En el Reino Unido, los **public schools** son colegios privados de prestigio y de mucha tradición; suelen ser internados. Los colegios públicos británicos se llaman **state schools**. En Estados Unidos los **public schools** son, sencillamente, colegios públicos.

---

publication [pʌblɪ'keɪʃ³n] *n* publicación *f*.

publicity [pʌ'blɪsɪtɪ] *n* publicidad *f*.

publish ['pʌblɪʃ] *vt* **1** *(book, newspaper)* publicar, editar. **2** *(make known)* divulgar.

publisher ['pʌblɪʃə'] *n (person)* editor,-ra. *(company)* editorial *f*.

pudding ['pʊdɪŋ] *n* **1** CULIN *(sweet)* budín *m*, pudín *m*; *(savoury)* pastel *m*. **2** GB *fam (dessert)* postre *m*.

puddle ['pʌd³l] *n* charco.

Puerto Rican [pweətəʊ'riːk³n] *adj* puertorriqueño,-a, portorriqueño,-a.
  ▶ *n* puertorriqueño,-a, portorriqueño,-a.

Puerto Rico [pweətəʊ'riːkəʊ] *n* Puerto Rico.

puff [pʌf] *n* **1** *(of wind, air)* soplo, racha, ráfaga; *(of smoke)* bocanada. **2** *(action)* soplo, soplido; *(at cigarette, pipe)* calada, chupada.
  ▶ *vt (blow - gen)* soplar; *(- smoke)* echar.
  ▶ *vi* **1** *(pipe, cigarette)* chupar (at/on, -), dar caladas (at/on, a). **2** *(pant)* jadear, resoplar. **3** *(train)* echar humo, echar vapor.

puke [pjuːk] *vi fam* devolver, vomitar.

pull [pʊl] *n* **1** *(tug)* tirón *m*. **2** *(of moon, current)* fuerza. **3** *(attraction)* atracción *f*; *(influence)* influencia.
  ▶ *vt* **1** *(draw)* tirar de; *(drag)* arrastrar: *the horse was pulling a cart* el caballo tiraba de una carreta. **2** *(tug forcefully)* tirar de, dar un tirón a: *don't pull my hair!* ¡no me tires del pelo! **3** *(remove, draw out)* sacar. **4** *(damage - muscle)* sufrir un tirón. **5**

fam (attract - crowd, audience) atraer; *(boy, girl)* ligarse, ligar con.
▸ *vi* **1** *(tug)* tirar *(at/on, de)*. **2** *(on pipe, cigarette)* chupar, dar caladas a. **3** *(of vehicle - veer)* tirar.
◆ **to pull down** *vt sep* derribar, tirar (abajo).
◆ **to pull in** *vt sep* **1** *(crowd)* atraer. **2** *(money)* sacar, ganar.
▸ *vi (train)* entrar en la estación; *(bus, car)* parar.
◆ **to pull out** *vt sep (gun, tooth, plug, etc)* sacar; *(troops)* retirar.
▸ *vi* **1** *(train)* salir de la estación; *(bus, car)* salir. **2** *(withdraw)* retirarse.

pulley ['pulɪ] *n* polea.

pullover ['pulǝʊvǝ^r] *n* pullover *m*, jersey *m*.

pulmonary ['pʌlmǝn^ǝrɪ] *adj* pulmonar.

pulse[1] [pʌls] *n* **1** ANAT pulso. **2** PHYS pulsación *f*.
▸ *vi* palpitar, latir.

pulse[2] [pʌls] *n* BOT legumbre *f*.

puma ['pjuːmǝ] *n* puma *m*.

pumice stone ['pʌmɪsstǝʊn] *n* piedra pómez.

pump[1] [pʌmp] *n (machine)* bomba: *bicycle pump* bomba de aire, bombín *m*.
▸ *vt* bombear.
▸ *vi (of heart)* latir.
◆ **to pump up** *vt sep* inflar.

pump[2] [pʌmp] *n (plimsoll)* zapatilla de lona, playera; *(for dancing)* zapatilla de ballet.

pumpkin ['pʌmpkɪn] *n* calabaza.

punch[1] [pʌntʃ] *n* **1** *(blow)* puñetazo, golpe *m*; *(in boxing)* pegada. **2** *fig* fuerza, empuje *m*.
▸ *vt* dar un puñetazo a, pegar a.

punch[2] [pʌntʃ] *n (for making holes)* perforadora, taladro; *(in leather)* punzón *m*; *(for tickets)* máquina de picar billetes.
▸ *vt (make a hole in)* perforar; *(leather)* punzar; *(ticket)* picar.

punch[3] [pʌntʃ] *n (drink)* ponche *m*.

punctual ['pʌŋktjʊǝl] *adj* puntual.

punctuality ['pʌŋktjʊælɪtɪ] *n* puntualidad *f*.

punctuate ['pʌŋktjʊeɪt] *vt* **1** LING puntuar. **2** *(interrupt)* interrumpir.

punctuation ['pʌŋktjʊ'eɪʃ^ǝn] *n* puntuación *f*. COMP **punctuation mark** signo de puntuación.

puncture ['pʌŋktʃǝ^r] *n* pinchazo.
▸ *vt (tyre, ball, etc)* pinchar.

punish ['pʌnɪʃ] *vt* castigar.

punishment ['pʌnɪʃmǝnt] *n* castigo.

punk [pʌŋk] *n (person)* punk *mf*; *(music)* punk *m*.

pupil[1] ['pjuːp^ǝl] *n* EDUC alumno,-a.

pupil[2] ['pjuːp^ǝl] *n* ANAT pupila.

puppet ['pʌpɪt] *n* **1** títere *m*. **2** *fig* títeres *m*. COMP **puppet show** teatro de títeres.

puppy ['pʌpɪ] *n* cachorro,-a.
ⓘ *pl* puppies.

purchase ['pɜːtʃǝs] *n fml* compra.
▸ *vt fml* comprar, adquirir.

pure ['pjʊǝ^r] *adj (gen)* puro,-a: *it was pure chance* fue pura casualidad.

purée ['pjʊǝreɪ] *n* puré *m*.

purification [pjʊǝrɪfɪ'keɪʃ^ǝn] *n* purificación *f*.

purify ['pjʊǝrɪfaɪ] *vt (gen)* purificar; *(water)* depurar, purificar.
ⓘ *pt & pp* purified, *ger* purifying.

puritan ['pjʊǝrɪt^ǝn] *adj* puritano,-a.
▸ *n* puritano,-a.

purple ['pɜːp^ǝl] *adj* morado,-a.
▸ *n (color m)* púrpura, (color *m*) morado.

purpose ['pɜːpǝs] *n* **1** *(aim, intention)* propósito, intención *f*, fin *m*; *(reason)* razón *f*, motivo: *what is the purpose of your visit?* ¿cuál es el motivo de su visita? **2** *(use)* uso, utilidad *f*. **3** *(determination)* resolución *f*. LOC **to no purpose** inútilmente, en vano. ‖ **on purpose** a propósito, adrede, a posta.

purr [pɜː^r] *n (of cat)* ronroneo.
▸ *vi (of cat)* ronronear.

purse [pɜːs] *n* **1** GB monedero, portamonedas *m*. **2** US bolso.
▸ *vt (lips)* fruncir.

pursue [pǝ'sjuː] *vt* **1** *(chase)* perseguir; *(follow)* seguir. **2** *(seek)* buscar; *(strive for)* esforzarse por conseguir, luchar por. **3** *(carry out - policy)* llevar a cabo; *(- mat-*

P

ter) investigar. **4** *(continue with)* seguir, dedicarse a, ejercer.

pursuit [pə'sjuːt] *n* **1** *(chase)* persecución *f*; *(hunt)* caza. **2** *(search)* búsqueda; *(striving)* lucha. **3** *(activity)* actividad *f*.

pus [pʌs] *n* pus *m*.

push [puʃ] *n* *(shove)* empujón *m*.
▶ *vt* **1** *(gen)* empujar. **2** *(press - button, bell, etc)* pulsar, apretar.
▶ *vi* **1** *(shove)* empujar. **2** *(move forward)* abrirse paso. **3** *(pressurize)* presionar, exigir.

pushchair ['puʃtʃeəʳ] *n* GB cochecito de niño, sillita de niño.

push-up ['puʃʌp] *n* US flexión *f*.

pussycat ['pusɪkæt] *n* *fam* minino,-a, gatito,-a.

put [put] *vt* **1** *(gen)* poner; *(place)* colocar; *(add)* echar, añadir; *(place inside)* meter, poner. **2** *(express)* expresar, decir: *you put that very well* lo has expresado muy bien. **3** *(calculate, estimate)* calcular: *I'd put the cost at 100 pounds* yo diría que cuesta 100 libras. [LOC] **to put STH right** arreglar ALGO. ‖ **to put the blame on SB** echar la culpa a ALGN.
◆ **to put down** *vt sep* **1** *(set down - gen)* dejar; *(- phone)* colgar. **2** *(payment)* entregar, dejar (en depósito); *(deposit)* dejar. **3** *(rebellion)* sofocar. **4** *(write)* apuntar, anotar, escribir.
▶ *vi* AV aterrizar.
◆ **to put forward** *vt sep* **1** *(idea, theory, plan)* proponer, presentar. **2** *(clock, meeting, wedding)* adelantar.
◆ **to put in** *vt sep* **1** *(install, fit)* instalar, poner. **2** *(include, insert)* poner, incluir; *(say)* agregar. **3** *(enter, submit - claim, request, bid)* presentar. **4** *(spend time working)* trabajar, hacer.
▶ *vi* *(ship)* hacer escala.
◆ **to put off** *vt sep* **1** *(postpone)* aplazar, posponer. **2** *(distract)* distraer. **3** *(discourage)* desanimar, disuadir, quitar las ganas a.
◆ **to put on** *vt sep* **1** *(clothes)* poner, ponerse: *put your coat on* ponte el abrigo. **2** *(expression, attitude)* fingir, adoptar. **3** *(gain, increase)* aumentar. **4** *(present - show)* presentar, montar; *(- exhibition)*

organizar. **5** *(switch on - light, television)* encender; *(- music, radio)* poner.
◆ **to put out** *vt sep* **1** *(fire, light, cigarette)* apagar. **2** *(put outside - cat, washing, rubbish)* sacar. **3** *(extend - hand)* tender, alargar; *(- tongue)* sacar; *(dislocate)* dislocar. **4** *(inconvenience)* molestar; *(upset, offend, annoy)* molestar, ofender. **5** *(publish, issue)* publicar; *(broadcast)* difundir.
◆ **to put up** *vt sep* **1** *(provide accommodation for)* alojar, hospedar. **2** *(erect - tent)* armar; *(- building, fence)* levantar, construir. **3** *(shelves, picture, decorations)* colocar; *(curtains, notice, poster)* colgar. **4** *(raise - hand)* levantar; *(flag)* izar; *(hair)* recoger; *(umbrella)* abrir. **5** *(increase - price, etc)* aumentar, subir. **6** *(present - candidate)* presentar, proponer.
▶ *vt insep* **1** *(resistence, struggle)* ofrecer, oponer: *they put up a good fight* ofrecieron mucha resistencia. **2** *(money)* poner, aportar.
◆ **to put up with** *vt insep* soportar, aguantar.
ⓘ *pt & pp* put, *ger* putting.

putt [pʌt] *n* tiro al hoyo.
▶ *vt* tirar al hoyo.

puzzle ['pʌzəl] *n* **1** *(jigsaw)* puzzle *m*; *(toy)* rompecabezas *m*; *(riddle)* adivinanza, acertijo; *(crossword)* crucigrama *m*. **2** *(mystery)* misterio, enigma *m*.
▶ *vt* dejar perplejo,-a, extrañar.
◆ **to puzzle out** *vt sep* *(problem)* resolver; *(mystery)* descifrar.

pygmy ['pɪgmɪ] *adj* pigmeo,-a, enano,-a.
▶ *n* *(small person)* pigmeo,-a, enano,-a.

pyjamas [pə'dʒɑːməz] *n pl* pijama *m sing*.

pylon ['paɪlən] *n* **1** ELEC torre *f* (de tendido eléctrico). **2** ARCH pilón *m*, pilar *m*.

pylorus ['paɪlərəs] *n* píloro.

pyramid ['pɪrəmɪd] *n* pirámide *f*.

pyrites [paɪ'raɪtiːz] *n* pirita.

pyromaniac [paɪrəʊ'meɪnɪæk] *n* pirómano,-a.

pyrotechnics [paɪrəʊ'teknɪks] *n* pirotecnia.
▶ *n pl* fuegos *mpl* artificiales.

python ['paɪθən] *n* pitón *m*.

Q

Q, q [kjuː] *n (the letter)* Q, q *f*.

quack [kwæk] *vi* graznar.

Qatar [kæ'tɑːʳ] *n* Qatar.

quadriceps ['kwɒdrɪseps] *n* ANAT cuádriceps *m*.

quail [kweɪl] *n* codorniz *f*.

quake [kweɪk] *n fam* terremoto.

qualification [kwɒlɪfɪ'keɪʃºn] *n* **1** *(for job)* requisito. **2** *(ability)* aptitud *f*, capacidad *f*. **3** *(paper)* diploma *m*, título. **4** *(reservation)* reserva, salvedad *f*. **5** *(restriction)* limitación *f*.

☒ Qualification no significa 'calificación (nota)', que se traduce por mark.

qualified ['kwɒlɪfaɪd] *adj* **1** *(for job)* capacitado,-a. **2** *(with qualifications)* titulado,-a: *qualified nurse* enfermero,-a titulado,-a. **3** *(limited, modified)* limitado,-a, restringido,-a.

qualify ['kwɒlɪfaɪ] *vt* **1** *(entitle, make eligible)* capacitar, dar derecho. **2** *(modify)* modificar, matizar, puntualizar. **3** LING calificar.
ⓘ *pt & pp* qualified, *ger* qualifying.

quality ['kwɒlɪti] *n* **1** *(degree of excellence)* calidad *f*: *of good quality* de buena calidad; *of poor quality* de poca calidad. **2** *(attribute)* cualidad *f*: *she has many qualities* tiene muchas cualidades. COMP **quality control** control *m* de calidad. ‖ **quality newspapers** prensa de calidad.
ⓘ *pl* qualities.

quantity ['kwɒntɪti] *n* **1** cantidad *f*. **2** MATH cantidad *f*.
ⓘ *pl* quantities.

quarrel ['kwɒrªl] *n* **1** riña, disputa, pelea. **2** *(disagreement)* desacuerdo. **3** *(complaint)* queja: *I have no quarrel with him* no tengo ninguna queja de él, no tengo nada contra él. LOC **to pick a quar-**

rel with SB meterse con ALGN, buscar pelea con ALGN.
▶ *vi (argue)* reñir, pelearse, disputar, discutir: *she is always quarrelling with her mother* siempre está discutiendo con su madre.
ⓘ *pt & pp* quarrelled *(US quarreled), ger* quarrelling *(US quarreling)*.

quarry ['kwɒri] *n* **1** cantera. **2** *(in hunting)* presa.
ⓘ *pl* quarries.
▶ *vt* extraer.
ⓘ *pt & pp* quarried, *ger* quarrying.

quart [kwɔːt] *n* cuarto de galón.

✎ En Gran Bretaña equivale a 1,14 litros; en Estados Unidos equivale a 0,95 litro.

quarter ['kwɔːtəʳ] *n* **1** cuarto. **2** *(area)* barrio: *the old quarter* el casco antiguo. **3** *(time)* cuarto: *it's a quarter to one* es la una menos cuarto. **4** *(of moon)* cuarto. **5** *(three months)* trimestre *m*. **6** US *(amount)* veinticinco centavos; *(coin)* moneda de veinticinco centavos. COMP **first quarter** cuarto creciente. ‖ **last quarter** cuarto menguante.
▶ *n pl* **quarters** alojamiento *m sing*. COMP **at close quarters** desde muy cerca. ‖ **to give no quarter** no dar cuartel.

quartz [kwɔːts] *n* cuarzo. COMP **quartz watch** reloj *m* de cuarzo.

quay [kiː] *n* muelle *m*.

queen [kwiːn] *n* **1** reina. **2** *(cards, chess)* dama, reina; *(chess)* reina. COMP **queen bee** abeja reina. ‖ **Queen Mother** reina madre.

queer [kwɪəʳ] *adj* **1** raro,-a, extraño,-a. **2** *(ill)* malucho,-a. **3** *fam* gay. **4** *(mad)* loco,-a, chiflado,-a.

quench [kwentʃ] *vt* **1** *(thirst)* saciar. **2** *(fire)* apagar.

query ['kwɪərɪ] *n* **1** pregunta, duda. **2** LING signo de interrogación. **3** *fig* interrogante *m*.
ⓘ *pl* queries.
► *vt* **1** *(doubt)* poner en duda. **2** *(ask)* preguntar.
ⓘ *pt & pp* queried, *ger* querying.

quest [kwest] *n* búsqueda, busca. LOC **in quest of** en busca de: *in quest of the Holy Grail* en busca del Santo Grial.

question ['kwestʃ°n] *n* **1** pregunta. **2** *(in exam)* pregunta, problema *m*. **3** *(problem, issue)* cuestión *f*, problema *m*. **4** *(topic, matter)* cuestión *f*, asunto. LOC **it's a question of** se trata de, es cuestión de: *it's a question of time* es cuestión de tiempo. ▌**out of the question** imposible, impensable. ▌**that is the question** de eso se trata. ▌**without question** sin rechistar: *she did it without question* lo hizo sin rechistar. COMP **question mark 1** *(punctuation mark)* signo de interrogación, interrogación *f*, interrogante *m*. **2** *(doubt)* interrogante *m*. ▌**question tag** coletilla.
► *vt* **1** hacer preguntas a, interrogar. **2** *(cast doubt on)* cuestionar, poner en duda.

questionnaire [kwestʃə'neəʳ] *n* cuestionario.

queue [kju:] *n* GB cola. LOC **to jump the queue** colarse.
► *vi* hacer cola.

quick [kwɪk] *adj* **1** *(fast)* rápido,-a: *let's have a quick look* echemos un vistazo. **2** *(clever)* espabilado,-a, listo,-a.

quickly ['kwɪklɪ] *adv* *(speed up)* rápido
► *vi* *(speed up)* acelerarse.

quicksand ['kwɪksænd] *n* arenas *fpl* movedizas.

quiet ['kwaɪət] *adj* **1** *(silent)* callado,-a, silencioso,-a: *he kept quiet all night* estuvo callado toda la noche. **2** *(peaceful, calm)* tranquilo,-a, sosegado,-a: *this is a very quiet village* éste es un pueblo muy tranquilo. **3** *(unobtrusive)* callado,-a, reservado,-a. **4** *(tranquil, without fuss)* tranquilo,-a. LOC **be quiet!** ¡cállate!
► *n* **1** *(silence)* silencio. **2** *(calm)* tranquilidad *f*, calma, sosiego.
► *vt* US calmar, silenciar: *she quieted the baby down* calmó a la criatura.

► *vi* US calmarse. LOC **on the quiet** a la chita callando, a hurtadillas: *he did it on the quiet* lo hizo en secreto.

quietly ['kwaɪətlɪ] *adv* **1** *(silently)* silenciosamente, sin hacer ruido; *(not loudly)* bajo: *she always speaks quietly* siempre habla en voz baja. **2** *(calmly)* tranquilamente. **3** *(discreetly)* discretamente, con discreción. **4** *(simply)* sencillamente, con sencillez.

quilt [kwɪlt] *n* edredón *m*.

quince [kwɪns] *n* membrillo.

quit [kwɪt] *vt* **1** dejar, abandonar: *he quit his job* dejó el trabajo. **2** *(stop)* dejar de: *she quit smoking* dejó de fumar.
► *vi* marcharse, irse.
ⓘ *pt & pp* quit, *ger* quitting.

❌ To quit no significa 'quitar', que se traduce por to remove.

quite [kwaɪt] *adv* **1** *(rather)* bastante: *they played quite well* jugaron bastante bien; *they're quite difficult exercises* son ejercicios bastante difíciles. **2** *(totally)* completamente, del todo: *I quite understand* lo entiendo perfectamente. **3** *(exceptional)* excepcional, increíble, original: *it's been quite a year* ha sido un año excepcional. **4** *(exactly)* exactamente: *it isn't quite what I was looking for* no es exactamente lo que buscaba.

quiver[1] ['kwɪvəʳ] *n* **1** *(tremble of lips, voice)* temblor *m*; *(of eyelids)* parpadeo; *(shiver)* estremecimiento.
► *vi* temblar, estremecerse.

quiz [kwɪz] *n* **1** *(competition)* concurso. **2** *(enquiry)* encuesta; *(exam)* examen *m*.
► *vt* preguntar, interrogar.

quotation [kwəʊ'teɪʃ°n] *n* **1** LING cita. **2** FIN cotización *f*. **3** COMM presupuesto. COMP **quotation marks** comillas *fpl*.

quote [kwəʊt] *n* **1** LING cita. **2** *(price - gen)* presupuesto; *(- for shares)* cotización *f*.
► *vt* **1** citar, entrecomillar. **2** *(price)* dar, ofrecer. **3** FIN cotizar.

quotient ['kwəʊʃ°nt] *n* **1** *(in mathematics)* cociente *m*. **2** *(degree)* coeficiente *m* grado. COMP **intelligence quotient** coeficiente intelectual *m*, coeficiente *m* de inteligencia.

R

R, r [ɑː] *n* **1** *(the letter)* R, r *f*.

rabbit ['ræbɪt] *n* conejo.

raccoon [rə'kuːn] *n* mapache *m*.

race¹ [reɪs] *n (people)* raza.

race² [reɪs] *n* **1** SP carrera. **2** *(current)* corriente *f* fuerte; *(channel)* canal *m*. LOC **to run a race** participar en una carrera.
  ▶ *vt* **1** *(person)* competir con, echar una carrera a. **2** *(engine)* acelerar.

racecourse ['reɪskɔːs] *n* GB hipódromo.

racehorse ['reɪhɔːs] *n* caballo de carreras.

racial ['reɪʃəl] *adj* racial.

racing ['reɪsɪŋ] *n* carreras *fpl*.
  ▶ *adj* de carreras. COMP **racing car** coche *m* de carreras. I **racing driver** piloto de carreras.

racism ['reɪsɪzəm] *n* racismo.

racist ['reɪsɪst] *adj* racista.
  ▶ *n* racista *mf*.

rack [ræk] *n* **1** estante *m*. **2** AUTO baca. **3** *(on train)* rejilla. **4** *(for torture)* potro.

racket¹ ['rækɪt] *n* SP raqueta.

racket² ['rækɪt] *n* **1** *(din)* alboroto, ruido. **2** *fam (fraud)* timo. **3** *fam (business)* asunto, negocio.

racoon [rə'kuːn] *n* mapache *m*.

racquet ['rækɪt] *n* raqueta.

radar ['reɪdɑːʳ] *n* radar *m*. COMP **radar trap** control *m* de velocidad por radar.

radiation [reɪdɪ'eɪʃən] *n* radiación *f*.

radiator ['reɪdɪeɪtəʳ] *n* radiador *m*.

radical ['rædɪkəl] *adj* radical.
  ▶ *n* radical *mf*.

radii ['reɪdɪaɪ] *n pl* → radius.

radio ['reɪdɪəʊ] *n* radio *f*. COMP **radio cassette** radiocasete *m*.
  ⓘ *pl* radios.

radioactive [reɪdɪəʊ'æktɪv] *adj* radiactivo,-a. LOC **radioactive waste** residuos *mpl* radiactivos.

radioactivity [reɪdɪəʊæk'tɪvɪtɪ] *n* radiactividad *f*.

radiography [reɪdɪ'ɒgrəfɪ] *n* radiografía.
  ⓘ *pl* radiographies.

radiologist [reɪdɪ'ɒlədʒɪst] *n* radiólogo,-a.

radiology [reɪdɪ'ɒlədʒɪ] *n* radiología.

radish ['rædɪʃ] *n* rábano.

radium ['reɪdɪəm] *n* radio.

radius ['reɪdɪəs] *n* radio.
  ⓘ *pl* radii ['reɪdɪaɪ].

radon ['reɪdɒn] *n* radón *m*.

raffle ['ræfəl] *n* rifa.
  ▶ *vt* rifar, sortear.

raft [rɑːft] *n* **1** balsa. **2** US *fam* montón *m*.

rag [ræg] *n* **1** harapo, andrajo,. **2** *(for cleaning)* trapo.

rage [reɪdʒ] *n* rabia, furor *m*, cólera.
  ▶ *vi* **1** *(person)* estar hecho,-a una furia. **2** *(fire, etc)* arder sin control; *(storm, sea)* rugir; *(debate, etc)* seguir candente.

ragout [ræ'guː] *n* ragú *m*.

raid [reɪd] *n* **1** MIL incursión *f*, ataque *m*. **2** *(by police)* redada. **3** *(robbery)* atraco.
  ▶ *vt* **1** MIL hacer una incursión en. **2** *(police)* hacer una redada en. **3** *(rob)* atracar, asaltar.

rail [reɪl] *n* **1** barra. **2** *(handrail)* pasamano, barandilla, baranda. **3** *(for train)* raíl *m*, carril *m*, riel *m*. **4** *(the railway)* ferrocarril *m*. LOC **by rail** por ferrocarril.

railing ['reɪlɪŋz] *n* verja.

railroad ['reɪlrəʊd] *n* US → railway.
  ▶ *vt* **1** *(person)* presionar. **2** *(measure, bill)* tramitar sin debate.

railway ['reɪlweɪ] n ferrocarril m. COMP
railway carriage vagón m. ▮ railway engine
locomotora. ▮ railway line vía férrea.
▮ railway station estación f de ferrocarril.
▮ railway track vía férrea.

rain [reɪn] n lluvia. COMP rain forest selva
tropical. ▮ rain gauge pluviómetro.
▸ vi llover: it's raining está lloviendo.

rainbow ['reɪnbəʊ] n arco iris m.

raincoat ['reɪnkəʊt] n impermeable m.

raindrop ['reɪndrɒp] n gota de lluvia.

rainfall ['reɪnfɔːl] n 1 precipitación f.
2 (quantity) pluviosidad f.

rainforest ['reɪnfɒrɪst] n selva tropical.

rainy ['reɪnɪ] adj lluvioso,-a.
ⓘ comp rainier, superl rainiest.

raise [reɪz] vt 1 (lift up) levantar: raise
your hands levantad la mano. 2 (move to a
higher position) subir. 3 (build, erect) erigir,
levantar. 4 (increase) subir, aumentar.
5 (improve) mejorar. 6 (laugh,
smile, etc) provocar; (doubt, fear) suscitar.
7 (children) criar, educar; (animals)
criar. 8 (matter, point) plantear. 9 (funds)
recaudar.
▸ n US aumento de sueldo.

✎ Raise en el sentido de 'levantar' siempre
va seguido de un complemento. Mientras
que rise (subir), nunca lleva complemento.

raisin ['reɪzᵊn] n pasa.

rake [reɪk] n (tool) rastrillo.

rally ['rælɪ] n 1 (public gathering) reunión
f; (political) mitin m; (demonstration) manifestación
f. 2 (car race) rally m. 3 (in
tennis) intercambio (de golpes).
ⓘ pl rallies.
▸ vi (recover) reponerse, recuperarse.
▸ vt (bring together) unir.
ⓘ pt & pp rallied, ger rallying.

ram [ræm] n ZOOL carnero.

ramp [ræmp] n 1 (slope) rampa. 2 (steps)
escalerilla. 3 GB (speed bump) badén m.
4 US (slip road) vía de acceso.

ran [ræn] pt → run.

ranch [rɑːntʃ] n rancho, hacienda. COMP
ranch house 1 (type of house) bungalow
m. 2 (house on ranch) hacienda.

random ['rændəm] adj aleatorio,-a. LOC
at random al azar. COMP random access
memory memoria de acceso directo.

rang [ræŋ] pt → ring.

range [reɪndʒ] n 1 (choice) gama, surtido;
(of products) gama; (of clothes) línea.
2 (reach) alcance m. 3 (of mountains) cordillera,
sierra. 4 US (prairie) pradera.
▸ vi 1 variar, oscilar: they range from ...
to... van desde ... hasta ... 2 (wander) vagar
(over, por).
▸ vt 1 (arrange) colocar, disponer. 2
(travel) recorrer, viajar por.

rank [ræŋk] n 1 (line) fila. 2 MIL (in hierarchy)
graduación f, rango.
▸ vi (be) figurar, estar
▸ vt (classify) clasificar, considerar.

ranking ['ræŋkɪŋ] n clasificación f,
ranking m.

ransom ['rænsəm] n rescate m. LOC to
hold to ransom 1 pedir rescate por. 2
fig chantajear. LOC ransom money rescate
m.
▸ vt rescatar.

rap [ræp] n 1 golpe m seco. 2 MUS rap m.
▸ vi 1 golpear. 2 MUS cantar rap.
ⓘ pt & pp rapped, ger rapping.

rape¹ [reɪp] n violación f.
▸ vt violar.

rape² [reɪp] n BOT colza.

rapid ['ræpɪd] adj rápido,-a.
▸ n pl rapids rápidos mpl.

rapper ['ræpəʳ] n cantante mf de rap
rapero,-a.

rare [reəʳ] adj 1 (uncommon) poco común,
raro,-a. 2 (air) enrarecido,-a. 3
CULIN poco hecho,-a. COMP rare earth
tierra rara. ▮ rare gas gas m raro.

✖ Rare no significa 'raro (extraño)', que
se traduce por strange.

rarely ['reəlɪ] adv rara vez, pocas veces.

rascal ['rɑːskᵊl] n bribón m, pillo.

rash¹ [ræʃ] n 1 MED sarpullido, erupción
f cutánea. 2 (series) sucesión f, serie f.

rash² [ræʃ] adj imprudente, precipitado,-a.

raspberry ['rɑːzbᵊrɪ] n 1 frambuesa. 2 fam (noise) pedorreta.
ⓘ pl raspberries.

rat [ræt] n 1 rata. 2 fam canalla m.

rate [reɪt] n 1 tasa, índice m 2 (speed) velocidad f, ritmo 3 (price) tarifa, precio. ᴸᴼᶜ at any rate 1 (anyway) de todos modos. 2 (at least) por lo menos, al menos. ‖ at the rate of a razón de. ‖ first/second rate de primera/segunda (categoría). ᶜᴼᴹᴾ rate of exchange tipo de cambio.
▶ vt 1 (consider) considerar 2 (deserve) merecer. 3 (fix value) tasar.
▶ n pl rates GB contribución f sing urbana.

rather ['rɑːðəʳ] adv 1 (a little) algo; (fairly) bastante; (very) muy. 2 (showing preference): I'd rather go out preferiría salir. 3 (more precisely) o mejor dicho: there was a river, or rather a stream había un río, o mejor dicho un arroyo

ratify ['rætɪfaɪ] vt ratificar.
ⓘ pt & pp ratified, ger ratifying.

ratings ['reɪtɪŋs] n pl TV índice m sing de audiencia.

ratio ['reɪʃɪəʊ] n razón f, relación f, proporción f.
ⓘ pl ratios.

ration ['ræʃᵊn] n ración f.
▶ vt racionar.
▶ n pl rations víveres mpl.

✗ Ration no significa 'ración (de comida)', que se traduce por portion.

rational ['ræʃᵊnəl] adj racional.

rattle ['rætᵊl] n 1 (object) carraca, matraca; (baby's) sonajero; (rattlesnake's) cascabel m. 2 (noise) ruido; (of train) traqueteo; (vibration) vibración f.
▶ vt hacer sonar, hacer vibrar.
▶ vi sonar, vibrar.

rattlesnake ['rætᵊlsneɪk] n serpiente f de cascabel.

ravage ['rævɪdʒ] vt devastar, asolar.
▶ n pl ravages estragos mpl.

rave [reɪv] n GB fiesta con música de baile y que puede durar toda la noche.

raven ['reɪvᵊn] n cuervo.

ravine [rəˈviːn] n barranco.

raw [rɔː] adj 1 (uncooked) crudo,-a. 2 (unprocessed) bruto,-a; (unrefined) sin refinar; (untreated) sin tratar. 3 (inexperienced) novato,-a. 4 (weather) crudo,-a. ᶜᴼᴹᴾ raw material materia prima.

ray¹ [reɪ] n (of light) rayo.

ray² [reɪ] n (fish) raya.

razor ['reɪzəʳ] n 1 (cutthroat) navaja de afeitar; (safety) maquinilla de afeitar. 2 (electric) máquina de afeitar. ᶜᴼᴹᴾ razor blade hoja de afeitar.

reach [riːtʃ] n alcance m. ᴸᴼᶜ beyond the reach of fuera del alcance de. ‖ out of reach of fuera del alcance de. ‖ within reach of 1 (at hand) al alcance de. 2 (near) cerca de
▶ vt 1 (arrive in/at, get to) llegar a. 2 (rise to, fall to) alcanzar. 3 (be able to touch) alcanzar, llegar a. 4 (contact) contactar, localizar. 5 (pass) alcanzar
▶ vi 1 (be long enough) llegar. 2 (extend) extenderse. 3 (take) extender la mano, tender la mano.

react [rɪˈækt] vi reaccionar.

reaction [rɪˈækʃᵊn] n reacción f.

reactor [rɪˈæktəʳ] n reactor m.

read [riːd] vt 1 (gen) leer. 2 (instrument) indicar, marcar. 3 (sign, notice) decir, poner.
◆ to read out vt sep leer en voz alta.
ⓘ pt & pp read [red].

readable ['riːdəbᵊl] adj 1 (handwriting) legible. 2 (style) ameno,-a.

reader ['riːdəʳ] n 1 (person - gen) lector,-ra; (- of proofs) corrector,-ra. 2 (at university) profesor,-ra adjunto,-a. 3 (apparatus) lector m.

readily ['redɪlɪ] adv 1 (easily) fácilmente. 2 (willingly) de buena gana.

reading ['riːdɪŋ] n 1 lectura. 2 (of bill, law) presentación f. 3 (of instrument) indicación f, lectura. 4 (interpretation) interpretación f.

readjust [riːəˈdʒʌst] vt reajustar.
▶ vi (readapt) readaptarse.

ready ['redɪ] adj 1 (prepared) preparado,-a, listo,-a. 2 (willing) dispuesto,-a. 3 (quick) rápido,-a; (easy) fácil. ᴸᴼᶜ to get ready prepararse. ‖ to get STH ready

R

preparar ALGO. ‖ **to make ready** preparar.

ready-made [redɪ'meɪd] *adj* hecho,-a, confeccionado,-a.

reafforestation [rɪəfɒrɪ'steɪʃ°n] *n* GB reforestación *f*, repoblación *f* forestal.

reagent [riː'eɪdʒənt] *n* reactivo.

real [rɪəl] *adj* **1** real, verdadero,-a. **2** *(genuine)* auténtico,-a. COMP **real estate** bienes *mpl* inmuebles.
► *adv* US *fam* muy

realise ['rɪəlaɪz] *vt* → realize.

reality [rɪ'ælɪtɪ] *n* realidad *f*.

realize ['rɪəlaɪz] *vt* **1** *(understand)* darse cuenta de, comprender. **2** *(know)* saber. **3** *(carry out)* realizar. **4** *(sell)* realizar, vender; *(fetch)* reportar

> ❌ To realize no significa 'realizar', que se traduce por to carry out.

really ['rɪəlɪ] *adv* **1** *(in fact)* en realidad. **2** *(very)* muy, realmente. **3** *(showing interest)* ¿ah sí?, ¿en serio? ¿de verdad?; *(showing surprise)* ¿de verdad?, ¡no me digas!; *(showing annoyance)* ¡vaya!

reap [riːp] *vt* cosechar.

rear¹ [rɪəʳ] *adj* trasero,-a, de atrás.
► *n* **1** *(back part)* parte *f* de atrás. **2** *(of room)* fondo. **3** *fam (of person)* trasero.

rearmament [riː'ɑːməmənt] *n* rearme *m*.

rearrange [riːə'reɪndʒ] *vt* **1** *(objects)* colocar de otra manera. **2** *(event)* cambiar la fecha de, cambiar la hora de.

rear-view mirror [rɪəvjuː'mɪrəʳ] *n* retrovisor *m*.

reason ['riːz°n] *n* **1** *(cause)* razón *f*, motivo. **2** *(faculty)* razón *f*.
► *vt* deducir, llegar a la conclusión de que
► *vi* razonar.

reasonable ['riːzənəb°l] *adj* **1** *(gen)* razonable. **2** *(acceptable)* aceptable.

reasonably ['riːz°nəblɪ] *adv* **1** *(gen)* razonablemente. **2** *(quite)* bastante.

reassure [riːə'ʃʊəʳ] *vt* **1** *(comfort)* tranquilizar. **2** *(assure again)* volver a asegurar.

rebate ['riːbeɪt] *n* **1** *(of tax)* devolución *f*. **2** *(discount)* descuento.

rebel [*(adj-n)* 'reb°l; *(vb)* rɪ'bel] *adj* rebelde.
► *n* rebelde *mf*.
► *vi* rebelarse (against, contra).
① *pt & pp* rebelled, *ger* rebelling.

rebellion [rɪ'beliən] *n* rebelión *f*.

rebound [*(n)* 'riːbaʊnd; *(vb)* rɪ'baʊnd] *n* rebote *m*
► *vi* rebotar.

recall [*(n)* rɪ'kɔːl; *(vb)* rɪ'kɔːl] *n* **1** *(memory)* memoria. **2** *(withdrawal)* retirada.
► *vt* **1** *(remember)* recordar. **2** *(withdraw)* retirar.

receipt [rɪ'siːt] *n* **1** *(document)* recibo. **2** *(act of receiving)* recepción *f*, recibo.
► *n pl* **receipts** COMM ingresos *mpl*, recaudación *f sing.*

receive [rɪ'siːv] *vt* **1** *(gen)* recibir. **2** *(wound)* sufrir. **3** *(radio signal)* recibir. **4** *(stolen goods)* comerciar con
► *vt (welcome)* recibir, acoger.

receiver [rɪ'siːvəʳ] *n* **1** *(of telephone)* auricular *m*. **2** *(of stolen goods)* perista *mf*. **3** JUR síndico,-a, síndico,-a de quiebras. **4** *(of radio signal)* receptor *m*. **5** *(in American football)* receptor,-ra.

recent ['riːs°nt] *adj* reciente: *in recent months/years* en los últimos meses/años.

recently ['riːs°ntlɪ] *adv* **1** *(lately)* recientemente, últimamente. **2** *(a short time ago)* hace poco

reception [rɪ'sepʃ°n] *n* **1** *(gen)* recepción *f*. **2** *(welcome)* acogida. **3** *(party)* recepción *f*; *(after wedding)* banquete *m*. COMP **reception desk** recepción *f*.

receptionist [rɪ'sepʃ°nɪst] *n* recepcionista *m & f*.

recharge [riː'tʃɑːdʒ] *vt* recargar.

rechargeable [riː'tʃɑːdʒəb°l] *adj* recargable.

recipe ['resəpɪ] *n* **1** receta. **2** *fig* fórmula. COMP **recipe book 1** *(personal collection)* recetario. **2** *(cookery book)* libro de cocina.

reckless ['rekləs] *adj* **1** *(hasty)* precipitado,-a. **2** *(careless)* imprudente, temerario,-a. COMP **reckless driving** conducción *f* temeraria.

reckon ['rek°n] *vt* **1** *(estimate)* calcular. **2** *(calculate)* calcular. **3** *(regard)* considerar. **4** *(think)* creer, considerar.

reckoning [ˈrekᵊnɪŋ] *n* cálculos *mpl*: *by my reckoning, ...* según mis cálculos,...

recognise [ˈrekəgnaɪz] *vt* → **recognize**.

recognition [rekəgˈnɪʃᵊn] *n* reconocimiento.

recognize [ˈrekəgnaɪz] *vt* reconocer.

recollect [rekəˈlekt] *vt* recordar.

☒ To recollect no significa 'recolectar', que se traduce por to **harvest**.

recollection [rekəˈlekʃᵊn] *n* recuerdo.

☒ Recollection no significa 'recolección', que se traduce por **harvest**.

recommend [rekəˈmend] *vt* recomendar.

recommendation [rekəmenˈdeɪʃᵊn] *n* recomendación *f*.

reconstruct [riːkənsˈtrʌkt] *vt* reconstruir.

record [(*n*) ˈrekɔːd; (*vb*) rɪˈkɔːd] *n* **1** *(written evidence)* constancia escrita **2** *(note)* relación *f*. **3** *(facts about a person)* historial *m*. **4** MUS disco. **5** SP récord *m*, marca, plusmarca. `LOC` **to break a record** batir un récord. `COMP` **medical record** historial *m* médico. ‖ **record holder** plusmarquista *mf*. ‖ **record player** tocadiscos *m sing*.

▶ *vt* **1** *(write down)* anotar, apuntar. **2** *(voice, music)* grabar. **3** *(instrument, gauge)* registrar

▶ *adj* récord.

▶ *n pl* **records** *(files)* archivos *mpl*

☒ Record no significa 'recordar', que se traduce por to **remember**.

recorded [rɪˈkɔːdɪd] *adj (written)* anotado,-a; *(on tape, etc)* grabado,-a. `COMP` **recorded delivery** correo certificado.

recorder [rɪˈkɔːdəʳ] *n* MUS flauta. `COMP` **cassette recorder** casete *m*.

recording [rɪˈkɔːdɪŋ] *n* grabación *f*. `COMP` **recording studio** estudio de grabación.

recover [rɪˈkʌvəʳ] *vt (gen)* recuperar; *(dead body)* rescatar.

▶ *vi* recuperarse, reponerse.

recovery [rɪˈkʌvəri] *n* recuperación *f*.

recreation [rekrɪˈeɪʃᵊn] *n* **1** *(free time)* esparcimiento. **2** *(hobby)* pasatiempo. **3** *(in school)* recreo.

recruit [rɪˈkruːt] *n (soldier)* recluta *m*.

▶ *vt (soldier)* reclutar.

recruitment [rɪˈkruːtmənt] *n (of soldiers)* reclutamiento; *(of employees)* contratación *f*.

recta [ˈrektə] *n pl* → **rectum**.

rectangle [ˈrektæŋgᵊl] *n* rectángulo.

rectangular [rektˈæŋgjʊləʳ] *adj* rectangular.

rectify [ˈrektɪfaɪ] *vt* rectificar.

rectum [ˈrektəm] *n* recto.
ⓘ *pl* **rectums** o **recta** [ˈrektə].

recur [rɪˈkɜːʳ] *vi* repetirse, reproducirse.
ⓘ *pt & pp* **recurred**, *ger* **recurring**.

☒ To recur no significa 'recurrir a', que se traduce por to **resort to**, to **turn to**.

recurrent [rɪˈkʌrənt] *adj* **1** MATH periódico,-a. **2** MED recurrente.

recycle [riːˈsaɪkᵊl] *vt* reciclar.

recycling [riːˈsaɪkᵊlɪŋ] *n* reciclaje *m*.

red [red] *n* **1** *(colour)* rojo. **2** *(left-winger)* rojo,-a.

▶ *adj* **1** rojo,-a **2** *(hair)* pelirrojo,-a.
ⓘ *comp* **redder**, *superl* **reddest**.

redbreast [ˈredbrest] *n* petirrojo.

redcurrant [redˈkʌrənt] *n* grosella.

redemption [rɪˈdempʃᵊn] *n* **1** *(of debt)* pago. **2** *(of voucher)* canje *m*. **3** REL redención *f*.

red-haired [ˈredˈheəd] *adj* pelirrojo,-a.

redhead [ˈredhed] *n* pelirrojo,-a.

redid [riːˈdɪd] *pt* → **redo**.

redo [riːˈduː] *vt* rehacer, volver a hacer.
ⓘ *pt* **redid** [riːˈdɪd], *pp* **redone** [riːˈdʌn], *ger* **redoing**.

redone [riːˈdʌn] *pt* → **redo**.

redskin [ˈredskɪn] *n* piel roja *mf*.

reduce [rɪˈdjuːs] *vt* **1** *(gen)* reducir, disminuir. **2** *(price, etc)* rebajar.

reduction [rɪˈdʌkʃᵊn] *n (gen)* reducción *f*; *(fall)* disminución *f*; *(in price)* rebaja.

redundancy [rɪˈdʌndənsi] *n* **1** *(dismissal)* despido. **2** *(superfluity)* superfluidad *f*. **3** LING redundancia.
ⓘ *pl* **redundancies**.

R

redundant [rɪ'dʌndənt] *adj* **1** *(dismissed)* despedido,-a. **2** *(superfluous)* superfluo,-a. **3** LING redundante.

redwood ['redwʊd] *n* secuoya.

reed [riːd] *n* **1** *(plant)* caña, junco. **2** MUS lengüeta.

reef [riːf] *n* arrecife *m*.

reel [riːl] *n* **1** *(of thread, cotton)* carrete *m*; *(of camera film)* carrete *m*, rollo; *(of cine film)* bobina; *(of wire, tape)* rollo. **2** *(for fishing)* carrete *m*.
  ◆ **to reel in** *vt sep (line)* recoger, cobrar; *(fish)* cobrar, sacar del agua.

refer [rɪ'fɜːʳ] *vt (send)* mandar, enviar
  ▶ *vi* **1** *(allude to)* referirse (**to**, a). **2** *(mention, name)* hacer referencia (**to**, a).
  ① *pt & pp* referred, *ger* referring.

referee [refə'riː] *n* SP árbitro,-a.
  ▶ *vt* arbitrar.

reference ['refʳrəns] *n* **1** referencia, mención **2** *(for job)* referencias *fpl*. COMP **reference book** libro de consulta.

referendum [refə'rendəm] *n* referéndum *m*.
  ① *pl* referendums o referenda [refə'rendə].

refill [*(n)* 'riːfɪl; *(vb)* riː'fɪl] *n (for pen, etc)* recambio; *(for lighter)* carga.
  ▶ *vt (glass, pen)* volver a llenar; *(lighter)* recargar.

refinery [rɪ'faɪnərɪ] *n* refinería.
  ① *pl* refineries.

reflect [rɪ'flekt] *vt* reflejar
  ▶ *vi (think)* reflexionar (**on**, sobre).
  ◆ **to reflect on** *vt insep* perjudicar

reflection [rɪ'flekʃʳn] *n* **1** *(image)* reflejo. **2** *(thought)* reflexión *f*. **3** *(aspersion)* descrédito. LOC **on reflection**, ... pensándolo bien, ...

reflector [rɪ'flektəʳ] *n (gen)* reflector *m*; *(on car)* catafaro.

reflex ['riːfleks] *n* reflejo.
  ① *pl* reflexes.

reflexive [rɪ'fleksɪv] *adj* reflexivo,-a.

reforest [riː'fɒrɪst] *vt* reforestar.

reforestation [riːfɒrɪ'steɪʃʳn] *n* reforestación *f*, repoblación *f* forestal.

reform [rɪ'fɔːm] *n* reforma.
  ▶ *vt* reformar.

refraction [rɪ'frækʃʳn] *n* refracción *f*.

refrain¹ [rɪ'freɪn] *n* MUS estribillo.

☒ Refrain no significa 'refrán', que se traduce por **proverb**, **saying**.

refrain² [rɪ'freɪn] *vi* abstenerse (**from**, de)

refresh [rɪ'freʃ] *vt* refrescar.

refreshing [rɪ'freʃɪŋ] *adj (gen)* refrescante; *(rest, sleep)* reparador,-ra.

refreshment [rɪ'freʃmənt] *n* refresco.

refrigerator [rɪ'frɪdʒəreɪtəʳ] *n* frigorífico, nevera.

refuge ['refjuːdʒ] *n* refugio.

refugee [refjuː'dʒiː] *n* refugiado,-a.

refund [*(n)* 'riːfʌnd; *(vb)* riː'fʌnd] *n* reembolso.
  ▶ *vt* reembolsar.

refusal [rɪ'fjuːzəl] *n* **1** *(negative reply)* negativa, respuesta negativa. **2** *(rejection)* rechazo.

refuse¹ ['refjuːs] *n* basura. COMP **refuse collection** recogida de basuras.

refuse² [rɪ'fjuːz] *vt* **1** *(reject)* rehusar, rechazar, no aceptar. **2** *(withhold)* negar, denegar, no conceder
  ▶ *vi* negarse (**to**, a)

regard [rɪ'gɑːd] *n* respeto, consideración. LOC **to hold in high regard** tener en gran estima. ▐ **without regard to** sin hacer caso de.
  ▶ *vt* **1** *(consider)* considerar. **2** *(look at)* mirar. **3** *(heed)* hacer caso a.
  ▶ *n pl* **regards** recuerdos *mpl*.

regarding [rɪ'gɑːdɪŋ] *prep* tocante a, respecto a.

regardless [rɪ'gɑːdləs] *adv fam* a pesar de todo.
  ▶ *prep* **regardless of** *fam* sin tener en cuenta.

regime [reɪ'ʒiːm] [also written régime] *n* régimen *m*.

regiment ['redʒɪmənt] *n* regimiento.
  ▶ *vt* **1** MIL regimentar. **2** *fig* disciplinar, reglamentar.

region ['riːdʒʳn] *n* región *f*.

regional ['riːdʒʳnəl] *adj* regional.

register ['redʒɪstəʳ] *n (gen)* registro; *(in school)* lista. COMP **register office** registro civil.

▶ vt **1** *(put on record, list)* registrar; *(car, student)* matricular; *(birth, death, marriage)* inscribir en el registro. **2** *(show - reading)* indicar, marcar; *(- feeling)* mostrar, reflejar. **3** *(make known)* hacer constar. **4** *(letter)* certificar.
▶ vi **1** *(for classes)* matricularse; *(at congress, with doctor)* inscribirse; *(at hotel)* registrarse.

☒ To register no significa 'registrar (cachear)', que se traduce por to frisk.

registered ['redʒɪstəd] *adj* **1** *(person)* inscrito,-a; *(student)* matriculado,-a. **2** *(letter)* certificado,-a. **3** *(car, etc)* matriculado,-a; *(ship)* de bandera. COMP **registered trademark** marca registrada.

registration [redʒɪs'treɪʃ°n] *n* **1** *(of birth, death, marriage)* inscripción *f*; *(of patent, etc)* registro. **2** *(enrolment)* inscripción *f*; *(of student)* matrícula. COMP **registration number** AUTO matrícula.

registry ['redʒɪstrɪ] *n* registro. COMP **registry office** registro civil

regret [rɪ'gret] *n* **1** *(remorse)* remordimiento. **2** *(sadness)* pesar *m*.
▶ vt **1** *(feel sorry)* lamentar, arrepentirse de. **2** *(express one's sadness)* lamentar. **3** *(miss)* echar de menos, echar en falta.
▶ *n pl* **regrets** excusas *mpl*

regular ['regjʊlə'] *adj*. **1** *(gen)* regular. **2** *(normal)* normal. **3** *(habitual)* habitual. **4** *(normal in size)* de tamaño normal. **5** US *(pleasant)* simpático,-a.
▶ *n fam* cliente *mf* habitual.

☒ Regular no significa 'regular (pasable)', que se traduce por so-so, not bad.

regularity [regjʊ'lærətɪ] *n* regularidad *f*.
regularly ['regjʊləlɪ] *adv* regularmente, con regularidad.
regulate ['regjʊleɪt] *vt* regular.
regulation [regjʊ'leɪʃ°n] *n* **1** *(control)* regulación *f*. **2** *(rule)* regla.
rehearsal [rɪ'hɜːs°l] *n* ensayo.
rehearse [rɪ'hɜːs] *vt* ensayar.
reign [reɪn] *n* reinado.
▶ *vi* reinar.
rein [reɪn] *n* rienda.
▶ *n pl* **reins** *(child's)* andadores *mpl*.

reindeer ['reɪndɪə'] *n* reno.
ⓘ *pl* **reindeer** o **reindeers**.
reject [*(n)* 'riːdʒekt; *(vb)* rɪ'dʒekt] *n (thing)* artículo defectuoso; *(person)* marginado,-a.
▶ vt *(gen)* rechazar, no aceptar; *(in law)* desestimar.
rejection [rɪ'dʒekʃ°n] *n (gen)* rechazo; *(negative reply)* respuesta negativa.
rejoice [rɪ'dʒɔɪs] *vi* alegrarse.
relapse [rɪ'læps] *n* **1** MED recaída. **2** *(crime)* reincidencia.
▶ *vi* **1** MED recaer. **2** *(crime)* reincidir. LOC **to suffer a relapse** tener una recaída.
relate [rɪ'leɪt] *vt* **1** *(tell)* relatar, contar. **2** *(connect)* relacionar (to, con).
▶ *vi (connect)* relacionarse.
related [rɪ'leɪtɪd] *adj* **1** *(connected)* relacionado,-a. **2** *(relatives)* emparentado,-a.
relation [rɪ'leɪʃ°n] *n* **1** *(connection)* relación *f*. **2** *(family)* pariente *mf*.
relationship [rɪ'leɪʃ°nʃɪp] *n* **1** *(connection)* relación *f*. **2** *(between people)* relaciones *fpl*.
relative ['relətɪv] *adj* relativo,-a.
▶ *n* pariente *mf*, familiar *mf*.
relatively ['relətɪvlɪ] *adv* relativamente.
relativity [relə'tɪvɪtɪ] *n* relatividad *f*.
relaunch [*(vb)* riː'lɔːntʃ; *(n)* 'riːlɔːntʃ] *vt* relanzar.
▶ *n* relanzamiento.
relax [rɪ'læks] *vt* **1** *(gen)* relajar. **2** *(grip, hold)* aflojar. **3** *(rules, control)* suavizar.
▶ *vi* **1** *(gen)* relajarse. **2** *(grip, hold)* aflojarse.
relaxation [riːlæk'seɪʃ°n] *n* **1** *(gen)* relajación *f*. **2** *(of grip, hold)* aflojamiento. **3** *(of rules, control)* suavización *f*.
relaxed [rɪ'lækst] *adj* **1** *(person)* relajado,-a. **2** *(atmosphere)* distendido,-a.
relaxing [rɪ'læksɪŋ] *adj* relajante.
relay ['riːleɪ] *n* **1** relevo. **2** ELEC relé *m*. COMP **relay race** carrera de relevos. ▌**relay station** estación *f* repetidora.
release [rɪ'liːs] *n* **1** *(setting free)* liberación *f*, puesta en libertad. **2** *(relief)* alivio. **3** *(of film)* estreno; *(of record)* lanzamiento. **4** *(of gas, etc)* emisión *f*.

R

5 *(new thing - film)* estreno, novedad *f* cinematográfica; *(- record)* nuevo disco, novedad *f* discográfica. **6** *(statement)* comunicado.
▸ *vt* **1** *(set free)* liberar, poner en libertad. **2** *(let go of)* soltar. **3** *(bring out - film)* estrenar; *(- record)* sacar. **4** *(gas, etc - give out)* emitir. **5** *(statement, information)* hacer público, dar a conocer.

relevant ['reləvənt] *adj* **1** *(connected)* pertinente. **2** *(important)* relevante.

reliable [rɪ'laɪəbəl] *adj* fiable.

relief [rɪ'liːf] *n* **1** *(from pain, etc)* alivio. **2** *(help)* auxilio, socorro, ayuda. **3** *(person)* relevo. **4** *(lifting of siege)* liberación *f*. **5** GEOG relieve *m*.

relieve [rɪ'liːv] *vt* **1** *(lessen)* aliviar. **2** *(take over from)* relevar. **3** *(help)* socorrer, ayudar. **4** *(lift siege of)* liberar.

religion [rɪ'lɪdʒ⁰n] *n* religión *f*.

religious [rɪ'lɪdʒəs] *adj* religioso,-a.

reload [riː'ləʊd] *vt* *(gun)* volver a cargar; *(program, page)* recargar.

reluctant [rɪ'lʌktənt] *adj* reacio,-a.

reluctantly [rɪ'lʌktəntlɪ] *adv* muy a mi *(tu, su, etc)* pesar.

rely on [rɪ'laɪ ɒn] *vt* *(trust)* confiar en.
ⓘ *pt & pp* relied.

remade [riː'meɪd] *pt & pp* → remake.

remain [rɪ'meɪn] *vi* **1** *(stay)* quedarse, permanecer. **2** *(be left)* quedar, sobrar. **3** *(continue)* seguir, continuar.
▸ *n pl* remains restos *mpl*.

remainder [rɪ'meɪndəʳ] *n* resto.

remake [*(n)* 'riː.meɪk; *(vb)* riː'meɪk] *n* nueva versión *f*.
▸ *vt* hacer una nueva versión de.
ⓘ *pt & pp* remade [riː'meɪd].

remark [rɪ'mɑːk] *n* observación *f*.
▸ *vt* **1** *(say)* observar, comentar. **2** *(notice)* advertir.
◆ **to remark on** *vt insep* comentar.

remarkable [rɪ'mɑːkəbəl] *adj* **1** *(exceptional)* extraordinario,-a, excepcional. **2** *(odd)* extraño,-a; *(surprising)* sorprendente, curioso,-a.

remedy ['remədɪ] *n* remedio.
ⓘ *pl* remedies.
▸ *vt* remediar.

remember [rɪ'membəʳ] *vt* **1** recordar, acordarse de. **2** *(commemorate)* recordar.
▸ *vi* acordarse, recordar.

✎ La diferencia entre remember y remind es que remember se refiere al acto de recordar algo (acordarse de) y remind se emplea cuando se le recuerda algo a alguien.

remind [rɪ'maɪnd] *vt* recordar.
✎ Consulta también remember.

reminder [rɪ'maɪndəʳ] *n* **1** *(note)* recordatorio. **2** *(of payment due)* aviso. **3** *(keepsake)* recuerdo.

remorse [rɪ'mɔːs] *n* remordimiento.

remote [rɪ'məʊt] *adj* **1** *(far away)* remoto,-a, lejano,-a. **2** *(lonely)* aislado,-a, apartado,-a. **3** *(person)* distante. COMP **remote control** mando a distancia.

removal [rɪ'muːv⁰l] *n* **1** *(getting rid of)* eliminación *f*; *(surgically)* extirpación *f*. **2** *(moving)* traslado; *(to another house)* traslado, mudanza. **3** *(from post)* destitución *f*.

remove [rɪ'muːv] *vt* **1** *(get rid of - gen)* quitar, eliminar; *(- surgically)* extirpar. **2** *(take out, take off)* quitar. **3** *(move)* trasladar. **4** *(dismiss)* destituir.
▸ *vi* *(change houses)* trasladarse.

renaissance [rə'neɪs⁰ns] *n* renacimiento. COMP **the Renaissance** el Renacimiento.
▸ *adj* **Renaissance** renacentista.

rename [riː'neɪm] *vt* renombrar.

rendezvous ['rɒndɪvuː] *n* **1** cita. **2** *(place)* lugar *m* de reunión.
ⓘ *pl* rendezvous.

renew [rɪ'njuː] *vt* **1** *(gen)* renovar; *(contract, permit, etc)* prorrogar. **2** *(start again)* reanudar. **3** *(replace)* sustituir.

renewable [rɪ'njuːəb⁰l] *adj* renovable. COMP **renewable energy** energía renovable.

renounce [rɪ'naʊns] *vt* renunciar a.

rent [rent] *n* **1** *(for flat, etc)* alquiler *m*. **2** *(for land)* arriendo.
▸ *vt* **1** *(flat)* alquilar. **2** *(land)* arrendar.
LOC **"For rent"** «Se alquila».

✗ Renta no significa 'renta (ingresos)', que se traduce por income.

rental ['rentəl] n **1** (for flat, etc) alquiler m. **2** (for land) arriendo.

rented ['rentɪd] adj de alquiler.

reorganise [riːˈɔːgənaɪz] vt → **reorganize**.

reorganize [riːˈɔːgənaɪz] vt reorganizar.

repaid [riːˈpeɪd] pt & pp → **repay**.

repair [rɪˈpeəʳ] n reparación f.
▶ vt reparar, arreglar.

repay [riːˈpeɪ] vt devolver.
ⓘ pt & pp repaid, ger repaying.

repeat [rɪˈpiːt] n **1** (gen) repetición f. **2** (on television) reposición f.
▶ vt & vi repetir.

repel [rɪˈpel] vt **1** (gen) repeler. **2** (disgust) repugnar, repeler.
ⓘ pt & pp repelled, ger repelling.

repellent [rɪˈpelənt] n repelente m.
▶ vt arrepentirse de.

repetition [repəˈtɪʃⁿn] n repetición f.

repetitive [rɪˈpetɪtɪv] adj repetitivo,-a.

replace [rɪˈpleɪs] vt **1** (put back) devolver a su sitio. **2** (substitute) reemplazar, sustituir; (change) cambiar.

replacement [rɪˈpleɪsmənt] n **1** (act) sustitución f, reemplazo. **2** (person) sustituto,-a. **3** (thing) otro,-a. **4** (spare part) recambio, pieza de recambio.

replay [(n) 'riːpleɪ; (vb) riːˈpleɪ] n **1** (of film sequence) repetición f de la jugada. **2** (match) partido de desempate.
▶ vt **1** (tape, film) volver a poner. **2** (match) volver a jugar.

reply [rɪˈplaɪ] n respuesta, contestación f. ᴸᴼᶜ **in reply to** en respuesta a.
ⓘ pl replies.
▶ vi responder (to, a), contestar (to, a).
ⓘ pt & pp replied.

report [rɪˈpɔːt] n **1** (informative document) informe m. **2** (school report) boletín m escolar, informe m escolar. **3** (piece of news) noticia. **4** (news story) reportaje m. **5** (rumour) rumor m. **6** (of gun) estampido.
▶ vi **1** (give information) informar (on, sobre). **2** (go in person) presentarse.
▶ vt **1** (say, inform) decir. **2** (to authority) informar de. **3** (to police - crime) denunciar; (- accident) dar parte de

reported speech [rɪpɔːtɪdˈspiːtʃ] n estilo indirecto.

reporter [rɪˈpɔːtəʳ] n reportero,-a.

represent [reprɪˈzent] vt representar.

representative [reprɪˈzentətɪv] adj representativo,-a.
▶ n **1** representante mf. **2** US diputado,-a.

reproach [rɪˈprəʊtʃ] n reproche m.
▶ vt reprochar (for, -).

reproduce [riːprəˈdjuːs] vt reproducir.
▶ vi reproducirse.

reproduction [riːprəˈdʌkʃⁿn] n reproducción f.

reproductive [riːprəˈdʌktɪv] adj reproductor,-ra.

reptile ['reptaɪl] n reptil m.

republic [rɪˈpʌblɪk] n república.

republican [rɪˈpʌblɪkən] adj republicano,-a.
▶ n republicano,-a.

repugnant [rɪˈpʌgnənt] adj repugnante.

repulsion [rɪˈpʌlʒən] vt **1** (reject) rechazar. **2** (drive back) repulsar.

repulsive [rɪˈpʌlsɪv] adj repulsivo,-a.

reputation [repjʊˈteɪʃⁿn] n reputación f, fama. ᴸᴼᶜ **to have a reputation for ...** tener fama de…

request [rɪˈkwest] n **1** solicitud f, petición f. **2** (on radio) canción f.
▶ vt **1** (gen) pedir, solicitar; (officially) rogar. **2** (on radio) pedir.

require [rɪˈkwaɪəʳ] vt **1** requerir, exigir. **2** (need) necesitar, requerir. ᴸᴼᶜ **to be required to do** STH estar obligado,-a a hacer ALGO.

requirement [rɪˈkwaɪəmənt] n **1** (demand) requisito. **2** (need) necesidad f.

reran [riːˈræn] pt → **rerun**.

rerun [(n) 'riːrʌn; (vb) riːˈrʌn] n (repetition) repetición f; (TV programme) reposición f; (film) reestreno.
▶ vt (repeat) repetir; (TV programme) reponer; (film) reestrenar.
ⓘ pt reran [riːˈræn], pp rerun [riːˈrʌn], ger rerunning.

resat ['riːsæt] pt & pp → **resit**.

rescue ['reskjuː] n rescate m.
▶ vt rescatar (from, de).

research [rɪˈsɜːtʃ] n investigación f.
▶ vi investigar (into, -).
▶ vt documentar.

R

researcher [rɪ'sɜːtʃəʳ] *n* investigador,-ra.

resemblance [rɪ'zembləns] *n* parecido, semejanza.

resemble [rɪ'zembᵊl] *vt* parecerse a.

resent [rɪ'zent] *vt* ofenderse por.

resentment [rɪ'zentmənt] *n* resentimiento, rencor *m*.

reservation [rezə'veɪʃᵊn] *n* reserva.

reserve [rɪ'zɜːv] *n (gen)* reserva.
  ▸ *vt* reservar.

reservoir ['rezəvwɑːʳ] *n* **1** *(lake)* embalse *m*. **2** *(store)* reserva.

reset [riː'set] *vt* **1** *(programmer, computer)* reinicializar; *(mechanism)* rearmar. **2** *(clock)* poner en hora. **3** *(bone)* componer. **4** *(book)* recomponer.
  ⓘ *pt & pp* reset, *ger* resetting.

residence ['rezidəns] *n* residencia.

resident ['rezidᵊnt] *adj* residente.
  ▸ *n (gen)* residente *mf; (of area)* vecino, -a; *(in hotel)* huésped,-da.

residential [rezi'denʃᵊl] *adj* residencial.

residual [rɪ'zidjuəl] *adj* residual.

resign [rɪ'zaɪn] *vi* dimitir (from, de), presentar la dimisión.
  ▸ *vt* dimitir de. [LOC] to resign os to STH resignarse a ALGO.

resignation [rezɪg'neɪʃᵊn] *n* **1** *(from post)* dimisión *f*. **2** *(acceptance)* resignación *f*. [LOC] to hand in one's resignation presentar la dimisión.

resilience [rɪ'zɪliəns] *n* **1** *(flexibility)* elasticidad *f*. **2** *(strength)* fuerza, resistencia.

resin ['rezɪn] *n* resina.

resist [rɪ'zɪst] *vt* **1** *(not give in to)* resistir. **2** *(oppose)* oponer resistencia a.

resistance [rɪ'zɪstəns] *n* **1** *(gen)* resistencia. **2** *(opposition)* oposición *f*. [LOC] to put up resistance oponer resistencia.

resistant [rɪ'zɪstənt] *adj* resistente.

resit [*(n)* 'riːsɪt; *(vb)* riː'sɪt] *n* examen *m* de repesca.
  ▸ *vt* volver a presentarse a.
  ⓘ *pt & pp* resat [riː'sɪt], *ger* resitting.

resolution ['rezəlu:ʃən] *n* resolución *f*.

resort [rɪ'zɔːt] *n* **1** *(place)* lugar *m* de vacaciones. **2** *(recourse)* recurso.
  ▸ *vi* recurrir (to, a).

resource [rɪ'zɔːs] *n* recurso.

respect [rɪ'spekt] *n* **1** *(admiration, consideration)* respeto. **2** *(aspect)* respecto
  ▸ *vt* respetar.

respectable [rɪ'spektəbᵊl] *adj* **1** *(gen)* respetable. **2** *(decent)* decente.

respiration [respɪ'reɪʃən] *n* respiración *f*.

respiratory ['respᵊrətᵊrɪ] *adj* respiratorio,-a. [COMP] respiratory system sistema *m* respiratorio.

respond [rɪ'spɒnd] *vi* responder.

response [rɪ'spɒns] *n* **1** *(gen)* respuesta. **2** *(reaction)* reacción *f*.

responsibility [rɪspɒnsɪ'bɪlɪtɪ] *n* responsabilidad *f*. [COMP] to accept responsibility for responsabilizarse de.
  ⓘ *pl* responsibilities.

responsible [rɪ'spɒnsəbᵊl] *adj* **1** *(gen)* responsable. **2** *(position)* de responsabilidad

rest¹ [rest] *n* **1** *(repose)* descanso, reposo. **2** *(peace)* paz *f*, tranquilidad *f*. **3** *(support)* soporte *m; (for head)* reposacabezas *m; (for arms)* apoyabrazos *m*.
  ▸ *vt* **1** *(relax)* descansar. **2** *(lean)* apoyar.
  ▸ *vi* **1** *(relax)* descansar. **2** *(be calm)* quedarse tranquilo,-a. **3** *(depend)* depender (on, de).
  ▸ *vt (lean)* apoyar.

> ☒ To rest no significa 'restar', que se traduce por to substract.

rest² [rest] *vi* quedar así.
  ▸ *n* the rest el resto.

restaurant ['restᵊrɒnt] *n* restaurante *m*.

restless ['restləs] *adj* inquieto,-a. [LOC] to grow restless impacientarse.

restoration [restə'reɪʃᵊn] *n* **1** *(gen)* restauración *f*. **2** *(return)* devolución *f*.

restore [rɪ'stɔːʳ] *vt* **1** *(gen)* restaurar. **2** *(return)* devolver. **3** *(order)* restablecer.

restrain [rɪ'streɪn] *vt* contener.

restrict [rɪ'strɪkt] *vt* restringir, limitar.

restriction [rɪ'strɪkʃən] *n* *(limited)* restricción *f*.

result [rɪ'zʌlt] *n* **1** resultado. **2** *(consequence)* consecuencia.
  ▸ *vi* to result from resultar de.
  ◆ to result in *vt insep* producir.

resume [rɪ'zjuːm] *vt* **1** *(begin again)* reanudar. **2** *(take over again)* volver a asumir.
▶ *vi* continuar.

❌ To resume no significa 'resumir', que se traduce por to **summarize**.

résumé ['rezjuːmeɪ] *n* **1** *(summary)* resumen *m*. **2** US *(curriculum vitae)* currículo, currículum vitae *m*.

resuscitate [rɪ'sʌsɪteɪt] *vt* reanimar.

retail ['riːteɪl] *n* venta al detalle, venta al por menor.
▶ *vt* vender al detalle, vender al por menor.
▶ *adv* al detalle, al por menor.

retailer ['riːteɪlə'] *n* detallista *mf*, minorista *mf*.

retain [rɪ'teɪn] *vt* **1** *(keep - power, moisture)* retener; *(- heat, charge)* conservar. **2** SP *(lead)* mantener; *(title)* revalidar. **3** *(possessions)* guardar. **4** *(remember)* retener, recordar. **5** *(hold back)* contener. **6** *(employ)* contratar.

retaliate [rɪ'tælɪeɪt] *vi* tomar represalias (**against**, contra).

retard [rɪ'taːd] *vt* retardar, retrasar.

retina ['retɪnə] *n* retina.
ⓘ *pl* retinas o retinae ['retɪniː].

retinue ['retɪnjuː] *n* séquito.

retire [rɪ'taɪə'] *vt* *(from work)* jubilar.
▶ *vi* **1** *(from work)* jubilarse. **2** *(withdraw)* retirarse. **3** *(go to bed)* acostarse.

retired [rɪ'taɪəd] *adj* jubilado,-a.

retirement [rɪ'taɪənt] *n* jubilación *f*.

retrace [rɪ'treɪs] *vt* desandar, volver sobre. LOC **to retrace one's steps** volver sobre sus pasos.

retreat [rɪ'triːt] *n* **1** *(withdrawal)* retirada. **2** *(place)* retiro, refugio.
▶ *vi* **1** *(withdraw)* retirarse. **2** *(back down)* dar marcha atrás.

retribution [retrɪ'bjuːʃ°n] *n* justo castigo.

❌ Retribution no significa 'retribución (pago)', que se traduce por **pay**.

retrospective [retrə'spektɪv] *adj* **1** *(exhibition, etc)* retrospectivo,-a. **2** *(law)* retroactivo,-a.

return [rɪ'tɜːn] *n* **1** *(coming or going back)* vuelta, regreso. **2** *(giving back)* devolución *f*. **3** SP *(of ball)* devolución *f*; *(of service)* resto. **4** *(on keyboard)* retorno. **5** *(ticket)* billete *m* de ida y vuelta. COMP **return ticket** billete *m* de ida y vuelta.
▶ *vi* **1** *(come back, go back)* volver, regresar. **2** *(reappear)* reaparecer.
▶ *vt* **1** *(give back)* devolver. **2** SP *(ball)* devolver; *(serve)* restar. **3** POL *(elect)* elegir. **4** *(verdict)* pronunciar. **5** *(interest)* producir.
▶ *n pl* **returns** resultados *mpl* electorales.

returnable [rɪ'tɜːnəb°l] *adj* retornable.

reunion [riː'juːnɪən] *n* reencuentro.

❌ Reunion no significa 'reunión', que se traduce por **meeting**.

reunite [riːjuː'naɪt] *vt* *(parts)* reunir.

reuse [riːjuːz] *vt* *(parts)* reutilizar.

reveal [rɪ'viːl] *vt* **1** *(make known)* revelar. **2** *(show)* dejar ver, mostrar.

❌ To reveal no significa 'revelar (una foto)', que se traduce por to **develop**.

revenge [rɪ'vendʒ] *n* venganza.
▶ *vt* vengar. LOC **to revenge os** vengarse.

revenue ['revənjuː] *n* ingresos *mpl*.

reverberation [rɪvɜːbəreɪʃən] *vt* resonar, retumbar.

reverse [rɪ'vɜːs] *adj* inverso,-a.
▶ *n* **1** *(back - of coin, paper)* reverso; *(- of cloth)* revés *m*. **2** AUTO marcha atrás. **3** *(setback)* revés *m*. COMP **reverse gear** marcha atrás. ❙ **the reverse side 1** *(of coin, paper)* reverso. **2** *(of cloth)* revés *m*.
▶ *vt* **1** *(positions, roles)* invertir. **2** *(decision)* revocar. **3** *(vehicle)* dar marcha atrás a.
▶ *vi* AUTO poner marcha atrás, dar marcha atrás.
▶ *n* **the reverse** lo contrario.

revert [rɪ'vɜːt] *vi* **1** volver (**to**, a). **2** JUR revertir.

review [rɪ'vjuː] *n* **1** *(magazine, show)* revista. **2** MIL revista. **3** *(examination)* examen *m*. **4** *(of film, book, etc)* crítica.
▶ *vt* **1** *(troops)* pasar revista a. **2** *(examine)* examinar. **3** *(film, book, etc)* hacer una crítica de. LOC **under review** bajo revisión.

R

revise [rɪ'vaɪz] *vt* **1** revisar. **2** *(correct)* corregir. **3** *(change)* modificar. **4** *(examination topic)* repasar.
▶ *vi (for exam)* repasar.

revision [rɪ'vɪʒ°n] *n* **1** revisión *f.* **2** *(correction)* corrección *f.* **3** *(change)* modificación *f.* **4** *(for exam)* repaso.

revival [rɪ'vaɪv°l] *n* **1** *(rebirth)* renacimiento. **2** *(of economy)* reactivación *f.* **3** *(of play)* reestreno.

revive [rɪ'vaɪv] *vt* **1** reanimar, reavivar, despertar. **2** *(economy)* reactivar. **3** *(play)* reestrenar. **4** MED reanimar.
▶ *vi* MED volver en sí.

revolt [rɪ'vəʊlt] *n (rising)* revuelta, rebelión *f.*
▶ *vi (rise)* sublevarse (against, contra), rebelarse (against, contra).
▶ *vt (disgust)* repugnar.

revolting [rɪ'vəʊltɪŋ] *adj* repugnante, asqueroso,-a.

revolution [revə'lu:ʃ°n] *n* revolución *f.*

revolutionary [revə'lu:ʃ°nərɪ] *adj* revolucionario,-a.
▶ *n* revolucionario,-a.

revolve [rɪ'vɒlv] *vi* girar.
▶ *vt* hacer girar.

revolver [rɪ'vɒlvə'] *n* revólver *m.*

revolving [rɪ'vɒlvɪŋ] *adj* giratorio,-a. COMP **revolving door** puerta giratoria.

reward [rɪ'wɔːd] *n* recompensa.
▶ *vt* recompensar.

rewind [riː'waɪnd] *vt* rebobinar.
ⓘ *pt & pp* rewound [riː'waʊnd].

rewound [riː'waʊnd] *pt & pp* → rewind.

rewrite [(vb) riː'raɪt; (n) 'riːraɪt] *vt* volver a escribir.
ⓘ *pt* rewrote [riː'rəʊt], *pp* rewritten [riː'rɪtən].
▶ *n* nueva versión *f.*

rewritten [riː'rɪtən] *pp* → rewrite.

rewrote [riː'rəʊt] *pt* → rewrite.

rheumatism ['ruːmətɪz°m] *n* reumatismo, reuma *m*, reúma *m.*

rhinoceros [raɪ'nɒsərəs] *n* rinoceronte *m.*
ⓘ *pl* rhinoceroses o rhinoceros.

rhizome ['raɪzəʊm] *n* rizoma *m.*

rhombus ['rɒmbəs] *n* rombo.
ⓘ *pl* rhombuses o rhombi ['rɒmbaɪ].

rhubarb ['ruːbɑːb] *n* ruibarbo.

rhyme [raɪm] *n* rima.
▶ *vi* rimar (with, con).

rhythm ['rɪð°m] *n* ritmo.

rhythmic ['rɪðmɪk] *adj* rítmico,-a. COMP **rhythmic gymnastics** gimnasia rítmica.

rib [rɪb] *n* costilla. COMP **rib cage** caja torácica.

ribbon ['rɪb°n] *n* **1** cinta. **2** *(for hair)* lazo.

ribonucleic [raɪbəʊnjuː'kleɪk] *adj* ribonucleico,-a.

rice [raɪs] *n* arroz *m.* COMP **rice field** arrozal *m.* ▌ **rice pudding** arroz *m* con leche.

rich [rɪtʃ] *adj* **1** rico,-a. **2** *(luxurious)* suntuoso,-a, lujoso,-a. **3** *(fertile)* fértil. **4** *(food)* fuerte, pesado,-a.
▶ *n pl* **riches** riqueza *f sing.*

> ✖ Rich no significa 'rico (sabroso)', que se traduce por tasty.

richness ['rɪtʃnəs] *n* **1** *(wealth)* riqueza. **2** *(fertility)* fertilidad *f.* **3** *(of voice)* sonoridad *f.* **4** *(of colour)* viveza.

rid [rɪd] *vt* librar. LOC **to get rid of** deshacerse de.
ⓘ *pt & pp* rid o ridded, *ger* ridding.

ridden ['rɪdən] *pp* → ride.

riddle ['rɪd°l] *n* acertijo, adivinanza.
▶ *vt* **1** cribar. **2** *(with bullets)* acribillar.

ride [raɪd] *n* **1** *(on bicycle, horse)* paseo. **2** *(in car)* paseo, vuelta; *(on bus, train)* viaje *m*, trayecto.
▶ *vi* **1** *(on horse)* montar a caballo; *(on bicycle)* ir en bicicleta. **2** *(in vehicle)* viajar.
▶ *vt* **1** *(horse)* montar. **2** *(bicycle)* montar en, andar en.
ⓘ *pt* rode [rəʊd], *pp* ridden ['rɪdən], *ger* riding.

rider ['raɪdə'] *n* **1** *(on horse - man)* jinete *m*, *(woman)* amazona. **2** *(on bicycle)* ciclista *mf.* **3** *(on motorcycle)* motorista *mf.* **4** *(clause)* cláusula adicional.

ridge [rɪdʒ] *n* **1** GEOG cresta. **2** *(of roof)* caballete *m.*

ridiculous [rɪ'dɪkjʊləs] *adj* ridículo,-a.

ridicule ['rɪdɪkjuːl] *n* ridículo.
▶ *vt* ridiculizar, poner en ridículo.

riding ['raɪdɪŋ] *n* equitación *f.*

rifle ['raɪf°l] *n* rifle *m*, fusil *m.*

rig [rɪg] *n* plataforma petrolífera.
▶ *vt* **1** MAR apañar. **2** *fam (fix)* amañar.
ⓘ *pt & pp* **rigged**, *ger* **rigging**.

right [raɪt] *adj* **1** *(not left)* derecho,-a. **2** *(correct)* correcto,-a. **3** *(just)* justo,-a. **4** *(suitable)* apropiado,-a, adecuado,-a. **5** *fam (total)* auténtico,-a, total. **6** *fam (okay)* bien. ⓁⓄⒸ **all right!** ¡bien!, ¡conforme!, ¡vale! ▌**right away** en seguida. ▌**right now** ahora mismo. ▌**to be right** tener razón. ▌**to get it right** acertar. ▌**to put right** arreglar, corregir. ⒸⓄⓂⓅ **right angle** ángulo recto. ▌**right wing** POL derecha.
▶ *adv* **1** a la derecha. **2** *(correctly)* bien, correctamente. **3** *(exactly)* justo. **4** *(well)* bueno, bien.
▶ *n* **1** *(not left)* derecha. **2** *(entitlement)* derecho.
▶ *vt* **1** corregir. **2** MAR enderezar.

right-hand [ˈraɪthænd] *adj* derecho,-a.

right-handed [raɪtˈhændɪd] *adj* diestro,-a.

right-wing [ˈraɪtwɪŋ] *adj* POL de derechas, derechista.

rigid [ˈrɪdʒɪd] *adj* rígido,-a.

rim [rɪm] *n* **1** *(gen)* borde *m*, canto. **2** *(of wheel)* llanta. **3** *(of spectacles)* montura.

rind [raɪnd] *n* corteza.

ring¹ [rɪŋ] *n* **1** *(for finger)* anillo, sortija. **2** *(hoop)* anilla, aro. **3** *(circle)* círculo; *(of people)* corro; *(of criminals)* red *f*. **4** *(of circus)* pista, arena. **5** *(for boxing)* ring *m*, cuadrilátero; *(for bullfighting)* ruedo. ⒸⓄⓂⓅ **ring road** cinturón *m* de ronda.
▶ *vt* **1** *(put a ring on)* anillar. **2** *(draw a ring round)* marcar con un círculo. **3** *(encircle)* rodear.

ring² [rɪŋ] *n* **1** *(of bell)* tañido, toque *m*; *(of doorbell)* llamada. **2** *(phone call)* llamada.
▶ *vi* **1** *(bell)* sonar. **2** *(ears)* zumbar.
▶ *vt* **1** *(call)* llamar. **2** *(bell)* tocar.
◆ **to ring off** *vt sep* colgar el teléfono.
◆ **to ring up** *vt sep* llamar por teléfono, telefonear.
ⓘ *pt* **rang** [ræŋ], *pp* **rung** [rʌŋ].

ringing [ˈrɪŋɪŋ] *n* **1** campaneo, repique *m*. **2** *(in ears)* zumbido.

rink [rɪŋk] *n* pista de patinaje. ⒸⓄⓂⓅ **ice rink** pista de hielo.

rinse [rɪns] *vt* **1** *(clothes, hair)* aclarar. **2** *(dishes, mouth)* enjuagar.
▶ *n* **1** *(of clothes)* aclarado. **2** *(of dishes)* enjuague *m*. **3** *(for hair)* tinte *m*.

riot [ˈraɪət] *n* **1** *(in street)* disturbio. **2** *(in prison)* motín *m*. ⒸⓄⓂⓅ **riot police** policía antidisturbios.
▶ *vi* **1** *(in street)* provocar disturbios. **2** *(in prison)* amotinarse.

rip [rɪp] *n* rasgón *m*, desgarrón *m*.
▶ *vt* rasgar, desgarrar.
ⓘ *pt & pp* **ripped**, *ger* **ripping**.

ripe [raɪp] *adj* maduro,-a.

rip-off [ˈrɪpɒf] *n fam* timo.

ripple [ˈrɪpəl] *n* **1** *(on water)* onda. **2** *(sound)* murmullo.
▶ *vt* rizar.
▶ *vi* rizarse.

rise [raɪz] *n* **1** ascenso, subida. **2** *(increase)* aumento. **3** *(slope)* subida, cuesta.
▶ *vi* **1** ascender, subir. **2** *(increase)* aumentar. **3** *(stand up)* ponerse de pie. **4** *(get up)* levantarse. **5** *(sun)* salir. **6** *(river)* nacer. **7** *(level of river)* crecer. **8** *(mountains)* elevarse.
ⓘ *pt* **rose** [rəʊz], *pp* **risen** [ˈrɪsən].

risen [ˈrɪsən] *pp* → **rise**.

rising [ˈraɪzɪŋ] *n (rebellion)* levantamiento.
▶ *adj* **1** *(prices)* en aumento. **2** *(sun)* naciente. **3** *(land)* en pendiente.

risk [rɪsk] *n* riesgo, peligro. ⓁⓄⒸ **to take a risk** correr un riesgo.
▶ *vt* arriesgar.

risky [ˈrɪskɪ] *adj* arriesgado,-a.
ⓘ *comp* **riskier**, *superl* **riskiest**.

ritual [ˈrɪtjʊəl] *adj* risorio.

rite [raɪt] *n* rito.

rival [ˈraɪvəl] *adj* competidor,-ra, rival.
▶ *n* competidor,-ra, rival *mf*.
▶ *vt* competir con, rivalizar con.

river [ˈrɪvəʳ] *n* río.

river-bed [ˈrɪvəbed] *n* lecho.

riverside [ˈrɪvəsaɪd] *n* ribera, orilla.

rivet [ˈrɪvɪt] *n* remache *m*.
▶ *vt* **1** remachar. **2** *fig* fijar, absorber.

road [rəʊd] *n* **1** carretera. **2** *(way)* camino. ⒸⓄⓂⓅ **road sign** señal *f* de tráfico.

R

roadway ['rəʊdweɪ] *n* calzada.
roadworks ['rəʊdwe:ks] *n pl* obras.
roam [rəʊm] *vt* vagar por.
▶ *vi* vagar.
roar [rɔːʳ] *n* **1** *(of bull, person)* bramido. **2** *(of lion, sea)* rugido. **3** *(of traffic)* estruendo. **4** *(of crowd)* griterío, clamor *m*.
▶ *vi* **1** *(bull, person)* bramar. **2** *(lion, sea)* rugir.
roast [rəʊst] *adj* asado,-a. COMP **roast beef** rosbif *m*. ∎ **roast potato** patata al horno.
▶ *n* asado.
▶ *vt* **1** *(meat)* asar. **2** *(coffee, nuts, etc)* tostar.
▶ *vi* asarse.
rob [rɒb] *vt* **1** robar. **2** *(bank)* atracar; *(shop)* asaltar, robar.
ⓘ *pt & pp* **robbed**, *ger* **robbing**.

✎ Rob no es lo mismo que steal: rob se usa con la persona robada o con un sitio que se atraca; steal se usa con el dinero u objetos robados. Consulta también steal.

robber ['rɒbəʳ] *n* atracador,-a.
robbery ['rɒbərɪ] *n* atraco.
robin ['rɒbɪn] *n* petirrojo.
robot ['rəʊbɒt] *n* robot *m*.
rock [rɒk] *n* **1** *(gen)* roca. **2** US piedra. **3** MUS rock *m*, música rock.
▶ *vt* **1** *(chair)* mecer. **2** *(baby)* acunar. **3** *(upset)* sacudir, convulsionar.
▶ *vi* *(chair)* mecerse.
rocket ['rɒkɪt] *n* **1** *(missile)* cohete *m*. COMP **rocket launcher** lanzacohetes *m*.
▶ *vi* *(rise)* dispararse.
rocking-chair ['rɒkɪŋtʃeəʳ] *n* mecedora.
rocky ['rɒkɪ] *adj* rocoso,-a.
ⓘ *comp* **rockier**, *superl* **rockiest**.
rod [rɒd] *n* **1** *(thin)* vara. **2** *(thick)* barra. **3** *(for fishing)* caña.
rode [rəʊd] *pt* → **ride**.
rodent ['rəʊdˀnt] *n* roedor *m*.
roebuck ['rəʊbʌk] *n* corzo.
rogue [rəʊg] *n* bribón,-ona, pillo,-a.
role [rəʊl] *n* papel, interpretación *m*.
roll [rəʊl] *n* **1** *(gen)* rollo. **2** *(of film)* carrete *m*. **3** *(list)* lista. **4** *(of bread)* bollo, panecillo; *(sandwich)* bocadillo. COMP **to call the roll** pasar lista.

▶ *vt* **1** *(ball, coin)* hacer rodar. **2** *(flatten)* allanar, apisonar. **3** *(into a ball)* enroscar. **4** *(paper)* enrollar.
◆ **to roll up** *vt sep* **1** enrollar. **2** *(into a ball)* enroscar.
▶ *vi* enrollarse.
roller ['rəʊləʳ] *n* **1** *(for painting)* rodillo. **2** *(wave)* ola grande. **3** *(for hair)* rulo. COMP **roller coaster** montaña rusa. ∎ **roller skating** patinaje *m* sobre ruedas.
rollerblades ['rəʊləbleɪdz] *n pl* patines *mpl* en línea.
ROM [rɒm] *abbr* **(read-only memory)** memoria solo de lectura; *(abbreviation)* ROM *f*.
Roman ['rəʊmən] *adj* romano,-a.
▶ *n* romano,-a. COMP **Roman numeral** número romano.
Romance [rəʊˈmæns] *adj* románico,-a.
romance [rəʊˈmæns] *n* **1** romance *m*. **2** *(novel)* novela romántica.
Romania [ruːˈmeɪnɪə] *n* Rumanía.
Romanian [ruːˈmeɪnɪən] *adj* rumano,-a.
▶ *n* **1** *(person)* rumano,-a. **2** *(language)* rumano.
romanise ['rəʊmənaɪz] *vt* romanizar.
romantic [rəʊˈmæntɪk] *adj* romántico,-a.
roof [ruːf] *n* **1** tejado; *(tiled)* techado. **2** *(of mouth)* cielo. **3** *(of car, etc)* techo. COMP **flat roof** azotea. ∎ **roof rack** baca. ∎ **roof tiles** tejas *fpl*.
▶ *vt* techar.
rooftop ['ruːftɒp] *n* tejado.
rookie ['rʊkɪ] *n fam* novato,-a.
room [ruːm] *n* **1** habitación *f*, pieza. **2** *(space)* espacio, sitio, lugar *m*. COMP **room temperature** temperatura ambiente.
▶ *vi* **1** *(lodge)* alojarse. **2** *(share a room)* compartir una habitación.
roomy ['ruːmɪ] *adj* espacioso,-a.
ⓘ *comp* **roomier**, *superl* **roomiest**.
rooster ['ruːstəʳ] *n* gallo.
root¹ [ruːt] *n* raíz *f*.
▶ *vt* arraigar.
▶ *vi* arraigar.
rope [rəʊp] *n* *(gen)* cuerda; *(thicker)* soga.
▶ *vt* atar *(con cuerdas)*, amarrar.
◆ **to rope off** *vt sep* acordonar.

rosary [ˈrəʊzərɪ] n rosario.
ⓘ pl rosaries.

rose¹ [rəʊz] n 1 (flower) rosa. 2 (bush) rosal m. 3 (colour) rosa m. 4 (of shower, etc) alcachofa. COMP **rose garden** rosaleda. ‖ **rose window** rosetón m.

rose² [rəʊz] pt → rise.

rosé [ˈrəʊzeɪ] n vino rosado.

rosebud [ˈrəʊzbʌd] n capullo de rosa.

rosebush [ˈrəʊzbʌʃ] n rosal m.

rosemary [ˈrəʊzmərɪ] n romero.

rot [rɒt] n 1 (decay) putrefacción f. 2 (rubbish) tonterías fpl.
▶ vt pudrir.
▶ vi pudrirse.
ⓘ pt & pp rotted, ger rotting.

rotate [rəʊˈteɪt] vt 1 (spin) hacer girar, dar vueltas a. 2 (alternate) alternar.
▶ vi 1 (spin) girar, dar vueltas. 2 (alternate) alternarse.

rotation [rəʊˈteɪʃən] n rotación f.

rotten [ˈrɒtən] adj podrido,-a.

rough [rʌf] adj 1 (not smooth) áspero,-a, basto,-a. 2 (road) lleno,-a de baches. 3 (edge) desigual. 4 (rude) rudo,-a. 5 (approximate) aproximado,-a.

roughly [ˈrʌflɪ] adv 1 (about) aproximadamente; (more or less) más o menos. 2 (not gently) bruscamente.

round [raʊnd] adj redondo,-a.
▶ n 1 (circle) círculo. 2 (series) serie f, tanda; (one of a series) ronda. 3 SP (stage of competition) ronda; (boxing) asalto; (of golf) partido. 4 (of drinks) ronda. 5 (of policeman, etc) ronda. 6 (for gun) cartucho. 7 (of bread) rebanada. COMP **round trip** viaje m de ida y vuelta. ‖ **round number** número redondo.
▶ adv 1 (in circles): it goes round and round da vueltas y vueltas. 2 (about) por ahí. 3 (to somebody's house) a casa.
▶ prep alrededor de.
▶ vt doblar.

roundabout [ˈraʊndəbaʊt] n 1 tiovivo. 2 AUTO rotonda.

route [ruːt] n 1 ruta, camino. 2 (of bus) línea, trayecto.
▶ vt mandar.

router [ˈruːtər] n COMPUT direccionador m, enrutador m.

routine [ruːˈtiːn] n rutina.

row¹ [raʊ] n 1 (fight) riña, pelea. 2 (din, racket) jaleo.
▶ vi pelearse.

row² [rəʊ] n (line) fila, hilera.

row³ [rəʊ] vi (in a boat) remar.

rowing [ˈrəʊɪŋ] n remo. COMP **rowing boat** bote m de remos.

royal [ˈrɔɪəl] adj real.

royalty [ˈrɔɪəltɪ] n 1 realeza. 2 (people) miembros mpl de la familia real.
ⓘ pl royalties.
▶ n pl **royalties** (gen) royalties mpl; (of writer) derechos mpl de autor.

rub [rʌb] n friega.
▶ vt (gen) frotar; (hard) restregar.
▶ vi rozar.
◆ **to rub out** vt sep borrar.
▶ vi borrarse.
ⓘ pt & pp rubbed, ger rubbing.

rubber [ˈrʌbər] n 1 caucho, goma. 2 (eraser) goma de borrar. COMP **rubber band** goma elástica. ‖ **rubber ring** flotador m.

rubbish [ˈrʌbɪʃ] n 1 (refuse) basura. 2 (nonsense) tonterías fpl. COMP **rubbish bin** cubo de la basura. ‖ **rubbish dump** vertedero, basurero.

rubella [ruːˈbelə] n rubéola.

ruby [ˈruːbɪ] n rubí m.
ⓘ pl rubies.

rucksack [ˈrʌksæk] n mochila.

rudder [ˈrʌdər] n timón m.

rude [ruːd] adj 1 (person) maleducado, -a, grosero,-a; (behaviour) grosero,-a; (word) malsonante. 2 (improper) grosero,-a. 3 (crude) rudo,-a, tosco,-a.

rug [rʌg] n alfombra, alfombrilla.

rugby [ˈrʌgbɪ] n rugby m.

ruin [ˈruːɪn] n ruina.
▶ vt 1 arruinar. 2 (spoil) estropear.

ruined [ˈruːɪnd] adj 1 arruinado,-a. 2 (spoilt) estropeado,-a. 3 (building) en ruinas.
◆ **to rule out** vt sep excluir, descartar.

ruler [ˈruːlər] n 1 gobernante mf, dirigente mf. 2 (monarch) soberano,-a, monarca mf. 3 (instrument) regla.

R

ruling ['ruːlɪŋ] *adj (in charge)* dirigente; *(governing)* en el poder; *(reigning)* reinante.
▸ *n* JUR fallo.

rum [rʌm] *n* ron *m*.

Rumania [ruːˈmeɪnɪə] *n* → **Romania**.

Rumanian [ruːˈmeɪnɪən] *adj-n* → **Romanian**.

rumble ['rʌmbəl] *n (gen)* ruido sordo; *(of thunder)* estruendo.
▸ *vi (gen)* hacer un ruido sordo; *(thunder)* retumbar.

ruminant ['ruːmɪnənt] *adj* rumiante.
▸ *n* rumiante *m*.

run [rʌn] *n* **1** carrera. **2** *(trip)* viaje *m*; *(for pleasure)* paseo. **3** *(ski)* pista. **4** *(in stocking)* carrera. **4** *(in cricket)* carrera. **9** *(in printing)* tirada. **10** *(at cards)* escalera.
LOC **to go for a run** ir a correr.
▸ *vi* **1** *(gen)* correr. **2** *(flow)* correr. **3** *(operate)* funcionar. **4** *(trains, buses)* circular. **5** *(in election)* presentarse. **6** *(play)* estar en cartel; *(contract, etc)* seguir vigente. **7** *(colour)* correrse.
▸ *vt* **1** *(gen)* correr. **2** *(race)* correr en, participar en. **3** *(take by car)* llevar, acompañar. **4** *(manage)* dirigir, regentar. **5** *(organize)* organizar. **6** *(operate)* hacer funcionar. **7** *(pass, submit to)* pasar. **8** *(publish)* publicar. **9** *(water)* dejar correr.
◆ **to run after** *vt insep* perseguir.
◆ **to run away** *vi* **1** *(gen)* irse corriendo. **2** *(from home, etc)* fugarse, escaparse.
◆ **to run down** *vt sep* **1** *(knock down)* atropellar. **2** *(criticize)* criticar. **3** *(battery)* agotar.
▸ *vt insep* bajar corriendo.
▸ *vi* **1** bajar corriendo. **2** *(battery)* agotarse. **3** *(clock)* pararse.
◆ **to run into** *vt insep* **1** entrar corriendo en. **2** *(car)* chocar con. **3** *(meet)* tropezar con.
◆ **to run off** *vt sep (print)* imprimir.
▸ *vi* irse corriendo.
◆ **to run out** *vi* **1** salir corriendo. **2** *(be used up - gen)* acabarse; *(- stocks)* agotarse. **3** *(contract)* caducar.
ⓘ *pt* ran [ræn], *pp* run [rʌn], *ger* running.

rung¹ [rʌŋ] *n* escalón *m*.

rung² [rʌŋ] *pp* → **ring**.

runner ['rʌnəʳ] *n* **1** corredor,-ra. **2** *(of sledge)* patín *m*; *(of skate)* cuchilla. **3** *(carpet)* alfombrilla. **4** *(on furniture)* tapete *m*. COMP **runner bean** judía verde.

running ['rʌnɪŋ] *n* **1** *(action)* el correr; *(sport)* atletismo. **2** *(management)* dirección *f*.
▸ *adj* **1** *(water)* corriente. **2** *(continuous)* continuo,-a.

runny ['rʌnɪ] *adj* **1** *(liquid)* líquido,-a; *(egg)* poco hecho..
ⓘ *comp* runnier, *superl* runniest.

run-up ['rʌnʌp] *n* **1** *(period before)* etapa preliminar. **2** *(before jumping, etc)* carrerilla.

runway ['rʌnweɪ] *n* pista de aterrizaje.

rural ['ruːrəl] *adj* rural.

rush¹ [rʌʃ] *n* **1** prisa. **2** *(movement)* movimiento impetuoso. COMP **rush hour** hora punta. ‖ **rush job** trabajo urgente.
▸ *vt* **1** *(hurry - person)* apresurar, dar prisa a, meter prisa a. **2** *(send quickly)* enviar urgentemente. **3** *(attack)* abalanzarse sobre.
▸ *vi* ir deprisa, precipitarse.
◆ **to rush in** *vi* entrar corriendo.
◆ **to rush out** *vi* salir corriendo.

rush² [rʌʃ] *n (plant)* junco.

Russia ['rʌʃə] *n* Rusia.

Russian ['rʌʃ°n] *adj* ruso,-a.
▸ *n* **1** *(person)* ruso,-a. **2** *(language)* ruso.

rust [rʌst] *n* óxido, herrumbre *m*.
▸ *vt* oxidar.
▸ *vi* oxidar.

rustle ['rʌsəl] *n (of leaves, etc)* crujido; *(of silk)* frufrú *m*.
▸ *vt (leaves, etc)* hacer crujir.
▸ *vi (leaves, etc)* crujir.
▸ *vt (cattle)* robar.
▸ *vi (cattle)* robar ganado.

rusty ['rʌstɪ] *adj* **1** *(metal)* oxidado,-a. **2** *fig* oxidado,-a, olvidado,-a.
ⓘ *comp* rustier, *superl* rustiest.

ruthless ['ruːθləs] *adj* cruel, despiadado,-a.

Rwanda [ruˈændə] *n* Ruanda.

Rwandan [ruˈændən] *adj* ruandés,-esa.
▸ *n* ruandés,-esa.

rye [raɪ] *n* centeno. COMP **rye bread** pan *m* de centeno. ‖ **rye grass** ballica.

S

S, s [es] *n (the letter)* S, s *f*.

saber ['seɪbəʳ] *n* US → **sabre**.

sabotage ['sæbətɑːʒ] *n* sabotaje *m*.
▶ *vt* sabotear.

saboteur [sæbə'tɜːʳ] *n* saboteador,-ra.

sabre ['seɪbəʳ] *n* sable *m*.

saccharin ['sækərɪn] *n* sacarina.

sachet ['sæʃeɪ] *n* bolsita, sobrecito.

sack¹ [sæk] *n (bag)* saco.
▶ *vt* GB *fam* despedir a, echar a. LOC to get the sack ser despedido,-a. I to give SB the sack despedir a ALGN.

sack² [sæk] *vt* MIL saquear.
▶ *n* MIL saqueo.

❌ To sack no significa 'sacar', que se traduce por to take out.

sacrament ['sækrəmənt] *n* sacramento.

sacred ['seɪkrəd] *adj* sagrado,-a.

sacrifice ['sækrɪfaɪs] *n* **1** *(gen)* sacrificio. **2** *(offering)* ofrenda.
▶ *vt* sacrificar.

sacrum ['sækrəm] *n* ANAT sacro.
ⓘ *pl* sacra ['sækrə].

sad [sæd] *adj* **1** *(unhappy)* triste: *you look very sad* estás muy triste. **2** *(deplorable)* lamentable.
ⓘ *comp* sadder, *superl* saddest.

sadden ['sædən] *vt* entristecer.
▶ *vi* entristecerse.

saddle ['sædəl] *n (for horse)* silla (de montar); *(of bicycle, etc)* sillín *m*.
▶ *vt* ensillar (up, -).

sadism ['seɪdɪzəm] *n* sadismo.

sadist ['seɪdɪst] *n* sádico,-a.

sadly ['sædlɪ] *adv* tristemente.

sadness ['sædnəs] *n* tristeza.

safari [sə'fɑːrɪ] *n* safari *m*.

safe [seɪf] *adj* **1** *(gen)* seguro,-a; *(out of danger)* a salvo, fuera de peligro: *it's not safe to play in the road* es peligroso jugar en la calle. **2** *(unharmed)* ileso,-a, indemne. **3** *(not risky - method, investment, choice)* seguro,-a; *(subject)* no polémico,-a. LOC safe and sound sano,-a y salvo,-a.
▶ *n* caja fuerte, caja de caudales.

safe-conduct [seɪf'kɒndʌkt] *n* salvoconducto.

safely ['seɪflɪ] *adv* **1** *(for certain)* con toda seguridad: *we can safely say that...* podemos decir con toda seguridad que .... **2** *(without mishap)* sin contratiempos, sin accidentes. **3** *(securely)* de manera segura.

safety ['seɪftɪ] *n* seguridad *f*. COMP safety belt cinturón *m* de seguridad. I safety match cerilla, fósforo. I safety pin imperdible *m*.

saffron ['sæfrən] *n (plant, condiment)* azafrán *m*.

sag [sæg] *vi* **1** *(shelf, branch, beam, ceiling)* combarse; *(roof, bed)* hundirse. **2** *(demand, prices, etc)* caer, bajar. **3** *fig (spirits)* flaquear, decaer.
ⓘ *pt & pp* sagged, *ger* sagging.

sage¹ [seɪdʒ] *adj* sabio,-a.
▶ *n* sabio,-a.

sage² [seɪdʒ] *n* BOT salvia.

Sagittarius [sædʒɪ'teərɪəs] *n* Sagitario.

said [sed] *pt & pp* → **say**.

sail [seɪl] *n* **1** *(canvas)* vela. **2** *(of windmill)* aspa.
▶ *vt* **1** *(travel)* navegar; *(cross)* cruzar en barco: *she sailed the Atlantic single-handed* cruzó el Atlántico sola. **2** *(control ship)* gobernar. LOC in full sail a toda vela. I to set sail zarpar, hacerse a la mar.
▶ *vi* **1** *(ship, boat)* navegar. **2** *(begin journey)* zarpar, hacerse a la mar.

S

sailing ['seɪlɪŋ] n **1** (skill) navegación f. **2** (sport) vela: we go sailing every weekend hacemos vela todos los fines de semana. **3** (departure) salida; (crossing) travesía. COMP **sailing boat** barco de vela, velero.

sailor ['seɪlə'] n marinero.

saint [seɪnt] n (person) santo,-a.

sake [seɪk] n bien m: for your own sake por tu propio bien; for the kids' sake por los niños. LOC **for God's sake!** ¡por el amor de Dios!, ¡por Dios! ‖ **for Heaven's sake!** ¡por el amor de Dios!

salad ['sæləd] n ensalada. COMP **salad bowl** ensaladera. ‖ **salad dressing** aliño, aderezo.

salamander ['sæləmændə'] n salamandra.

salami [sə'lɑːmɪ] n salami m.

salary ['sælərɪ] n sueldo, salario.
 ⓘ pl salaries.

sale [seɪl] n **1** (act, transaction) venta. **2** (special offer) rebajas fpl, liquidación f: I bought it in a sale lo compré en las rebajas.
 ► n pl **sales** (amount sold) venta, ventas fpl; (reductions) rebajas fpl. LOC **for sale** en venta. ‖ **"For sale"** (sign on house, etc) «Se vende». ‖ **on sale 1** (available) en venta, a la venta. **2** (reduced) rebajado,-a. COMP **clearance sale** liquidación f. ‖ **sale goods** artículos mpl rebajados. ‖ **sales assistant** dependiente,-a.

salesclerk ['seɪlzklɑːk] n US dependiente,-a.

salesman ['seɪlzmən] n **1** (gen) vendedor m; (in shop) dependiente m. **2** (travelling) representante m.
 ⓘ pl salesmen ['seɪlzmən].

saleswoman ['seɪlzwʊmən] n **1** (gen) vendedora; (in shop) dependienta. **2** (travelling) representante f.
 ⓘ pl saleswomen ['seɪlzwɪmɪn].

saline ['seɪlaɪn] adj salino,-a.

saliva [sə'laɪvə] n saliva.

salivary [sə'laɪvərɪ] adj salival.

salmon ['sæmən] n **1** (fish) salmón m. **2** (colour) color m salmón.
 ⓘ pl salmon.

salmonella [sælmə'nelə] n **1** (bacteria) salmonella. **2** (food poisoning) intoxicación f.

saloon [sə'luːn] n **1** US taberna, bar m. **2** (public room) sala; (on ship) salón m.

salt [sɔːlt] n (gen) sal f. LOC **to be the salt of the earth** ser la sal de la tierra.► adj salado,-a.
 ► vt **1** (preserve, cure) salar. **2** (season) echar sal a.
 ► n pl **salts** sales fpl.

salted ['sɔːltɪd] adj salado,-a.

salpeter [sɔːlt'piːtə'] n US → saltpetre.

saltpetre [sɔːlt'piːtə'] n salitre m.

salty ['sɔːltɪ] adj salado,-a.
 ⓘ comp saltier, superl saltiest.

salute [sə'luːt] n MIL saludo; (firing of guns) salva.
 ► vt MIL saludar.

❌ To salute no significa 'saludar (decir hola)', que se traduce por to say hello.

Salvadorian [sælvə'dɔːrɪən] adj salvadoreño,-a.
 ► n salvadoreño,-a.

samba ['sæmbə] n (dance) samba.

same [seɪm] adj **1** (not different) mismo,-a: the same day el mismo día. **2** (alike) mismo,-a, igual, idéntico,-a: he's wearing the same tie as you lleva una corbata igual que la tuya. LOC **at the same time 1** (simultaneously) a la vez, al mismo tiempo. **2** (however) sin embargo, aun así.
 ► pron **the same** lo mismo: it won't be the same without you no será lo mismo sin ti.
 ► adv **the same** igual, del mismo modo: they talk the same hablan igual. LOC COMP **all the same** a pesar de todo. ‖ **it's all the same to me** me da igual, me da lo mismo. ‖ **the same as** igual que, como. ‖ **the same to you** ¡igualmente!

Samoa [sə'məʊə] n Samoa.

Samoan [sə'məʊən] adj samoano,-a.
 ► n **1** (person) samoano,-a. **2** (language) samoano.

sample ['sɑːmpəl] n muestra.
 ► vt probar.

sanatorium [sænə'tɔːrɪəm] n sanatorio.
 ⓘ pl sanatoriums o sanatoria [sænə'tɔːrɪə].

sanction ['sæŋkʃən] *n* sanción *f*.
▶ *vt fml* sancionar.

sanctuary ['sæŋktjʊərɪ] *n* **1** REL *(sacred place)* santuario. **2** *(gen)* refugio, protección *f*. **3** *(for animals)* reserva.
ⓘ *pl* sanctuaries.

sand [sænd] *n (gen)* arena.
▶ *vt (smooth)* lijar (**down**, -).
▶ *n pl* sands *(beach)* playa *f sing*; *(sandbank)* banco *m sing* de arena.

sandal ['sændəl] *n* sandalia.

sandbank ['sændbæŋk] *n* banco de arena.

sandcastle ['sænka:səl] *n* castillo de arena.

sander ['sændə'] *n (machine)* lijadora.

sandpaper ['sændpeɪpə'] *n* papel *m* de lija.
▶ *vt* lijar.

sandwich ['sænwɪdʒ] *n (French bread)* bocadillo; *(sliced bread)* sándwich *m*.
ⓘ *pl* sandwiches.

sandy ['sændɪ] *adj* **1** *(beach, etc)* arenoso,-a, de arena. **2** *(hair)* rubio,-a oscuro,-a.
ⓘ *comp* sandier, *superl* sandiest.

sane [seɪn] *adj* **1** *(person)* cuerdo,-a; *(mind)* sano,-a. **2** *fig (solution, decision, etc)* sensato,-a.

⊠ Sane no significa 'sano (con salud)', que se traduce por healthy.

sang [sæŋ] *pt* → sing.

sanitary ['sænɪtərɪ] *adj* **1** *(to do with health)* sanitario,-a, de sanidad. **2** *(hygienic)* higiénico,-a. COMP sanitary napkin / sanitary pad / sanitary towel compresa.

sanitation [sænɪ'teɪʃən] *n (public health)* sanidad *f* (pública); *(hygiene)* higiene *f*.

sank [sæŋk] *pt* → sink.

Santa Claus [sæntə'klɔ:z] *n* Papá *m* Noel.

sap [sæp] *n* BOT savia.

sapphire ['sæfaɪə'] *n* zafiro.

sarcasm ['sɑ:kæzəm] *n* sarcasmo.

sarcastic [sɑ:'kæstɪk] *adj* sarcástico,-a.

sarcophagus [sɑ:'kɒfəgəs] *n* sarcófago.
ⓘ *pl* sarcophaguses o sarcophagi [sɑ:'kɒfəgaɪ].

sardine [sɑ:'di:n] *n* sardina. COMP to be packed like sardines estar como sardinas en lata.

sat [sæt] *pt & pp* → sit.

satanic [sə'tænɪk] *adj* satánico,-a.

satchel ['sætʃəl] *n* cartera *(de colegial)*, mochila *(de colegial)*.

satellite ['sætəlaɪt] *n* satélite *m*. COMP satellite dish TV antena parabólica. I satellite television televisión *f* vía satélite.

satin ['sætɪn] *n* satén *m*, raso.
▶ *adj (made of satin)* de satén, de raso.

satisfaction [sætɪs'fækʃən] *n* satisfacción *f*.

satisfactory [sætɪs'fæktərɪ] *adj* **1** satisfactorio,-a. **2** EDUC suficiente.

satisfied ['sætɪsfaɪd] *adj* **1** satisfecho,-a, complacido,-a, contento,-a. **2** *(convinced)* convencido,-a.

satisfy ['sætɪsfaɪ] *vt* **1** *(please, make happy)* satisfacer, complacer, contentar: *does nothing satisfy you?* ¿no hay nada que te satisfaga? **2** *(fulfil)* satisfacer. **3** *(convince)* convencer.
ⓘ *pt & pp* satisfied, *ger* satisfying.

satisfying ['sætɪsfaɪɪŋ] *adj (gen)* satisfactorio,-a; *(meal)* bueno,-a, delicioso,-a.

satsuma [sæt'su:mə] *n* mandarina.

saturate ['sætʃəreɪt] *vt* saturar (**with**, de).

saturation [sætʃə'reɪʃən] *n* saturación *f*.

Saturday ['sætədɪ] *n* sábado: *next Saturday* el sábado que viene, el próximo sábado; *on Saturday morning* el sábado por la mañana; *the following Saturday* el sábado siguiente.

Saturn ['sætɜ:n] *n* Saturno.

sauce [sɔ:s] *n* CULIN salsa.

saucepan ['sɔ:spən] *n* cazo, cacerola.

saucer ['sɔ:sə'] *n* platillo.

Saudi ['saʊdɪ] *adj* saudí, saudita.
▶ *n* saudí *mf*, saudita *mf*. COMP Saudi Arabia Arabia Saudita.

sauna ['sɔ:nə] *n* sauna.

sausage ['sɒsɪdʒ] *n* salchicha.

sauté ['səʊteɪ] *vt* saltear.
ⓘ *pt & pp* sautéed o sautéd, *ger* sautéing.
▶ *adj* salteado,-a.

S

savage ['sævɪdʒ] *adj* **1** *(ferocious)* feroz; *(cruel)* cruel; *(violent)* violento,-a, salvaje: *a savage attack* un ataque duro. **2** *pej (primitive)* salvaje.

savanna [sə'vænə] *n* sabana.

save [seɪv] *vt* **1** *(gen)* salvar (from, de), rescatar (from, de): *you saved my life!* ¡me has salvado la vida! **2** *(not spend)* ahorrar: *I've saved $200 towards my holidays* he ahorrado 200 dólares para las vacaciones. **3** *(keep, put by - food, strength)* guardar, reservar; *(- stamps)* coleccionar. **4** SP *(goal)* parar. **5** COMPUT guardar, archivar.
▶ *vi (not spend)* ahorrar (up, -): *we're saving up to buy a flat* ahorramos para comprar un piso.
▶ *n* SP parada.

saving ['seɪvɪŋ] *n (of time, money)* ahorro, economía.
▶ *n pl* **savings** ahorros *mpl.* COMP **savings account** cuenta de ahorros.

savor ['seɪvəʳ] *n* US → **savour**.

savory ['seɪvərɪ] *adj* US → **savoury**.

savour ['seɪvəʳ] *vt* saborear.

savoury ['seɪvərɪ] *adj* **1** *(salty)* salado, -a; *(tasty)* sabroso,-a. **2** *(respectable, wholesome)* saludable, sano,-a.
▶ *n* entrante *m* salado, canapé *m.*

saw¹ [sɔː] *n (tool)* sierra, serrucho.
▶ *vt* serrar.
▶ *vi* serrar, cortar.
ⓘ *pt* sawed, *pp* sawed o sawn [sɔːn].

saw² [sed] *pt* → **see**.

sawdust ['sɔːdʌst] *n* serrín *m.*

sawn [sɔːn] *pp* → **saw¹**.

saxophone ['sæksəfəʊn] *n* saxofón *m.*

saxophonist [sæk'sɒfənɪst] *n* saxofonista *mf*, saxo *mf.*

say [seɪ] *vt* **1** *(gen)* decir: *what did he say?* ¿qué dijo?, ¿qué ha dicho? **2** *(prayer)* rezar; *(poem, lines)* recitar. **3** *(think)* pensar, opinar, decir: *I say we keep looking* creo que deberíamos seguir buscando. **5** *(suppose)* suponer, poner, decir: *come round at, say, 8.00 pm* pásate hacia las 8.00, ¿te parece? LOC **it is said that ...** dicen que ..., se dice que .... **not to say ...** por no decir .... **I that is to say** es decir.
ⓘ *pt & pp* said [sed].

saying ['seɪɪŋ] *n* dicho, decir *m.*

scab [skæb] *n* MED costra, postilla.

scabies ['skeɪbiːz] *n* MED sarna.

scaffold ['skæfəʊld] *n* **1** *(framework)* andamio. **2** *(for execution)* patíbulo, cadalso.

scaffolding ['skæfəldɪŋ] *n* andamiaje *m.*

scald [skɔːld] *n* escaldadura.
▶ *vt* escaldar.

scale¹ [skeɪl] *n* **1** *(of fish, reptile)* escama. **2** *(on skin)* escama.

scale² [skeɪl] *n* **1** *(measure)* escala: *a metric scale* una escala métrica. **2** *(size, amount)* escala, magnitud *f.* **3** MUS escala. LOC **on a large scale** a gran escala. COMP **scale model** maqueta.

scale³ [skeɪl] *n (pan)* platillo.
▶ *vi* SP *(weigh)* pesar.
▶ *n pl* **scales** *(for weighing in shop, kitchen)* balanza; *(bathroom, large weights)* báscula.

scallop ['skɒləp] *n (mollusc)* vieira, concha de peregrino.

scalp [skælp] *n* ANAT cuero cabelludo.

scalpel ['skælpəl] *n* **1** *(surgeon's)* bisturí *m*; *(for dissecting)* escalpelo. **2** *(tool)* escoplo, gubia.

scamper ['skæmpəʳ] *vi* corretear.

scampi ['skæmpɪ] *n* colas *fpl* de cigala rebozadas.

scan [skæn] *vt* **1** *(examine)* escrutar, escudriñar. **2** *(glance at)* echar un vistazo a. **3** TECH *(with radar)* explorar. **4** MED, INFORM escanear.
ⓘ *pt & pp* scanned, *ger* scanning.
▶ *n* **1** TECH *(with radar)* exploración *f.* **2** MED *(gen)* exploración *f* ultrasónica; *(in gynaecology, etc)* ecografía.

scandal ['skændəl] *n* **1** *(outrage)* escándalo; *(disgrace)* vergüenza. **2** *(gossip)* chismorreo.

ⓧ Scandal no significa 'escándalo (alboroto)', que se traduce por racket.

scandalous ['skændələs] *adj* escandaloso,-a.

ⓧ Scandalous no significa 'escandaloso (ruidoso)', que se traduce por noisy.

scanner ['skænəʳ] *n* **1** TECH *(radar)* antena direccional. **2** MED, INFORM escáner *m.*

scapula ['skæpjʊlə] *n* ANAT escápula.

scar [skɑːʳ] n **1** cicatriz f. **2** fig marca, señal f.

scarce [skeəs] adj (not plentiful) escaso,-a.

scarcely ['skeəslɪ] adv **1** (hardly) apenas: I scarcely know them apenas los conozco. **2** (surely not) ni mucho menos.

scare [skeəʳ] n **1** (fright) susto: what a scare you gave me! ¡vaya susto me has dado! **2** (widespread alarm) alarma, pánico.
▶ vt asustar, espantar: did I scare you? ¿te he asustado?
▶ vi asustarse, espantarse.

scarecrow ['skeəkrəʊ] n espantapájaros m.

scared [skeəd] adj asustado,-a, espantado,-a. LOC **to be scared** tener miedo (of, a/de): I'm scared of spiders tengo miedo a las arañas, las arañas me dan miedo.

scarf [skɑːf] n (small) pañuelo; (silk) fular m; (long, woollen) bufanda.
ⓘ pl scarfs o scarves [skɑːvz].

scarlet ['skɑːlət] adj escarlata.
▶ n escarlata m.

scary ['skeərɪ] adj fam (situation, etc) espantoso,-a; (film, story) de miedo, de terror.
ⓘ comp scarier, superl scariest.

scatter ['skætəʳ] vt **1** (crowd, birds) dispersar. **2** (papers, cushions, etc) esparcir, desparramar; (money) derrochar.
▶ vi dispersarse.

scenario [sɪˈnɑːrɪəʊ] n **1** (of film) guion m; (in theatre) argumento. **2** (situation) (posible) situación f, panorama m.
ⓘ pl scenarios.

☒ Scenario no significa 'escenario', que se traduce por stage.

scene [siːn] n **1** (place) lugar m, escenario; (sight, picture) escena. **2** (in play, book) escena. **3** (stage setting) decorado, escenario.

scenery ['siːnərɪ] n **1** (landscape) paisaje m. **2** THEAT (on stage) decorado.

scent [sent] n **1** (gen) olor m; (pleasant smell) aroma m. **2** (perfume) perfume m. **3** (track, trail) pista, rastro.
▶ vt **1** (animal) olfatear. **2** fig (suspect) intuir. **3** (perfume) perfumar (with, de).

scepter ['septəʳ] n US → sceptre.

sceptical ['skeptɪkəl] adj escéptico,-a.

sceptre ['septəʳ] n cetro.

schedule ['ʃedjuːl, US 'skedjuəl] n **1** (programme) programa m: a work schedule un programa de trabajo. **2** (list - gen) lista. **3** US (timetable) horario. LOC **on schedule 1** (flight) a la hora (prevista). **2** (work) al día. ‖ **to be ahead of schedule** ir adelantado,-a. ‖ **to be behind schedule** ir retrasado,-a.
▶ vt programar, fijar.

schematic [skiːˈmætɪk] adj esquemático,-a.

scheme [skiːm] n **1** (plan) plan m; (project) proyecto. **2** (system, order) sistema m, orden m; (arrangement) disposición f, combinación f: a colour scheme una combinación de colores. **3** (plot) complot m, conspiración f.
▶ vi (plot) conspirar, intrigar, confabularse.
▶ vt (plan deviously) tramar, maquinar.

☒ Scheme no significa 'esquema (resumen)', que se traduce por outline.

schism ['skɪzəm] n cisma m.

schizophrenia [skɪtsəʊˈfriːnɪə] n esquizofrenia.

schizophrenic [skɪtsəʊˈfrenɪk] adj esquizofrénico,-a.

scholar ['skɒləʳ] n **1** (learned person) erudito,-a; (specialist) especialista mf: Latin scholar latinista. **2** (scholarship holder) becario,-a. **3** (good learner) estudiante mf.

☒ Scholar no significa 'escolar (alumno)', que se traduce por pupil.

scholarship ['skɒləʃɪp] n **1** (grant, award) beca. **2** (learning) erudición f.

school¹ [skuːl] n **1** (gen) escuela, colegio: what are you going to do when you leave school? ¿qué harás cuando dejes el colegio? **2** (lessons) clase f: let's meet after school quedemos después de clase. **3** (university department) facultad f. **4** (group of artists, etc) escuela: the Dutch school of painting la escuela pictórica holandesa. COMP **school age** edad f escolar.
▶ vt **1** (teach) enseñar; (train) educar, formar. **2** (discipline) disciplinar.

S

school² ['skuːl] *n (of fish)* banco.

schoolbook ['skuːlbʊk] *n* libro de texto.

schoolboy ['skuːlbɔɪ] *n* alumno, escolar *m*.

schoolchild ['skuːltʃaɪld] *n* alumno,-a, escolar *mf*.
   ⓘ *pl* schoolchildren ['skuːltʃɪldrən].

schoolgirl ['skuːlgɜːl] *n* alumna, escolar *f*.

school-leaver ['skuːlliːvəʳ] *n* alumno,-a que está a punto de dejar la escuela.

schoolteacher ['skuːltiːtʃəʳ] *n (secondary school)* profesor,-ra; *(primary school)* maestro,-a.

science ['saɪəns] *n* **1** *(gen)* ciencia. **2** *(subject)* ciencias *fpl*. COMP **science fiction** ciencia ficción.

scientific [saɪən'tɪfɪk] *adj* científico,-a.

scientist ['saɪəntɪst] *n* científico,-a.

scissors ['sɪzəz] *n pl* tijeras *fpl*. COMP **a pair of scissors** unas tijeras.

scold [skəʊld] *vt* reñir, regañar.

scone [skəʊn, skɒn] *n* CULIN bollo *(que se suele comer con mantequilla, mermelada, nata, etc)*.

scoop [skuːp] *n* **1** *(for flour, rice, etc)* pala; *(for ice-cream)* cucharón *m*. **2** *(amount)* palada, cucharada. **3** *(news story)* primicia.
   ▶ *vt* **1** *(take out)* sacar con una pala. **2** *(beat rival)* vencer, pisar; *(get news first)* dar la primicia. **3** *(win)* ganar; *(make profit)* forrarse.

scooter ['skuːtəʳ] *n (child's)* patinete *m*, patineta; *(motorized)* escúter *m*, Vespa.

scope [skəʊp] *n* alcance *m*: *that is beyond the scope of this report* eso queda fuera del alcance de este informe.

scorch [skɔːtʃ] *vt* **1** *(singe)* chamuscar,. **2** *(burn)* quemar, abrasar.
   ▶ *vi* **1** *(singe)* chamuscarse. **2** GB *fam (travel fast)* ir a toda velocidad.

score [skɔːʳ] *n* **1** SP *(gen)* tanteo; *(in golf, cards)* puntuación *f*: *what's the score?* ¿cómo van? **2** *(in exam, test)* nota, calificación *f*. **3** MUS *(written version)* partitura; *(of film, play, etc)* música.
   ▶ *vt* **1** SP *(goal)* marcar, hacer, meter; *(point)* ganar; *(run)* hacer, realizar: *he scored the winning goal* marcó el gol decisivo. **2** *(in exam, test)* sacar, obtener,

conseguir. **3** *(give points to)* dar, puntuar: *this question scores 10 points* esta pregunta vale 10 puntos.
   ▶ *vi* SP *(gen)* marcar (un tanto); *(goal)* marcar (un gol); *(point)* puntuar, conseguir puntos.

scoreboard ['skɔːbɔːd] *n* marcador *m*.

scorer ['skɔːrəʳ] *n* **1** *(scorekeeper)* encargado,-a del marcador. **2** *(goal striker)* goleador,-ra.

scorn [skɔːn] *n* desdén *m*, desprecio.
   ▶ *vt* desdeñar, despreciar, menospreciar.

Scorpio ['skɔːpɪəʊ] *n* Escorpión *mf*.

scorpion ['skɔːpɪən] *n* escorpión *m*, alacrán *m*.

Scot [skɒt] *n* escocés,-esa.

Scotland ['skɒtlənd] *n* Escocia.

Scottish ['skɒtɪʃ] *adj* escocés,-esa.

scourer ['skaʊrəʳ] *n* estropajo.

scout [skaʊt] *n* **1** MIL *(person)* explorador,-ra; *(plane)* avión *m* de reconocimiento. **2** *(boy)* scout *m*.

scowl [skaʊl] *vi* fruncir el ceño.
   ▶ *n* ceño (fruncido).

scrabble ['skræbəl] *vi (among stones, etc)* escarbar; *(in bag, etc)* hurgar; *(on floor, etc)* rebuscar.

scramble ['skræmbəl] *vi* trepar *(over, por)* *(up, a)*, subir gateando. *(clamber)* moverse rápidamente.
   ▶ *vt* **1** *(mix, jumble)* revolver, mezclar. **2** *(eggs)* revolver.

scrambled eggs [skræmbəld 'egz] *n pl* huevos revueltos.

scrap [skræp] *n* **1** *(of paper, cloth, etc)* trozo, pedazo; *(of news, conversation)* fragmento, migaja. **2** *(of metal)* chatarra. **3** *(in negatives)* pizca, ápice *m*.
   ▶ *vt* **1** *(throw away)* desechar; *(cars, etc)* desguazar. **2** *fig (idea)* descartar; *(plan)* abandonar.
   ⓘ *pt & pp* scrapped, *ger* scrapping.
   ▶ *n pl* scraps *(gen)* restos *mpl*.

scrapbook ['skræpbʊk] *n* álbum *m* de recortes.

scrape [skreɪp] *vt* **1** *(surface, paint, etc)* raspar *(away/off, -)*, rascar *(away/off, -)*: *he scraped the paint off the door* raspó la pintura de la puerta. **2** *(graze skin)* arañarse. **3** *(rub against)* rozar, raspar, rascar.

▶ *vi* **1** *(grate)* chirriar. **2** *(rub against)* raspar, rozar. **3** *(economize)* hacer economías, ahorrar.

scratch [skrætʃ] *n* arañazo, rasguño: *there's a scratch on this record* este disco está rayado.

▶ *adj* **1** *(improvised)* improvisado,-a.

ⓘ *comp* **scratchier**, *superl* **scratchiest**.

▶ *vt* **1** *(with nail, claw)* arañar, rasguñar; *(paintwork, furniture, record)* rayar. **2** *(part of body)* rascar: *she scratched her leg* se rascó la pierna.

▶ *vi* **1** *(animal)* arañar, rascar, rasguñar; *(pen)* raspear; *(wool, sweater, towel)* raspar, picar. **2** *(itch)* rascarse.

scream [skriːm] *n* **1** *(of pain, fear)* grito, chillido, alarido; *(of laughter)* carcajada. **2** *fig (screech)* chirrido. **3** *fam (funny person)* persona divertida; *(funny thing)* cosa divertida: *your cousin's a scream* tu primo es la monda, tu primo es divertidísimo.

▶ *vi* **1** *(gen)* gritar, chillar,; *(wind, siren, etc)* aullar: *she screamed for help* pidió socorro a gritos; *he was screaming with laughter* se mondaba de risa, se tronchaba de risa. **2** *fig (need)* pedir (a gritos), clamar (a gritos).

screech [skriːtʃ] *n* *(of person)* grito, alarido, chillido; *(of tyres, brakes, birds, etc)* chirrido; *(of siren)* aullido. COMP **screech owl** lechuza.

▶ *vt* gritar, decir a gritos, chillar.

▶ *vi* *(person)* chillar; *(tyres, brakes, bird, etc)* chirriar; *(siren)* aullar; *(gate)* rechinar.

screen [skriːn] *n* **1** *(partition)* biombo, mampara. **2** *(for window)* mosquitera. **3** *(protection, cover)* cortina, pantalla. **4** *(of TV, for projection)* pantalla.

▶ *n* **the screen** la pantalla, el cine.

screenplay ['skriːnpleɪ] *n* guion *m*.

screensaver ['skriːnseɪvəʳ] *n* salvapantallas *m*.

screw [skruː] *n* **1** *(metal pin)* tornillo. **2** *(propeller)* hélice *f*. **3** *(turn)* vuelta.

▶ *vt* **1** *(fasten with screws)* atornillar; *(tighten)* enroscar, apretar: *screw the two pieces together* une las dos piezas con tornillos. **2** *(crumple)* arrugar. **3** *(cheat,*

swindle) timar; *(overcharge)* clavar; *(get money out of)* sacar.

▶ *vi* *(turn, tighten)* atornillarse, enroscarse.

screwdriver ['skruːdraɪvəʳ] *n* *(tool)* destornillador *m*.

scribble ['skrɪbəl] *n* garabato, garabatos *mpl*.

▶ *vt* garabatear, garrapatear.

scribe [skraɪb] *n* **1** *(copier)* escribiente *mf*, amanuense *mf*. **2** *(in Biblical times)* escriba *m*.

script [skrɪpt] *n* **1** *(of film, etc)* guion *m*. **2** *(writing)* escritura; *(text)* texto; *(handwriting)* letra.

scroll [skrəʊl] *n* COMPUT barra de desplazamiento.

◆ **to scroll down** *vi* COMPUT desplazarse hacia abajo.

◆ **to scroll up** *vi* COMPUT desplazarse hacia arriba.

scrooge [skruːdʒ] *n* *fam pej* tacaño,-a.

scrotum ['skrəʊtəm] *n* ANAT escroto.

ⓘ *pl* **scrotums** o **scrota** ['skrəʊtə].

scrounge [skraʊndʒ] *vi* *fam* gorrear **(from/off,** a**),** vivir de gorra.

▶ *vt* *(gen)* gorrear **(from/off,** a**),** gorronear **(from/off,** a**):** *he scrounges fags off his friends* gorronea pitillos a los amigos.

scrub¹ [skrʌb] *n* *(undergrowth)* maleza.

scrub² [skrʌb] *vt* **1** *(clean)* fregar bien, restregar. **2** *fam (cancel)* cancelar.

ⓘ *pt & pp* **scrubbed**, *ger* **scrubbing**.

scruffy ['skrʌfɪ] *adj* desaliñado,-a.

ⓘ *comp* **scruffier**, *superl* **scruffiest**.

scrupulous ['skruːpjʊləs] *adj* *(meticulous)* escrupuloso,-a.

scrutinize ['skruːtɪnaɪz] *vt* escudriñar.

scrutiny ['skruːtɪnɪ] *n* **1** *(examination)* examen *m* profundo. **2** GB *(of votes)* escrutinio. LOC **to be under scrutiny** ser analizado,-a.

scuba ['skjuːbə] *n* equipo de submarinismo. COMP **scuba diving** submarinismo, buceo con botellas de oxígeno.

sculptor ['skʌlptəʳ] *n* escultor,-ra.

sculpture ['skʌlptʃəʳ] *n* escultura.

▶ *vt* esculpir **(in,** en**).**

S

scythe [saɪð] *n* guadaña.

sea [siː] *n* **1** mar *m & f*: *we love swimming in the sea* nos encanta nadar en el mar. **2** *fig* mar *m*, multitud *f*: *a sea of faces* un mar de caras. ⌐LOC⌐ **at sea** en el mar. ▌**by sea** por mar, en barco. ▌**by the sea** a orillas del mar. ▌**out to sea** mar adentro. ▌**to go by sea** ir en barco. ⌐COMP⌐ **sea bird** ave *f* marina. ▌**sea lion** león marino. ▌**sea mile** milla marina. ▌**sea wall** dique *m*, rompeolas *m*.
▸ *adj* marítimo,-a, de mar.

seabed ['siːbed] *n* fondo marino.

seafood ['siːfuːd] *n* marisco, mariscos *mpl*.

seagull ['siːɡʌl] *n* gaviota.

seahorse ['siːhɔːs] *n* caballito de mar, hipocampo.

seal¹ [siːl] *n* ZOOL foca.

seal² [siːl] *n* **1** (*official stamp*) sello: *wax seal* sello de lacre. **2** (*on letter*) sello; (*on bottle, etc*) precinto.

seam [siːm] *n* **1** SEW costura. **2** GEOL (*of mineral*) veta, filón *m*: *coal seam* veta de carbón.

seaman ['siːmən] *n* marinero, marino.
ⓘ *pl* seamen ['siːmən].

search [sɜːtʃ] *n* (*gen*) búsqueda (for, de); (*of building*) registro; (*of person*) cacheo. ⌐LOC⌐ **in search of** en busca de. ⌐LOC⌐ **search warrant** orden *f* de registro.
▸ *vt* (*gen*) buscar (for, -); (*building, suitcase, etc*) registrar; (*person*) cachear, registrar: *they searched the house for clues* registraron la casa buscando pistas.
▸ *vi* (*gen*) buscar (through, entre); (*pockets*) registrar.

seashell ['siːʃel] *n* concha (de mar).

seashore ['siːʃɔːʳ] *n* (*coast*) orilla del mar.

seasick ['siːsɪk] *adj* mareado,-a.

seasickness ['siːsɪknəs] *n* mareo.

seaside ['siːsaɪd] *n* playa, costa. ⌐LOC⌐ ⌐COMP⌐ **seaside resort** lugar *m* de veraneo en la costa.

season ['siːzən] *n* (*of year*) estación *f*; (*time*) época; (*for sport, theatre, social activity*) temporada: *the tourist season* la temporada turística. ⌐LOC⌐ **to be in season 1** (*fresh food*) estar en sazón. **2** (*game*) ser temporada de: *strawberries are in season* es temporada de fresas. ▌**to go in season** ir en temporada alta. ▌**to go off/out of season** ir en temporada baja.
▸ *vt* **1** (*food*) sazonar (with, con), condimentar (with, con).

seasonal ['siːzənəl] *adj* estacional.

seasoning ['siːzənɪŋ] *n* CULIN condimento.

seat [siːt] *n* **1** (*chair - gen*) asiento; (*- in cinema, theatre*) butaca: *I'd like a window seat* quisiera un asiento al lado de la ventanilla. **2** (*place*) plaza; (*at theatre, opera, stadium*) localidad *f*. **3** POL (*in parliament*) escaño. ⌐LOC⌐ **to take a seat** sentarse, tomar asiento. ⌐COMP⌐ **seat belt** cinturón *m* de seguridad.
▸ *vt* **1** (*sit*) sentar. **2** (*accommodate*) tener sitio para; (*theatre, hall, etc*) tener cabida para. ⌐LOC⌐ **please be seated** siéntese/siéntense por favor. ▌**to seat os** sentarse.

seaweed ['siːwiːd] *n* alga (marina).

second¹ ['sekənd] *n* **1** (*time*) segundo: *Powell's time was 9.77 seconds* Powell hizo un tiempo de 9,77 segundos. **2** *fam* momento, momentito: *I'll be back in a second* enseguida vuelvo. ⌐COMP⌐ **second hand** (*of watch*) segundero. ▌**second name** apellido.

second² ['sekənd] *adj* (*gen*) segundo,-a; (*another*) otro,-a: *it's the second largest city in England* es la segunda ciudad más grande de Inglaterra. ⌐LOC⌐ **to have second helpings** repetir. ▌**to have second thoughts (about STH)** entrarle dudas a uno (sobre ALGO), cambiar de idea (sobre ALGO). ⌐COMP⌐ **second floor 1** GB segundo piso. **2** US primer piso. ▌**second name** apellido.
▸ *pron* segundo,-a.
▸ *n* **1** (*in series*) segundo,-a. **2** GB (*degree*) ≈ notable *m*.
▸ *adv* segundo, en segundo lugar: *he came second* llegó segundo, quedó en segundo lugar.

✎ Consulta también sixth.

secondary ['sekəndərɪ] *adj* secundario,-a. ⌐COMP⌐ **secondary school** colegio de enseñanza secundaria, instituto de bachillerato .

second-class [sekənd'klɑːs] *adj* de segunda (clase).

second-degree [sekənddɪ'griː] *adj* MED de segundo grado. COMP **second-degree burns** quemaduras *fpl* de segundo grado.

second-hand [sekənd'hænd] *adj* **1** *(used, not new)* de segunda mano, usado,-a, viejo,-a: *we bought a second-hand car* compramos un coche de segunda mano.
▶ *adv* **1** *(buy)* de segunda mano. **2** *(learn, find out)* por terceros.

secret ['siːkrət] *adj (gen)* secreto,-a: *this is my secret hiding-place* éste es mi escondite secreto.
▶ *n* **1** *(gen)* secreto; *(something confided)* secreto, confidencia. **2** *(method, key)* secreto, clave *f.* LOC **in secret** en secreto. I **to keep a secret** guardar un secreto.

secretary ['sekrətərɪ] *n* **1** secretario,-a. **2** *(non-elected official)* ministro,-a; *(representative below ambassador)* ministro,-a plenipotenciario,-a.
ⓘ *pl* secretaries.

secrete [sɪ'kriːt] *vt* **1** *(emit liquid)* secretar, segregar. **2** *fml (hide)* ocultar, esconder.

secretion [sɪ'kriːʃən] *n (of liquid)* secreción *f.*

secretly ['siːkrətlɪ] *adv* en secreto.

sect [sekt] *n* secta.

section ['sekʃən] *n* sección *f.*

sector ['sektə] *n (gen)* sector *m.*

secular ['sekjʊlə'] *adj (education)* laico,-a; *(art, music)* profano,-a.

☒ Secular no significa 'secular (antiguo)', que se traduce por **ancient**.

secure [sɪ'kjʊə'] *adj* **1** *(job, income, etc)* seguro,-a; *(relationship, etc)* estable. **2** *(ladder, shelf, foothold)* firme; *(stronghold)* seguro,-a; *(base, foundation)* sólido,-a.
▶ *vt* **1** *(make safe)* asegurar; *(protect)* proteger *(from, de)*; *(against, contra)*. **2** *(fasten)* cerrar bien. **3** *(obtain)* obtener, conseguir.

☒ Secure no significa 'seguro', que se traduce por **sure**.

securely [sɪ'kjʊəlɪ] *adv* bien.

security [sɪ'kjʊərətɪ] *n* **1** *(safety, confidence)* seguridad *f.* **2** *(protection)* seguridad *f.* COMP **security guard** guarda *mf* de seguridad. I **security service** servicio de seguridad. I **security van** furgoneta blindada.
ⓘ *pl* securities.

sedan [sɪ'dæn] *n* US *(car)* berlina.

sedate [sɪ'deɪt] *vt* MED sedar.

sedative ['sedətɪv] *n* sedante *m*, calmante *m.*
▶ *adj* sedante.

sedentary ['sedəntərɪ] *adj* sedentario,-a.

sediment ['sedɪmənt] *n* sedimento.

sedimentary [sedɪ'mentərɪ] *adj* sedimentario,-a.

sedimentation [sedɪmen'teɪʃən] *n* sedimentación *f.*

seduction [sɪ'dʌkʃən] *n (sexual)* seducción *f.*

see [siː] *vt* **1** *(gen)* ver: *you can see the sea from here* desde aquí se ve el mar; *see page 123* véase la página 123. **2** *(meet, visit)* ver; *(receive)* ver, atender; *(go out with)* salir con: *I'm seeing Pat on Friday* he quedado con Pat el viernes. **3** *(understand)* comprender, entender, ver: *I can see your point* entiendo tu punto de vista. **4** *(visualize, imagine)* imaginarse, ver; *(envisage)* creer: *I can't see him working in a factory* no me lo imagino trabajando en una fábrica. **5** *(find out, discover)* ver; *(learn)* oír, leer: *I'll see what I can do* veré lo que puedo hacer. **6** *(ensure, check)* asegurarse de, procurar: *see that you arrive on time* procura llegar a la hora. **7** *(accompany)* acompañar: *he saw me home* me acompañó a casa.
▶ *vi* **1** *(gen)* ver: *she can't see without her glasses* no ve sin las gafas. **2** *(find out, discover)* ver: *we'll have to see* ya veremos. **3** *(understand)* entender, ver: *oh, I see* ah, ya veo. LOC **I'll be seeing you!** ¡hasta luego! I **let me see/let's see** a ver, vamos a ver. I **seeing is believing** ver para creer. I **see you around** ya nos veremos. I **see you later/soon/Monday!** ¡hasta luego/pronto/el lunes! I **you see 1** *(in explanations)* verás. **2** *(in questions)* ¿sabes?, ¿ves?
ⓘ *pt* saw [sɔː], *pp* seen [siːn], *ger* seeing.

seed [siːd] *n* BOT *(gen)* semilla; *(of fruit)* pepita: *sunflower seeds* pipas.
▸ *vt* **1** *(plant seeds)* sembrar (with, de). **2** *(remove seed)* despepitar.

seek [siːk] *vt* **1** *(look for, try to obtain)* buscar: *the homeless seek food and shelter* la gente sin techo busca comida y alojamiento. **2** *(ask for)* pedir, solicitar. **3** *(attempt, try)* tratar de, intentar.
▸ *vi* *(look for, try to obtain)* buscar (after/for, -), ir en busca de.
ⓘ *pt & pp* sought [sɔːt].

seem [siːm] *vi* *(appear)* parecer: *she seems nice* parece maja; *it seems like there's going to be a storm* parece que va a haber una tormenta. LOC **so it seems** eso parece.

seemingly ['siːmɪŋlɪ] *adv* **1** *(used with adjective)* aparentemente. **2** *(used separately)* al parecer, según parece.

seen [siːn] *pp* → see.

seep [siːp] *vi* filtrarse.

seesaw ['siːsɔː] *n* *(for children)* balancín *m*, subibaja *m*.

see-through ['siːθruː] *adj* transparente.

segment ['segmənt] *n* *(gen)* segmento; *(of orange)* gajo.

seize [siːz] *vt* **1** *(grab)* asir, agarrar, coger: *he seized my arm* me agarró del brazo. **2** *(opportunity)* aprovechar. **3** *(take control of)* tomar, apoderarse de. **4** *(person - arrest)* detener; *(- take hostage)* secuestrar. LOC **to be seized with** STH *(pain, fear, panic, etc)* apoderarse ALGO de uno.

seldom ['seldəm] *adv* raramente, pocas veces: *we seldom eat out* pocas veces comemos fuera.

select [sɪ'lekt] *vt* *(thing)* escoger, elegir; *(team, player, candidate)* seleccionar.
▸ *adj* selecto,-a, escogido,-a.

selection [sɪ'lekʃən] *n* **1** *(people or things chosen)* selección *f*; *(choosing)* elección *f*. **2** *(range to choose from)* surtido, gama.

selective [sɪ'lektɪv] *adj* selectivo,-a.

self [self] *n* **1** ser *m*, uno,-a mismo,-a, sí mismo,-a: *he was his usual self again* volvió a ser él mismo. **2** *(in psychology)* yo: *my other self* mi otro yo.
ⓘ *pl* selves.

self-adhesive [selfəd'hiːsɪv] *adj* autoadhesivo,-a, autoadherente.

self-catering [self'keɪtərɪŋ] *adj* sin servicio de comidas.

self-confident [self'kɒnfɪdənt] *adj* seguro,-a de sí mismo,-a.

self-control [selfkən'trəʊl] *n* dominio de sí mismo,-a, autocontrol *m*.

self-defence [selfdɪ'fens] *n* defensa personal, autodefensa. LOC **to act in self-defence** actuar en defensa propia.

self-employed [selfɪm'plɔɪd] *adj* autónomo,-a, que trabaja por cuenta propia.

self-esteem [selfɪ'stiːm] *n* amor *m* propio.

self-government [self'gʌvənmənt] *n* autonomía, autogobierno.

self-help [self'help] *n* autoayuda.

selfish ['selfɪʃ] *adj* egoísta.

selfishness ['selfɪʃnəs] *n* egoísmo.

self-made [self'meɪd] *adj* *(man, woman)* que ha llegado donde está por sus propios esfuerzos, que se ha hecho a sí mismo,-a .

self-portrait [self'pɔːtreɪt] *n* autorretrato.

self-respect [selfrɪ'spekt] *n* amor *m* propio, dignidad *f*.

self-service [self'sɜːvɪs] *adj* de autoservicio.
▸ *n* autoservicio.

self-sufficient [selfsə'fɪʃənt] *adj* autosuficiente.

sell [sel] *vt* **1** *(gen)* vender: *he sold his bike to his neighbour* vendió la bici a su vecino. **2** *fam* *(convince)* convencer de.
▸ *vi* *(product)* venderse: *these plants sell at a pound each* estas plantas se venden a una libra cada una. LOC **to be sold out** estar agotado,-a.
◆ **to sell off** *vt sep* liquidar.
◆ **to sell out** *vi* **1** *(be disloyal)* claudicar, venderse. **2** COMM *(sell all of)* agotarse (of, -), acabarse (of, -).
▸ *vt sep* COMM *(sell all of)* agotar, agotar las existencias de.
ⓘ *pt & pp* sold [səʊld].

sell-by date ['selbaɪdeɪt] *n* fecha límite de venta, fecha de caducidad.

seller ['selə^r] n *(person)* vendedor,-ra.

Sellotape® ['seləteɪp] n celo®.

sell-out ['selaʊt] n **1** *(performance)* éxito de taquilla. **2** *fam (betrayal)* traición f, engaño.

semantic [sɪ'mæntɪk] *adj* semántico,-a.

semen ['siːmən] n semen m.

semester [sɪ'mestə^r] n semestre m.

semiautomatic [semɔːtə'mætɪk] *adj* semiautomático,-a.

semicircle ['semɪsɜːkəl] n semicírculo.

semicolon [semɪ'kəʊlən] n punto y coma m.

semidetached [semɪdɪ'tætʃt] *adj* pareado,-a.

▸ n *(house)* casa pareada.

semifinal [semɪ'faɪnəl] n semifinal f.

semifinalist [semɪ'faɪnəlɪst] n semifinalista mf.

seminal ['semɪnəl] *adj* seminal.

semiskimmed [semɪ'skɪmd] *adj* semidesnatado,-a, semidescremado,-a.

semolina [semə'liːnə] n sémola.

senate ['senət] n POL senado.

senator ['senətə^r] n senador,-ra.

send [send] *vt* **1** *(gen)* enviar, mandar; *(telex, telegram)* enviar, poner; *(radio signal, radio message)* transmitir, emitir: *he sent me some flowers* me mandó flores. **2** *(order to go)* mandar, enviar: *the doctor sent me to a specialist* el médico me mandó a un especialista. **3** *(cause to become)* volver, hacer: *the noise sent her mad* el ruido la volvió loca.

▸ *vi (send a message)* avisar.

◆ **to send away** *vt sep* despachar.

◆ **to send back** *vt sep* **1** *(goods, etc)* devolver. **2** *(person)* hacer volver.

◆ **to send for** *vt insep* **1** *(person)* llamar a, hacer llamar a. **2** *(thing)* pedir, encargar.

◆ **to send in** *vt sep (application, request)* mandar, enviar.

ⓘ *pt & pp* **sent** [sent].

sender ['sendə^r] n remitente mf.

Senegal [senɪ'gɔːl] n Senegal.

Senegalese [senɪgə'liːz] *adj* senegalés,-esa.

▸ n senegalés,-esa.

▸ n pl **the Senegalese** los senegaleses mpl.

senile ['siːnaɪl] *adj* senil.

senior ['siːnɪə^r] *adj* **1** *(in age)* mayor: *he's five years senior to me* es cinco años mayor que yo. **2** *(in rank)* superior; *(with longer service)* más antiguo,-a, de mayor antigüedad. COMP **senior citizen** jubilado,-a.

▸ n **1** *(in age)* mayor mf; *(in rank)* superior fm. **2** GB *(pupil)* mayor mf. **3** US estudiante mf del último curso.

☒ To accord no significa 'acordar', que se traduce por **to agree**.

sensation [sen'seɪʃən] n *(gen)* sensación f; *(ability to feel)* sensibilidad f.

sensational [sen'seɪʃənəl] *adj* **1** *fam (wonderful)* sensacional. **2** *(exaggerated)* sensacionalista.

sensationalist [sen'seɪʃənəlɪst] *adj* sensacionalista.

sense [sens] n **1** *(faculty)* sentido: *sense of smell* sentido del olfato. **2** *(feeling - of well-being, loss)* sensación f; *(awareness, appreciation - of justice, duty)* sentido. **3** *(wisdom, judgement)* sentido común. **4** *(meaning - gen)* sentido; *(- of word)* significado, acepción f: *in every sense of the word* en todos los sentidos. LOC **in a sense** hasta cierto punto, en cierto sentido. I **in no sense** de ninguna manera. I **to make sense 1** *(have clear meaning)* tener sentido. **2** *(be sensible)* ser razonable, ser sensato,-a. I **to talk sense** hablar con juicio. COMP **sense of humour** sentido del humor.

senseless ['sensləs] *adj* **1** *(unconscious)* inconsciente. **2** *(foolish, pointless)* absurdo,-a, sin sentido, insensato,-a.

sensibility [sensɪ'bɪlətɪ] n sensibilidad f.

▸ n pl **sensibilities** susceptibilidad f *sing*.

sensible ['sensɪbəl] *adj* **1** *(person)* sensato,-a; *(behaviour, decision)* razonable, prudente; *(choice)* acertado,-a. **2** *(clothes)* cómodo,-a.

☒ Sensible no significa 'sensible', que se traduce por **sensitive**.

sensitive ['sensɪtɪv] *adj* **1** *(person - perceptive)* sensible (**to**, a), consciente (**to**, de). **2** *(person - touchy)* susceptible (**to**, a), pre-

S

ocupado,-a (**about**, por). **3** *(teeth, paper, instrument, film)* sensible (**to**,-a).

sensitivity [sensɪ'tɪvətɪ] *n* **1** *(gen)* sensibilidad *f* (**to**, a/frente a). **2** *(touchiness)* susceptibilidad *f* (**to**, a). **3** *(of skin, issue)* delicadeza.

sensor ['sensə^r] *n* TECH sensor *m*, detector *m*.

sent [sent] *pt & pp* → **send**.

sentence ['sentəns] *n* **1** *(gen)* frase *f*; *(in grammar)* oración *f*. **2** JUR sentencia, fallo.
▶ *vt* JUR condenar.

⊠ Sentence no significa 'sentencia (máxima)', que se traduce por **saying**.

sentimental [sentɪ'mentəl] *adj* sentimental.

sentry ['sentrɪ] *n* centinela *m*.
ⓘ *pl* sentries.

sepal ['sepəl] *n* BOT sépalo.

separate [*(vb)* 'sepəreɪt; *(adj)* 'sepərət] *vt* separar (**from**, de).
▶ *vi* **1** *(gen)* separarse.
▶ *adj* **1** *(apart)* separado,-a: *keep the sheep separate from the goats* mantén a las ovejas separadas de las cabras. **2** *(not shared)* separado,-a, individual: *we had separate rooms* cada uno tenía su habitación. **3** *(different)* distinto,-a, diferente.

separately ['sepərətlɪ] *adv* por separado, aparte.

separation [sepə'reɪʃən] *n* separación *f*.

sepia ['si:pɪə] *adj* sepia.

September [səp'tembə^r] *n* septiembre *m*, setiembre *m*.

✎ Para ejemplos de uso, consulta **May**.

septic ['septɪk] *adj* séptico,-a.

septum ['septəm] *n* ANAT septo.
ⓘ *pl* septa ['septə].

sepulcher ['sepəlkə^r] *n* US → **sepulchre**.

sepulchre ['sepəlkə^r] *n* sepulcro.

sequel ['si:kwəl] *n* **1** *(result, consequence)* secuela. **2** *(book, film, etc)* segunda parte *f*.

sequence ['si:kwəns] *n* secuencia, orden *m*.

sequoia [sɪ'kwɔɪə] *n* secoya, secuoya.

Serb [sɜːb] *n* *(person)* serbio,-a.
▶ *adj* serbio,-a.

Serbia ['sɜːbɪə] *n* Serbia.

Serbian ['sɜːbɪən] *n* **1** *(person)* serbio, -a. **2** *(dialect)* serbio.
▶ *adj* serbio,-a.

serf [sɜːf] *n* siervo,-a.

sergeant ['sɑːdʒənt] *n* **1** MIL sargento *mf*. **2** *(of police)* cabo *mf*.

serial ['sɪərɪəl] *adj* **1** consecutivo,-a, en serie. **2** *(in parts)* seriado,-a, en capítulos.
▶ *n* *(gen)* serie *f*, serial *m*.

series ['sɪəri:z] *n* *(gen)* serie *f*, sucesión *f*. LOC **in series** TECH en serie.
ⓘ *pl* series.

serious ['sɪərɪəs] *adj* **1** *(solemn, earnest)* serio,-a: *you can't be serious!* ¡no lo dices en serio! **2** *(causing concern, severe)* grave, serio,-a: *no serious damage was caused* no hubo daños importantes.

seriously ['sɪərɪəslɪ] *adv* **1** *(in earnest)* en serio. **2** *(severely)* seriamente, gravemente.

seriousness ['sɪərɪəsnəs] *n* **1** *(severity)* seriedad *f*. **2** *(earnestness, solemnity)* seriedad *f*. LOC **in all seriousness** hablando (muy) en serio.

sermon ['sɜːmən] *n* sermón *m*.

serum ['sɪərəm] *n* MED suero.
ⓘ *pl* serums o sera ['sɪərə].

servant ['sɜːvənt] *n* sirviente *mf*.

serve [sɜːv] *vt* **1** *(work for)* servir (**as**, de). **2** *(customer)* servir: *dinner is served at 8.00 pm* se sirve la cena a les 8.00. **3** *(be useful to)* servir, ser útil: *it serves many different purposes* sirve para varias cosas. **4** *(provide with service)* prestar servicio a: *the new hospital will serve the whole region* el nuevo hospital prestará servicio a toda la región.
▶ *vi* **1** *(work for)* servir: *my father served in the army* mi padre sirvió en el ejército. **2** *(in shop)* atender; *(food, drink)* servir. **3** *(be useful to)* servir (**as**, de): *this will serve as an example* esto servirá de ejemplo.
▶ *n* *(tennis)* saque *m*.

server ['sɜːvə^r] *n* *(computer)* servidor *m*.

service ['sɜːvɪs] *n* **1** *(gen)* servicio. **2** *(maintenance of car, machine)* revisión *f*. **3** REL oficio. **4** *(tennis)* saque *m*, servicio.

▶ *adj (for use of workers)* de servicio: *service entrance* entrada de servicio. `COMP`
service area área de servicio. ▮ **service charge 1** *(on bill)* servicio. **2** *(in banking)* comisión *f.* ▮ **service station** estación *f* de servicio.

▶ *n pl* **services** *(work, act, help)* servicios *mpl.*

serviette [sɜːˈvɛt] *n* GB servilleta.

sesame [ˈsɛsəmɪ] *n* BOT sésamo, ajonjolí *m.*

session [ˈsɛʃən] *n* **1** *(gen)* sesión *f.* **2** EDUC *(term)* trimestre *m.*

set¹ [set] *n* **1** *(of golf clubs, brushes, tools, etc)* juego; *(books, poems)* colección *f*; *(of turbines)* equipo, grupo: *chess set* juego de ajedrez; *set of dishes* vajilla. **2** ELEC *(apparatus)* aparato: *they bought a TV set* compraron un televisor. **3** MATH conjunto. **4** SP *(tennis)* set *m.*

set² [set] *n* **1** *(in hairdressing)* marcado. **2** *(scenery)* decorado; *(place of filming)* plató *m.* **3** *(position, posture)* postura. `COMP`
set square cartabón *m*, escuadra.

▶ *vt* **1** *(put, place)* poner, colocar. **2** *(prepare - trap)* tender, preparar; *(- table)* poner; *(- camera, video)* preparar; *(- clock, watch, oven, etc)* poner: *set the table for dinner* pon la mesa para la cena. **3** *(date, time)* fijar, señalar, acordar: *have you set a date for the wedding?* ¿has fijado una fecha para la boda? **4** *(price)* fijar; *(value)* poner. **5** *(exam, test, problem)* poner; *(homework)* mandar, poner. **6** *(story, action)* ambientar: *the novel is set in Madrid* la novela está ambientada en Madrid.

◆ **to set off** *vi (begin journey)* salir.

▶ *vt sep* **1** *(bomb)* hacer estallar; *(alarm)* hacer sonar; *(firework)* lanzar, tirar. **2** *(cause, start)* provocar.

① *pt & pp* set.

◆ **to set up** *vt sep* **1** *(business)* establecer, montar. **2** *(machine)* instalar.

setback [ˈsetbæk] *n* revés *m*, contratiempo.

settee [seˈtiː] *n* sofá *m.*

settle¹ [ˈsetəl] *vt* **1** *(establish)* instalar, colocar; *(make comfortable)* poner cómodo,-a *he settled himself on the sofa* se puso cómodo en el sofá. **2** *(decide on, fix)* acordar, decidir, fijar. **3** *(sort out - problem, dis-*

pute) resolver, solucionar; *(- differences)* resolver, arreglar; *(- score)* arreglar, ajustar: *we need to settle an argument* tenemos que resolver una discusión. **4** *(calm - nerves)* calmar; *(- stomach)* asentar.

▶ *vi* **1** *(make one's home in)* establecerse, instalarse. **2** *(make os comfortable)* ponerse cómodo,-a *(into,* en). **3** *(bird, fly, etc)* posarse. **4** *(sediment, dregs)* precipitarse. **5** *(calm down)* calmarse. **6** *(pay)* pagar, saldar la deuda.

◆ **to settle down** *vi* **1** *(establish a home)* instalarse, afincarse, establecerse; *(lead settled way of life)* empezar a llevar una vida asentada. **2** *(calm down)* calmarse, tranquilizarse. **3** *(get comfortable)* ponerse cómodo,-a.

◆ **to settle in** *vi* **1** *(get used to)* acostumbrarse, adaptarse. **2** *(move in)* instalarse.

settle² [ˈsetəl] *n (wooden bench)* banco.

settlement [ˈsetəlmənt] *n* **1** *(village)* poblado, pueblo, asentamiento; *(colony)* colonia. **2** *(agreement)* acuerdo, convenio.

setup [ˈsetʌp] *n* **1** *(arrangement, organization)* sistema *m*, situación *f.* **2** *fam (trick)* montaje *m.*

seven [ˈsevən] *adj* siete.
▶ *n* siete *m.*

✎ Consulta también six.

seventeen [sevənˈtiːn] *adj* diecisiete.
▶ *n* diecisiete *m.*

✎ Consulta también six.

seventeenth [sevənˈtiːnθ] *adj* decimoséptimo,-a.
▶ *adv* en decimoséptimo lugar.
▶ *n* **1** *(in series)* decimoséptimo,-a. **2** *(fraction)* decimoséptimo; *(one part)* decimoséptima parte *f.*

✎ Consulta también sixth.

seventh [ˈsevənθ] *adj* séptimo,-a.
▶ *adv* en séptimo lugar.
▶ *n* **1** *(in series)* séptimo,-a. **2** *(fraction)* séptimo; *(one part)* séptima parte *f.*

✎ Consulta también sixth.

seventieth [ˈsevəntɪəθ] *adj* septuagésimo,-a.

S

▶ *adv* en septuagésimo lugar.

▶ *n* **1** *(in series)* septuagésimo,-a. **2** *(fraction)* septuagésimo; *(one part)* septuagésima parte *f*.

✎ Consulta también **sixtieth**.

seventy ['sevəntɪ] *adj* setenta.

▶ *n* setenta *m*.

✎ Consulta también **sixty**.

several ['sevərəl] *adj (some)* varios,-as: *we've been there several times* hemos ido varias veces.

▶ *pron (some)* varios,-as.

severe [sɪ'vɪər] *adj* **1** *(person, punishment, treatment)* severo,-a. **2** *(pain)* agudo,-a; *(injury, illness, damage)* grave, serio,-a.

severity [sɪ'verətɪ] *n* **1** *(of person, punishment, criticism)* severidad *f*. **2** *(of pain)* agudeza, intensidad *f*; *(of illness, wound)* gravedad *f*.

sew [səʊ] *vt* coser (onto, a).

▶ *vi* coser.

◆ **to sew up** *vt sep* **1** *(hole, tear, etc)* coser; *(mend)* remendar. **2** *fam (arrange, settle)* arreglar, acordar: *you've got everything sewn up!* ¡lo tienes todo arreglado!

ⓘ *pt* sewed, *pp* sewed o sewn [səʊn].

sewage ['sju:ɪdʒ] *n* aguas *fpl* residuales.

sewer [sjʊər] *n* alcantarilla, cloaca.

sewing ['səʊɪŋ] *n* costura. COMP **sewing machine** máquina de coser.

sewn [səʊn] *pp* → **sew**.

sex [seks] *n* sexo: *the opposite sex* el sexo opuesto. LOC **to have sex with sb** tener relaciones sexuales con ALGN.

sexism ['seksɪzəm] *n* sexismo.

sexist ['seksɪst] *adj* sexista.

▶ *n* sexista *mf*.

sexual ['seksjʊəl] *adj* sexual.

sexuality [seksjʊ'ælətɪ] *n* sexualidad *f*.

sexy ['seksɪ] *adj (sexually attractive)* sexy; *(erotic)* erótico,-a.

ⓘ *comp* sexier, *superl* sexiest.

shabby ['ʃæbɪ] *adj* **1** *(clothes)* gastado,-a, raído,-a, desharrapado,-a; *(furniture)* de aspecto lastimoso. **2** *(person)* mal vestido,-a, desaseado,-a.

ⓘ *comp* shabbier, *superl* shabbiest.

shack [ʃæk] *n* choza.

shade [ʃeɪd] *n* **1** *(shadow)* sombra: *a temperature of 30 degrees in the shade* una temperatura de 30 grados a la sombra. **2** *(for lamp)* pantalla; *(for eye)* visera; *(blind)* persiana. **3** *(of colour)* tono, matiz *m*.

▶ *vt* **1** *(shelter from light)* proteger de la luz. **2** ART *(darken)* sombrear (in, -).

▶ *vi (change gradually)* convertirse (into, en).

▶ *n pl* **shades** *fam* gafas *fpl* de sol.

shadow ['ʃædəʊ] *n* **1** *(dark shape)* sombra. **2** *(trace)* sombra, vestigio. **3** *(follower)* sombra.

▶ *adj* GB en la sombra.

shady ['ʃeɪdɪ] *adj* **1** *(place)* a la sombra; *(tree)* que da sombra. **2** *fam (person)* sospechoso,-a; *(deal, past)* turbio,-a.

ⓘ *comp* shadier, *superl* shadiest.

shaft [ʃɑːft] *n* **1** *(of axe, tool, golf club)* mango; *(of arrow)* astil *m*; *(of lance, spear)* asta. **2** *(of mine)* pozo; *(of lift)* hueco. **3** *(of light)* rayo.

shake [ʃeɪk] *n* **1** sacudida. **2** US *fam (milkshake)* batido.

▶ *vt* **1** *(move - carpet, person)* sacudir; *(- bottle, dice)* agitar: *shake well before use* agítese bien antes de usar. **2** *(upset, shock)* afectar, impresionar: *the news shook her badly* la noticia le afectó mucho. LOC **to shake hands** estrecharse la mano. ▌ **to shake one's head** negar con la cabeza.

▶ *vi (gen)* temblar: *she was shaking with fear* temblaba de miedo.

ⓘ *pt* shook [ʃʊk], *pp* shaken ['ʃeɪkən].

shaken ['ʃeɪkən] *pp* → **shake**.

▶ *adj (liquid)* agitado,-a.

shaker ['ʃeɪkər] *n (for cocktails)* coctelera; *(for salt)* salero.

shaky ['ʃeɪkɪ] *adj* **1** *(hand, voice)* tembloroso,-a; *(writing)* tamblón,-ona; *(step)* inseguro,-a. **2** *fig (argument, etc)* sin fundamento; *(government, currency)* débil.

ⓘ *comp* shakier, *superl* shakiest.

shall [ʃæl, *unstressed* ʃəl] *aux* **1** [usado con la primera persona del *sing* y el *pl*] *(future)*: *shall go tomorrow* iré mañana; *I shan't mention any names* no daré nombres. **2** [usado con la primera persona del *sing* y el *pl*] *(questions, offers, suggestions)*: *shall I close the window?* ¿cierro la ventana?; *I'll carry it, shall I?* lo llevaré yo, ¿quieres?

3 *fml (emphatic, command)*: *you shall leave immediately* te irás enseguida.

shallow ['ʃæləʊ] *adj* **1** *(water, pond, etc)* poco profundo,-a; *(dish, bowl)* llano, -a, plano,-a. **2** *fig* superficial.
ⓘ *comp* shallower, *superl* shallowest.
▶ *n pl* shallows bajío *m sing*.

shame [ʃeɪm] *n* **1** *(disgrace, humiliation)* vergüenza; *(dishonour)* deshonra. **2** *(pity)* pena, lástima: *what a shame you couldn't go* qué pena que no pudieras ir.
▶ *vt* avergonzar, deshonrar.

shameful ['ʃeɪmful] *adj* vergonzoso,-a.

shameless ['ʃeɪmləs] *adj* desvergonzado,-a.

shammy ['ʃæmɪ] *n* gamuza.
ⓘ *pl* shammies.

shampoo [ʃæm'puː] *n* **1** *(product)* champú *m*. **2** *(act)* lavado.
ⓘ *pl* shampoos.

shandy ['ʃændɪ] *n* GB cerveza con limonada.
ⓘ *pl* shandies.

shan't [ʃɑːnt] *aux* → shall.

shanty ['ʃæntɪ] *n (shack)* chabola.
ⓘ *pl* shanties.

shantytown ['ʃæntɪtaʊn] *n* chabolas *fpl*, barrio de chabolas.

shape [ʃeɪp] *n* **1** *(form, appearance)* forma: *in the shape of a heart* en forma de corazón. **2** *(outline, shadow)* figura. **3** *(state - of thing)* estado; *(- of person)* forma, condiciones *fpl*: *the team is in good shape* el equipo está en buena forma. **4** *(framework, character)* configuración *f*.
LOC in shape *(fit)* en forma. ‖ in the shape of **1** *(physically)* bajo la forma de. **2** *(figuratively)* en forma de. ‖ to take shape tomar forma.
▶ *vt* **1** *(gen)* dar forma a; *(clay)* modelar: *he shaped the dough into a ball* formó una bola con la masa. **2** *(character)* formar; *(future, destiny)* decidir, determinar.
◆ to shape up *vi* desarrollarse.

share [ʃeəʳ] *n* **1** *(portion)* parte *f*. **2** FIN acción *m*.
▶ *vt* **1** *(have or use with others)* compartir: *can you share one book between two?* ¿podéis compartir un libro entre los dos? **2**

(tell news, feelings, etc) compartir. **3** *(divide)* repartir, dividir.
▶ *vi* compartir: *there's only one bed so you'll have to share* solo hay una cama, así que tendréis que compartirla.

shareholder ['ʃeəhəʊldəʳ] *n* accionista *mf*.

shareware ['ʃeəweəʳ] *n* programas *mpl* compartidos.

shark [ʃɑːk] *n* ZOOL tiburón *m*.

sharp [ʃɑːp] *adj* **1** *(knife, etc)* afilado,-a; *(needle, pencil)* puntiagudo,-a. **2** *(angle)* agudo,-a; *(bend)* cerrado,-a; *(slope)* empinado,-a. **3** *(outline)* definido,-a; *(photograph, etc)* nítido,-a; *(contrast)* marcado, -a. **4** *(mind, wit)* perspicaz; *(eyes, ears)* agudo,-a, bueno,-a: *keep a sharp eye on those two* ten bien vigilados a esos dos. **5** *(person - clever)* listo,-a, vivo,-a. **6** *(pain)* agudo,-a, fuerte; *(cry, noise)* agudo,-a, estridente; *(frost)* fuerte; *(wind)* cortante, penetrante. **7** *(taste)* ácido,-a; *(smell)* acre. **8** *(change, etc)* brusco,-a, repentino,-a, súbito,-a. **9** MUS *(key)* sostenido, -a; *(too high)* desafinado,-a.
▶ *adv* **1** *(exactly)* en punto: *at ten o'clock sharp* a las diez en punto. **2** *(abruptly)* bruscamente.

sharpen ['ʃɑːpən] *vt* **1** *(knife, claws)* afilar; *(pencil)* sacar punta a. **2** *fig (feeling, intelligence)* agudizar; *(desire)* avivar; *(appetite)* abrir.
▶ *vi (voice)* agudizarse.

sharpener ['ʃɑːpənəʳ] *n (for knife)* afilador *m*; *(for pencil)* sacapuntas *m*.

sharply ['ʃɑːplɪ] *adv* **1** *(abruptly, suddenly)* repentinamente. **2** *(acutely)* agudamente. **3** *(clearly)* marcadamente, claramente.

shatter ['ʃætəʳ] *vt* **1** *(break into small pieces)* romper, hacer añicos, hacer pedazos. **2** *fig (health)* destrozar, quebrantar, minar; *(nerves)* destrozar.

shave [ʃeɪv] *n* afeitado. LOC to have a shave afeitarse.
▶ *vt* **1** *(face, legs, underarms)* afeitar; *(head)* rapar. **2** *(wood)* cepillar.
▶ *vi (person)* afeitarse: *he shaves every morning* se afeita cada mañana.

shaver ['ʃeɪvəʳ] *n* máquina de afeitar.

S

shaving [ˈʃeɪvɪŋ] n (of face) afeitado. COMP **shaving brush** brocha de afeitar. ▮ **shaving cream** crema de afeitar. ▮ **shaving foam** espuma de afeitar.
▸ n pl **shavings** (wood) virutas fpl.

shawl [ʃɔːl] n chal m, mantón m.

she [ʃiː] pron ella: she's called Nina se llama Nina; she's happy está contenta.
▸ n (animal) hembra; (baby) niña.

she- [ʃiː] pref hembra: she-bear osa.

shear [ʃɪəʳ] vt 1 (sheep) esquilar.
ⓘ pt sheared, pp sheared o shorn [ʃɔːn].
▸ n pl **shears** (gen) tijeras fpl (grandes); (for hedges) podadera f sing.

shearer [ˈʃɪərəʳ] n esquilador,-ra.

shed¹ [ʃed] n (in garden, for bicycles) cobertizo.

shed² [ʃed] vt 1 (leaves, horns, skin) mudar; (clothes) quitarse, despojarse de; (workers, jobs) deshacerse de; (load, weight) perder: the snake sheds its skin la serpiente muda la piel. 2 fig (inhibitions, etc) liberarse de. 3 (water) repeler. 4 (blood, tears, etc) derramar.
ⓘ pt & pp shed, ger shedding.

she'd [ʃiːd] contr 1 she had. 2 she would.

sheep [ʃiːp] n oveja.
ⓘ pl sheep.

sheepdog [ˈʃiːpdɒg] n perro pastor.

sheepfold [ˈʃiːpfəʊld] n redil m, aprisco.

sheer [ʃɪəʳ] adj 1 (total, utter) total, absoluto,-a, puro,-a: by sheer coincidence por pura casualidad. 2 (cliff) escarpado,-a; (drop) vertical.

sheet [ʃiːt] n 1 (on bed) sábana: bottom/top sheet sábana bajera/encimera. 2 (of paper) hoja; (of metal) lámina, chapa; (of glass) lámina, placa; (of tin) hoja. COMP **sheet music** hojas pl de partitura, papel pautado.

shelf [ʃelf] n estante. COMP (set of) **shelves** estantería.
ⓘ pl shelves.

shell [ʃel] n 1 (of egg, nut) cáscara; (of pea) vaina; (of tortoise, lobster, etc) caparazón m; (of snail, oyster, etc) concha: the children were collecting shells on the beach los niños recogían conchas en la playa. 2 (of building) armazón m, esqueleto,

estructura; (of vehicle) armazón m; (of ship) casco. 3 MIL (for explosives) proyectil m, obús m.

she'll [ʃiːl] contr 1 she will. 2 she shall.

shellfish [ˈʃelfɪʃ] n (individual) marisco; (as food) marisco, mariscos mpl.
ⓘ pl shellfish.

shelter [ˈʃeltəʳ] n 1 (protection) abrigo, protección f, cobijo: the climbers sought shelter from the storm los montañeros buscaron abrigo para protegerse de la tormenta. 2 (place) refugio, cobijo.
▸ vt (protect) proteger, resguardar; these trees should shelter us from the rain esos árboles nos resguardarán de la lluvia.
▸ vi (from weather, etc) resguardarse, guarecerse; (from danger) refugiarse.

shelve [ʃelv] vt 1 (put on shelf) poner en el estante, poner en la estantería. 2 fig (postpone, abandon) aparcar, archivar.

shepherd [ˈʃepəd] n pastor m.
▸ vt (guide, direct) guiar, conducir.

shelves [ʃelvz] pl → shelf.

sheriff [ˈʃerɪf] n 1 US sheriff mf, alguacil,-la. 2 GB gobernador,-ra civil.

sherry [ˈʃerɪ] n jerez m.
ⓘ pl sherries.

she's [ʃiːz] contr 1 she is. 2 she has.

shield [ʃiːld] n 1 (for protection) escudo. 2 TECH pantalla protectora. 3 (of animal) caparazón m.
▸ vt (protect) proteger (from, de).

shift [ʃɪft] n 1 (change) cambio: a shift in policy un cambio de política. 2 (of work, workers) turno: the day/night shift el turno de día/de noche. COMP **shift key** tecla de las mayúsculas.
▸ vt 1 (change) cambiar; (move) desplazar, mover: he shifted his feet movió sus pies. 2 (transfer) traspasar, transferir. 3 US (change gear) cambiar.
▸ vi 1 (change) cambiar: the wind shifted el viento cambió de dirección. 2 US (change gear) cambiar de marcha.

shilling [ˈʃɪlɪŋ] n chelín m.

shin [ʃɪn] n ANAT espinilla, canilla. COMP **shin guard / shin pad** espinillera.

shinbone [ˈʃɪnbəʊn] n ANAT tibia.

shine [ʃaɪn] n brillo, lustre m: *he gave his shoes a good shine* sacó brillo a sus zapatos.

▶ vi **1** *(sun, light, eyes)* brillar; *(metal, glass, shoes)* relucir, brillar; *(face)* resplandecer, irradiar: *her eyes shone with happiness* le brillaban los ojos de alegría. **2** *fig (excel)* sobresalir (at, en), destacar (at, en), brillar (at, en): *he shines at tennis* destaca en tenis.

ⓘ *pt & pp* **shone** [ʃɒn].

shiny [ˈʃaɪnɪ] adj brillante.

ⓘ *comp* **shinier**, *superl* **shiniest**.

ship [ʃɪp] n *(gen)* barco, buque m, embarcación f. COMP **passenger ship** buque m de pasajeros. ▌**ship's company** tripulación f.

▶ vt *(send - gen)* enviar, mandar; *(- by ship)* enviar por barco: *we had our luggage shipped to England* mandamos nuestro equipaje a Inglaterra por barco.

ⓘ *pt & pp* **shipped**, *ger* **shipping**.

shipbuilding [ˈʃɪpbɪldɪŋ] n construcción f naval.

shipment [ˈʃɪpmənt] n *(act)* embarque m, envío, transporte m (marítimo).

shipowner [ˈʃɪpəʊnəʳ] n armador,-a.

shipwreck [ˈʃɪprek] n naufragio. LOC **to be shipwrecked** naufragar.

shipyard [ˈʃɪpjɑːd] n astillero.

shirk [ʃɜːk] vt *(duty, etc)* esquivar, eludir.

shirt [ʃɜːt] n *(gen)* camisa; *(for sport)* camiseta.

shirtsleeve [ˈʃɜːtsliːv] n manga de camisa. LOC **in shirtsleeves** en mangas de camisa.

shiver [ˈʃɪvəʳ] n *(with cold)* escalofrío.

▶ vi *(with cold)* temblar, tiritar; *(with fear)* estremecerse.

▶ n pl **the shivers** escalofríos mpl.

shivery [ˈʃɪvərɪ] adj *(with cold)* estremecido,-a; *(feverish)* destemplado,-a.

shoal¹ [ʃəʊl] n *(underwater sandbank)* banco de arena.

shoal² [ʃəʊl] n *(of fish)* banco, cardumen m.

▶ n pl **shoals** fam montones mpl.

shock¹ [ʃɒk] n **1** *(jolt, blow)* choque m, impacto, golpe m; *(of explosion, etc)* sacudida; *(electric)* descarga. **2** *(upset, distress)* conmoción f, golpe m; *(fright, scare)* susto: *you gave me quite a shock* me has dado un buen susto. **3** MED shock m, choque m. COMP **shock absorber** amortiguador m. ▌**shock therapy / shock treatment** electrochoque m.

▶ vt **1** *(upset)* conmocionar, conmover, afectar. **2** *(startle)* asustar, sorprender; *(scandalize)* escandalizar, horrorizar.

▶ vi impresionar, impactar.

shock² [ʃɒk] n *(of hair)* mata.

shocked [ʃɒkt] adj horrorizado,-a, escandalizado,-a.

shocking [ˈʃɒkɪŋ] adj **1** *(disgraceful, offensive)* chocante, escandaloso,-a, vergonzoso,-a. **2** fam *(very bad)* espantoso,-a, pésimo,-a.

shoe [ʃuː] n **1** zapato: *I need a new pair of shoes* necesito unos zapatos nuevos. **2** *(for horse)* herradura. LOC **to put os in sb else's shoes** ponerse en el lugar de ALGN. COMP **shoe polish** betún m.

▌**shoe shop** zapatería.

shoebrush [ˈʃuːbrʌʃ] n cepillo para los zapatos.

shoehorn [ˈʃuːhɔːn] n calzador m.

shoelace [ˈʃuːleɪs] n cordón m (de zapato).

shoemaker [ˈʃuːmeɪkəʳ] n zapatero,-a.

shoeshine [ˈʃuːʃaɪn] n limpieza de zapatos. COMP **shoeshine boy** limpiabotas m.

shone [ʃɒn] pt → shine.

shook [ʃʊk] pt → shake.

shoot [ʃuːt] n BOT *(gen)* brote m, retoño, renuevo; *(of vine)* sarmiento.

▶ vt **1** *(person, animal)* pegar un tiro a, pegar un balazo a; *(hit, wound)* herir (de bala); *(kill)* matar de un tiro, matar a tiros; *(hunt)* cazar: *she was shot in the back* recibió un balazo en la espalda. **2** *(fire - missile)* lanzar; *(- arrow, bullet, weapon)* disparar; *(- glance)* lanzar: *they shot questions at her* la bombardearon a preguntas. **3** *(film)* rodar, filmar; *(photograph)* fotografiar. LOC **to shoot pool** jugar al billar. ▌**to shoot sb dead** matar a ALGN a tiros.

S

► *vi* **1** *(fire weapon)* disparar (**at**, a/sobre); *(hunt with gun)* cazar. **2** SP *(aim at goal)* tirar, disparar, chutar. **3** CINEM rodar, filmar. **5** BOT brotar.

◆ **to shoot down** *vt sep* **1** *(aircraft)* derribar, abatir; *(person)* matar a tiros. **2** *fig (argument, idea, etc)* rebatir.

ⓘ *pt & pp* **shot** [ʃɒt].

shooting [ˈʃuːtɪŋ] *n* **1** *(shots)* disparos *mpl*, tiros *mpl*; *(killing)* asesinato. **2** *(hunting)* caza. **3** CINEM rodaje *m*.

► *adj (pain)* punzante. COMP **shooting star** estrella fugaz.

shop [ʃɒp] *n* **1** *(gen)* tienda; *(business)* comercio, negocio: *I'm going to the shop* voy a la tienda. **2** *(workshop)* taller *m*. LOC **to keep shop** tener una tienda. COMP **repair shop** taller *m* de reparaciones. ❙ **shop assistant** dependiente,-a. ❙ **shop window** escaparate *m*.

► *vi (gen)* hacer la compra, comprar: *we usually shop on Saturday mornings* normalmente hacemos la compra los sábados por la mañana.

◆ **to shop around** *vi* ir de tienda en tienda y comparar precios.

ⓘ *pt & pp* **shopped**, *ger* **shopping**.

shopkeeper [ˈʃɒpkiːpəʳ] *n* tendero,-a.

shoplifter [ˈʃɒplɪftəʳ] *n* mechero,-a.

shoplifting [ˈʃɒplɪftɪŋ] *n* hurto (en las tiendas).

shopper [ˈʃɒpəʳ] *n* comprador,-ra.

shopping [ˈʃɒpɪŋ] *n (purchases)* compra, compras *fpl*; *(activity)* compra: *I had a bit of shopping to do* tuve que hacer unas compras. LOC **to do the shopping** hacer la compra. ❙ **to go shopping** ir de compras. COMP **shopping bag** cesta de la compra. ❙ **shopping basket** bolsa de la compra. ❙ **shopping centre** centro comercial. ❙ **shopping list** lista de la compra. ❙ **shopping mall** US centro comercial. ❙ **shopping precinct** zona comercial. ❙ **shopping trolley** carrito (de la compra).

shore [ʃɔːʳ] *n (of sea, lake)* orilla; *(coast)* costa; *(beach)* playa. LOC **on shore** en tierra.

shorn [ʃɔːn] *pp* → **shear**.

short [ʃɔːt] *adj* **1** *(not long)* corto,-a; *(not tall)* bajo,-a: *he's got short hair* lleva el pe-

lo corto; *Jo is short for Joanne* Jo es el diminutivo de Joanne. **2** *(brief - of time)* breve, corto,-a: *the days are shorter in winter* los días son más cortos en invierno **3** *(deficient)* escaso,-a: *water was short* escaseaba el agua. **4** *(curt)* seco,-a, brusco,-a. LOC **for short** para abreviar. ❙ **in short** en pocas palabras. ❙ **short of** a menos que, salvo que. ❙ **to be short of** STH andar escaso,-a de ALGO, estar falto,-a de ALGO: *I'm a bit short of money* ando ALGO escaso de dinero. ❙ **to run short of** STH acabarse ALGO: *we're running short of coffee* se nos está acabando el café. COMP **short circuit** cortocircuito. ❙ **short cut 1** *(route)* atajo. **2** *(method)* método fácil, fórmula mágica. ❙ **short order** US comida rápida. ❙ **short story** cuento.

► *adv (abruptly)* bruscamente: *the car stopped short* el coche se paró bruscamente.

► *n* **1** *(drink)* copa, chupito. **2** CINEM cortometraje *m*, corto. **3** ELEC cortocircuito.

shortage [ˈʃɔːtɪdʒ] *n* falta, escasez *f*.

shorten [ˈʃɔːtən] *vt* acortar.

► *vi* acortarse.

shorthand [ˈʃɔːthænd] *n* taquigrafía.

shortly [ˈʃɔːtlɪ] *adv* **1** *(soon)* dentro de poco, en breve: *shortly after/before* poco después/antes. **2** *(impatiently)* bruscamente.

shorts [ʃɔːts] *n pl* **1** pantalones *mpl* cortos, shorts *mpl*: *a pair of shorts* un pantalón corto. **2** US *(underpants)* calzoncillos *mpl*.

short-sighted [ˈʃɔːtsaɪtɪd] *adj* **1** MED miope, corto,-a de vista. **2** *(plan, policy, etc)* corto,-a de miras, estrecho,-a de miras.

short-sleeved [ˈʃɔːtsliːvd] *adj* de manga corta.

shot¹ [ʃɒt] *n* **1** *(act, sound)* tiro, disparo, balazo: *I thought I heard a shot* creo haber oído un disparo. **2** *(projectile)* bala, proyectil *m*. **3** *(person)* tirador,-ra. **4** s *(in football)* chut *m*, chute *m*; *(in tennis, golf, cricket, etc)* golpe *m*; *(in basketball)* tiro. **5** *(attempt, try)* intento. **6** *fam (injection)* inyección *f*, pinchazo. **7** *(drink* trago, chupito. **8** *(photo)* foto *f*; *(cinema)* toma. LOC **like a shot** *(without hesitation)* sin pensarlo dos veces, sin dudar.

shot² [sed] *pt & pp* → **shoot.**

shotgun ['ʃɒtgʌn] *n* escopeta.

should [ʃʊd] *aux* **1** *(duty, advisability, recommendation)* deber: *you should see the dentist* deberías ir al dentista. **2** *(probability)* deber de: *the clothes should be dry now* la ropa ya debe de estar seca. **3** *(subjunctive, conditional)*: *if you should see Janet by any chance* si por casualidad vieras a Janet. **4** *(conditional, 1st person)* : *I should like to ask a question* quisiera hacer una pregunta. **5** *(tentative statement)* : *I should think so* me imagino que sí. **6** *(disbelief, surprise)*: *how should I know!* ¡yo qué sé! LOC **I should have thought ...** hubiera pensado...

✎ **Should**, cuando expresa el condicional para la primera persona, equivale a **would.**

shoulder ['ʃəʊldəʳ] *n* **1** ANAT hombro: *she looked over her shoulder* miró por encima del hombro. **2** *(of meat)* paletilla. **3** *(of hill, mountain)* ladera; *(of road)* arcén *m*, andén *m*. LOC **a shoulder to cry on** un paño de lágrimas. ▌ **to rub shoulders with** SB codearse con ALGN. COMP **shoulder bag** bolso (de bandolera). ▌ **shoulder blade** omóplato. ▌ **shoulder strap 1** *(of garment)* tirante *m*. **2** *(of bag)* correa.

▶ *n pl* **shoulders** ANAT hombros *mpl*, espalda *f sing*.

shout [ʃaʊt] *n* grito.

▶ *vt* gritar (out, -): *get out! he shouted* ¡fuera! gritó.

▶ *vi* gritar: *I don't like it when you shout at me* no me gusta que me grites.

◆ **to shout down** *vt sep* abuchear.

shouting ['ʃaʊtɪŋ] *n* gritos *mpl*.

shove [ʃʌv] *n* empujón *m*: *we had to give the car a shove* tuvimos que dar un empujón al coche.

▶ *vt* **1** *(push)* empujar: *she shoved the plate away* apartó el plato de un empujón. **2** *(put casually)* meter.

▶ *vi* *(push)* empujar, dar empujones.

shovel ['ʃʌvəl] *n* **1** *(tool)* pala. **2** *(machine)* excavadora, pala mecánica.

show [ʃəʊ] *n* **1** THEAT *(entertainment)* espectáculo; *(performance)* función *f*: *let's go and see a show* vayamos a ver un espectáculo. **2** *(on TV, radio)* programa *m*, show *m*. **3** *(exhibition)* exposición *f*. **4** *(display)* muestra, demostración *f*: *a show of strength* una demostración de fuerza, una exhibición de fuerza. **5** *(outward appearance, pretence)* apariencia. LOC **the show must go on** el espectáculo debe continuar. ▌ **time will show** el tiempo lo dirá. COMP **fashion show** desfile *m* de modelos. ▌ **quiz show** programa *m* concurso. ▌ **show business** el mundo del espectáculo.

▶ *vt* **1** *(gen)* enseñar: *I showed her my photos* le enseñé mis fotos. **2** *(point out)* indicar, señalar. **3** *(reveal - feelings)* demostrar, expresar; *(- interest, enthusiasm, etc)* demostrar, mostrar: *she rarely shows his feelings* raras veces demuestra sus sentimientos. **4** *(allow to be seen)* dejar ver: *black doesn't show the dirt* el negro no deja ver la suciedad. **5** *(prove, demonstrate)* demostrar. **6** *(guide)* llevar, acompañar: *I'll show you to your room* te acompañaré a tu habitación. **7** *(painting, etc)* exponer, exhibir; *(film)* dar, poner, pasar, proyectar; *(slides)* pasar, proyectar; *(on TV)* dar, poner.

▶ *vi* **1** *(be perceptible)* verse, notarse: *the stain doesn't show* no se ve la mancha. **2** CINEM poner, dar, echar, proyectar, exhibir: *what's showing at the Odeon?* ¿qué dan en el Odeon?, ¿qué echan en el Odeon?

◆ **to show off** *vi (gen)* fanfarronear, presumir, lucirse; *(child)* hacerse el/la gracioso,-a.

▶ *vt sep* **1** *(set off)* hacer resaltar, realzar. **2** *(flaunt, parade)* hacer alarde de, presumir de.

◆ **to show up** *vt sep* **1** *(make visible)* hacer resaltar, hacer destacar. **2** *fam (embarrass)* dejar en ridículo, poner en evidencia.

▶ *vi* **1** *(be visible)* notarse, verse. **2** *fam (arrive)* acudir, presentarse, aparecer. ① *pt* **showed**, *pp* **showed** o **shown** [ʃəʊn].

shower [ˈʃaʊəʳ] n **1** METEOR chubasco, chaparrón m. **2** (of stones, blows, insults, etc) lluvia. **3** (in bathroom) ducha. ⎡LOC⎤ **to have a shower / take a shower** ducharse. ⎡COMP⎤ **shower cap** gorro de baño. ‖ **shower gel** gel m de baño, gel m de ducha.
▸ vt **1** (sprinkle) espolvorear; (spray) rociar. **2** fig (bestow, heap) inundar, colmar, llover.
▸ vi **1** (rain) llover; (objects) caer, llover. **2** (in bath) ducharse.

showing [ˈʃəʊɪŋ] n **1** (of film) pase m, sesión f, proyección f; (of paintings) exhibición f. **2** (performance) actuación f; (result) resultado.

showman [ˈʃəʊmən] n **1** (manager) empresario (de espectáculos). **2** (entertainer) artista m, showman m.
ⓘ pl showmen [ˈʃəʊmən].

shown [ʃəʊn] pp → show.

show-off [ˈʃəʊɒf] n fam fanfarrón, -ona.

showroom [ˈʃəʊruːm] n sala de exposiciones (de concesionario de coches).

showy [ˈʃəʊɪ] adj (thing) llamativo,-a, vistoso,-a; (person) ostentoso,-a.
ⓘ comp showier, superl showiest.

shrank [ʃræŋk] pt → shrink.

shrapnel [ˈʃræpnəl] n metralla.

shred [ʃred] n **1** (gen) triza; (of cloth) jirón m; (of paper) tira; (of tobacco) brizna, hebra. **2** fig (bit) pizca: not a shred of truth ni pizca de verdad. ⎡LOC⎤ **to tear** STH/ **sb to shreds** hacer trizas ALGO/a ALGN.
▸ vt (paper) hacer trizas, triturar; (vegetables - cut in strips) cortar en tiras; (- grate) rallar.
ⓘ pt & pp shredded, ger shredding.

shrew [ʃruː] n ZOOL musaraña.

shrewd [ʃruːd] adj **1** (person) astuto,-a, sagaz. **2** (decision) muy acertado,-a; (move) hábil, inteligente.

shrewdness [ˈʃruːdnəs] n (gen) astucia, sagacidad f.

shriek [ʃriːk] n chillido, grito agudo.
▸ vi chillar, gritar. ⎡LOC⎤ **to shriek with laughter** reírse a carcajadas.
▸ vt chillar, gritar.

shrill [ʃrɪl] adj **1** (voice, words, people) agudo,-a, estridente; (sound, whistle) agudo,-a, estridente, penetrante. **2** (demand, protest, criticism) frenético,-a, estridente.
▸ vi (whistle) pitar; (phone, alarm) sonar; (person, voice) chillar.

shrimp [ʃrɪmp] n camarón m, gamba.

shrine [ʃraɪn] n REL (holy place) santuario, lugar m sagrado.

shrink [ʃrɪŋk] vt (clothes, etc) encoger.
▸ vi **1** (clothes) encoger, encogerse; (meat) achicarse, reducirse. **2** (savings, numbers, profits, etc) disminuir, reducirse. **3** (move back) retroceder, echarse atrás.
ⓘ pt shrank [ʃræŋk], pp shrunk [ʃrʌŋk].

shroud [ʃraʊd] n **1** REL mortaja, sudario. **2** fig (of mist, secrecy) velo.

Shrove Tuesday [ʃrəʊvˈtjuːzdɪ] n martes m de carnaval.

shrub [ʃrʌb] n arbusto, mata.

shrug [ʃrʌg] vt encoger. ⎡LOC⎤ **to shrug one' shoulders** encogerse de hombros.
ⓘ pt & pp shrugged, ger shrugging.

shrunk [ʃrʌŋk] pp → shrink.

shudder [ˈʃʌdəʳ] n **1** (of person) escalofrío. **2** (of machine, engine) vibración, sacudida.
▸ vi **1** (person) estremecerse, temblar (with, de): I shudder to think of it me dan escalofríos solo de pensarlo. **2** (machinery, vehicle) vibrar, dar sacudidas.

shuffle [ˈʃʌfəl] n **1** (walk) arrastre m. **2** (of cards) baraje m, barajadura.
▸ vt **1** (feet - drag) arrastrar; (- move) mover. **2** (cards) barajar; (papers) revolver.
▸ vi (walk) andar arrastrando los pies; (in seat) revolverse.

shut [ʃʌt] vt (gen) cerrar: shut your eyes cierra los ojos.
▸ vi (gen) cerrar, cerrarse.
◆ **to shut down** vt sep (factory, business) cerrar.
▸ vi (factory, business) cerrar.
◆ **to shut up** vt sep **1** (close) cerrar. **2** (confine) encerrar. **3** fam (quieten) callar, hacer callar.
▸ vi **1** (close) cerrar. **2** (keep quiet) callarse: shut up! ¡cállate!
ⓘ pt & pp shut, ger shutting.

shutdown ['ʃʌtdaʊn] *n (of factory, etc)* cierre *m*.

shutter ['ʃʌtə'] *n* **1** *(on window)* postigo, contraventana; *(of shop)* cierre *m*. **2** *(of camera)* obturador *m*.

shuttle ['ʃʌtəl] *n* **1** AV puente *m* aéreo. **2** *(bus, train)* servicio regular de enlace. **3** *(in weaving)* lanzadera. COMP **shuttle service** servicio regular de enlace.

shuttlecock ['ʃʌtəlkɒk] *n* volante *m*.

shy [ʃaɪ] *adj* **1** *(person)* tímido,-a, vergonzoso,-a: *don't be shy* no seas tímido, no tengas vergüenza. **2** *(animal)* asustadizo,-a.
ⓘ *comp* **shyer** o **shier**, *superl* **shyest** o **shiest**.
▸ *vi (horse)* espantarse (at, de), respingar, asustarse.

shyness ['ʃaɪnəs] *n* timidez *f*.

sick [sɪk] *adj* **1** *(ill)* enfermo,-a. **2** *(nauseated, queasy)* mareado,-a. **3** *(fed up)* harto,-a; *(worried)* preocupado,-a: *I'm sick and tired of your moaning* estoy más que harto de tus quejas. LOC **to be sick** vomitar, devolver. ▪ **to feel sick** estar mareado,-a, tener náuseas. COMP **sick leave** baja por enfermedad.

sickle ['sɪkəl] *n* hoz *f*.

sickly ['sɪklɪ] *adj* **1** *(person)* enfermizo,-a. **2** *(smell, taste)* empalagoso,-a, dulzón, -ona; *(colour)* horrible, asqueroso,-a.
ⓘ *comp* **sicklier**, *superl* **sickliest**.

sickness ['sɪknəs] *n* **1** *(illness)* enfermedad *f*. **2** *(nausea)* náuseas *fpl*, ganas *fpl* de vomitar.

side [saɪd] *n* **1** *(gen)* lado; *(of coin, cube, record)* cara: *there's a garage at the side of the house* hay un garaje al lado de la casa; *write on one side of the paper only* solo escribir en una cara del papel. **2** *(of hill, mountain)* ladera, falda. **3** *(of body)* lado, costado: *she was lying on her side* estaba echada de lado. **4** *(edge - gen)* borde *m*; *(- of lake, river, etc)* orilla; *(- of page)* margen *m*. LOC **side by side** juntos,-as, uno,-a al lado del/de la otro,-a. ▪ **to keep on the right side of** SB tratar de llevarse bien con ALGN.
▸ *adj* lateral. COMP **side dish** guarnición *f*, acompañamiento. ▪ **side drum** tambor *m*. ▪ **side effect** efecto secundario. ▪ **side street** callejuela. ▪ **side view** vista de perfil.

sideboard ['saɪdbɔːd] *n (furniture)* aparador *m*.

sideboards ['saɪdbɔːdz] *n pl* patillas *fpl*.

sideburns ['saɪdbɜːnz] *n pl* patillas *fpl*.

sidecar ['saɪdkɑː'] *n* sidecar *m*.

sidelight ['saɪdlaɪt] *n* AUTO luz *f* de posición.

sidereal [saɪ'dɪərɪəl] *adj* sideral.

sidewalk ['saɪdwɔːk] *n* US acera.

sideways ['saɪdweɪz] *adj (movement, step)* lateral; *(look, glance)* de soslayo, de reojo.
▸ *adv* de lado.

siege [siːdʒ] *n* **1** MIL sitio, cerco. **2** *(by criminals, journalists)* asedio. LOC **to be under siege** estar sitiado,-a.

Sierra Leone [sɪeərəlɪ'əʊn] *n* Sierra Leona.

Sierra Leonean [sɪeərəlɪ'əʊnɪən] *adj* sierraleonés,-esa.
▸ *n* sierraleonés,-esa.

sieve [sɪv] *n (fine)* tamiz *m*; *(coarse)* criba; *(for liquids)* colador *m*.
▸ *vt (fine)* tamizar; *(coarse)* cribar.

sigh [saɪ] *n (of person)* suspiro.
▸ *vi (person)* suspirar (for, por); *(wind)* susurrar, gemir: *she sighed with relief* suspiró aliviada.

sight [saɪt] *n* **1** *(gen)* vista: *his sight is failing* le está fallando la vista; *we waited until he was out of sight* esperamos hasta que hubo desaparecido; *it was her first sight of the countryside* fue la primera vez que veía el campo. **2** *(thing seen, spectacle)* espectáculo. LOC **in/within sight** a la vista. ▪ **to come into sight** aparecer. ▪ **to know** SB **by sight** conocer a ALGN de vista.
▸ *vt* ver, divisar.
▸ *adv* **a sight** *fam (a great deal)* mucho: *a sight better* mucho mejor.
▸ *n pl* **sights** *(of city)* monumentos *mpl*, lugares *mpl* de interés.

sightseeing ['saɪtsiːɪŋ] *n* visita turística, turismo. LOC **to go sightseeing** visitar los monumentos y lugares de interés.

sign [saɪn] *n* **1** *(symbol)* signo, símbolo. **2** *(gesture)* gesto, seña; *(signal)* señal *f*:

S

wait until I give the sign espera hasta que dé la señal. LOC **as a sign of** como muestra de. COMP **sign language** lenguaje *m* por señas.

▶ *vt* **1** *(letter, document, cheque, etc)* firmar: *sign your name here, please* firme aquí, por favor. **2** *(player, group)* fichar *(on/up, -)*. **3** *(gesture)* hacer una seña/señal.

▶ *vi* **1** *(write name)* firmar. **2** *(player, group)* fichar *(for/with, por)*. **3** US *(use sign language)* comunicarse por señas, hablar por señas.

◆ **to sign up** *vt sep (soldier)* reclutar; *(worker)* contratar.

▶ *vi (soldier)* alistarse; *(student)* matricularse.

signal ['sɪɡnəl] *n* señal *f*: *traffic signal* señal de tráfico.

▶ *adj (achievement, triumph, success, etc)* señalado,-a, destacado,-a, notable.

▶ *vt* **1** *(indicate)* indicar, señalar, marcar; *(forecast)* pronosticar. **2** *(gesture)* hacer señas, hacer una seña: *he signalled the waiter to bring the bill* le hizo una seña al camarero para que trajera la cuenta.

▶ *vi* **1** *(gesture)* hacer señas, hacer una seña. **2** AUTO poner el intermitente.

signature ['sɪɡnɪtʃəʳ] *n (name)* firma.

significance [sɪɡ'nɪfɪkəns] *n* **1** *(meaning)* significado. **2** *(importance)* importancia: *it's of no significance* no tiene importancia.

significant [sɪɡ'nɪfɪkənt] *adj* **1** *(meaningful - gen)* significativo,-a. **2** *(important)* importante, trascendente, considerable.

signify ['sɪɡnɪfaɪ] *vt fml* significar.
ⓘ *pt & pp* **signified**, *ger* **signifying**.

signpost ['saɪnpəʊst] *n* poste *m* indicador.

silence ['saɪləns] *n (gen)* silencio: *we walked in silence* caminamos en silencio.
LOC **to reduce SB to silence** dejar a ALGN sin habla.

▶ *vt (person)* acallar, hacer callar; *(protest, opposition, criticism)* apagar, silenciar.

silencer ['saɪlənsəʳ] *n* silenciador *m*.

silent ['saɪlənt] *adj* **1** *(thing, place, taciturn person)* silencioso,-a. **2** *(not speaking)* callado,-a: *he was silent for a moment* se quedó callado un momento. **3** *(film, con-*

sonant) mudo,-a; *(prayer)* silencioso,-a. LOC **to be silent** callarse.

silhouette [sɪluːˈet] *n* silueta.

silicon ['sɪlɪkən] *n* silicio.

silicone ['sɪlɪkəʊn] *n* silicona.

silk [sɪlk] *n* seda.
▶ *adj* de seda.

silken ['sɪlkən] *adj (like silk)* sedoso,-a; *(of silk)* de seda.

silkworm ['sɪlkwɜːm] *n* gusano de seda.

silky ['sɪlkɪ] *adj (cloth, hair, fur, etc)* sedoso,-a; *(voice)* aterciopelado,-a; *(skin)* suave.
ⓘ *comp* **silkier**, *superl* **silkiest**.

sill [sɪl] *n (of window)* alféizar *m*, antepecho.

silly ['sɪlɪ] *adj* **1** *(stupid)* tonto,-a, estúpido,-a: *how silly of me!* ¡qué tonto soy! **2** *(unimportant)* trivial, sin importancia.
ⓘ *comp* **sillier**, *superl* **silliest**.
▶ *n* tonto,-a, bobo,-a.

silver ['sɪlvəʳ] *n* **1** *(metal)* plata: *sterling silver* plata de ley. **2** *(coins)* monedas *fpl* (de plata). **3** *(articles, ornaments, etc)* plata.
▶ *adj* **1** *(made of silver)* de plata. **2** *(in colour)* plateado,-a; *(hair)* canoso,-a, cano,-a. COMP **silver foil / silver paper** papel *m* de plata. ‖ **silver medal** medalla de plata. ‖ **silver screen** el cine *m*.
▶ *vt (metal)* dar un baño de plata a, platear.

similar ['sɪmɪləʳ] *adj* parecido,-a (to, a), similar (to, a), semejante (to, a): *those boys are very similar* esos chicos se parecen mucho.

similarity [sɪmɪˈlærətɪ] *n (likeness)* semejanza, parecido, similitud *f*.
ⓘ *pl* **similarities**.

simile ['sɪmɪlɪ] *n* símil *m*.

simmer ['sɪməʳ] *vt* CULIN hervir a fuego lento.
▶ *vi* CULIN hervir a fuego lento.

simple ['sɪmpəl] *adj* **1** *(gen)* sencillo,-a, simple: *a simple solution* una solución sencilla. **2** *(plain, pure, nothing more than)* sencillo,-a, puro,-a, mero,-a: *for the simple reason that...* por la sencilla razón que ...
ⓘ *comp* **simpler**, *comp* **simplest**.

simplicity [sɪmˈplɪsəti] n **1** (easiness, incomplexity) sencillez f, simplicidad f. **2** (lack of sophistication) sencillez f, naturalidad f.

simplify [ˈsɪmplɪfaɪ] vt simplificar.
ⓘ pt & pp simplified, ger simplifying.

simply [ˈsɪmplɪ] adv **1** (easily, plainly, modestly) simplemente, sencillamente: she lives very simply vive muy sencillamente. **2** (only) simplemente, solamente, solo; (just, merely) meramente: I simply don't know sencillamente, no lo sé. **3** (really, absolutely) francamente, realmente.

simulate [ˈsɪmjəleɪt] vt simular.

simultaneous [sɪməlˈteɪnɪəs] adj simultáneo,-a: simultaneous translation traducción simultánea.

sin [sɪn] n pecado.
▶ vi pecar (against, contra).
ⓘ pt & pp sinned, ger sinning.

since [sɪns] adv desde entonces: she arrived in 1988 and has lived here ever since llegó en 1988 y vive aquí desde entonces.
▶ prep desde: I've been here since four o'clock llevo aquí desde las cuatro.
▶ conj **1** (time) desde que: it's years since I went to the theatre hace años que no voy al teatro. **2** (because, seeing that) ya que, puesto que: since you're going to the shop ... ya que vas a la tienda ...

sincere [sɪnˈsɪəʳ] adj sincero,-a.

sincerely [sɪnˈsɪəlɪ] adv sinceramente.
ⓁⓄⒸ Yours sincerely (in letter) (le saluda) atentamente.

sincerity [sɪnˈserətɪ] n sinceridad f.

sinew [ˈsɪnjuː] n tendón m.

sing [sɪŋ] vt (gen) cantar.
▶ vi (person, bird) cantar; (wind, kettle, bullet) silbar; (ears, insect) zumbar.
ⓘ pt sang [sæŋ], pp sung [sʌŋ].

singer [ˈsɪŋəʳ] n (gen) cantante mf; (in choir) cantor,-ra: jazz singer cantante de jazz.

singing [ˈsɪŋɪŋ] n (act) canto, cantar m; (songs) canciones fpl: he loves singing in the shower le encanta cantar en la ducha.

single [ˈsɪŋɡəl] adj **1** (only one) solo,-a, único,-a: we heard a single scream oímos un solo grito. **2** (composed of one part) simple, sencillo,-a: single figures cifras de un solo dígito. **3** (for one person) indi-

vidual. **4** (separate, individual) cada: every single day todos los días. **5** (unmarried) soltero,-a. ⓁⓄⒸ in single file en fila india. ⒸⓄⓂⓅ single cream nata líquida. ▌ single parent **1** (mother) madre f soltera. **2** (father) padre m soltero. ▌ single room habitación f individual.
▶ n **1** GB (single ticket) billete m de ida, billete m sencillo. **2** (record) (disco) sencillo, single m.
▶ n pl singles SP (in tennis, badminton) individuales mpl.

single-parent [ˈsɪŋɡəlpeərənt] adj (family) monoparental.

singular [ˈsɪŋɡjʊləʳ] adj **1** (in grammar) singular. **2** fml (outstanding) extraordinario,-a.
▶ n LING singular m.

sinister [ˈsɪnɪstəʳ] adj siniestro,-a.

sink [sɪŋk] n (in kitchen) fregadero, pila; (in bathroom) lavabo, lavamanos m.
▶ vt **1** (ship) hundir. **2** fig (hopes, plans) acabar con.
▶ vi **1** (gen) hundirse. **2** (sun, moon) ponerse.
ⓘ pt sank [sæŋk], pp sunk [sʌŋk].

sinner [ˈsɪnəʳ] n pecador,-ra.

sip [sɪp] n sorbo.
▶ vt sorber, beber a sorbos.
ⓘ pt & pp sipped, ger sipping.

siphon [ˈsaɪfən] n sifón m.

sir [sɜːʳ] n **1** fml (gen) señor m: yes, sir sí, señor. **2** (title) sir m. ⓁⓄⒸ Dear Sir (in letter) muy señor mío, muy señores míos, estimado señor.

siren [ˈsaɪərən] n (gen) sirena.

sirloin [ˈsɜːlɔɪn] n solomillo.

sister [ˈsɪstəʳ] n **1** (relative) hermana. **2** (comrade) hermana, compañera.

sister-in-law [ˈsɪstərɪnlɔː] n cuñada.
ⓘ pl sisters-in-law.

sit [sɪt] vt **1** (child, etc) sentar (down, -): she sat him down on the table lo sentó en la mesa. **2** (room, hall, etc) tener cabida para; (table) ser para. **3** GB (exam) presentar a.
▶ vi **1** (action) sentarse (down, -): I sat next to Anna me senté junto a Anna. **2** (be seated) estar sentado,-a: they were sitting on the floor estaban sentados en el

suelo. **3** *(village, building)* estar, situarse; *(clothes)* sentar, quedar: *that dress sits well on you* aquel vestido te sienta bien.
▶ *vi fam (baby-sit)* hacer de canguro (for, a).

◆ **to sit back** *vi* **1** *(lean back)* recostarse; *(relax)* ponerse cómodo,-a. **2** *(take no active part)* cruzarse de brazos.

◆ **to sit out** *vt sep* **1** *(stay until end)* aguantar (hasta el final). **2** *(not dance)* no bailar.

◆ **to sit up** *vi* **1** *(in bed)* incorporarse (en la cama). **2** *(stay up late)* quedarse levantado,-a.
▶ *vt sep (child, etc)* sentar.
① *pt & pp* sat [sæt], *ger* sitting.

site [saɪt] *n (location)* situación *f*, emplazamiento, colocación *f*. COMP **archaeological site** yacimiento arqueológico.
▶ *vt* situar, ubicar, emplazar.

sit-in [ˈsɪtɪn] *n (protest)* sentada.

sitting [ˈsɪtɪŋ] *n (of meal)* turno; *(of committee, for portrait)* sesión *f*.
▶ *adj (position)* sentado,-a. COMP **sitting room** sala de estar.

situated [ˈsɪtjʊeɪtɪd] *adj (building, etc)* situado,-a, ubicado,-a.

situation [sɪtjʊˈeɪʃən] *n* **1** *(circumstances)* situación *f*: *we're in a difficult situation* estamos en una situación difícil. **2** *(location)* situación *f*, ubicación *f*.

sit-up [ˈsɪtʌp] *n* SP abdominal *m*.

six [sɪks] *adj* seis: *it costs six pounds* cuesta seis libras; *six hundred* seiscientos,-as; *six thousand* seis mil.
▶ *n* seis *m*: *she's six years old* tiene seis años; *it's six o'clock* son las seis.

sixteen [sɪksˈtiːn] *adj* dieciséis.
▶ *n* dieciséis *m*.

✎ Consulta también **six**.

sixteenth [sɪksˈtiːnθ] *adj* decimosexto,-a.
▶ *adv* en decimosexto lugar.
▶ *n* **1** *(in series)* decimosexto,-a. **2** *(fraction)* decimosexto; *(one part)* decimosexta parte *f*.

✎ Consulta también **sixth**.

sixth [sɪksθ] *adj* sexto,-a: *the sixth floor* la sexta planta, el sexto piso.
▶ *adv* sexto, en sexto lugar: *he came sixth* llegó en sexto lugar.
▶ *n* **1** *(in series)* sexto,-a; *(day)* el seis, el día seis: *the sixth of June* el seis de junio. **2** *(fraction)* sexto; *(one part)* sexta parte *f*. COMP **sixth form** GB ≈ segundo de bachillerato. ‖ **sixth form college** GB ≈ *instituto para estudiantes de segundo de bachillerato.*

sixtieth [ˈsɪkstɪəθ] *adj* sexagésimo,-a.
▶ *adv* en sexagésimo lugar.
▶ *n* **1** *(in series)* sexagésimo,-a. **2** *(fraction)* sexagésimo; *(one part)* sexagésima parte *f*.

sixty [ˈsɪkstɪ] *adj* sesenta: *there were about sixty people* había unas sesenta personas.
▶ *n* sesenta *m*.

size [saɪz] *n* **1** *(gen)* tamaño *f*; *(magnitude)* magnitud *f*: *it's the size of an egg* es del tamaño de un huevo. **2** *(of clothes)* talla; *(of shoes)* número; *(of person)* talla, estatura: *she's a size 12* gasta la talla 12.

skate¹ [skeɪt] *n* patín *m*.
▶ *vi* patinar.

skate² [skeɪt] *n (fish)* raya.

skateboard [ˈskeɪtbɔːd] *n* monopatín *m*.

skater [ˈskeɪtə'] *n* patinador,-ra.

skating [ˈskeɪtɪŋ] *n* patinaje *m*. COMP **ice skating** patinaje *m* sobre hielo. ‖ **skating rink** pista de patinaje.

skeleton [ˈskelɪtən] *n* **1** *(of person, animal)* esqueleto. **2** *(of building, ship)* armazón *m*, estructura.

sketch [sketʃ] *n* **1** *(drawing)* dibujo; *(preliminary drawing)* bosquejo, esbozo. **2** *(outline, rough idea)* esquema *m*, esbozo.
▶ *vt (draw)* dibujar; *(preliminary drawing)* bosquejar, hacer un bosquejo de.
▶ *vi* hacer bosquejos, hacer bocetos.

◆ **to sketch in/out**

skewer [ˈskjʊə'] *n* CULIN pincho, brocheta.

ski [skiː] *n (equipment)* esquí *m*.
▶ *vi* esquiar. LOC **to ski down** bajar esquiando. COMP **ski jump 1** *(slope)* pista de saltos, trampolín *m*. **2** *(competition)* saltos *mpl* de esquí. ‖ **ski lift** telesquí *m*.

ski resort estación *f* de esquí. **ski slope** pista de esquí.

skid [skɪd] *n* AUTO patinazo, derrapaje *m*. COMP **skid row** US barrios *mpl* bajos, barriadas *fpl*.

skier ['skiːəʳ] *n* esquiador,-ra.

skies [skaɪz] *pl* → **sky**.

skiing ['skiːɪŋ] *n* esquí *m*.

skilful ['skɪlfʊl] *adj (gen)* diestro,-a, hábil. LOC **to be skilful at STH** ser hábil para ALGO.

skilfully ['skɪlfʊlɪ] *adv* hábilmente.

skill [skɪl] *n* **1** *(ability)* habilidad *f*, destreza; *(talent)* talento, don *m*, dotes *fpl*. **2** *(technique)* técnica, arte *m*.
▶ *n pl* **skills** *(expertise)* capacidad *f sing*, aptitudes *fpl*: *a person with computer skills* una persona con algo informática.

skilled [skɪld] *adj* **1** *(specialized)* cualificado,-a, especializado,-a. **2** *(able)* hábil, diestro,-a; *(expert)* experto,-a.

skillful ['skɪlfʊl] *adj* US → **skilful**.

skillfully ['skɪlfʊlɪ] *adv* US → **skilfully**.

skimmed [skɪmd] *adj (milk)* desnatado,-a.

skimmer ['skɪməʳ] *n (spoon)* espumadera.

skin [skɪn] *n* **1** *(of person)* piel *f*; *(of face)* cutis *m*, piel *f*: *she has light/dark skin* tiene la piel clara/morena. **2** *(of animal)* piel *f*, pellejo. **3** *(of fruit, vegetable)* piel *f*. **4** *(on paint)* telilla, capa fina; *(on milk, custard, etc)* nata.

skinflint ['skɪnflɪnt] *n fam* tacaño,-a.

skinhead ['skɪnhed] *n* cabeza *mf* rapada, skin *mf*.

skinny ['skɪnɪ] *adj fam* flaco,-a.
ⓘ *comp* **skinnier**, *superl* **skinniest**.

skip¹ [skɪp] *n* salto, brinco.
▶ *vi* **1** *(move, jump)* saltar, brincar; *(with rope)* saltar a la comba. **2** *(jump, flit)* saltar.
▶ *vt (miss, omit)* saltarse: *she skipped a few pages* se saltó unas páginas.
ⓘ *pt & pp* **skipped**, *ger* **skipping**.

skip² [skɪp] *n (container)* contenedor *m*.

skipper ['skɪpəʳ] *n* **1** MAR patrón,-ona, capitán,-ana. **2** SP capitán,-ana.

skipping ['skɪpɪŋ] *n* COMP **skipping rope** comba, cuerda de saltar.

skirt [skɜːt] *n (garment)* falda.

skirting ['skɜːtɪŋ] [also **skirting board**] *n* GB zócalo, rodapié *m*.

skittle ['skɪtəl] *n (wooden pin)* bolo.
▶ *n pl* **skittles** bolos *mpl*, boliche *m sing*.

skull [skʌl] *n* **1** ANAT cráneo. **2** *(symbol)* calavera. COMP **skull and crossbones** bandera pirata.

skunk [skʌŋk] *n* ZOOL mofeta.

sky [skaɪ] *n (gen)* cielo; *(firmament)* firmamento.
ⓘ *pl* **skies**.

sky-blue ['skaɪbluː] *adj* azul celeste.

skylark ['skaɪlɑːk] *n* alondra.

skylight ['skaɪlaɪt] *n* tragaluz *m*, claraboya.

skyline ['skaɪlaɪn] *n* **1** *(horizon)* horizonte *m*. **2** *(of city)* perfil *m*.

skyscraper ['skaɪskreɪpəʳ] *n* rascacielos *m*.

slab [slæb] *n (of stone)* losa; *(of cake)* trozo; *(of chocolate)* tableta.

slack¹ [slæk] *adj* **1** *(not taut)* flojo,-a: *a slack rope* una cuerda floja. **2** *(careless, lax)* descuidado,-a. **3** *(not busy - trade, demand)* flojo,-a.
▶ *n (part of rope, wire, etc)* parte *f* floja.
◆ **to slack off**

slack² [slæk] *n (coal)* cisco.

slacken ['slækən] *vt* **1** *(rope, grip)* aflojar; *(reins)* soltar. **2** *(speed)* reducir, disminuir.
▶ *vi (speed)* reducirse, disminuir.

slalom ['slɑːləm] *n* SP slalom *m*, eslalon *m*.

slam [slæm] *n (of lid, book, etc)* golpe *m*; *(of door)* portazo.
▶ *vt* **1** *(shut forcefully)* cerrar de golpe: *she slammed the door in my face* me dio con la puerta en las narices. **2** *(throw noisily)* arrojar, lanzar. **3** *fig (criticize)* criticar duramente. **4** *(defeat)* dar una paliza a. LOC **to slam on the brakes** AUTO dar un frenazo. **to slam the phone down** colgar de golpe.
ⓘ *pt & pp* **slammed**, *ger* **slamming**.

slang [slæŋ] *n* argot *m*, jerga.
▶ *adj* de jerga, de argot.

slant [slɑ:nt] n **1** (gen) inclinación f. **2** (point of view) enfoque m, punto de vista.
▶ vt **1** (slope) inclinar. **2** fig (news, report, etc) presentar tendenciosamente.
▶ vi (slope) inclinarse.

slap [slæp] n (gen) palmada; (smack) cachete m; (in face) bofetada, bofetón m. COMP **a slap in the face** (rebuff) un desaire, una bofetada.
▶ adv **1** (straight) de lleno: we drove slap into a wall dimos de lleno contra una pared. **2** (right) justo.
▶ vt (gen) pegar (con la mano).
① pt & pp **slapped**, ger **slapping**.

slash [slæʃ] n **1** (with sword) tajo; (with knife) cuchillada. **2** fam (oblique) barra oblicua.
▶ vt **1** (with sword) dar un tajo a; (with knife) acuchillar, rajar. **2** fig (prices, wages) rebajar, reducir: prices slashed precios de remate.

slate [sleɪt] n (gen) pizarra. LOC **to wipe the slate clean** hacer borrón y cuenta nueva.

slaughter [ˈslɔ:tə'] n matanza.
▶ vt (animals) matar, sacrificar; (people) matar brutalmente.

slaughterhouse [ˈslɔ:təhaʊs] n matadero.

slave [sleɪv] n esclavo,-a. COMP **slave trade** trata de esclavos.

slavery [ˈsleɪvəri] n esclavitud f.

sledge [sledʒ] n GB trineo.
▶ vi ir en trineo.

sleep [sli:p] n sueño: I'm going to have a little sleep voy a dormir un poco. LOC **to go to sleep 1** (fall asleep) dormirse. **2** (become numb) dormirse, entumecerse.
▶ vi (gen) dormir: I slept well he dormido bien.
◆ **to sleep in** vi (sleep late) quedarse en la cama, dormir hasta tarde.
① pt & pp **slept** [slept].

sleeping [ˈsli:pɪŋ] adj durmiente, dormido,-a. COMP **sleeping bag** saco de dormir. ‖ **Sleeping Beauty** la Bella Durmiente. ‖ **sleeping car** coche cama m.

sleepless [ˈsli:pləs] adj insomne. LOC **to have a sleepless night** pasar la noche en blanco.

sleepy [ˈsli:pɪ] adj **1** (drowsy) soñoliento,-a. **2** (quiet, not busy) tranquilo,-a.
① comp **sleepier**, superl **sleepiest**.

sleet [sli:t] n aguanieve f.
▶ vi caer aguanieve.

sleeve [sli:v] n **1** (of garment) manga. **2** (of record) funda. LOC **to have STH up one's sleeve** guardarse una carta en la manga.

sleigh [sleɪ] n trineo. COMP **sleigh bell** cascabel m.

slender [ˈslendə'] adj **1** (person) delgado,-a, esbelto,-a. **2** fig (hope, chance) ligero,-a, remoto,-a; (income, majority) escaso,-a.
① comp **slenderer**, comp **slenderest**.

slept [slept] pt & pp → sleep.

slice [slaɪs] n **1** (of bread) rebanada; (thin - ham, etc) lonja, loncha; (- meat) tajada; (- of salami, lemon, etc) rodaja. **2** (portion - of cake, pie) porción f, trozo; (- of melon, etc) raja. **3** fig (share) parte f; (proportion) proporción f. COMP **sliced bread** pan m de molde.
▶ vt **1** (cut up) cortar a rebanadas, cortar a lonjas, cortar a rodajas: she sliced up the ham cortó el jamón en lonchas. **2** (cut off) cortar: can you slice me a piece of cake? ¿puedes cortarme un trozo de pastel?
◆ **to slick down** vt sep (hair) alisar.

slid [slɪd] pt & pp → slide.

slide [slaɪd] n **1** (act of sliding) deslizamiento, desliz m; (slip) resbalón m. **2** (in playground) tobogán m. **3** (photo) diapositiva. **4** (of microscope) platina, portaobjetos m. COMP **slide projector** proyector m de diapositivas.
▶ vt (gen) deslizar, pasar; (furniture) correr.
▶ vi **1** (slip deliberately) deslizar, deslizarse; (slip accidentally) resbalar: she slid on the ice resbaló en el hielo. **2** (move quietly) deslizarse: the drawer slid open el cajón se abrió con facilidad.
① pt & pp **slid** [slɪd].

slight [slaɪt] adj **1** (small in degree) pequeño,-a, ligero,-a; (not serious, unim-

portant) leve, insignificante: *a slight change of plan* un pequeño cambio de planes. **2** *(person)* menudo,-a. `LOC` **not in the slightest** en absoluto.

▶ *n (affront)* desaire *m*, desprecio.

slightly ['slaɪtlɪ] *adv (a little)* ligeramente, un poco, ALGO: *I know him slightly* apenas lo conozco. `LOC` **to be slightly built** ser de complexión menuda.

slim [slɪm] *adj* **1** *(person, build)* delgado,-a, esbelto,-a. **2** *(chance, hopes, prospect)* remoto,-a.

ⓘ *comp* **slimmer**, *superl* **slimmest**.

▶ *vi* adelgazar, hacer régimen: *I'm slimming* estoy a régimen.

ⓘ *pt & pp* **slimmed**, *ger* **slimming**.

sling [slɪŋ] *n* **1** MED cabestrillo. **2** *(catapult)* honda; *(child's)* tirador *m*. **3** *(device for lifting, carrying)* cuerda; *(for baby)* canguro.

▶ *vt* **1** *fam (throw)* tirar, arrojar: *sling it in the bin* tíralo a la basura. **2** *(lift, support)* colgar.

ⓘ *pt & pp* **slung** [slʌŋ].

slingshot ['slɪŋʃɒt] *n* tirachinas *m*.

slip [slɪp] *n* **1** *(slide)* resbalón *m*; *(trip)* traspiés *m*, tropezón *m*. **2** *(mistake)* error *m*, equivocación *f*; *(moral)* desliz *m*. **3** *(women's underskirt)* combinación *f*; *(petticoat)* enaguas *fpl*. `COMP` **a slip of the pen** un lapsus. ‖ **a slip of the tongue** un lapsus linguae.

▶ *vi* **1** *(slide)* resbalar; *(fall, get away, escape)* caer: *my foot slipped* se me fue el pie. **2** AUTO *(clutch, tyre)* patinar.

▶ *vt* **1** *(pass, give, put)* pasar, deslizar, dar a escondidas: *she slipped the note into her bag* disimuladamente metió la nota en el bolso. **2** *(overlook, forget)* escaparse.

◆ **to slip out** *vi (secret, comment, etc)* escaparse.

ⓘ *pt & pp* **slipped**, *ger* **slipping**.

slipper ['slɪpər] *n* zapatilla.

slippery ['slɪpərɪ] *adj (surface)* resbaladizo,-a

ⓘ *comp* **slipperier**, *superl* **slipperiest**.

slit [slɪt] *n (opening)* abertura, hendedura; *(cut)* corte *m*, raja: *light came*

through the slits in the blind entraba la luz por las ranuras de la persiana.

▶ *vt (cut)* cortar, rajar, hender.

ⓘ *pt & pp* **slit**, *ger* **slitting**.

slither ['slɪðər] *vi* deslizarse.

slogan ['sləʊgən] *n* eslogan *m*, lema *m*.

slope [sləʊp] *n* **1** *(incline)* cuesta, pendiente *f*; *(upward)* subida; *(downward)* bajada, declive *m*: *a steep slope* una cuesta empinada. **2** *(of mountain)* ladera, falda, vertiente *f*; *(of roof)* vertiente *f*.

▶ *vi* inclinarse.

sloppy ['slɒpɪ] *adj* **1** *(messy, careless - gen)* descuidado,-a; *(- manual work)* chapucero,-a; *(- appearance, dress)* desaliñado,-a, dejado,-a. **2** *(sentimental)* empalagoso,-a.

ⓘ *comp* **sloppier**, *superl* **sloppiest**.

slot [slɒt] *n* **1** *(for coin)* ranura; *(groove)* muesca; *(opening)* rendija, abertura. **2** *(programme)* espacio; *(position, place)* puesto, hueco. `COMP` **slot machine 1** *(vending machine)* distribuidor *m* automático. **2** *(for gambling)* máquina tragaperras.

▶ *vt (insert)* insertar, introducir: *slot the coin in the machine* insertar la moneda en la máquina.

ⓘ *pt & pp* **slotted**, *ger* **slotting**.

Slovak ['sləʊvæk] *adj* eslovaco,-a.

▶ *n* **1** *(person)* eslovaco,-a. **2** *(language)* eslovaco.

Slovakia [sləʊ'vækɪə] *n* Eslovaquia.

Slovene ['sləʊviːn] *adj* esloveno,-a.

▶ *n* **1** *(person)* esloveno,-a. **2** *(language)* esloveno.

Slovenia [sləʊ'viːnə] *n* Eslovenia.

slow [sləʊ] *adj* **1** *(gen)* lento,-a: *a slow recovery* una recuperación lenta. **2** *(clock, watch)* atrasado,-a: *my watch is slow* mi reloj va atrasado. **3** *(dull, not active)* aburrido,-a. **4** *(not quick to learn)* lento,-a, torpe; *(thick)* corto,-a de alcances: *he's a slow learner* le cuesta aprender. `COMP` **to be slow about/in doing** STH tardar en hacer ALGO.

▶ *adv* despacio, lentamente: *drive slow!* ¡conduce despacio!

▶ *vt (vehicle, machine)* reducir la marcha de.

S

▶ *vi (gen)* ir más despacio.

◆ **to slow down** *vt sep* hacer ir más despacio.

▶ *vi (gen)* ir más despacio.

slowdown ['sləʊdaʊn] *n* US *(workers)* huelga de celo.

slowly ['sləʊlɪ] *adv* despacio, lentamente.

sludge [slʌdʒ] *n* **1** *(mud)* fango, cieno, lodo, barro. **2** *(sewage)* aguas *fpl* residuales.

slug [slʌg] *n* ZOOL babosa.

slum [slʌm] *n* **1** *(place, house, etc)* casuca, casucha, tugurio. **2** *fam (tip)* pocilga.

▶ *vi fam* visitar los barrios bajos.

ⓘ *pt & pp* **slummed**, *ger* **slumming**.

▶ *n pl* **slums** *(area)* barrios *mpl* bajos.

slump [slʌmp] *n (recession)* crisis *f* económica; *(drop in demand, etc)* bajón *m*, baja repentina.

slung [slʌŋ] *pt & pp* → **sling**.

slurp [slɜːp] *vt* sorber ruidosamente.

sly [slaɪ] *adj* **1** *(cunning)* astuto,-a, ladino,-a; *(deceitful)* tramposo,-a. **2** *(secretive, knowing)* furtivo,-a: *a sly smile* una sonrisa maliciosa. **3** *(mischievous, playful)* travieso,-a, pícaro,-a. [LOC] **on the sly** a escondidas.

ⓘ *comp* **slyer** o **slier**, *superl* **slyest** o **sliest**.

smack¹ [smæk] *n* **1** *(slap)* bofetada, tortazo, azote *m*; *(blow)* golpe *m*. **2** *fam (loud kiss)* besote *m*, beso sonoro.

▶ *vt* **1** *(slap)* dar una bofetada a, abofetear, pegar a. **2** *(strike)* golpear.

smack² [smæk] *n* **1** *(flavour)* sabor *m*; *(smell)* olor *m*. **2** *(hint, suggestion)* pizca.

small [smɔːl] *adj* **1** *(not large)* pequeño, -a, chico,-a: *we live in a small flat* vivimos en un piso pequeño. **2** *(in height)* bajo,-a, pequeño,-a: *he's a small man* es un hombre bajito. **3** *(young)* joven, pequeño,-a: *when I was small* cuando era pequeño. [LOC] **in the small hours** a altas horas de la madrugada. ‖ [COMP] **small ads** anuncios *mpl* por palabras, pequeños anuncios *mpl*. ‖ **small change** cambio, monedas *fpl* sueltas. ‖ **small letter** letra minúscula. ‖ **small print** letra pequeña.

ⓘ *comp* **smaller**, *comp* **smallest**.

▶ *adv* pequeño: *cut it up small* córtalo en trocitos.

smallpox ['smɔːlpɒks] *n* viruela.

smart [smɑːt] *adj* **1** *(elegant)* elegante, fino,-a; *(chic)* fino,-a, de buen tono. **2** US *(clever)* listo,-a, inteligente; *(sharp)* agudo,-a, vivo,-a; *(impudent)* fresco,-a, descarado,-a: *he thinks he's so smart* se cree muy listo. **3** *(quick, brisk)* rápido,-a, ligero,-a.

smash [smæʃ] *n* **1** *(noise)* estrépito, estruendo. **2** *(collision)* choque *m* violento, colisión *f*. **3** *(blow)* golpe *m*. **4** SP *(tennis)* smash *m*, mate *m*. **5** *(success, hit)* exitazo, gran éxito. [COMP] **smash hit** gran éxito, exitazo.

▶ *vt* **1** *(break)* romper; *(shatter)* hacer pedazos, hacer añicos; *(destroy - car, room, etc)* destrozar: *the vandals smashed the place up* los vándalos destrozaron el local. **2** *(hit forcefully)* romper; *(crash, throw violently)* estrellar (into, contra). **3** *(defeat)* vencer, aplastar; *(destroy)* destrozar. **4** SP *(in tennis)* hacer un mate.

▶ *vi* **1** *(break)* romperse; *(shatter)* hacerse añicos: *the mirror smashed into tiny pieces* el espejo se hizo añicos. **2** *(crash)* estrellarse (into, contra), chocar (into, contra).

smashing ['smæʃɪŋ] *adj* GB *fam* estupendo,-a, fantástico,-a, genial, fenomenal.

smear [smɪər] *n* **1** *(smudge, stain)* mancha. **2** *fig (defamation)* calumnia.

▶ *vt* **1** *(spread - butter, ointment)* untar; *(-grease, paint)* embadurnar: *he smeared butter on the bread* untó el pan con mantequilla. **2** *(make dirty)* manchar. **3** *fig (defame)* calumniar, difamar.

smell [smel] *n* **1** *(sense)* olfato. **2** *(odour)* olor *m*; *(perfume)* perfume *m*, aroma *m*.

▶ *vt* **1** oler. **2** *fig* olfatear.

▶ *vi* **1** oler. **2** *(have particular smell)* oler (a).

ⓘ *pt & pp* **smelled** o **smelt** [smelt].

smelly ['smelɪ] *adj* apestoso,-a, maloliente.

smelt¹ [smelt] *vt (melt)* fundir.

smelt² [smelt] *pp* → **smell**.

smile [smaɪl] *n* sonrisa.

▶ *vi (gen)* sonreír.

▶ *vt (say with a smile)* decir sonriendo.
◆ **to smile on** *vi* sonreír a.

smiley ['smaɪlɪ] *n* COMPUT emoticón *m*.

smith [smɪθ] *n* herrero,-a.

smog [smɒg] *n* niebla tóxica, smog *m*.

smoke [sməʊk] *n* **1** *(gen)* humo. **2** *fam (cigarette)* cigarrillo, cigarro, pitillo.
▶ *vt* **1** *(person)* fumar. **2** *(meat, fish)* ahumar.
▶ *vi* **1** *(person)* fumar. **2** *(fire, chimney, etc)* echar humo, humear.

smoker ['sməʊkəʳ] *n* **1** *(person)* fumador,-ra. **2** *(on train)* vagón *m* de fumadores.

smoking ['sməʊkɪŋ] *adj* humeante.
▶ *n* fumar *m*.

smoky ['sməʊkɪ] *adj* lleno,-a de humo.
ⓘ *comp* smokier, *comp* smokiest.

smooth [smuːð] *adj* **1** *(surface, texture, tyre)* liso,-a; *(skin)* suave; *(road)* llano,-a, uniforme; *(sea)* tranquilo,-a, en calma. **2** *(liquid mixture, sauce)* sin grumos. **3** *(wine, beer, etc)* suave.
▶ *vt (gen)* alisar; *(with sandpaper)* lijar; *(polish)* pulir.

smother ['smʌðəʳ] *vt* **1** *(asphyxiate)* asfixiar, ahogar. **2** *(put out - fire)* sofocar, extinguir, apagar. **3** *(stifle - yawn, cough, laughter)* contener, reprimir; *(suppress - opposition)* acallar. **4** *(cover)* cubrir (in/with, de); *(heap)* colmar (in/with, de).
▶ *vi (asphyxiate)* asfixiarse, ahogarse.

smudge [smʌdʒ] *n (stain - gen)* mancha; *(- of ink)* borrón *m*.
▶ *vt (gen)* manchar; *(writing)* emborronar.
▶ *vi (ink, paint, etc)* correrse.

smuggle ['smʌgəl] *vt* **1** *(illegally)* pasar de contrabando. **2** *(sneak)* pasar a escondidas.

smuggler ['smʌgləʳ] *n* contrabandista *mf*.

snack [snæk] *n (light meal)* bocado, piscolabis *m*, tentempié *m*, refrigerio *m*; *(in afternoon)* merienda.
▶ *vi* comer, comerse. LOC **to have a snack** picar ALGO. COMP **snack bar** cafetería.

▶ *n pl* **snacks** *(gen)* cosas *fpl* para picar; *(in bar)* tapas *fpl*.

snail [sneɪl] *n* caracol *m*.

snake [sneɪk] *n (big)* serpiente *f*; *(small)* culebra.
▶ *vi fig (river, road, etc)* serpentear.

snap [snæp] *n* **1** *(sharp noise)* ruido seco; *(of fingers, branch)* chasquido. **2** *fam (snapshot)* foto *f*, instantánea.
▶ *vt* **1** *(break)* partir en dos, romper en dos. **2** *(close)* cerrar de golpe. **3** *(click)* chasquear. **4** *(say sharply)* decir bruscamente.
▶ *vi* **1** *(break)* romperse, partirse. **2** *fig (person)* perder los nervios, sufrir una crisis nerviosa. **3** *(speak sharply)* regañar (at, a), hablar con brusquedad (at, a).
ⓘ *pt & pp* snapped, *ger* snapping.

⊕ **Snap** es también un juego de cartas en el que los jugadores van poniendo cartas sobre la mesa, y si salen dos del mismo número el primero que cante snap se las lleva todas. El que se quede sin cartas es eliminado; gana el que queda cuando los demás están eliminados.

snapshot ['snæpʃɒt] *n* foto *f*, instantánea.

snarl [snɑːl] *n (growl)* gruñido.
▶ *vi (growl)* gruñir (at, a).
▶ *vt (say)* gruñir.

snatch [snætʃ]
vt **1** *(grab)* arrebatar, arrancar, coger; *(steal)* robar; *(kidnap)* secuestrar. **2** *(sleep, food, etc)* coger, pillar; *(opportunity, etc)* aprovechar.
▶ *vi* arrebatar, quitar.

sneak [sniːk] *n fam* acusica *mf*, acusón,-ona, chivato,-a, soplón,-ona.
▶ *vt (take out)* sacar (a escondidas); *(take in)* pasar (a escondidas), colar (de extranjis).
▶ *vi* **1** *(move)* moverse sigilosamente. **2** *(tell tales)* acusar (on, a), chivarse (on, de).

sneakers ['sniːkəz] *n pl* US zapatillas *fpl* de deporte.

sneer [snɪəʳ] *n* **1** *(look)* cara de desprecio; *(smile)* sonrisa burlona. **2** *(remark)* comentario desdeñoso.

S

▶ vi (mock) burlarse (at, de), mofarse (at, de); (scorn) desdeñar, despreciar.

sneeze [sni:z] n estornudo.
▶ vi estornudar.

sniff [snɪf] n 1 aspiración. 2 (inhalation) aspiración f (por la nariz), inhalación f.
▶ vt 1 (person - gen) oler; (animal) olfatear, husmear. 3 (drugs) esnifar.
◆ **to snip off** vt sep cortar con tijeras.

snob [snɒb] n esnob mf.

snooker ['snu:kər] n snooker m.

snoop [snu:p] vi 1 (search, investigate) husmear, fisgar. 2 (pry) entrometerse, meterse (into, en).
▶ n (person) fisgón,-ona.

snooze [snu:z] n fam cabezada, siestecilla.
▶ vi fam dormitar, echar una cabezada.

snore [snɔ:ʳ] n ronquido.
▶ vi roncar.

snorkel ['snɔ:kəl] n (of swimmer) tubo de respiración; (of submarine) esnórquel m.
▶ vi bucear con tubo de respiración.
ⓘ pt & pp snorkelled (US snorkeled), ger snorkelling (US snorkeling).

snorkelling ['snɔ:kəlɪŋ] n buceo (con tubo de respiración).

snort [snɔ:t] vi 1 (make noise - person) resoplar, bufar; (- animal) resoplar. 2 (say angrily, etc) bramar, gruñir.
▶ vt (drugs) esnifar.
▶ n 1 (person) resoplido, bufido; (animal) resoplido. 2 fam (drink) trago.

snout [snaut] n 1 (of animal) morro, hocico. 2 GB fam (of person) napias mf, narizotas mf. 3 (of gun, bottle, etc) morro. 4 GB sl (tobacco) tabaco. 5 GB sl (informer) soplón,-ona, chivato,-a.

snow [snəu] n 1 METEOR (gen) nieve f; (snowfall) nevada. 2 TV nieve f.
▶ vi nevar: it's snowing está nevando.

snowball ['snəubɔ:l] n bola de nieve.

snowboard ['snəubɔ:d] n snowboard.

snowdrop ['snəudrɒp] n BOT campanilla de invierno.

snowflake ['snəufleɪk] n copo de nieve.

snowman ['snəumæn] n muñeco de nieve.

snowplough ['snəuplau] n quitanieves m.

snowshoe ['snəuʃu:] n raqueta (de nieve).

snowstorm ['snəustɔ:m] n tormenta de nieve.

snowy ['snəuɪ] adj de nieve, nevado,-a.
ⓘ comp snowier, superl snowiest.
◆ **to snuff out** vt sep (rebellion) sofocar; (hopes) acabar con.

so [səu] conj 1 (therefore) así que, por lo tanto, de manera que. 2 (to express purpose) para, para que.
▶ adv 1 (introductory) así que, pues, bueno: so you've decided to come así que has decidido venir. 2 (very - before adj or adv) tan; (- before noun or with verb) tanto,-a: she's so bored está tan aburrida. 3 (unspecified number or amount, limit) tanto,-a: I can only do so much no puedo hacer más. 4 (thus, in this way) así, de esta manera, de este modo: he's about so tall es así de alto. 5 (to avoid repetition) que sí: I think/hope so creo/espero que sí. 6 (to express agreement, also) también: so am I/so do I/so can I/so have I yo también.
▶ adj (factual, true) así: it can't be so no puede ser. LOC and so on (and so forth) y así sucesivamente. I if so de ser así. I or so más o menos. I so far hasta ahora. I so long! ¡hasta luego! I so many tantos,-as. I so much tanto. I so much for STH: so much for your advice! ¡vaya consejo que me diste! I so that para que. I so what? ¿y qué?

soak [səuk] vt (put in liquid) poner en remojo, remojar; (saturate) empapar.
▶ vi 1 (washing, dried pulses) estar en remojo. 2 (bathe) bañarse. 3 (penetrate, empapar, calar.
▶ n 1 remojón m. 2 fam (drunkard) borracho,-a.

soap [səup] n jabón m: a bar/cake/tablet o soap una pastilla de jabón. COMP soap opera culebrón m, telenovela. I soap powder detergente m en polvo.
▶ vt enjabonar, jabonar.

soar [sɔːʳ] vi **1** *(bird, plane - fly)* volar; *(- rise)* remontar el vuelo, remontarse; *(- glide)* planear. **2** *fig (prices, costs, etc)* dispararse. **3** *(building)* elevarse, alzarse.

sob [sɒb] n sollozo.
▶ vi sollozar.
▶ vt decir sollozando, decir entre sollozos.
ⓘ pt & pp **sobbed**, ger **sobbing**.

sober ['səʊbəʳ] adj **1** *(not drunk)* sobrio,-a. **2** *(person)* serio,-a, formal; *(attitude)* sobrio,-a, moderado,-a, sensato,-a. **3** *(colour)* discreto,-a, sobrio,-a.

so-called ['səʊkɔːld] adj llamado,-a, supuesto,-a.

soccer ['sɒkəʳ] n fútbol m.

⊕ El soccer es la denominación que se utiliza en Estados Unidos para hablar nuestro fútbol. La palabra football está reservada al fútbol americano, uno de los deportes rey del país.

sociable ['səʊʃəbəl] adj sociable.

social ['səʊʃᵊl] adj **1** *(gen)* social. **2** *fam (sociable)* sociable.
▶ n *(informal meeting)* acto social, reunión f (social); *(party)* fiesta; *(dance)* baile m.

socialism ['səʊʃəlɪzəm] n socialismo.

socialist ['səʊʃəlɪst] adj & n socialista mf.

socialize ['səʊʃᵊlaɪz] vi *(mix socially)* relacionarse, alternar; *(at party)* mezclarse con la gente, hacer vida social.
▶ vt **1** TECH *(adapt to society)* socializar. **2** US *(nationalize)* nacionalizar.

society [sə'saɪətɪ] n **1** *(community, people)* sociedad f. **2** *(fashionable group, upper class)* (alta) sociedad f. **3** *(organization, club)* sociedad f, asociación f, club m, círculo m. **4** *fml (company)* compañía.
ⓘ pl **societies**.

sociology [səʊsɪ'ɒlədʒɪ] n sociología.

sock [sɒk] n calcetín m.

socket ['sɒkɪt] n **1** ANAT *(of eye)* cuenca, órbita; *(of joint)* glena. **2** ELEC *(for plug)* enchufe m, toma de corriente; *(for light bulb)* portalámparas m. COMP **socket wrench** llave f de tubo.

soda ['səʊdə] n **1** CHEM sosa, soda. **2** *(soda water)* soda, sifón m. **3** US *(pop)* refresco. **4** *(ice-cream soda)* soda con helado y almíbar.

sodium ['səʊdɪəm] n CHEM sodio. COMP **sodium bicarbonate** bicarbonato sódico.

sofa ['səʊfə] n sofá m.

soft [sɒft] adj **1** *(not hard)* blando,-a; *(spongy)* esponjoso,-a; *(flabby)* fofo,-a. **2** *(skin, hair, fur, etc)* suave. **3** *(light, music, colour)* suave; *(words)* tierno,-a; *(breeze, steps, knock)* ligero,-a; *(outline)* difuminado,-a; *(voz)* baja. **4** *fam (easy)* fácil. COMP **soft copy** datos mpl contenidos en la memoria del ordenador. ▌ **soft drink** refresco. ▌ **soft palate** velo del paladar.

soft-boiled ['sɒft'bɔɪld] adj *(egg)* pasado por agua.

soften ['sɒfᵊn] vt suavizar, ablandar.
▶ vi *(leather, heart, butter)* ablandarse; *(skin)* suavizarse.

softener ['sɒfənəʳ] n suavizante m.

software ['sɒftweəʳ] n COMPUT software m.

soggy ['sɒgɪ] adj **1** *(wet)* empapado,-a, saturado,-a. **2** *(too soft)* pastoso,-a, gomoso,-a.
ⓘ comp **soggier**, superl **soggiest**.

soil [sɔɪl] n **1** *(earth)* tierra. **2** *fml (country, territory)* tierra.
▶ vt **1** *(dirty)* ensuciar; *(stain)* manchar. **2** *fig (reputation)* manchar.
▶ vi ensuciarse.

soiled [sɔɪld] adj *(dirty)* sucio,-a; *(stained)* manchado,-a.

solar ['səʊlə] adj solar. COMP **solar cell** célula solar. ▌ **solar corona** corona solar. ▌ **solar energy** energía solar. ▌ **solar plexus** plexo solar.▌ **solar year** año solar. ▌ the **solar system** el sistema m solar.

sold [slept] pt & pp → **sell**.

solder ['sɒldəʳ] n soldadura.
▶ vt soldar.

soldier ['səʊldʒəʳ] n *(not officer)* soldado; *(military man)* militar m. COMP **a soldier of fortune** un mercenario.

sole¹ [səʊl] n *(fish)* lenguado.

S

sole² [səʊl] *adj* **1** *(only, single)* único,-a. **2** *(exclusive)* exclusivo,-a.

sole³ [səʊl] *n* *(of foot)* planta; *(of shoe, sock)* suela.
▸ *vt* poner suela a.

solicitor [səˈlɪsɪtəʳ] *n* **1** GB abogado,-a. **2** US oficial *mf* de justicia.

solid [ˈsɒlɪd] *adj* **1** *(not liquid or gas)* sólido,-a. **2** *(not hollow)* macizo,-a. **3** *(dense, compact)* compacto,-a. **4** *(unmixed)* puro,-a, macizo,-a. **5** *(strong)* sólido,-a, fuerte. **6** *(reliable)* sólido,-a, de confianza, de fiar. **7** *(unanimous)* unánime. **8** *(continuous)* seguido,-a, entero, -a; *(unbroken)* continuo,-a. **9** TECH *(three-dimensional)* tridimensional.
▸ *n* *(substance)* sólido.

solidarity [sɒlɪˈdærətɪ] *n* solidaridad *f*.

solidification [səlɪdɪfɪˈkeɪ[ə]n] *n* solidificación *f*.

solidify [səˈlɪdɪfaɪ] *vt* solidificar.
▸ *vi* solidificarse.
① *pt & pp* **solidified**, *ger* **solidifying**.

solitary [ˈsɒlɪt[ə]rɪ] *adj* **1** *(alone)* solitario, -a. **2** *(secluded, remote)* apartado,-a, retirado,-a. **3** *(only, sole)* solo,-a, único,-a.

solitude [ˈsɒlɪtjuːd] *n* soledad *f*.

solo [ˈsəʊləʊ] *n* **1** MUS solo. **2** AV vuelo en solitario. **3** *(card game)* solitario.
① *pl* **solos**.
▸ *adj* **1** MUS *(performance, album)* en solitario; *(instrument)* solo; *(piece)* para solista. **2** *(attempt, flight)* en solitario.
▸ *adv* **1** MUS *(play, sing)* solo,-a. **2** *(fly)* en solitario.

soloist [ˈsəʊləʊɪst] *n* MUS solista *mf*.

solstice [ˈsɒlstɪs] *n* solsticio.

soluble [ˈsɒljəbəl] *adj* soluble.

solution [səˈljuːʃən] *n* solución *m*.

solve [sɒlv] *vt* *(problem)* resolver, solucionar; *(case, equation)* resolver.

solvent [ˈsɒlvənt] *adj* **1** *(not in debt)* solvente. **2** *(that can dissolve)* soluble.
▸ *n* solvente *m*, disolvente *m*.

Somali [səˈmɑːlɪ] *adj* somalí.
▸ *n* somalí *mf*.

Somalia [səˈmɑːlɪə] *n* Somalia.

some [sʌm] *adj* **1** *(with plural noun)* unos, -as, algunos,-as; *(a few)* unos,-as

cuantos,-as, unos,-as pocos,-as: *there were some flowers on the table* había unas flores en la mesa. **2** *(with singular noun)* algún, alguna; *(a little)* algo de, un poco de: *would you like some coffee?* ¿quieres un poco de café? **3** *(certain)* cierto,-a, alguno,-a: *some days are better than others* algunos días son mejores que otros. **4** *(unknown, unspecified)* algún, alguna: *some day* un día de éstos. **5** *(quite a lot of)* bastante: *she's been gone some time* hace ya bastante tiempo que se ha ido. **6** *fam iron (none, not at all)* valiente, menudo,-a: *some help that was!* ¡valiente ayuda! **7** *fam (quite a, a fine)* menudo,-a: *that was some meal!* ¡menuda comida!
▸ *pron* **1** *(unspecified number)* unos,-as, algunos,-as: *I'll have to buy some potatoes* tendré que comprar patatas. **2** *(unspecified amount)* no se traduce: *if you want more paper, there's some in the drawer* si te hace falta más papel, hay en el cajón. **3** *(certain ones)* ciertos,-as, algunos,-as; *(a certain part)* algo, un poco, parte *f*: *some of my friends* algunos amigos míos.
▸ *adv* **1** *(approximately, about)* unos,-as, alrededor de, aproximadamente: *there were some twenty people* había unas veinte personas. **2** US *fam (rather, a little)* un poco: *they waited some* esperaron un poco.

somebody [ˈsʌmbədɪ] *pron* alguien: *somebody must have lost it* alguien debe haberlo perdido. LOC **somebody else** otro,-a, otra persona.

somehow [ˈsʌmhaʊ] *adv* **1** *(in some way)* de algún modo, de alguna manera. **2** *(for some reason)* por alguna razón.

someone [ˈsʌmwʌn] *pron* → **somebody**.

someplace [ˈsʌmpleɪs] *adv* US → **somewhere**.

somersault [ˈsʌməsɔːlt] *n* *(by acrobat)* salto mortal; *(by child)* voltereta; *(by car)* vuelta de campana.
▸ *vi* *(acrobat)* dar un salto mortal; *(child)* dar volteretas; *(car)* dar una vuelta de campana.

something [ˈsʌmθɪŋ] *pron* **1** algo. **2** *(a thing of value)* algo. **3** *(in vague or ill-defined statements)* algo.

▶ *adv*: it costs something like 100 pounds cuesta unas cien libras.

sometime ['sʌmtaɪm] *adv* algún día.
▶ *adj fml (former)* antiguo,-a, ex-.

sometimes ['sʌmtaɪmz] *adv* a veces, de vez en cuando.

somewhat ['sʌmwɒt] *adv* algo, un tanto.

somewhere ['sʌmweə'] *adv* 1 *(in some place)* en alguna parte; *(to some place)* a alguna parte. 2 *(approximately)* más o menos, alrededor de.
▶ *pron* un lugar, un sitio. LOC **somewhere else 1** *(in)* en otra parte, en otro sitio. 2 *(to)* a otra parte, a otro sitio.

son [sʌn] *n* hijo.

song [sɒŋ] *n (gen)* canción *f*; *(art, of bird)* canto.

songbird ['sɒŋbɜːd] *n* pájaro cantor, ave *f* canora.

songbook ['sɒŋbʊk] *n* cancionero.

songwriter ['sɒŋraɪtə'] *n* compositor, -ra (de canciones).

son-in-law ['sʌnɪnlɔː] *n* yerno.
ⓘ *pl* sons-in-law.

soon [suːn] *adv* 1 *(within a short time)* pronto, dentro de poco. 2 *(early)* pronto, temprano. 3 *(expressing preference, readiness, willingness)*: I'd (just) as soon eat in as... preferiría comer en casa que… LOC **as soon as** tan pronto como. ∎ **as soon as possible** cuanto antes. ∎ **soon afterwards** poco después.

sooner ['suːnə'] *adv* 1 *(earlier)* más temprano. 2 *(rather)* antes. LOC **no sooner said than done** dicho y hecho. ∎ **sooner or later** tarde o temprano. ∎ **the sooner the better** cuanto antes mejor.

soot [sʊt] *n* hollín *m*.

soothe [suːð] *vt* 1 *(calm)* calmar, tranquilizar, aplacar; *(quieten)* acallar. 2 *(ease pain)* aliviar, calmar.

sorcerer ['sɔːsərə'] *n* hechicero, brujo.

sorcery ['sɔːsərɪ] *n* hechicería, brujería.

sore [sɔː'] *adj* 1 *(aching)* dolorido,-a; *(painful)* doloroso,-a; *(inflamed)* inflamado,-a. 2 US *fam (angry)* enfadado,-a (about, por), picado,-a (about, por).

3 *lit (great)* enorme, gran; *(serious)* grave; *(urgent)* urgente.
▶ *n* MED llaga, úlcera.

sorrow ['sɒrəʊ] *n* 1 *(grief)* pena, pesar *m*, dolor *m*. 2 *(cause of sadness)* disgusto.
▶ *vi* llorar (at/over/for, por).

sorry ['sɒrɪ] *adj (pitiful, wretched)* triste, lamentable. LOC **to be sorry** *(grieved, feeling sadness)* sentir. ∎ **to feel sorry for SB** compadecer. ∎ **to say sorry** disculparse, pedir perdón.
ⓘ *comp* sorrier, *superl* sorriest.
▶ *interj* 1 *(apology)* ¡perdón!, ¡disculpe! 2 GB *(for repetition)* ¿perdón?, ¿cómo?

sort [sɔːt] *n* 1 *(type, kind)* clase *f*, tipo, género, suerte *f*; *(make, brand)* marca. 2 *fam (person)* tipo,-a, tío,-a. LOC **a sort of** una especie de. ∎ **of a sort / of sorts** una especie de. ∎ **nothing of the sort** nada semejante. ∎ **sort of** en cierto modo.
▶ *vt* 1 *(classify)* clasificar. 2 *(repair)* arreglar.
▶ *vi (check)* revisar (through, -).
◆ **to sort out** *vt sep* 1 *(classify)* clasificar; *(put in order)* ordenar, poner en orden. 2 *(separate)* separar (from, de). 3 *(solve - problem)* arreglar, solucionar; *(- misunderstanding)* aclarar. 4 *(arrange)* organizar, arreglar; *(set - date)* fijar. 5 *(deal with - person)* meter en vereda.

so-so ['səʊsəʊ] *adv fam* así así, regular.

sought [sɔːt] *pt & pp* → **seek**.

soul [səʊl] *n* 1 REL alma, espíritu *m*. 2 *(spirit)* espíritu *m*; *(feeling, character)* carácter *m*, personalidad *f*. 3 *(person)* alma, persona. 4 MUS soul *m*, música soul.

sound¹ [saʊnd] *adj* 1 *(healthy)* sano,-a. 2 *(solid)* sólido,-a, firme; *(in good condition)* en buen estado. 3 *(sensible)* sensato,-a, acertado,-a; *(valid)* sólido,-a, lógico,-a, razonable; *(responsible)* responsable, formal, de fiar; *(reliable, safe)* seguro,-a. 4 *(thorough)* completo,-a; *(severe)* severo,-a. 5 *(of sleep)* profundo,-a. LOC **to be sound asleep** estar dormido como un tronco.

sound² [saʊnd] *vt* 1 MAR sondar. 2 MED *(gen)* sondar; *(chest)* auscultar.
▶ *n* MED sonda.

sound³ [saʊnd] *n* GEOG estrecho, brazo de mar.

sound⁴ [saʊnd] *n* **1** (gen) sonido; (noise) ruido. **2** TV (volume) volumen *m.* **3** (impression, idea) idea. COMP **sound effects** efectos sonoros.
   ► *vt* **1** (bell, horn, trumpet) tocar, hacer sonar; (alarm) dar (la señal de); (retreat) tocar. **2** LING pronunciar.
   ► *vi* **1** (bell, horn, alarm, etc) sonar, resonar. **2** (seem) parecer; (give impression) sonar. **3** LING pronunciarse, sonar.

soundtrack ['saʊndtræk] *n* banda sonora.

soup [suːp] *n* CULIN (gen) sopa; (clear, thin) caldo, consomé *m.*

sour ['saʊər] *adj* **1** (fruit) ácido,-a, agrio, -a; (milk) cortado,-a, agrio,-a; (wine) agrio,-a. **2** (person) amargado,-a, avinagrado,-a; (behaviour, expression) agrio,-a, avinagrado,-a.
   ► *vt* **1** (milk) agriar, cortar. **2** (person, relationship) amargar.
   ► *vi* **1** (milk) agriarse, cortarse; (wine) agriarse. **2** (person, character) amargarse, avinagrarse.

source [sɔːs] *n* **1** (of river) fuente *f,* nacimiento. **2** (origin, cause) fuente *f,* origen *m.*

south [saʊθ] *n* sur *m.*
   ► *adj* sur, del sur, meridional. COMP **South American** sudamericano,-a. **the South Pole** el Polo Sur.
   ► *adv* (direction) hacia el sur; (location) al sur.
   ► *n* **the South** el Sur *m,* el sur *m.*

southeast [saʊθiːst] *n* sudeste *m.*
   ► *adj* sudeste, del sudeste.
   ► *adv* (direction) hacia el sudeste; (location) al sudeste.

southern ['sʌðᵊn] *adj* del sur, meridional, austral. COMP **Southern Europe** Europa del Sur.

southward ['saʊθwəd] *adj* hacia el sur, en dirección sur.
   ► *adv* al sur, hacia el sur.

southwards ['saʊθwədz] *adv* (direction) hacia el sur; (location) al sur.

southwest [saʊθwest] *n* suroeste *m.*
   ► *adj* suroeste, del suroeste.
   ► *adv* al suroeste, hacia el suroeste.

souvenir [suːvəˈnɪər] *n* recuerdo (of, de).

sovereign ['sɒvrɪn] *n* **1** soberano,-a. **2** GB (coin) soberano.
   ► *adj* soberano,-a.

sow¹ [saʊ] *n* ZOOL cerda, puerca.

sow² [səʊ] *vt* (gen) sembrar (with, de).
   ⓘ *pt* sowed, *pp* sowed o sown [səʊn].

sown [səʊn] *pp* → sow.

soy [sɔɪ] *n* US soja.

soya ['sɔɪə] *n* GB soja. COMP **soya bean** soja.

spa [spaː] *n* **1** (resort) balneario; (baths) baños *mpl,* termas *fpl.* **2** US (jacuzzi) jacuzzi *m.* **3** US (gymnasium) gimnasio.

space [speɪs] *n* **1** PHYS espacio. **2** (continuous expanse) espacio. **3** (room, unoccupied area) espacio, sitio, lugar *m.* **4** (gap, empty place) espacio, hueco. **5** (in time) espacio, lapso. COMP **space lab** laboratorio espacial. **space probe** sonda espacial. **space ship** nave *f* espacial. **space shuttle** transbordador *m* espacial.

space-bar ['speɪsbaːʳ] *n* barra espaciadora *m.*

spacecraft ['speɪskraːft] *n* nave *f* espacial.
   ⓘ *pl* spacecraft.

spaceship ['speɪsʃɪp] *n* nave *f* espacial.

spade¹ [speɪd] *n* (playing card - international pack) pica; (- Spanish pack) espada.

spade² [speɪd] *n* (for digging) pala.

   ☒ Spade no significa 'espada', que se traduce por sword.

spaghetti [spəˈgetɪ] *n* espagueti *m.*

Spain [speɪn] *n* España.

span¹ [spæn] *pt* → spin.

span² [spæn] *n* **1** (of wings) envergadura; (of arch, bridge) luz *f,* ojo; (of hand) palmo. **2** (of time) período, lapso.
   ► *vt* **1** (cross) atravesar, cruzar. **2** (extend over) abarcar, extenderse a.
   ⓘ *pt & pp* spanned, *ger* spanning.

Spaniard ['spænjəd] *n* (person) español,-la.

Spanish ['spænɪʃ] *adj* español,-la. [COMP] **Spanish America** Hispanoamérica. ▮ **Spanish guitar** guitarra clásica.
▶ *n* **1** *(person)* español,-la. **2** *(language)* español *m*, castellano.
▶ *n pl* **the Spanish** los españoles *mpl*.

spanner ['spænə^r] *n* llave *f* de tuerca.

spare [speə^r] *adj* **1** *(reserve)* de repuesto; *(free)* libre; *(extra)* de sobra. **2** *(thin, lean)* enjuto,-a.
▶ *n* *(spare part)* recambio, repuesto. [COMP] **spare room** habitación *f* de invitados. ▮ **spare time** tiempo libre. ▮ **spare tyre 1** *(wheel)* rueda de recambio. **2** *(stomach)* michelín *m*. ▮ **spare wheel** rueda de recambio.
▶ *vt* **1** *(do without)* prescindir de, pasar sin. **2** *(begrudge)* escatimar. **3** *(save, relieve)* ahorrar, evitar.

spark [spɑːk] *n* **1** *(from fire, electrical)* chispa. **2** *(trace)* chispa, pizca. **3** *(cause, trigger)* chispazo. [COMP] **spark plug** bujía.
▶ *vi* echar chispas, chispear.

sparking plug ['spɑːkɪŋplʌg] *n* AUTO bujía.

sparkle ['spɑːkəl] *n* **1** *(of diamond, glass)* centelleo, destello, brillo; *(of eyes)* brillo. **2** *fig (liveliness)* viveza; *(wit)* brillo.
▶ *vi* **1** *(gen)* brillar; *(firework)* echar chispas, chispear. **2** *fig (person)* brillar, lucirse; *(conversation)* brillar.

sparkler ['spɑːkələ^r] *n* **1** *(firework)* bengala. **2** *fam (gem)* brillante *m*.

sparrow ['spærəʊ] *n* gorrión *m*.

sparse [spɑːs] *adj* *(vegetation)* escaso,-a, poco denso,-a; *(population)* disperso,-a, esparcido,-a; *(hair)* ralo,-a; *(information)* escaso,-a.

spasm ['spæzəm] *n* **1** MED espasmo. **2** *(of coughing, laughing, etc)* ataque *m*, acceso; *(of anger)* arrebato, acceso.

spat [spæt] *pt & pp* → **spit²**.

spatter ['spætə^r] *vt* *(splash)* salpicar (with, de); *(sprinkle)* rociar (with, de).
▶ *vi* salpicar.
▶ *n* *(spattered spot)* salpicadura, manchita; *(small amount)* pizca.

speak [spiːk] *vi* **1** *(gen)* hablar. **2** *(make speech)* pronunciar un discurso. **3** *(on phone)* hablar.

▶ *vt* **1** *(utter, say)* decir. **2** *(language)* hablar. [LOC] **generally/roughly speaking** en términos generales. ▮ **personally speaking** personalmente. ▮ **speaking of...** a propósito de…
◆ **to speak for** *vt insep (state views, wishes of)* hablar en nombre de.
◆ **to speak out** *vi (speak openly)* hablar claro.
◆ **to speak up** *vi* **1** *(speak more loudly)* hablar más fuerte. **2** *(give opinion)* defender.
① *pt* **spoke** [spəʊk], *pp* **spoken** [spəʊkən].

speaker ['spiːkə^r] *n* **1** *(gen)* persona que habla, el que habla, la que habla; *(in dialogue)* interlocutor,-ra; *(in public)* orador,-ra; *(lecturer)* conferenciante *mf*. **2** *(of language)* hablante *mf*. **3** *(loudspeaker)* altavoz *m*.
▶ *n* **the Speaker 1** GB el/la presidente,-a de la Cámara de los Comunes. **2** US el/la presidente,-a de la Cámara de los Representantes.

spear [spɪə^r] *n* **1** *(gen)* lanza; *(javelin)* jabalina; *(harpoon)* arpón *m*. **2** BOT punta.
▶ *vt* *(with fork)* pinchar; *(with harpoon)* arponear; *(impale with spear)* atravesar con una lanza.

special ['speʃ^əl] *adj* **1** *(not ordinary or usual)* especial; *(exceptional)* extraordinario,-a. **2** *(specific)* específico,-a, particular.
▶ *n* **1** *(train)* tren *m* especial. **2** *(TV programme)* programa *m* especial. **3** US *(special offer)* oferta especial.

speciality [speʃɪˈælɪtɪ] *n* especialidad *f*.
① *pl* **specialities**.

specialize ['speʃəlaɪz] *vi* especiliazarse.

species ['spiːʃiːz] *n* especie *f*.
① *pl* **species**.

specific [spəˈsɪfɪk] *adj* **1** *(particular, not general)* específico,-a; *(definite)* concreto,-a. **2** *(exact, detailed, precise)* preciso,-a; *(clear in meaning)* explícito,-a.
▶ *n* MED *(drug)* específico.
▶ *n pl* **specifics** *(particulars, details)* datos *mpl* (concretos).

specify ['spesɪfaɪ] *vt* especificar, precisar, concretar.
① *pt & pp* **specified**, *ger* **specifying**.

S

specimen ['spesɪmən] *n* **1** *(sample)* espécimen *m*, muestra. **2** *(example)* ejemplar *m*. **3** *fam pej (person)* tipo,-a.

speck [spek] *n* **1** *(of dust, soot)* mota; *(stain)* manchita; *(dot)* punto negro. **2** *(trace)* pizca.

spectacle ['spektəkəl] *n (show, display)* espectáculo.
▸ *n pl* **spectacles** gafas *fpl.*

spectacular [spek'tækjələr] *adj* espectacular.

spectator [spek'teɪtər] *n* espectador,-ra.
▸ *n pl* **the spectators** el público *m sing.*

specter ['spektər] *n* US → **spectre**.

spectre ['spektər] *n* espectro.

spectrum ['spektrəm] *n* **1** PHYS espectro. **2** *(range)* espectro, gama.
ⓘ *pl* **spectra** ['spektrə].

sped [sped] *pt & pp* → **speed**.

speech [spi:tʃ] *n* **1** *(faculty, act)* habla. **2** *(spoken language, way of speaking)* habla, manera de hablar. **3** *(formal talk)* discurso, alocución *f*; *(informal talk)* charla; *(lectura)* conferencia; *(lines in play)* diálogo. COMP **direct speech** estilo directo. **indirect speech** estilo indirecto. **part of speech** parte de la oración.
ⓘ *pl* **speeches**.

speed [spi:d] *n* **1** *(rate of movement)* velocidad *f*; *(quickness)* rapidez *f*; *(haste)* prisa. **2** *(sensitivity of film)* sensibilidad *f*, velocidad *f*; *(time of shutter)* tiempo de exposición, abertura. **3** *(gear)* marcha, velocidad *f*. **4** *sl (drug)* speed *m*, anfetas *fpl.* COMP **speed limit** límite *m* de velocidad.
▸ *vi* **1** *(go fast)* ir corriendo, ir a toda prisa, ir a toda velocidad. **2** *(break limit)* ir a exceso de velocidad.
1 *(hurry - process, matter)* acelerar. **2** *(take quickly)* hacer llegar rápidamente.
◆ **to speed up** *vt sep (process, matter, production)* acelerar; *(person)* apresurar, meter prisa a.
▸ *vi (vehicle)* acelerar; *(person, process, production)* acelerarse, apresurarse, darse prisa.
ⓘ *pt & pp* **speeded** o **sped** [sped].

speedboat ['spi:dbəʊt] *n* lancha rápida.

speeding ['spi:dɪŋ] *n* AUTO exceso de velocidad.

speedometer [spɪ'dɒmɪtər] *n* velocímetro.

speedway ['spi:dweɪ] *n* **1** *(racing)* carreras *fpl* de moto. **2** *(track)* pista de carreras, circuito.

speedy ['spi:dɪ] *adj (quick)* rápido,-a, veloz; *(prompt)* pronto,-a, rápido,-a.
ⓘ *comp* **speedier**, *superl* **speediest**.

speleology [spi:lɪ'ɒlədʒɪ] *n* espeleología.

spell¹ [spel] *n (magical)* hechizo, encanto.

spell³ [spel] *vt* **1** *(orally)* deletrear; *(written)* escribir correctamente. **2** *fig (mean)* significar, representar; *(bring)* traer, acarrear; *(foretell)* anunciar, augurar, presagiar.
▸ *vi* saber escribir correctamente.
◆ **to spell out** *vt sep* **1** *(word)* deletrear. **2** *(explain in detail)* explicar con detalle, detallar, pormenorizar.
ⓘ *pt & pp* **spelled** o **spelt** [spelt].

spelling ['spelɪŋ] *n* ortografía. COMP **spelling mistake** falta de ortografía.

spelt [spelt] *pt & pp* → **spell**.

spend [spend] *vt* **1** *(money)* gastar (on, en). **2** *(pass time)* pasar. **3** *(devote time/energy)* dedicar (on, a), invertir (on, en). **4** *(use up, exhaust)* gastar, agotar.
▸ *vi (money)* gastar.
ⓘ *pt & pp* **spent** [spent].

spent [spent] *pt & pp* → **spend**.
▸ *adj* **1** *(used)* usado,-a, gastado,-a. **2** *(exhausted)* agotado,-a; *(finished)* acabado,-a.

sperm [spɜ:m] *n* esperma *mf.* COMP **sperm whale** cachalote *m.*

sphere [sfɪər] *n* **1** *(shape)* esfera. **2** *(area, range, extent)* esfera, ámbito.

spherical ['sferɪkəl] *adj* esférico,-a.

sphincter ['sfɪŋktər] *n* esfínter *m.*

sphinx [sfɪŋks] *n* esfinge *f.*

spice [spaɪs] *n* **1** especia. **2** *fig* sazón *m*, sal *f*, salsa, sabor *m.*
▸ *vt* **1** CULIN sazonar, condimentar. **2** *(story, etc)* echar salsa a (up, -).

spicy ['spaɪsɪ] *adj* **1** CULIN *(seasoned)* sazonado,-a, condimentado,-a; *(hot)* picante. **2** *fig (story, etc)* picante.
ⓘ *comp* spicier, *superl* spiciest.

spider ['spaɪdər] *n* araña. COMP **spider's web** telaraña.

spied [spaɪd] *pt & pp* → spy.

spike¹ [spaɪk] *n* **1** *(sharp point)* punta, pincho; *(sharp-pointed object)* objeto puntiagudo. **2** *(on running shoe)* clavo.
▸ *vt* **1** *(with shoes)* clavar. **2** *(drink)* echar alcohol a.

spike² [spaɪk] *n* BOT espiga.

spill [spɪl] *vt (liquid)* derramar, verter; *(knock over)* volcar.
▸ *vi* **1** *(liquid)* derramarse, verterse. **2** *(people)* salir en tropel.
◆ **to spill over** *vi (liquid)* salirse, desbordarse; *(people)* rebosar; *(conflict)* extenderse.
ⓘ *pt & pp* spilled o spilt [spɪlt].

spilt [spɪlt] *pt & pp* → spill.

spin [spɪn] *n* **1** *(turn)* vuelta, giro, revolución *f.* **2** *(of washing machine)* centrifugado. **3** SP *(of ball)* efecto. **4** *(of plane)* barrena; *(of car)* patinazo. **5** *(ride, trip)* vuelta, paseo *(en coche o en moto).*
▸ *vt* **1** *(make turn)* hacer girar, dar vueltas a. **2** *(washing)* centrifugar. **3** *(ball)* darle efecto a. **4** *(cotton, wool, etc)* hilar; *(spider's web)* tejer.
▸ *vi* **1** *(turn)* girar, dar vueltas. **2** *(washing machine)* centrifugar. **3** *(cotton, wool, etc)* hilar. **4** *(plane)* caer en barrena; *(car)* patinar. **5** *(move rapidly)* girar(se), darse la vuelta.
ⓘ *pt* spun [spʌn] o span [spæn], *pp* spun [spʌn], *ger* spinning.

spinach ['spɪnɪdʒ] *n* **1** BOT espinaca. **2** CULIN espinacas *fpl.*

spinal ['spaɪnəl] *adj* espinal, vertebral. COMP **spinal column** columna vertebral. ▮ **spinal cord** médula espinal.

spin-dryer [spɪn'draɪər] *n* secador *m* centrífuga, centrifugadora.

spine [spaɪn] *n* **1** ANAT columna vertebral, espina dorsal, espinazo. **2** *(of book)* lomo. **3** ZOOL *(of hedgehog, etc)* púa. **4** BOT espina.

spinning ['spɪnɪŋ] *n (action)* hilado; *(art)* hilandería. COMP **spinning top** peonza, trompo. ▮ **spinning wheel** rueca, torno de hilar.

spiny ['spaɪnɪ] *adj* espinoso,-a.
ⓘ *comp* spinier, *superl* spiniest.

spiral ['spaɪərəl] *n* espiral *f.*
▸ *adj* espiral, en espiral.
▸ *vi* **1** *(move in a spiral)* moverse en espiral. **2** *(increase rapidly)* dispararse.

spire ['spaɪər] *n* aguja.

spirit¹ ['spɪrɪt] *n* CHEM alcohol *m.*
▸ *n pl* spirits *(alcoholic drink)* bebidas *fpl* alcohólicas, licores *mpl.*

spirit² ['spɪrɪt] *n* **1** *(soul)* espíritu *m,* alma; *(ghost)* fantasma *m.* **2** *(person)* ser *m,* alma. **3** *(force, vigour)* vigor *m,* energía; *(personality)* carácter *m; (courage)* valor *m.*

spiritual ['spɪrɪtjʊəl] *adj* espiritual.
▸ *n (song)* espiritual *m* negro.

spit¹ [spɪt] *n* **1** CULIN asador *m,* espetón *m.* **2** GEOG *(of sand)* banco; *(of land)* punta, lengua.

spit² [spɪt] *n (saliva)* saliva, esputo.
▸ *vt (gen)* escupir.
▸ *vi* **1** *(gen)* escupir (at, a), (on, en). **2** *(rain)* chispear. **3** *(sputter)* chisporrotear.
◆ **to spit out** *vt sep* **1** *(gen)* escupir. **2** *fig (say sharply)* soltar.
ⓘ *pt & pp* spat [spæt].

spite [spaɪt] *n (ill will)* rencor *m,* ojeriza. LOC **in spite of** a pesar de, pese a
▸ *vt* fastidiar.

spiteful ['spaɪtfʊl] *adj (person)* rencoroso,-a, malévolo,-a; *(comment)* malicioso,-a.

spittle ['spɪtəl] *n* saliva, baba.

splash [splæʃ] *n* **1** *(noise)* chapoteo. **2** *(spray)* salpicadura, rociada. **3** *(small amount)* gota, chorrito, poco. **4** *fig (of light, colour, etc)* mancha.
▸ *vt* **1** *(gen)* salpicar (with, de), rociar (with, de). **2** *fam (of news, story, etc)* sacar, salir.
ⓘ *pl* splashes.
▸ *vi* **1** *(of liquid)* salpicar, esparcirse. **2** *(move noisily)* chapotear *(about/around, -).*
◆ **to splash down** *vi* amarar, amerizar.

◆ **to splash out** vi fam darse un lujo, gastarse un dineral.

spleen [spli:n] n ANAT bazo.

splendid ['splendɪd] adj **1** (excellent) estupendo,-a, maravilloso,-a. **2** (magnificent) espléndido,-a, magnífico,-a.

☒ Splendid no significa 'espléndido (generoso)', que se traduce por lavish.

splinter ['splɪntəʳ] n (of wood) astilla; (of metal, bone, stone) esquirla; (of glass) fragmento.

split [splɪt] n **1** (crack, cut, break) grieta, raja. **2** (tear - in garment) desgarrón m, rasgón m; (- in seam) descosido. **3** (division) división f, ruptura. **4** (division, sharing out) reparto.
▶ adj **1** (cracked) partido,-a, rajado,-a; (torn) desgarrado,-a, rasgado,-a. **2** (divided) dividido,-a.
▶ vt **1** (crack, break) agrietar; (cut) partir. **2** (tear - garment) rajar, desgarrar; (- seam) descoser. **3** PHYS (atom) desintegrar. **4** (divide, separate) dividir (up, -).
▶ vi **1** (crack) agrietarse, rajarse; (in two parts) partirse. **2** (tear - garment) rajarse, desgarrarse; (- seams) descoserse. **3** (divide) dividirse (up, -).
◆ **to split up** vt sep (friends, lovers) separar.
▶ vi (crowd, meeting) dispersarse; (couple) separarse, romper.
ⓘ pt & pp **split**, ger **splitting**.

spoil [spɔɪl] vt **1** (ruin) estropear, echar a perder, arruinar. **2** (invalidate) anular. **3** (make child selfish) mimar, consentir; (indulge) complacer.
▶ vi (food) estropearse, echarse a perder.
ⓘ pt & pp **spoiled** o **spoilt** [spɔɪlt].

spoilt [spɔɪlt] pp → **spoil**.
▶ adj **1** (food, etc) estropeado,-a. **2** (child) mimado,-a, consentido,-a. **3** (ballot paper) nulo,-a.

spoke¹ [spəʊk] n (of wheel) radio, rayo.

spoke² [spəʊk] pt → **speak**.

spoken ['spəʊkⁿn] pt & pp → **speak**.
▶ adj hablado,-a, oral.

spokesman ['spəʊksmən] n portavoz m
ⓘ pl **spokesmen** ['spəʊksmən].

spokesperson ['spəʊkspɜ:sⁿn] n portavoz mf.
ⓘ pl **spokespersons** o **spokespeople** ['spəʊksppi:pⁿl].

spokeswoman ['spəʊkswʊmən] n portavoz f.
ⓘ pl **spokeswomen** ['spəʊkswɪmɪn].

sponge [spʌndʒ] n **1** (gen) esponja. **2** GB (cake) bizcocho. COMP **sponge cake** bizcocho.

sponsor ['spɒnsəʳ] n **1** (gen) patrocinador,-ra, sponsor mf; (for arts) mecenas mf. **2** FIN avalador,-ra, garante mf.
▶ vt **1** (gen) patrocinar; (studies, research) subvencionar. **2** (support) apoyar, respaldar. **3** FIN avalar, garantizar.

spontaneous [spɒnˈteɪnɪəs] adj espontáneo,-a.

spooky ['spu:kɪ] adj fam escalofriante, espeluznante, horripilante.
ⓘ comp **spookier**, superl **spookiest**.

spool [spu:l] n carrete m, bobina.

spoon [spu:n] n cuchara.

spoonful ['spu:nfʊl] n cucharada.
ⓘ pl **spoonfuls** o **spoonsful**.

sport [spɔ:t] n **1** (gen) deporte m. **2** (person) buena persona. **3** (fun) diversión f. **4** fam (fellow) amigo,-a.
▶ vt (wear proudly) lucir.
▶ vi (frolic) retozar, juguetear.

sports [spɔ:ts] n pl deportes mpl.
▶ n (meeting) competición f deportiva.
▶ adj deportivo,-a, de deportes. COMP
sports car (coche m) deportivo. ▌ **sports centre/complex** polideportivo. ▌ **sports club** club deportivo. ▌ **sports commentator** comentarista deportivo. ▌ **sports event** evento deportivo. ▌ **sports ground** campo de deportes. ▌ **sports jacket** chaqueta (de) sport.

sportsman ['spɔ:tsmən] n deportista m.
ⓘ pl **sportsmen** ['spɔ:tsmən].

sportswear ['spɔ:tsweəʳ] n (for sport) ropa de deporte; (casual) ropa (de) sport.

sportswoman ['spɔ:tswʊmən] n deportista.
ⓘ pl **sportswomen** ['spɔ:tswɪmɪn].

sporty ['spɔ:tɪ] adj deportivo,-a, aficionado,-a a los deportes.
ⓘ comp **sportier**, superl **sportiest**.

spot [spɒt] n 1 (dot) punto; (on fabric) lunar m, mota; (on animal) mancha. 2 (mark, stain) mancha. 3 (blemish, pimple) grano. 4 (place) sitio, lugar m. 5 (area of body) punto; (flaw) mancha. 6 (fix, trouble) lío, aprieto, apuro. 7 (place in broadcast) espacio. 8 fam (small amount) poquito, poquitín m; (drop) gota. 9 (position) puesto. 10 fam (spotlight) foco. [LOC] **on the spot 1** (at once, then and there) en el acto, allí mismo. 2 (at the place of the action) en el lugar del los hechos. 3 (without moving away) en el lugar.
▸ vt 1 (notice) darse cuenta de, notar; (see) ver; (recognize) reconocer; (find) encontrar, descubrir; (catch out) pillar. 2 (mark with spots) motear; (stain) manchar, salpicar.
▸ vi GB (rain) chispear, lloviznar.
ⓘ pt & pp **spotted**, ger **spotting**.
▸ adj (price, cash) contante, al contado.

spotlight ['spɒtlaɪt] n (lamp) foco, proyector m, reflector m; (beam) luz f de foco.
▸ vt 1 iluminar, enfocar. 2 (draw attention to) poner de relieve, destacar.

spotted ['spɒtɪd] adj (with dots) con puntos; (fabric) de lunares; (speckled) moteado,-a; (stained) manchado,-a; (animal) con manchas.

spotty ['spɒtɪ] adj (person, face, complexion) con granos, lleno,-a de granos.
ⓘ comp **spottier**, superl **spottiest**.

spout [spaʊt] n 1 (of jug) pico; (of fountain) surtidor m, caño; (of roof-gutter) canalón m; (of teapot) pitorro m. 2 (jet of water) chorro.

sprain [spreɪn] n MED torcedura.
▸ vt torcer.

sprang [sræŋ] pt → **spring**.

spray¹ [spreɪ] n (of flowers) ramillete m.

spray² [spreɪ] n 1 (of water) rociada; (from sea) espuma; (from aerosol) pulverización f. 2 (aerosol) spray m; (atomizer) atomizador m, vaporizador m. [COMP] **spray can** aerosol m. ❙ **spray paint** pintura spray.
▸ vt (water) rociar; (crops) fumigar; (paint) pintar a pistola.
▸ vi (water) rociar.

spread [spred] vt 1 (lay out) extender, tender; (unfold) desplegar; (scatter) esparcir. 2 (butter, etc) untar, extender; (paint, glue, etc) extender, repartir. 3 (news, ideas, etc) difundir, divulgar; (rumour) hacer correr; (disease, fire) propagar; (panic, terror) sembrar. 4 (wealth, work, cost) distribuir, repartir.
▸ vi 1 (stretch out) extenderse; (open out, unfold) desplegarse; (widen) ensancharse. 2 (butter, etc) extenderse. 3 (news, ideas, etc) difundirse, divulgarse; (rumour) correr; (disease, fire) propagarse. 4 (in time) extenderse.
ⓘ pt & pp **spread**.

spreadsheet ['spredʃiːt] n hoja de cálculo.

spring [sprɪŋ] n 1 (season) primavera. 2 (of water) manantial m, fuente f. 3 (of mattress, seat) muelle m; (of watch, lock, etc) resorte m; (of car) ballesta. 4 (elasticity) elasticidad f; (active, healthy quality) energía, brío. 5 (leap, jump) salto, brinco. [COMP] **spring onion** cebolleta.
▸ vi 1 (jump) saltar. 2 (appear) aparecer (de repente).
▸ vt 1 (operate mechanism) accionar. 2 fig (news, surprise) espetar (on, a), soltar. 3 fam (help escape, set free) soltar.
ⓘ pt **sprang** [spræŋ], pp **sprung** [sprʌŋ].

springboard ['sprɪŋbɔːd] n trampolín m.

sprinkle ['sprɪŋkəl] vt 1 (with water) rociar (with, de/con), salpicar (with, de/con). 2 (with flour, sugar, etc) espolvorear (with, de/con). 3 fig salpicar (with, de/con).

sprint [sprɪnt] (dash) carrera corta.
▸ vi (dash) correr a toda velocidad.

sprocket ['sprɒkɪt] n TECH diente m de engranaje. [COMP] **sprocket wheel** rueda dentada.

sprout [spraʊt] n BOT (shoot) brote m, retoño. [COMP] **(Brussels) sprouts** coles fpl de Bruselas.
▸ vi brotar, salir.
▸ vt (leaves, shoots) echar; (beard, etc) salir.

sprung [sprʌŋ] pp → **spring**.

spud [spʌd] n fam patata.

spun [spʌn] pt & pp → **spin**.

S

spur [spɜː^r] *n* **1** *(horse rider's)* espuela. **2** ZOOL *(of cock)* espolón *m*.
▶ *vt* **1** *(horse)* espolear. **2** *fig (stimulate)* estimular, incitar.
ⓘ *pt & pp* spurred, *ger* spurring.

spy [spaɪ] *n (gen)* espía *mf*.
ⓘ *pl* spies.
▶ *vi* espiar (on, a).
ⓘ *pt & pp* spied, *ger* spying.

spyhole ['spaɪhəʊl] *n* mirilla.

squabble ['skwɒbəl] *n* riña, pelea.
▶ *vi* reñir, pelearse (over, por) (about, sobre).

squad [skwɒd] *n* **1** MIL pelotón *m*. **2** *(of police)* brigada. **3** SP *(team)* equipo; *(national)* selección *f*.

squadron ['skwɒdrən] *n (of soldiers)* escuadrón *m*; *(of planes)* escuadrilla; *(of ships)* escuadra.

square [skweə^r] *n* **1** *(shape)* cuadrado; *(on fabric)* cuadro; *(on chessboard, graph paper, crossword)* casilla. **2** *(in town)* plaza; *(block of houses)* manzana. **3** MATH cuadrado. **4** *(tool)* escuadra.
▶ *adj* **1** *(in shape)* cuadrado,-a; *(forming right angle)* en ángulo recto, a escuadra. **2** MATH cuadrado,-a. **3** *fam (fair)* justo, -a, equitativo,-a; *(honest)* honesto,-a, franco,-a. **4** *(equal in points)* igual, empatado,-a; *(not owing money)* en paz. COMP square metre metro cuadrado. ‖ square root raíz *f* cuadrada.
▶ *adv* directamente.

squared ['skweəd] *adj (paper)* cuadriculado,-a.

squash¹ [skwɒʃ] *n* **1** *(drink)* concentrado de frutas. **2** SP squash *m*.
▶ *vt* **1** *(crush, flatten)* aplastar, chafar. **2** *(squeeze)* apretar, apiñar.
▶ *vi* **1** *(crush, flatten)* aplastarse, chafarse. **2** *(squeeze)* apretujarse.

squash² [skwɒʃ] *n* BOT calabaza.

squat [skwɒt] *adj (person)* rechoncho, -a y bajo,-a, achaparrado,-a; *(building)* achaparrado,-a.
ⓘ *comp* squatter, *superl* squattest.
▶ *vi* **1** *(crouch)* agacharse, ponerse en cuclillas. **2** *(in building)* ocupar ilegalmente.
ⓘ *pt & pp* squatted, *ger* squatting.

squatter ['skwɒtə^r] *n* ocupante *mf* ilegal, okupa *mf*.

squeak [skwiːk] *n (of mouse)* chillido; *(of wheel, hinge, etc)* chirrido, rechinamiento; *(of shoes)* crujido.
▶ *vi (mouse)* chillar; *(wheel, hinge, etc)* chirriar, rechinar; *(shoes)* chirriar.

squeal [skwiːl] *n (of animal, person)* chillido, grito; *(of tyres, brakes)* chirrido.
▶ *vi* **1** *(animal, person)* chillar; *(tyres, brakes)* chirriar. **2** *fam (inform on)* cantar, chivarse.
▶ *vt (say)* decir chillando, gritar.

squeeze [skwiːz] *vt* **1** *(gen)* apretar; *(lemon, orange)* exprimir. **2** *(fit in)* meter. **3** *(force out)* extraer, sacar.

squeezer ['skwiːzə^r] *n* exprimidor *m*.

squid [skwɪd] *n (gen)* calamar *m*; *(small)* chipirón *m*.
ⓘ *pl* squid o squids.

squint [skwɪnt] *n* **1** MED bizquera, estrabismo. **2** *fam (quick look)* vistazo, ojeada, miradita.
▶ *vi* **1** MED bizquear, ser bizco,-a. **2** *(in sunlight)* entrecerrar los ojos.

squire [skwaɪə^r] *n* **1** HIST *(knight's armour-carrier)* escudero. **2** GB *fam* jefe *m*.

squirrel ['skwɪrəl] *n* ardilla.

Sri Lanka [sriː'læŋkə] *n* Sri Lanka.

stab [stæb] *n* **1** *(with knife)* puñalada, navajazo. **2** *(of pain)* punzada.
▶ *vt (with knife)* apuñalar, acuchillar.
ⓘ *pt & pp* stabbed, *ger* stabbing.

stability [stə'bɪlɪtɪ] *n* estabilidad *f*.

stabilizer ['steɪbɪəlaɪzə^r] *n* **1** *(on plane, ship, bicycle)* estabilizador *m*. **2** *(in food)* estabilizante *m*.

stable¹ ['steɪbəl] *adj* **1** estable.
ⓘ *comp* stabler, *comp* stablest.

stable² ['steɪbəl] *n (for horses)* cuadra; *(for other animals)* establo.

stack [stæk] *n* **1** *(pile, heap)* montón *m*. **2** *(of grass, grain, etc)* almiar *m*. **3** *(chimney)* cañón de chimenea.
▶ *vt* **1** *(pile up)* apilar, amontonar; *(fill)* llenar. **2** *fam (in cards)* arreglar.
▶ *n pl* **stacks** *fam* montón *m*, montones *mpl*.
▶ *n pl* **stacks** *(in library)* estanterías *fpl*.

stadium ['steɪdɪəm] *n* estadio.
① *pl* stadiums o stadia ['steɪdɪə].

staff [stɑːf] *n* **1** *(personnel - gen)* personal *m*, plantilla; *(- teachers)* profesorado. **2** MIL estado mayor. **3** *(stick)* bastón *m*; *(of shepherd)* cayado; *(of bishop)* báculo; *(flagpole)* asta. **4** [*n* staves ['steɪvz] MUS pentagrama *m*.

stag [stæg] *n* ZOOL ciervo, venado.

stage [steɪdʒ] *n* **1** *(point, period)* etapa, fase *f*. **2** *(of journey, race)* etapa; *(day's journey)* jornada. **3** *(in theatre)* escenario, escena; *(raised platform)* plataforma, tablado, estrado. **4** *fig (scene of action)* escena. **5** *(of rocket)* fase *f*. **6** *fam (stagecoach)* diligencia. LOC **by stages / in stages** por etapas.
▶ *vt* **1** THEAT poner en escena, montar. **2** *(hold, carry out)* llevar a cabo, efectuar; *(arrange)* organizar, montar.
▶ *n* **the stage** *(the theatre)* el teatro, las tablas *fpl*.

stagecoach ['steɪdʒkəʊtʃ] *n* diligencia.

stagger ['stægər] *vi (walk unsteadily)* tambalearse.
▶ *vt* **1** *(hours, work)* escalonar. **2** *(amaze)* asombrar, pasmar.
▶ *n (unsteady walk)* tambaleo.

stagnation [stæg'neɪʃən] *n (of water)* estancamiento; *(person)* anquilosamiento.

stain [steɪn] *n* **1** *(gen)* mancha. **2** *(dye)* tinte *m*, tintura.
▶ *vt* **1** *(gen)* manchar. **2** *(dye)* teñir. COMP **stain remover** quitamanchas *m*.
▶ *vi* mancharse.

stainless ['steɪnləs] *adj (spotless)* sin mancha. COMP **stainless steel** acero inoxidable.

stair [steər] *n* **1** *(single step)* escalón *m*, peldaño. **2** *lit* escalera.
▶ *n pl* **stairs** escalera *f sing*.

staircase ['steəkeɪs] *n* escalera.

stairway ['steəweɪ] *n* escalera.

stake [steɪk] *n* **1** *(bet)* apuesta. **2** *(investment, share)* interés *m*, participación *f*.
▶ *vt* **1** *(bet)* apostar, jugar(se); *(risk)* arriesgar, jugarse. **2** *(give financial support to)* invertir en.

stale [steɪl] *adj* **1** *(food - gen)* no fresco, -a, pasado,-a; *(- bread, cake)* duro,-a; *(tobacco)* rancio,-a; *(wine, beer)* picado, -a. **2** *(air)* viciado,-a; *(smell)* a cerrado. **3** *(news)* viejo,-a, pasado,-a; *(joke)* trillado,-a.

stalemate ['steɪlmeɪt] *n* **1** *(chess)* tablas *fpl*. **2** *fig* punto muerto, impasse *m*.

stalk [stɔːk] *n* **1** BOT *(of plant)* tallo; *(of fruit)* rabo, rabillo; *(of cabbage)* troncho. **2** ZOOL pedúnculo.

stall² [stɔːl] *n* **1** *(in market)* puesto, tenderete *m*; *(at fair)* caseta, barraca. **2** *(for animal - stable)* establo; *(- stable compartment)* compartimiento (en un establo). **3** *(row of seats)* sillería. **4** *(small room, compartment)* compartimiento.
▶ *vi* AUTO calarse, pararse.
▶ *n pl* **stalls** *(in theatre)* platea *f sing*.

stallion ['stælɪən] *n* semental *m*.

stamen ['steɪmən] *n* BOT estambre *m*.

stamina ['stæmɪnə] *n (endurance)* resistencia, aguante *m*.

stammer ['stæmər] *n* tartamudeo.
▶ *vi* tartamudear.
▶ *vt (say with a stammer)* decir tartamudeando, farfullar.

stamp [stæmp] *n* **1** *(postage)* sello; *(fiscal)* timbre *m*; *(trading stamp)* cupón *m*, vale *m*. **2** *(tool - gen)* sello; *(- rubber)* sello de goma, tampón *m*; *(- metal)* cuño, troquel *m*. **3** *(seal, mark)* sello. **4** *(with foot - act)* patada, pisotón *m*; *(- sound)* paso.
COMP **stamp collecting** filatelia.
▶ *vt* **1** *(letter)* franquear. **2** *(passport, document)* sellar, marcar con sello; *(metal, coin)* acuñar, troquelar.

☒ Stamp no significa 'estampa', que se traduce por picture.

stand [stænd] *n* **1** *(position)* lugar *m*, sitio; *(attitude, opinion)* posición *f*, postura; *(defence, resistance)* resistencia. **2** *(of lamp, sculpture, etc)* pie *m*, pedestal *m*, base *f*. **3** *(stall - in market)* puesto, tenderete *m*; *(- at exhibition)* stand *m*; *(- at fair)* caseta, barraca. **4** *(for taxis)* parada. **5** SP *(in stadium)* tribuna. **6** US *(witness box)* estrado.

► vi **1** (person - be on one's feet) estar de pie, estar; (- get up) ponerse de pie, levantarse; (- remain on one's feet) quedarse de pie, estar; (- take up position) ponerse. **2** (measure - height) medir; (- value, level) marcar, alcanzar. **3** (thing - be situated) estar, encontrarse.

► vt **1** (place) poner, colocar. **2** fam (bear, tolerate) aguantar, soportar. **3** fam (invite) invitar: I'll stand you a drink te invitaré a una copa. LOC not to stand a chance no tener ni la más remota posibilidad. ▮ to stand clear (of STH) apartarse (de algo). ▮ to stand in the way of impedir, obstaculizar, poner trabas a. ▮ to stand to reason ser lógico,-a. ▮ to stand trial ser procesado,-a.

◆ to stand back vi (move back) apartarse, echarse hacia atrás, alejarse; (be objective) distanciarse (from, de).

◆ to stand by vi **1** (do nothing) cruzarse de brazos, quedarse sin hacer nada. **2** (be ready for action - gen) estar preparado,-a, estar listo,-a; (- troops) estar en estado de alerta.

► vt insep **1** (not desert) no abandonar, respaldar, apoyar, defender. **2** (keep to - decision) atenerse a; (- promise) cumplir.

◆ to stand for vt insep **1** (mean) significar, querer decir; (represent) representar. **2** (support, be in favour of) defender, apoyar, ser partidario,-a de. **3** (tolerate) tolerar, permitir, consentir.

◆ to stand in for vt insep (substitute, deputize) sustituir, suplir.

◆ to stand up vi **1** (get up) ponerse de pie, levantarse; (be standing) estar de pie. **2** (withstand) resistir (to, -), soportar (to, -).

► vt sep **1** (place upright) poner en posición vertical. **2** fam (fail to keep appointment) dejar plantado,-a a, dar un plantón a.

◆ to stand up for vt insep (defend) defender; (support) apoyar.

ⓘ pt & pp **stood** [stud].

standard ['stændəd] n **1** (level, degree) nivel m; (quality) cualidad f. **2** (criterion, yardstick) criterio, valor m. **3** (norm, rule) norma, regla, estándar m. **4** (flag) estandarte m, bandera; (of ship) pabellón m. **5** (official measure) patrón m. COMP **standard of living** nivel m de vida.

► adj normal, estándar.

► n pl **standards** (moral principles) principios mpl, valores mpl.

standardize ['stændədaɪz] vt normalizar, estandarizar.

standby ['stændbaɪ] n **1** (person) suplente mf, sustituto,-a, reserva mf. **2** (thing) recurso.

stank [stæŋk] pt → stink.

stanza ['stænzə] n estrofa.

staple¹ ['steɪpəl] adj **1** (food, ingredient) básico,-a; (product, export) principal. **2** (usual) típico,-a, de siempre.

► n (main food) alimento básico; (main product) producto principal; (main thing) elemento principal.

staple² ['steɪpəl] n (fastener) grapa.

► vt grapar.

stapler ['steɪpələr] n grapadora.

star [stɑːr] n (gen) estrella; (person) estrella, astro. COMP **Stars and Stripes** la bandera de los Estados Unidos.

► vi CINEM protagonizar (in, -).

ⓘ pt & pp **starred**, ger **starring**.

⊕ La bandera de Estados Unidos se conoce como Stars and Stripes (barras y estrellas) porque está compuesta por 13 barras horizontales rojas y lleva en una esquina 50 estrellas blancas sobre un fondo azul.

starboard ['stɑːbəd] n MAR estribor m.

starch [stɑːtʃ] n (for laundry, in rice) almidón m; (in potatoes) fécula.

► vt (laundry) almidonar.

stare [steər] n mirada fija.

► vi mirar fijamente (at, -), clavar la vista (at, en).

starfish ['stɑːfɪʃ] n estrella de mar.

starlet ['stɑːlət] n aspirante f a estrella.

starling ['stɑːlɪŋ] n estornino.

start [stɑːt] n **1** (gen) principio, comienzo, inicio. **2** SP (of race) salida; (advantage) ventaja. **3** (fright, jump) susto, sobresalto.

► vt **1** (begin - gen) empezar, comenzar, iniciar; (- conversation) entablar. **2** (cause to begin - fire, epidemic) provocar; (- argu

ment, fight, war, etc) empezar, iniciar. **3** (set up - business) montar, poner; (- organization) fundar, establecer, crear. **4** (set in motion - machine) poner en marcha; (- vehicle) arrancar, poner en marcha.
▶ vi **1** (begin) empezar, comenzar. **2** (be set up - business) ser fundado,-a, fundarse, crearse. **3** (begin to operate) ponerse en marcha; (car) arrancar.
◆ **to start off** vi **1** (begin) empezar, comenzar. **2** (leave) salir, ponerse en camino.
▶ vt sep empezar, ayudar a empezar.
◆ **to start up** vt sep (car) arrancar; (engine) poner en marcha; (business) montar, poner en marcha; (conversation) entablar.

starter ['stɑːtə^r] n **1** SP (official) juez mf de salida. **2** SP (competitor) competidor,-ra, participante mf. **3** AUTO motor m de arranque. **4** CULIN fam primer plato, entrante m.

startle ['stɑːt^əl] vt asustar, sobresaltar: you startled me! ¡me has asustado!

starvation [stɑːˈveɪʃ^ən] n hambre f, inanición f.

starve [stɑːv] vi (feel hungry) pasar hambre; (die) morirse de hambre.
▶ vt **1** (deprive of food) privar de comida a, hacer pasar hambre a. **2** fig privar (of, de).

starving ['stɑːvɪŋ] adj muerto,-a de hambre, famélico,-a.

state [steɪt] n **1** (condition) estado. **2** POL (government) estado. **3** (country, division of country) estado. **4** (ceremony, pomp) ceremonia, pompa, solemnidad f.
▶ adj POL estatal, del estado.
▶ vt **1** (say, declare, express) exponer, declarar, afirmar. **2** (specify) fijar.

stated ['steɪtɪd] adj (specified) indicado,-a, señalado,-a.

statement ['steɪtmənt] n **1** (gen) declaración f, afirmación f; (official) comunicado. **2** FIN estado de cuentas, extracto de cuenta. COMP **to make a statement** JUR prestar declaración.

statesman ['steɪtsmən] n estadista m, hombre m de estado.
ⓘ pl **statesmen** ['steɪtsmən].

static ['stætɪk] adj **1** TECH estático,-a. **2** (not moving, not changing) estacionario,-a. COMP **static electricity** electricidad f estática.
▶ n (interference) interferencias fpl, parásitos mpl.
▶ n **statics** PHYS estática.

station ['steɪʃ^ən] n **1** (railway) estación f (de ferrocarril); (underground) estación f de metro; (bus, coach) estación f, terminal f. **2** (radio) emisora, estación f, radio f; (TV) canal m. **3** AGR granja. **4** (social rank) condición f social, posición f social.

stationary ['steɪʃ^ən^ərɪ] adj estacionario,-a.

stationer ['steɪʃ^ənə^r] n dueño,-a de una papelería. COMP **stationer's (shop)** papelería.

stationery ['steɪʃ^ən^ərɪ] n (paper) papel m de escribir; (pen, ink, etc) artículos mpl de escritorio.

statistics [stəˈtɪstɪks] n (science) estadística.
▶ n pl (data) estadísticas fpl.

statue ['stætjuː] n estatua.

statuette [stætjʊˈet] n estatuilla.

stature ['stætʃə^r] n **1** (height) estatura, talla. **2** fig (standing) talla.

statute ['stætjuːt] n estatuto.

staves [steɪvz] n pl → **staff**.

stay¹ [steɪ] n **1** (prop, support) sostén m, soporte m, puntal m. **2** (in corset) ballena.

stay² [steɪ] n (time) estancia, permanencia.
▶ vi (remain) quedarse, permanecer.
▶ vi (continue to be) seguir.
▶ vi (reside temporarily) alojarse, hospedarse.
▶ vt fml (stop) detener; (delay) aplazar, suspender; (calm) calmar.
◆ **to stay in** vi quedarse en casa, no salir.

steadily ['stedɪlɪ] adv **1** (grow, improve, rise) constantemente, a un ritmo constante; (rain, work) sin parar. **2** (gaze, stare) fijamente; (walk) con paso seguro, decididamente; (speak) firmemente.

S

steady ['stedɪ] *adj* **1** *(table, ladder, etc)* firme, seguro,-a; *(gaze)* fijo,-a; *(voice)* tranquilo,-a, firme. **2** *(regular, constant - heartbeat, pace)* regular; *(- demand, speed, improvement, decline, increase)* constante; *(- flow, rain)* continuo,-a; *(rhythm)* regular, constante; *(- prices, currency)* estable. **3** *(regular - job)* fijo,-a, estable; *(- income)* regular, fijo,-a. **4** *(student)* aplicado,-a; *(worker, person)* serio,-a, formal.
  ⓘ *comp* steadier, *superl* steadiest.
  ▶ *interj* ¡cuidado!, ¡ojo!
  ▶ *n (boyfriend)* novio; *(girlfriend)* novia.
  ▶ *vt* **1** *(hold firm - ladder, table, etc)* sujetar, sostener; *(stabilize)* estabilizar. **2** *(person, nerves)* calmar, tranquilizar.
  ⓘ *pt & pp* steadied, *ger* steadying.

steak [steɪk] *n* **1** *(of beef)* bistec *m*, filete *m*; *(of salmon)* rodaja. **2** *(meat for stewing)* carne *f* de vaca para estofar.

steal [sti:l] *vt* robar, hurtar.
  ▶ *vi* **1** *(rob)* robar, hurtar. **2** *(move quietly, creep)* moverse con sigilo.
  ⓘ *pt* stole [stəʊl], *pp* stolen ['stəʊlən].

steam [sti:m] *n* vapor *m*. [COMP] **steam engine 1** *(locomotive)* locomotora de vapor, máquina de vapor. **2** *(engine)* motor *m* de vapor. ❙ **steam iron** plancha de vapor.
  ▶ *vt* CULIN *(vegetables)* cocer al vapor.
  ▶ *vi (boat)* echar vapor; *(soup, drink, etc)* humear.

steamboat ['sti:mbəʊt] *n* vapor *m*.

steamer ['sti:mə'] *n* **1** MAR vapor *m*, buque *m* de vapor. **2** CULIN olla a vapor.

steamship ['sti:mʃɪp] *n* vapor *m*, buque *m* de vapor.

steel [sti:l] *n (gen)* acero.
  ▶ *adj (knife, girder, etc)* de acero. [COMP] **steel industry** industria del acero ❙ **steel mill** acerería, acería. ❙ **steel wool** estropajo de acero.

steelworks ['sti:lwɜ:ks] *n pl* acería, acerería.

steep¹ [sti:p] *vt (soak - washing)* remojar; *(- dried food)* poner en remojo; *(- fruit)* macerar.
  ▶ *vi (fruit)* macerarse.

steep² [sti:p] *adj* **1** *(hill, slope, stairs)* empinado,-a; *(rise, drop)* abrupto,-a, brusco,-a. **2** *fam (price, fee)* excesivo,-a; *(demand)* excesivo,-a, poco razonable.

steeple ['sti:pªl] *n* aguja, chapitel *m*.

steeplechase ['sti:pªlʃeɪs] *n* carrera de obstáculos.

steer¹ [stɪə'] *n* buey *m*.

steer² [stɪə'] *vt (gen)* dirigir, guiar; *(vehicle)* conducir, dirigir; *(ship)* gobernar; *(conversation)* llevar.
  ▶ *vi (vehicle)* ir al volante; *(ship)* llevar el timón, estar al timón.

steering ['stɪərɪŋ] *n* dirección *f*. [COMP] **steering column** columna de (la) dirección. ❙ **steering lock 1** *(device)* seguro antirrobo. **2** *(when turning)* radio de giro. ❙ **steering wheel** volante *m*.

stem [stem] *n* **1** BOT *(of plant, flower)* tallo; *(of leaf)* pecíolo; *(of fruit)* pedúnculo. **2** *(of glass)* pie *m*; *(of tobacco pipe)* boquilla, caña. **3** LING raíz *f*, radical *m*.
  ▶ *vt (stop - gen)* frenar, detener, parar; *(- bleeding)* contener, parar.
  ⓘ *pt & pp* stemmed, *ger* stemming.

stench [stentʃ] *n* hedor *m*, peste *f*, fetidez *f*.

stencil ['stensªl] *n* **1** *(template)* plantilla; *(design, pattern)* estarcido. **2** *(for typewriter)* cliché *m*, matriz *f*.

stenography [stə'nɒɡrəfɪ] *n* US taquigrafía.

step [step] *n* **1** *(gen)* paso. **2** *(measure)* medida; *(formality)* gestión *f*, trámite *m*. **3** *(stair)* escalón *m*, peldaño; *(of vehicle)* estribo.
  ▶ *vi* **1** *(move, walk)* dar un paso, andar. **2** *(tread)* pisar.
  ▶ *n pl* **steps** GB *(stepladder)* escalera de tijera. *(outdoor)* escalinata; *(indoor)* escalera; *(of plane)* escalerilla.
  ⓘ *pt & pp* stepped, *ger* stepping.

stepbrother ['stepbrʌðə'] *n* hermanastro.

stepchild ['steptʃaɪld] *n* hijastro,-a.
  ⓘ *pl* stepchildren ['steptʃɪldrən].

stepdaughter ['stepdɔ:tə'] *n* hijastra.

stepfather ['stepfɑ:ðə'] *n* padrastro.

stepladder ['steplædə'] *n* escalera de tijera.

stepmother ['stepmʌðə'] *n* madrastra.

steppe [step] *n* GEOG estepa.

stepsister ['stepsɪstə'] *n* hermanastra.

stepson ['stepsʌn] *n* hijastro.

stereo ['steriəʊ] *n* estéreo.

stereotype ['steriətaip] *n* estereotipo.
  ► *vt* estereotipar.

sterile ['stəraɪl] *adj* **1** *(barren)* estéril. **2** *(germfree)* esterilizado,-a.

sterility [stə'rɪlɪti] *n* esterilidad *f*.

sterilize ['sterəlaɪz] *vt* esterilizar.

sterling ['stɜːlɪŋ] *n* FIN libra esterlina, libras *fpl* esterlinas. LOC **the pound sterling** la libra esterlina.

stern[1] [stɜːn] *adj* severo,-a, austero,-a.

stern[2] [stɜːn] *n* MAR popa.

sternum ['stɜːnəm] *n* ANAT esternón *m*.
  ⓘ *pl* sternums o sterna ['stɜːnə].

steroid ['steroɪd] *n* esteroide *m*.

stethoscope ['steθəskəʊp] *n* estetoscopio.

stew [stjuː] *n* CULIN estofado, guisado.
  ► *vt (meat)* estofar, guisar; *(fruit)* hacer una compota de.

steward ['stjuːəd] *n* **1** *(on ship)* camarero; *(on plane)* auxiliar *m* de vuelo. **2** *(manager of estate)* administrador *m*. **3** *(of club, hotel)* mayordomo. **4** GB *(in horse racing)* comisario de carreras; *(in athletics)* juez *m*; *(at demonstration, etc)* oficial *mf*.

stewardess ['stjuːədes] *n (on ship)* camarera; *(on plane)* azafata, auxiliar *f* de vuelo.
  ⓘ *pl* stewardesses.

stick[1] [stɪk] *vt* **1** *(insert pointed object)* clavar, hincar. **2** *fam* poner, meter. **3** *(fix)* colocar, fijar; *(with glue)* pegar, fijar. **4** *fam (bear)* aguantar, soportar.
  ► *vi* **1** *(penetrate)* clavarse. **2** *(fix, become attached)* pegarse. **3** *(jam - drawer, key in lock)* atascarse; *(- machine part, lock)* atrancarse, encasquillarse; *(- vehicle in mud)* atascarse. **4** *(in cards)* plantarse.
  ◆ **to stick out** *vi* **1** *(project, protrude)* salir, sobresalir; *(be noticeable)* resaltar, destacarse. **2** *fam (be obvious)* ser obvio,-a, ser evidente.
  ► *vt sep* **1** *(tongue, hand)* sacar. **2** *(endure)* aguantar.
  ⓘ *pt & pp* stuck [stʌk].

stick[2] [stɪk] *n* **1** *(piece of wood)* trozo de madera, palo; *(twig)* ramita; *(for punishment)* palo, vara. **2** *(for walking)* bastón *m*. **3** *(for plants)* rodrigón *m*, tutor *m*. **4** MUS *(baton)* batuta; *(drumstick)* palillo. **5** SP *(for hockey)* palo.

sticker ['stɪkə'] *n* **1** *(label)* etiqueta adhesiva; *(with slogan, picture)* pegatina. **2** *(person)* persona tenaz.

sticking ['stɪkɪŋ] COMP **sticking plaster** *(small)* tirita®; *(on roll)* esparadrapo.

sticky ['stɪkɪ] *adj* pegajoso,-a. COMP **sticky tape** cinta adhesiva.
  ⓘ *comp* stickier, *comp* stickiest.

stiff [stɪf] *adj* **1** *(hair, fabric)* rígido,-a, tieso,-a; *(card, collar, brush, lock)* duro,-a. **2** *(joint)* entumecido,-a; *(muscle)* agarrotado,-a. **3** *(door, window)* difícil de abrir, difícil de cerrar. **4** *(not liquid)* espeso,-a, consistente. **5** *(person, manner)* estirado,-a, tieso,-a; *(smile)* forzado,-a. **6** *fig (climb, test, etc)* difícil, duro,-a; *(breeze)* fuerte; *(sentence, punishment)* severo,-a. **7** *fam (price, fee)* excesivo,-a. **8** *fam (drink)* fuerte, cargado,-a. LOC **to be stiff** tener agujetas.

stifle ['staɪfəl] *vt* ahogar, sofocar.

still [stɪl] *adj* **1** *(not moving)* quieto,-a, inmóvil; *(stationary)* parado,-a; *(water)* manso,-a; *(air)* en calma. **2** *(tranquil, calm)* tranquilo,-a; *(peaceful)* sosegado,-a; *(subdued)* callado,-a, apagado,-a; *(silent)* silencioso,-a. **3** *(not fizzy - water)* sin gas; *(soft drink)* sin burbujas.
  ► *adv* **1** *(so far)* todavía, aún. **2** *(even)* aún, todavía. **3** *(even so, nevertheless)* a pesar de todo, con todo, no obstante, sin embargo. **4** *fml (besides, yet, in addition)* aún, todavía. **5** *(quiet, without moving)* quieto,-a. COMP **still life** ART naturaleza muerta *m*.

stilt [stɪlt] *n* zanco.

stilted ['stɪltɪd] *adj* afectado,-a.

stimulant ['stɪmjʊlənt] *n* estimulante *m*.

stimulate ['stɪmjəleɪt] *vt (activate)* estimular; *(encourage)* animar, alentar.

stimulating ['stɪmjəleɪtɪŋ] *adj (gen)* estimulante; *(inspiring)* inspirador,-ra.

stimulation [stɪmjə'leɪʃən] *n (stimulus)* estímulo; *(action)* estimulación *f*.

S

stimulus ['stɪmjələs] *n* estímulo.
ⓘ *pl* stimuli ['stɪmjəliː].

sting [stɪŋ] *n* **1** *(organ - of bee, wasp)* aguijón *m*; *(- of scorpion)* uña; *(- of plant)* pelo urticante. **2** *(action, wound)* picadura. **3** *(pain)* escozor *m*, picazón *f*. **4** *fig (of remorse)* punzada. **5** US *(trick)* timo, golpe *m*.
▶ *vt* **1** *(gen)* picar. **2** *fig (remark)* herir en lo más hondo; *(conscience)* remorder. **3** *(provoke)* incitar, provocar (into/to, a). **4** *(overcharge, swindle)* clavar.
▶ *vi* **1** *(insects, nettles, etc)* picar; *(substance)* escocer. **2** *(be painful)* escocer.
ⓘ *pt & pp* stung [stʌŋ].

stink [stɪŋk] *n* **1** *(smell)* peste *f*, hedor *m*, hediondez *f*, fetidez *f*. **2** *fam (fuss, trouble)* escándalo, lío, follón *m*.
▶ *vi* **1** apestar (of, a), heder (of, a). **2** *fam (seem bad or dishonest)* dar asco.
ⓘ *pt* stank [stæŋk] o stunk [stʌŋk], *pp* stunk [stʌŋk].

stinking ['stɪŋkɪŋ] *adj* apestoso,-a.

stipulate ['stɪpjəleɪt] *vt* estipular, especificar.

stipulation [stɪpjə'leɪʃ°n] *n* estipulación *f*, condición *f*.

stir [stɜːʳ] *vt* **1** *(liquid, mixture)* remover, revolver. **2** *(move slightly)* mover, agitar. **3** *(curiosity, interest, etc)* despertar, excitar; *(anger)* provocar; *(imagination)* avivar, estimular; *(emotions)* conmover.
▶ *vi* **1** *(move)* moverse, agitarse; *(wake up)* despertarse; *(get up)* levantarse. **2** *(feelings)* despertarse. **3** *fam (cause trouble)* armar lío, meter cizaña.
ⓘ *pt & pp* stirred, *ger* stirring.

stirring ['stɜːrɪŋ] *adj (moving)* conmovedor,-ra; *(rousing, exciting)* emocionante.

stirrup ['stɪrəp] *n* **1** *(for riding)* estribo. **2** *(on trousers)* trabilla. COMP **stirrup pump** bomba de mano.

stitch [stɪtʃ] *n* **1** *(in sewing)* puntada; *(in knitting)* punto. **2** MED punto (de sutura). **3** *(sharp pain)* punzada; *(when running, etc)* flato.
▶ *vt* **1** SEW coser (on, a), (up, -). **2** MED suturar (up, -).
▶ *vi* SEW coser.

stoat [stəʊt] *n* armiño.

stock [stɒk] *n* **1** *(supply)* reserva. **2** COMM *(goods)* existencias *fpl*, stock *m*; *(variety)* surtido. **3** FIN *(company's capital)* capital *m* social. **4** AGR *(livestock)* ganado. **5** CULIN *(broth)* caldo. LOC **in stock** en existencia. ▌ **out of stock** agotado,-a. COMP **stock exchange** bolsa. ▌ **stock market** mercado bursátil.
▶ *vt* COMM *(keep supplies of)* tener en stock; *(sell)* vender.
▶ *n pl* **stocks** FIN *(shares)* acciones *fpl*, valores *mpl*.

stockbroker ['stɒkbrəʊkəʳ] *n* corredor,-ra de bolsa, agente *mf* de bolsa, bolsista *mf*.

stockholder ['stɒkhəʊldəʳ] *n* US accionista *mf*.

stocking ['stɒkɪŋ] *n* media.

stoic ['stəʊɪk] *n* estoico,-a.

stoical ['stəʊɪk°l] *adj* estoico,-a.

stoicism ['stəʊɪsɪz°m] *n* estoicismo.

stole¹ [stəʊl] *pt* → **steal**.

stole² [stəʊl] *n (garment)* estola.

stolen ['stəʊlən] *pp* → **steal**.

stomach ['stʌmək] *n* **1** ANAT estómago. **2** *fam (belly)* barriga; *(abdomen)* abdomen *m*, vientre *m*.
▶ *vt* *fig (bear, endure)* aguantar, soportar, tragar; *(eat, drink)* tolerar.

stomachache ['stʌməkeɪk] *n* dolor *n* de estómago.

stoma ['stəʊmə] *n* estoma *m*.
ⓘ *pl* stomas o stomata [s'təʊmətə].

stomp [stɒmp] *vi fam* pisar fuerte.

stone [stəʊn] *n* **1** *(gen)* piedra. **2** *(on grave)* lápida. **3** *(of fruit)* hueso. **4** MED cálculo, piedra. **5** GB *(measure of weight* unidad de peso que equivale a 6,348 kg.
▶ *adj* de piedra, pétreo,-a. COMP **Stone Age** Edad *f* de Piedra.
▶ *vt* **1** *(person)* apedrear, lapidar. **2** *(fruit* deshuesar.

stoneware ['stəʊnweəʳ] *n* gres *m*, cerá mica de gres.

stonework ['stəʊnwɜːk] *n* mampostería

stood [stʊd] *pt & pp* → **stand**.

stooge [stuːdʒ] *n* **1** THEAT comparsa *m* **2** *pej (person)* títere *mf*, pelele *mf*.

stool [stuːl] *n* **1** *(seat)* taburete *m*, banqueta. **2** MED *(faeces)* deposición *f*, heces *fpl*.

stoop¹ [stuːp] *n* US *(porch)* entrada.

stoop² [stuːp] *n* **1** *(of person)* encorvamiento, encorvadura; *(of shoulders)* espaldas *fpl* encorvadas.
▶ *vi* **1** *(bend)* inclinarse (**down**, -), agacharse (**down**, -). **2** *(have a stoop)* andar encorvado,-a.

stop [stɒp] *n* **1** *(halt)* parada, alto. **2** *(stopping place)* parada. **3** *(on journey)* parada; *(break, rest)* descanso, pausa. **4** *(punctuation mark)* punto; *(in telegram)* stop *m*. **5** MUS *(on organ)* registro; *(knob)* botón *m* de registro; *(on wind instrument)* llave *f*. **6** *(in camera)* diafragma *m*.
▶ *vt* **1** *(halt - vehicle, person)* parar, detener; *(- machine, ball)* parar. **2** *(end, interrupt - production)* parar; *(- inflation, advance)* parar, contener; *(- conversation, play)* interrumpir; *(- pain, etc)* poner fin a, acabar con. **3** *(pay, match, holidays)* suspender; *(cheque)* cancelar; *(money from wages)* retener. **4** *(cease)* dejar de, parar de. **5** *(prevent)* impedir, evitar. **6** *(block - hole)* tapar, taponar (**up**, -); *(- gap)* rellenar (**up**, -); *(- tooth)* empastar (**up**, -). **7** MUS *(string, key)* apretar; *(hole)* cubrir.
▶ *vi* **1** *(halt)* parar, pararse, detener, detenerse. **2** *(cease)* acabarse, terminar, cesar. **3** GB *fam (stay)* quedarse.
◆ **to stop over** *vi* **1** *(interrupt journey)* parar; *(overnight)* pasar la noche, hacer noche. **2** *(on flight)* hacer escala.
ⓘ *pt & pp* **stopped**, *ger* **stopping**.

topcock ['stɒpkɒk] *n* llave *f* de paso.

topover ['stɒpəʊvəʳ] *n* *(stop)* parada; *(on flight)* escala; *(stay)* estancia.

topper ['stɒpəʳ] *n* tapón *m*.

topping ['stɒpɪŋ] *adj* GB *(of train)* que para en todas las estaciones.

top-press [stɒp'pres] *adj* *(news)* de última hora.

topwatch ['stɒpwɒtʃ] *n* cronómetro.
ⓘ *pl* **stopwatches**.

torage ['stɔːrɪdʒ] *n* **1** *(act)* almacenaje *m*, almacenamiento. **2** *(place)* almacén *m*, depósito, guardamuebles *m*.

3 *(cost)* (gastos *mpl* de) almacenaje *m*. **4** COMPUT almacenamiento.

store [stɔːʳ] *n* **1** *(supply - gen)* reserva, provisión *f*; *(- of wisdom, knowledge)* reserva; *(- of jokes, etc)* colección *f*. **2** *(warehouse)* almacén *m*, depósito. **3** US *(shop)* tienda.
▶ *vt* **1** *(put away)* almacenar (**up**, -); *(keep)* guardar; *(amass)* acumular, hacer acopio de. **2** COMPUT almacenar. **3** *(put in storage)* guardar, almacenar, mandar a un depósito. **4** *fig (trouble, etc)* ir acumulando (**up**, -), ir almacenando (**up**, -). **5** *(fill with supplies)* abastecer (**with**, de).
▶ *n pl* **stores** *(provisions)* provisiones *fpl*, víveres *mpl*, MIL *(supplies, equipment)* pertrechos *mpl*; *(place)* intendencia *f sing*.

storehouse ['stɔːhaʊs] *n* almacén *m*, depósito.

storekeeper ['stɔːkiːpəʳ] *n* US tendero,-a.

storeroom ['stɔːruːm] *n* *(gen)* almacén *m*, depósito; *(for food)* despensa.

storey ['stɔːrɪ] *n* piso, planta.

stork [stɔːk] *n* cigüeña.

storm [stɔːm] *n* **1** *(thunderstorm)* tormenta; *(at sea)* tempestad *f*, temporal *m*; *(with wind)* borrasca. **2** *fig (uproar)* revuelo, escándalo; *(of missiles, insults)* lluvia, torrente *m*.

stormy ['stɔːmɪ] *adj* **1** *(weather)* tormentoso,-a. **2** *fig (meeting, discussion)* acalorado,-a; *(relationship)* tormentosa,-a, con muchos altibajos.
ⓘ *comp* **stormier**, *superl* **stormiest**.

story¹ ['stɔːrɪ] *n* US → **storey**.

story² ['stɔːrɪ] *n* **1** *(gen)* historia; *(tale)* cuento, relato; *(account)* relato. **2** *(anecdote)* anécdota; *(joke)* chiste *m*. **3** *(rumour)* rumor *m*; *(lie)* mentira, cuento. **4** *(newspaper article)* artículo; *(newsworthy item)* artículo de interés periodístico. **5** *(storyline, narrative, plot)* argumento, trama.
ⓘ *pl* **stories**.

storybook ['stɔːrɪbʊk] *n* libro de cuentos.

storyteller ['stɔːrɪteləʳ] *n* cuentista *mf*.

stout [staʊt] *adj* **1** *euph (fat)* corpulento,-a, robusto,-a. **2** *(strong)* sólido,-a, fuerte. **3** *(determined, resolute)* firme, resuelto,-a, tenaz; *(brave)* valiente.

S

▶ n (beer) cerveza negra.

stove [stəʊv] n **1** (for heating) estufa. **2** (cooker) cocina; (cooking ring) hornillo; (oven) horno.

straight [streɪt] adj **1** (not curved - gen) recto,-a; (- hair) liso,-a. **2** (level, upright) derecho,-a, recto,-a. **3** (tidy, neat) en orden. **4** (honest - person) honrado,-a, de confianza; (sincere) sincero,-a. **5** (direct - question) directo,-a; (- refusal, rejection) categórico,-a, rotundo,-a. **6** (correct, accurate) correcto,-a. **7** (consecutive) seguido,-a. **8** (drink) solo,-a.

▶ adv **1** (in a straight line) recto,-a. **2** (not in a curve) derecho,-a, recto,-a. **3** (directly) directamente. **4** (immediately) en seguida. **5** (frankly) francamente, con franqueza. **6** (clearly) claro, con claridad: LOC straight away en seguida. ‖ straight off en el acto. ‖ straight up en serio. ‖ to go straight (criminal) reformarse.

straightaway [streɪtəˈweɪ] adv en seguida, inmediatamente.

straighten [ˈstreɪtən] vt **1** (wire) enderezar; (- tie, skirt, picture) poner bien, poner recto,-a; (- hair) estirar, alisar. **2** (tidy) ordenar (up, -), arreglar (up, -).

▶ vi (road) hacerse recto,-a.

straightforward [streɪtˈfɔːwəd] adj **1** (honest) honrado,-a; (sincere, open) sincero,-a, franco,-a, abierto,-a. **2** (simple, easy) sencillo,-a, simple; (clear) claro,-a.

strain¹ [streɪn] n **1** (race, breed) raza; (descent) linaje m; (of plant, virus) cepa. **2** (streak) vena.

strain² [streɪn] n **1** PHYS (tension) tensión f; (pressure) presión f; (weight) peso. **2** (stress, pressure) tensión f, estrés m; (effort) esfuerzo; (exhaustion) agotamiento. **3** (tension) tirantez f, tensión f. **4** MED torcedura, esguince m.

▶ vt **1** (stretch) estirar, tensar. **2** (damage, weaken - muscle) torcer(se), hacerse un esguince en; (- back) hacerse daño en; (- voice, eyes) forzar; (ears) aguzar; (- heart) cansar. **3** (stretch - patience, nerves, credulity) poner a prueba; (- resources) estirar al máximo; (- relations) someter a demasiada tensión, crear tirantez en. **4** (filter - liquid) colar; (- vegetables, rice) escurrir.

strainer [ˈstreɪnər] n colador m.

strait [streɪt] n GEOG estrecho.

▶ n pl **straits** (difficulties) aprietos mpl, apuros mpl.

straitjacket [ˈstreɪtdʒækɪt] n **1** camisa de fuerza. **2** fig control m, limitaciones fpl.

strand¹ [strænd] n lit (beach) playa.

strand² [strænd] n **1** (of thread) hebra, hilo; (of rope, string) ramal m; (of hair) pelo; (of pearls) sarta. **2** fig (of story, argument) hilo, línea.

strange [streɪndʒ] adj **1** (odd, bizarre) extraño,-a, raro,-a. **2** (unknown) desconocido,-a; (unfamiliar) nuevo,-a. COMP strange to say aunque parezca mentira.

strangely [ˈstreɪndʒlɪ] adv extrañamente.

stranger [ˈstreɪndʒər] n (unknown person) extraño,-a, desconocido,-a; (outsider) forastero,-a.

☒ Stranger no significa 'extranjero', que se traduce por foreigner.

strangle [ˈstræŋɡəl] vt **1** (kill) estrangular. **2** fig (stifle) sofocar, ahogar.

stranglehold [ˈstræŋɡəlhəʊld] n **1** SP (wrestling) llave f al cuello. **2** pej (firm control) poder m, dominio.

strap [stræp] n (on watch, camera) correa; (on bag) asa; (on shoe) tira; (on dress, etc) tirante m.

▶ vt **1** (fasten) atar con correa. **2** (bandage) vendar.

ⓘ pt & pp strapped, ger strapping.

strapless [ˈstræpləs] adj sin tirantes.

strapping [ˈstræpɪŋ] adj (big, strong) fornido,-a, robusto,-a.

stratagem [ˈstrætədʒəm] n estratagema.

strategic [strəˈtiːdʒɪk] adj estratégico,-a.

strategist [ˈstrætədʒɪst] n estratega mf.

strategy [ˈstrætədʒɪ] n estrategia.

ⓘ pl strategies.

stratosphere [ˈstrætəsfɪər] n estratosfera.

stratum [ˈstrɑːtəm] n **1** GEOL estrato. (level, class) estrato, nivel m.

ⓘ pl strata [ˈstrɑːtə].

straw [strɔ:] n **1** (dried stalk(s)) paja. **2** (for drinking) paja, pajita.
► adj de paja.

strawberry ['strɔ:bərɪ] n (gen) fresa; (large) fresón m. COMP **strawberry jam** mermelada de fresa. ‖ **strawberry tree** madroño.
ⓘ pl strawberries.

stray [streɪ] adj **1** (lost) perdido,-a, extraviado,-a; (animal) callejero,-a. **2** (isolated, odd) perdido,-a.
► n (animal) animal m extraviado.
► vi **1** (get lost) extraviarse, perderse; (wander away) desviarse, apartarse, alejarse; (from group) separarse, apartarse, alejarse. **2** fig (digress, wander) divagar, apartarse del tema, desviarse del tema.

stream [stri:m] n **1** (brook) arroyo, riachuelo. **2** (current) corriente f. **3** (flow of liquid) flujo, chorro, río; (of blood, air) chorro; (of lava, tears) torrente m; (of light) raudal m. **4** fig (of people) oleada, torrente m; (of vehicles, traffic) desfile m continuo, caravana; (of abuse, excuses, insults) torrente m, sarta. **5** GB (class, pupils) clase f, grupo, nivel m (de alumnos seleccionados según su nivel académico).
► vi **1** (flow, pour out) manar, correr, chorrear; (gush) salir a chorros. **2** fig (people, vehicles, etc) desfilar. **3** (hair, banner, scarf) ondear.
► vt **1** (liquid) derramar. **2** GB poner en grupos según su nivel académico.

streamer ['stri:mər] n (decoration) serpentina; (flag) banderín m.

street [stri:t] n calle f. LOC **at street level** a nivel de la calle. ‖ **to walk the streets 1** (homeless) estar sin techo. **2** (prostitute) trabajar la calle. COMP **one-way street** calle de sentido único. ‖ **street cleaner** barrendero,-a. ‖ **street corner** esquina. ‖ **street directory** callejero. ‖ **street lamp** farola. ‖ **street lighting** alumbrado público. ‖ **street plan** plano de la ciudad. ‖ **street market** mercadillo. ‖ **street value** valor m (en el mercado).

streetcar ['stri:tka:] n US tranvía.

streetlamp ['stri:tlæmp] n farol m, farola.

streetlight ['stri:tlaɪt] n farol m, farola.

strength [streŋθ] n **1** (of person - physical) fuerza, fuerzas fpl, fortaleza; (- stamina) resistencia, aguante m. **2** (intellectual, spiritual) fortaleza, entereza, firmeza. **3** (of machine, object) resistencia; (of wind, current) fuerza; (of light, sound, magnet, lens) potencia. **4** (of solution) concentración f; (of drug) potencia; (of alcohol) graduación f. **5** (of currency) valor m, fortaleza; (of economy) solidez f, fortaleza. **6** (of argument, evidence, story) fuerza, validez f, credibilidad f; (of emotion, conviction, colour) intensidad f; (of protest) energía. **7** (strong point) punto fuerte, virtud f; (ability, capability) capacidad f; (advantage) ventaja. **8** (power, influence) poder m, potencia. **9** (force in numbers) fuerza numérica, número.

strengthen ['streŋθən] vt **1** (wall, glass, defence, etc) reforzar; (muscle) fortalecer. **2** (character, faith, love) fortalecer; (support) aumentar; (relationship, ties) consolidar, fortalecer; (resolve, determination) redoblar, intensificar.
► vi **1** (muscle) fortalecerse. **2** (economy, currency) reforzarse, fortalecerse; (relationship) consolidarse, reforzarse, fortalecerse; (support, opposition, feeling) intensificarse, aumentar.

stress [stres] n **1** MED tensión f (nerviosa), estrés m. **2** (pressure) presión f, tensión f. **3** TECH tensión f. **4** (emphasis) hincapié m (on, en), énfasis m (on, en). **5** LING (on word) acento (tónico). COMP **stress mark** acento.
► vt **1** (emphasize) hacer hincapié en, poner énfasis en, subrayar, enfatizar. **2** LING (word) acentuar.

stressed [strest] adj **1** MED (person) estresado,-a. **2** PHYS (object) tensado,-a.

stressful ['stresful] adj estresante, de mucho estrés.

stretch [stretʃ] n **1** (of land, water) extensión f; (of road) tramo, trecho. **2** (elasticity) elasticidad f. **3** (act of stretching) estiramiento. **4** (period of time) período, tiempo, intervalo; (in prison) condena. **5** SP (of racetrack) recta.
► vt **1** (extend - elastic, clothes, rope) estirar; (- canvas) extender; (- shoes) ensanchar;

S

(- arm, leg) alargar, estirar, extender; *(-wings)* desplegar, extender. **2** *(make demands on, make to use all abilities)* exigir a. **3** *(strain - money, resources)* estirar, emplear al máximo; *(- patience)* abusar; *(- meaning)* forzar, distorsionar.

▶ *vi* **1** *(elastic)* estirarse; *(fabric)* dar de sí; *(shoes)* ensancharse, dar de sí; *(person, animal - gen)* estirarse; *(person - when tired)* desperezarse. **2** *(extend - land, sea, etc)* extenderse (out, -); *(- in time)* alargarse, prolongarse. **3** *(reach)* llegar (to, para), alcanzar (to, para).

▶ *adj (material, jeans, etc)* elástico,-a.

◆ **to stretch out** *vi (person - gen)* estirarse; *(- lie down)* tumbarse.

▶ *vt sep (arm, leg)* alargar, estirar, extender. **2** *(money, resources)* estirar.

> ❌ To stretch no significa 'estrechar', que se traduce por to tighten, to narrow.

stretcher ['stretʃəʳ] *n* camilla.

stretchy ['stretʃɪ] *adj* elástico,-a.
ⓘ *comp* stretchier, *superl* stretchier.

strew [struː] *vt lit (scatter)* esparcir, desparramar; *(lie scattered)* sembrar, cubrir.
ⓘ *pt* strewed, *pp* strewed o strewn [struːn].

strict [strɪkt] *adj* **1** *(severe - person)* severo,-a, estricto,-a; *(- discipline)* riguroso,-a, severo,-a, estricto,-a; *(- rule, law, order, etc)* estricto,-a, riguroso,-a, rígido,-a. **2** *(exact, precise)* estricto,-a, riguroso,-a; *(complete, total)* absoluto,-a.

strictly ['strɪktlɪ] *adv* **1** *(severely)* severamente, estrictamente, de manera estricta. **2** *(rigorously, rigidly)* estrictamente; *(categorically)* terminantemente. **3** *(exactly, precisely)* estrictamente, exactamente; *(completely)* totalmente, del todo. **4** *(exclusively)* exclusivamente. LOC **strictly speaking** en realidad.

stride [straɪd] *n* **1** *(long step)* zancada; *(gait)* paso, manera de andar. **2** *(advance, development)* progresos *mpl*.

▶ *vi* andar a zancadas.
ⓘ *pt* strode [strəʊd], *pp* stridden ['strɪdən].

▶ *n pl* strides *fam (trousers)* pantalón *m sing*, pantalones *mpl*.

stridden ['strɪdən] *pp* → stride.

strike [straɪk] *n* **1** *(by workers, students, etc)* huelga. **2** SP *(blow - gen)* golpe *m*; *(- in tenpin bowling)* pleno; *(- in baseball)* strike *m*. **3** *(find)* hallazgo; *(of oil, gold, etc)* descubrimiento. **4** MIL ataque *m*: *air strike* ataque aéreo.

▶ *vt* **1** *(hit)* pegar, golpear. **2** *(knock against, collide with)* dar contra, chocar contra; *(ball, stone)* pegar contra, dar contra; *(lightning, bullet, torpedo)* alcanzar. **3** *(disaster, earthquake)* golpear, sobrevenir; *(disease)* atacar, golpear. **4** *(gold, oil)* descubrir, encontrar, dar con; *(track, path)* dar con. **5** *(coin, medal)* acuñar. **6** *(match)* encender. **7** *(of clock)* dar, tocar. **8** MUS *(note)* dar; *(chord)* tocar. **9** *(bargain, deal)* cerrar, hacer; *(balance)* encontrar, hallar; *(agreement)* llegar a. **10** *(pose, attitude)* adoptar. **11** *(give impression)* parecer, dar la impresión de. **12** *(occur to)* ocurrírsele a; *(remember)* acordarse de. **13** *(render)* dejar. **14** *(cause fear, terror, worry)* infundir. **15** *(take down - sail, flag)* arriar; *(- tent, set)* desmontar. **16** *(cutting)* plantar.

▶ *vi* **1** *(attack - troops, animal, etc)* atacar; *(- disaster, misfortune)* sobrevenir, ocurrir; *(- disease)* atacar, golpear; *(- lightning)* alcanzar, caer. **2** *(workers, etc)* declararse en huelga, hacer huelga. **3** *(clock)* dar la hora.

◆ **to strike back** *vi* **1** *(gen)* devolver el golpe. **2** MIL contraatacar.

◆ **to strike down** *vt sep (by illness, disease)* abatir, fulminar.

◆ **to strike off** *vt sep* **1** *(name from list)* tachar. **2** JUR *(doctor, lawyer, etc)* inhabilitar para ejercer.

◆ **to strike on** *vt insep (discover)* dar con, encontrar.

◆ **to strike out** *vt sep (remove, cross out)* tachar.

▶ *vi* **1** *(attack, hit out)* arremeter (at, contra). **2** *(set off)* emprender el camino.

◆ **to strike up** *vt insep (friendship)* entablar, trabar; *(conversation)* entablar, iniciar.

▶ *vi (band)* empezar a tocar.
ⓘ *pt & pp* struck [strʌk].

strikebreaker ['straɪkbreɪkəʳ] *n* esquirol *mf*, rompehuelgas *mf*.

striker ['straɪkəʳ] n **1** (worker) huelguista mf. **2** SP (football) delantero,-a; (cricket) bateador,-ra.

striking ['straɪkɪŋ] adj **1** (eye-catching) llamativo,-a; (stunning) atractivo,-a. **2** (similarity, resemblance) sorprendente, asombroso,-a; (feature, etc) impresionante, destacado,-a. **3** (on strike) en huelga.

string [strɪŋ] n **1** (cord) cuerda, cordel m; (lace) cordón m; (of puppet) hilo. **2** (on instrument, racket) cuerda. **3** (of garlic, onions) ristra; (of pearls, beads) sarta, hilo. **4** (of vehicles) fila, hilera; (of hotels) cadena; (of events) serie f, cadena, sucesión f; (of lies, complaints) sarta; (of insults) retahíla. COMP **string orchestra** orquesta de cuerda. ‖ **string quartet** cuarteto de cuerda.

▶ vt **1** (beads) ensartar, enhebrar. **2** (guitar, racket) encordar. **3** (beans) quitar la hebra a.

① pt & pp **strung** [strʌŋ].

▶ n pl **the strings** MUS los instrumentos mpl de cuerda.

strip¹ [strɪp] vt **1** (person) desnudar, quitarle la ropa a; (bed) quitar la ropa de; (room, house) vaciar; (wallpaper, paint) quitar; (leaves, bark) arrancar. **2** (property, rights, titles) despojar (of, de). **3** (engine) desarmar, desmontar (down, -); (ship) desaparejar.

▶ vi (undress) desnudarse (off, -), quitarse la ropa; (perform striptease) hacer un strip-tease.

① pt & pp **stripped**, ger **stripping**.

▶ n (striptease) strip-tease m.

strip² [strɪp] n **1** (of paper, leather) tira; (of land) franja; (of metal) tira, cinta. **2** SP (colours, kit) equipo. **3** (airstrip) pista (de aterrizaje). **4** [also strip (cartoon)] historieta, tira cómica. COMP **strip lighting** alumbrado fluorescente. ‖ **strip mining** US explotación f a cielo abierto.

stripe [straɪp] n **1** (gen) raya, lista. **2** MIL galón m. **3** (kind, type) tipo, clase f.

▶ vt pintar a rayas, dibujar a rayas.

striped [straɪpt] adj rayado,-a, a rayas: a striped shirt una camisa a rayas.

stripy ['staɪpɪ] adj rayado,-a, a rayas.

① comp **stripier**, superl **stripiest**.

strive [straɪv] vi esforzarse, procurar.

① pt **strove** [strəʊv], pp **striven** ['strɪvən].

striven ['strɪvən] pt → **strive**.

strode [strəʊd] pt → **stride**.

stroke [strəʊk] n **1** (blow) golpe m. **2** (caress) caricia. **3** SP (in tennis, cricket, golf) golpe m, jugada; (in billiards) tacada; (in rowing) palada; (in swimming - movement) brazada; (- style) estilo. **4** SP (oarsman) cabo. **5** (of pen) trazo; (of brush) pincelada. **6** (of bell) campanada. **7** (of engine) tiempo; (of piston) carrera. **8** MED ataque m de apoplejía, derrame m cerebral. **9** (oblique) barra (oblicua).

▶ vt **1** (caress) acariciar. **2** (ball) dar un golpe a.

stroll [strəʊl] n paseo, vuelta.

▶ vi dar un paseo, dar una vuelta.

stroller ['strəʊləʳ] n **1** (pushchair) cochecito, sillita de niño. **2** (person) paseante mf.

strong [strɒŋ] adj **1** (physically - person) fuerte; (- consitution) robusto,-a. **2** (material, furniture, shoes, etc) fuerte, resistente. **3** (country, army) poderoso,-a, fuerte. **4** (beliefs, views, principles) firme; (faith) firme, sólido,-a; (support) mucho, firme. **5** (argument, evidence) contundente, convincente; (influence) grande; (protest) enérgico,-a. **6** (colour) fuerte, intenso,-a, vivo,-a; (smell, food, drink) fuerte; (tea, coffee) fuerte, cargado,-a; (light) brillante. **7** (resemblance, accent) fuerte, marcado,-a. **8** (chance, likelihood, probability) bueno,-a. **9** (wind, current) fuerte. **10** (good - team) fuerte; (- cast) sólido,-a. **11** (currency, etc) fuerte.

▶ adv fuerte.

strongbox ['strɒŋbɒks] n caja fuerte.

stronghold ['strɒŋhəʊld] n **1** MIL fortaleza. **2** fig baluarte m.

strongroom ['strɒŋruːm] n cámara acorazada.

stroppy ['strɒpɪ] adj GB fam borde, de mala uva.

① comp **stroppier**, superl **stroppiest**.

strove [strəʊv] pt → **strive**.

struck [strʌk] pt & pp → **strike**.

structural ['strʌktʃ°rəl] adj (gen) estructural. COMP **structural engineer** ingeniero,-a de estructuras.

S

structure ['strʌktʃər] n **1** (organization, composition) estructura. **2** (thing constructed) construcción f; (building) edificio.
▶ vt (arguemnt, essay, report, etc) estructurar; (event) planificar.

struggle ['strʌgəl] n (gen) lucha; (physical fight) pelea, forcejeo.
▶ vi **1** (fight) luchar; (physically) forcejear. **2** (strive) luchar (for, por), esforzarse (for, por); (suffer) pasar apuros; (have difficulty) costar, tener problemas.

strum [strʌm] vt rasguear.
▶ vi rasguear (on, -).
ⓘ pt & pp strummed, ger strumming.

strung [strʌŋ] pt & pp → string. LOC to be highly strung estar muy nervioso, -a, estar muy tenso,-a.

strut [strʌt] n **1** ARCH (rod, bar) puntal m, riostra. **2** (way of walking) contoneo, pavoneo.
▶ vi pavonearse, contonearse.
ⓘ pt & pp strutted, ger strutting.

stub [stʌb] n (of cigarette) colilla; (of pencil, candle) cabo; (of cheque, etc) matriz f.
▶ vt darse un golpe.
ⓘ pt & pp stubbed, ger stubbing.
◆ to stub out vt sep apagar.

stubborn ['stʌbən] adj **1** (person, animal) terco,-a, testarudo,-a, tozudo,-a, obstinado,-a; (refusal, resistance) obcecado,-a. **2** (stain, cough, etc) rebelde.

stubbornly ['stʌbənlɪ] adv tercamente, cabezudamente.

stubby ['stʌbɪ] adj corto,-a y rechoncho,-a.
ⓘ comp stubbier, superl stubbiest.

stucco ['stʌkəʊ] n estuco.
ⓘ pl stuccoes o stuccos.

stuck [stʌk] pt & pp → stick.
▶ adj **1** (unable to move) atascado,-a. **2** (trapped) atrapado,-a; (in routine) estancado,-a. **3** fam (stumped) atascado,-a; (in difficulties) en apuros.

stuck-up [stʌk'ʌp] adj fam creído,-a, estirado,-a.

stud [stʌd] n semental m. COMP stud farm cuadra.

student ['stjuːdənt] n **1** (university) estudiante mf, universitario,-a; (school) alumno,-a. **2** fml (scholar) estudioso,-a.
▶ adj estudiantil.

studio ['stjuːdɪəʊ] n **1** (TV, radio) estudio. **2** (artist's) estudio, taller m.
ⓘ pl studios.
▶ n pl studios CINEM estudios mpl.

studious ['stjuːdɪəs] adj **1** (fond of studying) estudioso,-a, aplicado,-a. **2** fml (careful) esmerado,-a; (deliberate) deliberado,-a.

study ['stʌdɪ] n **1** (act of studying) estudio; (investigation, research) investigación f, estudio. **2** (room) despacho, estudio.
ⓘ pl studies.
▶ vt **1** (gen) estudiar; (university subject) estudiar, cursar; (investigate, research) estudiar, investigar. **2** (scrutinize) estudiar, examinar.
▶ vi estudiar.
ⓘ pt & pp studied, ger studying.
▶ n pl studies (work) estudios mpl; (subjects) estudios mpl, asignaturas fpl.

stuff [stʌf] n **1** fam (matter, material, substance) materia, material m. **2** fam (things, possesions) cosas fpl, trastos mpl. **3** fam (content) cuento, rollo, cosas fpl.
▶ vt **1** (fill - container, bag, box) llena (with, de); (- cushion, toy, food) rellena (with, de); (- hole) tapar. **2** (dead animal) disecar. **3** (push carelessly, shove) meter poner. **4** fam (beat, thrash) dar una pali za a. **5** sl (sod) meter.

stuffed [stʌft] adj **1** (full) relleno,-a (crammed) atiborrado,-a. **2** (animal) di secado,-a.

stuffing ['stʌfɪŋ] n relleno.

stuffy ['stʌfɪ] adj **1** (room) ma ventilado,-a; (atmosphere) cargado,-a **2** (person) estirado,-a, remilgado,-a (institution) tradicional; (ideas, manner formal, serio,-a, convencional.
ⓘ comp stuffier, superl stuffiest.

stumble ['stʌmbəl] n tropezón m, tra pié m, trompicón m.
▶ vi **1** (trip) tropezar (on/over, con dar un traspié. **2** (walk unsteadily) tan balearse. **3** (while speaking) atrancars atascarse.
◆ to stumble across / stumble on insep dar con, tropezar con.

stun [stʌn] vt **1** (make unconscious) dejar si sentido; (daze) aturdir, atontar, pa

mar. **2** *(surprise)* sorprender, dejar atónito,-a, dejar pasmado,-a; *(shock)* atolondrar, aturdir, dejar anonadado,-a.
ⓘ *pt & pp* stunned, *ger* stunning.

stung [stʌŋ] *pt & pp* → sting.

stunk [stʌŋk] *pt & pp* → stink.

stunning ['stʌnɪŋ] *adj* **1** *(surprising)* alucinante, apabullante; *(shocking)* asombroso,-a. **2** *(beautiful, impressive)* impresionante, imponente, fenomenal.

stunt¹ [stʌnt] *vt (growth)* atrofiar.

stunt² [stʌnt] *n* **1** *(dangerous act)* proeza; *(in film)* escena peligrosa. **2** *(trick)* truco, maniobra. COMP **stunt man** especialista *m*. ▍ **stunt woman** especialista *f*.

stunted ['stʌntɪd] *adj (tree, body)* raquítico,-a; *(growth)* atrofiado,-a.

stupefy ['stjuːpɪfaɪ] *vt* **1** *(alcohol, drugs)* atontar, aturdir, aletargar. **2** *(amaze)* dejar pasmado,-a, dejar estupefacto,-a.
ⓘ *pt & pp* stupefied, *ger* stupefying.

stupid ['stjuːpɪd] *adj* **1** tonto,-a, bobo,-a, imbécil, estúpido,-a. **2** *(senseless)* atontado,-a. **3** *fam (annoying)* maldito,-a.
ⓘ *comp* stupider, *comp* stupidest.
▶ *n* tonto,-a, imbécil *mf*.

stupidity [stjuːˈpɪdɪti] *n* estupidez *f*, tontería.

stupidly ['stjuːpɪdli] *adv* estúpidamente, tontamente.

stupor ['stjuːpə'] *n* estupor *m*.

sturdy ['stɜːdi] *adj* **1** *(strong)* robusto,-a, fuerte; *(solid)* sólido,-a. **2** *(opposition, resistence, defence)* enérgico,-a, férreo,-a, tenaz, inquebrantable.
ⓘ *comp* sturdier, *superl* sturdiest.

sturgeon ['stɜːdʒən] *n* esturión *m*.

stutter ['stʌtə'] *n* tartamudeo.
▶ *vi* tartamudear.
▶ *vt* decir tartamudeando, balbucear.

sty¹ [staɪ] *n (for pigs)* pocilga.
ⓘ *pl* sties.

sty² [staɪ] *n* → stye.
ⓘ *pl* sties.

stye [staɪ] *n (in eye)* orzuelo.

style [staɪl] *n* **1** *(gen)* estilo. **2** *(type, model)* modelo, diseño. **3** *(of hair)* peinado. **4** *(fashion)* moda. **5** *fml (correct title)* título. **6** BOT estilo.

▶ *vt* **1** *(gen)* diseñar; *(hair)* peinar. **2** *fml (name, title)* llamar.

stylish ['staɪlɪʃ] *adj* **1** *(elegant)* elegante, con mucho estilo. **2** *(fashionable)* a la moda, de última moda.

stylist ['staɪlɪst] *n* **1** *(hairdresser)* estilista *mf*, peluquero,-a. **2** *(writer)* estilista *mf*.

stylized ['staɪlaɪzd] *adj* estilizado,-a.

stylus ['staɪləs] *n* **1** *(of record player)* aguja. **2** *(for writing)* estilo.
ⓘ *pl* styluses o styli .

suave [swɑːv] *adj (charming, polite)* afable, cortés; *(slick, ingratiating)* zalamero,-a.

☒ Suave no significa 'suave', que se traduce por soft.

sub [sʌb] *n* **1** *(submarine)* submarino. **2** SP *(substitute)* sustituto,-a, suplente *mf*. **3** *(subscription)* cuota, subscripción *f*, suscripción *f*. **4** *(subeditor)* redactor,-ra. **5** GB *(advance from wages)* anticipo.
▶ *vi (act as substitute)* sustituir (for, a).
▶ *vt* **1** GB *(give an advance)* anticipar, dar un anticipo. **2** *(subedit)* corregir, revisar.
ⓘ *pt & pp* subbed, *ger* subbing.

subconscious [sʌbˈkɒnʃəs] *adj* subconsciente.
▶ *n* the subconscious el subconsciente *m*.

subcontinent [sʌbˈkɒntɪnənt] *n* subcontinente *m*.

subcontract [*(n)* sʌbˈkɒntrækt; *(vb)* sʌbkənˈtrækt] *n* subcontrato.
▶ *vt* subcontratar (to, a).

subculture ['sʌbkʌltʃə'] *n* subcultura.

subdivide [sʌbdɪˈvaɪd] *vt* subdividir (into, en).

subgroup ['sʌbɡruːp] *n* subgrupo.

subhuman [sʌbˈhjuːmən] *adj* infrahumano,-a.

subject [*(n-adj)* 'sʌbdʒekt; *(vb)* səbˈdʒekt] *n* **1** *(theme, topic)* tema *m*. **2** EDUC asignatura. **3** *(citizen)* súbdito, ciudadano,-a. **4** LING sujeto. **5** *(cause)* objeto *(of/for, de)*. **6** *(of experiment)* sujeto.
▶ *vt (bring under control)* someter, sojuzgar (to, a).
▶ *adj (subordinate, governed)* sometido,-a.
subject to *(bound by)* sujeto,-a a; *(prone to - floods, subsidence)* expuesto,-a a; *(- change, delay)* susceptible de, suje-

to,-a a; (- *illness*) propenso,-a a. COMP
subject matter 1 (*topic*) tema *m*, materia. **2** (*contents*) contenido.

▶ *prep* **subject to** (*conditional on*) previo, -a, supeditado,-a a.

◆ **to subject to** *vt sep* someter a.

subjective [səb'dʒektɪv] *adj* subjetivo,-a.

subjunctive [səb'dʒʌŋktɪv] *adj* LING subjuntivo,-a.

▶ *n* LING subjuntivo.

sublet [sʌb'let] *vt* realquilar, subarrendar.

▶ *vi* realquilar, subarrendar.

ⓘ *pt & pp* **sublet**, *ger* **subletting**.

sublime [sə'blaɪm] *adj* **1** (*beauty, music, compliment, etc*) sublime. **2** *fam* (*food, performance*) maravilloso,-a, sensacional. **3** *pej* (*indifference, ignorance, etc*) sumo,-a, supremo,-a, absoluto,-a, total.

▶ *n* **the sublime** lo sublime.

subliminal [sʌb'lɪmɪnəl] *adj* subliminal.

sub-machine-gun [sʌbmə'ʃiːngʌn] *n* ametralladora, metralleta.

submarine ['sʌbməriːn] *n* submarino.

▶ *adj* submarino,-a.

submerge [səb'mɜːdʒ] *vt* sumergir (in, en).

▶ *vi* sumergirse.

submission [səb'mɪʃən] *n* **1** (*subjection*) sumisión *f* (to, a). **2** SP (*in wrestling*) rendición *f*. **3** (*presentation*) presentación *f*. **4** (*report*) informe *m*; (*proposal*) propuesta.

submit [səb'mɪt] *vt* **1** (*present*) presentar. **2** (*subject*) someter (to, a). **3** JUR (*suggest*) sostener.

▶ *vi* (*admit defeat, surrender*) rendirse, ceder; (*to demand, wishes*) acceder.

ⓘ *pt & pp* **submitted**, *ger* **submitting**.

subnormal [sʌb'nɔːməl] *adj* **1** (*person*) subnormal, retrasado,-a. **2** (*temperatures*) por debajo de lo normal.

subordinate [(*adj-n*) sə'bɔːdɪnət; (*vb*) sə'bɔːdɪneɪt] *adj* **1** (*lower, less important*) subordinado,-a (to, a), secundario, -a. **2** LING subordinado,-a. COMP **subordinate clause** oración *f* subordinada.

▶ *n* (*person*) subordinado,-a, subalterno,-a.

▶ *vt* subordinar (to, a), supeditar (to, a).

subordination [səbɔːdɪ'neɪʃən] *n* subordinación *f*.

subscribe [səb'skraɪb] *vi* **1** (*to newspaper, etc*) suscribirse (to, a), abonarse (to, a). **2** (*to charity*) hacer donaciones, contribuir con donativos (to, a). **3** (*to opinion, theory*) suscribir (to, -), estar de acuerdo (to, con). **4** FIN (*shares*) suscribir (for, -).

▶ *vt* **1** (*contribute*) contribuir, donar. **2** *fml* (*sign*) suscribir.

subscriber [səb'skraɪbər] *n* (*to newspaper, etc*) suscriptor,-ra, abonado,-a; (*to telephone service, cable television*) abonado,-a.

subscription [səb'skrɪpʃən] *n* (*to newspaper, etc*) suscripción *f*, abono; (*to club*) cuota; (*to charity*) donativo, donación *f*.

subsection ['sʌbsekʃən] *n* JUR (*in document, text*) artículo.

subsequent ['sʌbsɪkwənt] *adj* subsiguiente, posterior. LOC **subsequent to** posterior a.

subside [səb'saɪd] *vi* **1** (*land, building, road*) hundirse. **2** *fig* (*person*) dejarse caer. **3** (*storm, wind*) amainar; (*floods*) decrecer, bajar; (*pain, fever*) disminuir; (*noise, applause*) irse apagando; (*anger, excitement*) calmarse.

subsidiary [səb'sɪdɪərɪ] *adj* **1** (*role, interest, issue*) secundario,-a. **2** (*income*) adicional, extra; (*payment, loan*) subsidiario,-a.

▶ *n* COMM filial *f*.

ⓘ *pl* **subsidiaries**.

subsidize ['sʌbsɪdaɪz] *vt* (*gen*) subvencionar; (*exports*) primar.

subsidy ['sʌbsɪdɪ] *n* subvención *f*, subsidio.

ⓘ *pl* **subsidies**.

subsist [səb'sɪst] *vi* subsistir.

subsistence [səb'sɪstəns] *n* subsistencia.

subsoil ['sʌbsɔɪl] *n* subsuelo.

substance ['sʌbstəns] *n* **1** (*matter*) sustancia. **2** (*real matter, solid content*) sustancia, solidez *f*. **3** (*essence, gist*) esencia, sustancia. **4** (*wealth*) riqueza.

substantial [səb'stænʃəl] *adj* **1** (*solid*) sólido,-a, fuerte. **2** (*large - sum, increase, loss, damage*) importante, considerable; (*- difference, change*) sustancial, notable. **3** *(meal - large)* abundante; *(nourishing)* sustancioso,-a. **4** *(wealthy)* acaudalado,-a. **5** *fml (real, tangible)* sustancial.

substantiate [səb'stænʃreɪt] *vt (gen)* confirmar, corroborar; *(accusation)* probar.

substantive ['sʌbstəntɪv] *adj fml (research, information, evidence)* sustantivo, -a; *(matter, issue)* fundamental.
▶ *n* LING sustantivo.

substitute ['sʌbstɪtjuːt] *n* **1** *(person)* sustituto,-a, suplente *mf*. **2** *(thing)* sucedáneo (for, de).
▶ *vt* sustituir, reemplazar.
▶ *vi* sustituir, suplir (for, a).

substitution [sʌbstɪ'tjuːʃ°n] *n* sustitución *f*.

subterranean [sʌbtə'reɪnɪən] *adj* subterráneo,-a.

subtitle ['sʌbtaɪt°l] *n* subtítulo.
▶ *vt* subtitular, poner subtítulos a.

subtle ['sʌt°l] *adj* **1** *(person - tactful)* delicado,-a, discreto,-a. **2** *(colour, difference, hint, joke)* sutil; *(taste)* delicado,-a, ligero,-a; *(lighting)* tenue, sutil. **3** *(remark, mind)* agudo,-a, perspicaz; *(plan, argument, analysis)* ingenioso,-a; *(irony)* fino,-a.
ⓘ *comp* subtler, *comp* subtlest.

subtotal ['sʌb'təʊt°l] *n* subtotal *m*.

subtract [səb'trækt] *vt* restar (from, de).

subtraction [səb'trækʃ°n] *n* resta.

subtropical [sʌb'trɒpɪk°l] *adj* subtropical.

suburb ['sʌbɜːb] *n* barrio residencial.
COMP **the suburbs** las afueras *fpl*.

❌ Suburb no significa 'suburbio (barrio desfavorecido', que se traduce por slums.

suburban [sə'bɜːb°n] *adj (area)* de los barrios residenciales; *(attitude)* convencional.

suburbia [sə'bɜːbɪə] *n* los barrios *mpl* residenciales.

subversion [sʌb'vɜːʃ°n] *n* subversión *f*.

subversive [sʌb'vɜːsɪv] *adj* subversivo,-a.
▶ *n (person)* elemento subversivo.

subway ['sʌbweɪ] *n* **1** GB *(underpass)* paso subterráneo. **2** US *(underground)* metro.

succeed [sək'siːd] *vi* **1** *(be successful - person)* tener éxito, triunfar; *(- plan, marriage)* salir bien; *(- strike)* surtir efecto, dar resultado. **2** *(manage)* lograr, conseguir. **3** *(throne)* subir (to, a); *(title)* heredar (to, -).
▶ *vt* **1** *(take place of)* suceder a. **2** *fml (follow after)* suceder a.

❌ To succeed no significa 'suceder', que se traduce por to happen.

succeeding [sək'siːdɪŋ] *adj* subsiguiente.

success [sək'ses] *n* **1** *(good result, achievement)* éxito. **2** *(successful person, thing)* éxito.

❌ Success no significa 'suceso', que se traduce por event.

successful [sək'sesful] *adj (person, career, film)* de éxito; *(plan, performance, attempt)* acertado,-a, logrado,-a; *(business)* próspero,-a; *(marriage)* feliz; *(meeting)* satisfactorio,-a, positivo,-a.

successfully [sʌk'sesfulɪ] *adv* con éxito, satisfactoriamente.

succession [sək'seʃ°n] *n* **1** *(act of following)* sucesión *f*. **2** *(series)* serie *f*, sucesión *f*. **3** *(to post, throne)* sucesión *f*.

successive [sək'sesɪv] *adj* sucesivo,-a, consecutivo,-a.

successor [sək'sesə'] *n* sucesor,-ra.

succulent ['sʌkjələnt] *adj* **1** *(juicy)* suculento,-a. **2** BOT carnoso,-a.
▶ *n* BOT planta carnosa, suculenta.

such [sʌtʃ] *adj* **1** *(of that sort)* tal, semejante. **2** *(so much, so great)* tal, tanto,-a.
▶ *adv (so very)* tan.
▶ *pron (of that specified sort)* tal. LOC **as such 1** *(strictly speaking)* propiamente dicho. **2** *(that way)* como tal. ▌**in such a way that...** de tal manera que… ▌**such as** *(like, for example)* como. ▌**such as?** ¿por ejemplo?

suck [sʌk] *vt* **1** *(person - liquid)* sorber; *(- lollipop, pencil, thumb, etc)* chupar; *(insect - blood, nectar)* chupar, succionar. **2** *(vacuum cleaner)* aspirar (in, -); *(pump)* succionar, aspirar (in, -); *(plant)* absorber (up, -). **3** *(draw powerfully)* arrastrar.
▶ *vi* **1** *(person)* chupar (at/on, -); *(baby)* mamar (at, -); *(vacuum cleaner)* aspirar (up,-); *(pump)* succionar, aspirar.

sucker [ˈsʌkəʳ] *n* **1** ZOOL ventosa. **2** BOT chupón *m*, mamón *m*. **3** *(rubber disc)* ventosa.

suckle [ˈsʌkəl] *vt* amamantar, dar de mamar a.
▸ *vi* mamar.

sucrose [ˈsjuːkrəʊz] *n* sacarosa.

suction [ˈsʌkʃən] *n (sticking together)* succión *f*; *(of water, air)* aspiración *f*. COMP **suction cup** ventosa. ‖ **suction pump** bomba de aspiración.

Sudan [suːˈdæn] [also the Sudan] *n* Sudán.

Sudanese [suːdəˈniːz] *adj* sudanés, -esa.
▸ *n* sudanés,-esa.
▸ *n pl* **the Sudanese** los sudaneses *mpl*.

sudden [ˈsʌdən] *adj* **1** *(quick)* súbito,-a, repentino,-a. **2** *(unexpected)* inesperado,-a, imprevisto,-a. **3** *(abrupt)* brusco,-a. LOC **all of a sudden** de repente. COMP **sudden death** muerte *f* súbita.

suddenly [ˈsʌdənlɪ] *adv* **1** *(unexpectedly)* de repente, de pronto. **2** *(abruptly)* bruscamente.

suds [sʌdz] *n pl* jabonaduras *fpl*, espuma *f sing* (de jabón).

sue [suː] *vt* JUR demandar.
▸ *vi* JUR entablar una demanda (for, por).

suede [sweɪd] *n* ante *m*, gamuza.
▸ *adj* de ante, de gamuza.

suet [ˈsuːɪt] *n* sebo.

suffer [ˈsʌfəʳ] *vt* **1** *(gen)* sufrir; *(pain)* padecer, sufrir; *(hunger)* padecer, pasar; *(losses)* sufrir, registrar. **2** *(bear, tolerate)* aguantar, soportar, tolerar.
▸ *vi* **1** *(gen)* sufrir. **2** *(be affected - work, studies, etc)* verse afectado,-a; *(- health)* resentirse: LOC **to suffer from 1** *(illness)* sufrir de, padecer. **2** *(shock)* sufrir los efectos de. **3** *(effects)* resentirse de.

sufferer [ˈsʌfərəʳ] *n* enfermo,-a.

suffering [ˈsʌfərɪŋ] *n (affliction)* sufrimiento, aflicción *f*; *(grief)* pena, dolor *m*; *(pain)* dolor *m*.

sufficient [səˈfɪʃənt] *adj* suficiente, bastante. LOC **to be sufficient** bastar.

suffix [ˈsʌfɪks] *n* sufijo.

suffocate [ˈsʌfəkeɪt] *vt* asfixiar, ahogar.
▸ *vi* asfixiarse, ahogarse.

❌ To **suffocate** no significa 'sofocar (un incendio)', que se traduce por **to put out**.

suffocation [sʌfəˈkeɪʃən] *n* asfixia, ahogo.

suffrage [ˈsʌfrɪdʒ] *n* sufragio.

sugar [ˈʃʊgəʳ] *n* **1** azúcar *m & f*. **2** US *fam (form of address)* cariño, cielo. COMP **sugar beet** remolacha azucarera.
▸ *vt* azucarar.

sugar-coated [ʃʊgəˈkəʊtɪd] *adj* cubierto,-a de azúcar.

suggest [səˈdʒest] *vt* **1** *(propose)* sugerir, proponer; *(advise)* sugerir, aconsejar. **2** *(imply)* insinuar. **3** *(indicate)* indicar. **4** *(evoke)* evocar, sugerir.

suggestion [səˈdʒestʃən] *n* **1** *(proposal)* sugerencia, propuesta. **2** *(insinuation)* insinuación *f*. **3** *(indication, hint)* indicio; *(slight trace)* sombra, traza, asomo, nota. **4** *(in psychology)* sugestión *f*.

suggestive [səˈdʒestɪv] *adj (with sexual connotations)* provocativo,-a, insinuante.

suicidal [suːɪˈsaɪdəl] *adj* suicida.

suicide [ˈsuːɪsaɪd] *n* **1** *(act)* suicidio. **2** *(person)* suicida *mf*. **3** *fig* suicidio. COMP **to commit suicide** suicidarse.

suit [suːt] *n* **1** *(man's)* traje *m*; *(woman's)* traje *m* de chaqueta. **2** JUR pleito, juicio. **3** *(in cards)* palo.
▸ *vt* **1** *(be convenient, acceptable)* convenir a, venir bien a; *(please)* satisfacer, agradar, contentar. **2** *(be right for)* ir bien a, sentar bien a; *(look good on)* quedar bien a, favorecer. **3** *(adapt)* adaptar (to, a), ajustar (to, a).

suitable [ˈsuːtəbəl] *adj* **1** *(appropriate)* adecuado,-a (for, para), apropiado, -a (for, para); *(for job, post)* adecuado,-a, indicado,-a, idóneo,-a. **2** *(acceptable, proper)* apropiado,-a, apto,-a. **3** *(convenient)* conveniente.

suitcase [ˈsuːtkeɪs] *n* maleta.

suite [swiːt] *n* **1** *(of furniture)* juego. **2** *(in hotel)* suite *f*. **3** MUS suite *f*. **4** *(retinue)* séquito, comitiva. **5** COMPUT juego.

suited ['su:tɪd] *adj* apropiado,-a (for, para), adecuado,-a (for, para).

sulk [sʌlk] *vi* enfurruñarse, estar de mal humor.
▸ *n* malhumor *m*.

sulky ['sʌlkɪ] *adj (look, mood)* malhumorado,-a; *(person)* con tendencia a enfurruñarse.
ⓘ *comp* sulkier, *superl* sulkiest.

sullen ['sʌlən] *adj* **1** *(person, mood)* hosco,-a, arisco,-a, huraño,-a; *(face)* adusto,-a.

sully ['sʌlɪ] *vt* **1** *(dirty)* ensuciar. **2** *fig (tarnish, spoil)* manchar, mancillar.
ⓘ *pt & pp* sullied, *ger* sullying.

sultan ['sʌlt°n] *n* sultán *m*.

sultry ['sʌltrɪ] *adj* **1** *(weather)* bochornoso,-a, sofocante. **2** *(person)* sensual.
ⓘ *comp* sultrier, *superl* sultriest.

sum [sʌm] *n* **1** MATH *(calculation)* cuenta; *(addition)* suma, adición *f*. **2** *(amount of money)* suma (de dinero), cantidad *f* (de dinero). **3** *(total amount)* suma, total *m*. COMP **in sum** en resumen. ┃ LOC **the sum total** total *m*.
▸ *n pl* **sums** aritmética *f sing*, cálculos *mpl*.
◆ **to sum up** *vt sep* **1** *(summarize)* resumir, hacer un resumen de, sintetizar. **2** *(size up - situation)* evaluar; *(- person)* catalogar.
▸ *vi (summarize)* resumir; *(of judge)* recapitular.
ⓘ *pt & pp* summed, *ger* summing.

summarize ['sʌməraɪz] *vt* resumir, hacer un resumen de.

summary ['sʌmərɪ] *n (gen)* resumen *m*.
ⓘ *pl* summaries.
▸ *adj* **1** JUR *(justice, punishment)* sumario, -a: *summary trial* juicio sumario. **2** *(immediate - dismissal)* inmediato,-a. **3** *(brief - account)* breve, corto,-a. LOC **in summary** en resumen.

summer ['sʌmə'] *n* **1** *(gen)* verano. **2** *lit* abril *m*.
▸ *adj (gen)* de verano; *(summery)* veraniego,-a.

summertime ['sʌmətaɪm] *n* verano, estío.

summit ['sʌmɪt] *n* **1** *(of mountain, career)* cumbre *f*, cima *f*. **2** *(meeting)* cumbre *f*.

summon ['sʌmən] *vt* **1** *(person)* llamar; *(meeting, parliament)* convocar. **2** JUR citar, emplazar.
◆ **to summon up** *vt insep* **1** *(courage)* armarse de; *(strength)* reunir, cobrar; *(support)* lograr, obtener; *(resources, help)* reunir, conseguir. **2** *(memories, thoughts)* evocar.

sumptuous ['sʌmptjuəs] *adj (gen)* suntuoso,-a; *(meal)* opíparo,-a.

sun [sʌn] *n (gen)* sol *m*.

sunbathe ['sʌnbeɪð] *vi* tomar el sol.

sunbeam ['sʌnbi:m] *n* rayo de sol.

sunbed ['sʌnbed] *n* cama solar.

sunburn ['sʌnbɜːn] *n* quemadura de sol.

sunburnt ['sʌnbɜːnt] *adj (burnt)* quemado,-a (por el sol); *(tanned)* bronceado, -a, moreno,-a.

Sunday ['sʌndɪ] *n* domingo.

✎ Para ejemplos de uso, consulta Saturday.

sundial ['sʌndaɪəl] *n* reloj *m* de sol.

sundown ['sʌndaʊn] *n* US puesta de(l) sol.

sun-dried ['sʌndraɪd] *adj* secado,-a al sol.

sunflower ['sʌnflaʊə'] *n* girasol *m*. COMP **sunflower seed** semilla de girasol, pipa.

sung [sʌŋ] *pp* → sing.

sunglasses ['sʌnglɑːsɪz] *n pl* gafas *fpl* de sol.

sunhat ['sʌnhæt] *n* pamela, sombrero de ala ancha.

sunk [sʌŋk] *pp* → sink.

sunken ['sʌnkən] *adj* **1** *(ship, treasure)* hundido,-a, sumergido,-a; *(eyes, cheeks)* hundido,-a. **2** *(terrace, bath)* a un nivel más bajo.

sunlight ['sʌnlaɪt] *n* sol *m*, luz *f* del sol.

sunlit ['sʌnlɪt] *adj* soleado,-a.

sunny ['sʌnɪ] *adj* **1** *(room, house, etc)* soleado,-a; *(day)* de sol. **2** *fig (person)* alegre, risueño,-a; *(future)* risueño,-a.
ⓘ *comp* sunnier, *superl* sunniest.

sunrise ['sʌnraɪz] *n (sun-up)* salida del sol; *(dawn)* amanecer *m*, alba *m*.

sunroof ['sʌnru:f] *n* **1** AUTO capota, techo corredizo. **2** *(on building)* azotea.

S

sunset ['sʌnset] *n (sundown)* puesta de(l) sol, ocaso; *(twilight)* crepúsculo, atardecer *m*.

sunshade ['sʌnʃeɪd] *n* **1** *(parasol)* sombrilla. **2** *(awning)* toldo.

sunshine ['sʌnʃaɪn] *n* **1** sol *m*, luz *f* de sol. **2** *fig* alegría. **3** GB *fam (friendly form of address)* corazón, majo,-a; *(sarcastic)* guapo,-a.

sunstroke ['sʌnstrəʊk] *n* insolación *f*.

suntan ['sʌntæn] *n* bronceado, moreno. COMP **suntan lotion** bronceador *m*.

sun-tanned ['sʌntænd] *adj* bronceado,-a, moreno,-a.

super ['suːpər] *adj fam* genial, súper, fenomenal, de primera.
▶ *n* **1** GB *(superintendent)* comisario,-a de policía. **2** US *(superintendent)* portero,-a.

superb [suːˈpɜːb] *adj* estupendo,-a, magnífico,-a, espléndido,-a, soberbio,-a.

superbly [suːˈpɜːblɪ] *adv* estupendamente, magníficamente, espléndidamente, soberbiamente.

supercilious [suːpəˈsɪlɪəs] *adj (condescending)* altanero,-a; *(disdainful)* desdeñoso,-a.

superficial [suːpəˈfɪʃəl] *adj (gen)* superficial.

superfluous [suːˈpɜːfluəs] *adj (gen)* superfluo,-a; *(remark, comment)* de más.

superhuman [suːpəˈhjuːmən] *adj* sobrehumano,-a.

superintendent [suːpərɪnˈtendənt] *n* **1** *(person in charge - gen)* director,-ra, inspector,-ra, supervisor,-ra. **2** GB *(in police)* comisario,-a de policía. **3** US *(in apartment building)* portero,-a, conserje *mf*. **4** *(of park)* encargado,-a.

superior [suːˈpɪərɪər] *adj* **1** *(gen)* superior **(to,** a). **2** *pej (attitude, tone, smile)* de superioridad.
▶ *n (senior)* superior *mf*.

superiority [suːpɪərɪˈɒrɪtɪ] *n* superioridad *f*.

superlative [suːˈpɜːlətɪv] *adj* **1** *(excellent)* superlativo,-a, de primera, excelente, excepcional. **2** LING superlativo,-a.
▶ *n* LING superlativo.

superman ['suːpəmæn] *n* superhombre *m*.
ⓘ *pl* **supermen** ['suːpəmən].

supermarket [suːpəˈmɑːkɪt] *n* supermercado, autoservicio.

supernatural [suːpəˈnætʃərəl] *adj* sobrenatural.
▶ *n* **the supernatural** lo sobrenatural *m*.

superpower ['suːpəpaʊər] *n* superpotencia.

supersonic [suːpəˈsɒnɪk] *adj* supersónico,-a.

superstar ['suːpəstɑːr] *n* superestrella.

superstition [suːpəˈstɪʃən] *n* superstición *f*.

superstitious [sjuːpəˈstɪʃəs] *adj* supersticioso,-a.

superstore ['suːpəstɔːr] *n* hipermercado.

superstructure ['suːpəstrʌktʃər] *n* superestructura.

supertanker ['suːpətæŋkər] *n* superpetrolero.

supervise ['suːpəvaɪz] *vt* **1** *(watch over)* vigilar. **2** *(keep check on)* supervisar; *(run)* dirigir.

supervision [suːpəˈvɪʒən] *n* supervisión *f*.

supervisor ['suːpəvaɪzər] *n* **1** *(gen)* supervisor,-ra. **2** GB *(of thesis)* director,-ra de tesis.

superwoman ['suːpəwʊmən] *n* supermujer *f*.
ⓘ *pl* **superwomen** ['suːpəwɪmɪn].

supper ['sʌpər] *n* cena. LOC **to have supper** cenar.

supper-time ['sʌpətaɪm] *n* hora de cenar.

supplement [*(n)* 'sʌplɪmənt]; *(vb)* 'sʌplɪment] *n* **1** *(charge)* suplemento. **2** *(dietary)* complemento. **3** LIT suplemento.
▶ *vt* complementar.

supplementary [sʌplɪˈmentərɪ] *adj* **1** *(gen)* suplementario,-a, adicional. **2** MATH suplementario,-a.

supplier [səˈplaɪər] *n* COMM proveedor,-ra, abastecedor,-ra.

supply [səˈplaɪ] *n* **1** *(provision)* suministro. **2** COMM *(provision - to markets, areas, etc)* abastecimiento; *(- to individuals,* *houses, shops, etc)* suministro. **3** *(amount available)* reserva.

ⓘ *pl* supplies.

▸ *vt* **1** *(goods, materials)* suministrar. **2** *(a person, company, city, etc)* abastecer (with, de), proveer (with, de). **3** *(give - information, proof, facts)* facilitar, proporcionar. **4** MIL *(with provisions)* aprovisionar. **5** *fml (need, requirement)* satisfacer.

ⓘ *pt & pp* supplied, *ger* supplying.

▸ *n pl* **supplies** *(food)* provisiones *fpl,* víveres *mpl; (stock)* existencias *fpl,* stock *m.* MIL pertrechos *mpl.*

support [sə'pɔːt] *n* **1** *(physical - gen)* apoyo, sostén *m; (- thing worn on body)* protector *m.* **2** *(of building)* soporte *m,* puntal *m.* **3** *(moral)* apoyo, respaldo. **4** *(financial)* ayuda económica, apoyo económico; *(sustenance)* sustento; *(person)* sostén *m.* **5** *(supporters)* afición *f.* **6** *(evidence)* pruebas *fpl.*

▸ *vt* **1** *(roof, bridge, etc)* sostener; *(weight)* aguantar, resistir; *(part of body)* sujetar. **2** *(back, encourage)* apoyar, respaldar, ayudar; *(cause, motion, proposal)* apoyar, estar de acuerdo con. **3** SP *(follow)* seguir; *(encourage)* animar. **4** *(keep, sustain)* mantener, sustentar, sostener; *(feed)* alimentar. **5** *(corroborate, substantiate)* confirmar, respaldar, apoyar, respaldar. **6** *fml (endure)* soportar, tolerar.

🗙 To support no significa 'soportar (sufrir)', que se traduce por to bear.

supporter [sə'pɔːtər] *n* **1** POL partidario,-a. **2** SP *(gen)* seguidor,-ra; *(fan)* hincha *mf,* forofo,-a.

▸ *n pl* **supporters** SP la afición *f sing.*

COMP **supporters' club** peña deportiva.

supporting [sə'pɔːtɪŋ] *adj (part, role)* secundario,-a.

suppose [sə'pəʊz] *vt* **1** *(assume, imagine)* suponer, imaginarse. **2** *(in polite requests):* I don't suppose you could lend me £10, could you? no podrías dejarme 10 libras, ¿no? **3** *(believe)* creer. **4** *(postulate)* suponer. **5** *fml (presuppose)* suponer. LOC **I suppose not** supongo que no. ▌ **I suppose so** supongo que sí.

▸ *conj* **1** *(hypothesis)* ¿y si…?, pongamos por caso, supongamos. **2** *(making suggestions)* ¿y si…?, ¿qué tal si…?

supposed [sə'pəʊzd] *adj* supuesto,-a. LOC **to be supposed to 1** *(supposition, reputation)* se supone que, dicen que. **2** *(obligation, responsibility)* deber, tener que. **3** *(intention)* se supone que.

supposing [sə'pəʊzɪŋ] *conj* **1** *(hypothesis)* ¿y si…?, suponiendo. **2** *(making suggestions)* ¿y si…?, ¿qué tal si…?

suppository [sə'pɒzɪtᵊrɪ] *n* supositorio.

ⓘ *pl* suppositories.

supremacy [suː'preməsɪ] *n* supremacía.

supreme [suː'priːm] *adj (highest)* supremo,-a, sumo,-a; *(greatest)* supremo,-a.

supremo [su'priːməʊ] *n* GB *fam* gran jefe,-a.

ⓘ *pl* supremos.

surcharge ['sɜːtʃɑːdʒ] *n* recargo, sobretasa.

▸ *vt (person)* aplicar un recargo a.

sure [ʃʊər] *adj* **1** *(positive, certain)* seguro,-a (about/of, de); *(convinced)* convencido,-a. **2** *(certain, inevitable)* seguro,-a. **3** *(reliable)* seguro,-a.

▸ *adv* **1** *(of course)* claro, por supuesto. **2** US *(as intensifier)* realmente, de verdad.

surely ['ʃʊəlɪ] *adv* **1** *(doubtless)* seguramente, sin duda. **2** *(as intensifier):* surely you haven't forgotten! ¡no se te habrá olvidado! **3** *(in a sure manner)* con seguridad. **4** US *(certainly)* por supuesto, desde luego, claro (que sí).

surf [sɜːf] *n (waves)* olas *fpl,* oleaje *m; (foam)* espuma.

▸ *vi* hacer surf. LOC **to surf the net** navegar en Internet.

surface ['sɜːfɪs] *n* **1** *(gen)* superficie *f; (of road)* firme *m.* **2** *fig (exterior)* apariencia.

▸ *adj (gen)* superficial.

▸ *vt (cover road)* pavimentar; *(with asphalt)* asfaltar.

▸ *vi* **1** *(submarine, etc)* salir a la superficie; *(problems, etc)* aflorar, aparecer, surgir. **2** *(from bed)* asomarse, dejarse ver; *(after disappearance)* reaparecer.

surfboard ['sɜːfbɔːd] *n* tabla de surf.

surfer ['sɜːfər] *n* surfista *mf.*

surfing ['sɜːfɪŋ] *n* surf *m.*

S

surgeon ['sɜːdʒən] *n* cirujano,-a.

surgery ['sɜːdʒərɪ] *n* **1** *(operating)* cirugía. **2** GB *(place)* consultorio, consulta; *(time)* consulta.
ⓘ *pl* surgeries.

surgical ['sɜːdʒɪkəl] *adj (instrument, treatment)* quirúrgico,-a.

Surinam [sʊərɪˈnæm] *n* Surinam.

surmount [sɜːˈmaʊnt] *vt* **1** *(overcome)* superar, vencer. **2** ARCH rematar, coronar.

surname ['sɜːneɪm] *n* apellido.

surpass [sɜːˈpɑːs] *vt (better)* superar; *(exceed)* superar, sobrepasar.

surplus ['sɜːpləs] *n (of goods, produce)* excedente *m*, sobrante *m*; *(of budget)* superávit *m*.
▸ *adj* sobrante, excedente.

surprise [səˈpraɪz] *n* sorpresa.
▸ *adj (visit, result)* inesperado,-a; *(attack, party)* sorpresa.
▸ *vt* **1** *(cause surprise to)* sorprender. **2** *(catch unawares)* sorprender, coger desprevenido,-a.

surprised [səˈpraɪzd] *adj (person)* sorprendido,-a; *(look)* de sorpresa.

surprising [səˈpraɪzɪŋ] *adj* sorprendente.

surreal [səˈrɪəl] *adj* surrealista.

surrealism [səˈrɪəlɪzəm] *n* surrealismo.

surrealist [səˈrɪəlɪst] *n* surrealista *mf*.
▸ *adj* surrealista.

surrender [səˈrendər] *n* **1** *(capitulation)* rendición *f*; *(submission)* sumisión *f*, claudicación *f*. **2** *(giving up - of arms)* entrega; *(- of rights)* renuncia.
▸ *vt* **1** MIL *(weapons, town)* rendir, entregar. **2** *fml (passport, ticket, etc)* entregar; *(claim, right, privilege)* renunciar a, ceder.
▸ *vi* rendirse, entregarse.

surround [səˈraʊnd] *vt (encircle)* rodear (with, de).
▸ *n* marco, borde *m*.

surrounding [səˈraʊndɪŋ] *adj* circundante.
▸ *n pl* **surroundings** *(of town, city, etc)* alrededores *mpl fpl*. *(environment)* entorno, ambiente *m*.

surveillance [sɜːˈveɪləns] *n* vigilancia.

survey [*(n)* 'sɜːveɪ; *(vb)* səˈveɪ] *n* **1** *(investigation - of opinion)* sondeo, encuesta; *(- of prices, trends, etc)* estudio; *(written report)* informe *m*. **2** *(of land)* inspección *f*, reconocimiento; *(in topography)* medición *f*. **3** *(general view)* visión *f* general, visión *f* de conjunto. **4** GB *(of house, building)* inspección *f*, peritaje *m*.
▸ *vt* **1** *(contemplate, look at)* contemplar, mirar. **2** *(study - gen)* examinar, analizar; *(- prices, trends, etc)* estudiar, hacer una encuesta sobre; *(investigate - people)* encuestar, hacer un sondeo de. **3** *(- land)* hacer un reconocimiento de; *(in topography)* medir. **4** *(house, building)* inspeccionar, hacer un peritaje de.

surveyor [səˈveɪər] *n (of land)* agrimensor,-ra, topógrafo,-a; *(of house, building)* perito,-a.

survival [səˈvaɪvəl] *n* **1** *(gen)* supervivencia. **2** *(relic)* reliquia, vestigio (from, de).

survive [səˈvaɪv] *vi* **1** *(gen)* sobrevivir; *(custom, tradition)* sobrevivir, perdurar; *(book, painting)* conservarse. **2** *fam (cope, get by)* ir tirando, arreglárselas.
▸ *vt* **1** *(disaster)* sobrevivir a. **2** *(person)*, sobrevivir a.

survivor [səˈvaɪvər] *n* superviviente *mf*, sobreviviente *mf*.

suspect [*(adj-n)* 'sʌspekt; *(vb)* səˈspekt] *adj (suspicious)* sospechoso,-a; *(dubious, questionable)* dudoso,-a.
▸ *n (person)* sospechoso,-a.
▸ *vt* **1** *(believe guilty)* sospechar de; *(mistrust)* recelar de, desconfiar de, dudar de. **2** *(think true)* sospechar. **3** *(suppose, guess)* imaginarse, creer.

suspend [səˈspend] *vt* **1** *(stop temporarily, suspender; (postpone)* posponer, aplazar. **2** *(remove)* suspender. **3** *(hang)* suspender, colgar.

☒ To suspend no significa 'suspender (un examen)', que se traduce por to fail.

suspense [səsˈpens] *n (anticipation)* incertidumbre *f*; *(intrigue)* suspense *m* intriga.

suspension [səˈspenʃən] *n* **1** *(halt)* suspensión *f*; *(postponement)* aplazamiento, postergación *f*. **2** *(of employee, player)* suspensión *f*; *(of pupil)* expulsión *f*.

CHEM suspensión f. **4** TECH suspensión f. COMP **suspension points** puntos suspensivos.

suspicion [sə'spɪʃᵊn] n **1** (gen) sospecha; (mistrust) recelo, desconfianza; (doubt) duda; (hunch) presentimiento. **2** (slight trace) pizca, asomo, atisbo.

suspicious [sə'spɪʃəs] adj **1** (arousing suspicion) sospechoso,-a. **2** (distrustful, wary) desconfiado,-a, suspicaz.

sustain [sə'steɪn] vt **1** (keep alive - gen) sustentar; (- spirits, hope) mantener. **2** (maintain - gen) sostener; (- interest, conversation) mantener; (- work) continuar. **3** MUS (note) sostener. **4** fml (suffer - loss, injury, wound, etc) sufrir. **5** fml (hold up) sostener. **6** JUR admitir.

sustainable [sə'steɪnəbᵊl] adj sostenible.

suture ['sʌtʃeʳ] n (thread) hilo de sutura; (stitch) punto de sutura.
▸ vt suturar.

swab [swɒb] n **1** MED (cotton wool) algodón m; (gauze) gasa. **2** MED (specimen) frotis m, muestra. **3** (cleaning cloth) paño, bayeta, trapo; (mop) fregona.
▸ vt **1** MED (wound) limpiar. **2** MAR (deck) limpiar, fregar.
① pt & pp swabbed, ger swabbing.

swallow¹ ['swɒləʊ] n (of drink, food) trago.
▸ vt **1** (food, etc) tragar. **2** fig (be taken in by) tragarse.
▸ vi tragar.
◆ **to swallow up** vt sep **1** (engulf) tragarse, engullir. **2** (use up) consumir, tragarse, comerse, absorber.

swallow² ['swɒləʊ] n (bird) golondrina.

swam [swæm] pt → swim.

swamp [swɒmp] n pantano, ciénaga.
▸ vt **1** (land) inundar, anegar; (boat) hundir. **2** fig (inundate) inundar (with/by, de); (overwhelm) agobiar, abrumar (with/by, de).

swan [swɒn] n (bird) cisne m.
▸ vi pavonearse.
① pt & pp swanned, ger swanning.

swap [swɒp] n canje m, cambalache m.
▸ vt fam cambiar, intercambiar.
▸ vi hacer un intercambio, cambiar.
① pt & pp swapped, ger swapping.

swarm [swɔːm] n **1** (of bees) enjambre m. **2** fig (of people) enjambre m, nube f, multitud f.
▸ vi **1** (bees) enjambrar. **2** fig (people) aglomerarse, apiñarse, arremolinarse.
◆ **to swarm with** vt insep rebosar de, estar plagado,-a de.

swathe¹ [sweɪð] n → swath.

swathe² [sweɪð] vt (wrap) envolver, vendar.
◆ **to swathe in** vt sep fig envolver.

sway [sweɪ] n **1** (movement) balanceo, vaivén m, movimiento. **2** fig (influence) dominio, influencia (over, sobre).
▸ vt **1** (swing) balancear, bambolear. **2** fig (influence) influir en, influenciar, convencer.
▸ vi **1** (person, tree, ladder) balancearse, bambolearse; (tower) bambolearse; (crops) mecerse; (person - totter) tambalearse. **2** fig (waver) vacilar (between, entre), oscilar (between, entre).

swear [sweəʳ] vt **1** (declare formally) jurar; (vow) juramentar. **2** fam (state firmly) jurar.
▸ vi **1** (declare formally) jurar, prestar juramento. **2** (curse) decir palabrotas, soltar tacos; (blaspheme) jurar, blasfemar.
◆ **to swear by** vt insep fam tener una fe absoluta en.
◆ **to swear in** vt sep (in court) tomarle juramento a.
◆ **to swear to** vt insep jurar.
① pt swore [swɔːʳ], pp sworn [swɔːn].

swearword ['sweəwɜːd] n palabrota.

sweat [swet] n **1** (perspiration) sudor m. **2** fam (hard work) paliza. **3** fam (anxious state) nerviosismo. COMP **sweat gland** glándula sudorípara.
▸ vi **1** (perspire) sudar. **2** (cheese) exudar humedad. **3** (work hard) sudar la gota gorda. **4** fam (worry) estar preocupado,-a, sufrir.
▸ vt GB (cook gently) rehogar.
◆ **to sweat out** vt sep (illness, cold) quitarse sudando; (toxins) eliminar.

sweater ['swetəʳ] n suéter m, jersey m.

sweatshirt ['swetʃɜːt] n sudadera.

Swede [swiːd] n (person) sueco,-a.

Sweden ['swiːdᵊn] n Suecia.

Swedish ['swiːdɪʃ] adj sueco,-a.

S

▶ *n (language)* sueco.

▶ *n pl* **the Swedish** los suecos *mpl*.

sweep [swiːp] *n* **1** *(with broom)* barrido. **2** *(of arm)* movimiento amplio, gesto amplio; *(with weapon)* golpe *m*. **3** *(curve)* curva; *(area, stretch)* extensión *f*. **4** *fig (range, extent)* abanico, alcance *m*. **5** *(by police, rescuers)* peinado, rastreo. **6** *fam (chimney cleaner)* deshollinador,-ra.

▶ *vt* **1** *(room, floor)* barrer; *(chimney)* deshollinar. **2** *(with hand)* quitar de un manotazo. **3** *(move over)* azotar, barrer. **4** *(remove by force)* arrastrar, llevarse. **5** *(pass over)* recorrer. **6** *fig (spread through)* recorrer, extenderse por. **7** *(touch lightly)* rozar, pasar por.

▶ *vi* **1** *(with broom)* barrer. **2** *(move quickly)* pasar rápidamente. **3** *(extend)* recorrer, extenderse.

◆ **to sweep aside** *vt sep* **1** *(objection, etc)* rechazar; *(suggestion)* descartar. **2** *(object)* apartar (bruscamente).

◆ **to sweep away** *vt sep* **1** *(privilege, etc)* erradicar. **2** *(by flood, storm)* arrastrar, llevarse.

◆ **to sweep up** *vt sep* **1** *(room, etc)* barrer; *(dust, etc)* (barrer y) recoger. **2** *(object, person)* recoger, levantar.

▶ *vi* barrer, limpiar.

ⓘ *pt & pp* swept [swept].

sweeping ['swiːpɪŋ] *adj* **1** *(broad)* amplio,-a; *(very general)* muy general. **2** *(overwhelming)* arrollador,-ra, aplastante; *(far-reaching)* radical; *(huge)* enorme. COMP **sweeping brush** escoba.

sweet [swiːt] *adj* **1** *(taste)* dulce; *(sugary)* azucarado,-a. **2** *(pleasant)* agradable; *(smell)* fragante, bueno,-a; *(sound, music, voice)* melodioso,-a, suave, dulce. **3** *(air)* limpio,-a; *(water)* dulce. **4** *(charming)* encantador,-ra, simpático,-a; *(cute)* rico,-a, mono,-a; *(gentle)* dulce. COMP **sweet corn** maíz *m* tierno. | **sweet pea** guisante *m* de olor. | **sweet pepper** pimiento morrón. | **sweet potato** boniato, batata.

▶ *n* **1** GB *(candy)* caramelo, golosina; *(chocolate)* bombón *m*. **2** GB *(dessert)* postre *m*. **3** *(form of address)* cariño, cielo, amor *m*, vida.

sweet-and-sour ['swiːtⁿsauəʳ] *adj* CULIN agridulce.

sweetcorn ['swiːtkɔːn] *n* maíz *m* tierno.

sweeten ['swiːtⁿn] *vt* **1** *(drink, etc)* endulzar, azucarar; *(air, breath)* refrescar. **2** *fig (person)* endulzar (el carácter de); *(temper)* aplacar, calmar. **3** *fam (make more attractive)* hacer más apetecible.

◆ **to sweeten up** *vt sep* ablandar.

sweetener ['swiːtⁿnəʳ] *n* **1** *(in food, drink)* edulcorante *m*, dulcificante *m*. **2** *fam (bribe)* soborno.

sweetheart ['swiːthɑːt] *n* **1** *(dear, love)* cariño, tesoro, amor *m*. **2** *(loved one)* novio,-a.

sweetness ['swiːtnəs] *n (taste)* dulzor *m*; *(smell)* fragancia; *(sound)* suavidad *f*; *(character)* dulzura, simpatía.

swell [swel] *n* **1** *(of sea)* marejada, oleaje *m*. **2** MUS *(crescendo)* crescendo.

▶ *vi* **1** *(gen)* hincharse (up, -); *(sea)* levantarse; *(river)* crecer, subir. **2** *(grow in number)* crecer, aumentar; *(- louder)* hacerse más fuerte.

▶ *vt* **1** *(gen)* hinchar; *(river)* hacer crecer. **2** *(increase in number)* aumentar, engrosar.

ⓘ *pt & pp* swelled o swollen ['swəʊlən].

swelling ['swelɪŋ] *n (swollen place)* hinchazón *f*, bulto; *(condition)* tumefacción *f*.

swept [swept] *pt & pp* → **sweep**.

swerve [swɜːv] *n* **1** AUTO viraje *m* brusco, desvío brusco. **2** SP *(by player)* regate *m*; *(of ball)* efecto.

▶ *vi* **1** AUTO virar bruscamente, dar un viraje brusco. **2** SP *(player)* dar un regate, regatear; *(ball)* llevar efecto. **3** *fig (veer, deviate)* desviarse (from, de).

swift [swɪft] *adj* **1** *(runner, horse)* rápido,-a, veloz. **2** *(reaction, reply)* pronto,-a, rápido,-a.

▶ *n (bird)* vencejo común.

swim [swɪm] *n* baño. LOC **to go for a swim** ir a nadar. | **to have a swim** bañarse, nadar.

▶ *vi* **1** *(gen)* nadar. **2** *(be covered in liquid)* nadar (in, en), flotar (in, en); *(be overflowing)* estar cubierto,-a (with, de), estar inundado,-a (with, de). **3** *(spin, whirl)* dar vueltas.

▶ vt (cross river) cruzar a nado, cruzar nadando; (cover distance) nadar, hacer; (use particular stroke) nadar.

ⓘ pt swam [swæm], pp swum [swʌm], ger swimming.

swimmer ['swɪmər] n nadador,-ra.

swimming ['swɪmɪŋ] n natación f. LOC to go swimming ir a nadar. COMP swimming baths piscina cubierta. I swimming costume bañador m. I swimming pool piscina. I swimming trunks bañador m (de hombre).

swimsuit ['swɪmsuːt] n bañador m.

swimwear ['swɪmweər] n bañadores mpl.

swindle ['swɪndəl] n (fiddle) estafa; (con) timo.

▶ vt estafar, timar.

swine [swaɪn] n 1 [pl swine] arch (pig) cerdo, puerco, cochino. 2 [pl swines] fam (person) cerdo,-a, canalla mf, marrano,-a.

swing [swɪŋ] n 1 (movement) balanceo, vaivén m; (of pendulum) oscilación f, vaivén m; (of hips) contoneo. 2 (plaything) columpio. 3 (change, shift) giro, viraje m, cambio. 4 SP (in golf, boxing) swing m. 5 MUS (jazz style) swing m; (rhythm) ritmo. COMP swing bridge puente m giratorio. I swing door puerta giratoria.

▶ vi 1 (hanging object) balancearse, bambolearse; (pendulum) oscilar; (arms, legs) menearse; (child on swing) columpiarse; (on a pivot) mecerse. 2 (drive) girar, doblar; (walk) caminar con energía; (jump) saltar. 3 (shift) cambiar, oscilar, virar. 4 (music, band) tener ritmo; (party) estar muy animado,-a.

▶ vt 1 (gen) balancear. 2 (cause to move) hacer girar. 3 (change) cambiar. 4 fam (arrange, achieve) arreglar.

ⓘ pt & pp swung [swʌŋ].

swipe [swaɪp] n 1 (blow) golpe m. 2 (verbal attack) ataque m. COMP swipe card tarjeta magnética.

▶ vt 1 pegarle a, darle a. 2 fam (pinch) birlar, mangar, afanar.

▶ vi asestar un golpe (at, a), intentar darle (at, a).

swirl [swɜːl] n 1 (gen) remolino; (of smoke, cream) voluta; (of skirt) vuelo. 2 (pattern) espiral f.

▶ vi (whirl) arremolinarse; (person) girar, dar vueltas.

▶ vt arremolinar.

Swiss [swɪs] adj suizo,-a.

▶ n suizo,-a.

▶ n pl the Swiss los suizos mpl.

switch [swɪtʃ] n 1 ELEC interruptor m, conmutador m. 2 US (on railway) agujas fpl. 3 (change, shift) cambio; (turnaround) viraje m. 4 (exchange, swap) intercambio, trueque m.

▶ vt 1 (change) cambiar de; (move) trasladar; (attention) desviar. 2 (exchange) intercambiar. 3 (setting) poner; (channel) cambiar de. 4 (train) desviar, cambiar de vía.

▶ vi (gen) cambiar (to, a).

◆ to switch off vt sep (light, TV, etc) apagar; (current, gas, electricity) cortar, desconectar; (engine) parar.

▶ vi (light, machine, heating) apagarse; (engine) parar; (person) distraerse, desconectar, dejar de prestar atención.

◆ to switch on vt sep (light, machine, engine) encender; (light, radio, TV) poner.

▶ vi (gen) encenderse.

◆ to switch over vi (gen) cambiar (to, a); (channel) cambiar de canal.

switchboard ['swɪtʃbɔːd] n centralita.

Switzerland ['swɪtsələnd] n Suiza.

swivel ['swɪvəl] vi girarse, volverse.

ⓘ pt & pp swivelled (US swiveled), ger swivelling (US swiveling).

▶ vt (head) girar; (chair) hacer girar. COMP swivel chair silla giratoria.

swollen ['swəʊlən] pp → swell.

▶ adj (ankle, face) hinchado,-a; (glands) inflamado,-a; (river, lake) crecido,-a.

swoop [swuːp] vi 1 (bird) abalanzarse (down on, sobre), abatirse (down on, sobre); (plane) bajar en picado. 2 fam (police) hacer una redada (on, en).

▶ n 1 (of bird, plane) descenso (en picado). 2 fam (by police) redada.

sword [sɔːd] n espada.

swordfish ['sɔːdfɪʃ] n pez m espada.

swore [swɔːr] pt → swear.

sworn [swɔːn] *pp* → swear.

swot [swɒt] *n* empollón,-ona.
▸ *vi* empollar.
ⓘ *pt & pp* swotted, *ger* swotting.

swum [swʌm] *pp* → swim.

swung [swʌŋ] *pt & pp* → swing.

sybarite ['sɪbəraɪt] *n lit* sibarita *mf*.

syllable ['sɪləbəl] *n* sílaba.

syllabus ['sɪləbəs] *n* programa *m* de estudios.
ⓘ *pl* syllabuses o syllabi.

sylph [sɪlf] *n* sílfide *f*.

symbiosis [sɪmbɪ'əʊsɪs] *n* simbiosis *f*.

symbol ['sɪmbəl] *n* símbolo (of, de).

symbolize ['sɪmbəlaɪz] *vt* simbolizar.

symmetrical [sɪ'metrɪkəl] *adj* simétrico,-a.

symmetry ['sɪmɪtrɪ] *n* simetría.

sympathetic [sɪmpə'θetɪk] *adj* **1** *(showing pity, compassion)* compasivo,-a; *(understanding)* comprensivo,-a (to, con); *(kind)* amable. **2** *(showing agreement, approval)* favorable (to, a).

✖ Sympathetic no significa 'simpático', que se traduce por **nice**.

sympathize ['sɪmpəθaɪz] *vi* **1** *(show pity, commiserate)* compadecer, compadecerse (with, de); *(understand)* comprender (with, -). **2** *(support - cause)* simpatizar (with, con).

sympathizer ['sɪmpəθaɪzəʳ] *n* simpatizante *mf*.

sympathy ['sɪmpəθɪ] *n* **1** *(pity, compassion)* compasión *f*, lástima; *(condolences)* condolencia, pésame *m*. **2** *(understanding)* comprensión *f*; *(affinity)* afinidad *f*. **3** *(agreement, support)* acuerdo *m*.
ⓘ *pl* sympathies.
▸ *n pl* **sympathies** *(condolences)* condolencia *f sing*, pésame *m sing*. *(loyalties, leanings)* simpatías *fpl*, tendencias *fpl*.

✖ Sympathy no significa 'simpatía (amabilidad)', que se traduce por **pleasantness**.

symphony ['sɪmfənɪ] *n* sinfonía. COMP **symphony orchestra** orquesta sinfónica.
ⓘ *pl* symphonies.

symposium [sɪm'pəʊzɪəm] *n* simposio.
ⓘ *pl* symposiums o symposia.

symptom ['sɪmptəm] *n* **1** MED síntoma *m*. **2** *(sign)* síntoma *m*, señal *f*, indicio.

synagogue ['sɪnəgɒg] *n* sinagoga.

synchronize ['sɪŋkrənaɪz] *vt* sincronizar.

syncopation [sɪŋkə'peɪʃən] *n* síncopa.

syndicalism ['sɪndɪkəlɪzəm] *n* sindicalismo.

syndicalist ['sɪndɪkəlɪst] *n* sindicalista *mf*.

syndicate ['sɪndɪkət] *n* **1** *(gen)* corporación *f*, agrupación *f*, empresa. **2** *(news agency)* agencia (de prensa).
▸ *vt (distribute)* distribuir; *(publish)* publicar.

✖ Syndicate no significa 'sindicato', que se traduce por **trade union**.

syndrome [sɪndrəʊm] *n* síndrome *m*.

synonym ['sɪnənɪm] *n* sinónimo.

synopsis [sɪ'nɒpsɪs] *n* sinopsis *f*, resumen *m*.
ⓘ *pl* synopses.

syntactic [sɪn'tæktɪk] *adj* sintáctico,-a.

syntax ['sɪntæks] *n* sintaxis *f inv*.

synthesis ['sɪnθəsɪs] *n* síntesis *f inv*.
ⓘ *pl* syntheses.

synthesize ['sɪnθəsaɪz] *vt* sintetizar.

synthesizer ['sɪnθəsaɪzəʳ] *n* sintetizador *m*.

synthetic [sɪn'θetɪk] *adj* sintético,-a.
▸ *n* fibra sintética.

syphilis ['sɪfɪlɪs] *n* sífilis *f*.

Syria ['sɪrɪə] *n* Siria.

Syrian ['sɪrɪən] *adj* sirio,-a.
▸ *n* sirio,-a.

syringe [sɪ'rɪndʒ] *n* MED jeringa, jeringuilla.
▸ *vt* MED *(ear)* hacer un lavado de.

syrup ['sɪrəp] *n* **1** MED jarabe *m*. **2** CULIN almíbar *m*.

system ['sɪstəm] *n* **1** *(gen)* sistema *m*: **2** *(body)* cuerpo, organismo.

systematic [sɪstə'mætɪk] *adj* sistemático,-a, metódico,-a.

systematize ['sɪstɪmətaɪz] *vt* sistematizar.

systemize ['sɪstəmaɪz] *vt* sistematizar.

systole ['sɪstəlɪ] *n* sístole *m*.

T, t [tiː] *n (the letter)* T, t *f*.

tab [tæb] *n* **1** *(flap)* lengüeta; *(on can)* anilla. **2** *(label)* etiqueta. **3** US *(bill)* cuenta. **4** *(on computer)* tabulador *m*.

table ['teɪbəl] *n* **1** *(gen)* mesa. **2** *(chart)* tabla, cuadro. **3** SP clasificación *f*. COMP **table football** futbolín *m*. ▪ **table of contents** índice *m* de materias. ▪ **table tennis** tenis *m* de mesa, pingpong *m*.
▶ *vt* GB *(motion, report, etc)* presentar.
▶ *n pl* **tables** tablas *fpl* de multiplicar.

🗙 Table no significa 'tabla (de madera)', que se traduce por **board, plank**.

tablecloth ['teɪbəlklɒθ] *n* mantel *m*.

tablespoon ['teɪbəlspuːn] *n* **1** cucharón *m*. **2** cuchara grande.

tablet ['tæblɪt] *n* **1** MED pastilla, comprimido. **2** *(of soap)* pastilla.

tabloid ['tæblɔɪd] *n* periódico de formato pequeño.

tabulate ['tæbjʊleɪt] *vt* tabular.

tachycardia [tækɪˈkɑːdɪə] *n* taquicardia.

tack [tæk] *n* **1** *(nail)* tachuela. **2** MAR bordada, viraje *m*. **3** *(approach)* táctica. **4** SEW hilván *m*.

tackle ['tækəl] *n* **1** *(equipment)* equipo, aparejos *mpl*. **2** MAR polea, aparejo. **3** SP *(football)* entrada; *(rugby)* placaje *m*.
▶ *vt* **1** *(deal with - problem)* abordar, encarar; *(- task)* emprender; *(person)* hablar con. **2** SP *(football)* entrarle a; *(rugby)* placar.

tact [tækt] *n* tacto, discreción *f*.

🗙 Tact no significa 'tacto (sentido)', que se traduce por **touch**.

tactful ['tæktfʊl] *adj* diplomático,-a.

tactic ['tæktɪk] *n* táctica.

tactical ['tæktɪkəl] *adj* táctico,-a.

tactics ['tæktɪks] *n pl* MIL táctica *f sing*.

tactless ['tæktləs] *adj (person)* falto,-a de tacto, poco diplomático,-a; *(remark, question)* indiscreto,-a.

tadpole ['tædpəʊl] *n* renacuajo.

Tadzhik ['tædʒɪk] *adj* tadjiko,-a.
▶ *n (person)* tadjiko,-a.
ⓘ *pl* Tadzhik.

Tadzhiki [tæˈdʒiːkɪ] *n (language)* tadjiko.

Tadzhikistan [tædʒiːkɪˈstæn] *n* Tadjikistán.

tag [tæg] *n* **1** *(label)* etiqueta. **2** *(phrase)* coletilla. **3** *(game)* el corre que te pillo.
▶ *vt* etiquetar.

Tahiti [təˈhiːtɪ] *n* Tahití.

Tahitian [təˈhiːʃən] *adj* tahitiano,-a.
▶ *n* **1** *(person)* tahitiano,-a. **2** *(language)* tahitiano.

4 ['teɪfə] *n* taifa.

tail [teɪl] *n (gen)* cola; *(of some four-legged animals)* cola, rabo.
▶ *n pl* **tails** *(of coin)* cruz *f sing*.

tailback ['teɪlbæk] *n (traffic jam)* caravana, cola, retención *f*.

tailbone ['teɪlbəʊn] *n* cóccix *m*.

tailor ['teɪlər] *n* sastre,-a.

Taiwan [taɪˈwæn] *n* Taiwán.

Taiwanese [taɪwæˈniːz] *adj* taiwanés,-esa.
▶ *n* taiwanés,-esa.

take [teɪk] *n* CINEM toma.
▶ *vt* **1** *(gen)* llevar. **2** *(remove)* llevarse, quitar, coger. **3** *(hold, grasp)* tomar, coger. **4** *(accept - money, etc)* aceptar. **5** *(win prize, competition)* ganar. **6** *(medicine, drugs)* tomar. **7** *(subject)* estudiar; *(course of study)* seguir, cursar. **8** *(bus, train, etc)* tomar, coger. **9** *(time)* tardar, llevar. LOC **not to take no for an answer** no

aceptar una respuesta negativa. **I take it or leave it** lo tomas o lo dejas. **I to take place** ocurrir. **I to take STH for granted** dar ALGO por sentado.

▶ *vi* **1** *(work - dye)* coger; *(- fire)* prender; *(- cutting)* prender; *(- seed)* germinar. **2** *(fish)* picar. **3** *(in draughts, etc)* comer.

◆ **to take after** *vi* parecerse.

◆ **to take apart** *vt sep* **1** *(machine, etc)* desmontar, deshacer. **2** *(argument)* echar por tierra.

◆ **to take away** *vt sep* **1** *(remove)* llevarse, quitar. **2** *(subtract)* restar.
▶ *vi (food)* llevar.

◆ **to take back** *vt sep* **1** *(accept back)* recibir otra vez, aceptar algo devuelto; *(employee)* readmitir. **2** *(return)* devolver. **3** *(retract)* retirar, retractar. **4** *(in time)* hacer recordar.

◆ **to take off** *vt sep* **1** *(clothes)* quitarse. **2** *(remove, detach)* quitar, sacar. **3** *(force to go)* llevar. **4** *(have as holiday)* tomarse. **5** *(imitate)* imitar. **6** *(deduct, discount)* descontar, rebajar.
▶ *vi* **1** *(plane)* despegar. **2** *(leave hurriedly)* irse, marcharse. **3** *(become popular)* tener éxito, ponerse de moda.

◆ **to take over** *vt sep* **1** *(country, party, etc)* tomar (posesión de), apoderarse de; *(building)* ocupar. **2** *(company, business)* absorber, adquirir; *(job, post)* hacerse cargo de; *(duty, responsibility)* asumir.
ⓘ *pt* **took** [tʊk], *pp* **taken** ['teɪkən].

take-away ['teɪkəweɪ] *n* **1** *(food)* comida para llevar. **2** *(restaurant)* restaurante *m* de comida para llevar.

taken ['teɪkᵊn] *pp* → **take**.
▶ *adj (seat)* ocupado,-a.

take-off ['teɪkɔ:f] *n* **1** *(aviation)* despegue *m*. **2** SP salto.

take-out ['teɪkaʊt] *n* US *(food)* comida para llevar.

takeover ['teɪkəʊvəʳ] *n* **1** POL toma de posesión. **2** *(of company)* adquisición *f*.

talc [tælk] *n* talco.

talcum powder ['tælkəmpaʊdəʳ] *n* polvos *mpl* de talco.

tale [teɪl] *n (story)* cuento.

talent ['tælənt] *n* **1** *(special ability)* talento, dotes *mpl*. **2** *(talented people)* gente *f*

de talento, gente *f* dotada. **3** *fam (attractive people)* gente *f* guapa.

talented ['tæləntɪd] *adj* de talento.

talk [tɔ:k] *vi* **1** *(gen)* hablar **(to**, con/a). **2** *(negotiate)* negociar.
▶ *vt* hablar **(about/of**, de).
▶ *n* **1** *(conversation)* conversación *f*. **2** *(lecture)* charla, conferencia.
▶ *n pl* **talks** negociaciones *fpl*.

◆ **to talk back** *vi* contestar, contestar de mala manera.

◆ **to talk down** *vt insep* **1** *(person)* hacer callar. **2** *(aircraft)* dirigir por radio.

talkative ['tɔ:kətɪv] *adj* hablador,-ra, parlanchín,-ina, charlatán,-ana.

tall [tɔ:l] *adj* alto,-a. COMP **tall story** cuento chino.

tallow ['tæləʊ] *n* sebo.

talon ['tælən] *n* garra.

tambourine [tæmbə'ri:n] *n* pandereta.

tame [teɪm] *adj* **1** *(by nature)* manso,-a, dócil. **2** *(tamed)* domesticado,-a.
▶ *vt* domar, domesticar.

tampon ['tæmpɒn] *n* tampón *m*.

tan¹ [tæn] *n* **1** *(colour)* color *m* marrón claro. **2** *(suntan)* bronceado, moreno. LOC **to get a tan** ponerse moreno.
▶ *adj* marrón claro.
▶ *vt* **1** *(leather)* curtir. **2** *(skin)* broncear, poner moreno,-a.
▶ *vi* broncearse, ponerse moreno,-a.
ⓘ *pt & pp* **tanned**, *ger* **tanning**.

tangent ['tændʒənt] *n* tangente *f*.

tangerine [tændʒə'ri:n] *n* **1** *(fruit)* clementina, mandarina. **2** *(colour)* naranja.
▶ *adj* naranja.

tangle ['tæŋgᵊl] *n* **1** *(confused mass)* enredo, embrollo; *(confusion)* enredo, lío.
▶ *vt* enredar, enmarañar.
▶ *vi* enredarse.

tank [tæŋk] *n* **1** *(for water)* depósito, tanque *m*; *(for fuel)* depósito. **2** MIL tanque *m*. COMP **think tank** grupo de expertos.

tanker ['tæŋkəʳ] *n* **1** *(ship)* buque *m* cisterna. **2** *(for oil)* petrolero. **3** *(lorry)* camión *m* cisterna.

tanned [tænd] *adj (person)* moreno,-a, bronceado,-a; *(leather)* curtido,-a.

tantrum ['tæntrəm] n berrinche m, rabieta.

Tanzania [tænzə'nɪə] n Tanzania.

Tanzanian [tænzə'nɪən] adj tanzano,-a.
▶ n tanzano,-a.

tap¹ [tæp] n **1** grifo. **2** (light blow) golpecito. **3** (on phone) micrófono de escucha. **4** (on barrel) espita; (for gas) llave f. COMP **tap water** agua del grifo.
▶ vt **1** (strike lightly) dar un golpecito a. **2** (on keyboard) teclear, pulsar. **3** (liquid) sacar. **4** (resources) explotar, utilizar. **5** (telephone) pinchar, intervenir.
◆ **to tap out** vt sep **1** teclear, escribir a máquina. **2** (in Morse code) enviar.
ⓘ pt & pp **tapped**, ger **tapping**.

❌ Tap no significa 'tapa', que se traduce por lid.

tap² [tæp] n claqué m. COMP **tap dance** claqué m.

tape [teɪp] n **1** (audio, visual) cinta. **2** (recorded material) grabación f. **3** SP cinta de llegada. **4** (sticky) cinta adhesiva. COMP **tape measure** cinta métrica. ‖ **tape recorder** magnetófono.
▶ vt **1** (fasten) pegar con cinta adhesiva. **2** (record) grabar.

tapestry ['tæpəstrɪ] n **1** (art) tapicería. **2** (cloth) tapiz m.
ⓘ pl **tapestries**.

tar [tɑːʳ] n **1** (for roads, in cigarettes) alquitrán m. **2** (in soap, etc) brea.
▶ vt alquitranar.
ⓘ pt & pp **tarred**, ger **tarring**.

target ['tɑːgɪt] n **1** (of missile, goal, aim) objetivo. **2** (in shooting, of criticism) blanco. **3** (board) diana.
▶ vt **1** (aim at target) apuntar. **2** (cause to have effect on) dirigir a, destinar a.
▶ adj (date, figure) fijado,-a; (audience, market) objetivo.

tariff ['tærɪf] n **1** (list of fixed charges) tarifa. **2** (duty to be paid on imports) arancel m.
▶ adj arancelario,-a.

tarmac ['tɑːmæk] n **1** asfalto. **2** (area) pista.
▶ vt asfaltar.

tarpaulin [tɑː'pɔːlɪn] n lona.

tarsus ['tɑːsəs] n ANAT tarso.
ⓘ pl **tarsi**.

tart [tɑːt] adj **1** (sour) acre, agrio,-a. **2** (reply) mordaz, áspero,-a, acre.
▶ n **1** (pie) tarta, pastel m.
◆ **to tart up** vt sep (building) renovar, remodelar; (person) emperifollar.

tartan ['tɑːtən] n tartán m.

tartar ['tɑːtəʳ] n **1** (on teeth) sarro. **2** (in wine) tártaro.

task [tɑːsk] n tarea, labor f.

Tasmania [tæz'meɪnɪə] n Tasmania.

Tasmanian [tæz'meɪnɪən] adj tasmano,-a.
▶ n tasmano,-a.

taste [teɪst] n **1** (faculty) gusto. **2** (flavour) sabor m. **3** (small sample) muestra, poquito; (experience) experiencia. **4** (ability to make good judgements) gusto; (liking) afición f (for, a), gusto (for, por). COMP **taste buds** papilas gustativas.
▶ vt **1** (try food) probar; (wine) catar, degustar. **2** (eat, drink) probar. **3** (experience) conocer. **4** (perceive flavour) notar.
▶ vi saber (of/like, a).

tasteful ['teɪstful] adj de buen gusto, elegante.

tasteless ['teɪstləs] adj **1** de mal gusto. **2** (insipid) insípido,-a, soso,-a.

tasty ['teɪstɪ] adj sabroso,-a, rico,-a.
ⓘ comp **tastier**, superl **tastiest**.

tattoo [tə'tuː] n **1** MIL retreta. **2** (on skin) tatuaje m.
ⓘ pl **tattoos**.
▶ vt tatuar.
ⓘ pt & pp **tattooed**, ger **tattooing**.

taught [tɔːt] pt & pp → **teach**.

taunt [tɔːnt] n mofa, pulla, insulto.
▶ vt bufarse de, mofarse de; (provoke) hostigar, provocar.

Taurus ['tɔːrəs] n Tauro.

taut [tɔːt] adj tirante, tenso,-a.

tavern ['tævəⁿn] n taberna, mesón m.

tax [tæks] n **1** impuesto, contribución f. **2** fig (burden, strain) carga (on, sobre), esfuerzo (on, para).
ⓘ pl **taxes**.
▶ vt **1** (impose a tax on - goods, profits) gravar; (- business, person) imponer contribuciones a. **2** fig (strain, test) poner a prueba.

T

taxation [tæk'seɪʃⁿn] *n (taxes)* impuestos *mpl*; *(system)* sistema *m* tributario.

tax-deductible ['tæksdɪ'dʌktəbⁿl] *adj* desgravable.

tax-free ['tæks'fri:] *adj* libre de impuestos, exento,-a de impuestos.

taxi ['tæksɪ] *n* taxi *m*. COMP **taxi driver** taxista *mf*.
ⓘ *pl* taxis.

taxonomy [tæk'sɒnəmɪ] *n* taxonomía.
ⓘ *pl* taxonomies.

taxpayer ['tækspeɪəʳ] *n* contribuyente *mf*.

tea [ti:] *n* **1** *(gen)* té *m*. **2** *(infusion)* infusión *f*.

tea-break ['ti:breɪk] *n* descanso *para tomar el té*.

teach [ti:tʃ] *vt (gen)* enseñar; *(subject)* dar clases. LOC **that'll teach you** así aprenderás.
▶ *vi* ser profesor,-ra, dar clases
ⓘ *pt & pp* taught [tɔ:t].

teacher ['ti:tʃəʳ] *n* maestro,-a, profesor,-ra.

teaching ['ti:tʃɪŋ] *n* enseñanza.
▶ *adj* docente. COMP **teaching staff** profesorado.
▶ *n pl* **teachings** enseñanzas *fpl*.

teacup ['ti:kʌp] *n* taza para té.

teak [ti:k] *n* teca.

team [ti:m] *n* **1** *(gen)* equipo. **2** *(of horses)* tiro; *(of oxen)* yunta.
▶ *adj* de equipo.
▶ *vi* combinar (with, con).

teamwork ['ti:mwɜ:k] *n* trabajo de equipo.

teapot ['ti:pɒt] *n* tetera.

tear¹ [teəʳ] *n (rip)* rasgón *m*, desgarrón *m*.
▶ *vt* **1** *(rip, make a hole)* rasgar, desgarrar; *(pull apart, into pieces)* romper, hacer pedazos. **2** *(remove by force)* arrancar.
▶ *vi* **1** romperse, rasgarse. **2** *(rush)* ir a toda velocidad, lanzarse, precipitarse. COMP **wear and tear** desgaste *m*.
◆ **to tear apart** *vt sep* **1** *(rip up)* despedazar, desgarrar; *(destroy)* destrozar. **2** *fig* destrozar, desgarrar.

◆ **to tear up** *vt sep (paper)* hacer pedazos; *(plant)* arrancar de raíz.
ⓘ *pt* tore [tɔ:ʳ], *pp* torn [tɔ:n].

tear² [tɪəʳ] *n* lágrima.

teardrop ['tɪədrɒp] *n* lágrima.

tearoom ['ti:rum] *n* salón *m* de té.

tease [ti:z] *vt* **1** *(make fun of - playfully)* tomar el pelo a, burlarse de; *(- annoyingly, unkindly)* molestar. **2** *(wool, etc)* cardar.
▶ *vi* tomar el pelo.
▶ *n* **1** *(joker)* bromista *mf*. **2** *fam (flirt)* coqueta.

teasel ['ti:zⁿl] *n* cardencha.

teashop ['ti:ʃɒp] *n* salón *m* de té.

teaspoon ['ti:spu:n] *n* cucharilla.

teat [ti:t] *n* **1** ZOOL tetilla. **2** *(on bottle)* tetina.

teatime ['ti:taɪm] *n* hora del té, hora de la merienda.

technical ['teknɪkⁿl] *adj* técnico,-a.
COMP **technical college** instituto de formación profesional.

technician [tek'nɪʃⁿn] *n* técnico,-a.

technique [tek'ni:k] *n* técnica.

technological [teknə'lɒdʒɪkⁿl] *adj* tecnológico,-a.

technology [tek'nɒlədʒɪ] *n* tecnología.
ⓘ *pl* technologies.

teddy bear ['tedɪbeəʳ] [also **teddy**] *n* osito de peluche.

tedious ['ti:dɪəs] *adj* tedioso,-a, aburrido,-a.

teenage ['ti:neɪdʒ] *adj* adolescente.

teenager ['ti:neɪdʒəʳ] *n* quinceañero,-a.

teens [ti:nz] *n pl* adolescencia.

tee-shirt ['ti:ʃɜ:t] *n* camiseta.

teeth [ti:θ] *n pl* → tooth.

teethe [ti:ð] *vi* echar los dientes.

teetotaller [ti:'təʊtⁿləʳ] *n* abstemio,-a.

telecommunications [telɪkəmju:-'keɪʃⁿnz] *n pl* telecomunicaciones *fpl*.

telegram ['telɪgræm] *n* telegrama *m*.

telegraph ['telɪgrɑ:f] *n* telégrafo.
▶ *vi* telegrafiar.

telepathy [tɪ'lepəθɪ] *n* telepatía.

telephone ['telɪfəʊn] *n* teléfono. COMP **telephone box** cabina telefónica. ▮ **telephone call** llamada telefónica. ▮

telephone directory listín *m* telefónico. ▪ **telephone number** número telefónico.
▸ *vt* telefonear, llamar por teléfono.
▸ *vi* hacer una llamada telefónica.

telephonist [təˈlefənɪst] *n* telefonista *mf*.

telephoto lens [telɪfəʊtəʊˈlenz] *n* teleobjetivo.

teleprinter [ˈtelɪprɪntəʳ] *n* teletipo.

telescope [ˈtelɪskəʊp] *n* telescopio.

telescopic [telɪˈskɒpɪk] *adj (aerial)* telescópico,-a; *(umbrella)* plegable.

televise [ˈtelɪvaɪz] *vt* televisar.

television [ˈtelɪvɪʒ°n] *n* **1** *(gen)* televisión *f*. **2** *(set)* televisor *m*.

telex® [ˈteleks] *n* télex *m*.
▸ *vt* enviar por télex.

tell [tel] *vt* **1** *(gen)* decir. **2** *(story, joke)* contar; *(truth, lies, secret)* decir. **3** *(talk about)* hablar de. **4** *fml* comunicar, informar. **5** *(distinguish)* distinguir.
◆ **to tell apart** *vt sep* (saber) distinguir.
◆ **to tell off** *vt sep* **1** regañar, reñir. **2** MIL destacar.
◆ **to tell on** *vt insep (inform on)* chivarse de.
ⓘ *pt & pp* told [təʊld].

teller [ˈteləʳ] *n (in bank)* cajero,-a.

telling-off [telɪŋˈɒf] *n fam* bronca.

telltale [ˈtelteɪl] *n* chivato,-a, acusica *mf*.
▸ *adj* revelador,-ra.

telly [ˈtelɪ] *n fam* tele *f*.
ⓘ *pl* tellies.

temper [ˈtempəʳ] *n* **1** *(mood)* humor *m*; *(nature)* genio. **2** *(of metal)* temple *m*.
▸ *vt* **1** *(metal)* templar. **2** *fig* atenuar.

tempera [ˈtempərə] *n* temple *m*. COMP **tempera paints** témperas.

temperate [ˈtemprɪt] *adj (gen)* moderado,-a; *(climate)* templado,-a.

temperature [ˈtemp°rɪtʃəʳ] *n* temperatura. LOC **to have/run a temperature** tener fiebre.

tempered [ˈtempəd] *adj* templado,-a.

tempest [ˈtempɪst] *n* tempestad *f*.

template [ˈtempleɪt] *n* plantilla.

temple [ˈtemp°l] *n* **1** *(building)* templo. **2** ANAT sien *f*.

temporary [ˈtemp°rərɪ] *adj* temporal.

tempt [tempt] *vt* tentar.

temptation [tempˈteɪʃ°n] *n* tentación *f*.
LOC **to yield to temptation** caer en la tentación.

tempting [ˈtemptɪŋ] *adj* tentador,-ra.

ten [ten] *n* diez *m*.
▸ *adj* diez.

✎ Consulta también six.

tenable [ˈtenəb°l] *adj* **1** *(theory, etc)* sostenible, defendible. **2** *(post, office)*: how long is the post tenable for? ¿durante cuántos años se puede ocupar el puesto?

tenacity [təˈnæsɪtɪ] *n* tenacidad *f*.

tenant [ˈtenənt] *n* inquilino,-a.

tend [tend] *vt (person)* cuidar de, atender; *(other)* ocuparse de.
▸ *vi (have tendency)* tender (**to**, a), tener tendencia (**to**, a).
◆ **to tend to** *vt insep* ocuparse de.

tendency [ˈtendənsɪ] *n* tendencia.
ⓘ *pl* tendencies.

tender¹ [ˈtendəʳ] *adj* **1** *(meat, etc)* tierno,-a. **2** *(loving)* tierno,-a, cariñoso,-a. **3** *(sore)* dolorido,-a. **4** *(delicate)* delicado,-a, sensible.
ⓘ *comp* tenderer, *comp* tenderest.

tender² [ˈtendəʳ] *n* COMM *(offer)* oferta.
▸ *vt* presentar, ofrecer.
▸ *vi* hacer una oferta (**for**, para).

tenderness [ˈtendənəs] *n* ternura.

tendon [ˈtendən] *n* tendón *m*.

tennis [ˈtenɪs] *n* tenis *m*. COMP **tennis court** pista de tenis. ▪ **tennis player** jugador,-a de tenis.

tenon [ˈtenən] *n* espiga.
▸ *vt* despatillar.

tenor [ˈtenəʳ] *n* tenor *m*.

tense [tens] *adj* **1** *(anxious)* tenso,-a. **2** *(taut)* tirante, tenso,-a.
▸ *n (of verb)* tiempo verbal.
▸ *vt* tensar.

tension [ˈtenʃ°n] *n* tensión *f*.

tent [tent] *n* tienda de campaña.

tentacle [ˈtentək°l] *n* tentáculo.

tenth [tenθ] *adj* décimo,-a.
▸ *adv* en décimo lugar.
▸ *n (fraction)* décimo; *(one part)* décima parte *f*.

✎ Consulta también sixth.

T

tepee ['ti:pi:] *n* tipi *m*.

tepid ['tepɪd] *adj* tibio,-a.

term [tɜ:m] *n* **1** EDUC trimestre *m*. **2** *(period of time)* período. **3** *(expression, word)* término.
  ▶ *n pl* **terms** *(sense)* términos *mpl*. COMM condiciones *fpl*, *(relations)* relaciones *fpl*.

terminal ['tɜ:mɪnəl] *adj* terminal.
  ▶ *n* **1** ELEC borne *m*. **2** COMPUT terminal *m*. **3** *(at airport, etc)* terminal *f*.

terminate ['tɜ:mɪneɪt] *vt* **1** *(gen)* terminar, poner fin a; *(contract)* rescindir. **2** *(pregnancy)* interrumpir.
  ▶ *vi* terminarse.

termini ['tɜ:mɪnaɪ] *n pl* → **terminus**.

terminology [tɜ:mɪ'nɒlədʒɪ] *n* terminología.

terminus ['tɜ:mɪnəs] *n* término.
  ⓘ *pl* **terminuses** o **termini** ['tɜ:mɪnaɪ].

termite ['tɜ:maɪt] *n* termita.

terrace ['terəs] *n* **1** *(of house, café, bar, etc)* terraza. **2** *(on hillside)* terraza, bancal *m*.
  ▶ *n pl* **terraces** SP gradas *fpl*.

terraced house [terəst'haʊs] *n* casa adosada.

terrain [tə'reɪn] *n* terreno.

terrible ['terɪbəl] *adj* **1** terrible, espantoso,-a. **2** *fam (as intensifier)* mucho,-a.

terribly ['terɪblɪ] *adv* **1** terriblemente. **2** *fam (very)* muy.

terrific [tə'rɪfɪk] *adj* **1** *(wonderful)* fabuloso,-a, estupendo,-a. **2** *(huge)* tremendo,-a.

> ✕ Terrific no significa 'terrorífico', que se traduce por **terrifying**.

terrify ['terɪfaɪ] *vt* aterrar, aterrorizar.
  ⓘ *pt & pp* **terrified**, *ger* **terrifying**.

terrifying ['terɪfaɪɪŋ] *adj* aterrador,-ra, espantoso,-a.

territory ['terɪtərɪ] *n* **1** *(gen)* territorio. **2** *(zone)* zona, área.
  ⓘ *pl* **territories**.

terror ['terəʳ] *n* **1** *(gen)* terror *m*, espanto. **2** *fam (child)* diablillo.

terrorism ['terərɪzəm] *n* terrorismo.

terrorist ['terərɪst] *n* terrorista *mf*.
  ▶ *adj* terrorista.

tertiary ['tɜ:ʃərɪ] *adj* terciario,-a.

test [test] *n* **1** *(trial)* prueba. **2** EDUC *(gen)* examen *m*; *(multiple choice)* test *m*. **3** MED análisis *m*. COMP **test tube** probeta.
  ▶ *vt* probar.

testicle ['testɪkəl] *n* testículo.

testify ['testɪfaɪ] *vt* JUR declarar.
  ▶ *vi* **1** *(bear witness)* dar fe (to, de). **2** JUR prestar declaración, testificar.
  ⓘ *pt & pp* **testified**, *ger* **testifying**.

testimony ['testɪmənɪ] *n* testimonio.
  ⓘ *pl* **testimonies**.

test-tube baby [testtju:b'beɪbɪ] *n* niño,-a probeta.

tetanus ['tetənəs] *n* tétanos *m inv*.

text [tekst] *n* texto.

textbook ['tekstbʊk] *n* libro de texto.

textile ['tekstaɪl] *adj* textil.
  ▶ *n* textil *m*.

texture ['tekstʃəʳ] *n* textura.

Thai [taɪ] *adj* tailandés,-esa.
  ▶ *n* **1** *(person)* tailandés,-esa. **2** *(language)* tailandés *m*.

Thailand ['taɪlænd] *n* Tailandia.

Thames [temz] *n* el Támesis *m*.

than [ðæn, *unstressed* ðən] *conj* **1** que: *he is taller than you are* él es más alto que tú. **2** *(with numbers)* de: *more than fifty* más de cincuenta. **3** *(followed by clause)* de lo que: *this is easier than we thought* esto es más fácil de lo que pensábamos.

thank [θæŋk] *vt* dar las gracias a, agradecer. LOC **no, thank you** no, gracias. ‖ **thank you** gracias.

thankful ['θæŋkfʊl] *adj* agradecido,-a.

thankless ['θæŋkləs] *adj* ingrato,-a.

thanks [θæŋks] *interj* gracias: *thanks to* gracias a. LOC **no, thanks** no, gracias.
  ▶ *n pl (gratitude)* agradecimiento.

thanksgiving [θæŋks'gɪvɪŋ] *n* acción *f* de gracias. COMP **Thanksgiving Day** Día *m* de Acción de Gracias.

> ⊕ **Thanksgiving Day** (Día de Acción de Gracias) se celebra en Estados Unidos el cuarto jueves de noviembre. Recuerda el día de 1621 en que los colonos ingleses dieron gracias a Dios por la cosecha que les permitiría sobrevivir su segundo invierno en el Nuevo Mundo.

that [ðæt *unstressed* ðət] *adj* ese, esa; *(remote)* aquel, aquella.
ⓘ *pl* those.
▸ *pron* **1** ése *m*, ésa; *(remote)* aquél *m*, aquélla. **2** *(indefinite)* eso; *(remote)* aquello. **3** *(relative)* que. **4** *(with preposition)* que, el/la que, el/la cual. LOC **that is to say** es decir. ‖ **that's it** *(that's all)* eso es todo. **2** *(that's right)* eso es. **3** *(that's enough)* se acabó. ‖ **that's right** así es. ‖ **that's that** se acabó. ‖ **who's that?** *(on 'phone)* ¿quién es?
ⓘ *pl* those.
▸ *adv fam* tan, tanto,-a, tantos,-as.

thatch [θætʃ] *n* **1** *(straw)* paja; *(roof)* tejado de paja. **2** *(hair)* mata.

thaw [θɔː] *n* deshielo.
▸ *vt (food)* descongelar; *(snow, ice)* derretir.
▸ *vi* **1** *(food)* descongelarse; *(snow, ice)* derretirse. **2** *(person)* ablandarse; *(relations)* distenderse, mejorar.
◆ **to thaw out** *vi* descongelarse.
▸ *vt sep* descongelar.

the [ðə] [delante de una vocal se pronuncia [ðɪ]; con énfasis [ðiː]] *def art* **1** el, la; *(plural)* los, las. **2** *(per)* por: *we are paid by the hour* nos pagan por horas. **3** *(emphasis)* el, la, los, las: *you're not the Paul Newman, are you?* no serás el auténtico Paul Newman, ¿verdad?
▸ *adv (with comparatives)*: *the more you have, the more you want* cuanto más se tiene, más se quiere.

theater [ˈθiːətəʳ] *n* US → theatre.

theatre [ˈθiːətəʳ] *n* **1** *(gen)* teatro. **2** MED quirófano. **3** US cine *m*. **4** *(scene of action)* escenario.
▸ *adj* teatral, de teatro.

theft [θeft] *n* robo, hurto.

their [ðeəʳ] *adj* su; *(plural)* sus: *they took their children and their dog* se llevaron a sus hijos y al perro.

theirs [ðeəz] *pron* (el) suyo, (la) suya; *(plural)* (los) suyos, (las) suyas: *that house is theirs* aquella casa es suya.

them [ðem, *unstressed* ðˀm] *pron* **1** *(direct object)* los, las; *(indirect object)* les; *(before another pronoun)* se: *the Smiths are coming, do you know them?* vienen los Smith, ¿los

conoces?; *take these flowers and give them to Mary* coge estas flores y se las das a Mary. **2** *(with preposition, stressed)* ellos, ellas: *don't speak to them* no hables con ellos. **3** *fam (used with singular meaning)* lo, la, le: *if anyone arrives, tell them to wait* si llega alguien, dile que espere.

thematic [θɪˈmætɪk] *adj* temático,-a.

theme [θiːm] *n* tema *m*. COMP **theme park** parque *m* temático.

themselves [ðəmˈselvz] *pron* **1** *(subject)* ellos/ellas mismos(as): *they made it themselves* lo hicieron ellos mismos. **2** *(object)* se: *they looked at themselves in the mirror* se miraron en el espejo. **3** *(after preposition)* sí mismos,-as: *they are old enough to look after themselves* son lo bastante mayores como para cuidar de sí mismos. LOC **by themselves** solos,-as: *don't leave the children by themselves* no dejes a los niños solos.

then [ðen] *adv* entonces, luego: *I was born in 1963, life was different then* nací en 1963, entonces la vida era distinta; *I'll have soup first and then steak* primero tomaré sopa y luego un filete.

theology [θɪˈblədʒɪ] *n* teología.

theorem [ˈθɪərəm] *n* teorema *m*.

theoretic [θɪəˈretɪk] *adj* teórico,-a.

theoretical [θɪəˈretɪkˀl] *adj* teórico,-a.

theory [ˈθɪərɪ] *n* teoría. LOC **in theory** en teoría.
ⓘ *pl* theories.

therapist [ˈθerəpɪst] *n* terapeuta *mf*.

therapy [ˈθerəpɪ] *n* terapia, terapéutica: *she's having therapy* está recibiendo terapia.
ⓘ *pl* therapies.

there [ðeəʳ] *adv* **1** allí, allá, ahí: *I often go there on holiday* voy de vacaciones allí a menudo. **2** *(in discussion)* acerca de eso: *I agree with you there* estoy de acuerdo contigo en eso. LOC **there and then** en el momento. ‖ **there is/are, etc** → be. ‖ **there you are** aquí tiene. ‖ **there you go** ya está.

thereafter [ðeəˈræftəʳ] *adv* a partir de entonces.

thereby [ˈðeəbaɪ] *adv* por eso, por ello.

T

therefore ['ðeəfɔːʳ] *adv* por tanto, por lo tanto, por consiguiente.

thermal ['θɜːməl] *adj* **1** *(stream, bath, spring)* termal; *(underwear)* térmico,-a. **2** PHYS térmico,-a.
▸ *n* corriente *f* térmica.

thermometer [θə'mɒmɪtəʳ] *n* termómetro.

thermos® ['θɜːmɒs] *n* termo.

thermostat ['θɜːməstæt] *n* termostato.

thesaurus [θɪ'sɔːrəs] *n* diccionario ideológico.

these [ðiːz] *adj* estos,-as: *these apples are cheaper than those* estas manzanas son más baratas que aquellas.
▸ *pron* éstos,-as: *which ones do you prefer?–these* ¿cuáles prefieres? –éstos.

they [ðeɪ] *pron* **1** *(plural)* ellos,-as: *where are the children? –they're in the garden* ¿dónde están los niños? –están en el jardín. **2** *fam (singular - substitutes* he *or* she*)* él, ella: *if anyone saw the accident, they should go to the police* si alguien vio el accidente, que vaya a la policía. LOC **they say that...** se dice que…

thick [θɪk] *adj* **1** *(solid things)* grueso,-a: *it's a thick book* es un libro grueso. **2** *(liquid, gas, vegetation, etc)* espeso,-a. **3** *(beard, eyebrows)* poblado,-a. **4** *(cloud, smoke, fog, forest)* denso,-a, espeso,-a. **5** *(fur, hedge)* tupido,-a. **6** *fam (stupid)* corto,-a, corto,-a de alcances; *(unable to think)* espeso,-a. **7** *(accent)* marcado,-a, cerrado,-a; *(of speech, voice)* poco claro,-a.
▸ *adv* espesamente, gruesamente.

thicken ['θɪkən] *vt* espesar.
▸ *vi* espesarse, hacerse más denso,-a.

thickness ['θɪknəs] *n* **1** *(in size)* espesor *m*, grosor *m*. **2** *(density - of liquid)* espesura; *(- of fog)* densidad *f*. **3** *(layer)* capa.

thief [θiːf] *n (gen)* ladrón,-ona; *(mugger)* atracador,-ra.
ⓘ *pl* **thieves** [θiːvz].

thieves [θiːvz] *pl* → **thief**.

thigh [θaɪ] *n* muslo.

thighbone ['θaɪbəʊn] *n* fémur *m*.

thimble ['θɪmbəl] *n* dedal *m*.

thin [θɪn] *adj* **1** *(gen)* delgado,-a, fino,-a, **2** *(liquid - soup, sauce)* poco espeso,-a, claro,-a; *(- rain)* fino,-a. **3** *(audience, crowd)* poco numeroso,-a; *(response, attendance)* escaso,-a. **4** *(voice)* débil. **5** *(excuse, argument)* pobre, poco convincente.
ⓘ *comp* **thinner**, *superl* **thinnest**.
▸ *adv* finamente.
▸ *vt (paint)* diluir; *(sauce)* hacer menos espeso,-a.
▸ *vi* **1** *(fog, mist)* disiparse. **2** *(audience, crowd, traffic)* hacerse menos denso,-a, disminuir.
◆ **to thin down** *vi* adelgazar.
▸ *vt sep (sauce)* hacer menos espeso,-a, aclarar; *(paint)* diluir.
◆ **to thin out** *vt insep (crowd, traffic)* mermar, disminuir.
▸ *vt sep (crops, plants)* entresacar.

thing [θɪŋ] *n* **1** *(object)* cosa, objeto. **2** *(non-material)* cosa. **3** *(affair)* asunto. **4** *(person, creature)*: *you poor little thing!* ¡pobrecito! **5** *(with negative)* nada: *I can't understand a thing you're saying* no entiendo nada de lo que dices.
▸ *n* **the thing** *(what)* lo que: *the thing I like most in life* lo que más me gusta en la vida.
▸ *n pl* **things** *(belongings)* cosas *fpl*, ropa *f sing*, equipaje *m sing*.

think [θɪŋk] *vi* **1** *(gen)* pensar. **2** *(remember)* acordarse (of, de), recordar. **3** *(imagine)* imaginarse, pensar.
▸ *vt* **1** *(gen)* pensar. **2** *(believe)* creer. **3** *(remember)* recordar, acordarse de.
◆ **to think ahead** *vi* prevenir.
◆ **to think back** *vi* hacer memoria.
◆ **to think out** *vt sep (consider carefully)* estudiar, pensar bien.
ⓘ *pt & pp* **thought** [θɔːt].

thinking ['θɪŋkɪŋ] *n* **1** *(opinion)* opinión *f*, parecer *m*. **2** *(thought)* pensamiento.
▸ *adj* pensante, inteligente.

third [θɜːd] *adj* tercero,-a. COMP **third person** LING tercera persona.
▸ *adv (in series)* tercero, en tercer lugar.
▸ *n* **1** tercero,-a. **2** *(fraction)* tercio; *(one part)* tercera parte *f*.

✎ Consulta también **sixth**.

third-party ['θɜːdpɑːtɪ] *adj (insurance)* a terceros.

third-world [ˈθɜːdwɜːld] *adj* (*in general*) del tercer mundo; (*pejorative use*) tercermundista.

thirst [θɜːst] *n* sed *f*.

thirsty [ˈθɜːstɪ] *adj* **1** sediento,-a: *I'm thirsty* tengo sed. **2** (*work, etc*) que da sed. **3** *fig* (*eager*) ansioso,-a (**for**, por).
LOC **to be thirsty** tener sed.
ⓘ *comp* thirstier, *superl* thirstiest.

thirteen [θɜːˈtiːn] *n* trece *m*.
▶ *adj* trece.

✎ Consulta también six.

thirteenth [θɜːˈtiːnθ] *adj* decimotercero,-a.
▶ *adv* en decimotercero lugar.
▶ *n* (*fraction*) decimotercero; (*one part*) decimotercera parte *f*.

✎ Consulta también sixth.

thirties [ˈθɜːtɪz] *n pl* **the thirties** los años *mpl* treinta. LOC **to be in one's thirties** tener treinta y tantos años.

✎ Consulta también sixties.

thirtieth [ˈθɜːtɪəθ] *adj* trigésimo,-a.
▶ *adv* en trigésimo lugar.
▶ *n* (*fraction*) trigésimo; (*one part*) trigésima parte *f*.

✎ Consulta también sixtieth.

thirty [ˈθɜːtɪ] *n* treinta *m*.
▶ *adj* treinta.

✎ Consulta también sixty.

this [ðɪs] *adj* este, esta: *whose is this book?* ¿de quién es este libro?
ⓘ *pl* these [ðiːs].
▶ *pron* éste, ésta; (*indefinite*) esto: *I prefer this one* prefiero éste. **2** (*on 'phone*): *this is Laura* soy Laura.
ⓘ *pl* these [ðiːs].
▶ *adv* tan, tanto,-a: *I didn't think it was this far* no creía que fuera tan lejos. LOC **this is** (*introducing*) te presento a.

thistle [ˈθɪsəl] *n* cardo.

thoracic [θəˈræsɪk] *adj* torácico,-a.

thorax [ˈθɔːræks] *n* tórax *m inv*.

thorn [θɔːn] *n* espina, pincho.

thorough [ˈθʌrə] *adj* **1** (*deep*) profundo,-a, a fondo. **2** (*careful*) cuidadoso,-a,

minucioso,-a. **3** (*person*) concienzudo,-a. **4** (*utter, complete*) total, verdadero,-a.

thoroughgoing [ˈθʌrəɡəʊɪŋ] *adj* profundo,-a, minucioso,-a.

thoroughly [ˈθʌrəlɪ] *adv* **1** (*carefully*) a fondo, meticulosamente. **2** (*completely*) totalmente, absolutamente.

those [ðəʊz] *adj* esos,-as; (*remote*) aquellos,-as: *could you pass me those plates?* ¿me podrías pasar esos platos?
▶ *pron* ésos,-as; (*remote*) aquéllos,-as: *if these are my books, whose are those?* si estos libros son míos, ¿de quién son aquellos?

though [ðəʊ] *conj* aunque, si bien, a pesar de que: *though he doesn't earn very much, he loves his job* aunque no gana mucho, le encanta su trabajo.
▶ *adv* sin embargo, a pesar de todo: *it's expensive –it's worth it though* es caro –sin embargo, vale lo que cuesta. LOC **even though** como si. ❙ **even though** aun cuando, a pesar de que.

thought [θɔːt] *pt & pp* → think.
▶ *n* **1** pensamiento **2** (*consideration*) consideración *f*. **3** (*idea, opinion*) idea, opinión *f*. **4** (*intention*) intención *f*.

thoughtful [ˈθɔːtfʊl] *adj* **1** (*considerate*) atento,-a, considerado,-a. **2** (*pensive*) pensativo,-a, meditabundo,-a. **3** (*considered*) serio,-a.

thoughtless [ˈθɔːtləs] *adj* **1** (*unthinking*) irreflexivo,-a, descuidado,-a. **2** (*inconsiderate*) desconsiderado,-a, poco considerado,-a.

thousand [ˈθaʊzənd] *n* mil *m*: *there were thousands of people* había miles de personas.
▶ *adj* mil: *it costs a thousand euros* cuesta mil euros.

thousandth [ˈθaʊzənθ] *adj* milésimo,-a.
▶ *adv* en milésimo lugar.
▶ *n* (*fraction*) milésimo; (*one part*) milésima parte *f*.

thrash [θræʃ] *vt* **1** (*beat*) azotar. **2** (*defeat*) derrotar, dar una paliza a. **3** (*arm, leg, etc*) sacudir.

thread [θred] *n* **1** SEW hilo, hebra. **2** (*of screw, bolt*) rosca. **3** (*of story*) hilo.
▶ *vt* **1** (*needle*) enhebrar. **2** (*beads*) ensartar.

threat [θret] *n* amenaza.

T

threaten [ˈθretᵊn] vt amenazar (with/to, con).
▶ vi amenazar.

threatening [ˈθretᵊnɪŋ] adj amenazador,-ra, intimidatorio,-a.

three [θriː] n tres m.
▶ adj tres. COMP **three quarters** tres cuartos. ‖ **Three Wise Men** los Reyes Magos.

✎ Consulta también six.

three-dimensional [θriːdɪˈmenʃənəl] adj tridimensional.

thresh [θreʃ] vt trillar.

thresher [ˈθreʃəʳ] n (machine) trilladora.

threshold [ˈθreʃəʊld] n 1 umbral m. 2 fig umbral m, límite m.

threw [θruː] pt → throw.

thrill [θrɪl] n (excitement) emoción f, ilusión f.
▶ vt (excite) entusiasmar, hacer ilusión a, ilusionar.
▶ vi (de excited) entusiasmarse.

thriller [ˈθrɪləʳ] n (novel) novela de suspense; (film) película de suspense; (play) obra de suspense.

thrilling [ˈθrɪlɪŋ] adj emocionante, apasionante.

throat [θrəʊt] n garganta.

thrombosis [θrɒmˈbəʊsɪs] n trombosis f inv.

throne [θrəʊn] n trono.

throttle [ˈθrɒtᵊl] n 1 válvula reguladora. 2 fam acelerador m. LOC **at full throttle** a toda pastilla.

through [θruː] prep 1 por, a través de. 2 (because of) por, a causa de. 3 (from beginning to the end) hasta el final de. 4 US terminado,-a, acabado,-a.
▶ adv 1 de un lado a otro. 2 (to the end) hasta el final. 3 GB (on phone) conectado,-a. 4 US terminado,-a, acabado,-a.
▶ adj (train) directo,-a; (traffic) de paso.

throughout [θruːˈaʊt] prep 1 por todo,-a, en todo,-a. 2 (time) a lo largo de.
▶ adv 1 (all over) por/en todas partes. 2 (completely) completamente. 3 (time) todo el tiempo.

throw [θrəʊ] n 1 lanzamiento, tiro. 2 (of dice) tirada, lance m; (in game) jugada, turno.

▶ vt 1 (gen) tirar, arrojar, lanzar. 2 fig (kiss) echar, tirar; (glance, look) lanzar, dirigir.

◆ **to throw away** vt sep 1 (get rid of, discard) tirar. 2 (waste) desaprovechar, perder; (money) malgastar, derrochar. 3 (speech) lanzar al aire.

◆ **to throw back** vt sep 1 (ball, etc) devolver. 2 (bedclothes) echar atrás.

◆ **to throw in** vt sep 1 fam (include) incluir gratis. 2 SP sacar de banda.

◆ **to throw out** vt sep 1 (expel) echar, expulsar. 2 (reject) rechazar. 3 (discard) tirar.

◆ **to throw up** vi vomitar, devolver.
ⓘ pt **threw** [θruː], pp **thrown** [θrəʊn].

throwaway [ˈθrəʊəweɪ] adj de usar y tirar.

throw-in [ˈθrəʊɪn] n SP saque m de banda.

thrown [θrəʊn] pp → throw.

thru [θruː] prep-adv US → through.

◆ **to thrust on** vt sep imponer.

thud [θʌd] n ruido sordo.
▶ vi caer con un ruido sordo.
ⓘ pt & pp **thudded**, ger **thudding**.

thumb [θʌm] n pulgar m.
▶ vt hacer autostop.

◆ **to thumb through** vt insep hojear.

thumbtack [ˈθʌmtæk] n US chincheta.

thump [θʌmp] n (blow) golpe m, puñetazo; (sound) golpazo.
▶ vt golpear, pegar un puñetazo.
▶ vi (gen) golpear; (heart) latir con fuerza; (feet) caminar con pasos pesados.

thunder [ˈθʌndəʳ] n trueno.
▶ vi tronar.
▶ vt (shout) bramar, rugir.

thunderstorm [ˈθʌndəstɔːm] n tormenta.

Thursday [ˈθɜːzdɪ] n jueves m.

✎ Para ejemplos de uso, consulta Saturday.

thus [ðʌs] adv 1 (in this way, like this) así, de este modo. 2 (consequently) así que, por lo tanto, por consiguiente. 3 (to this extent) hasta.

thwart [θwɔːt] vt desbaratar, frustrar.

thyme [taɪm] n tomillo.

thyroid [ˈθaɪrɔɪd] n tiroides m. COMP **thyroid gland** glándula tiroides.

Tibet [tɪˈbet] n Tíbet.

Tibetan [tɪˈbetᵊn] *adj* tibetano.
▶ *n* **1** *(person)* tibetano,-a. **2** *(language)* tibetano.

tibia [ˈtɪbɪə] *n* tibia.

tick¹ [tɪk] *n* ZOOL garrapata.

tick² [tɪk] *n* **1** *(noise)* tictac *m*. **2** *(mark)* marca, señal *f*.
▶ *vi (clock)* hacer tictac.
▶ *vt* señalar, marcar.

ticket [ˈtɪkɪt] *n* **1** *(for transport)* billete *m*. **2** *(for concert, cinema, etc)* entrada. **3** *(for library, etc)* carnet *m*. **4** *(label)* etiqueta. **5** *(for item deposited)* resguardo. **6** *fam (fine)* multa. **7** POL lista de candidatos. COMP **ticket collector** revisor,-a. ∥ **ticket inspector** revisor,-a. ∥ **ticket office** taquilla.

tickle [ˈtɪkᵊl] *n* cosquilleo.
▶ *vi (touch lightly)* hacer cosquillas; *(itch)* picar.

tidal [ˈtaɪdᵊl] *adj* de la marea. COMP **tidal wave 1** *(gen)* maremoto. **2** *fig* oleada.

tide [taɪd] *n* **1** marea. **2** *fig (trend)* corriente *f*. COMP **high tide** pleamar *f*. ∥ **low tide** bajamar *f*.

tidy [ˈtaɪdɪ] *adj* **1** *(place)* ordenado,-a, bien arreglado. **2** *(person - appearance)* arreglado,-a; *(- habits)* metódico,-a.
ⓘ *comp* **tidier**, *superl* **tidiest**.
▶ *n* organizador *m*.
▶ *vt [also tidy up]* ordenar.
▶ *vi [also tidy up]* poner las cosas en orden.
◆ **to tidy away** *vt sep* recoger, guardar.
◆ **to tidy out** *vt sep* limpiar, ordenar.
ⓘ *pt & pp* **tidied**, *ger* **tidying**.

tie [taɪ] *n* **1** *(of shirt)* corbata. **2** *(for fastening)* cierre *m*. **3** *(rod, beam)* tirante *m*. **4** *fig (bond)* lazo, vínculo: *family ties are strong* los lazos del parentesco son fuertes. **5** *fig (restriction)* atadura. **6** SP *(draw)* empate *m*; *(match)* partido.
▶ *vt* **1** *(fasten)* atar; *(knot, bow)* hacer. **2** *fig* ligar, vincular, relacionar. **3** *(restrict)* atar. **4** MUS ligar.
▶ *vi* **1** *(fasten)* atarse. **2** SP empatar.
◆ **to tie down** *vt sep* **1** atar, sujetar. **2** *(restrict)* atar; *(commit oneself)* comprometerse.
◆ **to tie up** *vt sep* **1** *(fasten)* atar; *(boat)* amarrar. **2** *(link)* conectar, ligar, rela-

cionar. **3** *(occupy)* liar, ocupar. **4** FIN *(capital)* inmovilizar, invertir. **5** *(finalize)* finalizar, concluir, cerrar.
ⓘ *pt & pp* **tied**, *ger* **tidying**.

tier [tɪəʳ] *n* **1** *(in stadium)* grada. **2** *(of cake)* piso. **3** *(in hierarchy)* nivel *m*.

tiger [ˈtaɪgəʳ] *n* tigre *m*.

tight [taɪt] *adj* **1** *(firmly fastened)* apretado,-a, duro,-a. **2** *(taut)* tirante, tenso,-a. **3** *(clothes)* ajustado,-a, ceñido,-a. **4** *(not leaky)* hermético,-a, impermeable. **5** *(hold)* estrecho,-a, fuerte. **6** *(packed together)* apretado,-a. **7** *(strict - schedule)* apretado,-a; *(- security)* estricto,-a, riguroso,-a. **8** *fam (mean)* agarrado,-a, tacaño,-a. **9** *fam (drunk)* borracho,-a. **10** *(bend)* cerrado,-a.
▶ *adv* firmemente, fuerte.

tighten [ˈtaɪtᵊn] *vt* **1** *(gen)* apretar, ajustar; *(rope)* tensar. **2** *(make stricter - security)* hacer más estricto, reforzar; *(- credit)* restringir.
▶ *vi (gen)* apretarse; *(rope, muscles)* tensarse.
◆ **to tighten up** *vt sep* intensificar, hacer más estricto,-a.
▶ *vi* ponerse más estricto,-a.

tightrope [ˈtaɪtrəʊp] *n* cuerda floja. COMP **tightrope walker** funámbulo.

tights [taɪts] *n pl* **1** *(gen)* pantys *mpl*, medias *fpl*. **2** *(thick)* leotardos *mpl*, mallas *fpl*.

tigress [ˈtaɪgrəs] *n* tigresa.

tile [taɪl] *n* *(wall)* azulejo; *(floor)* baldosa; *(roof)* teja.
▶ *vt* **1** *(wall)* alicatar, poner azulejos a. **2** *(floor)* embaldosar. **3** *(roof)* tejar.

till [tɪl] *prep* hasta.
▶ *conj* hasta que.
▶ *n (for cash)* caja.
▶ *vt (cultivate)* labrar, cultivar.

tiller [ˈtɪləʳ] *n* caña del timón.

tilt [tɪlt] *n* **1** inclinación *f*, ladeo *m*. **2** *(with lance)* acometida.
▶ *vt* inclinar, ladear.
▶ *vi* **1** *(slope, shift)* inclinarse. **2** *(with lance)* acometer.

timber [ˈtɪmbəʳ] *n* **1** *(wood)* madera (de construcción). **2** *(beam)* viga. **3** *(trees)*

T

árboles *mpl* maderables. COMP **timber mill** aserradero.

▶ *interj* ¡cuidado, que cae!, ¡allá va!

time [taɪm] *n* **1** *(period)* tiempo. **2** *(short period)* rato. **3** *(of day)* hora. **4** *(age, period, season)* época. **5** *(occasion)* vez *f*. **6** *(suitable moment)* momento. **7** MUS compás *m*. **8** GB la hora de cerrar.

▶ *vt* **1** *(measure time)* medir la duración de, calcular; *(races, etc)* cronometrar. **2** *(schedule)* estar previsto,-a. LOC **(and) about time** ya era hora. **I all the time** todo el tiempo. **I at any time** en cualquier momento. **I at no time** nunca. **I at one time** en un tiempo. **I at the same time** al mismo tiempo. **I for the time being** de momento. **I from time to time** de vez en cuando. **I in time 1** *(in the long run)* con el tiempo. **2** *(not late)* a tiempo. **I on time** puntual. **I time after time** una y otra vez. **I time's up** se acabó el tiempo. **I to be ahead of one's time** adelantarse a su época. **I to give SB a hard time** ponérselo difícil a ALGN. **I to have a bad time** pasarlas negras. **I to have a good time** pasarlo bien. **I to take one's time 1** *(not hurry)* hacer ALGO con calma. **2** *(be slow)* tardar mucho. **I to tell the time** decir la hora.

▶ *n pl* **times** veces *fpl*. LOC **at times** a veces. **I to keep up with the times** estar al día.

timeless ['taɪmləs] *adj* eterno,-a.

timely ['taɪmlɪ] *adj* oportuno,-a.

timer ['taɪmə^r] *n* temporizador *m*.

time-share ['taɪmʃeə^r] *adj (property)* en multipropiedad.

timetable ['taɪmteɪb^əl] *n* horario.

timid ['tɪmɪd] *n* tímido,-a.

timing ['taɪmɪŋ] *n* **1** *(time chosen)* momento escogido; *(judgement)* sentido de la oportunidad. **2** SP *(measurement of time)* cronometraje *m*.

tin [tɪn] *n* **1** *(metal)* estaño. **2** *(can)* lata, bote *m*. **3** *(for baking)* molde *m*.

▶ *vt* enlatar.

ⓘ *pt & pp* tinned, *ger* tinning.

tinfoil ['tɪnfɔɪl] *n* papel *m* de estaño.

tinkle ['tɪŋk^əl] *n* tintineo.

▶ *vt* hacer tintinear.

▶ *vi* **1** *(ring)* tintinear. **2** GB *fam (urinate)* hacer pipí.

tinned [tɪnd] *adj* enlatado,-a. COMP **tinned food** comida de lata.

tin-opener ['tɪnəʊpənə^r] *n* abrelatas *m inv*.

tinsel ['tɪns^əl] *n* espumillón *m*.

tiny ['taɪnɪ] *adj* diminuto,-a.

ⓘ *comp* tinier, *superl* tiniest.

tip¹ [tɪp] *n (gen)* extremo, punta, cabo; *(of cigarette)* boquilla, filtro. LOC **from tip to toe** de pies a cabeza.

tip² [tɪp] *n* **1** *(gratuity)* propina. **2** *(advice)* consejo, truco; *(confidential information)* soplo, confidencia; *(prediction)* pronóstico.

▶ *vt* **1** *(give gratuity to)* dar una propina a. **2** *(predict)* pronosticar.

tip³ [tɪp] *n (for rubbish)* vertedero, basurero; *(dirty place)* porquería, desorden *m*.

▶ *vt* **1** *(lean, tilt)* inclinar, ladear. **2** *(pour)* verter; *(throw)* tirar; *(empty)* vaciar. **3** *(rubbish)* verter.

◆ **to tip over** *vi (overturn)* volcarse, caerse; *(boat)* zozobrar.

▶ *vt sep* volcar.

ⓘ *pt & pp* tipped, *ger* tipping.

tipsy ['tɪpsɪ] *adj* achispado,-a, piripi.

ⓘ *comp* tipsier, *superl* tipsiest.

tiptoe ['tɪptəʊ] *vi* caminar de puntillas. LOC **on tiptoe** de puntillas.

tire¹ [taɪə^r] *vt* cansar.

▶ *vi* cansarse *(of, de)*.

◆ **to tire out** *vt sep* agotar.

tire² [taɪə^r] *n* US → tyre.

tired [taɪəd] *adj* **1** *(weary)* cansado,-a. **2** *(fed up)* harto,-a *(of, de)*. LOC **to get tired** cansarse.

tireless ['taɪələs] *adj* incansable.

tiresome ['taɪəsəm] *adj* molesto,-a, pesado,-a.

tiring ['taɪərɪŋ] *adj* cansado,-a, agotador,-ra.

tissue ['tɪʃuː] *n* **1** *(cloth)* tisú *m*. **2** *(handkerchief)* pañuelo de papel, kleenex. **3** BIOL tejido. COMP **tissue paper** papel *m* de seda.

title ['taɪt^əl] *n* título.

▶ *vt* titular.

▶ *n pl* **titles** *(film credits)* créditos *mpl*.

titleholder ['taɪtəlhəʊldəʳ] n campeón,-ona.

to [tʊ, *unstressed* tə] prep **1** *(with place)* a: *we're going to a concert* vamos a un concierto. **2** *(towards)* hacia: *the Labour party has moved to the right* el partido laborista se ha desplazado hacia la derecha. **3** *(as far as, until)* a, hasta: *from beginning to end* desde el principio hasta el final. **4** *(of time)* menos: *it's ten to two* son las dos menos diez. **5** *(with indirect object)* a: *I showed the letter to my mother* le enseñé la carta a mi madre. **6** *(indicating comparison)* a: *I prefer tea to coffee* prefiero el té al café. **7** *prep (ratio)* a: *they won by fourteen points to ten* ganaron por catorce puntos a diez. **8** *(in order to)* para, a fin de: *I worked overtime to earn some extra money* hice horas extras para ganar más dinero. **9** *(substituting infinitive)*: *would you like to dance? -I'd love to* ¿te gustaría bailar? -me encantaría.
► adv *(of door)* ajustada: *push the door to* ajusta la puerta. LOC **to and fro** ir y venir.

✎ Cuando se usa con la raíz del verbo para formar el infinitivo no se traduce: *I want to help you* quiero ayudarte.

toad [təʊd] n sapo.

toadstool ['təʊdstuːl] n hongo venenoso.

✎ Toadstool es el nombre en general de las setas no comestibles, las que sí se pueden comer se llaman mushrooms.

toast [təʊst] n **1** *(food)* pan m tostado, tostada. **2** *(drink)* brindis m.
► vt **1** *(cook)* tostar. **2** *(drink)* brindar por, beber a la salud de.

toaster ['təʊstəʳ] n tostadora.

tobacco [tə'bækəʊ] n tabaco.
① pl tobaccos o tobaccoes.

tobacconist's [tə'bækənɪsts] n estanco.

Tobago [tə'beɪgəʊ] n Tobago.

toboggan [tə'bɒgən] n trineo.

today [tə'deɪ] n hoy m.
► adv **1** hoy. **2** *(nowadays)* hoy en día.
◆ **to toddle off** vi marcharse, irse.

toddler ['tɒdləʳ] n niño,-a (que empieza a andar).

toe [təʊ] n **1** ANAT dedo del pie. **2** *(of shoe)* puntera; *(of sock)* punta.

toecap ['təʊkæp] n puntera.

toenail ['təʊneɪl] n uña del dedo del pie.

toffee ['tɒfɪ] n caramelo.
◆ **to tog out / tog up** vt sep vestir.
► vi vestirse.

together [tə'geðəʳ] adv **1** *(gen)* juntos, -as. **2** *(simultaneously)* a la vez, al mismo tiempo. **3** *(nonstop)* seguido,-a. LOC **to bring together** reunir. ‖ **to come together** juntarse.‖ **together with** junto con.
► adj fam *(confident, organized, capable)* seguro,-a de sí mismo,-a.

Togo ['təʊgəʊ] n Togo.

Togolese [təʊgə'liːz] adj togolés,-esa.
► n togolés,-esa.

toilet ['tɔɪlət] n **1** *(appliance)* váter m, inodoro; *(room)* lavabo, baño. **2** *(public)* servicios mpl, aseos mpl. **3** *(washing)* aseo personal, higiene m personal. COMP **toilet paper** papel m higiénico.

toiletries ['tɔɪlətrɪz] n pl artículos mpl de aseo.

token ['təʊkⁿn] n **1** *(sign, proof)* señal f, prueba. **2** *(memento, souvenir)* detalle m, recuerdo. **3** *(coupon)* vale m. **4** *(coin)* ficha. LOC **in token of** en recuerdo de.
► adj simbólico,-a.

told [təʊld] pt & pp → tell.

tolerance ['tɒlərəns] n tolerancia.

tolerant ['tɒlərənt] adj tolerante (of/towards, con).

tolerate ['tɒləreɪt] vt tolerar, aguantar, soportar.

toll¹ [təʊl] n **1** *(payment)* peaje m. **2** *(loss)* mortalidad f, número de víctimas mortales. LOC **to take its toll on** afectar negativamente.

toll² [təʊl] n *(of bell)* tañido.
► vt tañer, doblar.
► vi doblar.

tollgate ['təʊlgeɪt] n peaje m.

tom [tɒm] n gato (macho).

tomahawk ['tɒməhɔːk] n hacha de guerra.

tomato [tə'mɑːtəʊ, US tə'meɪtəʊ] n tomate m.
① pl tomatoes.

T

tomb [tuːm] *n* tumba, sepulcro.

tombstone ['tuːmstəʊn] *n* lápida (sepulcral).

tomcat ['tɒmkæt] *n* gato (macho).

tomorrow [təˈmɒrəʊ] *n* mañana.
▸ *adv* mañana: *tomorrow morning/afternoon* mañana por la mañana/tarde; *see you tomorrow!* ¡hasta mañana!

ton [tʌn] *n* tonelada.
▸ *n pl* **tons** *fam* montones *mpl*.

tone [təʊn] *n* tono.

Tonga ['tɒŋɡə] *n* Tonga.

Tongan ['tɒŋɡən] *adj* tongano,-a.
▸ *n* **1** *(person)* tongano,-a. **2** *(language)* tongano.

tongs [tɒŋz] *n pl* tenacillas *fpl*, pinzas *fpl*.

tongue [tʌŋ] *n* **1** ANAT lengua. **2** *(language)* lengua, idioma *m*. **3** *(of shoe)* lengüeta. **4** *(of bell)* badajo. **5** *(of land, flame)* lengua. LOC **to stick one's tongue out** sacar la lengua. COMP **tongue twister** trabalenguas *m*.

tonic ['tɒnɪk] *n* **1** MED tónico. **2** MUS tónica. **3** *(drink)* tónica.
▸ *adj* tónico,-a. COMP **tonic water** tónica.

tonight [təˈnaɪt] *n* esta noche *f*.
▸ *adv* esta noche *f*.

tonne [tʌn] *n* tonelada.

tonsil ['tɒnsəl] *n* amígdala.

tonsillitis [tɒnsəˈlaɪtəs] *n* amigdalitis *f*.

too [tuː] *adv* **1** *(excessively)* demasiado. **2** *(also)* también. **3** *(besides)* además. **4** *(very)* muy. LOC **too many** demasiados,-as. **too much** demasiado,-a.

took [tʊk] *pt* → take.

tool [tuːl] *n* *(gen)* herramienta; *(instrument)* instrumento.
▸ *vt* *(book)* estampar; *(leather)* labrar.
▸ *n pl* **tools** *(gardening, etc)* útiles *mpl*.
▸ **to tool up** *vt sep* equipar.

toolbar ['tuːlbɑːʳ] *n* barra de herramientas.

toolbox ['tuːlbɒks] *n* caja de herramientas.

toolkit ['tuːlkɪt] *n* juego de herramientas.

tooth [tuːθ] *n* **1** *(gen)* diente *m*; *(molar)* muela; *(front tooth)* incisivo. **2** *(of comb)* púa. **3** *(of saw)* diente *m*.
① *pl* teeth.

toothache ['tuːθeɪk] *n* dolor *m* de muelas.

toothbrush ['tuːθbrʌʃ] *n* cepillo de dientes.

toothless ['tuːθləs] *adj* desdentado,-a.

toothpaste ['tuːθpeɪst] *n* pasta de dientes.

toothpick ['tuːθpɪk] *n* mondadientes *m inv*, palillo.

top¹ [tɒp] *n* **1** *(highest/upper part)* parte *f* superior. **2** *(far end - of street)* final *m*; *(- of table)* cabecera. **3** *(of mountain)* cumbre *m*. **4** *(of tree)* copa. **5** *(surface)* superficie *f*. **6** *(of bottle)* tapón *m*; *(of pen)* capuchón *m*. **7** *(highest position)*: *she was top of the class* fue la primera de la clase. **8** *(of list)* cabeza. **9** *(of car)* capota. **10** *(clothes)* top *m*; *(of bikini)* parte de arriba. **11** *(beginning)* principio. **12** *(gear)* directa.
▸ *adj* **1** *(highest)* de arriba, superior, más alto,-a. **2** *(best, highest, leading)* mejor, principal. **3** *(highest, maximum)* principal, máximo,-a. COMP **top brass** altos mandos *mpl*. ‖ **top gear** directa.
▸ *vt* **1** *(cover)* cubrir, rematar. **2** *(remove top of plant/fruit)* quitar los rabillos. **3** sl *(kill)* cargarse. **4** *(come first, head)* encabezar. **5** *(better, surpass, exceed)* superar.
① *pt & pp* topped, *ger* topping.
▸ *n pl* **tops** *(of plant)* hojas *fpl*.

top² [tɒp] *n* peonza. LOC **to sleep like a top** dormir como un tronco.

topaz ['təʊpæz] *n* topacio.

topic ['tɒpɪk] *n* tema *m*.

☒ Tópico no significa 'tópico', que se traduce por commonplace.

topography [təˈpɒɡrəfɪ] *n* topografía.

toponym ['tɒpənɪm] *n* topónimo.

topping ['tɒpɪŋ] *n* *(for pizza)* ingrediente *m*; *(for ice-cream)* cubierta.
▸ *adj* excelente.

topple ['tɒpəl] *vt* **1** *(overturn)* volcar. **2** *fig (overthrow)* derribar, derrocar.
▸ *vi* *(fall)* caerse; *(lose balance)* tambalearse, perder el equilibrio.

torch [tɔːtʃ] n **1** (with naked flame) antorcha. **2** (electric) linterna.
▶ vt quemar, prender fuego a.

tore [tɔːʳ] pt → **tear**.

torment [(n) 'tɔːmənt; (vb) tɔː'ment] n (gen) tormento; (suffering) angustia.
▶ vt **1** (cause to suffer) atormentar, torturar. **2** (annoy) molestar.

torn [tɔːn] pp → **tear**.

tornado [tɔːˈneɪdəʊ] n tornado.
ⓘ pl tornados o tornadoes.

torpedo [tɔːˈpiːdəʊ] n torpedo.
ⓘ pl torpedos o torpedoes.

torrent ['tɒrənt] n torrente m.

torrential [təˈrenʃəl] adj torrencial.

torso ['tɔːsəʊ] n torso.
ⓘ pl torsos.

tort [tɔːt] n JUR agravio.

tortoise ['tɔːtəs] n tortuga (de tierra).

torture ['tɔːtəʳ] n tortura.

Tory ['tɔːrɪ] n GB conservador,-ra.
ⓘ pl Tories.
▶ adj GB conservador,-ra.

toss [tɒs] n **1** (shake) sacudida, movimiento. **2** (of coin) sorteo a cara o cruz.
▶ vt **1** (move, shake) mover, agitar, sacudir; (pancake) dar la vuelta a; (salad) mezclar. **2** (throw) arrojar, lanzar, tirar.
LOC **to toss a coin** echarlo a cara o cruz.
ⓘ pt & pp totted, ger totting.

total ['təʊtəl] adj (overall) total; (complete) completo,-a, rotundo,-a.
▶ n total m, suma.
▶ vt sumar.
▶ vi sumar, ascender a.

totalitarian [təʊtælɪˈteərɪən] adj totalitario,-a.

totally ['təʊtəlɪ] adv totalmente, completamente.

totem ['təʊtəm] n tótem m. COMP **totem pole** tótem m.

touch [tʌtʃ] n **1** (gen) toque m; (light touch) roce m. **2** (detail) detalle m, toque m. **3** (sense) tacto. **4** (connection) contacto, comunicación f. **5** (slight quantity) poquito, pizca. **6** fam (skill, ability) habilidad f. **7** (manner, style) toque m, sello. **9** SP toque m. LOC **to be in touch with STH** estar al corriente de ALGO. ‖

to get in touch ponerse en contacto (with, con).
▶ vt **1** (gen) tocar; (lightly) rozar. **2** (eat) probar. **3** (move) conmover. **4** (equal, rival) igualar.
▶ vi tocarse.
◆ **to touch down** vi **1** (plane) aterrizar.
◆ **to touch on / touch upon** vi mencionar.
◆ **to touch up** vt sep ART retocar.

touching ['tʌtʃɪŋ] adj conmovedor,-ra.

touch-screen ['tʌtʃskriːn] n pantalla táctil.

tough [tʌf] adj **1** (strong) fuerte, resistente. **2** (difficult) duro,-a, arduo,-a. **3** (rough, violent) violento,-a. **4** (severe) duro,-a, severo,-a. **5** (meat) duro,-a.
▶ n tipo duro.

tour [tʊəʳ] n **1** viaje m, excursión f. **2** (round building) visita. **3** (by performers) gira; (cycling) vuelta.
▶ vt **1** (gen) recorrer, viajar por. **2** (building) visitar. COMP **tour operator** agente m de viajes.
▶ vi (by performers) hacer una gira.

tourism ['tʊərɪzəm] n turismo.

tourist ['tʊərɪst] n turista mf.
▶ adj turístico,-a. COMP **tourist class** clase f turista. ‖ **tourist office** oficina de turismo.

tournament ['tʊənəmənt] n torneo.

tow [təʊ] vt remolcar.
▶ n remolque m. LOC **on tow** de remolque.

toward [təˈwɔːd] prep US → **towards**.

towards [təˈwɔːdz] prep **1** (in direction of) hacia. **2** (attitude) con, para con. **3** (payment) para. **4** (of time) hacia, cerca de.

towel ['taʊəl] n toalla.

tower ['taʊəʳ] n **1** (gen) torre f. **2** (of church) campanario. COMP **tower block** bloque m (de pisos).

town [taʊn] n **1** (large) ciudad f; (small) población f, municipio, pueblo. **2** (city centre) centro. **3** (people) ciudadanos mpl, ciudad f.
▶ adj urbano,-a, municipal. COMP **town council** ayuntamiento. ‖ **town hall** ayuntamiento.

T

township ['taʊnʃɪp] *n* **1** *(gen)* municipio, pueblo. **2** *(in South Africa)* distrito
segregado.

toxic ['tɒksɪk] *n* tóxico,-a.

toy [tɔɪ] *n* juguete *m*.
▶ *adj* **1** de juguete. **2** *(dog)* enano,-a.
COMP **toy shop** juguete *m*.

toyshop ['tɔɪʃɒp] *n* juguetería.

trace [treɪs] *n* **1** *(mark, sign)* indicio, rastro. **2** *(small amount - material)* pizca, vestigio; *(- non-material)* dejo, asomo, nota. COMP **trace element** oligoelemento.
▶ *vt* **1** *(sketch)* trazar, esbozar. **2** *(copy)*
calcar. **3** *(find)* encontrar, localizar;
(follow) seguir la pista de. **4** *(describe
development)* describir.

tracer ['treɪsər] *n* **1** MIL trazadora. **2**
MED trazador *m*. COMP **tracer bullet** bala trazadora.

trachea [trə'kɪə] *n* ANAT tráquea.

tracing ['treɪsɪŋ] *n* calco. COMP **tracing
paper** papel *m* de calco.

track [træk] *n* **1** *(mark)* pista, huellas
fpl, rastro; *(of wheels)* rodada. **2** *(of rocket, bullet, etc)* trayectoria. **3** *(path)* camino, senda, sendero. **4** SP pista. **5** *(for
motor-racing)* circuito. **6** *(of railway)* vía;
(platform) andén *m*. **7** *(on record, etc)* tema *m*, corte *m*, canción *f*. LOC **to be on
the right track** ir por buen camino. I
to keep track of seguir. COMP **track and
field** atletismo.
▶ *vt* **1** *(person, animal)* seguir la pista de.
2 TECH seguir la trayectoria de.
◆ **to track down** *vt sep* localizar.

tracksuit ['træksuːt] *n* chándal *m*.

tract¹ [trækt] *n* *(treatise)* tratado; *(pamphlet)* folleto.

traction ['trækʃən] *n* tracción *f*.

tractor ['træktər] *n* tractor *m*.

trade [treɪd] *n* **1** *(commerce)* comercio. **2**
(business) negocio; *(industry)* industria.
3 *(occupation)* oficio, profesión *f*.
▶ *adj* comercial. COMP **trade gap** déficit *m* comercial. I **trade fair** feria de
muestras. I **trade name** nombre *m*
comercial. I **trade union** sindicato. I
trade winds vientos *mpl* alisios.
▶ *vi* *(do business)* comerciar.
▶ *vt* *(exchange)* cambiar.

trademark ['treɪdmɑːk] *n* marca registrada, marca.

trader ['treɪdər] *n* comerciante *mf*.

tradesman ['treɪdzmən] *n* **1** *(businessman)* comerciante *m*; *(shopkeeper)* tendero. **2** *(deliveryman)* repartidor *m*.
ⓘ *pl* tradesmen ['treɪdɪŋ].

trading ['treɪdɪŋ] *n* comercio.

tradition [trə'dɪʃən] *n* tradición *f*.

traditional [trə'dɪʃənəl] *adj* tradicional.

traffic ['træfɪk] *n* tráfico.
▶ *adj* de la circulación, del tráfico. COMP
traffic circle US rotonda. I **traffic jam**
atasco, embotellamiento. I **traffic
lights** semáforo. I **traffic warden** guardia *mf* de tráfico.
▶ *vi* traficar (in, con).

⊕ Un **traffic warden** es un especie de
guardia urbano que vigila que los coches
estén bien aparcados y regula el tráfico de
las ciudades.

tragedy ['trædʒədɪ] *n* tragedia.
ⓘ *pl* tragedies.

tragic ['trædʒɪk] *adj* trágico,-a.

trail [treɪl] *n* **1** *(path)* camino, sendero.
2 *(track, mark, scent)* rastro, pista, huellas *fpl*. **3** *(of rocket, comet)* cola; *(of dust,
vapour)* estela; *(of blood)* reguero.
▶ *vt* **1** *(follow)* seguir la pista de. **2** *(drag)*
arrastrar.
▶ *vi* **1** *(lag behind)* ir rezagado,-a, quedarse atrás. **2** *(drag)* arrastrarse.

trailer ['treɪlər] *n* **1** AUTO remolque *m*. **2** US
caravana. **3** CINEM tráiler *m*, avance *m*.

train [treɪn] *n* **1** *(transport)* tren *m*. **2** *(of
dress)* cola. **3** *(line - of animals)* recua;
(- of vehicles) convoy *m*.
▶ *vt* **1** SP entrenar, preparar. **2** *(teach)*
enseñar. **3** *(animal)* amaestrar, adiestrar. COMP **train driver** maquinista *m*.
I **train station** estación *f* de tren.
▶ *vi* **1** SP entrenarse, prepararse. **2**
(teach) estudiar. **3** MIL adiestrarse.

trained [treɪnd] *adj* **1** *(worker - skilled)* ca-
lificado,-a, cualificado,-a. **2** *(animal)*
amaestrado,-a, adiestrado,-a.

trainee [treɪˈniː] *n* **1** *(manual work)* aprendiz,-za. **2** *(professional work)* persona que está haciendo prácticas.

trainer [ˈtreɪnəʳ] *n* **1** SP entrenador,-ra. **2** *(of dogs)* amaestrador,-ra; *(of circus animals)* domador,-ra; *(of race horses)* preparador,-ra. **3** *(shoe)* zapatilla de deporte.

training [ˈtreɪnɪŋ] *n* **1** formación *f* (profesional), capacitación *f*. **2** SP entrenamiento, preparación *f* física.
▸ *vi* MIL instrucción *f*.

traitor [ˈtreɪtəʳ] *n* traidor,-ra.

tram [træm] *n* tranvía *m*.

tramcar [ˈtræmkɑːʳ] *n* tranvía *m*.

tramp [træmp] *n* vagabundo,-a.

❌ Tramp no significa 'trampa', que se traduce por **trap**.

trample [ˈtræmpəl] *vt* pisotear.
▸ *vi* pisotear (on/over, -).

trampoline [ˈtræmpəliːn] *n* cama elástica.

tranquilliser [ˈtræŋkwɪlaɪzəʳ] *n* → **tranquillizer**.

tranquillizer [ˈtræŋkwɪlaɪzəʳ] *n* tranquilizante *m*, calmante *m*.

transcend [trænˈsend] *vt* **1** *(go beyond)* trascender. **2** *(surpass)* superar.

transept [ˈtrænsept] *n* crucero.

transfer [*(n)* ˈtrænsfɜːʳ; *(vb)* trænsˈfɜːʳ] *n* **1** FIN transferencia. **2** JUR *(of property)* traspaso. **3** *(of employee)* traslado. **4** SP *(of player)* traspaso; *(player)* fichaje *m*. **5** *(drawing)* cromo, calcomanía. **6** *(of airline passenger)* transbordo, trasbordo.
▸ *vt* **1** FIN transferir. **2** JUR *(property)* traspasar. **3** *(employee, prisoner)* trasladar. **4** SP *(player)* traspasar. **5** *(data, information, phone call)* pasar.
ⓘ *pt & pp* transferred, *ger* transferring.

transform [trænsˈfɔːm] *vt* transformar.
▸ *vi* transformarse (into, en), convertirse (into, en).

transistor [trænˈzɪstəʳ] *n* transistor.

transition [trænˈzɪʃən] *n* transición *f*.

transitive [ˈtrænsɪtɪv] *adj* transitivo,-a.

translate [trænsˈleɪt] *vt* **1** *(gen)* traducir (from, de) (into, a). **2** *(express, explain)* expresar. **3** *(transform)* transformar.
▸ *vi* *(person)* traducir; *(word, book, etc)* traducirse.

translation [trænsˈleɪʃən] *n* traducción *f*.

translator [trænsˈleɪtəʳ] *n* traductor,-ra.

translucent [trænzˈluːsənt] *adj* translúcido,-a.

transmission [trænzˈmɪʃən] *n* transmisión *f*.

transmit [trænzˈmɪt] *vt* transmitir (to, a).
ⓘ *pt & pp* transmitted, *ger* transmitting.

transmitter [trænzˈmɪtəʳ] *n* transmisor *m*.

transparency [trænsˈpeərənsɪ] *n* **1** *(quality)* transparencia. **2** *(slide)* diapositiva; *(acetate)* transparencia.
ⓘ *pl* transparencies.

transparent [trænsˈpeərənt] *adj* **1** transparente. **2** *fig* claro,-a, evidente.

transplant [*(n)* ˈtrænsplɑːnt; *(vb)* trænsˈplɑːnt] *n* trasplante *m*.
▸ *vt* trasplantar.

transport [*(n)* ˈtrænspɔːt; *(vb)* trænsˈpɔːt] *n* transporte *m*.
▸ *vt* **1** transportar. **2** HIST deportar.

trap [træp] *n* **1** *(gen)* trampa. **2** *(vehicle)* coche *m* ligero de dos ruedas. **3** *(of drain)* sifón *m*. ⌊LOC⌋ **to set a trap** tender una trampa.
▸ *vt* **1** *(catch - gen)* atrapar; *(snare - animal)* cazar; *(imprison)* entrampar; *(part of body)* pillar. **2** SP *(in football)* parar con el pie. **3** *fig (trick)* engañar, tender una trampa a. **4** *(heat, light, etc)* retener.
ⓘ *pt & pp* trapped, *ger* trapping.

trapdoor [ˈtræpdɔːʳ] *n* *(gen)* trampilla; *(in theatre)* escotillón *m*.

trapeze [trəˈpiːz] *n* *(of circus)* trapecio.

trapezium [trəˈpiːzɪəm] *n* trapecio.
ⓘ *pl* trapeziums o trapezia [trəˈpiːzɪə].

trapezoid [ˈtræpɪzɔɪd] *n* **1** GB trapecio *m*. **1** US trapezoide.

trash [træʃ] *n* basura. ⌊COMP⌋ **trash can 1** *(on computer)* papelera de reciclaje. **2** *(for waste)* US cubo de la basura.

trauma [ˈtrɔːmə] *n* trauma *m*.

T

travel ['trævəl] *n* viajes *mpl*, viajar *m*. COMP
travel agency agencia de viajes. ‖ **travel
sickness** mareo.
▶ *vt* viajar por, recorrer.
▶ *vi* **1** *(make a journey)* viajar; *(go)* ir. **2**
(move, go) ir. **3** *(go fast)* ir rápido, ir a
toda velocidad. **4** *(as salesperson)* ser
viajante, ser representante. **5** *(wine,
food, etc)* poderse transportar.
ⓘ *pt & pp* travelled (US traveled), *ger*
travelling (US traveling).
▶ *n pl* **travels** *(journeys)* viajes *mpl*.

traveler ['trævələr] *n* US → **traveller**.

traveller ['trævələr] *n* **1** *(gen)* viajero,-a.
2 *(representative)* viajante *mf*, representante *mf*. COMP **traveller's cheque** cheque
m de viaje.

trawler ['trɔːlər] *n* pesquero de arrastre.

tray [treɪ] *n* **1** *(for food)* bandeja. **2** *(for papers)* caja, cesta. **3** *(in photography)* cubeta.

treachery ['tretʃəri] *n* traición *f*.
ⓘ *pl* treacheries.

tread [tred] *n* **1** *(manner or sound of walking)*
paso, pasos *mpl*. **2** *(on stair)* escalón *m*.
▶ *vt* **1** *(gen)* pisar, pisotear. **2** *(walk on)*
andar por; *(make)* hacer.
ⓘ *pt* trod [trɒd], *pp* trodden [ˈtrɒdən] o
trod [trɒd].

treason ['triːzən] *n* traición *f*.

treasure ['treʒər] *n* *(gen)* tesoro.

treasurer ['treʒərər] *n* tesorero,-a.

treasury ['treʒəri] *n* tesorería.
ⓘ *pl* treasuries.

treat [triːt] *n* **1** *(meal, drink)* convite *m*. **2**
(present) regalo. **3** *(pleasure)* placer *m*,
gusto, deleite *m*.
▶ *vt* **1** *(gen)* tratar. **2** *(invite)* invitar; *(give)*
regalar.

treatment ['triːtmənt] *n* **1** MED tratamiento, cura. **2** *(manner of treating)* trato. **3** *(process)* tratamiento.

✕ Treatment no significa 'tratamiento
(forma de dirigirse a alguien)', que se traduce por form of address.

treaty ['triːti] *n* tratado.
ⓘ *pl* treaties.

treble ['trebəl] *adj* **1** *(threefold)* triple. **2** MUS
de tiple. COMP **treble clef** clave *f* de sol.
▶ *n* MUS tiple *mf*.

▶ *vt* triplicar.
▶ *vi* triplicarse.

tree [triː] *n* árbol *m*.

tree-top ['triːtɒp] *n* copa.

trekking ['trekɪŋ] *n* senderismo.

tremble ['trembəl] *n* temblor *m*.
▶ *vi* temblar.

tremendous [trɪˈmendəs] *adj* **1** *(huge)*
tremendo,-a, inmenso,-a. **2** *fam*
(great) fantástico,-a, estupendo,-a.

trench [trentʃ] *n* **1** *(ditch)* zanja. **2** MIL
trinchera.

trend [trend] *n* **1** *(tendency)* tendencia
(to/towards, hacia), tónica. **2** *(fashion)*
moda.

trendy ['trendi] *adj fam* moderno,-a,
de moda.
ⓘ *comp* trendier, *superl* trendiest.

trespass ['trespəs] *n* **1** entrada ilegal.
2 REL pecado.
▶ *vi* **1** *(on land)* entrar sin autorización; *(in affairs)* entrometerse. **2** REL
pecar (against, contra). LOC "No tres-
passing" «Prohibido el paso».

✕ To trespass no significa 'traspasar',
que se traduce por to go through.

trespasser ['trespəsər] *n* intruso,-a.

tress [tres] *n* mechón *m*.
▶ *n pl* **tresses** melena *f sing*, cabellera *f sing*

trestle ['tresəl] *n* caballete *m*.

trial ['traɪəl] *n* **1** JUR proceso, juicio. **2**
(test) prueba. **3** *(suffering)* aflicción *f*
sufrimiento; *(trouble)* molestia.
▶ *n pl* **trials** SP pruebas *fpl*.

triangle ['traɪæŋgəl] *n* triángulo.

triangular [traɪˈæŋgjʊlər] *adj* triangular.

tribal ['traɪbəl] *adj* tribal.

tribe [traɪb] *n* **1** tribu *f*. **2** *fam (family)*
tribu *f*, familia.

tribune ['trɪbjuːn] *n* **1** ARCH tribuna. **2**
(Roman magistrate) tribuno.

tributary ['trɪbjʊtəri] *n* afluente *m*.
ⓘ *pl* tributaries.
▶ *adj* tributario,-a.

tribute ['trɪbjuːt] *n* **1** *(homage)* homenaje *m*, tributo. **2** *(payment)* tributo.

triceps ['traɪseps] *n pl* tríceps *m inv*.

trick [trɪk] n **1** (gen) truco. **2** (prank, joke) broma. **3** (cards won) baza. LOC **to play a trick on** SB gastarle una broma a ALGN. ‖ **trick or treat** US frase de los niños que en Halloween van por las casas pidiendo un regalo a cambio de no hacer una jugarreta.
▸ adj de juguete, de mentira.
▸ vt (deceive) engañar, burlar.

trickle ['trɪkəl] n **1** goteo, hilo. **2** fig pequeña cantidad f, poco.
▸ vi **1** (liquid) gotear, salir gota a gota. **2** fig salir (entrar, llegar, etc) poco a poco.

tricky ['trɪkɪ] adj **1** (person) astuto,-a. **2** (problem, situation - difficult) difícil; (- delicate) delicado,-a.
① comp trickier, superl trickiest.

tricycle ['traɪsɪkəl] n triciclo.

trident ['traɪdənt] n tridente m.

trier [traɪəʳ] n persona que se esfuerza.

trifle ['traɪfəl] n **1** (unimportant thing) nimiedad f. **2** (little money) poco dinero. **3** GB postre de bizcocho. LOC **a trifle** un poco, algo.

trigger ['trɪgəʳ] n **1** (of gun) gatillo. **2** (of camera, machine) disparador m.

trigonometry [trɪgə'nɒmətrɪ] n trigonometría.

trillion ['trɪlɪən] n **1** billón m. **2** GB (formerly) trillón m.

✎ En el uso actual, tanto en EE UU como en Gran Bretaña, un **trillion** equivale al billón español, es decir, un millón de millones.

trim [trɪm] adj **1** (neat, tidy) (bien) arreglado,-a, ordenado,-a, cuidado,-a. **2** (person, figure) esbelto,-a, delgado,-a.
① comp trimmer, superl trimmest.
▸ n **1** (cut) recorte m. **2** (decoration - on clothes) adornos mpl; (- along edges) ribete m; (upholstery) tapicería.
▸ vt **1** (make neat) arreglar; (cut - hair) cortar, recortar; (- hedge, etc) podar. **2** (reduce by cutting back) recortar, reducir. **3** (decorate) adornar (with, con); (upholster) tapizar.
◆ **to trim off** vt sep recortar, quitar.
① pt & pp trimmed, ger trimming.

trimmings ['trɪmɪŋz] n pl **1** CULIN (accompaniments) guarnición f sing. **2** (deco-

rations) adornos mpl. **3** (after cutting) recortes mpl.

Trinidad ['trɪnɪdæd] n Trinidad. COMP **Trinidad and Tobago** Trinidad y Tobago.

trip [trɪp] n **1** (journey) viaje m. **2** (excursion) excursión f.
▸ vi **1** (stumble) tropezar (over, con). **2** (move lightly) ir con paso ligero.
① pt & pp tripped, ger tripping.

tripe [traɪp] n **1** CULIN callos mpl. **2** fam tonterías fpl, bobadas fpl.

triple ['trɪpəl] adj triple.

triplet ['trɪplət] n (child) trillizo,-a.

triumph ['traɪəmf] n **1** triunfo, éxito. **2** (joy) júbilo, alegría.
▸ vi triunfar (over, de/sobre), vencer.

trivial ['trɪvɪəl] adj trivial.

trod [trɒd] pt → tread.

trodden ['trɒdən] pp → tread.

troll [trəʊl] n duende m.

trolley ['trɒlɪ] n **1** (in supermarket, at airport) carro, carrito. **2** (in hospital) cama con ruedas. **3** (for food) mesita de ruedas. **4** US tranvía. COMP **trolley bus** trolebús mf. ‖ **trolley car** tranvía mf.

trombone [trɒm'bəʊn] n trombón m.

trophy ['trəʊfɪ] n trofeo.
① pl trophies.

tropic ['trɒpɪk] n trópico.
▸ n pl **the tropics** los trópicos mpl.

tropical ['trɒpɪkəl] adj tropical.

tropism [trə'pɪzəm] n tropismo.

troposphere ['trɒpəsfɪəʳ] n troposfera.

trot [trɒt] n trote m.
▸ vi (gen) trotar, ir al trote; (on horse) cabalgar al trote.
① pt & pp trotted, ger trotting.
▸ n pl **the trots** fam diarrea f sing.

trouble ['trʌbəl] n **1** (problems) problema m, problemas mpl. **2** (inconvenience, bother) molestia, esfuerzo. **3** (unrest, disturbance) conflictos mpl, disturbios mpl. LOC **to be in trouble** tener problemas. ‖ **to get in trouble** meterse en un lío.
▸ vt **1** (cause worry, distress) preocupar, inquietar. **2** (hurt) dar problemas a, doler. **3** (bother) molestar, incomodar.
▸ vi molestarse, preocuparse (about, por).

T

troublemaker ['trʌbªlmeɪkəʳ] n alborotador,-ra.

trough [trɒf] n (for drinking) abrevadero; (for eating) comedero, pesebre m.

trousers ['trauzəz] n pl pantalón m sing, pantalones mpl.

trout [traut] n trucha.

trowel ['trauəl] n 1 (bricklaying tool) paleta. 2 (garden tool) desplantador m.

truant ['truːənt] n (from school) persona que hace novillos. LOC **to play truant** hacer novillos.

truce [truːs] n tregua.

truck [trʌk] n 1 (lorry) camión m. 2 GB (railway wagon) vagón m.

trucker ['trʌkəʳ] n US camionero,-a.

true [truː] adj 1 (not false) verdadero,-a, cierto,-a. 2 (genuine, real) auténtico,-a, genuino,-a, real. 3 (faithful) fiel, leal. 4 (exact) exacto,-a. LOC **to come true** hacerse realidad.
► adv 1 (truthfully) sinceramente. 2 (accurately) bien.

truffle ['trʌfªl] n trufa.

truly ['truːlɪ] adv 1 (really) verdaderamente, de verdad, realmente. 2 (sincerely) sinceramente. 3 (faithfully) fielmente, lealmente. LOC **yours truly** (in letters) atentamente.
◆ **to trump up** vt sep inventar, falsificar.

trumpet ['trʌmpɪt] n MUS trompeta.
► vi 1 fanfarronear. 2 (elephant) barritar.

truncheon ['trʌntʃªn] n porra (de policía).

trunk [trʌŋk] n 1 (of tree, body) tronco. 2 (large case) baúl m. 3 (elephant's) trompa. 4 US (of car) maletero.

trunks [trʌŋks] n pl bañador m sing (de hombre).

trust [trʌst] n 1 (confidence) confianza. 2 (responsibility) responsabilidad f. 3 FIN (money, property) fondo de inversión.
► vt 1 (have faith in, rely on) confiar en, fiarse de. 2 (hope, expect) esperar.
► vi confiar (in, en), tener confianza (in, en).

trustful ['trʌstful] adj confiado,-a.

trustworthy ['trʌstwɜːðɪ] adj 1 (person) digno,-a de confianza, honrado,-a. 2 (news, etc) fidedigno,-a.

truth [truːθ] n verdad f.

truthful ['truːθful] adj 1 (account, etc) verídico,-a, veraz. 2 (person) sincero,-a, veraz.

try [traɪ] n 1 intento. 2 SP (rugby) ensayo.
① pl tries.
► vt 1 (attempt) intentar. 2 (test, use) probar, ensayar; (food) probar. 3 JUR juzgar, procesar.
► vi (make an attempt) intentar.
◆ **to try for** vi tratar de obtener.
◆ **to try on** vt sep (clothes) probarse.
◆ **to try out** vt sep probar, ensayar.
① pt & pp **tried**, ger **trying**.

tsar [zɑːʳ] n zar m.

tsarina [zɑːˈriːnə] n zarina.

tsetse fly ['tsetsɪflaɪ] n mosca tsetsé.

T-shirt ['tiːʃɜːt] n camiseta.

tub [tʌb] n 1 (for washing clothes) balde m. 2 (bath) bañera. 3 (food container) tarrina.

tuba ['tjuːbə] n tuba.

tube [tjuːb] n 1 (pipe, container) tubo. 2 AUTO cámara de aire.
► n **the tube** la televisión f.
► n **the Tube** (underground) el metro.

⊕ The Tube es el nombre con el que se conoce al metro de Londres.

tuck [tʌk] n 1 (fold) pliegue m. 2 GB (sweets etc) golosinas fpl, chucherías fpl.

Tuesday ['tjuːzdɪ] n martes m inv.

✎ Para ejemplos de uso, consulta Saturday.

tuft [tʌft] n 1 (of feathers) penacho. 2 (of hair) mechón m. 3 (of grass) mata.

tug [tʌg] n 1 (pull) tirón m, estirón m. 2 (boat) remolcador m.
► vt 1 (pull) tirar de, dar un estirón de. 2 (boat) remolcar.
① pt & pp **tugged**, ger **tugging**.
► vi tirar (at, de).
① pt & pp **tugged**, ger **tugging**.

tuition [tjuːˈɪʃªn] n enseñanza, instrucción f. COMP **private tuition** clases fpl particulares. ‖ **tuition fees** EDUC matrícula.

tulip ['tjuːlɪp] n tulipán m.

tumble ['tʌmbªl] n caída, tumbo. COMP **tumble drier** secadora.
► vi 1 (fall) caerse. 2 (in acrobatics) dar volteretas.

tumbler ['tʌmbᵊləʳ] n **1** (glass) vaso. **2** (acrobat) volteador,-ra. **3** (toy) tentetieso.

tummy ['tʌmɪ] n barriga.
ⓘ pl tummies.

tumor ['tjuːməʳ] n US → tumour.

tumour ['tjuːməʳ] n barriga.

tuna ['tjuːnə] n atún m, bonito.
ⓘ pl tuna o tunas.

tune [tjuːn] n melodía. ⌊LOC⌋ **in tune** afinado,-a. ‖ **out of tune** desafinado,-a.
▶ vt **1** MUS afinar. **2** (radio, etc) sintonizar. **3** (engine) poner a punto.

tuner ['tjuːnəʳ] n **1** (of piano) afinador,-ra. **2** (on radio) sintonizador m.

tungsten ['tʌŋstən] n tungsteno.

tunic ['tjuːnɪk] n túnica.

tuning ['tjuːnɪŋ] n **1** (of instrument) afinación f. **2** (of radio) sintonización f. **3** (of engine) puesta a punto. ⌊COMP⌋ **tuning fork** diapasón m.

Tunis ['tjuːnɪs] n Túnez.

Tunisia [tjuːˈnɪsɪə] n Túnez.

Tunisian [tjuːˈnɪsɪən] adj tunecino,-a.
▶ n tunecino,-a.

tunnel ['tʌnᵊl] n túnel m.
▶ vt excavar un túnel.
ⓘ pt & pp tunnelled (US tunneled), ger tunnelling (US tunneling).

turban ['tɜːbᵊn] n turbante m.

turbojet ['tɜːbəʊdʒet] n turborreactor m.

turbot ['tɜːbət] n rodaballo.
ⓘ pl turbot o turbots.

turbulence ['tɜːbjʊləns] n turbulencia.

turf [tɜːf] n césped m. ⌊COMP⌋ **the turf** las carreras de caballos, el turf m.
◆ **to turf out** vt sep fam poner de patitas en la calle, echar.

Turk [tɜːk] n (person) turco,-a.

Turkey ['tɜːkɪ] n Turquía.

turkey ['tɜːkɪ] n pavo. ⌊LOC⌋ **to talk turkey** hablar a las claras.

Turkish ['tɜːkɪʃ] adj turco,-a.
▶ n (language) turco.
▶ n pl **the Turkish** los turcos mpl.

turn [tɜːn] n **1** (gen) vuelta. **2** (change of direction) giro, vuelta; (bend) curva, recodo. **3** (chance, go) turno. **4** (change) cambio, giro.
⌊LOC⌋ **to turn a corner** doblar la esquina.

▶ vt **1** (rotate) girar, hacer girar. **2** (page) pasar, volver; (soil) revolver; (ankle) torcer. **3** (change) convertir, transformar; (milk) agriar; (stomach) revolver.
▶ vi **1** (revolve) girar, dar vueltas. **2** (change direction - person) girarse, volverse. **3** (become) hacerse, ponerse, volverse; (milk) agriarse, cortarse.
◆ **to turn back** vt sep **1** (make return) hacer volver. **2** (clock) retrasar.
▶ vi (return) volverse atrás.
◆ **to turn down** vt sep **1** (reject) rechazar; (request) denegar. **2** (radio, etc) bajar. **3** (fold) doblar.
◆ **to turn into** vt sep convertir.
◆ **to turn off** vt sep **1** (electricity) desconectar; (light, gas, appliance) apagar; (tap) cerrar. **2** (dislike) repugnar, dar asco a.
▶ vt insep (off road) salir de.
▶ vi **1** (switch off) apagarse. **2** (off road) salir.
◆ **to turn on** vt sep **1** (electricity) conectar; (light, gas, appliance) encender; (tap) abrir; (engine) poner en marcha, encender. **2** (attack) atacar, arremeter contra; (aim, point at) apuntar, dirigir. **3** fam (excite) excitar, entusiasmar.
▶ vt insep (hinge on) depender de, girar en torno a.
▶ vi encenderse.
◆ **to turn out** vt sep **1** (light) apagar. **2** (produce) producir, fabricar. **3** (empty) vaciar; (cake, jelly, etc) desmoldar. **4** (expel) expulsar, echar.
▶ vi **1** (prove to be, happen) salir, resultar. **2** (go out) salir; (attend) asistir, acudir; (crowds) salir a la calle.
◆ **to turn round** vi dar la vuelta.
◆ **to turn up** vi (arrive) llegar, presentarse; (appear) aparecer.
▶ vt sep **1** (fold upwards) doblar hacia arriba, levantar; (shorten) acortar. **2** (radio, gas, heat, etc) subir.
▶ vt insep (find) descubrir, encontrar.

turnabout ['tɜːnəbaʊt] n giro, cambio.

turning ['tɜːnɪŋ] n bocacalle f, esquina. ⌊COMP⌋ **turning lathe** torno.

turnip ['tɜːnɪp] n nabo.

turnover ['tɜːnəʊvəʳ] n **1** (sales, business) facturación f. **2** (movement of employees) movimiento; (of stock) rotación f. **3** CULIN pastelito relleno.

T

turnpike ['tɜːnpaɪk] *n* US autopista de peaje.

turquoise ['tɜːkwɔɪz] *n* **1** *(gem)* turquesa. **2** *(colour)* azul *m* turquesa.
▶ *adj* azul turquesa.

turtle ['tɜːtəl] *n* tortuga marina.

tusk [tʌsk] *n* colmillo.

tutor ['tjuːtəʳ] *n* **1** *(private teacher)* profesor,-ra particular. **2** *(at university)* profesor,-ra, tutor,-ra.
▶ *vt* dar clases particulares a (in, de).

Tuvalu [tuːvəˈluː] *n* Tuvalu.

tuxedo [tʌkˈsiːdəʊ] *n* US esmoquin *m*.
ⓘ *pl* tuxedos.

TV ['tiːbjuːəns] *abbr* (television) televisión *f*, tele *f*.

tweezers ['twiːzəz] *n pl* pinzas *fpl*.

twelfth [twelfθ] *adj* duodécimo,-a.
▶ *adv* en duodécimo lugar.
▶ *n (fraction)* duodécimo; *(one part)* duodécima parte *f*.

✎ Consulta también sixth.

twelve [twelv] *n* doce *m*.
▶ *adj* doce.

✎ Consulta también six.

twenties ['twentɪz] *n pl* the twenties los años *mpl* veinte. ᴸᴼᶜ to be in one's twenties tener veintitantos años.

✎ Consulta también sixties.

twentieth ['twentɪəθ] *adj* vigésimo,-a.
▶ *adv* en vigésimo lugar.
▶ *n (fraction)* vigésimo; *(one part)* vigésima parte *f*.

✎ Consulta también sixtieth.

twenty ['twentɪ] *n* veinte *m*.
▶ *adj* veinte.

✎ Consulta también sixty.

twice [twaɪs] *adv* dos veces. ᴸᴼᶜ twice over dos veces.

twig¹ [twɪg] *n* ramita.

twilight ['twaɪlaɪt] *n* crepúsculo.

twin [twɪn] *n* gemelo,-a, mellizo,-a.
▶ *adj* gemelo,-a, mellizo,-a. ᶜᴼᴹᴾ twin bed cama doble.
▶ *vt* hermanar.
ⓘ *pt & pp* twinned, *ger* twinning.

twinkle ['twɪŋkəl] *n* **1** *(of light, stars)* centelleo. **2** *(in eye)* brillo.
▶ *vi* **1** *(lights, stars)* centellear, destellar. **2** *(eyes)* brillar.

twirl [twɜːl] *n* giro, vuelta.
▶ *vt* **1** girar rápidamente, dar vueltas a. **2** *(twist, fiddle with)* retorcer, juguetear con.
▶ *vi* girar rápidamente, dar vueltas.

twist [twɪst] *n* **1** *(in road)* recodo, vuelta. **2** *(action)* torsión *m*. **3** MED torcedura, esguince *m*. **4** *(dance)* twist *m*.
▶ *vt* **1** *(sprain)* torcer. **2** *(screw, coil)* retorcer. **3** *(turn, wind)* girar, dar vueltas a.
▶ *vi* **1** *(turn)* girarse. **2** *(wind, coil)* enroscarse, enrollarse. **3** *(road)* serpentear.

twitch [twɪtʃ] *n* **1** *(pull)* tirón *m*. **2** *(nervous tic)* tic *m* nervioso.
▶ *vt* mover.
▶ *vi* moverse nerviosamente.

twitter ['twɪtəʳ] *n* gorjeo.
▶ *vt* gorjear.

two [tuː] *n* dos *m*. ᴸᴼᶜ in two por la mitad. ▌ in twos de dos en dos. ▌ it takes two es cosa de dos. ▌ to put two and two together atar cabos. ▌ that makes two of us ya somos dos.
▶ *adj* dos.

tycoon [taɪˈkuːn] *n* magnate *m*.

type [taɪp] *n* **1** *(kind)* tipo, clase *f*. **2** *(letter)* letra, carácter *m*.
▶ *vt & vi* escribir a máquina.
◆ to type up *vt sep* pasar a máquina.

❌ Type no significa 'tipo (persona)', que se traduce por guy.

typewriter ['taɪpraɪtəʳ] *n* máquina de escribir.

typhoid ['taɪfɔɪd] *n* fiebre *f* tifoidea.

typhus ['taɪfəs] *n* tifus *m*.

typical ['tɪpɪkəl] *adj* típico,-a.

typing ['taɪpɪŋ] *n* mecanografía.

typist ['taɪpɪst] *n* mecanógrafo,-a.

tyranny ['tɪrənɪ] *n* tiranía.
ⓘ *pl* tyrannies.

tyrant ['taɪərənt] *n* tirano,-a.

tyre [taɪəʳ] *n* neumático.

Tyrrhenian [tɪriːniən] *adj* tirreno,-a. ᶜᴼᴹᴾ the Tyrrhenian Sea el (mar) *m* Tirreno.

tzar [zɑːʳ] *n* zar *m*, czar *m*.

U

U, u [juː] *n (the letter)* U, u *f.*

udder ['ʌdəʳ] *n* ubre *f.*

UFO ['juːˈefəʊ] *abbr* (unidentified flying object) ovni *m f*, objeto volador no identificado.

Uganda [juːˈgændə] *n* Uganda.

Ugandan [juːˈgændn] *adj* ugandés, -esa.
► *n* ugandés,-esa.

ugly ['ʌglɪ] *adj* **1** feo,-a. **2** *(situation, etc)* desagradable. **3** *(custom, vice)* repugnante.
ⓘ *comp* uglier, *superl* ugliest.

Ukraine [juːˈkreɪn] *n* Ucrania.

Ukranian [juːˈkeɪnɪən] *adj* ucraniano,-a.
► *n* **1** *(person)* ucraniano,-a. **2** *(language)* ucraniano.

ulcer ['ʌlsəʳ] *n* **1** *(external)* llaga. **2** *(in stomach)* úlcera.

ulna ['ʌlnə] *n* cúbito.
ⓘ *pl* ulnae ['ʌlniː].

ultimate ['ʌltɪmət] *adj* **1** *(final)* final. **2** *(basic)* esencial, fundamental.
► *n* **the ultimate** *(good)* el último grito; *(bad)* el colmo.

ⓧ Ultimate no significa 'último', que se traduce por last.

ultrasound ['ʌltrəsaʊnd] *n* ultrasonido.

ultraviolet [ʌltrəˈvaɪələt] *adj* ultravioleta.

umbilical [ʌmˈbɪlɪkəl] *adj* umbilical.
COMP **umbilical cord** cordón *m* umbilical.

umbrella [ʌmˈbrelə] *n* **1** paraguas *m.* **2** *fig (protection)* manto *f*; *(patronage)* patrocinio.

umpire ['ʌmpaɪəʳ] *n* árbitro,-a.

► *vt* arbitrar.

✎ El término **umpire** se emplea sobre todo para hablar de árbitros de deportes como el cricket o el tenis. La palabra usual para 'árbitro' es referee.

unable [ʌnˈeɪbəl] *adj* incapaz.

unacceptable [ʌnəkˈseptəbəl] *adj* inaceptable, inadmisible.

unaccountable [ʌnəˈkaʊntəbəl] *adj* inexplicable.

unaccustomed [ʌnəˈkʌstəmd] *adj* desacostumbrado,-a.

unaffected [ʌnəˈfektɪd] *adj* **1** *(unchanged)* no afectado,-a. **2** *(for person)* afable, campechano. **3** *(indifferent)* inmutable. **4** *(style)* llano,-a.

unanimous [juːˈnænɪməs] *adj* unánime.

unashamed [ʌnəˈʃeɪmd] *adj* descarado,-a.

unattended [ʌnəˈtendɪd] *adj* **1** *(children)* sin vigilar. **2** *(not looked after)* desatendido,-a. **3** *(alone)* solo,-a.

unavailable [ʌnəˈveɪləbəl] *adj* **1** no disponible. **2** *(busy)* ocupado,-a. **3** *(out of print)* agotado,-a. **4** *(not for sale)* que no está en venta.

unaware [ʌnəˈweəʳ] *adj* ignorante, inconsciente.

unbearable [ʌnˈbeərəbəl] *adj* inaguantable, insoportable, intolerable.

unbeatable [ʌnˈbiːtəbəl] *adj* **1** *(competition)* invencible. **2** *(price, quality)* insuperable, inigualable, inmejorable.

unbelievable [ʌnbɪˈliːvəbəl] *adj* increíble.

unbiased [ʌnˈbaɪəst] *adj* imparcial.

unbiassed [ʌnˈbaɪəst] *adj* → **unbiased**.

unblock [ʌn'blɒk] vt **1** (pipe, drain) desatascar. **2** (street, road) desobstruir. **3** (nose) destaponar.

unbreakable [ʌn'breɪkəbəl] adj **1** irrompible. **2** fig inquebrantable. **3** (horse) indomable.

unbutton [ʌn'bʌtən] vt desabrochar.
▸ vi fam relajarse.

uncertain [ʌn'sɜːtən] adj **1** (not certain) incierto,-a, dudoso,-a. **2** (unspecified) indeterminado,-a. **3** (indecisive) indeciso,-a. **4** (changeable) variable.

unchanged [ʌn'tʃeɪndʒd] adj igual, sin alterar.

unchecked [ʌn'tʃekt] adj **1** no comprobado,-a. **2** (unrestrained) libre, libremente.

uncivilized [ʌn'sɪvəlaɪzd] adj **1** (tribe) salvaje. **2** (not cultured) inculto,-a. **3** fig poco ortodoxo,-a.

uncle ['ʌnkəl] n tío.

unclear [ʌn'klɪər] adj confuso,-a.

uncoil [ʌn'kɔɪl] vt desenrollar.
▸ vi **1** (snake) desenroscarse. **2** (rope) desenrollarse.

uncomfortable [ʌn'kʌmfətəbəl] adj **1** (physical) incómodo,-a. **2** (worrying) inquietante. **3** (unpleasant) desagradable.

uncommon [ʌn'kɒmən] adj **1** (rare) poco común. **2** (strange) insólito,-a; (unusual) extraordinario,-a. **3** (excessive) desmesurado,-a.

unconcerned [ʌnkən'sɜːnd] adj despreocupado, indiferente.

unconscious [ʌn'kɒnʃəs] adj **1** MED inconsciente. **2** (unaware) inconsciente. **3** (not on purpose) involuntario,-a.
▸ n the unconscious el inconsciente.

🗵 Unconscious no significa 'inconsciente (irresponsable)', que se traduce por thoughtless.

uncontrollable [ʌnkən'trəʊləbəl] adj **1** (general) incontrolable. **2** (people) ingobernable. **3** (desire) irresistible. **4** (child) indisciplinado,-a.

uncountable [ʌn'kaʊntəbəl] adj incontable.

uncover [ʌn'kʌvər] vt **1** destapar. **2** (secret) revelar, descubrir.

unction ['ʌŋkʃən] n **1** REL (act, ointment) unción f. **2** (balm) ungüento.

uncultivated [ʌn'kʌltɪveɪtɪd] adj **1** (land) yermo,-a, baldío,-a. **2** (person) inculto,-a.

undamaged [ʌn'dæmɪdʒd] adj **1** (goods) sin desperfectos, intacto,-a. **2** (person) indemne, ileso,-a.

undefeated [ʌndɪ'fiːtɪd] adj invicto,-a.

undeniable [ʌndɪ'naɪəbəl] adj innegable.

under ['ʌndər] prep **1** (below) bajo, debajo de. **2** (less than) menos de. **3** (controlled, affected, influenced by) bajo. **4** (suffering, subject to) bajo. **5** (according to) conforme a, según. **6** (known by) con, bajo.
▸ adv **1** (below) debajo. **2** (less) menos.

undercarriage ['ʌndəkærɪdʒ] n tren m de aterrizaje.

underclothes ['ʌndəkləʊðz] n pl ropa f sing interior.

undercover [ʌndə'kʌvər] adj clandestino,-a, secreto,-a,.
▸ adv en la clandestinidad.

underdeveloped [ʌndədɪ'veləpt] adj **1** subdesarrollado,-a. **2** (of photo) insuficientemente revelado,-a.

underestimate [(n) ʌndər'estɪmət; (vb) ʌndər'estɪmeɪt] n menosprecio.
▸ vt infravalorar, subestimar.

undergo [ʌndə'geʊ] n cúbito.
ⓘ pt underwent [ʌndə'went], pp undergone [ʌndə'gɒn].

undergone [ʌndə'gɒn] pp → undergo.

underground [(adj-n) 'ʌndəgraʊnd; (adv) ʌndə'graʊnd] adj **1** subterráneo, -a. **2** fig clandestino,-a. **3** fig (cinema, music) underground.
▸ n **1** (railway) metro. **2** (resistance) resistencia.
▸ adv **1** bajo tierra. **2** fig (secretly) en la clandestinidad, clandestinamente.

undergrowth ['ʌndəgrəʊθ] n maleza, monte m bajo.

underline [ʌndə'laɪn] vt subrayar.

underneath [ʌndə'niːθ] prep bajo, debajo de.
▸ adv abajo, debajo, por debajo.
▸ adj de abajo, inferior.
▸ n parte f inferior, fondo.

undernourished [ˌʌndəˈnʌrɪʃt] *adj* desnutrido,-a, subalimentado,-a.

underpants [ˈʌndəpænts] *n pl* calzoncillos *mpl*, eslip *m sing*.

understand [ˌʌndəˈstænd] *vt* **1** entender. **2** *(believe)* tener entendido. **3** *(to get on with sb)* entenderse. **4** *(take for granted)* sobreentender.
ⓘ *pt & pp* understood [ˌʌndəˈstʊd].

understanding [ˌʌndəˈstændɪŋ] *n* comprensión.

understatement [ˌʌndəˈsteɪtmənt] *n* eufemismo.

understood [ˌʌndəˈstʊd] *pt & pp* → understand.

undertake [ˌʌndəˈteɪk] *vt* *(take on - job, task)* emprender; *(- responsibility)* asumir.
▶ *vi* *(promise)* comprometerse (**to**, a).
ⓘ *pt* undertook [ˌʌndəˈtʊk], *pp* undertaken [ˌʌndəˈteɪkən].

undertaken [ˌʌndəˈteɪkən] *pp* → undertake.

undertaker [ˈʌndəteɪkəʳ] *n* empresario,-a de pompas fúnebres.
▶ *n pl* *(undertaker's)* funeraria, pompas *fpl* fúnebres.

undertook [ˌʌndəˈtʊk] *pt* → undertake.

undervalue [ˌʌndəˈvæljuː] *vt* subvalorar.

underwater [ˌʌndəˈwɔːtəʳ] *adj* submarino,-a, subacuático,-a.
▶ *adv* bajo el agua.

underwear [ˈʌndəwɛəʳ] *n* ropa interior.

underwent [ˌʌndəˈwent] *pt* → undergo.

underworld [ˈʌndəwɜːld] *n* *(of criminals)* hampa, bajos fondos *mpl*, inframundo.

undesirable [ˌʌndɪˈzaɪərəbəl] *adj* indeseable.
▶ *n* indeseable *mf*.

undetermined [ˌʌndɪˈtɜːmaɪnd] *adj* indeterminado,-a, indefinido,-a.

undid [ʌnˈdɪd] *pt* → undo.

undisputed [ˌʌndɪsˈpjuːtɪd] *adj* **1** *(unquestionable)* indiscutible, incuestionable. **2** *(unchallenged)* incontestable.

undo [ʌnˈduː] *vt* **1** *(knot)* deshacer, desatar. **2** *(button)* desabrochar. **3** *(arrange-*

ment) anular. **4** *(destroy)* deshacer, destruir. **5** *(to set right)* enmendar, reparar.
ⓘ *pt* undid [ʌnˈdɪd], *pp* undone [ʌnˈdʌn].

undone [ʌnˈdʌn] *pp* → undid.
▶ *adj* *(incomplete)* inacabado,-a.

undoubted [ʌnˈdaʊtɪd] *adj* indudable.

undress [ʌnˈdres] *vt* desnudar.
▶ *vi* desnudarse.

undrinkable [ʌnˈdrɪnkəbəl] *adj* imbebible.

uneasy [ʌnˈiːzɪ] *adj* **1** *(worried)* intranquilo,-a, inquieto,-a, preocupado,-a; *(disturbing)* inquietante. **2** *(annoying)* incómodo,-a.
ⓘ *comp* uneasier, *superl* uneasiest.

unemployed [ˌʌnɪmˈplɔɪd] *adj* parado,-a, sin trabajo, en paro.

unemployment [ˌʌnɪmˈplɔɪmənt] *n* **1** paro, desempleo. **2** *(percentage)* número de parados.

unequal [ʌnˈiːkwəl] *adj* **1** *(not the same)* desigual, distinto,-a; *(pulse)* irregular. **2** *(not adequate)* poco apto, inadecuado,-a.

unequivocal [ˌʌnɪˈkwɪvəkəl] *adj* inequívoco,-a, claro,-a.

uneven [ʌnˈiːvən] *adj* **1** *(not level)* desigual; *(bumpy)* accidentado,-a. **2** *(varying)* irregular, variable. **3** *(road)* lleno,-a de baches. **4** *(unfairly matched)* desigual. **5** MATH impar.

unexpected [ˌʌnɪkˈspektɪd] *adj* **1** inesperado,-a. **2** *(event)* imprevisto,-a.

unfair [ʌnˈfɛəʳ] *adj* injusto,-a.

unfaithful [ʌnˈfeɪθful] *adj* **1** *(husband, wife)* infiel. **2** *(friend)* desleal.

unfamiliar [ˌʌnfəˈmɪlɪəʳ] *adj* *(unknown)* desconocido,-a.

unfashionable [ʌnˈfæʃnəbəl] *adj* *(fashion, trends, etc)* pasado,-a de moda; *(ideas, measures)* poco popular.

unfasten [ʌnˈfɑːsən] *vt* **1** *(vest, button)* desabrochar. **2** *(untie)* desatar. **3** *(open)* abrir.

unfavorable [ʌnˈfeɪvərəbəl] *adj* US → unfavourable.

unfavourable [ʌnˈfeɪvərəbəl] *adj* **1** *(gen)* desfavorable; *(criticism)* adverso,-a. **2** *(winds)* contrario,-a.

U

unfinished [ʌnˈfɪnɪʃt] *adj* inacabado, -a, incompleto,-a, sin acabar.

unfit [ʌnˈfɪt] *adj* **1** *(person)* no apto,-a, incapaz. **2** *(physically)* incapacitado,-a, inútil. **3** *(injured)* lesionado,-a. **4** *(incompetent)* incompetente. ⊡ **to be unfit** no estar en forma.

unfold [ʌnˈfəʊld] *vt* **1** *(paper)* desplegar; *(sheet)* desdoblar. **2** *(newspaper)* abrir; *(map)* extender. **3** *(outline)* exponer; *(reveal)* revelar. **4** *(secret)* descubrir.
▶ *vi* **1** *(open up)* desdoblarse; *(landscape)* extenderse. **2** *(ideas, etc)* desarrollarse. **3** *(secret)* descubrirse, revelarse.

unforgettable [ʌnfəˈgetəbəl] *adj* inolvidable.

unfortunate [ʌnˈfɔːtʃənət] *adj* **1** *(person, event)* desgraciado,-a. **2** *(remark)* desafortunado,-a.

unfriendly [ʌnˈfrendlɪ] *adj* poco amistoso,-a, antipático,-a, hostil.
ⓘ *comp* **unfriendlier**, *superl* **unfriendliest**.

unfulfilled [ʌnfʊlˈfɪld] *adj* **1** *(not carried out)* incumplido,-a, frustrado,-a. **2** *(not satisfied)* insatisfecho,-a. **3** *(ambition)* frustrado,-a; *(dream)* irrealizado,-a.

ungrateful [ʌnˈgreɪtfʊl] *adj* **1** *(unthankful)* desagradecido,-a. **2** *(thankless)* ingrato,-a.

unhappy [ʌnˈhæpɪ] *adj* **1** *(sad)* infeliz. **2** *(miserable)* desdichado,-a. **3** *(unsuitable)* desafortunado,-a, poco afortunado,-a.
ⓘ *comp* **unhappier**, *superl* **unhappiest**.

unharmed [ʌnˈhɑːmd] *adj* ileso,-a.

unhealthy [ʌnˈhelθɪ] *adj* **1** *(place)* malsano,-a, insalubre. **2** *(ill)* enfermizo, -a, enfermo,-a. **3** *fig (unnatural)* morboso,-a, malsano,-a.
ⓘ *comp* **unhealthier**, *superl* **unhealthiest**.

unhelpful [ʌnˈhelpfʊl] *adj (advice)* inútil, vano,-a; *(person)* poco servicial.

unhurt [ʌnˈhɜːt] *adj* ileso,-a, indemne.

unicorn [ˈjuːnɪkɔːn] *n* unicornio.

uniform [ˈjuːnɪfɔːm] *adj* **1** uniforme. **2** *(temperature)* constante.
▶ *n* uniforme *m*.

unify [ˈjuːnɪfaɪ] *vt* unificar.
ⓘ *pt & pp* **unified**, *ger* **unifying**.

unimportant [ʌnɪmˈpɔːtənt] *adj* insignificante, sin importancia, poco importante.

uninhabited [ʌnɪnˈhæbɪtɪd] *adj* **1** deshabitado,-a. **2** *(deserted)* despoblado,-a.

uninteresting [ʌnˈɪntrəstɪŋ] *adj* sin interés.

union [ˈjuːnɪən] *n* **1** unión *f*. **2** *fig (marriage)* enlace *m*. **3** *(of workers)* sindicato. **4** TECH unión *f*.
▶ *adj* sindical, del sindicato. COMP **Union Jack** *la bandera del Reino Unido*.

⊕ La **Union Jack** es la bandera del Reino Unido y está formada por la combinación de las enseñas de Inglaterra, Escocia e Irlanda.

unionize [juːnjəˈnaɪz] *vt* sindicalizar.
▶ *vi* agremiarse, sindicalizarse.

unirrigated [ʌnɪrɪgeɪtəd] *adj* de secano.

unique [juːˈniːk] *adj* **1** *(singular)* único, -a. **2** *(outstanding)* extraordinario,-a.

unit [ˈjuːnɪt] *n* **1** unidad *f*. **2** *(furniture)* módulo, elemento. **3** MIL unidad *f*. **4** MATH unidad *f*. **5** TECH grupo. **6** *(centre)* centro; *(department)* servicio. **7** *(team)* equipo.

unite [juːˈnaɪt] *vt (join)* unir; *(assemble)* reunir.
▶ *vi* unirse, reunirse.

unity [ˈjuːnɪtɪ] *n* *(union)* unidad *f*; *(harmony)* armonía.

universal [juːnɪˈvɜːsəl] *adj* universal.

universe [ˈjuːnɪvɜːs] *n* universo.

university [juːnɪˈvɜːsətɪ] *n* universidad *f*.
ⓘ *pl* **universities**.
▶ *adj* universitario,-a.

unkempt [ʌnˈkempt] *adj* **1** *(general)* descuidado,-a. **2** *(hair)* despeinado,-a. **3** *(appearance)* desaliñado,-a.

unkind [ʌnˈkaɪnd] *adj* **1** *(unpleasant)* desconsiderado,-a. **2** *(cruel)* cruel; *(criticism)* despiadado,-a.

unknown [ʌnˈnəʊn] *adj* desconocido,-a.
▶ *n* lo desconocido.

unleash [ʌnˈliːʃ] *vt* **1** *(dog)* soltar. **2** *fig (free - gen)* liberar; *(- passions)* desatar. **3** *(fury)* provocar.

unless [ənˈles] *conj* a menos que, a no ser que.

▸ *prep* salvo, excepto.

unlike [ʌnˈlaɪk] *adj (different)* diferente a, distinto de; *(not characteristic)* impropio,-a.

▸ *prep* a diferencia de

unlikely [ʌnˈlaɪklɪ] *adj (improbable)* improbable, poco probable; *(unexpected, unusual)* inverosímil.

ⓘ *comp* unlikelier, *superl* unlikeliest.

unlimited [ʌnˈlɪmɪtɪd] *adj* ilimitado,-a.

unload [ʌnˈləʊd] *vt* **1** *(gen)* descargar. **2** *(get rid of)* deshacerse de.

▸ *vi* descargar.

unlock [ʌnˈlɒk] *vt* **1** *(door)* abrir (con llave). **2** *fig (secret)* revelar; *(enigma)* resolver.

unlucky [ʌnˈlʌkɪ] *adj* **1** *(unfortunate)* desafortunado,-a, desgraciado,-a. **2** *(fateful)* aciago,-a, nefasto,-a.

ⓘ *comp* unluckier, *superl* unluckiest.

unmarried [ʌnˈmærɪd] *adj* soltero,-a.

unmistakable [ʌnmɪsˈteɪkəbəl] *adj* inconfundible, inequívoco,-a.

unnecessary [ʌnˈnesəsərɪ] *adj* innecesario,-a.

unnoticed [ʌnˈnəʊtɪst] *adj* inadvertido,-a, desapercibido,-a.

unoccupied [ʌnˈɒkjʊpaɪd] *adj* **1** *(house)* deshabitado,-a. **2** *(person)* desocupado,-a. **3** *(post)* vacante. **4** *(area)* despoblado,-a. **5** *(seat)* libre. **6** MIL no ocupado,-a.

unofficial [ʌnəˈfɪʃəl] *adj* extraoficial, oficioso,-a.

unpack [ʌnˈpæk] *vt* **1** *(objects)* desempaquetar, desenvolver. **2** *(suitcase)* deshacer. **3** *(boxes)* desembalar.

▸ *vi* deshacer las maletas.

unpardonable [ʌnˈpɑːdənəbəl] *adj* imperdonable.

unpleasant [ʌnˈplezənt] *adj* **1** *(disagreeable, nasty)* desagradable, molesto,-a. **2** *(unfriendly)* antipático,-a. **3** *(words)* grosero,-a, mal educado,-a.

unplug [ʌnˈplʌg] *vt* desenchufar.

ⓘ *pt & pp* unplugged, *ger* unplugging.

unpopular [ʌnˈpɒpjələr] *adj* impopular.

unpredictable [ʌnprɪˈdɪktəbəl] *adj* **1** imprevisible. **2** *(of person)* de reacciones imprevisibles. **3** *(whimsical)* antojadizo,-a.

unproductive [ʌnprəˈdʌktɪv] *adj* **1** *(inefficient)* improductivo,-a. **2** *fig (fruitless)* infructuoso,-a.

unprovable [ʌnˈpruːvəbəl] *adj* indemostrable.

unpublished [ʌnˈpʌblɪʃt] *adj* inédito,-a, no publicado,-a.

unreachable [ʌnˈriːtʃəbəl] *adj* inalcanzable.

unreadable [ʌnˈriːdəbəl] *adj* **1** *(handwriting)* ilegible. **2** *(book)* imposible de leer; *(understand)* incomprensible.

unreal [ʌnˈrɪəl] *adj* irreal.

unrealistic [ʌnrɪəˈlɪstɪk] *adj* poco realista.

unreasonable [ʌnˈriːzənəbəl] *adj* **1** irrazonable. **2** *(irrational)* irracional. **3** *(excessive)* desmesurado,-a; *(prices)* exorbitante. **4** *(hour)* inoportuno,-a.

unrecognizable [ʌnrekəgˈnaɪzəbəl] *adj* irreconocible.

unreliable [ʌnrɪˈlaɪəbəl] *adj* **1** *(person)* de poca confianza, poco formal, que no es de fiar. **2** *(information)* que no es de fiar, poco seguro,-a. **3** *(machine)* poco fiable, poco seguro,-a. **4** *(news)* poco fidedigno,-a.

unrest [ʌnˈrest] *n* **1** *(uneasiness)* malestar *m*. **2** *(restlessness)* inquietud *f*; *(political disturbance)* agitación *f*, disturbios *mpl*.

unroll [ʌnˈrəʊl] *vt* desenrollar.

▸ *vi* desenrollarse.

unsaddle [ʌnˈsædəl] *vt* **1** *(horse)* desensillar. **2** *(horseman)* desmontar.

unsafe [ʌnˈseɪf] *adj* **1** *(risky)* inseguro,-a, arriesgado,-a. **2** *(dangerous)* peligroso,-a.

unsatisfactory [ʌnsætɪsˈfæktərɪ] *adj* insatisfactorio,-a, poco satisfactorio,-a.

unsavory [ʌnˈseɪvərɪ] *adj* US → **unsavoury**.

unsavoury [ʌnˈseɪvərɪ] *adj* **1** *(taste, etc)* desagradable; *(tasteless)* insípido,-a. **2** *(morally not right)* deshonroso,-a, infame, sospechoso,-a; *(person)* indeseable.

U

unscrew [ʌnˈskruː] vt destornillar, desatornillar.

unseen [ʌnˈsiːn] adj (invisible) no visto, -a, invisible; (unnoticed) inadvertido,-a.

unselfish [ʌnˈselfɪʃ] adj desinteresado,-a.

unsettled [ʌnˈsetˀld] adj 1 (weather) inestable. 2 (person) nervioso,-a, intranquilo; (situation) inestable. 3 (country, etc) agitado,-a. 4 (question, matter) pendiente; (account, etc) sin saldar. 5 (land) sin colonizar, sin poblar.

unshaven [ʌnˈʃeɪvˀn] adj sin afeitar.

unsheathe [ʌnˈʃiːð] vt desenvainar.

unshrinkable [ʌnˈʃrɪŋkəbˀl] adj inencogible, que no encoge.

unskilled [ʌnˈskɪld] adj 1 (worker) no cualificado,-a. 2 (job) no especializado,-a. 3 (untalented) inexperto,-a.

unsolved [ʌnˈsɒlvd] adj sin resolver.

unstable [ʌnˈsteɪbˀl] adj inestable.

unsteady [ʌnˈstedɪ] adj 1 (not firm) inseguro,-a, inestable; (furniture) cojo,-a, inestable. 2 (voice, hand) tembloroso, -a, poco firme. 3 (weather conditions) variable; (pulse) irregular.
ⓘ comp unsteadier, superl unsteadiest.

unstressed [ʌnˈstrest] adj LING átono,-a.

unsuccessful [ʌnsəkˈsesfʊl] adj 1 fracasado,-a, sin éxito. 2 (useless) inútil, infructuoso,-a; (examination) suspendido,-a. 3 (candidate in elections) derrotado,-a, vencido,-a.

unsuited [ʌnˈsuːtɪd] adj 1 (person) no apto,-a; (thing) impropio,-a, inadecuado,-a. 2 (people) incompatible.

unsure [ʌnˈʃʊəʳ] adj inseguro,-a, poco seguro,-a.

unsympathetic [ʌnsɪmpəˈθetɪk] adj (unfeeling) poco compasivo, sin compasión f, indiferente; (lacking understanding) poco comprensivo,-a.

untamable [ʌnˈteɪməbˀl] adj indomable.

untangle [ʌnˈtæŋgˀl] vt desenredar.

untidy [ʌnˈtaɪdɪ] adj 1 (room, person) desordenado,-a. 2 (scruffy) desaliñado,-a, desaseado,-a; (hair) despeinado,-a.
ⓘ comp untidier, superl untidiest.

untie [ʌnˈtaɪ] vt 1 (unfasten) desatar. 2 (liberate) soltar, desligar.

until [ʌnˈtɪl] prep hasta.
▶ conj hasta que.

untrue [ʌnˈtruː] adj 1 falso,-a. 2 (unfaithful) infiel, desleal. 3 (inexact) inexacto,-a, erróneo,-a.

unusable [ʌnˈjuːzəbˀl] adj inservible.

unused adj 1 [ʌnˈjuːzd] (new) nuevo,-a, sin estrenar; (not in use) que no se utiliza. 2 [ʌnˈjuːst] (unaccustomed) desacostumbrado,-a.

unusual [ʌnˈjuːʒʊəl] adj 1 (rare, strange) insólito,-a, poco común. 2 (different) original; (exceptional) extraordinario,-a.

unveil [ʌnˈveɪl] vt 1 (uncover) descubrir. 2 fig (reveal) descubrir, desvelar; (secret) revelar.

unwanted [ʌnˈwɒntɪd] adj 1 (child) no deseado,-a. 2 (advice, etc) no solicitado,-a, no pedido,-a. 3 (superfluous) superfluo,-a.

unwelcome [ʌnˈwelkəm] adj 1 (guest) inoportuno,-a, molesto,-a; (news) desagradable. 2 (uncomfortable) incómodo,-a.

unwell [ʌnˈwel] adj (sick, ill) indispuesto,-a, malo,-a.

unwilling [ʌnˈwɪlɪŋ] adj reacio,-a, poco dispuesto,-a.

unwind [ʌnˈwaɪnd] vt desenrollar.
▶ vi 1 desenrollarse. 2 fam (relax) relajarse.
ⓘ pt & pp unwound [ʌnˈwaʊnd].

unwise [ʌnˈwaɪz] adj 1 (foolish) imprudente; (senseless) insensato,-a. 2 (ill-advised) desaconsejable, poco aconsejable.

unwound [ʌnˈwaʊnd] pt & pp → unwind.

unwrap [ʌnˈræp] vt (present) desenvolver; (parcel, package) abrir, deshacer.
ⓘ pt & pp unwrapped, ger unwrapping.

unzip [ʌnˈzɪp] vt 1 bajar la cremallera de. 2 COMPUT descomprimir.
ⓘ pt & pp unzipped, ger unzipping.

up [ʌp] adv 1 (upwards) hacia arriba, arriba. 2 (out of bed) levantado,-a. 3 (sun, moon): the sun is up ha salido el sol. 4 (roadworks) levantado,-a, en obras. 5 (towards)

hacia. **6** *(northwards)* ir hacia el norte. **7** *(totally finished)* acabado,-a. **8** *(into pieces)* a trozos, a porciones, a raciones.
▶ *prep* **1** *(movement)*: *to go up the stairs* subir la escalera. **2** *(position)* en lo alto de.
▶ *vt* subir, aumentar.
ⓘ *pt & pp* upped, *ger* upping.

up-and-coming [ˌʌpənˈkʌmɪŋ] *adj* prometedor,-ra, que promete mucho.

up-and-down [ˌʌpˈnˈdaʊn] *adj* **1** *(motion)* vertical; *(varying)* variable. **2** *(eventful)* accidentado,-a; *(period)* con altibajos.

upbringing [ˈʌpbrɪŋɪŋ] *n* educación *f*.

upcoming [ˈʌpkʌmɪŋ] *adj* próximo,-a.

update [*(n)* ˈʌpdeɪt; *(vb)* ʌpˈdeɪt] *n* actualización *f*, puesta al día.
▶ *vt* actualizar, modernizar.

upfront [ʌpˈfrʌnt] *adj* sincero,-a, franco,-a.

upgrade [*(vb)* ʌpˈgreɪd; *(n)* ˈʌpgreɪd] *vt* **1** *(promote)* ascender, subir de categoría. **2** *(improve)* mejorar.
▶ *n* mejora.

uphekd [ʌpˈhæeld] *pt & pp* → uphold.

uphill [*(adj)* ˈʌphɪl; *(adv)* ʌpˈhɪl] *adj* **1** ascendente. **2** *fig (task, struggle)* arduo,-a, difícil, duro,-a, penoso,-a.
▶ *adv* cuesta arriba.

uphold [ʌpˈhəʊld] *vt* **1** *(opinion)* sostener, mantener; *(to support)* apoyar. **2** *(defend)* defender. **3** *(confirm)* confirmar.
ⓘ *pt & pp* upheld [ʌpˈhæeld].

upholster [ʌpˈhəʊlstəʳ] *vt* tapizar.

upkeep [ˈʌpkiːp] *n (maintenance)* conservación *f*; *(costs)* gastos *mpl* de mantenimiento.

uplift [ʌpˈlɪft] *vt (lift up)* elevar, levantar; *(soul, voice)* inspirar, elevar, alzar.
▶ *n fig* edificación *f*, inspiración *f*.

upload [ʌpˈləʊd] *vt (Internet)* publicar en la red, subir a la red.

up-market [ˈʌpmɑːkɪt] *adj* de calidad *f* superior, de categoría.

upon [əˈpɒn] *prep fml* en, sobre. Consulta también on.

upper [ˈʌpəʳ] *adj* **1** *(position)* superior. **2** *(in geography)* alto,-a; superior.
▶ *n (of shoe)* pala.

uppermost [ˈʌpəməʊst] *adj* **1** más alto,-a. **2** *fig* principal, dominante.

upright [ˈʌpraɪt] *adj* **1** derecho,-a, vertical. **2** *(honest)* recto,-a, honrado,-a.
▶ *adv* derecho, en posición *f* vertical.
▶ *n SP* poste *m*, palo.

uprising [ʌpˈraɪzɪŋ] *n* alzamiento, levantamiento, sublevación *f*.

uproar [ˈʌprɔːʳ] *n* alboroto, tumulto.

uproot [ʌpˈruːt] *vt* **1** *(plant, etc)* desarraigar, arrancar; *(people)* desarraigar. **2** *(eliminate)* eliminar, extirpar.

upset [*(adj-vb)* ʌpˈset; *(n)* ˈʌpset] *adj* **1** *(angry)* disgustado,-a, contrariado,-a. **2** *(mentally or physically)* trastornado,-a; *(worried)* preocupado,-a. **3** *(nerves)* desquiciado,-a; *(a little unwell)* indispuesto,-a. **4** *(stomach)* trastornado,-a. **5** *(overturned)* volcado,-a; *(spoiled)* desbaratado,-a.
▶ *n* **1** *(reversal)* revés *m*, contratiempo; *(slight ailment)* malestar *m*. **2** *(emotion, stomach, etc)* trastorno; *(plans, etc)* trastorno. **3** *(trouble, difficulty)* molestia *f*. **4** *(sport)* un resultado inesperado.
▶ *vt* **1** *(overturn)* volcar; *(capsize)* hacer zozobrar. **2** *(spill)* derramar. **3** *(shock)* trastornar. **4** *(person)* contrariar; *(worry)* preocupar; *(displease)* disgustar. **5** *(stomach)* sentar mal. **6** *(plans)* desbaratar. **7** *(to cause disorder)* desordenar, revolver.
ⓘ *pt & pp* upset [ʌpˈset], *ger* upsetting.

upsetting [ʌpˈsetɪŋ] *adj* desconcertante, inquietante, preocupante.

upside down [ˌʌpsaɪdˈdaʊn] *adv* **1** al revés. **2** *fig (disorder)* patas arriba.

upstairs [*(adv)* ʌpˈsteəz; *(n)* ˈʌpsteəz] *adv* *(direction)* al piso de arriba; *(position)* en el piso de arriba.
▶ *adj* de arriba.
▶ *n* piso de arriba, piso superior.

upstream [ʌpˈstriːm] *adv* **1** aguas arriba. **2** *(against the current)* a contracorriente.

upsurge [ˈʌpsɜːdʒ] *n* **1** *(increase)* aumento; *(anger)* acceso. **2** *fig (strong increase in feelings, etc)* resurgimiento; *(of violence)* ola.

up-to-date [ˌʌptəˈdeɪt] *adj* **1** al día. **2** *(modern)* moderno,-a, a la moda; *(informed)* al tanto, al corriente, al día.

U

upward ['ʌpwəd] *adj* hacia arriba.
▸ *adv* hacia arriba.
▸ *adj* COMM *(tendency)* al alza *m*.

upwards ['ʌpwədz] *adv* **1** hacia arriba.
2 *fam* algo más de.

uranium [ju'reɪnɪəm] *n* CHEM uranio.

Uranus [ju'reɪnəs] *n* Urano.

urban ['ɜːbən] *adj* urbano,-a.

urbane [ɜː'beɪn] *adj* cortés, urbano,-a.

ureter [juə'riːtər] *n* uréter *m*.

urethra [ju'riːθrə] *n* uretra.

urge [ɜːdʒ] *n* impulso, deseo.
▸ *vt* **1** encarecer, preconizar, instar, insistir. **2** *(incite)* incitar; *(plead)* exhortar. **3** *(encourage)* animar.

urgency ['ɜːdʒənsɪ] *n* urgencia.

urgent ['ɜːdʒənt] *adj* urgente.

urinary ['juərɪnərɪ] *adj* urinario,-a.
COMP **urinary tract** tracto urinario.

urinate ['juərɪneɪt] *vi* orinar.

urine ['juərɪn] *n* orina.

urn [ɜːn] *n* urna.

urology [ju'rɒlədʒɪ] *n* MED urología.

Ursa ['ɜːrsə] *(constellation) n* la Osa.

Uruguay ['juərəgwaɪ] *n* Uruguay.

Uruguayan [juərə'gwaɪən] *adj* uruguayo,-a.
▸ *n* uruguayo,-a.

us [ʌs, ʌz] *pron* **1** nos; *(with preposition)* nosotros,-as. **2** *fam* me.

usable ['juːzəbəl] *adj* utilizable, aprovechable.

usage ['juːsɪdʒ] *n* **1** uso, manejo. **2** *(custom)* uso, costumbre *f*, usanza. **3** LING uso. **4** *(way of speaking)* habla *m*, lenguaje *m*.

use [*(n)* juːs; *(vb)* juːz] *n* **1** uso, empleo, utilización *f*. **2** *(handling)* manejo. **3** *(usefulness)* utilidad *f*. **4** *(right to use, power to use)* uso.
▸ *vt* **1** utilizar. **2** *(consume)* gastar, consumir. **3** *(exploit unfairly)* aprovecharse de. **4** *fam (need)* necesitar.

▸ *aux* **to use to** *(past habits)* soler, acostumbrar: *we used to go fishing in the lake* solíamos ir a pescar al lago.

✎ Como auxiliar, si la frase no indica una costumbre, se debe traducir con el imperfecto.

◆ **to use up** *vt sep* gastar, acabar.

useable ['juːzəbəl] *adj* → usable.

used ['juːst] *adj* **1** [juːzd] *(second-hand)* usado,-a. **2** [juːst] *(accustomed)* acostumbrado,-a. COMP **to be used to** estar acostumbrado,-a a. ‖ **to get used to** acostumbrarse a.

✎ Consulta también use.

useful ['juːsful] *adj* útil.

useless ['juːsləs] *adj* **1** inútil. **2** *fam (person)* inepto,-a, incompetente.

user ['juːzər] *n* usuario,-a.

usual ['juːʒuəl] *adj* habitual, corriente.
▸ *n* **1** lo habitual. **2** *fam (drink, etc)* lo de siempre.

utensil [juː'tensəl] *n* utensilio.

uterus ['juːtərəs] *n* útero.
ⓘ *pl* **uteruses o uteri** ['juːtəraɪ].

utility [juː'tɪlɪtɪ] *n* **1** utilidad *f*. **2** *(company)* empresa de servicio público.
ⓘ *pl* **utilities**.

utmost ['ʌtməust] *adj* sumo,-a, extremo,-a.
▸ *n* máximo.

utter ['ʌtər] *vt* **1** *(words)* pronunciar, articular; *(feelings)* expresar. **2** *(lies curses, etc)* soltar; *(shouts, cries, etc)* lanzar, dar. **3** *(theatre)* proferir; *(sounds)* emitir.

utterly ['ʌtəlɪ] *adv* totalmente.

uvula ['juːvjʊlə] *n* úvula, campanilla.
ⓘ *pl* **uvulas o uvulae** ['juːvjʊliː].

Uzbek ['ʊzbek] *adj* uzbeco,-a.
▸ *n* **1** *(person)* uzbeco,-a. **2** *(language)* uzbeco.

Uzbekistan [ʊzbekɪ'stæn] *n* Uzbekistán.

V

V, v [viː] *n (the letter)* V, v *f.*

vacancy [ˈveɪkənsɪ] *n* **1** *(job)* vacante *f.* **2** *(room)* habitación *f* libre. LOC **"No vacancies"** «Completo».
ⓘ *pl* vacancies.

vacant [ˈveɪkənt] *adj* **1** *(gen)* vacío. **2** *(job)* vacante. **3** *(room)* libre. **4** *(mind, expression)* vacío,-a.

vacation [vəˈkeɪʃən] *n* vacaciones *fpl.*

vaccinate [ˈvæksɪneɪt] *vt* vacunar.

vaccination [væksɪˈneɪʃən] *n* vacunación *f.*

vaccine [ˈvæksiːn] *n* vacuna.

vacuum [ˈvækjʊəm] *n* **1** vacío. **2** *fam (vacuum cleaner)* aspiradora. COMP **vacuum cleaner** aspirador *m.* ∎ **vacuum flask** termo.
▶ *vt* limpiar con aspiradora, pasar la aspiradora por.

vacuum-packed [ˈvækjʊəmpækt] *adj* envasado,-a al vacío.

vagina [vəˈdʒaɪnə] *n* vagina.
ⓘ *pl* vaginas o vaginae [vəˈdʒaɪniː].

vaginae [vəˈdʒaɪniː] *n pl* → **vagina**.

vague [veɪg] *adj* **1** *(imprecise)* vago,-a, impreciso. **2** *(indistinct)* borroso,-a.

❌ Vague no significa 'vago (holgazán)', que se traduce por lazy.

vain [veɪn] *adj* **1** *(conceited)* vanidoso,-a. **2** *(hopeless)* vano,-a, inútil. LOC **in vain** en vano.

valence [ˈveɪləns] *n* US valencia.

valency [ˈveɪlənsɪ] *n* GB valencia.
ⓘ *pl* valencies.

valid [ˈvælɪd] *adj* **1** válido,-a. **2** *(ticket)* valedero,-a.

validate [ˈvælɪdeɪt] *vt fml* validar.

valley [ˈvælɪ] *n* valle *m.*

valor [ˈvælər] *n* US → **valor**.

valour [ˈvælər] *n* valor *m*, valentía *f.*

❌ Valour no significa 'valor (valía)', que se traduce por value.

valuation [væljʊˈeɪʃən] *n* **1** *(act)* valoración *f.* **2** *(price)* valor *m.*

value [ˈvæljuː] *n* valor *m.*
▶ *vt* **1** *(estimate value of)* valorar, tasar. **2** *(appreciate)* valorar, apreciar.

valve [vælv] *n* **1** *(in general)* válvula. **2** RAD lámpara. **3** ZOOL valva. **4** MUS llave *f.*

vampire [ˈvæmpaɪər] *n* urgencia.

van [væn] *n* **1** camioneta, furgoneta. **2** GB *(on train)* furgón *m.*

vanadium [vəˈneɪdɪəm] *n* vanadio.

Vandal [ˈvændəl] *adj* vándalo,-a.
▶ *n* vándalo,-a.

vandalism [ˈvændəlɪzəm] *n* vandalismo.

vandalize [ˈvændəlaɪz] *n* urgencia.

vane [veɪn] *n* **1** *(weather, etc)* veleta. **2** *(of fan, etc)* aspa.

vanilla [vəˈnɪlə] *n* vainilla.

vanish [ˈvænɪʃ] *vi* desaparecer.

vanity [ˈvænɪtɪ] *n* vanidad.

vapor [ˈveɪpər] *n* US → **vapour**.

vapour [ˈveɪpər] *n* **1** vapor *m.* **2** *(on windowpane)* vaho.

variable [ˈveərɪəbəl] *adj* variable.
▶ *n* variable *f.*

variant [ˈveərɪənt] *n* variante *f.*

varicose [ˈværɪkəʊs] *adj* varicoso,-a.
COMP **varicose veins** varices *fpl.*

varied [ˈveərɪd] *adj* variado,-a, diverso,-a.

variety [vəˈraɪətɪ] *n* **1** *(diversity)* variedad *f.* **2** *(assortment)* surtido.
ⓘ *pl* varieties.

various ['veərɪəs] *adj* **1** *(different)* diverso,-a, distinto,-a. **2** *(several)* varios,-as.

varnish ['vɑːnɪʃ] *n* **1** *(for wood, metals)* barniz *m*. **2** *(for nails)* esmalte *m*.
► *vt* **1** *(wood, metals)* barnizar. **2** *(nails)* pintar.

vary ['veərɪ] *vi* variar.
► *vt* variar de.
ⓘ *pt & pp* varied, *ger* varying.

vascular ['væskjələ'] *adj* vascular.

vas deferens ['væs 'defərenz] *n* ANAT conducto deferente.

vase [vɑːz, US veɪz] *n* jarrón *m*, florero.

vassal ['væsəl] *n* vasallo,-a.

vast [vɑːst] *adj* *(extensive)* vasto,-a, inmenso,-a; *(huge)* inmenso,-a, enorme.

Vatican ['vætɪkən] *adj* vaticano,-a.
COMP **Vatican City** Ciudad *f* del Vaticano.
► *n* the Vatican el Vaticano.

vault¹ [vɔːlt] *n* **1** *(ceiling)* bóveda. **2** *(in bank)* cámara acorazada. **3** *(for dead)* panteón *m*; *(in church)* cripta. **4** *(cellar)* sótano; *(for wine)* bodega.

vault² [vɔːlt] *vt* saltar.
► *vi* saltar.
► *n* *(gymnastics)* salto.

veal [viːl] *n* ternera.

vector ['vektə'] *n* vector *m*.

vegetable ['vedʒtəbəl] *n* **1** *(as food)* verdura, hortaliza. **2** *(as plant)* vegetal *m*. **3** *fam* *(person)* vegetal *m*.

vegetarian [vedʒɪ'teərɪən] *adj* vegetariano,-a.
► *n* vegetariano,-a.

vegetation [vedʒɪ'teɪʃən] *n* vegetación *f*.

vehicle ['viːəkəl] *n* **1** TECH vehículo. **2** *fig* medio, vehículo.

veil [veɪl] *n* velo.
► *vt* velar.

vein [veɪn] *n* **1** ANAT vena. **2** BOT vena, nervio. **3** *(of mineral)* veta, vena, filón *m*. **4** *(mood)* humor *m*, vena.

velum ['viːləm] *n* velo (del paladar).
ⓘ *pl* vela ['viːlə].

velvet ['velvɪt] *n* terciopelo.

vena cava ['viːnə 'keɪvə] *n* ANAT vena cava.

vending machine ['vendɪŋməʃiːn] *n* máquina expendedora.

vendor ['vendə'] *n* vendedor,-ra.

Venezuela [venə'zweɪlə] *n* Venezuela.

Venezuelan [venə'zweɪlən] *adj* venezolano,-a.
► *n* venezolano,-a.

vengeance ['vendʒəns] *n* venganza.

venous ['viːnəs] *adj* venoso,-a.

ventilate ['ventɪleɪt] *vt* ventilar.

ventricle ['ventrɪkəl] *n* ventrículo.

venture ['ventʃə'] *vt* arriesgar, aventurar.
► *vi* arriesgarse.
► *n* aventura, empresa arriesgada.
COMP **business venture** empresa comercial. ▌ **joint venture** empresa conjunta. ▌ **venture capital** capital *m* riesgo.

venue ['venjuː] *n* **1** *(place)* local *m*. **2** *(scene)* escenario.

Venus ['viːnəs] *n* Venus *f*. COMP **Venus flytrap** dionea.

veranda [və'rændə] *n* porche *m*.

verb [vɜːb] *n* verbo.

verbal ['vɜːbəl] *adj* verbal. COMP **verbal noun** gerundio.

verdict ['vɜːdɪkt] *n* **1** veredicto, fallo. **2** *(opinion)* opinión *f*, juicio.

verge [vɜːdʒ] *n* **1** borde *m*, margen *m*. **2** *(of road)* arcén *m*.
◆ **to verge on** *vt insep* **1** *(condition)* rayar en. **2** *(age)* rondar.

verify ['verɪfaɪ] *vt* verificar, comprobar.
ⓘ *pt & pp* verified, *ger* verifying.

vermicelli [vɜːmɪ'selɪ] *n* fideos *mpl*.

vermin ['vɜːmɪn] *n pl* **1** *(small animals)* alimañas *fpl*. **2** *(insects)* bichos *mpl*, sabandijas *fpl*. **3** *(people)* gentuza *f sing*, chusma *f sing*.

verruca [və'ruːkə] *n* verruga.
ⓘ *pl* verrucas o verrucae [və'ruːkiː].

verse [vɜːs] *n* **1** *(poetry)* versos *mpl*, poesía. **2** *(set of lines)* estrofa. **3** *(song, set of lines)* estrofa. **4** *(in Bible)* versículo.

❌ Verse no significa 'verso (parte del poema)', que se traduce por line.

version ['vɜːʒ³n] *n* **1** versión *f.* **2** MUS interpretación *f.* **3** AUTO modelo. COMP **stage version** THEAT adaptación *f* teatral.

versus ['vɜːsəs] *prep* **1** *(against)* contra. **2** *(as opposed to)* frente a.

vertebra ['vɜːtɪbrə] *n* vértebra.
ⓘ *pl* vertebrae ['vɜːtɪbriː].

vertebral ['vɜːtɪbrəl] *adj* vertebral.

vertebrate ['vɜːtɪbrət, 'vɜːtɪbreɪt] *adj* vertebrado,-a.
▶ *n* vertebrado.

vertex ['vɜːteks] *n* vértice *m.*
ⓘ *pl* vertexes o vertices ['vɜːtɪsiːz].

vertical ['vɜːtɪkəl] *adj* vertical.

very ['verɪ] *adv* **1** *(extremely)* muy. **2** *(emphatic)* muy.
▶ *adj* **1** *(extreme)* de todo. **2** *(precise)* mismo,-a, exacto,-a. LOC **the very best** el/la mejor, lo mejor.

vesicle ['vesɪk³l] *n* vesícula.

vessel ['ves³l] *n* **1** *(ship)* nave *f,* buque *m.* **2** *(container)* recipiente *m,* vasija. **3** ANAT vaso. COMP **cargo vessel** buque *m* de carga.

vest [vest] *n* **1** GB camiseta. **2** US chaleco.

vestibule ['vestɪbjuːl] *n* **1** *(entrance hall)* vestíbulo, entrada. **2** ANAT vestíbulo.

vet [vet] *n fam* veterinario,-a.

veteran ['vet³rən] *adj* veterano,-a.
▶ *n* **1** veterano,-a. **2** *(soldier, etc)* excombatiente *mf.*

veterinary ['vet³rɪn³rɪ] *adj* veterinario,-a. COMP **veterinary surgeon** veterinario,-a.

veto ['viːtəʊ] *n* veto.
ⓘ *pl* vetoes.
▶ *vt* vetar; *(forbid)* prohibir, vedar.
ⓘ *pt & pp* vetoed, *ger* vetoing.

vexed [vekst] *adj* disgustado,-a. COMP **vexed question** tema *m* controvertido.

via ['vaɪə] *prep* **1** *(through)* vía, por. **2** *(by means of)* por medio de, a través de.

vibrate [vaɪ'breɪt, US 'vaɪbreɪt] *vi* vibrar (with, con).
▶ *vt* hacer vibrar.

vibration [vaɪ'breɪʃ³n] *n* vibración *f.*

vicar ['vɪkə'] *n* párroco.

vice¹ [vaɪs] *n* vicio.

vice² [vaɪs] *n (tool)* torno de banco, tornillo de banco.

vice³ [vaɪs] *pref* vice-. COMP **vice admiral** MIL vicealmirante *m.* ▮ **vice chancellor** EDUC rector,-ra. ▮ **vice president** vicepresidente,-ta.

vicereine [vaɪs'reɪn] *n* virreina.

viceroy ['vaɪsrɔɪ] *n* virrey *m.*

vicinity [və'sɪnətɪ] *n* **1** inmediaciones *fpl.* **2** *fml* proximidad *f.*

vicious ['vɪʃəs] *adj* **1** *(cruel)* cruel; *(malicious)* malintencionado,-a. **2** *(violent)* virulento,-a, violento,-a. **3** *(dangerous)* peligroso,-a.

✗ Vicious no significa 'vicioso', que se traduce por depraved.

victim ['vɪktɪm] *n* víctima.

victory ['vɪkt³rɪ] *n* victoria, triunfo.
ⓘ *pl* victories.

victuals ['vɪt³lz] *n pl* vituallas *fpl,* víveres *mpl.*

vicuna [vɪ'kjuːnə] *n* vicuña.

video ['vɪdɪəʊ] *n* **1** *(in general)* vídeo. **2** *(pop video)* videoclip *m.* COMP **video game** videojuego.
ⓘ *pl* videos.

videoconference [vɪdɪəʊk'kɒnfərəns] *n* videoconferencia.

videodisc ['vɪdɪəʊdɪsk] *n* videodisco.

videorecorder [vɪdɪəʊrɪ'kɔːdə'] *n* vídeo.

videotape ['vɪdɪəʊteɪp] *n* cinta de vídeo
▶ *vt* grabar en vídeo.

videotext ['vɪdɪəʊtekst] *n* videotexto.

Vietnam [vjet'næm] *n* Vietnam.

Vietnamese [vjetnə'miːz] *adj* vietnamita.
▶ *n* **1** *(person)* vietnamita *mf.* **2** *(language)* vietnamita *m.*
▶ *n pl* the Vietnamese los vietnamitas *mpl.*

view [vjuː] *n* **1** vista, panorama *m.* **2** *(opinion)* opinión *f,* parecer *m.*
▶ *vt* **1** *(consider)* considerar, ver. **2** *(regard, think about)* enfocar. **3** *(examine)* ver; *(visit)* visitar. **4** *(watch)* ver; *(critically)* visionar.

V

viewer ['vjuːər] n **1** TV telespectador,-ra, televidente mf. **2** (photography) visionadora.

viewpoint ['vjuːpɔɪnt] n punto de vista.

vignette [vɪn'jet] n **1** (artwork) viñeta. **2** (description) estampa.

vigor ['vɪɡər] n US → vigour.

vigour ['vɪɡər] n vigor m, energía.

Viking ['vaɪkɪŋ] adj vikingo,-a.
▶ n vikingo,-a.

villa ['vɪlə] n **1** (for holidays) chalet m; (in country) casa de campo. **2** (Roman) villa. **3** GB (large house) villa, quinta.

village ['vɪlɪdʒ] n (gen) pueblo; (small) pueblecito. COMP **village idiot** el tonto del pueblo. I **village life** la vida de pueblo.

villager ['vɪlɪdʒər] n habitante m del pueblo, aldeano,-a.

villain ['vɪlən] n **1** (bad character) malo,-a, malo,-a de la película. **2** GB fam malvado,-a. LOC **the villain of the piece** fam el malo de la película.

vine [vaɪn] n **1** vid f. **2** (made to climb) parra. COMP **vine grower** viticultor,-ra. I **vine growing** viticultura. I **vine leaf** hoja de parra. I **vine shoot** sarmiento.

vinegar ['vɪnɪɡər] n vinagre m. COMP **vinegar bottle** vinagrera. I **wine vinegar** vinagre m de vino.

vineyard ['vɪnjəd] n viña, viñedo.

vintage ['vɪntɪdʒ] n cosecha.
▶ adj **1** (wine) de añada. **2** (classic) clásico,-a; (high-quality) glorioso,-a, maravilloso,-a. **3** fam lo mejor de. COMP **vintage car** coche m de época construido entre 1919 y 1930.

viola[1] [vaɪˈəʊlə] n MUS viola.

viola[2] [vaɪˈəʊlə] n BOT violeta.

violate ['vaɪəleɪt] vt violar; (law) infringir, transgredir.

violation [vaɪəˈleɪʃən] n violación f; (of law) infracción f, transgresión f.

violence ['vaɪələns] n violencia.

violet ['vaɪələt] n **1** BOT violeta f. **2** (colour) violeta m, violado,-a, violáceo,-a.
▶ adj (de color) violeta, violado,-a.

violin [vaɪəˈlɪn] n violín.

violinist [vaɪəˈlɪnɪst] n violinista mf.

viper ['vaɪpər] n víbora.

viral ['vaɪrəl] adj viral, vírico,-a.

virgin ['vɜːdʒɪnɪst] adj virgen.
▶ n virgen f.

Virgo ['vɜːɡəʊ] n Virgo.

virtual ['vɜːtʃʊəl] adj virtual. COMP **virtual reality** realidad f virtual.

virtue ['vɜːtʃuː] n **1** virtud f. **2** (advantage) ventaja. LOC **by virtue of** en virtud de. I **in virtue of** en virtud de.

virus ['vaɪrəs] n virus m. COMP **virus infection** infección f vírica.
① pl viruses.

visa ['viːzə] n visado, am visa. COMP **entry visa** visado de entrada. I **exit visa** visado de salida.

viscosity [vɪsˈkɒsɪti] n viscosidad f.

visibility [vɪzɪˈbɪlɪti] n visibilidad f.

visible ['vɪzɪbəl] adj visible.

Visigoth ['vɪzɪɡɒθ] n visigodo,-a.

Visigothic ['vɪzɪɡɒθɪk] adj visigodo,-a.

vision ['vɪʒən] n **1** (gen) visión f. **2** (eyesight) vista. LOC **a man of vision** un hombre con visión de futuro.

visit ['vɪzɪt] vt **1** (person) visitar, hacer una visita a. **2** (place) visitar, ir a.
▶ vi estar de visita.
▶ n visita. LOC **to pay sb a visit** hacer una visita a algn. I **to visit with sb** US charlar con algn.

visiting ['vɪzɪtɪŋ] adj **1** (for visiting) de visita. **2** (guest) visitante. COMP **visiting card** tarjeta de visita. I **visiting hours** horas fpl de visita. I **visiting lecturer** profesor,-ra invitado,-a. I **visiting team** equipo visitante.

visitor ['vɪzɪtər] n **1** (at home) invitado,-a, visita. **2** (tourist) turista mf, visitante mf. COMP **visitors' book** libro de visitas.

visor ['vaɪzər] n visera.

visual ['vɪʒʊəl] adj visual. COMP **visual aid** medio visual. I **visual arts** artes mpl visuales. I **visual display unit** pantalla.

vital ['vaɪtəl] adj **1** vital. **2** (essential) esencial, imprescindible. COMP **vital organ** órgano vital. I **vital signs** señales fpl de vida.

► *n pl* órganos *mpl* vitales. LOC **of vital importance** de suma importancia.

vitamin ['vɪtəmɪn, 'vaɪtəmɪn] *n* vitamina. COMP **vitamin C** vitamina C. ‖ **vitamin content** contenido vitamínico. ‖ **vitamin deficiency** avitaminosis *f*.

vitro ['vi:trəʊ] LOC **in vitro** in vitro.

viva ['vaɪvə] *n* GB *fam (abbr of* viva voce*)* examen *m* oral.

vivid ['vɪvɪd] *adj* **1** vivo,-a, intenso,-a. **2** *(description)* gráfico,-a. LOC **to have a vivid imagination** tener mucha imaginación.

viviparous [vɪ'vɪpərəs] *adj* vivíparo,-a.

vixen ['vɪksⁿn] *n* zorra.

V-neck ['vi:nek] *n* cuello de pico.

vocabulary [və'kæbjʊlərɪ] *n* vocabulario.
ⓘ *pl* vocabularies.

vocal ['vəʊkⁿl] *adj* **1** vocal. **2** *fam (noisy)* escandaloso,-a. COMP **vocal cords** cuerdas *fpl* vocales.

vocational [vəʊ'keɪʃⁿəl] *adj* profesional. COMP **vocational guidance** orientación *f* profesional.

vocative ['vɒkətɪv] *n* vocativo.
► *adj* vocativo,-a.

vogue [vəʊg] *n* boga, moda. LOC **to be all the vogue** estar muy en boga. COMP **to be in vogue** estar en boga.

voice [vɔɪs] *n* voz *f*. LOC **at the top of one's voice** a voz en grito. ‖ **in a loud voice** en voz alta. ‖ **in a low/soft voice** en voz baja, a media voz. ‖ **to lose one's voice** quedarse afónico,-a, quedarse sin voz. ‖ **to lower/raise one's voice** bajar/levantar la voz. ‖ **with one voice** de una voz, a una, a coro. COMP **voice box** laringe *f*. ‖ **voice offstage** THEAT voz *f* en off.
► *vt* **1** expresar. **2** LING sonorizar.

voiceless ['vɔɪsləs] *adj* **1** *(hoarse)* afónico,-a. **2** LING sordo,-a.

voice-over [vɔɪs'əʊvəʳ] *n* voz *f* en off.

void [vɔɪd] *adj* **1** vacío,-a (of, de): *void of interest* falto,-a de interés. **2** JUR nulo, -a, inválido,-a.
► *n* vacío.
► *vt* **1** *(empty)* vaciar. **2** JUR anular.

volcano [vɒl'keɪnəʊ] *n* volcán *m*.
ⓘ *pl* volcanos o volcanoes.

volley ['vɒlɪ] *n* **1** MIL descarga. **2** *fig (of stones)* aluvión *m*; *(of blows)* tanda; *(of applause)* salva. **3** *(tennis)* volea.
► *vi* **1** MIL lanzar una descarga. **2** *(tennis)* hacer una volea.
► *vt (sp)* volear.

volleyball ['vɒlɪbɔ:l] *n* voleibol *m*.

volt [vəʊlt] *n* voltio.

voltage ['vəʊltɪdʒ] *n* voltaje *m*, tensión *f*.

voltmeter ['vəʊltmi:təʳ] *n* voltímetro.

voluble ['vɒljəbⁿl] *adj* locuaz, hablador,-ra.

❌ Voluble no significa 'voluble', que se traduce por changeable.

volume ['vɒljʊm] *n* **1** volumen *m*. **2** *(book)* tomo. LOC **to speak volumes** decirlo todo. ‖ **to turn down/up the volume** bajar/subir el volumen.

voluntary ['vɒlⁿtⁿrɪ] *adj* voluntario,-a. COMP **voluntary organization** organización *f* benéfica. ‖ **voluntary society** sociedad *f* benéfica. ‖ **voluntary work** obras *fpl* benéficas. ‖ **voluntary helper/worker** voluntario,-a.

volunteer [vɒlən'tɪəʳ] *n* voluntario,-a.
► *vt* ofrecer.
► *vi* **1** ofrecerse (for, para). **2** MIL alistarse como voluntario,-a (for, en).

vomit ['vɒmɪt] *n* vómito.
► *vi* vomitar, devolver.
► *vt* vomitar, devolver.

vote [vəʊt] *n* **1** voto. **2** *(voting)* voto, votación *f*. **3** *(right to vote)* sufragio.
► *vi* votar. COMP **vote of censure** voto de censura. ‖ **vote of confidence** voto de confianza.
► *vt* **1** votar. **2** *(elect)* elegir. **3** *fam* considerarse: *the party was voted a complete flop* la fiesta se consideró un desastre total. LOC **to be voted into/out of office** ganar/perder las elecciones. ‖ **to vote by a show of hands** votar a mano alzada. ‖ **to vote on sth / take a vote on sth** someter algo a votación.
◆ **to vote down** *vt sep* rechazar.
◆ **to vote through** *vt sep* aprobar.

voter ['vəʊtəʳ] *n* votante *mf*.

voucher ['vaʊtʃəʳ] *n* GB vale *m*, bono. JUR comprobante *m*, justificante *m*.

V

vow [vaʊ] *n* **1** promesa solemne. **2** REL voto. LOC **to take a vow of chastity/ poverty** hacer voto de castidad/pobreza. ▌ **to take one's vows** pronunciar sus votos. COMP **vow of silence** voto de silencio.

vowel ['vaʊəl] *n* vocal *f*.

voyage ['vɔɪɪdʒ] *n* viaje *m*; *(by sea)* viaje *m* en barco; *(crossing)* travesía.
▶ *vi fml* viajar.

✎ Voyage se refiere a un viaje generalmente largo por mar o en el espacio. La palabra más usual para 'viaje' es journey.

vulgar ['vʌlgəʳ] *adj* **1** *(in poor taste)* de mal gusto. **2** *(coarse)* grosero,-a, ordinario,-a. **3** LING vulgar. COMP **vulgar fraction** fracción *f* común.

☒ Vulgar no significa 'vulgar (corriente', que se traduce por common.

vulgarity [vʌl'gærɪtɪ] *n* **1** *(poor taste)* mal gusto. **2** *(coarseness)* vulgaridad *f*, ordinariez *f*, grosería.

vulnerable ['vʌlnərəbəl] *adj* vulnerable.

vulture ['vʌltʃəʳ] *n* buitre *m*.

vulva ['vʌlvə] *n* vulva.
ⓘ *pl* vulvas o vulvae ['vʌlviː].

W

W, w ['dʌbəlju:] *n (the letter)* W, w *f.*

W [west] *abbr* (west) oeste *m; (abbreviation)* O.

wade [weɪd] *vi* caminar por el agua.
▶ *vt* vadear.

wafer ['weɪfəʳ] *n (for ice cream)* barquillo; *(biscuit)* galleta de barquillo.

wage [weɪdʒ] *n* sueldo, salario *m.*
▶ *n pl* **wages** sueldo *m sing,* salario *m sing.*

waggon ['wægən] *n* GB → wagon.

wagon ['wægən] *n* **1** *(cart)* carro; *(covered)* carromato. **2** GB *(railway truck)* vagón *m.* **3** US *(trolley)* carrito, mesa camarera.

wagon-lit [vægɒn'li:] *n* coche-cama *m.*
ⓘ *pl* wagons-lits.

wail [weɪl] *n (of pain, grief)* lamento, gemido; *(of siren)* aullido.
▶ *vi* **1** *(person - cry)* gemir, llorar; *(- complain)* quejarse (about/over, de), lamentarse (about/over, de). **2** *(siren)* aullar, ulular; *(wind)* ulular.

waist [weɪst] *n* **1** ANAT cintura. **2** *(of garment)* talle *m.* **3** *(of guitar, etc)* parte estrecha.

waistcoat ['weɪskəut] *n* chaleco.

waistline ['weɪstlaɪn] *n* **1** ANAT cintura. **2** SEW talle *m.*

wait [weɪt] *n (gen)* espera; *(delay)* demora.
▶ *vi* esperar (for, -), aguardar (for, -).
LOC **to wait at table** servir la mesa.
▶ *vt* esperar, aguardar.
◆ **to wait about / wait around** *vi* esperar, perder el tiempo.
◆ **to wait on** *vt insep* servir.

waiter ['weɪtəʳ] *n* camarero. COMP **head waiter** maitre *m.*

waiting ['weɪtɪŋ] *n* espera. COMP **waiting room** sala de espera.

waitress ['weɪtrəs] *n* camarera.
ⓘ *pl* waitresses.

wake [weɪk] *vt* despertar (up, -).
▶ *vi* despertarse (up, -).
◆ **to wake up to** *vt insep (become aware)* darse cuenta de.
ⓘ *pt* woke [wəuk], *pp* woken ['wəukən].

Wales [weɪlz] *n* País *m* de Gales.

walk [wɔːk] *n* **1** *(gen)* paseo; *(distance)* camino; *(long)* caminata, excursión *f; (sport)* marcha. **2** *(path, route)* paseo, ruta; *(long)* excursión *f.* **3** *(gait)* modo de andar *mpl.*
▶ *vi* andar, caminar, pasear.
▶ *vt* **1** *(cover on foot)* ir a pie, ir andando, andar. **2** *(person)* acompañar; *(animal)* pasear.
◆ **to walk away** *vi* alejarse.
◆ **to walk into** *vt insep* **1** *(get caught)* caer en. **2** *(bump into)* tropezar con.
◆ **to walk out** *vi* **1** *(leave suddenly)* marcharse. **2** *(go on strike)* ir a la huelga.
◆ **to walk out on** *vt insep (abandon)* abandonar a.

walker ['wɔːkəʳ] *n* **1** *(gen)* paseante *mf; (hiker)* excursionista *mf.* **2** *(athlete)* marchador,-ra. **3** *(for babies)* andador *m; (for disabled)* andador *m.*

walkie-talkie [wɔːkɪ'tɔːkɪ] *n* walkie-talkie *m.*

walkman® [wɔːkmən] *n* walkman® *m.*
ⓘ *pl* walkmen [wɔːkmən].

wall [wɔːl] *n* **1** *(exterior)* muro; *(defensive, city)* muralla; *(garden)* tapia; *(sea)* dique *m.* **2** *(interior)* pared *f; (partition)* tabique *m.* **3** ANAT *(of artery, blood vessel)* pared *f; (of abdomen)* pared *f* abdominal. **4** SP barrera.

wallet [ˈwɒlɪt] *n* cartera.

wallpaper [ˈwɔːlpeɪpəʳ] *n* **1** papel *m* pintado. **2** *(for computer screen)* papel *m* tapiz.
▸ *vt* empapelar.

wally [ˈwɒlɪ] *n fam* idiota *mf*, inútil *mf*.
ⓘ *pl* wallies.

walnut [ˈwɔːlnʌt] *n (fruit)* nuez *f*; *(wood)* nogal *m*. COMP **walnut tree** nogal *m*.

walrus [ˈwɔːlrəs] *n* morsa.
ⓘ *pll* walruses.

waltz [wɔːls] *n* vals *m*.
ⓘ *pl* waltzes.

wand [wɒnd] *n* varita.

wander [ˈwɒndəʳ] *vi* **1** *(roam)* deambular, errar, vagar; *(stroll)* pasear, caminar. **2** *(stray)* apartarse, desviarse, alejarse; *(get lost)* extraviarse.
▸ *n* vuelta, paseo.

want [wɒnt] *n* **1** *(lack)* falta, carencia. **2** *(desire, need)* necesidad *f*.
▸ *vt* **1** *(gen)* querer. **2** *fam (need)* necesitar. **3** *fam (ought to)* deber. **4** *fml (lack)* necesitar, carecer de,.

wanted [ˈwɒntɪd] *adj* **1** *(for work)* necesario,-a. **2** *(by police)* buscado,-a.

war [wɔːʳ] *n* guerra.

ward [wɔːd] *n* **1** *(in hospital)* sala. **2** GB *(for elections)* distrito electoral.

warden [ˈwɔːdᵊn] *n* **1** *(of hostel, home)* encargado,-a. **2** US *(of prison)* alcaide *m*, director,-ra. **3** *(of university)* rector,-ra.

wardrobe [ˈwɔːdrəʊb] *n* **1** armario (ropero), guardarropa *m*. **2** *(clothes)* vestuario. **3** *(theatre)* vestuario.

warehouse [ˈweəhaʊs] *n* almacén *m*, depósito.
▸ *vt* almacenar, depositar.

warfare [ˈwɔːfeəʳ] *n* **1** *(war)* guerra. **2** *(conflict, struggle)* lucha, batalla.

warhead [ˈwɔːhed] *n* ojiva, cabeza.

warm [wɔːm] *adj* **1** *(climate, wind)* cálido,-a; *(day)* caluroso,-a, de calor. **2** *(hands, etc)* caliente; *(liquid)* tibio,-a, templado,-a. **3** *(clothing)* de abrigo, que abriga. **4** *(colour)* cálido,-a. **5** *(welcome, applause, etc)* cálido,-a, caluroso,-a. **6** *(character)* afectuoso,-a.
▸ *vt (gen)* calentar.

▸ *vi* calentarse.
◆ **to warm up** *vt sep* **1** *(food)* calentar, recalentar; *(engine)* calentar. **2** *(audience, party)* animar.
▸ *vi* **1** *(food, engine, etc)* calentarse. **2** *(audience, party)* animarse. **3** SP hacer ejercicios de calentamiento.

warm-blooded [ˈwɔːmˈblʌdɪd] [se escribe warm blooded cuando no se usa para calificar a un nombre] *adj* de sangre caliente.

warmly [ˈwɔːmlɪ] *adv* **1** *(with heat)* con ardor. **2** *(thank)* con efusión; *(recommend)* con entusiasmo; *(welcome, greet)* calurosamente. **3** *(dress)* con ropa de abrigo.

warmth [wɔːmθ] *n* **1** *(heat)* calor *m*. **2** *fig* afecto, cordialidad *f*.

warm-up [ˈwɔːmʌp] *n* SP calentamiento, precalentamiento.

warn [wɔːn] *vt* **1** avisar (of, de), advertir (of, de), prevenir (about, sobre), (against, contra). **2** *(instead of punishing)* amonestar.

warning [ˈwɔːnɪŋ] *n* **1** *(of danger)* aviso, advertencia. **2** *(instead of punishment)* amonestación *f*. **3** *(advance notice)* aviso.
▸ *adj (shot, glance)* de aviso, de advertencia.

warrant [ˈwɒrənt] *n* **1** JUR orden *f* judicial, mandamiento judicial. **2** *(voucher)* bono, vale *m*. **3** *fml (justification)* justificación *f*. COMP **warrant officer** suboficial *m*.
▸ *vt* **1** *fml (justify)* justificar; *(deserve)* merecer, ser digno,-a de. **2** *(guarantee)* garantizar.

warranty [ˈwɒrəntɪ] *n* **1** COMM *(guarantee)* garantía. **2** *fml (authority)* autorización *f*.
ⓘ *pl* warranties.

warrior [ˈwɒrɪəʳ] *n* guerrero,-a.

warship [ˈwɔːʃɪp] *n* buque *m* de guerra.

wart [wɔːt] *n* verruga.

warthog [ˈwɔːthɒg] *n* jabalí *m* verrugoso.

wartime [ˈwɔːtaɪm] *n* tiempos *mpl* de guerra.
▸ *adj* de guerra.

was [wɒz, *unstressed* wəz] *pt* → **be.**

wash [wɒʃ] *n* **1** *(act)* lavado. **2** *(laundry)* ropa sucia, colada. **3** *(of ship)* estela; *(of water)* remolinos *mpl*; *(sound)* chapoteo.
▸ *vt* **1** *(gen)* lavar; *(dishes)* fregar. **2** *(carry)* llevar, arrastrar.
▸ *vi* **1** *(gen)* lavarse. **2** *(flow, lap)* batir.
◆ **to wash away** *vt sep* **1** *(destroy and carry away)* llevarse, arrastrar. **2** *(remove)* borrar.
◆ **to wash up** *vt sep* **1** fregar. **2** arrastrar a la playa.
▸ *vi* **1** fregar los platos. **2** US lavarse las manos y la cara, lavarse rápidamente.

washable ['wɒʃəbəl] *adj* lavable.

washbasin ['wɒʃbeɪsən] *n* *(fixed to wall)* lavabo; *(bowl)* palangana.

washbowl ['wɒʃbəʊl] *n* US palangana.

washer ['wɒʃəʳ] *n* **1** TECH *(metal)* arandela; *(rubber)* junta. **2** *fam* *(machine)* lavadora.

washing ['wɒʃɪŋ] *n* **1** *(action)* lavado, el lavar *m*. **2** *(dirty clothes)* colada, ropa sucia; *(clean clothes)* colada; *(clothes hanging out)* ropa tendida. LOC **to do the washing** hacer la colada. LOC **washing machine** lavadora. ▮ **washing powder** detergente *m*.

washing-up [wɒʃɪŋˈʌp] *n* **1** *(action)* fregado, el fregar *m*. **2** *(dishes)* platos *mpl*. LOC **to do the washing-up** fregar los platos. COMP **washing-up liquid** lavavajillas *m*.

wasp [wɒsp] *n* avispa. COMP **wasp's nest** avispero.

waste [weɪst] *n* **1** *(gen)* derroche *m*; *(of money, energy)* despilfarro; *(of time)* pérdida,. **2** *(matter)* desechos *mpl*, desperdicios *mpl*; *(rubbish)* basura.
▸ *adj* **1** *(unwanted)* desechado,-a. **2** *(land)* yermo,-a, baldío,-a.
▸ *vt* *(gen)* desperdiciar, malgastar; *(resources)* derrochar; *(time, chance)* desaprovechar, perder.

wastepaper basket [weɪstˈpeɪpə-bɑː-kɪt] *n* papelera.

watch [wɒtʃ] *n* **1** *(timepiece)* reloj *m*. **2** *(look-out)* vigilancia, guardia; *(person)* vigilante *mf*, guardia *mf*, centinela *mf*, guarda *mf*. **3** MAR *(period, body)* guardia; *(individual)* vigía *mf*. **4** HIST ronda.
① *pl* **watches**.
▸ *vt* **1** *(look at, observe)* mirar, observar; *(television, sport)* ver. **2** *(keep an eye on)* vigilar, observar; *(spy on)* espiar, vigilar. **3** *(be careful about)* tener cuidado con, cuidar de.
▸ *vi* *(look)* mirar, observar. LOC **watch out!** ¡cuidado!
◆ **to watch out for** *vt insep* **1** *(look out for, be alert)* estar alerta, estar pendiente de. **2** *(be careful of)* tener cuidado con.

watchdog ['wɒtʃdɒg] *n* **1** perro guardián. **2** *fig* guardián,-ana.

watcher ['wɒtʃəʳ] *n* observador,-ra, espectador,-ra.

water ['wɔːtəʳ] *n* **1** *(gen)* agua: *drinking water* agua potable; *mineral water* agua mineral; *running water* agua corriente; *spring water* agua de manantial. **2** *(tide)* marea. COMP **water bottle** *(flask)* cantimplora. ▮ **water polo** waterpolo. ▮ **water power** energía hidráulica. ▮ **water supply** abastecimiento de agua, suministro de agua. ▮ **water tank** depósito de agua. ▮ **water vapour** vapor *m* de agua. ▮ **water wheel** **1** *(for power)* rueda hidráulica. **2** *(for irrigation)* noria.
▸ *vt* **1** *(plant, river)* regar. **2** *(animals)* abrevar.
◆ **to water down** *vt sep* **1** *(drink)* aguar, mezclar con agua. **2** *fig* descafeinar.

watercolor ['wɔːtəkʌləʳ] *n* → **watercolour.**

watercolour ['wɔːtəkʌləʳ] *n* acuarela.
▸ *n pl* **watercolours** acuarelas *fpl*.

watercress ['wɔːtkres] *n* berro.

waterfall ['wɔːtəfɔːl] *n* cascada, salto de agua, catarata.

watering ['wɔːtərɪŋ] *n* riego.

watermark ['wɔːtəmɑːk] *n* filigrana.

watermelon ['wɔːtəmelən] *n* sandía.

watermill ['wɔːtəmɪl] *n* molino de agua.

waterpark ['wɔːtəpɑːk] *n* parque *m* acuático.

waterpipe ['wɔːtəpaɪp] *n* cañería.

W

waterproof ['wɔ:təpru:f] *adj* **1** *(material)* impermeable. **2** *(watch)* sumergible.
▸ *n (coat)* impermeable *m*.
▸ *vt* impermeabilizar.

water-ski ['wɔ:təski:] *n* esquí *m* acuático.
▸ *vi* hacer esquí acuático.

water-skiing ['wɔ:təski:ɪŋ] *n* esquí *m* acuático.

watersports ['wɔ:təspɔ:ts] *n pl* deportes *mpl* acuáticos.

watertight ['wɔ:tətaɪt] *adj* **1** estanco,-a, hermético,-a. **2** *fig* irrefutable, irrebatible.

water-wheel ['wɔ:təwi:l] *n* **1** *(for power)* rueda hidráulica. **2** *(for irrigation)* noria.

waterworks ['wɔ:təwɜ:ks] *n* depuradora, planta de tratamiento de aguas.
▸ *n pl* GB *fam euph* aparato urinario.

watt [wɒt] *n* ELEC watt *m*, vatio.

wave [weɪv] *n* **1** *(in sea)* ola. **2** *(in hair)* onda. **3** PHYS onda. **4** *(of hand)* ademán *m*, movimiento; *(in greeting)* saludo con la mano. **5** *(steady increase)* ola, oleada. **6** *(influx)* oleada; *(sudden increase)* oleada, ola.
▸ *vi* **1** *(greet)* saludar (con la mano). **2** *(flag)* ondear; *(corn)* ondular. **3** *(hair)* ondular.
▸ *vt* **1** *(brandish)* agitar. **2** *(direct)* indicar con la mano. **3** *(hair)* marcar, ondular.

wavelength ['weɪvleŋθ] *n* RAD longitud *f* de onda.

wavy ['weɪvɪ] *adj* ondulado,-a.
ⓘ *comp* wavier, *superl* waviest.

wax [wæks] *n* **1** *(gen)* cera. **2** *(in ear)* cerumen *m*.
▸ *vt* *(polish)* encerar. COMP **paraffin wax** parafina. **I sealing wax** lacre *m*. **I wax candle** vela. **I wax crayons** ceras *fpl*. **I wax paper** papel *m* encerado.

way [weɪ] *n* **1** *(right route, road, etc)* camino. **2** *(direction)* dirección *f*. **3** *(distance)* distancia. **4** *(manner, method)* manera, modo.
▸ *adv fam* muy. LOC **all the way 1** *(distance)* todo el viaje. **2** *(completely)* totalmente. **I by the way** *(incidentally)* a propósito, por cierto. **I in a way** en cierto modo, en cierta manera. **I in some ways** en algunos aspectos. **I in this way** *(thus)* de este modo, de esta manera. **I one way or the other** *(somehow)* de algún modo, de una manera u otra, como sea. **I out of the way 1** *(remote)* apartado,-a, remoto,-a. **2** *(exceptional)* excepcional, particular, original. **I that way 1** *(direction)* por allá. **2** *(like that)* así. **I the right way round** bien puesto. **I the wrong way round** al revés. **I to be in the way** estorbar, estar por en medio. **I to be on the way** *(coming)* estar en camino, estar al llegar, avecinarse. **I to get out of the way** apartarse. **I to find your way** encontrar el camino. **I to give way 1** *(collapse)* ceder, hundirse. **2** *(yield)* ceder (to, a). **3** *(when driving)* ceder el paso. **I to loose your way** perderse. LOC **way in** entrada. **I way out 1** *(exit)* salida. **2** *(solution)* solución *f*, remedio.
▸ *n pl* **ways** *(customs)* costumbres *fpl*; *(habits, behaviour)* manías *fpl*.

WC ['wɔ:təski:ɪŋ] *abbr* water closet váter *m*, retrete *m*.

we [wi:, *unstressed* wɪ] *pron* nosotros, -as.

weak [wi:k] *adj* **1** *(gen)* débil. **2** *(tea, coffee, etc)* aguado,-a, poco cargado,-a.
▸ *n pl* **the weak** los necesitados *mpl*, los inválidos *mpl*.

weaken ['wi:kən] *vt* **1** *(gen)* debilitar. **2** *(argument)* quitar fuerza a; *(morale)* socavar.
▸ *vi* **1** *(person)* debilitarse, desfallecer. **2** *(resolve, influence)* flaquear. **3** *(currency)* aflojar, caer. **4** *(give in)* ceder.

weakness ['wi:knəs] *n* **1** *(gen)* debilidad *f*, flaqueza. **2** *(lack of conviction)* falta de peso, pobreza. **3** *(defect, fault, flaw)* flaqueza, punto flaco.
ⓘ *pl* weaknesses.

wealth [welθ] *n* **1** *(riches)* riqueza. **2** *fig* abundancia, profusión *f*.

wealthy ['welθɪ] *adj* rico,-a, adinerado,-a, acaudalado,-a.
ⓘ *comp* wealthier, *superl* wealthiest.

weapon ['wepən] *n* arma.

wear [weə^r] *n* **1** *(clothing)* ropa: *evening wear* traje de noche; *ladies' wear* ropa para señoras; *men's wear* ropa para hombres. **2** *(use)* uso: *for everyday wear* para todos los días. **3** *(deterioration)* desgaste *m*, deterioro. **4** *(capacity for being used)* durabilidad *f*. COMP **wear and tear** desgaste *m*.

▸ *vt* **1** *(clothing, jewellery, etc)* llevar, vestir; *(shoes)* calzar. **2** *(accept, tolerate)* tolerar, aceptar, soportar. **3** *(damage by use)* desgastar.

▸ *vi* **1** *(become damaged by use)* desgastarse. **2** *(endure)* durar.

◆ **to wear out** *vt sep* **1** *(shoes, etc)* gastar, desgastar, romper con el uso. **2** *(person)* agotar, rendir.

▸ *vi (shoes, etc)* gastarse, desgastarse, romperse con el uso.

ⓘ *pt* **wore** [wɔ:^r], *pp* **worn** [wɔ:n].

wearable ['weərəb^əl] *adj* que se puede llevar, que se puede poner.

weary ['wɪərɪ] *adj* **1** *(exhausted)* cansado, -a, agotado,-a. **2** *(fed up)* cansado,-a, harto,-a.

ⓘ *comp* **wearier**, *superl* **weariest**.

▸ *vt* cansar.

▸ *vi* cansarse de.

weasel ['wi:z^əl] *n* comadreja.

weather ['weðə^r] *n (gen)* tiempo. COMP **weather forecast** parte *m* meteorológico.

weather-vane ['weðəveɪn] *n (clothing)* veleta.

weave [wi:v] *n* tejido.

▸ *vt* **1** *(gen)* tejer. **2** *fig (plot, story)* tramar, urdir.

ⓘ *pt* **wove** [wəʊv], *pp* **woven** ['wəʊv^ən], *ger* **weaving**.

weaver ['wi:və^r] *n* tejedor,-ra.

web [web] *n* **1** *(spider's)* telaraña. **2** *fig* red *f*, sarta, embrollo. **3** *(of animals' feet)* membrana interdigital. **4** *(Internet)* web *f*.

webmaster ['webmɑ:stə^r] *n* administrador,-ra de web.

website ['websaɪt] *n* web *f*, sitio web.

wed [wed] *vt* casarse con.

ⓘ *pt & pp* **wedded** o **wed**, *ger* **wedding**.

we'd [wi:d] *contr* (we had, we would) → **have**, **would**.

wedding ['wedɪŋ] *n* boda, casamiento. COMP **wedding anniversary** aniversario de bodas. ▮ **wedding ring** anillo de bodas.

wedge [wedʒ] *n* **1** *(gen)* cuña, calza. **2** *(of cake, cheese)* trozo grande. **3** *(golf)* wedge *m*.

▸ *vt* **1** *(force apart)* acuñar, calzar. **2** *(pack tightly)* apretar.

Wednesday ['wenzdɪ] *n* miércoles *m inv*.

✎ Para ejemplos de uso, consulta **Saturday**.

weed [wi:d] *n* **1** BOT *(in garden)* mala hierba; *(in water)* algas *fpl*. **2** *fam pej (person)* debilucho,-a, canijo,-a.

weedkiller ['wi:dkɪlə^r] *n* herbicida *m*.

week [wi:k] *n* semana.

weekend ['wi:kend, wi:'kend] *n* fin *m* de semana. COMP **long weekend** puente *m*.

▸ *vi* pasar el fin de semana.

weekly ['wi:klɪ] *adj* semanal.

▸ *adv* semanalmente, cada semana: *twice weekly* dos veces por semana.

▸ *n (press)* semanario.

weep [wi:p] *vi* **1** *fml (person)* llorar. **2** *(wound)* supurar.

ⓘ *pt & pp* **wept** [wept].

weigh [weɪ] *vt* **1** *(gen)* pesar. **2** *fig (consider carefully)* ponderar, sopesar (up, -); *(compare carefully)* contraponer (with/against, a).

▸ *vi* **1** *(gen)* pesar. **2** *(be important to, have influence on)* influir en, pesar.

weight [weɪt] *n* **1** *(gen)* peso. **2** *(of scales, clock, gym)* pesa; *(heavy object)* peso, cosa pesada. **3** *fig (burden, worry)* peso, carga. **4** *fig (importance, influence)* peso, importancia, influencia. LOC **to lose weight** perder peso, adelgazar. ▮ **to put on weight** engordar, ganar peso. COMP **weights and measures** pesos *mpl* y medidas.

▸ *vt* **1** *(make heavy)* cargar con peso, poner peso en, añadir peso a; *(fishing net)* lastrar. **2** *fig (statistics, etc)* ponderar.

W

weightlifter ['weɪtlɪftəʳ] *n* SP levantador,-ra de pesas, halterófilo,-a.

weird [wɪəd] *adj* **1** *(bizarre)* raro,-a, extraño,-a. **2** *(eerie)* siniestro,-a.

welcome ['welkəm] *adj* **1** *(gen)* bienvenido,-a. **2** *(news, sight, etc)* grato,-a, agradable; *(change)* oportuno,-a, beneficioso,-a. |LOC| **you're welcome** *(not at all)* no hay de qué, de nada.
▶ *interj* bienvenido,-a (**to**, a).
▶ *n* bienvenida, acogida.
▶ *vt* **1** *(greet)* acoger, recibir; *(officially)* dar la bienvenida a. **2** *(approve of, support)* aplaudir, acoger con agrado.

welcoming ['welkəmɪŋ] *adj* *(smile)* acogedor,-ra; *(speech)* de bienvenida.

weld [weld] *n* soldadura.
▶ *vt* **1** soldar. **2** *fig* soldar, unir.
▶ *vi* soldarse.

welfare ['welfeəʳ] *n* **1** *(well-being)* bienestar *m*; *(health)* salud *f*. **2** *(care, help)* protección *f*. **3** US *(money)* seguridad *f* social. |COMP| **welfare state** estado de bienestar. ‖ **welfare worker** asistente *mf* social.

well¹ [wel] *n* **1** *(for water)* pozo. **2** *(of staircase)* hueco de la escalera; *(of lift)* hueco del ascensor. **3** GB *(in court)* área de los abogados.
▶ *vi* *(tears, blood)* brotar (**up**, -), manar (**up**, -).

well² [wel] *adj* **1** *(in good health)* bien. **2** *(satisfactory, right)* bien.
▶ *adv* **1** *(gen)* bien. **2** *(with modals)* bien. **3** *(much, quite)* bien. |LOC| **as well** *(also, too)* también. ‖ **as well as** además de. ‖ **very well** muy bien, bueno. ‖ **well done!** ¡muy bien!, ¡así se hace! ‖ **well I never!** ¡vaya!, ¡habráse visto! ‖ **well off** *(comfortable, rich)* acomodado,-a.
▶ *interj* **1** *(gen)* bueno, bien, pues. **2** *(surprise)* ¡vaya!

well-balanced ['wel'bælənst] [se escribe well balanced cuando no se usa para calificar a un nombre] *adj* equilibrado,-a.

well-behaved ['welbɪ'heɪvd] [se escribe well behaved cuando no se usa para calificar a un nombre] *adj* formal, educado,-a.

well-being [wel'biːɪŋ] *n* bienestar *m*.

well-done ['wel'dʌn] [se escribe well done cuando no se usa para calificar a un nombre] *adj* muy hecho,-a.

well-founded ['wel'faʊndɪd] [se escribe well founded cuando no se usa para calificar a un nombre.] *adj* bien fundado,-a.

wellington ['welɪŋtən] [a veces Wellington] *n* botas de agua.

well-known [wel'nəʊn] *adj* (bien) conocido,-a.

well-off ['wel'ɒf] [se escribe well off cuando no se usa para calificar a un nombre] *adj* rico,-a, acomodado,-a, pudiente.

Welsh [welʃ] *adj* galés,-esa.
▶ *n* *(language)* galés *m*.
▶ *n pl* **the Welsh** los galeses *mpl*.

Welshman ['welʃmən] *n* galés *m*.
ⓘ *pl* **Welshmen** ['welʃmən].

Welshwoman ['welʃwʊmən] *n* galesa.
ⓘ *pl* **Welshwomen** ['welʃwɪmɪn].

went [went] *pt* → **go.**

wept [wept] *pt & pp* → **weep.**

were [wɜːʳ] *pt* → **be.**

we're [wɪəʳ] *contr* (we are) → **be.**

werewolf ['wɪəwʊlf] *n* hombre *m* lobo.
ⓘ *pl* **werewolves** ['wɪəwʊlvz].

west [west] *n* oeste *m*, occidente *m*.
▶ *adj* occidental, del oeste. |COMP| **West Indies** las Antillas. ‖ **West Indian** antillano,-a.
▶ *adv* al oeste, hacia el oeste.
▶ *n* **the West** POL Occidente *m*, los países *mpl* occidentales.

western ['westən] *adj* del oeste, occidental.
▶ *n* *(cinema)* western *m*.

westerner ['westənəʳ] *n* occidental *mf*.

westward ['westwəd] *adj* hacia el oeste.

westwards ['westwədz] *adv* hacia el oeste.

wet [wet] *adj* **1** *(gen)* mojado,-a; *(damp)* húmedo,-a. **2** *(weather)* lluvioso,-a. **3** *(paint, ink)* fresco,-a. **4** *fam* *(person)* apocado,-a, soso,-a.
ⓘ *comp* **wetter**, *superl* **wettest.**
▶ *n* **1** *(damp)* humedad *f*. **2** *(rain)* lluvia **3** *fam* *(person)* apocado,-a; *(politician)* moderado,-a.

▸ *vt* mojar, humedecer.

ⓘ *pt & pp* wet o wetted, *ger* wetting.

wetness ['wetnəs] *n* humedad *f.*

wetsuit ['wetsu:t] *n* traje *m* isotérmico.

we've [wi:v] *contr* (we have) → **have.**

whale [weɪl] *n* ballena.

whalebone ['weɪlbəʊn] *n* (barba de) ballena.

whaler ['weɪlər] *n* (gen) ballenero,-a.

whaling ['weɪlɪŋ] *n* caza de ballenas.
[COMP] **whaling industry** industria ballenera.

wharf [wɔ:f] *n* muelle *m,* embarcadero.

ⓘ *pl* wharfs o wharves.

wharves [wɔ:vz] *pl* → **wharf.**

what [wɒt] *adj* **1** (direct questions) qué: *what time is it?* ¿qué hora es?. **2** (indirect questions) qué: *I don't know what to do* no sé qué hacer. **3** (exclamations) qué: *what a man!* ¡qué hombre! **4** (all the) todo,-a: *what money we have is in the drawer* todo el aceite que tenemos está aquí.

▸ *pron* **1** (direct questions) qué: *what is it?* ¿qué es?. **2** (indirect questions) qué: *he didn't know what to say* no sabía qué decir. **3** lo que: *that's what he told me* eso es lo que me dijo. [LOC] **guess what?** ¿sabes qué? ∥ **what about...?** ¿qué te parece...?. ∥ **what for?** **1** (why) ¿por qué? **2** (for what purpose) ¿para qué? ∥ **what if...?** ¿y si...? ∥ **what is it? 1** (what's wrong?) ¿qué pasa? **2** (definition) ¿qué es?

▸ *interj* ¡cómo!: *what! you've lost it!* ¡cómo! ¡lo has perdido!

whatever [wɒt'evər] *adj* **1** (any) cualquiera que. **2** (at all) en absoluto.

▸ *pron* **1** (anything, all that) (todo) lo que. **2** (no matter what): *whatever happens* pase lo que pase. **3** (surprise) qué. **4** *fam* (show indifference) lo que sea.

whatsoever [wɒtsəʊ'evər] *adj* en absoluto.

wheat [wi:t] *n* trigo.

wheatmeal ['wi:tmi:l] *n* [COMP] **wheatmeal flour** harina integral de trigo.

wheel [wi:l] *n* **1** rueda. **2** (steering wheel) volante *m.*

▸ *vt* (push) empujar.

▸ *vi* **1** girar. **2** (birds) revolotear.

▸ *n pl* **wheels** *fam* coche *m* sing.

wheelbarrow ['wi:lbærəʊ] *n* carretilla de mano.

wheelchair ['wi:ltʃeər] *n* silla de ruedas.

when [wen] *adv* **1** (direct questions) cuándo: *when did it happen?* ¿cuándo pasó? **2** (indirect questions) cuándo: *tell me when you're ready* dime cuándo estés listo. **3** (at which, on which) cuando, en que: *there are times when I can't cope* hay momentos en que no puedo más.

▸ *conj* **1** (at the time that) cuando: *when I arrived* cuando llegué yo. **2** (whenever) cuando, siempre que: *when I have a free moment* cuando tenga un momento libre. **3** (considering) cuando, si: *why do you want to move?* ¿por qué te quieres mudar? **4** (although) cuando, aunque: *they said it was red when in fact it was blue* dijeron que era roja cuando en realidad era azul.

▸ *pron* cuando: *that was when it broke* fue entonces cuando se rompió.

whenever [wen'evər] *conj* **1** (at any time, when) cuando quiera que. **2** (every time that) siempre que.

▸ *adv* (surprise) cuándo.

where [weər] *adv* **1** (direct question - place) dónde; (- direction) adónde: *where is it?* ¿dónde está?. **2** (indirect question) dónde, adónde: *tell me where it is* dime dónde está. **3** (at, in or which) donde, en que; (to which) adonde, a donde: *this is where it all happened* es aquí donde pasó todo.

▸ *conj* **1** donde: *where I come from we don't do that* de donde soy yo eso no se hace. **2** (when) cuando: *where possible* cuando sea posible.

whereabouts [(n) 'weərəbaʊts; (adv) weərə'baʊts] *n* paradero.

▸ *adv* (por) dónde.

whereas [weər'æz] *conj* **1** mientras que. **2** JUR considerando que.

whereby [weə'baɪ] *adv fml* por el/la/lo cual.

wherein [weə'rɪn] *adv* en donde.

whereupon ['weərəpɒn] *adv* con lo cual.

W

wherever [weər'evər] *conj* **1** *(in any place, where)* dondequiera que. **2** *(everywhere)* dondequiera.

▶ *adv* **1** *(in questions)* dónde, adónde. **2** *(unspecified place)* en cualquier parte.

whether ['weðər] *conj* **1** si. **2** *(no matter if)* aunque.

which [wɪtʃ] *adj* **1** *(direct questions)* qué, cuál, cuáles: *which size?* ¿qué tamaño/ talla? **2** *(indirect questions)* qué: *I can't remember which department she's in* no recuerdo en qué sección trabaja.

▶ *pron* **1** *(questions)* cuál, cuáles: *which do you want?* ¿cuál quieres? **2** *(indirect questions)* cuál: *ask him which is his* pregúntale cuál es el suyo. **3** *(defining relative)* que; *(with preposition)* que, el/la que, el/la cual, los/las que, los/las cuales: *the shoes which I bought* los zapatos que compré. **4** *(non-defining relative)* el/la cual, los/las cuales: *two glasses, one of which was dirty* dos copas, una de las cuales estaba sucia. **5** *(referring to a clause)* lo que, lo cual: *he lost, which was sad* perdió, lo cual era triste.

whichever [wɪtʃ'evər] *adj* **1** *(any one)* cualquier, el/la que. **2** *(no matter which)* cualquiera que, no importa. **3** *(interrogative)* cuál.

▶ *pron* **1** cualquiera, el/la que. **2** *(interrogative)* cuál.

while [waɪl] *n* *(time)* rato, tiempo: *we talked for a while* charlamos durante un rato.

▶ *conj* **1** *(when)* mientras: *somebody stole our car while we were on holiday* nos robaron el coche mientras estábamos de vacaciones. **2** *(although)* aunque: *while I sympathize with the cause, I cannot support your methods* aunque simpatizo con la causa, no puedo apoyar tus métodos. **3** *(whereas)* mientras que: *he prefers to go out, while I like staying in* él prefiere salir mientras que a mí me gusta quedarme en casa.

whim [wɪm] *n* antojo, capricho.

whimsical ['wɪmsɪkəl] *adj* *(person, idea, etc)* caprichoso,-a; *(smile)* enigmático,-a; *(story, etc)* fantástico,-a.

whip [wɪp] *n* **1** *(for animals)* látigo; *(for punishment)* azote *m*; *(for riding)* fusta. **2** CULIN *(desert)* batido.

▶ *vt* **1** *(person)* azotar; *(horse)* fustigar. **2** *(wind)* azotar. **3** CULIN *(ingredients)* batir; *(cream, egg whites)* montar. **4** GB *fam (steal)* birlar, mangar. **5** *(act quickly)* hacer algo deprisa.

ⓘ *pt & pp* whipped, *ger* whipping.

whipping ['wɪpɪŋ] *n* azotaina, paliza.

COMP whipping cream nata para montar.

whirl [wɜːl] *n* **1** *(movement)* giro, vuelta. **2** *fig* torbellino.

▶ *vi* **1** *(move round)* girar, dar vueltas; *(of dust, leaves, etc)* arremolinarse. **2** *(move quickly)* ir como un relámpago.

whisk [wɪsk] *n* **1** *(quick movement)* movimiento brusco, sacudida. **2** CULIN *(hand)* batidor *m*; *(electric)* batidora.

▶ *vt* **1** *(of animal's tail)* sacudir (la cola). **2** CULIN batir. **3** *(take quickly)* llevar rápidamente.

whisker ['wɪskər] *n* *(single hair)* pelo (de la barba).

▶ *n pl* whiskers *(man's)* patillas *fpl*. *(of cat, etc)* bigote *m*, bigotes *mpl*.

whiskey [wɪskɪ] *n* → whisky.

whisky [wɪskɪ] *n* whisky *m*.

ⓘ *pl* whiskies.

whisper ['wɪspər] *n* **1** *(quiet voice)* susurro. **2** *(rumour)* rumor *m*, voz *f*.

▶ *vt* **1** *(gen)* susurrar, decir en voz baja. **2** *(rumour)* correr la voz, rumorearse.

whispering ['wɪspərɪŋ] *n* *(gen)* cuchicheo; *(of leaves)* murmullo.

whistle ['wɪsəl] *n* **1** *(instrument)* silbato, pito. **2** *(noise)* silbido, pitido; *(of train)* pitido; *(of wind)* silbido.

▶ *vt* *(tune)* silbar.

▶ *vi* *(person, kettle, wind)* silbar; *(referee, police, train)* pitar.

white [waɪt] *adj* **1** blanco,-a. **2** *(pale)* pálido,-a.

▶ *n* **1** blanco, color *m* blanco. **2** *(person)* blanco,-a. **3** *(of egg)* clara. **4** *(of eye)* blanco. COMP white (blood) cell glóbulo blanco. ‖ the White House la Casa Blanca.

▶ *n pl* **whites** *(linen)* ropa *f sing* blanca; *(for tennis)* ropa *f sing* de jugar al tenis.

🌐 La **White House** es la residencia oficial del presidente de Estados Unidos y se usa como sinónimo del gobierno de este país.

white-collar [waɪtˈkɒləʳ] *adj* administrativo,-a; oficinista *mf*.

whiten [ˈwaɪtªn] *vt* blanquear, emblanquecer.

◆ **to whittle away** *vt sep* mermar, ir reduciendo, ir disminuyendo.

◆ **to whittle down** *vt sep* reducir.

whiz [wɪz] *n* → whizz.

whizz [wɪz] *n (sound)* zumbido, silbido.

▶ *vi* **1** *(make sound)* zumbar, silbar. **2** *(car, bullet)* pasar zumbando, pasar silbando; *(time)* pasar volando.

who [huː] *pron* **1** *(direct questions)* quién, quiénes: *who is it?* ¿quién es? **2** *(indirect questions)* quién, quiénes: *I don't know who they are* no sé quiénes son. **3** *(defining relative)* que: *you're the only one who can help me* eres el único que puede ayudarme. **4** *(non-defining relative)* que, quien, quienes, el/la cual, los/las cuales: *the workers, who were on strike,...* los trabajadores, los cuales estaban en huelga,...

whoever [huːˈevəʳ] *pron* **1** *(the person who)* quien, quienquiera que, el que. **2** *(no matter who)* quienquiera que, cualquiera que. **3** *(questions, exclamations)* quién?

whole [həʊl] *adj* **1** *(entire, all (the), the full amount of)* entero,-a, íntegro,-a, todo,-a. **2** *(intact, not broken)* intacto,-a, sano,-a; *(in one piece, complete)* entero, -a. ⸂COMP⸃ **whole number** número entero.

▶ *n* conjunto, todo. ⸂LOC⸃ **as a whole** en conjunto, en su totalidad. ▌**on the whole** en general.

wholemeal [ˈhəʊlmiːl] *adj* integral.

wholesale [ˈhəʊlseɪl] *adj* **1** COMM al por mayor. **2** *(complete, indiscriminate)* total,

general, masivo,-a, sistemático,-a, absoluto,-a, indiscriminado, -a.

▶ *adv* **1** COMM al por mayor. **2** *(on a large scale)* de modo general, en su totalidad, en masa, de manera sistemática.

▶ *n* COMM venta al por mayor.

whom [huːm] *pron* **1** *fml (direct questions)* a quién/quiénes: *to whom should I address it?* ¿a quién debería ir dirigido? **2** *fml (relative - defining)* que, quien, quienes; *(- after preposition)* quien, quienes, el cual, la cual, los cuales, las cuales: *pupils whom I have taught* alumnos a quienes he dado clase. **3** *(relative - non-defining)* quien, quienes, el cual, la cual, los cuales, las cuales: *our guest, of whom you must all have heard,...* nuestro invitado, de quien todos deben haber oído hablar,...

whopper [ˈwɒpəʳ] *n* **1** *fam (large thing)* cosa enorme, cosa descomunal. **2** *fam (lie)* trola, bola.

whose [huːz] *pron* **1** *(direct questions)* de quién/quiénes: *whose is this?* ¿de quién es esto? **2** *(indirect questions)* de quién/quiénes: *I don't know whose it is* no sé de quién es.

▶ *adj* **1** *(direct questions)* de quién/quiénes: *whose dog is this?* de quién es este perro? **2** *(indirect questions)* de quién/quiénes: *I wonder whose books these are* me pregunto de quién serán estos libros. **3** *(relative)* cuyo,-a, cuyos,-as: *the woman whose car was stolen* la mujer cuyo coche fue robado.

why [waɪ] *adv* **1** *(direct questions - for what reason)* por qué; *(- for what purpose)* para qué: *why didn't you go?* ¿por qué no fuiste? **2** *(indirect questions - for what reason)* por qué; *(- for what purpose)* para qué: *I asked him why he did it* le pregunté por qué lo hizo. **3** *(relative)* por eso: *that is why he left* por eso se fue. ⸂COMP⸃ **why not?** ¿por qué no?

▶ *interj* ¡vaya!, ¡anda!, ¡toma!

▶ *n* porqué *m*.

wick [wɪk] *n* mecha.

wicked [ˈwɪkɪd] *adj* **1** *(evil - person)* malvado,-a, malo,-a; *(- action)* malo,-a, perverso,-a, inicuo,-a. **2** *(harmful)* peligroso,-a, dañino,-a, nocivo,-a. **3** *(mischievous)* travieso,-a, pícaro,-a. **4** *fam fig (very bad - gen)* malísimo,-a; *(- weather)* feo,-a, horrible; *(- temper, price)* terrible; *(- waste)* vergonzoso,-a; *(humour)* cruel.

▶ *n pl* **the wicked** los malos.

wicker ['wɪkə'] *n* mimbre *m*.

▶ *adj* de mimbre.

wide [waɪd] *adj* **1** *(broad)* ancho,-a; *(space, hole, gap)* grande. **2** *(having specified width)* de ancho. **3** *(large - area)* amplio,-a, extenso,-a; *(- knowledge, experience, repercussions)* amplio,-a; *(- coverage, range, support)* extenso,-a. **4** *(eyes, smile)* abierto,-a. **5** *(off target)* desviado,-a.

▶ *adv* **1** *(fully - gen)* completamente. **2** *(off target)* desviado.

wide-angle ['waɪdæŋgəl] *adj* amplio,-a. COMP **wide-angle lens** objetivo gran angular.

widely ['waɪdlɪ] *adv* **1** *(over wide area or range of things)* extensamente; *(generally)* generalmente. **2** *(to a large degree)* mucho.

widen ['waɪdən] *vt* **1** *(road, etc)* ensanchar. **2** *fig (knowledge, etc)* ampliar, extender.

▶ *vi* **1** *(road, etc)* ensancharse; *(eyes)* abrirse. **2** *(project, etc)* extenderse; *(difference, gap)* aumentar.

widescreen ['waɪdskriːn] *adj* TV pantalla panorámica.

widespread ['waɪdspred] *adj (concern, confusion, unrest, use, belief)* generalizado,-a; *(damage, disease, news)* extenso, -a, extendido,-a. LOC **to become widespread 1** *(gen)* generalizarse. **2** *(illness, news)* extenderse, difundirse.

widow ['wɪdəʊ] *n* viuda.

widower ['wɪdəʊə'] *n* viudo.

width [wɪdθ] *n* **1** *(gen)* anchura. **2** *(of material)* ancho. **3** *(of swimming pool)* ancho.

wield [wiːld] *vt* **1** *(weapon, tool, etc)* empuñar, blandir, manejar. **2** *fig (power, control, etc)* ejercer.

wife [waɪf] *n* esposa, mujer *f*.
ⓘ *pl* **wives**.

wig [wɪg] *n* **1** *(gen)* peluca. **2** JUR peluquín *m*.

wild [waɪld] *adj* **1** *(gen)* salvaje. **2** *(plant, flower)* silvestre; *(vegetation)* salvaje. **3** *(country, landscape)* agreste. **4** *(weather - wind)* borrascoso,-a; *(- sea)* bravo,-a; *(- night)* tempestuoso,-a. **5** *(very excited - person)* loco,-a (with, de), alocado, -a. **6** *(showing lack of thought - thoughts, talk)* disparatado,-a; *(- guess)* al azar; *(- idea, scheme)* descabellado,-a. **7** *fam (fantastic, crazy)* bárbaro,-a, salvaje. LOC **wild boar** jabalí *m*.

▶ *n* **the wild** estado salvaje, estado natural, naturaleza.

wildcat ['waɪldkæt] *n* gato,-a montés. COMP **wildcat strike** huelga espontánea.

wildebeest ['wɪldəbiːst] *n* ñu *m*.

wildlife ['waɪldlaɪf] *n* fauna. COMP **wildlife park** reserva natural.

will¹ [wɪl] *n* **1** *(control, volition)* voluntad *f*; *(free will)* voluntad *f*. **2** JUR testamento, últimas *fpl* voluntades. LOC **against one's will** contra su voluntad. COMP **last will and testament** última voluntad *f*.

▶ *vt* **1** *(make or intend to happen by power of mind)* desear, querer. **2** *fml (intend, desire)* querer, ordenar, mandar. **3** JUR legar, dejar en testamento.

will² [wɪl] *aux* **1** *(future)*: *she will be here tomorrow* estará aquí mañana. **2** *(be disposed to, be willing to)*: *(no), I won't* no quiero. **3** *(requests)* querer: *will you do me a favour?* ¿quieres hacerme un favor? **4** *(general truths, custom)*: *accidents will happen* siempre habrá accidentes. **5** *(orders, commands)*: *will you be quiet!* ¡quieres callarte! **6** *(insistence, persistence)* insistir en: *she will play her music at full volume* insiste en poner la música a tope. **7** *(can, possibility)* poder: *this phone will accept credit cards* este teléfono va con tarjetas de crédito. **8** *(supposition, must, probability)* deber de: *that'll be John* será John, debe de ser John.

willing ['wɪlɪŋ] *adj* **1** *(without being forced)* complaciente, de gran voluntad dispuesto,-a; *(eager)* entusiasta. **2**

(ready, prepared, disposed) dispuesto,-a (to, a). **3** *(given/done gladly)* voluntario, -a. comp **to show willing** dar pruebas de buena voluntad.

willingly [ˈwɪlɪŋlɪ] *adv* de buena gana, de buen grado.

willow [ˈwɪləʊ] *n* sauce *m*.

willpower [ˈwɪlpaʊəʳ] *n* (fuerza de) voluntad *f*.

wilt [wɪlt] *vt* marchitar, secar.
  ▶ *vi* **1** *(plant)* marchitarse, secarse. **2** *(person - become weak or tired)* debilitarse, decaer, languidecer; *(- lose confidence)* desanimarse.

wimp [wɪmp] *n fam pej* debilucho,-a, esmirriado,-a, canijo,-a.

win [wɪn] *n* victoria.
  ▶ *vt* **1** *(gen)* ganar; *(victory)* conseguir, ganar. **2** *(prize, cup, etc)* ganar, llevarse. **3** *(gain, obtain, achieve - gen)* conseguir, obtener, ganar; *(- friendship, respect)* granjearse; *(- sympathy, affection)* ganarse, granjearse; *(- support)* atraer, captar; *(- heart, love)* conquistar.
  ▶ *vi* ganar.
  ① *pt & pp* **won**, *ger* **winning**.

wind¹ [wɪnd] *n* **1** METEOR viento, aire *m*. **2** *(breath)* aliento. **3** *(flatulence)* gases *mpl*, flato; *(air)* gases *mpl* del estómago. **4** *pej (talk)* palabrería.
  ▶ *adj* MUS de viento. comp **wind instrument** instrumento de viento.
  ▶ *vt* **1** dejar sin aliento, cortar la respiración. **2** *(baby)* hacer eructar.

wind² [waɪnd] *vt* **1** *(handle)* dar vueltas a, girar. **2** *(on reel)* arrollar, devanar. **3** *(tape, film)* bobinar. **4** *(clock)* dar cuerda a *(up, -)*. **5** *(bandage, scarf)* envolver; *(wool)* ovillar.
  ▶ *vi (road, river)* serpentear, zigzaguear; *(staircase)* formar una espiral.
  ① *pt & pp* **wound** [waʊnd].
  ▶ *n (bend)* curva, recodo, vuelta.

windlass [ˈwɪndləs] *n* torno.

windmill [ˈwɪndmɪl] *n* molino de viento.

window [ˈwɪndəʊ] *n* **1** *(gen)* ventana. **2** *(in vehicle, bank, theatre, etc)* ventanilla. **3** *(of shop)* escaparate *m*. **4** *(glass)* cristal *m*. **5** COMPUT ventana.

window-dressing [ˈwɪndəʊdresɪŋ] *n* **1** decoración *f* de escaparates, escaparatismo. **2** *fig* fachada, apariencias *fpl*.

windowpane [ˈwɪndəʊpeɪn] *n* cristal *m*.

windpipe [ˈwɪndpaɪp] *n* tráquea.

windscreen [ˈwɪndskriːn] *n* AUTO parabrisas *m inv*. comp **windscreen wiper** limpiaparabrisas *m*.

windshield [ˈwɪndʃiːld] *n* US→ **windscreen**.

windsurf [ˈwɪndsɜːf] *vi* hacer windsurfing.

windsurfing [ˈwɪndsɜːfɪŋ] *n* windsurf *m*.

windy [ˈwɪndɪ] *adj* **1** *(day, weather)* ventoso,-a; *(place)* expuesto,-a al viento. **2** *(speech)* rimbombante.
  ① *comp* **windier**, *superl* **windiest**.

wine [waɪn] *n* **1** vino: *red/rosé/white wine* vino tinto/rosado/blanco. **2** *(colour)* (color *m*) morado, granate *m*. comp **wine cellar** bodega. ▌ **wine grower** vinicultor,-ra. ▌ **wine taster** catavinos *mf*.

winery [ˈwaɪnərɪ] *n* bodega.
  ① *pl* **wineries**.

wineskin [ˈwaɪnskɪn] *n* odre *m*, bota.

wing [wɪŋ] *n* **1** *(gen)* ala. **2** AUTO aleta. **3** SP *(side)* banda; *(player)* extremo,-a.
  ▶ *vi* volar.
  ▶ *n pl* **wings** THEAT bastidores *mpl*.

winged [wɪŋd] *adj* alado,-a, con alas.

winger [ˈwɪŋəʳ] *n* SP extremo,-a.

wingspan [ˈwɪŋspæn] *n* envergadura.

wink [wɪŋk] *n* guiño.
  ▶ *vi* **1** *(person)* guiñar el ojo. **2** *(of light, star)* titilear, parpadear.
  ◆ **to wink at** *vt insep (pretend not to notice)* hacer la vista gorda.

winker [ˈwɪŋkəʳ] *n* GB *(indicator)* intermitente *m*.

winkle [ˈwɪŋkəl] *n* bígaro, bigarro.

winner [ˈwɪnəʳ] *n* **1** ganador,-ra, vencedor,-ra. **2** *fam (idea, etc)* éxito.

winning [ˈwɪnɪŋ] *adj* **1** *(person, team, etc)* ganador,-ra. **2** *(ticket, number, etc)* premiado,-a. **3** *(stroke, goal)* decisivo,-a. **4** *(smile, ways)* atractivo,-a, encantador,-ra.
  ▶ *n pl* **winnings** ganancias *fpl*.

W

winter ['wɪntər] n invierno.
▸ vi fml invernar, pasar el invierno.
COMP **winter solstice** solsticio de invierno.

wipe [waɪp] vt (clean) limpiar; (dry) enjugar.
▸ vi (dishes) enjugar.
▸ n **1** (clean) lavado, fregado. **2** (cloth) paño, trapo.
◆ **to wipe out** vt sep **1** (destroy - army) aniquilar; (- population, species) exterminar. **2** (clean inside) limpiar el interior de. **3** (cancel - debts) saldar, liquidar, cancelar; (- profit) borrar, anular.

wiper ['waɪpər] n AUTO limpiaparabrisas m inv.

wire ['waɪər] n **1** (metal) alambre m. **2** ELEC cable m, hilo. **3** (fence) alambrada, valla. **4** US telegrama m. COMP **wire cutters** cortaalambres m inv.
▸ vt **1** (fasten, join) atar con alambre. **2** (house) hacer la instalación eléctrica de; (equipment, appliance) conectar (a la toma eléctrica). **3** US (telegram) enviar un telegrama a; (money) mandar un giro telegráfico a.

wired ['waɪəd] adj conectado,-a.

wireless ['waɪələs] n **1** (set) radio f. **2** (system) radiofonía. COMP **wireless operator** radiotelegrafista mf.

wiring ['waɪrɪŋ] n cableado.

wisdom ['wɪzdəm] n **1** (knowledge) sabiduría, saber m. **2** (good sense - of person) cordura, (buen) juicio, tino; (- of action) prudencia, sabiduría, sensatez f. COMP **wisdom tooth** muela del juicio.

wise [waɪz] adj **1** (learned, knowledgeable) sabio,-a. **2** (sensible, prudent - person) prudente, sensato,-a; (- action, remark) prudente; (- advice) sabio,-a; (- decision, choice, move) atinado,-a, acertado,-a. COMP **the Three Wise Men** los Reyes Magos. ‖ **wise guy** sabelotodo.

✎ Consulta three.

◆ **to wise up** vi (realize, become aware) darse cuenta; (become informed) enterarse; (wake up) espabilarse.

wish [wɪʃ] vt **1** (want) querer, desear. **2** fml (demand, want) querer. **3** (hope) desear.
▸ vi **1** desear (for, -). **2** fml (want) querer.
▸ n deseo.
▸ n pl **wishes** (greeting) deseos mpl; (in letter) saludos mpl, recuerdos mpl.
◆ **to wish on** vt sep: I wouldn't wish that on anyone eso no se lo desearía a nadie.

wishful ['wɪʃful] adj fml de ensueño. COMP **wishful thinking** ilusiones fpl.

wisp [wɪsp] n **1** (of grass, straw, etc) brizna; (of hair, wool, etc) mechón m; (of smoke, cloud) voluta. **2** (person) persona menuda.

wistful ['wɪstful] adj pensativo,-a, nostálgico,-a, melancólico,-a.

wit [wɪt] n **1** (clever humour) agudeza, ingenio. **2** (intelligence) inteligencia. **3** (person) persona salada, chistoso,-a.

witch [wɪtʃ] n bruja. COMP **witch doctor** hechicero.
① pl witches.

witchcraft ['wɪtʃkrɑːft] n brujería.

witch-hunt ['wɪtʃhʌnt] n caza de brujas.

with [wɪð, wɪθ] prep **1** (accompanying) con: come with me ven conmigo. **2** (having, possessing) con, de; (including, and also) con, incluido: the man with the beard el hombre de la barba. **3** (using, by means of) con: cut it with a knife córtalo con un cuchillo. **4** (cover, fill, contain) de: you fill it with water lo llenas de agua. **5** (agreeing, in support of) con: we're with you all the way! ¡estamos contigo hasta el final! **6** (against) con: I've had a row with Daniel he discutido con Daniel. **7** (because of, on account of) de: trembling with fear temblando de miedo. **8** (indicating manner) con: with pleasure con mucho gusto. **9** (in same direction as) con: with the flow con la corriente. **10** (at the same time and rate as) con: wine improves with age el vino mejora con los años. **11** (regarding, concerning) con: this has nothing to do with you esto no tiene nada que ver contigo. **12** (in the case of, as regards) con respecto a, en cuanto a: with Mrs Smith what happened was that... er el caso de la Señora Smith lo que pasó fue que... **13** *(as an employee or client of)* en: *she's with the council now* trabaja en el ayuntamiento ahora. **14** *(remaining)*: *with only half an hour to go* cuando tan sólo falta media hora. **15** *(despite, in spite of)* con: *with all his faults* con todos sus defectos. **16** *(in comparisons)* con: *if we compare this brand with a cheaper one* si comparamos esta marca con una más barata. **17** *(illness)* con: *he's in bed with flu* está en cama con la gripe. **18** *(according to)* según, de acuerdo con: *prices vary with the seasons* los precios varían según la temporada.

withdraw [wɪð'drɔː] *vt* **1** *(take out)* retirar, sacar. **2** *fml (retract, take back - statement)* retractarse de, retirar; *(- offer)* renunciar a; *(- charge, support)* retirar.
ⓘ *pt* withdrew [wɪð'druː], *pp* withdrawn [wɪð'drɔːn].
▸ *vi (retire, not take part in)* retirarse. ［COMP］
to withdraw into oneself retraerse.

withdrawal [wɪð'drɔːəl] *n* **1** *(gen)* retirada. **2** *(of words)* retractación *f*. **3** *(psychology, behaviour)* retraimiento. ［COMP］
withdrawal symptoms síndrome *m* de abstinencia.

withdrawn [wɪð'drɔːn] *pp* → **withdraw**.

withdrew [wɪð'druː] *pt* → **withdraw**.

wither ['wɪðəʳ] *vt* **1** *(plant)* marchitar, secar. **2** *(crush)* fulminar, aplastar, intimidar.
▸ *vi* **1** *(plant)* marchitarse (away, -), secarse (away, -). **2** *fig (hopes, etc)* desvanecerse, menguar.

within [wɪ'ðɪn] *prep* **1** *fml (inside)* dentro de. **2** *(inside range or limits of)* al alcance de. **3** *(less than - distance)* a menos de. **4** *(less than - time)* dentro de.
▸ *adv fml* dentro, en el interior.

without [wɪ'ðaʊt] *prep* **1** sin. **2** *arch* fuera de.
▸ *adv* **1** fuera. **2** sin.

withstand [wɪð'stænd] *vt (gen)* resistir; *(pain)* aguantar, soportar.
ⓘ *pt & pp* withstood [wɪð'stʊd].

withstood [wɪð'stʊd] *pt & pp* → **withstand**.

witness ['wɪtnəs] *n* **1** *(person)* testigo *mf*. **2** *fml (testimony, evidence)* testimonio.
ⓘ *pl* witnesses.
▸ *vt* **1** *(see)* presenciar, ver. **2** *(document)* firmar como testigo. **3** *(be a sign or proof of)* testimoniar; *(look at the example of)* ver, notar, considerar.
▸ *vi* JUR *fml (give evidence, testify)* atestiguar (to, -), declarar (to, -).

witty ['wɪtɪ] *adj (person)* ingenioso,-a, agudo,-a, salado,-a; *(remark)* agudo,-a; *(speech)* gracioso,-a.
ⓘ *comp* wittier, *superl* wittiest.

wives [waɪvz] *n pl* → **wife**.

we'd [wiːd] *contr* (we had, we would) → **have, would**.

wizard ['wɪzəd] *n* **1** *(male witch)* brujo, hechicero. **2** *(genius)* lince *mf*, genio, experto,-a.

woeful ['wəʊfʊl] *adj* **1** *fml (very sad)* afligido,-a, apenado,-a, triste. **2** *(deplorable)* lamentable, deplorable, penoso,-a, malísimo,-a.

woke [wəʊk] *pt* → **wake**.

woken [wəʊkən] *pp* → **have, wake**.

wolf [wʊlf] *n* lobo. ［COMP］ **wolf cub** lobezno.
ⓘ *pl* wolves.
▸ *vt* [also wolf down] tragarse, zamparse, devorar.

wolfhound ['wʊlfhaʊnd] *n* perro lobo.

wolfram ['wʊlfrəm] *n* wolframio, volframio, wolfram *m*.

wolves [wʊlvz] *pl* → **wolf**.

woman ['wʊmən] *n* mujer *f*, señora.
ⓘ *pl* women ['wɪmɪn].

womb [wuːm] *n* útero, matriz *f*.

women ['wɪmɪn] *n pl* → **woman**.

won [wʌn] *pt & pp* → **win**.

wonder ['wʌndəʳ] *n* **1** *(thing)* maravilla, milagro. **2** *(feeling)* admiración *f*, asombro.
▸ *adj* milagroso,-a.
▸ *vt* **1** *fml (be surprised)* sorprenderse, extrañarse. **2** *(ask oneself)* preguntarse. **3** *(polite request)*: *I wonder if you can help me* a ver si puede ayudarme.

W

▶ vi **1** (reflect, ponder) pensar (about, en); (doubt) tener dudas. **2** fml (marvel) asombrarse, maravillarse, admirarse. COMP I shouldn't wonder if + indic no me extrañaría que + subj. ▌ it's a wonder (that) + indic es un milagro que + subj. ▌ no/little/small wonder (that) + indic no es de extrañar que + subj.

wonderful ['wʌndəful] adj maravilloso,-a, estupendo,-a.

wont [wəunt] n costumbre f, hábito.

won't [wəunt] contr (will not) → will.

wood [wud] n **1** (material) madera. **2** (for fire) leña. **3** (forest) bosque m. **4** SP (golf) palo de madera; (bowling) bola.
▶ n pl **woods** bosque m sing.

wooden ['wudⁿn] adj **1** de madera. **2** fig (expression, style) rígido,-a; (movement) tieso,-a; (acting) sin expresión.

woodland ['wudlənd] n bosque m, arbolado, monte m.

woodpecker ['wudpekəʳ] n pico, pájaro carpintero.

woodwork ['wudwɜːk] n **1** (craft) carpintería. **2** (of building) maderaje m, maderamen m.

woodworm ['wudwɜːm] n carcoma: it has woodworm está carcomido,-a.

woody ['wudɪ] adj **1** (wooded) arbolado,-a. **2** (like wood) leñoso,-a.
ⓘ comp **woodier**, superl **woodiest**.

wool [wul] n lana.
▶ adj **1** (made of wool) de lana. **2** COMM lanero,-a.

woolen ['wulən] adj-n US → woollen.

woollen ['wulən] adj **1** (made of wool) de lana. **2** COMM lanero,-a.
▶ n pl **woollens** géneros mpl de lana.

word [wɜːd] n **1** (gen) palabra: tell me what happened in your own words explícame con tus propias palabras lo que pasó. **2** (message, news) noticia: word came that... llegó noticia (de) que... **3** (promise) palabra: I give you my word te doy mi palabra. **4** (command) orden f: wait until I give the word espera hasta que dé la orden. **5** LING palabra, vocablo, voz f. **6 the word** (rumour) voz f, rumor m: the word is that Macy is pregnant corre la voz de que Macy

está embarazada. LOC **in a word** en una palabra. ▌ **in other words** o sea, es decir. ▌ **not in so many words** no exactamente. ▌ **to keep one's word** cumplir su palabra. ▌ **to put sth into words** expresar ALGO con palabras. ▌ **word for word** palabra por palabra. COMP **a word of advice** un consejo. ▌ **a word of warning** una advertencia. ▌ **word processor** procesador m de textos.
▶ n pl **words** (lyrics) letra f sing. (discussion, talk) palabras fpl.
▶ vt expresar, formular, redactar: a well-worded letter una carta bien redactada.

wording ['wɜːdɪŋ] n redacción f, expresión f, palabras fpl, términos mpl.

wore [wɔːʳ] pt → wear.

work [wɜːk] n **1** (gen) trabajo. **2** (employment) empleo, trabajo. **3** (building work, roadworks) obras fpl. **4** (product, results) trabajo, obra. **5** (literary, etc) obra. ▶ vt **1** (person) hacer trabajar. **2** (machine) manejar; (mechanism) accionar. **3** (mine, oil well) explotar; (land, fields) trabajar, cultivar. **4** (produce) hacer. **5** (wood, metal, clay) trabajar; (dough) amasar. **6** (make by work or effort) trabajar. **7** fam (arrange) arreglar. **8** (move gradually) work the butter into the flour vaya mezclando la mantequilla con la harina. COMP **to be in work** tener trabajo. ▌ **to be out of work** estar en el paro. ▌ **to get down/set to work** ponerse a trabajar. ▌ **to get worked up** exaltarse.
▶ vi **1** (gen) trabajar. **2** (machine, system) funcionar. **3** (medicine, cleaner) surtir efecto; (plan) tener éxito. **4** (move) they eventually worked round to my way of thinking finalmente coincidieron con mi parecer.
▶ n pl **works** (factory) fábrica f sing.
◆ **to work out** vt sep **1** (calculation, sum) calcular, hacer. **2** (plan, scheme) planear, elaborar, pensar; (itinerary) planear; (details, idea) desarrollar. **3** (problem) solucionar, resolver; (solution) encontrar. **4** (person) calar, entender.
▶ vi **1** (calculation) salir (at, por), resultar. **2** (turn out well - things) salir bien,

(- problem) resolverse. **3** SP hacer ejercicio.

workaholic [wɜːkəˈhɒlɪk] *n fam* adicto,-a al trabajo.

workbench [ˈwɜːkbentʃ] *n* banco de trabajo.

workbook [ˈwɜːkbʊk] *n* cuaderno, libreta de ejercicios.

workday [ˈwɜːkdeɪ] *n* US día *m* laborable.

worker [ˈwɜːkəʳ] *n (gen)* trabajador,-ra; *(manual)* obrero,-a, operario,-a; *(office)* oficinista *mf*, administrativo,-a. COMP **worker bee** abeja obrera.

workforce [ˈwɜːkfɔːs] *n (of company, factory, etc)* personal *m*, plantilla; *(of country)* población *f* activa.

working [ˈwɜːkɪŋ] *adj* **1** *(clothes, conditions, surface)* de trabajo; *(week, day, life)* laborable. **2** *(population, partner, etc)* activo,-a; *(person, mother)* que trabaja. COMP **the working class** la clase trabajadora.

▶ *n (machine, model)* que funciona; *(part)* móvil.

▶ *adj* **1** *(majority)* suficiente. **2** *(hypothesis, etc)* de trabajo.

▶ *n (of machine)* funcionamiento; *(of pit)* explotación *f*.

▶ *n pl* **workings** *(of mine, quarry)* pozos *mpl. (mechanics)* funcionamiento.

working-class [wɜːkɪŋˈklɑːs] *adj (person)* de clase obrera, de clase trabajadora; *(area)* obrero,-a.

workman [ˈwɜːkmən] *n (gen)* trabajador *m*; *(manual)* obrero, operario. ① *pl* **workmen** [ˈwɜːkmən].

workmate [ˈwɜːkmeɪt] *n* compañero, -a de trabajo.

workplace [ˈwɜːkpleɪs] *n* lugar *m* de trabajo.

workshop [ˈwɜːkʃɒp] *n* taller *m*.

worktop [ˈwɜːktɒp] *n* encimera.

world [wɜːld] *n* **1** *(earth)* mundo: *I'd love to travel round the world* me encantaría dar la vuelta al mundo. **2** *(sphere)* mundo: *the world of show business* el mundo del espectáculo. **3** *(life)* mundo, vida: *in this world* en esta vida. **4** *(people)* mundo: *in the eyes of the world* a los ojos del mundo. **5** *(large amount, large number)*: *this will make a world of difference to the disabled* esto cambiará totalmente la vida de los minusválidos. LOC **out of this world** fenomenal.

▶ *adj (population, peace)* mundial; *(politics, trade)* internacional: *world record* récord mundial; *world power* potencia mundial. COMP **World Bank** Banco Mundial. ‖ **world champion** campeón,-ona mundial. ‖ **World Cup** el Mundial, los Mundiales. ‖ **world fair** exposición *f* internacional. ‖ **world music** música étnica. ‖ **World Wusic** guerra mundial.

worldwide [wɜːldˈwaɪd] *adj* mundial, universal.

▶ *adv* mundialmente.

worm [wɜːm] *n* **1** *(grub, maggot)* gusano; *(earthworm)* lombriz *f*. **2** *pej (person)* gusano, canalla. **3** TECH *(of screw)* tornillo.

▶ *vt* **1** *(make one's way)* deslizarse; *(insinuate)* insinuarse (into, en). **2** MED quitar las lombrices a, desparasitar.

▶ *n pl* **worms** MED lombrices *fpl*.

worn [wɔːn] *pp* → wear.

worn-out [ˈwɔːnˈaʊt] [se escribe worn out cuando no se usa para calificar a un nombre] *adj* **1** *(thing)* gastado,-a, estropeado,-a. **2** *(person)* rendido,-a, agotado,-a.

worried [ˈwʌrɪd] *adj (person)* inquieto,-a, preocupado,-a (about, por); *(look, voice)* de preocupación.

worry [ˈwʌrɪ] *n (state, feeling)* preocupación *f*, inquietud *f*, intranquilidad *f*; *(problem)* preocupación *f*, problema *m*; *(responsibility)* responsabilidad *f*. ① *pl* **worries**.

▶ *vt* **1** inquietar, preocupar. **2** *(annoy, disturb)* molestar. **3** *(of dog)* acosar, perseguir.

▶ *vi* inquietarse, preocuparse (about/ over, por). ① *pt & pp* **worried**, *ger* **worrying**.

worrying [ˈwʌrɪɪŋ] *adj* inquietante, preocupante, desconcertante.

W

worse [wɜːs] *adj (comp of* **bad**) peor.
▸ *adv (comp of badly)* peor; *(more intensely)* más. [LOC] **to be worse off 1** *(financially)* andar peor de dinero. **2** *(physically)* estar peor. ❙ **to get worse** empeorar. ❙ **to get worse and worse** ir de mal en peor. ❙ **to go from bad to worse** ir de mal en peor. ❙ **to make matters worse** por si fuera poco. ❙ **worse still** lo que es peor.
▸ *n* lo peor.

worsen [ˈwɜːsən] *vt* empeorar.
▸ *vi* empeorarse.

worship [ˈwɜːʃɪp] *n* **1** REL adoración *f*, veneración *f*, culto; *(service)* culto, oficio. **2** *(devotion, love)* amor *m*, culto, idolatría.
▸ *vt* **1** REL adorar, venerar. **2** *(idolize)* rendir culto a, idolatrar.
ⓘ *pt & pp* worshipped, *ger* worshipping.

worst [wɜːst] *adj (superl of* **bad**) peor.
▸ *adv (superl)* peor.
▸ *n (indefinite)* lo peor; *(person)* el/la peor, los/las peores. [LOC] **at (the) worst** en lo peor de los casos. ❙ **if the worst comes to the worst** si pasa lo peor.

worth [wɜːθ] *n* **1** *(in money)* valor *m*. **2** *(of person)* valía; *(of thing)* valor *m*.
▸ *adj* **1** *(having certain value)* que vale, que tiene un valor de. **2** *(deserving of)* que vale la pena, que merece la pena. [LOC] **to get one's money's worth** sacarle jugo al dinero. ❙ **to be worth SB's while** valer la pena.

worthless [ˈwɜːθləs] *adj* **1** *(gen)* sin valor. **2** *(useless)* inútil, sin ningún valor. **3** *(person)* despreciable.

worthwhile [wɜːθˈwaɪl] *adj* **1** *(gen)* que vale la pena, que merece la pena.

worthy [ˈwɜːðɪ] *adj* **1** *(deserving)* digno,-a *(of*, de), merecedor,-ra *(of*, de); *(winner, opponent, successor)* digno,-a. **2** *(action, cause)* meritorio,-a, bueno,-a, justo,-a.
ⓘ *comp* worthier, *superl* worthiest.

would [wʊd] *aux* **1** *(conditional)*: I would love to me encantaría. **2** *(polite requests)*: would you be so kind as to close the window? ¿me haría usted el favor de cerrar la ven-tana? **3** *(offers, invitations)*: would you like a drink? ¿quieres tomar algo? **4** *(willing-ness)*: he wouldn't help me se negó a ayu-darme, no quiso ayudarme. **5** *(giving ad-vice)*: I wouldn't dwell on it yo que tú no pensaría en ello. **6** *(conjecture)*: that would have been in 1978 eso debe haber sido en 1978. **7** *(past habit, custom)* soler: we would often go out together a menudo sa-líamos juntos. **8** *(insistence, persistence)*: you would say that! ¡es típico de ti decir eso!

wound¹ [wuːnd] *n* herida.
▸ *vt* herir.

wound² [waʊnd] *pt & pp* → **wind²**

wounded [ˈwuːndɪd] *adj* herido,-a.
▸ *n pl* the wounded los heridos.

wove [wəʊv] *pt* → **weave**.

woven [ˈwəʊvən] *pp* → **weave**.

wrap [ræp] *vt* **1** *(cover)* envolver. **2** *fig (surround, immerse)* envolver (in, de), rodear (in, de).
◆ **to wrap up** *vi* **1** *(wear warm clothes)* abrigarse. **2** *(shut up)* callarse, cerrar el pico.
▸ *vt sep (complete)* conseguir; *(conclude)* concluir, dar fin a.
ⓘ *pt & pp* wrapped, *ger* wrapping.

wrapper [ˈræpə*r*] *n (of food)* envoltorio, envoltura; *(of book)* sobrecubierta.

wrapping [ˈræpɪŋ] *n* envoltura, en-voltorio. [COMP] **wrapping paper 1** *(plain)* papel *m* de envolver. **2** *(fancy)* papel *m* de regalo.

wrath [rɒθ] *n* cólera, ira.

wreak [riːk] *vt* causar, provocar, sem-brar. [COMP] **to wreak damage/havoc o**n STH hacer estragos en ALGO.

wreath [riːθ] *n (of flowers)* corona.

wreck [rek] *n* **1** MAR *(action)* naufragio; *(ship)* barco naufragado o hundido. **2** *(of car, plane)* restos *mpl*; *(of building)* rui-nas *fpl*, escombros *mpl*. **3** *fig (person)* ruina.
▸ *vt* **1** MAR *(ship)* hacer naufragar. **2** *(car, plane)* destrozar; *(machine)* desbaratar, estropear. **3** *fig (health, career)* arruinar; *(life, marriage)* destrozar; *(hopes)* destruir, echar por tierra; *(plans)* estropear, des-baratar; *(chances)* echar a perder.

wreckage ['rekɪdʒ] *n* **1** *(of vehicle)* restos *mpl*; *(of building)* ruinas *fpl*, escombros *mpl*. **2** *fig* ruina.

wrecked [rekt] *adj* **1** MAR *(ship)* naufragado,-a; *(sailor)* náufrago,-a. **2** *(car, plane)* destrozado,-a; *(building)* destruido,-a.
▶ *n fig (life, career, hopes)* arruinado,-a, destrozado,-a; *(plans)* estropeado,-a.
▶ *adj fam fig (stoned)* ciego,-a, colocado,-a, pasado,-a.

wrench [rentʃ] *n* **1** *(pull)* tirón *m*, arranque *m*. **2** MED torcedura. **3** *fig* separación *f* dolorosa. **4** GB *(tool)* llave *f* inglesa. **5** US *(tool)* llave *f*.
ⓘ *pl* wrenches.
▶ *vt* **1** *(pull)* arrancar (de un tirón), arrebatar. **2** MED torcer.

wrestle ['resəl] *vi* **1** *(fight)* luchar (with, con/contra). **2** *fig (problem, conscience)* luchar (with, con), lidiar (with, con).
▶ *vt* luchar contra.
▶ *n* lucha.

wrestler ['resələr] *n* SP luchador,-ra.

wrestling ['reslɪŋ] *n* lucha.

wretch [retʃ] *n* **1** *(unfortunate person)* desdichado,-a, infeliz, desgraciado,-a. **2** *fam (rascal)* pillo,-a, pícaro,-a, granuja *mf*. **3** *(bad person)* canalla *mf*, malvado,-a.

wriggle ['rɪgəl] *vi* retorcerse, menearse, moverse.
▶ *vt* menear, mover.
▶ *n* meneo.

wriggly ['rɪgəlɪ] *adj* sinuoso,-a.
ⓘ *comp* wrigglier, *superl* wriggliest.

wring [rɪŋ] *vt* **1** *(one's hands)* torcer, retorcer; *(bird's neck)* retorcer. **2** *(clothes)* escurrir (out, -), retorcer (out, -). **3** *fig (heart)* partir. **4** *fig (confession, truth, etc)* sonsacar, arrancar, sacar.
ⓘ *pt & pp* wrung [rʌŋ].
▶ *n (of clothes)*: give it a good wring escúrrelo bien.

wringer ['rɪŋər] *n* escurridor *m*, rodillo.

wrinkle ['rɪŋkəl] *n* arruga.
▶ *vt* arrugar.
▶ *vi* arrugarse.

wrinkled ['rɪŋkld] *adj* arrugado,-a.

wrist [rɪst] *n* **1** ANAT muñeca. **2** *(of clothes)* puño.

wristband ['rɪstbænd] *n* **1** *(of clothes)* puño. **2** *(sweatband)* muñequera.

wristwatch ['rɪstwɒtʃ] *n* reloj *m* de pulsera.
ⓘ *pl* wristwatches.

write [raɪt] *vt (gen)* escribir; *(article)* redactar; *(cheque)* extender.
▶ *vi (gen)* escribir (about, sobre).
◆ **to write back** *vi* contestar (por carta).
◆ **to write down** *vt sep (note)* anotar, apuntar.
ⓘ *pt* wrote [rəʊt], *pp* written ['rɪtən], *ger* writing.

writer ['raɪtər] *n* **1** *(by profession)* escritor,-ra; *(of book, letter)* autor,-ra. **2** *(of handwriting)*: she's a neat writer tiene buena letra.

writhe [raɪð] *vi (physically)* retorcerse, contorsionarse.

writing ['raɪtɪŋ] *n* **1** *(script)* escritura; *(handwriting)* letra. **2** *(written work)* composición *f*, trabajo. **3** *(occupation)* profesión *f* de escritor,-ra, trabajo literario; *(activity)* escribir *m*. LOC in writing por escrito. COMP writing desk escritorio. | writing materials objetos *mpl* de escritorio. | writing paper papel *m* de escribir.
▶ *n pl* writings obra, escritos *mpl*.

written ['rɪtən] *pp* → write.
▶ *adj* escrito,-a. LOC the written word la palabra escrita. COMP written consent consentimiento por escrito. | written exam examen *m* escrito.

wrong [rɒŋ] *adj* **1** *(erroneous)* erróneo,-a, equivocado,-a, incorrecto,-a: a wrong answer una respuesta incorrecta. **2** *(mistaken)* equivocado,-a: we proved him wrong demostramos que estaba equivocado. **3** *(evil, immoral)* malo,-a; *(unacceptable, unfair)* injusto,-a: stealing is wrong robar es malo. **4** *(amiss)* mal: is anything wrong? ¿pasa algo? **5** *(unsuitable)* inadecuado,-a, impropio,-a; *(time)* inoportuno,-a: she's the wrong person for the job no es la persona adecuada para el puesto; I think I said the wrong thing creo que he dicho algo que no debía; *he was in the wrong place at the wrong time* estaba en el sitio equivocado en el momento inoportuno. `LOC` **to be in the wrong 1** *(mistaken)* estar equivocado,-a. **2** *(at fault)* tener la culpa. **I to be wrong** *(person)* estar equivocado,-a, no tener razón, equivocarse. **I to have/get the wrong number** *(tel)* confundirse de número, equivocarse de número. **I to get sb wrong** malinterpretar a ALGN. **I to get sth wrong** equivocarse, no acertar. **I to go wrong 1** *(things in general)* salir mal. **2** *(make a mistake)* equivocarse. **3** *(go wrong way)* equivo-carse de camino. *(machine, device)* romperse, estropearse. *(plan)* fallar, fracasar. **I wrong side out** al revés. **I you can't go wrong** *(giving directions)* no tiene pérdida.

▸ *adv* mal, incorrectamente, equivo-cadamente.

▸ *n* **1** *(evil, bad action)* mal *m*. **2** *(injustice)* injusticia; *(offence)* agravio.

▸ *vt* *(treat unfairly)* ser injusto,-a con; *(judge unfairly)* juzgar mal; *(offend)* agra-viar.

wrote [rəut] *pt* → write.

wrung [rʌŋ] *pt & pp* → wring.

wry [raɪ] *adj* irónico,-a, sardónico,-a.

X, x [eks] *n (the letter)* X, x *f.*
xenon [ˈzenɒn] *n* xenón *m.*
xenophobia [zenəˈfəʊbɪə] *n* xenofobia.
xenophobic [zenˈfəʊbɪk] *adj* xenófobo,-a.
xerography [zɪˈrɒgrəfɪ] *n* xerografía.
Xerox® [ˈzɪərɒks] *n* xerocopia, fotocopia.

▶ *vt* xerocopiar, fotocopiar.
X-ray [ˈeksreɪ] *n* **1** rayo X. **2** *(photograph)* radiografía.

▶ *vt* radiografiar.
xylene [ˈzaɪliʌn] *n* xileno.
xylography [zaɪˈlɒgrəfɪ] *n* xilografía.
xylophone [ˈzaɪləfəʊn] *n* xilófono.

Y

Y, y [waɪ] *n (the letter)* Y, y *f.*

yacht [jɒt] *n* **1** yate *m.* **2** *(with sails)* velero, yate *m.* [COMP] **yacht club** club *m* náutico. **I yacht race** regata.

yachting ['jɒtɪŋ] *n* deporte *m* de la vela, vela.

yak [jæk] *n* yac *m*, yak *m.*

yank [jæŋk] *n fam* tirón *m.*
▶ *vt fam* tirar de.
◆ **to yank out** *vt sep* arrancar, sacar de un tirón.

yard [jɑːd] *n* **1** *(measure)* yarda. **2** GB *(of house)* patio. **3** US *(of house)* jardín *m.* **4** *(industrial)* almacén *m.* **5** *(naut)* verga.
[COMP] **Scotland Yard** *oficina central de la policía británica en Londres.*

✎ Una yarda equivale a 0,914 metros.

yarn [jɑːn] *n* **1** hilo. **2** *(story)* cuento.
[COMP] **to spin a yarn 1** *(story)* contar un cuento. **2** *(lie)* venir con cuentos.

yawn [jɔːn] *vi* **1** bostezar. **2** *(gap, etc)* abrirse.
▶ *n* **1** bostezo. **2** *fam (boring event)* rollo.

year [jɪəʳ] *n* **1** año. **2** EDUC curso. [LOC] **all the year round** durante todo el año. **I year in, year out** año tras año.

yearbook ['jɪəbʊk] *n* anuario.

yearly ['jɪəlɪ] *adj* anual.
▶ *adv* anualmente.

yearn [jɜːn] *vi (desire)* anhelar (for, -), ansiar (for, -); *(nostalgically)* añorar. [LOC] **to yearn to do** STH suspirar por hacer ALGO.

yearning ['jɜːnɪŋ] *n (desire)* anhelo (for, de); *(nostalgia)* añoranza (for, de).
▶ *adj* anhelante.

yeast [jiːst] *n* levadura.

yell [jel] *n* grito, alarido.
▶ *vi* gritar, dar alaridos.

yellow ['jeləʊ] *adj* **1** amarillo,-a. **2** *(cowardly)* cobarde.
▶ *n* amarillo.
▶ *vt* ponerse amarillo.
▶ *vi* amarillear. [COMP] **yellow card** *(sp)* tarjeta amarilla. **I yellow fever** fiebre *f* amarilla. **I yellow jersey** *(sp)* maillot *m* amarillo. **I Yellow Pages** páginas amarillas. **I yellow press** prensa sensacionalista.

yelp [jelp] *n* gañido.
▶ *vi* gañir.

Yemen ['jemən] *n* Yemen.

Yemeni ['jemənɪ] *adj* yemení.
▶ *n* yemení *mf.*

yeoman ['jəʊmən] *n* HIST pequeño terrateniente *m.* [COMP] **yeoman of the guard** alabardero de la Torre de Londres.

yes [jes] *adv* **1** sí. **2** *(answering person)* dime; *(answering phone)* ¿dígame?
▶ *n* sí *m.* [LOC] **to say yes** decir que sí.

yesterday ['jestədɪ] *adv* ayer.
▶ *n* ayer *m.* [LOC] **the day before yesterday** anteayer.

yesteryear ['jestəjɪəʳ] *adv lit* antaño.

yet [jet] *adv* **1** todavía, aún. **2** *(until now)* hasta la fecha, hasta ahora. **3** *(even)* aún, todavía. **4** *(expressing future possibility, hope, etc)* aún: *don't give up, you may win yet* no te rindas, aún puedes ganar.
[COMP] **yet again** otra vez. **I yet another…** otro,-a… más: *yet another gold medal for Broddle* otra medalla de oro más para Broddle.
▶ *conj* pero, aunque: *a cheap yet effective solution to the problem* una solución barata pero efectiva para el problema.

yew [juː] *n* tejo.

yield [jiːld] *n* **1** *(harvest)* cosecha. **2** FIN *(return)* rendimiento, rédito.

▶ *vt* **1** *(produce)* producir, dar. **2** *(give, hand over)* entregar. **3** FIN rendir.

▶ *vi* **1** *(surrender)* rendirse (to, ante), ceder (to, a). **2** *(break)* ceder. **3** US ceder el paso.

◆ **to yield up** *vt sep (secrets)* revelar.

yoghourt ['jɒgət] *n* → yoghurt.

yoghurt ['jɒgət] *n* yogur *m*. COMP yoghurt maker yogurtera.

yogurt ['jɒgət] *n* → yoghurt.

yoke [jəʊk] *n* **1** *(for carrying, pulling)* yugo. **2** *(pair of oxen)* yunta. **3** SEW canesú *m*.

▶ *vt* **1** *(oxen)* uncir. **2** *fig* unir.

yolk [jəʊk] *n* yema.

you [juː] *pron* **1** *(subject, familiar, singular)* tú: *and what did you say?* y tú, ¿qué dijiste? **2** *(subject, familiar, plural - men)* vosotros; *(- women)* vosotras: *you two, where are you going?* vosotros dos, ¿adónde vais? **3** *(subject, polite, singular)* usted, Vd., Ud.: *you must wait here until the doctor arrives* usted debe esperar aquí hasta que llegue el médico. **4** *(subject, polite, plural)* ustedes, Vds., Uds.: *you must both wait here* ustedes dos deben esperar aquí. **5** *(subject, impersonal)* se, uno: *you can go by coach or train* se puede ir en tren o en autocar. **6** *(object, familiar, singular)* te; *(with prep)* ti; *(if prep is* con*)* contigo: *I'm going with you* voy contigo. **7** *(object, familiar, plural)* os; *(with preposition)* vosotros,-as: *I'll go with you* iré con vosotros. **8** *(direct object, polite, singular - man)* lo, le; *(- woman)* la; *(with preposition)* usted: *good morning, sir, can I help you?* buenos días, señor, ¿puedo ayudarlo? **9** *(direct object, polite, plural - men)* los; *(- women)* las; *(with preposition)* ustedes: *I wanted to talk to you two ladies* quería hablar con ustedes dos. **10** *(indirect object, polite, singular)* le: *I'll send you a letter* le mandaré una carta. **11** *(indirect object, polite, plural)* les: *I sent both of you a card* les mandé una felicitación a los dos. **12** *(object, impersonal)*: *cyanide kills you* el cianuro mata.

young [jʌŋ] *adj (gen)* joven; *(brother, sister)* menor. LOC **to be young at heart** ser joven de espíritu. COMP **young lady 1** *(woman)* señorita. **2** *(girlfriend)* novia. ▌ **young man 1** *(man)* joven *m*, muchacho. **2** *(boyfriend)* novio. ▌ **young woman** joven *f*, muchacha.

▶ *n* **the young** *(humans)* los jóvenes *mpl*, la juventud *f*, la gente *f* joven; *(animals)* las crías *fpl*.

youngish ['jʌŋɪʃ] *adj* bastante joven, juvenil.

youngster ['jʌŋstəʳ] *n* joven *mf*.

your [jɔːʳ] *adj* **1** *(familiar, singular)* tu, tus; *(plural)* vuestro,-a, vuestros,-as. **2** *(polite)* su, sus. **3** *fml (address)* Su: *Your Majesty* Su Majestad.

yours [jɔːz] *pron* **1** *(familiar, singular)* (el) tuyo, (la) tuya, (los) tuyos, (las) tuyas; *(plural)* (el) vuestro, (la) vuestra, (los) vuestros, (las) vuestras. **2** *(polite)* (el) suyo, (la) suya, (los) suyos, (las) suyas. **3** *(letters)* le saluda…: *Yours sincerely...* le saluda atentamente…

yourself [jɔːˈself] *pron* **1** *(familiar singular)* te; *(emphatic)* tú mismo,-a. **2** *(polite singular)* se; *(emphatic)* usted mismo,-a.

yourselves [jɔːˈselvz] *pron* **1** *(familiar plural)* os; *(emphatic)* vosotros,-as mismos,-as. **2** *(polite plural)* se; *(emphatic)* ustedes mismos,-as.

youth [juːθ] *n* **1** *(period)* juventud *f*. **2** *(young person)* joven *mf*. **3** *(young people)* juventud *f*, los jóvenes *mpl*. COMP **youth club** club *m* juvenil. ▌ **youth hostel** albergue *m* juvenil.

youthful ['juːθfʊl] *adj* joven, juvenil.

yowl [jaʊl] *n* aullido.

▶ *vi* aullar.

yucca ['jʌkə] *n* yuca.

Yugoslav ['juːgəslɑːv] *n (person)* yugoslavo,-a.

Yugoslavia [juːgəˈslɑːvɪə] *n* Yugoslavia.

Yugoslavian [juːgəˈslɑːvɪən] *adj* yugoslavo,-a.

▶ *n* yugoslavo,-a.

yuppie ['jʌpɪ] *n* yuppie *mf*.

Z

Z, z [zed] *n (the letter)* Z, z *f.*
Zaire [zɑːˈɪə] *n* Zaire.
Zairean [zɑːˈɪrɪən] *adj* zaireño,-a.
▸ *n* zaireño,-a.
Zambia [ˈzæmbɪə] *n* Zambia.
Zambian [ˈzæmbɪən] *adj* zambiano,-a.
▸ *n* zambiano,-a.
zap [zæp] *vt* **1** *fam (kill)* cargarse. **2** *(attack)* atacar.
▸ *vi (hurry)* apresurarse.
ⓘ *pt & pp* **zapped**, *ger* **zapping**.
▸ *n* marcha.
zeal [ziːl] *n* celo, entusiasmo.
zebra [ˈziːbrə, ˈzebrə] *n* cebra. [COMP] **zebra crossing** paso de peatones, paso de cebra.
zebu [ˈziːbuː, ˈziːbjuː] *n* cebú *m.*
zed [zed] *n* GB zeta.
zee [ziː] *n* US zeta.
zenith [ˈzenɪθ] *n* cenit *m.*
zephyr [ˈzefər] *n* céfiro *m.*
zeppelin [ˈzepəlɪn] *n* zepelín *m.*
zero [ˈzɪərəʊ] *n* cero.
ⓘ *pl* **zeros** o **zeroes**.
zest [zest] *n* **1** *(eagerness)* brío, entusiasmo. **2** *(spice)* emoción *f.* **3** *(of lemon, etc)* cáscara.
zigzag [ˈzɪɡzæɡ] *n* zigzag *m.*
▸ *vi* zigzaguear.
ⓘ *pt & pp* **zigzagged**, *ger* **zigzagging**.

Zimbabwe [zɪmˈbɑːbweɪ] *n* Zimbabwe.
Zimbabwean [zɪmˈbɑːbwɪən] *adj* zimbabwense, zimbabuo,-a.
▸ *n* zimbabwense *mf*, zimbabuo,-a.
zinc [zɪŋk] *n* cinc *m*, zinc *m.*
zip [zɪp] *n* **1** cremallera. **2** *fam (energy)* vigor *m*, energía. **3** *fam (hiss)* zumbido.
▸ *vt* COMPUT comprimir. [COMP] **zip code** US código postal. ‖ **zip fastener** cremallera.
◆ **to zip by** *vt insep* pasar como un rayo.
▸ *vi* pasar como un rayo.
◆ **to zip past** *vt-vi* → **zip by.**
◆ **to zip up** *vt sep* cerrar con cremallera.
zipped [zɪpt] *adj* COMPUT comprimido,-a.
zipper [ˈzɪpər] *n* US cremallera.
zodiac [ˈzəʊdɪæk] *n* zodiaco, zodíaco.
zombie [ˈzɒmbɪ] *n* zombi *mf*, zombie *mf.*
zonal [ˈzəʊnəl] *adj* zonal.
zone [zəʊn] *n* zona.
▸ *vt* dividir en zonas.
zoo [zuː] *n* zoo *m*, parque *m* zoológico, zoológico.
ⓘ *pl* **zoos.**
zoological [zuːəˈlɒdʒɪkəl] *adj* zoológico,-a.
zoologist [zuˈɒlədʒɪst] *n* zoólogo,-a.
zoology [zuˈɒlədʒɪ] *n* zoología.
zucchini [zuːˈkiːnɪ] *n* US calabacín *m.*
ⓘ *pl* **zucchini** o **zucchinis.**
zygote [ˈzaɪɡəʊt] *n* cigoto.

LEARNING IN SPANISH

LA COMUNICACIÓN EN CLASE

- ¡Buenos días a todos!
- ¿Cómo estáis esta mañana?
- ¿Qué quiere decir...?
- ¿Cómo se pronuncia esta palabra?
- ¿Podrías repetir eso, por favor?
- ¿Podría hablar más despacio?
- Lo siento, no lo entiendo

COMMUNICATION IN CLASS

- Good morning everybody!
- How are you this morning?
- What does... mean?
- How do you pronounce this word?
- Could you repeat that, please?
- Could you speak more slowly?
- Sorry, I don't understand

PASANDO LISTA

- Voy a pasar lista
- ¿Dónde está Pedro? Hoy no ha venido...
- Kevin no ha venido porque está enfermo
- Marta no está porque ha ido al médico

TAKING THE ROLL

- I'm going to take the roll
- Where's Peter? —He's not here today...
- Kevin isn't here because he's ill
- Marta is absent because she's gone to the doctor's

Vocabulario / Vocabulary

lista de alumnos de clase	roll	silla	chair
		limpiar	clean
		borrar	rub off
tiempo climatológico	weather	leer	read
caliente	hot	responder	answer
frío	cold	repartir	hand out
estufa	heater	sacar	take out
aparato de aire acondicionado	air conditioner	encender	switch on
		apagar	switch off
		abrir	open
pizarra	blackboard	cerrar	close

Preguntando sobre cosas que se hacen en clase

► ¿Podrías limpiar la pizarra?

► ¿Podrías borrar esas frases?

► Por favor, levantad esas sillas

Requesting actions in class

► Would you clean the blackboard?

► Could you erase those sentences?

► Please, lift those chairs up

Organizar la clase

► Sacad los libros de matemáticas, por favor

► ¿Podrías repartir estas hojas, por favor?

► Colocaos en grupos de 2,3,4...

► Voy a dividir la clase en dos grupos

Organizing the class

► Take your math books out, please

► Could you hand out these papers, please?

► Put yourselves into groups of 2,3,4...

► I'm going to divide the class in two groups

Poner deberes

► En casa, leed este fragmento

► Revisad estos ejercicios

► Completad las siguientes actividades...

Assigning homework

► Read this passage at home

► Go over these exercises

► Complete the following activities...

Hablar sobre la lección

► En unos minutos vamos a practicar...

► Al final de la clase vamos a leer una historia

► María, por favor, ¿podrías responder a esta pregunta?

► ¿Podrías traerme los diccionarios?

► ¿Podrías pasarme la goma?

Talking about the lesson

► In a few minutes we're going to practice...

► At the end of the class we're going to read a story

► Mary, please, could you answer this question?

► Could you bring me the dictionaries?

► Could you pass me the eraser?

Vocabulario / Vocabulary

papel de lija	sandpaper
papel higiénico	toilet paper
papel de periódico	newspaper
papel de colores	colored paper
papel charol	glazed paper
maqueta	model
retrato	portrait
dibujo	drawing
contorno	outline
esquema	diagram
fondo	background
paisaje	landscape

Diseños / Patterns

tela vaquera	denim
liso	plain
a rayas	striped
a cuadros	checked
de lunares	spotted

Texturas / Textures

liso	smooth
rugoso	rough
suave	soft
áspero	coarse
duro	hard

marquetería
marquetry

tejer
knitting

cerámica
pottery

bordado
embroidery

costura
sewing

collage
collage

mosaicos
mosaics

decoración de huevos
egg decorating

encuadernado
de libros
bookbinding

construcción
de collares
beadwork

diseño de postales
cardmaking

FRASES COMUNICATIVAS EN CLASE DE MANUALIDADES

COMMUNICATIVE SENTENCES IN THE ARTS & CRAFTS CLASS

- ► Vete a buscar las ceras, por favor
- ► Fetch the crayons, please

- ► Que los responsables repartan los pinceles, por favor
- ► Students in charge, please, hand out the brushes

- ► ¡Arreglad ese desorden!
- ► Tidy up that mess!

- ► ¿Puedo sacar punta a los lápices de colores?
- ► May I sharpen the crayons?

- ► Hoy vamos a hacer dos talleres en clase
- ► Today we are going to do two workshops in class

- ► Traed toallas para secar la mesa
- ► Fetch some towels to dry the table

- ► Calcad la plantilla en la cartulina
- ► Trace round the template onto the card

- ► Colgad esos dibujos para que se sequen
- ► Hang up those printings to dry them

- ► Este pegamento se seca enseguida
- ► This glue sets right away

- ► Lavaos las manos antes de salir de clase
- ► Wash your hands before leaving the class

Verbos en la clase de manualidades			
pegar	stick	cortar	cut out
calcar	trace	doblar	fold
sombrear	shade	difuminar	diffuse
mirar	look	acabar	finish
dibujar	draw	crear	create
colorear	color	pulir	polish
seguir	follow	pintar	paint
completar	complete	hacer punto	knit
comenzar de nuevo	start over	bordar	embroider
		coser	sew

FRASES COMUNICATIVAS EN CLASE DE MATEMÁTICAS

- ►¿Puedes resolver esta multiplicación?
  - 7 × 3 = (siete por tres igual a ____)
- ►Dime el resultado de esta suma
- ►¿Cuál es el dividendo de esta división?
  - ¿y el resto?
- ►¿Cuántas caras tiene un hexágono?
- ►Dibuja una línea recta
- ►Coge una regla y comprueba esta medida
- ►¿Cómo se leen estos números?
  - 6.5 seis coma cinco
  - 1 $^2/_3$ uno y dos tercios
  - 8^2 ocho al cuadrado
  - 5^3 cinco al cubo
  - 3^4 tres elevado a cuatro

COMMUNICATIVE SENTENCES IN THE MATH CLASS

- ► Can you solve this multiplication?
  - 7 × 3 = (seven times three equals _____)
- ► Tell me the answer to this sum
- ► What is the dividend of this division?
  - and the remainder?
- ► How many sides does a hexagon have?
- ► Draw a straight line
- ► Take a ruler and check this measurement
- ► How do you read these numbers?
  - six point five
  - one and two thirds
  - eight squared
  - five cubed
  - three to the power of four

Vocabulario / Vocabulary

operación	operation
resultado	result
problema	problem
conmutativa	commutative
asociativa	associative
distributiva	distributive
resto	remainder
divisor	divisor
cociente	quotient

Don't forget

In English we use a comma (,) to separate thousands, but in Spanish we use a period (.):

1.532.620   **1,532,620**

However, the Spanish use a comma to separate decimals, not a period, like we do:

23,45   **23.45**

+	más plus	$7 + 2 = 9$	**suma** / addition
−	menos minus	$7 - 2 = 5$	**resta** / subtraction
X	multiplicado por multiplied by	$7 \times 2 = 14$	**multiplicación** / multiplication
/	dividido entre divided by	$7/2 = 3,5$	**división** / division

=	es igual a is equal to	**≠**	no es igual a is not equal to
1/2	fracción fraction	**3.5**	parte decimal decimal part
()	paréntesis parenthesis	**√**	raíz cuadrada de square root of
%	porcentaje percentage	**∅**	conjunto vacío empty set
>	es mayor que is greater than	**≥**	es igual o mayor que is equal to or greater than
<	es menor que is less than	**≤**	es igual o menor que is equal to or less than
∈	pertenece a belongs to	**π**	pi pi

Números / Numbers

1	uno	one	21	veintiuno	twenty-one
2	dos	two	22	veintidós	twenty-two
3	tres	three	30	treinta	thirty
4	cuatro	four	31	treinta y uno	thirty-one
5	cinco	five	40	cuarenta	forty
6	seis	six	50	cincuenta	fifty
7	siete	seven	60	sesenta	sixty
8	ocho	eight	70	setenta	seventy
9	nueve	nine	80	ochenta	eighty
10	diez	ten	90	noventa	ninety
11	once	eleven	100	cien	one hundred
12	doce	twelve	101	ciento uno	one hundred one
13	trece	thirteen			
14	catorce	fourteen	200	doscientos	two hundred
15	quince	fifteen	300	trescientos	three hundred
16	dieciséis	sixteen			
17	diecisiete	seventeen	1.000	mil	one thousand
18	dieciocho	eighteen			
19	diecinueve	nineteen	1.000.000	un millón	one million
20	veinte	twenty			

Ordinales / Ordinal numbers

primero	first	undécimo	eleventh
segundo	second	duodécimo	twelfth
tercero	third	decimotercero	thirteenth
cuarto	fourth	decimocuarto	fourteenth
quinto	fifth	decimoquinto	fifteenth
sexto	sixth	vigésimo	twentieth
séptimo	seventh	vigésimo primero	twenty-first
octavo	eighth		
noveno	ninth	trigésimo	thirtieth
décimo	tenth	centésimo	hundredth

1.345.36**5**	unidad unit	**1/2**	medio a half
1.345.3**6**5	decenas tens	**1/3**	un tercio a third
1.345.**3**65	centenas hundreds	**1/4**	un cuarto a quarter
1.34**5**.365	millares thousands		
1.345.365	millones millions	**3/4**	tres cuartos three quarters

Medidas de longitud / Linear measures

1 milímetro	1 millimeter	= 0.04 inches
1 centímetro	1 centimeter	= 0.39 inches
1 metro	1 meter	= 1.09 yards
1 kilómetro	1 kilometer	= 1,093.61 yards / 0.62 miles

Medidas de capacidad / Measures of capacity

1 mililitro	1 mililiter	= 0.002 pints
1 centilitro	1 centiliter	= 0.02 pints
un litro	1 liter	= 2.113 pints

Pesos / Weights

1 gramo	1 gram	= 0,035 ounces
1 kilo	1 kilogram	= 2.204 pounds
1 tonelada	1 ton	= 2204 pounds

FRASES COMUNICATIVAS EN FÚTBOL Y BALONCESTO

- ► Venga, hagamos diez flexiones
- ► Botad el balón
- ► Haz una finta y lanza el balón
- ► Penalización por más de 3 segundos
- ► Parad el partido
- ► Id a la línea de tiros libres
- ► Bloquead el tiro
- ► ¡Pasos!
- ► Dobles
- ► Id al punto de penalty
- ► Id a la línea de banda
- ► Id a la línea de fondo
- ► Pasad el balón
- ► Coged el rebote
- ► Salto entre dos
- ► Detén el balón en la línea de medio campo

COMMUNICATIVE SENTENCES IN SOCCER AND BASKETBALL

- ► Come on! Let's do ten push-ups
- ► Bounce the ball
- ► Fake and shoot the ball
- ► Three-second violation
- ► Stop the game
- ► Go to the free-throw line
- ► Block the shot
- ► Traveling!
- ► Double dribble
- ► Go to the penalty spot
- ► Go to the side line
- ► Go to the end line
- ► Pass the ball
- ► Get the rebound
- ► Jump ball
- ► Stop the ball at the midfield line

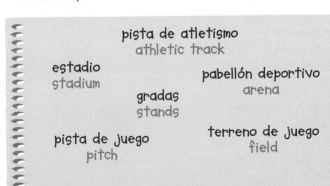

pista de atletismo
athletic track

estadio
stadium

pabellón deportivo
arena

gradas
stands

pista de juego
pitch

terreno de juego
field

Verbos en la clase de educación física

caminar	walk	usar	blow a
hacer footing	jog	el silbato	whistle
nadar	swim	arrodillarse	kneel
bucear	dive	hacer una finta	fake
saltar	jump	hacer	do push-ups
placar	tackle	flexiones	
patinar	skate	hacer el pino	do a
esquiar	ski		handstand
hacer esquí acuático	water-ski	botar	bounce
apuntar	aim	lanzar	throw
correr	run	coger	catch
golpear	punch	balancearse	swing
pedalear	cycle	escalar	climb
montar	ride	hacer estiramientos	stretch
chutar	hit (the ball)	flexionar hacia delante	bend over
chutar	kick		
saltar a la comba	jump rope	flexionar hacia atrás	bend backwards
caer	fall		

cuerda
rope

balón
ball

colchoneta
mat

palo de hockey
hockey stick

raqueta
racket

potro
vaulting-horse

silbato
whistle

bate
bat

FRASES COMUNICATIVAS

COMMUNICATIVE SENTENCES

- ► ¡Mirad, está lloviendo a cántaros!
- ► Look, it's pouring down rain!

- ► Ayer un rayo cayó en la antena
- ► Yesterday, lightning struck the antenna

- ► Vamos a mirar la estación meteorológica y comprobar la humedad
- ► Let's look at the weather station and check the humidity

- ► ¡Estamos a dos grados bajo cero!
- ► It's two degrees below zero!

- ► Hala! ¡Acaba de salir un arco iris!
- ► Wow, a rainbow has just appeared!

- ► Se aproxima un frente frío
- ► A cold front is approaching

Estaciones / Seasons	
primavera	spring
verano	summer
otoño	fall
invierno	winter

Temperatura / Temperature	
cálido	hot
templado	warm
fresco	cool
frío	cold
helado	freezing

Vocabulario / Vocabulary			
soleado	sunny	atardecer	dusk
lluvioso	rainy	nubes	clouds
nevado	snowy	nieve	snow
ventoso	windy	lluvia	rain
nebuloso	foggy	granizo	hail
nublado	cloudy	niebla	fog
tormentoso	stormy	trueno	thunder
amanecer	dawn	arco iris	rainbow

FRASES COMUNICATIVAS EN EL LABORATORIO

COMMUNICATIVE SENTENCES AT THE LAB

- ► Examinad ese insecto con el microscopio
- ► Look at that insect under the microscope

- ► Ajustad el objetivo si está borroso
- ► Adjust the lens if it's blurred

- ► Tened mucho cuidado con esas probetas
- ► Be very careful with those test tubes

- ► Colocad bien los taburetes
- ► Put those stools back properly

- ► No os llevéis las batas a casa
- ► Don't take the lab coats home

- ► Conectad esos electrodos
- ► Connect those electrodes

El microscopio / The microscope

prismáticos binoculares	prismatic binoculars
rueda de enfoque	focusing wheel
lente convexa	convex lens
lente cóncava	concave lens

Vocabulario / Vocabulary

probeta	test tube	alambre	wire
llama	flame	electrodo	electrode
frasco	flask	imán	magnet
embudo	funnel	espátula	spatula
filtro de papel	filter paper	pipeta	pipette
pinzas	tongs	peso	weight
lupa	magnifying glass	batería	battery
		temporizador	timer
jeringuilla	syringe	microscopio	microscope
termómetro	thermometer	ocular	eyepiece
gasa	gauze	transparencia	slide
trípode	tripod	báscula	balance/ scales
bata de laboratorio	lab coat	objetivo	objective lens

La cara / The face

ojo	eye
nariz	nose
oreja	ear
boca	mouth
mejilla	cheek
barbilla	chin
frente	forehead
mandíbula	jaw
bigote	mustache
barba	beard
diente	tooth
labio	lip
lengua	tongue

El ojo / The eye

globo ocular	eyeball
ceja	eyebrow
párpado	eyelid
pestaña	eyelash
pupila	pupil
iris	iris

Los órganos / The organs

cerebro	brain
tráquea	windpipe
intestino	bowel
vejiga	bladder

Peinados / Hairstyles

rubio	blonde/fair	calvo	bald
moreno	dark	entradas	receding hairline
gris, canoso	gray		
liso	straight	trenzas	plaits
rizado	curly	coleta	ponytail
ondulado	wavy	flequillo	bangs
en punta	spiky		
a la altura de los hombros	shoulder-length		
		perilla	goatee
largo	long	barba de 3 días	stubble
corto	short		

FRASES COMUNICATIVAS

► ¿Cuántos huesos crees que tiene el cuerpo humano?

► ¿Eres miope/hipermétrope?

► ¿Te han operado alguna vez?

COMMUNICATIVE SENTENCES

► How many bones do you think the human body has?

► Are you near–/far–sighted?

► Have you ever had surgery?

FRASES COMUNICATIVAS EN CLASE DE INFORMÁTICA

COMMUNICATIVE SENTENCES IN THE COMPUTER SCIENCE CLASS

- ▸ Imprimid los textos después de corregirlos
- ▸ Print the texts after you've corrected them

- ▸ Encended los monitores
- ▸ Switch the monitors on

- ▸ Id a la carpeta 'Mis documentos' y abridla
- ▸ Go to the 'My documents' folder and open it

- ▸ Preparad una breve presentación visual
- ▸ Prepare a short visual presentation

- ▸ Ahora no hay conexión a Internet
- ▸ There's no Internet connection available now

Partes de un e-mail / Parts of an email

correo basura	spam
tema	subject
herramientas	tools
borrador	draft
archivo	file
adjuntar	attach
guardar	save
eliminar	delete
enviar	send
archivo adjunto	attachment
libreta de direcciones	address book

Vocabulario / Vocabulary

dominio	domain	palanca de mando	joystick
enlace	link		
contraseña	password	impresora de inyección	inkjet printer
motor de búsqueda	search engine		
		impresora láser	laser printer
descarga	download	cartucho	cartridge

Meses / Months

enero	January
febrero	February
marzo	March
abril	April
mayo	May
junio	June
julio	July
agosto	August
septiembre	September
octubre	October
noviembre	November
diciembre	December

Días / Days

lunes	Monday
martes	Tuesday
miércoles	Wednesday
jueves	Thursday
viernes	Friday
sábado	Saturday
domingo	Sunday

Don't forget

In Spanish, never write days and months with a capital letter.

FRASES COMUNICATIVAS

▶ ¿Qué fecha es hoy?

▶ El año 2013 no es un año bisiesto

▶ ¿Qué día de la semana es el 13?

▶ El último fin de semana de marzo iremos de excursión

▶ Nos quedan 10 minutos

▶ Tenemos que cambiar las pilas al reloj de pared

▶ ¿Qué hora es?

COMMUNICATIVE SENTENCES

▶ What's today's date?

▶ The year 2013 is not a leap year

▶ What day of the week is the 13th?

▶ We're going on a field trip on the last weekend in March

▶ We have 10 minutes left

▶ We need to replace the batteries in the clock

▶ What's the time? / What time is it?

Vocabulario / Vocabulary

reloj de pulsera	watch	agujas del reloj	the hands of a clock
reloj de pared	clock	calendario	calendar
		año bisiesto	leap year

**son las nueve
en punto**
it's nine o'clock

son las 9 y cinco
it's five past nine

son las 9 y diez
it's ten past nine

son las nueve y cuarto
it's a quarter past nine

**son las nueve
y media**
it's half past nine

**son las diez
menos veinte**
it's twenty to ten

**son las diez
menos cuarto**
it's a quarter to ten

**son las diez
menos diez**
it's ten to ten

09:15 **son las nueve
y quince**
it's nine fifteen

09:10 **son las nueve y diez**
it's nine ten

09:30 **son las nueve treinta**
it's nine thirty

son las nueve y cuarenta
it's nine forty **09:40**

Carta informal / Informal letter

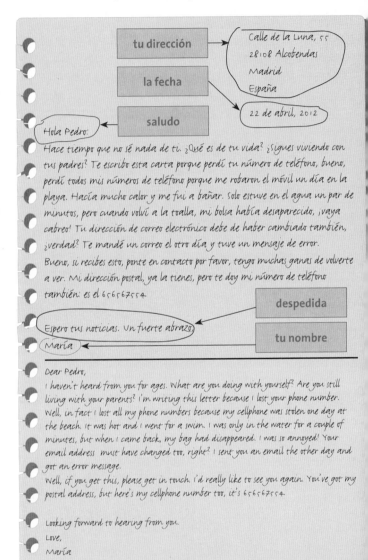

tu dirección → Calle de la Luna, 55
28108 Alcobendas
Madrid
España

la fecha → 22 de abril, 2012

saludo → Hola Pedro:

Hace tiempo que no sé nada de ti. ¿Qué es de tu vida? ¿Sigues viviendo con tus padres? Te escribo esta carta porque perdí tu número de teléfono, bueno, perdí todos mis números de teléfono porque me robaron el móvil un día en la playa. Hacía mucho calor y me fui a bañar. Solo estuve en el agua un par de minutos, pero cuando volví a la toalla, mi bolsa había desaparecido, ¡vaya cabreo! Tu dirección de correo electrónico debe de haber cambiado también, ¿verdad? Te mandé un correo el otro día y tuve un mensaje de error.

Bueno, si recibes esto, ponte en contacto por favor, tengo muchas ganas de volverte a ver. Mi dirección postal, ya la tienes, pero te doy mi número de teléfono también: es el 65656 7554

despedida

Espero tus noticias. Un fuerte abrazo,

tu nombre

María

Dear Pedro,

I haven't heard from you for ages. What are you doing with yourself? Are you still living with your parents? I'm writing this letter because I lost your phone number. Well, in fact I lost all my phone numbers because my cellphone was stolen one day at the beach. It was hot and I went for a swim. I was only in the water for a couple of minutes, but when I came back, my bag had disappeared. I was so annoyed! Your email address must have changed too, right? I sent you an email the other day and got an error message.

Well, if you get this, please get in touch. I'd really like to see you again. You've got my postal address, but here's my cellphone number too, it's 65656 7554.

Looking forward to hearing from you.

Love,

María

Frases útiles en cartas y correos electrónicos / Useful phrases in letters and emails

SALUDOS FORMALES

- Estimado Sr. García
- Apreciada Sra. Gutiérrez
- Muy Sr mío / Muy Sra. mía
- Muy Sres. míos

FORMAL GREETINGS

- Dear Mr. García
- Dear Mrs Gutiérrez
- Dear Sir / Dear Madam
- Dear Sirs

SALUDOS INFORMALES

- Querida Paloma
- Hola Felipe

INFORMAL GREETINGS

- Dear Paloma
- Hi Felipe, Dear Felipe

DESPEDIDAS FORMALES

- Le agradezco de antemano su atención
- Le saluda atentamente
- Reciba un cordial saludo
- Quedo a la espera de recibir sus noticias

FORMAL CLOSING PHRASES

- I thank you in advance for your attention
- Yours faithfully, Yours sincerely
- Yours faithfully, Yours sincerely
- I look forward to hearing from you.

DESPEDIDAS INFORMALES

- Saludos cordiales
- Un saludo / Saludos
- Un abrazo
- Hasta pronto

INFORMAL CLOSING PHRASES

- Kind regards
- Yours / Yours
- Best wishes
- See you soon

DESPEDIDAS ENTRE AMIGOS Y FAMILIARES

- Con cariño / Con amor
- Un (fuerte) abrazo
- Un beso / Besos
- Un besazo / Un besote

CLOSING PHRASES FOR FRIENDS AND FAMILY

- Yours affectionately / Love
- Best wishes / Love
- Love / Lots of love
- Love / Lots of love

OTRAS EXPRESIONES

- Me dirijo a Usted ...
- Dale recuerdos a ...
- Saludos a ...
- María te manda recuerdos

OTHER EXPRESSIONS

- I am writing to you ...
- Give my greetings to ...
- Give my love to ...
- María sends her greetings/love

AL TELÉFONO

- ► ¿Puedo hablar con Juan? / ¿Está Juan?
- ► ¿Podría dejarle un mensaje, por favor?
- ► ¿De parte de quién?
- ► Hola, soy Belén
- ► Un momento, por favor
- ► Ahora no está
- ► Te has equivocado de número
- ► ¿Puede deletrear su nombre?
- ► Está comunicando / Comunica
- ► No hay línea
- ► Mi dirección de correo electrónico es I, N, F, O, 'arroba', A, B, C, 'punto' E, S

ON THE PHONE

- ► Can I speak to John, please? / Is John there, please?
- ► Could I leave a message for him, please?
- ► Who's calling?
- ► Hello, it's Belén speaking
- ► Hold on, please
- ► He/she's not in at the moment
- ► Wrong number / You've dialled the wrong number
- ► Could you spell your name?
- ► The line's engaged / The line's busy
- ► There's no tone
- ► My email address is info@abc.es

SMS / SMS		
xa	para	for
xo	pero	but
xq, xk	porque	because
ad+	además	what's more / also
nls	no lo sé	I don't know
tkm	te quiero mucho	I love you a lot
a2	adiós	bye
salu2	saludos	regards
tvl	te veo luego	see you later

PRONUNCIACIÓN / PRONUNCIATION

In general, Spanish words are pronounced as they are written,
there is a closer correspondence between the pronunciation
and the written word than there is in English. So, if you learn
a few easy rules, you will be able to pronounce Spanish correctly
when you read it.

Of course, people from different countries have different
pronunciations, but the differences do not usually prevent
understanding. Here we give you both European and Latin American
Spanish, although the main differences in pronunciation,
as opposed to accent, are confined to the letters **c** and **z**.

VOCALES / VOWELS

Spanish has 5 pure vowels:

a   **casa** – similar to the *a* in *father*, but shorter
e   **Pepe** – similar to the *e* in *went*, but a little longer
i   similar to *ee* in *feel*, but a little shorter
o   similar to the *o* in British English *lost*
u   similar to *oo* in *root*

DIPTONGOS / DIPHTHONGS

ai   like the *y* in *pylon*.
au   like *ow* in *cow*.
ei   like *ay* in *day*.
eu   this does now exist in English, it is similar to a combination
     of *e* as in *get* and *w* as in *wet*.
oi /oy   like *oy* in *boy*.
ui /uy   like *wee* in *sweet*.
uo   similar to *wo* in *woke*.

CONSONANTES / CONSONANTS

b, v   these are pronounced exactly the same, but they do have
     two pronunciations:
     – at the start of a sentence and after **m**, like the *b* in *bubble*
     – in other positions, the lips vibrate, but do not close
       entirely. It's like an English *v*, but with the top and
       bottom lips instead of the top teeth and bottom lips.
c   – before **a**, **o** and **u**, like the *c* in *cat*.
     – before **e** and **i**, like *th* in *thin* [in American Spanish like
       s in *sister*]
d   – at the start of a sentence, and after **l**, like *d* in *dad*.
     – in all other positions, like *th* in *this*.

f	as in English.
g	– before **a**, **o** and **u**, like *g* in *gang*.
	– before **e** and **i**, like Scottish *ch* as in *loch*.
	– remember that in the combinations **gue** and **gui**, the **u** is not pronounced unless it is written with a diaresis (**ü**), so in **guerra**, the first syllable **gue** is pronounced like *ge* in *get*, and in **guitarra**, **gui** is pronounced like *gi* in *give*.
h	always silent.
j	like Scottish *ch* as in *loch*.
k	as in English.
l	as in English.
ll	like *lli* as in *billion* [in some pronunciations, like *y* in *yes*].
m	as in English.
n	as in English.
ñ	like *ny* as in *canyon*.
p	as in English.
qu	like *c* in *cat*
r	a single tap of the tongue behind the teeth.
rr	a strongly trilled *r*, as in Scottish pronunciation.
s	as in English.
t	as in English.
w	this only occurs in foreign words, it is pronounced like *b* and *v* (see above).
z	like *th* in *thin* [in American Spanish like *s* in *sister*].

Acentuación / Accentuation

To pronounce Spanish properly, you also need to know which syllable to stress, a change in stress can sometimes change the meaning of a word! Here are the basic rules:
 – words ending in a consonant except **–n** or **–s** are stressed on the last syllable: comer (to eat), ciudad (city), continental (continental).
 – words ending in a vowel or **–n** or **–s** are stressed on the next to last syllable: comen (they eat), ciudades (cities), terraza (terrace), jarabe (syrup).

All words which are exceptions to these two rules have a written accent over the stressed vowel; the accent shows you where the stress falls, it does not change the quality of the vowel: árbol (tree), águila (eagle), acabé (I finished), jamón (ham).

Spanish verbs are conjugated in three moods: the indicative, the subjunctive and the imperative. In the indicative and subjunctive there are simple tenses and compound tenses. Compound tenses for all verbs are formed with the auxiliary verb *haber*, which accompanies the invariable participle of the verb to be conjugated.

The following table shows the conjugation of compound tenses, which is, as stated above, the same for all verbs, the only difference being the participle which follows the auxiliary. Following on from that come the simple tenses; firstly the three regular conjugations and then the models for the conjugation of the irregular verbs.

Tiempos compuestos / Compound Tenses

AMAR / TEMER / PARTIR					
indicative			**subjunctive**		
Present Perfect	he	amado / temido / partido	Present Perfect	haya	amado / temido / partido
	has	amado / temido / partido		hayas	amado / temido / partido
	ha	amado / temido / partido		haya	amado / temido / partido
	hemos	amado / temido / partido		hayamos	amado / temido / partido
	habéis	amado /temido / partido		hayáis	amado / temido / partido
	han	amado / temido / partido		hayan	amado / temido / partido
Pluperfect	había	amado / temido / partido	Pluperfect	hubiera o hubiese	amado / temido / partido
	habías	amado / temido / partido		hubieras o hubieses	amado / temido / partido
	había	amado / temido / partido		hubiera o hubiese	amado / temido / partido
	habíamos	amado / temido / partido		hubiéramos o hubiésemos	amado / temido / partido
	habíais	amado / temido / partido		hubierais o hubieseis	amado / temido / partido
	habían	amado / temido / partido		hubieran o hubiesen	amado / temido / partido
Past Anterior	hube	amado / temido / partido			
	hubiste	amado / temido / partido			
	hubo	amado / temido / partido			
	hubimos	amado / temido / partido			
	hubisteis	amado / temido / partido			
	hubieron	amado / temido / partido			
Future Perfect	habré	amado / temido / partido	Future Perfect	hubiere	amado / temido / partido
	habrás	amado / temido / partido		hubieres	amado / temido / partido
	habrá	amado / temido / partido		hubiere	amado / temido / partido
	habremos	amado / temido / partido		hubiéremos	amado / temido / partido
	habréis	amado / temido / partido		hubiereis	amado / temido / partido
	habrán	amado / temido / partido		hubieren	amado / temido / partido
Future Perfect	habría	amado / temido / partido			
	habrías	amado / temido / partido			
	habría	amado / temido / partido			
	habríamos	amado / temido / partido			
	habríais	amado / temido / partido			
	habría	amado / temido / partido			

Tiempos simples / Simple Tenses

Modelos de conjugación de los verbos regulares / Models for the Conjugation of Regular Verbs

-AR VERB AMAR			
indicative		**subjunctive**	
Present	am–o	**Present**	am–e
	am–as / (vos) am–ás		am–es
	am–a		am–e
	am–amos		am–emos
	am–áis		am–éis
	am–an		am–en
Imperfect	am–aba	**Imperfect**	am–ara o am–ase
	am–abas		am–aras o am–ases
	am–aba		am–ara o am–ase
	am–ábamos		am–áramos o am–ásemos
	am–abais		am–arais o am–aseis
	am–aban		am–aran o am–asen
Preterite	am–é	**Future**	am–are
	am–aste		am–ares
	am–ó		am–are
	am–amos		am–áremos
	am–asteis		am–aréis
	am–aron		am–aren
Future	am–aré		
	am–arás		
	am–ará		
	am–aremos		
	am–aréis		
	am–arán		
Conditional	am–aría		
	am–arías		
	am–aría		
	am–aríamos		
	am–aríais		
	am–arían		
imperative		**non–personal forms**	
Imperativo	am–a (tú)	**Infinitve**	am–ar
	am–e (él/Vd.)		
	am–emos (nos.)	**Gerund**	am–ando
	am–ad (vos.)		
	am–en (ellos/Vds.)	**Past participle**	am–ado

-ER VERB TEMER

	indicative		subjunctive
Present	tem-o	**Present**	tem-a
	tem-es / (vos) tem-és		tem-as
	tem-e		tem-a
	tem-emos		tem-amos
	tem-éis		tem-áis
	tem-en		tem-an
Imperfect	tem-ía	**Imperfect**	tem-iera *o* tem-iese
	tem-ías		tem-ieras *o* tem-ieses
	tem-ía		tem-iera *o* tem-iese
	tem-íamos		tem-iéramos *o* tem-iésemos
	tem-íais		tem-ierais *o* tem-ieseis
	tem-ían		tem-ieran *o* tem-iesen
Preterite	tem-í	**Future**	tem-iere
	tem-iste		tem-ieres
	tem-ió		tem-iere
	tem-imos		tem-iéremos
	tem-isteis		tem-iereis
	tem-ieron		tem-ieren
Future	tem-eré		
	tem-erás		
	tem-erá		
	tem-eremos		
	tem-eréis		
	tem-erán		
Conditional	tem-ería		
	tem-erías		
	tem-ería		
	tem-eríamos		
	tem-eríais		
	tem-erían		

	imperative		non-personal forms
Imperativo	tem-e (tú)	**Infinitve**	tem-er
	tem-a (él/Vd.)		
	tem-amos (nos.)	**Gerund**	tem-iendo
	tem-ed (vos.)		
	tem-an (ellos/Vds.)	**Past participle**	tem-ido

-IR VERB PARTIR			
indicative		**subjunctive**	
Present	part–o	**Present**	part–a
	part–es / (vos)part–ís		part–as
	part–e		part–a
	part–imos		part–amos
	part–ís		part–áis
	part–en		part–an
Imperfect	part–ía	**Imperfect**	part–iera o part–iese
	part–ías		part–ieras o part–ieses
	part–ía		part–iera o part–iese
	part–íamos		part–iéramos o part–iésemos
	part–íais		part–ierais o part–ieseis
	part–ían		part–ieran o part–iesen
Preterite	part–í	**Future**	part–iere
	part–iste		part–ieres
	part–ió		part–iere
	part–imos		part–iéremos
	part–isteis		part–iereis
	part–ieron		part–ieren
Future	part–iré		
	part–irás		
	part–irá		
	part–iremos		
	part–iréis		
	part–irán		
Conditional	part–iría		
	part–irías		
	part–iría		
	part–iríamos		
	part–iríais		
	part–irían		
imperative		**non–personal forms**	
Imperativo	part–e (tú)	**Infinitve**	part–ir
	part–a (él/Vd.)		
	part–amos (nos.)	**Gerund**	part–iendo
	part–id (vos.)		
	part–an (ellos/Vds.)	**Past participle**	part–ido

ESPAÑOL
INGLÉS

A, a *nf (la letra)* A, a.

a *prep* **1** *(dirección)* to, on , in: *girar a la derecha* to turn (to the) right; *irse a casa* to go home; *subir al autobús* to get on the bus; *llegar a Barcelona* to arrive in Barcelona. **2** *(destino)* to, towards. **3** *(distancia)* away: *a diez kilómetros de casa* ten kilometres (away) from home. **4** *(lugar)* at, on: *a la entrada* at the entrance; *a la izquierda* on the left. **5** *(tiempo)* at: *a las once* at eleven; *a tiempo* in time; *al final* in the end. **6** *(modo)* by, in: *a ciegas* blindly; *a oscuras* in the dark. **7** *(instrumento)* by, in: *a mano* by hand; *a pie* on foot. **8** *(precio)* a: *a tres euros el kilo* three euros a kilo. **9** *(medida)* at: *a 90 kilómetros por hora* at 90 kilometres an hour. **10** *(finalidad)* to: *él vino a vernos* he came to see us. **11** *(complemento directo persona)*: *vi a Juanita* I saw Juanita. **12** *(complemento indirecto)* to: *dámelo* give it to me. **13** *verbo + a + inf* to: *aprender a nadar* to learn (how) to swim.

✎ Consulta también al.

ábaco *nm* abacus.

abad *nm* abbot.

abadesa *nf* abbess.

abadía *nf* abbey.

abajo *adv* **1** *(lugar)* below, down: *ahí abajo* down there. **2** *(en una casa)* downstairs. **3** *(dirección)* down, downward: *calle abajo* down the street.
  ▶ *interj* down with!: *¡abajo el dictador!* down with the dictator!

abalanzarse *vpr* **1** *(lanzarse)* to rush forward, spring forward. **2** abalanzarse sobre to rush at; *(león, tigre)* to pounce on; *(águila, etc)* to swoop down on.

abandonado,-a *pp* → abandonar.
  ▶ *adj* **1** abandoned: *un barco abandonado* an abandoned ship. **2** *(descuidado)* neglected: *tiene el despacho abandonado* his office hasn't been looked after. **3** *(desaseado)* untidy, unkempt.

abandonar *vt* **1** *(desamparar)* to abandon, forsake: *la suerte le ha abandonado* luck has forsaken him. **2** *(lugar)* to leave, quit: *abandonar el barco* to abandon ship. **3** *(descuidar)* to neglect. **4** DEP *(retirarse)* to withdraw from.
  ▶ *vpr* abandonarse to neglect OS.

abanicar *vt* to fan.

abanico *nm* **1** fan. **2** *fig* range: *un abanico de posibilidades* a range of possibilities.

abaratar *vt* to reduce the price of, make cheaper.
  ▶ *vpr* abaratarse *(precio)* to come down; *(artículo)* to become cheaper.

abarcar *vt* **1** *(englobar)* to cover, embrace: *sus conocimientos abarcan el campo de la psicología* her knowledge covers the field of psychology. **2** *(abrazar)* to embrace.

abarrotado,-a *adj* packed (de, with).

abastecer *vt* to supply, provide.

abastecimiento *nm* supplying.

abasto LOC dar abasto *fam* to be sufficient for: *no doy abasto para corregir tantos ejercicios* I've got so many exercises to correct that I just can't cope.

abatible *adj* folding, collapsible: *asiento abatible* folding seat.

abatido,-a *pp* → abatir.
  ▶ *adj (deprimido)* dejected, depressed.

abatir *vt* **1** *(derribar)* to knock down, pull down. **2** *(matar)* to kill; *(herir)* to wound. **3** *(bajar)* to lower, take down.

abdicar *vt & vi* to abdicate, renounce.

abdomen *nm* abdomen.

abdominal *adj* abdominal.
► *nm pl* **abdominales** *(ejercicios)* sit-ups.

abductor *adj* abductor.

abecedario *nm* alphabet.

abedul *nm* birch tree, birch.

abeja *nf* bee. COMP **abeja obrera** worker bee. ‖ **abeja reina** queen bee.

abejorro *nm* bumblebee.

abertura *nf* **1** *(agujero)* opening, gap; *(grieta)* crack, slit. **2** *(en óptica)* aperture.

abeto *nm* fir tree, fir.

abierto,-a *pp* → abrir.
► *adj* **1** open, unlocked. **2** *(grifo)* (turned) on: *dejó el grifo abierto* she left the tap running. **3** *fig (sincero)* open, frank. **4** *(tolerante)* open-minded.

abisal *adj* abyssal.

abismo *nm* abyss.

ablación *nf* ablation.

ablandar *vt* **1** to soften. **2** *fig (persona)* to soothe, soften up, appease.
► *vpr* **ablandarse** to soften, get softer.

ablativo *nm* ablative (case).

abofetear *vt* to slap.

abogacía *nf* legal profession.

abogado,-a *nm & nf* lawyer, solicitor; *(tribunal supremo)* barrister. COMP **abogado de oficio** legal-aid lawyer. ‖ **abogado defensor** counsel for the defence. ‖ **abogado del diablo** devil's advocate.

abolición *nf* abolition.

abolir *vt* to abolish.

abolladura *nf (hundimiento)* dent; *(bollo)* bump.

abollar *vt* to dent.

abominable *adj* abominable, loathsome.

abonado,-a *pp* → abonar.
► *adj* **1** *(tierra)* fertilized. **2** FIN paid.
► *nm & nf (al teléfono, a revista)* subscriber; *(a teatro, tren, etc)* season ticket holder.

abonar *vt* **1** FIN to pay. **2** *(tierra)* to fertilize. **3** *(subscribir)* to subscribe.
► *vpr* **abonarse** *(a una revista)* to subscribe (a, to); *(al teatro, tren, etc)* to buy a season ticket (a, for).

abono *nm* **1** *(pago)* payment. **2** *(fertilizante)* fertilizer; *(acción)* fertilizing. **3** *(a revista)* subscription; *(a teatro, tren, etc)* season-ticket.

abordaje *nm* boarding. LOC ¡al abordaje! stand by to board!

abordar *vt* **1** MAR *(chocar)* to run foul of, collide with; *(atacar)* to board. **2** *fig (persona)* to approach; *(asunto, tema)* to tackle.

aborigen *adj* aboriginal, native.
► *nm* aborigine, native.

aborrecer *vt* **1** to abhor, hate, detest. **2** *(aves)* to abandon.

abortar *vi (voluntariamente)* to abort, have an abortion; *(involuntariamente)* to miscarry, have a miscarriage.
► *vt (interrumpir)* to stop; *(frustrar)* to foil, thwart.

aborto *nm* **1** *(provocado)* abortion; *(espontáneo)* miscarriage. **2** *pey (persona)* ugly person, freak; *(cosa)* abortion.

abotonar *vt (ropa)* to button, button up.
► *vpr* **abotonarse** to do one's buttons up.

abovedado,-a *adj* vaulted, arched.

abrasador,-ra *adj* burning, scorching.

abrasar *vt (quemar)* to burn, scorch.
► *vi* to burn (up): *esta sopa abrasa* this soup is scalding hot.
► *vpr* **abrasarse** to burn. LOC **abrasarse de calor** *fig* to be sweltering.

abrazadera *nf* clamp, brace.

abrazar *vt* to embrace, hug.

abrazo *nm* hug, embrace. LOC **dar un abrazo a** ALGN to embrace SB. ‖ **un abrazo (de)** *(en carta)* with best wishes from.

abrebotellas *nm inv* bottle opener.

abrecartas *nm inv* letter-opener, paper knife.

abrelatas *nm inv* tin-opener, US can-opener.

abrevadero *nm* drinking trough.

abreviar *vt* **1** *(acortar)* to shorten, cut short. **2** *(texto)* to abridge; *(palabra)* to abbreviate.

abreviatura *nf* abbreviation.

abridor *nm* opener.

abrigar *vt* **1** *(contra el frío)* to wrap up; *(ropa)* to be warm. **2** *(proteger)* to shelter, protect. **3** *fig (sospechas)* to harbour (US harbor), have.

▶ *vpr* **abrigarse** *(uso reflexivo)* to wrap os up.

abrigo *nm* **1** *(prenda)* coat, overcoat. **2** *(refugio)* shelter. LOC **ropa de abrigo** warm clothing, warm clothes *pl*.

abril *nm* April.

✎ Para ejemplos de uso, consulta marzo.

abrillantador *nm* polish.

abrillantar *vt* to polish, make shine, burnish.

abrir *vt* **1** *(gen)* to open. **2** *(cremallera)* to undo: *abrió la cremallera de la maleta* she undid the zip on the case, she unzipped the case. **3** *(luz)* to switch on, turn on; *(gas, grifo)* to turn on.

▶ *vpr* **abrirse 1** *(gen)* to open. **2** *(dar)* to open (a, onto), look (a, onto): *la casa se abre al mar* the house looks onto the sea. **3** *fig (sincerarse)* to open out. **4** *argot (largarse)* to clear off, be off. LOC **abrir fuego** MIL to open fire. ∎ **abrir paso** to make way. ∎ **en un abrir y cerrar de ojos** *fam* in the twinkling of an eye.

abrochar *vt* **1** *(camisa)* to button (up); *(zapato)* to tie up. **2** *(botones)* to do up; *(broche, corchete)* to fasten: *abróchense los cinturones* please fasten your seat belts.

absceso *nm* abscess.

abscisa *nf* abscissa.

ábside *nm* apse.

absolución *nf* **1** REL absolution. **2** JUR acquittal.

absolutismo *nm* absolutism.

absoluto,-a *adj* absolute. LOC **en absoluto** not at all, by no means. ∎ **nada en absoluto** nothing at all.

absolver *vt* **1** REL to absolve. **2** JUR to acquit.

absorbente *adj* **1** absorbent. **2** *fig (trabajo)* absorbing; *(exigente)* demanding. **3** *fig (persona)* overbearing.

▶ *nm* absorbent.

absorber *vt* to absorb, soak up.

absorción *nf* absorption.

absorto,-a *adj* **1** *(pasmado)* amazed. **2** *(ensimismado)* absorbed (en, in).

abstemio,-a *adj* abstemious, teetotal.

▶ *nm & nf* teetotaller.

abstención *nf* abstention.

abstenerse *vpr* to abstain (de, from), refrain (de, from).

abstinencia *nf* abstinence. COMP **síndrome de abstinencia** withdrawal symptoms *pl*.

abstracción *nf* abstraction.

abstracto,-a *adj* abstract.

absurdo,-a *adj* absurd.

abuchear *vt* to boo, jeer at.

abuela *nf* grandmother; *(familiarmente)* grandma, granny.

abuelo *nm* grandfather; *(familiarmente)* granddad, grandpa.

▶ *nm pl* **abuelos** grandparents.

abundancia *nf* abundance, plenty.

abundante *adj* abundant, plentiful.

abundar *vi* to abound, be plentiful.

aburrido,-a *pp* → aburrir.

▶ *adj* **1** *(con ser)* boring, tedious. **2** *(con estar)* bored, weary; *(cansado)* tired of; *(harto)* fed up with.

aburrimiento *nm* boredom.

aburrir *vt* **1** to bore. **2** *(cansar)* to tire.

▶ *vpr* **aburrirse** to get bored (con/de/ por, with).

abusar *vi* **1** *(propasarse)* to go too far, abuse (de, -): *abusar de algn* to take unfair advantage of sb. **2** *(usar mal)* to misuse (de, -): *abusar de la comida* to eat too much.

abusivo,-a *adj* excessive, exorbitant.

abuso *nm* **1** abuse, misuse. **2** *(injusticia)* injustice.

a.C. *abrev* (antes de Cristo) before Christ; *(abreviatura)* BC.

acá *adv* **1** *(lugar)* here, over here. **2** *(tiempo)* now, at this time. LOC **de acá para allá** to and fro, up and down.

acabado,-a *pp* → acabar.

▶ *adj* **1** *(terminado)* finished; *(perfecto)* perfect, complete: *acabado,-a de hacer* freshly made. **2** *fig (malparado)* worn-out, spent: *una persona acabada* a has-been; *un actor acabado* a burnt-out actor.

▶ *nm* **acabado** finish.

acabar *vt* **1** *(gen)* to finish; *(completar)* to complete. **2** *(consumir)* to use up.

► *vi* **1** *(gen)* to finish, end; *acaba en punta* it has a pointed end. **2 acabar por +** *gerundio* to end up + *-ing*: *acabé por comprar el vestido* I ended up buying the dress.
► *vpr* **acabarse** to end, finish, come to an end; *(no quedar)* to run out. LOC **acabar bien** to have a happy ending. ‖ **acabar con 1** *(destruir)* to destroy, put an end to. **2** *(terminar)* to finish, finish off. ‖ **acabar de +** *inf* to have just + *pp*: *no lo toques, acabo de pintarlo ahora mismo* don't touch it, I've just painted it. ‖ **acabar mal 1** *(cosa)* to end badly. **2** *(persona)* to come to a bad end. ‖ **¡se acabó!** that's it!

academia *nf* **1** *(institución)* academy. **2** *(escuela)* school, academy.

acalorado,-a *adj* **1** hot; *(cara)* flushed. **2** *fig* *(persona)* excited, worked up; *(debate)* heated, angry.

acampada *nf* camping.

acampar *vt & vi* to camp.

acantilado *nm* cliff.

acaparar *vt* **1** *(productos)* to hoard; *(mercado)* to corner, buy up. **2** *(monopolizar)* to monopolize, keep for os.

acariciar *vt* **1** to caress, fondle. **2** *(pelo, animal)* to stroke. **3** *fig* *(esperanzas, etc)* to cherish; *(idea, plan)* to have in mind.

ácaro *nm* mite.

acarrear *vt* **1** *(transportar)* to carry, transport. **2** *fig* *(producir)* to cause, bring, give rise to.

acaso *adv* perhaps, maybe: *acaso esté enfermo* maybe he's ill. LOC **por si acaso** just in case.

acatar *vt* **1** *(leyes, etc)* to obey, observe, comply with. **2** *(respetar)* to respect.

acatarrarse *vpr* to catch a cold.

acceder *vi* **1** *(consentir)* to consent (a, to), agree (a, to). **2** *(tener entrada)* to enter. **3** *(alcanzar)* to accede (a, to).

accesible *adj* accessible; *(persona)* approachable.

acceso *nm* **1** *(entrada)* access, entry. **2** *(de tos)* fit; *(de fiebre)* attack, bout. **3** INFORM access: *acceso aleatorio* random access.

accidental *adj* accidental: *no fue más que un encuentro accidental* it was nothing but a chance meeting.

accidente *nm* **1** accident: *sufrir un accidente* to have an accident. **2** *(terreno)* unevenness, irregularity. LOC **por accidente** by chance. COMP **accidente de trabajo** industrial accident. ‖ **accidente de tráfico** road accident. ‖ **accidentes geográficos** geographical features.

acción *nf* **1** action; *(acto)* act, deed. **2** COM share. **3** TEAT plot. LOC **entrar en acción** MIL to go into action. ‖ **ponerse en acción** to start doing sth. COMP **película de acción** adventure film.

accionar *vt* *(máquina)* to drive, work, activate.

accionista *nm o nf* shareholder, stockholder.

acechar *vt* **1** *(vigilar)* to watch, spy on; *(esperar)* to lie in wait for. **2** *(caza)* to stalk.

acecho LOC **estar al acecho de 1** *(vigilar)* to be on the lookout for. **2** *(esperar)* to lie in wait for.

aceite *nm* oil. COMP **aceite de girasol** sunflower oil. ‖ **aceite de maíz** corn oil. ‖ **aceite de oliva** olive oil. ‖ **aceite de ricino** castor oil.

aceitera *nf* **1** oil bottle. **2** AUTO oil can.
► *nf pl* **aceiteras** oil and vinegar set *sing*, cruet *sing*.

aceituna *nf* olive.

aceleración *nf* acceleration. COMP **poder de aceleración** AUTO acceleration.

acelerador,-ra *adj* accelerating.
► *nm* **acelerador** AUTO accelerator.

acelerar *vt* **1** to accelerate; *(paso)* to quicken. **2** *fig* to speed up.

acelga *nf* chard.

acento *nm* **1** *(tilde)* accent (mark). **2** *(tónico)* stress. **3** *(pronunciación)* accent: *acento andaluz* Andalusian accent. **4** *(énfasis)* emphasis, stress. COMP **acento ortográfico** written accent, accent.

acentuación *nf* accentuation.

acentuar *vt* **1** *(tilde)* to accentuate; *(tónico)* to stress. **2** *(resaltar)* to emphasize, stress.

▶ *vpr* **acentuarse** to become more pronounced, become more marked.

acepción *nf* meaning, sense.

aceptable *adj* acceptable.

aceptación *nf* **1** acceptance. **2** *(aprobación)* approval; *(éxito)* success: *la película tuvo poca aceptación* the film wasn't popular, the film met with little success.

aceptar *vt* **1** to accept, receive. **2** *(aprobar)* to approve of.

acequia *nf* irrigation channel, ditch.

acera *nf* pavement, US sidewalk.

acerca de *adv* about, concerning, on.

acercar *vt* to bring near, bring nearer, draw up: *acércate* come closer; *¿me acercas el agua?* can you pass the water?
▶ *vpr* **acercarse 1** *(aproximarse)* to be near: *se acerca el verano* summer is near. **2** *(ir)* to go: *acércate a la esquina* go to the corner. **3** *(visitar)* to drop in, drop by.

acero *nm* steel. COMP **acero inoxidable** stainless steel.

acertado,-a *pp* → acertar.
▶ *adj* **1** *(opinión, etc)* right, correct; *(comentario)* fitting; *(idea, decisión)* clever; *(palabra)* exact. **2** *(conveniente)* suitable. LOC **estar acertado,-a** to be wise.

acertante *nm o nf* winner.

acertar *vt* **1** *(en un objetivo)* to hit. **2** *(dar con lo cierto)* to get right: *solo acertó cinco preguntas* she only got five questions right. **3** *(por azar)* to guess correctly; *(concurso, quinielas)* to win.
▶ *vi* to get right, be right.

acertijo *nm* riddle.

acético,-a *adj* acetic.

acetileno *nm* acetylene.

achacar *vt* to impute, attribute.

achaque *nm* ailment, complaint.

achatado,-a *adj* flattened.

achicar *vt* **1** *(hacerse más pequeño)* to diminish, reduce, make smaller. **2** *(agua)* to drain; *(en barco)* to bale out.
▶ *vpr* **achicarse 1** *(amenguarse)* to get smaller. **2** *(amilanarse)* to lose heart.

achicharrar *vt* to scorch; *(comida)* to burn.
▶ *vpr* **achicharrarse** to roast.

achicoria *nf* chicory.

achuchar *vt* **1** *(azuzar)* to nag at. **2** *(abrazar)* to hug, squeeze: *había una pareja achuchándose en el rincón* there was a couple having a cuddle in the corner. **3** *(empujar)* to shove.

achuchón *nm* **1** *fam (empujón)* push, shove. **2** *fam (indisposición)* ailment: *le dio un achuchón* he had a funny turn. **3** *fam (abrazo)* hug, squeeze.

acicalarse *vpr* to dress up, smarten up.

acicate *nm* spur.

acidez *nf* **1** *(sabor)* sourness, sharpness. **2** QUÍM acidity. COMP **acidez de estómago** heartburn.

ácido,-a *adj* **1** *(sabor)* sharp, tart. **2** QUÍM acidic. **3** *(tono)* harsh.
▶ *nm* **ácido** QUÍM acid. COMP **ácido sulfúrico** sulphuric acid. ❙ **ácido úrico** uric acid.

acierto *nm* **1** *(adivinación)* correct guess, right answer. **2** *(buena idea)* good choice/idea.

aclamar *vt* to acclaim.

aclaración *nf* explanation.

aclarar *vt* **1** *(cabello, color)* to lighten, make lighter. **2** *(líquido)* to thin (down). **3** *(enjuagar)* to rinse. **4** *(explicar)* to explain.
▶ *vi (mejorar el tiempo)* to clear (up).
▶ *vpr* **aclararse 1** *(entender)* to understand: *no me aclaro con esta lección* I can't understand this lesson. **2** *(decidirse)* to make up one's mind.

aclimatación *nf* acclimatization, US acclimation.

aclimatarse *vpr* to become acclimatized (a, to), become US acclimated (a, to).

acné *nf* acne.

acobardarse *vpr* to become frightened, lose one's nerve, shrink back (ante, from).

acogedor,-ra *adj* **1** *(persona)* welcoming, friendly. **2** *(lugar)* cosy, warm.

acoger *vt (recibir)* to receive; *(a invitado)* to welcome.

acogida *nf* **1** reception, welcome. **2** *(aceptación)* popularity. LOC **tener buena acogida** to be welcomed.

acometer *vt* **1** *(embestir)* to attack. **2** *(emprender)* to undertake.

acometida *nf* **1** *(ataque)* attack, assault. **2** *(derivación)* connection.

acomodado,-a *adj* *(rico)* well-to-do, well off.

acomodador,-ra *nm & nf* *(hombre)* usher; *(mujer)* usherette.

acompañamiento *nm* **1** accompaniment. **2** *(guarnición de plato)* accompaniment to a main dish, side dish. **3** MÚS accompaniment.

acompañante *nm o nf* **1** companion, escort. **2** MÚS accompanist.

acompañar *vt* **1** to accompany, go with: *te acompaño a la puerta* I'll see you to the door; *nos acompañó al cine* she came with us to the cinema. **2** *(adjuntar)* to enclose, attach. **3** MÚS to accompany. LOC **acompañar en el sentimiento** *fml* to express one's condolences to.

acondicionado,-a *pp* → acondicionar.
▶ *adj* equipped, fitted-out.

acondicionador *nm* conditioner. COMP **acondicionador de aire** air conditioner. ‖ **acondicionador del cabello** hair conditioner.

acondicionar *vt* **1** to fit up, set up. **2** *(mejorar)* to improve.

aconsejable *adj* advisable.

aconsejar *vt* to advise.

acontecimiento *nm* event, happening.

acopio LOC **hacer acopio de** to store up.

acoplamiento *nm* **1** fitting, adaptation. **2** *(de naves espaciales)* docking.

acoplar *vt* **1** *(juntar)* to fit (together), join, adjust. **2** TÉC to couple, connect.
▶ *vpr* **acoplarse 1** to fit, join. **2** *(naves espaciales)* to dock.

acorazado,-a *adj* armoured (US armored), armour-plated (US armor-plated).
▶ *nm* **acorazado** battleship.

acordar *vt* **1** to agree. **2** *(decidir)* to decide.
▶ *vpr* **acordarse** to remember (de, -): *no se acuerda de nada* she can't remember anything.

acorde *adj* in agreement, agreed.
▶ *nm* MÚS chord.

acordeón *nm* accordion.

acorralar *vt* to corner.

acortar *vt & vi* to shorten, make shorter.

acosar *vt* to pursue, chase.

acoso *nm* **1** pursuit, chase. **2** *fig* hounding. COMP **acoso sexual** sexual harassment.

acostarse *vpr* **1** *(estirarse)* to lie down. **2** *(irse a dormir)* to go to bed: *es hora de acostarse* it's bedtime. LOC **acostarse con** *fam* to sleep with, go to bed with.

acostumbrado,-a *pp* → acostumbrar.
▶ *adj* **1** *(persona)* accustomed (a, to), used (a, to). **2** *(hecho)* usual, customary: *es lo acostumbrado* it is the custom.

acostumbrar *vt* **1** *(habituar)* to accustom to. **2** *(soler)* to be in the habit of.
▶ *vpr* **acostumbrarse** *(habituarse)* to become accustomed (a, to), get used (a, to).

acre *nm* *(medida)* acre.

acreditado,-a *adj* **1** *(prestigioso)* reputable, well-known, prestigious. **2** *(representante, embajador)* accredited.

acreedor,-ra *adj* deserving: *ser/hacerse acreedor a* to be worthy of.
▶ *nm & nf* FIN creditor.

acribillar *vt* to riddle, pepper.

acrílico,-a *adj* acrylic.

acrobacia *nf* acrobatics.

acróbata *nm o nf* acrobat.

acta *nf* **1** *(relación)* minutes *pl*, record (of proceedings); *(publicación)* transactions *pl*. **2** *(certificado)* certificate, official document. LOC **levantar acta** to draw up the minutes. COMP **acta notarial** affidavit.

actinia *nf* sea anemone.

actitud *nf* *(disposición)* attitude; *(postura)* position.

activar *vt* **1** TÉC to activate. **2** INFORM to enable. **3** *fig* *(avivar)* to liven up, quicken.

actividad *nf* activity.

activo,-a *adj* active: *estar en activo* to be on active service.
▶ *nm* **activo** FIN asset, assets *pl*.

acto *nm* **1** act, action. **2** *(ceremonia)* ceremony. **3** TEAT act. LOC **en el acto** at once.

actor *nm* actor.

actriz *nf* actress.

actuación *nf* **1** *(en cine, teatro)* performance. **2** *(intervención)* intervention, action.

actual *adj* **1** present, current: *dadas las circunstancias actuales* under the present circumstances. **2** *(actualizado)* up-to-date: *tiene un diseño muy actual* it has a very up-to-date design.

actualidad *nf* **1** present (time). **2** *(hechos)* current affairs *pl*; *(estado)* the current state of things: *este programa te da toda la actualidad cinematográfica* this programme gives you all the latest cinema news. LOC **en la actualidad** at present.

actualizar *vt* **1** *(poner al día)* to bring up to date, update. **2** *(filosofía)* to actualize.

actualmente *adv* *(hoy en día)* nowadays, these days; *(ahora)* at present, at the moment.

actuar *vi* **1** *(gen)* to act (como/de, as). **2** *(en obra, película)* to perform, act.

acuarela *nf* watercolour (US watercolor).

acuario *nm* aquarium.

Acuario *nm inv* Aquarius.

acuático,-a *adj* aquatic, water.

acudir *vi* **1** *(ir)* to go; *(venir)* to come, arrive. **2** *(presentarse)* to come back.

acueducto *nm* aqueduct.

acuerdo *nm* agreement. LOC **¡de acuerdo!** all right!, O.K.! **‖ de acuerdo con** in accordance with. **‖ estar de acuerdo** to agree (con, with). **‖ llegar a un acuerdo** to come to an agreement. **‖ ponerse de acuerdo** to agree.

acumulación *nf* accumulation.

acumular *vt* to accumulate; *(datos)* to gather; *(dinero)* to amass.

acunar *vt* to rock.

acuñar *vt* **1** *(monedas)* to strike, coin, mint. **2** *(una frase)* to coin.

acupuntura *nf* acupuncture.

acurrucarse *vpr* to curl up, snuggle up.

acusación *nf* **1** accusation. **2** JUR charge.

acusado,-a *pp* → acusar.
  ► *nm & nf* accused, defendant.

acusar *vt* **1** *(echar la culpa)* to accuse (de, of). **2** JUR to charge (de, with). **3** *(manifestar)* to give away.

acusativo *nm* accusative.

acuse COMP acuse de recibo acknowledgement of receipt.

acústica *nf* acoustics.

acutángulo COMP triángulo acutángulo acute triangle.

adaptación *nf* adaptation.

adaptar *vt* **1** *(acomodar)* to adapt. **2** *(ajustar)* to adjust, fit.
  ► *vpr* **adaptarse** *(persona)* to adapt OS (a, to); *(cosa)* to fit, adjust.

adecuado,-a *pp* → adecuar.
  ► *adj* adequate, suitable.

adecuar *vt* to adapt, make suitable.

a. de J.C. *abrev* (antes de Jesucristo) before Christ; *(abreviatura)* BC.

adelantado,-a LOC por adelantado in advance.

adelantamiento *nm* overtaking. LOC hacer un adelantamiento to overtake.

adelantar *vt* **1** to move forward. **2** *(reloj)* to put forward. **3** *(pasar delante)* to pass. **4** AUTO to overtake. **5** *(dinero)* to pay in advance.
  ► *vi (reloj)* to be fast.
  ► *vpr* **adelantarse 1** *(ir delante)* to go ahead. **2** *(llegar temprano)* to be early. **3** *(anticiparse)* to get ahead (a, of). **4** *(reloj)* to gain, be fast.

adelante *adv* forward, further.
  ► *interj* **1** *(pase)* come in! **2** *(siga)* go ahead!, carry on! LOC de aquí en adelante from here on. **‖ en adelante** henceforth. **‖ más adelante 1** *(tiempo)* later on. **2** *(espacio)* further on.

adelanto *nm* **1** *(avance)* advance. **2** *(tiempo)* advance. **3** *(pago)* advance; *(técnicamente)* advance payment.

adelgazar *vt (afinar)* to make slim.
  ► *vi (perder peso)* to slim, lose weight.

ademán *nm (gesto)* gesture.
  ► *nm pl* **ademanes** manners.

además *adv* **1** *(también)* also, as well. **2** *(es más)* furthermore, what is more: *¡y además, el coche es mío!* and what's more, the car's mine! LOC **además de** as well as, in addition to: *además de amable es guapo* as well as being kind, he's handsome.

adenoides *nm* adenoids.

adentro *adv* inside.
▶ *nm pl* **adentros** inward mind *sing*: *para sus adentros* in his heart. LOC **mar adentro** out to sea.

adepto,-a *nm & nf* follower, supporter.

aderezar *vt (condimentar)* to season; *(ensalada)* to dress.

adeudar *vt* **1** *(deber)* to owe, have a debt of. **2** FIN to debit, charge.

adherente *adj* adherent, adhesive.

adherir *vt (pegar)* to stick on.
▶ *vi (pegarse)* to stick (a, to).
▶ *vpr* **adherirse 1** *(pegarse)* to stick (a, to). **2** *fig (unirse)* to adhere to, follow.

adhesivo,-a *adj* adhesive.
▶ *nm* **adhesivo** adhesive.

adición *nf* addition.

adicción *nf* addiction. LOC **crear adicción** to be addictive.

adicional *adj* additional.

adictivo,-a *adj* addictive.

adicto,-a *adj* addicted (a, to).
▶ *nm & nf* **1** *(drogas)* addict. **2** *(partidario)* supporter, follower.

adiestrar *vt* to train, instruct.

adinerado,-a *adj* rich, wealthy.

adiós *interj* **1** *(gen)* goodbye!; *(familiarmente)* bye!, bye-bye! **2** *(al cruzarse con alguien)* hello!
▶ *nm* goodbye.

adiposo,-a *adj* adipose.

aditivo,-a *adj* additive.
▶ *nm* **aditivo** additive.

adivinanza *nf* riddle, puzzle.

adivinar *vt* **1** *(descubrir)* to guess: *le adivinó el pensamiento* she read his mind. **2** *(predecir)* to forecast, foretell. **3** *(enigma)* to solve.

adivino,-a *nm & nf* fortune-teller.

adjetivo,-a *adj* adjective, adjectival.
▶ *nm* **adjetivo** adjective.

adjudicar *vt* **1** *(premio)* to award. **2** *(venta)* to sell, knock down: *¡adjudicado!* sold! **3** *(obras)* to award a contract to.
▶ *vpr* **adjudicarse 1** *(apropiarse)* to appropriate, take over. **2** *(obtener)* to win.

adjunto,-a *adj* **1** *(en carta)* enclosed. **2** *(asistente)* assistant.

administración *nf* **1** *(gen)* administration. **2** *(de medicamento)* administering. COMP **administración de lotería** lottery office. ∎ **administración pública** public administration.

administrador,-ra *nm & nf* **1** administrator. **2** *(manager)* manager. COMP **administrador,-ra de fincas** estate agent. ∎ **administrador de web** webmaster.

administrar *vt* **1** *(bienes, justicia)* to administer. **2** *(dirigir)* to manage, run. **3** *(suministrar)* to give: *le administró una aspirina* she gave him an aspirin.
▶ *vpr* **administrarse** to manage one's own money, manage one's own affairs.

administrativo,-a *adj* administrative.
▶ *nm & nf (funcionario)* official, civil servant; *(de empresa, banco)* office worker.

admirable *adj* admirable.

admiración *nf* **1** admiration. **2** *(signo)* exclamation mark.

admirador,-ra *nm & nf* admirer.

admirar *vt* **1** *(estimar)* to admire. **2** *(sorprender)* to amaze, surprise, astonish.

admisión *nf* **1** admission. **2** *(aceptación)* acceptance. **3** TÉC inlet, intake. LOC «Reservado el derecho de admisión» "The management reserves the right to refuse admission". COMP **plazo de admisión** closing date.

admitir *vt* **1** *(dar entrada)* to admit, let in. **2** *(aceptar)* to accept, admit: *«No se admiten propinas»* "No tipping", "Tipping not allowed". **3** *(permitir)* to allow: *su obra admite varias interpretaciones* his work is open to various interpretations. **4** *(reconocer)* to admit. **5** *(tener capacidad)* to hold.

ADN *abrev* MED (ácido desoxirribonucleico) desoxyribonucleic acid; *(abreviatura)* DNA.

adobar *vt* **1** CULIN to marinate, marinade. **2** *(pieles)* to tan.

adobe *nm* adobe.

adolescencia *nf* adolescence.

adolescente *adj* adolescent.
▶ *nm o nf* adolescent.

adonde *adv* where.

adónde *adv* where.

adopción *nf* adoption.

adoptar *vt* to adopt.

adoptivo,-a *adj* adoptive.

adoquín *nm* cobble, paving stone.

adorable *adj* adorable.

adoración *nf* adoration, worship.

adorar *vt* **1** REL to worship. **2** *fig* to adore.

adormecerse *vpr* to doze off.

adormilarse *vpr* to doze, drowse.

adornar *vt* to adorn, decorate.

adorno *nm* decoration, adornment. LOC **de adorno** decorative.

adosado,-a *adj* semidetached: *casas adosadas* semidetached houses.

adquirir *vt* to acquire; *(comprar)* to buy.

adquisición *nf* acquisition; *(compra)* buy, purchase.

adrede *adv* deliberately, on purpose, purposely.

adrenalina *nf* adrenalin.

aduana *nf* **1** customs *pl*. **2** *(oficinas)* customs building. LOC **pasar (por) la aduana** to go through customs.

aducir *vt* to adduce, allege.

adueñarse *vpr* to take possession (de, of).

adulación *nf* adulation, flattery.

adular *vt* to adulate, flatter.

adulterar *vt* to adulterate.

adulterio *nm* adultery.

adulto,-a *adj* adult.
▶ *nm & nf* adult.

adverbio *nm* adverb.

adversario,-a *adj* opposing.
▶ *nm & nf* adversary, opponent.

adversidad *nf* adversity, misfortune.

adverso,-a *adj* adverse.

advertencia *nf* **1** warning. **2** *(consejo)* piece of advice.

advertir *vt* **1** *(darse cuenta)* to notice, realize. **2** *(llamar la atención)* to warn: *ya te lo advertí* I told you. **3** *(aconsejar)* to advise.

adviento *nm* Advent.

adyacente *adj* adjacent.

aéreo,-a *adj* **1** aerial. **2** AV air.

aerobic *nm* aerobics.

aerobio,-a *adj* aerobic.

aerodeslizador *nm* hovercraft.

aerodinámico,-a *adj* aerodynamic.

aeródromo *nm* aerodrome, US airfield.

aeroespacial *adj* aerospace.

aerofagia *nf* aerophagia.

aerógrafo *nm* airbrush.

aerolínea *nf* airline.

aeronáutica *nf* aeronautics.

aeronaval *adj* air-sea.

aeronave *nf* airship. COMP **aeronave espacial** spaceship.

aeroplano *nm* aeroplane, US airplane.

aeropuerto *nm* airport.

aerosol *nm* aerosol, spray.

aerostático,-a *adj* aerostatic.

aerotaxi *nm* air taxi.

afable *adj* affable, kind.

afamado,-a *adj* famous, well-known.

afán *nm* **1** *(celo)* zeal; *(interés)* keenness, eagerness. **2** *(esfuerzo)* effort.

afanar *vt* *fam* *(robar)* to nick, pinch.
▶ *vpr* **afanarse** to work with zeal. LOC **afanarse en** to work hard at. **afanarse por** to strive to, do one's best to.

afección *nf* *(enfermedad)* complaint, disease.

afectado,-a *pp* → **afectar**.
▶ *adj* affected.

afectar *vt* **1** *(impresionar)* to move. **2** *(dañar)* to damage. **3** *(concernir)* to concern.

afectivo,-a *adj* **1** *(sensible)* sensitive. **2** *(psicología)* affective.

afecto *nm* affection: *con todo mi afecto* with all my love. LOC **tomarle afecto a** ALGN to become fond of SB.

afectuoso,-a *adj* affectionate.

afeitar *vt* to shave.

afeminado,-a *adj* effeminate.

aferrarse *vpr* to clutch (a, to), cling (a, to).

Afganistán *nm* Afghanistan.

afgano,-a *adj* Afghan.
► *nm & nf (persona)* Afghan.
► *nm* **afgano** *(idioma)* Afghan.

afianzar *vt* **1** *(sujetar)* to strengthen, reinforce. **2** *fig* to support, back.
► *vpr* **afianzarse** *(estabilizarse)* to steady OS.

afición *nf* **1** *(inclinación)* liking, penchant: *tener afición por algo* to be fond of sth. **2 la afición** the fans *pl*, the supporters *pl*.

aficionado,-a *pp* → aficionarse.
► *adj* **1** keen, fond: *ser aficionado a algo* to be fond of STH. **2** *(no profesional)* amateur.
► *nm & nf* **1** fan, enthusiast. **2** *(no profesional)* amateur.

aficionarse *vpr* to become fond (a, of), take a liking (a, to).

afijo *nm* affix.

afilar *vt* to sharpen.

afiliarse *vpr* to join (a, to), become affiliated (a, to).

afín *adj* **1** *(semejante)* similar, kindred. **2** *(relacionado)* related. **3** *(próximo)* adjacent, next.

afinar *vt* **1** MÚS to tune. **2** *(puntería)* to sharpen.

afinidad *nf* **1** affinity. **2** QUÍM similarity.

afirmación *nf* statement, assertion.

afirmar *vt* **1** *(afianzar)* to strengthen, reinforce. **2** *(aseverar)* to state, say, declare.
► *vpr* **afirmarse** *(ratificarse)* to maintain (en, -).

afirmativo,-a *adj* affirmative. LOC **en caso afirmativo** if the answer is yes.

aflicción *nf* affliction, grief, suffering.

afligir *vt* to afflict, grieve, trouble.
► *vpr* **afligirse** to grieve, be distressed.

aflojar *vt* **1** *(soltar)* to loosen. **2** *fig (esfuerzo)* to relax. **3** *fam fig (dinero)* to pay up.

aflorar *vi* **1** *(mineral)* to crop out/up, outcrop. **2** *fig (aparecer)* to come up to the surface, appear.

afluencia *nf* inflow, influx: *afluencia de público* flow of people.

afluente *nm (río)* tributary.

afonía *nf* loss of voice.

afónico,-a *adj* hoarse, voiceless. LOC **estar afónico** to have lost one's voice.

aforo *nm (capacidad)* seating capacity.

afortunado,-a *adj* **1** lucky, fortunate: *fue una pregunta poco afortunada* it was a rather inappropriate question. **2** *(dichoso)* happy.

afrenta *nf fml* affront, outrage.

africano,-a *adj* African.
► *nm & nf* African.

afrontar *vt* to face, confront.

afterhours *nm* after-hours club.

afuera *adv* outside: *la parte de afuera* the outside; *salir afuera* to come/go out.
► *nm pl* **afueras** outskirts.

agacharse *vpr* **1** *(encogerse)* to cower. **2** *(agazaparse)* to crouch (down), squat.

agalla *nf* **1** *(de pez)* gill. **2** *(de ave)* temple. **3** BOT gall, oak apple.
► *nf pl* **agallas** *fam* courage *sing*, guts, pluck *sing*: *tener agallas* to have guts.

agarrado,-a *pp* → agarrar.
► *adj fam* stingy, tight. LOC **bailar agarrado** to dance cheek to cheek.

agarrar *vt* **1** *(con la mano)* to clutch, seize, grasp: *agárrala fuerte* hold it tight. **2** *fam (pillar)* to catch.
► *vpr* **agarrarse** *(cogerse)* to hold on, cling (a, to).

agarrotado,-a *adj (músculo)* stiff.

ágata *nf* agate.

agencia *nf* agency; *(sucursal)* branch. COMP **agencia de turismo** tourist office. ‖ **agencia de viajes** travel agency.

agenda *nf* **1** *(libro)* diary. **2** *(orden del día)* agenda.

agente *nm o nf* agent.
► *nm* agent. COMP **agente de cambio y bolsa** stockbroker. ‖ **agente de policía** **1** *(hombre)* policeman. **2** *(mujer)* policewoman.

ágil *adj* agile.

agilidad *nf* agility.

agilizar *vt* to speed up.

agitar *vt* **1** *(mover)* to agitate, shake; *(pañuelo)* to wave: «*Agítese antes de usarlo*» «Shake before use». **2** *(intranquilizar)* agitate, excite.

aglomeración *nf* **1** agglomeration. **2** *(de gente)* crowd.

aglomerado *nm (madera)* chipboard.

agnosticismo *nm* agnosticism.

agobiado,-a *pp* → agobiar.
▶ *adj fig (abrumado)* overwhelmed: *agobiado de trabajo* up to one's eyes in work.

agobiar *vt (abrumar)* to overwhelm.
▶ *vpr* **agobiarse** *(angustiarse)* to worry too much, get worked up.

agobio *nm* burden, fatigue, suffocation.

agonía *nf* **1** dying breath, last gasp: *murió después de una larga agonía* she died after a long illness; *en su agonía* on her deathbed. **2** *(sufrimiento)* agony, grief, sorrow.

agonizar *vi* to be dying: *está agonizando* she could die any moment now.

agosto *nm* August. LOC **hacer su agosto** *fig* to make a packet/pile, feather one's nest.

✎ Para ejemplos de uso, consulta marzo.

agotado,-a *pp* → agotar.
▶ *adj* **1** *(cansado)* exhausted, worn out. **2** *(libros)* out of print; *(mercancías)* sold out.

agotador,-ra *adj* exhausting.

agotamiento *nm* exhaustion. COMP **agotamiento físico** physical strain.

agotar *vt* to exhaust, tire/wear out.
▶ *vpr* **agotarse** **1** *(cansarse)* to become exhausted, become tired out. **2** COM to be sold out.

agraciado,-a *adj* **1** *(bello)* attractive, beautiful. **2** *(ganador)* winning.
▶ *nm & nf* lucky winner. LOC **ser poco agraciado, -a** to be unattractive/plain.

agradable *adj* nice, pleasant.

agradar *vi* to please.

agradecer *vt* **1** to thank for, be grateful for. **2** *(uso impersonal)* to be welcome: *siempre se agradece una ayuda* help is always welcome.

agradecido,-a *pp* → agradecer.
▶ *adj* grateful, thankful: *le quedaría muy agradecido si...* I should be very much obliged if…

agradecimiento *nm* gratefulness, gratitude, thankfulness.

agrado *nm* pleasure: *no es de su agrado* it isn't to his liking.

agrandar *vt* to enlarge, make larger.

agrario,-a *adj* agrarian, land, agricultural.

agravante *adj* aggravating.
▶ *nm & nf* **1** added difficulty. **2** JUR aggravating circumstance.

agravar *vt* to aggravate, worsen.
▶ *vpr* **agravarse** to get worse, worsen.

agravio *nm* offence, insult.

agredir *vt* to attack.

agregar *vt* to add.

agresión *nf* aggression, attack.

agresividad *nf* aggressiveness.

agresivo,-a *adj* aggressive.

agresor,-ra *nm & nf* aggressor, attacker.

agreste *adj* **1** *(salvaje)* wild. **2** *(abrupto)* rugged; *(rocoso)* rocky. **3** *(sin cultivar)* uncultivated.

agrícola *adj* agricultural, farming.

agricultor,-ra *nm & nf* farmer.

agricultura *nf* agriculture, farming.

agridulce *adj* **1** bittersweet. **2** CULIN sweet and sour.

agrietarse *vpr* to crack; *(piel)* to get chapped.

agrio,-a *adj* sour.
▶ *nm pl* **agrios** citrus fruits.

agronomía *nf* agronomy.

agrónomo,-a *adj* farming.
▶ *nm & nf* agronomist.

agropecuario,-a *adj* agricultural, farming.

agrupación *nf* **1** grouping, group. **2** *(asociación)* association.

agrupar *vt* to group, put into groups.
▶ *vpr* **agruparse** **1** to group together, form a group. **2** *(asociarse)* to associate.

agua *nf* **1** water: *echarse al agua* to dive in. **2** *(lluvia)* rain. **3** ARQUIT slope of a roof: *tejado a dos aguas* pitched roof. COMP **agua dulce** fresh water. ▌ **agua corriente** running water. ▌ **agua de colonia** (eau de) cologne. ▌ **agua del grifo** tap water. ▌ **agua mineral con gas** sparkling mineral water. ▌ **agua oxigenada** hydrogen peroxide. ▌ **agua potable** drinking water. ▌ **aguas jurisdiccionales** territorial waters.

aguacate *nm (árbol)* avocado; *(fruto)* avocado (pear).

aguacero *nm* heavy shower, downpour.

aguado,-a *pp* → aguar.
▶ *adj* watered down, wishy-washy.

aguafiestas *nm o nf inv* killjoy, spoilsport, wet blanket.

aguafuerte *nm & nf* **1** ARTE etching. **2** QUÍM nitric acid.

aguamarina *nf* aquamarine.

aguanieve *nf* sleet.

aguantar *vt* **1** *(contener)* to hold (back). **2** *(sostener)* to hold, support. **3** *(soportar)* to tolerate: *no aguanto más* I can't stand any more, I can't take any more.
▶ *vpr* **aguantarse 1** *(contenerse)* to keep back; *(risa, lágrimas)* to hold back. **2** *(resignarse)* to resign OS.

aguante *nm* **1** *(paciencia)* patience, endurance. **2** *(fuerza)* strength. LOC **tener mucho aguante 1** *(paciente)* to be very patient. **2** *(resistente)* to be strong, have a lot of stamina.

aguar *vt* to water down, add water to. LOC **aguar la fiesta a ALGN** to spoil SB's fun.

aguardar *vt* to wait (for), await.
▶ *vi* to wait.

aguardiente *nm* eau de vie, spirit, liquor.

aguarrás *nm* turpentine.

agudo,-a *adj* **1** *(afilado)* sharp. **2** *(dolor)* acute. **3** *fig (ingenioso)* witty; *(mordaz)* sharp. **4** *(voz)* high-pitched. **5** *(sonido)* treble, high. **6** LING *(palabra)* oxytone; *(acento)* acute. **7** MAT *(ángulo)* acute.

agüero *nm* omen, presage. LOC **ser de mal agüero** to be ill-omened. **I ser pájaro de mal agüero** *fig* to be bird of ill omen.

aguijón *nm* **1** ZOOL sting. **2** BOT thorn, prickle. **3** *fig (estímulo)* sting, spur.

águila *nf* eagle.

aguilucho *nm* *(cría del águila)* eaglet.

aguinaldo *nm* Christmas bonus/box.

aguja *nf* **1** needle; *(de tricotar)* knitting needle. **2** *(de reloj)* hand; *(de tocadiscos)* stylus. **3** *(de arma)* firing pin. **4** *(de tren)* point, US switch.

agujerear *vt* to make holes in.

agujero *nm* **1** hole. **2** *fig (falta de dinero)* shortfall: *encontraron un agujero de varios millones de euros* they found that several million euros were missing. COMP
agujero negro black hole.

agujetas *nf pl* stiffness *sing*: *tener agujetas* to be stiff.

ah *interj* **1** *(caer en la cuenta)* ah!, oh! **2** *(sorpresa, admiración)* oh!

ahí *adv* there, in that place. LOC **de ahí que** hence, therefore. **I por ahí 1** *(lugar)* round there. **2** *(aproximadamente)* more or less.

ahijado,-a *nm & nf* **1** godchild; *(chico)* godson; *(chica)* goddaughter. **2** *(adoptivo)* adopted child.

ahínco *nm* eagerness.

ahogado,-a *pp* → ahogar.
▶ *adj* **1** drowned. **2** *(asfixiado)* asphyxiated, suffocated.
▶ *nm & nf* drowned person.

ahogar *vt* **1** *(asfixiar)* to choke, suffocate. **2** *(en el agua)* to drown. **3** *(motor)* to flood.
▶ *vpr* **ahogarse 1** to be drowned, drown: *se cayó al río y se ahogó* he fell into the river and drowned. **2** *(sofocarse)* to choke, suffocate. **3** *(motor)* to flood. LOC **ahogarse en un vaso de agua** *fig* to make a mountain out of a molehill.

ahora *adv* **1** *(en este momento)* now: *ahora no tengo tiempo* I haven't got time now. **2** *(hace un momento)* just a moment ago: *lo acabo de ver ahora* I've just seen it. **3** *(dentro de un momento)* in a minute, shortly: *ahora te lo preparo* I'll get it ready for you in a minute. LOC **de ahora en adelante** from now on. **I hasta ahora** until now, so far. **I por ahora** for the time being.

ahorcar *vt* to hang.
▶ *vpr* **ahorcarse** to hang oneself.

ahorrador,-ra *adj* thrifty.
▶ *nm & nf* thrifty person.

ahorrar *vt* to save.
▶ *vpr* **ahorrarse** to save OS: *te ahorrarás problemas si lo haces como yo te digo* you'l save yourself problems if you do it the way I say.

ahorro *nm* saving: *me supone un ahorro de 60 euros al mes* it represents a saving of 60 euros a month.
▶ *nm pl* **ahorros** savings.

ahumado,-a *pp* → ahumar.
▶ *adj* smoked; *(bacon)* smoky.

ahumar *vt* to smoke.

ahuyentar *vt* **1** to drive away, scare away. **2** *fig* to dismiss.

airbag® *nm* airbag®.

aire *nm* **1** air. **2** *(viento)* wind; *(corriente)* draught. **3** *fig (aspecto)* air, appearance: *tiene un aire cansado* she looks tired. **4** *fig (parecido)* resemblance, likeness: *tienen un aire de familia* there's a family likeness to them. **5** *fig (estilo)* style, manner, way: *lo hizo a su aire* he did it his way. **6** MÚS air, melody. LOC **al aire libre** in the open air, outdoors. ▌**tomar el aire** to take the air, get some fresh air. COMP **aire acondicionado** air conditioning. ▌**aire puro** clean air.

airear *vt* **1** *(ventilar)* to air. **2** *fig (un asunto)* to publicize.
▶ *vpr* **airearse** to get some fresh air.

airoso,-a LOC **salir airoso,-a** to do well, be successful: *salió airoso de la entrevista* he did well in the interview.

aislado,-a *pp* → aislar.
▶ *adj* **1** *(suelto)* isolated. **2** TÉC insulated.

aislante *adj* insulating.
▶ *nm* insulator.

aislar *vt* **1** *(dejar separado)* to isolate. **2** TÉC to insulate.

a. J.C. *abrev* → a. de J.C.

ajedrez *nm* **1** *(juego)* chess. **2** *(tablero y piezas)* chess set.

ajeno,-a *adj* **1** *(de otro)* another's, belonging to other people. **2** *(extraño)* not involved.

ajetreo *nm* activity, bustle.

ajo *nm* garlic. LOC **estar en el ajo** *fam fig* to be involved, be in the thick of it. COMP **ajo tierno** young garlic.

ajustado,-a *pp* → ajustar.
▶ *adj* **1** *(precio)* very low, rock-bottom; *(presupuesto)* tight. **2** *(apretado)* tight-fitting, tight.

ajustar *vt* **1** *(adaptar)* to adjust, regulate. **2** *(apretar)* to tighten. **3** *(encajar)* to fit, fit tight.

ajuste *nm* **1** *(unión)* adjustment, fitting. **2** TÉC assembly. **3** COM settlement, fixing. COMP **ajuste de cuentas** *fig* settling of scores.

al *contr* → a. LOC **al +** *inf* on + *ger*: *me lo encontré al salir de casa* I met him when I was leaving, I met him on leaving.

ala *nf* **1** wing. **2** DEP winger.
▶ *nf pl* **alas** *(atrevimiento)* daring *sing*. COMP **ala delta 1** *(aparato)* hang glider. **2** *(deporte)* hang gliding.

alabanza *nf* praise.

alabar *vt* *(elogiar)* to praise.

alabastro *nm* alabaster.

alacena *nf* cupboard.

alacrán *nm* scorpion.

alambique *nm* still.

alambre *nm* wire.

alameda *nf* **1** poplar grove. **2** *(paseo)* avenue, promenade, boulevard.

álamo *nm* poplar.

alano,-a *adj* mastiff, wolfhound.

alarde *nm* display, bragging, boasting. LOC **hacer alarde de** to flaunt, show off, parade.

alardear *vi* to boast, brag, show off.

alargador *nm* extension lead.

alargar *vt* **1** to lengthen. **2** *(estirar)* to stretch. **3** *(prolongar)* to prolong. **4** *(dar)* to hand, pass.

alarido *nm* screech, yell, shriek.

alarma *nf* alarm. LOC **dar la alarma** to give the alarm, raise the alarm.

alarmante *adj* alarming.

alarmar *vt* to alarm.
▶ *vpr* **alarmarse** to be alarmed, alarm os.

alarmista *nm o nf* alarmist.

alazán,-ana *adj* light chestnut, sorrel.

alba *nf* dawn, daybreak.

albacea *nm o nf* JUR *(hombre)* executor; *(mujer)* executrix.

albahaca *nf* basil.

albanés,-esa *adj* Albanian.
▶ *nm & nf (persona)* Albanian.
▶ *nm* **albanés** *(idioma)* Albanian.

Albania *nf* Albania.

albañil *nm* (*de ladrillos*) bricklayer; (*en general*) building worker.

albarán *nm* delivery note, despatch note.

albaricoque *nm* **1** (*fruta*) apricot. **2** (*árbol*) apricot tree.

alberca *nf* reservoir.

albergar *vt* **1** (*alojar*) to lodge, house, accommodate. **2** *fig* (*sentimientos*) to cherish, harbour (*us* harbor).

albergue *nm* **1** (*hostal*) hostel. **2** (*refugio*) shelter, refuge. COMP **albergue juvenil** youth hostel.

albino,-a *adj* albino.
  ▶ *nm & nf* albino.

albóndiga *nf* meatball.

albornoz *nm* bathrobe.

alborotador,-ra *nm & nf* troublemaker, agitator.

alborotar *vt* **1** (*agitar*) to agitate, excite. **2** (*desordenar*) to make untidy, turn upside down. **3** (*sublevar*) to incite to rebel.
  ▶ *vi* to make a racket.

alboroto *nm* **1** (*gritería*) din, racket, row. **2** (*desorden*) uproar, commotion, disturbance.

albufera *nf* lagoon.

álbum *nm* album.

albúmina *nf* albumin.

alcachofa *nf* **1** (*planta*) artichoke. **2** (*pieza*) rose, sprinkler.

alcalde *nm* mayor.

alcaldesa *nf* **1** (*cargo*) lady mayor, mayoress. **2** (*mujer del alcalde*) mayoress.

alcaldía *nf* **1** (*cargo*) mayorship. **2** (*oficina*) mayor's office, mayoralty.

alcalino,-a *adj* alkaline.

alcaloide *nm* alkaloid.

alcance *nm* **1** reach, grasp: *está al alcance de todo el mundo* it's within everyone's reach. **2** (*de arma*) range. **3** (*trascendencia*) scope, importance. **4** (*inteligencia*) intelligence: *persona de pocos alcances* person of low intelligence.

alcanfor *nm* camphor.

alcantarilla *nf* **1** (*conducto*) sewer. **2** (*boca*) drain.

alcantarillado *nm* sewer system.

alcanzar *vt* **1** (*gen*) to reach. **2** (*persona*) to catch up, catch up with. **3** (*pasar*) to pass, hand over: *alcánzame el agua* pass me some water. **4** (*conseguir*) to attain, achieve: *alcanzamos los objetivos* we achieved the goals.
  ▶ *vi* **1** (*ser suficiente*) to be sufficient (*para*, for), be enough (*para*, for): *eso no alcanza para todos* that's not enough for all of us. **2** (*ser capaz*) to manage, succeed: *no alcanzo a verlo* I can't see it.

alcaparra *nf* **1** (*fruto*) caper. **2** (*planta*) caper bush.

alcayata *nf* hook.

alcázar *nm* **1** (*fortaleza*) fortress, citadel. **2** (*palacio*) palace, castle.

alce *nm* elk, moose.

alcoba *nf* bedroom.

alcohol *nm* **1** (*sustancia*) alcohol. **2** (*bebida*) alcohol, spirits *pl*.

alcoholemia *nf* alcohol: *tasa/nivel de alcoholemia* blood alcohol level.

alcohólico,-a *adj* alcoholic.
  ▶ *nm & nf* alcoholic.

alcoholímetro *nm* breathalyzer®.

alcoholismo *nm* alcoholism.

alcornoque *nm* **1** BOT cork oak. **2** *fig* blockhead, idiot, dimwit.

aldaba *nf* **1** (*llamador*) door knocker. **2** (*barra*) bar. **3** (*pestillo*) bolt.

aldea *nf* hamlet, small village.

aldeano,-a *nm & nf* villager.

aldehído *nm* aldehyde.

aleación *nf* alloy.

aleatorio,-a *adj* random, chance.

alegar *vt* to allege, plead, claim.

alegoría *nf* allegory.

alegórico,-a *adj* allegorical, allegoric.

alegrar *vt* **1** (*causar alegría*) to make happy, make glad, cheer up. **2** *fig* (*avivar*) to brighten (up), enliven. **3** *fam* (*achispar*) to make tipsy.
  ▶ *vpr* **alegrarse 1** to be pleased, be glad. **2** *fam* (*achisparse*) to get tipsy.

alegre *adj* **1** (*contento*) happy, glad. **2** (*color*) bright. **3** (*música*) lively. **4** (*espacio*) cheerful, pleasant. **5** *fam* (*achispado*) tipsy.

alegría *nf* happiness, joy.

alejar *vt* to remove, move away.
  ► *vpr* **alejarse** to go/move away.

alemán,-ana *adj* German.
  ► *nm & nf (persona)* German.
  ► *nm* **alemán** *(idioma)* German.

Alemania *nf* Germany.

alentar *vt* **1** *(animar)* to encourage. **2** *(tener)* to harbour (US harbor), cherish.

alérgeno *nm* allergen.

alergia *nf* allergy.

alérgico,-a *adj* allergic (a, to).

alero *nm* **1** ARQUIT eaves *pl*. **2** DEP forward.

alerta *adv (vigilante)* on the alert.
  ► *nf (atención)* alert.
  ► *interj* look/watch out!

alertar *vt* to alert (de, to).

aleta *nf* **1** *(de pez)* fin; *(de mamífero, de nadador)* flipper. **2** *(de nariz)* wing, ala. **3** *(de avión)* aileron; *(de coche)* wing.

aletear *vi* **1** *(ave)* to flutter, flap its wings. **2** *(pez)* to move its fins.

alfabetizar *vt* **1** *(enseñar)* to teach to read and write. **2** *(ordenar)* to alphabetize, put in alphabetic order.

alfabeto *nm* **1** *(abecedario)* alphabet. **2** *(código)* code. COMP **alfabeto Morse** Morse code.

alfalfa *nf* alfalfa, lucerne.

alfarería *nf* **1** *(arte)* pottery. **2** *(taller)* potter's workshop.

alféizar *nm* sill, windowsill.

alférez *nm* second lieutenant.

alfil *nm* bishop.

alfiler *nm* **1** *(costura)* pin. **2** *(joya)* brooch, pin. **3** *(del pelo)* clip. **4** *(de corbata)* tiepin.

alfombra *nf* **1** carpet, rug. **2** *(de baño)* bath mat.

alfombrilla *nf* **1** rug, mat. **2** *(de ordenador)* mousemat, mousepad.

alforja *nf* saddlebag.

alga *nf* alga; *(marina)* seaweed.

algarroba *nf* **1** *(fruto)* carob bean. **2** *(planta)* vetch.

algarrobo *nm* carob tree.

álgebra *nf* algebra.

algo *pron (afirmación)* something; *(negación, interrogación)* anything: *vamos a tomar algo* let's have something to drink; *¿quieres algo?* do you want anything? LOC **algo es algo** something is better than nothing.
  ► *adv (un poco)* a bit, a little, somewhat: *te queda algo grande* it's a bit too big for you.

algodón *nm* cotton. COMP **algodón dulce/de azúcar** candyfloss, (US cotton candy). ▌ **algodón hidrófilo** cotton wool.

algoritmo *nm* algorithm.

alguacil *nm* bailiff.

alguien *pron (afirmativo)* somebody, someone; *(interrogativo, negativo)* anybody, anyone: *preguntemos a alguien* let's ask someone; *¿hay alguien?* is anyone there?

algún *adj* → alguno,-a.

alguno,-a *adj (afirmativo)* some; *(interrogativo, negativo)* any: *alguna noche voy al cine* some nights I go to the cinema; *¿ha habido alguna llamada?* has anyone phoned?, have there been any phone calls?; *el ministro no facilitó dato alguno* the minister didn't provide any information.
  ► *pron (afirmativo)* someone, somebody; *(interrogativo, negativo)* anybody: *que venga alguno que sepa francés* get someone who speaks French. LOC **alguno que otro** some, a few.

alhaja *nf* **1** jewel, gem. **2** *fig (cosa, persona)* gem, treasure.

aliado,-a *pp* → aliar.
  ► *adj* allied.
  ► *nm & nf* ally.

alianza *nf* **1** *(pacto)* alliance. **2** *(anillo)* wedding ring.

aliar *vt* to ally.
  ► *vpr* **aliarse** to become allies, form an alliance (con, with).

alias *adv* alias.
  ► *nm inv* alias.

alicates *nm pl* pliers.

aliciente *nm* incentive, inducement.

alienígena *nm o nf* alien.

aliento *nm* **1** *(respiración)* breath, breathing. **2** *fig (ánimo)* spirit, courage. LOC **quedarse sin aliento 1** *(respi-*

rando mal) to be breathless, be out of breath. **2** *(sorprendido)* to gasp.

alijo *nm* consignment: *un alijo de armas* a consignment of smuggled arms, an arms cache.

alimaña *nf* pest.

alimentación *nf* **1** *(acción)* feeding. **2** *(alimento)* food; *(dieta)* diet. **3** TÉC feed. COMP **bomba de alimentación** feed pump.

alimentar *vt* **1** *(dar alimento)* to feed. **2** *(mantener)* to keep, support. **3** *(uso técnico)* to feed.
▶ *vpr* **alimentarse** to live (de/con, on).

alimento *nm* **1** *(comida)* food. **2** *(valor nutritivo)* nutritional value, nourishment.

alineación *nf* **1** *(colocación)* alignment, lining up. **2** *(equipo)* line-up.

alinear *vt* **1** *(poner en línea)* to align, line up. **2** DEP to pick, select.

aliñar *vt* *(gen)* to season, flavour (US flavor); *(ensalada)* to dress.

aliño *nm* *(gen)* seasoning; *(para ensalada)* dressing.

alisar *vt* to smooth.

alistarse *vpr* to enlist, join up, enrol (US enroll).

aliviar *vt* **1** fig *(enfermedad, dolor)* to relieve, ease, alleviate, soothe. **2** *(consolar)* to comfort, console.

alivio *nm* **1** *(mejoría)* relief: *¡qué alivio!* what a relief! **2** *(consuelo)* comfort, consolation.

aljibe *nm* cistern, tank.

allá *adv* **1** *(lugar)* there, over there: *más allá* further (on); *allá va tu madre* there goes your mother. **2** *(tiempo)* back: *allá por los años sesenta* back in the sixties.

allanamiento COMP **allanamiento de morada 1** unlawful entry. **2** *(robo)* housebreaking, breaking and entering.

allanar *vt* **1** *(aplanar)* to level, flatten. **2** *(dificultad, etc)* to smooth out, solve, resolve.

allegado,-a *adj* close, related.
▶ *nm & nf (familia)* relative; *(amigo)* close friend.

allí *adv* **1** *(lugar)* there, over there: *allí abajo/arriba* down/up there; *por allí* over

there, round there. **2** *(tiempo)* then, at that moment.

alma *nf* soul. LOC **no había ni una alma** there wasn't a soul, there was nobody there. **I no poder** ALGN **con su alma** to be absolutely exhausted.

almacén *nm* **1** *(local)* warehouse, storehouse. **2** *(habitación)* storeroom.
▶ *nm pl* **almacenes** department store *sing.* COMP **grandes almacenes** department store *sing.*

almacenar *vt* **1** to store, warehouse. **2** *(acumular)* to store up, keep.

almeja *nf* clam.

almena *nf* merlon.
▶ *nf pl* **almenas** battlements.

almendra *nf* almond.

almendro *nm* almond tree.

almíbar *nm* syrup.

almidón *nm* starch.

almirante *nm* admiral.

almizcle *nm* musk.

almohada *nf* pillow. LOC **consultar** ALGO **con la almohada** *fam* to sleep on STH.

almohadilla *nf* **1** *(gen)* small cushion. **2** COST *(para coser)* sewing cushion; *(para alfileres)* pincushion. **3** *(de teclado)* number sign, pound. **4** *(de animal)* pad. **5** ARQUIT *(de capitel)* volute cushion.

almohadón *nm* cushion, large pillow.

almorrana *nf* fam pile.

almorzar *vi* *(al mediodía)* to have lunch; *(de desayuno)* to have breakfast; *(a media mañana)* to have elevenses, have a mid-morning snack.
▶ *vt (al mediodía)* to have for lunch; *(de desayuno)* to have for breakfast; *(a media mañana)* to have for elevenses, have for a mid-morning snack.

almuerzo *nm* **1** *(a mediodía)* lunch. **2** *(a media mañana)* mid-morning snack, elevenses *pl.* **3** *(desayuno)* breakfast.

alojamiento *nm* lodging, accommodation.

alojar *vt* **1** *(hospedar)* to lodge, put up, accommodate; *(dar vivienda a)* to house. **2** *(meter)* to put, place.
▶ *vpr* **alojarse** *(persona)* to stay; *(bala, etc)* to be lodged.

alondra *nf* lark.

alopecia *nf* alopecia.

alpaca¹ *nf (animal, tela)* alpaca.

alpaca² *nf (metal)* nickel silver, German silver, alpaca.

alpargata *nf* rope-soled sandal, espadrille.

Alpes *nm pl* los Alpes the Alps.

alpinismo *nm* mountaineering, mountain climbing.

alpinista *nm o nf* mountaineer, mountain climber.

alpiste *nm* birdseed, canary grass.

alquilar *vt* **1** *(dar en alquiler - período largo)* to rent, rent out, let; *(- período corto)* to hire out. **2** *(recibir en alquiler - período largo)* to rent; *(- período corto)* to hire. LOC «Se alquila» "To let".

alquiler *nm* **1** *(acción - de casa)* renting, letting; *(- de coche)* hire. **2** *(cuota - de casa)* rent; *(- de TV, etc)* rental. LOC «En alquiler» "To let", US "For rent".

alquimia *nf* alchemy.

alquitrán *nm* tar.

alrededor *adv* **1** *(lugar)* round, around: *mira alrededor* look around. **2** alrededor de *(tiempo)* around: *alrededor de las cuatro* around four o'clock. **3** *(aproximadamente)* about: *alrededor de veinte* about twenty.
▶ *nm pl* **alrededores** surrounding area *sing*: *en los alrededores de Sevilla* in the vicinity of Seville, just outside Seville.

alta *nf* **1** *(de un enfermo)* discharge: *dieron de/el alta al enfermo* the patient was discharged from hospital. **2** *(de un empleado)* registration *with Social Security*. **3** *(entrada, admisión)* admission; *(ingreso)* membership.

altar *nm* altar.

altavoz *nm* loudspeaker.

alteración *nf* **1** *(cambio)* alteration, change. **2** *(excitación)* agitation, uneasiness, restlessness. COMP alteración del orden público breach of the peace, disturbance of the peace.

alterar *vt* **1** *(cambiar)* to change, modify, alter. **2** *(enfadar)* to annoy, upset.
▶ *vpr* **alterarse 1** *(cambiar)* to change. **2** *(enfadarse)* to lose one's temper, get upset.

altercado *nm* argument, quarrel.

alternar *vt (gen)* to alternate.
▶ *vi* **1** *(turnar)* to alternate. **2** *(relacionarse)* to meet people, socialize (con, with), mix (con, with). **3** *(en salas de fiesta, bar)* to entertain.

alternativa *nf* alternative, option, choice.

alternativo,-a *adj* alternative.

alterno,-a *adj* alternate, alternating: *días alternos* alternate days.

Alteza *nf* Highness. LOC Su Alteza Real **1** *(hombre)* His Royal Highness. **2** *(mujer)* Her Royal Highness.

altibajos *nm pl* ups and downs.

altiplano *nm* high plateau.

altitud *nf* height, altitude.

alto¹ *nm (parada)* stop: *hicieron un alto para comer* they stopped for lunch.
▶ *interj* halt!; *(policía)* stop!

alto,-a² *adj* **1** *(persona, edificio, árbol)* tall. **2** *(montaña, pared, techo, precio)* high. **3** *(elevado)* top, upper: *viven en los pisos altos* they live on the upper floors. **4** *(voz, sonido)* loud: *lo dijo en voz alta* she said it aloud. LOC a altas horas de la noche late at night. COMP alta cocina haute cuisine. ▌ alta sociedad high society.
▶ *adv* **alto 1** high (up). **2** *(voz)* loud, loudly. LOC pasar por alto to pass over.
▶ *nm* **1** *(altura)* height: *solo hace dos metros de alto* it's only two metres high. **2** *(elevación)* hill, high ground. LOC en lo alto de on the top of. ▌ por todo lo alto *fig* in a grand way.

altramuz *nm* lupin.

altruismo *nm* altruism.

altura *nf* **1** *(gen)* height: *el edificio tiene una altura de 80 metros* the building is 80 metres high. **2** *(altitud)* altitude. **3** *(nivel)* level, par; *(punto)* point: *¿a qué altura de la calle vives?* how far up the street do you live? LOC estar a la altura de to measure up to, match up to, be on a par with. ▌ a estas alturas by now, at this stage.

alubia *nf* bean.

alucinación *nf* hallucination.

alucinado,-a *pp* → alucinar.
▶ *adj argot* amazed, stunned, gobsmacked.

alucinante *adj* **1** hallucinatory. **2** *argot (extraordinario)* brilliant, fantastic, amazing, incredible, mind-blowing.

alucinar *vt* **1** *(producir sensaciones)* to hallucinate. **2** *fig (cautivar)* to fascinate, amaze, astound, flip out, stun.
‣ *vi argot* to be amazed, be gobsmacked: *¡alucinas!* you're out of your mind!, you're crazy!

alud *nm* avalanche.

aludido,-a *pp* → aludir.
‣ *adj* above-mentioned, in question.
LOC **darse por aludido,-a** to take the hint.

aludir *vi* to allude (a, to), mention (a, -), refer (a, to).

alumbrado,-a *nm* lighting, lights *pl*; *(coche)* lights *pl*.

alumbramiento *nm* afterbirth.

alumbrar *vt* **1** *(iluminar)* to light, give light to, illuminate. **2** *fig (enseñar)* to enlighten.
‣ *vi* **1** *(iluminar)* to give light. **2** *(parir)* to give birth to.

aluminio *nm* aluminium, US aluminum.

alumnado *nm (de colegio)* pupils *pl*; *(de universidad)* student body.

alumno,-a *nm & nf (de colegio)* pupil; *(de universidad)* student. COMP **alumno externo** day pupil. ‖ **alumno interno** boarder. ‖ **antiguo alumno 1** *(de colegio)* old boy, former pupil. **2** *(de universidad)* old student, former student.

alunizar *vi* to land on the moon.

alusión *nf* allusion, reference.

aluvión *nm* **1** alluvion: *tierra de aluvión* alluvium, alluvial soil. **2** *fig* flood: *un aluvión de insultos* a barrage of insults.

alveolar *adj* alveolar.

alveolo *nm* **1** ANAT alveolus. **2** *(de panal)* cell.

alza *nf (aumento)* rise, increase. LOC **al alza / en alza** rising.

alzamiento *nm* **1** *(aumento)* raising, lifting. **2** *(rebelión)* uprising, insurrection.

alzar *vt* **1** *(levantar)* to raise, lift. **2** *(construir)* to build, erect. **3** *(un plano)* to draw up, make out. LOC **alzar el vuelo** to take off.

‣ *vpr* **alzarse 1** *(levantarse)* to rise up, get up. **2** *(sublevarse)* to rise, rebel.

a.m. *abrev* (ante meridiem) ante meridiem; *(abreviatura)* a.m.

ama *nf (propietaria)* landlady. COMP **ama de casa** housewife.

amabilidad *nf* kindness, affability.

amable *adj* kind, nice: *¿sería usted tan amable de...?* would you be so kind as to...?

amaestrar *vt (adiestrar)* to train; *(domar)* to tame.

amainar *vi (viento)* to die down, drop.

amamantar *vt* to breast-feed, suckle.

amanecer *vi* **1** to dawn, get light: *en verano amanece pronto* day breaks early in summer. **2** *(estar)* to be at dawn, be at daybreak: *amanecimos en Barcelona* we were in Barcelona at dawn.
‣ *nm* dawn, daybreak. LOC **al amanecer** at daybreak.

amanerado,-a *adj* affected, mannered.

amante *adj* loving, fond (de, of).
‣ *nm o nf* lover.

amañar *vt (falsear)* to fiddle, fix; *(cuentas)* to cook; *(elecciones)* to rig.

amapola *nf* poppy.

amar *vt* to love.
‣ *vpr* **amarse** to love each other, be in love (with each other).

amarar *vi (hidroavión)* to land at sea; *(nave espacial)* to splash down.

amargado,-a *pp* → amargar.
‣ *adj* embittered, resentful: *estar amargado,-a* to feel very bitter.
‣ *nm & nf* bitter person.

amargar *vi (tener sabor amargo)* to taste bitter.
‣ *vt* **1** *(hacer amargo)* to make bitter. **2** *fig (disgustos, etc)* to embitter, make bitter. **3** *fig (estropear)* to spoil, ruin: *la lluvia nos amargó el día* the rain put a damper on our day.
‣ *vpr* **amargarse** *fig* to become embittered, become bitter. LOC **a nadie le amarga un dulce** a gift is always welcome.

amargo,-a *adj* **1** *(sabor)* bitter. **2** *fig (carácter)* sour; *(experiencia)* bitter, sour, painful.

amargura *nf* **1** bitterness. **2** *(dolor)* sorrow, grief, sadness.

amarillo,-a *adj* yellow.
▶ *nm* amarillo yellow. COMP **prensa amarilla** sensationalist press.

amarra *nf* mooring rope.
▶ *nf pl* **amarras** *fam fig* connections. LOC **soltar las amarras 1** MAR to cast off, let go. **2** *fig* to break loose.

amarrar *vt* **1** *(atar)* to tie (up), fasten. **2** MAR to moor, tie up.

amarre *nm* mooring.

amasar *vt* **1** CULIN to knead. **2** *fig (reunir)* to amass.

amasijo *nm fam (mezcolanza)* hotchpotch, jumble.

amateur *adj* amateur.
▶ *nm o nf* amateur.

amatista *nf* amethyst.

amazona *nf* **1** *(mitología)* Amazon. **2** *(jinete)* horsewoman.

Amazonas *nm* **el Amazonas** the Amazon.

amazónico,-a *adj* Amazonian.

ámbar *nm* amber.

ambición *nf* ambition, aspiration.

ambicioso,-a *adj (plan, etc)* ambitious; *(persona)* ambitious, enterprising.

ambidextro,-a *adj* ambidextrous.
▶ *nm & nf* ambidextrous person.

ambientación *nf* **1** *(ambiente)* atmosphere. **2** *(localización)* setting.

ambientador *nm* air freshener.

ambiental *adj* **1** *(del ambiente)* environmental. **2** *(de fondo)* background.

ambientar *vt* **1** *(dar ambiente)* to give atmosphere to. **2** *(localizar)* to set.
▶ *vpr* **ambientarse** to adapt, get used (a, to).

ambiente *nm* **1** *(aire)* air, atmosphere. **2** *(entorno)* environment, atmosphere: *no hay mucho ambiente de noche* there is not much going on at night. LOC **cambiar de ambiente** to have a change of scene.

ambigüedad *nf* ambiguity.

ambiguo,-a *adj* ambiguous.

ámbito *nm* **1** *(espacio)* sphere, space. **2** *(marco)* field: *en el ámbito de la informática* in the computer science field.

ambivalente *adj* ambivalent.

ambos,-as *adj* both: *por ambos lados* on both sides.
▶ *pron* both: *me gustan ambos* I like both of them, I like them both.

ambulancia *nf* ambulance.

ambulante *adj* itinerant, travelling.

ambulatorio,-a *adj* ambulatory.
▶ *n* ambulatorio surgery, clinic.

ameba *nf* amoeba *(US* ameba*)*.

amedrentar *vt* to frighten, scare.
▶ *vpr* **amedrentarse** *(asustarse)* to be frightened, be scared; *(acobardarse)* to become intimidated.

amén *nm* REL amen. LOC **decir amén a todo/todos** *fam* to agree with everything/everybody.

amenaza *nf* threat, menace.

amenazar *vt & vi* to threaten.

amenizar *vt* to liven up, make entertaining, make enjoyable.

ameno,-a *adj* lively, entertaining, enjoyable.

América *nf* America. COMP **América Central** Central America. ▌**América del Norte** North America. ▌**América del Sur** South America. ▌**América Latina** Latin America.

americana *nf* jacket.

americano,-a *adj* American.
▶ *nm & nf* American.

amerizar *vi* → amarar.

ametralladora *nf* machine gun.

ametrallar *vt* **1** to machine-gun. **2** *fig (acosar)* to chase, pursue, besiege.

amianto *nm* asbestos.

amígdala *nf* tonsil.

amigdalitis *nf inv* tonsillitis.

amigo,-a *adj* **1** *(amigable)* friendly: *es muy amigo de Julio* he's very friendly with Julio. **2** *(aficionado)* fond (de, of): *no es muy amiga de discotecas* she's not keen on discos.
▶ *nm & nf* **1** friend: *una amiga mía* a friend of mine; *son amigos íntimos* they are close friends. **2** *(novio)* boyfriend; *(novia)* girlfriend. **3** *(amante)* lover.

amigote *nm fam* pal, mate, chum.

amiguismo *nm* contacts *pl*, string-pulling.

aminoácido *nm* amino acid.

aminorar *vt* to reduce, decrease. LOC aminorar el paso to slow down.

amistad *nf* friendship.
▶ *nf pl* amistades friends. LOC hacer amistades to make friends.

amistoso,-a *adj* friendly: *partido amistoso* friendly match.

amnesia *nf* amnesia.

amniótico,-a *adj* amniotic.

amnistía *nf* amnesty.

amo *nm* 1 *(señor)* master. 2 *(dueño)* owner. 3 *(jefe)* boss.

amoldarse *vpr* to adapt, adjust (a, to).

amonestación *nf* 1 *(represión)* reprimand, admonition, admonishment. 2 DEP caution, booking.

amonestar *vt* 1 *(reprender)* to reprimand, admonish. 2 DEP to caution, book.

amoníaco *nm* ammonia.

amontonar *vt* 1 to heap up, pile up. 2 *(juntar)* to collect, gather, accumulate.
▶ *vpr* amontonarse 1 to heap up, pile up. 2 *(gente)* to crowd together.

amor *nm* 1 *(gen)* love. 2 *(cuidado)* loving care; *(devoción)* devotion. LOC con/de mil amores *fam* willingly, with pleasure. ∎ hacer el amor to make love. COMP amor propio self-esteem.

amoral *adj* amoral.

amoratado,-a *adj* 1 *(de frío)* blue with cold. 2 *(de un golpe)* bruised, black and blue.

amordazar *vt (persona)* to gag; *(perro)* to muzzle.

amorfo,-a *adj* amorphous.

amoroso,-a *adj* loving, affectionate.

amortiguador *nm* 1 AUTO shock absorber. 2 TÉC damper.

amortiguar *vt (golpe)* to cushion; *(dolor)* to alleviate, ease, soothe; *(ruido)* to muffle; *(luz)* to subdue, dim.

amotinarse *vpr* 1 to rebel, rise up, riot. 2 MIL to mutiny.

amparar *vt* to protect, shelter.

▶ *vpr* ampararse 1 *(protegerse)* to take shelter, protect OS. 2 *(acogerse)* to avail OS of the protection (en, of), seek protection (en, in).

amparo *nm* protection, shelter.

amperio *nm* ampere.

ampliación *nf* 1 enlargement, extension. 2 ARQUIT extension. 3 *(fotografía)* enlargement.

ampliar *vt* 1 to enlarge, extend. 2 ARQUIT to build an extension onto. 3 *(fotografía)* to enlarge. 4 *(capital)* to increase. 5 *(estudios)* to further. 6 *(tema, idea)* to develop, expand on.

amplificación *nf* amplification.

amplio,-a *adj* 1 *(extenso)* large. 2 *(espacioso)* roomy, spacious. 3 *(ancho)* wide, broad. 4 *(holgado)* loose.

amplitud *nf* 1 *(extensión)* extent, range. 2 *(espacio)* room, space, spaciousness. 3 *(anchura)* width. 4 *(holgadura)* looseness. 5 FÍS amplitude.

ampolla *nf* 1 MED blister. 2 *(burbuja)* bubble. 3 *(tubito)* ampoule, phial.

amputar *vt* to amputate.

amueblar *vt* to furnish. LOC sin amueblar unfurnished.

amuleto *nm* amulet, charm.

amurallar *vt* to wall.

anabolizante *adj* anabolic.

anaconda *nf* anaconda.

anacoreta *nm o nf* anchorite.

anacronismo *nm* anachronism.

anaerobio,-a *adj* anaerobic.

anagrama *nm* anagram.

anal *adj* anal.

analfabetismo *nm* illiteracy.

analfabeto,-a *adj* 1 illiterate. 2 *fig* stupid.
▶ *nm & nf* 1 illiterate person. 2 *fig* stupid person, ignoramus.

analgésico,-a *adj* analgesic.
▶ *nm* analgésico analgesic, painkiller.

análisis *nm inv* analysis. COMP análisis de orina urine test. ∎ análisis de sangre blood test.

analizar *vt* to analyse (US analyze).

analogía *nf* analogy.

analógico,-a *adj* analogical.

análogo,-a *adj* analogous, similar.

anaquel *nm* shelf.

anarquía *nf* anarchy.

anárquico,-a *adj* anarchic, anarchical.

anarquista *adj* anarchist.

▶ *nm o nf* anarchist.

anatomía *nf* anatomy.

anca *nf* haunch. COMP **ancas de rana** frogs' legs.

ancestral *adj* ancestral, ancient.

ancho,-a *adj* **1** *(gen)* broad, wide. **2** *(prenda - holgada)* loose-fitting; *(- grande)* too big.

▶ *nm* **ancho 1** *(anchura)* breadth, width: *¿qué ancho tiene?* how wide is it?; *tiene cuatro metros de ancho* it's four metres wide. **2** *(en costura)* width. LOC **a sus anchas** *fam* comfortable, at ease. ‖ **estar más ancho,-a que largo,-a** to be full of os. ‖ **quedarse tan ancho,-a** *fam* to behave as if nothing had happened, not bat an eyelid.

anchoa *nf* anchovy.

anchura *nf* breadth, width.

anciano,-a *adj* very old, elderly, aged.

▶ *nm & nf* old person, elderly person.

ancla *nf* anchor.

anclar *vi* MAR to anchor.

▶ *vt* TÉC to anchor.

andadas LOC **volver a las andadas** to go back to one's old tricks.

Andalucía *nf* Andalusia.

andaluz,-za *adj* Andalusian.

▶ *nm & nf (persona)* Andalusian.

▶ *nm* **andaluz** *(dialecto)* Andalusian.

andamio *nm* scaffold.

andanada *nf* MAR broadside.

andante COMP **caballero andante** knight errant.

andanzas *nf pl* adventures.

andar *vi* **1** *(moverse)* to walk. **2** *(funcionar)* to work, run, go: *este reloj no anda* this watch doesn't work. **3** *(estar)* to be: *¿cómo andas?* how are you?, how's it going? **4** *(juntarse)* to mix (con, with). LOC **andar a gatas** to crawl. ‖ **andar de puntillas** to tiptoe. ‖ **andar con rodeos** to beat about the bush. ‖ **andar con cuidado / andarse con cuidado** to be careful. ‖ **andarse por las ramas** *fig* to beat about the bush.

▶ *interj* **¡anda!** well!, oh!: *¡anda ya!* come off it!.

andén *nm* platform.

Andes *nm pl* **los Andes** the Andes.

andino,-a *adj* Andean.

▶ *nm & nf* Andean.

Andorra *nm* Andorra.

andorrano,-a *adj* Andorran.

▶ *nm & nf* Andorran.

androide *nm* android.

anécdota *nf* anecdote.

anélido *nm* annelid.

anemia *nf* anaemia (US anemia).

anemona *nf* anemone. COMP **anemona de mar** sea anemone.

anestesia *nf* anaesthesia (US anesthesia).

anestésico,-a *adj* anaesthetic (US anesthetic).

▶ *nm* **anestésico** anaesthetic (US anesthetic).

anexión *nf* annexation.

anexo,-a *adj* adjoining, attached (a, to).

▶ *nm* **anexo** annexe (US annex).

anfetamina *nf* amphetamine.

anfibio,-a *adj* amphibious.

▶ *nm* **anfibio** amphibian.

▶ *nm pl* **los anfibios** amphibia *pl*.

anfiteatro *nm* **1** amphitheatre (US amphitheater). **2** *(en universidad)* lecture theatre (US theater). **3** *(en teatro, cine)* circle.

anfitrión,-ona *nm & nf (hombre)* host; *(mujer)* hostess.

ángel *nm* angel.

angina *nf* angina. LOC **tener anginas** to have a sore throat. COMP **angina de pecho** angina pectoris.

anglosajón,-ona *adj* Anglo-Saxon.

▶ *nm & nf (persona)* Anglo-Saxon.

▶ *nm* **anglosajón** *(idioma)* Anglo-Saxon.

Angola *nf* Angola.

angosto,-a *adj* narrow.

ángstrom *nm* angstrom.

anguila *nf* eel.

angula *nf* elver.

ángulo *nm* **1** angle. **2** *(rincón)* corner. COMP **ángulo recto** right angle.

angustia *nf* anguish, distress.

angustiar *vt* **1** *(afligir)* to distress, upset. **2** *(preocupar)* to worry, make anxious.

angustioso,-a *adj* *(situación)* distressing, worrying; *(mirada)* anguished.

anhelar *vt* to long for, yearn for.

anhelo *nm* longing, yearning.

anhídrido *nm* anhydride.

anilla *nf* *(aro)* ring.
▶ *nf pl* **anillas** DEP rings.

anillo *nm* **1** ring. **2** ARQUIT annulet. **3** *(de gusano)* annulus; *(de culebra)* coil. LOC **venir como anillo al dedo** to be just what SB needed, suit SB fine.

animación *nf* **1** *(actividad)* activity, movement, bustle. **2** *(viveza)* liveliness. **3** CINE animation.

animado,-a *pp* → animar.
▶ *adj* **1** *(movido)* animated, lively, jolly. **2** *(concurrido)* bustling, full of people. **3** *(alegre)* cheerful, in high spirits, excited.

animador,-ra *nm & nf* **1** *(artista)* entertainer. **2** *(de un equipo)* cheerleader.

animadversión *nf* antagonism, hostility, ill will, animosity.

animal *adj* animal.
▶ *nm* **1** animal. **2** *fig* *(basto)* rough person, brute, lout; *(necio)* dunce. COMP **animal doméstico** pet. ‖ **reino animal** animal kingdom.

animar *vt* **1** *(alegrar a algn)* to cheer up. **2** *(alegrar algo)* to brighten up, liven up. **3** *(alentar)* to encourage.
▶ *vpr* **animarse 1** *(persona)* to cheer up. **2** *(fiesta, etc)* to brighten up, liven up. **3** *(decidirse)* to make up one's mind.

ánimo *nm* **1** *(espíritu)* spirit; *(mente)* mind; *(alma)* soul. **2** *(intención)* intention, purpose: *sin ánimo de ofender* no offence intended. **3** *(valor)* courage: *no tengo ánimos de nada* I don't feel up to anything. **4** *(aliento)* encouragement.
▶ *interj* cheer up!

anión *nm* anion.

aniquilar *vt* to annihilate, destroy.

anís *nm* **1** *(planta)* anise; *(grano)* aniseed. **2** *(bebida)* anisette.

aniversario *nm* anniversary.

ano *nm* anus.

anoche *adv* *(late)* last night; *(early)* yesterday evening.

anochecer *vi* **1** to get dark: *cuando anocheció* when it got dark. **2** to be at nightfall, reach at nightfall.
▶ *nm* nightfall, dusk, evening. LOC **al anochecer** at nightfall, at dusk.

ánodo *nm* anode.

anofeles *nm inv* anopheles.

anomalía *nf* anomaly.

anómalo,-a *adj* anomalous.

anonimato *nm* anonymity.

anónimo,-a *adj* **1** *(desconocido)* anonymous. **2** *(sociedad)* limited, US incorporated.
▶ *nm* **anónimo** *(carta)* anonymous letter.

anorak *nm* anorak.

anorexia *nf* anorexia.

anormal *adj* **1** *(no normal)* abnormal. **2** *(inhabitual)* unusual. **3** MED subnormal.

anotación *nf* **1** *(acotación)* annotation. **2** *(nota)* note. **3** *(apunte)* noting.

anotar *vt* **1** *(acotar)* to annotate, add notes to. **2** *(apuntar)* to take down, jot down, make a note of.

ansia *nf* **1** *(ansiedad)* anxiety; *(angustia)* anguish. **2** *(deseo)* eagerness, longing, yearning: *tener ansia de poder* to be longing for power.

ansiar *vt* to long for, yearn for.

ansiedad *nf* **1** anxiety. **2** MED nervous tension.

ansioso,-a *adj* **1** *(desasosegado)* anguished, anxious, desperate. **2** *(deseoso)* eager, longing (por/de, to).

antagónico,-a *adj* antagonistic.

antaño *adv* formerly, in olden times, long ago.

antártico,-a *adj* Antarctic.

Antártida *nf* Antarctica.

ante¹ *prep* **1** before, in the presence of. **2** *(considerando)* in the face of: *ante estas circunstancias* under the circumstances. LOC **ante todo 1** *(primero)* first of all. **2** *(por encima de)* above all.

ante² *nm* **1** ZOOL elk, moose. **2** *(piel)* suede.

anteayer *adv* the day before yesterday.

antebrazo *nm* forearm.

antecedente *nm* **1** precedent. **2** GRAM antecedent. **3** MED history.
▶ *nm pl* **antecedentes** record *sing*.

antecesor,-ra *nm & nf* **1** *(en un cargo)* predecessor. **2** *(antepasado)* ancestor.

antelación *nf* precedence: *con cinco días de antelación* five days beforehand. LOC **con antelación** in advance.

antemano, in LOC **de antemano** beforehand, in advance.

antena *nf* **1** RAD TV aerial, antenna. **2** ANAT antenna, feeler. LOC **estar en antena** to be on the air. COMP **antena parabólica** satellite dish.

anteojos *nm pl* **1** *(binóculos)* binoculars, field glasses. **2** *(gafas)* glasses, spectacles.

antepasado *nm* ancestor.
▶ *nm pl* **antepasados** forefathers, forbears.

antepenúltimo,-a *adj* antepenultimate.

anteponer *vt* **1** *(poner delante)* to place in front (a, of), put in front (a, of); *(poner antes)* to put before. **2** *(preferir)* to prefer (a, to).

antera *nf* anther.

anterior *adj* **1** *(tiempo)* previous, preceding, before: *el día anterior* the day before. **2** *(lugar)* front: *la parte anterior* the front part.
▶ *nm o nf* the previous one.

anterioridad *nf* priority. LOC **con anterioridad** previously. | **con anterioridad a** prior to, before.

antes *adv* **1** *(tiempo)* before, earlier: *llámame antes de salir* ring me before you leave; *deberías estar allí antes de las nueve* you should be there before nine. **2** *(en el pasado)* before, in the past. **3** *(lugar)* in front, before. LOC **antes de nada** first of all. | **lo antes posible** as soon as possible.
▶ *adj* before.

antesala *nf* anteroom, antechamber.

antiadherente *adj* nonstick.

antiaéreo,-a *adj* anti-aircraft.

antibalas *adj* bullet-proof.

antibiótico,-a *adj* antibiotic.
▶ *nm* **antibiótico** antibiotic.

anticaspa *adj* anti-dandruff: *champú anticaspa* dandruff shampoo.

anticiclón *nm* anticyclone, high pressure area.

anticipación *nf* anticipation, advance. LOC **con anticipación** in advance.

anticipado,-a *pp* → anticipar.
▶ *adj* brought forward; *(temprano)* early: *gracias anticipadas* thanks in advance; *pago anticipado* payment in advance. LOC **por anticipado** in advance.

anticipar *vt* **1** to anticipate, advance, bring forward. **2** *(dinero)* to advance.
▶ *vpr* **anticiparse 1** *(llegar antes)* to come early. **2** *(adelantarse)* to beat to it: *él se me anticipó* he beat me to it.

anticipo *nm* **1** *(gen)* foretaste, preview. **2** *(pago)* advance, advance payment.

anticlinal *nm* anticline.

anticonceptivo,-a *adj* contraceptive.
▶ *nm* **anticonceptivo** contraceptive.

anticongelante *adj* antifreeze.
▶ *nm* **anticongelante** antifreeze.

anticorrosivo,-a *adj* anticorrosive.
▶ *nm* **anticorrosivo** anticorrosive.

anticuado,-a *adj* antiquated, old-fashioned, obsolete, out-of-date.

anticuario *nm* *(conocedor)* antiquary, antiquarian; *(comerciante)* antique dealer.

anticuerpo *nm* antibody.

antidepresivo,-a *adj* antidepressant.
▶ *nm* **antidepresivo** antidepressant.

antidisturbios *adj* riot. COMP **material antidisturbios** riot gear. | **policía antidisturbios** riot police.

antidoping *adj* anti-doping, anti-drug.

antídoto *nm* antidote.

antifaz *nm* mask.

antígeno *nm* antigen.

antigüedad *nf* **1** *(período)* antiquity. **2** *(en empleo)* seniority. **3** *(objeto)* antique. LOC **en la antigüedad** in olden days, in former times. COMP **tienda de antigüedades** antique shop.

antiguo,-a *adj* **1** *(gen)* ancient, old; *(coche)* vintage, old. **2** *(en empleo)* senior. **3** *(pasado)* old-fashioned. **4** *(anterior)* former: *el antiguo primer ministro* the former Prime Minister.

antihéroe *nm* antihero.

antihistamínico *nm* antihistamine.

antiinflamatorio *nm* anti-inflammatory.

antílope *nm* antelope.

antimonio *nm* antimony.

antiniebla *adj inv* anti-fog. [COMP] **faros antiniebla** foglamps. ‖ **luces antiniebla** foglamps.

antipatía *nf* antipathy, dislike.

antipático,-a *adj* unfriendly, unpleasant, unkind.
▶ *nm & nf* unpleasant person.

antípoda *nm & nf* *(punto)* antipode, antipodes *pl*.

antirrobo *adj inv* anti-theft.

antisemitismo *nm* anti-Semitism.

antiséptico,-a *adj* antiseptic.
▶ *nm* **antiséptico** antiseptic.

antiterrorista *adj* antiterrorist.

antítesis *nf inv* antithesis.

antitetánico,-a *adj* anti-tetanus.

antitranspirante *adj* antiperspirant.
▶ *nm* antiperspirant.

antivirus *nm* **1** *(fármaco)* antivirus drug. **2** INFORM antivirus.

antojo *nm* **1** *(capricho)* whim, fancy; *(de embarazada)* craving. **2** *(en la piel)* birthmark.

antología *nf* anthology.

antónimo *nm* antonym.

antonomasia *nf* antonomasia. [LOC] **por antonomasia** par excellence.

antorcha *nf* torch.

antracita *nf* anthracite.

ántrax *nm inv* anthrax.

antro *nm* **1** *(caverna)* cavern. **2** *(tugurio)* dump, hole, dive.

antropoide *nm o nf* anthropoid.

antropología *nf* anthropology.

anual *adj* annual, yearly.

anuario *nm* yearbook.

anudar *vt* *(atar)* to knot, tie, fasten.

anulación *nf* **1** *(gen)* annulment, cancellation; *(de ley)* repeal; *(de sentencia)* quashing, overturning. **2** DEP *(de gol)* disallowing. [COMP] **anulación de matrimonio** annulment of marriage.

anular¹ *adj* ring-shaped.
▶ *nm* ring finger.

anular² *vt* **1** *(matrimonio)* to annul; *(una ley)* to repeal; *(una sentencia)* to quash. **2** *(un pedido, viaje)* to cancel; *(un contrato)* to invalidate, cancel. **3** DEP *(un gol)* to disallow.

anunciar *vt* **1** *(avisar)* to announce, make public. **2** *(hacer publicidad)* to advertise.
▶ *vpr* **anunciarse** to put an advert (en, in).

anuncio *nm* **1** *(aviso)* announcement; *(signo)* sign. **2** *(publicidad)* advertisement, advert, ad. **3** *(valla publicitaria)* hoarding, US billboard. [COMP] **anuncios por palabras** classified adverts, small ads.

anverso *nm* **1** *(de moneda)* obverse. **2** *(de página)* recto.

anzuelo *nm* **1** fish-hook. **2** *fig* lure, bait. [LOC] **tragar/morder/picar el anzuelo** to swallow the bait.

añadidura *nf* addition, addendum. [LOC] **por añadidura** besides, in addition.

añadir *vt* to add (a, to).

añejo,-a *adj* **1** *(vino, queso)* mature; *(jamón)* cured. **2** *(viejo)* old.

añicos *nm pl* bits, pieces. [LOC] **hacer añicos** to smash to pieces. ‖ **hacerse añicos** to shatter, smash to bits.

año *nm* year: *el año pasado* last year; *el año que viene* next year; *los años sesenta* the sixties. [COMP] **año escolar** school year. ‖ **año luz** light year.
▶ *nm pl* years, age *sing*: *¿cuántos años tienes?* how old are you?; *tengo 20 años* I'm 20 years old. [LOC] **hace años** a long time ago, years ago.

añorar *vt* **1** *(gen)* to long for, miss, yearn for. **2** *(país)* to be homesick for, miss.

aorta *nf* aorta.

aovar *vi* to lay eggs.

apacible *adj* *(persona)* gentle, calm, placid; *(vida)* quiet, peaceful; *(clima, tiempo)* mild; *(mar)* calm.

apaciguar *vt* to pacify, appease, placate, calm down.

apadrinar *vt* **1** *(en bautizo)* to act as godfather to. **2** *(en boda)* to be the best man for. **3** *(artista)* to sponsor.

apagar *vt* **1** *(fuego)* to extinguish, put out. **2** *(luz)* to turn out, turn off, put out. **3** *(televisión, etc)* to switch off, turn off. **4** *fig (sed)* to quench.

apagón *nm* power cut, blackout.

apaisado,-a *adj* **1** oblong. **2** INFORM landscape.

apalancarse *vpr argot* to settle OS, settle down.

apalear *vt (pegar)* to beat, cane, thrash.

apañarse [LOC] apañárselas to manage, get by.

apaño *nm* **1** *(remiendo, compostura)* repair, mend, patch. **2** *(acuerdo)* agreement, deal.

aparador *nm* **1** *(escaparate)* shop window. **2** *(mueble)* sideboard, cupboard, buffet.

aparato *nm* **1** *(mecanismo)* (piece of) apparatus, set; *(eléctrico)* appliance. **2** *(dispositivo)* device; *(instrumento)* instrument. **3** *(teléfono)* telephone: *está al aparato* he's on the phone. **4** *(avión)* plane. [COMP] aparato de radio radio set. **‖** aparato digestivo ANAT digestive system.

aparcamiento *nm* **1** *(acción)* parking. **2** *(en la calle)* place to park, parking place. **3** *(parking)* car park, US parking lot.

aparcar *vt* to park.
▶ *vi* to park. [LOC] «Prohibido aparcar» «No parking».

aparearse *vpr* to mate.

aparecer *vi* **1** to appear: *no aparece en la lista de invitados* she's not on the guest list. **2** *(dejarse ver)* to show up, turn up: *espero que no aparezca por mi casa* I hope he doesn't show his face near my house.

aparejador,-ra *nm & nf (de obras)* clerk of works; *(perito)* quantity surveyor.

aparentar *vt* **1** *(simular)* to pretend, affect: *aparenta indiferencia* she pretends not to care, she affects indifference. **2** *(tener aspecto de)* to look: *no aparenta la edad que tiene* he doesn't look his age.
▶ *vi* to show off.

aparente *adj* apparent.

aparición *nf* **1** appearance. **2** *(visión)* apparition.

apariencia *nf* appearance, aspect. [LOC] **en apariencia** apparently, by all appearances. **‖** guardar las apariencias *fig* to keep up appearances.

apartado,-a *pp* → apartar.
▶ *adj* **1** *(alejado)* remote, distant; *(aislado)* isolated, cut off. **2** *(retirado)* retired.
▶ *nm* **apartado 1** post office box. **2** *(párrafo)* section.

apartamento *nm* small flat, apartment.

apartar *vt* **1** *(alejar)* to move away. **2** *(reservar)* to put aside, set aside.
▶ *vpr* **apartarse 1** *(alejarse)* to move away. **2** *(separarse)* to withdraw, move away.

aparte *adv* apart, aside, separately.
▶ *adj (distinto)* special: *eso es caso aparte* that's completely different.
▶ *nm* **1** TEAT aside. **2** LING paragraph: *punto y aparte* full stop, new paragraph. [LOC] **aparte de** *(excepto)* apart from. *(además de)* as well as, besides.

apasionante *adj* exciting, fascinating.

apasionarse *vpr* to get excited, become enthusiastic (por/de, about).

apatía *nf* apathy.

apátrida *adj* stateless.
▶ *nm o nf* stateless person.

apeadero *nm* halt.

apearse *vpr (del tren, autobús, etc.)* to get off; *(del coche)* to get out of; *(del caballo)* to dismount.

apedrear *vt* **1** *(tirar piedras)* to throw stones at. **2** *(matar a pedradas)* to stone (to death).

apego *nm* attachment, affection, liking, fondness.

apelación *nf* **1** JUR appeal. **2** *(llamamiento)* appeal, call.

apelar *vi* **1** JUR to appeal. **2** *fig (recurrir)* to resort to.

apelativo *nm* appellative, name.

apellidarse *vpr* to be called, have as a surname.

apellido *nm* family name, surname, (US last name).

apenas *adv* **1** *(casi no)* scarcely, hardly: *apenas lo conozco* I hardly know him. **2** *(con dificultad)* only just. **3** *(tan pronto como)* as soon as, no sooner: *apenas entramos, sonó el teléfono* no sooner had we had come in than the phone rang.

apéndice *nm* **1** *(órgano interno)* appendix. **2** *(de libro)* appendix.

apendicitis *nf inv* appendicitis.

aperitivo *nm* **1** *(bebida)* apéritif. **2** *(comida)* appetizer, snack.

apertura *nf* **1** *(comienzo)* opening, beginning. **2** POL liberalization.

apestar *vi* *(oler mal)* to stink.

apetecer *vi* *(agradar)* to feel like, fancy: *¿te apetece ir al teatro?* do you fancy going to the theatre?

apetecible *adj* **1** *(empleo)* desirable; *(idea)* appealing. **2** *(comida)* tasty, appetizing.

apetito *nm* appetite. LOC **abrir el apetito** to whet one's appetite.

apetitoso,-a *adj* **1** *(aspecto de comida)* appetizing; *(comida)* tasty, delicious. **2** *(oferta)* tempting.

apiadarse *vpr* to take pity (de, on).

ápice *nm* **1** *(punta)* apex. **2** *fig* tiny bit, speck, iota. LOC **ni un ápice** not one bit.

apicultura *nf* beekeeping, apiculture.

apilar *vt* to pile up, heap up.

apio *nm* celery.

apisonadora *nf* steamroller, roadroller.

aplacar *vt* to placate, calm, soothe.

aplanar *vt* to smooth, level, make even.

aplastante *adj* crushing, overwhelming. COMP **triunfo/victoria aplastante** *(electoral)* landslide victory.

aplastar *vt* **1** *(gen)* to flatten, squash, crush. **2** *fig (destruir)* to crush, destroy.

aplaudir *vt* to clap, applaud.

aplauso *nm* applause.

aplazamiento *nm (gen)* adjournment, postponement; *(de pago)* deferment.

aplazar *vt (gen)* to adjourn, postpone, put off; *(un pago)* to defer.

aplicación *nf* application.

aplicado,-a *pp →* aplicar.
▶ *adj (estudioso)* studious, diligent, hard-working.

aplicar *vt* to apply.
▶ *vpr* **aplicarse** *(esforzarse)* to apply OS, work hard.

aplique *nm* **1** *(adorno)* appliqué. **2** *(lámpara)* wall light, wall lamp.

aplomo *nm* composure, self-possession.

apocado,-a *adj* **1** *(intimidado)* intimidated, frightened. **2** *(tímido)* shy, timid.

apocalipsis *nm inv* apocalypse.

apócope *nm* apocope.

apodarse *vpr* to be nicknamed.

apoderado,-a *pp →* apoderarse.
▶ *nm & nf* **1** agent, representative. **2** *(de torero, deportista)* manager.

apoderarse *vpr* to take possession (de, of), seize (de, -): *el miedo se apoderó de é* he was seized by fear.

apodo *nm* nickname.

apogeo *nm* **1** *(de órbita)* apogee. **2** *fig (punto culminante)* summit, height, climax, peak.

apolítico,-a *adj* apolitical.

apología *nf* apology, defence (US defense).

apoplejía *nf* apoplexy, stroke.

aporrear *vt (persona)* to beat, hit thrash; *(puerta)* to bang on; *(piano)* to bang (away) on.

aportación *nf* contribution.

aportar *vt* **1** *(contribuir)* to contribute. **2** *(proporcionar)* to give, provide.

aposento *nm* **1** *(cuarto)* room. **2** *(hospedaje)* lodgings *pl.*

apósito *nm* dressing.

aposta *adv* on purpose, deliberately, intentionally.

apostar *vt* to bet (por, on).
▶ *vpr* **apostarse** to bet.

apóstol *nm* **1** apostle. **2** *fig (defensor* apostle, champion.

apóstrofe *nm & nf* **1** GRAM apostrophe **2** *(reprimenda)* reprimand, rebuke.

apotema *nf* apothem.

apoteósico,-a *adj* enormous, tremendous.

apoyar *vt* **1** to lean, rest. **2** *(fundar)* to base, found. **3** *fig (defender algo)* to support; *(defender a alguien)* to back, support.
▶ *vpr* **apoyarse 1** *(descansar)* to lean (en, on), rest (en, on), stand (en, on). **2** *fig (basarse)* to be based (en, on).

apoyo *nm* support.

apreciable *adj* **1** *(perceptible)* appreciable, noticeable. **2** *(estimable)* valuable, precious.

apreciar *vt* **1** *(valorar)* to appraise (en, at). **2** *(sentir aprecio)* to regard highly, hold in high esteem. **3** *(reconocer valor)* to appreciate. **4** *(percibir)* to notice, see, perceive.

aprecio *nm* esteem, regard. [LOC] **sentir aprecio por** ALGN to be fond of SB.

aprender *vt* **1** to learn. **2** *(memorizar)* to learn by heart.
▶ *vpr* **aprenderse** learn by heart.

aprendiz,-za *nm & nf* apprentice, trainee.

aprendizaje *nm* **1** *(situación)* apprenticeship. **2** *(tiempo)* training period. **3** *(en pedagogía)* learning.

aprensión *nf (miedo)* apprehension; *(asco)* squeamishness.

aprensivo,-a *adj* apprehensive.

apresar *vt* **1** *(tomar por fuerza)* to seize, capture. **2** *(asir)* to clutch.

apresurarse *vpr* to hurry, hurry up.

apretar *vt* **1** *(estrechar)* to squeeze, hug. **2** *(tornillo)* to tighten; *(cordones, nudo)* to do up tight. **3** *(comprimir)* to compress, press together, pack tight. **4** *(botón)* to press, push.
▶ *vi* **1** *fig (aumentar)* to increase, get worse: *el calor aprieta* it's getting hotter and hotter. **2** *(prendas)* to fit tight, be tight on.

apretón [COMP] **apretón de manos** handshake.

aprieto *nm* tight spot, difficulty, scrape, fix. [LOC] **poner a** ALGN **en un aprieto** to put SB in an awkward situation.

aprisa *adv* quickly.

aprobación *nf (gen)* approval; *(ley)* passing.

aprobado,-a *pp* → aprobar.
▶ *adj* approved, passed.
▶ *nm* **aprobado** EDUC pass (mark). [LOC] **sacar/tener un aprobado** to get a pass.

aprobar *vt* **1** *(gen)* to approve; *(ley)* to pass. **2** *(estar de acuerdo)* to approve of. **3** EDUC *(examen, asignatura)* to pass.
▶ *vi* to pass.

apropiación *nf* appropriation. [COMP] **apropiación indebida** JUR theft.

apropiado,-a *pp* → apropiarse.
▶ *adj* suitable, fitting, appropriate.

apropiarse *vpr* to appropriate (de, -), take possession (de, of).

aprovechable *adj* usable.

aprovechado,-a *pp* → aprovechar.
▶ *adj* **1** *(espacio)* well-planned. **2** *pey (egoísta)* selfish; *(gorrón)* sponging, scrounging. [LOC] **mal aprovechado,-a** wasted.
▶ *nm & nf fam (gorrón)* sponger, scrounger; *(oportunista)* opportunist.

aprovechamiento *nm* **1** *(uso)* use, exploitation: *el aprovechamiento de los recursos naturales* the exploitation of natural resources. **2** *(provecho)* improvement, progress.

aprovechar *vt* **1** *(emplear útilmente)* to make good use of, make the most of. **2** *(sacar provecho)* to benefit from, take advantage of.
▶ *vpr* **aprovecharse** *(de alguien)* to take advantage (de, of); *(de algo)* to make the most (de, of). [LOC] **¡que aproveche!** enjoy your meal!

aproximación *nf* **1** *(gen)* approximation. **2** *(acercamiento)* bringing together; *(de países)* rapprochement.

aproximado,-a *pp* → aproximar.
▶ *adj* approximate, estimated. [COMP] **cálculo aproximado** rough estimate.

aproximar *vt* to bring near, put near.
▶ *vpr* **aproximarse** to come near, come closer.

aptitud *nf* aptitude, ability.

apto,-a *adj* **1** *(apropiado)* suitable, appropriate: *no es apto para este trabajo* he's not suitable for this job. **2** *(capaz)* capable, able.

apuesta *nf* bet, wager.

apuesto,-a *adj* (*gen*) good-looking; (*hombre*) handsome.

apuntador,-ra *nm & nf* TEAT prompter.

apuntar *vt* **1** (*señalar*) to point (a, at). **2** (*arma*) to aim. **3** (*anotar*) to note down, make a note of. **4** TEAT to prompt.
▸ *vpr* **apuntarse 1** (*inscribirse*) to enrol. **2** *fam* (*participar*) to take part (a, in): ¿*te apuntas?* are you game?

apunte *nm* **1** note. **2** (*dibujo*) sketch.
▸ *nm pl* **apuntes** (*de clase*) notes.

apuñalar *vt* to stab.

apurar *vt* **1** (*terminar*) to finish up. **2** AM (*dar prisa*) to hurry, rush.
▸ *vpr* **apurarse 1** (*preocuparse*) to get worried, be worried. **2** AM (*darse prisa*) to hurry, rush.

apuro *nm* **1** fix, tight spot; (*de dinero*) hardship. **2** (*vergüenza*) embarrassment. LOC **estar/encontrarse en un apuro** to be in a tight spot. ‖ **pasar apuros 1** (*económicos*) to be hard up. **2** (*dificultades*) to be in a tight spot.

aquejado,-a *adj* suffering (de, from).

aquel,-ella *adj* **1** that. **2** **aquellos,-as** those.

aquél,-élla *pron* **1** that one; (*el anterior*) the former: *aquél es el mío* that one is mine. **2** **aquéllos,-as** those; (*los anteriores*) the former. LOC **aquél que...** he who... ‖ **todo aquél que...** anyone who..., whoever...

aquella *adj* → aquel.

aquélla *pron* → aquél.

aquello *pron* that, it.

aquellos,-as *adj* → aquel,-ella.

aquéllos,-as *pron* → aquél,-éllas.

aquí *adv* **1** (*lugar*) here: *por aquí por favor* this way please. **2** (*tiempo*) now: *de aquí en adelante* from now on.

árabe *adj* (*gen*) Arab; (*de Arabia*) Arabian.
▸ *nm & nf* Arab.

Arabia *nf* Arabia. COMP **Arabia Saudita** Saudi Arabia.

arácnido *nm* arachnid.

arado *nm* plough (US plow).

arancel *nm* tariff, customs duty.

arándano *nm* bilberry, blueberry.

arandela *nf* washer.

araña *nf* **1** (*arácnido*) spider. **2** (*pez*) weever. **3** (*lámpara*) chandelier. COMP **araña de mar** spider crab. ‖ **tela de araña** spider's web.

arañar *vt* **1** (*raspar*) to scratch. **2** *fig* (*recoger*) to scrape together.
▸ *vpr* **arañarse** to scratch.

arañazo *nm* scratch.

arar *vt* to plough (US plow).

arbitraje *nm* **1** (*en un desacuerdo*) arbitration. **2** DEP (*en fútbol, boxeo*) refereeing (*en cricket, tenis*) umpiring.

arbitrar *vt* **1** to arbitrate. **2** DEP (*en fútbol, boxeo*) to referee; (*en cricket, tenis*) to umpire.

arbitrario,-a *adj* arbitrary.

árbitro,-a *nm & nf* **1** arbiter, arbitrator. **2** DEP (*fútbol, boxeo*) referee; (*cricket, tenis*) umpire.

árbol *nm* **1** BOT tree. **2** TÉC axle, shaft. **3** MAR mast. **4** (*gráfico*) tree (diagram).

arboleda *nf* grove, wood, copse.

arbusto *nm* shrub, bush.

arca *nf* chest. COMP **arca de Noé** Noah's ark. ‖ **arcas públicas** Treasury *sing*.

arcada *nf* **1** (*conjunto de arcos*) arcade. (*de puente*) arch. **3** (*vómitos*) retching.

arcaico,-a *adj* archaic.

arce *nm* maple (tree).

arcén *nm* side of the road, verge; (*de autopista*) hard shoulder.

archipiélago *nm* archipelago.

archivador *nm* (*mueble*) filing cabinet. (*carpeta*) file.

archivar *vt* **1** (*ordenar*) to file (away). INFORM to save. **3** (*arrinconar*) to shelve.

archivo *nm* **1** (*informe, ficha*) file. **2** (*documentos*) files *pl*, archives *pl*. **3** INFORM file. **4** (*lugar*) archive. **5** (*archivador*) filing cabinet.

arcilla *nf* clay.

arco *nm* **1** ARQUIT arch. **2** (*en geometría*) arc. **3** (*arma*) bow. **4** (*de violín, etc*) bow. COMP **arco de medio punto** semicircular arch. ‖ **arco iris** rainbow. ‖ **arco voltaico** electric arc.

arder *vi* to burn; (*completamente*) to burn down; (*sin llama*) to smoulder.

ardid *nm* scheme, trick.

ardilla *nf* squirrel.

ardor *nm* **1** burning sensation, burn; *(calor)* heat. **2** *fig (ansia)* ardour (US ardor), fervour (US fervor). COMP **ardor de estómago** heartburn.

arduo,-a *adj* arduous.

área *nf* **1** *(zona)* area, zone. **2** *(medida)* are. **3** *(superficie)* area.

arena *nf* sand. COMP **arenas movedizas** quicksand *sing*.

arenisca *nf* sandstone.

arenoso,-a *adj* sandy.

arenque *nm* herring.

argamasa *nf* mortar.

Argelia *nm* Algeria.

argelino,-a *adj* Algerian.
► *nm & nf* Algerian.

Argentina *nf* Argentina, the Argentine.

argentino,-a *adj* Argentinian.
► *nm & nf* Argentinian.

argón *nm* argon.

argot *nm* **1** *(popular)* slang. **2** *(técnico)* jargon.

argucia *nf* sophism, subtlety.

argumentación *nf* **1** *(proceso)* arguing, argument. **2** *(argumento)* argument.

argumentar *vt* to deduce.

argumento *nm* **1** argument. **2** *(de novela, obra, etc)* plot.

aria *nf* aria.

aridez *nf* **1** aridity. **2** *fig* dryness.

árido,-a *adj* **1** arid. **2** *fig* dry.
► *nm pl* **áridos** dry goods.

Aries *nm inv* Aries.

ariete *nm* **1** *(fútbol)* centre (US center) forward. **2** *(máquina)* battering ram.

ario,-a *adj* Aryan.

arisco,-a *adj* **1** *(persona - altiva)* unsociable, unfriendly; *(- áspera)* surly, gruff; *(- huidiza)* shy. **2** *(animal)* unfriendly.

arista *nf* **1** *(línea)* edge. **2** *(filamento del trigo)* beard. **3** ARQUIT *(de viga)* arris; *(de bóveda)* groin. **4** *(de montaña)* arête.

aristocracia *nf* aristocracy.

aristócrata *nm o nf* aristocrat.

aritmético,-a *adj* arithmetical, arithmetic.

arma *nf* weapon, arm. LOC **alzarse en armas** to rise up in arms. ‖ **ser de armas tomar** *fig* to be formidable. COMP **arma blanca** knife. ‖ **arma de fuego** firearm.

armada *nf* navy, naval forces *pl*.

armadillo *nm* armadillo.

armador,-ra *nm & nf* shipowner.

armadura *nf* **1** *(traje)* suit of armour (US armor). **2** *(armazón)* frame. **3** ARQUIT framework.

armamento *nm* *(acción)* armament, arming.

armar *vt* **1** *(dar armas)* to arm. **2** *(cargar)* to load; *(bayoneta)* to fix. **3** *(montar - mueble)* to assemble. **4** *fam (causar, originar)* to cause, kick up, create: *armó un lío tremendo* he kicked up a tremendous fuss. LOC **armarla** *fam* to cause trouble, kick up a fuss.
► *vpr* **armarse 1** *(proveerse)* to provide OS (de, with), arm OS (de, with): *se armó de pintura y pincel y se puso a pintar* he provided himself with paint and paintbrush and began to paint. **2** *(producirse)* to be, break out: *se armó un jaleo* there was a right row. LOC **armarse de paciencia** to summon up patience. ‖ **armarse de valor** to pluck up courage.

armario *nm* *(para ropa)* wardrobe, US closet; *(de cocina)* cupboard. COMP **armario empotrado** built-in wardrobe, built-in cupboard.

armatoste *nm* *(cosa)* monstrosity; *(máquina)* useless contraption.

armazón *nm & nf* **1** frame, framework; *(de madera)* timberwork. **2** ARQUIT shell; *(de escultura)* armature.

armiño *nm* ermine.

armisticio *nm* armistice.

armonía *nf* harmony.

armónica *nf* harmonica, mouth organ.

armonioso,-a *adj* harmonious.

aro *nm* **1** hoop, ring. **2** *(juego)* hoop.

aroma *nm* aroma; *(del vino)* bouquet.

aromático,-a *adj* aromatic, fragrant.

arpa *nf* harp.

arpón *nm* harpoon.

arqueología *nf* archaeology (US archeology).

arqueólogo,-a *nm & nf* archaeologist (US archeologist).

arquero,-a *nm & nf* archer.

arquetipo *nm* archetype.

arquitecto,-a *nm & nf* architect.

arquitectura *nf* architecture.

arquitrabe *nm* architrave.

arquivolta *nf* archivolt.

arrabales *nm pl* outskirts.

arraigar *vi* to take root.
▶ *vpr* **arraigarse** *(establecerse)* to settle down.

arraigo *nm* **1** *(acción)* act of taking root. **2** *fig (raíces)* roots: *con mucho arraigo* deeply-rooted.

arrancar *vt* **1** *(árbol)* to uproot; *(flor)* to pull up. **2** *(plumas, cejas)* to pluck; *(cabello, diente)* to pull out; *(con violencia - página)* to tear out. **3** *(obtener - aplausos, sonrisa)* to get; *(- confesión, información)* to extract. **4** *(coche)* to start.
▶ *vi* **1** *(partir)* to begin, start. **2** *(salir)* to go, leave. **3** *(coche)* to start; *(tren)* to pull out.

arranque *nm* **1** TÉC starting mechanism. **2** *(comienzo)* start. **3** *fig (arrebato)* outburst, fit.

arrasar *vt* **1** *(destruir)* to raze, destroy. **2** *(allanar)* to level, smooth.
▶ *vi (disco, libro, película)* to be a smash hit, sweep the board; *(deportista)* to sweep to victory.

arrastrar *vt* **1** *(gen)* to drag, pull, **2** *(corriente, aire)* to sweep along. **3** *(traer como consecuencia)* to cause, bring, lead to.
▶ *vpr* **arrastrarse 1** to drag OS, crawl. **2** *fig (humillarse)* to creep, crawl.

arrastre *nm* **1** *(acción)* dragging, pulling. **2** *(telesquí)* drag lift. **3** *(en naipes)* lead.

arre *interj* gee up!, giddy up!

arrear *vt* **1** *(animales)* to spur on, urge on. **2** *(apresurar)* to hurry up. **3** *fam (pegar)* to hit: *le arreó una bofetada* she slapped him round the face.

arrebatar *vt* **1** *(quitar)* to grab, snatch. **2** *fig (cautivar)* to captivate, fascinate.

arrebato *nm (arranque)* fit, outburst.

arreciar *vi* to get stronger, get worse.

arrecife *nm* reef.

arreglado,-a *pp* → arreglar.
▶ *adj* **1** *(solucionado)* settled, fixed, sorted out. **2** *(ordenado)* tidy, neat, arranged, orderly. **3** *(bien vestido)* well dressed, smart.

arreglar *vt* **1** *(gen)* to settle, sort out, fix. **2** *(ordenar)* to tidy up, clear up. **3** *(reparar)* to mend, fix, repair. **4** MÚS to arrange. **5** *fam* to sort out: *¡ya te arreglaré!* I'll teach you!, I'll sort you out.
▶ *vpr* **arreglarse 1** *(componerse)* to get ready, dress up; *(cabello)* to do. **2** *(solucionarse)* to get sorted out, work out; *(pareja)* to get back together again. LOC **arreglárselas** to manage, cope: *arregla telas como puedas* do the best you can.

arreglo *nm* **1** *(acuerdo)* arrangement, agreement, settlement. **2** *(reparación)* repair. **3** MÚS arrangement. COMP **arreglo de cuentas** settling of scores, settling-up.

arremangarse *vpr* to roll up one's sleeves.

arremeter *vi* **1** *(gen)* to attack, charge; *(toro)* to charge. **2** *(verbalmente)* to attack.

arrendamiento *nm* **1** renting, leasing, letting. **2** *(precio)* rent.

arrendar *vt (dar en alquiler)* to let, lease; *(tomar en alquiler)* to rent, lease.

arrendatario,-a *nm & nf* **1** *(que da en arriendo)* leaseholder, lessee. **2** *(inquilino)* tenant.

arrepentido,-a *pp* → arrepentirse.
▶ *adj* regretful, repentant.
▶ *nm & nf* penitent.

arrepentimiento *nm* regret, repentance.

arrepentirse *vpr* **1** *(gen)* to regret (de, -). REL to repent (de, of).

arrestar *vt* **1** to arrest, detain. **2** *(poner en prisión)* to imprison, jail, put in prison.

arresto *nm* arrest.

arriar *vt* **1** *(velas)* to lower. **2** *(bandera)* to strike.

arriba *adv* **1** up; *(encima)* on (the) top: *ponlo más arriba* put it higher up. **2** *(piso)* upstairs: *vive arriba* he/she lives upstairs. **3** *(en escritos)* above: *véase más arriba* see above.

▶ *interj* up!: ¡arriba la República! long live the Republic!, up the Republic! |LOC| **de arriba abajo** from top to bottom. ▪ **hacia arriba** upwards.

arriesgado,-a *pp* → arriesgar.
▶ *adj* **1** *(peligroso)* risky, dangerous. **2** *(temerario)* bold, daring, fearless.

arriesgar *vt* **1** to risk; *(dinero)* to stake. **2** *(aventurar)* to venture.
▶ *vpr* **arriesgarse** to risk.

arrimar *vt* *(acercar)* to move closer.
▶ *vpr* **arrimarse** to move close, get close.

arrinconar *vt* **1** *(poner en un rincón)* to put in a corner. **2** *(retirar)* to lay aside, put away. **3** *(acorralar)* to corner.

arritmia *nf* arrhythmia.

arroba *nf* **1** *(medida de peso)* measure of weight equal to 11.502 kg, 25.3 lbs; *(medida de capacidad)* variable liquid measure. **2** *(Internet)* at, @.

arrodillarse *vpr* to kneel down, get down on one's knees.

arrogancia *nf* arrogance.

arrogante *adj* arrogant.

arrojar *vt* **1** *(tirar)* to throw, fling. **2** *(echar con violencia)* to throw out, kick out. **3** *(vomitar)* to vomit, throw up. **4** *(cuentas, etc)* to show, produce, give.
▶ *vpr* **arrojarse** to throw os.

arrojo *nm* boldness, dash, bravery, daring.

arrollador,-ra *adj* overwhelming, irresistible.

arrollar *vt* **1** *(envolver)* to roll (up). **2** *(al enemigo)* to crush, rout.

arropar *vt* to wrap up.

arroyo *nm* **1** *(corriente de agua)* stream, brook. **2** *(en la calle)* gutter.

arroz *nm* rice. |COMP| **arroz blanco 1** *(seco)* white rice. **2** *(hervido)* boiled rice. ▪ **arroz con leche** rice pudding. ▪ **arroz integral** brown rice.

arruga *nf* *(piel)* wrinkle; *(ropa)* crease.

arrugar *vt* *(piel)* to wrinkle; *(ropa)* to crease; *(papel)* to crumple (up).
▶ *vpr* **arrugarse 1** *(piel)* to wrinkle; *(ropa)* to crease; *(papel)* to crumple (up). **2** *fam* *(acobardarse)* to get the wind up.

arruinar *vt* **1** to bankrupt, ruin. **2** *(estropear)* to damage: *la tormenta ha arruinado la cosecha* the storm has ruined the crops.
▶ *vpr* **arruinarse** to be bankrupt, be ruined.

arrullar *vt* **1** *(ave)* to coo. **2** *(adormecer)* to lull.

arsenal *nm* **1** MAR shipyard. **2** *(de armas)* arsenal. **3** *fig* *(cantidad)* storehouse, mine.

arsénico *nm* arsenic.

arte *nm* **1** art. **2** *(habilidad)* craft, skill. **3** *(astucia)* cunning. **4** *(pesca)* fishing gear.

artefacto *nm* device, appliance; *(explosivo)* explosive device.

arteria *nf* artery. |COMP| **arteria carótida** carotid artery. ▪ **arteria coronaria** coronary artery.

artesa *nf* trough.

artesanal *adj* *(objeto)* handmade; *(comida)* home-made.

artesanía *nf* **1** *(calidad)* craftsmanship. **2** *(arte, obra)* crafts *pl*, handicrafts *pl*.

artesano,-a *adj* handmade.
▶ *nm & nf* *(hombre)* craftsman; *(mujer)* craftswoman.

artesonado *nm* panelled ceiling, coffered ceiling.

ártico,-a *adj* Arctic.
▶ *nm* **el Ártico** the Arctic. |COMP| **el Círculo Ártico** the Arctic Circle. ▪ **el océano Ártico** the Arctic Ocean.

articulación *nf* **1** LING articulation. **2** ANAT joint, articulation. **3** TÉC joint.

articulado,-a *pp* → articular.
▶ *adj* **1** *(lenguaje)* articulate. **2** *(objeto)* articulated.

articular *adj* articulated.
▶ *vt* **1** to articulate. **2** JUR to article.

artículo *nm* **1** article. **2** *(mercancía)* article, product. |COMP| **artículos de primera necesidad** basic commodities.

artífice *nm o nf* **1** *(artista)* craftsman, artist. **2** *(autor)* author: *Pepe ha sido el artífice de todo esto* this is all Pepe's doing.

artificial *adj* artificial.

artificioso,-a *adj* affected.

artillería *nf* artillery.

artilugio *nm* device, gadget.

artimaña *nf* artifice, trick, ruse.

artista *nm o nf* artist.

artístico,-a *adj* artistic.

artritis *nf inv* arthritis.

artrópodo *nm* arthropod.

artrosis *nf inv* arthrosis.

arzobispo *nm* archbishop.

as *nm* **1** *(naipes)* ace. **2** *(dados)* one. **3** *fig* ace, star, wizard.

asa *nf* handle.

asado,-a *pp* → asar.
▶ *adj* roast, roasted.
▶ *nm* **asado** roast.

asador *nm* **1** *(utensilio)* roaster. **2** *(establecimiento)* grill room, grill house.

asalariado,-a *nm & nf* wage earner, salaried worker.

asalmonado,-a *adj* salmon-pink.

asaltante *adj* assaulting, attacker.
▶ *nm o nf* attacker; *(en robo)* raider, robber.

asaltar *vt* **1** to assault, attack; *(para robar)* to raid, rob. **2** *(abordar)* to approach, come up to.

asalto *nm* **1** assault, attack; *(con robo)* raid, robbery. **2** *(boxeo)* round.

asamblea *nf* assembly, meeting.

asar *vt* to roast.
▶ *vpr* **asarse 1** *(cocerse)* to roast. **2** *fig* *(pasar calor)* to be roasting, be boiling hot. [LOC] asar a la parrilla to grill. ▌asar al horno to roast.

ascendencia *nf* **1** ancestry, ancestors *pl*: *era alemán, pero de ascendencia polaca* he was German, but of Polish descent. **2** *(influencia)* ascendancy.

ascender *vt* to promote.
▶ *vi* **1** *(subir)* to climb. **2** *(de categoría)* to be promoted (a, to). **3** *(sumar)* to amount (a, to).

ascendiente *nm o nf* *(antepasado)* ancestor.
▶ *nm* *(influencia)* ascendancy, power.

ascensión *nf* *(subida)* climb, climbing.

ascenso *nm* **1** *(subida)* climb, ascent. **2** *(aumento)* rise (de, in). **3** *(promoción)* promotion.

ascensor *nm* lift, US elevator.

asco *nm* disgust, repugnance. [LOC] dar asco to be disgusting. ▌hacer ascos a AL-GO to turn up one's nose at STH. ▌¡qué asco! how disgusting!, how revolting!

ascua *nf* live coal.

asear *vt* *(adecentar)* to clean, tidy up.
▶ *vpr* **asearse** *(arreglarse)* to wash, get washed.

asediar *vt* to besiege.

asedio *nm* siege.

asegurado,-a *pp* → asegurar.
▶ *adj* **1** *(con seguro)* insured. **2** *(garantizado)* secure: *tiene el futuro asegurado* his future is secure.

asegurar *vt* **1** *(fijar)* to secure. **2** COM to insure. **3** *(garantizar)* to assure, guarantee.
▶ *vpr* **asegurarse 1** *(cerciorarse)* to make sure. **2** COM to insure OS.

asemejarse *vpr* to look like, be like.

asentir *vi* to assent, agree; *(con la cabeza)* to nod.

aseo *nm* **1** *(acción)* cleaning, tidying up. **2** *(limpieza)* cleanliness, tidiness. **3** *(habitación)* bathroom, toilet.

aséptico,-a *adj* **1** aseptic. **2** *fig* cold, indifferent.

asequible *adj* accessible: *a un precio asequible* at a reasonable price, at an affordable price.

aserrar *vt* to saw (up).

asesinar *vt* **1** to kill, murder. **2** *(a un personaje importante)* to assassinate.

asesinato *nm* **1** killing, murder. **2** *(de un pesonaje importante)* assassination.

asesino,-a *nm & nf* killer; *(hombre)* murderer; *(mujer)* murderess.

asesor,-ra *adj* advisory.
▶ *nm & nf* adviser, consultant.

asesorar *vt* **1** *(dar consejo)* to advise, give advice. **2** COM to act as a consultant to.
▶ *vpr* **asesorarse** *(tomar consejo)* to take advice, consult (de, -).

asesoría *nf* **1** *(cargo)* consultancy. **2** *(oficina)* consultant's office.

aseveración *nf* asseveration, assertion.

asfalto *nm* asphalt.

asfixia *nf* asphyxia, suffocation.

asfixiar *vt* to asphyxiate, suffocate.

▶ *vpr* **asfixiarse** to asphyxiate, suffocate.

así *adv* **1** *(de esta manera)* thus, (in) this way. **2** *(de esa manera)* (in) that way: *por decirlo así* so to speak; *y así sucesivamente* and so on. **3** *(tanto)* as: *así usted como yo* both you and I. **4** *(por tanto)* therefore. **5** *(tan pronto como)* as soon as: *así que lo sepa* as soon as I know. LOC **así así** so-so. ▮ **así que** so.
▶ *adj* such: *un hombre así* a man like that, such a man.

Asia *nf* Asia.

asiático,-a *adj* Asian.
▶ *nm & nf* Asian.

asiduidad *nf* assiduity, frequency.

asiduo,-a *adj* assiduous, frequent.

asiento *nm* **1** *(silla, etc)* seat. **2** *(emplazamiento)* site. **3** COM entry, registry. LOC **tomar asiento** to take a seat.

asignación *nf* **1** *(acción)* assignment, allocation. **2** *(nombramiento)* appointment, assignment. **3** *(remuneración)* allocation, allowance; *(sueldo)* wage, salary.

asignar *vt* **1** to assign, allot, allocate. **2** *(nombrar)* to appoint, assign.

asignatura *nf* subject.

asilo *nm* **1** *(institución)* asylum, home, institution. **2** *fig (protección)* protection, assistance. LOC **dar asilo** to shelter. COMP **asilo de ancianos** old people's home. ▮ **asilo político** political asylum.

asimetría *nf* asymmetry.

asimilar *vt* to assimilate.

asimismo *adv* **1** *(también)* also, as well. **2** *(de esta manera)* likewise. **3** *(además)* moreover.

asir *vt* *(agarrar)* to grab, seize, grasp, take hold of.

asistencia *nf* **1** *(presencia)* attendance, presence. **2** *(público)* audience. **3** *(ayuda)* assistance, help, aid. COMP **asistencia médica** medical assistance. ▮ **asistencia técnica** technical backup. ▮ **falta de asistencia** absence.

asistenta *nf* cleaning lady.

asistente *adj* **1** *(que está)* attending. **2** *(que ayuda)* assistant.

▶ *nm o nf* **1** *(que está)* member of the audience. **2** *(que ayuda)* assistant. COMP **asistente social** social worker.

asistir *vi* *(ayudar)* to attend, be present.
▶ *vt* *(ayudar)* to help, assist; *(a los enfermos)* to attend, care for.

asma *nf* asthma.

asno *nm* ass, donkey.

asociación *nf* association.

asociado,-a *pp* → asociar.
▶ *adj* associated, associate.
▶ *nm & nf* associate, partner.

asociar *vt* to associate (a/con, with), connect, link.
▶ *vpr* **asociarse** **1** *(relacionarse)* to be associated (a/con, with). **2** COM to form a partnership, become partners.

asociativo,-a *nf* associative. COMP **propiedad asociativa** associativity.

asomar *vi* *(empezar a aparecer)* to appear, begin to show, come out.
▶ *vt* *(mostrar)* to stick out.
▶ *vpr* **asomarse** **1** *(a ventana)* to stick one's head out (a, of), lean out (a, of); *(a balcón)* to come out (a, onto). **2** *(aparecer)* to appear.

asombrar *vt* to amaze, astonish.
▶ *vpr* **asombrarse** to be astonished, be amazed, be surprised.

asombro *nm* amazement, astonishment, surprise.

asombroso,-a *adj* amazing, astonishing, surprising.

asomo *nm* sign, trace, hint. LOC **ni por asomo** by no means.

asonante *adj* assonant.

aspa *nf* **1** *(cruz)* cross. **2** *(de molino)* sail; *(de ventilador)* blade; *(armazón)* arms *pl*.

aspaviento *nm* fuss. LOC **hacer aspavientos** to make a great fuss.

aspecto *nm* **1** *(faceta)* aspect, side, angle. **2** *(apariencia)* look, appearance: *¿qué aspecto tenía?* what did he look like?

aspereza *nf* roughness, coarseness.

áspero,-a *adj* **1** *(cosa)* rough, coarse. **2** *fig (persona)* surly.

aspersión *nf* sprinkling.

aspersor *nm* sprinkler.

aspiración *nf* **1** *(al respirar)* inhalation, breathing in. **2** LING aspiration. **3** TÉC intake. **4** *fig (ambición)* aspiration, ambition.

aspirador *nm* vacuum cleaner, Hoover.

aspirante *nm o nf* candidate, applicant.

aspirar *vt* **1** *(al respirar)* to inhale, breathe in. **2** *(absorber)* to suck in, draw in. **3** LING to aspirate.
▶ *vi fig (desear)* to aspire (a, to).

aspirina® *nf* aspirin.

asquear *vt* to disgust, revolt.

asqueroso,-a *adj* **1** *(sucio)* dirty, filthy. **2** *(desagradable)* disgusting, revolting, foul.
▶ *nm & nf (sucio)* filthy person, revolting person.

asta *nf* **1** *(de bandera)* staff, pole. **2** *(de lanza)* shaft; *(pica)* lance, pike. **3** *(cuerno)* horn.

asterisco *nm* asterisk.

asteroide *adj* asteroid.
▶ *nm* asteroid.

astigmatismo *nm* astigmatism.

astilla *nf* splinter, chip.

astillero *nm* shipyard, dockyard.

astrágalo *nm* **1** ANAT astragalus. **2** ARQUIT astragal.

astro *nm* star.

astrofísica *nf* astrophysics.

astrología *nf* astrology.

astrólogo,-a *nm & nf* astrologer.

astronauta *nm o nf* astronaut.

astronomía *nf* astronomy.

astrónomo,-a *nm & nf* astronomer.

astucia *nf* **1** astuteness, cunning, shrewdness. **2** *(treta)* trick, ruse.

astuto,-a *adj* astute, cunning, shrewd.

asumir *vt* to assume, take on, take upon OS.

asunto *nm* **1** *(cuestión)* matter, issue; *(tema)* subject; *(de obra)* theme: *no quiero hablar del asunto* I don't want to discuss the matter. **2** *(negocio)* affair, business: *no es asunto tuyo* it's none of your business. **3** *(aventura)* affair, love affair.
COMP **asuntos exteriores** POL Foreign Affairs.

asustado,-a *adj* frightened, scared.

asustar *vt* to frighten, scare.
▶ *vpr* **asustarse** to be frightened, be scared.

atacar *vt* to attack.

atajar *vi* to take a short cut.

atajo *nm* **1** *(camino)* short cut. **2** *fig (grupo)* bunch.

atalaya *nf* *(torre)* watchtower, lookout; *(mirador)* vantage point.

ataque *nm* **1** attack. **2** MED fit. COMP **ataque de nervios** nervous breakdown.

atar *vt* to tie. LOC **atar cabos** *fig* to put two and two together.

atardecer *vi* to get dark, grow dark.
▶ *nm* evening, dusk.

atareado,-a *adj* busy, occupied.

atascar *vt* **1** *(bloquear)* to block up, clog. **2** *fig (obstaculizar)* to hamper, hinder, obstruct.
▶ *vpr* **atascarse 1** *(bloquearse)* to get blocked. **2** *(mecanismo)* to get stuck.

atasco *nm* **1** *(acción)* obstruction, blockage. **2** *(de tráfico)* traffic jam.

ataúd *nm* coffin.

ataviar *vt* **1** *(arreglar)* to dress up. **2** *(adornar)* to adorn, deck.

ateísmo *nm* atheism.

atemorizar *vt* to frighten, scare.

atención *nf* **1** *(gen)* attention. **2** *(detalle)* nice thought: *fue una atención por su parte* it was a nice thought, it was very kind of him. LOC **a la atención de** ALGN *(en cartas)* for the attention of SB. ‖ **llamar la atención** to attract attention. ‖ **llamar la atención a** ALGN to take SB to task. ‖ **prestar atención** to pay attention (a, to).
▶ *interj* **¡atención!** *(gen)* your attention please!; *(cuidado)* watch out!, look out!

atender *vt* **1** *(servir - cliente)* to serve, attend to, see to: *¿ya la atienden?* are you being served? **2** *(cuidar)* to take care of, look after. **3** *(negocio)* to take care of; *(teléfono)* to answer. **4** *(consejo, advertencia)* to heed, pay attention to; *(ruego, deseo, protesta)* to attend to; *(instrucción)* to follow, carry out.

▶ *vi* **1** *(prestar atención)* to pay attention (a, to), attend (a, to). **2** *(tener en cuenta)* to bear in mind.

atenerse *vpr* **1** *(ajustarse)* to abide (a, by), comply (a, with). **2** *(acogerse)* to rely (a, on).

atentado *nm* **1** *(ataque)* attack, assault. **2** *(afrenta)* affront. COMP **atentado terrorista** terrorist attack.

atentamente *adv* **1** attentively, carefully. **2** *(amablemente)* politely; *(en carta)* sincerely, faithfully: «*Le saluda atentamente*» "Yours sincerely", "Yours faithfully".

atentar *vi (físicamente - a una institución)* to attack (a/contra, -), make an attack (a/contra, on); *(- a una persona)* to attempt to kill, make an attempt on sb's life.

atento,-a *adj* **1** attentive. **2** *(amable)* polite, courteous.

atenuante *adj* **1** attenuating. **2** JUR extenuating.

▶ *nm* JUR extenuating circumstance.

atenuar *vt* **1** to attenuate. **2** JUR to extenuate.

ateo,-a *adj* atheistic.

▶ *nm & nf* atheist.

aterrador,-ra *adj* terrifying, frightful.

aterrizaje *nm* landing. COMP **aterrizaje forzoso** emergency landing.

aterrizar *vi* to land.

aterrorizar *vt* to terrify.

atesorar *vt* **1** *(acumular)* to hoard, accumulate, store up. **2** *fig* to possess.

atestado[1] *nm* JUR affidavit, statement.

atestado,-a[2] *adj* packed (de, with), crammed (de, with).

atestiguar *vt* **1** JUR to testify to, bear witness to, give evidence of. **2** *(ofrecer muestras)* to attest, testify, vouch for.

atiborrarse *vpr fam (de comida)* to stuff OS (de, with).

ático *nm* **1** *(vivienda)* penthouse, attic flat. **2** ARQUIT attic, loft.

atinar *vi* **1** *(dar con)* to hit upon, find. **2** *(acertar)* to get it right, be right, succeed.

atípico,-a *adj* atypical.

atisbo *nm* **1** *(acción)* spying, watching. **2** *fig (indicio)* inkling, slight sign.

atizar *vt* **1** *(fuego)* to poke; *(vela)* to snuff. **2** *fig (pasiones)* to rouse, excite; *(rebelión)* to stir up. **3** *(dar - golpe)* give, deal.

atlántico,-a *adj* Atlantic. COMP **el (océano) Atlántico** the Atlantic (Ocean).

atlas *nm inv* atlas.

atleta *nm o nf* athlete.

atlético,-a *adj* athletic.

atletismo *nm* athletics.

atmósfera *nf* atmosphere.

atolondrado,-a *adj* **1** *(desatinado)* scatterbrained, reckless, silly. **2** *(aturdido)* stunned, bewildered.

atómico,-a *adj* atomic.

atomizador *nm* atomizer, spray.

átomo *nm* atom.

atónito,-a *adj* astonished, amazed.

átono,-a *adj* atonic, unstressed.

atontado,-a *adj* **1** *(aturdido)* stunned, confused, bewildered. **2** *(tonto)* stupid, silly, foolish.

atormentar *vt* **1** *(torturar)* to torture. **2** *fig (causar disgusto)* to torment, harass.

▶ *vpr* **atormentarse** *(sufrir)* to torment OS.

atornillar *vt* to screw on, screw down.

atracador,-ra *nm & nf (de banco)* (bank) robber; *(en la calle)* attacker, mugger, thief.

atracar *vt (robar - banco, tienda)* to hold up, rob; *(- persona)* to mug.

▶ *vi* MAR *(a otra nave)* to come alongside; *(a tierra)* to tie up, dock, berth.

▶ *vpr* **atracarse** *(de comida)* to gorge OS (de, on), stuff OS (de, with).

atracción *nf (gen)* attraction.

▶ *nf pl* **atracciones** *(de feria)* rides *pl*.

atraco *nm* hold-up, robbery.

atracón *nm fam* binge, blowout.

atractivo,-a *adj* attractive, charming.

▶ *nm* **atractivo** attraction, charm, appeal.

atraer *vt* to attract.

atragantarse *vpr (no poder tragar)* to choke (con, on), swallow the wrong way.

atrapar *vt* to seize, capture, catch.

atrás adv **1** back: *dio un salto atrás* she jumped back. **2** *(tiempo)* ago: *días atrás* several days ago.

atrasado,-a pp → atrasar.
- ► adj **1** *(desfasado)* outdated. **2** *(pago)* overdue. **3** *(reloj)* slow. **4** *(país)* backward, underdeveloped; *(alumno)* slow, backward.

atrasar vt *(gen)* to delay, postpone, put back; *(reloj)* to put back.
- ► vi *(reloj)* to be slow.
- ► vpr **atrasarse 1** *(tren, etc)* to be late. **2** *(quedarse atrás)* to fall behind.

atraso nm **1** delay. **2** *(de reloj)* slowness: *el tren lleva mucho atraso* the train is very late. **3** *(de un país)* backwardness.

atravesar vt **1** *(cruzar)* to cross, go across, go over; *(pasar por)* to go through, pass through. **2** *(experimentar - gen)* to go through, experience; *(enfermedad, etc)* to suffer. **3** *(poner oblicuamente)* to put across, lay across. **4** *(con bala, etc)* to go through; *(con espada)* to run through. **5** *(situación)* to go through.

atrayente adj attractive.

atreverse vpr to dare, venture.

atrevido,-a pp → atreverse.
- ► adj **1** *(osado)* daring, bold. **2** *(insolente)* insolent, impudent. **3** *(indecoroso)* daring, risqué.

atribuir vt to attribute (a, to), ascribe.

atributo nm attribute, quality.

atril nm *(para libros)* lectern, bookrest; *(para música)* music stand.

atrio nm **1** *(patio)* atrium. **2** *(vestíbulo)* vestibule, entrance hall.

atrocidad nf **1** *(barbaridad)* atrocity, outrage. **2** *(disparate - acción)* something stupid, foolish thing; *(- dicho)* silly remark, stupid remark.

atropellar vt **1** AUTO to knock down, run over. **2** *(arrollar)* to trample over.

atropello nm **1** *(accidente)* accident, collision; *(de coche)* knocking down, running over. **2** *(apresuramiento)* haste. **3** fig *(agravio)* outrage, abuse; *(de derecho)* violation.

atroz adj atrocious, outrageous.

atuendo nm attire, dress, outfit.

atún nm tuna, tuna fish, tunny.

aturdido,-a adj **1** *(confundido)* stunned, dazed, bewildered. **2** *(atolondrado)* reckless, harebrained.

audacia nf audacity, boldness, daring.

audaz adj audacious, bold, daring.

audición nf **1** *(acción)* hearing; *(radio, televisión)* reception. **2** TEAT audition. **3** MÚS concert.

audiencia nf **1** *(recepción)* audience, hearing. **2** *(entrevista)* formal interview. **3** JUR high court. **4** *(público)* audience.

audífono nm hearing aid, deaf aid.

audiovisual adj audio-visual.
- ► nm audio-visual.

auditar vt to audit.

auditivo,-a adj auditory.

auditor,-ra nm & nf FIN auditor.

auditorio nm **1** *(público)* audience. **2** *(lugar)* auditorium, hall.

auge nm **1** *(del mercado)* boom. **2** *(de precios)* boost. **3** *(de fama, etc)* peak, summit.

augurio nm augury.

aula nf *(en escuela)* classroom; *(en universidad)* lecture room.

aullar vi to howl, yell, bay.

aullido nm howl, yell.

aumentar vt **1** to augment, increase; *(precios)* to put up; *(producción)* to step up. **2** *(óptica)* to magnify. **3** *(fotos)* to enlarge. **4** *(sonido)* to amplify.

aumento nm **1** increase, growth. **2** *(óptica)* magnification. **3** *(fotos)* enlargement. **4** *(sonido)* amplification. **5** *(salario)* rise, US raise.

aun adv even: *aun los tontos lo saben* even a fool knows that.
- ► conj *(+ gerundio o participio)* although, even though: *aun llegando tarde, lo recibieron amablemente* although he was late, he was given a warm reception. LOC **aun así** even so, even then. ‖ **aun cuando** although, even though.

aún adv *(afirmación)* still; *(negación, interrogación)* yet: *aún no ha llamado* he hasn't phoned yet. LOC **aún más** even more.

aunque conj **1** *(valor concesivo)* although, though; *(con énfasis)* even if, even though. **2** *(valor adversativo)* but.

aupar *vt* to help up.

aureola *nf* aureole, halo.

aurícula *nf* auricle.

auricular *adj* auricular, of the ear.
▶ *nm* **1** *(teléfono)* receiver, earpiece. **2** *(dedo)* little finger.
▶ *nm pl* **auriculares** earphones, headphones.

aurora *nf* dawn, daybreak. COMP **aurora boreal/borealis** aurora borealis, northern lights *pl*.

auscultar *vt* to sound.

ausencia *nf* absence.

ausentarse *vpr* **1** *(faltar)* to be absent. **2** *(irse)* to leave.

ausente *adj* **1** absent. **2** *(distraído)* lost in thought.
▶ *nm o nf* absentee.

austeridad *nf* austerity.

austero,-a *adj* austere.

Australia *nf* Australia.

australiano,-a *adj* Australian.
▶ *nm & nf (persona)* Australian.

australopiteco *nm* australopithecine.

Austria *nf* Austria.

austríaco,-a *adj* Austrian.
▶ *nm & nf* Austrian.

auténtico,-a *adj* authentic, genuine, real.

auto¹ *nm (coche)* car. COMP **autos de choque** bumper cars.

auto² *nm* **1** JUR decree, writ. **2** LIT mystery play, religious play.

autoadhesivo,-a *adj* self-adhesive.

autobiografía *nf* autobiography.

autobús *nm* bus.

autocar *nm* coach.

autocontrol *nm* self-control.

autóctono,-a *adj* indigenous.

autodefensa *nf* self-defence (US self-defense).

autodeterminación *nf* self-determination.

autodidacta *nm o nf* self-taught person.

autoescuela *nf* driving school, school of motoring.

autoestop *nm* → autostop.

autoestopista *nm o nf* → autostopista.

autógrafo,-a *nm* autograph.

autómata *nm* automaton.

automático,-a *adj* automatic.

automóvil *nm* automobile, car.

automovilismo *nm* **1** motoring. **2** DEP motor racing.

automovilista *nm o nf* motorist, driver.

automovilístico,-a *adj* car.

autonomía *nf* **1** *(gen)* autonomy. **2** *(capacidad para funcionar sin recargar)* range.

autonómico,-a *adj* autonomous, self-governing.

autónomo,-a *adj* **1** *(región)* autonomous. **2** *(trabajador)* self-employed.
▶ *nm & nf* COM self-employed person.

autopista *nf* motorway, US highway.

autopsia *nf* **1** autopsy, postmortem. **2** *fig* postmortem.

autor,-ra *nm & nf* **1** *(escritor)* writer, author; *(hombre)* author; *(mujer)* authoress. **2** *(responsable - gen)* person responsible; *(- de delito)* perpetrator.

autoridad *nf* authority.

autoritario,-a *adj* authoritarian.

autorización *nf* authorization.

autorizado,-a *pp* → autorizar.
▶ *adj* **1** *(oficial)* authorized, official. **2** *(experto)* authoritative, expert.

autorizar *vt* **1** to authorize. **2** JUR to legalize. **3** *(aprobar)* to approve of, give authority to.

autorretrato *nm* self-portrait.

autoservicio *nm* **1** *(restaurante)* self-service restaurant, cafeteria. **2** *(supermercado)* supermarket.

autostop *nm* hitchhiking.

autostopista *nm o nf* hitch-hiker.

autosuficiencia *nf* self-sufficiency.

autovía *nf* dual carriageway, US highway.

auxiliar *adj* auxiliary, assistant.
▶ *nm* **1** *(persona)* auxiliary, assistant. **2** GRAM *(verbo)* auxiliary.
▶ *vt (ayudar)* to help, assist; *(a un enfermo)* to attend; *(a un país)* to give aid to.
COMP **auxiliar administrativo** administrative assistant.

auxilio *nm* help, aid, assistance, relief.
▶ *interj* help! COMP **primeros auxilios** first aid *sing*.

aval *nm* endorsement, guarantee.

avalancha *nf* avalanche.

avalar *vt* to guarantee, endorse.

avance *nm* 1 *(acción)* advance. 2 *(pago)* advance payment. 3 *(de película)* trailer. [COMP] avance informativo TV news preview, US news brief.

avanzar *vi* to advance, go forward.
▶ *vt* 1 *(mover adelante)* to advance, move forward. 2 *(dinero)* to advance. 3 *(una propuesta)* to put forward.

avaricia *nf* avarice.

avaro,-a *adj (tacaño)* avaricious, miserly, mean; *(codicioso)* greedy, avaricious.
▶ *nm & nf (tacaño)* miser; *(codicioso)* greedy person.

avasallar *vt* to subjugate, subdue.

ave *nf* bird. [COMP] ave de rapiña bird of prey. I aves de corral poultry *sing*.

avecinarse *vpr* to approach (a, -).

avellana *nf* hazelnut.

avemaría *nf* Ave Maria, Hail Mary.

avena *nf* oats *pl*.

avenida *nf* 1 *(calle)* avenue. 2 *(riada)* flood, spate.

aventajar *vt* 1 *(exceder)* to surpass, beat. 2 *(ir en cabeza)* to lead, be ahead; *(llegar)* to come first, come ahead (a, of).

aventura *nf* 1 adventure. 2 *(riesgo)* hazard, risk. 3 *(relación amorosa)* (love) affair.

aventurado,-a *pp* → aventurar.
▶ *adj* 1 *(arriesgado)* dangerous, risky. 2 *(atrevido)* daring, bold.

aventurar *vt (idea, opinión, etc)* to venture, dare, hazard.
▶ *vpr* aventurarse to venture, dare.

aventurero,-a *nm & nf (hombre)* adventurer; *(mujer)* adventuress.

avergonzado,-a *pp* → avergonzar.
▶ *adj* embarrassed, ashamed.

avergonzar *vt (causar vergüenza)* to shame, put to shame; *(turbar)* to embarrass.
▶ *vpr* avergonzarse to be ashamed (de, of), be embarrassed (de, about).

avería *nf* 1 *(en productos)* damage. 2 TÉC failure. 3 AUTO breakdown.

averiado,-a *pp* → averiar.
▶ *adj* 1 *(en productos)* damaged. 2 TÉC faulty, not working, out of order. 3 AUTO broken down.

averiar *vt* 1 *(productos)* to damage, spoil. 2 TÉC to cause to malfunction. 3 AUTO to cause a breakdown to.
▶ *vpr* averiarse 1 *(productos)* to get damaged. 2 TÉC to malfunction, go wrong. 3 AUTO to break down.

averiguación *nf* inquiry, investigation.

averiguar *vt* to inquire, investigate, find out about: *averigua quién viene* find out who's coming.

aversión *nf* aversion. [LOC] sentir aversión por to loathe.

avestruz *nm* ostrich.

aviación *nf* 1 aviation. 2 MIL air force. [COMP] accidente de aviación air crash.

aviador,-ra *nm & nf* aviator, flier; *(hombre)* airman; *(mujer)* airwoman.

avidez *nf* avidity, eagerness.

ávido,-a *adj* avid, eager: *el chico estaba ávido de aventuras* the boy was thirsty for adventure.

avión *nm* aeroplane (US airplane), plane, aircraft.

avioneta *nf* light plane, light aircraft.

avisar *vt* 1 *(informar)* to inform, notify, announce. 2 *(advertir)* to warn. 3 *(mandar llamar)* to call for.

aviso *nm* 1 *(información)* notice. 2 *(advertencia)* warning. [LOC] hasta nuevo aviso until further notice. I sin previo aviso without prior notice.

avispa *nf* wasp.

avispero *nm* 1 *(conjunto de avispas)* swarm of wasps. 2 *(nido de avispas)* wasp's nest. 3 *fig (lío)* tight spot, mess.

avivar *vt* 1 *(fuego)* to stoke (up). 2 *(anhelos, deseos)* to enliven. 3 *(pasiones, dolor)* to intensify. 4 *(paso)* to quicken. 5 *(colores, luz)* to brighten up.

axial *adj* axial.

axila *nf* 1 *(del cuerpo)* armpit, underarm. 2 MED axilla. 3 *(de planta)* axil.

axioma *nm* axiom.

ay *interj* **1** *(dolor)* ouch!, ow! **2** *(pena)* alas!: *¡ay de mí!* woe is me!, poor me! **3** *(temor)* oh!

ayer *adv* **1** *(el día anterior)* yesterday. **2** *(en el pasado)* in the past, formerly.
▶ *nm* past. LOC **ayer por la mañana/tarde** yesterday morning/afternoon. ‖ **ayer por la noche** last night.

ayuda *nf* **1** help, aid, assistance. **2** *(lavativa)* enema. LOC **ir en ayuda de** ALGN to come to SB's assistance. ‖ **prestar ayuda** to help (a, -).

ayudar *vt* to help, aid, assist: *¿en qué podemos ayudarte?* how can we help you?
▶ *vpr* **ayudarse** *(apoyarse)* to make use (de/con, of).

ayunar *vi* to fast.

ayunas LOC **en ayunas** on an empty stomach: *tómalo en ayunas* take it on an empty stomach.

ayuno *nm* fast, fasting.

ayuntamiento *nm* **1** *(corporación)* town council, city council. **2** *(edificio)* town hall, city hall.

azabache *nm* jet. LOC **negro,-a como el azabache** jet-black.

azada *nf* hoe.

azafata *nf* **1** *(de avión)* air hostess, stewardess. **2** *(de congresos)* hostess.

azafrán *nm* saffron.

azahar *nm* *(de naranjo)* orange blossom; *(de limonero)* lemon blossom. COMP **agua de azahar** orange flower water.

azalea *nf* azalea.

azar *nm* **1** chance. **2** *(percance)* misfortune, accident. **3** *(en probabilidad)* event. LOC **al azar** at random. ‖ **por puro azar** by pure chance.

azotar *vt* **1** *(con látigo)* to whip, flog. **2** *(golpear)* to beat down on. **3** *(viento, olas)* to lash. **4** *fig (peste, hambre, etc)* to ravage.

azote *nm* **1** *(instrumento)* whip, scourge. **2** *(golpe)* lash, stroke (of the whip). **3** *(manotada)* smack. **4** *(del viento, del agua)* lashing. **5** *fig* scourge.

azotea *nf* flat roof. LOC **estar mal de la azotea** *fam* to have a screw loose.

azteca *adj* Aztec.
▶ *nm o nf* Aztec.

azúcar *nm & nf* sugar. COMP **azúcar blanco** refined sugar. ‖ **azúcar moreno/negro** brown sugar.

azucarado,-a *pp* → azucarar.
▶ *adj* **1** *(con azúcar)* sugared, sweetened. **2** *(como el azúcar)* sugar-like; *(dulce)* sweet. **3** *fig* sugary.

azucarero *nm* *(vasija)* sugar bowl.

azucarillo *nm* *(terrón)* sugar lump.

azucena *nf* white lily.

azufre *nm* sulphur (US sulfur).

azul *adj* blue.
▶ *nm* blue. COMP **azul celeste** sky blue, light blue. ‖ **azul cielo** sky blue, light blue. ‖ **azul eléctrico** electric blue. ‖ **azul marino** navy blue. ‖ **azul turquesa** turquoise. ‖ **sangre azul** blue blood.

azulejo *nm* *(baldosa)* tile, glazed tile.

azuzar *vt* to egg on.

B

B, b *nf (la letra)* B, b.

baba *nf* **1** *(de animal, adulto)* spittle, saliva; *(de niño)* dribble. **2** *(de caracol, babosa)* slime. LOC **caérsele a uno la baba** *fam* to drool.

babear *vi* **1** *(adulto, animal)* to slobber, slaver; *(niño)* to dribble. **2** *fig* to drool, slobber.

babero *nm* **1** bib. **2** *(babi)* child's overall.

babosa *nf* slug.

baca *nf* rack, roof rack, luggage rack.

bacalao *nm* cod.

bache *nm* **1** *(en carretera)* pothole. **2** *(de aire)* air pocket. **3** *fig* bad patch.

bachillerato *nm* **1** Spanish certificate of secondary education. **2** Spanish non-compulsory secondary education.

bacilo *nm* bacillus.

bacón *nm* bacon.

bacteria *nf* bacterium.

bádminton *nm* badminton.

bafle *nm* loudspeaker.

Bahamas *nf pl* **las Bahamas** the Bahamas.

bahía *nf* bay.

bailaor,-ra *nm & nf* flamenco dancer.

bailar *vt* **1** to dance. **2** *(hacer girar)* to spin: *bailó una moneda en la mesa* she spun a coin on the table.
▶ *vi* **1** to dance: *¿bailas?* do you want to dance?, would you like to dance? **2** *(girar)* to spin. **3** *(ser grande)* to be too big: *me bailan estos zapatos* these shoes are too big for me. **4** *(moverse - cosa)* to wobble; *(- persona)* to move about, fidget: *esta silla baila* this chair wobbles.
5 *(estar suelto)* to be loose: *este tornillo baila* this screw is loose.

bailarín,-ina *nm & nf* dancer.

baile *nm* **1** dance. **2** *(de etiqueta)* ball. **3** *(sala)* dance hall.

baja *nf* **1** *(descenso)* fall, drop. **2** *(por enfermedad)* sick leave.

bajada *nf* **1** *(disminución)* drop, fall. **2** *(descenso)* descent; *(de telón, barrera)* lowering. **3** *(camino)* way down. **4** *(en carretera, etc)* slope, hill.

bajar *vt* **1** *(coger algo de un lugar alto)* to get down. **2** *(dejar más abajo)* to lower. **3** *(reducir)* to lower, reduce, bring down. **4** *(recorrer de arriba abajo)* to go down. **5** *(en informática)* to download.
▶ *vi* **1** to come down. **2** *(reducirse)* to fall, drop: *ha bajado la temperatura* the temperature has dropped. **3** *(marea)* to go out. **4** *(apearse - de coche)* to get out (de, of); *(de bicicleta, caballo)* to get off (de, -).
▶ *vpr* **bajarse** to come down, to get out (de, -), to get off (de, -).

bajo,-a *adj* **1** *(gen)* low: *precios bajos* low prices. **2** *(persona)* short, not tall. **3** *(cabeza)* bowed, held low; *(ojos)* lowered, downcast. **4** *(marea)* out: *la marea está baja* the tide is out. **5** *(época)* late: *la Baja Edad Media* the late Middle Ages.

bajo *nm* **1** *(piso)* ground floor, US first floor. **2** *(de prenda)* bottoms *pl*, US cuff. **3** MÚS *(instrumento)* bass; *(contrabajo)* double bass.
▶ *nm o nf* MÚS *(músico)* bass player.
▶ *adv* low, softly, quietly.
▶ *prep* under, below.
▶ *nm pl* **bajos** ground floor;

bajura LOC **de bajura** inshore.

bala *nf* **1** bullet. **2** *(paquete)* bale.

balada *nf* ballad.

balancear *vt* to rock, swing.
▶ *vi* to rock, to swing.
▶ *vpr* **balancearse** *(mecerse)* to rock; *(columpio, brazo)* to swing.

balanceo *nm (gen)* swinging.

balancín *nm* **1** *(mecedora)* rocking chair. **2** *(columpio)* seesaw.

balanza *nf (aparato)* scales *pl*.

balar *vi* to bleat, baa.

balcón *nm (en edificio)* balcony.

balde *nm* bucket, pail. LOC **de balde** free, for nothing.

baldío,-a *adj* uncultivated, barren.
▶ *nm* **baldío** wasteland.

baldosa *nf* floor tile.

baldosín *nm* tile, wall tile.

balido *nm* bleat, baa.

balín *nm* pellet.

baliza *nf* **1** *(de mar)* buoy. **2** *(de tierra)* beacon.

ballena *nf* whale.

ballesta *nf (arma)* crossbow.

ballet *nm* ballet.

balneario,-a *adj* spa.

balón *nm* DEP ball.

baloncesto *nm* basketball.

balonmano *nm* handball.

balonvolea *nm* volleyball.

balsa *nf* **1** pool. **2** MAR raft.

bálsamo *nm* balsam, balm.

bambolear *vi* to sway.
▶ *vpr* **bambolearse** to sway.

bamboleo *nm* swaying.

bambú *nm* bamboo.

banal *adj* trivial.

banana *nf* banana.

banca *nf* **1** COM banking; *(bancos)* (the) banks *pl*. **2** *(en juego)* bank.

bancada *nf* **1** *(banco)* long bench. **2** *(superficie)* work surface.

bancal *nm* **1** *(en pendiente)* terrace. **2** *(en llano)* plot.

bancarrota *nf* bankruptcy. LOC **estar en bancarrota** to be bankrupt.

banco *nm* **1** bank. **2** *(asiento)* bench; *(de iglesia)* pew. **3** *(mesa)* bench, work bench. **4** *(de peces)* shoal. COMP **banco de datos** data bank.

banda¹ *nf* **1** *(faja)* sash. **2** *(lista)* band. **3** *(tira)* strip. **4** *(lado)* side. **5** *(en billar)* cushion. COMP **banda magnética** magnetic strip.

banda² *nf* **1** *(músicos)* band. **2** *(maleantes)* gang.

bandada *nf* **1** *(de pájaros)* flock; *(de insectos)* swarm; *(de peces)* shoal. **2** *(de personas)* horde.

bandeja *nf (gen)* tray; *(para diapositivas)* magazine.

bandera *nf* flag. COMP **bandera nacional** national flag.

banderilla *nf* **1** *(tauromaquia)* banderilla *(barbed dart stuck into the bull's back)*. **2** *(tapa)* pickled onion, carrot, gherkin, pepper, etc on a cocktail stick.

banderín *nm* pennant.

bandido,-a *nm & nf* bandit.

bando *nm* **1** *(facción)* faction, party, camp. **2** *(de aves)* flock; *(de insectos)* swarm; *(de peces)* shoal.

bandolera *nf* bandolier.

bandolero *nm* bandit.

banjo *nm* banjo.

banquero,-a *nm & nf* banker.

banqueta *nf* **1** *(taburete)* stool; *(para los pies)* footstool. **2** *(banco)* little bench.

banquete *nm* banquet, feast.

bañador *nm (gen)* swimsuit; *(de mujer)* swimming costume; *(de hombre)* swimming trunks *pl*.

bañar *vt* **1** *(lavar)* to bath: *me baño cada mañana* I have a bath every morning. **2** *(cubrir)* to coat: *bañó los pasteles en chocolate* she coated the cakes in chocolate.
▶ *vpr* **bañarse** to bathe; *(nadar)* to have a swim, go for a swim.

bañera *nf* bath, bathtub.

bañista *nm o nf* bather, swimmer.

baño *nm* **1** *(gen)* bath; *(en piscina, mar)* dip, swim. **2** *(cuarto)* bathroom; *(servicio)* toilet. **3** *(bañera)* bath, bathtub.
▶ *nm pl* **baños** *(balneario)* spa *sing*.

bar *nm* **1** *(cafetería)* café, snack bar; *(de bebidas alcohólicas)* bar. **2** FÍS bar.

baraja *nf (naipes)* pack, deck.

barajar *vt (naipes)* to shuffle.
baranda *nf* handrail, banister.
barandilla *nf* handrail, banister.
barato,-a *adj* cheap.
► *adv* **barato** cheaply, cheap.
barba *nf* **1** ANAT chin. **2** *(pelo)* beard.
barbacoa *nf* barbecue.
barbaridad *nf* **1** *(crueldad - cualidad)* cruelty; *(- acto)* atrocity, act of cruelty. **2** *(disparate)* piece of nonsense.
barbarismo *nm* barbarism.
bárbaro,-a *adj* **1** HIST barbarian. **2** *(cruel)* barbaric, savage, cruel. **3** *fam (espléndido)* fantastic, terrific.
► *nm & nf* HIST barbarian.
► *adv* **bárbaro**: *lo pasamos bárbaro* we had a great time.
barbecho *nm* fallow land.
barbería *nf* barber's shop, barber's.
barbero *nm* barber.
barbilla *nf* chin.
barbo *nm* barbel.
barca *nf* boat, small boat.
barcaza *nf* lighter.
barco *nm (gen)* boat; *(grande)* ship.
bardo *nm* bard.
baremo *nm* **1** *(para calcular)* ready reckoner. **2** *(tarifas)* scale, table.
barítono *nm* baritone.
barman *nm* barman, US bartender.
barniz *nm (para madera)* varnish; *(para cerámica)* glaze.
barnizar *vt (madera)* to varnish; *(cerámica)* to glaze.
barómetro *nm* barometer.
barón *nm* baron.
barquero,-a *nm & nf (hombre)* boatman; *(mujer)* boatwoman.
barquillo *nm (gen)* wafer; *(cucurucho)* cornet.
barra *nf* **1** *(en bar, cafetería)* bar. **2** *(vara)* bar; *(para cortinas)* rod; *(de bicicleta)* crossbar. **3** *(de helado)* block. **4** *(de pan)* loaf. COMP **barra de labios** lipstick.
barrabasada *nf* dirty trick.
barraca *nf* **1** *(casita)* cottage *(typical in Valencia and Murcia)*. **2** *(puesto)* stall; *(caseta de feria)* booth. **3** *(chabola)* shack.

barracón *nm* hut, large hut.
barranco *nm* **1** *(precipicio)* precipice. **2** *(torrentera)* gully; *(más profunda)* ravine.
barranquismo *nm* canyoning.
barrendero,-a *nm & nf* road sweeper.
barreno *nm* **1** *(barrena)* large drill. **2** *(agujero)* drill hole, bore hole.
barreño *nm* large bowl.
barrer *vt* **1** *(suelo)* to sweep; *(hojas, migas, etc)* to sweep up. **2** *(limpiar)* to sweep away: *el viento barrió las nubes del cielo* the wind swept the clouds from the sky.
barrera *nf* **1** *(gen)* barrier. **2** *(en plaza de toros - valla)* barrier; *(- asientos)* front row. **3** *fig* obstacle.
barricada *nf* barricade.
barriga *nf* belly, stomach, tummy.
barril *nm* barrel, keg.
barrio *nm* neighbourhood (US neighborhood); *(zona)* district, area.
barrizal *nm* quagmire.
barro *nm* **1** *(lodo)* mud. **2** *(arcilla)* clay: *objetos de barro* earthenware *sing*. **3** *(objeto)* earthenware object.
barroco,-a *adj* **1** ARTE baroque. **2** *fig* ornate.
barrote *nm* **1** bar. **2** *(de escalera, silla)* rung.
barullo *nm* noise, din, racket.
basar *vt* to base *(en, on)*.
► *vpr* **basarse** *(cosa)* to be based *(en, on)*; *(persona)* to base oneself on.
báscula *nf (gen)* scales *pl*; *(de farmacia)* weighing machine.
bascular *vi* **1** to tilt. **2** *(oscilar)* to swing. **3** *(variar)* to swing, alternate.
base *nf* **1** *(gen)* base. **2** *fig* basis. **3** QUÍM base, alkali. **4** MAT base. **5** *(en béisbol)* base. COMP **base de datos** database.
► *nf pl* **bases 1** *(de concurso)* rules. **2 las bases** *(de partido, etc)* grass roots.
básico,-a *adj (gen)* basic.
basílica *nf* basilica.
basta¹ *nf* tacking stitch.
basta² *interj* enough!, stop it!

bastante *adj* **1** enough, sufficient. **2** *(abundante)* quite a lot of: *había bastante gente* there were quite a lot of people.
▶ *adv* **1** enough: *son lo bastante ricos como para poder permitírselo* they're rich enough to be able to afford it. **2** *(un poco)* fairly, quite: *es bastante alto* it's fairly high. **3** *(tiempo)* some time, quite a while.

bastar *vi* to be enough, be sufficient, suffice: *mi sueldo no basta para pagar el alquiler* my salary is not enough to pay the rent. LOC **bastar con** to be enough: *es muy concentrado, basta con una gota* it's highly concentrated, one drop is enough.

bastidor *nm* **1** frame. **2** *(de lienzo)* stretcher. **3** *(de coche)* chassis. **4** TEAT wing.

basto¹ *nm* ≈ club.
▶ *nm pl* **bastos** ≈ clubs: *el as de bastos* ≈ the ace of clubs.

basto,-a² *adj* **1** *(grosero)* coarse, rough. **2** *(sin pulimentar)* rough, unpolished.

bastón *nm* **1** stick, walking stick, US cane. **2** *(de esquí)* stick, ski stick.

basura *nf* **1** *(cosa)* rubbish, US garbage. **2** *(persona despreciable)* swine. LOC **sacar la basura** to put the rubbish out.

basurero *nm* **1** *(persona)* dustman, US garbage man. **2** *(lugar)* tip, rubbish dump.

bata *nf* **1** *(prenda ligera)* housecoat; *(albornoz)* dressing gown, US robe. **2** *(de trabajo)* overall; *(de médicos, etc)* white coat.

batalla *nf* battle.

batallar *vi* to battle, fight.

batallón *nm* **1** MIL battalion. **2** *(multitud)* horde.

batata *nf* BOT sweet potato.

bate *nm* bat.

batear *vi* to bat.
▶ *vt* to hit.

batería *nf* **1** *(eléctrica)* battery. **2** TEAT footlights *pl*. **3** *(conjunto de cosas)* set; *(de preguntas)* barrage. **4** MÚS drums *pl*.
▶ *nm o nf* drummer. LOC **recargar las baterías** to recharge one's batteries. COMP **batería de cocina** pots and pans *pl*.

batido,-a *nm* batido **1** CULIN beaten eggs. **2** *(bebida)* milk shake.

batidor,-ra *nf* CULIN *(manual)* whisk.

batidora *nf* blender, mixer.

batir *vt* **1** *(huevos)* to beat; *(nata, claras)* to whip. **2** *(palmas)* to clap. **3** *(metales)* to beat. **4** *(alas)* to flap, beat. **5** *(derribar)* to knock down. **6** *(vencer)* to beat, defeat. **7** DEP *(marca, récord)* to break.
▶ *vpr* **batirse** to fight.

batracio,-a *adj* batrachian.
▶ *nm* batracio batrachian.

batuta *nf* baton. LOC **llevar la batuta** to be the boss.

baúl *nm* *(cofre)* chest; *(de viaje)* trunk.

bautismo *nm* baptism, christening.

bautizar *vt* **1** to baptize, christen. **2** *(poner nombre a)* to name.

bautizo *nm* baptism, christening.

bauxita *nf* bauxite.

baya *nf* berry.

bayeta *nf* **1** baize. **2** *(paño)* cloth.

bayo,-a *adj* bay, whitish yellow.
▶ *nm* bayo *(caballo)* bay.

baza *nf* **1** *(naipes)* trick. **2** *(ventaja)* asset, advantage. **3** *(ocasión)* chance. LOC **meter baza** *fig* to butt in, stick one's oar in.

bazar *nm* **1** *(oriental)* bazaar. **2** *(tienda)* electrical goods and hardware shop.

beatificar *vt* to beatify.

beato,-a *adj* **1** *(beatificado)* blessed. **2** *(devoto)* devout.

bebé *nm* baby. COMP **bebé probeta** test-tube baby.

bebedero,-a *nm* **1** *(abrevadero)* water trough. **2** *(vasija)* drinking dish.

beber *vt* to drink.
▶ *vi* **1** to drink. **2** *(emborracharse)* to drink, drink heavily: *bebe mucho* he's a heavy drinker.

bebida *nf* drink, beverage.

beca *nf* *(gen)* grant; *(concedida por méritos)* scholarship, award.

becar *vt* *(gen)* to award a grant to; *(por méritos)* to award a scholarship to.

becario,-a *nm & nf* grant holder, scholarship holder.

becerro,-a *nm & nf* calf *(up to one year old)*.

bechamel *nf* béchamel sauce, white sauce.

bedel,-la *nm & nf* porter.

beduino,-a *nm & nf* Bedouin.

begonia *nf* begonia.

beicon *nm* bacon.

beige *adj* beige.
▶ *nm* beige.

béisbol *nm* baseball.

belén *nm* REL nativity scene, crib.

belga *adj* Belgian.
▶ *nm & nf* Belgian.

Bélgica *nf* Belgium.

Belice *nm* Belize.

bélico,-a *adj* military. COMP **conflicto bélico** armed conflict, war.

belleza *nf* beauty.

bello,-a *adj* beautiful.

bellota *nf* acorn.

bemol *adj* MÚS flat.
▶ *nm* MÚS flat.

bencina *nf* benzine.

bendecir *vt* to bless.

bendición *nf* blessing.
▶ *nf pl* **bendiciones** wedding ceremony *sing*.

bendito,-a *adj* **1** *(bienaventurado)* blessed. **2** *(feliz)* happy: *¡bendita la hora en que la conocí!* happy the hour I met her! **3** *(poco inteligente)* simple.
▶ *nm & nf* simple soul.

benefactor,-ra *adj* beneficent.
▶ *nm & nf* *(hombre)* benefactor; *(mujer)* benefactress.

beneficiar *vt* **1** to benefit, favour (US favor). **2** *(mina)* to work. **3** COM to sell below par.
▶ *vpr* **beneficiarse 1** to benefit. **2** COM to profit. LOC **beneficiarse de ALGO** to do well out of STH, benefit from STH.

beneficiario,-a *nm & nf* beneficiary.

beneficio *nm* **1** *(ganancia)* profit. **2** *(bien)* benefit. LOC **a beneficio de** in aid of.
❙ **sacar beneficio de** to profit from.

beneficioso,-a *adj* beneficial.

benéfico,-a *adj* charitable. COMP **función benéfica** charity performance.

benevolencia *nf* **1** benevolence, kindness. **2** *(comprensión)* understanding.

benévolo,-a *adj* **1** benevolent, kind. **2** *(comprensivo)* understanding.

bengala *nf* *(para fiestas, etc)* sparkler.

benigno,-a *adj* **1** *(persona)* benign, gentle. **2** *(tumor)* benign. **3** *(clima)* mild.

benjamín,-ina *nm & nf* *(en familia - gen)* youngest child.
▶ *adj* DEP of the youngest age group *(9 or 10 years old)*.

berberecho *nm* cockle, common cockle.

berenjena *nf* aubergine, US eggplant.

berilo *nm* beryl.

bermudas *nm pl* Bermudas, Bermuda shorts.

berrear *vi* **1** *(becerro)* to bellow. **2** *(persona)* to bawl; *(niño)* to howl, bawl.

berrido *nm* **1** *(de becerro)* bellow. **2** *(de persona)* howl.

berrinche *nm* rage, tantrum, anger. LOC **coger un berrinche** to throw a tantrum.

berro *nm* watercress.

berza *nf* cabbage.

besamel *nf* bechamel, white sauce.

besar *vt* to kiss.
▶ *vpr* **besarse** *(uso recíproco)* to kiss.

beso *nm* kiss.

bestia *nf* *(animal)* beast.
▶ *nm o nf* *(persona - bruto)* brute; *(- ignorante)* ignorant fool; *(- torpe)* clumsy oaf.
▶ *adj* **1** *(bruto)* brutish. **2** *(ignorante)* ignorant; *(grosero)* rude; *(torpe)* clumsy. **3** *(asombroso)* fantastic, amazing. LOC **a lo bestia 1** *(fuerte)* hard. **2** *(a lo loco)* like a madman. **3** *(en cantidad)* in enormous amounts.

bestial *adj* **1** *(brutal)* beastly, bestial. **2** *fam (enorme)* enormous.

bestiario *nm* bestiary.

best-seller *nm* best-seller.

besucón,-ona *adj* fond of kissing.

besugo *nm (pez)* sea bream.

besuquear *vt* to kiss again and again.

betún *nm (para zapatos)* shoe polish.

bianual *adj* biannual.

biberón *nm* baby's bottle, bottle.

Biblia *nf* Bible.

bibliografía *nf* bibliography.

biblioteca *nf* **1** library. **2** *(mueble)* bookcase, bookshelf.

bibliotecario,-a *nm & nf* librarian.

bicarbonato *nm* bicarbonate.

bicentenario,-a *nm* bicentenary, US bicentennial.

bíceps *nm inv* biceps.

bicho *nm (animal)* animal, creature; *(insecto)* bug, creepy-crawly.

bici *nf fam* bike.

bicicleta *nf* bicycle. COMP **bicicleta de carreras** racing bike. ‖ **bicicleta de montaña** mountain bike.

bicolor *adj* two-coloured (US two-colored).

bidé *nm* bidet.

bidón *nm* drum.

biela *nf* AUTO connecting rod.

bien *adv* **1** *(gen)* well: *canta bien* she sings well. **2** *(como es debido)* properly, right: *si no pronuncias bien, no te van a entender* if you don't pronounce the words properly, they won't understand you. **3** *(acertadamente)* right, correctly: *contestó bien a todas las preguntas* she answered all the questions correctly. **4** *(de acuerdo)* O.K., all right: *ven mañana a las dos, -bien* -come tomorrow at two, -all right. **5** *(mucho)* very: *es bien sencillo* it's really simple. **6** *(de gusto, olor, aspecto, etc)* good, nice, lovely: *esta cerveza está muy bien* this beer's very good. **7** *(de salud)* well: *¿te encuentras bien?* are you feeling all right? **8** *(físicamente)* good-looking: *su novio está muy bien* her boyfriend's very good-looking. LOC **hacer bien** to do good. ‖ **¡ya está bien!** that's enough!

▶ *nm pl* **bienes** property *sing*, possessions. COMP **bienes inmuebles** real estate *sing*.

▶ *conj* **bien... bien** either... or: *se lo enviaremos bien por correo, bien por mensajero* we'll send it to you either by post or by messenger.

bienal *adj* biennial.

▶ *nf* biennial exhibition, biennial festival.

bienestar *nm* wellbeing, welfare: *bienestar social* social welfare.

bienhechor,-ra *adj* beneficent, beneficial.

bienio *nm (periodo)* two-year period, biennium.

bienvenido,-a *adj* welcome.

bífido,-a *adj* forked.

bifocal *adj* bifocal. COMP **gafas bifocales** bifocals.

bifurcación *nf (de la carretera)* fork; *(de ferrocarril)* junction.

bigamia *nf* bigamy.

bigote *nm* **1** moustache (US mustache). **2** *(de gato)* whiskers *pl*.

bigotudo,-a *adj* mustachioed.

bikini® *nm* → biquini®.

bilabial *adj* bilabial.

bilateral *adj* bilateral.

biliar *adj* biliary, bile.

bilingüe *adj* bilingual.

bilingüismo *nm* bilingualism.

bilis *nf inv* **1** bile. **2** *fig* spleen.

billar *nm* **1** billiards. **2** *(mesa)* billiard table. COMP **billar americano** pool.

▶ *nm pl* **billares** billiard room.

billete *nm* **1** *(moneda)* note, US bill: *un billete de cincuenta euros* a fifty-euro note. **2** *(de transporte, sorteo, teatro, etc)* ticket. COMP **billete de ida y vuelta** return ticket, US round-trip ticket.

billetera *nf* wallet, US billfold.

billetero *nm* purse, US change purse.

billón *nm* trillion.

✎ El uso español coincide con el antiguo significado británico en el que un billion era a million million.

binario,-a *adj* binary.

bingo *nm* **1** *(juego)* bingo. **2** *(sala)* bingo hall. LOC **¡bingo!** bingo!

binóculo *nm* pince-nez.

binomio *nm* binomial.

biodegradable *adj* biodegradable.

biografía *nf* biography.

biográfico,-a *adj* biographical.

biógrafo,-a *nm & nf* biographer.

biología *nf* biology.

biológico,-a *adj* biological.

biólogo,-a *nm & nf* biologist.

biomasa *nf* biomass.

biombo *nm* screen, folding screen.

biopsia *nf* biopsy.

bioquímica *nf* biochemistry.

biosfera *nf* biosphere.

bióxido *nm* dioxide.

bípedo,-a *adj* biped.

biplaza *nm* two-seater.

bipolar *adj* bipolar.

biquini *nm (traje de baño)* bikini.

Birmania *nf* Burma.

birria *nf* rubbish.

bis *adv* **1** *(en dirección):* viven en el 23 bis they live at 23A. **2** MÚS repeat, bis.

bisabuelo,-a *nm & nf* great-grandparent; *(hombre)* great-grandfather; *(mujer)* great-grandmother.

bisagra *nf* hinge.

biscote *nm* piece of Melba toast.

bisección *nf* bisection.

bisectriz *nf* bisector.

bisel *nm* bevel.

biselado,-a *adj* bevelled (US beveled).

bisiesto *adj* leap. COMP **año bisiesto** leap year.

bisílabo,-a *adj* two-syllabled.

bismuto *nm* bismuth.

bisnieto,-a *nm & nf* great-grandchild; *(chico)* great-grandson; *(chica)* great-granddaughter.

bisonte *nm* bison.

bistec *nm* steak.

bisturí *nm* scalpel.

bisutería *nf* costume jewellery (US jewelry).

bit *nm* bit.

biunívoco,-a *adj* one-to-one.

bivalente *adj* bivalent.

bivalvo,-a *adj* bivalve, bivalvular.

bizco,-a *adj* cross-eyed.

bizcocho *nm* sponge, sponge cake.

biznieto,-a *nm & nf* → bisnieto,-a.

bizquear *vi* to squint, be cross-eyed.

blanco,-a *adj* white.
▶ *nm & nf (gen)* white; *(hombre)* white man; *(mujer)* white woman.
▶ *nm* **blanco 1** *(color)* white. **2** *(objetivo)* target, mark. **3** *fig* object: fue el blanco de todas sus críticas he was the target of all their criticism. **4** *(hueco)* blank, gap; *(en escrito)* blank space. **5** *(vino)* white wine.

blancura *nf* whiteness.

blando,-a *adj (gen)* soft.

blandura *nf* softness.

blanquear *vt* **1** to whiten, make white. **2** *(con cal)* to whitewash. **3** *(con lejía)* to bleach.
▶ *vi* to whiten, turn white.

blanquecino,-a *adj* whitish, off-white.

blanqueo *nm* **1** whitening. **2** *(con cal)* whitewashing.

bledo *nm* common amaranth. LOC **me importa un bledo** *fam* I don't care less, I couldn't give a damn.

blindado,-a *adj* armoured (US armored). COMP **puerta blindada** reinforced door.

blindaje *nm* **1** armour (US armor), armour-plating (US armor-plating). **2** *(de puerta)* reinforcing.

blindar *vt* **1** to armour-plate (US armor-plate). **2** *(puerta)* to reinforce.

bloc *nm* notepad, pad.

bloque *nm* **1** block. **2** *(papel)* pad, notepad. LOC **en bloque** en bloc.

bloquear *vt (gen)* to block: esto podría bloquear el proceso de paz this could block the peace process.
▶ *vpr* **bloquearse** *(persona)* to have a mental block.

bloqueo *nm* **1** *(gen)* blocking. **2** MIL blockade. **3** *(precios, cuenta)* freezing.

blues *nm inv* blues.

blusa *nf* blouse.

boa *nf (serpiente)* boa.

bobada *nf* silliness, foolishness. LOC **decir bobadas** to talk nonsense.

bobina *nf* **1** reel, bobbin. **2** ELEC coil.
bobo,-a *adj* silly, foolish.
 ▶ *nm & nf* fool.
boca *nf* **1** ANAT mouth. **2** *(abertura)* entrance, opening: *hay una boca de metro en la esquina* there's an entrance to the underground on the corner. LOC **boca abajo** face downwards. ‖ **callarse la boca** to shut up, shut one's mouth. COMP **boca a boca** kiss of life.
bocacalle *nf* entrance to a street.
bocadillo *nm* sandwich.
bocado *nm* **1** mouthful. **2** *(piscolabis)* snack, bite to eat. **3** *(mordedura)* bite.
bocajarro LOC **a bocajarro 1** *(disparar)* at point-blank range. **2** *(decir algo)* point-blank.
bocata *nm fam* sandwich, sarnie.
boceto *nm* sketch; *(proyecto)* outline.
bochorno *nm* **1** *(calor)* sultry weather, close weather; *(viento)* hot wind. **2** *fig (rubor)* embarrassment, shame.
bochornoso,-a *adj* **1** *(sofocante)* hot, sultry. **2** *fig (vergonzoso)* disgraceful, shameful.
bocina *nf* horn.
boda *nf* marriage, wedding.
bodega *nf* **1** *(almacén)* wine cellar. **2** *(tienda)* wine shop. **3** *(de barco)* hold.
bodegón *nm* still life.
body *nm* body.
bofetada *nf* slap, slap in the face.
bofetón *nm* hard slap.
boga *nf* vogue.
bogavante *nm* lobster.
bohemio,-a *adj (vida, etc)* bohemian.
 ▶ *nm & nf (artista, etc)* bohemian.
boicot *nm (no participación)* boycott.
boicotear *vt (no participar)* to boycott.
boina *nf* beret.
boj *nm* **1** *(árbol)* box tree. **2** *(madera)* boxwood.
bol *nm* bowl.
bola *nf* **1** *(gen)* ball. **2** *fam* fib, lie.
bolera *nf* bowling alley.
boletín *nm* **1** *(revista)* periodical. **2** *(de noticias)* bulletin, news bulletin. **3** *(impreso)* form. **4** *(de colegio)* report.

boleto *nm* **1** ticket. **2** *(quiniela)* coupon.
boli *nm fam* ballpen, biro.
bólido *nm fam (coche)* racing car.
bolígrafo *nm* ballpoint pen.
bolívar *nm* bolivar *(monetary unit of Venezuela).*
Bolivia *nf* Bolivia.
boliviano,-a *adj* Bolivian.
 ▶ *nm & nf* Bolivian.
bollo *nm* **1** *(dulce)* pastry, bun. **2** *(abolladura)* dent.
bolo *nm* skittle, ninepin.
 ▶ *nm pl* **bolos** skittles.
bolsa¹ *nf (gen)* bag: *¿tiene una bolsa de plástico?* have you got a plastic bag? COMP **bolsa de aseo** toilet bag. ‖ **bolsa de deportes** sports bag.
bolsa² *nf* stock exchange.
bolsillo *nm* pocket. LOC **de bolsillo** pocket: *una calculadora de bolsillo* a pocket calculator.
bolso *nm* handbag, US purse.
bomba *nf* **1** *(explosivo)* bomb. **2** *(noticia)* bombshell. **3** pump. LOC **pasarlo bomba** to have a whale of a time.
bombardear *vt* **1** *(desde el aire)* to bomb. **2** *fig* to bombard: *me bombardearon a preguntas* they bombarded me with questions.
bombardeo *nm (desde el aire)* bombing.
bombardero *nm* bomber.
bombear *vt (agua)* to pump.
bombero,-a *nm (gen)* firefighter; *(hombre)* fireman; *(mujer)* firewoman.
bombilla *nf* light bulb, bulb.
bombín *nm (sombrero)* bowler hat.
bombo *nm (tambor)* bass drum.
bombón *nm* chocolate.
bombona *nf* cylinder. COMP **bombona de butano** butane cylinder.
bonachón,-ona *adj* kind.
bondad *nf* kindness.
bondadoso,-a *adj* kind, good.
boniato *nm* sweet potato.
bonito *nm (pez)* bonito.
bonito,-a *adj* lovely, nice.

bono *nm* **1** *(vale)* voucher. **2** *(billete)* ticket.

bonobús *nm multiple-journey* bus ticket.

bonoloto *nm Spanish state-run* lottery.

boñiga *nf* cow dung.

boquerón *nm (pez)* anchovy.

boquete *nm* hole.

boquiabierto,-a *adj* open-mouthed, agape.

boquilla *nf* **1** *(de pipa, instrumento)* mouthpiece. **2** *(filtro de cigarrillo)* tip.

borbotear *vi* to bubble.

borbotón *nm* bubbling.

bordado,-a *nm* embroidery.

bordar *vt* to embroider.

borde¹ *adj (antipático)* unpleasant.

borde² *nm* **1** *(extremo)* edge. **2** *(de vaso, taza)* rim.

bordear *vt* to skirt, go round.

bordillo *nm* kerb, US curb.

bordo *nm* MAR board. LOC **a bordo** on board.

boreal *adj* boreal, northern.

bórico,-a *adj* boric.

borla *nf* tassel.

borrachera *nf* drunken state.

borracho,-a *adj (persona)* drunk.
▶ *nm & nf* drunkard, drunk.

borrador *nm.* **1** *(de pizarra)* duster. **2** *(goma)* eraser, GB rubber.

borrar *vt* **1** to erase, rub out. **2** INFORM to delete.

borrasca *nf (tormenta)* storm.

borrego,-a *nm & nf* lamb.

borrón *nm* blot, ink blot.

borroso,-a *adj (visión)* blurred, hazy.

Bosnia *nf* Bosnia. COMP **Bosnia-Herzegovina** Bosnia Herzegovina.

bosnio,-a *adj* Bosnian.
▶ *nm & nf* Bosnian.

bosque *nm* wood, forest.

bosquejar *vt* to sketch, outline.

bosquejo *nm (dibujo)* sketch; *(plan, etc)* outline.

bostezar *vi* to yawn.

bostezo *nm* yawn.

bota¹ *nf* boot. COMP **botas de agua** gum boots, US rubber boots.

bota² *nf (de vino)* wineskin.

botánico,-a *adj* botanical.

botar *vi* **1** *(pelota)* to bounce. **2** *(persona)* to jump, jump up and down.

bote¹ *nm* MAR small boat. COMP **bote salvavidas** lifeboat.

bote² *nm (salto)* bounce.

bote³ *nm* **1** *(lata)* tin, can. **2** *(tarro)* jar. **3** *(para propinas)* jar for tips, box for tips. **4** *(fondo)* kitty.

botella *nf* **1** bottle. **2** *(de gas)* cylinder.

botellín *nm* small bottle.

botijo *nm* earthenware jar *(with spout and handle for drinking)*.

botín¹ *nm (zapato)* ankle boot.

botín² *nm* **1** *(de guerra)* spoils *pl*, booty. **2** *(de robo)* haul.

botiquín *nm* first-aid kit.

botón *nm (gen)* button.

bóveda *nf* vault.

boxeador,-ra *nm & nf* boxer.

boxear *vi* to box.

boxeo *nm* boxing.

bóxer *nm (perro)* boxer.

boya *nf* **1** MAR buoy. **2** *(corcho)* float.

boyante *adj fig* prosperous.

bozal *nm* muzzle.

bracear *vi (nadar)* to swim.

braga *nf (prenda)* panties *pl*, knickers *pl*.

bragueta *nf* fly, flies *pl*.

braille *nm* Braille.

bramar *vi* to bellow.

branquia *nf* gill.

brasa *nf* ember, live coal.

brasero *nm* brazier.

Brasil *nm* Brazil.

brasileño,-a *adj* Brazilian.
▶ *nm & nf* Brazilian.

bravío,-a *adj (animal)* wild, fierce.

bravo,-a *adj (fiero)* fierce, ferocious.
▶ *interj* ¡bravo! well done!, bravo!

bravura *nf (fiereza)* fierceness.

braza *nf (natación)* breaststroke.

brazada *nf (natación)* stroke.

brazalete *nm* bracelet, bangle.

brazo *nm (de persona)* arm.
▶ *nm pl* **brazos** hands, workers.

brea *nf* tar, pitch.

brebaje *nm* brew, potion.

brecha *nf* **1** break, opening. **2** *fig* breach.

breve *adj* short, brief. LOC **en breve** soon, shortly.

brevedad *nf* brevity, briefness.

brezo *nm* heather, heath.

bricolaje *nm* do-it-yourself, DIY.

brida *nf* *(de caballo)* bridle.

bridge *nm* bridge.

brigada *nf* *(unidad militar)* brigade.

brillante *adj* **1** *(extraordinario)* brilliant: *un alumno brillante* a brilliant student. **2** *(pelo, metal, zapatos)* shiny; *(ojos)* sparkling; *(luz, color)* bright; *(pintura)* gloss.
▶ *nm (diamante)* diamond.

brillantina *nf* brilliantine.

brillar *vi* **1** *(luz, sol, luna, pelo, zapatos)* to shine. **2** *(ojos)* to sparkle; *(estrella)* to twinkle; *(metal, dientes)* to gleam; *(cosa húmeda)* to glisten. **3** *fig* to be outstanding.

brillo *nm* **1** *(gen)* shine. **2** *(de estrella)* twinkling; *(de ojos)* sparkle; *(de pelo, zapatos)* shine. **3** *(en televisor)* brightness.

brincar *vi (cabra, etc)* to skip; *(persona)* to leap, bound.

brinco *nm (de cabra)* skip, hop; *(de persona)* leap, bound.

brindar *vi (cabra, etc)* to toast (por, to), drink (por, to): *¡brindemos por el futuro!* let's drink to the future!
▶ *vt (ofrecer)* to offer, provide.
▶ *vpr* **brindarse** to offer (a, to), volunteer (a, to).

brindis *nm inv* toast.

brisa *nf* breeze.

británico,-a *adj* British.
▶ *nm & nf* British person, Briton, Britisher.

brizna *nf (gen)* bit; *(de hierba)* blade.

broca *nf (barrena)* drill, bit.

brocha *nf* brush, paintbrush.

brochazo *nf* brushstroke.

broche *nm* **1** *(cierre)* fastener. **2** *(joya)* brooch.

broma *nf* joke: *no es broma* It's not a joke.

bromear *vi* to joke.

bromista *nm o nf* joker.

bronca *nf* **1** *(lío)* row. **2** *(riña)* quarrel; *(discusión)* argument. **3** *(reprimenda)* telling-off.

bronce *nm* bronze.

bronceado,-a *adj* bronzed.
▶ *nm* **bronceado** tan, suntan.

bronceador,-ra *nm* suntan lotion.

broncear *vt (persona)* to tan, suntan.
▶ *vpr* **broncearse** to tan, get a tan.

bronquio *nm* bronchus.

bronquitis *nf inv* bronchitis.

brotar *vi (plantas - nacer)* to sprout; *(- echar brotes)* to come into bud.

brote *nm* shoot, sprout.

broza *nf* **1** *(hojas)* dead leaves; *(ramitas)* dead twigs. **2** *(maleza)* scrub, brush.

bruces LOC **caerse de bruces** to fall flat on one's face.

bruja *nf (hechicera)* witch.

brujería *nf* witchcraft, sorcery.

brujo,-a *nm* wizard, sorcerer.

brújula *nf* compass.

bruma *nf* mist.

bruñido,-a *adj* burnished.

brusco,-a *adj* **1** *(repentino)* sudden. **2** *(persona)* abrupt.

brusquedad *nf* **1** *(de carácter)* abruptness. **2** *(rapidez)* suddenness.

brutal *adj (cruel)* brutal, savage.

brutalidad *nf (crueldad)* brutality.

bruto,-a *adj* **1** *(cruel)* brutal. **2** *(necio)* stupid, thick. **3** *(tosco)* rough, coarse.
▶ *nm & nf (persona - violenta)* brute, beast; *(necio)* ignoramus.

bucal *adj* oral, mouth.

bucanero *nm* buccaneer.

bucear *vi* to dive.

bucle *nm* **1** curl. **2** INFORM loop.

bucólico,-a *adj* bucolic.

budismo *nm* Buddhism.

budista *adj* Buddhist.
▶ *nm o nf* Buddhist.

buen *adj* → **bueno,-a.**

bueno,-a *adj* **1** *(gen)* good. **2** *(persona - amable)* kind; *(- agradable)* nice. **3** *(tiempo)* good, nice. **4** *(apropiado)* right, suitable. **5** *(de salud)* well.
▶ *interj* **¡bueno!** *(sorpresa)* well, very well; *(de acuerdo)* all right!

buey *nm* ox, bullock.

búfalo *nm* buffalo.

bufanda *nf* scarf.

bufar *vi (toro)* to snort.

bufé *nm* buffet.

bufete *nm (de abogado)* lawyer's office.

bufido *nm* snort.

bufón,-ona *nm & nf* buffoon, jester.

buhardilla *nf* attic.

búho *nm* owl.

buitre *nm* vulture.

bujía *nf (de motor)* spark plug.

bulbo *nm* bulb.

bulevar *nm* boulevard.

Bulgaria *nf* Bulgaria.

búlgaro,-a *adj* Bulgarian.
▶ *nm & nf (persona)* Bulgarian.
▶ *nm* **búlgaro** *(idioma)* Bulgarian.

bulldozer *nm* bulldozer.

bullicio *nm* **1** *(ruido)* noise, racket. **2** *(tumulto)* bustle, hustle and bustle.

bullicioso,-a *adj (ruidoso)* noisy.

bulto *nm* **1** *(tamaño)* volume, size, bulk. **2** *(forma)* shape, form. **3** *(abultamiento - en cosa)* bulge; *(- en piel)* lump.

bum *interj* boom!

bumerán *nm* boomerang.

bungalow *nm* bungalow.

búnker *nm* bunker.

buñuelo *nm* fritter.

BUP *abrev* EDUC (Bachillerato Unificado Polivalente) former General Certificate of Secondary Education studies.

buque *nm* MAR ship, vessel.

burbuja *nf* bubble. LOC **con burbujas** *(bebida)* fizzy.

burbujear *vi* to bubble.

burdo,-a *adj* **1** *(tejido)* coarse, rough. **2** *(persona)* coarse, crude.

burgués,-esa *nm & nf* middle-class.

burguesía *nf* middle class.

burla *nf* **1** *(mofa)* mockery, gibe. **2** *(broma)* joke. **3** *(engaño)* deception, trick.

burlar *vt* **1** to deceive, trick. **2** *(eludir)* to dodge, evade.
▶ *vpr* **burlarse** to mock (de, -), make fun (de, of), laugh (de, at).

burlón,-ona *nm & nf* joker.

burocracia *nf* bureaucracy.

burócrata *nm o nf* bureaucrat.

burrada *nf* **1** drove of asses. **2** *fam* a lot: *me gusta una burrada* I love it.

burro,-a *adj* stupid.
▶ *nm & nf* **1** *(animal)* donkey, ass. **2** *(persona ignorante)* ass.

bus *nm* **1** AUTO bus. **2** INFORM bus.

busca *nf* search, hunt.

buscapersonas *nm* bleeper, pager.

buscar *vt* **1** *(gen)* to look for, search for. **2** *(en lista, índice, etc)* to look up: *búscalo en el diccionario* look it up in the dictionary. **3** *(ir a coger)* to go and get, fetch. **4** *(recoger)* to pick up.

búsqueda *nf* search.

busto *nm (figura)* bust.

butaca *nf (sillón)* armchair.

butacón *nm* easy chair.

butano *nm* butane.

buzo *nm* diver.

buzón *nm* letter box, US mailbox.

byte *nm* INFORM byte.

C

C, c *nf (la letra)* C, c.

C¹ *sím* **(Celsius)** Celsius; *(símbolo)* C.

C² *sím* **(centígrado)** centigrade; *(símbolo)* C.

cabal *adj* **1** *(exacto)* exact, precise. **2** *fig (persona)* honest, upright.

cábala *nf* **1** *(ciencia oculta)* cabala, cabbala. **2** [en este sentido, también se usa en plural con el mismo significado] *fig (conjetura)* guess, divination. **3** *fig (intriga)* plot.

cabalgar *vi* to ride (en/sobre, -).

cabalgata *nf* cavalcade.

caballa *nf* mackerel.

caballería *nf* **1** MIL cavalry. **2** HIST knighthood.

caballero,-a *nm* **1** gentleman, sir. **2** HIST knight.

caballete *nm* easel.

caballito *nm* small horse. COMP **caballito de mar** sea horse.
  ► *nm pl* **caballitos** *(tiovivo)* merry-go-round *sing*, US carrousel *sing*.

caballo *nm* **1** ZOOL horse. **2** *(ajedrez)* knight.

cabaña *nf (choza)* cabin, hut, shack.

cabecear *vi* **1** to move one's head, shake one's head. **2** *(dar cabezadas)* to nod.

cabecera *nf* **1** *(gen)* top, head. **2** *(de un periódico)* headline.

cabecilla *nm o nf* leader.

cabellera *nf* hair, head of hair.

cabello *nm* hair.

caber *vi* **1** *(encajar)* to fit (en, into): *cabe ahí arriba* it'll fit up there. **2** *(pasar)* to fit, go. **3** MAT to go: *ocho entre dos caben a cuatro* two into eight goes four times, eight divided by two is four.

cabeza *nf* **1** *(gen)* head: *diez mil por cabeza* ten thousand a head. **2** *fig (juicio)* good judgement; *(talento)* talent, intelligence. LOC **cabeza abajo** upside down. ▮ **estar mal de la cabeza** *fig* not to be right in the head. ▮ **meterse ALGO en la cabeza** *fam* to get STH into one's head. COMP **cabeza cuadrada** *fam* bigot. ▮ **cabeza de ajo** bulb of garlic. ▮ **cabeza rapada** skinhead.

cabezada *nf (golpe recibido)* blow on the head; *(golpe dado)* butt, head butt. LOC **dar cabezadas** *fam* to nod.

cabezal *nm* TÉC head, headstock.

cabina *nf (gen)* cabin, booth. COMP **cabina telefónica** telephone box, US telephone booth.

cable *nm (maroma)* cable.

cabo *nm* **1** *(extremo)* end, stub. **2** *fig* end: *al cabo de un mes* in a month's time. **3** *(cuerda)* rope, line. **4** GEOG cape. LOC **al cabo** finally. ▮ **llevar a cabo** to carry out.

cabra *nf* goat. LOC **estar como una cabra** *fam* to be off one's rocker, be nuts.

cabrito *nm* ZOOL kid.

caca *nf* **1** *fam euf (excremento)* pooh. **2** *fam (en lenguaje infantil)* dirt.

cacahuete *nm (fruto)* peanut.

cacao *nm* **1** BOT cacao. **2** *(polvo, bebida)* cocoa. **3** *fam (jaleo)* mess, cockup.

cacarear *vi (gallina)* to cluck; *(gallo)* to crow.

cacatúa *nf (ave)* cockatoo.

cacería *nf* hunting, hunt.

cacerola *nf* saucepan, casserole.

cachalote *nm* sperm whale.

cacharro *nm* **1** *(de cocina)* crock, piece of crockery. **2** *fam (cosa)* piece of junk. **3** *fam pey (coche)* banger.

cachemira *nf (tejido)* cashmere.

cachete *nm (bofetada)* slap.

cacho *nm fam* bit, piece.

cachorro,-a *nm & nf (de perro)* pup, puppy; *(de gato)* kitten; *(de león, oso, zorro, tigre)* cub; *(de otros mamíferos)* young.

cacique *nm* **1** *(jefe indio)* chief, cacique. **2** POL local political boss.

caco *nm fam* thief.

cacto *nm* cactus.

cada *adj* **1** *(de dos)* each; *(de varios)* every. **2** *fam (intensificador)* such: *¡dice cada cosa!* he says such strange things! LOC **cada día** every day.

cadáver *nm* corpse, cadaver, body, dead body.

cadena *nf* **1** *(gen)* chain; *(de perro)* leash, lead. **2** *(montañosa)* range. **3** *(musical)* music centre (US center). **4** TV channel. **5** RAD chain of stations. COMP **trabajo en cadena** assembly-line work.

cadera *nf* hip.

caducar *vi* **1** *(documento, etc)* to expire: *mi pasaporte caduca este año* my passport expires this year. **2** *(alimento)* to pass its sell-by date.

caducidad *nf* expiry.

caer *vi* **1** *(gen)* to fall: *caer de espalda* to fall on one's back. **2** *(derrumbar)* to fall down, collapse. **3** *(hallarse)* to be: *el camino cae a la derecha* the road is on the right. **4** *(coincidir fechas)* to fall on, be: *el día cuatro cae en jueves* the fourth falls on a Thursday. LOC **dejar caer** to drop: *dejé caer el vaso* I dropped the glass.
▶ *vpr* **caerse 1** *(gen)* to fall, fall down. **2** *(desprenderse)* to fall out: *se le cae el pelo* he's losing his hair. LOC **caerse de sueño** *fig* to be dead on one's feet, be ready to drop.

café *nm* **1** *(gen)* coffee. **2** *(cafetería)* café, coffee bar, coffee shop. COMP **café con leche** white coffee.

cafeína *nf* caffeine.

cafetera *nf* **1** *(para hacer café)* coffeemaker. **2** *(para servir café)* coffeepot.

cafetería *nf (gen)* snack bar, coffee bar.

caimán *nm* alligator, cayman.

caja *nf* **1** *(gen)* box. **2** *(de madera)* chest; *(grande)* crate. **3** *(de bebidas)* case. **4** *(en comercio)* cash desk, till; *(en banco)* cashier's desk; *(en supermercado)* checkout. **5** *(banco)* bank: *caja de ahorros* savings bank. COMP **caja registradora** cash register.

cajero,-a *nm & nf* cashier. COMP **cajero automático** cash point, automatic cash dispenser.

cajetilla *nf* **1** *(de tabaco)* packet, US pack. **2** *(de cerillas)* box.

cajón *nm* **1** *(en mueble)* drawer. **2** *(caja grande)* crate.

cal *nf* lime. COMP **cal viva** quicklime.

cala *nf* **1** *(ensenada)* cove, creek. **2** *(planta)* arum lily.

calabacín *nm* **1** *(pequeño)* courgette, US zucchini. **2** *(grande)* marrow, US squash.

calabaza *nf* gourd, pumpkin.

calabozo *nm* **1** *(prisión)* jail, prison. **2** *(celda)* cell.

calamar *nm* squid.

calambre *nm* **1** *(contracción)* cramp. **2** *(descarga eléctrica)* electric shock.

calamidad *nf (desgracia)* calamity, disaster.

calar *vt (mojar)* to soak through, soak, drench.
▶ *vpr* **calarse 1** *(mojarse)* to get soaked. **2** AUTO to stop, stall.

calavera *nf (cabeza del esqueleto)* skull.

calcetín *nm* sock.

cálcico,-a *adj* calcium, calcic.

calcinar *vt* **1** to calcine. **2** *fig* to burn.

calcio *nm* calcium.

calcita *nf* calcite.

calcomanía *nf* transfer.

calculador,-ra *adj* calculating.
▶ *nm & nf* calculator. COMP **calculadora de bolsillo** pocket calculator.

calcular *vt* **1** to calculate, work out: *calcular una suma* to calculate a figure. **2** *(suponer)* to think, suppose, figure, guess.

cálculo *nm* calculation, estimate.

caldera *nf* boiler.

calderilla *nf* small change.

caldo *nm* **1** CULIN stock, broth. **2** *(sopa)* consommé.

calefacción *nf* heating. COMP **calefacción central** central heating.

calefactor *nm (máquina)* heater.

calendario *nm* calendar. COMP **calendario académico** school year.

calentador,-ra *nm* heater.

calentar *vt* **1** *(comida, habitación, cuerpo)* to warm up; *(agua, horno)* to heat. **2** DEP to warm up, tone up.

calibre *nm* **1** *(de arma)* calibre. **2** *fig (importancia)* importance.

calidad *nf* **1** quality. **2** *(cualidad)* kind, types. LOC **de primera calidad** first-class.

cálido,-a *adj* warm: *un clima cálido* a warm climate.

caliente *adj (mayor intensidad)* hot; *(menor intensidad)* warm.

calificación *nf (nota)* mark.

calificar *vt* **1** *(determinar las cualidades)* to describe, qualify. **2** EDUC to mark, grade.

caligrafía *nf* **1** *(arte)* calligraphy. **2** *(escritura de una persona)* handwriting. COMP **ejercicios de caligrafía** handwriting exercises.

cáliz *nm* **1** REL chalice. **2** BOT calyx. **3** *lit (copa)* cup.

caliza *nf* limestone.

callar *vi (no hablar)* to be quiet, keep quiet. LOC **¡cállate!** keep quiet!, be quiet!

calle *nf* **1** street, road. **2** DEP lane. LOC **dejar a** ALGN **en la calle 1** *(sin trabajo)* to fire SB. **2** *(sin casa)* to leave SB homeless.

callejero,-a *adj (que gusta de callejear)* fond of wandering about.
▶ *nm* **callejero** *(de calles)* street directory.

callo *nm* MED callus, corn.

calma *nf* calmness, calm, tranquillity (US tranquility). LOC **tomárselo con calma** to take it easy.

calmante *adj* soothing, sedative, tranquillizing (US tranquilizing).

calmar *vt* **1** *(persona)* to calm (down). **2** *(dolor)* to relieve, soothe.
▶ *vpr* **calmarse 1** *(persona)* to calm down. **2** *(dolor, etc)* to abate, ease off.

calor *nm* heat, warmth: *hace calor* it is hot.

caloría *nf* calorie.

caluroso,-a *adj* **1** *(tiempo)* warm, hot. **2** *fig* warm, enthusiastic.

calva *nf* **1** *(de la cabeza)* bald patch. **2** *(de un bosque)* clearing.

calvo,-a *adj (persona)* bald.

calzada *nf* road, US pavement.

calzado *nm* footwear, shoes *pl*.

calzar *vt* **1** *(poner calzado)* to put shoes on. **2** *(llevar calzado)* to wear: *¿qué número calzas?* what size do you take?
▶ *vpr* **calzarse** *(forma reflexiva)* to put (one's shoes) on.

calzoncillos *nm pl* pants.

cama *nf (gen)* bed. LOC **guardar cama** to be confined to bed, stay in bed. I **hacer la cama** to make the bed. I **irse a la cama** to go to bed. COMP **cama de matrimonio** double bed. I **cama individual** single bed.

camada *nf (gen)* litter.

camaleón *nm* chameleon.

cámara *nf* **1** *(de parlamento)* house. **2** *(de rueda)* inner tube. **3** TÉC chamber. **4** *(fotográfica, de cine)* camera. **5** ANAT cavity. COMP **cámara alta** POL upper house. I **cámara baja** POL lower house. I **cámara de aire** air chamber. I **cámara de cine** cine camera, (US movie camera).
▶ *nm o nf (hombre)* cameraman; *(mujer)* camerawoman.

camarero,-a *nm & nf (de bar, restaurante - hombre)* waiter; *(mujer)* waitress.

camarón *nm* common prawn.

camarote *nm* cabin.

cambiar *vt* **1** *(gen)* to change: *han cambiado las sillas* the chairs have been changed. **2** *(intercambiar)* to exchange. **3** *(moneda extranjera)* to change, exchange.

▶ *vi* **1** *(gen)* to change: *has cambiado mucho* you have changed a lot.

▶ *vpr* **cambiarse 1** *(mudarse de ropa)* to change, get changed. **2** *(mudarse de casa)* to move.

cambio *nm* **1** change, changing. **2** *(intercambio)* exchange, exchanging. ᴸᴼᶜ **a cambio de** in exchange for. ▌**en cambio** on the other hand, but, whereas.

camelia *nf* camellia.

camello *nm* ᶻᴼᴼᴸ camel.

camerino *nm* dressing room.

camilla *nf (para enfermos)* stretcher.

caminar *vi (andar)* to walk.

▶ *vt (recorrer)* to cover, travel: *he caminado cinco kilómetros* I have covered five kilometres.

caminata *nf* long walk, trek.

camino *nm* **1** *(vía)* path, track. **2** *(ruta)* way, route. ᴸᴼᶜ **ir camino de** to be on one's way to. ▌**ponerse en camino** to set off (on a journey).

camión *nm* lorry, ᴜˢ truck. ᶜᴼᴹᴾ **camión de mudanzas** removal van.

camionero,-a *nm & nf* lorry driver, ᴜˢ truck driver.

camioneta *nf* van.

camisa *nf* shirt.

camiseta *nf* **1** *(ropa interior)* vest, ᴜˢ undershirt. **2** *(niqui)* T-shirt. **3** ᴰᴱᴾ shirt, jersey.

camisón *nm* nightdress, nightie.

campamento *nm* **1** *(acción de acampar)* camping. **2** *(lugar)* camp.

campana *nf* **1** *(gen)* bell. **2** *fam (extractora)* extractor hood, (ᴜˢ stove extractor hood).

campanada *nf* stroke of a bell.

campanario *nm* belfry, bell tower.

campanilla *nf* **1** *(gen)* small bell. **2** ᴬᴺᴬᵀ uvula. **3** *(flor)* morning glory.

campaña *nf* **1** campaign: *campaña electoral* election campaign.

campechano,-na *adj fam* frank.

campeón,-ona *nm & nf* champion.

campeonato *nm* championship.

campesino,-a *nm & nf (gen)* peasant; *(hombre)* countryman; *(mujer)* countrywoman.

camping *nm* camp site. ᴸᴼᶜ **hacer camping / ir de camping** to go camping.

campiña *nf* countryside.

campo *nm* **1** *(campiña)* country, countryside: *vivir en el campo* to live in the country. **2** *(agricultura)* field. **3** *(de deportes)* field, pitch. **4** *(espacio)* space: *en el campo de la medicina* in the field of medicine.

campus *nm inv* campus.

camuflaje *nm* camouflage.

cana *nf* grey hair, white hair.

Canadá *nm* Canada.

canadiense *adj* Canadian.
▶ *nm & nf* Canadian.

canal *nm* **1** *(artificial)* canal. **2** *(natural)* channel.
▶ *nm & nf* ᵀᴱᶜ channel.

canalizar *vt* to channel.

canalla *nm o nf* swine.

canalón *nm (por el borde del tejado)* gutter.

Canarias *fpl* **las (islas) Canarias** the Canary Islands, the Canaries.

canario,-a *adj* Canarian.
▶ *nm & nf* Canarian.
▶ *nm* **canario** *(pájaro)* canary.

canasto *nm (cesto)* basket, hamper.

cancelar *vt* **1** *(anular)* to cancel. **2** *(saldar una deuda)* to settle, pay.

cáncer *nm* cancer.

cancerígeno,-a *adj* carcinogenic.

cancha *nf (gen)* ground; *(tenis)* court.

canciller *nm* chancellor.

canción *nf* song. ᶜᴼᴹᴾ **canción de cuna** lullaby.

candado *nm* padlock.

candidato,-a *nm & nf* candidate.

candidatura *nf* **1** *(aspiración)* candidacy, candidature: *presentó su candidatura* she put forward her candidature. **2** *(lista de candidatos)* list of candidates.

candidez *nf* ingenuousness, innocence.

cándido,-a *adj* ingenuous, innocent.

candil *nm* oil lamp.

canela *nf* cinnamon.

cangrejo *nm (de mar)* crab.

canguro *nm* ᶻᴼᴼᴸ kangaroo.
▶ *nm o nf fam* baby-sitter.

caníbal *nm o nf* cannibal.

canica *nf* marble: *jugar a las canicas* to play marbles.

canino,-a *adj* canine.

canjear *vt* to exchange.

canoa *nf* canoe; *(bote)* boat.

canon *nm* 1 *(regla)* canon, norm. 2 *(cantidad de dinero)* tax.

canoso,-a *adj* grey-haired (US grayhaired).

cansado,-a *adj* 1 *(gen)* tired, weary: *estoy cansada* I'm tired. 2 *(que fatiga)* tiring: *es un trabajo muy cansado* it's a very tiring job. 3 *(harto)* tired (de, of), fed up (de, with).

cansancio *nm* tiredness, weariness.

cansar *vt* 1 *(causar cansancio)* to tire, tire out, make tired. 2 *(molestar)* to annoy; *(aburrir)* to tire, bore.
▶ *vi (causar cansancio)* to be tiring.
▶ *vpr* **cansarse** *(padecer cansancio)* to get tired, tire: *se cansó de correr* he got tired of running.

cantante *nm o nf* singer.

cantaor,-ra *nm & nf* flamenco singer.

cantar *vt* 1 to sing: *cantó una canción preciosa* she sang a beautiful song. 2 *(en juegos de naipes)* to call.
▶ *vi* 1 to sing. 2 *(pájaros)* to sing, chirp; *(insectos)* to chirp.

cántaro *nm (vasija)* pitcher. LOC **llover a cántaros** *fig* to rain cats and dogs.

cante *nm* MÚS singing.

cantera *nf (de piedra)* quarry.

cantero *nm* stonemason.

cántico *nm* canticle.

cantidad *nf (gen)* quantity; *(de dinero)* amount, sum.
▶ *adv fam* a lot: *llovía cantidad* it was pouring with rain.

cantimplora *nf* water bottle.

cantina *nf* 1 *(comedor)* canteen. 2 *(de estación)* buffet.

canto *nm* 1 *(arte)* singing. 2 *(canción)* song. 3 *(de cuchillo)* blunt edge. 4 *(esquina)* corner. 5 *(piedra)* stone, pebble. COMP **canto rodado** 1 *(grande)* boulder. 2 *(pequeño)* pebble.

cantor,-ra *adj* singing. LOC **pájaro cantor** songbird.
▶ *nm & nf* singer.

caña *nf* 1 *(planta)* reed. 2 *(tallo)* cane, stem. 3 *(de pescar)* rod. 4 *(de cerveza)* small glass of draught beer. COMP **caña de azúcar** sugar cane.

cañada *nf* 1 GEOG glen, dell, hollow. 2 *(sendero)* cattle track.

cáñamo *nm* BOT hemp.

cañería *nf* piping.

caño *nm (tubo)* tube.

cañón *nm* 1 *(de artillería)* gun; *(antiguamente)* cannon. 2 *(de arma)* barrel. 3 GEOG canyon.

caoba *nf* mahogany.

caolín *nm* kaolin.

caos *nm inv* chaos.

caótico,-a *adj* chaotic.

capa *nf* 1 *(prenda)* cloak, cape. 2 GEOL stratum, layer. 3 *(de pintura)* coat; *(de polvo)* layer; *(de chocolate, etc)* coating, layer.

capacidad *nf* 1 *(gen)* capacity: *hay capacidad para cinco personas* there's room for five people. 2 *fig (habilidad)* capability, ability.

capacitar *vt* 1 *(instruir)* to train, qualify. 2 *(autorizar)* to qualify, entitle.

caparazón *nm* shell, carapace.

capataz,-za *nm & nf (hombre)* foreman; *(mujer)* forewoman.

capaz *adj* 1 *(competente)* capable, able: *es una persona muy capaz* she's very capable. 2 *(cualificado)* qualified. 3 *(capaz)* capable (de, of): *no es capaz de eso* he's incapable of doing that.

capazo *nm* 1 *(cesto)* basket. 2 *(para bebé)* carry cot.

capellán *nm* chaplain.

capicúa *adj* reversible.

capilla *nf (iglesia)* chapel.

capital *nf* capital, chief town.

capitalismo *nm* capitalism.

capitalista *adj* capitalist.
▶ *nm o nf* capitalist.

capitán,-ana *nm & nf* 1 *(oficial)* captain. 2 *(jefe)* leader, chief. 3 DEP captain.

capitanear *vt* **1** *(gen)* to lead; *(tropas)* to command. **2** *(equipo)* to captain. **3** *(buque)* to captain.

capitel *nm* capital, chapter.

capítulo *nm* **1** *(gen)* chapter. **2** *fig (tema)* subject, matter.

capó *nm* bonnet, US hood.

capota *nf (cubierta plegadiza)* folding hood, folding top.

capricho *nm (deseo)* whim, fancy.

caprichoso,-a *adj* capricious, whimsical, fanciful.
▶ *nm & nf* whimsical person.

cápsula *nf (gen)* capsule.

captar *vt* **1** *(ondas)* to receive. **2** *(entender)* to understand, grasp. **3** *(atraer a personas)* to attract, recruit.

captura *nf* capture.

capturar *vt* to capture, seize.

capucha *nf* hood.

capuchón *nm (de estilográfica, etc)* cap.

capullo *nm* **1** *(de insectos)* cocoon. **2** BOT bud.

caqui *adj* khaki.

cara *nf* **1** *(rostro)* face. **2** *(expresión)* face, expression. **3** *(lado)* side; *(de moneda)* right side. **4** *(superficie)* face. **5** *fig (aspecto)* look. **6** *fam fig (desvergüenza)* cheek, nerve: *¡vaya cara!* what a cheek! LOC **dar la cara** *fig* to face the consequences. **poner buena cara** to look pleased. ‖ COMP **cara de circunstancias** *fig* serious look. ‖ **cara dura** *fig* cheek, nerve.

carabina *nf (arma)* carbine, rifle.

caracol *nm (de tierra)* snail.

caracola *nf* conch.

carácter *nm* **1** *(personalidad)* character. **2** *(condición)* nature, kind. LOC **tener buen carácter** to be good-natured.

característico,-a *adj* characteristic.

carambola *nf (billar)* cannon, US carom.

caramelo *nm (dulce)* sweet, US candy.

caravana *nf (expedición)* caravan. *(atasco)* traffic jam, tailback.

caray *interj* good heavens!, God!

carbón *nm (gen)* coal.

carboncillo *nm* charcoal.

carbónico,-a *adj* carbonic. COMP **anhídrido carbónico** carbon dioxide.

carbonífero,-a *adj* carboniferous.

carbonilla *nf (residuo de carbón)* coal dust.

carbonizar *vt* **1** *(reducir a carbón)* to carbonize. **2** *(quemar)* to burn, char.

carbono *nm* carbon. COMP **dióxido de carbono** carbon dioxide.

carburador *nm* carburettor (US carburetor).

carcajada *nf* burst of laughter, guffaw. LOC **reír(se) a carcajadas** to laugh one's head off, roar with laughter.

cárcel *nf* jail, gaol, prison.

carcelero,-a *adj* prison, goal, jail.

carcoma *nf (insecto)* woodworm.

cardamomo *nm* cardamom.

cardenal *(hematoma)* bruise. *nm* REL cardinal.

cardiaco,-a *adj* cardiac, heart.

cardinal *adj* cardinal.

cardiología *nf* cardiology.

cardiólogo,-a *nm & nf* cardiologist.

cardo *nm* **1** BOT *(espinoso)* thistle; *(comestible)* cardoon.

carecer *vi* to lack (de, -).

carencia *nf* lack (de, of).

careta *nf (máscara)* mask. COMP **careta antigás** gas mask.

carey *nm* **1** *(animal)* sea turtle. **2** *(concha)* tortoiseshell.

carga *nf* **1** *(acción)* loading. **2** *(lo cargado)* load; *(de avión, barco)* cargo, freight.

cargado,-a *adj* **1** *(atmósfera)* heavy, dense. **2** strong. **3** *fig* burdened, weighed down: *cargado,-a de responsabilidades* weighed down with responsibility.

cargador,-ra *nm* **1** *(de arma)* magazine. **2** *(de batería)* battery charger. **3** *(de pluma, etc)* filler.

cargamento *nm (gen)* load; *(de avión, barco)* cargo, freight.

cargar *vt* **1** *(poner peso)* to load. **2** *(arma, máquina de fotos)* to load. **3** ELEC to charge: *cargar las pilas* to charge the batteries. **4** *(pluma, etc)* to fill. **5** INFORM to load.
▶ *vi* **1** *(gen)* to load. **2** *(batería)* to charge. **3** *(toro, elefante, etc)* to charge **4** *(atacar)* to charge (contra/sobre, -). **5**

cargar con *(algo que pesa)* to carry; *(una obligación)* to shoulder, take on.
▶ *vpr* **cargarse 1** *(llenarse)* to load OS (de, with): *cargarse de trabajo* to burden OS with work. **2** ELEC to become charged. **3** EDUC *fam (suspender)* to fail. **4** *fam (destrozar)* to smash, ruin. **5** *fam (matar)* to knock off.

cargo *nm* **1** *(peso)* load, weight. **2** *(empleo)* post, position. **3** *(gobierno, custodia)* charge, responsibility. LOC **hacerse cargo de 1** *(responsabilizarse de)* to take charge of. **2** *(entender)* to realize: *me hago cargo* I realize that.

caricatura *nf* caricature.

caricia *nf* caress, stroke.

caridad *nf* charity.

caries *nf inv (enfermedad)* tooth decay, caries *pl*; *(lesión)* cavity.

cariño *nm* **1** *(amor)* love, affection. **2** *(esmero)* loving care. **3** *(apelativo)* darling, love, US honey. LOC **coger/tomar cariño a** ALGN/ALGO to grow fond of SB/STH.

cariñoso,-a *adj* loving, affectionate.

carisma *nm* charisma.

carismático,-a *adj* charismatic.

carmín *nm (pintalabios)* lipstick.

carnada *nf* bait.

carnaval *nm* carnival.

carne *nf* **1** ANAT flesh. **2** CULIN meat. **3** *(de fruta)* pulp. **4** *fig (cuerpo)* flesh. COMP **carne de cerdo** pork. ‖ **carne de cordero** lamb. ‖ **carne de ternera** veal. ‖ **carne de vaca** beef. ‖ **carne picada** mince, mincemeat, US ground meat, loose meat.

carné *nm* card. COMP **carné de conducir** driving licence. ‖ **carné de identidad** identity card..

carnicería *nf* butcher's, butcher's shop.

carnicero,-a *nm & nf (profesión)* butcher.

carnívoro,-a *adj* carnivorous.
▶ *nm & nf* carnivore.

caro,-a *adj (costoso)* expensive, dear.
▶ *adv* **caro** at a high price. LOC **costar caro,-a / salir caro,-a 1** *(ser costoso)* to cost a lot. **2** *(causar daño)* to cost dear.

carpa *nf* **1** *(pez)* carp. **2** *(de circo)* big top, marquee.

carpeta *nf (archivador)* folder, file; *(informática)* folder.

carpintería *nf (obra y oficio)* carpentry.

carpintero,-a *nm & nf* carpenter.

carraca *nf (instrumento)* rattle.

carrera *nf* **1** *(acción)* run. **2** *(trayecto - de desfile)* route; *(- de taxi)* ride, journey. **3** *(camino)* road. **4** DEP race. **5** *(estudios)* degree course, university education. COMP **carrera contra reloj** race against the clock. ‖ **carrera diplomática** diplomatic career.

carreta *nf* cart.

carrete *nm* **1** *(de hilo)* bobbin, reel. **2** ELEC coil. **3** *(de caña de pescar)* reel. **4** *(de película)* spool; *(de fotos)* film, roll of film. **5** *(de máquina de escribir)* cartridge.

carretera *nf* road. COMP **carretera nacional** A road, main road. ‖ **carretera de circunvalación** ring road.

carretilla *nf* wheelbarrow.

carril *nm* **1** *(de ferrocarril)* rail. **2** *(de carretera)* lane. COMP **carril bus** bus lane.

carrillo *nm* cheek.

carrito *nm (para la compra)* trolley, US cart.

carro *nm* **1** *(vehículo)* cart. **2** *(de supermercado, aeropuerto)* trolley, US cart.

carrocería *nf* body, bodywork.

carromato *nm* covered wagon.

carroña *nf* carrion.

carroñero,-a *adj* carrion-eating.

carroza *adj fam* old, old-fashioned.
▶ *nf (tirado por caballos)* coach, carriage.

carruaje *nm* carriage, coach.

carrusel *nm (tiovivo)* merry-go-round, US carrousel.

carta *nf* **1** *(misiva)* letter. **2** *(naipe)* card. **3** *(minuta)* menu. LOC **a la carta** à la carte. ‖ **echar una carta** to post a letter, US mail a letter.

cartabón *nm* set square, triangle.

cartel *nm* poster, bill.

cartelera *nf (en periódicos)* entertainment section. LOC **en cartelera** running, on.

C

cartera *nf* **1** *(monedero)* wallet. **2** *(de colegial)* satchel, school bag. **3** *(de ejecutivo)* briefcase.

carterista *nm o nf* pickpocket.

cartero,-a *nm & nf (hombre)* postman; *(mujer)* postwoman.

cartílago *nm* cartilage.

cartilla *nf* **1** *(para aprender)* first reader. **2** *(cuaderno)* book.

cartón *nm* **1** *(material)* cardboard. **2** *(de cigarrillos)* carton. COMP **cartón piedra** papier-mâché.

cartucho *nm (de explosivo)* cartridge.

cartulina *nf* thin cardboard.

casa *nf* **1** *(vivienda)* house. **2** *(piso)* flat. **3** *(edificio)* building. **4** *(hogar)* home: *nos quedamos en casa* we stayed at home. **5** *(empresa)* firm, company. LOC **buscar casa** to go house-hunting.

casaca *nf* fitted short coat.

casado,-a *adj* married.

casar *vt* to marry.
 ▶ *vi (casarse)* to marry (con, -), get married (con, to).
 ▶ *vpr* **casarse** to get married (con, to) marry (con, -).

cascabel *nm* bell.

cascada *nf* cascade, waterfall.

cascanueces *nm inv* nutcrackers *pl.*

cascar *vt (romper)* to crack.
 ▶ *vpr* **cascarse** *(romperse)* to crack.

cáscara *nf* **1** *(de huevo, nuez)* shell. **2** *(de fruta)* skin, peel.

cascarón *nm* eggshell.

cascarrabias *nm o nf inv fam* grumpy person, bad-tempered person.

casco *nm* **1** *(para la cabeza)* helmet. **2** *(envase)* empty bottle. **3** *(de barco)* hull. **4** *(de caballería)* hoof.

caserío *nm* **1** *(casa)* country house. **2** *(pueblo)* hamlet, small village.

casero,-a *adj* **1** *(persona)* home-loving. **2** *(productos)* home-made: *pan casero* home-made bread.
 ▶ *nm & nf (dueño - hombre)* landlord; *(mujer)* landlady.

caseta *nf* **1** *(casita)* hut, booth. **2** *(de feria)* stall, stand. **3** *(de bañistas)* bathing hut, US bath house. **4** *(de perro)* kennel, doghouse.

casete *nm (magnetófono)* cassette player, cassette recorder.
 ▶ *nf (cinta)* cassette, cassette tape.

casi *adv* almost, nearly: *había casi cincuenta personas* there were almost fifty people. LOC **casi nunca** hardly ever.

casilla *nf* **1** *(casita)* hut, lodge. **2** *(de casillero)* pigeonhole. **3** *(cuadrícula)* square.

casillero *nm* pigeonholes *pl.*

casino *nm* casino.

casis *nm inv* blackcurrant bush.

caso *nm* **1** *(ocasión)* case, occasion. **2** *(gramatical)* case. LOC **en caso de que** if *en caso de que te pierdas, llámame* if you get lost, call me. ∥ **en cualquier caso** in any case. ∥ **en todo caso** anyhow, at any rate.

caspa *nf* dandruff.

casquete *nm (prenda)* skullcap.

casquillo *nm* **1** TÉC ferrule, metal tip. **2** *(de cartucho)* case.

casta *nf (linaje)* lineage, descent.

castaña *nf* BOT chestnut.

castañetear *vi (dientes)* to chatter.

castaño,-a *adj (pelo)* brown.
 ▶ *nm* **castaño 1** BOT *(árbol)* chestnut tree. **2** *(madera)* chestnut.

castañuela *nf* castanet.

castellano,-a *adj* Castilian.
 ▶ *nm & nf (persona)* Castilian.
 ▶ *nm* **castellano** *(idioma)* Castilian, Spanish.

castigar *vt (aplicar una pena)* to punish.

castigo *nm* **1** *(gen)* punishment. **2** *(en deporte)* penalty.

castillo *nm* castle.

casting *nm* casting, audition.

castizo,-a *adj* pure, authentic.

casto,-a *adj* chaste.

castor *nm* beaver.

casual *adj* accidental, chance.

casualidad *nf* **1** chance, accident. **2** *(coincidencia)* coincidence. LOC **de casualidad / por casualidad** by chance

cataclismo *nm* cataclysm.

catacumbas *nf pl* catacombs.

catalán,-ana *adj* Catalan, Catalonian.
► *nm & nf (persona)* Catalan.
► *nm* **catalán** *(idioma)* Catalan.

catalejo *nm* telescope.

catalogar *vt* **1** to catalogue (US catalog). **2** *fig* to classify, class.

catálogo *nm* catalogue (US catalog).

catamarán *nm* catamaran.

cataplasma *nf* poultice, cataplasm.

catapulta *nf* catapult.

catar *vt* **1** *(probar)* to taste. **2** *(examinar)* to examine, inspect.

catarata *nf* **1** waterfall. **2** MED cataract.

catarro *nm* cold, catarrh: *cogí un catarro* I caught a cold.

catástrofe *nf* catastrophe.

catastrófico,-a *adj* catastrophic.

catear *vt* EDUC *fam* to fail, US flunk.

catecismo *nm* catechism.

cátedra *nf (cargo de universidad)* professorship; *(de instituto)* post of head of department.

catedral *nf* cathedral.

catedrático,-a *nm & nf (de universidad)* professor; *(de instituto)* head of department.

categoría *nf* category, class; *(social)* class: *un restaurante de primera categoría* a first-class restaurant.

catequesis *nf inv* catechism.

cateto *nm (de triángulo)* side of a right-angled triangle forming the right angle.

catolicismo *nm* Catholicism.

católico,-a *adj* Catholic.

catorce *adj (cardinal)* fourteen; *(ordinal)* four.

catorceavo,-a *adj* fourteenth.
► *nm & nf* fourteenth.
🔖 Consulta también sexto,-a.

catre *nm (cama plegable)* folding bed; *(de campaña)* camp bed.

cauce *nm* **1** *(de río)* bed. **2** *fig (canal)* channel, way.

caucho *nm* rubber.

caudal *nm (de río)* flow.

caudaloso,-a *adj (río)* deep, plentiful.

causa *nf* **1** *(gen)* cause. **2** *(motivo)* cause, reason, motive. ⌐LOC¬ **a causa de** because of, on account of.

causar *vt* **1** *(provocar)* to cause, bring about. **2** *(proporcionar)* to make, give.

cáustico,-a *adj* caustic.

cautela *nf* caution, cautiousness.

cauteloso,-a *adj* cautious, wary.

cauterizar *vt* to cauterize, fire.

cautivar *vt* to take prisoner, capture.

cautivo,-a *adj* captive.

cauto,-a *adj* cautious, wary.

cava *nm (bebida)* cava, champagne.

cavar *vt* to dig.

caverna *nf* cavern, cave.

cavernícola *nm o nf* cave dweller, caveman.

caviar *nm* caviar.

cavidad *nf* cavity.

cavilar *vi* think about, brood over.

caza *nf* **1** *(acción)* hunting. **2** *(de animales)* game. ⌐LOC¬ **ir de caza** to go hunting.

cazador,-ra *nm & nf* hunter.

cazadora *nf (chaqueta)* jacket.

cazar *vt* **1** to hunt. **2** *fam (conseguir)* to catch, land.

cazo *nm* **1** *(cucharón)* ladle. **2** *(cacerola)* saucepan.

cazuela *nf* **1** *(utensilio)* casserole, saucepan. **2** *(guiso)* casserole, stew.

CE *abrev* **(Comunidad Europea)** European Community; *(abreviatura)* EC.

cebada *nf* barley.

cebar *vt* **1** *(animal)* to fatten, fatten up. **2** *(poner cebo)* to bait.
► *vpr* **cebarse** *fig (ensañarse)* to show no mercy (en/con, towards), take it out (en/con, on), vent one's anger (en/con, on).

cebo *nm* **1** *(para animales)* food. **2** *(para pescar)* bait.

cebolla *nf* **1** onion. **2** *(bulbo)* bulb. **3** *(de ducha)* rose, nozzle.

cebolleta *nf* **1** *(especia)* chives *pl*. **2** *(cebolla)* spring onion.

cebollino *nm* **1** *(especia)* chives *pl*. **2** *(cebolla)* spring onion.

cebra *nf* zebra. COMP **paso cebra** zebra crossing, US crosswalk.

ceceo *nm* lisp.

cecina *nf* cured meat.

ceder *vt* **1** *(dar)* to cede, give: **2** DEP *(balón)* to pass.
▶ *vi* **1** *(rendirse)* to yield (a, to), give way (a, to). **2** *(disminuir)* to diminish, slacken, go down: *la fiebre ha cedido* his temperature has gone down. LOC **ceder el paso** AUTO to give way, US yield.

cedro *nm* cedar.

CEE *abrev* (Comunidad Económica Europea) European Economic Community; *(abreviatura)* EEC.

cefalópodo,-a *adj* cephalopod.
▶ *nm* **cefalópodo** cephalopod.

cefalotórax *nm* cephalothorax.

cegar *vt (gen)* to blind: *el sol me cegó* the sun blinded me.
▶ *vpr* **cegarse** *fig* to become blind, be blinded.

ceguera *nf* blindness.

ceja *nf* eyebrow. LOC **tener** ALGO **entre ceja y ceja** *fig* to have STH in one's head.

celda *nf* cell.

celebración *nf (fiesta)* celebration.

celebrar *vt* **1** *(festejar)* to celebrate. **2** *(organizar)* to hold: *celebraron el debate ayer* the debate was held yesterday.
▶ *vpr* **celebrarse** *(tener lugar)* to take place, be held.

célebre *adj* famous, celebrated.

celeste *adj (color)* sky-blue.
▶ *nm (color)* sky blue.

celestial *adj* celestial, heavenly.

celibato *nm* celibacy.

celo®¹ *nm fam* sellotape, US Scotch tape.

celo² *nm* **1** *(cuidado)* zeal, fervour (US fervor). **2** BIOL *(macho)* rut; *(hembra)* heat.
▶ *nm pl* **celos** jealousy *sing*. LOC **dar celos** to make jealous.

celofán® *nm* cellophane®.

celosía *nf* **1** *(reja)* lattice. **2** *(ventana)* lattice window.

celoso,-a *adj (envidioso)* jealous.

Celsius *nm* Celsius.

célula *nf* cell.

celular *adj* cell, cellular.

celulosa *nf* cellulose.

cementerio *nm* cemetery.

cemento *nm (gen)* concrete, cement. COMP **cemento armado** reinforced concrete.

cena *nf (gen)* supper; *(formal)* dinner.

cenar *vi* to have supper, have dinner.
▶ *vt* to have for supper, have for dinner.

cencerro *nm* cowbell. LOC **estar como un cencerro** to be nuts, be crackers.

cenefa *nf* **1** *(sobre tejido)* edging, trimming. **2** *(sobre muro, pavimento, etc)* ornamental border, frieze.

cenicero *nm* ashtray.

cenit *nm* zenith.

ceniza *nf* ash, ashes *pl*.

censar *vt (hacer el censo)* to take a census of.

censo *nm (padrón)* census. COMP **censo electoral** electoral roll.

censura *nf* **1** censorship.

censurar *vt* to censor: *el libro fue censurado* the book was censored.

centavo,-a *nm* **1** *(parte)* hundredth, hundredth part. **2** *(moneda)* cent, centavo.

✎ Consulta también sexto,-a.

centella *nf* **1** *(rayo)* lightning. **2** *(chispa)* spark, flash.

centellear *vi* **1** *(gen)* to sparkle, flash. **2** *(estrellas)* to twinkle.

centena *nf* hundred.

centenar *nm* hundred. LOC **a centenares / por centenares** in hundreds.

centenario,-a *nm & nf (persona)* centenarian.
▶ *nm* **centenario** *(aniversario)* centenary, centennial, hundredth anniversary.

centeno *nm* rye.

centésimo,-a *adj* hundredth.
▶ *nm & nf* hundredth.

▶ nm **centésimo** *(moneda)* cent, centesimo.

✎ Consulta también sexto,-a.

centígrado,-a *adj* centigrade.
centigramo *nm* centigram, centigramme.
centilitro *nm* centilitre (US centiliter).
centímetro *nm* centimetre (US centimeter).
céntimo *nm* cent, centime. LOC **estar sin un céntimo** *fam* to be penniless.
centinela *nm & nf* **1** MIL sentry. **2** *(guardián)* watch, lookout.
centollo *nm* spider crab.
central *adj* central.
▶ *nf* **1** *(oficina principal)* head office, headquarters *pl*. **2** *(eléctrica)* power station. COMP **central telefónica** telephone exchange.
centralita *nf* switchboard.
centralizar *vt* to centralize.
centrar *vt* **1** *(gen)* to centre (US center). **2** *fig (atención, etc)* to centre (US center), focus.
▶ *vpr* **centrarse** to centre (US center) (en, on), focus (en, on): *se centró en el tema principal* he focused on the main topic.
céntrico,-a *adj* central, US downtown.
centrifugadora *nf (para ropa)* spin-dryer.
centrifugar *vt (ropa)* to spin-dry.
centrífugo,-a *adj* centrifugal.
centrípeto,-a *adj* centripetal.
centro *nm* **1** centre (US center), middle. **2** *(de ciudad)* town centre, city centre, US downtown area. **3** *(asociación)* centre (US center), association, institution. COMP **centro comercial** shopping centre, US mall. ❙ **centro cultural** cultural centre (US center).
centrocampista *nm o nf* midfield player.
céntuplo,-a *adj* centuple, hundred-fold.
▶ *nm* **céntuplo** centuple, hundred-fold.

centuria *nf* century.
ceñir *vt* **1** *(estrechar)* to cling to, be tight on. **2** *(rodear)* to surround, encircle.
▶ *vpr* **ceñirse 1** *(atenerse)* to keep (a, to), limit OS (a, to): *ceñirse al tema* to keep to the subject. **2** *(ajustarse una prenda)* to cling.
ceño *nm* frown. LOC **fruncir el ceño** to frown.
cepa *nf (de vid)* vine.
cepillar *vt (gen)* to brush.
cepillo *nm* **1** brush. **2** *(de carpintería)* plane. COMP **cepillo de dientes** toothbrush. ❙ **cepillo del pelo** hairbrush.
cepo *nm* **1** *(rama)* bough, branch. **2** *(de yunque)* stock. **3** *(de reo)* pillory, stocks *pl*. **4** *(trampa)* trap. **5** *(para auto)* clamp.
cera *nf* **1** wax; *(de abeja)* beeswax. **2** *(pulimento)* wax, polish.
cerámica *nf* **1** *(arte)* ceramics, pottery. **2** *(objeto)* piece of pottery.
ceramista *nm o nf* ceramist, potter.
cerca¹ *nf (vallado)* fence, wall.
cerca² *adv (lugar y tiempo)* near, close: *aquí cerca* near here. LOC **cerca de 1** *(cercano a)* near, close. **2** *(aproximadamente)* nearly, about, around.
cercado *nm* **1** *(lugar)* enclosure. **2** *(cerca)* fence, wall.
cercano,-a *adj* **1** *(inmediato)* near, close: *el fin está cercano* the end is near. **2** *(vecino)* nearby, neighbouring (US neighboring). **3** *(pariente)* close.
cercar *vt (poner una cerca)* to fence in, enclose: *cercaron la hacienda* they fenced in the property.
cerco *nm* **1** *(lo que rodea)* circle, ring. **2** *(aureola)* halo. **3** *(asedio)* siege.
cerdo,-a *nm & nf fam pey (persona sucia)* pig, slob.
▶ *nm* **cerdo 1** *(animal)* pig. **2** *(carne)* pork.
cereal *nm* cereal.
cerebro *nm* **1** ANAT brain. **2** *fig* brains *pl*: *es el cerebro de la banda* he's the brains behind the gang.
ceremonia *nf* ceremony.
ceremonial *adj* ceremonial.

ceremonioso,-a *adj* ceremonious, formal.

cereza *nf* cherry.

cerezo *nm* cherry tree.

cerilla *nf (fósforo)* match.

cero *nm* **1** MAT zero. **2** *(cifra)* nought, zero. **3** DEP nil: *ganamos tres a cero* we won three nil.

cerrado,-a *adj* **1** shut, closed. **2** LING close, closed: *vocal cerrada* close vowel. **3** *(acento)* broad, thick. **4** *(curva)* tight, sharp. **5** *fig (persona introvertida)* uncommunicative, reserved.

cerradura *nf* lock.

cerrajería *nf (negocio)* locksmith's shop.

cerrajero,-a *nm & nf* locksmith.

cerrar *vt* **1** to close, shut: *cierra la puerta* close the door. **2** *(grifo, gas)* to turn off; *(luz)* to turn off, switch off. **3** *(cremallera)* to zip (up). **4** *(frontera, puerto)* to close; *(camino)* to block. **5** *(en dominó)* to block.
▶ *vi* **1** to close, shut. **2** *(punto)* to cast off. **3** *(una herida)* to close up, heal.
▶ *vpr* **cerrarse 1** to close, shut. **2** *(una herida)* to close up, heal.

cerro *nm* hill.

cerrojo *nm* bolt. [LOC] **correr el cerrojo** to bolt.

certamen *nm* competition, contest.

certeza *nf* certainty.

certificado,-a *adj (envío)* registered.
▶ *nm* **certificado 1** *(documento)* certificate. **2** *(carta)* registered letter.

certificar *vt* **1** *(gen)* to certify. **2** *(carta, paquete)* to register.

cerumen *nm* earwax, cerumen.

cervato *nm* fawn.

cervecería *nf* **1** *(bar)* pub, bar. **2** *(destilería)* brewery.

cerveza *nf* beer, ale. [COMP] **cerveza de barril** draught (US draft) beer. ‖ **cerveza negra** stout.

cervical *adj* cervical, neck.

cesar *vi* to cease, stop: *cesó de llover* it stopped raining. [LOC] **sin cesar** incessantly.

cesárea *nf* caesarean (US Cesarean), Caesarean (US Cesarean) section.

cese *nm* **1** cessation. **2** *(despido)* dis missal.

cesión *nf* cession.

césped *nm* lawn, grass.

cesta *nf* **1** basket. **2** DEP *(baloncesto)* bas ket. [COMP] **cesta de la compra** shoppin basket.

cesto *nm* basket. [COMP] **cesto de los pa peles** wastepaper basket.

cetáceo,-a *nm* cetacean.

cetro *nm* sceptre (US scepter).

CFC *abrev (clorofluorocarbono)* chloro fluorocarbon; *(abreviatura)* CFC.

cg *sím (centigramo)* centigram, cent gramme; *(símbolo)* cg.

chabola *nf* shack: *un barrio de chabolas* shanty town.

chacal *nm* jackal.

chacha *nf* **1** *fam (niñera)* nanny, nurse maid. **2** *fam (sirvienta)* maid.

chacinería *nf* pork butcher's shop.

chador *nm* chuddar, chudder, chud dah.

chafar *vt* **1** *(aplastar)* to squash, crush flatten. **2** *(arrugar)* to crumple crease.
▶ *vpr* **chafarse** *(aplastarse)* to b squashed, be crushed, be flattene *(arrugarse)* to become creased, be come crumpled.

chaflán *nm* **1** *(bisel)* chamfer. **2** *(esquin* corner.

chal *nm* shawl.

chalado,-a *adj (loco)* mad, crazy, nut

chalar *vt fam (enloquecer)* to drive cr zy.
▶ *vpr* **chalarse** *fam* to go mad, go cr zy, go nuts.

chaleco *nm* waistcoat, US vest. [COMP] **chaleco salvavidas** life jacket.

chalet *nm* **1** *(casa individual)* house, d tached house. **2** *(adosado)* semid tached house.

chalupa *nf (embarcación)* boat, launch

chamán *nm* sorcerer, wizard, sh man.

chamarra *nf (zamarra)* sheepskin jacket.

champaña *nm* champagne.

champiñón *nm* mushroom.

champú *nm* shampoo.

chamuscar *vt* to singe, scorch.
▶ *vpr* **chamuscarse** to be singed, get scorched.

chamusquina *nf* scorching, singeing.

chancho *nm* AM *(animal)* pig; *(carne)* pork.

chanchullo *nm fam* fiddle, wangle, racket.

chancla *nf (chancleta)* flip-flop.

chancleta *nf* flip-flop.

chándal *nm* track suit, jogging suit.

chanquete *nm* transparent goby.

chantaje *nm* blackmail.

chantajear *vt* to blackmail.

chao *interj fam* bye-bye!, cheerio!, so long!, ciao!

chapa *nf* 1 *(de metal)* sheet, plate. 2 *(de madera)* panel, sheet; *(contrachapado)* plywood. 3 *(tapón)* bottle top, cap. 4 *(medalla)* badge, disc.
▶ *nf pl* **chapas** game *sing* of tossing up coins.

chapado,-a *adj* 1 *(metal)* plated: *chapado,-a en plata* silver-plated. 2 *(madera)* veneered, finished.

chaparrón *nm (lluvia)* downpour, heavy shower: *cayó un buen chaparrón* there was a downpour.

chapista *nm o nf* 1 sheet metal worker. 2 AUTO panel beater.

chapotear *vi (agitar en el agua)* to splash about.

chapurrear *vt* to speak a little, have a smattering of: *chapurreo el inglés* I have a smattering of English, I speak a little English.

chapuza *nf* 1 *(trabajo sin importancia)* odd job. 2 *(trabajo mal hecho)* botched job, shoddy piece of work.

chapuzón *nm (baño)* dip. LOC **darse un chapuzón** to have a dip.

chaqueta *nf* jacket. COMP **chaqueta de punto** cardigan.

chaquetón *nm* winter jacket.

charanga *nf* 1 brass band. 2 *fam (bulla)* din, racket.

charca *nf* pool, pond.

charco *nm* puddle, pond.

charcutería *nf* pork butcher's shop, delicatessen.

charla *nf* 1 *(conversación)* talk, chat. 2 *(conferencia)* talk, informal lecture.

charlar *vi* to chat, talk.

charlatán,-ana *adj* 1 *(hablador)* talkative. 2 *(chismoso)* gossipy.
▶ *nm & nf* 1 *(parlanchín)* chatterbox. 2 *(chismoso)* gossip.

charloteo *nm fam* chatter, prattle.

chárter *adj inv* charter.
▶ *nm* charter.

chasco *nm fig (decepción)* disappointment. LOC **llevarse un chasco** to be disappointed.

chasis *nm (del coche)* chassis.

chasquear *vi* 1 *(lengua)* to click; *(dedos)* to snap. 2 *(látigo, madera)* to crack.

chasquido *nm* 1 *(de la lengua)* click; *(de los dedos)* snap. 2 *(de látigo, madera)* crack.

chat *nm* INFORM chat.

chatarra *nf* 1 *(hierro viejo)* scrap iron, scrap. 2 *fam pey (calderilla)* small change.

chatear *vi* INFORM *fam* to chat (con, with/to).

chateo *nm* INFORM *fam* chat, chatting.

chato,-a *adj (nariz)* snub; *(persona)* snub-nosed.

chaval,-la *nm & nf (joven)* kid, youngster; *(chico)* lad, boy; *(chica)* lass, girl.

chavo *nm pl* **chavos** *(dinero)* money *sing*, cash *sing*.

checo,-a *adj* Czech.
▶ *nm & nf (persona)* Czech.
▶ *nm* **checo** *(idioma)* Czech. COMP **República Checa** Czech Republic.

chef *nm* chef.

chelín *nm* shilling.

cheque *nm* cheque (US check). LOC **cobrar un cheque** to cash a cheque (US check).

chequear *vt* **1** *(controlar)* to check. **2** *(comprobar)* to check up on.

chequeo *nm* MED checkup.

Chequia *nf* Czechia.

chica *nf* girl.

chicharra *nf (cigarra)* cicada.

chicharro *nm* **1** *(chicharrón)* pork crackling, fried pork rind. **2** *(pez)* scad, horse mackerel.

chicharrón *nm (de cerdo)* pork crackling, fried pork rind.

chichón *nm* bump, lump.

chicle *nm* chewing gum.

chico,-a *nm & nf (gen)* kid, youngster.

chiflado,-a *adj fam* mad, crazy, barmy, nuts, bonkers.

chiflar *vi (silbar)* to hiss, whistle.
▶ *vt* **1** *(silbar)* to hiss, boo. **2** *fam (gustar)* to fascinate, enchant.

chiflido *nm* whistle, whistling.

chií *adj* Shiite.
▶ *nm o nf* Shiite.

chiíta *adj-nm o nf* → **chií.**

chilaba *nf* jellabah, jellaba.

chile *nm (pimiento)* chili, chili pepper.

Chile *nm* Chile.

chileno,-a *adj* Chilean.
▶ *nm & nf* Chilean.

chillar *vi* **1** *(persona)* to scream, shriek, shout: **2** *(cerdo)* to squeal; *(ratón)* to squeak; *(pájaro)* to squawk, screech. **3** *(radio)* to blare; *(frenos)* to screech, squeal. **4** *(colores)* to be loud, be gaudy, clash. **5** *fam (reñir)* to tell off.

chillido *nm* **1** *(de persona)* shriek, scream, cry. **2** *(de cerdo)* squeal; *(de ratón)* squeak; *(de pájaro)* squawk, screech.

chillón,-ona *adj* **1** *(que chilla mucho)* screaming, loud. **2** *(voz)* shrill, high-pitched; *(sonido)* harsh, strident. **3** *fig (color)* loud, gaudy.

chimenea *nf* **1** chimney. **2** *(hogar)* fireplace, hearth. **3** *(de barco)* funnel, stack.

chimpancé *nm* chimpanzee.

china *nm (piedrecita)* pebble.

China *nf* China.

chinchar *vt fam* to annoy, pester, bug.
▶ *vpr* **chincharse** *fam* to grin and bear it, put up with it, lump it. LOC **¡chínchate!** *fam* hard luck!, tough luck!

chinche *nm & nf* ZOOL bedbug, bug.

chincheta *nf* drawing pin, US thumbtack.

chinchilla *nf* chinchilla.

chino,-a *adj* Chinese.
▶ *nm & nf (persona)* Chinese person.
▶ *nm* **chino** **1** *(idioma)* Chinese. **2** *(colador)* sieve.
▶ *nm pl* **chinos** guessing game *sing.*

chip *nm* INFORM chip.

chipirón *nm* baby squid.

Chipre *nm* Cyprus.

chipriota *adj* Cypriot.
▶ *nm o nf* Cypriot.

chiquillo,-a *nm & nf* kid, youngster.

chiquito,-a *adj* tiny, very small, weeny.
▶ *nm & nf* tiny tot, kid.

chirimoya *nf* custard apple.

chiringuito *nm fam (en playa)* refreshment stall, refreshment stand; *(en carretera)* roadside snack bar, hot food stand.

chirla *nf* small clam.

chirriar *vi* **1** *(al freír comida, etc)* to sizzle. **2** *(rueda, frenos)* to screech, squeal; *(puerta)* to creak. **3** *(aves)* to squawk.

chirrido *nm* **1** *(de rueda, frenos)* screech; *(de puerta)* creak, creaking. **2** *(de aves)* squawk, squawking.

chisme *nm* **1** *(comentario)* piece of gossip. **2** *(trasto)* knick-knack; *(de cocina, etc)* gadget; *(cosa)* thing, thingamajig.

chismoso,-a *nm & nf* gossip.

chispa *nf* **1** *(de lumbre, eléctrica, etc)* spark. **2** *fig (ingenio, gracia)* wit, sparkle; *(inteligencia)* intelligence; *(viveza)* liveliness.

chispear *vi* **1** *(echar chispas)* to spark, throw out sparks. **2** [en este sentido se usa sólo en tercera persona; no lleva sujeto] METEOR to drizzle, spit.

chistar *vi* to speak. LOC **sin chistar** without saying a word.

chiste *nm* **1** *(dicho)* joke, funny story. **2** *(dibujo)* cartoon. `LOC` **contar un chiste** to tell a joke.

chistera *nf fig (sombrero)* top hat.

chistoso,-a *adj* **1** *(persona)* witty, funny, fond of joking. **2** *(suceso)* funny, amusing.

chivar *vt* **1** *fam (molestar)* to annoy, pester. **2** *fam (delatar)* to squeal on, tell on.
▶ *vpr* **chivarse** *fam* to tell, squeal, split.

chivato,-a *nm & nf fam (acusica)* telltale.

chivo,-a *nm & nf (cría macho)* kid, young goat; *(cría hembra)* kid, young she-goat.

choc *nm* shock.

chocar *vi* **1** *(colisionar con algo)* to collide (contra/con, with), crash (contra/con, into), run (contra/con, into). **2** *(una pelota)* to hit (contra, -), strike (contra, -).
▶ *vt* **1** *fig (sorprender)* to surprise; *(extrañar)* to shock. **2** *(las manos)* to shake.

choco *nm* small cuttlefish.

chocolate *nm* **1** *(sólido)* chocolate. **2** *(líquido)* drinking chocolate, cocoa. `COMP` **chocolate con leche** milk chocolate.

chocolatería *nf* **1** *(fábrica)* chocolate factory. **2** *(tienda)* chocolate shop. **3** *(donde se toma)* café specializing in drinking chocolate.

chocolatero,-a *adj (aficionado al chocolate)* fond of chocolate, chocolate-loving.
▶ *nm & nf* **1** *(fabricante)* chocolate maker. **2** *(vendedor)* chocolate seller.

chocolatina *nf* bar of chocolate.

chófer *nm* **1** *(particular)* chauffeur. **2** *(de autocar, etc)* driver.

chollo *nm* **1** *fam (ganga)* bargain, snip, gift. **2** *(trabajo)* cushy job.

chopera *nf* poplar grove.

chopo *nm (árbol)* poplar.

choque *nm* **1** *(gen)* collision, impact; *(de coche, tren, etc)* crash, smash, collision. **2** *(discusión)* dispute, quarrel. **3** MED shock.

chorizo,-a *nm* chorizo *(highly-seasoned pork sausage)*.

chorrear *vi* **1** *(caer a chorro)* to spout, gush, spurt. **2** *(gotear)* to drip.

chorro *nm* **1** *(de líquido)* jet, spout, spurt, gush. **2** *(de gas)* jet, blast. `LOC` **a chorros** in abundance: *tiene dinero a chorros* he's got plenty of money, he's loaded (with money).

choto,-a *nm & nf* **1** *(cabrito)* kid, young goat; *(cabrita)* female kid, young she-goat. **2** *(ternero)* sucking calf.

choza *nf* hut, shack.

christmas *nm inv* Christmas card.

chubasco *nm (chaparrón)* heavy shower, downpour.

chubasquero *nm* raincoat.

chuche *nm fam* sweet, US candy.

chuchería *nf fam (golosina)* sweet, US candy.

chucho,-a *nm & nf fam (perro)* mutt, US pooch.

chucrut *nm* sauerkraut.

chufa *nf (planta)* chufa; *(fruto)* tiger nut.

chulear *vi fam (presumir)* to brag, show off: *mira a Felipe cómo chulea con su coche nuevo* look at Felipe showing off his new car.

chuleta *nf* **1** *(costilla)* chop, cutlet. **2** *fam fig (entre estudiantes)* crib, crib note, US trot.

chulo,-a *adj* **1** *fam (descarado)* cocky, cheeky. **2** *fam (vistoso)* showy, flashy. **3** *fam (bonito)* nice, pretty.

chupado,-a *adj* **1** *fig (muy flaco)* skinny, thin; *(mejillas, cara)* hollow. **2** *argot fig (muy fácil)* dead easy.

chupar *vt* **1** to suck. **2** *(absorber)* to absorb, soak up, suck up.

chupete *nm* dummy, US pacifier.

churrería *nf* fritter shop.

churro *nm (dulce)* fritter, US cruller.

chusma *nf* riffraff, rabble, mob.

chut *nm* DEP shot, kick.

chutar *vi* DEP to shoot, kick.

chute *nm argot* fix.

cianita *nf* cyanite.

cianuro *nm* cyanide. COMP **cianuro potásico** potassium cyanide.

cibercafé *nm* Internet café.

ciberespacio *nm* cyberspace.

cibernauta *nm o nf* Net user.

cibernética *nf* cybernetics.

cicatriz *nf* scar.

cicatrizar *vi* to heal, cicatrize.

cíclico,-a *adj* cyclic, cyclical.

ciclismo *nm* cycling.

ciclista *adj* cycle, cycling.
▶ *nm o nf* cyclist.

ciclomotor *nm* moped.

ciclón *nm* cyclone.

ciego,-a *adj (persona)* blind. LOC **a ciegas 1** *(sin ver)* blindly. **2** *(sin pensar)* without thinking.

cielo *nm* **1** *(gen)* sky. **2** *(clima)* weather, climate. **3** REL heaven.
▶ *interj* **cielos** good heavens! LOC **llovido,-a del cielo** *fig* heaven-sent. ‖ **ser un cielo (de persona)** *fam* to be an angel.

ciempiés *nm inv* centipede.

cien *adj* [se usa sólo antes de los nombres en plural] one hundred, a hundred.
▶ *nm* one hundred, a hundred. LOC **cien por cien** one hundred per cent.

✎ Consulta también **ciento y seis**.

ciénaga *nf* marsh, bog.

ciencia *nf (disciplina)* science. COMP **ciencia ficción** science fiction. ‖ **ciencias naturales** natural sciences.

cienmilésimo,-a *adj* hundred thousandth.
▶ *nm & nf* hundred thousandth.

✎ Consulta también **sexto,-a**.

cienmillonésimo,-a *adj* hundred millionth.
▶ *nm & nf* hundred millionth.

✎ Consulta también **sexto,-a**.

científico,-a *adj* scientific.
▶ *nm & nf* scientist.

ciento *adj* one hundred, a hundred:
▶ *nm* **1** *(número)* hundred. **2** **un ciento** *(centena)* about a hundred. LOC **por ciento** per cent.

✎ Consulta también **cien**.

cierre *nm* **1** *(acción)* closing, shutting; *(de fábrica)* shutdown; *(de radio, etc)* close-down. **2** *(de prenda)* fastener; *(de bolso)* clasp; *(de cinturón)* buckle, clasp. COMP **cierre patronal** lockout.

cierto,-a *adj* **1** *(seguro)* certain, sure. **2** *(verdadero)* true: *no es cierto* that's not true. LOC **estar en lo cierto** to be right. ‖ **por cierto** by the way.
▶ *adv* **cierto** certainly.

ciervo,-a *nm & nf (gen)* deer; *(macho)* stag, hart; *(hembra)* doe, hind.

cifra *nf* **1** *(número)* figure, number. **2** *(cantidad)* amount, number. **3** *(código)* cipher, code.

cifrar *vt (codificar)* to encode; *(en informática)* to encrypt.

cigala *nf* Dublin Bay prawn.

cigarra *nf* cicada.

cigarrillo *nm* cigarette.

cigarro *nm* **1** *(puro)* cigar. **2** *(cigarrillo)* cigarette.

cigoto *nm* zygote.

cigüeña *nf (ave)* stork.

cilindrada *nf* cylinder capacity.

cilíndrico,-a *adj* cylindric, cylindrical.

cilindro *nm* cylinder.

cima *nf* **1** *(de montaña)* summit, top; *(de árbol)* top. **2** *fig (cumbre)* summit, peak.

cimentar *vt* **1** ARQUIT to lay the foundations of. **2** *fig (afianzar)* to strengthen, consolidate.

cimiento [se usa sólo en plural con el mismo significado] *nm* **1** ARQUIT foundation, foundations *pl*. **2** *fig* basis, origin. LOC **poner los cimientos** to lay the foundations.

cinabrio *nm* cinnabar.

cinc *nm* zinc.

cincel *nm* chisel.

cincelar *vt* to chisel, engrave.

cincha *nf (de caballo)* girth, US cinch.

cinco *adj (cardinal)* five; *(ordinal)* fifth.
▶ *nm (número)* five. LOC **¡choca esos cinco!** *fam* put it there!, give me five!

✎ Consulta también **seis**.

cincuenta *adj (cardinal)* fifty; *(ordinal)* fiftieth.
▶ *nm (número)* fifty.
✎ Consulta también seis.

cincuentavo,-a *adj* fiftieth.
▶ *nm & nf* fiftieth.
✎ Consulta también sexto,-a.

cine *nm* **1** *(local)* cinema, US movie theater: *ir al cine* to go to the cinema, US go to the movies. **2** *(arte)* cinema.

cineasta *nm o nf* film director, filmmaker.

cineclub *nm* **1** *(organización)* film society, film club. **2** *(local)* cinema, US movie theater.

cinematografía *nf* film-making, cinematography, US movie-making.

cinematográfico,-a *adj* cinematographic.

cinematógrafo *nm* film projector, US movie projector.

cinética *nf* kinetics.

cinético,-a *adj* kinetic.

cínico,-a *adj* cynical.
▶ *nm & nf* cynic.

cinismo *nm* cynicism.

cinta *nf* **1** *(gen)* band, strip; *(decorativa)* ribbon. **2** COST braid, edging. **3** TÉC tape. **4** *(de máquina de escribir)* ribbon. **5** *(casete)* tape. COMP **cinta adhesiva** adhesive tape. ‖ **cinta magnética** magnetic tape. ‖ **cinta métrica** tape measure.

cintura *nf* waist.

cinturilla *nf* waistband.

cinturón *nm* belt. COMP **cinturón de seguridad** safety belt, seat belt.

ciprés *nm* cypress.

circo *nm* **1** *(gen)* circus. **2** GEOG cirque.

circonita *nf* zirconite.

circuito *nm* **1** *(eléctrico)* circuit. **2** *(recorrido)* tour, circuit. **3** *(de carreras)* track, circuit.

circulación *nf* **1** *(gen)* circulation. **2** *(de vehículos)* traffic. COMP **circulación sanguínea** blood circulation. ‖ **código de (la) circulación** highway code.

circular *adj* circular.
▶ *vi* **1** *(gen)* to circulate, move, go round. **2** *(líquido, electricidad)* to circulate, flow. **3** *(coche)* to drive; *(trenes, autobuses)* to run; *(peatón)* to walk. **4** *fig (rumor, etc)* to spread, get round.

círculo *nm* *(gen)* circle. COMP **círculo familiar** family circle. ‖ **círculo polar antártico** Antarctic Circle. ‖ **círculo polar ártico** Arctic Circle. ‖ **círculo vicioso** *fig* vicious circle.

circunferencia *nf* circumference.

circunflejo,-a *adj* circumflex.
▶ *nm* **circunflejo** circumflex.

circunscribir *vt* to circumscribe.
▶ *vpr* **circunscribirse** *(ceñirse)* to confine OS (a, to), limit OS (a, to).

circunscripción *nf* district, area. COMP **circunscripción electoral** constituency.

circunstancia *nf* circumstance. LOC **en estas circunstancias** under the circumstances.

circunstancial *adj* circumstantial.

circunvalar *vt* to go round.

cirio *nm* long wax candle. LOC **armar un cirio** *fam* to kick up a rumpus.

cirrosis *nf inv* cirrhosis.

ciruela *nf* plum. COMP **ciruela claudia** greengage. ‖ **ciruela pasa** prune.

ciruelo *nm* plum tree.

cirugía *nf* surgery. COMP **cirugía estética** plastic surgery.

cirujano,-a *nm & nf* surgeon.

cisma *nm* REL schism.

cisne *nm* swan.

cisterna *nf* cistern, tank.

cita *nf* **1** *(para negocios, médico, etc)* appointment: *tengo una cita con mi abogado* I have an appointment with my lawyer. **2** *(amorosa)* date. **3** *(mención)* quotation. LOC **tener una cita** to have an appointment, have an engagement.

citación *nf* **1** *(mención)* quotation. **2** JUR citation, summons.

citar *vt* **1** *(dar cita)* to make an appointment with, arrange to meet. **2** *(mencionar)* to quote.

citoplasma *nm* cytoplasm.

cítrico,-a *adj* citric.
► *nm pl* **cítricos** citrus fruits.

ciudad *nf* city, town. COMP **ciudad dormitorio** dormitory town. ‖ **ciudad universitaria** university campus.

ciudadanía *nf* citizenship.

ciudadano,-a *adj* civic.
► *nm & nf* citizen.

ciudadela *nf* citadel, fortress.

cívico,-a *adj* civic.

civil *adj* **1** civil. **2** *(no militar)* civilian. **3** *(no eclesiástico)* lay, secular.

civilización *nf* civilization.

civilizar *vt* to civilize.

civismo *nm* **1** good citizenship, community spirit. **2** *(al servicio de los demás)* civility.

cizalla [también se usa en plural con el mismo significado.] *nf (tijeras)* metal shears *pl*, wire cutters *pl*.

cl *sím* (centilitro) centilitre (US centiliter); (símbolo) cl.

clamor *nm (griterío)* shouting, din, noise.

clan *nm* clan.

clandestino,-a *adj* clandestine, underground, secret.

claqué *nm* tap dancing.

claraboya *nf* skylight.

claridad *nf (luminosidad)* light, brightness. LOC **con claridad** clearly.

clarín *nm (instrumento)* bugle.
► *nm o nf (músico)* bugler.

clarinete *nm (instrumento)* clarinet.

clarinetista *nm o nf* clarinettist, clarinetist.

claro,-a *adj* **1** *(gen)* clear. **2** *(iluminado)* bright, well-lit. **3** *(color)* light: *azul claro* light blue. **4** *(salsa, etc)* thin; *(café, chocolate, etc)* weak. LOC **dejar ALGO claro** to make STH clear. ‖ **estar claro** to be clear.
► *adv* clearly.
► *interj* **¡claro!** of course!.

clase *nf (grupo, categoría)* class. **2** *(aula)* classroom; *(de universidad)* lecture hall. **3** *(tipo)* type, sort. LOC **asitir a clase** to attend class. COMP **clase media** middle class. ‖ **clase particular** private class, private lesson. ‖ **primera clase** first class.

clasicismo *nm* classicism.

clásico,-a *adj* **1** *(de los clásicos)* classical: *literatura clásica* classical literature. **2** *(tradicional)* classic.
► *nm* **clásico** classic: *este libro es un clásico de la ciencia ficción* this book is a science-fiction classic.

clasificación *nf* **1** *(gen)* classification. **2** *(distribución)* sorting, filing. **3** DEP league, table. **4** *(de discos)* top twenty, hit parade.

clasificar *vt* **1** to class, classify. **2** *(distribuir)* to sort, file.
► *vpr* **clasificarse 1** DEP to qualify. **2** *(llegar)* to come.

claustro *nm* ARQUIT cloister.

claustrofobia *nf* claustrophobia.

claustrofóbico,-a *adj* claustrophobic.

cláusula *nf* clause.

clausura *nf* **1** *(cierre)* closure. **2** *(acto)* closing ceremony, closing session.

clausurar *vt* **1** *(poner fin)* to close, conclude. **2** *(cerrar)* to close (down).

clavar *vt* **1** *(con clavos)* to nail. **2** *(un clavo)* to bang, hammer in; *(estaca)* to drive. **3** *fig (atención)* to fix; *(ojos)* to rivet.
► *vpr* **clavarse** *(gen)* to stick.

clave *nf* **1** *(de un enigma, etc)* key, clue: *la clave del éxito* the key to success. **2** *(de signos)* code, key, cipher: *un mensaje en clave* a coded message. **3** MÚS key: **4** ARQUIT keystone.
► *nm (instrumento)* harpsichord.

clavel *nm* carnation.

clavicémbalo *nm* harpsichord.

clavicordio *nm* clavichord.

clavícula *nf* clavicle, collarbone.

clavija *nf* **1** TÉC peg. **2** ELEC *(de enchufe)* pin.

clavo *nm* **1** nail. **2** BOT clove. LOC **dar en el clavo** *fig* to hit the nail on the head.

claxon® *nm* horn, hooter.

clemencia *nf* clemency, mercy.

clerical *adj* clerical.

clérigo *nm* priest.

clero *nm* clergy.

clic *nm* click. LOC **hacer clic 1** *(hacer ruido)* to click, go click. **2** INFORM to click.

clicar *vt* to click on.
▶ *vi* to click.

clienta *nf* client, customer.

cliente *nm o nf* client, customer.

clientela *nf* customers *pl*, clients *pl*, clientele.

clima *nm* climate.

climático,-a *adj* climatic, climatical.

climatizado,-a *adj* air-conditioned.

climatizar *vt* to air-condition.

climatología *nf* climatology.

clínica *nf* *(hospital)* clinic, private hospital.

clínico,-a *adj* clinical: *muerte clínica* clinical death.

clip *nm* **1** *(para papel)* paper clip. **2** *(para pelo)* hair-grip, US bobby pin. **3** *(pendiente)* clip-on earring.

cloaca *nf* sewer, drain.

clon *nm* clone.

clonación *nf* cloning.

clonar *vt* to clone.

clónico,-a *adj* cloned.
▶ *nm* **clónico** *(ordenador)* clone.

cloquear *vi* to cluck.

cloro *nm* chlorine.

clorofila *nf* chlorophyll.

clorofílico,-a *adj* chlorophyllous.

cloroformo *nm* chloroform.

clown *nm* clown..

club *nm* club, society. COMP **club de fútbol** football club. ▌ **club de tenis** tennis club. ▌ **club náutico** yacht club.

cm *sím* (centímetro) centimetre (US centimeter); *(símbolo)* cm.

coaccionar *vt* to coerce, compel.

coagular *vt* *(gen)* to coagulate, clot; *(leche)* to curdle.
▶ *vpr* **coagularse** to coagulate, clot; *(leche)* to curdle.

coágulo *nm* coagulum, clot.

coala *nm* koala, koala bear.

coartada *nf* alibi.

coba *nf fam* soft soap. LOC **dar coba a ALGN** *fam* to soft-soap SB.

cobalto *nm* cobalt.

cobarde *adj* cowardly.
▶ *nm o nf* coward.

cobardía *nf* cowardice.

cobaya *nm* guinea pig.

cobertizo *nm* shed, shack.

cobertura *nf* **1** *(gen)* cover. **2** *(de una red, servicio)* coverage. COMP **cobertura de chocolate** chocolate coating. ▌ **cobertura de seguros** insurance cover.

cobijar *vt* **1** *(cubrir)* to cover. **2** *fig* to shelter.
▶ *vpr* **cobijarse** to take shelter.

cobijo *nm* **1** *(hospedaje)* lodging. **2** *(refugio)* shelter. **3** *fig* protection, refuge.

cobol *nm* INFORM COBOL.

cobra *nf* *(serpiente)* cobra.

cobrador,-ra *nm & nf* **1** *(de luz, etc)* collector. **2** *(de transporte - hombre)* conductor; *(- mujer)* conductress.

cobrar *vt* **1** *(fijar precio por)* to charge; *(cheques)* to cash; *(salario)* to earn. **2** to get: *si no te estás quieto vas a cobrar una torta* if you don't keep still you'll get a smack. **3** *fig (adquirir)* to gain, get.
▶ *vi* to be in for it.
▶ *vpr* **cobrarse 1** *(dinero)* to take, collect. **2** *(víctimas)* to claim. **3** *(recuperar)* to recover (de, from); *(volver en sí)* to come round.

cobre *nm* *(metal)* copper.

cobro *nm* **1** *(pago)* payment. **2** *(cobranza)* collection; *(de cheque)* cashing. COMP **cobro revertido** reverse-charge, US collect.

coca *nf* **1** *(arbusto)* coca. **2** *argot* coke. **3** *fam (bebida)* Coke®.

cocción *nf* *(gen)* cooking; *(en agua)* boiling; *(en horno)* baking.

cóccix *nm inv* coccyx.

cocear *vi* to kick.

cocer *vt* *(gen)* to cook; *(hervir)* to boil; *(al horno)* to bake.
▶ *vpr* **cocerse 1** *(gen)* to cook; *(hervir)* to boil; *(al horno)* to bake. **2** *fam (de calor)* to be roasting, be boiling.

coche *nm* **1** *(automóvil)* car, automobile, motorcar: *fuimos en coche* we went by car. **2** *(de tren, de caballos)* carriage, coach. **3** *(de niño)* pram, US baby carriage. COMP **coche cama** sleeping car. ▌ **coche de alquiler** hired car, US rented car. ▌ **coche de bomberos** fire engine. ▌ **coche de carreras** racing car.

cochera *nf* depot.

cochino,-a *adj* *(sucio)* filthy, disgusting.
▶ *nm & nf* **1** ZOOL *(gen)* pig; *(macho)* swine; *(hembra)* sow. **2** *fam (persona)* dirty person, filthy person, pig.

cocido,-a *adj* cooked; *(en agua)* boiled; *(al horno)* baked.
▶ *nm* **cocido** CULIN stew.

cociente *nm* quotient.

cocina *nf* **1** *(lugar)* kitchen. **2** *(gastronomía)* cooking: *cocina española* Spanish cooking, Spanish cuisine. **3** *(aparato)* cooker, US stove. COMP **cocina casera** home cooking. ▌ **cocina de gas** gas cooker, US gas stove. ▌ **cocina de mercado** seasonal produce. ▌ **cocina eléctrica** electric cooker, US electric stove.

cocinar *vt* to cook.
▶ *vi* to cook.

cocinero,-a *nm & nf* cook. COMP **primer cocinero** chef.

coco¹ *nm* **1** BOT *(árbol)* coconut palm. **2** *(fruta)* coconut. COMP **coco rallado** desiccated coconut.

coco² *nm* **1** *fam (fantasma)* bogeyman. **2** *argot (cabeza)* noddle, noggin, nut. LOC **comerse el coco** *fam* to get worked up, worry about it.

cocodrilo *nm* crocodile.

cocotero *nm* coconut palm.

cóctel *nm* *(bebida)* cocktail.

codazo *nm* *(golpe)* poke with one's elbow, blow with one's elbow: *le pegó un codazo* she poked him with her elbow. LOC **abrirse paso a codazos** to elbow one's way through.

codear *vi* *(empujar)* to elbow.
▶ *vpr* **codearse** to rub shoulders (con, with), hobnob (con, with).

codera *nf* elbow patch.

codicia *nf* greed, coveting.

codiciar *vt* to covet, desire, crave for.

codicioso,-a *adj* covetous, greedy.

codificación *nf* **1** *(de mensajes)* encoding. **2** INFORM coding, code.

codificar *vt* **1** *(leyes)* to codify. **2** *(mensajes)* to encode. **3** INFORM to code.

código *nm* code. COMP **código de barras** bar code. ▌ **código de la circulación** highway code. ▌ **código de señales** MAR flag signals. ▌ **código Morse** Morse code.

codillo *nm* **1** *(del brazo)* elbow. **2** *(en cocina)* shoulder. **3** *(de tubería)* elbow.

codo *nm* **1** ANAT elbow. **2** TÉC bend. LOC **alzar el codo / empinar el codo** *fam* to have a few drinks, knock them back. ▌ **codo a codo / codo con codo** *fig* side by side, closely. ▌ **de codos** on one's elbows. ▌ **hablar por los codos** *fam* to talk nineteen to the dozen, talk nonstop. ▌ **romperse los codos** *fig* to study a lot, swot, cram.

codorniz *nf* quail.

coeficiente *nm* **1** MAT coefficient. **2** *(grado)* degree, rate. COMP **coeficiente de inteligencia** intelligence quotient, IQ.

cofia *nf* bonnet.

coexistir *vi* to coexist.

cofradía *nf* **1** *(hermandad)* brotherhood. **2** *(asociación)* association. **3** *(gremio)* guild.

cofre *nm* *(grande)* trunk, chest; *(pequeño)* box, casket.

coger *vt* **1** *(asir)* to seize, take hold of: *coge al bebé* hold the baby. **2** *(apresar)* to capture, catch. **3** *(tomar)* to take: *coge algo para beber* take a drink. **4** *(tren, etc)* to catch. **5** *(tomar prestado)* to borrow: *te he cogido el libro* I've borrowed your book. **6** *(recolectar frutos, etc)* to pick; *(del suelo)* to gather. **7** *(enfermedad, balón)* to catch: *cogí un resfriado* I caught a cold. **8** *(velocidad, fuerza)* to gather. **9** *(emisora, canal)* to pick up, get: *coger la BBC* to get the BBC. **10** *(notas)* to take, take down. **11** *(entender)* to understand, get: *no cogí el final* I didn't get the end. LOC **coger cariño a** ALGO/ALGN to become fond of STH/SB, take a liking to STH/SB. **| coger por sorpresa** to catch by surprise.

▶ *vpr* **cogerse** *(agarrarse)* to hold on: *cógete fuerte* hold on tight. LOC **cogerse un cabreo** *fam* to get very angry.

cogollo *nm (de lechuga, etc)* heart.

cogote *nm* back of the neck.

coherencia *nf* coherence, coherency.

coherente *adj* coherent, connected.

cohete *nm* rocket.

cohibir *vt* to inhibit, restrain.

▶ *vpr* **cohibirse** to feel inhibited, feel embarrassed.

coincidir *vi* **1** *(estar de acuerdo)* to agree (en, on), coincide (en, in). **2** *(ajustarse)* to coincide. **3** *(ocurrir al mismo tiempo)* to be at the same time (con, as), coincide (con, with); *(en el mismo lugar)* to meet.

cojear *vi* **1** *(persona)* to limp, hobble. **2** *(muebles)* to wobble. LOC **cojear del mismo pie** *fam* to have the same faults.

cojera *nf* limp, lameness.

cojín *nm* cushion.

cojo,-a *adj* **1** *(persona)* lame, crippled. **2** *(mueble)* wobbly. **3** *fig (defectuoso)* faulty, incomplete.

col *nf* cabbage. COMP **col de Bruselas** Brussels sprout.

cola¹ *nf* **1** *(gen)* tail. **2** *(de vestido)* train; *(de chaqueta)* tail. **3** *(fila)* queue, US line. LOC **hacer cola** to queue up, US stand in line. **| COMP cola de caballo** *(peinado)* ponytail.

cola² *nf (pegamento)* glue.

colaboración *nf* **1** collaboration. **2** *(prensa)* contribution.

colaborador,-ra *adj* collaborating.

▶ *nm & nf* **1** collaborator. **2** *(prensa)* contributor.

colaborar *vi* **1** to collaborate (con, with). **2** *(prensa)* to contribute (en, to).

colada *nf* **1** *(lavado)* washing, laundry; *(con lejía)* bleaching. **2** *(ropa)* washing, wash. **3** *(volcánica)* outflow. LOC **hacer**

la colada to do the washing, do the laundry.

colador *nm* **1** *(de té, café)* strainer. **2** *(de caldo, alimentos)* colander, sieve.

colapsar *vt (ciudad, aeropuerto, etc)* to paralyse; *(tráfico)* to bring to a standstill, bring to a halt.

▶ *vi* to collapse.

colar *vt (líquido)* to strain, filter.

▶ *vi fam* to wash: *veremos si cuela* we'll see if it washes.

▶ *vpr* **colarse 1** *(escabullirse)* to slip in, gatecrash. **2** *(en una cola)* to push in, jump the queue, US jump the line. **3** *fam (equivocarse)* to slip up, make a mistake.

colcha *nf* bedspread.

colchón *nm* mattress. COMP **colchón neumático** air mattress.

colchoneta *nf* small mattress.

cole *nm fam* school.

colear *vi (perro, etc)* to wag its tail; *(vaca, caballo, etc)* to swish its tail.

colección *nf* collection.

coleccionar *vt* to collect.

coleccionista *nm o nf* collector.

colectividad *nf* community.

colectivo,-a *adj* collective, group.

▶ *nm* **colectivo 1** *(asociación)* association, guild. **2** LING collective noun.

colegio *nm (escuela)* school: *van al colegio en autobús* they go to school by bus. COMP **colegio público** state school.

coleóptero *nm* coleopteran.

cólera *nf* **1** *(bilis)* bile. **2** *fig (ira)* anger, rage.

▶ *nm* MED cholera.

colérico,-a *adj* furious, irascible.

colesterol *nm* cholesterol.

coleta *nf* pigtail, ponytail.

colgado,-a *adj* hanging (de, from).

colgador *nm* (coat) hanger.

colgante *adj* hanging.

▶ *nm* **1** ARQUIT festoon. **2** *(joya)* pendant.

colgar *vt* **1** *(gen)* to hang (up). **2** *(la colada)* to hang out. **3** *(atribuir)* to pin. **4** *(el teléfono)* to put down.

▶ *vi* **1** *(estar colgado)* to hang (de, from): *cuelga del techo* it hangs from the ceiling. **2** *(una prenda)* to hang down, be crooked. **3** *(teléfono)* to hang up, ring off: *¡no cuelgue!* please hold!, hold the line, please!

colibrí *nm* humming bird.

cólico *nm* colic.

coliflor *nf* cauliflower.

colilla *nf* cigarette end, cigarette butt, butt.

colina *nf* hill, slope.

colirio *nm* eye drops *pl*.

colisión *nf* *(de vehículos)* collision, crash.

colisionar *vi* *(chocar)* to collide (con/contra, with), crash (con/contra, into).

colitis *nf inv* colitis.

collar *nm* **1** *(adorno)* necklace. **2** *(de animal)* collar.

colmar *vt* *(gen)* to fill (de, with); *(vaso, copa)* to fill to the brim.

colmena *nf* beehive.

colmillo *nm* **1** eye tooth, canine tooth. **2** *(de carnívoro)* fang; *(de jabalí, elefante, morsa)* tusk.

colmo *nm* height, summit. LOC *¡esto es el colmo!* this is the last straw!, this is the limit!

colocar *vt* **1** *(gen)* to place, put. **2** *(dar empleo)* to get a job for.
▶ *vpr* **colocarse 1** *(situarse)* to place os, put os, find os a place. **2** *(trabajar)* to find a job (de, as), get a job (de, as).

Colombia *nf* Colombia.

colombiano,-a *adj* Colombian.
▶ *nm & nf* Colombian.

colon *nm* ANAT colon.

colonia *nf* **1** *(grupo)* colony. **2** [normalmente en plural] *(vacaciones infantiles)* summer camp. **3** *(perfume)* cologne.

colonial *adj* POL colonial.

colonialismo *nm* colonialism.

colonización *nf* colonization.

colonizar *vt* to colonize, settle.

colono *nm* **1** *(habitante)* colonist, settler. **2** AGR tenant farmer.

coloquial *adj* colloquial.

coloquio *nm* talk, discussion.

color *nm* **1** colour (US color): *es de color verde* it's green. LOC **de color 1** *(en color)* in colour (US color), coloured (US colored). **2** *(persona)* coloured (US colored). ‖ **en color / en colores** *(cine, foto)* in colour (US color).

colorado,-a *adj* **1** coloured (US colored). **2** *(rojo)* red. LOC **ponerse colorado,-a** to blush, go red.

colorante *nm* colouring (US coloring), dye.

colorear *vt* to colour (US color).

colorete *nm* rouge, blusher.

colorido *nm* colour (US color).

coloso *nm* colossus.

columna *nf* **1** *(gen)* column. **2** ANAT spine. **3** *(elemento central)* backbone. COMP **columna vertebral** vertebral column, spinal column.

columpiar *vt* to swing.
▶ *vpr* **columpiarse** to swing (de, on).

columpio *nm* swing.

colza *nf* rape. COMP **aceite de colza** rapeseed oil, US canola oil.

coma[1] *nf* **1** *(puntuación)* comma. **2** *(en música)* comma. **3** MAT point: *cuatro coma cinco* four point five.

coma[2] *nm* MED coma. LOC **entrar en coma** to go into a coma.

comadreja *nf* weasel.

comadrona *nm & nf* midwife.

comandante *nm* **1** *(oficial)* commander, commanding officer. **2** *(graduación)* major. **3** *(piloto)* pilot.

comando *nm* **1** MIL commando. **2** INFORM command.

comarca *nf* area, region.

comba *nf* **1** *(de cuerda, cable)* bend, curve. **2** *(cuerda)* skipping rope. **3** *(juego)* skipping. LOC **saltar a la comba** to skip, US skip rope.

combar *vt* to bend.
▶ *vpr* **combarse** *(una cuerda)* to bend; *(viga, pared)* to sag, bulge.

combate *nm* **1** *(gen)* combat, battle. **2** MIL battle. **3** *(boxeo)* fight, contest.

combatiente *adj* fighting.
▶ *nm o nf* fighter, combatant.

combatir *vi* to fight (contra, against /-), struggle (contra, against).
▶ *vt* **1** *(luchar contra)* to fight: *combatir el cáncer* to fight cancer. **2** *fig* to combat, fight. **3** *fig (batir, golpear)* to beat, lash.

combativo,-a *adj* spirited, aggressive.

combinación *nf* **1** combination. **2** *(prenda)* slip.

combinar *vt* **1** *(gen)* to combine. **2** QUÍM to combine. **3** *(colores)* to match (con, -), go (con, with).

combustible *adj* combustible.
▶ *nm* fuel.

comedero *nm* feeding trough, manger.

comedia *nf* **1** TEAT comedy, play. **2** *fig* farce, pretence (US pretense).

comediante,-a *nm & nf* **1** *(hombre)* actor; *(mujer)* actress. **2** *fig* hypocrite, comedian.

comedor,-ra *nm (sala)* dining room; *(en una fábrica, un colegio, etc)* canteen.

comensal *nm o nf* person at the table, diner.

comentar *vt* **1** *(texto)* to comment on. **2** *(expresar una opinión)* to talk about, discuss.

comentario *nm* **1** *(observación)* remark, comment. **2** *(explicación, narración)* commentary.
▶ *nm pl* **comentarios** *(murmuración)* gossip *sing*.

comentarista *nm o nf* commentator.

comenzar *vt* to begin, start.
▶ *vi* to begin, start: *comenzó a reír* he began to laugh, he began laughing. LOC **comenzar con** to begin with. ‖ **comenzar + ger** to start by + ger: *comenzó explicando...* he started by explaining...

comer *vt* **1** to eat. **2** *(en ajedrez)* to take, capture.
▶ *vi (gen)* to eat; *(a mediodía)* to have lunch, lunch; *(por la noche)* to have dinner, dine.
▶ *nm* eating.
▶ *vpr* **comerse 1** to eat. **2** *fig (saltarse)* to omit; *(párrafo)* to skip; *(palabra)* to swallow.

comercial *adj* **1** *(del comercio)* commercial. **2** *(de tiendas)* shopping.
▶ *nm o nf (vendedor)* seller; *(hombre)* salesman; *(mujer)* saleswoman.

comerciante *adj* business-minded.
▶ *nm o nf* merchant. **2** *(interesado)* moneymaker.

comerciar *vi* **1** *(comprar y vender)* to trade, deal, buy and sell. **2** *(hacer negocios)* to do business (con, with).

comercio *nm* **1** *(ocupación)* commerce, trade. **2** *(tienda)* shop, store. LOC **comercio al por mayor** wholesale trade. COMP **comercio exterior** foreign trade. ‖ **libre comercio** free trade.

comestible *adj* edible, eatable.
▶ *nm pl* **comestibles** groceries, food *sing*, foodstuffs *pl*.

cometa *nm (cuerpo celeste)* comet.
▶ *nf (juguete)* kite.

cometer *vt (crimen)* to commit; *(falta, error)* to make.

cómic *nm* comic.

cómico,-a *adj* **1** *(divertido)* comic, comical, funny. **2** *(de comedia)* comedy.
▶ *nm & nf (actor)* comedian, comic.

comida *nf* **1** *(alimento)* food: **2** *(desayuno, etc)* meal. **3** *(almuerzo)* lunch.

comienzo *nm* start, beginning. LOC **a comienzos de** at the beginning of. ‖ **dar comienzo** to begin, start.

comillas *nf pl* inverted commas. LOC **entre comillas** in inverted commas.

comilona *nf* big meal, blowout.

comino *nm* BOT cumin, cummin. LOC **me importa un comino** *fam* I don't give a damn.

comisaría *nf (de policía)* police station.

comisario *nm (de policía)* police inspector.

comisión *nf* **1** *(retribución)* commission. **2** *(comité)* committee. LOC **a comisión / con comisión** on a commission basis. COMP **comisión bancaria** service charge, bank commission.

comité *nm* committee.

comitiva *nf* suite, retinue.

como *adv* **1** *(modo)* how: *lo hizo como quiso* he did it the way he wanted to. **2** *(com-*

paración) as, like: *negro como la noche* as dark as night. **3** *(en calidad de)* as: *como invitado* as a guest. **4** *(según)* as: *como dice tu amigo* as your friend says. **5** *fam (aproximadamente)* about: *había como unos cien* there were about a hundred. LOC **como quiera que 1** *(no importa cómo)* however. **2** *(ya que)* since, as, inasmuch as. ▌**como sea** whatever happens, no matter what. ▌**hacer como si** to pretend to +inf: *hace como si no viese nada* he's pretending not to see anything.
▶ *conj* **1** *(así que)* as: *como llegaban se presentaban* they introduced themselves as they arrived. **2** *(si)* if: *como lo vuelvas a hacer...* if you do it again.... **3** *(porque)* as, since: *como llegamos tarde no pudimos entrar* since we arrived late we couldn't get in.

cómo *adv* **1** *(interrogativo)* how. **2** *(por qué)* why. **3** *(admiración)* how: *¡cómo pasa el tiempo!* how time flies! LOC **¿cómo?** *fam* what? ▌**¿cómo es que...?** how is it that...? ▌**¡cómo no!** but of course!, certainly!

cómoda *nf* chest of drawers, commode.

comodidad *nf* **1** *(confort)* comfort. **2** *(facilidad)* convenience. LOC **con comodidad** comfortably.

comodín *nm (mono)* joker; *(otra carta)* wild card.

cómodo,-a *adj* **1** comfortable, cosy. **2** *(útil)* convenient, handy.

compactar *vt* to compact, compress.

compadecer *vt* to pity, feel sorry for.
▶ *vpr* **compadecerse** to take pity (de, on), pity (de, -), feel sorry (de, for).

compaginar *vt (combinar)* to combine, make compatible.
▶ *vpr* **compaginarse** to go together, be compatible.

compañerismo *nm* companionship, fellowship, comradeship.

compañero,-a *nm & nf* **1** *(sentimental, pareja)* partner. **2** *(colega)* companion, mate; *(camarada)* comrade. **3** *fig (guante, zapato, etc)* the other one, the one that goes with this one. COMP **compa-**

ñero,-a de colegio schoolmate. ▌**compañero,-a de piso** flatmate. ▌**compañero,-a de trabajo** workmate, colleague.

compañía *nf* company. LOC **en compañía de** in the company of. ▌**hacer compañía a ALGN** to keep SB company.

comparación *nf* comparison. LOC **en comparación con** compared to, in comparison to.

comparar *vt* to compare:

comparativo,-a *adj* comparative.

compartimento *nm* compartment: *compartimento de primera clase* first-class compartment.

compartir *vt* **1** *(dividir)* to divide (up), split, share (out). **2** *(poseer en común)* to share.

compás *nm* **1** *(instrumento)* compass, compasses *pl.* **2** *(brújula)* compass. **3** MÚS *(división)* time; *(intervalo)* beat; *(ritmo)* rhythm. LOC **al compás de** in time to. ▌**llevar el compás 1** *(con la mano)* to beat time. **2** *(al bailar)* to keep time. ▌**perder el compás** to lose the beat.

compasión *nf* compassion, pity.

compasivo,-a *adj* compassionate, sympathetic.

compatibilidad *nf* compatibility.

compatibilizar *vt* to make compatible.

compatible *adj* compatible.

compendio *nm* summary, digest, précis, synopsis.

compenetrarse *vpr (uso recíproco)* to understand each other.

compensar *vt* **1** *(pérdida, error)* to make up for. **2** *(indemnizar)* to compensate, indemnify. **3** TÉC to balance, compensate. **4** *fam (merecer la pena)* to be worth one's while.

competencia *nf* **1** *(rivalidad)* competition, rivalry: **2** *(competidores)* competitors *pl*, rival company. **3** *(habilidad)* competence, ability, proficiency. **4** *(incumbencia)* responsibility.

competente *adj* **1** *(capaz)* competent, capable, proficient. **2** *(adecuado)* adequate.

competición *nf* competition, contest.

competidor,-ra *adj* **1** *(que compite)* competing. **2** *(rival)* rival.
▶ *nm & nf* **1** *(rival)* competitor. **2** *(en competición deportiva)* competitor.

competir *vi* to compete.

competitividad *nf* competitiveness.

competitivo,-a *adj* competitive.

complacer *vt* **1** *(satisfacer)* to satisfy, gratify, oblige. **2** *(agradar)* to please. **3** *fml* to please, give pleasure.

complejo,-a *adj* complex.
▶ *nm* **complejo** complex.

complementar *vt* to complement.
▶ *vpr* **complementarse** to complement each other, be complementary to each other.

complementario,-a *adj* complementary.

complemento *nm* **1** *(gen)* complement. **2** GRAM object, complement. COMP **complemento circunstancial** adverbial complement. I **complemento directo** direct object. I **complemento indirecto** indirect object.

completamente *adv* completely.

completar *vt* **1** *(gen)* to complete. **2** *(acabar)* to finish; *(perfeccionar)* to round off.

completo,-a *adj* **1** *(terminado)* finished, completed. **2** *(lleno)* full. LOC **al completo** full up, filled to capacity. I **por completo** completely.

complexión *nf* constitution, build: *su hermano es de complexión fuerte* his brother is well-built.

complicación *nf* complication.

complicado,-a *adj* **1** *(gen)* complicated, complex. **2** *(carácter)* complex.

complicar *vt* **1** *(gen)* to complicate, make complicated. **2** *(implicar)* to involve (en, in).

cómplice *nm o nf* accomplice.

complicidad *nf* complicity.

complot *nm* plot, conspiracy.

componente *adj* component, constituent.
▶ *nm* **1** *(pieza)* component, constituent; *(ingrediente)* ingredient. **2** *(miembro)* member.

componer *vt* **1** *(formar)* to compose, make up, form. **2** *(reparar)* to fix, repair, mend. **3** *(adornar)* to adorn, decorate. **4** *(música, versos)* to compose.
▶ *vpr* **componerse** *(consistir)* to consist (de, of), be made up (de, of): *las palabras se componen de sílabas* words are made up of syllables.

comportamiento *nm* behaviour (US behavior), conduct.

comportar *vt* *(implica)* to involve, entail: *eso comporta un cambio de planes* that involves a change of plan.
▶ *vpr* **comportarse** *(portarse)* to behave: *se comportó mal* she misbehaved.

composición *nf* **1** *(gen)* composition. **2** *(arreglo)* arrangement.

compositor,-ra *nm & nf* composer.

compota *nf* compote.

compra *nf* purchase, buy. LOC **hacer la compra** to do the shopping, go shopping. I **ir de compras** to go shopping. COMP **compra a plazos** hire purchase, US instalment buying.

comprador,-ra *nm & nf* purchaser, buyer, shopper.

comprar *vt* to buy.

compraventa *nf* buying and selling, dealing.

comprender *vt* **1** *(entender)* to understand: *lo comprendiste mal* you misunderstood it. **2** *(contener)* to comprise, include. LOC **¿comprendes?** *(en conversación)* you see?

comprensión *nf* understanding.

comprensivo,-a *adj* **1** *(tolerante)* understanding. **2** *(que comprende o incluye)* comprehensive.

compresa *nf* **1** *(higiénica)* sanitary towel. **2** *(vendaje)* compress.

comprimido,-a *adj* compressed.
▶ *nm* **comprimido** tablet.

comprimir *vt (apretar)* to compress; *(gente)* to cram together.

comprobante *nm (recibo)* receipt, voucher.

comprobar *vt* **1** *(verificar)* to verify, check. **2** *(observar)* to see, observe: *como podrán ustedes comprobar* as you can see for yourselves. **3** *(confirmar)* to confirm.

comprometer *vt* **1** *(exponer a riesgo)* to endanger, jeopardize, risk; *(a una persona)* to compromise. **2** *(implicar)* to involve, implicate. **3** *(obligar)* to commit. **4** *(poner en un aprieto)* to embarrass.
  ▶ *vpr* **comprometerse** **1** *(contraer una obligación)* to commit os, pledge. **2** *(involucrarse)* to get involved. **3** *(establecer relaciones formales)* to get engaged. [LOC] **comprometerse a hacer** ALGO to undertake to do STH.

comprometido,-a *adj* **1** *(difícil, arriesgado)* difficult, in jeopardy. **2** *(escritor, artista, etc)* committed. **3** *(involucrado)* involved. **4** *(para casarse)* engaged.

compromiso *nm* **1** *(obligación)* commitment, obligation: *cumplió sus compromisos* she fulfilled her obligations. **2** *(cita)* appointment; *(amorosa)* date. **3** *(apuro)* difficult situation, bind. **4** *(matrimonial)* engagement.

compuesto,-a *adj (gen)* compound.

compulsar *vt* **1** *(cotejar)* to collate. **2** JUR to make a certified true copy of.

compulsivo,-a *adj* compelling, compulsive.

compungido,-a *adj* **1** *(arrepentido)* remorseful. **2** *fig (triste)* sorrowful, sad.

compungir *vt fml (entristecer)* to sadden, make sad.
  ▶ *vpr* **compungirse** *(entristecerse)* to be saddened, feel sad.

computación *nf* computing.

computador *nm* computer.

computadora *nf* computer.

computar *vt* **1** *(calcular)* to compute, calculate. **2** *fml (tomar en cuenta)* to take into account, count.

computarizar *vt* to computerize.

computerizar *vt* to computerize.

cómputo *nm* computation, calculation.

comulgar *vi* REL to receive Holy Communion.

común *adj* **1** *(gen)* common: *eso es poco común* that's unusual. **2** *(compartido)* shared, communal.

comuna *nf* commune.

comunal *adj* communal.

comunicación *nf* **1** *(gen)* communication. **2** *(comunicado)* communication; *(oficial)* communiqué. **3** *(telefónica)* connection. **4** *(unión)* link, connection.
  ▶ *nf pl* **comunicaciones** communications.

comunicado,-a *adj* served. [COMP] **comunicado de prensa** press release.

comunicar *vt* **1** *(hacer partícipe)* to communicate, convey, transmit. **2** *(hacer saber)* to communicate, make known, tell. **3** *(conectar)* to connect.
  ▶ *vi* **1** *(ponerse en comunicación)* to communicate; *(por carta)* to correspond. **2** *(teléfono)* to be engaged, US be busy. **3** *(estar conectado)* to communicate, be connected.
  ▶ *vpr* **comunicarse** **1** *(tener relación)* to communicate; *(ponerse en contacto)* to get in touch, get in contact (con, with). **2** *(estar conectado)* to be connected (con, to).

comunicativo,-a *adj* **1** *(actitud, sentimiento)* catching, infectious. **2** *(persona)* communicative, sociable, open.

comunidad *nf* community. [COMP] **comunidad autónoma** autonomous region. ▌ **Comunidad Económica Europea** European Economic Community.

comunión *nf* **1** communion, fellowship. **2** REL Holy Communion.

comunismo *nm* communism.

comunista *adj* communist.
  ▶ *nm o nf* communist.

comunitario,-a *adj (gen)* of the community, relating to the community.

con *prep* **1** *(instrumento, medio)* with. **2** *(modo, circunstancia)* in, with. **3** *(juntamente, en compañía)* with. **4** *(contenido)* with. **5** *(relación)* to. **6** *(comparación)*

compared to. **7 con +** *inf* by + *ger.*
8 *(aunque)* in spite of. LOC **con que /**
con tal de que / con tal que provided,
as long as. ‖ **con todo (y eso)** nevertheless, even so.

concavidad *nf* concavity.

cóncavo,-a *adj* concave.

concebir *vt* **1** *(engendrar)* to conceive. **2**
fig (comprender) to understand.
▶ *vi (quedarse embarazada)* to become
pregnant, conceive.

conceder *vt* **1** *(otorgar)* to grant, concede; *(premio)* to award. **2** *(atribuir)* to
give, attach. **3** *(oportunidad, tiempo)* to
give. **4** *(admitir)* to concede, admit.

concejal,-la *nm & nf* town councillor.

concejo *nm* town council, council.

concentración *nf* **1** *(gen)* concentration. **2** *(de gente)* gathering, rally.

concentrar *vt* to concentrate.
▶ *vpr* **concentrarse 1** *(reunirse)* to concentrate. **2** *(fijar la atención)* to concentrate (en, on).

concéntrico,-a *adj* concentric.

concepción *nf* conception.

concepto *nm* **1** *(idea)* concept, conception, idea. **2** *(opinión)* opinion, view.
LOC **bajo ningún concepto** under no
circumstances. ‖ **en concepto de** by
way of.

conceptual *adj* conceptual.

concernir *vi* [se usa sólo en tercera persona de presente de indicativo, imperfecto de
indicativo y presente de subjuntivo; y en
formas impersonales] *(afectar)* to concern, touch. LOC **en lo que a mí** *(ti, él,*
etc) **concierne** as far as I am *(you are, he*
is, etc) concerned.

concertado,-a *adj* concerted.

concertar *vt* **1** *(planear)* to plan, coordinate. **2** *(entrevista)* to arrange; *(acuer-*
do) to reach; *(tratado, negocio)* to conclude, settle. **3** *(precio)* to agree on.
▶ *vi* **1** *(concordar)* to agree, match up;
(números) to tally. **2** LING to agree.

concertino *nm* first violin.

concertista *nm o nf* soloist.

concesión *nf* **1** concession, granting.
2 *(de premio)* awarding.

concesionario,-a *nm & nf* concessionaire, licence holder, licensee.
▶ *nm* **concesionario** *(de coches)* dealer.

concesivo,-a *adj* LING concessive.

concha *nf* **1** *(caparazón)* shell. **2** *(carey)*
tortoiseshell. **3** *(ostra)* oyster.

conciencia *nf* **1** *(moral)* conscience. **2**
(conocimiento) consciousness, aware-
ness. LOC **a conciencia** conscientious-
ly. ‖ **remorderle a** ALGN **la conciencia** to
weigh on SB's conscience.

concienciar *vt* to make aware (de,
of).
▶ *vpr* **concienciarse** to become aware
(de, of).

concienzudo,-a *adj* conscientious.

concierto *nm* **1** MÚS *(sesión)* concert;
(composición) concerto. **2** *(acuerdo)*
agreement. **3** *(armonía)* concert, concord.

conciliación *nf* conciliation, recon-
ciliation.

conciliador,-ra *adj* conciliatory, con-
ciliating.

conciliar *adj* conciliar.
▶ *vt* **1** *(gen)* to conciliate, bring together. **2** *(enemigos)* to reconcile.

concilio *nm* council.

concisión *nf* concision, conciseness.

conciso,-a *adj* concise, brief.

conciudadano,-a *nm & nf* fellow citizen.

concluir *vt* **1** *(terminar)* to finish. **2** *(trato,*
negocio) to close.
▶ *vi (finalizar)* to finish, come to an
end, conclude.

conclusión *nf* **1** *(final)* conclusion, end.
2 *(deducción)* conclusion. LOC **en con-**
clusión in conclusion. ‖ **llegar a una**
conclusión to come to a conclusion.

concluyente *adj* conclusive, decisive.

concordancia *nf* **1** concordance,
agreement. **2** LING agreement.

concordante *adj* concordant.

concordar *vt* **1** *(poner de acuerdo)* to
bring into agreement, reconcile. **2**
LING to make agree.

▸ *vi* **1** *(convenir)* to agree, coincide, match. **2** LING to agree.

concordia *nf* concord, harmony.

concreción *nf (concisión)* concision, conciseness.

concretar *vt* **1** *(precisar)* to specify, state explicitly. **2** *(hora, precio)* to fix, set. **3** *(resumir)* to sum up.

▸ *vpr* **concretarse** *(tomar forma)* to take shape.

concreto,-a *adj* **1** *(real)* concrete, real. **2** *(particular)* particular, specific. LOC **en concreto** *(en particular)* in particular, specifically.

concurrencia *nf* **1** *(confluencia)* combination, concurrence. **2** *(participación)* participation.

concurrido,-a *adj* **1** *(lugar público)* busy, crowded. **2** *(espectáculo)* well-attended, popular.

concurrir *vi* **1** *(juntarse en un lugar - gente)* to gather, come together, meet. **2** *(tomar parte - concurso, etc)* to compete, take part.

concursante *nm o nf* **1** *(a concurso)* contestant, participant, competitor. **2** *(a empleo)* candidate.

concursar *vi* **1** *(competir)* to compete, take part. **2** *(para un empleo)* to be a candidate.

concurso *nm* **1** *(gen)* competition; *(de belleza, deportivo)* contest; *(en televisión)* quiz. **2** *(para puestos)* public examination: **3** *fml (concurrencia)* gathering.

condado *nm* county.

conde *nm* count.

condecoración *nf* decoration.

condecorar *vt* to decorate.

condena *nf* JUR sentence.

condenado,-a *adj* **1** JUR convicted. **2** *(sin remedio)* hopeless.

condenar *vt* **1** JUR *(declarar culpable)* to convict, find guilty. **2** JUR *(decretar condena)* to sentence, condemn. **3** *(desaprobar)* to condemn.

condensación *nf* **1** *(acción)* condensing. **2** *(efecto)* condensation.

condensado,-a *adj* condensed.

condensador,-ra *adj* condensing.

condensar *vt* to condense.

condescender *vi (adaptarse)* to comply (a, with), consent (a, to).

condescendiente *adj (complaciente)* obliging.

condición *nf* **1** *(naturaleza)* nature, condition. **2** *(carácter)* nature, character. **3** *(circunstancia)* circumstance, condition. **4** *(estado social)* status, position. **5** *(calidad)* capacity. **6** *(exigencia)* condition. LOC **a condición de que...** provided (that)… ‖ **con la condición de que...** on the condition that…

▸ *nf pl* **condiciones 1** *(estado)* condition *sing*, state *sing*. **2** *(aptitud)* aptitude *sing*, talent *sing*. LOC **estar en condiciones de hacer** ALGO **1** *(físicas)* to be fit to do STH. **2** *(posición, autoridad)* to be in a position to do STH.

condicionado,-a *adj* conditioned.

condicional *adj* conditional.

▸ *nm* conditional.

condicionar *vt* **1** *(influir en)* to condition, determine. **2** *(supeditar)* to make conditional.

condimentar *vt* to season, flavour (US flavor).

condimento *nm* seasoning, flavouring (US flavoring).

condolerse *vpr* to sympathize (de, with), feel sorry (de, for), feel pity (de, for).

cóndor *nm* condor.

conducir *vt* **1** *(guiar)* to lead, take, show. **2** *(coche, animales)* to drive.

▸ *vi* **1** *(un coche)* to drive. **2** *(llevar)* to lead (a, -).

conducta *nf* conduct, behaviour (US behavior).

conductividad *nf* conductivity.

conductivo,-a *adj* conductive.

conducto *nm (tubería)* pipe, conduit.

conductor,-ra *adj* FÍS conductive.

▸ *nm & nf* AUTO driver.

▸ *nm* **conductor** FÍS conductor.

conectar *vt (gen)* to connect (up).

▸ *vi* **1** RAD TV *(coger)* to tune in (con, to); *(dar conexión)* to tune in (con, with). **2** *fam (llevarse bien)* to hit it off, get on well.

conector *nm* connector.

conejera *nf* **1** *(conejal)* rabbit hutch. **2** *(madriguera)* rabbit warren, rabbit burrow.

conejero,-a *nm & nf* rabbit breeder.

conejillo *nm* young rabbit. COMP **conejillo de Indias** guinea pig.

conejo,-a *nm & nf* rabbit.

conexión *nf* TÉC connection.

conexo,-a *adj* connected, related.

confabulación *nf* conspiracy, plot.

confabular *vi* to confabulate, discuss.
  ▶ *vpr* **confabularse** to conspire, plot.

confección *nf* **1** *(acción)* dressmaking, tailoring; *(ropa)* off-the-peg clothes *pl*, ready-to-wear clothes *pl*. **2** *(realización)* making, making up.

confeccionar *vt (vestido)* to make, make up; *(plato)* to prepare.

confederación *nf* confederation, confederacy.

confederar *vt* to confederate.

conferencia *nf* **1** *(charla)* talk, lecture. **2** POL conference, meeting. **3** *(teléfono)* long-distance call. LOC **dar una conferencia sobre** ALGO to lecture on STH, give a lecture on STH.

conferenciante *nm o nf* lecturer.

conferenciar *vi* to confer.

conferir *vt* **1** *(conceder)* to confer, bestow, award. **2** *(dar)* to give.

confesar *vt (reconocer)* to confess, admit.
  ▶ *vpr* **confesarse** to go to confession, confess.

confesión *nf (expresión)* confession, admission.

confesional *adj* denominational.

confesionario *nm* confessional.

confeso,-a *adj* JUR self-confessed.

confesor *nm* confessor.

confeti *nm* confetti.

confiado,-a *adj* **1** *(crédulo)* unsuspecting, gullible. **2** *(seguro)* confident, self-confident.

confianza *nf* **1** *(seguridad)* confidence. **2** *(familiaridad)* familiarity, intimacy. **3** *(presunción)* conceit. LOC **de confianza 1** *(fiable)* reliable. **2** *(de responsabilidad)* trustworthy. ▌ **en confianza** confidentially, in confidence. ▌ **tener confianza en uno mismo** to be self-confident.

confiar *vi* **1** *(tener fe)* to trust (en, -), confide (en, in). **2** *(estar seguro)* to be confident, trust. **3** *(contar)* to count (en, on), rely (en, on).
  ▶ *vt* **1** *(depositar)* to entrust. **2** *(secretos, problemas, etc)* to confide.
  ▶ *vpr* **confiarse** *(entregarse)* to entrust os.

confidencia *nf* confidence, secret.

confidencial *adj* confidential.

confidencialidad *nf* confidentiality.

configurar *vt* **1** to form, shape. **2** INFORM to configure.

confinar *vt (recluir)* to confine.

confirmación *nf* confirmation.

confirmar *vt* to confirm.

confiscar *vt* to confiscate.

confitado,-a *adj (fruta)* candied, glacé. COMP **frutas confitadas** candied fruit *sing*.

confitar *vt (frutas)* to candy; *(carne)* to preserve.

confitería *nf* confectioner's, sweet shop, US candy shop.

confitero,-a *nm & nf* confectioner.

confitura *nf* preserve, jam.

conflictividad *nf* disputes *pl*.

conflictivo,-a *adj (situación)* difficult; *(tema)* controversial.

conflicto *nm* **1** *(choque)* conflict. **2** *fig (apuro)* dilemma. COMP **conflicto laboral** industrial dispute.

confluencia *nf* confluence.

confluir *vi (personas)* to converge, come together; *(ríos, caminos, etc)* to meet, converge.

conformar *vt* **1** *(dar forma)* to shape. **2** *(adaptar)* to conform, adjust.
  ▶ *vpr* **conformarse** *(contentarse)* to resign os (con, to), be content (con, with), make do (con, with).

conforme *adj* **1** *(satisfecho)* satisfied. **2** *(de acuerdo)* in accordance with, in keeping with. **3** *(resignado)* resigned. LOC **conforme a** in accordance with, according to.
▶ *adv* **1** *(según, como)* as. **2** *(en cuanto)* as soon as. **3** *(a medida que)* as.

conformidad *nf* *(aprobación)* approval, consent. LOC **en conformidad con** ALGO in conformity with STH, in agreement with.

conformismo *nm* conformism.

conformista *nm o nf* conformist.

confort *nm* comfort.

confortable *adj* comfortable.

confraternizar *vi* to fraternize.

confrontación *nf* *(enfrentamiento)* confrontation.

confrontar *vt* **1** *(gen)* to confront; *(carear)* to bring face to face. **2** *(cotejar)* to compare (con, with), collate (con, with).

confundir *vt* **1** *(equivocar)* to confuse (con, with), mistake (con, for). **2** *(turbar)* to confound, embarrass.
▶ *vpr* **confundirse 1** *(mezclarse)* to mingle; *(colores, formas)* to blend. **2** *(equivocarse)* to get mixed up, make a mistake. **3** *(turbarse)* to be confused, be embarrassed.

confusión *nf* **1** *(desorden)* confusion, chaos. **2** *(equivocación)* mistake, confusion.

confuso,-a *adj* **1** *(ideas)* confused. **2** *(estilo, etc)* obscure, confused. **3** *fig (turbado)* confused, embarrassed.

congelación *nf* **1** *(gen)* freezing. **2** *(precios, salarios, etc)* freeze. **3** MED *(gen)* exposure; *(extremidades)* frostbite.

congelado,-a *adj* **1** *(gen)* frozen. **2** MED frostbitten.
▶ *nm pl* **congelados** frozen food *sing*.

congelador *nm* freezer.

congelar *vt* **1** *(gen)* to freeze. **2** MED to cause frostbite on.
▶ *vpr* **congelarse 1** to freeze. **2** MED to get frostbite.

congeniar *vi* to get on.

congénito,-a *adj* **1** congenital. **2** *fig* innate.

congestión *nf* congestion.

congestionar *vt* to congest.
▶ *vpr* **congestionarse** to become congested.

conglomerado *nm* **1** TÉC conglomerate. **2** *fig* conglomeration, collection.

conglomerar *vt* to conglomerate.

congratular *vt fml* to congratulate on.
▶ *vpr* **congratularse** *fml* to congratulate OS (de/por, on).

congregación *nf* **1** *(reunión)* assembly. **2** REL congregation.

congregar *vt* to congregate, assemble.
▶ *vpr* **congregarse** to congregate, assemble.

congresista *nm o nf* **1** *(que asiste a un congreso)* congress participant. **2** *(diputado)* member of congress; *(hombre)* congressman; *(mujer)* congresswoman.

congreso *nm* congress. COMP **congreso de los Diputados** Parliament, US Congress.

congrio *nm* conger, conger eel.

congruencia *nf* **1** *(conveniencia)* congruity. **2** MAT congruence.

congruente *adj* **1** *(coherente)* coherent, suitable. **2** MAT congruent.

cónico,-a *adj* **1** conical. **2** *(en geometría)* conic.

conífera *nf* conifer.

conjetura *nf* conjecture. LOC **hacer conjeturas** to make conjectures.

conjeturar *vt* to conjecture.

conjugación *nf* conjugation.

conjugado,-a *adj* *(enlazado)* combined.

conjugar *vt* to conjugate.

conjunción *nf* conjunction.

conjuntamente *adv* jointly, together.

conjuntar *vt* to coordinate.

conjuntivitis *nf inv* conjunctivitis.

conjunto,-a *adj* **1** *(compartido)* joint. **2** *(combinado)* combined. LOC **en conjunto** altogether, on the whole.

▶ *nm* **conjunto 1** *(grupo)* group, collection. **2** *(todo)* whole: **3** *(prenda)* outfit, ensemble. **4** MÚS *(clásico)* ensemble; *(pop)* band, group. **5** MAT set. **6** DEP team.

conjura *nf* plot, conspiracy.

conjuración *nf* plot, conspiracy.

conjurar *vt (gen)* to exorcise; *(peligro)* to avert, stave off, ward off.
▶ *vi (conspirar)* to conspire (contra, against).
▶ *vpr* **conjurarse** to conspire (contra, against).

conjuro *nm* **1** *(exorcismo)* exorcism. **2** *(encantamiento)* spell, incantation.

conmemorar *vt* to commemorate.

conmemorativo,-a *adj* commemorative.

conmigo *pron* with me, to me.

conmoción *nf* **1** commotion, shock: *causar conmoción* to cause a commotion. **2** MED concussion. **3** *(levantamiento)* riot. COMP **conmoción cerebral** concussion.

conmocionar *vt* **1** to shock. **2** MED to concuss. **3** *fig* to trouble, disturb.

conmovedor,-ra *adj* moving, touching.

conmover *vt* **1** *(persona)* to move, touch. **2** *(cosa)* to shake.

conmutador *nm* switch.

conmutar *vt* **1** *(cambiar)* to exchange. **2** JUR to commute. **3** ELEC to commutate.

conmutativo,-a *adj* commutative.

connivencia *nf* connivance, collusion.

cono *nm* cone.

conocedor,-ra *nm & nf* expert (de, on), connoisseur (de, of).

conocer *vt* **1** *(gen)* to know; *(noticia)* to hear. **2** *(persona)* to meet, get to know. **3** *(reconocer)* to recognize. **4** *(país, lugar)* to have been to. LOC **dar a conocer** to make known.
▶ *vi* **1** *(saber)* to know (de, about). **2** JUR to hear (de, -).
▶ *vpr* **conocerse** *(a sí mismo)* to know os; *(dos o más personas)* to know each other; *(por primera vez)* to meet, get to know.

conocido,-a *adj* **1** known. **2** *(famoso)* well-known.

conocimiento *nm* **1** [en 1, también se usa en plural con el mismo significado] *(saber)* knowledge. **2** *(sensatez)* good sense. **3** *(conciencia)* consciousness. LOC **tener conocimiento de** ALGO to know about STH.

conquista *nf* conquest. LOC **hacer una conquista** *(amorosa)* to make a conquest.

conquistador,-ra *adj* conquering.

conquistar *vt (con las armas)* to conquer.

consagración *nf* **1** *(artista, etc)* recognition. **2** *(de una costumbre)* establishment. **3** *(dedicación)* dedication.

consagrado,-a *adj (reconocido)* recognized, established.

consagrar *vt* **1** *(palabra, expresión)* to establish. **2** *(dedicar)* to dedicate. **3** *(artista, etc)* to confirm, establish.

consanguíneo,-a *adj* consanguineous.
▶ *nm & nf* blood relation.

consanguinidad *nf* consanguinity, blood relationship.

consciente *adj* **1** conscious, aware. **2** MED conscious. **3** *(responsable)* reliable, responsible. LOC **estar consciente** to be conscious. I **ser consciente de** ALGO to be aware of STH.

consecuencia *nf* **1** consequence, result. **2** *(coherencia)* consistency. LOC **a consecuencia de** as a consequence of, as a result of. I **como consecuencia de** as a consequence of, as a result of.

consecuente *adj* **1** *(siguiente)* consequent. **2** *(resultante)* resulting. **3** *(coherente)* consistent.

consecutivamente *adv* consecutively.

consecutivo,-a *adj* consecutive.

conseguir *vt* **1** *(cosa)* to obtain, get; *(objetivo)* to attain, achieve. **2** *(lograr)* to manage, succeed in.

consejería *nf* **1** *(lugar)* Council. **2** *(cargo)* councillor.

consejero,-a *nm & nf* **1** *(asesor)* adviser, advisor, counsellor. **2** POL councillor.

consejo *nm* **1** *(recomendación)* advice. **2** *(junta)* council, board. LOC **pedir consejo a** ALGN to ask SB for advice. COMP **consejo de ministros** cabinet.

consenso *nm* **1** *(acuerdo)* consensus. **2** *(consentimiento)* consent, assent.

consensuar *vt* to reach a consensus on.

consentido,-a *adj (mimado)* spoiled, spoilt.
▶ *nm & nf (persona)* spoiled person, spoilt person; *(niño)* spoiled child, spoilt child.

consentimiento *nm* consent.

consentir *vt* **1** *(tolerar)* to allow, permit, tolerate. **2** *(mimar)* to spoil.
▶ *vi* **1** *(admitir)* to consent (en, to), agree (en, to). **2** *(ceder)* to weaken.

conserje *nm* **1** *(portero)* porter; *(de hotel)* hall porter. **2** *(de escuela)* caretaker.

conserva [también se usa en plural con el mismo significado] *nf* **1** *(en lata)* tinned food, canned food. **2** *(dulces)* preserves *pl*.

conservación *nf (de alimentos)* preservation.

conservador,-ra *adj* POL conservative.
▶ *nm & nf* **1** POL conservative. **2** *(de museos)* curator.

conservadurismo *nm* conservatism.

conservante *nm* preservative.

conservar *vt* **1** *(alimentos)* to preserve. **2** *(guardar)* to keep, save.
▶ *vpr* **conservarse** **1** *(tradición, etc)* to survive. **2** *fig (mantenerse)* to keep well.

conservatorio *nm* conservatory, conservatoire, school of music.

conservero,-a *adj* canning: *industria conservera* canning industry.

considerable *adj* considerable.

considerablemente *adv* considerably.

consideración *nf* **1** *(reflexión)* consideration, attention: *este tema merece nuestra consideración* this subject deserves our attention. **2** *(respeto)* regard. LOC **con consideración** *(respeto)* respectfully. ▌**en consideración a** considering.

considerar *vt (reflexionar)* to consider, think over, think about.

consigna *nf (en estación, etc)* left-luggage office, US check-room.

consignar *vt* **1** *(mercancías)* to consign, ship, dispatch. **2** *(destinar - dinero, etc)* to allocate. **3** *(anotar)* to note down.

consigo *pron* **1** *(3ª persona singular - hombre)* with him; *(- mujer)* with her; *(- cosa, animal)* with it. **2** *(usted)* with you. **3** *(3ª persona plural)* with them. **4** *(ustedes)* with you.

consiguiente *adj* consequent, resulting, resultant. LOC **por consiguiente** therefore, consequently.

consistencia *nf (dureza)* consistency.

consistente *adj* **1** *(firme)* firm, solid. **2** *fig* sound, solid. **3** CULIN thick. LOC **consistente en** consisting of.

consistir *vi* **1** *(estribar)* to lie (en, in), consist (en, in). **2** *(estar formado)* to consist (en, of).

consistorial *adj* REL consistorial. COMP **casa consistorial** town hall.

consola *nf* **1** *(mueble)* console table. **2** *(de ordenador, etc)* console. COMP **consola de videojuegos** games console.

consolar *vt* to console, comfort.

consolidación *nf* consolidation.

consolidar *vt* to consolidate.

consomé *nm* clear soup, consommé.

consonante *nf* consonant.

consonántico,-a *adj* consonantal, consonant.

conspiración *nf* conspiracy, plot.

conspirador,-ra *nm & nf* conspirator.

conspirar *vi* to conspire, plot.

constancia *nf* **1** *(perseverancia)* constancy, perseverance. **2** *(evidencia)* evidence, proof. LOC **dejar constancia de** ALGO *(probar)* to prove STH.

constante *adj* **1** *(invariable)* constant. **2** *(persona)* steadfast.
▶ *nf* MAT constant.

constantemente *adv* constantly.

constar *vi* **1** *(consistir en)* to consist (de, of), be made up (de, of), comprise (de, -). **2** *(figurar)* to figure, be included, appear. **3** *(ser cierto)* to be a fact. **4** *(quedar claro)* to be clear, be known. LOC **hacer constar 1** *(señalar)* to point out, state. **2** *(escribir)* to put down, include.

constatar *vt* to verify, confirm.

constelación *nf* constellation.

consternar *vt* to dismay, shatter.

constipado,-a *nm* MED cold. LOC **estar constipado,-a** to have a cold.

constiparse *vpr* to catch a cold.

constitución *nf* constitution.

constitucional *adj* constitutional.

constituyente *adj* constituent.

construcción *nf* **1** construction: *la industria de la construcción* the construction industry. **2** *(edificio)* building. LOC **en construcción** under construction.

constructivo,-a *adj* constructive.

constructor,-ra *adj* construction, building.
▶ *nm & nf (de edificios)* builder; *(de barcos)* shipbuilder.

construir *vt* to construct, build.

consuelo *nm* consolation, comfort.

cónsul *nm o nf* consul.

consulado *nm* **1** *(oficina)* consulate. **2** *(cargo)* consulship.

consular *adj* consular.

consulta *nf* **1** *(acción)* consultation. **2** MED surgery, US doctor's office; *(consultorio)* consulting room. LOC **pasar consulta** to see patients, hold surgery.

consultar *vt* **1** *(pedir opinión)* to consult (con, with/-), seek advice (con, from): *consulté con mis padres* I consulted with my parents. **2** *(buscar en un libro)* to look up. LOC **consultar con un abogado** to consult a lawyer, take legal advice.

consultor,-ra *nm & nf* consultant.

consultorio *nm* MED *(consulta)* surgery, US doctor's office; *(habitación)* consulting room.

consumar *vt (terminar)* to complete, carry out.

consumición *nf* **1** consumption. **2** *(bebida)* drink.

consumidor,-ra *nm & nf* consumer.

consumir *vt* **1** *(gastar, usar)* to consume, use. **2** *(destruir)* to destroy, consume.
▶ *vpr* **consumirse 1** *(extinguirse)* to burn out. **2** *fig (afligirse)* to waste away.

consumismo *nm* consumerism.

consumista *nm o nf* consumerist.

consumo *nm* consumption.

contabilidad *nf* **1** *(profesión)* accountancy; *(carrera)* accounting. **2** *(de empresa, etc)* accounting, bookkeeping. LOC **llevar la contabilidad** to keep the books.

contabilizar *vt* to enter in the books.

contable *nm o nf* bookkeeper, accountant.
▶ *adj* countable.

contactar *vt* to contact, get in touch (con, with).

contacto *nm* **1** contact. **2** AUTO ignition. LOC **ponerse en contacto con** to get in touch with, get in contact with.

contado,-a *adj* few. COMP **en contadas ocasiones** seldom, rarely.

contador,-ra *nm* meter.

contagiar *vt* **1** *(enfermedad)* to transmit, pass on. **2** *fig* to infect, pass on, give.
▶ *vpr* **contagiarse 1** *(enfermar)* to get infected. **2** *(transmitirse)* to be contagious: *esta enfermedad no se contagia* this disease is not contagious.

contagio *nm* MED contagion, infection.

contagioso,-a *adj* infectious, contagious: *enfermedad contagiosa* infectious disease; *risa contagiosa* infectious laugh.

contáiner *nm* container.

contaminación *nf* contamination; *(de agua, aire)* pollution.

contaminante *nm* polluting agent.

contaminar *vt* to contaminate; *(agua, aire)* to pollute.

contar vt 1 *(calcular)* to count. 2 *(explicar)* to tell: *me contó un cuento* she told me a story.
▶ vi to count: *los niños saben contar* the children know how to count.

contemplación nf *(acción)* contemplation.

contemplar vt *(mirar)* to contemplate.

contemplativo,-a adj contemplative.

contemporáneo,-a adj contemporary.

contenedor,-ra adj containing.
▶ nm **contenedor** container.

contener vt 1 *(incluir)* to contain, hold. 2 *(detener)* to hold back, restrain. 3 *(respiración)* to hold.

contenido,-a adj *(moderado)* moderate, reserved.
▶ nm **contenido** content, contents pl.

contentar vt *(satisfacer)* to please, content.
▶ vpr **contentarse** *(conformarse)* to make do (con, with), be satisfied (con, with).

contento,-a adj happy, pleased: *estoy contento de conocerle* I'm pleased to meet you.

contestación nf *(respuesta)* answer, reply.

contestador nm answering machine.

contestar vt *(responder)* to answer.

contienda nf contest, dispute, struggle.

contigo pron with you.

contiguo,-a adj contiguous (a, to), adjoining, adjacent (a, to).

continental adj continental.

continente nm GEOG continent.

continuación nf continuation, follow-up. LOC **a continuación** next.

continuador,-ra adj continuing.
▶ nm & nf continuator.

continuamente adv continuously.

continuar vt *(proseguir)* to continue, carry on.

continuidad nf continuity.

continuo,-a adj 1 *(seguido)* continuous. 2 *(continuado)* continual, constant.

contornar vt 1 *(dar vueltas)* to skirt. 2 *(hacer los perfiles)* to trace the outline of.

contorno nm 1 *(perfil)* outline; *(perímetro)* perimeter. 2 *(canto)* rim, edge.

contorsionarse vpr to contort os, twist os.

contorsionista nm o nf contortionist.

contra prep 1 against: *tres contra uno* three against one. 2 for: *un producto contra las picaduras de mosquitos* a product for mosquito bites. LOC **en contra** against: *estaba en contra* he was against it.

contraatacar vt to counterattack.

contraataque nm counterattack.

contrabajo nm *(instrumento)* double bass.

contrabandista nm o nf smuggler.

contrabando nm 1 smuggling, contraband. 2 *(mercancías)* smuggled goods pl, contraband. LOC **pasar** ALGO **de contrabando** to smuggle STH in.

contracción nf contraction.

contrachapado nm plywood.

contracorriente nf crosscurrent.

contractura nf contracture.

contradecir vt *(decir lo contrario)* to contradict.

contradicción nf contradiction. LOC **estar en contradicción con** to be inconsistent with, contradictory to.

contradictorio,-a adj contradictory.

contraer vt 1 *(encoger)* to contract: *contraer un músculo* to contract a muscle. 2 *(enfermedad)* to catch. 3 *(deuda)* to contract, incur; *(hábito)* to pick up. 4 LING to contract.

contrafuerte nm ARQUIT buttress.

contrahecho,-a adj deformed, hunchbacked.

contraindicación nf MED contraindication.

contraindicar vt MED to contraindicate.

contralto nm o nf contralto.

contraluz nm o nf view against the light, back light. LOC **a contraluz** against the light.

contraofensiva *nf* counteroffensive.

contraorden *nf* countermand.

contrapartida *nf* **1** COM balancing entry. **2** *fig* compensation.

contrapesar *vt* **1** to counterbalance, counterpoise. **2** *fig* to balance, offset.

contrapeso *nm* **1** counterweight. **2** *fig* counterbalance.

contraponer *vt* **1** *(oponer)* to set in opposition (a, to). **2** *fig (contrastar)* to contrast (a, with).

contraportada *nf* back page, back cover.

contraposición *nf* **1** *(contraste)* contrast. **2** *(oposición)* conflict, clash: *contraposición de intereses* conflict of interests. LOC **estar en contraposición** to clash.

contraprestación *nf* contractual obligation.

contraproducente *adj* counterproductive.

contrapuesto,-a *adj* opposed.

contrapunto *nm* counterpoint.

contra-reloj *adj* against the clock.
▶ *nm (en ciclismo)* time trial.

contrariamente *adv* contrary (a, to).

contrariar *vi* **1** *(oponerse)* to oppose, go against. **2** *(disgustar)* to annoy, upset: *no quería contrariarte* I didn't want to upset you.

contrario,-a *adj* **1** *(opuesto)* contrary, opposite: *iba en sentido contrario* he was going in the opposite direction. **2** *(perjudicial)* harmful (a, to), bad (a, for): *el fumar es contrario a la salud* smoking is bad for your health. LOC **al contrario** on the contrary. **de lo contrario** otherwise. **llevar la contraria a** ALGN to oppose SB. **por el contrario** on the contrary. **todo lo contrario** quite the opposite.
▶ *nm & nf* opponent, adversary, rival.

contrarreloj *adj* against the clock.
▶ *nf* race against the clock. COMP **(etapa) contrarreloj** time trial.

contrarrestar *vt (hacer frente)* to resist, oppose.

contrasentido *nm* **1** *(contradicción)* contradiction. **2** *(disparate)* piece of nonsense: *eso es un contrasentido* that's nonsense.

contraseña *nf (seña)* secret sign; *(palabra)* password.

contrastar *vt (comprobar)* to check, verify.
▶ *vi (oponerse)* to contrast (con, with).

contraste *nm (oposición)* contrast.

contratación *nf* **1** *(contrato - obrero)* hiring; *(- empleado)* engagement. **2** *(pedido)* total orders *pl*, volume of business.

contratar *vt* **1** *(servicio, etc)* to sign a contract for. **2** *(obrero)* to hire; *(empleado)* to engage.

contratiempo *nm (contrariedad)* setback, hitch; *(accidente)* mishap.

contratista *nm o nf* contractor. COMP **contratista de obras** building contractor.

contrato *nm* contract. COMP **contrato de alquiler** lease, leasing agreement. **contrato de compraventa** contract of sale. **contrato de trabajo** work contract. **contrato temporal** temporary contract.

contraventana *nf* shutter.

contrayente *adj* contracting.
▶ *nm o nf (en matrimonio)* contracting party.

contribución *nf* **1** contribution. **2** *(impuesto)* tax.

contribuir *vt (pagar)* to pay.
▶ *vi* **1** *(aportar)* to contribute: *contribuir a los gastos* to contribute to the expenses. **2** *(pagar impuestos)* to pay taxes.

contribuyente *nm o nf* taxpayer.

contrincante *nm* opponent, rival.

control *nm* **1** *(gen)* control. **2** *(comprobación)* check. **3** *(sitio)* checkpoint. LOC **estar bajo control** to be under control. **estar fuera de control** to be out of control. COMP **control a distancia** remote control. **control de natalidad** birth control.

controlador,-ra *adj* control.
▶ *nm & nf (aéreo)* air traffic controller.

controlar *vt* **1** *(gen)* to control. **2** *(comprobar)* to check.
▶ *vpr* **controlarse** *(moderarse)* to control os.

contundente *adj fig (categórico)* convincing, overwhelming, weighty: *un «no» contundente* a firm «no».

contusión *nf* contusion, bruise.

contusionar *vt* to contuse, bruise.

convalecencia *nf* convalescence.

convalecer *vi* to convalesce (de, after), recover (de, from).

convaleciente *adj* convalescent.
▶ *nm o nf* convalescent.

convalidación *nf* **1** EDUC validation. **2** *(documentos)* ratification, authentication.

convalidar *vt* **1** EDUC to validate. **2** *(documentos)* to ratify, authenticate.

convencer *vt* **1** *(de algo)* to convince; *(para hacer algo)* to persuade: *lo convencieron de su error* they convinced him of his mistake. **2** *fam (en frases negativas)* to like, be keen on: *ese color no me acaba de convencer* I'm not sure about that colour.
▶ *vi* to be convincing: *el equipo local no convenció con su actuación* the local team's performance was not very convincing.
▶ *vpr* **convencerse** to become convinced, be convinced, convince os: *se convenció de que era guapo* he convinced himself that he was good-looking.

convencimiento *nm* conviction. LOC **llegar al convencimiento de que...** to be convinced that...

convención *nf* **1** *(congreso)* convention, congress. **2** *(acuerdo)* convention, treaty. **3** *(costumbre)* convention.

convencional *adj* conventional.

convencionalismo *nm* conventionalism, conventionality.

conveniencia *nf* **1** *(utilidad)* usefulness. **2** *(oportunidad)* suitability, advisability: *la conveniencia de estas medidas* the advisability of these measures. **3** *(provecho)* interest, benefit: *solo se preocupa de su propia conveniencia* he only looks out for his own interests. COMP **conve-**

niencias sociales social conventions. ▌ **matrimonio de conveniencia** marriage of convenience.

conveniente *adj* **1** *(útil)* useful. **2** *(oportuno)* suitable, convenient. **3** *(ventajoso)* advantageous. **4** *(aconsejable)* advisable. **5** *(precio)* good, fair. LOC **creer conveniente** to think advisable, be better.

convenientemente *adv (adecuadamente)* suitably; *(bien)* properly.

convenio *nm* agreement, treaty. COMP **convenio colectivo / convenio laboral** collective agreement.

convenir *vt (acordar)* to agree, arrange: *convenimos el precio* we agreed the price.
▶ *vi* **1** *(acordar)* to agree: *convinimos en la fecha* we agreed on the date. **2** *(ser oportuno o conveniente)* to be good for: *no te conviene hacer esfuerzos* it's not good for you to exert yourself. **3** *(ser adecuado o propio)* to suit: *ese chico no te conviene* that boy is not right for you. LOC **conviene + inf** it is as well to + inf: *conviene mencionar que...* it's as well to mention that... ▌ **conviene que + subj** it is better that, it is advisable + inf: *conviene que te vayas* it is better that you go.

convento *nm (de monjas)* convent; *(de monjes)* monastery.

converger *vi* to converge, come together.

convergir *vi* to converge, come together.

conversación *nf* conversation, talk. LOC **dar conversación a** ALGN to talk to SB, keep SB chatting. ▌ **entablar conversación con** ALGN to get into conversation with SB, engage SB in conversation.

conversador,-ra *adj* talkative.
▶ *nm & nf* conversationalist, talker.

conversar *vi* to converse (con, with), talk (con, to).

conversión *nf* conversion.

convertir *vt (transformar)* to change, turn, transform, convert.
▶ *vpr* **convertirse 1** *(transformarse)* to turn (en, into), change (en, into). **2** *(volverse)* to become (en, -), turn (en,

into): *su sueño se convirtió en realidad* his dream came true.

convexo,-a *adj* convex.

convicción *nf* conviction: *tengo la convicción de que vendrán* I firmly believe that they'll come.

convidado,-a *adj* invited.
▶ *nm & nf* guest.

convidar *vt* **1** *(invitar)* to invite: *me convidó a una fiesta* he invited me to a party. **2** *(ofrecer)* to offer: *nos convidó a pastel* he offered us some cake.

convincente *adj* convincing.

convincentemente *adv* convincingly.

convite *nm* **1** *(invitación)* invitation. **2** *(comida)* meal; *(fiesta)* party.

convivencia *nf* **1** living together. **2** *fig* coexistence.

convivir *vi* **1** to live together. **2** *fig* to coexist. LOC **saber convivir** to give and take.

convocar *vt* to convoke, summon, call together. LOC **convocar una reunión** to call a meeting.

convocatoria *nf* **1** *(citación)* convocation, summons *sing*, call to a meeting. **2** EDUC examination: *convocatoria de septiembre* (September) resits *pl*.

convoy *nm* **1** *(escolta)* convoy. **2** *(tren)* train.

conyugal *adj* conjugal. COMP **vida conyugal** married life.

cónyuge *nm o nf (gen)* spouse, partner; *(marido)* husband; *(mujer)* wife.
▶ *nm pl* **cónyuges** husband and wife, married couple *sing*.

coñac *nm* cognac, brandy.

cooperación *nf* cooperation.

cooperar *vi* to cooperate.

cooperativa *nf* cooperative.

coordenada *nf* coordinate.

coordinación *nf* coordination.

coordinador,-ra *adj* coordinating.
▶ *nm & nf* coordinator.

coordinadora *nf (comité)* coordinating committee.

coordinar *vt* to coordinate: *coordinaron la campaña* they coordinated the campaign.

copa *nf* **1** *(vaso)* glass; *(bebida)* drink: *¿te apetece una copa?* do you fancy a drink? **2** *(de árbol)* top. **3** *(trofeo)* cup.
▶ *nf pl* **copas** *(naipes)* hearts.

copete *nm* **1** *(cabello)* tuft. **2** *(penacho)* crest. **3** *(de montaña, helado)* top.

copia *nf* **1** *(gen)* copy. **2** *(de fotografía)* print. **3** *fig (persona)* image: *es la copia de su padre* he's the image of his father. LOC **sacar una copia** to make a copy.

copiadora *nf* photocopier.

copiar *vt* **1** *(gen)* to copy: *lo copió del libro* he copied it from the book. **2** EDUC to cheat, copy. **3** *(escribir)* to take down. LOC **copiar al pie de la letra** to copy word for word.

copiloto *nm* **1** AV copilot. **2** AUTO co-driver.

copioso,-a *adj* **1** *fml (abundante)* plentiful, abundant, copious. **2** *fml (lluvia)* heavy; *(cabello)* long.

copista *nm o nf* copyist.

copla *nf* **1** *(verso, estrofa)* verse, stanza. **2** *(canción)* popular folk song.

copo *nm (gen)* flake; *(de nieve)* snowflake; *(de algodón)* ball (of cotton). COMP **copos de avena** rolled oats.

coproducción *nf* co-production, joint production.

coproductor,-ra *nm & nf* co-producer.

copropiedad *nf* joint ownership.

coprotagonizar *vt* to co-star (-, in).

copulativo,-a *adj* copulative.

coque *nm* coke.

coqueta *nf* **1** *(mujer)* flirt, coquette. **2** *(mueble)* dressing table.

coquetear *vi* to flirt.

coqueteo *nm* flirtation.

coquetería *nf* coquetry, flirting, flirtation.

coraje *nm* **1** *(valor)* courage, toughness. **2** *(ira)* anger. LOC **dar coraje** *fam* to infuriate, make furious: *me da coraje que haya ganado él* it makes me furious that he won. ▪ **echarle coraje a** ALGO to put some spirit into STH.

coral¹ *adj* MÚS choral.
▸ *nf* MÚS *(grupo)* choir, choral society.
▸ *nm* MÚS *(composición)* choral, chorale.

coral² *nm* ZOOL coral.
▸ *nm pl* **corales** coral beads.

coralina *nf* coralline.

coralino,-a *adj* coral.

Corán *nm* Koran.

coránico,-a *adj* Koranic.

coraza *nf* **1** *(armadura)* armour (US armor), cuirass. **2** *(caparazón)* shell, carapace. **3** *fig (protección)* armour (US armor), protection.

corazón *nm* **1** ANAT heart. **2** *fig (parte central)* heart, core: *en el corazón de la ciudad* in the heart of the city. **3** *(de fruta)* core. **4** *(apelativo)* darling, dear, sweetheart. LOC **abrir el corazón a** ALGN *fig* to open one's heart to SB. ▪ **de todo corazón** *fig* sincerely, in all sincerity. ▪ **estar con el corazón en un puño** *fig* to have one's heart in one's mouth. ▪ **estar enfermo del corazón** to have heart trouble.
▸ *nm pl* **corazones** *(naipes)* hearts.

corazonada *nf (sentimiento)* hunch, feeling, inkling: *tuve la corazonada de que él no estaba* I had a hunch that he wasn't there.

corbata *nf* tie, US necktie: *iba con corbata* he was wearing a tie.

corcel *nm* lit steed, charger.

corchea *nf* quaver.

corchete *nm* **1** COST hook and eye, snap fastener. **2** *(signo impreso)* square bracket.

corcho *nm* **1** cork; *(corteza)* cork bark. **2** *(tapón)* cork. **3** *(para pescar, nadar)* float. **4** *(tabla)* cork mat. **5** *(tablón para anuncios, notas)* cork board.

cordada *nf* rope.

cordel *nm* rope, cord.

cordelería *nf* **1** *(oficio)* ropemaking. **2** *(cuerdas)* ropes *pl*.

cordero,-a *nm & nf* **1** lamb. **2** *fig (persona dócil)* lamb, angel.

▸ *nm* **cordero 1** *(piel)* lambskin. **2** *(carne - joven)* lamb; *(- crecido)* mutton. LOC **ser manso como un cordero** to be as gentle as a lamb.

cordial *adj (afectuoso)* cordial, friendly, warm: *una bienvenida cordial* a warm welcome.

cordialidad *nf* cordiality, warmth, friendliness.

cordialmente *adv* **1** cordially, warmly. **2** *(despedida en carta)* sincerely.

cordillera *nf* mountain range, mountain chain.

cordón *nm* **1** *(cuerda)* string. **2** *(de zapatos)* shoelace, shoestring.

cordoncillo *nm* **1** *(en tejido)* rib, ribbing. **2** *(bordado)* braid, piping.

cordura *nf* good sense. LOC **con cordura** sensibly, prudently, wisely.

Corea *nf* Korea. COMP **Corea del Norte** North Korea. ▪ **Corea del Sur** South Korea.

coreano,-a *adj* Korean.
▸ *nm & nf (persona)* Korean.
▸ *nm* **coreano** *(idioma)* Korean.

corear *vt* **1** *(cantar)* to chorus, sing in chorus. **2** *(hablar)* to chorus, speak in chorus. **3** *fig (aclamar)* to applaud.

coreografía *nf* choreography.

coreografiar *vt* to choreograph.

coreógrafo,-a *nm & nf* choreographer.

corindón *nm* corundum.

corinto,-a *adj* maroon.
▸ *nm* **corinto** *(color)* maroon.

cormorán *nm* cormorant.

cornada *nf* goring.

cornalina *nf* cornelian, carnelian.

cornamenta *nf (gen)* horns *pl*; *(del ciervo)* antlers *pl*.

cornamusa *nf* bagpipe.

córnea *nf* cornea.

cornear *vt* to gore.

corneja *nf* crow.

cornejo *nm* dogwood.

córneo,-a *adj* hornlike, corneous.

córner *nm* DEP *(lugar)* corner; *(golpe)* corner, corner kick. LOC **lanzar un córner**

/ **sacar un córner** / **tirar un córner** to take a corner.

corneta *nf (instrumento)* bugle.

cornisa *nf* ARQUIT cornice.

coro *nm* **1** MÚS choir. **2** TEAT chorus. LOC **a coro** *fig* all together. I **hacer coro** *fig* to join in the chorus.

corola *nf* corolla.

corona *nf* **1** *(aro, cerco)* crown. **2** *(de flores, etc)* wreath, garland, crown. **3** *fig (dignidad real)* King's, Queen's: *el discurso de la corona* the King's speech. **4** *fig (reino)* crown, kingdom. **5** *(aureola)* halo. **6** *(en geometría)* annulus, ring. COMP **corona solar** solar corona.

coronación *nf* **1** coronation. **2** *fig (culminación)* crowning.

coronar *vt* to crown.
▶ *vi* to crown.

coronel *nm* colonel.

coronilla *nf (parte de la cabeza)* crown of the head. LOC **estar hasta la coronilla** *fam* to be fed up (de, with).

corpiño *nm* bodice.

corporación *nf* corporation. COMP **corporación metropolitana** city corporation.

corporativo,-a *adj* corporative, corporate. COMP **imagen corporativa** corporate image.

corpulencia *nf* corpulence, stoutness.

corpulento,-a *adj* corpulent, stocky, stout.

corral *nm* **1** *(de casa)* yard, courtyard. **2** *(de granja)* farmyard, US corral.

correa *nf* **1** *(tira de piel)* strap, leather strip. **2** *(de perro)* lead, leash. **3** *(de reloj)* watchstrap. **4** *(cinturón)* belt. **5** TÉC belt.

corrección *nf* **1** *(rectificación)* correction. **2** *(educación)* courtesy, correctness, politeness, good manners *pl*. LOC **tratar con corrección** to be polite.

correccional *adj* correctional.
▶ *nm* detention centre, reformatory.

correctamente *adv* **1** *(sin errores)* correctly, accurately. **2** *(con educación)* correctly, politely, properly.

correcto,-a *adj* **1** *(sin errores)* correct, accurate. **2** *(adecuado)* suitable. **3** *(educado)* polite, courteous. **4** *(conducta)* proper.

corrector,-ra *adj* corrective.
▶ *nm & nf (de pruebas impresas)* proofreader.

corredero,-a *adj* sliding: *ventana corredera* sliding window.

corredor,-ra *adj* **1** running. **2** *(ave)* flightless: *ave corredora* flightless bird.
▶ *nm & nf* **1** DEP runner; *(de coches)* driver. **2** FIN broker. COMP **corredor,-ra de bolsa** stockbroker. I **corredor,-ra de coches** racing driver. I **corredor,-ra de fondo** long-distance runner.▶ *nm* **corredor** *(pasillo)* corridor, gallery.

corregir *vt* **1** *(amendar)* to correct, rectify. **2** *(reprender)* to reprimand, scold, tell off. **3** EDUC to mark.

correlación *nf* correlation.

correlativo,-a *adj* correlative.

correo *nm* **1** *(servicio, correspondencia)* post, US mail. **2** *(persona)* courier. LOC **echar al correo** to post, US mail. I **por correo** by post, US by mail. COMP **apartado de correos** (post office) box. I **correo aéreo** airmail. I **correo certificado** registered post, US registered mail. I **correo electrónico** electronic mail, e-mail. I **correo urgente** special delivery.
▶ *nm pl* **correos** *(oficina)* post office *sing*.

correr *vi* **1** *(gen)* to run: *se marchó corriendo* she ran off. **2** *(darse prisa)* to rush, hurry: *¡corre, es tarde!* hurry up, it's late! **3** *(viento)* to blow. **4** *(agua)* to flow, run. **5** *(tiempo)* to pass, fly. **6** *(conductor)* to drive fast. **7** *(coche)* to go fast. **8** *(puerta, ventana)* to slide.
▶ *vt* **1** *(distancia)* to cover; *(país)* to travel through. **2** *(carrera)* to run; *(caballo)* to race, run. **3** *(echar)* to close; *(cortina)* to draw; *(cerrojo)* to bolt. **4** *(mover)* to pull up, move, draw up: *corre la mesa* move the table. **5** *(estar expuesto)* to run: *correr un peligro* to run a risk. **6** *(aventura)* to have. LOC **a todo correr** at full speed. I **correr mundo** to be a globe-

trotter. **I correr un peligro** to be in danger.

▶ *vpr* **correrse 1** *(persona)* to move over; *(objeto)* to shift, slide. **2** *(color, tinta)* to run. **3** *(media)* to ladder. **4** *(avergonzarse)* to blush, go red.

correspondencia *nf* **1** *(gen)* correspondence. **2** *(cartas)* post, US mail. **3** *(de trenes, etc)* connection. [LOC] **mantener correspondencia con ALGN** to correspond with SB. [COMP] **curso por correspondencia** correspondence course.

corresponder *vi* **1** *(ser adecuado)* to become, befit; *(color, aspecto)* to match, go with: *los zapatos no corresponden al vestido* the shoes don't go with the dress. **2** *(encajar)* to correspond (a, to), tally (a, with); *(descripción)* to fit. **3** *(pertenecer)* to belong, pertain: *esta mesa corresponde a mi habitación* this table belongs in my bedroom.

▶ *vt* **1** *(ser el turno)* to be one's turn: *me corresponde a mí* it's my turn. **2** *(en un reparto)* to get. **3** *(incumbir)* to be the job of, be the responsibility of: *eso te corresponde a ti* that's your job. **4** *(devolver)* to return; *(amabilidad)* to repay.

▶ *vpr* **corresponderse 1** *(ajustarse)* to correspond; *(cifras)* to tally: *la dirección que te dio no se corresponde con la que yo tengo* the address he gave you doesn't correspond to the one I have. **2** *(armonizar)* to be in harmony, go with. **3** *(amarse)* to love each other.

correspondiente *adj* **1** *(que corresponde)* corresponding (a, to). **2** *(apropiado)* suitable, appropriate. **3** *(respectivo)* own.

corresponsal *nm o nf* correspondent.

corretear *vi* **1** *fam (correr)* to run about. **2** *fam (vagar)* to hang about.

corrida *nf* **1** *(carrera)* run, race. **2** *(de toros)* bullfight.

corriente *adj* **1** *(común)* ordinary, average: *personas corrientes* ordinary people. **2** *(agua)* running. **3** *(fecha)* current, present: *el cinco del corriente mes* the fifth of this month. **4** *(cuenta)* current. [LOC] **al corriente 1** *(actualizado)* up to date. **2** *(enterado)* aware. **3** *(informado)*

informed, in the know: *¿estás al corriente de lo que ha pasado?* do you know what's happened? **I ir a contra corriente** *fig* to go against the tide. **I seguirle la corriente a ALGN** to humour (US humor) SB. **I tener al corriente** to keep informed. **I corriente sanguínea** bloodstream.

▶ *nm (mes)* current month, this month.

▶ *nf* **1** *(masa de agua)* current, stream, flow. **2** *(de aire)* draught (US draft). **3** ELEC current.

corrientemente *adv* usually, normally.

corro *nm* **1** *(cerco)* circle, ring. **2** *(juego)* ring-a-ring o'roses. **3** *(en la bolsa)* round enclosure.

corroer *vt* **1** *(desgastar)* to corrode. **2** GEOL to erode.

corromper *vt* **1** *(pudrir)* to turn bad. **2** *(pervertir)* to corrupt, pervert. **3** *(sobornar)* to bribe.

▶ *vpr* **corromperse 1** *(pudrirse)* to go bad, rot. **2** *(pervertirse)* to become corrupted.

corrosivo,-a *adj* **1** corrosive. **2** *fig* caustic.

▶ *nm* **corrosivo** corrosive.

corrupción *nf* **1** *(putrefacción)* rot, decay. **2** *fig* corruption, degradation. **3** *fig (soborno)* bribery.

corrupto,-a *adj* corrupt.

corruptor,-ra *adj* corrupting.

▶ *nm & nf* corrupter, perverter.

corsario,-a *adj* privateer.

▶ *nm* **corsario** privateer.

corsé *nm* corset.

corsetería *nf* ladies' underwear shop.

corta *nf* tree felling.

cortacésped *nm & nf* lawnmower.

cortacircuitos *nm inv* circuit breaker.

cortado,-a *adj* **1** *(troceado)* cut; *(en lonchas)* sliced. **2** *(leche)* sour. **3** *fam (aturdido)* dumbfounded. [LOC] **quedarse cortado,-a 1** *fam (sin palabras)* to be speechless, be lost for words. **2** *(avergonzado)* to become embarrassed.

▶ *nm* **cortado** *(café)* coffee with a dash of milk.

cortador,-ra *adj* cutting.
▶ *nm & nf (sastre, zapatero)* cutter.

cortadora *nf* cutting machine.

cortafrío *nm* cold chisel.

cortafuego *nm* **1** *(en el campo)* firebreak. **2** *(en un edificio)* firewall. **3** INFORM firewall.

cortante *adj* **1** *(que corta)* cutting, sharp. **2** *fig (aire)* biting. **3** *fig (persona, estilo)* sharp, brusque.

cortaplumas *nm inv* penknife.

cortar *vt* **1** *(gen)* to cut. **2** *(pelo)* to cut, trim. **3** *(árbol)* to cut down. **4** *(carne)* to carve. **5** *(pastel)* to cut up. **6** *(cabeza, teléfono, gas)* to cut off. **7** *(mayonesa, leche)* to curdle. **8** *(piel)* to chap, crack. **9** *(viento, frío)* to chill, bite. **10** COST to cut out. **11** *(interrumpir)* to cut off, interrupt. **12** *(bloquear)* to block: *cortaron la carretera* the road was blocked. **13** *(suprimir)* to cut out. **14** *fig (separar)* to divide, split, cut. LOC **¡corta el rollo!** *fam* knock it off! ▮ **cortar con ALGN** to split up with SB. ▮ **cortar el bacalao** *fam* to be the boss. ▮ **cortar en seco** *fig* to cut short. ▮ **cortar la digestión** to give one indigestion, upset one's stomach. ▮ **cortar la palabra** to interrupt. ▮ **cortar por lo sano** *fam* to take drastic measures.
▶ *vpr* **cortarse 1** to cut: *este metal se corta fácilmente* this metal cuts easily. **2** *(herirse)* to cut, cut os: *me he cortado* I've cut myself. **3** *(el pelo - por otro)* to have one's hair cut; *(- uno mismo)* to cut one's hair: *¿te has cortado el pelo?* have you had your hair cut? **4** *(piel)* to become chapped. **5** *(leche)* to go off, curdle; *(mayonesa)* to curdle. **6** *(comunicación)* to be cut off.

cortaúñas *nm inv* nail clippers.

corte¹ *nf* **1** *(del rey, etc)* court. **2** *(séquito)* retinue. **3** AM *(tribunal)* court.
▶ *nf pl* **las Cortes** the Spanish Parliament *sing.*

corte² *nm* **1** *(gen)* cut: *me he hecho un corte en el dedo* I've cut my finger. **2** *(filo)* edge. **3** *(sección)* section: *corte horizontal* horizontal section. **4** *(de pelo)* cut, haircut. **5** *(de helado)* wafer, US ice-cream sandwich. **6** *fam fig (vergüenza)* embarrassment: *le daba corte entrar y se quedó fuera* he was too embarrassed to go in so he stayed outside. LOC **dar un corte a ALGN** *fam* to cut SB dead.

cortejar *vt* to court.

cortejo *nm* **1** *(acompañantes)* entourage, retinue. **2** *(galanteo)* courting.

cortés *adj* courteous, polite.

cortesano,-a *adj* **1** *(de la corte)* court. **2** *(cortés)* courteous, courtly.
▶ *nm & nf (de la corte)* courtier.

cortesía *nf* **1** *(educación)* courtesy, politeness. **2** *(en cartas)* formal ending. **3** *(tratamiento)* title. **4** *(reverencia)* bow, curtsy. **5** *(regalo)* present: *esta bolsa es una cortesía de la empresa* this bag is courtesy of the company.

cortina *nf* **1** curtain. **2** *fig* curtain, screen. LOC **correr las cortinas** to draw the curtains. COMP **cortina de humo** *fig* smoke screen.

cortinaje *nm* drapery.

corto,-a *adj* **1** *(extensión)* short: *distancia corta* short distance. **2** *(duración)* short, brief: *una película corta* my short film. **3** *(escaso)* scant, meagre (US meager). **4** *fig (tonto)* thick, dim. **5** *fig (tímido)* shy, timid. LOC **corto,-a de miras** *fam* narrow-minded. ▮ **corto,-a de vista** short-sighted. ▮ **quedarse corto,-a 1** *(ropa)* to become too short: *el pantalón se me ha quedado corto* my trousers have become too short for me. **2** *(calcular mal)* to underestimate, miscalculate: *te quedaste corto con los bocadillos* you didn't make enough sandwiches.
▶ *nm* **corto** short film, short.

cortocircuito *nm* short circuit.

cortometraje *nm* short film, short.

corva *nf* back of the knee.

corzo,-a *nm & nf (macho)* roe buck; *(hembra)* roe deer.

cosa *nf* **1** *(gen)* thing: *coge tus cosas* take your things, take your stuff. **2** *(asunto)* matter, business: *es cosa tuya* it's your business. **3** *(nada)* nothing, not anything: *no hay cosa igual* there's nothing like it. LOC **como cosa tuya** as if it were your idea. **como si tal cosa** just like that. **es cosa de... 1** *(tiempo)* it's time to... **2** *(cuestión)* it's a matter of... **no valer gran cosa** not to be worth much. **ser cosa hecha** *fam* to be no sooner said than done.

▸ *nf pl* **cosas** *fam (manías)* hang-ups: *son cosas de niños* kids do that kind of thing.

cosaco,-a *adj* Cossack.
▸ *nm* **cosaco** Cossack.

coscorrón *nm* blow on the head, knock on the head.

cosecante *nf* cosecant.

cosecha *nf* **1** harvest, crop. **2** *(tiempo)* harvest time. **3** *(año del vino)* vintage. LOC **de cosecha propia 1** *(hortalizas, fruta)* home-grown. **2** *fig (ideas, etc)* of one's own invention.

cosechadora *nf* combine harvester.

cosechar *vi* to harvest, reap.
▸ *vt* **1** *(recoger)* to harvest. **2** *(cultivar)* to grow.

coseno *nm* cosine.

coser *vt* **1** *(unir)* to sew; *(un botón)* to sew on; *(pespuntes, etc)* to stitch: *le cosí los pantalones* I sewed up her trousers. **2** MED to stitch up. **3** *(grapar)* to staple together. **4** *fig (unir)* to join.

cosido *nm* **1** sewing. **2** MED stitching.

cosificar *vt* to trivialize, belittle.

cosmética *nf* cosmetics *pl.*

cosmético,-a *adj* cosmetic.
▸ *nm* **cosmético** cosmetic.

cósmico,-a *adj* cosmic.

cosmogonía *nf* cosmogony.

cosmografía *nf* cosmography.

cosmográfico,-a *adj* cosmographic, cosmographical.

cosmología *nf* cosmology.

cosmológico,-a *adj* cosmologic, cosmological.

cosmonauta *nm o nf* cosmonaut.

cosmonave *nf* spaceship, spacecraft.

cosmopolita *adj* cosmopolitan.
▸ *nm o nf* cosmopolitan.

cosmos *nm inv* cosmos.

cosquillas *nf pl* tickling *sing.* LOC **hacer cosquillas a** ALGN to tickle SB. **tener cosquillas** to be ticklish. **buscarle las cosquillas a** ALGN *fam* to needle SB, annoy SB.

cosquilleo *nm* tickling.

costa¹ *nf (litoral)* coast, coastline; *(playa)* beach, seaside, US shore: *tenemos una casa en la costa* we have a house at the seaside, US we have a house on the shore.

costa² *nf* FIN cost, price. LOC **a costa de 1** *(aprovechándose)* at the expense of. **2** *(a base de)* by, by dint of, by means of: *lo consiguió a costa de muchos sacrificios* he managed it by making a lot of sacrifices. **a toda costa** at all costs, at any price.
▸ *nf pl* **costas** JUR costs.

Costa de Marfil *nf* Ivory Coast.

costado *nm* side.
▸ *nm pl* **costados** lineage *sing.* LOC **por los cuatro costados** through and through.

costar *vi* **1** *(valer)* to cost: *¿cuánto costó?* how much was it? **2** *(ser difícil)* to be hard, be difficult; *(resultar difícil)* to be difficult for: *cuesta encontrar trabajo* it's hard to find a job. **3** *(tiempo)* to take: *me costó cuatro horas* it took me four hours. LOC **costar barato,-a** to be cheap. **costar caro,-a 1** to be expensive, cost a lot. **2** to pay dearly for STH: *esa afirmación le costará cara* he'll pay dearly for saying that. **costar mucho / costar trabajo** to be difficult, be hard work.

Costa Rica *nf* Costa Rica.

costarricense *adj* Costa Rican.
▸ *nm o nf* Costa Rican.

coste *nm* cost, price, expense. COMP **coste de la vida** cost of living.

costear *vt (pagar)* to pay for, afford: *su padre le costeó el viaje* his father paid for his journey.
▸ *vpr* **costearse** to pay one's way.

costero,-a *adj* coastal, coast.

costilla *nf* **1** ANAT rib. **2** CULIN cutlet.
▸ *nf pl* **costillas** *fam (espalda)* back *sing.*

costillar *nm* ribs *pl.*

costo *nm* cost, price.

costoso,-a *adj* **1** *(caro)* costly, expensive. **2** *(difícil)* hard, difficult.

costra *nf* **1** crust. **2** MED scab.

costumbre *nf* **1** *(hábito)* habit: *tengo la costumbre de comer temprano* I'm in the habit of having lunch early. **2** *(tradición)* custom: *es una costumbre rusa* it's a Russian custom. **3** JUR usage. LOC **como de costumbre** as usual. ‖ **tener por costumbre** + *inf* to be in the habit of + *ger*. COMP **la fuerza de la costumbre** the force of habit.
► *nf pl* **costumbres** *(personales)* ways, manner *sing*; *(de un pueblo)* customs.

costumbrismo *nm* folk literature.

costumbrista *adj* about local customs.
► *nm o nf* writer of folk literature.

costura *nf* **1** *(cosido)* sewing. **2** *(línea de puntadas)* seam: *medias sin costura* seamless stockings. **3** *(confección)* dressmaking. COMP **cesto de la costura** sewing basket.

costurera *nf* seamstress.

costurero *nm* **1** *(estuche)* sewing basket, sewing kit. **2** *(mueble)* workbox.

cota¹ *nf* *(traje)* tabard. COMP **cota de malla** coat of mail.

cota² *nf* **1** *(altura)* height above sea level: *la cota mil* one thousand metres above sea level. **2** *(número en mapa)* spot height. **3** *fig (nivel)* level: *la xenofobia está llegando a cotas muy altas* xenophobia is showing an alarming increase.

cotangente *nf* cotangent.

cotejar *vt (gen)* to compare; *(textos)* to collate, compare.

cotejo *nm (gen)* comparison; *(textos)* collation, comparison.

cotidiano,-a *adj* daily, everyday: *la vida cotidiana* everyday life.

cotiledón *nm* cotyledon.

cotilla *nf (faja)* corset.
► *nm o nf fam* busybody, gossip.

cotillear *vi fam* to gossip, tittle-tattle.

cotilleo *nm fam* gossip, gossiping, tittle-tattle.

cotillón *nm* **1** *(danza)* cotillion, cotillon. **2** *(fiesta)* party, celebration *especially on New Year's Eve.*

cotización *nf* **1** FIN quotation, market price. **2** *(cuota)* membership fee, subscription.

cotizar *vt* FIN to quote, price.
► *vi (pagar cuota)* to pay a subscription.
► *vpr* **cotizarse 1** *(acciones)* to sell (a, at): *las acciones del banco se cotizan a diez euros con veintitrés* the bank's shares are selling at ten euros twenty-three. **2** *fig (valorarse)* to be valued, be in demand: *este pintor se cotiza mucho* this painter is in great demand.

coto¹ *nm* **1** *(terreno)* enclosure, reserve. **2** *(poste)* boundary mark. **3** *(límite)* restriction. LOC **poner coto a** ALGO to put a stop to STH. COMP **coto de caza** game preserve.

coto² *nm (pez)* miller's thumb.

cotorra *nf* **1** *(ave)* parrot. **2** *fam fig* chatterbox. LOC **hablar como una cotorra** to be a chatterbox.

cotorrear *vi fam fig* to chatter, prattle (on).

cotorreo *nm fam fig* chatter, prattle.

COU *abrev* EDUC (Curso de Orientación Universitaria) ≈ *former pre-university course.*

cowboy *nm* cowboy.

coxis *nm inv* coccyx.

coyote *nm* coyote.

coyuntura *nf* **1** ANAT joint, articulation. **2** *fig (circunstancia)* moment, juncture. COMP **coyuntura económica** economic situation.

coz *nf* kick. LOC **dar una coz** to kick.

crac *nm* **1** *(quiebra)* crash, bankruptcy: *el crac de la bolsa de Nueva York* the Wall Street crash. **2** *(onomatopeya)* crack, snap: *el brazo me hizo crac* my arm gave a crack.

crack *nm (persona)* star, ace: *es un auténtico crack del fútbol* he's a crack football player.

craneal *adj* cranial.

craneano,-a *adj* cranial.

cráneo *nm* cranium, skull. [LOC] **ir de cráneo** *fam* to have a lot on one's plate, have one's work cut out.

cráter *nm* crater.

crawl *nm* crawl.

creación *nf* 1 *(gen)* creation. 2 *(fundación)* foundation, establishment, setting up.

creador,-ra *adj* creative.
▶ *nm & nf* creator, maker.

crear *vt* 1 *(gen)* to create: *crear problemas* to create problems. 2 *(fundar)* to found, establish; *(partido)* to set up. 3 *(inventar)* to invent.
▶ *vpr* **crearse** to make, make for os: *crearse enemigos* to make enemies for os.

creatividad *nf* creativity.

creativo,-a *adj* creative.

crecer *vi* 1 *(persona, planta)* to grow: *has crecido mucho* you've grown a lot. 2 *(incrementar)* to increase, grow, get bigger: *la población ha crecido un uno por ciento* the population has grown by one per cent. 3 *(corriente, marea)* to rise. 4 *(luna)* to wax.
▶ *vpr* **crecerse** *(tomar mayor fuerza)* to grow in confidence: *se crece ante las dificultades* he comes into his own when faced with problems.

crecido,-a *adj* 1 *(persona)* grown, grown-up. 2 *(cantidad)* big, large. 3 *(río)* in flood, in spate.

creciente *adj* 1 *(que crece)* growing; *(que aumenta)* increasing: *un interés creciente* an increasing interest. 2 *(precios)* rising. 3 *(luna)* crescent (in the first quarter).
▶ *nf (de agua)* flood, spate.

crecimiento *nm* 1 *(desarrollo)* growth, increase. 2 *(subida)* rise. 3 *(de un río)* flooding, rising.

credibilidad *nf* credibility.

crédito *nm* 1 COM credit. 2 *(confianza)* credit, belief, credence. 3 *(fama)* reputation, standing. [LOC] **a crédito** on credit. ▌**dar crédito a** *(creer)* to believe (in): *no doy crédito a mis oídos* I can't believe what I'm hearing. ▌**ser digno,-a de crédito** to be reliable. [COMP] **crédito hi-**

potecario debt secured by a mortgage.

credo *nm fig (creencias)* credo, creed.

credulidad *nf* credulity, gullibility.

crédulo,-a *adj* credulous, gullible.

creencia *nf* belief.

creer *vt* 1 *(dar por cierto)* to believe: *si no lo veo no lo creo* I've got to see it to believe it. 2 *(suponer, opinar)* to think, suppose: *¿y tú que crees?* what do you think? 3 *(tener fe)* to believe. [LOC] **creer a ciencia cierta** to be convinced. ▌**¡no creas!** do you really think so?, I'm not so sure. ▌**¡ya lo creo!** of course!
▶ *vpr* **creerse** 1 *(aceptar)* to believe: *no me lo creo* I don't believe it, I can't believe it. 2 *(considerarse)* to think: *¿quién te has creído que eres?* who do you think you are? [LOC] **¡que te crees tú eso!** that's what you think!

creíble *adj* credible, believable.

creído,-a *adj* arrogant, vain, conceited. [LOC] **ser un creído,-a** to be full of os.

crema *nf* 1 *(de leche, licor, ungüento)* cream. 2 *(natillas)* custard. 3 *(betún)* shoe polish. 4 *fig (lo mejor)* cream. [COMP] **crema bronceadora** suntan cream. ▌**crema de afeitar** shaving cream. ▌**crema hidratante** moisturizing cream.
▶ *adj* cream, cream coloured (US cream colored).

cremación *nf* cremation.

crematorio *nm* crematorium.

cremoso,-a *adj* creamy: *queso cremoso* full-fat cheese.

crepe *nf (torta)* pancake, crepe.

crepé *nm (tejido, caucho)* crepe.

crepería *nf* creperie.

crepitar *vi* to crackle.

crepúsculo *nm* twilight.

cresta *nf* 1 *(de ave)* crest; *(de gallo)* comb. 2 *(de pelo)* toupée. 3 *(de montaña, ola)* crest. [LOC] **estar en la cresta de la ola** *fam* to be on the crest of a wave.

Creta *nf* Crete.

cretense *adj* Cretan.
▶ *nm o nf* Cretan.

cretino,-a *adj* stupid, cretinous.
▶ *nm & nf* cretin, idiot.

creyente *adj* believing.
▶ *nm o nf* believer.

cría *nf* **1** *(acto de criar)* nursing; *(de animal)* breeding, raising. **2** *(cachorro)* young. **3** *(camada - ovíparos)* brood; *(- mamíferos)* litter.

criada *nf* maid.

criadero *nm* **1** *(de plantas)* nursery; *(de animales)* breeding farm; *(de peces)* hatchery. **2** *(mina)* seam. COMP **criadero de ostras** oyster bed.

criado,-a *adj* *(animal)* reared, raised; *(persona)* bred, brought up.
▶ *nm & nf* servant.

criador *nm & nf* breeder.

criar *vt* **1** *(educar niños)* to bring up, rear, care for: *lo crió una tía* his aunt brought him up. **2** *(nutrir)* to feed (con, -); *(con pecho)* to suckle, nurse, breast-feed. **3** *(animales)* to breed, raise, rear. **4** *(producir)* to have, grow; *(vinos)* to make, mature.
▶ *vpr* **criarse 1** *(crecer)* to grow; *(formarse)* to be brought up. **2** *(producirse)* to grow.

criatura *nf* **1** creature. **2** *(niño)* baby, child. **3** *fig* baby.

cribar *vt* **1** *(colar)* to sift, sieve. **2** *fig (seleccionar)* to screen.

cric *nm* jack.

cricquet *nm* cricket.

crimen *nm* **1** *(delito)* crime. **2** *(asesinato)* murder.

criminal *adj* **1** criminal. **2** *fam (muy malo)* awful, criminal, appalling.
▶ *nm o nf* criminal.

criminalista *nm o nf (abogado)* criminal lawyer.

criminología *nf* criminology.

crin [también se usa en plural con el mismo significado] *nf* mane.

crío,-a *nm & nf fam* kid, child.
▶ *adj fam* young: *todavía eres muy crío* you're still too young. LOC **ser un crío,-a** *fam* to be childish.

criollo,-a *adj* Creole.
▶ *nm & nf (persona)* Creole.
▶ *nm (idioma)* Creole.

cripta *nf* crypt.

críquet *nm* cricket.

crisálida *nf* chrysalis.

crisantemo *nm* chrysanthemum.

crisis *nf inv* **1** *(dificultad)* crisis. **2** *(ataque)* fit, attack: *crisis de asma* asthma attack. **3** *(escasez)* shortage: *crisis de alimentos* food shortage. LOC **estar en crisis** to be in crisis, reach crisis point. COMP **crisis de gobierno** cabinet crisis. **I crisis nerviosa** nervous breakdown.

crisma *nm & nf fam (cabeza)* head, nut.

crisol *nm* **1** crucible. **2** *fig* melting pot.

crispación *nf fig* tension: *un clima de crispación* a tense atmosphere.

crispar *vt fig (irritar)* to irritate, annoy, infuriate: *ese tipo me crispa* that guy infuriates me. LOC **crispar los nervios a** ALGN *fig* to get on SB's nerves.
▶ *vpr* **crisparse** *fig (irritarse)* to get annoyed, get angry.

cristal *nm* **1** *(mineral)* crystal. **2** *(vidrio)* glass. **3** *(de ventana)* window pane, pane. **4** *(de lente)* lens. **5** *(de coche)* window.
▶ *nm pl* **cristales 1** *(trozos)* glass *sing*: *ten cuidado, hay cristales por el suelo* be careful, there's some broken glass on the floor. **2** *(ventanas)* windows. COMP **botella de cristal** glass bottle. **I cristal de cuarzo** quartz crystal.

cristalera *nf* **1** *(mueble)* display cabinet. **2** *(escaparate)* window, shop window. **3** *(conjunto de cristales)* windows *pl*; *(puertas)* glass doors *pl*; *(techo)* glass roof.

cristalería *nf* **1** *(fábrica)* glassworks. **2** *(tienda)* glassware shop. **3** *(conjunto)* glassware; *(vasos)* glasses *pl*.

cristalero,-a *nm & nf* glazier.

cristalino,-a *adj* transparent, crystal-clear.
▶ *nm* **cristalino** crystalline lens.

cristalización *nf* **1** crystallization. **2** *fig* consolidation.

cristalizar *vt* to crystallize.
▶ *vi* **1** to crystallize. **2** *fig* to crystallize (en, into).
▶ *vpr* **cristalizarse** to crystallize.

cristalografía *nf* crystallography.

cristiandad *nf* Christendom.

cristianismo *nm* Christianity.

cristiano,-a *adj* Christian.
  ▶ *nm* Christian.

criterio *nm* **1** *(en lógica)* criterion. **2** *(juicio)* judgement, discernment. **3** *(opinión)* opinion, point of view.

criticar *vt* to criticize.
  ▶ *vi (murmurar)* to gossip.

crítico,-a *adj* critical.
  ▶ *nm & nf* critic.

Croacia *nf* Croatia.

croar *vi* to croak.

croata *adj* Croatian, Croat.
  ▶ *nm o nf (persona)* Croat, Croatian.
  ▶ *nm (idioma)* Croat, Croatian.

crocante *nm* almond brittle.

crocanti *nm* almond brittle.

croché *nm* crochet.

croissant *nm* croissant.

croissantería *nf* croissant shop.

crol *nm* crawl.

cromado,-a *adj* chrome.
  ▶ *nm* **cromado** chroming.

cromar *vt* to chrome.

cromático,-a *adj* chromatic.

cromatismo *nm* chromatism.

cromo *nm* **1** *(metal)* chromium, chrome. **2** *(estampa)* picture card, sticker: *un álbum de cromos* a picture-card album. LOC **ir hecho,-a un cromo** *fam* to look a sight.

cromosoma *nm* chromosome.

crónica *nf* **1** *(gen)* account, chronicle. **2** *(en periódico)* article, column, feature. **3** RAD TV *(programa)* programme (US program); *(reportaje)* feature, report. **4** HIST chronicle.

crónico,-a *adj* **1** chronic. **2** *fig* deeply rooted.

cronista *nm o nf* **1** HIST chronicler. **2** *(de prensa)* columnist, feature writer. **3** RAD TV commentator.

cronología *nf* chronology.

cronológico,-a *adj* chronological.

cronometrar *vt* to time.

cronómetro *nm* **1** chronometer. **2** DEP stopwatch.

croqueta *nf* croquette.

croquis *nm inv* sketch, outline.

cros *nm inv (a pie)* cross-country race; *(en moto)* motocross race.

cruasán *nm* croissant.

cruce *nm* **1** cross, crossing. **2** AUTO crossroads. **3** *(de razas)* crossbreeding. **4** *(interferencia telefónica, etc)* crossed line: *hay un cruce* there's a crossed line. **5** ELEC short circuit.

crucero *nm* **1** *(buque)* cruiser. **2** *(viaje)* cruise.

crucial *adj* **1** crucial. **2** *fig* crucial, critical.

crucifijo *nm* crucifix.

crucifixión *nf* crucifixion.

crucigrama *nm* crossword (puzzle).

crudeza *nf* **1** *(rudeza)* crudeness, rudeness, coarseness. **2** *(del clima)* harshness.

crudo,-a *adj* **1** *(sin cocer)* raw; *(poco hecho)* underdone: *la carne está cruda* the meat is underdone, the meat isn't cooked enough. **2** *fig (duro)* crude, coarse. **3** *(color)* natural, unbleached. **4** *(clima)* harsh. LOC **verlo muy crudo** *fam* not to hold out much hope.
  ▶ *nm* **crudo** *(petróleo)* crude oil, crude.

cruel *adj (persona)* cruel (con/para, to).

crueldad *nf* **1** cruelty. **2** *(dureza)* harshness, severity.

cruelmente *adv* cruelly.

crujido *nm* **1** *(de puerta)* creak, creaking. **2** *(de patatas fritas)* crunching. **3** *(seda, papel)* rustle, rustling. **4** *(de dientes)* grinding.

crujiente *adj* **1** *(alimentos)* crunchy. **2** *(seda)* rustling.

crujir *vi* **1** *(puerta)* to creak. **2** *(patatas fritas)* to crunch. **3** *(seda, hojas)* to rustle. **4** *(dientes)* to grind.

crustáceo *nm* crustacean.

cruz *nf* **1** *(gen)* cross. **2** *(de moneda)* tails *pl*: *¿cara o cruz?* heads or tails?

cruzada *nf* **1** HIST crusade. **2** *(campaña)* campaign.

cruzar *vt* **1** *(gen)* to cross: *cruzar una calle* to cross a street. **2** *(poner atravesado)* to lay across; *(estar atravesado)* to lie across. **3** *(en geometría)* to intersect. **4** *(animales)* to cross. **5** *(miradas, palabras)* to exchange. [LOC] **cruzar a nado** to swim across. **cruzar los brazos** to fold one's arms.
▶ *vpr* **cruzarse 1** *(encontrarse)* to cross each other. **2** *(intercambiarse)* to exchange.

cuaderno *nm* *(libreta)* notebook, journal; *(escolar)* exercise book.

cuadra *nf* **1** *(establo)* stable. **2** AM *(manzana)* block, block of houses.

cuadrado,-a *adj* **1** *(forma)* square. **2** *fam* *(persona)* broad, stocky. **3** *fig (mente)* rigid, one-track.
▶ *nm* **cuadrado** square. [LOC] **elevar al cuadrado** to square.

cuadragésimo,-a *adj* fortieth.
▶ *nm & nf* fortieth.

✎ Consulta también sexto,-a.

cuadrangular *adj* quadrangular.

cuadrángulo *nm* quadrangle.

cuadrante *nm* **1** *(reloj)* sundial. **2** *(instrumento)* quadrant. **3** *(cojín)* square pillow.

cuadrar *vt* **1** *(dar figura cuadrada)* to square, make square. **2** *(geometría, matemáticas)* to square. **3** COM to balance.
▶ *vi* **1** *(coincidir)* to square, agree. **2** COM to tally, add up: *las cuentas de este mes no cuadran* the accounts don't add up this month. **3** *fig (ir bien)* to suit: *el estilo no cuadra con el tema* the style doesn't suit the subject.

cuádriceps *nm inv* quadriceps.

cuadrícula *nf* squares *pl*, grid.

cuadriculado,-a *adj* squared.
▶ *nm* **cuadriculado** squares *pl*, grid.

cuadricular *vt* to square, divide into squares.
▶ *adj* squared.

cuadrienio *nm* quadrennium.

cuadriga *nf* chariot.

cuadrilátero,-a *adj* quadrilateral, four-sided.
▶ *nm* **cuadrilátero** *(boxeo)* ring.

cuadrilla *nf* **1** *(grupo)* party, gang. **2** *(de bandidos, etc)* gang, band. **3** *(de obreros)* gang, team.

cuadro *nm* **1** *(cuadrado)* square. **2** *(pintura)* painting, picture. **3** TEAT scene. **4** *(descripción)* description, picture. **5** *(dirigentes)* leaders *pl*; *(personal)* staff. **6** *(conjunto de datos)* chart, graph. [LOC] **a cuadros** checked, US checkered: *tela a cuadros* checked (US checkered) cloth. [COMP] **cuadro clínico** clinical pattern. **cuadro sinóptico** diagram, chart.

cuadrúpedo,-a *adj* quadruped.
▶ *nm* **cuadrúpedo** quadruped.

cuádruple *adj* quadruple, fourfold.

cuadruplicar *vt* to quadruple.
▶ *vi* to quadruple.

cuajada *nf* *(leche)* curd; *(requesón)* cottage cheese.

cuajar *vt* **1** *(gen)* to coagulate; *(leche)* to curdle; *(sangre)* to clot. **2** *(huevo)* to set.
▶ *vi* **1** *(nieve)* to lie. **2** *fig (tener éxito)* to be a success, come off: *la cosa no cuajó* it didn't come off.
▶ *vpr* **cuajarse 1** to coagulate; *(leche)* to curdle; *(sangre)* clot. **2** *(huevo)* to set.

cual *pron* **1** *(precedido de artículo - persona)* who, whom: *la gente a la cual preguntamos* the people whom we asked. **2** *(precedido de artículo - cosa)* which: *la ciudad en la cual nací* the city where I was born. [LOC] **cada cual** everyone, everybody.
▶ *adv fml* as, like: *se enamoró cual si tuviese quince años* he fell in love like a teenager.

cuál *pron* **1** *(interrogativo)* which, which one, what: *¿cuál es el más alto?* which one is the tallest? **2** *(valor distributivo)* some. **3** *(exclamativo)* how, what: *¡cuál no sería mi asombro!* imagine my amazement! [LOC] **a cuál más** equally: *a cuál más listo* each as clever as the other.
▶ *adj (interrogativo)* which.

cualidad *nf* **1** *(de persona)* quality, attribute. **2** *(de cosa)* quality, property.

cualitativo,-a *adj* qualitative.

cualquier *adj (indefinido)* any: *cualquier otro día* any other day; *cualquier cosa* anything; *cualquier persona* anyone.

✎ Consulta también cualquiera.

cualquiera *adj* **1** *(indefinido)* any: *un día cualquiera* any day. **2** *(ordinario)* ordinary: *no es una corbata cualquiera* it's not an ordinary tie.

▸ *pron* **1** *(persona indeterminada)* anybody, anyone; *(cosa indeterminada)* any, any one: *cualquiera lo compraría* anybody would buy it. **2** *(nadie)* nobody: *¡cualquiera lo coge!* nobody would take it!

▸ *nf* **cualquiera que** *(persona)* whoever; *(cosa)* whatever, whichever: *cualquiera que diga eso, miente* whoever says that is lying.

cuan *adv* [se usa sólo antes de adjetivo y de adverbio] *fml* as: *cayó cuan largo era* he fell flat on the floor.

✎ Consulta también **cuanto**.

cuán *adv* [se usa sólo antes de adjetivo y de adverbio] *(interrogativo)* how: *¡cuán idiota!* how stupid!

✎ Consulta también **cuanto**.

cuando *adv* *(tiempo)* when: *cuando tenía diez años* when he was ten.

▸ *conj* **1** *(temporal)* when, whenever: *ven a verme cuando quieras* come and see me whenever you want. **2** *(condicional)* if: *cuando él lo dice* if he says so. **3** *(causal)* since. LOC **de vez en cuando** now and then, from time to time. **I hasta cuando** until.

▸ *prep* during, at the time of: *cuando la guerra* during the war.

cuándo *adv* *(interrogativo)* when: *¿cuándo es tu cumpleaños?* when is your birthday?

▸ *nm* when: *no sé el cómo ni el cuándo* I don't know how or when.

cuantía *nf* **1** *(cantidad)* quantity; *(importe)* amount: *la cuantía de una factura* the amount of a bill. **2** *(dimensión)* extent: *la cuantía del desastre ecológico* the extent of the ecological disaster.

cuantitativo,-a *adj* quantitative.

cuanto *nm* Fís quantum: *la teoría de los cuantos* the quantum theory.

cuánto,-a *adj* **1** *(pregunta - singular)* how much; *(- plural)* how many: *¿cuántos años tienes?* how old are you? **2** *(exclama-*

ción) what a lot of, so many, so much: *¡cuánta gente!* there are so many people!, what a lot of people!

▸ *pron* *(singular)* how much; *(plural)* how many: *¿cuánto es?* how much is it?

▸ *adv* how, how much: *¡cuánto me alegro!* I'm so glad!

cuanto,-a³ *adj* *(singular)* as much as; *(plural)* as many as: *puedes beber cuanta agua quieras* you can drink as much water as you want. LOC **cuanto antes** as soon as possible. **I en cuanto** as soon as, when: *en cuanto llegue dile...* as soon as he arrives tell him... **I unos,-as cuantos,-as** some, a few.

▸ *pron* **1** *(singular)* everything, all: *escribe cuanto quieras* write as much as you want. **2** *(plural)* all who, everybody who: *cuantos entraron se asustaron* everybody who came in was frightened.

cuarcita *nf* quartzite.

cuarenta *adj* *(cardinal)* forty; *(ordinal)* fortieth. LOC **cantarle las cuarenta a ALGN** to give SB a piece of one's mind.

▸ *nm* *(número)* forty.

✎ Consulta también **seis**.

cuarentavo,-a *adj* fortieth.

▸ *nm & nf* fortieth.

✎ Consulta también **sexto,-a**.

cuarentena *nf* **1** *(exacto)* forty; *(aproximado)* about forty. **2** MED quarantine. LOC **poner a ALGN en cuarentena** MED to quarantine SB, put SB in quarantine.

cuaresma *nf* Lent.

cuarta *nf* **1** *(palmo)* span. **2** *(cuadrante)* quadrant.

✎ Consulta también **cuarto,-a**.

cuartear *vt* **1** *(dividir en cuatro)* to quarter, divide into four. **2** *(descuartizar)* to quarter. **3** *(rajar)* to crack.

▸ *vpr* **cuartearse** *(rajarse)* to crack, split.

cuartel *nm* MIL barracks *pl.*

cuarteto *nm* quartet.

cuartilla *nf* sheet of paper.

cuarto *nm* **1** *(parte)* quarter: *un cuarto de hora* a quarter of an hour. **2** *(de animal)* quarter. **3** *(de ropa)* quarter: *un chaquetón tres cuartos* a three-quarter length jacket. **4** *(habitación)* room. LOC **de tres al cuarto** *fam* worthless, third-rate. ▎**estar sin un cuarto** *fam* to be broke. ▎**tres cuartos de lo mismo** *fam* almost exactly the same. COMP **cuarto creciente** first quarter. ▎**cuarto de baño** bathroom. ▎**cuartos de final** DEP quarter finals.
▶ *nm pl* **cuartos** *fam (dinero)* money *sing*, dough *sing*.

cuarto,-a *adj (ordinal)* fourth: *llegó cuarto* he arrived in fourth place, he came fourth.
▶ *nm & nf* fourth.
✎ Consulta también **sexto,-a**.

cuarzo *nm* quartz.

cuaternario,-a *adj* quaternary.
▶ *nm* **el cuaternario** the quaternary.

cuatrienio *nm* quadrennium, four-year period.

cuatrimestral *adj (en frecuencia)* four-monthly; *(en duración)* four-month.

cuatrimestre *nm* four-month period: *en el primer cuatrimestre de 2007* in the first four months of 2007.

cuatrisílabo,-a *adj* quadrisyllabic.
▶ *nm* **cuatrisílabo** quadrisyllable.

cuatro *adj (cardinal)* four; *(ordinal)* fourth. LOC **caer cuatro gotas** *fam* to rain very lightly, spit. ▎**decirle cuatro cosas a** ALGN to tell SB off. COMP **cuatro gatos** *fam* just a few people, hardly anyone.
▶ *nm (número)* four.
✎ Consulta también **seis**.

cuatrocientos,-as *adj* four hundred.
▶ *nm* **cuatrocientos** *(número)* four hundred.
✎ Consulta también **seis**.

cuba *nf* cask, barrel.
Cuba *nf* Cuba.
cubano,-a *adj* Cuban.
▶ *nm & nf* Cuban.

cubertería *nf* cutlery.

cubeta *nf* **1** *(rectangular)* tray, tank, dish. **2** *(cubo)* bucket.

cúbico,-a *adj* cubic: *raíz cúbica* cube root.

cubierta *nf* **1** *(gen)* cover, covering. **2** *(de libro)* cover. **3** ARQUIT roof. **4** *(de neumático)* tyre (US tire). **5** *(de barco, avión)* deck. LOC **en cubierta** on deck.

cubierto,-a *adj* **1** *(gen)* covered. **2** *(cielo)* overcast. **3** *(plaza)* filled.
▶ *nm* **cubierto 1** *(techumbre)* cover. **2** *(en la mesa)* place setting. LOC **ponerse a cubierto** to take cover. ▎**tener las espaldas cubiertas** *fam* to be well-heeled.
▶ *nm pl* **cubiertos** cutlery *sing*.

cubilete *nm* **1** *(molde)* mould (US mold). **2** *(de dados)* dice cup, dice shaker; *(juego)* cup.

cubismo *nm* cubism.

cubista *adj* cubist.
▶ *nm o nf* cubist.

cubito *nm* **1** little cube. **2** *(de hielo)* ice cube.

cúbito *nm* cubitus.

cubo¹ *nm* **1** *(recipiente)* bucket. **2** *(de rueda)* hub. COMP **cubo de la basura** rubbish bin, US garbage can.

cubo² *nm* MAT cube. LOC **elevar al cubo** to cube.

cubrecama *nm* bedspread.

cubrir *vt* **1** *(gen)* to cover. **2** CULIN to coat (de, with). **3** *(poner tejado)* to put a roof on. **4** *(niebla, etc)* to shroud (de, in), cloak. **5** *(ocultar)* to hide. **6** *(llenar)* to fill (de, with), cover (de, with): *cubrir de agua* to fill with water. **7** *(alcanzar)* to come up: *el agua le cubría hasta los tobillos* the water came up to his ankles.
▶ *vpr* **cubrirse 1** *(abrigarse)* to cover os. **2** *(la cabeza)* to put one's hat on. **3** *fig (protegerse)* to protect os. **4** *(cielo)* to become overcast. **5** *(llenarse)* to be filled.

cucaña *nf (palo, juego)* greasy pole.

cucaracha *nf* cockroach.

cuchara *nf* spoon.

cucharada *nf* spoonful. COMP **cucharada colmada** heaped spoonful. I **cucharada rasa** level spoonful.

cucharadita *nf* teaspoonful.

cucharilla *nf* teaspoon. COMP **cucharilla de café** coffee spoon.

cucharita *nf* teaspoon.

cucharón *nm* ladle.

cuchichear *vi* to whisper.

cuchicheo *nm* whispering.

cuchilla *nf (hoja)* blade. COMP **cuchilla de afeitar** razor blade.

cuchillada *nf (golpe)* stab, slash; *(herida)* stab wound, knife wound.

cuchillería *nf* cutler's shop.

cuchillo *nm* **1** knife. **2** ARQUIT support.

cuclillas LOC **en cuclillas** crouching. I **ponerse en cuclillas** to crouch down.

cuclillo *nm* cuckoo.

cuco *nm (insecto)* caterpillar.

cuco,-a *adj fam (coquetón)* cute. **2** *(taimado)* shrewd, crafty.
▶ *nm* **cuco** *(ave)* cuckoo.

cucú *nm* **1** *(canto)* cuckoo. **2** *(reloj)* cuckoo clock.

cucurucho *nm* **1** *(de papel)* paper cone. **2** *(helado)* cornet, cone. **3** *(capirote)* pointed hood.

cuello *nm* **1** ANAT neck. **2** *(de camisa, vestido, abrigo)* collar; *(de jersey)* neck: *un jersey de cuello alto* a polo neck jumper, US a turtleneck jumper. **3** *(de botella)* bottleneck.

cuenca *nf* **1** *(escudilla)* wooden bowl. **2** ANAT socket. **3** GEOG basin. **4** *(minera)* coalfield.

cuenco *nm (vasija)* earthenware bowl.

cuenta *nf* **1** *(bancaria)* account. **2** *(factura)* bill. **3** *(cálculo)* count, counting. **4** *(de collar, etc)* bead. LOC **caer en la cuenta** to realize: *y entonces caí en la cuenta de que...* and then I realized that..., and then it dawned on me that.... I **en resumidas cuentas** in short. I **hacer cuentas** to do sums. I **más de la cuenta** too much, too many: *comió más de la cuenta* she ate too much. I **pedir cuentas** to ask for an explanation. I **por la cuenta que le trae** in one's own interest. I

sacar cuentas to work out. I **tener en cuenta** to take into account. COMP **cuenta atrás** countdown. I **cuenta corriente** current account. I **cuenta de correo electrónico** e-mail account.

cuentagotas *nm inv* dropper.

cuentakilómetros *nm inv (de velocidad)* speedometer; *(de distancia)* mileometer.

cuentarrevoluciones *nm inv* rev counter.

cuentavueltas *nm inv* rev counter.

cuentista *adj fam* overdramatic.
▶ *nm o nf* **1** *(autor)* story writer; *(narrador)* storyteller. **2** *fam (que exagera)* over-dramatic person; *(que miente)* fibber, liar.

cuento *nm* **1** *(relato)* story, tale. **2** LIT short story. **3** *fam (chisme)* gossip. **4** *fam (embuste)* fib, story. LOC **dejarse de cuentos 1** *fam (ir al grano)* to get to the point. **2** *(decir mentiras)* to stop telling fibs. I **ir con el cuento a** ALGN to go and tell SB. I **tener mucho cuento** *fam* to make a lot of fuss. I **venir a cuento** to be pertinent. COMP **cuento chino** tall story. I **cuento de hadas** fairy tale.

cuerda *nf* **1** *(cordel)* rope, string. **2** *(instrumento)* string, cord; *(voz)* voice. **3** *(de reloj)* spring: *dar cuerda a un reloj* to wind up a watch. **4** *(en geometría)* chord. **5** DEP interior. COMP **cuerdas vocales** vocal chords.
▶ *nf pl* **cuerdas 1** *(boxeo)* ropes. **2** MÚS strings.

cuerdo,-a *adj* **1** *(persona)* sane. **2** *(acción)* prudent, sensible.
▶ *nm & nf (persona)* sane person, person in one's right mind.

cuerno *nm* **1** horn; *(de ciervo)* antlers *pl*. **2** *(de antena)* antlers *pl*. **3** MÚS horn.
▶ *interj* golly!, gosh!

cuero *nm* **1** *(de animal)* skin, hide. **2** *(curtido)* leather: *pantalón de cuero* leather trousers. **3** *(odre)* wineskin. **4** *(balón)* ball. LOC **quedarse en cueros** *fam* to strip off.

cuerpo *nm* **1** ANAT body. **2** *(constitución)* build. **3** *(figura)* figure. **4** *(tronco)* trunk.

5 *(grupo)* body, force, corps: *el cuerpo de bomberos* the fire brigade (US the fire department). **6** *(cadáver)* corpse, body. **7** QUÍM substance. **8** FÍS body. **9** DEP length. LOC **cuerpo a cuerpo** hand-to-hand. ▮ **de cuerpo entero** full-length. ▮ **en cuerpo y alma** *fig* heart and soul, body and soul. COMP **cuerpo diplomático** diplomatic corps. ▮ **cuerpo geométrico** regular solid. ▮ **cuerpos celestes** heavenly bodies.

cuervo *nm (córvido en general)* crow; *(específico)* raven.

cuesta *nf (pendiente)* slope. LOC **a cuestas** on one's back, on one's shoulders. ▮ **hacérsele a uno** ALGO **cuesta arriba** *fig* to find STH an uphill struggle, find STH very difficult. ▮ **ir cuesta abajo** *fig* to go downhill.

cuestión *nf* **1** *(pregunta)* question. **2** *(asunto)* business, matter, question. **3** *(discusión)* dispute, quarrel, argument. LOC **en cuestión** in question. ▮ **en cuestión de...** *(tiempo)* in just a few..., in a matter of... ▮ **eso es otra cuestión** that's a whole different matter.

cuestionable *adj* questionable.

cuestionar *vt* to question.

cuestionario *nm* questionnaire.

cueva *nf* cave.

cuidado *nm* **1** *(atención)* care, carefulness. **2** *(recelo)* worry.
▶ *interj* look out!, watch out!: *¡cuidado con la moto!* mind the motorbike! LOC **andarse con cuidado** to go carefully. ▮ «**Cuidado con el perro**» «Beware of the dog». ▮ **con cuidado** carefully. ▮ **tener cuidado** to be careful. ▮ **traer sin cuidado** not to care. COMP **cuidados intensivos** intensive care *sing*.

cuidador,-ra *nm & nf* keeper.

cuidadoso,-a *adj* **1** *(atento)* careful. **2** *(celoso)* cautious.

cuidar *vt* to look after, take care of, care for.
▶ *vpr* **cuidarse** to take care of os, look after os: *¡cuídate mucho!* take good care of yourself!

culebra *nf* snake.

culinario,-a *adj* culinary, cooking: *arte culinario* cuisine.

culminación *nf* culmination, climax.

culminante *adj (momento)* culminating, climatic; *(punto)* highest.

culminar *vi* **1** to reach a peak. **2** *fig (acabar)* to finish, end.

culpa *nf* **1** *(culpabilidad)* guilt, blame. **2** *(falta)* fault: *esto es culpa mía* it's my fault. LOC **echar la culpa a** ALGN to put the blame on SB. ▮ **tener la culpa** to be to blame (de, for): *yo no tengo la culpa* I'm not to blame, it's not my fault.

culpabilidad *nf* guilt, culpability.

culpable *adj* guilty.
▶ *nm o nf* offender, culprit.

culpar *vt* **1** *(gen)* to blame (de, for). **2** *(de un delito)* to accuse (de, of).

cultivar *vt* **1** to cultivate, farm. **2** *(ejercitar facultades)* to work at, practise (US practice), improve: *cultivar la memoria* to improve one's memory. **3** *(en biología)* to produce. LOC **cultivar las amistades** *fig* to cultivate friendships.

cultivo *nm* **1** *(acción)* cultivation, farming. **2** *(cosecha)* crop. **3** BIOL culture. **4** *fig (desarrollo)* development, growth.

culto,-a *adj* **1** *(persona)* cultured, educated. **2** *(estilo)* refined.
▶ *nm* **culto** worship.

cultura *nf* culture. LOC **de cultura** educated.

cultural *adj* cultural.

cumbre *nf* **1** *(de montaña)* summit, top. **2** *fig (culminación)* pinnacle. **3** *(reunión)* summit conference, summit meeting.

cumpleaños *nm inv* birthday.

cumplido,-a *adj* **1** *(completo)* complete, full. **2** *(abundante)* large, ample. **3** *(perfecto)* perfect. **4** *(educado)* polite, courteous.
▶ *nm* **cumplido** compliment. LOC **sin cumplidos** informally.

cumplidor,-ra *adj (que cumple)* who delivers the goods: *es una chica muy cumplidora* she always delivers the goods, she always fulfils her promises.

C

cumplir *vt* **1** *(orden)* to carry out; *(deseo)* to fulfil; *(US* fulfill); *(deber)* to do. **2** *(promesa)* to keep. **3** JUR *(ley)* to observe, abide by; *(pena)* to serve. **4** *(años)* to be, turn: *¡que cumplas muchos más!* many happy returns! **5** *(satisfacer)* to do, carry out, fulfil *(US* fulfill). LOC **cumplir con el deber** to do one's duty. ‖ **cumplir con su palabra** to keep one's word. ‖ **para cumplir** as a formality.
▸ *vi* **1** *(plazo)* to expire, end. **2** *(deuda, pago)* to fall due.
▸ *vpr* **cumplirse 1** *(realizarse)* to be fulfilled, come true: *se cumplió la profecía* the prophecy came true. **2** *(fecha)* to be: *se cumple una semana del comienzo del curso* it's a week since the course began.

cúmulo *nm* **1** *(montón)* load, pile, heap; *(cantidad)* series, host, string: *un cúmulo de desgracias* a series of misfortunes. **2** METEOR cumulus.

cumulonimbo *nm* cumulonimbus.

cuna *nf* **1** *(cama)* cradle. **2** *(linaje)* birth, lineage, stock. **3** *fig (origen)* cradle, birthplace: *la cuna de la filosofía* the cradle of philosophy. **4** *(lugar de nacimiento)* birthplace.

cundir *vi* **1** *(extenderse)* to spread: *cundió el pánico* panic spread. **2** *(dar de sí)* to go a long way, go far: *una hora cunde muy poco* you can't do much in an hour. **3** *(aumentar de volumen)* to swell, expand: *los fideos cunden al cocerse* noodles expand when cooked.

cuneta *nf* **1** *(de carretera)* verge. **2** *(zanja)* ditch.

cuña *nf* *(pieza)* wedge.

cuñado,-a *nm & nf (hombre)* brother-in-law; *(mujer)* sister-in-law.

cuño *nm* **1** *(troquel)* die, stamp. **2** *(sello)* stamp, mark.

cuota *nf* **1** *(pago)* membership fee, dues *pl.* **2** *(porción)* quota, share.

cupo *nm (cuota)* quota.

cupón *nm* **1** *(vale)* coupon, voucher. **2** *(de lotería)* ticket.

cúpula *nf* cupola, dome.

cura *nm* REL priest.
▸ *nf* **1** cure, healing. **2** *(tratamiento)* treatment: *cura de adelgazamiento* slim-ming treatment. LOC **hacer las primeras curas** to give first aid.

curable *adj* curable.

curación *nf* **1** *(gen)* cure. **2** *(de herida)* healing. **3** *(recuperación)* recovery.

curandero,-a *nm & nf* **1** *(charlatán)* quack. **2** *(curador)* folk healer.

curar *vt* **1** *(sanar)* to cure. **2** *(herida)* to dress; *(enfermedad)* to treat.
▸ *vi* **1** *(cuidar)* to take care *(de,* of). **2** *(recuperarse)* to recover, get well. **3** *(herida)* to heal (up).
▸ *vpr* **curarse 1** *(recuperarse)* to recover *(de,* from), get well. **2** *(herida)* to heal up.

curativo,-a *adj* curative: *poder curativo* healing power.

curia *nf* **1** REL curia. **2** JUR Bar.

curiosamente *adv* **1** *(con curiosidad)* curiously, strangely. **2** *(limpiamente)* cleanly.

curiosear *vi* **1** *(fisgar)* to pry, nose around. **2** *(mirar)* to look around.
▸ *vt (fisgar)* to pry into.

curiosidad *nf* **1** *(gen)* curiosity. **2** *(aseo)* cleanliness, tidiness. **3** *(cuidado)* care. LOC **tener curiosidad de** ALGO to be curious about STH.

currículo *nm* curriculum, curriculum vitae.

curry *nm* curry.

cursar *vt* **1** *(estudiar)* to study. **2** *(enviar)* to send, dispatch; *(orden)* to give. **3** *(tramitar)* to make an application.

cursi *adj fam (afectado)* pretentious, affected, twee.
▸ *nm o nf fam* pretentious person, affected person.

cursilada *nf* **1** *(cualidad)* affectation, pretentiousness. **2** *(hecho)* pretentious thing to do, posh thing to do. **3** *(obra, cosa)* pretentious thing: *las películas románticas me parecen una cursilada* for me romantic films are just sentimental slush.

cursillo *nm* short course, training course.

cursiva *nf (escritura)* cursive; *(tipografía)* italics *pl.*

curso *nm* **1** *(dirección)* course, direction: *el curso de los acontecimientos* the course of events. **2** EDUC *(nivel)* year, class; *(materia)* course; *(escolar)* school year: *vamos al mismo curso* we are in the same class. **3** *(río)* flow, current. COMP **curso acelerado** crash course.

cursor *nm* **1** INFORM cursor. **2** TÉC slide.

curtido,-a *adj* **1** *(por el sol)* tanned, sunburnt. **2** *(cuero)* tanned. **3** *fig (endurecido)* hardened.
▶ *nm* **curtido** *(operación)* tanning.
▶ *nm pl* **curtidos** tanned leather *sing*.

curtidor,-ra *nm & nf* tanner.

curtir *vt* **1** *(piel)* to tan. **2** *fig (acostumbrar)* to harden, toughen.
▶ *vpr* **curtirse 1** *(por el sol)* to get tanned. **2** *fig (acostumbrarse)* to become hardened.

curva *nf* **1** *(gen)* curve. **2** *(de carretera)* bend. **3** *(gráfico)* curve, graph. LOC **trazar una curva** to draw a curve.

curvar *vt* **1** *(gen)* to curve, bend. **2** *(espalda)* to arch.

curvilíneo,-a *adj* **1** curvilinear, curvilineal. **2** *fam (del cuerpo)* curvaceous, shapely.

curvo,-a *adj* curved, bent.

cuscús *nm* couscous.

cúspide *nf* **1** *(cumbre)* summit, peak. **2** *(en geometría)* apex. **3** *fig* peak.

custodia *nf* **1** custody, care. **2** REL monstrance. LOC **bajo custodia** in custody.

custodiar *vt* **1** *(proteger)* to keep, take care of. **2** *(vigilar)* to guard, watch over.

cutáneo,-a *adj* cutaneous, skin: *enfermedad cutánea* skin disease.

cúter *nm* **1** *(barco)* cutter. **2** *(cuchillo)* cutter.

cutícula *nf* cuticle.

cutis *nm inv* skin, complexion.

cuyo,-a *pron* **1** *(personas)* whose, of whom: *esta mujer, cuya hermana trabaja en Alemania...* this woman, whose sister works in Germany..., this woman, the sister of whom works in Germany... **2** *(cosas)* whose, of which: *un árbol cuyas hojas presentan esta enfermedad* a tree with leaves that show signs of this disease. LOC **en cuyo caso** in which case.

CV¹ *sím* (caballos de vapor) horse power; *(símbolo)* HP.

CV² *abrev* (currículum vítae) curriculum vitae; *(abreviatura)* CV.

D

D, d *nf (la letra)* D, d.

dado *nm* **1** *(para jugar)* die. **2** TÉC block. **3** ARQUIT dado. LOC **echar los dados** to throw the dice.

dado,-a *adj* **1** given: *dada la base y la altura, hallar la superficie* given the base and the height, find the area. **2** *(en vista de)* in view of: *dada su experiencia* in view of his experience. LOC **dado que** since, as, given that: *dado que llueve no saldremos* as it's raining we won't go out.

daga *nf* dagger.

dalai lama *nm* Dalai Lama.

dalia *nf* dahlia.

dálmata *adj* Dalmatian.
▶ *nm* Dalmatian.

daltónico,-a *adj* colour-blind, daltonic.

daltonismo *nm* colour (US color) blindness, daltonism.

dama *nf* **1** *(señora)* lady. **2** *(en el juego de damas)* king; *(en ajedrez)* queen.
▶ *nf pl* **damas** draughts, (US checkers).
COMP **tablero de damas** draughtboard, (US checkerboard).

damero *nm* draughtboard, US checkerboard.

damnificar *vt* **1** *(a una persona)* to injure, harm. **2** *(cosa)* to damage.

dandy *nm* dandy.

danés,-esa *adj* Danish.
▶ *nm & nf (persona)* Dane.
▶ *nm* **danés** *(idioma)* Danish.

danza *nf* **1** *(baile)* dance. **2** *fig (negocio sucio)* shady business, shady deal; *(lío)* mess: *no te metas en esa danza* don't get mixed up in a deal like that. **3** *fam fig (riña)* row.

danzante *adj* dancing.
▶ *nm o nf* dancer.

danzar *vt (bailar)* to dance.
▶ *vi (bailar)* to dance (con, with).

danzarín,-ina *nm & nf* dancer.

dañado,-a *adj* damaged, spoiled.

dañar *vt* **1** *(causar dolor)* to hurt, harm. **2** *(estropear)* to damage, spoil. **3** *fig* to damage, stain: *ese asunto dañará su reputación* that affair will damage his reputation.
▶ *vpr* **dañarse** *(estropearse)* to get damaged, spoil; *(alimentos)* to go bad, go off.

dañino,-a *adj* harmful (para, to), damaging (para, to).

daño *nm (a una persona)* harm, injury; *(a una cosa)* damage; *(perjuicio)* wrong. LOC **hacer daño 1** *(doler)* to hurt. **2** *(causar dolor a ALGN)* to hurt. **3** *(ser malo para ALGO)* to damage, harm. *(ser malo para ALGN)* to do SB harm: *me hizo daño con sus palabras* her words hurt me. ‖ **hacerse daño** to hurt OS: *se hizo daño en la mano* she hurt her hand.

dar *vt* **1** *(gen)* to give: *te daré un libro* I'll give you a book. **2** *(poner en las manos, entregar)* to deliver, hand over; *(poner al alcance)* to pass, hand: *dame la sal* pass me the salt. **3** *(proporcionar, ofrecer, procurar algo no material a una persona - noticia)* to tell, announce, report; *(- consejo)* to give; *(- recuerdos, recado)* to pass on, give. **4** *(permitir tener algo, conceder)* to give. **5** *(pagar a cambio)* to give, pay: *¿cuánto me daría por esto?* how much would you give me for it? **6** *(realizar una acción)*. **7** *(producir - cosecha)* to produce, yield; *(- fruto, flores)* to bear, produce; *(- beneficio)* to produce, yield: *la higuera da higos* the fig tree bears figs. **8** *(celebrar,* *tener lugar - película*) to show, screen; (*- obra de teatro*) to perform, put on; (*- concierto*) to give, perform, put on; (*- fiesta*) to give, throw: *daremos una fiesta* we'll have a party. **9** (*pegar*) to hit. **10** (*sonar el reloj las horas*) to strike. **11** (*untar, recubrir una superficie*) to apply, give. **12** (*abrir el paso de conductos*) to turn on: *he dado el gas* I've turned the gas on. LOC **dar a entender que...** to give to understand that..., imply that...: *dio a entender que no vendría* she implied she wouldn't come. **dar a luz** to give birth (a, to). **dar ALGO por** to assume, consider. **dar de sí 1** (*ropa*) to stretch, give. **2** (*dinero, comida*) to go a long way. **dar igual** to be all the same, not matter: *le daba igual* it didn't matter to him, he didn't care. **dar la mano a ALGN** to shake hands with SB.

▶ *vi* **1** (*pegar, golpear*) to hit: *la pelota le dio en toda la cara* the ball hit him right in the face. **2** (*en naipes*) to deal. **3** **dar a** (*botón, interruptor*) to press: *dale al botón* press the button. **4** (*mirar una cosa hacia una parte*) to look out onto, overlook. **5** **dar de** (*caer*) to fall: *dio de narices en el suelo* he fell flat on his face. **6** **dar de** (*suministrar*) to give. **7** **dar en** (*acertar*) to find, hit on. **8** **dar para** (*ser suficiente*) to be enough for, be sufficient for: *la sopa da para cuatro* the soup serves four.

dardo *nm* (*arma*) dart, arrow.

dársena *nf* dock, basin.

darvinismo *nm* Darwinism.

datar *vt* (*poner la data*) to date, put a date on.
▶ *vi* (*tener origen*) to date (de, from), date back (de, to): *esa iglesia data del siglo XI* that church dates from the eleventh century.

dátil *nm* date.

datilera *nf* date palm.

dativo,-a *adj* dative.
▶ *nm* **dativo** dative. LOC **en dativo** in the dative.

dato *nm* (*información*) fact, piece of information, datum. COMP **datos personales** personal details.

dB *sím* (*decibelio*) decibel; (*símbolo*) dB.

d.C. *abrev* (*después de Cristo*) Anno Domini; (*abreviatura*) AD.

DDT *abrev* (*diclorodifeniltricloroetano*) dichlorodiphenyltrichloroethane; (*abreviatura*) DDT.

de *prep* **1** (*posesión, pertenencia*) of, in: *la mesa de mi habitación* the table in my bedroom. **2** (*procedencia, origen*) from, in: *viene de Barcelona* she comes from Barcelona. **3** (*descripción*) with: *el señor del abrigo azul* the man in the blue coat. **4** (*tema*) of, on, about: *hablaron del tiempo* they talked about the weather. **5** (*materia*) made of, of: *un anillo de oro* a gold ring. **6** (*contenido*) of: *un vaso de agua* a glass of water. **7** (*oficio*) by, as: *trabaja de profesor* he works as a teacher. **8** (*modo*) on, in, as: *de pie* standing up. **9** (*tiempo*) at, by, in: *de día* by day, during the day. **10** (*lugar*) *varias traducciones*: *la vecina de arriba* our upstairs neighbour. **11** (*medida*) measuring: *una botella de dos litros* a two litre bottle. **12** (*causa*) with, because of, of: *llorar de alegría* to cry with joy. **13** (*agente*) by: *es una obra de Lope* a play by Lope. **14** (*con superlativo*) in, of: *el mayor de los tres* the eldest of the three. **15** (*en una aposición*) of: *la ciudad de Barcelona* the city of Barcelona.

✎ Consulta también del.

deambular *vi* to saunter, stroll.

debajo *adv* below, underneath: *el libro verde está debajo* the green book is underneath. LOC **por debajo** underneath: *tuvieron que pasar por debajo* they had to go underneath.

debate *nm* debate, discussion.

debatir *vt* to debate, discuss.

debe *nm* debit side.

deber *vt* **1** (*estar obligado a algo*) to owe: *debemos respeto a nuestros padres* we owe respect to our parents. **2** (*dinero, cosa*) to owe: *te debo cincuenta euros* I owe you fifty euros.
▶ *aux* **1** (*obligación presente*) must, have to, have got to: *debo ir a comprar* I must go shopping. **2** (*obligación pasada*) should, ought to: *debía haberlo comprado ayer* I should have bought it yester-

day. **3** *(obligación futura)* must, have to, have got to: *deberás tenerlo a las cinco* you must have it ready by five o'clock. **4** *(obligación moral)* should, ought to: *no deberías haberlo hecho* you shouldn't have done it. **5 deber de** *(probabilidad)* must; *(negativa)* can't: *deben de ser las seis* it must be six o'clock; *no deben de haber llegado* they can't have arrived.

▶ *vpr* **deberse 1** *(ser consecuencia)* to be due (a, to). **2** *(tener una obligación)* to have a duty (a, to).

▶ *nm* **deber** *(obligación)* duty, obligation. LOC **cumplir con su deber** to do one's duty. ‖ **hacer los deberes** to do one's homework.

▶ *nm pl* **deberes** *(escolares)* homework *sing.*

debidamente *adv* duly, properly.

debido,-a *adj* **1** *(merecido)* due: *con el debido respeto,...* with all due respect,... **2** *(conveniente)* right. LOC **como es debido 1** *(correctamente)* right, properly. **2** *(como es merecido)* deservedly: *siéntate en la silla como es debido* sit properly on the chair.

débil *adj* **1** *(persona)* weak, feeble. **2** *(ruido)* faint; *(luz)* dim, feeble. **3** LING weak.

▶ *nm o nf* weak person.

debilidad *nf* **1** *(de una persona)* weakness, feebleness. **2** *fig* weakness: *los coches de carreras son su debilidad* he has a weakness for racing cars. LOC **tener debilidad por 1** *(algo)* to have a weakness for. **2** *(alguien)* to have a soft spot for.

debilitamiento *nm* weakening.

debilitar *vt* to weaken, debilitate.

▶ *vpr* **debilitarse** to weaken, get weak, become weak.

debut *nm* debut, début.

debutante *nm o nf (actor)* first-time actor; *(actriz)* first-time actress.

debutar *vi* to make one's debut, make one's début.

década *nf* decade.

decadencia *nf* decadence, decline, decay.

decadente *adj* decadent.

decaedro *nm* decahedron.

decaer *vi (perder fuerzas)* to weaken; *(- entusiasmo, interés)* to flag; *(- salud)* to go down, deteriorate, decay; *(- belleza, etc)* to lose: *su interés está decayendo* his interest is flagging.

decagonal *adj* decagonal.

decágono *nm* decagon.

decagramo *nm* decagram, decagramme.

decaído,-a *adj* **1** *(débil)* weak. **2** *(triste)* sad, depressed, low.

decalitro *nm* decalitre (US decaliter).

decálogo *nm* Decalogue.

decámetro *nm* decametre (US decameter).

decano,-a *nm & nf (cargo)* dean.

decantar¹ *vt (verter)* to decant, pour off.

decantar² *vt (alabar)* to praise, laud.

▶ *vpr* **decantarse** *(preferir)* to prefer (hacia/por, -): *el público se decantó por el equipo local* the spectators were on the side of the local team.

decapar *vt (pintura)* to strip (off).

decapitar *vt* to behead, decapitate.

decápodo *nm* decapod.

decasílabo,-a *adj* decasyllabic.

decatlón *nm* decathlon.

decena *nf* **1** *(exacto)* ten. **2** *(aproximado)* about ten: *he invitado a una decena de personas* I have invited ten or so people.

decenal *adj* ten-year, decennial.

decencia *nf* **1** *(decoro)* decency, propriety. **2** *(honestidad)* honesty.

decenio *nm* decade.

decente *adj* **1** *(decoroso)* decent, proper. **2** *(honesto)* honest, upright; *(respetable)* decent, respectable.

decentemente *adv* decently.

decepción *nf* disappointment.

decepcionado,-a *adj* disappointed.

decepcionar *vt* to disappoint, let down: *no nos decepciones* don't disappoint us.

decibelio *nm* decibel.

decididamente *adv (con determinación)* resolutely, with determination: *soli-*

citó el trabajo decididamente he applied for the job with determination.

decidido,-a *adj* determined, resolute: *está decidido a acabar el trabajo* he's determined to finish the job.

decidir *vt (gen)* to decide; *(asunto)* to settle.
▶ *vi* to decide, choose: *tuvo que decidir entre los dos* she had to decide between the two.
▶ *vpr* **decidirse** to make up one's mind. LOC **decidirse por** to decide on: *se decidió por la falda roja* she decided on the red skirt.

decigramo *nm* decigram, decigramme.

decilitro *nm* decilitre (US deciliter).

décima *nf* LIT stanza of ten octosyllabic lines. LOC **tener (unas) décimas** *fam* to have a slight temperature.

decimal *adj* decimal.
▶ *nm* decimal.

decímetro *nm* decimetre (US decimeter).

décimo,-a *adj* tenth.
▶ *nm & nf* tenth.

✎ Consulta también sexto,-a.

decimoctavo,-a *adj* eighteenth.
▶ *nm & nf* eighteenth.

✎ Consulta también sexto,-a.

decimocuarto,-a *adj* fourteenth.
▶ *nm & nf* fourteenth.

✎ Consulta también sexto,-a.

decimonónico,-a *adj* nineteenth-century: *un escritor decimonónico* a nineteenth-century writer.

decimonono,-a *adj* nineteenth.
▶ *nm & nf* nineteenth.

✎ Consulta también sexto,-a.

decimonoveno,-a *adj-nm & nf* → decimonono,-a.

✎ Consulta también sexto,-a.

decimoquinto,-a *adj* fifteenth.
▶ *nm & nf* fifteenth.

✎ Consulta también sexto,-a.

decimoséptimo,-a *adj* seventeenth.
▶ *nm & nf* seventeenth.

✎ Consulta también sexto,-a.

decimosexto,-a *adj* sixteenth.
▶ *nm & nf* sixteenth.

✎ Consulta también sexto,-a.

decimotercero,-a *adj* thirteenth.
▶ *nm & nf* thirteenth.

✎ Consulta también sexto,-a.

decir *vt* **1** *(gen)* to say. **2** *(contar, revelar)* to tell: *dijo la verdad* she told the truth. **3** *(nombrar, llamar)* to call: *le dicen Cuca* she's called Cuca. **4** *(opinar)* to have to say. **5** *(un texto)* to read, say: *el texto dice lo siguiente* the text reads as follows. LOC **digo yo** in my opinion, I think. **|** **el qué dirán** what people say. **|** **es decir** that is (to say). **|** **¡no me digas!** really! **|** **querer decir** to mean: *quiero decir,...* I mean,… **|** **se dice...** they say…, it is said…

decisión *nf* **1** *(resolución)* decision: *sus padres tuvieron que tomar una decisión* his parents had to make a decision. **2** *(determinación)* determination, resolution.

decisivo,-a *adj (importante)* decisive.

declamar *vi* to declaim, recite.
▶ *vt* to declaim, recite.

declamatorio,-a *adj* declamatory.

declaración *nf* **1** *(gen)* declaration: *declaración de renta* income tax return. **2** [también se usa en plural con el mismo significado] *(explicación pública)* statement, comment. **3** JUR evidence. **4** *(en bridge)* bid. LOC **prestar declaración** JUR to give evidence.

declarar *vt* **1** *(gen)* to declare; *(manifestar)* to state: *lo declararon vencedor* he was declared the winner. **2** JUR to find.
▶ *vi* **1** to declare. **2** JUR to testify.
▶ *vpr* **declararse 1** *(amor)* to declare one's love (a, for). **2** *(fuego, guerra, etc)* to break out, start: *se declaró un incendio en el monte* a fire broke out on the mountain.

declinación *nf (gramatical)* declension.

declinar vi 1 *(disminuir)* to decline, come down. 2 *(acercarse al fin)* to end, draw to an end.
▶ vt GRAM to decline.

declive nm fig *(decadencia)* decline. LOC **en declive** *fig* on the decline.

decodificar vt to decode.

decolorar vt *(perder el color)* to discolour (US discolor).
▶ vpr **decolorarse** *(perder el color)* to fade, become discoloured (US discolored).

decoración nf 1 *(gen)* decoration. 2 TEAT scenery, set.

decorador,-ra nm & nf 1 decorator. 2 TEAT set designer.

decorar vt *(gen)* to decorate, adorn, embellish; *(una casa)* to decorate.

decorativo,-a adj decorative.

decoroso,-a adj 1 *(digno)* decent, respectable. 2 *(respetable)* respectable, honourable (US honorable): *un trabajo decoroso* an honourable job.

decrecer vi *(gen)* to decrease, diminish; *(aguas)* to subside, go down.

decretar vt 1 *(con decreto)* to decree. 2 *(ordenar)* to ordain, order.

decreto nm decree, order.

décuplo,-a adj tenfold.
▶ nm **décuplo** ten times.

dedal nm thimble.

dedicación nf dedication, devotion. LOC **de dedicación exclusiva** full-time.

dedicar vt 1 *(una dedicatoria)* to dedicate, inscribe. 2 *(tiempo, dinero)* to devote (a, to). 3 *(palabras)* to address.

dedicatoria nf dedication, inscription.

dedo nm 1 *(de la mano)* finger; *(del pie)* toe. 2 *(medida)* finger, digit. LOC **hacer dedo** *fam* to hitchhike. ‖ **no tener dos dedos de frente** *fig* to be as thick as two short planks. COMP **dedo anular** ring finger, third finger. ‖ **dedo gordo** 1 *(de la mano)* thumb. 2 *(del pie)* big toe. ‖ **dedo índice** forefinger, index finger. ‖ **dedo meñique** little finger. ‖ **dedo pulgar** thumb. ‖ **yema del dedo** fingertip.

deducción nf deduction.

deducir vt 1 to deduce, infer. 2 *(dinero)* to deduct, subtract.
▶ vpr **deducirse** to follow: *de aquí se deduce que...* from this it follows that…

deductivo,-a adj deductive.

defecto nm 1 *(gen)* defect, fault; *(de una joya)* imperfection, flaw. 2 *(de persona - moral)* fault, shortcoming; *(- física)* handicap. LOC **por defecto** INFORM default: *la impresora por defecto* the default printer.

defectuoso,-a adj defective, faulty.

defender vt 1 *(gen)* to defend (contra/de, against). 2 *(mantener una opinión, afirmación)* to defend, uphold; *(respaldar a ALGN)* to stand up for, support. 3 *(proteger)* to protect (contra/de, against/from). 4 JUR *(algo)* to argue, plead; *(a alguien)* to defend.
▶ vpr **defenderse** *(espabilarse)* to manage, get by, get along: *¿qué tal se defiende en inglés?* how does she get by in English?, what's her English like?

defensa nf defence (US defense).
▶ nm o nf DEP *(jugador)* back, defender.

defensiva nf defensive. LOC **estar a la defensiva** to be on the defensive.

defensor,-ra adj defending.
▶ nm & nf 1 defender. 2 JUR counsel for the defence (US defense). COMP **defensor del pueblo** ombudsman.

deficiente adj 1 *(defectuoso)* deficient, faulty. 2 *(insuficiente)* lacking, insufficient.
▶ nm o nf mentally retarded person. COMP **deficiente mental** mentally retarded person.

déficit nm inv COM deficit.

deficitario,-a adj showing a deficit.

definición nf definition. LOC **por definición** by definition.

definir vt to define.

definitivamente adv *(para siempre)* for good, once and for all: *se marchó definitivamente* she left for good.

definitivo,-a adj definitive, final. LOC **en definitiva** finally, in short, all in all.

deforestación nf deforestation.

deforestar *vt* to deforest.

deformación *nf* deformation, distortion.

deformar *vt* (*gen*) to deform, put out of shape; (*cara*) to disfigure; (*realidad, imagen, etc*) to distort.

deforme *adj* (*persona*) deformed; (*cosa*) misshapen, out of shape; (*imagen, cara*) distorted.

deformidad *nf* deformity, malformation.

defraudar *vt* **1** (*estafar*) to defraud, cheat. **2** (*decepcionar*) to disappoint, deceive. **3** *fig* (*frustrar*) to betray: *defraudar las esperanzas* to dash one's hopes.

defunción *nf fml* death, decease.

degenerar *vi* to degenerate.

degenerativo,-a *adj* degenerative.

deglutir *vt* to swallow.
▶ *vi* to swallow.

degradante *adj* degrading, humiliating.

degradar *vt* to degrade, debase.
▶ *vpr* **degradarse** to demean OS, degrade OS.

degustación *nf* tasting.

degustar *vt* to taste, sample, try.

dehesa *nf* pasture, meadow.

deidad *nf* deity, divinity.

dejadez *nf* **1** (*negligencia*) negligence, carelessness. **2** (*pereza*) laziness, apathy.

dejado,-a *adj* **1** (*descuidado*) untidy, slovenly. **2** (*perezoso*) lazy.
▶ *nm & nf* untidy person, slovenly person.

dejar *vt* **1** (*colocar*) to leave, put. **2** (*abandonar - persona, lugar*) to leave; (*- hábito, cosa, actividad*) to give up: *dejó el tabaco* he gave up smoking. **3** (*permitir*) to allow, let: *déjale jugar* let him play. **4** (*prestar*) to lend. **5** (*ceder*) to give. **6** (*aplazar*) to put off: *dejémoslo hasta mañana* let's leave it till tomorrow. **7** (*causar un efecto*) to make: *le película me ha dejado triste* the film made me sad. **8** (*legar*) to bequeath, leave.

▶ *aux* **1** dejar de + *inf* (*cesar - voluntariamente*) to stop + *ger*, give up + *ger*; (*- involuntariamente*) to stop + *ger*: *ha dejado de llover* it's stopped raining. **2 no dejar de** + *inf* not to fail *to* + *inf*: *no deja de sorprenderme* she never fails to surprise me. **3** dejar + *pp*: *lo dejó escrito en su agenda* he wrote it down in his diary.
▶ *vpr* **dejarse** (*olvidar*) to forget, leave behind: *me he dejado las llaves en casa* I've left my keys at home.

▶ *vpr* **dejarse de** (*cesar*) to stop: *déjate de tonterías* don't be silly. LOC **dejar ALGO por imposible** to give up on STH. ▐ **dejar en paz** to leave alone. ▐ **dejar preocupado,-a** to worry. ▐ **dejarse llevar por ALGN** to be influenced by SB.

del *contr* (*de + el*)→ **de**.

delantal *nm* apron, pinafore.

delante *adv* **1** (*enfrente*) in front; (*adelantado*) in front, ahead. **2 de delante** in front. **3 delante de** in front of, ahead of, before: *delante de mis ojos* before my eyes. **4 por delante** in front, ahead: *tenemos mucho tiempo por delante* we've got plenty of time ahead.

delantera *nf* **1** (*frente*) front (part). **2** DEP forward line, forwards *pl*. **3** (*ventaja*) lead, advantage. LOC **llevar la delantera** to be in the lead, be ahead.

delantero,-a *adj* front, front part: *el asiento delantero* the front seat.
▶ *nm* **delantero** DEP forward. COMP **delantero centro** centre (US center) forward.

delatar *vt* to inform on.
▶ *vpr* **delatarse** to give OS away.

delator,-ra *adj* accusing, denouncing.
▶ *nm & nf* accuser, denouncer.

delegación *nf* **1** (*gen*) delegation. **2** (*cargo*) office.

delegado,-a *nm & nf* **1** delegate. **2** COM representative.

delegar *vt* to delegate.

deletrear *vt* to spell, spell out.

deletreo *nm* spelling (out).

delfín *nm* (*animal*) dolphin.

delgado,-a *adj* **1** (*poco ancho*) thin. **2** (*esbelto*) slim, slender. **3** (*flaco*) thin.

deliberación *nf* deliberation.

deliberadamente *adv* deliberately.

deliberar *vt* to decide.
▶ *vi* to deliberate (sobre, on).

delicadeza *nf* 1 *(finura)* delicacy, daintiness. 2 *(tacto)* thoughtfulness; *(refinamiento)* refinement.

delicado,-a *adj* 1 *(fino)* delicate; *(refinado)* refined. 2 *(difícil)* delicate, difficult: *una situación delicada* a delicate situation. 3 *(frágil)* fragile.

delicia *nf* delight, pleasure.

delicioso,-a *adj* delightful, charming; *(una comida)* delicious.

delimitar *vt* 1 *(terreno)* to delimit, mark off. 2 *(definir)* to define, specify.

delincuencia *nf* delinquency.

delincuente *nm o nf* delinquent.

delineante *nm o nf (hombre)* draughtsman; *(mujer)* draughtswoman.

delinear *vt* to delineate, outline, sketch.

delirar *vi* to be delirious.

delirio *nm* 1 *(desvarío)* delirium. 2 *fig (disparate)* nonsense.

delito *nm* offence (US offense), crime.

delta *nf* 1 *(letra)* delta. 2 *(ala delta)* hanggliding.
▶ *nm* GEOG delta.

demacrado,-a *adj (gen)* emaciated; *(cara)* haggard, drawn.

demagogia *nf* demagoguery, demagogy.

demagógico,-a *adj* demagogic, demagogical.

demagogo,-a *nm & nf* demagogue.

demanda *nf* 1 *(petición)* petition, request. 2 COM *(pedido de mercancías)* demand. 3 JUR lawsuit. [LOC] **en demanda de** asking for.

demandado,-a *nm & nf* defendant.

demandante *nm o nf* 1 JUR plaintiff. 2 *(persona que busca)* seeker, hunter. *(persona que compra)* buyer. [COMP] **demandante de empleo** job hunter.

demandar *vt* 1 *(pedir)* to request, ask for; *(desear)* to desire. 2 JUR to sue.

demarcar *vt* to demarcate.

demás *adj* other, rest of.

▶ *pron* the other, the rest: *los demás llegaron tarde* the others arrived late.
▶ *adv* besides, moreover. [LOC] **por lo demás** apart from that, otherwise. **todo lo demás** everything else.

demasiado,-a *adj (singular)* too much; *(plural)* too many.
▶ *adv (modificador de adjetivo)* too; *(modificador de verbo)* too much: *es demasiado gordo* he's too fat.

demencia *nf* 1 insanity, madness, dementia. 2 *fig (disparate)* silly thing. [COMP] **demencia senil** senile dementia.

demente *adj* mad, insane.
▶ *nm o nf* 1 *(persona enferma)* mental patient. 2 *(loco, chalado)* lunatic.

democracia *nf* democracy.

demócrata *nm o nf* democrat.

democrático,-a *adj* democratic.

demografía *nf* demography.

demográfico,-a *adj* demographic.

demoler *vt* to demolish, pull down, tear down.

demolición *nf* demolition.

demoniaco,-a *adj* demoniacal, demonic, possessed by the devil.

demonio *nm* demon, devil. [LOC] **¡demonios!** *fam* hell!, damn!

demora *nf* delay.

demorar *vt (retrasar)* to delay, hold up.
▶ *vpr* **demorarse** *(retrasarse)* to be delayed, be held up.

demostración *nf* 1 *(gen)* demonstration. 2 MAT proof.

demostrar *vt* 1 *(probar)* to prove, show. 2 *(hacer una demostración)* to demonstrate, show. 3 MAT to prove.

demostrativo,-a *adj* demonstrative.
▶ *nm* demonstrative.

denegar *vt (desestimar)* to refuse; *(negar)* to deny.

denigrante *adj* denigrating, disparaging.

denigrar *vt* 1 to denigrate, disparage, run down. 2 *(insultar)* to insult, revile.

denominación *nf* 1 *(acción)* denomination, naming. 2 *(nombre)* denomination, name. COMP **denominación de origen** *(vinos)* guarantee of origin.

denominador,-ra *adj* denominative.
▶ *nm* **denominador** MAT denominator.
COMP **mínimo común denominador** lowest common denominator.

denominar *vt* to denominate, name.

densidad *nf* **1** *(gen)* density. **2** *fig (espesura)* thickness, denseness. COMP **densidad de población** population density.

denso,-a *adj (gen)* dense; *(espeso)* dense, thick.

dentado,-a *adj* **1** *(con dientes)* toothed. **2** BOT dentate.

dentadura *nf* teeth *pl*, set of teeth. COMP **dentadura postiza** false teeth *pl*, dentures *pl*.

dental *adj* dental. COMP **cepillo dental** toothbrush.

dentellada *nf* **1** *(mordisco)* bite. **2** *(señal)* tooth mark.

dentera *nf fig (envidia)* envy. LOC **dar dentera a** ALGN **1** *(dar grima)* to set SB's teeth on edge. **2** *(dar envidia)* to make SB green with envy.

dentición *nf* **1** *(acción de dentar)* teething, dentition, cutting of the teeth. **2** *(época en que dentan los niños)* dentition.

dentífrico,-a *adj* tooth.
▶ *nm* **dentífrico** toothpaste. COMP **pasta dentífrica** toothpaste.

dentista *nm o nf* dentist. LOC **ir al dentista** to go to the dentist's.

dentro *adv* inside; *(de edificio)* indoors, inside: *está ahí dentro* it's in there. LOC **dentro de 1** *(lugar)* in, inside: *dentro de la casa* in the house; *dentro de una semana* in a week, in a week's time. **2** *(tiempo)* in. ▌**dentro de lo posible** as far as possible. ▌**dentro de poco** soon, shortly. ▌**por dentro 1** *(de una cosa)* (on the) inside. **2** *(de una persona)* deep down, inside, inwardly.

denuncia *nf* **1** *(acusación)* accusation, formal complaint, report. **2** JUR *(acción)* reporting; *(documento)* report. LOC **presentar una denuncia contra** ALGN to

lodge a complaint against SB, bring an action against SB, report SB.

denunciar *vt* **1** *(poner una denuncia)* to report. **2** *(dar noticia)* to denounce.

deparar *vt* **1** *(presentar)* to bring, hold in store: *nadie sabe lo que el destino nos deparará* nobody knows what fate holds in store for us. **2** *(proporcionar)* to give, afford.

departamento *nm* **1** *(sección)* department, section. **2** *(de tren)* compartment.

dependencia *nf* **1** *(hecho de depender)* dependence. **2** *(habitación)* room, outbuilding.

depender *vi* **1** to depend (de, on): *depende de ti* it's up to you. **2** *(estar bajo el mando o autoridad)* to be under, be answerable to; *(necesitar)* to be dependent on: *aún depende de sus padres* she's still dependent on her parents.

dependienta *nf* shop assistant, salesgirl, saleswoman.

dependiente *adj* dependent (de, on).
▶ *nm o nf* shop assistant, salesman.

depilación *nf* depilation, hair removal. LOC **depilación a la cera** waxing.

depilar *vt* to depilate, remove the hair from; *(cejas)* to pluck.

depilatorio,-a *adj* depilatory. COMP **crema depilatoria** hair-removing cream.

deplorable *adj* deplorable, regrettable.

deplorar *vt* to deplore, lament, regret deeply.

deponer *vt* **1** *(dejar)* to lay down, set aside. **2** *(destituir)* to remove from office; *(a un rey)* to depose.

deportación *nf* deportation.

deportar *vt* to deport.

deporte *nm* sport: *¿practicas algún deporte?* do you do any sport?, do you play any sport? LOC **hacer deporte** to do some sport.

deportista *adj* sporty, keen on sport.
▶ *nm o nf (hombre)* sportsman; *(mujer)* sportswoman.

deportividad *nf* sportsmanship.

deportivo,-a *adj* **1** *(aficionado al deporte)* sporting, sporty. **2** *(relacionado con el deporte)* sports: *club deportivo* sports club. **3** *(informal)* casual: *ropa deportiva* casual clothes.
▸ *nm* **deportivo** *(coche)* sports car.

depositar *vt* **1** *(dinero, joyas)* to deposit. **2** *(colocar)* to place, put. **3** *(sedimentar)* to deposit.
▸ *vpr* **depositarse** *(caer en el fondo)* to settle.

depositario,-a *nm & nf (de algo material)* depositary, trustee; *(de algo inmaterial)* repository.

depósito *nm* **1** *(recipiente)* tank. **2** *(almacén)* store, warehouse, depot. **3** *(sedimento)* deposit, sediment. LOC **en depósito** in bond. COMP **depósito de gasolina** petrol tank.

depreciar *vt* to depreciate.
▸ *vpr* **depreciarse** to depreciate.

depredador,-ra *adj* depredatory.
▸ *nm & nf* depredator, pillager.

depredar *vt* to depredate, pillage.

depresión *nf* depression: *depresión atmosférica* atmospheric depression. COMP **depresión nerviosa** nervous breakdown.

depresivo,-a *adj* **1** *(deprimente)* depressing. **2** MED depressive.

deprimente *adj* depressing.

deprimido,-a *adj* depressed.

deprimir *vt* to depress.
▸ *vpr* **deprimirse** to get depressed.

deprisa *adv* quickly.

depuración *nf (del agua)* purification; *(de la sangre)* cleansing.

depurador,-ra *adj* purifying.
▸ *nm* **depurador** *(sustancia)* depurative; *(aparato)* purifier.

depurar *vt* **1** *(purificar agua)* to purify, depurate; *(sangre)* to cleanse. **2** POL to purge. **3** *fig (perfeccionar)* to purify, refine.

derecha *nf* **1** *(mano)* right hand. **2** *(lugar)* right: *dame el de la derecha* give me the one on the right. **3 la derecha** POL the right, the right wing.

derechista *adj* right-wing, rightist.

derecho,-a *adj* **1** right: *la mano derecha* the right hand. **2** *(recto)* straight, upright.
▸ *adv* **derecho** straight: *se fue derecho a la cama* he went straight to bed.
▸ *nm* **derecho 1** *(leyes)* law. **2** *(privilegio)* right: *todos los niños tienen derecho a la enseñanza gratuita* all children have a right to free education. **3** *(de una tela, calcetín, etc)* right side.
▸ *nm pl* **derechos** *(impuestos)* duties, taxes; *(tarifa)* fees. LOC **¡no hay derecho!** it's not fair! **I tener derecho a** to be entitled to, have the right to. COMP **derecho civil** civil law. **I derecho de admisión** right *sing* to refuse admission. **I derechos de matrícula** registration fees. **I derechos humanos** human rights.

deriva *nf* drift. LOC **ir a la deriva** to drift.

derivada *nf* MAT derivative.

derivado,-a *adj* derived, derivative.
▸ *nm* **derivado 1** LING derivative. **2** *(subproducto)* derivative, byproduct.

derivar *vi* **1** *(proceder)* to spring, arise, come, stem. **2** MAR to drift. **3** LING to be derived (de, from), derive (de, from).
▸ *vt* **1** *(dirigir)* to direct, divert. **2** LING to derive. **3** MAT to derive.
▸ *vpr* **derivarse 1** *(proceder)* to result (de, from), stem (de, from). **2** LING to be derived (de, from).

dermatología *nf* dermatology.

dermatólogo,-a *nm & nf* dermatologist.

dérmico,-a *adj* dermal, dermic, skin.

dermis *nf inv* dermis.

dermoprotector,-ra *adj* which is kind to the skin.

derogar *vt* **1** JUR to abolish, repeal. **2** *(contrato)* to rescind, cancel.

derramar *vt* to pour out, spill.

derrame *nm* pouring out, spilling. COMP **derrame cerebral** MED brain haemorrhage.

derrapar *vi* to skid.

derredor *nm* surroundings *pl*. LOC **al/en derredor** round, around.

✎ Consulta también **alrededor**.

derretir *vt (gen)* to melt; *(hielo, nieve)* to melt, thaw; *(metal)* to melt down.
▶ *vpr* **derretirse** *(fundirse)* to melt; *(hielo, nieve)* to melt, thaw.

derribar *vt* **1** *(demoler)* to pull down, demolish, knock down. **2** *(hacer caer a una persona)* to knock over; *(de un caballo)* to throw.

derribo *nm (demolición)* demolition, knocking down, pulling down.

derrocar *vt* **1** *(demoler)* to pull down, demolish, knock down. **2** *(gobierno)* to overthrow, bring down.

derrochar *vt (dilapidar)* to waste, squander.

derroche *nm (despilfarro)* waste, squandering.

derrota *nm* **1** *(de un ejército)* defeat. **2** *(fracaso)* failure, setback.

derrotar *vt* to defeat, beat: *me derrotó al tenis* he beat me at tennis.

derruido,-a *adj* in ruins.

derruir *vt* to pull down, demolish, knock down.

derrumbar *vt (demoler)* to pull down, demolish, knock down.
▶ *vpr* **derrumbarse 1** *(un edificio)* to collapse, fall down; *(un techo)* to fall in, cave in. **2** *fig* to collapse.

desabotonar *vt (desabrochar)* to unbutton, undo.

desabrigar *vt (ropa)* to take someone's coat off.
▶ *vpr* **desabrigarse** *(uso reflexivo)* to take off one's coat.

desabrochar *vt* to undo, unfasten.
▶ *vpr* **desabrocharse** *(una prenda)* to come undone, come unfastened.

desacato *nm* **1** *(falta de respeto)* lack of respect (a, for), disrespect (a, for). **2** JUR contempt (a, for). LOC **desacato a la autoridad** contempt.

desacelerar *vi* to decelerate.

desaconsejar *vt* to advise against.

desacostumbrado,-a *adj* unusual, strange.

desacostumbrar *vt (hacer perder un uso)* to break of a habit, get out of a habit.
▶ *vpr* **desacostumbrarse** *(perder la costumbre)* to get out of the habit (de, of), lose the habit (de, of), give up (de, -).

desacreditar *vt* to discredit, bring discredit on, bring into discredit.

desactivar *vt* to defuse.

desacuerdo *nm* disagreement. LOC **estar en desacuerdo con** to be in disagreement with.

desafiar *vt* **1** *(gen)* to defy. **2** *(no hacer caso a)* to flout; *(no obedecer)* to defy. **3** *(plantar cara a - persona)* to defy, stand up to; *(- dificultad)* to brave. LOC **desafiar a ALGN a hacer ALGO** to challenge SB to do STH, dare SB to do STH.

desafilar *vt* to blunt.

desafinado,-a *adj* out of tune.

desafinar *vi (gen)* to be out of tune; *(cantar)* to sing out of tune; *(tocar)* to play out of tune.
▶ *vt* to put out of tune.

desafío *nm* **1** *(reto)* challenge. **2** *(provocación)* provocation, defiance.

desafortunadamente *adv* unfortunately.

desafortunado,-a *adj (sin suerte)* unlucky, unfortunate.

desagradable *adj* disagreeable, unpleasant.

desagradar *vi* to displease: *me desagrada su música* I don't like his music.

desagradecido,-a *adj* ungrateful.

desagrado *nm* displeasure, discontent. LOC **con desagrado** reluctantly.

desagraviar *vt (reparar el agravio)* to make amends for, make up for.

desagravio *nm* amends *pl*, compensation.

desagüe *nm* **1** *(acción)* draining, drainage. **2** *(cañería)* waste pipe, drainpipe.

desahogado,-a *adj* **1** *(espacioso)* roomy, spacious. **2** *(con dinero)* well-off, well-to-do, comfortable: *una posición desahogada* comfortable circumstances.

desahogar *vt* **1** *(consolar)* to comfort; *(aliviar)* to relieve. **2** *fig (mostrar)* to

D

vent, pour out: *desahogó sus penas* he vented his grief.

▶ *vpr* **desahogarse** *(desfogarse)* to let off steam: *¡desahógate!* don't bottle it up!

desahogo *nm* **1** *(alivio)* relief. **2** *fig (económico)* comfort, ease: *viven con desahogo* they live comfortably.

desahuciado,-a *adj* **1** *(enfermo)* hopeless. **2** *(inquilino)* evicted.

desahuciar *vt* **1** to deprive of all hope. **2** JUR *(inquilino)* to evict.

desahucio *nm* eviction.

desajuste *nm (mal funcionamiento)* maladjustment; *(avería)* breakdown.

desalar *vt* to desalt.

desalentador,-ra *adj* discouraging, disheartening.

desalentar *vt fig (quitar el ánimo)* to discourage, dishearten.

▶ *vpr* **desalentarse** get discouraged.

desaliento *nm* discouragement.

desalinear *vt* to put out of line.

desaliñado,-a *adj* untidy, unkempt, scruffy.

desalojar *vt* **1** *(marcharse)* to evacuate, clear, move out of. **2** *(inquilino)* to evict (de, from).

desamortización *nf* disentailment.

desamortizar *vt* to disentail.

desamparado,-a *adj (persona)* helpless, unprotected.

desamparar *vt* to abandon, desert, leave helpless.

desamparo *nm* **1** *(abandono)* abandonment, desertion. **2** *(falta de ayuda)* helplessness.

desandar *vt* to go back over, retrace.

desangrar *vt (sangrar)* to bleed.

▶ *vpr* **desangrarse** to bleed heavily, lose blood.

desanimado,-a *adj (decaído)* dejected, downhearted.

desanimar *vt* to discourage, dishearten.

▶ *vpr* **desanimarse** to be discouraged, be disheartened, lose heart.

desánimo *nm* despondency, discouragement, dejection.

desaparecer *vi (dejar de estar)* to disappear.

desaparecido,-a *adj* missing.

▶ *nm & nf* missing person: *había diez desaparecidos* there were ten missing.

desaparición *nf* disappearance.

desapasionado,-a *adj* dispassionate, objective, impartial.

desapego *nm* **1** *(indiferencia)* indifference. **2** *(falta de afecto)* coolness, lack of affection.

desapercibido,-a *adj (inadvertido)* unnoticed. LOC **pasar desapercibido,-a** to go unnoticed.

desaprensivo,-a *adj* unscrupulous.

▶ *nm & nf* unscrupulous person.

desaprobación *nf* disapproval.

desaprobar *vt* to disapprove of.

desaprovechado,-a *adj (desperdiciado)* wasted.

desaprovechar *vt* **1** *(no sacar suficiente provecho)* not to take advantage of. **2** *(desperdiciar)* to waste. LOC **desaprovechar una ocasión** to miss an opportunity, waste an opportunity.

desarmado,-a *adj* **1** *(sin armas)* unarmed. **2** *(desmontado)* dismantled, taken to pieces.

desarmar *vt* **1** *(quitar las armas)* to disarm. **2** *(desmontar)* to dismantle, take apart, take to pieces: *el mecánico desmontó el motor* the mechanic stripped the engine down.

desarme *nm* disarmament. COMP **desarme nuclear** nuclear disarmament.

desarraigado,-a *adj fig (persona)* rootless, without roots, uprooted.

desarraigar *vt (árbol, persona)* to uproot.

▶ *vpr* **desarraigarse** *fig (persona)* to pull up one's roots.

desarraigo *nm (de árbol, persona)* uprooting.

desarreglar *vt (desordenar)* make untidy, mess up, untidy.

desarrollado,-a *adj* developed: *es un país desarrollado* it's a developed country.

desarrollar *vt* **1** *(gen)* to develop. *(deshacer un rollo)* to unroll, unfold. **2** *(exponer)* to expound, explain. **3** *(llevar a cabo)* to carry out: *desarrollar un proyecto* to carry out a project. **4** MAT to expand, develop.
▶ *vpr* **desarrollarse** *(crecer)* to develop.

desarrollo *nm* **1** *(gen)* development. **2** MAT expansion.

desarticulado,-a *adj* disjointed.

desarticular *vt* **1** MED to disarticulate, put out of joint, dislocate. **2** *(un mecanismo)* to take to pieces.

desaseado,-a *adj* **1** *(sucio)* untidy, dirty. **2** *(dejado)* untidy, slovenly, unkempt, scruffy.

desasosegado,-a *adj* restless, anxious.

desasosegar *vt* to make restless, make uneasy.
▶ *vpr* **desasosegarse** to become restless, become uneasy.

desasosiego *nm* uneasiness, anxiety, restlessness.

desastrado,-a *adj* *(desaseado)* untidy, slovenly, unkempt, scruffy.

desastre *nm* **1** *(catástrofe)* disaster, catastrophe. **2** *fam (calamidad)* disaster, flop: *la excursión fue un desastre* the trip was a washout.

desastroso,-a *adj* disastrous.

desatar *vt* **1** *(soltar - gen)* to untie, undo, unfasten; *(- perro, etc)* to let loose: *desata al perro* let the dog loose. **2** *fig (desencadenar)* to spark off, give rise to; *(pasiones)* to unleash.
▶ *vpr* **desatarse 1** *(soltarse)* to come untied, come undone, come unfastened. **2** *fig (desencadenarse)* to break, explode: *se desató una gran tormenta* a great storm broke.

desatascador *nm* plunger.

desatascar *vt* to unblock, clear.

desatender *vt* *(no prestar atención)* to pay no attention to.

desatento,-a *adj (descortés)* discourteous, impolite.
▶ *nm & nf (descortés)* impolite person, discourteous person.

desatornillar *vt* to unscrew.

desautorización *nf* disapproval.

desautorizado,-a *adj* unauthorized.

desautorizar *vt* **1** *(desaprobar)* to disapprove. **2** *(prohibir)* to ban, forbid: *el gobierno desautorizó la manifestación* the Government banned the demonstration.

desavenencia *nf (desacuerdo)* disagreement, discord.

desavenir *vt* to cause to quarrel.
▶ *vpr* **desavenirse** to quarrel.

desayunar *vi* to have breakfast, breakfast.
▶ *vt* to have for breakfast.

desayuno *nm* breakfast.

desazón *nf fig (disgusto)* grief, affliction, worry.

desazonado,-a *adj* **1** *fig (disgustado)* upset. **2** *fig (inquieto)* anxious, uneasy.

desazonar *vt* **1** *fig (disgustar)* to annoy, upset. **2** *fig (inquietar)* to make uneasy, worry.
▶ *vpr* **desazonarse 1** *fig (disgustarse)* to get upset. **2** *fig (inquietarse)* to worry.

desbandada *nf* scattering.

desbandarse *vpr* to scatter, disperse.

desbaratar *vt (frustrar)* to spoil, ruin: *nos desbarató los planes* she spoilt our plans.

desbloquear *vt* **1** TÉC to free. **2** FIN to unfreeze.

desbloqueo *nm* **1** TÉC freeing. **2** FIN unfreezing.

desbocado,-a *adj (caballo)* runaway.

desbocar *vi (desembocar)* to flow (en, into).
▶ *vpr* **desbocarse** *(caballo)* to run away, bolt.

desbordar *vt* **1** *(sobrepasar)* to overflow. **2** *fig (exceder)* to surpass, exceed: *eso desborda mis conocimientos* that's way over my head.
▶ *vi (salirse)* to overflow: *el río desbordó* the river overflowed.
▶ *vpr* **desbordarse 1** *(salirse)* to overflow, flood. **2** *fig* to burst.

desbrozar *vt (terreno)* to clear of weeds, clear of undergrowth.

descabalgar *vi* to dismount.

descabellado,-a *adj fig* wild, crazy: *una idea descabellada* a crackpot idea.

descacharrar *vt fam (romper)* to break; *(estropear)* to ruin, mess up, spoil.

descafeinado,-a *adj* decaffeinated.
▶ *nm* **descafeinado** decaffeinated coffee.

descalabrar *vt (herir)* to injure; *(en la cabeza)* to injure in the head.
▶ *vpr* **descalabrarse** to injure one's head.

descalabro *nm* misfortune, damage, loss.

descalcificación *nf* decalcification.

descalcificar *vt* to decalcify.

descalificación *nf* **1** disqualification. **2** *(descrédito)* discredit.

descalificar *vt* **1** to disqualify. **2** *(desacreditar)* to discredit.

descalzar *vt (zapatos)* to take off SB's shoes.
▶ *vpr* **descalzarse** to take off one's shoes.

descalzo,-a *adj* barefoot, barefooted.

descamación *nf* desquamation.

descamarse *vpr* to desquamate.

descampado,-a *nm* open space, open field.

descansado,-a *adj* **1** rested, refreshed. **2** *(tranquilo)* easy, effortless.

descansar *vi* **1** *(gen)* to rest, have a rest; *(un momento)* to take a break. **2** *(dormir)* to sleep: *¡que descanses!* sleep well!

descansillo *nm* landing.

descanso *nm* **1** rest, break. **2** *(en un espectáculo)* interval; *(en un partido)* interval, half-time. **3** *(alivio)* relief, comfort: *¡qué descanso!* what a relief! **4** *(rellano)* landing.

descapitalizar *vt (perder el capital)* to undercapitalize.

descapotable *adj* convertible.
▶ *nm* convertible.

descarado,-a *adj (actitud)* shameless, brazen, insolent; *(persona)* cheeky.
▶ *nm & nf* shameless person, cheeky person.

descarga *nf* **1** *(acción)* unloading. **2** *(eléctrica)* discharge. **3** INFORM download.

descargar *vt* **1** *(disparar una arma)* to fire, discharge, shoot; *(vaciar una arma)* to unload. **2** INFORM to download.
▶ *vi (tormenta)* to break; *(nubes)* to burst.
▶ *vpr* **descargarse** *(pilas, baterías)* to discharge.

descargo *nm (descarga)* unloading.

descaro *nm* impudence, cheek, nerve.
LOC *¡qué descaro!* what a cheek!

descarriado,-a *adj fig* lost. LOC ser la oveja descarriada *fig* to be the lost sheep.

descarriar *vt* **1** *(apartar del camino)* to send the wrong way, put on the wrong road, misdirect. **2** *fig* to lead astray.
▶ *vpr* **descarriarse** **1** *(perderse)* to lose one's way, get lost, go the wrong way. **2** *fig* to go astray.

descarrilar *vi* to be derailed, run off the rails, go off the rails .

descartar *vt* to discard, reject, rule out: *descartamos esa posibilidad* we ruled out that possibility.

descastado,-a *adj (poco cariñoso)* unaffectionate, cold.
▶ *nm & nf (poco cariñoso)* unaffectionate person.

descendencia *nf* offspring, descendants *pl.*

descender *vi* **1** to descend, go down, come down. **2** *(temperatura, nivel, etc)* to drop, fall, go down. **3** *(ser descendiente)* to descend (de, from), issue (de, from).
▶ *vt (bajar)* to go down: *descendió la escalera muy rápidamente* he went down the stairs very quickly.

descendiente *nm o nf* descendant; *(hijos)* offspring.

descenso *nm* **1** *(acción)* descent, lowering. **2** *(de temperatura)* drop, fall. **3** *fig (declive)* decline, fall. **4** DEP *(de división)* relegation.

descentralización *nf* decentraliza-
tion.

descentralizar *vt* to decentralize.

descentrar *vt fig* to disorientate,
throw, put off.
▶ *vpr* **descentrarse** *fig* to become dis-
orientated.

descifrar *vt* **1** to decipher, decode. **2**
fig (llegar a comprender) to solve, figure
out.

desclavar *vt (desprender)* to take off.

descodificar *vt* to decode.

descolgar *vt* **1** *(cuadro, etc)* to take
down. **2** *(bajar)* to lower, let down. **3**
(el teléfono) to pick up, lift: *dejó el teléfono descolgado* she left the telephone off
the hook.

descollar *vi* to stand out, excel.

descolonización *nf* decolonization.

descolonizar *vt* to decolonize.

descolorar *vt* to discolour (US discolor), fade.

descolorido,-a *adj* discoloured (US
discolored), faded.

descombro *nm* clearing.

descompensar *vt* to unbalance, upset, throw out of kilter.

descomponer *vt* **1** *(separar)* to break
down, split up. **2** *(estropear)* to break.
3 FÍS to resolve. **4** QUÍM to decompose. **5** MAT to split up. **6** *fig (molestar)*
to disturb, upset; *(irritar)* irritate. **7**
(pudrir) to rot.
▶ *vpr* **descomponerse 1** *(pudrirse)* to decompose, rot. **2** *(estropearse)* to break
down. **3** FÍS to resolve. **4** QUÍM to decompose. **5** MAT to split.

descomposición *nf* **1** *(pudrimiento)* de-
composition, decay. **2** *fam (diarrea)*
diarrhoea (US diarrhea).

descompresión *nf* decompression.

descomprimir *vt* to decompress, de-
pressurize.

descompuesto,-a *adj* **1** *(podrido)* de-
composed, decayed, rotten. **2** *(estropeado)* out of order, broken down. **3**
fig (alterado) upset. LOC **estar
descompuesto,-a** to have diarrhoea
(US diarrhea).

descomunal *adj* huge, enormous.

desconcertado,-a *adj* disconcerted,
confused, upset.

desconcertante *adj* disconcerting,
upsetting.

desconcertar *vt (perturbar)* to discon-
cert, upset, disturb.
▶ *vpr* **desconcertarse** *(perturbarse)* to be
disconcerted.

desconchado,-a *nm (pared)* flaking,
peeling; *(loza)* chipping.

desconchar *vt (pared)* to peel off,
flake; *(loza)* to chip.
▶ *vpr* **desconcharse** to peel off, flake
off; *(loza)* to chip.

desconchón *nm (en pared)* bare patch.

desconcierto *nm* disorder, confusion,
chaos.

desconectado,-a *adj fig* cut off (de,
from).

desconectar *vt* **1** ELEC to disconnect. **2**
(un aparato) to switch off, turn off. **3**
(desenchufar) to unplug. **4** *fam fig* to
turn off, switch off.

desconexión *nf* disconnection.

desconfiado,-a *adj* distrustful, suspicious, wary.
▶ *nm & nf* distrustful person, suspicious person, wary person.

desconfianza *nf* distrust, mistrust,
suspicion.

desconfiar *vi* **1** *(faltar la confianza)* to
distrust (de, -), mistrust (de, -), be
suspicious (de, of). **2** *(tener cuidado)* to
beware (de, of).

descongelar *vt* **1** *(comida)* to thaw,
thaw out. **2** *(nevera)* to defrost.

descongestión *nf (nasal)* unblocking,
clearing, decongestion.

descongestionar *vt* to clear.

desconocer *vt* not to know, be unaware of: *desconozco su nombre* I don't
know her name.

desconocido,-a *adj* **1** *(no conocido)* unknown. **2** *(extraño)* strange, unfamiliar.
▶ *nm & nf* stranger, unknown person.
▶ *nm* **lo desconocido** the unknown.

desconocimiento *nm* ignorance (de, of).

desconsideración *nf* thoughtlessness .

desconsiderado,-a *adj* thoughtless.
▶ *nm & nf* thoughtless person.

desconsolado,-a *adj* disconsolate, grief-stricken, inconsolable.

desconsolar *vt* to distress, grieve.

desconsuelo *nm* affliction.

descontar *vt (restar)* to deduct, take off, knock off.

descontento,-a *adj* displeased, unhappy, dissatisfied, discontented.
▶ *nm & nf* malcontent.

descontrol *nm fam* lack of control, chaos.

descontrolado,-a *adj* 1 uncontrolled, out of control. 2 *fam fig* out of control, wild.

descontrolarse *vpr (persona)* to lose control.

desconvocar *vt* to cancel, call off.

descorazonador,-ra *adj* disheartening, discouraging.

descorazonar *vt* to dishearten, discourage.
▶ *vpr* **descorazonarse** to lose heart, get discouraged.

descorchar *vt* to uncork.

descorrer *vt (cortinas)* to draw; *(cerrojo)* to unbolt.

descortés *adj* impolite, rude, discourteous.

descortesía *nf* impoliteness, rudeness, discourtesy.

descoser *vt* to unpick.
▶ *vpr* **descoserse** to come unstitched.

descosido,-a *nm* open seam.

descoyuntar *vt* 1 *(hueso)* to dislocate, disjoint. 2 *fig (cansar)* to exhaust, tire out.
▶ *vpr* **descoyuntarse** to become dislocated. LOC **descoyuntarse de risa** *fam* to split one's sides laughing.

descreído,-a *adj* disbelieving, unbelieving.
▶ *nm & nf* disbeliever, unbeliever.

descremado,-a *adj* skimmed. COMP **yogur descremado** low-fat yoghurt.

describir *vt* to describe.

descripción *nf* description.

descriptivo,-a *adj* descriptive.

descrito,-a *adj* described.

descuartizar *vt (persona)* to quarter; *(animal)* to quarter, cut up.

descubierto,-a *adj* open, uncovered: *el cielo está descubierto* the sky is clear.

descubrimiento *nm* discovery.

descubrir *vt* 1 *(gen)* to discover; *(petróleo, oro, minas)* to find; *(conspiración)* to uncover; *(crimen)* to bring to light. 2 *(averiguar)* to find out, discover: *descubrimos sus intenciones* we found out his intentions.
▶ *vpr* **descubrirse** *(la cabeza)* to take off one's hat.

descuento *nm* 1 discount, reduction, deduction. 2 DEP injury time. LOC **con descuento** at a discount, on offer.

descuidado,-a *adj* 1 *(negligente)* careless, negligent. 2 *(desprevenido)* unprepared.

descuidar *vt* 1 to neglect, overlook. 2 *(distraer)* to distract.
▶ *vpr* **descuidarse** *(no tener cuidado)* to be careless. LOC **¡descuida!** don't worry!

descuido *nm* 1 *(negligencia)* negligence, carelessness, neglect. 2 *(distracción)* oversight, slip, mistake. LOC **por descuido** inadvertently, by mistake.

desde *prep* 1 *(tiempo)* since: *desde 1992* since 1992. 2 *(lugar)* from: *desde allí* from there. LOC **desde ahora** from now on. ‖ **desde luego** 1 *(en realidad)* really. 2 *(como respuesta)* of course, certainly.

desdentado,-a *adj* toothless.

desdibujar *vt* to blur.
▶ *vpr* **desdibujarse** to become blurred, become faint.

desdicha *nf* misfortune, misery, adversity.

desdichado,-a *adj* unfortunate, wretched, unlucky.

desdoblar *vt* to unfold.

desdramatizar *vt* to make less traumatic, play down.

deseado,-a *adj* desired: *en el momento deseado* at the right time.

desear *vt* **1** *(querer)* to want: *deseo que venga* I want him to come. **2** *(anhelar)* to long for, wish for, desire; *(para alguien)* to wish: *¿qué desea?* can I help you?, what can I do for you?

desecar *vt* **1** *(gen)* to dry up. **2** *(pantano, laguna, etc)* to drain.
► *vpr* **desecarse** to dry up.

desechable *adj* disposable.

desechar *vt* **1** *(tirar)* to discard, throw out, throw away. **2** *(rechazar)* to refuse, reject; *(proyecto, idea)* to drop, discard.

desecho *nm (residuo)* reject.
► *nm pl* **desechos** waste *sing*, rubbish *sing*.

desembalar *vt* to unpack.

desembarazar *vt (dejar libre)* to free.
► *vpr* **desembarazarse** *(librarse)* to rid os (de, of), get rid (de, of).

desembarcar *vi* to disembark, land, go ashore.
► *vt (mercancías)* to unload; *(personas)* to disembark, put ashore.

desembarco *nm (mercancías)* landing, unloading; *(personas)* disembarkation, landing.

desembocadura *nf (de río)* mouth, outlet.

desembocar *vi* **1** *(río)* to flow (en, into). **2** *(calle)* to end (en, at), lead (en, into).

desembolso *nm (gasto)* expense, outlay, expenditure.

desembozar *vt fig* to uncover, bring out into the open.

desembrujar *vt* to remove a spell from.

desembuchar *vi* to come clean, spill the beans: *¡desembucha de una vez!* come out with it once and for all!

desempañar *vt* to wipe the steam from, demist.

desempaquetar *vt* to unpack, unwrap.

desemparejar *vt* to separate.

desempatar *vt* to break a tie between.
► *vi* DEP *(desempatar un resultado)* to break the deadlock.

desempate *nm* **1** tie-break, tiebreaker. **2** DEP play-off, tie-break. COMP **partido de desempate** play off, deciding match.

desempeñar *vt* **1** *(cumplir una obligación)* to discharge, fulfil (US fulfill), carry out; *(un cargo)* to fill, hold, occupy. **2** *(papel)* to play: *desempeña un papel vital* she plays a vital role.

desempeño *nm* **1** *(obligaciones, cargo)* carrying out, fulfilment (US fulfillment). **2** TEAT performance, acting.

desempleado,-a *adj* unemployed, out of work.
► *nm & nf* unemployed person.

desempleo *nm* unemployment. LOC **cobrar el desempleo** to be on the dole, (US be on welfare).

desempolvar *vt* **1** *(quitar el polvo)* to dust. **2** *fig (volver a usar)* to unearth.

desencadenar *vt fig (producir)* to spark off, give rise to.
► *vpr* **desencadenarse** **1** *(desatarse)* to break loose. **2** *(guerra, tormenta)* to break out: *se desencadenó una tormenta* a storm broke. **3** *(acontecimientos)* to start.

desencajar *vt (desunir)* to take apart, disjoint.
► *vpr* **desencajarse** *(desunirse)* to come apart, come loose.

desencallar *vt* to refloat.

desencantar *vt (desilusionar)* to disillusion, disappoint.
► *vpr* **desencantarse** to be disappointed, be disillusioned.

desencanto *nm (desilusión)* disillusionment, disappointment.

desenchufar *vt* to unplug, disconnect.

desencolar *vt* to unglue, unstick.
► *vpr* **desencolarse** to come unglued, come unstuck.

desencuadernar *vt* to unbind.
► *vpr* **desencuadernarse** to come unbound.

desenfadado,-a *adj* **1** *(despreocupado)* free and easy, carefree. **2** *(ropa)* casual.

desenfadar *vt* to calm down.
▸ *vpr* **desenfadarse** to calm down.

desenfado *nm* **1** *(soltura)* self-confidence, assurance. **2** *(franqueza)* frankness, openness.

desenfocado,-a *adj* out of focus.

desenfocar *vt* to take out of focus.

desenfoque *nm* incorrect focusing.

desenfrenado,-a *adj (gen)* frantic, uncontrolled, wild.

desenfreno *nm (falta de control)* lack of control, wild abandon.

desenfundar *vt (quitar)* to draw out, pull out.

desenganchar *vt (gen)* to unhook, unfasten; *(despegar)* to unstick.

desengañado,-a *adj* **1** *(desilusionado)* disillusioned. **2** *(decepcionado)* disappointed, let down.

desengañar *vt* **1** *(decepcionar)* to disappoint. **2** *(desilusionar)* to disillusion.
▸ *vpr* **desengañarse 1** *(ver la verdad)* to have one's eyes opened (de, about). **2** *(tener una decepción)* to be disappointed.

desengaño *nm (desilusión)* disillusion; *(decepción)* disappointment. LOC **sufrir un desengaño** to be disappointed.

desengrasar *vt* to remove the grease from.

desenhebrar *vt* to unthread.

desenjaular *vt* to let out of a cage, release.

desenlace *nm* **1** *(resultado)* outcome, result. **2** *(final)* end.

desenlazar *vt (desatar)* to untie, undo.

desenmarañar *vt* **1** *(desenredar)* to untangle, unravel. **2** *fig (poner en claro)* to unravel, clear up; *(un asunto)* to sort out.

desenmascarar *vt* to unmask.

desenredar *vt* to untangle, disentangle.
▸ *vpr* **desenredarse** to get out (de, of), extricate OS (de, from).

desenrollar *vt* to unroll, unwind.

desenroscar *vt* to unscrew, uncoil.

desentenderse *vpr (afectar ignorancia)* to pretend not to know (de, -/about), ignore (de, -), feign ignorance (de, of): *se desentiende de mí* she ignores me.

desenterrar *vt (un objeto)* to unearth, dig up; *(cadáver)* to disinter, exhume.

desentonar *vi* **1** MÚS *(instrumento)* to be out of tune; *(cantante)* to sing out of tune. **2** *fig (combinar)* not to match (con, -).

desentrenado,-a *adj* out of training.

desentrenarse *vpr* to be out of training, get out of training.

desenvainar *vt* to unsheathe, draw.

desenvoltura *nf fig (soltura)* confidence, assurance.

desenvolver *vt* **1** *(quitar lo que envuelve)* to unwrap. **2** *(aclarar)* to clear up.
▸ *vpr* **desenvolverse** *(manejarse)* to manage, cope: *se desenvuelve muy bien en los negocios* he manages very well in business.

desenvuelto,-a *adj (seguro)* confident, self-assured.

deseo *nm* wish, desire. LOC **formular un deseo** to make a wish. COMP **buenos deseos** good intentions.

deseoso,-a *adj* desirous, eager, anxious. LOC **estar deseoso,-a de hacer** ALGO to be eager to do STH.

desequilibrado,-a *adj* **1** unbalanced, out of balance. **2** *(persona)* mentally unbalanced.

desequilibrar *vt* **1** to unbalance, throw off balance. **2** *fig* to unbalance.
▸ *vpr* **desequilibrarse** *fig* to become unbalanced.

desequilibrio *nm* **1** lack of balance, imbalance. **2** *fig (mental)* unbalanced state of mind.

desertar *vi* **1** MIL to desert. **2** *fig (abandonar)* to abandon, desert.

desértico,-a *adj* desert.

desertización *nf* desertification.

desertor,-ra *nm & nf* deserter.

desesperación *nf* despair, desperation.

desesperadamente *adv* desperately, frantically.

desesperado,-a *adj (sin esperanza)* hopeless, desperate.

desesperanza *nf* despair, desperation, hopelessness.

desesperanzar *vt* to drive to despair.
▶ *vpr* **desesperanzarse** to despair, lose hope, give up hope (de, of).

desesperar *vt* **1** *(hacer perder la paciencia)* to drive to despair. **2** *(exasperar)* to exasperate.
▶ *vpr* **desesperarse 1** *(desesperanzar)* to lose hope, despair. **2** *(irritarse)* to get irritated, become exasperated: *se desespera por todo* everything exasperates her.

desestabilización *nf* destabilization.

desestabilizar *vt* to destabilize.

desestimar *vt* to disregard, underestimate.

desfachatez *nf* cheek, nerve.

desfalco *nm* embezzlement.

desfallecer *vt (disminuir las fuerzas)* to weaken.
▶ *vi* **1** *(debilitar)* to weaken, lose strength. **2** *(decaer)* to lose heart.

desfallecido,-a *adj* weak, faint.

desfallecimiento *nm* faintness.

desfasado,-a *adj* outdated, out of date; *(persona)* old-fashioned, behind the times.

desfasar *vt* TÉC to phase out.
▶ *vpr* **desfasarse 1** TÉC to change phase. **2** *(persona)* to be out of synch.

desfase *nm* **1** *(diferencia)* imbalance, gap. **2** TÉC phase difference. COMP **desfase horario 1** *(entre países)* time difference. **2** *(al volar en avión)* jet lag.

desfavorable *adj* unfavourable (US unfavorable).

desfavorecer *vt (perjudicar)* to disadvantage, put at a disadvantage.

desfigurado,-a *adj (persona)* disfigured.

desfigurar *vt (cara)* to disfigure.
▶ *vpr* **desfigurarse** *(descomponerse)* to become distorted.

desfiladero *nm* defile, gorge, narrow pass.

desfilar *vi* **1** *(gen)* to march. **2** MIL to march, march past, parade. **3** *(moda)* to parade, walk up and down.

desfile *nm* **1** *(gen)* parade, procession. **2** MIL parade. **3** *(moda)* fashion show.

desfogar *vt (descargar)* to give vent to, vent.
▶ *vpr* **desfogarse** to let off steam, vent one's anger.

desgajar *vt* **1** *(rama)* to tear off; *(página)* to rip out, tear out. **2** *(romper)* to break.

desgana *nf (inapetencia)* lack of appetite. LOC **con desgana** reluctantly.

desganado,-a *adj* **1** *(sin gana)* not hungry: *está desganado* he has no appetite. **2** *(apático)* apathetic, half-hearted.

desganar *vt* **1** *(quitar el apetito)* to spoil the appetite of. **2** *(quitar las ganas)* to turn off.
▶ *vpr* **desganarse 1** *(perder el apetito)* to lose one's appetite. **2** *(perder el interés)* to lose interest (de, in), go off (de, -).

desgañitarse *vpr fam* to shout os hoarse, shout one's head off.

desgarbado,-a *adj* ungainly, ungraceful, clumsy.

desgarrador,-ra *adj* heartbreaking, heart-rending.

desgarrar *vt (rasgar)* to tear, rip.
▶ *vpr* **desgarrarse** *(rasgarse)* to tear, rip.

desgarro *nm (rompimiento)* tear, rip.

desgastar *vt (ropa)* to wear out, wear away; *(tacones)* to wear down.
▶ *vpr* **desgastarse** *(gastarse)* to wear out, get worn.

desgaste *nm (gen)* wear.

desglosar *vt* **1** *(escrito)* to detach. **2** *(gastos)* to break down.

desglose *nm* breakdown, separation.

desgracia *nf* **1** *(desdicha)* misfortune. **2** *(mala suerte)* bad luck, mischance. LOC **por desgracia** unfortunately.

desgraciado,-a *adj* **1** *(sin suerte)* unfortunate, unlucky. **2** *(infeliz)* unhappy.
▶ *nm & nf* wretch, unfortunate person.

desgraciar *vt (echar a perder)* to spoil.
▶ *vpr* **desgraciarse** *(malograrse)* to fail, be spoiled; *(plan, proyecto)* to fall through.

desgranar *vt (guisante, maíz)* to shell; *(trigo)* to thresh.

desgravar *vt* to deduct.

desguace *nm* **1** *(de barco)* breaking up; *(coche)* car breaking, scrapping. **2** *(lugar)* breaker's yard, scrapyard.

desguazar *vt (barco)* to break up; *(coche)* to scrap.

deshabitado,-a *adj (pueblo, lugar)* uninhabited; *(casa, piso)* unoccupied.

deshabitar *vt* to leave, abandon, vacate.

deshabituar *vt (hacer perder el hábito)* to break from the habit.
▶ *vpr* **deshabituarse** to get out of the habit (a, of), give up (a, -).

deshacer *vt* **1** *(estropear)* to ruin, damage; *(romper)* to break; *(desordenar)* to upset. **2** *(nudo)* to untie, loosen; *(paquete)* to undo, unwrap; *(cama)* to strip; *(equipaje)* to unpack; *(puntadas)* to unpick. **3** *(romper un acuerdo)* to break off. **4** *(disolver)* to dissolve; *(derretir)* to melt. **5** *(desandar)* to retrace. **6** *(planes, proyectos)* to spoil, ruin.
▶ *vpr* **deshacerse 1** *(nudo)* to come undone, come untied; *(puntada)* to come unsewn. **2** *(disolverse)* to dissolve; *(derretirse)* to melt.

desharrapado,-a *adj* ragged, in tatters.

deshecho,-a *adj* **1** *(destruido)* destroyed. **2** *(estropeado)* damaged, ruined. **3** *(nudo)* untied, undone; *(paquete)* unwrapped; *(cama)* unmade; *(equipaje)* unpacked. **4** *(disuelto)* dissolved; *(derretido)* melted.

deshelar *vt* **1** to thaw, melt. **2** *(congelador)* to defrost. **3** *(coche)* to de-ice.
▶ *vpr* **deshelarse** to thaw out, melt.

desherbar *vt* to weed.

desheredar *vt* to disinherit.

deshidratación *nf* dehydration.

deshidratado,-a *adj* dehydrated.

deshidratar *vt* to dehydrate.
▶ *vpr* **deshidratarse** to become dehydrated.

deshielo *nm* thaw; *(de congelador)* defrosting; *(de parabrisas)* de-icing.

deshilachado,-a *adj* frayed.

deshilachar *vt* to fray.

deshilvanar *vt* to untack.

deshinchado,-a *adj* **1** *(neumático, etc)* flat, deflated. **2** *(sin hinchazón)* not swollen: *la rodilla ya la tienes deshinchada* the swelling in your knee has gone down.

deshinchar *vt* **1** *(neumático, etc)* to deflate, let down. **2** *(reducir la hinchazón)* to reduce the swelling of.
▶ *vpr* **deshincharse 1** to deflate, go down. **2** *(reducirse la hinchazón)* to go down.

deshojar *vt (flor)* to strip the petals off; *(árbol)* to strip the leaves off.
▶ *vpr* **deshojarse** *(flor)* to lose its petals; *(árbol)* to lose its leaves.

deshollinador *nm* chimney sweep.

deshollinar *vt* to sweep.

deshonestidad *nf (sin honestidad)* dishonesty.

deshonesto,-a *adj (sin honestidad)* dishonest.

deshonra *nf* dishonour (US dishonor), disgrace.

deshonrar *vt (gen)* to dishonour (US dishonor), disgrace.

deshonroso,-a *adj* dishonourable (US dishonorable).

desidia *nf* negligence.

desierto,-a *adj (sin habitantes)* uninhabited, deserted: *una isla desierta* a desert island.
▶ *nm* **desierto** desert.

designar *vt* **1** *(denominar)* to designate. **2** *(nombrar para un cargo)* to appoint, name, assign.

desigual *adj* **1** *(gen)* unequal, uneven. **2** *(diferente)* different, unequal. **3** *(irregular)* uneven, irregular. **4** *(no liso)* uneven, rough. **5** *(variable)* changeable *tiene un carácter muy desigual* she is very changeable.

desigualdad *nf (gen)* inequality, difference.

desilusión *nf* disappointment.

desilusionar *vt* to disappoint.
  ▶ *vpr* **desilusionarse** to be disappointed.

desincrustar *vt* to descale.

desinencia *nf* ending, desinence.

desinfectante *adj* disinfectant.
  ▶ *nm* disinfectant.

desinfectar *vt* to disinfect.

desinflamar *vt* to reduce the inflammation in.
  ▶ *vpr* **desinflamarse** to go down.

desinflar *vt (gen)* to deflate; *(una rueda)* to let down.
  ▶ *vpr* **desinflarse** to go down.

desinformar *vi* to misinform.

desinsectar *vt* to fumigate.

desintegrar *vt* **1** to disintegrate. **2** *fig* to disintegrate, break up. **3** FÍS to split.
  ▶ *vpr* **desintegrarse 1** to disintegrate. **2** *fig* to break up. **3** FÍS to split.

desinterés *nm (falta de interés)* lack of interest, indifference.

desinteresarse *vpr* **1** *(perder el interés)* to lose interest (de, in), go off (de, -). **2** *(desentenderse)* to have nothing to do (de, with).

desintoxicación *nf* detoxication.

desintoxicar *vt* to detoxicate.

desistir *vi (gen)* to desist, give up.

deslavar *vt* to half-wash.

desleal *adj* disloyal.

deslealtad *nf* disloyalty.

deslenguado,-a *adj fig (descarado)* insolent, cheeky.

desligar *vt* **1** *(desatar)* to untie, unfasten. **2** *fig (separar)* to separate (de, from). **3** *fig (librar de una obligación)* to release (de, from), free (de, from).
  ▶ *vpr* **desligarse 1** *(desatarse)* to break away (de, from). **2** *(librarse)* to release OS (de, from), free OS (de, from).

deslindar *vt* to delimit, mark the boundaries of.

desliz *nm* **1** *(resbalón)* slide, slip. **2** *fig (error)* slip, mistake error. LOC **tener un desliz** *fig* to slip up, make a slip.

deslizamiento *nm* slipping, slip. COMP **deslizamiento de tierra** landslide.

deslizar *vt (pasar)* to slide, slip.
  ▶ *vi (resbalar)* to slide, slip.
  ▶ *vpr* **deslizarse** *(gen)* to slide; *(sobre agua)* to glide.

deslucir *vt fig (quitar la gracia)* to mar, spoil.

deslumbrar *vt* to dazzle.

deslustrar *vt (metal)* to tarnish.

desmadejar *vt fig* to tire out, exhaust.

desmagnetizar *vt* to demagnetize.

desmantelar *vt* to dismantle.

desmaquillar *vt* to remove make-up from.
  ▶ *vpr* **desmaquillarse** to remove one's make-up.

desmarcarse *vpr* **1** DEP to get into an unmarked position. **2** *(distanciarse)* to distance OS (de, from), disassociate OS (de, from) .

desmayar *vt (causar desmayo)* to make faint.
  ▶ *vpr* **desmayarse** *(perder el sentido)* to faint.

desmayo *nm (pérdida del conocimiento)* faint, fainting fit. LOC **sufrir/tener un desmayo** to faint.

desmejorar *vt* to spoil, make worse, damage.
  ▶ *vi* to deteriorate, get worse, go downhill.
  ▶ *vpr* **desmejorarse** to deteriorate, get worse, go downhill.

desmelenar *vt (desgreñar)* to tousle, dishevel.
  ▶ *vpr* **desmelenarse** *fam (desmadrarse)* to let one's hair down.

desmemoriado,-a *adj* forgetful, absent-minded.

desmentir *vt* **1** *(negar)* to deny. **2** *(contradecir)* to contradict, belie.

desmenuzar *vt (gen)* to break into little pieces.

desmirriado,-a *adj fam* weedy, puny.

desmitificar *vt* to demystify.

desmoldar *vt* to remove from a mould, turn out.

desmontable *adj* that can be taken to pieces.

desmontar *vt* **1** *(desarmar)* to take to pieces, take down, dismantle. **2** *(motor)* to strip.
▸ *vi (del caballo)* to dismount (de, -).

desmoralizar *vt* to demoralize.
▸ *vpr* **desmoralizarse** to become demoralized.

desmoronamiento *nm* crumbling, disintegration, fall.

desmoronar *vt* to crumble, destroy.
▸ *vpr* **desmoronarse** to crumble, collapse, fall to pieces.

desnatado,-a *adj (leche)* skimmed; *(yogur)* low-fat.

desnaturalización *nf* **1** QUÍM denaturation. **2** *(adulteración)* adulteration.

desnaturalizar *vt* **1** *(adulterar)* to adulterate. **2** QUÍM to denature, denaturize.

desnivel *nm* **1** unevenness. **2** *(cuesta)* slope, drop. **3** *fig* difference.

desnivelar *vt* **1** *(sacar de nivel)* to make uneven. **2** *(desequilibrar)* to throw out of balance; *(balanza)* to tip.

desnudar *vt* **1** to undress. **2** *fig (despojar)* to strip.
▸ *vpr* **desnudarse** *(persona)* to get undressed, take one's clothes off.

desnudez *nf* nudity, nakedness.

desnudo,-a *adj (persona)* naked, nude; *(parte del cuerpo)* bare.

desnutrición *nf* malnutrition, undernourishment.

desnutrido,-a *adj* undernourished.

desobedecer *vt* to disobey.

desobediente *adj* disobedient.

desocupado,-a *adj* **1** *(ocioso)* free, not busy. **2** *(desempleado)* unemployed, out of work.

desocupar *vt* to vacate, leave, empty.

desodorante *nm* deodorant.

desolación *nf* **1** desolation. **2** *(tristeza)* affliction, grief.

desolado,-a *adj (triste)* distressed, heartbroken.

desolador,-ra *adj (desconsolador)* heartbreaking, devastating.

desorden *nm* disorder, disarray, mess, untidiness.

desordenado,-a *adj* **1** *(habitación, etc)* untidy, messy. **2** *(persona)* slovenly.

desordenar *vt* to untidy, disarrange, mess up.

desorganizar *vt* to disorganize, disrupt.

desorientar *vt* **1** to disorientate. **2** *fig (confundir)* to confuse.
▸ *vpr* **desorientarse** to lose one's bearings, lose one's sense of direction, get lost.

desovar *vi (insectos)* to lay eggs; *(peces)* to spawn.

desove *nm (insectos)* egg-laying; *(peces)* spawning.

desoxidante *adj* deoxidizing.

desoxirribonucleico,-a *adj* deoxyribonucleic.

despabilado,-a *adj fig (listo)* smart, sharp, quick.

despabilar *vt fig (despertar)* to wake up.
▸ *vpr* **despabilarse** **1** *(despertarse)* to wake up. **2** *(avivarse)* to wise up.

despachar *vt* **1** *(resolver)* to resolve, get through; *(tratar un asunto)* to deal with, attend. **2** *(despedir)* to dismiss, sack, fire. **3** *(en tienda)* to serve; *(vender)* to sell.

despacho *nm (oficina)* office; *(estudio)* study. COMP **despacho de billetes/localidades** ticket/box office.

despacio *adv (gen)* slowly.

desparasitar *vt (piojos)* to delouse; *(lombrices)* to worm.

desparramar *vt* to spread, scatter; *(un líquido)* to spill.

despectivo,-a *adj* **1** contemptuous, disparaging. **2** GRAM pejorative, derogatory.

despedida *nf* farewell, goodbye.

despedir *vt* **1** *(echar)* to throw out. **2** *(del trabajo)* to dismiss, fire, sack.

(decir adiós) to see off, say goodbye to.

► *vpr* **despedirse** *(decirse adiós)* to say goodbye (de, to).

despegar *vt (desenganchar)* to unstick, take off, detach.

► *vi (avión)* to take off.

► *vpr* **despegarse** *(separarse)* to come unstuck.

despegue *nm (avión)* takeoff.

despeinar *vt* to dishevel, ruffle.

► *vpr* **despeinarse** to mess up one's hair.

despejar *vt* **1** *(desalojar)* to clear. **2** MAT to find. **3** INFORM to clear.

► *vpr* **despejarse** **1** METEOR to clear up. **2** *(espabilarse)* to wake OS up, clear one's head.

despenalizar *vt* to legalize.

despensa *nf (lugar)* pantry, larder.

despeñar *vt* to throw over a cliff.

► *vpr* **despeñarse** *(caer)* to fall over a cliff.

desperdiciar *vt* to waste, squander; *(oportunidad)* to throw away.

desperdicio *nm* waste.

► *nm pl* **desperdicios** *(basura)* rubbish *sing; (desechos)* scraps, leftovers.

desperdigar *vt* to scatter, disperse.

desperezarse *vpr* to stretch.

desperfecto *nm* **1** *(daño)* damage. **2** *(defecto)* flaw, defect.

despertador *nm* alarm clock.

despertar *vt* to wake, wake up, awaken.

► *vi* to wake up, awake.

► *vpr* **despertarse** to wake up, awake.

despiadado,-a *adj* ruthless, merciless.

despido *nm* dismissal, sacking.

despierto,-a *adj* **1** awake. **2** *(espabilado)* lively, smart, sharp, bright.

despilfarrar *vt* to waste, squander.

despilfarro *nm* waste.

despistado,-a *adj (distraído)* absent-minded.

despistar *vt fig (desorientar)* to mislead, confuse.

► *vpr* **despistarse** **1** *(perderse)* to get lost.. **2** *(distraerse)* to get confused.

despiste *nm* **1** *(distracción)* absent-mindedness. **2** *(error)* mistake, slip.

desplazamiento *nm (traslado)* moving, removal.

desplazar *vt* **1** *(mover)* to move, shift. **2** *fig (sustituir)* to replace, take over from.

► *vpr* **desplazarse** to travel.

desplegar *vt (extender)* to unfold, spread (out).

despliegue *nm fig (exhibición)* display, show, manifestation.

desplomar *vt (hacer perder la verticalidad)* to put out of plumb.

► *vpr* **desplomarse** *(caer algo de peso)* to fall down, collapse, topple over.

despoblar *vt* to depopulate.

► *vpr* **despoblarse** to become depopulated, become deserted.

despojar *vt (quitar)* to deprive (de, of), strip.

► *vpr* **despojarse** *(desposeerse voluntariamente)* to forsake (de, -), give up (de,-).

despojo *nm (botín)* plunder, booty.

► *nm pl* **despojos** *(sobras)* leavings, scraps, leftovers.

desposeer *vt (gen)* to dispossess.

déspota *nm o nf* despot, tyrant.

despreciar *vt* **1** *(desdeñar)* to despise, scorn, look down on. **2** *(ignorar)* to disregard, ignore.

desprecio *nm (desestima)* contempt, scorn, disdain.

desprender *vt* **1** *(soltar)* to release. **2** *(emanar)* to give off.

► *vpr* **desprenderse** *(soltarse)* to come off, come away.

desprendimiento *nm (acción de desprenderse)* detachment, loosening.

despreocupado,-a *adj (tranquilo)* unconcerned, unworried.

despreocuparse *vpr* **1** *(dejar de preocuparse)* to stop worrying. **2** *(desentenderse)* to be unconcerned (de, about), be indifferent (de, to).

desprestigiar *vt* to discredit, ruin the reputation of.

desprevenido,-a *adj* unprepared, unready. LOC **coger/pillar a** ALGN **desprevenido,-a** to catch SB unawares, take SB by surprise.

desproporcionado,-a *adj* disproportionate, out of proportion.

después *adv* 1 afterwards, later. 2 *(entonces)* then. 3 *(luego)* next. LOC **después de** 1 *(tiempo)* after. 2 *(desde)* since. 3 *(+ pp)* after, once: *después de la cena* after supper. ❙ **después de todo** after all: *después de todo no está tan mal* it's not that bad after all.

despuntar *vt (quitar la punta)* to blunt, make blunt.

destacamento *nm* detachment.

destacar *vi (despuntar)* to stand out.
▶ *vt fig (dar énfasis)* to point out, emphasize.
▶ *vpr* **destacarse** to stand out.

destajo *nm* piecework. LOC **a destajo** by the piece.

destapar *vt* 1 *(gen)* to open: *destapé la caja y vi que estaba vacía* I opened the box and saw it was empty. 2 *(tapón)* to uncork; *(tapa)* to take the lid off. 3 *fig (descubrir)* to reveal, uncover.
▶ *vpr* **destaparse** *(en la cama)* to take the covers off.

destellar *vi (estrella)* to twinkle.

destello *nm (resplandor)* sparkle, flash; *(brillo)* gleam, shine.

destemplado,-a *adj* 1 *(carácter)* irritable, tetchy. 2 *(tiempo)* unpleasant.

desteñir *vt* to discolour (US discolor), fade.
▶ *vi* to lose colour (US color), fade, run.

desternillarse LOC **desternillarse de risa** *fam* to split one's sides laughing, be in stitches.

desterrar *vt* to exile, banish.

destiempo LOC **a destiempo** inopportunely, at the wrong moment: *llegó a destiempo* he arrived at the wrong moment.

destierro *nm* 1 *(pena)* banishment, exile. 2 *(lugar)* place of exile.

destilar *vt* to distil (US distill).

destilería *nf* distillery.

destinar *vt* 1 *(asignar)* to assign, set aside, destine; *(dinero)* to allocate, set aside. 2 *(persona)* to assign, post.

destinatario,-a *nm & nf* 1 *(de carta)* addressee. 2 *(de mercancías)* consignee.

destino *nm* 1 *(sino)* destiny, fate. 2 *(uso)* purpose, use. 3 *(lugar)* destination. LOC **con destino a** bound for, going to.

destitución *nf* dismissal, removal.

destituir *vt* to dismiss.

destornillador *nm* screwdriver.

destornillar *vt* to unscrew.

destrabar *vt (quitar las trabas)* to unfetter.

destreza *nf* skill.

destronar *vt* 1 to dethrone. 2 *fig* to overthrow, unseat.

destrozar *vt* 1 *(romper)* to destroy, wreck; *(despedazar)* to tear to pieces, tear to shreds. 2 *fig (causar daño moral)* to crush, shatter, devastate.

destrozo *nm (acción)* destruction.

destrucción *nf* destruction.

destruir *vt* to destroy.

desunir *vt (separar)* to divide, separate.

desuso *nm* disuse: *eso está en desuso* that's obsolete, that's outdated.

desvalido,-a *adj* needy, destitute.

desvalijar *vt* 1 *(a alguien)* to rob. 2 *(un lugar)* to burgle.

desván *nm* loft, attic.

desvanecer *vt* 1 *(hacer desaparecer)* to clear, dispel, disperse. 2 *fig (recuerdo etc)* to dispel, banish.
▶ *vpr* **desvanecerse** 1 *(disiparse)* to disperse, clear. 2 *fig (desaparecer)* to vanish, disappear; *(recuerdos)* to fade.

desvanecimiento *nm (desmayo)* faint, fainting fit.

desvariar *vi* to be delirious, rave.

desvarío *nm* 1 *(delirio)* delirium, raving. 2 *(disparate)* nonsense, act of madness. 3 *(capricho)* fancy, whim.

desvelar *vt* 1 *(quitar el sueño)* to keep awake. 2 *fig (revelar)* to reveal, dis close: *nos desveló el secreto* she revealed the secret to us.

▶ *vpr* **desvelarse 1** to be unable to sleep. **2** *fig* *(dedicarse)* to devote os (por, to): *siempre se ha desvelado por su familia* she has always devoted herself to her family.

desvelo *nm* *(dedicación)* devotion, dedication.

desventaja *nf* **1** disadvantage, drawback. **2** *(problema)* problem. LOC **estar en desventaja** to be at a disadvantage.

desvergonzado,-a *adj* *(sinvergüenza)* shameless, brazen.

desvergüenza *nf* *(falta de decoro)* shamelessness.

desvestir *vt* to undress.

▶ *vpr* **desvestirse** to undress, get undressed.

desviación *nf* **1** deviation. **2** *(de carretera)* diversion, detour.

desviar *vt* **1** *(gen)* to deviate, change the course of: *desvió la mirada* she looked away. **2** *(golpe, balón)* to deflect. **3** *(carretera, río, barco, avión)* to divert. **4** *fig* *(tema)* to change.

▶ *vpr* **desviarse 1** *(avión, barco)* to go off course; *(coche)* to make a detour. **2** *(golpe, balón)* to be deflected. **3** *(persona, camino)* to leave.

desvío *nm* diversion, detour.

desvivirse *vpr* **1** *(desvelarse)* to do one's utmost (por, for), be devoted (por, to). **2** *(desear)* to be mad (por, about).

detallado,-a *adj* detailed, thorough.

detallar *vt* **1** to detail, give the details of, tell in detail. **2** *(especificar)* to specify.

detalle *nm* **1** *(pormenor)* detail, particular. **2** *(delicadeza)* nice gesture, nice thought. **3** *(toque decorativo)* touch. LOC **al detalle** COM retail. ‖ **tener un detalle** to be considerate, be thoughtful.

detallista *nm o nf* COM retailer, retail trader.

detectar *vt* to detect.

detective *nm o nf* detective.

detener *vt* **1** *(parar)* to stop, halt; *(proceso, negociación)* to hold up. **2** *(retener)* to keep, delay, detain.

▶ *vpr* **detenerse 1** *(pararse)* to stop, halt: *el tren se detuvo* the train stopped. **2** *(entretenerse)* to hang about, linger.

detenidamente *adv* carefully, thoroughly.

detenido,-a *adj* **1** *(parado)* held up. **2** JUR under arrest: *está detenido* he's under arrest.

▶ *nm & nf* JUR prisoner.

detergente *nm* detergent.

deteriorar *vt* *(estropear)* to damage, spoil; *(gastar)* to wear out.

▶ *vpr* **deteriorarse** *(estropearse)* to get damaged; *(gastarse)* to wear out.

deterioro *nm* **1** *(daño)* damage, deterioration; *(desgaste)* wear and tear. **2** *fig* *(empeoramiento)* deterioration, worsening.

determinado,-a *adj* **1** *(preciso)* definite, precise, certain, given, particular. **2** *(día, hora, etc)* fixed, set, appointed. **3** GRAM definite. **4** MAT determinate.

determinante *adj* decisive, determinant.

▶ *nm* MAT determinant.

determinar *vt* **1** *(decidir)* to resolve, decide, determine. **2** *(fijar)* to fix, set, appoint. **3** *(estipular)* to stipulate, specify.

▶ *vpr* **determinarse** *(decidirse)* to make up one's mind, decide.

detestar *vt* to detest, hate, abhor.

detonación *nf* detonation.

detonador *nm* detonator.

detonante *adj* detonating, explosive.

▶ *nm* **1** detonator. **2** *fig* trigger.

detrás *adv* **1** behind: *detrás de la puerta* behind the door. **2** *(en la parte posterior)* at the back, in the back. **3** *(después)* then, afterwards. LOC **ir detrás de** to go after.

deuda *nf* **1** debt. **2** REL trespass. COMP **deuda pública** national debt.

deudor,-ra *nm & nf* debtor.

devaluación *nf* devaluation.

D

devaluar *vt* to devalue.

devoción *nf* **1** devotion, devoutness. **2** *(afición)* devotion, dedication.

devolver *vt* **1** *(volver algo a un estado anterior)* to put back, return. **2** *(por correo)* to send back, return. **3** *(restituir un dinero)* to refund, return. **4** *(una visita, un cumplido, etc)* to return, pay back. **5** *fam (vomitar)* to vomit, throw up, bring up.
▶ *vi fam (vomitar)* to throw up, be sick.

devorar *vt* to devour.

devuelto,-a *nm (vómito)* vomit.

Dg *sím (decagramo)* decagram; *(símbolo)* Dg.

dg *sím (decigramo)* decigram; *(símbolo)* dg.

día *nm* **1** day. **2** *(con luz)* daylight, daytime: *ya es de día* it's daylight. **3** *(tiempo)* day, weather.
▶ *nm pl* **días** *(vida)* days. [LOC] **al día siguiente** the following day. ▌ **¡buenos días!** good morning! ▌ **todos los días** each day, every day. ▌ **dar los buenos días** to say good morning. ▌ **de día** during the day. ▌ **estar al día** *fig* to be up to date. ▌ **hacer buen/mal día** to be a nice/horrible day. ▌ **ser de día** to be daylight. [COMP] **día de año nuevo** New Year's Day. ▌ **día de descanso** day off. ▌ **día festivo** holiday, bank holiday. ▌ **día de paga** payday. ▌ **día entre semana** weekday.

diabetes *nf inv* diabetes.

diabético,-a *adj* diabetic.

diablo *nm* devil, demon. [COMP] **un diablillo** a little devil.

diablura *nf* mischief, naughtiness.

diacrítico,-a *adj* diacritic, diacritical.

diadema *nf* **1** *(joya)* diadem. **2** *(adorno para el pelo)* hairband.

diafragma *nm* **1** ANAT diaphragm. **2** *(en fotografía)* aperture. **3** MED diaphragm, cap.

diagnóstico,-a *nm* diagnosis.

diagonal *adj* diagonal. [LOC] **en diagonal** diagonally.

diagrama *nm* diagram. [COMP] **diagrama de flujo** INFORM flow chart.

dial *nm* dial.

dialecto *nm* dialect.

dialogar *vi* **1** *(conversar)* to talk, have a conversation. **2** *fig (negociar)* to negotiate, hold talks **(sobre,** on).

diálogo *nm* dialogue, conversation.

diamante *nm* diamond.

diámetro *nm* diameter.

diana *nf* DEP *(objeto)* target; *(para dardos)* dartboard; *(blanco)* bull's eye.

diapositiva *nf* slide.

diario,-a *adj* daily, everyday.
▶ *nm* **diario 1** *(prensa)* daily, paper, daily newspaper. **2** *(íntimo)* diary, journal. [LOC] **a diario** daily, every day.

diarrea *nf* diarrhoea (US diarrhea).

dibujante *nm o nf* **1** artist, drawer. **2** *(de dibujos animados)* cartoonist. **3** TÉC *(hombre)* draughtsman (US draftsman); *(mujer)* draughtswoman (US draftswoman).

dibujar *vt* **1** to draw, sketch. **2** TÉC to design. **3** *fig (describir)* to describe.

dibujo *nm* **1** *(arte)* drawing, sketching. **2** *(imagen)* drawing. **3** *(motivo)* pattern, design. [COMP] **dibujo artístico** artistic drawing. ▌ **dibujo lineal** draughtsmanship (US draftsmanship). ▌ **dibujos animados** cartoons.

diccionario *nm* dictionary.

dicho,-a *adj* said, mentioned: *dicha casa...* the said house…; *dicho esto se marchó* having said this he left. [LOC] **dicho y hecho** no sooner said than done.

diciembre *nm* December.

✎ Consulta también **marzo**.

dictado,-a *nm* dictation.

dictador,-ra *nm & nf* dictator.

dictadura *nf* dictatorship.

dictar *vt* **1** to dictate. **2** JUR *(ley)* to enact, decree, announce; *(sentencia)* to pronounce, pass.

didáctico,-a *adj* didactic.

diecinueve *adj (cardinal)* nineteen; *(ordinal)* nineteenth.

▶ *nm* **1** *(número)* nineteen. **2** *(fecha)* nineteenth.

✎ Consulta también seis.

dieciocho *adj (cardinal)* eighteen; *(ordinal)* eighteenth.
▶ *nm* **1** *(número)* eighteen. **2** *(fecha)* eighteenth.

✎ Consulta también seis.

dieciséis *adj (cardinal)* sixteen; *(ordinal)* sixteenth.
▶ *nm* **1** *(número)* sixteen. **2** *(fecha)* sixteenth.

✎ Consulta también seis.

diecisiete *adj (cardinal)* seventeen; *(ordinal)* seventeenth.
▶ *nm* **1** *(número)* seventeen. **2** *(fecha)* seventeenth.

✎ Consulta también seis.

diente *nm* **1** *(gen)* tooth. **2** *(de ajo)* clove. LOC **echar los dientes** to teethe. ‖ **hablar entre dientes** *fig* to mumble, mutter. COMP **diente de leche** milk tooth.

diéresis *nf inv* diaeresis, dieresis.

diesel *adj* diesel.

diestro,-a *adj* **1** *lit* right. **2** *(hábil)* skilful (US skillful).

dieta *nf (régimen, alimentación)* diet.

diez *adj (cardinal)* ten; *(ordinal)* tenth.
▶ *nm* **1** *(número)* ten. **2** *(fecha)* tenth.

✎ Consulta también seis.

diezmilésimo,-a *adj* ten-thousandth.
▶ *nm & nf* ten-thousandth.

✎ Consulta también sexto,-a.

diferencia *nf* difference.

diferenciar *vt (distinguir)* to differentiate, distinguish (entre, between).
▶ *vpr* **diferenciarse** to differ, be different (por, because of).

diferente *adj* different.

difícil *adj* difficult, hard.

dificultad *nf* **1** difficulty. **2** *(obstáculo)* obstacle; *(problema)* trouble, problem.

difunto,-a *nm & nf* deceased.

difusión *nf* **1** *(de luz, calor)* diffusion. **2** *fig (de noticia, enfermedad, etc)* spreading. **3** RAD broadcast, broadcasting.

digestión *nf* digestion.

digestivo,-a *adj* digestive.

digital *adj* digital.

dígito *nm* digit.

dignarse *vpr* to deign (a, to), condescend (a, to).

dignidad *nf* **1** *(cualidad)* dignity. **2** *(cargo)* rank, office, post.

digno,-a *adj* **1** *(merecedor)* worthy, deserving. **2** *(respetable)* worthy, honourable (US honorable). LOC **digno,-a de admiración** worthy of admiration, admirable.

dilatado,-a *adj* **1** dilated. **2** *(vasto)* vast, extensive, large. **3** FÍS expanded.

dilatar *vt* **1** to dilate. **2** FÍS to expand. **3** *(prolongar)* to prolong, extend.

diligencia *nf* **1** *(cuidado)* diligence, care. **2** *(rapidez)* rapidity, speed. **3** *(carreta)* stagecoach.

diluir *vt* **1** *(un sólido)* to dissolve. **2** *(un líquido)* to dilute.
▶ *vpr* **diluirse 1** *(un sólido)* to dissolve. **2** *(un líquido)* to dilute.

diluviar *vi* [se emplea sólo en tercera persona del singular; no lleva sujeto] to pour with rain, pour down.

diluvio *nm* flood.

dimensión *nf* **1** [también se usa en plural con el mismo significado] dimension, size. **2** *fig (importancia)* importance.

diminutivo,-a *adj* diminutive.
▶ *nm* **diminutivo** diminutive.

diminuto,-a *adj* tiny, minute.

dimisión *nf* resignation.

dimitir *vi* to resign (de, from).

Dinamarca *nf* Denmark.

dinamita *nf* dynamite.

dinastía *nf* dynasty.

dinero *nm* **1** money. **2** *(fortuna)* wealth. LOC **andar mal/escaso,-a de dinero** to be short of money. ‖ **tirar el dinero por la ventana** to throw money down the drain. COMP **dinero en metálico** cash.

dinosaurio *nm* dinosaur.

dioptría *nf* dioptre (US diopter).

dios *nm* god.

diosa *nf* goddess.

diploma *nm* diploma.

diplomacia *nf* diplomacy.

diplomático,-a *adj* diplomatic.
▶ *nm & nf* diplomat.

diptongo *nm* diphthong.

diputado,-a *nm & nf (miembro del Congreso)* deputy, *member of the Spanish Parliament.*

dique *nm (muro)* dike, breakwater.

dirección *nf* **1** *(acción de dirigir)* management, running. **2** *(cargo)* directorship, position of manager. **3** *(sentido)* direction, way. **4** *(destino)* destination: *salió con dirección a Cádiz* he left for Cádiz. **5** *(domicilio)* address. **6** TÉC steering. COMP **calle de dirección única** one-way street.

directivo,-a *adj* directive, managing.
▶ *nm & nf* director, manager, board member.

directo,-a *adj* direct, straight.
▶ *nm* **directo** DEP straight hit. LOC **en directo** TV live.

director,-ra *nm & nf* **1** director, manager. **2** *(de colegio - hombre)* headmaster; *(- mujer)* headmistress. **3** *(de orquesta)* conductor. COMP **director,-ra de cine** film director.

directorio,-a *nm* **1** *(gobierno)* governing body. **2** *(de direcciones)* directory, guide. **3** INFORM directory.

dirigente *adj* leading, directing.
▶ *nm o nf* **1** leader. **2** *(de empresa)* manager.

dirigir *vt* **1** *(empresa)* to manage; *(negocio, escuela)* to run; *(un periódico)* to edit. **2** *(orquesta)* to conduct; *(película)* to direct. **3** *(coche)* to drive, steer; *(barco)* to steer; *(avión)* to pilot. **4** *(un partido)* to lead. **5** *(carta, protesta)* to address.
▶ *vpr* **dirigirse 1** *(ir)* to go (a, to), make one's way (a, to), make (a, for). **2** *(hablar)* to address (a, -), speak (a, to): *se dirigió a su padre* she addressed her father.

discapacitado,-a *adj* handicapped, disabled.

disciplina *nf* **1** *(conjunto de reglas)* discipline. **2** *(doctrina)* doctrine. **3** *(asignatura)* subject.

disciplinado,-a *adj* disciplined.

discípulo,-a *nm & nf* **1** *(seguidor)* disciple, follower. **2** *(alumno)* pupil, student.

disc-jockey *nm o nf* disc jockey, DJ.

disco *nm* **1** disc. **2** DEP discus. **3** *(de música)* record. **4** INFORM disk. COMP **disco duro** hard disk.

discoteca *nf (local)* discotheque, nightclub.

discreción *nf* **1** *(sensatez)* discretion, tact. **2** *(agudeza)* wit. LOC **a discreción** *(a voluntad)* at one's discretion.

discreto,-a *adj (prudente)* discreet, prudent, tactful.

discriminación *nf* discrimination. COMP **discriminación racial** racial discrimination.

discriminar *vt* **1** *(diferenciar)* to discriminate, distinguish. **2** *(por raza, religión, etc)* to discriminate against.

disculpa *nf* excuse, apology. LOC **pedir disculpas a** ALGN to apologize to SB.

disculpar *vt* **1** *(descargar de culpa)* to excuse: *disculpe el retraso* please excuse the delay. **2** *(perdonar)* to excuse, forgive: *¡disculpe!* excuse me!
▶ *vpr* **disculparse** to apologize (por, for), excuse OS.

discurrir *vi* **1** *(andar)* to walk, wander. **2** *(fluir)* to flow, run. **3** *(transcurrir)* to pass, go by. **4** *fig (reflexionar)* to think (sobre, about), ponder (sobre, on/over), meditate (sobre, on).

discurso *nm (conferencia)* speech.

discusión *nf* **1** *(charla)* discussion. **2** *(disputa)* argument.

discutir *vi* **1** *(examinar)* to discuss (de, -). **2** *(contender)* to argue.

diseminar *vt* to disseminate, scatter, spread.
▶ *vpr* **diseminarse** to spread.

diseñador,-ra *nm & nf* designer.

diseñar *vt* to design.

diseño *nm* design.

disfraz *nm* **1** *(para engañar)* disguise. **2** *(para una fiesta, etc)* fancy dress outfit, fancy dress costume.

disfrazar *vt (persona)* to disguise, dress up.
▶ *vpr* **disfrazarse 1** *(para engañar)* to disguise os (de, as). **2** *(para una fiesta, etc)* to dress up (de, as).

disfrutar *vt* **1** *(poseer)* to own, enjoy, possess; *(pensión, renta)* to receive. **2** *(aprovechar)* to make the most of.
▶ *vi* **1** *(poseer)* to enjoy (de, -), have (de, -), possess (de, -): *disfruta de buena salud* he enjoys good health. **2** *(gozar)* to enjoy, enjoy os: *disfruté mucho en el cine* I enjoyed myself very much at the cinema.

disgustar *vt* **1** *(molestar)* to displease, annoy, upset. **2** *(desagradar)* to dislike: *me disgusta ese sabor dulce* I don't like that sweet taste.
▶ *vpr* **disgustarse 1** *(enfadarse)* to get angry, get upset. **2** *(pelearse)* to quarrel (con, with).

disgusto *nm* **1** *(enfado)* displeasure, annoyance, anger. **2** *fig (pelea)* argument, quarrel. LOC **a disgusto** against one's will, reluctantly, unwillingly. ∥ **dar un disgusto** to upset. ∥ **llevarse un disgusto** to get upset.

disimular *vt (ocultar)* to hide, conceal.
▶ *vi* to pretend, dissemble: *no disimules* stop pretending.

disimulo *nm* pretence (us pretense), dissemblance.

dislocar *vt (sacar de lugar)* to dislocate.

disminución *nf* decrease, reduction.

disminuido,-a *adj* disabled.

disminuir *vt* **1** *(gen)* to decrease. **2** *(medidas, velocidad)* to reduce.
▶ *vi* **1** *(gen)* to diminish. **2** *(temperatura, precios)* to drop, fall.

disolución *nf* **1** *(gen)* dissolution. **2** QUÍM solution, dissolution.

disolver *vt (gen)* to dissolve.
▶ *vpr* **disolverse 1** *(gen)* to dissolve. **2** *fig* to be dissolved.

dispar *adj* unlike, different.

disparar *vt* **1** *(arma)* to fire; *(bala, flecha)* to shoot. **2** *(lanzar)* to hurl, throw. **3** DEP to shoot.

disparatado,-a *adj* absurd, foolish, ridiculous.

disparo *nm* **1** *(acción)* firing. **2** *(efecto)* shot. **3** DEP shot.

dispersar *vt (gen)* to disperse, scatter.
▶ *vpr* **dispersarse** *(gen)* to disperse, scatter.

disperso,-a *adj (esparcido)* scattered.

disponer *vt* **1** *(colocar)* to dispose, arrange, set out. **2** *(preparar)* to prepare, get ready. **3** *(ordenar)* to order, decree.
▶ *vi* **1** *(tener)* to have (de, -). **2** *(hacer uso)* to make use (de, of), have the use (de, of).
▶ *vpr* **disponerse** *(prepararse)* to get ready (a, to), prepare (a, to).

disponibilidad *nf* availability.

disponible *adj (gen)* available.

dispositivo *nm* device, gadget.

dispuesto,-a *adj* **1** *(decidido)* determined. **2** *(preparado)* prepared, ready, willing.

disputa *nf (discusión)* dispute, argument, quarrel.

disputar *vt* **1** *(competir)* to compete for, contend for. **2** DEP to play: *los equipos disputaron un partido amistoso* the teams played a friendly match.

disquete *nm* diskette, floppy disk.

disquetera *nf* disk drive.

distancia *nf* **1** distance. **2** *fig (diferencia)* difference, gap. LOC **a distancia** from a distance: *lo vimos a distancia* we saw it from a distance.

distanciar *vt* to distance, separate.
▶ *vpr* **distanciarse** to move away, become separated.

distante *adj* **1** *(en el espacio)* distant, far; *(en el tiempo)* distant, remote. **2** *fig* distant.

distinción *nf* **1** *(gen)* distinction. **2** *(elegancia)* distinction, elegance, refinement.

distinguido,-a *adj* **1** distinguished. **2** *(elegante)* elegant.

D

distinguir *vt* **1** *(diferenciar)* to distinguish. **2** *(caracterizar)* to mark, distinguish. **3** *(ver)* to see, make out.
▶ *vpr* **distinguirse** *(destacar)* to stand out, distinguish os.

distinto,-a *adj (diferente)* different.
▶ *adj vpr* **distintos,-as** various, several.

distracción *nf* **1** *(divertimiento)* amusement, pastime, recreation, entertainment. **2** *(despiste)* distraction, absent-mindedness.

distraer *vt* **1** *(divertir)* to amuse, entertain. **2** *(atención)* to distract.
▶ *vpr* **distraerse 1** *(divertirse)* to amuse os, enjoy os. **2** *(despistarse)* to get distracted, be inattentive, be absent-minded .

distraído,-a *adj* **1** *(desatento)* absent-minded. **2** *(entretenido)* entertaining, fun.

distribuir *vt* **1** *(repartir)* to distribute. **2** *(correo)* to deliver; *(trabajo)* to share, allot.

distrito *nm* district.

disturbio *nm* disturbance, riot.

diurno,-a *adj* daily, daytime.

divagar *vi* to digress, ramble.

diván *nm* divan, couch.

divergente *adj* divergent, diverging.

divergir *vi* to diverge.

diversidad *nf* diversity, variety.

diversificar *vt* to diversify, vary.

diversión *nf* fun, amusement, entertainment.

diverso,-a *adj* different.
▶ *adj vpr* **diversos,-as** several, various.

divertido,-a *adj* **1** *(gracioso)* funny, amusing. **2** *(entretenido)* fun, entertaining, enjoyable.

divertir *vt* to amuse, entertain.
▶ *vpr* **divertirse** to enjoy os, have a good time: ¡diviértete! enjoy yourself!

dividir *vt* **1** to divide. **2** *(separar)* to divide, separate: *el río divide las dos comarcas* the river separates the two counties. **3** *(repartir)* to divide, split.
▶ *vpr* **dividirse** *(separarse)* to divide, split up.

divino,-a *adj* divine.

divisible *adj* **1** dividable. **2** MAT divisible.

división *nf* **1** división. **2** *fig* division, divergence.

divisor *nm* **1** divider. **2** MAT divisor. COMP máximo común divisor MAT highest common factor, (US highest common denominator). ▌ mínimo común divisor MAT lowest common factor, (US lowest common denominator) .

divo,-a *nm & nf* star.

divorciado,-a *adj* divorced.
▶ *nm & nf (hombre)* divorcé; *(mujer)* divorcée.

divorciar *vt* to divorce.
▶ *vpr* **divorciarse** to get divorced (de, from).

divorcio *nm* divorce.

divulgar *vt* **1** *(difundir)* to divulge, spread, disclose. **2** *(por radio)* to broadcast. **3** *(propagar)* to popularize.
▶ *vpr* **divulgarse** to become known, spread.

Djibouti *nm* Djibouti, Jibouti.

dl *sím (decilitro)* decilitre (US deciliter); *(símbolo)* dl.

Dl *sím (decalitro)* decalitre (US decaliter); *(símbolo)* Dl.

dm *sím (decímetro)* decimetre (US decimeter); *(símbolo)* dm.

Dm *sím (decámetro)* decametre (US decameter); *(símbolo)* Dm.

do *nm (de solfa)* doh, do; *(de escala diatónica)* C.

dobladillo *nm* **1** *(de vestido, etc)* hem. **2** *(de pantalones)* turn-up, US cuff.

doblaje *nm* dubbing.

doblar *vt* **1** *(duplicar)* to double: *le doblo la edad* I'm twice as old as she is. **2** *(plegar)* to fold. **3** *(torcer)* to bend: *doblar un dedo* to bend a finger. **4** *(esquina)* to turn, go round. **5** *(película)* to dub.
▶ *vpr* **doblarse** *(plegarse)* to fold.

doble *adj* **1** double. **2** *(nacionalidad)* dual.
▶ *nm* **1** double: *tiene el doble que yo* he's got twice as much as I have. **2** *(duplicado)*

duplicate. LOC **ver doble** to see double.

▶ *nm o nf* CINE stand-in, double; *(hombre)* stunt man; *(mujer)* stunt woman.

▶ *adv* double.

▶ *nm pl* **dobles** *(tenis)* doubles.

doce *adj (cardinal)* twelve; *(ordinal)* twelfth.

▶ *nm* **1** *(número)* twelve. **2** *(fecha)* twelfth.

✎ Consulta también seis.

docena *nf* dozen. LOC **a docenas** COM by the dozen.

dócil *adj* docile, obedient.

doctor,-ra *nm & nf* doctor.

doctrina *nf* **1** doctrine. **2** *(enseñanza)* teachings *pl*.

documentación *nf* **1** documentation, documents *pl*. **2** *(para identificar)* papers *pl*, identification.

documental *adj* documentary.

▶ *nm* documentary.

documento *nm* document.

dodecaedro *nm* dodecahedron.

dodecasílabo,-a *nm* dodecasyllable, Alexandrine.

dólar *nm* dollar.

doler *vi* **1** to ache, hurt. **2** *(afligir)* to distress, sadden, upset, hurt: *me duele tal pobreza* such poverty distresses me. **3** *(sentir)* to be sorry, be sad: *me duele habérselo dicho* I'm sorry I told her about it.

dolido,-a *adj fig* hurt.

dolor *nm* **1** pain, ache. **2** *fig* pain, sorrow, grief. COMP **dolor de cabeza** headache.

dolorido,-a *adj* sore, aching.

doloroso,-a *adj* **1** painful. **2** *fig* painful, distressing.

domador,-ra *nm & nf* tamer; *(de caballos)* horse breaker.

domar *vt* **1** to tame; *(caballos)* to break in. **2** *fig* to tame, control.

domesticar *vt* **1** to domesticate, tame. **2** *(adiestrar)* to train. **3** *fig* to subdue.

doméstico,-a *adj* domestic.

domicilio *nm* **1** residence, home, abode. **2** *(dirección)* address.

dominante *adj* dominant, dominating.

dominar *vt* **1** *(tener bajo dominio)* to dominate. **2** *(conocer a fondo)* to master: *domina el inglés* she has a good command of English.

▶ *vi* **1** *(ser superior)* to dominate. **2** *(destacar)* to stand out: *domina mucho el rojo* red is the predominant colour. **3** *(predominar)* to predominate.

▶ *vpr* **dominarse** *(controlarse)* to control os, restrain os.

domingo *nm* Sunday.

✎ Consulta también jueves.

Dominica *nf* Dominica.

dominicano,-a *adj* Dominican.

▶ *nm & nf* Dominican. COMP **República Dominicana** Dominican Republic.

dominio *nm* **1** *(soberanía)* dominion. **2** *(poder)* power, control. **3** *(supremacía)* supremacy. **4** *(de conocimientos)* mastery, good knowledge; *(de un idioma)* good command. **5** *(territorio)* domain. **6** INFORM domain.

dominó *nm* **1** *(juego)* dominoes *pl*. **2** *(fichas)* set of dominoes.

don¹ *nm (talento)* talent, natural gift.

don² *nm* Mr: *Señor Don Juan Pérez* Mr Juan Pérez.

donante *nm o nf* donor. COMP **donante de sangre** blood donor.

donar *vt fml* to donate, give.

donativo *nm* donation.

donde *adv* where, in which. LOC **de donde / desde donde** from where, whence.

dónde *pron* where: *¿dónde está?* where is it?; *no sé dónde está* I don't know where it is; *¿a dónde va?* where is he going?; *¿hasta dónde?* how far?

dondequiera *adv (en cualquier parte)* anywhere; *(en todas partes)* everywhere: *dondequiera que esté lo encontraremos* wherever he is we'll find him.

dónut® *nm* doughnut.

doña *nf* Mrs: *Doña Elena Suárez* Mrs Elena Suárez.

D

dorado,-a *adj* golden.

dormido,-a *adj* **1** asleep. **2** *(soñoliento)* sleepy: *tengo el brazo dormido* my arm has gone numb, my arm has gone to sleep. LOC **quedarse dormido,-a 1** *(dormir)* to fall asleep. **2** *(dormirse más de la cuenta)* to oversleep.

dormir *vi* **1** to sleep: *tengo ganas de dormir* I feel sleepy. **2** *(pernoctar)* to spend the night.
► *vt* to put to sleep.
► *vpr* **dormirse 1** to fall asleep, nod off. **2** *fig* to go to sleep: *se me ha dormido el pie* my foot has gone to sleep. LOC **¡a dormir!** to bed! ▌ **dormir como un lirón** *fam* to sleep like a log. ▌ **dormir la siesta** to have a nap.

dormitorio *nm* **1** *(en una casa)* bedroom. **2** *(colectivo)* dormitory.

dorsal *adj* **1** dorsal, back. **2** LING dorsal.
► *nm* DEP number.

dorso *nm* back, reverse. COMP **dorso de la mano** back of the hand.

dos *adj (cardinal)* two; *(ordinal)* second: *entre ellas dos* between the two of them.
► *nm (número)* two; *(fecha)* second. LOC **cada dos por tres** *fam* every five minutes. COMP **dos veces** twice: *es dos veces mayor que su hermana* she's twice as old as her sister.

✎ Consulta también seis.

doscientos,-as *adj (numeral)* two hundred; *(cardinal)* two-hundredth.
► *nm & nf* two hundred.

✎ Consulta también seis.

dosificar *vt* **1** *(gen)* to dose. **2** *(esfuerzos, etc)* to measure.

dosis *nf inv* dose.

dotado,-a *adj* **1** *(equipado)* equipped, provided: *está dotado con airbag* it's equipped with an airbag. **2** *(con dotes)* gifted: *está muy dotado para las matemáticas* he has a talent for mathematics.

dotar *vt* **1** *(proveer de personal)* to staff (de, with); *(de material)* to equip (de, with). **2** *(bienes, dinero)* to assign. **3** *fig (dones y cualidades)* to endow (de,

with), provide (de, with): *la naturaleza la dotó de un sexto sentido* nature endowed her with a sixth sense.

dragón *nm* **1** *(reptil)* flying dragon. **2** *(animal fabuloso)* dragon.

drama *nm* drama.

dramático,-a *adj* dramatic.

drenar *vt* to drain.

drive *nm* drive.

droga *nf* **1** drug. **2** *fig (cosa desagradable)* nuisance. COMP **droga blanda/dura** soft/hard drug.

drogadicto,-a *nm & nf* drug addict.

drogar *vt* to drug.
► *vpr* **drogarse** to take drugs.

droguería *nf* hardware shop.

dromedario *nm* dromedary.

dualidad *nf* duality.

ducentésimo,-a *adj* two-hundredth.
► *nm & nf* two-hundredth.

ducha *nf* shower. LOC **darse/tomar una ducha** to take a shower, have a shower.

duchar *vt* to give a shower.
► *vpr* **ducharse** to take a shower, have a shower.

duda *nf* doubt. LOC **no hay duda** there is no doubt. ▌ **salir de dudas** to shed one's doubts. ▌ **sin duda** no doubt, without a doubt.

dudar *vi* **1** to doubt, have doubts. **2** *(titubear)* to hesitate: *dudo entre quedarme o marcharme* I'm not sure whether to stay or leave.
► *vt* to doubt: *lo dudo* I doubt it. LOC **dudar de** ALGN to doubt SB, mistrust SB.

dudoso,-a *adj* **1** *(incierto)* doubtful, uncertain. **2** *(vacilante)* hesitant, undecided. **3** *(poco seguro)* questionable.

duende *nm* *(espíritu travieso)* goblin, elf.

dueño,-a *nm & nf* **1** *(propietario)* owner: *¿quién es la dueña?* who is the owner? **2** *(de casa, piso - hombre)* landlord; *(mujer)* landlady. LOC **ser dueño,-a de sí mismo,-a** to be self-possessed.

dulce *adj* **1** *(gen)* sweet. **2** *fig* soft, gentle.

▸ *nm* CULIN *(caramelo)* sweet; *(pastel)* cake. COMP **dulce de membrillo** quince jelly.

dulzura *nf* **1** sweetness. **2** *fig* softness, gentleness, sweetness.

duna *nf* dune.

dúo *nm* duet.

duodécimo,-a *adj* twelfth.
▸ *nm & nf* twelfth.

✎ Consulta también sexto,-a.

duodeno *nm* duodenum.

duplicar *vt (gen)* to duplicate; *(cantidad)* to double.
▸ *vpr* **duplicarse** to double.

duque *nm* duke.

duquesa *nf* duchess.

duración *nf* **1** duration, length: *¿cuál es la duración de la obra?* how long is the play? **2** *(coche, máquina, etc)* life. LOC **de larga duración 1** *(periodo de tiempo)* long, long-term. **2** *(bombilla, etc)* long-life.

duradero,-a *adj* durable, lasting.

duramente *adv* **1** *(con dificultad)* hard. **2** *(con severidad)* harshly.

durante *adv* during, in, for: *viví allí durante un año* I lived there for a year.

durar *vi* **1** to last, go on for: *la película duró tres horas* the film went on for three hours. **2** *(ropa, calzado)* to wear well, last: *ese abrigo le duró mucho* he got a lot of wear out of that coat.

durazno *nm* **1** *(fruto)* peach. **2** *(árbol)* peach tree.

dureza *nf* **1** hardness, toughness. **2** *fig (de carácter)* toughness, harshness, severity. **3** *(callosidad)* corn.

duro,-a *adj* **1** hard. **2** *(carne)* tough; *(pan)* stale. **3** *(difícil)* hard, difficult.
▸ *nm* **duro** *(antiguamente)* five pesetas; *(moneda)* five-peseta coin.
▸ *adv* hard: *dale duro* hit him hard.

DVD *nm* (Disco Versátil Digital) DVD.

E

E, e *nf (la letra)* E, e.

e *conj* and.

✎ Usado en vez de y antes de palabras que empiezan por i o hi: *compramos manzanas e higos* we bought some apples and figs.

EAU *abrev* (Emiratos Árabes Unidos) United Arab Emirates; *(abreviatura)* UAE.

ebanista *nm o nf* cabinet-maker.

ebullición *nf (hervor)* boil, boiling.

echado,-a *adj (tumbado)* lying down.

echar *vt* **1** *(lanzar)* to throw. **2** *(dejar caer)* to put, drop. **3** *(líquido)* to pour; *(comida)* to give; *(sal)* to add, put in. **4** *(carta)* to post, US mail. **5** *(expulsar)* to throw out: *lo han echado del cine* he was thrown out of the cinema. **6** *(despedir de empleo)* to sack, dismiss, fire. **7** *(brotar, salir - plantas)* to sprout; *(- dientes)* to cut; *(- pelo)* to grow. **8** *(decir)* to tell. **9** *(emanar)* to give out, give off: *la caja de fusibles echa chispas* sparks are coming out of the fuse box. **10** *(suponer, calcular)* to guess: *yo le echo 40* I think she's 40. **11** *(poner, aplicar)* to put on, apply. **12** *(llave)* to lock, turn; *(cerrojo)* to bolt, fasten. **13** *fam (en el cine, teatro)* to show, put on: *echan una buena película en la tele* there's a good film on TV.
    ▶ *vi* **1** echar a + *inf (empezar)* to begin to: *echó a correr* she ran off. **2** echar de + *inf (dar)*: *echar de comer* to feed.
    ▶ *vpr* **echarse 1** *(arrojarse)* to throw os. **2** *(tenderse)* to lie down. **3** *(ponerse)* to put on. **4** *(novio, novia)* to get os. **5** echarse a + *inf (empezar)* to begin to: *se echó a reír* he burst out laughing.

eclipsar *vt* **1** *(astro)* to eclipse. **2** *fig* to eclipse, outshine.

eclipse *nm* eclipse.

eco *nm* echo.

ecografía *nf* ultrasound scan.

ecología *nf* ecology.

ecológico,-a *adj* ecological.

ecologista *adj* ecological.
    ▶ *nm o nf* ecologist.

economato *nm* company store.

economía *nf* **1** *(administración)* economy. **2** *(ciencia)* economics. **3** *(ahorro)* economy, saving.

económico,-a *adj* **1** *(gen)* economic. **2** *(barato)* cheap, economical, inexpensive. COMP **crisis económica** economic crisis, recession.

economista *nm o nf* economist.

economizar *vt (ahorrar)* to economize, save.
    ▶ *vi* to economize, save.

ecosistema *nm* ecosystem.

ecuación *nf* equation. COMP **ecuación de primer grado** simple equation. **ecuación de segundo grado** quadratic equation.

ecuador *nm* GEOG equator.

Ecuador *nm* Ecuador.

ecuatoguineano,-a *adj* of Equatorial Guinea, from Equatorial Guinea.
    ▶ *nm & nf* person from Equatorial Guinea, inhabitant of Equatorial Guinea.

ecuatorial *adj* equatorial.

ecuatoriano,-a *adj* Ecuadorian.
    ▶ *nm & nf* Ecuadorian.

ecuestre *adj* equestrian.

edad *nf* **1** age. **2** *(tiempo, época)* time, period.

edén *nm* **1** Eden. **2** *fig* paradise, heaven.

edición *nf* **1** *(ejemplares)* edition. **2** *(publicación)* publication. **3** INFORM editing.

edificar *vt* *(construir)* to build, construct.

edificio *nm* building.

edil,-la *nm & nf* *(concejal)* town councillor.
▶ *nm* edil *(magistrado romano)* aedile.

edredón *nm* eiderdown, US comforter.

educación *nf* **1** *(preparación)* education. **2** *(crianza)* upbringing, breeding. **3** *(modales)* manners *pl*, politeness.

educado,-a *adj* polite.

educar *vt* **1** *(enseñar)* to educate, teach. **2** *(criar)* to bring up. **3** *(en la cortesía, etc)* to teach manners.

educativo,-a *adj* educational: *sistema educativo* education system.

edulcorar *vt* **1** to sweeten. **2** *fig* to soften, alleviate.

EE UU *abrev* (Estados Unidos) the United States of America; *(abreviatura)* USA.

efe *nf* name of the letter f.

efectivamente *adv* **1** *(realmente)* in fact, actually. **2** *(de verdad)* indeed.

efectivo,-a *adj (que tiene efecto)* effective.
▶ *nm* efectivo *(dinero)* cash.

efecto *nm* **1** *(resultado)* effect, result, end. **2** *(impresión)* impression: *la escena le hizo un gran efecto* the scene made a great impression on her. **3** DEP spin: *dio efecto a la pelota* he put some spin on the ball.

efectuar *vt* **1** *(gen)* to carry out, perform, make, do. **2** *(pago)* to make; *(pedido)* to place. **3** *(suma, etc)* to do. **4** *(viaje, visita, etc)* to make.

efervescente *adj* **1** *(gen)* effervescent. **2** *(bebida)* sparkling, fizzy. **3** *(pastilla)* soluble.

eficacia *nf* **1** *(persona)* efficiency, effectiveness; *(cosas)* efficacy, effectiveness. **2** *(rendimiento)* efficiency.

eficaz *adj* **1** *(eficiente)* efficient. **2** *(cosa)* efficacious, effective. **3** *(que produce rendimiento)* efficient.

eficiente *adj* efficient.

EGB *abrev* EDUC (Enseñanza General Básica) ≈ *former Primary School Education*.

egipcio,-a *adj* Egyptian.
▶ *nm & nf (persona)* Egyptian.
▶ *nm* egipcio *(idioma)* Egyptian.

Egipto *nm* Egypt.

egoísmo *nm* selfishness, egoism.

egoísta *adj* selfish, egoistic, egoistical.
▶ *nm o nf* egoist, selfish person.

eje *nm* **1** *(línea, recta)* axis. **2** TÉC shaft, spindle. **3** AUTO axle.

ejecución *nf* **1** *(de una orden, etc)* carrying out, execution. **2** MÚS performance. **3** *(ajusticiamiento)* execution.

ejecutar *vt* **1** *(una orden, etc)* to carry out. **2** MÚS to perform, play. **3** *(ajusticiar)* to execute. **4** INFORM to run.

ejecutivo,-a *adj* executive.
▶ *nm & nf* executive.
▶ *nm* el ejecutivo *(gobierno)* the government. COMP poder ejecutivo the executive.

ejemplar *nm (copia)* copy, number, issue.

ejemplo *nm* **1** example. **2** *(modelo)* model. LOC dar ejemplo to set an example. ‖ por ejemplo for example, for instance.

ejercer *vt* **1** *(profesión, etc)* to practise (US practice), be in practice as. **2** *(influencia)* to exert.

ejercicio *nm* **1** *(de profesión)* practice; *(de derecho)* use, exercise; *(de función)* performance. **2** EDUC exercise; *(examen)* test; *(pregunta de examen)* question; *(deberes)* homework. **3** DEP exercise.

ejército *nm* army.

el *determinante* **1** the: *el agua* water. **2** el de the one: *el de hoy* today's. **3** el que *(persona - sujeto)* the one who; *(- objeto)* the one, the one that, the one whom: *el que vi* the one I saw. **4** *(cosa)* the one, the one that, the one which: *el que me diste* the one (that) you gave me.

él *pron* **1** *(sujeto - persona)* he; *(- cosa, animal)* it: *él vive aquí* he lives here. **2** *(objeto - persona)* him; *(- cosa, animal)* it: *comió con él* she had lunch with him. LOC de él *(posesivo)* his: *es de él* it's his. ‖ él mismo himself.

elaborar *vt* **1** *(producto)* to make, manufacture, produce. **2** *(madera, metal, etc)* to work.

elástico,-a *adj* elastic.
▶ *nm* elástico elastic.

ele *nf name of the letter* l.

elección *nf* **1** *(nombramiento)* election. **2** *(opción)* choice: *lo dejamos a tu elección* we'll leave it up to you.
▸ *nf pl* **elecciones** elections.

electricidad *nf* electricity.

electricista *nm o nf* electrician.

eléctrico,-a *adj* electric, electrical.

electrodoméstico *nm* electrical appliance.

electrón *nm* electron.

electrónica *nf* electronics.

electrónico,-a *adj* electronic.

elefante,-a *nm & nf (macho)* elephant; *(hembra)* cow elephant, female elephant. COMP **elefante marino** elephant seal.

elegancia *nf* elegance.

elegante *adj* elegant, smart, stylish.

elegir *vt* **1** *(escoger)* to choose. **2** POL to elect.

elemental *adj* **1** *(del elemento)* elemental. **2** *(obvio)* elementary, basic.

elemento *nm* **1** *(gen)* element. **2** *(parte)* component, part. **3** *(individuo)* type, sort. LOC **¡menudo elemento!** *fam* he's a right one!

elevación *nf* **1** *(de terreno)* elevation, rise. **2** *(precios)* rise, raising, increasing; *(voz, tono)* raising; *(peso)* raising, lifting. **3** MAT raising.

elevado,-a *adj (gen)* high. LOC **elevado,-a a** MAT raised to: *elevado a la quinta potencia* raised to the power of five; *elevado al cubo* cubed.

elevalunas *nm inv* window winder. COMP **elevalunas eléctrico** electric window.

elevar *vt* **1** *(peso, etc)* to elevate, raise, lift. **2** *(precios)* to raise, increase, put up; *(tono, voz)* to raise. **3** MAT to raise.
▸ *vpr* **elevarse 1** *(subir)* to rise (up): *el humo se elevaba* the smoke was rising up. **2** *(alcanzar)* to reach: *se eleva hasta el techo* it reaches the ceiling.

eliminación *nf* elimination.

eliminar *vt* **1** *(gen)* to eliminate, exclude. **2** *(esperanzas, miedos, etc)* to get rid of, cast aside. **3** *fam (matar)* to kill, eliminate.

eliminatoria *nf* heat, qualifying round.

eliminatorio,-a *adj* eliminatory.

elipse *nf* ellipse.

elíptico,-a *adj* elliptic, elliptical.

elite *nf* elite.

ella *pron* **1** *(sujeto - persona)* she; *(- cosa, animal)* it. **2** *(objeto - persona)* her; *(- cosa, animal)* it: *vino con ella* he came with her.

elle *nf name of the digraph* ll.

ello *pron* it: *no me digas nada de ello* don't tell me anything about it.

ellos,-as *pron* **1** *(sujeto)* they. **2** *(objeto)* them: *vino con ellos* she came with them. LOC **de ellos,-as** theirs: *el coche es de ellos* the car is theirs. ‖ **ellos,-as mismos,-as** themselves.

elocuente *adj* eloquent.

elogiar *vt* to praise, eulogize.

elogio *nm* praise, eulogy.

eludir *vt* **1** *(responsabilidad, justicia, etc)* to evade. **2** *(pregunta)* to avoid, evade; *(persona)* to avoid.

emanar *vi* **1** *(olor, etc)* to emanate. **2** *(derivar)* to derive (de, from), come (de, from).

emancipar *vt* to emancipate, free.
▸ *vpr* **emanciparse** to become emancipated, become free.

embajada *nf (edificio)* embassy.

embajador,-ra *nm & nf* ambassador.

embalar *vt (empaquetar)* to pack, wrap.
▸ *vpr* **embalarse** *(acelerar)* to speed up.

embalse *nm* **1** *(acción)* damming. **2** *(presa)* dam, reservoir.

embarazada *adj-nf* pregnant woman.

embarazo *nm (preñez)* pregnancy.

embarazoso,-a *adj* embarrassing.

embarcación *nf (nave)* boat, vessel, craft.

embarcadero *nm* pier, jetty, quay.

embarcar *vt (personas)* to embark, put on board; *(mercancías)* to load.
▸ *vpr* **embarcarse** *(en barco)* to embark, go on board; *(en avión)* to board.

embargar *vt* **1** JUR to seize, seques-trate, impound. **2** *(emociones)* to over-come.

embargo *nm* *(de bienes)* seizure of prop-erty, sequestration. LOC **sin embargo** nevertheless, however.

embarque *nm* *(de personas)* boarding; *(de mercancías)* loading.

embaucar *vt* to deceive, trick, dupe, cheat, swindle.

embelesar *vt* to charm, delight, fas-cinate.

embellecer *vt* to make beautiful, beautify.
▶ *vpr* **embellecerse** to make os beau-tiful, beautify os.

embestir *vt* *(toro)* to charge.

émbolo *nm* TÉC piston; *(de cafetera)* plunger.

emborrachar *vt* to make drunk.
▶ *vpr* **emborracharse** to get drunk.

emboscada *nf* ambush. LOC **tender una emboscada** to lay an ambush.

embotellamiento *nm* AUTO *fig* traffic jam.

embrague *nm* clutch.

embrión *nm* **1** embryo. **2** *fig (idea, etc)* beginnings *pl*, embryo.

embrujar *vt* **1** *(persona)* to bewitch; *(lu-gar)* to haunt. **2** *fig (fascinar)* to be-witch, enchant.

embrujo *nm* **1** spell, charm. **2** *fig (fasci-nación)* fascination, attraction.

embudo *nm* funnel.

embuste *nm* *(mentira)* lie; *(engaño)* trick.

embustero,-a *nm & nf* liar.

embutido *nm* *(alimento)* processed cold meat, cold cut.

eme *nf* *name of the letter* m.

emergencia *nf* **1** *(imprevisto)* emergen-cy. **2** *(salida)* emergence. LOC **en caso de emergencia** in case of emergency.

emerger *vi* to emerge.

emigración *nf* **1** emigration. **2** *(aves, pueblo)* migration.

emigrante *nm o nf* emigrant.

emigrar *vi* to emigrate; *(aves, pueblo)* to migrate.

emirato *nm* emirate. COMP **Emiratos Árabes Unidos** United Arab Emir-ates.

emisión *nf* **1** *(gen)* emission. **2** *(bonos, sellos, monedas)* issue. **3** RAD TV *(progra-ma)* broadcast; *(transmisión)* transmis-sion.

emisora *nf* radio station.

emitir *vt* **1** *(sonido, luz)* to emit; *(olor)* to give off. **2** *(manifestar)* to express. **3** *(bonos, monedas, sellos)* to issue. **4** RAD TV to broadcast, transmit.
▶ *vi* RAD TV to transmit.

emoción *nf* **1** *(sentimiento)* emotion, feeling. **2** *(excitación)* excitement.

emocionado,-a *adj* (deeply) moved, (deeply) touched.

emocionante *adj* **1** *(conmovedor)* mov-ing, touching. **2** *(excitante)* exciting, thrilling.

emocionar *vt* **1** *(conmover)* to move, touch. **2** *(excitar)* to excite, thrill.
▶ *vpr* **emocionarse 1** *(conmoverse)* to be moved, be touched. **2** *(excitarse)* to get excited.

emoticono *nm* INFORM emoticon.

emotivo,-a *adj (persona)* emotional; *(acto, etc)* moving, touching; *(palabras)* emotive.

empachar *vt* *(comer demasiado)* to give indigestion.
▶ *vpr* **empacharse** *(de comer)* to have in-digestion, get indigestion.

empacho *nm* *(indigestión)* indigestion.

empalagoso,-a *adj* **1** *(dulces)* too sweet, sickly. **2** *fig (persona)* sickly sweet, cloying.

empalmar *vt* *(unir)* to join, connect.
▶ *vi* **1** *(enlazar)* to join, connect. **2** *(se-guir)* to follow on from.

empanada *nf* pasty, pie.

empanadilla *nf* pasty.

empañar *vt* *(cristal)* to steam up.
▶ *vpr* **empañarse** *(cristal)* to steam up.

empapar *vt* **1** *(humedecer)* to soak; *(pe-netrar)* to soak, drench. **2** *(absorber)* to soak up.

▶ *vpr* **empaparse 1** *(humedecerse)* to get soaked. **2** *(persona)* to get soaked, get drenched, be soaked, be drenched.

empapelar *vt (una pared)* to wallpaper.

empaquetar *vt (hacer paquetes)* to pack (up), wrap (up).

empastar *vt (diente)* to fill.

empaste *nm (de diente)* filling.

empatar *vt* to draw.

empate *nm (en fútbol, rugby)* draw, US tie; *(en carrera, votación)* tie: *el gol del empate* the equalizer.

empedrado,-a *adj (calle)* cobbled.
▶ *nm* **empedrado 1** *(adoquines)* cobbles *pl*, cobblestones *pl*. **2** *(acción)* cobbling, paving.

empeine *nm (pie, zapato)* instep.

empeñar *vt* **1** *(objetos)* to pawn, US hock. **2** *(palabra)* to pledge.
▶ *vpr* **empeñarse 1** *(endeudarse)* to get into debt. **2** *(insistir)* to insist (en, on).

empeño *nm (insistencia)* determination.

empeorar *vi* to worsen, deteriorate.

emperador *nm* **1** emperor. **2** *(pez)* swordfish.

emperatriz *nf* empress.

empezar *vt* to begin, start.

empinado,-a *adj (alto)* very high.

emplazar *vt (situar)* to locate, place, situate.

empleado,-a *nm & nf* employee, clerk.

emplear *vt* **1** *(dar empleo)* to employ. **2** *(usar)* to use: *empleó un cuchillo* he used a knife. **3** *(dinero)* to spend. **4** *(tiempo)* to invest, spend.
▶ *vpr* **emplearse 1** *(usarse)* to be used: *este tipo de ordenador ya no se emplea* this type of computer is no longer used. **2** *(tener trabajo)* to be employed.

empleo *nm* **1** *(trabajo)* occupation, job. **2** POL employment. **3** *(uso)* use.

empobrecer *vi* to impoverish.
▶ *vpr* **empobrecerse** to become poor, become impoverished.

empollar *vt* **1** *(huevos)* to hatch. **2** *fam (estudiar)* to swot, swot up, US bone up on.

empollón,-ona *nm & nf fam pey* swot.

emprendedor,-ra *adj* enterprising, resourceful.

emprender *vt* **1** *(gen)* to start. **2** *(misión)* to tackle; *(viaje)* to set off on; *(tarea)* to undertake. LOC **emprender el vuelo** to take flight.

empresa *nf (compañía)* firm, company. COMP **empresa multinacional** multinational company.

empresario,-a *nm & nf (gen)* employer, manager; *(hombre)* businessman, manager; *(mujer)* businesswoman, manageress.

empujar *vt* to push, shove, thrust.

empuje *nm* **1** push, thrust, drive. **2** *fig (energía)* energy, drive.

empujón *nm* push, shove. LOC **abrirse paso a empujones** to push one's way through.

en *prep* **1** *(lugar - gen)* in, at: *en Valencia* in Valencia; *en casa* at home; *en el trabajo* at work. **2** *(- en el interior)* in, inside: *en el cajón* in the drawer. **3** *(lugar - sobre)* on: *en la mesa* on the table. **4** *(año, mes, estación)* in; *(día)* on; *(época, momento)* at: *en 1994* in 1994; *en aquel momento* at that moment. **5** *(dirección)* into: *entró en su casa* he went into his house. **6** *(transporte)* by: *ir en coche* to go by car. **7** *(tema, materia)* at, in: *experto en economía* expert in economics; *bueno en ajedrez* good at chess. **8** *(modo, manera)* in: *en inglés* in English. LOC **en cuanto** as soon as. ∎ **en camino** on the way.

enajenar *vt (propiedad)* to alienate.

enamorado,-a *nm & nf* lover, sweetheart.

enamoramiento *nm* infatuation, falling in love.

enamorar *vt* to win the heart of.
▶ *vpr* **enamorarse** to fall in love (de, with).

enano,-a *adj* dwarf.
▶ *nm & nf* dwarf.

encabezamiento *nm* **1** *(gen)* heading. **2** *(fórmula)* form of address.

encabezar *vt* **1** *(carta, lista)* to head. **2** *(acaudillar)* to lead. **3** DEP *(carrera)* to lead; *(clasificación)* to head, top.

encadenar vt 1 *(poner cadenas)* to chain (up). 2 *fig (enlazar)* to connect, link up.

encajar vt 1 *(ajustar)* to fit. 2 *(recibir)* to take, withstand. 3 *(soportar)* to bear. 4 *(indirecta, comentario)* to get in. 5 *(dar un golpe)* to land: *le encajó un golpe* he landed him a blow. 6 TÉC to gear.

encaje nm 1 *(acto)* fit, fitting. 2 *(hueco)* socket; *(caja)* housing. 3 COST lace.

encalar vt to whitewash.

encallar vi 1 MAR to run aground. 2 *fig* to flounder, fail.

encaminar vt *(guiar, orientar)* to direct, guide, set on the right road, put on the right road.
▶ vpr **encaminarse** *(dirigirse)* to head (a, for) (hacia, towards). LOC **estar bien encaminado,-a** to be on the right track.

encantador,-ra adj enchanting, charming, delightful.

encantar vt 1 *(hechizar)* to cast a spell on, bewitch. 2 *fam (gustar)* to delight, love.

encanto nm 1 *(hechizo)* spell, enchantment, charm. 2 *fig (cosa)* delight, enchantment; *(persona)* charm.

encapricharse vpr 1 *(empeñarse)* to set one's mind (con/en, on). 2 *(encariñarse)* to take a fancy (con, to).

encarar vt *(afrontar)* to face, face up to, confront.
▶ vpr **encararse 1** *(situación, problema)* to face up (a/con, to). 2 *(persona)* to stand up (a/con, to).

encarcelar vt to imprison.

encarecer vt *(precios)* to put up the price of.

encargado,-a adj in charge.
▶ nm & nf **1** COM *(hombre)* manager; *(mujer)* manageress. 2 *(empleado)* person in charge.

encargar vt 1 *(encomendar)* to entrust, put in charge of. 2 *(recomendar)* to recommend, advise. 3 COM *(pedir)* to order, place an order for: *encargó 4 kilos de naranjas* he ordered 4 kilos of oranges.
▶ vpr **encargarse de** to take charge of, look after, see to, deal with.

encargo nm 1 *(recado)* errand. 2 COM order, commission. LOC **hacer un encargo** *(recado)* to run an errand.

encariñarse vpr to become fond (con, of), get attached (con, to).

encauzar vt 1 to channel. 2 *fig* to direct, guide.

encéfalo nm encephalon.

encendedor nm lighter.

encender vt 1 *(hacer arder)* to light, set fire to; *(cerilla)* to strike, light; *(vela)* to light. 2 *(luz, radio, tv)* to turn on, switch on, put on; *(gas)* to turn on, light.
▶ vpr **encenderse** *(luz)* to go on, come on; *(llama)* to flare up.

encerado nm *(pizarra)* blackboard.

encerar vt to wax, polish.

encerrar vt 1 *(gen)* to shut in, shut up. 2 *(con llave)* to lock in, lock up.

encestar vt to score a basket.

enchufado,-a adj *fam* well-connected, with friends in the right places.
▶ nm & nf *fam (gen)* person with friends in the right places, US wirepuller; *(en la escuela)* teacher's pet.

enchufar vt 1 ELEC to connect, plug in. 2 *(unir)* to join, connect, fit. 3 *fam fig* to pull strings for: *enchufó a su hija en la empresa* he got his daughter a job in the company.

enchufe nm 1 ELEC *(hembra)* socket; *(macho)* plug. 2 *fam fig (trabajo)* easy job; *(influencias)* contacts pl, friends pl in high places. LOC **tener enchufe** *fam* to have contacts.

encía nf gum.

enciclopedia nf encyclopaedia, encyclopedia.

encima adv 1 *(más arriba)* above, overhead; *(sobre)* on top. 2 *(ropa, etc)* on, on top: *ponte algo encima* put something on. 3 *(además)* in addition, besides. 4 *fam (por si fuera poco)* what's more, on top of that, besides. LOC **encima de 1** *(a más altura)* over, above. 2 *(sobre)* on. 3 *(además)* besides, as well as, on top of that. ▮ **por encima de 1** *(más importante)* above. 2 *(más allá)* beyond: *está por encima de sus posibilidades* it's beyond her capabilities.

encina *nf* holm oak, evergreen oak.

encoger *vt* **1** *(contraer)* to contract. **2** *(tejido)* to shrink.
▶ *vi* *(tejido)* to shrink.
▶ *vpr* **encogerse 1** *(contraerse)* to contract. **2** *(tejido)* to shrink.

encolar *vt* *(dar cola)* to glue.

encontrar *vt* **1** *(gen)* to find. **2** *(una persona sin buscar)* to come across, meet, bump into. **3** *(dificultades)* to run into, come up against.
▶ *vpr* **encontrarse 1** *(estar)* to be: *se encuentra enfermo* he's ill. **2** *(persona)* to meet; *(por casualidad)* to bump into, run into, meet: *nos encontraremos allí* we'll meet there. **3** *(dificultades)* to run into. **4** *fig (sentirse)* to feel, be: *me encuentro mal* I feel bad.

encrucijada *nf* **1** crossroads, intersection. **2** *fig* crossroads.

encuadernación *nf* *(arte)* bookbinding.

encuadernar *vt* to bind.

encuadrar *vt* **1** *(cuadro, etc)* to frame. **2** *fig (encajar)* to fit in, insert.
▶ *vpr* **encuadrarse** *(incorporarse)* to join.

encuadre *nm* framing.

encubrir *vt* **1** *(ocultar)* to conceal, hide. **2** JUR *(delito)* to cover up; *(criminal)* to cover up for.

encuentro *nm* **1** *(de personas)* meeting. **2** DEP meeting, clash; *(partido)* match, game.

encuesta *nf* *(sondeo)* poll, survey. LOC **hacer una encuesta** to carry out an opinion poll.

encuestador,-ra *nm & nf* pollster.

encuestar *vt* to poll.

encurtidos *nm pl* pickles.

endecasílabo,-a *adj* hendecasyllabic.

enderezar *vt* **1** *(poner derecho)* to straighten out. **2** *(poner vertical)* to set upright. **3** *fig (situación, etc)* to put right.
▶ *vpr* **enderezarse** *(ponerse recto)* to straighten up.

endeudarse *vpr* to get into debt, fall into debt.

endibia *nf* endive.

endulzar *vt* to sweeten.

endurecer *vt* **1** to harden, make hard. **2** *fig* to harden, toughen.

ene *nf* name of the letter n.
▶ *adj (indeterminado)* n: *ene veces* n times.

enebro *nm* juniper.

eneldo *nm* dill.

enemigo,-a *adj* enemy, hostile.
▶ *nm & nf* enemy, foe.

enemistar *vt* to make enemies of, set at odds, cause a rift between.
▶ *vpr* **enemistarse** to become enemies.

energía *nf* **1** energy, power. **2** *fig* vigour (US vigor). COMP **energía cinética** kinetic energy.

enérgico,-a *adj* **1** energetic, vigorous. **2** *fig (decisión)* firm; *(palabra)* strong.

enero *nm* January.

✎ Consulta también **marzo**.

enervar *vt* **1** MED to enervate. **2** *fam (irritar)* to irritate, exasperate, get on one's nerves.
▶ *vpr* **enervarse** *fam* to get flustered, get worked up.

enfadado,-a *adj* angry, cross, annoyed, US mad.

enfadar *vt* to make angry, make cross, annoy.
▶ *vpr* **enfadarse 1** to get angry (con, with), get cross (con, with). **2** *(pelearse)* to fall out (con, with) (por, about).

enfado *nm* anger, irritation.

énfasis *nm & nf inv* emphasis, stress.

enfermar *vi* to fall ill, become ill, be taken ill.

enfermedad *nf* illness, disease, sickness. COMP **enfermedad contagiosa** contagious disease.

enfermería *nf* infirmary, sick bay.

enfermero,-a *nm & nf (hombre)* male nurse; *(mujer)* nurse.

enfermizo,-a *adj* sickly, unhealthy.

enfermo,-a *adj* sick, ill.

enfilar *vt* **1** *(poner en fila)* to line up. **2** *(una calle)* to go along, go down.

enfocar *vt* **1** to focus, focus on, get into focus. **2** *(luz)* to shine a light on.

3 *fig (problema, etc)* to focus on, approach, look at.

enfoque *nm* **1** *(acción)* focus, focusing. **2** *fig* focus, approach, angle.

enfrascarse *vpr* **1** *fig* to become absorbed (en, in), become engrossed (en, in). **2** *fig (en lectura)* to bury os (en, in).

enfrentamiento *nm* confrontation.

enfrentar *vt* **1** *(poner frente a frente)* to bring face to face, confront. **2** *(encarar)* to face, confront.
▶ *vpr* **enfrentarse** **1** *(hacer frente)* to face (a/con, -), confront (a/con, -). **2** DEP to meet (a/con, -). **3** *(pelearse)* to have an argument (a, with), fall out (a, with); *(chocar)* to clash (a/con, with).

enfrente *adv* opposite, in front, facing.

enfriar *vt* **1** to cool (down), chill. **2** *fig* to cool down.
▶ *vpr* **enfriarse** **1** *(lo demasiado caliente)* to cool down. **2** *(tener frío)* to get cold; *(resfriarse)* to catch a cold, get a cold.

enfurecer *vt* to infuriate, enrage.
▶ *vpr* **enfurecerse** **1** to get furious, lose one's temper. **2** *(mar)* to become rough.

enfurruñarse *vpr fam* to sulk, get in a huff.

engalanar *vt (cosa)* to festoon, deck out.
▶ *vpr* **engalanarse** *(persona)* to dress up, get dressed up.

enganchar *vt* **1** *(agarrar con gancho)* to hook. **2** *(colgar)* to hang, hang up. **3** *(vagones)* to couple.
▶ *vpr* **engancharse** **1** to get caught (en, on), snag (en, on). **2** MIL to enlist, join up. **3** *argot (drogas)* to get hooked (a, on).

engañar *vt* **1** *(gen)* to deceive, mislead, fool, take in. **2** *(estafar)* to cheat, trick.
▶ *vpr* **engañarse** **1** *(ilusionarse)* to deceive os. **2** *(equivocarse)* to be mistaken, be wrong.

engaño *nm* **1** deceit, deception. **2** *(estafa)* fraud, trick, swindle. **3** *(mentira)* lie.

engañoso,-a *adj (gen)* deceptive.

engarzar *vt* **1** *(perlas, etc)* to string, thread. **2** *fig (palabras, frases)* to string together.

engatusar *vt fam* to get round, coax, cajole.

engendrar *vt* to engender, beget.

engendro *nm* **1** *(feto)* foetus (US fetus). **2** *fam fig (persona)* freak. **3** *fig (cosa)* monstrosity.

englobar *vt* **1** *(incluir)* to include, comprise. **2** *(reunir)* to bring together, lump together.

engomar *vt* to gum, glue, stick.

engominarse *vpr (brillantina)* to put hair cream on; *(fijador)* to gel one's hair, put hair gel on.

engordar *vt* to fatten, fatten up, make fat.
▶ *vi* **1** *(persona)* to put on weight, get fatter. **2** *(alimento)* to be fattening.

engorroso,-a *adj fam* bothersome, annoying, awkward.

engranaje *nm* **1** TÉC gears *pl*. **2** *(de reloj)* cogs *pl*. **3** *fig* machinery.

engrasar *vt (dar grasa)* to grease, oil, lubricate.

engrescar *vt (incitar)* to cause trouble between; *(animar)* to get going, arouse, excite.
▶ *vpr* **engrescarse** to get embroiled.

engrosar *vt* **1** *(hacer grueso)* to thicken. **2** *fig (aumentar)* to increase, swell.

engullir *vt* to swallow.

enharinar *vt (cubrir)* to flour; *(manchar)* to sprinkle with flour.

enhebrar *vt* **1** to thread. **2** *fig* to connect, link.

enhorabuena *nf* congratulations *pl*.
▶ *adv* thank God.

enigma *nm* enigma, puzzle, mystery.

enigmático,-a *adj* enigmatic, mysterious, puzzling.

enjabonar *vt* **1** to soap. **2** *fig* to soft-soap, butter-up.

enjambre *nm* **1** swarm. **2** *fig* swarm, throng, crowd.

enjaular *vt* **1** to cage. **2** *fam fig* to put in jail, put inside.

enjoyar *vt* to adorn with jewels.

▸ *vpr* **enjoyarse** *fam* to put on lots of jewellery (US jewelry), be dripping with jewels.

enjuagar *vt* to rinse.
▸ *vpr* **enjuagarse** to rinse one's mouth out.

enjugar *vt (secar)* to dry, wipe (away), mop up.

enjuiciar *vt* **1** *(juzgar)* to judge; *(examinar)* to examine. **2** JUR *(civil)* to sue; *(criminal)* to indict, prosecute.

enlace *nm* **1** *(conexión)* link, connection. **2** *(boda)* marriage. **3** *(tren, etc)* connection. **4** QUÍM bond.

enlatado,-a *adj* canned, tinned.

enlatar *vt* to can, tin.

enlazar *vt* **1** *(unir)* to link, connect, tie (together). **2** *(ideas, etc)* to link, connect, relate. **3** *(carreteras, etc)* to connect.
▸ *vi (trenes, etc)* to connect (**con**, with).
▸ *vpr* **enlazarse 1** *(unirse)* to be linked, be connected. **2** *(casarse)* to get married, marry.

enlodar *vt* to muddy, cover with mud.

enloquecedor,-ra *adj* maddening.

enloquecer *vt* **1** *(volver loco)* to drive mad. **2** *fam (gustar)* to be mad/crazy about, be wild about.
▸ *vi (volverse loco)* to go mad/crazy, go out of one's mind.

enlosado *nm (de losas)* paving; *(de baldosas)* tiling.

enlosar *vt (losas)* to pave; *(baldosas)* to tile.

enlucir *vt (paredes, etc)* to plaster.

enmadrado,-a *adj* tied to one's mother's apron strings.

enmadrarse *vpr* to be tied to one's mother's apron strings.

enmarañar *vt* **1** *(enredar)* to tangle. **2** *fig* to embroil, muddle up, confuse.
▸ *vpr* **enmarañarse 1** *(enredarse)* to get tangled. **2** *fig* to get into a muddle, get confused.

enmarcar *vt* to frame.

enmascarado,-a *adj* masked.
▸ *nm & nf* masked person.

enmascarar *vt* **1** to mask. **2** *fig* to mask, disguise, conceal.

enmendar *vt* **1** to correct, put right. **2** *(un daño)* to repair, put right.
▸ *vpr* **enmendarse** to reform, mend one's ways.

enmienda *nf* **1** correction. **2** *(de daño)* repair, indemnity, compensation. LOC **hacer propósito de enmienda** to turn over a new leaf.

enmohecer *vt (pan, queso, etc)* to make mouldy (US moldy); *(metal)* to rust.
▸ *vpr* **enmohecerse** *(pan, queso, etc)* to go mouldy (US moldy); *(metal)* to rust, go rusty.

enmoquetar *vt* to carpet.

enmudecer *vt (hacer callar)* to silence.
▸ *vi* **1** *(quedar mudo)* to be struck dumb; *(perder la voz)* to lose one's voice. **2** *(callar)* to fall silent, keep quiet.

enojado,-a *adj* angry, cross.

enojar *vt* to anger, annoy, make angry.
▸ *vpr* **enojarse** to get angry (**con**, with), get annoyed (**con**, with), lose one's temper (**con**, with).

enojo *nm* anger, annoyance.

enojoso,-a *adj* annoying, irritating.

enorgullecer *vt* to fill with pride.
▸ *vpr* **enorgullecerse** to be proud (**de**, of), pride os (**de**, on).

enorme *adj (grande)* enormous, huge, vast.

enormidad *nf (grandeza)* enormity, hugeness.

enquistarse *vpr* to encyst.

enrabiar *vt* to enrage, infuriate.
▸ *vpr* **enrabiarse** to become enraged.

enraizar *vi* **1** BOT to take root. **2** *fig (persona)* to put down roots.
▸ *vpr* **enraizarse** *(planta, árbol)* to take root; *(persona)* to put down roots.

enredadera *nf* creeper, climbing plant.

enredar *vt* **1** *(engatusar)* to involve, implicate. **2** *(meter cizaña)* to sow discord, cause trouble. **3** *(enmarañar)* to tangle up, entangle. **4** *fig (asunto, etc)* to confuse, complicate.

▶ *vpr* **enredarse 1** *(hacerse un lío)* to get tangled up, get entangled, get into a tangle.

enredo *nm* **1** *(maraña)* tangle. **2** *(confusión)* mess, muddle, confusion, mix-up. **3** *(engaño)* deceit. **4** *(travesura)* mischief.

enrejado *nm* *(reja)* railings *pl*, grating.

enrejar *vt* **1** *(puerta, ventana)* to put a grating on. **2** *(vallar)* to fence, put railings round.

enrevesado,-a *adj* complicated, difficult.

enriquecer *vt* **1** *(hacer rico)* to make rich. **2** *fig* to enrich.
▶ *vpr* **enriquecerse** to get rich.

enriquecimiento *nm* enrichment.

enrocar *vi* *(ajedrez)* to castle.
▶ *vt* *(ajedrez)* to castle.

enrojecimiento *nm* *(rostro)* blushing.

enrollado,-a *adj* **1** *(papel)* rolled up; *(cable)* coiled. **2** *fam (guay)* cool, great.

enrollar *vt* **1** *(papel)* to roll up; *(hilo)* to wind up. **2** *(a alguien)* to involve.
▶ *vpr* **enrollarse 1** *fam fig (hablar)* to go on and on (con, to), chatter (con, to). **2** *fam fig (tener relaciones)* to have an affair (con, with). **3** *fam fig (liarse)* to get involved (con, with).

enroque *nm* castling.

enroscar *vt* *(tornillo)* to screw in.
▶ *vpr* **enroscarse** to wind, coil; *(cable)* to roll up; *(serpiente)* to coil itself (up).

ensaimada *nf* spiral-shaped pastry made of light dough.

ensalada *nf* salad.

ensaladera *nf* salad bowl.

ensaladilla *nf* vegetable salad.

ensamblar *vt* to join, assemble.

ensanchar *vt* **1** *(gen)* to widen, enlarge, extend. **2** COST to let out.
▶ *vpr* **ensancharse** to get wider, expand, spread, stretch.

ensanche *nm* **1** *(gen)* widening, enlargement, extension. **2** *(de ciudad)* urban development.

ensartar *vt* *(cuentas)* to string (together), thread; *(aguja)* to thread.

ensayar *vt* **1** TEAT to rehearse. **2** MÚS to practise (US practice). **3** *(probar)* to try out, test.

ensayo *nm* **1** TEAT rehearsal. **2** MÚS practice. **3** *(prueba)* test, experiment, trial, attempt. **4** *(literario, etc)* essay.

enseguida *adv* at once, straight away, immediately.

✎ También se escribe en seguida.

enseñante *nm o nf* teacher.

enseñanza *nf* **1** *(educación)* education, teaching. **2** *(doctrina)* teaching, doctrine. COMP **enseñanza general básica** general basic education. ǀ **enseñanza primaria** primary education.

enseñar *vt* **1** *(en escuela, etc)* to teach, train, instruct. **2** *(educar)* to educate. **3** *(mostrar, dejar ver)* to show: *me enseñó el libro* he showed me the book.

ensillar *vt* put a saddle on.

ensimismado,-a *adj* engrossed, absorbed, lost.

ensimismarse *vpr* *(abstraerse)* to become lost in thought.

ensoñar *vt* to daydream about.

ensordecedor,-ra *adj* deafening.

ensordecer *vt* to deafen.
▶ *vi* to go deaf.

ensortijado,-a *adj* curly.

ensuciar *vt* to dirty, make dirty.
▶ *vpr* **ensuciarse** *(mancharse)* to get dirty.

ensueño *nm* dream, fantasy. LOC **de ensueño** dream.

entablar *vt* **1** *(poner tablas)* to plank, board. **2** *(conversación)* to begin, start, open; *(amistad)* to strike up.

entallar *vt* COST to take in at the waist.

entarimado *nm* parquet floor.

ente *nm* *(ser)* being.

entender *nm* *(opinión)* understanding, opinion.
▶ *vt* **1** *(comprender)* to understand. **2** *(darse cuenta)* to realize. **3** *(discurrir)* to think, believe: *entiendo que sería mejor ir* I think it would be better to go. **4** *(interpretar)* to understand, take it.

▶ *vi (tener conocimiento)* to know (de, about).

▶ *vpr* **entenderse 1** *(comprenderse)* to be understood. **2** *fam (conocerse)* to know what one is doing: *yo ya me entiendo* I have my reasons. **3** *fam (llevarse bien)* to get along.

entendido,-a *nm & nf* expert.

entendimiento *nm* **1** *(comprensión)* understanding, comprehension. **2** *(sentido común)* understanding, sense, judgement. **3** *(inteligencia)* intelligence.

enterado,-a *nm & nf fam* expert, authority. LOC **darse por enterado,-a de** ALGO to be aware of STH. ▮ **estar enterado,-a** to be in the know.

enterar *vt* to inform (de, about/of); *(poner al corriente)* to acquaint (de, with), tell (de, about).

▶ *vpr* **enterarse 1** *(averiguar)* to find out (de, about). **2** *(tener conocimiento)* to learn, hear. **3** *(darse cuenta)* to realize.

enternecer *vt (conmover)* to move, touch.

▶ *vpr* **enternecerse** to be moved, be touched.

entero,-a *adj (completo)* entire, whole, complete.

▶ *nm* **entero** MAT whole number.

enterrar *vt* **1** to bury, inter. **2** *fig (olvidar)* to forget, give up.

entierro *nm* **1** *(acción)* burial. **2** *(ceremonia)* funeral.

entonar *vt* **1** *(nota)* to pitch; *(canción)* to sing, intone. **2** *(colores)* to match.

▶ *vi* **1** MÚS to intone. **2** *(colores)* to match. **3** *fig (armonizar)* to be in harmony (con, with), be in tune (con, with).

entonces *adv* **1** *(en aquel momento)* then. **2** *(en tal caso)* so, then: *entonces no lo quieres* so you don't want it. LOC **desde entonces** since then.

entornado,-a *adj (ojos, etc)* half-closed; *(puerta)* ajar.

entornar *vt* **1** *(ojos, etc)* to half-close. **2** *(puerta)* to leave ajar.

entorno *nm* **1** environment, surroundings *pl*. **2** INFORM environment.

entorpecer *vt* **1** to make numb, make dull. **2** *fig (dificultar)* to obstruct.

entorpecimiento *nm* **1** dullness, numbness. **2** *fig (obstrucción)* obstruction, hindrance.

entrada *nf* **1** *(gen)* entrance, entry. **2** *(vestíbulo)* hall, entrance. **3** *(billete)* ticket, admission. **4** *(público)* audience. **5** *(de libro, oración, etc)* opening; *(de año, mes)* beginning: *la entrada de la primavera* the beginning of spring. **6** *(pago inicial)* down payment, deposit. **7** CULIN entrée, starter. **8** INFORM input. **9** DEP tackle. LOC **de entrada 1** *(desde el principio)* straight away, from the outset. **2** *(en comida)* for starters. ▮ «**Prohibida la entrada**» "No admittance".

entramado *nm* wooden framework.

entrante *adj* entering, coming, incoming: *el año entrante* the coming year; *el mes entrante* next month.

▶ *nm* CULIN starter.

entrañable *adj* **1** *(amistad)* intimate, close. **2** *(amigo)* dear. **3** *(recuerdo)* fond.

entrar *vi* **1** *(ir adentro)* to come in, go in. **2** *(tener entrada)* to be welcome. **3** *(en una sociedad, etc)* to join; *(en una profesión)* to take up, join. **4** *(encajar, caber)* to fit: *este tornillo no entra* this screw doesn't fit. **5** *(empezar - año, estación)* to begin, start; *(- período, época)* to enter; *(- libro, carta)* to begin, open: *ya ha entrado el verano* summer has begun. **6** *(venir)* to come over, come on: *me entraron ganas de llorar* I felt like crying. **7** *(alcanzar)* to reach: *ha entrado en los cuarenta* he has reached forty. **8** INFORM to access.

▶ *vt (meter)* to put.

entre *prep* **1** *(dos términos)* between. **2** *(varios)* among, amongst: *entre los periódicos* among the newspapers. **3** *(entremedio)* somewhere between: *entre azul y verde* somewhere between blue and green. LOC **de entre** from among, out of: ▮ **entre tanto** meanwhile, in the meantime.

entreabierto,-a *adj (ojos, etc)* half-open; *(puerta)* ajar.

entreabrir *vt* **1** *(ojos)* to half open. **2** *(puerta, etc)* to leave ajar.

entreacto *nm* interval.

entrecejo *nm* space between the eyebrows; *(ceño)* frown.

entrecot *nm* entrecôte.

entredicho *nm* *(duda)* doubt, question. LOC **poner** ALGO **en entredicho** to have one's doubts about STH.

entrega *nf* **1** *(gen)* handing over. **2** *(de premios)* presentation. **3** COM delivery. **4** *(de posesiones)* surrender. **5** *(fascículo)* instalment (US installment), part. **6** DEP pass. COMP **entrega a domicilio** home delivery.

entregar *vt* **1** *(dar)* to hand over. **2** *(deberes, ejercicios)* to hand in, give in; *(premios)* to present, award. **3** COM to deliver.
► *vpr* **entregarse 1** *(rendirse)* to give in (a, to), surrender. **2** *(dedicarse)* to devote os (a, to), be devoted (a, to). **3** *pey (caer en)* to give os over (a, to), take (a, to).

entrelazar *vt* to entwine, interweave, interlace.

entremedias *adv* **1** in between. **2** *(mientras tanto)* meanwhile, in the meantime. LOC **entremedias de** between, among.

entremés *nm* hors d'oeuvre *pl*.

entremezclar *vt* to intermingle.
► *vpr* **entremezclarse** to intermingle.

entrenador,-ra *nm & nf* trainer, coach.

entrenamiento *nm* training.

entrenar *vt* to train, coach.
► *vpr* **entrenarse** to train.

entreno *nm* training.

entresijo *nm fig* secret, mystery. LOC **conocer todos los entresijos** *fig* to know all the ins and outs.

entresuelo *nm* mezzanine, GB first floor, US second floor.

entretanto *adv* meanwhile.

entretejer *vt* to interweave, intertwine.

entretener *vt* **1** *(detener)* to hold up, detain; *(retrasar)* to delay. **2** *(ocupar)* to keep busy. **3** *(distraer)* to occupy, keep occupied. **4** *(divertir)* to entertain, amuse, distract.
► *vpr* **entretenerse 1** *(retrasarse)* to be delayed, be held up. **2** *(distraerse)* to keep os occupied. **3** *(divertirse)* to amuse os.

entretenido,-a *adj* *(divertido)* entertaining, amusing.

entretenimiento *nm* *(distracción)* entertainment, distraction, amusement.

entretiempo *nm* period between seasons; *(primavera)* spring; *(otoño)* autumn. LOC **un traje de entretiempo** a lightweight suit.

entrevista *nf* **1** *(prensa)* interview. **2** *(reunión)* meeting. LOC **hacer una entrevista a** ALGN to interview SB.

entrevistador,-ra *nm & nf* interviewer.

entrevistar *vt* to interview.
► *vpr* **entrevistarse 1** *(prensa)* to have an interview (con, with). **2** *(reunirse)* to have a meeting (con, with).

entristecer *vt* to make sad.
► *vpr* **entristecerse** to be sad (por, about).

entrometerse *vpr* to meddle, interfere.

entrometido,-a *adj* nosy.
► *nm & nf* meddler, nosy parker.

entroncar *vt* to relate, link, connect.
► *vi (parentesco)* to be related.

entumecido,-a *adj* numb.

entumecimiento *nm* numbness.

enturbiar *vt* **1** to make muddy, make cloudy, cloud. **2** *fig* to cloud, muddle, obscure.
► *vpr* **enturbiarse 1** to get muddy, become cloudy. **2** *fig* to get confused, get muddled.

entusiasmado,-a *adj* excited.

entusiasmar *vt* **1** *(causar entusiasmo)* to fill with enthusiasm, excite. **2** *(gustar)* to like, love: *me entusiasma la ópera* I love opera.
► *vpr* **entusiasmarse 1** to get enthusiastic (con, about), get excited (con, about). **2** *(gustar)* to love (con, -), like (con, -).

entusiasmo *nm* enthusiasm. LOC **con entusiasmo** keenly, enthusiastically.

entusiasta *adj* enthusiastic.

enumeración *nf (cómputo)* enumeration, count, reckoning.

enumerar *vt* to enumerate.

enunciado *nm* **1** *(teoría, etc)* enunciation. **2** LING statement. **3** *(problema, etc)* wording.

enunciar *vt* **1** *(teoría)* to enunciate. **2** *(expresar)* to express, state, word.

envalentonar *vt* to make bold, make daring.
▶ *vpr* **envalentonarse** *(volverse valiente)* to become bold, become daring.

envasado,-a *adj (bebidas)* bottled; *(conservas)* canned, tinned; *(paquetes)* packed.
▶ *nm* **envasado** *(bebidas)* bottling; *(conservas)* canning; *(paquetes)* packing. COMP **envasado al vacío** vacuum-packed.

envasar *vt (botellas)* to bottle; *(latas)* to can, tin; *(paquetes)* to pack.

envase *nm* **1** *(acción - paquetes)* packing; *(- botellas)* bottling; *(- latas)* canning. **2** *(recipiente)* container. **3** *(botella vacía)* empty. COMP **envase de cartón** carton. ‖ **envase de plástico** plastic container. ‖ **envase sin retorno** nonreturnable bottle.

envejecer *vt* to age, make look old.
▶ *vi* to get old, grow old.

envejecido,-a *adj* aged, old, old-looking: *Pablo está muy envejecido* Pablo looks very old.

envejecimiento *nm* ageing.

envenenamiento *nm* poisoning.

envenenar *vt* to poison.

envés *nm inv* **1** *(de página)* back, reverse. **2** *(de tela)* wrong side. **3** BOT reverse.

enviado,-a *nm & nf* messenger, envoy. COMP **enviado,-a especial** special correspondent.

enviar *vt* **1** *(gen)* to send. **2** COM to dispatch, remit; *(por barco)* to ship.

enviciar *vt (pervertir)* to corrupt, pervert.
▶ *vi* BOT to produce too many leaves and not enough fruit.
▶ *vpr* **enviciarse** *(pervertirse)* to become corrupted, fall into bad habits.

envidar *vi* to bid, bet.

envidia *nf* envy. LOC **dar envidia** to make envious. ‖ **tener envidia de** ALGO/ALGN to envy STH/SB.

envidiable *adj* enviable.

envidiar *vt* to envy.

envidioso,-a *adj* envious.

envío *nm* **1** *(acción)* sending, dispatch. **2** COM dispatch, shipment. **3** *(paquete)* parcel. **4** *(mensaje electrónico)* posting. LOC **hacer un envío** COM to dispatch an order. ‖ **envío contra reembolso** cash on delivery. ‖ COMP **gastos de envío** postage and packing.

envite *nm (apuesta)* bet.

enviudar *vi (hombre)* to become a widower, lose one's wife; *(mujer)* to become a widow, lose one's husband.

envoltorio *nm (de caramelo, etc)* wrapper.

envolver *vt (con papel)* to wrap, wrap up.

enyesado *nm* **1** plastering. **2** MED plaster cast.

enyesar *vt* **1** to plaster. **2** MED to put in plaster.

enzarzar *vt* **1** *(de zarzas)* to cover with brambles. **2** *fig (engrescar)* to sow discord among, set at odds.
▶ *vpr* **enzarzarse** **1** *(enredarse en zarzas)* to get entangled in brambles. **2** *fig (discusión, asunto)* to get involved (en, in).

enzima *nm & nf* enzyme.

eñe *nf name of the letter* ñ.

eoceno,-a *adj* Eocene.
▶ *nm* **eoceno** Eocene.

eólico,-a *adj* wind: *energía eólica* wind power.

épica *nf* epic poetry.

epiceno *adj* epicene.

epicentro *nm* epicentre (US epicenter).

épico,-a *adj* epic, heroic.

epicureísmo *nm* Epicureanism.

epicúreo,-a *adj* Epicurean.

epidemia *nf* epidemic.

epidémico,-a *adj* epidemic.

epidérmico,-a *adj* epidermic, skin: *enfermedad epidérmica* skin disease.

epidermis *nf inv* epidermis, skin.

epígrafe *nm* **1** *(cita)* epigraph. **2** *(título)* title, heading.

epilepsia *nf* epilepsy.

epiléptico,-a *adj* epileptic.

epílogo *nm* *(parte final)* epilogue (US epilog).

episcopado *nm* *(obispos)* episcopacy.

episcopal *adj* episcopal.

episodio *nm* **1** *(literario)* episode. **2** *(suceso)* incident, event.

epístola *nf fml* epistle, letter.

epitelio *nm* epithelium.

epíteto *nm* epithet.

época *nf* **1** time, age. **2** HIST period, epoch: *muebles de época* period furniture. **3** AGR season, time: *la época de la recolección* harvest time. LOC **por aquella época** about that time. ▌**ser de su época** to be with the times.

epopeya *nf* **1** LIT epic poem. **2** *(hecho)* heroic deed.

equidad *nf* *(moderación)* fairness, reasonableness.

equidistancia *nf* equidistance.

equidistante *adj* equidistant.

equidistar *vi* to be equidistant (de, from).

equilátero,-a *adj* equilateral.

equilibrado,-a *adj* **1** balanced. **2** *(persona)* sensible, well-balanced.

equilibrar *vt* **1** to balance, poise. **2** *fig* to balance, adjust.
▶ *vpr* **equilibrarse** **1** to balance (en, on). **2** *fig* to recover one's balance.

equilibrio *nm* **1** *(estabilidad)* balance: *perdió el equilibrio* he lost his balance. **2** FÍS equilibrium. **3** *fig* *(armonía)* balance, harmony. LOC **hacer equilibrios** *fig* to perform a balancing act. ▌**mantener el equilibrio** to keep one's balance.

equilibrismo *nm* *(gen)* balancing act; *(de funámbulo)* tightrope walking.

equilibrista *nm o nf* *(funámbulo)* tightrope walker.

equino,-a *adj* equine, horse.

equinoccio *nm* equinox.

equinodermo *nm* echinoderm.

equipaje *nm* luggage, baggage. COMP **equipaje de mano** hand luggage.

equipar *vt* to equip, furnish.
▶ *vpr* **equiparse** *(uso reflexivo)* to kit os out (con/de, with), equip os (con/de, with).

equiparable *adj* comparable (a/con, to/with).

equiparar *vt* to compare (a/con, with), liken (a/con, to).

equipo *nm* **1** *(prestaciones)* equipment. **2** *(ropas, utensilios)* outfit, kit. **3** *(de personas)* team. COMP **equipo de alta fidelidad** hi-fi system. ▌**equipo de fútbol** football team. ▌**equipo de música** music centre, stereo system.

equis *nf inv* **1** *name of the letter* x. **2** MAT x, unknown quantity.

equitación *nf* horsemanship, horse riding, US horseback riding.

equitativo,-a *adj* equitable, fair.

equivalencia *nf* **1** *(igualdad)* equivalence. **2** *(sustitución)* compensation.

equivalente *adj* *(igual)* equivalent.
▶ *nm* equivalent.

equivaler *vi* **1** *(ser igual)* to be equivalent (a, to), be equal (a, to). **2** *(significar)* to be tantamount (a, to), amount (a, to), mean (a, -).

equivocación *nf* **1** *(error)* mistake, error. **2** *(malentendido)* misunderstanding. LOC **cometer una equivocación** to make a mistake.

equivocado,-a *adj* mistaken, wrong.

equivocar *vt* **1** to mistake, get wrong. **2** *(cambiar)* to get mixed up: *equivoqué vuestros regalos* I got your presents mixed up.
▶ *vpr* **equivocarse** to make a mistake, be mistaken, be wrong; *(de dirección, camino, etc)* to go wrong; get wrong: *me equivoqué de calle* I got the wrong street.

equívoco,-a *adj* equivocal, misleading, ambiguous.
▶ *nm* **equívoco** **1** ambiguity, double meaning. **2** *(malentendido)* misunderstanding.

era *nf* *(tiempo)* era, age.

erario *nm* exchequer, treasury.

erasmismo *nm* Erasmianism.

ere *nf name of the letter* r.

erecto,-a *adj* erect.

eremita *nm* hermit, eremite.

ergonómico,-a *adj* ergonomic.

erguido,-a *adj* erect, upright, straight.

erguir *vt* to raise (up straight), erect, lift up.
► *vpr* **erguirse** *(ponerse derecho)* to straighten up, stand up straight.

erial *adj* uncultivated, untilled.
► *nm* uncultivated land.

erigir *vt (alzar)* to erect, build.

Eritrea *nf* Eritrea.

eritreo,-a *adj* Eritrean.
► *nm & nf (persona)* Eritrean.

erizado,-a *adj* bristly, prickly.

erizar *vt (pelo - animal)* to bristle; *(- persona)* make stand on end.
► *vpr* **erizarse** *(pelo - de animal)* to bristle; *(- de persona)* to stand on end: *el pelo se le erizó* his hair stood on end.

erizo *nm (animal)* hedgehog. [COMP] **erizo de mar** sea urchin.

ermita *nf* hermitage, shrine.

ermitaño,-a *adj* recluse.
► *nm & nf (persona solitaria)* hermit.
► *nm* **ermitaño** ZOOL hermit crab.

erosión *nf* erosion, wearing away.

erosionar *vt* to erode.

erosivo,-a *adj* erosive.

erradicar *vt* **1** to eradicate. **2** *(enfermedad)* to stamp out.

errado,-a *adj* mistaken, wrong.

errante *adj* wandering, errant.

errar *vt (objetivo)* to miss, get wrong.
► *vi* **1** *(vagar)* to wander, rove, roam. **2** *(equivocarse)* to be mistaken, be wrong.

errata *nf* erratum, misprint.

errático,-a *adj* erratic.

erre *nf name of the digraph* rr.

erróneo,-a *adj* erroneous, wrong, mistaken, unsound: *explicación errónea* wrong explanation.

error *nm* error, mistake.

eructar *vi* to belch, burp.

eructo *nm* belch, burp.

erudición *nf* erudition, learning.

erudito,-a *adj* erudite, learned.
► *nm & nf* scholar, expert.

erupción *nf* **1** *(volcánica)* eruption. **2** *(cutánea)* rash. [LOC] **entrar en erupción** to erupt.

eruptivo,-a *adj* eruptive.

esbelto,-a *adj* slim, slender.

esbozar *vt* to sketch, outline. [LOC] **esbozar una sonrisa** *fig* to force a smile, smile weakly.

esbozo *nm* sketch, outline.

escabechado,-a *adj* pickled, in brine.

escabechar *vt* to pickle, preserve in brine; *(arenque)* to souse, pickle.

escabeche *nm* brine, pickle.

escabechina *nf fam* massacre.

escabroso,-a *adj* **1** *(desigual)* uneven, rough: *terreno escabroso* rough terrain. **2** *fig (difícil)* tough, difficult.

escabullirse *vpr* **1** *(entre las manos)* to slip through. **2** *fig (persona)* to slip away, sneak off, disappear.

escacharrar *vt* **1** *fam (romper)* to break. **2** *fam (estropear)* to ruin, spoil.

escafandra *nf* diving suit.

escafandrista *nm o nf* diver.

escala *nf* **1** *(escalera - de mano)* ladder; *(- de tijera)* stepladder. **2** *(mapa, plano, etc)* scale: *lo dibujó a escala* he drew it to scale. **3** *(puerto)* port of call; *(aeropuerto)* stopover. **4** MÚS scale.

escalada *nf (montaña)* climb, climbing.

escalador,-ra *nm & nf* climber.

escalafón *nm (de personas)* roll, promotion list.

escalar *vt (montaña)* to climb.

escaldado,-a *adj* scalded.

escaleno *adj* scalene.

escalera *nf* **1** stairs *pl*, staircase. **2** *(escala)* ladder.

escalerilla *nf (de barco)* gangway; *(de avión)* steps *pl*.

escalfar *vt* to poach: *huevos escalfados* poached eggs.

escalinata *nf* outside steps *pl*.

escalofriante *adj* chilling, bloodcurdling, hair-raising.

escalofrío *nm (de frío)* shiver. [LOC] **tener escalofríos** to shiver.

escalón *nm* **1** *(peldaño)* step, stair; *(de escala)* rung. **2** *fig (grado)* degree, level, grade. **3** *fig (paso, medio)* stepping stone.

escalonado,-a *adj (espaciado)* spaced out, at regular intervals.

escalonar *vt* **1** *(espaciar)* to place at intervals, space out. **2** *(cabello)* cut in layers.

escama *nf* **1** scale. **2** *fig (de piel, de jabón)* flake.

escamado,-a *adj fam fig* wary, suspicious.

escamar *vt* **1** *(quitar escamas)* to scale, remove the scales from. **2** *fam fig* to make suspicious, make wary.

escampar *vt* to clear out.
▶ *vi* [se emplea sólo en tercera persona; no lleva sujeto] METEOR to stop raining, clear up.

escandalizar *vt* to shock.
▶ *vpr* **escandalizarse** to be shocked (de/por, at), be scandalized (de/por, by).

escándalo *nm* **1** scandal. **2** *(alboroto)* racket, fuss, din, uproar. [LOC] **armar un escándalo** to kick up a fuss.

escandaloso,-a *adj* **1** scandalous, shocking, outrageous. **2** *(alborotado)* noisy, rowdy.

Escandinavia *nf* Scandinavia.

escandinavo,-a *adj* Scandinavian.
▶ *nm & nf* Scandinavian.

escanear *vt* to scan.

escáner *nm* scanner.

escaño *nm* **1** *(banco)* bench. **2** POL seat.

escapada *nf* **1** *fam (salida)* quick trip. **2** *(huida)* escape.

escapar *vi* **1** *(huir)* to escape, get away, run away. **2** *(librarse)* to escape.
▶ *vpr* **escaparse** **1** *(huir)* to escape, run away, get away. **2** *(librarse)* to escape, avoid. **3** *(gas, etc)* to leak.

escaparate *nm* shop window.

escapatoria *nf* **1** *(huida)* escape, flight. **2** *(excusa)* excuse, way out.

escape *nm* **1** *(huida)* escape, flight, getaway. **2** *(de gas, etc)* leak.

escarabajo *nm* beetle.

escaramujo *nm* **1** *(rosal)* wild rose, dog rose. **2** *(fruto)* rosehip.

escaramuza *nf (riña)* run-in, squabble.

escarbar *vt* **1** *(suelo)* to scratch. **2** *(bolsillo, papeles)* to rummage in.

escarcha *nf* frost, hoarfrost.

escarlata *adj* scarlet.

escarlatina *nf* scarlet fever.

escarmentar *vt* teach a lesson to.
▶ *vi* to learn one's lesson: *a ver si escarmientas* that'll teach you (a lesson).

escarmiento *nm* lesson.

escarola *nf* curly endive.

escarpado,-a *adj* **1** *(inclinado)* steep, sheer. **2** *(abrupto)* craggy.

escarpia *nf* spike, hook.

escasear *vi (faltar)* to be scarce.

escasez *nf (carencia)* scarcity, lack, shortage.

escaso,-a *adj* **1** *(insuficiente)* scarce, scant, very little, small. **2** *(recursos)* slender; *(dinero)* tight; *(público)* small; *(lluvias, salario)* low; *(tiempo)* very little. **3** *(poco de algo)* few: *escasos días* few days. **4** *(que le falta poco)* hardly, scarcely, barely: *un kilo escaso* barely a kilo.

escayola *nf* **1** *(yeso)* plaster of Paris; *(estuco)* stucco. **2** MED plaster.

escayolar *vt* to put in plaster, plaster.

escena *nf* **1** TEAT *(parte)* scene; *(lugar)* stage. **2** *fig* scene.

escenario *nm* **1** TEAT stage. **2** CINE scenario. **3** *fig* scene, setting.

escenificar *vt* **1** *(novela)* to dramatize. **2** *(obra de teatro)* to stage.

escenografía *nm* **1** CINE set design. **2** TEAT stage design.

escenógrafo,-a *nm & nf* **1** CINE set designer. **2** TEAT stage designer.

escepticismo *nm* scepticism (US skepticism).

escéptico,-a *adj* sceptic (US skeptic).

escindir *vt* to split, divide.
▶ *vpr* **escindirse** to split (off) (en, into).

escisión *nf* **1** split, division. **2** FÍS fission. **3** MED excision.

esclavitud *nf* slavery, servitude.

esclavizar *vt* to enslave.

E

esclavo,-a *adj* enslaved.
▶ *nm & nf (gen)* slave.

esclusa *nf* lock, sluicegate, floodgate.

escoba *nf* brush, broom.

escobilla *nf* small brush.

escobón *nm* large brush.

escocer *vi* **1** to smart, sting: *le escuecen sus heridas* his cuts sting. **2** *fig* to hurt.

escocés,-a *adj* Scottish.
▶ *nm & nf (persona)* Scot; *(hombre)* Scotsman; *(mujer)* Scotswoman.
▶ *nm* **escocés** *(idioma)* Scottish Gaelic.

Escocia *nf* Scotland. COMP **Nueva Escocia** Nova Scotia.

escoger *vt* to choose, pick out, select.

escogido,-a *adj* chosen, selected; *(selecto)* choice, select.

escolar *adj* school, scholastic.
▶ *nm o nf (chico)* schoolboy; *(chica)* schoolgirl.

escolástico,-a *adj* scholastic.

escollera *nf* breakwater, jetty.

escollo *nm fig* difficulty, pitfall, snag.

escolopendra *nf* centipede.

escolta *nf* escort.

escoltar *vt* **1** to escort. **2** MAR to convoy.

escombros *nm pl* rubble *sing*, debris *sing*.

esconder *vt* to hide, conceal.
▶ *vpr* **esconderse** to hide.

escondidas LOC **hacer** ALGO **a escondidas de** ALGN to do STH behind SB's back.

escondite *nm* **1** *(lugar)* hiding place. **2** *(juego)* hide-and-seek.

escopeta *nf* shotgun.

escorpión *nm* scorpion.

escorzo *nm* foreshortening.

escote *nm* COST low neckline.

escozor *nm* **1** stinging, smarting. **2** *fig* pain, grief.

escribir *vt* **1** *(gen)* to write. **2** *(deletrear)* to spell, write.
▶ *vi* to write.
▶ *vpr* **escribirse 1** *(deletrear)* to spell, be spelt: *¿cómo se escribe?* how do you spell it? **2** *(uso recíproco)* to write to each other. LOC **escribir a mano** to write in longhand, write by hand. ‖ **escribir a máquina** to type.

escrito,-a *adj* written; *(mencionado)* stated.
▶ *nm* **escrito 1** *(documento)* writing, document, text. **2** *(obra)* work, writing: *los escritos de Orwell* Orwell's writings.

escritor,-ra *nm & nf* writer.

escritorio *nm* **1** *(mueble)* writing desk, bureau. **2** *(oficina)* office.

escritura *nf* **1** *(gen)* writing: *escritura fonética* phonetic script. **2** *(caligrafía)* handwriting, writing. **3** JUR deed, document.

escrúpulo *nm* **1** [también se usa en plural con el mismo significado] *(recelo)* scruple, doubt, qualm. **2** [también se usa en plural con el mismo significado] *(aprensión)* fussiness: *eso me da escrúpulos* I'm finicky about it, I'm fussy about it. **3** *fig (cuidado)* extreme care: *lo hizo con escrúpulo* he did it with extreme care.

escrupuloso,-a *adj* **1** scrupulous. **2** *(aprensivo)* finicky, fussy. **3** *fig (exacto)* scrupulous, meticulous.

escrutinio *nm* **1** *(examen)* scrutiny, examination. **2** *(de votos)* count.

escuadra *nf* **1** *(instrumento -de dibujo)* set square; *(-de carpintería)* square; *(pieza de metal)* bracket. **2** *(de tropas)* squad; *(de buques)* squadron, fleet. **3** *(fútbol)* angle.

escuadrilla *nf* squadron.

escuadrón *nm* squadron.

escuálido,-a *adj* **1** *(delgado)* emaciated, extremely thin, skinny. **2** *(sucio)* squalid, filthy.

escucha *nf (acción)* listening. LOC **estar a la escucha de** to be listening out for. ‖ COMP **escuchas telefónicas** phone tapping *sing*.

escuchar *vt* **1** to listen to; *(oír)* to hear. **2** *(atender)* to listen to, pay attention to: *no escuchaba mis consejos* he didn't listen to my advice.

escudo *nm* **1** *(arma)* shield. **2** *(de armas)* coat of arms. **3** *(moneda)* escudo. **4** *fig (amparo)* protection, shield.

escuela *nf* **1** *(gen)* school. **2** *(experiencia)* experience, instruction.

esculpir *vt (gen)* to sculpt, sculpture; *(madera)* to carve; *(metal)* to engrave.

escultor,-ra *nm & nf (hombre)* sculptor; *(mujer)* sculptress.

escultura *nf (gen)* sculpture; *(en madera)* carving; *(en metal)* engraving.

escupir *vi* to spit.
▶ *vt* **1** to spit out. **2** *fig (despedir)* to belch out: *la fábrica escupía humo* the factory belched out smoke.

escurreplatos *nm inv* plate rack.

escurridizo,-a *adj* **1** slippery. **2** *fig* slippery, elusive.

escurridor *nm* **1** *(colador)* strainer, colander. **2** *(de platos)* plate rack. **3** *(para ropa)* wringer, mangle.

escurrir *vt (platos, etc)* to drain; *(ropa)* to wring out; *(comida)* to strain.
▶ *vi* **1** *(destilar)* to drip, trickle. **2** *(deslizar)* to slip, slide.
▶ *vpr* **escurrirse** **1** *(platos, etc)* to drain. **2** *(líquido)* to drip, trickle. **3** *(deslizarse)* to slip, slide. **4** *fam (escapar)* to run away, slip away.

esdrújulo,-a *adj* proparoxytone, stressed on the antepenultimate syllable.

ese *nf name of the letter* s.
▶ *nf pl* **eses** zigzags.

ese,-a *adj* that; *(plural)* those.

ése,-a *pron* **1** *(cosa)* that one. **2** *(hombre - sujeto)* he; *(mujer - sujeto)* she: *ése me lo dijo* he told me so. **3** *(hombre - complemento)* him; *(mujer - complemento)* her: *se lo dio a ésa* he gave it to her. **4** *(anterior)* the former.

✎ Cuando no se produzca confusión con el adjetivo se puede omitir el acento.

esencia *nf* **1** essence. **2** *(perfume)* essence, perfume, scent.

esencial *adj* essential. ⸢LOC⸣ **lo esencial** the main thing.

esfera *nf* **1** sphere, globe. **2** *(de reloj)* dial, face. **3** *fig (campo)* field, sphere; *(ambiente)* sphere, circle.

esférico,-a *adj* spherical.
▶ *nm* **esférico** *(balón)* ball.

esfinge *nf* sphinx.

esforzar *vt* **1** *(forzar)* to strain. **2** *(animar)* to encourage, spur on.
▶ *vpr* **esforzarse** *(físicamente)* to make an effort, exert os; *(moralmente)* to try hard, strive: *se ha esforzado para llegar a la cumbre* she has striven to get to the top.

esfuerzo *nm* **1** effort, endeavour (US endeavor). **2** *(valor)* courage, spirit. ⸢LOC⸣ **sin esfuerzo** effortlessly.

esfumar *vt* **1** *(esfuminar)* to stump, blend. **2** *(colores)* to tone down.
▶ *vpr* **esfumarse** *fam (largarse)* to disappear, fade away.

esgrima *nf* fencing.

esguince *nm* MED sprain.

eslabón *nm* link.

eslalon *nm* slalom.

eslip *nm* **1** *(ropa interior)* men's briefs *pl*, underpants *pl*. **2** *(bañador)* trunks *pl*. s *pl* **eslips**.

eslogan *nm* slogan. ⸢COMP⸣ **eslogan publicitario** advertising slogan.

eslovaco,-a *adj* Slovak.
▶ *nm & nf (persona)* Slovak.
▶ *nm* **eslovaco** *(idioma)* Slovak.

Eslovaquia *nf* Slovakia.

Eslovenia *nf* Slovenia.

esloveno,-a *adj* Slovene.
▶ *nm & nf (persona)* Slovene.
▶ *nm* **esloveno** *(idioma)* Slovene.

esmaltar *vt* **1** to enamel. **2** *(uñas)* to varnish. **3** *fig (adornar)* to decorate, adorn.

esmalte *nm* **1** *(gen)* enamel. **2** *(de uñas)* nail varnish, nail polish. **3** *(objeto esmaltado)* enamelled object. **4** *(color)* smalt.

esmeralda *nf* emerald.

esmerar *vt (pulir)* to polish.
▶ *vpr* **esmerarse** to do one's best (en/ por, to), take great pains (en/por, over).

esmero *nm* great care, neatness.

esnob *adj (persona)* snobbish; *(lugar, etc)* posh.
▶ *nm o nf* snob.

esnobismo *nm* snobbery, snobbishness.

eso *pron* that: *eso es lo que dijo* that's what she said.

ESO *abrev* EDUC (Enseñanza Secundaria Obligatoria) *compulsory secondary education up to 16.*

esófago *nm* oesophagus (US esophagus), gullet.

esos,-as *adj* those.

✎ Consulta también ese,-a.

ésos,-as *pron* those (ones).

✎ Consulta también ése,-a.

espacial *adj* **1** MAT spatial, spacial. **2** *(del cosmos)* space.

espaciar *vt* to space out.

espacio *nm* **1** *(gen)* space. **2** *(que se ocupa)* space, room: *necesitamos más espacio* we need more room. **3** *(de tiempo)* period, space. **4** *(programa)* programme (US program).

espacioso,-a *adj* *(ancho)* spacious, roomy.

espada *nf* **1** *(arma)* sword. **2** *(naipe)* spade.
▶ *nf pl* **espadas** *(palo de baraja)* spades.

espaguetis *nm pl* spaghetti *sing*.

espalda *nf* **1** [también se usa en plural con el mismo significado] *(gen)* back. **2** *(natación)* backstroke.

espantapájaros *nm inv* scarecrow.

espantar *vt* **1** *(asustar)* to frighten, scare, scare off. **2** *(ahuyentar)* to frighten away.
▶ *vpr* **espantarse 1** *(asustarse)* to be frightened, be scared. **2** *(asombrarse)* to be amazed, be astonished.

espanto *nm* **1** *(miedo)* fright, dread, terror. **2** *(asombro)* astonishment, amazement. LOC **¡qué espanto!** how awful!

espantoso,-a *adj* **1** *(terrible)* frightful, dreadful. **2** *(asombroso)* astonishing, amazing. **3** *(desmesurado)* dreadful, terrible.

España *nf* Spain.

español,-la *adj* Spanish.
▶ *nm & nf (persona)* Spaniard.
▶ *nm* **español** *(idioma)* Spanish, Castilian.

esparadrapo *nm* sticking plaster.

esparcir *vt* **1** *(desparramar)* to scatter. **2** fig *(divulgar)* to spread.
▶ *vpr* **esparcirse 1** *(desparramarse)* to scatter, be scattered. **2** fig *(divulgarse)* to spread out.

espárrago *nm* asparagus.

esparto *nm* esparto grass.

espátula *nf* **1** *(gen)* spatula. **2** *(de pintor)* palette knife; *(de cristalero)* putty knife. **3** TÉC stripping knife. **4** *(ave)* spoonbill.

especia *nf* spice.

especial *adj* **1** *(gen)* special. **2** *(remilgado)* fussy (para, about), finicky (para, about): *es un poco especial para la comida* she's a bit finicky about food. LOC **en especial** especially.

especialidad *nf* **1** *(gen)* speciality (US specialty). **2** EDUC main subject, specialized field.

especialista *adj* specialist.
▶ *nm o nf* **1** specialist. **2** CINE stand-in; *(hombre)* stunt man; *(mujer)* stunt woman.

especialización *nf* specialization.

especialmente *adv* **1** *(exclusivamente)* specially. **2** *(particularmente)* especially.

especie *nf* **1** *(de animales, plantas)* species. **2** *(tipo)* kind, sort. **3** *(tema)* matter, notion, idea; *(noticia)* piece of news. LOC **en especie** in kind: *pagar en especie* to pay in kind.

especiero,-a *nm & nf* grocer.
▶ *nm* **especiero** spice rack.

especificar *vt* to specify.

específico,-a *adj* specific.
▶ *nm* **específico** *(medicamento)* specific; *(especialidad)* patent medicine. COMP **peso específico** specific gravity.

espécimen *nm* specimen.

espectacular *adj* spectacular.

espectáculo *nm* **1** spectacle, sight. **2** *(diversión)* entertainment. **3** *(TV, radio, etc)* performance, show.

espectador,-ra *nm & nf* **1** *(de deportes)* spectator. **2** *(de obra, película)* member of the audience; *(de televisión)* viewer.

▶ *nm pl* **espectadores** *(de obra, película)* audience *sing*; *(de programa televisivo)* viewers.

espectro *nm* **1** FÍS spectrum. **2** *(fantasma)* spectre (US specter), ghost, apparition. **3** *fig (persona)* ghost. **4** *(conjunto, serie)* range.

especulador,-ra *adj* speculating.
▶ *nm & nf* speculator.

especular *vt fig (reflexionar)* to speculate about.
▶ *vi* **1** *(comerciar)* to speculate (en, in); *(en bolsa)* to speculate (en, on). **2** *(conjeturar)* to speculate (sobre, about).

espejismo *nm* **1** mirage. **2** *fig* mirage, illusion.

espejo *nm* **1** mirror. **2** *fig (imagen)* mirror, reflection.

espeleología *nf* potholing, speleology.

espeleólogo,-a *nm & nf* potholer, speleologist.

espeluznante *adj* hair-raising, terrifying, horrifying.

espeluznar *vt* to horrify, terrify, make one's hair stand on end.

espera *nf* **1** wait, waiting. **2** *(paciencia)* patience. LOC **en espera de...** waiting for.... ❙ **estar a la espera** to be waiting, be expecting.

esperanza *nf* hope, expectance. LOC **con la esperanza de...** in the hope of.... ❙ **tener muchas esperanzas** to have high hopes. COMP **esperanza de vida** life expectancy.

esperanzador,-ra *adj* encouraging.

esperanzar *vt* to give hope to.
▶ *vpr* **esperanzarse** to have hope.

esperar *vt* **1** *(tener esperanza)* to hope for, expect: *esperan un milagro* they're hoping for a miracle. **2** *(contar, creer)* to expect: *no te esperábamos hasta mañana* we didn't expect you till tomorrow. **3** *(aguardar)* to wait for, await: *espera un momento* wait a moment. **4** *(desear)* to hope: *espero verlo* I hope to see him. **5** *fig (bebé)* to expect.
▶ *vi* to wait: *esperaré hasta que lleguen* I'll wait until they get here.

▶ *vpr* **esperarse 1** *(aguardar)* to wait: *espérense en recepción* please wait in reception. **2** *(creer, contar)* to expect: *se espera que seas puntual* you're expected to be punctual. **3** *(desear)* to hope: *se espera que lo hayan pasado bien* we hope you've had a good time.

espermatozoide *nm* spermatozoon, sperm.

espesar *vt (salsa, etc)* to thicken; *(tejido, etc)* to make thicker.
▶ *vpr* **espesarse 1** *(gen)* to get thicker. **2** *(salsa, etc)* to thicken.

espeso,-a *adj* **1** *(líquido, sustancia, objeto)* thick. **2** *(bosque, niebla)* thick, dense. **3** *(pasta, masa)* stiff. LOC **estar espeso,-a** *fam* not to be able to think straight.

espesor *nm* thickness.

espesura *nf* **1** *(de líquido, objeto)* thickness. **2** *(de niebla, etc)* denseness. **3** *fig (en bosque)* thicket, dense wood.

espía *nm o nf* spy.

espiar *vt* to spy on, watch.

espiga *nf* **1** *(gen)* spike; *(de trigo)* ear. **2** *(de tejido)* herringbone. **3** *(clavija)* peg, pin.

espigado,-a *adj* **1** BOT ripe. **2** *(en forma de espiga)* ear-shaped. **3** *fig (persona)* tall, lanky.

espigón *nm* **1** MAR breakwater, jetty. **2** *(punta)* sharp point, spike.

espina *nf* **1** *(de planta)* thorn. **2** *(de pez)* fishbone. **3** *(columna vertebral)* spine, backbone. **4** *fig (pesar)* sadness, sorrow, grief.

espinaca *nf* spinach.

espinal *adj* spinal: *médula espinal* spinal marrow.

espinilla *nf* **1** *(de la pierna)* shinbone. **2** *(grano)* blackhead.

espino *nm* **1** *(árbol)* hawthorn. **2** *(alambre)* barbed wire. COMP **espino albar** common hawthorn. ❙ **espino negro** blackthorn.

espinoso,-a *adj* **1** *(planta)* thorny. **2** *(pez)* spiny. **3** *fig* thorny, prickly, difficult, tricky.

espionaje *nm* spying, espionage: *película de espionaje* spy film.

E

espiral adj spiral: *escalera espiral* spiral staircase.
▶ nf **1** spiral. **2** *(de reloj)* hairspring.

espirar vt to exhale, breathe out.
▶ vi to breathe.

espiritismo nm spiritualism.

espiritista adj spiritualistic.
▶ nm o nf spiritualist.

espíritu nm **1** *(gen)* spirit. **2** *(alma)* soul, spirit. **3** *(fantasma)* ghost, spirit. **4** *(licores)* spirits pl. **5** fig *(idea central)* spirit, essence, soul.

espiritual adj spiritual.

espiritualidad nf spirituality.

espléndido,-a adj **1** *(magnífico)* splendid, magnificent. **2** *(generoso)* generous, lavish.

esplendor nm **1** *(resplandor)* brilliance, shining. **2** fig *(magnificencia)* magnificence, splendour (US splendor). **3** *(auge)* glory.

esplendoroso,-a adj **1** *(resplandeciente)* brilliant, radiant, shining. **2** *(grandioso)* magnificent, lavish.

espliego nm lavender.

espolear vt **1** to spur on. **2** fig to spur on, encourage.

espolón nm **1** *(de ave)* spur. **2** *(de caballería)* fetlock. **3** *(de nave)* ram. **4** *(malecón)* sea wall. **5** fam *(sabañón)* chilblain.

espolvorear vt **1** *(despolvorear)* to dust. **2** *(esparcir)* to powder, sprinkle.

esponja nf **1** sponge. **2** fig *(gorrón)* sponger.

esponjar vt *(ahuecar)* to fluff up; *(tierra)* to loosen.
▶ vpr **esponjarse 1** fig *(envanecerse)* to swell with pride. **2** fig *(físicamente)* to glow with health.

esponjoso,-a adj *(gen)* spongy; *(bizcocho)* light.

espontáneamente adv spontaneously.

espontaneidad nf spontaneity.

espontáneo,-a adj **1** *(cosa)* spontaneous; *(discurso)* impromptu, unprepared. **2** *(persona)* natural, unaffected.

espora nf spore.

esporádicamente adv sporadically.

esporádico,-a adj sporadic.

esposa nf wife.

esposado,-a adj **1** *(casado)* married. **2** *(con esposas)* handcuffed.

esposar vt to handcuff, put handcuffs on.

esposas nf pl handcuffs.

esposo nm husband.

esprint nm sprint.

esprintar vi to sprint.

esprínter nm o nf sprinter.

espuela nf **1** spur. **2** fig spur, stimulus.

espuerta nf two-handled rush basket.

espuma nf **1** *(gen)* foam; *(de jabón)* lather; *(de cerveza)* froth, head; *(olas)* surf. **2** *(impurezas)* scum. **3** *(tejido)* foam.

espumadera nf skimmer.

espumar vt *(quitar espuma)* to skim.
▶ vi *(hacer espuma - jabón)* to lather; *(- cerveza)* to froth; *(- vino)* to sparkle; *(- olas)* to foam.

espumillón nm tinsel.

espumoso,-a adj *(ola)* foamy, frothy; *(jabón)* lathery; *(vino)* sparkling.

esqueje nm cutting.

esquela nf **1** *(carta)* short letter. **2** *(mortuoria)* obituary notice.

esqueleto nm **1** ANAT skeleton. **2** ARQUIT framework.

esquema nm **1** *(gráfica)* diagram. **2** *(plan)* outline, plan.

esquemático,-a adj schematic, diagrammatic.

esquematizar vt **1** *(plan, idea)* to outline. **2** *(plano, etc)* to sketch.

esquí nm **1** *(tabla)* ski. **2** DEP skiing.
s pl **esquís**. COMP **esquí acuático** water-skiing. ‖ **esquí alpino** alpine skiing. **esquí náutico** water-skiing.

esquiador,-ra nm & nf skier.

esquiar vi to ski.

esquilador,-ra nm & nf sheepshearer.

esquiladora nf shears pl.

esquilar vt **1** *(pelo)* to clip. **2** *(ovejas)* to shear.

esquimal adj Eskimo.
▶ nm o nf Eskimo.
▶ nm *(idioma)* Eskimo.

esquina *nf* corner.
▸ *vt* **1** *(hacer esquina)* to form a corner with, be on the corner of. **2** *(poner en esquina)* to put in a corner.

esquinazo *nm* corner. ⌐LOC⌐ **dar el esquinazo a** ALGN *fam* to give SB the slip.

esquirla *nf* splinter.

esquirol *nm* blackleg, scab.

esquisto *nm* shale.

esquivar *vt* **1** *(persona)* to avoid, shun. **2** *(golpe)* to dodge, elude.

esquivo,-a *adj* cold, aloof.

esquizofrenia *nf* schizophrenia.

esquizofrénico,-a *adj* schizophrenic.
▸ *nm & nf* schizophrenic.

estabilidad *nf* stability.

estabilización *nf* stabilization.

estabilizar *vt* to stabilize, make stable.
▸ *vpr* **estabilizarse** to become stable, become stabilized.

estable *adj* stable, steady.

establecer *vt* **1** *(gen)* to establish; *(fundar)* to found, set up. **2** *(récord)* to set. **3** *(ordenar)* to state, lay down, establish.
▸ *vpr* **establecerse** *(en un lugar)* to settle; *(en un negocio)* to set up in business.

establecimiento *nm* **1** *(acto)* establishment, founding, setting-up. **2** *(de gente)* settlement. **3** *(local)* establishment, shop, store.

establo *nm* **1** stable, cowshed, stall. **2** *fig* filthy place, pigsty.

estabular *vt* to stable.

estaca *nf* **1** *(palo con punta)* stake, post; *(para tienda de campaña)* peg. **2** *(garrote)* stick, cudgel. **3** *(rama)* cutting. **4** *(clavo)* spike.

estacada *nf* *(obra)* fence, fencing.

estacazo *nm* blow with a stick.

estación *nf* **1** *(del año, temporada)* season. **2** *(de tren, radio)* station.

estacional *adj* seasonal.

estacionamiento *nm* **1** AUTO *(acción)* parking; *(lugar)* car park, US parking lot. **2** *fig (estancamiento)* impasse.

estacionar *vt* **1** *(colocar)* to position, place. **2** AUTO to park.
▸ *vpr* **estacionarse 1** *(estancarse)* to be stationary, remain in the same place. **2** AUTO to park.

estacionario,-a *adj* stationary, stable.

estadio *nm* **1** *(lugar)* stadium. **2** *(fase)* stage, phase. **3** *arc (medida)* stadium, furlong.

estadista *nm o nf* **1** POL *(hombre)* statesman; *(mujer)* stateswoman. **2** MAT statistician.

estadística *nf* **1** *(ciencia)* statistics. **2** *(dato)* statistic, figure.

estadístico,-a *adj* statistical.
▸ *nm & nf* statistician.

estado *nm* **1** *(situación)* state, condition: *su estado es delicado* his condition is delicate. **2** *(en orden social)* status. **3** HIST estate. **4** POL state.

Estados Unidos *nm pl* The United States.

estadounidense *adj* American, from the United States.
▸ *nm o nf* American, person from the United States.

estafa *nf* fraud, swindle.

estafador,-ra *nm & nf* racketeer, swindler, trickster.

estafar *vt* to swindle, trick, cheat, defraud.

estafilococo *nm* staphylococcus.

estalactita *nf* stalactite.

estalagmita *nm* stalagmite.

estallar *vi* **1** *(reventar)* to explode, blow up. **2** *(neumático)* to burst; *(bomba)* to explode, go off; *(cristal)* to shatter. **3** *(volcán)* to erupt. **4** *(látigo)* to crack. **5** *fig (rebelión, epidemia)* to break out. **6** *fig (pasión, sentimientos)* to burst: *estallar en lágrimas* to burst into tears.

estallido *nm* **1** *(explosión)* explosion. **2** *(de trueno)* crash; *(de látigo)* crack. **3** *fig* outbreak.

estambre *nm* **1** COST worsted, woollen yarn (US woolen yarn). **2** BOT stamen.

estamento *nm* class, stratum.

estampa *nf* **1** *(imagen)* picture. **2** *fig (aspecto)* appearance, look, aspect.

estampación *nf* printing.

estampado,-a *adj (gen)* patterned, print; *(tela)* printed; *(metal)* stamped.
▶ *nm* **estampado** *(tela)* print.

estampar *vt* **1** *(imprimir)* to print. **2** *(metales)* to stamp. **3** *(dejar huella)* to stamp. LOC **estampar la firma** to sign.

estampida *nf* **1** *(ruido)* bang. **2** *(de animales)* stampede.

estampilla *nf* stamp, rubber stamp.

estampita *nf* religious print.

estancado,-a *adj* **1** *(agua)* stagnant. **2** *fig (asunto, negocio)* at a standstill; *(negociaciones)* deadlocked; *(persona)* stuck, bogged down.

estancamiento *nm* **1** stagnation. **2** *fig* deadlock, standstill.

estancar *vt* **1** *(aguas)* to hold up, hold back, dam; *(flujo)* to check. **2** *fig (progreso)* to check, block, hold up.
▶ *vpr* **estancarse 1** *(líquido)* to stagnate, become stagnant. **2** *fig* to stagnate, get bogged down.

estanco,-a *adj* watertight.
▶ *nm* **estanco** *(tienda)* tobacconist's.

estándar *adj* standard, standardized: *modelo estándar* standard model; *reglas estándar* set rules.

estandarte *nm* standard, banner.

estanque *nm* **1** *(de peces, etc)* pool, pond. **2** *(para proveer agua)* reservoir, tank.

estanquero,-a *nm & nf* tobacconist.

estante *nm* **1** *(anaquel)* shelf; *(para libros)* bookcase. **2** *(de máquina)* stand.

estantería *nf* shelving, shelves *pl*.

estaño *nm* tin.

estar *vi* **1** *(lugar, posición)* to be: *estamos en casa* we are at home. **2** *(permanecer)* to be, stay: *estuvimos allí diez días* we stayed there for ten days. **3** *(cualidades transitorias)* to be: *está cansado* he's tired. **4** *(una prenda)* to suit, be: *te está grande* it's too big for you.
▶ *aux* **1** *estar + gerundio* to be: *estaban cantando* they were singing. **2** *estar a (precio)* to be, sell at; *(fecha)* to be: *estamos a 15 de marzo* it's the 15th of March. **3**

estar con *(tener)* to have; *(estar de acuerdo)* to agree with: *estoy con Ana* I agree with Ana. **4 estar de** *(gen)* to be; *(trabajar)* to be, be working as; *(ir vestido)* to be, be dressed in: *estar de vacaciones* to be on holiday; *está de uniforme* he's in uniform. **5 estar en** *(consistir)* to be, lie; *(entender)* to understand; *(creer)* to think, believe; *(depender de uno)* to be up to. **6 estar para** *(estar a punto)* to be about to; *(estar acabado)* to be finished, be ready; *(estar de humor)* to feel like, be in the mood for. **7 estar por** *(no haberse ejecutado)* to remain to be; *(estar determinado)* to be for; *(ir a)* to be going to; *(a favor)* to be for. **8 estar que** *fam* to be nearly, be really, be practically: *está que se hunde* it's practically ruined. **9 estar sin + inf** not to have been + *pp*: *el coche está sin lavar* the car hasn't been washed, the car still needs washing.
▶ *vpr* **estarse** *(permanecer)* to spend, stay: *se estuvo todo el día leyendo* she spent all day reading.

estarcido *nm* stencil.

estarcir *vt* to stencil.

estasis *nf inv* stasis.

estatal *adj* state.

estático,-a *adj* static.

estatua *nf* statue.

estatuilla *nf* statuette, figurine.

estatura *nf* height, stature.

estatuto *nm* statute. COMP **estatuto de autonomía** statute of autonomy.

este *adj* **1** east, eastern. **2** *(dirección)* easterly; *(viento)* east, easterly.
▶ *nm* **1** east. **2** *(viento)* east wind.

este,-a *adj* this; *(plural)* these: *este libro* this book; *estas manzanas* these apples.

éste,-a *pron* **1** *(cosa)* this one: *dame éste* give me this one. **2** *(hombre - sujeto)* he; *(mujer - sujeto)* she: *ésta me lo dijo* she told me. **3** *(hombre - complemento)* him; *(mujer - complemento)* her: *se lo dio a éste* she gave it to him. **4** *(este último)* the latter. *pey* this one.

🖎 Cuando no se produzca confusión con el adjetivo se puede omitir el acento.

estela¹ *nf* **1** *(de barco)* wake, wash; *(de avión)* vapour (US vapor) trail; *(de cometa)* tail. **2** *fig* trail.

estela² *nf* *(monumento)* stela, stele.

estelar *adj* **1** *(sideral)* stellar. **2** *fig* star.

estenordeste *nm* **1** east-northeast. **2** *(viento)* east-northeast wind.

estepa¹ *nf* *(llanura)* steppe.

estepa² *nf* *(planta)* rockrose.

estepario,-a *adj* steppe, from the steppes.

éster *nm* ester.

estera *nf* rush mat.

estercolero *nm* **1** dunghill, dung heap. **2** *fig* pigsty.

estéreo *nm* stereo.

estereofónico,-a *adj* stereo, stereophonic.

estereoscopio *nm* stereoscope.

estereotipado,-a *adj fig* stereotyped, standard, set.

estereotipo *nm* stereotype.

estéril *adj* **1** *(tierra)* sterile, barren. **2** *(hombre)* sterile; *(mujer)* sterile, infertile. **3** *(aséptico)* sterile. **4** *fig* futile, useless.

esterilidad *nf* **1** *(de terreno)* sterility, barrenness. **2** *(de hombre)* sterility; *(de mujer)* sterility, infertility. **3** *fig* futility, uselessness.

esterilización *nf* sterilization.

esterilizador,-ra *nm* sterilizer.

esterilizar *vt* to sterilize.

esterilla *nf* **1** *(felpudo)* small mat. **2** *(de cañamazo)* rush matting, wickerwork.

esterlina *adj* sterling.
▶ *nf* sterling.

esternocleidomastoideo *nm* sternocleidomastoid.

esternón *nm* sternum, breastbone.

estesudeste *nm* **1** east-southeast. **2** *(viento)* east-southeast wind.

esteta *nm o nf* aesthete (US esthete).

estética *nf* aesthetics (US esthetics).

estéticamente *adv* aesthetically.

estético,-a *adj* aesthetic (US esthetic).

estetoscopio *nm* stethoscope.

estiércol *nm* dung, manure.

estilete *nm* **1** *(punzón)* stylus. **2** *(puñal)* stiletto. **3** MED probe.

estilismo *nm* stylism.

estilista *nm o nf* **1** *(escritor)* stylist. **2** *(diseñador)* stylist, designer.

estilístico,-a *adj* stylistic.

estilización *nf* stylization.

estilizar *vt* **1** to stylize. **2** *(hacer delgado)* to make thinner.

estilo *nm* **1** *(gen)* style. **2** *(modo)* manner, fashion. **3** GRAM speech. **4** *(natación)* stroke.

estilográfica *nf* fountain pen.

estima *nf* esteem, respect.

estimable *adj* **1** esteemed, reputable, worthy. **2** *(cantidad)* considerable.

estimación *nf* **1** *(afecto)* esteem, respect. **2** *(valoración)* estimation, evaluation. **3** *(cálculo)* estimate. COMP **propia estima** self-esteem.

estimado,-a *adj* **1** *(apreciado)* esteemed, respected. **2** *(valorado)* valued, estimated: *el precio estimado* the estimated price.

estimar *vt* **1** *(apreciar)* to esteem, respect, hold in esteem, admire. **2** *(valorar)* to value. **3** *(juzgar, creer)* to consider, think, reckon.

estimulación *nf* stimulation.

estimulante *adj* stimulating, encouraging.
▶ *nm* stimulant.

estimular *vt* **1** *(animar)* to encourage, stimulate. **2** *(apetito, pasiones)* to whet.

estímulo *nm* **1** stimulus, stimulation. **2** *fig* encouragement. **3** COM incentive.

estío *nm* summer.

estipendio *nm* stipend, fee, remuneration.

estipular *vt* to stipulate.

estirado,-a *adj* **1** *fig (en el vestir)* stiff, formal, starchy. **2** *fig (orgulloso)* stiff, conceited, haughty.
▶ *nm* **estirado 1** *(textil)* drawing. **2** *(del pelo)* straightening; *(de la piel)* lift.

estiramiento *nm* stretch.

estirar *vt* **1** *(gen)* to stretch. **2** *(cuello)* to crane. **3** *(medias)* to pull up; *(falda)* to pull down. **4** *fig (dinero)* to spin out, make go further.
▶ *vi (crecer)* to shoot up.
▶ *vpr* **estirarse 1** *(crecer)* to shoot up. **2** *(desperezarse)* to stretch.

estirón *nm* pull, jerk, tug.

estirpe *nf* stock, lineage, race.

estival *adj* summer.

esto *pron* this: *esto me gusta* I like this.

estocada *nf* stab, thrust.

estofa *nf fig* class, type.

estofado *nm* CULIN stew.

estofar *vt* CULIN to stew.

estoicismo *nm* stoicism.

estoico,-a *adj* stoic, stoical.
▶ *nm & nf* stoic.

estoma *nm* stoma.

estomacal *adj* **1** *(del estómago)* stomach, of the stomach. **2** *(digestivo)* digestive.
▶ *nm (bebida)* digestive liqueur.

estómago *nm* stomach. COMP dolor de estómago stomachache.

Estonia *nf* Estonia.

estonio,-a *adj* Estonian.
▶ *nm & nf (persona)* Estonian.
▶ *nm* estonio *(idioma)* Estonian.

estopa *nf* **1** *(fibra)* tow. **2** *(tela)* burlap.
COMP estopa de acero steel wool.

estoque *nm (espada)* sword.

estor *nm* roller blind.

estorbar *vt* **1** *(dificultar)* to hinder, get in the way; *(obstruir)* to obstruct, block, hold up. **2** *fig (molestar)* to annoy, bother, disturb.
▶ *vi (ser obstáculo)* to be in the way.

estorbo *nm* **1** *(obstáculo)* obstruction, obstacle. **2** *(molestia)* hindrance, encumbrance; *(persona)* nuisance.

estornino *nm* starling.

estornudar *vi* to sneeze.

estornudo *nm* sneeze.

estos,-as *adj* these.

✎ Consulta también este,-a.

éstos,-as *pron* these (ones).

✎ Consulta también éste,-a.

estrabismo *nm* strabismus, squint: *tengo estrabismo* I have a squint.

estrado *nm* stage, platform; *(tarima)* dais.
▶ *nm pl* estrados JUR courtrooms.

estrago *nm* havoc, ruin, ravage.

estragón *nm* tarragon.

estrangular *vt* **1** *(ahogar)* to strangle. **2** MED to strangulate. **3** AUTO to throttle.

estratagema *nf* **1** MIL stratagem. **2** *fam fig* trick.

estratega *nm o nf* strategist.

estrategia *nf* strategy.

estratégicamente *adv* strategically.

estratégico,-a *adj* strategic.

estratificar *vt* to stratify.
▶ *vpr* **estratificarse** to be stratified.

estrato *nm* **1** GEOL stratum. **2** *(capa)* stratum. **3** *(nivel social)* stratum, class. **4** *(nube)* stratus.

estratosfera *nf* stratosphere.

estraza *nf* rag, piece of cloth.

estrechamente *adv* **1** *(con estrechez)* narrowly, tightly. **2** *fig (con intimidad)* closely, intimately: *están estrechamente unidos* they're very close.

estrechar *vt* **1** *(carretera)* to make narrower. **2** *(prenda)* to take in. **3** *(abrazar)* to squeeze, hug; *(mano)* to shake: *nos estrechamos las manos* we shook hands. **4** *fig (obligar)* to compel, constrain. **5** *fig (relaciones, lazos)* to strengthen.
▶ *vpr* **estrecharse 1** *(valle, etc)* to narrow, become narrower. **2** *(apretarse)* to squeeze together, squeeze up. **3** *fig (relaciones, etc)* to strengthen, get stronger.

estrechez *nf* **1** *(poco ancho)* narrowness. **2** *(falta espacio)* lack of space. **3** *(prendas)* tightness. **4** *fig (económica)* want, need. **5** *fig (amistad)* closeness, intimacy. **6** *fig (apuro)* tight spot. LOC pasar estrecheces *fig* to be hard up.

estrecho,-a *adj* **1** *(poco ancho)* narrow. **2** *(ropa)* tight; *(calzado)* tight, small. **3** *(habitación)* cramped, poky, small. **4** *(sin espacio)* packed, jam-packed. **5** *fig (amistad, etc)* close, intimate.
▶ *nm* estrecho GEOG strait, straits *pl*.

estrella *nf* **1** *(gen)* star. **2** *fig (destino)* destiny, fate.

estrellado,-a *adj* **1** *(cielo)* starry, star-spangled, full of stars. **2** *(forma)* star-shaped. **3** *(hecho pedazos)* smashed, shattered.

estrellar *vt* **1** *(llenar de estrellas)* to cover with stars. **2** *fam (hacer pedazos)* to smash (to pieces), shatter. **3** *(freír)* to fry.
▶ *vpr* **estrellarse 1** *(llenarse de estrellas)* to be full of stars. **2** *(hacerse pedazos)* to smash, shatter. **3** *(chocar)* to crash.

estremecedor,-ra *adj* **1** startling. **2** *(grito)* bloodcurdling.

estremecer *vt* **1** *(gen)* to shake. **2** *fig (asustar)* to startle, frighten.
▶ *vpr* **estremecerse 1** *(temblar)* to shake. **2** *(de miedo)* to tremble, shudder; *(de frío)* to shiver, tremble. **3** *fig* to shudder.

estrenar *vt* **1** *(gen)* to use for the first time; *(ropa)* to wear for the first time. **2** *(obra)* to perform for the first time, give the first performance of; *(película)* to release, put on release.
▶ *vpr* **estrenarse** to make one's debut.

estreno *nm* **1** *(de algo)* first use. **2** *(persona)* début, first appearance. **3** *(de obra)* first performance; *(de película)* premiere.

estreñido,-a *adj* **1** constipated. **2** *fig* mean, stingy.

estreñimiento *nm* constipation.

estreñir *vt* to constipate, make constipated.
▶ *vpr* **estreñirse** to become constipated.

estrépito *nm* **1** din, racket, clatter. **2** *fig* ostentation, fuss.

estrepitoso,-a *adj* **1** noisy, clamorous. **2** *(ruido)* deafening. **3** *fig (éxito)* resounding; *(fracaso)* spectacular.

estreptococo *nm* streptococcus.

estrés *nm* stress.

estresado,-a *adj* under stress.

estresante *adj* stressful.

estría *nf* **1** *(ranura)* groove. **2** ARQUIT flute. **3** *(en la piel)* stretch mark.

estriar *vt* **1** *(hacer ranuras)* to groove. **2** ARQUIT to flute. **3** *(piel)* to give stretch marks.
▶ *vpr* **estriarse** *(piel)* to get stretch marks.

estribillo *nm* **1** *(de poesía)* refrain; *(de canción)* chorus. **2** *(muletilla)* pet phrase, pet saying.

estribo *nm* **1** *(de jinete)* stirrup. **2** *(de carruaje, tren)* step. **3** AUTO running board; *(de moto)* footrest. **4** ARQUIT buttress; *(de puente)* pier, support. **5** *(del oído)* stirrup bone.

estribor *nm* starboard.

estricto,-a *adj* strict, rigorous.

estridencia *nf* **1** *(ruido)* stridency, shrillness. **2** *(color, etc)* loudness, garishness, gaudiness.

estridente *adj* **1** *(ruido)* strident, shrill. **2** *(color, etc)* loud, garish, gaudy.

estroboscópico,-a *adj* stroboscopic.

estroboscopio *nm* stroboscope, strobe.

estrofa *nf* stanza, verse.

estrógeno *nm* oestrogen (US estrogen).

estropajo *nm* **1** *(para fregar)* scourer. **2** *fig (desecho)* useless thing.

estropajoso,-a *adj* **1** *(lengua)* furry. **2** *(carne, etc)* gristly, tough. **3** *(pelo)* straw-like.

estropear *vt* **1** *(máquina)* to damage, break, ruin. **2** *(cosecha)* to spoil, ruin. **3** *(plan, etc)* to spoil, ruin.
▶ *vpr* **estropearse 1** *(máquina)* to break down. **2** *(cosecha)* to be spoiled, get damaged. **3** *(plan, etc)* to fail, fall through, go wrong. **4** *(comida)* to go bad.

estropicio *nm* **1** *fam (rotura)* breakage, damage; *(ruido producido)* crash, clatter, smash. **2** *fam (desorden)* mess; *(jaleo)* fuss, rumpus.

estructura *nf* **1** *(gen)* structure. **2** *(armazón)* frame, framework.

estructurado,-a *adj* structured, organized.

estructurar *vt* to structure, organize.
▶ *vpr* **estructurarse** to be structured, be organized.

estruendo *nm* 1 *(ruido)* great noise, din. 2 *(confusión)* uproar, tumult.

estruendoso,-a *adj (ruido)* noisy, deafening; *(aplauso)* thunderous.

estrujar *vt* 1 *(exprimir)* to squeeze. 2 *(apretar - alguien)* to crush; *(- algo)* to screw up. 3 *(ropa)* to wring. 4 *fig (sacar partido)* to drain, bleed dry.
▶ *vpr* **estrujarse** *(apretujarse)* to crowd, throng.

estuario *nm* estuary.

estucado *nm* stucco, stucco work.

estucar *vt* to stucco.

estuche *nm* 1 *(caja)* case, box. 2 *(conjunto)* set.

estuco *nm* stucco.

estudiante *nm o nf* student.

estudiar *vt* to study, learn.
▶ *vi* to study: *estudia para maestro* he's training to be a teacher.
▶ *vpr* **estudiarse** to consider.

estudio *nm* 1 *(gen)* study. 2 *(apartamento)* studio flat (US apartment), bedsit.
▶ *nm pl* **estudios** *(conocimientos)* studies, education *sing*.

estudioso,-a *adj* studious.

estufa *nf (calentador)* heater, stove; *(de gas, eléctrica)* fire.

estupa *nf argot (grupo)* drug squad.
▶ *nm o nf (oficial)* drug-squad officer.

estupefaciente *adj* stupefying.
▶ *nm* drug, narcotic.

estupefacto,-a *adj* astounded, dumbfounded, flabbergasted.

estupendamente *adv* marvellously (US marvelously), wonderfully.

estupendo,-a *adj* marvellous (US marvelous), wonderful, super.

estupidez *nf* stupidity, stupid thing.

estúpido,-a *adj* stupid, silly.
▶ *nm & nf* berk, idiot.

estupor *nm* stupor, amazement, astonishment. LOC **causar estupor** to astonish.

esturión *nm* sturgeon.

etapa *nf* 1 period, stage. 2 *(parada)* stop, stage. 3 DEP leg, stage.

éter *nm* QUÍM ether.

etéreo,-a *adj* ethereal.

eternamente *adv* eternally.

eternidad *nf* 1 eternity. 2 *fam* ages *pl*.

eternizar *vt* 1 to eternize, eternalize. 2 *fam* to prolong endlessly.
▶ *vpr* **eternizarse** 1 *fam (ser interminable)* to be interminable, be endless; *(discusión)* to drag on. 2 *fam (tardar mucho)* to take ages.

eterno,-a *adj* eternal, everlasting, endless.

ética *nf* ethics *pl*, ethic.

éticamente *adv* ethically.

ético,-a *adj* ethical.

etílico,-a *adj* ethylic.

etimología *nf* etymology.

etimológico,-a *adj* etymological.

etíope *adj* Ethiopian.
▶ *nm o nf (persona)* Ethiopian.
▶ *nm* **etíope** *(idioma)* Ethiopian, Ethiopic.

Etiopía *nf* Ethiopia.

etiqueta *nf* 1 *(rótulo)* label, tag. 2 *(formalidad)* etiquette, formality, ceremony.

etiquetar *vt* to label, put a label on.

etnia *nf* ethnic group.

étnico,-a *adj* ethnic.

etnografía *nf* ethnography.

etnología *nf* ethnology.

etnólogo,-a *nm & nf* ethnologist.

eucalipto *nm* eucalyptus.

eufemismo *nm* euphemism.

euforia *nf* euphoria, elation.

eufórico,-a *adj* euphoric, elated.

eunuco *nm* eunuch.

eureka *interj* eureka!

euritmia *nf* eurythmics.

euro *nm* euro.

euroasiático,-a *adj* Eurasian.
▶ *nm & nf* Eurasian.

eurodiputado,-a *nm & nf* Member of the European Parliament, MEP, Euro MP.

Europa *nf* Europe.

europeísta *adj* pro-European.
▶ *nm o nf* pro-European.

europeo,-a *adj* European.
▶ *nm & nf* European. COMP **Comunidad Europea** European Community. ∥ **Unión Europea** European Union.

eurovisión *nf* Eurovision.

Euskadi *nm* the Basque Country.

euskera *nm (idioma)* Basque.

eutanasia *nf* euthanasia.

evacuación *nf* evacuation.

evacuar *vt* **1** *(lugar)* to evacuate. **2** ANAT to empty.

evadir *vt* **1** *(peligro, respuesta)* to avoid; *(responsabilidad)* to shirk. **2** *(capital, impuestos)* to evade.
▶ *vpr* **evadirse** *(escaparse)* to escape.

evaluación *nf* **1** evaluation, assessment. **2** EDUC *(acción)* assessment; *(examen)* exam.

evaluar *vt* to evaluate, assess.

evangélico,-a *adj* evangelical.

evangelio *nm* gospel.

evangelista *nm* evangelist.

evaporación *nf* evaporation.

evaporar *vt* to evaporate.
▶ *vpr* **evaporarse 1** to evaporate. **2** *fig* to vanish, disappear.

evasión *nf* **1** *(fuga)* escape, flight. **2** *fig* escape, escapism.

evasivo,-a *adj* evasive.

eventual *adj* **1** *(casual)* chance; *(probable)* possible. **2** *(trabajo)* casual, temporary, provisional. **3** *(ingresos, gastos)* incidental.
▶ *nm o nf* casual worker, temporary worker.

eventualidad *nf* eventuality, contingency.

evidencia *nf (claridad)* obviousness, clearness; *(certeza)* certainty.

evidenciar *vt* to show, make evident, prove, make obvious.

evidente *adj* evident, obvious.

evidentemente *adv* evidently, obviously.

evitar *vt* **1** *(gen)* to avoid. **2** *(impedir)* to prevent, avoid. **3** *(ahorrar)* to spare, save.

evocar *vt* **1** *(recuerdo)* to evoke, call up. **2** *(recordar)* to evoke, bring to mind.

evolución *nf* **1** *(cambio)* evolution; *(desarrollo)* development. **2** *(vuelta)* turn.

evolucionar *vi* **1** *(gen)* to evolve, develop. **2** *(dar vueltas)* to turn.

evolucionismo *nm* evolutionism.

evolutivo,-a *adj* evolutionary, evolving.

ex- *pref* ex-, former: *el ex primer ministro* the former prime minister.

exacerbar *vt* **1** *(agravar)* to exacerbate, aggravate, make worse. **2** *(irritar)* to exacerbate, exasperate, irritate.

exactamente *adv* exactly, precisely.

exactitud *nf (fidelidad)* exactness; *(precisión)* accuracy.

exacto,-a *adj* **1** *(fiel)* faithful, true; *(preciso)* accurate, exact. **2** *(verdad)* true: *eso no es exacto* that's not true.

exageración *nf* exaggeration.

exagerado,-a *adj* exaggerated.

exagerar *vt* to exaggerate.
▶ *vi* **1** to exaggerate. **2** *(abusar)* to overdo it, do too much.

exaltado,-a *adj* **1** *(discusión, etc)* heated, impassioned. **2** *(persona)* hot-headed, worked up.

exaltar *vt* **1** *(elevar)* to raise, promote. **2** *fig (alabar)* to exalt, praise, extol.
▶ *vpr* **exaltarse** *(excitarse)* to get overexcited, get worked up, get carried away.

examen *nm* **1** examination, exam. **2** *(estudio)* consideration, examination, study. COMP **examen final** final examination. ∥ **examen oral** oral examination.

examinar *vt (gen)* to examine.
▶ *vpr* **examinarse** to take an examination, sit an examination.

exasperante *adj* exasperating.

exasperar *vt* to exasperate.
▶ *vpr* **exasperarse** to get exasperated.

excavación *nf* **1** excavation, digging. **2** *(arqueológica)* dig.

excavadora *nf (máquina)* digger.

excavar *vt* to excavate, dig.

excedencia *nf* **1** *(de funcionario, etc)* leave. **2** *(de profesor)* sabbatical leave.

excedente *adj* *(sobrante)* excess, surplus.
▶ *nm* COM surplus, excess.

exceder *vt* **1** *(superar)* to excel, surpass. **2** *(sobrepasar)* to exceed, be in excess of.
▶ *vpr* **excederse 1** *(pasarse)* to overdo it, go too far. **2** *(en atenciones, etc)* to be extremely kind.

excelente *adj* excellent, first-rate.

excentricidad *nf* eccentricity.

excéntrico,-a *adj* eccentric.

excepción *nf* exception. LOC **a excepción de** with the exception of, except for. ‖ **de excepción** exceptional.

excepcional *adj* **1** *(extraordinario)* exceptional, outstanding. **2** *(raro)* exceptional, unusual.

excepto *adv* except (for), apart from, excepting.

exceptuar *vt* to except, leave out, exclude.

excesivo,-a *adj* excessive.

exceso *nm* **1** excess. **2** COM surplus. COMP **exceso de equipaje** excess baggage.

excipiente *nm* excipient.

excisión *nf* excision.

excitación *nf* **1** *(acción)* excitation. **2** *(sentimiento)* excitement.

excitante *adj* **1** exciting. **2** MED stimulating.

excitar *vt* **1** to excite. **2** *(emociones)* to stimulate, arouse.
▶ *vpr* **excitarse** to get excited, get worked up, get carried away.

exclamación *nf* exclamation; *(grito)* cry.

exclamar *vt* to exclaim, cry out.
▶ *vi* to exclaim, cry out.

exclamativo,-a *adj* exclamatory.

exclamatorio,-a *adj* exclamatory.

excluir *vt* **1** to exclude, shut out. **2** *(rechazar)* to reject; *(descartar)* to rule out; *(expulsar)* to throw out.

exclusión *nf* exclusion, shutting out.

exclusiva *nf* **1** COM sole right. **2** *(prensa)* exclusive, scoop.

exclusividad *nf* exclusiveness, exclusivity.

exclusivo,-a *adj* exclusive.

excluyente *adj* exclusive.

excremento *nf* excrement.

excretor,-ra *adj* excretory.

exculpar *vt* **1** to exonerate. **2** JUR to acquit.

excursión *nf* excursion, trip.

excursionismo *nm* hiking, rambling.

excursionista *nm o nf* tripper; *(a pie)* hiker, rambler.

excusa *nf* **1** *(pretexto)* excuse. **2** *(disculpa)* excuse, apology.

excusar *vt* **1** *(justificar)* to excuse. **2** *(disculpar)* to pardon, forgive, excuse.
▶ *vpr* **excusarse** *(justificarse)* to excuse os; *(disculparse)* to apologize.

exención *nf* exemption.

exento,-a *adj* **1** free (de, from), exempt (de, from). **2** *(descubierto)* open.

exfoliación *nf* exfoliation.

exfoliar *vt* to exfoliate.
▶ *vpr* **exfoliarse** to exfoliate.

exhalación *nf* **1** exhalation. **2** *(estrella)* shooting star; *(rayo)* flash of lightning.

exhalar *vt* **1** *(gases, vapores, etc)* to give off; *(aire)* to exhale, breathe out. **2** *fig* *(suspiros, etc)* to heave, let out; *(quejas)* to utter.

exhaustivo,-a *adj* exhaustive, thorough, comprehensive.

exhausto,-a *adj* exhausted.

exhibición *nf* **1** *(exposición)* exhibition, show. **2** CINE showing.

exhibicionismo *nm* exhibitionism.

exhibir *vt* **1** to exhibit, show, display. **2** *(ostentar)* to show off.
▶ *vpr* **exhibirse** *(ostentar)* to show off, make an exhibition of os.

exhortar *vt* to exhort.

exhumación *nf* exhumation.

exhumar *vt* **1** to exhume. **2** *fig* to revive, recall.

exigencia *nf* **1** demand, exigency. **2** *(requisito)* requirement.

exigente *adj* demanding, exacting.

exigir *vt* **1** *(pedir por derecho)* to demand. **2** *fig (necesitar)* to require, call for.

exilado,-a *nm & nf* exile.

exilio *nm* exile.

existencia *nf (vida)* existence, life.
▶ *nf pl* **existencias** stock *sing*, stocks.

existencial *adj* existential.

existencialismo *nm* existentialism.

existencialista *adj* existentialist.
▶ *nm o nf* existentialist.

existente *adj* **1** existing, existent. **2** COM in stock.

existir *vi* to exist, be.

éxito *nm* success.

exitoso,-a *adj* successful.

éxodo *nm* exodus.

exogamia *nf* exogamy.

exorcismo *nm* exorcism.

exorcista *nm o nf* exorcist.

exotérico,-a *adj* exoteric.

exótico,-a *adj* exotic.

exotismo *nm* exoticism.

expandir *vt* **1** *(dilatar)* to expand. **2** *fig (divulgar)* to spread.
▶ *vpr* **expandirse 1** *(dilatarse)* to expand. **2** *fig (divulgarse)* to spread.

expansión *nf* **1** *(dilatación)* expansion. **2** *(difusión)* spreading. **3** *(aumento)* expansion, increase, growth.

expansionista *adj* expansionist.

expansivo,-a *adj* **1** *(gas, etc)* expansive. **2** *fig (franco)* expansive, open, frank.

expatriar *vt* to expatriate, banish.
▶ *vpr* **expatriarse** *(emigrar)* to emigrate, become an expatriate; *(exilarse)* to go into exile.

expectativa *nf* **1** *(esperanza)* expectation, hope. **2** *(posibilidad)* prospect.

expectoración *nf* **1** *(acción)* expectoration. **2** *(flema)* sputum, phlegm.

expectorar *vt* to expectorate.
▶ *vi* to expectorate.

expedición *nf* **1** *(gen)* expedition. **2** *(grupo de personas)* expedition, party.

3 *(acción de expedir)* dispatch, shipping; *(remesa)* shipment.

expedientar *vt* to take disciplinary action against, open a file on.

expediente *nm* **1** JUR proceedings *pl*, action: *expediente judicial* legal proceedings. **2** *(informe)* dossier, record; *(ficha)* file. **3** *(recurso)* expedient.

expedir *vt* **1** *(mercancías)* to send, dispatch, ship; *(correo)* to send, dispatch. **2** *(pasaporte, título)* to issue. **3** *(contrato, documento)* to draw up.

expeditivamente *adv* expeditiously.

expeditivo,-a *adj* expeditious.

expendedor,-ra *adj* selling, retailing, retail.
▶ *nm & nf* dealer, retailer, seller.

expender *vt* **1** *(gastar)* to spend. **2** *(vender)* to sell. **3** *(vender al menudeo)* to retail, sell.

expensas *nf pl* expenses, charges, costs.

experiencia *nf* **1** *(gen)* experience. **2** *(experimento)* experiment.

experimentación *nf* experimentation, experimenting, testing.

experimentado,-a *adj* **1** *(persona)* experienced. **2** *(método)* tested, tried.

experimental *adj* experimental.

experimentar *vt* **1** *(hacer experimentos)* to experiment, test. **2** *(probar)* to test, try out. **3** *(sentir, notar)* to experience, feel; *(- cambio)* to undergo; *(- aumento)* to show; *(- pérdida, derrota)* to suffer.

experimento *nm* experiment, test.

experto,-a *adj* expert.
▶ *nm & nf* expert.

expiar *vt* to expiate, atone for.

expirar *vi* to expire.

explanada *nf* esplanade.

explayar *vt* *fml (extender)* to extend, spread out.
▶ *vpr* **explayarse** *(dilatarse al hablar)* to dwell (en, on), talk at length (en, about).

explicable *adj* explicable, explainable.

explicación *nf* **1** explanation. **2** *(motivo)* reason.

explicar *vt* **1** *(gen)* to explain, expound, tell. **2** *(justificar)* to justify.
▶ *vpr* **explicarse** *(expresarse)* to explain os, make os understood, make os clear.

explicativo,-a *adj* explanatory.

explícito,-a *adj* explicit.

exploración *nf* **1** *(gen)* exploration. **2** TÉC scanning. **3** MIL reconnaissance.

explorador,-ra *nm & nf* **1** *(persona)* explorer. **2** *(niño)* boy scout; *(niña)* girl guide, US girl scout.

explorar *vt* **1** *(gen)* to explore. **2** MED to probe. **3** MIL to reconnoitre. **4** TÉC to scan. **5** *(de mina)* to drill, prospect.

exploratorio,-a *adj* **1** exploratory. **2** MED exploratory, probing.

explosión *nf* **1** explosion, blast, blowing up. **2** *fig* outburst.

explosionar *vt* to explode.
▶ *vi* to explode, blow up.

explosiva *nf* LING plosive.

explosivo,-a *adj* **1** explosive. **2** LING plosive.
▶ *nm* **explosivo** explosive.

explotación *nf* **1** *(gen)* exploitation. **2** *(de terreno)* cultivation, farming. **3** *(de industria)* running, operating. **4** *(de recursos)* tapping, exploitation.

explotador,-ra *nm & nf pey* exploiter.

explotar *vt* **1** *(sacar provecho)* to exploit; *(mina)* to work; *(tierra)* to cultivate; *(industria)* to operate, run; *(recursos)* to tap, exploit.
▶ *vi* *(explosionar)* to explode, blow up.

expoliación *nf* plundering, pillaging, despoiling.

expoliar *vt* to plunder, pillage, despoil.

expolio *nm* **1** *(acción)* plundering, pillaging, despoiling. **2** *(botín)* loot, booty.

exponencial *adj* exponential.

exponente *adj* exponent, expounding.
▶ *nm* **1** MAT index, exponent. **2** *(prototipo)* exponent.

exponer *vt* **1** *(explicar)* to expound, explain; *(propuesta)* to put forward; *(he-*

chos) to state, set out. **2** *(mostrar)* to show, exhibit; *(mercancías)* to display. **3** *(arriesgar)* to expose, risk, endanger.
▶ *vpr* **exponerse** *(arriesgarse)* to expose os (a, to), run the risk (a, of).

exportable *adj* exportable, for exportation.

exportación *nf* export, exportation.

exportador,-ra *adj* exporting.
▶ *nm & nf* exporter.

exportar *vt* to export.

exposición *nf* **1** *(de arte)* exhibition, show; *(de mercancías)* display. **2** *(explicación)* account, explanation; *(hechos, ideas)* exposé. **3** *(al sol, etc)* exposure.

expositivo,-a *adj* explanatory.

exprés *adj* **1** *(tren)* express. **2** *(café)* expresso. **3** *(olla)* pressure.

expresar *vt* **1** *(gen)* to express. **2** *(manifestar)* to state; *(comunicar)* to convey.
▶ *vpr* **expresarse** to express os.

expresión *nf* expression.

expresionismo *nm* expressionism.

expresionista *adj* expressionist.
▶ *nm o nf* expressionist.

expresividad *nf* expressivity.

expresivo,-a *adj* **1** *(elocuente)* expressive. **2** *(mirada)* meaningful; *(silencio)* eloquent.

expreso,-a *adj* *(especificado)* express.

exprimidor *nm* lemon squeezer, US juicer.

exprimir *vt* *(fruto)* to squeeze; *(zumo)* to squeeze out.

expropiación *nf* expropriation.

expropiar *vt* to expropriate.

expuesto,-a *adj* *(peligroso)* dangerous, risky; *(sin protección)* exposed.

expulsar *vt* **1** *(expeler)* to expel, eject, throw out; *(humo, etc)* to belch out. **2** DEP to send off.

expulsión *nf* **1** expulsion, ejection. **2** DEP sending off. **3** *(alumno)* expulsion.

expurgar *vt* **1** to expurgate. **2** *fig* to purge.

exquisitez *nf* **1** exquisiteness. **2** *(manjar)* delicacy.

exquisito,-a *adj* **1** *(gen)* exquisite. **2** *(gusto)* refined; *(sabor)* delicious, exquisite.

extasiado,-a *adj* ecstatic.

extasiar *vt* to enrapture.
▶ *vpr* **extasiarse** to go into ecstasies, go into raptures.

éxtasis *nm inv* ecstasy, rapture.

extático,-a *adj* extatic.

extender *vt* **1** *(mapa, papel)* to spread (out), open (out). **2** *(brazo, etc)* to stretch (out); *(alas)* to spread. **3** *(mantequilla, etc)* to spread. **4** *(documento)* to draw up; *(cheque)* to make out; *(pasaporte, certificado)* to issue.
▶ *vpr* **extenderse 1** *(durar)* to extend, last. **2** *(terreno)* to stretch. **3** *fig (difundirse)* to spread, extend.

extendido,-a *adj* **1** *(difundido)* widespread. **2** *(mano, etc)* outstretched.

extensible *adj* extendable.

extensión *nf* **1** *(gen)* extension. **2** *(dimensión)* extent, size; *(superficie)* area, expanse. **3** *(duración)* duration, length.

extensivo,-a *adj* extendable, extensive.

extenso,-a *adj* **1** *(amplio)* extensive, vast; *(grande)* large. **2** *(largo)* lengthy, long.

extenuado,-a *adj* **1** *(agotado)* exhausted. **2** *(débil)* weak. **3** *(flaco)* emaciated.

extenuante *adj* exhausting.

extenuar *vt* **1** *(agotar)* to exhaust. **2** *(debilitar)* to weaken.
▶ *vpr* **extenuarse** *(agotarse)* to exhaust os, wear os out.

exterior *adj* **1** *(gen)* exterior, outer, external. **2** *(ventana, puerta)* outside; *(pared)* outer. **3** *(aspecto)* outward. **4** *(extranjero)* foreign.
▶ *nm* **1** *(superficie externa)* exterior, outside. **2** *(extranjero)* abroad, overseas. **3** *(de una persona)* appearance. **4** DEP outside.
▶ *nm pl* **exteriores** CINE location shots.

exteriorización *nf* manifestation, externalization.

exteriorizar *vt* to show, reveal, express outwardly.

exterminación *nf* *(supresión)* extermination, wiping out; *(destrucción)* destruction.

exterminador,-ra *adj* exterminating.
▶ *nm & nf* exterminator.

exterminar *vt* *(suprimir)* to exterminate, wipe out; *(destruir)* to destroy.

exterminio *nm* extermination, wiping out; *(destrucción)* destruction.

externado *nm* day school.

externo,-a *adj* **1** external, outward: *parte externa* outside. **2** *(alumno)* day.

extinción *nf* extinction.

extinguir *vt* **1** *(fuego, etc)* to extinguish, put out. **2** *(especie, deuda, epidemia)* to wipe out.
▶ *vpr* **extinguirse 1** *(fuego, etc)* to go out. **2** *(especie, etc)* to become extinct, die out. **3** *(plazo)* to expire, run out.

extintor *nm* fire extinguisher.

extirpación *nf* **1** MED removal, extraction. **2** *fig* eradication, wiping out, stamping out.

extirpar *vt* **1** MED to remove, extract. **2** *fig* to eradicate, wipe out, stamp out.

extorsión *nf* **1** *(usurpación)* extortion. **2** *fig (molestia)* inconvenience, trouble.

extorsionar *vt* **1** *(usurpar)* to extort, exact. **2** *fig (molestar)* to inconvenience, cause inconvenience to.

extra *adj* **1** *fam* extra. **2** *fam (superior)* top-quality, best-quality. **3** *(paga)* bonus.
▶ *nm* **1** *fam (gasto)* additional expense. **2** *fam (plus)* bonus.

extracción *nf* **1** *(gen)* extraction; *(de lotería)* draw. **2** *(origen)* descent, extraction. COMP **extracción de datos** INFORM data retrieval.

extracto *nm* **1** *(sustancia)* extract. **2** *(trozo)* extract, excerpt. **3** *(resumen)* summary.

extractor *nm* extractor.

extradición *nf* extradition.

extraditar *vt* to extradite.

extraer *vt* **1** *(gen)* to extract. **2** *(conclusión)* to draw.

extraescolar *adj* out of school, extra-curricular. COMP **actividades extraescolares** extracurricular activities.

extrafino,-a *adj* superfine, best quality.

extralargo,-a *adj* king-size.

extralimitarse *vpr* *fig* to go too far, overstep.

extranjero,-a *adj* foreign, alien.
▶ *nm & nf* foreigner.
▶ *nm* **extranjero** foreign countries *pl*, abroad.

extrañar *vt* *(sorprender)* to surprise. **2** *(notar extraño)* to find strange, not to be used to.
▶ *vpr* **extrañarse 1** *(desterrarse)* to go into exile. **2** *(sorprenderse)* to be surprised (de/por, at).

extraño,-a *adj* **1** *(no conocido)* alien, foreign. **2** *(particular)* strange, peculiar, odd, funny.

extraordinaria *nf* *(paga)* bonus payment.

extraordinariamente *adv* extraordinarily, unusually.

extraordinario,-a *adj* **1** *(fuera de lo común)* extraordinary, unusual; *(sorprendente)* surprising; *(admirable)* outstanding, exceptional. **2** *(raro)* queer, odd. **3** *(gastos, etc)* additional, extra; *(paga)* bonus. **4** *(revista, etc)* special.
▶ *nm* **extraordinario 1** *(correo)* special delivery. **2** *(revista, etc)* special issue.

extraplano,-a *adj* slimline.

extrapolar *vt* to extrapolate.

extrarradio *nm* outskirts *pl*, suburbs *pl*.

extraterrestre *adj* extramundane, extraterrestrial.
▶ *nm o nf* alien.

extravagancia *nf* extravagance, eccentricity.

extravagante *adj* extravagant outrageous.

extraviado,-a *adj* **1** *(disoluto)* dissolute. **2** *(perdido - persona, objeto)* missing, lost; *(- perro, niño)* stray.

extraviar *vt* **1** *(persona)* to mislead. **2** *(objeto)* to mislay, lose.
▶ *vpr* **extraviarse 1** *(persona)* to get lost, lose one's way. **2** *(objeto)* to get mislaid.

extravío *nm* *(persona)* misleading; *(cosa)* loss, mislaying.

extremado,-a *adj* extreme.

extremar *vt* to carry to extremes, carry to the limit, overdo.
▶ *vpr* **extremarse** to do one's best, do one's utmost, take great pains.

extremidad *nf* **1** *(parte extrema)* extremity; *(punta)* end, tip. **2** ANAT limb, extremity.

extremismo *nm* extremism.

extremista *adj* extremist.
▶ *nm o nf* extremist.

extremo,-a *adj* **1** *(exagerado)* extreme. **2** *(distante)* further. **3** *fig* *(intenso)* utmost.
▶ *nm* **extremo 1** *(punta)* extreme, end. **2** *(asunto, materia)* matter, question. **3** DEP wing.

extrínseco,-a *adj* extrinsic.

extrovertido,-a *adj* extroverted.
▶ *nm & nf* extrovert.

exuberante *adj* **1** exuberant. **2** *(vegetación)* lush, abundant.

F

F, f *nf (la letra)* F, f.

F *sím (Fahrenheit)* Fahrenheit; *(símbolo)* F.

fa *nm* F.

fabada *nf* bean stew *including pork sausage and bacon.*

fábrica *nf* **1** *(industria)* factory, plant. **2** *(fabricación)* manufacture.

fabricación *nf* manufacture, production, making.

fabricante *nm o nf* manufacturer, maker.

fabricar *vt* **1** *(producir)* to make, manufacture, produce. **2** *fig (inventar)* to fabricate, invent.

fábula *nf* **1** LIT fable. **2** *(mito)* myth, legend. **3** *(mentira)* invention.

fabular *vt* **1** *(contar fábulas)* to fable. **2** *(imaginar)* to imagine.

fabuloso,-a *adj* **1** *(fantástico)* fabulous, fantastic. **2** LIT fabulous, mythical.

faceta *nf* facet.

fachada *nf* **1** ARQUIT façade, front. **2** *fam (apariencia)* outward show.

facial *adj* facial.

fácil *adj* **1** easy. **2** *(probable)* probable, likely.

facilidad *nf* **1** *(simplicidad)* ease, facility. **2** *(aptitud)* talent, gift: *tiene facilidad para la música* he has a gift for music. COMP **facilidad de palabra** fluency.
▶ *nf pl* **facilidades** *(medios que facilitan)* facilities.

facilitar *vt* **1** *(simplificar)* to make easy, make easier, facilitate. **2** *(proporcionar)* to provide with, supply with.

factor *nm (gen)* factor.

factoría *nf* **1** COM trading post. **2** *(fábrica)* factory, mill.

factura *nf* invoice, bill.

facturación *nf* **1** COM invoicing. **2** *(de equipajes)* registration, check-in.

facturar *vt* **1** COM to invoice, charge for. **2** *(equipaje)* to register, check in.

facultad *nf* **1** *(capacidad)* faculty, ability. **2** *(poder)* faculty, power. **3** *(universitaria)* faculty, school.

faena *nf* **1** *(tarea)* task, job. **2** *fam (mala pasada)* dirty trick.

fagocito *nm* phagocyte.

fagot *nm (instrumento)* bassoon.
▶ *nm o nf (músico)* bassoonist.

faisán *nm* pheasant.

faja *nf* **1** *(cinturón)* band, belt. **2** *(ropa interior)* corset, girdle.

fajo *nm* bundle; *(de billetes)* wad.

falda *nf* **1** *(prenda)* skirt. **2** *(regazo)* lap. **3** *(ladera)* slope. **4** *(corte de carne)* brisket.

faldón *nm* **1** *(de traje)* coat-tail; *(de camisa)* shirt-tail. **2** *(prenda de bebé)* wraparound skirt. **3** *(de tejado)* gable.

falible *adj* fallible.

falla *nf* **1** *(defecto)* defect, fault. **2** GEOG fault.

fallar *vi* **1** *(premio)* to award a prize. **2** *(fracasar, no funcionar)* to fail. **3** *(puntería)* to miss; *(plan)* to go wrong.
▶ *vt (premio)* to award.

fallecer *vi fml* to pass away, die.

fallo *nm* **1** *(en concurso)* decision. **2** *(error)* mistake, blunder; *(fracaso)* failure. **4** *(defecto)* fault, defect.

falsear *vt (falsificar)* to counterfeit, forge.

falsedad *nf* **1** *(hipocresía)* falseness, hypocrisy. **2** *(mentira)* falsehood, lie.

falsete *nm* falsetto.

falsificador,-ra *adj (de firma, cuadro)* forging; *(de dinero)* counterfeiting.

▶ *nm & nf (de firma, cuadro)* forger; *(de dinero)* counterfeiter.

falsificar *vt* **1** *(gen)* to falsify. **2** *(firma, cuadro)* to forge; *(dinero)* to counterfeit, forge.

falso,-a *adj* **1** *(no verdadero)* false, untrue. **2** *(moneda)* false, counterfeit. **3** *(persona)* insincere, false.

falta *nf* **1** *(carencia)* lack: *falta de sensibilidad* lack of sensitivity. **2** *(escasez)* shortage: *existe una falta de agua* there is a water shortage. **3** *(ausencia)* absence. **4** *(error)* mistake: *has hecho una falta de ortografía* you've made a spelling mistake. **5** *(defecto)* fault, defect. **6** DEP *(fútbol)* foul; *(tenis)* fault. LOC **echar en falta** to miss. ‖ **sin falta** without fail.

faltar *vi* **1** *(haber poco)* to be lacking, be needed: *falta (más) leche* we need (more) milk. **2** *(no tener)* to lack, not have (enough). **3** *(quedar)* to remain, be left: *falta poco para que...* it won't be long till...

falto,-a LOC **estar falto,-a de** to lack, be short of, be without: *estamos faltos de dinero* we're short of money.

fama *nf (renombre)* fame, renown.

famélico,-a *adj* starving, famished.

familia *nf* **1** family. **2** *(prole)* children *pl*, family.

familiar *adj* **1** *(de la familia)* family, of the family. **2** *(conocido)* familiar, well-known. **3** LING colloquial.
▶ *nm o nf* relation, relative.

familiaridad *nf* familiarity.

familiarizar *vt* to familiarize (con, with), make familiar (con, with).
▶ *vpr* **familiarizarse** to get to know: *familiarízate con el teclado* get to know the keyboard.

familiarmente *adv* familiarly.

famoso,-a *adj* famous, well-known.

fan *nm o nf* fan, admirer. LOC **ser un,-a fan de** ALGO to be mad about STH.

fanático,-a *adj* fanatic, fanatical.

fanatismo *nm* fanaticism.

fanerógamo,-a *adj* phanerogamic, phanerogamous.

fanfarrón,-ona *adj fam* swanky.

fanfarronear *vi fam (chulear)* to show off, swank.

fango *nm (barro)* mud, mire.

fantasear *vi* **1** *(forjar en la imaginación)* to daydream, dream. **2** *(presumir)* to boast, show off.
▶ *vt (imaginar)* dream.

fantasía *nf* **1** fantasy. **2** fancy.

fantasioso,-a *adj* imaginative.

fantasma *nm* **1** *(espectro)* phantom, ghost. **2** *fam (fanfarrón)* braggart, show-off.

fantasmal *adj* ghostly.

fantástico,-a *adj* **1** fantastic. **2** *(estupendo)* wonderful.

fantoche *nm* **1** *(títere)* puppet, marionette. **2** *pey (fanfarrón)* braggart.

faquir *nm* fakir.

faradio *nm* farad.

farándula *nf* **1** *(compañía de teatro)* group of strolling players. **2** *(profesión, mundo del teatro)* acting, the stage.

faraón *nm* Pharaoh.

faraónico,-a *adj* Pharaonic.

fardar *vi argot (presumir)* to show off, swank.

fardo *nm (paquete)* bundle, pack.

fardón,-ona *adj argot* classy, flash.

farero,-a *nm & nf* lighthouse keeper.

faringe *nf* pharynx.

faringitis *nf inv* pharyngitis.

farmacéutico,-a *adj* pharmaceutical.
▶ *nm & nf* pharmacist.

farmacia *nf* **1** *(estudios)* pharmacy. **2** *(tienda)* chemist's (shop), US drugstore, pharmacy.

fármaco *nm* medicine, medication.

farmacología *nf* pharmacology.

faro *nm* **1** *(torre)* lighthouse, beacon. **2** *(coche)* headlight. **3** *fig (guía)* guiding light, guide.

farol *nm* **1** *(farola)* streetlamp, streetlight. **2** *argot (fardada)* bragging, swank.

farola *nf* streetlight, streetlamp; *(de gas)* gas lamp.

farolero,-a *adj fam* boastful.
▶ *nm & nf fam (fanfarrón)* show-off.
▶ *nm* **farolero** *(de profesión)* lamplighter.

farolillo *nm* **1** *(farol de papel)* Chinese lantern. **2** BOT Canterbury bell.

farra *nf fam* binge, spree.

farruco,-a *adj fam* conceited, cocky.

farsa *nf* TEAT farce.

farsante *adj* lying, deceitful.

fascículo *nm* instalment (US installment), fascicule, fascicle.

fascinación *nf* fascination.

fascinante *adj* fascinating.

fascinar *vt* to fascinate, captivate.

fascismo *nm* fascism.

fascista *adj* fascist.

fase *nf (etapa)* phase, stage.

fastidiado,-a *adj* **1** *(hastiado)* sickened, disgusted. **2** *(molesto)* annoyed. **3** *fam (estropeado)* ruined, spoilt. **4** *fam (mal de salud)* ill, sick, in a bad way.

fastidiar *vt* **1** *(hastiar)* to sicken, disgust. **2** *(molestar)* to annoy, bother. **3** *(partes del cuerpo)* to hurt: *le fastidia el estómago* he's got a bad stomach. **4** *fam (estropear)* to damage, ruin; *(planes)* to spoil.
▶ *vpr* **fastidiarse** **1** *(aguantarse)* to put up with, grin and bear it. **2** *fam (estropearse)* to go wrong, break down: *se ha fastidiado la tele* the telly has gone wrong.

fastidio *nm* **1** *(molestia)* bother, nuisance. **2** *(aburrimiento)* boredom.

fastidioso,-a *adj* **1** *(molesto)* annoying, irksome. **2** *(aburrido)* boring, tedious.

fastuoso,-a *adj* **1** *(cosa)* splendid, lavish. **2** *(persona)* lavish, ostentatious.

fatal *adj* **1** *(inexorable)* fateful. **2** *(mortal)* deadly, fatal.
▶ *adv fam* awfully, terribly.

fatalidad *nf* **1** *(destino)* fate. **2** *(desgracia)* misfortune.

fatalismo *nm* fatalism.

fatalista *adj* fatalistic.

fatídico,-a *adj (desastroso)* disastrous, calamitous.

fatiga *nf (cansancio)* fatigue.

fatigar *vt* **1** *(cansar)* to wear out, tire. **2** *(molestar)* to annoy.

fatigoso,-a *adj (cansado)* tiring, exhausting.

fauces *nf pl (en anatomía)* gullet *sing*.

fauna *nf* fauna.

fauvismo *nm* fauvism.

fauvista *adj o nf* fauvist.

favor *nm* favour (US favor). LOC **a favor de** in favour (US favor) of. ▌**hacer un favor** to do a favour (US favor). ▌**por favor** please.

favorable *adj* favourable (US favorable). LOC **mostrarse favorable a ALGO** to be in favour (US favor) of STH.

favorecer *vt* **1** *(ayudar)* to favour (US favor), help. **2** *(agraciar)* suit: *el azul no me favorece* blue doesn't suit me.

favoritismo *nm* favouritism (US favoritism).

favorito,-a *adj* favourite (US favorite).

fax *nm (sistema, documento)* fax.

fe *nf* faith.

fealdad *nf* ugliness.

febrero *nm* February.

✎ Para ejemplos de uso consulta marzo.

febril *adj* MED feverish.

fecha *nf* **1** date: *¿qué fecha es hoy?* what's the date today? **2** *(día)* day. LOC **fijar la fecha** to fix a date. COMP **fecha de nacimiento** date of birth.
▶ *nf pl* **fechas** *(época)* time *sing*: *por esas fechas* at that time.

fécula *nf* starch.

fecundación *nf* fertilization.

fecundar *vt* to fertilize.

fecundidad *nf (fertilidad)* fertility.

federación *nf* federation.

federal *adj* federal.

federalismo *nm* federalism.

federalista *adj* federalist.

federar *vt* to federate.

feldespato *nm* feldspar, felspar.

felicidad *nf* happiness. LOC **¡(muchas) felicidades!** **1** *(éxitos)* congratulations! **2** *(cumpleaños)* happy birthday!

felicitación *nf* **1** *(acción)* congratulation. **2** *(tarjeta)* greetings card.

felicitar *vt* to congratulate (por, on).

felino,-a *adj* feline.

feliz *adj* happy.

felizmente *adv (con felicidad)* happily.

felpa *nf* plush.

felpudo,-a *adj (textil)* plushy, velvety.

femenino,-a *adj* 1 feminine. 2 *(sexo)* female; *(equipo, asociación)* women's.

feminidad *nf* femininity.

feminismo *nm* feminism.

feminista *adj* feminist.

femoral *adj* femoral.

fémur *nm* femur.

fenomenal *adj fam (fantástico)* great, terrific.
▶ *adv* wonderfully, marvellously.

fenómeno *nm* phenomenon.
▶ *adj fam (fantástico)* fantastic, terrific.

fenotipo *nm* phenotype.

feo,-a *adj (persona - nada atractiva)* ugly; *(- poco atractiva)* plain. 2 *(aspecto, situación, tiempo, etc)* nasty, horrible, unpleasant, awful.

féretro *nm* coffin.

feria *nf* 1 COM fair. 2 *(fiesta)* fair.

fermentación *nf* fermentation.

fermentar *vi* to ferment.

fermento *nm* ferment.

ferocidad *nf* ferocity, fierceness.

feroz *adj* fierce, ferocious.

ferretería *nf* ironmonger's.

ferretero,-a *nm & nf* ironmonger.

férrico,-a *adj* ferric.

ferrocarril *nm* railway, US railroad.

ferroviario,-a *adj* railway.

fértil *adj* fertile, rich.

fertilidad *nf* fertility, fecundity.

fertilización *nf* fertilization.

fertilizante *adj* fertilizing.
▶ *nm (abono)* fertilizer.

fertilizar *vt* to fertilize.

ferviente *adj* fervent, passionate.

fervor *nm* fervour (US fervor).

festejar *vt (celebrar)* to celebrate.

festejo *nm* feast, entertainment.

festival *nm* festival.

festividad *nf* 1 *(fiesta)* festivity, celebration. 2 *(día)* feast day, holiday.

festivo,-a *adj* 1 *(alegre)* festive, merry. 2 *(humorístico)* witty.

fétido,-a *adj* stinking, fetid.

feto *nm* foetus (US fetus).

feudal *adj* feudal.

feudalismo *nm* feudalism.

feudo *nm* fief, feud.

fiable *adj* reliable, trustworthy.

fiambre *nm* 1 CULIN cold meat, cold cut. 2 *fam (cadáver)* stiff, corpse.

fiambrera *nf* lunch box.

fianza *nf (depósito)* deposit.

fiar *vt* 1 *(vender)* to sell on credit. 2 *(confiar)* to confide, entrust. LOC de fiar trustworthy, reliable.
▶ *vpr* **fiarse** *(confiarse)* to trust (de, -).

fibra *nf* fibre (US fiber). COMP **fibra óptica** optical fibre (US fiber).

fibroso,-a *adj* fibrous.

ficción *nf* fiction.

ficha *nf* 1 *(tarjeta)* index card, file card. 2 *(de teléfono)* token. 3 *(en juegos)* counter; *(naipes)* chip; *(ajedrez)* piece, man; *(dominó)* domino.

fichaje *nm* signing (up).

fichar *vt* 1 *(anotar)* to put on an index card; *(registrar)* to open a file on. 2 DEP to sign up, sign on.
▶ *vi* DEP to sign up (por, with): *finalmente fichó por el Barcelona* he finally signed up with Barcelona F.C.

fichero *nm* 1 *(archivo)* card index. 2 *(mueble)* filing cabinet, file. 3 INFORM file.

ficticio,-a *adj* fictitious.

ficus *nm inv* rubber plant.

fidelidad *nf* 1 *(lealtad)* fidelity, faithfulness. 2 *(exactitud)* accuracy. COMP **alta fidelidad** high fidelity, hi-fi.

fideo *nm* noodle.

fiebre *nf (enfermedad)* fever, temperature. LOC **tener fiebre** to have a temperature.

fiel *adj* 1 *(leal)* faithful, loyal. 2 *(exacto)* accurate.

fieltro *nm* felt.

fiera *nf* wild animal, wild beast.

fiero,-a *adj* wild, fierce, ferocious.

fiesta *nf* 1 *(día no laborable)* holiday: *el viernes es fiesta* Friday's a holiday. 2 *(reunión)* party.
▶ *nf pl* **fiestas** festivity, fiesta.

figura *nf* **1** *(gen)* figure. **2** *(forma)* shape.

figurar *vi* **1** *(encontrarse)* to appear, be, figure: *figura como director* he appears as director. **2** *(destacar)* to stand out, be important.
▶ *vpr* **figurarse** *(imaginarse)* to imagine, suppose.

fijador,-ra *nm (para pelo)* hairspray, hair gel.

fijar *vt (sujetar)* to fix, fasten; *(puerta)* to hang; *(ventana)* to put in.
▶ *vpr* **fijarse 1** *(darse cuenta)* to notice. **2** *(poner atención)* to pay attention, watch: *fíjate cómo se hace* watch how it's done.

fijo,-a *adj* **1** *(sujeto)* fixed, fastened. **2** *(establecido)* set, definite, firm: *fecha fija* set date. **3** *(firme)* steady, stable, firm. **4** *(permanente)* permanent.

fila *nf (línea)* file, line, row.
▶ *nf pl* **filas** *(de ejército, partido)* ranks.

filamento *nm* filament.

filete *nm (de carne, pescado)* fillet (us fillet).

Filipinas *nf pl* **las Filipinas** the Philippines.

filipino,-a *adj* Filipino.
▶ *nm & nf (persona)* Filipino.
▶ *nm* **filipino** *(idioma)* Filipino.

film *nm* film, us movie.

filmar *vt* to film, shoot.

filmina *nf* slide, transparency.

filmoteca *nf* film institute.

filo *nm* cutting edge, edge.

filo- *pref* philo-.

filología *nf* philology.

filólogo,-a *nm & nf* philologist.

filón *nm (mineral)* seam, vein.

filosofar *vi* to philosophize.

filosofía *nf* philosophy.

filósofo,-a *nm & nf* philosopher.

filoxera *nf* phylloxera.

filtrar *vt* to filter, to leak.
▶ *vpr* **filtrarse** *(pasar a través)* to filter.

filtro *nm (material)* filter.

fin *nm* **1** *(final)* end. **2** *(objetivo)* purpose, aim. [LOC] **a fin de** in order to, so as to. ▌**a fin de que** so that. ▌**en fin** anyway. [COMP] **fin de semana** weekend.

final *adj (último)* final, last.
▶ *nm* end. [COMP] **final feliz** happy ending.
▶ *nf* DEP final.

finalidad *nf* purpose, aim.

finalista *nm o nf* finalist.

finalizar *vt* to end, finish.
▶ *vi* to end, finish.

financiación *nf* financing.

financiar *vt* to finance.

finanzas *nf pl* finances.

finca *nf* property, estate. [COMP] **finca rústica** country property.

fingir *vt* to feign, pretend: *fingió indiferencia* he feigned indifference.

finito,-a *adj* finite.

finlandés,-esa *adj* Finnish.
▶ *nm & nf (persona)* Finn.
▶ *nm* **finlandés** *(idioma)* Finnish.

Finlandia *nf* Finland.

fino,-a *adj* **1** *(delicado)* fine, delicate. **2** *(delgado)* thin. **3** *(educado)* refined, polite.

fiordo *nm* fiord, fjord.

firma *nf* **1** *(acto)* signing. **2** *(empresa)* firm.

firmamento *nm* firmament.

firmar *vt* to sign.

firme *adj (estable)* firm, steady.

firmeza *nf* firmness, steadiness.

fiscal *adj* fiscal, tax.
▶ *nm o nf* JUR public prosecutor, us district attorney.

fisco *nm* exchequer, us treasury.

fisgar *vt fam* to pry, snoop.

fisgón,-ona *adj* snooper, busybody.

fisgonear *vt* to pry, snoop.

física *nf* physics.

físico,-a *adj* physical.
▶ *nm & nf (profesión)* physicist.
▶ *nm* **físico** *(aspecto)* physique.

fisioterapeuta *nm o nf* physiotherapist.

fisioterapia *nf* physiotherapy.

fisonomía *nf* appearance.

fisura *nf* fissure.

fito- *pref* phyto-.

Fiyi *nm* Fiji.

fiyiano,-a *adj* Fijian.
▶ *nm & nf (persona)* Fijian.
▶ *nm* **fiyiano** *(idioma)* Fijian.

F

fláccido,-a *adj* flaccid, flabby.

flaco,-a *adj* **1** *(delgado)* thin, skinny. **2** *(débil)* weak, frail.

flagelo *nm* **1** whip. **2** BIOL flagellum.

flamenco,-a *adj* **1** *(gitano)* Andalusian gypsy. **2** *(música)* flamenco.
► *nm* **flamenco 1** *(idioma)* Flemish. **2** *(música)* flamenco music. **3** *(ave)* flamingo.

flan *nm* *(dulce)* crème caramel. LOC **estar como un flan** to be shaking like a leaf.

flanco *nm* flank, side.

flanera *nf* mould (US mold).

flaquear *vi* to weaken, give in, to fail.

flaqueza *nf* weakness, frailty.

flash *nm* flash, flashlight.

flato *nm* *(dolor)* stitch.

flauta *nf* flute.

flautista *o nf* flute player.

flecha *nf* arrow.

flechazo *nm* fig *(enamoramiento)* love at first sight.

fleco *nm* *(adorno)* fringe.

flemón *nm* abscess.

flequillo *nm* fringe, US bangs *pl*.

flexibilidad *nf* flexibility.

flexible *adj* flexible.

flexionar *vt* *(cuerpo)* to bend.

flexo *nm* adjustable table lamp.

flipar *vt* argot *(gustar)* to drive wild.
► *vi* **1** *(asombrarse)* to be amazed, be stunned. **2** *(pasárselo bien)* to freak out.

flirtear *vi* to flirt.

flojear *vi* **1** *(disminuir)* to go down. **2** *(debilitarse)* to weaken, grow weak.

flojera *nf* fam weakness, faintness.

flojo,-a *adj* **1** *(suelto)* loose; *(no tensado)* slack. **2** *(débil)* weak. **3** *(mediocre)* poor: *es un estudiante flojo* he's a poor student.

flor *nf* BOT flower, bloom. LOC **en flor** in bloom.

florecer *vi* **1** *(plantas)* to flower, bloom; *(árboles)* to blossom. **2** *(prosperar)* to flourish, thrive.

floreciente *adj* prosperous.

florería *nf* florist's (shop).

florero *nm* vase.

florista *nm o nf* florist.

floristería *nf* florist's (shop).

flota *nf* fleet.

flotador *nm* *(de niño)* rubber ring.

flotar *vi* to float.

flote LOC **a flote** afloat.

fluctuar *vi* *(variar)* to fluctuate.

fluido,-a *adj* *(sin obstáculos)* fluid.
► *nm* **fluido** FÍS fluid. COMP **fluido eléctrico** current, power.

fluir *vi* to flow.

flúor *nm* fluorine.

fluorescente *adj* fluorescent.
► *nm* fluorescent light.

fluvial *adj* fluvial, river.

fobia *nf* phobia.

foca *nf* seal.

foco *nm* **1** *(en física)* focus. **2** *(lámpara)* spotlight, floodlight.

fofo,-a *adj* flabby.

fogata *nf* bonfire.

fogón *nm* *(de cocina)* kitchen range, stove.

fogueo LOC **de fogueo** blank.

folclore *nm* folklore.

folclórico,-a *adj* folkloric, popular.

folio *nm* folio, leaf.

folk *nm* folk music.

folleto *nm* pamphlet, leaflet, brochure; *(explicativo)* instruction leaflet.

follón *nm* **1** fam *(alboroto)* rumpus, shindy. **2** fam *(enredo, confusión)* mess, trouble. LOC **armar (un) follón** fam to kick up a rumpus.

fomentar *vt* to promote.

fonda *nf* inn.

fondo *nm* **1** *(parte más baja)* bottom: *en el fondo del pozo* at the bottom of the well. **2** *(parte más lejana)* end, back: *al fondo de la sala* at the back of the hall. **3** *(segundo término)* background. LOC **a fondo 1** *(adjetival)* thorough. **2** *(adverbial)* thoroughly. ‖ **en el fondo** fig deep down, at heart. COMP **fondo del mar** sea bed.
► *nm pl* **fondos** funds, money *sing*.

fonema *nm* phoneme.

fonético,-a *adj* phonetic.

fónico,-a *adj* phonic.

fono- *pref* phono-.

fonología *nf* phonology.

fonoteca *nf* record library.

fontanería *nf* plumbing.

fontanero,-a *nm & nf* plumber.

footing *nm* jogging. [LOC] hacer footing to go jogging.

forastero,-a *nm & nf* stranger.

forcejear *vi* to wrestle, struggle.

forcejeo *nm* struggle, struggling.

forestal *adj* forest.

forja *nf (fragua)* forge.

forjado *nm* ARQUIT framework.

forjar *vt (metales)* to forge.

forma *nf* **1** *(gen)* form, shape: *en forma de X* X-shaped. **2** *(manera)* way. **3** DEP form. [LOC] de todas formas anyway, in any case. ‖ estar en forma to be in shape, be fit.

formación *nf* **1** *(gen)* formation. **2** *(educación)* upbringing. [COMP] formación profesional vocational training.

formal *adj* **1** *(con los requisitos necesarios)* formal. **2** *(serio)* serious, serious-minded. **3** *(cumplidor)* reliable, dependable.

formalizar *vt* to make formal.

formalmente *adv* formally.

formar *vt* **1** *(gen)* to form. **2** *(integrar, constituir)* to form, constitute: *formar parte de algo* to be a part of sth. **3** *(educar)* to bring up.
▶ *vpr* **formarse** *(educarse)* to be educated, be trained.

formatear *vt* to format.

formato *nm (gen)* format.

formidable *adj* tremendous, formidable.

formón *nm* firmer chisel.

fórmula *nf (gen)* formula.

formular *vt* **1** *(una teoría)* to formulate. **2** *(quejas, peticiones)* to express, make.
▶ *vi* QUÍM to write formulae.

formulario,-a *nm (documento)* form: *formulario de solicitud* application form.

forofo,-a *nm & nf fam* fan, supporter.

forraje *nm (pienso)* fodder, forage.

forrar *vt* **1** *(por dentro)* to line. **2** *(por fuera)* to cover. **3** *(tapizar)* to upholster.
▶ *vpr* **forrarse** *fam (de dinero)* to make a fortune, make a packet.

forro *nm* **1** *(interior)* lining. **2** *(funda)* cover, case. **3** *(tapizado)* upholstery.

fortalecer *vt* to fortify, strengthen.
▶ *vpr* **fortalecerse** to strengthen.

fortaleza *nf* **1** *(vigor)* strength. **2** *(recinto fortificado)* fortress.

fortificación *nf* fortification.

fortuito,-a *adj* chance, fortuitous.

fortuna *nf* **1** *(destino)* fortune, fate. **2** *(suerte)* luck.

forzado,-a *adj* **1** *(obligado)* forced. **2** *(rebuscado)* forced, strained. [COMP] risa forzada forced laugh.

forzar *vt* **1** *(persona)* to force, compel. **2** *(cosa)* to force open, break open.

forzoso,-a *adj* **1** *(inevitable)* inevitable, unavoidable. **2** *(obligatorio)* obligatory, compulsory.

forzudo,-a *adj* strong, brawny.

fosa *nf* **1** *(sepultura)* grave. **2** *(hoyo)* pit, hollow. **3** ANAT cavity, fossa. **4** *(en el océano)* trench, deep. [COMP] fosas nasales nostrils.

fosfato *nm* phosphate. [COMP] fosfato de cal calcium phosphate.

fosforescente *adj* phosphorescent.

fósforo *nm* **1** QUÍM phosphorus. **2** *(cerilla)* match.

fósil *nm* fossil.

foso *nm* **1** *(hoyo)* hole, pit. **2** *(de fortaleza)* moat.

foto *nf fam* photo, picture.

fotocopia *nf* photocopy.

fotocopiadora *nf* photocopier, photocopying machine.

fotocopiar *vt* to photocopy.

fotografía *nf* **1** *(proceso)* photography. **2** *(retrato)* photograph. [LOC] hacer fotografías to take photographs.

fotografiar *vt* to photograph, take a photograph of.

fotógrafo,-a *nm & nf* photographer.

fotón *nm* photon.

fotosíntesis *nf inv* photosynthesis.

FP *abrev* EDUC **(Formación Profesional)** Professional Formation *(vocational training)*.

fracasar *vi* to fail, be unsuccessful, fall through.

fracaso *nm* failure.

fracción *nf* **1** *(gen)* fraction. **2** POL faction.

fraccionar *vt* to divide, break up, split up.

fractura *nf* fracture.

fragancia *nf* fragrance.

fragata *nf* frigate.

frágil *adj* **1** *(quebradizo)* fragile, breakable. **2** *(débil)* frail, weak.

fragilidad *nf* **1** *(cualidad)* fragility. **2** *(debilidad)* frailty, weakness.

fragmento *nm* **1** *(pedazo)* fragment, piece. **2** *(literario)* passage.

fragua *nf* forge.

fraguar *vt* **1** *(metal)* to forge. **2** *fig (plan)* to dream up, fabricate; *(conspiración)* to hatch.
► *vi (endurecerse)* to set, harden.

fraile *nm* friar, monk.

frambuesa *nf* raspberry.

francamente *adv* frankly.

francés,-esa *adj* French.
► *nm & nf (persona)* French person; *(hombre)* Frenchman; *(mujer)* Frenchwoman.
► *nm* **francés** *(idioma)* French.

Francia *nf* France.

franco,-a[1] *nm & nf* HIST *(persona)* Frank.
► *nm* **franco** HIST *(idioma)* Frankish; *(moneda)* franc.

franco,-a[2] *adj* **1** *(persona)* frank, open. **2** *(cosa)* clear, obvious. **3** COM free.

francotirador,-ra *nm & nf* sniper.

franela *nf* flannel.

franja *nf* **1** *(banda)* band, strip. **2** *(de tierra)* strip. **3** COST fringe, border.

franquear *vt* **1** *(dejar libre)* to free, clear. **2** *(atravesar)* to cross. **3** *(obstáculo)* to overcome. **4** *(carta)* to frank.

franqueo *nm* postage.

franqueza *nf* **1** *(sinceridad)* frankness, openness. **2** *(confianza)* familiarity, intimacy.

frasco *nm* flask.

frase *nf* **1** *(oración)* sentence. **2** *(expresión)* phrase. COMP **frase hecha** set phrase, set expression, idiom.

fraternal *adj* fraternal, brotherly.

fraternidad *nf* fraternity, brotherhood.

fraude *nm* fraud. COMP **fraude fiscal** tax evasion.

fray *nm* Brother.

frecuencia *nf* frequency. LOC **con frecuencia** frequently, often.

frecuentar *vt* to frequent, visit.

frecuente *adj* **1** *(repetido)* frequent. **2** *(usual)* common.

frecuentemente *adv* frequently, often.

fregadero *nm* kitchen sink.

fregar *vt* **1** *(lavar)* to wash. **2** *(el suelo)* to mop. LOC **fregar los platos** to wash the dishes, GB do the washing up, wash up.

fregona *nf (utensilio)* mop.

freidora *nf* fryer, deep fryer.

freír *vt* **1** *(guisar)* to fry. **2** *fig* to annoy, exasperate.

frenar *vt* **1** to brake. **2** *fig* to restrain, check.
► *vi* to brake: *frenó de golpe* he jammed on the brakes.

frenazo *nm* sudden braking. LOC **dar un frenazo** to jam on the brakes.

freno *nm* **1** *(de auto)* brake. **2** *fig (contención)* curb, check. LOC **poner freno a ALGO** *fig* to curb STH.

frente *nm* **1** *(gen)* front. **2** MIL front, front line.
► *nf* ANAT forehead. LOC **de frente 1** *(hacia adelante)* straight ahead. **2** *(sin rodeos)* straight. ▌ **ponerse al frente de ALGO** to take command of STH.

fresa *nf* **1** *(planta)* strawberry plant. **2** *(fruto)* strawberry.
► *adj* strawberry.

fresco,-a *adj* **1** *(temperatura)* cool, cold: *viento fresco* cool wind; *agua fresca* cold water. **2** *(tela, vestido)* light, cool. **3** *(comida)* fresh. **4** *(reciente)* fresh, new: *noticias frescas* latest news *sing*. **5** *(desvergonzado)* cheeky, shameless.
► *nm* **fresco 1** *(frescor)* fresh air, cool air. **2** ARTE fresco. LOC **al fresco** in the cool. ▌ **quedarse tan fresco,-a** not to

bat an eyelid. **tomar el fresco** to get some fresh air.

frescor *nm* coolness, freshness.

frescura *nf* **1** *(frescor)* freshness, coolness. **2** *(desvergüenza)* cheek, nerve. LOC **¡qué frescura!** what a nerve!

fresno *nm* ash tree.

frialdad *nf* **1** *(frío)* coldness. **2** *(indiferencia)* coldness, indifference.

fricativo,-a *adj* fricative.

fricción *nf* **1** *(roce)* friction. **2** *(desacuerdo)* friction, discord.

frigorífico *nm* **1** *(electrodoméstico)* refrigerator, fridge. **2** *(cámara frigorífica)* cold store.

frijol *nm* bean, kidney bean.

frío,-a *adj* **1** *(gen)* cold. **2** *(indiferente)* cold, cool, indifferent; *(pasmado)* stunned: *la película me dejó frío* the film left me cold.
▶ *nm* **frío** cold. LOC **coger a ALGN en frío** *fig* to catch SB on the hop. **hace un frío que pela** *fam* it's freezing cold. **hacer frío** to be cold. **tener frío / pasar frío** to be cold.

friolero,-a *adj* sensitive to the cold.

friso *nm* **1** ARQUIT frieze. **2** *(zócalo)* skirting board.

frito,-a *adj* **1** CULIN fried. **2** *fam* fed up, sick: *este niño me tiene frita* I'm sick and tired of this kid.
▶ *nm* **frito** piece of fried food. LOC **quedarse frito,-a** *fam* *(dormido)* to fall fast asleep.

frívolo,-a *adj* frivolous.

frondoso,-a *adj* leafy, luxuriant.

frontera *nf* **1** frontier, border. **2** *fig* limit, bounds *pl*, borderline.

frontón *nm* **1** *(juego)* pelota. **2** *(edificio)* pelota court. **3** ARQUIT pediment.

frotar *vt* to rub. LOC **frotarse las manos** to rub one's hands together.

fruncir *vt* COST to gather. LOC **fruncir el ceño** to frown, knit one's brow.

frustración *nf* frustration.

frustrar *vt* **1** *(cosa)* to frustrate, thwart. **2** *(persona)* to disappoint.

▶ *vpr* **frustrarse 1** *(proyectos, planes)* to fail, come to nothing. **2** *(persona)* to get frustrated, get disappointed.

fruta *nf* fruit.

frutería *nf* fruit shop.

frutero,-a *adj & nf* fruit seller, fruiterer.
▶ *nm* **frutero** fruit dish, fruit bowl.

fruto *nm* **1** *(fruta)* fruit. **2** *(resultado)* fruit, result, product. LOC **dar fruto** to bear fruit. **sacar fruto de ALGO** to profit from STH. COMP **frutos secos 1** *(almendras, etc)* nuts. **2** *(pasas, etc)* dried fruit *sing*.

fucsia *nf* fuchsia.

fuego *nm* **1** fire. **2** *(lumbre)* light. **3** *(cocina)* burner, ring. LOC **a fuego lento 1** on a low flame. **2** *(al horno)* in a slow oven. **poner las manos en el fuego por ALGO/ALGN** to stake one's life on STH/SB. **prender fuego a ALGO** to set fire to STH. COMP **fuegos artificiales** fireworks.

fuel *nm* fuel oil.

fuelle *nm* *(aparato)* bellows *pl*.

fuente *nf* **1** *(manantial)* spring. **2** *(artificial)* fountain. **3** *(recipiente)* serving dish, dish. **4** *fig* source.

fuera *adv* **1** *(exterior)* out, outside: *salimos fuera* we went out, we went outside. **2** *(alejado)* away; *(en el extranjero)* abroad.
▶ *interj* get out!
▶ *prep* **fuera de** *(un lugar)* out of; *(más allá de)* outside, beyond; *(excepto)* except for, apart from. LOC **estar fuera de sí** to be beside os. **fuera de lo normal** extraordinary, very unusual. **fuera de serie** extraordinary. COMP **fuera de juego** offside.

fuerte *adj* **1** *(gen)* strong: *tiene un sabor fuerte* it has a strong taste. **2** *(en asignatura)* strong, good: *está muy fuerte en historia* she's very strong on history. **3** *(viento)* strong; *(lluvia, nevada)* heavy; *(tormenta, seísmo)* severe; *(calor)* intense. **4** *(dolor, enfermedad)* severe, bad. **5** *(golpe)* hard, heavy. **6** *(sonido)* loud. **7** *(subida)* steep, sharp; *(bajada)* sharp: *un fuerte descenso en el precio del petróleo* a sharp fall in the price of oil. **8** *(discusión)*

heated, violent; *(aplauso)* loud, thunderous. **9** *(comida - pesado)* heavy; *(- cargado)* rich. **10** *(color)* intense.
▶ *nm* **1** *(fortificación)* fort. **2** *(punto fuerte)* forte, strong point.
▶ *adv* **1** *(mucho)* a lot. **2** *(con fuerza)* hard: *empuja fuerte* push hard. **3** *(volumen)* loud: *la música sonaba fuerte* the music was loud.

fuerza *nf* **1** *(gen)* strength. **2** *(violencia)* force, violence. **3** *(militar)* force. **4** *(en física)* force. **5** *(electricidad)* power, electric power. **6** *(poder)* power. LOC **a fuerza de** by dint of, by force of. ‖ **a la fuerza** by force. ‖ **con fuerza 1** *(gen)* strongly. **2** *(llover)* heavily. **3** *(apretar, agarrar)* tightly; *(pegar, empujar)* hard. ‖ **por fuerza** by force. COMP **fuerza de voluntad** willpower.

fuga *nf* **1** *(huida)* flight, escape. **2** *(escape)* leak.

fugarse *vpr (gen)* to flee, escape; *(de casa)* to run away from home.

fugaz *adj* fleeting, brief.

fugitivo,-a *adj (en fuga)* fleeing.
▶ *nm & nf* fugitive, runaway.

fulano,-a *nm & nf* so-and-so; *(hombre)* what's his name; *(mujer)* what's her name.
▶ *nm* **fulano** *fam pey* guy, GB bloke.

fulminar *vt* **1** to strike with lightning. **2** *fig* to strike dead. LOC **fulminar a** ALGN **(con la mirada)** to look daggers at SB.

fumador,-ra *nm & nf* smoker. LOC **los no fumadores** nonsmokers.

fumar *vt* to smoke.

fumigar *vt* to fumigate.

funámbulo,-a *nm & nf* tightrope walker.

función *nf* **1** *(gen)* function. **2** *(cargo)* duty. **3** *(espectáculo)* performance, show. LOC **en función de** according to. ‖ **en funciones** acting. ‖ **entrar en función** *(persona)* to take up one's post. ‖ **estar en funciones** to be in office. COMP **función de noche** evening performance. ‖ **función de tarde** matinée.

funcional *adj* functional.

funcionamiento *nm* operation, working.

funcionar *vi (desempeñar una función)* to work, function: *funciona con gasolina/diesel* it runs on petrol/diesel.

funcionario,-a *nm & nf* functionary, employee. COMP **funcionario,-a público,-a** civil servant, government employee.

funda *nf* **1** *(flexible)* cover. **2** *(rígida)* case. **3** *(de disco)* sleeve. COMP **funda de almohada** pillowcase.

fundación *nf* foundation.

fundador,-ra *nm & nf* founder.

fundamental *adj* fundamental.

fundamentalismo *nm* fundamentalism.

fundamentalista *adj* fundamentalist.
▶ *nm o nf* fundamentalist.

fundamentalmente *adv* fundamentally, basically.

fundamento *nm* **1** *(base)* basis, grounds *pl.* **2** *(seriedad)* seriousness; *(confianza)* reliability. LOC **sin fundamento** unfounded.

fundar *vt* **1** *(crear)* to found; *(erigir)* to raise: *su padre fundó la empresa* her father founded the company. **2** *(basar)* to base, found.
▶ *vpr* **fundarse 1** *(crearse)* to be founded. **2** *(teoría, afirmación)* to be based (en, on); *(persona)* to base os (en, on).

fundición *nf* **1** *(derretimiento)* melting. **2** *(de metales)* smelting. **3** *(lugar)* foundry, smelting works.

fundir *vt* **1** *(derretir)* to melt: *el sol funde la nieve* the sun melts the snow. **2** *(separar mena y metal)* to smelt. **3** *(dar forma)* to cast: *fundir una figura en bronce* to cast a figure in bronze. **4** *(bombilla, plomos)* to blow.
▶ *vpr* **fundirse 1** *(derretirse)* to melt: *la nieve se funde* snow melts. **2** *(bombilla, plomos)* to fuse, go, blow, burn out: *se han fundido los plomos* the fuses have gone. **3** *(unirse)* to merge.

fúnebre *adj* **1** *(mortuorio)* funeral. **2** *(lúgubre)* mournful, lugubrious.

funeral *nm* [también se usa en plural con el mismo significado] **1** *(entierro)* funeral. **2** *(conmemoración)* memorial service.

funerala COMP ojo a la funerala *fam* black eye.

funeraria *nf* undertaker's, US funeral parlor.

funerario,-a *adj* funerary, funeral.

funesto,-a *adj* ill-fated, fatal.

fungicida *adj* fungicidal.
▶ *nm* fungicide.

funicular *nm* funicular, funicular railway.

furgón *nm* **1** AUTO van, truck. **2** *(de tren)* (goods) wagon, US boxcar. COMP **furgón de cola** guard's van.

furgoneta *nf* van.

furia *nf* fury, rage.

furibundo,-a *adj* furious, enraged.

furiosamente *adv* furiously.

furioso,-a *adj* **1** *(colérico)* furious. **2** *(tempestad, vendaval)* raging. LOC **ponerse furioso,-a** to get angry.

furor *nm* fury, rage. LOC **hacer furor** *fig* to be all the rage.

furtivamente *adv* furtively.

furtivo,-a *adj* furtive.

furúnculo *nm* boil.

fusa *nf* demisemiquaver, US thirty-second note.

fuseaux *nm* ski pants *pl.*

fuselaje *nm* fuselage.

fusible *nm* fuse.

fusil *nm* rifle, gun.

fusilamiento *nm* shooting, execution.

fusilar *vt* **1** *(ejecutar)* to shoot, execute. **2** *(plagiar)* to plagiarize.

fusión *nf* **1** *(de metales)* fusion, melting; *(de hielo)* thawing, melting. **2** *(de intereses, partidos, ideas)* fusion. **3** *(de empresas)* merger, amalgamation.

fusionar *vt* **1** *(fundir)* to fuse. **2** *(unir)* to join, unite. **3** COM to merge: *proponen fusionar ambas empresas* they propose to merge the two companies.
▶ *vpr* **fusionarse** *(unir)* to join, unite; *(empresas)* to merge.

fusta *nf* riding whip.

fuste *nm* **1** *(palo)* stick. **2** *(de columna)* shaft.

futbito *nm* five-a-side football.

fútbol *nm* football, soccer. COMP **fútbol americano** American football.

futbolín® *nm* table football.

futbolista *nm o nf* footballer, football player, soccer player.

futbolístico,-a *adj* football.

futón *nm* futon.

futurista *adj* futuristic.

futuro,-a *adj* future.
▶ *nm* **futuro** future. LOC **en un futuro próximo** in the near future. COMP **futuro imperfecto** future. ∎ **futuro perfecto** future perfect.

F

G

G, g *nf (la letra)* G, g.

g *sím (gramo)* gram, gramme; *(símbolo)* g.

gabán *nm* overcoat.

gabardina *nf (impermeable)* raincoat.

gabinete *nm* **1** *(habitación)* study. **2** POL cabinet. **3** *(despacho)* office.

Gabón *nm* Gabon.

gabonés,-esa *adj* Gabonese.
  ▶ *nm & nf* Gabonese.

gacela *nf* gazelle.

gacha *nf (masa)* paste.
  ▶ *nf pl* **gachas** *(papilla)* porridge *sing*.

gafas *nf pl* **1** spectacles, glasses. **2** *(de motorista, esquí, natación)* goggles. COMP **gafas de bucear** diving mask *sing*. ▌ **gafas de sol** sunglasses.

gafe *adj fam* jinx.
  ▶ *nm o nf fam* jinx.

gaita *nf* **1** bagpipes *pl*, pipes *pl*. **2** *fam* bother, drag, pain.

gaitero,-a *nm & nf* MÚS piper, bagpipe player.

gajo *nm (de fruta)* segment.

gala *nf* **1** *(espectáculo)* gala. **2** *(vestido)* best dress. LOC **hacer gala de** to make a show of. COMP **cena de gala** gala dinner.
  ▶ *nf pl* **galas** *(adorno)* finery *sing*. LOC **lucir sus mejores galas** to be dressed in all one's finery.

galáctico,-a *adj* galactic.

galán *nm (atractivo)* handsome young man; *(mujeriego)* ladies' man.

galardón *nm* prize.

galaxia *nf* galaxy.

galera *nf (mar)* galley.

galería *nf* **1** *(gen)* gallery. **2** *(corredor descubierto)* balcony, verandah. **3** TEAT gallery, balcony. COMP **galerías comerciales** shopping centre *sing*.

galés,-a *adj* Welsh.
  ▶ *nm & nf (persona)* Welsh person; *(hombre)* Welshman; *(mujer)* Welshwoman.
  ▶ *nm* **galés** *(idioma)* Welsh.

Gales *nm* Wales. COMP **País de Gales** Wales.

galgo,-a *nm & nf* greyhound.

galleta *nf* CULIN biscuit, US cookie.

gallina *nf* hen.
  ▶ *nm o nf fam* chicken, coward. LOC **jugar a la gallina ciega** to play blind man's buff.

gallinero *nm* **1** henhouse. **2** *fam* bedlam, madhouse. **3** **el gallinero** TEAT the gods *pl*.

gallo *nm* **1** cock, rooster. **2** *(pez)* John Dory. **3** *fig (al cantar)* false note; *(al hablar)* squeak. LOC **en menos que canta un gallo** in a flash.

galón¹ *nm* **1** *(cinta)* braid. **2** MIL stripe, chevron.

galón² *nm (medida)* gallon.

galopar *vi* to gallop.

galope *nm* gallop. LOC **a galope / al galope** **1** at a gallop. **2** *fig* in a rush. ▌ **a galope tendido** at full gallop.

gama *nf* **1** MÚS scale. **2** *(gradación, variedad)* range.

gamba¹ *nf* ZOOL prawn; *(pequeña)* shrimp.

gamba² *nf argot (pierna)* leg. LOC **meter la gamba** *fam* to put one's foot in it.

gamberrada *nf* act of hooliganism.

gamberro,-a *adj* loutish, rowdy.
  ▶ *nm & nf* vandal, hooligan, lout.

Gambia *nf* Gambia.

gambiano,-a *adj* Gambian.
▶ *nm & nf* Gambian.

gamo *nm* fallow deer.

gamuza *nf* **1** ZOOL chamois. **2** *(piel)* chamois leather. **3** *(paño)* duster.

gana *nf* **1** *(deseo)* wish (de, for), desire. **2** *(apetito)* appetite; *(hambre)* hunger.
LOC **dar a** ALGN **la gana de hacer** ALGO *fam* to feel like doing STH. ∥ **tener ganas de (hacer)** ALGO to feel like (doing) STH.

ganadería *nf* **1** *(crianza)* cattle raising, stockbreeding. **2** *(ganado)* cattle, livestock.

ganadero,-a *nm & nf* **1** *(propietario)* cattle breeder, stockbreeder. **2** *(cuidador de ganado)* herdsman, US herder.

ganado *nm* livestock, stock; *(vacas)* cattle. COMP **ganado bovino** cattle *pl.* ∥ **ganado vacuno** cattle *pl.*

ganador,-ra *adj* winning.
▶ *nm & nf* winner.

ganancia *nf* gain, profit.

ganar *vt* **1** *(partido, concurso, premio)* to win. **2** *(dinero)* to earn: *¿cuánto ganas al año?* how much do you earn a year? **3** *(alcanzar)* to reach. **4** *(lograr)* to win.
▶ *vi* **1** *(mejorar)* to improve. **2** *(cambiar favorablemente)* to gain:
▶ *vpr* **ganarse 1** to earn. **2** *(ser merecedor)* to deserve: *se lo han ganado* they deserve it. LOC **ganar a** ALGN **en** ALGO to be better than SB at STH.

ganchillo *nm* **1** *(aguja)* crochet hook. **2** *(labor)* crochet work. LOC **hacer ganchillo** to crochet.

gancho *nm* **1** hook. **2** *(para ropa)* peg. **3** *fam (atractivo)* attractiveness, charm. *(en boxeo)* hook. **4** *(en baloncesto)* hook shot. LOC **tener gancho** *fam* to be attractive, have charm.

gandul,-la *adj* lazy, idle.
▶ *nm & nf* idler, loafer, lazybones.

gandulear *vi* to idle, loaf around.

ganga *nf* *(algo barato)* bargain, good buy. COMP **precio de ganga** bargain price.

gángster *nm* gangster.

gansada *nf fam* silly thing to say, silly thing to do.

ganso,-a *nm & nf* ZOOL goose; *(macho)* gander.

ganzúa *nf* **1** *(garfio)* picklock. **2** *(ladrón)* burglar.

garabatear *vt (escribir)* to scribble, scrawl; *(dibujar)* to doodle.

garabato *nm* **1** *(gancho)* hook. **2** *(dibujo)* doodle; *(escritura)* scrawl, scribble.

garaje *nm* garage.

garantía *nf* **1** *(seguridad)* guarantee, security. **2** COM guarantee, warranty.

garantizado,-a *adj* guaranteed.

garantizar *vt* **1** to guarantee. **2** COM to warrant.

garbanzo *nm* chickpea.

garbeo *nm fam* walk, stroll.

garbo *nm* **1** *(airosidad al andar)* gracefulness. **2** *(gracia)* grace, stylishness.

garboso,-a *adj (airoso)* graceful.

gardenia *nf* gardenia.

garfio *nm* hook, grapple.

garganta *nf* **1** *(cuello)* throat. **2** *(desfiladero)* gorge, narrow pass.

gargantilla *nf* short necklace.

gárgola *nf* gargoyle.

garita *nf* **1** *(caseta)* box, cabin, hut; *(de centinela)* sentry box. **2** *(portería)* porter's lodge.

garito *nm* **1** *(casa de juego)* gambling dene. **2** *(antro de diversión)* dive, joint.

garra *nf (de mamífero)* paw, claw; *(de ave)* talon.
▶ *nf pl* **garras** *(poder)* clutches. LOC **caer en las garras de** ALGN *fig* to fall into SB's clutches. ∥ **tener garra 1** *(relato, etc)* to be compelling. **2** *(persona)* to have charisma.

garrafa *nf* carafe.

garrafal *adj* monumental, huge.

garrafón *nm* demijohn, large carafe.

garrapata *nf* tick.

garrotazo *nm* blow with a stick.

garrote *nm* thick stick, cudgel, club.

garza *nf* heron. COMP **garza real** grey heron.

gas *nm (gen)* gas.

▶ *nm pl* **gases** *(flatulencias)* wind *sing*, flatulence *sing*, US gas *sing*.

gasa *nf* gauze.

gaseosa *nf* GB lemonade, US soda.

gasóleo *nm* diesel oil.

gasolina *nf* petrol, US gasoline, gas. LOC **poner gasolina** to get some petrol.

gasolinera *nf* **1** petrol station, US gas station. **2** *(lancha)* motorboat.

gastado,-a *adj* **1** *(desgastado)* worn-out. **2** *(acabado)* finished, empty, used up.

gastador,-ra *adj (derrochador)* spendthrift.

gastar *vt* **1** *(consumir dinero, tiempo)* to spend; *(gasolina, electricidad)* to use (up), consume: *este coche gasta mucha gasolina* this car uses a lot of petrol. **2** *(malgastar)* to waste. **3** *(usar perfume, jabón)* to use; *(ropa)* to wear.
▶ *vpr* **gastarse 1** *(desgastarse)* to wear out. **2** *(consumirse)* to run out.

gasto *nm* expenditure, expense. COMP **gastos de mantenimiento** running costs, maintenance costs. **❙ gastos diarios** daily expenses.

gastronomía *nf* gastronomy.

gastronómico,-a *adj* gastronomic, gastronomical.

gata *nf* she-cat, cat.

✎ Véase también **gato**.

gatas LOC **a gatas** on all fours. **❙ andar a gatas** to crawl.

gatear *vi (andar a gatas)* to crawl.

gatera *nf* cat door, cat flap.

gatillo *nm* trigger.

gatito,-a *nm & nf fam* kitty, pusy.

gato *nm* **1** cat, tomcat. **2** *(de coche)* jack. LOC **buscarle tres/cinco pies al gato** *fam* to split hairs, complicate things. **❙ dar gato por liebre** *fam* to take SB in, con SB. **❙ hay gato encerrado** *fam* there's something fishy going on.

gatuno,-a *adj* catlike, feline.

gavilán *nm* sparrowhawk.

gavilla *nf (de ramas, etc)* sheaf.

gaviota *nf* seagull, gull.

gay *adj* gay, homosexual.
▶ *nm* gay, homosexual.

gaznate *nm* gullet.

gazpacho *nm* cold soup made of tomatoes and other vegetables.

ge *nf* name of the letter g.

gel *nm* gel.

gelatina *nf* **1** *(sustancia)* gelatine. **2** *(preparado alimenticio)* jelly.

gelatinoso,-a *adj* gelatinous, jelly-like.

gélido,-a *adj* icy, icy cold.

gema *nf* **1** BOT bud. **2** *(piedra)* gem.

gemelo,-a *adj* twin.
▶ *nm & nf* twin.
▶ *nm* **gemelo** *(músculo)* calf muscle.
▶ *nm pl* **gemelos 1** *(botones)* cufflinks. **2** *(anteojos)* binoculars.

gemido *nm (quejido)* groan, moan.

gemir *vi (quejarse)* to moan, groan.

gen *nm* gene.

genciana *nf* gentian.

generación *nf* generation.

generacional *adj* generation, generational.

generador,-ra *nm (máquina)* generator.

general *adj* **1** general. **2** *(común)* common, usual, widespread.
▶ *nm (oficial)* general. LOC **en general** in general, generally.

generalidad *nf* **1** *(gen)* generality. **2** *(mayoría)* majority. **3** *(generalización)* general statement.
▶ *nf pl* **generalidades** *(nociones)* basic knowledge *sing*.

generalización *nf* **1** *(gen)* generalization. **2** *(extensión)* spread, spreading.

generalizado,-a *adj* widespread, common.

generalizar *vt* **1** *(gen)* to generalize. **2** *(extender)* to spread, popularize.
▶ *vpr* **generalizarse** to spread, become widespread, become common.

generalmente *adv* usually.

generar *vt* to generate.

genéricamente *adv* generically.

genérico,-a *adj* generic.

género *nm* **1** *(clase)* kind, sort. **2** *(tela)* cloth. **3** *(mercancía)* article. **4** GRAM gender. **5** BIOL genus.

generosamente *adv* generously.

generosidad *nf* generosity, unselfishness.

generoso,-a *adj* generous (con/para, to).

génesis *nf inv* genesis.

genética *nf* genetics *sing*.

genial *adj* **1** brilliant, inspired. **2** *fam* terrific, great, smashing.
▶ *adv fam* great.

genialidad *nf* **1** *(idea)* brilliant idea, stroke of genius. **2** *(cualidad)* genius.

genio *nm* **1** *(carácter)* temper, disposition. **2** *(facultad)* genius: *Einstein fue un genio* Einstein was a genius. **3** *(espíritu)* spirit: *el genio del Renacimiento* the Renaissance spirit. LOC **estar de mal genio** to be in a bad mood. ‖ **tener mal genio** to have a bad temper.

genital *adj* genital.
▶ *nm pl* **genitales** genitals.

genocidio *nm* genocide.

gente *nf* **1** people *pl*. **2** *(familia)* family, folks *pl*, people *pl*: *me gusta estar con mi gente* I like being with my family. COMP **gente menuda** *fam* nippers *pl*, kids *pl*.

gentil *adj* *(amable)* kind.

gentileza *nf* **1** *(gracia)* grace, elegance. **2** *(cortesía)* politeness, kindness.

gentilicio *adj* gentile.
▶ *nm* gentile.

gentío *nm* crowd.

gentuza *nf pey* mob, rabble, riffraff.

genuino,-a *adj* genuine, authentic.

geografía *nf* geography.

geógrafo,-a *nm & nf* geographer.

geología *nf* geology.

geológico,-a *adj* geologic, geological.

geólogo,-a *nm & nf* geologist.

geometría *nf* geometry.

geométrico,-a *adj* geometric, geometrical.

Georgia *nf* Georgia.

georgiano,-a *adj* Georgian.
▶ *nm & nf (persona)* Georgian.
▶ *nm* **georgiano** *(idioma)* Georgian.

geranio *nf* geranium.

gerencia *nf (actividad)* management.

gerente *nm o nf (hombre)* manager; *(mujer)* manageress.

geriatría *nf* geriatrics *sing*.

geriátrico,-a *adj* geriatric.
▶ *nm* **geriátrico** *(sanatorio)* geriatric hospital; *(residencia)* old people's home.

germano,-a *adj* Germanic.

germen *nm* germ.

germinar *vi* to germinate.

gerundio *nm* gerund.

gesta *nf* arc heroic deed, exploit.

gestación *nf* **1** gestation. **2** *(período)* gestation period.

gestante *adj* gestating.
▶ *nf* expectant mother.

gesticular *vi* to gesticulate.

gestión *nf* [también se usa en plural con el mismo significado] *(trámite)* step, measure, move. COMP **gestión de datos** data management.

gestionar *vt* **1** *(negociar)* to negotiate. **2** *(administrar)* to manage, run.

gesto *nm* **1** *(movimiento)* gesture. **2** *(mueca)* grimace. LOC **hacer gestos a** *fam* to make gestures at.

gestor,-ra *nm & nf* **1** *(administrador)* manager, director. **2** *person who transacts official business on his clients' behalf*, ≈ solicitor.

Ghana *nf* Ghana.

ghanés,-a *adj* Ghanaian.
▶ *nm & nf* Ghanaian.

giba *nf* hump, hunch.

giga *nf (gigabyte)* giga, gigabyte.

gigabyte *nm* gigabyte.

gigante *nm & nf (hombre)* giant; *(mujer)* giantess.
▶ *adj* giant, gigantic, huge.

gigantesco,-a *adj* giant, gigantic.

gimnasia *nf* gymnastics *sing*.

gimnasio *nm* gymnasium, gym.

gincana *nf* gymkhana.

G

ginebra nf gin.

ginecología nf gynaecology.

ginecólogo,-a nm & nf gynaecologist.

gineta nf genet.

gira nf tour.

girar vi 1 *(dar vueltas)* to rotate, whirl, spin. 2 *(torcer)* to turn: *girar a la izquierda* to turn left. 3 *fig (versar)* to deal with: *la conversación giró en torno al teatro* the conversation evolved around theatre.
▶ vt 1 COM to issue: *girar una letra* to issue a draft. 2 *(cambiar de sentido)* to turn, turn around: *girar el cuerpo* to turn one's body.

girasol nm sunflower.

giratorio,-a adj rotating, gyratory.

giro nm 1 *(vuelta)* turn, turning. 2 *(dirección)* course, direction. 3 COM draft. COMP **giro postal** money order.

gitano,-a nm & nf gypsy, gipsy.

glaciación nf glaciation.

glacial adj 1 glacial. 2 *fig* glacial, icy: *tuvo un recibimiento glacial* he had an icy reception.

glaciar nm glacier.

gladiador nm gladiator.

gladiolo nm gladiolus.

glándula nf gland.

glicerina nf glycerin, glycerine.

global adj global, comprehensive.

globo nm 1 *(esfera)* globe, sphere. 2 *(tierra)* globe. 3 *(de aire)* balloon.

glóbulo nm globule. COMP **glóbulo blanco** white corpuscle. ‖ **glóbulo rojo** red corpuscle.

gloria nf 1 *(bienaventuranza)* glory. 2 *(fama)* fame, honour (US honor).

glorieta nf 1 *(en un jardín)* arbour. 2 *(plazoleta)* small square.

glorificar vt to glorify.

glorioso,-a adj glorious.

glosar vt 1 *(explicar)* to gloss. 2 *(interpretar)* to interpret.

glosario nm glossary.

glotón,-ona adj greedy, gluttonous.
▶ nm & nf glutton.

glotonería nf gluttony, greed.

glúcido nm glucide.

glucosa nf glucose.

gluten nm gluten.

gnomo nm gnome.

gobernador,-ra nm & nf governor.

gobernante adj ruling, governing.
▶ nm o nf ruler, leader.

gobernar vt 1 *(gen)* to govern. 2 *(un país)* to rule. 3 *(un negocio)* to run, handle. 4 *(un barco)* to steer.

gobierno nm 1 POL government. 2 *(mando)* command, running. 3 *(conducción)* direction, control; *(de un barco)* steering; *(de timón)* rudder.

goce nm pleasure, enjoyment.

godo,-a adj Gothic.
▶ nm & nf *(persona)* Goth.

gofre nm waffle.

gol nm goal.

goleador,-ra nm & nf scorer. COMP **el máximo goleador** the top scorer.

golear vt to hammer.

golf nm *(deporte)* golf.

golfista nm o nf golfer.

golfo nm gulf, large bay.

golfo,-a nm & nf *(holgazán)* good-for-nothing; *(niño)* rascal, little devil.

golondrina nf *(ave)* swallow.

golosina nf sweet, US candy.

goloso,-a adj sweet-toothed.

golpe nm 1 blow, knock; *(puñetazo)* punch: *le dio un golpe* he hit him. 2 *(de coche)* collision; *(fuerte)* bang; *(ligero)* bump. 3 *fig (desgracia)* blow, misfortune. LOC **de golpe** suddenly, all of a sudden. ‖ **no dar golpe** *fam* not to lift a finger, not do a blessed thing. COMP **golpe bajo** *fig* punch below the belt. ‖ **golpe de Estado** coup, coup d'état. ‖ **golpe de vista** quick glance.

golpear vt *(gen)* to hit, strike; *(personas)* to thump, hit, punch; *(puerta)* to knock on.

golpista nm o nf person involved in a coup d'état.

goma nf 1 *(material)* gum, rubber. 2 *(de borrar)* rubber, US eraser. 3 *(de pegar)* glue, gum. 4 *(banda elástica)* rubber band. COMP **goma arábiga** gum arabic. ‖ **goma de mascar** chewing gum.

gomaespuma *nf* foam rubber.

gomina *nf* hair cream.

gominola *nf* jelly bean, jelly.

gong *nm* gong.

gordo,-a *adj* 1 *(carnoso)* fat: *se puso gordo* he got fat. 2 *(grueso)* thick. 3 *(grave)* serious. 4 *(importante)* big: *¡qué mentira tan gorda!* what a big lie!
▶ *nm & nf* fat person, fatty.
▶ *nm* **gordo** 1 *fam (grasa)* fat. 2 **el gordo** the first prize *in the lottery.*

gordura *nf* fatness.

gorila *nm (animal)* gorilla.

gorjear *vi* to chirp, twitter.

gorra *nf* 1 *(gen)* cap. 2 *(con visera)* peaked cap. loc **de gorra** *fam* free.

gorrión,-ona *nm & nf* sparrow.

gorro *nm* 1 cap. 2 *(de bebé)* bonnet. 3 *(de cocinero)* chef's hat.

gorrón,-ona *adj fam* scrounging, sponging.
▶ *nm & nf* sponger, scrounger.

gorronear *vi* to scrounge.

gota *nf* 1 drop. 2 *(de sudor)* bead. 3 *(de aire)* breath. loc **caer cuatro gotas** to be spitting with rain. | **gota a gota** drop by drop. | **ni gota** not a bit, nothing at all. comp **gota fría** cold air pool.

gotear *vi* 1 *(grifo)* to drip; *(tejado)* to leak. 2 [sólo se usa en tercera persona; no lleva sujeto] *(lluvia)* to drizzle.

gotera *nf* 1 *(agujero)* leak. 2 *(agua)* drip.

gótico,-a *adj* Gothic.

gozar *vi* 1 *(poseer, disfrutar)* to enjoy (de, -): *goza de muy buena salud* he enjoys very good health. 2 *(sentir placer)* to enjoy os: *gozamos con su presencia* we really enjoy her company.

gozne *nm* hinge.

gozo *nm* joy, delight, pleasure.

grabación *nf* recording.

grabado,-a *nm* 1 *(arte)* engraving. 2 *(dibujo)* picture, drawing.

grabar *vt* 1 ARTE to engrave. 2 *(registrar)* to record. 3 INFORM to save. loc **grabarse en la memoria** *fig* to be engraved on one's memory.

gracia *nf* 1 *(favor)* favour (US favor). 2 *(atractivo)* grace, charm. 3 *(chiste)* joke. loc **hacer gracia, tener gracia** *(diversión)* to be funny. | **¡qué gracia!** how funny!
▶ *nf pl* **gracias** thank you, thanks. loc **dar gracias a** ALGN to thank SB. | **gracias a** thanks to.

gracioso,-a *adj* 1 *(atractivo)* graceful, charming. 2 *(bromista)* witty, facetious. 3 *(divertido)* funny, amusing.
▶ *nm & nf* TEAT jester, clown, fool. loc **hacerse el gracioso** to try to be funny.

grada *nf* 1 *(peldaño)* step, stair. 2 *(gradería)* tier.
▶ *nf pl* **gradas** stands, terraces.

gradería *nf* stands *pl*, terraces *pl*.

grado *nm* 1 *(gen)* degree: *estábamos a 27 grados* it was 27 degrees. 2 *(estado)* stage. 3 EDUC *(curso)* class, year. 4 EDUC *(título)* degree. 5 *(peldaño)* step.

graduación *nf* 1 *(gen)* graduation. 2 *(de alcohol)* strength. 3 EDUC graduation.

graduado,-a *nm & nf* EDUC graduate. comp **gafas graduadas** prescription glasses. | **graduado escolar** *certificate of elementary school studies.*

gradual *adj* gradual.

graduar *vt* 1 *(termómetro)* to graduate, calibrate. 2 *(regular)* to adjust, regulate. 3 *(conceder un diploma)* to confer a degree on, US graduate. 4 *(medir)* to gauge, measure; *(la vista)* to test, check.
▶ *vpr* **graduarse** to graduate, get one's degree. loc **graduarse la vista** to have one's eyes tested.

grafía *nf* 1 *(signo)* graphic symbol. 2 *(escritura)* writing. 3 *(ortografía)* spelling.

gráficamente *adv* graphically.

grafía *nf* graph, diagram.

gráfico,-a *adj* graphic.
▶ *nm* **gráfico** *(dibujo)* sketch, chart.

grafiti *nm pl* graffiti.

grafito *nm* graphite.

gragea *nf* pill, tablet.

grajo,-a *nm & nf* rook.

G

gramática *nf* grammar.

gramo *nm* gram, gramme.

gramófono *nm* gramophone.

gramola® *nf* gramophone.

gran *adj* [se usa delante de nombres masculinos en singular] **1** *(fuerte, intenso)* great: *se llevaron un gran susto* they were terribly shocked. **2** *(excelente)* great: *aquél era un gran libro* that was a great book.

✎ Consulta también **grande**.

granada *nf* BOT pomegranate.

granate *adj* maroon, claret.
► *nm* **1** *(color)* maroon, claret. **2** *(mineral)* garnet.

grande *adj* **1** *(tamaño)* large, big. **2** *(fuerte, intenso)* great: *su partida les produjo una pena muy grande* his departure caused them great sorrow. **3** *(mayor)* grown-up, old, big.
► *nm* *(de elevada jerarquía)* great. LOC **a lo grande** on a grand scale, in a big way. ▮ **estar grande una cosa a ALGN** to be too big on SB. ▮ **pasarlo en grande** *fam* to have a great time.

✎ Consulta también **gran**.

grandeza *nf* **1** *(tamaño)* size. **2** *(generosidad)* generosity.

grandioso,-a *adj* grandiose, grand, magnificent.

granel LOC **a granel 1** *(sin envase)* in bulk. **2** *(en abundancia)* lots of.

granero *nm* granary, barn.

granito *nm* granite.

granizada *nf* **1** hailstorm. **2** *fig (lluvia)* hail, shower.

granizado,-a *nm* iced drink.

granizar *vi* [sólo se usa en tercera persona; no lleva sujeto] to hail.

granizo *nm* hail, hailstone.

granja *nf* farm.

granjero,-a *nm & nf* farmer.

grano *nm* **1** grain; *(de café)* bean. **2** MED pimple, spot. LOC **ir al grano** *fam* to come to the point, get to the point.
► *nm pl* **granos** cereals.

granuja *nm* **1** *(pilluelo)* ragamuffin, urchin. **2** *(estafador)* crook, trickster.

granulado,-a *adj* granulated.

granuloso,-a *adj* **1** *(superficie)* granular. **2** *(piel)* pimply.

grapa *nf* *(para papel)* staple.

grapadora *nf* stapler.

grapar *vt* to staple.

grasa *nf* grease, fat.

grasiento,-a *adj* greasy, oily.

graso,-a *adj* greasy, oily, fatty.

gratamente *adv* pleasantly.

gratén *nm* gratin.

gratificación *nf* **1** *(satisfacción)* gratification. **2** *(recompensa)* reward.

gratificador,-ra *adj* gratifying, rewarding.

gratificante *adj* gratifying, rewarding.

gratificar *vt* **1** *(satisfacer)* to gratify. **2** *(recompensar)* to reward, tip.

gratinador *nm* grill.

gratinar *vt* to brown under the grill.

gratis *adv* free.

gratitud *nf* gratitude.

grato,-a *adj* pleasant, pleasing (para, to).

gratuidad *nf* gratuitousness.

gratuitamente *adv* *(de balde)* free of charge, free.

gratuito,-a *adj* *(de balde)* free.

grava *nf* **1** *(guijas)* gravel. **2** *(piedra machacada)* crushed stone.

gravable *adj* taxable.

gravar *vt* to tax.

grave *adj* **1** *(pesado)* heavy. **2** *(serio)* grave, serious. **3** *(voz, nota)* deep, low. LOC **estar grave** to be seriously ill.

gravedad *nf* **1** FÍS gravity. **2** *(importancia)* gravity, seriousness.

gravemente *adv* **1** *(seriamente)* seriously. **2** *(solemnemente)* solemnly, gravely.

gravilla *nf* fine gravel.

gravitar *vi* **1** FÍS to gravitate. **2** *(apoyarse en)* to rest (sobre, on).

graznar *vi* **1** *(cuervo)* to caw, croak. **2** *(oca)* to honk. **3** *(pato)* to quack.

graznido *nm* **1** *(de cuervo)* caw, croak. **2** *(de oca)* honk. **3** *(de pato)* quack.

greca *nf* fret, fretwork.

Grecia *nf* Greece.

greda *nf* fuller's earth, clay.

gregario,-a *adj* gregarious.

gremial *adj* **1** trade union, union. **2** HIST guild.

gremio *nm* **1** HIST guild, corporation. **2** *(sindicato)* union. **3** *(profesión)* profession.

greña *nf* lock of entangled hair.
▶ *nf pl* **greñas** untidy mop of hair.

gres *nm* stoneware.

gresca *nf* **1** *(bulla)* racket. **2** *(riña)* row.

griego,-a *adj* Greek.
▶ *nm & nf (persona)* Greek.
▶ *nm* **griego** *(idioma)* Greek.

grieta *nf* crack, crevice.

grifería *nf* taps *pl*, US faucets *pl*.

grifo *nm (llave)* tap, US faucet.

grill *nm* grill.

grillete *nm* shackle.

grillo *nm* ZOOL cricket.

grima *nf* displeasure, disgust.

gripal *adj* related to flu.

gripe *nf* flu, influenza. LOC **tener la gripe** to have (the) flu.

griposo,-a *adj* flu. LOC **estar griposo** to have (the) flu.

gris *adj* **1** grey (US gray). **2** *fig (mediocre)* mediocre, third-rate. **3** *fig (triste)* grey (US gray), gloomy.
▶ *nm (color)* grey (US gray).

grisáceo,-a *adj* greyish.

gritar *vi (gen)* to shout; *(chillar)* cry out, scream: *¡no me grites!* don't shout at me!

griterío *nm* shouting, uproar.

grito *nm* shout; *(chillido)* cry, scream. LOC **a grito limpio** at the top of one's voice. ▌**dar un grito 1** to shout. **2** *(chillar)* to scream. ▌**el último grito** *fig* the latest thing, the last word. ▌**pedir** ALGO **a gritos** *fig* to be crying out for STH, be badly in need of STH. ▌**pegar un grito 1** to shout. **2** *(chillar)* to scream.

gritón,-ona *adj* noisy, loudmouthed.
▶ *nm & nf* loudmouth.

grogui *adj* **1** DEP punch-drunk, groggy. **2** *fig* groggy, half-asleep.

grosella *nf* redcurrant.

grosellero *nm* redcurrant bush.

groseramente *adv* crudely, rudely.

grosería *nf* **1** *(ordinariez)* rude word, rude expression. **2** *(rusticidad)* rudeness, coarseness. LOC **decir una grosería** to say something rude.

grosero,-a *adj* **1** *(tosco)* coarse, crude. **2** *(maleducado)* rude.
▶ *nm & nf* rude person.

grosor *nm* thickness.

grotesco,-a *adj* ridiculous.

grúa *nf* **1** *(construcción)* crane, derrick. **2** AUTO breakdown van, US tow truck.

gruesa *nf (doce docenas)* gross.

grueso,-a *adj* **1** *(objeto)* thick. **2** *(persona)* fat, stout.
▶ *nm* **grueso 1** *(grosor)* thickness. **2** *(parte principal)* bulk.

grulla *nf* crane.

grumete *nm* cabin boy.

grumo *nm* lump; *(de sangre)* clot; *(de leche)* curd.

grumoso,-a *adj* lumpy, clotted.

gruñido *nm* grunt, growl.

gruñir *vi* to grunt.

gruñón,-ona *adj* grumbling, grumpy.

grupa *nf* croup, hindquarters *pl*.

grupo *nm* **1** group. **2** TÉC unit, set. COMP **grupo electrógeno** power plant. ▌**grupo sanguíneo** blood group.

gruta *nf* cavern, grotto, cave.

gua *nm* **1** *(juego)* marbles *pl*. **2** *(hoyo)* hole for the marbles.

guacamayo *nm* macaw.

guache *nm* gouache.

guadaña *nf* scythe.

guantada *nf* slap.

guantazo *nm* slap.

guante *nm* glove. LOC **echar el guante a** ALGO *fam* to nick STH.

guantera *nf* glove compartment.

guaperas *adj inv fam* good-looking.
▶ *nm o nf* good looker, looker.

guapetón,-ona *adj fam* good-looking.

G

guapo,-a *adj* **1** good-looking; *(hombre)* handsome; *(mujer)* beautiful, pretty. **2** *argot (bonito)* nice, smart.

guapote,-a *adj fam* good-looking.

guapura *nf fam* good looks *pl*.

guarda *nm o nf (persona)* guard, keeper. ▸ *nf* **1** *(custodia)* custody, care. **2** *(de la ley, etc)* observance. **3** *(de libro)* flyleaf.

guardabarrera *nm o nf* gatekeeper.

guardabarros *nm inv* mudguard, US fender.

guardabosque *nm* forester.

guardacoches *nm o nf inv* parking attendant.

guardacostas *nm o nf inv (persona)* coastguard. ▸ *nm* coastguard vessel.

guardaespaldas *nm o nf inv* bodyguard.

guardafrenos *nm o nf inv* guard.

guardagujas *nm o nf inv (hombre)* pointsman, US switchman; *(mujer)* pointswoman, US switchwoman.

guardameta *nm o nf* goalkeeper.

guardamuebles *nm inv* furniture warehouse.

guardapolvo *nm* **1** *(cubierta)* dust cover. **2** *(mono)* overalls *pl*.

guardar *vt* **1** *(cuidar)* to keep, watch over, keep an eye on. **2** *(conservar)* to keep, hold. **3** *(la ley)* to observe, obey; *(un secreto)* to keep. **4** *(poner en un sitio)* to put away: *guárdatelo en el bolsillo* put it in your pocket. **5** *(reservar)* to save, keep: *le guardaron el mejor sitio* they saved the best seat for him. **6** INFORM to save. **7 guardarse de** *(precaverse, evitar)* to guard against, avoid, be careful not to. LOC **guardar las formas** to be polite.

guardarropa *nm* **1** *(armario)* wardrobe. **2** *(cuarto)* cloakroom.

guardarropía *nf* wardrobe for props.

guardavía *nm (hombre)* signalman.

guardería *nf* **1** crèche, nursery. **2** *(oficio de guarda)* keeping. COMP **guardería infantil** nursery, nursery school.

guardia *nf* **1** *(vigilancia)* watch, lookout. **2** *(servicio)* duty, call. ▸ *nm o nf (hombre)* policeman; *(mujer)* policewoman. LOC **estar de guardia 1** *(doctor)* to be on duty, be on call. **2** *(soldado)* to be on guard duty. **3** *(marino)* to be on watch. COMP **farmacia de guardia** duty chemist's. **I médico de guardia** doctor on duty.

guardián,-ana *nm & nf* guardian, keeper, custodian.

guarecer *vt* to take shelter (de, from), shelter (de, from).

guarida *nf* ZOOL haunt, den, lair.

guarnecer *vt* **1** *(decorar)* to adorn, decorate; *(en cocina)* to garnish. **2** *(proveer)* to provide (de, with).

guarnición *nf* **1** *(gen)* decoration, trimmings *pl*. **2** CULIN accompaniment to a main dish. **3** MIL garrison.

guarrada *nf* **1** *fam* something dirty, disgusting thing: *¡no hagas guarradas!* don't do such filthy things! **2** *fam (mala pasada)* dirty trick.

guarro,-a *adj* dirty, filthy. ▸ *nm & nf* pig, dirty pig.

guasa *nf* jest, fun, mockery. LOC **estar de guasa** to be joking.

guasón,-ona *adj* funny, joking. ▸ *nm & nf* jester, joker.

guata *nf* **1** *(algodón)* raw cotton. **2** *(relleno)* padding.

guateado,-a *adj* padded, quilted.

Guatemala *nf* Guatemala.

guatemalteco,-a *adj* Guatemalan. ▸ *nm & nf* Guatemalan.

guateque *nm* party.

guay *adj fam* great, cool.

gubernamental *adj* government, governmental.

gubernativo,-a *adj* government, governmental.

gubia *nf* gouge.

guepardo *nm* cheetah.

guerra *nf* war. LOC **dar guerra** *fam* to cause trouble. **I declarar la guerra a** to declare war on. COMP **guerra civil** civil war. **I guerra fría** cold war. **I guerra mundial** world war.

guerrear *vi* to war.

guerrera *nf (chaqueta)* army jacket.

guerrero,-a *adj* **1** warlike. **2** *fam (niño)* difficult. ▸ *nm & nf* warrior, soldier.

guerrilla *nf* **1** *(guerra)* guerrilla warfare. **2** *(banda)* guerrilla band.

guerrillero,-a *nm & nf* guerrilla.

gueto *nm* ghetto.

guía *nm o nf (persona)* guide, leader.
► *nf* **1** *(norma)* guidance, guideline. **2** *(libro)* guidebook. [COMP] **guía de teléfonos** telephone directory, phone book.

guiar *vt* **1** to guide, lead. **2** *(conducir automóvil)* to drive; *(barco)* to steer; *(avión)* to pilot; *(caballo, bici)* to ride.
► *vpr* **guiarse** to be guided.

guijarro *nm* pebble, stone.

guillotina *nf* guillotine.

guillotinar *vt* to guillotine.

guinda *nf* **1** *(fruta)* sour cherry, morello cherry. **2** *(remate)* final touch.

guindilla *nf* **1** red pepper, chilli. **2** *fam (policía)* cop.

guindo *nm* morello cherry tree. [LOC] **caerse** ALGN **del guindo** *fam* to cotton on, twig.

guinea *nf* guinea.

Guinea *nf* Guinea. [COMP] **Guinea Ecuatorial** Equatorial Guinea. **I Guinea-Bissau** Guinea-Bissau. **I Nueva Guinea** New Guinea.

guineano,-a *adj* Guinean.
► *nm & nf* Guinean.

guiñapo *nm* **1** *(andrajo)* rag, tatter. **2** *fig (persona)* wreck.

guiñar *vt* **1** to wink: *me guiñó un ojo* he winked at me. **2** MAR to yaw.

guiño *nm* wink.

guiñol *nm* puppet theatre.

guion *nm* **1** *(esquema)* notes *pl*, sketch, outline. **2** GRAM hyphen, dash. **3** CINE script.

guionista *nm o nf* scriptwriter.

guirigay *nm* **1** *(lenguaje)* gibberish. **2** *(griterío)* racket, noise, din.

guirlache *nm* almond brittle.

guirnalda *nf* garland, wreath.

guisa *nf* manner, way.

guisado,-a *adj* cooked, stewed.
► *nm* **guisado** stew.

guisante *nm* pea.

guisar *vt* to cook, stew.
► *vpr* **guisarse** to cook, stew.

guiso *nm* stew.

guitarra *nf* guitar.

guitarrero,-a *nm & nf* **1** *(vendedor)* guitar seller. **2** *(fabricante)* guitar maker.

guitarrista *nm o nf* guitarist.

gula *nf* gluttony.

gurú *nm* guru.

gusanillo *nm* **1** little worm. **2** *(espiral)* spiral binding. **3** *(intranquilidad)* niggling doubt. [LOC] **matar el gusanillo** *fam* to have a snack.

gusano *nm* **1** worm; *(oruga)* caterpillar. **2** *fig (persona)* worm. [COMP] **gusano de seda** silkworm.

gustar *vt* **1** *(agradar)* to like. **2** *(probar)* to taste, try.

gustativo,-a *adj* gustative. [COMP] **papila gustativa** taste bud.

gustillo *nm* **1** *fam (regusto)* aftertaste. **2** *fam (satisfacción)* satisfaction, pleasure.

gusto *nm* **1** *(sentido, sabor)* taste. **2** *(inclinación)* liking, taste. **3** *(placer)* pleasure: *tengo el gusto de presentarle a mi hermano* may I introduce you to my brother? **4** *(capricho)* whim, fancy. [LOC] **con mucho gusto** with pleasure. **I dar gusto** to please, delight: *me da gusto verla comer* I enjoy watching her eat. **I estar a gusto** to feel comfortable, feel at ease. **I hacer** ALGO **a gusto** to enjoy doing STH. **I hacer** ALGO **por gusto** to do STH for fun. **I ¡qué gusto!** how lovely! **I tanto gusto** pleased to meet you. **I tener buen gusto** to have good taste.

gustosamente *adv* with pleasure, gladly, willingly.

gustoso,-a *adj* **1** *(sabroso)* tasty, savoury, palatable. **2** *(agradable)* agreeable, pleasant. **3** *(con gusto)* glad, willing, ready: *aceptó gustosa* she accepted willingly.

gutural *adj* guttural.

Guyana *nf* Guyana.

guyanés,-esa *adj* Guyanese.
► *nm & nf* Guyanese.

G

H, h *nf (la letra)* H, h.

haba *nf (legumbre)* broad bean.

haber *vi (impersonal)* to be: *hay un coche* there's a car.
► *aux* **1** *(en tiempos compuestos)* to have: *lo has hecho* you have done it. **2 haber de + inf** *(obligación)* to have to, must, should: *han de venir hoy* they must come today. **3 haber que + inf** *(obligación)* must, have to: *habrá que hacerlo* we'll have to do it. [LOC] **¡haberlo dicho!** why didn't you say so! **▌ había una vez...** once upon a time there was... **▌ ¡habráse visto!** what a cheek! **▌ ¡hay que ver!** well, really!, well, I never! **▌ no hay de qué** you're welcome, don't mention it. **▌ no hay (nada) como...** there's nothing like... **▌ ¿qué hay?** hello!, hi!, how are you doing?
► *nm* COM credit, assets *pl*.
► *nm pl* **haberes** *(posesiones)* property *sing*, assets.

habichuela *nf (gen)* bean; *(judía blanca)* haricot bean; *(judía verde)* French bean, green bean.

hábil *adj* **1** *(diestro)* skilful (US skillful). **2** *(despabilado)* clever, smart. **3** *(acto)* clever. **4** *(apto, adecuado)* good, suitable. [LOC] **ser hábil en ALGO / ser hábil para ALGO** *(persona)* to be good at STH. [COMP] **día hábil** working day.

habilidad *nf* **1** *(aptitud)* skill. **2** *(astucia)* cleverness, smartness. [LOC] **tener habilidad para ALGO** to be good at STH.

habilidoso,-a *adj* skilful (US skillful).

habilitar *vt* **1** *(espacio)* to fit out; *(tiempo)* to set aside: *habilitó una habitación para consulta* he fitted a bedroom out as a consulting room. **2** *(capacitar)* to entitle, qualify; *(autorizar)* to empower.

habitable *adj* habitable, liveable.

habitación *nf* **1** *(gen)* room. **2** *(dormitorio)* bedroom. [COMP] **habitación doble** double room. **▌ habitación individual** single room.

habitante *nm o nf* inhabitant.

habitar *vt* to live in, inhabit.
► *vi* to live.

hábitat *nm* habitat.

hábito *nm* **1** *(costumbre)* habit, custom. **2** *(vestido)* habit. [LOC] **tener el hábito de...** to be in the habit of...

habitual *adj* usual, habitual.

habitualmente *adv (repetidamente)* usually; *(regularmente)* regularly.

habituar *vt* to accustom (a, to).
► *vpr* **habituarse** to become accustomed (a, to), get used (a, to).

habla [va precedido de el en singular] *nf* **1** *(facultad)* speech. **2** *(idioma)* language; *(dialecto)* dialect. [LOC] **de habla española / de habla hispana** Spanish-speaking. **▌ estar al habla con ALGN** to be in touch with SB. **▌ perder el habla** to lose one's power of speech.

hablado,-a *adj* spoken, oral: *francés hablado* spoken French.

hablador,-ra *adj* **1** *(parlanchín)* talkative. **2** *(chismoso)* gossipy.

habladuría [también se usa en plural con el mismo significado] *nf (chisme)* piece of gossip; *(rumor)* rumour (US rumor).

hablante *nm o nf* speaker.

hablar *vi* **1** *(gen)* to speak, talk: *habló conmigo* he spoke to me. **2** *(mencionar)* to talk, mention: *no me habló de eso* she didn't mention that. [LOC] **hablar a solas** to talk to os. **▌ hablar bajo** to speak softly. **▌ hablar claro** to speak plainly.

❚ **hablar en broma** to be joking. ❚
¡quién fue a hablar! look who's
talking!► *vt* **1** *(idioma)* to speak: *habla
francés* he speaks French. **2** *(tratar)*
to talk over, discuss: *ya lo hablaremos después*
we'll discuss it later. **LOC** «**Se habla
inglés**» "English spoken".
► *vpr* **hablarse** *(uso recíproco)* to speak,
talk: *ayer nos hablamos por teléfono* we
spoke on the 'phone yesterday. **LOC no
hablarse con** ALGN not to be on speaking
terms with SB.

hacendado,-a *nm & nf* landowner.
hacendoso,-a *adj* house-proud.
hacer *vt* **1** *(producir, fabricar, crear)* to
make: *hice un pastel* I made a cake. **2**
(arreglar, disponer - uñas) to do; *(- barba)*
to trim; *(- cama)* to make; *(- maleta)* to
pack. **3** *(obrar, ejecutar)* to do: *haz lo que
quieras* do what you want. **4** *(conseguir -
amigos, dinero)* to make. **5** *(obligar)* to
make: *nos hizo leer* she made us read. **6**
(recorrer) to do: *hacer noventa kilómetros
por hora* to do ninety kilometres per
hour. **7** *(en suma)* to make: *con esta hacen
ochenta* that makes eighty. **8** *(ocupar
un lugar)* to be: *él hace el número cuatro*
he's the fourth on the list. **9** *(hacer parecer)*
to make look: *ese vestido te hace mayor*
that dress makes you look older. **10**
(acostumbrar) to accustom. **11** *(practicar)*
to do: *¿haces deporte?* do you do any
sport? **LOC a medio hacer** half-done,
half-finished. ❚ **¡así se hace!** that's it! ❚
hace mucho a long time ago. ❚ **hacer
bien en...** to be right to...: *hice bien en ir* I
was right to go. ❚ **hacer mal** to do the
wrong thing. ❚ **hacer tiempo** to kill
time.
► *vi* **1** *(actuar)* to play (de, -); *(representar)*
to act: *hizo de abuela* she played the
grandmother. **2** *(comportarse)* to pretend
to be, act: *hacer el tonto* to act the fool.
3 *(clima)* to be: *hace buen día* it's a fine
day. **4** *(tiempo pasado)* ago: *hace tres años*
three years ago. **LOC hacer como que +
ind** to pretend, act as if: *hizo como que
no sabía nada* he acted as if he knew
nothing. ❚ **hacer como si + subj** to pretend, act as if.

► *vpr* **hacerse 1** *(volverse)* to become,
get: *hacerse rico* to get rich. **2** *(crecer)* to
grow: *se ha hecho mucho* he's grown a
lot. **3** *(resultar)* to become, go on,
seem: *la película se hizo muy larga* the
film went on too long. **4** *(simular)* to
pretend: *se hizo la elegante* she pretended
to be elegant. **5** *(mandar hacer)* to
have made, have done: *me hice un
vestido en la modista* I had a dress made at
the dressmaker's. **LOC hacerse el/la sordo,-a**
fig to turn a deaf ear. ❚ **hacerse
una idea de** ALGO to imagine STH.

hacha [va precedido de el en singular] *nf*
(instrumento) axe (US ax).
hache *nf (la letra)* aitch.
hacia *prep* **1** *(dirección)* towards, to. **2**
(tiempo) at about, at around: *estaremos
ahí hacia las dos* we'll be there at about
two. **LOC hacia abajo** downward(s),
down. ❚ **hacia acá** this way. ❚ **hacia
adelante** forward(s): *inclínate hacia delante*
lean forward. ❚ **hacia allá** that
way. ❚ **hacia atrás** backward(s), back.
❚ **hacia casa** home, homeward.
hacienda *nf* **1** *(bienes)* property,
wealth, possessions *pl*. **2** *(finca)* estate,
property, US ranch. **3** FIN Treasury.
COMP hacienda pública public
funds *pl*, public finances *pl*.
hada [va precedido de el en singular] *nf*
fairy.
Haití *nm* Haiti.
haitiano,-a *adj* Haitian.
► *nm & nf* Haitian.
halagador,-ra *adj* flattering.
halagar *vt* **1** *(lisonjear)* to flatter. **2** *(satisfacer)*
to please.
halago *nm* compliment, flattery.
halcón *nm* falcon.
hallar *vt* **1** *(encontrar)* to find. **2** *(averiguar)*
to find out.
► *vpr* **hallarse** *(estar)* to be: *se hallaba enfermo*
he was ill.
hallazgo *nm* **1** *(descubrimiento)* finding,
discovery. **2** *(cosa descubierta)* find.
halo *nm* halo, aura.
halógeno,-a *adj* halogenous.

H

hamaca *nf* **1** *(de red)* hammock. **2** *(tumbona)* deck chair.

hambre [va precedido de el en singular] *nf* hunger, starvation, famine. [LOC] **matar el hambre** *fig* to stave off hunger. ▌**ser más listo,-a que el hambre** *fig* to be a cunning devil. ▌**tener hambre** to be hungry.

hambriento,-a *adj* **1** hungry, starving. **2** *fig* hungry, longing: *hambriento de justicia* longing for justice.

hambruna *nf* famine.

hamburguesa *nf* hamburger.

hamburguesería *nf* hamburger restaurant.

hámster *nm* hamster.

harapiento,-a *adj* ragged, tattered.

harapo *nm* rag, tatter.

hardware *nm* hardware.

harén *nm* harem.

harina *nf* flour.

hartar *vt* **1** *(atiborrar)* to satiate, fill up. **2** *fig (deseo, etc)* to satisfy. **3** *(fastidiar)* to annoy, irritate: *me harta con sus tonterías* his silly remarks get on muy nerves. **4** *(cansar)* to tire, bore.
▸ *vpr* **hartarse 1** *(atiborrarse)* to eat one's fill, stuff os. **2** *(cansarse)* to get fed up (de, with), get tired (de, of): *me harté de esperarla* I got tired of waiting for her. [LOC] **hasta hartarse** to repletion.

harto,-a *adj* **1** *(repleto)* full, satiated. **2** *fam (cansado)* tired (de, of), fed up (de, with).

hasta *prep* **1** *(tiempo)* until, till, up to: *hasta el sábado* until Saturday; *desde las diez hasta las dos* from ten to two. **2** *(lugar)* as far as, up to, down to. **3** *(cantidad)* up to, as many as. **4** *(incluso)* even: *hasta sabe escribir* she even knows how to write. **5** *(como despedida)* see you: *¡hasta mañana!* see you tomorrow! [LOC] **desde... hasta...** from... to... ▌ **¿hasta cuándo?** until when?, how long? ▌ **hasta que** until.

hastiar *vt* to bore.
▸ *vpr* **hastiarse** to get sick (de, of), get tired (de, of).

hastío *nm* **1** *(repugnancia)* disgust. **2** *fig (aburrimiento)* boredom.

hatajo *nm fig* heap, lot, bunch: *un hatajo de disparates* a load of nonsense.

hatillo *nm* small bundle.

haya *nf* BOT beech.

hayedo *nm* beech groove.

haz *nm* **1** *(de cosas)* bundle. **2** *(de luz)* shaft, beam.

hazaña *nf* deed, exploit, heroic feat.

hazmerreír *nm* laughing stock.

hebilla *nf* buckle.

hebra *nf* **1** *(de hilo)* thread. **2** *(de carne)* sinew; *(de legumbre)* string; *(de madera)* grain; *(de planta)* strand.

hebreo,-a *adj* Hebrew.
▸ *nm & nf (persona)* Hebrew.
▸ *nm* **hebreo** *(idioma)* Hebrew.

hechicería *nf* **1** *(arte)* sorcery, witchcraft. **2** *(hechizo)* spell, charm.

hechicero,-a *adj & nf (hombre)* sorcerer, wizard; *(mujer)* sorceress, witch.

hechizar *vt* **1** *(embrujar)* cast a spell on. **2** *fig (cautivar)* to charm, bewitch.

hechizo *nm* **1** *(embrujo)* charm, spell. **2** *fig (embelesamiento)* fascination, charm.

hecho,-a *adj* **1** *(carne)* done. **2** *(persona)* mature. **3** *(frase, expresión)* set. **4** *(ropa)* ready-made. [LOC] **muy hecho,-a 1** *(carne)* well-cooked. **2** *(pasada)* overdone. ▌ **ser un hombre hecho y derecho** to be a real man.
▸ *nm* **hecho 1** *(realidad)* fact. **2** *(suceso)* event. [LOC] **de hecho** in fact.

hectárea *nf* hectare.

hectogramo *nm* hectogramme.

hectolitro *nm* hectolitre.

hectómetro *nm* hectometre.

hediondo,-a *adj (apestoso)* stinking, foul-smelling, smelly.

hedor *nm* stink, stench.

helada *nf* METEOR frost.

heladería *nf* ice-cream parlour.

helado,-a *adj* **1** *(gen)* frozen: *estoy helado* I'm frozen. **2** *(muy frío)* icy, freezing cold. **3** *(café, té)* iced.

▶ *nm* helado ice-cream. LOC dejar a ALGN helado,-a to stun SB.

helador,-ra *adj* icy, freezing.

helar *vt (congelar)* to freeze.
▶ *vi* [sólo se usa en tercera persona; no lleva sujeto] METEOR to freeze: *anoche heló* it froze last night.
▶ *vpr* **helarse 1** *(congelarse)* to freeze: *el estanque se ha helado* the pond has frozen over. **2** *(persona)* to freeze, freeze to death: *me estoy helando* I'm freezing.

helecho *nm* fern.

hélice *nf* **1** *(espiral)* helix. **2** *(propulsor)* propeller.

helicóptero *nm* helicopter.

helio *nm* helium.

helipuerto *nm* heliport.

hematoma *nm* bruise.

hembra *nf* **1** *(animal)* female. **2** *(mujer)* woman. **3** TÉC female.

hemeroteca *nf* newspaper library.

hemiciclo *nm (parlamento)* floor.

hemisferio *nm* hemisphere.

hemorragia *nf* haemorrhage. COMP hemorragia nasal nosebleed.

hemorroide *nf* haemorrhoid.
▶ *nf pl* **hemorroides** piles, haemorrhoids.

henchir *vt (llenar)* to fill (de, with), stuff (de, with), cram (de, with).

hender *vt (cortar)* to cleave, split, crack.

hendidura *nf* cleft, crack.

heno *nm* hay.

hepatitis *nf inv* hepatitis.

heptaedro *nm* heptahedron.

heptagonal *adj* heptagonal.

heptágono,-a *adj* heptagonal.
▶ *nm* **heptágono** heptagon.

heráldica *nf* heraldry.

herbario,-a *adj* herbal.
▶ *nm & nf (botánico)* botanist.
▶ *nm* **herbario** *(colección)* herbarium.

herbicida *nm* weedkiller, herbicide.

herbívoro,-a *adj* herbivorous, grass-eating.
▶ *nm & nf* herbivore.

herbolario,-a *nm & nf (persona)* herbalist.
▶ *nm* **herbolario** *(tienda)* herbalist's (shop).

herboristería *nf* herbalist's (shop).

hercio *nm* hertz.

heredad *nf (terreno)* country estate.

heredar *vt* **1** to inherit. **2** *fig* to inherit: *ha heredado los ojos de su padre* he's got his father's eyes.

heredero,-a *nm & nf (hombre)* heir; *(mujer)* heiress.

hereditario,-a *adj* hereditary.

hereje *nm o nf* heretic.

herejía *nf* heresy.

herencia *nf* **1** inheritance, legacy. **2** *(genética)* heredity.

herético,-a *adj* heretical.

herida *nf* wound.

herido,-a *adj* **1** *(físicamente)* wounded, injured, hurt: *el niño resultó herido* the boy was injured. **2** *fig (emocionalmente)* hurt, wounded. LOC herido,-a de gravedad badly injured.
▶ *nm & nf* wounded person, injured person.

herir *vt* **1** *(dañar)* to wound, injure, hurt. **2** *fig (ofender)* to hurt, offend.

hermafrodita *adj* hermaphrodite.

hermanado,-a *adj (ciudad, pueblo)* twinned.

hermanar *vt* **1** *(unir)* to unite, join. **2** *(combinar)* to combine. **3** *(personas)* to unite spiritually. **4** *(ciudades)* to twin.

hermanastro,-a *nm & nf (hombre)* stepbrother; *(mujer)* stepsister.

hermandad *nf (de hermanos)* fraternity, brotherhood; *(de hermanas)* fraternity, sisterhood.

hermano,-a *nm & nf (hombre)* brother; *(mujer)* sister: *¿cuántos hermanos tienes?* how many brothers and sisters have you got?

hermético,-a *adj* **1** hermetic, airtight. **2** *fig* impenetrable, secretive.

hermoso,-a *adj* **1** *(gen)* beautiful, lovely: *hace un día hermoso* it's a lovely day. **2** *(hombre)* handsome.

H

hermosura *adj (cualidad - de mujer, lugar)* beauty, loveliness; *(- de hombre)* handsomeness.
▶ *nf* **1** *(mujer hermosa)* beautiful woman, beauty. **2** *(persona, cosa)* beautiful thing.

hernia *nf* hernia, rupture.

héroe *nm* hero.

heroicamente *adv* heroically.

heroico,-a *adj* heroic.

heroína *nf* **1** *(mujer)* heroine. **2** *(droga)* heroin.

heroísmo *nm* heroism.

herpes *nm inv* herpes, shingles.

herradura *nf* horseshoe.

herraje *nm* iron fittings *pl*, ironwork.

herramienta *nf* tool.

herrar *vt (caballo)* to shoe.

herrería *nf* **1** *(fábrica)* ironworks *pl*. **2** *(taller)* forge, smithy, blacksmith's.

herrero *nm* blacksmith, smith.

herrumbre *nf (óxido)* rust.

hervir *vt* to boil.
▶ *vi* **1** to boil: *el agua ya hierve* the water is boiling. **2** *fig (el mar)* to surge.

hervor *nm* boiling, bubbling. LOC **dar un hervor a** ALGO to blanch STH.

heterogéneo,-a *adj* heterogeneous.

heterosexual *adj* heterosexual.
▶ *nm o nf* heterosexual.

hexaedro *nm* hexahedron.

hexagonal *adj* hexagonal.

hexágono *nm* hexagon.

hexámetro *nm* hexameter.

hiato *nm* hiatus.

hibernación *nf* hibernation.

hibernar *vi* to hibernate.

hibisco *nm* hibiscus.

híbrido,-a *adj* hybrid.
▶ *nm & nf* hybrid.

hidalgo,-a *nm* nobleman.

hidratante *adj* moisturizing.

hidratar *vt* **1** to hydrate. **2** *(piel)* to moisturize.

hidráulico,-a *adj* hydraulic.

hídrico,-a *adj* hydric.

hidroavión *nm* seaplane.

hidrocarburo *nm* hydrocarbon.

hidroeléctrico,-a *adj* hydroelectric.

hidrógeno *nm* hydrogen.

hidromasaje COMP **bañera de hidromasaje** Jacuzzi®, whirlpool bath.

hidroterapia *nf* hydrotherapy.

hiedra *nf* ivy.

hiel *nf* **1** bile. **2** *fig* bitterness, gall.

hielo *nm* **1** ice. **2** *fig (frialdad)* coldness. COMP **cubito de hielo** ice cube.

hiena *nf* hyaena, hyena.

hierático,-a *adj (rígido)* rigid.

hierba *nf* **1** grass. **2** CULIN herb. COMP **finas hierbas** mixed herbs.

hierbabuena *nf* mint.

hierro *nm (metal)* iron. COMP **hierro forjado** wrought iron. ❙ **hierro fundido** cast iron.

hígado *nm* liver.

higiene *nf* hygiene.

higiénico,-a *adj* hygienic.

higo *nm* fig. LOC **de higos a brevas** *fig* once in a blue moon. COMP **higo chumbo** prickly pear.

higuera *nf* fig tree.

hijastro,-a *nm & nf (niño, niña)* stepchild; *(hijo)* stepson; *(hija)* stepdaughter.

hijo,-a *nm & nf (niño, niña)* child; *(chico)* son; *(chica)* daughter: *tiene dos hijos y dos hijas* he has two sons and two daughters. COMP **hijo,-a único,-a 1** *(niño, niña)* only child. **2** *(chico)* only son. **3** *(chica)* only daughter.
▶ *nm pl* **hijos** children: *tiene cuatro hijos* she has four children.

hilacha *nf* **1** *(hilacho)* loose thread. **2** *(resto)* rest.

hilado,-a *adj* spun.
▶ *nm* **hilado 1** *(operación)* spinning. **2** *(hilo)* thread.

hilandería *nf* **1** *(arte)* spinning. **2** *(fábrica)* spinning mill.

hilandero,-a *nm & nf* spinner.

hilar *vt* **1** to spin. **2** *fig* to work out.

hilarante *adj* hilarious.

hilaridad *nf fml* hilarity, mirth.

hilatura *nf* **1** *(arte)* spinning. **2** *(industria)* spinning mill.

hilera *nf (línea)* line, row.

hilo *nm* **1** thread; *(grueso)* yarn. **2** *(lino)* linen. **3** *(alambre, cable)* wire. **4** *fig (de luz)* thread, thin beam; *(de líquido)* trickle, thin stream. **5** *fig (de historia, discurso)* thread; *(de pensamiento)* train. LOC **estar pendiente de un hilo** *fig* to be hanging by a thread. **I mover los hilos** *fig* to pull the strings. **I perder el hilo** *fig* to lose the thread.

hilvanar *vt* **1** to tack, baste. **2** *fig* to put together, outline.

himno *nm* hymn. COMP

hincapié LOC **hacer hincapié** *(insistir)* to insist on. *(subrayar)* to emphasize (en, -), stress (en, -).

hincar *vt (clavar)* to drive (in).

hincha *nm o nf* DEP fan, supporter.

hinchado,-a *adj (inflado)* blown up. **2** *(piel)* swollen, puffed up.

hinchar *vt* **1** *(inflar)* to blow up; *(con bomba)* to pump up: *hinchar un globo* to blow up a balloon. **2** *fig (exagerar)* to blow up.
▶ *vpr* **hincharse 1** MED to swell (up): *se me ha hinchado el pie* my foot has swollen up. **2** *fam (comer)* to stuff os.

hinchazón *nf* swelling, inflation.

hindú *adj* Hindu.
▶ *nm o nf* Hindu.

hinduismo *nm* Hinduism.

hinojo *nm* BOT fennel.

hipar *vi (tener hipo)* to hiccup, have the hiccups.

hiperactivo,-a *adj* hyperactive.

hipermercado *nm* hypermarket.

hipersensible *adj* hypersensitive.

hipertensión *nf* high blood pressure.

hipertenso,-a *adj* hypertensive.
▶ *nm & nf* hypertensive.

hípica *nf* horse riding.

hípico,-a *adj* horse, equestrian.

hipnosis *nf inv* hypnosis.

hipnótico,-a *adj* hypnotic.

hipnotismo *nm* hypnotism.

hipnotizador,-ra *adj* hypnotizing.
▶ *nm & nf* hypnotist.

hipnotizar *vt* to hypnotize.

hipo *nm* hiccup. LOC **quitar el hipo** *fig* to take one's breath away.

hipocondríaco,-a *adj* hypochondriac.

hipocresía *nf* hypocrisy.

hipócrita *adj* hypocritical.
▶ *nm o nf* hypocrite.

hipódromo *nm* racetrack, racecourse.

hipopótamo *nm* hippopotamus.

hipoteca *nf* mortgage.

hipotecar *vt* to mortgage.

hipotecario,-a *adj* mortgage.

hipotensión *nf* low blood pressure.

hipotenso,-a *adj* hypotensive.

hipotenusa *nf* hypotenuse.

hipótesis *nf inv* hypothesis.

hipotético,-a *adj* hypothetic, hypothetical.

hippie *adj* hippy.
▶ *nm o nf* hippy.

hiriente *adj* **1** wounding. **2** *fig* hurtful, cutting, wounding.

hirsuto,-a *adj* **1** hairy; *(cerdoso)* bristly. **2** *fig (persona)* rough, brusque, surly.

hispánico,-a *adj* Hispanic, Spanish.

hispano,-a *adj* **1** *(de España)* Spanish, Hispanic. **2** *(de América)* Spanish-American.
▶ *nm & nf* **1** *(de España)* Spaniard. **2** *(de América)* Spanish American, US Hispanic.

hispanoamericano,-a *adj* Spanish American, Latin American.

Hispanoamérica *nf* Spanish America, Latin America.

hispanohablante *adj* Spanish-speaking.
▶ *nm o nf* Spanish speaker.

histeria *nf* hysteria.

histérico,-a *adj* hysterical.
▶ *nm & nf* hysteric. LOC **poner histérico,-a a ALGN** *fam* to drive SB mad.

histerismo *nm* hysteria.

historia *nf* **1** *(estudio)* history. **2** *(narración)* story, tale. LOC **pasar a la historia** to go down in history. COMP **historia natural** natural history. **I historia universal** world history.

historiado,-a *adj fig* overelaborate.

H

historiador,-ra *nm & nf* historian.
historial *nm* **1** MED medical record, case history. **2** *(currículo)* curriculum vitae.
historiar *vt* **1** *(contar)* to tell the story of; *(acontecimientos)* to recount. **2** *(escribir)* to write the history of.
histórico,-a *adj* **1** *(relativo a la historia)* historical. **2** *(importante)* historic, memorable. **3** *(cierto)* factual, true.
historieta *nf* **1** *(cuento)* short story, anecdote. **2** *(viñetas)* comic strip.
hito *nm* **1** *(mojón)* milestone. **2** *fig (hecho importante)* milestone, landmark.
hobby *nm* hobby.
hocico *nm* *(de animal)* snout, muzzle.
hockey *nm* hockey. COMP **hockey sobre hielo** ice hockey.
hogar *nm* **1** *(de chimenea)* hearth, fireplace. **2** *fig (casa)* home. **3** *fig (familia)* family.
hogareño,-a *adj* **1** *(vida)* family. **2** *(persona)* home-loving, stay-at-home.
hogaza *nf* large loaf (of bread).
hoguera *nf* **1** bonfire. **2** *fig* blaze.
hoja *nf* **1** *(gen)* leaf. **2** *(pétalo)* petal. **3** *(de papel)* sheet. **4** *(de libro)* leaf, page. **5** *(de cuchillo, etc)* blade. **6** *(de puerta, ventana)* leaf: *una ventana de dos hojas* a double-leaf window. LOC **de hoja perenne** BOT evergreen. ▌ COMP **hoja de afeitar** razor blade.
hojalata *nf* tin, tin plate.
hojalatería *nf* *(taller, tienda)* tinsmith's.
hojalatero *nm* tinsmith.
hojaldrado,-a *adj* puff: *pasta hojaldrada* puff pastry.
hojaldre *nm & nf* [suele utilizarse más como masculino] puff pastry.
hojarasca *nf* dead leaves *pl*.
hojeada *nf* flick.
hojear *vt* to leaf through.
hola *interj fam* hello!, hullo!, US hi!
Holanda *nf* Holland.
holandés,-esa *adj* Dutch.
▶ *nm & nf (persona)* Dutch person; *(hombre)* Dutchman; *(mujer)* Dutchwoman.
▶ *nm* **holandés** *(idioma)* Dutch.

holandesa *nf (papel)* quarto sheet.
holgado,-a *adj* **1** *(ropa)* loose. **2** *(espacio)* roomy. **3** *(posición)* comfortable.
holgar *vi* **1** *(descansar)* to rest. **2** *(estar ocioso)* to be idle. LOC **huelga decir que...** needless to say (that)...
holgazán,-ana *adj* idle, lazy.
▶ *nm & nf* lazybones, layabout.
holgazanear *vi* to laze around.
holgazanería *nf* idleness, laziness.
holgura *nf* **1** *(ropa)* looseness. **2** *(espacio)* room, spaciousness. **3** *fig (bienestar)* affluence, comfort.
hollar *vt (comprimir)* to tread (on).
hollín *nm* soot.
holocausto *nm* holocaust.
hombre *nm* **1** *(individuo)* man. **2** *(especie)* man, mankind. **3** *fam (marido)* husband.
▶ *interj (asombro)* hey!, hey there!, well!: *¡hombre, Pedro, no te esperaba!* hey, Pedro, I didn't expect you! COMP **hombre orquesta** one-man band. ▌ **hombre rana** frogman.
hombrera *nf* shoulder pad.
hombría *nm* manliness, virility.
hombro *nm* shoulder. LOC **a hombros** on one's shoulders. ▌ **arrimar el hombro** to help out, lend a hand.
hombruno,-a *adj* mannish, manly.
homenaje *nm* homage, tribute. LOC **en homenaje a** in honour of. ▌ **rendir homenaje a** ALGN to pay tribute to SB.
homenajear *vt* to pay tribute to.
homeopatía *nf* homeopathy.
homicida *adj* homicidal, murder: *el arma homicida* the murder weapon.
▶ *nm o nf (hombre)* murderer; *(mujer)* murderess.
homicidio *nm* homicide, murder.
homínido *nm* hominid, hominoid.
homogéneo,-a *adj* homogeneous.
homologado,-a *adj* **1** *(centro, estudios)* officially approved, officially recognized. **2** *(productos)* authorized.
homologar *vt (comprobar)* to approve, recognize, authorize.
homosexual *adj* homosexual.
▶ *nm o nf* homosexual.

homosexualidad *nf* homosexuality.

honda *nf* sling.

hondo,-a *adj* **1** deep. **2** *fig* profound.

hondonada *nf* hollow, depression.

hondura *nf* depth.

Honduras *nm* Honduras.

hondureño,-a *adj* Honduran.
▶ *nm & nf* Honduran.

honestidad *nf* **1** *(honradez)* honesty, uprightness. **2** *(decencia)* decency.

honesto,-a *adj* **1** *(honrado)* honest, upright. **2** *(decente)* decent.

hongo *nm* *(gen)* fungus; *(comestible)* mushroom; *(venenoso)* toadstool.

honor *nm* *(virtud)* honour. LOC **en honor a la verdad** to be fair, in all fairness. **hacer honor a** to live up to.
▶ *nm pl* **honores** *(agasajo)* honours.

honorable *adj* honourable.

honorario,-a *adj* honorary.
▶ *nm pl* **honorarios** fees.

honorífico,-a *adj* honorary.

honra *nf* **1** *(honor)* honour. **2** *(buena reputación)* reputation, good name.
▶ *nf pl* **honras** *(fúnebres)* last honours.

honradez *nf* honesty, integrity.

honrado,-a *adj* *(honesto)* honest.

honrar *vt* *(gen)* to honour: *nos honró con su presencia* he honoured us with his presence.
▶ *vpr* **honrarse** to be honoured.

honroso,-a *adj* **1** *(que honra)* honourable. **2** *(decoroso)* respectable.

hora *nf* **1** *(unidad de tiempo)* hour: *media hora* half an hour. **2** *(tiempo)* time: *¿qué hora es?* what time is it? **3** *(cita)* appointment: *tengo hora para las cuatro y media* I have an appointment at half past four. LOC **a altas horas** in the small hours. **¡a buenas horas!** and about time too! **a la hora** at the proper time, on time. **a primera hora** first thing in the morning. **dar la hora** to strike the hour. **de última hora** last-minute: *una noticia de última hora* some last-minute news. **pedir hora** to make an appointment. **por horas** by the hour: *cobro por horas* I get paid by the hour. COMP **hora de comer** lunch time, dinner time. **hora punta** rush hour.

horadar *vt* **1** *(perforar)* to pierce. **2** *(taladrar)* to bore (through).

horario,-a *adj* time.
▶ *nm* **horario** **1** timetable. **2** *(jornada laboral)* hours *pl*, timetable: *tengo horario de mañana* I work mornings. COMP **horario comercial** *(tienda)* opening hours *pl*. **horario laboral** working hours *pl*.

horca *nf* **1** *(patíbulo)* gallows *pl*, gibbet. **2** AGR hayfork, pitchfork.

horcajadas LOC **a horcajadas** astride.

horchata *nf* sweet milky drink made from tiger nuts or almonds.

horchatería *nf* bar where *horchata* is sold.

horda *nf* **1** horde, mob. **2** *fig* gang.

horizontal *adj* horizontal.

horizonte *nm* horizon.

horma *nf* **1** mould. **2** *(de zapato)* last.

hormiga *nf* ant.

hormigón *nm* concrete. COMP **hormigón armado** reinforced concrete.

hormigonera *nf* concrete mixer.

hormiguear *vi* to itch, tingle: *me hormigueaba la mano* I had pins and needles in my hand.

hormigueo *nm* pins and needles *pl*.

hormiguero *nm* ant hill, ant's nest.

hormona *nf* hormone.

hormonal *adj* hormonal.

hornacina *nf* niche.

hornada *nf* **1** batch. **2** *fig* set, batch.

hornear *vt* to bake.

hornillo *nm* **1** TÉC small furnace. **2** *(para cocinar)* stove.

horno *nm* **1** *(de cocina)* oven. **2** TÉC furnace. **3** *(cerámica, ladrillos)* kiln. **4** *(panadería)* bakery. COMP **horno (de) microondas** microwave oven. **horno eléctrico** electric oven.

horóscopo *nm* horoscope.

horquilla *nf* *(de pelo)* hairgrip, hairclip.

horrendo,-a *adj* horrible, awful.

hórreo *nm* granary.

horrible *adj* horrible, awful.

H

horripilante *adj* hair-raising, horrifying, terrifying.

horripilar *vt* to horrify, scare stiff.

horror *nm* **1** *(repulsión)* horror, terror. **2** *(temor)* hate. **3** *fig (atrocidad)* atrocity. LOC ¡qué horror! how awful!

horrorizar *vt (causar horror)* to horrify, terrify.
▶ *vpr* **horrorizarse** to be horrified.

horroroso,-a *adj* **1** *(que causa miedo)* horrifying. **2** *fam (feo)* hideous.

hortaliza *nf* vegetable.

hortelano,-a *nm & nf* market gardener.

hortensia *nf* hydrangea.

hortera *adj fam* common, tasteless.

hortícola *adj* horticultural.

horticultor,-ra *nm & nf* horticulturist.

horticultura *nf* horticulture.

hosco,-a *adj* **1** *(insociable)* sullen, surly. **2** *(lugar)* gloomy, dark.

hospedaje *nm* **1** *(acción)* lodging; *(precio)* cost of lodging. **2** *(lugar)* lodgings *pl*, accommodation.

hospedar *vt* to lodge, put up.
▶ *vpr* **hospedarse** to stay (en, at).

hospicio *nm* **1** *(de huérfanos)* orphanage. **2** *(de pobres)* poorhouse.

hospital *nm* hospital, infirmary.

hospitalidad *nf* hospitality.

hospitalizar *vt* to send into hospital, hospitalize.

hostal *nm* hostel, hotel.

hostelería *nf* catering.

hostia *nf* **1** REL host. **2** *tabú (choque)* bump, bash; *(torta)* slap, punch.

hostigar *vt* **1** *(azotar)* to whip. **2** *fig (perseguir)* to plague, persecute.

hostil *adj* hostile.

hostilidad *nf* hostility.
▶ *nf pl* **hostilidades** hostilities.

hotel *nm (establecimiento)* hotel.

hotelero,-a *adj* hotel.
▶ *nm & nf* hotel manager, hotelier.

hoy *adv* **1** *(día)* today. **2** *fig (actualmente)* now, nowadays. LOC de hoy en adelante from now on. ▌ hoy (en) día nowadays, today, these days.

hoyo *nm* **1** *(agujero)* hole, pit. **2** *(sepultura)* grave.

hoyuelo *nm* dimple.

hoz¹ *nf* agr sickle.

hoz² *nf* geog ravine, gorge.

hucha *nf* moneybox, piggy bank.

hueco,-a *adj* **1** hollow: pared hueca hollow wall, stud wall. **2** *(vacío)* empty. **3** *(cóncavo)* concave.
▶ *nm* **hueco** **1** *(cavidad)* hollow, hole. **2** *(de tiempo)* slot, free time; *(de espacio)* empty space. **3** *fig (vacante)* vacancy.

huelga *nf* strike. LOC estar en huelga / estar de huelga to be on strike. COMP huelga de brazos caídos go-slow. ▌ huelga de celo work-to-rule. ▌ huelga general general strike. ▌ huelga de hambre hunger strike.

✎ Consulta también **holgar**.

huelguista *nm o nf* striker.

huella *nf* **1** *(de pie)* footprint; *(de ruedas)* track. **2** *fig (vestigio)* trace, sign: las huellas del tiempo the traces of time. LOC dejar huella to leave one's mark (en, on). COMP huella dactilar fingerprint.

huérfano,-a *adj* orphan, orphaned.
▶ *nm & nf* orphan.

huerta *nf (terreno)* market garden.

huerto *nm (de verduras)* vegetable garden; *(de frutas)* orchard.

hueso *nm* **1** ANAT bone. **2** *(de fruta)* stone, US pit. **3** *fam fig (cosa difícil)* struggle, problem: las mates son un hueso para mí I find maths really hard. LOC ser un hueso duro de roer *fig* to be a hard nut to crack.

huésped,-da *nm & nf (invitado)* guest.

hueste *nf* [también se usa en plural con el mismo significado] MIL army, host.

huesudo,-a *adj* bony.

hueva *nf* roe, spawn.

huevera *nf* **1** *(copa)* egg cup. **2** *(cartón)* egg box.

huevería *nf* egg shop.

huevero,-a *nm & nf (persona)* egg seller.

huevo *nm* egg. COMP huevo duro hard-boiled egg. ▌ huevo frito fried egg. ▌ huevo pasado por agua soft-boiled egg.

huida *nf* flight, escape.

huidizo,-a *adj* fleeting, elusive.

huir *vi* **1** *(escapar)* to flee, run away. **2** *(evitar)* to avoid (de, -).

hule *nm* oilcloth, oilskin.

hulla *nf* coal.

humanidad *nf* **1** *(género humano)* humanity, mankind. **2** *(cualidad)* humanity, humaneness.
  ▶ *nf pl* **humanidades** EDUC humanities.

humanismo *nm* humanism.

humanista *nm o nf* humanist.

humanístico,-a *adj* humanistic.

humanitario,-a *adj* humanitarian.

humanizar *vt* to humanize.
  ▶ *vpr* **humanizarse** to become more human.

humano,-a *adj* **1** human. **2** *(benigno)* humane.

humareda *nf* cloud of smoke.

humeante *adj* **1** *(de humo)* smoky, smoking. **2** *(de vaho)* steaming.

humear *vi* **1** *(humo)* to smoke. **2** *(vaho)* to steam.

humectante *adj* moistening.

humedad *nf* **1** humidity. **2** *(de vapor)* moisture.

humedecer *vt* to moisten, dampen.
  ▶ *vpr* **humedecerse** to become moist.

húmedo,-a *adj* **1** *(clima)* humid, damp. **2** *(impregnado)* damp, moist, wet.

húmero *nm* humerus.

humidificador *nm* humidifier.

humidificar *vt* to humidify.

humildad *nf* humility, humbleness.

humilde *adj* humble, modest.

humildemente *adv* humbly.

humillación *nf* humiliation.

humillante *adj* humiliating.

humillar *vt* to humiliate, humble.
  ▶ *vpr* **humillarse** to humble os.

humo *nm* **1** smoke. **2** *(gas)* fumes *pl*. **3** *(vapor)* steam.
  ▶ *nm pl* **humos** *fig* airs. LOC **bajarle los humos a** ALGN *fig* to put SB in his/her place.

humor *nm* **1** *(ánimo)* mood. **2** *(carácter)* temper. **3** *(gracia)* humour. LOC **estar de buen humor** to be in a good mood.

humorada *nf* joke, witticism.

humorismo *nm* humour.

humorista *adj* humorous.
  ▶ *nm o nf (cómico)* comedian.

humorístico,-a *adj* humorous.

humus *nm inv* humus.

hundible *adj* sinkable.

hundido,-a *adj* **1** *(barco, etc)* sunken. **2** *(ojos)* deep-set; *(mejillas)* hollow.

hundimiento *nm* **1** *(barco)* sinking. **2** *(tierra)* subsidence. **3** *(edificio)* collapse.

hundir *vt* **1** *(sumir)* plunge: *hundió la mano en la arena* she plunged her hand into the sand. **2** *(barco)* to sink. **3** *(derrumbar)* to demolish, ruin: *el terremoto hundió el edificio* the earthquake caused the building to collapse.
  ▶ *vpr* **hundirse 1** *(barco)* to sink. **2** *(derrumbarse)* to collapse, fall down.

húngaro,-a *adj* Hungarian.
  ▶ *nm & nf (persona)* Hungarian.
  ▶ *nm* **húngaro** *(idioma)* Hungarian.

Hungría *nf* Hungary.

huracán *nm* hurricane.

huracanado,-a *adj* hurricane: *vientos huracanados* hurricane winds.

huraño,-a *adj* sullen, unsociable.

hurgar *vt* **1** *(remover)* to poke, rake. **2** *(bolsillo, bolso, etc)* to rummage in.
  ▶ *vpr* **hurgarse** to pick.

hurón,-ona *nm (animal)* ferret.

hurra *interj* hurray!, hurrah!

hurraca *nf* magpie.

hurtadillas LOC **a hurtadillas** stealthily, on the sly.

hurtar *vt (robar)* to steal, pilfer.

hurto *nm* petty theft, pilfering.

husmeador,-ra *adj* **1** *(con la nariz)* sniffing. **2** *fig (fisgón)* prying.

husmear *vt* **1** *(con el olfato)* to sniff, scent. **2** *fig (indagar)* to pry (en, into).
  ▶ *vi* **1** to sniff. **2** *fig* to snoop around.

huso *nm (para hilar)* spindle, bobbin. COMP **huso horario** time zone.

I

I, i *nf* (la letra) I, i.
COMP **i griega** *name of the letter* y. ∥ **i latina** *name of the letter* i.

ibérico,-a *adj* Iberian.

íbero,-a *adj* Iberian.
▶ *nm & nf* (persona) Iberian.

iberoamericano,-a *adj* Latin American.
▶ *nm & nf* Latin American.

iceberg *nm* iceberg.

icono *nm* icon.

ida *nf* (acción) going; (salida) departure.
LOC **de ida sola** single. ∥ **de ida y vuelta** (billete) return.

idea *nf* **1** idea. **2** (noción) notion. **3** (ingenio) imagination.

ideal *adj* ideal.
▶ *nm* ideal.

idealismo *nm* idealism.

idealista *adj* idealistic.
▶ *nm o nf* idealist.

idealizar *vt* to idealize.

idear *vt* **1** (concebir) to conceive. **2** (inventar) to design.

ideario *nm* ideology.

idéntico,-a *adj* identical.

identidad *nf* identity. COMP **carnet de identidad** identity card.

identificar *vt* to identify.
▶ *vpr* **identificarse** (solidarizarse) to identify (con, with).

ideología *nf* ideology.

ideólogo,-a *nm & nf* ideologist.

idílico,-a *adj* idyllic.

idilio *nm* **1** *lit* idyll. **2** *fam* romance.

idioma *nm* language.

idiosincrasia *nf* idiosyncrasy.

idiota *adj* **1** MED idiotic. **2** *fam* (tonto) stupid.
▶ *nm o nf* idiot.

idiotez *nf* **1** MED idiocy. **2** (estupidez) stupid thing to say, stupid thing to do.

idiotizar *vt* to turn into an idiot.

ido,-a *adj* **1** (loco) mad. **2** (despistado) absent-minded. LOC **estar ido,-a 1** *fam* (loco) to be mad. **2** (despistado) to be miles away.

idolatrar *vt* **1** to worship. **2** *fig* to idolize.

ídolo *nm* idol.

idóneo,-a *adj* suitable.

iglesia *nf* **1** (edificio) church. **2** (institución) Church.

iglú *nm* igloo.

ignorancia *nf* ignorance.

ignorante *adj* ignorant.
▶ *nm o nf* ignoramus.

ignorar *vt* **1** (desconocer) not to know, not be aware of. **2** (no hacer caso) to ignore.

igual *adj* **1** (parte) equal. **2** (lo mismo) the same. **3** (muy parecido) just like.
▶ *adj* (persona) equal.
▶ *adv* **1** (en comparativas) the same. **2** *fam* maybe, perhaps: *igual no vienen* they may well not come.

igualar *vt* **1** to make equal. **2** (allanar) to level; (pulir) to smooth. **3** (comparar) to match: *no hay nadie que lo iguale* nobody can match him, he has no equal.
▶ *vpr* **igualarse 1** (ser iguales) to be equal. **2** (compararse) to be compared.

igualdad *nf* equality.

iguana *nf* iguana.

ilegal *adj* illegal.

ilegalidad *nf* illegality.

ilegible *adj* unreadable, illegible.

ilegítimo,-a *adj* illegitimate.

ileso,-a *adj* unharmed, unhurt. LOC salir ileso,-a to escape unharmed.

iletrado,-a *adj* illiterate.

ilícito,-a *adj* unlawful, illicit.

ilimitado,-a *adj* unlimited.

ilógico,-a *adj* illogical.

iluminación *nf (de una sala)* lighting; *(de una feria)* illumination; *(de una película, un espectáculo)* lighting.

iluminar *vt* to light, light up.

ilusión *nf* **1** *(no real)* illusion. **2** *(esperanza)* hope. **3** *(emoción)* excitement.

ilusionado,-a *adj* excited.

ilusionar *vt* **1** *(crear ilusiones)* to raise hopes. **2** *(entusiasmar)* to excite.
▶ *vpr* **ilusionarse 1** *(esperanzarse)* to build up one's hopes. **2** *(entusiasmarse)* to be excited (**con**, about).

ilusionismo *nm* conjuring.

ilusionista *nm o nf* conjurer, illusionist.

iluso,-a *adj* naive, gullible.

ilustración *nf* **1** *(de un texto)* illustration. **2** *(erudición)* learning. **3 la Ilustración** HIST the Enlightenment.

ilustrado,-a *adj* **1** *(texto)* illustrated. **2** *(culto)* learned. **3** HIST of the Enlightenment.

ilustrar *vt* **1** *(texto)* to illustrate. **2** *(instruir)* to enlighten.

ilustre *adj* **1** *(célebre)* renowned, illustrious. **2** *(distinguido)* distinguished.

imagen *nf* **1** image. **2** TV picture. LOC ser la viva imagen de ALGN to be the spitting image of SB.

imaginación *nf* imagination, fantasy.

imaginar *vt* **1** *(gen)* to imagine. **2** *(idear)* to devise, think up.

✎ También se usa la forma imaginarse, sobre todo en el lenguaje coloquial.

imaginario,-a *adj* imaginary.

imaginativo,-a *adj* imaginative.

imán¹ *nm* magnet.

imán² *nm* REL imam.

imantar *vt* to magnetize.

imbatible *adj* unbeatable.

imbécil *adj* **1** MED *(retrasado)* imbecile. **2** *fam* stupid, imbecile.
▶ *nm o nf* **1** MED imbecile. **2** *fam* idiot.

imbecilidad *nf* **1** MED imbecility. **2** *fam* stupid thing to do.

imberbe *adj* beardless.

imborrable *adj* indelible.

imbuir *vt* to imbue.

imitación *nf* **1** *(copia)* imitation. **2** *(parodia)* impression.

imitador,-ra *adj* imitative.
▶ *nm & nf* **1** imitator. **2** *(cómico)* impressionist.

imitar *vt* to copy, imitate; *(gestos)* to mimic; *(persona)* to mimic, do an impression of.

impaciencia *nf* impatience.

impacientar *vt* to make lose one's patience, exasperate.
▶ *vpr* **impacientarse** to get impatient.

impaciente *adj* impatient, anxious.

impactado,-a *adj* impacted.

impactante *adj* striking, powerful.

impactar *vt* **1** *(físicamente)* to hit. **2** *(impresionar)* to make an impression on: *esa escena me impactó mucho* that scene made a deep impression on me.

impacto *nm* **1** *(choque)* impact. **2** *(marca)* mark; *(agujero)* hole.

impar *adj* odd.

imparable *adj* unstoppable.

imparcial *adj* impartial, fair.

imparcialidad *nf* impartiality.

impartir *vt (lección)* to give.

impasible *adj* impassive.

impávido,-a *adj* dauntless.

impecable *adj* impeccable, faultless.

impedido,-a *adj* disabled.
▶ *nm & nf* disabled person.

impedimento *nm* impediment, obstacle.

impedir *vt (hacer imposible)* to prevent, stop: *¿hay algo que te lo impida?* is there anything stopping you?

impeler *vt* to drive forward, propel.

impenetrable *adj* impenetrable.

impensable *adj* unthinkable.

imperar *vi* to rule, prevail.

imperativo,-a *adj* imperative.
▶ *nm* **imperativo** LING imperative.

imperceptible *adj* imperceptible.

imperdible *nm* safety pin.

imperdonable *adj* unforgivable.

imperfección *nf* **1** imperfection. **2** *(defecto)* defect, fault.

imperfecto,-a *adj* **1** imperfect. **2** LING imperfect.
▶ *nm* **imperfecto** imperfect.

imperialismo *nm* imperialism.

imperio *nm* empire.

imperioso,-a *adj* **1** *(autoritario)* imperious. **2** *(necesario)* urgent, pressing.

impermeabilizar *vt* to waterproof.

impermeable *adj* waterproof.
▶ *nm* raincoat.

impersonal *adj* impersonal.

impertérrito,-a *adj* imperturbable.

impertinencia *nf* **1** impertinence. **2** *(palabras)* impertinent remark.

impertinente *adj* impertinent.
▶ *nm pl* **impertinentes** lorgnette *sing*.

imperturbable *adj* imperturbable.

ímpetu *nm* **1** *(fuerza)* vigour; *(entusiasmo)* enthusiasm; *(energía)* energy. **2** *(impulso)* impetus; *(fuerza)* force.

impetuoso,-a *adj* **1** *(persona)* impetuous. **2** *(viento)* violent.

implacable *adj* implacable, relentless.

implantar *vt* **1** to introduce. **2** MED to implant.

implante *nm* implant.

implicar *vt* **1** *(conllevar)* to imply. **2** *(involucrar)* to involve (en, in).

implícito,-a *adj* implicit.

implorar *vt* to implore, entreat, beg.

impoluto,-a *adj* spotless.

imponderable *adj* *(factor)* imponderable; *(valor)* incalculable.

imponente *adj* impressive.

imponer *vt* **1** *(ley, límite, sanción)* to impose. **2** *(respeto)* to inspire.
▶ *vi* *(asustar)* to be frightening.
▶ *vpr* **imponerse 1** to impose one's authority (a, on). **2** *(obligarse)* to force os to. **3** *(prevalecer)* to prevail.

impopular *adj* unpopular.

importación *nf* **1** *(acción)* importation, import. **2** *(productos)* imports *pl*.

importancia *nf* importance.

importante *adj* **1** *(gen)* important; *(por su gravedad)* serious; *(por su cantidad)* considerable.

importar *vt* **1** COM *(traer de fuera)* to import. **2** *(valer)* to amount to.
▶ *vi* **1** *(tener importancia)* to matter. **2** *(molestar)* to mind.

importe *nm* *(gen)* price, cost.

importunar *vt* *(molestar)* to pester.

imposible *adj* impossible.

imposición *nf* *(gen)* imposition.

impostor,-ra *nm & nf* **1** *(farsante)* impostor. **2** *(difamador)* slanderer.

impotencia *nf* impotence.

impotente *adj* impotent.

impreciso,-a *adj* imprecise, vague.

impredecible *adj* *(persona)* unpredictable; *(circunstancia)* unforeseeable.

imprenta *nf* **1** *(arte)* printing. **2** *(taller)* printer's, printing house.

imprescindible *adj* essential, indispensable.

impresión *nf* **1** *(en imprenta)* printing. **2** *(huella)* impression, imprint. **3** *fig* *(efecto)* impression; *(negativo)* shock.

impresionable *adj* impressionable.

impresionante *adj* **1** *(admirable)* impressive. **2** *fam* *(gen)* incredible; *(enorme)* tremendous.

impresionar *vt* **1** *(causar admiración)* to impress: *me impresionó el paisaje* the scenery impressed me. **2** *(afectar)* to affect; *(inquietar)* to disturb.

impresionismo *nm* impressionism.

impresionista *adj* impressionist.
▶ *nm o nf* impressionist.

impreso,-a *adj* printed.
▶ *nm* **impreso** *(formulario)* form.

impresor,-ra *nm & nf* *(persona)* printer.

impresora *nf* *(máquina)* printer.

imprevisible *adj* *(hecho)* unforeseeable; *(persona)* unpredictable.

imprevisto,-a *adj* unexpected.

▶ *nm pl* **imprevistos** *(gastos)* incidental expenses.

imprimir *vt* **1** *(gen)* to print. **2** *(dejar huella)* to stamp. **3** *fig (grabar)* to fix.

improbable *adj* improbable, unlikely.

improductivo,-a *adj* unproductive.

improperio *nm* insult.

impropio,-a *adj (inadecuado)* unsuitable, inappropriate. LOC **ser impropio,-a de** ALGN not to be worthy of SB.

improvisado,-a *adj (gen)* improvised.

improvisar *vt* to improvise.
▶ *vi* to improvise.

improviso LOC **de improviso** suddenly, unexpectedly.

imprudencia *nf* **1** *(falta de prudencia)* carelessness. **2** *(acción imprudente)* rash move; *(indiscreción)* indiscretion.

imprudente *adj* careless.
▶ *nm o nf (imprudente)* careless person; *(indiscreto)* indiscreet person.

impúdico,-a *adj (indecente)* immodest, indecent.

impuesto,-a *nm* **impuesto** tax, duty.

impugnar *vt* **1** *(resultado)* to contest. **2** *(teoría)* to refute.

impulsar *vt* **1** to impel. **2** TÉC to drive forward. **3** *(incitar)* to drive.

impulsivo,-a *adj* impulsive.
▶ *nm & nf* impulsive person.

impulso *nm* **1** impulse. **2** *(fuerza, velocidad)* momentum.

impune *adj* unpunished.

impunidad *nf* impunity.

impureza *nf* impurity.

impuro,-a *adj* impure.

imputación *nf* accusation.

imputar *vt* to impute.

inabarcable *adj* huge, vast.

inaccesible *adj* inaccessible.

inaceptable *adj* unacceptable.

inadaptado,-a *adj* maladjusted.
▶ *nm & nf* misfit.

inadvertido,-a *adj* unnoticed.

inagotable *adj* inexhaustible.

inaguantable *adj* unbearable.

inalámbrico,-a *adj* cordless.

inanición *nf* starvation.

inanimado,-a *adj* inanimate, lifeless.

inapreciable *adj* **1** *(insignificante)* imperceptible. **2** *(valioso)* invaluable.

inaudible *adj* inaudible.

inaudito,-a *adj (nunca oído)* unheard-of.

inauguración *nf* opening, inauguration.

inaugurar *vt* to inaugurate, open.

inca *adj* Inca.
▶ *nm o nf* Inca.

incalculable *adj* incalculable.

incalificable *adj (intolerable)* unspeakable.

incandescente *adj* incandescent.

incansable *adj* tireless.

incapacidad *nf* **1** *(gen)* incapacity, inability. **2** *(insuficiencia)* disability.

incapacitado,-a *adj (físicamente)* disabled; *(mentalmente)* incapacitated, unfit.

incapacitar *vt* **1** *(impedir)* to incapacitate.

incapaz *adj* **1** incapable (de, of). **2** *(incompetente)* incompetent.

incauto,-a *adj (crédulo)* gullible.
▶ *nm & nf* gullible person.

incendiar *vt* to set on fire, set fire to.
▶ *vpr* **incendiarse** to catch fire.

incendiario,-a *adj* incendiary.
▶ *nm & nf* arsonist.

incendio *nm* fire.

incentivo *nm* incentive.

incertidumbre *nf* uncertainty.

incesto *nm* incest.

incestuoso,-a *adj* incestuous.

incidente *nm* incident, event.

incidir *vi* **incidir en 1** *(repercutir en)* to have an effect on, affect. **2** *(incurrir en)* to fall into. **3** *(tratar)* to touch upon; *(insistir en)* to stress.

incienso *nm* incense.

incierto,-a *adj* uncertain, doubtful.

incinerar *vt (basura)* to incinerate; *(cadáveres)* to cremate.

incipiente *adj* incipient.

incisión *nf* incision.

inciso,-a *nm* passing remark.

incitante *adj* **1** *(estimulante)* inciting. **2** *(provocativo)* provocative.

incitar *vt* to incite (a, to).

inclemencia *nf* harshness.

inclinación *nf* **1** *(desviación)* slant. **2** *(tendencia)* leaning. **3** *(afición)* penchant.

inclinar *vt* **1** *(ladear)* to tilt. **2** *fig (persuadir)* to dispose, move.
▶ *vpr* **inclinarse 1** *(doblarse)* to bend, lean; *(como saludo)* to bow. **2** **inclinarse a** *fig (propender a)* to incline to. **3** **inclinarse por** *(escoger)* to choose, opt for.

incluir *vt* **1** to include. **2** *(adjuntar - en carta, etc)* to enclose.

incluso *adv* even.
▶ *prep* even.

incógnita *nf fig (misterio)* mystery.

incógnito,-a *adj* unknown.

incoherencia *nf (falta de coherencia)* incoherence.

incoherente *adj* incoherent.

incomodar *vt* **1** *(causar molestia)* to inconvenience. **2** *(fastidiar)* to annoy, bother. **3** *(enojar)* to anger.
▶ *vpr* **incomodarse** *(enfadarse)* to get annoyed, get angry.

incómodo,-a *adj* uncomfortable. [LOC] **sentirse incómodo,-a** to feel awkward.

incomparable *adj* incomparable.

incompetencia *nf* incompetence.

incompetente *adj* incompetent.

incompleto,-a *adj* **1** incomplete. **2** *(inacabado)* unfinished.

incomprensión *nf* lack of understanding.

incomunicado,-a *adj* **1** *(por la nieve)* cut off. **2** *(preso)* in solitary confinement.

inconcebible *adj* inconceivable.

incondicional *adj (rendición)* unconditional.
▶ *nm o nf* staunch supporter.

inconexo,-a *adj* disconnected.

inconformista *adj* nonconformist.
▶ *nm o nf* nonconformist.

inconfundible *adj* unmistakable.

incongruencia *nf* incongruity.

inconsciencia *nf* **1** MED unconsciousness. **2** *(irreflexión)* thoughtlessness.

inconsciente *adj* **1** MED unconscious. **2** *(irreflexivo)* thoughtless.

inconstante *adj (variable)* inconstant, changeable.

incontable *adj* countless.

incontinencia *nf* incontinence.

incontrolable *adj* uncontrollable.

inconveniente *adj* inappropriate.
▶ *nm (desventaja)* drawback.

incordiar *vt* to pester, bother.

incorporación *nf (llegada)* arrival; *(inclusión)* inclusion; *(unión)* joining.

incorporar *vt* **1** *(añadir)* to incorporate, include. **2** CULIN *(añadir)* to add.
▶ *vpr* **incorporarse 1** *(levantarse)* to sit up. **2** *(a un trabajo)* to start; *(a una empresa, equipo, etc)* to join.

incorrección *nf* **1** *(falta de corrección)* incorrectness. **2** *(error)* mistake.

incorrecto,-a *adj* **1** *(inexacto)* incorrect. **2** *(descortés)* impolite.

incorregible *adj* incorrigible.

incrédulo,-a *adj* incredulous.

increíble *adj* incredible.

incrementar *vt* to increase.

incremento *nm* increase, rise.

increpar *vt (insultar)* to abuse.

incriminar *vt* to incriminate.

incrustar *vt* **1** to incrust, encrust. **2** *(arte)* to inlay.

incubar *vt* to incubate.

inculcar *vt* to inculcate, instil: *les inculcaron la necesidad de tener estudios* they instilled in them the need to study.

inculpar *vt* to accuse (de, of).

inculto,-a *adj (persona)* uneducated.
▶ *nm & nf (persona)* ignoramus.

incumbir *vi* to be incumbent (a, upon).

incumplir *vt (promesa)* to break; *(deber)* to fail to fulfil; *(contrato)* to break; *(orden)* to disobey, fail to comply with.

incurable *adj* incurable.

incurrir *vi* **incurrir en** *(error)* to fall into; *(delito)* to commit.

indagar *vt* to investigate, inquire into.

indecencia *nf* **1** indecency. **2** *(acción indecente)* scandal, outrage.

indecente *adj* **1** *(impúdico)* indecent. **2** *(indigno)* miserable.

indecible *adj* indescribable.

indecisión *nf* indecision.

indeciso,-a *adj* **1** *(persona)* indecisive, undecided. **2** *(asunto no resuelto)* undecided.

indecoroso,-a *adj* indecorous.

indefenso,-a *adj* defenceless.

indefinido,-a *adj* **1** *(período de tiempo)* indefinite; *(contrato)* open-ended. **2** *(impreciso)* indefinite. **3** LING indefinite.

indemne *adj* unharmed, unhurt.

indemnización *nf* compensation, indemnity.

indemnizar *vt* to compensate (de/por, for), indemnify (de/por, for).

independencia *nf* independence.

independiente *adj* **1** independent. **2** *(individualista)* self-sufficient.

independizar *vt* to make independent.
 ▶ *vpr* **independizarse** to become independent (de, of).

indeterminado,-a *adj* **1** *(gen)* indeterminate; *(en tiempo, número)* indefinite. **2** *(impreciso)* vague.

India *nf* India.

indicación *nf* **1** *(gesto, señal)* sign. **2** *(instrucción)* instruction.

indicado,-a *adj* appropriate, suitable.

indicador,-ra *adj (gen)* indicating.
 ▶ *nm (gen)* indicator; *(con aguja, escala)* gauge.

indicar *vt* to indicate, point out.

indicativo,-a *adj* indicative.
 ▶ *nm* **indicativo** LING indicative.

índice *nm* **1** *(gen)* index. **2** *(de un libro)* index, table of contents; *(catálogo)* catalogue. **3** *(dedo)* index finger.

indicio *nm* **1** *(señal)* sign. **2** *(resto)* trace.

indiferencia *nf* indifference.

indiferente *adj* indifferent.

indigente *nm o nf* poor person: *los indigentes* the needy.

indigestión *nf* indigestion.

indigesto,-a *adj (alimento)* indigestible.

indignación *nf* indignation.

indignar *vt* to infuriate.
 ▶ *vpr* **indignarse** to become indignant (por, at/about).

indigno,-a *adj* **1** unworthy (de, of). **2** *(vil)* low, contemptible.

indio,-a *adj* Indian.
 ▶ *nm & nf* Indian. LOC **hacer el indio** *fam* to play the fool.

indirecto,-a *adj* indirect.

indiscreción *nf* indiscretion.

indiscreto,-a *adj* indiscreet.
 ▶ *nm & nf* indiscreet person.

indispensable *adj* essential.

indisponer *vt* MED to upset, make unwell.
 ▶ *vpr* **indisponerse** *(enfermarse)* to be unwell.

indispuesto,-a *adj* MED indisposed, unwell.

individual *adj* individual.
 ▶ *nm pl* **individuales** DEP singles.

individualista *adj* individualistic.
 ▶ *nm o nf* individualist.

individuo,-a *nm & nf pey (gen)* character, individual.
 ▶ *nm* **individuo** person.

indocumentado,-a *adj (sin documentación)* without means of identification.

índole *nf* **1** *(carácter)* disposition, nature. **2** *(tipo)* type, kind.

indolente *adj* indolent.

indoloro,-a *adj* painless.

indómito,-a *adj* indomitable.

Indonesia *nf* Indonesia.

indonesio,-a *adj* Indonesian.
 ▶ *nm & nf* Indonesian.

inducir *vt* **1** to induce. **2** ELEC to induce.

indulgencia *nf* indulgence, leniency.

indultar *vt* JUR to pardon.

indulto *nm* pardon, amnesty.

indumentaria *nf* clothing, clothes *pl*.

industria *nf* **1** *(gen)* industry. **2** *(fábrica)* factory.

industrial *adj* industrial.
 ▶ *nm o nf* industrialist, manufacturer.

industrializar *vt* to industrialize.

inédito,-a *adj (libro)* unpublished.

inepto,-a *adj (persona)* incompetent.
 ▶ *nm & nf* incompetent person.

inercia *nf* inertia.

inerte *adj* **1** *(materia, gas)* inert. **2** *(cadáver)* lifeless.

inesperado,-a *adj* unexpected.

inestable *adj* unstable, unsteady.

inevitable *adj* inevitable.

inexistente *adj* nonexistent.

inexorable *adj* inexorable.

inexperto,-a *adj* inexperienced.

inexplicable *adj* inexplicable.

inexpresivo,-a *adj* expressionless.

infalible *adj* infallible.

infame *adj* *(vil)* despicable, vile.

infamia *nf* disgrace.

infancia *nf* **1** *(gen)* childhood. **2** *(los niños)* children *pl*.

infante *nm* **1** *lit (niño)* infant. **2** *(soldado)* infantryman.

infantería *nf* infantry.

infantil *adj* **1** *(literatura, juego)* children's; *(equipo)* junior. **2** *(inmaduro)* childish.

infarto *nm (de miocardio)* heart attack. COMP **infarto de miocardio** heart attack.

infatigable *adj* indefatigable, tireless.

infección *nf* infection.

infectar *vt* to infect (de, with).
▶ *vpr* **infectarse** to become infected (de, with).

infeliz *adj* **1** *(desdichado)* unhappy. **2** *(ingenuo)* ingenuous.

inferior *adj* **1** *(situado debajo)* lower. **2** *(cantidad)* less, lower. **3** *(en calidad)* inferior (a, to).
▶ *nm o nf (en rango)* subordinate; *(en calidad)* inferior.

inferioridad *nf* inferiority.

infernal *adj* infernal.

infidelidad *nf* **1** *(sexual)* infidelity, unfaithfulness. **2** *(de un amigo)* disloyalty.

infiel *adj (esposo)* unfaithful (a/con/para, to); *(amigo)* disloyal (a, to).

infiernillo *nm* portable stove.

infierno *nm* hell. LOC **¡vete al infierno!** go to hell!, get lost!

infiltrar *vt* to infiltrate.
▶ *vpr* **infiltrarse** to infiltrate (en, -).

ínfimo,-a *adj (en calidad)* lowest, poorest; *(precio)* ridiculous.

infinidad *nf* **1** *(infinito)* infinity. **2** *(gran cantidad)* infinite number.

infinitivo *nm* infinitive.

infinito,-a *adj* infinite.
▶ *nm* **el infinito** the infinite, infinity.

inflamable *adj* inflammable.

inflamación *nf* MED inflammation.

inflamar *vt* MED to inflame.
▶ *vpr* **inflamarse** MED to become inflamed.

inflar *vt* **1** *(balón)* to blow up, inflate. **2** *fig (hechos, noticias)* to exaggerate. **3** *(precios)* to inflate.
▶ *vpr* **inflarse 1** to inflate one's opinion of os. **2** *fam (hartarse de comer)* to stuff os (de, with).

inflexible *adj* inflexible.

influencia *nf* influence.

influir *vt* to influence.
▶ *vi* to have influence.

influyente *adj* influential.

información *nf* **1** *(conocimiento)* information. **2** *(noticia)* piece of news; *(conjunto de noticias)* news. **3** *(en telefónica)* directory enquiries *pl*.

informal *adj* **1** *(desenfadado)* informal. **2** *(persona)* unreliable.

informar *vt (dar noticia)* to inform (de, about).
▶ *vi* to inform (de, about), tell (de, about).
▶ *vpr* **informarse** to find out (de, about).

informática *nf* computing.

informático,-a *adj* computer.
▶ *nm & nf* computer expert.

informativo,-a *adj (ilustrativo)* informative: *una campaña con carácter informativo* a public awareness campaign.
▶ *nm* **informativo** news programme.

informatizar *vt* to computerize.

informe *nm* report.
▶ *nm pl* **informes** references.

infracción *nf* infringement.

infractor,-ra *adj* offending.
▶ *nm & nf* offender.

infraestructura *nf* infrastructure.

infranqueable *adj* **1** impassable. **2** *fig* insurmountable.

infrarrojo,-a *adj* infrared.

infravalorar *vt* to underestimate.

infrecuente *adj* infrequent.

infringir *vt* (gen) to infringe; (ley) to break.

infructuoso,-a *adj* fruitless, unsuccessful.

infundado,-a *adj* unfounded.

infundir *vt* (respeto) to command; (miedo) to fill with; (valor) to instil.

infusión *nf* infusion.

ingeniar *vt* to devise.
▶ *vpr* **ingeniárselas** to manage, find a way, contrive.

ingeniería *nf* engineering.

ingeniero,-a *nm & nf* engineer.

ingenio *nm* **1** (talento) talent; (chispa) wit. **2** (habilidad) ingenuity.

ingenioso,-a *adj* (inteligente) ingenious, clever; (con chispa) witty.

ingenuo,-a *adj* naive, ingenuous.
▶ *nm & nf* naive person.

ingerir *vt* (alimentos) to eat; (bebida) to drink.

Inglaterra *nf* England.

ingle *nf* groin.

inglés,-esa *adj* English.
▶ *nm & nf* (persona) English person; (hombre) Englishman; (mujer) Englishwoman.
▶ *nm* **inglés** (idioma) English.

ingratitud *nf* ingratitude, ungratefulness.

ingrato,-a *adj* **1** (persona) ungrateful. **2** (trabajo, tarea) thankless.

ingrediente *nm* ingredient.

ingresar *vt* (dinero) to pay in, deposit.
▶ *vi* **ingresar en 1** (entrar) to join. **2** (hospital) to be admitted to.

ingreso *nm* **1** (en club, ejército) joining; (en hospital) admission; (en universidad) entrance. **2** (entrada) entry.
▶ *nm pl* **ingresos** (sueldo, renta) income *sing*; (beneficios) revenue *sing*.

inhabitable *adj* uninhabitable.

inhalar *vt* to inhale, breathe in.

inherente *adj* inherent (a, in).

inhibir *vt* (reprimir) to inhibit.

▶ *vpr* **inhibirse 1** (reprimirse) to be inhibited. **2** (abstenerse) to refrain (de, from); (negarse) to refuse (de, to).

inhóspito,-a *adj* inhospitable.

inhumano,-a *adj* **1** (persona) inhuman, cruel. **2** (dolor, sufrimiento) inhuman.

iniciación *nf* **1** (comienzo) start, beginning. **2** (de una persona) initiation.

inicial *adj* initial.
▶ *nf* initial.

iniciar *vt* **1** (empezar) to start, begin. **2** (introducir) to initiate (en, in).
▶ *vpr* **iniciarse** (empezar) to start, begin.

iniciativa *nf* initiative.

inicio *nm* beginning, start.

inimitable *adj* inimitable.

injertar *vt* to graft.

injerto *nm* graft.

injuria *nf* insult, affront.

injuriar *vt* (insultar) to insult.

injusticia *nf* injustice, unfairness.

injusto,-a *adj* unfair, unjust.

inmadurez *nf* immaturity.

inmaduro,-a *adj* immature.

inmediaciones *nf pl* (de una zona) surrounding area *sing*; (de una casa) vicinity *sing*.

inmediato,-a *adj* **1** (poco después) immediate. **2** (contiguo) next (a, to), adjoining (a, -).

inmejorable *adj* (gen) unbeatable.

inmensidad *nf* **1** immensity. **2** (gran cantidad) great number.

inmenso,-a *adj* immense, vast.

inmersión *nf* (gen) immersion; (de un buceador, submarino) dive.

inmerso,-a *adj* immersed (en, in).

inmigración *nf* immigration.

inmigrante *adj* immigrant.
▶ *nm o nf* immigrant.

inmigrar *vi* to immigrate.

inminente *adj* imminent.

inmobiliario,-a *adj* property, US real estate.
▶ *nf* **(agencia) inmobiliaria** estate agency, US real estate company.

inmolar *vt* to immolate, sacrifice.

inmoral *adj* immoral.

inmoralidad *nf* immorality.

inmortal *adj* immortal.

inmortalidad *nf* immortality.

inmortalizar *vt* to immortalize.

inmóvil *adj* still, motionless.

inmovilizar *vt* to immobilize.

inmueble *nm* building.

inmundo,-a *adj (sucio)* dirty, filthy.

inmune *adj* MED immune (a, to).

inmunidad *nf* immunity.

inmutar *vt* to affect.
  ▸ *vpr* **inmutarse** to react.

innato,-a *adj* innate, inborn.

innecesario,-a *adj* unnecessary.

innegable *adj* undeniable.

innovación *nf* innovation.

innovador,-ra *adj* innovatory.
  ▸ *nm & nf* innovator.

innovar *vi* to innovate.

innumerable *adj* innumerable, countless.

inocencia *nf* innocence.

inocentada *nf* practical joke.

inocente *adj* **1** innocent. **2** *(ingenuo)* naive, innocent.
  ▸ *nm o nf* naive person, innocent person.

inocuo,-a *adj* innocuous, harmless.

inodoro,-a *adj* odourless.
  ▸ *nm* **inodoro** toilet.

inofensivo,-a *adj* harmless, inoffensive.

inolvidable *adj* unforgettable.

inoperante *adj* ineffective, inoperative.

inopia LOC **estar en la inopia 1** *fam (distraído)* to have one's head in the clouds. **2** *(ignorante)* to be in the dark.

inoportuno,-a *adj* inopportune.

inorgánico,-a *adj* inorganic.

inoxidable *adj* rustproof.

input *nm* input.

inquebrantable *adj (promesa)* unbreakable; *(fe)* unshakeable.

inquietante *adj* disturbing.

inquietar *vt* to worry.

  ▸ *vpr* **inquietarse** to worry (por, about).

inquieto,-a *adj* **1** *(agitado)* restless. **2** *(preocupado)* worried, anxious.

inquietud *nf* **1** *(agitación)* restlessness. **2** *(preocupación)* worry, anxiety.

inquilino,-a *nm & nf* tenant.

inquina *nf* animosity, antipathy. LOC **tener inquina a** ALGN to feel animosity towards SB.

insaciable *adj* insatiable.

insalubre *adj* unhealthy.

insano,-a *adj* **1** *(no sano)* unhealthy. **2** *(loco)* insane.

insatisfecho,-a *adj* dissatisfied, unsatisfied.

inscribir *vt* **1** *(grabar)* to inscribe. **2** *(apuntar)* to register; *(en un curso)* to enrol.
  ▸ *vpr* **inscribirse** *(gen)* to register; *(para un curso)* to enrol.

inscripción *nf* **1** *(grabado)* inscription. **2** *(registro)* registration; *(en un curso)* enrolment.

insecticida *adj* insecticidal.
  ▸ *nm* insecticide.

insecto *nm* insect.

inseguridad *nf* **1** *(falta de confianza)* insecurity. **2** *(duda)* uncertainty. **3** *(peligro)* lack of safety.

inseguro,-a *adj* **1** *(sin confianza)* insecure. **2** *(que duda)* uncertain. **3** *(peligroso)* unsafe.

insensato,-a *adj* foolish.
  ▸ *nm & nf* fool.

insensible *adj* **1** insensitive, unfeeling, thoughtless. **2** MED insensible.

inseparable *adj* inseparable.

insertar *vt* to insert (en, into).

inservible *adj* useless.

insigne *adj* distinguished, eminent.

insignia *nf (distintivo)* badge.

insignificante *adj* insignificant.

insinuación *nf* **1** *(indicación)* insinuation, hint. **2** *fam (amorosa)* overture. LOC **hacerle insinuaciones a** ALGN *(insinuarse)* to make a pass at SB.

insinuar *vt* to insinuate, hint.

insípido,-a *adj* insipid.

insistencia *nf* insistence.

insistente *adj* insistent.

insistir *vi* **1** to insist (en, on). **2** *(enfatizar)* to stress (en, -).

insobornable *adj* incorruptible.

insolación *nf* MED sunstroke.

insolencia *nf* **1** *(atrevimiento)* insolence. **2** *(palabra)* cheeky remark.

insolente *adj* **1** *(descarado)* insolent. **2** *(soberbio)* haughty.

insolidario,-a *adj* unsupportive.

insólito,-a *adj* extremely unusual.

insolvente *adj* insolvent.

insomne *adj* sleepless.
▶ *nm o nf* insomniac.

insomnio *nm* insomnia.

insondable *adj* unfathomable.

insonorizado,-a *adj* soundproof.

insonorizar *vt* to soundproof.

insoportable *adj* unbearable.

insospechado,-a *adj* unexpected.

insostenible *adj* untenable.

inspección *nf* *(gen)* examination, inspection; *(policial)* search.

inspeccionar *vt* *(gen)* to inspect; *(zona, lugar del crimen)* to search.

inspector,-ra *nm & nf* inspector.

inspiración *nf* **1** inspiration. **2** *(inhalación)* inhalation.

inspirado,-a *adj* inspired.

inspirar *vt* **1** *(aspirar)* to inhale, breathe in. **2** *(infundir)* to inspire.
▶ *vpr* **inspirarse** to be inspired (en, by).

instalación *nf* installation.
▶ *nf pl* **instalaciones** *(de un servicio)* facilities *pl*.

instalador,-ra *nm & nf* installer, fitter.

instalar *vt* **1** *(colocar)* to install. **2** *(equipar)* to fit out.
▶ *vpr* **instalarse** *(persona)* to settle; *(empresa)* to set up.

instancia *nf* *(petición)* request; *(solicitud)* form.

instantánea *nf* *(foto)* snapshot, snap.

instantáneo,-a *adj* **1** *(inmediato)* instantaneous, immediate. **2** *(momentáneo)* brief, fleeting.

instante *nm* moment, instant.

instar *vi* *(insistir)* to press, urge.

instauración *nf* establishment.

instaurar *vt* to establish.

instigar *vt* to instigate.

instintivo,-a *adj* instinctive.

instinto *nm* instinct.

institución *nf* **1** *(organismo)* institution. **2** *(creación)* establishment, institution; *(introducción)* introduction.

institucional *adj* institutional.

instituir *vt* **1** *(crear)* to institute, establish. **2** *(nombrar)* to appoint.

instituto *nm* **1** *(asociación)* institute. **2** EDUC state secondary school, US high school. COMP **instituto de bachillerato** state secondary school, US high school.

institutriz *nf* governess.

instrucción *nf* **1** *(enseñanza)* instruction; *(cultura)* education. **2** MIL military training.
▶ *nf pl* **instrucciones** *(indicaciones)* instructions.

instructivo,-a *adj* *(conferencia)* instructive; *(juguete)* educational.

instructor,-ra *adj* *(gen)* instructing.
▶ *nm & nf* instructor.

instruido,-a *adj* well-educated.

instruir *vt* **1** *(enseñar)* to instruct. **2** MIL to train. **3** JUR to investigate.

instrumental *adj* *(música)* instrumental.
▶ *nm* instruments *pl*.

instrumentar *vt* *(gen)* to arrange; *(para orquesta)* to orchestrate.

instrumentista *nm o nf* *(músico)* instrumentalist.

instrumento *nm* instrument.

insubordinado,-a *adj* insubordinate.
▶ *nm & nf* insubordinate person.

insubordinar *vt* to stir up.
▶ *vpr* **insubordinarse** to rebel.

insuficiente *adj* insufficient.
▶ *nm* EDUC fail.

insufrible *adj* insufferable.

insular *adj* insular.
▶ *nm o nf* islander.

insulina *nf* insulin.

insulso,-a *adj* insipid, tasteless.

insultante *adj* insulting.

insultar *vt* to insult.

insulto *nm* insult.

insumisión *nf (gen)* rebelliousness.

insumiso,-a *adj* rebellious.
▶ *nm & nf* MIL *person who refuses to do military service or community service in lieu*.

insuperable *adj (calidad, capacidad)* unbeatable; *(obstáculo, miedo, complejo)* unsurmountable, insuperable.

insurgente *adj* insurgent.

insurrección *nf* insurrection.

intachable *adj* irreproachable.

intacto,-a *adj* intact.

integración *nf* integration.

integral *adj* **1** *(completo)* full. **2** *(pan, pasta)* wholemeal; *(arroz)* brown.

integrante *adj* integral.
▶ *nm o nf* member.

integrar *vt (formar)* to make up.
▶ *vpr* **integrarse** to integrate.

integridad *nf* integrity.

integrismo *nm (gen)* reaction; *(religioso)* fundamentalism.

integrista *adj (gen)* reactionary; *(religioso)* fundamentalist.
▶ *nm o nf (gen)* reactionary; *(en religión)* fundamentalist.

íntegro,-a *adj* **1** *(completo)* whole, entire; *(versión)* unabridged. **2** *(honrado)* honest, upright.

intelecto *nm* intellect.

intelectual *adj* intellectual.
▶ *nm o nf* intellectual.

inteligencia *nf* intelligence. COMP **inteligencia artificial** artificial intelligence.

inteligente *adj* intelligent.

intemperie *nf* bad weather. LOC **a la intemperie** in the open (air).

intempestivo,-a *adj* inopportune.

intemporal *adj* timeless.

intención *nf (propósito)* intention.

intencionado,-a *adj* deliberate!.

intendencia *nf* MIL *(cuerpo)* ≈ service corps, US quartermaster corps.

intendente *nm* **1** supervisor. **2** MIL quartermaster general.

intensidad *nf* **1** *(gen)* intensity. **2** *(de una enfermedad)* severity; *(del dolor)* acuteness. **3** *(de la luz, del color)* brightness, intensity; *(del amor, de la fe)* strength.

intensificar *vt* to intensify.

intensivo,-a *adj* intensive.

intenso,-a *adj* **1** *(gen)* intense. **2** *(dolor)* acute. **3** *(luz, color)* bright, intense. **4** *(amor)* passionate.

intentar *vt* to try.

intento *nm* attempt, try.

interactivo,-a *adj* interactive.

intercalar *vt* to insert.

intercambiar *vt* to exchange.

intercambio *nm* exchange.

interceder *vi* to intercede.

interceptar *vt* **1** *(mensaje, correspondencia)* to intercept. **2** *(obstruir)* to block.

interceptor *adj* intercepting.
▶ *nm* interceptor.

intercesión *nf* intercession.

intercesor,-ra *adj* interceding.
▶ *nm & nf* intercessor.

interconexión *nf* interconnection.

interés *nm* **1** *(gen)* interest; *(propio)* self-interest. **2** FIN interest.

interesado,-a *adj* **1** *(gen)* interested. **2** *(egoísta)* selfish, self-interested.
▶ *nm & nf* **1** *(gen)* interested party. **2** *(egoísta)* selfish person.

interesante *adj* interesting.

interesar *vt* **1** to interest. **2** *(afectar)* to concern.
▶ *vpr* **interesarse** to take an interest (por, in).

interfaz *nf* interface.

interferencia *nf* **1** *(gen)* interference; *(intencionada)* jamming. **2** *fig* interference.

interferir *vt* **1** *(transmisión, programa)* to jam. **2** *(obstaculizar)* to interfere in.
▶ *vi* to meddle, interfere.

interfono *nm* intercom.

interino,-a *adj* **1** temporary, provisional. **2** *(director, presidente)* acting.
▶ *nm & nf (sustituto)* stand-in.

interior *adj* **1** *(bolsillo)* inside; *(habitación)* without a view, interior; *(jardín)* interior. **2** *(del país)* domestic, internal. **3** GEOG inland.

▶ *nm* **1** *(en una vivienda)* inside: *pasemos al interior* let's go inside. **2** *(conciencia)* inside. **3** GEOG interior.

interiorismo *nm* interior design.

interiorista *nm o nf* interior designer.

interiorizar *vt (creencia, principio)* to internalize.

interjección *nf* interjection.

interlocutor,-ra *nm & nf* speaker, interlocutor.

intermediario,-a *nm & nf (gen)* intermediary; *(en disputas)* mediator.

intermedio,-a *adj (gen)* intermediate; *(tamaño)* medium; *(calidad)* average; *(tiempo)* intervening; *(espacio)* between.
▶ *nm* **intermedio** *(de un espectáculo)* interval, intermission.

interminable *adj* endless, interminable.

intermitencia *nf* intermittence.

intermitente *adj (gen)* intermittent.
▶ *nm* AUTO indicator, US blinker.

internacional *adj* international.

internado *nm* boarding school.

internar *vt (en un colegio)* to send to boarding school; *(en un hospital)* to confine (en, to).
▶ *vpr* **internarse** *(penetrar)* to penetrate.

internauta *nm o nf* internaut, netsurfer.

interno,-a *adj* **1** *(órgano)* internal. **2** *(alumno)* boarding.
▶ *nm & nf* **1** *(alumno)* boarder. **2** *(médico)* intern. **3** *(preso)* prisoner.

interpelar *vt* POL to interpellate.

interponer *vt* to interpose.
▶ *vpr* **interponerse 1** *(físicamente)* to interpose os. **2** *fig* to intervene.

interpretación *nf* **1** *(gen)* interpretation. **2** *(de pieza, obra)* performance.

interpretar *vt* **1** to interpret. **2** *(obra, pieza)* to perform; *(papel)* to play.

intérprete *nm o nf* **1** *(traductor)* interpreter. **2** *(actor, músico)* performer.

interrelación *nf* interrelation.

interrelacionar *vt* to interrelate.

interrogación *nf* **1** *(acción)* interrogation, questioning. **2** *(signo)* question mark. **3** *(pregunta)* question.

interrogador,-a *nm & nf* interrogator.

interrogante *nm (incógnita)* question mark.

interrogar *vt* **1** to question. **2** *(a testigo, etc)* to interrogate.

interrogativo,-a *adj* interrogative.

interrogatorio *nm* interrogation.

interrumpir *vt* **1** *(gen)* to interrupt. **2** *(tráfico)* to block.

interrupción *nf* interruption.

interruptor *nm* switch.

intersección *nf* intersection.

interurbano,-a *adj (gen)* inter-city; *(llamada)* trunk, long-distance.

intervalo *nm* **1** *(de tiempo)* interval. **2** *(de espacio)* gap.

intervención *nf* **1** *(gen)* intervention. **2** *(discurso)* speech. **3** MED operation.

intervenir *vi* **1** *(tomar parte)* to take part (en, in). **2** *(hablar)* to speak (en, at).
▶ *vt* **1** MED to operate on. **2** *(alijo, mercancía)* to seize.

interventor,-ra *nm & nf (gen)* inspector, auditor.

intestinal *adj* intestinal.

intestino *nm* intestine.

intimar *vi* to become close (con, to).

intimidación *nf* intimidation.

intimidad *nf* **1** *(amistad)* intimacy. **2** *(vida privada)* privacy, private life.

intimidar *vt* to intimidate.

íntimo,-a *adj* **1** *(vida)* private. **2** *(amigo, relación)* close. **3** *(sentimiento, emoción)* most intimate. **4** *(higiene)* personal.
▶ *nm & nf (amigo)* close friend.

intocable *adj* untouchable.

intolerable *adj* intolerable.

intolerancia *nf* intolerance: *intolerancia a la lactosa* intolerance of lactose.

intolerante *adj* intolerant.

intoxicación *nf* poisoning.

intoxicar *vt* to poison.
▶ *vpr* **intoxicarse** to poison os.

intraducible *adj* untranslatable.

intranquilidad *nf* worry, uneasiness.

intranquilizar *vt* to worry.
▶ *vpr* **intranquilizarse** to get worried.
intranquilo,-a *adj* worried, uneasy.
intransferible *adj* nontransferable.
intransigencia *nf* intransigence.
intransigente *adj* intransigent.
intransitable *adj* impassable.
intransitivo,-a *adj* intransitive.
intrascendente *adj* unimportant, in-significant.
intratable *adj (persona)* unsociable.
intrépido,-a *adj* intrepid.
intriga *nf (maquinación secreta)* intrigue. **2** *(curiosidad)* curiosity. **3** *(de una narración, película)* intrigue.
intrigado,-a *adj* intrigued.
intrigante *adj* intriguing.
intrigar *vt (interesar)* to intrigue.
intrínseco,-a *adj* intrinsic.
introducción *nf* introduction.
introducir *vt* **1** *(gen)* to introduce; *(legislación)* to introduce, bring in. **2** *(meter)* to put, place; *(insertar)* insert. **3** *(importar)* to bring in, import.
▶ *vpr* **introducirse** *(entrar)* to get in.
intromisión *nf* interference, meddling.
introspectivo,-a *adj* introspective.
introvertido,-a *adj* introverted.
▶ *nm & nf* introvert.
intruso,-a *adj* intrusive.
▶ *nm & nf* intruder.
intuición *nf* intuition.
intuir *vt* to sense, feel.
intuitivo,-a *adj* intuitive.
inundación *nf* flood, flooding.
inundar *vt* **1** to flood. **2** *fig* to inundate.
inusitado,-a *adj* uncommon, rare.
inusual *adj* unusual.
inútil *adj* **1** *(gen)* useless. **2** *(intento)* vain.
▶ *nm o nf fam (persona)* hopeless case.
inutilizar *vt* **1** to render useless. **2** *(máquina)* to put out of action.
invadir *vt* to invade.
inválido,-a *adj* disabled, handicapped.
▶ *nm & nf* disabled person.
invariable *adj* invariable.
invasión *nf* invasion.

invasor,-ra *adj* invading.
▶ *nm & nf* invader.
invencible *adj (ejército)* invincible; *(obstáculo)* unsurmountable.
invención *nf* invention.
invendible *adj* unsaleable.
inventar *vt* **1** *(crear)* to invent. **2** *(mentir)* to make up, fabricate.
inventario *nm* inventory.
inventiva *nf* inventiveness.
invento *nm* invention.
inventor,-ra *nm & nf* inventor.
invernadero *nm* greenhouse.
invernal *adj* winter, wintry.
invernar *vi (animales)* to hibernate.
inverosímil *adj* unlikely.
inversión *nf* **1** *(gen)* inversion. **2** FIN investment.
inverso,-a *adj* inverse, opposite.
invertebrado,-a *adj* invertebrate.
▶ *nm* **invertebrado** invertebrate.
invertido,-a *adj* reversed, inverted.
invertir *vt* **1** *(orden)* to invert, reverse. **2** *(dirección)* to reverse. **3** *(tiempo)* to spend (en, on). **4** FIN to invest (en, in).
investidura *nf* investiture.
investigación *nf* **1** *(indagación)* investigation, enquiry. **2** *(estudio)* research.
investigador,-ra *adj* **1** *(que indaga)* investigating. **2** *(que estudia)* research.
▶ *nm & nf* **1** *(científico)* researcher. **2** *(detective)* investigator.
investigar *vt* **1** *(indagar)* to investigate. **2** *(campo)* to do research on.
investir *vt* to invest.
inviable *adj* non-viable, unfeasible.
invidente *adj* blind.
▶ *nm o nf* blind person.
invierno *nm* winter.
invisible *adj* invisible.
invitación *nf* invitation.
invitado,-a *adj* invited.
▶ *nm & nf* guest.
invitar *vt* to invite.
▶ *vi (incitar)* to encourage.
invocar *vt* to invoke.
involucrar *vt* to involve (en, in).

involuntario,-a *adj (reflejo, movimiento)* involuntary; *(error)* unintentional.

invulnerable *adj* invulnerable.

inyección *nf* injection.

inyectable *adj* injectable.
▶ *nm* injection.

inyectar *vt* to inject (en, into).

iodo *nm* iodine.

ir *vi* **1** *(gen)* to go; *(acudir)* to come. **2** *(camino, etc)* to lead. **3** *(funcionar)* to work, go. **4** *(sentar bien)* to suit; *(agradar)* to like. **5** *(tratar)* to be about.
▶ *aux* ir + a + **1** going to: *voy a venderlo* I'm going to sell it. **2** ir + : *fuimos andando* we walked, we went on foot. **3** ir + to be: *ir cansado,-a* to be tired.
▶ *vpr* **irse 1** *(marcharse)* to go away, leave. **2** *(deslizarse)* to slip. **3** *(gastarse)* to go, disappear.

ira *nf* wrath, rage.

iracundo,-a *adj* irritable, irate.

Irak *nm* Iraq.

Irán *nm* Iran.

iraní *adj* Iranian.
▶ *nm o nf* Iranian.

iranio,-a *adj* Iranian.
▶ *nm & nf (persona)* Iranian.
▶ *nm* iranio *(idioma)* Iranian.

iraquí *adj* Iraqi.
▶ *nm o nf (persona)* Iraqi.
▶ *nm (idioma)* Iraqi.

irascible *adj* irascible, irritable.

iris *nm inv* iris.

Irlanda *nf* Ireland. COMP **Irlanda del Norte** Northern Ireland.

irlandés,-esa *adj* Irish.
▶ *nm & nf (persona - hombre)* Irishman; *(- mujer)* Irish woman.
▶ *nm* irlandés *(idioma)* Irish.

ironía *nf* irony.

irónico,-a *adj* **1** ironic. **2** *(burlón)* mocking.

irracional *adj* irrational.

irradiar *vt* to irradiate, radiate.

irreal *adj* unreal.

irreconocible *adj* unrecognizable.

irreflexivo,-a *adj (acto)* rash; *(persona)* impetuous.

irregular *adj* irregular.

irregularidad *nf* irregularity.

irrelevante *adj* irrelevant.

irremediable *adj (daño)* irremediable.

irrepetible *adj* unrepeatable.

irreprochable *adj* irreproachable.

irresistible *adj* **1** irresistible. **2** *pey (insoportable)* unbearable.

irrespetuoso,-a *adj* disrespectful.

irresponsable *adj* irresponsible.
▶ *nm o nf* irresponsible person.

irreversible *adj* irreversible.

irrigar *vt* to irrigate.

irrisorio,-a *adj* derisory, ridiculous.

irritable *adj* irritable.

irritación *nf* irritation.

irritante *adj* irritating, annoying.

irritar *vt* to irritate.
▶ *vpr* **irritarse** to get annoyed.

irrumpir *vi* to burst (en, into).

irrupción *nf* irruption.

isla *nf* island.

islam *nm* Islam.

islámico,-a *adj* Islamic.

islandés,-esa *adj* Icelandic.
▶ *nm & nf (persona)* Icelander.
▶ *nm* islandés *(idioma)* Icelandic.

Islandia *nf* Iceland.

isleño,-a *adj* island.
▶ *nm & nf* islander.

islote *nm* small unhinhabited island.

isósceles *adj* isosceles.

Israel *nm* Israel.

israelí *adj* Israeli.
▶ *nm o nf* Israeli.

istmo *nm* isthmus.

Italia *nf* Italy.

italiano,-a *adj* Italian.
▶ *nm & nf (persona)* Italian.
▶ *nm* italiano *(idioma)* Italian.

itinerante *adj* itinerant.

itinerario *nm* itinerary.

izar *vt* to hoist.

izquierda *nf* **1** *(mano)* left hand; *(pierna)* left leg. **2** POL the left.

izquierdista *adj* left-wing.

izquierdo,-a *adj* left.

J

J, j *nf (la letra)* J, j.

jabalí *nm* wild boar.

jabalina *nf* DEP javelin.

jabato *nm* ZOOL young wild boar.

jabón *nm* soap. COMP **jabón de tocador** toilet soap.

jabonera *nf* soap dish.

jabonoso,-a *adj* soapy.

jaca *nf* cob, small horse.

jacinto *nm* hyacinth.

jactarse *vpr* to boast, brag (de, about).

jacuzzi® *nm* jacuzzi®.

jade *nm* jade.

jadear *vi* to pant.

jadeo *nm* panting.

jaguar *nm* jaguar.

jalea *nf* jelly. COMP **jalea real** royal jelly.

jalear *vt* **1** *(animar)* to cheer (on), clap and shout at. **2** *(caza)* to urge on.

jaleo *nm* **1** *(alboroto)* din, racket: *no se oye nada con este jaleo* I can't hear a thing with all this racket. **2** *(escándalo)* fuss, commotion.

jalón *nm* **1** *(estaca)* stake, post. **2** *fig* milestone, landmark.

jalonar *vt (con estacas)* to stake out.

Jamaica *nf* Jamaica.

jamaicano,-a *adj* Jamaican.
  ▶ *nm & nf* Jamaican.

jamás *adv (+ indic)* never; *(+ subj)* ever: *jamás volveré* I shall never return. LOC **jamás de los jamases** never ever. ‖ **por siempre jamás** for ever (and ever).

jamba *nf* jamb.

jamón *nm (curado)* cured ham; *(pata del cerdo)* leg of ham. COMP **jamón de York/ jamón en dulce** boiled ham. ‖ **jamón serrano** cured ham.

Japón *nm* Japan.

japonés,-esa *adj* Japanese.
  ▶ *nm & nf (persona)* Japanese.
  ▶ *nm* **japonés** *(idioma)* Japanese.

jaque *nm* check. COMP **jaque mate** checkmate.

jaqueca *nf* migraine, headache.

jarabe *nm* MED syrup, mixture. COMP **jarabe para la tos** cough syrup.

jardín *nm* garden. COMP **jardín botánico** botanical garden. ‖ **jardín de infancia** nursery school.

jardinera *nf* **1** *(mujer)* gardener. **2** *(mueble para tiestos)* plant stand; *(en ventana)* window box.

jardinería *nf* gardening.

jardinero,-a *nm & nf* gardener.

jarra *nf* **1** *(para servir)* jug, US pitcher. **2** *(para beber)* tankard, beer mug.

jarro *nm* **1** *(recipiente)* jug. **2** *(contenido)* jugful.

jarrón *nm* **1** vase. **2** ARTE urn.

jaspeado,-a *adj* mottled, speckled.

jaula *nf* cage.

jauría *nf* pack of hounds.

Java *nf* Java.

javanés,-esa *adj* Javanese.
  ▶ *nm & nf* Javanese.

jazmín *nm* jasmine.

jazz *nm* jazz.

jeep® *nm* jeep.

jefatura *nf (sede)* central office; *(militar)* headquarters.

jefe,-a *nm & nf* **1** boss, head, chief. **2** COM *(hombre)* manager; *(mujer)* manageress. **3** POL leader. **4** *(de una tribu)* chief. COMP **jefe de cocina** chef. ‖ **jefe de estación** station master. ‖ **jefe de Estado** Head of State.

jengibre *nm* ginger.

jeque *nm* sheik, sheikh.

jerarquía *nf* **1** hierarchy. **2** *(grado)* scale. **3** *(categoría)* rank.

jerárquico,-a *adj* hierarchical.

jerez *nm* sherry.

jerga *nf (lenguaje)* jargon.

jergón *nm (colchón)* pallet.

jeringuilla *nf* syringe.

jeroglífico,-a *adj* hieroglyphic.
▶ *nm* **jeroglífico 1** hieroglyph, hieroglyphic. **2** *(juego)* rebus.

jersey *nm* sweater, pullover, jumper.

jesuita *nm o nf* Jesuit.

jet *nm* jet.

jilguero *nm* goldfinch.

jinete *nm* rider, horseman.

jirafa *nf* giraffe.

jirón *nm* shred: *una camisa hecha jirones* a tattered shirt.

jocoso,-a *adj (persona)* jocular; *(tono)* humorous, jokey.

jofaina *nf* washbasin.

jogging *nm* jogging: *practican el jogging* they go jogging.

jolgorio *nm* **1** *(juerga)* binge. **2** *(algazara)* party.

Jordania *nf* Jordan.

jordano,-a *adj* Jordanian.
▶ *nm & nf* Jordanian.

jornada *nf* **1** *(día de trabajo)* working day: *una jornada de ocho horas* an eight-hour day. **2** *(camino recorrido)* day's journey. **3** *(en periodismo)* day: *las noticias de la jornada* today's news. COMP **media jornada** half-day.

jornal *nm* day's wage.

jornalero,-a *nm & nf* day labourer.

joroba *nf (deformidad)* hump.

jorobado,-a *adj* hunchbacked.
▶ *nm & nf* hunchback.

jorobar *vt* **1** *fam (fastidiar)* to bother, annoy. **2** *fam (romper)* to smash up, break. **3** *fam (estropear)* to ruin, wreck.

jota *nf popular Spanish dance and music.*

joven *adj* young.
▶ *nm o nf (hombre)* youth, young man; *(mujer)* young lady, girl.

jovial *adj* jovial, cheerful.

jovialidad *nf* joviality, cheerfulness.

joya *nf* jewel, piece of jewellery.

joyería *nf (tienda)* jewellery shop, jeweller's shop.

joyero,-a *nm & nf* jeweller.
▶ *nm* **joyero** jewellery case.

juanete *nm (en el pie)* bunion.

jubilación *nf* **1** *(acción)* retirement. **2** *(dinero)* pension.

jubilado,-a *adj* retired.
▶ *nm o nf* pensioner, retired person.

jubilar *vt* **1** *(retirar)* to retire. **2** *(persona)* to pension off; *(objeto)* to get rid of.
▶ *vpr* **jubilarse** *(retirarse)* to retire.

júbilo *nm* jubilation, joy.

jubiloso,-a *adj* jubilant, joyful.

jubón *nm arc* doublet.

judaico,-a *adj* Judaic.

judaísmo *nm* Judaism.

judería *nf* Jewish quarter.

judía *nf (planta)* bean. COMP **judía verde** French bean, green bean.

judicatura *nf* **1** *(profesión)* judgeship. **2** *(cuerpo)* judiciary, judicature.

judicial *adj* judicial.

judío,-a *adj (gen)* Jewish.
▶ *nm & nf (persona)* Jew.

judo *nm* judo.

judoca *nm o nf* judoka.

juego *nm* **1** *(gen)* game; *(actividad deportiva)* sport. **2** *(con dinero)* gambling. **3** *(acción de jugar)* playing. **4** *(conjunto de piezas)* set: *un juego de llaves* a set of keys. COMP **juego de azar** game of chance. ❙ **juego de café/té** coffee/tea service.

juerga *nf fam* rave-up, bash.

juerguista *adj* fun-loving.
▶ *nm o nf* raver.

jueves *nm inv* Thursday: *todos los jueves* every Thursday; *el jueves que viene* next Thursday; *el jueves pasado* last Thursday; *el jueves por la mañana/tarde/noche* Thursday morning/afternoon/night.

juez,-za *nm & nf* judge. COMP **juez de línea** linesman. ❙ **juez de paz** justice of the peace.

J

jugada *nf* **1** *(en ajedrez)* move; *(en billar)* shot; *(en dardos)* throw. **2** *(momento del juego)* move, piece of play. **3** *fam* dirty trick.

jugador,-ra *nm & nf* **1** player. **2** *(apostador)* gambler.

jugar *vi* to play.
   ▶ *vt (intervenir)* to play, go: *¿quién juega?* whose go is it?
   ▶ *vpr* **jugarse 1** *(arriesgar)* to risk. **2** *(apostarse)* to bet: *¿cuánto te juegas a que no viene?* what's the betting he won't come?

jugarreta *nf fam* dirty trick.

juglar *nm* minstrel.

jugo *nm* **1** *(gen)* juice. **2** *(interés)* substance.

jugoso,-a *adj (fruta, carne)* juicy.

juguete *nm* **1** toy. **2** *fig* plaything.

juguetear *vi* to play (con, with).

juguetería *nf (tienda)* toy shop.

juguetón,-ona *adj* playful.

juicio *nm* **1** *(gen)* judgement: *a mi juicio* in my opinion. **2** *(sensatez)* reason, common sense. **3** JUR trial. LOC **en su sano juicio** in one's right mind. ‖ **llevar a** ALGN **a juicio** to take legal action against SB. ‖ **perder el juicio** to go mad.

juicioso,-a *adj (persona)* sensible, wise.

juliana *nf* damewort.

julio¹ *nm* July.

✎ Para ejemplos de uso, consulta marzo.

julio² *nm* Fís joule.

jumbo *nm* jumbo jet.

juncal *nm* BOT reedbed.

junco *nm* BOT rush, reed.

jungla *nf* jungle.

junio *nm* June.

✎ Para ejemplos de uso, consulta marzo.

júnior *adj* DEP junior.

junta *nf (reunión)* meeting, assembly.

juntar *vt* **1** *(unir)* to put together; *(piezas)* to assemble. **2** *(reunir - dinero)* to raise; *(- gente)* to gather together.
   ▶ *vpr* **juntarse 1** *(unirse)* to join, get together; *(ríos, caminos)* to meet. **2** *(acercarse)* to squeeze up: *juntaos un poco que no quepo* squeeze up, I can't get in.

junto,-a *adj* together. LOC **junto a** next to. ‖ **junto con** along with, together with.

jura *nf (acción)* oath; *(ceremonia)* swearing-in, pledge.

jurado,-a *adj* sworn.
   ▶ *nm* **jurado** JUR *(tribunal)* jury; *(miembro del tribunal)* juror, member of the jury.

juramentar *vt* to swear in.

juramento *nm* **1** JUR oath. **2** *(blasfemia)* swearword.

jurar *vt* to swear, take an oath.
   ▶ *vi (blasfemar)* to curse, swear.

jurásico,-a *adj* Jurassic.

jurel *nm* scad, horse mackerel.

jurídico,-a *adj* legal, juridical.

jurisdicción *nf* jurisdiction.

jurisprudencia *nf* jurisprudence.

jurista *nm o nf* jurist, lawyer.

justicia *nf* **1** *(equidad, derecho)* justice, fairness. **2 la justicia** *(organismo)* the law.

justiciero,-a *adj* avenging.

justificable *adj* justifiable.

justificación *nf* justification.

justificante *adj* justifying.
   ▶ *nm (prueba)* written proof.

justificar *vt* **1** *(acción)* to justify. **2** *(persona)* to excuse.
   ▶ *vpr* **justificarse** *(persona)* to justify os; *(acción)* to be justified.

justo,-a *adj* **1** *(persona, decisión)* just, fair. **2** *(ropa)* tight. **3** *(exacto)* exact: *tengo el dinero justo para el autobús* I have the exact money for the bus. **4** *(escaso)* just enough: *me queda lo justo para llegar a fin de mes* I have just enough money to get by.
   ▶ *adv* **justo** *(en el preciso momento)* just; *(en el preciso lugar)* right: *vivo justo en el centro de la ciudad* I live right in the centre of town.

juvenil *adj* **1** young, youthful. **2** DEP junior, youth.

juventud *nf* **1** *(período)* youth. **2** *(los jóvenes)* young people *pl*, youth *pl*.

juzgado *nm (local)* court. COMP **juzgado de guardia** court, police court.

juzgar *vt* **1** *(formar juicio)* to judge. **2** *(considerar)* to consider, think.

K

K, k *nf (la letra)* K, k.
kaki *nm* **1** *(árbol)* persimmon tree. **2** *(fruta)* persimmon.
Kampuchea *nf* Kampuchea.
kampucheo,-a *adj* Kampuchean.
▶ *nm & nf* Kampuchean.
karst *nm* karst.
kárstico,-a *adj* karstic.
kart® *nm* go-kart, kart.
karting *nm* go-kart racing, karting.
Kathmandu *nm* Katmandu, Kathmandu.
kayac *nm* kayak.
kazajio,-a *adj* Kazakh.
▶ *nm & nf (persona)* Kazakh.
▶ *nm* **kazajio** *(idioma)* Kazakh.
Kazajstán *nm* Kazakhstan.
Kenia *nf* Kenya.
keniano,-a *adj* Kenyan.
▶ *nm & nf* Kenyan.
keroseno *nm* kerosene.
Khartum *nm* Khartoum.
kilo *nm* **1** kilogram. **2** *argot (antiguamente)* million pesetas.
kilobyte *nm* kilobyte.
kilocaloría *nf* kilocalorie.

kilogramo *nm* kilogram.
kilohertz *nm inv* kilohertz.
kilolitro *nm* kilolitre, US kiloliter.
kilometraje *nm* ≈ mileage.
kilómetro *nm* kilometre, US kilometer.
kilowatt *nm* kilowatt.
kirguís *adj* Kirghiz.
▶ *nm o nf (persona)* Kirghiz.
▶ *nm (idioma)* Kirghiz.
Kirguizistán *nm* Kirghizstan, Kirghizia.
Kiribati *nm* Kiribati.
kiwi *nm* **1** *(ave)* kiwi. **2** *(fruta)* kiwi, kiwi fruit.
km/h *abrev* **(kilómetros hora)** kilometres (US kilometers) per hour; *(abreviatura)* kph.
knock-out *nm* knockout.
koala *nm* koala.
kurdo,-a *adj* Kurdish.
▶ *nm & nf (persona)* Kurd.
▶ *nm* **kurdo** *(idioma)* Kurdish.
Kuwait *nm* Kuwait.
kuwaití *adj* Kuwaiti.
▶ *nm & nf* Kuwaiti.
kW/h *abrev* **(kilovatios hora)** kilowatts per hour; *(abreviatura)* kWh.

L

L, l *nf (la letra)* L, l.

la¹ *art def* the: *la casa* the house.

la² *pron (persona)* her; *(cosa)* it: *la invité a cenar* I invited her to supper; *no la he leído* I haven't read it.

✎ Consulta también **las**.

la³ *nm* MÚS la, lah, A.

laberíntico,-a *adj* labyrinthic.

laberinto *nm* labyrinth, maze.

labial *adj (gen)* labial.
▶ *nf* LING labial.

labio *nm* lip.

labor *nf* **1** *(gen)* work: *las labores del campo* farm work.

✎ Consulta también **las**.

laborable *adj (de trabajo)* working.

laboral *adj* labour.

laboratorio *nm* laboratory.

laborioso,-a *adj (trabajoso)* laborious.

labrador,-ra *nm & nf* farmer.

labranza *nf* farming.

labrar *vt* AGR *(campo)* to work; *(con arado)* to plough (US plow).

labriego,-a *nm & nf* farm worker.

lacio,-a *adj (cabello)* straight.

lacón *nm* ham.

lacónico,-a *adj* laconic.

lacra *nf* **1** *(señal)* mark, scar. **2** *(defecto)* fault.

lacrado,-a *adj (sobre)* sealed with wax.

lacrar *vt* to seal (with sealing wax).

lacre *nm* sealing wax.

lacrimal *adj* tear, lacrimal, lachrymal.

lacrimoso,-a *adj* tearful.

lactancia *nf* lactation.

lactante *nm o nf* unweaned baby.

lácteo,-a *adj* milk, milky. COMP productos lácteos dairy products.

láctico,-a *adj* lactic.

lactosa *nf* lactose.

lacustre *adj* lake.

ladear *vt* to tilt.

ladeo *nm* tilt.

ladera *nf* hillside.

lado *nm (gen)* side. LOC al lado de ALGN next to SB: *me puse a su lado* I sat next to her. **l estar al lado** *(muy cerca)* to be very near. **l por un lado... por otro...** on the one hand… on the other hand…

ladrador,-ra *adj* barking.

ladrar *vi* to bark.

ladrido *nm* bark.

ladrillo *nm* brick.

ladrón,-ona *nm & nf (persona - que roba)* thief; *(- que tima, engaña)* crook.

lagartija *nf* small lizard.

lagarto,-a *nm & nf (animal)* lizard.

lago *nm* lake.

lágrima *nf* tear. LOC llorar a lágrima viva *fam* to cry one's eyes out.

lagrimal *adj* tear, lachrymal.
▶ *nm* corner of the eye.

lagrimear *vi* to run, water.

lagrimeo *nm* watering.

lagrimón *nm* large teardrop, large tear.

laguna *nf* small lake, lagoon.

laico,-a *adj* lay, secular.

laja *nf* slab.

lama¹ *nm* REL lama.

lama² *nf* **1** *(lámina)* slat. **2** *(barro)* slime.

lamentable *adj (injusticia)* regrettable, deplorable; *(estado)* sorry, pitiful.

lamentar *vt* to regret.
▶ *vpr* **lamentarse** to complain.

lamento *nm* moan, cry.

lamer *vt* to lick.

lametazo *nm* lick.

lametón *nm* lick.

lámina *nf* 1 *(gen)* sheet, plate. 2 *(ilustración)* illustration; *(grabado)* engraving.

laminado,-a *adj* laminated.

laminar *vt* to laminate.

lámpara *nf* lamp.

lamparón *nm fam* stain.

lamprea *nf* lamprey.

lana *nf* wool. LOC **de lana** woollen (US woolen).

lanar *adj* wool-bearing.

lance *nm* 1 *(suceso)* event. 2 *(pelea)* quarrel.

lanceolado,-a *adj* lanceolate.

lancero *nm* lancer.

lanceta *nf* lancet, lance.

lancha *nf (bote)* launch, boat. COMP **lancha salvavidas** lifeboat.

landa *nf* moor.

lanero,-a *adj* wool.

langosta *nf* 1 *(crustáceo)* crawfish, spiny lobster. 2 *(insecto)* locust.

langostino *nm type of* prawn.

languidecer *vi* to languish.

languidez *nf (falta de vigor)* languor.

lánguido,-a *adj (falto de vigor)* languid, languorous.

lanilla *nf (tejido)* flannel.

lanza *nf* lance, spear.

lanzadera *nf* shuttle.

lanzado,-a *adj (impetuoso)* impetuous; *(decidido)* determined.

lanzador,-ra *nm & nf (de jabalina)* thrower; *(de béisbol)* pitcher; *(de cricket)* bowler.

lanzamiento *nm* 1 *(acción de lanzar)* throwing. 2 *(de cohete)* launching. COMP **lanzamiento de peso** shot put.

lanzar *vt* 1 *(gen)* to throw. 2 *(cohete)* to launch. 3 *fig (grito)* to let out.
▶ *vpr* **lanzarse** *(actuar decididamente)* to throw os, launch os into.

Laos *nm* Laos.

laosiano,-a *adj* Laotian.
▶ *nm & nf (persona)* Laotian.
▶ *nm* **laosiano** *(idioma)* Laotian.

lapa *nf (molusco)* limpet.

laparoscopia *nf* laparoscopy.

lapicero *nm* pencil.

lápida *nf* tombstone, slab.

lápiz *nm* pencil. COMP **lápiz de ojos** eyeliner. ▌ **lápiz óptico** light pen.

lapso *nm (de tiempo)* period of time.

lapsus *nm inv (error)* slip; *(de memoria)* memory lapse, lapse of memory.

laquear *vt* to lacquer.

largar *vt* 1 *fam (dar)* to give: *le largó un discurso de media hora* he gave him a half-hour speech. 2 *fam (contar)* to tell: *esa lo larga todo* she can't keep anything to herself.
▶ *vpr* **largarse** *fam (irse)* to go, leave: *me largo* I'm off, US I'm out of here.

largo,-a *adj (en longitud)* long. LOC **a lo largo de** along, throughout: *a lo largo del año* throughout the year. ▌ **dar largas a** ALGN to put SB off. ▌ **pasar de largo** to pass by.
▶ *nm* **largo** 1 length: *¿qué mide de largo?* how long is it?, what length is it? 2 *(de piscina)* length, US lap.

largometraje *nm* feature film.

larguero *nm (en fútbol)* crossbar.

larguirucho,-a *adj fam* lanky.

largura *nf* length.

laringe *nf* larynx.

laríngeo,-a *adj* laryngeal.

laringitis *nf inv* laryngitis.

laringología *nf* laryngology.

laringólogo,-a *nm & nf* laryngologist.

larva *nf* larva.

larvario,-a *adj* larval.

las *art def* the: *las casas* the houses.
▶ *pron (objeto directo)* them: *las vi* I saw them.

✎ Consulta también **la**.

lasca *nf* chip.

láser *nm inv* laser.

lasitud *nf* lassitude, weariness.

lástima *nf* pity.

lastimar *vt (herir)* to hurt, injure.
▶ *vpr* **lastimarse** to hurt os.

lastimero,-a *adj* pitiful.

lastimoso,-a *adj* pitiful, sorry.

lastrar *vt* MAR to ballast.

lastre *nm* MAR ballast.

lata *nf* **1** *(hojalata)* tin plate. **2** *(envase)* tin, can. **3** *(fastidio)* bore, drag, pain: *es una lata tener que estudiar los fines de semana* it's a pain having to study at weekends.

latente *adj* latent.

lateral *adj* *(gen)* side.

látex *nm inv* latex.

latido *nm* beat.

latifundio *nm (finca)* latifundium.

latigazo *nm* lash.

látigo *nm* whip.

latín *nm* Latin.

latino,-a *adj* Latin.
▶ *nm & nf* Latin.

Latinoamérica *nf* Latin America.

latinoamericano,-a *adj* Latin American.
▶ *nm & nf* Latin American.

latir *vi* to beat.

latitud *nf* latitude.

latitudinal *adj* latitudinal.

latón *nm* brass.

latoso,-a *adj fam* annoying, boring.

laúd *nm* lute.

laudatorio,-a *adj* laudatory.

laureada *nf* MIL *(insignia)* decoration.

laureado,-a *adj* prizewinning.

laurear *vt* **1** to award a prize to. **2** *(militar)* to decorate.

laurel *nm (árbol)* bay.

lava *nf* lava.

lavable *adj* washable.

lavabo *nm* **1** *(pila)* washbasin. **2** *(cuarto de baño)* washroom. **3** *(público)* toilet.

lavada *nf* big wash.

lavadero *nm* **1** *(en casa)* laundry room. **2** *(público)* public washing place.

lavado *nm* wash.

lavadora *nf* washing machine.

lavafrutas *nm inv* finger bowl.

lavamanos *nm inv* washbasin.

lavanda *nf* lavender.

lavandería *nf (automática)* launderette, US laundromat; *(con servicio)* laundry.

lavaplatos *nm inv* dishwasher.

lavar *vt* **1** *(ropa, cuerpo, etc)* to wash. **2** *(platos)* to wash up.
▶ *vpr* **lavarse** to wash os.

lavativa *nf* enema.

lavavajillas *nm inv* dishwasher.

laxante *nm* laxative.

laxitud *nf* laxity, laxness.

laxo,-a *adj (sin tensión)* slack.

lazada *nf* **1** *(nudo)* knot. **2** *(lazo)* bow.

lazar *vt* to lasso.

lazarillo *nm* guide. COMP **perro lazarillo** guide dog.

lazo *nm* **1** *(cinta)* ribbon; *(de adorno)* bow. **2** *fig (vínculo)* tie, bond.

le *pron* **1** *(objeto directo)* him; *(usted)* you: *¿quién le sirvió?* who served you? **2** *(objeto indirecto - a él)* him; *(- a ella)* her; *(- a usted)* you: *le regalaron un perrito* they gave him a puppy; *le repito la pregunta* I'll repeat the question for you.

✎ Consulta también **les** y **leísmo**.

leal *adj* **1** loyal, faithful. **2** *(justo)* fair.

lealtad *nf* loyalty, faithfulness.

lebrel *nm* greyhound.

lebrillo *nm* bowl.

lección *nf* lesson. LOC **dar una lección a** ALGN *fig* to teach SB a lesson.

lechada *nf* whitewash.

lechal *adj* sucking.

lechazo *nm (cordero)* sucking lamb.

leche *nf* milk. COMP **leche desnatada** skimmed milk.

lechera *nf (recipiente)* milk churn.

lechería *nf* dairy.

lechero,-a *nm* milkman, dairyman.

lecho *nm (gen)* bed; *(de un río)* river bed.

lechón *nm (animal)* piglet.

lechuga *nf* lettuce.

lechuza *nf* owl.

lectivo,-a *adj* school.

lector,-ra *nm & nf* reader. COMP **lector óptico** optical scanner.

leer *vt (gen)* to read.
▶ *vi* to read.

legado,-a *nm* **1** *(herencia)* legacy, bequest. **2** *(persona)* legate.

legajo *nm* dossier.

legal *adj* (gen) legal.

legalidad *nf* (de una acción, etc) legality.

legalista *adj* legalistic.

legalización *nf* **1** (de una situación) legalization. **2** (de documento) to authenticate.

legalizar *vt* **1** (situación) to legalize. **2** (documento) to authenticate.

legaña *nf* sleep.

legar *vt* to bequeath.

legendario,-a *adj* legendary.

legibilidad *nf* legibility.

legible *adj* legible.

legión *nf* MIL legion.

legionario,-a *nm* legionary.

legislación *nf* legislation.

legislador,-ra *adj* legislative.

legislar *vi* to legislate.

legislativo,-a *adj* legislative.

legislatura *nf* (período) term of office.

legitimación *nf* legitimization.

legitimar *vt* to legitimate.

legitimidad *nf* legitimacy.

legítimo,-a *adj* (genuino) real, authentic.

legua *nf* (medida) league.

legumbre *nf* **1** (planta) legume. **2** (fruto) pulse.

leguminoso,-a *nf pl* leguminous plants.

leído,-a *adj* well-read.

leísmo *nm* incorrect use of **le** and **les** as direct object instead of **lo** and **los**.

leísta *adj* given to leísmo.
▶ *nm o nf* person who is given to leísmo.

lejanía *nf* distance.

lejano,-a *adj* (tierra, país) distant.

lejía *nf* bleach.

lejos *adv* far, far away, far off. LOC **a lo lejos** in the distance, far away. | **de lejos** from a distance.

lelo,-a *adj fam* gormless, stupid.

lema *nm* (gen) motto; (en publicidad) slogan.

lencería *nf* (ropa interior) lingerie.

lengua *nf* **1** ANAT tongue. **2** (idioma) language. LOC **irse de la lengua** *fam* to let the cat out of the bag. | **tener ALGO en la punta de la lengua** *fig* to have

STH on the tip of one's tongue. | COMP **lengua materna** mother tongue.

lenguado *nm* sole.

lenguaje *nm* **1** (gen) language. **2** (habla) speech.

lenguaraz *adj* (hablador) garrulous.

lengüeta *nf* (de zapato) tongue.

lente *nm & nf* lens.
▶ *nm pl* **lentes** lenses. COMP **lentes de contacto** contact lenses.

lenteja *nf* lentil.

lentejuela *nf* sequin.

lentilla *nf* contact lens.

lentitud *nf* slowness.

lento,-a *adj* slow.
▶ *adv* **lento** slowly.

leña *nf* wood, firewood.

leñador,-ra *nm & nf* woodcutter.

leñera *nf* woodshed.

leño *nm* log.

leñoso,-a *adj* ligneous, woody.

león,-ona *nm & nf* (animal - macho) lion; (- hembra) lioness. COMP **león marino** sea lion.

leonera *nf* lion's den.

leonino,-a *adj* **1** (de león) lion-like.

leopardo *nm* leopard.

leotardos *nm pl* thick woollen tights.

lepra *nf* leprosy.

leproso,-a *adj* leprous.

lerdo,-a *adj fam* slow-witted.

les *pron* **1** (objeto directo) them; (ustedes) you: *dice que les vio ayer* she says she saw them yesterday; *no les entiendo* I don't understand you. **2** (objeto indirecto) them; (a ustedes) you: *entraron en casa ladrones y les robaron* burglars broke in and robbed them; *les doy una oportunidad más* I'll give you one more chance.

✎ Consulta también le.

lesión *nf* (daño físico) wound, injury.

lesionado,-a *adj* injured.

lesionar *vt* (herir) to injure.
▶ *vpr* **lesionarse** to get injured.

lesivo,-a *adj* damaging, injurious.

Lesotho *nm* Lesotho.

letal *adj* lethal, deadly.

L

letanía *nf fam (lista)* long list.
letargo *nm* lethargy.
letón,-ona *adj* Latvian.
▶ *nm & nf (persona)* Latvian.
▶ *nm* **letón** *(idioma)* Latvian.
Letonia *nf* Latvia.
letra *nf* **1** *(del alfabeto)* letter. **2** *(de impren-ta)* character. **3** *(escritura)* handwrit-ing. **4** *(de canción)* lyrics *pl*, words *pl*. COMP **letra de imprenta** block capitals *pl*. ▌ **letra mayúscula** capital letter.
letrado,-a *nm & nf* lawyer.
letrero *nm* sign, notice.
letrina *nf* latrine.
leucemia *nf* leukaemia, US leukemia.
leucocito *nm* white blood cell.
leva *nf* MIL levy.
levadizo,-a *adj* which can be raised.
levadura *nf* yeast.
levantamiento *nm (de objeto, etc)* lifting.
levantar *vt (alzar)* to raise, lift: *no lo pue-do levantar, pesa mucho* I can't lift it, it's heavy. LOC **levantar la vista** to look up.
▶ *vpr* **levantarse 1** *(alzarse)* to rise. **2** *(po-nerse de pie)* to stand up. **3** *(dejar la cama)* get out of bed. **4** *(viento)* to get up.
levante *nm (este)* East.
levar *vt (ancla)* to weigh.
leve *adj* **1** slight, light.
levedad *nf* lightness, insignificance.
levitar *vi* to levitate.
léxico,-a *adj* lexical.
lexicón *nm (diccionario)* lexicon.
ley *nf* law.
leyenda *nf (narración)* legend.
lezna *nf* awl.
liado,-a *adj (ocupado)* busy.
liana *nf* liana.
liar *vt* **1** *(atar)* to tie up, bind; *(envolver)* to wrap up. **2** *fam (complicar)* to mix up, make a mess of; *(confundir)* to confuse: *cuéntale la verdad y no lo líes más* tell him the truth and stop messing him about.
▶ *vpr* **liarse a +** *sustantivo* to start + *ger*: *se liaron a discutir* they started arguing.
libanés,-esa *adj* Lebanese.
▶ *nm & nf* Lebanese.
Líbano *nm* **el Líbano** the Lebanon.

libar *vt (néctar)* to suck.
libélula *nf* dragonfly.
liberación *nf (de una persona)* release.
liberado,-a *adj* liberated.
liberador,-ra *adj* liberating.
liberal *adj* liberal.
▶ *nm o nf* liberal.
liberalismo *nm* liberalism.
liberalización *nf* liberalization.
liberar *vt* to free.
Liberia *nf* Liberia.
liberiano,-a *adj* Liberian.
▶ *nm & nf* Liberian.
libertad *nf (gen)* freedom, liberty. LOC **poner en libertad** to free, release. COMP **libertad de expresión** freedom of expression.
libertar *vt* to liberate.
libertario,-a *adj* libertarian.
Libia *nf* Libya.
libio,-a *adj* Libyan.
▶ *nm & nf* Libyan.
libra *nf (moneda, medida)* pound. COMP **li-bra esterlina** pound sterling.
librar *vt* to save (de, from): *me libraron de toda responsabilidad* they absolved me of all responsibility.
▶ *vi fam (tener libre)* to be off: *libro todo los lunes* I've got Mondays off.
▶ *vpr* **librarse** to escape (de, from).
libre *adj (gen)* free. COMP **entrada libre** free admittance.
librecambio *nm* free trade.
librería *nf (tienda)* bookshop.
librero,-a *nm & nf* bookseller.
libreta *nf (para anotar)* notebook.
libreto *nm* libretto.
libro *nm (gen)* book. COMP **libro de bolsillo** paperback. ▌ **libro de consulta** refer-ence book. ▌ **libro de texto** textbook.
licencia *nf (permiso)* licence.
licenciado,-a *nm & nf* EDUC graduate.
licenciar *vt* EDUC to award a degree to.
▶ *vpr* **licenciarse** to graduate.
licenciatura *nf* university degree.
liceo *nm (colegio)* secondary school.
lícito,-a *adj* **1** *(legal)* licit. **2** *(justo)* fair.

licor *nm (dulce)* liqueur; *(bebida alcohólica)* liquor, spirits *pl*.

licuadora *nf* juice extractor.

licuar *vt* to liquefy.

lid *nf fig (controversia)* dispute.

líder *nm o nf* leader.

liderar *vt* to lead.

liderazgo *nm* leadership.

lidia *nf (de toros)* bullfight.

liebre *nf (animal)* hare.

Liechtenstein *nm* Liechtenstein.

lienzo *nm* ARTE *(tela)* canvas.

liga *nf* **1** *(asociación)* league, alliance. **2** DEP league.

ligadura *nf (atadura)* tie, bond.

ligamento *nm* ligament.

ligar *vt* **1** *(atar)* to tie, bind. **2** *(unir)* to link, connect.

ligero,-a *adj* **1** *(liviano)* light. **2** *(sin importancia)* minor, light.

lignito *nm* lignite.

lija *nf (papel)* sandpaper.

lijar *vt* to sand.

lila *adj (color)* lilac.
▶ *nf (flor)* lilac.

lima *nf* **1** *(herramienta)* file; *(para uñas)* nail file. **2** *(fruta)* lime; *(árbol)* lime tree.

limar *vt (pulir)* to file.

limitación *nf* limitation.

limitado,-a *adj* limited.

limitar *vt (gen)* to limit.
▶ *vi* **limitar con** to border with. LOC **limitarse a + *inf*** to restrict os to + *ger*, do no more than + *inf* : *una persona inteligente no se limita a ver la televisión* an intelligent person does not restrict himself to watching television.

límite *nm* **1** *(extremo)* limit. **2** *(frontera)* boundary. COMP **límite de velocidad** speed limit.

limítrofe *adj* bordering.

limo *nm* slime.

limón *nm* lemon.

limonada *nf* lemonade.

limonero *nm* lemon tree.

limonita *nf* limonite.

limosna *nf* alms *pl*, charity. LOC **pedir limosna** to beg.

limpiabotas *nm inv* bootblack.

limpiacristales *nm inv (producto)* window cleaning fluid.

limpiador,-ra *adj* cleaning.
▶ *nm & nf (persona)* cleaner.

limpiamente *adv* cleanly.

limpiaparabrisas *nm inv* windscreen wiper, US windshield wiper.

limpiar *vt (gen)* to clean, cleanse.

limpieza *nf (acción de limpiar)* cleaning.

limpio,-a *adj (sin suciedad)* clean.
▶ *adv* fairly: *no juegan limpio, hacen trampa* they don't play fair, they cheat.

linaje *nm (ascendencia)* lineage.

linaza *nf* linseed.

lince *nm* ZOOL lynx.

linchar *vt* to lynch.

lindar *vi* to border (**con**, on), adjoin (**con**, -).

linde *nm & nf* boundary.

lindo,-a *adj* pretty, nice, lovely.

línea *nf (gen)* line. COMP **línea aérea** airline. ‖ **línea recta** straight line.

lineal *adj* linear.

linfático,-a *adj* lymphatic.

lingote *nm* ingot.

lingüística *nf* linguistics.

lino *nm* **1** *(tela)* linen. **2** BOT flax.

linterna *nf (de pilas)* torch.

lío *nm (embrollo)* mess. LOC **hacerse un lío 1** *(uso literal)* to get tangled up. **2** *(uso figurado)* to get muddled up.

lípido *nm* lipid.

lipotimia *nf* blackout.

liquen *nm* lichen.

liquidación *nf (venta)* sale.

liquidar *vt* **1** *(deuda)* to settle, liquidate. **2** *(mercancías)* to sell off.

líquido,-a *nm* liquid.

lira *nf* **1** MÚS lyre. **2** *(moneda)* lira.

lírica *nf* poetry, lyric poetry.

lirio *nm* lily.

lirón *nm* dormouse. LOC **dormir como un lirón** to sleep like a log.

lis *nf (planta)* lily.

liso,-a *adj* **1** smooth. **2** *(pelo)* straight.

lista *nf (relación)* list.

listo,-a *adj* **1** *(inteligente)* clever, smart. **2** *(preparado)* ready: *¿estás lista?* are you ready?

litera *nf* bunk bed; *(tren)* couchette.

literal *adj* literal.

literario,-a *adj* literary.

literatura *nf* literature.

litigar *vi (disputar)* to argue, dispute.

litigio *nm (disputa)* dispute.

litio *nm* lithium.

litoral *nm* coast.

litosfera *nf* lithosphere.

litro *nm* litre, US liter.

Lituania *nf* Lithuania.

lituano,-a *adj* Lithuanian.
▶ *nm & nf (persona)* Lithuanian.
▶ *nm* **lituano** *(idioma)* Lithuanian.

liviano,-a *adj (ligero)* light.

lívido,-a *adj* livid.

llaga *nf (gen)* sore; *(en la boca)* ulcer.

llagar *vt* to cover with ulcers.

llama *nf* **1** *(de fuego)* flame. **2** ZOOL llama.

llamada *nf (gen)* call.

llamamiento *nm (convocatoria)* call.

llamar *vt* **1** *(gen)* to call. **2** *(dar nombre)* to name. **3** *(atraer)* to appeal to. LOC llamar por teléfono to call, phone, GB ring, ring up.
▶ *vi (a la puerta)* to knock; *(al timbre)* to ring; *(al teléfono)* to ring, call, phone.
▶ *vpr* **llamarse** *(tener nombre)* to be called.

llamativo,-a *adj* showy, flashy.

llamear *vi* to blaze.

llano,-a *adj* **1** *(plano)* flat. **2** *(sencillo)* simple.
▶ *nm* **llano** *(llanura)* plain.

llanta *nf* wheel rim, rim.

llanto *nm* crying, weeping.

llanura *nf (llano)* plain.

llave *nf (de puerta, etc)* key.

llavero *nm* key ring.

llegada *nf* **1** arrival. **2** DEP finishing line.

llegar *vi* **1** to arrive (a, at/in), get (a, at), reach (a, -): *llegó el primero* he arrived first. **3** *(alcanzar)* to reach: *¿llegas a ese estante?* can you reach that shelf? **4** *(ser suficiente)* to be enough, suffice:

¿te llega con diez euros? is ten euros enough? **5** *(cantidad)* to amount (a, to). **6** llegar a + *inf (uso enfático)*: *llegó a llamarme tonto* he even called me a silly.

llenar *vt* **1** *(espacio, recipiente)* to fill. **2** *(formulario)* to fill in. **3** *(tiempo)* to fill, occupy. **4** llenar de *(alegría)* to fill with.
▶ *vpr* **llenarse 1** *(gen)* to fill. **2** *(de gente)* to fill up.

lleno,-a *adj* **1** full (de, of): *está lleno de gente* it's full of people. **2** *(cubierto)* covered (de, with).

llevadero,-a *adj* bearable.

llevar *vt* **1** *(gen)* to take: *llévale esto a tu abuela* take this to your granny. **2** *(tener)* to have; *(tener encima)* to have, carry: *¿qué llevas ahí?* what's that you've got there? **3** *(prenda)* to wear, have on: *no me gusta llevar sombrero* I don't like wearing a hat. **4** *(aguantar)* to cope with. **5** *(dirigir)* to be in charge of: *¿quién lleva los pedidos?* who's in charge of orders? **6** *(conducir - coche)* to drive: *lleva un Seat azul* he drives a blue Seat. **7** *(años)* to be older: *te llevo tres años* I'm three years older than you.
▶ *vi* **1** llevar a *(conducir)* to take, lead: *esta senda lleva a la cima* this path takes you to the summit. **2** llevar a + *inf (inducir)* to lead to, make: *esto me lleva a pensar que...* this leads me to think that...
▶ *vpr* **llevarse 1** *(obtener)* to get; *(ganar)* to win: *los rusos se llevaron todas las medallas* the Russians won all the medals. **2** *(recibir)* to get: *se llevó un buen susto* he got quite a shock. **3** *(estar de moda)* to be fashionable: *este color ya no se lleva* this colour is not fashionable any more. **4** *(entenderse)* to get on (con, with), get along (con, with): *se lleva bien con sus padres* he gets on well with his parents. **5** MAT to carry over.

llorar *vi* to cry, weep.
▶ *vt* to mourn.

llorón,-ona *nm & nf fam* crybaby.

lloroso,-a *adj* tearful, weeping.

llover *vi* [se usa sólo en tercera persona; no lleva sujeto] to rain: *llueve* it's raining.

lloviznar *vi* [se usa sólo en tercera persona; no lleva sujeto] to drizzle.

lluvia *nf* **1** rain. **2** *fig* shower, barrage.
lo *art neut* the: *dime lo que quieres* tell me what you want. LOC **lo que** what.
▶ *pron* **1** *(objeto directo - él)* him; *(- usted)* you: *no lo conozco de nada* I don't know him from Adam. **2** *(objeto directo - cosa, animal)* it: *¿lo has probado?* have you tried it?
loar *vt* to praise, extol.
lobezno,-a *nm & nf* ZOOL wolf cub.
lobo,-a *nm & nf (macho)* wolf; *(hembra)* she-wolf.
lóbulo *nm* lobe.
local *adj* local.
▶ *nm (para negocio)* premises *pl*.
localidad *nf* **1** *(ciudad)* town. **2** TEAT *(asiento)* seat; *(billete)* ticket.
localizar *vt* **1** *(encontrar)* to locate, find. **2** *(infección, incendio)* to localize.
locativo,-a *adj* locative.
loción *nf* lotion.
loco,-a *adj (gen)* mad, crazy, insane.
▶ *nm & nf* lunatic.
locomoción *nf* locomotion.
locomotor,-ra *adj* locomotive.
locomotora *nf* locomotive.
locución *nf* phrase, locution.
locura *nf (perturbación)* madness.
locutor,-ra *nm & nf* announcer.
locutorio *nm* telephone booth.
lodo *nm* mud.
logarítmico,-a *adj* logarithmic.
logaritmo *nm* logarithm.
lógica *nf* logic.
lógico,-a *adj* **1** *(de la lógica)* logical. **2** *(natural)* normal, to be expected.
logística *nf* logistics.
logopeda *nm o nf* speech therapist.
logotipo *nm* logo, logotype.
logrado,-a *adj (conseguido)* successful.
lograr *vt (conseguir)* to get, achieve.
logro *nm (éxito)* achievement.
loísmo *nm incorrect use of* lo *and* los *as indirect objects instead of* le *and* les.
loma *nf* hill.
lombriz *nf (intestinal)* worm.
lomo *nm* **1** CULIN *(de cerdo)* loin; *(de ternera)* sirloin. **2** ANAT back.
lona *nf* canvas.

loncha *nf (de jamón, queso, etc)* slice.
londinense *adj* of London.
▶ *nm o nf* Londoner.
Londres *nm* London.
longaniza *nf cured pork sausage*.
longitud *nf* **1** length. **2** GEOG longitude.
lonja *nf (mercado)* exchange, market.
lontananza *nf (fondo)* background.
loor *nm lit* praise.
lord *nm* lord.
loriga *nf* HIST cuirass.
loro *nm (pájaro)* parrot.
los *art def* the: *los niños* the boys.
▶ *pron (objeto directo)* them; *(ustedes)* you: *los vi* I saw them; *a ustedes dos no los quiero volver a ver* I don't want to see you two again.

✎ Consulta también lo, el.

losa *nf* flagstone, slab.
loseta *nf* floor tile.
lotería *nf* lottery.
loto *nm (flor)* lotus.
loza *nf (cerámica)* china.
lozanía *nf (de persona)* healthiness.
lozano,-a *adj* **1** *(persona)* healthy, lusty. **2** *(planta)* fresh.
lubina *nf* bass.
lubricante *nm* lubricant.
lubricar *vt* to lubricate.
lucerna *nf* skylight.
lucero *nm* bright star.
lucha *nf* **1** *(gen)* fight, struggle. **2** DEP wrestling. COMP **lucha libre** free-style wrestling.
luchador,-ra *nm & nf* **1** *(gen)* fighter. **2** DEP wrestler.
luchar *vi* **1** to fight. **2** DEP to wrestle.
lucidez *nf* lucidity.
lucido,-a *adj* beautiful.
lúcido,-a *adj* lucid, clear-headed.
luciérnaga *nf* glow-worm.
lucífero,-a *adj lit* resplendent.
lucimiento *nm* showing off.
lucio *nm* pike.
lución *nm* slowworm.

lucir *vt (mostrar)* to show, display; *(ropa)* to wear, sport.
▶ *vpr* **lucirse** *(sobresalir)* to be brilliant.

lucrarse *vpr* to make a profit.

lucrativo,-a *adj* lucrative, profitable.

lucro *nm* gain, profit.

luctuoso,-a *adj lit* mournful, sorrowful.

lúdico,-a *adj* recreational.

ludópata *nm o nf* compulsive gambler.

ludopatía *nf* compulsive gambling.

luego *adv* **1** *(después)* then, afterwards, next. **2** *(más tarde)* later.
▶ *conj* so, therefore.

lugar *nm* **1** *(sitio, ciudad)* place. **2** *(posición, situación)* place, position: *llegó en quinto lugar* he finished in fifth place. **3** *(espacio)* room, space: *ya no hay lugar para más muebles* there's no room for any more furniture. LOC **en lugar de** instead of.

lugareño,-a *adj* local.
▶ *nm & nf* local.

lugarteniente *nm* deputy.

lúgubre *adj (triste)* bleak, lugubrious.

lujo *nm* luxury.

lujosamente *adv* luxuriously.

lujoso,-a *adj* luxurious.

lumbago *nm* lumbago.

lumbar *adj* lumbar.

lumbre *nf (fuego)* fire.

lumbrera *nf (persona)* genius, luminary.

luminaria *nf (en fiestas)* light.

lumínico,-a *adj* light.

luminiscencia *nf* luminiscence.

luminiscente *adj* luminiscent.

luminosidad *nf* luminosity.

luminoso,-a *adj* bright, luminous.

luminotecnia *nf* lighting.

luminotécnico,-a *adj* lighting.

luna *nf* **1** *(satélite)* moon. **2** *(cristal)* window pane; *(de ventana)* glass. **3** *(espejo)* mirror. COMP **luna llena** full moon. ‖ **luna de miel** honey moon.

lunación *nf* lunation.

lunar *adj* lunar, moon: *las fases lunares* the phases of the moon.
▶ *nm (en la piel)* beauty spot. LOC **de lunares** spotted.

lunático,-a *nm & nf* lunatic.

lunes *nm inv* Monday.

✎ Consulta también **jueves**.

luneta *nf car* window. COMP **luneta térmica** heated rear windscreen.

lúnula *nf* half-moon, lunule.

lupa *nf* magnifying glass. LOC **con lupa** meticulously.

lúpulo *nm* hop.

lustrabotas *nm o nf* bootblack.

lustrar *vt* to polish.

lustre *nm (brillo)* polish, shine, lustre, US luster.

lustro *nm* five years *pl*.

lustroso,-a *adj* shiny.

luto *nm* **1** mourning. **2** *fig* grief.

luxación *nf* dislocation.

Luxemburgo *nm* Luxembourg.

luxemburgués,-esa *adj* of Luxembourg, from Luxembourg.
▶ *nm & nf* Luxembourger.

luz *nf* **1** *(gen)* light. **2** *fam (electricidad)* electricity. **3** *(iluminación)* lighting. LOC **dar a luz** to give birth. ‖ **salir a la luz** to come out. COMP **luces de posición** sidelights. ‖ **luz del sol** sunlight.

M, m *nf (la letra)* M, m.

m¹ *sím (metro)* metre (US meter); *(símbolo)* m.

m² *sím (milla)* mile; *(símbolo)* m.

m³ *abrev (minuto)* minute; *(abreviatura)* min.

maca *nf (en fruta)* bruise.

macabro,-a *adj* macabre.

macaco,-a *nm & nf* ZOOL macaque.

macarrón *nm (pasta italiana)* piece of macaroni.
▸ *nm pl* **macarrones** macaroni.

macedonia *nf* fruit salad. COMP **macedonia de frutas** fruit salad.

maceración *nf (remojo - de fruta)* maceration, soaking; *(- de carne, pescado)* marinading.

macerar *vt (poner en remojo - fruta)* to macerate, soak; *(- carne, pescado)* to marinade.

maceta *nf* flowerpot.

macetero *nm* flowerpot holder.

macha *adj (almeja) type of* clam.

machacar *vt* **1** *(triturar)* to crush. **2** *fam (vencer)* to hammer, thrash. **3** *fam (insistir en)* to harp on about, go on about.
▸ *vi* **1** *(estudiar)* to swot up, cram, US grind. **2** *(insistir en)* to go on (con, about), harp on (con, about).

machacón,-ona *adj fam* insistent, repetitive.

machaque *nm* beating.

machetazo *nm* blow with a machete.

machete *nm* machete.

machihembrado,-a *nm* tongue and groove joint.

machismo *nm* male chauvinism.

machista *adj* male chauvinist.

macho *adj* **1** *(animal, planta)* male. **2** *(persona)* macho, tough.
▸ *nm* **1** *(animal, planta)* male. **2** *fam (hombre)* macho man, tough guy.

macilento,-a *adj* wan, pallid.

macizo,-a *adj* solid.
▸ *nm* **macizo** *(montañoso)* massif, mountain mass.

macro *nf* INFORM macro.

macrocefalia *nf* macrocephaly..

macrocosmos *nm inv* macrocosm.

macroeconomía *nf* macroeconomics.

macroeconómico,-a *adj* macroeconomic.

macroscópico,-a *adj* macroscopic.

mácula *nf lit* blemish.

macuto *nm* knapsack, rucksack.

Madagascar *nm* Madagascar.

madeja *nf (de lana)* skein, hank.

madera *nf (en el árbol)* wood; *(cortada)* timber, US lumber: **es de madera** it's made of wood, it's wooden.

maderero,-a *adj (industria)* timber.

madero *nm* piece of timber.

madona *nf* Madonna.

madrastra *nf* stepmother.

madraza *nf fam* doting mother.

madre *nf* mother. COMP **madre soltera** single mother.

madreselva *nf* honeysuckle.

madrigal *nm* madrigal.

madriguera *nf (de conejo)* burrow, warren; *(de zorro)* den, lair.

madrina *nf* godmother.

madroño *nm* strawberry tree.

madrugada *nf (después de medianoche)* early morning: *a las cinco de la madrugada* at five o'clock in the morning.

madrugador,-ra *nm & nf* early riser.
madrugar *vi (levantarse pronto)* to get up early.
madrugón LOC pegarse un madrugón *fam* to get up at the crack of dawn.
madurar *vi* 1 *(fruto)* to ripen. 2 *(persona)* to mature.
▶ *vt* 1 *(fruto)* to ripen. 2 *(plan, proyecto)* to think about carefully.
madurez *nf (de la persona)* maturity.
maduro,-a *adj* 1 *(persona)* mature. 2 *(fruta)* ripe.
maestre *nm* HIST master.
maestría *nf (destreza)* mastery, skill.
maestro,-a *adj (principal)* master; *(pared, viga)* main, supporting.
▶ *nm & nf* 1 *(de primaria - hombre)* schoolmaster; *(- mujer)* schoolmistress. 2 *(instructor)* teacher. COMP **maestro de escuela** schoolteacher.
magacín *nm (revista)* magazine.
magdalena *nf* small sponge cake.
magenta *nf* magenta.
magia *nf* magic.
mágico,-a *adj (pócima, palabra)* magic.
magisterio *nm (profesión)* teaching profession.
magistrado,-a *nm & nf (juez)* judge.
magistral *adj* masterly, masterful.
magistratura *nf (cuerpo)* judges *pl.*
magma *nf* magma.
magnanimidad *nf* magnanimity.
magnánimo,-a *adj* magnanimous.
magnate *nm* tycoon, magnate.
magnesio *nm* magnesium.
magnético,-a *adj* magnetic.
magnetismo *nm* magnetism.
magnetización *nf* magnetization.
magnetizar *vt* to magnetize.
magnetofónico,-a *adj* sound recording.
magnetófono *nm* tape recorder.
magnicidio *nm* assassination.
magnificar *vt (ensalzar)* to praise.
magnificencia *nf* magnificence, splendour.
magnífico,-a *adj* splendid.
magnitud *nf* FÍS magnitude.

magno,-a *adj* great.
magnolia *nf (árbol, flor)* magnolia.
magnolio *nm* magnolia.
mago,-a *nm & nf (gen)* magician, conjurer; *(de los cuentos)* wizard.
magro,-a *adj* lean.
magulladura *nf* bruise, contusion.
magullar *vt* to bruise.
maicena *nf* cornflour.
mailing *nm* mailshot.
maitre *nm o nf* head waiter, maître.
maíz *nm* 1 *(planta)* maize, US corn. 2 *(grano)* sweet corn, US corn.
maizal *nm* maize field, US corn field.
majada *nf* sheepfold.
majadería *nf* nonsense, balderdash.
majadero,-a *adj* stupid, dim-witted.
majar *vt* to crush.
majestad *nf (distinción)* majesty.
majestuoso,-a *adj* majestic.
majo,-a *adj (simpático)* nice.
majuelo *nm (viña)* young vine.
mal *nm* 1 evil. 2 *(daño)* harm. 3 *(enfermedad)* sickness.
▶ *adj (forma apocopada de malo)* bad.
▶ *adv* 1 *(no adecuadamente)* badly: *se portó mal con nosotros* he treated us badly. 2 *(enfermo)* ill, sick: *me encuentro mal* I feel ill, I don't feel well. 3 *(incorrectamente)* wrong: *lo has hecho mal* you've done it wrong. 4 *(en frases negativas)* bad, badly: *la película no está mal* the film's not bad.
malabarismo *nm* juggling. LOC **hacer malabarismos** to juggle.
malabarista *nm o nf* juggler.
malacostumbrado,-a *adj* spoilt.
malacostumbrar *vt* to spoil.
malaria *nf* malaria.
malasio,-a *adj* Malaysian.
▶ *nm & nf* Malaysian.
malaventura *nf* misfortune.
malaventurado,-a *adj* unfortunate.
Malawi *nm* Malawi.
malawiano,-a *adj* Malawian.
▶ *nm & nf* Malawian.
malayo,-a *adj* Malay.
▶ *nm & nf (persona)* Malay.
▶ *nm* **malayo** *(idioma)* Malay.

Malaysia *nf* Malaysia.

malcarado,-a *adj* grim-faced.

malcomer *vi* not to eat enough.

malcriado,-a *adj (mimado)* spoilt.

malcriar *vt* to spoil.

maldad *nf* **1** *(cualidad)* evil, wickedness. **2** *(acto)* evil thing, wicked thing.

maldecir *vt* to curse, damn.
▶ *vi* to curse.

maldiciente *adj* slanderous.

maldición *nf* curse.

maldito,-a *adj* damned.

Maldivas *nm* Maldives.

maldivo,-a *adj* Maldivian.
▶ *nm & nf* Maldivian.

maleabilidad *nf* malleability.

maleable *adj* malleable.

maleante *nm o nf* delinquent.

malear *vt (dañar)* to spoil, damage.

malecón *nm* mole, jetty.

maledicencia *nf* evil talk, gossip.

maleducado,-a *adj* rude.
▶ *nm & nf* rude person: *es una maleducada* she's really rude.

maleducar *vt (niño)* to spoil.

maleficio *nm* curse, evil spell.

maléfico,-a *adj* evil, harmful.

malentendido *nm* misunderstanding.

malestar *nm* fig unrest.

maleta *nf* suitcase, case. LOC **hacer la maleta 1** *(empacar)* to pack. **2** *(irse)* to pack up.

maletero *nm* AUTO boot, US trunk.

maletín *nm* briefcase.

malévolo,-a *adj* malevolent.

maleza *nf (malas hierbas)* weeds *pl*.

malformación *nf* malformation.

malgache *adj* Madagascan, Malagsy.
▶ *nm o nf* Madagascan.

malgastador,-ra *nm & nf* squanderer.

malgastar *vt* to waste, squander.

malhablado,-a *adj* foul-mouthed.

malhecho,-a *adj* deformed.

malhechor,-ra *nm & nf* criminal.

malherir *vt* to wound badly.

malhumor *nm* bad temper.

malhumorado,-a *adj* bad-tempered.
LOC **estar malhumorado,-a** to be in a bad mood.

Malí *nm* Mali.

malicia *nf (mala intención)* malice.

maliciosamente *adv* maliciously.

malicioso,-a *adj* malicious, spiteful.

maliense *adj* Malian.
▶ *nm o nf* Malian.

maligno,-a *adj* malignant.

malintencionado,-a *adj* malicious.
▶ *nm & nf* malicious person.

malinterpretar *vt* to misinterpret.

malísimo,-a *adj* terrible.

malla *nf (red)* mesh.
▶ *nf pl* **mallas** *(medias sin pie)* leggings.

malnacido,-a *nm & nf* despicable person.

malnutrición *nf* malnutrition.

malnutrido,-a *adj* malnourished.

malo,-a *adj* **1** bad: *¡qué día tan malo hace!* what dreadful weather! **2** *(malvado)* wicked, evil: *es muy mala persona* he's a nasty piece of work. **3** *(travieso)* naughty: *¡qué niño más malo!* what a naughty child! **4** *(nocivo)* harmful: *el tabaco es malo para la salud* smoking is bad for you. **5** *(enfermo)* ill, sick: *no ha venido a trabajar porque está malo con gripe* he's off sick with flu. **6** *(estropeado)* off: *este pescado ya está malo* this fish has gone off already.
▶ *nm & nf (en la ficción)* baddy, villain: *¿quién es el malo?* who's the baddy?

malogrado,-a *adj* wasted.

malograr *vt (desaprovechar)* to waste.

maloliente *adj* foul-smelling.

malparado,-a LOC **salir malparado,-a** to come off badly.

malpensado,-a *adj* nasty-minded.

malsano,-a *adj (ambiente, vida)* unhealthy; *(curiosidad)* morbid, unhealthy; *(mente)* sick.

malsonante *adj* offensive, rude.

malta *nf* malt.

Malta *nf* Malta.

maltear *vt* to malt.

maltés *adj* Maltese.
▶ *nm & nf (persona)* Maltese.
▶ *nm* **maltés** *(idioma)* Maltese.

M

maltratar vt (tratar mal) to ill-treat, mistreat; (pegar) to batter.

maltrato nm mistreatment.

maltrecho,-a adj 1 (persona) battered. 2 (cosa) damaged, destroyed.

malva adj (color) mauve.
▶ nf mallow.

malvado,-a adj wicked, evil.

malvarrosa nf hollyhock.

malvasía nf (uva) malvasia.

malvavisco nm marshmallow.

malvender vt to sell at a loss.

malversar vt to embezzle.

Malvinas nf pl **Islas Malvinas** Falkland Islands, Falklands.

malvinense adj of the Falklands.
▶ nm o nf Falklander, Falkland islander.

malvivir vi to live very badly.

mama nf (pecho) breast.

mamá nf fam mummy, US mom.

mamar vt (succionar) to suck.
▶ vi (bebé) to feed. [LOC] **dar de mamar** to breast-feed.

mamario,-a adj mammary.

mambo nm mambo.

mamífero,-a adj mammalian.

mamografía nf mammography.

mamotreto nm (armatoste) monstrosity.

mampara nf screen.

mampostería nf masonry.

mamut nm mammoth.

maná nm manna.

manada nf (vacas, elefantes) herd; (ovejas) flock; (lobos, perros) pack. [LOC] **en manada** en masse.

mánager nm o nf manager.

manantial nm spring.

manar vi (salir) to flow (de, from), pour (de, from), well (de, from).

manatí nm manatee.

manazas adj inv clumsy.

mancha nf stain, spot.

manchado,-a adj stained.

manchar vt to stain, dirty.
▶ vpr **mancharse** to get dirty.

mancillar vt arc to sully.

manco,-a adj (sin un brazo) one-armed; (sin una mano) one-handed.

mancomunidad nf association.

mandamiento nm REL commandment.

mandar vt 1 (ordenar) to order, tell. 2 (enviar) to send.
▶ vi (dirigir - un grupo) to be in charge.

mandarina nf mandarin, tangerine.

mandatario,-a nm & nf POL leader.

mandato nm (orden) order.

mandíbula nf jaw.

mandil nm apron.

mandioca nf manioc, cassava.

mando nm 1 (autoridad) command: le han relevado en el mando he's been dismissed. 2 (dispositivo) control. [COMP] **mando a distancia** (sistema) remote control.

mandolina nf mandolin.

mandón,-ona adj fam bossy.
▶ nm & nf fam bossy boots.

mandrágora nf mandrake.

mandril nm ZOOL mandril.

manecilla nf (de reloj) hand.

manejable adj easy-to-handle.

manejar vt to handle, operate, use.

manejo nm (uso) handling, use.

manera nf way, manner. [LOC] **de cualquier manera** 1 (en cualquier caso) in any case. 2 (sin cuidado, consideración, interés) carelessly. ▌**de ninguna manera** certainly not. ▌**de todas maneras** in any case.

manga nf sleeve: en mangas de camisa in shirt sleeves.

manganeso nm manganese.

mangar vt fam to pinch, nick, swipe.

manglar nm mangrove swamp.

mango¹ nm handle.

mango² nm BOT mango.

mangonear vt fam to boss about.

mangoneo nm fam meddling.

mangosta nf mongoose.

manguera nf (de riego) hose.

manguito nm (de manos) muff.

maní nm peanut.

manía nf 1 MED mania. 2 (ojeriza) dislike, grudge. 3 (costumbre) habit; (obsesión) obsession, mania: tiene la manía de morderse las uñas she has a habit of biting her nails.

maníaco,-a *adj* MED manic.
▶ *nm & nf fam* maniac.

maniatar *vt* to tie up.

maniático,-a *adj (raro)* cranky.
▶ *nm & nf (quisquilloso)* fusspot.

manicomio *nm* mental hospital.

manicura *nf* manicure.

manido,-a *adj (tema)* stale.

manifestación *nf* demonstration.

manifestante *nm o nf* demonstrator.

manifestar *vt (expresar)* to express.
▶ *vpr* **manifestarse** to demonstrate: *se manifestaron a favor del desarme nuclear* they demonstrated in favour of nuclear disarmament.

manifiesto,-a *adj* obvious, evident.
▶ *nm* **manifiesto** manifesto.

manija *nf* handle.

manilla *nf (de reloj)* hand.

manillar *nm* handlebars *pl*.

maniobra *nf* manoeuvre.

maniobrar *vi* to manoeuvre.

manipulación *nf* manipulation.

manipulador,-ra *adj* manipulative.
▶ *nm & nf* manipulator.

manipular *vt* to manipulate.

maniqueísmo *nm (doctrina)* Manichaeism.

maniquí *nm (muñeco)* dummy.

manirroto,-a *adj fam* spendthrift.
▶ *nm & nf fam* spendthrift.

manitas *nm o nf* handyman.

manivela *nf* crank, handle.

manjar *nm* delicious dish, delicacy.

mano *nf* **1** ANAT hand. **2** *(de pintura)* coat. LOC **a mano 1** *(escrito)* handwritten, by hand. **2** *(hecho)* handmade, by hand. **3** *(cerca)* to hand, handy, near. ▌**echar una mano** to give a hand, lend a hand.

manojo *nm* bunch.

manómetro *nm* pressure gauge.

manopla *nf (guante)* mitten.

manotazo *nm* slap, smack, swipe.

mansarda *nf* attic.

mansedumbre *nf* meekness, docility.

mansión *nf* mansion.

manso,-a *adj (animal)* tame.

manta *nf (gen)* blanket.

mantear *vt* to toss in a blanket.

manteca *nf (elaborado)* lard. COMP **manteca de cacao** cocoa butter. ▌**manteca de cerdo** lard.

mantecado *nm (helado)* dairy ice cream.

mantecoso,-a *adj* greasy.

mantel *nm* tablecloth.

mantelería *nf* table linen.

mantener *vt* **1** *(conservar)* to keep. **2** *(sustentar)* to support, maintain: *ella sola mantiene a toda la familia* she supports the whole family by herself. **3** *(conversación, relaciones)* to have; *(correspondencia)* to keep up.
▶ *vpr* **mantenerse 1** *(sostenerse)* to remain, stand. **2** *(continuar en un estado, una posición)* to keep: *se mantuvo a distancia* she kept her distance. **3** *(sostenerse)* to manage, maintain os, ssupport os.

mantenimiento *nm* maintenance.

mantequera *nf* butter dish.

mantequería *nf (tienda)* delicatessen.

mantequilla *nf* butter.

mantilla *nf* **1** *(de mujer)* mantilla. **2** *(de niño)* shawl.

mantillo *nm (abono del suelo)* humus.

mantis *nf* mantis. COMP **mantis religiosa** praying mantis.

manto *nm (capa)* cloak.

mantón *nm* large shawl.

manual *adj* manual.
▶ *nm* manual, handbook.

manualidad *nf* handicraft.
▶ *nf pl* **manualidades** arts and crafts.

manubrio *nm* crank, crankhandle.

manufacturar *vt* to manufacture.

manuscrito,-a *adj* handwritten.
▶ *nm* **manuscrito** manuscript.

manutención *nf (gen)* maintenance.

manzana *nf* BOT apple.

manzanilla *nf (planta)* camomile.

manzano *nm* apple tree.

maña *nf (habilidad)* skill, knack.

mañana *nf* morning: *hace una mañana preciosa* it's a beautiful morning. LOC **por la mañana** in the morning.
▶ *adv* tomorrow: *mañana no tengo que ir al cole* I don't have to go to school to-

M

morrow. LOC **¡hasta mañana!** see you tomorrow!

mañoso,-a *adj (habilidoso)* skilful.

maorí *adj* Maori.
▶ *nm & nf (persona)* Maori.
▶ *nm (idioma)* Maori.

mapa *nm* map.

mapache *nm* racoon.

mapamundi *nm* map of the world.

maqueta *nf (de edificio, monumento, etc)* scale model.

maquetar *vt* to do the page layout of.

maquetista *nm o nf* **1** *(de maquetas)* model maker. **2** *(de libros)* page designer.

maquiavélico,-a *adj* Machiavellian.

maquillador,-ra *nm & nf* make-up assistant.

maquillaje *nm* make-up.

maquillar *vt* to make up.
▶ *vpr* **maquillarse** *(ponerse maquillaje)* to make os up.

máquina *nf* **1** *(gen)* machine. **2** *(de un tren)* engine. COMP **máquina de afeitar** shaver, electric razor. ∣ **máquina de coser** sewing machine. ∣ **máquina de escribir** typewriter. ∣ **máquina de fotos** camera. ∣ **máquina de lavar** washing machine.

maquinar *vt* to scheme, plot.

maquinaria *nf* **1** machinery. **2** mechanism.

maquinilla *nf* razor.

maquinista *nm o nf (de tren)* engine driver, US engineer.

mar *nm & nf (gen)* sea. LOC **en alta mar** on the high sea, on the open sea. ∣ **la mar de...** *(muy)* very, really.

marabunta *nf* **1** swarm of ants. **2** *fam fig* mob, crowd.

maraca *nf* maraca.

maracuyá *nf* passion fruit.

marajá *nm* maharajah.

maraña *nf (espesura)* thicket.

maratón *nm* marathon.

maratoniano,-a *adj* marathon.

maravilla *nf* wonder, marvel. LOC **de maravilla** wonderfully.

maravillar *vt* to astonish, amaze.
▶ *vpr* **maravillarse** to marvel (de, at).

maravilloso,-a *adj* wonderful.

marca *nf* **1** *(señal)* mark, sign. **2** *(en comestibles, productos del hogar)* brand; *(en otros productos)* make. **3** DEP record. COMP **marca registrada** registered trademark.

marcado,-a *adj* **1** *(señalado)* marked. **2** *(acento)* marked, pronounced.

marcador *nm* **1** DEP scoreboard. **2** INFORM bookmark.

marcapasos *nm inv* pacemaker.

marcar *vt* **1** *(señalar)* to mark; *(ganado)* to brand. **2** DEP *(gol, canasta)* to score. **3** *(en teléfono)* to dial.

marcha *nf* **1** *(de protesta, soldados)* march. **2** *(progreso)* course, progress. **3** *(abandono)* leaving. **4** AUTO gear. **5** DEP walk. **6** *fam (de persona)* go, energy; *(de lugar, ambiente)* life. LOC **dar marcha atrás 1** *(coche)* to reverse. **2** *(proyecto)* to fall through. ∣ **ir de marcha** *(por la noche)* go out on the town. ∣ **poner en marcha 1** *(coche)* to start. **2** *(proyecto)* to start up.

marchar *vi* **1** *(ir)* to go, walk. **2** *(funcionar)* to work, run. **3** MIL to march.
▶ *vpr* **marcharse** to leave.

marchitar *vt* to wither.
▶ *vpr* **marchitarse** to wither.

marchito,-a *adj (planta)* withered; *(belleza)* faded.

marchoso,-a *adj fam (persona)* fun-loving, wild; *(música, sitio)* lively.
▶ *nm & nf* raver, fun-lover.

marcial *adj* martial.

marciano,-a *adj* Martian.
▶ *nm & nf* Martian.

marco *nm* **1** *(de cuadro, ventana)* frame. **2** *(moneda)* mark.

marea *nf* tide. COMP **marea alta** high tide. ∣ **marea baja** low tide. ∣ **marea negra** oil slick.

mareado,-a *adj (en general)* sick: *estoy mareado* I feel sick.

mareante *adj (que marea)* sickening.

marear *vt* to make sick.
▶ *vpr* **marearse 1** to get sick. **2** *(sentir vértigo)* to get dizzy.

marejada *nf* swell.

marejadilla *nf* slight swell.

maremoto *nm* tidal wave.

mareo *nm* sickness.

marfil *nm* ivory.

marfileño,-a *adj (de Costa de Marfil)* of the Ivory Coast.
▸ *nm & nf* native of the Ivory Coast.

marga *nf* marl.

margarina *nf* margarine.

margarita *nf* 1 BOT daisy. 2 *(de máquina)* daisywheel.

margen *nm (del papel)* margin.

marginación *nf* exclusion.

marginado,-a *adj* marginalized.
▸ *nm & nf* social outcast.

marginal *adj* 1 *(asunto)* marginal, minor. 2 *(persona)* marginalized.

marginar *vt (persona)* exclude; *(grupo social)* marginalize.

marido *nm* husband.

marimandón,-ona *nm & nf fam* bossy boots.

marina *nf (flota)* navy.

marinar *vt* to marinate.

marine *nm* marine.

marinero,-a *nm* sailor.

marino,-a *adj (corriente, animal)* marine.

marioneta *nf* puppet. COMP **(teatro de) marionetas** puppet show.

mariposa *nf (insecto)* butterfly.

mariposear *vi (andar alrededor)* to buzz around.

mariquita *nf* ZOOL ladybird, US ladybug.

marisabidilla *nf fam* know-all.

mariscada *nf (comida)* seafood dish.

mariscal *nm* marshal.

mariscar *vi* to fish for shellfish.

marisco *nm* seafood, shellfish.

marisma *nf* salt marsh.

marismeño,-a *adj (cultivo)* marshy.

marisquería *nf* seafood restaurant.

marital *adj* marital.

marítimo,-a *adj* maritime, sea.

marketing *nm* marketing.

marmita *nf* casserole, cooking pot.

mármol *nm* marble.

marmolería *nf (taller)* marble cutter's workshop.

marmóreo,-a *adj* marmoreal.

marmota *nf* ZOOL marmot.

maroma *nf* thick rope.

marqués,-esa *nm & nf (hombre)* marquis, marquess; *(mujer)* marchioness.

marquesina *nf* bus shelter.

marquetería *nf* marquetry.

marrano,-a *adj fam* filthy, dirty.
▸ *nm & nf fam (sucio)* filthy pig, dirty pig.
▸ *nm* **marrano** ZOOL pig.

marrón *adj* brown.
▸ *nm (color)* brown.

marroquí,-ina *adj* Moroccan.
▸ *nm & nf* Moroccan.

marroquinería *nf (artículos)* leather goods *pl*.

Marruecos *nm* Morocco.

marrullero,-a *adj fam* crafty.

marsupial *nm* marsupial.

marsupio *nm* marsupium.

marta *nf* marten.

Marte *nm* Mars.

martes *nm* Tuesday.

✎ Consulta también jueves.

martillazo *nm* blow with a hammer.

martillear *vt* to hammer.

martilleo *nm* hammering.

martillo *nm* hammer.

martinete *nm (ave)* heron.

martingala *nf fam (artimaña)* ruse.

Martinica *nf* Martinique.

martín pescador *nm* kingfisher.

mártir *nm o nf* martyr.

martirio *nm* 1 martyrdom. 2 *fig* torture, torment.

martirizar *vt* 1 to martyr. 2 *fig* to torment, torture.

marzo *nm* March: *el día 16 de marzo* March the sixteenth, the sixteenth of March; *nací el 6 de marzo de 1993* I was born on March 6th 1993; *durante el mes de marzo* in March; *en marzo del año pasado* last March; *en marzo del año que viene* next March; *a principios de marzo* at the beginning of March; *a mediados de marzo* in mid-March; *a finales de marzo* at the end of March.

mas *conj* but.

M

más adv 1 (comparativo) more: este año ha llovido más it has rained more this year. 2 (con números o cantidades) more: más de tres more than three. 3 (superlativo) most: es la más guapa she's the prettiest. 4 (después de pron interrog e indef) else: ¿algo más? anything else? 5 (exclamativo) so: ¡qué película más buena! what a wonderful film! LOC de más spare, extra. I más bien rather. I más o menos more or less.
▶ prep MAT plus: dos más dos igual a cuatro two plus two is four.
▶ nm (signo) plus sign.

masa nf 1 (en general) mass. 2 FÍS mass: unidad de masa unit of mass. 3 CULIN (para pan) dough; (para tartas) pastry. 4 (de gente) mass, crowd.

masacre nf massacre.

masaje nm massage.

masajear vt to massage.

masajista nm o nf (hombre) masseur; (mujer) masseuse.
▶ nm & nf DEP (en fútbol) physiotherapist, physio.

mascar vt to chew.

máscara nf (careta) mask.

mascarilla nf (de belleza) face mask.

mascota nf 1 (figura) mascot. 2 (animal doméstico) pet.

masculinidad nf masculinity.

masculino,-a adj 1 male: la población masculina the male population. 2 (propio de hombres) masculine. 3 GRAM masculine.

mascullar vt to mumble, mutter.

masificado,-a adj overcrowded.

masilla nf putty.

masivo,-a adj mass, massive.

master nm EDUC Master's degree.

máster nm (estudios) master's degree.

masticar vt to chew, masticate.

mástil nm 1 (asta) mast. 2 MAR mast.

mastodóntico,-a adj fam enormous.

mastoides nf inv mastoid.

mata nf (arbusto) shrub, bush.

matadero nm slaughterhouse.

matador,-ra adj fam (agotador) killing.

matalahúva nf (planta) anise.

matamoscas nm 1 (insecticida) fly spray. 2 (pala) fly swat.

matanza nf (gen) slaughter.

matar vt 1 (persona - gen) to kill.
▶ vpr **matarse** (involuntariamente) to die; (voluntariamente) to kill os.

matasellos nm inv (marca) postmark.

mate[1] adj (sin brillo) matt.

mate[2] nm (ajedrez) mate.

mate[3] nm (hierba) maté.

matemática nf (ciencia) mathematics.

matemáticas nf pl mathematics sing.

matemático,-a adj mathematical.
▶ nm & nf mathematician.

materia nf 1 (sustancia) matter. 2 (asignatura) subject. COMP **materia prima** raw material.

material adj (en general) material.
▶ nm (conjunto de cosas) equipment.

materialismo nm materialism.

materialista adj materialistic.

materializar vt to put into practice.

maternal adj maternal, motherly.

maternidad nf maternity.

materno,-a adj (abuelo, etc) maternal.

matinal adj morning.

matiz nm 1 (color) shade, tint. 2 (variación) nuance.

matizar vt 1 ARTE (colores) to blend. 2 (sonido) to modulate. 3 (añadir un matiz) to tinge (de, with).

matojo nm small shrub, bush.

matón,-ona nm & nf fam bully, thug.

matorral nm (maleza) bushes pl.

matraca nf wooden rattle.

matraz nm flask.

matriarca nf matriarch.

matriarcado nm matriarchy.

matriarcal adj matriarchal.

matrícula nf 1 (registro - de personas) registration, enrollment: plazo de matrícula registration period. 2 (tasa) registration fee(s), tuition fee(s). 3 AUTO (placa) number plate, US license plate. COMP **matrícula de honor** distinction.

matricular vt (persona) to register.

▶ *vpr* **matricularse** to register, enroll: *me he matriculado en Informática* I've enrolled for computer science.

matrimonial *adj (derecho)* matrimonial.

matrimonio *nm* **1** *(estado)* marriage. **2** *(pareja)* married couple.

matriz *nf* **1** ANAT womb. **2** MAT matrix.

matrona *nf (comadrona)* midwife.

matutino,-a *adj* morning.
▶ *nm* **matutino** *(periódico)* morning paper.

maullar *vi* miaow, US meow.

Mauritania *nf* Mauritania.

mauritano,-a *adj* Mauritanian.
▶ *nm & nf* Mauritanian.

mausoleo *nm* mausoleum.

maxilar *nm* jaw, jawbone.

máxima *nf (temperatura)* maximum temperature.

máxime *adv fml* especially.

maximizar *vt* to maximize.

máximo,-a *adj (velocidad)* maximum; *(puntuación, condecoración)* highest.
▶ *nm* **máximo** maximum: *tenéis una hora como máximo para acabar* you must be finished in an hour.

maya *adj* Mayan.
▶ *nm o nf (persona)* Mayan.
▶ *nm* **maya** *(idioma)* Mayan.

mayestático,-a *adj* majestic.

mayo *nm* May.

🖎 Para ejemplos de uso, consulta marzo.

mayólica *nf* majolica.

mayonesa *nf* mayonnaise.

mayor *adj* **1** *(comparativo)* bigger, greater, larger; *(persona)* older; *(hermanos, hijos)* elder, older. **2** *(superlativo)* biggest, greatest, largest; *(persona)* oldest; *(hermanos, hijos)* eldest, oldest. **3** *(de edad)* mature, elderly: *la gente mayor* elderly people. **4** *(adulto)* grown-up. **5** *(principal)* main. **6** MÚS major.
▶ *nm pl* **los mayores** *(adultos)* grown-ups, adults.
▶ *nm & nf* **el/la mayor** *(entre varios)* the oldest.

mayoral *nm (capataz)* foreman.

mayordomo *nm* butler.

mayoría *nf* majority: *la mayoría de los hombres...* most men…

mayorista *nm o nf* wholesaler.

mayoritario,-a *adj* majority.

mayúscula *nf* capital, capital letter.

mayúsculo,-a *adj (enorme)* enormous, gigantic

maza *nf* HIST *(arma)* mace.

mazapán *nm* marzipan.

mazmorra *nf* dungeon.

mazo *nm (martillo)* mallet.

mazorca *nf* cob. COMP **mazorca de maíz** corncob.

me *pron* **1** me: *no me lo dijo* she didn't tell me; *dámelo* give it to me. **2** *(reflexivo)* myself: *me veo en el espejo* I can see myself in the mirror.

meandro *nm* meander.

meca *nf* mecca, Mecca.

mecánica *nf (ciencia)* mechanics.

mecánico,-a *adj* mechanical.
▶ *nm & nf* mechanic.

mecanismo *nm* mechanism.

mecanización *nf* mechanization.

mecanizado,-a *adj* mechanized.

mecanizar *vt* to mechanize.

mecano® *nm* Meccano.

mecanografía *nf* typing.

mecanografiar *vt* to type.

mecedora *nf* rocking chair.

mecenas *nm o nf* patron.

mecer *vt* to rock.
▶ *vpr* **mecerse** *(en una silla)* to rock; *(en un columpio)* to swing.

mecha *nf* **1** *(de vela)* wick. **2** MIL fuse.

mechado,-a *adj* larded.

mechar *vt (carne)* to lard.

mechero *nm (cigarette)* lighter.

mechón *nm (de pelo)* lock, strand.

medalla *nf* medal.

medallero *nm* DEP medals table.

medallista *nm o nf* DEP medal winner.

medallón *nm (joya)* medallion.

media *nf* **1** *(calcetín)* sock. **2** *(promedio)* average. **3** MAT mean. **4** **la media** *(hora)* half past, half past the hour. COMP **media aritmética** arithmetic mean.

M

▶ *nf pl* **medias** *(enteras)* tights, pantihose; *(no enteras)* stockings.
mediación *nf* mediation.
mediado,-a *adj (recipiente)* half-empty; LOC **a mediados de** halfway through.
mediador,-ra *adj* mediating.
▶ *nm & nf* mediator.
mediana *nf* MAT median.
medianero,-a *adj* dividing.
mediano,-a *adj (de calidad)* average; *(de tamaño)* medium, medium-sized.
medianoche *nf* midnight.
mediante *adj* by means of.
mediar *vi* **1** *(interceder)* to intercede (en favor de, on behalf of). **2** *(interponerse)* to mediate (en, in), intervene (en, in). **3** *(estar en medio)* to be. **4** *(llegar a la mitad)*.
medicación *nf* medicines *pl.*
medicamento *nm* medicine, drug.
medicar *vt (recetar)* to prescribe.
▶ *vpr* **medicarse** to take medicine.
medicina *nf* medicine.
medicinal *adj* medicinal.
medición *nf (acción)* measuring.
médico,-a *adj* medical.
▶ *nm & nf* doctor. COMP **médico,-a de cabecera** general practitioner, GP. ▌**médico,-a de familia** family doctor.
medida *nf* **1** *(acción)* measuring; *(dato, número)* measurement. **2** *(disposición)* measure. LOC **a medida que** as.
medidor,-ra *nm AM (contador)* meter.
medieval *adj* medieval.
medievalista *nm o nf* medievalist.
medievo *nm* Middle Ages *pl.*
medio,-a *adj* **1** *(mitad)* half: *las dos y media* half past two; *un año y medio* a year and a half. **2** *(intermedio)* middle: *a media tarde* in the middle of the afternoon. **3** *(de promedio)* average.
▶ *adv* half: *medio terminado,-a* half-finished.
▶ *nm* **medio 1** *(mitad)* half. **2** *(centro)* middle. **3** *(contexto - físico)* environment. COMP **medio ambiente** environment.
▶ *nm pl* **medios** *(recursos)* means.
medioambiental *adj* environmental.
mediocampista *nm o nf* midfield player.

mediocre *adj* mediocre.
mediocridad *nf* mediocrity.
mediodía *nm (las doce)* midday.
mediopensionista *nm o nf* day student.
medir *vt* to measure.
▶ *vpr* **medirse** to measure os.
meditación *nf* meditation.
meditar *vt* to meditate, think.
▶ *vi* to meditate (sobre, over).
mediterráneo,-a *adj* Mediterranean.
▶ *nm & nf* Mediterranean. COMP **el (mar) Mediterráneo** the Mediterranean (Sea).
médium *nm o nf* medium.
medrar *vi (mejorar socialmente)* to get rich.
médula *nf* **1** ANAT marrow. **2** BOT pith. COMP **médula espinal** spinal cord.
medular *adj* ANAT marrow.
medusa *nf* jellyfish.
megabyte *nm* megabyte.
megafonía *nf* sound amplification.
megáfono *nm* megaphone.
megahercio *nm* megahertz.
megalítico,-a *adj* megalithic.
megalito *nm* megalith.
megalómano,-a *nm & nf* megalomaniac.
megatón *nm* megaton.
megavatio *nm* megawatt.
megavoltio *nm* megavolt.
mejicano,-a *adj* Mexican.
▶ *nm & nf* Mexican.
Méjico *nm* Mexico.
mejilla *nf* cheek.
mejillón *nm* mussel.
mejor *adj* **1** *(comparativo)* better: *este libro es mejor que aquél* this book is better than that one. **2** *(superlativo)* best: *mi mejor amigo,-a* my best friend. LOC **a lo mejor** perhaps, maybe.
▶ *adv* **1** *(comparativo)* better: *cada vez mejor* better and better every day. **2** *(superlativo)* best.
▶ *nm & nf* **el/la mejor** the best (one).
mejora *nf (progreso)* improvement.
mejorable *adj* which could be improved.
mejorar *vt* to improve.

▶ *vi* to improve, get better.
▶ *vpr* **mejorarse** to get better: *¡que te mejores!* I hope you get better.

mejoría *nf* improvement.

melancolía *nf* melancholy, sadness.

melancólico,-a *adj* melancholic.

melanina *nf* melanin.

melaza *nf* molasses.

melena *nf* 1 *(de persona)* hair. 2 *(de león)* mane.

melisa *nf* lemon balm.

mella *nf (hendedura)* nick, notch.

mellar *vt* 1 *(objeto)* to chip, nick. 2 *fig* to dent, damage.

mellizo,-a *adj* twin.
▶ *nm & nf* twin.

melocotón *nm* peach.

melocotonero *nm* peach tree.

melodía *nf* melody.

melódico,-a *adj* melodic.

melodrama *nm* melodrama.

melodramático,-a *adj* melodramatic.

melómano,-a *adj* music lover.

melón *nm (fruto)* melon.

meloso,-a *adj (dulce)* sweet, honeyed.

membrana *nf* membrane.

membrillo *nm (fruta)* quince.

memo,-a *adj fam* stupid, dim.

memorable *adj* memorable.

memorándum *nm (cuaderno)* notebook.

memoria *nf* 1 *(gen)* memory. 2 *(informe)* report. 3 *(inventario)* inventory.
▶ *nf pl* **memorias** *(biografía)* memoirs.
[LOC] **de memoria** (off) by heart, by memory. **I hacer memoria** to try to remember. [COMP] **memoria RAM** RAM memory.

memorial *nm (acto)* conmemoration.

memorizar *vt* to memorize.

mena *nf* ore.

menaje *nm* household goods. [COMP] **menaje de cocina** kitchen equipment.

mención *nf* mention.

mencionar *vt* to mention, cite.

mendelismo *nm* Mendelism.

mendicante *adj* mendicant.

mendicidad *nf* begging.

mendigar *vi* to beg.

mendigo,-a *nm & nf* beggar.

mendrugo *nm* hard crust (of bread).

menear *vt (cabeza)* to shake; *(cola)* to wag; *(cuerpo, caderas)* to wiggle.

menestra *nf* vegetable stew.

mengua *nf (disminución)* decrease.

menguado,-a *adj* diminished.

menguante *adj (luna)* waning.

menguar *vi* 1 *(cantidad)* to decrease. 2 *(luna)* to wane.

menhir *nm* menhir.

meninge *nm* meninx.

meningitis *nm inv* meningitis.

menisco *nm* meniscus.

menopausia *nf* menopause.

menopáusico,-a *adj* menopausal.

menor *adj* 1 *(comparativo - en tamaño)* smaller; *(- en calidad, importancia)* lesser; *(- en edad)* younger. 2 *(superlativo - en tamaño)* smallest; *(- en calidad, importancia)* least; *(- en edad)* youngest. 3 *(inferior)* minor. 4 MÚS minor.
▶ *nm o nf* JUR minor. [COMP] **menor de edad** minor.

menos *adj* 1 *(comparativo - en cantidad)* less; *(- en número)* fewer: *yo tengo menos años que tú* I'm younger than you. 2 *(superlativo - de cantidad)* least; *(- de número)* fewest: *yo soy la que menos culpa tiene* I'm the least guilty.
▶ *adv* 1 *(comparativo - de cantidad)* less; *(- de número)* fewer: *voy al gimnasio menos que antes* I go to the gym less than before. 2 *(superlativo)* least: *es el menos guapo* he's the least good-looking. 3 *(con horas)* to: *las tres menos cuarto* a quarter to three. 4 MAT minus. [LOC] **a menos que** unless. **I al menos** at least. **I por lo menos** at least.
▶ *prep* but, except: *todo menos eso* anything but that.
▶ *pron (cantidad)* less; *(número)* fewer: *me pagó menos* he paid me less.
▶ *nm* MAT minus sign.

menospreciar *vt* 1 *(despreciar)* to despise, scorn. 2 *(no valorar)* to undervalue, underrate.

M

menosprecio *nm (poco aprecio)* underestimation, lack of appreciation.

mensaje *nm* 1 *(en general)* message. 2 *(envío electrónico)* posting.

mensajería *nf* courier service.

mensajero,-a *nm & nf* courier.

menstruación *nf* menstruation.

menstrual *adj* menstrual.

menstruar *vi* to menstruate.

mensual *adj* monthly.

mensualidad *nf (que se cobra)* monthly salary; *(que se paga)* monthly instalment.

mensurable *adj* measurable.

menta *nf (hierba)* mint.

mental *adj* mental.

mentalidad *nf* mentality.

mentalizar *vt* to make aware.
 ▶ *vpr* **mentalizarse** *(hacerse a la idea)* to get used to the idea.

mente *nf* 1 *(pensamiento)* mind. 2 *(facultades)* mind, intelligence, intellect.

mentir *vi* to lie.

mentira *nf* lie.

mentiroso,-a *nm & nf* liar.

mentón *nm* chin.

mentor *nm* mentor.

menú *nm* 1 CULIN menu. 2 INFORM menu. COMP **menú del día** set menu.

menudo,-a *adj* 1 *(pequeño)* small, tiny. 2 *(enfático)* what a…: ¡menudo lío! what a mess! LOC **a menudo** often.

meñique *adj* little. COMP **(dedo) meñique** little finger.

meollo *nm (lo esencial)* core, heart, crux.

mercader *nm arc* merchant.

mercadería *nf* merchandise.

mercadillo *nm* flea market, bazaar.

mercado *nm* market. COMP **Mercado Común** Common Market. ▌ **mercado de abastos** wholesale food market.

mercancía *nf (gen)* goods.

mercante *adj* merchant.

mercantil *adj* commercial.

mercantilismo *nm* mercantilism.

mercenario,-a *nm & nf* mercenary.

mercería *nf (tienda)* haberdasher's shop, US notions store.

mercurio *nm* QUÍM mercury.

merecedor,-ra *adj* worthy.

merecer *vt* to deserve, be worth: *merece la pena verlo* it's worth a visit.

merecido,-a *nm (just)* come-uppance. LOC **llevar su merecido** to get one's come-uppance.

merendar *vi* to have tea.
 ▶ *vt* to have something for tea.

merendero *nm* open-air snack bar.

merengue *nm* CULIN meringue.

meridiano,-a *nm* meridian.

meridional *adj* southern.

merienda *nf* afternoon snack, tea.

merina *nf* merino sheep.

mérito *nm (de alguien)* merit.

merluza *nf* hake.

mermar *vt* to reduce.
 ▶ *vi* to decrease, diminish.

mermelada *nf* jam; *(de cítricos)* marmalade.

mero *nm (pez)* grouper.

merodear *vi (curiosear)* to prowl about.

mes *nm* month.

mesa *nf (gen)* table; *(de oficina)* desk. LOC **poner la mesa** to set the table, lay the table. ▌ **quitar/recoger la mesa** to clear the table.

meseta *nf* GEOG plateau.

mesianismo *nm* Messianism.

mesías *nm inv* Messiah.

mesilla *nf* small table. COMP **mesilla de noche** bedside table.

mesocarpio *nm* mesocarp.

mesolítico,-a *nm* the Mesolithic.

mesón *nm* old-style restaurant.

mestizaje *nm* crossbreeding.

mestizo,-a *adj* of mixed race.
 ▶ *nm & nf* person of mixed race.

mesura *nf* restraint, moderation.

meta *nf* 1 *(en una carrera)* finishing line. 2 *(portería)* goal. 3 *fig* purpose.

metabolismo *nm* metabolism.

metabolizar *vt* to metabolize.

metafísica *nf* metaphysics.

metáfora *nf* metaphor.

metafórico,-a *adj* metaphorical.

metal *nm* metal.

metálico,-a *adj* metallic.
▶ *nm* **metálico** cash.

metalista *nm o nf* metal worker.

metalistería *nf* metal work.

metalizado,-a *adj* metallic.

metalizar *vt* to metallize (US metalize).

metalurgia *nf* metallurgy.

metalúrgico,-a *adj* metallurgical.
▶ *nm & nf* metallurgist.

metamórfico,-a *adj* metamorphic.

metamorfosis *nf inv* metamorphosis.

metano *nm* methane.

metanol *nm* methanol.

metástasis *nf inv* metastasis.

metatarso *nm* metatarsus.

meteórico,-a *adj* meteoric.

meteorito *nm* meteorite.

meteoro *nm* meteor.

meteorología *nf* meteorology.

meteorológico,-a *adj* meteorological.

meteorólogo,-a *nm & nf* meteorologist.

metepatas *nm o nf fam* bigmouth.

meter *vt* **1** *(introducir)* to put. **2** *(implicar)* to put into (en, -), get into (en, -), involve in (en, -).
▶ *vpr* **meterse 1** *(introducirse en)* to get in: *se metió en la cama* he got into bed. **2** *(tomar parte - negocio)* to go into (en, -); *(involucrarse en)* to get involved (en, in/with), get mixed up (en, in/with). **3** *(introducirse)* to get involved (en, in): *me metí totalmente en el papel* I got completely into in the role. **4** *(ir)* to go: *¿dónde se habrá metido?* where can he have got to?

meticuloso,-a *adj (cuidadoso)* meticulous.

metido,-a *adj (envuelto, implicado)* involved (en, in).

metileno *nm* methylene.

metílico,-a *adj* methylic.

metódico,-a *adj* methodical.

método *nm* method.

metodología *nf* methodology.

metodológico,-a *adj* methodological.

metonimia *nf* metonymy.

metraje *nm (película rodada)* footage. ᴄᴏᴍᴾ **largo metraje** (full-length) feature film.

metralla *nf* shrapnel.

metralleta *nf* sub-machine-gun.

métrica *nf* metrics *pl*.

métrico,-a *adj* **1** *(sistema, unidad)* metric. **2** *(del verso)* metrical, metric. ᴄᴏᴍᴾ **sistema métrico** metric system.

metro *nm* **1** metre (US meter). **2** *(cinta)* tape measure. **3** *(transporte)* underground, tube, US subway. ᴄᴏᴍᴾ **metro cuadrado** square metre.

metrónomo *nm* metronome.

metrópoli *nf* metropolis.

metropolitano,-a *adj* metropolitan.
▶ *nm* **metropolitano** *fml* underground, tube, US subway.

mexicano,-a *adj* Mexican.
▶ *nm & nf* Mexican.

México *nm* Mexico.

mezcla *nf* **1** *(acción)* mixing, blending. **2** *(producto)* mixture, blend.

mezclar *vt* **1** *(incorporar, unir)* to mix, blend. **2** *(desordenar)* to mix up.
▶ *vpr* **mezclarse 1** *(personas)* to mix (con, with). **2** *(cosas)* to get mixed up.

mezquindad *nf* **1** meanness, stinginess. **2** *(acción)* mean thing.

mezquino,-a *adj* low, base.

mezquita *nf* mosque.

mi *nm* MÚS E.

mí *pron* me: *éste es para mí* this one is for me.

miau *nm* miaow, meow, mew.

mica *nf* GEOL mica.

michelín *nm fam* spare tyre.

mico *nm (animal)* monkey.

micología *nf* mycology.

micosis *nf inv* mycosis.

micra *nf* micron.

micro *nm fam* mike, microphone.

microbio *nm* microbe.

microbiología *nf* microbiology.

M

microchip *nm* microchip.

microclima *nm* microclimate.

microcomputador *nm* microcomputer.

microcosmos *nm inv* microcosm.

microeconomía *nf* microeconomics.

microelectrónica *nf* microelectronics.

microfilme *nm* microfilm.

micrófono *nm* microphone.

microondas *nm* microwave. COMP horno microondas microwave oven.

microordenador *nm* microcomputer.

microprocesador *nm* microprocessor.

microscópico,-a *adj* microscopic.

microscopio *nm* microscope.

miedo *nm* fear. LOC **tener miedo** to be scared, be frightened, be afraid: *tiene miedo a la oscuridad* he's afraid of the dark.

miedoso,-a *adj* easily frightened.

miel *nf* honey.

miembro *nm* **1** *(extremidad)* limb. **2** *(socio)* member. **3** MAT member.

mientras *adv* meanwhile.
▶ *conj* **1** *(temporal)* while, whilst: *mientras estés de vacaciones no pienses en el trabajo* while you're on holiday, don't think about work. **2** *(adversativa)* whereas: *yo al menos he estudiado, mientras que tú no* at least I have studied, whereas you haven't.

miércoles *nm* Wednesday.

✎ Consulta también jueves.

mies *nf* corn, grain.

miga *nf* *(parte blanda del pan)* crumb.

migración *nf* migration.

migraña *nf* migraine.

migrar *vi* to migrate.

migratorio,-a *adj* migratory.

mijo *nm* millet.

mil *adj* **1** thousand. **2** *(milésimo)* thousandth.
▶ *nm* a thousand, one thousand.

✎ Consulta también seis y sexto,-a.

milagro *nm* miracle.

milagroso,-a *adj* miraculous.

milanesa LOC **a la milanesa** done in breadcrumbs.

milano *nm* kite.

milenario,-a *adj* millennial.
▶ *nm* milenario millennium.

milenio *nm* millennium.

milésimo,-a *adj* thousandth.
▶ *nm & nf* thousandth.

✎ Consulta también sexto,-a.

milhojas *nm inv* CULIN millefeuille.

mili *nf fam* military service. LOC **hacer la mili** *fam* to do one's military service.

milicia *nf* *(gente armada)* militia.

miliciano,-a *adj* of the militia.
▶ *nm & nf (hombre)* militiaman; *(mujer)* militiawoman.

miligramo *nm* milligram.

mililitro *nm* millilitre (US milliliter).

milimétrico,-a *adj* pinpoint.

milímetro *nm* millimetre (US millimeter).

militante *adj* militant.

militar *adj* military.
▶ *nm* military man, soldier.

milla *nf* mile. COMP **milla náutica** nautical mile.

millar *nm* thousand.

millón *nm* million.

millonario,-a *nm & nf (hombre)* millionaire; *(mujer)* millionairess.

mimar *vt (consentir)* to spoil.

mimbre *nm* wicker.

mimetismo *nm* mimicry.

mímico,-a *adj* mimic.

mimo *nm* **1** *(actor)* mime artist. **2** *(cariño)* pampering. **3** *(cuidado)* care. LOC **hacerle mimos a ALGN** to pamper SB.

mimosa *nf* BOT mimosa.

mimoso,-a *adj (cariñoso)* loving.

mina *nf* **1** mine. **2** *(explosivo)* mine. **3** *(de lápiz)* lead. COMP **mina de carbón** coal mine.

minar *vt (terreno)* to mine.

minarete *nm* minaret.

mineral *adj* mineral. COMP **agua mineral** mineral water.
▶ *nm* mineral.

minería *nf (técnica)* mining.

minero,-a *adj* mining.
▶ *nm & nf* miner.

miniatura *nf* miniature.

minifalda *nf* mini skirt.

minifundio *nm* smallholding.

minigolf *nm* crazy golf.

mínima *nf (temperatura)* minimum temperature.

minimizar *vt* to minimize.

mínimo,-a *adj* minimum, lowest.
▶ *nm* **mínimo** minimum: *pon el gas en el mínimo* turn the gas right down. LOC **como mínimo** at least. COMP **mínimo común múltiplo** lowest common multiple.

minino *nm fam* pussy, kitty.

minio *nm* red lead, minium.

ministerio *nm* POL ministry, US department.

ministro,-a *nm & nf* POL minister, US secretary. COMP **primer,-ra ministro,-a** prime minister.

minoría *nf* minority.

minorista *adj* retail.

minoritario,-a *adj* minority.

minucia *nf* trifle.

minucioso,-a *adj* meticulous.

minúscula *nf (letra)* small letter.

minúsculo,-a *adj (letra)* small; *(detalle)* insignificant.

minusvalía *nf* handicap, disability.

minusválido,-a *adj* disabled, handicapped.
▶ *nm & nf* disabled person.

minuta *nf (factura)* bill.

minutero *nm* minute hand.

minuto *nm* minute.

mío,-a *adj* my, of mine: *es muy amiga mía* she's a good friend of mine.
▶ *pron* mine: *este abrigo es mío* this coat is mine.

miocardio *nm* myocardium.

miope *adj* short-sighted, myopic.
▶ *nm o nf* short-sighted person.

miopía *nf* short-sightedness.

mira *nf* **1** *(dispositivo)* sight. **2** *fig* intention.

mirada *nf (gen)* look; *(vistazo)* glance. LOC **echar una mirada a** ALGO/ALGN to take a look at STH/SB.

mirador *nm* **1** *(balcón)* glassed-in balcony. **2** *(lugar)* viewing point.

miramiento *nm* consideration.

mirar *vt* **1** *(observar)* to look at; *(con atención)* to watch. **2** *(buscar)* to look; *(registrar)* to search: *me miraron todo al pasar por la aduana* they went through everything at customs. **3** *(tener cuidado con)* to watch: *mira bien lo que haces* watch what you do.
▶ *vi* **1** *(gen)* to look. **2** *(buscar)* to look: *mira debajo de la cama* look under the bed. **3** *(tener cuidado)* to mind, watch, be careful: *mira que no te engañen* mind they don't cheat you. LOC **¡mira!** look!

miríada *nf* myriad.

mirilla *nf* peephole, spyhole.

miriópodo *nm* myriapod.

mirlo *nm* blackbird.

mirón,-ona *nm & nf fam pey (curioso)* nosy parker.

mirra *nf* myrrh.

mirto *nm* myrtle.

misa *nf* mass.

misal *nm* missal.

misántropo,-a *nm & nf* misanthrope, misanthropist.

miscelánea *nf* miscellany.

miserable *adj* **1** *(tacaño)* mean. **2** *(malvado)* wretched.
▶ *nm o nf* **1** *(malvado)* wretch. **2** *(tacaño)* miser.

miseria *nf (pobreza)* extreme poverty.

misericordia *nf* mercy.

mísero,-a *adj* miserable.

misil *nm* missile.

misión *nf (tarea)* mission, task.

misionero,-a *nm & nf* missionary.

mismo,-a *adj* **1** *(idéntico)* same: *el mismo color* the same colour. **2** *(enfático)* very: *en esta misma casa nací yo* I was born in this very house.
▶ *pron* same: *es el mismo del año pasado* it's the same one as last year.
▶ *adv* **mismo** same: *piensa lo mismo que tu* he thinks the same as you. LOC **es lo mismo 1** *(la misma cosa)* it amounts to the same thing. **2** *(no importa)* it doesn't matter.

M

misógino,-a *adj* misogynous.

míster *nm (en fútbol)* manager, coach.

misterio *nm* mystery.

misterioso,-a *adj* mysterious.

mística *nf* 1 *(misticismo)* mysticism. 2 *(teología)* mystic theology.

misticismo *nm* mysticism.

místico,-a *adj* mystic, mystical.
▶ *nm & nf (persona)* mystic.

mitad *nf* 1 half: *me llevo la mitad* I'll take half. 2 *(medio)* middle: *en mitad de la plaza* in the middle of the square.

mítico,-a *adj* mythical.

mitificar *vt (convertir en mito)* to mythicize.

mitin *nm* meeting, rally.

mito *nm* myth.

mitología *nf* mythology.

mitológico,-a *adj* mythological.

mitosis *nf inv* mitosis.

mixto,-a *adj* mixed.

mobiliario *nm* furniture.

moca *nf (café)* mocha.

mocasín *nm* moccasin.

mochila *nf* rucksack, backpack.

mochuelo *nm* ZOOL little owl.

moción *nf* motion.

moco *nm* 1 *(mucosidad)* mucus; *(familiarmente)* snot. LOC **limpiarse los mocos** *fam* to blow one's nose.

mocoso,-a *nm & nf fam* brat.

moda *nf* fashion.

modales *nm pl* manners.

modalidad *nf* form, means, way.

modelado *nm* modelling (US modeling).

modelar *vt* to model, shape.

modélico,-a *adj* model.

modelismo *nm (de arcilla, etc)* modelling.

modelo *adj* model.
▶ *nm o nf (persona)* (fashion) model.

módem *nm* modem.

moderación *nf* moderation.

moderado,-a *adj* moderate.

moderador,-ra *nm & nf (de reunión)* chairperson.

moderar *vt* to moderate.

modernismo *nm (arte, literatura)* Modernism.

modernista *adj* Modernist.
▶ *nm o nf* Modernist.

modernizar *vt* to modernize.

moderno,-a *adj* modern.

modestia *nf* modesty.

modesto,-a *adj* modest.

modificar *vt* to alter, modify.

modista *nm o nf (de ropa para mujer)* dressmaker.

modisto *nm* 1 *(diseñador)* fashion designer. 2 *(sastre)* tailor.

modo *nm* 1 way, manner. 2 LING mood: *el modo subjuntivo* the subjunctive mood. LOC **de modo que** so: *de modo que ya lo sabes* so now you know. ▮ **en cierto modo** in a way.
▶ *nm pl* **modos** manners. LOC **de todos modos** anyhow, at any rate.

modorra *nf fam* drowsiness.

modular *vt* to modulate.
▶ *adj* modular.

módulo *nm* 1 *(gen)* module. 2 *(mueble)* unit.

mofa *nf* mockery, derision.

mofarse *vpr* to scoff, mock.

mofeta *nf* skunk.

moflete *nm fam* chubby cheek.

mogollón *nm fam* loads *pl.*
▶ *adv fam* a lot: *nos gustó mogollón* it was dead brilliant.

mohair *nm* mohair.

moho *nm* mould, (US mold).

mohoso,-a *adj* mouldy (US moldy).

mojado,-a *adj (húmedo)* wet, moist.

mojama *nf* dried salted tuna.

mojar *vt* 1 *(gen)* to wet. 2 *(alimento)* to dip
▶ *vpr* **mojarse** 1 to get wet. 2 *fam (comprometerse)* to commit os.

mojigato,-a *adj (gazmoño)* prudish.

mojón *nm (poste - de distancia)* milepost.

molar *nm (diente)* molar.

molde *nm* mould (US mold).

moldeable *adj* mouldable.

moldeado,-a *adj* moulded (US molded).

moldear *vt* ARTE *(dar forma)* to mould (US mold).

moldura *nf* moulding (US molding).
mole *nf* mass, bulk, hulk.
molécula *nf* molecule.
molecular *adj* molecular.
moler *vt* **1** *(gen)* to grind. **2** *(cansar)* to wear out.
molestar *vt* **1** *(interrumpir)* to disturb. **2** *(perturbar)* to bother, upset: *me molestan los ruidos* noise bothers me. **3** *(importunar)* to pester: *¡deja de molestarme ya!* stop pestering me! **4** *(hacer daño - apretar)* to hurt: *estos zapatos me molestan* these shoes hurt my feet.
▶ *vpr* **molestarse** to bother: *perdone que le moleste* I'm sorry to bother you.
molestia *nf* **1** *(incomodidad)* bother, trouble; *(fastidio)* nuisance. **2** MED trouble.
molesto,-a *adj* **1** annoying. **2** *(enfadado)* annoyed.
molido,-a *adj* **1** *(café)* ground. **2** *fam (cansado)* worn-out. LOC **estar molido,-a** *fam* to be worn-out.
molienda *nf* *(de café)* grinding.
moliente LOC **corriente y moliente** run of the mill, common or garden.
molinero,-a *nm & nf* miller.
molinillo *nm* grinder, mill.
molino *nm* mill. COMP **molino de viento** windmill.
molla *nf* *(pulpa)* flesh.
molleja *nf* *(de ave)* gizzard.
mollera *nf* *fam (inteligencia)* brains *pl*.
molón,-na *adj* *argot* cool, brill, fab.
molusco *nm* mollusc (US mollusk).
momentáneo,-a *adj* momentary.
momento *nm* **1** moment. **2** *(período)* time.
momia *nf* mummy.
momificación *nf* mummification.
momificar *vt* to mummify.
monacal *adj* monastic.
monacato *nm* *(institución)* monastic community.
Mónaco *nm* Monaco.
monada *nf* *(cosa bonita)* beauty, lovely thing; *(persona)* gorgeous person.
monaguillo *nm* altar boy.
monarca *nm* monarch.

monarquía *nf* monarchy.
monárquico,-a *adj* monarchic.
monasterio *nm* monastery.
monástico,-a *adj* monastic.
monda *nf* *(piel)* peel, skin.
mondadientes *nm inv* toothpick.
mondadura *nf* *(piel - de fruta)* peel.
mondar *vt* *(pelar)* to peel.
mondo,-a *adj* *(limpio)* bare.
mondongo *nm* innards *pl*.
moneda *nf* *(pieza)* coin.
monedero *nm* purse.
monegasco,-a *adj* Monegasque.
▶ *nm & nf* Monegasque.
monetario,-a *adj* monetary.
monetarismo *nm* monetarism.
monetarista *adj* monetarist.
mongólico,-a *adj* affected by Down's syndrome.
▶ *nm & nf* person affected by Down's syndrome.
mongolismo *nm* Down's syndrome, mongolism.
monicaco *nm* *fam* dodgy geezer.
monigote *nm* **1** *(figura)* rag doll, paper doll. **2** *(dibujo)* matchstick man.
monismo *nm* monism.
monista *adj* monistic.
monitor,-ra *nm & nf (profesor)* instructor.
▶ *nm* **monitor** *(pantalla)* screen.
monja *nf* nun.
monje *nm* monk.
mono,-a *adj (bonito)* nice, lovely, cute.
▶ *nm & nf* ZOOL monkey.
▶ *nm* **mono** *(prenda de trabajo)* overalls *pl*.
monocarril *nm* monorail.
monocolor *adj* monochrome.
monocorde *adj fig (monótono)* dull.
monocotiledónea *nf* monocotyledon.
monocotiledóneo,-a *adj* monocotyledonous.
monocromático,-a *adj* monochromatic.
monocromía *nf* monochrome.
monocromo,-a *adj* monochrome.
monocular *adj* monocular.
monóculo *nm* monocle.

M

monocultivo *nm* monoculture.
monódico,-a *adj* monodic.
monofásico,-a *adj* single-phase.
monofonía *nm* mono.
monofónico,-a *adj* mono.
monogamia *nf* monogamy.
monógamo,-a *adj* monogamous.
monografía *nf* monograph.
monográfico,-a *adj* monographic.
monograma *nm* monogram.
monolingüe *adj* monolingual.
monolítico,-a *adj* monolithic.
monolito *nm* monolith.
monologar *vi* to soliloquize.
monólogo *nm (reflexión)* monologue.
monomanía *nf* **2** *fam* obsession.
monomaníaco,-a *adj* MED monomaniac.
monomio *n* MAT monomial.
monoparental *adj* one-parent.
monopatín *nm* skateboard.
monoplano *nm* monoplane.
monoplaza *adj* single-seat.
monopolio *nm* monopoly.
monopolista *adj* monopolistic.
monopolización *nf* monopolization.
monopolizador,-ra *adj* monopolizing.
monopolizar *vt* to monopolize.
monorraíl *nm* monorail.
monosilábico,-a *adj* monosyllabic.
monosílabo,-a *adj* monosyllabic.
▶ *nm* **monosílabo** monosyllable.
monoteísmo *nm* monotheism.
monoteísta *adj* monotheistic.
▶ *nm o nf* monotheist.
monotonía *nf* monotony.
monótono,-a *adj* monotonous.
monovolumen *nm* people carrier.
monóxido *nm* monoxide. COMP monóxido de carbono carbon monoxide.
monseñor *nm* Monsignor.
monserga *nf fam (lección)* nagging.
monstruo *adj fam* fantastic, terrific.
▶ *nm* **1** monster. **2** *fam (genio)* genius.
monstruosidad *nf (cosa)* monstrosity.
monstruoso,-a *adj* monstrous.

monta *nf* **1** *(importancia)* value, account, importance. **2** *(de un caballo)* riding.
montacargas *nm* service lift.
montador,-ra *nm & nf (operario)* fitter.
montadora *nf* splicing machine.

✎ Consulta también **montador,-a.**

montaje *nm* **1** *(de piezas)* assembly. **2** *(en foto)* montage. **3** *fam (farsa)* setup.
montante *nm* **1** *(total)* total, total amount. **2** *(pieza vertical)* upright. **3** *(ventana)* skylight.
montaña *nf* mountain.
montañero,-a *nm & nf* mountaineer.
montañés,-esa *nm & nf* highlander.
montañismo *nm* mountaineering.
montañoso,-a *adj* mountainous.
montaplatos *nm inv* dumb waiter.
montar *vi* **1** *(subir - caballo, bicicleta)* to mount, get on; *(- coche)* to get in; *(- avión)* to get on, board. **2** *(ir en bicicleta)* to ride: *¿sabes montar en bicicleta?* can you ride bicycle?
▶ *vt* **1** *(subir - caballo)* to mount, get on. **2** *(subir - persona)* to put on: *monté al niño en la bicicleta* I lifted the kid onto his bike. **3** *(ensamblar)* to assemble, put together; *(tienda de campaña)* to put up. **4** *(nata)* to whip; *(claras)* to whisk.
▶ *vpr* **montarse 1** *(subirse)* to get on; *(- en un coche)* to get in; *(- en un caballo)* to mount, get on. **2** *fam (armarse)* to break out: *se montó un buen jaleo* there was a real to-do.
montaraz *adj (de montaña)* mountain.
monte *nm* **1** mountain, mount. **2** *(bosque)* wild, woodland.
montenegrino,-a *adj* Montenegrin.
▶ *nm & nf* Montenegrin.
Montenegro *nm* Montenegro.
montepío *nm* friendly society.
montera *nf* bullfighter's hat.
montería *nf (caza)* hunt.
montero,-a *nm & nf* hunter.
montés *adj* wild.
montículo *nm* mound, hillock.
monto *nm* total, total amount.
montón *nm* **1** heap, pile. **2** *fam (gran cantidad)* stacks *pl*, loads *pl*, heaps *pl*:

vino un montón de gente loads of people came.

montura *nf* **2** *(silla)* saddle. **3** *(armazón - de gafas)* frame.

monumental *adj* monumental.

monumento *nm* ARTE monument.

monzón *nm* monsoon.

monzónico,-a *adj* monsoon.

moña *nf fam (borrachera)* bender.

moño *nm* bun.

moquear *vi* to have a runny nose.

moqueta *nf* fitted carpet.

moquillo *nm (de perro)* distemper.

mora *nf* **1** *(de moral)* mulberry. **2** *(zarza-mora)* blackberry.

morada *nf* adobe, dwelling.

morado,-a *adj (color)* purple.
▶ *nm* **morado** *(color)* purple.

morador,-ra *nm & nf* dweller.

moral¹ *adj* moral.
▶ *nf* **1** *(reglas)* morals *pl*. **2** *(ánimo)* morale, spirits *pl*.

moral² *nm* BOT mulberry tree.

moraleja *nf* moral.

moralidad *nf* morality.

moralina *nf* false morals *pl*.

moralista *adj* moralistic.

moralizador,-ra *adj* moralizing.

moralizar *vi* to moralize.
▶ *vt* to moralize.

morar *vi* to reside, dwell.

moratón *nm fam* bruise.

moratoria *nf* moratorium.

morbidez *nf* softness, tenderness.

morbo *nm fam* thrill.

morbosidad *nf (interés)* morbid curiosity.

morboso,-a *adj fam* kinky.

morcilla *nf* black pudding.

mordaz *adj* mordant, sarcastic.

mordaza *nf* gag.

mordedura *nf* bite.

morder *vt* to bite: *le ha mordido mi perro* my dog's bitten him.
▶ *vi* to bite: *ten cuidado que muerde* be careful, it bites.
▶ *vpr* **morderse** to bite. LOC **morderse la lengua** *(callarse)* to hold one's tongue.

mordida *nf fam (soborno)* bribe.

mordiente *nm* mordant.

mordisco *nm* bite.

mordisquear *vt* to nibble.

morena *nf (pez)* moray eel.

moreno,-a *adj* **1** *(pelo)* dark. **2** *(pan, azúcar)* brown.
▶ *nm* **moreno** suntan.

morera *nf* white mulberry.

moretón *nm* bruise.

morfema *nm* morpheme.

morfina *nf* morphine.

morfinómano,-a *nm & nf* morphine addict.

morfología *nf* morphology.

morfológico,-a *adj* morphological.

morganático,-a *adj* morganatic.

morgue *nf* morgue.

moribundo,-a *adj* moribund.

morir *vi (ser vivo)* to die.
▶ *vpr* **morirse** to die.

mormón,-ona *adj* Mormon.
▶ *nm & nf* Mormon.

mormónico,-a *adj* Mormon.

moro,-a *adj* Moorish.
▶ *nm & nf* Moor.

morosidad *nf* **1** *(tardanza)* delay; *(- en un pago)* arrears *pl*.

moroso,-a *adj* FIN *(cliente)* in arrears.
▶ *nm & nf* defaulter.

morral *nm* haversack.

morralla *nf* **1** *(pescado)* small fish. **2** *pey (gente)* riffraff.

morrazo LOC **pegarse un morrazo** *fam* to give os a bash.

morrena *nf* moraine.

morriña *nf* homesickness.

morrión *nm* helmet.

morro *nm* **1** *fam (de persona - boca)* lips *pl*, mouth; *(cara)* face. **2** *fam (cara dura)* cheek. **3** *(de animal)* snout, nose.

morrocotudo,-a *adj fam* terrific.

morrón *adj* COMP **pimiento morrón** sweet red pepper.

morrudo,-a *adj fam* thick-lipped.

morsa *nf* walrus.

Morse *nm* Morse code.

mortadela *nf* mortadella.

M

mortaja *nf* shroud.

mortal *adj* **1** *(criatura, ser)* mortal. **2** *(peligro, herida)* fatal. **3** *(aburrimiento, susto)* deadly.
▶ *nm o nf* mortal.

mortalidad *nf* mortality.

mortandad *nf* death toll.

mortecino,-a *adj* **1** *(luz)* faint, dull. **2** *(color)* lifeless, dull.

mortero *nm* mortar.

mortífero,-a *adj* deadly, lethal.

mortificación *nf* mortification.

mortificante *adj* mortifying.

mortificar *vt* to mortify.

mortuorio,-a *adj* mortuary.

moruno,-a *adj* Moorish.

mosaico *nm* mosaic.

mosca *nf* fly.

moscada COMP nuez moscada nutmeg.

moscardón *nm* **1** blowfly. **2** *(persona)* pest.

moscatel *nm* muscatel.

mosconear *vt fam* to pester.
▶ *vi fam* to be a pest, be a pain.

mosquear *vt fam* to annoy.
▶ *vpr* **mosquearse** *fam (enfadarse)* to get cross.

mosquete *nm* musket.

mosquetero *nm* musketeer.

mosquetón *nm* **1** *(arma)* short carbine. **2** *(cierre)* snap link.

mosquitera *nf* mosquito net.

mosquitero *nm* mosquito net.

mosquito *nm* mosquito.

mostacera *nf* mustard pot.

mostacho *nm* moustache.

mostaza *nf* mustard.

mosto *nm* *(zumo)* grape juice.

mostrador *nm* *(de tienda)* counter.

mostrar *vt* to show.
▶ *vpr* **mostrarse** to appear.

mostrenco,-a *adj (grande)* mammoth.

mota *nf (partícula)* speck.

mote *nm* nickname.

moteado,-a *adj* dotted, speckled.

motear *vt* to fleck, speck.

motejar *vt* to nickname.

motel *nm* motel.

motilidad *nf* motility.

motín *nm (levantamiento)* riot, uprising.

motivación *nf* motivation, motive.

motivar *vt* **1** *(causar)* to cause, give rise to. **2** *(estimular)* to motivate.

motivo *nm* motive, reason, cause.

moto *nf fam (motocicleta)* motorbike.

motocarro *nm* three-wheeled van.

motocicleta *nf* motorcycle.

motociclismo *nm* motorcycling.

motociclista *nm o nf* motorcyclist.

motocross *nm* motocross.

motocultivo *nm* mechanised agriculture.

motonáutica *nf* speedboat racing.

motonáutico,-a *adj* speedboat.

motor,-ra *adj* **1** motive. **2** BIOL motor: *función motora* motor function.
▶ *nm* **motor** TÉC engine.

motora *nf* small motorboat.

motorismo *nm* motorcycling.

motorista *nm o nf* motorcyclist.

motorizado,-a *adj* motorized.

motorizar *vt* to motorize.

motosierra *nf* power saw.

motriz *adj* [sólo se usa con monbres en femenino] motive.

mousse *nf* CULIN mousse.

mouton *nm (piel)* sheepskin.

movedizo,-a *adj (inestable)* unstable.

mover *vt* **1** to move.
▶ *vpr* **moverse 1** *(gen)* to move. **2** *fam (darse prisa)* to get a move on.

movible *adj* movable.

movida *nf fam (animación)* action.

movido,-a *adj* **1** *(día, temporada)* busy. **2** *(fiesta, concurso)* lively. **3** *(foto)* blurred.

móvil *adj* movable, mobile.
▶ *nm* **1** FÍS moving body. **2** *(motivo)* motive. **3** *(decoración, juguete)* mobile. **4** *(teléfono)* mobile (phone), cell phone.

movilidad *nf* mobility.

movilización *nf* mobilization.

movilizar *vt* to mobilize.

movimiento *nm* **1** *(gen)* movement; *(técnicamente)* motion. **2** *(de gente, ideas)* activity. **3** *(artístico, político)* movement.

moviola® *nf (máquina)* Moviola.

moza *nf (chica)* lass.

Mozambique *nm* Mozambique.

mozambiqueño,-a *adj* Mozambiquean.
▶ *nm & nf* Mozambiquean.

mozárabe *adj* Mozarab.
▶ *nm o nf* Mozarab.

mozo,-a *adj* young.
▶ *nm* **mozo 1** *(joven)* young man, lad. **2** *(camarero)* waiter. **3** *(de estación)* porter.

MP3 *abrev* (Moving Pictures Experts Group Audio Layer 3) MP3.

mu *interj (mugido)* moo.

muaré *nm* moiré.

muchacho,-a *nm & nf (chico)* boy; *(chica)* girl.

muchedumbre *nf (de personas)* crowd.

mucho,-a *adj* **1** *(singular - en afirmativas)* a lot of; *(- en negativas, interrogativas)* a lot of, much: *hicieron mucho ruido* they made a lot of noise; *no tiene mucho dinero* he hasn't got a lot of/much money. **2** *(plural - en afirmativas)* a lot of, lots of; *(- en negativas, interrogativas)* a lot of, many: *¿tienes muchos libros?* have you got a lot of/many books? **3** *(demasiado - singular)* too much; *(- plural)* too many.
▶ *pron (singular)* a lot, much; *(plural)* a lot, many: *muchos de sus amigos acudieron* many of his friends came.
▶ *adv* **1** *(de cantidad)* a lot, much: *mucho mejor/peor* much better/worse. **2** *(de tiempo)*: *mucho antes/después* much earlier/later. **3** *(de frecuencia)* often: *no vienen mucho por aquí* they don't come here often. LOC **como mucho** at the most: *te pagarán como mucho treinta euros* they'll pay you thirty euros at the most.

mucosa *nf* mucous membrane.

mucosidad *nf* mucus.

mucoso,-a *adj* mucous.

muda *nf (de ropa)* change of clothes.

mudable *adj* **1** changeable. **2** *(carácter)* fickle.

mudanza *nf (de residencia)* moving.

mudar *vt* **1** to change, alter. **2** *(plumas)* to moult (US molt). **3** *(voz)* to break: *le está mudando la voz* his voice is breaking. **4** *(piel)* to shed.
▶ *vpr* **mudarse 1** to change. **2** *(de residencia)* to move.

mudez *nf* dumbness, muteness.

mudo,-a *adj* **1** *(por defecto)* dumb; *(por voluntad)* silent, quiet. **2** *(vocal, consonante)* mute.

mueble *nm* piece of furniture.
▶ *nm pl* **muebles** furniture *sing*.

mueca *nf* **1** *(de burla)* mocking gesture, face. **2** *(de dolor)* grimace.

muela *nf (diente)* tooth, molar.

muelle *nm* **1** *(elástico)* spring. **2** MAR dock, wharf; *(malecón)* pier, jetty.

muérdago *nm* mistletoe.

muerdo *nm fam* bite.

muermo *nm fam* drag, pain, bore.

muerte *nf* **1** death. **2** *(asesinato)* murder.

muerto,-a *adj* **1** *(sin vida)* dead; *(sin actividad)* lifeless. **2** *fam (cansado)* tired.
▶ *nm & nf* dead person.

muesca *nf (corte)* nick, notch.

muesli *nm* muesli.

muestra *nf* **1** *(ejemplar)* sample. **2** *(modelo)* pattern. **3** *(señal)* proof, sign: *daba muestras de alegría* she looked happy. **4** *(exposición)* show, display.

muestrario *nm* collection of samples.

muestreo *nm (gen)* sampling.

mugido *nm (de vaca - uno)* moo.

mugir *vi (vaca)* to moo.

mugre *nf* grime, filth.

mugriento,-a *adj* grimy, filthy.

muguete *nm* lily of the valley.

mujer *nf* **1** woman. **2** *(esposa)* wife.

mujeriego,-a *adj pey* fond of the ladies.

mujerona *nf fam* big woman.

mújol *nm* grey mullet.

muladar *nm* dump.

mulato,-a *adj* mulatto.
▶ *nm & nf* mulatto.

mulero *nm* muleteer.

muleta *nf (para andar)* crutch.

M

muletilla *nf* **1** *(bastón)* cross-handled cane. **2** *(frase repetida)* pet phrase.

muletón *nm* flannelette.

mullido,-a *adj* soft, springy.

mullir *vt (lana)* to soften; *(almohada, colchón)* to fluff up.

mulo,-a *nm & nf (macho)* mule; *(hembra)* she-mule. LOC **ser más terco,-a que una mula** to be as stubborn as a mule.

multa *nf (gen)* fine; *(de tráfico)* ticket.

multar *vt* to fine: *¿cuánto te multaron?* how much did they fine you?

multiacceso *nm* multiaccess.

multicines *nm pl* multiplex *sing*.

multicolor *adj* multicoloured.

multicopiar *vt* to duplicate.

multicopista *nf* duplicator.

multicultural *adj* multicultural.

multidimensional *adj* multidimensional.

multidireccional *adj* multidirectional.

multidisciplinar *adj* multidisciplinary.

multifacético,-a *adj* multifaceted.

multiforme *adj* multiform.

multigrado *adj* multigrade.

multilateral *adj* multilateral.

multimedia *adj* multimedia.

multimillonario,-a *adj (de libras)* multimillion-pound; *(de dólares)* multimillion-dollar: *un contrato multimillonario* a multimillion-dollar contract.
▶ *nm & nf* multimillionaire.

multinacional *adj* multinational.
▶ *nf* multinational.

multípara *nf* multiparous.

múltiple *adj* **1** multiple. **2** *(muchos)* many, a number of, numerous: *opiniones múltiples* a number of opinions.

multiplicable *adj* multipliable.

multiplicación *nf* multiplication.

multiplicador,-ra *adj* multiplying.
▶ *nm* multiplicador multiplier.

multiplicar *vt* to multiply *(por, by)*.

multiplicidad *nf* multiplicity.

múltiplo *adj* multiple.
▶ *nm* multiple.

multipropiedad *nf* time-share.

multirracial *adj* multiracial.

multirriesgo *adj* fully comprehensive.

multitud *nf* **1** *(de personas)* crowd. **2** *(de cosas, ideas)* multitude.

multitudinario,-a *adj* multitudinous.

multiuso *adj* multipurpose.

mundanal *adj* of the world, mundane. LOC **huir del mundanal ruido** to get away from it all.

mundano,-a *adj* of the world.

mundial *adj* worldwide, world.
▶ *nm* world championship. LOC **de fama mundial** world-famous. COMP **mundial de fútbol** World Cup.

mundialmente *adv* worldwide. LOC **mundialmente conocido,-a** world-famous.

mundillo *nm* world, circles *pl*: *el mundillo teatral* theatrical circles.

mundo *nm* world: *ha dado la vuelta al mundo dos veces* he's been around the world twice; *vive aislado en su propio mundo* he's isolated himself in his own little world; *el mundo del cine* the cinema, the world of cinema. LOC **no ser nada del otro mundo** to be nothing to write home about. ‖ **por nada del mundo** not for all the world. ‖ **tener mundo** to know the ways of the world. ‖ **venir al mundo** to come into the world. ‖ **el fin del mundo** the end of the world. COMP **el Nuevo Mundo** the New World. ‖ **el Tercer Mundo** the Third World.

mundología *nf fam* worldliness.

munición *nf* ammunition.

municipal *adj (gobierno)* town, municipal; *(instalaciones)* council.
▶ *nm o nf (hombre)* policeman; *(mujer)* policewoman.
▶ *nf pl* **las municipales** local elections.

municipio *nm* **1** municipality. **2** *(ayuntamiento)* town council.

muñeca *nf* **1** ANAT wrist. **2** *(juguete)* doll. COMP **muñeca de trapo** rag doll.

muñeco *nm (juguete)* doll. COMP **muñeco de nieve** snowman.

muñequera *nf* wristband.

muñir *vt (amañar)* to fix.

muñón *nm* ANAT stump.

mural *adj* mural.
▸ *nm* mural.

muralla *nf* city wall.

murciélago *nm* bat.

murga *nf fam* nuisance. LOC **dar la murga** *fam* to be a pain in the neck.

murmullante *adj* babbling.

murmullo *nm (susurro)* whisper, whispering; *(voz baja)* murmur, murmuring.

murmuración *nf* gossip, backbiting.

murmurador,-ra *adj* gossipy.
▸ *nm & nf* gossip.

murmurar *vt (susurrar)* to murmur, whisper.
▸ *vi* **1** *(criticar)* to gossip. **2** *(decir en voz baja)* to murmur.

muro *nm* wall.

murria *nf* sadness, melancholy.

mus *nm* card game in which players use signs to communicate.

musa *nf* muse.
▸ *nf pl* **las musas** the Arts.

musaraña *nf* ZOOL shrew. LOC **estar pensando en las musarañas** to daydream.

musculación *nf* body-building.

muscular *adj* muscular.

musculatura *nf* muscles *pl*.

músculo *nm* muscle.

musculoso,-a *adj* muscular.

muselina *nf* muslin.

museo *nm* museum. COMP **museo de arte** art museum.

musgo *nm* moss. LOC **cubierto,-a de musgo** mossy, moss-covered.

musgoso,-a *adj* mossy.

música *nf* music. COMP **música de fondo** background music. ‖ **música clásica** classical music.

musical *adj* musical.
▸ *nm* musical.

musicalidad *nf* musicality.

musicar *vt* to write the music for, set to music.

músico,-a *nm & nf* musician.

musicología *nf* musicology.

musicólogo,-a *nm & nf* musicologist.

musiquilla *nf fam pey* tacky music.

musitar *vi (susurrar)* to whisper.

muslo *nm* **1** thigh. **2** CULIN *(de ave)* drumstick.

mustiarse *vi* to wilt, wither.

mustio,-a *adj* **1** *(plantas)* withered, faded. **2** *(persona)* down, downcast.

musulmán,-ana *adj* Muslim.
▸ *nm & nf* Muslim.

mutabilidad *nf* changeability.

mutable *adj* mutable.

mutación *nf* **1** change. **2** BIOL mutation.

mutante *adj* mutant.
▸ *nm o nf* mutant.

mutilación *nf* mutilation.

mutilado,-a *adj (persona)* disabled.
▸ *nm & nf* cripple.

mutilar *vt* to cripple

mutis *nm* TEAT exit.

mutismo *nm* silence.

mutua *nf* mutual benefit society. COMP **mutua de seguros** mutual insurance company.

mutualidad *nf (asociación)* mutual benefit society.

mutualista *nm o nf* member of a mutual benefit society.

mutuamente *adv* mutually: *se quieren mutuamente* they love each other.

mutuo,-a *adj* mutual, reciprocal: *por mutuo acuerdo* by mutual agreement.

muy *adv* very: *es muy difícil* it's very difficult; *se levantó muy temprano* he got up very early; *lo has hecho muy bien* you've done it very well. LOC **muy de mañana** very early in the morning. ‖ **por muy que...** however…: *por muy tarde que sea* however late it is.

M

N

N, n *nf (la letra)* N, n.
N *sím* **(norte)** north; *(símbolo)* N.
nabo *nm (planta)* turnip.
nácar *nm* mother-of-pearl.
nacarado,-a *adj* nacred.
nacer *vi* **1** *(persona)* to be born; *(ave)* to hatch out; *(semilla, planta)* to sprout. **2** *(río)* to rise; *(agua)* to spring; *(camino)* to start, begin. **3** *(sol)* to rise. LOC **al nacer** at birth.
nacido,-a *adj* born. LOC **bien nacido,-a** *(de buen corazón)* kind-hearted. ‖ **mal nacido,-a** despicable.
naciente *adj* **1** *(nuevo)* new. **2** *(creciente)* growing.
  ▶ *nm (este)* East.
nacimiento *nm* **1** birth. **2** *fig* origin, beginning. LOC **de nacimiento** from birth.
nación *nf* nation. COMP **Naciones Unidas** United Nations.
nacional *adj* national.
nacionalidad *nf* nationality.
nacionalismo *nm* nationalism.
nacionalista *adj* nationalist.
  ▶ *nm o nf* nationalist.
nacionalización *nf* naturalization.
nacionalizar *vt* **1** *(persona)* to naturalize. **2** *(empresa)* to nationalize.
  ▶ *vpr* **nacionalizarse** *(persona)* to become naturalized: *nacionalizarse español/británico/etc* to take up Spanish/British/etc citizenship.
nada *pron* nothing: *no quiero nada* I don't want anything.
  ▶ *adv* (not) at all: *no me gusta nada* I don't like it at all.
  ▶ *nf* nothingness. LOC **de nada 1** *(no hay de qué)* don't mention it, think

nothing of it, (US you're welcome). **2** *(insignificante)* insignificant: *gracias, –de nada* thanks, – don't mention it. ‖ **nada más…** as soon as…, no sooner…
nadador,-ra *nm & nf* swimmer.
nadar *vi* to swim.
nadería *nf* trifle.
nadie *pron* nobody, not… anybody: *aquí no hay nadie* there's nobody here.
nado LOC **a nado** swimming: *cruzaron el río a nado* they swam across the river.
nafta *nf* naphtha.
naftalina *nf* naphthalene. COMP **bola de naftalina** mothball.
naif *adj* naïf, naive.
  ▶ *nm* naïf art.
nailon® *nm* nylon®.
naipe *nm* playing card.
nalga *nf* buttock.
Namibia *nf* Namibia.
namibio,-a *adj* Namibian.
  ▶ *nm & nf* Namibian.
nana *nf* lullaby.
naranja *nf (fruto)* orange.
  ▶ *adj (color)* orange.
naranjada *nf* orangeade, orange drink.
naranjal *nm* orange grove.
naranjo *nm* orange tree.
narcisismo *nm* narcissism.
narcisista *adj* narcissistic.
  ▶ *nm o nf* narcissist.
narciso *nm* **1** *(flor)* daffodil, narcissus **2** *(hombre)* narcissist.
narcótico,-a *adj* narcotic.
  ▶ *nm* **narcótico** *(medicamento)* narcotic *(droga)* drug.
narcotraficante *adj* drug trafficking.
  ▶ *nm o nf* drug trafficker.

narcotráfico *nm* drug trafficking.

nardo *nm* nard, spikenard.

narigón,-ona *adj fam* big-nosed.

nariz *nf* **1** ANAT nose. **2** *fig (sentido)* sense of smell. LOC **meter las narices en** ALGO to poke one's nose into STH.
▶ *interj* ¡**narices**! *fam* not on your life!

narración *nf (historia)* story.

narrador,-ra *nm & nf* storyteller.

narrar *vt (gen)* to tell, relate, narrate.

narrativa *nf (género)* fiction.

narval *nm* narwhal.

nasa *nf (aparejo)* keepnet; *(cesta)* creel.

nasal *adj* nasal.
▶ *nf (letra)* nasal.

nata *nf* **1** cream. **2** *(de leche hervida)* skin. COMP **nata montada** whipped cream.

natación *nf* swimming.

natal *adj* native. COMP **ciudad natal** home town: l **país natal** native country.

natalicio *nm* birthday.

natalidad *nf* birth rate.

natillas *nf pl* custard *sing*.

natividad *nf* nativity.

nativo,-a *adj* native.

nato,-a *adj* born.

natural *adj* **1** *(no artificial)* natural. **2** *(fruta, flor)* fresh. LOC **al natural** CULIN in its own juice.
▶ *nm (nativo)* native, inhabitant. LOC **ser natural de** to be a native of, come from.

naturaleza *nf* **1** nature. **2** *(complexión)* physical constitution.

naturalidad *nf* **1** *(sencillez)* naturalness. **2** *(espontaneidad)* ease, spontaneity.

naturalismo *nm* naturalism.

naturalista *adj* naturalist.
▶ *nm o nf* naturalist.

naturalizar *vt* to naturalize.
▶ *vpr* **naturalizarse** to become naturalized: *se ha naturalizado español* he has taken up Spanish citizenship.

naturista *adj* naturist.
▶ *nm o nf* naturist.

naturopatía *nf* naturopathy.

naufragar *vi* **1** *(barco)* to sink, be wrecked; *(persona)* to be shipwrecked. **2** *fig* to fail.

naufragio *nm* shipwreck.

náufrago,-a *adj* shipwrecked.
▶ *nm & nf* shipwrecked person.

Nauru *nm* Nauru.

nauruano,-a *adj* Nauruan.
▶ *nm & nf* Nauruan.

náusea [también se usa en plural con el mismo significado] *nf* nausea, sickness.

nauseabundo,-a *adj* nauseating.

náutica *nf* navigation, seamanship.

náutico,-a *adj* nautical. COMP **deportes náuticos** water sports.

navaja *nf (cuchillo)* penknife.

naval *adj* naval.

nave *nf* **1** *(náutica)* ship, vessel. **2** *(espacial)* spaceship, spacecraft. **3** *(almacén)* industrial warehouse.

navegable *adj (río)* navigable.

navegación *nf (arte)* navigation.

navegador *nm (de internet)* browser.

navegante *nm o nf* navigator.

navegar *vi* **1** *(barco)* to sail. **2** *(avión)* to fly.

Navidad *nf* Christmas. LOC **felicitar las Navidades a** ALGN to wish SB a merry Christmas.

navideño,-a *adj* Christmas.

naviera *nf (empresa)* shipping company.

navío *nm* vessel, ship.

Neanderthal *adj* Neanderthal.

neblina *nf* mist.

neblinoso,-a *adj* misty.

nebulizador *nm* nebulizer.

nebulosa *nf* nebula.

nebulosidad *nf* nebulosity.

nebuloso,-a *adj* cloudy, hazy.

necedad *nf (ignorancia)* stupidity.

necesario,-a *adj* necessary.

neceser *nm (bolsa de aseo)* toilet bag.

necesidad *nf* **1** necessity, need. **2** *(pobreza)* poverty, want. LOC **pasar necesidades** to be in need.

necesitado,-a *adj* needy, poor.

necesitar *vt* to need.

necio,-a *adj* stupid.

nécora *nf* fiddler crab.

N

necrología *nf (biografía)* obituary.
necrológico,-a *adj* obituary.
▶ *nf pl* **necrológicas** *(sección prensa)* obituaries *pl.*
necrópolis *nf inv* necropolis.
necrosis *nf inv* necrosis.
néctar *nm* nectar.
nectarina *nf* nectarine.
neerlandés,-esa *adj* Dutch.
▶ *nm & nf* **1** *(persona - hombre)* Dutchman; *(- mujer)* Dutch woman. **2** *(idioma)* Dutch.
nefasto,-a *adj* unlucky, ill-fated.
nefrítico,-a *adj* nephritic. COMP **cólico nefrítico** nephrocolic.
negación *nf* **1** *(de un derecho)* negation. **2** refusal. **3** *(en gramática)* negative.
negado,-a *adj (inepto)* hopeless.
negar *vt* **1** *(rechazar)* to deny. **2** *(no conceder)* to refuse.
▶ *vpr* **negarse** to refuse (a, to): *se negó a devolverme el dinero* he refused to give me my money back.
negativa *nf (rechazo)* refusal.
negativo,-a *adj* negative.
▶ *nm* **negativo** *(en fotografía)* negative.
negligencia *nf* negligence.
negligente *adj* negligent.
▶ *nm o nf* negligent person.
negociable *adj* negotiable.
negociación *nf* negotiation.
negociado *nm (sección)* department.
negociador,-ra *adj* negotiating.
▶ *nm & nf* negotiator.
negociante *nm o nf* dealer, merchant.
negociar *vi (comerciar)* to do business, deal (con, in).
▶ *vt* POL to negotiate.
negocio *nm* **1** *(actividad)* business. **2** *(gestión)* deal, transaction.
negra *nf* MÚS crotchet, US quarter note.
negro,-a *adj* **1** *(gen)* black. **2** *(cine, novela)* detective.
▶ *nm & nf (hombre)* black (man); *(mujer)* black (woman).
▶ *nm* **negro** *(color)* black.
negrura *nf* blackness.
negruzco,-a *adj* blackish.

nene,-a *nm & nf* baby.
nenúfar *nm* water lily.
neoclasicismo *nm* neoclassicism.
neoclásico,-a *adj* neoclassical.
neocolonialismo *nm* neocolonialism.
neófito,-a *nm & nf* neophyte.
neolítico,-a *adj* neolithic.
▶ *nm* **neolítico** Neolithic.
neologismo *nm* neologism.
neón *nm* neon.
neonatal *adj* neonatal.
neorrealismo *nm* neorealism.
neozelandés,-esa *adj* of New Zealand, from New Zealand.
▶ *nm & nf* New Zealander.
Nepal *nm* Nepal.
nepalés,-esa *adj* Nepalese, Nepali.
▶ *nm & nf (persona)* Nepalese, Nepali.
▶ *nm* **nepalés** *(idioma)* Nepalese, Nepali.
nepotismo *nm* nepotism.
nereida *nf* nereid.
nervadura *nf* BOT nervures *pl.*
nervio *nm* ANAT nerve.
▶ *nm pl* **nervios** nerves. LOC **tener los nervios de punta** to be on edge.
nerviosismo *nm* nervousness.
nervioso,-a *adj (gen)* nervous. LOC **ponerse nervioso,-a** to get nervous.
neto,-a *adj (peso, cantidad)* net.
neumático,-a *nm* tyre (US tire).
neumonía *nf* pneumonia.
neura *nf* fam obsession.
neurálgico,-a *adj fig (fundamental)* key.
neurocirujano,-a *nm & nf* neurosurgeon.
neurología *nf* neurology.
neurólogo,-a *nm & nf* neurologist.
neurona *nf* neuron, neurone.
neurosis *nf inv* neurosis.
neurótico,-a *adj* neurotic.
▶ *nm & nf* neurotic.
neutral *adj* neutral.
neutralidad *nf* neutrality.
neutralizar *vt* to neutralize.
neutro,-a *adj* **1** neutral. **2** LING neuter.
▶ *nm* **neutro** neuter.
neutrón *nm* neutron.
nevada *nf* snowfall.

evado,-a *adj* covered with snow.

evar *vi* [se usa sólo en tercera persona; no lleva sujeto] to snow.

evera *nf (eléctrica)* fridge, refrigerator.

evero *nm* ice field.

ewton *nm* newton.

exo *nm* **1** link. **2** LING connective.

i *conj* **1** neither, nor. **2** not even.

icaragua *nf* Nicaragua.

icaragüense *adj* Nicaraguan.
▶ *nm o nf* Nicaraguan.

icho *nm* niche.

icotina *nf* nicotine.

idada *nf (polluelos)* brood.

idificar *vi* to nest.

ido *nm* nest.

iebla *nf* **1** *(nubes)* fog. **2** *fig* mist.

ieto,-a *nm & nf* grandchild; *(niño)* grandson; *(niña)* granddaughter.

ieve *nf* snow.

igeria *nf* Nigeria.

igeriano,-a *adj* Nigerian.
▶ *nm & nf* Nigerian.

igromancia *nf* necromancy.

ihilismo *nm* nihilism.

ihilista *adj* nihilistic.

ilón® *nm* nylon®.

imbo *nm* nimbus.

imiedad *nf (cosa nimia)* trifle.

imio,-a *adj* insignificant, trivial.

infa *nf* nymph.

ingún *adj* [se usa ante un nombre masculino en singular] → ninguno,-a.

inguno,-a *adj* no, not any.
▶ *pron* **1** *(persona)* nobody, no one. **2** *(objeto)* not any, none: *ninguno me gusta* I don't like any of them.

✎ Consulta también ningún.

iñato,-a *nm & nf fam* brat.

iñera *nf* nanny.

iñería *nf (chiquillada)* childishness.

iñez *nf (de una persona)* childhood.

iño,-a *nm & nf* **1** *(gen)* child; *(chico)* boy, little boy; *(chica)* girl, little girl.
▶ *nm pl* **niños** children, kids.

ipón,-ona *adj* Nipponese.
▶ *nm & nf* Nipponese.

níquel *nm* nickel.

niquelado,-a *adj* nickel-plated.

niquelar *vt* to nickel.

niqui *nm* T-shirt.

nirvana *nm* nirvana.

níscalo *nm* milk cap.

níspero *nm (fruto)* medlar.

nitidez *nf (transparencia)* clearness.

nítido,-a *adj (claro)* accurate.

nitrato *nm* nitrate.

nítrico,-a *adj* nitric.

nitrito *nm* nitrite.

nitrógeno *nm* nitrogen.

nitroglicerina *nf* nitroglycerine.

nitroso,-a *adj* nitrous.

nivel *nm* **1** *(altura)* level. **2** *(categoría)* standard. COMP **nivel del mar** sea level.

nivelación *nf (de un terreno)* levelling.

nivelado,-a *adj* level.

nivelar *vt (gen)* to level out, level off.

níveo,-a *adj lit* snow-white.

no *adv* no, not.
▶ *nm* no: *un no rotundo* a definite no.

nobel *nm* Nobel prize.

nobiliario,-a *adj* noble.

noble *adj (gen)* noble; *(madera)* fine.
▶ *nm o nf* noble.

nobleza *nf* **1** honesty. **2** nobility.

noche *nf* night. LOC **buenas noches 1** *(saludo)* good evening. **2** *(despedida)* good night. **‖ por la noche** at night, after dark.

Nochebuena *nf* Christmas Eve.

Nochevieja *nf* New Year's Eve.

noción *nf* notion, idea.

nocividad *nf* noxiousness.

nocivo,-a *adj* noxious, harmful.

noctámbulo,-a *adj* nocturnal.
▶ *nm & nf fam (trasnochador)* night owl.

nocturno,-a *adj (gen)* nocturnal; *(vida)* night; *(clase)* evening.

nodo *nm* node.

nodriza *nf* wet nurse.

nodular *adj* nodular, nodulated.

nódulo *nm* nodule.

nogal *nm* walnut tree.

nogalina *nf* walnut dye.

N

nómada *adj* nomadic.
► *nm o nf* nomad.
nomadismo *nm* nomadism.
nombrado,-a *adj* well-known.
nombramiento *nm* appointment.
nombrar *vt* to name.
nombre *nm* **1** name. **2** LING noun.
nomenclatura *nf* nomenclature.
nomeolvides *nm inv (flor)* forget-me-not.
nómina *nf* pay cheque (US check).
nominación *nf* nomination.
nominal *adj* nominal.
nominalismo *nm* nominalism.
nominalista *adj* nominalist.
nominalizar *vt* to substantivize.
nominalmente *adv* nominally.
nominar *vt* to nominate.
nominativo,-a *adj* **1** *(cheque)* personal.
2 LING nominative.
non *nm* odd number.
nonagenario,-a *nm & nf* nonagenarian.
nonagésimo,-a *nm & nf* ninetieth.
► *adj* ninetieth.
nones *interj* no way!
noquear *vt* to knock out.
norcoreano,-a *adj* North Korean.
► *nm & nf* North Korean.
nordeste *nm* northeast.
nórdico,-a *adj* **1** *(del norte)* northern. **2**
(de los países del norte) Nordic.
► *nm & nf (persona)* Scandinavian.
noreste *nm* → nordeste.
noria *nf* **1** *(para agua)* water wheel.
2 *(de feria)* big wheel.
norma *nf* norm, rule.
normal *adj (habitual)* normal, usualy.
► *nf (gasolina)* two-star petrol.
normalidad *nf* normality.
normalización *nf* normalization.
normalizar *vt* to normalize.
normativa *nf* rules *pl*, regulations *pl*.
normativo,-a *adj* normative.
noroeste *nm* northwest.
norte *nm* north.
Norteamérica *nf* North America.
norteamericano,-a *adj* North American.
► *nm & nf* North American.

Noruega *nf* Norway.
noruego,-a *adj* Norwegian.
► *nm & nf (persona)* Norwegian.
► *nm* **noruego** *(idioma)* Norwegian.
nos *pron* **1** *(complemento)* us: *nos dijo qu*
no nos moviéramos he told us not t
move. **2** *(uso reflexivo)* ourselves: *nos l*
vamos we wash ourselves. **3** *(uso recípr*
co) each other: *nos vemos mucho* we se
each other often.
nosotros,-as *pron* **1** *(sujeto)* we: *nosotr*
no fuimos we didn't go. **2** *(complement*
us: *con nosotros,-as* with us.
nostalgia *nf* homesickness.
nostálgico,-a *adj* nostalgic.
nota *nf* **1** *(anotación)* note. **2** *(calificació*
mark, grade. **3** MÚS note.
notable *adj* considerable, remarkable
notación *nf* notation.
notar *vt* **1** *(percibir)* to notice. **2** *(sentir)* t
feel: *noto un poco de calor* I feel a bit ho
► *vpr* **notarse 1** *(percibirse)* to show
apenas se le nota la cicatriz you can hard
see his scar. **2** *(sentirse)* to feel.
notario,-a *nm & nf* notary public.
noticia *nf (información)* news *pl*.
► *nf pl* **las noticias** the news.
noticiario *nm* news.
notición *nm fam* bombshell.
notificación *nf* notification.
notificar *vt* to notify, inform.
notoriedad *nf (fama)* fame, prestige.
notorio,-a *adj* well-known.
novatada *nf (broma)* practical joke.
novato,-a *nm & nf (principiante)* beginne
novecientos,-as *adj* nine hundre
(ordinal) nine-hundredth.

Consulta también seis.

novedad *nf* **1** *(cualidad)* newness.
(cambio) change, innovation.
novedoso,-a *adj* novel.
novel *adj (escritor, escultor)* novice.
novela *nf* novel.
novelar *vt* to novelize.
novelesco,-a *adj (de novela)* fiction-like
novelista *nm o nf* novelist.
novena *nf* REL novena.

noveno,-a *adj* ninth.
▶ *nm & nf* ninth.

✎ Consulta también sexto.

noventa *adj* ninety.
▶ *nm* ninety.

✎ Consulta también sesenta.

novia *nf (amiga)* girlfriend.
noviazgo *nm* engagement.
novicio,-a *nm & nf* REL novice.
noviembre *nm* November.

✎ Para ejemplos de uso, consulta marzo.

novillada *nf* bullfight with young bulls.
novillero,-a *nm & nf* novice bullfighter.
novillo *nm* young bull.
novio *nm* boyfriend.
nubarrón *nm* storm cloud.
nube *nf* cloud.
núbil *adj* nubile.
nublado,-a *adj* cloudy, overcast.
▶ *nm* **nublado** storm cloud.
nubosidad *nf* cloudiness.
nuboso,-a *adj* cloudy.
nuca *nf* nape (of the neck).
nuclear *adj* nuclear.
núcleo *nm* nucleus.
nudillo *nm* knuckle.
nudismo *nm* nudism.
nudo *nm* knot.
nudoso,-a *adj (madera)* knotty.
nuera *nf* daughter-in-law.
nuestro,-a *adj* our, of ours.
▶ *pron* ours.
nueva *nf* tidings *pl*, news *sing*.
nueve *adj* nine; *(noveno)* ninth.
▶ *nm* nine.

✎ Consulta también seis.

nuevo,-a *adj* new. LOC **de nuevo** again.
nuez *nf* BOT walnut.
nulidad *nf* **1** *(ineptitud)* incompetence. **2** JUR nullity.
nulo,-a *adj (sin valor)* invalid.

numeración *nf* **1** *(proceso)* numbering. **2** *(conjunto)* numbers *pl*. **3** *(sistema)* numbers *pl*, numerals *pl*.
numerador *nm* numerator.
numeral *adj* numeral.
▶ *nm* numeral.
numerar *vt* to number.
numérico,-a *adj* numerical.
número *nm* **1** *(gen)* number. **2** *(de una publicación)* number, issue. **3** *(de zapatos)* size: *¿qué número calzas?* what's your shoe size?, what size shoe do you take? **4** *(de un espectáculo)* act. **5** *(de lotería)* lottery ticket number. **7** LING number. COMP **número impar** odd number. ❙ **número ordinal** ordinal number. ❙ **número par** even number. ❙ **número primo** prime number. ❙ **número quebrado** fraction. ❙ **número romano** Roman numeral.
numeroso,-a *adj* numerous: *son familia numerosa* they're a large family.
numismática *nf* numismatics.
numismático,-a *adj* numismatic.
nunca *adv* **1** never. **2** *(en interrogativa)* ever. LOC **más que nunca** more than ever. ❙ **nunca más** never again. ❙
nupcial *adj (marcha, tarta)* wedding; *(misa)* nuptial; *(lecho)* marriage.
nupcias *nf pl fml* wedding *sing*, nuptials.
nurse *nf* nanny.
nutria *nf* otter.
nutrición *nf* nutrition.
nutrido,-a *adj (alimentado)* nourished.
nutriente *adj* nutrient.
▶ *nm* nutrient.
nutrir *vt* **1** *(alimentar)* to feed, nourish. **2** *fig* to encourage. **3** *(abastecer)* to supply (de, with).
▶ *vpr* **nutrirse 1** *(alimentarse)* to receive nourishment (de, from). **2** *fig (abastecerse)* to draw (de, on).
nutritivo,-a *adj* nutritious, nourishing. COMP **sustancia nutritiva** nutrient. ❙ **valor nutritivo** nutritional value.

N

Ñ, ñ *nf the fifteenth letter of the Spanish alphabet.*

ñandú *nm* AM rhea.

ñoñería *nf (tontería)* inanity, nonsense.

ñoño ,-a *adj* **1** *(soso)* insipid, dull. **2** *(tímido)* shy. **3** *(remilgado)* fussy. **4** *(poco seguro)* wet, drippy, wimpish: *no seas ñoño, no es más que un rasguño* don't be such a wimp, it's no more than a scratch. **5** AM old.

ñoqui *nm* gnocchi *pl*.

ñora *nf type of* red pepper.

ñu *nm* gnu.

O, o *nf (la letra)* O, o.

o *conj* **1** or: *¿té o café?* tea or coffee? **2** *(concesiva)* whether... or: *estudie o no, tiene que aprobar* whether he studies or not, he has to pass.

O *sím (oeste)* west; *(símbolo)* W.

oasis *nm inv* oasis.

obcecado,-a *adj* blind.

obcecar *vt* to blind.
▶ *vpr* **obcecarse** to be obstinate.

obedecer *vt (regla, ley)* to obey.
▶ *vi (persona)* to obey.

obediencia *nf* obedience.

obediente *adj* obedient.

obertura *nf* MÚS overture.

obesidad *nf* obesity.

obeso,-a *adj* obese.

obispo *nm* bishop.

objeción *nf* objection.

objetar *vt* to object.

objetividad *nf* objectivity.

objetivo,-a *adj* objective.
▶ *nm* **objetivo 1** *(fin)* aim, objective. **2** *(lente)* lens.

objeto *nm* **1** *(cosa)* object. **2** *(fin)* aim, purpose, object.

objetor,-ra *adj* objecting, dissenting.
▶ *nm & nf* objector.

oblea *nf* wafer.

oblicuo,-a *adj* oblique.

obligación *nf (deber)* duty, obligation.

obligado,-a *adj (forzoso)* required.

obligar *vt* to force, make.
▶ *vpr* **obligarse** to undertake, promise.

obligatorio,-a *adj* compulsory.

obnubilar *vt (fascinar)* to fascinate.

oboe *nm* oboe.

obra *nf* **1** *(trabajo)* work. **2** *(construcción)* building site. COMP **obra de teatro** play.
▶ *nf pl* **obras** *(en casa)* repairs.

obrar *vi (proceder)* to act, behave.

obrero,-a *adj* working.
▶ *nm & nf* worker, labourer.

obscenidad *nf* obscenity.

obsceno,-a *adj* obscene.

obscurantismo *nm* obscurantism.

obscurantista *adj* obscurantist.

obscurecer *vt* to darken.
▶ *vpr* **obscurecerse** *(día)* to get cloudy.

obscuridad *nf* darkness.

obscuro,-a *adj* **1** *(cielo, color)* dark. **2** *(idea, razonamiento)* obscure.

obsequiar *vt (regalar)* to give, offer.

obsequio *nm* gift, present.

observación *nf (acción)* observation.

observador,-ra *adj* observant.
▶ *nm & nf* observer.

observar *vt* **1** *(mirar)* to observe, watch. **2** *(notar)* to notice.

observatorio *nm* observatory.

obsesión *nf* obsession.

obsesionar *vt* to obsess.
▶ *vpr* **obsesionarse** to get obsessed.

obseso,-a *nm & nf* maniac.
▶ *adj* obsessed.

obsidiana *nf* obsidian.

obsoleto,-a *adj* obsolete.

obstáculo *nm (inconveniente)* objection.

obstante *adv* **no obstante** nevertheless, however.

obstetricia *nf* obstetrics.

obstinado,-a *adj* obstinate.

obstinarse *vpr* to persist (en, in), insist (en, on).

obstrucción *nf* obstruction.

obstruir *vt* to obstruct, block.
▶ *vpr* **obstruirse** to get blocked up.
obtener *vt (beca, resultados)* to get, obtain; *(premio)* to win.
obturador *nm* shutter.
obtuso,-a *adj* obtuse.
obviar *vt fml* to obviate, remove.
obvio,-a *adj* obvious.
oca *nf* goose.
ocasión *nf (oportunidad)* opportunity.
ocasional *adj (gen)* occasional.
ocasionar *vt (causar)* to cause.
ocaso *nm (anochecer)* sunset.
occidental *adj* western, occidental.
occidente *nm* the West.
Oceanía *nf* Oceania.
océano *nm* ocean.

✎ En poesía también se escribe oceano.

oceanografía *nf* oceanography.
ochenta *adj* eighty; *(octagésimo)* eightieth.
▶ *nm* eighty.

✎ Consulta también sesenta.

ocho *adj* eight; *(octavo)* eighth.
▶ *nm* eight.

✎ Consulta también seis.

ochocientos,-as *adj* eight hundred; *(ordinal)* eight hundredth.
▶ *nm & nf* eight hundred.
ocio *nm (tiempo libre)* leisure.
ocioso,-a *adj (desocupado)* idle.
ocre *adj* ochre.
octagonal *adj* octagonal.
octágono,-a *nm* octagon.
octano *nm* octane.
octava *nf (en música)* octave.
octavilla *nf (impreso)* pamphlet.
octavo,-a *adj* eighth: *llegó en octavo lugar* he came eighth.
▶ *nm & nf* eighth: *era la octava en la lista* she was the eighth on the list.
▶ *nm* **octavo** *(parte)* eighth.

✎ Consulta también sexto.

octeto *nm* octet.
octogésimo,-a *adj* eightieth.

octogonal *adj* octagonal.
octógono *nm* octagon.
octosílabo,-a *adj* octosyllabic.
▶ *nm* **octosílabo** octosyllable.
octubre *nm* October.

✎ Para ejemplos de uso, consulta marzo.

ocular *adj* eye, ocular.
oculista *nm o nf* eye specialist.
ocultar *vt (gen)* to hide, conceal.
oculto,-a *adj (escondido)* hidden.
ocupación *nf (empleo)* occupation, employment.
ocupado,-a *adj* **1** *(persona)* busy. **2** *(asiento)* taken; *(teléfono)* engaged.
ocupante *nm o nf* occupant.
ocupar *vt* **1** to occupy, take. **2** *(llenar)* to take up. **3** *(habitar)* occupy. **4** *(estar - en un cargo)* to hold, fill.
▶ *vpr* **ocuparse de** to take care of.
ocurrencia *nf* idea.
ocurrir *vi* to happen: *¿qué fue lo que ocurrió?* what happened?
▶ *vpr* **ocurrirse** to occur to: *no se me ocurre nada* nothing occurs to me.
odiar *vt* to hate, loathe.
odio *nm* hatred, loathing.
odioso,-a *adj* hateful, despicable.
odontólogo,-a *nm & nf* odontologist.
odorífico,-a *adj* odoriferous.
odre *nm* wineskin.
oeste *nm* west.
ofender *vt (herir)* to offend: *no quisiera ofenderte, pero...* no offence, but...
▶ *vpr* **ofenderse** to get offended.
ofendido,-a *adj* offended.
ofensa *nf* offence.
ofensivo,-a *adj* offensive.
oferta *nf* **1** offer. **2** *(suministro)* supply.
ofertar *vt (ofrecer)* to offer.
oficial *adj* official.
▶ *nm o nf* office worker, officer.
oficiala *nf (operaria)* assistant.
oficialmente *adv* officially.
oficiante *nm o nf* officiant.
oficiar *vi (ejercer)* to act (de, as).
oficina *nf* office.
oficinista *nm o nf* office worker, clerk.

oficio *nm (ocupación)* job.
oficioso,-a *adj (noticia)* unofficial.
ofidio *nm* snake.
ofimática *nf* office automation.
ofrecer *vt (dar)* to offer.
▶ *vpr* **ofrecerse** *(prestarse)* to offer.
ofrecimiento *nm* offer, offering.
ofrenda *nf* offering.
ofrendar *vt* to make an offering of.
oftalmología *nf* ophthalmology.
oftalmólogo,-a *nm & nf* eye specialist.
ofuscar *vt (confundir)* to muddle.
▶ *vpr* **ofuscarse** to get muddled.
ogro *nm* ogre.
oh *interj* oh!
ohm *nm* ohm.
ohmio *nm* ohm.
oídas LOC **de oídas** by hearsay.
oído *nm* **1** *(sentido)* hearing. **2** *(órgano)* ear.
oiga *interj (para llamar la atención)* excuse me!; *(por teléfono)* hello?
oír *vt* **1** *(percibir)* to hear: *no oí nada* I didn't hear anything. **2** *(atender)* to answer.
ojal *nm* buttonhole.
ojalá *interj* I hope so: *¡ojalá sea verdad!* I hope it's true!
ojeada *nf* glance, quick look.
ojear *vt (mirar)* to have a quick look at.
ojeras *nf pl* dark rings under the eyes.
ojeriza *nf fam* dislike.
ojeroso,-a *adj* haggard.
ojival *adj (arte)* ogival.
ojo *nm* **1** eye. **2** *(agujero)* hole; *(de aguja)* eye. COMP
okupa *nm o nf argot* squatter.
ola *nf* wave. COMP **ola de frío** cold spell.
oleáceo,-a *adj* oleaceous.
oleada *nf* **1** big wave. **2** *fig* wave.
oleaginoso,-a *adj* oleaginous.
oleaje *nm* swell.
oleicultura *nf (cultivo)* olive-growing.
óleo *nm (material)* oil; *(obra)* oil painting.
oleoducto *nm* pipeline.
oleoso,-a *adj* oily.
oler *vt* to smell.
▶ *vi* to smell: *huele a gas* it smells of gas in here.

▶ *vpr* **olerse** to sense: *se ha olido que nos vamos* she has sensed that we are leaving.
olfatear *vt (oler)* to sniff, smell.
olfateo *nm* sniffing.
olfativo,-a *adj* olfactory.
olfato *nm* sense of smell.
olfatorio,-a *adj* olfactory.
oligarca *nm o nf* oligarch.
oligarquía *nf* oligarchy.
oligárquico,-a *adj* oligarchic.
oligoelemento *nm* trace element.
oligofrenia *nf* **1** *(enfermedad)* mental handicap. **2** *pey* mental deficiency.
oligofrénico,-a *adj* mentally retarded.
▶ *nm & nf* mentally retarded person.
olimpiada *nf* HIST Olympiad.

✎ También se escribe **olimpíada**.

olisquear *vt (olfatear)* to sniff.
oliva *nf* olive.
olivar *nm* olive grove.
olivarero,-a *adj (industria)* olive.
▶ *nm & nf* olive grower.
olivo *nm* olive tree.
olla *nf (utensilio)* pan.
olmo *nm* elm tree.
olor *nm* smell.
oloroso,-a *adj* fragrant.
olvidadizo,-a *adj* forgetful.
olvidar *vt* to forget.
▶ *vpr* **olvidarse** to forget (de, -).
olvido *nm* **1** *(desmemoria)* oblivion. **2** *(lapsus)* oversight, lapse.
Omán *nm* Oman.
omaní *adj* Omani.
▶ *nm o nf* Omani.
ombligo *nm* navel.
omega *nf (letra)* omega.
omisión *nf* omission.
omitir *vt (no decir)* to omit, leave out.
ómnibus *nm inv* bus.
omnipotente *adj* omnipotent.
omnipresente *adj* omnipresent.
omnívoro,-a *adj* omnivorous.
omoplato *nm* shoulder blade.

✎ También se escribe **omóplato**.

O

once *adj* eleven; *(undécimo)* eleventh.
▶ *nm* eleven.

✎ Consulta también **seis**.

onceavo,-a *adj (parte)* eleventh: *la onceava parte de...* an eleventh of...
▶ *nm* eleventh: *tres onceavos* three elevenths.

✎ Consulta también **sexto**.

oncología *nf* oncology.
oncólogo,-a *nm & nf* oncologist.
onda *nf* wave.
ondear *vi (bandera)* to fly, flutter.
ondina *nf* water nymph, undine.
ondulación *nf* undulation, wave.
ondulado,-a *adj (pelo)* wavy.
ondulante *adj (movimiento)* rolling.
ondular *vt (pelo)* to wave.
ondulatorio,-a *adj* undulatory.
oneroso,-a *adj* onerous.
ónice *nm* onyx.
onírico,-a *adj* dream, of dreams.
ónix *nm* onyx.
onomástica *nf* saint's day.
onomástico,-a *adj* onomastic.
onomatopeya *nf* onomatopoeia.
onomatopéyico,-a *adj* onomatopoeic.
ontología *nf* ontology.
ontológico,-a *adj* ontological.
ONU *abrev* (Organización de las Naciones Unidas) United Nations Organization; *(abreviatura)* UNO.
onza *nf (peso)* ounce.
opacidad *nf* opaqueness, opacity.
opaco,-a *adj* opaque.
opalino,-a *adj (de ópalo)* opal.
ópalo *nm* opal.
opción *nf (en general)* option.
opcional *adj* optional.
open *nm inv* DEP open.
ópera *nf* opera.
operación *nf (gen)* operation.
operador,-ra *nm & nf* operator.
operando *nm* operand.
operante *adj* operative.
operar *vt* MED to operate (a, on).

▶ *vpr* **operarse** MED to have an operation.

operario,-a *nm & nf* operator, worker.
operativo,-a *adj* operative.
opereta *nf* operetta.
operístico,-a *adj* operatic.
opinable *adj* debatable.
opinar *vi* to think (de, about).
opinión *nf (juicio)* opinion.
opio *nm* opium.
opíparo,-a *adj fml* lavish.
oponente *nm o nf* opponent.
oponer *vt* to reply with.
▶ *vpr* **oponerse** *(estar en contra)* to oppose (a, -), be against (a, -).
oporto *nm* port.
oportunidad *nf* opportunity, chance.
oportunismo *nm* opportunism.
oportunista *nm o nf* opportunist.
oportuno,-a *adj (a tiempo)* opportune.
oposición *nf (antagonismo)* opposition.
opresión *nf* oppression.
opresivo,-a *adj* oppressive.
opresor,-ra *nm & nf* oppressor.
oprimido,-a *nm & nf* oppressed person.
oprimir *vt* **1** *(botón)* to press: *oprima el botón* press the button. **2** *fig* to oppress.
oprobio *nm* opprobrium.
optar *vi (elegir)* to choose (entre, from).
optativa *nf* EDUC *(asignatura)* optional subject.
optativo,-a *adj* **1** optional. **2** LING *(oración, modo)* optative.
óptica *nf* **1** *(tienda)* optician's. **2** FÍS optics.
óptico,-a *nm & nf* optician.
optimismo *nm* optimism.
optimista *adj* optimistic.
optimizar *vt* to optimize.
óptimo,-a *adj* very best, optimum.
opuesto,-a *adj* **1** *(contrario)* contrary, opposed. **2** *(de enfrente)* opposite.
opulencia *nf* opulence.
opulento,-a *adj* opulent.
oquedad *nf (hueco)* cavity.
oración *nf* **1** REL *(plegaria)* prayer. **2** LING clause, sentence. COMP
oráculo *nm* oracle.

orador,-ra *nm & nf* speaker, orator.
oral *adj* oral.
orangután *nm* ZOOL orang-utan.
orar *vi* to pray.
oratoria *nf* oratory.
oratorio,-a *adj (estilo, arte)* oratorical.
orbe *nm (esfera)* orb; *(mundo)* world.
órbita *nf (de un astro)* orbit.
orbital *adj* orbital.
orca *nf* killer whale, orc.
orden *nm (ordenación)* order.
  ▶ *nf (mandato)* order.
ordenación *nf* arrangement.
ordenada *nf* MAT ordinate.
ordenado,-a *adj* tidy.
ordenador,-ra *nm* INFORM computer.
ordenamiento *nm* ordering.
ordenanza *nf (norma)* ordinance.
ordenar *vt* **1** *(arreglar)* to put in order; *(habitación)* to tidy up. **2** *(mandar)* to order.
ordeñar *vt* to milk.
ordinal *adj* ordinal.
  ▶ *nm* ordinal.
ordinariez *nf (defecto)* vulgarity.
ordinario,-a *adj* **1** *(corriente)* ordinary, common. **2** *(grosero)* vulgar, common.
orégano *nm* oregano.
oreja *nf* ear.
orejera *nf* earflap.
orejero *nm (sillón)* wing chair.
orfanato *nm* orphanage.
orfandad *nf* orphanage.
orfebre *nm* goldsmith, silversmith.
orfebrería *nf (en oro)* gold work.
orfeón *nm* choral society.
órfico,-a *adj* lit orphic.
organdí *nm* organdie.
orgánico,-a *adj* organic.
organigrama *nm* organization chart.
organillero,-a *nm & nf* organ-grinder.
organillo *nm* barrel organ.
organismo *nm* **1** *(humano)* organism. **2** *(institucional)* organization, body.
organista *nm o nf* organist.
organización *nf* organization.
organizar *vt* to organize.
organizativo,-a *adj* organizational.

órgano *nm* organ.
orgullo *nm (propia estima)* pride.
orgulloso,-a *adj* proud.
orientación *nf* aspect.
oriental *adj* eastern, oriental.
  ▶ *nm o nf* Oriental.
orientar *vt* **1** *(antena)* to point. **2** *(esfuerzos)* to direct. **3** *(aconsejar)* to advise.
  ▶ *vpr* **orientarse** to find one's bearings.
oriente *nm* East.
orificio *nm (agujero)* hole.
origen *nm (causa)* cause, origin.
original *adj (gen)* original.
  ▶ *nm* original.
originalidad *nf* originality.
originar *vt* to cause, give rise to.
originario,-a *adj* original.
orilla *nf* **1** *(borde)* edge. **2** *(del río)* bank; *(del mar)* shore.
orillar *vt (sortear)* to get round.
orina *nf* urine.
orinar *vi* to urinate.
oriundo,-a *adj* native of.
orla *nf (adorno)* edging.
ornamentación *nf* ornamentation.
ornamental *adj* ornamental.
ornamentar *vt* to adorn, decorate.
ornamento *nm* ornament.
ornitología *nf* ornithology.
ornitológico,-a *adj* ornithological.
ornitólogo,-a *nm & nf* ornithologist.
ornitorrinco *nm* platypus.
oro *nm* gold.
orografía *nf* orography.
orográfico,-a *adj* orographic.
orondo,-a *adj* hearty, plump.
orquesta *nf* orchestra, dance band.
orquestal *adj* orchestral.
orquestar *vt* to orchestrate.
orquídea *nf* orchid.
ortiga *nf* nettle.
ortodoncia *nf* orthodontics.
ortodoxia *nf* orthodoxy.
ortodoxo,-a *adj* orthodox.
  ▶ *nm & nf* orthodox.
ortografía *nf* spelling.
ortográfico,-a *adj* spelling.

O

ortopedia *nf* orthopaedics.

ortopédico,-a *adj* orthopaedic.

ortopedista *nm o nf* orthopaedist.

oruga *nf* caterpillar.

orzuelo *nm* sty.

os *pron* **1** *(complemento directo)* you: *os escucho* I am listening to you. **2** *(complemento indirecto)* you: *os traje un libro* I brought you a book. **3** *(reflexivo)* yourselves: *¿ya os estáis vistiendo?* are you getting dressed already? **4** *(recíproco)* each other: *os parecéis mucho* you look very much alike.

osadía *nf (audacia)* audacity, daring.

osado,-a *adj (audaz)* audacious.

osamenta *nf (esqueleto)* skeleton.

osar *vi lit* to dare, have the audacity to.

oscilación *nf (de precios)* fluctuation.

oscilar *vi (variar)* to vary, fluctuate.

oscilatorio,-a *adj* oscillating.

oscurantismo *nm* obscurantism.

oscuras LOC *a oscuras* in the dark.

óseo,-a *adj (tejido, estructura)* bone.

osera *nf* bear's den.

osezno *nm* bear cub.

osificación *nf* ossification.

osificar *vt* to ossify.

osmio *nm* osmium.

ósmosis *nf inv* osmosis.

oso *nm* bear.

ostentación *nf* ostentation.

ostentar *vt (poseer)* to hold.

ostentoso,-a *adj* ostentatious.

osteópata *nm o nf* osteopath.

osteopatía *nf* osteopathy.

osteopático,-a *adj* osteopathic.

ostra *nf* oyster.

ostracismo *nm* ostracism.

ostrero,-a *adj* oyster.

ostrícola *adj* oyster.

OTAN *abrev* (Organización del Tratado del Atlántico Norte) North Atlantic Treaty Organization; *(abreviatura)* NATO.

otear *vt (horizonte)* to scan.

otero *nm* hillock.

otitis *nf inv* ear infection, otitis.

otomano,-a *adj* Ottoman.
▶ *nm & nf (persona)* Ottoman.

otoñal *adj* autumnal, autumn, US fall.

otoño *nm* autumn, US fall.

otorgante *adj (de un premio)* awarding.

otorgar *vt (conceder)* to grant, give (a, to); *(premio)* to award (a, to).

otorrinolaringólogo,-a *nm & nf* ear, nose and throat specialist.

otorrinolaringología *nf* ear, nose and throat, ENT.

otro,-a *adj* other, another.
▶ *pron* other, another: *otros* others.

ovación *nf* ovation, applause.

ovacionar *vt* to give an ovation (a, to).

oval *adj* oval.

ovalado,-a *adj* oval.

óvalo *nm* oval.

ovario *nm* ovary.

oveja *nf* sheep, ewe.

overtura *nf* MÚS overture.

ovillar *vt* to roll into a ball.

ovillo *nm* ball of wool.

ovino,-a *adj* ovine, sheep.

ovíparo,-a *adj* oviparous.

ovulación *nf* ovulation.

ovular *adj* ovular.
▶ *vi* to ovulate.

óvulo *nm* ovule.

oxiacetilénico,-a *adj* oxyacetylene.

oxiacetileno *nm* oxyacetylene.

oxidable *adj* oxidizable.

oxidación *nf* **1** QUÍM oxidation. **2** *(proceso)* rusting.

oxidado,-a *adj* rusty.

oxidar *vt* to rust.
▶ *vpr* **oxidarse** to rust, go rusty.

óxido *nm (herrumbre)* rust.

oxigenado,-a *adj* QUÍM oxygenated.

oxigenar *vt* to get some fresh air in.
▶ *vpr* **oxigenarse** to get some fresh air.

oxígeno *nm* oxygen.

oye *interj fam (para llamar la atención)* hey!

oyente *nm o nf* RAD listener.

ozono *nm* ozone. COMP *capa de ozono* ozone layer.

P

P, p *nf (la letra)* P, p.
pabellón *nm (en una feria)* stand.
pabilo *nm* wick.
pábulo *nm* fuel.
pacana *nf* pecan nut.
pacer *vi* to graze.
pachón,-ona *adj (perro)* pointer.
paciencia *nf* patience.
paciente *nm o nf* patient.
pacificación *nf* pacification.
pacíficamente *adv* peacefully.
pacificar *vt* to pacify.
pacífico,-a *adj* peaceful.
pacifismo *nm* pacifism.
pacifista *adj* pacifist.
▶ *nm o nf* pacifist.
pactar *vt* to agree (to).
▶ *vi* to come to an agreement.
pacto *nm* pact, agreement.
padecer *vt* to suffer.
▶ *vi (sufrir)* to suffer (de, from).
padecimiento *nm* suffering.
padrastro *nm (padre)* stepfather.
padrazo *nm fam* loving father.
padre *nm* father.
▶ *nm pl* **padres** parents.
padrino *nm (de bautizo)* godfather.
▶ *nm pl* **padrinos** godparents.
padrón *nm (censo)* census.
paella *nf (comida)* paella.
paellera *nf* paella pan.
paga *nf* **1** *(sueldo)* pay. **2** *(de los niños)* pocket money.
pagadero,-a *adj* payable.
pagador,-ra *adj* paying.
▶ *nm & nf (gen)* payer.
paganismo *nm* paganism.
pagano,-a *nm & nf* REL pagan.

pagar *vt* to pay: *ya he pagado lo que debía* I've already paid what I owed.
▶ *vi* to pay: *en esta empresa pagan muy bien* this company pays very well.
página *nf* page.
paginación *nf* pagination.
pago *nm* payment.
paguro *nm (ermitaño)* hermit crab.
país *nm* country.
paisaje *nm* landscape.
paisajista *nm o nf (pintor)* landscape artist.
paisajístico,-a *adj* landscape.
paisano,-a *nm & nf* **1** *(compatriota)* fellow countryman. **2** *(campesino)* countryman.
paja *nf* **1** straw. **2** *fig (relleno)* waffle.
pajar *nm (lugar)* hayloft.
pajarera *nf* aviary.
pajarería *nf (tienda)* caged-bird shop.
pajarero,-a *adj* of birds.
pajarita *nf (de cuello)* bow tie.
pájaro *nm (animal)* bird.
paje *nm* page.
pajita *nf (para beber)* straw.
pajizo,-a *adj* straw-coloured (US straw-colored).
Pakistán *nm* Pakistan.
pakistaní *adj* Pakistani.
▶ *nm o nf* Pakistani.
pala *nf* **1** shovel. **2** DEP *(de ping-pong)* bat.
palabra *nf* word.
palacete *nm* mansion.
palaciego,-a *adj* palatial.
palacio *nm* palace.
palada *nf (gen)* shovelful.
paladar *nm* **1** palate. **2** *fig* taste.
paladear *vt* to savour, relish.
paladín *nm fig* champion.

palafito *nm* house on stilts.

palanca *nf (gen)* lever. LOC hacer palanca to lever.

palangana *nf* bowl.

palangre *nm (arte de pesca)* boulter.

palatal *adj* palatal.
▶ *nf* palatal.

palco *nm (en el teatro)* box.

paleografía *nf* palaeography.

paleógrafo,-a *nm & nf* palaeographer.

paleolítico,-a *adj* Palaeolithic.
▶ *nm* el paleolítico the Palaeolithic.

paleontología *nf* palaeontology.

paleontólogo,-a *nm & nf* palaeontologist.

Palestina *nf* Palestine.

palestino,-a *adj* Palestinian.
▶ *nm & nf* Palestinian.

palestra *nf* arena, forum.

paleta *nf* 1 *(de pintor)* palette. 2 *(de albañil)* trowel.

paletada *nf (de albañil)* going over with a trowel.

paletilla *nf* 1 ANAT shoulder blade. 2 CULIN shoulder.

paliar *vt* to palliate, alleviate.

paliativo,-a *adj* palliative.
▶ *nm* paliativo palliative.

palidecer *vi* 1 to turn pale. 2 *fig* to fade.

palidez *nf* paleness, pallor.

pálido,-a *adj* pale.

palillero *nm* toothpick holder.

palillo *nm (mondadientes)* toothpick.

palio *nm* canopy.

palisandro *nm* rosewood.

paliza *nf* beating, thrashing.

palma *nf* 1 BOT palm (tree). 2 *(de la mano)* palm.
▶ *nf pl* palmas *(aplausos)* clapping *sing*.

palmada *nf (golpe)* slap, pat.

palmar *nm* palm grove.

palmarés *nm (lista)* list of winners.

palmatoria *nf* candlestick.

palmeado,-a *adj* 1 BOT palmate. 2 ZOOL *(dedos)* webbed.

palmear *vi* to clap.

palmera *nf* BOT palm tree, palm.

palmeral *nm* palm grove.

palmetazo *nm* stroke of the cane.

palmípedo,-a *adj* web-footed.
▶ *nf pl* palmípedas ZOOL *(género)* web-footed birds.

palmito *nm* 1 CULIN palm heart. 2 BOT palmetto.

palmo *nm (medida)* span.

palmotear *vi* to clap.

palmoteo *nm* clapping.

palo *nm* 1 *(estaca)* stick; *(de valla)* post; *(de telégrafos)* pole. 2 *(golpe)* blow.

paloma *nf (gen)* pigeon; *(blanca)* dove.

palomar *nm* dovecote.

palometa *nf* Ray's bream.

palomilla *nf (tuerca)* wing nut.

palomino *nm* young pigeon.

palomitas COMP palomitas de maíz popcorn *sing*.

palomo *nm* cock pigeon.

palote *nm (dibujo)* stroke.

palpable *adj* palpable.

palpar *vt* MED to palpate.

palpitación *nf* palpitation.

palpitante *adj (tema, cuestión)* burning.

palpitar *vi* to palpitate, throb.

pálpito *nm* hunch, feeling.

paludismo *nm* malaria.

palurdo,-a *nm & nf* country bumpkin.

palustre *adj (de las lagunas)* lake.

pamela *nf* wide-brimmed straw hat.

pampa *nf* pampas *pl*.

pámpano *nm* vine shoot.

pamplina *nf (tontería)* daft thing.

pamplinero,-a *adj* sweet-talking.

pan *nm* 1 *(masa)* bread; *(hogaza)* loaf of bread. 2 *(alimento)* food, bread. COMP barra de pan loaf of bread. ▮ pan integral wholemeal bread.

pana *nf* corduroy.

panacea *nf* panacea.

panadería *nf* bakery, baker's.

panadero,-a *nm & nf* baker.

panal *nm* honeycomb.

Panamá *nm* Panama.

panameño,-a *adj* Panamanian.
▶ *nm & nf* Panamanian.

panamericano,-a *adj* Pan-American.

pancarta *nf* **1** placard. **2** INFORM banner.
panceta *nf* bacon.
páncreas *nm inv* pancreas.
pancreático,-a *adj* pancreatic.
panda *nm* ZOOL panda.
pandemónium *nm* pandemonium.
pandeo *nm (torcedura)* warp.
pandereta *nf* small tambourine.
pandero *nm* tambourine.
pandilla *nf* group of friends.
panecillo *nm* bread roll.
panel *nm (gen)* panel.
panera *nf* breadbasket.
panfleto *nm fig* propaganda.
pánico *nm* panic.
panificadora *nf* industrial bakery.
panocha *nf (de maíz)* corncob.
panorama *nm* panorama, view.
panorámica *nf* panorama.
panorámico,-a *adj* panoramic.
pantalla *nf* screen.
pantalón [también se usa en plural con el mismo significado] *nm* trousers *pl*, US pants. COMP **pantalón vaquero** jeans *pl*.
pantano *nm* **1** *(artificial)* reservoir. **2** *(natural)* marsh.
pantanoso,-a *adj* marshy.
panteísmo *nm* pantheism.
panteón *nm* pantheon.
pantera *nf* panther.
panties *nm pl* tights.
pantomima *nf* **1** *(representación)* pantomime, mime. **2** *fig* farce, pretence.
pantorrilla *nf* calf.
pantufla *nf* slipper.
panza *nf* belly.
panzada *nf (en el agua)* belly flop.
pañal *nm* nappy, US diaper.
pañería *nf* draper's, draper's shop.
paño *nm* cloth.
pañoleta *nf* shawl.
pañuelo *nm* handkerchief.
papa¹ *nm* **1** *fam* dad. **2** **el Papa** the Pope.
papa² *nf (patata)* potato. COMP **papas fritas** chips, US French fries.

papá *nm fam* dad, daddy. COMP **Papá Noel** Santa Claus.
papada *nf* double chin.
papagayo *nm* parrot.
papaya *nf* papaya.
papayo *nm* papaya tree.
papel *nm* **1** *(gen)* paper. **2** *(en película)* role, part. COMP **papel higiénico** toilet paper. ‖ **papel pintado** wallpaper.
▶ *nm pl* **papeles** *fam (documentación)* papers.
papeleo *nm fam* paperwork.
papelera *nf* **1** wastepaper basket. **2** *(en la calle)* litter bin.
papelería *nf* stationer's.
papelero,-a *adj (del papel)* paper: *la industria papelera* the paper industry.
papeleta *nf* **1** *(de voto)* ballot paper. **2** *(de examen)* results slip.
paperas *nf pl* mumps.
papi *nm fam* dad, daddy.
papila *nf* papilla.
papilla *nf (infantil)* baby food.
papiro *nm* papyrus.
papú *adj* Papuan.
▶ *nm o nf* Papuan.
Papúa *nf* Papua. COMP **Papúa Nueva Guinea** Papua New Guinea.
paquete *nm* **1** *(cajita)* packet, pack. **2** *(conjunto)* set, packet: *un paquete de galletas* a package of biscuits. COMP **paquete postal** parcel.
paquidermo *nm* pachyderm.
Paquistán *nm* Pakistan.
paquistaní *adj* Pakistani.
▶ *nm o nf* Pakistani.
par *adj* **1** equal. **2** MAT even.
▶ *nm (dos)* couple; *(pareja)* pair.
para *prep* **1** *(finalidad)* for: *es para su cumpleaños* it's for her birthday. **2** *(uso, utilidad)* for: *¿tienes algo para el dolor de cabeza?* have you got anything for a headache? **3** *(destino, dirección)* for, to: *¿para dónde vas?* where are you going? **4** *(tiempo, fechas límites)* by, before: *lo necesito para el viernes* I need it by Friday.
▶ *conj (finalidad)* to, in order to: *lo hice para ahorrar tiempo* I did it to save time.
parábola *nf* MAT parabola.

P

parabólica *nf* satellite dish.
parabólico,-a *adj* parabolic. COMP antena parabólica satellite dish.
parabrisas *nm inv* windscreen.
paracaídas *nm inv* parachute.
paracaidismo *nm* parachuting.
paracaidista *nm o nf* DEP parachutist.
parachoques *nm inv* AUTO bumper.
parada *nf* **1** (*gen*) stop, halt. **2** (*de autobús, etc*) stop. **3** (*pausa*) pause. COMP parada de autobús bus stop.
paradero *nm* whereabouts *pl*.
paradigmático,-a *adj* paradigmatic.
paradisíaco,-a *adj* heavenly.
parado,-a *adj* **1** (*quieto*) still. **2** (*sin trabajo*) unemployed.
▶ *nm & nf* unemployed person.
paradójico,-a *adj* paradoxical.
parador *nm* (*hotel*) state-run hotel.
parafina *nf* paraffin.
paraguas *nm inv* umbrella.
Paraguay *nm* Paraguay.
paraguaya *nf type of* peach.
paraguayo,-a *adj* Paraguayan.
▶ *nm & nf* Paraguayan.
paraíso *nm* paradise.
paraje *nm* spot.
paralela *nf* (*línea*) parallel line.
▶ *nf pl* **paralelas** DEP parallel bars.
paralelo,-a *adj* parallel.
▶ *nm* paralelo parallel.
paralelogramo *nm* parallelogram.
parálisis *nf inv* paralysis.
paralítico,-a *adj* paralytic.
▶ *nm & nf* paralytic.
paralización *nf* paralysis.
paralizar *vt* **1** MED to paralyse. **2** (*circulación*) to bring to a standstill.
parámetro *nm* parameter.
páramo *nm* moor.
paranoia *nf* paranoia.
paranoico,-a *nm & nf* paranoic.
parapente *nm* paragliding.
parapeto *nm* parapet.
parapléjico,-a *nm & nf* paraplegic.
parapsicología *nf* parapsychology.

parapsicológico,-a *adj* parapsychological.
parar *vt* **1** to stop. **2** DEP to save: *ha parado tres disparos* he's made three saves.
▶ *vi* to stop: *aquí no para el tren* the train doesn't stop here.
▶ *vpr* **pararse** to stop.
pararrayos *nm inv* lightning conductor.
parasitario,-a *adj* parasitic.
parásito,-a *nm* BIOL parasite.
parasol *nm* parasol, sunshade.
parcela *nf* (*de tierra*) plot (of land).
parcelar *vt* (*finca*) to divide into plots.
parche *nm* patch.
parchís *nm inv* ludo.
parcial *adj* (*gen*) partial.
▶ *nm* (*examen*) *examination covering part of the course and counting towards the final mark*.
parcialidad *nf* (*injusticia*) bias, partiality.
parco,-a *adj* (*escaso*) frugal, sparing.
pardo,-a *adj* (*color tierra*) brown.
pareado,-a *adj* (*casa*) semidetached.
parecer *nm* (*opinión*) opinion, mind.
▶ *vi* **1** to seem, look (like): *parece un oso* it looks like a bear. **2** (*opinar*) to think: *¿qué te parece?* what do you think?
▶ *vpr* **parecerse** to be alike, look like: *se parecen mucho* they're very much alike.
parecido,-a *adj* similar.
▶ *nm* parecido resemblance, likeness.
pared *nf* **1** wall. **2** (*de una montaña*) side.
paredón *nm* execution wall.
pareja *nf* **1** (*gen*) pair: *he perdido la pareja de este calcetín* I've lost the other sock. **2** (*de personas*) couple; (*de baile*) partner.
parejo,-a *adj* (*sin diferencia*) the same; (*por igual*) even.
parentela *nf* relatives *pl*, relations *pl*.
parentesco *nm* kinship, relationship.
paréntesis *nm inv* **1** (*gen*) parenthesis. **2** fig (*interrupción*) break, interruption.
paria *nm o nf* pariah.
paridad *nf* (*gen*) parity, equality.
pariente,-a *nm & nf* relative.
parir *vt* fam to give birth to.
▶ *vi* to give birth.
parlamentario,-a *adj* parliamentary.
▶ *nm & nf* member of parliament.

parlamento *nm* parliament.
parlante *adj* talking.
parlotear *vi fam* to chatter, prattle on.
parmesan *nm (queso)* Parmesan cheese.
paro *nm* 1 stop. 2 *(desempleo)* unemployment.
parodia *nf* parody.
parodiar *vt* to parody.
paroxismo *nm* paroxysm.
parpadear *vi (ojos)* to blink, wink.
párpado *nm* eyelid.
parque *nm (jardines)* park. COMP **parque de atracciones** amusement park.
parqué *nm* parquet.
parquímetro *nm* parking meter.
parra *nf* grapevine.
parrafada *nf fam (conversación)* chat.
párrafo *nm* paragraph.
parranda *nf fam* spree.
parrilla *nf* 1 grill, US broiler, barbecue. LOC **a la parrilla** CULIN grilled.
parrillada *nf* mixed grill *(of meat or fish)*.
párroco *nm* parish priest.
parroquia *nf (iglesia)* parish church.
parsimonia *nf (lentitud)* slowness.
parsimonioso,-a *adj (tranquilo)* slow.
parte *nf* 1 *(gen)* part; *(en una partición)* portion: *divide el pastel en tres partes* cut the cake into three (slices). 2 *(en negocio)* share. 3 *(lugar)* place: *no lo venden en ninguna parte* they don't sell it anywhere. 4 *(en un conflicto)* side: *las dos partes quieren llevar la razón* both sides believe they are right.
▸ *nm (comunicado)* official report.
▸ *nf pl* **partes** *fam* privates, private parts. LOC **en parte** partly. ‖ **por una parte,... por otra...** on the one hand…, on the other hand…
partera *nf* midwife.
parterre *nm* flowerbed.
partición *nf (de una herencia)* partition.
participación *nf* involvement.
participante *nm o nf* participant.
participar *vi* to participate, take part.
▸ *vt (notificar)* to notify, inform.
partícipe *adj* participating.
▸ *nm o nf* participant.

participio *nm* participle.
partícula *nf* particle.
particular *adj (concreto)* particular.
▸ *nm* 1 private individual. 2 *(asunto)* matter, subject.
particularidad *nf (gen)* peculiarity.
particularizar *vt* to distinguish.
partida *nf* 1 *(remesa)* consignment, lot. 2 *(documento)* certificate. 3 *(juego)* game. LOC **jugar una partida** to play a game. COMP **partida de nacimiento** birth certificate.
partidario,-a *adj* supporting.
▸ *nm & nf* supporter.
partidista *adj* biased, partisan.
partido,-a *adj* 1 divided. 2 *(roto)* broken.
▸ *nm* **partido** 1 *(grupo político)* party, group. 2 DEP *(equipo)* team; *(juego)* game, match. COMP **partido amistoso** friendly game.
partir *vt* 1 *(dividir)* to divide, cut: *voy a partir pan* I'll cut some bread. 2 *(romper)* to break; *(nueces, almendras)* to crack.
▸ *vi (irse)* to leave, set out, set off.
▸ *vpr* **partirse** to break: *se ha partido la pierna* he's broken his leg.
partitivo,-a *adj* partitive.
▸ *nm* **partitivo** partitive.
partitura *nf* score.
parto *nm* childbirth: *fue un parto difícil* it was a difficult birth. LOC **estar de parto** to be in labour (US labor).
parvulario *nm* nursery school.
párvulo,-a *nm & nf* infant.
pasa *nf* raisin.
pasable *adj* passable.
pasadizo *nm* passage.
pasado,-a *adj* 1 past. 2 *(año, semana, etc)* last. 3 *(después)* after: *pasadas las once* after eleven. 4 *(estropeado)* bad. COMP **pasado mañana** the day after tomorrow.
▸ *nm* **pasado** 1 *(tiempo)* past. 2 LING past, past tense.
pasador *nm* slide.
pasaje *nf* 1 *(tarifa)* fare, ticket. 2 *(pasajeros)* passengers *pl*. 3 *(fragmento)* passage.
pasajero,-a *nm & nf* passenger.
pasamanos *nm inv* handrail.

P

pasamontañas *nm inv* balaclava.

pasaporte *nm* passport.

pasapurés *nm inv* vegetable mill.

pasar *vi* **1** *(ir)* to pass, pass by, go: *pasa de un idioma a otro sin darse cuenta* he goes from one language to another without realizing. **2** *(tiempo)* to pass, go by: *¡cómo pasa el tiempo!* doesn't time fly! **3** *(entrar)* to come in, go in: *pasa, está abierto* come in, it's not locked. **4** *(cesar)* to pass, cease: *en cuanto pase la tormenta salimos* we'll go out when the storm has passed. **5** *(límite)* to exceed *(de, -)*. **6** *(ocurrir)* to happen. **7** *(sufrir)* to suffer.

▶ *vt* **1** *(trasladar)* to move, transfer: *pasa este documento al otro CD* move this file to the other CD. **2** *(comunicar, dar)* to give: *pásale el informe al jefe* give this report to the boss. **3** *(cruzar)* to cross: *pasamos la frontera ayer* we crossed the border yesterday. **4** *(alcanzar)* to pass, reach: *pásame la sal, por favor* pass me the salt, please. **5** *(aventajar)* to surpass, be better than: *tu hermano ya te pasa en matemáticas* your brother is better than you at maths. **6** *(adelantar)* to overtake: *me pasó un deportivo rojo en una curva* a red sports car overtook me on a bend. **7** *(deslizar)* to run: *pasó el dedo por el estante* he ran his finger along the shelf. **8** *(tolerar)* to overlook: *esta te la paso, pero que no se repita* I'll overlook it this time, but don't let it happen again. **9** *(aprobar)* to pass: *pasé el examen a la primera* I passed my test first time. **10** *(proyectar)* to show: *pasaron unas diapositivas* they showed some slides. **11** *(tiempo - estar)* to spend; *(- disfrutar, padecer)* to have: *pasamos unas vacaciones estupendas* we had a wonderful holiday.

▶ *vpr* **pasarse 1** *(cambiar)* to pass over *(a, to)*: *se ha pasado al otro bando* she's gone over to the other side. **2** *(pudrirse)* to go off. **3** *(olvidarse)* to forget: *se me pasó la fecha de entrega* I forgot about the deadline. **4** *(ir)* to go by *(por, -)*, call in *(por, at)*: *pásate por casa cuando quieras* pop in any time.

pasarela *nf (puente)* footbridge.

pasatiempos *nm pl* puzzles.

pascua *nf* Easter.

▶ *nf pl* **pascuas** Christmas *sing*.

pase *nm (permiso)* pass.

pasear *vi* to stroll, go for a walk.

▶ *vt* to take for a walk.

paseo *nm* **1** *(a pie)* walk; *(a caballo)* ride. **2** *(en coche)* drive; *(en bicicleta, moto)* ride. LOC **dar un paseo** to go for a walk.

pasillo *nm* corridor.

pasión *nf* passion.

pasividad *nf* passiveness, passivity.

pasmado,-a *adj* flabbergasted.

pasmar *vt* to astonish, amaze.

▶ *vpr* **pasmarse** *fam (asombrarse)* to be astonished, be amazed.

pasmo *nm (asombro)* amazement.

pasmoso,-a *adj* astonishing.

paso *nm* **1** *(movimiento)* step, footstep. **2** *(camino)* passage. LOC **abrirse paso** to force one's way through. **I estar de paso** to be passing through. COMP **paso de peatones** pedestrian crossing.

pasta *nf* **1** *(masa)* paste. **2** CULIN *(italiana)* pasta. **3** *(croissant, etc)* pastry; *(de té)* biscuit.

pastar *vt* to pasture, graze.

▶ *vi* to pasture, graze.

pastel *nm* CULIN *(dulce)* cake; *(salado)* pie.

pastelería *nf (tienda)* cake shop.

pastelero,-a *nm & nf* pastrycook.

pasteurizado,-a *adj* pasteurized.

pasteurizar *vt* to pasteurize.

pastilla *nf* **1** *(medicina)* tablet, pill. **2** *(de chocolate, jabón)* bar.

pasto *nm (pastizal)* pasture.

pastor,-ra *nm & nf* shepherd.

pastoso,-a *adj (sustancia)* pasty.

pata *nf* **1** *(gen)* leg. **2** *(garra)* paw. **3** *(pezuña)* hoof. LOC **a cuatro patas** on all fours. **I meter la pata** *fam* to put one's foot in it. **I patas arriba** upside down.

patada *nf* kick.

patalear *vi* **1** *(con enfado)* to stamp one's feet. **2** *(protestar)* to kick up a fuss.

pataleo *nm* **1** *(con los pies)* stamping. **2** *(protesta)* complaining.

pataleta *nf fam* tantrum.

patata *nf* potato. COMP **patatas fritas 1** *(de bolsa)* crisps. **2** *(de sartén)* chips.

paté *nm* pâté.

patear *vt* **1** to kick. **2** *(andar)* to walk.

patentado,-a *adj* patented.

patentar *vt* to patent.

patente *adj (evidente)* obvious, patent.

patera *nf* boat.

paternal *adj* paternal.

paternalista *adj* paternalistic.

paternidad *nf* paternity.

paterno,-a *adj* paternal.

patético,-a *adj* pathetic.

patíbulo *nm* gallows *sing*.

patilla *nf* **1** *(pata)* leg. **2** *(de las gafas)* arm.
▶ *nf pl* sideboards, US sideburns.

patín *nm* **1** *(de ruedas)* roller skate, skate; *(de hielo)* ice skate. **2** *(tabla)* skateboard. **3** *(patinete)* scooter. **4** *(en el mar)* pedalo.

pátina *nf* patina.

patinador,-ra *nm & nf* skater.

patinaje *nm* skating. COMP **patinaje artístico** figure skating. | **patinaje sobre hielo** ice-skating. | **patinaje sobre ruedas** roller skating.

patinar *vi* **1** *(como diversión)* to skate. **2** *(vehículo)* to skid.

patinazo *nm* **1** skid. **2** *fam (error)* boob.

patinete *nm* scooter.

patio *nm* **1** *(de una casa)* courtyard; *(de un colegio)* playground. **2** TEAT pit.

pato,-a *nm & nf (ave)* duck.
▶ *nm* **pato** *fam (persona)* clumsy person.

patológico,-a *adj* pathological.

patria *nf* homeland.

patriarca *nm* patriarch.

patriarcado *nm* patriarchy.

patrimonio *nm* patrimony.

patrio,-a *adj* of one's homeland.

patriota *nm o nf* patriot.

patriótico,-a *adj* patriotic.

patriotismo *nm* patriotism.

patrocinador,-ra *nm & nf* sponsor.

patrocinar *vt* to sponsor.

patrocinio *nm* sponsorship.

patrón,-ona *nm & nf* **1** *(dueño de una casa)* landlord. **2** *(jefe)* employer. **3** REL patron saint.
▶ *nm* **patrón 1** *(en costura)* pattern. **2** *(de barco)* skipper. **3** *(modelo)* standard.

patronal *adj (fiesta)* of one's patron saint.
▶ *nf (institución)* employers' association.

patronato *nm (patronal)* employers' association.

patrulla *nf (de vigilancia)* patrol.

patrullar *vt* to patrol.

paulatino,-a *adj* gradual.

pausa *nf* **1** pause. **2** MÚS rest.

pausado,-a *adj* unhurried, slow.

pauta *nf (norma)* rule, guideline.

pavimentar *vt (con losas)* to pave.

pavimento *nm (de losas)* pavement.

pavo,-a *nm & nf (ave - macho)* turkey; *(- hembra)* turkey hen. COMP **pavo real** peacock.
▶ *nm* **pavo** *fam (timidez)* shyness.

pavonearse *vpr* to brag, swagger.

pavoneo *nm* strutting.

pavor *nm* terror.

pavoroso,-a *adj* frightful.

payasada *nf* **1** buffoonery. **2** *fam* silly thing.

payaso,-a *nm & nf* **1** *(artista de circo)* clown. **2** *fam* joker.

paz *nf* peace. LOC **dejar en paz** to leave alone. | **hacer las paces** to make up.

peaje *nm* **1** *(dinero)* toll. **2** *(lugar)* toll-booth.

peana *nf* pedestal, stand.

peatón *nm* pedestrian.

peatonal *adj (calle, zona)* pedestrian.

peca *nf* freckle.

pecado *nm* sin.

pecador,-ra *nm & nf* sinner.

pecaminoso,-a *adj* sinful, wicked.

pecar *vi* to sin.

pecera *nf* fishbowl, fish tank.

pechera *nf (de camisa)* shirt front.

pechina *nf* scallop.

pecho *nm* **1** *(gen)* chest. **2** *(seno)* breast. LOC **dar el pecho** to breast-feed.

pechuga *nf (de un ave)* breast.

pecíolo *nm* petiole.

pecoso,-a *adj (persona)* freckly.

pectina *nf* pectin.

pectoral *nm (músculo)* pectoral muscle.

P

pecuario,-a *adj* cattle.

peculiar *adj (característico)* particular.

peculiaridad *nf* peculiarity.

pecuniario,-a *adj* pecuniary.

pedagogía *nf* pedagogy.

pedagógico,-a *adj* pedagogic(al).

pedagogo,-a *nm & nf* educator.

pedal *nm* **1** pedal. **2** *fam* bender.

pedalear *vi* to pedal.

pedaleo *nm* pedalling.

pedanía *nf* hamlet.

pedante *adj* pedantic, pompous.

pedantería *nf* pedantry, pomposity.

pedazo *nm* piece, bit.

pedernal *nm* **1** *(sílex)* flint. **2** *fig* rock.

pedestal *nm* pedestal.

pedestre *adj (a pie)* on foot.

pediatra *nm o nf* paediatrician.

pediatría *nf* paediatrics.

pedicuro,-a *nm & nf* chiropodist.

pedido *nm (de mercancías)* order. LOC hacer un pedido to place an order.

pedigrí *nm* pedigree.

pedigüeño,-a *nm & nf* pest.

pedir *vt* **1** *(gen)* to ask for: *me pidió que la acompañara* she asked me to go with her. **2** *(mercancías, en restaurante)* to order: *¿qué has pedido de postre?* what did you order for dessert?
▶ *vi (por la calle)* to beg.

pedrada *nf* blow with a stone.

pedregal *nm* rocky ground.

pedregoso,-a *adj* stony, rocky.

pedrera *nf* stone quarry.

pedrería *nf* precious stones *pl*.

pedrisco *nm (granizo)* hail.

pedrusco *nm* rough stone.

pedúnculo *nm (de planta)* stem.

pega *nf fam (dificultad)* snag: *me pusieron muchas pegas* they made it difficult for me.

pegadizo,-a *adj* **1** *(canción, música)* catchy. **2** *(sustancia)* sticky, adhesive.

pegajoso,-a *adj* **1** *(mano)* sticky. **2** *pey (persona)* clingy.

pegamento *nm* glue.

pegar¹ *vt* **1** *(gen)* to stick. **2** *(contagiar)* to give: *me has pegado la gripe* you've given

me your flu. **3** *(acercar)* to move close to: *pega la estantería a la pared* move the bookcase against the wall. **4** INFORM to paste.
▶ *vi (combinar)* to match: *esta blusa no pega con la falda* this blouse doesn't go with the skirt.
▶ *vpr* **pegarse 1** *(quemarse)* to stick: *se me ha vuelto a pegar el arroz* the rice has stuck again. **2** *(persona)* to latch onto.

pegar² *vt* **1** *(golpear)* to hit: *mamá, Pablo me ha pegado* mum, Pablo hit me. **2** *(dar)* to give: *¡vaya susto me has pegado!* you didn't half scare me!

pegatina *nf* sticker.

pego LOC dar el pego *fam* to look like the real thing.

pegote *nm fam (masa)* sticky dollop.

peinado *nm* combing.

peinado,-a *adj* combed.

peinar *vt* **1** *(gen)* to comb; *(con cepillo)* to brush. **2** *(registrar)* to comb, search.

peine *nm* comb.

peineta *nf* ornamental comb.

peladilla *nf* sugared almond.

pelado,-a *adj* **1** bald, bare. **2** *(cabeza)* hairless, bald.

peladuras *nf pl* peelings.

pelaje *nm (de animal)* coat, fur.

pelambrera *nf fam* hair.

pelapatatas *nm inv* potato peeler.

pelar *vt* **1** *(persona)* to cut sb's hair. **2** *(fruta, patata, etc)* to peel.
▶ *vpr* **pelarse 1** *(cortarse el pelo)* to get one's hair cut. **2** *(piel)* to be peeling.

peldaño *nm* step.

pelea *nf (física)* fight; *(verbal)* quarrel.

peleador,-ra *adj* argumentative.

pelear *vi* to fight, to quarrel, argue.
▶ *vpr* **pelearse** to fight, to quarrel.

peleón,-ona *nm & nf* quarrelsome.

peletería *nf (establecimiento)* fur shop.

peletero,-a *adj (industria)* fur.
▶ *nm & nf* furrier.

peliagudo,-a *adj* tricky.

pelícano *nm* pelican.

película *nf* film. COMP película de suspense thriller. ‖ película muda silent movie.

peligrar *vi* to be in danger.

peligro *nm* danger. `LOC` **correr peligro de** to be in danger of. **I estar fuera de peligro** to be out of danger.

peligroso,-a *adj* dangerous.

pelín *nm fam* teeny bit.

pelirrojo,-a *adj* red-haired.

pellejo *nm (piel)* skin.

pelliza *nf (forrada de piel)* fur-lined coat.

pellizcar *vt* to pinch, nip.

pellizco *nm* pinch, nip.

pelo *nm* **1** hair. **2** *(de animal)* coat, fur. **3** *fam* bit: *perdí el tren por un pelo* I missed the train by seconds. `LOC` **no tener un pelo de tonto,-a** *fam* to be nobody's fool. **I poner los pelos de punta** to make one's hair stand on end. **I tomar el pelo a** ALGN to pull sb's leg.

pelota *nf* ball. `COMP` **pelota de fútbol** football.
▶ *nm o nf fam* creep.

pelotazo *nm* blow with a ball.

pelotilla *nf* small ball.

pelotón *nm* **1** *fig (grupo)* bunch. **2** *(de ciclistas)* pack, peloton.

peltre *nm* pewter.

peluca *nf* wig.

peluche *nm (muñeco)* teddy bear.

peludo,-a *adj* hairy.

peluquería *nf* hairdresser's.

peluquero,-a *nm & nf* hairdresser.

peluquín *nm* hairpiece.

pelusa *nf (pelo)* fluff.

pélvico,-a *adj* pelvic.

pelvis *nf inv* pelvis.

pena *nf* **1** *(castigo)* sentence, punishment. **2** *(tristeza)* grief, sorrow. **3** *(lástima)* pity: *¡qué pena que no podáis venir!* it's a shame you can't make it! **4** *(dificultad)* hardship, trouble.

penado,-a *nm & nf* convict.

penal *adj (derecho)* criminal.
▶ *nm (prisión)* prison, US penitentiary.

penalidad *nf* trouble, hardship.

penalización *nf (acción)* penalization.

penalizar *vt* to penalize.

penalti *nm* penalty.

penar *vt (castigar)* to punish, penalize.
▶ *vi (padecer)* to suffer, grieve.

pender *vi* to hang (de, from).

pendiente *adj* **1** hanging. **2** *(asunto)* pending, outstanding. `LOC` **estar pendiente de** ALGO *(a la espera)* to be waiting for STH.
▶ *nf (cuesta)* slope; *(inclinación)* gradient.
▶ *nm (joya)* earring.

pendular *adj* pendular.

péndulo *nm* pendulum.

penetración *nf* penetration.

penetrante *adj* penetrating.

penetrar *vi* **1** *(introducirse - en un territorio)* to penetrate (en, -); *(- en propiedad)* to enter. **2** *(atravesar)* to penetrate, seep through: *la humedad ha penetrado por el suelo* damp has seeped through the floor.
▶ *vt (atravesar)* to penetrate; *(ruido)* to pierce.

penicilina *nf* penicillin.

península *nf* peninsula. `COMP` **la Península Ibérica** the Iberian Peninsula.

penique *nm* penny.

penitencia *nf* REL *(virtud)* penitence; *(castigo, sacramento)* penance.

penitenciaría *nf* penitentiary.

penitenciario,-a *adj (institución, sistema)* prison.

penoso,-a *adj (doloroso)* painful.

pensador,-ra *nm & nf* thinker.

pensamiento *nm (idea)* thought.

pensante *adj* thinking.

pensar *vi* **1** *(gen)* to think (en, of/about): *estuvo pensando en sus amigos* he was thinking about his friends. **2** *(considerar)* to consider, think (en, about). **3** *(creer)* to think, think about. **4** *(opinar)* to think (de, about). **5** *(decidir)* to decide. **6** *(tener la intención)* to intend to, plan, think of.

pensativo,-a *adj* pensive.

pensión *nf* **1** *(para jubilados)* pension. **2** *(casa de huéspedes)* boarding house. `COMP` **pensión completa** full board.

pensionista *nm o nf (jubilado)* pensioner.

pentagonal *adj* pentagonal.

pentágono *nm* pentagon.

pentagrama *nm* MÚS stave, staff.

pentatlón *nm* pentathlon.

penúltimo,-a *adj* penultimate.
▶ *nm & nf* last but one, next to last.

P

penumbra *nf (gen)* semidarkness.

penuria *nf (escasez)* shortage.

peña¹ *nf (piedra)* rock; *(monte)* crag.

peña² *nf (grupo)* group of friends; *(asociación)* club.

peñasco *nm* crag.

peñón *nm* craggy rock. LOC **el Peñón de Gibraltar** the Rock of Gibraltar.

peón *nm* **1** *(trabajador)* unskilled labourer (US laborer). **2** *(en el ajedrez)* pawn.

peonía *nf* BOT peony.

peonza *nf* top, spinning top.

peor *adj* **1** *(comparativo)* worse: *tu coche es peor que el mío* your car is worse than mine. **2** *(superlativo)* worst.

pepinillo *nm* gherkin.

pepino *nm* cucumber.

pepita *nf (de fruta)* → seed, pip.

peque *nm* kid.

pequeñez *nf* **1** *(de tamaño)* smallness. **2** *(insignificancia)* trifle.

pequeñito,-a *adj fam* teeny, wee.

pequeño,-a *adj* **1** *(de tamaño)* little, small: *este jersey me está pequeño* this jumper is too small for me. **2** *(de edad)* young. **3** *(en tiempo)* short: *nos hemos tomado unas pequeñas vacaciones* we've taken a short holiday.
► *nm & nf (niño)* little one: *a esta hora los pequeños tienen que estar en la cama* kids should be in bed by now. LOC **de pequeño,-a** as a child.

pequinés,-esa *adj* Pekinese.
► *nm* **pekinés** *(perro)* Pekinese.

pera *nf (fruta)* pear.

peral *nm* pear tree.

perca *nf* perch.

percance *nm* mishap.

percatarse *vpr* to notice (de, -).

percebe *nm* goose barnacle.

percepción *nf* perception.

perceptible *adj* perceptible.

perceptivo,-a *adj* perceptive.

percha *nf* **1** *(de ropa)* hanger. **2** *(perchero de pared)* rack; *(gancho)* hook.

perchero *nm (de pie)* coat stand.

percherón,-ona *adj (caballo)* Percheron.

percibir *vt (notar)* to perceive, notice.

percusión *nf* percussion.

percusionista *nm o nf* percussionist.

percutir *vt (golpear)* to strike.

perdedor,-ra *nm & nf* loser.

perder *vt* **1** *(gen)* to lose. **2** *(malgastar, desperdiciar)* to waste: *se pasa el día perdiendo el tiempo* he's always wasting time. **3** *(tren, etc)* to miss.
► *vi* **1** *(gen)* to lose; *(salir perdiendo)* to lose out. **2** *(empeorar)* to get worse.
► *vpr* **perderse 1** *(extraviarse - persona)* to get lost; *(- cosa, etc)* to go missing: *se me ha perdido un pendiente* I've lost an earring. **2** *(dejar escapar)* to miss: *¡no te lo pierdas!* don't miss it!

perdición *nf (moral)* undoing, ruin.

pérdida *nf* **1** *(daño)* loss: *las tormentas han originado muchas pérdidas materiales* the storms have caused serious damage. **2** *(desperdicio)* waste. **3** *(escape)* leak.

perdido,-a *adj* **1** *(extraviado)* lost. **2** *(desperdiciado)* wasted. **3** *(bala)* stray.

perdigón *nm* pellet.

perdiguero *nm* gun dog.

perdiz *nf* partridge.

perdón *nm* pardon, forgiveness. LOC **pedir perdón** to apologize, say sorry.

perdonable *adj* excusable, forgivable.

perdonar *vt* **1** *(gen)* to forgive. **2** *(excusar)* to excuse: *perdona que te interrumpa* excuse me for interrupting. **3** *(deuda)* to write off.

perdurar *vi* to last, continue to exist.

perecedero,-a *adj* perishable.

perecer *vi* to perish, die.

peregrinación *nf* pilgrimage.

peregrinar *vi* to go on a pilgrimage.

peregrino,-a *nm & nf* REL pilgrim.

perejil *nm* parsley.

perenne *adj* perennial.

pereza *nf* laziness. LOC **tener pereza** to feel lazy.

perezoso,-a *adj* lazy.
► *nm* **perezoso** ZOOL sloth.

perfección *nf* perfection. LOC **a la perfección** perfectly: *habla inglés a la perfección* he speaks perfect English.

perfeccionar *vt* **1** *(mejorar)* to improve. **2** *(hacer perfecto)* to perfect.

perfeccionista *adj* perfectionist.
▶ *nm o nf* perfectionist.

perfecto,-a *adj* perfect.

perfidia *nf* perfidy.

pérfido,-a *adj* perfidious.

perfil *nm* **1** *(gen)* profile. **2** *(silueta)* outline.

perfilar *vt* *(dar forma)* to outline.

perforación *nf* *(gen)* perforation.

perforadora *nf* **1** *(en una mina)* drill. **2** *(de papeles)* punch.

perforar *vt* **1** *(gen)* to perforate. **2** *(terreno)* to drill, bore. **3** *(papel)* to punch.

perfumar *vt* to perfume, scent.

perfume *nm* perfume.

perfumería *nf* *(tienda)* perfumery.

pergamino *nm* parchment.

pérgola *nf* pergola.

pericardio *nm* pericardium.

pericarpio *nm* pericarp.

pericia *nf* skill.

periferia *nf* *(de una ciudad)* outskirts *pl*.

periférico,-a *adj* **1** *(gen)* peripheral. **2** *(barrio, zona)* outlying.
▶ *nm* **periférico** INFORM peripheral unit.

perifollo *nm* BOT common chervil.

perífrasis *nf* periphrasis.

perifrástico,-a *adj* periphrastic.

perilla *nf* goatee.

perímetro *nm* perimeter.

periodicidad *nf* periodicity.

periódico,-a *adj* periodical.
▶ *nm* **periódico** newspaper.

periodismo *nm* journalism.

periodista *nm o nf* journalist.

período *nm* period.

peripecia *nf* incident.

peripuesto,-a *adj fam* all dressed up.

periquito,-a *nm o nf* parakeet.

periscopio *nm* periscope.

peristilo *nm* peristyle.

peritaje *nm* *(informe)* expert's report.

perito,-a *nm & nf* *(experto)* expert.

perjudicado,-a *nm & nf* person who loses out, person affected: *los más perjudicados han sido los campesinos* farmers have been worst affected.

perjudicar *vt* to adversely affect.

perjudicial *adj* harmful.

perjuicio *nm* *(material)* damage; *(económico)* loss.

perjurio *nm* perjury.

perla *nf* **1** pearl. **2** *fig* gem.

permanecer *vi* to stay, remain.

permanencia *nf* *(estancia)* stay.

permanente *adj* permanent, lasting.

permanganato *nm* permanganate.

permeabilidad *nf* permeability.

permeable *adj* permeable.

permisividad *nf* permissiveness.

permisivo,-a *adj* permissive.

permiso *nm* **1** permission. **2** *(documento)* permit. **3** leave. COMP **permiso de conducir** driving licence, US driver's licence.

permitir *vt* to allow, let: *permitió que sus hijas fueran al concierto* he let his daughters go to the concert.
▶ *vpr* **permitirse** to allow OS, afford.
LOC ¿me permite? may I?

permuta *nf* exchange.

permutación *nf* permutation.

permutar *vt* **1** to exchange. **2** MAT to permute.

pernicioso,-a *adj* pernicious, harmful.

pernoctar *vi* to spend the night.

pero *conj* but.

perol *nm* cooking pot.

peroné *nm* fibula.

perorata *nf* spiel.

peróxido *nm* peroxide. COMP **peróxido de hidrógeno** hydrogen peroxide.

perpendicular *adj* perpendicular.

perpetrar *vt* to perpetrate, commit.

perpetuación *nf* perpetuation.

perpetuar *vt* to perpetuate.
▶ *vpr* **perpetuarse** to be perpetuated.

perpetuidad *nf* perpetuity.

perpetuo,-a *adj* *(gen)* perpetual; *(cargo)* permanent. COMP **nieves perpetuas** perpetual snows.

perplejidad *nf* perplexity.

perplejo,-a *adj* perplexed.

P

perrera *nf (lugar)* dog pound.
perro,-a *nm* perro ZOOL dog. COMP **perro caliente** hot dog. ▌**perro pastor** sheepdog.
persecución *nf* **1** pursuit. **2** *(represión)* persecution.
perseguidor,-ora *nm & nf* pursuer.
perseguir *vt* **1** to pursue, chase. **2** *fig (seguir)* to follow: *este perro me persigue* this dog follows me everywhere.
perseverante *adj* persevering.
perseverar *vi* to persevere.
persiana *nf* blind.
persignarse *vpr* to cross OS.
persistente *adj* persistent.
persistir *vi (mantenerse firme)* to persist, persevere.
persona *nf* person. LOC **en persona** in person.
personaje *nm* **1** *(famoso)* celebrity. **2** *(en obra, película)* character.
personal *nm (de una empresa)* staff.
personalidad *nf (carácter)* personality.
personalizar *vt* to personalize.
▶ *vi* to get personal.
personarse *vpr* to appear in person.
personificación *nf* personification.
personificar *vt* to personify.
perspectiva *nf* **1** ARTE perspective. **2** *(posibilidad)* prospect: *este negocio presenta muy buenas perspectivas* this business has good prospects. **3** *(vista)* view, perspective. **4** *(punto de vista)* point of view.
perspicacia *nf* sharpness.
perspicaz *adj* sharp, perspicacious.
persuadir *vt* to persuade, convince.
▶ *vpr* **persuadirse** to be convinced.
persuasión *nf* persuasion.
persuasivo,-a *adj* persuasive.
pertenecer *vi* to belong (a, to).
perteneciente *adj* belonging (a, to).
pertenencia *nf* **1** *(propiedad)* property: *esto es de mi pertenencia* this belongs to me. **2** *(afiliación)* membership.
▶ *nf pl* **pertenencias** *(bienes)* belongings.
pértiga *nf* pole. COMP **salto de pértiga** pole vault.

pertinaz *adj* **1** *(sequía, frío)* prolonged, persistent. **2** *(persona)* obstinate.
pertinente *adj* **1** *(oportuno)* appropriate. **2** *(relevante)* pertinent, relevant.
pertrechar *vt* to supply (de, with).
▶ *vpr* **pertrecharse** to equip OS.
pertrechos *nm pl* equipment *sing.*
perturbación *nf* disruption.
perturbado,-a *adj* **1** *(trastornado)* mentally disturbed. **2** *(intranquilo)* perturbed.
perturbar *vt* **1** *(alterar)* to disturb, perturb. **2** *(inquietar)* to perturb.
Perú *nm* Peru.
peruano,-a *adj* Peruvian.
▶ *nm & nf* Peruvian.
perversidad *nf (maldad)* wickedness.
perversión *nf (maldad)* wickedness.
perverso,-a *adj (malvado)* evil, wicked.
▶ *nm & nf* evil person.
pervertir *vt (gen)* to corrupt.
pervivencia *nf* survival.
pervivir *vi* to live on, persist.
pesa *nf* weight.
pesadez *nf* **1** *(lentitud)* sluggishness. **2** *(molestia)* bore.
pesadilla *nf* nightmare.
pesado,-a *adj* **1** *(gen)* heavy. **2** *(molesto)* tiresome; *(aburrido)* boring.
▶ *nm & nf (persona)* bore, pain. LOC **ponerse pesado,-a** to get boring.
pesadumbre *nf* sorrow, grief.
pésame *nm* condolences *pl.* LOC **dar el pésame** to offer your condolences.
pesar *vi* **1** to weigh: *¿cuánto pesas?* how much do you weigh? **2** *(tener mucho peso)* to be heavy. **3** *(sentir)* to be sorry, regret: *me pesa mucho no haberle invitado* I really regret not having invited him.
▶ *vt* to weigh.
▶ *nm (pena)* sorrow, grief. LOC **a pesar de** despite, in spite of.
pesca *nf (actividad)* fishing.
pescadería *nf* fishmonger's.
pescadero,-a *nm & nf* fishmonger.
pescadilla *nf* young hake.
pescado *nm* fish. COMP **pescado azul** blue fish. ▌**pescado blanco** white fish.

pescador *nm & nf* fisherman.

pescar *vi (ir a pescar)* to fish, go fishing. LOC ir a pescar to go fishing.
► *vt* **1** *(sacar del agua)* to get, catch. **2** *fam (agarrar)* catch: *he pescado un buen resfriado* I've caught a really nasty cold.

pescuezo *nm* neck.

pesebre *nm* manger, stall.

pesimismo *nm* pessimism.

pesimista *adj* pessimistic.
► *nm o nf* pessimist.

pésimo,-a *adj* dreadful, awful.

peso *nm* **1** *(gen)* weight. **2** *(balanza)* scales *pl*. **3** *(carga)* load, burden. LOC de peso **1** *(pesado)* heavy. **2** *(importante)* important. **3** *(convincente)* strong, powerful.

pespunte *nm* backstitch.

pesquero,-a *nm* fishing boat.

pesquisa *nf* inquiry.

pestaña *nf (del ojo)* eyelash.

pestañear *vi* to blink.

peste *nf (mal olor)* stink, stench.

pesticida *nm* pesticide.

pestilente *adj (apestoso)* stinking.

pestillo *nm* bolt. LOC cerrar con pestillo to bolt.

pétalo *nm* petal.

petanca *nf* petanque, boules.

petardo *nm (de verbena)* firecracker.

petate *nm (de soldado, marinero)* kit bag.

petición *nf* **1** *(gen)* request. **2** plea.

petirrojo *nm* robin.

peto *nm (pantalón)* pair of dungarees.

pétreo,-a *adj* stony.

petrificar *vt (fosilizar)* to petrify.

petróleo *nm* oil.

petrolero,-a *adj* oil.
► *nm* petrolero oil tanker.

petrolífero,-a *adj* oil-bearing.

petroquímica *nf* petrochemistry.

petroquímico,-a *adj* petrochemical.

petulancia *nf* vanity.

petulante *adj* vain.

petunia *nf* petunia.

peyorativo,-a *adj* pejorative.

pez *nm* fish.

pezón *nm* nipple.

pezuña *nf* hoof.

piadoso,-a *adj* pious, devout.

pianista *nm o nf* pianist.

piano *nm* piano.

pianola® *nf* Pianola.

piar *vi* to chirp, tweet.

piara *nf* herd of pigs.

pica *nf* **1** *(lanza)* pike. **2** *(de la baraja)* spade.

picada *nf (picadura - de avispa)* sting; *(- de mosquito)* bite.

picadero *nm (escuela)* riding school.

picadillo *nm (de carne)* minced meat; *(de verduras)* chopped vegetables.

picado,-a *adj* **1** CULIN *(cortado - verdura)* finely chopped; *(- carne)* minced. **2** *(diente)* decayed. **3** *fam (ofendido)* offended.

picador *nm (minero)* face worker.

picadora *nf* mincer.

picadura *nf (de insecto, serpiente)* bite; *(de abeja, avispa)* sting.

picante *adj* **1** *(comida)* hot. **2** *fig (chiste)* spicy.

picapedrero *nm* stonecutter.

picaporte *nm* **1** *(para llamar)* door knocker. **2** *(para abrir)* door handle.

picar *vt* **1** *(morder - insecto)* to bite; *(- abeja, avispa)* to sting. **2** *(perforar - papel, tarjeta)* to punch. **3** *(dar con un pico)* to jab, goad. **4** CULIN *(cortar)* to chop finely; *(carne)* to mince. **5** *(comida)* to nibble: *vamos a salir a picar algo* we're going to get a bite to eat.
► *vi* **1** *(sentir escozor)* to itch: *me pica todo el cuerpo* I'm itching all over. **2** *(estar picante)* to be hot. **3** *(pez)* to bite; *(persona)* to fall for it. **4** *(comer)* to have a nibble.
► *vpr* picarse **1** *(muela)* to decay, go bad. **2** *(mar)* to get choppy. **3** *(ofenderse)* to take offence.

picardía *nf (astucia)* craftiness.

picaresco,-a *nf* picaresque genre.

pícaro,-a *adj (astuto)* crafty, sly.
► *nm & nf (persona astuta)* slyboots.

picazón *nf (picor)* itch.

pichichi *nm (goleador)* top goal scorer.

P

pichón,-ona *nm & nf* pigeon.

pico *nm* **1** *(de ave)* beak. **2** *(herramienta)* pickaxe, pick. **3** *(de montaña)* peak. **4** *(punta)* corner. LOC **y pico** *(cantidad)*: *llegaremos sobre las seis y pico* we'll be there just after six.

picor *nm* itch.

picotazo *nm* **1** *(de ave)* peck. **2** *(de insecto, reptil)* bite; *(de abeja, avispa)* sting.

picotear *vt* to peck, peck at.

picoteo *nm* **1** *(de ave)* pecking. **2** *(acción de comer)* nibbling, snacking.

pictórico,-a *adj* pictorial.

picudo,-a *adj* pointed.

pie *nm* **1** ANAT foot. **2** *(base - de una lámpara)* base; *(- de una escultura)* plinth. **3** *(medida de longitud)* foot. LOC **a pie** on foot. ▌**ponerse de pie** to get to one's feet, stand up.

piedad *nf (misericordia)* pity, mercy.

piedra *nf* stone. COMP **piedra preciosa** gem, precious stone.

piel *nf* **1** *(de persona)* skin. **2** *(de la fruta, patatas)* peel.

pienso *nm* fodder.

pierna *nf* leg.

pieza *nf* **1** *(gen)* piece; *(de un aparato)* part. **2** MÚS piece, piece of music. **3** TEAT play. **4** *(de un juego de tablero)* piece.

pigmentación *nf* pigmentation.

pigmento *nm* pigment.

pigmeo,-a *adj (raza)* Pygmy.
▶ *nm & nf (raza)* Pygmy.

pijama *nm* pyjamas (US pajamas) *pl*.

pila *nf* **1** ELEC battery. **2** *(de fregar)* sink. **3** *fam (montón)* pile, heap: *tengo una pila de cosas que hacer* I've got piles of work to do. LOC **ponerse las pilas** *fam* to get one's act together.

pilar *nm* pillar.

pilastra *nf* pilaster.

píldora *nf* pill, tablet.

pileta *nf* AM swimming pool.

pillaje *nm* looting.

pillar *vt* **1** *(coger)* to catch. **2** *fam (robar)* to nick. **3** *fam (atropellar)* to run over. **4** *fam (entender)* to catch, get, grasp.
▶ *vi fam (encontrarse)* to be: *me pilla muy cerca de casa* it's very near home.

pillo,-a *nm & nf (niño)* little monkey, little devil.

pilón *nm (de una fuente)* basin.

píloro *nm* pylorus.

pilotar *vt (avión)* to pilot, fly; *(coche)* to drive; *(barco)* to sail.

pilote *nm* pile.

piloto *nm (conductor - de avión)* pilot; *(- de coche)* driver; *(- de barco)* pilot.

pimentero *nm* **1** *(recipiente)* pepper pot. **2** *(planta)* pepper plant.

pimentón *nm* paprika. COMP **pimentón picante** cayenne pepper.

pimienta *nf (especia)* pepper.

pimiento *nm (gen)* pepper; *(rojo)* red pepper; *(verde)* green pepper.

pinacoteca *nf* art gallery.

pináculo *nm* pinnacle.

pinar *nm* pine grove.

pincel *nm* paintbrush.

pincelada *nf* brush stroke.

pinchadiscos *nm o nf* disc jockey, DJ.

pinchar *vt* **1** *(punzar)* to prick. **2** MED *(poner inyección)* to give a injection. **3** *(sujetar)* to spear, jab. **4** *(enfadar)* to needle.

pinchazo *nm* **1** *(de neumático)* puncture. **2** *(inyección)* injection, jab, US shot.

pinche *nm & nf (de cocina)* kitchen assistant.

pincho *nm* **1** *(de una planta)* thorn. **2** *(de un erizo)* spine, prickle. **3** *(de aperitivo)* snack. **4** *(brocheta)* skewer. COMP **pincho moruno** shish kebab.

pineda *nf* pine grove.

pingo *nm fam (de ropa)* rag.

ping-pong *nm* table tennis, ping-pong.

pingüe *adj* substantial.

pingüino *nm* penguin.

pino *nm (árbol)* pine tree; *(madera)* pine.

pinta *nf* **1** *(mancha)* dot. **2** *(medida)* pint. **3** *fam (aspecto)* look.

pintada *nf* graffiti.

pintado,-a *adj (maquillado)* made-up.

pintalabios *nm inv* lipstick.

pintar *vt* **1** *(gen)* to paint; *(dibujar)* to draw. **2** *(maquillar)* to make up.
▶ *vi* **1** *(gen)* to paint. **2** *(marcar)* to write.

▶ *vpr* **pintarse** *(maquillarse)* to put one's make up on.

pintarrajear *vt fam* to daub.

pintarrajo *nm fam* daub.

pintaúñas *nm inv* nail varnish.

pinto,-a *adj* spotted.

pintor,-ra *nm & nf* artist, painter.

pintoresco,-a *adj* **1** *(lugar)* picturesque. **2** *(persona)* bizarre.

pintura *nf* **1** *(arte)* painting. **2** *(producto)* paint: *un bote de pintura* a tin of paint.

pinza *nf* **1** *(de cangrejo)* pincer. **2** *(de la ropa)* clothes peg.
▶ *nf pl* **pinzas** **1** *(de depilar)* tweezers. **2** *(de servir hielo)* tongs.

pinzamiento *nm* trapped nerve.

pinzón *nm* finch.

piña *nf* **1** *(fruta)* pineapple. **2** *(del pino)* pine cone.

piñata *nf hollow figure filled with sweets (which children try to break open at parties).*

piñón *nm (comestible)* pine nut kernel.

pío *nm* chirp.

pío,-a *adj* pious.

piojo *nm* louse.

piolet *nm* ice axe (US ax).

pionero,-a *nm & nf* pioneer.

pipa¹ *nf (de tabaco)* pipe.

pipa² *nf (de girasol)* sunflower seed.

pipeta *nf* pipette.

pique *nm (rivalidad)* rivalry, needle.

piqueta *nf* pickaxe.

piquete *nm (de huelga)* picket.

pira *nf* pyre.

pirado,-a *adj fam (loco)* loony, wacky.

piragua *nf* canoe.

piragüismo *nm* canoeing.

piragüista *nm o nf* canoeist.

piramidal *adj* pyramidal.

pirámide *nf* pyramid.

piraña *nf* piranha.

pirata *adj* pirate.
▶ *nm o nf (de la informática)* hacker.

piratear *vt* **1** *(gen)* to pirate. **2** *(informática)* to hack.

piratería *nf (gen)* piracy.

pirita *nf* pyrite.

pirómano,-a *nm & nf* pyromaniac.

piropear *vt* to make flirtatious comments to.

piropo *nm* compliment.

pirotecnia *nf* fireworks *pl*.

pirotécnico,-a *adj* pyrotechnic.
▶ *nm & nf* fireworks expert.

pirueta *nf* pirouette.

piruleta *nf* lollipop.

pirulí *nm fam (de caramelo)* lollipop.

pisada *nf (huella)* footprint.

pisapapeles *nm inv* paperweight.

pisar *vt* **1** *(gen)* to tread on. **2** *(acelerador, embrague)* to put one's foot on. **3** *fig (entrar)* to set foot in.
▶ *vi* to tread, walk, step: *no pises muy fuerte que nos oyen los vecinos* tread more quietly, the neighbours will hear us.

piscifactoría *nf* fish farm.

piscina *nf* swimming pool.

piso *nm* **1** *(para vivir)* flat. **2** *(planta)* floor.

pisotear *vt (pisar)* to trample.

pisotón *nm* stamp.

pista *nf* **1** *(rastro)* trail, track. **2** *(indicio)* clue. **3** *(de baile)* dance floor. **4** *(camino)* track. **5** *(de tenis)* court. **6** *(de circo)* ring. **7** *(de aterrizaje)* runway. COMP **pista de esquí** ski slope.

pistachero *nm* pistachio tree.

pistacho *nm* pistachio (nut).

pistilo *nm* pistil.

pistola *nf* gun.

pistolera *nf* holster.

pistolero *nm* gunman.

pistoletazo *nm* gunshot.

pistón *nm (de un motor)* piston.

pita *nf* BOT pita.

pitada *nf* **1** *(bocinazo)* hoot. **2** *(pitido)* whistle.

pitar *vi* **1** *(silbar)* to blow a whistle. **2** *(tocar la bocina)* to hoot. **3** *(abuchear)* to boo and hiss. LOC **ir/irse pitando** *fam* to rush out, dash off.
▶ *vt* DEP *(falta)* to whistle.

pitido *nm* **1** *(silbido)* whistle. **2** *(bocinazo)* hoot, honk.

pitillera *nf* cigarette case.

pitillo *nm* cigarette.

pito *nm (silbato)* whistle.

pitón[1] *nf* ZOOL python.

pitón[2] *nm (del toro)* horn.

pitonisa *nf* fortune teller.

pitorro *nm* spout.

pituitaria *nf* pituitary (gland).

pívot *nm o nf* centre.

pivotar *vi* to pivot.

pivote *nm* pivot.

pizarra *nf* **1** *(mineral)* slate. **2** *(para escribir)* blackboard.

pizca *nf fam (gen)* bit; *(de sal)* pinch.

pizza *nf* pizza.

pizzería *nf* pizzeria, pizza parlour.

placa *nf* **1** *(de metal)* sheet. **2** *(con el nombre)* plaque. **3** *(de matrícula)* number plate. **4** *(de hielo)* sheet.

placaje *nm* tackle.

placar *vt (en rugby)* to tackle.

placebo *nm* placebo.

placenta *nf* placenta.

placentero,-a *adj* pleasant.

placer *nm* pleasure.
▶ *vi* to please: *haz lo que te plazca* do as you please.

placidez *nf* placidity.

plácido,-a *adj* placid, calm.

plafón *nm (lámpara de techo)* ceiling light.

plaga *nf* **1** *(epidemia)* plague. **2** *(de insectos)* plague, pest. **3** *fig* invasion.

plagar *vt* to plague, infest.

plagiar *vt* to plagiarize.

plagio *nm* plagiarism.

plaguicida *nm* pesticide.

plan *nm* **1** *(intención)* plan. **2** *(programa)* project.

plana *nf (página)* page: *la noticia viene en primera plana* the news is on the front page.

plancha *nf* **1** *(de metal)* plate. **2** *(electrodoméstico)* iron. LOC **a la plancha** grilled.

planchado,-a *nm (acción)* ironing.

planchar *vt* to iron, press.

planchista *nm o nf* panel beater.

plancton *nm* plankton.

planeador *nm* glider.

planear *vt (futuro, idea)* to plan.
▶ *vi (en el aire)* to glide.

planeo *nm* gliding, glide.

planeta *nm* planet.

planetario,-a *adj* planetary.
▶ *nm* **planetario** planetarium.

planicie *nf* plain.

planificación *nf* planning.

planificador,-ra *adj* planning.
▶ *nm & nf* planner.

planificar *vt* to plan.

plano,-a *adj (superficie)* flat.
▶ *nm* **plano** **1** *(de una ciudad)* street plan, map. **2** *(de una casa)* plan. **3** *(nivel)* level. **4** MAT plane.

planta *nf* **1** BOT plant. **2** *(del pie)* sole. **3** *(de un edificio)* floor. COMP **planta baja** ground floor, US first floor.

plantación *nf* **1** *(terreno)* plantation. **2** *(acción)* planting.

plantar *vt* **1** AGR to plant. **2** *(colocar - gen)* to put, place; *(- tienda de campaña)* to pitch, put up.
▶ *vpr* **plantarse** *fam (colocarse)* to place OS, position OS: *se plantó en la esquina* she positioned herself on the corner.

plante *nm (laboral)* protest action.

planteamiento *nm* **1** MAT *(formulación - de un problema)* formulation.

plantear *vt* **1** *(pregunta)* to pose, raise. **2** *(problema)* to cause. **3** MAT *(problema)* to formulate.
▶ *vpr* **plantearse** to consider.

plantel *nm* cadre.

plantilla *nf* **1** *(patrón)* model, pattern. **2** *(personal)* staff.

plantón LOC **darle plantón a** ALGN *fam (no presentarse)* to stand SB up.

plañidero,-a *adj* plaintive, mournful.

plañir *vi* to mourn.

plaqueta *nf (de sangre)* platelet.

plasma *nm* plasma.

plasmar *vt fig* to give expression to.

plastelina *nf* Plasticine.

plástica *nf* plastic arts *pl*.

plasticidad *nf* plasticity.

plástico,-a *adj* plastic.
▶ *nm* **plástico** *(material)* plastic.

plastificado,-a *adj* laminated.

plastificar *vt* to laminate.

plastilina® *nf* Plasticine®.

plata *nf* silver.

plataforma *nf* platform. COMP plataforma petrolífera oil rig.

platanal *nm* banana plantation.

platanero,-a *nm* banana tree.

plátano *nm* banana.

platea *nf* stalls *pl*.

plateado,-a *adj (color)* silvery.

platear *vt* to silver-plate.

plateresco,-a *adj* platersque.

platería *nf (taller)* silversmith's.

platero,-a *nm & nf* silversmith.

plática *nf* talk.

platicar *vi* to chat, talk.

platillo *nm* **1** *(de postre)* dessert plate; *(de café)* saucer. COMP platillo volante flying saucer.

platina *nf* MÚS → pletina.

platino *nm* platinum.

plato *nm* **1** *(recipiente)* plate, dish. **2** CULIN dish. **3** *(en comida)* course: *de primer plato hay sopa* we've got soup for starters.

plató *nm (de cine)* set, film set; *(de televisión)* floor.

platónico,-a *adj* platonic.

plausible *adj (probable)* plausible.

playa *nf* **1** *(superficie de arena)* beach. **2** *(costa)* seaside.

playeras *nf pl* canvas shoes.

plaza *nf* **1** *(de una población)* square. **2** *(mercado)* marketplace. **3** *(puesto de trabajo)* position. COMP plaza de parking parking space.

plazo *nm* **1** *(periodo de tiempo)* time. **2** *(de compra)* instalment, US installment. LOC comprar ALGO a plazos to buy STH on hire purchase, US buy STH on an installment plan.

plazoleta *nf* small square.

pleamar *nf* high tide.

plebe *nf (gen)* common people.

plebeyo,-a *nm & nf* plebeian.

plebiscito *nm* plebiscite.

plegable *adj* folding, collapsible.

plegamiento *nm* folding.

plegar *vt* to fold.
▶ *vpr* **plegarse** to yield, give in.

plegaria *nf* prayer.

pleitear *vi* to sue.

pleito *nm* litigation, lawsuit.

plenamente *adv* fully.

plenario,-a *adj* plenary.

plenilunio *nm* full moon.

plenitud *nf (sensación física)* fullness.

pleno,-a *adj (gen)* full, complete: *en pleno centro de la ciudad* right in the centre of the city.

pleonasmo *nm* pleonasm.

pletina *nf* deck, cassette deck.

pletórico,-a *adj* full. LOC pletórico de alegría jubilant, euphoric.

pleura *nf* pleura.

plexiglás® *nm* Perspex®.

plexo *nm* plexus.

pliego *nm (papel)* sheet of paper.

pliegue *nm* **1** fold. **2** *(en la ropa)* pleat.

plinto *nm (en gimnasia)* vaulting horse.

plisado,-a *adj* pleated.

plomada *nf* **1** *(de albañil)* plumb line. **2** *(sonda)* lead. **3** *(para pescar)* weights *pl*.

plomazo *nm o nf fam* bore.

plomizo,-a *adj (color)* lead-coloured.

plomo *nm* **1** lead. **2** *(pesa)* lead weight. **3** ELEC fuse. **4** *fam fig* bore. LOC sin plomo *(gasolina)* unleaded, lead-free.

pluma *nf* **1** *(de ave)* feather. **2** *(de escribir)* fountain pen.

plumaje *nm (de ave)* plumage.

plumero *nm (para el polvo)* feather duster.

plumilla *nf* nib.

plumón *nm* **1** *(de un ave)* down. **2** *(anorak)* down-filled anorak.

plural *adj* plural.
▶ *nm* plural.

pluralidad *nf (gen)* multiplicity; *(diversidad)* diversity.

pluralismo *nm* pluralism.

pluralista *adj* pluralist.

pluralizar *vt* LING to pluralize.
▶ *vi (generalizar)* to generalize.

pluriempleo *nm* having more than one job.

plurilingüe *adj* multilingual.

pluscuamperfecto *nm* pluperfect.

plusmarca *nf* record.

P

plusmarquista *nm o nf* record holder.
plusvalía *nf* **1** *(aumento)* appreciation.
2 *(impuesto)* capital gains tax.
plutocracia *nf* plutocracy.
Plutón *nm* Pluto.
plutonio *nm* plutonium.
pluvial *adj* rain, pluvial.
pluviómetro *nm* rain gauge.
pluviosidad *nf* rainfall.
población *nf* **1** *(número de habitantes)* population. **2** *(lugar - ciudad)* town; *(- pueblo)* village.
poblado,-a *adj (zona)* populated.
poblamiento *nm* settlement.
poblar *vt* **1** *(ocupar territorio)* to settle. **2** *(habitar)* to inhabit. **3** *(llenar)* to fill: *han poblado de árboles el campo* they've planted the field with trees.
pobre *adj* **1** *(gen)* poor. **2** *(infeliz)* poor.
▶ *nm o nf* **1** *(con poco dinero)* poor person; *(mendigo)* beggar. **2** *(infeliz)* poor thing: *la pobre se cree que le van a devolver el dinero* the poor thing thinks she is going to get her money back.
pobreza *nf (escasez de dinero)* poverty.
pocilga *nf* pigsty.
pócima *nf (preparado)* potion.
poción *nf* potion.
poco,-a *adj* little; *(plural)* few, not many: *hago muy poco ejercicio últimamente* I do very little exercise these days. [LOC] **hace poco** not long ago. ▌ **poco antes** shortly before. ▌ **poco después** shortly afterwards. ▌ **por poco** nearly.
▶ *pron* **poco** little; *(en plural)* not many: *lo poco que aprendí se me ha olvidado* what little I learned I've forgotten.
▶ *adv* little, not much: *voy poco por allí* I rarely go there.
▶ *nm* **un poco** a little, a bit: *¿me das un poco?* could you give me a little?
poda *nf* pruning.
podadera *nf* pruning shears *pl*.
podar *vt* to prune.
podenco *nm* hound.
poder *vt* **1** *(de facultad)* can, be able to: *¿puedes echarme una mano?* can you lend me a hand?; *no pude abrirlo* I couldn't open it, I was unable to open it. **2** *(de per-*

miso) may, can: *pueden pagar en efectivo o con tarjeta* you can pay in cash or by credit card; *puede retirarse* you may leave. **3** *(conjetura)* may, might: *podría haberlo dejado sobre la mesa* I may have left it on the table. **4** *(sugerencias)* can: *podríamos ir a esquiar* we could go skiing. [LOC] **puede que** maybe, perhaps: *puede que venga más tarde* she may come later.
▶ *vi (superar)* to be stronger than: *tú puedes a todos* you can beat all of them.
▶ *nm* **1** *(gen)* power. **2** *(posesión)* possession, hands *pl*: *la pelota está ahora en mi poder* the ball is now in my hands.
poderío *nm (autoridad)* power.
poderoso,-a *adj* powerful.
podio *nm* podium.
podólogo,-a *nm & nf* chiropodist.
podredumbre *nf* rottenness.
podrido,-a *adj* **1** rotten. **2** *fig* corrupt.
poema *nm* poem.
poesía *nf* **1** poetry. **2** *(poema)* poem.
poeta *nm o nf* poet.
poético,-a *adj* poetic.
poetisa *nf* poetess.
polaco,-a *adj* Polish.
▶ *nm & nf (persona)* Pole.
▶ *nm* **polaco** *(idioma)* Polish.
polar *adj* polar. [COMP] **estrella polar** Pole Star, Polaris.
polaridad *nf* polarity.
polarizar *vt* **1** Fís to polarize. **2** *(atención)* to focus.
polaroid® *nf* Polaroid.
polea *nf* pulley.
polémica *nf* controversy.
polémico,-a *adj* controversial.
polemizar *vi* to debate.
polen *nm* pollen.
poleo *nm* **1** *(planta)* pennyroyal. **2** *(infusión)* mint tea.
policía *nf* police, police force.
▶ *nm o nf (gen)* police officer; *(hombre)* policeman; *(mujer)* policewoman.
policíaco,-a *adj* detective.
policial *adj* police.
policromía *nf* polychromy.
policromo,-a *adj* polychrome.

polideportivo *nm* sports centre.
poliedro *nm* polyhedron.
poliéster *nm* polyester.
poliestireno *nm* polystyrene.
polietileno *nm* polythene.
polifacético,-a *adj* versatile.
polifónico,-a *adj* polyphonic.
poligamia *nf* polygamy.
polígamo,-a *adj* polygamous.
▶ *nm & nf* polygamist.
polígloto,-a *adj* polyglot.
▶ *nm & nf* polyglot.
poligonal *adj* polygonal.
polígono *nm* 1 *(figura)* polygon. 2 *(gen)* area. COMP **polígono industrial** industrial estate.
polígrafo,-a *nm & nf* polygraph.
poliinsaturado,-a *adj* polyunsaturated.
polilla *nf* moth.
polímero *nm* polymer.
polimorfo,-a *adj* polymorphic.
polinización *nf* pollination.
polinizar *vt* to pollinate.
polinomio *nm* polynomial.
poliomielitis *nf inv* poliomyelitis.
polisemia *nf* polysemy.
polisémico,-a *adj* polysemous.
polisílabo,-a *adj* polysyllabic.
politécnico,-a *adj (gen)* polytechnic.
▶ *nm* **politécnico** *(instituto)* technical college.
politeísmo *nm* polytheism.
politeísta *adj* polytheistic.
▶ *nm o nf* polytheist.
política *nf* politics.
político,-a *adj* 1 political. 2 *(por matrimonio)* -in-law: *madre política* mother-in-law; *padre político* father-in-law.
▶ *nm & nf* politician.
politizar *vt* to politicize.
poliuretano *nm* polyurethane.
polivalente *adj fig (versátil)* versatile.
polivinilo *nm* polyvinyl.
póliza *nf* 1 *(de seguros)* policy. 2 *(sello)* official tax stamp.
polizón *nm* stowaway.
pollera *nf* AM skirt.

pollería *nf (tienda)* poultry shop; *(sección de supermercado)* poultry section.
pollino,-a *nm & nf* ZOOL donkey.
pollo *nm* chicken.
polluelo *nm* chick.
polo *nm* 1 TÉC pole. 2 *(caramelo)* ice lolly. 3 DEP polo. COMP **Polo Norte** North Pole. ∥ **Polo Sur** South Pole.
Polonia *nf* Poland.
poltrona *nf* easy chair.
poltrón,-ona *adj* lazy.
polución *nf (atmosférica)* pollution.
polucionar *vt* to pollute.
polvareda *nf (de polvo)* cloud of dust.
polvera *nf (powder)* compact.
polvo *nm* 1 *(suciedad)* dust. 2 *(medicamento, etc)* powder. LOC **en polvo** 1 *(leche, cacao)* powdered. 2 *(nieve)* powdery. COMP **polvos de talco** talcum powder *sing*.
pólvora *nf* gunpowder.
polvoriento,-a *adj* dusty.
pomada *nf* cream.
pomelo *nm (fruto)* grapefruit; *(árbol)* grapefruit tree.
pómez *nf* pumice stone.
pomo *nm (de puerta)* knob.
pompa *nf* 1 *(de jabón, chicle)* bubble. 2 *(ostentación)* pomp. COMP **pompas de jabón** soap bubbles.
pomposo,-a *adj* pompous.
pómulo *nm* 1 *(hueso)* cheekbone. 2 *(mejilla)* cheek.
ponche *nm* punch.
ponderado,-a *adj (prudente)* measured.
ponderar *vt* 1 *(sopesar)* to ponder, consider, think over, weigh up. 2 *(alabar)* to praise highly.
ponedero *nm* nest box.
ponedora *adj (gallina)* laying.
ponencia *nf (académica)* paper; *(parlamentaria)* address, speech.
ponente *nm o nf* speaker.
poner *vt* 1 *(gen)* to place, put, set. 2 *(prenda)* to put on: *me pondré el pantalón negro* I'll put my black trousers on, I'll wear my black trousers. 3 *(encender)* to turn on, put on: *puso la radio* she put the radio on. 4 *(programar)* to set: *he*

P

puesto el despertador a las siete I've set the alarm clock for seven. **5** *(escribir)* to put, write: *pon tu nombre aquí* put your name here. **6** *(decir)* to say: *¿qué pone ese letrero?* what does that sign say? **7** *(en cine, televisión)* to show: *lo ponen mañana a las tres* it's on tomorrow at three o'clock. **8** *(dar nombre)* to name, call: *le pusieron Laura* they called her Laura. **9** *(dinero)* to put in: *pusimos veinte euros cada uno* we put in twenty euros each. **10** *(telegrama, fax)* to send; *(nota)* to leave. **11** *(deber, multa)* to give: *nos han puesto deberes para las vacaciones* they've given us homework for the holidays. **12** poner + *adj* to make, turn: *la has puesto triste* you've made her sad.

▶ *vpr* **ponerse 1** *(sol)* to set. **2** *(volverse)* to become, get, turn: *se puso muy contenta con la noticia* the news made her very happy. **3** *(contestar al teléfono)* to answer the phone; *(hablar por teléfono)* to come to the phone: *en este momento no se puede poner* he can't come to the phone right now. **4** ponerse a + *inf* to start + *to* + *inf*/-*ing*: *se puso a cantar* he started to sing, he started singing.

poniente *nm (dirección)* west.

pontificar *vi* to pontificate.

pontífice *nm* pope, pontiff.

pontón *nm* pontoon.

ponzoña *nf* venom.

ponzoñoso,-a *adj* venomous.

popa *nf* stern.

populacho *nm* mob, masses *pl*.

popular *adj* **1** *(del pueblo)* traditional. **2** *(muy conocido)* popular.

popularizar *vt* to popularize.

populista *adj* populist.

populoso,-a *adj* populous.

popurrí *nm* potpourri.

póquer *nm* poker.

por *prep* **1** *(gen)* for: *lo hice por ti* I did it for you. **2** *(a través de)* through, by: *iremos por la autopista* we'll go on the motorway. **3** *(calle, carretera)* along, down, up: *íbamos por la calle cuando…* we were walking along the street when… **4** *(lugar aproximado)* in, near, round: *está por aquí* it's somewhere round here. **5** *(cau-*

sa) because of: *suspendieron el concierto por la lluvia* they cancelled the concert because of the rain. **6** *(tiempo)* at, for: *nos veremos por vacaciones* I'll see you during the holidays. **7** *(medio)* by: *llegó por correo* it arrived by post. **8** *(autoría)* by: *fue escrito por Azorín* it was written by Azorín. **9** *(distribución)* per: *cinco por ciento* five per cent. **10** *(tras)* by: *les interrogó uno por uno* he interrogated each one in turn. **11** *(con pasiva)* by: *fue comprado por la reina* it was bought by the queen. **12** *(en calidad de)* as: *la tomó por esposa* he took her as his wife. **13** *(en lugar de)* instead of, in the place of: *ve tú por mí* you go in my place. **14** *(multiplicado por)* times, multiplied by: *tres por cuatro, doce* three fours are twelve, three times four is twelve. LOC **estar por + inf** *(a punto de)* to be on the point of + -*ing*. ‖ **por más que + *subj*** however much, no matter how much. ‖ **por mucho que + *subj*** however much, no matter how much.

porcelana *nf* china, porcelain: *una porcelana* a piece of china.

porcentaje *nm* percentage.

porcentual *adj* percentage.

porche *nm* veranda(h), US porch.

porcino,-a *adj* porcine. COMP **ganado porcino** pigs *pl*, US hogs *pl*.

porción *nf (gen)* portion, part.

pordiosero,-a *nm & nf* beggar.

porfiar *vi (insistir)* to insist (en, on).

pormenor *nm* detail. LOC **al pormenor** retail.

pormenorizar *vt* to detail.

poro *nm* pore.

poroso,-a *adj* porous.

porque *conj* **1** *(de causa)* because: *no voy porque no quiero* I'm not going because I don't want to. **2** *(de finalidad)* in order that, so that.

porqué *nm* cause, reason: *nunca sabremos el porqué* we'll never know why.

porquería *nf (suciedad)* dirt, filth.

porqueriza *nf* pigsty.

porra *nf (de policía)* truncheon. LOC **mandar a la porra a** ALGN *fam* to tell SB to get lost, send SB packing.

porrazo *nm (con bastón)* blow; *(al caer)* bump, knock.

porrón *nm* typical glass drinking vessel with a thin spout used for pouring wine into the mouth.

portaaviones *nm inv* aircraft carrier.

portada *nf (de revista, periódico)* front page; *(de libro)* title page.

portador,-ra *adj* carrying.
▶ *nm & nf (de un virus)* carrier.

portaequipajes *nm inv* **1** *(de un coche - maletero)* boot, US trunk; *(- en el techo)* roof rack. **2** *(de un tren)* luggage rack.

portafolios *nm inv* **1** portfolio, folder. **2** *(maletín)* briefcase.

portal *nm (entrada de edificio)* hallway.

portalámparas *nm* bulbholder.

portaminas *nm inv* propelling pencil.

portamonedas *nm inv* purse.

portar *vt* to carry.
▶ *vpr* **portarse** to behave. LOC **portarse bien** to be good, behave OS.

portátil *adj* portable.

portavoz *nm o nf (gen)* spokesperson.

portazo *nm* bang, slam *(of a door)*.

porte *nm (transporte)* carriage, freight. COMP **portes debidos** carriage due.

porteador,-ra *nm & nf* porter.

portentoso,-a *adj* prodigious.

portería *nf* **1** *(de un edificio)* porter's lodge. **2** DEP goal.

portero,-a *nm & nf* **1** *(de un edificio)* porter. **2** DEP goalkeeper. COMP **portero automático** entryphone.

pórtico *nm* portico.

portillo *nm* breach.

portón *nm* large door.

Portugal *nm* Portugal.

portugués,-esa *adj* Portuguese.
▶ *nm & nf (persona)* Portuguese.
▶ *nm* portugués *(idioma)* Portuguese.

porvenir *nm* future.

pos LOC **en pos de** after, in pursuit of.

posada *nf* inn.

posar *vi (para foto, etc)* to pose.
▶ *vt (colocar)* to rest.

▶ *vpr* **posarse 1** *(pájaro)* to alight, perch, sit. **2** *(sedimento)* to settle.

posavasos *nm inv* coaster.

posdata *nf* postscript.

pose *nf (postura)* pose.

poseedor,-ra *nm & nf* owner.

poseer *vt* **1** *(propiedad)* to own. **2** *(conocimientos, talento, etc)* to have.

posesión *nf* possession. LOC **tomar posesión** *(de un cargo)* to take up.

posesivo,-a *adj* possessive.

poseso,-a *nm & nf* possessed person.

posguerra *nf* postwar period.

posibilidad *nf* possibility.

posible *adj* possible. LOC **hacer todo lo posible** to do one's best.

posición *nf (postura, situación)* position.

positivo,-a *adj* positive.

poso *nm* **1** *(del café)* dregs *pl*. **2** *fig* trace.

posología *nf* dosage.

posparto *nm* postpartum.

posponer *vt (en el tiempo)* to postpone.

posta *nf (de caballos)* change of horses. LOC **a posta** on purpose.

postal *nf* postcard.

poste *nm* post.

póster *nm* poster.

postergar *vt (retrasar)* to postpone.

posteridad *nf* posterity.

posterior *adj* **1** *(en el espacio)* back, rear: *en la parte posterior del edificio* at the back of the building. **2** *(en el tiempo)* later.

posteriori LOC **a posteriori** a posteriori.

postgrado *nm* postgraduate course.

postgraduado,-a *nm & nf* postgraduate student.

postigo *nm (de ventana)* shutter.

postilla *nf* scab.

postizo,-a *adj* false.

postor,-ra *nm & nf* bidder.

postrar *vt* to prostrate.
▶ *vpr* **postrarse** to prostrate OS.

postre *nm* dessert.

postular *vt (defender)* to postulate.

póstumo,-a *adj* posthumous.

postura *nf* **1** *(de un cuerpo)* posture, position. **2** *(actitud)* attitude.

P

potable *adj* drinkable.

potaje *nm* CULIN hotpot.

potasio *nm* potassium.

pote *nm (vasija)* pot.

potencia *nf* **1** *(capacidad)* power: *este coche tiene mucha potencia* this car is very powerful. **2** *(país)* power. **3** *(en matemática)* power: *elevamos seis a la tercera potencia* we raise six to the power of three.

potencial *adj* potential.
 ▶ *nm* **1** potential. **2** LING conditional tense.

potenciar *vt* to strengthen.

potentado,-a *nm* tycoon, potentate.

potente *adj* powerful.

potestad *nf* power.

potestativo,-a *adj* optional.

potingue *nm fam (crema)* face cream.

potrero *nm (lugar)* paddock.

potro,-a *nm & nf* ZOOL *(macho)* colt.

poza *nf (en un río)* pool.

pozo *nm (de agua, petróleo)* well.

práctica *nf* practice.
 ▶ *nf pl* **prácticas** practical *sing.* LOC **en la práctica** in practice.

practicable *adj (realizable)* feasible.

practicante *nm o nf (persona)* nurse.

practicar *vt* **1** *(gen)* to practise (US practice). **2** *(hacer)* to make; *(deporte)* to play.
 ▶ *vi* to practise (US practice).

práctico,-a *adj* **1** *(gen)* practical. **2** *(hábil)* skilful (US skillful).

pradera *nf* prairie, grassland.

prado *nf* meadow.

pragmático,-a *adj* pragmatic.

pragmatismo *nm* pragmatism.

preámbulo *nm* preamble.

preaviso *nm* notice.

precalentamiento *nm* DEP warming up.

precalentar *vt* to pre-heat.

precariedad *nf* precariousness.

precario,-a *adj* precarious.

precaución *nf* precaution.

precavido,-a *adj* cautious.

precedente *adj* preceding.
 ▶ *nm* precedent.

preceder *vt* to precede.

preceptiva *nf* precepts *pl.*

preceptivo,-a *adj* compulsory.

precepto *nm* precept.

preceptor,-ra *nm & nf* EDUC tutor.

preciado,-a *adj* precious.

preciarse *vpr* to be proud (de, of).

precintar *vt* to seal.

precinto *nm* seal.

precio *nm* **1** *(coste)* price. **2** *fig (valor)* value.

preciosidad *nf (belleza)* loveliness.

precioso,-a *adj (bello)* beautiful.

precipicio *nm* cliff, precipice.

precipitación *nf* **1** *(prisa)* rush, haste. **2** METEOR precipitation, rainfall.

precipitado,-a *adj (apresurado)* hasty.

precipitar *vt* **1** *(apresurar)* to rush. **2** QUÍM to precipitate.
 ▶ *vpr* **precipitarse** **1** *(apresurarse)* to rush, be hasty. **2** *(caer)* to fall.

precisar *vt* **1** to say exactly. **2** *(necesitar)* to need.

precisión *nf* precision, accuracy.

preciso,-a *adj* **1** precise. **2** *(necesario)* necessary.

precocinado,-a *adj* precooked.

preconcebido,-a *adj* preconceived.

preconizar *vt* to advocate.

precoz *adj* **1** *(persona)* precocious. **2** *(cosecha)* early. **3** *(diagnóstico)* early.

precursor,-ra *nm & nf* precursor.

predador,-ra *adj* predatory.

predecesor,-ra *nm & nf* predecessor.

predecir *vt* to predict.

predestinado,-a *adj* predestined.

predestinar *vt* to predestine.

predeterminar *vt* to predetermine.

prédica *nf* sermon.

predicación *nf* preaching.

predicado *nm* predicate.

predicador,-ra *nm & nf* preacher.

predicar *vt* to preach.

predicativo,-a *adj* predicative.

predicción *nf* prediction.

predilección *nf* predilection.

predilecto,-a *adj* favourite.

predisponer *vt* to predispose.

predisposición *nf* predisposition.

predominante *adj* predominant.

predominar *vt* to predominate.

predominio *nm* predominance.

preeminente *adj* pre-eminent.

preescolar *adj (enseñanza, edad, etapa)* preschool, nursery-school.

preestablecer *vt* to pre-establish.

preestablecido,-a *adj* pre-established.

preestreno *nm* preview.

prefabricado,-a *adj* prefabricated.

prefacio *nm* preface.

preferencia *nf* preference.

preferente *adj* preferential.

preferible *adj* preferable.

preferido,-a *adj* favourite (US favorite).

preferir *vt* to prefer.

prefijo *nm* 1 LING prefix. 2 *(telefónico)* dialling code, US area code.

pregón *nm (discurso de fiestas)* opening address.

pregonar *vt (noticia)* to announce, make public.

pregonero *nm* town crier.

pregunta *nf* question. LOC **hacer una pregunta a** ALGN to ask SB a question.

preguntar *vt* to ask.
► *vpr* **preguntarse** to wonder: *me pregunto si vendrá* I wonder if he'll come.

preguntón,-ona *adj fam* inquisitive.

prehistoria *nf* prehistory.

prehistórico,-a *adj* prehistoric.

prejuicio *nm* prejudice.

prejuzgar *vt* to prejudge.

preliminar *adj* preliminary.

preludio *nm* prelude.

prematrimonial *adj* premarital.

prematuro,-a *adj* premature.

premeditación *nf* premeditation.

premeditado,-a *adj* premeditated.

premeditar *vt* to premeditate.

premiado,-a *adj* prizewinning.
► *nm & nf* prizewinner.

premiar *vt* to award a prize to.

premio *nm* prize.

premisa *nf* premise.

premonición *nf* premonition.

premonitorio,-a *adj* premonitory.

premura *nf (prisa)* urgency.

prenatal *adj* antenatal.

prenda *nf* 1 *(de vestir)* garment. 2 *(en juego)* forfeit.

prendarse *vpr* to fall in love (de, with).

prendedor *nm (broche)* brooch; *(alfiler)* pin.

prender *vt* 1 *(sujetar)* to attach; *(con agujas)* to pin. 2 *(encender - fuego)* to light; *(- luz)* to turn on.
► *vi* 1 *(arraigar - planta, costumbre)* to take root. 2 *(fuego, madera, etc)* to catch light, catch fire.

prensa *nf* 1 *(máquina)* press. 2 *(periódicos)* papers *pl*.

prensar *vt* to press.

preñado,-a *adj* pregnant.

preñar *vt (mujer)* to make pregnant; *(animal)* to impregnate.

preocupación *nf* worry.

preocupado,-a *adj* worried.

preocupar *vt* to worry.
► *vpr* **preocuparse** 1 *(sentir preocupación)* to worry (por, about).

preparación *nf* 1 *(gen)* preparation. 2 *(física, deportiva)* training.

preparado,-a *adj* ready, prepared.

preparador,-ra *nm & nf* DEP coach.

preparar *vt* 1 to prepare, get ready: *voy a preparar el desayuno* I'll get breakfast ready. 2 DEP *(entrenar)* to train, coach: *se está preparando para el maratón* she's training for the marathon. 3 *(estudiar)* to revise for, work for.

preparativos *nm pl* arrangements.

preposición *nf* preposition.

prepotencia *nf (arrogancia)* arrogance.

prepotente *adj* arrogant.

prerrogativa *nf* prerogative.

presa *nf* 1 *(embalse)* dam. 2 *(acción)* capture. COMP **ave de presa** bird of prey.

presagiar *vt* to be a warning of.

presagio *nm (señal)* omen.

presbítero *nm* priest.

prescindir *vi* **prescindir de** *(pasar sin)* to do without.

prescribir *vt (recetar)* to prescribe.

prescripción *nf* prescription.

P

presencia *nf (gen)* presence.

presenciar *vt (acontecimiento)* to be present at.

presentación *nf* 1 *(de un objeto, documento, etc)* presentation, showing: *la presentación del carné es imprescindible para entrar* passes must be shown to allow access. 2 *(de personas)* introduction.

presentador,-ra *nm & nf* presenter.

presentar *vt* 1 *(gen)* to present; *(mostrar)* to show. 2 *(entregar)* to hand in. 3 *(sacar al mercado)* to launch. 4 *(personas)* to introduce: *¿te han presentado ya?* have you been introduced yet? 5 TV to present.
▶ *vpr* **presentarse** 1 *(comparecer)* to turn up. 2 *(para elección)* to stand.

presente *adj* present.
▶ *nm* 1 *(tiempo)* present. 2 LING present tense. 3 *(obsequio)* gift.
▶ *nm pl* **presentes** those present.

presentimiento *nm* premonition.

presentir *vt* to have a feeling (que, that).

preservar *vt* to preserve.

preservativo *nm* condom.

presidencia *nf* 1 POL presidency. 2 *(de una empresa)* chairmanship.

presidente,-ta *nm & nf* 1 POL president. 2 chairman, US president.

presidiario,-a *nm & nf* convict.

presidio *nm* prison, penitentiary.

presidir *vt (reunión)* to chair.

presilla *nf* fastener.

presión *nf* pressure.

presionar *vt* 1 *(objeto)* to press. 2 *(persona)* to pressure, put pressure on.

preso,-a *nm & nf* prisoner.

prestación *nf* 1 *(servicio)* service. 2 *(de la Seguridad Social)* benefit, allowance. COMP **prestación por desempleo** unemployment benefit.

prestado,-a *adj* lent, on loan.

prestamista *nm o nf* moneylender.

préstamo *nm (crédito)* loan. LOC **pedir un préstamo** to ask for a loan.

prestar *vt (dejar prestado)* to lend, loan.

prestidigitador,-ra *nm & nf* conjuror.

prestigio *nm* prestige.

prestigioso,-a *adj* prestigious.

presto,-a *adj* 1 *(preparado)* ready. 2 *(rápido)* quick.

presumible *adj* probable, likely.

presumido,-a *adj (en el vestir)* vain.

presumir *vi* 1 *(vanagloriarse)* to boast (de, about), show off (de, about). 2 *(ser presumido)* to be vain.
▶ *vt (suponer)* to suppose, assume.

presunto,-a *adj* presumed, alleged.

presuntuoso,-a *adj (presumido)* vain.

presuponer *vt* to presuppose.

presupuestar *vt (proyecto)* to budget for; *(construcción, obra, etc)* to estimate.

presupuesto *nm (en finanzas)* budget; *(de una obra)* estimate.

pretencioso,-a *adj* pretentious.
▶ *nm & nf* pretentious person.

pretender *vt* 1 *(querer)* to want to: *pretende ganar el concurso* he wants to win the contest. 2 *(intentar)* to try to: *no sé qué pretende hacer* I don't know what he's trying to do. 3 *(cortejar)* to court.

pretendido,-a *adj* supposed.

pretendiente *nm (enamorado)* suitor.

pretensión *nf* 1 *(intención)* aim; *(ambición)* ambition. 2 *(derecho)* claim.

pretérito,-a *adj* past: *en tiempos pretéritos* in the past.
▶ *nm* **pretérito** simple past, preterite.

pretexto *nm* pretext.

prevalecer *vi* to prevail.

prevención *nf (precaución)* prevention.

prevenido,-a *adj* forewarned.

prevenir *vt (evitar)* to avoid, prevent.

preventivo,-a *adj (medicina)* preventive.

prever *vt (anticipar)* to foresee.

previo,-a *adj* previous.

previsible *adj* foreseeable.

previsión *nf* forecast. COMP **previsión meteorológica** weather forecast.

previsor,-ra *adj* farsighted.

prieto,-a *adj* tight.

prima *nf (gratificación)* bonus.

primacía *nf* primacy.

primar *vi (predominar)* to be important.

primaria *nf* primary education.

primario,-a *adj* primary.

primate *nm* primate.

primavera *nf* **1** spring. **2** *lit (año)* year.

primaveral *adj* spring, spring-like.

primera *nf* **1** AUTO first gear. **2** *(en transportes)* first class.

primerizo,-a *nm & nf* beginner.

primero,-a *adj* first: *el primer día del año* the first day of the year.
▶ *nm & nf* first: *es la primera de la clase* she's top of the class.
▶ *adv* **primero** *(en primer lugar)* first: *primero vamos a mirarlo en el diccionario* let's look it up in the dictionary first.

✎ Antes de los nombres masculinos en singular se usa primer.

primicia *nf (noticia)* scoop.

primigenio,-a *adj* original.

primitiva *nf* ≈ National Lottery.

primitivo,-a *adj* HIST primitive.

primo,-a *nm & nf (familiar)* cousin.

primogénito,-a *adj* first-born, eldest.
▶ *nm & nf* first-born, eldest.

primor *nm (delicadeza)* delicateness.

primordial *adj* essential.

primoroso,-a *adj* delicate.

princesa *nf* princess.

principado *nm* principality.

principal *adj* main: *lo principal es que duerma* the main thing is that he sleeps.
▶ *nm (piso)* first floor, US second floor.

príncipe *nm* prince.

principiante,-a *nm & nf* beginner.

principio *nm* **1** *(inicio)* beginning, start: *me voy de vacaciones a principios de mes* I'm going on holiday at the beginning of the month. **2** *(moral)* principle.

pringar *vt (ensuciar)* to make greasy: *me he puesto las manos pringando de grasa* I've got my hands covered in grease.

pringoso,-a *adj* greasy.

prior,-ra *nm & nf (hombre)* prior; *(mujer)* prioress.

prioridad *nf* priority.

prioritario,-a *adj* priority.

prisa *nf* hurry: *¡date prisa que no llegamos!* hurry up or we'll never make it! LOC correr prisa to be urgent. | tener prisa to be in a hurry.

prisión *nf* prison.

prisionero,-a *nm & nf* prisoner.

prisma *nm* prism.

prismáticos *nm pl* binoculars.

privacidad *nf* privacy.

privación *nf* deprivation, privation.

privado,-a *adj* private.

privar *vt (despojar)* to deprive (de, of).

privativo,-a *adj (exclusivo)* exclusive.

privatizar *vt* to privatize.

privilegiado,-a *adj* privileged.

privilegiar *vt* to privilege.

privilegio *nm* privilege.

pro *nm* advantage. COMP los pros y los contras the pros and cons.

proa *nf* bow, prow.

probabilidad *nf* probability.

probable *adj (posible)* probable, likely.

probado,-a *adj* proven.

probador *nm* changing room.

probar *vt* **1** *(demostrar)* to prove. **2** *(comprobar)* to test, check: *prueba el coche a ver cómo responde* check the car to see how it performs. **3** *(vino, comida, etc)* to taste, try. **4** *(prenda, zapato)* to try on.
▶ *vi* to try: *prueba a cambiarle la pila* try changing the battery.

probeta *nf* test tube.

problema *nm* problem. LOC tener problemas con to have trouble with.

problemático,-a *adj* problematic.

procedencia *nf* **1** origin.

procedente *adj* coming (de, from): *el tren procedente de Sevilla* the train arriving from Seville.

proceder LOC proceder de to come: *el queso procede de la leche* cheese comes from milk.

procedimiento *nm (método)* procedure.

procesado,-a *adj* **1** INFORM processed. **2** JUR tried.
▶ *nm & nf* **el/la procesado,-a** the accused.

procesador *nm* processor. COMP procesador de textos INFORM word processor.

P

procesar *vt* **1** *(gen)* to process. **2** JUR to try.

procesión *nf* procession.

proceso *nm* *(gen)* process. COMP **proceso de datos** data processing.

proclamar *vt* to proclaim.
▶ *vpr* **proclamarse** to proclaim OS.

proclive *adj* prone.

procreación *nf* procreation.

procrear *vi* to procreate.

procurador,-ra *nm & nf* JUR procurator.

procurar *vt* **1** to try. **2** *(proporcionar)* to get.

prodigar *vt* to be lavish with.

prodigio *nm* prodigy, miracle.

prodigioso,-a *adj* prodigious.

pródigo,-a *adj (generoso)* lavish.

producción *nf* production.

producir *vt* **1** *(gen)* to produce. **2** *(causar)* to cause.
▶ *vpr* **producirse** to happen.

productividad *nf* productivity.

productivo,-a *adj* productive.

producto *nm (gen)* product.

productor,-ra *adj* producing.
▶ *nm & nf* producer.

productora *nf* CINE production company.

proeza *nf* feat, heroic deed.

profanar *vt* to desecrate, profane.

profano,-a *adj (no sagrado)* profane.

profecía *nf* prophecy.

proferir *vt (palabra, sonido, etc)* to utter.

profesión *nf* profession.

profesional *adj* professional: *es futbolista profesional* he's a professional footballer.
▶ *nm o nf* professional: *es todo un profesional* he's a real professional.

profesionalidad *nf* professionalism.

profesor,-ra *nm & nf* teacher. COMP **profesor,-ra particular** private tutor.

profesorado *nm* teaching staff.

profeta *nm* prophet.

profético,-a *adj* prophetic.

profetizar *vt* to prophesy.

prófugo,-a *nm & nf* fugitive.

profundidad *nf* depth: *tiene cuatro metros de profundidad* it's four metres deep.

profundizar *vt* profundizar en *(tema, cuestión)* to look deeply into.

profundo,-a *adj (gen)* deep.

profuso,-a *adj* profuse.

progenitor,-ra *nm & nf (padre)* father; *(madre)* mother.
▶ *nm pl* **progenitores** parents.

programa *nm* **1** *(gen)* programme (US program). **2** INFORM program. **3** EDUC *(de un curso)* syllabus.

programación *nf* **1** *(de televisión, radi, etco)* programming (US programing). **2** *(de teatro)* billing. **3** INFORM programming.

programador,-ra *nm & nf* INFORM programmer.

programar *vt* **1** *(gen)* to programme (US program). **2** INFORM to program. **3** *(organizar, planear, etc)* to plan.

progresar *vi* to progress.

progresión *nf* progression. COMP **progresión aritmética** arithmetic progression.

progresista *adj* progressive.
▶ *nm o nf* progressive.

progresivo,-a *adj* progressive.

progreso *nm* progress.

prohibición *nf* prohibition, ban.

prohibido,-a *adj* forbidden.

prohibir *vt* to forbid.

prohibitivo,-a *adj* prohibitive.

prójimo *nm* fellow man, neighbour (US neighbor).

prole *nf* offspring.

proletariado *nm* proletariat.

proletario,-a *nm & nf* proletarian.

proliferar *vi* to proliferate.

prolijo,-a *adj (meticuloso)* meticulous.

prólogo *nm* prologue, US prolog.

prolongación *nf (gen)* prolongation.

prolongado,-a *adj (largo)* prolonged.

prolongar *vt* **1** *(en el tiempo, etc)* to prolong. **2** *(en el espacio)* to extend.
▶ *vpr* **prolongarse** to go on.

promedio *nm* average.

promesa *nf* promise.

prometedor,-ra *adj* promising.

prometer *vt* to promise: *¿lo prometes?* promise?
▶ *vi* to be promising: *esta chica es una pintora que promete* this girl is a promising artist.

prometido,-a *nm & nf (hombre)* fiancé; *(mujer)* fiancée.

prominente *adj* prominent.

promiscuo,-a *adj* promiscuous.

promoción *nf* promotion.

promocionar *vt* (to promote.

promontorio *nm* promontory.

promotor,-ra *nm & nf (inmobiliario)* developer.

promover *vt* to promote.

promulgar *vt* to enact, promulgate.

pronombre *nm* pronoun.

pronosticar *vt* to predict.

pronóstico *nm (del tiempo)* forecast. COMP **pronóstico meteorológico** weather forecast.

pronto,-a *adv* **1** *(rápido)* soon: *no llores que pronto vendrá tu mamá* don't cry, your mummy will be here soon. **2** *(temprano)* early: *has llegado demasiado pronto* you've arrived too early. LOC **de pronto** suddenly.

pronunciación *nf* pronunciation.

pronunciado,-a *adj (marcado)* marked.

pronunciar *vt* **1** *(gen)* to pronounce. **2** *(discurso)* to make.

propagación *nf* propagation.

propaganda *nf* **1** *(publicidad)* advertising. **2** *(electoral)* propaganda.

propagar *vt* to propagate, spread.

propano *nm* propane.

propasarse *vpr* to go too far.

propensión *nf* inclination, tendency.

propenso,-a *adj* inclined. LOC **ser propenso,-a a** ALGO to be prone to sth.

propiciar *vt (favorecer)* contribute to.

propiciatorio,-a *adj* propitiatory.

propicio,-a *adj (gen)* suitable.

propiedad *nf (bien inmueble)* property. COMP **propiedad privada** private property.

propietario,-a *nm & nf* owner.

propina *nf* tip.

propinar *vt* to give.

propio,-a *adj* **1** *(de nuestra propiedad)* own. **2** *(indicado)* appropriate. **3** *(mismo - él)* himself; *(- ella)* herself; *(- cosa, animal)* itself; *(- en plural)* themselves.

proponer *vt (persona, plan, etc)* to propose.
▶ *vpr* **proponerse** to intend.

proporción *nf* proportion.

proporcionado,-a *adj* in proportion.

proporcional *adj* proportionate.

proporcionar *vt (ayuda, etc)* to supply.

proposición *nf (idea)* proposal.

propósito *nm* **1** *(intención)* intention. **2** *(objetivo)* aim.

propuesta *nf* proposal.

propugnar *vt* to advocate.

propulsar *vt (medida, idea, etc)* to promote.

propulsión *nf* propulsion.

propulsor,-ra *nm (motor)* motor.

prórroga *nf (de un plazo)* extension.

prorrogable *adj* renewable.

prorrogar *vt (alargar)* to extend.

prosa *nf* prose.

prosaico,-a *adj* prosaic.

proscribir *vt (prohibir)* to proscribe.

proscrito,-a *nm & nf (criminal)* outlaw.

proseguir *vt* to continue, carry on.

proselitismo *nm* proselytism.

proselitista *adj* proselytic.
▶ *nm o nf* proselytizer.

prosodia *nf* prosody.

prosopopeya *nf (figura retórica)* prosopopoeia.

prospección *nf (del suelo)* surveying; *(para minerales)* prospecting.

prospecto *nm* leaflet, prospectus.

prosperar *vi* to prosper, thrive.

prosperidad *nf* prosperity.

próspero,-a *adj* prosperous.

próstata *nf* prostate, prostate gland.

prostitución *nf* prostitution.

prostituir *vt* to prostitute.
▶ *vpr* **prostituirse** to prostitute os.

prostituta *nf* prostitute.

protagonismo *nm* leading role.

P

protagonista *adj* main, leading.
▶ *nm o nf (de película - actor)* leading man; *(- actriz)* leading lady.

protagonizar *vt (película, etc)* to star in.

protección *nf* protection.

proteccionismo *nm* protectionism.

proteccionista *adj* protectionist.

protector,-ra *nm & nf (persona)* protector.

proteger *vt* to protect.

protegido,-a *nm & nf (hombre)* protégé; *(mujer)* protégée.

proteína *nf* protein.

proteínico,-a *adj* proteinic.

prótesis *nf* MED *(uso formal)* prosthesis. COMP **prótesis dental** denture.

protesta *nf* protest.

protestante *adj* Protestant.
▶ *nm o nf* Protestant.

protestar *vi (mostrar disconformidad)* to protest (contra, against).

protocolo *nm (gen)* protocol.

protón *nm* proton.

protoplasma *nm* protoplasm.

prototipo *nm* prototype.

protozoo *nm* protozoan.

protuberancia *nf* protuberance.

provecho *nm (beneficio)* benefit. LOC ¡buen provecho! enjoy your meal!

provechoso,-a *adj (beneficioso)* beneficial.

proveedor,-ra *nm & nf* supplier.

proveer *vt (suministrar)* to provide (de, with).

provenir *vi* to come (de, from).

proverbial *adj* proverbial.

proverbio *nm* proverb, saying.

providencia *nf* JUR ruling.

providencial *adj* providential.

provincia *nf* province. LOC **de provincias** provincial.

provinciano,-a *adj pey* provincial.

provisión *nf (suministro)* provision.

provisional *adj* provisional.

provisto,-a *adj* provided (de, with), equipped (de, with).

provocación *nf (gen)* provocation.

provocar *vt* to incite, to provoke.

provocativo,-a *adj* provocative.

próximamente *adv* shortly, soon.

proximidad *nf* proximity.

próximo,-a *adj* **1** *(cerca)* near. **2** *(siguiente)* next: *el mes próximo* next month.

proyección *nf* **1** *(gen)* projection. **2** CINE screening, showing.

proyectar *vt (película)* to show.

proyectil *nm* projectile, missile.

proyecto *nm* **1** *(propósito)* plan. **2** *(plan)* project.

proyector *nm (de cine)* film projector.

prudencia *nf (cuidado)* care, caution; *(moderación)* moderation.

prudente *adj* sensible, prudent.

prueba *nf* **1** *(demostración)* proof. **2** *(experimento)* experiment, trial: *haz la prueba* try it. **3** *(examen)* test. **4** MED test. **5** DEP event. LOC **poner a prueba** to put to the test. COMP **prueba de acceso** entrance examination.

psicoanálisis *nm inv* psychoanalysis.

psicología *nf* psychology.

psicopatía *nf* psychopathy.

psicosis *nf inv* psychosis.

psique *nf* psyche.

psiquiatría *nf* psychiatry.

psiquiátrico,-a *adj* psychiatric.

psíquico,-a *adj* psychic, psychical.

pterodáctilo *nm* pterodactyl.

púa *nf* **1** *(de peine, cepillo)* tooth. **2** *(de erizo)* quill. **3** MÚS plectrum.

pubertad *nf* puberty.

pubis *nm inv* **1** pubes *pl*. **2** *(hueso)* pubis.

publicable *adj* publishable.

publicación *nf* publication.

publicar *vt (libro, etc)* to publish.

publicidad *nf (comercial)* advertising.

publicista *nm o nf* advertising executive.

publicitario,-a *adj* advertising.

público,-a *adj* public.
▶ *nm* **público** *(de un espectáculo)* audience; *(de televisión)* audience, viewers *pl*: *el público aplaudió entusiasmado* the audience applauded warmly. LOC **en público** in public.

publirreportaje *nm (documentary style)* television advertisement.

puchero *nm (olla)* cooking pot.

púdico,-a *adj* chaste, decent.

pudiente *adj* wealthy, rich.

pudor *nm (decencia)* decency.

pudoroso,-a *adj* decent, chaste.

pudrir *vt* to rot.
  ▶ *vpr* **pudrirse** to rot.

pueblerino,-a *adj (de pueblo)* village.

pueblo *nm* **1** *(población)* village. **2** *(gente)* people.

puente *nm (sobre un río, etc)* bridge.

puerco,-a *nm & nf* pig. COMP **puerco espín** porcupine.

puericultor,-ora *nm & nf* child care specialist.

puericultura *nf* child care.

pueril *adj (infantil)* puerile, childish.

puerro *nm* leek.

puerta *nf* **1** door. **2** *(verja)* gate. **3** DEP *(portería)* goal. COMP **puerta de embarque** gate.

puerto *nm* **1** MAR port, harbour. **2** *(de montaña)* (mountain) pass. COMP **puerto deportivo** marina.

Puerto Rico *nm* Puerto Rico.

puertorriqueño,-a *adj* Puerto Rican.
  ▶ *nm & nf* Puerto Rican.

pues *conj* **1** *(ya que)* since, as. **2** *(por lo tanto)* therefore, so. **3** *(repetitivo)* then. **4** *(enfático)* well: *pues bien* well then; *¡pues claro!* of course!; *pues no* well no.

puesta *nf* **1** *(colocación)* setting. **2** *(de huevos)* laying. COMP **puesta de sol** sunset.

puesto,-a *nm* **1** *(sitio)* place: *ya han llegado al primer puesto* they've made it to the top. **2** *(de mercado)* stall; *(de feria, etc)* stand. **3** *(empleo)* position, post. LOC **puesto que** since, as.

púgil *nm* boxer.

pugnar *vi* to fight, struggle.

puja *nf (acción)* bidding.

pujante *adj* thriving.

pujar *vt (en subasta)* to bid higher.

pulcritud *nf* neatness.

pulcro,-a *adj* neat.

pulga *nf* flea.

pulgada *nf* inch.

pulgar *nm* thumb.

pulgón *nm* aphid.

pulimentar *vt* to polish.

pulir *vt (superficie)* to polish.

pullover *nm* pullover.

pulmón *nm* lung.

pulmonar *adj* lung, pulmonary.

pulmonía *nf* pneumonia.

pulpa *nf* pulp.

púlpito *nm* pulpit.

pulpo *nm* ZOOL octopus.

pulsación *nf* **1** pulsation. **2** *(de corazón)* beat. **3** *(en mecanografía)* stroke.

pulsador *nm (gen)* push button.

pulsar *vt* **1** *(botón, timbre, etc)* to press. **2** *(tecla - de máquina de escribir)* to tap; *(- de piano)* to play.

pulsera *nf* **1** bracelet. **2** *(de reloj)* watch strap.

pulso *nm* **1** *(presión sanguínea)* pulse: *déjame que te tome el pulso* let me take your pulse. **2** *(firmeza en la mano)* steady hand: *para dibujar hay que tener buen pulso* to be able to draw you need a steady hand.

pulular *vi* to swarm.

pulverizador *nm* spray, atomizer.

pulverizar *vt* **1** *(líquido)* to atomize, spray. **2** *(sólido)* to pulverize. **3** *(enemigo)* to crush, wipe out.

puma *nm* puma, mountain lion.

punción *nf* puncture.

punitivo,-a *adj* punitive.

punta *nf (extremo)* tip; *(extremo afilado)* point. LOC **sacar punta a** *(lápiz)* to sharpen.

puntada *nf* stitch.

puntal *nm* **1** prop. **2** *fig* support.

puntapié *nm* kick.

puntear *vt* **1** *(dibujar)* to dot. **2** MÚS to pluck.

punteo *nm* MÚS plucking, US picking.

puntera *nf (de zapato, calcetín, etc)* toe.

puntería *nf* aim: *¡qué buena puntería!* what a good shot!

puntero,-a *adj* leading.
  ▶ *nm* **puntero** *(para señalar)* pointer.

puntiagudo,-a *adj* pointed.

P

puntilla *nf* COST lace. LOC **de puntillas** on tiptoe.

puntilloso,-a *adj (exigente)* punctilious.

punto *nm* **1** *(gen)* point. **2** *(tanto)* point: *nos llevan cinco puntos de ventaja* they're five points ahead of us. **3** *(detrás de abreviatura)* dot; *(al final de la oración)* full stop, US period. **4** *(lugar)* spot: *¿en qué punto de la carretera se encuentran?* exactly where on the road are they? **5** *(tejido)* knitwear: *me he comprado una falda de punto* I bought a knitted skirt. **6** *(en costura, sutura, etc)* stitch: *me caí y me dieron tres puntos en la barbilla* I fell and needed three stitches on my chin. LOC **en punto** sharp, on the dot: *son las tres en punto* it's exactly three o'clock. COMP **dos puntos** colon. ▍ **punto cardinal** cardinal point. ▍ **punto de vista** point of view. ▍ **punto débil** weak point. ▍ **punto y coma** semicolon. ▍ **punto y seguido** full stop, new sentence, US period, new sentence.

puntuable *adj* valid.

puntuación *nf* **1** *(en ortografía)* punctuation. **2** *(acción de puntuar)* scoring; *(total de puntos)* score. **3** EDUC *(acción)* marking; *(nota)* mark: *obtuvo una puntuación muy alta* she got a very high mark.

puntual *adj (que llega a su hora)* punctual: *han llegado muy puntuales* they've arrived right on time.

puntualidad *nf* punctuality.

puntualización *nf* remark.

puntualizar *vt (especificar)* to point out.

puntuar *vt* **1** LING to punctuate. **2** EDUC to mark.
▶ *vi* DEP to score.

punzada *nf* sharp pain, stab of pain.

punzante *adj* stabbing.

punzar *vt* to prick.

punzón *nm* punch.

puñado *nm* handful.

puñal *nm* dagger.

puñalada *nf (herida)* stab wound.

puñetazo *nm* punch.

puño *nm* **1** *(mano)* fist. **2** *(de arma)* handle. **3** *(de camisa, abrigo, etc)* cuff.

pupila *nf* pupil.

pupilaje *nm (de persona)* board and lodging; *(de coche)* garaging.

pupilo,-a *nm & nf (de un tutor)* pupil.

pupitre *nm* school desk.

purasangre *adj* thoroughbred.
▶ *nm (caballo)* thoroughbred.

puré *nm (espeso)* purée; *(sopa)* thick soup: *hoy tenemos puré de zanahoria* today we've got thick carrot soup. COMP **puré de patatas** mashed potatoes.

pureza *nf* purity.

purga *nf* purge.

purgación *nf (acción)* purging.

purgante *nm* purgative, laxative.

purgar *vt* to purge (de, of).

purgatorio *nm* purgatory.

purificación *nf* purification.

purificador,-ra *adj* purifying.
▶ *nm* **purificador** purifier.

purificante *adj* purifying.

purificar *vt* to purify.

purismo *nm* purism.

purista *adj* purist.
▶ *nm o nf* purist.

puritano,-a *adj* puritan, puritanic.
▶ *nm & nf* puritan.

puro,-a *adj* **1** *(sin mezcla)* pure: *tiene un perro de pura raza* he has a purebred dog. **2** *(mero)* sheer, mere, pure: *me enteré por pura casualidad* I found out by pure chance.
▶ *nm* **puro** cigar.

púrpura *adj* purple.
▶ *nm* purple.

purulento,-a *adj* purulent.

pus *nm* pus.

pusilánime *adj* faint-hearted.

pusilanimidad *nf* faint-heartedness.

pústula *nf* pustule.

putrefacción *nf* putrefaction.

putrefacto,-a *adj* putrefied, rotten.

pútrido,-a *adj* putrefied, rotten.

puya *nf (comentario)* gibe.

puyazo *nm (comentario)* gibe.

puzzle *nm* jigsaw, puzzle.

Q, q *nf (la letra)* Q, q.
Qatar *nm* Qatar.
quásar *nm* quasar.
que¹ *pron* **1** *(sujeto, persona)* who, that; *(cosa)* that, which: *la chica que vino ayer está enferma* the girl who came yesterday is ill. **2** *(complemento, persona)* whom, who; *(cosa)* that, which: *el coche que me prestaste está ahí* the car (that) you lent me is there. **3** *prep + que (complemento circunstancial)* which; *(lugar)* where; *(tiempo)* when: *la casa en que vivía estaba lejos* the house where he lived was far away. **4** *art def + que* the one which, the one that: *ese libro es el que me gusta* that's the book I like.
que² *conj* **1** that: *dice que no vendrá* he says (that) he won't come. **2** *(en comparaciones)* than: *es más alto que su padre* he is taller than his father. **3** *(deseo, mandato)*: *¡que te diviertas!* enjoy yourself! **4** *(duda, extrañeza)*: *¿que no te hicieron pagar nada?* (you say) they didn't make you pay anything? **5** *(causal, consecutiva)*: *¡arriba, que ya son las ocho!* get up, it's eight o'clock! **6** *(tanto si... como si...)* whether... or not...: *que llueva que no llueva, iremos de excursión* whether it rains or not, we're going on a trip. **7** *(reiterativo)* and: *charla que charla se nos pasó la hora* we were so busy talking that the hour just flew by. **8** *(final)* so that: *ven aquí que te vea bien* come here so that I can see you properly. **9** *fam (condicional)* if: *que te gusta, te lo quedas; que no te gusta, lo cambias* if you like it, keep it; if you don't, you can change it. **10** *que no (adversativa)* not: *justicia pido, que no perdón* I want justice, not mercy.

qué *pron* what: *no sé qué hacer* I don't know what to do; *¿qué querías?* what did you want?
▶ *adj* **1** *(cuál)* which: *no sé qué libro quiere* I don't know which book he wants. **2** *(en frases interrogativas)* how, what: *¿qué años tienes?* how old are you?; *¿qué has dicho?* what did you say? **3** *(en frases exclamativas)* how, what: *¡qué bonito!* how nice!; *¡qué flor más bonita!* what a lovely flower! **4** *(cantidad)* what: *¡qué de gente!* what a crowd!

quebrada *nf* GEOL *(paso)* gorge, ravine.
quebradizo,-a *adj* **1** *(frágil)* fragile, brittle; *(pastel)* short. **2** *fig (débil moralmente)* weak, frail.
quebrado,-a *adj* **1** *(terreno)* rugged, rough, uneven; *(camino)* tortuous. **2** *(número)* fractional.
quebrantar *vt* **1** *(cascar)* to crack. **2** *(romper)* to break, shatter; *(machacar)* to grind. **3** *(debilitar)* to weaken. **4** *fig (salud, posición, fortuna)* to undermine, shatter. **5** *fig (incumplir)* to break, violate. **6** *fig (suavizar)* to take the edge off, temper; *(ablandar)* to soften. **7** *fig (causar lástima)* to wound, shatter.
▶ *vpr* **quebrantarse 1** *(cascarse)* to crack. **2** *(romperse)* to break. **3** *(la salud)* to be shattered.
quebrar *vt (romper, incumplir)* to break.
▶ *vi* **1** FIN to go bankrupt. **2** *fig (flaquear)* to weaken.
▶ *vpr* **quebrarse 1** *(romperse)* to break. **2** *(herniarse)* to rupture os. **3** *(interrumpirse)* to be broken, open up. **4** *fig (ánimo)* to break, crack.
quedar *vi* **1** *(permanecer)* to remain, stay. **2** *fig (terminar)* to end. **3** *(cita)* to arrange to meet. **4** *(resultado de algo)* to

be. **5** *(favorecer)* to look, fit. **6** *(estar situado)* to be. **7** *(restar)* to be left, remain. **8** *(faltar)* to be, be still. **9 quedar en** *(convenir)* to agree to. **10 quedar por + inf** not to have been + *pp*: *la cama quedó por hacer* the bed had not been made, the bed was left unmade. **11 quedar + ger** to be, remain: *cuando me fui el niño quedaba durmiendo* when I left the child was sleeping.
▸ *vpr* **quedarse 1** *(permanecer)* to remain, stay, be. **2** *(resultado de algo)* to be, remain. **3** *euf (morirse)* to die. **4** *(mar, viento)* to become calm; *(viento)* to drop. **5 quedarse con** *(retener algo)* to keep.

quehacer *nm* task, chore, job.

queja *nf* **1** *(descontento)* complaint. **2** *(de dolor)* moan, groan.

quejarse *vpr* **1** *(de descontento)* to complain (de, about). **2** *(de dolor)* to moan, groan.

quejido *nm* groan, moan.

quejumbroso,-a *adj* **1** *(persona)* whining, plaintive. **2** *(tono)* querulous.

quemado,-a *adj* **1** burnt; *(por el sol)* sunburnt. **2** *fig (resentido)* embittered. **3** *fam (acabado)* spent, burnt-out.

quemador,-ra *nm* burner.

quemadura *nf* **1** *(acción)* burning. **2** *(herida)* burn; *(de sol)* sunburn; *(escaldadura)* scald.

quemar *vt* **1** *(gen)* to burn; *(plantas)* to scorch. **2** *(incendiar)* to set on fire. **3** *fam (acabar)* to burn out.
▸ *vi (estar muy caliente)* to be burning hot.
▸ *vpr* **quemarse** *(persona)* to burn os; *(cosa)* to be burnt.

querella *nf* **1** JUR action, lawsuit. **2** *(queja)* complaint. **3** *(enfrentamiento)* dispute, quarrel.

querencia *nf* **1** *(acción)* love. **2** *(inclinación del animal)* homing instinct; *(inclinación del hombre)* homesickness.

querer *vt* **1** *(amar)* to love. **2** *(desear)* to want. **3** *(buscar)* to be asking for, be looking for. **4** *(petición)* would. **5** *(verificarse)* may, might.
▸ *nm* love, affection.

querido,-a *adj (amado)* dear, beloved; *(en carta)* dear.
▸ *nm & nf* **1** *(amante)* lover; *(mujer)* mistress. **2** *fam (apelativo)* darling.

quesera *nf* **1** *(fábrica)* cheese factory. **2** *(para servirlo)* cheese dish.

queso *nm* cheese.

quicio *nm* pivot hole.

quid *nm* crux.

quiebra *nf* **1** *(rotura)* break, crack. **2** *(bancarrota)* failure, bankruptcy; *(crack)* crash, collapse. **3** *(pérdida)* loss. **4** GEOG gorge. **5** *fig (fracaso)* failure.

quien *pron* **1** *(sujeto)* who: *me encontré a Toni, quien me dijo que estabas enfermo* I met Toni, who told me you were ill. **2** *(complemento)* who, whom: *las personas a quienes me encontré ayer están aquí* the people (whom) I met yesterday are here. **3** *(indefinido)* whoever, anyone who: *quien sepa la respuesta que me lo diga* anyone who knows the answer tell me.

quién *pron* **1** *(sujeto)* who: *¿quién te lo dijo?* who told you? **2** *(complemento)* who, whom: *¿con quién hablas?* who are you talking to? **3 de quién** *(posesivo)* whose: *¿de quién es esto?* whose is this?

quienquiera *pron* whoever: *entre, quienquiera que sea* come in, whoever you may be.

quieto,-a *adj* **1** *(sin movimiento)* still, motionless. **2** *fig (sosegado)* quiet, calm.

quilate *nm* **1** *(unidad de peso)* carat. **2** *(unidad del oro)* carat (US karat).

quilogramo *nm* → kilogramo.

quilométrico,-a *adj* → kilométrico,-a.

quilómetro *adj* → kilómetro.

quimera *nf* **1** *(mitología)* chimera. **2** *fig (ilusión)* wild fancy, fantasy. **3** *fig (preocupación)* worry; *(sospecha infundada)* unfounded suspicion.

quimérico,-a *adj* unrealistic, fantastic.

química *nf* chemistry.

químicamente *adv* chemically.

químico,-a *adj* chemical.
▸ *nm & nf* chemist.

quincalla *nf (objetos de metal)* cheap metalware; *(baratija)* trinket.

quincallero,-a *nm & nf (de objetos de metal)* seller of cheap metalware; *(de baratijas)* trinket seller.

quince *adj (cardinal)* fifteen; *(ordinal)* fifteenth.
▶ *nm* fifteen.

✎ Consulta también seis.

quinceañero,-a *adj* **1** *(de quince años)* fifteen-year-old. **2** *(adolescente)* teenage.
▶ *nm & nf* **1** *(de quince años)* fifteen-year-old. **2** *(adolescente)* teenager.

quinceavo,-a *adj* fifth.
▶ *nm & nf* fifth.

✎ Consulta también sexto,-a.

quincena *nf* **1** *(tiempo)* fortnight. **2** *(paga)* fortnightly pay.

quincenal *adj* fortnightly.

quincuagenario,-a *adj* quinquagenarian.
▶ *nm & nf* quinquagenarian.

quincuagésimo,-a *adj* fiftieth.
▶ *nm & nf* fiftieth.

✎ Consulta también sexto,-a.

quingentésimo,-a *adj* five hundredth.
▶ *nm & nf* five hundredth.

✎ Consulta también sexto,-a.

quiniela *nf* football pools *pl.*

quinientos,-as *adj (cardinal)* five hundred; *(ordinal)* five-hundredth.
▶ *nm* **quinientos** *(número)* five hundred.

✎ Consulta también seis.

quinina *nf* quinine.

quinqué *nm* oil lamp.

quinquenal *adj* quinquennial, five-year.

quinquenio *nm* quinquennium, five-year period.

quinta *nf* **1** *(casa)* country house. **2** *(reemplazo militar)* call-up, conscript, US draft. **3** MÚS fifth.

quintal *nm* quintal *(46 kilograms).*

quinteto *nm* quintet.

quintilla *nf* five-line stanza.

quintillizo,-a *nm & nf* quintuplet, quin.

quinto,-a *adj* fifth.
▶ *nm & nf* fifth.
▶ *nm* **quinto 1** MIL conscript, recruit. **2** *fam (de cerveza)* small bottle of beer (= 20 cl).

✎ Consulta también sexto,-a.

quintuplicación *nf* quintupling.

quintuplicar *vt* to quintuple.

quíntuplo,-a *adj* quintuple.
▶ *nm* **quíntuplo** quintuple.

quinzavo,-a *adj-nm & nf* → quinceavo, -a.

quiosco *nm* kiosk; *(de periódicos)* newsstand; *(de música)* bandstand.

quiosquero,-a *nm & nf* newsagent.

quirófano *nm* operating theatre (US theater).

quirúrgico,-a *adj* surgical.

quitaesmaltes *nm inv* nail polish remover.

quitamanchas *nm inv* stain remover.

quitamiedos *nm inv* handrail.

quitanieves *nm inv* snowplough (US snowplow).

quitapinturas *nm inv* paint stripper.

quitar *vt* **1** *(separar)* to remove, take off. **2** *(sacar)* to take off, take out; *(prendas)* to take off; *(tiempo)* to take up. **3** *(apartar)* to take away, take off. **4** *(hacer desaparecer)* to remove; *(dolor)* to relieve; *(sed)* to quench. **5** *(despojar)* to take; *(robar)* to steal. **6** *(restar)* to subtract; *(descontar)* to take off. **7** *(prohibir)* to forbid, rule out. **8** *(impedir)* to prevent. **9** *(disminuir)* to take away. **10** *fam (radio, agua, etc)* to turn off.
▶ *vpr* **quitarse 1** *(desaparecer)* to go away, come out. **2 quitarse de** *(del juego, bebida, etc)* to give up.

quizá *adv* → quizás.

quizás *adv* perhaps, maybe.

Q

R

R, r *nf (la letra)* R, r.

rábano *nm* radish. LOC ¡me importa un rábano! I don't give a toss!, I couldn't care less!

rabí *nm* rabbi.

rabia *nf* **1** MED rabies. **2** *fig (enfado)* rage, fury, anger. LOC dar rabia to make furious.

rabiar *vi* **1** *(enfadarse)* to rage, be furious: *Elena está que rabia* Elena is furious. **2** *fig (padecer)* to suffer (de, from): *rabiar de dolor* to writhe in pain. LOC hacer rabiar a ALGN to make SB see red.

rabieta *nf fam* tantrum. LOC coger una rabieta *fam* to throw a tantrum.

rabillo *nm (pecíolo)* stalk, stem. LOC mirar por el rabillo del ojo to look out of the corner of one's eye.

rabino *nm* rabbi.

rabioso,-a *adj fig (airado)* furious, angry. LOC ponerse rabioso,-a to fly into a rage.

rabo *nm (gen)* tail.

rácano,-a *adj fam (tacaño)* mean, stingy.

racha *nf* **1** *(ráfaga)* gust, squall. **2** *fig (período)* spell, patch. **3** *fig (serie)* string, run, series *sing*: *hubo una racha de incendios* there was a series of fires. LOC a rachas in fits and starts, on and off. ▪ tener una buena racha to have a run of good luck.

racimo *nm* bunch, cluster.

ración *nf* **1** *(parte)* portion, share. **2** *(de comida)* portion, serving, helping: *«Cuatro raciones»* «Serves four».

racional *adj* rational.

racionar *vt (limitar)* to ration.

racismo *nm* racism, racialism.

radiación *nf* radiation.

radiactivo,-a *adj* radioactive.

radiador *nm* radiator.

radiante *adj fig* radiant: *radiante de alegría* radiant with joy.

radiar *vt* **1** *(irradiar)* to radiate, irradiate. **2** *(retransmitir)* to broadcast, transmit.

radical *adj* radical.

radicalizar *vt* **1** to radicalize. **2** *(postura)* to harden.
▪ *vpr* **radicalizarse** **1** *(conflicto)* to intensify. **2** *(postura)* to harden.

radio¹ *nm* **1** *(de círculo)* radius: *en un radio de 10 metros* within a radius of 10 metres. **2** *(de rueda)* spoke. **3** *(campo)* scope. COMP radio de acción *fig* field of action, scope.

radio² *nf* **1** *(radiodifusión)* radio: *lo oí por la radio* I heard it on the radio. **2** *(aparato)* radio, wireless.

radioactivo,-a *adj* radioactive.

radioaficionado,-a *nm & nf* radio ham.

radiocasete *nm* radio cassette.

radiodifusión *nf* broadcasting.

radiofónico,-a *adj* radio: *concurso radiofónico* radio quiz programme.

radiografía *nf* **1** *(técnica)* radiography. **2** *(imagen)* X-ray, radiograph. LOC hacerse una radiografía to have an X-ray taken.

radionovela *nf* serial.

radiorreceptor *nm* radio, radio set.

radioterapia *nf* radiotherapy.

radiotransmisión *nf* broadcasting.

radiotransmitir *vt* to broadcast.

radioyente *nm o nf* listener.

raer *vt* to scrape (off).

ráfaga *nf* **1** *(de viento)* gust, squall. **2** *(de disparos)* burst. **3** *(de luz)* flash.

rafia *nf* raffia.

raid *nm (incursión)* raid.

raigambre *nf* **1** *(raíces)* roots *pl*, root system. **2** *fig* tradition, history.

raíl *nm* rail.

raíz *nf* root. ⃞LOC de raíz entirely. ▌ echar raíces **1** *(planta)* to take root. **2** *(persona)* to settle, put down roots. ⃞COMP raíz cuadrada square root.

raja *nf* **1** *(corte)* cut, slit. **2** *(hendidura)* crack, split. **3** *(tajada)* slice.

rajá *nm* rajah.

rajar *vt* **1** *(hender)* to split, crack. **2** *(hacer tajadas)* to slice.
  ▶ *vpr* **rajarse 1** *(partirse)* to split, crack. **2** *fam (desistir)* to back out, quit.

rajatabla ⃞LOC a rajatabla strictly.

ralentí *nm* CINE slow motion. ⃞LOC al ralentí *(motor)* ticking over.

ralentizar *vt* to slow down.

rallado,-a *adj (queso, etc)* grated.

rallador *nm* grater.

ralladura *nf* grated rind: *ralladura de limón* grated lemon rind.

rallar *vt* to grate.

rally *nm* rally.

rama *nf* branch. ⃞LOC andarse por las ramas *fam* to beat about the bush. ▌ en rama raw: *canela en rama* cinnamon stick.

ramaje *nm* foliage, branches *pl*.

ramal *nm (de camino, etc)* branch.

ramalazo *nm fam (ataque)* fit.

rambla *nf (paseo)* boulevard, avenue.

ramificación *nf* ramification.

ramificarse *vpr* to ramify, branch (out).

ramillete *nm* **1** posy. **2** *fig (conjunto)* bunch, group, collection.

ramo *nm* **1** *(de flores)* bunch, bouquet. **2** *fig (sector)* field: *el ramo de la alimentación* the food sector, the food industry.

rampa *nf (pendiente)* ramp. ⃞COMP rampa de lanzamiento launching pad.

rana *nf* frog.

rancho *nm* AM *(granja)* ranch, farm.

rancio,-a *adj* **1** *(comestibles)* stale. **2** *fig (antiguo)* old, ancient: *de rancio abolengo* of ancient lineage.

rand *nm* rand.

rango *nm* rank.

ranking *nm* ranking.

ranura *nf (para monedas, fichas)* slot.

rapapolvo *nm fam* dressing-down, ticking off, talking-to.

rapar *vt (pelo)* to crop.

rapaz *adj* ZOOL predatory, of prey: *ave rapaz* bird of prey.

rape¹ *nm (pez)* angler fish.

rape² *nm fam (rasura)* quick shave. ⃞LOC al rape close-cropped, short.

rapero,-a *nm & nf* rapper.

rapidez *nf* speed, rapidity: *con rapidez* quickly.

rápido,-a *adj* quick, fast.
  ▶ *adv* quickly: *¡rápido!* hurry up!
  ▶ *nm* rápido *(tren)* fast train.
  ▶ *nm pl* rápidos *(del río)* rapids.

rapiñar *vt fam* to pinch, steal.

rappel *nm* abseiling. ⃞LOC hacer rappel to abseil.

raptar *vt* to kidnap, abduct.

rapto *nm (secuestro)* kidnapping.

raqueta *nf (de tenis)* racket; *(de pingpong)* bat, US paddle.

raquítico,-a *adj* **1** *fig (exiguo)* meagre (US meager), small. **2** *fig (débil)* weak.

rareza *nf* **1** *(poco común)* rarity, rareness. **2** *(extravagancia)* eccentricity.

raro,-a *adj* **1** *(escaso)* scarce, rare: *los gorilas albinos son animales raros* albino gorillas are rare animals. **2** *(peculiar)* odd, strange, weird: *últimamente la encuentro rara* I think she's been acting a little strange recently. ⃞LOC ¡qué raro! how odd!, that's strange!

ras ⃞LOC a ras de (on a) level with. ▌ a ras de tierra at ground level.

rasante *adj (vuelo)* low, skimming.
  ▶ *nf (inclinación)* slope. ⃞COMP cambio de rasante brow of a hill.

rascacielos *nm inv* skyscraper.

rascador *nm (para rascar)* scraper.

rascar *vt* **1** *(la piel)* to scratch. **2** *(con rascador)* to scrape, rasp.

R

rasero *nm* strickle. LOC **por el mismo rasero** *fig* equally.

rasgado,-a *adj (roto)* torn, ripped.

rasgar *vt* to tear, rip.

rasgo *nm* **1** *(facción del rostro)* feature. **2** *(peculiaridad)* characteristic, feature. LOC **explicar a grandes rasgos** to outline.

rasguear *vt (instrumento)* to strum.

rasguñar *vt* to scratch, scrape.

rasguño *nm (arañazo)* scratch, scrape.

raso,-a *adj* **1** *(plano)* flat, level; *(liso)* smooth: *una cucharada rasa* a level spoonful. **2** *(atmósfera)* clear.
▶ *nm* **raso** *(tejido)* satin.

raspa *nf (de pescado)* bone, backbone.

raspar *vt* **1** *(rascar)* to scrape (off); *(dañar)* to scratch, graze. **2** *(rasar)* to graze, skim.

rasposo,-a *adj* rough, sharp.

rasqueta *nf* scraper.

rastra *nf (rastro)* trail, track. LOC **a rastras** **1** *(arrastrando)* dragging. **2** *(sin querer)* unwillingly, grudgingly: *llevar a rastras* to drag along.

rastrear *vt (seguir el rastro)* to trail, track.

rastrillar *vt (hojas, etc)* to rake.

rastrillo *nm* **1** *(rastro)* rake. **2** *fam (mercadillo)* flea market.

rastro *nm* **1** *(señal)* trace, track: *ni rastro de sangre* not a trace of blood. **2** *(vestigio)* vestige. **3** *(mercado)* flea market. LOC **seguir el rastro de** ALGN to follow SB's trail.

rastrojo *nm (paja)* stubble.

rasurar *vt* to shave.

rata *nf* ZOOL rat.

ratero,-a *nm & nf* pickpocket.

ratificar *vt* to ratify.
▶ *vpr* **ratificarse** to be confirmed.

rato *nm* **1** *(tiempo)* time, while, moment: *charlamos un rato* we chatted for a while. **2** *(espacio)* way: *hay un buen rato hasta Vigo* it's a long way to Vigo. **3** *fam (mucho)* very, a lot: *sabe un rato de deportes* she's a mine of information about sports. LOC **a ratos** at times. ▌ **pasar un buen rato** to have a good time. COMP **ratos libres** free time *sing*.

ratón *nm* mouse.

ratonera *nf (trampa)* mousetrap.

raudal *nm* **1** *(agua)* torrent, flood. **2** *fig (abundancia)* flood, wave. LOC **a raudales** in torrents.

raudo,-a *adj lit* swift, rapid.

raviolis *nm pl* ravioli.

raya¹ *nf* **1** *(línea)* line. **2** *(de color)* stripe: *pantalón a rayas* striped trousers.

raya² *nf (pez)* skate.

rayado,-a *adj* **1** *(tejido)* striped. **2** *(papel)* ruled.
▶ *nm* **rayado** stripes *pl*.

rayar *vt* **1** *(líneas)* to draw lines on, line, rule. **2** *(superficie)* to scratch.

rayo *nm* **1** ray, beam: *rayo de sol* sunbeam; *rayo de luz* ray of light. **2** *(relámpago)* lightning. COMP **rayo de luna** moonbeam. ▌ **rayos ultravioletas/UVA** ultraviolet rays. ▌ **rayos X** X-rays.

rayuela *nf* hopscotch.

raza *nf* **1** race. **2** *(animal)* breed. LOC **de raza** **1** *(perro)* pedigree. **2** *(caballo)* thoroughbred. COMP **raza humana** human race.

razón *nf* **1** *(facultad)* reason. **2** *(motivo)* reason, cause. **3** *(mensaje)* message. **4** *(justicia)* justice. **5** MAT ratio, rate. LOC **dar la razón a** ALGN to agree with SB, say that SB is right. ▌ **perder la razón** to lose one's reason. ▌ **tener razón** to be right.

razonable *adj* reasonable.

razonamiento *nm* reasoning.

razonar *vi* **1** *(discurrir)* to reason. **2** *(hablar)* to talk.
▶ *vt (explicar)* to reason out.

re *nm* re, ray, D.

reacción *nf* reaction. LOC **reacción en cadena** chain reaction.

reaccionar *vi* to react.

reacio,-a *adj* reluctant, unwilling.

reactivar *vt* to reactivate.

reactor *nm* **1** reactor. **2** AV jet, jet plane.

readmitir *vt (gen)* to readmit; *(un trabajador)* to reinstate.

reafirmar *vt* to reaffirm, reassert.

reagrupar *vt* to regroup.
▶ *vpr* **reagruparse** to regroup.

reajustar *vt* to readjust.

real¹ *adj (verdadero)* real: *en la vida real* in real life.

real² *adj (regio)* royal.

realce *nm (adorno)* relief.

realeza *nf* royalty.

realidad *nf* reality. LOC **en realidad** actually, in fact.

realista *adj (de la realidad)* realistic.
▶ *nm o nf (de la realidad)* realist.

realización *nf* **1** *(de un deseo)* fulfilment (US fulfillment). **2** *(ejecución)* execution, carrying out.

realizador,-ra *nm & nf* producer.

realizar *vt* **1** *(ambición)* to realize, fulfil, achieve; *(deseo, esperanza)* to fulfil. **2** *(llevar a cabo)* to accomplish, carry out, do, fulfil. **3** *(un viaje)* to make.
▶ *vpr* **realizarse 1** *(ambición, deseo)* to be fulfilled, be achieved; *(sueño)* to come true. **2** *(llevarse a cabo)* to be executed, be carried out.

realmente *adv* **1** *(de verdad)* really, truly. **2** *(en realidad)* actually, in fact: *realmente no hacía tanto frío* in fact it wasn't too cold.

realzar *vt* **1** *(elevar)* to raise, lift. **2** *fig (engrandecer)* to enhance, heighten.

reanimar *vt* **1** *(persona)* to revive. **2** *(fiesta, conversación)* to liven up.
▶ *vpr* **reanimarse** *(persona)* to revive.

reanudar *vt (gen)* to renew, resume.

reaparecer *vi* **1** *(gen)* to reappear. **2** *(un artista, etc)* to make a comeback. **3** *(un fenómeno)* to recur.

reavivar *vt* **1** *(fuego)* to stoke. **2** *(dolor)* to intensify; *(interés)* to revive.

rebaba *nf* rough edge.

rebaja *nf (descuento)* discount, reduction.
▶ *nf pl* **rebajas** sales.

rebajado,-a *adj* **1** *(precio)* reduced. **2** *(humillado)* humbled.

rebajar *vt* **1** *(nivel)* to lower. **2** *(precio)* to reduce. **3** *(color)* to soften. **4** *fig (humillar)* to humiliate.
▶ *vpr* **rebajarse** *fig (humillarse)* to humble os.

rebanada *nf* slice.

rebañar *vt (comida)* to finish off.

rebaño *nm (gen)* herd; *(de ovejas)* flock.

rebeca *nf* cardigan.

rebelarse *vpr* to rebel, revolt.

rebelde *adj* **1** rebellious. **2** *fig (tos, etc)* persistent.
▶ *nm o nf* rebel.

rebelión *nf* rebellion, revolt.

reblandecer *vt* to soften.
▶ *vpr* **reblandecerse** to soften.

rebobinar *vt* to rewind.

reborde *nm (de mesa)* edge; *(de taza, de tela)* edging.

rebosar *vi* **1** *(derramarse)* to overflow, brim over. **2** *fig* to brim (**de**, with), burst (**de**, with): *rebosar de alegría* to be brimming with joy.
▶ *vt fig (sentimiento)* to brim with; *(salud)* to exude.

rebotar *vi (pelota)* to bounce, rebound.

rebote *nm (de balón)* bounce, rebound. LOC **de rebote** *fig* on the rebound.

rebozado,-a *adj* coated in batter.

rebozar *vt* CULIN to coat in batter.

rebrotar *vi* to shoot, sprout.

rebuscado,-a *adj* affected, recherché.

rebuscar *vt* to search carefully for.

rebuznar *vi* to bray.

rebuzno *nm* bray, braying.

recabar *vt* **1** *(solicitar)* to ask for, entreat. **2** *(obtener)* to manage to get.

recadero,-a *nm & nf (gen)* messenger.

recado *nm* **1** *(mensaje)* message. **2** *(encargo)* errand: *me hizo un recado* she ran the errand for me.
▶ *nm pl* **recados** *(compras)* shopping sing.

recaer *vi (enfermedad)* to relapse, have a relapse.

recaída *nf (enfermedad)* relapse. LOC **sufrir una recaída** to have a relapse.

recalcar *vt fig* to emphasize, stress.

recalentar *vt* **1** *(volver a calentar)* to warm up. **2** *(calentar demasiado)* to overheat.

recámara *nf* **1** *(cuarto)* dressing room. **2** *(de arma)* chamber.

recambio *nm* spare, spare part; *(de pluma, bolígrafo)* refill.

recapacitar *vi* to think (**sobre**, over).

R

recapitular vt to recapitulate, sum up.

recargado,-a adj fig (exagerado) overe-laborate, exaggerated, contrived.

recargar vt **1** (volver a cargar) to reload; (pilas) to recharge; (mechero) to refill. **2** (sobrecargar) to overload. **3** fig (exage-rar) to overelaborate, exaggerate.

recargo nm extra charge, surcharge.

recatado,-a adj **1** (prudente) cautious, prudent. **2** (decente) decent.

recauchutar vt to retread, remould.

recaudar vt to collect.

recelar vt (sospechar) to suspect, dis-trust. **2** (temer) to fear.
▶ vi (desconfiar) to be suspicious (de, of): recela de todos he is suspicious of everybody.

recelo nm suspicion.

recepción nf **1** (gen) reception. **2** (de documento, carta, etc) receipt.

recepcionista nm o nf receptionist.

receptivo,-a adj receptive (a, to).

receptor,-ra nm & nf receiver, recipi-ent.
▶ nm receptor (de radio, etc) receiver.

receta nf **1** MED prescription. **2** CULIN recipe.

recetar vt to prescribe.

rechazar vt **1** (gen) to reject, turn down. **2** (ataque) to repel, drive back.

rechazo nm **1** rejection, refusal. **2** (ne-gativa) denial, rejection.

rechinar vi (madera) to creak; (metal) to squeak, screech; (dientes) to grind.

rechistar vi to say, reply.

rechoncho,-a adj fam chubby, tubby.

rechupete LOC de rechupete fam (muy bien) super, brill, fantastic. (comida) delicious, scrumptious.

recibidor nm (de casa) entrance hall.

recibimiento nm reception, wel-come.

recibir vt **1** (gen) to receive. **2** (salir al encuentro) to meet: nos recibió en la puer-ta he met us at the door.

recibo nm **1** (resguardo) receipt. **2** (factu-ra) invoice, bill.

reciclar vt (materiales) to recycle.

recién adv [se usa sólo ante un participio pasado] recently, newly; (café, pan) freshly: un pastel recién hecho a freshly baked cake. LOC «Recién pintado» "Wet paint".

reciente adj recent.

recinto nm grounds pl, precincts pl.

recio,-a adj (fuerte) strong, robust.

recipiente nm container, receptacle.

recíproco,-a adj reciprocal, mutual: un sentimiento recíproco a mutual feeling.

recital nm **1** MÚS recital, concert. **2** LIT reading: recital de poesía poetry reading.

recitar vt to recite.

reclamación nf **1** (demanda) claim, de-mand. **2** (queja) complaint. LOC pre-sentar una reclamación to lodge a complaint.

reclamar vt (pedir) to demand, claim.
▶ vi (protestar) to protest (contra, against): reclamaron contra aquella medi-da they protested against the measure.

reclamo nm **1** (para cazar) decoy bird, lure. **2** (anuncio) advertisement; (eslo-gan) advertising slogan.

reclinar vt to lean.
▶ vpr reclinarse to lean back, recline: se reclinó sobre la almohada he lent back on the pillow.

recluir vt (encerrar) to shut in.

recluso,-a nm & nf prisoner.

recluta nm o nf recruit.

reclutar vt to recruit.

recobrar vt **1** (gen) to recover. **2** (aliento) to get back. **3** (tiempo) to make up.
▶ vpr recobrarse (recuperarse) to recover (de, from).

recodo nm twist.

recogedor nm dustpan.

recoger vt **1** (volver a coger) to take again, take back. **2** (coger) to pick up, take back. **3** (ir a buscar) to pick up, collect: me recogerá a las cuatro he'll pick me up at four o'clock. **4** (cosecha) to har-vest, gather; (fruta) to pick. **5** (juntar) to gather, collect. **6** (velas) to take in; (cortinas) to draw. **7** (dar asilo) to take in, shelter: lo recogieron sus abuelos he

was taken in by his grandparents. **8** *(ordenar)* to clear up, tidy up.
► *vpr* **recogerse 1** *(irse a casa)* to go home. **2** *(irse a dormir)* to go to bed.

recolectar *vt* **1** *(reunir)* to gather, collect. **2** *(cosechar)* to harvest.

recomendar *vt* to recommend, advise: *te recomiendo que estudies más* I recommend that you study harder.

recompensa *nf* reward, recompense. LOC **en recompensa** in return.

recompensar *vt* **1** *(compensar)* to compensate. **2** *(remunerar)* to reward.

recomponer *vt* to repair, mend.

reconcentrar *vt* **1** *(concentrar)* to concentrate (en, to). **2** *(reunir)* to bring together.
► *vpr* **reconcentrarse** *(ensimismarse)* to become absorbed in thought, concentrate.

reconciliar *vt* to reconcile.
► *vpr* **reconciliarse** *(uso recíproco)* to be reconciled.

recóndito,-a *adj* hidden, secret.

reconfortar *vt* **1** *(confortar)* to comfort. **2** *(animar)* to cheer up.

reconocer *vt* **1** *(gen)* to recognize. **2** *(admitir)* to recognize, admit: *reconoció su error* she admitted her mistake. **3** *(afrontar)* to face: *reconozcámoslo* let's face it. **4** MIL *(terreno)* to reconnoitre (US reconnoiter). **5** MED *(paciente)* to examine.
► *vpr* **reconocerse 1** to recognize each other. **2** *(admitirse)* to admit: *se reconoció culpable* he admitted his guilt.

reconocimiento *nm* **1** *(gen)* recognition. **2** *(admisión)* admission. **3** MIL reconnaissance. **4** MED checkup.

reconstituyente *nm* tonic.

reconstruir *vt* to reconstruct.

reconvertir *vt* to restructure.

recopilar *vt* to compile, collect.

récord *adj* record: *en un tiempo récord* in record time.
► *nm* record.

recordar *vt* **1** *(rememorar)* to remember: *¿recuerdas?* do you remember? **2** *(traer a la memoria)* to remind (a, of): *me recuer-* *da a mi hermano* he reminds me of my brother.

recorrer *vt* **1** *(distancia)* to cover, travel. **2** *(país)* to tour, travel over, travel round. **3** *(ciudad)* to visit, walk round.

recorrido *nm* **1** *(trayecto)* journey, trip. **2** *(distancia)* distance travelled: *un tren de largo recorrido* a long-distance train. **3** *(itinerario)* itinerary, route.

recortar *vt* **1** *(muñecos, telas, etc)* to cut out. **2** *(lo que sobra)* to cut off. **3** *(el pelo)* to trim. **4** *fig* to cut, restrict: *han recortado los gastos* expenses have been cut.

recorte *nm* **1** *(acción)* cutting. **2** *(trozo)* cutting, clipping. **3** *(de periódico)* press clipping, newspaper cutting. **4** *(de pelo)* trim, cut. **5** *fig (reducción)* cut, reduction: *recorte del presupuesto* budget cut.

recostar *vt* to lean.
► *vpr* **recostarse 1** *(apoyarse)* to lean. **2** *(tumbarse)* to lie down.

recoveco *nm* turn, bend.

recrear *vt* *(divertir)* to amuse, entertain.
► *vpr* **recrearse** to amuse OS, enjoy OS.

recreo *nm* *(en la escuela)* playtime, break.

recriminar *vt* **1** *(reprender)* to recriminate. **2** *(reprochar)* to reproach.

recrudecer *vi* *(empeorar)* to worsen, aggravate.
► *vpr* **recrudecerse 1** *(empeorar)* to worsen. **2** *(aumentar)* to be increasing.

recta *nf* **1** *(línea)* straight line. **2** *(en carretera)* straight.

rectangular *adj* rectangular.

rectángulo,-a *adj* rectangular: *triángulo rectángulo* right-angled triangle.
► *nm* **rectángulo** rectangle.

rectificar *vt* **1** to rectify. **2** *(corregir)* to correct.

recto,-a *adj* **1** *(derecho)* straight. **3** *(ángulo)* right.
► *adv* straight, straight on: *vaya todo recto* go straight on.

recuadro *nm* box.

recubrir *vt* to cover **(con/de,** with).

recuento *nm* recount, count.

recuerdo *nm* **1** *(imagen)* memory. **2** *(regalo)* souvenir, keepsake.
LOC **en recuerdo de** in memory of.

▶ *nm pl* **recuerdos** *(saludos)* regards: *me dio recuerdos para ti* he sends you his regards.

recular *vi (retroceder)* to go back.

recuperación *nf* recovery.

recuperar *vt* **1** *(gen)* to recover. **2** *(afecto)* to win back; *(conocimiento)* to regain; *(tiempo, clases)* to make up.
▶ *vpr* **recuperarse** to recover (de, from).

recurrir *vi (acogerse - a algo)* to resort (a, to); *(- a algn)* to turn (a, to): *recurrió a sus padres* she turned to her parents.

recurso *nm (medio)* resort.
▶ *nm pl* **recursos** resources, means.

red *nf* **1** *(gen)* net. **2** *(sistema)* network, system. **3** ELEC mains *pl*. **4** INFORM network. **5** *fig (trampa)* trap. COMP **red de carreteras** road network.

redacción *nf* **1** *(escritura)* writing. **2** *(escrito)* composition, essay. **3** *(estilo)* wording. **4** *(oficina)* editorial office. **5** *(redactores)* editorial staff.

redactar *vt (escribir)* to write.

redactor,-ra *nm & nf* editor. COMP **redactor jefe** editor in chief.

redada *nf fig* raid.

redención *nf* redemption.

redescubrir *vt* to rediscover.

redil *nm* fold, sheepfold.

redimir *vt* to redeem.
▶ *vpr* **redimirse** to redeem OS.

redoblar *vt (aumentar)* to redouble: *redoblar esfuerzos* to redouble one's efforts.
▶ *vi (tambores)* to roll.

redoble *nm* roll.

redonda LOC **a la redonda** around.

redondear *vt* **1** *(poner redondo)* to round, make round. **2** *(cantidad)* to round up.

redondo,-a *adj* **1** *(circular)* round. **2** *fig (perfecto)* perfect, excellent: *un beneficio redondo* an excellent profit. **3** *fig (cantidad)* round: *en números redondos* in round figures.

reducción *nf* reduction.

reducir *vt* **1** *(gen)* to reduce: *reducir a cenizas* to reduce to ashes. **2** *(disminuir)* to reduce, cut, cut down on: *reducir gastos* to cut down on expenses.

▶ *vpr* **reducirse 1** *(gen)* to be reduced. **2** *(resultar)* to come down (a, to): *todo se redujo a una equivocación* it all came down to a mistake.

redundante *adj* redundant.

redundar *vi* **1** *(abundar)* to abound. **2** *(resultar)* to redound (en, to): *redundó en nuestro beneficio* it was to our advantage.

reembolsar *vt* **1** *(pagar)* to reimburse. **2** *(devolver)* to refund.

reembolso *nm* **1** *(pago)* reimbursement. **2** *(devolución)* refund. COMP **contra reembolso** cash on delivery.

reemplazar *vt* to replace.

reemplazo *nm* **1** replacement. **2** MIL call-up.

reencarnación *nf* reincarnation.

reencuentro *nm* reunion.

reestreno *nm (teatro)* revival; *(cine)* rerelease, rerun.

reestructurar *vt* to restructure.

referencia *nf (relación)* reference. LOC **hacer referencia a** ALGO to refer to STH.
▶ *nf pl* **referencias** *(informes)* references.

referéndum *nm inv* referendum.

referente *adj* concerning (a, -), regarding (a, -).

referir *vt* **1** *(expresar)* to tell, relate. **2** *(remitir)* to refer.
▶ *vpr* **referirse** to refer (a, to).

refilón LOC **mirar** ALGO **de refilón** to look at STH out of the corner of one's eye.

refinado,-a *adj (gen)* refined.

refinamiento *nm* refinement.

refinar *vt (azúcar, etc)* to refine.

refinería *nf* refinery.

reflector,-ra *adj* reflecting.
▶ *nm* **reflector 1** *(cuerpo)* reflector. **2** ELEC searchlight, spotlight.

reflejar *vt* **1** *(gen)* to reflect. **2** *(mostrar)* to show: *su rostro refleja sus sentimientos* her face shows her feelings.
▶ *vpr* **reflejarse** to be reflected.

reflejo,-a *adj (movimiento)* reflex.
▶ *nm* **reflejo 1** *(imagen)* reflection. **2** *(destello)* gleam, glint.

reflexión *nf* reflection.

reflexionar *vi* to reflect (**sobre**, on), think (**sobre**, about): *reflexionamos sobre el tema* we reflected on the subject.

reflexivo,-a *adj* reflective, thoughtful.

reforma *nf* 1 (*gen*) reform. 2 (*mejora*) improvement.
▶ *nf pl* **reformas** (*en construcción*) alterations, repairs, improvements. COMP **reforma agraria** agrarian reform.

reformar *vt* 1 (*gen*) to reform. 2 ARQUIT to renovate, do up.
▶ *vpr* **reformarse** (*corregirse*) to reform os.

reformatear *vt* INFORM to reformat.

reformatorio *nm* reformatory, reform school. COMP **reformatorio de menores** remand home.

reforzar *vt* to reinforce, strengthen.

refracción *nf* refraction. COMP **ángulo de refracción** angle of refraction.

refrán *nm* proverb, saying.

refregar *vt* 1 to rub hard. 2 *fam fig* to rub in: *me refregó mi error* he kept on about my mistake.

refrenar *vt* to restrain, curb, control.

refrescante *adj* refreshing.

refrescar *vt* 1 (*poner fresco*) to cool, refresh. 2 *fig* (*la memoria*) to refresh; (*idiomas*) to brush up on.
▶ *vi* 1 (*el tiempo*) to get cooler, cool down, turn cooler. 2 (*comida, bebida*) to be refreshing.
▶ *vpr* **refrescarse** 1 (*gen*) to cool down, cool off; (*lavarse*) to freshen up; (*tomar el fresco*) to get a breath of fresh air. 2 (*beber*) to have a cold drink.

refresco *nm* (*bebida*) soft drink.

refriega *nf* (*lucha*) scuffle, brawl.

refrigeración *nf* 1 refrigeration. 2 (*aire acondicionado*) air conditioning. 3 (*sistema*) cooling system.

refrigerador *nm* fridge, refrigerator.

refrigerar *vt* 1 (*enfriar*) to refrigerate. 2 (*con aire acondicionado*) to air-condition.

refrigerio *nm* refreshments *pl*, snack.

refuerzo *nm* (*fortalecimiento*) reinforcement, strengthening.

refugiado,-a *nm & nf* refugee. COMP **refugiado político** political refugee.

refugiar *vt* to shelter, give refuge to.

▶ *vpr* **refugiarse** (*gen*) to take refuge; (*de la lluvia*) to shelter.

refugio *nm* (*gen*) shelter, refuge.

refunfuñar *vi* *fam* to grumble, moan.

refutar *vt* to refute, disprove.

regadera *nf* watering can.

regadío,-a *adj* irrigable.
▶ *nm* **regadío** 1 (*acción*) irrigation, watering. 2 (*tierras*) irrigated land. COMP **cultivo de regadío** irrigation farming.

regalar *vt* (*dar un regalo*) to give as a present: *le podemos regalar un libro para su cumpleaños* we can get him a book for his birthday.

regaliz *nm* liquorice (US licorice).

regalo *nm* 1 (*obsequio*) gift, present. 2 (*ganga*) bargain, steal.

regañadientes LOC **a regañadientes** reluctantly, grudgingly, unwillingly.

regañar *vt* to scold, tell off.
▶ *vi* (*reñir*) to argue, quarrel, fall out: *no hacen más que regañar* they're always quarrelling.

regar *vt* 1 (*plantas, tierra, río*) to water. 2 (*calle*) to wash down, hose down.

regata *nf* MAR regatta, boat race.

regatear *vt* 1 (*un precio*) to haggle over, barter for. 2 (*escatimar*) to be sparing with. LOC **no regatear esfuerzos** to spare no effort.
▶ *vi* 1 (*comerciar*) to haggle, bargain. 2 DEP to dribble. 3 MAR to race.

regateo *nm* 1 (*precios*) haggling, bargaining. 2 DEP dribbling.

regazo *nm* lap.

regenerar *vt* to regenerate.

regentar *vt* 1 POL to govern, rule. 2 (*cargo*) to hold. 3 (*dirigir*) to manage.

regente,-a *adj* ruling, governing.
▶ *nm o nf* POL regent.

reggae *nm* reggae.

régimen *nm* 1 POL regime. 2 MED diet. 3 (*condiciones*) system, regime, rules *pl*. LOC **estar a régimen** to be on a diet.

regimiento *nm* regiment.

regio,-a *adj* (*real*) royal, regal.

región *nf* region.

regir *vt* 1 (*gobernar*) to govern, rule. 2 (*dirigir*) to manage, direct, run.

R

▶ *vi (ley, etc)* to be in force, apply: *esta ley aún rige* this law is still in force.

▶ *vpr* **regirse** *(guiarse)* to follow, abide (por, by), go (por, by): *se rige por la opinión de su padre* he goes by his father's opinion.

registrador,-ra *adj* registering, recording: *caja registradora* cash register.

▶ *nm & nf* registrar.

registrar *vt* **1** *(inspeccionar)* to search. **2** *(cachear)* to frisk. **3** *(inscribir)* to register, record, note.

▶ *vpr* **registrarse 1** *(matricularse)* to register, enrol (US enroll). **2** *(detectarse)* to be recorded. **3** *(ocurrir)* to happen: *se ha registrado un terremoto* there has been an earthquake.

registro *nm* **1** *(inspección)* search, inspection. **2** *(inscripción)* registration, recording. **3** JUR *(oficina)* registry. COMP **registro civil** *(oficina)* registry office.

regla *nf* **1** *(norma)* rule. **2** *(pauta)* pattern, rule. **3** *(instrumento)* ruler. **4** *(menstruación)* period. LOC **en regla** in order.

reglamentar *vt* to regulate.

reglamentario,-a *adj* statutory, prescribed, required; *(arma)* regulation.

reglamento *nm* regulations *pl*, rules *pl*.

reglar *vt (regular)* to regulate.

regocijarse *vpr* **1** *(alegrarse)* to be delighted (con, by). **2** *(regodearse)* to delight (de, in), take pleasure (de, in).

regocijo *nm (placer)* delight, joy.

regresar *vi* to return, come back, go back.

regreso *nm* return. LOC **estar de regreso** to be back.

reguero *nm* **1** *(corriente)* trickle of water. **2** *(señal)* trail, trickle.

regular *adj* **1** *(gen)* regular. **2** *fam (pasable)* so-so, average, not bad.

▶ *vt* **1** *(gen)* to regulate. **2** *(ajustar)* to adjust.

regularizar *vt* to regularize; *(normalizar)* to standardize; *(arreglar)* to sort out.

rehabilitar *vt* to rehabilitate.

▶ *nf (en rango)* to reinstate.

rehacer *vt (volver a hacer)* to do again.

▶ *vpr* **rehacerse** *(recuperarse)* to recover, recuperate.

rehén *nm o nf* hostage.

rehogar *vt* to fry lightly.

rehuir *vt* to avoid, shun.

rehusar *vt* to refuse, decline: *rehusé la invitación* I declined the invitation.

reimprimir *vt* to reprint.

reina *nf (gen)* queen.

reinado *nm* reign.

reinar *vi* **1** to reign. **2** *fig (prevalecer)* to reign, prevail: *reina el desconcierto* disorder reigns.

reincidente *adj* **1** relapsing. **2** JUR reoffending, recidivist.

▶ *nm o nf* JUR reoffender, recidivist.

reincidir *vi* **1** to relapse (en, into), fall back (en, into). **2** JUR to reoffend.

reincorporar *vt* to reincorporate.

▶ *vpr* **reincorporarse** to rejoin (a, -): *se reincorporará al trabajo el lunes* she will go back to work on Monday.

reiniciar *vt* to restart.

reino *nm* kingdom, reign.

reinserción *nf* reintegration, rehabilitation: *la reinserción social* social rehabilitation.

reinsertar *vt* to reintegrate.

▶ *vpr* **reinsertarse** to reintegrate.

reintegrar *vt* **1** *(reincorporar)* to reinstate, restore. **2** *(pagar)* to refund, reimburse.

▶ *vpr* **reintegrarse** *(volver a ejercer)* to return (a, to): *se reintegró a su puesto* he returned to his job.

reintegro *nm* **1** FIN reimbursement, repayment, refund. **2** *(de lotería)* refund of the price of the ticket.

reír *vt* to laugh at: *reír las gracias* to laugh at jokes.

▶ *vi* to laugh.

▶ *vpr* **reírse** to laugh (de, at): *¿de qué te ríes?* what are you laughing at?

reiterar *vt* to reiterate, repeat.

reiterativo,-a *adj* repetitive.

reivindicación *nf* claim, demand.

reivindicar *vt* to claim, demand.

reivindicativo,-a *adj* protest.

reja *nf (de ventana)* grill, grille, bar.

rejilla *nf* **1** *(celosía)* grill, grille. **2** *(de chimenea)* grate. **3** *(de silla)* wickerwork. **4** *(de horno)* grid iron. **5** *(de ventilador)* grill. **6** *(para equipaje)* luggage rack.

rejuvenecer *vt* to rejuvenate.
▶ *vpr* **rejuvenecerse** to become rejuvenated.

relación *nf* **1** *(correspondencia)* relation, relationship. **2** *(conexión)* link, connection. **3** *(lista)* list, record. **4** *(relato)* account, telling. **5** *(en matemática)* ratio.
▶ *nf pl* **relaciones** *(conocidos)* acquaintances; *(contactos)* contacts, connections. LOC **con relación a / en relación a** with regard to, regarding.

relacionar *vt* **1** *(poner en relación)* to relate, connect, associate. **2** *(relatar)* to tell, list.
▶ *vpr* **relacionarse 1** *(estar conectado)* to be related (con, to), be connected (con, with). **2** *(alternar)* to get acquainted (con, with), mix (con, with), meet (con, -).

relajante *adj* relaxing.

relajar *vt* *(gen)* to relax.
▶ *vpr* **relajarse** *(descansar)* to relax.

relamer *vt* to lick.
▶ *vpr* **relamerse** to lick one's lips repeatedly.

relamido,-a *adj* *(pulcro)* prim and proper.

relámpago *nm* flash of lightning.

relampaguear *vi* [se usa sólo en tercera persona; no lleva sujeto] to flash.

relatar *vt* **1** *(una historia)* to narrate, tell. **2** *(un suceso)* to report, tell.

relativizar *vt* to lessen the importance of, play down.

relativo,-a *adj* relative.

relato *nm* **1** *(narración)* story, tale. **2** *(informe)* report, account.

relegar *vt* to relegate (a, to).

relente *nm* dew.

relevante *adj* **1** *(significativo)* relevant. **2** *(importante)* excellent, outstanding.

relevar *vt* **1** *(sustituir)* to relieve, take over from. **2** *(eximir)* to exempt (de, from). **3** *(destituir)* to dismiss, relieve.

relevo *nm* **1** MIL relief, change of the guard. **2** DEP relay.

relieve *nm* **1** relief. **2** *fig (renombre)* renown, fame. LOC **en relieve** in relief. ∎ **poner de relieve** *fig* to emphasize, highlight, underline.

religión *nf* religion.

religioso,-a *adj* religious.
▶ *nm & nf (hombre)* monk; *(mujer)* nun.

relinchar *vi* to neigh, whinny.

reliquia *nf* relic.

rellano *nm* landing.

rellenar *vt* **1** *(volver a llenar)* to refill, fill again. **2** *(cuestionario)* to fill in, fill out. **3** CULIN *(ave)* to stuff; *(pastel)* to fill.

relleno,-a *adj* **1** *(totalmente lleno)* stuffed. **2** CULIN stuffed; *(pasteles)* filled.
▶ *nm* **relleno** CULIN *(aves)* stuffing; *(pasteles)* filling.

reloj *nm* clock; *(de pulsera)* watch. LOC **contra reloj** against the clock. COMP **reloj de arena** hourglass. ∎ **reloj de pulsera** wristwatch.

relojería *nf* **1** *(arte)* watchmaking. **2** *(tienda)* watchmaker's, jeweller's.

relojero,-a *nm & nf* watchmaker.

reluciente *adj* shining, gleaming.

relucir *vi* *(brillar)* to shine, gleam. LOC **sacar a relucir** ALGO to bring up STH.

relumbrar *vi* to shine, dazzle, gleam.

remachar *vt* *(clavo, etc)* to clinch; *(metal)* to rivet.

remangar *vt* *(mangas, pantalones)* to roll up; *(faldas, vestidos)* to pull up, hitch up.
▶ *vpr* **remangarse** *fig* to decide quickly, make a snap decision.

remanso *nm* **1** *(estanque)* pool. **2** *(lugar tranquilo)* quiet place.

remar *vi* to row.

remarcar *vt* to stress, underline.

rematado,-a *adj* **1** absolute, utter, out-and-out. **2** convicted.

rematar *vt* **1** *(acabar)* to finish off, round off. **2** *(precios)* to knock down. **3** DEP to shoot.
▶ *vi* DEP to take a shot at goal, shoot.

remate *nm* **1** *(final)* end, finish. **2** DEP shot. LOC **de remate** *fam* utter, out-and-out, total.

R

remediar *vt* **1** *(poner remedio)* to remedy. **2** *(reparar)* to repair, make good. **3** *(resolver)* to solve.

remedio *nm* **1** *(cura)* remedy, cure. **2** *fig (solución)* solution. LOC **como último remedio** as a last resort. ‖ **no tener más remedio que** to have no choice but to.

rememorar *vt* to remember, recall.

remendar *vt* COST to mend; *(ropas)* to patch; *(calcetines)* to darn.

remero,-a *nm & nf* DEP rower; *(hombre)* oarsman; *(mujer)* oarswoman.

remesa *nf* **1** *(de dinero)* remittance. **2** *(de mercancías)* consignment, shipment.

remeter *vt* *(meter adentro)* to tuck in.

remiendo *nm* mend, darn.

remilgado,-a *adj* **1** *(afectado)* affected. **2** *(con la comida)* fussy, finicky.

remite *nm* sender's name and address.

remitente *nm o nf* sender.

remitir *vt* **1** *(enviar)* to remit, send. **2** *(referir)* to refer.
▶ *vi (ceder)* to subside: *la fiebre ha remitido* the fever has subsided.
▶ *vpr* **remitirse** *(atenerse)* to refer (a, to): *se remitió a su propio acuerdo* he referred to his own agreement.

remo *nm* **1** *(pala)* oar, paddle. **2** DEP rowing.

remodelar *vt* *(modificar)* to reshape.

remojar *vt* *(empapar)* to soak (en, in).

remojo *nm* soaking. LOC **poner en remojo** to soak, leave to soak.

remolacha *nf* beetroot. COMP **remolacha azucarera** sugar beet.

remolcador *nm* **1** MAR tug, tugboat. **2** AUTO breakdown truck.

remolcar *vt* to tow.

remolino *nm* **1** *(de polvo)* whirl, cloud; *(de agua)* whirlpool, eddy; *(de aire)* whirlwind. **2** *(de pelo)* tuft.

remolón,-ona *adj* lazy, slack.

remolonear *vi* to shirk, slack.

remolque *nm* **1** *(acción)* towing. **2** *(vehículo)* trailer.

remontar *vt* **1** *(elevar)* to raise. **2** *(subir)* to go up. **3** *(río)* to sail up; *(vuelo)* to soar.

▶ *vpr* **remontarse 1** *(al volar)* to soar. **2** *(datar)* to go back (a, to).

remorder *vt* *fig (desasosegar)* to trouble, worry.

remordimiento *nm* remorse.

remoto,-a *adj* remote, far-off.

remover *vt* **1** *(trasladar)* to move. **2** *(tierra)* to turn over, dig up. **3** *(líquido)* to stir. **4** *(comida)* to stir; *(ensalada)* to toss. **5** *fig (agitar)* to get moving, stir up.
▶ *vpr* **removerse** to stir, shift.

remunerar *vt* to remunerate, reward.

renacimiento *nm* **1** *(vuelta a nacer)* rebirth. **2** *fig* revival, renaissance. **3** **el Renacimiento** HIST the Renaissance.

renacuajo *nm* **1** ZOOL tadpole. **2** *fam (niño)* shrimp.

rencor *nm* **1** *(odio)* rancour (US rancor). **2** *(resentimiento)* resentment.

rencoroso,-a *adj* **1** *(hostil)* rancorous. **2** *(resentido)* resentful.

rendido,-a *adj* **1** *(sumiso)* humble, submissive. **2** *(muy cansado)* worn out, exhausted.

rendija *nf* crack, split.

rendimiento *nm* **1** *(producción - de terreno)* yield; *(- de máquina)* output; *(- de persona)* progress, performance; *(- de inversión)* yield, return. **2** *(trabajo - de motor, máquina)* performance.

rendir *vt* **1** *(vencer)* to defeat, conquer. **2** *(cansar)* to exhaust, wear out. **3** *(producir)* to yield, produce; *(progresar)* to progress.
▶ *vi (dar fruto)* to pay.
▶ *vpr* **rendirse 1** *(entregarse al enemigo)* to surrender, give in. **2** *(darse por vencido)* to give up: *¡me rindo!* I give up!

renegar *vt* *(negar)* to deny vigorously.
▶ *vi* **1** *(gen)* to renounce (de, -). **2** *(protestar)* to grumble, complain.

renglón *nm* *(línea)* line.

reno *nm* reindeer.

renombre *nm* renown, fame.

renovación *nf* **1** *(de contrato, etc)* renewal. **2** *(de casa)* renovation.

renovar *vt* **1** *(gen)* to renew. **2** *(casa)* to renovate; *(de decoración)* to redecorate.

renta *nf* **1** *(ingresos)* income. **2** *(declaración de renta)* tax return. **3** *(beneficio)* interest, return. **4** *(alquiler)* rent. COMP **renta per cápita** per capita income.

rentable *adj* profitable.

rentar *vt* to produce, yield.

renuncia *nf* **1** renunciation. **2** *(dimisión)* resignation.

renunciar *vi* **1** *(abandonar)* to give up (a, -), abandon (a, -). **2** *(dimitir)* to resign. **3** to renounce (a, -).

reñido,-a *adj* **1** *(enemistado)* on bad terms, at odds. **2** *(de rivalidad)* bitter, tough, hard-fought.

reñir *vi* **1** *(discutir)* to quarrel, argue. **2** *(desavenirse)* to fall out.
▶ *vt (reprender)* to scold, tell off.

reojo LOC **de reojo** out of the corner of one's eye.

repantigarse *vpr fam* to lounge, loll.

reparación *nf* **1** *(arreglo)* repair. **2** *fig (desagravio)* reparation, redress *pl*.

reparar *vt* **1** *(arreglar)* to repair, mend, fix. **2** *(remediar - daño)* to make good; *(- perjuicio, insulto)* to make up for.

reparo *nm* objection. LOC **no tener reparos en** not to hesitate to.

repartición *nf* distribution.

repartidor,-ra *nm & nf (hombre)* delivery man; *(mujer)* delivery woman; *(chico)* delivery boy; *(chica)* delivery girl.

repartir *vt* **1** *(dividir)* to distribute, divide, share out. **2** *(entregar)* to give out, hand out; *(correo, leche)* to deliver; *(premios)* to give out. **3** *(comida)* to hand out. **4** *(distribuir)* to spread out.

reparto *nm* **1** *(división)* sharing out, division; *(distribución)* distribution. **2** *(de un terreno)* parcelling out; *(de un país)* partition. **3** *(entrega)* handing out; *(de mercancías)* delivery. **4** *(de obra, película)* cast.

repasar *vt (volver a examinar)* to revise, go over.

repaso *nm* check; *(lección)* review. COMP **curso de repaso** refresher course.

repatriar *vt* to repatriate.

repecho *nm* short steep slope.

repelente *adj* repellent, repulsive.

repeler *vt* **1** *(rechazar)* to repel, repulse. **2** *(repugnar)* to disgust, repel.

repente *nm* **1** *fam (movimiento)* sudden movement. **2** *fam (ataque)* fit. LOC **de repente** suddenly, all of a sudden.

repentino,-a *adj* sudden.

repercusión *nf* repercussion.

repercutir *vi fig (trascender)* to have repercussions (en, on), affect.

repertorio *nm* **1** *(resumen)* list, index. **2** TEAT repertoire, repertory.

repesca *nf fam* second chance; *(examen)* resit. LOC **hacer un examen de repesca** to resit an exam.

repetición *nf (gen)* repetition.

repetido,-a *adj* repeated.

repetidor,-ra *nm & nf* EDUC repeat student.
▶ *nm* **repetidor** TÉC relay, booster station.

repetir *vt* **1** *(gen)* to repeat: *se lo repetí dos veces* I told him twice. **2** *(volver a hacer)* to do again, do over again.
▶ *vi* **1** *(volver a servirse)* to have a second helping. **2** EDUC to repeat a year.
▶ *vpr* **repetirse 1** *(persona)* to repeat OS. **2** *(hecho)* to recur.

repetitivo,-a *adj* repetitive.

repicar *vt (campanas)* to peal, ring out.

repique *nm* peal, ringing.

repisa *nf* ledge, shelf.

replantear *vt (asunto, problema)* to reconsider, rethink.

replegarse *vpr* to withdraw, retreat.

repleto,-a *adj* jam-packed (de, with).

réplica *nf* **1** *(respuesta)* answer, reply.

replicar *vt (contestar)* to answer, reply.
▶ *vi* to argue, answer back.

repliegue *nm (pliegue)* fold, crease.

repoblar *vt* to repopulate; *(bosque)* to reafforest, reforest.

repollo *nm* cabbage.

reponer *vt* **1** *(reemplazar)* to replace. **2** *(en el cine)* to rerun.
▶ *vpr* **reponerse** *(salud, susto)* to recover.

reportaje *nm* **1** *(prensa, radio)* report. **2** *(noticias)* article, news item.

reportero,-a *nm & nf* reporter.

R

reposar *vi* **1** *(descansar)* to rest, take a rest. **2** *(yacer)* to rest, lie, be buried. **3** *(un líquido)* to settle. LOC **dejar reposar** CULIN to leave to stand.

reposo *nm* **1** *(descanso)* rest. **2** *(tranquilidad)* peace.

repostar *vt* **1** *(provisiones)* to stock up with. **2** *(coche)* to fill up.

repostería *nf* *(pastas)* cakes *pl*; *(chocolate, bombones)* confectionery.

reprender *vt* to reprimand, scold.

represa *nf* dam.

represalia *nf* reprisal, retaliation.

representación *nf* **1** *(gen)* representation. **2** performance. LOC **en representación de** as a representative of.

representante *adj* representative.
▶ *nm o nf* representative.

representar *vt* **1** *(gen)* to represent. **2** *(símbolo)* to represent, stand for: *una paloma representa la paz* a dove stands for peace. **3** TEAT *(obra)* to perform; *(papel)* to play (the part of).

representativo,-a *adj* representative.

represión *nf* repression.

represivo,-a *adj* repressive.

reprimenda *nf* reprimand.

reprimido,-a *adj* repressed.
▶ *nm & nf* repressed person.

reprimir *vt* *(gen)* to repress, suppress.
▶ *vpr* **reprimirse** to control OS.

reprochar *vt* to reproach, censure.

reproche *nm* reproach, criticism.

reproducción *nf* reproduction.

reproducir *vt* to reproduce, repeat.
▶ *vpr* **reproducirse** **1** *(gen)* to reproduce. **2** *(volver a ocurrir)* to recur.

reproductor,-ra *adj* **1** *(gen)* reproducing. **2** ANAT reproductive.

reptar *vi* *(arrastrarse)* to crawl, slither.

reptil *nm* reptile.

república *nf* republic.

republicano,-a *adj* republican.
▶ *nm & nf* republican.

repudiar *vt* to repudiate.

repuesto,-a *nm* **1** *(prevención)* store, supply, stock. **2** *(recambio)* spare, spare part. LOC **de repuesto** spare, in reserve.

repugnante *adj* repugnant, disgusting.

repugnar *vt* **1** *(negar)* to deny. **2** *(contradecir)* to contradict.

repujado,-a *adj* embossed, repoussé.

repujar *vt* to emboss.

repulsión *nf* repulsion, repugnance.

repulsivo,-a *adj* repulsive, revolting.

repuntar *vi* **1** *(la marea)* to turn. **2** *(economía)* to recover, pick up.

reputación *nf* reputation.

requemado,-a *adj* scorched, burnt.

requemar *vt* *(gen)* to scorch, burn.

requerimiento *nm* **1** *(súplica)* request. **2** JUR *(aviso)* summons *pl*; *(intimación)* injunction.

requerir *vt* **1** *(necesitar)* to require, need: *esto requiere gran paciencia* this requires a lot of patience. **2** *(decir con autoridad)* to demand, call for. **3** *(solicitar)* to request.

requesón *nm* cottage cheese.

réquiem *nm* requiem.

requisar *vt* **1** MIL to requisition. **2** *fam (apropiarse)* to grab, swipe.

requisito *nm* requisite, requirement.

res *nf* *(gen)* beast, animal; *(cabeza de ganado)* head.

resaca *nf* **1** *(de las olas)* undertow, undercurrent. **2** *(de borrachera)* hangover.

resaltar *vi* fig *(distinguirse)* to stand out (de, from).
▶ *vt* to highlight, stress, emphasize.

resbaladizo,-a *adj* slippery.

resbalar *vi* **1** *(deslizarse)* to slide. **2** *(sin querer - persona)* to slip.

resbalón *nm* slip.

rescatar *vt* **1** *(rehén, náufrago, persona atrapada, etc)* to rescue; *(cadáver)* to recover; *(ciudad)* to recapture. **2** *(recuperar)* to recover.

rescate *nm* **1** *(salvamento)* rescue; *(de ciudad)* recapture. **2** *(dinero)* ransom. **3** *(recuperación)* recovery, recapture.

resecar *vt* to dry up.
▶ *vpr* **resecarse** to dry up.

reseco,-a *adj (seco)* very dry, parched.
resentido,-a *adj* resentful. [LOC] estar
resentido,-a con ALGN to bear resentment towards SB.
resentimiento *nm* resentment.
reseña *nf* **1** *(crítica)* review; *(en prensa)*
write-up. **2** *(descripción)* description.
reseñar *vt* **1** *(crítica)* to review. **2** *(describir)* to describe.
reserva *nf* **1** *(de plazas, entradas)* booking, reservation. **2** *(provisión)* reserve;
(existencias) stock. **3** *(cautela)* reservation. **4** *(discreción)* discretion, reserve.
5 *(vino)* vintage. **6** *(de animales)* reserve;
(de personas) reservation. **7** MIL reserve, reserves *pl*.
▶ *nf pl* **reservas** COM reserves, stock
sing.
reservado,-a *adj* **1** *(persona)* reserved.
2 *(asunto)* confidential.
▶ *nm* **reservado** *(en local)* private room;
(en tren) reserved compartment.
reservar *vt* **1** *(plazas, etc)* to book, reserve. **2** *(guardar)* to keep, save. **3**
(ocultar) to withhold, keep to OS.
▶ *vpr* **reservarse 1** *(conservarse)* to save
OS (para, for). **2** to withhold, keep to
OS: *se reservó su opinión* she kept her
opinion to herself.
resfriado,-a *adj* with a cold.
▶ *nm* **resfriado** cold.
resfriar *vt (enfriar)* to cool.
▶ *vpr* **resfriarse** MED to catch a cold.
resguardar *vt* **1** *(proteger)* to protect
(de, from), shelter (de, from). **2** *(salvaguardar)* to safeguard (de, against).
▶ *vpr* **resguardarse** *(protegerse)* to protect OS.
resguardo *nm* **1** *(protección)* protection,
shelter. **2** *(garantía)* safeguard, guarantee. **3** *(recibo)* receipt, ticket.
residencia *nf (gen)* residence. [COMP] residencia de ancianos old people's
home.
residir *vi* **1** to reside (en, in), live (en,
in). **2** *fig* to lie (en, in).
residuo *nm* residue.
▶ *nm pl* **residuos** waste *sing*, refuse *sing*.
resignación *nf* resignation.

resignado,-a *adj* resigned.
resignar *vt* to resign, relinquish.
▶ *vpr* **resignarse** to resign OS (a, to).
resina *nf* resin.
resistencia *nf* **1** *(gen)* resistance. **2**
(aguante) endurance, stamina. **3** *(oposición)* resistance, opposition. **4** ELEC
resistance. **5** *(de materiales)* strength.
resistente *adj* **1** *(que resiste)* resistant (a,
to). **2** *(fuerte)* tough, strong.
resistir *vi* **1** *(aguantar - algo)* to hold
(out); *(- alguien)* to hold out, take (it),
have endurance. **2** *(durar)* to endure,
last. **3** *(ejército)* to hold out, resist.
▶ *vt* **1** *(soportar)* to stand, tolerate. **2**
(peso, etc) to bear, withstand, take.
3 *(tentación, etc)* to resist.
▶ *vpr* **resistirse 1** *(rechazar)* to resist. **2**
fam (costar) to be difficult, be hard: *la
física se le resiste* he's struggling with
physics. **3** *(negarse)* to refuse: *me resisto
a creerlo* I find it hard to believe.
resolución *nf* **1** *(decisión)* resolution,
decision; *(determinación)* determination, resolve. **2** *(solución)* solution; *(de
un conflicto)* settlement; *(en técnica)* resolution.
resolver *vt* **1** *(solucionar - gen)* to resolve,
solve; *(- asunto, conflicto)* to resolve, settle; *(- dificultad)* to overcome. **2** *(decidir)*
to resolve, decide (-, to). **3** *(deshacer)* to
resolve. **4** QUÍM to dissolve.
▶ *vpr* **resolverse 1** *(solucionarse)* to be
solved; *(resultar)* to work out. **2** *(reducirse)* to end up (en, in), turn out.
resonancia *nf* **1** resonance. **2** *(eco)*
echo. **3** *fig (importancia)* importance;
(consecuencias) repercussions *pl*.
resorte *nm* **1** spring. **2** *fig* means *pl*.
respaldar *vt* to support, back (up).
▶ *vpr* **respaldarse 1** to lean back (en,
on). **2** *(apoyarse)* to lean (en, on).
respaldo *nm* **1** back. **2** *fig* support,
backing.
respectivamente *adv* respectively.
respectivo,-a *adj* respective. [LOC] en lo
respectivo a with regard to, regarding.
respetar *vt* to respect.

R

respeto *nm* **1** (*gen*) respect. **2** *fam (miedo)* fear.
▸ *nm pl* **respetos** respects. [COMP] **falta de respeto** lack of respect.

respetuoso,-a *adj* respectful.

respiración *nf* **1** (*acción*) breathing, respiration. **2** (*aliento*) breath more easily, breathe.

respirar *vi* **1** to breathe. **2** (*estar vivo*) to be breathing. **3** *fig (relajarse)* to breathe more easily, breathe a sigh of relief: *al oír al doctor, respiramos* when we heard what the doctor had to say we breathed a sigh of relief. [LOC] **sin respirar** **1** (*sin descanso*) nonstop. **2** (*con atención*) attentively.
▸ *vt (absorber)* to breathe, breathe in, inhale.

respiratorio,-a *adj* respiratory.

respiro *nm* **1** (*resuello*) breathing. **2** *fig (descanso)* breather, break. **3** *fig (alivio)* relief, respite.

resplandor *nm* (*de luz*) brightness, brilliance; (*de metales, cristales*) gleam, glitter; (*del fuego*) glow, blaze.

responder *vt (contestar)* to answer.
▸ *vi* **1** (*contestar*) to answer, reply. **2** (*replicar*) to answer back. **3** (*corresponder*) to answer, respond to: *tengo que responder a su amabilidad* I have to respond to his kindness. **4** (*tener el efecto deseado*) to respond: *el motor respondió bien* the engine responded well. **5** (*ser responsable*) to answer (de, for), accept responsibility (de, for).

responsabilidad *nf* responsibility.

responsable *adj* responsible.
▸ *nm o nf* **1** (*encargado*) person in charge. **2** (*de un crimen*) perpetrator, culprit, person responsible. [LOC] **hacerse responsable de** ALGO to assume responsibility for STH.

respuesta *nf* **1** (*gen*) answer, reply. **2** (*reacción*) response. [LOC] **en respuesta a** in response to.

resquebrajar *vt* to crack.
▸ *vpr* **resquebrajarse** to crack.

resta *nf* subtraction.

restablecer *vt* (*gen*) to reestablish; (*orden, monarquía*) to restore.

▸ *vpr* **restablecerse** **1** (*gen*) to be reestablished; (*orden, etc*) to be restored. **2** MED to recover, get better.

restablecimiento *nm* **1** (*gen*) reestablishment; (*orden, etc*) restoration. **2** MED recovery.

restante *adj* remaining.
▸ *nm* **lo restante** the rest, the remainder, what is left over.

restar *vt* **1** MAT to subtract, take (away). **2** *fig (quitar)* to reduce, deduct. **3** DEP to return.
▸ *vi (quedar)* to be left, remain. [LOC] **restar importancia a** ALGO to play STH down, play down the importance of STH.

restauración *nf* (*restablecimiento*) restoration.

restaurante *nm* restaurant.

restaurar *vt (obra, etc)* to restore.

resto *nm* **1** remainder, rest. **2** MAT remainder.
▸ *nm pl* **restos** **1** (*gen*) remains; (*ruinas*) ruins. **2** (*de comida*) leftovers.

restricción *nf* restriction.

restringir *vt* **1** (*limitar*) to restrict, limit. **2** (*astringir*) to contract.

resucitar *vt* **1** to resuscitate. **2** *fig* to revive.
▸ *vi* to resuscitate.

resuelto,-a *adj (decidido)* resolute, determined.

resultado *nm* result.

resultar *vi* **1** (*gen*) to result, be the result of. **2** (*ser*) to be: *resultó vencedor* he won. **3** (*acabar siendo*) to turn out to be: *resultó ser muy agradable* he turned out to be very nice. **4** (*salir*) to come out, turn out, work out: *todo resultó como esperábamos* it all worked out as we expected. **5** (*ocurrir*) to turn out: *resulta que está enfermo y no puede venir* it turns out that he's ill and can't come. **6** (*ser conveniente*) to be advisable. **7** (*tener éxito*) to be a success, come off: *el negocio resultó* the business was a success. [LOC] **resulta que** it turns out that.

resumen *nm* summary.

resumir *vt* **1** (*reducir*) to summarize. **2** (*concluir*) to sum up: *resumiendo, es una* *novela excelente* in short, it's an excellent novel.

▸ *vpr* **resumirse 1** to be summarized, be summed up. **2** *(venir a ser)* to be reduced (en, to), boil down (en, to).

resurgir *vi* **1** *(volver a aparecer)* to reappear. **2** *(revivir)* to revive.

retablo *nm* altarpiece, reredos.

retaguarda *nf* rearguard. LOC **ir a la retaguarda** to bring up the rear.

retal *nm* *(de tela)* offcut, remnant.

retama *nf* broom.

retar *vt* **1** *(desafiar)* to challenge. **2** *fam* *(reprender)* to scold.

retazo *nm* remnant, fragment.

retención *nf* **1** *(gen)* retention. **2** FIN withholding, deduction. **3** *(de tráfico)* traffic jam, (traffic) hold-up.

retener *vt* **1** *(contener)* to restrain, hold back. **2** *(no dejar marchar)* to keep, keep back: *no quiero retenerte* I don't want to keep you. **3** *(no devolver)* to keep. **4** *(en la memoria)* to retain, remember. **5** *(detener)* to detain; *(arrestar)* to arrest. **6** FIN to deduct, withhold. **7** *(absorber)* to retain, hold: *el algodón retiene el agua* cotton holds water.

▸ *vpr* **retenerse** to restrain os, hold os back.

retina *nf* retina.

retirada *nf* MIL retreat, withdrawal.

retirado,-a *adj* **1** *(apartado)* remote. **2** *(tranquilo)* secluded, quiet. **3** *(jubilado)* retired.

▸ *nm & nf* retired person, US retiree.

retirar *vt* **1** *(apartar - gen)* to take away, remove; *(- un mueble)* to move away. **2** *(un carnet)* to take away. **3** *(algo dicho)* to take back. **4** *(dinero, ley, moneda)* to withdraw. **5** *(jubilar)* to retire.

▸ *vpr* **retirarse 1** MIL to retreat, withdraw. **2** *(apartarse del mundo)* to go into seclusion. **3** *(apartarse)* to withdraw, draw back, move back: *retírate, no veo* move back, I can't see. **4** *(alejarse)* to move away: *retírate de la ventana* move away from the window. **5** *(irse a descansar)* to retire: *se retiró a su habitación* she retired to her bedroom. **7** *(jubilarse)* to

retire. LOC **no se retire** *(al teléfono)* hold on, don't hang up.

retiro *nm* **1** *(jubilación)* retirement. **2** *(pensión)* pension.

reto *nm* challenge.

retocar *vt* *(dibujo, fotografía)* to touch up, retouch.

retoque *nm* finishing touch.

retorcer *vt* **1** *(gen)* to twist. **2** *(ropa)* to wring (out).

▸ *vpr* **retorcerse 1** *(gen)* to become twisted, twist. **2** *(doblarse)* to bend. LOC **retorcerse de risa** *fig* to double up with laughter.

retorcido,-a *adj fig* twisted: *mente retorcida* warped mind.

retornable *adj* returnable. LOC «**Envase no retornable**» "Non-returnable".

retorno *nm* **1** return. **2** *(recompensa)* reward.

retortijón *nm* *(de tripas)* stomach cramp.

retozar *vi* to frolic, gambol.

retraído,-a *adj* **1** *(tímido)* shy, reserved. **2** *(poco comunicativo)* unsociable, withdrawn.

retraimiento *nm* *(timidez)* shyness, reserve, retiring nature.

retransmisión *nf* broadcast, transmission.

retransmitir *vt* RAD TV to broadcast. LOC **retransmitir** ALGO **en directo** to broadcast STH live.

retrasado,-a *adj* **1** *(en conocimientos, trabajo)* behind. **2** *(pagos)* late. **3** *(reloj)* slow. **4** *(tren, avión, etc)* delayed. **5** *(país)* backward, underdeveloped.

▸ *nm & nf* mentally retarded person.

retrasar *vt* **1** *(atrasar)* to delay, put off, postpone. **2** *(reloj)* to put back. **3** DEP to pass back.

▸ *vpr* **retrasarse 1** *(atrasarse)* to be late, arrive late, be delayed. **2** *(reloj)* to be slow. **3** *(trabajo, conocimientos, pagos)* to fall behind.

retraso *nm* **1** *(demora)* delay. **2** *(subdesarrollo)* backwardness, underdevelopment.

R

retratar *vt* **1** *(pintura)* to portray, paint a portrait of. **2** *(foto)* to photograph, take a photograph of. **3** *fig* to describe, portray, depict.
▶ *vpr* **retratarse** *(darse a conocer)* to be described, be portrayed.

retrato *nm* **1** *(pintura)* portrait. **2** *(foto)* photograph. **3** *fig (descripción)* description, depiction, portrayal. ⎣LOC⎦ **ser el vivo retrato de** ALGN to be the spitting image of SB.

retrete *nm* toilet, lavatory.

retribución *nf* **1** *(pago)* pay, payment. **2** *(recompensa)* recompense, reward.

retribuir *vt* **1** *(pagar)* to pay. **2** *(recompensar)* to remunerate, reward.

retroceder *vi* **1** *(recular)* to go back, move back. **2** *(bajar de nivel)* to go down.

retroceso *nm* **1** *(movimiento)* backward movement. **2** *(económico)* recession.

retrógrado,-a *adj* **1** *(que retrocede)* retrograde. **2** *fig (reaccionario)* reactionary.
▶ *nm & nf (reaccionario)* reactionary.

retrospectivo,-a *adj* retrospective.

retumbar *vi* **1** *(resonar)* to resound, echo. **2** *(tronar)* to thunder, boom.

reuma *nm* rheumatism.

reúma *nm* rheumatism.

reumático,-a *adj* rheumatic.
▶ *nm & nf* rheumatic.

reumatismo *nm* rheumatism.

reunificar *vt* to reunify.

reunión *nf (gen)* meeting, gathering.

reunir *vt* **1** *(congregar)* get together. **2** *(juntar algo)* to put together: *reunimos todos nuestros libros* we put all our books together. **3** *(recoger)* to gather (together); *(dinero)* to raise. **4** *(coleccionar)* to collect. **5** *(tener)* to have, possess. **6** *(requisitos)* to satisfy, meet, fulfil (US fulfill).
▶ *vpr* **reunirse** to meet (con, -), get together, have a meeting with.

reutilizar *vt* to reuse.

reválida *nf* final examination.

revalidar *vt* to confirm, ratify, validate.

revalorización *nf (de moneda)* revaluation; *(de precio)* appreciation, increase in value.

revalorizar *vt (moneda)* to revalue; *(precio)* to increase the value of.
▶ *vpr* **revalorizarse** *(moneda)* to revalue; *(precio)* to appreciate, go up in value.

revancha *nf* **1** revenge. **2** *(en naipes)* return game. **3** DEP return match.

revelación *nf* revelation.

revelado *nm* developing.

revelador,-ra *adj* revealing.
▶ *nm* **revelador** developer.

revelar *vt* **1** to reveal, disclose. **2** *(fotos)* to develop.

revender *vt* **1** *(gen)* to resell. **2** *(al por menor)* to retail. **3** *(entradas)* to tout.

reventa *nf* **1** *(gen)* resale. **2** *(al por menor)* retail. **3** *(de entradas)* touting.

reventar *vt* **1** *(gen)* to burst. **2** *(neumático)* to puncture, burst. **3** *(romper)* to break, smash. **4** *(estropear)* to ruin, spoil. **5** *fig (agotar)* to exhaust, tire out.
▶ *vi* **1** *fam (fastidiar)* to annoy: *me revientan sus preguntas* her questions get on my nerves. **2** *(estallar)* to burst: *la cañería reventó* the pipe burst.
▶ *vpr* **reventarse 1** *(estallar)* to burst. **2** *fam (cansarse)* to tire OS out.

reventón,-ona *nm* **1** *(de cañería)* burst. **2** *(de neumático)* blowout.

reverendo,-a *adj* **1** reverend. **2** *fam (enorme)* enormous, great.
▶ *nm & nf* reverend.

reversible *adj* reversible.

reverso *nm* reverse, back.

revés *nm* **1** *(reverso)* back, reverse, wrong side; *(de tela)* wrong side. **2** *(bofetada)* slap; *(golpe)* backhander. **3** *(en tenis)* backhand (stroke). **4** *fig (contrariedad)* misfortune, setback, reverse. ⎣LOC⎦ **al revés** *(al contrario)* the other way round.

revestimiento *nm* covering, coating.

revestir *vt* **1** *(recubrir)* to cover (de, with), coat (de, with), line (de, with). **3** *fig (presentar)* to take on: *la* *ceremonia revistió gran solemnidad* the ceremony took on great solemnity.

▶ *vpr* **revestirse** to arm OS: *revestirse de paciencia* to arm OS with patience.

revisar *vt* **1** *(gen)* to revise, go through, check. **2** *(examen, etc)* to check, look over. **3** *(cuentas)* to check, audit.

revisión *nf* **1** *(gen)* revision, checking. **2** *(de billetes)* inspection. **3** *(de coche)* service, overhaul. COMP **revisión médica** checkup.

revisor,-ra *nm & nf* ticket inspector.

revista *nf* **1** *(publicación)* magazine, review, journal. **2** *(inspección)* inspection. **3** MIL review. **4** TEAT revue: *chica de revista* chorus girl.

revistero *nm* magazine rack.

revitalizar *vt* to revitalize.

revivir *vi* to revive.

▶ *vt* to revive, bring back to life.

revocar *vt* *(ley)* to revoke, repeal; *(orden)* to cancel, rescind.

revolcar *vt* *(derribar al suelo)* to knock down, knock over.

▶ *vpr* **revolcarse** *(echarse)* to roll about.

revolotear *vi* to fly about, flutter about, hover.

revoloteo *nm* fluttering, hovering.

revoltijo *nm* *(mezcla)* mess, clutter, jumble.

revoltoso,-a *adj* **1** *(rebelde)* rebellious.

▶ *nm & nf* rebel, troublemaker.

revolución *nf* revolution.

revolucionario,-a *adj* revolutionary.

▶ *nm & nf* revolutionary.

revolver *vt* **1** *(agitar)* to stir. **2** *(mezclar)* to mix. **3** *(ensalada)* to toss. **4** *(habitación, casa, etc)* to turn upside down. **5** *(papeles)* to rummage through; *(bolso, bolsillo, etc)* to rummage in. **6** *(producir náuseas)* to upset, turn: *le revolvió el estómago* it turned his stomach.

▶ *vpr* **revolverse 1** *(moverse)* to fidget; *(en la cama)* to toss and turn. **2** *(volverse con rapidez)* to turn around, spin round. **3** *(tiempo)* to turn stormy; *(mar)* to become rough.

revólver *nm* revolver.

revoque *nm* *(enlucido)* plastering.

revuelta *nf* *(revolución)* revolt, riot.

revuelto,-a *adj* **1** *(desordenado)* confused, mixed up, in a mess. **2** *(gente)* agitated, restless, up in arms. **3** *(tiempo)* stormy, unsettled; *(mar)* rough. **4** *(época)* turbulent: *tiempos revueltos* turbulent times.

rey *nm* king.

rezar *vi* **1** *(orar)* to pray. **2** *(decir)* to say, read.

ría *nf* *(gen)* estuary, river mouth; *(técnicamente)* ria.

riachuelo *nm* brook, stream.

riada *nf* **1** flood, flooding. **2** *fig* flood.

ribera *nf* **1** *(de río)* bank. **2** *(del mar)* shore, seashore. **3** *(tierra cercana a un río)* riverside, waterfront.

ribete *nm* *(cinta)* border, trimming, edging.

ribetear *vt* to edge, border.

ribonucleico,-a *adj* ribonucleic.

rico,-a *adj* **1** *(acaudalado)* rich, wealthy. **2** *(abundante)* rich: *rico en potasio* rich in potassium. **3** *(sabroso)* tasty, delicious. **4** *(tierra)* rich, fertile. **5** *(excelente)* rich, excellent. **6** *fam (bonito)* lovely, adorable: *tiene un niño muy rico* she's got a lovely boy.

▶ *nm & nf* rich person.

ridiculizar *vt* to ridicule, deride.

ridículo,-a *adj* ridiculous, absurd.

▶ *nm* **ridículo** ridicule. LOC **hacer el ridículo** to make a fool of OS.

riego *nm* irrigation, watering. COMP **riego sanguíneo** blood circulation.

riel *nm* rail.

rienda *nf* **1** rein. **2** *fig (control)* restraint. LOC **llevar las riendas** *fig* to hold the reins, be in control.

riesgo *nm* risk, danger. LOC **a todo riesgo** *(seguro)* fully-comprehensive.

rifa *nf* raffle.

rifar *vt* to raffle (off).

▶ *vpr* **rifarse 1** MAR to split. **2** *(solicitar, desear)* to fight over.

rifle *nm* rifle.

rigidez *nf* **1** *(dureza)* stiffness, rigidity. **2** *fig (rectitud)* strictness, firmness, inflexibility.

R

rígido,-a *adj* **1** *(duro)* rigid, stiff. **2** *fig (severo)* strict, firm, inflexible.

rigor *nm* **1** *(severidad)* rigour (US rigor), strictness, severity. **2** *(dureza)* rigour (US rigor), harshness. **3** *(exactitud)* precision, exactness.

rigurosamente *adv* **1** *(con severidad)* rigorously, severely, strictly. **2** *(con exactitud)* accurately. **3** *(minuciosamente)* meticulously. **4** *(totalmente)* absolutely.

rigurosidad *nf* rigorousness, strictness.

riguroso,-a *adj* **1** *(severo)* rigorous, severe, strict. **2** *(clima)* rigorous, severe, harsh. **3** *(exacto)* exact. **4** *(minucioso)* meticulous.

rima *nf* rhyme.
▶ *nf pl* **rimas** poem *sing*.

rimar *vt* to rhyme.
▶ *vi* to rhyme.

rincón *nm* corner.

rinconera *nf* corner unit.

ring *nm* ring.

rinoceronte *nm* rhinoceros.

riña *nf* **1** *(pelea)* fight. **2** *(discusión)* quarrel.

riñón *nm* **1** kidney.

río *nm* **1** river. **2** *fig* stream, river: *un río de sangre* a river of blood.

riqueza *nf (cualidad)* richness, wealthiness.

risa *nf* **1** laugh. **2** *(risas)* laughter. [LOC] **darle risa a ALGN** to make SB laugh. ‖ **entrar la risa** to begin to laugh: ‖ **ser cosa de risa** to be laughable. [COMP] **ataque de risa** fit of laughter.

risco *nm* crag, cliff.

ristra *nf* string.

risueño,-a *adj* **1** *(sonriente)* smiling. **2** *(animado)* cheerful.

rítmico,-a *adj* rhythmic, rhythmical.

ritmo *nm* **1** rhythm. **2** *fig* pace, speed.

rito *nm* **1** REL rite. **2** *fig (costumbre)* ritual.

ritual *adj* ritual.
▶ *nm* ritual.

rival *adj* rival.
▶ *nm o nf* rival.

rivalidad *nf* rivalry.

rivalizar *vi* to rival.

rivera *nf* brook, stream.

rizado,-a *adj* **1** *(pelo)* curly. **2** MAR choppy.
▶ *nm* **rizado** *(de pelo)* curling.

rizar *vt (pelo)* to curl.
▶ *vpr* **rizarse 1** *(pelo)* to curl, go curly. **2** *(el mar)* to ripple.

rizo *nm* **1** *(de pelo)* curl. **2** *(en el agua)* ripple. **3** *(tejido)* towelling (US toweling), terry towelling. **4** AV loop.

rizoma *nm* rhizome.

robar *vt* **1** *(banco, persona)* to rob; *(objeto)* to steal; *(casa)* to break into, burgle. **2** *(raptar)* to kidnap. **3** *(en naipes)* to draw. **4** *fig (cobrar muy caro)* to rip off. **5** *fig (corazón, alma)* to steal.

robinia *nf* robinia, false acacia.

roble *nm* oak, oak tree.

robledal *nm* oak grove, oak wood.

robo *nm* **1** *(gen)* theft, robbery; *(en casa)* burglary; *(en banco)* robbery. **2** *(en naipes)* draw. **3** *fig (estafa)* robbery.

robot *nm* robot.

robótica *nf* robotics.

robótico,-a *adj* robotic, robot-like.

robotizar *vt* to automate.

robustecer *vt* to strengthen.
▶ *vpr* **robustecerse** to grow stronger, gain strength.

robusto,-a *adj* robust, strong, sturdy.

roca *nf* rock.

roce *nm* **1** *(fricción)* rubbing; *(en piel)* chafing. **2** *(señal - en zapatos)* scuff mark; *(- en piel)* graze; *(- en coche, etc)* mark. **3** *(contacto físico)* light touch, brush. **4** *fam (trato)* contact. **5** *fam (disensión)* friction, brush.

rociar *vt* **1** *(salpicar)* to spray, sprinkle. **2** *fig (esparcir)* to scatter, strew.

rocín *nm (caballo)* nag, hack.

rocío *nm* dew.

rock *nm* rock.

rockero,-a *nm & nf (músico)* rock musician; *(fan)* rock fan.

rococó *adj* rococo.

rocoso,-a *adj* rocky, stony.

rodaballo *nm* turbot.

rodaja *nf* slice. LOC **en rodajas** sliced.

rodaje *nm* **1** CINE filming, shooting. **2** AUTO running-in.

rodamiento *nm* bearing.

rodapié *nm* skirting board, US baseboard.

rodar *vi* **1** *(dar vueltas)* to roll; *(rueda)* to turn. **2** *(caer rodando)* to roll down. **3** *fig (ir de un lado a otro)* to roam. **4** *(vehículos)* to run; *(velocidad)* to do.
▶ *vt* **1** *(hacer que de vueltas)* to roll. **2** CINE to film, shoot. **3** AUTO to run in. **4** *(recorrer)* to travel.

rodear *vt (cercar)* to surround, encircle.
▶ *vpr* **rodearse** to surround OS (de, with).

rodela *nf* round shield.

rodeno,-a *adj* red.

rodeo *nm* **1** *(desviación)* detour. **2** *fig (elusión)* evasiveness.

rodera *nf* tyre (US tire) mark, track.

rodilla *nf* **1** ANAT knee. **2** *(paño)* cloth, floorcloth.

rodillazo *nm* blow with the knee, blow to the knee.

rodillera *nf* **1** DEP knee pad. **2** COST knee patch.

rodillo *nm* **1** roller. **2** CULIN rolling pin.

rododendro *nm* rhododendron.

rodomiel *nm* rose honey.

roedor,-ra *adj* rodent.
▶ *nm* **roedor** rodent.

roer *vt* **1** *(hueso)* to gnaw. **2** *fig (desgastar)* to wear away.

rogar *vt (pedir)* to request, ask; *(implorar)* to beg, implore, plead.

rogativa *nf* rogation.

roído,-a *adj* gnawed, eaten away.

rojear *vi* to redden, turn red.

rojez *nf* redness.

rojizo,-a *adj* reddish.

rojo,-a *adj (color)* red.
▶ *nm & nf* POL *(gen)* red, Communist.
▶ *nm* **rojo** red.

rol *nm (papel)* role.

rollista *nm o nf fam (cuentista)* over-dramatic person.

rollizo,-a *adj* plump, chubby.

rollo *nm* **1** *(gen)* roll. **2** *fam (aburrimiento)* drag, bore, pain: *esta peli es un rollo* this film is a drag. **3** *fam (discurso, explicación, etc)* long drawn-out speech, boring lecture. **4** *fam (amorío)* affair. **5** *fam (asunto)* business.

romance *adj* LING Romance.
▶ *nm* **1** LING *(gen)* Romance language; *(castellano)* Spanish. **2** *(amorío)* romance.

romancero *nm* collection of romances.

románico,-a *adj* **1** *(arquitectura, arte - gen)* Romanesque. **2** *(lengua)* Romance.

romanizar *vt* to Romanize.

romanticismo *nm* romanticism.

romántico,-a *adj* romantic.
▶ *nm & nf* romantic.

rómbico,-a *adj* rhombic.

rombo *nm* **1** rhombus. **2** *(naipes)* diamond.

romboedro *nm* rhombohedron.

romboide *nm* rhomboid.

romería *nf* pilgrimage.

romero *nm* BOT rosemary.

romo,-a *adj (sin punta)* blunt, dull.

rompecabezas *nm inv* **1** *(juego)* (jigsaw) puzzle. **2** *fig (problema)* riddle, puzzle, conundrum.

rompecocos *nm inv* brain-teaser.

rompecorazones *nm o nf inv fam* heart-throb, heartbreaker.

rompehielos *nm inv* icebreaker.

rompeolas *nm inv* breakwater, jetty.

romper *vt* **1** *(gen)* to break; *(papel, tela)* to tear. **2** *(rajar, reventar)* to split. **3** *(gastar)* to wear out. **4** *fig (relaciones)* to break off. **5** *fig (ley)* to break. **6** *fig (cerca, límite)* to break through, break down.
▶ *vi* **1** *fig (acabar - con algo)* to break; *(-con alguien)* to split up, US break up. **2** *(olas, día)* to break. **3** **romper a** + *inf fig (empezar)* to burst out: *romper a reír* to burst out laughing. **4** **romper en** + *sust fig (prorrumpir)* to burst into: *romper en llanto* to burst into tears.
▶ *vpr* **romperse 1** *(gen)* to break: *se me ha roto esta uña* I've broken this nail. **2** *(papel, tela)* to tear, rip. **3** *(rajarse, reven-*

R

tarse) to split. **4** *(desgastarse)* to wear out: *se me han roto los zapatos* my shoes are worn out. **5** *(coche)* to break down.

ron *nm* rum.

roncar *vi* to snore.

roncha *nf (en la piel)* swelling, lump, spot.

ronco,-a *adj* hoarse.

ronda *nf* **1** *(patrulla)* patrol, watch. **2** *(de policía)* beat. **3** *(vuelta)* round. **4** *(de bebidas, cartas)* round. **5** *(negociaciones)* round. LOC **hacer la ronda** to do one's rounds.

rondar *vt* **1** *(vigilar)* to patrol, do the rounds of. **2** *(merodear)* to prowl around, hang about, haunt: *siempre ronda la casa* he's always prowling around the house. **3** *fig (años)* to be about: *ronda los cincuenta* she's about fifty.
► *vi* **1** *(vigilar)* to patrol. **2** *(merodear)* to prowl around, roam around.

ronquera *nf* hoarseness.

ronquido *nm* snore, snoring.

ronronear *vi* to purr.

ronroneo *nm* purring.

roña *nf (suciedad)* filth, dirt.

roñería *nf fam* meanness, stinginess.

roñica *nm o nf fam* scrooge, miser.

roñoso,-a *adj* **1** *(sucio)* filthy, dirty. **2** *fam (tacaño)* mean, stingy.
► *nm & nf fam* scrooge, miser.

ropa *nf* clothing, clothes *pl*: *ropa de invierno* winter clothes; *ropa de esquí* ski wear. COMP **ropa blanca** linen, household linen. ❙ **ropa interior** underwear.

ropero *nm* wardrobe, US closet.

roquefort *nm (específicamente)* Roquefort; *(en general)* blue cheese.

roquero,-a *adj-nm & nf →* rockero,-a.

rosa *nf (flor)* rose.
► *nm (color)* pink.
► *adj* **1** *(color)* pink. **2** *fig (novela)* romantic. LOC **fresco,-a como una rosa** *fig* as fresh as a daisy.

rosado,-a *adj* **1** *(color)* rosy, pink. **2** *(vino)* rosé.
► *nm* **rosado** *(vino)* rosé.

rosal *nm* rosebush.

rosaleda *nf* rose garden.

rosario *nm* **1** REL rosary, beads *pl*. **2** *fig* string, series: *rosario de mentiras* string of lies. LOC **rezar el rosario** to say the rosary.

rosbif *nm* roast beef.

rosca *nf* **1** *(de tornillo)* thread. **2** CULIN doughnut. **3** *(carnosidad)* roll of fat. **4** *(anilla)* ring.

rosco *nm* ring-shaped bread roll.

roscón *nm* ring-shaped pastry; *(de Pascua)* Easter ring.

rosetón *nm* rose window.

rosquilla *nf* doughnut, ring-shaped pastry.

rostro *nm fml (cara)* face.

rotación *nf* rotation.

rotativo,-a *adj* rotary, revolving.
► *nm* **rotativo** newspaper.

roto,-a *adj* **1** *(gen)* broken. **2** *(tela, papel)* torn. **3** *(gastado)* worn out. **4** *(cansado)* tired.
► *nm* **roto** *(agujero)* hole, tear.

rotonda *nf (plaza)* roundabout, US traffic circle.

rótula *nf* ANAT kneecap.

rotulación *nf* lettering, labelling.

rotulador *nm* felt-tip pen.

rotular *vt* to label.

rotulista *nm o nf* signwriter.

rótulo *nm* **1** *(letrero)* sign; *(luminoso)* neon sign. **2** *(titular)* heading, title.

rotundo,-a *adj* **1** *(redondo)* round. **2** *fig (éxito)* resounding. **3** *(negativa)* flat, categorical; *(afirmación)* categorical, emphatic: *un no rotundo* a flat refusal.

rotura *nf* **1** *(gen)* break, breaking, crack. **2** *(en tela, papel)* tear, rip. **3** MED fracture.

roturar *vt* to plough (US plow).

roulotte *nf* caravan.

rozadura *nf* scratch, abrasion.

rozamiento *nm (roce)* rubbing, friction.

rozar *vt* **1** *(tocar ligeramente)* to touch lightly, brush. **2** *(raspar)* to rub against

brush against; *(herir)* to graze: *el zapato me roza el pie* my shoe's rubbing my foot.
► vi **1** *(raspar)* to rub. **2** *fig (tener relación)* to border (con, on), verge (con, on).
► vpr **rozarse 1** *(rasparse)* to rub (con, against), brush (con, against). **2** *(desgastarse)* to wear (out). **3** *fig (tratarse)* to come into contact (con, with), rub shoulders (con, with).

Ruanda *nf* Rwanda.

ruandés,-esa *adj* Rwandan.
► *nm & nf* Rwandan.

rubeola *nf* German measles, rubella.

rubí *nm* ruby.

rubia *nf* blonde.

rubio,-a *adj* **1** *(cabello)* fair; *(persona)* fair-haired; *(hombre)* blond; *(mujer)* blonde. **2** *(tabaco)* Virginia.
► *nm & nf (hombre)* blond; *(mujer)* blonde.

rublo *nm* rouble.

rubor *nm* blush, flush.

ruborizarse *vpr* to blush, go red, redden.

rúbrica *nf* **1** *(de firma)* flourish (in signature). **2** *(título)* title, heading.

ruda *nf* rue.

rudeza *nf* roughness, coarseness.

rudimentario,-a *adj* rudimentary.

rudo,-a *adj* rough, coarse.

rueca *nf* distaff.

rueda *nf* **1** *(gen)* wheel: *de cuatro ruedas* four-wheeled. **2** *(círculo)* circle, ring. COMP **rueda de la fortuna** wheel of fortune. | **rueda de molino** millstone. | **rueda de prensa** press conference. | **rueda de recambio** spare wheel. | **rueda delantera** front wheel.

ruedo *nm (en las plazas de toros)* bullring, arena.

ruego *nm* request, petition. COMP **ruegos y preguntas** any other business.

rufián *nm (canalla)* scoundrel, villain, ruffian.

rugby *nm* rugby.

rugido *nm* roar, bellow.

rugir *vi* to roar, bellow; *(viento)* to howl; *(tripas)* to rumble.

rugosidad *nf* rugosity.

rugoso,-a *adj* rough, wrinkled.

ruibarbo *nm* rhubarb.

ruido *nm* **1** *(gen)* noise. **2** *(sonido)* sound. **3** *(jaleo)* din, row. **4** *fig* stir, commotion. LOC **hacer ruido 1** to make a noise. **2** *fig* to cause a stir. | **mucho ruido y pocas nueces** *fam* much ado about nothing.

ruidoso,-a *adj* **1** noisy, loud. **2** *fig* sensational.

ruin *adj* **1** *pey (vil)* mean, base, despicable, vile. **2** *(pequeño)* petty, insignificant. **3** *(tacaño)* stingy, mean.

ruina *nf* **1** ruin, collapse. **2** *fig* fall, end, downfall.
► *nf pl* **ruinas** ruins. LOC **estar hecho,-a una ruina** *fig* to be a wreck.

ruindad *nf* **1** *(maldad)* meanness, vileness. **2** *(acto)* mean act, low trick.

ruinoso,-a *adj* **1** ruinous, disastrous. **2** *fig* tumbledown, dilapidated.

ruiseñor *nm* nightingale.

rular *vt (funcionar)* to work.

ruleta *nf* roulette.

rulot *nf* caravan.

Rumanía *nf* Romania.

rumano,-a *adj* Romanian, Rumanian.
► *nm & nf (persona)* Romanian, Rumanian.
► *nm* **rumano** *(idioma)* Romanian, Rumanian.

rumba *nf* rumba, rhumba.

rumbo *nm* **1** *(dirección)* course, direction. **2** *fam fig (pompa)* pomp, show. **3** *fam fig (generosidad)* lavishness, generosity. LOC **perder el rumbo 1** to go off course. **2** *fig* to lose one's bearings.

rumiante *adj* ruminant.
► *nm* ruminant.

rumiar *vi (animal)* to ruminate, chew the cud.
► *vt* **1** *(mascar)* to chew. **2** *fig (pensar)* to ruminate, chew over, reflect on.

rumor *nm* **1** *(murmullo)* murmur. **2** *(noticia, voz)* rumour (US rumor).

rumorearse *vpr* [se usa sólo en tercera persona; no lleva sujeto] to be rumoured (US rumored): *se rumorea que está enfer-*

R

mo it is rumoured that he's ill, he's rumoured to be ill.

rupestre *adj* rock. COMP **pintura rupestre** cave painting.

rupia *nf* rupee.

ruptura *nf* 1 *(rotura)* breaking, breakage, break. 2 *fig* breaking-off, break-up.

rural *adj* rural, country: *médico rural* country doctor.

Rusia *nf* Russia.

ruso,-a *adj* Russian.
▶ *nm & nf (persona)* Russian.
▶ *nm* **ruso** *(idioma)* Russian.

rústico,-a *adj* rustic, rural.
▶ *nm* **rústico** peasant. LOC **en rústica** in paperback.

ruta *nf* route, way, road. COMP **ruta aérea** air route, airway.

rutina *nf* routine: *la rutina diaria* the daily routine.

rutinario,-a *adj* 1 *(gen)* routine. 2 *(persona)* unimaginative, dull.

S

S, s *nf (la letra)* S, s.

S *sím* (sur) south; *(símbolo)* S.

sábado *nm* Saturday.

📎 Para ejemplos de uso, consulta **jueves.**

sábana *nf* sheet.

sabelotodo *nm o nf inv pey* know-all, know-it-all.

saber *nm* knowledge.
- ▶ *vt* **1** *(gen)* to know. **2** *(tener habilidad)* to be able to, know how to. **3** *(enterarse)* to learn, find out.
- ▶ *vi (tener sabor)* to taste (a, of).
- ▶ *vpr* **saberse** to know.

sabido,-a *adj* known.

sabiduría *nf* **1** *(conocimientos)* knowledge. **2** *(prudencia)* wisdom.

sabio,-a *adj* **1** *(con conocimientos)* learned, knowledgeable. **2** *(con prudencia)* wise, sensible.
- ▶ *nm & nf* **1** *(instruido)* learned person. **2** *(prudente)* sage, wise person.

sable *nm* sabre (US saber).

sabor *nm* **1** taste, flavour (US flavor). **2** *fig* feeling.

saborear *vt* **1** to taste. **2** *fig* to savour (US savor), relish.

sabroso,-a *adj* **1** *(con mucho sabor)* tasty, delicious. **2** *(agradable)* pleasant, delightful.

sabueso *nm* **1** *(perro)* bloodhound. **2** *fig (persona)* sleuth.

sacacorchos *nm inv* corkscrew.

sacapuntas *nm inv* pencil sharpener.

sacar *vt* **1** *(poner en el exterior)* to take out, pull out, get out. **2** *(obtener - gen)* to get; *(- premio)* to win; *(- dinero)* to get, make, earn; *(- billete)* to get, buy. **3** *(dinero del banco)* to draw, withdraw, take out. **4** *(resolver)* to work out, solve. **5** *(encontrar)* to get, find. **6** *(enseñar)* to show. **7** *(quitar)* to remove. **8** *(extraer de algo)* to extract, obtain. **9** *(agua)* to draw. **10** *(llevar fuera)* to take out. **11** *(fotografía)* to take; *(fotocopia, copia)* to make. **12** *(producir)* to produce. **13** *(moda)* to introduce, set; *(nuevo producto)* to bring out. **14** *(publicar)* to publish, bring out. **15** *fam (ir por delante)* to be ahead. **16** *fam (ser más alto)* to be taller. **17** DEP *(tenis)* to serve; *(fútbol)* to kick off. **18** MAT *(restar)* to subtract; *(raíz)* to extract, find out. **19** *(mineral)* to extract. **20** QUÍM to extract.
- ▶ *vpr* **sacarse 1** *(desvestirse)* to take off. **2** *(fotografía)* to have taken.

saciar *vt* **1** *(hambre)* to satiate; *(sed)* to quench. **2** *fig (deseos)* to satisfy; *(ambiciones)* to fulfil (US fulfill).
- ▶ *vpr* **saciarse** to satiate os, be satiated.

saco *nm* **1** *(bolsa)* sack, bag. **2** AM *(americana)* jacket.

sacrificar *vt* **1** *(gen)* to sacrifice. **2** *fig (reses)* to slaughter; *(animal doméstico)* to destroy, put down.
- ▶ *vpr* **sacrificarse** to sacrifice os (por, for).

sacrificio *nm* sacrifice.

sacro,-a *adj* **1** *(sagrado)* sacred. **2** ANAT sacrum.
- ▶ *nm* **sacro** *(hueso)* sacrum.

sacudida *nf* **1** *(gen)* shake. **2** *(movimiento violento)* jolt, jerk. **3** *(terremoto)* earthquake.

sacudir *vt* **1** *(gen)* to shake. **2** *(alfombra, etc)* to shake out; *(polvo, arena)* to shake off. **3** *(golpear algo)* to beat. **4** *(cabeza)* to shake. **5** *(dar una paliza)* to beat up. **6** *fig (emocionar, alterar)* to shake.

sagacidad *nf* **1** sagacity, cleverness. **2** *(astucia)* shrewdness, astuteness.

sagaz *adj* **1** clever, sagacious. **2** *(astuto)* shrewd, astute.

sagrado,-a *adj* sacred, holy.

Sáhara *nm* Sahara.

saharaui *adj* Saharaui, Sahrawi.
▶ *nm o nf* Saharaui, Sahrawi.

sahariana *nf* safari shirt, safari jacket.

sahariano,-a *adj* Saharan.

sal *nf* salt. COMP **sal fina** table salt.
▶ *nf pl* **sales** smelling salts.

sala *nf* **1** *(aposento)* room; *(grande)* hall. **2** *(sala de estar)* lounge, living room. **3** *(de hospital)* ward; *(de cine)* cinema; *(de teatro)* theatre. **4** JUR *(lugar)* courtroom; *(tribunal)* court.

salado,-a *adj* **1** *(con sal)* salted; *(con demasiada sal)* salty. **2** *fam fig (agudo)* witty; *(gracioso)* funny; *(encantador)* charming, attractive.

salamandra *nf* salamander.

salamanquesa *nf* ZOOL gecko.

salar *vt* **1** *(curar)* to salt. **2** *(sazonar)* to salt, add salt to.

salarial *adj* salary, wage.

salario *nm* salary, wages *pl*, wage.

salazón *nf* **1** *(acción)* salting. **2** *(carne)* salted meat; *(pescado)* salted fish.

salchicha *nf* sausage.

salchichón *nm* salami-type sausage.

saldo *nm* **1** *(de una cuenta)* balance. **2** *(pago)* liquidation, settlement. **3** *(resto de mercancía)* remnant, leftover, remainder. **4** *(venta a bajo precio)* sale.

salero *nm* **1** *(recipiente)* saltcellar, US salt shaker. **2** *fig (gracia)* charm, wit.

salida *nf* **1** *(partida)* departure. **2** *(puerta, etc)* exit, way out. **3** *(momento de salir)*. **4** *(viaje corto)* trip. **5** *(de un astro)* rising. **6** DEP start. **7** COM outlet, market. **8** FIN outlay, expenditure. **9** *fig (ocurrencia)* witty remark, witticism. **10** *fig (escapatoria)* solution, way out. **11** *fig (perspectiva)* opening. **12** TÉC outlet. **13** INFORM output.

saliente *adj* **1** *(que sobresale)* projecting. **2** *(cesante)* outgoing.
▶ *nm* projection, overhang, ledge.

salina *nf* **1** *(mina)* salt mine. **2** *(establecimiento)* salt works.

salir *vi* **1** *(ir hacia afuera)* to go out (de, of). **2** *(venir de dentro)* to come out. **3** *(partir)* to leave. **4** *(no estar)* to be out. **5** *(amigos, novios)* to go out. **6** *(aparecer)* to appear, be. **7** *(revista, novela, etc)* to come out; *(moda)* to come in. **8** *(proceder)* to come (de, from). **9** *(resultar)* to turn out, turn out to be. **10** *(examen, prueba)* to go, turn out. **11** *(venir a costar)* to come to, cost, work out. **12** *(sobresalir)* to project, stick out. **13** *(sol, etc)* to rise, come out; *(vegetales)* to come up; *(flores)* to come out. **14** *(granos)* to get, break out in, come out in; *(pelo)* to grow; *(diente)* to cut. **15** *(mancha)* to come out, come off. **16** *(parecerse)* to take after (a, -). **17** *(al azar)* to be drawn. **18** *(nombre, palabra)* to be able to think of. **19** *(solucionar)* to work out. **20** *(librarse)* to get out (de, of). **21** *(trabajo, oportunidad)* to come up. **22** *(dar a)* to open (a, onto), come out (a, at).
▶ *vpr* **salirse 1** *(líquido, gas)* to leak, leak out; *(río)* to overflow. **2** *(al hervir)* to boil over. **3** *(tornillo, etc)* to come off, come out. **4** *(de la carretera)* to go off (de, -).

salitre *nm* saltpetre (US saltpeter).

saliva *nf* saliva.

salmón *nm (pez)* salmon.
▶ *adj (color)* salmon, salmon pink.

salmonete *nm* red mullet.

Salomón *nm* Solomon. COMP **Islas Salomón** Solomon Islands.

salón *nm* **1** *(en casa)* sitting room, drawing room, lounge. **2** *(en edificio público)* hall. **3** *(exposición)* show, exhibition.

salpicar *vt* **1** *(rociar)* to sprinkle. **2** *(caer gotas)* to splash.

salpullido *nm* rash.

salsa *nf* **1** sauce. **2** *fam fig (gracia)* zest, spice. **3** MÚS salsa.

saltamontes *nm inv* grasshopper.

saltar *vi* **1** *(gen)* to jump, leap. **2** *(en paracaídas)* to parachute. **3** *(romperse)* to break; *(estallar)* to burst. **4** *(desprenderse)* to come off. **5** *(tapón, corcho)* to pop out, pop off. **6** *fig (enfadarse)* to blow up, explode. **7** *fig (de una cosa a otra)* to jump, skip. **8** *fig (decir)* to come out (con, with); *(contestar)* to answer (con, with).
▶ *vt* **1** *fig (salvar de un salto)* to jump (over), leap (over). **2** *(arrancar)* to pull off. **3** *(ajedrez, etc)* to jump. **4** *fig (omitir)* to skip, miss out.
▶ *vpr* **saltarse 1** *(ley, etc)* to ignore. **2** *(omitir)* to skip, miss out. **3** *(desprenderse)* to come off; *(- lentilla)* to fall out.

salto *nm* **1** *(gen)* jump, leap. **2** DEP jump; *(natación)* dive. **3** *(de agua)* waterfall. **4** *(despeñadero)* precipice. **5** *fig (omisión)* gap.

salubridad *nf (estado de salud)* healthiness; *(de lugar, clima)* salubriousness, salubrity.

salud *nf* health.

saludable *adj* **1** *(sano)* healthy, wholesome. **2** *fig (beneficioso)* good, beneficial.

saludar *vt* **1** *(demostrar cortesía)* to greet. **2** *(decir hola)* to say hello to. **3** MIL to salute.

saludo *nm* **1** greeting. **2** MIL salute.

salvación *nf* **1** *(gen)* salvation, rescue. **2** REL salvation.

salvado *nm* bran.

Salvador *nm* **El Salvador 1** El Salvador. **2** REL the Saviour (US Savior).

salvadoreño,-a *adj* Salvadorian, Salvadoran.
▶ *nm & nf* Salvadorian, Salvadoran.

salvaguardar *vt* to safeguard (de, from).

salvaje *adj* **1** *(planta)* wild. **2** *(animal)* wild. **3** *(pueblo, tribu)* savage, uncivilized. **4** *fam fig (violento)* savage, wild. **5** *(bruto)* uncouth, boorish.
▶ *nm o nf* **1** *(no civilizado)* savage. **2** *(bruto)* brute, boor.

salvamento *nm* rescue.

salvar *vt* **1** *(librar de peligro)* to save, rescue. **2** *(barco)* to salvage. **3** *(honor, ruina)* to save. **4** *(obstáculo)* to clear. **5** *(dificultad)* to overcome, get round. **6** *(distancia)* to cover.
▶ *vpr* **salvarse 1** *(sobrevivir)* to survive, come out alive. **2** *(escaparse)* to escape (de, from). **3** REL to be saved, save one's soul.

salvapantallas *nm inv* INFORM screensaver.

salvavidas *nm inv* life belt.

salvedad *nf (excepción)* exception.

salvia *nf* sage.

salvo,-a *adj (ileso)* unharmed, safe.
▶ *adv* **salvo** except, except for.

salvoconducto *nm* safe-conduct.

Samoa *nf* Samoa.

samoano,-a *adj* Samoan.
▶ *nm & nf (persona)* Samoan.
▶ *nm* **samoano** *(idioma)* Samoan.

san *adj* saint.

✎ Se usa delante de nombres de santos masculinos, excepto Tomás, Tomé, Toribio y Domingo. Consulta también **santo,-a**.

sanar *vt* to heal, cure.
▶ *vi* **1** *(enfermo)* to recover, get better. **2** *(herida)* to heal.

sanatorio *nm* clinic, nursing home; *(hospital)* hospital.

sanción *nf* **1** *(aprobación)* sanction, approval. **2** *(pena)* sanction, penalty.

sandalia *nf* sandal.

sándalo *nm* sandalwood.

sandía *nf* watermelon.

sándwich *nm* sandwich.

sanear *vt* **1** *(limpiar)* to clean; *(desinfectar)* to disinfect. **2** *(económicamente)* to make financially viable.

sangrado *nm* indention, indentation, indent.

sangrar *vt* **1** *(abrir una vena)* to bleed. **2** *(dar salida a un líquido)* to drain. **3** *fam fig (dejar sin dinero)* to bleed dry. **4** *(en impresión)* to indent.

sangre *nf* blood.

sangría *nf* **1** *(bebida)* sangria. **2** MED bleeding, bloodletting. **3** *fig (de dinero, etc)* drain.

S

sangriento,-a *adj* **1** *(que echa sangre)* bleeding. **2** *(con sangre)* bloody.

sanguijuela *nf* leech, bloodsucker.

sanidad *nf* **1** *(calidad de sano)* health, healthiness. **2** *(servicios)* health: *sanidad pública* public health.

sanitario,-a *adj* sanitary, health.
▶ *nm & nf* health officer.
▶ *nm pl* **sanitarios** bathroom fittings.

sano,-a *adj* **1** *(con salud)* healthy, fit. **2** *(saludable)* healthy, wholesome. **3** *fig (sin corrupción)* sound.

santo,-a *adj* **1** *(gen)* holy, sacred. **2** *(persona)* holy, saintly. **3** *fam (para enfatizar)* hell of a, real, right. **4** *(como título)* saint: *Santa Elena* Saint Helen.
▶ *nm & nf* saint.
▶ *nm* **santo 1** *(imagen)* image of a saint. **2** *fam (dibujo)* picture. **3** *(onomástica)* saint's day.

✎ Consulta también **san**.

santuario *nm* sanctuary, shrine.

saña *nf* **1** *(enojo)* rage, fury. **2** *(crueldad)* cruelty, viciousness.

sapiencia *nf* **1** *fml (sabiduría)* wisdom. **2** *(conocimiento)* knowledge.

saque *nm* **1** *(tenis)* service. **2** *(fútbol)* kick-off. [COMP] **saque de banda** *(fútbol)* throw-in.

saquear *vt (casas)* to plunder, pillage; *(casas, comercios)* to loot.

sarampión *nm* measles *pl*.

sarcasmo *nm* sarcasm.

sarcástico,-a *adj* sarcastic.

sarcófago *nm* sarcophagus.

sardina *nf* sardine.

sarga *nf* serge, twill.

sargento *nm* **1** MIL sergeant. **2** *fig* tyrant.

sarmiento *nm* vine shoot.

sarna *nf* MED *(en personas)* scabies; *(en animales)* mange.

sarpullido *nm* rash.

sarro *nm* **1** *(en los dientes)* tartar. **2** *(sedimento)* deposit.

sarta *nf* string.

sartén *nf* frying pan, US fry pan.

sastre,-a *nm & nf* tailor.

satélite *nm* satellite.

satén *nm* satin.

satisfacción *nf (gen)* satisfaction.

satisfacer *vt* **1** *(gen)* to satisfy. **2** *(deuda)* to pay. **3** *(requisitos, exigencias)* to meet, fulfil satisfy. **4** *(agravio, ofensa)* to make amends for.

satisfactorio,-a *adj* satisfactory.

satisfecho,-a *adj* **1** *(contento)* satisfied, pleased. **2** *(pagado de sí mismo)* self-satisfied.

saturación *nf* saturation.

saturado,-a *adj* **1** saturated. **2** *fig* sick, tired.

saturnismo *nm* lead poisoning.

Saturno *nm* Saturn.

sauce *nm* willow.

saúco *nm* elder.

saudí *adj* Saudi.
▶ *nm o nf* Saudi.

saudita *adj-nm o nf* → **saudí**.

sauna *nf* sauna.

saurio,-a *adj* saurian.
▶ *nm & nf* saurian.

savia *nf* **1** BOT sap. **2** *fig* sap, vitality.

saxofón *nm (instrumento)* saxophone, sax.
▶ *nm o nf (músico)* saxophonist, sax player.

saya *nf* **1** *(falda)* skirt. **2** *(enagua)* petticoat.

sazón *nf* **1** *(madurez)* ripeness. **2** *(sabor)* taste, flavour (US flavor). **3** *(aderezo)* seasoning.

sazonar *vt* **1** *(madurar)* to ripen, mature. **2** *(comida)* to season, flavour (US flavor).

se¹ *pron* **1** *(reflexivo - él)* himself; *(- ella)* herself; *(- usted, ustedes)* yourself, yourselves; *(- ellos, ellas)* themselves; *(- esto)* itself. **2** *(recíproco)* each other, one another: *se quieren* they love each other. **3** *(pasiva)*: *se han abierto las puertas* the doors have been opened. **4** *(impersonal)*: *se ve que no* apparently not.

se² *pron (objeto indirecto - a él)* him, to him; *(- a ella)* her, to her; *(- a ellos, ellas)* them, to them; *(- a esto)* it, to it; *(- a* *usted, ustedes)* you, to you: *se lo dije* I told her.

✎ Se usa delante de los pronombres la, las, lo y los en vez de les o las.

sé¹ *pres indic* → **saber.**

sé² *imperat* → **ser.**

sebo *nm* **1** *(grasa)* fat. **2** CULIN suet. **3** *(para velas)* tallow.

seca *nf (sequía)* drought.

secado *nm* drying.

secador *nm* **1** dryer, drier. **2** *(de pelo)* hairdryer.

secadora *nf* tumble dryer, dryer.

secano *nm* dry land.

secante *adj (geometría)* secant.
  ▶ *nf* secant.

secar *vt* **1** *(gen)* to dry. **2** *(lágrimas, vajilla)* to wipe; *(líquido)* to wipe up, mop up. **3** *(planta)* to wither, dry up; *(río, fuente, etc)* to dry up.
  ▶ *vpr* **secarse 1** *(gen)* to dry. **2** *(líquido, río, etc)* to dry up; *(planta)* to wither, dry up.

sección *nf* **1** *(corte)* section, cut. **2** *(geometría)* section. **3** *(departamento)* section, department. **4** *(en periódico, revista)* page, section.

seco,-a *adj* **1** *(gen)* dry. **2** *(frutos, flores)* dried. **3** *(marchito)* withered, dried up. **4** *fig (carácter)* dry; *(tono, respuesta)* curt, sharp. **5** *fig (golpe, ruido)* sharp.

secreción *nf* secretion.

secretaría *nf* **1** *(cargo)* secretaryship, office of secretary. **2** *(oficina)* secretary's office; *(en la administración)* secretariat.

secretario,-a *nm & nf* secretary.

secreteo *nm* whispering.

secreto,-a *adj* secret.
  ▶ *nm* **secreto 1** *(lo reservado)* secret. **2** *(reserva)* secrecy.

secta *nf* sect.

sector *nm* **1** *(gen)* sector. **2** *fig (zona)* area. **3** *fig (parte)* section.

secuela *nf* consequence, result.

secuencia *nf* sequence.

secuenciar *vt* to arrange in sequence, put in sequence.

secuestrar *vt* **1** *(personas)* to kidnap; *(avión)* to hijack. **2** JUR to sequester, seize, confiscate.

secuestro *nm* **1** *(personas)* kidnapping; *(de avión)* hijacking. **2** JUR sequestration, seizure, confiscation.

secundar *vt* to support, second.

secundaria *nf* EDUC secondary education.

secundario,-a *adj* secondary.
  ▶ *nm* **secundario** GEOL secondary.

secuoya *nf* sequoia, redwood.

sed *nf* thirst.

seda *nf* silk.

sede *nf* **1** *(oficina central)* headquarters, central office. **2** *(del gobierno)* seat.

sedentario,-a *adj* sedentary.

sediento,-a *adj* **1** thirsty. **2** *fig (poder, etc)* hungry (**de**, for), thirsty (**de**, for).

sedimentar *vt* to settle, deposit.
  ▶ *vpr* **sedimentarse** to settle.

sedimento *nm* sediment, deposit.

seductor,-ra *adj* **1** seductive. **2** *(atractivo)* captivating. **3** *(persuasivo)* tempting.
  ▶ *nm & nf* seducer.

segador,-ra *nm & nf* harvester, reaper.

segadora *nf* harvester, reaper; *(de césped)* lawnmower.

segar *vt* **1** *(gen)* to reap, cut; *(césped)* to mow. **2** *fig (matar)* to mow down, cut down. **3** *fig (truncar)* to cut off.

segmento *nm* **1** *(gen)* segment. **2** INFORM overlay.

segregar *vt* **1** *(separar)* to segregate. **2** *(secretar)* to secrete.

segueta *nf* fret saw.

seguido,-a *adj* **1** *(continuo)* continuous. **2** *(consecutivo)* consecutive, successive. **3** *(en línea recta)* straight, direct.
  ▶ *adv* **seguido** straight.

seguidor,-ra *nm & nf* **1** follower. **2** DEP follower, supporter, fan.

seguir *vt* **1** *(gen)* to follow. **2** *(perseguir)* to pursue, chase. **3** *(continuar)* to continue, carry on. **4** *(un camino)* to continue

S

on. **5** (curso, etc) to do; (explicaciones) to follow.
▶ vi **1** (proseguir) to go on, carry on. **2** (continuar) to follow on, continue. **3** (permanecer, mantenerse) to continue to be, be still.
▶ vpr **seguirse 1** (inferirse) to deduce. **2** (suceder a continuación) to follow.

según prep **1** (conforme) according to. **2** (dependiendo) depending on. **3** (como) just as. **4** (a medida que) as. **5** (tal vez) it depends.

segunda nf **1** (tren, etc) second class. **2** (marcha del auto) second, second gear. **3** fig (intención) ulterior motive.

segundero nm second hand.

segundo,-a adj second.
▶ nm & nf second.
▶ nm **segundo** (tiempo) second.

✎ Para ejemplos de uso, consulta seis.

seguridad nf **1** (gen) security. **2** (física) safety. **3** (certeza) certainty, sureness. **4** (confianza) confidence.

seguro,-a adj **1** (asegurado) secure. **2** (a salvo) safe. **3** (firme) firm, steady. **4** (cierto) certain, sure. **5** (de fiar) reliable. **6** (confiado) confident.
▶ nm **seguro 1** (contrato, póliza) insurance. **2** (mecanismo) safety device, safety catch.
▶ adv for sure, definitely.

seis adj **1** six: pesa seis kilos it weighs six kilos; son las seis en punto it's exactly six o'clock; el seis de junio the six of june; tienen un hijo de seis años they have a boy of six; somos seis there are six of us. **2** (sexto) sixth: soy el seis de la lista I'm sixth on the list.
▶ nm six: el seis number six; seis por seis treinta y seis six times six is thirty-six, six sixes are thirty-six.

seisavo,-a adj-nm & nf → sexto,-a.

seiscientos,-as adj (cardinal) six hundred; (ordinal) six hundredth.
▶ nm **seiscientos** (número) six hundred.

seísmo nm (terremoto) earthquake.

selección nf **1** (gen) selection. **2** DEP (gen) team; (fútbol) squad.

seleccionar vt to select.

selectividad nf EDUC university entrance examination.

selenio nm selenium.

sellar vt **1** (timbrar) to stamp; (oficial) to seal. **2** (monedas, etc) to hallmark, stamp. **3** fig (habitación, etc) to close (up), seal up. **4** fig (dejar señal) to stamp, brand. **5** fig (concluir) to seal, settle, conclude.
▶ vi to sign on.

sello nm **1** (de correos) stamp. **2** (de estampar, precinto) seal.

selva nf **1** (bosque) forest. **2** (jungla) jungle.

selvicultura nf forestry.

semáforo nm traffic lights pl.

semana nf **1** (tiempo) week. **2** fig (salario) weekly wage.

semanal adj weekly.

semanario,-a adj weekly.
▶ nm weekly magazine.

semántica nf semantics.

sembrado,-a adj fig (cubierto) covered (de, with), full (de, of).
▶ nm **sembrado** sown field.

sembrador,-ra nm & nf sower.

sembradora nf seed drill.

sembrar vt **1** AGR to sow. **2** fig (esparcir) to scatter, spread.

semejante adj **1** (parecido) similar. **2** pey (tal) such, like that. **3** (geometría) similar.
▶ nm fellow being.

semejanza nf similarity, likeness.

semen nm semen.

semental nm stud.

semestral adj half-yearly, semestral.

semestre nm **1** six-month period, semester. **2** EDUC semester.

semicírculo nm semicircle.

semicircunferencia nf semicircumference.

semiconductor nm semiconductor.

semicorchea nf semiquaver, sixteenth note.

semiesférico,-a adj hemispheroidal.

semifinal nf semifinal.

semifusa *nf* hemidemisemiquaver, sixty-fourth note.

semilla *nf* 1 seed. 2 *fig* seed, seeds.

semillero *nm* 1 seedbed. 2 *fig* hotbed, breeding ground.

seminal *adj* seminal.

semiología *nf* semiology.

semiótica *nf* semiotics.

semiseco,-a *adj* medium dry.

semitono *nm* semitone, half-step.

semivocal *adj* semivocal.
> *nf* semivowel.

sémola *nf* semolina.

senado *nm* 1 senate. 2 *fig (reunión)* assembly.

senador,-ra *nm & nf* senator.

sencillez *nf* 1 *(gen)* simplicity. 2 *(naturalidad)* simplicity, lack of affectation, unpretentiousness. 3 *(ingenuidad)* gullibility, naivety.

sencillo,-a *adj* 1 *(sin adornos)* simple, plain. 2 *(fácil)* simple, easy. 3 *(no compuesto)* single. 4 *fig (persona - natural)* natural, unaffected, unpretentious; *(- ingenua)* naive, gullible.

senderismo *nm* trekking.

sendero *nm* path.

sendos,-as *adj* each, either.

Senegal *nm* Senegal.

senegalés,-esa *adj* Senegalese.
> *nm & nf* Senegalese.

seno *nm* 1 *(pecho)* breast, bosom. 2 *(hueco entre el pecho y la ropa)* bosom. 3 *(matriz)* womb. 4 *(cavidad)* cavity, hollow, hole. 5 MAT sine. 6 ANAT sinus.

sensación *nf* 1 *(impresión)* sensation, feeling: *sensación de calor* feeling of warmth. 2 *(emoción)* sensation.

sensacional *adj* sensational.

sensatez *nf* good sense.

sensato,-a *adj* sensible.

sensibilidad *nf* 1 *(percepción, sentido artístico)* sensitivity, feeling. 2 *(emotividad)* sensibility. 3 *(precisión)* sensitivity.

sensible *adj* 1 *(capaz de sentir)* sentient. 2 *(impresionable)* sensitive. 3 *(piel, oído)* sensitive. 4 *(perceptible)* perceptible, appreciable, noticeable. 5 *(considerable)* significant, considerable, sizea-

ble. 6 *(que causa pena)* terrible, sad. 7 TÉC *(preciso)* sensitive.

sensorial *adj* sensory.

sentado,-a *adj* 1 seated, sitting. 2 *(establecido)* established, settled.

sentar *vt* 1 *(en silla, etc)* to sit, seat. 2 *fig (establecer)* to establish.
> *vi* 1 *(color, ropa, etc)* to suit. 2 *(comida, etc)* to do; *(comentario, etc)* to take.
> *vpr* **sentarse** 1 *(en silla, etc)* to sit, sit down. 2 *(líquido)* to settle. 3 *(tiempo)* to settle, settle down.

sentencia *nf* 1 JUR *(decisión)* judgement; *(condena)* sentence. 2 *(aforismo)* proverb, maxim, saying, motto.

sentenciar *vt* to sentence (a, to).

sentido,-a *adj* 1 *(muerte, etc)* deeply felt. 2 *(sensible)* touchy, sensitive.
> *nm* **sentido** 1 *(gen)* sense. 2 *(significado)* sense, meaning. 3 *(conocimiento)* consciousness. 4 *(dirección)* direction.

sentimental *adj* sentimental.
> *nm o nf* sentimental person.

sentimiento *nm* 1 *(gen)* feeling. 2 *(pena)* sorrow, grief.

sentir *nm* 1 *(sentimiento)* feeling. 2 *(opinión)* opinion, view.
> *vt* 1 *(gen)* to feel. 2 *(lamentar)* to regret, be sorry about, feel sorry. 3 *(oír)* to hear. 4 *(presentir)* to feel, think, have a feeling that.
> *vpr* **sentirse** to feel.

seña *nf* 1 *(indicio, gesto)* sign. 2 *(señal)* mark.
> *nf pl* **señas** address *sing.*

señal *nf* 1 *(signo)* sign, indication. 2 *(marca)* mark; *(en libro)* bookmark. 3 *(aviso, comunicación)* signal. 4 *(placa, letrero)* sign. 5 *(vestigio)* trace. 6 *(cicatriz)* scar. 7 *(de teléfono)* tone. 8 *(de pago)* deposit.

señalado,-a *adj* 1 *(famoso)* distinguished, famous. 2 *(fijado)* appointed, fixed. 3 *(significativo)* noticeable. 4 *(marcado)* marked, scarred.

señalar *vt* 1 *(marcar)* to mark. 2 *(hacer notar)* to point out. 3 *(apuntar hacia)* to point to, show. 4 *(con el dedo)* to point at. 5 *(fijar - cita)* to arrange, make; *(fecha, lugar, precio)* to set, fix.

S

señalización *nf* **1** *(señales)* road signs *pl*; *(de aeropuerto, estación)* signposting, signs *pl*. **2** *(colocación)* signposting.

señalizar *vt* to signpost.

señor,-ra *adj* **1** *(noble)* distinguished, noble. **2** *fam* fine.
▶ *nm & nf* **1** *(hombre)* man, gentleman; *(mujer)* woman, lady. **2** *(amo - hombre)* master; *(- mujer)* mistress. **3** *(tratamiento - hombre)* sir; *(- mujer)* madam, US ma'am. **4** *(ante apellido - hombre)* Mr; *(- mujer)* Mrs.

señora *nf* *(esposa)* wife.

señorita *nf* **1** *(mujer joven)* young woman; *(con más formalidad)* young lady. **2** *(tratamiento)* Miss. **3** *fam* *(puro)* small cigar. **4** **la señorita** EDUC the teacher, Miss.

señuelo *nm* **1** decoy. **2** *fig* bait.

sépalo *nm* sepal.

separación *nf* **1** separation. **2** *(espacio)* space, gap.

separado,-a *adj* **1** separate. **2** *(divorciado)* separated. LOC **por separado** separately, individually.

separar *vt* **1** *(gen)* to separate. **2** *(hacer grupos)* to separate, sort out. **3** *(guardar aparte)* to set aside, put aside. **4** *(apartar)* to move away (de, from). **5** *(de empleo, cargo)* to remove (de, from), dismiss (de, from). **6** *fig* *(mantener alejado)* to keep away (de, from).
▶ *vpr* **separarse 1** *(tomar diferente camino)* to separate, part company. **2** *(matrimonio)* to separate. **3** *(apartarse)* to move away (de, from). **4** *(desprenderse)* to separate (de, from), come off (de, -). **5** *(de amigo, etc)* to part company (de, with). **6** **separarse de** *(dejar algo)* to part with.

sepia *nf* *(pez)* cuttlefish.

septenario,-a *adj* septenary.
▶ *nm* **septenario** septenary.

septenio *nm* septennium.

septentrional *adj* northern.

septeto *nm* septet.

septicemia *nf* septicaemia (US septicemia).

séptico,-a *adj* septic.

septiembre *nm* September.

✎ Para ejemplos de uso, consulta **marzo**.

séptimo,-a *adj* seventh.

✎ Para ejemplos de uso, consulta **sexto,-a**.

septuagenario,-a *nm & nf* septuagenarian.

septuagésimo,-a *adj* seventieth.

✎ Para ejemplos de uso, consulta **sexto,-a**.

sepulcro *nm* tomb.

sepultar *vt* to bury.

sepultura *nf* **1** *(lugar)* grave. **2** *(acto)* burial.

sequía *nf* drought.

ser *vi* **1** *(gen)* to be: *Sócrates era filósofo* Socrates was a philosopher. **2** *(pertenecer)* to be, belong (de, to): *estas sillas son nuestras* these chairs are ours. **3** *(ser propio)* to be like (de, -): *es muy de Pilar* it's just like Pilar. **4** *(costar)* to be, cost: *¿cuánto es?* how much is it? **5** *(causar)* to cause, be. **6** *(consistir en)* to lie in, consist of. **7** *(suceder)* to happen (de, to): *¿qué fue de Iván?* what happened to Iván? **8** *(ocurrir, tener lugar)* to take place, be held: *la reunión será en el salón de actos* the meeting will be held in the assembly hall. **9 ser de** *(proceder)* to be from, come from: *Santi es de Cáceres* Santi is from Cáceres. **10** *(indica material)* to be made of: *la puerta es de madera* the door is made of wood. **11** *(devenir)* to become of: *¡qué sería de nosotros sin ti!* what would become of us without you! **12** *(estar escrito)* to be by, be written by: *es de García Márquez* it's by García Márquez. **13 ser de +** *inf* *(ser digno)* to be worth: *es de ver* it's worth seeing; *es de admirar* she's to be admired.
▶ *aux* *(pasiva)* to be: *fue encontrado por Raúl* it was found by Raúl.
▶ *nm* **1** *(ente)* being. **2** *(esencia)* essence, substance. **3** *(valor)* core, heart. **4** *(vida)* life, existence. COMP **ser humano** human being.

serbal *nm* service tree.

serbio,-a *adj* Serb, Serbian.
▶ *nm & nf* Serb, Serbian.
▶ *nm* **serbio** *(idioma)* Serbian.

serenar *vt* **1** *(gen)* to calm. **2** *fig* *(a alguien)* to calm down.

▶ *vpr* **serenarse 1** METEOR to clear up. **2** *(mar)* to grow calm. **3** *fig (persona)* to calm down.

serenidad *nf* serenity, calm. LOC conservar la serenidad to keep calm.

sereno,-a *adj* **1** METEOR *(cielo)* clear; *(tiempo)* fine, good. **2** *fig (persona - tranquila)* calm. **3** *fig (ambiente, etc)* calm, peaceful, quiet.
▶ *nm* **sereno 1** *(vigilante)* night watchman. **2** *(ambiente de la noche)* night air, night dew.

serie *nf* **1** *(gen)* series. **2** *(conjunto)* series, string, succession.

seriedad *nf* **1** *(gravedad)* seriousness, gravity. **2** *(formalidad)* reliability, dependability. LOC con seriedad seriously.

serio,-a *adj* **1** *(importante)* serious, grave. **2** *(severo)* serious. **3** *(formal)* reliable, responsible, dependable. **4** *(color)* sober; *(traje, etc)* formal. LOC tomar en serio to take seriously.

sermón *nm* **1** REL sermon. **2** *fam* sermon, ticking-off, lecture.

seropositivo,-a *adj* **1** seropositive. **2** *(con el VIH)* HIV positive.

serpentear *vi* **1** *(gen)* to crawl, wriggle. **2** *(camino)* to wind, twist; *(río)* to wind, meander.

serpentín *nm*

serpentina *nf (de papel)* streamer.

serpiente *nf* snake.

serpol *nm* wild thyme.

serranía *nf* mountain range, mountains *pl*.

serrar *vt* to saw.

serrería *nf* sawmill.

serrín *nm* sawdust.

serrucho *nm* handsaw.

servicial *adj* obliging, helpful, accommodating.

servicio *nm* **1** *(gen)* service. **2** *(criados)* servants *pl*; *(asistente)* domestic help. **3** *(juego, conjunto)* set. **4** *(favor)* service, favour (US favor). **5** DEP service, serve. **6** [también servicios.] *(retrete)* toilet, US rest room.

servidor,-ra *nm & nf* **1** servant. **2** *euf* myself.
▶ *nm* **servidor 1** MIL gunner. **2** INFORM server.

servilleta *nf* napkin, serviette.

servio,-a *adj* Serb, Serbian.
▶ *nm & nf* Serb, Serbian.
▶ *nm* **servio** *(idioma)* Serbian.

servir *vt* **1** *(gen)* to serve. **2** *(comida, bebida)* to serve, wait on. **3** *(ayudar)* to help. **4** COM *(suministrar)* to serve, supply with; *(entregar)* to deliver.
▶ *vi* **1** *(gen)* to serve. **2** *(ser útil)* to be useful, be helpful, be a help. **3** *(objeto)* to be no good: *esto no sirve* this is no good. **4** *(estar al servicio de otro)* to be a servant, be in service. **5** *(asistir a la mesa)* to serve (en, at), wait (en, at): *servir en la mesa* to wait at table.
▶ *vpr* **servirse 1** *(comida, etc)* to serve os, help os. **2** *(usar)* to use (de, -), make use of (de, -).

sésamo *nm* sesame.

sesenta *adj (cardinal)* sixty; *(ordinal)* sixtieth.
▶ *nm (número)* sixty.

✎ Para ejemplos de uso, consulta **seis**.

sesentavo,-a *adj* sixtieth.

✎ Para ejemplos de uso, consulta **sexto,-a**.

sesión *nf* **1** *(reunión)* session, meeting. **2** CINE showing. COMP sesión continua continuous session. ‖ sesión plenaria plenary session.

seso *nm* **1** brain. **2** *fam fig* brains *pl*, grey matter, sense.
▶ *nm pl* **sesos** CULIN brains.

seta *nf (comestible)* mushroom; *(no comestible)* toadstool.

setecientos,-as *adj (cardinal)* seven hundred; *(ordinal)* seven-hundredth.
▶ *nm* **setecientos** *(número)* seven hundred.

✎ Para ejemplos de uso, consulta **seis**.

setenta *adj (cardinal)* seventy; *(ordinal)* seventieth.
▶ *nm (número)* seventy.

✎ Para ejemplos de uso, consulta **seis**.

S

setentavo,-a *adj* seventieth.
▶ *nm & nf* seventieth.

✎ Para ejemplos de uso, consulta **sexto,-a.**

setiembre *nm* September.

✎ Para ejemplos de uso, consulta **marzo.**

seto *nm* hedge.
severidad *nf* **1** *(gravedad)* severity, harshness. **2** *(rigurosidad)* strictness.
severo,-a *adj* **1** *(grave)* severe, harsh. **2** *(riguroso)* strict.
sexagenario,-a *adj* sexagenarian.
▶ *nm & nf* sexagenarian.
sexagesimal *adj* sexagesimal.
sexagésimo,-a *adj* sixtieth.
▶ *nm & nf* sixtieth.

✎ Para ejemplos de uso, consulta **sexto,-a.**

sexenio *nm* six-year period.
sexismo *nm* sexism.
sexista *adj* **1** sexist. **2** *(machista)* chauvinistic.
▶ *nm* **1** sexist. **2** *(machista)* male chauvinist.
sexo *nm* **1** sex. **2** *(órganos)* sexual organs *pl*, genitals *pl*.
sextante *nm* sextant.
sexteto *nm* sextet.
sexto,-a *adj* sixth: *una sexta parte* a sixth; *el siglo sexto* the sixth century; *Alfonso sexto* Alfonso the sixth; *vive en un sexto piso* he lives in a sixth-floor flat; *acabó en sexto lugar* he finished in sixth palce. **2** *(sexto)* sixth: *soy el seis de la lista* I'm sixth on the list.
▶ *nm & nf* sixth: *le correspondió un sexto del pastel* he got a sixth of the cake.
sextuplicar *vt* to multiply by six, sextuplicate.
séxtuplo,-a *adj* sextuple.
▶ *nm* **séxtuplo** six times as much, six times as many.
sexual *adj (gen)* sex; *(relaciones)* sexual: *vida sexual* sex life.
sexualidad *nf* sexuality.
Seychelles *nm pl* **las (islas) Seychelles** the Seychelles.
sha *nm* shah.
shérif *nm* sheriff.

si¹ *conj* **1** *(condicional)* if: *si quieres puedes venir con nosotros* you can come with us if you want to. **2** *(disyuntiva, duda)* if, whether: *no sé si decírselo (o no)* I don't know whether to tell her (or not). **3** *(énfasis)* but: *¡pero si es facilísimo!* ¡but it's really easy! ⎵LOC⎵ **como si** as if. ▌ **por si acaso** just in case: *llévatelo por si acaso* take it with you just in case.
si² *nm* MÚS ti, si, B.
sí¹ *pron* **1** *(él)* himself; *(ella)* herself; *(cosa)* itself; *(ellos, ellas)* themselves; *(usted)* yourself; *(ustedes)* yourselves: *lo hizo por sí misma* she did it by herself; *hablaban para sí* they were talking to themselves. **2** *(uno mismo)* oneself. **3** *(recíproco)* each other: *hablaban entre sí* they were talking to each other.
sí² *adv* **1** yes: *dijo que sí* she said yes. **2** *(enfático)* of course: *sí que me gusta* of course I like it. ⎵LOC⎵ **creo que sí** I think so. ▌ **porque sí 1** *(sin razón)* just because I *(you, etc)* say so. **2** *(por naturaleza)* that's the way it is: *no puedes marcharte porque sí* you can't leave just because you feel like it.
siberiano,-a *adj* Siberian.
▶ *nm & nf* Siberian.
sicoanálisis *nm inv* psychoanalysis.
sicodélico,-a *adj* psychedelic.
sicología *nf* psychology.
sida *abrev* MED **(síndrome de inmunodeficiencia adquirida)** acquired immune deficiency syndrome; *(abreviatura)* AIDS.
siderurgia *nf* iron and steel industry.
sidra *nf* cider, US hard cider.
siega *nf* **1** *(acción)* harvesting, reaping. **2** *(época)* harvest, harvest time. **3** *(mieses)* harvest.
siembra *nf* **1** *(acción)* sowing. **2** *(época)* sowing time. **3** *(sembrado)* sown field.
siempre *adv* always: *siempre recordaré sus palabras* I'll always remember her words.
siempreviva *nf* everlasting flower, immortelle.
sien *nf* temple.
sierra *nf* **1** TÉC saw. **2** GEOG mountain range.

Sierra Leona *nf* Sierra Leone.
sierraleonés,-esa *adj* Sierra Leonean.
▸ *nm & nf* Sierra Leonean.
siesta *nf* siesta, afternoon nap.
siete *adj (cardinal)* seven; *(séptimo)* seventh.
▸ *nm* **1** *(número)* seven. **2** *fam (rasgón)* tear.

✎ Para ejemplos de uso, consulta seis.

sigilo *nm* **1** *(secreto)* secrecy. **2** *(discreción)* discretion.
sigla *nf* acronym, abbreviation.
siglo *nm* **1** century. **2** *fig (vida mundana)* world. COMP **el Siglo de Oro** the Golden Age.
significación *nf* **1** *(sentido)* meaning. **2** *(trascendencia)* significance.
significado,-a *adj* well-known, important.
▸ *nm* **significado 1** meaning. **2** LING signifier.
significar *vt* **1** to mean: *no sé lo que significa* I don't know what it means. **2** *(hacer saber)* to make known, express.
significativo,-a *adj (que da a entender)* meaningful. **2** *(importante)* significant.
signo *nm* **1** *(gen)* sign. **2** GRAM mark. **3** *(destino)* fate, destiny. **4** *(tendencia)* tendency.
siguiente *adj* following, next: *vamos a leer el capítulo siguiente* we're going to read the next chapter. LOC **¡el siguiente!** next, please!
sílaba *nf* syllable.
silbar *vi* **1** to whistle. **2** *(abuchear)* to hiss, boo.
silbato *nm* whistle.
silbido *nm* **1** *(acción)* whistle, whistling. **2** *(abucheo)* hissing.
silenciar *vt* **1** *(ocultar)* to hush up. **2** *(pasar por alto)* not to mention.
silencio *nm* silence. LOC **guardar silencio** to keep quiet.
silencioso,-a *adj (persona)* quiet; *(objeto)* silent.
silepsis *nf inv* syllepsis.
sílex *nm inv* flint.

silicato *nm* silicate.
sílice *nf* silica.
silíceo,-a *adj* flinty.
silícico,-a *adj* silicic.
silicio *nm* silicon.
silla *nf* **1** chair. **2** *(de montar)* saddle.
sillar *nm (piedra)* ashlar.
sillín *nm* saddle.
sillón *nm* armchair.
silueta *nf* **1** *(contorno)* silhouette. **2** *(figura)* figure, shape.
silvestre *adj* wild.
silvicultura *nf* forestry.
sima *nf* abyss, chasm.
simbiosis *nf inv* symbiosis.
simbólico,-a *adj* symbolic, symbolical.
simbolizar *vt* to symbolize.
símbolo *nm* symbol.
simetría *nf* symmetry.
simétrico,-a *adj* symmetric.
simiente *nf* seed.
simiesco,-a *adj* simian, apelike.
símil *nm* **1** *(comparación)* comparison. **2** *(semejanza)* resemblance. **3** LIT simile.
similar *adj* similar.
simio *nm* simian, monkey.
simpatía *nf* **1** *(cordialidad)* affection (por, for), liking (por, for). **2** *(amabilidad)* warmth, pleasantness. **3** *(afinidad)* affinity (por, with). **4** *(solidaridad)* sympathy (por, towards), solidarity (con, with). **5** MED sympathy.
simpático,-a *adj* **1** *(amable)* nice, likeable; *(agradable)* kind, friendly; *(encantador)* charming. **2** MED sympathetic.
simpatizante *nm o nf* supporter.
simpatizar *vi* **1** *(con persona)* to get on (con, with). **2** *(con idea, etc)* to sympathize (con, with).
simple *adj* **1** *(gen)* simple. **2** *(único)* single, just one. **3** *(mero)* mere. **4** *(persona)* simple, simple-minded.
simplicidad *nf* **1** simplicity. **2** *(ingenuidad)* naivety, ingenuousness.
simplificar *vt* to simplify.
simposio *nm* symposium.
simulación *nf* simulation.

S

simulacro *nm* sham, pretence (US pretense): *simulacro de incendio* fire drill.

simulado,-a *adj* simulated.

simulador,-ra *adj* simulative.
> *nm & nf* pretender.
> *nm* **simulador** TÉC simulator.

simular *vt* **1** to simulate. **2** *(fingir)* to pretend.

simultanear *vt* **1** *(hacer dos cosas)* to do simultaneously, do at the same time. **2** *(combinar)* to combine.

simultaneidad *nf* simultaneity.

simultáneo,-a *adj* simultaneous.

sin *prep* **1** *(carencia)* without. **2** *(además de)* not counting. LOC **estar sin + inf** not to have been + *pp*: *está sin planchar* it hasn't been ironed. **‖ sin querer** accidentally, by mistake: *lo hizo sin querer* he didn't mean to do it.

sinagoga *nf* synagogue.

sinalefa *nf* synalepha, synaloepha, elision.

sincerarse *vpr* *(abrirse)* to open one's heart (con, to).

sinceridad *nf* sincerity.

sincero,-a *adj* sincere.

sinclinal *nm* syncline.

síncopa *nf* **1** MÚS syncopation. **2** LING syncope.

sincopado,-a *adj* MÚS syncopated.

sincopar *vt* **1** *(notas, palabras)* to syncopate. **2** *fig (abreviar)* to abridge.

síncope *nm* syncope.

sincretismo *nm* syncretism.

sincronía *nf* synchrony.

sincrónico,-a *adj* synchronic.

sincronismo *nm* synchronism.

sincronización *nf* synchronization.

sincronizar *vt* to synchronize.

sindicado,-a *adj* who belongs to a trade union.

sindical *adj* trade union, union.

sindicalismo *nm* trade unionism, unionism.

sindicalista *nm o nf* trade unionist, unionist.

sindicar *vt* to unionize.

> *vpr* **sindicarse** *(unirse a un sindicato)* to join a trade union.

sindicato *nm* trade union, union.

síndico *nm* **1** POL elected representative. **2** *(depositario)* trustee.

síndrome *nm* syndrome.

sinéresis *nf inv* syneresis, synaeresis.

sinergia *nf* synergy.

sinfín *nm* endless number.

sinfonía *nf* symphony.

sinfónico,-a *adj* symphonic.

Singapur *nm* Singapore.

singular *adj* **1** *(único)* singular, single. **2** *(excepcional)* extraordinary, exceptional.
> *nm* GRAM singular. LOC **en singular** GRAM in the singular.

singularidad *nf* **1** *(unicidad)* singularity. **2** *(excepcionalidad)* strangeness, uniqueness.

singularizar *vt* **1** *(distinguir)* to distinguish, single out. **2** GRAM to use in the singular.
> *vpr* **singularizarse** to distinguish os (por, by/with), stand out ((por, for).

siniestra *nf (izquierda)* left hand.

siniestrado,-a *adj lit* damaged.

siniestro,-a *adj* **1** *lit (izquierdo)* left, lefthand. **2** *(malo)* sinister, ominous.
> *nm* **siniestro** disaster, catastrophe; *(accidente)* accident; *(incendio)* fire.

sinnúmero *nm* endless number.

sino¹ *conj* **1** *(contraposición)* but: *no es blanco sino negro* it isn't white but black. **2** *(excepción)* but, except for: *nadie lo sabe sino Antonio* nobody knows except for Antonio.

sino² *nm (destino)* fate, destiny.

sinonimia *nf* synonymy.

sinónimo,-a *adj* synonymous.
> *nm* **sinónimo** synonym.

sinopsis *nf inv* synopsis.

sinóptico,-a *adj* synoptic, synoptical.

sinrazón *nf* wrong, injustice.

sinsabor *nm fig* worry, trouble, heartache.

sintáctico,-a *adj* syntactic, syntactical.

sintagma *nm* phrase. COMP sintagma nominal noun phrase.

sintaxis *nf inv* syntax.

síntesis *nf inv* synthesis.

sintético,-a *adj* synthetic.

sintetizador *nm* synthesizer.

sintetizar *vt* **1** to synthesize. **2** *(resumir)* to summarize: *sintetizando diría que...* to sum up, I'd like to say that...

síntoma *nm* symptom.

sintomático,-a *adj* **1** symptomatic. **2** *fig* significant.

sintomatología *nf* symptomatology.

sintonía *nf* **1** *(de radio)* tuning. **2** *(música)* signature tune. **3** *fig (armonía)* harmony. LOC estar en sintonía con ALGN *fig* to be in tune with SB, be on SB's wavelength.

sintonizador *nm* **1** *(botón)* tuning knob. **2** *(de cadena de sonido)* tuner.

sintonizar *vt (radio)* to tune in to: *sintonizó una emisora local* he tuned in to a local radio station.
▶ *vi fig (llevarse bien)* to get on well, be on the same wavelength.

sinuosidad *nf* **1** *(cualidad)* sinuosity. **2** *(curva)* bend, curve. **3** *fig (de argumento, etc)* tortuousness; *(de persona)* deviousness.

sinuoso,-a *adj* **1** *(camino)* winding. **2** *fig (argumento)* tortuous; *(persona)* devious.

sinvergüenza *nm o nf* **1** *(pícaro)* rotter, swine, louse. **2** *(descarado)* cheeky devil.

siquiatra *nm o nf* psychiatrist.

siquiatría *nf* psychiatry.

síquico,-a *adj* → psíquico,-a.

siquiera *conj* **1** *(adversativa)* even though, even if: *quisiera hablar contigo, siquiera fuera un momento* I would like to speak to you, even if it's only for a moment. **2** *(distributiva)* whether.
▶ *adv (por lo menos)* at least: *dame siquiera la mitad* give me at least half of it.

sirena *nf* **1** *(ninfa)* siren, mermaid. **2** *(alarma)* siren.

Siria *nf* Syria.

sirio,-a *adj* Syrian.
▶ *nm & nf* Syrian.

sirviente,-a *nm & nf* servant.

sisa *nf* COST armhole.

sisal *nm* sisal.

sisar *vt* **1** COST to dart, take in. **2** *(hurtar)* to pilfer, pinch, nick; *(estafar)* to cheat.

sisear *vi* to hiss.
▶ *vt* to hiss.

siseo *nm* hiss, hissing.

sísmico,-a *adj* seismic.

sismo *nm* earthquake, tremor.

sismógrafo *nm* seismograph.

sismología *nf* seismology.

sismólogo,-a *nm & nf* seismologist.

sistema *nm* system. COMP sistema de ecuaciones simultaneous equations *pl*. ❙ sistema métrico decimal decimal metric system. ❙ sistema nervioso nervous system. ❙ sistema operativo operative system.

sistemático,-a *adj* systematic.

sistematizar *vt* to systematize.

sístole *nf* systole.

sistólico,-a *adj* systolic.

sitiado,-a *adj* besieged.
▶ *nm & nf* besieged.

sitial *nm* seat of honour (US honor).

sitiar *vt* to besiege, lay siege to.

sitio *nm* **1** *(lugar)* place. **2** *(espacio)* space, room. **3** *(asiento)* seat. **4** MIL siege. COMP sitio web website.

sito,-a *adj fml* located, situated.

situación *nf* **1** *(circunstancia)* situation. **2** *(posición)* position. **3** *(emplazamiento)* situation, location.

situado,-a *adj* situated, located.

situar *vt* to place, locate, situate, put.
▶ *vpr* situarse **1** *(colocarse)* to be placed, be located, be situated. **2** *(lograr una posición)* to get on, do well, be successful.

soasar *vt* to roast lightly.

sobaco *nm* armpit.

sobado,-a *adj* **1** *(desgastado)* worn, shabby. **2** *(manoseado)* well-thumbed, dog-eared. **3** *fig (manido)* well-worn.

S

sobar *vt* **1** *(ablandar)* to knead. **2** *fig* *(manosear - objeto)* to finger; *(- persona)* to grope, paw, touch up.

soberanía *nf* sovereignty.

soberano,-a *adj* **1** sovereign. **2** *fig* extreme, supreme. **3** *fam* huge, great.
► *nm & nf* sovereign.

soberbia *nf* **1** *(orgullo)* pride; *(arrogancia)* arrogance, haughtiness. **2** *(cólera)* rage, anger.

soberbio,-a *adj* **1** *(orgulloso)* proud; *(arrogante)* arrogant, haughty. **2** *(suntuoso)* sumptuous, magnificent. **3** *(magnífico)* superb, splendid, magnificent.

sobornable *adj* bribable, venal.

sobornar *vt* to bribe, suborn.

soborno *nm* **1** *(acción)* bribery. **2** *(regalo, etc)* bribe.

sobra *nf* *(exceso)* excess, surplus. ⌜LOC⌝ saber ALGO de sobra to know STH only too well.
► *nf pl* sobras *(desperdicios)* leftovers.

sobrado,-a *adj* *(que sobra)* ample, more than enough, plenty of.

sobrante *adj* leftover, remaining, spare.

sobrar *vi* **1** *(haber más de lo necesario)* to be more than enough, be too much. **2** *(estar de más)* to be superfluous, be unnecessary. **3** *(quedar)* to have left over, be left over.

sobre *prep* **1** *(encima)* on, upon, on top of. **2** *(por encima)* over, above. **3** *(acerca de)* about, on. **4** *(alrededor de)* about, around.
► *nm* **1** *(de correo)* envelope. **2** *(de sopa, etc)* packet. ⌜LOC⌝ sobre todo above all, especially.

sobre- *pref* super-, over-.

sobreabundancia *nf* superabundance, overabundance.

sobrealimentar *vt* to overfeed.

sobreático *nm* penthouse.

sobrecarga *nf* **1** overload. **2** *fig* additional burden, further worry.

sobrecargar *vt* **1** to overload. **2** *fig* to overburden.

sobrecogedor,-ra *adj* **1** *(conmovedor)* dramatic, awesome. **2** *(que da miedo)* frightening.

sobrecoger *vt* **1** *(coger de repente)* to startle, take by surprise. **2** *(asustar)* to frighten, scare.

sobrecubierta *nf* jacket, dust cover.

sobredosis *nf inv* overdose.

sobreentender *vt* **1** *(comprender)* to understand. **2** *(deducir)* to deduce.
► *vpr* **sobreentenderse** to be implied, be inferred: *se sobreentiende que su respuesta será afirmativa* one assumes that she will say yes.

sobreexcitación *nf* overexcitement.

sobreexcitar *vt* to overexcite.
► *vpr* **sobreexcitarse** to get overexcited.

sobreexponer *vt* to overexpose.

sobreexposición *nf* overexposure.

sobrehilar *vt* COST to whipstitch.

sobrehumano,-a *adj* superhuman.

sobreimpresión *nf* overprint.

sobrellevar *vt* to bear, endure.

sobremanera *adv* exceedingly.

sobremesa *nf* **1** *(período)* afternoon: *la programación de la sobremesa* the afternoon's television programmes. **2** *(charla)* table talk.

sobrenadar *vi* to float.

sobrenatural *adj* supernatural.

sobrenombre *nm* nickname.

sobrentender *vt-vpr* → sobreentender.

sobrepaga *nf* bonus.

sobrepasar *vt* **1** to exceed, surpass, be in excess of. **2** *(competición)* to beat.

sobrepeso *nm* **1** overload, excess weight. **2** *(de persona)* excess weight.

sobreponer *vt* to put on top (en, of), superimpose (en, on).
► *vpr* **sobreponerse** **1** *fig* *(al dolor, etc)* to overcome (a, -). **2** *fig* *(animarse)* to pull os together.

sobreproducción *nf* excess production, overproduction.

sobresaliente *adj* **1** sticking out, protruding. **2** *fig* outstanding, excellent.
► *nm* *(calificación - colegio)* A; *(- universidad)* first, US A.

sobresalir *vi* **1** to stick out, protrude. **2** *fig* to stand out, excel.

sobresaltar *vt* to startle.

▶ *vpr* **sobresaltarse** to be startled.

sobresalto *nm* start; *(de temor)* fright, shock.

sobresdrújulo,-a *adj* accented on the antepenultimate syllable.

sobrestimar *vt* to overestimate.

sobretodo *nm (abrigo)* overcoat.

sobrevalorar *vt* to overestimate.

sobrevenir *vi* to happen to, befall: *no sabremos nunca lo que le sobrevino* we'll never know what happened to her.

sobreviviente *nm o nf* survivor.

sobrevivir *vi* **1** *(gen)* to survive. **2** *(a alguien)* to outlive.

sobrevolar *vt* to fly over.

sobrexcitación *nf* overexcitement.

sobrexcitar *vt-vpr* → sobreexcitar.

sobrexponer *vt* → sobreexponer.

sobriedad *nf* sobriety, moderation, restraint.

sobrino,-a *nm & nf (hombre)* nephew; *(mujer)* niece.

sobrio,-a *adj* **1** *(estilo, color, etc)* sober, plain. **2** *(persona)* sober, moderate.

socavar *vt* **1** *(excavar)* to dig under. **2** *fig* to undermine.

socavón *nm* **1** *(cueva excavada)* excavation. **2** *(bache)* hollow, hole. **3** *(de una mina)* gallery, tunnel.

sociabilidad *nf* sociability.

sociable *adj* sociable, friendly.

social *adj* social.

socialdemocracia *nf* social democracy.

socialdemócrata *adj* social democratic.

▶ *nm o nf* social democrat.

socialismo *nm* socialism.

socialista *adj* socialist.

▶ *nm o nf* socialist.

socializar *vt* **1** *(gen)* to socialize. **2** *(nacionalizar)* to nationalize.

sociedad *nf* **1** *(gen)* society. **2** COM company. **3** *(asociación)* society, association.

socio,-a *nm & nf* **1** *(miembro)* member. **2** COM partner, associate. **3** *(accionista)* shareholder, member.

socioeconómico,-a *adj* socioeconomic.

sociología *nf* sociology.

sociólogo,-a *nm & nf* sociologist.

socorrer *vt* to help, assist, come to the aid of, go to the aid of.

socorrista *nm o nf* life-saver, lifeguard.

socorro *nm* **1** *(ayuda)* help, aid, assistance. **2** *(provisiones)* supplies *pl*, provisions *pl*.

▶ *interj* help!

soda *nf* **1** *(bebida)* soda water. **2** QUÍM soda.

sódico,-a *adj* sodium.

sodio *nm* sodium.

sofá *nm* sofa, settee.

sofá-cama *nm* sofa bed, studio couch.

sofisticación *nf* sophistication.

sofisticado,-a *adj* sophisticated.

sofocante *adj* suffocating, stifling.

sofocar *vt* **1** *(ahogar)* to suffocate, stifle, smother. **2** *fig (incendio)* to put out, extinguish; *(rebelión)* to suppress, put down.

▶ *vpr* **sofocarse 1** *(de calor, etc)* to suffocate. **2** *fig (ruborizarse)* to blush.

sofoco *nm* **1** *(ahogo)* suffocation, stifling sensation. **2** *fig (vergüenza)* embarrassment; *(rubor)* blushing. **3** *fam (disgusto)* shock.

sofocón *nm fam* shock. LOC **llevarse un sofocón** *fam* to get into a state.

sofreír *vt* to fry lightly, brown.

sofrito *nm* fried tomato and onion sauce.

software *nm* software.

soga *nf* rope, cord.

soja *nf* soya bean, US soybean. COMP **salsa de soja** soy sauce.

sojuzgar *vt* to subjugate.

sol[1] *nm* **1** *(estrella)* sun. **2** *(luz)* sun, sunlight, sunshine. **3** *fam (persona)* darling. **4** *(moneda de Perú)* sol, standard monetary unit of Peru. LOC **hace sol** it's sunny, the sun's shining. I **tomar**

el sol 1 *(tendido)* to sunbathe. **2** *(al caminar)* to get some sun.

sol² *nm* MÚS sol, G.

solapa *nf* **1** *(de prenda)* lapel. **2** *(de sobre, libro)* flap.

solapado,-a *adj fig* sly, evasive.

solapar *vt* **1** COST to put lapels on. **2** *fig (ocultar)* to conceal, cover up.
▶ *vi (cubrir)* to overlap.

solar¹ *adj (del sol)* solar.

solar² *nm* **1** *(terreno)* plot, lot; *(en obras)* building site. **2** *(casa solariega)* ancestral home.

solar³ *vt (suelo)* to floor.

solaz *nm* **1** *(esparcimiento)* recreation, entertainment. **2** *(descanso)* rest, relaxation.

solazar *vt* **1** *(entretener)* to amuse, entertain. **2** *(descansar)* to rest, relax.
▶ *vpr* **solazarse 1** *(divertirse)* to enjoy os. **2** *(relajarse)* to relax.

soldado *nm* soldier. COMP **soldado raso** private.

soldador,-ra *nm & nf* welder.
▶ *nm* **soldador** soldering iron.

soldadura *nf* **1** *(acción)* welding, soldering. **2** *(unión)* weld, soldered joint.

soldar *vt* **1** *(metal)* to weld, solder. **2** *fig (enmendar)* to mend.
▶ *vpr* **soldarse** *(huesos)* to knit.

soleado,-a *adj* sunny.

solear *vt* to expose to the sun, put in the sun.

soledad *nf* **1** *(estado)* solitude. **2** *(sentimiento)* loneliness. **3** *(lugar)* lonely place.

solemne *adj* **1** solemn, majestic. **2** *pey* downright: *es una solemne tontería* it's downright stupidity.

solemnidad *nf* **1** *(pompa)* solemnity, pomp, formality. **2** *(acto, ceremonia)* solemn ceremony, ceremonial occasion.

solemnizar *vt (celebrar)* to solemnize, celebrate; *(conmemorar)* to commemorate.

soler *vi (acostumbrar - presente)* to be in the habit of + *-ing*; *(- pasado)* used to:

solía venir cada martes she used to come every Tuesday.

solicitante *nm o nf* applicant.

solicitar *vt* **1** *(pedir)* to request. **2** *(trabajo)* to apply for; *(permiso, etc)* to ask for; *(votos)* to canvass for. **3** *(persona)* to chase after. **4** *(cortejar)* to woo, court.

solícito,-a *adj* obliging, attentive.

solicitud *nf* **1** *(petición)* request; *(de trabajo)* application; *(- impreso)* application form. **2** *(instancia)* petition. **3** *(diligencia)* solicitude, care. COMP **solicitud de empleo** job application.

solidaridad *nf* solidarity.

solidario,-a *adj* **1** *(ligado)* united. **2** *(responsabilidad, causa)* common.

solidarizarse *vpr* **1** *(gen)* to show one's solidarity (con, with). **2** *(apoyar)* to support (con, -).

solidez *nf (resistencia)* solidity, strength; *(firmeza)* firmness.

solidificación *nf* solidification.

solidificar *vt* **1** *(líquido)* to solidify. **2** *(pasta)* to harden, set.
▶ *vpr* **solidificarse 1** *(líquido)* to solidify. **2** *(pasta)* to harden, set.

sólido,-a *adj* **1** *(fuerte)* solid, strong; *(firme)* firm. **2** *fig (color)* fast. **3** *fig (principios, etc)* sound.
▶ *nm* **sólido** solid.

solista *nm o nf* soloist.

solitaria *nf* MED tapeworm.

solitario,-a *adj* **1** *(que está solo)* solitary, lone. **2** *(que se siente solo)* lonely. **3** *(lugar)* deserted, lonely.
▶ *nm & nf (persona)* solitary person.
▶ *nm* **solitario** *(diamante, naipes)* solitaire.

sólito,-a *adj* usual, customary.

soliviantar *vt* **1** *(inducir)* to rouse, stir up. **2** *(irritar)* to irritate.

sollozar *vi* to sob.

sólo *adv* → **solo¹**.

solo¹ *adv* [sólo se usa si se puede producir confusión con el adjetivo o con el nombre] only, just: *solo quiero café* I just want a coffee.

solo,-a *adj* **1** *(sin compañía)* alone, on one's own, by os; *(sin ayuda)* (by) os, (for) os. **2** *(solitario)* lonely. **3** *(único)* only, sole, single. **4** *(café)* black.

▸ *nm* **solo 1** *(naipes)* solitaire. **2** *fam (café)* black coffee. **3** MÚS solo. LOC **a solas** alone, by os.

solomillo *nm* sirloin.

soltar *vt* **1** *(desasir)* to let go of, release, drop. **2** *(desatar)* to untie, unfasten, undo; *(aflojar)* to loosen. **3** *(preso)* to release, free, set free. **4** *(animal)* to let out; *(perro)* to unleash. **5** *(humo, olor)* to give off. **6** *(puntos)* to drop. **7** *(de vientre)* to loosen. **8** *fam (arrear)* to give, deal. **9** *fam (decir)* to come out with, blurt out.

▸ *vpr* **soltarse 1** *(desatarse)* to come untied, come unfastened. **2** *(desprenderse)* to come off. **3** *(tornillo, etc)* to come loose. **4** *(animal)* to get loose, break loose. **5** *(puntos)* to come undone. **6** *(vientre)* to loosen. **7** *fig (adquirir habilidad)* to become proficient, get the knack. **8** *fig (desenvolverse)* to become self-confident, loosen up.

soltero,-a *adj* single, unmarried.

▸ *nm & nf (hombre)* bachelor, single man; *(mujer)* single woman.

soluble *adj* soluble.

solución *nf* solution.

solucionar *vt* **1** *(problema)* to solve. **2** *(huelga, asunto)* to settle.

solventar *vt* **1** *(dificultad, problema)* to solve, resolve. **2** *(deuda, asunto)* to settle.

solvente *adj* **1** FIN solvent. **2** *(fiable)* reliable.

▸ *nm* QUÍM solvent.

somalí *adj* Somali.

▸ *nm o nf* Somali.

Somalia *nf* Somalia.

sombra *nf* **1** *(falta de sol)* shade. **2** *(silueta)* shadow. **3** *(espectro)* ghost, shade. **4** *fig (persona que sigue a otra)* shadow. **5** *fam fig (gracia)* wit. **6** *fig (parte pequeña)* trace, shadow, bit. **7** *fig (clandestinidad)* secrecy.

sombreado *nm* shading.

sombrero *nm* **1** *(prenda)* hat.

sombrilla *nf* parasol, sunshade.

sombrío,-a *adj* **1** *(lugar)* dark. **2** *fig (tenebroso)* gloomy, sombre (US somber). **3** *fig (persona)* gloomy, sullen.

someter *vt* **1** *(rebeldes)* to subdue, put down; *(rebelión)* to quell. **2** *(hacer recibir)* to subject (a, to). **3** *(pasiones)* to subdue. **4** *(proponer, presentar)* to submit.

▸ *vpr* **someterse 1** *(rendirse)* to surrender (a, to). **2** *(tratamiento, etc)* to undergo (a, -). LOC **someter a prueba** to test, put to the test. ‖ **someter** ALGO **a votación** to put STH to the vote.

somnolencia *nf* sleepiness, drowsiness, somnolence.

somnoliento,-a *adj* sleepy, drowsy.

son *nm* **1** *(sonido)* sound. **2** *fig (modo)* manner, way: *a mi son* my way. LOC **en son de paz** in peace.

sonado,-a *adj* **1** *(conocido)* famous. **2** *(escándalo, etc)* much talked-about. **3** *fam fig (loco)* mad, crazy.

sonámbulo,-a *nm & nf* sleepwalker, somnambulist.

sonar¹ *vi* **1** *(hacer ruido)* to sound. **2** *(timbre, teléfono, etc)* to ring. **3** *(alarma, reloj)* to go off. **4** *(instrumento)* to play. **5** *(letra)* to be pronounced.

▸ *vt* **1** *(conocer vagamente)* to sound familiar, ring a bell. **2** *(timbre, etc)* to ring; *(bocina)* to blow, sound; *(instrumento)* to play.

▸ *vpr* **sonarse** *(nariz)* to blow.

sonar² *nm* MAR sonar.

sonda *nf* **1** MED *(para intervenciones quirúrgicas)* probe; *(para evacuar líquidos)* catheter. **2** MAR sounding line. **3** *(barreno)* drill, bore. **4** *(atmosférica)* sonde; *(espacio)* probe.

sondear *vt* **1** MED to sound, probe. **2** MAR to sound. **3** *(subsuelo)* to drill, bore. **4** *fig (encuestar)* to sound out.

sondeo *nm* **1** MED sounding, probing. **2** MAR sounding. **3** *(del subsuelo)* drilling, boring. **4** *fig (encuesta)* poll.

soneto *nm* sonnet.

sónico,-a *adj* sonic.

sonido *nm* sound.

sonoridad *nf* sonority.

S

sonoro,-a *adj* **1** *(resonante)* loud, resounding. **2** LING sound.

sonreír *vi* to smile.
▶ *vt* **1** to smile at. **2** *fig (favorecer)* to smile on, smile upon.
▶ *vpr* **sonreírse** to smile.

sonriente *adj* smiling.

sonrisa *nf* smile.

sonrojar *vt* to make blush.
▶ *vpr* **sonrojarse** to blush.

sonsacar *vt* **1** *(gen)* to wheedle. **2** *fig (secreto)* to get out of, worm out.

soñador,-ra *nm & nf* dreamer.

soñar *vt* **1** *(al dormir)* to dream. **2** *fig (fantasear)* to daydream, dream.
▶ *vi* **1** *(al dormir)* to dream (con, about/of). **2** *fig (fantasear)* to daydream (con, about), dream (con, about/of).

soñolencia *nf* sleepiness.

soñoliento,-a *adj* drowsy, sleepy.

sopa *nf (plato)* soup.

sopesar *vt* **1** to try the weight of. **2** *fig* to weigh up.

soplar *vi* **1** *(viento, etc)* to blow. **2** *fam (denunciar)* to squeal.
▶ *vt* **1** *(polvo, etc)* to blow away, blow off; *(vela)* to blow out; *(sopa)* to blow on; *(globo)* to blow up. **2** *(vidrio)* to blow. **3** *fam fig (delatar)* to split on, grass on. **4** *fam fig (en un examen, etc)* to whisper the answer, tell the answer.

soplete *nm* blowtorch, blowlamp.

soplido *nm* blow, puff.

soplo *nm* **1** *(con la boca)* blow, puff. **2** *(de viento)* puff. **3** *fig (momento)* moment, minute. **4** MED murmur. **5** *fam (de secreto, etc)* tip-off.

soportar *vt* **1** *(aguantar)* to support, bear. **2** *fig (sufrir)* to stand, bear, endure. **3** *fig (lluvia, tormenta, etc)* to weather.

soporte *nm* support. COMP **soporte de datos** INFORM data carrier.

sorbo *nm* **1** *(acción)* sip. **2** *(trago)* gulp.

sordera *nf* deafness.

sordidez *nf* **1** *(suciedad)* squalor. **2** *(mezquindad)* meanness.

sórdido,-a *adj* **1** *(sucio)* squalid, sordid. **2** *(mezquino)* mean.

sordo,-a *adj* **1** *(persona)* deaf. **2** *(sonido, dolor, golpe)* dull. **3** LING voiceless.
▶ *nm & nf (persona)* deaf person.

sordomudez *nf* deaf-mutism.

sordomudo,-a *adj* deaf and dumb.
▶ *nm & nf* deaf mute.

sorgo *nm* sorghum.

sorprendente *adj* surprising, amazing, astonishing.

sorprender *vt* **1** *(coger desprevenido)* to catch unawares, take by surprise. **2** *fig (descubrir)* to discover; *(conversación)* to overhear. **3** *fig (maravillar)* to surprise, astonish, amaze.
▶ *vpr* **sorprenderse** *fig* to be surprised.

sorpresa *nf* surprise.

sortear *vt* **1** *(echar a suertes)* to draw lots for, cast lots for. **2** *(rifar)* to raffle. **3** MIL to draft. **4** *fig (obstáculos, dificultad)* to get round, overcome; *(preguntas)* to dodge, evade, get round.

sorteo *nm* draw; *(rifa)* raffle.

sortija *nf (anillo)* ring.

sortilegio *nm* **1** *(hechicería)* sorcery, witchcraft. **2** *(hechizo)* spell.

sosa *nf* **1** QUÍM soda. **2** BOT saltwort.

sosegado,-a *adj* calm, quiet.

sosegar *vt (aplacar)* to calm, quieten.
▶ *vpr* **sosegarse** *(calmarse)* to calm down.

sosiego *nm* calmness, peace.

soso,-a *adj* **1** *(insípido)* tasteless; *(sin sal)* unsalted. **2** *fig* dull, insipid.

sospecha *nf* suspicion.

sospechar *vt (imaginar)* to suspect, think, suppose.
▶ *vi (desconfiar)* to suspect (de, -).

sospechoso,-a *adj* suspicious.
▶ *nm & nf* suspect.

sostén *nm* **1** *(apoyo)* support. **2** *(sustento)* sustenance. **3** [también se usa en plural con el mismo significado] *(prenda)* bra.

sostener *vt* **1** *(mantener firme)* to support, hold up. **2** *(sujetar)* to hold. **3** *fig (apoyar)* to support, back. **4** *fig (afirmar)* to maintain, affirm. **5** *fig (alimentar)* to support, keep. **6** *fig (velocidad, correspondencia, relación, etc)* to keep up.
▶ *vpr* **sostenerse** **1** *(mantenerse)* to support os; *(de pie)* to stand up. **2** *(permanecer)* to stay, remain.

sostenibilidad *nf* sustainability.

sostenible *adj (gen)* sustainable; *(argumento)* tenable.

sostenido,-a *adj* **1** *(continuado)* sustained; *(constante)* steady. **2** MÚS sharp: *fa sostenido* F sharp.
► *nm* **sostenido** MÚS sharp.

sota *nf (cartas)* jack, knave.

sótano *nm (gen)* basement; *(de casa)* cellar, basement.

sotavento *nm* lee, leeward.

soterrar *vt* **1** to bury. **2** *fig* to hide.

soto *nm* **1** *(arboleda)* grove, copse.

Sri Lanka *nf* Sri Lanka.

stop *nm* **1** *(señal)* stop sign. **2** *(parada)* stop.

su *adj (de él)* his; *(de ella)* her; *(de usted, de ustedes)* your; *(de ellos, de ellas)* their; *(de animales, cosas)* its; *(de uno)* one's.

suave *adj* **1** *(agradable al tacto)* soft, smooth. **2** *(liso, llano)* smooth, even. **3** *fig (apacible)* gentle, mild. **4** *fig (tranquilo)* easy. **5** *fig (música, palabras, voz, luz, movimiento, viento)* soft, gentle. **6** *fig (clima)* mild, clement.

suavizante *nm* **1** *(de pelo)* hair conditioner. **2** *(de ropa)* fabric softener.

suavizar *vt* **1** *(hacer agradable)* to soften. **2** *(alisar)* to smooth (out). **3** *fig* to soften.

subacuático,-a *adj* underwater.

subafluente *nm* tributary.

subalimentación *nf* undernourishment.

subalimentar *vt* to underfeed.

subalterno,-a *nm & nf* subordinate.

subasta *nf* **1** *(venta)* auction. **2** *(adjudicación de obra)* invitation to tender.

subastador,-ra *nm & nf* auctioneer.

subastar *vt* to auction (off).

subatómico,-a *adj* subatomic.

subcampeón,-ona *nm & nf (en competición)* runner-up; *(en ránking)* number two.

subdesarrollo *nm* underdevelopment.

subdirector,-ra *nm & nf* assistant director, assistant manager.

súbdito,-a *nm & nf* **1** *(de un rey)* subject. **2** *(ciudadano)* citizen.

subida *nf* **1** *(ascenso)* ascent, climb. **2** *(pendiente)* slope, hill. **3** *fig (aumento - gen)* increase; *(- de temperatura)* rise; *(- de precios, salario)* rise, increase.

subíndice *nm* subscript, subindex.

subir *vi* **1** *(ir hacia arriba - gen)* to go up, come up; *(- avión)* to climb. **2** *(en un vehículo - coche)* to get in; *(autobús, avión, barco, tren)* to get on, get onto. **3** *(montar - bicicleta)* to get on; *(- caballo)* to get on, mount. **4** *(a un árbol)* to climb up. **5** *fig (elevarse, aumentar)* to rise. **6** *fig (categoría, puesto)* to be promoted.
► *vt* **1** *(escaleras, calle)* to go up, climb; *(montaña)* to climb. **2** *(mover arriba)* to carry up, take up, bring up; *(poner arriba)* to put upstairs. **3** *(cabeza, etc)* to lift, raise. **4** *(pared)* to raise. **5** *fig (precio, salario, etc)* to raise, put up. **6** *fig (subir el volumen - voz)* to raise; *(- aparato)* to turn up. **7** *fig (color)* to strengthen.
► *vpr* **subirse 1** *(piso, escalera)* to go up. **2** *(árbol, muro, etc)* to climb up (a, -). **3** *(en un vehículo - coche)* to get in (a, -); *(autobús)* to get on (a, -); *(avión, barco, tren)* to get on (a, -), get onto (a,-): *¡súbete, súbete al coche!* get in, get into the car! **4** *(en animales, bicicleta)* to get on (a, -), mount. **5** *(ropa, calcetines)* to pull up; *(cremallera)* to do up, zip up; *(mangas)* to roll up.

súbito,-a *adj* sudden.

subjetivo,-a *adj* subjective.

subjuntivo,-a *adj* subjunctive.
► *nm* **subjuntivo** subjunctive.

sublevación *nf* uprising, revolt.

submarinismo *nm* skin diving.

submarinista *nm o nf* skin-diver.

submarino,-a *adj* underwater.
► *nm* **submarino** submarine.

submúltiplo,-a *adj* submultiple.
► *nm* **submúltiplo** submultiple.

suboficial *nm* **1** MIL noncommissioned officer. **2** MAR petty officer.

subordinación *nf* subordination.

subordinado,-a *adj* subordinate.
► *nm & nf* subordinate.

subordinar *vt* to subordinate.
► *vpr* **subordinarse** to subordinate os.

S

subproducto *nm* by-product.
subrayar *vt* **1** to underline. **2** *fig* to emphasize, underline, stress.
subreino *nm* subkingdom.
subrepticio,-a *adj* surreptitious.
subrogar *vt* to subrogate, substitute.
subsanar *vt* **1** *(remediar)* to rectify, correct. **2** *(dificultad, etc)* to overcome.
subscribir *vt-vpr* → suscribir.
subscriptor,-ra *nm & nf* subscriber.
subscrito,-a *adj-nm & nf* → suscrito,-a.
subsecretaría *nf* **1** *(cargo)* under-secretaryship. **2** *(oficina)* under-secretary's office.
subsecretario,-a *nm & nf* under-secretary.
subsidiario,-a *adj* subsidiary.
subsidio *nm* allowance, benefit.
subsistencia *nf* **1** *(hecho)* subsistence. **2** *(lo necesario para vivir)* sustenance.
  ▶ *nf pl* **subsistencias** *(provisiones)* food *sing*, provisions, supplies.
subsistir *vi* **1** *(conservarse)* to subsist, last. **2** *(vivir)* live on, survive.
substancia *nf* → sustancia.
substancial *adj* → sustancial.
substanciar *vt* to condense, abridge.
substancioso,-a *adj* → sustancioso,-a.
substantivar *vt* to use as a noun.
substantivo,-a *adj-nm* → sustantivo.
substitución *nf* substitution.
substituible *adj* replaceable.
substituir *vt* → sustituir.
substituto,-a *nm & nf* → sustituto,-a.
substracción *nf* → sustracción.
substraendo *nm* subtrahend.
substraer *vt-vpr* → sustraer.
substrato *nm* substratum.
subsuelo *nm* subsoil.
subterfugio *nm* *(escapatoria)* subterfuge; *(pretexto)* pretext.
subterráneo,-a *adj* underground.
  ▶ *nm* **subterráneo** underground passage, tunnel, subway.
subtítulo *nm* **1** subtitle. **2** LIT subhead.
subtotal *nm* subtotal.
subtropical *adj* subtropical.

suburbano,-a *adj* suburban.
  ▶ *nm* suburbano suburban train.
suburbio *nm* *(periferia)* suburb.
subvención *nf* subsidy, grant.
subvencionar *vt* to subsidize.
subversión *nf* subversion.
subversivo,-a *adj* subversive.
subyacente *adj* underlying.
subyacer *vi* to underlie (en, -).
subyugar *vt* **1** to subjugate. **2** *fig* to captivate.
succionar *vt* to suck up.
suceder *vi* **1** [sólo se usa en tercera persona; no lleva sujeto] *(acontecer)* to happen, occur: ¿qué sucede? what's the matter? **2** *(seguir)* to follow (a, -), succeed (a, -). **3** *(heredar)* to succeed.
  ▶ *vpr* **sucederse** to follow one another.
sucesión *nf* **1** *(herencia)* succession, inheritance. **2** *(descendencia)* issue, heirs *pl*. **3** *(al trono)* succession. **4** *(serie)* series, succession.
sucesivo,-a *adj* **1** *(siguiente)* following, successive. **2** *(consecutivo)* consecutive, running.
suceso *nm* **1** *(hecho)* event, happening, occurrence. **2** *(incidente)* incident. **3** *(delito)* crime.
sucesor,-ra *nm & nf* successor.
suciedad *nf* **1** *(inmundicia)* dirt, filth. **2** *(calidad)* dirtiness, filthiness.
sucio,-a *adj* **1** *(con manchas)* dirty, filthy. **2** *(que se ensucia fácilmente)* which dirties easily. **3** *fig (deshonesto)* shady, underhand. **4** DEP *fig* foul, dirty, unfair. **5** *fig (trabajo, lenguaje)* dirty, filthy.
  ▶ *adv* **sucio** *fig* in an underhand way, dirty. [LOC] **en sucio** in rough.
sucumbir *vi* **1** *(rendirse)* to succumb (a, to), yield (a, to). **2** *(morir)* to perish. **3** *fig (tentación, etc)* to give in (a, to), yield (a, to).
sucursal *nf* **1** *(oficina)* branch, branch office. **2** *(delegación)* subsidiary.
sudadera *nf* **1** *(prenda)* sweatshirt. **2** *fam (acción)* sweat.
Sudáfrica *nf* South Africa.
sudafricano,-a *adj* South African.
Sudamérica *nf* South America.

sudamericano,-a *adj* South American.

Sudán *nm* Sudan.

sudanés,-esa *adj* Sudanese.
▶ *nm & nf* Sudanese.

sudar *vi (transpirar)* to sweat, perspire.

sudario *nm* shroud.

sudeste *adj* **1** *(del sudeste)* southeast, southeastern; *(hacia el sudeste)* southeasterly. **2** *(viento)* southeast.
▶ *nm* **1** *(punto cardinal)* southeast. **2** *(viento)* southeast wind.

sudoeste *adj* **1** *(del sudoeste)* southwest, southwestern; *(hacia el sudoeste)* southwesterly. **2** *(viento)* southwest.
▶ *nm* **1** *(punto cardinal)* southwest. **2** *(viento)* southwest wind.

sudor *nm* **1** sweat. **2** *fig* effort.

sudoríparo,-a *adj* sweat. COMP **glándulas sudoríparas** sweat glands.

sudoroso,-a *adj* sweaty.

Suecia *nf* Sweden.

sueco,-a *adj* Swedish.
▶ *nm & nf (persona)* Swede.
▶ *nm* **sueco** *(idioma)* Swedish.

suegro,-a *nm & nf (hombre)* father-in-law; *(mujer)* mother-in-law.

suela *nf (del calzado)* sole.

sueldo *nm* salary, pay, wages *pl*.

suelo *nm* **1** *(superficie)* ground; *(de interior)* floor. **2** *fig (tierra)* soil, land; *(mundo)* earth. **3** *(territorio)* soil, land. **4** *(terreno)* land. **5** *(pavimento)* surface. **6** *fig (de vasija, etc)* bottom.

suelto,-a *adj* **1** *(no sujeto)* loose. **2** *(desatado)* undone, untied. **3** *(no envasado o empaquetado)* loose. **4** *(desaparejado)* odd. **5** *(dinero)* in change. **6** *(en libertad)* free; *(huido)* at large. **7** *(disgregado)* scattered. **8** *(con diarrea)* loose. **9** *(prenda)* loose, loose-fitting. **10** *fig (ligero)* agile, nimble; *(veloz)* swift.
▶ *nm* **suelto** *(cambio)* change, small change, loose change.

sueño *nm* **1** *(acto)* sleep. **2** *(ganas de dormir)* sleepiness. **3** *(lo soñado)* dream. **4** *fig (ilusión)* dream, illusion.

suero *nm* **1** MED serum. **2** *(de la leche)* whey.

suerte *nf* **1** *(fortuna)* luck, fortune. **2** *(azar)* chance. **3** *(destino)* destiny, fate. **4** *(estado, condición)* lot, situation. **5** *fml (tipo)* sort, kind, type. LOC **¡buena suerte!** good luck!

suéter *nm* sweater.

suficiente *adj* **1** *(bastante)* sufficient, enough. **2** *(apto)* suitable. **3** *fig (engreído)* smug, complacent.

sufijo,-a *adj* suffixal.
▶ *nm* **sufijo** suffix.

sufragar *vt (costear - gastos)* to defray, pay; *(- empresa)* to finance.

sufragio *nm* **1** suffrage. **2** *(voto)* vote.

sufrido,-a *adj* **1** *(persona)* patient, long-suffering. **2** *(color)* practical; *(tejido)* hardwearing.

sufrimiento *nm* suffering.

sufrir *vt* **1** *(padecer)* to suffer. **2** *(accidente, ataque)* to have; *(operación)* to undergo. **3** *(dificultades, cambios)* to experience; *(derrota, consecuencias)* to suffer. **4** *(aguantar)* to bear put up with.
▶ *vi (padecer)* to suffer.

sugerencia *nf* suggestion.

sugerente *adj* suggestive.

sugerir *vt* **1** to suggest. **2** *(insinuar)* to hint. **3** *(suscitar)* to suggest.

sugestión *nf* suggestion.

sugestionar *vt* to influence.

sugestivo,-a *adj (que atrae)* fascinating, attractive.

suicidarse *vpr* to commit suicide.

suicidio *nm* suicide.

Suiza *nf* Switzerland.

suizo,-a *adj* Swiss.
▶ *nm & nf* Swiss.

sujeción *nf (acción)* subjection.

sujetador,-ra *adj* fastening.
▶ *nm* **sujetador** bra.

sujetar *vt* **1** *(fijar)* to fix, secure, hold. **2** *(agarrar, sostener)* hold on to. **3** *(papeles)* to fasten; *(pelo)* to hold in place. **4** *fig (dominar, someter)* to control.
▶ *vpr* **sujetarse** **1** *(agarrarse)* to hold on, hold tight. **2** *fig (someterse)* to subject os (a, to).

S

sujeto,-a *adj* **1** *(sometido)* subject (a, to), liable (a, to). **2** *(agarrado, atado)* fastened, secure.
▶ *nm* **sujeto 1** LING subject. **2** *(individuo)* fellow, individual, character.

sulfato *nm* sulphate (US sulfate).

sulfhídrico,-a *adj* sulphuretted (US sulfureted).

sulfito *nm* sulphite (US sulfite).

sulfurar *vt* **1** QUÍM to sulphurate (US sulfurate). **2** *fam fig (irritar)* to infuriate.
▶ *vpr* **sulfurarse** *fam fig* to blow one's top, lose one's rag.

sulfúrico,-a *adj* sulphuric (US sulfuric).

sulfuro *nm* sulphide (US sulfide).

sulfuroso,-a *adj* sulphurous (US sulfurous).

sultán,-ana *nm & nf (hombre)* sultan; *(mujer)* sultana.

suma *nf* **1** *(cantidad)* sum, amount. **2** MAT sum, addition. **3** *(resumen)* summary.

sumando *nm* addend.

sumar *vt* **1** MAT to add, add up. **2** *(componer una cantidad)* to total, amount to, come to. **3** *(compendiar)* to sum up.
▶ *vpr* **sumarse** *(unirse)* to join (a, in).

sumario,-a *adj* **1** summary, brief. **2** JUR summary.
▶ *nm* **sumario 1** *(resumen)* summary. **2** JUR legal proceedings *pl*, indictment.

sumergible *adj* submersible.
▶ *nm* submarine.

sumergir *vt* **1** *(meter bajo líquido)* to submerge, submerse, immerse. **2** *fig (hundir)* to plunge, sink.
▶ *vpr* **sumergirse 1** *(meterse bajo líquido)* to submerge (en, in), go underwater. **2** *fig* to become immersed (en, in).

sumidero *nm* drain, sewer.

suministrador,-ra *nm & nf* supplier.

suministrar *vt* to provide, supply.

suministro *nm* supply, supplying.

sumisión *nf* **1** *(acto)* submission. **2** *(carácter)* submissiveness.

sumiso,-a *adj* submissive, obedient.

sumo,-a *adj* **1** *(supremo)* supreme, highest. **2** *fig (muy grande)* greatest.

suntuario,-a *adj* sumptuary.

suntuoso,-a *adj* sumptuous.

supeditar *vt* **1** *(subordinar)* to subordinate (a, to). **2** *(condicionar)* to subject (a, to).
▶ *vpr* **supeditarse** *(someterse)* to subject os (a, to), bow (a, to).

súper *nm fam (supermercado)* supermarket.
▶ *nf fam (gasolina)* four-star.

superable *adj* surmountable.

superabundante *adj* superabundant.

superar *vt* **1** *(exceder)* to surpass, exceed, excel. **2** *(obstáculo, etc)* to overcome, surmount.
▶ *vpr* **superarse 1** *(sobrepasarse)* to excel os. **2** *(mejorarse)* to improve os, better os.

superconductividad *nf* superconductivity.

superconductor *nm* superconductor.

superdotado,-a *nm & nf* genius.

superestrato *nm* superstratum.

superestructura *nf* superstructure.

superficial *adj* superficial.

superficialidad *nf* superficiality.

superficie *nf* **1** *(parte externa)* surface. **2** *(área)* area.

superfluo,-a *adj* superfluous.

superhombre *nm* superman.

superíndice *nm* superscript.

superintendente *nm o nf* superintendent.

superior *adj* **1** *(encima de)* upper, top: *labio superior* upper lip. **2** *(por encima de)* greater (a, than), higher (a, than), above (a, -). **3** *fig (persona - que supera)* superior; *(- mejor)* better. **4** *fig (calidad, etc)* superior, high, excellent. **5** EDUC higher.
▶ *nm* **1** *(jefe)* superior. **2** REL superior.

superioridad *nf (persona)* superiority.

superlativo,-a *adj* superlative.
▶ *nm* **superlativo** superlative.

supermercado *nm* supermarket.

supernova *nf* supernova.

superpoblación *nf* overpopulation.

superpoblado,-a *adj* overpopulated.

superponer *vt* **1** to superimpose, lay on top. **2** *fig* to put before.

superposición *nf* superimposition.

superpotencia *nf* superpower.

superpuesto,-a *pp* → superponer.

supersónico,-a *adj* supersonic.

superstición *nf* superstition.

supersticioso,-a *adj* superstitious.

supervisar *vt* to supervise.

supervisión *nf* supervision, control.

supervisor,-ra *nm & nf* supervisor.

supervivencia *nf* survival.

superviviente *adj* surviving.

▶ *nm o nf* survivor.

suplemento *nm* **1** *(de revista, etc)* supplement. **2** *(de dinero)* extra charge. **3** *(geometría)* supplement.

suplencia *nf* substitution.

suplente *nm o nf* **1** *(gen)* substitute. **2** DEP reserve player. **3** TEAT understudy.

súplica *nf* **1** request, entreaty, plea. **2** JUR petition.

suplicar *vt* **1** to beseech, beg, implore. **2** JUR to appeal to.

suplicio *nm* *(castigo)* torture.

suplir *vt* **1** *(reemplazar)* to replace, substitute. **2** *(compensar)* to make up for.

suponer *vt* **1** *(gen)* to suppose, assume. **2** *(significar)* to mean. **3** *(conllevar)* to mean, entail, require. **4** *(adivinar)* to guess; *(imaginar)* to imagine, think. **5** *(creer)* to think.

▶ *nm fam* supposition.

suposición *nf* supposition, assumption.

suprarrenal *adj* suprarenal.

supremo,-a *adj* **1** *(gen)* supreme. **2** *(decisivo)* decisive. **3** *(último)* last, final.

suprimir *vt* **1** *(libertad, etc)* to suppress; *(ley, impuestos)* to abolish; *(dificultades)* to eliminate, remove; *(restricciones)* to lift. **2** *(tabaco, alcohol)* to cut out. **3** *(palabra)* to delete, take out, leave out. **4** *(omitir)* to omit.

supuesto,-a *adj* **1** *(que se supone)* supposed, assumed. **2** *(pretendido)* so-called, self-styled.

▶ *nm* **supuesto 1** *(suposición)* supposition, assumption. **2** *(hipótesis)* hypothesis.

supurar *vi* to suppurate.

sur *nm* **1** south. **2** *(viento)* south wind.

Suramérica *nf* South America.

suramericano,-a *adj-nm & nf* → sudamericano,-a.

surcar *vt* **1** AGR to plough (US plow). **2** *(agua)* to cut through, cross; *(aire)* to fly through.

surco *nm* **1** *(en tierra)* furrow. **2** *(arruga)* wrinkle. **3** *(de disco)* groove.

surcoreano,-a *adj* South Korean.

▶ *nm & nf* South Korean.

sureste *adj-nm* → sudeste.

surfista *nm o nf* surfer.

surgir *vi* **1** *(agua)* to spring forth, spurt up. **2** *fig (aparecer - gen)* to appear, emerge; *(- dificultades)* to crop up, arise, come up. **3** MAR to anchor.

Surinam *nm* Surinam.

suroeste *adj-nm* → sudoeste.

surtido,-a *adj* **1** *(variado)* assorted. **2** *(bien provisto)* well stocked.

▶ *nm* **surtido** assortment, selection.

surtidor *nm* **1** *(fuente)* fountain. **2** *(chorro)* jet, spout.

surtir *vt* *(proveer)* to supply (de, with), provide (de, with).

▶ *vi (brotar)* to spout, spurt.

▶ *vpr* **surtirse** to supply os, provide os.

susceptibilidad *nf* **1** *(gen)* susceptibility. **2** *(sensibilidad)* sensitivity.

susceptible *adj* **1** *(gen)* susceptible. **2** *(sensible)* oversensitive.

suscitar *vt* **1** *(gen)* to cause, provoke. **2** *(rebelión)* to stir up, arouse; *(discusión)* to start; *(problemas)* to cause, raise; *(interés)* to arouse.

suscribir *vt* **1** FIN to subscribe. **2** *fig (convenir con alguien)* to subscribe to, endorse. **3** *(a una revista, etc)* to take out a subscription for. **4** *fml (firmar)* to subscribe.

▶ *vpr* **suscribirse** *(abonarse)* to subscribe.

suscripción *nf* subscription.

suscriptor,-ra *nm & nf* subscriber.

S

suscrito,-a *adj* **1** *(abonado)* subscribed. **2** *(firmado)* undersigned.
▸ *nm & nf* undersigned.

suspender *vt* **1** *(levantar)* to hang, hang up, suspend. **2** *(aplazar - gen)* to postpone, put off, delay; *(- reunión)* to adjourn. **3** EDUC *fig* to fail. **4** *fig* *(pagos)* to suspend; *(servicio)* to discontinue.

suspensión *nf* **1** *(acto de levantar)* hanging, hanging up, suspension. **2** AUTO suspension. **3** *(aplazamiento - gen)* delay, postponement; *(- de reunión)* adjournment. **4** *(supresión)* suspension, discontinuation.

suspenso,-a *adj* **1** *(colgado)* hanging, suspended. **2** REL *fig* *(alumno)* failed. **3** *fig* *(asombrado)* bewildered, amazed.
▸ *nm* **suspenso** EDUC fail.

suspicacia *nf* *(sospecha)* suspicion.

suspicaz *adj* **1** *(desconfiado)* mistrustful, distrustful. **2** *(que sospecha)* suspicious.

suspirar *vi* to sigh.

suspiro *nm* sigh.

sustancia *nf* **1** *(gen)* substance. **2** *(esencia)* substance, essence.

sustancial *adj* **1** *(gen)* substantial. **2** *(fundamental)* essential, fundamental. **3** *(importante)* important, substantial.

sustanciar *vt* to condense, abridge.

sustancioso,-a *adj* **1** *(nutritivo)* wholesome. **2** *fig* *(libro, etc)* meaty.

sustantivar *vt* to use as a noun.

sustantivo,-a *nm* noun, substantive.

sustentable *adj* tenable.

sustentación *nf* **1** *(soporte)* support. **2** *(mantenimiento)* sustenance, maintenance.

sustentar *vt* **1** *(familia, etc)* to maintain, support, sustain. **2** *(sostener)* to hold up, support. **3** *(teoría, opinión)* to support, defend.

sustento *nm* **1** *(alimento)* sustenance, food. **2** *(apoyo)* support.

sustitución *nf* substitution, replacement.

sustituible *adj* replaceable, expendable.

sustituir *vt* *(reemplazar)* to substitute (por, with), replace (por, with).

sustitutivo,-a *adj* substitutive.
▸ *nm* **sustitutivo** substitute.

sustituto,-a *nm & nf* substitute, stand-in, replacement.

susto *nm* fright, scare, shock.

sustracción *nf* **1** *(robo)* theft. **2** MAT subtraction.

sustraendo *nm* subtrahend.

sustraer *vt* **1** *(robar)* to steal. **2** MAT to subtract.
▸ *vpr* **sustraerse** *(faltar al cumplimiento)* to evade (a, -), elude (a, -); *(tentaciones)* to resist (a, -).

sustrato *nm* substratum.

susurrar *vi* to whisper.

susurro *nm* **1** whisper. **2** *fig* *(agua)* murmur; *(hojas)* rustle.

sutil *adj* **1** *(delgado)* thin, fine. **2** *(aroma)* delicate; *(color)* soft. **3** *(brisa)* gentle. **4** *fig* subtle.

suturar *vt* to stitch.

suyo,-a *adj* *(de él)* his, of his; *(de ella)* her, of hers; *(de animales, cosas)* its; *(de usted, de ustedes)* yours, of yours; *(de ellos, de ellas)* theirs, of theirs: *este libro es suyo* this book is hers; *aquel amigo suyo* that friend of yours.
▸ *pron* *(de él)* his; *(de ella)* hers; *(de usted, de ustedes)* yours; *(de ellos, de ellas)* theirs: *éstos son los míos, los suyos están sobre la mesa* there are mine, hers are on the table.
▸ *nf* **la suya** *(ocasión, oportunidad)* one's chance, one's opportunity.
▸ *nm* **lo suyo 1** *(lo que toca)* what one deserves. **2** *(habilidad)* forte, one's thing: *lo suyo es el tenis* tennis is his thing. **3** *fam* *(mucho)* a lot: *comió lo suyo* he ate a lot.
▸ *nm pl* **los suyos** *(familiares)* his *(her, your, etc)* family *sing*; *(amigos)* his *(her, your, etc)* friends, his *(her, your, etc)* people.

Swazilandia *nf* Swaziland.

T

T, t *nf (la letra)* T, t.

tabaco *nm* **1** *(gen)* tobacco. **2** *(cigarrillos)* cigarettes *pl*; *(cigarro)* cigar. **3** *(enfermedad)* black rot. COMP **tabaco rubio** Virginia tobacco.

tábano *nm* horsefly.

taberna *nf* pub, bar.

tabique *nm* partition, partition wall.

tabla *nf* **1** *(de madera)* board, plank. **2** *(de piedra)* slab; *(de metal)* sheet. **3** *(estante)* shelf. **4** ARTE panel. **5** COST pleat. **6** *(índice)* index. **7** *(lista)* list; *(catálogo)* catalogue (US catalog). **8** MAT table. COMP **tabla de multiplicar** multiplication table.
▶ *nf pl* **tablas 1** TEAT stage *sing*, boards. **2** *(ajedrez)* stalemate *sing*, draw *sing*.

tablado *nm* **1** *(suelo)* wooden floor. **2** *(entarimado)* wooden platform. **3** *(del escenario)* stage.

tablero *nm* **1** *(tablón)* panel, board. **2** *(en juegos)* board. **3** *(encerado)* blackboard. **4** AUTO dashboard. **5** INFORM display board. COMP **tablero de ajedrez** chessboard.

tableta *nf* **1** *(pastilla)* tablet. **2** *(de chocolate)* bar.

tablón *nm* **1** plank. **2** *(en construcción)* board. COMP **tablón de anuncios** notice board, US bulletin board.

tabulación *nf* tabulation.

tacaño,-a *adj* mean, stingy.

tacha *nf* **1** *(defecto)* flaw, blemish, defect. **2** *(descrédito)* blemish.

tachadura *nf* crossing out.

tachar *vt* **1** *(borrar)* to cross out. **2** *(culpar)* to accuse (de, of): *lo tachan de fascista* they accuse him of being a fascist.

tachuela *nf* tack, stud.

tacita *nf* little cup.

tácito,-a *adj* tacit.

taco *nm* **1** *(tarugo)* plug, stopper. **2** *(para pared)* plug, Rawlplug. **3** *(bloc de notas)* notepad, writing pad; *(calendario)* tear-off calendar. **4** *(de entradas)* book; *(de billetes)* wad. **5** *(de billar)* cue. **6** CULIN *(de queso, etc)* cube, piece; *(en Méjico)* taco, rolled-up tortilla. **7** *fam (palabrota)* swearword.

tacón *nm* heel.

táctica *nf* tactic, tactics *pl*, strategy.

tacto *nm* **1** *(sentido)* touch. **2** *(acción)* touch, touching. **3** *fig (delicadeza)* tact. LOC **tener tacto** to be tactful.

Tadjikistán *nm* Tadzhikistan.

tadjiko,-a *adj* Tadzhiki.
▶ *nm o nf (persona)* Tadzhik.
▶ *nm* **tadjiko** *(idioma)* Tadzhiki.

Tahití *nm* Tahiti.

tahitiano,-a *adj* Tahitian.
▶ *nm & nf (persona)* Tahitian.
▶ *nm* **tahitiano** *(idioma)* Tahitian.

tailandés,-esa *adj* Thai.
▶ *nm & nf (persona)* Thai.
▶ *nm* **tailandés** *(idioma)* Thai.

Tailandia *nf* Thailand.

Taiwan *nm* Taiwan.

taiwanés,-esa *adj* Taiwanese.
▶ *nm & nf* Taiwanese.

tajada *nf* **1** *(rodaja)* slice. **2** *(corte)* cut; *(cuchillada)* stab.

tajo *nm* **1** *(corte)* cut, slash. **2** *(filo)* cutting edge. **3** *(escarpa)* steep cliff.

tal *adj* **1** *(semejante)* such: *en tales condiciones* in such conditions. **2** *(tan grande)* such, so: *tal es su ignorancia que...* he is so ignorant that... **3** *(cosa sin especificar)* such and such: *tal día* such and such a

day. **4** *(persona sin especificar)* someone called, a certain: *vino un tal Alberto* someone called Alberto came.
▶ *pron (alguno - cosa)* such a thing, something; *(- persona)* someone, somebody: *yo no dije tal cosa* I didn't say such a thing.
▶ *adv (así)* in such a way, so: *tal me contestó que no supe cómo reaccionar* he answered in such a way that I didn't know how to react. LOC **tal como 1** *(ejemplos)* such as. **2** *(de la misma manera)* just as. ‖ **tal cual** just as it is.

tala *nf* tree felling.

taladrar *vt* **1** *(gen)* to drill; *(pared)* to bore through. **2** *fig (los oídos)* to pierce.

taladro *nm* **1** *(herramienta)* drill, bore. **2** *(agujero)* hole.

talar *vt* **1** *(cortar)* to fell, cut down. **2** *(destruir)* to devastate.

talento *nm* **1** *(entendimiento)* talent, intelligence. **2** *(aptitud)* gift, talent: *tiene talento para las matemáticas* she has a gift for mathematics.

talla *nf* **1** *(estatura)* height. **2** *fig (moral, intelectual)* stature. **3** *(de prenda)* size: *¿qué talla usa?* what size is he? **4** *(escultura)* carving, sculpture. **5** *(tallado - piedras)* cutting; *(- metal)* engraving.

tallar *vt* **1** *(madera, piedra)* to carve, shape; *(piedras preciosas)* to cut; *(metales)* to engrave. **2** *(medir)* to measure the height of.

talle *nm* **1** *(cintura)* waist. **2** *(figura - de hombre)* build, physique; *(- de mujer)* figure, shape.

taller *nm* **1** *(obrador)* workshop. **2** *(de artista)* studio. **3** *(en fábrica)* shop, workshop. **4** AUTO garage, repair shop.

tallo *nm* BOT stem, stalk; *(renuevo)* sprout, shoot.

talón *nm* **1** *(de pie, zapato, etc)* heel. **2** *(cheque)* cheque (US check). COMP **talón bancario** counter cheque (US check). ‖ **talón de Aquiles** Achilles' heel.

talonario *nm (de cheques)* cheque book (US check book); *(de recibos)* stub book.

tamaño,-a *adj (semejante)* such a, so big a: *no pude aguantar tamaña imperti-* *nencia* I couldn't tolerate such an impertinent remark.
▶ *nm* **tamaño** *(medida)* size: *¿de qué tamaño es?* what size is it?

tamarindo *nm* tamarind.

tambalearse *vpr* **1** *(persona)* to stagger; *(mueble)* to wobble. **2** *fig* to be shaky.

también *adv* **1** *(igualmente)* also, too, as well, so: *Pedro también estaba* Pedro was also there, Pedro was there too, Pedro was there as well. **2** *(además)* besides, in addition.

tambor *nm* **1** *(instrumento)* drum. **2** *(maquinaria)* drum. **3** *(de arma)* cylinder, barrel. **4** *(de lavadora)* drum. **5** *(de freno)* brake drum.

tamiz *nm* sieve.

tamizar *vt* **1** *(harina, tierra)* to sieve. **2** *(luz)* to filter. **3** *fig (seleccionar)* to screen.

tampoco *adv* neither, nor, not... either: *no quiere estudiar y tampoco quiere ir al cine* he doesn't want to study and he doesn't want to go to the cinema either.

tan *adv* **1** *(tanto)* such, such a, so: *no seas tan cruel* don't be so cruel. **2** *(comparativo - como)* as... as, so... (that); *(- que)* so..., so... (that): *está tan gordo como tú* he's as fat as you (are). LOC **tan solo** only, just: *tan solo quiero uno* I only want one.

tanda *nf* **1** *(conjunto)* batch, lot; *(serie)* series, course. **2** *(turno)* shift. **3** *(en billar)* game.

tangente *adj* tangent.
▶ *nf* tangent.

tanque *nm* **1** *(depósito)* tank, reservoir. **2** MIL tank. **3** *(vehículo cisterna)* tanker.

tantear *vt* **1** *(calcular)* to estimate, guess. **2** *(probar medidas)* to size up. **3** *fig (ensayar)* to try out, put to the test. **4** *fig (persona)* to sound out. **5** *(dibujo)* to sketch.
▶ *vi* **1** DEP to score, keep score. **2** *(andar a tientas)* to feel one's way.

tanto,-a *adj* **1** *(incontables)* so much; *(contables)* so many: *no comas tantos caramelos* don't eat so many sweets. **2** *(comparación - incontable)* as much; *(- contables)* as many: *tengo tantos libros como tú* I've got as many books as you.

► *pron (incontable)* so much; *(contable)* so many: *no había tantos* there weren't so many.

► *adv* **1** *(cantidad)* so much: *¡te quiero tanto!* I love you so much! **2** *(tiempo)* so long: *esperamos tanto* we waited for so long. **3** *(frecuencia)* so often: *no los telefonees tanto* don't phone them so often.

► *nm* **tanto 1** *(punto)* point; *(fútbol)* goal. **2** *(cantidad imprecisa)* so much, a certain amount: *percibes un tanto al mes* you get so much a month. **3** *(poco)* bit: *es un tanto estrecho* it's a bit narrow. `LOC` **a las tantas** *fam* very late, at an unearthly hour. **‖ por lo tanto** therefore.

Tanzania *nf* Tanzania.

tanzano,-a *adj* Tanzanian.
► *nm & nf* Tanzanian.

tapa *nf* **1** *(cubierta)* lid, top; *(de botella)* cap, top, stopper. **2** *(de libro)* cover. **3** *(de zapato)* heel-plate. **4** CULIN *(comida)* appetizer, savoury (US savory), tapa.

tapadera *nf* **1** cover, lid. **2** *fig* cover.

tapar *vt* **1** *(cubrir)* to cover; *(con tapa)* to put the lid on. **2** *(con ropas, etc)* to wrap up. **3** *(obstruir)* to obstruct; *(tubería)* to block. **4** *(ocultar)* to hide; *(a la vista)* to block. **5** *fig (encubrir)* to cover up.

► *vpr* **taparse 1** *(abrigarse)* to wrap up. **2** *(la nariz)* to be blocked up.

tapia *nf (cerca)* garden wall; *(de adobe)* mud wall, adobe wall.

tapiar *vt* **1** *(área)* to wall in, wall off. **2** *fig (puerta, ventana)* to wall up, close up.

tapicería *nf* **1** ARTE tapestry making. **2** *(tapices)* tapestries *pl*. **3** *(de muebles, etc)* upholstery. **4** *(tienda)* upholsterer's, upholsterer's workshop.

tapiz *nm* **1** *(de pared)* tapestry. **2** *(alfombra)* rug, carpet.

tapón *nm* **1** stopper, plug; *(de botella)* cap. **2** *(del oído)* wax in the ear. **3** *(baloncesto)* block. **4** *(embotellamiento)* traffic jam.

taponar *vt* **1** *(orificio, etc)* to plug, stop. **2** *(atascar)* to block. **3** *(poner el tapón)* to put the plug in. **4** MED to tampon, plug.

taquilla *nf* **1** *(de tren, etc)* ticket office; *(de cine, teatro)* box office. **2** *(recaudación)* takings *pl*, returns *pl*. **3** *(casillero)* pigeonholes *pl*. **4** *(armario)* locker.

tara *nf* **1** *(peso)* tare. **2** *(defecto)* defect, blemish, fault.

tardar *vt (emplear tiempo)* to take: *tardé cuatro horas* it took me four hours.
► *vi (demorar)* to take a long time: *se tarda más a pie* it takes longer on foot.

tarde *nf* **1** *(hasta las cinco aprox.)* afternoon. **2** *(después de las cinco aprox.)* evening.
► *adv* **1** *(hora avanzada)* late: *se está haciendo tarde* it's getting late. **2** *(demasiado tarde)* too late: *es tarde para salir* it's too late to go out.

tarea *nf* task, job.

tarifa *nf* **1** *(precio)* tariff, rate; *(de transporte)* fare. **2** *(lista de precios)* price list.

tarima *nf* platform, dais.

tarjeta *nf* card. `COMP` **tarjeta de crédito** credit card. **‖ tarjeta de memoria** memory card, chip card. **‖ tarjeta postal** postcard.

tarro *nm* **1** *(vasija)* jar, pot, tub. **2** *fam (cabeza)* bonce.

tarta *nf* flan, tart, pie: *tarta de manzana* apple pie.

tartamudear *vi* to stammer, stutter.

tartamudez *nf* stammering.

tartamudo,-a *nm & nf* stutterer.

tasa *nf* **1** *(valoración)* valuation. **2** *(precio)* fee, charge. **3** *(impuesto)* tax, levy. **4** *(límite)* limit; *(medida)* measure. **5** *(índice)* rate. `COMP` **tasa de natalidad** birth rate.

tasar *vt* **1** *(valorar)* to value. **2** *(poner precio)* to set the price of, fix the price of.

Tasmania *nf* Tasmania.

tasmano,-a *adj* Tasmanian.
► *nm & nf* Tasmanian.

tata *nf fam* nanny.

tatarabuelo,-a *nm & nf (hombre)* great-great-grandfather; *(mujer)* great-great-grandmother.

tataranieto,-a *nm & nf (hombre)* great-great-grandson; *(mujer)* great-great-granddaughter.

tatuaje *nm* **1** *(dibujo)* tattoo. **2** *(técnica)* tattooing.

tatuar *vt* to tattoo.

tauromaquia *nf* bullfighting, art of bullfighting, tauromachy.

taxi *nm* taxi, cab.

T

taxista *nm o nf* taxi driver.

taza *nf* **1** *(recipiente)* cup. **2** *(contenido)* cupful. **3** *(de retrete)* bowl.

te¹ *nf* **1** *name of the letter* t. **2** *(regla)* T-square.

te² *pron* **1** you, to you, for you: *te mandaré una carta* I'll send you a letter. **2** *(uso reflexivo)* yourself: *ponte el abrigo* put your coat on. **3** *(uso pronominal) no se traduce: vete a casa* go home.

té *nm* tea. COMP **la hora del té** teatime.

teatral *adj* **1** *(del teatro)* theatrical, dramatic. **2** *fig (exagerado)* stagy, stagey, theatrical.

teatro *nm* **1** theatre (US theater). **2** ARTE theatre (US theater), acting, stage. **3** *fig (exageración)* show, play-acting.

tebeo *nm* children's comic.

teca *nf (árbol, madera)* teak.

techo *nm* **1** *(interior)* ceiling; *(de coche, tejado)* roof. **2** *fig (límite superior)* ceiling.

tecla *nf* key.

teclado *nm* keyboard.

teclear *vi (piano)* to press the keys; *(máquina de escribir, ordenador)* to type, tap the keys.

técnica *nf* **1** *(tecnología)* technique, technology. **2** *(habilidad)* technique, method. **3** *(ingeniería)* engineering.

técnico,-a *adj* technical.
▶ *nm & nf* technician, technical expert.

tecnología *nf* technology.

tectónica *nf* tectonics.

tedio *nm* tedium, boredom.

teja *nf (de barro)* tile.

tejado *nm* roof.

tejano,-a *adj* Texan.
▶ *nm & nf* Texan.
▶ *nm pl* **tejanos** *(pantalón)* jeans.

tejar *vt* to tile.

tejer *vt* **1** *(en telar)* to weave. **2** *(hacer punto)* to knit. **3** *(araña)* to spin. **4** *fig (plan)* to weave, plot, scheme.

tejido *nm* **1** *(tela)* textile. **2** ANAT tissue.

tejo *nm (árbol)* yew tree.

tejón *nm* badger.

tela *nf* **1** *(textil)* material, fabric, cloth. **2** *(de araña)* cobweb. **3** ARTE *(lienzo)* canvas; *(cuadro)* painting. **4** *fam (dinero)* dough. **5** *fam (asunto, tema)* subject, matter. COMP **tela metálica** wire gauze.

telar *nm* **1** *(para tejer)* loom. **2** *(para encuadernar)* sewing press.

telaraña *nf* cobweb, spider's web.

tele *nf fam* telly, TV.

telecomunicación *nf* telecommunication.

telediario *nm* television news bulletin, TV news.

teleférico *nm* cable car.

telefilm *nm* TV film.

telefonear *vi* to phone.

teléfono *nm* telephone, phone. COMP **teléfono móvil** mobile phone.

telegrafiar *vt* to telegraph, wire.

telégrafo *nm* telegraph.

telegrama *nm* telegram, cable.

telemando *nm* remote control.

telenovela *nf* soap opera.

teleobjetivo *nm* telephoto lens.

telepatía *nf* telepathy.

telescopio *nm* telescope.

telesilla *nm* chair lift.

telespectador,-ra *nm & nf* TV viewer.

telesquí *nm* ski lift, drag lift.

teletexto *nm* teletext.

televisar *vt* to televise.

televisión *nf* **1** *(sistema)* television. **2** *fam (aparato)* television set.

televisor *nm* television set.

télex® *nm* telex.

telón *nm* curtain. COMP **telón de acero** POL iron curtain. ‖ **telón de fondo** TEAT backdrop.

tema *nm* **1** *(de discurso, escrito, etc)* topic, subject, theme. **2** MÚS theme.

temario *nm (de examen)* programme (US program); *(de conferencia)* agenda.

temática *nf* subject matter.

temático,-a *adj* **1** thematic. **2** LING stem.

temblar *vi* **1** *(de frío)* to shiver (de, with); *(de miedo)* to tremble (de, with). **2** *(voz)* to quiver.

temblor *nm* **1** *(gen)* tremor; *(de frío)* shivering, shivers *pl*. **2** *fig* shiver.

temer *vt* **1** *(tener miedo)* to fear, be afraid of. **2** *(sospechar)* to fear, be afraid.
▶ *vi* **1** *(tener miedo)* to be afraid. **2** *(preocuparse)* to worry.
▶ *vpr* **temerse** to be afraid: *me temo que sí* I'm afraid so.

temerario,-a *adj* reckless, rash.

temible *adj* dreadful, fearful.

temor *nm* fear.

temperamento *nm* temperament.

temperatura *nf* temperature.

tempestad *nf* **1** storm. **2** *fig* turmoil.

templado,-a *adj* **1** *(agua)* warm, lukewarm; *(clima, temperatura)* mild, temperate. **2** *(moderado)* moderate; *(sereno)* composed, unruffled. **3** *(valiente)* brave. **4** MÚS tuned. **5** *(metal)* tempered.

templar *vt* **1** *(moderar)* to moderate, temper. **2** *(algo frío)* to warm up; *(algo caliente)* to cool down. **3** *fig (cólera)* to appease; *(apaciguar)* to calm down. **4** *(cuerda, tornillo)* to tighten (up). **5** MÚS to tune. **6** TÉC to temper. **7** *(colores)* to match.
▶ *vpr* **templarse** *(contenerse)* to control os.

templo *nm* temple.

temporada *nf* **1** *(en artes, deportes, moda)* season. **2** *(período)* period, time. COMP **temporada alta** high season. **temporada baja** low season.

temporal¹ *adj* *(transitorio)* temporary.
▶ *nm* METEOR storm.

temporal² *adj* ANAT temporal.
▶ *nm* ANAT temporal bone.

temprano,-a *adj* early.
▶ *adv* early: *nunca se levanta temprano* he never gets up early.

tenaza *nf* [también se usa en plural con el mismo sigificado] *(herramienta)* pliers *pl*, pincers *pl*; *(para el fuego)* tongs *pl*.

tendedero *nm* *(cuerda)* clothesline; *(lugar)* drying place.

tendencia *nf* *(inclinación)* tendency, inclination, leaning; *(movimiento)* trend.

tender *vt* **1** *(extender - mantel, etc)* to spread; *(- red)* to cast. **2** *(puente)* to throw; *(vía, cable)* to lay; *(cuerda)* to stretch. **3** *(ropa, colada)* to hang out. **4** *(mano)* to stretch out. **5** *(emboscada, trampa)* to lay, set.

▶ *vi* *(tener tendencia)* to tend (a, to), have a tendency (a, to): *tiende al aburrimiento* it tends to be boring.
▶ *vpr* **tenderse** *(tumbarse)* to lie down.

tendero,-a *nm & nf* shopkeeper.

tendón *nm* tendon, sinew.

tenedor,-ra *nm (utensilio)* fork.

tener *vt* **1** *(gen)* to have, have got: *tuvimos un día estupendo* we had a wonderful day. **2** *(poseer)* to own. **3** *(sostener)* to hold: *¿qué tienes en la mano?* what are you holding? **4** *(coger)* to take: *ten tu copa* take your glass. **5** *(sensación, sentimiento)* to be, feel: *tengo hambre* I'm hungry. **6** *(mantener)* to keep: *la lluvia me ha tenido despierta toda la noche* the rain has kept me up all night. **7** *(medir)* to measure. **8** *(contener)* to hold, contain. **9** *(edad)* to be. **10** *(un hijo)* to have. **11** *(celebrar)* to hold: *tener una reunión* to hold a meeting. **12** *(considerar)* to consider, think: *lo tienen por muy listo* they think he's very smart. LOC **¡ahí tienes!** so, there you are! ∥ **tener cariño a** to be fond of. ∥ **tener compasión** to take pity (de, on). ∥ **tener ilusión** to be enthusiastic.
▶ *aux* **tener que** *(obligación)* to have to, have got to, must: *tengo que quedarme* I must stay.
▶ *vpr* **tenerse** *(sostenerse)* to stand up. LOC **tenerse por** to consider os: *se tiene por guapo* he thinks he's handsome.

tenia *nf* tapeworm.

teniente *nm* lieutenant.

tenis *nm (deporte)* tenis. COMP **tenis de mesa** table tennis, ping-pong.

tenista *nm o nf* tennis player.

tensar *vt* **1** *(cable, cuerda)* to tauten. **2** *(arco)* to draw.

tensión *nf* **1** ELEC tension, voltage. **2** *(de materiales)* stress; *(de gases)* pressure. **3** MED pressure. **4** *fig (de una situación)* tension; *(de una persona)* stress, strain. COMP **alta tensión** ELEC high tension. ∥ **tensión arterial** blood pressure.

tenso,-a *adj* **1** *(cuerda)* tense. **2** *fig (relaciones)* strained. **3** *fig (persona)* tense.

tentación *nf* temptation.

tentáculo *nm* tentacle.

tentador,-ra *adj* tempting, enticing.

T

tentar *vt* **1** *(palpar)* to feel, touch. **2** *(incitar)* to tempt, entice.

tentempié *nm fam (refrigerio)* snack.

teñir *vt* **1** *(dar un color)* to dye. **2** *(rebajar un color)* to tone down.
► *vpr* **teñirse** *(el pelo)* to dye one's hair.

teoría *nf* theory. ⓛⓞⒸ **en teoría** theoretically.

teórica *nf* theory, theoretics.

teórico,-a *adj* theoretic, theoretical.
► *nm & nf* theoretician, theorist.

terapeuta *nm o nf* therapist.

terapia *nf* therapy.

tercer *adj* [se usa ante nombres en masculino singular] third: *el tercer mundo* the third world.

✎ Consulta también tercero,-a.

tercera *nf* **1** *(clase)* third class. **2** *(marcha de auto)* third gear, third. **3** MÚS third.

tercermundista *adj* third-world.

tercero,-a *adj (ordinal)* third.
► *nm & nf (parte)* third.
► *nm* **tercero 1** *(mediador)* mediator. **2** *(persona ajena)* outsider.

✎ Consulta también sexto,-a.

tercio,-a *adj* third.
► *nm* **tercio 1** *(parte)* third. **2** *(en tauromaquia)* stage, part.

terciopelo *nm* velvet.

terco,-a *adj* obstinate, stubborn.

termal *adj* thermal.

termas *nf pl (baños)* spa *sing*, hot baths.

térmico,-a *adj* thermal.

terminación *nf* **1** *(acción)* ending, termination. **2** *(conclusión)* completion. **3** *(parte final)* end. **4** GRAM ending.

terminal *adj (último)* final, terminal.
► *nf* **1** *(estación)* terminus. **2** *(en aeropuerto)* terminal.
► *nm (de ordenador)* terminal.

terminar *vt* **1** *(acabar)* to finish, complete. **2** *(dar fin)* to end.
► *vi* **1** *(acabar)* to finish, end: *terminó a las cuatro* it finished at four. **2** *(acabar de)* to have just *(de, -)*: *termina de marchar* he has just left. **3** *(final de una acción, de un estado)* to end up: *terminó por marcharse* he ended up leaving. **4** *(eliminar)* to put an end *(con, to)*. **5** *(estropear)* to damage *(con, -)*, ruin *(con, -)*: *la lluvia terminó con la cosecha* the rain damaged the crops. **6** *(reñir)* to break up *(con, with)*. **7** *(enfermedad)* to come to the final stage.
► *vpr* **terminarse 1** *(acabarse)* to finish. **2** *(agotarse)* to run out: *se ha terminado el azúcar* the sugar has run out.

término *nm* **1** *(fin)* end, finish. **2** *(estación)* terminus, terminal. **3** *(límite)* limit, boundary; *(hito)* boundary marker. **4** *(plazo)* term, time, period. **5** *(palabra)* term, word: *término técnico* technical term. **6** *(estado)* condition, state. **7** *(lugar, posición)* place. **8** *(en matemáticas, gramática)* term. ⓛⓞⒸ **dar término a** ALGO to conclude STH.
► *nm pl* **términos** *(condiciones)* conditions, terms.

terminología *nf* terminology.

termita *nf* termite.

termitero *nm* termite's nest.

termo *nm (recipiente)* flask, thermos flask.

termómetro *nm* thermometer.

termostato *nm* thermostat.

ternera *nf* CULIN veal, beef.

ternero,-a *nm & nf (animal)* calf.

ternura *nf* tenderness, gentleness.

terraplén *nm* embankment.

terráqueo,-a *adj* earth.

terrateniente *nm o nf* landowner.

terraza *nf* **1** *(balcón)* terrace. **2** *(azotea)* roof terrace. **3** *(de un café)* terrace.

terremoto *nm* earthquake.

terrenal *adj* earthly, worldly.

terreno,-a *adj* worldly, earthly.
► *nm* **terreno 1** *(tierra)* land, piece o land, ground; *(solar)* plot, site. **2** GEO terrain. **3** AGR *(de cultivo)* soil; *(campo)* field. **4** DEP field, ground.

terrestre *adj* **1** *(de la tierra)* terrestrial, earthly. **2** *(por tierra)* by land.

terrible *adj* terrible, awful.

terrícola *nm o nf (habitante)* earth dweller; *(en ciencia ficción)* earthling.

territorial *adj* territorial.

territorio *nm* territory.

terrón *nm* **1** *(de tierra)* clod. **2** *(de azúcar, etc)* lump.

terror *nm* **1** *(gen)* terror. **2** CINE horror.

terrorismo *nm* terrorism.

terrorista *adj* terrorist.
▸ *nm o nf* terrorist.

tesoro *nm* **1** *(gen)* treasure. **2** *fig* treasure.

testamento *nm* **1** JUR will, testament. **2** REL Testament. LOC **hacer testamento** to make one's will.

testarudo,-a *adj* obstinate, stubborn.

testigo *nm o nf* witness.
▸ *nm* **1** *(prueba)* proof. **2** DEP baton.

testimonio *nm* **1** JUR testimony, evidence. **2** *(prueba)* evidence, proof.

tétanos *nm inv* tetanus.

tetera *nf* teapot.

tetraedro *nm* tetrahedron.

textil *adj* textile.
▸ *nm* textile.

texto *nm* text.

textura *nf* **1** *(textil)* texture. **2** *(minerales)* structure.

tez *nf* complexion.

ti *pron* [se usa sólo después de una preposición] you: *te lo doy a ti* I'll give it to you.

tía *nf* *(pariente)* aunt.

tibio,-a *adj* **1** tepid. **2** *fig* cool.

tiburón *nm* shark.

tic *nm* **1** tic, twitch. **2** *fig (manía)* habit.

ticket *nm* → tique.

tiempo *nm* **1** *(gen)* time. **2** *(época)* time, period, age, days *pl*: *en tiempo de los romanos* in Roman times. **3** METEOR weather: *¿qué tiempo hace?* what's the weather like? **4** *(edad)* age: *¿qué tiempo tiene el niño?* how old is your baby? **5** *(temporada)* season: *fruta del tiempo* fruit in season. **6** *(momento)* moment, time: *no es tiempo de preguntarle eso* it's not the time to ask him that. **7** MÚS tempo, movement. **8** DEP *(parte)* half. **9** GRAM tense. **10** TÉC stroke. LOC **hacer buen tiempo** the weather is good. COMP **tiempo libre** free time.

tienda *nf* **1** *(establecimiento)* shop, US store. **2** *(de campaña)* tent. **3** *(de carro)* cover. LOC **ir de tiendas** to go shopping. COMP **tienda de campaña** tent.

tierno,-a *adj* **1** *(blando)* tender, soft. **2** *fig (reciente)* fresh: *pan tierno* fresh bread. **3** *fig (cariñoso)* affectionate.

tierra *nf* **1** *(planeta)* earth. **2** *(superficie sólida)* land. **3** *(terreno cultivado)* soil, land. **4** *(país)* country, land. **5** *(suelo)* ground. **6** ELEC earth, US ground.
▸ *nf pl* **tierras** land *sing*. LOC **tierra adentro** inland. COMP **tierra de nadie** no-man's-land. ‖ **tierra firme** terra firma.

tieso,-a *adj* **1** *(rígido)* stiff, rigid. **2** *(erguido)* upright, erect. **3** *(tenso)* taut, tight.

tiesto *nm* flowerpot.

tifón *nm* typhoon.

tigre *nm* tiger.

tijera *nf* [se suele usar en plural] *(instrumento)* scissors *pl*, pair of scissors.

tila *nf* **1** *(tilo)* lime. **2** *(flor)* lime blossom. **3** *(infusión)* lime-blossom tea.

tilde *nf* **1** *(gen)* written accent; *(de la ñ)* tilde. **2** *fig (tacha)* fault, flaw.

tilo *nm* lime tree.

timar *vt* to swindle, cheat, trick.

timbre *nm* **1** *(de la puerta)* bell. **2** *(sello)* stamp, seal. **3** MÚS timbre.

timidez *nf* shyness, timidity.

tímido,-a *adj* shy, timid.

timo¹ *nm* *(estafa)* swindle.

timo² *nm* *(glándula)* thymus.

timón *nm* **1** *(barco, avión)* rudder. **2** *(del arado)* beam. **3** *fig (negocio, etc)* helm.

Timor Oriental *nm* East Timor.

tímpano *nm* *(del oído)* eardrum.

tiniebla *nf* [también se usa en plural con el mismo significado] *(oscuridad)* darkness.
▸ *nf pl* **tinieblas** *fig (ignorancia)* ignorance *sing*, confusion *sing*.

tinta *nf* **1** *(gen)* ink. **2** *(tinte)* dyeing.
▸ *nf pl* **tintas** colours (US colors). COMP **tinta china** Indian ink.

tinte *nm* **1** *(colorante)* dye. **2** *(proceso)* dyeing. **3** *(tintorería)* dry-cleaner's. **4** *fig (aspecto)* shade.

tintero *nm* inkwell.

tintinear *vi* → tintinar.

tinto,-a *adj* **1** *(teñido)* dyed. **2** *(vino)* red.
▸ *nm* **tinto** *(vino)* red wine.

tintorería *nf* dry-cleaner's.

T

tío *nm* **1** *(pariente)* uncle. **2** *fam (hombre)* guy.
▶ *nm pl* **tíos** aunt and uncle.

tiovivo *nm* merry-go-round.

típico,-a *adj* **1** *(característico)* typical, characteristic. **2** *(pintoresco)* picturesque; *(tradicional)* traditional: *un plato típico* a traditional dish, a local dish.

tipo *nm* **1** *(clase)* type, kind. **2** FIN rate. **3** ANAT *(de hombre)* build, physique; *(de mujer)* figure. **4** *fam (persona)* guy, fellow, bloke. **5** *(en impresión)* type. COMP **tipo de interés** FIN rate of interest.

tíquet → tique.

tira *nf* **1** *(cinta, banda)* strip. **2** *(de dibujos)* comic strip. LOC **la tira** *(cantidad)* a lot, loads; *(mucho tiempo)* for yonks, for ages: *comimos la tira* we ate loads.

tirada *nf* **1** *(acción)* throw: *en la segunda tirada le salieron dos seises* he got two sixes on the second throw. **2** *(impresión)* print run: *una tirada de cinco mil ejemplares* a print run of five thousand. **3** *(distancia)* stretch: *hay una buena tirada hasta allí* it's a good few miles away. **4** *(serie)* series.

tirado,-a *adj* **1** *fam (precio)* dirt cheap. **2** *fam (problema, asunto)* dead easy. **3** *fam (abandonado)* let down.

tirador,-ra *nm & nf (persona)* shooter.
▶ *nm (de puerta, cajón)* knob, handle.

tirano,-a *nm & nf* tyrant.

tirante *adj* **1** taut. **2** *fig (situación)* tense.
▶ *nm* **1** *(de ropa en general)* strap. **2** TÉC brace, stay. **3** ARQUIT beam.
▶ *nm pl* **tirantes** *(de pantalón)* braces, US suspenders.

tirar *vt* **1** *(echar)* to throw, fling. **2** *(dejar caer)* to drop. **3** *(desechar)* to throw away. **4** *(derribar)* to knock down; *(casa, árbol)* to pull down. **5** *(derramar)* to spill. **6** *(vaso, botella)* to knock over. **7** *(estirar)* to pull. **8** *(imprimir)* to print. **9** *(un tiro)* to fire; *(una bomba)* to drop; *(cohete)* to launch. **10** DEP to take. **11** *fig (malgastar)* to waste, squander.
▶ *vi* **1** *(cuerda, puerta)* to pull (de, -). **2** *(estufa, chimenea)* to draw. **3** *(en juegos)* to be a player's move, be a player's turn: *tira él* it's his turn. **4** *fam (funcionar)* to work, run: *esto ya no tira* this doesn't

work any more. **5** *fam (durar)* to last: *con esta reparación tirará un par de meses* after these repairs it'll last for a couple of months. **6** *fam fig (atraer)* to attract, appeal: *no le tira la mecánica* mechanics doesn't appeal to him. **7** *fig (inclinarse)* to be attracted (a/hacia, to), be drawn (a/hacia, to): *esta chica tira hacia las artes* this girl is drawn to the arts. **8** *fig (parecerse)* to take after (a, -): *tira a su padre* she takes after her father. **9** *fig (mantenerse)* to get by, get along: *ella tira con poco dinero* she gets by with little money. **10** *(disparar)* to shoot, fire. **11** DEP *(fútbol)* to shoot; *(ciclismo)* to set the pace.
▶ *vpr* **tirarse 1** *(lanzarse)* to throw os. **2** *(abalanzarse)* to rush (sobre, at), jump (sobre, on). **3** *(tumbarse)* to lie down. **4** *fam (tiempo)* to spend: *se tiró una hora en la ducha* he spent an hour in the shower.

tirita® *nf* sticking plaster, plaster.

tiritar *vi (gen)* to shiver, shake.

tiro *nm* **1** *(lanzamiento)* throw. **2** *(disparo, ruido)* shot. **3** *(galería de tiro)* shooting gallery. **4** DEP shooting. **5** *(caballerías)* team. **6** COST *(de pantalón)* distance between waist and crotch. **7** *(de chimenea)* draught (US draft). **8** *(fútbol, etc)* shot. COMP **tiro al blanco** target shooting.

tirón *nm* pull, tug. LOC **de un tirón** *fam* in one go.

tiroteo *nm* shooting.

títere *nm* **1** *(marioneta)* puppet, marionette. **2** *fig (persona)* puppet, dupe.
▶ *nm pl* **títeres** puppet show *sing*. LOC **no dejar títere con cabeza 1** *fam (destruir)* to break everything in sight. **2** *(criticar)* to spare nobody.

titulado,-a *adj* **1** *(llamado)* called. **2** EDUC *(diplomado)* qualified.

titular *vt* to entitle, title, call.
▶ *adj* regular.
▶ *nm o nf* **1** *(poseedor)* holder. **2** *(de un puesto)* office holder.
▶ *nm (prensa)* headline.
▶ *vpr* **titularse 1** *(llamarse)* to be called, be titled. **2** EDUC to graduate (en, in).

título *nm* **1** *(de obra)* title. **2** *(de texto legal)* heading. **3** *(dignidad)* title. **4** *(persona noble)* noble (person). **5** EDUC *(licenciatura)*

degree; *(diploma)* certificate. **6** *(documento)* title. **7** *(titular de prensa)* headline.
▶ *nm pl* **títulos** *(titulación)* qualifications; *(méritos)* qualities. COMP **título de propiedad** deeds *pl*.

tiza *nf* chalk.

toalla *nf* towel. COMP **toalla de baño** bath towel.

toallero *nm* towel rail, towel rack.

tobillera *nf* ankle sock.

tobillo *nm* ankle.

tobogán *nm* **1** *(rampa)* slide, chute. **2** *(trineo)* toboggan, sledge.

tocadiscos *nm inv* record player.

tocado *nm* **1** *(peinado)* coiffure, hairdo. **2** *(prenda)* headdress, hat.

tocado,-a *adj* **1** *(fruta)* bad, rotten. **2** *fam (perturbado)* crazy, touched.

tocador *nm* **1** *(mueble)* dressing-table. **2** *(habitación)* dressing-room, boudoir.

tocar *vt* **1** *(gen)* to touch: *no tocar la mercancía* do not handle the goods. **2** *(sentir por el tacto)* to feel: *tócalo, está frío* feel it, it's cold. **3** *(revolver)* to rummage amongst, root around: *no toques mis papeles* leave my papers alone. **4** *(hacer sonar - instrumento, canción)* to play; *(timbre)* to ring; *(bocina)* to blow, honk; *(campanas)* to strike. **5** *(la hora)* to strike. **6** DEP *(diana)* to hit; *(esgrima)* to touch. **7** *fig (mencionar)* to touch on. **8** *fig (impresionar)* to touch, reach: *me tocó el corazón* he touched my heart.
▶ *vi* **1** *(ser el turno)* to be one's turn: *le toca a él* it's his turn. **2** *(corresponder)* to be up to: *le toca a él explicarse* it's up to him to explain himself. **3** *(ganar)* to win. **4** *(en un reparto, etc)* to be: *le tocó en Cartagena* he was posted to Cartagena. **6** *(tener que)* to have to: *nos tocó llevarla* we had to take her. **7** *(afectar)* to concern, affect: *le toca directamente* it directly concerns you. **8** *(entrar en contacto)* to touch.
▶ *vpr* **tocarse** *(uso reflexivo)* to touch os; *(uso recíproco)* to touch each other.

tocino *nm* **1** *(carne)* bacon. **2** *(grasa)* fat.

todavía *adv* **1** *(a pesar de ello)* still. **2** *(tiempo)* still, yet: *todavía están allí* they're still there. **3** *(para reforzar)* even: *esto todavía está mejor* this is even better.

todo,-a *adj* **1** *(sin excluir nada)* all: *todos los vecinos lo vieron* all the neighbours saw it. **2** *(verdadero)* real: *era todo un reto* it was a real challenge. **3** *(cada)* every: *todos los días* every day.
▶ *pron* **1** *(sin excluir nada)* all, everything: *llamaron todos* they all phoned. **2** *(cualquiera)* anybody: *todo el que yo diga* anybody I say.
▶ *nm* **todo** *(totalidad)* whole.
▶ *adv* completely, totally, all: *está todo mojado* it's all wet.

todoterreno *adj* four-wheel-drive.
▶ *nm* four-wheel-drive vehicle.

Togo *nm* Togo.

togolés,-esa *adj* Togolese.
▶ *nm & nf* Togolese.

toldo *nm* **1** *(cubierta)* awning. **2** *(de playa)* sunshade.

tolerancia *nf* tolerance.

tolerante *adj* tolerant, lenient.

tolerar *vt* **1** *(permitir, soportar)* to tolerate, put up with: *no te toleraré esa actitud* I won't put up with that attitude. **2** *(inconvenientes)* to stand.

toma *nf* **1** *(acción)* taking. **2** MED dose. **3** MIL capture. **4** *(de aire)* intake, inlet; *(de agua)* outlet, tap; *(de electricidad)* plug, socket. **5** *(grabación)* recording. **6** CINE take, shot. COMP **toma de posesión** takeover.

tomar *vt* **1** *(gen)* to take: *lo tomó en broma* she took it as a joke. **2** *(baño, ducha)* to have, take; *(foto)* to take. **3** *(comer, beber)* to have; *(beber)* to drink; *(comer)* to eat: *tómate la leche* drink your milk. **4** *(el autobús, el tren)* to catch. **5** *(aceptar)* to accept, take. **6** *(comprar)* to buy, get, have: *tomaré manzanas* I'll get some apples. **7** *(adquirir)* to acquire, get into: *tomar una costumbre* to acquire a habit. **8** MIL to capture, take.
▶ *vi* *(encaminarse)* to go, turn.
▶ *vpr* **tomarse** **1** *(gen)* to take: *me tomé una aspirina* I took an aspirin. **2** *(beber)* to drink; *(comer)* to eat. LOC **tomarse las cosas con calma** to take it easy.

tomate *nm* *(fruto)* tomato.

tómbola *nf* tombola.

T

tomillo *nm* thyme.

tomo *nm* (*volumen*) volume.

tonel *nm* barrel, cask.

tonelada *nf* ton. [COMP] **tonelada métrica** metric ton, tonne.

Tonga *nf* Tonga.

tongano,-a *adj* Tongan.
▶ *nm & nf* (*persona*) Tongan.
▶ *nm* **tongano** (*idioma*) Tongan.

tónica *nf* **1** (*tendencia*) tendency, trend. **2** (*bebida*) tonic, tonic water.

tónico,-a *adj* **1** (*sílaba*) tonic, stressed. **2** (*nota musical*) tonic.
▶ *nm* **tónico** MED tonic.

tono *nm* **1** (*gen*) tone: *el tono de su discurso* the tone of her speech. **2** (*energía*) energy. [LOC] **fuera de tono** *fig* inappropriate, out of place.

tontear *vi* (*decir tonterías*) to act the clown, fool about.

tontería *nf* **1** (*calidad de tonto*) stupidity, silliness. **2** (*dicho, hecho*) silly thing, stupid thing. **3** (*insignificancia*) trifle. [LOC] **hacer tonterías** to mess about, fool around.

tonto,-a *adj* silly, stupid, US dumb: *¡qué idea más tonta!* what a stupid idea!
▶ *nm & nf* fool, idiot. [LOC] **hacerse el tonto** to play dumb.

topacio *nm* topaz.

topar *vi* **1** (*chocar*) to bump into: *el coche topó contra un poste* the car bumped into a pole. **2** (*encontrar - algo*) to come across, find; (*- alguien*) to bump into, run into. **3** *fig* (*dificultades, etc*) to come up against, run into.

tope *nm* **1** (*límite*) limit, end. **2** TÉC stop, check. **3** (*de ferrocarril*) buffer, bumping post, bumper. **4** MAR masthead.
▶ *adj fig* top, maximum.
▶ *adv argot* really, absolutely: *la fiesta fue tope divertida* the party was absolutely brilliant. [LOC] **a tope 1** *argot* (*al límite*) flat out. **2** (*lleno*) jam-packed, chock-a-block.

tópico,-a *adj* MED external: *uso tópico* external use.
▶ *nm* **tópico** commonplace, cliché.

topo *nm* mole.

toque *nm* **1** (*acto*) touch. **2** (*de campana*) ringing, peal, pealing; (*de trompeta*) blare, sounding; (*de claxon*) honk; (*de sirena*) hoot; (*de tambor*) beat, beating. **3** (*pincelada*) touch. **4** *fig* (*advertencia*) warning. [LOC] **dar un toque a ALGN 1** (*llamar*) to take SB to task. **2** (*llamar la atención*) to call sb's attention.

tórax *nm inv* thorax.

torcer *vt* **1** (*gen*) to twist. **2** (*doblar*) to bend; (*madera*) to warp.
▶ *vi* (*girar*) to turn: *torció a la derecha* he turned right.
▶ *vpr* **torcerse 1** (*gen*) to twist. **2** (*doblarse*) to bend; (*madera*) to warp. **3** (*ladearse*) to become slanted. **4** MED to sprain, twist. **5** *fig* (*plan*) to fall through.

torcido,-a *adj* **1** (*que no es recto*) twisted. **2** (*madera*) warped; (*metal*) bent. **3** (*ladeado*) slanted, crooked, lopsided: *el cuadro está torcido* the painting is crooked.

torear *vt* **1** (*lidiar*) to fight. **2** *fig* (*entretener*) to put off. **3** *fig* (*burlar*) to tease, confuse. **4** *fig* (*asunto, etc*) to tackle skilfully. **5** *fig* (*evitar*) to avoid.
▶ *vi* (*lidiar*) to fight.

torero,-a *nm & nf* bullfighter.

tormenta *nf* storm.

tornado *nm* tornado.

torneo *nm* **1** (*justa*) tourney, joust. **2** DEP tournament, competition.

tornillo *nm* screw, bolt.

toro *nm* (*animal*) bull.
▶ *nm pl* **los toros** (*corrida*) bullfight *sing*; (*arte*) bullfighting *sing*.

torpe *adj* **1** (*poco hábil*) clumsy. **2** (*de movimiento*) slow, awkward. **3** (*poco inteligente*) dim, thick.

torpedo *nm* MIL torpedo.

torpeza *nf* **1** (*falta de habilidad*) clumsiness, awkwardness. **2** (*mental*) dimness, stupidity. **3** (*de movimiento*) slowness, heaviness. **4** (*error*) blunder.

torre *nf* **1** (*gen*) tower. **2** (*campanario*) bell tower. **3** (*chalé*) country house, house, villa. **4** (*ajedrez*) rook, castle.

torrencial *adj* torrential.

torrente *nm* **1** *(de agua)* mountain stream. **2** *fig (abundancia)* flood, stream.

torta *nf* **1** CULIN cake. **2** *fam (golpe)* blow, crack; *(bofetada)* slap, wallop. LOC **ni torta** *fam* not a thing: *no ve ni torta* he can't see a thing.

tortazo *nm* **1** *fam (golpe)* whack, thump. **2** *fam (bofetada)* slap, punch.

tortícolis *nf inv* stiff neck.

tortilla *nf* **1** omelette (US omelet). **2** AM tortilla, pancake. COMP **tortilla de patatas** potato omelette.

tórtola *nf* → tórtolo,-a.

tortuga *nf* **1** *(de tierra)* tortoise. **2** *(marina)* turtle.

torturar *vt* to torture.

tos *nf* cough, coughing. LOC **tener tos** to have a cough.

toser *vi* to cough.

tostada *nf* toast, slice of toast.

tostador,-ra *nm & nf (de pan)* toaster; *(de café)* roaster.

tostar *vt* **1** *(pan)* to toast; *(café)* to roast; *(carnes)* to brown. **2** *fig (piel)* to tan.
▶ *vpr* **tostarse** *fig (la piel)* to get brown, turn brown, tan.

total *adj* total, complete, overall: *anestesia total* general anaesthetic.
▶ *nm* **1** *(totalidad)* whole: *el total de la población* the whole population. **2** *(suma)* total, sum.
▶ *adv* **1** *(en conclusión)* in short, so: *total, que se fueron porque quisieron* they left because they wanted to. **2** *(al fin y al cabo)* after all.

totalitario,-a *adj* totalitarian.

totalitarismo *nm* totalitarianism.

tótem *nm* totem; *(efigie)* totem pole.

tóxico,-a *adj* toxic, poisonous.
▶ *nm* **tóxico** toxicant, poison.

toxicómano,-a *nm & nf* drug addict.

tozudo,-a *adj* stubborn, obstinate.

trabajador,-ra *adj* **1** *(que trabaja)* working. **2** *(laborioso)* hard-working.
▶ *nm & nf* worker (US laborer).

trabajar *vi* **1** *(gen)* to work: *trabaja mucho* she works hard. **2** *(en obra, película)* to act, perform: *¿quién trabaja en la obra?* who's in the play?
▶ *vt* **1** *(materiales)* to work (on). **2** *(idea, idioma, etc)* to work on. **3** *(la tierra)* to till. **4** CULIN *(pasta)* to knead.

trabajo *nm* **1** *(ocupación)* work. **2** *(tarea)* task, job. **3** *(empleo)* job. **4** *(esfuerzo)* effort. **5** EDUC report.
▶ *nm pl* **trabajos** *fig (penalidades)* hardships. COMP **trabajos manuales** arts and crafts, handicrafts.

trabalenguas *nm inv* tongue twister.

trabar *vt* **1** *(unir)* to join, link. **2** *(sujetar)* to lock, fasten. **3** *(mecanismo)* to jam. **4** *(prender a alguien)* to shackle. **5** *(caballería)* to hobble. **6** *fig (empezar)* to start. **7** *fig (conversación, amistad)* to strike up. **8** *fig (impedir)* to impede.
▶ *vpr* **trabarse** *(enredarse)* to get tangled up. LOC **trabársele la lengua a ALGN** to get tongue-tied.

tractor *nm* tractor.

tradición *nf* tradition.

tradicional *adj* traditional.

traducción *nf* translation.

traducir *vt* **1** *(gen)* to translate. **2** *(expresar)* to express, show.
▶ *vpr* **traducirse** *(resulta)* to result in.

traductor,-ra *adj* translating.
▶ *nm & nf* translator.

traer *vt* **1** *(gen)* to bring. **2** *(llevar consigo)* to carry: *traía un bolso* she was carrying a bag. **3** *(vestir)* to wear: *traía una falda verde* she was wearing a green skirt. **4** *(causar)* to cause, bring: *esto le trajo muchos problemas* it caused him a lot of problems. **5** *(contener)* to contain: *el paquete trae un regalo* the package contains a gift.
▶ *vpr* **traerse** *(llevar consigo)* to bring along: *tráete al bebé* bring your baby along.

traficante *nm o nf* **1** trader, dealer. **2** *(ilegal)* trafficker.

traficar *vi* **1** to deal. **2** *(de forma ilegal)* to traffic (en, in), deal (en, in): *trafica en/con drogas* he traffics in drugs.

tráfico *nm* **1** AUTO traffic. **2** COM traffic.

tragaperras COMP **máquina tragaperras** slot machine.

tragar *vt* **1** *(ingerir)* to swallow. **2** *(absorber)* to soak up. **3** *fig (hacer desaparecer)* to swallow up. **4** *fig (gastar, consumir)*

T

to eat up, guzzle: *este coche traga mucha gasolina* this car guzzles petrol. **5** *fig (creer)* to swallow, believe. **6** *fig (aguantar)* to put up with; *(disimular)* to hide: *tuvo que tragar sus exigencias* she had to put up with his demands. **7** *fig (soportar a alguien)* to stand, stomach: *no trago a Pedro* I can't stand Pedro.

▶ *vi* to swallow, swallow up.

▶ *vpr* **tragarse** *(ingerir)* to swallow: *se tragó un botón* he swallowed a button.

tragedia *nf* tragedy.

trágico,-a *adj* tragic.

trago *nm* **1** *(sorbo)* swig, drop. **2** *fam (bebida)* drink. **3** *fam fig (adversidad)* rough time.

traición *nf* treason, betrayal. [LOC] **a traición** treacherously.

traicionar *vt* **1** *(gen)* to betray. **2** *fig (delatar)* to give away, betray: *su expresión traicionó sus pensamientos* his expression gave away his thoughts.

traidor,-ra *adj* treacherous.

▶ *nm & nf* traitor.

traje *nm* **1** *(de hombre)* suit. **2** *(de mujer)* dress. [COMP] **traje de chaqueta** tailored suit. ‖ **traje de noche** evening dress.

trama *nf* **1** *(textil)* weft, woof. **2** *(argumento)* plot.

tramar *vt* **1** *(tejidos)* to weave. **2** *fig (maquinar)* to plot, cook up.

tramitación *nf* JUR procedure.

tramitar *vt* **1** *(gestionar)* to deal with, process: *tramitaremos su pasaporte* we'll get your passport sorted out. **2** *(solicitar, negociar)* to arrange, negotiate: *tramitar un préstamo* to negotiate a loan.

trámite *nm* **1** *(paso)* step. **2** *(formalidad)* formality, requirement.

tramo *nm* **1** *(camino, etc)* stretch. **2** *(de escalera)* flight. **3** *(de terreno)* lot.

trampa *nf* **1** *(abertura)* trapdoor, hatch. **2** *(para cazar)* trap. **3** *fig (engaño)* fiddle; *(truco)* trick. **4** *fig (deuda)* debt. [LOC] **tender una trampa** to set a trap.

trampolín *nm* **1** *(de piscina)* springboard. **2** *(de esquí)* ski jump.

tramposo,-a *adj* deceitful, tricky.

▶ *nm & nf* trickster, cheat; *(en las cartas)* cardsharp.

trancazo *nm* **1** *(golpe)* blow with a cudgel. **2** *fam fig (resfriado)* cold; *(gripe)* flu.

trance *nm* **1** *(momento crítico)* critical moment. **2** *(dificultad)* fix, tight spot. **3** *(éxtasis)* trance.

tranquilidad *nf* *(quietud)* calmness; *(sosiego)* peace and quiet. [COMP] **paz y tranquilidad** peace and quiet.

tranquilizante *nm* tranquillizer (US tranquilizer).

tranquilizar *vt* **1** *(calmar)* to calm down, tranquillize (US tranquilize). **2** *(dar confianza)* to reassure, set one's mind at rest.

▶ *vpr* **tranquilizarse 1** *(calmarse)* to calm down. **2** to set one's mind at rest.

tranquilo,-a *adj* **1** *(sin inquietud)* calm, relaxed, tranquil. **2** *(sin preocupación)* reassured. **3** *(sin movimiento)* calm, still, quiet. **4** *(sin ruidos)* quiet, still, peaceful. **5** *(persona)* calm, easy-going, placid. **6** *(agua)* still; *(conciencia)* clear.

transacción *nf* transaction, deal.

transatlántico,-a *adj* transatlantic.

▶ *nm* **transatlántico** liner, ocean liner.

transbordar *vt* to transfer.

▶ *vi* change *(de tren, etc)*.

transbordador *nm* ferry. [COMP] **transbordador espacial** space shuttle.

transbordo *nm* **1** *(de vehículo)* change, US transfer. **2** *(de barco)* transshipment.

transcribir *vt* to transcribe.

transcripción *nf* transcription.

transcurrir *vi* **1** *(tiempo)* to pass, elapse. **2** *(acontecer)* to take place, go off.

transcurso *nm* **1** *(paso)* course. **2** *(duración)* space, period: *en el transcurso de dos años* in the space of two years.

transeúnte *nm o nf (peatón)* pedestrian.

transferencia *nf* FIN transfer.

transferible *adj* transferable.

transferir *vt* FIN to transfer, convey.

transformación *nf* transformation.

transformador,-ra *adj* transforming.

▶ *nm* **transformador** transformer.

transformar *vt* to transform, change.

▶ *vpr* **transformarse** to change, be transformed: *se transformó completamente* he was completely transformed. [LOC] **transformarse en 1** *(persona)* to become. **2** *(objeto)* to convert into.

transfusión *nf* transfusion. [COMP] **transfusión de sangre** blood transfusion.

transgénico,-a *adj* genetically modified.

transgresión *nf* transgression.

transgresor,-ra *nm & nf* transgressor, law-breaker.

transición *nf* transition.

transigencia *nf* **1** *(actitud)* tolerance, lenience. **2** *(concesión)* compromise.

transigente *adj* accommodating, tolerant, lenient.

transigir *vi* **1** *(ceder)* to compromise, give in, yield. **2** *(tolerar)* to tolerate.

transistor *nm* transistor.

transitable *adj* passable.

transitado,-a *adj* busy.

transitar *vi* **1** *(viajar)* to travel, travel about. **2** *(pasar)* to pass, go, walk.

transitivo,-a *adj* transitive.

tránsito *nm* **1** *(acción)* passage, transit, movement. **2** AUTO traffic. **3** *euf (muerte)* death, passing. **4** *(lugar de parada)* stopping place.

transitoriedad *nf* transience.

transitorio,-a *adj (pasajero)* transitory; *(de transición)* transitional, interim.

transmediterráneo,-a *adj* trans-Mediterranean.

transmisible *adj* transmissible.

transmisión *nf* **1** *(propagación)* transmission. **2** JUR transfer, transference. **3** RAD TV broadcast. **4** TÉC drive.
▶ *nf pl* **transmisiones** MIL signals. [COMP] **derechos de transmisión 1** JUR *(de herencia)* succession duty. **2** *(de televisión, etc)* broadcasting rights. **‖ transmisión en directo** RAD TV live broadcast.

transmisor,-ra *adj* transmitting.
▶ *nm & nf* transmitter.

transmitir *vt* **1** *(gen)* to transmit. **2** RAD TV to broadcast. **3** *(enfermedad)* to transmit, pass on. **4** JUR to transfer, hand down.

transmutar *vt* to transmute.
▶ *vpr* **transmutarse** to change, transform.

transoceánico,-a *adj* transoceanic.

transparencia *nf* **1** transparency. **2** *(diapositiva)* transparency.

transparentar *vt fig (emociones, etc)* to reveal.
▶ *vpr* **transparentarse 1** *(ser transparente)* to be transparent, show through. **2** *fig (emociones, etc)* to show.

transparente *adj* **1** *(gen)* transparent. **2** *(tela, vestido)* transparent. **3** *fig* straight, plain.

transpiración *nf* perspiration.

transpirar *vi* to perspire, transpire.

transplantar *vt* **1** *(gen)* to transplant. **2** *(trasladar)* to transfer.

transplante *nm* transplant.

transportable *adj* transportable.

transportar *vt* **1** *(gen)* to transport. **2** *(pasajeros)* to carry; *(mercancías en barco)* to ship. **3** MAT to transfer. **4** MÚS to transpose. **5** *fig (hacer perder la razón)* to carry away, send into raptures.
▶ *vpr* **transportarse** *fig* to be transported, be enraptured.

transporte *nm* **1** *(medio)* transport. **2** *(acción)* transport, US transportation. **3** COM freight, freightage. **4** MÚS transposition. **5** *fig* transport, ecstasy, bliss. [COMP] **transporte público** public transport.

transportista *nm o nf* carrier.

transvasar *vt* **1** *(líquidos)* to decant. **2** *(entre ríos)* to transfer.

transvase *nm* **1** *(de líquidos)* decanting. **2** *(de ríos)* transfer.

transversal *adj* transverse.

transverso,-a *adj* transverse.

tranvía *nm* **1** *(sistema)* tramway. **2** *(vehículo)* tram, tramcar, US streetcar.

trapecio *nm* **1** DEP trapeze. **2** *(geometría)* trapezium, US trapezoid. **3** ANAT *(hueso)* trapezium; *(músculo)* trapezius.

trapecista *nm o nf* trapeze artist.

trapería *nf* secondhand clothes shop.

T

trapero,-a *nm & nf (hombre)* rag-and-bone man, US junkman; *(mujer)* rag-and-bone woman.

trapezoide *nm* trapezoid, US trapezium.

trapo *nm* **1** *(tela vieja)* rag. **2** *(paño, bayeta)* cloth. **3** MAR sails *pl*. **4** *(telón)* curtain. **5** *(del torero)* red cape.
▶ *nm pl* **trapos** clothes, rags. LOC **poner a** ALGN **como un trapo (sucio)** *fam* to tear SB apart. COMP **trapo del polvo** duster.

tráquea *nf* trachea, windpipe.

traqueal *adj* tracheal.

traqueotomía *nf* tracheotomy.

tras *prep* **1** *(después de)* after: *tras la salida del avión* after the departure of the plane. **2** *(detrás)* behind: *tras el muro* behind the wall. **3** *(en pos de)* after, in pursuit of: *iba siempre tras el éxito* he was always in pursuit of success. LOC **día tras día** day after day.

trasbordador *nm* ferry, car ferry.

trascendencia *nf* **1** *(importancia)* significance, importance. **2** *(filosofía)* transcendence, transcendency.

trascendental *adj* **1** *(importante)* significant, very important, consequential; *(de gran alcance)* far-reaching. **2** *(filosofía)* transcendent, transcendental.

trascendente *adj* → trascendental.

trascender *vi* **1** *(olor - despedir)* to smell; *(- llegar hasta)* to reach. **2** *(darse a conocer)* to become known, leak out: *el resultado trascendió* the result leaked out. **3** *(extenderse)* to spread, have a wide effect.

trascribir *vt* to transcribe.

trascripción *nf* transcription.

trasegar *vt* **1** *(mudar)* to move about, shuffle. **2** *(líquidos)* to decant.

trasero,-a *adj* back, rear.
▶ *nm* **trasero** *fam euf* bottom, bum.

trasferencia *nf* → transferencia.

trasferible *adj* transferable.

trasferir *vt* → transferir.

trasfondo *nm* **1** background. **2** *fig* undertone.

trasformación *nf* transformation.

trasformador,-ra *adj-nm* → transformador,-ra.

trasgresión *nf* transgression.

trasgresor,-ra *nm & nf* transgressor, law-breaker.

trashumancia *nf* transhumance, seasonal migration.

trashumante *adj* transhumant.

trasiego *nm* comings and goings *pl*, hustle and bustle.

traslación *nf* **1** *(de la Tierra)* passage, movement. **2** *(en matemáticas)* translation.

trasladar *vt* **1** *(cambiar de sitio)* to move. **2** *(de cargo, etc)* to transfer. **3** *(aplazar)* to postpone, put off.
▶ *vpr* **trasladarse 1** *(ir)* to go. **2** *(cambiar de residencia)* to move.

traslado *nm* **1** *(cambio de lugar)* move, moving; *(de residencia)* removal. **2** *(de cargo, etc)* transfer. **3** *(copia)* copy. **4** JUR notification.

traslúcido,-a *adj* translucent, semi-transparent.

traslucir *vt fig* to show, reveal, betray.
▶ *vpr* **traslucirse 1** *(material)* to be translucent. **2** *fig (dejar ver)* to show, show through.

trasluz *nm* diffused light, reflected light. LOC **mirar** ALGO **al trasluz** to look at STH against the light.

trasmano *nm o nf* second hand.

trasnochado,-a *adj* **1** *fig (viejo)* old, hackneyed. **2** *fig (desmejorado)* haggard, bleary-eyed.

trasnochador,-ra *nm & nf* night bird, nighthawk.

trasnochar *vi* to stay up late, stay up until the early hours.

traspapelado,-a *adj* mislaid, misplaced.

traspapelar *vt* to mislay, misplace.
▶ *vpr* **traspapelarse** to get mislaid, get misplaced.

traspasar *vt* **1** *(atravesar)* to go through, cross. **2** *(cambiar de lugar)* to move. **3** *(perforar)* to go through, pierce. **4** *(dar,* *pasar)* to transfer; *(vender)* to sell. **5** *fig (exceder)* to exceed, go beyond.

traspaso *nm* **1** *(de negocio, etc)* transfer, sale. **2** *(precio)* transfer fee.

traspié *nm* **1** *(tropezón)* stumble, trip. **2** *fig (equivocación)* blunder.

trasponer *vt-vpr* → transponer.

trasportista *nm o nf* carrier.

trasposición *nf* transposition.

traspuesto,-a LOC quedarse traspuesto,-a to nod off, doze off.

traspunte *nm* callboy.

trasquilado,-a *adj* **1** *(oveja)* sheared; *(pelo)* hacked, unevenly cut. **2** *fam fig* curtailed, cut down.

trasquilar *vt* **1** *(animales)* to shear. **2** *(pelo)* to hack, cut unevenly. **3** *fig* to curtail.

trastabillar *vi* **1** *(dar traspiés)* to stumble, trip. **2** *(tambalearse)* to stagger, totter.

trastada *nf fam (mala pasada)* dirty trick.

trastazo *nm fam* whack, wallop, thump. LOC darse un trastazo *fam* to come a cropper.

traste *nm* MÚS fret. LOC irse al traste *fig* to fall through.

trastear *vt* **1** MÚS to play. **2** *(revolver)* to rummage in. **3** *fig (manejar)* to twist around one's little finger.
► *vi (revolver)* to rummage.

trastero,-a *nm* junk room.

trastienda *nf* **1** *(de tienda)* back room. **2** *fig (astucia)* cunning.

trasto *nm* **1** *(algo inútil)* piece of junk. **2** *fam (niño)* little devil. **3** *fam (persona)* useless person, good-for-nothing, dead loss.
► *nm pl* **trastos 1** *(utensilios)* tackle *sing*, gear *sing*. **2** *fam (pertenencias)* belongings, things. LOC tirarse los trastos a la cabeza *fig* to have a blazing row.

trastocar *vt (cambiar)* to change.
► *vpr* **trastocarse** *(trastornarse)* to go mad.

trastornado,-a *adj* **1** *(preocupado)* upset. **2** *(loco)* mad. **3** *(mente)* unbalanced.

trastornar *vt* **1** *(revolver)* to turn round, turn upside down. **2** *(alterar - planes)* to disrupt; *(- paz, orden)* to disturb. **3** *(estómago)* to upset. **4** *fig (enloquecer)* to drive crazy.
► *vpr* **trastornarse** *(perturbarse)* to go mad, go out of one's mind.

trastorno *nm* **1** *(desorden)* confusion. **2** *(molestia)* trouble, inconvenience. **3** *(perturbación)* disruption, upheaval, upset. **4** MED upset.

trastrocar *vt* **1** *(gen)* to switch around, change around. **2** *(orden)* to invert, reverse; *(significado)* to change.

trasunto *nm* **1** *(copia)* copy. **2** *(representación)* representation.

trata *nf* slave trade.

tratable *adj* friendly, congenial, easy to get along with.

tratadista *nm o nf* treatise writer.

tratado *nm* **1** *(pacto)* treaty. **2** *(estudio)* treatise.

tratamiento *nm* **1** *(gen)* treatment. **2** *(de datos, materiales)* processing. **3** *(título)* title, form of address. COMP tratamiento de textos word processing.

tratar *vt* **1** *(gen - objeto)* to treat, handle; *(- persona)* to treat: *nos trató bien* he treated us well. **2** *(asunto, tema)* to discuss, deal with. **3** *(gestionar)* to handle, run. **4** *(dar tratamiento)* to address as. **5** *(calificar, considerar)* to consider, call: *lo trató de idiota* she called him an idiot. **6** MED to treat. **7** *(datos, texto)* to process. **8** QUÍM to treat.
► *vi* **1** *(relacionarse)* to be acquainted (con, with), know (con, -). **2** *(tener tratos)* to deal with (con, with). **3** *(negociar)* to negotiate (con, with). **4** *(intentar)* to try (de, to): *trata de hacerlo* try to do it. **5** *(versar)* to be about: *trata de/sobre espías* it's about spies.
► *vpr* **tratarse 1** *(relacionarse)* to talk to each other, be on speaking terms: *no se tratan* they're not on speaking terms. **2** *(llamarse)* to address each other as, call each other. **3** *(referirse)* to be about: *se trataba de un atraco* it was about a robbery.

T

trato *nm* **1** *(acción)* treatment. **2** *(modales)* manner. **3** *(contacto)* contact. **4** *(acuerdo)* agreement. **5** COM deal. **6** *(tratamiento)* title. LOC **cerrar un trato** to close a deal. ▌**¡trato hecho!** it's a deal!

trauma *nm* trauma.

traumático,-a *adj* traumatic.

traumatismo *nm* traumatism.

traumatizar *vt* **1** MED to traumatize. **2** *fam* to shock.

través *nm* **1** *(inclinación)* slant. **2** *(pieza de madera)* crosspiece, crossbeam. **3** MAR beam. **4** *fig (desgracia)* misfortune. LOC **a través de 1** *(de un lado a otro)* across, over. **2** *(por dentro)* through. **3** *(mediante)* through, from.

travesaño *nm* **1** ARQUIT crosspiece. **2** DEP crossbar.

travesía *nf* **1** *(viaje)* crossing; *(por mar)* voyage, crossing. **2** *(calle)* crossstreet, passage. **3** *(distancia)* distance.

travesura *nf* piece of mischief, childish prank. LOC **hacer travesuras** to get into mischief.

traviesa *nf* **1** *(de ferrocarril)* sleeper, US tie. **2** *(en construcción)* trimmer.

travieso,-a *adj* mischievous, naughty.

trayecto *nm* **1** *(distancia)* distance, way. **2** *(recorrido)* route, itinerary.

trayectoria *nf* **1** trajectory. **2** *fig* line, course, path.

traza *nf fig (apariencia)* looks *pl*, appearance.

trazado *nm* **1** *(plano)* layout, plan. **2** *(dibujo)* drawing, sketch. **3** *(de carretera, ferrocarril)* route, course.

trazar *vt* **1** *(línea, plano, dibujo)* to draw, draw up. **2** *(parque)* to lay out; *(edificio)* to design. **3** *(itinerario)* to trace. **4** *fig (plan, etc)* to outline, draft.

trazo *nm* **1** *(línea)* line. **2** *(de una letra)* stroke. **3** *fig (rasgo facial)* feature.

trébol *nm* **1** *(planta)* clover, trefoil. **2** *(naipes)* club.

trece *adj (cardinal)* thirteen; *(ordinal)* thirteenth.

▶ *nm (número)* thirteen; *(fecha)* thirteenth.

✎ Consulta también seis.

treceavo,-a *adj* thirteenth.
▶ *nm & nf* thirteenth.

✎ Consulta también sexto,-a.

trecho *nm* **1** *(espacio)* distance, way; *(tiempo)* while, time. **2** *(de camino, ruta)* stretch. **3** AGR plot, patch. **4** *fam (parte)* piece, bit.

tregua *nf* **1** truce. **2** *fig* respite, rest.

treinta *adj (cardinal)* thirty; *(ordinal)* thirtieth.
▶ *nm (número)* thirty; *(fecha)* thirtieth.

✎ Consulta también seis.

treintañero,-a *adj* thirty-year-old.
▶ *nm & nf* thirty-year-old person.

treintavo,-a *adj* thirtieth.
▶ *nm & nf* thirtieth.

✎ Consulta también sexto,-a.

tremendo,-a *adj* **1** *(terrible)* terrible, dreadful, frightful. **2** *(muy grande)* huge, enormous, tremendous. **3** *(travieso)* terrible. LOC **tomarse** ALGO **por la tremenda** *fig* to make a great fuss about STH.

trementina *nf* turpentine.

tremolar *vt* to wave.
▶ *vi* to wave, flutter.

trémulo,-a *adj* **1** *(tembloroso)* tremulous, quivering. **2** *(luz, llama)* flickering.

tren *nm* **1** *(ferrocarril)* train. **2** *(conjunto de máquinas)* convoy, line. **3** *fig (ritmo, modo)* speed, pace. LOC **coger el tren / tomar el tren** to catch a train. COMP **tren de alta velocidad** high-speed train.

trenca *nf (abrigo)* duffel coat, duffle coat.

trenza *nf* **1** *(peluquería)* plait, US braid. **2** COST braid.

trenzado *nm* **1** *(trenza - de pelo)* plait, US braid; *(- de costura)* braid. **2** *(en danza)* entrechat. **3** *(de caballo)* crossover step.

trenzar *vt* **1** to plait, braid. **2** *(peluquería)* to plait, us braid.

trepador,-ra *adj (planta)* climbing.
▶ *nm & nf fam pey* go-getter, social climber.

trepanación *nf* trepanation, trephination.

trepanar *vi* to trepan, trephine.

trépano *nm* **1** MED trephine. **2** TÉC bit.

trepar¹ *vt (escalar)* to climb.
▶ *vi (escalar)* to climb.

trepar² *vt* **1** *(taladrar)* to drill. **2** *(un bordado)* to trim.

trepidante *adj* **1** vibrating, shaking. **2** *fig (vida, etc)* hectic, frantic.

trepidar *vi* to vibrate, shake.

tres *adj (cardinal)* three; *(ordinal)* third.
▶ *nm (número)* three; *(fecha)* third. COMP **tres en raya** noughts and crosses, us tick-tack-toe.

✎ Consulta también **seis**.

trescientos,-as *adj (cardinal)* three hundred; *(ordinal)* three hundredth.
▶ *nm (número)* three hundred.

✎ Consulta también **seis**.

tresillo *nm (mueble)* suite, three-piece suite.

treta *nf* trick, ruse.

tríada *nf* triad.

triangular *adj* triangular.

triángulo,-a *adj* triangular.
▶ *nm* **triángulo** triangle. COMP **triángulo equilátero** equilateral triangle. ‖ **triángulo isósceles** isosceles triangle. ‖ **triángulo rectángulo** right-angled triangle.

triatlón *nm* triathlon.

tribal *adj* tribal, tribe.

tribu *nf* tribe.

tribuna *nf* **1** *(plataforma)* rostrum, dais. **2** DEP grandstand.

tribunal *nm* **1** JUR court. **2** *(de examen)* board of examiners. LOC **llevar a los tribunales** to take to court. COMP **Tribunal Supremo** High Court, us Supreme Court.

tributación *nf* taxation, levy.

tributar *vt* to pay.

tributario,-a *adj* tributary, tax.
▶ *nm & nf* taxpayer.

tributo *nm* **1** *(impuesto)* tax. **2** *(a cambio de algo)* tribute. **3** *fig (carga)* price. **4** *fig (de sentimiento)* token.

tricéfalo,-a *adj* tricephalous.

tríceps *nm inv* triceps.

triciclo *nm* tricycle.

tricornio *nm (sombrero)* three-cornered hat.

tricotar *vt* to knit.

tridente *nm* trident.

tridimensional *adj* three-dimensional.

triedro *nm* trihedron.

trienal *adj* triennial.

trienio *nm* triennium.

trifásico,-a *adj* ELEC three-phase.

trigal *nm* wheat field.

trigésimo,-a *adj* thirtieth.
▶ *nm & nf* thirtieth.

✎ Consulta también **sexto,-a**.

triglifo *nm* triglyph.

trigo *nm (cereal)* wheat.

trigonometría *nf* trigonometry.

trigonométrico,-a *adj* trigonometric, trigonometrical.

trigueño,-a *adj* **1** *(pelo)* corn-coloured (us corn-colored), dark blonde. **2** *(piel)* dark, swarthy. **3** *(persona)* olive-skinned.

triguero,-a *adj* wheat.

trilateral *adj* three-sided, trilateral.

trilingüe *adj* trilingual.

trilita *nf* TNT, trinitrotoluene.

trilla *nf* threshing.

trillado,-a *adj* **1** *(camino)* beaten, well-trodden. **2** *fig (expresión, etc)* overworked, well-worn.

trilladora *nf* threshing machine.

trillar *vt* **1** to thresh. **2** *fig* to wear out.

trillizo,-a *nm & nf* triplet.

trilogía *nf* trilogy.

trimestral *adj* quarterly, three-monthly, trimestral.

trimestre *nm* **1** quarter, trimester. **2** EDUC term.

trimotor *nm* three-engined aircraft.

trinar *vi* **1** *(ave)* to warble, trill. **2** MÚS to trill. **3** *fam (enfadarse)* to rage, fume: *Pedro está que trina* Pedro is fuming.

trinchar *vt* to carve, slice (up).

trinchera *nf* trench.

trineo *nm* sleigh, sled, sledge.

Trinidad *nf* Trinidad. COMP **Trinidad y Tobago** Trinidad and Tobago.

trinitrotolueno *nm* trinitrotoluene.

trino *nm* **1** *(ave)* warble, trill. **2** MÚS trill.

trino,-a *adj* trine.

trinomio *nm* trinomial.

trinquete¹ *nm (lengüeta)* pawl; *(mecanismo)* ratchet.

trinquete² *nm* **1** *(frontón)* pelota court. **2** MAR *(palo)* foremast; *(vela)* foresail.

trío *nm* trio.

tripa *nf* **1** *(intestino)* gut, intestine. **2** *(barriga)* gut, stomach. **3** *(de vasija)* belly. **4** *fam (embarazo)* belly.
  ▶ *nf pl* **tripas** *fam (interior)* innards.

tripartito,-a *adj* tripartite.

triple *adj* **1** triple. **2** *(tres veces)* three times: *pagamos el triple del precio real* we paid three times the real price.
  ▶ *nm* triple. COMP **triple salto** triple jump.

triplicado *nm* triplicate.

triplicar *vt* to triple, treble.

trípode *nm* tripod.

tríptico *nm* triptych.

triptongo *nm* triphthong.

tripulación *nf* crew.

tripulante *nm* crew member.

tripular *vt* to man.

tris *nm fam fig* bit; *(sonido)* crack. LOC **en un tris** *fam* in a jiffy: *lo hizo en un tris* he did it in a jiffy.

trisílabo,-a *adj* trisyllabic.
  ▶ *nm* **trisílabo** trisyllable.

triste *adj* **1** *(infeliz)* sad, unhappy; *(futuro)* bleak. **2** *(oscuro, sombrío)* gloomy, dismal. **3** *(único)* single, only: *ni un triste libro* not a single book. **4** *(insignificante)* poor, humble. LOC **es triste que...** it's a pity...: *es triste que no los podamos ayudar* it's a pity we can't help them.

tristeza *nf* sadness.
  ▶ *nf pl* **tristezas** problems, sufferings.

tristón,-ona *adj fam* gloomy, sad, melancholy.

tritón *nm* **1** *(anfibio)* newt. **2** Tritón *(mitología)* Triton.

triturado,-a *adj* **1** ground, crushed. **2** *fig* crumpled up.

triturador,-ra *adj* grinding, crushing, triturating.
  ▶ *nm* **triturador** waste disposal unit, US garbage disposal unit.

trituradora *nf* grinder, crushing machine. COMP **trituradora de papel** paper shredder.

triturar *vt* **1** to grind (up), crush; *(papel)* to shred. **2** *fig (físicamente)* to beat (up); *(moralmente)* to tear apart.

triunfador,-ra *adj* winning.
  ▶ *nm & nf* winner.

triunfal *adj* triumphant.

triunfalismo *nm* **1** triumphalism. **2** POL jingoism.

triunfalista *adj* **1** triumphalist. **2** POL jingoistic.
  ▶ *nm o nf* **1** triumphalist. **2** POL jingoist.

triunfar *vi* to triumph. LOC **triunfar en la vida** to succeed in life.

triunfo *nm* **1** *(victoria)* triumph, victory. **2** DEP win. **3** *(éxito)* success. **4** *(naipes)* trump.

trivial *adj* trivial, petty.

trivialidad *nf* triviality, pettiness.

trivializar *vt* to trivialize, minimize.

triza *nf* bit, fragment. LOC **estar hecho, -a trizas** *fam* to feel washed out.

trocar *vt* **1** *(permutar)* to exchange, swap: *trocar un lápiz por un bolígrafo* to exchange a pencil for a biro. **2** *(transformar)* to turn (en, into), convert (en, into).

trocear *vt* to cut up.

trofeo *nm* trophy.

trófico,-a *adj* food.

troglodita *nm o nf* troglodyte.

trolebús *nm* trolley bus.

tromba *nf* waterspout. COMP **tromba de agua** downpour.

trombo *nm* thrombus.

trombón *nm* MÚS trombone.
▸ *nm o nf* trombonist. COMP **trombón de varas** slide trombone.

trombosis *nf inv* thrombosis.

trompa *nf* 1 MÚS horn. 2 *(de elefante)* trunk. 3 *(de insecto)* proboscis. 4 ANAT tube. 5 *fam fig (nariz)* hooter, snout. LOC **estar trompa** *fam* to be plastered. COMP **trompa de Eustaquio** Eustachian tube. ‖ **trompa de Falopio** Fallopian tube.
▸ *nm o nf* MÚS horn player.

trompazo *nm* bump. LOC **darse un trompazo** to have a bump, have a crash.

trompeta *nf* MÚS trumpet.
▸ *nm o nf* trumpet player.

trompetista *nm o nf* trumpet player, trumpeter.

trompicón *nm* 1 *(tropezón)* trip, stumble. 2 *(golpe)* blow, hit. LOC **a trompicones** in fits and starts.

trompo *nm* top, spinning top.

tronar *vi* 1 [se usa sólo en tercera persona; no lleva sujeto] *(trueno)* to thunder. 2 *(cañón, etc)* to thunder.

tronchar *vt* 1 *(árboles)* to cut down, fell. 2 *fig* to destroy. LOC **troncharse de risa** *fam* to split one's sides with laughter.

troncho *adj* stem, stalk.

tronco *nm* 1 ANAT trunk, torso. 2 BOT *(tallo de árbol)* trunk; *(leño)* log. 3 *fig (linaje)* family stock. 4 *fig (persona inútil)* blockhead. 5 *(geometría)* frustum. 6 *argot (compañero)* mate, pal, chum. LOC **dormir como un tronco** *fam* to sleep like a log. COMP **tronco de cono** truncated cone.

tronera *nf* 1 *(de fortificación)* loophole, embrasure. 2 *(de barco)* porthole. 3 *(de billar)* pocket.

trono *nm* throne.

tropa *nf* 1 MIL troops *pl*, soldiers *pl*. 2 *(muchedumbre)* crowd.

▸ *nf pl* **tropas** MIL troops, fighting soldiers.

tropel *nm* throng, mob. LOC **en tropel** in a mad rush.

tropelía *nf* 1 *(atropello)* outrage. 2 *(tropel)* throng, mob. 3 *(delito)* crime.

tropezar *vi* 1 *(trompicar)* to trip, stumble: *tropezó con mi pie* he tripped over my foot. 2 *fig (encontrar a alguien)* to come (con, across), bump (con, into). 3 *fig (encontrar dificultades, etc)* to come up (con, against), run (con, into).

tropezón *nm* 1 *(traspié)* trip, stumble. 2 *fig (error)* slip-up, faux pas. 3 *fam (de comida)* chunk of food. LOC **dar un tropezón** to trip.

tropical *adj* tropical.

trópico *nm* tropic.
▸ *nm pl* **trópicos** tropics.

tropiezo *nm* 1 *(obstáculo)* trip. 2 *fig (error)* blunder; *(revés)* setback, mishap. 3 *(riña)* quarrel.

tropismo *nm* tropism.

tropo *nm* trope.

troposfera *nf* troposphere.

troquel *nm* die.

troqueladora *nf* stamping machine.

troquelar *vt (gen)* to stamp; *(monedas)* to strike; *(cuero)* to emboss.

trotamundos *nm o nf inv* globe-trotter; *(mochilero)* backpacker.

trotar *vi* 1 to trot. 2 *fig (andar)* to bustle, run, run about.

trote *nm* 1 *(de caballo)* trot. 2 *fam fig (actividad)* chasing about, hustle and bustle, bustle. LOC **al trote** at a trot.

trovador,-ra *nm & nf* troubadour, minstrel.

trozo *nm* piece, chunk.

trucaje *nm* trick photography.

trucar *vt* 1 *(foto, etc)* to doctor, alter, tamper with. 2 AUTO to soup up.

trucha *nf* trout.

truco *nm* 1 *(ardid)* trick. 2 *(fotográfico)* trick effect, trick camera shot. 3 *(tranquillo)* knack. LOC **coger el truco a ALGO** *fam* to get the knack of STH, get the hang of STH.

T

truculencia *nf* 1 cruelty. 2 *fig* sensationalism.

truculento,-a *adj* 1 *(cruel)* cruel. 2 *fig (excesivo)* sensationalistic.

trueno *nm* 1 thunder, thunderclap. 2 *fam (joven)* hare brain.

trueque *nm* exchange, swap.

trufa *nf* 1 *(hongo)* truffle. 2 *(de chocolate)* chocolate truffle.

trufar *vt* to stuff with truffles.
▶ *vi fig* to tell lies.*f*

truhan,-ana *nm & nf* rogue, crook.

truncado,-a *adj (geometría)* truncated.

truncar *vt* 1 *(cortar)* to truncate. 2 *fig (ilusiones, esperanzas)* to shatter, cut short. 3 *fig (escrito)* to leave unfinished; *(sentido)* to upset.
▶ *vpr* **truncarse** *fig (ilusiones, etc)* to cut short.

trust *nm* trust, cartel.

tu *adj* your: *tu coche* your car; *tus coches* your cars.

tú *pron* 1 you. 2 REL Thou. [LOC] **tratar de tú** to address as *tú*.

tuareg *adj* Tuareg.
▶ *nm* Tuareg.

tuba *nf* tuba.

tubérculo *nm* 1 BOT tuber. 2 MED tubercle.

tuberculosis *nf inv* tuberculosis.

tuberculoso,-a *adj* 1 BOT tuberous. 2 MED tubercular, tuberculous.

tubería *nf* 1 *(de agua)* piping, pipes *pl*, plumbing. 2 *(de gas, petróleo)* pipeline.

tuberoso,-a *adj* tuberous.

tubo *nm* 1 *(de ensayo, etc)* tube. 2 *(tubería)* pipe. 3 ANAT tube. [COMP] **tubo de ensayo** test tube. ▌**tubo de escape** exhaust pipe, exhaust. ▌**tubo digestivo** alimentary canal.

tubular *adj* tubular.
▶ *nm* bicycle tyre.

tucán *nm* toucan.

tuerca *nf* nut.

tuerto,-a *adj* one-eyed, blind in one eye.
▶ *nm & nf* one-eyed person.

tuétano *nm* 1 marrow. 2 *fig* essence, core.

tufo *nm* 1 *(mal olor)* pong, foul smell, stink. 2 *(emanación)* fume, vapour (US vapor).

tugurio *nm* 1 *(choza)* shepherd's hut. 2 *(casucha)* hovel, shack. 3 *fig* hole, dive.

tul *nm* tulle.

tulipa *nf* 1 *(bot)* small tulip. 2 *(lámpara)* tulip-shaped lampshade.

tulipán *nm* tulip.

tullido,-a *adj* crippled, disabled.
▶ *nm & nf* cripple.

tumbado,-a *adj (estirado)* lying, stretched out: *tumbado al sol* lying in the sun.

tumbar *vt* 1 *(derribar)* to knock out, knock over. 2 EDUC *fam* to fail.
▶ *vpr* **tumbarse** *(acostarse)* to lie down, stretch out.

tumbo *nm* jolt, bump. [LOC] **dar tumbos** to jolt, bump along.

tumbona *nf* 1 *(hamaca)* deck-chair. 2 *(silla extensible)* lounger.

tumor *nm* tumour (US tumor).

túmulo *nm* 1 *(montecillo)* tumulus, burial mound, barrow. 2 *(catafalco)* catafalque.

tumulto *nm* tumult, commotion.

tumultuoso,-a *adj* tumultuous, riotous.

tuna *nf* student minstrel group.

tunda *nf* 1 *fam* thrashing, beating. 2 *fig (trabajo agotador)* exhausting job, drag.

tundra *nf* tundra.

tunecino,-a *adj* Tunisian.
▶ *nm & nf* Tunisian.

túnel *nm* tunnel.

Túnez *nm* 1 *(ciudad)* Tunis. 2 *(país)* Tunisia.

tungsteno *nm* tungsten.

túnica *nf* tunic.

tuno *nm* BOT prickly pear.

tupí *adj* Tupi.
▶ *nm & nf* Tupi.
▶ *nm (idioma)* Tupi.

tupido,-a *adj* 1 dense, thick. 2 *fig (torpe)* clumsy, dense.

tupir *vi (apretar)* to pack tight, press down.
▶ *vpr* **tupirse 1** *(comiendo)* to stuff os. **2** *(ofuscarse)* to get muddled up, get in a muddle.

turba¹ *nf* **1** *(combustible)* peat, turf. **2** *(abono)* peat, peat moss.

turba² *nf (muchedumbre)* mob, crowd.

turbación *nf* **1** *(alteración)* disturbance. **2** *(preocupación)* anxiety, worry. **3** *(desconcierto)* confusion, uneasiness.

turbado,-a *adj* **1** *(alterado)* disturbed, unsettled. **2** *(preocupado)* worried, upset. **3** *(desconcertado)* confused.

turbador,-ra *adj* **1** *(que altera)* disturbing, unsettling. **2** *(preocupante)* worrying, upsetting. **3** *(desconcertante)* confusing, disconcerting.

turbante *nm* turban.

turbar *vt* **1** *(alterar)* to unsettle, disturb. **2** *(enturbiar)* to stir up. **3** *(preocupar)* to upset, worry. **4** *(desconcertar)* to baffle, put off.
▶ *vpr* **turbarse 1** *(preocuparse)* to be upset, become upset. **2** *(desconcertarse)* to be confused, be baffled.

turbera *nf* peat bog.

turbina *nf* turbine.

turbio,-a *adj* **1** *(oscurecido)* cloudy, muddy, turbid. **2** *fig (dudoso)* shady, dubious. **3** *fig (turbulento)* turbulent. **4** *fig (confuso)* confused. **5** *fig (vista)* blurred.

turbo *nm* turbo.

turbogenerador *nm* turbogenerator.

turbohélice *nm* turboprop.

turborreactor *nm* turbojet, turbojet engine.

turbulencia *nf* turbulence.

turbulento,-a *adj* turbulent, troubled.

turco,-a *adj* Turkish.
▶ *nm & nf (persona)* Turk.
▶ *nm* **turco** *(idioma)* Turkish.

turgencia *nf* turgidity, turgidness.

turgente *adj* turgid.

turismo *nm* **1** *(gen)* tourism. **2** *(industria)* tourist trade, tourist industry. **3** AUTO private car, saloon. LOC **hacer**

turismo 1 *(país)* to go touring. **2** *(ciudad, pueblo)* to go sightseeing.

turista *nm o nf* tourist.

turístico,-a *adj* tourist. LOC **de interés turístico** of interest to tourists.

Turkmenistán *nm* Turkmenistan.

túrmix® *nm inv* liquidizer, blender.

turnar *vi* to alternate.
▶ *vpr* **turnarse** to take turns.

turno *nm* **1** *(tanda)* turn, go: *es mi turno* it's my turn; *¿a quién le toca el turno?* who's next? **2** *(período de trabajo)* shift. LOC **estar de turno** to be on duty. COMP **turno de día / turno de noche** day shift / night shift.

turquesa *adj* turquoise.
▶ *nf (piedra)* turquoise.
▶ *nm (color)* turquoise.

Turquía *nf* Turkey.

turrón *nm type of* nougat.

turronería *nf* shop selling nougat.

tute *nm* **1** *(naipes)* card game. **2** *fig (esfuerzo)* beating, thrashing.

tutear *vt* **1** to address as *tú*. **2** *fig* to be on familiar terms with.
▶ *vpr* **tutearse** *(uso recíproco)* to address each other as *tú*.

tutela *nf* **1** JUR guardianship, tutelage. **2** *fig* protection, guidance. LOC **bajo la tutela de** under the protection of.

tutelar *adj* tutelary.

tuteo *nm* use of the *tú* form of address.

tutor,-ra *nm & nf* **1** JUR guardian. **2** *fig* protector, guide. **3** EDUC tutor.
▶ *nm* tutor AGR stake, prop.

tutoría *nf* **1** JUR guardianship, tutelage. **2** EDUC post of tutor.

Tuvalu *nm* Tuvalu.

tuyo,-a *adj* of yours, one of your: *¿es primo tuyo?* is he a cousin of yours?, is he your cousin?
▶ *pron* yours, your own: *el tuyo está allí* yours is there.
▶ *nm* **lo tuyo** *(lo que es tuyo)* what is yours; *(lo que te concierne)* your business, your own business.
▶ *nm pl* **los tuyos** *(familiares)* your family *sing*; *(amigos)* your friends.

T

U

U, u *nf (la letra)* U, u.

u [se usa ante palabras que empiezan por o u ho] *conj* or: *diez u once* ten or eleven.

✎ Consulta también **o**.

ubre *nf* udder.

ucraniano,-a *adj* Ukranian.
▶ *nm & nf (persona)* Ukranian.

Uganda *nf* Uganda.

ugandés,-esa *adj* Ugandan.
▶ *nm & nf* Ugandan.

úlcera *nf* ulcer. COMP **úlcera de estómago** stomach ulcer.

ulceración *nf* ulceration.

ultimar *vt* to finish, complete.

ultimátum *nm inv* **1** ultimatum. **2** *fam* final word.

último,-a *adj* **1** last. **2** *(más reciente)* latest; *(de dos)* latter. **3** *(más alejado)* furthest; *(más abajo)* bottom, lowest; *(más arriba)* top; *(más atrás)* back. **4** *(definitivo)* final. LOC **por último** finally.

ultraje *nm* outrage, insult.

ultraligero *adj* ultralight.
▶ *nm* **ultraligero** *(avión)* microlight.

ultramar *nm* overseas: *viene de ultramar* it comes from overseas, it's imported.

ultramarino,-a *adj* overseas.
▶ *nm pl* **ultramarinos** groceries.

ultrasonido *nm* ultrasound.

ultravioleta *adj inv* ultraviolet.

ulular *vi* **1** *(animal)* to howl; *(búho)* to hoot. **2** *fig* to howl.

umbilical *adj* umbilical.

umbral *nm* **1** threshold. **2** *fig* threshold, outset.

un,-na *art indef* a, an: *un libro* a book; *un ojo* an eye.

▶ *adj* **1** *(numeral)* one: *tiene un año* he's one year old. **2** *(indef)* some: *un día volverá* he'll come some day.

✎ Consulta también **uno,-a**.

unánime *adj* unanimous.

unanimidad *nf* unanimity.

undécimo,-a *adj* eleventh.
▶ *nm & nf (ordinal, partitivo)* eleventh.

✎ Consulta también **sexto,-a**.

ungüento *nm* ointment.

ungulado,-a *adj* ungulate, hoofed.
▶ *nm* **ungulado** ungulate.

unicelular *adj* unicellular, single-cell.

único,-a *adj* **1** *(solo)* only, sole: *la única persona* the only person. **2** *(extraordinario)* unique.

unicornio *nm* unicorn.

unidad *nf* **1** unit. **2** *(barco)* vessel; *(avión)* aircraft; *(de tren)* carriage, coach. **3** *(cohesión)* unity.

unido,-a *adj* **1** *(junto)* united. **2** *(avenido)* attached: *estar muy unidos* to be very close.

unifamiliar COMP **vivienda unifamiliar** detached house.

unificación *nf* unification.

unificador,-ra *adj* unifying.
▶ *nm & nf* unifier.

unificar *vt* to unify.

uniformado,-a *adj* in uniform.

uniformar *vt* **1** *(igualar)* to make uniform, standardize. **2** *(poner un uniforme)* to put into uniform, give a uniform.

uniforme *adj* **1** uniform. **2** *(superficie)* even.
▶ *nm (prenda)* uniform.

uniformidad *nf* **1** *(igualdad)* uniformity. **2** *(de superficie)* evenness.

uniformizar *vt* to standardize.

unilateral *adj* unilateral.

unión *nf* **1** union. **2** TÉC *(acoplamiento)* joining; *(junta)* joint.

unir *vt* **1** *(juntar)* to unite, join. **2** *(combinar)* to combine (a, with).

unitario,-a *adj* unitary.

univalvo,-a *adj* univalve.

universal *adj* universal.

universidad *nf* university.

universitario,-a *adj* university.
▶ *nm & nf (que está estudiando)* university student; *(licenciado)* university graduate.

universo *nm* universe.

unívoco,-a *adj* univocal.

uno,-a *adj (numeral)* one: *el número uno* number one.
▶ *pron* **1** one: *uno (de ellos)* one of them. **2** *(impersonal)* one, you: *uno tiene que velar por sus intereses* one has to look after one's own interests. **3** *fam (persona)* someone, somebody: *estaba hablando con una* he was talking to some woman.
▶ *nm* **uno** *(número)* one.
▶ *nf* **la una** *(hora)* one o'clock.
▶ *adj vpr* **unos,-as** *(indefinido)* some; *(aproximado)* about, around: *unas cajas* some boxes; *habrá unos treinta* there must be around thirty. LOC **a (la) una** together. ‖ **de uno,-a en uno,-a** one by one.

untar *vt* **1** to grease, smear: *untar pan con mantequilla* to spread butter on bread. **2** *fam (sobornar)* to bribe.

uña *nf* **1** nail; *(del dedo)* fingernail; *(del dedo del pie)* toenail. **2** *(garra)* claw; *(pezuña)* hoof.

uralita® *nf* uralite.

uranio *nm* uranium.

Urano *nm* Uranus.

urbanismo *nm* town planning.

urbanización *nf* **1** *(proceso)* urbanization. **2** *(conjunto residencial)* housing development, housing estate.

urbanizar *vt* to urbanize, develop.

urbano,-a *adj* urban, city.

urbe *nf* large city, metropolis.

uréter *nm* ureter.

uretra *nf* urethra.

urgencia *nf* urgency, emergency.
▶ *nf pl* **urgencias** *(servicio)* casualty department *sing*, casualty *sing*, US emer-

gency room. LOC **en (un) caso de urgencia** in an emergency.

urgente *adj* **1** urgent. **2** *(correo)* express (post, US mail), first-class (post, US mail).

urgir *vi* to be urgent, be pressing.

urinario,-a *adj* urinary.
▶ *nm* **urinario** *(retrete)* urinal.

urna *nf* **1** POL ballot box. **2** *(vasija)* urn. **3** *(caja)* glass case.

urraca *nf* **1** magpie. **2** *fig (cotorra)* chatterbox.

urticaria *nf* hives *pl*, urticaria.

Uruguay *nm* Uruguay.

uruguayo,-a *adj* Uruguayan.
▶ *nm & nf* Uruguayan.

usado,-a *adj* **1** *(gastado)* worn out, old. **2** *(de segunda mano)* second-hand, used.

usar *vt* **1** to use. **2** *(prenda)* to wear.
▶ *vi* to use (de, -).
▶ *vpr* **usarse** *(estar de moda)* to be used, be in fashion.

uso *nm* **1** use. **2** *(ejercicio)* exercise. **3** *(de prenda)* wearing. **4** *(costumbre)* usage, custom. **5** GRAM usage.

usted *pron fml* you.

usual *adj* usual, common.

usuario,-a *nm & nf* user.

usurero,-a *nm & nf* usurer.

usurpar *vt* to usurp.

utensilio *nm* **1** *(herramienta)* tool, utensil. **2** *(aparato)* device, implement.

uterino,-a *adj* uterine.

útero *nm* uterus, womb.

útil¹ *adj* useful.

útil² *nm* *(herramienta)* tool, instrument.

utilidad *nf* **1** utility, usefulness. **2** *(beneficio)* profit.

utilitario,-a *adj* utilitarian.
▶ *nm* **utilitario** *(coche)* utility vehicle.

utilizar *vt* to use, make use of.

utopía *nf* utopia.

utópico,-a *adj* utopian.

uva *nf* grape.

uve *nf name of the letter* v.

uzbeco,-a *adj* Uzbek.
▶ *nm & nf (persona)* Uzbek.
▶ *nm* **uzbeco** *(idioma)* Uzbek.

Uzbekistán *nm* Uzbekistan.

U

V

V, v *nf (la letra)* V, v.

V *sím (voltio)* volt; *(símbolo)* V.

vaca *nf* **1** *(carne)* beef. **3** *(cuero)* cowhide.

vacaciones *nf pl* holiday, holidays *pl*, US vacation: *se fueron de vacaciones a Mallorca* they went to Majorca for their holidays. LOC **irse de vacaciones** to go on holiday.

vacante *adj* vacant.
▶ *nf* vacancy.

vaciar *vt* **1** *(recipiente)* to empty; *(local)* to empty, clear. **2** *(contenido)* to pour away. **3** *(dejar hueco)* to hollow out. **4** *(moldear)* to cast, mould (US mold).

vacilación *nf* **1** *(duda)* hesitation. **2** *(oscilación)* swaying, vacillation.

vacilar *vi* **1** *(oscilar)* to sway, vacillate. **2** *(estar poco firme)* to wobble. **3** *(al andar)* to sway, stagger; *(al hablar)* to falter. **4** *(luz)* to flicker. **5** *fig (dudar)* to hesitate, waver. **6** *fam (tomar el pelo)* to joke, tease: *¡no me vaciles!* don't tease me! **7** *fam (presumir)* to show off.

vacío,-a *adj* **1** *(gen)* empty: *el cine está vacío* the cinema is empty. **2** *(no ocupado)* vacant, unoccupied; *(sin muebles)* unfurnished. **3** *(hueco)* hollow.
▶ *nm* **vacío 1** *(gen)* emptiness, void. **2** *(hueco)* gap; *(espacio)* space, empty space; *(espacio en blanco)* blank space. **3** *(vacante)* vacancy. **4** FÍS vacuum. **5** *fig (falta)* emptiness, void.

vacuna *nf* MED vaccine.

vacunación *nf* MED vaccination.

vado *nm* **1** *(de río)* ford. **2** *(de acera)* dropped kerb. COMP **«Vado permanente»** "Keep clear".

vagabundo,-a *adj* **1** wandering, roving. **2** *pey* vagrant.
▶ *nm & nf* **1** *(trotamundos)* wanderer, rover. **2** *pey* vagrant, tramp, US hobo. **3** *(sin casa)* tramp, US hobo.

vagar¹ *vi (estar ocioso)* to idle about.

vagar² *vi (errar)* to wander (por, about), roam (por, about): *pasa su tiempo vagando por el pueblo* he spends his time wandering about town.

vago,-a¹ *adj* **1** *(vacío)* empty; *(desocupado)* vacant. **2** *(holgazán)* lazy, idle.

vago,-a² *adj (impreciso)* vague: *idea vaga* vague idea.

vagón *nm* **1** *(para pasajeros)* carriage, coach, US car. **2** *(para mercancías)* wagon, goods van, truck, US boxcar.

vaho *nm* **1** *(vapor)* vapour (US vapor), steam. **2** *(aliento)* breath.

vaina *nf* **1** *(de espada, etc)* sheath. **2** *(de instrumento, etc)* case. **3** BOT pod.

vainilla *nf* vanilla.

vajilla *nf* tableware, dishes *pl*, crockery. COMP **una vajilla** a dinner service.

vale *nm* **1** *(comprobante)* voucher; *(recibo)* receipt. **2** *(pagaré)* promissory note.
▶ *interj fam* OK!

valedor,-ra *nm & nf* protector.

valentía *nf (valor)* bravery, courage.

valer *vt* **1** *(tener un valor de)* to be worth: *no vale nada* it is worthless. **2** *(costar)* to cost, be: *vale siete euros el kilo* it costs seven euros a kilo **3** *(hacer merecedor)* to win, earn, get: *el suspenso le valió un rapapolvo* failing the exam earned him a good ticking-off. **4** *(ocasionar)* to cause: *me ha valido muchos problemas* he's caused me a lot of problems. **5** MAT to equal.
▶ *vi* **1** *(tener un valor de)* to be worth. **2** *(ser útil, adecuado)* to be useful, be of use, be good for: *¿te vale este libro?* is this book any use (to you)? **3** *(costar)* to cost,

be worth. **4** *(ser válido, contar)* to count. **5** *(tener validez)* to be valid; *(monedas)* to be legal tender: *ese billete aún vale* that ticket is still valid. **6** *(ser suficiente, bastar)* to do, be enough: *con esto ya me vale* this will be enough for me. **7** *(estar permitido)* to be allowed, be permitted.
▶ *nm (valía)* value.
▶ *vpr* **valerse 1** *(utilizar)* to use (de, of), make use (de, of): *se valió de un bastón* he used a stick. **2** *(espabilarse)* to manage, cope. LOC **valerse por sí mismo** to be able to manage on one's own.

valeroso,-a *adj* courageous, brave.

validez *nf* validity.

válido,-a *adj* valid.

valiente *adj* **1** *(valeroso)* brave, courageous, bold. **2** *(fuerte)* strong.

valioso,-a *adj* valuable, precious.

valla *nf* **1** *(cerca)* fence; *(construcción)* wall. **2** MIL stockade. **3** DEP hurdle. **4** *(para publicidad)* hoarding, US billboard. **5** *fig* obstacle. COMP **valla publicitaria** hoarding, US billboard.

vallado *nm* **1** *(cerca)* fence. **2** MIL stockade.

vallar *vt* to fence (in).

valle *nm* valley.

valor *nm* **1** *(valía)* value, worth, merit: *una persona de gran valor* a person of great merit. **2** *(precio)* price. **3** *(validez)* value: *estas monedas dejarán de tener valor muy pronto* these coins will soon be of no value. **4** *(importancia)* importance. **5** *(coraje)* courage. **6** MAT value.
▶ *nm pl* **valores 1** FIN securities, bonds. **2** *(principios)* values.

valorar *vt* **1** *(tasar)* to value, calculate the value of. **2** *(aumentar el valor)* to raise the value of.

vals *nm* waltz.

válvula *nf* valve. COMP **válvula de seguridad** safety valve.

vampiro *nm* **1** *(espectro)* vampire. **2** *(mamífero)* vampire bat. **3** *fig* parasite.

vandalismo *nm* vandalism.

vándalo,-a *adj* Vandal.
▶ *nm & nf* **1** Vandal. **2** *fig* vandal.

vanidad *nf* vanity, conceit.

vanidoso,-a *adj* vain, conceited.

Vanuatu *nm* Vanuatu.

vapor *nm* **1** *(gas)* vapour (US vapor), steam. **2** *(barco)* steamship, steamer. LOC **al vapor** CULIN steamed. COMP **vapor de agua** water vapour (US vapor).

vaquero,-a *adj* cow, cattle.
▶ *nm & nf (pastor)* cowherd, US cowboy; *(pastora)* cowherd, US cowgirl.
▶ *nm pl* **vaqueros** *(pantalones)* jeans, pair of jeans.

vara *nf* **1** *(palo)* staff, rod, pole. **2** *(de mando)* staff, mace. **3** *(medida de longitud)* unit of length equal to approximately 33 inches. **4** *(tauromaquia)* lance, pike.

variable *adj* variable, changeable.
▶ *nf* MAT variable.

variación *nf* variation, change.

variado,-a *adj* **1** varied, mixed. **2** *(galletas, helados)* assorted.

variante *adj* variable.
▶ *nf* **1** *(versión)* variant. **2** *(diferencia)* difference.

variar *vt* **1** *(cambiar)* to change. **2** *(dar variedad)* to vary, give some variety to.
▶ *vi* **1** *(cambiar)* to change: *han variado de planes* they have changed their plans. **2** *(diferir)* to be different (de, to), differ (de, from): *lo que dices varía de tus primeras declaraciones* what you're saying differs from your first statement. **3** MAT to vary. LOC **para variar** *irón* as usual, just for a change.

varicela *nf* MED chickenpox, varicella.

variedad *nf* **1** *(diversidad)* variety, diversity: *una gran variedad de productos* a wide variety of products. **2** *(clase, tipo)* variety.
▶ *nf pl* **variedades** *(espectáculo)* variety show *sing*.

varilla *nf* **1** *(vara)* stick, rod. **2** *(de paraguas, abanico)* rib; *(de corsé)* stay.

vario,-a *adj* **1** *(diverso)* different, diverse. **2** *(variado)* varied, assorted. **3** *(mudable)* changeable, variable.
▶ *nm pl* **varios** *(algunos)* some, several.

varita *nf* small stick. COMP **varita mágica** magic wand.

varón *nm* **1** *(hombre)* man; *(chico)* boy. **2** *(sexo)* male.

V

vasco,-a *adj* Basque.
▸ *nm & nf (persona)* Basque.
▸ *nm* **vasco** *(idioma)* Basque. COMP **País Vasco** Basque Country.

vasija *nf* vessel, pot, jar.

vaso *nm* **1** *(para beber)* glass. **2** *(para flores)* vase. **3** ANAT vessel. COMP **vaso capilar** capillary. ‖ **vasos sanguíneos** blood vessels.

vasto,-a *adj* vast, immense, huge.

váter *nm fam* toilet.

vatio *nm* watt.

vaya *interj* what a: *¡vaya idea!* what an idea!

vecindario *nm* **1** *(lugar)* neighbourhood (US neighborhood). **2** *(vecinos)* neighbours *pl* (US neighbors *pl*), community, residents *pl*.

vecino,-a *adj* nearby, next, neighbouring (US neighboring).
▸ *nm & nf* **1** *(del barrio)* neighbour (US neighbor). **2** *(residente)* resident. **3** *(habitante)* inhabitant.

vegetación *nf* vegetation.
▸ *nf pl* **vegetaciones** MED adenoids.

vegetal *adj* vegetable.
▸ *nm* **1** vegetable, plant. **2** *(persona)* vegetable.

vegetariano,-a *adj* vegetarian.
▸ *nm & nf* vegetarian.

vehículo *nm* **1** *(gen)* vehicle. **2** *(coche)* car. **3** *fig* vehicle. **4** *fig (enfermedades)* transmitter, carrier.

veinte *adj (cardinal)* twenty; *(vigésimo)* twentieth.
▸ *nm (número)* twenty; *(fecha)* twentieth. COMP **los años veinte** the twenties.

✎ Consulta también seis.

veinteavo,-a *adj* twentieth.
▸ *nm & nf* twentieth.

✎ Consulta también sexto.

veintena *nf (exacto)* twenty; *(aproximado)* about twenty.

veinticinco *adj (cardinal)* twenty-five; *(ordinal)* twenty-fifth.
▸ *nm (número)* twenty-five; *(fecha)* twenty-fifth.

veinticuatro *adj (cardinal)* twenty-four; *(ordinal)* twenty-fourth.

▸ *nm (número)* twenty-four; *(fecha)* twenty-fourth.

veintidós *adj (cardinal)* twenty-two; *(ordinal)* twenty-second.
▸ *nm (número)* twenty-two; *(fecha)* twenty-second.

veintinueve *adj (cardinal)* twenty-nine; *(ordinal)* twenty-ninth.
▸ *nm (número)* twenty-nine; *(fecha)* twenty-ninth.

veintiocho *adj (cardinal)* twenty-eight; *(ordinal)* twenty-eighth.
▸ *nm (número)* twenty-eight; *(fecha)* twenty-eighth.

veintiséis *adj (cardinal)* twenty-six; *(ordinal)* twenty-sixth.
▸ *nm (número)* twenty-six; *(fecha)* twenty-sixth.

veintisiete *adj (cardinal)* twenty-seven; *(ordinal)* twenty-seventh.
▸ *nm (número)* twenty-seven; *(fecha)* twenty-seventh.

veintitrés *adj (cardinal)* twenty-three; *(ordinal)* twenty-third.
▸ *nm (número)* twenty-three; *(fecha)* twenty-third.

veintiún *adj* [se usa sólo ante nombres en masculino] twenty-one.

veintiuna *nf* pontoon, blackjack.

veintiuno,-a *adj (cardinal)* twenty-one; *(ordinal)* twenty-first.
▸ *nm (número)* twenty-one; *(fecha)* twenty-first.

vejar *vt* **1** *(molestar)* to vex, annoy. **2** *(humillar)* to humiliate.

vejez *nf* old age.

vejiga *nf* bladder.

vela¹ *nf* **1** *(vigilia)* watch, vigil; *(de muerto)* wake. **2** *(desvelo)* wakefulness. **3** *(candela)* candle. LOC **pasar la noche en vela** to have a sleepless night.

vela² *nf* **1** *(de barco)* sail. **2** DEP sailing. **3** *fig (barco de vela)* sailing ship.

velamen *nm* sails *pl*.

velar¹ *vi* **1** *(no dormir)* to stay awake; *(no acostarse)* to stay up. **2** *fig (cuidar)* to watch (por, over), look (por, after): *velaron por él* they looked after him.

▶ vt *(enfermo)* to sit up with, watch over; *(muerto)* to keep vigil over.

velar² adj LING velar.

▶ vt **1** fig *(cubrir)* to hide, cover, veil. **2** *(fotografía)* to fog. **3** *(pintura)* to glaze.

▶ vpr **velarse** *(fotografía)* to become fogged, get exposed.

velero,-a nm & nf *(fabricante de velas)* sailmaker.

▶ nm **velero** sailing ship, sailing boat.

veleta nf *(para el viento)* weathercock, weather vane.

▶ nm o nf fam fig *(persona)* fickle person.

vello nm **1** *(de persona - pelusa)* down; *(- en las piernas, etc)* hair. **2** *(de fruta, planta)* down, bloom.

velo nm **1** *(gen)* veil. **2** ANAT velum.

velocidad nf **1** *(rapidez)* speed, velocity. **2** AUTO *(marcha)* gear. COMP **velocidad de la luz** speed of light. ‖ **velocidad de transmisión** INFORM bit rate.

velocímetro nm speedometer.

velódromo nm cycle track, US velodrome.

veloz adj fast, quick, swift, rapid.

vena nf **1** ANAT vein. **2** *(yacimiento)* vein, seam. **3** BOT vein. **4** *(en mármol, etc)* vein, streak. **5** fig *(disposición)* mood. LOC **tener vena de...** to have a gift for...: *tiene vena de cantante* he has a gift for singing.

venado nm **1** ZOOL stag, deer. **2** CULIN venison.

vencedor,-ra adj winning.

▶ nm & nf **1** *(equipo, etc)* winner, victor.

vencejo nm *(ave)* swift.

vencer vt **1** DEP to beat. **2** *(exceder)* to outdo, surpass: *la vence en belleza* she surpasses her in beauty. **3** *(problema, etc)* to overcome, surmount. **4** *(ser dominado)* to overcome: *la venció el cansancio* she was overcome by tiredness.

▶ vi **1** *(ganar)* to win. **2** *(deuda, etc)* to fall due, be payable. **3** *(plazo)* to expire.

▶ vpr **vencerse 1** *(romperse)* to break; *(doblarse)* to bend, incline. **2** fig *(reprimir)* to control OS.

venda nf bandage.

vendaje nm dressing.

vendar vt to bandage.

vendaval nm strong wind, gale.

vendedor,-ra adj selling.

▶ nm & nf **1** *(gen)* seller; *(hombre)* salesman; *(mujer)* saleswoman. **2** *(dependiente)* shop assistant.

vender vt **1** *(gen)* to sell. **2** fig *(traicionar)* to betray.

▶ vpr **venderse 1** *(uso impersonal)* to be on sale, be sold: *se vende en farmacias* on sale at your chemist's. **2** *(dejarse sobornar)* to sell OS. LOC **«Se vende»** "For sale".

vendimia nf *(cosecha)* grape harvest.

veneno nm *(química, vegetal)* poison; *(animal)* venom.

venenoso,-a adj **1** poisonous, venomous. **2** fig spiteful, venomous.

venezolano,-a adj Venezuelan.

▶ nm & nf Venezuelan.

Venezuela nf Venezuela.

venganza nf revenge, vengeance.

vengar vt to avenge.

▶ vpr **vengarse** to take revenge (de, on).

venir vi **1** *(gen)* to come: *el mes que viene* next month. **2** *(llegar)* to arrive: *vino tarde* he arrived late. **3** *(proceder)* to come (de, from): *viene de París* it comes from Paris. **4** *(estar, aparecer)* to be, come: *las explicaciones vienen en español* the instructions are in Spanish. **5** *(ser)* to be: *eso te viene grande* that's too big for you.

▶ aux **1** venir a + inf *(aproximación)* to be about; *(alcanzar, llegar a)* to arrive at; *(terminar por)* to end up. **2** venir + ger *(acción durativa)*: *lo venía avisando desde hace tiempo* he has been warning us about it for a long time. **3** venir + pp *(ser, estar)* to be: *eso viene motivado por la inflación* it's caused by inflation.

▶ vpr **venirse** to come back, go back.

venoso,-a adj **1** *(sangre)* venous. **2** *(manos, etc)* veined, veiny.

venta nf **1** *(acción)* sale, selling. **2** *(hostal)* country inn; *(restaurante)* restaurant.

ventaja nf **1** *(gen)* advantage. **2** *(provecho)* profit LOC **llevar ventaja a** ALGN to have the advantage over SB.

ventajoso,-a adj **1** advantageous. **2** *(beneficioso)* profitable.

ventana nf **1** ARQUIT window. **2** *(de la nariz)* nostril.

V

ventanilla *nf* **1** *(banco, coche, sobre, etc)* window. **2** *(barco)* porthole. **3** *(de taquilla)* window, ticket window.

ventilación *nf* ventilation.

ventilador *nm* ventilator, fan.

ventilar *vt* **1** *(lugar)* to air, ventilate. **2** *(agitar al viento)* to air. **3** *fig (dar a conocer)* to air. **4** *fig (discutir)* to discuss, clear up.
▶ *vpr* **ventilarse 1** *(lugar)* to be ventilated. **2** *(objeto)* to be aired. **3** *fam (terminar)* to finish off: *se ventiló el pastel en un minuto* he finished off the cake in a minute.

ventisca *nf* snowstorm, blizzard.

ventoso,-a *adj* windy.

ver *vt* **1** *(gen)* to see: *no te veo* I can't see you. **2** *(mirar)* to look (at). **3** *(televisión)* to watch. **4** *fig (entender)* understand: *no veo por qué lo hizo* I can't understand why she did it. **5** *(visitar)* to visit, see: *ven a verme* come and see me. **6** JUR to try, hear. **7** *(parecer)* to look: *te veo triste* you look sad. LOC **a ver** let's see, let me see.
▶ *nm* **1** *(vista)* sight, vision. **2** *(apariencia)* looks *pl*, appearance.
▶ *vpr* **verse 1** *(ser visto)* to be seen: *aquí dentro no se ve nada* you can't see a thing in here. **2** *(con algn)* to meet, see each other. **3** *(en una situación, etc)* to find os, be: *se vio en un apuro* he was in a fix. **4** *(imaginarse)* to imagine os.

veranear *vi* to spend the summer (holiday) (en, in/at).

veraneo *nm* summer holiday. LOC **ir de veraneo** to go on holiday.

veraniego,-a *adj* summer, summery.

verano *nm* summer.

veras LOC **de veras** really, seriously.

veraz *adj* truthful, veracious.

verbal *adj* verbal, oral.

verbena *nf* **1** BOT verbena. **2** *(fiesta)* night party.

verbo *nm* verb.

verdad *nf* **1** truth, truthfulness: *es verdad* it's true. **2** *(confirmación)*: *es bonita, ¿verdad?* she's pretty, isn't she?

verdadero,-a *adj* true, real.

verde *adj* **1** *(color)* green. **2** *(fruta)* unripe, green; *(madera)* unseasoned. **3** fig *(persona)* green, immature. **4** *fam (chiste)* blue, dirty.
▶ *nm* **1** *(color)* green. **2** *(hierba)* grass. **3** POL green: *los verdes* the Greens.

verdugo *nm* **1** *(persona)* executioner. **2** *(prenda)* balaclava, balaclava helmet.

verdulera *nf* fig coarse woman, foul-mouthed woman.

verdulería *nf* greengrocer's (shop).

verdulero,-a *nm & nf* greengrocer.

verdura *nf* **1** *(hortaliza)* vegetables *pl*, greens *pl*. **2** *(color)* greenness, greenery.

vereda *nf* footpath, path.

veredicto *nm* verdict.

vergonzoso,-a *adj* **1** *(acto)* shameful, shocking: *un asunto vergonzoso* a shocking business. **2** *(persona)* bashful, shy.

vergüenza *nf* **1** *(deshonor, etc)* shame, sense of shame: *sus palabras me dan vergüenza* her words make me feel ashamed. **2** *(timidez)* bashfulness, shyness; *(turbación)* embarrassment: *me da vergüenza bailar* I'm too shy to dance. **3** *(escándalo)* disgrace, shame: *lo que han hecho es una vergüenza* what they did is a disgrace. LOC **¡qué vergüenza!** it's a disgrace!, how disgraceful!

verídico,-a *adj* truthful, true.

verificar *vt* **1** *(comprobar)* to verify, check. **2** *(probar)* to prove. **3** *(efectuar)* to carry out, perform.
▶ *vpr* **verificarse 1** *(comprobarse)* to come true. **2** *(efectuarse)* to take place.

verja *nf* **1** *(reja)* grating, grille. **2** *(cerca)* railing, railings *pl*. **3** *(puerta)* iron gate.

verruga *nf* wart.

versión *nf* **1** *(gen)* version, account. **2** *(traducción)* translation. **3** *(adaptación)* adaptation. LOC **en versión original** in the original language.

verso *nm* **1** LIT verse. **2** *fam (poema)* poem.

vértebra *nf* vertebra.

vertebrado,-a *adj* vertebrate.
▶ *nm pl* **los vertebrados** the vertebrates.

vertebral *adj* vertebral, spinal.

vertedero *nm* rubbish dump, rubbish tip.

verter vt **1** *(líquido - voluntariamente)* to pour, pour out. **2** *(derramar)* to spill. **3** *(vaciar)* to empty, empty out. **4** *(basura)* to dump. **5** *fig (conceptos, ideas, etc)* to express, voice.

vertical adj vertical: *lo puso vertical* she put it upright.
▶ nf vertical, vertical line.
▶ nm vertical.

vértice nm vertex.

vertiente nf **1** *(gen)* slope. **2** *fig (aspecto)* angle.

vértigo nm **1** MED vertigo. **2** *(mareo)* dizziness, giddiness: *me da vértigo* it makes me feel dizzy. **3** *fig* frenzy.

vesícula nf vesicle. COMP **vesícula biliar** gall bladder.

vestíbulo nm **1** *(de casa)* hall, entrance. **2** *(de hotel, etc)* hall, lobby, vestibule, foyer.

vestido,-a adj dressed: *vestida de blanco* dressed in white.
▶ nm **vestido 1** *(indumentaria)* clothes pl, dress, costume. **2** *(de mujer)* dress; *(de hombre)* suit.

vestigio nm vestige, trace, remains pl.

vestimenta nf clothes pl, garments pl.

vestir vt **1** *(llevar)* to wear, be dressed in: *vestía un vestido rojo* she was wearing a red dress. **2** *(ayudar a vestirse)* to dress; *(hacer vestidos)* to make clothes for: *la vistió su madre* her mother dressed her. **3** *(cubrir)* to cover (de, with).
▶ vi **1** to dress: *vestir de negro* to dress in black. **2** *(ser elegante, lucir)* to be classy, look smart: *esa falda viste mucho* that skirt is very classy.
▶ vpr **vestirse 1** *(uso reflexivo)* to dress OS, get dressed. **2** *(comprarse la ropa)* to buy one's clothes: *se viste en Milán* she buys her clothes in Milan.

vestuario nm **1** *(ropas)* wardrobe, clothes pl. **2** TEAT *(ropa)* wardrobe, costumes pl; *(camerino)* dressing room. **3** DEP changing room.

veta nf **1** *(de mármol, roca)* seam, vein; *(de madera)* streak. **2** *fig* streak.

vetar vt to veto, put a veto on.

veterinario,-a adj veterinary.

▶ nm & nf veterinary surgeon, vet, US veterinarian.

veto nm veto. LOC **poner el veto a** to put a veto on, veto.

vez nf **1** time: *fue la única vez que la vi* it was the only time I saw her; *una vez* once; *dos veces* twice; *cuatro veces* four times. **2** *(turno)* turn; *(ocasión)* occasion. LOC **a veces** sometimes. **otra vez** again.

vía nf **1** *(camino)* road, way; *(calle)* street; *(carril)* lane. **2** *(de tren)* track, line; *(en la estación)* platform: *el tren de la vía uno* the train at platform one. **3** ANAT passage, canal, track. **4** *fig (modo)* way, manner, means. **5** JUR procedure. **6** *(rumbo, dirección)* via, through: *Barcelona-Singapur vía Frankfurt* Barcelona-Singapore via Frankfurt. LOC **dar vía libre a** to leave the way open for. **por vía aérea 1** *(gen)* by air. **2** *(correo)* airmail. COMP **transmisión vía satélite** satellite transmission.

viajante nm commercial traveller (US traveler), travelling (US traveling) salesman.

viajar vi to travel: *ha viajado por el mundo entero* she's travelled all over the world.

viaje nm **1** *(gen)* journey, trip. **2** *(en coche)* drive, journey. **3** *(travesía por mar)* voyage. **4** [se suele usar en plural] *(concepto de viajar)* travel. **5** *(carga)* load. LOC **¡buen viaje!** bon voyage!, have a good trip! **estar de viaje** to be away, be away on a trip. COMP **viaje de ida y vuelta** return trip, US round trip.

viajero,-a adj travelling (US traveling).
▶ nm & nf **1** traveller (US traveler). **2** *(en transporte público)* passenger.

víbora nf viper.

vibración nf **1** vibration. **2** LING rolling, trilling.

vibrar vi **1** *(gen)* to vibrate; *(pulsar)* to throb, pulsate: *toda la ciudad vibraba de actividad* the whole city throbbed with activity. **2** *fig (conmover)* to be moved, be overcome with emotion: *el cantante hizo vibrar al público* the singer thrilled the audience. **3** LING to roll, trill.

vibratorio,-a adj vibratory.

V

viciar vt 1 (corromper) to corrupt, lead astray. 2 (aire) to pollute.
▶ vpr **viciarse** 1 (enviciarse) to take to vice, become corrupted. 2 (objeto) to go out of shape.

vicio nm 1 (corrupción) vice, corruption. 2 (mala costumbre) bad habit; (inmoralidad) vice. 3 (del lenguaje) incorrect usage. 4 (defecto) defect.

vicioso,-a adj 1 (cosa) faulty, defective. 2 (persona) depraved, perverted.
▶ nm & nf depraved person.

víctima nf victim, casualty.

victoria nf victory, triumph. [LOC] cantar victoria to proclaim a victory.

victorioso,-a adj victorious, triumphant.

vid nf grapevine, vine.

vida nf 1 (gen) life. 2 (viveza) liveliness. 3 (tiempo) lifetime, life. 4 (modo de vivir) life, way of life. 5 (medios) living, livelihood. [LOC] darse la gran vida / pegarse la gran vida / darse la vida padre fam to live it up. ‖ de por vida for life. ‖ de toda la vida lifelong: un amigo de toda la vida a lifelong friend. ‖ estar con vida / estar sin vida to be alive / be dead. ‖ ganarse la vida to earn one's living. ‖ quitarle la vida a ALGN to take SB's life. [COMP] vida familiar family life.

vídeo nm (aparato) video, video recorder; (cinta) video, video tape.

videoconferencia nf videoconference.

videoclip nm video, pop video.

videoclub nm video club.

videojuego nm video game.

vidriera nf 1 (ventana) picture window. 2 (puerta) glass door. 3 (de balcón, galería) French window. 4 (vitral) stained-glass window. 5 (escaparate) shop window.

vidriero,-a nm & nf 1 (fabricante) glassmaker. 2 (colocador) glazier.

vidrio nm (material) glass.

viejo,-a adj 1 (gen) old: un coche viejo an old car. 2 (desgastado) old, worn-out. 3 (antiguo) old, ancient.
▶ nm & nf (hombre) old man; (mujer) old woman. [LOC] hacerse viejo,-a to grow old.

viento nm 1 (gen) wind. 2 (rumbo) direction. 3 (de caza) scent. 4 (cuerda) rope, guy. 5 fam (flatulencia) wind, flatulence. [LOC] contra viento y marea fig come hell or high water. ‖ hacer viento / soplar viento to be windy. ‖ ir viento en popa 1 MAR to sail before the wind. 2 fig to do very well.

vientre nm 1 ANAT belly, abdomen. 2 (vísceras) bowels pl. 3 (de embarazada) womb.

viernes nm inv Friday. [COMP] Viernes Santo Good Friday.

✎ Consulta también jueves.

Vietnam nm Vietnam.

vietnamita adj Vietnamese.
▶ nm & nf (persona) Vietnamese.
▶ nm vietnamita (idioma) Vietnamese.

viga nf 1 (de madera) beam, rafter. 2 (de acero, etc) girder.

vigésimo,-a adj twentieth: vigésimo primero twenty-first.
▶ nm & nf twentieth.

✎ Consulta también sexto,-a.

vigía nm o nf lookout.

vigilante adj 1 (que vigila) vigilant, watchful. 2 (alerta) alert.
▶ nm o nf (hombre) guard, watchman; (mujer) guard. [COMP] vigilante nocturno night watchman.

vigilar vt 1 (cuidar) to watch (over), look after: vigila al niño look after the baby. 2 (con armas, etc) to guard. 3 (supervisar) to oversee. 4 (estar atento) to keep an eye on, take care of: vigila la puerta, que no entre nadie keep an eye on the door and see nobody gets in.
▶ vi (gen) to keep watch.

vigor nm 1 (fuerza) vigour (US vigor), strength. 2 (validez) force, effect. [LOC] en vigor in force.

vigoroso,-a adj vigorous, strong.

VIH abrev MED (virus de inmunodeficiencia humana) Human Immune Deficiency Virus; (abreviatura) HIV.

vil *adj* vile, base, despicable.

vileza *nf* **1** *(cualidad)* vileness, baseness. **2** *(acto)* vile act, despicable deed.

villa *nf* **1** *(casa)* villa, country house. **2** *(pueblo)* small town; *(ciudad)* town.

villancico *nm* carol, Christmas carol.

villano,-a *nm & nf* HIST villein, serf. **2** *fig (persona ruin)* villain.

vinagre *nm* **1** vinegar. **2** *fig* sourpuss.

vinculación *nf* **1** *(acción)* linking, binding. **2** *(vínculo)* link, bond.

vincular *vt* **1** *(unir)* to link (a, to), bind (a, to). **2** *(relacionar)* to relate (con, to), connect (con, with), link (con, with). **3** JUR to entail.
▶ *vpr* **vincularse** to link OS (a, to).

vínculo *nm* **1** tie, bond, link. **2** *fig* link.

vinícola *adj* wine-producing.

vinicultor,-ra *nm & nf* wine producer.

vinicultura *nf* wine production, wine growing.

vino *nm* wine. COMP **vino blanco** white wine. **▌vino tinto** red wine.

viña *nf* vineyard.

viñedo *nm* vineyard.

viñeta *nf* **1** *(en impresión)* vignette. **2** *(dibujo humorístico)* cartoon.

viola *nf* viola.

violáceo,-a *adj* violaceous, violet.

violencia *nf* **1** *(fuerza)* violence. **2** *(embarazo)* embarrassment. **3** *(situación embarazosa)* embarrassing situation. **4** *(violación)* rape.

violentar *vt* **1** *(forzar algo)* to force, break open. **2** *(obligar a alguien)* to force, use force on. **3** *fig (entrar)* to break into, enter by force.
▶ *vpr* **violentarse 1** *fig (molestarse)* to get annoyed. **2** *fig (avergonzarse)* to feel ashamed.

violento,-a *adj* **1** *(gen)* violent. **2** *(molesto)* embarrassed, awkward, ill at ease.

violeta *adj (color)* violet.
▶ *nm (color)* violet.
▶ *nf* BOT violet.

violín *nm* violin.

violinista *nm o nf* violinist.

violón *nm* double bass.

violoncelista *nm o nf* cellist.

violoncelo *nm* cello.

violonchelista *nm o nf* cellist.

violonchelo *nm* cello.

viraje *nm* **1** *(curva)* turn, bend. **2** *(en coche)* turn. **3** MAR tack. **4** *(fotografía)* toning.

viral *adj* viral.

virar *vi* **1** MAR to tack, put about. **2** AUTO to turn round.

virgen *adj* **1** *(persona)* virgin. **2** *(puro)* virgin, pure.
▶ *nm o nf* virgin. COMP **la Santísima Virgen** the Blessed Virgin.

vírico,-a *adj* viral.

virtual *adj* virtual.

virtud *nf* **1** *(cualidad)* virtue. **2** *(propiedad, eficacia)* property, quality: *con virtudes curativas* with medicinal properties. LOC **en virtud de** by virtue of.

virtuosismo *nm* virtuosity.

virtuoso,-a *adj* virtuous.
▶ *nm & nf* virtuous person.

viruela *nf* **1** MED smallpox. **2** *(marca)* pockmark. LOC **picado,-a de viruelas** pockmarked.

virulencia *nf* virulence.

virulento,-a *adj* virulent.

virus *nm inv* virus.

viruta *nf* shaving.

visado,-a *adj* endorsed with a visa.
▶ *nm* **visado** visa.

visar *vt* **1** *(pasaporte)* to endorse with a visa. **2** *(documento)* to endorse, approve.

víscera *nf* internal organ.
▶ *nf pl* **vísceras** viscera, entrails.

visceral *adj* **1** visceral. **2** *fig* profound, deep-rooted.

viscosa *nf* viscose.

viscoso,-a *adj* viscous.

visera *nf* **1** *(de gorra)* peak; *(de casco)* visor. **2** *(suelta)* eyeshade. **3** AUTO sun visor.

visibilidad *nf* visibility.

visigodo,-a *nm & nf* Visigoth.

visillo *nm* small lace curtain.

visión *nf* **1** *(acción)* vision. **2** *(vista)* sight. **3** *(ilusión)* vision. **4** *fig (persona fea)*

V

fright, sight. [LOC] **ver visiones** to dream, see things.

visita *nf* **1** *(acción)* visit. **2** *(invitado)* visitor, guest; *(invitados)* visitors *pl*, guests *pl*. [LOC] **estar de visita en** to be visiting. [COMP] **horas de visita** MED surgery hours.

visitante *nm o nf* visitor.

visitar *vt* **1** *(ir a ver a alguien)* to visit, pay a visit to, call on, go and see: *vamos a ver a la abuela* let's go and visit grandma. **2** *(lugar)* to visit, see. **3** *(inspeccionar)* to inspect, visit, examine.

vislumbrar *vt* **1** *(ver)* to glimpse, catch a glimpse of, make out. **2** *fig (conjeturar)* to begin to see: *vislumbraron una solución al problema* they began to see a solution to the problem.

viso *nm* **1** *(reflejo)* sheen, shimmer. **2** *(ropa interior)* underskirt. **3** *fig (apariencia)* appearance. [LOC] **tener visos de** to seem, appear.

visón *nm* mink.

visor *nm* **1** *(de arma)* sight. **2** *(de máquina fotográfica)* viewfinder.

víspera *nf* **1** *(día anterior)* day before. **2** *(de fiesta)* eve.
▶ *nf pl* **vísperas** REL vespers.

vista *nf* **1** *(visión)* sight, vision. **2** *(ojo)* eye, eyes *pl*. **3** *(panorama)* view. **4** *(aspecto)* appearance, aspect, look. **5** *(dibujo, cuadro, foto)* view. **6** *(intención)* intention. **7** *(propósito)* outlook, prospect. **8** JUR trial, hearing.
▶ *nf pl* **vistas** view *sing*: *la habitación tiene vistas al mar* the room has a view of the sea. [LOC] **a primera vista / a simple vista** at first sight: *a primera vista parecía más complicado* at first sight it looked more complicated. ▌ **con vistas a 1** *(hacia)* overlooking. **2** *(pensando en)* with a view to, in anticipation of. ▌ **en vista de** in view of, considering. ▌ **hacer la vista gorda** *fam* to turn a blind eye. ▌ **ser corto,-a de vista** to be short-sighted. ▌ **tener vista de lince** *fig* to be eagle-eyed, have eyes like a hawk.

vistazo *nm* glance. [LOC] **dar un vistazo a ALGO / echar un vistazo a ALGO 1** *(mirar)* to have a look at STH. **2** *(vigilar)* to keep an eye on.

visto,-a *adj* **1** *(anticuado)* old-fashioned. **2** *(dado)* in view of, considering. **3** *(corriente)* common. **4** *(ladrillo, viga, obra)* exposed. **5** JUR *(dictaminado)*: *el caso está visto para sentencia* the case has been heard and a verdict may be decided upon.
▶ *nm* **visto** approval. [LOC] **dar el visto bueno a ALGO** to approve STH, O.K. STH. ▌ **estar bien visto,-a** to be well looked upon, be considered acceptable. ▌ **por lo visto** apparently. ▌ **visto que...** in view of the fact that..., given that..., seeing that...

vistoso,-a *adj* **1** *(llamativo)* showy, flashy. **2** *(colorido)* bright, colourful (US colorful).

visual *adj* visual.
▶ *nf (línea)* line of vision, line of sight.

visualización *nf* display.

visualizar *vt* **1** to visualize. **2** INFORM to display.

vital *adj* **1** *(de la vida)* vital. **2** *fig (esencial)* essential, vital.

vitalicio,-a *adj* life, for life: *un cargo vitalicio* a post held for life.

vitalidad *nf* vitality.

vitalizar *vt* to vitalize.

vitamina *nf* vitamin.

vitícola *adj* wine-growing, wine-producing, viticultural.

viticultor,-ra *nm & nf* wine grower, viticulturist.

viticultura *nf* wine-growing, viticulture.

vitorear *vt (aclamar)* to cheer, acclaim.

vitral *nm* stained-glass window.

vítreo,-a *adj* vitreous.

vitrina *nf* **1** *(armario)* glass cabinet, display cabinet. **2** *(de exposición)* glass case, showcase. **3** *(escaparate)* shop window.

vitro *loc* in vitro in vitro. [COMP] **fecundación in vitro** in vitro fertilization.

vitrocerámica [COMP] **encimera vitrocerámica** ceramic hob.

vitualla *nf* [generalmente se usa en plural] provisions *pl*, food.

viudedad *nf* **1** *(estado)* widowhood. **2** *(pensión - hombre)* widower's pension; *(- mujer)* widow's pension.

viudez *nf* widowhood.

viudo,-a *adj* widowed.
▶ *nm & nf (hombre)* widower; *(mujer)* widow.

viva *nm* cheer, shout.

vivaz *adj* **1** *(vivo)* vivacious, lively. **2** *(perspicaz)* sharp, quick-witted.

víveres *nm pl* food *sing*, provisions, supplies.

vivero *nm* **1** *(de plantas)* nursery. **2** *(de peces)* fish farm, fish hatchery; *(de moluscos)* bed.

viveza *nf* **1** *(persona)* liveliness, vivacity. **2** *(color, relato)* vividness. **3** *(al hablar)* vehemence. **4** *(agudeza)* sharpness, quick-wittedness.

vivienda *nf* **1** *(gen)* housing, accommodation. **2** *(morada)* dwelling. **3** *(casa)* house. **4** *(piso)* flat.

vivir *vi* **1** *(tener vida)* to live; *(estar vivo)* to be alive: *vivió hasta los ochenta años* he lived to the age of eighty. **2** *(habitar)* to live: *vive en Barcelona* she lives in Barcelona. **3** *(mantenerse)* to live, live on, make a living: *ese trabajo no le da para vivir* he can't live on what that job pays. **4** *fig (durar)* to last, live on.
▶ *vt (pasar por, experimentar)* to live through, go through, experience: *mi abuelo vivió la guerra* my grandfather lived through the war.

vivo,-a *adj* **1** *(que tiene vida)* living; *(que está)* alive: *materia viva* living matter; *Pepe está vivo* Pepe is alive. **2** *(fuego, llama)* live, burning. **3** *(lengua)* living. **4** *fig (color, etc)* bright, vivid. **5** *fig (animado)* lively, vivacious. **6** *fig (dolor, emoción, etc)* acute, deep, intense. **7** *fig (descripción, etc)* lively, graphic. **8** *fig (carácter)* quick, irritable. **9** *fig (listo)* quick-witted. **10** *fig (astuto)* shrewd, sly. **11** *fig (llaga, herida)* open. LOC **en vivo** TV live.
▶ *nm & nf* **1** living person: *los vivos* the living. **2** *fam fig (astuto)* quick-witted person.

vocablo *nm* word, term.

vocabulario *nm* vocabulary.

vocación *nf* vocation, calling.

vocacional *adj* vocational.

vocal *adj* vocal.
▶ *nf* vowel.
▶ *nm o nf (de junta, etc)* member.

vocativo *nm* vocative.

vocear *vi (dar voces)* to shout, cry out.
▶ *vt* **1** *(divulgar)* to publish. **2** *(gritar)* to shout, cry out. **3** *(divulgar)* to publish, proclaim. **4** *(aclamar)* to cheer, acclaim.

vocero,-a *nm & nf (gen)* spokesperson; *(hombre)* spokesman; *(mujer)* spokeswoman.

voladizo,-a *adj* projecting, jutting out.
▶ *nm* **voladizo** projection.

volador,-ra *adj* flying.

volante *adj (que vuela)* flying.
▶ *nm* **1** COST flounce; *(adorno)* frill, ruffle. **2** AUTO steering wheel. **3** TÉC flywheel.

volar *vi* **1** *(ir por el aire)* to fly. **2** *fig (papeles, etc)* to be blown away. **3** *fig (ir deprisa)* to fly: *el tiempo vuela* time flies. **4** *fam fig (desaparecer)* to disappear, vanish. **5** *fig (sobresalir de un edificio)* to jut out, project. **6** *fig (noticia, etc)* to spread rapidly.
▶ *vt* **1** *fig (hacer explotar - edificio)* to blow up, demolish; *(- caja fuerte)* to blow open; *(- en minería)* to blast. **2** *fig (en impresión)* to raise. **3** *(en caza)* to flush.
▶ *vpr* **volarse** *(papeles, etc)* to be blown away. LOC **echarse a volar** to fly away, fly off.

volcán *nm* volcano.

volcánico,-a *adj* volcanic.

volcar *vi* **1** *(coche, etc)* to turn over, overturn. **2** MAR to capsize.
▶ *vt* **1** *(gen)* to turn over, knock over, upset. **2** *(vaciar)* to empty out, pour out. **3** *fig (hacer cambiar de parecer)* to make change one's mind.
▶ *vpr* **volcarse** *fig (entregarse)* to do one's utmost.

volear *vt* to volley.

voleibol *nm* volleyball.

voleo *nm* DEP volley. LOC **a voleo / al voleo** *fig* at random, haphazardly.

volquete *nm* dumper-truck.

voltaje *nm* voltage.

voltear *vt* **1** *(dar vueltas)* to whirl, twirl. **2** *(poner al revés)* to turn over, toss. **3** *(campanas)* to peal, ring out. **4** *(a una persona)* to toss up in the air.

voltereta *nf* somersault. LOC **dar volteretas** to do somersaults.

voltímetro *nm* voltmeter.

voltio *nm* volt.

voluble *adj* changeable, fickle.

volumen *nm* **1** *(gen)* volume. **2** *(tamaño)* size. COMP **volumen de negocios** turnover.

voluminoso,-a *adj* **1** voluminous. **2** *(enorme)* bulky, massive.

voluntad *nf* **1** *(cualidad)* will. **2** *(fuerza de voluntad)* willpower: *tiene mucha voluntad* she's very strong-willed. **3** *(deseo)* wish. **4** *(propósito)* intention, purpose: *tiene buena voluntad* her intentions are good. **5** *(afecto)* affection. LOC **a voluntad** at will. ▌ **buena voluntad** goodwill. COMP **voluntad de hierro / voluntad férrea** will of iron, iron will.

voluntariado *nm* **1** MIL voluntary enlistment. **2** *(civil)* group of volunteers.

voluntario,-a *adj* voluntary.
  ▶ *nm & nf* volunteer.

voluntarioso,-a *adj (con voluntad)* willing.

voluta *nf* **1** ARQUIT volute, scroll. **2** *(espiral)* spiral, column. **3** *(de humo)* ring.

volver *vt* **1** *(dar vuelta a)* to turn, turn over; *(hacia abajo)* to turn upside down; *(de dentro afuera)* to turn inside out; *(lo de atrás hacia delante)* to turn back to front: *volver la tortilla* to turn the omelette. **2** *(convertir)* to turn, make, change: *el dinero ha vuelto tonto a Paco* money has made Paco foolish. **3** *(devolver)* to give back; *(a su lugar)* to put back.
  ▶ *vi* **1** *(regresar)* to return; *(ir)* to go back; *(venir)* to come back: *vuelve*

cuando quieras come back whenever you want. **2** *(a un tema, etc)* to return, revert. **3** **volver a** *(hacer otra vez)* to do again: *volver a leer* to read again. LOC **volver a las andadas** to fall back into one's old habits. ▌ **volver del revés** to turn inside out. ▌ **volver en sí** to regain consciousness, come round. ▌
  ▶ *vpr* **volverse 1** *(regresar - ir)* to go back; *(- venir)* to come back. **2** *(darse la vuelta)* to turn. **3** *(convertirse)* to turn, become. LOC **volverse atrás** *fig* to go back on one's word, back out. ▌ **volverse en contra de** ALGN to turn against SB.

vomitar *vt* **1** to vomit, bring up. **2** *fig* to belch, spew out.
  ▶ *vi* to be sick, vomit: *tengo ganas de vomitar* I feel sick.

vómito *nm* **1** *(resultado)* vomit. **2** *(acción)* vomiting.

voracidad *nf* voracity, voraciousness.

vorágine *nf* vortex, whirlpool.

voraz *adj* **1** voracious. **2** *fig* fierce, raging.

vórtice *nf* **1** vortex, whirlpool. **2** *(de ciclón)* centre (US center) of a cyclone.

vos *pron* **1** *arc (usted)* thou, you. **2** AM *(tú)* you.

vosotros,-as *pron (sujeto)* you; *(objeto)* you, yourselves: *con vosotros* with you; *entre vosotras* among yourselves; *¿cómo lo sabéis vosotros?* how do you know?

votación *nf* **1** *(voto)* vote, ballot. **2** *(acto)* vote, voting. LOC **someter** ALGO **a votación** to put STH to the vote, take a ballot on STH. COMP **votación a mano alzada** voting by a show of hands.

votante *nm o nf* voter.

votar *vi (dar el voto)* to vote.
  ▶ *vt (proponer para aprobar)* to pass.

voto *nm* **1** *(gen)* vote: *tres votos a favor* three votes for. **2** REL vow. **3** *(deseo)* wish. **4** *(blasfemia)* curse, oath. COMP **derecho al voto** the right to vote. ▌ **voto de censura** vote of no confidence. ▌ **voto de confianza** vote of confidence.

voz *nf* **1** *(sonido)* voice. **2** *(grito)* shout. **3** *(vocablo, palabra)* word. **4** GRAM voice: *voz activa* active voice. **5** MÚS *(de instrumento)* tone; *(cantante)* voice: *canción a tres voces* three-part song. **6** *fig (rumor)* rumour (US rumor). **7** *fig (en asamblea - facultad de hablar)* voice, say; *(- voto)* vote. LOC **alzar la voz / levantar la voz** to raise one's voice. **I dar voces** to shout. **I en voz alta** aloud. **I en voz baja** in a low voice. **I tener voz y voto 1** *fam* to have a say. **2** *fml* to be a voting member.

vuelco *nm* **1** *(gen)* tumble, upset. **2** *(barco)* capsizing. **3** *fig* change. LOC **dar un vuelco** *(coche)* to overturn. **2** *(empresa)* to go to ruin. **I me dio un vuelco el corazón** my heart missed a beat.

vuelo *nm* **1** *(acto, espacio, etc)* flight. **2** *(acción)* flying. **3** ARQUIT *(voladizo)* projection. LOC **al vuelo** in flight. **I alzar el vuelo / emprender el vuelo / levantar el vuelo** to take flight. **I cazarlas al vuelo / cogerlas al vuelo** *fig* to be quick on the uptake. COMP **vuelo chárter / vuelo regular** charter flight / scheduled flight.

vuelta *nf* **1** *(giro)* turn. **2** *(en un circuito)* lap, circuit. **3** *(paseo)* walk, stroll: *vamos a dar una vuelta* let's go for a walk. **4** *(regreso, retorno)* return; *(viaje de regreso)* return journey, journey back: *a la vuelta de las vacaciones* after the holidays. **5** *(dinero de cambio)* change: *quédese con la vuelta* keep the change. **6** *(curva)* bend, curve. **7** *(reverso)* back, reverse. **8** *(de torneo, etc)* round. **9** *(cambio)* change, alteration. **10** COST *(de pantalón)* turn-up; *(forro)* lining. **11** *(al hacer punto)* row. LOC **a vuelta de correo** by return of post. **I dar la vuelta a 1** *(alrededor)* to go round. **2** *(girar)* to turn (round). **3** *(de arriba abajo)* to turn upside down. **4** *(de dentro a fuera)* to turn inside out. **5** *(cambiar de lado)* to turn over. **I dar la vuelta al mundo** to go round the world. **I dar vueltas a ALGO** *fig* to worry about STH: *¡no lo des más vueltas!* don't worry about it! **I dar media vuelta** to turn round. **I estar de vuelta de todo** to have seen it all before. **I ¡hasta la vuelta!** see you when I get back! COMP **la vuelta al colegio 1** *(en publicidad)* "Back to school". **2** *(primer día)* first day back at school.

vuelto,-a *adj (cuello)* roll: *jersey de cuello vuelto* roll-neck sweater.

vuestro,-a *adj* your, of yours: *vuestra casa* your house; *un amigo vuestro* a friend of yours.
▶ *pron* yours: *éstas son las vuestras* these are yours.
▶ *nm* **lo vuestro** what is yours, what belongs to you.

vulgar *adj* **1** *(grosero)* vulgar, coarse, common: *lenguaje vulgar* coarse language. **2** *(general)* common, general. **3** *(banal)* banal, ordinary; *(idea)* commonplace. **4** *(no técnico)* lay: *término vulgar* lay term.

vulgaridad *nf* **1** *(grosería)* vulgarity, coarseness. **2** *(banalidad)* banality, triviality.

vulgarismo *nm* vulgarism.

vulgarización *nf* vulgarization, popularization.

vulgarizar *vt* **1** *(popularizar)* to popularize, vulgarize. **2** *(hacer vulgar)* to make common.
▶ *vpr* **vulgarizarse** *(popular)* to become popular, become common; *(grosero)* to become vulgar, become common.

vulgo *nm pey* common people *pl*, masses *pl*.

vulnerable *adj* vulnerable.

vulneración *nf* **1** *(gen)* violation. **2** *fig (reputación)* damaging, harming.

vulnerar *vt* **1** *(ley, etc)* to violate. **2** *fig (honor, etc)* to damage, harm.

V

W, w *nf (la letra)* W, w.
W *sím* (vatio) watt; *(símbolo)* W.
wáter *nm fam* toilet.
waterpolo *nm* water polo.
watt *nm* watt.

✎ Consulta también **vatio**.

web *nf* website.
whisky *nm* whisky; *(irlandés)* whiskey.
COMP **whisky escocés** Scotch, Scotch whisky.
windsurfing *nm* windsurfing.
wolframio *nm* wolfram.

X, x *nf (la letra)* X, x.
xenofobia *nf* xenophobia.
xenófobo,-a *adj* xenophobic.
 ▶ *nm & nf* xenophobe.

xerocopia *nf* Xerox, photocopy.
xerografía *nf* xerography.
xilófono *nm* xylophone.
xilografía *nf* xylography.

Y, y *nf (la letra)* Y, y.

y *conj* **1** and: *Alberto y María* Alberto and María. **2** *(hora)* past: *son las tres y cuarto* it's a quarter past three. **3** *(en pregunta)* what about: *¿y Pepe, se viene?* what about Pepe, is he coming? **4** *(repetición)* after: *veces y veces* time after time, time and time again. LOC **y eso que** even though. ▌ **¿y (qué)?** so (what)? ▌ **¿y si... ?** what if… ? ▌ **¡y tanto!** you bet!, and how!

✎ Consulta también e.

ya *adv* **1** already: *esa película ya la he visto* I've already seen that film. **2** *(más tarde)* later: *ya lo haré* I'll do it later. **3** *(ahora mismo)* at once, right now, straightaway: *tienes que mandarlo ya* you must send it at once. **4** *(ahora)* now: *ya viven en el piso nuevo* they're living in the new flat now. **5** *(uso enfático)* *ya lo sé* I know that; *es facilísimo, ya verás* it's dead easy, you'll see. **6** *(denota satisfacción)*: *¡ya tenemos coche nuevo!* we've got the new car! **7** *(con tono amenazante)*: *¡ya verás ya!* just you wait! **8** *(con indignación)*: *¡ya está bien!* enough is enough! **9** *(para tranquilizar)*: *ya encontrarás trabajo, ya verás como sí* you'll find a job, you'll see. **10** *(para afirmar)* I know, yes: *tienes que estudiar –ya, pero...* you have to study – I know, but… LOC **¡ya está!** there we are!, all done! ▌ **ya que** since, seeing that: *ya que estás aquí, quédate a cenar* seeing that you're here, why don't you stay for supper?
▶ *interj irón* oh yes!

yacer [92] *vi* **1** *(estar enterrado)* to lie. **2** *fml (hallarse)* to lie. **3** *lit (dormir)* to be lying; *(acostarse)* to lie (**con**, with): *Aquí yace...* Here lies…

yacimiento *nm* bed, deposit. COMP **yacimiento petrolífero** oilfield.

yarda *nf* yard.

yate *nm* yacht.

yedra *nf* ivy.

yegua *nf* mare.

yeísmo *nm* pronunciation of ll as y.

yema *nf* **1** *(de huevo)* yolk. **2** BOT bud. **3** *(del dedo)* fingertip. COMP **yema de huevo** egg yolk.

Yemen *nm* Yemen.

yemení *adj* Yemeni.
▶ *nm o nf* Yemeni.

yerba *nf* → hierba.

yermo ,-a *adj* **1** *(estéril)* barren. **2** *(despoblado)* deserted, uninhabited.

yerno *nm* son-in-law.

yesca *nf* tinder.

yeso *nm* **1** *(mineral)* gypsum. **2** *(para la construcción)* plaster. **3** *(tiza)* chalk. **4** *(escultura)* plaster cast.

yeyuno *nm* jejunum.

yihad *nf* jihad.

yo *pron* I: *el jefe soy yo* I'm the boss; *soy yo* it's me; *entre tú y yo* between you and me; *yo en tu lugar...* if I were you…; *yo que tú...* if I were you…
▶ *nm* **el yo** the ego, the self.

yodo *nm* iodine.

yogur *nm* yoghurt.
▶ *pl* yogures.

yogurt *nm* yoghurt.
▶ *pl* yogurts.

yóquey *nm* jockey.

yugo *nm* yoke.

yugular *adj* jugular.
▶ *nf* jugular vein.

yunque *nm* anvil.

yunta *nf* team of oxen, yoke.

yuxtaposición *nf* juxtaposition.

Z

Z, z *nf (la letra)* Z, z.

zafarrancho *nm* **1** MIL clearing for action. **2** *(jaleo)* commotion. **3** *(desorden)* mess.

zafarse *vpr* to get away (de, from), free OS (de, from), escape (de, from): *logró zafarse de la policía* he managed to get away from the police.

zafiro *nm* sapphire.

zaga *nf* **1** rear. **2** *(en deporte)* defence (US defense). LOC **a la zaga** behind. ∎ **no irle a la zaga a** ALGN not to lag behind SB: *es muy travieso, pero su hermano no le va a la zaga* he's really naughty, but his brother's every bit as bad.

zagal,-la *nm & nf* **1** *(muchacho)* lad; *(muchacha)* lass. **2** *(pastor)* shepherd; *(pastora)* shepherdess.

zaguán *nm* hall, hallway.

zaherir *vt* **1** to wound, hurt. **2** *(sentimientos)* to hurt.

Zaire *nm* Zaire.

zaireño,-a *adj* Zairean.
▶ *nm & nf* Zairean.

zalamero,-a *adj* charming, winning.
▶ *nm & nf* charmer. LOC **ponerse zalamero,-a** to turn on the charm.

zamarra *nf* sheepskin jacket.

Zambia *nf* Zambia.

zambiano,-a *adj* Zambian.
▶ *nm & nf* Zambian.

zambo,-a *adj* knock-kneed.
▶ *nm (mono)* spider monkey.

zambullida *nf* plunge, dive. LOC **darse una zambullida** to take a dip.

zambullir *vt* to plunge.

zampar *vi fam* to stuff oneself.

zampoña *nf* panpipes.

zanahoria *nf* carrot.

zanca *nf (de pájaro)* leg; *(de persona)* long leg.

zancada *nf* stride. LOC **en dos zancadas** in two shakes.

zancadilla *nf* **1** trip. **2** *fam (engaño)* ruse, trick. LOC **ponerle la zancadilla a** ALGN to trip SB up.

zanco *nm* stilt.

zancudo,-a *adj* **1** long-legged. **2** *(ave)* wading. COMP **aves zancudas** waders, wading birds.
▶ *nm* **zancudo** AM mosquito.

zángano,-a *nm & nf fam (persona)* loafer.
▶ *nm (insecto)* drone.

zanja *nf* trench. LOC **abrir una zanja** to dig a trench.

zanjar *vt fig (asunto)* to settle.

zapata *nf* **1** *(arandela)* washer. **2** TÉC shoe. **3** *(de cámara fotográfica)* hot shoe. COMP **zapata de freno** brake shoe.

zapatear *vi (bailar)* to stamp one's feet rhythmically.

zapateo *nm* rhythmic stamping.

zapatería *nf* **1** *(tienda)* shoe shop. **2** *(taller de reparación)* shoe repairer's, cobbler's; *(taller de fabricación)* shoemaker's. **3** *(oficio)* shoemaking.

zapatero,-a *nm & nf* **1** *(que arregla)* shoe repairer, cobbler. **2** *(que fabrica)* shoemaker. **3** *(que vende)* shoe seller. COMP **zapatero remendón** cobbler.

zapatilla *nf* **1** *(de estar en casa)* slipper. **2** *(de loneta)* plimsoll. COMP **zapatilla de ballet** ballet shoe. ∎ **zapatilla de deporte** trainer, running shoe.

zapato *nm* shoe. COMP **zapatos de tacón** high-heeled shoes.

zar *nm* tsar, czar.

zarabanda *nf* **1** MÚS saraband. **2** *fam (jaleo)* bustle, confusion.

zarandear *vt* **1** *(sacudir)* to shake; *(empujar)* to jostle, knock about. **2** *(cribar)* to sieve.

zarandeo *nm* **1** *(sacudida)* shaking; *(empujones)* jostling about. **2** *(criba)* sieving. **3** *(contoneo)* swaggering, strutting.

zarcillo *nm* **1** *(pendiente)* earring. **2** BOT tendril.

zarigüeya *nf* opossum.

zarina *nf* tsarina, czarina.

zarpa *nf* claw, paw. LOC **echarle la zarpa a** ALGO **1** *(animal)* to pounce on STH. **2** *(persona)* to grab STH.

zarpar *vi* to weigh anchor, set sail.

zarza *nf* bramble, blackberry bush.

zarzal *nm* bramble patch.

zarzamora *nf (zarza)* blackberry bush; *(fruto)* blackberry.

zarzuela *nf* **1** MÚS zarzuela, *Spanish operetta*. **2** CULIN fish stew.

zenit *nm* zenith.

zeta *nf (letra)* zed, US zee.
▶ *nm argot* police car.

Zimbabwe *nm* Zimbabwe.

zimbabwense *adj* Zimbabwean.
▶ *nm o nf* Zimbabwean.

zinc *nm* zinc.

zócalo *nm* **1** *(de habitación)* skirting board; *(de edificio)* plinth course, plinth. **2** *(pedestal)* plinth, socle.

zodiaco *nm* zodiac.

zona *nf* **1** area. **2** *(fronteriza, militar)* zone.
▶ *nm* MED *(herpes)* shingles. COMP **zona azul** parking meter zone. **zona edificada** built-up area. **zona fronteriza** border zone. **zona glacial** frigid zone. **zona templada** temperate zone. **zona tórrida** torrid zone. **zona verde** green zone.

zoología *nf* zoology.

zoológico,-a *adj* zoological.
▶ *nm* zoo.

zoólogo,-a *nm & nf* zoologist.

zorra *nf* **1** *(animal)* vixen. **2** *tabú (mujer)* bitch.

zorro,-a *adj (astuto)* cunning, sly.
▶ *nm* **zorro 1** *(animal)* fox; *(macho)* dog fox, fox. **2** *(piel)* fox-fur, fox-skin. **3** *(persona)* old fox. COMP **zorro viejo** sly old fox.
▶ *nm pl* **zorros** *(para el polvo)* duster *sing*.

zorzal *nm (ave)* thrush.

zozobrar *vi* **1** *(barco)* to sink, capsize. **2** *(persona)* to worry, be anxious. **3** *(proyecto)* to fail, be ruined.

zueco *nm* clog.

zulo *nm* hide-out.

zumbar *vi (abejorro, oídos)* to buzz: *me zumban los oídos* my ears are buzzing.
▶ *vt fam (pegar)* to thrash.

zumo *nm* juice: *zumo de naranja* orange juice.

zurcir *vt* to darn, mend.

zurdo,-a *adj (persona)* left-handed; *(mano)* left.
▶ *nm & nf* left-hander, left-handed person.
▶ *nf (mano)* left hand: *un golpe con la zurda* a left-handed blow.

zurra *nf fam* thrashing.

zurrar *vt* **1** *fam* to thrash. **2** *fam (cuero)* to tan.

zurrón *nm* shepherd's pouch, shepherd's bag.